wwnorton.com/nawol

The StudySpace site that accompanies *The Norton Anthology of World Literature* is FREE, but you will need the code below to register for a password that will allow you to access the copyrighted materials on the site.

READ-WELL

THE NORTON ANTHOLOGY OF

WORLD
LITERATURE

SHORTER THIRD EDITION

VOLUME 1

THE NORTON ANTHOLOGY OF

WORLD

LITERATURE

SHORTER THIRD EDITION

MARTIN PUCHNER, *General Editor*
HARVARD UNIVERSITY

SUZANNE AKBARI
UNIVERSITY OF TORONTO

WIEBKE DENECKE
BOSTON UNIVERSITY

VINAY DHARWADKER
UNIVERSITY OF WISCONSIN, MADISON

BARBARA FUCHS
UNIVERSITY OF CALIFORNIA, LOS ANGELES

CAROLINE LEVINE
UNIVERSITY OF WISCONSIN, MADISON

PERICLES LEWIS
YALE UNIVERSITY

EMILY WILSON
UNIVERSITY OF PENNSYLVANIA

VOLUME 1

W. W. NORTON & COMPANY | New York · London

W. W. Norton & Company has been independent since its founding in 1923, when William Warder Norton and Mary D. Herter Norton first published lectures delivered at the People's Institute, the adult education division of New York City's Cooper Union. The firm soon expanded its program beyond the Institute, publishing books by celebrated academics from America and abroad. By midcentury, the two major pillars of Norton's publishing program—trade books and college texts—were firmly established. In the 1950s, the Norton family transferred control of the company to its employees, and today—with a staff of four hundred and a comparable number of trade, college, and professional titles published each year—W. W. Norton & Company stands as the largest and oldest publishing house owned wholly by its employees.

Editor: Peter Simon
Assistant Editor: Conor Sullivan
Editorial Assistant: Quynh Do
Managing Editor, College: Marian Johnson
Manuscript Editors: Barney Latimer, Alice Falk, Katharine Ings, Michael Fleming, Susan Joseph, Pamela Lawson
Project Editor: Diane Cipollone
Electronic Media Editor: Eileen Connell
Print Ancillary Editor: Laura Musich
Editorial Assistant, Media: Jennifer Barnhardt
Marketing Manager, Literature: Kimberly Bowers
Production Manager, College: Sean Mintus
Photo Editor: Patricia Marx
Permissions Manager: Megan Jackson
Permissions Clearing: Margaret Gorenstein
Text Design: Jo Anne Metsch
Art Director: Rubina Yeh
Cartographer: Adrian Kitzinger
Composition: Jouve North America, Brattleboro, VT
Manufacturing: R. R. Donnelley & Sons—Crawfordsville, IN

The text of this book is composed in Fairfield Medium with the display set in Aperto.

Library of Congress Cataloging-in-Publication Data

The Norton anthology of world literature / Martin Puchner, General Editor.—Shorter Third edition.
    pages cm
    Includes bibliographical references and index.
    ISBN 978-0-393-91960-8 (paperback, v. 1)—ISBN 978-0-393-91961-5 (paperback, v. 2)
1. Literature—Collections.   I. Puchner, Martin, 1969–   II. Norton anthology of world masterpieces
    PN6014.N66 2013
    808.8—dc23

                                                                        2012044551

W. W. Norton & Company, Inc., 500 Fifth Avenue, New York, NY 10110-0017
wwnorton.com
W. W. Norton & Company Ltd., Castle House, 75/76 Wells Street, London W1T 3QT

2 3 4 5 6 7 8 9 0

Contents

III. EARLY CHINESE LITERATURE AND THOUGHT 747

VII. JAPAN'S CLASSICAL AGE

Preface

In 1665, a Turkish nobleman traveled from his native Istanbul to Europe and recorded with disarming honesty his encounter with an alien civilization. Over the course of his life, Evliya Çelebi would crisscross the Ottoman Empire from Egypt all the way to inner Asia, filling volume after volume with his reports of the cities, peoples, and legends he came across. This was his first journey to Vienna, a longtime foe of the Ottoman Empire. Full of confidence about the superiority of his own culture, Evliya was nevertheless impressed by Vienna's technical and cultural achievements. One episode from his *Travels,* a charming moment of self-deprecation, tells us how, during his tour of Vienna's inner city, Evliya sees what he believes to be "captives from the nation of Muhammad" sitting in front of various shops, toiling away at mind-numbing, repetitive tasks. Feeling pity for them, he offers them some coins, only to find that they are in fact mechanical automatons. Embarrassed and amazed at the same time, Evliya ends this tale by embracing the pleasure of seeing something new: "This was a marvelous and wonderful adventure indeed!"

Throughout his travels, Evliya remained good-humored about such disorienting experiences, and he maintained an open mind as he compared the cultural achievements of his home with those of Vienna. The crowning achievement of Vienna is the cathedral, which towers over the rest of the city. But Evliya found that it couldn't compare with the architectural wonders of Istanbul's great mosques. As soon as he was taken to the library, however, he was awestruck: "There are God knows how many books in the mosques of Sultan Barqūq and Sultan Faraj in Cairo, and in the mosques of [Sultan Meḥmed] The Conqueror and Sultan Süleymān and Sultan Bāyezīd and the New Mosque, but in this St. Stephen's Monastery in Vienna there are even more." He admired the sheer diversity and volume of books: "As many nations and different languages as there are, of all their authors and writers in their languages there are many times a hundred thousand books here." He was drawn, naturally enough, to the books that make visible the contours and riches of the world: atlases, maps, and illustrated books. An experienced travel writer, he nonetheless struggled to keep his equilibrium, saying finally that he was simply "stunned."

Opening *The Norton Anthology of World Literature* for the first time, a reader may feel as overwhelmed by its selection of authors and works (from "as many different languages as there are") as Evliya was by the cathedral library. For most students, the world literature course is a semester- or year-long encounter with the unknown—a challenging and rewarding journey, not a stroll down familiar, well-worn paths. Secure in their knowledge of the culture of their upbringing, and perhaps even proud of its accomplishments, most students will discover in world literature a bewildering variety of similarly rich and admirable cultures about which they know little, or nothing. Setting off on an imaginative journey in an unfamiliar text, readers may ask themselves questions similar to those a traveler in a strange land might ponder: How should I orient myself in this unfamiliar culture? What am I not seeing that someone raised in this culture would recognize right away? What can I learn here? How can I relate to the people I meet? Students might imagine the perils of the encounter, wondering if they will embarrass themselves in the process, or simply find themselves "stunned" by the sheer number of things they do not know.

But as much as they may feel anxiety at the prospect of world literature, students may also feel, as Evliya did, excitement at the discovery of something new, the exhilaration of having their horizons expanded. This, after all, is why Evliya traveled in the first place. Travel, for him, became almost an addiction. He sought again and again the rush of the unknown, the experience of being stunned, the feeling of marveling over cultural achievements from across the world. Clearly Evliya would have liked to linger in the cathedral library and immerse himself in its treasures. This experience is precisely what *The Norton Anthology of World Literature* offers to you and your students.

As editors of the Shorter Third Edition, we celebrate the excitement of world literature, but we also acknowledge that the encounter with the literary unknown is a source of anxiety. From the beginning of our collaboration, we have set out to make the journey more enticing and less intimidating for our readers.

First, we have made the introductory matter clearer and more informative by shortening headnotes and by following a consistent pattern of presentation, beginning with the author's biography, then moving to the cultural context, and ending with a brief introduction to the work itself. The goal of this approach is to provide students with just enough information to prepare them for their own reading of the work, but not so much information that their sense of discovery is numbed.

The mere presentation of an anthology—page after page of unbroken text— can feel overwhelming to anyone, but especially to an inexperienced student of literature. To alleviate this feeling, and to provide contextual information that words might not be able to convey, we have added hundreds of images and other forms of visual support to the anthology. Most of these images are integrated into the introductions to each major section of the anthology, providing context and visual interest. More than fifty of these images are featured in two newly conceived color inserts that offer pictures of various media, utensils, tools, technologies, and types of writing, as well as scenes of writing and reading from different epochs. The result is a rich visual overview of the material and cultural importance of writing and texts. Recognizing the importance of geography to many of the works in the anthology, the editors have revised the map program so that it complements the literature more directly. Each of the twenty-six maps has been redrawn to help readers orient themselves in the many corners of the world to which this anthology will take them. Finally, newly redesigned timelines at the end of each volume help students see at a glance the temporal relationships among literary works and historical events. Taken together, all of these visual elements make the anthology not only more inviting but also more informative than ever before.

The goal of making world literature a pleasurable adventure also guided our selection of translations. World literature gained its power from the way it reflected and shaped the imagination of peoples, and from the way it circulated outside its original context. For this, it depends on translation. While purists sometimes insist on studying literature only in the original language, a dogma that radically shrinks what one can read, world literature not only relies on translation but actually thrives on it. Translation is a necessity, the only thing that enables a worldwide circulation of literature. It also is an art. One need only think of the way in which translations of the Bible shaped the history of Latin or English. Translations are re-creations of works for new readers. Our edition pays keen attention to translation, and we feature dozens of new translations that make classical texts newly readable and capture the originals in compelling ways. With each choice of translation, we sought a version that would spark a sense of wonder while still being accessible to a contemporary reader. Many of the anthology's most fundamental classics—from *Gilgamesh*, Homer's epics, the Greek dramatists, Virgil, the Bible, the *Bhagavad-gītā*, and the Qur'an to *The Canterbury Tales*, *The Tale of Genji*, Goethe's *Faust*, Ibsen's *Hedda Gabler*, and Kafka's *Metamorphosis*—are presented in new translations that are both exciting works in English and skillful echoes of the spirit and flavor of the original. In some cases, we commissioned new translations—for instance, for the work of the South Asian poet Kabir, rendered beautifully by our South Asian editor and prize-winning translator Vinay Dharwadker, and for a portion of Çelebi's travels to Vienna by our Ottoman expert Gottfried Hagen that has never before been translated into English.

Finally, the editors decided to make some of the guiding themes of the world literature course, and this anthology, more visible. Experienced teachers know about these major themes and use them to create linked reading assignments, and the anthology has long touched on these topics, but with the Shorter Third Edition, these themes rise to the surface, giving all readers a clearer sense of the ties that bind diverse works together. Following is a discussion of each of these organizing themes.

Contact and Culture

Again and again, literature evokes journeys away from home and out into the world, bringing its protagonists—and thus its readers—into contact with peoples who are different from them. Such contact, and the cross-pollination it fosters, was crucial for the formation of cultures. The earliest civilizations—the civilizations that invented writing and hence literature—sprang up where they did because they were located along strategic trading and migration routes. Contact was not just something that happened between fully formed cultures, but something that made these cultures possible in the first place.

Committed to presenting the anthology's riches in a way that conveys this central fact of world literature, we have created new sections that encompass broad contact zones—areas of intense trade in peoples, goods, art, and ideas. The largest such zone is centered on the Mediterranean basin and reaches as far as the Fertile Crescent. It is in this large area that the earliest literatures emerged and intermingled. For the Mediterranean Sea was not just a hostile environment that could derail a journey home, as it did for Odysseus, who took ten years to find his way back to Greece from the Trojan War in Asia Minor; it was a connecting tissue as well, allowing for intense contact around its harbors. Medieval maps of the Mediterranean pay tribute to this fact: so-called portolan charts show a veritable mesh of lines connecting hundreds of ports. In the reorganized Mediterranean sections, we have placed together texts from this broad region, the location of intense conflict as well as friendly exchange, rather than isolating them from each other.

One of the many ways that human beings have bound themselves to each other and have attempted to bridge cultural and geographic distances is through religion. As a form of cultural exchange, and an inspiration for cultural conflict, religion is an important part of the deep history of contact and encounter presented in the anthology, and the editors have taken every opportunity to call attention to this fact. This is nowhere more visible than in a new section in volume 1 called "Encounters with Islam," which follows the cultural influence of Islam beyond its point of origin in Arabia and Persia. Here we draw together works from western Africa, Asia Minor, and South Asia, each of them blending the ideas and values of Islam with indigenous folk traditions to create new forms of cultural expression. The original oral stories of the extraordinary Mali epic *Sunjata* (in a newly established version and translation) incorporate elements of Islam much the way the Anglo-Saxon epic *Beowulf* incorporates elements of Christianity. In a different way, the encounter of Islam with other cultures emerges at the eastern end of its sphere of influence, in South Asia, where a multireligious culture absorbs and transforms Islamic material, as in the philosophical poems of Tukaram and Kabir (both presented in new selections and translations). Evliya Çelebi, with his journey to Vienna, belongs to this larger history as well, giving us another lens through which to view the encounter of Islam and Christianity that is dramatized by so many writers elsewhere in the anthology (most notably, in the *Song of Roland*).

The greatest story of encounter between peoples to be told in the first half of the anthology is the encounter of Europe (and thus of Eurasia) with the Americas. To tell this story properly, the editors decided to eliminate the old dividing line between the European Renaissance and the New World that had prevailed in previous editions and instead created one broad cultural sphere that combines the two. A (newly expanded) cluster within this section gathers texts immediately relevant to this encounter, vividly chronicling all of its willful violence and its unintended consequences in the "New" World. This section also reveals the ways in which the European discovery of the Americas wrought violence in Europe. Old certainties and authorities overthrown, new worlds imagined, the very concept of being human revised—nothing that happened in the European Renaissance was untouched by the New World. Rarely had contact between two geographic zones had more consequences: henceforth, the Americas would be an important part of the story of Europe.

In Volume 2, another new section, "Realism across the Globe," traces perhaps the first truly global artistic movement, one that found expression in France, Britain, Russia, Brazil, and Japan.

In the twentieth century, the pace of cultural exchange and contact, so much swifter than in preceding centuries, transformed most literary movements, from modernism to postcolonialism, into truly global phenomena. At the end of the second volume, we encounter Elizabeth Costello, the title character in J. M. Coetzee's novel. A writer herself, Costello has been asked to give lectures on a cruise ship; mobile and deracinated, she and a colleague deliver lectures on the novel in Africa, including the role of geography and oral literature. The scene captures many themes of world literature—and serves as an image of our present stage of globalization. World literature is a story about the relation between the world and literature, and we tell this story partly by paying attention to this geographic dimension.

Worlds of the Imagination

Literature not only moves us to remote corners of the world and across landscapes; it also presents us with whole imagined worlds to which we as readers can travel. The construction of literary, clearly made-up worlds has always been a theme of world literature, which has suggested answers to fundamental questions, including how the world came into being. The Mayan epic *Popol Vuh,* featured in volume 1, develops one of the most elaborate creation myths, including several attempts at creating humans (only the fourth is successful). Other texts underline this theme, including the newly added Babylonian creation epic, the *Enuma Elish,* at the very beginning of the anthology. The myths in this epic and other texts in the first section of the anthology resonate throughout the history of world literature, providing imaginative touchstones for later authors (such as Virgil, Dante, and Goethe) to adapt and use in their own imaginative world-creation.

But world-creation not only operates on a grand scale. It also occurs at moments when literature restricts itself to small, enclosed universes that are observed with minute attention. The great eighteenth-century Chinese novel *The Story of the Stone* by Cao Xueqin (presented in a new selection) withdraws to a family compound, whose walls it almost never leaves, to depict life in all its subtlety within this restricted space for several thousand pages. Sometimes we are invited into the even more circumscribed space of the narrator's own head, where we encounter strange and surreal worlds, as in the great modernist and postmodernist fictions from Franz Kafka and Jorge Luis Borges. By providing a thematic through-line, the new edition of the anthology reveals the myriad ways in which authors not only seek to explain our world but also compete with it by imagining new and different ones.

Genres

Over the millennia, literature has developed a set of rules and conventions that authors work with and against as they make decisions about subject matter, style, and form. These rules help us distinguish between different types of literature—that is, different genres. The broad view of literature afforded by the anthology, across both space and time, is particularly capable of showing how genres emerge and are transformed as they are used by different writers and for different purposes. The new edition of the anthology underscores this crucial dimension of literature by tracking the movement of genres—of, for example, the frame-tale narration from South Asia to northern Europe. To help readers recognize this theme, we have created ways of making genre visible. Lyric poetry is found everywhere in the anthology, and it is the focus of specially designed sections that cast light on classical Sanskrit lyric; China's T'ang poetry; Japan's classical poetry anthologies, the *Kokinshū* and *Man'yōshū* (as well as one of the world's most successful poetic genres, the haiku); and on the poetry of modernism. By the same token, a cluster on manifestos highlights modernism's most characteristic invention, with its shrill demands and aggressive layout. Among the genres, drama is perhaps the most difficult to grapple with because it is so closely entangled with theatrical performance. You don't understand a play unless you understand what kind of theater it was intended for, how it was performed, and how audiences watched it. To capture this dimension, we have grouped one of the most prominent regional drama traditions—Athenian drama of the 5th century B.C.E.—in its own section.

Oral Literature

The relation of the spoken word to literature is perhaps the most important theme that emerges from these pages. All literature goes back to oral storytelling—all the foundational epics, from South Asia via Greece and Africa to Central America, are deeply rooted in oral storytelling; poetry's rhythms are best appreciated when heard; and drama, a form that comes alive in performance, continues to be engaged with an oral tradition. Throughout the anthology, we connect works to the oral traditions from which they sprang and remind readers that writing has coexisted with oral storytelling since the invention of the former. A new and important cluster in volume 2 on oral literature foregrounds this theme and showcases the nineteenth-century interest in oral traditions such as fairy and folk tales and slave stories. At the same time, this cluster, and the anthology as a whole, shows the importance of gaining literacy.

Varieties of Literature

In presenting everything from the earliest literatures to a (much-expanded) selection of contemporary literature reaching to the early twenty-first century, and from oral storytelling to literary experiments of the avant-garde, the anthology confronts us with the question not just of world literature, but of literature as such. The world of Greek myth, for example, is seen by almost everyone as literary, even though it arose from ritual practices that are different from what we associate with literature. But this is even more the case with other texts, such as the Qur'an or the Bible, which still function as religious texts for many, while others appreciate them primarily or exclusively as literature. Some texts, such as the *Daodejing* or *Bhagavad-gītā* belong in philosophy. Our modern conception of literature as imaginative literature, as fiction, is very recent, about two hundred years old. *The Norton Anthology of World Literature* offers a much-expanded conception of literature that includes creation myths, wisdom literature, religious texts, philosophy, and fairy tales in addition to plays, poems, and narrative fiction. This answers to an older definition of literature as writing of high quality.

This brings us to the last and perhaps most important question: When we study the world, why study it through its literature? Hasn't literature lost some of its luster for us, we who are faced with so many competing media and art forms? Like no other art form or medium, literature offers us a deep history of human thinking. As our illustration program shows, writing was invented not for the composition of literature, but for much more mundane purposes, such as the recording of ownership, contracts, or astronomical observations. But literature is writing's most glorious side-product. Because language expresses human consciousness, no other art form can capture the human past with the precision and scope of literature. Language shapes our thinking, and literature, the highest expression of language, plays an important role in that process, pushing the boundaries of what we can think, and how we think it. The other great advantage of literature is that it can be reactivated with each reading. The great architectural monuments of the past are now in ruins. Literature, too, often has to be excavated, as with many classical texts. But once a text has been found or reconstructed it can be experienced as if for the first time by new readers. Even though many of the literary texts collected in this anthology are at first strange, because they originated so very long ago, they still speak to today's readers with great eloquence and freshness.

Because works of world literature are alive today, they continue to elicit strong emotions and investments. The epic *Rāmāyana*, for example, plays an important role in the politics of India, where it has been used to bolster Hindu nationalism, just as the *Bhagavad-gītā*, here in a new translation, continues to be a moral touchstone in the ethical deliberation about war. And the three religions of the book, Judaism, Christianity, and Islam, make our selections from their scriptures a more than historical exercise. China has recently elevated the sayings of Confucius, whose influence on Chinese attitudes about the state had waned in the twentieth century, creating Confucius Institutes all over the world to promote Chinese culture in what is now called New Confucianism. The debates about the role of the church and secularism, which we highlight through a new cluster and selections in all volumes, have become newly important in current deliberations on the relation between church and state. World literature is never neutral. We know its relevance precisely by the controversies it inspires.

Going back to the earliest moments of cultural contact and moving forward to the global flows of the twenty-first century, *The Norton Anthology of World Literature* attempts to provide a deep history. But it is a special type of history: a literary one. World literature is grounded in the history of the world, but it is also the history of imagining this world; it is a history not just of what happened, but also of how humans imagined their place in the midst of history. We, the editors of this Shorter Third Edition, can think of no better way to prepare young people for a global future than through a deep and meaningful exploration of world literature. Evliya Çelebi sums up his exploration of Vienna as a "marvelous and wonderful adventure"—we hope that readers will feel the same about the adventure in reading made possible by this anthology and will return to it for the rest of their lives.

About the Shorter Third Edition

New Selections and Translations

This Shorter Third Edition represents a thoroughgoing, top-to-bottom revision of the anthology that altered nearly every section in important ways. Following is a list of the new sections and works, in order:

VOLUME I

New translations of Egyptian love poems • Benjamin R. Foster's translation of *Gilgamesh* • Selections from chapters 12, 17, 28, 29, 31, 32, and 33 of Genesis, and from chapters 19 and 20 of Exodus • All selections from Genesis, Exodus, and Job are newly featured in Robert Alter's translation, and chapter 25 of Genesis (Esau spurning his birthright) is presented in a graphic visualization by R. Crumb based on Alter's translation • Homer's *Iliad* and *Odyssey* are now featured in Stanley Lombardo's highly regarded translations • A new selection and a new translation of Sappho's lyrics • New translations of *Oedipus the King* (by Robert Bagg), and *Medea* (by Diane Arnson Svarlien) • A new selection of Catullus's poems, in a new translation by Peter Green • *The Aeneid* is now featured in Robert Fagles's career-topping translation, and book II is newly added • New selections from book 1 of Ovid's *Metamorphoses* join the previous selection, now featured in Charles Martin's recent translation • New selections from the Chinese *Classic of Poetry* • Confucius's *Analects* now in a new translation by Simon Leys • The *Daodejing* is newly added • Selections from the Christian Bible now featured in a new translation by Richmond Lattimore • Selections from the Qur'an now featured in M. A. S. Abdel Haleem's translation • A new selection from Abolqasem Ferdowsi's *Shahnameh*, in a new translation by Dick Davis • Additional material from Marie de France's *Lais*, in a translation by Robert Hanning and Joan Ferrante • Dante's *Divine Comedy* now featured in Mark Musa's translation • A new translation by Sheila Fisher of Chaucer's *Canterbury Tales* and "The Wife of Bath's Tale" newly included • New selections in fresh translations of classical Tamil and Sanskrit lyric poetry • New selections and translations of Chinese lyric poetry• Refreshed selections and new translations of lyric poetry in "Japan's Classical Age" • A new, expanded selection from, and a new translation of, Murasaki Shikibu's *The Tale of Genji* • A new translation by David C. Conrad of the West African epic *Sunjata* • A new selection from Evliya Çelebi's *The Book of Travels*, never before translated into English, now in Gottfried Hagen's translation • New selection of Indian lyric poetry by Kabir, Mīrabāī, and Tukaram, in fresh new translations • new selections from, and a new translation of, Michiavelli's *The Prince* • Marguerite de Navarre, *Heptameron*, newly included • A new cluster, "The Encounter of Europe and the New World."

VOLUME 2

Molière's *Tartuffe* now featured in a new translation by Constance Congdon and Virginia Scott • New selections by Sor Juana Inés de la Cruz, in a new translation by Electa Arenal and Amanda Powell • Alexander Pope's "An Essay on Man" • Mary Wollstonecraft's *A Vindication of the Rights of Woman*, newly included • Wu Cheng'en's *The Journey to the West* in a new translation by Anthony Yu • An expanded, refreshed selection from Cao Xueqin's *The Story of the Stone*, part of which is now featured in John Minford's translation • A new cluster, "The World of Haiku," features work by Kitamura Kigin, Matsuo Bashō, Morikawa Kyoriku, Yosa Buson, and Chikamatsu Monzaemon • New selection from book 2 of Rousseau's *Confessions* • A new grouping, "Lyric Poetry in the Long Nineteenth Century," features a generous sampling of lyric poetry from the period, including new poems by William Wordsworth, Anna Bunina, Andrés Bello, John Keats, Heinrich Heine, Elizabeth Barrett Browning, Tennyson, Walt Whitman, and José Martí, as well as an exciting new translation of Arthur Rimbaud's *Illuminations* by John Ashbery • A new selection and all new translations of Ghalib's poetry by Vinay Dharwadker • Flaubert's *A Simple Heart* • Ibsen's *Hedda Gabler*, now featured in a new translation by Rick Davis and Brian Johnston • Machado de Assis's *The Rod of Justice* • Chekhov's *The Cherry Orchard*, now featured in a new translation by Paul Schmidt • Higuchi Ichiyō's *Separate Ways* • A new cluster, "Orature," with a German folktale; Anansi stories from Ghana, Jamaica, and the United States; as well as slave songs, stories, and spirituals, Malagasy wisdom poetry, and the Navajo Night Chant • Thomas Mann's *Death in Venice*, complete • Selection from Marcel Proust's *Remembrance of Things Past*, featured in Lydia Davis's critically acclaimed translation • James Joyce's "The Dead" • Franz Kafka's *The Metamorphosis* now featured in Michael Hofmann's translation • Akutagawa's *In a Bamboo Grove* • Premchand's "The Road to Salvation" • Chapter 1 of Woolf's *A Room of One's Own* newly added to the selection from chapter 3 • Zhang Ailing's *Sealed Off* • Constantine Cavafy • Pablo Neruda • Octavio Paz • Léopold Sédar Senghor • Tadeusz Borowski's *This Way for the Gas, Ladies and Gentlemen* • Paul Celan • Doris Lessing • Saadat Hasan Manto • James Baldwin • Samuel Beckett's *Endgame* • Clarice Lispector's "The Daydreams of a Drunk Woman" • Chinua Achebe's *Chike's School Days* • Alexander Solzhenitsyn's "Matryona's Home" • Mahmoud Darwish • Yehuda Amichai • Derek Walcott • Seamus Heaney • V. S. Naipaul • Ngugi Wa Thiong'o • Bessie Head • Salman Rushdie • Jamaica Kincaid • Hanan Al-Shaykh • Isabel Allende • Chu T'ien-Hsin • J. M. Coetzee.

Supplements for Instructors and Students

Norton is pleased to provide instructors and students with several supplements to make the study and teaching of world literature an even more interesting and rewarding experience:

Instructor Resource Folder

A new Instructor Resource Folder features images and video clips that allow instructors to enhance their lectures with some of the sights and sounds of world literature and its contexts.

Instructor Course Guide

Teaching with The Norton Anthology of World Literature: *A Guide for Instructors* provides teaching plans, suggestions for in-class activities, discussion topics and writing projects, and extensive lists of scholarly and media resources.

Coursepacks

Available in a variety of formats, Norton coursepacks bring digital resources into a new or existing online course. Coursepacks are free to instructors, easy to download and install, and available in a variety of formats, including Blackboard, Desire2Learn, Angel, and Moodle.

StudySpace (*wwnorton.com/nawol*)

This free student companion site features a variety of complementary materials to help students read and study world literature. Among them are reading-comprehension quizzes, quick-reference summaries of the anthology's introductions, review quizzes, an audio glossary to help students pronounce names and terms, tours of some of the world's important cultural landmarks, timelines, maps, and other contextual materials.

Writing about World Literature

Written by Karen Gocsik, Executive Director of the Writing Program at Dartmouth College, in collaboration with faculty in the world literature program at the University of Nevada, Las Vegas, *Writing about World Literature* provides course-specific guidance for writing papers and essay exams in the world literature course.

For more information about any of these supplements, instructors should contact their local Norton representative.

Acknowledgments

The editors would like to thank the following people, who have provided invaluable assistance by giving us sage advice, important encouragement, and help with the preparation of the manuscript: Sara Akbari, Alannah de Barra, Wendy Belcher, Jodi Bilinkoff, Freya Brackett, Psyche Brackett, Michaela Bronstein, Amanda Claybaugh, Rachel Carroll, Lewis Cook, David Damrosch, Dick Davis, Amanda Detry, Anthony Domestico, Merve Emre, Maria Fackler, Guillermina de Ferrari, Karina Galperín, Stanton B. Garner, Kimberly Dara Gordon, Elyse Graham, Stephen Greenblatt, Sara Guyer, Langdon Hammer, Iain Higgins, Mohja Kahf, Peter Kornicki, Paul Kroll, Lydia Liu, Bala Venkat Mani, Ann Matter, Barry McCrea, Alexandra McCullough-Garcia, Rachel McGuiness, Jon McKenzie, Mary Mullen, Djibril Tamsir Niane, Felicity Nussbaum, Andy Orchard, John Peters, Daniel Taro Poch, Daniel Potts, Megan Quigley, Imogen Roth, Catherine de Rose, Ellen Sapega, Jesse Schotter, Stephen Scully, Brian Stock, Tomi Suzuki, Joshua Taft, Sara Torres, Lisa Voigt, Kristen Wanner, and Emily Weissbourd.

All the editors would like to thank the wonderful people at Norton, principally our editor Pete Simon, the driving force behind this whole undertaking, as well as Marian Johnson (Managing Editor, College), Alice Falk, Michael Fleming, Katharine Ings, Susan Joseph, and Barney Latimer (Copyeditors), Conor Sullivan (Assistant Editor), Quynh Do (Editorial Assistant), Diane Cipollone (Copyeditor and Project Editor), Megan Jackson (College Permissions Manager), Margaret Gorenstein (Permissions), Patricia Marx (Art Research Director), Debra Morton Hoyt (Art Director; cover design), Rubina Yeh (Design Director), Jo Anne Metsch (Designer; interior text design), Adrian Kitzinger (cartography), Agnieszka Gasparska (timeline design), Eileen Connell, (Media Editor), Jennifer Barnhardt (Editorial Assistant, Media), Laura Musich (Associate Editor; Instructor's Guide), Benjamin Reynolds (Production Manager), and Kim Bowers (Marketing Manager, Literature) and Ashley Cain (Humanities Sales Specialist).

This anthology represents a collaboration not only among the editors and their close advisors, but also among the thousands of instructors who teach from the anthology and provide valuable and constructive guidance to the publisher and editors. *The Norton Anthology of World Literature* is as much their book as it is ours, and we are grateful to everyone who has cared enough about this anthology to help make it better. We're especially grateful to the more than five hundred professors of world literature who responded to an online survey in early 2008, whom we have listed below. Thank you all.

Michel Aaij (Auburn University Montgomery); Sandra Acres (Mississippi Gulf Coast Community College); Larry Adams (University of North Alabama);

Mary Adams (Western Carolina University); Stephen Adams (Westfield State College); Roberta Adams (Roger Williams University); Kirk Adams (Tarrant County College); Kathleen Aguero (Pine Manor College); Richard Albright (Harrisburg Area Community College); Deborah Albritton (Jefferson Davis Community College); Todd Aldridge (Auburn University); Judith Allen-Leventhal (College of Southern Maryland); Carolyn Amory (Binghamton University); Kenneth Anania (Massasoit Community College); Phillip Anderson (University of Central Arkansas); Walter Anderson (University of Arkansas at Little Rock); Vivienne Anderson (North Carolina Wesleyan College); Susan Andrade (University of Pittsburgh); Kit Andrews (Western Oregon University); Joe Antinarella (Tidewater Community College); Nancy Applegate (Georgia Highlands College); Sona Aronian (University of Rhode Island); Sona Aronian (University of Rhode Island); Eugene Arva (University of Miami); M. G. Aune (California University of Pennsylvania); Carolyn Ayers (Saint Mary's University of Minnesota); Diana Badur (Black Hawk College); Susan Bagby (Longwood University); Maryam Barrie (Washtenaw Community College); Maria Baskin (Alamance Community College); Samantha Batten (Auburn University); Charles Beach (Nyack College); Michael Beard (University of North Dakota); Bridget Beaver (Connors State College); James Bednarz (C. W. Post College); Khani Begum (Bowling Green State University); Albert Bekus (Austin Peay State University); Lynne Belcher (Southern Arkansas University); Karen Bell (Delta State University); Elisabeth Ly Bell (University of Rhode Island); Angela Belli (St. John's University); Leo Benardo (Baruch College); Paula Berggren (Baruch College, CUNY); Frank Bergmann (Utica College); Nancy Blomgren (Volunteer State Community College); Scott Boltwood (Emory & Henry College); Ashley Bonds (Copiah-Lincoln Community College); Thomas Bonner (Xavier University of Louisiana); Debbie Boyd (East Central Community College); Norman Boyer (Saint Xavier University); Nodya Boyko (Auburn University); Robert Brandon (Rockingham Community College); Alan Brasher (East Georgia College); Harry Brent (Baruch College); Charles Bressler (Indiana Wesleyan University); Katherine Brewer; Mary Ruth Brindley (Mississippi Delta Community College); Mamye Britt (Georgia Perimeter College); Gloria Brooks (Tyler Junior College); Monika Brown (University of North Carolina–Pembroke); Greg Bryant (Highland Community College); Austin Busch (SUNY Brockport); Barbara Cade (Texas College); Karen Caig (University of Arkansas Community College at Morrilton); Jonizo Cain-Calloway (Del Mar College); Mark Calkins (San Francisco State University); Catherine Calloway (Arkansas State University); Mechel Camp (Jackson State Community College); Robert Canary (University of Wisconsin–Parkside); Stephen Canham (University of Hawaii at Manoa); Marian Carcache (Auburn University); Alfred Carson (Kennesaw State University); Farrah Cato (University of Central Florida); Biling Chen (University of Central Arkansas); Larry Chilton (Blinn College); Eric Chock (University of Hawaii at West Oahu); Cheryl Clark (Miami Dade College–Wolfson Campus); Sarah Beth Clark (Holmes Community College); Jim Cody (Brookdale Community College); Carol Colatrella (Georgia Institute of Technology); Janelle Collins (Arkansas State University); Theresa Collins (St. John's University); Susan Comfort (Indiana University of Pennsylvania); Kenneth Cook (National Park Community College); Angie Cook (Cisco Junior College); Yvonne Cooper (Pierce College); Brenda Cornell (Central Texas College); Judith Cortelloni (Lincoln College); Robert

Cosgrove (Saddleback College); Rosemary Cox (Georgia Perimeter College); Daniel Cozart (Georgia Perimeter College); Brenda Craven (Fort Hays State University); Susan Crisafulli (Franklin College); Janice Crosby (Southern University); Randall Crump (Kennesaw State University); Catherine Cucinella (California State University San Marcos); T. Allen Culpepper (Manatee Community College–Venice); Rodger Cunningham (Alice Lloyd College); Lynne Dahmen (Purdue University); Patsy J. Daniels (Jackson State University); James Davis (Troy University); Evan Davis (Southwestern Oregon Community College); Margaret Dean (Eastern Kentucky University); JoEllen DeLucia (John Jay College, CUNY); Hivren Demir-Atay (Binghamton University); Rae Ann DeRosse (University of North Carolina–Greensboro); Anna Crowe Dewart (College of Coastal Georgia); Joan Digby (C. W. Post Campus Long Island University); Diana Dominguez (University of Texas at Brownsville); Dee Douglas-Jones (Winston-Salem State University); Jeremy Downes (Auburn University); Denell Downum (Suffolk University); Sharon Drake (Texarkana College); Damian Dressick (Robert Morris University); Clyburn Duder (Concordia University Texas); Dawn Duncan (Concordia College); Kendall Dunkelberg (Mississippi University for Women); Janet Eber (County College of Morris); Emmanuel Egar (University of Arkansas at Pine Bluff); David Eggebrecht (Concordia University of Wisconsin); Sarah Eichelman (Walters State Community College); Hank Eidson (Georgia Perimeter College); Monia Eisenbraun (Oglala Lakota College/Cheyenne-Eagle Butte High School); Dave Elias (Eastern Kentucky University); Chris Ellery (Angelo State University); Christina Elvidge (Marywood University); Ernest Enchelmayer (Arkansas Tech University); Niko Endres (Western Kentucky University); Kathrynn Engberg (Alabama A&M University); Chad Engbers (Calvin College); Edward Eriksson (Suffolk Community College); Donna Estill (Alabama Southern Community College); Andrew Ettin (Wake Forest University); Jim Everett (Mississippi College); Gene Fant (Union University); Nathan Faries (University of Dubuque); Martin Fashbaugh (Auburn University); Donald J. Fay (Kennesaw State University); Meribeth Fell (College of Coastal Georgia); David Fell (Carroll Community College); Jill Ferguson (San Francisco Conservatory of Music); Susan French Ferguson (Mountain View Comumunity College); Robyn Ferret (Cascadia Community College); Colin Fewer (Purdue Calumet); Hannah Fischthal (St. John's University); Jim Fisher (Peninsula College); Gene Fitzgerald (University of Utah); Monika Fleming (Edgecombe Community College); Phyllis Fleming (Patrick Henry Community College); Francis Fletcher (Folsom Lake College); Denise Folwell (Montgomery College); Ulanda Forbess (North Lake College); Robert Forman (St. John's University); Suzanne Forster (University of Alaska–Anchorage); Patricia Fountain (Coastal Carolina Community College); Kathleen Fowler (Surry Community College); Sheela Free (San Bernardino Valley College); Lea Fridman (Kingsborough Community College); David Galef (Montclair State University); Paul Gallipeo (Adirondack Community College); Jan Gane (University of North Carolina–Pembroke); Jennifer Garlen (University of Alabama–Huntsville); Anita Garner (University of North Alabama); Elizabeth Gassel (Darton College); Patricia Gaston (West Virginia University, Parkersburg); Marge Geiger (Cuyahoga Community College); Laura Getty (North Georgia College & State University); Amy Getty (Grand View College); Leah Ghiradella (Middlesex County College); Dick Gibson (Jacksonville University); Teresa

Gibson (University of Texas–Brownsville); Wayne Gilbert (Community College of Aurora); Sandra Giles (Abraham Baldwin Agricultural College); Pamela Gist (Cedar Valley College); Suzanne Gitonga (North Lake College); James Glickman (Community College of Rhode Island); R. James Goldstein (Auburn University); Jennifer Golz (Tennessee Tech University); Marian Goodin (North Central Missouri College); Susan Gorman (Massachusetts College of Pharmacy and Health Sciences); Anissa Graham (University of North Alabama); Eric Gray (St. Gregory's University); Geoffrey Green (San Francisco State University); Russell Greer (Texas Woman's University); Charles Grey (Albany State University); Frank Gruber (Bergen Community College); Alfonso Guerriero Jr. (Baruch College, CUNY); Letizia Guglielmo (Kennesaw State University); Nira Gupta-Casale (Kean University); Gary Gutchess (SUNY Tompkins Cortland Community College); William Hagen (Oklahoma Baptist University); John Hagge (Iowa State University); Julia Hall (Henderson State University); Margaret Hallissy (C. W. Post Campus Long Island University); Laura Hammons (Hinds Community College); Nancy Hancock (Austin Peay State University); Carol Harding (Western Oregon University); Cynthia Hardy (University of Alaska–Fairbanks); Steven Harthorn (Williams Baptist College); Stanley Hauer (University of Southern Mississippi); Leean Hawkins (National Park Community College); Kayla Haynie (Harding University); Maysa Hayward (Ocean County College); Karen Head (Georgia Institute of Technology); Sandra Kay Heck (Walters State Community College); Frances Helphinstine (Morehead State University); Karen Henck (Eastern Nazarene College); Betty Fleming Hendricks (University of Arkansas); Yndaleci Hinojosa (Northwest Vista College); Richard Hishmeh (Palomar College); Ruth Hoberman (Eastern Illinois University); Rebecca Hogan (University of Wisconsin–Whitewater); Mark Holland (East Tennessee State University); John Holmes (Virginia State University); Sandra Holstein (Southern Oregon University); Fran Holt (Georgia Perimeter College–Clarkston); William Hood (North Central Texas College); Glenn Hopp (Howard Payne University); George Horneker (Arkansas State University); Barbara Howard (Central Bible College); Pamela Howell (Midland College); Melissa Hull (Tennessee State University); Barbara Hunt (Columbus State University); Leeann Hunter (University of South Florida); Gill Hunter (Eastern Kentucky University); Helen Huntley (California Baptist University); Luis Iglesias (University of Southern Mississippi); Judith Irvine (Georgia State University); Miglena Ivanova (Coastal Carolina University); Kern Jackson (University of South Alabama); Kenneth Jackson (Yale University); M. W. Jackson (St. Bonaventure University); Robb Jackson (Texas A&M University–Corpus Christi); Karen Jacobsen (Valdosta State University); Maggie Jaffe (San Diego State University); Robert Jakubovic (Raymond Walters College); Stokes James (University of Wisconsin–Stevens Point); Beverly Jamison (South Carolina State University); Ymitri Jayasundera-Mathison (Prairie View A&M University); Katarzyna Jerzak (University of Georgia); Alice Jewell (Harding University); Elizabeth Jones (Auburn University); Jeff Jones (University of Idaho); Dan Jones (Walters State Community College); Mary Kaiser (Jefferson State Community College); James Keller (Middlesex County College); Jill Keller (Middlesex Community College); Tim Kelley (Northwest-Shoals Community College); Andrew Kelley (Jackson State Community College); Hans Kellner (North Carolina State); Brian Kennedy (Pasadena City College); Shirin Khanmohamadi

(San Francisco State University); Jeremy Kiene (McDaniel College); Mary Catherine Kiliany (Robert Morris University); Sue Kim (University of Alabama–Birmingham); Pam Kingsbury (University of North Alabama); Sharon Kinoshita (University of California, Santa Cruz); Lydia Kualapai (Schreiner University); Rita Kumar (University of Cincinnati); Roger Ladd (University of North Carolina–Pembroke); Daniel Lane (Norwich University); Erica Lara (Southwest Texas Junior College); Leah Larson (Our Lady of the Lake University); Dana Lauro (Ocean County College); Shanon Lawson (Pikes Peak Community College); Michael Leddy (Eastern Illinois University); Eric Leuschner (Fort Hays State University); Patricia Licklider (John Jay College, CUNY); Pamela Light (Rochester College); Alison Ligon (Morehouse College); Linda Linzey (Southeastern University); Thomas Lisk (North Carolina State University); Matthew Livesey (University of Wisconsin–Stout); Vickie Lloyd (University of Arkansas Community College at Hope); Judy Lloyd (Southside Virginia Community College); Mary Long (Ouachita Baptist University); Rick Lott (Arkansas State University); Scott Lucas (The Citadel); Katrine Lvovskaya (Rutgers University); Carolin Lynn (Mercyhurst College); Susan Lyons (University of Connecticut—Avery Point); William Thomas MacCary (Hofstra University); Richard Mace (Pace University); Peter Marbais (Mount Olive College); Lacy Marschalk (Auburn University); Seth Martin (Harrisburg Area Community College–Lancaster); Carter Mathes (Rutgers University); Rebecca Mathews (University of Connecticut); Marsha Mathews (Dalton State College); Darren Mathews (Grambling State University); Corine Mathis (Auburn University); Ken McAferty (Pensacola State College); Jeff McAlpine (Clackamas Community College); Kelli McBride (Seminole State College); Kay McClellan (South Plains College); Michael McClung (Northwest-Shoals Community College); Michael McClure (Virginia State University); Jennifer McCune (University of Central Arkansas); Kathleen McDonald (Norwich University); Charles McDonnell (Piedmont Technical College); Nancy McGee (Macomb Community College); Gregory McNamara (Clayton State University); Abby Mendelson (Point Park University); Ken Meyers (Wilson Community College); Barbara Mezeske (Hope College); Brett Millan (South Texas College); Sheila Miller (Hinds Community College); David Miller (Mississippi College); Matt Miller (University of South Carolina–Aiken); Yvonne Milspaw (Harrisburg Area Community College), Ruth Misheloff (Baruch College); Lamata Mitchell (Rock Valley College); D'Juana Montgomery (Southwestern Assemblies of God University); Lorne Mook (Taylor University); Renee Moore (Mississippi Delta Community College); Dan Morgan (Scott Community College); Samantha Morgan-Curtis (Tennessee State University); Beth Morley (Collin College); Vicki Moulson (College of the Albemarle); L. Carl Nadeau (University of Saint Francis); Wayne Narey (Arkansas State University); LeAnn Nash (Texas A&M University–Commerce); Leanne Nayden (University of Evansville); Jim Neilson (Wake Technical Community College); Jeff Nelson (University of Alabama–Huntsville); Mary Nelson (Dallas Baptist University); Deborah Nester (Northwest Florida State College); William Netherton (Amarillo College); William Newman (Perimeter College); Adele Newson-Horst (Missouri State University); George Nicholas (Benedictine College); Dana Nichols (Gainesville State College); Mark Nicoll-Johnson (Merced College); John Mark Nielsen (Dana College); Michael Nifong (Georgia College & State University); Laura Noell (North Virginia Community College);

Bonnie Noonan (Xavier University of Louisiana); Patricia Noone (College of Mount Saint Vincent); Paralee Norman (Northwestern State University–Leesville); Frank Novak (Pepperdine University); Kevin O'Brien (Chapman University); Sarah Odishoo (Columbia College Chicago); Samuel Olorounto (New River Community College); Jamili Omar (Lone Star College–CyFair); Michael Orlofsky (Troy University); Priscilla Orr (Sussex County Community College); Jim Owen (Columbus State University); Darlene Pagan (Pacific University); Yolanda Page (University of Arkansas–Pine Bluff); Lori Paige (Westfield State College); Linda Palumbo (Cerritos College); Joseph Parry (Brigham Young University); Carla Patterson (Georgia Highlands College); Andra Pavuls (Davenport University); Sunita Peacock (Slippery Rock University); Velvet Pearson (Long Beach City College); Joe Pellegrino (Georgia Southern University); Sonali Perera (Rutgers University); Clem Perez (St. Philip's College); Caesar Perkowski (Gordon College); Gerald Perkus (Collin College); John Peters (University of North Texas); Lesley Peterson (University of North Alabama); Judy Peterson (John Tyler Community College); Sandra Petree (Northwestern Oklahoma State University); Angela Pettit (Tarrant County College NE); Michell Phifer (University of Texas–Arlington); Ziva Piltch (Rockland Community College); Nancy Popkin (Harris-Stowe State University); Marlana Portolano (Towson University); Rhonda Powers (Auburn University); Lisa Propst (University of West Georgia); Melody Pugh (Wheaton College); Jonathan Purkiss (Pulaski Technical College); Patrick Quinn (College of Southern Nevada); Peter Rabinowitz (Hamilton College); Evan Radcliffe (Villanova University); Jody Ragsdale (Northeast Alabama Community College); Ken Raines (Eastern Arizona College); Gita Rajan (Fairfield University); Elizabeth Rambo (Campbell University); Richard Ramsey (Indiana University–Purdue University Fort Wayne); Jonathan Randle (Mississippi College); Amy Randolph (Waynesburg University); Rodney Rather (Tarrant County College Northwest); Helaine Razovsky (Northwestern State University); Rachel Reed (Auburn University); Karin Rhodes (Salem State College); Donald R. Riccomini (Santa Clara University); Christina Roberts (Otero Junior College); Paula Robison (Temple University); Jean Roelke (University of North Texas); Barrie Rosen (St. John's University); James Rosenberg (Point Park University); Sherry Rosenthal (College of Southern Nevada); Daniel Ross (Columbus State University); Maria Rouphail (North Carolina State University); Lance Rubin (Arapahoe Community College); Mary Ann Rygiel (Auburn University); Geoffrey Sadock (Bergen Community College); Allen Salerno (Auburn University); Mike Sanders (Kent State University); Deborah Scally (Richland College); Margaret Scanlan (Indiana University South Bend); Michael Schaefer (University of Central Arkansas); Tracy Schaelen (Southwestern College); Daniel Schenker (University of Alabama–Huntsville); Robyn Schiffman (Fairleigh Dickinson University); Roger Schmidt (Idaho State University); Robert Schmidt (Tarrant County College–Northwest Campus); Adrianne Schot (Weatherford College); Pamela Schuman (Brookhaven College); Sharon Seals (Ouachita Technical College); Su Senapati (Abraham Baldwin Agricultural College); Phyllis Senfleben (North Shore Community College); Theda Shapiro (University of California–Riverside); Mary Sheldon (Washburn University); Donald Shull (Freed-Hardeman University); Ellen Shull (Palo Alto College); Conrad Shumaker (University of Central Arkansas); Sara Shumaker (University of Central Arkansas); Dave Shuping (Spartanburg Methodist College);

Horacio Sierra (University of Florida); Scott Simkins (Auburn University); Bruce Simon (SUNY Fredonia); LaRue Sloan (University of Louisiana–Monroe); Peter Smeraldo (Caldwell College); Renee Smith (Lamar University); Victoria Smith (Texas State University); Connie Smith (College of St. Joseph); Grant Smith (Eastern Washington University); Mary Karen Solomon (Coloardo NW Community College); Micheline Soong (Hawaii Pacific University); Leah Souffrant (Baruch College, CUNY); Cindy Spangler (Faulkner University); Charlotte Speer (Bevill State Community College); John Staines (John Jay College, CUNY); Tanja Stampfl (Louisiana State University); Scott Starbuck (San Diego Mesa College); Kathryn Stasio (Saint Leo University); Joyce Stavick (North Georgia College & State University); Judith Steele (Mid-America Christian University); Stephanie Stephens (Howard College); Rachel Sternberg (Case Western Reserve University); Holly Sterner (College of Coastal Georgia); Karen Stewart (Norwich University); Sioux Stoeckle (Palo Verde College); Ron Stormer (Culver-Stockton College); Frank Stringfellow (University of Miami); Ayse Stromsdorfer (Soldan I. S. H. S.); Ashley Strong-Green (Paine College); James Sullivan (Illinois Central College); Zohreh Sullivan (University of Illinois); Richard Sullivan (Worcester State College); Duke Sutherland (Mississippi Gulf Coast Community College/Jackson County Campus); Maureen Sutton (Kean University); Marianne Szlyk (Montgomery College); Rebecca Taksel (Point Park University); Robert Tally (Texas State University); Tim Tarkington (Georgia Perimeter College); Patricia Taylor (Western Kentucky University); Mary Ann Taylor (Mountain View College); Susan Tekulve (Converse College); Stephen Teller (Pittsburgh State University); Stephen Thomas (Community College of Denver); Freddy Thomas (Virginia State University); Andy Thomason (Lindenwood University); Diane Thompson (Northern Virginia Community College); C. H. Thornton (Northwest-Shoals Community College); Elizabeth Thornton (Georgia Perimeter); Burt Thorp (University of North Dakota); Willie Todd (Clark Atlanta University); Martin Trapp (Northwestern Michigan College); Brenda Tuberville (University of Texas–Tyler); William Tucker (Olney Central College); Martha Turner (Troy University); Joya Uraizee (Saint Louis University); Randal Urwiller (Texas College); Emily Uzendoski (Central Community College–Columbus Campus); Kenneth Van Dover (Lincoln University); Kay Walter (University of Arkansas–Monticello); Cassandra Ward-Shah (West Chester University); Gina Weaver (Southern Nazarene University); Cathy Webb (Meridian Community College); Eric Weil (Elizabeth City State University); Marian Wernicke (Pensacola Junior College); Robert West (Mississippi State University); Cindy Wheeler (Georgia Highlands College); Chuck Whitchurch (Golden West College); Julianne White (Arizona State University); Denise White (Kennesaw State University); Amy White (Lee University); Patricia White (Norwich University); Gwen Whitehead (Lamar State College–Orange); Terri Whitney (North Shore Community College); Tamora Whitney (Creighton University); Stewart Whittemore (Auburn University); Johannes Wich-Schwarz (Maryville University); Charles Wilkinson (Southwest Tennessee Community College); Donald Williams (Toccoa Falls College); Rick Williams (Rogue Community College); Lea Williams (Norwich University); Susan Willis (Auburn University–Montgomery); Sharon Wilson (University of Northern Colorado); J. D. Wireman (Indiana State University); Rachel Wiren (Baptist Bible College); Bertha Wise (Oklahoma City Community College); Sallie Wolf (Arapahoe

Community College); Rebecca Wong (James Madison University); Donna Woodford-Gormley (New Mexico Highlands University); Paul Woodruff (University of Texas–Austin); William Woods (Wichita State University); Marjorie Woods (University of Texas–Austin); Valorie Worthy (Ohio University); Wei Yan (Darton College); Teresa Young (Philander Smith College); Darcy Zabel (Friends University); Michelle Zenor (Lon Morris College); and Jacqueline Zubeck (College of Mount Saint Vincent).

THE NORTON ANTHOLOGY OF

WORLD
LITERATURE

SHORTER THIRD EDITION

VOLUME 1

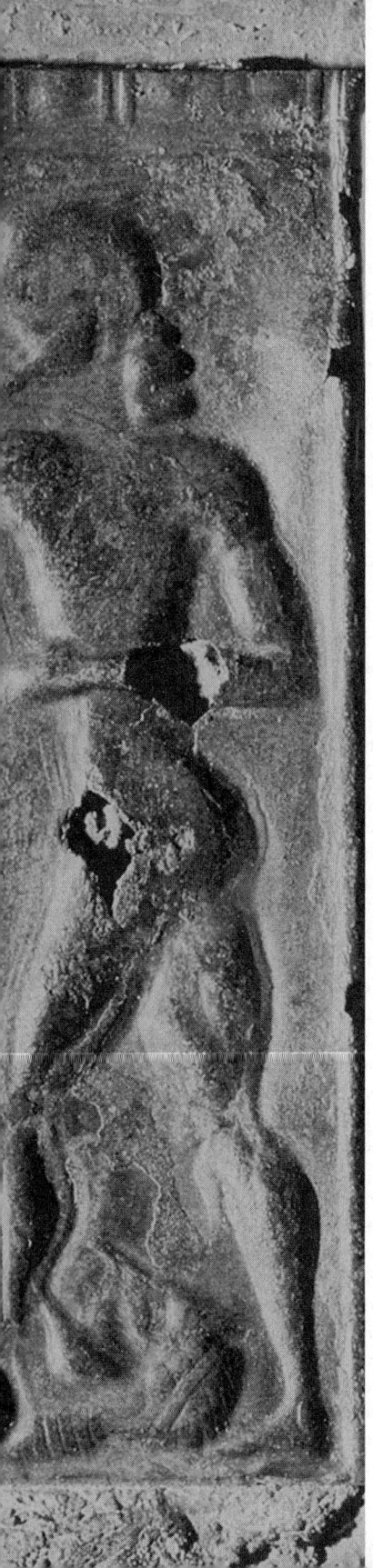

I

Ancient Mediterranean and Near Eastern Literature

THE INVENTION OF WRITING AND THE EARLIEST LITERATURES

The word "literature" comes from the Latin for "letters." "Oral literature" is therefore a contradiction in terms. Most modern westerners assume that literature is something we read in books; it is, by definition, written language. But people told stories and sang songs long before they had any means to record them. Oral types of song, poetry, and storytelling are quite different from those produced by writing, and it is difficult for us, living in an age dominated by printed and digital language, to imagine a world where nobody could read or write. Preliterate societies had different intellectual values from our own. We tend to think that a "good" story or essay is one that is neatly organized, original, and free from obvious repetition; we think of clichés as a mark of bad writing. But people without literacy tend to love stock phrases, traditional sayings, and proverbs. They are an essential mechanism by which cultural memory is preserved. Before writing, there was no such thing as an "author"—a single individual who, all alone, creates a text to be experienced by a solitary, silent reader. Instead,

King Priam asks Achilles for the body of his son, Hector. From an archaic Greek bronze relief, ca. 570–560 B.C.E.

3

poets, singers, and storytellers echoed and manipulated the old tales and the inherited wisdom of their people.

Of course, without either writing or recording equipment, all oral storytelling is inevitably lost. The tales that were told before there was writing cannot be collected in any anthology. But they left their mark on the earliest works of written literature—and many subsequent ones as well. As one would expect, literacy did not take hold all at once; the transition was partial and gradual, and in much of the ancient world, poetry and storytelling were less closely associated with written texts than they are for us. Plato's *Phaedrus* gives us some indication that the ancient Athenians were conscious of the enormous cultural change involved in the invention of writing. Nostalgia for the days before literacy continued into the later ancient world. By the time of the early Roman Empire—whose culture was much more literate than that of classical Athens—poets could make self-conscious efforts to imitate oral gestures, as when **Virgil**, writing his ultraliterate epic, the *Aeneid*, pretends to be an oral poet: "Wars and a man I sing."

An administrative tablet from Mesopotamia, ca. 3100–2900 B.C.E.

Writing was not originally invented to preserve literature. The earliest written documents we have contain commercial, administrative, political, and legal information. It was in the region of the Tigris and Euphrates rivers, Mesopotamia (which means "the place between the rivers"), that writing was first developed; the earliest texts date from around 3300 to 2990 B.C.E. The characters of this writing were inscribed on tablets of wet clay with a pointed stick; the tablets were then left in the sun to bake hard. The characters are pictographic: the sign for *ox* looks like an ox head and so on. The bulk of the texts are economic—lists of food, textiles, and cattle. But the script cannot handle anything much more complicated than lists, and by 2800 B.C.E. scribes began to use the wedge-shaped end of the stick to make marks rather than the pointed end to draw pictures. The resulting script is known as cuneiform, from the Latin word *cuneus*, "a wedge." By 2500 B.C.E. cuneiform was used for many things beyond administrative lists: the texts preserved historical events and even, finally, literature. It was on clay tablets and in cuneiform script that the great Sumerian epic poem *Gilgamesh* was written down. This writing system was not, however, designed for a large reading public. Each sign denoted a syllable—consonant plus a vowel—which meant that the reader had to be familiar with a large number of signs. Furthermore, the same sign often represented two or more different sounds, and the same sound could be represented by several different signs. It is a script that could be written and read only by experts, the scribes, who often proudly recorded their own names on the tablets.

The writing system invented by the Egyptians was even more

A limestone stele (ca. fourth century B.C.E.) in the shape of the symbol of the Phoenician goddess Tanit, with Punic script (a derivative of Phoenician) carved into its surface.

esoteric than cuneiform. It is called hieroglyphic, an adjective formed from the Greek words for "sacred" and "carving." Although it appears on many different materials, its most conspicuous and continuous use was for inscriptions carved on temple walls and public monuments. It was pictographic, like the earliest Sumerian script, but the pictures were more elaborate and artistic. Unlike the Sumerian pictographs, they were not replaced by a more efficient system; the pictures remained in use for the walls of temples and tombs, while more cursive versions of hieroglyphics—the hieratic and demotic scripts—were developed for faster writing. But the Egyptians soon developed their system to include signs standing for sounds, as well as for single objects: for instance, the same sign could mean either "house," pr, or simply the sound pr. This was only one of many complications that made even the modified versions of the script a difficult medium of communication for anyone not trained in its intricacies. It is no wonder that one of the

frequent figures to appear in Egyptian sculpture and painting is the professional scribe, his legs tucked underneath him, his writing material in his lap, and his brush in his hand.

There was one ancient writing system that, unlike cuneiform and hieroglyphic, survived in modified forms, until the present day. It was developed by the Phoenicians, a Semitic trading people. The script consisted of twenty-two simple signs for consonantal sounds. Through trade, the Phoenician script spread all over the Mediterranean. It was adopted by the ancient Hebrews, among others. The obvious advantage of this system was that it was so easy to learn. But there was still one area of inefficiency in this system—namely, that the absence of notation for the vowels made for ambiguity. We still do not know, for example, what the vowel sounds were in the sacred name of God, often called the Tetragrammaton, because it consists of four letters; in our alphabet the name is written as YHWH. The usual surmise is Jahweh (yá-way), but for a long time the traditional English-language version was Jehovah.

One thing was needed to make the script even more efficient: signs for the vowels. This was the contribution of the Greeks, who, in the eighth or possibly the ninth century B.C.E., adopted the Phoenician script for their own language but used for the vowels some Phoenician signs that stood for consonantal combinations not native to Greek. They took over (but soon modified) the Phoenician letter shapes and also their names: alpha, a meaningless word in Greek, represents the original aleph ("ox"), and beta represents the original beta ("house"). The Greeks admitted their indebtedness; Greek myths told the story of Cadmus, king of Tyre, who taught the Greeks how to write, and, as the historian Herodotus tells us, the letters were called Phoenician.

The Romans, who adapted the Greek alphabet for their own language, carved their inscriptions on stone in the same capital letters that we still use today.

ANCIENT NEAR EASTERN AND MEDITERRANEAN CULTURES

Modern, postindustrial societies depend, economically, on machines and sources of energy to operate them. We use complex devices to produce food and clothes, to build roads and cities, to excavate natural resources (such as oil or coal), to construct nonnatural materials (such as plastics), to get from place to place, and to communicate with others across the globe: by phone, television, computers, and the Internet. In the ancient world, though metal was mined and worked, what we know as heavy industry did not exist. Coal and oil were not exploited for energy. War galleys were propelled by sail and human oarsmen;

armies moved, sometimes vast distances, on foot. People therefore relied far more heavily on the kind of natural resources that can be easily accessed by human labor: no ancient city could be built far from fresh water and fertile soil, on which to grow crops and graze animals for meat and wool. Where we use machines and fossil fuel, all the advanced civilizations of the ancient world depended for their existence on slaves, who worked the land; took care of animals and children; dug the mines; built houses, temples, cities and pyramids; manufactured household goods (ranging from basic tableware to decorative artwork); performed housework; and provided entertainment. Modern Western societies exploit natural resources and harness them by using the cheap human labor available in less "developed" countries; most of the time, we do not even think about the people who made our clothes, phones, or cars or about the energy it takes to produce them and dispose of them. Similarly, elite ancient Hebrews, Greeks, and Romans seem to

A relief from the Palace of Sargon, from the eighth century B.C.E. It shows the transport of large logs fueled by human rowers.

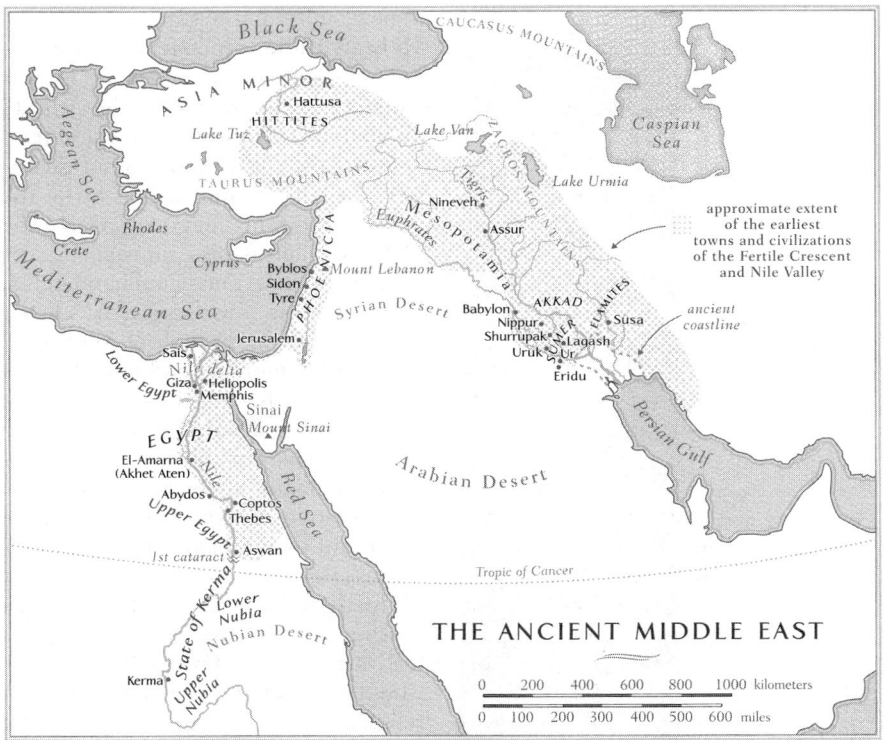

approximate extent
of the earliest
towns and civilizations
of the Fertile Crescent
and Nile Valley

ancient
coastline

THE ANCIENT MIDDLE EAST

| 0 | 200 | 400 | 600 | 800 | 1000 kilometers |

| 0 | 100 | 200 | 300 | 400 | 500 | 600 miles |

have taken slaves almost entirely for granted. The existence of ancient slavery should remind us not to idealize ancient cultures (even those of the "great Western tradition") and to remember how easily human beings, ourselves included, can be blinkered about the forms of injustice and exploitation that are essential to their cultural existence.

Because ancient societies depended on the proximity of natural resources, especially well-irrigated, fertile soil, the first civilizations of the Mediterranean basin developed in two regions that were particularly receptive to agriculture and animal husbandry. These areas were the valley of the Nile, where annual floods left large tracts of land moist and fertile under the Egyptian sun, and the valleys of the Euphrates and Tigris rivers, which flowed through the Fertile Crescent, a region centered on modern Iraq. Great cities—Thebes and Memphis in Egypt

and Babylon and Nineveh in the Fertile Crescent—came into being as centers for the complicated administration of the irrigated fields. Supported by the surplus the land produced, they became centers also for government, religion, and culture.

Later, from the second millennium B.C.E. onward, more cultures developed around the Mediterranean, including those of the Hebrews, the Greeks, and the Romans. These societies remained distinct from one another, and each included many separate social groups: we should be wary of generalizing about what "people in antiquity" believed or did. But it does make sense to consider the ancient Mediterranean and Near East as a single, albeit complex, unit, because there were large-scale cultural exchanges between these various peoples, as a result of trade, colonization, and imperialism. Greek sculpture

An archaic Greek grave stele of Aristion, ca. 510 B.C.E. This piece, although Greek, exhibits characteristics common to Egyptian and other Mediterranean and near Eastern sculpture.

a new cult to the sun god; and the **Hebrew Bible**, which featured the singular and "jealous" god that is now worshipped by many of the world's populations. But neither of these texts suggests that other gods do not exist— only that the creator deity is by far the most important and powerful. The Hebrew Bible is also unusual in suggesting, in the Ten Commandments, that religious observance is closely connected with the observance of a moral code; morality and religion were not necessarily linked in the ancient world, and gods of ancient literature often behave in obviously immoral ways. In many ancient cultures, religious practice ("orthopraxy") was more important than religious belief ("orthodoxy"). Religion involved a shared set of rituals and practices, which united a community in shared activities such as festivals and song; few ancient cultures would have understood the idea of a religious "creed" (a text outlining the specific beliefs of a particular religious community, to which all members must subscribe). Cult practices were often highly localized. We should, then, be wary of assuming that the stories about gods that appear in literary texts are necessarily a record of the religious beliefs of a whole culture. Myths circulated in many different forms, changing from one place and time to another; in most ancient cultures, composing alternative stories about the gods does not seem to have been regarded as "heretical," as it might seem to a modern Jewish, Christian, or Muslim reader.

and architecture of the seventh century B.C.E., for instance, show heavy debts to Egypt, and striking similarities between Greek and Near Eastern myths are probably the result of Mesopotamian influence.

Most ancient cultures were polytheistic (they believed in many gods); and since crosscultural religious influence was common, gods were often reinvented from one place to another. Ancient texts that emphasize a single deity over all others are rare: the most important exceptions to the polytheistic rule are the Egyptian *Great Hymn to the Aten*, composed at a time when the Egyptian monarchy was setting up

THE GREEKS

The origin of the peoples who eventually called themselves Hellenes is still a mystery. The language they spoke belongs clearly to the Indo-European family (which includes the Germanic,

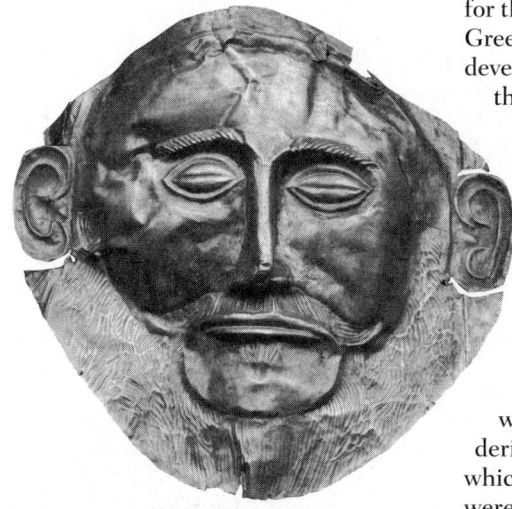

A gold "death mask" from Mycenae, ca. 1550–1500 B.C.E., sometimes referred to as the "mask of Agamemnon."

Celtic, Italic, and Sanskrit language groups), but many of the ancient Greek words and place names have terminations that are definitely not Indo-European—the word for sea (*thalassa*), for example. The Greeks of historic times were presumably a blend of native tribes and Indo-European invaders.

In the second millennium B.C.E., a brilliant culture, called Minoan after the mythical king Minos, flourished on the large island of Crete, centered around enormous palace structures; and the citadel of Mycenae and the palace at Pylos show that mainland Greece, in that same period, had a comparably rich culture, which included knowledge of a writing system called Linear B. But some time in the last century of the millennium, the great palaces were destroyed by fire. With them disappeared not only the arts and skills that had created Mycenean wealth but even the system of writing. For the next few hundred years, the Greeks were illiterate and so no written evidence survives

for this time, known as the Dark Ages of Greece. During this time, the Greeks developed the oral tradition of poetry that would culminate in the *Iliad* and the *Odyssey*.

The Dark Ages ended in the eighth century B.C.E., when Greece again became literate—but with a quite different alphabet, borrowed from the Phoenicians. At this time, Greece was still a highly fragmented place, made up of many small independent cities. These were known as "city-states" (a rendering of the Greek term *polis*, from which we get "politics"), because they were independent political and economic entities—not, like modern cities, ruled by a centralized national government. The geography of Greece—a land of mountain barriers and scattered islands—encouraged this fragmentation. The cities differed from each other in custom, political constitution, and even dialect: their relations with each other were those of rivals and fierce competitors. In the eighth and seventh centuries B.C.E., Greeks founded many new cities all over the Mediterranean coast, including some along the coast of Asia Minor. Many of these new outposts of Greek civilization experienced a faster economic and cultural development than the older cities of the mainland. It was in the cities founded on the Asian coast that the Greeks adapted to their own language the Phoenician system of writing, adding signs for the vowels to create their alphabet. The Greeks probably first used their new written language for commercial records and transactions, but as literacy became more widespread all over the Greek world in the course of the seventh century B.C.E., treaties and political decrees were inscribed on stone and literary works written on rolls of paper made from the Egyptian papyrus plant.

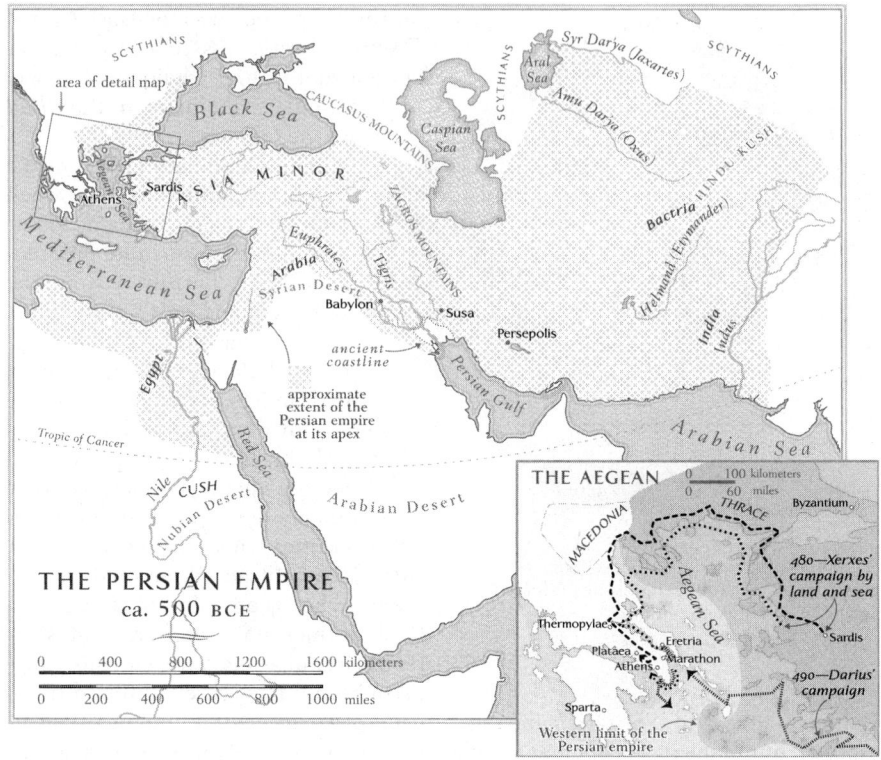

In the sixth century B.C.E., the Persian Empire dominated the Near East and Mediterranean areas, eventually becoming the largest empire in the ancient world. Millions of people lived under Persian control, and the ruling dynasty of Persia (the Achaemenids) conducted an expansionist policy, extending their domain from their center in Pasargadae (in modern Iran) east, as far as the Indus river, and west, into Egypt and Libya, as well as into the eastern parts of Greece, such as the cities of Ionia (in Asia Minor). The Persians had a sophisticated and globalized culture, influenced by the many other peoples they had encountered; their art was rich and intricate, and their architecture was impressively monumental. The empire was governed by a complex and highly developed political system, with the emperor at the top. The Persian army was huge and expertly trained, and it included vast numbers of skilled cavalrymen and archers. By the beginning of the fifth century B.C.E., the Persian Empire must have seemed all but unstoppable; it would have been reasonable for the Persians to assume that they could dominate the remaining parts of Greece. But surprisingly, the Greeks—led by Athens and Sparta—managed to repel repeated Persian invasions in the years 490 to 479 B.C.E., winning decisive naval battles at Marathon and Salamis. Their astonishing victory over Persia boosted the confidence of the Greek cities in the fifth century. Free from the fear of foreign invasion, the Athenians produced their most important literary and cultural achievements.

Sparta was governed by a ruling elite, an oligarchy ("rule of the few") that used strict military discipline to maintain control over a majority underclass. By contrast, Attica—the city-state of which Athens was the leading city—was at this time a democracy, one of the first such states in the world. "Democracy," which means "rule by the people," did not imply that all adult inhabitants had the chance to vote; "the people" were a small subset of the population, since women, slaves, and metics (resident aliens) were all excluded from the rights of citizenship. The citizens of Attica in the fifth century probably numbered only about thirty thousand, while the total population may have been ten times that. Slaves had no rights at all; they were the property of their masters. Women, even free-born women, could not own property, hold office, or vote. The elite women of Athens had less autonomy than those in most Greek city-states, including Sparta (where women were allowed to exercise outside in the gymnasium); in Athens, they were expected to remain inside the house except for funerals and religious festivals, rarely seen by men other than

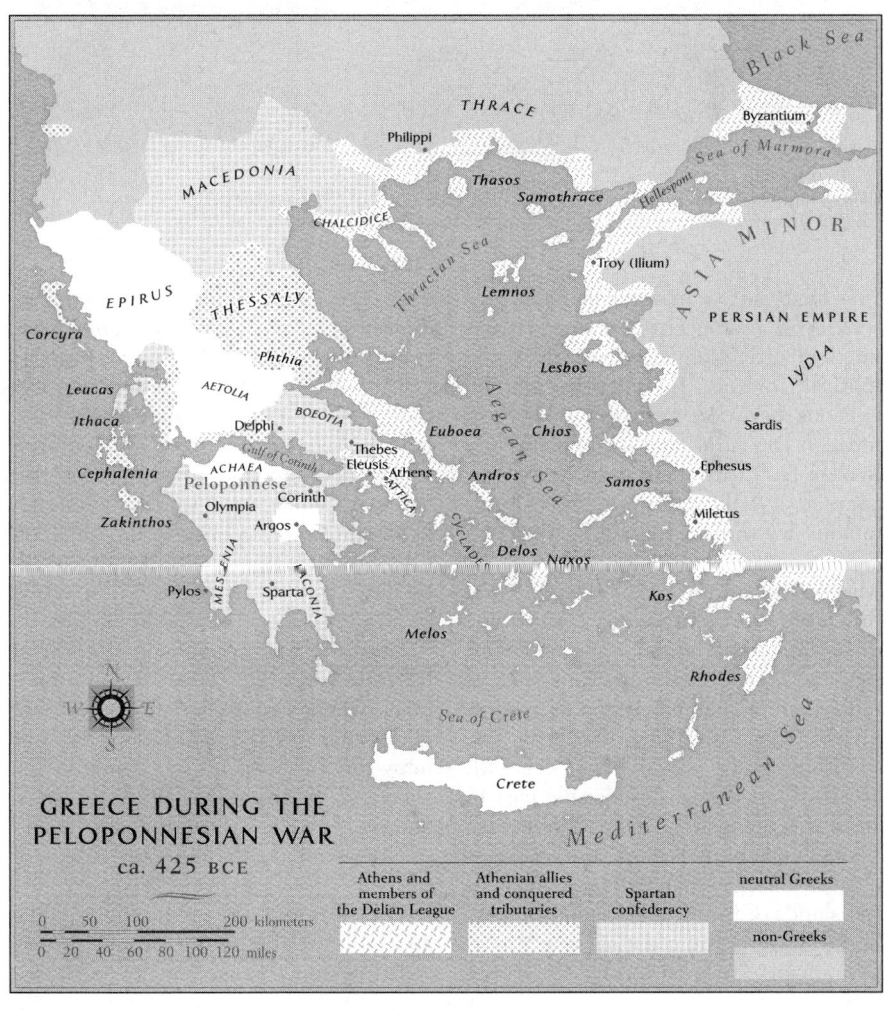

GREECE DURING THE
PELOPONNESIAN WAR
ca. 425 BCE

Athens and members of the Delian League	Athenian allies and conquered tributaries	Spartan confederacy	neutral Greeks
			non-Greeks

A contemporary artist's reconstruction of the Acropolis in fifth-century Athens. The Parthenon temple is the large structure near the top of the image.

their husbands or male relatives. Moreover, even among citizens who participated in civic life on a roughly equal political footing, there were marked divisions between rich and poor, and between the rural peasant and the city dweller. Still, Athenian democracy represented a bold achievement of civic equality for those who belonged. Since the voting population was so small, it was possible for the city to function as a direct, not representational, democracy: any citizen could attend assembly meetings and vote directly on the issues at hand—rather than electing a representative to vote in his place.

Athens' power lay in the fleet with which it had played its decisive part in the struggle against Persia, and with this fleet it rapidly became the leader of a naval alliance that included most of the islands of the Aegean Sea and many Greek cities on the coast of Asia Minor. This alliance, formed to defend Greece

from Persia, soon became an empire, and Athens, with its formidable navy, received an annual tribute from its "allies." Unlike Athens, Sparta was rigidly conservative in government and policy. Because the individual citizen was reared and trained by the state for the state's business, war, the Spartan land army was superior to any other in Greece, and the Spartans controlled, by direct rule or by alliance, a majority of the city-states of the Peloponnese. Athens and Sparta, allies in the war of liberation against Persia, became enemies when the external danger was eliminated. As the years went by, war between the two cities came to be accepted as inevitable by both sides, and in 431 B.C.E. it began. It was to end in 404 B.C.E. with the total defeat of Athens.

The fifth century saw many political and cultural changes in Athens, as the self-confidence roused by Persian victories, and celebrated by monumental displays of civic pride (such as the famous Parthenon temple to the city's goddess, Athena, completed in 438 B.C.E.), gave way to the increasing social tensions and anxieties of the war years. But fifth-century Athens was also at the center of cultural and intellectual changes that were without precedent in the ancient world. In the sixth century, Greeks on the Ionian coast had already begun to develop new, protoscientific ideas, alternatives to the old myths about how the world was made. Now many of the most original thinkers and writers from all over the Greek world began to gather in Athens. This time marked the beginning of new ways of thinking in many different areas. Greek doctors began to ask new questions about how the body works, including how environmental factors (such as climate and diet) affect health, and they supported their theories by observation. The first anthropological historian, Herodotus, analyzed and described how one culture differs from another (focusing on differences between Greeks, Persians, and Egyptians), while the first political historian, Thucydides, showed how economic and political factors could combine to cause war. These years marked the dawning of prose literature, in medicine, history, and philosophy. The fifth century was also the great age of Athenian theater: both tragedy and comedy developed and flourished at this time, and drama provided an essential outlet for the cultural confusions of the age.

Literary and intellectual changes accompanied changes in the ways that elite young men were educated. Throughout the Greek world, during the fifth century and beyond, children's education was based on the poems of Homer; Greek boys learned the tales of the *Iliad* and the *Odyssey* along with the alphabet, often from an educated slave tutor; sections of these poems were also performed, by trained actors (rhapsodes), as adult entertainment. But in the fifth century the education of adolescent boys changed. Intellectuals immigrating to Athens from other Greek cities met a new demand for their services as teachers, to train young men for public life, especially for the art of public speaking. These professional tutors, or Sophists ("wisdom teachers"), taught the techniques of rhetoric, as well as more substantial subjects like political science, ethics, literary criticism, even astronomy.

The Sophists were popular, and many parents were willing to spend large sums to have their sons trained by them. But, perhaps inevitably, the new educational methods, combined with the new intellectual trends sweeping the city, resulted in a generation gap. Older men felt that the new teachers had corrupted their sons and led them to question the value of traditional religious beliefs and practices. These fathers saw the intellectual advances of the fifth century as morally corrupting: some feared the corrosion of moral certainty when teachers made claims like that of the Sophist Protagoras, that "Man is the measure of all things." The most famous of the Sophists, in his own day as well as later, was Socrates. Socrates was in some ways an unusual Sophist: unlike the majority of these teachers, he was an Athenian citizen, not an immigrant from another city; and unlike other Sophists he seems to have demanded no fee for his teaching. But we should not be too quick to accept the sharp distinction that his pupil and defender, Plato, made between the (supposedly fraudulent) Sophists and the (genuinely philosophical) Socrates. Contemporaries—including the comedian Aristophanes, who wrote a play attacking Socrates' dangerous sophistry (*Clouds*)—made no such distinction. Socrates's interests and methods seemed to overlap with those of other wisdom teachers: like Protagoras, he investigated ethics, politics, and

A mosaic from a villa in Pompeii from ca. 100 B.C.E. depicts a philosophical discussion in the Academy of Plato.

truth through "dialectics," a method of question and answer—although, unlike Protagoras, he apparently believed in the possibility of true goodness. Still, his extraordinary mind and personality made him by far the most influential intellectual of his time, and—largely through the work of his most brilliant student, Plato—Socrates became the starting point for all later Western philosophy.

In the last quarter of the fifth century, the whole traditional basis of individual conduct, which had been concern for the unity and cohesion of the city-state, was undermined. "In peace and prosperity," says Thucydides, "both states and individuals are actuated by higher motives; . . . but war, which takes away the comfortable provision of daily life, is a hard master, and tends to assimilate men's characters to their conditions." Growing aggressive in their desperation, the Athenians were aware that they were faring badly in the war and launched a disastrous naval campaign in Sicily (413 B.C.E.), in which many ships were lost and many men lost their freedom and their lives. Unstable political conditions followed, leading to a short-lived oligarchic revolution at home

(411 B.C.E.). The war dragged on for another seven years, until finally Athens, her last fleet gone, surrendered to the Spartans. A pro-Spartan antidemocratic regime, the Thirty Tyrants, was installed but soon overthrown. Athens became a democracy again, but the confidence and unity of its great age were gone forever. One of the first actions of the new democratic government was to execute Socrates, who had been associated with Alcibiades and Critias and whose "corruption of the young" and unusual religious beliefs must have seemed to represent everything the city wanted to forget.

In the fourth century B.C.E., the Greek city-states became involved in constant internecine warfare. Politically and economically bankrupt, they fell under the power of Macedon in the north, whose king, Philip, combined a ferocious energy with a cynicism that enabled him to take full advantage of the disunity of the city-states. Greek liberty ended at the battle of Chaeronea in 338 B.C.E., and Philip's son Alexander inherited a powerful army and the political control of all Greece. He led his Macedonian and Greek armies against Persia, and in a few brilliant campaigns became master of an empire that extended into Egypt in the south and to the borders of India in the east. He died at Babylon in 323 B.C.E., and his empire broke up into a number of independent kingdoms ruled by his generals; modern scholars refer to the period that followed (323–146 B.C.E.) as the Hellenistic age. One of these generals, Ptolemy, founded a Greek dynasty that ruled Egypt until after the Roman conquest and ended only with the death of Cleopatra. The results of Alexander's fantastic achievements were more durable than might have been expected. Into the newly conquered territories came thousands of Greeks who wished to escape from the political futility and economic crisis of the homeland. Wherever they went, they took with them their language, their culture, and their typical buildings— the gymnasium and the theater. The great Hellenistic cities, though now part of kingdoms, grew out of the earlier city-state model and continued many of its civic and political institutions. At

A detail from a mosaic (dating from ca. 80 B.C.E.) discovered in Pompeii that shows Alexander the Great on horseback in battle.

ROMAN EXPANSION
through the 1st century CE

Roman influence at the beginning
of the First Punic War (3rd c. BCE)

Roman influence at the end
of the Punic Wars (2nd c. BCE)

The Roman Empire at the
death of Augustus (14 CE)

Designation of
broad regional
area of the empire

Designation of
region that came under
direct Roman rule
after 14 CE

Designation of neighboring
region that remained
independent or came
under direct Roman
rule only temporarily

Major provincial capital	▣ **Narbo**
Important provincial capital	◉ **Sirmium**
Important trading city	• **Aquileia**
Other city	○ **Verona**
Major trade route	— — —
Main road	·········
Naval bases	♨ **Misenum**
Legionary base	■
Fortified lines (to height of empire, 120 CE)	

0   200   400   600   800 kilometers

0   100   200   300   400   500 miles

Italia

Thracia

GERMANIA

Vistula

Dneiper

Prut

Dneister

SARMATIA

D a c i a

CARPATHIAN MOUNTAINS

Sirmium

Danube

Caspian Sea

CAUCASUS MOUNTAINS

Istrus/Tomis

Black Sea

ARMENIA

Sinope

Trapezus

P E R S I A

Amasia

Byzantium

T h r a c i a

Ancyra

A s i a

C a p p a d o c i a

ZAGROS MOUNTAINS

Thessalonica

M E S O P O T A M I A

Aegean Sea

Athens

Corinthus

TAURUS MOUNTAINS

Tarsus

Tigris

Rhodes

Antiochia

Euphrates

Cyprus

S e a

Crete

Damascus

Syrian Desert

Cyrene

Caesarea

Alexandria

Jerusalem

A e g y p t u s

Nile

Arabian Desert

Red Sea

Tropic of Cancer

A sculpture of a Roman nobleman of the first century B.C.E. holding the busts of two of his ancestors. Honoring one's ancestors was a core virtue in Roman life.

Alexandria, in Egypt, the Ptolemies formed a Greek library to preserve the texts of Greek literature for the scholars who studied and edited them, a school of Greek poetry flourished, and Greek geographers and mathematicians made new advances in science. The Middle East became, as far as the cities were concerned, a Greek-speaking region; and when, some two or three centuries later, the first accounts of the life and teaching of Jesus of Nazareth were recorded, they were written in the simple vernacular Greek known as *koine* ("the common language"), on which the cultural homogeneity of the whole area was based.

ROME

When Alexander died in 323 B.C.E., the city of Rome was engaged in a struggle for the control of the surrounding areas. By the middle of the third century B.C.E., Rome dominated most of the Italian peninsula. Expansion southward brought Rome into collision with Carthage, a city in North Africa that was then the greatest power in the western Mediterranean. Two protracted wars resulted (264–241 and 218–201 B.C.E.), and it was only at the end of a third, shorter war (149–146 B.C.E.) that the Romans destroyed their great rival. The second Carthaginian (or Punic) War was particularly hard fought, both in Spain and in Italy itself, where the Carthaginian general Hannibal, having made a spectacular crossing of the Alps, operated for years, and where Rome's southern Italian allies defected to Carthage and had to be slowly won over again. Rome, however, emerged from this war in 201 B.C.E. not merely victorious but a world power. The next two decades saw frequent wars—in Spain, in Greece, and in Asia Minor—that laid the foundations of the Roman Empire.

Unlike Athens, Rome was never a democracy. Instead, from around 509 B.C.E.—when, according to legend, the last tyrannical king of Rome had been overthrown—the state was governed by a complex political system (which changed and developed over time) known as a republic. Power was shared among several different official groups of people, which included the Senate, a body that controlled money and administration, and that was traditionally dominated by the upper classes;

the Assemblies, gathered from the people, including lower class or "plebeian" citizens; and elected officials called Magistrates, the most important of whom were the two Consuls, elected every year. The system (one of the most important models for the United States Constitution many centuries later) was designed, above all, to prevent any single person or group from seizing total control. The republic would last until the time of the Roman civil wars, in the first century B.C.E.

The Greeks believed that arguing, strife, and competition can be good, since they inspire us to outdo others and improve ourselves. The Romans, by contrast, saw conflict as deadly: it was what, in Roman mythology, led the founder of their city, Romulus, to kill his twin brother, Remus. Whereas the Athenians prided themselves on adaptability, versatility, and grace, the Roman idea of personal and civic virtue was based on a sense of tradition, a myth of old Roman virtue and integrity. "By her ancient customs and her men the Roman state stands," wrote Ennius, a Roman epic poet, capturing an ethos that emphasized tradition (known as the *mos maiorum*, the custom of predecessors) and commended "seriousness" (*gravitas*), "manly courage" (*virtus*), "industry" (*diligentia*), and above all, "duty" (*pietas*). Roman power was built on efficiency, and strength through unity. The Romans organized a complicated yet stable federation that held Italy loyal to them in the presence of invading armies, and they developed a legal code that formed the model for all later European and American law. The achievements of the Romans, in conquest and in organizing their empire after victory, were due in large part to their talent for practical affairs. They built sewers, baths with hot and cold water, straight roads, and aqueducts to last two thousand years.

A Roman aqueduct, built in the first century B.C.E., still standing at Pont du Gard in France.

Given the Romans' pragmatism and adherence to tradition, one might expect their literature to be very dull. But this is not true at all. Roman poets often struggled with, or frankly rejected, the moral codes of their society. The poems of **Catullus**, an aristocratic young man who lived in the last years of the Roman Republic (first century B.C.E.), suggest a deliberate attempt to thumb his nose at the serious Roman topics of politics, war, and tradition. Instead, Catullus writes about love, sex, and feelings and satirizes the people he finds most annoying. A generation or two later, both Virgil and **Ovid** also question—in very different ways—whether unthinking loyalty to the Roman state is a desirable goal.

By the end of the first century B.C.E., Rome was the capital of an empire that stretched from the Straits of Gibraltar to Mesopotamia and the frontiers of Palestine, and as far north as Britain. While Greek history began with the epics of Homer (instrumental in creating a sense of Greek national identity that transcended the divisions of the many city-states), the Romans had conquered half the world before they began to write. Latin literature began with a translation of the *Odyssey,* made by a Greek prisoner of war; and, with the exception of satire, the model was always Greek. Roman authors borrowed wholesale from Greek originals, not furtively but openly and proudly, as a tribute to the source. But this frank acknowledgment of indebtedness should not blind us to the fact that Latin literature is original, and sometimes profoundly so. Catullus translated the Greek lyric poet **Sappho**, but he added to her evocation of agonizing jealousy a distinctively Roman anxiety about idleness. Ovid retold Greek myths, making them funnier by giving

them a Roman rhetorical punch. Virgil based his epic, the *Aeneid*, on Homer, but he chose as his theme the coming of the Trojan prince Aeneas to Italy, where he was to found a city from which, in the fullness of time, would come "the Latin race . . . and the high walls of Rome."

The institutions of the Roman city-state proved inadequate for world government. The second and first centuries B.C.E. were dominated by civil war, between various factions vying for power: generals against senators and populists against aristocrats. Coalitions were formed, but each proved unstable. Julius Caesar, a successful Roman general, seized power (although he refused the title "king"); but he was assassinated in 44 B.C.E. by a party hoping to restore the old system of shared rule. More years of civil war followed, until finally, in 31 B.C.E., Julius's adoptive nephew, Octavian—who later titled himself Augustus—managed to defeat the ruler of the eastern half of the empire, Mark Antony, along with Antony's ally and lover, Cleopatra, queen of Egypt. Augustus played his hand carefully, claiming that he was restoring the Republic; but he assumed primary control of the state and became the first in the long line of Roman emperors.

For the next two hundred years the successors of Augustus, the Roman emperors, ruled the Mediterranean and Near Eastern world. The empire covered a vast area that included Britain, France, all southern Europe, the Middle East, and the whole of North Africa. Some native inhabitants, in all these areas, were killed by the Romans; others were enslaved; many, both slave and free, were Romanized, acculturated into the norms of the Roman people. Roman culture stamped this whole area of the world in ways that can still be discerned today: the Romans built roads, cities, public baths and theaters and brought their literature and language—Latin—to the provinces they ruled. All modern Romance languages, including Spanish, French, and Italian, developed from the language spoken throughout the Roman Empire.

But controlling so many people, in so many different areas, from the central government in Rome was difficult and expensive. It could not be done forever. Marcus Aurelius (121–180 C.E.), who in his spare time wrote a beautiful book of thoughts about his struggle to live a good life (the *Meditations*), was the first emperor to share his power with a partner; this was the first official recognition that the empire was too big to be ruled by one man. The Romans fought a long losing battle against invading tribes from the north and east. When it finally fell, the empire left behind it the idea of the world-state, later adopted by the medieval church, which ruled from the same center, Rome, and which claimed a spiritual authority as great as the secular authority it replaced.

THE BABYLONIAN CREATION EPIC
(*ENUMA ELISH*)

Enuma Elish ("When on high"), titled from the opening words of the poem, is an Akkadian poem that may have originated as early as the eighteenth century B.C.E. (although some have dated it to the twelfth century B.C.E.). Even this ancient story combined several other, much earlier cosmogonies, from Sumerian, Old Akkadian, and West Semitic cultures, that told of the warrior god's struggle against the primeval female sea monster (Tiamat). The narrative structure of our text reflects a clear agenda: the author gives pride of place to the Babylonian god, Marduk, whose temple in Babylon becomes the religious and political center of the world. The story traces the world's creation: from the two primary personifications of ocean (fresh and salt, Apsu and Tiamat) out of which emerge the earliest gods—who fight against the fresh ocean, the father-figure Apsu, when he wants to destroy them and restore primeval silence. Then Marduk, the creator god, kills Tiamat and from her body fashions the world; he establishes the first city, Babylon, where he has his cosmic home in the Esagila temple. Marduk's father, Ea, creates the first humans out of the blood of Qingu, Tiamat's consort and general, and these are to serve the gods' many needs. Finally, Marduk creates the netherworld, providing a mythic space for human existence after death.

From The Babylonian Creation Epic (*Enuma Elish*)[1]

From *Tablet I*

When on high no name was given to heaven,
Nor below was the netherworld called by name,
Primeval Apsu was their progenitor.
And matrix-Tiamat was she who bore them all,[2]
They were mingling their waters together,   5
No canebrake was intertwined nor thicket matted close.[3]
When no gods at all had been brought forth,
Nor called by names, none destinies ordained,
Then were the gods formed within the(se two).

* * *

From *Tablet V*

Marduk creates Babylon as the terrestrial counterpart to Esharra, abode of the gods in heaven. The gods are to repose there during their earthly sojourns.

Marduk made ready to speak and said
(These) words to the gods his fathers,
"Above Apsu, the azure dwelling,
"As a counterpart to Esharra, which I built for you,
"Below the firmament, whose grounding I made firm.   5
"A house I shall build, let it be the abode of my pleasure.
"Within it I shall establish its holy place.
"I shall appoint my (holy) chambers.
        I shall establish my kingship.
"When you go up from Apsu to assembly,
"Let your stopping places be here, before your assembly.[4]   10
"When you come down from heaven to [assembly],
"Let your stopping places be there to receive all of you.
"I shall call [its] name [Babylon],
        Houses of the Great Gods,[5]
"We shall all hold fe[stival]s with[in] it."
When the gods his fathers heard what he commanded,   15
They [. . .]
"Over all things that your hands have created,
"Who has [authority, save for you]?
"Over the earth that you have created,
"Who has [authority, save for] you?   20
"Babylon, to which you have given name,
"Make our [stopping place] there forever."

* * *

---

1. Translated by and with footnotes adapted from Benjamin R. Foster.
2. Before anything existed in the world, Mother Ocean, Tiamat, and Fresh Water, Apsu, mingled to produce the first pairs of gods.
3. Nothing divided or covered the waters.
4. When the gods or their cult images traveled to Babylon, they could stay in chambers at Marduk's temple.
5. Original meaning of the name Babylon.

From *Tablet VI*

The rebellious gods are offered a general pardon if they will produce their leader. They produce Qingu, claiming that he started the war. He is sacrificed, and his blood is used to make a human being.

When [Mar]duk heard the speech of the gods,
He was resolving to make artful things:
He would tell his idea to Ea,[6]
What he thought of in his heart he proposes,
"I shall compact blood, I shall cause bones to be,   5
"I shall make stand a human being, let 'Man' be its name.
"I shall create humankind,
"They shall bear the gods' burden that those may rest.
"I shall artfully double the ways of the gods:
"Let them be honored as one but divided in twain."[7]   10
Ea answered him, saying these words,
He told him a plan to let the gods rest,
"Let one, their brother, be given to me,
"Let him be destroyed so that people can be fashioned.
"Let the great gods convene in assembly,   15
"Let the guilty one be given up that they may abide."
Marduk convened the great gods in assembly,
He spoke to them magnanimously as he gave the command,
The gods heeded his utterance,
As the king spoke to the Anunna-gods (these) words,   20
"Let your first reply be the truth!
"Do you speak with me truthful words!
"Who was it that made war,
"Suborned Tiamat and drew up for battle?
"Let him be given over to me, the one who made war,   25
"I shall make him bear his punishment, you shall be released."
The Igigi, the great gods answered him,
To Lugaldimmerankia, counsellor of all the gods, their lord,
"It was Qingu who made war,
"Suborned Tiamat and drew up for battle."   30
They bound and held him before Ea.
They imposed the punishment on him and shed his blood.
From his blood he made humankind.
He imposed the burden of the gods and exempted the gods.
After Ea the wise had made humankind,   35
They imposed the burden of the gods on them!
That deed is beyond comprehension.
By the artifices of Marduk did Nudimmud create!

Marduk divides the gods of heaven and netherworld.
The gods build Esagila, Marduk's temple in Babylon

---

6. Before this text was written, creation in the Mesopotamian tradition was usually attributed to the Mother Goddess and Ea (or Enki), the god of wisdom and magic. In order to insert Marduk, the Babylonian city god, into this tra- dition, the text credits Marduk with giving Ea the idea for creating humankind.

7. Reference to the two main divisions of the Mesopotamian pantheon: the supernatural "Anunna-gods" and the infernal "Igigi-gods."

Marduk the king divided the gods,
The Anunna-gods, all of them, above and below,   40
He assigned to Anu[8] for duty at his command.
He set three hundred in heaven for (their) duty,
A like number he designated for the ways of the netherworld:
He made six hundred dwell in heaven and netherworld.
After he had given all the commands,   45
And had divided the shares of the Anunna-gods
        of heaven and netherworld,
The Anunna-gods made ready to speak.
To Marduk their lord they said,
"Now, Lord, you who have liberated us.
"What courtesy may we do you?   50
"We will make a shrine, whose name will be a byword,
"Your chamber that shall be our stopping place,
        we shall find rest therein.
"We shall lay out the shrine, let us set up its emplacement,
"When we come (to visit you), we shall find rest therein."
When Marduk heard this,   55
His features glowed brightly, like the day,
"Then make Babylon the task that you requested,
"Let its brickwork be formed, build high the shrine."
The Anunna-gods set to with hoes,
One (full) year they made its bricks.   60
When the second year came,
They raised the head of Esagila,[9] the counterpart to Apsu,
They built the upper ziggurat of Apsu,
For Anu-Enlil-Ea[1] they founded his [. . .] and dwelling,
He took his seat in sublimity before them,   65
Its pinnacles were facing toward the base of Esharra.
After they had done the work of Esagila,
All the Anunna-gods devised their own shrines.

* * *

Marduk is made supreme god. Anshar gives him a second name, Asalluhi. Anshar
explains Marduk's role among gods and men with respect to this second name.

After Anu had ordained the destinies of the bow,[2]
He set out the royal throne
        that stood highest among the gods,   70
Anu had him sit there, in the assembly of the gods.
Then the great gods convened,
They made Marduk's destiny highest, they prostrated themselves.

8. The sky god who is supreme in the pantheon but remote from human affairs. The
ancient city-state Uruk, where the great hero
Gilgamesh was king, was known for its temple
to Anu.
9. Wordplay on the name of Marduk's temple,

which means "house whose head is high."
1. Here three major gods of the Mesopotamian pantheon probably stand for the powerful Marduk.
2. Right before this passage, Marduk's bow is
made into a star constellation by the god Anu.

They laid upon themselves a curse (if they broke the oath),
With water and oil they swore, they touched their throats.³   75
They granted him exercise of kingship over the gods,
They established him forever
        for lordship of heaven and netherworld.
Anshar⁴ gave him an additional name, Asalluhi,
"When he speaks, we will all do obeisance,
"At his command the gods shall pay heed.   80

                              *   *   *

*Beginning of the explanation of Marduk's fifty names. Names 1–9 are those borne by
Marduk prior to this point in the narrative. Each of them is correlated with crucial
points in the narrative as follows: his birth, his creation of the human race to provide
for the gods, his terrible anger but his willingness to spare the rebellious gods, his
proclamation by the gods as supreme among them, his organization of the cosmos,
his saving the gods from danger, his sparing the gods who fought on the side of Tiamat, but his killing of Tiamat and Qingu, and his enabling the gods to proceed with
the rest of what is narrated.*

"Let us pronounce his fifty names,
"That his ways shall be (thereby) manifest, his deeds likewise(?):
        MARDUK!
"Who, from his birth, was named by his forefather Anu,
"Establisher of pasture and watering place,
        who enriches (their) stables,
"Who by his Deluge weapon subdued the stealthy ones,   85
"Who saved the gods his forefathers from danger.
"He is indeed the Son, the Sun,
        the most radiant of the gods,
"They shall walk in his brilliant light forever.
"On the people whom he made,
        creatures with the breath of life,
"He imposed the gods' burden, that those be released.   90
"Creation, destruction, absolution, punishment:
"Each shall be at his command, these shall gaze upon him.
"MARUKKA shall he be,
        the god who created them (humankind),
"Who granted (thereby) the Anunna-gods contentment,
        who let the Igigi-gods rest.
"MARUTUKKU shall be the trust of his land,
        city, and people,   95
"The people shall heed him forever."
The rest of the fifty names of Marduk follow here.

                              *   *   *

3. A slashing gesture people performed when
taking an oath to show what should happen to
those who break it.
4. God of the second generation after the

creator couple Tiamat and Apsu. Anshar,
"Whole Heaven," is coupled with Kishar,
"Whole Earth."

From *Tablet VII*

Composition and purpose of this text, its approval by Marduk.

They must be grasped: the "first one"[5] should reveal (them),
The wise and knowledgeable should ponder (them) together,
The master should repeat, and make the pupil understand.
The "shepherd," the "herdsman" should pay attention,[6]
He must not neglect the Enlil of the gods, Marduk,   5
So his land may prosper and he himself be safe.
His word is truth, what he says is not changed,
Not one god can annul his utterance.
If he frowns, he will not relent,
If he is angry, no god can face his rage.   10
His heart is deep, his feelings all encompassing,
He before whom crime and sin must appear for judgment.
The revelation (of the names) that the "first one"
        discoursed before him (Marduk),
He wrote down and preserved for the future to hear,
The [wo]rd of Marduk who created the Igigi-gods,   15
[His/Its   ] let them [   ], his name let them invoke.
Let them sound abroad the song of Marduk,
How he defeated Tiamat and took kingship.

5. As in other Mesopotamian mythical stories, this part explains how the text originated
and how it should be used by later ages. The
"first one" probably refers to somebody who
recites or "reveals" the text during a religious
ceremony. This epilogue emphasizes the
sacredness of the text—approved by Marduk
himself—which should not be changed by
future generations.
6. "Shepherd" is a cliché for king.

EGYPTIAN LOVE POEMS

ca. 1300–1100 B.C.E.

Ancient Egypt has one of the world's oldest literary traditions. The only others that can match its antiquity and longevity are those of ancient Mesopotamia, China, and India. Stretching over almost three millennia, from perhaps as early as 2700 B.C.E. to the common era, the texts that emerged from ancient Egypt display a remarkable range of themes, genres, and styles: biographical inscriptions honoring the dead from tombs, stone stelae, and statutes; hymns to the gods; accounts of travel adventures; laments of life and loss; wisdom texts advising future generations on how to live a good life in a flawed world; passionate love poetry; fantastic tales; and satirical fables.

For much of the Common Era, the literature of ancient Egypt was virtually unknown. Except for a few motifs and narratives that passed into Greek and from there into medieval European texts, the Egyptian literary tradition disappeared in the late fourth century C.E., and hieroglyphs, the "sacred engraved signs" of the Egyptian writing system, as the Greeks called them, could not be read. It was not until the nineteenth century that European scholars deciphered the forgotten language and gradually recovered Egypt's written heritage, including the rich body of its literature.

THE ORAL AND WRITTEN IN EGYPTIAN LITERARY CULTURE

Egyptian texts were written in successive forms of the ancient Egyptian language, a member of the Afroasiatic-language family that was distantly related to ancient Semitic languages such as Hebrew and Akkadian. The classical form of the language is Middle Egyptian, written from about 2000 B.C.E. onward; although Middle Egyptian continued to be used as an elevated literary language, it was partly displaced by Late Egyptian (ca. 1300–900 B.C.E.), and later by Demotic (ca. 650 B.C.E.–third century C.E.). For most of its history, Egyptian was written in two main scripts: the more ceremonial and elaborate hieroglyphic script and the cursive form using ink on papyrus, called "hieratic" or "priestly writing" by the Greeks, which was used for everyday affairs and for religious texts.

Literacy was restricted to elites in ancient Egypt; perhaps as few as one in a hundred people could read and write. Thus, literature was not a medium for broad consumption by reading but was enjoyed mostly through oral delivery.

The earliest longer texts come from the Old Kingdom in the third millennium B.C.E. Inscriptions carved in the tombs of high-ranking officials praise the moral worth of their occupants and sometimes tell of memorable events in their lives. They are in metrical form and carefully crafted. Thousands of such texts survive from the three millennia of ancient Egyptian history, and they constitute the largest category of continuous composition surviving from ancient Egypt.

THE CLASSICAL PERIODS OF EGYPTIAN LITERATURE

Kings of the Middle Kingdom (ca. 1940–1650 B.C.E.) expanded the use of writing and scribal schools. The first great period of Egyptian literature, which formed part of this development, saw the production of tales, wisdom texts, dialogues, and complaints. These genres employ complex imaginary settings and narrative frames such as cycles of stories.

During the New Kingdom era (ca. 1500–1000 B.C.E.), motifs deriving from the Near East became more prominent in Egyptian literature, part of a larger cosmopolitanism that resulted from Egypt's active relations with other countries. A bold affirmation of this life and its pleasures appears in a new genre of the New Kingdom, short poems performed at social gatherings, poems in praise of city life, and "harpist's songs," depicted as being performed by harpists, which meditate on the next life. In defiance of Egypt's traditional lavish tomb culture, some of these poems claim that constructing a monumental tomb with expensive grave goods is worthless and that one should instead enjoy this life on earth to the full. The passionate love lyrics featured in our selections appear only during the New Kingdom and are another expression of a forceful embracing of pleasures in this life.

THE LATE PERIOD (CA. 1000–30 B.C.E.)

The first millennium B.C.E. Egypt brought major upheavals to Egyptian society and literature. Egypt lost its imperial power and became the target of foreign invasions: as Nubians, Assyrians, Persians, and Alexander the Great's Macedonians swept through Egypt, ruling dynasties, the ethnic make-up of society, and religious beliefs and literary production changed drastically. Finally, in 30 B.C.E., Egypt lost its political independence; when Roman armies conquered the country, Queen Cleopatra, its last independent ruler, notoriously committed suicide by snakebite, and Egypt became a province of the Roman Empire.

Egypt is one of the world's great civilizations. Its culture faded during the third century C.E. and became overshadowed by the Hellenistic and Roman cultures that increasingly permeated Egypt's society. By that date, Egyptian literature had flourished for three millennia, three times longer than the most ancient European literary traditions today. With its fabulous age and rich record of innovation, Egypt's literature uniquely showcases the dynamics of change over time. It humbles us as we think about whether and how the world's literary traditions stand the test of time.

Although love poetry must have existed in oral form in earlier periods, love poems only survive on papyri, potsherds, and flakes of limestone from the later part of the New Kingdom. Looking at the women musicians and nearly nude girls singing and dancing in the paintings on tomb walls, we can imagine that love songs were performed with music and dance at banquets. Composed in rather informal, at times sexually explicit language, similar texts were also used in the cult of goddesses and in praise of royal women. Egyptian love poetry shows striking parallels with love poetry of other Near Eastern traditions, such as the somewhat later Song of Songs in the **Hebrew Bible**.

The lovers in the poems are young and often not yet free from parental supervision. As a gesture of endearment, they address each other as "brother" and "sister," words that have a broad meaning in ancient Egyptian. Roughly half of the poems are spoken by the girl, and half by the boy. (A small group, not represented in this selection, gives the words of the garden tree in whose shade the girl and boy have a tryst.) Many poems imagine situations in which the lovers might meet and make themselves attractive to each other: by going into the water to retrieve a fish— an erotic symbol—the girl, for example, can make her dress transparent and expose her charms. Many of the poems brim with imagery of the pleasures of desire and sex, but some also remind us how fleeting love can be: in one poem the girl worries, after the lovers have spent the night together, that the boy is now more interested in breakfast than in staying with her.

The Beginning of the Song That Diverts the Heart[1]

(*Girl*)
How beautiful is your beloved,[2]
    the one adored of your heart,
        when she has returned from the meadow!
My beloved, my darling,
    my heart longs for your love—   5
        all that you created!

1. All selections translated by Michael V. Fox.
2. In the original, this is literally "your sister." *Sister* and *brother* are frequent terms of affec-

tion in the Egyptian love songs. The terms imply intimacy, not consanguinity.

I say to you:
      See what happened!
I came ready to trap birds,
      my snare in one hand,   10
my cage in the other,
      together with my mat.[3]
All the birds of the land Punt[4]
      have descended on Egypt,
           anointed with myrrh.   15
The first to come
      takes my bait.
Its fragrance comes from Punt,
      its claws full of balm.[5]
My heart desires you.   20
      Let us release it[6] together.
I am with you, I alone,
      to let you hear the sound of my call,[7]
           for my lovely myrrh-anointed one.
You are here with me,   25
      as I set the snare.
Going to the field is pleasant (indeed)
      for one who loves it.[8]

[My god, my lotus . . .]

(*Girl*)
My god, my lotus . . .[1]
The north wind blows . . .
      How pleasant it is to go to the river. . . .
My heart longs to go down
      to bathe before you,   5
that I may show you my beauty
      in a tunic of the finest royal linen,
drenched in fragrant oils,
      my hair plaited in reeds.
I'd go down to the water with you,   10
      and come out to you carrying a red fish,[2]
           which feels just right in my fingers.

3. Perhaps to be placed as a cover over the birdcage.
4. A region bordering on the southern Red Sea from which aromatics came, as well as an ideal location known as "God's Land."
5. Or "its claws are caught by the balm." (The Egyptian can be read as a double entendre.) Birds were sometimes trapped by pitch smeared on a tree.
6. "It" is the "bait" mentioned before. This probably refers to the fulfilment of sexual desire.
7. Fowlers imitated bird calls to lure birds to the trap.
8. Just what "it" refers to is vague, perhaps intentionally so. Is it bird trapping? Lovemaking?
1. The lotus was the most important Egyptian flower, whose aroma was held to excite the senses. The "north wind" is the breeze that makes the heat bearable and brings the breath of life.
2. A tilapia, a well-known erotic symbol that was also used as an amulet made of red stone.

I'd set it before you,
    while gazing at your beauty.
O my hero, my beloved,   15
    come and see me!

(*Boy*)
My beloved's love
    is over there, on the other side,
The river surrounds my body.[3]
    The flood waters are powerful in this season,
        and a crocodile waits on the sandbank.   5
Yet I went down to the water
    to wade through the flood,
        my heart brave in the channel.
I found the crocodile to be like a mouse,[4]
    and the surface of the water like dry land to my feet.   10
It is her love
    that makes me strong.
        She casts a water spell for me!
I see my heart's beloved
    standing right before me!   15

(*Boy*)
My beloved has come,
    my heart rejoices,
        my arms are open to embrace her.
My heart is as happy in its place
    as a fish in its pond.   5
O night, you are mine forever,
    since my lady came to me!

[I wish I were her Nubian maid]

(*Boy*)
I wish I were her Nubian maid,
    her attendant in secret,
        as she brings her a bowl of mandragoras.[1]
It is in her hand,
    while she gives pleasure.   5
In other words:
she would grant me
    the hue of her whole body.[2]

---

3. He has—at least in imagination—stepped into the Nile, braving its dangers to reach the girl on the other side.
4. This alludes to tales of magic in which a magician can turn a tiny figure into a crocodile and vice versa.
1. The mandragora fruit was thought to be an aphrodisiac. It was also an erotic symbol, both for its flower and probably for its long taproot.
2. In the boy's fantasy, he is a maidservant in the girl's bedchamber. He would offer fruit while the girl gave him pleasure. That is to say, she would let him see her naked.

(*Boy*)
I wish I were the laundryman
    of my beloved's clothes,
        for even just a month!
I would be strengthened
    by grasping the garments   5
        that touch her body.
For I would be washing out the moringa oils[3]
    that are in her kerchief.
Then I'd rub my body
    with her castoff garments,   10
        and she . . .
O how I would be in joy and delight,
    my body vigorous!

(*Boy*)
I wish I were her little signet ring,
    the keeper of her finger!
I would see her love[4]
    each and every day,
And I would steal her heart.   5

[I passed close by his house]

Sixth Stanza[1]

(*Girl*)
I passed close by his house,
    and found his door ajar.
My beloved was standing beside his mother,
    and with him all his brothers and sisters.
Love of him captures the heart   5
    of all who walk along the way—
a precious youth without peer,
    a lover excellent of character!
He gazed at me when I passed by,
    but I must exult alone.   10
How joyfully does my heart rejoice, my beloved,
    since I first saw you!
If only mother knew my heart
    she would go inside for a while.
        O Golden One,[2] put that in her heart!   15
Then I could hurry to my beloved
    and kiss him in front of everyone,
        and not be ashamed because of anyone.

3. Moringa oil was the normal ancient Egyptian oil, and evidently could be perfumed.
4. Her capacity to inspire love.

1. This poem and the next are excerpted from a set of numbered stanzas.
2. Hathor, the goddess of love.

I would be happy to have them see
                that you know me,   20
                        and would hold festival to my Goddess.
My heart leaps up to go forth
                that I may gaze on my beloved.
How lovely it is to pass by!³

[Seven whole days]

Seventh Stanza

(*Boy*)
Seven whole days¹ I have not seen my beloved.
Illness has invaded me,
                my limbs have grown heavy,
                        and I barely sense my own body.
Should the master physicians come to me,   5
                their medicines could not ease my heart.
The lector priests² have no good treatment,
                because my illness cannot be diagnosed.
But if someone tells me, "Here she is!"—that will revive me.
                Her name—that is what will get me up.   10
The coming and going of her messengers—
                that's what will revive my heart.
More potent than any medicine is my beloved for me;
                more powerful than the *Physician's Manual*.
Her coming in from outside is my amulet.³   15
                If I see her, I'll become healthy.
If she but gives me a glance, my limbs will regain vigor.
                If she speaks, I'll grow strong.
If I hug her, she'll drive illness from me.
                But she has been gone for seven days.   20

[Am I not here with you?]

(*Girl*)
Am I not here with you?
                Then why have you set your heart to leave?
                        Why don't you embrace me?
Has my deed come back upon me?
If you seek to caress my thighs.   5
Is it because you are thinking of food
                that you would go away?
                        Or because you are a slave to your belly?

---

3. Each stanza in this seven-stanza song starts
and ends by punning on a word. In Egyptian
six and *pass by* sound alike.
1. The number seven is used because this is
the seventh stanza. Ancient Egypt did not have
a seven-day week.
2. Specialists in religious and magical texts.
Here the term means "magicians."
3. *Amulet* also means "well-being," and both
senses apply here.

Is it because you care about clothes?
  Well, I have a bedsheet!   10
Is it because you are hungry that you would leave?
  Then take my breasts
    that their gift may flow forth to you.
Better a day in the embrace of my beloved
  than thousands on thousands anywhere else!   15

THE EPIC OF GILGAMESH
ca. 1900–250 B.C.E.

The *Epic of Gilgamesh* is the greatest work of ancient Mesopotamia and one of the earliest pieces of world literature. The story of its main protagonist, King Gilgamesh, and his quest for immortality touches on the most fundamental questions of what it means to be human: death and friendship, nature and civilization, power and violence, travel adventures and homecoming, love and sexuality. Because of the appeal of its central hero and his struggle with the meaning of culture in the face of human mortality, the epic spread throughout the ancient Near East and was translated into various regional languages during the second millennium B.C.E. As far as we know, no other literary work of the ancient world spread so widely across cultures and languages. And yet, after a long period of popularity, *Gilgamesh* was forgotten, seemingly for good: after circulating in various versions for many centuries, it vanished from human memory for over two thousand years. Its rediscovery by archeologists in the nineteenth century was a sensation and allows us to read a story that for many centuries was known to many cultures and people throughout the Near East but has come down to us today only by chance on brittle clay tablets.

KING GILGAMESH AND HIS STORY

Gilgamesh was thought to be a priest-king of the city-state of Uruk in Southern Mesopotamia, the lands around the rivers Euphrates and Tigris in modern-day Iraq. He probably ruled around 2700 B.C.E. and was remembered for the building of Uruk's monumental city walls, which were ten kilometers long and fitted with nine hundred towers; portions of these walls are still visible today. We will never know for sure how the historical king compares to the epic hero Gilgamesh. But soon after his death, he was venerated as a great king and judge of the Underworld. In the epic he appears as "two-thirds divine and one-third human," the offspring of Ninsun, a goddess in the shape of a wild cow, and of a human father named Lugalbanda. By some accounts, *Gilgamesh* means "the offspring is a hero," or, according to another etymology, "the old man is still a young man."

Gilgamesh was not written by one specific author but evolved gradually over the long span of a millennium. The earliest story of Gilgamesh appears around 2100 B.C.E. in a cycle of poems in the Sumerian language. Sumerian is the earliest Mesopotamian language. It is written in "cuneiform" script—wedge-shaped characters incised in clay or stone—and has no connection to any other known language. About six hundred years after Gilgamesh's death, kings of the third dynasty of Ur, another Mesopotamian city-state, claimed descent from the legendary king of Uruk and enjoyed hearing of the great deeds of Gilgamesh at court; the earliest cycle of Gilgamesh poems was written for these rulers. As in the later epic, in the Sumerian cycle of poems Gilgamesh is a powerful king and an awe-inspiring warrior. Gilgamesh's shattering realization that he will die and can attain immortality only by making a name for himself appears already in this earliest version of the Gilgamesh story, where he exclaims:

> I have peered over the city wall,
> I have seen the corpses floating in
> the river's water.
> So too it will come to pass for me,
> so it will happen to me . . .
> Since no man can avoid life's end,
> I would enter the mountain land
> and set up my name.

The Sumerian poetry cycle became the basis for the old version of *Gilgamesh,* written in Babylonian, a variant of the Akkadian language—a transnational written language that was widely used throughout the Ancient Near East. The traditional Babylonian epic version of *Gilgamesh,* which adapted the Sumerian poems into a connected narrative, circulated for more than fifteen hundred years. It was read widely from Mesopotamia to Syria, the Levant, and Anatolia and was translated into non-Mesopotamian languages such as Hittite, the language of an empire that controlled Turkey and Northern Syria in the latter half of the second millennium B.C.E.

The definitive revision of the epic is attributed to a Babylonian priest and scholar named Sin-leqi-unninni. He lived around 1200 B.C.E., and by his time King Gilgamesh had been dead for about fifteen hundred years. He carefully selected elements from the older traditions, inserted new plot elements, and added a preface to the epic. His version, included here in translation, is divided into eleven chapters recorded on eleven clay tablets. New fragments of *Gilgamesh* continue to surface from archaeological excavations; some pieces are still missing, and some passages are fragmentary and barely legible, but thanks to the painstaking work of scholars of Ancient Mesopotamia we can today read an extended, gripping narrative.

THE WORLD'S OLDEST EPIC HERO

The Gilgamesh of the epic is an awe-inspiring, sparkling hero, but at first also the epitome of a bad ruler: arrogant, oppressive, and brutal. As the epic begins, the people of Uruk complain to the Sumerian gods about Gilgamesh's overbearing behavior, and so the gods create the wild man Enkidu to confront Gilgamesh. While Gilgamesh is a mixture of human and divine, Enkidu is a blend of human and wild animal, though godlike in his own way. He is raised by beasts in the wilderness and eats what they eat. When he breaks hunters' traps for the sake of his animal companions he becomes a threat to human society and Gilgamesh decides to tame him with the attractions of urban life and civilization: for seven days Enkidu makes love to a harlot (prostitute), sent out for the purpose, and at her urging he takes a cleansing bath and accepts clothing and a first meal of basic human foodstuff, bread, and beer. Shamhat, the prostitute, leads him to the city of Uruk. Although he and Gilgamesh are at first bent on competing with each other, they quickly develop a deep bond of friendship.

Their friendship established, Gilgamesh proposes to Enkidu the first of their epic adventures: to travel to the great Cedar Forest and slay the giant Humbaba, who guards the forest for the harsh god Enlil. With the blessing of the sun god Shamash they succeed, and they cut down some magnificent trees that they float down the Euphrates River to Mesopotamia. But their violent act has its consequence: the dying giant curses them and Enlil is enraged. Their second adventure leads to a yet more ambiguous success, which will set in motion the tragic end of their friendship. Gilgamesh, cleansed from battle and radiant in victory, attracts the desire of Ishtar, goddess of love and warfare. Instead of politely resisting her advances, Gilgamesh makes the fatal error of chiding her for her fickle passions and known cruelty toward her lovers, and heaps insults on the goddess. Scandalized by Gil-

gamesh's accusations, she unleashes the Bull of Heaven against the two friends, and it wreaks havoc in Uruk. After the heroic duo kills the Bull of Heaven, a council of the gods convenes to avoid further disaster. The gods decide that Gilgamesh and Enkidu have gone too far; one of them must die. The lot falls to Enkidu, because Gilgamesh is the king.

Enkidu's death brings Gilgamesh face to face with mortality. He mourns for Enkidu bitterly for seven days and nights and only when a worm creeps out of the corpse's nose does he accept that his friend is dead. Terrified that he too will die, Gilgamesh forsakes the civilized world to find the one human being known to have achieved immortality: Utanapishtim, survivor of the Great Flood. Like Enkidu in his days as a wild man, Gilgamesh roams the steppe, disheveled and clad in a lion-skin, and sets out on a quest to ask Utanapishtim for the secret of eternal life. He braves monsters, runs along the sun's path under the earth at night,

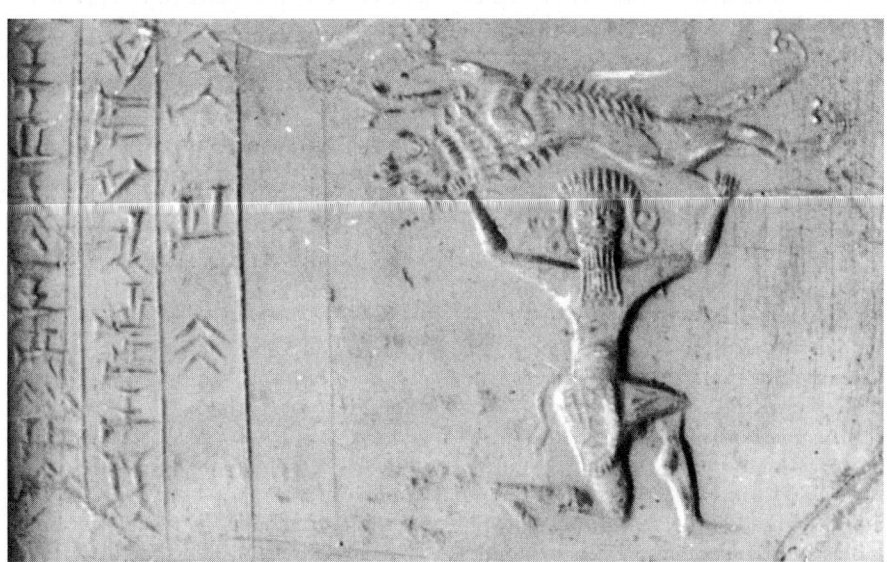

This modern impression of an ancient cylinder seal shows a bearded hero, kneeling and raising an outstretched lion above his head.

encounters a mysterious woman who keeps a tavern at the edge of the world, passes a garden of jeweled trees, crosses the waters of death, and finally arrives at the doorstep of Utanapishtim and his wife. Utanapishtim's dramatic account of their experience and survival of the flood resembles the biblical story of Noah and the Great Flood in Genesis. At his wife's request, Utanapishtim gives Gilgamesh the chance to attain immortality by eating a magic plant, but he is afraid to try it and a serpent steals the magic plant and gains the power of immortality for itself. In the end Gilgamesh returns to Uruk, empty-handed. Although in the final moments of the epic he proudly surveys the mighty city walls of his making, he is a profoundly changed man.

AN ANCIENT EPIC

The word *epic* comes from a Greek term meaning simply "speech" or "song." It has come to refer to long poems that use elevated language to describe a panoramic sweep of action, spanning the divine and human worlds. Greek epics usually invoke the Muses, goddesses in charge of the arts and a poet's inspiration who inform the poets of past events and the world of the gods. They often include long speeches, in which protagonists remember past events or justify future actions. And they rely heavily on the repetition of lines with variation and on a rhetoric of parallels and contrasts. Scholars of Homeric epic have argued that repetition and formulaic expression helped the bards to remember and recite extensive storylines and point to the poems' oral and performative roots.

Gilgamesh shares certain important features with Greek epic. Certainly, the verse form is different: a verse line is not defined by a fixed number of syllables or stresses but varies in length, which can only be inferred by context,

such as through patterns of parallelism. Still, in contrast to the literary works of other civilizations of the ancient world that had no epic, like China and East Asia, *Gilgamesh* can be considered part of a larger Near Eastern and Mediterranean epic tradition. Although *Gilgamesh* was only translated into cuneiform languages and never directly entered the epic repertoire of alphabet languages like Greek, it shared with the Greek tradition a number of classically epic motifs. In Achilles' mourning for his friend Patroclus (in Homer's *Iliad*) we can recognize Gilgamesh's desperation at the loss of Enkidu. Just as Gilgamesh finally returns to Uruk after challenging adventures, Odysseus (in Homer's *Odyssey*) returns to Ithaca from the Trojan War in the guise of a destitute stranger after performing dangerous feats. In *Gilgamesh* and Greek epics, scenes featuring councils of the gods who decide the fate of their heroes reflect religious beliefs about the intersection between human limitations and divine powers but are also astute plot devices that sharpen the profile of the heroes and their ways of confronting divine antagonism. We can see a parallel to the wiliness of the Greek gods and their personal preferences in the opposition of Shamash and Enlil, in particular in Enlil's argument that Enkidu should be sacrificed and Gilgamesh spared.

In contrast to the orally rooted Homeric epic, *Gilgamesh* was from the outset conceived as a literary work. With its elevated style, geometrically parallel phrases, and moments of complex word play, *Gilgamesh* was addressed to the sophisticated ears and minds of scholars and members of the royal court. We know that it was used in Babylonian schools to teach literature. This hypothesis is further supported when we look at the nuanced use of speech registers in the epic's portrayal of its protagonists. Utanapishtim speaks in an obscure archaic style that befits a sage from before the Great Flood, and he has a solemn way of rolling and doubling his consonants. The goddess Ishtar appears in an unfavorable light, talking like a low-class streetwalker. In contrast, Shamhat, the prostitute who brings Enkidu to the city, speaks with unexpected eloquence and distinction.

Shamhat is a thought-provoking example of the several powerful female protagonists in *Gilgamesh*. Much of what Gilgamesh accomplishes is ultimately due to women: his mother's pleas with the sun god Shamash allow him to kill Humbaba; the wife of the scorpion monster persuades her husband to give Gilgamesh entrance to the tunnel leading to the jeweled garden; and the mysterious woman he finds at the end of the world, the tavern keeper Siduri, helps him find Utanapishtim, whose wife persuades her husband to give Gilgamesh the plant of rejuvenation. In some of Gilgamesh's encounters there are touches of wit and parody. It is stunning to find this blend of epic grandeur and comic sobriety in the world's earliest epic. Part of the epic's subtlety is invisible today, because we know so much less about the historical and literary context of *Gilgamesh* than we know about the context of Greek epic. Still, the glimpses we get show the sophistication of the early Mesopotamian states and the art of literary narrative they developed.

Like Mesopotamian civilization and its cuneiform writing system, *Gilgamesh* eventually disappeared. In the seventh century B.C.E., when an invading force of ancient Iranian people called Medians sacked Nineveh, one of the capitals of the Assyrian Empire, copies of the epic written on clay tablets, which had been preserved in the palace library of Ashurbanipal, the last great Assyrian king (reigned 668–627 B.C.E.), vanished in the destruction. Although the epic did not disappear completely and still circulated until the third century B.C.E., it was only rediscovered in the 1850s, when an English explorer, Austen Henry Layard, dug up thousands of tablets from the site at Nineveh. They were later deciphered at the British Museum in London, and when the young curator George Smith made the stunning discovery that this epic contained a version of the biblical story of the flood, which had hitherto been considered unique to the book of Genesis, this challenged conceptions about the origin of biblical narrative. *Gilgamesh* was suddenly propelled into the canon of world literature.

The Epic of Gilgamesh took shape many centuries before the Greeks and Hebrews learned how to write, and it circulated in the Near East and Levant long before the book of Genesis and the Homeric epics took shape. The rediscovery of the names of the gods and humans who people the epic and of the history of the cities and lands in which they lived is a gradual, ongoing process. And the meaning of the epic itself is tantalizingly ambiguous. Has Gilgamesh succeeded or failed in his quest? What makes us human? Can civilization bring immortality? Whatever we decide to believe, the story of Gilgamesh and his companion Enkidu, of their quest for fame and immortality, speaks to contemporary readers with an urgency and immediacy that makes us forget just how ancient it is.

The Epic of Gilgamesh[1]

Tablet I

He who saw the wellspring, the foundations of the land,
Who knew the ways, was wise in all things,
Gilgamesh, who saw the wellspring, the foundations of the land,
He knew the ways, was wise in all things,
He it was who inspected holy places everywhere,   5
Full understanding of it all he gained,
He saw what was secret and revealed what was hidden,
He brought back tidings from before the flood,
From a distant journey came home, weary, at peace,
Engraved all his hardships on a monument of stone,   10
He built the walls of ramparted Uruk,[2]
The lustrous treasury of hallowed Eanna!
See its upper wall, whose facing gleams like copper,
Gaze at the lower course, which nothing will equal,
Mount the stone stairway, there from days of old,   15
Approach Eanna, the dwelling of Ishtar,
Which no future king, no human being will equal.
Go up, pace out the walls of Uruk,
Study the foundation terrace and examine the brickwork.
Is not its masonry of kiln-fired brick?   20
And did not seven masters lay its foundations?
One square mile of city, one square mile of gardens,
One square mile of clay pits, a half square mile of Ishtar's dwelling,
Three and a half square miles is the measure of Uruk!
Search out the foundation box of copper,   25
Release its lock of bronze,
Raise the lid upon its hidden contents,
Take up and read from the lapis tablet
Of him, Gilgamesh, who underwent many hardships.
Surpassing all kings, for his stature renowned,   30
Heroic offspring of Uruk, a charging wild bull,
He leads the way in the vanguard,
He marches at the rear, defender of his comrades.
Mighty floodwall, protector of his troops,
Furious flood-wave smashing walls of stone,   35
Wild calf of Lugalbanda, Gilgamesh is perfect in strength,
Suckling of the sublime wild cow, the woman Ninsun,[3]
Towering Gilgamesh is uncannily perfect.
Opening passes in the mountains,
Digging wells at the highlands' verge,   40
Traversing the ocean, the vast sea, to the sun's rising,
Exploring the furthest reaches of the earth,

1. Translated by and with footnotes adapted from Benjamin R. Foster.
2. City-state ruled by King Gilgamesh. It was the largest city of Mesopotamia at the time and among its important temples featured Eanna, a sanctuary for the goddess of love and warfare, Ishtar.
3. Lugalbanda, Gilgamesh's father, was an earlier king of Uruk. His mother was Ninsun, a goddess called "the wild cow."

Seeking everywhere for eternal life,
Reaching in his might Utanapishtim the Distant One,
Restorer of holy places that the deluge had destroyed,   45
Founder of rites for the teeming peoples,
Who could be his like for kingly virtue?
And who, like Gilgamesh, can proclaim, "I am king!"
Gilgamesh was singled out from the day of his birth,
Two-thirds of him was divine, one-third of him was human!   50
The Lady of Birth drew his body's image,
The God of Wisdom brought his stature to perfection.

He was perfection in height,
Ideally handsome
In the enclosure of Uruk he strode back and forth,   55
Lording it like a wild bull, his head thrust high.
The onslaught of his weapons had no equal.
His teammates stood forth by his game stick,
He was harrying the young men of Uruk beyond reason.
Gilgamesh would leave no son to his father,   60
Day and night he would rampage fiercely.
This was the shepherd of ramparted Uruk,
This was the people's shepherd,
Bold, superb, accomplished, and mature!
Gilgamesh would leave no girl to her mother!   65
The warrior's daughter, the young man's spouse,
Goddesses kept hearing their plaints.
The gods of heaven, the lords who command,
Said to Anu:[4]

    You created this headstrong wild bull in ramparted Uruk,   70
    The onslaught of his weapons has no equal.
    His teammates stand forth by his game stick,
    He is harrying the young men of Uruk beyond reason.
    Gilgamesh leaves no son to his father!
    Day and night he rampages fiercely.   75
    This is the shepherd of ramparted Uruk,
    This is the people's shepherd,
    Bold, superb, accomplished, and mature!
    Gilgamesh leaves no girl to her mother!

The warrior's daughter, the young man's spouse,   80
Anu kept hearing their plaints.

[*Anu speaks.*]

    Let them summon Aruru,[5] the great one,
    She created the boundless human race.

---

4. The sky god who is supreme in the pantheon but remote from human affairs. Uruk

was known for its temples for Anu and Ishtar.
5. Goddess of birth.

Let her create a partner for Gilgamesh, mighty in strength,
Let them contend with each other, that Uruk may have peace.   85

They summoned the birth goddess, Aruru:

You, Aruru, created the boundless human race,
Now, create what Anu commanded,
To his stormy heart, let that one be equal,
Let them contend with each other, that Uruk may have peace.   90

When Aruru heard this,
She conceived within her what Anu commanded.
Aruru wet her hands,
She pinched off clay, she tossed it upon the steppe,
She created valiant Enkidu in the steppe,   95
Offspring of potter's clay, with the force of the hero Ninurta.[6]
Shaggy with hair was his whole body,
He was made lush with head hair, like a woman,
The locks of his hair grew thick as a grainfield.
He knew neither people nor inhabited land,   100
He dressed as animals do.
He fed on grass with gazelles,
With beasts he jostled at the water hole,
With wildlife he drank his fill of water.

A hunter, a trapping-man,   105
Encountered him at the edge of the water hole.
One day, a second, and a third he encountered him at the edge
    of the water hole.
When he saw him, the hunter stood stock-still with terror,
As for Enkidu, he went home with his beasts.
Aghast, struck dumb,   110
His heart in a turmoil, his face drawn,
With woe in his vitals,
His face like a traveler's from afar,
The hunter made ready to speak, saying to his father:

My father, there is a certain fellow who has come
    from the uplands,   115
He is the mightiest in the land, strength is his,
Like the force of heaven, so mighty is his strength.
He constantly ranges over the uplands,
Constantly feeding on grass with beasts,
Constantly making his way to the edge of the water hole.   120
I am too frightened to approach him.
He has filled in the pits I dug,
He has torn out my traps I set,
He has helped the beasts, wildlife of the steppe, slip
    from my hands,
He will not let me work the steppe.   125

6. A god of agriculture and war. Son of Enlil.

His father made ready to speak, saying to the hunter:

My son, in Uruk dwells Gilgamesh,
There is no one more mighty than he.
Like the force of heaven, so mighty is his strength.
Take the road, set off towards Uruk, 130
Tell Gilgamesh of the mightiness-man.
He will give you Shamhat the harlot, take her with you,
Let her prevail over him, instead of a mighty man.
When the wild beasts draw near the water hole,
Let her strip off her clothing, laying bare her charms. 135
When he sees her, he will approach her.
His beasts that grew up with him on the steppe will deny him.

Giving heed to the advice of his father,
The hunter went forth.
He took the road, set off towards Uruk, 140
To the king, Gilgamesh, he said these words:

There is a certain fellow who has come from the uplands,
He is mightiest in the land, strength is his,
Like the force of heaven, so mighty is his strength.
He constantly ranges over the uplands, 145
Constantly feeding on grass with his beasts,
Constantly making his way to the edge of the water hole.
I am too frightened to approach him.
He has filled in the pits I dug,
He has torn out my traps I set, 150
He has helped the beasts, wildlife of the steppe, slip
    from my hands,
He will not allow me to work the steppe.

Gilgamesh said to him, to the hunter:

Go, hunter, take with you Shamhat the harlot,
When the wild beasts draw near the water hole, 155
Let her strip off her clothing, laying bare her charms.
When he sees her, he will approach her,
His beasts that grew up with him on the steppe will deny him.

Forth went the hunter, taking with him Shamhat the harlot,
They took the road, going straight on their way. 160
On the third day they arrived at the appointed place.
Hunter and harlot sat down to wait.
One day, a second day, they sat by the edge of the water hole,
The beasts came to the water hole to drink,
The wildlife came to drink their fill of water. 165
But as for him, Enkidu, born in the uplands,
Who feeds on grass with gazelles,
Who drinks at the water hole with beasts,
Who, with wildlife, drinks his fill of water,

Shamhat looked upon him, a human-man, 170
A barbarous fellow from the midst of the steppe:

> There he is, Shamhat, open your embrace,
> Open your embrace, let him take your charms!
> Be not bashful, take his vitality!
> When he sees you, he will approach you, 175
> Toss aside your clothing, let him lie upon you,
> Treat him, a human, to woman's work!
> His wild beasts that grew up with him will deny him,
> As in his ardor he caresses you!

Shamhat loosened her garments, 180
She exposed her loins, he took her charms.
She was not bashful, she took his vitality.
She tossed aside her clothing and he lay upon her,
She treated him, a human, to woman's work,
As in his ardor he caressed her. 185
Six days, seven nights was Enkidu aroused, flowing into Shamhat.
After he had his fill of her delights,
He set off towards his beasts.
When they saw him, Enkidu, the gazelles shied off,
The wild beasts of the steppe shunned his person. 190
Enkidu had spent himself, his body was limp,
His knees stood still, while his beasts went away.
Enkidu was too slow, he could not run as before,
But he had gained reason and expanded his understanding.

He returned, he sat at the harlot's feet, 195
The harlot gazed upon his face,
While he listened to what the harlot was saying.
The harlot said to him, to Enkidu:

> You are handsome, Enkidu, you are become like a god,
> Why roam the steppe with wild beasts? 200
> Come, let me lead you to ramparted Uruk,
> To the holy temple, abode of Anu and Ishtar,
> The place of Gilgamesh, who is perfect in strength,
> And so, like a wild bull, he lords it over the young men.

As she was speaking to him, her words found favor, 205
He was yearning for one to know his heart, a friend.
Enkidu said to her, to the harlot:

> Come, Shamhat, escort me
> To the lustrous hallowed temple, abode of Anu and Ishtar,
> The place of Gilgamesh, who is perfect in strength, 210
> And so, like a wild bull, he lords it over the young men.
> I myself will challenge him, I will speak out boldly,
> I will raise a cry in Uruk: I am the mighty one!
> I am come forward to alter destinies!
> He who was born in the steppe is mighty, strength is his! 215

[*Shamhat speaks.*]

Come then, let him see your face,
I will show you Gilgamesh, where he is I know full well.
Come then, Enkidu, to ramparted Uruk,
Where fellows are resplendent in holiday clothing,
Where every day is set for celebration,   220
Where harps and drums are played.
And the harlots too, they are fairest of form,
Rich in beauty, full of delights,
Even the great gods are kept from sleeping at night!
Enkidu, you who have not learned to live,   225
Oh, let me show you Gilgamesh, the joy-woe man.
Look at him, gaze upon his face,
He is radiant with virility, manly vigor is his,
The whole of his body is seductively gorgeous.
Mightier strength has he than you,   230
Never resting by day or night.
O Enkidu, renounce your audacity!
Gilgamesh is beloved of Shamash,
Anu, Enlil, and Ea broadened his wisdom.[7]
Ere you come down from the uplands,   235
Gilgamesh will dream of you in Uruk.

[*The scene shifts to Uruk.*]

Gilgamesh went to relate the dreams, saying to his mother:

Mother, I had a dream last night:
There were stars of heaven around me,
Like the force of heaven, something kept falling upon me!   240
I tried to carry it but it was too strong for me,
I tried to move it but I could not budge it.
The whole of Uruk was standing by it,
The people formed a crowd around it,
A throng was jostling towards it,   245
Young men were mobbed around it,
Infantile, they were groveling before it!
[I fell in love with it], like a woman I caressed it,
I carried it off and laid it down before you,
Then you were making it my partner.   250

The mother of Gilgamesh, knowing and wise,
Who understands everything, said to her son,
Ninsun the wild cow, knowing and wise,
Who understands everything, said to Gilgamesh:

The stars of heaven around you,   255
Like the force of heaven, what kept falling upon you,

7. Shamash was god of the sun and of oracles, overseeing matters of justice and right dealing; Enlil was supreme god on earth; Ea, a god of wisdom and magic, is known for his beneficence to the human race.

Your trying to move it but not being able to budge it,
Your laying it down before me,
Then my making it your partner,
Your falling in love with it, your caressing it like a woman,   260
Means there will come to you a strong one,
A companion who rescues a friend.
He will be mighty in the land, strength will be his,
Like the force of heaven, so mighty will be his strength.
You will fall in love with him and caress him like a woman.   265
He will be mighty and rescue you, time and again.

He had a second dream,
He arose and went before the goddess, his mother,
Gilgamesh said to her, to his mother:

    Mother, I had a second dream.   270
    An axe was thrown down in a street of ramparted Uruk,
    They were crowding around it,
    The whole of Uruk was standing by it,
    The people formed a crowd around it,
    A throng was jostling towards it.   275
    I carried it off and laid it down before you,
    I fell in love with it, like a woman I caressed it,
    Then you were making it my partner.

The mother of Gilgamesh, knowing and wise,
Who understands everything, said to her son,   280
Ninsun the wild cow, knowing and wise,
Who understands everything, said to Gilgamesh:

    My son, the axe you saw is a man.
    Your loving it like a woman and caressing it,
    And my making it your partner   285
    Means there will come to you a strong one,
    A companion who rescues a friend,
    He will be mighty in the land, strength will be his,
    Like the strength of heaven, so mighty will be his strength.

Gilgamesh said to her, to his mother: 290

    Let this befall according to the command of the great
      counselor Enlil,
    I want a friend for my own counselor,
    For my own counselor do I want a friend!

Even while he was having his dreams,
Shamhat was telling the dreams of Gilgamesh to Enkidu,
Each was drawn by love to the other.

Tablet II

While Enkidu was seated before her,
Each was drawn by love to the other.

Enkidu forgot the steppe where he was born,
For six days, seven nights Enkidu was aroused and flowed
   into Shamhat.
The harlot said to him, to Enkidu: 5

   You are handsome, Enkidu, you are become like a god,
   Why roam the steppe with wild beasts?
   Come, let me lead you to ramparted Uruk,
   To the holy temple, abode of Anu,
   Let me lead you to ramparted Uruk,   10
   To hallowed Eanna, abode of Ishtar,
   The place of Gilgamesh, who is perfect in strength,
   And so, like a wild bull, he lords it over the people.
   You are just like him,
   You will love him like your own self.   15
   Come away from this desolation, bereft even of shepherds.

He heard what she said, accepted her words,
He was yearning for one to know his heart, a friend.
The counsel of Shamhat touched his heart.
She took off her clothing, with one piece she dressed him,   20
The second she herself put on.
Clasping his hand, like a guardian deity she led him,
To the shepherds' huts, where a sheepfold was,
The shepherds crowded around him,
They murmured their opinions among themselves: 25

   This fellow, how like Gilgamesh in stature,
   In stature tall, proud as a battlement.
   No doubt he was born in the steppe,
   Like the force of heaven, mighty is his strength.

They set bread before him,   30
They set beer before him.
He looked uncertainly, then stared,
Enkidu did not know to eat bread,
Nor had he ever learned to drink beer!
The harlot made ready to speak, saying to Enkidu: 35

   Eat the bread, Enkidu, the staff of life,
   Drink the beer, the custom of the land.

Enkidu ate the bread until he was sated,
He drank seven juglets of the beer.
His mood became relaxed, he was singing joyously,   40
He felt lighthearted and his features glowed.
He treated his hairy body with water,
He anointed himself with oil, turned into a man,
He put on clothing, became like a warrior.
He took his weapon, hunted lions,   45
The shepherds lay down to rest at night.
He slew wolves, defeated lions,
The herdsmen, the great gods, lay down to sleep.

Enkidu was their watchman, a wakeful man,
He was tall.   50

He was making love with Shamhat.
He lifted his eyes, he saw a man.
He said to the harlot:

> Shamhat, bring that man here!
> Why has he come?   55
> I will ask him to account for himself.

The harlot summoned the man,
He came over, Enkidu said to him:

> Fellow, where are you rushing?
> What is this, your burdensome errand?   60

The man made ready to speak, said to Enkidu:

> They have invited me to a wedding,
> Is it not people's custom to get married?
> I have heaped high on the festival tray
> The fancy dishes for the wedding.   65
> People's veils are open for the taking.
> For Gilgamesh, king of ramparted Uruk,
> People's veils are open for the taking!
> He mates with the lawful wife,
> He first, the groom after.   70
> By divine decree pronounced,
> From the cutting of his umbilical cord, she is his due.[8]

At the man's account, his face went pale.

Enkidu was walking in front, with Shamhat behind him.

When he entered the street of ramparted Uruk,   75
A multitude crowded around him.
He stood there in the street of ramparted Uruk,
With the people crowding around him.
They said about him:

> He is like Gilgamesh in build,   80
> Though shorter in stature, he is stronger of frame.
> This man, where he was born,
> Ate the springtime grass,
> He must have nursed on the milk of wild beasts.

The whole of Uruk was standing beside him,   85
The people formed a crowd around him,

---

8. This means that by his birthright Gilgamesh can take brides on their wedding nights, then leave them to their husbands.

A throng was jostling towards him,
Young men were mobbed around him,
Infantile, they groveled before him.

In Uruk at this time sacrifices were underway,   90
Young men were celebrating.
The hero stood ready for the upright young man,
For Gilgamesh, as for a god, the partner was ready.
For the goddess of lovemaking, the bed was made,
Gilgamesh was to join with the girl that night.   95

Enkidu approached him,
They met in the public street.
Enkidu blocked the door to the wedding with his foot,
Not allowing Gilgamesh to enter.
They grappled each other, holding fast like wrestlers,   100
They shattered the doorpost, the wall shook.
Gilgamesh and Enkidu grappled each other,
Holding fast like wrestlers,
They shattered the doorpost, the wall shook!
They grappled each other at the door to the wedding,   105
They fought in the street, the public square.
It was Gilgamesh who knelt for the pin, his foot on the ground.
His fury abated, he turned away.
After he turned away,
Enkidu said to him, to Gilgamesh: 110

> As one unique did your mother bear you,
> The wild cow of the ramparts, Ninsun,
> Exalted you above the most valorous of men!
> Enlil has granted you kingship over the people.

They kissed each other and made friends.   115

[*Gilgamesh speaks.*]

> Enkidu has neither father nor mother,
> His hair was growing freely
> He was born in the steppe.

Enkidu stood still, listening to what he said,
He shuddered and sat down.   120
Tears filled his eyes,
He was listless, his strength turned to weakness.
They clasped each other,
They joined hands.

Gilgamesh made ready to speak,   125
Saying to Enkidu:

> Why are your eyes full of tears,
> Why are you listless, your strength turned to weakness?

Enkidu said to him, to Gilgamesh:

> Cries of sorrow, my friend, have cramped my muscles,   130
> Woe has entered my heart.

Gilgamesh made ready to speak,
Saying to Enkidu:

> There dwells in the forest the fierce monster Humbaba,
> You and I shall kill him   135
> And wipe out something evil from the land.

Enkidu made ready to speak,
Saying to Gilgamesh:

> My friend, I knew that country
> When I roamed with the wild beasts.   140
> The forest is sixty double leagues in every direction,
> Who can go into it?
> Humbaba's cry is the roar of a deluge,
> His maw is fire, his breath is death.
> Why do you want to do this?   145
> The haunt of Humbaba is a hopeless quest.

Gilgamesh made ready to speak,
Saying to Enkidu:

> I must go up the mountain forest,
> I must cut a cedar tree   150
> That cedar must be big enough
> To make whirlwinds when it falls.

Enkidu made ready to speak,
Saying to Gilgamesh:

> How shall the likes of us go to the forest of cedars, my friend?   155
> In order to safeguard the forest of cedars,
> Enlil has appointed him to terrify the people,
> Enlil has destined him seven fearsome glories.⁹
> That journey is not to be undertaken,
> That creature is not to be looked upon.   160
> The guardian of [. . .], the forest of cedars,
> Humbaba's cry is the roar of a deluge,
> His maw is fire, his breath is death.
> He can hear rustling in the forest for sixty double leagues.
> Who can go into his forest?   165
> Adad is first and Humbaba is second.
> Who, even among the gods, could attack him?
> In order to safeguard the forest of cedars,

---

9. It was believed that divine beings were surrounded by an awe-inspiring radiance. In the older versions of *Gilgamesh*, this radiance was considered removable, like garments or jewelry.

Enlil has appointed him to terrify the people,
Enlil has destined him seven fearsome glories.   170
Besides, whosoever enters his forest is struck down by disease.

Gilgamesh made ready to speak,
Saying to Enkidu:

Why, my friend, do you raise such unworthy objections?
Who, my friend, can go up to heaven?   175
The gods dwell forever in the sun,
People's days are numbered,
Whatever they attempt is a puff of air.
Here you are, even you, afraid of death,
What has become of your bravery's might?   180
I will go before you,
You can call out to me, "Go on, be not afraid!"
If I fall on the way, I'll establish my name:
"Gilgamesh, who joined battle with fierce Humbaba" they'll say.

You were born and grew up on the steppe,   185
When a lion sprang at you, you knew what to do.
Young men fled before you

You speak unworthily,
How you pule! You make me ill.
I must set my hand to cutting a cedar tree,
I must establish eternal fame.   190
Come, my friend, let's both be off to the foundry,
Let them cast axes such as we'll need.

Off they went to the craftsmen,
The craftsmen, seated around, discussed the matter.   195
They cast great axes,
Axe blades weighing 180 pounds each they cast
They cast great daggers,
Their blades were 120 pounds each,
The cross guards of their handles thirty pounds each.   200
They carried daggers worked with thirty pounds of gold,
Gilgamesh and Enkidu bore ten times sixty pounds each.

Gilgamesh spoke to the elders of ramparted Uruk:

Hear me, O elders of ramparted Uruk,
The one of whom they speak   205
I, Gilgamesh, would see!
The one whose name resounds across the whole world,
I will hunt him down in the forest of cedars.
I will make the land hear
How mighty is the scion of Uruk.   210

I will set my hand to cutting a cedar,
An eternal name I will make for myself!

The elders of ramparted Uruk arose,
They responded to Gilgamesh with their advice:

> You are young, Gilgamesh, your feelings carry you away,   215
> You are ignorant of what you speak, flightiness has taken you,
> You do not know what you are attempting.
> We have heard of Humbaba, his features are grotesque,
> Who is there who could face his weaponry?
> He can hear rustling in the forest for sixty double leagues.   220
> Who can go into it?
> Humbaba's cry is the roar of a deluge,
> His maw is fire, his breath is death.
> Adad is first and Humbaba is second.
> Who, even among the gods, could attack him?   225
> In order to safeguard the forest of cedars,
> Enlil has appointed him to terrify the people,
> Enlil has destined him seven fearsome glories.
> Besides, whosoever enters his forest is struck down by disease.

When Gilgamesh heard the speech of his counselors,   230
He looked at his friend and laughed:

> Now then, my friend, do you say the same?:
> "I am afraid to die"?

Tablet III

The elders spoke to him, saying to Gilgamesh:

> Come back safely to Uruk's haven,
> Trust not, Gilgamesh, in your strength alone,
> Let your eyes see all, make your blow strike home.
> He who goes in front saves his companion,   5
> He who knows the path protects his friend.
> Let Enkidu walk before you,
> He knows the way to the forest of cedars,
> He has seen battle, been exposed to combat.
> Enkidu will protect his friend, safeguard his companion,   10
> Let him return, to be a grave husband.[1]
> We in our assembly entrust the king to you,
> On your return, entrust the king again to us.

Gilgamesh made ready to speak,
Saying to Enkidu: 15

> Come, my friend, let us go to the sublime temple,
> To go before Ninsun, the great queen.

---

1. "Grave husband" plays on the words for "bride" and "interment" (grave); the phrase seems to portend Enkidu's death.

Ninsun the wise, who is versed in all knowledge,
Will send us on our way with good advice.

Clasping each other, hand in hand,   20
Gilgamesh and Enkidu went to the sublime temple,
To go before Ninsun, the great queen.
Gilgamesh came forward and entered before her:

> O Ninsun, I have taken on a noble quest,
> I travel a distant road, to where Humbaba is,   25
> To face a battle unknown,
> To mount a campaign unknown.
> Give me your blessing, that I may go on my journey,
> That I may indeed see your face safely again,
> That I may indeed reenter joyfully the gate of ramparted Uruk,   30
> That I may indeed return to hold the festival for the new year,
> That I may indeed celebrate the festival for the new year twice over.
> May that festival be held in my presence, the fanfare sound!
> May their drums resound before you!

Ninsun the wild cow heard them out with sadness,   35
The speeches of Gilgamesh, her son, and Enkidu.
Ninsun entered the bathhouse seven times,
She bathed herself in water with tamarisk and soapwort.[2]
She put on a garment as beseemed her body,
She put on an ornament as beseemed her breast,   40
She set [. . .] and donned her tiara.
She climbed the stairs, mounted to the roof terrace,
She set up an incense offering to Shamash.
She made the offering, to Shamash she raised her hands in prayer:

> Why did you endow my son Gilgamesh with a restless heart?   45
> Now you have moved him to travel
> A distant road, to where Humbaba is,
> To face a battle unknown,
> To mount an expedition unknown.
> Until he goes and returns,   50
> Until he reaches the forest of cedars,
> Until he has slain fierce Humbaba,
> And wipes out from the land the evil thing you hate,
> In the day, when you traverse the sky,
> May Aya, your bride, not fear to remind you,   55
> "Entrust him to the watchmen of the night."

> While Gilgamesh journeys to the forest of cedars,
> May the days be long, may the nights be short,
> May his loins be girded, his arms strong!
> At night, let him make a camp for sleeping,   60
> Let him make a shelter to fall asleep in.

---

2. A medicinal plant used in cleansing and magic.

May Aya,[3] your bride, not fear to remind you,
When Gilgamesh, Enkidu, and Humbaba meet,
Raise up for his sake, O Shamash, great winds against Humbaba,
South wind, north wind, east wind, west wind, moaning wind,   65
Blasting wind, lashing wind, contrary wind, dust storm,
Demon wind, freezing wind, storm wind, whirlwind:
Raise up thirteen winds to blot out Humbaba's face,
So he cannot charge forward, cannot retreat,
Then let Gilgamesh's weapons defeat Humbaba.   70
As soon as your own [radiance] flares forth,
At that very moment heed the man who reveres you.
May your swift mules [. . .] you,
A comfortable seat, a bed is laid for you,
May the gods, your brethren, serve you your favorite foods,   75
May Aya, the great bride, dab your face with the fringe of her
    spotless garment.

Ninsun the wild cow made a second plea to Shamash:

O Shamash, will not Gilgamesh [. . .] the gods for you?
Will he not share heaven with you?
Will he not share tiara and scepter with the moon?   80
Will he not act in wisdom with Ea in the depths?
Will he not rule the human race with Irnina?[4]
Will he not dwell with Ningishzida[5] in the Land of No Return?

[*Ninsun apparently inducts Enkidu into the staff of her temple.*]

After Ninsun the wild cow had made her plea,
Ninsun the wild cow, knowing and wise, who understands everything,   85
She extinguished the incense, [she came down from the roof terrace],
She summoned Enkidu to impart her message:

Mighty Enkidu, though you are no issue of my womb,
Your little ones shall be among the devotees of Gilgamesh,
The priestesses, votaries, cult women of the temple.   90

She placed a token around Enkidu's neck:

As the priestesses take in a foundling,
And the daughters of the gods bring up an adopted child,
I herewith take Enkidu, as my adopted son,
    may Gilgamesh treat him well.   95

His dignitaries stood by, wishing him well,
In a crowd, the young men of Uruk ran along behind him,

---

3. Goddess of dawn and wife of Shamash, the sun god, often called upon in prayers to intercede with her husband.
4. Another name for Ishtar and a local form of the goddess.
5. Literally "Lord of the Upright Tree," a netherworld deity.

While his dignitaries made obeisance to him:

> Come back safely to Uruk's haven!
> Trust not, Gilgamesh, in your strength alone,   100
> Let your eyes see all, make your blow strike home.
> He who goes in front saves his companion,
> He who knows the path protects his friend.
> Let Enkidu walk before you,
> He knows the way to the forest of cedars.   105
> He has seen battle, been exposed to combat.
> Enkidu will protect his friend, safeguard his companion,
> Let him return, to be a grave husband.
> We in our assembly entrust the king to you,
> On your return, entrust the king again to us.   110

The elders hailed him,
Counseled Gilgamesh for the journey:

> Trust not, Gilgamesh, in your own strength,
> Let your vision be clear, take care of yourself.
> Let Enkidu go ahead of you,   115
> He has seen the road, has traveled the way.
> He knows the ways into the forest
> And all the tricks of Humbaba.
> He who goes first safeguards his companion,
> His vision is clear, he protects himself.   120
> May Shamash help you to your goal,
> May he disclose to you what your words propose,
> May he open for you the barred road,
> Make straight the pathway to your tread,
> Make straight the upland to your feet.   125
> May nightfall bring you good tidings,
> May Lugalbanda stand by you in your cause.
> In a trice accomplish what you desire,
> Wash your feet in the river of Humbaba whom you seek.
> When you stop for the night, dig a well,   130
> May there always be pure water in your waterskin.[6]
> You should libate cool water to Shamash
> And be mindful of Lugalbanda.

Tablet IV

At twenty double leagues they took a bite to eat,
At thirty double leagues they made their camp,
Fifty double leagues they went in a single day,
A journey of a month and a half in three days.
They approached Mount Lebanon.   5
Towards sunset they dug a well,
Filled their waterskin with water.

---

6. Travelers carried drinking water in leather bags.

Gilgamesh went up onto the mountain,
He poured out flour for an offering, saying.

     O mountain, bring me a propitious dream!   10

Enkidu made Gilgamesh a shelter for receiving dreams,
A gust was blowing, he fastened the door.
He had him lie down in a circle of flour,
And spreading out like a net, Enkidu lay down in the doorway.
Gilgamesh sat there, chin on his knee.   15
Sleep, which usually steals over people, fell upon him.
In the middle of the night he awoke,
Got up and said to his friend:

     My friend, did you not call me? Why am I awake?
     Did you not touch me? Why am I disturbed?   20
     Did a god not pass by? Why does my flesh tingle?
     My friend, I had a dream,
     And the dream I had was very disturbing.

The one born in the steppe,
Enkidu explained the dream to his friend: 25

     My friend, your dream is favorable,
     The dream is very precious as an omen.
     My friend, the mountain you saw is Humbaba,
     We will catch Humbaba and kill him,
     Then we will throw down his corpse on the field of battle.   30
     Further, at dawn the word of Shamash will be in our favor.

At twenty double leagues they took a bite to eat,
At thirty double leagues they made their camp,
Fifty double leagues they went in a single day,
A journey of a month and a half in three days.   35
They approached Mount Lebanon.
Towards sunset they dug a well,
They filled their waterskin with water.
Gilgamesh went up onto the mountain,
He poured out flour for an offering, saying: 40

     O mountain, bring me a propitious dream!

Enkidu made Gilgamesh a shelter for receiving dreams,
A gust was blowing, he fastened the door.
He had him lie down in a circle of flour,
And spreading out like a net, Enkidu lay down in the doorway.   45
Gilgamesh sat there, chin on his knee.
Sleep, which usually steals over people, fell upon him.
In the middle of the night he awoke,

Got up and said to his friend:

> My friend, did you not call me? Why am I awake?   50
> Did you not touch me? Why am I disturbed?
> Did a god not pass by? Why does my flesh tingle?
> My friend, I had a second dream,
> And the dream I had was very disturbing.
> A mountain was in my dream, an enemy.   55
> It threw me down, pinning my feet,
> A fearsome glare grew ever more intense.
> A certain young man, handsomest in the world, truly handsome he was,
> He pulled me out from the base of the mountain,
> He gave me water to drink and eased my fear,   60
> He set my feet on the ground again.

The one born in the steppe,
Enkidu explained the dream to his friend:

> My friend, your dream is favorable,
> The dream is very precious as an omen.   65
> My friend, we will go [. . .]
> The strange thing was Humbaba,
> Was not the mountain, the strange thing, Humbaba?
> Come then, banish your fear.

At twenty double leagues they took a bite to eat,   70
At thirty double leagues they made their camp,
Fifty double leagues they went in a single day,
A journey of a month and a half in three days.
They approached Mount Lebanon.
Towards sunset they dug a well,   75
They filled their waterskin with water.
Gilgamesh went up onto the mountain,
He poured out flour as an offering, saying:

> O mountain, bring me a propitious dream!

Enkidu made Gilgamesh a shelter for receiving dreams,   80
A gust was blowing, he fastened the door.
He had him lie down in a circle of flour,
And spreading out like a net, Enkidu lay down in the doorway.
Gilgamesh sat there, chin on his knee.
Sleep, which usually steals over people, fell upon him.   85
In the middle of the night he awoke,
Got up and said to his friend:

> My friend, did you not call me? Why am I awake?
> Did you not touch me? Why am I disturbed?
> Did a god not pass by? Why does my flesh tingle?   90
> My friend, I had a third dream,
> And the dream I had was very disturbing.

The heavens cried out, the earth was thundering,
Daylight faded, darkness fell,
Lightning flashed, fire shot up,   95
The flames burgeoned, spewing death.
Then the glow was dimmed, the fire was extinguished,
The burning coals that were falling turned to ashes.
You who were born in the steppe, let us discuss it.

Enkidu [explained], helped him accept his dream,   100
Saying to Gilgamesh:

[*Enkidu's explanation is mostly lost, but perhaps it was that the volcanolike
explosion was Humbaba, who flared up, then died.*]

Humbaba, like a god [. . .]
[. . .] the light flaring [. . .]
We will be victorious over him.
Humbaba aroused our fury   105
we will prevail over him.
Further, at dawn the word of Shamash will be in our favor.

At twenty double leagues they took a bite to eat,
A thirty double leagues they made their camp.
Fifty double leagues they went in a single day,   110
A journey of a month and a half in three days.
They approached Mount Lebanon.[7]
Towards sunset they dug a well,
They filled their waterskin with water.
Gilgamesh went up onto the mountain,   115
He poured out flour as an offering, saying:

O mountain, bring me a propitious dream!

Enkidu made Gilgamesh a shelter for receiving dreams,
A gust was blowing, he fastened the door.
He had him lie down in a circle of flour,   120
And spreading out like a net, Enkidu lay down in the doorway.
Gilgamesh sat there, chin on his knee.
Sleep, which usually steals over people, fell upon him.
In the middle of the night he awoke,

My friend, did you not call me? Why am I awake?   125
Did you not touch me? Why am I disturbed?
Did a god not pass by? Why does my flesh tingle?
My friend, I had a [fourth] dream,
The dream I had was very disturbing.
My friend, I saw a fourth dream,   130
More terrible than the other three.
I saw the lion-headed monster-bird Anzu[8] in the sky.

7. Mountain ranges along the Mediterranean
coast of present-day Lebanon.
8. Monstrous bird with the head of a lion. He
appears in a mythological story, where he
steals power from the god Enlil but is defeated
in battle by Enlil's son Ninurta.

He began to descend upon us, like a cloud.
He was terrifying, his appearance was horrible!
His maw was fire, his breath death.   135

[*Enkidu explains the fourth dream.*]

The lion-headed monster-bird Anzu who descended upon us, like a cloud,
Who was terrifying, whose appearance was horrible,
Whose maw was fire, whose breath was death,
Whose dreadful aura frightens you.
The young man you saw was mighty Shamash   140

[*It is not clear how many dreams there were in all though one version refers
to five. A poorly preserved manuscript of an old version includes the following
dream that could be inserted here, as portions of it are fulfilled in
Tablet VI.*]

I was grasping a wild bull of the steppe!
As it bellowed, it split the earth,
It raised clouds of dust, blotting out the sky.
I crouched down before it,
It seized my hands, pinioned my arms.   145
Someone pulled me out
He stroked my cheeks, he gave me to drink from his waterskin.

[*Enkidu explains the dream.*]

It is the god, my friend, to whom we go,
The wild bull was no enemy at all,
The wild bull you saw is Shamash, the protector,   150
He will take our hands in need.
The one who gave you water to drink from his waterskin
Is your god who proclaims your glory, Lugalbanda.
We should rely on one another,
We will accomplish together a deed unheard of in the land.   155

[*Something has happened to discourage Gilgamesh, perhaps an unfavorable
oracle. Shamash comes to their aid with timely advice, just before they hear
Humbaba's cry.*]

[Before Shamash his tears flowed down]:

Remember, stand by me, hear [my prayer],
Gilgamesh, scion of [ramparted Uruk]!

Shamash heard what he said,
From afar a warning voice called to him from the sky: 160

Hurry, confront him, do not let him go off into the forest,
Do not let him enter the thicket!

He has not donned all of his seven fearsome glories,
One he has on, six he has left off!

They charged forward like wild bulls.   165
He let out a single bloodcurdling cry,
The guardian of the forest shrieked aloud,
Humbaba was roaring like thunder.

Gilgamesh made ready to speak,
Said to Enkidu: 170

Humbaba [. . .]
We cannot confront him separately.

Gilgamesh spoke to him, said to Enkidu:

My friend, why do we raise such unworthy objections?
Have we not crossed all the mountains?   175
The end of the quest is before us.
My friend knows battle,
You rubbed on herbs, you did not fear death,
Your battle cry should be dinning like a drum!
Let the paralysis leave your arm, let weakness quit your knees,   180
Take my hand, my friend, let us walk on together!
Your heart should be urging you to battle.
Forget about death,
He who marches first, protects himself,
Let him keep his comrade safe!   185
Those two will have established fame down through the ages.

The pair reached the edge of the forest,
They stopped their talk and stood there.

Tablet V

They stood at the edge of the forest,
They gazed at the height of the cedars,
They gazed at the way into the forest.
Where Humbaba would walk, a path was made,
Straight were the ways and easy the going.   5
They saw the cedar mountain, dwelling of the gods, sacred to the
    goddess Irnina.
On the slopes of that mountain, the cedar bears its abundance,
Agreeable is its shade, full of pleasures.
The undergrowth is tangled, the [thicket] interwoven.

[*In older versions, they begin to cut trees and Humbaba hears the noise. In the
standard version, they meet Humbaba first.*]

Humbaba made ready to speak, saying to Gilgamesh: 10

> How well-advised they are, the fool Gilgamesh and the yokelman!
> Why have you come here to me?
> Come now, Enkidu, small-fry, who does not know his father,
> Spawn of a turtle or tortoise, who sucked no mother's milk!
> I used to see you when you were younger but would not go near you.   15
> Had I killed the likes of you, would I have filled my belly?
> you have brought Gilgamesh before me,
> you stand there, a barbarian foe!
> I should cut off your head, Gilgamesh, throat and neck,
> I should let cawing buzzard, screaming eagle, and vulture feed
>   on your flesh.   20

Gilgamesh made ready to speak, saying to Enkidu:

> My friend, Humbaba's features have grown more grotesque,
> We strode up like heroes to vanquish him.

Enkidu made ready to speak, saying to Gilgamesh:

> Why, my friend, do you raise such unworthy objections?   25
> How you pule! You make me ill.
> Now, my friend, this has dragged on long enough.
> The time has come to pour the copper into the mold.
> Will you take another hour to blow the bellows,
> An hour more to let it cool?   30
> To launch the flood weapon, to wield the lash,
> Retreat not a foot, you must not turn back,
> Let your eyes see all, let your blow strike home!

[*In the combat with Humbaba, the rift valley of Lebanon is formed by their
circling feet.*]

He struck the ground to confront him.
At their heels the earth split apart,   35
As they circled, the ranges of Lebanon were sundered!
The white clouds turned black,
Death rained down like fog upon them.
Shamash raised the great winds against Humbaba,
South wind, north wind, east wind, west wind, moaning wind,   40
Blasting wind, lashing wind, contrary wind, dust storm,
Demon wind, freezing wind, storm wind, whirlwind:
The thirteen winds blotted out Humbaba's face,
He could not charge forward, he could not retreat.
Then Gilgamesh's weapons defeated Humbaba.   45

Humbaba begged for life, saying to Gilgamesh:

> You were once a child, Gilgamesh, you had a mother who bore you,
> You are the offspring of Ninsun the wild cow.
> You grew up to fulfill the oracle of Shamash, lord of the mountain:
> "Gilgamesh, scion of Uruk, is to be king."   50
>
> O Gilgamesh, spare my life!
> Let me dwell here for you [as your . . .],
> Say however many trees you [require . . .],
> For you I will guard the myrtle wood [. . .].

Enkidu made ready to speak, saying to Gilgamesh: 55

> My friend! Do not listen to what Humbaba says,
> Do not heed his entreaties!

[*Humbaba is speaking to Enkidu.*]

> You know the lore of my forest,
> And you understand all I have to say.
> I might have lifted you up, dangled you from a twig at the entrance
>   to my forest,   60
> I might have let cawing buzzard, screaming eagle, and vulture feed
>   on your flesh.
> Now then, Enkidu, mercy is up to you,
> Tell Gilgamesh to spare my life!

Enkidu made ready to speak, saying to Gilgamesh:

> My friend! Humbaba is guardian of the forest of cedars,   65
> Finish him off for the kill, put him out of existence.
> Humbaba is guardian of the forest of cedars,
> Finish him off for the kill, put him out of existence,
> Before Enlil the foremost one hears of this!
> The great gods will become angry with us,   70
> Enlil in Nippur, Shamash in Larsa.[9]
> Establish your reputation for all time:
> "Gilgamesh, who slew Humbaba."
>
> May the pair of them never reach old age!
> May Gilgamesh and Enkidu come across no graver friend to bank on![1]   75

9. Nippur and Larsa are cities in Babylonia with important temples to Enlil and Shamash, respectively.
1. This is one of the elaborate, sometimes obscure wordplays in *Gilgamesh*. In Humbaba's curse, *cross* sounds like *friend* and *bank* echoes *grave*, so that the giant's words can mean either "May they not cross water safely to the opposite bank" or "May they not find a friend to rely on."

[*An old version contains the following exchange between Gilgamesh and Enkidu concerning the seven fearsome glories of Humbaba.*]

Gilgamesh said to Enkidu:

> Now, my friend, let us go on to victory!
> The glories will be lost in the confusion,
> The glories will be lost and the brightness will [. . .].

Enkidu said to him, to Gilgamesh: 80

> My friend, catch the bird and where will its chicks go?
> Let us search out the glories later,
> They will run around in the grass like chicks.
> Strike him again, then kill his retinue.

[*Gilgamesh kills Humbaba. In some versions he has to strike multiple blows before the monster falls.*]

Gilgamesh heeded his friend's command,   85
He raised the axe at his side,
He drew the sword at his belt.
Gilgamesh struck him on the neck,
Enkidu, his friend, [. . .].
They pulled out [. . .] as far as the lungs,   90
He tore out the [. . .],
He forced the head into a cauldron.
[. . .] in abundance fell on the mountain,
He struck him, Humbaba the guardian, down to the ground.
His blood [. . .]   95
For two leagues the cedars [. . .].
He killed the glories with him.
He slew the monster, guardian of the forest,
At whose cry the mountains of Lebanon trembled,
At whose cry all the mountains quaked.   100
He slew the monster, guardian of the forest,
He trampled on the broken [. . .],
He struck down the seven glories.
The battle net [. . .], the sword weighing eight times sixty pounds,
He took the weight of ten times sixty pounds upon him,   105
He forced his way into the forest,
He opened the secret dwelling of the supreme gods.
Gilgamesh cut down the trees,
Enkidu chose the timbers.
Enkidu made ready to speak, said to Gilgamesh: 110

> You killed the guardian by your strength,
> Who else could cut through this forest of trees?
> My friend, we have felled the lofty cedar,
> Whose crown once pierced the sky.
> I will make a door six times twelve cubits high, two times twelve
>   cubits wide,   115

One cubit shall be its thickness,
Its hinge pole, ferrule, and pivot box shall be unique.[2]
Let no stranger approach it, may only a god go through.
Let the Euphrates bring it to Nippur,
Nippur, the sanctuary of Enlil.   120
May Enlil be delighted with you,
May Enlil rejoice over it!

They lashed together a raft
Enkidu embarked
And Gilgamesh [. . .] the head of Humbaba.   125

Tablet VI

He washed his matted locks, cleaned his head strap,
He shook his hair down over his shoulders.
He threw off his filthy clothes, he put on clean ones,
Wrapping himself in a cloak, he tied on his sash,
Gilgamesh put on his kingly diadem.   5
The princess Ishtar coveted Gilgamesh's beauty:

Come, Gilgamesh, you shall be my bridegroom!
Give, oh give me of your lusciousness!
You shall be my husband and I shall be your wife.
I will ready for you a chariot of lapis and gold,   10
With golden wheels and fittings of gemstones,
You shall harness storm demons as if they were giant mules.
Enter our house amidst fragrance of cedar,
When you enter our house,
The splendid exotic doorsill shall do you homage,   15
Kings, nobles, and princes shall kneel before you,
They shall bring you gifts of mountain and lowland as tribute.
Your goats shall bear triplets, your ewes twins,
Your pack-laden donkey shall overtake the mule,
Your horses shall run proud before the wagon,   20
Your ox in the yoke shall have none to compare!

Gilgamesh made ready to speak,
Saying to the princess Ishtar:
What shall I give you if I take you to wife?
Shall I give you a headdress for your person, or clothing?   25
Shall I give you bread or drink?
Shall I give you food, worthy of divinity?
Shall I give you drink, worthy of queenship?
What would I get if I marry you?
You are a brazier that goes out when it freezes,   30

2. Mesopotamian doors did not use hinges but were made of a panel attached to a post. It was this post, or "hinge pole," that rotated when the door was opened or closed, some-times on a piece of metal, or "ferrule," at the bottom. The top of the post was cased or enclosed so the hinge pole would not slip off its pivot point.

A flimsy door that keeps out neither wind nor draught,
A palace that crushes a warrior,
A mouse that gnaws through its housing,
Tar that smears its bearer,
Waterskin that soaks its bearer,   35
Weak stone that undermines a wall,
Battering ram that destroys the wall for an enemy,
Shoe that pinches its wearer!
Which of your lovers lasted forever?
Which of your heroes went up to heaven?   40
Come, I call you to account for your lovers:
He who had jugs of cream on his shoulders and [. . .] on his arm,
For Dumuzi,[3] your girlhood lover,
You ordained year after year of weeping.
You fell in love with the brightly colored roller bird,   45
Then you struck him and broke his wing.
In the woods he sits crying "My-wing!"
You fell in love with the lion, perfect in strength,
Then you dug for him ambush pits, seven times seven.
You fell in love with the wild stallion, eager for the fray,   50
Whip, goad, and lash you ordained for him,
Seven double leagues of galloping you ordained for him,
You ordained that he muddy his water when he drinks,
You ordained perpetual weeping for his mother, divine Silili.
You fell in love with the shepherd, keeper of herds,   55
Who always set out cakes baked in embers for you,
Slaughtered kids for you every day.
You struck him and turned him into a wolf,
His own shepherd boys harry him off,
And his own hounds snap at his heels!   60
You fell in love with Ishullanu,[4] your father's gardener,
Who always brought you baskets of dates,
Who daily made your table splendid.
You wanted him, so you sidled up to him:
"My Ishullanu, let's have a taste of your vigor!   65
Bring out your member, touch our sweet spot!"
Ishullanu said to you,
"Me? What do you want of me?
Hath my mother not baked? Have I not eaten?
Shall what I taste for food be insults and curses?   70
In the cold, is my cover to be the touch of a reed?"
When you heard what he said,
You struck him and turned him into a scarecrow,
You left him stuck in his own garden patch,
His well sweep goes up no longer, his bucket does not descend.   75
As for me, now that you've fallen in love with me, you will treat me
    like them!

---

3. Shepherd god. He was a youthful lover of
Ishtar, who let him be taken to the netherworld when she had to provide a substitute for
herself.

4. According to a Sumerian myth, Ishtar
seduced a gardener named Ishullanu whom
she then sought to kill.

When Ishtar heard this,
Ishtar was furious and went up to heaven,
Ishtar went sobbing before Anu, her father,
Before Antum, her mother, her tears flowed down: 80

> Father, Gilgamesh has said outrageous things about me,
> Gilgamesh's been spouting insults about me,
> Insults and curses against me!

Anu made ready to speak,
Saying to the princess Ishtar: 85

> Well now, did you not provoke the king, Gilgamesh,
> And so Gilgamesh spouted insults about you,
> Insults and curses against you?

Ishtar made ready to speak,
Saying to Anu, her father: 90

> Well then, Father, pretty please, the Bull of Heaven,
> So I can kill Gilgamesh on his home ground.
> If you don't give me the Bull of Heaven,
> I'll strike [. . .] to its foundation,
> I'll raise up the dead to devour the living,   95
> The dead shall outnumber the living!

Anu made ready to speak,
Saying to the princess Ishtar:

> If you insist on the Bull of Heaven from me,
> Let the widow of Uruk gather seven years of chaff,   100
> Let the farmer of Uruk raise seven years of hay.

Ishtar made ready to speak,
Saying to Anu, her father:

> The widow of Uruk has gathered seven years of chaff,
> The farmer of Uruk has raised seven years of hay.   105
> With the Bull of Heaven's fury I will kill him!

When Anu heard what Ishtar said,
He placed the lead rope of the Bull of Heaven in her hand,
Ishtar led the Bull of Heaven away.

When it reached Uruk,   110
It dried up the groves, reedbeds, and marshes,
It went down to the river, it lowered the river by seven cubits.
At the bull's snort, a pit opened up,
One hundred young men of Uruk fell into it.
At its second snort, a pit opened up,   115
Two hundred young men of Uruk fell into it.

At its third snort, a pit opened up,
Enkidu fell into it, up to his middle.
Enkidu jumped out and seized the bull by its horns, ✳
The bull spewed its foam in his face,   120
Swished dung at him with the tuft of its tail.
Enkidu made ready to speak,
Saying to Gilgamesh:

> I have seen, my friend, the strength of the Bull of Heaven,
> So knowing its strength, I know how to deal with it.   125
> I will get around the strength of the Bull of Heaven,
> I will circle behind the Bull of Heaven,
> I will grab it by the tuft of its tail,
> I will set my feet on its [. . .],
> Then you, like a strong, skillful slaughterer,   130
> Thrust your dagger between neck, horn, and tendon!

Enkidu circled behind the Bull of Heaven,
He grabbed it by the tuft of its tail,
He set his feet on its [. . .],
And Gilgamesh, like a strong, skillful slaughterer,   135
Thrust his dagger between neck, horn, and tendon!

After they had killed the Bull of Heaven,
They ripped out its heart and set it before Shamash.
They stepped back and prostrated themselves before Shamash,
Then the two comrades sat down beside each other.   140
Ishtar went up on the wall of ramparted Uruk,
She writhed in grief, she let out a wail:

> That bully Gilgamesh who demeaned me, he's killed the Bull of Heaven!

When Enkidu heard what Ishtar said, ✳
He tore off the bull's haunch and flung it at her: 145

> If I could vanquish you, I'd turn you to this,
> I'd drape the guts beside you!

Ishtar convened the cult women, prostitutes, harlots,
She set up a lament over the haunch of the bull.

Gilgamesh summoned all the expert craftsmen,   150
The craftsmen marveled at the massiveness of its horns,
They were molded from thirty pounds each of lapis blue,
Their outer shell was two thumbs thick!
Six times three hundred quarts of oil, the capacity of both,
He donated to anoint the statue of his god, Lugalbanda.   155
He brought them inside and hung them up in his master bedroom.

They washed their hands in the Euphrates,
Clasping each other, they came away,

Paraded through the streets of Uruk.
The people of Uruk crowded to look upon them.   160
Gilgamesh made a speech
To the servant-women of his palace:

> Who is the handsomest of young men?
> Who is the most glorious of males?
> Gilgamesh is the handsomest of young men!   165
> Gilgamesh is the most glorious of males!
> She at whom we flung the haunch in our passion,
> Ishtar, she has no one in the street to satisfy her,

Gilgamesh held a celebration in his palace.
The young men slept stretched out on the couch of night.   170
While Enkidu slept, he had a dream.

Tablet VII

> My friend, why were the great gods in council?

Enkidu raised,
spoke to the door as if it were human:[5]

> O bosky door, insensate,
> Which lends an ear that is not there,   5
> I sought your wood for twenty double leagues,
> Till I beheld a lofty cedar
> No rival had your tree in the forest.
> Six times twelve cubits was your height, two times twelve cubits was
>   your width,
> One cubit was your thickness,   10
> Your hinge pole, ferrule, and pivot box were unique.
> I made you, I brought you to Nippur, I set you up.
> Had I known, O door, how you would requite me,
> And that this your goodness towards me [. . .],
> I would have raised my axe, I would have chopped you down,   15
> I would have floated you as a raft to the temple of Shamash,
> I would have set up the lion-headed monster-bird Anzu at its gate,
> Because Shamash heard my plea
> He gave me the weapon to kill Humbaba.
> Now then, O door, it was I who made you, it was I who set you up. 20
> I will tear you out!
> May a king who shall arise after me despise you,
> May he alter my inscription and put on his own![6]

He tore out his hair, threw away his clothing.

5. Because there is a gap in the text, it is unclear why Enkidu curses the door so violently. Since it is made of cedar wood from the forest, it might embody the adventure that results in Enkidu's death.

6. These concluding words of Enkidu's curse of the cedar door parody traditional Mesopotamian inscriptions affixed to monuments, which called the wrath of the gods upon anyone who damaged, removed, or usurped the monument.

When he heard out this speech, swiftly, quickly his tears flowed down,   25
When Gilgamesh heard out Enkidu's speech, swiftly, quickly, his tears
  flowed down.

Gilgamesh made ready to speak, saying to Enkidu:

> My friend, you are rational but you say strange things,
> Why, my friend, does your heart speak strange things?
> The dream is a most precious omen, though very frightening,   30
> Your lips are buzzing like flies.
> Though frightening, the dream is a precious omen.
> The gods left mourning for the living,
> The dream left mourning for the living,
> The dream left woe for the living!   35
> Now I shall go pray to the great gods,
> I will be assiduous to my own god, I will pray to yours,
> To Anu, father of the gods,
> To Enlil, counselor of the gods,
> I will make your image of gold beyond measure.   40
> You can pay no silver, no gold can you [. . .],
> What Enlil commanded is not like the [. . .] of the gods,
> What he commanded, he will not retract.
> The verdict he has scrivened, he will not reverse nor erase.
> People often die before their time.   45

At the first glimmer of dawn,
Enkidu lifted his head, weeping before Shamash,
Before the sun's fiery glare, his tears flowed down:

> I have turned to you, O Shamash, on account of the precious days
>   of my life,
> As for that hunter, the entrapping-man,   50
> Who did not let me get as much life as my friend,
> May that hunter not get enough to make him a living.
> Make his profit loss, cut down his take,
> May his income, his portion evaporate before you,
> Any wildlife that enters his traps, make it go out the window!   55

When he had cursed the hunter to his heart's content,
He resolved to curse the harlot Shamhat:

> Come, Shamhat, I will ordain you a destiny,
> A destiny that will never end, forever and ever!
> I will lay on you the greatest of all curses,   60
> Swiftly, inexorably, may my curse come upon you.
> May you never make a home that you can enjoy,
> May you never caress a child of your own,
> May you never be received among decent women.
> May beer sludge impregnate your lap,   65
> May the drunkard bespatter your best clothes with vomit.
> May your swain prefer beauties,

May he pinch you like potter's clay.
May you get no alabaster,
May no table to be proud of be set in your house.   70
May the nook you enjoy be a doorstep,
May the public crossroads be your dwelling,
May vacant lots be your sleeping place,
May the shade of a wall be your place of business.
May brambles and thorns flay your feet,   75
May toper and sober slap your cheek.[7]
May riffraff of the street shove each other in your brothel,
May there be a brawl there.
When you stroll with your cronies, may they catcall after you.
May the builder not keep your roof in repair,   80
May the screech owl roost in the ruins of your home.
May a feast never be held where you live.

May your purple finery be expropriated,
May filthy underwear be what you are given,
Because you diminished me, an innocent,   85
Yes me, an innocent, you wronged me in my steppe.

When Shamash heard what he said,
From afar a warning voice called to him from the sky:

O Enkidu, why curse Shamhat the harlot,
Who fed you bread, fit for a god,   90
Who poured you beer, fit for a king,
Who dressed you in a noble garment,
And gave you handsome Gilgamesh for a comrade?
Now then, Gilgamesh is your friend and blood brother!
Won't he lay you down in the ultimate resting place?   95
In a perfect resting place he will surely lay you down!
He will settle you in peaceful rest in that dwelling sinister,
Rulers of the netherworld will do you homage.
He will have the people of Uruk shed bitter tears for you,
He will make the pleasure-loving people burdened down for you,   100
And, as for him, after your death, he will let his hair grow
    matted,
He will put on a lion skin and roam the steppe.

When Enkidu heard the speech of the valiant Shamash,
His raging heart was calmed,
his fury was calmed: 105

Come, Shamhat, I will ordain you a destiny,
My mouth that cursed you, let it bless you instead.
May governors and dignitaries fall in love with you,
May the man one double league away slap his thighs in excitement,
May the man two double leagues away let down his hair.   110

7. That is, may anyone hit her, drunk or not.

May the subordinate not hold back from you, but open his trousers,
May he give you obsidian, lapis, and gold,
May ear bangles be your gift.
To the man whose wealth is secure, whose granaries are full,
May Ishtar of the gods introduce you,   115
For your sake may the wife and mother of seven be abandoned.

Enkidu was sick at heart,
He lay there lonely.
He told his friend what weighed on his mind:

    My friend, what a dream I had last night!   120
Heaven cried out, earth made reply,
I was standing between them.
There was a certain man, his face was somber,
His face was like that of the lion-headed monster-bird Anzu,
His hands were the paws of a lion,   125
His fingernails were the talons of an eagle.
He seized me by the hair, he was too strong for me,
I hit him but he sprang back like a swing rope,
He hit me and capsized me like a raft.
Like a wild bull he trampled me,   130
"Save me, my friend!"—but you did not save me!
He trussed my limbs like a bird's.
Holding me fast, he took me down to the house of shadows,
    the dwelling of hell,
To the house whence none who enters comes forth,
On the road from which there is no way back,   135
To the house whose dwellers are deprived of light,
Where dust is their fare and their food is clay.
They are dressed like birds in feather garments,
Yea, they shall see no daylight, for they abide in darkness.
Dust lies thick on the door and bolt,   140
When I entered that house of dust,
I saw crowns in a heap,
There dwelt the kings, the crowned heads who once ruled the land,
Who always set out roast meat for Anu and Enlil,
Who always set out baked offerings, libated cool water from
    waterskins.   145
In that house of dust I entered,
Dwelt high priests and acolytes,
Dwelt reciters of spells and ecstatics,[8]
Dwelt the anointers of the great gods,
Dwelt old King Etana[9] and the god of the beasts,   150
Dwelt the queen of the netherworld, Ereshkigal.[1]

---

8. Reciters of spells were learned scholars, while prophets, or "ecstatics," were people who spoke in a trance without having studied their words. Ecstatics were sometimes social outcasts or people without education.

9. Ancient king who was said to have flown up to heaven on an eagle to find a plant that would help him and his wife have a child.
1. Queen of the netherworld and jealous sister of the goddess Ishtar.

Belet-seri,[2] scribe of the netherworld, was kneeling before her,
She was holding a tablet and reading to her,
She lifted her head, she looked at me:
"Who brought this man?"   155
I who went with you through all hardships,
Remember me, my friend, do not forget what I have undergone!
My friend had a dream needing no interpretation.

Enkidu

The day he had the dream, his strength ran out.
Enkidu lay there one day, a second day he was ill,   160
Enkidu lay in his bed, his illness grew worse.
A third day, a fourth day, Enkidu's illness grew worse.
A fifth, a sixth, a seventh,
An eighth, a ninth, a tenth day,
Enkidu's illness grew worse.   165
An eleventh, a twelfth day,
Enkidu lay in his bed.
He called for Gilgamesh, roused him with his cry:

My friend laid on me the greatest curse of all!
I feared the battle but will die in my bed,   170
My friend, he who falls quickly in battle is glorious.

[*Enkidu dies.*]

Tablet VIII

At the first glimmer of dawn,
Gilgamesh lamented his friend:

Enkidu, my friend, your mother the gazelle,
Your father the wild ass brought you into the world,
Onagers raised you on their milk,   5
And the wild beasts taught you all the grazing places.
The pathways, O Enkidu, to the forest of cedars,
May they weep for you, without falling silent, night and day.
May the elders of the teeming city, ramparted Uruk, weep for you,
May the crowd who blessed our departure weep for you.   10
May the heights of highland and mountain weep for you,
May the lowlands wail like your mother.
May the forest of balsam and cedar weep for you,
Which we slashed in our fury.
May bear, hyena, panther, leopard, deer, jackal,   15
Lion, wild bull, gazelle, ibex, the beasts and creatures of the steppe,
    weep for you.[3]
May the sacred Ulaya River[4] weep for you, along whose banks we once
    strode erect,
May the holy Euphrates weep for you,
Whose waters we libated from waterskins.

2. Literally "Lady of the Steppe," scribe and
bookkeeper in the netherworld.
3. This refers to an episode that does not

appear in the extant portions of the epic.
4. Karun River in the southwest of modern
Iran.

May the young men of ramparted Uruk weep for you,   20
Who watched us slay the Bull of Heaven in combat.
May the plowman weep for you at his plow,
Who extolled your name in the sweet song of harvest home.
May they weep for you, of the teeming city of Uruk,
Who exalted your name at the first [. . .].   25
May the shepherd and herdsman weep for you,
Who held the milk and buttermilk to your mouth,
May the nurse weep for you,
Who treated your rashes with butter.
May the harlot weep for you,   30
Who massaged you with sweet-smelling oil.
Like brothers may they weep for you,
Like sisters may they tear out their hair for your sake.
Enkidu, as your father, your mother,
I weep for you bitterly.   35

Hear me, O young men, listen to me,
Hear me, O elders of Uruk, listen to me!
I mourn my friend Enkidu,
I howl as bitterly as a professional keener.
Oh for the axe at my side, oh for the safeguard by my hand,   40
Oh for the sword at my belt, oh for the shield before me,
Oh for my best garment, oh for the raiment that pleased me most!
An ill wind rose against me and snatched it away!
O my friend, swift wild donkey, mountain onager, panther of the steppe,
O Enkidu my friend, swift wild donkey, mountain onager, panther
    of the steppe!   45
You who stood by me when we climbed the mountain,
Seized and slew the Bull of Heaven,
Felled Humbaba who dwelt in the forest of cedar,
What now is this sleep that has seized you?
Come back to me! You hear me not.   50

But, as for him, he did not raise his head.
He touched his heart but it was not beating.
Then he covered his friend's face, like a bride's.
He hovered round him like an eagle,
Like a lioness whose cubs are in a pitfall,   55
He paced to and fro, back and forth,
Tearing out and hurling away the locks of his hair,
Ripping off and throwing away his fine clothes like something foul.

At the first glimmer of dawn,
Gilgamesh sent out a proclamation to the land: 60

Hear ye, blacksmith, lapidary,[5] metalworker, goldsmith, jeweler!
Make an image of my friend,
Such as no one ever made of his friend!

5. Gem carver.

I will lay you down in the ultimate resting place,
In a perfect resting place I will surely lay you down.   65
I will settle you in peaceful rest in that dwelling sinister,
Rulers of the netherworld will do you homage.
I will have the people of Uruk shed bitter tears for you,
I will make the pleasure-loving people burdened down for you,
And, as for me, now that you are dead, I will let my hair grow
     matted,   70
I will put on a lion skin and roam the steppe!

He slaughtered fatted cattle and sheep, heaped them high for his friend,
They carried off all the meat for the rulers of the netherworld.
He displayed in the open for Ishtar, the great queen,
Saying: "May Ishtar, the great queen, accept this,   75
May she welcome my friend and walk at his side."

He displayed in the open for Ninshuluhha,[6] housekeeper of the
     netherworld,
Saying: "May Ninshuluhha, housekeeper of the crowded netherworld,
     accept this,
May she welcome my friend and walk at his side.
May she intercede on behalf of my friend, lest he lose courage."   80
The obsidian knife with lapis fitting,
The sharpening stone pure-whetted with Euphrates water,
He displayed in the open for Bibbu, meat carver of the netherworld,
Saying: "May Bibbu, meat carver of the crowded netherworld,
     accept this,
Welcome my friend and walk at his side."   85

Tablet IX purpose of life

Gilgamesh was weeping bitterly for Enkidu, his friend,
As he roamed the steppe:

Shall I not die too? Am I not like Enkidu?
Oh woe has entered my vitals!
I have grown afraid of death, so I roam the steppe.   5
noah-like Having come this far, I will go on swiftly
Towards Utanapishtim,[7] son of Ubar-Tutu.
I have reached mountain passes at night.
I saw lions, I felt afraid,
I looked up to pray to the moon,   10
To the moon, beacon of the gods, my prayers went forth:
"Keep me safe!"

6. A netherworld deity in charge of ritual washing.
7. Akkadian name for the sage who, together with his wife, survived the Great Flood and became immortal. He resembles the biblical Noah and his name literally means "He Found Life." He is called "Ziusudra" in Sumerian and "Ullu" in Hittite.

[At night] he lay down, then awoke from a dream.
He rejoiced to be alive.
He raised the axe at his side,   15
He drew the sword from his belt,
He dropped among them like an arrow,
He struck the lions, scattered, and killed them.

[*Gilgamesh approaches the scorpion monsters who guard the gateway to the sun's
passage through the mountains.*]

The twin peaks are called Mashum.
When he arrived at the twin peaks called Mashum,   20
Which daily watch over the rising and setting of the sun,
Whose peaks thrust upward to the vault of heaven,
Whose flanks reach downward to hell,
Where scorpion monsters guard its gateway,
Whose appearance is dreadful, whose venom is death,   25
Their fear-inspiring radiance spreads over the mountains,
They watch over the sun at its rising and setting,
When Gilgamesh saw their fearsomeness and terror,
He covered his face.
He took hold of himself and approached them.   30

The scorpion monster called to his wife:

    This one who has come to us, his body is flesh of a god!

The wife of the scorpion monster answered him:

    Two-thirds of him is divine, one-third is human.

The scorpion monster, the male one, called out,   35
To Gilgamesh, scion of the gods, he said these words:

    Who are you who have come this long way?

[*The scorpion monster apparently warns Gilgamesh that he has only twelve hours
to get through the sun's tunnel before the sun enters it at nightfall.*]

The scorpion monster made ready to speak, spoke to him,
Said to Gilgamesh, [scion of the gods]:

    Go, Gilgamesh!   40

He opened to him the gateway of the mountain,
Gilgamesh entered the mountain.
He heeded the words of the scorpion monster,
He set out on the way of the sun.
When he had gone one double hour,   45
Dense was the darkness, no light was there,
It would not let him look behind him.

When he had gone two double hours,
Dense was the darkness, no light was there,
It would not let him look behind him.   50
When he had gone three double hours,
Dense was the darkness, no light was there,
It would not let him look behind him.
When he had gone four double hours,
Dense was the darkness, no light was there,   55
It would not let him look behind him.
When he had gone five double hours,
Dense was the darkness, no light was there,
It would not let him look behind him.
When he had gone six double hours,   60
Dense was the darkness, no light was there,
It would not let him look behind him.
When he had gone seven double hours,
Dense was the darkness, there was no light,
It would not let him look behind him.   65
When he had gone eight double hours, he rushed ahead,
Dense was the darkness, there was no light,
It would not let him look behind him.
When he had gone nine double hours, he felt the north wind,
Dense was the darkness, there was no light,   70
It would not let him look behind him.
When he had gone ten double hours,
The time for the sun's entry was drawing near.
When he had gone eleven double hours, just one double hour was left,
When he had gone twelve double hours, he came out ahead of the sun!   75
He had run twelve double hours, bright light still reigned!
He went forward, seeing the trees of the gods.
The carnelian bore its fruit,
Like bunches of grapes dangling, lovely to see,
The lapis bore foliage,   80
Fruit it bore, a delight to behold.

[*The fragmentary lines that remain continue the description of the wonderful grove.*]

Tablet X

[*Gilgamesh approaches the tavern of Siduri, a female tavern keeper who lives at the end of the earth. This interesting personage is unknown outside this poem, nor is it clear who her clientele might be in such a remote spot.*]

Siduri[8] the tavern keeper, who dwells at the edge of the sea,
For her was wrought the cuprack,[9] for her the brewing vat of gold,
Gilgamesh made his way towards her,

---

8. Literally "Maiden" in Hurrian, a language of northern Syria and northern Mesopotamia that was not related to Sumerian or Akkadian.

9. Some Mesopotamian drinking cups were conical, with pointed bottoms, so they were set on a wooden rack to hold them up.

He was clad in a skin,
He had flesh of gods in his body.   5
Woe was in his vitals,
His face was like a traveler's from afar.
The tavern keeper eyed him from a distance,
Speaking to herself, she said these words,
She debated with herself: 10

> This no doubt is a slaughterer of wild bulls!
> Why would he make straight for my door?

At the sight of him the tavern keeper barred her door,
She barred her door and mounted to the roof terrace.
But he, Gilgamesh, put his ear to the door,   15
He lifted his chin.

Gilgamesh said to her, to the tavern keeper:

> Tavern keeper, when you saw me why did you bar your door,
> Bar your door and mount to the roof terrace?
> I will strike down your door, I will shatter your doorbolt,   20

Gilgamesh said to her, to the tavern keeper:

> I am Gilgamesh, who killed the guardian,
> Who seized and killed the bull that came down from heaven,
> Who felled Humbaba who dwelt in the forest of cedars,
> Who killed lions at the mountain passes.   25

The tavern keeper said to him, to Gilgamesh:

> If you are indeed Gilgamesh, who killed the guardian,
> Who felled Humbaba who dwelt in the forest of cedars,
> Who killed lions at the mountain passes,
> Who seized and killed the bull that came down from heaven,   30
> Why are your cheeks emaciated, your face cast down,
> Your heart wretched, your features wasted,
> Woe in your vitals,
> Your face like a traveler's from afar,
> Your features weathered by cold and sun,   35
> Why are you clad in a lion skin, roaming the steppe?

Gilgamesh said to her, to the tavern keeper:

> My cheeks would not be emaciated, nor my face cast down,
> Nor my heart wretched nor my features wasted,
> Nor would there be woe in my vitals,   40
> Nor would my face be like a traveler's from afar,
> Nor would my features be weathered by cold and sun,
> Nor would I be clad in a lion skin, roaming the steppe,
> But for my friend, swift wild donkey, mountain onager, panther of the steppe,

But for Enkidu, swift wild donkey, mountain onager, panther
   of the steppe,   45
My friend whom I so loved, who went with me through every
   hardship,
Enkidu, whom I so loved, who went with me through every hardship,
The fate of mankind has overtaken him.
Six days and seven nights I wept for him,
I would not give him up for burial,   50
Until a worm fell out of his nose.
I was frightened.
I have grown afraid of death, so I roam the steppe,
My friend's case weighs heavy upon me.
A distant road I roam over the steppe,   55
My friend Enkidu's case weighs heavy upon me!
A distant road I roam over the steppe,
How can I be silent? How can I hold my peace?
My friend whom I loved is turned into clay,
Enkidu, my friend whom I loved, is turned into clay!   60
Shall I too not lie down like him,
And never get up forever and ever?

[*An old version adds the following episode.*]

After his death I could find no life,
Back and forth I prowled like a bandit in the steppe.
Now that I have seen your face, tavern keeper,   65
May I not see that death I constantly fear!

The tavern keeper said to him, to Gilgamesh:

Gilgamesh, wherefore do you wander?
The eternal life you are seeking you shall not find.
When the gods created mankind,   70
They established death for mankind,
And withheld eternal life for themselves.
As for you, Gilgamesh, let your stomach be full,
Always be happy, night and day.
Make every day a delight,   75
Night and day play and dance.
Your clothes should be clean,
Your head should be washed,
You should bathe in water,
Look proudly on the little one holding your hand,   80
Let your mate be always blissful in your loins,
This, then, is the work of mankind.

Gilgamesh said to her, to the tavern keeper:

What are you saying, tavern keeper?
I am heartsick for my friend.   85
What are you saying, tavern keeper?
I am heartsick for Enkidu!

[*The standard version resumes.*]

Gilgamesh said to her, to the tavern keeper:

> Now then, tavern keeper, what is the way to Utanapishtim?
> What are its signs? Give them to me.   90
> Give, oh give me its signs!
> If need be, I'll cross the sea,
> If not, I'll roam the steppe.

The tavern keeper said to him, to Gilgamesh:

> Gilgamesh, there has never been a place to cross,   95
> There has been no one from the dawn of time who could ever cross
>   this sea.
> The valiant Shamash alone can cross this sea,
> Save for the sun, who could cross this sea?
> The crossing is perilous, highly perilous the course,
> And midway lie the waters of death, whose surface is impassable.   100
> Suppose, Gilgamesh, you do cross the sea,
> When you reach the waters of death, what will you do?
> Yet, Gilgamesh, there is Ur-Shanabi,[1] Utanapishtim's boatman,
> He has the Stone Charms with him as he trims pine trees in the forest.
> Go, show yourself to him,   105
> If possible, cross with him, if not, then turn back.

[*Gilgamesh advances and without preamble attacks Ur-Shanabi and smashes the
Stone Charms.*]

When Gilgamesh heard this,
He raised the axe at his side,
He drew the sword at his belt,
He crept forward, went down towards them,   110
Like an arrow he dropped among them,
His battle cry resounded in the forest.
When Ur-Shanabi saw the shining [. . .],
He raised his axe, he trembled before him,
But he, for his part, struck his head [. . .] Gilgamesh,   115
He seized his arm [. . .] his chest.
And the Stone Charms, the protection . . . of the boat,
Without which no one crosses the waters of death,
He smashed them and threw them into the broad sea,
Into the channel he threw them, his own hands foiled him,   120
He smashed them and threw them into the channel!

Gilgamesh said to him, to Ur-Shanabi:

> Now then, Ur-Shanabi, what is the way to Utanapishtim?
> What are its signs? Give them to me,
> Give, oh give me its signs!   125

1. Servant of Utanapishtim, ferryman who crosses the ocean and the waters of death.

> If need be, I'll cross the sea,
> If not, I'll roam the steppe.

Ur-Shanabi said to him, to Gilgamesh:

> Your own hands have foiled you, Gilgamesh,
> You have smashed the Stone Charms, you have thrown them into
>   the channel.   130

[*An old version has the following here.*]

> The Stone Charms, Gilgamesh, are what carry me,
> Lest I touch the waters of death.
> In your fury you have smashed them,
> The Stone Charms, they are what I had with me to make the crossing!

> Gilgamesh, raise the axe in your hand,   135
> Go down into the forest, cut twice sixty poles each five times twelve
>   cubits long,
> Dress them, set on handguards,
> Bring them to me.

When Gilgamesh heard this,
He raised the axe at his side,   140
He drew the sword at his belt,
He went down into the forest, cut twice sixty poles each five times
   twelve cubits long,
He dressed them, set on handguards,
He brought them to him.
Gilgamesh and Ur-Shanabi embarked in the boat,   145
They launched the boat, they embarked upon it.
A journey of a month and a half they made in three days!
Ur-Shanabi reached the waters of death,
Ur-Shanabi said to him, to Gilgamesh:

> Stand back, Gilgamesh! Take the first pole,   150
> Your hand must not touch the waters of death,
> Take the second, the third, the fourth pole, Gilgamesh,
> Take the fifth, sixth, and seventh pole, Gilgamesh,
> Take the eighth, ninth, and tenth pole, Gilgamesh,
> Take the eleventh and twelfth pole, Gilgamesh.   155

With twice sixty Gilgamesh had used up the poles.
Then he, for his part, took off his belt,
Gilgamesh tore off his clothes from his body,
Held high his arms for a mast.
Utanapishtim was watching him from a distance,   160
Speaking to himself, he said these words,
He debated to himself:

> Why have the Stone Charms, belonging to the boat, been smashed,
> And one not its master embarked thereon?
> He who comes here is no man of mine.   165

[In the fragmentary lines that follow, Gilgamesh lands at Utanapishtim's wharf and questions him.]

Utanapishtim said to him, to Gilgamesh:

> Why are your cheeks emaciated, your face cast down,
> Your heart wretched, your features wasted,
> Woe in your vitals,
> Your face like a traveler's from afar, 170
> Your features weathered by cold and sun,
> Why are you clad in a lion skin, roaming the steppe?

Gilgamesh said to him, to Utanapishtim:

> My cheeks would not be emaciated, nor my face cast down,
> Nor my heart wretched, nor my features wasted, 175
> Nor would there be woe in my vitals,
> Nor would my face be like a traveler's from afar,
> Nor would my features be weathered by cold and sun,
> Nor would I be clad in a lion skin, roaming the steppe,
>
> But for my friend, swift wild donkey, mountain onager, panther
>   of the steppe, 180
> But for Enkidu, my friend, swift wild donkey, mountain onager, panther
>   of the steppe,
> He who stood by me as we ascended the mountain,
> Seized and killed the bull that came down from heaven,
> Felled Humbaba who dwelt in the forest of cedars,
> Killed lions at the mountain passes, 185
> My friend whom I so loved, who went with me through every hardship,
> Enkidu, whom I so loved, who went with me through every hardship,
> The fate of mankind has overtaken him.
> Six days and seven nights I wept for him,
> I would not give him up for burial, 190
> Until a worm fell out of his nose.
> I was frightened.
> I have grown afraid of death, so I roam the steppe,
> My friend's case weighs heavy upon me.
> A distant road I roam over the steppe, 195
> My friend Enkidu's case weighs heavy upon me!
> A distant path I roam over the steppe,
> How can I be silent? How can I hold my peace?
> My friend whom I loved is turned into clay,
> Enkidu, my friend whom I loved, is turned into clay! 200
> Shall I too not lie down like him,
> And never get up, forever and ever?

Gilgamesh said to him, to Utanapishtim:

> So it is to go find Utanapishtim, whom they call the "Distant One,"
> I traversed all lands, 205
> I came over, one after another, wearisome mountains,

Then I crossed, one after another, all the seas.
Too little sweet sleep has smoothed my countenance,
I have worn myself out in sleeplessness,
My muscles ache for misery,   210
What have I gained for my trials?
I had not reached the tavern keeper when my clothes were worn out,
I killed bear, hyena, lion, panther, leopard, deer, ibex, wild beasts
      of the steepe,
I ate their meat, I [. . .] their skins.
Let them close behind me the doors of woe,   215
Let them seal them with pitch and tar.

Utanapishtim said to him, to Gilgamesh:

Why, O Gilgamesh, did you prolong woe,
You who are formed of the flesh of gods and mankind,
You for whom the gods acted like fathers and mothers?   220
When was it, Gilgamesh, you [. . .] to a fool?

You strive ceaselessly, what do you gain?
When you wear out your strength in ceaseless striving,
When you torture your limbs with pain,
You hasten the distant end of your days.   225
Mankind, whose descendants are snapped off like reeds in a canebrake!
The handsome young man, the lovely young woman, death [. . .]
No one sees death,
No one sees the face of death,
No one hears the voice of death,   230
But cruel death cuts off mankind.
Do we build a house forever?
Do we make a home forever?
Do brothers divide an inheritance forever?
Do disputes prevail in the land forever?   235
Do rivers rise in flood forever?
Dragonflies drift downstream on a river,
Their faces staring at the sun,
Then, suddenly, there is nothing.
The sleeper and the dead, how alike they are!   240
They limn not death's image,
No one dead has ever greeted a human in this world.
The supreme gods, the great gods, being convened,
Mammetum, she who creates destinies, ordaining destinies with them,
They established death and life,   245
They did not reveal the time of death.

Tablet XI

Gilgamesh said to him, to Utanapishtim the Distant One:

As I look upon you, Utanapishtim,
Your limbs are not different, you are just as I am.
Indeed, you are not different at all, you are just as I am!

Yet your heart is drained of battle spirit,   5
You lie flat on your back, your arm idle.
You then, how did you join the ranks of the gods and find
    eternal life?

Utanapishtim said to him, to Gilgamesh:

I will reveal to you, O Gilgamesh, a secret matter,
And a mystery of the gods I will tell you.   10
The city Shuruppak,[2] a city you yourself have knowledge of,
Which once was set on the bank of the Euphrates,
That aforesaid city was ancient and gods once were within it.
The great gods resolved to send the deluge,
Their father Anu was sworn,   15
The counselor the valiant Enlil,
Their throne-bearer Ninurta,
Their canal-officer Ennugi,[3]
Their leader Ea was sworn with them.
He repeated their plans to the reed fence: 20
"Reed fence, reed fence, wall, wall!
Listen, O reed fence! Pay attention, O wall!
O Man of Shuruppak, son of Ubar-Tutu,
Wreck house, build boat,
Forsake possessions and seek life,   25
Belongings reject and life save!
Take aboard the boat seed of all living things.
The boat you shall build,
Let her dimensions be measured out:
Let her width and length be equal,   30
Roof her over like the watery depths."
I understood full well, I said to Ea, my lord:
"Your command, my lord, exactly as you said it,
I shall faithfully execute.
What shall I answer the city, the populace, and the elders?"   35
Ea made ready to speak,
Saying to me his servant;
"So, you shall speak to them thus:
'No doubt Enlil dislikes me,
I shall not dwell in your city.   40
I shall not set my foot on the dry land of Enlil,
I shall descend to the watery depths and dwell with my lord Ea.
Upon you he shall shower down in abundance,
A windfall of birds, a surprise of fishes,
He shall pour upon you a harvest of riches,   45
In the morning cakes in spates,
In the evening grains in rains.'"

At the first glimmer of dawn,

2. City in Babylonia reputed to antedate the   written.
flood, long abandoned at the time the epic was   3. Minor deity in charge of water courses.

The land was assembling at the gate of Atrahasis:[4]
The carpenter carried his axe,   50
The reed cutter carried his stone,
The old men brought cordage,
The young men ran around,
The wealthy carried the pitch,
The poor brought what was needed.   55
In five days I had planked her hull:
One full acre was her deck space,
Ten dozen cubits, the height of each of her sides,
Ten dozen cubits square, her outer dimensions.[5]
I laid out her structure, I planned her design: 60
I decked her in six,
I divided her in seven,
Her interior I divided in nine.
I drove the water plugs into her,
I saw to the spars and laid in what was needful.   65
Thrice thirty-six hundred measures of pitch I poured in the oven,
Thrice thirty-six hundred measures of tar I poured out inside her.
Thrice thirty-six hundred measures basket-bearers brought
    aboard for oil,
Not counting the thirty-six hundred measures of oil that the offering
    consumed,
And the twice thirty-six hundred measures of oil that the boatbuilders
    made off with.   70
For the builders I slaughtered bullocks,
I killed sheep upon sheep every day,
Beer, ale, oil, and wine
I gave out to the workers like river water,
They made a feast as on New Year's Day,   75
I dispensed ointment with my own hand.
By the setting of Shamash,[6] the ship was completed.
Since boarding was very difficult,
They brought up gangplanks, fore and aft,
They came up her sides two-thirds of her height.   80
Whatever I had I loaded upon her:
What silver I had I loaded upon her,
What gold I had I loaded upon her,
What living creatures I had I loaded upon her,
I sent up on board all my family and kin,   85
Beasts of the steppe, wild animals of the steppe, all types of skilled
    craftsmen I sent up on board.

---

4. Literally "Super-wise," another Akkadian name of the immortal flood hero Utanapishtim.
5. The proportions of the boat suggest standard measures of both ship building and the construction of ziggurats, pyramidal temple towers.
6. The references to Shamash here and below suggest that in some now lost version of this story, Shamash, the god of justice, rather than Ea, the god of wisdom, warned Utanapishtim of the flood and told him how much time he had to build his ship. This substitution of one god for the other might be due to Shamash's role in the epic as protector of Gilgamesh. In the oldest account of the Babylonian story of the flood, Ea sets a timing device, apparently a water clock, to inform Utanapishtim of the time left before the onset of the deluge.

Shamash set for me the appointed time:
"In the morning, cakes in spates, ?
In the evening, grains in rains,
Go into your boat and caulk the door!"   90
That appointed time arrived,
In the morning cakes in spates,
In the evening grains in rains,
I gazed upon the face of the storm,
The weather was dreadful to behold!   95
I went into the boat and caulked the door.
To the caulker of the boat, to Puzur-Amurri the boatman,
I gave over the edifice, with all it contained.

At the first glimmer of dawn,
A black cloud rose above the horizon.   100
Inside it Adad[7] was thundering,
While the destroying gods Shullat and Hanish[8] went in front,
Moving as an advance force over hill and plain.
Errakal[9] tore out the mooring posts of the world,
Ninurta[1] came and made the dikes overflow.   105
The supreme gods held torches aloft,
Setting the land ablaze with their glow.
Adad's awesome power passed over the heavens,
Whatever was light was turned into darkness.
He flooded the land, he smashed it like a clay pot!   110
For one day the storm wind blew,
Swiftly it blew, the flood came forth,
It passed over the people like a battle,
No one could see the one next to him,
The people could not recognize one another in the downpour.   115
The gods became frightened of the deluge,
They shrank back, went up to Anu's highest heaven.
The gods cowered like dogs, crouching outside.
Ishtar screamed like a woman in childbirth,
And sweet-voiced Belet-ili[2] wailed aloud: 120
"Would that day had come to naught,
When I spoke up for evil in the assembly of the gods!
How could I have spoken up for evil in the assembly of the gods,
And spoken up for battle to destroy my people?
It was I myself who brought my people into the world,   125
Now, like a school of fish, they choke up the sea!"
The supreme gods were weeping with her,
The gods sat where they were, weeping,
Their lips were parched, taking on a crust.
Six days and seven nights   130

---

7. God of thunder.
8. Gods of destructive storms.
9. God of death.
1. God of war.

2. A goddess of birth, who in one version of
the flood story was said to have collaborated
with the god Ea in creating the human
race.

The wind continued, the deluge and windstorm leveled the land.
When the seventh day arrived,
The windstorm and deluge left off their battle,
Which had struggled, like a woman in labor.
The sea grew calm, the tempest stilled, the deluge ceased.   135

I looked at the weather, stillness reigned,
And the whole human race had turned into clay.
The landscape was flat as a rooftop.
I opened the hatch, sunlight fell upon my face.
Falling to my knees, I sat down weeping,   140
Tears running down my face.
I looked at the edges of the world, the borders of the sea,
At twelve times sixty double leagues the periphery emerged.
The boat had come to rest on Mount Nimush,[3]
Mount Nimush held the boat fast, not letting it move.   145
One day, a second day Mount Nimush held the boat fast, not letting
    it move.
A third day, a fourth day Mount Nimush held the boat fast, not letting
    it move.
A fifth day, a sixth day Mount Nimush held the boat fast, not letting
    it move.

When the seventh day arrived,
I brought out a dove and set it free.   150
The dove went off and returned,
No landing place came to its view, so it turned back.
I brought out a swallow and set it free,
The swallow went off and returned,
No landing place came to its view, so it turned back.   155
I brought out a raven and set it free,
The raven went off and saw the ebbing of the waters.
It ate, preened, left droppings, did not turn back.
I released all to the four directions,
I brought out an offering and offered it to the four directions.   160
I set up an incense offering on the summit of the mountain,
I arranged seven and seven cult vessels,
I heaped reeds, cedar, and myrtle in their bowls.
The gods smelled the savor,
The gods smelled the sweet savor,   165
The gods crowded round the sacrificer like flies.

As soon as Belet-ili arrived,
She held up the great fly-ornaments that Anu had made
    in his ardor:
"O gods, these shall be my lapis necklace, lest I forget,
I shall be mindful of these days and not forget, not ever!   170
The gods should come to the incense offering,

---

3. High peak sometimes identified with Pir Omar Gudrun in Kurdistan. Landing place of the
ark in the Gilgamesh epic.

But Enlil should not come to the incense offering,
For he, irrationally, brought on the flood,
And marked my people for destruction!"
As soon as Enlil arrived,   175
He saw the boat, Enlil flew into a rage,
He was filled with fury at the gods:
"Who came through alive? No man was to survive destruction!"
Ninurta made ready to speak,
Said to the valiant Enlil: 180
"Who but Ea could contrive such a thing?
For Ea alone knows every artifice."

Ea made ready to speak,
Said to the valiant Enlil:
"You, O valiant one, are the wisest of the gods,   185
How could you, irrationally, have brought on the flood?
Punish the wrongdoer for his wrongdoing,
Punish the transgressor for his transgression,
But be lenient, lest he be cut off,
Bear with him, lest he [. . .].   190
Instead of your bringing on a flood,
Let the lion rise up to diminish the human race!
Instead of your bringing on a flood,
Let the wolf rise up to diminish the human race!
Instead of your bringing on a flood,   195
Let famine rise up to wreak havoc in the land!
Instead of your bringing on a flood,
Let pestilence rise up to wreak havoc in the land!
It was not I who disclosed the secret of the great gods,
I made Atrahasis have a dream and so he heard the secret   200
    of the gods.
Now then, make some plan for him."
Then Enlil came up into the boat,
Leading me by the hand, he brought me up too.
He brought my wife up and had her kneel beside me.
He touched our brows, stood between us to bless us: 205
"Hitherto Utanapishtim has been a human being,
Now Utanapishtim and his wife shall become like us gods.
Utanapishtim shall dwell far distant at the source of the
    rivers."
Thus it was that they took me far distant and had me dwell at the
    source of the rivers.
Now then, who will convene the gods for your sake,   210
That you may find the eternal life you seek?
Come, come, try not to sleep for six days and seven nights.

As he sat there on his haunches,
Sleep was swirling over him like a mist.
Utanapishtim said to her, to his wife: 215

Behold this fellow who seeks eternal life!
Sleep swirls over him like a mist.

[*Utanapishtim's wife, taking pity on Gilgamesh, urges her husband to awaken him and let him go home*].

His wife said to him, to Utanapishtim the Distant One:

> Do touch him that the man may wake up,
> That he may return safe on the way whence he came,   220
> That through the gate he came forth he may return to his land.

Utanapishtim said to her, to his wife:

> Since the human race is duplicitous, he'll endeavor to dupe you.
> Come, come, bake his daily loaves, put them one after another by his
>   head,
> Then mark the wall for each day he has slept.   225

She baked his daily loaves for him, put them one after another by
    his head,
Then dated the wall for each day he slept.
The first loaf was dried hard,
The second was leathery, the third soggy,
The crust of the fourth turned white,   230
The fifth was gray with mold, the sixth was fresh,
The seventh was still on the coals when he touched him, the man
    woke up.

Gilgamesh said to him, to Utanapishtim the Distant One:

> Scarcely had sleep stolen over me,
> When straightaway you touched me and roused me.   235

Utanapishtim said to him, to Gilgamesh:

> Up with you, Gilgamesh, count your daily loaves,
> That the days you have slept may be known to you.
> The first loaf is dried hard,
> The second is leathery, the third soggy,   240
> The crust of the fourth has turned white,
> The fifth is gray with mold,
> The sixth is fresh,
> The seventh was still in the coals when I touched you and
>   you woke up.

Gilgamesh said to him, to Utanapishtim the Distant One: 245

> What then should I do, Utanapishtim, whither should I go,
> Now that the Bereaver has seized my flesh?
> Death lurks in my bedchamber,
> And wherever I turn, there is death!

Utanapishtim said to him, to Ur-Shanabi the boatman: 250

> Ur-Shanabi, may the harbor offer you no haven,
> May the crossing point reject you,
> Be banished from the shore you shuttled to.
> The man you brought here,
> His body is matted with filthy hair,   255
> Hides have marred the beauty of his flesh.
> Take him away, Ur-Shanabi, bring him to the washing place.
> Have him wash out his filthy hair with water, clean as snow,
> Have him throw away his hides, let the sea carry them off,
> Let his body be rinsed clean.   260
> Let his headband be new,
> Have him put on raiment worthy of him.
> Until he reaches his city,
> Until he completes his journey,
> Let his garments stay spotless, fresh and new.   265

Ur-Shanabi took him away and brought him to the washing place.
He washed out his filthy hair with water, clean as snow,
He threw away his hides, the sea carried them off,
His body was rinsed clean.
He renewed his headband,   270
He put on raiment worthy of him.
Until he reached his city,
Until he completed his journey,
His garments would stay spotless, fresh and new.

Gilgamesh and Ur-Shanabi embarked on the boat,   275
They launched the boat, they embarked upon it.
His wife said to him, to Utanapishtim the Distant One:

> Gilgamesh has come here, spent with exertion,
> What will you give him for his homeward journey?

At that he, Gilgamesh, lifted the pole,   280
Bringing the boat back by the shore.
Utanapishtim said to him, to Gilgamesh:

> Gilgamesh, you have come here, spent with exertion,
> What shall I give you for your homeward journey?
> I will reveal to you, O Gilgamesh, a secret matter,   285
> And a mystery of the gods I will tell you.
> There is a certain plant, its stem is like a thornbush,
> Its thorns, like the wild rose, will prick [your hand].
> If you can secure this plant, [. . .]

No sooner had Gilgamesh heard this,   290
He opened a shaft, flung away his tools.
He tied heavy stones to his feet,

They pulled him down into the watery depths.
He took the plant though it pricked his hand.
He cut the heavy stones from his feet,   295
The sea cast him up on his home shore.

Gilgamesh said to him, to Ur-Shanabi the boatman:

> Ur-Shanabi, this plant is cure for heartache,
> Whereby a man will regain his stamina.
> I will take it to ramparted Uruk,   300
> I will have an old man eat some and so test the plant.
> His name shall be "Old Man Has Become Young-Again-Man."
> I myself will eat it and so return to my carefree youth.

At twenty double leagues they took a bite to eat,
At thirty double leagues they made their camp.   305

Gilgamesh saw a pond whose water was cool,
He went down into it to bathe in the water.
A snake caught the scent of the plant,
Stealthily it came up and carried the plant away,
On its way back it shed its skin.   310

Thereupon Gilgamesh sat down weeping,
His tears flowed down his face,
He said to Ur-Shanabi the boatman:

> For whom, Ur-Shanabi, have my hands been toiling?
> For whom has my heart's blood been poured out?   315
> For myself I have obtained no benefit,
> I have done a good deed for a reptile!
> Now, floodwaters rise against me for twenty double leagues,
> When I opened the shaft, I flung away the tools.
> How shall I find my bearings?   320
> I have come much too far to go back, and I abandoned the boat on
>   the shore.

At twenty double leagues they took a bite to eat,
At thirty double leagues they made their camp.
When they arrived in ramparted Uruk,
Gilgamesh said to him, to Ur-Shanabi the boatman: 325

> Go up, Ur-Shanabi, pace out the walls of Uruk.
> Study the foundation terrace and examine the brickwork.
> Is not its masonry of kiln-fired brick?
> And did not seven masters lay its foundations?
> One square mile of city, one square mile of gardens,   330
> One square mile of clay pits, a half square mile of Ishtar's
>   dwelling,
> Three and a half square miles is the measure of Uruk!

THE HEBREW BIBLE

ca. 1000–300 B.C.E.

The sacred writings of the ancient Hebrew people are arguably the world's most influential texts. They have remained the sacred text of Judaism and have inspired two other major world religions: Christianity and Islam. Because these texts have been so influential in human affairs, and have become central to so many people's core religious beliefs, they are not often read in the same way as "literary" texts. But studying the books of the Hebrew Bible as literature— paying close attention to their narrative techniques, their imagery, characterization, and point of view—is not incompatible with religious faith. Close reading enriches our understanding and appreciation of these texts as supremely important cultural and historical documents, for readers of any religious background or belief.

The Hebrew Bible encompasses a rich variety of texts from different periods, composed in both poetry and prose. One of the obvious differences between the Bible and most works of "literature"—such as Aeschylus's *Agamemnon* or **Virgil's *Aeneid***—is that no single human hand composed the whole Bible, or even the whole of Genesis or Job. Traditionally, Moses is thought to have been the author of the first five books of the Bible and also, according to some traditions, the book of Job. But modern Bible scholars agree that these books, in their current form, must have been woven together from several different earlier sources. This theory explains the otherwise puzzling fact that there are often odd contradictions and repetitions in the narrative. For example, God tells Noah to take two of every kind of animal into the ark; but a little later, the Lord tells Noah to take seven pairs of each animal. The simplest explanation for this kind of discrepancy is that the text we have is a collage built of several earlier narratives, put together, or "redacted," into a single master story. Many scholars believe that it is possible to distinguish between the different original strands, each of which has its distinct stylistic features and perspectives on the narrative. For instance, one strand of the text is identified by the name that it uses for God, *YHWH* (a personal name for the Hebrew god: in English, *Jehovah*, and hence the strand is called *J*); in another strand (dubbed *E*), God is called *Elohim* (which comes from the standard Semitic term for any god, *el*).

The various sources have been put together with great skill, and the result is a text of extraordinary literary, philosophical, and theological richness. The lengthiest selections included here are abridged versions of the books of Genesis and Job. Perhaps the most important element running through the two is a complex ethical concern with how human suffering and prosperity come about and what role God plays in shaping human lives. The books resist easy answers to these questions. We might expect that God would simply punish wrongdoers and reward the righteous; and indeed, he does punish Adam and Eve for their disobedience. But often the relation between human behavior and divine favor is shown to be deeply mysterious. God favors Abel over Cain, blesses Noah and Abraham over all other humans, seems to pay more attention to Isaac than Ishmael, favors Jacob over Esau and Joseph over his brothers, and blesses the Hebrew people over all other inhabitants of the Middle East; but in none of these cases are we given an explanation, let alone a moral justification. Moreover, God allows even his favorites, such as Jacob, Joseph, and Job, to suffer terrible hardship before restoring them to prosperity. The book of Job brings this issue explicitly to the forefront. God's ways are mysterious, and instead of reinforcing a simple moral (like "Be good and God will bless you"), the Bible constantly undercuts it. But throughout these texts, we see that God's power is the major force in all of human history. It is no accident that the book of Genesis—unlike other ancient creation stories—begins not with earth, sky, and sea but with God himself, the originator of everything.

GENESIS

The first book of the Bible takes its name from the Greek word for "origin" or "birth"—*genesis*. The book tells a story of how the world, and the human race, came into existence; how humans first disobeyed God; and how God began to establish a special relationship with a series of chosen men and their families: Noah, Abraham, Isaac, Jacob, and Joseph. The book was probably redacted in the fifth century B.C.E., a period when the people of Judah were in exile in Babylon. One can understand Genesis in this context, as an attempt to consolidate Jewish identity in the midst of an alien culture.

The first section (chapters 1–11) recounts "creation history"—God's creation of the world and of humankind, and the development of early human society. Human beings occupy center stage in this account of the world's origin, as they do not in, for example, Mesopotamian and Greek creation stories. This early age is marked especially by God's anger at humanity, from his expulsion of Adam and Eve from Eden to his destruction of the Tower of Babel, which scatters human beings and divides their single language into many languages. God's decision to destroy humanity is presented as a reversal of the original act of creation. The flood mixes together again the waters that were separated on the second day of creation, and it destroys almost all the different kinds of animals created on the fifth and sixth days, together with almost all humans.

But not quite all animals and humans are destroyed. Noah and his family, and the animals taken onto the ark, are spared, because Noah has found favor in God's eyes; Noah's various wives and the chosen animals, it seems, have attracted no particular divine attention but benefit by association with Noah. This dramatic demonstration of God's power and willingness to favor certain members of the human race while destroying others leads to a new beginning. The second part of Genesis (chapters 12–50) moves from humanity in general to the stories of four men and their families: Abraham and his wife, Sarah; Isaac and his wife, Rebekah; Jacob and his wives, Leah and Rachel; and Joseph and his brothers. The transition is marked by God's first declaration of his commitment to the people of Israel. When he tells Noah's descendant Abram (who will be renamed Abraham) to leave his home in Mesopotamia, he declares, "I will make you a great nation and I will bless you and make your name great, and you shall be a blessing." Showing him the land of Canaan, he promises, "To your seed I will give this land." This positive covenant builds on the merely negative promise God has already made to humanity in general: that he will never again destroy the world by flood (chapter 9). Now there is a purpose in history: other peoples will be blessed through the people of Israel, who are chosen for a particularly close relationship with God.

Many complications arise that seem to threaten the fulfillment of the covenant—and add narrative excitement to the story. God has promised "this land" to Abraham's children, but repeatedly, Abraham's descendants—Jacob, and later Joseph and his brothers—must leave the land of their fathers, deferring the hope of a settled home in the promised land. The pattern of exile from home recurs again and again in the book of Genesis and recalls the expulsion of Adam and Eve from the Garden of Eden, while the strife between family members, especially brothers, and the theme of the triumph of a younger brother over an elder, constantly recall the story of Cain and Abel. Repeatedly, we see God's covenant fulfilled in unexpected ways, revealing his power and his surpassing of merely human expectations.

God himself can be seen as the most vivid and complex character of the book of Genesis. He, like the humans made in his image, enjoys an evening stroll through a cool garden; he is willing to scheme and make deals; he has his particular friends and his favorites; and he is capable of emotions: pleasure, hope, anger, and regret. But the human characters in this book, both men and women, are also strikingly vivid. They are people of intense feelings, and their relationships with one another, their loves, hatreds, fears, and desires, are evoked in compelling detail.

It is worthwhile to pay close attention to the way the text brings people's feelings, characters, and motivations to life, in just a few simple words. We often seem to be invited to ponder several possible layers of meaning in what people say, as when Abraham loads up Isaac with wood for the fire, takes the cleaver in his hand, and leads him into the mountain. Isaac says simply, "Father!" Is he scared? Does he know what his father plans to do? Does the

word fill Abraham himself with guilt and horror? Or is he unshaking in his resolve to obey? A world of family conflict is opened up in the text's simple observations. "And Isaac loved Esau for the game that he brought him, but Rebekah loved Jacob" and "The LORD regarded Abel and his offering but He did not regard Cain and his offering." Reasons for these preferences seem to exist, but they are often deeply hidden.

The tale of Jacob, who is renamed "Israel," is central to this text and forms one of its most gripping story lines. Jacob and Esau are twins who fight each other even in the womb: as shown in Robert Crumb's memorable image, Jacob emerges already grabbing hold of his brother's heel—a detail reminiscent of the everlasting "enmity" between humanity and the serpent, which bites the heels of the children of Adam. As they grow older, the brothers grow ever more different: Esau is a wild, hairy man, while Jacob, the mother's boy, the clever one, likes to stay home. Jacob plays a pair of tricks on his brother, first duping him out of his birthright and then robbing him of his dying father's blessing. Understandably enough, Esau wants to kill him. And yet when Jacob travels away from home, he is granted a vision from God, who promises him protection, the inheritance of the land, and blessing for himself and for his "seed." Why, we may wonder, does God prefer the trickster Jacob over the loyal, filial Esau? Is he rewarded for his brains, which he certainly has in abundance? Or for his unstoppable drive to get ahead, evident even from the womb? Or is it his capacity to love, shown in his relationships with his mother, his favorite wife, and his favorite sons? Is it his willingness to engage directly with God and God's messengers, as when he wrestles with the angel all night and emerges declaring, "I have seen God face to face"? Whatever we decide, it is striking that Jacob, or "Israel," the father of the Jewish people, is presented in such fascinatingly unidealized terms. He is a fully human, rounded, and believable character.

Joseph, the firstborn of Jacob's favorite wife, Rachel, is a very different but equally fascinating character. Whereas Jacob's intelligence is practical, focused on the present—combining an acute ability to judge other people with a keen eye for how to protect and promote himself—Joseph is a dreamer, whose mind can read symbols and look to the future. He has a sense of his own great destiny, confirmed by his dreams, which represent him as the first of all his race. Dreams occupy an interesting middle ground in this story, between internal and external worlds: on the one hand, Joseph's dreams are a clue to his state of mind, his hopes for greatness; on the other, his dreams are a sign of the fact that God has favored him and will set him above his brothers. Like later prophets, Joseph suffers many tribulations. As Pharaoh's dream interpreter, Joseph becomes a prototype for the later priests and prophets of Israel: he can discern divine purpose in the signs that remain mysterious to ordinary humans. Joseph's story forms a bridge to the book of Exodus, in which the Hebrew people will need long-term faith in God and in their destiny to survive the years of exile.

Like the *Odyssey*, the book of Genesis is about the search for a homeland, a special place of belonging—although here the quest belongs not to a single man but to a whole people. As in the *Odyssey*, hospitality plays an essential part in the value structure of the text. It is often through human hospitality that God's plan can succeed. Abraham, sitting by his tent flap in the alien land of Mamre, passes a test of his hospitality with flying colors when he offers a lavish feast to the "three men" who turn out to be messengers of the Lord. We see the descendants of Abraham negotiate their relationships with the various other peoples who inhabit the area that God seems to have promised as their inherit-

ance. At the same time, they must try to avoid total assimilation: Isaac insists, for example, that Jacob must not "take a wife from the daughters of Canaan"; in terms of culture, worship, and "seed," the people must remain distinct. Circumcision, which God enjoins on Abraham and his family, marks this male line off from its neighbors. But the story of Joseph illustrates the advantages of at least partial assimilation. Joseph dresses as an Egyptian, marries an Egyptian woman, and has children by her, even as he remembers his family, his father, and the land of his birth; it is, indeed, through his power in the land of Egypt, and his willingness to serve Pharoah, that Joseph manages to save his family and preserve the future of Israel.

EXODUS

After the death of Joseph, the Hebrew people remain in Egypt and multiply, and the Egyptians become increasingly hostile toward this alien population. Moses, along with his brother Aaron, is chosen by God as the savior of the people, the man who will lead them out of slavery and exile and back to their homeland in Canaan. They escape from Egypt, crossing the waters of the Red Sea, which miraculously part to let them through and then wash back to drown Pharoah and his army. In the wilderness, Moses goes to hear the word of God at the top of Mount Sinai, and the Ten Commandments are revealed to him: ten rules of ethical and religious conduct, to be carved on stone tablets, that will form the basis for the new law of the Hebrew people and their covenant with God.

PSALMS

The book of Psalms is a collection of 150 poems or hymns. Traditionally, King David was imagined as the author, though modern scholars believe that the various poems come from different time periods, some from before Jerusalem was besieged

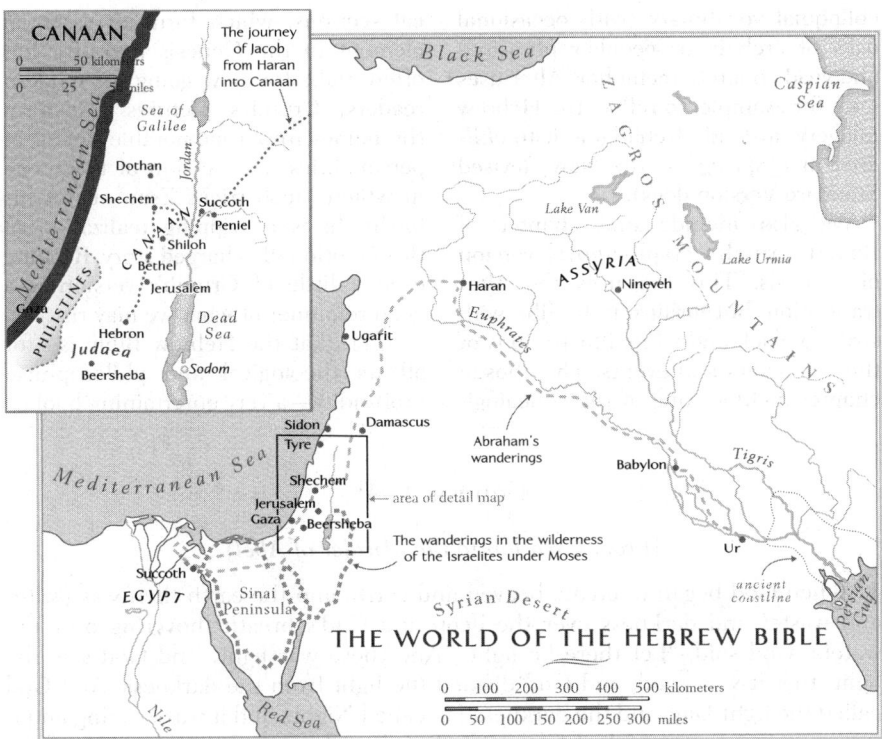

and finally destroyed by the Babylonians (in 587 B.C.E.), while others (such as "By the Rivers of Babylon") were clearly composed afterward, at a time when the Hebrew people were exiled to the city of their conquerors. Most were composed to be used in worship, and they range in theme and mood, from hymns of praise or joyful thanksgiving to desperate songs of lament expressing the sorrows of a people in exile or the bitterness of a person unjustly wronged. The rich, vivid imagery of the Psalms—especially in the language of the King James translation, used here—has had an essential influence on the development of literature in English.

A NOTE ON THE TRANSLATION

Except for the Psalms, presented in the King James version, the biblical text given here is from the recent modern translations by Robert Alter. Alter's language is mostly contemporary, but he is conscious of the need to be faithful to the poetic rhythms of the original. Far more than other translators, Alter preserves the simple syntax and verbal repetitions of the Hebrew—for instance, by repeating *and* no less than twenty times in the first eight verses of Genesis. The lack of subordination is an essential feature of the text's style, as are other kinds of word order that Alter tries to imitate in English, like emphatic inversion (God says, "To your seed I will give" rather than "I will give to your seed"). The Bible tells its complex story in a surprisingly small number of words, and nouns may take on greater power through their repetition in a number of different contexts: it is worthwhile to trace, for example, the use of *hand* or *house* or *brother* throughout the book of Genesis. Alter does not manage to retain every repetition or verbal effect of the Hebrew, but the translation comes close to mirroring the Bible's combination of simple, colloquial vocabulary (with occasional uses of archaic or peculiar phrasing) and vivid concrete metaphor. Alter uses *seed*, for example, to reflect the Hebrew imagery, instead of changing it to *children* or *offspring* (as the New Revised Standard Version does).

We also include one chapter of Robert Crumb's graphic-novel version of Genesis. This too uses the Alter translation but brings it to life with striking black-and-white illustrations of the characters and events. The chosen chapter includes one of the genealogi-

cal sections, which form an essential element in the Genesis narrative but often make for slow going for modern readers; Crumb's pictures transform the names into a memorable lineup of personalities. His version of the scene in which Jacob tricks Esau out of his birthright is a gripping realization of this emotionally charged story. Reading even a little of Crumb's version is a good reminder of what we may risk forgetting: that the Hebrew Bible is—for all its theological and philosophical profundity—a very entertaining book.

Genesis 1–4[1]

[From Creation to the Murder of Abel]

1. When God began to create heaven and earth, and the earth then was welter and waste[2] and darkness over the deep and God's breath[3] hovering over the waters, God said, "Let there be light." And there was light. And God saw the light, that it was good, and God divided the light from the darkness. And God called the light Day, and the darkness He called Night. And it was evening and it was morning, first day. And God said, "Let there be a vault in the midst of the waters, and let it divide water from water."[4] And God made the vault and it divided the water beneath the vault from the water above the vault, and so it was. And God called the vault Heavens, and it was evening and it was morning, second day. And God said, "Let the waters under the heavens be gathered in one place so that the dry land will appear," and so it was. And God called the dry land Earth and the gathering of waters He called Seas, and God saw that it was good. And God said, "Let the earth grow grass, plants yielding seed of each kind and trees bearing fruit of each kind, that has its seed within it upon the earth." And so it was. And the earth put forth grass, plants yielding seed, and trees bearing fruit of each kind, and God saw that it was good. And it was evening and it was morning, third day. And God said, "Let there be lights in the vault of the heavens to divide the day from the night, and they shall be signs for the fixed times and for days and years, and they shall be lights in the vault of the heavens to light up the earth." And so it was. And God made the two great lights, the great light for dominion of day and the small light for dominion of night, and the stars. And God placed them in the vault of the heavens to light up the earth and to have dominion over day and night and to divide the light from the darkness. And God saw that it was good. And it was evening and it was morning, fourth day. And

1. Excerpts from Genesis are translated by Robert Alter. The notes are indebted to Alter's annotations.
2. The translator combines a rare English word (*welter*, meaning chaos, or the turmoil of rolling waves) with *waste* to render a

phrase that is very rare in the Hebrew, *tohu wabohu*.
3. The Hebrew word for "breath," *ruah*, may also mean "spirit."
4. The water below the vault, or sky, is the ocean; the water above the vault is the rain.

God said, "Let the waters swarm with the swarm of living creatures and let fowl fly over the earth across the vault of the heavens." And God created the great sea monsters and every living creature that crawls, which the water had swarmed forth of each kind, and the winged fowl of each kind, and God saw that it was good. And God blessed them, saying, "Be fruitful and multiply and fill the water in the seas and let the fowl multiply in the earth." And it was evening and it was morning, fifth day. And God said, "Let the earth bring forth living creatures of each kind, cattle and crawling things and wild beasts of each kind. And so it was. And God made wild beasts of each kind and cattle of every kind and all crawling things on the ground of each kind, and God saw that it was good. And God said, "Let us make a human in our image,[5] by our likeness, to hold sway over the fish of the sea and the fowl of the heavens and the cattle and the wild beasts and all the crawling things that crawl upon the earth.

> And God created the human in his image,
> in the image of God He created him,
> male and female He created them.[6]

And God blessed them, and God said to them, "Be fruitful and multiply and fill the earth and conquer it, and hold sway over the fish of the sea and the fowl of the heavens and every beast that crawls upon the earth." And God said, "Look, I have given you every seed-bearing plant on the face of all the earth and every tree that has fruit bearing seed, yours they will be for food. And to all the beasts of the earth and to all the fowl of the heavens and to all that crawls on the earth, which has the breath of life within it, the green plants for food." And so it was. And God saw all that He had done, and, look, it was very good. And it was evening and it was morning, the sixth day.

2.[7] Then the heavens and the earth were completed, and all their array. And God completed on the seventh day the task He had done, and He ceased on the seventh day from all the task He had done. And God blessed the seventh day and hallowed it, for on it He had ceased from all His task that He had created to do. This is the tale of the heavens and the earth when they were created.

On the day the LORD God made earth and heavens, no shrub of the field being yet on the earth and no plant of the field yet sprouted, for the LORD God had not caused rain to fall on the earth and there was no human to till the soil, and wetness would well from the earth to water all the surface of the soil, then the LORD God fashioned the human, humus from the soil,[8] and blew into his nostrils the breath of life, and the human became a living creature. And the LORD God planted a garden in Eden, to the east, and He placed there the human He had fashioned. And the LORD God caused to sprout from the soil every tree lovely to look at and good for food, and the tree of life was in the midst of the garden, and the tree of knowledge, good and evil. Now a river runs out of Eden to water the

5. The Hebrew word for "human" is 'adam, which also means "dust"; it is not the first man's name, but the noun denoting all humanity. It does not necessarily imply that the human is male.

6. Here and elsewhere in the translation, the indentation marks a shift into a brief passage

of verse in the translation, reflecting a shift in the original.

7. This is the beginning of a different account of the Creation, which does not agree in all respects with the first.

8. There is a pun in the Hebrew on 'adam, "human," and 'adamah, "humus" or "soil."

garden and from there splits off into four streams. The name of the first is Pishon, the one that winds through the whole land of Havilah, where there is gold. And the gold of that land is goodly, bdellium[9] is there, and lapis lazuli. And the name of the second river is Gihon, the one that winds through all the land of Cush. And the name of the third river is Tigris, the one that goes to the east of Ashur. And the fourth river is Euphrates. And the LORD God took the human and set him down in the garden of Eden to till it and watch it. And the LORD God commanded the human, saying, "From every fruit of the garden you may surely eat. But from the tree of knowledge, good and evil, you shall not eat, for on the day you eat from it, you are doomed to die." And the LORD God said, "It is not good for the human to be alone, I shall make him a sustainer beside him." And the LORD God fashioned from the soil each beast of the field and each fowl of the heavens and brought each to the human to see what he would call it, and whatever the human called a living creature, that was its name. And the human called names to all the cattle and to the fowl of the heavens and to all the beasts of the field, but for the human no sustainer beside him was found. And the LORD God cast a deep slumber on the human, and he slept, and He took one of his ribs and closed over the flesh where it had been, and the LORD God built the rib He had taken from the human into a woman and He brought her to the human. And the human said:

> "This one at last, bone of my bones
>   and flesh of my flesh,
> This one shall be called Woman,
>   for from man was this one taken."[1]

Therefore does a man leave his father and his mother and cling to his wife and they become one flesh. And the two of them were naked, the human and his woman, and they were not ashamed.

3. Now the serpent was most cunning of all the beasts of the field that the LORD God had made. And he said to the woman, "Though God said, you shall not eat from any tree of the garden—" And the woman said to the serpent, "From the fruit of the garden's trees we may eat, but from the fruit of the tree in the midst of the garden God has said, 'You shall not eat from it and you shall not touch it, lest you die.'" And the serpent said to the woman, "You shall not be doomed to die. For God knows that on the day you eat of it your eyes will be opened and you will become as gods knowing good and evil." And the woman saw that the tree was good for eating and that it was lust to the eyes and the tree was lovely to look at, and she took of its fruit and ate, and she also gave to her man, and he ate. And the eyes of the two were opened, and they knew they were naked, and they sewed fig leaves and made themselves loincloths.

And they heard the sound of the LORD God walking about in the garden in the evening breeze, and the human and his woman hid from the LORD God in the midst of the trees of the garden. And the LORD God called to the human and said to him, "Where are you?" And he said, "I heard Your sound in the garden and I was afraid, for I was naked, and I hid." And He said, "Who told you that you were naked? From the tree I commanded you not to eat have you eaten?" And the human said, "The woman whom you gave by me, she gave me

---

9. A fragrant tree.   1. "Man" is ish in Hebrew; "woman" is ishshah.

from the tree, and I ate." And the Lord God said to the woman, "What is this you have done?" And the woman said, "The serpent beguiled me and I ate." And the Lord God said to the serpent, "Because you have done this,

> Cursed be you
>> of all cattle and all beasts of the field.
> On your belly shall you go
>> and dust shall you eat all the days of your life.
> Enmity will I set between you and the woman,
>> between your seed and hers.
> He will boot your head
>> and you will bite his heel."[2]

To the woman He said,

> "I will terribly sharpen your birth pangs,
>> in pain shall you bear children.
> And for your man shall be your longing,
>> and he shall rule over you."

And to the human He said, "Because you listened to the voice of your wife and ate from the tree that I commanded you. 'You shall not eat from it,'

> Cursed be the soil for your sake,
>> with pangs shall you eat from it all the days of your life.
> Thorn and thistle shall it sprout for you
>> and you shall eat the plants of the field.
> By the sweat of your brow shall you eat bread
>> till you return to the soil,
>>> for from there were you taken,
> for dust you are
>> and to dust shall you return."

And the human called his woman's name Eve, for she was the mother of all that lives.[3] And the Lord God made skin coats for the human and his woman, and He clothed them. And the Lord God said, "Now that the human has become like one of us, knowing good and evil, he may reach out and take as well from the tree of life and live forever." And the Lord God sent him from the garden of Eden to till the soil from which he had been taken. And He drove out the human and set up east of the garden of Eden the cherubim and the flame of the whirling sword to guard the way to the tree of life.

4. And the human knew Eve his woman and she conceived and bore Cain, and she said, "I have got me a man with the Lord." And she bore as well his brother, Abel, and Abel became a herder of sheep while Cain was a tiller of the soil. And it happened in the course of time that Cain brought from the fruit of the soil an offering to the Lord. And Abel too had brought from the choice firstlings of his flock, and

---

2. "Boot . . . bite" represents a pun in Hebrew: the word for trampling, or "booting," is repeated to refer to the snake's reaction; it may refer to the snake's hiss just before it bites.

3. The name *Hawah*, Eve, is similar to the verbal root *hayah*, "to live."

the Lord regarded Abel and his offering but He did not regard Cain and his offering, and Cain was very incensed, and his face fell. And the Lord said to Cain,

> "Why are you incensed,
>   and why is your face fallen?
> For whether you offer well,
>   or whether you do not,
> at the tent flap sin crouches
>   and for you is its longing
>   but you will rule over it."[4]

And Cain said to Abel his brother, "Let us go out to the field." And when they were in the field, Cain rose against Abel his brother and killed him. And the Lord said to Cain, "Where is Abel your brother?" And he said, "I do not know. Am I my brother's keeper?" And He said, "What have you done? Listen! your brother's blood cries out to me from the soil. And so, cursed shall you be by the soil that gaped with its mouth to take your brother's blood from your hand. If you till the soil, it will no longer give you its strength. A restless wanderer shall you be on the earth." And Cain said to the Lord, "My punishment is too great to bear. Now that You have driven me this day from the soil and I must hide from Your presence, I shall be a restless wanderer on the earth and whoever finds me will kill me." And the Lord said to him, "Therefore whoever kills Cain shall suffer sevenfold vengeance." And the Lord set a mark upon Cain so that whoever found him would not slay him.

And Cain went out from the Lord's presence and dwelled in the land of Nod east of Eden. And Cain knew his wife and she conceived and bore Enoch. Then he became the builder of a city and called the name of the city, like his son's name, Enoch. And Irad was born to Enoch,[5] and Irad begot Mehujael and Mehujael begot Methusael and Methusael begot Lamech. And Lamech took him two wives, the name of the one was Adah and the name of the other was Zillah. And Adah bore Jabal: he was the first of tent dwellers with livestock. And his brother's name was Jubal: he was the first of all who play on the lyre and pipe. As for Zillah, she bore Tubal-Cain, who forged every tool of copper and iron. And the sister of Tubal-Cain was Naamah. And Lamech said to his wives,

> "Adah and Zillah, O hearken my voice,
>   You wives of Lamech, give ear to my speech.
> For a man have I slain for my wound,
>   a boy for my bruising.
> For sevenfold Cain is avenged,
>   and Lamech seventy and seven."

And Adam again knew his wife and she bore a son and called his name Seth, as to say, "God has granted me[6] other seed in place of Abel, for Cain has killed him." As for Seth, to him, too, a son was born, and he called his name Enosh. It was then that the name of the Lord was first invoked.

---

4. Obscure; it seems to mean something like "Sin shall be eager for you, but you must master it."

5. This is the first of many lists of genealogies in the book of Genesis. Genealogy is one of the major ways in which the text evokes and orders historical time and creates a connection between past and present.

6. The pun in Hebrew is between the name *Shet* and the verb *shat*, "granted."

Genesis 6–9

[Noah and the Flood]

6. And it happened as humankind began to multiply over the earth and daughters were born to them, that the sons of God saw that the daughters of man were comely, and they took themselves wives howsoever they chose.[7] And the LORD said, "My breath shall not abide in the human forever, for he is but flesh. Let his days be a hundred and twenty years."

The Nephilim[8] were then on the earth, and afterward as well, the sons of God having come to bed with the daughters of man who bore them children: they are the heroes of yore, the men of renown.

And the LORD saw that the evil of the human creature was great on the earth and that every scheme of his heart's devising was only perpetually evil. And the LORD regretted having made the human on earth and was grieved to the heart. And the LORD said, "I will wipe out the human race I created from the face of the earth, from human to cattle to crawling thing to the fowl of the heavens, for I regret that I have made them." But Noah found favor in the eyes of the LORD. This is the lineage of Noah—Noah was a righteous man, he was blameless in his time, Noah walked with God—and Noah begot three sons, Shem and Ham and Japheth. And the earth was corrupt before God and the earth was filled with outrage. And God saw the earth and, look, it was corrupt, for all flesh had corrupted its ways on the earth. And God said to Noah, "The end of all flesh is come before me, for the earth is filled with outrage by them, and I am now about to destroy them, with the earth. Make yourself an ark of cypress wood, with cells you shall make the ark, and caulk it inside and out with pitch. This is how you shall make it: three hundred cubits, the ark's length; fifty cubits, its width; thirty cubits, its height. Make a skylight in the ark, within a cubit of the top you shall finish it, and put an entrance in the ark on one side. With lower and middle and upper decks you shall make it. As for me, I am about to bring the Flood, water upon the earth, to destroy all flesh that has within it the breath of life from under the heavens, everything on the earth shall perish. And I will set up my covenant with you, and you shall enter the ark, you and your sons and your wife and the wives of your sons, with you. And from all that lives, from all flesh, two of each thing you shall bring to the ark to keep alive with you, male and female they shall be. From the fowl of each kind and from the cattle of each kind and from all that crawls on the earth of each kind, two of each thing shall come to you to be kept alive. As for you, take you from every food that is eaten and store it by you, to serve for you and for them as food." And this Noah did; as all that God commanded him, so he did.

7. And the LORD said to Noah, "Come into the ark, you and all your household, for it is you I have seen righteous before Me in this generation. Of every clean animal take you seven pairs, each with its mate, and of every animal that is not

---

7. The passage is based on archaic myths (perhaps from an old Hittite tradition) about male gods ("the sons of God") having sex with mortal women.
8. This appears to mean "the fallen ones."

The allusion seems cryptic, perhaps because the monotheistic writer is avoiding explicit discussion of multiple semidivine or divine figures, although the idea of such beings would have been familiar to the ancient reader.

clean, one pair, each with its mate.[9] Of the fowl of the heavens as well seven pairs, male and female, to keep seed alive over all the earth. For in seven days' time I will make it rain on the earth forty days and forty nights and I will wipe out from the face of the earth all existing things that I have made." And Noah did all that the LORD commanded him.

Noah was six hundred years old when the Flood came, water over the earth. And Noah and his sons and his wife and his sons' wives came into the ark because of the waters of the Flood. Of the clean animals and of the animals that were not clean and of the fowl and of all that crawls upon the ground two each came to Noah into the ark, male and female, as God had commanded Noah. And it happened after seven days, that the waters of the Flood were over the earth. In the six hundredth year of Noah's life, in the second month, on the seventeenth day of the month, on that day,

> All the wellsprings of the great deep burst
> and the casements of the heavens were opened.

And the rain was over the earth forty days and forty nights. That very day, Noah and Shem and Ham and Japheth, the sons of Noah, and Noah's wife, and the three wives of his sons together with them, came into the ark, they as well as beasts of each kind and cattle of each kind and each kind of crawling thing that crawls on the earth and each kind of bird, each winged thing. They came to Noah into the ark, two by two of all flesh that has the breath of life within it. And those that came in, male and female of all flesh they came, as God had commanded him, and the LORD shut him in. And the Flood was forty days over the earth, and the waters multiplied and bore the ark upward and it rose above the earth. And the waters surged and multiplied mightily over the earth, and the ark went on the surface of the water. And the waters surged most mightily over the earth, and all the high mountains under the heavens were covered. Fifteen cubits above them the waters surged as the mountains were covered. And all flesh that stirs on the earth perished, the fowl and the cattle and the beasts and all swarming things that swarm upon the earth, and all humankind. All that had the quickening breath of life in its nostrils, of all that was on dry land, died. And He wiped out all existing things from the face of the earth, from humans to cattle to crawling things to the fowl of the heavens, they were wiped out from the earth. And Noah alone remained, and those with him in the ark. And the waters surged over the earth one hundred and fifty days.

8. And God remembered Noah and all the beasts and all the cattle that were with him in the ark. And God sent a wind over the earth and the waters subsided. And the wellsprings of the deep were dammed up, and the casements of the heavens, the rain from the heavens held back. And the waters receded from the earth little by little, and the waters ebbed. At the end of a hundred and fifty days the ark came to rest, on the seventeenth day of the seventh month, on the

9. "Clean" and "not clean" refer to the categories of animals that might or might not be sacrificed; it does not refer to dietary restrictions, which came later in the tradition. There is clearly a discrepancy in the narratives here, between the previous chapter's specification of "two of each thing" and this chapter's requirement of "seven pairs."

mountains of Ararat. The waters continued to ebb, until the tenth month, on
the first day of the tenth month, the mountaintops appeared. And it happened,
at the end of forty days, that Noah opened the window of the ark he had made.
And he sent out the raven and it went forth to and fro until the waters should
dry up from the earth. And he sent out the dove to see whether the waters had
abated from the surface of the ground. But the dove found no resting place for
its foot and it returned to him to the ark, for the waters were over all the earth.
And he reached out and took it and brought it back to him into the ark. Then
he waited another seven days and again sent the dove out from the ark. And
the dove came back to him at eventide and, look, a plucked olive leaf was in its
bill, and Noah knew that the waters had abated from the earth. Then he waited
still another seven days and sent out the dove, and it did not return to him
again. And it happened in the six hundred and first year, in the first month, on
the first day of the month, the waters dried up from the earth, and Noah took
off the covering of the ark and he saw and, look, the surface of the ground was
dry. And in the second month, on the twenty-seventh day of the month, the
earth was completely dry. And God spoke to Noah, saying, "Go out of the ark,
you and your wife and your sons and your sons' wives, with you. All the animals
that are with you of all flesh, fowl and cattle and every crawling thing that
crawls on the earth, take out with you, and let them swarm through the earth
and be fruitful and multiply on the earth." And Noah went out, his sons and
his wife and his sons' wives with him. Every beast, every crawling thing, and
every fowl, everything that stirs on the earth, by their families, came out of the
ark. And Noah built an altar to the LORD and he took from every clean cattle
and every clean fowl and offered burnt offerings on the altar. And the LORD
smelled the fragrant odor and the LORD said in His heart, "I will not again
damn the soil on humankind's score. For the devisings of the human heart are
evil from youth. And I will not again strike down all living things as I did. As
long as all the days of the earth—

> seedtime and harvest
> and cold and heat
> and summer and winter
> and day and night
> shall not cease."

9. And God blessed Noah and his sons and He said to them, "Be fruitful and
multiply and fill the earth. And the dread and fear of you shall be upon all the
beasts of the field and all the fowl of the heavens, in all that crawls on the
ground and in all the fish of the sea. In your hand they are given. All stirring
things that are alive, yours shall be for food, like the green plants, I have given
all to you. But flesh with its lifeblood still in it you shall not eat. And just so,
your lifeblood I will requite, from every beast I will requite it, and from humankind, from every man's brother. I will requite human life.

> He who sheds human blood
> by humans his blood shall be shed,[1]

---

1. There is wordplay in the original, between *'adam*, "human," and *dam*, "blood."

> for in the image of God
>   He made humankind.
> As for you, be fruitful and multiply,
>   swarm through the earth, and hold sway over it."

And God said to Noah and to his sons with him, "And I, I am about to establish My covenant with you and with your seed after you, and with every living creature that is with you, the fowl and the cattle and every beast of the earth with you, all that have come out of the ark, every beast of the earth. And I will establish My covenant with you, that never again shall all flesh be cut off by the waters of the Flood, and never again shall there be a Flood to destroy the earth." And God said, "This is the sign of the covenant that I set between Me and you and every living creature that is with you, for everlasting generations: My bow I have set in the clouds to be a sign of the covenant between Me and the earth, and so, when I send clouds over the earth, the bow will appear in the cloud. Then I will remember My covenant, between Me and you and every living creature of all flesh, and the waters will no more become a Flood to destroy all flesh. And the bow shall be in the cloud and I will see it, to remember the everlasting covenant between God and all living creatures, all flesh that is on the earth." And God said to Noah, "This is the sign of the covenant I have established between Me and all flesh that is on the earth."

And the sons of Noah who came out from the ark were Shem and Ham and Japheth, and Ham was the father of Canaan. These three were the sons of Noah, and from these the whole earth spread out. And Noah, a man of the soil, was the first to plant a vineyard. And he drank of the wine and became drunk, and exposed himself within his tent. And Ham the father of Canaan saw his father's nakedness and told his two brothers outside. And Shem and Japheth took a cloak and put it over both their shoulders and walked backward and covered their father's nakedness, their faces turned backward so they did not see their father's nakedness. And Noah woke from his wine and he knew what his youngest son had done to him.[2] And he said,

> "Cursed be Canaan,
>   the lowliest slave shall he be
>   to his brothers."[3]

And he said,

> "Blessed be the LORD
>   the God of Shem,
>   unto them shall Canaan be slave.

2. The text leaves it unclear what Ham has done. Perhaps simply seeing his father naked is breaking a taboo.
3. An obvious purpose of this story is to justify the idea that the Israelites, rather than the Canaanites, ought to control the land of Canaan—an important issue in later Israelite history. After antiquity, Noah's three sons were often believed to have been the ancestors of the three supposed racial groups in the world: Japheth was the ancestor of European and Asian peoples, Shem was the ancestor of the Semitic races, and Ham was the ancestor of Africans. This interpretation goes well beyond the text itself and has often been motivated, implicitly or explicitly, by racism.

May God enlarge Japheth,
    may he dwell in the tents of Shem,
        unto them shall Canaan be slave."

And Noah lived after the Flood three hundred and fifty years. And all the days of Noah were nine hundred and fifty years. Then he died.

From Genesis 11

[The Tower of Babel]

11. And all the earth was one language, one set of words. And it happened as they journeyed from the east that they found a valley in the land of Shinar and settled there. And they said to each other, "Come, let us bake bricks and burn them hard." And the brick served them as stone, and bitumen served them as mortar. And they said, "Come, let us build us a city and a tower with its top in the heavens, that we may make us a name, lest we be scattered over all the earth." And the LORD came down to see the city and the tower that the human creatures had built. And the LORD said, "As one people with one language for all, if this is what they have begun to do, now nothing they plot to do will elude them. Come, let us go down and baffle their language there so that they will not understand each other's language." And the LORD scattered them from there over all the earth and they left off building the city. Therefore it is called Babel, for there the LORD made the language of all the earth babble.[4] And from there the LORD scattered them over all the earth.

*   *   *

From Genesis 12, 17, 18

[God's Promise to Abraham]

12. And the LORD said to Abram,[5] "Go forth from your land and your birthplace and your father's house to the land I will show you. And I will make you a great nation and I will bless you and make your name great, and you shall be a blessing. And I will bless those who bless you, and those who damn you I will curse, and all the clans of the earth through you shall be blessed." And Abram went forth as the LORD had spoken to him and Lot went forth with him, Abram being seventy-five years old when he left Haran. And Abram took

4. The pun in Hebrew is between *balal*, "to mix" or "to confuse," and the Akkadian place name *Babel* (or *Babylon*), which probably originally meant "gate of heaven." The "tower" is presumably a ziggurat, the type of tall building surrounding temple complexes in many ancient Mesopotamian cultures.
5. Ten generations and hundreds of years have passed since the time of Noah. Abram is a descendant of Noah's son Shem.

Sarai his wife and Lot his nephew and all the goods they had gotten and the folk they had bought in Haran,⁶ and they set out on the way to the land of Canaan, and they came to the land of Canaan. And Abram crossed through the land to the site of Shechem, to the Terebinth of Moreh. The Canaanite was then in the land. And the LORD appeared to Abram and said, "To your seed I will give this land." And he built an altar there to the LORD who had appeared to him.

* * *

17. And Abram was ninety-nine years old, and the LORD appeared to Abram and said to him, "I am El Shaddai.⁷ Walk in My presence and be blameless, and I will grant My covenant between Me and you and I will multiply you very greatly." And Abram flung himself on his face, and God spoke to him, saying, "As for Me, this is My covenant with you: you shall be father to a multitude of nations. And no longer shall your name be called Abram but your name shall be Abraham, for I have made you father to a multitude of nations.⁸ And I will make you most abundantly fruitful and turn you into nations, and kings shall come forth from you. And I will establish My covenant between Me and you and your seed after you through their generations as an everlasting covenant to be God to you and to your seed after you. And I will give unto you and your seed after you the land in which you sojourn, the whole land of Canaan, as an everlasting holding, and I will be their God."

And God said to Abraham, "As for you, you shall keep My commandment, you and your seed after you through their generations."

* * *

18. And the LORD appeared to him in the Terebinths of Mamre⁹ when he was sitting by the tent flap in the heat of the day. And he raised his eyes and saw, and, look, three men were standing before him. He saw, and he ran toward them from the tent flap and bowed to the ground. And he said, "My lord, if I have found favor in your eyes, please do not go on past your servant. Let a little water be fetched and bathe your feet and stretch out under the tree, and let me fetch a morsel of bread, and refresh yourselves. Then you may go on, for have you not come by your servant?" And they said, "Do as you have spoken." And Abraham hurried to the tent to Sarah and he said, "Hurry! Knead three *seahs* of choice semolina flour and make loaves."¹ And to the herd Abraham ran and fetched a tender and goodly calf and gave it to the lad, who

6. Slaves. Slavery was a common institution in the ancient Near East. The slave girl Hagar will play an important part in the story, since she is the mother of Abram's first son, Ishmael.
7. *El* means God; the meaning of *Shaddai* is obscure.
8. The names *Abram* and *Abraham* both mean "exalted father." Abram and Sarai (later Sarah) have to change their names, not to gain titles with new meaning but as a sign of

taking on their new roles as instruments of God's purpose.
9. Terebinths are small trees that produce turpentine; the word used here is sometimes interpreted to mean "oak trees." Mamre was the site of a cult shrine to the major Canaanite sky god.
1. A *seah* is a dry measure equal to about thirty cups; three *seah*s is almost five gallons—a lot of food for three people.

hurried to prepare it. And he fetched curds and milk and the calf that had been prepared and he set these before them, he standing over them under the tree, and they ate. And they said to him, "Where is Sarah your wife?" And he said, "There, in the tent." And he said, "I will surely return to you at this very season and, look, a son shall Sarah your wife have," and Sarah was listening at the tent flap, which was behind him. And Abraham and Sarah were old, advanced in years, Sarah no longer had her woman's flow. And Sarah laughed inwardly, saying, "After being shriveled, shall I have pleasure, and my husband is old?" And the LORD said to Abraham, "Why is it that Sarah laughed, saying, 'Shall I really give birth, old as I am?' Is anything beyond the LORD? In due time I will return to you, at this very season, and Sarah shall have a son." And Sarah dissembled, saying, "I did not laugh," for she was afraid. And He said, "Yes, you did laugh."

*　*　*

From Genesis 21, 22

[*Abraham and Isaac*]

21. And the LORD singled out Sarah as He had said, and the LORD did for Sarah as He had spoken. And Sarah conceived and bore a son to Abraham in his old age at the set time that God had spoken to him. And Abraham called the name of his son who was born to him, whom Sarah bore him, Isaac.[2] And Abraham circumcised Isaac his son when he was eight days old, as God had charged him. And Abraham was a hundred years old when Isaac his son was born to him. And Sarah said,

> "Laughter has God made me,
> Whoever hears will laugh at me."

*　*　*

22. And it happened after these things that God tested Abraham. And He said to him, "Abraham!" and he said, "Here I am." And He said, "Take, pray, your son, your only one, whom you love, Isaac, and go forth to the land of Moriah and offer him up as a burnt offering on one of the mountains which I shall say to you." And Abraham rose early in the morning and saddled his donkey and took his two lads with him, and Isaac his son, and he split wood for the offering, and rose and went to the place that God had said to him. On the third day Abraham raised his eyes and saw the place from afar. And Abraham said to his lads, "Sit you here with the donkey and let me and the lad walk ahead and let us worship and return to you." And Abraham took the wood for the offering and put it on Isaac his son and he took in his hand the fire and the cleaver, and the two of them went

---

2. "He who laughs."

together. And Isaac said to Abraham his father, "Father!" and he said, "Here I am, my son." And he said, "Here is the fire and the wood but where is the sheep for the offering?" And Abraham said, "God will see to the sheep for the offering, my son." And the two of them went together. And they came to the place that God had said to him, and Abraham built there an altar and laid out the wood and bound Isaac his son and placed him on the altar on top of the wood. And Abraham reached out his hand and took the cleaver to slaughter his son. And the LORD's messenger called out to him from the heavens and said, "Abraham, Abraham!" and he said, "Here I am." And he said, "Do not reach out your hand against the lad, and do nothing to him, for now I know that you fear God and you have not held back your son, your only one, from Me." And Abraham raised his eyes and saw and, look, a ram was caught in the thicket by its horns, and Abraham went and took the ram and offered him up as a burnt offering instead of his son. And Abraham called the name of that place YHWH-Yireh, as is said to this day, "On the mount of the LORD there is sight."[3] And the LORD's messenger called out to Abraham once again from the heavens, and He said, "By My own Self I swear, declares the LORD, that because you have done this thing and have not held back your son, your only one, I will greatly bless you and will greatly multiply your seed, as the stars in the heavens and as the sand on the shore of the sea, and your seed shall take hold of its enemies' gate. And all the nations of the earth will be blessed through your seed because you have listened to my voice." And Abraham returned to his lads, and they rose and went together to Beersheba, and Abraham dwelled in Beersheba.

* * *

Genesis 25

[Esau Spurns His Birthright]

We give chapter 25 of Genesis in the graphic-novel version by Robert Crumb. The words are based on Robert Alter's translation. Readers are invited to think about how the extra visual material contributes to the text and how these pictures might change one's interpretation of the Bible. We have chosen this chapter partly because it includes one of the many genealogies in Genesis, which are an essential feature of the Hebrew Bible's narrative method but hard for modern readers to appreciate; they are made vivid by Crumb's pictures. Moreover, Crumb's powerful depiction of Rebekah's conversation with the Lord is a good reminder of how important the female characters (the Matriarchs) are in this narrative. The chapter also marks the beginning of the story of Jacob and Esau; illustrations emphasize the textual, visual distinction between the hairy, wild hunter Esau and the smooth-skinned, smooth-talking Jacob.

3. The place name means "The Lord (Yaweh) sees" or "The Lord is seen."

Chapter 25

AND ABRAHAM TOOK ANOTHER WIFE, AND HER NAME WAS KETURAH. AND SHE BORE HIM ZIMRAN AND JOKSHAN AND MEDAN AND MIDIAN AND ISHBAK AND SHUAH.

AND JOKSHAN BEGOT SHEBA AND DEDAN. AND THE SONS OF DEDAN WERE THE ASHURIM AND THE LETUSHIM AND THE LEUMMIM. AND THE SONS OF MIDIAN WERE EPHAH AND EPHER AND ENOCH AND ABIDA AND ELDAAH. ALL THESE WERE THE DESCENDANTS OF KETURAH.

AND ABRAHAM GAVE EVERYTHING HE HAD TO ISAAC. AND TO THE SONS OF HIS CONCUBINES ABRAHAM GAVE GIFTS WHILE HE WAS STILL ALIVE, AND SENT THEM AWAY FROM ISAAC, HIS SON, EASTWARD, TO THE LAND OF THE EAST.

AND THESE ARE THE DAYS OF THE YEARS OF THE LIFE OF ABRAHAM, WHICH HE LIVED: 175 YEARS. ABRAHAM BREATHED HIS LAST AND DIED AT A RIPE OLD AGE, OLD AND SATED WITH YEARS, AND HE WAS GATHERED TO HIS KINFOLK.

AND ISAAC AND ISHMAEL, HIS SONS, BURIED HIM IN THE MACHPELAH CAVE IN THE FIELD OF EPHRON, SON OF ZOHAR THE HITTITE, WHICH FACES MAMRE, THE FIELD THAT ABRAHAM HAD BOUGHT FROM THE HITTITES. THERE ABRAHAM WAS BURIED, WITH SARAH, HIS WIFE.

AND IT CAME TO PASS AFTER THE DEATH OF ABRAHAM THAT GOD BLESSED HIS SON ISAAC, AND ISAAC SETTLED NEAR BEER-LAHAI-ROI.

AND THIS IS THE LINEAGE OF ISHMAEL, SON OF ABRAHAM WHOM HAGAR, THE EGYPTIAN, SARAH'S SLAVEGIRL, BORE TO ABRAHAM. AND THESE ARE THE NAMES OF THE SONS OF ISHMAEL ACCORDING TO THEIR LINEAGE...

NEBAIOTH, THE FIRSTBORN OF ISHMAEL...

AND KEDAR...

AND ADBEEL...

AND MIBSAM...

AND MISHMA...

AND DUMA...

AND MASSA...

HADAD...

AND TEMA...

JETUR...

NAPHISH...

AND KEDMAH.

THESE ARE THE SONS OF ISHMAEL, AND THESE ARE THEIR NAMES, BY THEIR TOWNS AND BY THEIR STRONGHOLDS, TWELVE CHIEFTAINS ACCORDING TO THEIR CLANS.

AND THESE ARE THE YEARS OF THE LIFE OF ISHMAEL: 137 YEARS. AND HE BREATHED HIS LAST AND DIED AND HE WAS GATHERED TO HIS KINFOLK. AND THEY RANGED FROM HAVILAH TO SHUR, WHICH FACES EGYPT, AND TILL YOU COME TO ASSHUR.

AND THIS IS THE LINEAGE OF ISAAC, SON OF ABRAHAM. ABRAHAM BEGOT ISAAC. AND ISAAC WAS FORTY YEARS OLD WHEN HE TOOK AS WIFE REBEKAH, DAUGHTER OF BETHUEL THE ARAMEAN FROM PADDAN-ARAM, SISTER OF LABAN THE ARAMEAN. AND ISAAC PLEADED WITH THE LORD ON BEHALF OF HIS WIFE, FOR SHE WAS BARREN.

IN THE FACE OF ALL HIS KIN HE WENT DOWN.

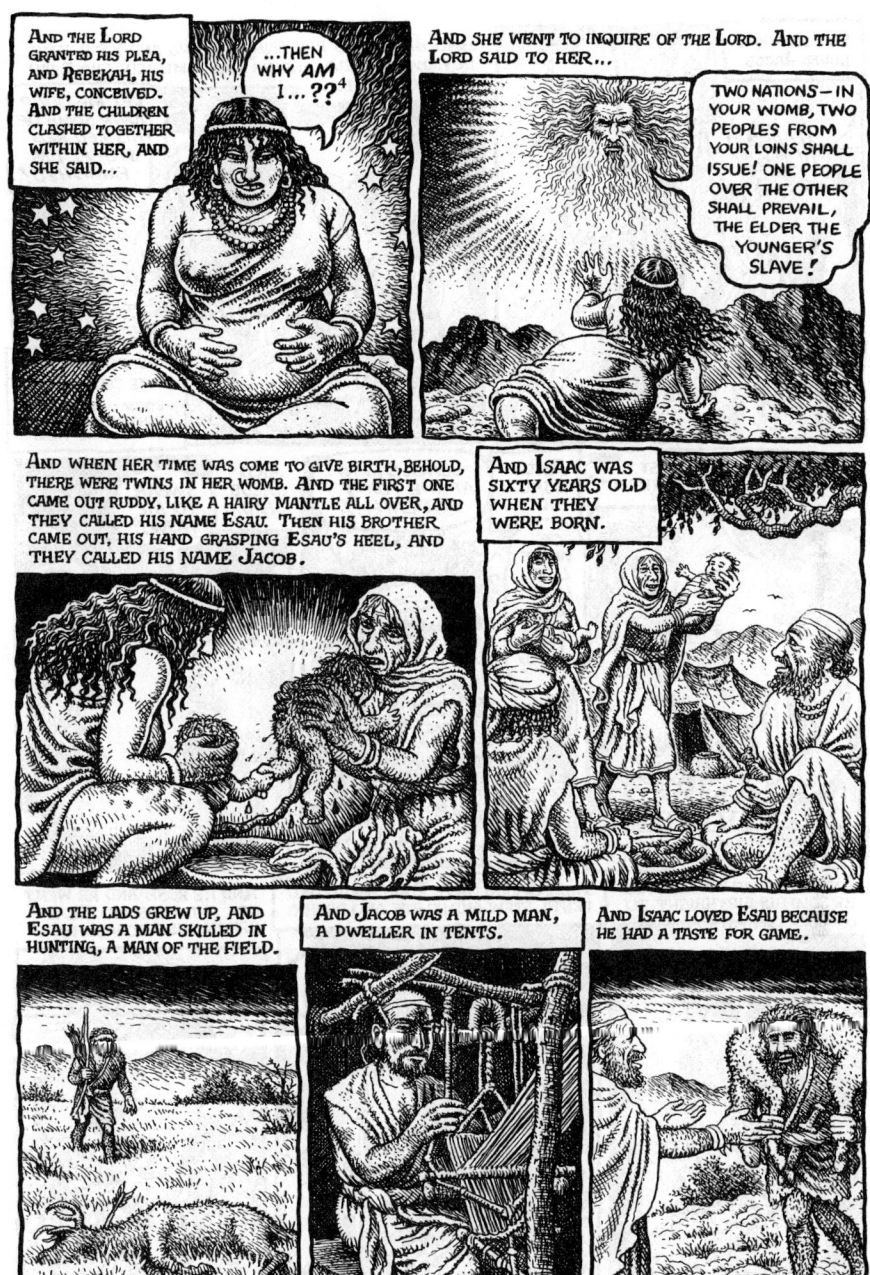

4. Rebekah's question is terse and open to interpretation. It may be elliptical (perhaps "Why am I . . . even having these babies?"), or it may imply, "Why me?"

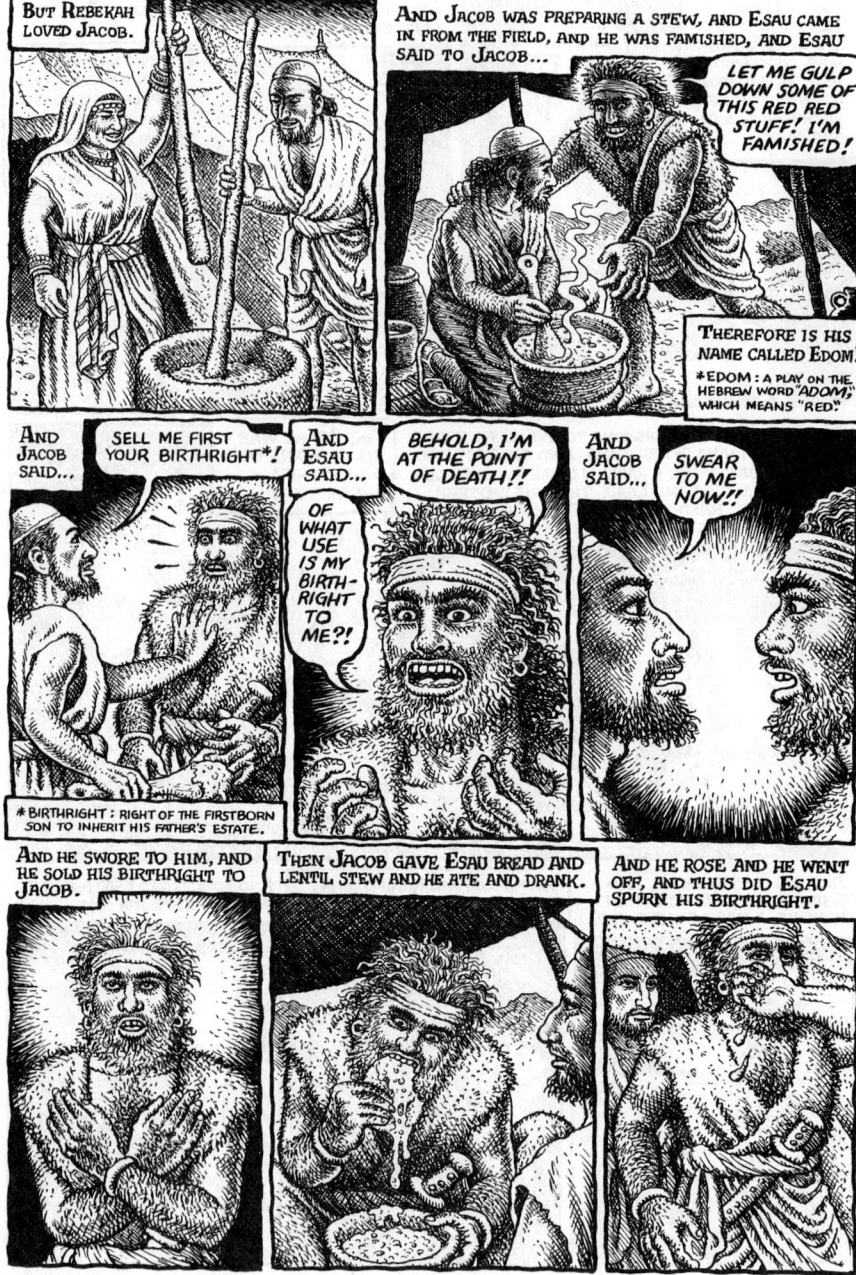

Genesis 27

[*Jacob and Esau*]

27. And it happened when Isaac was old, that his eyes grew too bleary to see, and he called to Esau his elder son and said to him, "My son!" and he said, "Here I am." And he said, "Look, I have grown old; I know not how soon I shall die. So now, take up, pray, your gear, your quiver and your bow, and go out to the field, and hunt me some game, and make me a dish of the kind that I love and bring it to me that I may eat, so that I may solemnly bless you before I die." And Rebekah was listening as Isaac spoke to Esau his son, and Esau went off to the field to hunt game to bring.

And Rebekah said to Jacob her son, "Look, I have heard your father speaking to Esau your brother, saying, 'Bring me some game and make me a dish that I may eat, and I shall bless you in the LORD's presence before I die.' So now, my son, listen to my voice, to what I command you. Go, pray, to the flock, and fetch me from there two choice kids that I may make them into a dish for your father of the kind he loves. And you shall bring it to your father and he shall eat, so that he may bless you before he dies." And Jacob said to Rebekah his mother, "Look, Esau my brother is a hairy man and I am a smooth-skinned man. What if my father feels me and I seem a cheat to him and bring on myself a curse and not a blessing?" And his mother said, "Upon me your curse, my son. Just listen to my voice and go, fetch them for me." And he went and he fetched and he brought to his mother, and his mother made a dish of the kind his father loved. And Rebekah took the garments of Esau her elder son, the finery that was with her in the house, and put them on Jacob her younger son, and the skins of the kids she put on his hands and on the smooth part of his neck. And she placed the dish, and the bread she had made, in the hand of Jacob her son. And he came to his father and said, "Father!" And he said, "Here I am. Who are you, my son?" And Jacob said to his father, "I am Esau your firstborn. I have done as you have spoken to me. Rise, pray, sit up, and eat of my game so that you may solemnly bless me." And Isaac said to his son, "How is it you found it this soon, my son?" And he said, "Because the LORD your God gave me good luck." And Isaac said to Jacob, "Come close, pray, that I may feel you, my son, whether you are my son Esau or not." And Jacob came close to Isaac his father and he felt him and he said, "The voice is the voice of Jacob and the hands are Esau's hands." But he did not recognize him for his hands were, like Esau's hands, hairy, and he blessed him. And he said, "Are you my son Esau?" And he said, "I am." And he said, "Serve me, that I may eat of the game of my son, so that I may solemnly bless you." And he served him and he ate, and he brought him wine and he drank. And Isaac his father said to him, "Come close, pray, and kiss me, my son." And he came close and kissed him, and he smelled his garments and he blessed him and he said, "See, the smell of my son is like the smell of the field that the LORD has blessed.

> May God grant you
>> from the dew of the heavens and the fat of the earth,
>>> and abundance of grain and drink.
> May peoples serve you,
>> and nations bow before you.

Be overlord to your brothers,
    may your mother's sons bow before you.
Those who curse you be cursed,
    and those who bless you, blessed."

And it happened as soon as Isaac finished blessing Jacob, and Jacob barely had left the presence of Isaac his father, that Esau his brother came back from the hunt. And he, too, made a dish and brought it to his father and he said to his father, "Let my father rise and eat of the game of his son so that you may solemnly bless me." And his father Isaac said, "Who are you?" And he said, "I am your son, your firstborn, Esau." And Isaac was seized with a very great trembling and he said, "Who is it, then, who caught game and brought it to me and I ate everything before you came and blessed him? Now blessed he stays." When Esau heard his father's words, he cried out with a great and very bitter outcry and he said to his father, "Bless me, too, Father!" And he said, "Your brother has come in deceit and has taken your blessing." And he said,

"Was his name called Jacob
    that he should trip me now twice by the heels?
My birthright he took,
    and look, now, he's taken my blessing."

And he said, "Have you not kept back a blessing for me?"
   And Isaac answered and said to Esau, "Look, I made him overlord to you, and all his brothers I gave him as slaves, and with grain and wine I endowed him. For you, then, what can I do, my son?" And Esau said to his father, "Do you have but one blessing, my father? Bless me, too, Father." And Esau raised his voice and he wept. And Isaac his father answered and said to him,

"Look, from the fat of the earth be your dwelling
    and from the dew of the heavens above.
By your sword shall you live
    and your brother shall you serve.
And when you rebel
    you shall break off his yoke from your neck."

And Esau seethed with resentment against Jacob over the blessing his father had blessed him, and Esau said in his heart, "As soon as the time for mourning my father comes round, I will kill Jacob my brother." And Rebekah was told the words of Esau her elder son, and she sent and summoned Jacob her younger son and said to him, "Look, Esau your brother is consoling himself with the idea he will kill you. So now, my son, listen to my voice, and rise, flee to my brother Laban in Haran, and you may stay with him a while until your brother's wrath subsides, until your brother's rage against you subsides and he forgets what you did to him, and I shall send and fetch you from there. Why should I be bereft of you both on one day?" And Rebekah said to Isaac, "I loathe my life because of the Hittite women! If Jacob takes a wife from Hittite women like these, from the native girls, what good to me is life?"

From Genesis 28

[*Jacob's Dream*]

28. ✳ ✳ ✳ And Jacob left Beersheba and set out for Haran. And he came upon a certain place and stopped there for the night, for the sun had set, and he took one of the stones of the place and put it at his head and he lay down in that place, and he dreamed, and, look, a ramp was set against the ground with its top reaching the heavens, and, look, messengers of God were going up and coming down it. And, look, the LORD was poised over him and He said, "I, the LORD, am the God of Abraham your father and the God of Isaac. The land on which you lie, to you I will give it and to your seed. And your seed shall be like the dust of the earth and you shall burst forth to the west and the east and the north and the south, and all the clans of the earth shall be blessed through you, and through your seed. And, look, I am with you and I will guard you wherever you go, and I will bring you back to this land, for I will not leave you until I have done that which I have spoken to you." And Jacob awoke from his sleep and he said, "Indeed, the LORD is in this place, and I did not know." And he was afraid and he said,

> "How fearsome is this place!
> This can be but the house of God,
>   and this is the gate of the heavens."

And Jacob rose early in the morning and took the stone he had put at his head, and he set it as a pillar and poured oil over its top. And he called the name of that place Bethel, though the name of the town before had been Luz. And Jacob made a vow, saying, "If the LORD God be with me and guard me on this way that I am going and give me bread to eat and clothing to wear, and I return safely to my father's house, then the LORD will be my God. And this stone that I set as a pillar will be a house of God, and everything that You give me I will surely tithe it to You."

From Genesis 29

[*Rachel and Leah*]

29. And Jacob lifted his feet and went on to the land of the Easterners. And he saw and, look, there was a well in the field, and, look, three flocks of sheep were lying beside it, for from that well they would water the flocks, and the stone was big on the mouth of the well. And when all the flocks were gathered there, they would roll the stone from the mouth of the well and would water the sheep and put back the stone in its place on the mouth of the well. And Jacob said to them, "My brothers, where are you from?" And they said, "We are from Haran." And he said to them, "Do you know Laban son of Nabor?" And they said, "We know him." And he said to them, "Is he well?" And they said, "He is well, and, look, Rachel his daughter is coming with the sheep." And he said, "Look, the day is still long. It is not time to gather in the herd. Water the sheep and take them to graze." And they said, "We cannot until all the flocks have gathered and the stone is rolled from the mouth of the well and we water

the sheep." He was still speaking with them when Rachel came with her father's sheep, for she was a shepherdess. And it happened when Jacob saw Rachel daughter of Laban his mother's brother and the sheep of Laban his mother's brother that he stepped forward and rolled the stone from the mouth of the well and watered the sheep of Laban his mother's brother. And Jacob kissed Rachel and lifted his voice and wept. And Jacob told Rachel that he was her father's kin, and that he was Rebekah's son, and she ran and told her father. And it happened, when Laban heard the report of Jacob his sister's son, he ran toward him and embraced him and kissed him and brought him to his house. And he recounted to Laban all these things. And Laban said to him, "Indeed, you are my bone and my flesh."

And he stayed with him a month's time, and Laban said to Jacob, "Because you are my kin, should you serve me for nothing? Tell me what your wages should be." And Laban had two daughters. The name of the elder was Leah and the name of the younger Rachel. And Leah's eyes were tender, but Rachel was comely in features and comely to look at, and Jacob loved Rachel. And he said, "I will serve seven years for Rachel your younger daughter." And Laban said, "Better I should give her to you than give her to another man. Stay with me." And Jacob served seven years for Rachel, and they seemed in his eyes but a few days in his love for her. And Jacob said to Laban, "Give me my wife, for my time is done, and let me come to bed with her." And Laban gathered all the men of the place and made a feast. And when evening came, he took Leah his daughter and brought her to Jacob, and he came to bed with her. And Laban gave Zilpah his slavegirl to Leah his daughter as her slavegirl. And when morning came, look, she was Leah. And he said to Laban, "What is this you have done to me? Was it not for Rachel that I served you, and why have you deceived me?" And Laban said, "It is not done thus in our place, to give the younger girl before the firstborn. Finish out the bridal week of this one and we shall give you the other as well for the service you render me for still another seven years." And so Jacob did. And when he finished out the bridal week of the one, he gave him Rachel his daughter as wife. And Laban gave to Rachel his daughter Bilhah his slavegirl as her slavegirl. And he came to bed with Rachel, too, and, indeed, loved Rachel more than Leah, and he served him still another seven years.

* * *

From Genesis 31

[*Jacob's Flight Back to Canaan*]

31. And he[5] heard the words of Laban's sons, saying, "Jacob has taken everything of our father's, and from what belonged to our father he has made all this wealth." And Jacob saw Laban's face and, look, it was not disposed toward him as in time past. And the LORD said to Jacob, "Return to the land of your fathers and to your birthplace and I will be with you."

* * *

5. Jacob.

From Genesis 32

[*Jacob Is Renamed Israel*]

32. * * * And he rose on that night and took his two wives and his two slave-girls and his eleven boys and he crossed over the Jabbok ford. And he took them and brought them across the stream, and he brought across all that he had. And Jacob was left alone, and a man wrestled with him until the break of dawn. And he saw that he had not won out against him and he touched his hip-socket and Jacob's hip-socket was wrenched as he wrestled with him. And he said, "Let me go, for dawn is breaking." And he said, "I will not let you go unless you bless me." And he said to him, "What is your name?" And he said, "Jacob." And he said, "Not Jacob shall your name hence be said, but Israel, for you have striven with God and men, and won out." And Jacob asked and said, "Tell your name, pray." And he said, "Why should you ask my name?" and there he blessed him. And Jacob called the name of the place Peniel, meaning, "I have seen God face to face and I came out alive." And the sun rose upon him as he passed Penuel[6] and he was limping on his hip. Therefore the children of Israel do not eat the sinew of the thigh which is by the hip-socket to this day, for he had touched Jacob's hip-socket at the sinew of the thigh.

From Genesis 33

[*Jacob and Esau Reconciled*]

33. And Jacob raised his eyes and saw and, look, Esau was coming, and with him were four hundred men. And he divided the children between Leah and Rachel, and between the two slavegirls. And he placed the slavegirls and their children first, and Leah and her children after them, and Rachel and Joseph[7] last. And he passed before them and bowed to the ground seven times until he drew near his brother. And Esau ran to meet him and embraced him and fell upon his neck and kissed him, and they wept. And he raised his eyes and saw the women and the children and he said, "Who are these with you?" And he said, "The children with whom God has favored your servant," And the slave-girls drew near, they and their children, and they bowed down. And Leah, too, and her children drew near, and they bowed down, and then Joseph and Rachel drew near and bowed down. And he said, "What do you mean by all this camp I have met?" And he said, "To find favor in the eyes of my lord." And Esau said, "I have much, my brother. Keep what you have." And Jacob said, "O, no, pray, if I have found favor in your eyes, take this tribute from my hand, for have I not seen your face as one might see God's face, and you received me in kindness? Pray, take my blessing that has been brought you, for God has favored me and I have everything." And he pressed him, and he took it.

* * *

6. "Penuel" is an alternate spelling of "Peniel." It is not clear why the text uses both.

7. Joseph is the first-born son of Rachel and Jacob.

From Exodus 19–20[1]

[*Moses Receives the Law*]

19. On the third new moon of the Israelites' going out from Egypt, on this day did they come to the Wilderness of Sinai. And they journeyed onward from Rephidim and they came to the Wilderness of Sinai, and Israel camped there over against the mountain. And Moses had gone up to God, and the LORD called out to him from the mountain, saying, "Thus shall you say to the house of Jacob, and shall you tell to the Israelites: 'You yourselves saw what I did to Egypt, and I bore you on the wings of eagles[2] and I brought you to Me. And now, if you will truly heed My voice and keep My covenant, you will become for Me a treasure among all the peoples, for Mine is all the earth. And as for you, you will become for Me a kingdom of priests and a holy nation.' These are the words that you shall speak to the Israelites."

And Moses came and he called to the elders of the people, and he set before them all these words that the LORD had charged him. And all the people answered together and said, "Everything that the LORD has spoken we shall do." And Moses brought back the people's words to the LORD. And the LORD said to Moses, "Look, I am about to come to you in the utmost cloud, so that the people may hear as I speak to you, and you as well they will trust for all time." And Moses told the people's words to the LORD. And the LORD said to Moses, "Go to the people and consecrate them today and tomorrow, and they shall wash their cloaks. And they shall ready themselves for the third day, for on the third day the LORD will come down before the eyes of all the people on Mount Sinai. And you shall set bounds for the people all around, saying, 'Watch yourselves not to go up on the mountain or to touch its edge. Whosoever touches the mountain is doomed to die. No hand shall touch him,[3] but He shall surely be stoned or be shot, whether beast or man, he shall not live. When the ram's horn blasts long, they[4] it is who will go up the mountain.'" And Moses came down from the mountain to the people, and he consecrated the people, and they washed their cloaks. And he said to the people, "Ready yourselves for three days. Do not go near a woman."[5] And it happened on the third day as it turned morning, that there was thunder and lightning and a heavy cloud on the mountain and the sound of the ram's horn, very strong, and all the people who were in the camp trembled. And Moses brought out the people toward God from the camp and they stationed themselves at the bottom of the mountain. And Mount Sinai was all in smoke because the LORD had come down on it in fire, and its smoke went up like the smoke from a kiln, and the whole mountain trembled greatly. And the sound of the ram's horn grew stronger and stronger. Moses would speak, and God would answer him with

1. Translated by Robert Alter, to whose notes some of the following annotations are indebted.
2. A metaphor for salvation. "What I did unto the Egyptians" refers to the plagues that afflicted Egypt and to the destruction of the Egyptian army, as it pursued the departing Israelites, at the Red Sea.

3. Whoever violates the ban on touching the mountain will be impure and an outcast from the community. Therefore he has to be killed at a distance, with stones or arrows.
4. I.e., Moses and Aaron.
5. Sexual abstinence and the washing of clothes were methods of ritual purification.

voice.[6] And the LORD came down on Mount Sinai, to the mountaintop, and the LORD called Moses to the mountaintop, and Moses went up. And the LORD said to Moses, "Go down, warn the people, lest they break through to the LORD to see and many of them perish. And the priests, too, who come near to the LORD, shall consecrate themselves,[7] lest the LORD burst forth against them." And Moses said to the Lord, "The people will not be able to come up to Mount Sinai, for You Yourself warned us, saying, 'Set bounds to the mountain and consecrate it.'" And the LORD said to him, "Go down, and you shall come up, you and Aaron[8] with you, and the priests and the people shall not break through to go up to the LORD, lest He burst forth against them." And Moses went down to the people and said it to them.

20. And God spoke all these words, saying: "I am the LORD your God Who brought you out of the land of Egypt, out of the house of slaves. You[9] shall have no other gods beside Me. You shall make you no carved likeness and no image of what is in the heavens above or what is on the earth below or what is in the waters beneath the earth. You shall not bow to them and you shall not worship them, for I am the LORD your God, a jealous god, reckoning the crime of fathers with sons, with the third generation and with the fourth, for My foes and doing kindness to the thousandth generation for My friends and for those who keep My commands. You shall not take the name of the LORD your God in vain, for the LORD will not acquit whosoever takes His name in vain. Remember the sabbath day to hallow it. Six days you shall work and you shall do your tasks, but the seventh day is a sabbath to the LORD your God. You shall do no task, you and your son and your daughter, your male slave and your slavegirl and your beast and your sojourner who is within your gates. For six days did the LORD make the heavens and the earth, the sea and all that is in it, and He rested on the seventh day. Therefore did the LORD bless the sabbath day and hallow it. Honor your father and your mother, so that your days may be long on the soil that the LORD your God has given you. You shall not murder. You shall not commit adultery. You shall not steal. You shall not bear false witness against your fellow man. You shall not covet your fellow man's wife, or his male slave, or his slavegirl, or his ox, or his donkey, or anything that your fellow man has."

And all the people were seeing the thunder and the flashes and the sound of the ram's horn and the mountain in smoke, and the people saw and they drew back and stood at a distance. And they said to Moses, "Speak you with us that we may hear, and let not God speak with us lest we die." And Moses said to the people, "Do not fear, for in order to test you God has come and in order that His fear be upon you, so that you do not offend." And the people stood at a distance, and Moses drew near the thick cloud where God was.

* * *

6. I.e., with words.

7. I.e., they are to purify themselves and remain at the bottom of the mountain as the rest of the people do.

8. Moses' closest companion and in an early tradition his brother; Aaron was Israel's first

High Priest.

9. Here and throughout this passage, the Hebrew text uses the singular of "you" (formulations of law elsewhere in the Hebrew Bible use the plural). The commandments are thus addressed to each person individually.

Psalm 8[1]

1. O Lord our Lord, how excellent is thy name in all the earth! who hast set thy glory above the heavens.

2. Out of the mouth of babes and sucklings hast thou ordained strength because of thine enemies, that thou mightest still the enemy and the avenger.

3. When I consider thy heavens, the work of thy fingers, the moon and the stars, which thou hast ordained;

4. What is man, that thou art mindful of him? and the son of man, that thou visitest him?

5. For thou hast made him a little lower than the angels, and hast crowned him with glory and honour.

6. Thou madest him to have dominion over the works of thy hands; thou hast put all things under his feet:

7. All sheep and oxen, yea, and the beasts of the field;

8. The fowl of the air, and the fish of the sea, and whatsoever passeth through the paths of the seas.

9. O Lord our Lord, how excellent is thy name in all the earth!

Psalm 19

1. The heavens declare the glory of God; and the firmament sheweth his handywork.

2. Day unto day uttereth speech, and night unto night sheweth knowledge.

3. There is no speech nor language, where their voice is not heard.

4. Their line is gone out through all the earth, and their words to the end of the world. In them hath he set a tabernacle for the sun,

5. Which is as a bridegroom coming out of his chamber, and rejoiceth as a strong man to run a race.

6. His going forth is from the end of the heaven, and his circuit unto the ends of it: and there is nothing hid from the heat thereof.

7. The law of the Lord is perfect, converting the soul: the testimony of the Lord is sure, making wise the simple.

8. The statutes of the Lord are right, rejoicing the heart: the commandment of the Lord is pure, enlightening the eyes.

9. The fear of the Lord is clean, enduring for ever: the judgments of the Lord are true and righteous altogether.

10. More to be desired are they than gold, yea, than much fine gold: sweeter also than honey and the honeycomb.

11. Moreover by them is thy servant warned: and in keeping of them there is great reward.

12. Who can understand his errors? cleanse thou me from secret faults.

13. Keep back thy servant also from presumptuous sins; let them not have dominion over me: then shall I be upright, and I shall be innocent from the great transgression.

---

1. The text of the Psalms is that of the King James version.

14. Let the words of my mouth, and the meditation of my heart, be acceptable in thy sight, O Lord, my strength, and my redeemer.

Psalm 23

1. The Lord is my shepherd; I shall not want.

2. He maketh me to lie down in green pastures: he leadeth me beside the still waters.

3. He restoreth my soul: he leadeth me in the paths of righteousness for his name's sake.

4. Yea, though I walk through the valley of the shadow of death, I will fear no evil: for thou art with me; thy rod and thy staff they comfort me.

5. Thou preparest a table before me in the presence of mine enemies: thou anointest my head with oil; my cup runneth over.

6. Surely goodness and mercy shall follow me all the days of my life: and I will dwell in the house of the Lord for ever.

Psalm 104

1. Bless the Lord, O my soul. O Lord my God, thou art very great; thou art clothed with honour and majesty.

2. Who coverest thyself with light as with a garment: who stretchest out the heavens like a curtain:

3. Who layeth the beams of his chambers in the waters: who maketh the clouds his chariot: who walketh upon the wings of the wind:

4. Who maketh his angels spirits; his ministers a flaming fire:

5. Who laid the foundations of the earth, that it should not be removed for ever.

6. Thou coveredst it with the deep as with a garment: the waters stood above the mountains.

7. At thy rebuke they fled; at the voice of thy thunder they hasted away.

8. They go up by the mountains; they go down by the valleys unto the place which thou hast founded for them.

9. Thou hast set a bound that they may not pass over; that they turn not again to cover the earth.

10. He sendeth the springs into the valleys, which run among the hills.

11. They give drink to every beast of the field: the wild asses quench their thirst.

12. By them shall the fowls of the heaven have their habitation, which sing among the branches.

13. He watereth the hills from his chambers: the earth is satisfied with the fruit of thy works.

14. He causeth the grass to grow for the cattle, and herb for the service of man: that he may bring forth food out of the earth;

15. And wine that maketh glad the heart of man, and oil to make his face to shine, and bread which strengtheneth man's heart.

16. The trees of the Lord are full of sap; the cedars of Lebanon, which he hath planted;

17. Where the birds make their nests: as for the stork, the fir trees are her house.

18. The high hills are a refuge for the wild goats; and the rocks for the conies.

19. He appointed the moon for seasons: the sun knoweth his going down.

20. Thou makest darkness, and it is night: wherein all the beasts of the forest do creep forth.

21. The young lions roar after their prey, and seek their meat from God.

22. The sun ariseth, they gather themselves together, and lay them down in their dens.

23. Man goeth forth unto his work and to his labour until the evening.

24. O Lord, how manifold are thy works! in wisdom hast thou made them all: the earth is full of thy riches.

25. So is this great and wide sea, wherein are things creeping innumerable, both small and great beasts.

26. There go the ships: there is that leviathan, whom thou hast made to play therein.

27. These wait all upon thee; that thou mayest give them their meat in due season.

28. That thou givest them they gather: thou openest thine hand, they are filled with good.

29. Thou hidest thy face, they are troubled: thou takest away their breath, they die, and return to their dust.

30. Thou sendest forth thy spirit, they are created: and thou renewest the face of the earth.

31. The glory of the Lord shall endure for ever: the Lord shall rejoice in his works.

32. He looketh on the earth, and it trembleth: he toucheth the hills, and they smoke.

33. I will sing unto the Lord as long as I live: I will sing praise to my God while I have my being.

34. My meditation of him shall be sweet: I will be glad in the Lord.

35. Let the sinners be consumed out of the earth, and let the wicked be no more. Bless thou the Lord, O my soul. Praise ye the Lord.

Psalm 137

1. By the rivers of Babylon,[1] there we sat down, yea, we wept, when we remembered Zion.

2. We hanged our harps upon the willows in the midst thereof.

3. For there they that carried us away captive required of us a song; and they that wasted us required of us mirth, saying, Sing us one of the songs of Zion.

---

1. On the Euphrates River. Jerusalem was captured and sacked by the Babylonians in 586 B.C.E. The Hebrews were taken away into captivity in Babylon.

4. How shall we sing the Lord's song in a strange land?

5. If I forget thee, O Jerusalem, let my right hand forget her cunning.

6. If I do not remember thee, let my tongue cleave to the roof of my mouth; if I prefer not Jerusalem above my chief joy.

7. Remember, O Lord, the children of Edom[2] in the day of Jerusalem; who said, Rase it, rase it, even to the foundation thereof.

8. O daughter of Babylon, who art to be destroyed; happy shall he be, that rewardeth thee as thou hast served us.

9. Happy shall he be, that taketh and dasheth thy little ones against the stones.

---

2. The Edomites helped the Babylonians capture Jerusalem.

HOMER

eighth century B.C.E.

The *Iliad* and the *Odyssey* tell the story of the clash of two great civilizations, and the effects of war on both the winners and the losers. Both poems are about the Trojan War, a mythical conflict between a coalition of Greeks and the inhabitants of Troy, a city in Asia Minor. These are the earliest works of Greek literature, composed almost three thousand years before our time. Yet they are rich and sophisticated in their narrative techniques, and they provide extraordinarily vivid portrayals of people, social relationships, and feelings, especially our incompatible desires for honor and violence, and for peace and a home.

HISTORICAL CONTEXTS

On the Greek island of Crete is an enormous palace, dominated by monumental arches adorned with fierce lions, built by the earliest Greek-speaking people: the Myceneans, who probably inspired the Trojan legends. About 2000 B.C.E., they began building big, fortified cities around central palaces in the south of Greece. The Myceneans had a form of writing—not an alphabet but a "syllabary" (in which a symbol corresponds to each syllable, not to each letter)—as well as a centralized, tightly controlled economy and sophisticated artistic and architectural traditions. The metal they used for weapons, armor, and tools was predominantly bronze, and their time is therefore known as the Bronze Age.

After dominating the region for around six hundred years, Mycenean civilization came to an end in around 1200 B.C.E. Archaeological investigations suggest that the great cities were burnt or destroyed around this time, perhaps by invasion or war. The next few hundred years are known as the Dark Ages of Greece: people seem to have been less wealthy, and the cultural knowledge of the Myceneans, including the knowledge of writing, was lost.

Greeks of this time spoke many different dialects and lived in small towns and villages scattered across a wide area. They did not regain their knowledge of reading or writing until an alphabet, invented by a trading people called the Phoenicians, was adopted in the eighth century B.C.E.

One might think that an illiterate society could have nothing like "literature," a word based on the Latin for "letters" (*litterae*). In the centuries of Greek illiteracy, however, there developed a thriving tradition of oral poetry, especially on the Ionian coast, in modern-day Turkey. Travelling bards told tales of the lost age of heroes who fought with bronze, and of the great cities besieged and destroyed by war. The Homeric poems make use of folk memories of a real conflict or conflicts between the Mycenean Greeks and inhabitants of one or more cities in Asia Minor. The world of Homer is neither historical in a modern sense, nor purely fictional. Through poetry, the Greeks of the Dark Ages created and preserved their own past.

Oral poets in ancient Greece used a traditional form (a six-part line called hexameter), fitting their own riffs into the rhythm, with musical accompaniment. They also relied on common themes, traditional stories, traditional characters, traditional adjectives (such as "swift Achilles" or "black ships"), phrases that fit the rhythm of the line, and even whole scenes that follow a set pattern, such as the way a warrior gets dressed or the way that meals are prepared. Fluent poetic ad-libbing is very difficult; these techniques gave each performer a structure, so that stories and lines did not have to be generated entirely on the spot. We know that the tradition of this type of composition must have gone back hundreds of years, because the *Iliad* and the *Odyssey*

include details that would have been anachronistic by the time these poems were written down, such as the use of bronze weapons: by the eighth century, soldiers fought with iron. Details from different periods are jumbled together, so that even in the eighth century B.C.E. the heroic, mythic world of the Homeric poems must have seemed quite distinct from everyday reality. In addition, the poems mix different Greek dialects, the speech of many different areas in the Greek-speaking world, into a language unlike anything anyone ever spoke.

It is hard to understand the relation between the heroic poetry composed and sung by illiterate bards in archaic Greece, and the written texts of the *Odyssey* and the *Iliad*. The question is made all the more difficult because the poems are far longer than most instances of oral poetic performance, including that of the oral poets living in the former Yugoslavia, who were studied by classicists in the twentieth century as the closest living analogy to ancient Greek bards. Good bards may be able to keep going for an hour or two: in the Homeric poems themselves, there are accounts of singers performing for a while after dinner. But a complete performance of either of these poems would have lasted at least twenty hours. This is much too long for an audience to sit through in an evening. It would also have been difficult for any poet, even a genius, to compose at this length without the use of writing. Perhaps, then, these poems are the work of an oral poet, or poets, who became literate. Or perhaps they represent a collaboration between one or more oral poets, and a scribe. In any case, soon after the Greeks developed their alphabet, they found a way to preserve their oral tradition in two monumental written poems.

These works make use of tradition in strikingly original ways, creating just two coherent stories out of the mass of legends that surrounded the Trojan War. They are long poems about heroes, a genre that later came to be called "epic"—from the Greek for "story" or "word." Throughout the ancient world, for hundreds of years to come, everybody knew the *Iliad* and the *Odyssey*. The poems were performed out loud, illustrated in paintings on vases or on walls, read, learned by heart, remembered, reworked, and imitated by everyone in the Greek and Roman worlds, from the Athenian tragedians to the Roman poet **Virgil**.

THE *ILIAD*

The title *Iliad* suggests a work about the Trojan War, since *Ilias* is another name for Troy. Greek readers or listeners would have been familiar with the background myths. Paris, a prince of Troy, son of King Priam, had to judge which of three goddesses should be awarded a golden apple: Athena, goddess of wisdom; Hera, the queen of the gods—a representative of power; or Aphrodite, goddess of sexual desire. He chose Aphrodite, and as his reward she gave him the most beautiful woman in the world, Helen of Sparta, as his wife. Unfortunately, Helen already had a husband: Menelaus, brother of the powerful general Agamemnon. When Paris took Helen with him back to Troy from Mycenae, Agamemnon and Menelaus mustered a great army, a coalition drawn from many Greek cities, including the great heroes Achilles, the fastest runner and best fighter, and Odysseus, the cleverest of the Greeks. So began a war that lasted ten years, until Odysseus finally found a stratagem to enter the city walls of Troy. He built a wooden horse, filled it with Greek armed men, and tricked the Trojans into taking the horse into the city. The Greek soldiers leaped from the horse and killed the male inhabi-

tants, captured the women, and razed the city to the ground.

Surprisingly, none of these events play any part in the main narrative of the *Iliad*, which begins when the war is already in its tenth year and ends before the capture of the city. Moreover, the central focus is not on the conflict between Greeks and Trojans, but on a conflict among the Greek commanders. The first word of the *Iliad* is "Rage," and the rage of Achilles—first against his comrade Agamemnon, and only later against the enemy Trojans—is the central subject of the poem. In Greek, the word used is *menis*, a term otherwise applied only to the wrath of the gods. Achilles' rage is an extraordinary thing, which sets him apart from the rest of humanity—Greeks and Trojans. The poem tells how Achilles, the greatest Greek hero and the son of a goddess, becomes alienated from his society, how his rage against the Greeks shifts into an inhuman aggression against the Trojans, and how he is at last willing to return to the human world.

The *Iliad* is about war, honor, and aggression. There are moments of graphic violence, when we are told exactly where the point of a spear or sword penetrates vulnerable human flesh: as when Achilles' friend Patroclus throws his spear at another warrior, Sarpedon, and catches him "just below the rib cage / where it protects the beating heart"; or when Hector rams his spear into Patroclus, "into the pit of his belly and all the way through"; or when Achilles' spear "pierced the soft neck but did not slit the windpipe." The precise anatomical detail reminds us of how vulnerable these warriors are, because they have mortal bodies—in contrast to the gods, who may participate in battle but can never die.

The plot deals with the exchange or ransoming of human bodies. Achilles' anger at Agamemnon is roused by a quarrel about who owns Briseis, a girl Achilles has seized as a prize of war but whom Agamemnon takes as recompense for the loss of his own girl, Chryseis. The story also hinges on the ownership of dead male bodies: the corpses, in turn, of Sarpedon, Patroclus, and Hector. War seems to produce its own kind of economy, a system of exchange: a live girl for a dead warrior, one life for another, or death for undying fame.

The *Iliad* is a violent poem, and, on one level, the violence simply contributes to the entertainment: it is exciting to hear or read about slaughter. But it would be a mistake to see the *Iliad* as pure military propaganda. At times, the poem brings out the terrible pity of war: the city of Troy will be ruined, the people killed or enslaved, and the poet looks back with regret to "the days of peace, before the Greeks came." Some similes compare the violence on the battlefield to the events of the world of peace, where people can plough the fields, build homes, and watch their sheep. But these similes may suggest that violence and the threat of pain and death are facts of life: even when people are at peace, there is murder, and lions or wolves leap into the fold to kill the sheep.

Within the narrow world of the battlefield, Homer's vividly imagined characters have choices to make. They cannot choose, like gods, to avoid death; but they can choose how they will die. The poem itself acknowledges that the exchange of honor for death may seem inadequate. After Agamemnon has treated him dishonorably, Achilles begins to question the whole heroic code, and its system of trading death for glory: "Nothing is worth my life," he declares, since prizes of honor can always be replaced but "a man's life cannot be won back." Unlike the other fighters, Achilles knows for sure—thanks to the goddess Thetis, his

mother—that staying at Troy will mean his death. But all the warriors of the *Iliad* are conscious that in fighting they risk their own deaths. Achilles' choices—to fight and die soon, in this war, or go home and live a little longer—are therefore a starker version of the decision faced by all these warriors.

Fascinatingly, the *Iliad* makes the Trojans as fully human as the Greeks. The Trojan hero, Hector, seems to many readers the most likeable character in the poem, fighting not for honor or vengeance but to protect his wife and their infant son. One of the most touching moments comes as Hector says goodbye to his tearful wife before going into battle; a deep tenderness connects Hector and his family—in contrast to the more shallow associations of the Greeks with their female prisoners of war. As Hector reaches down to kiss his son, the child screams, frightened at seeing his father in his helmet. The parents laugh together, and Hector takes off the helmet so the baby will not be scared as he swings him in his arms. The moment is both heartwarming and chilling, since we know—and his wife knows—that this devoted father will never see his son again; the baby is right to be frightened, since he will soon be swung headlong from the city walls by the victorious Greeks.

The *Iliad* culminates in an astonishing encounter, between Priam, king of Troy, and Achilles, who has killed his son Hector. Priam goes to plead with Achilles to return his son's body, and the two enemies end up sitting together, each weeping for those they have lost. The experience of grief is common to all humans, even those who kill each other in war. The major contrast drawn by the *Iliad* is not between Greek and Trojan, but between the humans and the immortal gods. The gods play an important role in the action of the poem, sometimes intervening to cause or

Achilles (left) slays Hector. From a red-figured volute-krater (a large ceramic wine decanter), ca. 500–480 B.C.E.

prevent a hero's death or dishonor. We are told at the beginning that there is a connection between all the deaths caused by Achilles' rage and the will of Zeus: the whole action of the poem happened "as Zeus' will was done." But the presence of the gods does not turn the human characters into puppets, controlled only by the gods or by fate. Human characters are never forced by gods to act out of character. Rather, human action and divine action work together, and the gods provide a way of talking about the elements of human experience that are otherwise incomprehensible.

Moreover, the presence of the gods—like the similes—makes us particularly aware of what is distinctive about human life in war. In the world of the gods, there are conflicts about hierarchy, just as there are on earth: sometimes the lesser gods refuse to recognize the authority of Zeus, just as some Greek chieftains sometimes refuse to bow to Agamemnon. But on Olympus, all quarrels end in laughter and drinking, not death. The most important fact about all the warriors in the *Iliad* is that they die. Moreover, before death humans have to face grief, dishonor, loss, and pain—things that

play little or no part in any god's life. Achilles in his rage refuses to accept the horror of loss: loss of honor, and the loss of his dearest friend, Patroclus. His rage can end, and he can eat again, only when he realizes that all humans, even the greatest warriors, have to have "hearts of iron," the ability to endure unendurable loss and keep on living. The *Iliad* provides a bleak but inspiring account of human suffering as a kind of power, which the gods themselves cannot achieve.

THE *ODYSSEY*

The *Odyssey*, which is included in its entirety in this anthology, has a special place in the study of world literature, since it deals explicitly with the relationship between the kind of people we know and those who are strange to us. It is about a journey that spans most of the world as it was known to Greeks at the time, and deals with issues that any student of world literature must confront, including the place of literature and memory in the formation of cultural identity. The poem shows us, in depth and in detail, the complex relationships between one westerner, a Greek man, and the other cultures that he encounters—not in war, but in the course of a long journey, where the worst enemies may lie inside his own household. The poem tells the story of Odysseus's homecoming from Troy, tracing his reclamation of a household from which he has been absent for the past twenty years. It is a gripping and varied tale, which includes fantasy and magic but also focuses on domestic details and on the human need for a family and a home.

The *Odyssey* is set after the *Iliad*, and was probably produced a little later, since it seems deliberately to avoid repeating anything that had been included in the *Iliad*, and fills in many important details that had been absent from the earlier poem—including allusions to the actual fall of Troy, and its aftermath. The *Odyssey* creates a different but complementary vision of the Trojan War, showing how the Greeks faced further danger in the long voyage back to Greece, and in their return to homes from which they had been absent for many years.

In the Greek original, the first word of the *Odyssey*—our first clue to the poem's subject—is *andra* ("man"). One man, Odysseus himself, is the center of the poem, in a way that no single hero, not even Achilles, is the center of the *Iliad*. The journey from war to peace requires different skills from those needed on the battlefield, and through the figure of Odysseus the poem shows us what those skills might be. He has strength and physical courage, but he also has brains: "the cunning hero" is the cleverest of those who fought at Troy. He is famously adaptable, a "man of many turns," able to deal with any eventuality, no matter how difficult or unexpected. He has psychological strength, an ability both to endure and to inflict pain without flinching; more than once, the poem connects the name *Odysseus* with the Greek word for "to be angry" or "hate"

(*odyssomai*): Odysseus is the man hated by the god Poseidon. He has the patience and self-restraint required to bide his time until the moment comes for him to reveal himself to his household. Most of all, he has the will to go home, and to restore his home to its proper order. It is no accident that Odysseus's favorite weapon is not the sword or the spear but the bow, which shoots from a distance at the target of his choice.

"Man" is also the subject of the *Odyssey* in a broader sense, because the poem has a particular interest in the diversity of cultures and ways of life. The *Iliad* is set almost exclusively on the battlefield of Troy, and focused on the relationships between the aristocratic male warriors. By contrast, the *Odyssey* shows us a multitude of distinct worlds and cultures, including non-human cultures. Odysseus spends years on the luxurious island of the nymph Calypso; he encounters the sweet-singing Sirens, the monster Scylla, and the Lotus-eaters; and he disembarks on the island of the sun, with its tempting, delicious cows, and of the witch Circe, who can turn men to pigs. He is almost killed on the island of the shepherd-giants, the Cyclopes, and he is welcomed in the magical land of Phaeacia, where fruits flourish all season long, and where he meets the king, the queen, and the princess, Nausicaa, who is out to do laundry and play ball with her girlfriends, while day-dreaming about her future husband. The many cultures of the poem include both the exotic and the ordinary.

Even in the Greek world, we are given glimpses of several distinct ways of life. The rich land of Sparta, ruled by Menelaus and his recovered wife, the beautiful, sophisticated Helen, with her fancy embroidery and her narcotics, contrasts with the poor island of Ithaca, Odysseus's homeland, which is too stony to raise horses or plentiful crops. In Ithaca, we see the lives of women as well as men; of old Laertes, Odysseus's father, as well as his insecure young son, Telemachus; and of the poor as well as the rich— including the old nurse who washes Odysseus and the pig-keeper, Eumaeus, who gives him shelter. In showing multiple encounters between the Greek hero and people who are very different from him, the Homeric poem invites us to think about how we ought to behave toward people who are not the same as ourselves.

The *Odyssey* is particularly concerned with the laws of hospitality, which in Greek is *xenia*—a word that covers the whole relationship between guests and hosts, and between strangers and those who take them in. Hospitality is the fundamental criterion for civilized society in this poem. Cultures may vary in other respects, but any good society will accommodate the wandering guest. Odysseus encounters many strange peoples in the course of his wanderings. Some, like the goddess Calypso, are almost too welcoming: she invites him into her home and her bed, and keeps him there even when he longs to go home. Odysseus acknowledges that Calypso is far more beautiful than his own wife and that her island is more lush than his own stony home; but, movingly, he still wants to go back. This poem deals with the fundamental desire we feel for our own people and our own place, not because they are better than any other, but simply because they are ours. Similarly, Odysseus rejects the possibility of starting his life over in the hospitable land of the Phaeacians. The monstrous one-eyed Cyclops, Polyphemus, is a grotesque counterpart to the good Phaeacian hosts: instead of welcoming and feeding his guests, the Cyclops wants to eat them for dinner. This encounter is a reminder of how distinctive, and unheroic, are the skills Odysseus needs to survive the journey home. Heroes in battle, in the *Iliad*,

are always concerned that their names be remembered in times to come. But Odysseus defeats Polyphemus— whose name suggests "Much-named"— by denying his own name, calling himself "Noman." The journey home has to trump even Odysseus's heroic identity.

At times, Odysseus's own men seem to transgress the laws of hospitality, as when they kill the cattle of the Sun, which they have been expressly forbidden to touch. We see further variations on the theme of hospitality in the visits that Odysseus's son, Telemachus, pays to his father's friends. The account in the first four books of Telemachus' activities—short journeys to visit uncles, cousins, and kinsmen in the surrounding neighborhood—may seem oddly inconsequential, and even unheroic. But a great deal of the *Odyssey*'s attraction lies in the way it values the little details of human relationships and human feelings over grand tales of honor and killing in war.

Hospitality is tested most severely when Odysseus arrives back as a stranger in his own home. The suitors have seized control of his house and are abusing his unwitting hospitality, in his absence, by courting his wife, devouring his food and drink, and ruining his property. There are repeated references in the *Odyssey* to the nightmare double of Odysseus's return: the homecoming of Agamemnon, who came back from Troy only to be killed in his bath by his wife, Clytemnestra, and her lover, Aegisthus. Zeus, the king of the gods, insists at the beginning of the poem that Aegisthus is hated by the gods, and he praises Agamemnon's son, Orestes, who avenges his father's death by killing the adulterous murderer.

First-time readers may be surprised that the wanderings of Odysseus, across the sea from Troy back to his stony Greek homeland, Ithaca, occupy only a short part of the whole poem. In the second half of the poem, beginning at book 13,

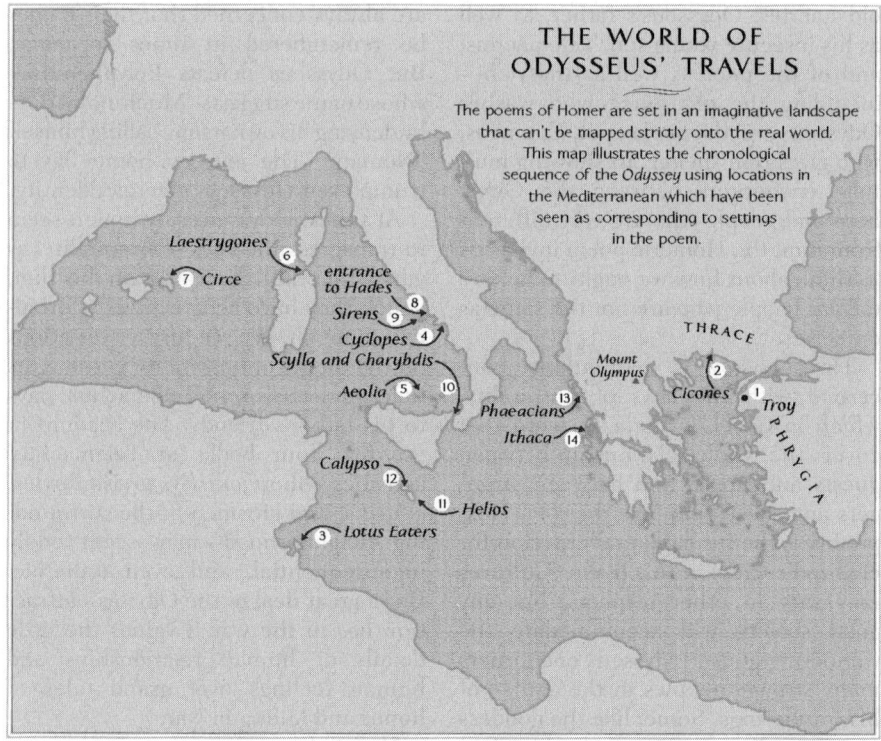

THE WORLD OF ODYSSEUS' TRAVELS

The poems of Homer are set in an imaginative landscape that can't be mapped strictly onto the real world. This map illustrates the chronological sequence of the *Odyssey* using locations in the Mediterranean which have been seen as corresponding to settings in the poem.

Laestrygones
6
7 Circe
entrance to Hades
8
Sirens 9
Cyclopes 4
Scylla and Charybdis
Aeolia 5 10
THRACE
Mount Olympus
2
Cicones
Troy
PHRYGIA
Phaeacians 13
Ithaca 14
Calypso 12
11 Helios
3 Lotus Eaters

Odysseus is back home in Ithaca. But his journey is only half complete. He arrives home as a stranger, disguised as a poor beggar. The act of homecoming seems to require several stages, beyond merely reaching a geographic location. Odysseus comes up with multiple tales to explain his presence in Ithaca; he uses his many disguises to test the loyalty of those he meets—and, as in the encounter with Polyphemus, he must show enormous self-control in his willingness to suppress his identity, at least temporarily. Throughout the poem, Odysseus has a particularly close affinity with poets and storytellers; he himself narrates his wanderings to the Phaeacians, and, once back on Ithaca, he tells a series of false stories about who he is and where he comes from. Controlling and multiplying stories is one of the most important ways in which Odysseus is a "man of many turns," able to see the multiplicity of the world and constantly to redefine his own place in it.

In the course of his homecoming, Odysseus passes a series of tests, and gets tests of his own. He must show his mastery of weapons (such as the strongbow) and his knowledge of the people who make up his household. Odysseus has to win the peace by reconnecting with each loyal member of his home: his servants, his son, his father, and—most memorably—his wife, Penelope. He tests her loyalty by refusing to reveal himself to her right away. But she shows herself a perfect match for her trickster husband, putting him to yet another test. When it is bedtime, she asks the servant to bring out the bed—the bed that, as only Odysseus himself could know, is formed from a tree growing right through the house; if Odysseus were an imposter, he would think the bed could be moved. The immovable bed is, of course, an image for the permanence of Penelope and Odysseus's marriage. When they talk in the bed that night after sex, a simile suggests that now, at last, both Odysseus and Penelope have come home; he, weeping, and she, clinging to him, are like sailors saved from drowning, "glad / To be alive and set foot on dry land." The image first seems to apply to Odysseus, and then to Penelope—a shift that suggests the dynamic intimacy between husband and wife.

The *Odyssey* has elements we associate with many other types of literature: romance, folklore, heroism, mystery, travellers' tales, magic, military exploits, and family drama. It is a text that can be enjoyed on any number of levels: as a feminized version of epic—a heroic story focused not on men fighting wars, but a journey home; as a love story; as a fantasy about fathers, sons, and patriarchy; as an account of Greek identity; as a work of primitive anthropology; as a meditation on cultural difference; as a morality tale; or as a pilgrim's progress. As the first word indicates, this is a poem about "man": about humanity. An extraordinarily rich work, as multilayered and intelligent as its hero, the *Odyssey* is enjoyable on first reading, and worth rereading over and over again.

From The Iliad[1]

BOOK I

[*The Rage of Achilles*]

Rage:
        Sing; Goddess,[2] Achilles' rage,
Black and murderous, that cost the Greeks
Incalculable pain, pitched countless souls
Of heroes into Hades' dark,
And left their bodies to rot as feasts   5
For dogs and birds, as Zeus' will was done.
   Begin with the clash between Agamemnon—
The Greek warlord—and godlike Achilles.

   Which of the immortals set these two
At each other's throats?   10
               Apollo,
Zeus' son and Leto's, offended
By the warlord. Agamemnon had dishonored
Chryses,[3] Apollo's priest, so the god
Struck the Greek camp with plague,   15
And the soldiers were dying of it.
                    Chryses
Had come to the Greek beachhead camp
Hauling a fortune for his daughter's ransom.

---

1. Translated by Stanley Lombardo.
2. The Muse, inspiration for epic poetry.
3. Chryses is from the town of Chryse near Troy. The Greeks had captured his daughter when they sacked Thebes (see below) and had given her to Agamemnon as his share of the booty.

Displaying Apollo's sacral ribbons   20
On a golden staff, he made a formal plea
To the entire Greek army, but especially
The commanders, Atreus' two sons:

"Sons of Atreus and Greek heroes all:
May the gods on Olympus grant you plunder   25
Of Priam's city[4] and a safe return home.
But give me my daughter back and accept
This ransom out of respect for Zeus' son,
Lord Apollo, who deals death from afar."—

A murmur rippled through the ranks: 30
"Respect the priest and take the ransom."
But Agamemnon was not pleased
And dismissed Chryses with a rough speech:

"Don't let me ever catch you, old man, by these ships again,
Skulking around now or sneaking back later.   35
The god's staff and ribbons won't save you next time.
The girl is mine, and she'll be an old woman in Argos[5]
Before I let her go, working the loom in my house
And coming to my bed, far from her homeland.
Now clear out of here before you make me angry!"   40

The old man was afraid and did as he was told.
He walked in silence along the whispering surf line,
And when he had gone some distance the priest
Prayed to Lord Apollo, son of silken-haired Leto:

"Hear me, Silverbow, Protector of Chryse,   45
Lord of Holy Cilia, Master of Tenedos,[6]
And Sminthian[7] God of Plague!
If ever I've built a temple that pleased you
Or burnt fat thighbones of bulls and goats[8]—
    Grant me this prayer: 50
Let the Danaans[9] pay for my tears with your arrows!"

Apollo heard his prayer and descended Olympus' crags
Pulsing with fury, bow slung over one shoulder,
The arrows rattling in their case on his back
As the angry god moved like night down the mountain.   55

4. Troy; Priam is its king. Olympus is the mountain in northern Greece that was supposed to be the home of the gods.
5. Agamemnon's home in the northeastern Peloponnesus, the southern part of mainland Greece.
6. An island off the Trojan coast. Like Chryse, Cilla is a town near Troy.
7. A cult epithet of Apollo, probably a reference to his role as the destroyer of field mice (the Greek *sminthos* means "mouse").
8. In sacrifice to Apollo.
9. The Greeks. Homer also calls them Achaeans and Argives.

He settled near the ships and let loose an arrow.
Reverberation from his silver bow hung in the air.
He picked off the pack animals first, and the lean hounds,
But then aimed his needle-tipped arrows at the men
And shot until the death-fires crowded the beach.   60

  Nine days the god's arrows rained death on the camp.
On the tenth day Achilles called an assembly.
Hera,[1] the white-armed goddess, planted the thought in him
Because she cared for the Greeks and it pained her
To see them dying. When the troops had all mustered,   65
Up stood the great runner Achilles, and said:

"Well, Agamemnon, it looks as if we'd better give up
And sail home—assuming any of us are left alive—
If we have to fight both the war and this plague.
But why not consult some prophet or priest   70
Or a dream interpreter, since dreams too come from Zeus,
Who could tell us why Apollo is so angry,
If it's for a vow or a sacrifice he holds us at fault.
Maybe he'd be willing to lift this plague from us
If he savored the smoke from lambs and prime goats."   75

Achilles had his say and sat down. Then up rose
Calchas, son of Thestor, bird-reader supreme,
Who knew what is, what will be, and what has been.
He had guided the Greek ships to Troy
Through the prophetic power Apollo   80
Had given him, and he spoke out now:

"Achilles, beloved of Zeus, you want me to tell you
About the rage of Lord Apollo, the Arch-Destroyer.
And I will tell you. But you have to promise me and swear
You will support me and protect me in word and deed.   85
I have a feeling I might offend a person of some authority
Among the Greeks, and you know how it is when a king
Is angry with an underling. He might swallow his temper
For a day, but he holds it in his heart until later
And it all comes out. Will you guarantee my security?"   90

Achilles, the great runner, responded:

"Don't worry. Prophesy to the best of your knowledge.
I swear by Apollo, to whom you pray when you reveal
The gods' secrets to the Greeks, Calchas, that while I live
And look upon this earth, no one will lay a hand   95
On you here beside these hollow ships, no, not even
Agamemnon, who boasts he is the best of the Achaeans."

1. Sister and wife of Zeus; she was hostile to the Trojans and therefore favored the Greeks.

And Calchas, the perfect prophet, taking courage:

"The god finds no fault with vow or sacrifice.
It is for his priest, whom Agamemnon dishonored   100
And would not allow to ransom his daughter,
That Apollo deals and will deal death from afar.
He will not lift this foul plague from the Greeks
Until we return the dancing-eyed girl to her father
Unransomed, unbought, and make formal sacrifice   105
On Chryse. Only then might we appease the god."

He finished speaking and sat down. Then up rose
Atreus' son, the warlord Agamemnon,
Furious, anger like twin black thunderheads seething
In his lungs, and his eyes flickered with fire   110
As he looked Calchas up and down, and said:

                    "You damn soothsayer!
You've never given me a good omen yet.
You take some kind of perverse pleasure in prophesying
Doom, don't you? Not a single favorable omen ever!   115
Nothing good ever happens! And now you stand here
Uttering oracles before the Greeks, telling us
That your great ballistic god is giving us all this trouble
Because I was unwilling to accept the ransom
For Chryses' daughter but preferred instead to keep her   120
In my tent! And why shouldn't I? I like her better than
My wife Clytemnestra. She's no worse than her
When it comes to looks, body, mind, or ability.
Still, I'll give her back, if that's what's best.
I don't want to see the army destroyed like this.   125
But I want another prize ready for me right away.
I'm not going to be the only Greek without a prize,
It wouldn't be right. And you all see where mine is going."

And Achilles, strong, swift, and godlike:

"And where do you think, son of Atreus,   130
You greedy glory-hound, the magnanimous Greeks
Are going to get another prize for you?
Do you think we have some kind of stockpile in reserve?
Every town in the area has been sacked and the stuff all divided.
You want the men to count it all back and redistribute it? 135
All right, you give the girl back to the god. The army
Will repay you three and four times over—when and if
Zeus allows us to rip Troy down to its foundations."

The warlord Agamemnon responded:

"You may be a good man in a fight, Achilles,   140
And look like a god, but don't try to put one over on me—

It won't work. So while you have your prize,
You want me to sit tight and do without?
Give the girl back, just like that? Now maybe
If the army, in a generous spirit, voted me   145
Some suitable prize of their own choice, something fair—
But if it doesn't, I'll just go take something myself,
Your prize perhaps, or Ajax's, or Odysseus',[2]
And whoever she belongs to, it'll stick in his throat.

But we can think about that later.   150
                          Right now we launch
A black ship on the bright salt water, get a crew aboard,
Load on a hundred bulls, and have Chryseis[3] board her too,
My girl with her lovely cheeks. And we'll want a good man
For captain, Ajax or Idomeneus[4] or godlike Odysseus—   155
Or maybe you, son of Peleus, our most formidable hero—
To offer sacrifice and appease the Arch-Destroyer for us."

Achilles looked him up and down and said:

"You shameless, profiteering excuse for a commander!
How are you going to get any Greek warrior   160
To follow you into battle again? You know,
I don't have any quarrel with the Trojans,
They didn't do anything to *me* to make me
Come over here and fight, didn't run off *my* cattle or horses
Or ruin *my* farmland back home in Phthia,[5] not with all   165
The shadowy mountains and moaning seas between.
It's for *you*, dogface, for your precious pleasure—
And Menelaus'[6] honor—that we came here,
A fact you don't have the decency even to mention!
And now you're threatening to take away the prize   170
That I sweated for and the Greeks gave me.
I never get a prize equal to yours when the army
Captures one of the Trojan strongholds.
No, I do all the dirty work with my own hands,
And when the battle's over and we divide the loot   175
You get the lion's share and I go back to the ships
With some pitiful little thing, so worn out from fighting
I don't have the strength left even to complain.
Well, I'm going back to Phthia now. Far better
To head home with my curved ships than stay here,   180
Unhonored myself and piling up a fortune for you."

2. Ajax, son of Telamon, was the bravest of the Greeks after Achilles, Odysseus the most crafty of the Greeks.
3. Daughter of Chryses.
4. King of Crete and a prominent leader on the Greek side.
5. Achilles' home in northern Greece.
6. Agamemnon's brother. The aim of the expedition against Troy was to recover his wife, Helen, who had run off with Paris, a son of Priam.

The warlord Agamemnon responded:

"Go ahead and desert, if that's what you want!
I'm not going to beg you to stay. There are plenty of others
Who will honor me, not least of all Zeus the Counselor.   185
To me, you're the most hateful king under heaven,
A born troublemaker. You actually *like* fighting and war.
If you're all that strong, it's just a gift from some god.
So why don't you go home with your ships and lord it over
Your precious Myrmidons.[7] I couldn't care less about you   190
Or your famous temper. But I'll tell you this:
Since Phoebus Apollo is taking away my Chryseis,
Whom I'm sending back aboard ship with my friends,
I'm coming to your hut and taking Briseis,[8]
Your own beautiful prize, so that you will see just how much   195
Stronger I am than you, and the next person will wince
At the thought of opposing me as an equal."

Achilles' chest was a rough knot of pain
Twisting around his heart: should he
Draw the sharp sword that hung by his thigh,   200
Scatter the ranks and gut Agamemnon,
Or control his temper, repress his rage?
He was mulling it over, inching the great sword
From its sheath, when out of the blue
Athena[9] came, sent by the white-armed goddess   205
Hera, who loved and watched over both men.
She stood behind Achilles and grabbed his sandy hair,
Visible only to him: not another soul saw her.
Awestruck, Achilles turned around, recognizing
Pallas Athena at once—it was her eyes—   210
And words flew from his mouth like winging birds:

"Daughter of Zeus! Why have you come here?
To see Agamemnon's arrogance, no doubt.
I'll tell you where I place my bets, Goddess:
Sudden death for this outrageous behavior."   215

Athena's eyes glared through the sea's salt haze.

"I came to see if I could check this temper of yours,
Sent from heaven by the white-armed goddess
Hera, who loves and watches over both of you men.
Now come on, drop this quarrel, don't draw your sword.   220
Tell him off instead. And I'll tell you,

7. The contingent led by Achilles.
8. A captive woman who had been awarded to
Achilles.
9. A goddess, daughter of Zeus, and a patron of
human ingenuity and resourcefulness, whether
exemplified by handicrafts (such as carpentry
or weaving) or cunning in dealing with others.
One of her epithets is Pallas. Like Hera, she
sided with the Greeks in the war.

Achilles, how things will be: You're going to get
Three times as many magnificent gifts
Because of his arrogance. Just listen to us and be patient."

Achilles, the great runner, responded: 225

"When you two speak, Goddess, a man has to listen
No matter how angry. It's better that way.
Obey the gods and they hear you when you pray."

With that he ground his heavy hand
Onto the silver hilt and pushed the great sword   230
Back into its sheath. Athena's speech
Had been well-timed. She was on her way
To Olympus by now, to the halls of Zeus
And the other immortals, while Achilles
Tore into Agamemnon again: 235

                    "You bloated drunk,
With a dog's eyes and a rabbit's heart!
You've never had the guts to buckle on armor in battle
Or come out with the best fighting Greeks
On any campaign! Afraid to look Death in the eye,   240
Agamemnon? It's far more profitable
To hang back in the army's rear—isn't it?—
Confiscating prizes from any Greek who talks back
And bleeding your people dry. There's not a real man
Under your command, or this latest atrocity   245
Would be your last, son of Atreus.
Now get this straight. I swear a formal oath:
  By this scepter,[1] which will never sprout leaf
Or branch again since it was cut from its stock
In the mountains, which will bloom no more   250
Now that bronze has pared off leaf and bark,
And which now the sons of the Greeks hold in their hands
At council, upholding Zeus' laws—
                    By this scepter I swear:
When every last Greek desperately misses Achilles,   255
Your remorse won't do any good then,
When Hector[2] the man-killer swats you down like flies.
And you will eat your heart out
Because you failed to honor the best Greek of all."

Those were his words, and he slammed the scepter,   260
Studded with gold, to the ground and sat down.

---

1. A wooden staff that symbolized authority. authority to speak.
It was handed by a herald to whichever leader 2. Son of Priam; he was the foremost warrior
rose to speak in an assembly as a sign of his among the Trojans.

Opposite him, Agamemnon fumed.
                                    Then Nestor
Stood up, sweet-worded Nestor, the orator from Pylos[3]
With a voice high-toned and liquid as honey.   265
He had seen two generations of men pass away
In sandy Pylos and was now king in the third.
He was full of good will in the speech he made:

"It's a sad day for Greece, a sad day.
Priam and Priam's sons would be happy indeed,   270
And the rest of the Trojans too, glad in their hearts,
If they learned all this about you two fighting,
Our two best men in council and in battle.
Now you listen to me, both of you. You are both
Younger than I am, and I've associated with men   275
Better than you, and they didn't treat me lightly.
I've never seen men like those, and never will,
The likes of Peirithous and Dryas, a shepherd to his people,
Caineus and Exadius and godlike Polyphemus,
And Aegeus' son, Theseus,[4] who could have passed for a god,   280
The strongest men who ever lived on earth, the strongest,
And they fought with the strongest, with wild things
From the mountains, and beat the daylights out of them.
I was their companion, although I came from Pylos,
From the ends of the earth—they sent for me themselves.   285
And I held my own fighting with them. You couldn't find
A mortal on earth who could fight with them now.
And when I talked in council, they took my advice.
So should you two now: taking advice is a good thing.
    Agamemnon, for all your nobility, don't take his girl.   290
Leave her be: the army originally gave her to him as a prize.
Nor should you, son of Peleus, want to lock horns with a king.
A scepter-holding king has honor beyond the rest of men,
Power and glory given by Zeus himself.
You are stronger, and it is a goddess[5] who bore you.   295
But he is more powerful, since he rules over more.
Son of Atreus, cease your anger. And I appeal
Personally to Achilles to control his temper, since he is,
For all Greeks, a mighty bulwark in this evil war."

And Agamemnon, the warlord: 300

"Yes, old man, everything you've said is absolutely right.
But this man wants to be ahead of everyone else,

---

3. A territory on the western shore of the Peloponnesus.
4. Heroes of an earlier generation. Except for the Athenian Theseus, these are the Lapiths from Thessaly in northern Greece. At the wedding of Peirithous, the mountain-dwelling centaurs (half human, half horse) got drunk and tried to rape the women who were present. The Lapiths killed them after a fierce fight.
5. The sea nymph Thetis, who was married to the mortal Peleus (Achilles' father). She later left him and went to live with her father, Nereus, in the depths of the Aegean Sea.

He wants to rule everyone, give orders to everyone,
Lord it over everyone, and he's not going to get away with it.
If the gods eternal made him a spearman, does that mean   305
They gave him permission to be insolent as well?"

And Achilles, breaking in on him:

"Ha, and think of the names people would call me
If I bowed and scraped every time you opened your mouth.
Try that on somebody else, but not on me.   310
I'll tell you this, and you can stick it in your gut:
I'm not going to put up a fight on account of the girl.
You, all of you, gave her and you can all take her back.
But anything else of mine in my black sailing ship
You keep your goddamn hands off, you hear?   315
Try it. Let everybody here see how fast
Your black blood boils up around my spear."

    So it was a stand-off, their battle of words,
And the assembly beside the Greek ships dissolved.
Achilles went back to the huts by his ships   320
With Patroclus[6] and his men. Agamemnon had a fast ship
Hauled down to the sea, picked twenty oarsmen,
Loaded on a hundred bulls due to the god, and had Chryses' daughter,
His fair-cheeked girl, go aboard also. Odysseus captained,
And when they were all on board, the ship headed out to sea.   325

Onshore, Agamemnon ordered a purification.
The troops scrubbed down and poured the filth
Into the sea. Then they sacrificed to Apollo
Oxen and goats by the hundreds on the barren shore.
The smoky savor swirled up to the sky.   330

That was the order of the day. But Agamemnon
Did not forget his spiteful threat against Achilles.
He summoned Talthybius and Eurybates,
Faithful retainers who served as his heralds:

"Go to the hut of Achilles, son of Peleus;   335
Bring back the girl, fair-cheeked Briseis.
If he won't give her up, I'll come myself
With my men and take her—and freeze his heart cold."

It was not the sort of mission a herald would relish.
The pair trailed along the barren seashore   340
Until they came to the Myrmidons' ships and encampment.
They found Achilles sitting outside his hut
Beside his black ship. He was not glad to see them.

6. Achilles' closest friend.

They stood respectfully silent, in awe of this king,
And it was Achilles who was moved to address them first: 345

"Welcome, heralds, the gods' messengers and men's.
Come closer. You're not to blame, Agamemnon is,
Who sent you here for the girl, Briseis.
                              Patroclus,
Bring the girl out and give her to these gentlemen.   350
You two are witnesses before the blessed gods,
Before mortal men and that hard-hearted king,
If ever I'm needed to protect the others
From being hacked to bits. His mind is murky with anger,
And he doesn't have the sense to look ahead and behind   355
To see how the Greeks might defend their ships."

Thus Achilles.
              Patroclus obeyed his beloved friend
And brought Briseis, cheeks flushed, out of the tent
And gave her to the heralds, who led her away.   360
She went unwillingly.
                    Then Achilles, in tears,
Withdrew from his friends and sat down far away
On the foaming white seashore, staring out
At the endless sea. Stretching out his hands,   365
He prayed over and over to his beloved mother:

"Mother, since you bore me for a short life only,
Olympian Zeus was supposed to grant me honor.
Well, he hasn't given me any at all. Agamemnon
Has taken away my prize and dishonored me."   370

His voice, choked with tears, was heard by his mother
As she sat in the sea-depths beside her old father.
She rose up from the white-capped sea like a mist,
And settling herself beside her weeping child
She stroked him with her hand and talked to him: 375

"Why are you crying, son? What's wrong?
Don't keep it inside. Tell me so we'll both know."

And Achilles, with a deep groan:

"You already know. Why do I have to tell you?
We went after Thebes, Eëtion's[7] sacred town,   380
Sacked it and brought the plunder back here.
The army divided everything up and chose
For Agamemnon fair-cheeked Chryseis.
Then her father, Chryses, a priest of Apollo,

---

7. Eëtion was king of the Cilicians in Asia Minor and father of Hector's wife, Andromache.
"Thebes" (or Thebe): the Cilicians' capital city, not the Greek or Egyptian city of the same name.

Came to our army's ships on the beachhead,   385
Hauling a fortune for his daughter's ransom.
He displayed Apollo's sacral ribbons
On a golden staff and made a formal plea
To the entire Greek army, but especially
The commanders, Atreus' two sons.   390
You could hear the troops murmuring,
'Respect the priest and take the ransom.'
But Agamemnon wouldn't hear of it
And dismissed Chryses with a rough speech.
The old man went back angry, and Apollo   395
Heard his beloved priest's prayer.
He hit the Greeks hard, and the troops
Were falling over dead, the god's arrows
Raining down all through the Greek camp.
A prophet told us the Arch-Destroyer's will,   400
And I demanded the god be appeased.
Agamemnon got angry, stood up
And threatened me, and made good his threat.
The high command sent the girl on a fast ship
Back to Chryse with gifts for Apollo,   405
And heralds led away my girl, Briseis,
Whom the army had given to me.
Now you have to help me, if you can.
    Go to Olympus
And call in the debt that Zeus owes you.   410
I remember often hearing you tell
In my father's house how you alone managed,
Of all the immortals, to save Zeus' neck
When the other Olympians wanted to bind him—
Hera and Poseidon[8] and Pallas Athena.   415
You came and loosened him from his chains,
And you lured to Olympus' summit the giant
With a hundred hands whom the gods call
Briareus but men call Aegaeon, stronger
Even than his own father Uranus,[9] and he   420
Sat hulking in front of cloud-black Zeus,
Proud of his prowess, and scared all the gods
Who were trying to put the son of Cronus in chains.
    Remind Zeus of this, sit holding his knees,
See if he is willing to help the Trojans   425
Hem the Greeks in between the fleet and the sea.
Once they start being killed, the Greeks may
Appreciate Agamemnon for what he is,
And the wide-ruling son of Atreus will see
What a fool he's been because he did not honor   430
The best of all the fighting Achaeans."

8. Brother of Zeus and god of the sea.
9. The Sky, husband of Earth and the first divine   ruler. He was overthrown by his son Cronus, who
in turn was overthrown by his son Zeus.

And Thetis, now weeping herself:

"O my poor child. I bore you for sorrow,
Nursed you for grief. Why? You should be
Spending your time here by your ships   435
Happily and untroubled by tears,
Since life is short for you, all too brief.
Now you're destined for both an early death
And misery beyond compare. It was for this
I gave birth to you in your father's palace   440
Under an evil star.
                    I'll go to snow-bound Olympus
And tell all this to the Lord of Lightning.
I hope he listens. You stay here, though,
Beside your ships and let the Greeks feel   445
Your spite; withdraw completely from the war.
Zeus left yesterday for the River Ocean
On his way to a feast with the Ethiopians.[1]
All the gods went with him. He'll return
To Olympus twelve days from now,   450
And I'll go then to his bronze threshold
And plead with him. I think I'll persuade him."

And she left him there, angry and heartsick
At being forced to give up the silken-waisted girl.

    Meanwhile, Odysseus was putting in   455
At Chryse with his sacred cargo on board.
When they were well within the deepwater harbor
They furled the sail and stowed it in the ship's hold,
Slackened the forestays and lowered the mast,
Working quickly, then rowed her to a mooring, where   460
They dropped anchor and made the stern cables fast.
The crew disembarked on the seabeach
And unloaded the bulls for Apollo the Archer.
Then Chryses' daughter stepped off the seagoing vessel,
And Odysseus led her to an altar   465
And placed her in her father's hands, saying:

"Chryses, King Agamemnon has sent me here
To return your child and offer to Phoebus
Formal sacrifice on behalf of the Greeks.
So may we appease Lord Apollo, and may he   470
Lift the afflictions he has sent upon us."

Chryses received his daughter tenderly.

---

1. A people believed to live at the extreme edges of the world. Ocean was thought of as a river
that encircled the earth.

Moving quickly, they lined the hundred oxen
Round the massive altar, a glorious offering,
Washed their hands and sprinkled on the victims   475
Sacrificial barley. On behalf of the Greeks
Chryses lifted his hands and prayed aloud:

"Hear me, Silverbow, Protector of Chryse,
Lord of Holy Cilla, Master of Tenedos,
As once before you heard my prayer,   480
Did me honor, and smote the Greeks mightily,
So now also grant me this prayer:
                              Lift the plague
From the Greeks and save them from death."

Thus the old priest, and Apollo heard him.   485

After the prayers and the strewing of barley
They slaughtered and flayed the oxen,
Jointed the thighbones and wrapped them
In a layer of fat with cuts of meat on top.
The old man roasted them over charcoal   490
And doused them with wine. Younger men
Stood by with five-tined forks in their hands.
When the thigh pieces were charred and they had
Tasted the tripe, they cut the rest into strips,
Skewered it on spits and roasted it skillfully.   495
When they were done and the feast was ready,
Feast they did, and no one lacked an equal share.
When they had all had enough to eat and drink,
The young men topped off mixing bowls with wine
And served it in goblets to all the guests.   500
All day long these young Greeks propitiated
The god with dancing, singing to Apollo
A paean[2] as they danced, and the god was pleased.
When the sun went down and darkness came on,
They went to sleep by the ship's stern-cables.   505

Dawn came early, a palmetto of rose,
Time to make sail for the wide beachhead camp.
They set up mast and spread the white canvas,
And the following wind, sent by Apollo,
Boomed in the mainsail. An indigo wave   510
Hissed off the bow as the ship surged on,
Leaving a wake as she held on course through the billows.
When they reached the beachhead they hauled the black ship
High on the sand and jammed in the long chocks;
Then the crew scattered to their own huts and ships.   515

All this time Achilles, the son of Peleus in the line of Zeus,[3]
Nursed his anger, the great runner idle by his fleet's fast hulls.

---

2. A song of praise to Apollo.   3. Peleus was the son of Aeacus, son of Zeus.

He was not to be seen in council, that arena for glory,
Nor in combat. He sat tight in camp consumed with grief,
His great heart yearning for the battle cry and war.   520

    Twelve days went by. Dawn.
The gods returned to Olympus,
Zeus at their head.
               Thetis did not forget
Her son's requests. She rose from the sea   525
And up through the air to the great sky
And found Cronus' wide-seeing son
Sitting in isolation on the highest peak
Of the rugged Olympic massif.
She settled beside him, and touched his knees   530
With her left hand, his beard with her right,[4]
And made her plea to the Lord of Sky:

"Father Zeus, if I have ever helped you
In word or deed among the immortals,
  Grant me this prayer: 535
Honor my son, doomed to die young
And yet dishonored by King Agamemnon,
Who stole his prize, a personal affront.
Do justice by him, Lord of Olympus.
Give the Trojans the upper hand until the Greeks   540
Grant my son the honor he deserves."

Zeus made no reply but sat a long time
In silence, clouds scudding around him.
Thetis held fast to his knees and asked again:

"Give me a clear yes or no. Either nod in assent   545
Or refuse me. Why should you care if I know
How negligible a goddess I am in your eyes."

This provoked a troubled, gloomy response:

"This is disastrous. You're going to force me
Into conflict with Hera. I can just hear her now,   550
Cursing me and bawling me out. As it is,
She already accuses me of favoring the Trojans.
Please go back the way you came. Maybe
Hera won't notice. I'll take care of this.
And so you can have some peace of mind,   555
I'll say yes to you by nodding my head,
The ultimate pledge. Unambiguous,
Irreversible, and absolutely fulfilled,
Whatever I say yes to with a nod of my head."

---

4. She takes on the posture of the suppliant, which physically emphasizes the desperation and
urgency of her request. Zeus was, above all other gods, the protector of suppliants.

And the Son of Cronus nodded. Black brows   560
Lowered, a glory of hair cascaded down from the Lord's
Immortal head, and the holy mountain trembled.

   Their conference over, the two parted. The goddess
Dove into the deep sea from Olympus' snow-glare
And Zeus went to his home. The gods all   565
Rose from their seats at their father's entrance. Not one
Dared watch him enter without standing to greet him.
And so the god entered and took his high seat.
                                 But Hera
Had noticed his private conversation with Thetis,   570
The silver-footed daughter of the Old Man of the Sea,
And flew at him with cutting words:

"Who was that you were scheming with just now?
You just love devising secret plots behind my back,
Don't you? You can't bear to tell me what you're thinking,   575
Or you don't dare. Never have and never will."

The Father of Gods and Men answered:

"Hera, don't hope to know all my secret thoughts.
It would strain your mind even though you are my wife.
What it is proper to hear, no one, human or divine,   580
Will hear before you. But what I wish to conceive
Apart from the other gods, don't pry into that."

And Lady Hera, with her oxen eyes wide:

"Oh my. The awesome son of Cronus has spoken.
Pry? You know that I never pry. And you always   585
Cheerfully volunteer—whatever information you please.
It's just that I have this feeling that somehow
The silver-footed daughter of the Old Man of the Sea
May have won you over. She *was* sitting beside you
Up there in the mists, and she did touch your knees.   590
And I'm pretty sure that you agreed to honor Achilles
And destroy Greeks by the thousands beside their ships."

And Zeus, the master of cloud and storm:

"You witch! Your intuitions are always right.
But what does it get you? Nothing, except that   595
I like you less than ever. And so you're worse off.
If it's as you think it is, it's my business, not yours.
So sit down and shut up and do as I say.
You see these hands? All the gods on Olympus
Won't be able to help you if I ever lay them on you."   600

Hera lost her nerve when she heard this.
She sat down in silence, fear cramping her heart,

And gloom settled over the gods in Zeus' hall.
Hephaestus,[5] the master artisan, broke the silence,
Out of concern for his ivory-armed mother: 605

"This is terrible; it's going to ruin us all.
If you two quarrel like this over mortals
It's bound to affect us gods. There'll be no more
Pleasure in our feasts if we let things turn ugly.
Mother, please, I don't have to tell you,   610
You have to be pleasant to our father Zeus
So he won't be angry and ruin our feast.
If the Lord of Lightning wants to blast us from our seats,
He can—that's how much stronger he is.
So apologize to him with silken-soft words,   615
And the Olympian in turn will be gracious to us."

He whisked up a two-handled cup, offered it
To his dear mother, and said to her:

"I know it's hard, mother, but you have to endure it.
I don't want to see you getting beat up, and me   620
Unable to help you. The Olympian can be rough.
Once before when I tried to rescue you
He flipped me by my foot off our balcony.
I fell all day and came down when the sun did
On the island of Lemnos[6] scarcely alive.   625
The Sintians had to nurse me back to health."

By the time he finished, the ivory-armed goddess
Was smiling at her son. She accepted the cup from him.
Then the lame god turned serving boy, siphoning nectar[7]
From the mixing bowl and pouring the sweet liquor   630
For all of the gods, who couldn't stop laughing
At the sight of Hephaestus hustling through the halls.

And so all day long until the sun went down
They feasted to their hearts' content,
Apollo playing beautiful melodies on the lyre,   635
The Muses singing responsively in lovely voices.
And when the last gleams of sunset had faded,
They turned in for the night, each to a house
Built by Hephaestus, the renowned master craftsman,
The burly blacksmith with the soul of an artist.   640
And the Lord of Lightning, Olympian Zeus, went to his bed,
The bed he always slept in when sweet sleep overcame him.
He climbed in and slept, next to golden-throned Hera.

---

5. The lame god of fire and the patron of   the Sintians.
craftspeople, especially metalworkers.   7. The drink of the gods.
6. An island in the Aegean Sea, inhabited by

Summary   As Achilles, angry with Agamemnon, stays out of the fighting, the Trojans make a series of successful attacks against the Greek forces. They are led by the greatest of the Trojan heroes, Hector, son of Priam and brother of Paris, who leaves behind his wife and infant son to challenge the invading army and defend his home. When Hector brings the Trojan soldiers right up to the Greek ships, ready to set them on fire, Agamemnon acknowledges that he made a mistake to alienate Achilles, and sends messengers (including Odysseus) to try to persuade the hero to return to the war. But Achilles holds out, and the fighting continues. Many men die on both sides. Finally Achilles' friend, Patroclus, volunteers to fight in his place, borrowing Achilles' own armor. He is killed by Hector, who strips him of the borrowed armor. When Achilles hears of his friend's death, he is overwhelmed with grief and savage rage. His mother, Thetis, has the god Hephaestus provide Achilles with new armor, and the warrior returns to battle. He slaughters many Trojans, and shows no pity even to those who beg him for mercy. He even tries to fight against divine forces, challenging the river of Troy, the Scamander, and chasing Apollo, who is fighting on the Trojan side. When we pick up the story, Achilles is desperate to kill Hector, the man who killed his friend.

BOOK XXII

[*The Death of Hector*]

Everywhere you looked in Troy, exhausted
Soldiers, glazed with sweat like winded deer,
Leaned on the walls, cooling down
And slaking their thirst.
                         Outside, the Greeks   5
Formed up close to the wall, locking their shields.
In the dead air between the Greeks
And Troy's Western Gate, Destiny
Had Hector pinned, waiting for death.

Then Apollo called back to Achilles: 10

"Son of Peleus, you're fast on your feet,
But you'll never catch me, man chasing god.
Or are you too raging mad to notice
I'm a god? Don't you care about fighting
The Trojans anymore? You've chased them back   15
Into their town, but now you've veered off here.
You'll never kill me. You don't hold my doom."

And the shining sprinter, Achilles:

"That was a dirty trick, Apollo,
Turning me away from the wall like that!   20
I could have ground half of Troy face down
In the dirt! Now you've robbed me
Of my glory and saved them easily
Because you have no retribution to fear.
I swear, I'd make you pay if I could!"   25

His mind opened to the clear space before him,
And he was off toward the town, moving

   Like a thoroughbred stretching it out
   Over the plain for the final sprint home—

Achilles, lifting his knees as he lengthened his stride.   30

Priam saw him first, with his old man's eyes,
A single point of light on Troy's dusty plain.

> *Sirius[8] rises late in the dark, liquid sky*
> *On summer nights, star of stars,*
> *Orion's Dog they call it, brightest*   35
> *Of all, but an evil portent, bringing heat*
> *And fevers to suffering humanity.*

Achilles' bronze gleamed like this as he ran.

And the old man groaned, and beat his head
With his hands, and stretched out his arms   40
To his beloved son, Hector, who had
Taken his stand before the Western Gate,
Determined to meet Achilles in combat.

Priam's voice cracked as he pleaded:

"Hector, my boy, you can't face Achilles   45
Alone like that, without any support—
You'll go down in a minute. He's too much
For you, son, he won't stop at anything!
O, if only the gods loved him as I do:
Vultures and dogs would be gnawing his corpse.   50
Then some grief might pass from my heart.
So many fine sons he's taken from me,
Killed or sold them as slaves in the islands.
Two of them now, Lycaon and Polydorus,
I can't see with the Trojans safe in town,   55
Laothoë's boys.[9] If the Greeks have them
We'll ransom them with the gold and silver
Old Altes gave us.[1] But if they're dead
And gone down to Hades, there will be grief
For myself and the mother who bore them.   60
The rest of the people won't mourn so much
Unless *you* go down at Achilles' hands.
So come inside the wall, my boy.
Live to save the men and women of Troy.
Don't just hand Achilles the glory   65
And throw your life away. Show some pity for me
Before I go out of my mind with grief
And Zeus finally destroys me in my old age,
After I have seen all the horrors of war—

8. The Dog Star, the brightest star in the constellation Canis Major. In Greece it rises in late summer, the hottest time of the year.
9. Laothoë was one of Priam's wives. Achilles killed Polydorus and Lycaon in the fighting outside the city (books 20 and 21).
1. The dowry of Laothoë, Altes' daughter.

My sons butchered, my daughters dragged off, 70
Raped, bedchambers plundered, infants
Dashed to the ground in this terrible war,
My sons' wives abused by murderous Greeks.
And one day some Greek soldier will stick me
With cold bronze and draw the life from my limbs, 75
And the dogs that I fed at my table,
My watchdogs, will drag me outside and eat
My flesh raw, crouched in my doorway, lapping
My blood.
                    When a young man is killed in war, 80
Even though his body is slashed with bronze,
He lies there beautiful in death, noble.
But when the dogs maraud an old man's head,
Griming his white hair and beard and private parts,
There's no human fate more pitiable." 85

And the old man pulled the white hair from his head,
But did not persuade Hector.
                                His mother then,
Wailing, sobbing, laid open her bosom
And holding out a breast spoke through her tears: 90

"Hector, my child, if ever I've soothed you
With this breast, remember it now, son, and
Have pity on me. Don't pit yourself
Against that madman. Come inside the wall.
If Achilles kills you I will never 95
Get to mourn you laid out on a bier, O
My sweet blossom, nor will Andromache,
Your beautiful wife, but far from us both
Dogs will eat your body by the Greek ships."

So the two of them pleaded with their son, 100
But did not persuade him or touch his heart.
Hector held his ground as Achilles' bulk
Loomed larger. He waited as a snake waits,

    Tense and coiled
    As a man approaches 105
    Its lair in the mountains,
    Venom in its fangs
    And poison in its heart,
    Glittering eyes
    Glaring from the rocks: 110

So Hector waited, leaning his polished shield
Against one of the towers in Troy's bulging wall,
But his heart was troubled with brooding thoughts:

"Now what? If I take cover inside,
Polydamas will be the first to reproach me. 115

He begged me to lead the Trojans back
To the city on that black night when Achilles rose.
But I wouldn't listen, and now I've destroyed
Half the army through my recklessness.
I can't face the Trojan men and women now,   120
Can't bear to hear some lesser man say,
'Hector trusted his strength and lost the army.'
That's what they'll say. I'll be much better off
Facing Achilles, either killing him
Or dying honorably before the city.   125
 But what if I lay down all my weapons,
Bossed shield, heavy helmet, prop my spear
Against the wall, and go meet Achilles,
Promise him we'll surrender Helen
And everything Paris brought back with her   130
In his ships' holds to Troy—that was the beginning
Of this war—give all of it back
To the sons of Atreus and divide
Everything else in the town with the Greeks,
And swear a great oath not to hold   135
Anything back, but share it all equally,
All the treasure in Troy's citadel.
 But why am I talking to myself like this?
I can't go out there unarmed. Achilles
Will cut me down in cold blood if I take off   140
My armor and go out to meet him
Naked like a woman. This is no time
For talking, the way a boy and a girl
Whisper to each other from oak tree or rock,
A boy and a girl with all their sweet talk.   145
Better to lock up in mortal combat
As soon as possible and see to whom
God on Olympus grants the victory."

Thus spoke Hector.
      And Achilles closed in   150
Like the helmeted God of War himself,
The ash-wood spear above his right shoulder
Rocking in the light that played from his bronze
In gleams of fire and the rising sun.
And when Hector saw it he lost his nerve,   155
Panicked, and ran, leaving the gates behind,
With Achilles on his tail, confident in his speed.

 You have seen a falcon
 In a long, smooth dive
 Attack a fluttering dove   160
 Far below in the hills.
 The falcon screams,
 Swoops, and plunges
 In its lust for prey.

So Achilles swooped and Hector trembled 165
In the shadow of Troy's wall.
                              Running hard,
They passed Lookout Rock and the windy fig tree,
Following the loop of the wagon road.
They came to the wellsprings of eddying 170
Scamander,[2] two beautiful pools, one
Boiling hot with steam rising up,
The other flowing cold even in summer,
Cold as freezing sleet, cold as tundra snow.
There were broad basins there, lined with stone, 175
Where the Trojan women used to wash their silky clothes
In the days of peace, before the Greeks came.

They ran by these springs, pursuer and pursued—
A great man out front, a far greater behind—
And they ran all out. This was not a race 180
For such a prize as athletes compete for,
An oxhide or animal for sacrifice, but a race
For the lifeblood of Hector, breaker of horses.

But champion horses wheeling round the course,
Hooves flying, pouring it on in a race for a prize— 185
A woman or tripod—at a hero's funeral games

Will give you some idea of how these heroes looked
As they circled Priam's town three times running
    While all the gods looked on.

Zeus, the gods' father and ours, spoke: 190

"I do not like what I see, a man close
To my heart chased down around Troy's wall.
Hector has burned many an ox's thigh
To me, both on Ida's peaks and in the city's
High holy places, and now Achilles 195
Is running him down around Priam's town.
Think you now, gods, and take counsel whether
We should save him from death or deliver him
Into Achilles' hands, good man though he be."

The grey-eyed goddess Athena answered: 200

    "O Father,
You may be the Lord of Lightning and the Dark Cloud,
But what a thing to say, to save a mortal man,
With his fate already fixed, from rattling death!
Do it. But don't expect us all to approve." 205

2. One of the two rivers in the plain of Troy.

Zeus loomed like a thunderhead, but answered gently:

"There, there, daughter, my heart wasn't in it.
I did not mean to displease you, my child. Go now,
Do what you have in mind without delay."

Athena had been longing for action   210
And at his word shot down from Olympus,

As Achilles bore down on Hector.

   A hunting hound starts a fawn in the hills,
   Follows it through brakes and hollows,
   And if it hides in a thicket, circles,   215
   Picks up the trail, and renews the chase.

No more could Hector elude Achilles.
Every time Hector surged for the Western Gate
Under the massive towers, hoping for
Trojan archers to give him some cover,   220
Achilles cut him off and turned him back
Toward the plain, keeping the inside track.

   Running in a dream, you can't catch up,
   You can't catch up and you can't get away.

No more could Achilles catch Hector   225
Or Hector escape.
                        And how could Hector
Have ever escaped death's black birds
If Apollo had not stood by his side
This one last time and put life in his knees?   230
Achilles shook his head at his soldiers:
He would not allow anyone to shoot
At Hector and win glory with a hit,
Leaving him only to finish him off.

But when they reached the springs the fourth time,   235
Father Zeus stretched out his golden scales
And placed on them two agonizing deaths,
One for Achilles and one for Hector.
When he held the beam, Hector's doom sank down
Toward Hades. And Phoebus Apollo left him.   240

By now the grey-eyed goddess Athena
Was at Achilles' side, and her words flew fast:

"There's nothing but glory on the beachhead
For us now, my splendid Achilles,
Once we take Hector out of action, and   245
There's no way he can escape us now,

Not even if my brother Apollo has a fit
And rolls on the ground before the Almighty.
You stay here and catch your breath while I go
To persuade the man to put up a fight."   250

Welcome words for Achilles. He rested,
Leaning on his heavy ash and bronze spear,
While the goddess made her way to Hector,
The spitting image of Deïphobus.[3]
And her voice sounded like his as she said: 255

"Achilles is pushing you hard, brother,
In this long footrace around Priam's town.
Why don't we stand here and give him a fight?"

Hector's helmet flashed as he turned and said:

"Deïphobus, you've always been my favorite   260
Brother, and again you've shown me why,
Having the courage to come out for me,
Leaving the safety of the wall, while all
Priam's other sons are cowering inside."

And Athena, her eyes as grey as winter moons: 265

"Mother and father begged me by my knees
To stay inside, and so did all my friends.
That's how frightened they are, Hector. But I
Could not bear the pain in my heart, brother.
Now let's get tough and fight and not spare   270
Any spears. Either Achilles kills us both
And drags our blood-soaked gear to the ships,
Or he goes down with your spear in his guts."

That's how Athena led him on, with guile.
And when the two heroes faced each other,   275
Great Hector, helmet shining, spoke first.

"I'm not running any more, Achilles.
Three times around the city was enough.
I've got my nerve back. It's me or you now.
But first we should swear a solemn oath.   280
With all the gods as witnesses, I swear:
If Zeus gives me the victory over you,
I will not dishonor your corpse, only
Strip the armor and give the body back
To the Greeks. Promise you'll do the same."   285

And Achilles, fixing his eyes on him:

3. Hector's brother.

"Don't try to cut any deals with me, Hector.
Do lions make peace treaties with men?
Do wolves and lambs agree to get along?
No, they hate each other to the core,   290
And that's how it is between you and me,
No talk of agreements until one of us
Falls and gluts Ares with his blood.
By God, you'd better remember everything
You ever knew about fighting with spears.   295
But you're as good as dead. Pallas Athena
And my spear will make you pay in a lump
For the agony you've caused by killing my friends."

With that he pumped his spear arm and let fly.
Hector saw the long flare the javelin made, and ducked.   300
The bronze point sheared the air over his head
And rammed into the earth. But Athena
Pulled it out and gave it back to Achilles
Without Hector noticing. And Hector,
Prince of Troy, taunted Achilles: 305

"Ha! You missed! Godlike Achilles! It looks like
You didn't have my number after all.
You said you did, but you were just trying
To scare me with big words and empty talk.
Did you think I'd run and you'd plant a spear   310
In my back? It'll take a direct hit in my chest,
Coming right at you, that and a god's help too.
Now see if you can dodge this piece of bronze.
Swallow it whole! The war will be much easier
On the Trojans with you dead and gone."   315

And Hector let his heavy javelin fly,
A good throw, too, hitting Achilles' shield
Dead center, but it only rebounded away.
Angry that his throw was wasted, Hector
Fumbled about for a moment, reaching   320
For another spear. He shouted to Deïphobus,
But Deïphobus was nowhere in sight.
It was then that Hector knew in his heart
What had happened, and said to himself:

"I hear the gods calling me to my death.   325
I thought I had a good man here with me,
Deïphobus, but he's still on the wall.
Athena tricked me. Death is closing in
And there's no escape. Zeus and Apollo
Must have chosen this long ago, even though   330
They used to be on my side. My fate is here,
But I will not perish without some great deed
That future generations will remember."

And he drew the sharp broadsword that hung
By his side and gathered himself for a charge.   335

   A high-flying eagle dives
   Through ebony clouds down
   To the sun-scutched⁴ plain to claw
   A lamb or a quivering hare

Thus Hector's charge, and the light   340
That played from his blade's honed edge.

Opposite him, Achilles exploded forward, fury
Incarnate behind the curve of his shield,
A glory of metalwork, and the plumes
Nodded and rippled on his helmet's crest,   345
Thick golden horsehair set by Hephaestus,
And his spearpoint glinted like the Evening Star

   In the gloom of night
   Star of perfect splendor,

A gleam in the air as Achilles poised   350
His spear with murderous aim at Hector,
Eyes boring into the beautiful skin,
Searching for the weak spot. Hector's body
Was encased in the glowing bronze armor
He had stripped from the fallen Patroclus,   355
But where the collarbones join at the neck
The gullet offered swift and certain death.
It was there Achilles drove his spear through
As Hector charged. The heavy bronze apex
Pierced the soft neck but did not slit the windpipe,   360
So that Hector could speak still.

He fell back in the dust.

                And Achilles exulted.

"So you thought you could get away with it
Didn't you, Hector? Killing Patroclus   365
And ripping off his armor, *my* armor,
Thinking I was too far away to matter.
You fool. His avenger was far greater—
And far closer—than you could imagine,
Biding his time back in our beachhead camp.   370
And now I have laid you out on the ground.
Dogs and birds are going to draw out your guts
While the Greeks give Patroclus burial."

4. Sun-beaten.

And Hector, barely able to shake the words out:

"I beg you, Achilles, by your own soul   375
And by your parents, do not
Allow the dogs to mutilate my body
By the Greek ships. Accept the gold and bronze
Ransom my father and mother will give you
And send my body back home to be burned   380
In honor by the Trojans and their wives."

And Achilles, fixing him with a stare:

"Don't whine to me about my parents,
You dog! I wish my stomach would let me
Cut off your flesh in strips and eat it raw   385
For what you've done to me. There is no one
And no way to keep the clogs off your head,
Not even if they bring ten or twenty
Ransoms, pile them up here and promise more,
Not even if Dardanian Priam weighs your body   390
Out in gold, not even then will your mother
Ever get to mourn you laid out on a bier.
No, dogs and birds will eat every last scrap."

Helmet shining, Hector spoke his last words:

"So this is Achilles. There was no way   395
To persuade you. Your heart is a lump
Of iron. But the gods will not forget this,
And I will have my vengeance on that day
When Paris and Apollo destroy you
In the long shadow of Troy's Western Gate."   400

Death's veil covered him as he said these things,
And his soul, bound for Hades, fluttered out
Resentfully, forsaking manhood's bloom.

He was dead when Achilles spoke to him:

"Die and be done with it. As for my fate,   405
I'll accept it whenever Zeus sends it."

And he drew the bronze spear out of the corpse,
Laid it aside, then stripped off the blood-stained armor.
The other Greeks crowded around
And could not help but admire Hector's   410
Beautiful body, but still they stood there
Stabbing their spears into him, smirking.

"Hector's a lot softer to the touch now
Than he was when he was burning our ships,"

One of them would say, pulling out his spear.   415

After Achilles had stripped the body
He rose like a god and addressed the Greeks:

"Friends, Argive commanders and councillors,
The gods have granted us this man's defeat,
Who did us more harm than all the rest   420
Put together. What do you say we try
Laying a close siege on the city now
So we can see what the Trojans intend—
Whether they will give up the citadel
With Hector dead, or resolve to fight on?   425
    But what am I thinking of? Patroclus' body
Still lies by the ships, unmourned, unburied,
Patroclus, whom I will never forget
As long as I am among the living,
Until I rise no more; and even if   430
In Hades the dead do not remember,
Even there I will remember my dear friend.
    Now let us chant the victory paean, sons
Of the Achaeans, and march back to our ships
With this hero in tow. The power and the glory   435
Are ours. We have killed great Hector,
Whom all the Trojans honored as a god."

But it was shame and defilement Achilles
Had in mind for Hector. He pierced the tendons
Above the heels and cinched them with leather thongs   440
To his chariot, letting Hector's head drag.
He mounted, hoisted up the prize armor,
And whipped his team to a willing gallop
Across the plain. A cloud of dust rose
Where Hector was hauled, and the long black hair   445
Fanned out from his head, so beautiful once,
As it trailed in the dust. In this way Zeus
Delivered Hector into his enemies' hands
To be defiled in his own native land.

Watching this from the wall, Hector's mother   450
Tore off her shining veil and screamed,
And his old father groaned pitifully,
And all through town the people were convulsed
With lamentation, as if Troy itself,
The whole towering city, were in flames.   455
They were barely able to restrain
The old man, frantic to run through the gates,
Imploring them all, rolling in the dung,
And finally making this desperate appeal:

"Please let me go, alone, to the Greek ships.   460
I don't care if you're worried. I want to see

If that monster will respect my age, pity me
For the sake of his own father, Peleus,
Who is about my age, old Peleus
Who bore him and bred him to be a curse   465
For the Trojans, but he's caused me more pain
Than anyone, so many of my sons,
Beautiful boys, he's killed. I miss them all,
But I miss Hector more than all of them.
My grief for him will lay me in the earth.   470
Hector! You should have died in my arms, son!
Then we could have satisfied our sorrow,
Mourning and weeping, your mother and I."

The townsmen moaned as Priam was speaking.
Then Hecuba raised the women's lament: 475

"Hector, my son, I am desolate!
How can I live with suffering like this,
With you dead? You were the only comfort
I had, day and night, wherever you were
In the town, and you were the only hope   480
For Troy's men and women. They honored you
As a god when you were alive, Hector.
Now death and doom have overtaken you."

    And all this time Andromache had heard
Nothing about Hector—news had not reached her   485
That her husband was caught outside the walls.
She was working the loom in an alcove
Of the great hall, embroidering flowers
Into a purple cloak, and had just called
To her serving women, ordering them   490
To put a large cauldron on the fire, so
A steaming bath would be ready for Hector
When he came home from battle. Poor woman,
She had little idea how far from warm baths
Hector was, undone by the Grey-Eyed One   495
And delivered into the hands of the Greeks.

Then she heard the lamentation from the tower.

She trembled, and the shuttle fell
To the floor. Again she called her women:

"Two of you come with me. I must see   500
What has happened. That was Hecuba's voice.
My heart is in my throat, my knees are like ice.
Something terrible has happened to one
Of Priam's sons. O God, I'm afraid
Achilles has cut off my brave Hector   505
Alone on the plain outside the city

And has put an end to my husband's
Cruel courage. Hector never held back
Safe in the ranks; he always charged ahead,
Second to no one in fighting spirit."   510

With these words on her lips Andromache
Ran outdoors like a madwoman, heart racing,
Her two waiting-women following behind.
She reached the tower, pushed through the crowd,
And looking out from the wall saw her husband   515
As the horses dragged him disdainfully
Away from the city to the hollow Greek ships.

Black night swept over her eyes.
She reeled backward, gasping, and her veil
And glittering headbands flew off,   520
And the diadem golden Aphrodite
Gave her on that day when tall-helmed Hector
Led her from her father's house in marriage.
And now her womenfolk were around her,
Hector's sisters and his brother's wives,   525
Holding her as she raved madly for death,
Until she caught her breath and her distraught
Spirit returned to her breast. She moaned then
And, surrounded by Trojan women, spoke:

"Hector, you and I have come to the grief   530
We were both born for, you in Priam's Troy
And I in Thebes in the house of Eëtion
Who raised me there beneath wooded Plakos
Under an evil star. Better never to have been born.
And now you are going to Hades' dark world,   535
Underground, leaving me in sorrow,
A widow in the halls, with an infant,
The son you and I bore but cannot bless.
You can't help him now you are dead, Hector,
And he can never help you. Even if   540
He lives through this unbearable war,
There's nothing left for him in life but pain
And deprivation, all his property
Lost to others. An orphan has no friends.
He hangs his head, his cheeks are wet with tears.   545
He has to beg from his dead father's friends,
Tugging on one man's cloak, another's tunic,
And if they pity him he gets to sip
From someone's cup, just enough to moisten
His lips but not enough to quench his thirst.   550
Or a child with both parents still alive
Will push him away from a feast, taunting him,
'Go away, your father doesn't eat with us.'
And the boy will go to his widowed mother

In tears, Astyanax, who used to sit   555
In his father's lap and eat nothing, but
Mutton and marrow. When he got sleepy
And tired of playing he would take a nap
In a soft bed nestled in his nurse's arms
His dreaming head filled with blossoming joy.   560
But now he'll suffer, now he's lost his father.
The Trojans called him Astyanax
Because you alone were Troy's defender,
You alone protected their walls and gates.
Now you lie by the curved prows of the ships,   565
Far from your parents. The dogs will glut
On your naked body, and shiny maggots
Will eat what's left.
                    Your clothes are stored away,
Beautiful, fine clothes made by women's hands—   570
I'll burn them all now in a blazing fire.
They're no use to you, you'll never lie
On the pyre in them. Burning them will be
Your glory before Trojan men and women."

And the women's moans came in over her lament.   575

Summary   Achilles buries Patroclus, and the Greeks celebrate the dead hero's fame with
athletic games, for which Achilles awards prizes.

BOOK XXIV

[Achilles and Priam]

   The funeral games were over.
The troops dispersed and went to their ships,
Where they turned their attention to supper
And a good night's sleep. But sleep
That masters all had no hold on Achilles.   5
Tears wet his face as he remembered his friend.
He tossed and turned, yearning for Patroclus,
For his manhood and his noble heart,
And all they had done together, the shared pain,
The battles fought, the hard times at sea.   10
Thinking on all this, he would weep softly,
Lying now on his side, now on his back,
And now face down. Then he would rise
To his feet and wander in a daze along the shore.
Dawn never escaped him. As soon as she appeared   15
Over the sea and the dunes, he would hitch
Horses to his chariot and drag Hector behind.
When he had hauled him three times around
Patroclus' tomb, he would rest again in his hut,
Leaving Hector stretched face down in the dust.   20
But Apollo kept Hector's flesh undefiled,

Pitying the man even in death. He kept him
Wrapped in his golden aegis, so that Achilles
Would not scour the skin as he dragged him.

So Achilles defiled Hector in his rage.   25
The gods, looking on, pitied Hector,
And urged Hermes to steal the body,
A plan that pleased all but Hera,
Poseidon, and the Grey-Eyed One,
Who were steady in their hatred   30
For sacred Ilion and Priam's people
Ever since Paris in his blindness
Offended these two goddesses
And honored the one who fed his fatal lust.[5]

    Twelve days went by. Dawn.   35
Phoebus Apollo addressed the immortals:

"How callous can you get? Has Hector
Never burned for you thighs of bulls and goats?
Of course he has. But now you cannot
Bring yourselves to save even his bare corpse   40
For his wife to look upon, and his mother,
And child, and Priam, and his people, who would
Burn him in fire and perform his funeral rites.
No, it's the dread Achilles that you prefer.
His twisted mind is set on what he wants,   45
As savage as a lion bristling with pride,
Attacking men's flocks to make himself a feast.
Achilles has lost all pity and has no shame left.
Shame sometimes hurts men, but it helps them too.
A man may lose someone dearer than Achilles has,   50
A brother from the same womb, or a son,
But when he has wept and mourned, he lets go.
The Fates have given men an enduring heart.
But this man? After he kills Hector,
He ties him behind his chariot   55
And drags him around his dear friend's tomb.
Does this make him a better or nobler man?
He should fear our wrath, good as he may be,
For he defiles the dumb earth in his rage."

This provoked an angry response from Hera: 60

"What you say might be true, Silverbow,
If we valued Achilles and Hector equally.
But Hector is mortal and suckled at a woman's breast,
While Achilles is born of a goddess whom I

---

5. Aphrodite, whom Paris judged more beautiful than Athena and Hera because he found the
bribe that she offered him—Helen—the most attractive.

Nourished and reared myself, and gave to a man,   65
Peleus, beloved of the gods, to be his wife.
All of you gods came to her wedding,
And you too were at the feast, lyre in hand,
Our forever faithless and fair-weather friend."

And Zeus, who masses the thunderheads: 70

"Calm down, Hera, and don't be so indignant.
Their honor will not be the same. But Hector
Was dearest to the gods of all in Ilion,
At least to me. He never failed to offer
A pleasing sacrifice. My altar never lacked   75
Libation or burnt savor, our worship due.
But we will not allow his body to be stolen—
Achilles would notice in any case. His mother
Visits him continually night and day.
But I would have one of you summon Thetis   80
So that I might have a word with her. Achilles
Must agree to let Priam ransom Hector."

   Thus spoke Zeus,
And Iris stormed down to deliver his message.
Midway between Samos[6] and rocky Imbros,   85
She dove into the dark sea. The water moaned
As it closed above her, and she sank into the deep

> *Like a lead sinker on a line*
> *That takes a hook of sharpened horn*
> *Down to deal death to nibbling fish.*   90

She found Thetis in a cave's hollow, surrounded
By her saltwater women and wailing
The fate of her faultless son, who would die
On Trojan soil, far from his homeland.
Iris, whose feet are like wind, stood near her: 95

"Rise, Thetis. Zeus in his wisdom commands you."

And the silver-footed goddess answered her:

"Why would the great god want me? I am ashamed
To mingle with the immortals, distraught as I am.
But I will go, and he will not speak in vain."   100

And she veiled her brightness in a shawl.
Of midnight blue and set out with Iris before her.
The sea parted around them in waves.
They stepped forth on the beach

---

6. I.e., Samothrace. It and Imbros are islands in the northeast Aegean Sea.

And sped up the sky, and found themselves   105
Before the face of Zeus. Around him
Were seated all the gods, blessed, eternal.
Thetis sat next to him, and Athena gave place.
Hera put in her hand a fine golden cup
And said some comforting words. Thetis drank   110
And handed the cup back. Then Zeus,
The father of gods and men, began to speak:

"You have come to Olympus, Thetis,
For all your incurable sorrow. I know.
Even so, I will tell you why I have called you.   115
For nine days the gods have argued
About Hector's corpse and about Achilles.
Some want Hermes to steal the body away,
But I accord Achilles the honor in this, hoping
To retain your friendship along with your respect.   120
Go quickly now and tell your son our will.
The gods are indignant, and I, above all,
Am angry that in his heart's fury
He holds Hector by the beaked ships
And will not give him up. He may perhaps fear me   125
And so release the body. Meanwhile,
I will send Iris to great-souled Priam
To have him ransom his son, going to the ships
With gifts that will warm Achilles' heart."

Zeus had spoken, and the silver-footed goddess   130
Streaked down from the peaks of Olympus
And came to her son's hut. She found him there
Lost in grief. His friends were all around,
Busily preparing their morning meal,
For which a great, shaggy ram had been slaughtered.   135
Settling herself beside her weeping child,
She stroked him with her hand and talked to him:

"My son, how long will you let this grief
Eat at your heart, mindless of food and rest?
It would be good to make love to a woman.   140
It hurts me to say it, but you will not live
Much longer. Death and Doom are beside you.
Listen now, I have a message from Zeus.
The gods are indignant, and he, above all,
Is angry that in your heart's fury   145
You hold Hector by these beaked ships
And will not give him up. Come now,
Release the body and take ransom for the dead."

And Achilles, swift of foot, answered her:

"So be it. Let them ransom the dead,   150
If the god on Olympus wills it so."

So mother and son spoke many words
To each other, with the Greek ships all around.

Meanwhile, Zeus dispatched Iris to Troy:

"Up now, swift Iris, leave Olympus   155
For sacred Ilion and tell Priam
He must go to the Greek ships to ransom his son
With gifts that will soften Achilles' heart.
Alone he must go, with only one attendant,
An elder, to drive the mule cart and bear the man   160
Slain by Achilles back to the city.
He need have no fear. We will send
As his guide and escort Hermes himself,
Who will lead him all the way to Achilles.
And when he is inside Achilles' hut,   165
Achilles will not kill him, but will protect him
From all the rest, for he is not a fool,
Nor hardened, nor past awe for the gods.[7]
He will in kindness spare a suppliant."

Iris stormed down to deliver this message.   170
She came to the house of Priam and found there
Mourning and lamentation. Priam's sons
Sat in the courtyard around their father,
Fouling their clothes with tears. The old man,
Wrapped in his mantle, sat like graven stone.   175
His head and neck were covered with dung
He had rolled in and scraped up with his hands.
His daughters and sons' wives were wailing
Throughout the house, remembering their men,
So many and fine, dead by Greek hands.   180
Zeus' messenger stood near Priam,
Who trembled all over as she whispered:

"Courage, Priam, son of Dardanus,
And have no fear. I have come to you
Not to announce evil, but good.   185
I am a messenger from Zeus, who
Cares for you greatly and pities you.
You must go to the Greek ships to ransom Hector
With gifts that will soften Achilles' heart.
You must go alone, with only one attendant,   190
An elder, to drive the mule cart and bear the man
Slain by Achilles back to the city.
You need have no fear. We will send
As your guide and escort Hermes himself,

7. Suppliants were under the protection of the gods, especially of Zeus.

Who will lead you all the way to Achilles. 195
And when you are inside Achilles' hut,
Achilles will not kill you, but will protect you
From all the rest, for he is not a fool,
Nor hardened, nor past awe for the gods.
He will in kindness spare a suppliant." 200

Iris spoke and was gone, a blur in the air.
Priam ordered his sons to ready the mule cart
And fasten onto it the wicker trunk.
He himself went down to a high-vaulted chamber,
Fragrant with cedar, that glittered with jewels. 205
And he called to Hecuba, his wife, and said:

"A messenger has come from Olympian Zeus.
I am to go to the ships to ransom our son
And bring gifts that will soften Achilles' heart.
What do you make of this, Lady? For myself, 210
I have a strange compulsion to go over there,
Into the wide camp of the Achaean ships."

Her first response was a shrill cry, and then:

"This is madness. Where is the wisdom
You were once respected for at home and abroad? 215
How can you want to go to the Greek ships alone
And look into the eyes of the man who has killed
So many of your fine sons? Your heart is iron.
If he catches you, or even sees you,
He will not pity you or respect you, 220
Savage and faithless as he is. No, we must mourn
From afar, sitting in our hall. This is how Fate
Spun her stern thread[8] for him in my womb,
That he would glut lean hounds far from his parents,
With that violent man close by. I could rip 225
His liver bleeding from his guts and eat it whole
That would be at least some vengeance
For my son. He was no coward, but died
Protecting the men and women of Troy
Without a thought of shelter or flight." 230

And the old man, godlike Priam:

"Don't hold me back when I want to go,
And don't be a bird of ill omen
In my halls. You will not persuade me!
If anyone else on earth told me to do this, 235

8. Fate or the Fates were often pictured as spinning the thread of a person's life.

A seer, diviner, or priest, we would
Set it aside and count it false.
But I heard the goddess myself and saw her face.
I will go, and her word will not be in vain.
If I am fated to die by the Achaean ships,   240
It must be so. Let Achilles cut me down
As soon as I have taken my son in my arms
And have satisfied my desire for grief."

He began to lift up the lids of chests
And took out a dozen beautiful robes,   245
A dozen single-fold cloaks, as many rugs,
And added as many white mantles and tunics.
He weighed and brought out ten talents of gold,
Two glowing tripods and four cauldrons with them,
And an exquisite cup, a state gift from the Thracians   250
And a great treasure. The old man spared nothing
In his house, not even this, in his passion
To ransom his son. Once out in the portico,
He drove off the men there with bitter words:

"Get out, you sorry excuses for Trojans!   255
Don't you have enough grief at home that you
Have to come here and plague me? Isn't it enough
That Zeus has given me the pain and sorrow
Of losing my finest son? You'll feel it yourselves
Soon enough. With him dead you'll be much easier   260
For the Greeks to pick off. But may I be dead and gone
Before I see my city plundered and destroyed."

And he waded through them, scattering them
With his staff. Then he called to his sons
In a harsh voice—Helenus and Paris,   265
Agathon, Pammon, Antiphonus, Polites,
Deïphobus, Hippothous, and noble Dius—
These nine, and shouted at them:

"Come here, you miserable brats. I wish
All of you had been killed by the ships   270
Instead of Hector. I have no luck at all.
I have fathered the best sons in all wide Troy,
And not one, not one I say, is left. Not Mestor,
Godlike Mestor, not Troilus, the charioteer,
Not Hector, who was like a god among men,   275
Like the son of a god, not of a mortal.
Ares killed them, and now all I have left
Are these petty delinquents, pretty boys, and cheats,
These dancers, toe-tapping champions,
Renowned throughout the neighborhood for filching goats!   280
Now will you please get the wagon ready
And load all this on, so I can leave?"

They cringed under their father's rebuke
And brought out the smooth-rolling wagon,
A beauty, just joinered,[9] and clamped on   285
The wicker trunk. They took the mule yoke
Down from its peg, a knobbed boxwood yoke
Fitted with guide rings, and the yoke-band with it,
A rope fifteen feet long. They set the yoke with care
Upon the upturned end of the polished pole,   290
Placing the ring on the thole-pin, and lashed it
Tight to the knob with three turns each way,
Then tied the ends to the hitch under the hook.
This done, they brought from the treasure chamber
The lavish ransom for Hector's head and heaped it   295
On the hand-rubbed wagon. Then they yoked the mules,
Strong-hooved animals that pull in harness,
Splendid gifts of the Mysians[1] to Priam.
And for Priam they yoked to a chariot horses
Reared by the king's hand at their polished stall.   300

So Priam and his herald, their minds racing,
Were having their rigs yoked in the high palace
When Hecuba approached them sorrowfully.
She held in her right hand a golden cup
Of honeyed wine for them to pour libation   305
Before they went. Standing by the horses she said:

"Here, pour libation to Father Zeus, and pray
For your safe return from the enemy camp,
Since you are set on going there against my will.
Pray to Cronion, the Dark Cloud of Ida,   310
Who watches over the whole land of Troy,
And ask for an omen, that swiftest of birds
That is his messenger, the king of birds,
To appear on the right before your own eyes,
Something to trust in as you go to the ships.   315
But if Zeus will not grant his own messenger,
I would not advise or encourage you
To go to the ships, however eager you are."

And Priam, with grave dignity:

"I will not disregard your advice, my wife.   320
It is good to lift hands to Zeus for mercy."
And he nodded to the handmaid to pour
Pure water over his hands, and she came up
With basin and pitcher. Hands washed,
He took the cup from his wife and prayed,   325
Standing in the middle of the courtyard
And pouring out wine as he looked up to heaven:

9. I.e., new-made.   1. A people of central Asia Minor.

"Father Zeus, who rules from Ida,
Most glorious, most great,
Send me to Achilles welcome and pitied.   330
And send me an omen, that swiftest of birds
That is your messenger, the king of birds,
To appear on the right before my own eyes,
That I may trust it as I go to the ships."

Zeus heard his prayer and sent an eagle,   335
The surest omen in the sky, a dusky hunter
Men call the dark eagle, a bird as large
As a doorway, with a wingspan as wide
As the folding doors to a vaulted chamber
In a rich man's house. It flashed on the right   340
As it soared through the city, and when they saw it
Their mood brightened.

        Hurrying now, the old man
Stepped into his chariot and drove off
From the gateway and echoing portico.   345
In front of him the mules pulled the wagon
With Idaeus at the reins. Priam
Kept urging his horses with the lash
As they drove quickly through the city.
His kinsmen trailed behind, all of them   350
Wailing as if he were going to his death.
When they had gone down from the city
And onto the plain, his sons and sons-in-law
Turned back to Troy. But Zeus saw them
As they entered the plain, and he pitied   355
The old man, and said to his son, Hermes:

"Hermes, there's nothing you like more
Than being a companion to men,[2] and you do obey—
When you have a mind to. So go now
And lead Priam to the Achaean ships, unseen   360
And unnoticed, until he comes to Achilles."

Thus Zeus, and the quicksilver courier complied,
Lacing on his feet the beautiful sandals,
Immortal and golden, that carry him over
Landscape and seascape in a rush of wind.   365
And he took the wand he uses to charm
Mortal eyes asleep and make sleepers awake.
Holding this wand, the tough quicksilver god
Flew down to Troy on the Hellespont,

---

2. Among his many functions, Hermes is an escort to travelers (in particular, he guides the souls of the dead to the underworld). He is also a trickster and will put the guards at the Greek wall to sleep so that Priam can pass through.

And walked off as a young prince whose beard   370
Was just darkening, youth at its loveliest.

Priam and Idaeus had just driven past
The barrow of Ilus[3] and had halted
The mules and horses in the river to drink.
By now it was dusk. Idaeus looked up   375
And was aware of Hermes close by.
He turned to Priam and said:

"Beware, son of Dardanus, there's someone here,
And if we're not careful we'll be cut to bits.
Should we escape in the chariot   380
Or clasp his knees and see if he will pity us?"

But the old man's mind had melted with fear.
The hair bristled on his gnarled limbs,
And he stood frozen with fear. But the Helper came up
And took the old man's hand and said to him: 385

"Sir, where are you driving your horses and mules
At this hour of the night, when all else is asleep?
Don't you fear the fury of the Achaeans,
Your ruthless enemies, who are close at hand?
If one of them should see you bearing such treasure   390
Through the black night, what would you do?
You are not young, sir, and your companion is old,
Unable to defend you if someone starts a fight.
But I will do you no harm and will protect you
From others. You remind me of my own dear father."   395

And the old man, godlike Priam, answered:

"Yes, dear son, it is just as you say.
But some god has stretched out his hand
And sent an auspicious wayfarer to meet me:
You have an impressive build, good looks,   400
And intelligence. Blessed are your parents."

And the Guide, limned in silver light:

"A very good way to put it, old sir.
But tell me this now, and tell me the truth:
Are you taking all of this valuable treasure   405
For safekeeping abroad or are you
All forsaking sacred Ilion in fear?
You have lost such a great warrior, the noblest,
Your son. He never let up against the Achaeans."

3. Priam's grandfather. The tomb was a landmark on the Trojan plain.

And the old man, godlike Priam, answered: 410

"Who are you, and from what parents born,
That you speak so well about my ill-fated son?"

And Hermes, limned in silver, answered:

"Ah, a test! And a question about Hector.
I have often seen him win glory in battle   415
He would drive the Argives back to their ships
And carve them to pieces with his bronze blade.
And we stood there and marvelled, for Achilles,
Angry with Agamemnon, would not let us fight.
I am his comrade in arms, from the same ship,   420
A Myrmidon. My father is Polyctor,
A wealthy man, and about as old as you.
He has six other sons, seven, counting me.
We cast lots, and I was chosen to come here.
Now I have come out to the plain from the ships   425
Because at dawn the Achaeans
Will lay siege to the city. They are restless,
And their lords cannot restrain them from battle."

And the old man, godlike Priam, answered him:

"If you really are one of Achilles' men,   430
Tell me this, and I want the whole truth.
Is my son still by the ships, or has Achilles
Cut him up by now and thrown him to the dogs?"

And Hermes, limned in silver light:

"Not yet, old sir. The dogs and birds have not   435
Devoured him. He lies beside Achilles' ship
Amid the huts just as he was at first. This is now
The twelfth day he has been lying there,
But his flesh has not decayed at all, nor is it
Consumed by worms that eat the battle-slain.   440
Achilles does drag him around his dear friend's tomb,
And ruthlessly, every morning at dawn,
But he stays unmarred. You would marvel, if you came,
To see him lie as fresh as dew, washed clean of blood,
And uncorrupted. All the wounds he had are closed,   445
And there were many who drove their bronze in him.
This is how the blessed gods care for your son,
Corpse though he be, for he was dear to their hearts."

And the old man was glad, and answered:

"Yes, my boy. It is good to offer   450
The immortals their due. If ever

There was anyone in my house
Who never forgot the Olympian gods,
It was my son. And so now they have
Remembered him, even in death.   455
But come, accept from me this fine cup,
And give me safe escort with the gods
Until I come to the hut of Peleus' son."

And Hermes, glimmering in the dark:

"Ah, an old man testing a young one.   460
But you will not get me to take gifts from you
Without Achilles' knowledge. I respect him
And fear him too much to defraud him.
I shudder to think of the consequences.
But I would escort you all the way to Argos,   465
With attentive care, by ship or on foot,
And no one would fight you for scorn of your escort."

And he leapt onto the chariot,
Took the reins and whip, and breathed
Great power into the horses and mules.   470
When they came to the palisade and trench
Surrounding the ships, the guards were at supper.
Hermes sprinkled them with drowsiness,
Then opened the gates, pushed back the bars,
And led in Priam and the cart piled with ransom.   475
They came to the hut of the son of Peleus
That the Myrmidons had built for their lord.
They built it high, out of hewn fir beams,
And roofed it with thatch reaped from the meadows.
Around it they made him a great courtyard   480
With thick-set staves. A single bar of fir
Held the gate shut. It took three men
To drive this bar home and three to pull it back,
But Achilles could work it easily alone.
Hermes opened the gate for Priam   485
And brought in the gifts for Peleus' swift son.
As he stepped to the ground he said:

"I am one of the immortals, old sir—the god
Hermes. My father sent me to escort you here.
I will go back now and not come before   490
Achilles' eyes. It would be offensive
For a god to greet a mortal face to face.
You go in, though, and clasp the knees
Of the son of Peleus, and entreat him
By his father and rich-haired mother   495
And by his son, so you will stir his soul."

And with that Hermes left and returned
To high Olympus. Priam jumped down

And left Idaeus to hold the horses and mules.
The old man went straight to the house   500
Where Achilles, dear to Zeus, sat and waited.

    He found him inside. His companions sat
Apart from him, and a solitary pair,
Automedon and Alcimus, warriors both,
Were busy at his side. He had just finished   505
His evening meal. The table was still set up.
Great Priam entered unnoticed. He stood
Close to Achilles, and touching his knees,
He kissed the dread and murderous hands
That had killed so many of his sons.   510

    Passion sometimes blinds a man so completely
    That he kills one of his own countrymen.
    In exile, he comes into a wealthy house,
    And everyone stares at him with wonder.

So Achilles stared in wonder at Priam.   515
Was he a god?
                And the others there stared
And wondered and looked at each other.
But Priam spoke, a prayer of entreaty:

"Remember your father, godlike Achilles.   520
He and I both are on the doorstep
Of old age. He may well be now
Surrounded by enemies wearing him down
And have no one to protect him from harm.
But then he hears that you are still alive   525
And his heart rejoices, and he hopes all his days
To see his dear son come back from Troy.
But what is left for me? I had the finest sons
In all wide Troy, and not one of them is left.
Fifty I had when the Greeks came over,   530
Nineteen out of one belly, and the rest
The women in my house bore to me.
It doesn't matter how many they were,
The god of war has cut them down at the knees.
And the only one who could save the city   535
You've just now killed as he fought for his country,
My Hector. It is for him I have come to the Greek ships,
To get him back from you. I've brought
A fortune in ransom. Respect the gods, Achilles.
Think of your own father, and pity me.   540
I am more pitiable. I have borne what no man
Who has walked this earth has ever yet borne.
I have kissed the hand of the man who killed my son."

He spoke, and sorrow for his own father
Welled up in Achilles. He took Priam's hand   545

And gently pushed the old man away.
The two of them remembered. Priam,
Huddled in grief at Achilles' feet, cried
And moaned softly for his man-slaying Hector.
And Achilles cried for his father and   550
For Patroclus. The sound filled the room.

When Achilles had his fill of grief
And the aching sorrow left his heart,
He rose from his chair and lifted the old man
By his hand, pitying his white hair and beard.   555
And his words enfolded him like wings:

"Ah, the suffering you've had, and the courage.
To come here alone to the Greek ships
And meet my eye, the man who slaughtered
Your many fine sons! You have a heart of iron.   560
But come, sit on this chair. Let our pain
Lie at rest a while, no matter how much we hurt.
There's nothing to be gained from cold grief.
Yes, the gods have woven pain into mortal lives,
While they are free from care.   565
                              Two jars
Sit at the doorstep of Zeus, filled with gifts
That he gives, one full of good things,
The other of evil. If Zeus gives a man
A mixture from both jars, sometimes   570
Life is good for him, sometimes not.
But if all he gives you is from the jar of woe,
You become a pariah, and hunger drives you
Over the bright earth, dishonored by gods and men.
Now take Peleus. The gods gave him splendid gifts   575
From the day he was born. He was the happiest
And richest man on earth, king of the Myrmidons,
And although he was a mortal, the gods gave him
An immortal goddess to be his wife.
But even to Peleus the god gave some evil: 580
He would not leave offspring to succeed him in power,
Just one child, all out of season. I can't be with him
To take care of him now that he's old, since I'm far
From my fatherland, squatting here in Troy,
Tormenting you and your children. And you, old sir,   585
We hear that you were prosperous once.
From Lesbos down south clear over to Phrygia
And up to the Hellespont's boundary,
No one could match you in wealth or in sons.
But then the gods have brought you trouble,   590
This constant fighting and killing around your town.
You must endure this grief and not constantly grieve.
You will not gain anything by torturing yourself
Over the good son you lost, not bring him back.
Sooner you will suffer some other sorrow."   595

And Priam, old and godlike, answered him:

"Don't sit me in a chair, prince, while Hector
Lies uncared for in your hut. Deliver him now
So I can see him with my own eyes, and you—
Take all this ransom we bring, take pleasure in it,   600
And go back home to your own fatherland,
Since you've taken this first step and allowed me
To live and see the light of day."

Achilles glowered at him and said:

"Don't provoke me, old man. It's my own decision   605
To release Hector to you. A messenger came to me
From Zeus—my own natural mother,
Daughter of the old sea god. And I know you,
Priam, inside out. You don't fool me one bit.
Some god escorted you to the Greek ships.   610
No mortal would have dared come into our camp,
Not even your best young hero. He couldn't have
Gotten past the guards or muscled open the gate.
So just stop stirring up grief in my heart,
Or I might not let you out of here alive, old man—   615
Suppliant though you are—and sin against Zeus."

The old man was afraid and did as he was told.

The son of Peleus leapt out the door like a lion,
Followed by Automedon and Alcimus, whom Achilles
Honored most now that Patroclus was dead.   620
They unyoked the horses and mules, and led
The old man's herald inside and seated him on a chair.
Then they unloaded from the strong-wheeled cart
The endless ransom that was Hector's blood price,
Leaving behind two robes and a fine-spun tunic   625
For the body to he wrapped in and brought inside.
Achilles called the women and ordered them
To wash the body well and anoint it with oil,
Removing it first for fear that Priam might see his son
And in his grief be unable to control his anger   630
At the sight of his child, and that this would arouse
Achilles' passion and he would kill the old man
And so sin against the commandments of Zeus.

After the female slaves had bathed Hector's body
And anointed it with olive, they wrapped it 'round   635
With a beautiful robe and tunic, and Achilles himself
Lifted him up and placed him on a pallet
And with his friends raised it onto the polished cart.
Then he groaned and called out to Patroclus:

"Don't be angry with me, dear friend, if somehow   640
You find out, even in Hades, that I have released
Hector to his father. He paid a handsome price,
And I will share it with you, as much as is right."

Achilles reentered his hut and sat down again
In his ornately decorated chair   645
Across the room from Priam, and said to him:

"Your son is released, sir, as you ordered.
He is lying on a pallet. At dawn's first light
You will go see him yourself.
     Now let's think about supper.   650
Even Niobe[4] remembered to eat
Although her twelve children were dead in her house,
Six daughters and six sturdy sons.
Apollo killed them with his silver bow,
And Artemis, showering arrows, angry with Niobe   655
Because she compared herself to beautiful Leto.
Leto, she said, had borne only two, while she
Had borne many. Well, these two killed them all.
Nine days they lay in their gore, with no one
To bury them, because Zeus had turned   660
The people to stone. On the tenth day
The gods buried them. But Niobe remembered
She had to eat, exhausted from weeping.
Now she is one of the rocks in the lonely hills
Somewhere in Sipylos, a place they say is haunted   665
By nymphs who dance on the Achelous' banks,
And although she is stone she broods on the sorrows
The gods gave her.[5]
                    Well, so should we, old sir,
Remember to eat. You can mourn your son later   670
When you bring him to Troy. You owe him many tears."

A moment later Achilles was up and had slain
A silvery sheep. His companions flayed it
And prepared it for a meal, sliced it, spitted it,
Roasted the morsels and drew them off the spits.   675
Automedon set out bread in exquisite baskets
While Achilles served the meat. They helped themselves
And satisfied their desire for food and drink.
Then Priam, son of Dardanus, gazed for a while
At Achilles, so big, so much like one of the gods,   680

4. Wife of Amphion, one of the two founders of the great Greek city of Thebes.
5. The legend of Niobe being turned into stone is thought to have had its origin in a rock face of Mount Sipylus (in Asia Minor) that resembled a woman who wept inconsolably for the loss of her children. The Achelous River runs near Mount Sipylus.

And Achilles returned his gaze, admiring
Priam's face, his words echoing in his mind.
When they had their fill of gazing at each other,
Priam, old and godlike, broke the silence:

"Show me to my bed now, prince, and quickly,   685
So that at long last I can have the pleasure of sleep.
My eyes have not closed since my son lost his life
Under your hands. I have done nothing but groan
And brood over my countless sorrows,
Rolling in the dung of my courtyard stables.   690
Finally I have tasted food and let flaming wine
Pass down my throat. I had eaten nothing till now."

Achilles ordered his companions and women
To set bedsteads on the porch and pad them
With fine, dyed rugs, spread blankets on top,   695
And cover them over with fleecy cloaks.
The women went out with torches in their hands
And quickly made up two beds. And Achilles,
The great sprinter, said in a bitter tone:

"You will have to sleep outside, dear Priam.   700
One of the Achaean counselors may come in,
As they always do, to sit and talk with me,
As well they should. If one of them saw you here
In the dead of night, he would tell Agamemnon,
And that would delay releasing the body.   705
But tell me this, as precisely as you can.
How many days do you need for the funeral?
I will wait that long and hold back the army."

And the old man, godlike Priam, answered:

"If you really want me to bury my Hector,   710
Then you could do this for me, Achilles.
You know how we are penned in the city,
Far from any timber, and the Trojans are afraid.
We would mourn him for nine days in our halls,
And bury him on the tenth, and feast the people.   715
On the eleventh we would heap a barrow over him,
And on the twelfth day fight, if fight we must."

And Achilles, strong, swift, and godlike:

"You will have your armistice."

And he clasped the old man's wrist   720
So he would not be afraid.
                    And so they slept,
Priam and his herald, in the covered courtyard,
Each with a wealth of thoughts in his breast.

But Achilles slept inside his well-built hut,   725
And by his side lay lovely Briseis.

Gods and heroes slept the night through,
Wrapped in soft slumber. Only Hermes
Lay awake in the dark, pondering how
To spirit King Priam away from the ships   730
And elude the strong watchmen at the camp's gates.
He hovered above Priam's head and spoke:

"Well, old man, you seem to think it's safe
To sleep on and on in the enemy camp
Since Achilles spared you. Think what it cost you   735
To ransom your son. Your own life will cost
Three times that much to the sons you have left
If Agamemnon and the Greeks know you are here."

Suddenly the old man was afraid. He woke up the herald.
Hermes harnessed the horses and mules   740
And drove them through the camp. No one noticed.
And when they reached the ford of the Xanthus,
The beautiful, swirling river that Zeus begot,
Hermes left for the long peaks of Olympus.

    Dawn spread her saffron light over earth,   745
And they drove the horses into the city
With great lamentation. The mules pulled the corpse.
No one in Troy, man or woman, saw them before
Cassandra, who stood like golden Aphrodite
On Pergamon's height. Looking out she saw   750
Her dear father standing in the chariot
With the herald, and then she saw Hector
Lying on the stretcher in the mule cart.
And her cry went out through all the city:

"Come look upon Hector, Trojan men and women,   755
If ever you rejoiced when he came home alive
From battle, a joy to the city and all its people."

She spoke. And there was not a man or woman
Left in the city, for an unbearable sorrow
Had come upon them. They met Priam by the gates   760
As he brought the body through, and in the front
Hector's dear wife and queenly mother threw themselves
On the rolling cart and pulled out their hair
As they clasped his head amid the grieving crowd.
They would have mourned Hector outside the gates   765
All the long day until the sun went down,
Had not the old man spoken from his chariot:

"Let the mules come through. Later you will have
Your fill of grieving, after I have brought him home."

He spoke, and the crowd made way for the cart.   770
And they brought him home and laid him
On a corded bed, and set around him singers
To lead the dirge and chant the death song.
They chanted the dirge, and the women with them.
White-armed Andromache led the lamentation   775
As she cradled the head of her man-slaying Hector:

"You have died young, husband, and left me
A widow in the halls. Our son is still an infant,
Doomed when we bore him. I do not think
He will ever reach manhood. No, this city   780
Will topple and fall first. You were its savior,
And now you are lost. All the solemn wives
And children you guarded will go off soon
In the hollow ships, and I will go with them.
And you, my son, you will either come with me   785
And do menial labor for a cruel master,
Or some Greek will lead you by the hand
And throw you from the tower, a hideous death,[6]
Angry because Hector killed his brother,
Or his father, or son. Many, many Greeks   790
Fell in battle under Hector's hands.
Your father was never gentle in combat.
And so all the townspeople mourn for him,
And you have caused your parents unspeakable
Sorrow, Hector, and left me endless pain.   795
You did not stretch your hand out to me
As you lay dying in bed, nor did you whisper
A final word I could remember as I weep
All the days and nights of my life."

The women's moans washed over her lament,   800
And from the sobbing came Hecuba's voice:

"Hector, my heart, dearest of all my children,
The gods loved you when you were alive for me,
And they have cared for you also in death.
My other children Achilles sold as slaves   805
When he captured them, shipped them overseas
To Samos, Imbros, and barren Lemnos.
After he took your life with tapered bronze
He dragged you around Patroclus' tomb, his friend
Whom you killed, but still could not bring him back.   810
And now you lie here for me as fresh as dew,
Although you have been slain, like one whom Apollo
Has killed softly with his silver arrows."

The third woman to lament was Helen.

---

6. Astyanax was, in fact, hurled from Troy's walls after the city fell.

"Oh, Hector, you were the dearest to me by far   815
Of all my husband's brothers. Yes, Paris
Is my husband, the godlike prince
Who led me to Troy. I should have died first.
This is now the twentieth year
Since I went away and left my home,   820
And I have never had an unkind word from you.
If anyone in the house ever taunted me,
Any of my husband's brothers or sisters,
Or his mother—my father-in-law was kind always—
You would draw them aside and calm them   825
With your gentle heart and gentle words.
And so I weep for you and for myself,
And my heart is heavy, because there is no one left
In all wide Troy who will pity me
Or be my friend. Everyone shudders at me."   830

And the people's moan came in over her voice.

Then the old man, Priam, spoke to his people:

"Men of Troy, start bringing wood to the city,
And have no fear of an Argive ambush.
When Achilles sent me from the black ships,   835
He gave his word he would not trouble us
Until the twelfth day should dawn."

He spoke, and they yoked oxen and mules
To wagons, and gathered outside the city.
For nine days they hauled in loads of timber.   840
When the tenth dawn showed her mortal light,
They brought out their brave Hector
And all in tears lifted the body high
Onto the bier, and threw on the fire.

Light blossomed like roses in the eastern sky.   845

The people gathered around Hector's pyre,
And when all of Troy was assembled there
They drowned the last flames with glinting wine.
Hector's brothers and friends collected
His white bones, their cheeks flowered with tears.   850
They wrapped the bones in soft purple robes
And placed them in a golden casket, and laid it
In the hollow of the grave, and heaped above it
A mantle of stones. They built the tomb
Quickly, with lookouts posted all around   855
In case the Greeks should attack early.
When the tomb was built, they all returned
To the city and assembled for a glorious feast
In the house of Priam, Zeus' cherished king.

That was the funeral of Hector, breaker of horses.   860

The Odyssey[1]

BOOK I

Speak, Memory[2]—
             Of the cunning hero,[3]
The wanderer, blown off course time and again
After he plundered Troy's sacred heights.
                   Speak
Of all the cities he saw, the minds he grasped,
The suffering deep in his heart at sea   5
As he struggled to survive and bring his men home
But could not save them, hard as he tried—
The fools—destroyed by their own recklessness
When they ate the oxen of Hyperion the Sun,[4]
And that god snuffed out their day of return.   10

        Of these things,

Speak, Immortal One,[5]
And tell the tale once more in our time.

By now, all the others who had fought at Troy—
At least those who had survived the war and the sea—
Were safely back home. Only Odysseus   15
Still longed to return to his home and his wife.
The nymph Calypso,[6] a powerful goddess—
And beautiful—was clinging to him
In her caverns and yearned to possess him.
The seasons rolled by, and the year came   20
In which the gods spun the thread
For Odysseus to return home to Ithaca,
Though not even there did his troubles end,
Even with his dear ones around him.
All the gods pitied him, except Poseidon,[7]   25
Who stormed against the godlike hero
Until he finally reached his own native land.

But Poseidon was away now, among the Ethiopians,
Those burnished people at the ends of the earth—
Some near the sunset, some near the sunrise—   30
To receive a grand sacrifice of rams and bulls.

---

1. Translated by Stanley Lombardo.
2. In the original, the first word is *andra* (man)—translated here as "hero"—and the first words rendered literally are "Man to me sing, Muse." Lombardo emphasizes the theme of memory, an important one in the poem, and reminds us that memory is, in Greek myth, the mother of the Muses.
3. Odysseus, who is not named until several lines later.

4. Hyperion was, in Greek mythology, a Titan, one of the generation of gods that preceded the Olympians. He was associated with the sun. The story of how Odysseus's men ate the cattle of the sun will be told in book 12.
5. The Muse.
6. Goddess, daughter of the Titan Atlas, who holds up the sky; her name connotes "hiding" or "secrecy."
7. God of the sea, brother of Zeus.

There he sat, enjoying the feast.
                                    The other gods
Were assembled in the halls of Olympian Zeus,[8]
And the Father of Gods and Men was speaking.
He couldn't stop thinking about Aegisthus,   35
Whom Agamemnon's son, Orestes, had killed:[9]

"Mortals! They are always blaming the gods
For their troubles, when their own witlessness
Causes them more than they were destined for!
Take Aegisthus now. He marries Agamemnon's   40
Lawful wife and murders the man on his return
Knowing it meant disaster—because we did warn him,
Sent our messenger, quicksilver Hermes,[1]
To tell him not to kill the man and marry his wife,
Or Agamemnon's son, Orestes, would pay him back   45
When he came of age and wanted his inheritance.
Hermes told him all that, but his good advice
Meant nothing to Aegisthus. Now he's paid in full."

Athena[2] glared at him with her owl-grey eyes:

"Yes, O our Father who art most high—   50
That man got the death he richly deserved,
And so perish all who would do the same.
But it's Odysseus I'm worried about,
That discerning, ill-fated man. He's suffered
So long, separated from his dear ones,   55
On an island that lies in the center of the sea,
A wooded isle that is home to a goddess,
The daughter of Atlas, whose dread mind knows
All the depths of the sea and who supports
The tall pillars that keep earth and heaven apart.   60
His daughter detains the poor man in his grief,
Sweet-talking him constantly, trying to charm him
Into forgetting Ithaca. But Odysseus,
Longing to see even the smoke curling up
From his land, simply wants to die. And yet you   65
Never think of him, Olympian. Didn't Odysseus
Please you with sacrifices beside the Greek ships
At Troy? Why is Odysseus so odious,[3] Zeus?"

Zeus in his thunderhead had an answer for her:

8. King of the gods.
9. Agamemnon was the leader of the Greek
armies in the Trojan War. In his ten-year
absence, his wife, Clytemnestra, took a lover,
Aegisthus; when Agamemnon returned from
the war, Aegisthus and Clytemnestra killed
him in his bath. Orestes, Agamemnon's son,
avenged his father by killing his killers. Other

versions of the myth, including that of Aeschylus (in his *Oresteia* plays), make Clytemnestra
more important in the story than Aegisthus;
perhaps deliberately, she is not named here.
1. Messenger god.
2. Goddess of wisdom, who favors Odysseus.
3. There is a pun on Odysseus's name in the
original Greek.

"Quite a little speech you've let slip through your teeth,   70
Daughter. How could I forget godlike Odysseus?
No other mortal has a mind like his, or offers
Sacrifice like him to the deathless gods in heaven.
But Poseidon is stiff and cold with anger
Because Odysseus blinded his son, the Cyclops   75
Polyphemus, the strongest of all the Cyclopes,
Nearly a god. The nymph Thoösa bore him,
Daughter of Phorcys, lord of the barren brine,
After mating with Poseidon in a scalloped sea-cave.[4]
The Earthshaker[5] has been after Odysseus   80
Ever since, not killing him, but keeping him away
From his native land. But come now,
Let's all put our heads together and find a way
To bring Odysseus home. Poseidon will have to
Put aside his anger. He can't hold out alone   85
Against the will of all the immortals."

And Athena, the owl-eyed goddess, replied:

"Father Zeus, whose power is supreme,
If the blessed gods really do want
Odysseus to return to his home,   90
We should send Hermes, our quicksilver herald,
To the island of Ogygia without delay
To tell that nymph of our firm resolve
That long-suffering Odysseus gets to go home.
I myself will go to Ithaca   95
To put some spirit into his son—
Have him call an assembly of the long-haired Greeks
And rebuke the whole lot of his mother's suitors.
They have been butchering his flocks and herds.
I'll escort him to Sparta and the sands of Pylos   100
So he can make inquiries about his father's return
And win for himself a name among men."

Athena spoke, and she bound on her feet
The beautiful sandals, golden, immortal,
That carry her over landscape and seascape   105
On a puff of wind. And she took the spear,
Bronze-tipped and massive, that the Daughter uses
To level battalions of heroes in her wrath.
She shot down from the peaks of Olympus
To Ithaca, where she stood on the threshold   110
Of Odysseus' outer porch. Holding her spear,
She looked like Mentes,[6] the Taphian captain,
And her eyes rested on the arrogant suitors.

---

4. The Cyclopes are one-eyed giants. Phorcys
is a minor sea god.
5. The Earthshaker is Poseidon, who had
power over earthquakes.
6. Friend of Odysseus.

They were playing dice in the courtyard,
Enjoying themselves, seated on the hides of oxen   115
They themselves had slaughtered. They were attended
By heralds and servants, some of whom were busy
Blending water and wine in large mixing bowls,
Others wiping down the tables with sponges
And dishing out enormous servings of meat.   120

Telemachus spotted her first.
He was sitting with the suitors, nursing
His heart's sorrow, picturing in his mind
His noble father, imagining he had returned
And scattered the suitors, and that he himself,   125
Telemachus, was respected at last.
Such were his reveries as he sat with the suitors.
And then he saw Athena.
                        He went straight to the porch,
Indignant that a guest had been made to wait so long.
Going up to her he grasped her right hand in his   130
And took her spear, and his words had wings:

"Greetings, stranger. You are welcome here.
After you've had dinner, you can tell us what you need."

Telemachus spoke, and Pallas Athena
Followed him into the high-roofed hall.   135
When they were inside he placed her spear
In a polished rack beside a great column
Where the spears of Odysseus stood in a row.
Then he covered a beautifully wrought chair
With a linen cloth and had her sit on it   140
With a stool under her feet. He drew up
An intricately painted bench for himself
And arranged their seats apart from the suitors
So that his guest would not lose his appetite
In their noisy and uncouth company—   145
And so he could inquire about his absent father.
A maid poured water from a silver pitcher
Into a golden basin for them to wash their hands
And then set up a polished table nearby.
Another serving woman, grave and dignified,   150
Set out bread and generous helpings
From the other dishes she had. A carver set down
Cuts of meat by the platter and golden cups.
Then a herald came by and poured them wine.

Now the suitors swaggered in. They sat down   155
In rows on benches and chairs. Heralds
Poured water over their hands, maidservants
Brought around bread in baskets, and young men
Filled mixing bowls to the brim with wine.
The suitors helped themselves to all this plenty,   160

And when they had their fill of food and drink,
They turned their attention to the other delights,
Dancing and song, that round out a feast.
A herald handed a beautiful zither
To Phemius, who sang for the suitors,   165
Though against his will. Sweeping the strings
He struck up a song. And Telemachus,
Putting his head close to Pallas Athena's
So the others wouldn't hear, said this to her:

"Please don't take offense if I speak my mind.   170
It's easy for them to enjoy the harper's song,
Since they are eating another man's stores
Without paying anything—the stores of a man
Whose white bones lie rotting in the rain
On some distant shore, or still churn in the waves.   175
If they ever saw him make landing on Ithaca
They would pray for more foot speed
Instead of more gold or fancy clothes.
But he's met a bad end, and it's no comfort to us
When some traveler tells us he's on his way home.   180
The day has long passed when he's coming home.
But tell me this, and tell me the truth:
Who are you, and where do you come from?
Who are your parents? What kind of ship
Brought you here? How did your sailors   185
Guide you to Ithaca, and how large is your crew?
I don't imagine you came here on foot.
And tell me this, too. I'd like to know,
Is this your first visit here, or are you
An old friend of my father's, one of the many   190
Who have come to our house over the years?"

Athena's seagrey eyes glinted as she said:

"I'll tell you nothing but the unvarnished truth.
I am Mentes, son of Anchialus, and proud of it.
I am also captain of the seafaring Taphians.   195
I just pulled in with my ship and my crew,
Sailing the deep purple to foreign ports.
We're on our way to Cyprus with a cargo of iron
To trade for copper. My ship is standing
Offshore of wild country away from the city,   200
In Rheithron harbor under Neion's woods.
You and I have ties of hospitality,
Just as our fathers did, from a long way back.
Go and ask old Laertes.[7] They say he never
Comes to town any more, lives out in the country,   205
A hard life with just an old woman to help him.
She gets him his food and drink when he comes in

_____
7. Odysseus's father.

From the fields, all worn out from trudging across
The ridge of his vineyard plot.
               I have come
Because they say your father has returned,   210
But now I see the gods have knocked him off course.
He's not dead, though, not godlike Odysseus,
No way in the world. No, he's alive all right.
It's the sea keeps him back, detained on some island
In the middle of the sea, held captive by savages.   215
And now I will prophesy for you, as the gods
Put it in my heart and as I think it will be,
Though I am no soothsayer or reader of birds.
Odysseus will not be gone much longer
From his native land, not even if iron chains   220
Hold him. He knows every trick there is
And will think of some way to come home.
But now tell me this, and I want the truth:
Tall as you are, are you Odysseus' son?
You bear a striking resemblance to him,   225
Especially in the head and those beautiful eyes.
We used to spend quite a bit of time together
Before he sailed for Troy with the Argive fleet.
Since then, we haven't seen each other at all."

Telemachus took a deep breath and said: 230

"You want the truth, and I will give it to you.
My mother says that Odysseus is my father.
I don't know this myself. No one witnesses
His own begetting. If I had my way, I'd be the son
Of a man fortunate enough to grow old at home.   235
But it's the man with the most dismal fate of all.
They say I was born from—since you want to know."

Athena's seagrey eyes glinted as she said:

"Well, the gods have made sure your family name
Will go on, since Penelope has borne a son like you.   240
But there is one other thing I want you to tell me.
What kind of a party is this? What's the occasion?
Some kind of banquet? A wedding feast?
It's no neighborly potluck, that's for sure,
The way this rowdy crowd is carrying on   245
All through the house. Any decent man
Would be outraged if he saw this behavior."

Telemachus breathed in the salt air and said:

"Since you ask me these questions as my guest—
This, no doubt, was once a perfect house,   250
Wealthy and fine, when its master was still home.
But the gods frowned and changed all that

When they whisked him off the face of the earth.
I wouldn't grieve for him so much if he were dead,
Gone down with his comrades in the town of Troy,   255
Or died in his friends' arms after winding up the war.
The entire Greek army would have buried him then,
And great honor would have passed on to his son.
But now the whirlwinds have snatched him away
Without a trace. He's vanished, gone, and left me   260
Pain and sorrow. And he's not the only cause
I have to grieve. The gods have given me other trials.
All of the nobles who rule the islands—
Doulichium, Samê, wooded Zacynthus—
And all those with power on rocky Ithaca   265
Are courting my mother and ruining our house.
She refuses to make a marriage she hates
But can't stop it either. They are eating us
Out of house and home, and will kill me someday."

And Pallas Athena, with a flash of anger: 270

"Damn them! You really do need Odysseus back.
Just let him lay his hands on these mangy dogs!
If only he would come through that door now
With a helmet and shield and a pair of spears,
Just as he was when I saw him first,   275
Drinking and enjoying himself in our house
On his way back from Ephyre. Odysseus
Had sailed there to ask Mermerus' son, Ilus,
For some deadly poison for his arrowheads.
Ilus, out of fear of the gods' anger,   280
Would not give him any, but my father
Gave him some, because he loved him dearly.
That's the Odysseus I want the suitors to meet.
They wouldn't live long enough to get married!
But it's on the knees of the gods now   285
Whether he comes home and pays them back
Right here in his halls, or doesn't.
                              So it's up to you
To find a way to drive them out of your house.
Now pay attention and listen to what I'm saying.
Tomorrow you call an assembly and make a speech   290
To these heroes, with the gods as witnesses.
The suitors you order to scatter, each to his own.
Your mother—if in her heart she wants to marry—
Goes back to her powerful father's house.
Her kinfolk and he can arrange the marriage,   295
And the large dowry that should go with his daughter.
And my advice for you, if you will take it,
Is to launch your best ship, with twenty oarsmen,
And go make inquiries about your long-absent father.
Someone may tell you something, or you may hear   300
A rumor from Zeus, which is how news travels best.

Sail to Pylos first and ask godly Nestor,
Then go over to Sparta and red-haired Menelaus.[8]
He was the last home of all the bronzeclad Greeks.
If you hear your father's alive and on his way home,   305
You can grit your teeth and hold out one more year.
If you hear he's dead, among the living no more,
Then come home yourself to your ancestral land,
Build him a barrow and celebrate the funeral
Your father deserves. Then marry off your mother.   310
After you've done all that, think up some way
To kill the suitors in your house either openly
Or by setting a trap. You've got to stop
Acting like a child. You've outgrown that now.
Haven't you heard how Orestes won glory   315
Throughout the world when he killed Aegisthus,
The shrewd traitor who murdered his father?
You have to be aggressive, strong—look at how big
And well-built you are—so you will leave a good name.
Well, I'm off to my ship and my men,   320
Who are no doubt wondering what's taking me so long.
You've got a job to do. Remember what I said."

And Telemachus, in his clear-headed way:

"My dear guest, you speak to me as kindly
As a father to his son. I will not forget your words.   325
I know you're anxious to leave, but please stay
So you can bathe and relax before returning
To your ship, taking with you a costly gift,
Something quite fine, a keepsake from me,
The sort of thing a host gives to his guest."   330

And Athena, her eyes grey as saltwater:

"No, I really do want to get on with my journey.
Whatever gift you feel moved to make,
Give it to me on my way back home,
Yes, something quite fine. It will get you as good."   335

With these words the Grey-eyed One was gone,
Flown up and away like a seabird. And as she went
She put courage in Telemachus' heart
And made him think of his father even more than before.
Telemachus' mind soared. He knew it had been a god,   340
And like a god himself he rejoined the suitors.

They were sitting hushed in silence, listening
To the great harper as he sang the tale
Of the hard journeys home that Pallas Athena
Ordained for the Greeks on their way back from Troy.   345

8. Brother of Agamemnon, husband of Helen, whose abduction by Paris caused the Trojan War.

His song drifted upstairs, and Penelope,
Wise daughter of Icarius, took it all in.
She came down the steep stairs of her house—
Not alone, two maids trailed behind—
And when she had come among the suitors   350
She stood shawled in light by a column
That supported the roof of the great house,
Hiding her cheeks behind her silky veils,
Grave handmaidens standing on either side.
And she wept as she addressed the brilliant harper: 355

"Phemius, you know many other songs
To soothe human sorrows, songs of the exploits
Of gods and men. Sing one of those
To your enraptured audience as they sit
Sipping their wine. But stop singing this one,   360
This painful song that always tears at my heart.
I am already sorrowful, constantly grieving
For my husband, remembering him, a man
Renowned in Argos and throughout all Hellas."

And Telemachus said to her coolly: 365

"Mother, why begrudge our singer
Entertaining us as he thinks best?
Singers are not responsible; Zeus is,
Who gives what he wants to every man on earth.
No one can blame Phemius for singing the doom   370
Of the Danaans:[9] it's always the newest song
An audience praises most. For yourself,
You'll just have to endure it and listen.
Odysseus was not the only man at Troy
Who didn't come home. Many others perished.   375
You should go back upstairs and take care of your work,
Spinning and weaving, and have the maids do theirs.
Speaking is for men, for all men, but for me
Especially, since I am the master of this house."

Penelope was stunned and turned to go,   380
Her son's masterful words pressed to her heart.
She went up the stairs to her room with her women
And wept for Odysseus, her beloved husband,
Until grey-eyed Athena cast sleep on her eyelids.

All through the shadowy halls the suitors   385
Broke into an uproar, each of them praying
To lie in bed with her. Telemachus cut them short:

"Suitors of my mother—you arrogant pigs—
For now, we're at a feast. No shouting, please!

9. Danaans are Greeks. Homer does not use a general term for the Greeks, instead referring to
three Greek tribes: Danaans, Argives, and Achaeans.

There's nothing finer than hearing 390
A singer like this, with a voice like a god's.
But in the morning we will sit in the meeting ground,
So that I can tell all of you in broad daylight
To get out of my house. Fix yourselves feasts
In each others' houses, use up your own stockpiles. 395
But if it seems better and more profitable
For one man to be eaten out of house and home
Without compensation—then eat away!
For my part, I will pray to the gods eternal
That Zeus grant me requital: Death for you 400
Here in my house. With no compensation."

Thus Telemachus. And they all bit their lips
And marveled at how boldly he had spoken to them.
Then Antinous, son of Eupeithes, replied:

"Well, Telemachus, it seems the gods, no less, 405
Are teaching you how to be a bold public speaker.
May the son of Cronus[1] never make you king
Here on Ithaca, even if it is your birthright."

And Telemachus, taking in a breath:

"It may make you angry, Antinous, 410
But I'll tell you something. I wouldn't mind a bit
If Zeus granted me this—if he made me king.
You think this is the worst fate a man can have?
It's not so bad to be king. Your house grows rich,
And you're held in great honor yourself. But, 415
There are many other lords on seawashed Ithaca,
Young and old, and any one of them
Could get to be king, now that Odysseus is dead.
But I will be master of my own house
And of the servants that Odysseus left me." 420

Then Eurymachus, Polybus' son, responded:

"It's on the knees of the gods, Telemachus,
Which man of Greece will rule this island.
But you keep your property and rule your house,
And may no man ever come to wrest them away 425
From you by force, not while men live in Ithaca.
But I want to ask you, sir, about your visitor.
Where did he come from, what port
Does he call home, where are his ancestral fields?
Did he bring news of your father's coming 430
Or was he here on business of his own?
He sure up and left in a hurry, wouldn't stay
To be known. Yet by his looks he was no tramp."

1. Zeus.

And Telemachus, with a sharp response:

"Eurymachus, my father is not coming home.   435
I no longer trust any news that may come,
Or any prophecy my mother may have gotten
From a seer she has summoned up to the house.
My guest was a friend of my father's from Taphos.
He says he is Mentes, son of Anchialus   440
And captain of the seafaring Taphians."

Thus Telemachus. But in his heart he knew
It was an immortal goddess.

                    And now
The young men plunged into their entertainment,
Singing and dancing until the twilight hour.   445
They were still at it when the evening grew dark,
Then one by one went to their own houses to rest.

Telemachus' room was off the beautiful courtyard,
Built high and with a surrounding view.
There he went to his bed, his mind teeming,   450
And with him, bearing blazing torches,
Went true-hearted Eurycleia, daughter of Ops
And Peisenor's granddaughter. Long ago,
Laertes had bought her for a small fortune
When she was still a girl. He paid twenty oxen   455
And honored her in his house as he honored
His wedded wife, but he never slept with her
Because he would rather avoid his wife's wrath.
Of all the women, she loved Telemachus the most
And had nursed him as a baby. Now she bore   460
The blazing torches as Telemachus opened
The doors to his room and sat on his bed.
He pulled off his soft tunic and laid it
In the hands of the wise old woman, and she
Folded it and smoothed it and hung it on a peg   465
Beside the corded bed. Then she left the room,
Pulled the door shut by its silver handle,
And drew the bolt home with the strap.

                    There Telemachus
Lay wrapped in a fleece all the night through,
Pondering the journey Athena had shown him.   470

BOOK II

Dawn's pale rose fingers brushed across the sky,
And Odysseus' son got out of bed and dressed.
He slung his sharp sword around his shoulder,
Then tied oiled leather sandals onto his feet,
And walked out of the bedroom like a god.   5

Wasting no time, he ordered the heralds
To call an assembly. The heralds' cries
Rang out through the town, and the men
Gathered quickly, their long hair streaming.
Telemachus strode along carrying a spear   10
And accompanied by two lean hounds.
Athena shed a silver grace upon him,
And everyone marveled at him as he entered.
The elders made way as he took his father's seat.

First to speak was the hero Aegyptius,   15
A man bowed with age and wise beyond telling.
His son, Antiphus, had gone off to Troy
In the ships with Odysseus (and was killed
In the cave of the Cyclops, who made of him
His last savage meal). Of three remaining sons,   20
One, Eurynomus, ran with the suitors,
And the other two kept their father's farm.
But Aegyptius couldn't stop mourning the one that was lost
And was weeping for him as he spoke out now:

"Hear me now, men of Ithaca.   25
We have never once held assembly or sat
In council since Odysseus left.
Who has called us together today?
Which of the young men, or of the elders,
Has such urgent business as this?   30
Has he had news of the army's return,
Some early report he wants to tell us about?
Or is there some other public matter
He wants to address? He's a fine man
In my eyes, and may Zeus bless him."   35

Telemachus was glad to hear these words,
And he rose from his seat, eager to speak.
There he stood, in the midst of the assembly,
And the herald Peisenor, a wise counselor,
Placed the staff in the hands of Odysseus' son.   40
In his speech he addressed old Aegyptius first:

"You won't have to look very far to find out
Who called this assembly. I called it myself.
No, I have not had news of the army's return,
Any early report I could tell you about.   45
Nor is there any other public matter
I want to address. It's a private matter,
My own need. Trouble has come to my house
In two forms. First, I have lost my noble father.
He was your king once, and like a father   50
To all of you, gentle and kind. And now,
There is even greater trouble, far greater,
Which will destroy my house and home.

Suitors have latched on to my mother,
Against her will, and they are the sons   55
Of the noblest men here. They shrink
From going to her father Icarius' house
So that he could arrange his daughter's dowry
And give her away to the man he likes best.
Instead, they gather at our house day after day,   60
Slaughtering our oxen and sheep and fat goats,
Living high and drinking wine recklessly.
We've lost almost everything, because
We don't have Odysseus to protect our house.
We can't defend ourselves. If it came to a fight   65
We would only show how pathetic we are.
Not that I wouldn't defend myself
If I had the power. Things have gone too far.
The ruin of my house has become a public disgrace.
You should all be indignant, and feel shame   70
Before your neighbors, and fear the wrath
Of the gods, who may yet turn against you.
I beg you by Olympian Zeus and by Themis,[2]
Who calls and dismisses assemblies of men,
Stop this, my friends, and let me be alone   75
In my grief—unless my father, Odysseus,
Was your enemy and did you some harm
And now you are paying me back in malice
By urging these suitors on. Better for me
If you yourselves, Ithacans all,   80
Were to eat up my treasures and flocks.
Then I might get restitution someday.
I'd go through the town and bend people's ears
And ask for our goods until they were all given back.
But there is nothing I can do now. There's no cure   85
For what you are making me suffer now."

He spoke in anger, bursting into tears
As he threw the scepter onto the ground.
The crowd was motionless with pity. No one
Had the heart to respond to him harshly,   90
Except Antinous, who now said:

"Well, the big speaker, the mighty orator.
You've got some nerve, Telemachus,
Laying the blame on us. It's not the suitors
Who are at fault, but your own mother,   95
Who knows more tricks than any woman alive.
It's been three years now, almost four,
Since she's been toying with our affections.
She encourages each man, leading us on,

2. Goddess whose name means "right" or "justice."

Sending messages. But her mind is set elsewhere.   100
Here's just one of the tricks she devised:
She set up a great loom in the main hall
And started weaving a sizeable fabric
With a very fine thread, and she said to us:

'Young men—my suitors, since Odysseus is dead—   105
Eager as you are to marry me, you must wait
Until I finish this robe—it would be a shame
To waste my spinning—a shroud for the hero
Laertes, when death's doom lays him low.
I fear the Achaean women would reproach me   110
If he should lie in death shroudless for all his wealth.'

"We were persuaded by this appeal to our honor.
Every day she would weave at the great loom,
And every night she would unweave by torchlight.
She fooled us for three years with her craft.   115
But in the fourth year, as the seasons rolled by,
And the moons waned, and the days dragged on,
One of her women who knew all about it
Told us, and we caught her unweaving
The gloried shroud. Then we forced her to finish it.   120
Now here is the suitors' answer to you,
And let every Achaean hear it as well:
Send your mother away with orders to marry
Whichever man her father likes best.
But if she goes on like this much longer,   125
Torturing us with all she knows and has,
All the gifts Athena has given her,
Her talent for handiwork, her good sense,
Her cleverness—all of which go far beyond
That of any of the heroines of old,   130
Tyro or Alcmene or garlanded Mycene,
Not one of whom had a mind like Penelope's,
Even though now she is not thinking straight—
We will continue to eat you out of house and home
For as long as she holds to this way of thinking   135
Which the immortal gods have put in her breast.
She is building quite a reputation for herself,
But at your expense. As for us, we're staying put
Until she chooses one of the Achaeans to marry."

Telemachus, drawing a deep breath, responded: 140

"Antinous, I cannot throw out of my house
The mother who bore me and raised me.
As for my father, he may be alive or dead
But he is not here. It would not be fair
If I had to pay a great price to Icarius,   145
As I would if I sent my mother back to him

On my own initiative. And the spirits would send me
Other evils, for my mother would curse me
As she left the house, and call on the Furies.[3]
And men all over would hold me at fault.   150
So I will never tell my mother to leave.
As for you, if you don't like it,
If this offends your sense of fairness,
Get out of my house! Fix yourselves feasts
In each others' houses, use up your own stockpiles.   155
But if it seems better and more profitable
For one man to be eaten out of house and home
Without compensation—then eat away!
But I will pray to the gods eternal
That Zeus grant me requital: Death for you   160
Here in my house. With no compensation."

Telemachus spoke, and Zeus in answer
Sent forth two eagles from a mountain peak.
They drifted lazily for a while on the wind,
Side by side, with wings outstretched.   165
But when they were directly above the assembly
With its hub-bub of voices, they wheeled about
And beat their wings hard, looking down
On the heads of all with death in their eyes.
Then they savaged each others' craws   170
With their talons and veered off to the east
Across the city and over the houses
Of the men below. Everyone was amazed,
And they all wondered what these birds portended.
Then the old hero Halitherses stepped forth,   175
Mastor's son, the best man of his time
In reading bird flight and uttering oracles.
He was full of good will in the speech that he made.
"Hear me men of Ithaca, and I mean
The suitors especially, since a great tide of woe   180
Is rising to engulf them. Odysseus
Shall not be away from his home much longer.
Even now he is near, sowing death for the suitors,
One and all, grim for them and grim for many others
Who dwell on Ithaca. But let us take thought now   185
Of how to make an end of this. Or better,
Let the suitors themselves make an end.
I am no inexperienced prophet,
But one who knows well, and I declare
That everything is coming true for that man,   190
Just as I told him when he left for Troy:
That after bitter pain and loss of all comrades
He would finally reach home after twenty years
Unknown to anyone. Now it is all coming true."

3. Spirits of vengeance.

Eurymachus, Polybus' son, answered him: 195

"Get out of here, old man. Go home and prophesy
For your own children—you don't want them to get hurt.
I'm a better prophet than you when it comes to this.
There are lots of birds under the sun, flying
All over the place, and not all of them are omens.   200
As for Odysseus, he died a long way from here,
And you should have died with him.
Then you wouldn't spout so many prophecies,
Or be egging Telemachus on in his anger,
Hoping he'll give you a gift to take home.   205
I'll tell you this, and I guarantee it'll be done:
If you, with all your experience and lore,
Talk a younger man into getting angry,
First, we'll go harder on him, and second,
We'll slap you with a fine so big   210
It'll make you choke when you have to pay it.
And this is my advice to Telemachus:
Send your mother back to her father's house
And have them prepare a wedding feast
And all the gifts that go with a beloved daughter.   215
Until then, the sons of the Achaeans will not stop
Their bitter courtship. One thing's for sure,
We fear no man, no, not even Telemachus
With all his big talk. We don't give a damn
For your prophecies, old man, and when they don't   220
Come true, you'll be more despised than ever.
And you, Telemachus, your inheritance
Is going down the drain and will never be restored
As long as your mother puts off this marriage.
After all, we wait here patiently day after day   225
Competing for her, and do not go after
Other women who might make us good wives."

And Telemachus, keeping his wits about him:

"I'm done pleading with you, Eurymachus,
And all the rest of you suitors. I've had my say.   230
Now the gods know all this, and so do the Achaeans.
All I want now is a fast ship and twenty men
Who will crew for me as I sail here and there.
I'm going to Sparta and to sandy Pylos
For news of my father, who has been long gone.   235
Someone may tell me something, or I may hear
A rumor from Zeus, which is how news travels best.
If I hear my father's alive and on his way home,
I can grit my teeth and hold out one more year.
If I hear he's dead, among the living no more,   240
I'll come home myself to my ancestral land,
Build him a barrow and celebrate the funeral
My father deserves. Then I'll marry off my mother."

He spoke and sat down. Then up rose Mentor,
An old friend of Odysseus. It was him,   245
Old Mentor, that Odysseus had put in charge
Of all his house when he left with the ships.
He spoke out now with good will to all:

"Hear me now, men of Ithaca.
Kings might as well no longer be gentle and kind   250
Or understand the correct order of things.
They might as well be tyrannical butchers
For all that any of Odysseus' people
Remember him, a godly king as kind as a father.
I have no quarrel with the suitors. True,   255
They are violent and malicious men,
But at least they are risking their own lives
In devouring the house of Odysseus,
Who, they say, will never return.
It is the rest of the people I am angry with.   260
You all sit here in silence and say nothing,
Not a word of rebuke to make the suitors quit,
Although you easily outnumber them."

Leocritus, Evenor's son, answered him:

"What kind of thing is that to say, Mentor,   265
You stubborn old fool, telling us to stop?
And do you think that even with superior numbers
People are going to fight us over a dinner?
Even if Odysseus, your Ithacan hero himself
Showed up, all hot to throw the suitors   270
Out of his house—well, let's just say
His wife wouldn't be too happy to see him,
No matter how much she missed him, that's how ugly
His death would be. No, you're way off the mark.
Now let's everybody scatter and go home.   275
Mentor and Halitherses can outfit Telemachus.
They're old friends of his father. But I think
He'll be getting his news sitting here in Ithaca
For a long time to come. He's not going anywhere."

With those words the brief assembly was over.   280
Everyone returned to their homes, but the suitors
Went off to the house of godlike Odysseus.

Telemachus, though, went down to the shore,
Washed his hands in the surf, and prayed to Athena:

"Hear me, god of yesterday. You came to our house   285
And commanded me to sail the misty sea
In search of news of my long-absent father.
Now the townspeople are blocking all that,
Especially the suitors, those arrogant bastards."

He prayed, and Athena was with him,   290
Looking just like Mentor and with Mentor's voice.
Her words flew to Telemachus on wings:

"You won't turn out to be a fool or a coward,
Telemachus, not if any of Odysseus' spirit
Has been instilled in you. Now there was a man   295
Who made sure of his words and deeds! Don't worry,
You'll make this journey, and it won't be in vain.
If you're really Odysseus' and Penelope's son,
You'll finish whatever you set your mind to.
You know, few sons turn out to be like their fathers;   300
Most turn out worse, a few better.
No, you don't have it in you to be a fool or a coward,
And you've got something of Odysseus' brains,
So there's reason to think you'll finish this job.
Never mind, then, about the suitors' schemes.   305
They're mad, not an ounce of sense or justice in them,
And they have no idea of the dark death
Closing in on them, doomed all to die on a single day.
As for you, the journey you have your heart set on
Won't be delayed. I myself, your father's old comrade,   310
Will equip a fast ship and sail along with you.
You get the provisions and stow them aboard,
Wine in jars and barley meal in tight skins,
Food that will stick to men's ribs. I'll go through town
And round up a volunteer crew. There are plenty of ships   315
In Ithaca, old and new. I'll scout out the best one,
Get her rigged, and launch her onto the open sea."

Thus Athena, daughter of Zeus.

And Telemachus, the voice of the goddess
Ringing in his ears, went on to his house   320
With a troubled heart. There he found
The haughty suitors, flaying goats
And singeing swine in the courtyard.
Antinous came up to him with a laugh
And clasped his hand and said to him: 325

"Ah, Telemachus, the dauntless orator,
That's the spirit! No hard feelings now!
Let's just eat and drink as we always have.
The townspeople will provide you with everything—
A ship, a crew—to speed you on to sacred Pylos   330
In your search for news of your noble father."

And Telemachus, drawing in his breath:

"Antinous, there is no way I can relax
Or enjoy myself with you arrogant bastards.
Isn't it bad enough that you have eaten through   335

Much of my wealth while I was still a child?
Now that I'm grown, and hear things from others,
And get angrier and angrier at what I see and hear,
I'm going to do my best to nail you to the wall,
Either by going to Pylos or staying here in this land.   340
But I am going, and I'll make the journey count,
Even though I have to sail in another man's ship
And can't captain my own, which I'm sure suits you fine."

And he withdrew his hand from Antinous'.
The suitors, busy with preparing the feast,   345
Jeered at him as they swaggered through the hall:

"Hey, everybody! Telemachus is planning to murder us!
He'll bring reinforcements from sandy Pylos,
Or even from Sparta. He's really serious.
Or he'll go to Ephyre and get deadly poisons   350
To put in our wine-bowl and kill us all."

And another would sneer:

                    "Who knows?
If he goes off wandering in a hollow ship,
He may die as Odysseus did, far from his friends.
That would mean more work for us, dividing   355
All his possessions and giving his house
Over to his mother—and the man she marries."

That's how their talk went. But Telemachus
Went down to his father's treasure chamber,
A large room where there lay gold and bronze   360
Piled to the ceiling. And there were clothes in chests,
Fragrant olive oil, and great jars of wine,
Old and sweet, an undiluted, heavenly drink,
Ranged in rows along the wall, ready for Odysseus
Should he ever return after all his suffering.   365
The close-fitting, double doors were locked,
And the room was watched day and night
By a wise old stewardess, Eurycleia,
Daughter of Ops, son of Peisenor. Telemachus
Had summoned her and now spoke to her there: 370

"Nurse, siphon me off some wine in jars,
The sweetest, mellowest wine we have
After what you are holding in reserve
For Odysseus, that unlucky man,
Should he ever return from the jaws of death.   375
Fill twelve jars and fit them with lids,
And pour some barley meal into well-sewn skins.
I'll need twenty quarts of ground barley meal.
But don't let anyone know. Just have all this
Ready to go. I'll pick it up this evening   380

After my mother has gone to bed upstairs.
I'm off to Sparta and to sandy Pylos
To see if I can get some news of my father."

He spoke, and Eurycleia gave a shrill cry.
She sobbed as her words went out to him: 385

"Ah, where did you get this idea, child?
Why would you want to travel abroad, you,
A beloved only son? Zeus-born Odysseus
Perished far from home, in a strange land.
These men, as soon as you are gone, will plot   390
To have you killed by treachery, and then divide
All these things among themselves. No, stay here
With what is yours. There is no need for you
To wander and suffer on the barren sea."

And Telemachus, in his cool-headed way: 395

"Don't worry, nurse. There is a god
Behind all this. But swear you won't say
Anything to my mother for a dozen days or so,
Or until she misses me herself or has heard
That I am gone. I don't want her crying."   400

And the old woman swore to the gods
That she would say nothing. That done,
She drew the wine for him in jars
And poured the barley meal into skins,
While Telemachus went back to join the suitors.   405

Owl-eyed Athena saw what to do next.
Assuming the form of Telemachus,
She went through the town recruiting sailors,
Telling them to gather by the ship at dusk.
Then she asked Noemon, Phronius' son,   410
For a fast ship, and he cheerfully agreed.

When the sun set and shadows hung everywhere,
She drew the swift ship down to the sea,
Put in all the gear a benched sailing ship needs,
And then moored it at the harbor's mouth. The crew   415
Gathered around, and the goddess encouraged each man.

Then she moved on, making her way
To the house of godlike Odysseus. There
She shed sweet sleep on the suitors
And made their minds wander in their wine   420
And knocked the cups from their hands. Eyelids heavy,
They stumbled to their feet and one by one
Staggered through the city home and to bed.

Athena's eyes flashed in the dark.
She looked like Mentor now, and in his voice   425
She called Telemachus out from the hall:

"Telemachus, your crew is ready with the oars
And waiting for you. It's time to set forth."

Pallas Athena led the way quickly,
And the man followed in the deity's footsteps.   430
They came down to the ship and the sea
And found the crew standing on the beach,
Their hair blowing in the offshore breeze.
And Telemachus, feeling his father's blood:

"This way, men! We have provisions to haul.   435
Everything's ready at my house. My mother
Knows nothing of all this, nor do any
Of the women, except for one I told."

He led the way, and they brought the provisions
Down to the ship and stowed them below.   440
Athena went aboard, followed by Telemachus,
And they sat side by side on the stern of the ship
As the men untied the cables and then came aboard
To sit at their benches. The Grey-eyed One⁴
Put the wind at their backs, a strong gust from the West   445
That came in chanting over the wine-dark water.
Telemachus called to the crew to rig the sail.
Falling to, they raised the fir mast,
Set it in its socket, braced it with forestays
And hauled up the white sail. The wind   450
Bellied the canvas, and an indigo wave
Hissed off the bow as the ship sped on.
When they had made all the tackle secure
In their swift black ship, they set out bowls
Brimming with wine, and poured libations   455
To the immortal gods, most of all
To the daughter of Zeus with seagrey eyes.

The ship bore through the night and into the dawn.

BOOK III

The sun rose from the still, beautiful water
Into the bronze sky, to shine upon the gods
And upon men who die on the life-giving earth.

The ship came to Pylos, Nestor's great city.
Onshore, black bulls were being sacrificed   5
To the blue-maned Lord of the Sea.⁵

---

4. Athena.   5. Poseidon.

Nine companies of five hundred men
Were each assigned nine bulls for sacrifice.
They had just tasted the innards and were burning
The thigh pieces for the god when the ship   10
Pulled in to shore. The crew furled the sail,
Moored the vessel and disembarked.
Telemachus stepped off the ship behind Athena,
And the goddess, eyes glinting, said to him:

"There's no need to feel embarrassed, Telemachus,   15
Not at all. This is why you have sailed the sea—
To get news of your father, to find out his fate
And where the earth conceals him. Come on, now,
Go straight up to Nestor. Let's see what he knows.
Ask him yourself, so he'll tell you the truth.   20
Not that he would lie. He's very wise."

And Telemachus, taking in a breath:

"How should I go up to him, Mentor,
And what should I say? I'm not used
To making clever speeches. And besides,   25
A young man just doesn't question an elder."

Athena's eyes glinted in the morning light:

"You'll come up with some things yourself, Telemachus,
And a god will suggest others. I do not think
You were born and bred without the gods' good will."   30

Thus Pallas Athena. She led the way quickly,
And the man followed in the deity's footsteps.
They came to the great company of Pylians
And there found Nestor sitting with his sons.
All around him were men preparing for the feast,   35
Skewering meat on spits and roasting it.
But when they saw the new arrivals, they all
Crowded around, clasping their hands in welcome
And inviting them to sit down. Nestor's son
Peisistratus was first, taking them both by the hand   40
And having them sit down at the feast
On soft fleeces spread on the sandy beach
Beside his father and Thrasymedes his brother.
Then he gave them servings of the inner organs
And poured wine into a golden cup. Passing it on   45
To Pallas Athena, he spoke directly to her,
The daughter of Zeus, who wields the aegis:

"Pray now, stranger, to Lord Poseidon,
For it is his feast you have happened upon.
When you have poured libations and have said   50
The ritual prayers, pass the cup of sweet wine

On to your friend, so that he too may pour,
Since I have no doubt he also prays to the gods.
All men have need of the immortal gods.
But he is younger than you, about my age,   55
So to you I will give the golden cup first."

He spoke, and handed her the cup of sweet wine,
And Athena rejoiced at his respect for custom
In handing her the golden cup first.
Without hesitation she prayed to Poseidon: 60

"Hear me, Poseidon who laps all the earth,
And do not refuse to fulfill my prayer.
Bring renown to Nestor first, and his sons,
And grant your grace to all the men of Pylos
In return for this glorious sacrifice.   65
And grant also to Telemachus and to me
A safe return home, having accomplished
All that we came for in our swift black ship."

Thus Athena's prayer, which she herself granted.
Then she gave Telemachus the beautiful cup,   70
And Odysseus' true son prayed the same way.

The meat was roasted now. They drew it
Off the spits and served it up for the feast.
When they had eaten and drunk all that they wanted,
Nestor, the Gerenian horseman, spoke: 75

"It is seemlier to ask our guests who they are
Now that they have enjoyed some food with us.
Who are you, strangers? Where do you sail from?
Are you on some business, or are you adventurers
Wandering the seas, risking your own lives   80
And bringing trouble to men in foreign lands?"

Telemachus felt a sudden surge of courage,
Implanted in his heart by Athena herself
So that he would inquire about his absent father
And win for himself a name among men: 85

"Nestor, son of Neleus, glory of the Achaeans,
You ask where we are from, and I will tell you.
We have come from Ithaca, under Mount Neion,
But my business is my own, not the Ithacans'.
I come for news of my father, any news at all   90
About noble Odysseus, who once, they say,
Fought beside you and sacked the city of Troy.
We have heard where each of the other heroes
Who fought the Trojans met his bitter end.
But Zeus has placed Odysseus' death   95

Beyond hope of knowing. No one can say
Exactly where Odysseus died,
Whether it was on land, overcome by enemies,
Or on the deep sea in Amphtrite's[6] waves.
And so I am at your knees, to see if you   100
Can tell me how my father met his end,
Whether you saw it with your own eyes,
Or heard about it from someone else,
Some wanderer. He was born to sorrow,
More than any man on earth. And do not,   105
Out of pity, spare me the truth, but tell me
Whatever you have seen, whatever you know.
I beseech you, if my father, noble Odysseus,
Ever fulfilled a promise he made to you
In the land of Troy, where the Achaeans suffered,   110
Remember it now, and tell me the truth."

And Nestor, the Gerenian horseman, answered:

"Ah, my friend, you bring to my mind
The sorrow we bravely endured in that land,
Heroes all and the sons of heroes—   115
Everything we suffered on the misty sea,
Looting and plundering wherever Achilles led,
And all of our battles around Priam's great city,
Where our best were killed. There lies
Ajax, dear to Ares, there great Achilles,   120
There Patroclus, like a god in council,
There my own dear son, Antilochus,
Strong and swift, a peerless warrior.
And there were many more losses we suffered.
No mortal man could recount them all.   125
Even if you stayed for five or six years
And wanted to hear the whole tale of woe,
You would return home weary before the end.
For nine years we devised all sorts of strategies
To bring Troy down—which the son of Cronus[7]   130
Scarcely brought to pass. In that effort
No man could match Odysseus for cunning.
Your father was the master of all strategies—
If indeed you are his son. I am amazed
As I look upon you. The way you speak   135
Is very much like him. One would not think
A younger man could speak so appropriately.
Now all that time Odysseus and I
Never disagreed in assembly or council.
We had one heart, and with our wisdom   140
We advised the Argives on the best course to take.
But when we had sacked Priam's tall town,

6. Amphtrite is a sea goddess.   7. Zeus.

Zeus planned in his heart a bitter journey home
For the Greeks—who were not all prudent or just,
Which is why the wrath of the Grey-eyed One   145
Brought many of them to an evil end.
She caused a quarrel between Atreus' two sons,
Agamemnon and Menelaus. It happened this way:
These two called an assembly of the entire army
In a reckless manner, toward sunset   150
And all out of order. We had all been drinking.
They made their speeches, and announced their purpose
In assembling the troops. Menelaus wanted
The entire army to set their sights homeward,
To begin shipping out on the open sea,   155
But this was not at all to Agamemnon's liking.
He wanted to delay their departure
And offer formal sacrifice to appease
The wrath of Athena—the fool,
He had no idea she would never relent.   160
The minds of the eternal ones are not quickly turned.
So these two stood there exchanging insults,
And the soldiers rose up with one huge roar
And took sides. We spent that night
Nursing our resentment against each other,   165
For Zeus was bringing on our doom.
At dawn some of us hauled our ships
To the bright water and loaded on board
Our goods and our softly belted women.
Half of the army held back, remaining   170
With King Agamemnon, son of Atreus,
But half of us embarked and launched our ships,
Which pulled away swiftly, for some god
Had made the teeming water smooth as glass.
We pulled in to Tenedos and offered sacrifice,   175
Eager to reach home, but Zeus held firm
Against our immediate return and stirred up
Still more dissension. Some now turned back
Their curved ships, following Odysseus,
A wise leader with a flexible mind,   180
Out of respect for Lord Agamemnon.
But I fled on with all my ships,
For I knew that Zeus had evil in mind.
Diomedes also got his men out then,
And Menelaus brought up the rear.   185
He caught up with us in Lesbos
As we were debating the long journey ahead,
Whether we should sail above rugged Chios
And on to Psyria, keeping Chios on our left,
Or go below Chios past windy Mimas.   190
We asked the god to give us a sign
And he showed us one, telling us
To cut through the sea straight to Euboea,
The sooner to get ourselves out of danger.

A shrill wind rose up and started to blow,   195
And the ships flew over the teeming brine.
We put in at Geraestus that night,
And, with all that water behind us,
We sacrificed many bulls to Poseidon.
On the fourth day Diomedes made Argos,   200
But I held on toward Pylos, and the wind
Did not die down once since it began to blow.

"And so I came home, dear child, knowing nothing
Of who survived and who was lost.
But what I have heard sitting here in my halls   205
You too shall hear, as is only right.
The Myrmidons, they say, made it safely home,
Led by the son of great-souled Achilles;
Philoctetes too; and Idomeneus
Brought back to Crete all of his men   210
Who survived the war; he lost none at sea.
Of Agamemnon you have already heard,
Far off though you be, how he came home
And how Aegisthus plotted his grisly death
And then paid for it in a horrible way.   215
How good it is for a son to be left
When a man dies! Agamemnon's son
Avenged his death, killing his murderer,
The treacherous Aegisthus. You too, my friend—
For I see that you are handsome and tall—   220
Should be brave and strong, and win a name for yourself."

And Telemachus, in his clear-headed way:

"Nestor, son of Neleus, glory of the Achaeans,
Truly, Orestes was a son who took vengeance,
And the Achaeans will spread his fame   225
To future generations. I wish the gods
Would clothe me in such strength, that I
Might take vengeance on the suitors
For their transgressions against me.
They are violent and malicious men.   230
But the gods have spun into the web of my life
No such happiness for me or my father,
And so I will simply have to endure."

Nestor, the Gerenian horseman, answered:

"Now that you've mentioned it, I recall hearing   235
That a crowd of suitors for your mother's hand,
Uninvited by you, are causing you trouble.
Why do you put up with this? Has some god
Turned the townspeople against you?
Who knows but that Odysseus may come some day,   240
Alone or with an army, and make them pay in blood.

Ah, if only grey-eyed Athena chose to love you
The way she did glorious Odysseus
In the land of Troy! I have never seen
A god show love so openly   245
As Athena did to him. You could see her
Standing at his side! If she would choose
To love you like that and take care of you,
Some of those suitors might forget about marriage!"

And Telemachus answered him: 250

"I do not think, sir, this will ever happen.
The very thought amazes me. It is too much
To hope for, even if the gods willed it."

Then Athena, eyes flashing, put in:

"Telemachus, what a thing to say!   255
It is easy for a god to bring a man safely home,
Even from far away. And speaking for myself,
I would rather suffer on my homeward journey
Than be killed at my hearth, as Agamemnon was—
By the treachery of Aegisthus and of his own wife.   260
But even the gods cannot ward off death,
The great leveler, from a man they love,
Not when destiny comes to lay him low."

And Telemachus answered him:

"Mentor, let us speak of this no longer,   265
For all our grief. He cannot return.
The gods have already devised his death.
But now I have another question for Nestor,
Steeped as he is in knowledge and wisdom.
He has been king for three generations   270
And has the look of an immortal god.
Nestor, son of Neleus, tell me this:
How was Agamemnon, son of Atreus, slain?
Where was Menelaus? How could Aegisthus
Dare to plot the murder of a king, a man   275
Far more powerful than he himself was?
Was Menelaus not in Argos, and did his absence
Encourage Aegisthus to commit the murder?"

And Nestor, the Gerenian horseman:

"Well then, my child, I will tell you all.   280
You yourself have guessed what would have happened
If Atreus' son, red-haired Menelaus,
Had come back from Troy and found Aegisthus
Still alive in his halls. His dead body

Would never have been buried in earth;   285
Dogs and birds would have ripped it apart
As it lay on the plain far from the city,
Nor would any Greek woman have wept for him,
So monstrous was the crime he planned and committed.
While we toiled and sweated over there in Troy,   290
He relaxed in a corner of bluegrass Argos
Sweet-talking the wife of Agamemnon,
Noble Clytemnestra. At first she refused
The whole sordid affair. She had good sense,
And with her was a singer whom Agamemnon,   295
When he left for Troy, had strictly ordered
To guard his wife. But when the gods doomed her
To be undone, Aegisthus took the singer of tales
To a desert island and left him there
For the dogs and birds. And he led her off,   300
Just as willing as he was, to his own house.
Many an ox's thigh he burned on the altars,
Many an offering he made of tapestries and gold
When he accomplished the great deed
He had never hoped in his heart to achieve.   305
          Menelaus and I were sailing then
On our way back from Troy, the best of friends.
But when we came to holy Sunium,
The cape of Athens, Phoebus Apollo
Shot Menelaus' pilot with his arrows,   310
Killing him softly as he held the tiller
Of the speeding ship—Phrontis his name,
The best rough-weather pilot in all the world.
So Menelaus stopped, eager though he was
To press on, and gave his comrade a funeral.   315
When he got his ships on the deep purple again
He made good time to Malea's steep height,
But then Zeus put trouble in his way, shearing
Blasts of shrill winds down from the sky,
And the waves swelled to the size of mountains.   320
Then he split the fleet into two, bringing some
To the part of Crete where the Cydonians live,
Near the Iardanus river. There is a smooth cliff
Sheer to the misty sea on the border of Gortyn,
Where the Southwest Wind drives huge waves   325
Against the headland on the left, toward Phaestus.
The only breakwater is a small rock offshore.
So, some of the fleet came there. The men
Barely escaped with their lives, but the ships
Were broken to pieces against the reef.   330
Five other black ships, though, were blown
All the way to Egypt, and Menelaus
Wandered up and down that coast with his ships,
A stranger in a strange land, amassing
A fortune in gold and goods. Aegisthus,   335

Meanwhile, was working his evil at home.
Having killed the son of Atreus
And subdued the people, he reigned
For seven years in gold-crusted Mycenae.
In the eighth year, though, he met his doom   340
In the person of Orestes, come back from Athens.
Orestes killed his father's murderer,
The treacherous Aegisthus, and, having killed him,
Invited all the Argives to a funeral feast
For his hateful mother and her craven lover.   345
On that very day Menelaus arrived,
Bearing all the treasure his ships could hold.
          So don't you wander long from home, my friend,
Leaving your wealth behind, and in your house
Insolent men who might divide up your goods   350
While you are gone on a useless journey.
Still, I think you should visit Menelaus,
For he has just lately returned from abroad,
From a country no one would hope to return to
Once a storm has driven him off course   355
Into a sea so wide that not even migrating birds
Make the trip more than once a year,
So great is that sea and so terrible.
                              So then,
Go off now with your ship and your crew.
Or if you would rather travel by land,   360
We have chariots and horses at your disposal.
My sons are at your service, ready to guide you
To gleaming Lacedaemon, where Menelaus lives.
Beseech him yourself, so he'll tell you the truth.
Not that he would lie. He's very wise."   365

The sun set on his words, and darkness came on.
Athena's eyes flashed grey as she said:

"You have told the tale well, old man.
But come, cut the tongues and mix the wine
So we can pour libations to Poseidon   370
And the other gods, and then think of sleep.
It is late. Twilight has faded to dark,
And it is not right to linger at feasts of the gods."

Thus Zeus' daughter, and they did as she said.
Heralds poured water over their hands   375
And youths filled bowls to the brim with drink
And served it to all, first pouring into each cup
A few drops for libation. They cut the tongues,
Threw them on the fire, and standing up in turn
Poured libations upon them. Having done so,   380
And having drunk to their heart's content,
Athena and godlike Telemachus

Both started to head for their hollow ship,
But Nestor prevailed upon them to stay:

"God forbid you should go to your ship—   385
As if I were poor and didn't have enough
Cloaks and blankets for myself and my guests
To sleep softly upon! I have plenty of cloaks and blankets,
And Odysseus' son shall never lie down
On the deck of a ship while I am alive,   390
Or any child of mine is left in the halls
To entertain strangers who come to my house."

And Athena, her eyes flecked with dark gold:

"Well spoken, old friend, and Telemachus
Would do well to accept your invitation.   395
It is better that way. So he will go with you
To sleep in your house, but I will go back
To the black ship and have a word with the crew
To raise their spirits. I am the only
Older man among them. They are all youngsters,   400
Telemachus' age, and sail with us as friends.
I will spend this night down there by the ship,
But at dawn I am off to the Cauconians
To collect an old debt, and not a small one at that.
But send this young man on his way   405
In a chariot, and send your son with him,
And the fastest, strongest horses you have."

Thus Athena, her eyes flashing in the dark,
And as she left they saw only a vulture
Beating its long, dusky wings.
                              Their jaws dropped   410
And the old man could scarcely believe his eyes.
He grabbed Telemachus' hand and said to him:

"If you have gods as escorts when you are so young,
I do not think you will turn out badly at all!
This was no other of the Olympian gods   415
But the daughter of Zeus, Tritogeneia,[8]
Most glorious Athena, who also honored
Your noble father among the Argive forces.
Be gracious, Lady, and grant me renown—
Me, my sons, and my venerable wife.   420
And in return I will sacrifice to you
A yearling heifer, broad of brow and unbroken,
Which no man has ever led beneath the yoke.
And I will plate her horns with gold for sacrifice."

8. This title for Athena seems to mean "third-born."

Thus Nestor, and Pallas Athena heard his prayer.   425
Then the old Gerenian horseman led his sons
And daughters' husbands to his beautiful palace,
Where they sat down in rows on benches and chairs.
The housekeeper opened a jar of wine
Eleven years old. The old man mixed a bowl   430
Of this sweet wine, and as he poured libations
He prayed over and over to Pallas Athena,
Daughter of Zeus who holds the aegis.

When they had all poured libations
And drunk wine to their hearts' content,   435
They went home to their houses to take their rest.
But Nestor told Telemachus to sleep
Under the echoing portico on a corded bed
Next to Peisistratus, a good man with a spear
And the only of Nestor's sons still unmarried.   440
Nestor himself slept in an inner room
With his wife, the lady of the house, beside him.

As soon as Dawn appeared in the sky
Nestor, the Gerenian horseman, rose
And went to sit on the polished stones   445
Outside his high doors, the white stones,
Glistening with oil, upon which of old
Neleus would sit, like a god in counsel.
Neleus had met his fate long ago
And gone down to Hades' undergloom,   450
And now upon these stones in his turn
Sat Nestor of Gerenia, holding a scepter.
His sons came out and gathered about him,
Echephron and Stratius and Perseus,
Aretus and godlike Thrasymedes,   455
And as the sixth, the hero Peisistratus.
And they brought godlike Telemachus
And had him sit beside Gerenian Nestor,
Who then spoke:

                    "Quickly now, my sons,
That I may propitiate Athena,   460
Who came to me at the feast of the god
As clear as day. One of you go to the plain
For a heifer, and have the cowherd
Drive her here speedily. Let another go
To the black ship of great-hearted Telemachus   465
And bring his crew, leaving only two behind.
And someone go fetch the goldsmith Laerces
To plate the horns of the heifer with gold.
The rest of you stay here, and have the serving women
Prepare a feast throughout our glorious halls,   470
And bring seats, plenty of logs, and fresh water."

Thus Nestor, and they all set to work. The heifer
Came from the plain, and from the sailing ship
Came Telemachus' crew. The smith came
With the tools of his trade, a bronze hammer,   475
An anvil, and a pair of well-made tongs
With which he wrought gold. And Athena came
To accept the sacrifice.
                                  Nestor, the old charioteer,
Gave the smith gold, and the smith worked it
And leafed it around the heifer's horns   480
To make the goddess rejoice at the offering.
Stratius and Echephron led the heifer up
By the horns, and Aretus came from the chamber
Carrying water for their hands in a basin
Embossed with flowers. In his other hand he held   485
A basket of barley. Thrasymedes stood by
With a sharp axe to strike down the heifer,
And Perseus held the blood-bowl. Nestor began
The washing of hands and sprinkling of barley,
Praying hard to Athena as he cut the first hairs   490
From the victim's head and threw them on the fire.
These rites done, high-hearted Thrasymedes
Came up and struck. When the axe severed
The sinews of the neck, and the heifer collapsed,
The women raised the ritual cry, Nestor's daughters,   495
The wives of his sons, and his august wife,
Eurydice, eldest of Clymenus' daughters.
Then the men raised the heifer's head from the ground
And held it for Peisistratus to cut the throat.
When the black blood had flowed out, and the life   500
Left the bones, they butchered the heifer,
Jointing the thigh pieces in ritual order
And covering them with a double layer of fat
And with bits cut raw from the rest of the carcass.
These the old man burned on split logs   505
And poured bright wine over them. At his side
Were young men holding five-tined forks.
When the thigh pieces were burned and the innards tasted,
They carved up the rest, skewered the pieces,
And roasted them holding the spits in their hands.   510

Meanwhile, Telemachus was being bathed
By Polycaste, Nestor's youngest daughter.
When this lovely girl had bathed him, rubbed him with oil,
And thrown on his shoulders a tunic and cloak,
Telemachus came forth like an immortal god   515
And took his seat beside Nestor, shepherd of the people.

When they had roasted the meat and drawn it
Off the spits, they sat down and feasted,
Waited upon by worthy men who poured their wine

Into golden cups. When they had enough   520
To eat and drink, Gerenian Nestor spoke:

"My sons, yoke the combed horses to the chariot
So that Telemachus may begin his journey."

He spoke, and they did as he said,
Quickly yoking the horses. The housekeeper   525
Placed in the chariot bread and wine
And the sort of fare kings and lords eat.
Telemachus mounted the beautiful chariot,
And Peisistratus, Nestor's son,
Stepped in beside him and took the reins.   530
He flicked the lash and the horses took off,
Eating up the plain and leaving behind them
The high rock of Pylos. All day long
They jostled the yoke that held them together.

As the sun set and the world grew dark   535
They came to Pherae and pulled up at the house
Of Diocles, son of Ortilochus,
Himself a son of the river Alpheus.
There they spent the night, and Diocles
Gave them the hospitality due to guests.   540

When Dawn brushed the pale sky with rose,
They yoked the horses, stepped up into
The inlaid chariot and drove out through the gate
And echoing portico. Peisistratus
Flicked the lash and the horses took off.   545
When they reached the level, wheat-bearing plains
They kept pushing on—so strong were their horses—
Until the sun set and the world grew dark.

BOOK IV

They came to the hollows of Lacedaemon[9]
And drove to Menelaus' palace,
Which they found filled with guests. Menelaus
Was hosting a double wedding party
For his son and his daughter. He was sending her   5
To wed the son of Achilles, as he had promised
Long ago in Troy, and now the gods
Were bringing the marriage to pass.
He was sending her off with horses and chariots
For her journey to the city of the Myrmidons,   10
Over whom her husband-to-be was lord.
For his son he was bringing a bride
From Sparta, the daughter of Alector.

9. Sparta.

This son, Megapenthes, was born from a slave woman,
For the gods had made Helen barren   15
After the birth of her daughter Hermione,
Who had the beauty of golden Aphrodite.
So Menelaus' kinsfolk and neighbors
Were feasting in the great hall. A bard
Was singing and playing the lyre,   20
And two tumblers whirled among the guests
And led them in the dancing.
                                    Telemachus
And Nestor's son halted their horses
At the gate, and Eteoneus,
Menelaus' right-hand man, came out and saw them   25
And went through the hall to bring the news
To the shepherd of the people. He stood
At Menelaus' shoulder and his words flew fast:

"Two strangers have arrived, Lord Menelaus,
Two men in the line of Zeus by their looks.   30
Should we unyoke their horses, or should we
Send them elsewhere for hospitality?"

And red-haired Menelaus, greatly displeased:

"It's not like you to talk nonsense like this,
Eteoneus. How many times have you and I   35
Enjoyed the hospitality of others,
Hoping that Zeus would someday put an end
To our hard traveling? Unyoke their horses
And bring our new guests in to the feast."

He spoke, and Eteoneus hurried through the halls,   40
Calling other attendants to come along with him.
They unyoked the sweating horses and tied them
At the stalls, where they threw before them
A mixture of spelt and white barley. They leaned
The chariot against the gleaming entrance walls   45
And led the men into the palace. Their eyes
Went wide as they looked around the mansion
Of this sky-bred king, for a light as of the sun
Or the moon played over the high-roofed home
Of glorious Menelaus. When they had taken it all in,   50
They went into the polished tubs. When the maids
Had bathed them and rubbed them down with oil,
And clothed them in tunics and fleecy cloaks,
They sat down on chairs beside Menelaus.
A maid poured water from a golden pitcher   55
Into a silver basin for them to wash their hands
And then set up a polished table nearby.
Another serving woman, grave and dignified,
Set out bread and served generous helpings
From the other dishes she had; a carver set down   60

Cuts of meat by the platter and golden cups;
And a herald came by and poured them wine.
Then red-haired Menelaus said in greeting:

"Enjoy yourselves and eat. After supper
We will ask who you are—your bloodlines   65
Have not been lost in you. You belong
To the race of men who are sceptered kings,
Bred from Zeus. You're not just anybody."

And he set before them the prime cut of roast beef
That had been served to him as a mark of honor.   70
They helped themselves to the feast before them,
And when they had enough of food and drink,
Telemachus spoke to Nestor's son, holding
His head close so the others wouldn't hear:

"Do you see all this, Peisistratus, my friend,   75
These echoing halls flashing with bronze,
With gold, amber, silver, and ivory?
This must be what the court of Olympian Zeus
Looks like. This is unimaginable wealth!"

Menelaus, the red-haired king, overheard him,   80
And, speaking to both of them, had this to say:

"No mortal man could challenge Zeus, my boys.
His halls and possessions are everlasting.
My wealth may be matched by another man's
Or maybe not. For it is true I brought home   85
Shiploads after wandering for eight hard years.
Cyprus, Phoenicia, Egypt—I went all over,
Came to the Ethiopians, the Sidonians,
The Erembi, even to Libya,
Where the lambs have horns soon after they're born.   90
The ewes give birth three times a year there,
And neither shepherd nor lord ever runs short
Of cheese, meat or milk; the flocks are milked year round.
While I wandered through those lands amassing wealth
My brother was murdered, caught off guard   95
By treachery and the guile of his accursed wife.
So I do not enjoy being lord of this wealth.
You may have heard of all this from your fathers,
Whoever they may be, for I suffered greatly
And saw my house ruined, with all its treasures.   100
I would gladly live with a third of my wealth
And have those men back who perished in Troy
Far from the bluegrass pastures of Argos. And yet,
Though I weep for them often in my halls,
Easing my heart, I do not grieve constantly—   105

A man can get too much of chill grief.
I miss them all, but there is one man I miss
More than all the others. When I think of him
I don't want to sleep or eat, for no one
In the entire Greek army worked as hard   110
As Odysseus, and all he ever got for it
Was pain and sorrow, and I cannot forget
My sorrow for him. He has been gone so long,
And we do not know whether he is alive or dead.
Old Laertes must mourn for him, Penelope too,   115
And Telemachus, who was an infant when he left."

His words roused in Telemachus the desire
To weep for his father. Hot tears
Fell from his eyes when he heard his father's name,
And he pulled his purple cloak over his face.   120
Seeing this, Menelaus wondered
Whether he should allow Telemachus
To bring up his father himself, or whether
He should draw him out with pointed questions.

While Menelaus pondered this,   125
Helen came from her fragrant bedroom
Like gold-spindled Artemis. Adraste,
Her attendant, drew up a beautiful chair for her,
And Alcippe brought her a soft wool rug.
Another maid, Phylo, brought a silver basket—   130
A gift from Alcandre, wife of Polybus,
Who lived in Thebes, the city in Egypt
That has the wealthiest houses in the world.
Polybus had given Menelaus two silver baths,
Two tripods, and ten bars of gold.   135
And his wife, Alcandre, gave to Helen
Beautiful gifts of her own—a golden spindle
And a silver basket with gold-rimmed wheels.
This basket Phylo now placed beside her,
Filled with fine-spun yarn, and across it   140
Was laid the spindle, twirled with violet wool.
Helen sat upon the chair, a footstool
Under her feet, and questioned her husband:

"Do we know, Menelaus, who our guests
Claim to be? Shall I speak my mind or not?   145
My heart urges me to speak. I have never seen
Such a resemblance between any two people,
Man or woman, as between this man
And Odysseus' son—as I imagine him now—
Telemachus, who was a newborn baby   150
When for my sake, shameless thing that I was,
The Greeks came to Troy with war in their hearts."

And Menelaus, the red-haired king:

"Now that you mention it, I see
The resemblance myself—the feet, the hands,   155
The way he looks at you, that head of hair.
And just now when I was talking about Odysseus,
Saying how much he went through for my sake,
Tears welled up in his eyes, bitter tears,
And he covered his face with his purple cloak."   160

At this Nestor's son Peisistratus spoke up:

"Menelaus, son of Atreus, Zeus-bred king,
This is indeed, as you say, Odysseus' son.
But he is prudent and would not think it proper,
When he just got here, to make a big speech   165
Before you—whose voice delights us as a god's.
Nestor of Gerenia sent me with him as a guide,
For he was eager to see you, hoping that
You could suggest something he could do or say.
A son has many problems to face at home   170
When his father is gone and there is no one else
To help him. So it is now with Telemachus,
Whose father is gone, and there is no one else
Among the people to keep him from harm."

And Menelaus, the red-haired king: 175

"What's this? Here in my house, the son
Of my dear friend who did so much for me!
I used to think that if he came back
I would give him a welcome no other Greek
Could ever hope to have—if Olympian Zeus   180
Had brought us both home from over the sea
In our swift ships. I would have given him
A city of his own in Argos, built him a house,
Brought him over from Ithaca with his goods,
His son and all of his people—a whole city   185
Cleared out just for him! We would have been together,
Enjoying each other's company, and nothing
Would have parted us until death's black cloud
Finally enfolded us. But I suppose Zeus himself
Begrudged us this, for Odysseus alone,   190
That unlucky man, was never brought home."

His words aroused in all of them
A longing for lamentation. Argive Helen,
A child of Zeus, wept; Telemachus wept;
And Menelaus wept, the son of Atreus.   195
Nor could Nestor's son keep his eyes dry,
For he remembered Antilochus,
His flawless brother, who had been killed

By Memnon, Dawn's resplendent son,
And this memory gave wings to his words: 200

"Son of Atreus, old Nestor used to say,
Whenever we talked about things like this,
That no one could match your understanding.
So please understand me when I say
That I do not enjoy weeping after supper—   205
And it will be dawn before we know it.
Not that I think it's wrong to lament the dead.
This is all we can do—cut our hair
And shed some tears. I lost someone myself
At Troy, my brother, not the least hero there.   210
You probably knew him. I am too young
Ever to have seen him, but men say Antilochus
Could run and fight as well as any man alive."

And Menelaus, the red-haired king:

"No one could have put that better, my friend,   215
Not even someone much older. Your speech,
Wise and clear, shows the sort of father you have.
It's easy to spot a man for whom Zeus
Has spun out happiness in marriage and children,
As he has done for Nestor throughout his life.   220
And now he has reached a sleek old age in his halls,
And his sons are wise and fight with the best.
So we will stop this weeping, and once more
Think of supper. Let the servants pour water
Over our hands. Telemachus and I will have   225
Much to say to each other come morning."

So he spoke, and Asphalion,
Menelaus' attendant, poured water
Over their hands, and they reached out
For all the good cheer spread out before them.   230

But Helen, child of Zeus, had other ideas.
She threw a drug into the wine bowl
They were drinking from, a drug
That stilled all pain, quieted all anger
And brought forgetfulness of every ill.   235
Whoever drank wine laced with this drug
Would not be sad or shed a tear that day,
Not even if his own father and mother
Should lie there dead, or if someone killed
His brother, or son, before his eyes.   240
Helen had gotten this potent, cunning drug
From Polydamna, the wife of Thon,
A woman in Egypt, where the land
Proliferates with all sorts of drugs,
Many beneficial, many poisonous.   245

Men there know more about medicines
Than any other people on earth,
For they are of the race of Paeeon, the Healer.
When she had slipped the drug into the wine,
Helen ordered another round to be poured,   250
And then she turned to the company and said:

"Menelaus, son of Atreus in the line of Zeus,
And you sons of noble fathers, it is true
That Zeus gives easy lives to some of us
And hard lives to others—he can do anything, after all—   255
But you should sit now in the hall and feast
And entertain yourselves by telling stories.
I'll start you off. I couldn't begin to tell you
All that Odysseus endured and accomplished,
But listen to what that hero did once   260
In the land of Troy, where the Achaeans suffered.
First, he beat himself up—gave himself some nasty bruises—
Then put on a cheap cloak so he looked like a slave,
And in this disguise he entered the wide streets
Of the enemy city. He looked like a beggar,   265
Far from what he was back in the Greek camp,
And fooled everyone when he entered Troy.
I alone recognized him in his disguise
And questioned him, but he cleverly put me off.
It was only after I had bathed him   270
And rubbed him down with oil and clothed him
And had sworn a great oath not to tell the Trojans
Who he really was until he got back to the ships,
That he told me, at last, what the Achaeans planned.
He killed many Trojans before he left   275
And arrived back at camp with much to report.
The other women in Troy wailed aloud,
But I was glad inside, for my heart had turned
Homeward, and I rued the infatuation
Aphrodite gave me when she led me away   280
From my native land, leaving my dear child,
My bridal chamber, and my husband,
A man who lacked nothing in wisdom or looks."

And Menelaus, the red-haired king:

"A very good story, my wife, and well told.   285
By now I have come to know the minds
Of many heroes, and have traveled far and wide,
But I have never laid eyes on anyone
Who had an enduring heart like Odysseus.
Listen to what he did in the wooden horse,   290
Where all we Argive chiefs sat waiting
To bring slaughter and death to the Trojans.
You came there then, with godlike Deiphobus.
Some god who favored the Trojans

Must have lured you on. Three times you circled 295
Our hollow hiding place, feeling it
With your hands, and you called out the names
Of all the Argive leaders, making your voice
Sound like each of our wives' in turn.
Diomedes and I, sitting in the middle 300
With Odysseus, heard you calling
And couldn't take it. We were frantic
To come out, or answer you from inside,
But Odysseus held us back and stopped us.
Then everyone else stayed quiet also, 305
Except for Anticlus, who wanted to answer you,
But Odysseus saved us all by clamping
His strong hands over Anticlus' mouth
And holding them there until Athena led you off."

Then Telemachus said in his clear-headed way: 310

"Menelaus, son of Atreus in the line of Zeus,
It is all the more unbearable then, isn't it?
My father may have had a heart of iron,
But it didn't do him any good in the end.
Please send us to bed now. It is time 315
We rested and enjoyed some sweet sleep."

He spoke, and Helen of Argos told her maids
To place beds on the porch and spread upon them
Beautiful purple blankets and fleecy cloaks.
The maids went out of the hall with torches 320
And made up the beds, and a herald
Led the guests out to them. So they slept there
On the palace porch, the hero Telemachus
And Nestor's glorious son. But Menelaus slept
In the innermost chamber of that high house 325
Next to Helen, Zeus' brightness upon her.

Dawn brushed her pale rose fingers across the sky,
And Menelaus got out of bed and dressed.
He slung his sharp sword around his shoulder,
Tied oiled leather sandals onto his feet, 330
And walked out of the bedroom like a god.
Then he sat down next to Telemachus and said:

"Tell me, Telemachus, what has brought you here
To gleaming Sparta over the sea's broad back?
Public business or private? Tell me the truth." 335

Telemachus took a deep breath and said:

"Menelaus, son of Atreus in the line of Zeus,
I came to see if you could tell me anything
About my father. My land is in ruin.

I'm being eaten out of house and home   340
By hostile men who constantly throng my halls
Slaughtering my sheep and horned cattle
In their arrogant courtship of my mother.
And so I am at your knees. Tell me
How my father, Odysseus, met his end,   345
Whether you saw it with your own eyes,
Or heard about it from someone else,
Some wanderer. He was born to sorrow,
More than any man on earth. And do not,
Out of pity, spare me the truth, but tell me   350
Whatever you have seen, whatever you know.
I beseech you, if my father, noble Odysseus,
Ever fulfilled a promise he made to you
In the land of Troy, where the Achaeans suffered,
Remember it now, and tell me the truth."   355
And Menelaus, deeply troubled by this:

"Those dogs! Those puny weaklings,
Wanting to sleep in the bed of a hero!
A doe might as well bed her suckling fawns
In the lair of a lion, leaving them there   360
In the bush and then going off over the hills
Looking for grassy fields. When the lion
Comes back, the fawns die an ugly death.
That's the kind of death these men will die
When Odysseus comes back. O Father Zeus,   365
And Athena and Apollo, bring Odysseus back
With the strength he showed in Lesbos once
When he wrestled a match with Philomeleides
And threw him hard, making all of us cheer—
That's the Odysseus I want the suitors to meet!   370
They'd get married all right—to bitter death.
But, as to what you ask me about,
I will not stray from the point or deceive you.
No, I will tell you all that the infallible
Old Man of the Sea told me, and hide nothing.   375
        I was in Egypt, held up by the gods
Because I failed to offer them sacrifice.
The gods never allow us to forget them.
There is an island in the whitecapped sea
Just north of Egypt. Men call it Pharos,   380
And it lies one hard day's sailing offshore.
There is a good harbor there where ships
Take on fresh water before heading out to sea.
The gods kept me stuck in that harbor
For twenty days. A good sailing breeze   385
Never rose up, and all my supplies
Would have been exhausted, and my crew spent,
Had not one of the gods taken pity on me
And saved me. This was Eidothea,
Daughter of Proteus, the Old Man of the Sea.   390

Somehow I had moved her heart. She met me
As I wandered alone, apart from my crew,
Who roamed the island continually, fishing
With bent hooks, their bellies cramped with hunger.
She came close to me and spoke: 395

'Are you completely out of your mind, stranger,
Or do you actually like suffering like this?
You've been marooned on this island a long time
With no end in sight, and your crew's fading fast.'

"She spoke like this, and I answered her: 400

'I tell you, goddess—whichever goddess you are—
That I am not stranded here of my own free will.
I must have offended one of the immortals.
But you tell me—for gods know everything—
Which of the immortals is pinning me down here   405
And won't let me go. And tell me how
I can sail back home over the teeming sea.'

"And the shining goddess answered me:

'Well, all right, stranger, since you ask.
This is the haunt of an unerring immortal,   410
Egyptian Proteus, the Old Man of the Sea,
Who serves Poseidon and knows all the deeps.
They say he's my father. If you can
Somehow catch him in ambush here,
He will tell you the route, and the distance too,   415
Of your journey home over the teeming sea.
And he will tell you, prince, if you so wish,
What has been done in your house for better or worse
While you have been gone on your long campaign.'

"So she spoke, and I answered her: 420

'Show me yourself how to ambush
The old god, or he may give me the slip.
It's hard for a mortal to master a god.'

"And the shining goddess answered me:

'I'll tell you exactly what you need to know.   425
When the sun is at high noon, the unerring
Old Man of the Sea comes from the salt water,
Hidden in dark ripples the West Wind stirs up,
And then lies down to sleep in the scalloped caves.
All around him seals, the brine-spirit's brood,   430
Sleep in a herd. They come out of the grey water
With breath as fetid as the depths of the sea.
I will lead you there at break of day
And lay you in a row, you and three comrades

Chosen by you as the best on your ship.   435
Now I'll tell you all the old man's wiles.
First, he will go over the seals and count them,
And when he has counted them off by fives,
He will lie down like a shepherd among them.
As soon as you see him lying down to rest,   440
Screw up your courage to the sticking point
And pin him down, no matter how he struggles
And tries to escape. He will try everything,
And turn into everything that moves on the earth,
And into water also, and a burning flame.   445
Just hang on and grip him all the more tightly.
When he finally speaks to you of his own free will
In the shape you saw him in when he lay down to rest,
Then ease off, hero, and let the old man go,
And ask him which of the gods is angry with you,   450
And how you can sail home over the teeming sea.'

"And with that she slipped into the surging sea.
I headed for my ships where they stood on the sand
And brooded on many things as I went.
When I had come down to the ships and the sea,   455
We made supper, and when night came on,
We lay down to take our rest on the beach.
When dawn came, a palmetto of rose,
I went along the shore of the open sea
Praying over and over to the immortal gods,   460
Taking with me the three of my crew
I trusted the most for any adventure.

"The goddess, meanwhile, dove underwater
And now came back with the skins of four seals,
All newly flayed. She was out to trick her father.   465
She scooped out hiding places for us in the sand
And sat waiting as we cautiously drew near.
Then she had us lie down in a row, and threw
A seal skin over each of us. It would have been
A gruesome ambush—the stench of the seals   470
Was unbearable—but the goddess saved us
By putting ambrosia under each man's nose,
Drowning out the stench with its immortal fragrance.
So we waited patiently all morning long,
And then the seals came from the water in throngs.   475
They lay down in rows along the seashore,
And at noon the Old One came from the sea.
He found the fat seals and went over the herd,
Counting them up. He counted us first,
Never suspecting any kind of trick,   480
And then he lay down. We rushed him
With a shout and got our hands on him,
And the Old One didn't forget his wiles,
Turning first into a bearded lion,

Then a serpent, a leopard, and a huge boar.   485
He even turned into flowing water,
And into a high, leafy tree. But we
Held on, gritting our teeth, and at last
The wily Old One grew weary, and said to me:

'Which god have you plotted with, son of Atreus,   490
To catch me off-guard? What do you want?'

"He spoke, and I answered him:

'You know, old man—don't try to put me off—
How long I have been stuck on this island
With no end in sight. I'm losing heart.   495
Just tell me this—you gods know everything—
Which of the immortals has marooned me here?
How can I sail home over the teeming sea?'

"When I said this, he answered:

'You should have offered noble sacrifice to Zeus   500
And the other gods before embarking
If you wanted a speedy journey home
Over the deep purple sea. It is not your fate
To come home to your friends and native land
Until you go once more to the waters of the Aegyptus,   505
The sky-fed river, and offer holy hecatombs[1]
To the immortal gods who hold high heaven.
Only then will they grant the journey you desire.'

"When he said this my spirit was crushed.
It was a long, hard pull over the misty deep   510
Back to the Aegyptus. Still, I answered:

'I will do all these things, just as you say.
But tell me this, and tell me the truth:
Did all the Achaeans make it home in their ships,
All those whom Nestor and I left at Troy?   515
Or did any die on shipboard, or in their friends' arms,
After winding up the war?'

            "To which Proteus said:

'Why, son of Atreus, ask me about this?
You don't need to know. Nor do I think
You will be free from tears once you have heard it.   520
Many were killed in the war. You were there
And know who they were. Many, too, survived.
On the homeward journey two heroes died.
Another still lives, perhaps, held back by the sea.

---

1. A sacrifice of a hundred cattle.

'Ajax went down among his long-oared ships.   525
Poseidon had driven him onto Gyrae's rocks
But saved him from the sea. He would have escaped,
Despite Athena's hatred, but he lost his wits
And boasted loudly that he had survived the deep
In spite of the gods. Poseidon heard this boast,   530
And with his trident he struck Gyrae's rock
And broke it asunder. One part held firm,
But the other part, upon which Ajax sat
In his blind arrogance, fell into the gulf
And took Ajax with it. And so he perished,   535
His lungs full of saltwater.
                        Your brother, though,
Outran the fates in his hollow ships,
With the help of Hera. But when he was nearing
Malea's heights, a stormwind caught him
And carried him groaning over the teeming sea   540
To the frontier of the land where Thyestes once lived
And after him Thyestes' son, Aegisthus.[2]
Then the gods gave him a following wind
And safe passage homeward. Agamemnon
Rejoiced to set foot on his ancestral land.   545
He fell to the ground and kissed the good earth
And hot tears of joy streamed from his eyes,
So glad was he to see his homeland again.
But from a high lookout a watchman saw him.
Aegisthus had treacherously posted him there   550
And promised a reward of two bars of gold.
He had been keeping watch for a year by then
So that Agamemnon would not slip by unseen
And unleash his might, and now he reported
His news to Aegisthus, who acted quickly   555
And set a trap. He chose his twenty best men
And had them wait in ambush. Opposite them,
On the hall's farther side, he had a feast prepared,
And then he drove off in his chariot,
Brooding darkly, to invite Agamemnon.   560
So he brought Agamemnon up to the palace
Unaware of his doom and slaughtered him
The way an ox is slaughtered at the stall.
None of Agamemnon's men was left alive,
Nor any of Aegisthus'. All were slain in the hall.'   565

"Proteus spoke, and my heart was shattered.
I wept and wept as I sat on the sand, losing
All desire to live and see the light of the sun.
When I could not weep or flail about any more,
The unerring Old Man of the Sea addressed me: 570
'Weep no more, son of Atreus. We gain nothing
By such prolonged bouts of grief. Instead,

---

2. Thyestes was the brother of Atreus, father of Agamemnon and Menelaus.

Go as quickly as you can to your native land.
Either Aegisthus will still be alive, or
Orestes may have beat you to it and killed him,   575
And you may happen to arrive during his funeral.'

"These words warmed my heart, although
I was still in shock. Then I asked him:

'I know now what became of these two,
But who is the third man, the one who's alive,   580
But held back by the sea, or perhaps is dead.
I want to hear about him, despite my grief.'

"Proteus answered me without hesitation:

'It is Laertes' son, whose home is in Ithaca.
I saw him on an island, shedding salt tears,   585
In the halls of Calypso, who keeps him there
Against his will. He has no way to get home
To his native land. He has no ships left,
No crew to row him over the sea's broad back.
As for you, Menelaus, Zeus' cherished king,   590
You are not destined to die and to meet your fate
In bluegrass Argos. The immortals will take you
To the ends of the earth and the Elysian Fields,
Where Rhadamanthus lives and life is easiest.
No snow, nor storm, nor heavy rain comes there,   595
But a sighing wind from the West always blows
Off the Ocean, a cooling breeze for men.
For Helen is your wife, and in the gods' eyes
You are the son-in-law of great Zeus himself.'³

"And with that he dove into the surging sea.   600
I went back to the ships with my godlike companions
And brooded on many things as I went.
When we had come down to the ships and the sea,
And had made supper, immortal night came on,
And we lay down to take our rest on the beach.   605
When dawn came with palmettoes of rose,
We hauled our ships down to the shining water,
And set up the masts and sails in the hulls.
The crews came aboard, and sitting in rows
They beat the sea white with their churning oars.   610
And so I sailed back to the rain-fed Aegyptus,
Moored my ships, and offered perfect sacrifice.
When I had appeased the everlasting gods
I heaped up a barrow for Agamemnon
So that his memory would not fade. Only then   615
Did I set sail for home, and the gods gave me

---

3. Helen was the daughter of Zeus, who made love to Leda in the guise of a swan.

A following wind that brought me back swiftly.
     Well, now, I want you to stay in my halls
Until eleven or twelve days have passed,
And then I will give you a royal send-off
And these splendid gifts: three horses
And a polished chariot, and a beautiful cup,
So that you can pour libations to the deathless gods
And remember me all the days of your life."

Telemachus answered in his clear-headed way:

"Son of Atreus, do not keep me here long.
I could spend a year in your house
And never miss my home or my parents.
That's how much I enjoy listening to you
And hearing your tales. But even now
My crew is getting restless back in Pylos
And you are keeping me long here.
               As for gifts,
Give me whatever treasure you will,
But I will not take horses to Ithaca.
They are better off here for you to enjoy,
For you rule a wide plain, with lotus
Everywhere, and galingale, and wheat and spelt,
And heavy ears of white barley. But Ithaca
Has no broad horse-runs or meadowlands at all.
Its pasture is for goats, and more lovely
Than horse pasture. None of the islands
That slope to the sea has rich meadows, or is good
For driving horses, and Ithaca least of all."

And Menelaus, who could make his voice
Carry in battle, said to Telemachus:

"You are of good blood, my boy, to talk like that!
All right, I will change my gifts, as I easily can.
Of all the gifts that lie stored in my house
I will give you the most beautiful—
And the most valuable—a well-wrought bowl,
Solid silver, with the lip finished in gold,
The work of Hephaestus. The hero Phaedimus,
King of the Sidonians, gave it to me
When I stayed at his house on my way home.
Now I want you to take it home with you."

And while they talked to each other,
The banqueters came to their lord's palace,
Driving sheep with them and bringing wine,
And bread that their veiled wives had sent with them.
And so they were busy with the feast in Menelaus' halls.

Meanwhile, back in Ithaca,
The suitors were entertaining themselves

620

625

630

635

640

645

650

655

660

In front of Odysseus' palace again,
Throwing the javelin and discus
On the level terrace, arrogant as ever.   665
Antinous and Eurymachus, who were
Their natural leaders, were sitting there,
And Noemon, son of Phronius,
Came up to them and asked Antinous:

"Antinous, do we have any idea   670
When Telemachus will return from Pylos?
He's gone off with a ship of mine,
And I need her to cross over to Elis,
Where I have twelve brood mares
And ten mules still at the teat. I would like   675
To drive one of them off and break him in."

When he said this, Antinous and Eurymachus
Just looked at each other. They had no idea
Telemachus had gone to Neleian Pylos.
They thought he was somewhere out in the field   680
With the sheep flocks, or off with the swineherd.
Antinous questioned Noemon closely:

"Tell me exactly when Telemachus left
And who went with him, a hand-picked crew
From the island, or his own fieldhands and slaves?   685
He could have done it either way. And tell me this,
So I'll have it right. Did he force you to give him
The ship, or were you just doing him a favor?"

And Noemon answered him:

"I gave it freely. What else could I do,   690
When a man like that, with all his troubles,
Asks me? It would be hard to refuse him.
Those who went with him are the best in town,
After ourselves, and when they boarded
I noticed Mentor going on board, too,   695
As their leader, either Mentor or a god
Who looked just like him. I wonder about this,
Because I saw Mentor here yesterday morning,
After he had set sail for sandy Pylos."

With that, Noemon left for his father's house.   700
Antinous and Eurymachus were furious.
They made the suitors stop their games
And had them sit down. Antinous
Addressed them. His black heart was seething
With anger, and his eyes burned like fire: 705

"Unbelievable! Telemachus has some nerve,
Pulling off this voyage. We never thought

We'd see it happen, and the boy is up and gone,
Just like that, with all of us against it,
Launching a ship and picking the best crew around.   710
He's going to start giving us trouble soon.
May Zeus cripple him before he reaches manhood!
All right, now, give me a ship and twenty men
So I can lie in ambush and watch for him
As he comes through the strait between Ithaca   715
And rocky Samos. He'll be sorry
He ever made this voyage in search of his father."

They all praised his speech and urged him on.
Then they stood up and went to Odysseus' palace.

It did not take Penelope long to find out   720
The suitors' dark intentions. The herald,
Medon, was the one who brought her word.
He had overheard the suitors talking
As he stood outside the courtyard
Where they were weaving their plots, and now   725
He went through the hall to tell Penelope.
As he crossed the threshold, she asked him:

"Medon, why have the suitors sent you here?
To tell the handmaids of divine Odysseus
To drop everything and prepare a feast for them?   730
May this be their last courtship, their last party,
Oh, may this latest feast be their last of all!
Do you hear me, you thronging leeches
Who are eating away Telemachus' property?
You surely weren't listening to your fathers   735
When you were children, or you would have heard
What kind of man Odysseus was to them,
How he never wronged anyone in word or deed,
How he was fair to everyone, unlike
Most sceptered kings, who all have their favorites.   740
He never lost his temper with any man at all.
But your vile deeds and hearts are plain to see,
And there is no gratitude for kindness past."

Then Medon, the tactful herald:

"If only this were the greatest evil, Lady,   745
But there is a greater and more grievous.
The suitors are planning—and may Zeus
Never bring their plans to pass—to kill Telemachus
On his way back home. He went to sandy Pylos
And gleaming Lacedaemon for news of his father."   750

When Medon said these things, Penelope felt
That her heart had been unstrung. Her eyes

Filled with tears, and she was unable to speak
For a long time. Finally she said to the herald:

"Medon, why is my son gone? There was no need   755
For him to board any sea-going ships,
Which men use to cross the wide water
As they use horses on land. Why did he go?
So that not even his name would be left among men?"

And Medon, the tactful herald: 760

"I do not know whether a god urged him on,
Or his own heart moved him to go to Pylos
To learn either of his father's return
Or of the manner in which he met his fate."

So saying, Medon went into Odysseus' house.   765
Pain washed over Penelope and seeped
Into her bones. She could not bring herself
To sit down in one of the many chairs
That were there in the house, but sat curled
On the worn threshold of her bedroom   770
And wept. Around her the women of the house
Moaned softly, the old and the young,
And Penelope spoke to them through her tears:

"Hear me, my friends, for the god on Olympus
Has given me pain beyond all other women   775
Of my generation. I have lost a fine husband
With a heart like a lion, the glory of the Danaans,
The pride of all Hellas, a man of many virtues.
And now the winds have ripped my beloved son
From my house. I never even heard him leave.   780
You were cruel, each of you, not to think
Of getting me from bed, for you must have known
He was going aboard that hollow black ship.
If I had known he was setting out on this journey,
He would have stayed here, despite his willfulness,   785
Or else he would have left me dead in our halls.
Quick now, someone go get old Dolios,
The servant whom my father gave me
Before I left home and who now tends my orchards.
He should sit with Laertes and tell him all this.   790
Laertes may be able to weave some plan
And complain to the people about these men
Who want to destroy his and Odysseus' line."

And her beloved nurse, Eurycleia, said:

"Child, you can spare me or stab me   795
With a sword, but I will not hide what I know.

I was in on all this. I got his provisions,
Bread and sweet wine. He made me swear
Not to tell you until twelve days had passed
Or until you missed him yourself or heard   800
He had gone. He didn't want you crying.
Now take a bath and put on some clean clothes.
Then go upstairs with the serving women
And pray to Athena, daughter of Zeus.
No matter what, she can save your son from death.   805
But do not trouble the old man. He has
Troubles enough. Yet I do not think
The line of Laertes, son of Arcesius,
Is entirely hated by the blessed gods.
There may still be someone in that line to own   810
This high hall and all the rich fields around."

So the old nurse soothed Penelope's grief
And kept her eyes dry. Penelope bathed
And put on clean clothes. Then she went upstairs
With the serving women, put barley for strewing   815
In a basket, and prayed to Athena:

"Hear me, Mystic Daughter of Zeus.
If ever in these halls my cunning Odysseus
Burned fat thighbones of bulls or sheep for you,
Remember it now and save my beloved son.   820
Protect him from the arrogant suitors' violence."

Penelope voiced this prayer, and Athena heard it,
While down in the shadowy halls below
These same suitors were talking noisily,
Making crude comments such as these: 825

"So while the lady upstairs gets ready to marry
One of her suitors, she has no idea
That her suitors are arranging to murder her son!"

But they had no idea of what was being arranged.
Antinous had some words for all of them: 830

"Are you crazy? Stow that kind of talk,
Or someone may report it to those inside.
We're going to do what we said we would
Under cover of silence. We're all in this together."

And he picked out the twenty best men there.   835
They went down to the shore of the sea
And hauled a fast ship out onto the water.
They set up mast and sail in that black ship
And fit the oars into the leather thole-straps,
All in due order. Then they unfurled the white sails.   840
Their attendants brought all their gear aboard,
And they moored the ship where she would catch

The evening breeze. Then they disembarked,
Ate their dinner, and waited for twilight.

Penelope lay in her room upstairs.   845
She would not touch any food or drink
But only lay there worrying about her son,
Wondering whether he would escape from death
Or be killed by the insolent suitors.

    Surrounded by men, a lion broods and then panics   850
    When they begin to tighten their crafty ring.

So too Penelope, until sleep drifted over her,
And she sank back with all her body relaxed.

Athena's eyes were flashing in the dark.
She made a phantom in the form of a woman,   855
Iphthime, daughter of great Icarius,
Now wed to Eumelus, whose home was in Pherae.
She sent the phantom into Odysseus' house
To stop Penelope's weeping and sobbing.
It drifted into her room through the keyhole   860
And stood above her head, and spoke to her:

"Asleep, Penelope, and broken-hearted?
The blessed gods are unwilling that you
Should weep and be sad, for your son will return.
He has not offended the gods at all."   865

And Penelope, slumbering sweetly
At the gate of dreams, answered her:

"Why have you come here, sister? You live
Far away and have seldom come before.
You tell me to stop grieving, tell me to rest   870
From the sorrows that plague my mind and heart.
Long ago now I lost my fine husband,
A lion-hearted man, the glory of the Danaans,
The pride of Hellas, a man of many virtues.
And now my beloved son has gone away   875
In a hollow ship, a mere child, who knows nothing
Of the world of men. I grieve for him even more
Than for my husband. I am trembling with fear
That he will get hurt, either among the people
He has gone off to visit, or on the open sea.   880
For his many enemies are plotting against him
And mean to kill him before he gets home."

The glimmering phantom answered her:

"Take heart, and don't be so afraid. The guide
Who goes with him is one many men pray for   885

To stand at their side, a powerful ally—
Pallas Athena. And she pities you in your grief,
For it is she who sent me to tell you this."

And Penelope, in her circumspect way:

"If you are truly a god and have heard a god's voice,   890
Tell me also of that man of many sorrows,
Whether he still lives and sees the light of the sun,
Or whether he is dead and in Hades' dark world."

The glimmering phantom answered her:

"No, I will not speak of him, whether he be   895
Alive or dead. Empty words are ill spoken."

And the phantom slipped through the keyhole
And became a sigh in the air. Penelope
Started up from sleep, and her heart was warmed
By the clear dream that had come in the soft black night.   900

By now the suitors had embarked and set sail,
Their hearts set on murdering Telemachus.
There is a rocky island out in the sea,
Midway between Ithaca and rugged Samos.
Asteris is its name, not very big,   905
But it has a harbor with outlets on either side
Where a ship can lie. There the suitors waited.

BOOK V

    Dawn reluctantly
Left Tithonus⁴ in her rose-shadowed bed,
Then shook the morning into flakes of fire.

Light flooded the halls of Olympus
Where Zeus, high Lord of Thunder,   5
Sat with the other gods, listening to Athena
Reel off the tale of Odysseus' woes.
It galled her that he was still in Calypso's cave:

"Zeus, my father—and all you blessed immortals—
Kings might as well no longer be gentle and kind   10
Or understand the correct order of things.
They might as well be tyrannical butchers
For all that any of Odysseus' people
Remember him, a godly king as kind as a father.
No, he's still languishing on that island, detained   15
Against his will by that nymph Calypso,

---

4. Dawn's lover, a mortal man whom she made immortal (though not ageless) and brought to
live with her in the sky.

No way in the world for him to get back to his land.
His ships are all lost, he has no crew left
To row him across the sea's crawling back.
And now the islanders are plotting to kill his son   20
As he heads back home. He went for news of his father
To sandy Pylos and white-bricked Sparta."

Storm Cloud Zeus had an answer for her:

"Quite a little speech you've let slip through your teeth,
Daughter. But wasn't this exactly your plan   25
So that Odysseus would make them pay for it later?
You know how to get Telemachus
Back to Ithaca and out of harm's way
With his mother's suitors sailing in a step behind."

Zeus turned then to his son Hermes and said: 30

"Hermes, you've been our messenger before.
Go tell that ringleted nymph it is my will
To let that patient man Odysseus go home.
Not with an escort, mind you, human or divine,
But on a rickety raft—tribulation at sea—   35
Until on the twentieth day he comes to Schería
In the land of the Phaeacians, our distant relatives,
Who will treat Odysseus as if he were a god
And take him on a ship to his own native land
With gifts of bronze and clothing and gold,   40
More than he ever would have taken back from Troy
Had he come home safely with his share of the loot.
That's how he's destined to see his dear ones again
And return to his high-gabled Ithacan home."

Thus Zeus, and the quicksilver messenger   45
Laced on his feet the beautiful sandals,
Golden, immortal, that carry him over
Landscape and seascape on a puff of wind.
And he picked up the wand he uses to charm
Mortal eyes to sleep and make sleepers awake.   50

Holding this wand the tough quicksilver god
Took off, bounded onto Pieria
And dove through the ether down to the sea,

   Skimming the waves like a cormorant,
   The bird that patrols the saltwater billows   55
   Hunting for fish, seaspume on its plumage,

Hermes flying low and planing the whitecaps.

When he finally arrived at the distant island
He stepped from the violet-tinctured sea

On to dry land and proceeded to the cavern   60
Where Calypso lived. She was at home.
A fire blazed on the hearth, and the smell
Of split cedar and arbor vitae⁵ burning
Spread like incense across the whole island.
She was seated inside, singing in a lovely voice   65
As she wove at her loom with a golden shuttle.
Around her cave the woodland was in bloom,
Alder and poplar and fragrant cypress.
Long-winged birds nested in the leaves,
Horned owls and larks and slender-throated shorebirds   70
That screech like crows over the bright saltwater.
Tendrils of ivy curled around the cave's mouth,
The glossy green vine clustered with berries.
Four separate springs flowed with clear water, criss-
Crossing channels as they meandered through meadows   75
Lush with parsley and blossoming violets.
It was enough to make even a visiting god
Enraptured at the sight. Quicksilver Hermes
Took it all in, then turned and entered
The vast cave.

          Calypso knew him at sight.   80
The immortals have ways of recognizing each other,
Even those whose homes are in outlying districts.
But Hermes didn't find the great hero inside.
Odysseus was sitting on the shore,
As ever those days, honing his heart's sorrow,   85
Staring out to sea with hollow, salt-rimmed eyes.

Calypso, sleek and haloed, questioned Hermes
Politely, as she seated him on a lacquered chair:

"My dear Hermes, to what do I owe
The honor of this unexpected visit? Tell me   90
What you want, and I'll oblige you if I can."

The goddess spoke, and then set a table
With ambrosia and mixed a bowl of rosy nectar.⁶
The quicksilver messenger ate and drank his fill,
Then settled back from dinner with heart content   95
And made the speech she was waiting for:

"You ask me, goddess to god, why I have come.
Well, I'll tell you exactly why. Remember, you asked.
Zeus ordered me to come here; I didn't want to.
Who would want to cross this endless stretch   100
Of deserted sea? Not a single city in sight
Where you can get a decent sacrifice from men.

---

5. An evergreen, whose name means "tree of   6. Magic food of the gods.
life."

But you know how it is: Zeus has the aegis,
And none of us gods can oppose his will.
He says you have here the most woebegone hero   105
Of the whole lot who fought around Priam's city
For nine years, sacked it in the tenth, and started home.
But on the way back they offended Athena,[7]
And she swamped them with hurricane winds and waves.
His entire crew was wiped out, and he   110
Drifted along until he was washed up here.
Anyway, Zeus wants you to send him back home. Now.
The man's not fated to rot here far from his friends.
It's his destiny to see his dear ones again
And return to his high-gabled Ithacan home."   115

He finished, and the nymph's aura stiffened.
Words flew from her mouth like screaming hawks:

"You gods are the most jealous bastards in the universe—
Persecuting any goddess who ever openly takes
A mortal lover to her bed and sleeps with him.   120
When Dawn caressed Orion[8] with her rosy fingers,
You celestial layabouts gave her nothing but trouble
Until Artemis finally shot him on Ortygia—
Gold-throned, holy, gentle-shafted assault goddess!
When Demeter followed her heart and unbound   125
Her hair for Iasion and made love to him
In a late-summer field, Zeus was there taking notes
And executed the man with a cobalt lightning blast.[9]
And now you gods are after me for having a man.
Well, I was the one who saved his life, unprying him   130
From the spar he came floating here on, sole survivor
Of the wreck Zeus made of his streamlined ship,
Slivering it with lightning on the wine-dark sea.
I loved him, I took care of him, I even told him
I'd make him immortal and ageless all of his days.   135
But you said it, Hermes: Zeus has the aegis
And none of us gods can oppose his will.
So all right, he can go, if it's an order from above,
Off on the sterile sea. How I don't know.
I don't have any oared ships or crewmen   140
To row him across the sea's broad back.
But I'll help him. I'll do everything I can.
To get him back safely to his own native land."

The quicksilver messenger had one last thing to say:

---

7. This passage is unusual in ascribing the deaths of Odysseus's companions to Athena, not Poseidon. In most versions of the myth, the Greeks offended Athena during the sack of the city, by various war crimes including the rape of the prophetess Cassandra by the Greek hero Ajax, in Athena's temple.

8. Orion was a human hunter with whom Dawn fell in love; the huntress goddess, Artemis, shot and killed him.

9. Demeter, goddess of the harvest, fell in love with Iasion (and in some versions had two sons by him); Zeus killed him with a thunderbolt.

"Well send him off now and watch out for Zeus' temper.   145
Cross him and he'll really be rough on you later."

With that the tough quicksilver god made his exit.

Calypso composed herself and went to Odysseus,
Zeus' message still ringing in her ears.
She found him sitting where the breakers rolled in.   150
His eyes were perpetually wet with tears now,
His life draining away in homesickness.
The nymph had long since ceased to please.
He still slept with her at night in her cavern,
An unwilling lover mated to her eager embrace.   155
Days he spent sitting on the rocks by the breakers,
Staring out to sea with hollow, salt-rimmed eyes.
She stood close to him and started to speak:

"You poor man. You can stop grieving now
And pining away. I'm sending you home.   160
Look, here's a bronze axe. Cut some long timbers
And make yourself a raft fitted with topdecks,
Something that will get you across the sea's misty spaces.

I'll stock it with fresh water, food and red wine—
Hearty provisions that will stave off hunger—and   165
I'll clothe you well and send you a following wind
To bring you home safely to your own native land,
If such is the will of the gods of high heaven,
Whose minds and powers are stronger than mine."

Odysseus' eyes shone with weariness. He stiffened,   170
And shot back at her words fletched like arrows:

"I don't know what kind of send-off you have in mind,
Goddess, telling me to cross all that open sea on a raft,
Painful, hard sailing. Some well-rigged vessels
Never make it across with a stiff wind from Zeus.   175
You're not going to catch me setting foot on any raft
Unless you agree to swear a solemn oath
That you're not planning some new trouble for me."

Calypso's smile was like a shower of light.
She touched him gently, and teased him a little: 180

"Blasphemous, that's what you are—but nobody's fool!
How do you manage to say things like that?
All right. I swear by Earth and Heaven above
And the subterranean water of Styx[1]—the greatest
Oath and the most awesome a god can swear—   185
That I'm not planning more trouble for you, Odysseus.

---

1. River of the underworld.

I'll put my mind to work for you as hard as I would
For myself, if ever I were in such a fix.
My heart is in the right place, Odysseus,
Nor is it a cold lump of iron in my breast."   190

With that the haloed goddess walked briskly away
And the man followed in the deity's footsteps.
The two forms, human and divine, came to the cave
And he sat down in the chair which moments before
Hermes had vacated, and the nymph set out for him   195
Food and drink such as mortal men eat.
She took a seat opposite godlike Odysseus
And her maids served her ambrosia and nectar.
They helped themselves to as much as they wanted,
And when they had their fill of food and drink   200
Calypso spoke, an immortal radiance upon her:
"Son of Laertes in the line of Zeus, my wily Odysseus,
Do you really want to go home to your beloved country
Right away? Now? Well, you still have my blessings.
But if you had any idea of all the pain   205
You're destined to suffer before getting home,
You'd stay here with me, deathless—
Think of it, Odysseus!—no matter how much
You missed your wife and wanted to see her again.
You spend all your daylight hours yearning for her.   210
I don't mind saying she's not my equal
In beauty, no matter how you measure it.
Mortal beauty cannot compare with immortal."

Odysseus, always thinking, answered her this way:

"Goddess and mistress, don't be angry with me.   215
I know very well that Penelope,
For all her virtues, would pale beside you.
She's only human, and you are a goddess,
Eternally young. Still, I want to go back.
My heart aches for the day I return to my home.   220
If some god hits me hard as I sail the deep purple,
I'll weather it like the sea-bitten veteran I am.
God knows I've suffered and had my share of sorrows
In war and at sea. I can take more if I have to."

The sun set on his words, and the shadows darkened.   225
They went to a room deep in the cave, where they made
Sweet love and lay side by side through the night.

Dawn came early, touching the sky with rose.

Odysseus put on a shirt and cloak,
And the nymph slipped on a long silver robe   230
Shimmering in the light, cinched it at the waist
With a golden belt and put a veil on her head.

What to do about sending Odysseus off?
She handed him an axe, bronze, both edges honed.
The olive-wood haft felt good in his palms.   235
She gave him a sharp adze, too, then led the way
To the island's far side where the trees grew tall,
Alder and poplar and silver fir, sky-topping trees
Long-seasoned and dry that would keep him afloat.
Calypso showed him where the trees grew tall   240
Then went back home, a glimmer in the woods,
While Odysseus cut timber.
                         Working fast,
He felled twenty trees, cut them to length,
Smoothed them skillfully and trued them to the line.
The glimmer returned—Calypso with an auger—   245
And he drilled the beams through, fit them up close
And hammered them together with joiners and pegs.
About the size of a deck a master shipwright
Chisels into shape for a broad-bowed freighter
Was the size Odysseus made his wide raft.   250
He fit upright ribs close-set in the decking
And finished them with long facing planks.
He built a mast and fit in a yardarm,
And he made a rudder to steer her by.
Then he wove a wicker-work barrier   255
To keep off the waves, plaiting it thick.
Calypso brought him a large piece of cloth
To make into a sail, and he fashioned that, too.
He rigged up braces and halyards and lines,
Then levered his craft down to the glittering sea.   260

Day four, and the job was finished.
Day five, and Calypso saw him off her island,
After she had bathed him and dressed him
In fragrant clothes. She filled up a skin
With wine that ran black, another large one   265
With water, and tucked into a duffel
A generous supply of hearty provisions.
And she put a breeze at his back, gentle and warm.

Odysseus' heart sang as he spread sail to the wind,
And he steered with the rudder, a master mariner   270
Aboard his craft. Sleep never fell on his eyelids
As he watched the Pleiades and slow-setting Boötes
And the Bear (also known as the Wagon)
That pivots in place and chases Orion
And alone is aloof from the wash of Ocean.[2]   275
Calypso, the glimmering goddess, had told him
To sail with the stars of the Bear on his left.
Seventeen days he sailed the deep water,
And on the eighteenth day the shadowy mountains

2. The constellation Ursa Major remains above the horizon.

Of the Phaeacians' land loomed on the horizon,   280
To his eyes like a shield on the misty sea.

And Poseidon saw him.
                        From the far Solymi Mountains
The Lord of Earthquake, returning from Ethiopia,
Saw him, an image in his mind bobbing on the sea.
Angrier than ever, he shook his head   285
And cursed to himself:

                        "Damn it all, the gods
Must have changed their minds about Odysseus
While I was away with the Ethiopians.
He's close to Phaeacia, where he's destined to escape
The great ring of sorrow that has closed around him.   290
But I'll bet I can still blow some trouble his way."

He gathered the clouds, and gripping his trident
He stirred the sea. And he raised all the blasts
Of every wind in the world and covered with clouds
Land and sea together. Night rose in the sky.   295
The winds blew hard from every direction,
And lightning-charged Boreas[3] rolled in a big wave.
Odysseus felt his knees and heart weaken.
Hunched over, he spoke to his own great soul:

"Now I'm in for it.   300
I'm afraid that Calypso was right on target
When she said I would have my fill of sorrow
On the open sea before I ever got home.
It's all coming true. Look at these clouds
Zeus is piling like flowers around the sky's rim,   305
And he's roughened the sea, and every wind
In the world is howling around me.
Three times, four times luckier than I
Were the Greeks who died on Troy's wide plain!
If only I had gone down on that day   310
When the air was whistling with Trojan spears
In the desperate fight for Achilles' dead body.
I would have had burial then, honored by the army.
As it is I am doomed to a wretched death at sea."

His words weren't out before a huge cresting wave   315
Crashed on his raft and shivered its timbers.
He was pitched clear of the deck. The rudder flew
From his hands, the mast cracked in two
Under the force of the hurricane winds,
And the yardarm and sail hove into the sea.   320
He was under a long time, unable to surface
From the heaving swell of the monstrous wave,

3. The North Wind.

Weighed down by the clothes Calypso had given him.
At last he came up, spitting out saltwater,
Seabrine gurgling from his nostrils and mouth.   325
For all his distress, though, he remembered his raft,
Lunged through the waves, caught hold of it
And huddled down in its center shrinking from death.

An enormous wave rode the raft into cross-currents.

    The North Wind in autumn sweeps through a field   330
    Rippling with thistles and swirls them around.

So the winds swirled the raft all over the sea,
South Wind colliding at times with the North,
East Wind shearing away from the West.

And the White Goddess saw him, Cadmus' daughter   335
Ino,[4] once a human girl with slim, beautiful ankles
Who had won divine honors in the saltwater gulfs.
She pitied Odysseus his wandering, his pain,
And rose from the water like a flashing gull,
Perched on his raft, and said this to him: 340

"Poor man. Why are you so odious to Poseidon,
Odysseus,[5] that he sows all this grief for you?
But he'll not destroy you, for all of his fury.
Now do as I say—you're in no way to refuse:
Take off those clothes and abandon your raft   345
To the winds' will. Swim for your life
To the Phaeacians' land, your destined safe harbor.
Here, wrap this veil tightly around your chest.
It's immortally charmed: Fear no harm or death.
But when with your hands you touch solid land   350
Untie it and throw it into the deep blue sea
Clear of the shore so it can come back to me."

With these words the goddess gave him the veil
And slipped back into the heavy seas
Like a silver gull. The black water swallowed her.   355
Godlike Odysseus brooded on his trials
And spoke these words to his own great soul:

"Not this. Not another treacherous god
Scheming against me, ordering me to abandon my raft.
I will not obey. I've seen with my own eyes   360
How far that land is where she says I'll be saved.
I'll play it the way that seems best to me.
As long as the timbers are still holding together
I'll hang on and gut it out right here where I am.

4. Human girl transformed into a sea nymph.
5. There is a pun on Odysseus's name in the Greek, similar to "odious . . . Odysseus."

When and if a wave shatters my raft to pieces,   365
Then I'll swim for it. What else can I do?"

As he churned these thoughts in the pit of his stomach
Poseidon Earthshaker raised up a great wave—
An arching, cavernous, sensational tsunami—
And brought it crashing down on him.   370

    As storm winds blast into a pile of dry chaff
    And scatter the stuff all over the place,

So the long beams of Odysseus' raft were scattered.
He went with one beam and rode it like a stallion,
Stripping off the clothes Calypso had given him   375
And wrapping the White Goddess' veil round his chest.
Then he dove into the sea and started to swim
A furious breaststroke. The Lord of Earthquake saw him
And said to himself with a slow toss of his head:

"That's right. Thrash around in misery on the open sea   380
Until you come to human society again.
I hope that not even then will you escape from evil."

With these words he whipped his sleek-coated horses
And headed for his fabulous palace on Aegae.

But Zeus' daughter Athena had other ideas.   385
She barricaded all the winds but one
And ordered them to rest and fall asleep.
Boreas, though, she sent cracking through the waves,
A tailwind for Odysseus until he was safe on Phaeacia,
And had beaten off the dark birds of death.   390

Two nights and two days the solid, mitered waves
Swept him on, annihilation all his heart could foresee.
But when Dawn combed her hair in the third day's light,
The wind died down and there fell
A breathless calm. Riding a swell   395
He peered out and saw land nearby.

    You know how precious a father's life is
    To children who have seen him through a long disease,
    Gripped by a malevolent spirit and melting away,
    But then released from suffering in a spasm of joy.   400

The land and woods were that welcome a sight
To Odysseus. He kicked hard for the shoreline,
But when he was as close as a shout would carry
He heard the thud of waves on the rocks,
Thundering surf that pounded the headland   405
And bellowed eerily. The sea churned with foam.
There were no harbors for ships, no inlets or bays,

Only jutting cliffs and rocks and barnacled crags.
Odysseus' heart sank and his knees grew weak.
With a heavy sigh he spoke to his own great soul: 410

"Ah, Zeus has let me see land I never hoped to see
And I've cut my way to the end of this gulf,
But there's no way to get out of the grey saltwater.
Only sharp rocks ahead, laced by the breakers,
And beyond them slick stone rising up sheer   415
Right out of deep water, no place for a foothold,
No way to stand up and wade out of trouble.
If I try to get out here a wave might smash me
Against the stone cliff. Some mooring that would be!
If I swim around farther and try to find   420
A shelving shore or an inlet from the sea,
I'm afraid that a squall will take me back out
Groaning deeply on the teeming dark water,
Or some monster will attack me out of the deep
From the swarming brood of great Amphtrite.   425
I know how odious I am to the Earthshaker."

As these thoughts welled up from the pit of his stomach
A breaker bore him onto the rugged coast.
He would have been cut to ribbons and his bones crushed
But grey-eyed Athena inspired him.   430
Slammed onto a rock he grabbed it with both hands
And held on groaning until the breaker rolled by.
He had no sooner ducked it when the backwash hit him
And towed him far out into open water again.

    It was just like an octopus pulled out of its hole   435
    With pebbles stuck to its tentacles,

Odysseus' strong hands clinging to the rocks
Until the skin was ripped off. The wave
Pulled him under, and he would have died
Then and there. But Athena was with him.   440
He surfaced again: the wave spat him up landwards,
And he swam along parallel to the coast, scanning it
For a shelving beach, an inlet from the sea,
And when he swam into the current of a river delta
He knew he had come to the perfect spot,   445
Lined with smooth rocks and sheltered from the wind.
He felt the flowing of the rivergod, and he prayed:

"Hear me, Riverlord, whoever you are
And however men pray to you:
I am a fugitive from the sea   450
And Poseidon's persecution,
A wandering mortal, pitiful
To the gods, I come to you,
To your water and your knees.

I have suffered much, O Lord,   455
Lord, hear my prayer."

At these words the god stopped his current,
Made his waters calm and harbored the man
In his river's shallows. Odysseus crawled out
On hands and knees. The sea had broken his spirit.   460
His whole body was swollen, and saltwater trickled
From his nose and mouth. Breath gone, voice gone,
He lay scarcely alive, drained and exhausted.
When he could breathe again and his spirit returned
He unbound the goddess' veil from his body   465
And threw it into the sea-melding river
Where it rode the crest of a wave down the current
And into Ino's own hands. He turned away from the river,
Sank into a bed of rushes, and kissed the good earth.
Huddled over he spoke to his own great soul: 470

"What am I in for now? How will this end?
If I keep watch all night here by the river
I'm afraid a hard frost—or even a gentle dew—
Will do me in, as weak as I am.
The wind blows cold from a river toward dawn.   475
But if I climb the bank to the dark woods up there
And fall asleep in a thicket, even if I survive
Fatigue and cold and get some sweet sleep,
I'm afraid I'll fall prey to some prowling beast."

He thought it over and decided it was better   480
To go to the woods. They were near the water
On an open rise. He found two olive trees there,
One wild, one planted, their growth intertwined,
Proof against blasts of the wild, wet wind,
The sun unable to needle light through,   485
Impervious to rain, so thickly they grew
Into one tangle of shadows. Odysseus burrowed
Under their branches and scraped out a bed.
He found a mass of leaves there, enough to keep warm
Two or three men on the worst winter day.   490
The sight of these leaves was a joy to Odysseus,
And the godlike survivor lay down in their midst
And covered himself up.

                    A solitary man
        Who lives on the edge of the wilderness
        And has no neighbors, will hide a charred log   495
        Deep in the black embers and so keep alive
        The fire's seed and not have to rekindle it
        From who knows where.

                        So Odysseus buried
Himself in the leaves. And Athena sprinkled

His eyes with sleep for quickest release   500
From pain and fatigue.
                    And she closed his eyelids.

                              BOOK VI

        So Odysseus slept, the godlike survivor
Overwhelmed with fatigue.
                        But the goddess Athena
Went off to the land of the Phaeacians,
A people who had once lived in Hypereia,
Near to the Cyclopes, a race of savages   5
Who marauded their land constantly. One day
Great Nausithous led his people
Off to Schería, a remote island,
Where he walled off a city, built houses
And shrines, and parceled out fields.   10
After he died and went to the world below,
Alcinous ruled, wise in the gods' ways.
Owl-eyed Athena now came to his house
To devise a passage home for Odysseus.
She entered a richly decorated bedroom   15
Where a girl as lovely as a goddess was sleeping,
Nausicaa, daughter of noble Alcinous.
Two maids, blessed with the beauty of Graces,
Slept on either side of the closed, polished doors.
Athena rushed in like a breath of wind,   20
Stood over Nausicaa's head, and spoke to her
In the guise of her friend, the daughter
Of the famed mariner Dymas. Assuming
This girl's form, the owl-eyed goddess spoke:

"Nausicaa, how could your mother have raised   25
Such a careless child? Your silky clothes
Are lying here soiled, and your wedding is near!
You'll have to dress yourself and your party well,
If you want the people to speak highly of you
And make your mother and father glad.   30
We'll wash these clothes at the break of dawn.
I'll go with you and help so you'll get it done quickly.
You're not going to be a virgin for long, you know!
All the best young men in Phaeacia are eager
To marry you—as well they should be.   35
Wake up now, and at dawn's first blush
Ask your father if he will hitch up the mulecart
To carry all these sashes and robes and things.
It'll be much more pleasant than going on foot.
The laundry pools are a long way from town."   40

The grey-eyed goddess spoke and was gone,
Off to Olympus, which they say is forever
The unmoving abode of the gods, unshaken

By winds, never soaked by rain, and where the snow
Never drifts, but the brilliant sky stretches   45
Cloudless away, and brightness streams through the air.
There, where the gods are happy all the world's days,
Went the Grey-eyed One after speaking to the girl.

Dawn came throned in light, and woke Nausicaa,
Who wondered at the dream as it faded away.   50
She went through the house to tell her parents,
Her dear father and mother. She found them within,
Her mother sitting by the hearth with her women,
Spinning sea-blue yarn. Her father she met
As he headed for the door accompanied by elders   55
On his way to a council the nobles had called.
She stood very close to her father and said:

"Daddy, would you please hitch up a wagon for me—
A high one that rolls well—so I can go to the river
And wash our good clothes that are all dirty now.   60
You yourself should wear clean clothes
When you sit among the first men in council.
And you have five sons who live in the palace,
Two married and three still bachelors.
They always want freshly washed clothes   65
To wear to the dances. This has been on my mind."

She was too embarrassed to mention marriage
To her father, but he understood and said:

"Of course you can have the mules, child,
And anything else. Go on. The servants will rig up   70
A high, smooth-rolling wagon fitted with a trunk."

He called the servants, and they got busy
Rolling out a wagon and hitching up mules.
Nausicaa brought out a pile of laundry
And loaded it into the polished cart,   75
While her mother packed a picnic basket
With all sorts of food and filled a goatskin with wine.
The girl put these up on the cart, along with
A golden flask of oil her mother gave her
For herself and her maids to rub on their skin.   80
She took the lash and the glossy reins
And had the mules giddyup. They jangled along
At a steady pace, pulling the clothes and the girl,
While the other girls, her maids, ran alongside.

They came to the beautiful, running river   85
And the laundry pools, where the clear water
Flowed through strongly enough to clean
Even the dirtiest clothes. They unhitched the mules
And shooed them out along the swirling river's edge

To munch the sweet clover. Then they unloaded   90
The clothes, brought them down to the water,
And trod them in the trenches, working fast
And making a game of it. When the clothes were washed
They spread them out neatly on the shore of the sea
Where the waves scoured the pebbled beach clean.   95
Then they bathed themselves and rubbed rich olive oil
Onto their skin, and had a picnic on the river's banks
While they waited for the sun to dry the clothes.
When the princess and her maids had enough to eat
They began to play with a ball, their hair streaming free.   100

> Artemis sometimes roams the mountains—
> Immense Taygetus, or Erymanthus—
> Showering arrows upon boars or fleet antelope,
> And with her play the daughters of Zeus
> Who range the wild woods—and Leto is glad   105
> That her daughter towers above them all
> With her shining brow, though they are beautiful all—

So the unwed princess among her attendants.

But when she was about to fold the clothes,
Yoke the mules, and head back home,   110
The Grey-eyed One sprung her plan:
Odysseus would wake up, see the lovely girl,
And she would lead him to the Phaeacians' city.
The princess threw the ball to one of the girls,
But it sailed wide into deep, swirling water.   115
The girls screamed, and Odysseus awoke.
Sitting up, he tried to puzzle it out:

"What kind of land have I come to now?
Are the natives wild and lawless savages,
Or godfearing men who welcome strangers?   120
That sounded like girls screaming, or the cry
Of the spirit women who hold the high peaks,
The river wells, and the grassy meadows.
Can it be I am close to human voices?
I'll go have a look and see for myself."   125

With that Odysseus emerged from the bushes.
He broke off a leafy branch from the undergrowth
And held it before him to cover himself.

> A weathered mountain lion steps into a clearing,
> Confident in his strength, eyes glowing.   130
> The wind and rain have let up, and he's hunting
> Cattle, sheep, or wild deer, but is hungry enough
> To jump the stone walls of the animal pens.

So Odysseus advanced upon these ringleted girls,
Naked as he was. What choice did he have? 135
He was a frightening sight, disfigured with brine,
And the girls fluttered off to the jutting beaches.
Only Alcinous' daughter stayed. Athena
Put courage in her heart and stopped her trembling.
She held her ground, and Odysseus wondered 140
How to approach this beautiful girl. Should he
Fall at her knees, or keep his distance
And ask her with honeyed words to show him
The way to the city and give him some clothes?
He thought it over and decided it was better 145
To keep his distance and not take the chance
Of offending the girl by touching her knees.
So he started this soft and winning speech:

"I implore you, Lady: Are you a goddess
Or mortal? If you are one of heaven's divinities 150
I think you are most like great Zeus' daughter
Artemis. You have her looks, her stature, her form.
If you are a mortal and live on this earth,
Thrice blest is your father, your queenly mother,
Thrice blest your brothers! Their hearts must always 155
Be warm with happiness when they look at you,
Just blossoming as you enter the dance.
And happiest of all will be the lucky man
Who takes you home with a cartload of gifts.
I've never seen anyone like you, 160
Man or woman. I look upon you with awe.
Once, on Delos, I saw something to compare—
A palm shoot springing up near Apollo's altar.
I had stopped there with the troops under my command
On what would prove to be a perilous campaign. 165
I marveled long and hard when I saw that tree,
For nothing like it had ever grown from the earth.
And I marvel now, Lady, and I am afraid
To touch your knees. Yet my pain is great.
Yesterday, after twenty days, I pulled myself out 170
Of the wine-dark sea. All that time, wind and wave
Bore me away from Ogygia Island,
And now some spirit has cast me up here
To suffer something new. I do not think
My trials will end soon. The gods have much more 175
In store for me before that ever happens.
Pity me, mistress. After all my hardships
It is to you I have come first. I don't know
A soul who lives here, not a single one.
Show me the way to town, and give me 180
A rag to throw over myself, some piece of cloth
You may have brought along to bundle the clothes.
And for yourself, may the gods grant you
Your heart's desire, a husband and a home,

And the blessing of a harmonious life.   185
For nothing is greater or finer than this,
When a man and woman live together
With one heart and mind, bringing joy
To their friends and grief to their foes."

And white-armed Nausicaa answered him: 190

"Stranger, you do not seem to be a bad man
Or a fool. Zeus himself, the Olympian god,
Sends happiness to good men and bad men both,
To each as he wills. To you he has given these troubles,
Which you have no choice but to bear. But now,   195
Since you have come to our country,
You shall not lack clothing, nor anything needed
By a sore-tried suppliant who presents himself.
I will show you where the city is and tell you
That the people here are called Phaeacians.   200
This is their country, and I am the daughter
Of great-hearted Alcinous, the Phaeacians' lord."

Then the princess called to the ringleted girls:

"Stop this now. Running away at the sight of a man!
Do you think he is part of an enemy invasion?   205
There is no man on earth, nor will there ever be,
Slippery enough to invade Phaeacia,
For we are very dear to the immortal gods,
And we live far out in the surging sea,
At the world's frontier, out of all human contact.   210
This poor man comes here as a wanderer,
And we must take care of him now. All strangers,
All beggars, are under the protection of Zeus,
And even small gifts are welcome. So let's feed
This stranger, give him something to drink,   215
And bathe him in the river, out of the wind."

The girls stopped, turned, and urged each other on.
They took Odysseus to a sheltered spot,
As Nausicaa, Alcinous' daughter, had ordered.
They set down a mantle and a tunic,   220
Gave him a golden flask of olive oil,
And told him to wash in the river.
Then sunlit Odysseus said to them:

"Stay off a ways there, girls, and let me
Wash the brine off my shoulders myself   225
And rub myself down. It's been a long time
Since my skin has felt oil. But I don't want
To wash in front of you. I'd be ashamed
To come out naked in front of young girls."

The girls went off and talked with Nausicaa,   230
And Odysseus rinsed off with river water
All the brine that caked his shoulders and back,
And he scrubbed the salty scurf from his scalp.
He finished his bath, rubbed himself down with oil,
And put on the clothes the maiden had given him.   235
Then Athena, born from Zeus, made him look
Taller and more muscled, and made his hair
Tumble down his head like hyacinth flowers.

> Imagine a craftsman overlaying silver
> With pure gold. He has learned his art   240
> From Pallas Athena and Lord Hephaestus,
> And creates works of breathtaking beauty.

So Athena herself made Odysseus' head and shoulders
Shimmer with grace. He walked down the beach
And sat on the sand. The princess was dazzled,   245
And she said to her white-armed serving girls:

"Listen, this man hasn't come to Phaeacia
Against the will of the Olympian gods.
Before, he was a terrible sight, but now,
He's like one of the gods who live in the sky.   250
If only such a man would be called my husband,
Living here, and content to stay here.
Well, go on, give him something to eat and drink."

They were only too glad to do what she said.
They served Odysseus food and drink,   255
And the long-suffering man ate and drank
Ravenously. It had been a long fast.

Nausicaa had other things on her mind.
She folded the clothes and loaded the wagon,
Hitched up the mules and climbed aboard.   260
Then she called to Odysseus and said:

"Get ready now, stranger, to go to the city,
So I can show you the way to my father's house,
Where I promise you will meet the best of the Phaeacians.
Now this is what you must do—and I think you understand: 265
As long as we're going through countryside and farms,
Keep up with my handmaidens behind the wagon.
Just jog along with them. I'll lead the way,
And we'll soon come to the city. It has a high wall
Around it, and a harbor on each side.   270
The isthmus gets narrow, and the upswept hulls
Are drawn up to the road. Every citizen
Has his own private slip. The market's there, too,
Surrounding Poseidon's beautiful temple

And bounded by stones set deep in the earth.   275
There men are always busy with their ships' tackle,
With cables and sails, and with planing their oars.
Phaeacians don't care for quivers and bows
But for oars and masts and streamlined ships
In which they love to cross the grey, salt sea.   280
It's their rude remarks I would rather avoid.
There are some insolent louts in this town,
And I can just hear one of them saying:
'Well, who's this tall, handsome stranger trailing along
Behind Nausicaa? Where'd she pick him up?   285
She'll probably marry him, some shipwreck she's taken in
From parts unknown. He's sure not local.
Maybe a god has come to answer her prayers,
Dropped out of the sky for her to have and to hold.
It's just as well she's found herself a husband   290
From somewhere else, since she turns up her nose
At the many fine Phaeacians who woo her.'
That's what they'll say, and it will count against me.
I myself would blame anyone who acted like this,
A girl who, with her father and mother to tell her better,   295
Kept the company of men before her wedding day.
No, stranger, be quick to understand me,
So that you can win from my father an escort home,
And soon at that.
              Close by the road you will find
A grove of Athena, beautiful poplars   300
Surrounded by a meadow. A spring flows through it.
Right there is my father's estate and vineyard,
About as far from the city as a shout would carry.
Sit down there and wait for a while, until
We reach the city and arrive at my house.   305
When you think we've had enough time to get there,
Go into the city and ask any Phaeacian
For the house of my father, Lord Alcinous.
It's very easy to spot, and any child
Can lead you there. There's no other house   310
In all Phaeacia built like the house
Of the hero Alcinous. Once you're safely within
The courtyard, go quickly though the hall
Until you come to my mother. She'll be sitting
By the hearth in the firelight, spinning   315
Sea-blue yarn—a sight worth seeing—
As she leans against a column, her maids behind her.
Right beside her my father sits on his throne,
Sipping his wine like an immortal god.
Pass him by and throw your arms   320
Around my mother's knees, if you want to see
Your homeland soon, however far it may be.
If she smiles upon you, there is hope that you will
Return to your home and see your loved ones again."

And she smacked the mules with the shining lash.   325
They trotted on smartly, leaving the river behind.
She drove so that Odysseus and the girls
Could keep up, and used the lash with care.
The sun had set when they reached the grove
Sacred to Athena. Odysseus sat down there   330
And said this prayer to great Zeus' daughter:

"Hear me, mystic child of the Storm God,[6]
O hear me now, as you heard me not
When I was shattered by the Earthshaker's blows.
Grant that I come to Phaeacia pitied and loved."   335

Thus his prayer, and Pallas Athena heard it
But did not appear to him face to face, not yet,
Out of respect for her uncle,[7] who would rage against
Godlike Odysseus until he reached home.

BOOK VII

While Odysseus was praying in the grove,
The strong mules bore Nausicaa to the city.
She pulled up at the gate of her father's palace,
And her brothers, men like gods, crowded around,
Unhitched the mules, and took the clothes inside.   5
Nausicaa went to her bedroom, where Eurymedusa,
Her waiting-woman, kindled a fire for her.
Eurymedusa had come from Apeire
In the curved ships, long ago, and had been chosen
From the spoils of war for Alcinous,   10
Who ruled the Phaeacians as if he were a god.
It was this old woman who had reared
White-armed Nausicaa in the palace
And who now prepared her supper on the fire.

As Odysseus started out for the city,   15
Athena enveloped him in magic mist,
So that none of the Phaeacians he might meet
Along the way would challenge him
And ask him who he was.
                    He was about to enter
The lovely city when the Grey-eyed One   20
Came up to him. She looked like a young girl
Carrying a pitcher, standing there before him,
And godlike Odysseus questioned her:

"My child, I wonder if you could guide me
To the house of Alcinous, the man   25
Who is lord of this people? I am a traveler

6. Zeus.   7. Poseidon.

From a far land, a stranger in need,
And I know no one in this city."

Athena's eyes flashed in the blue sealight:

"Well of course, grandad, I'll show you   30
Where Alcinous lives. His house is close to ours.
Come on, I'll lead the way. But you'll have to be quiet.
Don't look at anyone or ask any questions.
The people here aren't very tolerant of strangers
Or very welcoming. All they trust are their ships,   35
In which they cross the great ocean, because
Poseidon lets them. Their ships are very fast,
Fast as a flying bird, or even a thought."

Thus Pallas Athena, and she led the way
Quickly, while Odysseus followed   40
In the goddess' footsteps. None of the Phaeacians
Noticed him as he moved through their city,
For the dread goddess, her hair done up in braids,
Would not allow them, shedding around him
A magical mist that made him invisible.   45
She had a soft spot in her heart for the hero.

Odysseus marveled at the harbors
And the shapely ships, at the meeting grounds
And the long walls capped with palisades.
When they came to the king's palace,   50
The Grey-eyed One was the first to speak:

"Here you are, grandad, the house you asked for.
You will find the lords feasting at a banquet.
Go inside and don't be afraid of anything.
Things turn out better for a man who is bold,   55
Especially if he's a stranger from a distant land.
The first person you'll meet is the queen. Arete
Is her name, and she's from the same line
As King Alcinous. It goes like this:
First Nausithous was born from Poseidon   60
And Periboea, a most beautiful woman,
The youngest daughter of Eurymedon,
Who once was king of the arrogant Giants.
He brought destruction down on his reckless people
And on himself. Well, anyway, Poseidon   65
Lay with Periboea and she bore a son,
Nausithous, who ruled the Phaeacians.
Nausithous fathered Rhexenor and Alcinous.
Rhexenor had just got married when Apollo
Shot him with his silver bow in his hall.   70
He didn't leave a son, but did leave a daughter,
Only one, Arete. Alcinous married her
And honored her as no other woman on earth

Is honored, of all the women who keep house
For their husbands—that's how she is honored,   75
From the heart, and always has been,
Both by her children and by Alcinous himself
As by the people, who look to her as a goddess
And greet her as one when she goes through the city.
She understands everything, and has sound judgment   80
And settles quarrels with a generous heart.
If she likes you, there is a very good chance
You will get to see your dear ones again
And the high-roofed hall in your own native land."

Thus the goddess with the seagrey eyes,   85
And then she was off over the desolate water,
Leaving lovely Schería. She came to Marathon
And the wide streets of Athens, and she disappeared
Into the great house of Erechtheus.

       But Odysseus
Went to the glorious palace of Alcinous.   90
There he stood, heart pounding as he took it all in
Before crossing the bronze threshold. Gleams
As of the sun or the moon played over the high roof
Of Alcinous' house. The bronze walls, surmounted
With a blue enamel frieze, stretched from the threshold   95
To the inner hall. The outer doors were golden,
And silver doorposts were set in the bronze threshold.
The lintel was silver and the door handle gold.
Flanking the door were two gold and silver dogs
Made by Hephaestus[8] with all his art   100
To guard the palace, and they were immortal
And ageless. Inside, seats were built flush to the walls
On either side, stretching from the threshold
To the inner hall, and upon them were flung
Robes of a fine, soft weave, the craft of women.   105
The Phaeacian leaders would sit on these seats
Eating and drinking, and they lacked for nothing.
Golden statues of young men stood on pedestals
Holding torches to light the night for banqueters.
There were fifty slave women scattered through the house,   110
Some grinding yellow grain on the millstone,
Others weaving cloth or twirling yarn on spindles
As they sat, fluttering like so many leaves on a poplar,
And the finely woven fabric glistened with oil.
For just as the Phaeacian men outstrip all others   115
In sailing ships on the sea, so too are the women
Skilled above all others in working the loom.
Athena has given them a deep understanding
Of beautiful handiwork.
       Outside the courtyard,

8. God of fire and metalworking.

Just beyond the doors, are four acres, of orchard   120
Surrounded by a hedge. The trees there grow tall,
Blossoming pear trees and pomegranates,
Apple trees with bright, shiny fruit, sweet figs
And luxuriant olives. The fruit of these trees
Never perishes nor fails, summer or winter—   125
It lasts year round, and the West Wind's breath
Continually ripens apple after apple, pear upon pear,
Fig after fig, and one bunch of grapes after another.
The fruitful vineyard is planted there, too.
One warm, level spot is for drying grapes   130
In the sun; elsewhere, some grapes are being gathered
And others trod upon. In front, the unripe clusters
Are losing their bloom, and others are turning purple.
By the last row of vines are trim garden plots
With rich blooms of all sorts throughout the year.   135
Two separate springs flow through the orchard,
One of them meandering throughout the garden,
While the other flows under the courtyard threshold,
And from this spring the townspeople draw their water.

Odysseus stood and gazed at all of the blessings   140
The gods had lavished on the house of Alcinous.
When he had taken it all in, he passed quickly
Over the threshold and entered the house.
There he found the Phaeacian nobles
Tipping their cups in honor of Hermes,   145
To whom they poured libations last of all
When they thought it was time to take their rest.
Odysseus, the godlike survivor, went through the hall
In the heavy mist Athena had wrapped him in,
Until he came to Arete and Lord Alcinous.   150
There he threw his arms around Arete's knees,
And the magical mist melted away at that moment.
They were all hushed to silence, marveling
At the sight of Odysseus, who now made his prayer:

"Arete, daughter of godlike Rhexenor,   155
To your husband and to your knees I come
In great distress, and to these banqueters also—
May the gods grant prosperity to them
In this life, and may each of them hand down
Their wealth and honor to their children after them.   160
Grant me but this: a speedy passage home,
For I have suffered long, far from my people."

And with that he sat down in the ashes
By the fireside. The hall fell silent.
Finally Echeneus, a Phaeacian elder,   165
Wise in the old ways and the ways of words,
Spoke out with good will among them:

"Alcinous, this will not do at all. It is not proper
That a guest sit in the ashes on the hearth.
We are all holding back, waiting on your word.   170
Come, help the stranger up and have him sit
Upon a silver-studded chair. And bid the heralds
Mix wine, so we may pour libations also to Zeus,
Lord of Thunder, who walks beside suppliants.
And let the housekeeper bring out food for our guest."   175

When the sacred King Alcinous heard this,
He took the hand of Odysseus, the cunning hero,
And raised him from the fireside and had him sit
On a polished chair from which he asked his son
Laodamas to rise, for he was Alcinous'   180
Best beloved son, and sat at his right hand.
A maid poured water from a golden pitcher
Into a silver basin for him to wash his hands
And then set up a polished table nearby.
Another serving woman, grave and dignified,   185
Set out bread and generous helpings
From the other dishes she had. So Odysseus,
Who had endured much, ate and drank.
And the sacred King Alcinous spoke to the herald:

"Pontonous, mix the bowl and serve wine   190
To all, so we may pour libations also to Zeus,
Lord of Thunder, who walks beside suppliants."

Pontonous mixed the mellow wine
And served it to all, pouring out first
Drops for libation, which they all tipped out.   195
When they had drunk to their heart's content,
Alcinous addressed them and said:

"Hear me, Phaeacian lords and counselors,
So I may speak to you what is in my heart.
Now that you have feasted, go home to your rest.   200
In the morning we will invite more of the elders
And entertain the stranger in our halls
And offer fine sacrifices to the gods.
Then we will think of how to convey our guest
To his own native land, so he may come home   205
Speedily and with joy, be it ever so far.
Nor shall he suffer any harm or misfortune
Before he sets foot upon his own land. Thereafter,
He shall suffer whatever fate
The Spinners⁹ spun for him when he was born.   210
But if he is one of the immortals
Come down from heaven, then the gods

9. The Fates, who spin the threads of human lives.

Have changed their ways. Always before this,
Whenever we offered sacrifice to them,
They appeared to us in their own bright forms,   215
And they sat with us and shared the feast.
Even when one of us meets them on the road
They do not conceal themselves, for we are kin,
Just like the Cyclopes and savage Giants."

Odysseus, always thinking, answered him: 220

"Don't worry about that, Alcinous. I am not like
The immortals, either in build or looks.
I am completely human. Better to liken me
To the most woebegone man you ever knew.
That's who I'd compare myself to.   225
I could tell you much more, a long tale
Of the suffering I've had by the will of the gods,
But all I want now is to be allowed to eat,
Despite my grief. There is nothing more shameless
Than this belly of ours, which forces a man   230
To pay attention to it, no matter how many
Troubles he has, how much pain is in his heart.
I have pain in my heart, but my belly always
Makes me eat and drink and forget my troubles,
Pestering me to keep it filled. So then,   235
Please do move quickly at break of day
To set me ashore on my own native land,
Even though it be after all my suffering.
I'd die gladly once I've seen my home again,
My household servants and my high-roofed hall."   240

They praised him, and urged that the stranger
Be sped on his way. He had said all the right things.
Then, when they had poured libations and drunk
To their heart's content, they went home to rest.
Odysseus was left behind in the hall   245
Sitting beside Arete and godlike Alcinous.
The serving women cleared away the dishes,
And then white-armed Arete broke the silence.
She had recognized the mantle and tunic
As soon as she saw them, for she had made   250
These beautiful clothes herself, with her handmaids,
And when she spoke her words flew on wings:

"Stranger, I myself will ask you this first.
Who are you, and where do you come from?
And who gave you these clothes? Did you not say   255
That you came here wandering over the sea?"

And Odysseus, never at a loss for words:

"It would be hard, my lady, to tell the tale
Of all my troubles, since the heavenly gods

Have given me many. But I will tell you what   260
You ask me about.
                              There is an island,
Ogygia, that lies far off in the sea.
Atlas' daughter lives there, guileful Calypso,
Her hair rich as sea-foam, a dread goddess.
No one, mortal or divine, ever visits her.   265
It was my bad luck to be led to her hearth
By some mysterious force, all alone,
Washed up there after Zeus shattered my ship,
Slivering it with lightning on the wine-dark sea.
My whole crew went down in that wreck,   270
But I hung on to the curved keel of my ship,
Adrift for nine days. The tenth black night
Brought me to the island of Ogygia
And the awesome goddess. She took me in,
Gave me food, and said she would make me   275
Immortal and ageless for all of my days.
But she never touched my heart. I spent
Seven years with Calypso. The immortal clothes
She gave me were always wet with my tears.
Then, when the eighth year came around, she told me   280
I could go, either because of some message from Zeus,
Or because she herself had changed her mind.
She sent me off on a sturdy raft, well stocked
With bread and wine, and she clothed me well,
And put a breeze at my back, gentle and warm.   285
Seventeen days I sailed the deep water,
And on the eighteenth day the shadowy mountains
Of your land appeared, and my heart was glad.
But my luck turned sour, and I was soon engulfed
In suffering sent by the Earthshaker Poseidon.   290
He stirred up the winds, blocking my course,
And roused up huge seas that left me groaning
And unable to stay with my raft, which was
Shattered to pieces by the hurricane winds.
I swam my way through all that saltwater   295
Until wind and wave brought me here to your coast.
But if I had tried to come ashore, the pounding surf
Would have smashed me to bits on the beetling crags.
I swam back out and then along the coast
Until I came to a river, the perfect spot,   300
Lined with smooth stones and sheltered from the wind.
I staggered out, exhausted. Night was coming on.
I climbed the river bank and lay down to sleep
In the bushes, covering myself with dry leaves.
Some god shed upon me boundless slumber,   305
And I slept in the leaves, my heart troubled—
Slept through the night, through dawn and high noon,
And did not wake until the sun was going down.
When I awoke I saw your daughter's handmaids
Playing on the shore, and saw your daughter   310

Like a goddess among them. It was she
I supplicated, and she understood
Everything perfectly. You would not expect
Anyone so young to act with such grace,
For the young are thoughtless. She gave me bread   315
And bright red wine, bathed me in the river
And gave me these clothes.
                       As much as it pains me
To recall it, all I have told you is true."

And Alcinous responded:

                       "Stranger,
My daughter was out of line in not bringing you   320
Here to our house along with her handmaids,
Since you went to her first as a suppliant."

And Odysseus, with his usual presence of mind:

"Do not rebuke your blameless daughter for this,
My lord. She did tell me to follow along   325
With the girls, but I refused out of fear and shame,
Thinking your heart might cloud over with anger.
People everywhere, I have found, have tempers."

Alcinous answered him:

                       "Stranger,
My heart is not like that, to grow angry   330
Without cause. Better to give all things their due.
I would wish, by Zeus, by Athena and Apollo,
That you, being the kind of man you are—
My kind of man—would marry my daughter
And stay here and be called my son. I would   335
Give you a house filled with possessions
If you chose to remain, but no Phaeacian
Will ever keep you here against your will—
And may such a thing never please Father Zeus.
As for your send-off, so you can be sure of it,   340
It will be tomorrow. You will lie down and sleep
While they row you over the calm water
Until you come to your home, or wherever you will,
Even if it is much farther away than Euboea,
Which our sailors say is the farthest of lands.   345
They went there once when they took Rhadamanthus
To visit Tityus, the son of Earth.[1]
They made the round trip in a single day
Without even trying. But you will see for yourself
How good our ships and rowers are."   350

---

1. Rhadamanthus was a just king; Tityus was a giant, son of Gaia (Earth).

Odysseus, the godlike survivor, was glad,
And he spoke in prayer:

                    "Father Zeus,
Let Alcinous accomplish all that he says.
May his fame never fade over all the earth,
And may I reach at last my own native land."   355

So they spoke, and white-armed Arete told her maids
To place a bed on the porch and spread upon it
Beautiful purple blankets and fleecy cloaks.
The maids went out of the hall with torches
And made up the bed. Then they called to Odysseus: 360

"You may lie down, stranger. Your bed is made."

These were welcome words, and Odysseus,
Who had suffered much, fell asleep on the bed
Under the echoing portico. But Alcinous lay down
In the innermost chamber of that lofty house,   365
And his lady shared his bed and slept beside him.

                    BOOK VIII

        Dawn spread her roselight over the sky,
And Alcinous awoke in all his sacred might,
As did Zeus-born Odysseus, sacker of cities.
Alcinous led the way to the Phaeacian assembly,
Which was built near the harbor. The Phaeacians   5
Filed in and sat on the polished stones
Close by each other, and Pallas Athena,
Disguised as Alcinous' herald, went through the city
To lay the groundwork for Odysseus' trip home,
Going up to each man and saying to him: 10

"Gather round, Phaeacian leaders and counselors,
And go to the assembly to learn of the stranger
Who has just arrived at Alcinous' palace,
Driven over the sea, a man like a god."

This got their attention, and the seats   15
In the assembly filled up quickly with men
Who marveled at the sight of Laertes' son,
For Athena poured on his shoulders and head
A shimmering grace and made him taller
And more heavily muscled, so that he would be   20
Welcomed by the Phaeacians as a man to respect,
And so he would be able to accomplish the feats
The Phaeacians would use to test his mettle.
When the men were all gathered, Alcinous spoke:

"Hear me, Phaeacian lords and counselors,   25
So I may speak what is in my heart.

This stranger has come to my house
In his wanderings. I don't know who he is,
Or if he has come from the east or the west.
He asks for passage home, and asks us to set   30
A firm time for departure. Let us speed him
On his way, as we have always done.
No one has ever come to my house
And languished here long for lack of transport.
Haul a black ship, then, onto the bright saltwater   35
For her maiden voyage. And pick two and fifty
Of the best young sailors in all the land.
When you have lashed the oars well at the benches,
Disembark and hurry to my house. We have a feast
To prepare, and I will provide well for all!   40
Those are my orders for the younger men.
But you others, all the sceptered kings,
Come to my palace and help me entertain
The stranger in the hall. Let no one refuse.
And summon the godlike singer of tales,   45
Demodocus. For the god has given him,
Beyond all others, song that delights
However his heart urges him to sing."

So saying, he led the way, followed
By the sceptered kings. A herald went   50
For the godlike singer, and two and fifty
Chosen young sailors went, as he ordered,
Down to the shore of the barren sea.
There they hauled a ship out onto the water.
They set up mast and sail in that swift, black ship,   55
Fit the oars into the leather thole-straps,
All in due order, and then unfurled the white sails.
They moored the ship where her sails would catch
The evening breeze, and then went their way
To the great palace of wise Alcinous.   60
The porticoes, courtyards, and rooms were filled
With crowds of men both young and old.
Alcinous sacrificed for them a dozen sheep,
Eight white-tusked boars, and two shambling oxen,
Which they flayed and dressed for the feast.   65
Then the herald came up leading Demodocus.
The Muse loved this man, but gave him
Good and evil both, snuffing out the light
Of his eyes as she opened his heart to sweet song.
Pontonous, the herald, had the bard sit   70
Among the banqueters on a silver-studded chair
Propped against a column, and he hung the clear-toned lyre
On a peg above Demodocus' head
And showed him how to reach it with his hands.
He set up a table and basket beside the bard   75
And a cup of wine ready at hand.

They all reached out to the feast before them,
And when they had satisfied their appetites,
The Muse moved the bard to sing of heroes.
The piece that he sang was already famed   80
Throughout the world—the quarrel
Odysseus once had with Achilles,
Going head to head at a feast of the gods
With violent words, and Agamemnon,
The warlord, rejoiced that these two,   85
The best of the Greeks, were at each other's throats.
For long ago, when he crossed the stone threshold
In sacred Pytho to consult the oracle,
Apollo had prophesied that this would happen.[2]
That was in the days when the great tide of woe   90
Was rolling in upon Trojans and Greeks alike
Through the will of great Zeus.
                              This was the song
The renowned bard sang. But Odysseus
Pulled his great purple cloak over his head
And hid his handsome face. He was ashamed   95
To let the Phaeacians see his tears falling down.
Whenever the singer paused, Odysseus
Would wipe away his tears, pick up his great cup
And pour libations to the gods. But when the singer
Started again, urged on by the Phaeacian lords,   100
Who delighted in his words, Odysseus
Would cover his head again and moan.
He managed to conceal his tears from everyone
Except Alcinous, who sat at his elbow
And could not help but hear his heavy sighs.   105
Alcinous acted quickly and said to his guests:

"Hear me, Phaeacian nobles and lords.
We have had enough of feasting now,
And of the lyre that complements a feast.
We should go outdoors for some contests now,   110
All the athletic events, so that this stranger
Can tell his friends back home how good we are
In boxing, wrestling, jumping, and footraces."

And with that he led them outdoors. The herald
Hung the clear-toned lyre on its peg   115
And led Demodocus by the hand
Out of the hall and along the road
The nobles had gone down to see the games.
They made their way to the assembly grounds,
And huge crowds trailed along, thousands   120
Past counting.
                    Then up rose the young heroes.

2. Pytho is Delphi, home to an oracle of Apollo, god of prophecy.

Up rose Acroneus and Ocyalus and Elatreus;
Nauteus, Prymneus, Anchialus, and Eretmeus;
Ponteus, Proreus, Thoön, and Anabesineus;
Amphialus, Polyneus' son and Tecton's grandson;   125
And Euryalus, a match for the War God
And son of Naubolus. He was the handsomest
Of the Phaeacians, after peerless Laodamas.
And up rose the three sons of Alcinous,
Laodamas, Halius, and godlike Clytoneus.   130

The first contest was a footrace. The course
Stretched out before them from the starting post,
And they were off, raising dust from the plain
As they sped along. No one could keep up
With Clytoneus, who extended his lead   135
To the length of a furrow a mule-team plows.
That's how far ahead he was when he reached the crowd,
Leaving the rest of the field far behind.
Wrestling was next, and in this painful sport
Euryalus outdid the other young princes.   140
The best jumper proved to be Amphialus;
Elatreus took the discus throw; and Laodamas,
Alcinous' son, outboxed all comers.
Everyone had enjoyed the games, and then
Alcinous' son Laodamas said to his friends: 145

"Come on, now. We should ask the stranger
Whether he is skilled in any sport. His build
Is impressive enough, his thighs and calves,
His arms and stout neck. This man is strong!
He's still got what it takes, but he has been broken   150
By many hardships. Nothing's worse than the sea
To get a man out of shape, no matter how strong he is."

And Euryalus answered him:

"Well spoken, Laodamas. Go ahead
And challenge him yourself, in public."   155

When Laodamas heard this, he strode out
Front and center and spoke to Odysseus:

"You should come forward, too, as our guest,
And try your hand at one of the sports,
If you are skilled in any. I'm sure you are,   160
For there is no greater glory a man can win in life
Than the glory he wins with his hands and feet.
So shrug off your cares and give it a try.
It won't delay your journey. Your ship
Is already launched and the crew is ready."   165

Odysseus, always thinking, answered him this way:

"Laodamas, why do you provoke me like this?
I have more serious things on my mind
Than track and field. I've had my share of suffering,
And paid my dues. Now I sit in the middle   170
Of your assembly, longing to return home,
A suppliant before your king and all the people."

Then Euryalus taunted him to his face:

"You know, stranger, I've seen a lot of sportsmen,
And you don't look like one to me at all.   175
You look more like the captain of a merchant ship,
Plying the seas with a crew of hired hands
And keeping a sharp eye on his cargo,
Greedy for profit. No, you're no athlete."

Odysseus stared the man down and said: 180

"That's an ugly thing to say, stranger,
And it makes you look like a reckless fool.
The sad truth is that the gods don't give anyone
All their gifts, whether it's looks, intelligence,
Or eloquence. One man might not have good looks,   185
But the gods crown his words with beauty,
And men look at him with delight. He speaks
With unfaltering grace and sweet modesty,
And stands out in any crowd. When he walks
Through town, men look upon him as a god.   190
Another man might look like an immortal,
But his words are not crowned with beauty.
That's how it is with you. Your looks
Are outstanding. Not even a god
Could improve them. But your mind is crippled.   195
And now you've got my blood pumping
With your rude remarks. I'm no novice in sports,
As you suggest. No, I was one of the best,
When I could trust my youth and my hands.
Now I'm slowed down by my aches and pains   200
And the suffering I've had in war and at sea.
Even so, even with all I've been through,
I'll give your games a try. Your words
Cut deep, and now you've got me going."

He jumped up, cloak still on, and grabbed a discus   205
Larger than the others, thicker and much heavier
Than the one the Phaeacians used for competition.
Winding up, he let it fly, and the stone,
Launched with incredible force from his hand,
Hummed as it flew. The Phaeacians ducked   210

As the discus zoomed overhead and finally landed
Far beyond the other marks. Pallas Athena,
Who looked like a man now, marked the spot
Where it came down, and she called out to him:

"Even a blind man could find your mark, stranger,   215
For it's not all mixed up with the others
But way out front. You can be confident
No Phaeacian will come close to this throw."

Odysseus cheered up at this, glad to see
A loyal supporter out on the field.   220
In a lighter mood now, he spoke to the Phaeacians:

"Match that if you can, boys. In a minute
I'll get another one out just as far or farther.
And if anyone else has the urge to try me,
Step right up—I'm angry now—   225
I don't care if it's boxing, wrestling,
Or even running. Come one, come all—
Except Laodamas, who is my host.
Only a fool would challenge the man
Who gives him hospitality in a distant land.   230
He would only wind up hurting himself.
But I wouldn't turn down anyone else,
Or take any of you lightly. I only want
To see what you're made of, and to test myself.
I'm not weak in any athletic event,   235
And I really know how to handle a bow.
I'm always the first to hit my man
In the enemy lines, no matter how many archers
Are standing with me and getting off shots.
Only Philoctetes, of all the Greeks,   240
Outshot me at Troy. No one else came close,
Nor could any man now alive on this earth.
I do not compare myself to the men of old,
To Heracles, or Oechalian Eurytus,
Who tried to outshoot the immortal gods.   245
Eurytus died young, killed by Apollo,
Who was angry that he had challenged him
To a contest with the bow.
                             As for the spear,
I can throw it farther than you can shoot an arrow.
It's only in running that I fear some Phaeacian   250
May beat me to the line. I've taken a pounding
Out in the waves, and didn't come here aboard
A well-stocked ship, so my legs are still shaky."

He spoke, and they were all stunned to silence.
Only Alcinous was able to answer: 255

"Your words, stranger, are not ungracious.
You want only to demonstrate your prowess,

Angry that this man stood up at the games
And taunted you in a way no one ever would
Who knew in his heart how to speak fitly.   260
But now listen to my words, so that one day,
As you sit feasting with your wife and children,
You may tell another hero what you remember
Of the Phaeacians' skill in the feats that Zeus
Established as ours in our forefathers' days.   265
For we are not flawless boxers or wrestlers,
But we are swift of foot, and the best sailors,
And we love feasts and the lyre and dancing,
Fresh clothes, warm baths, and soft beds.
Up now, let the best dancers in Phaeacia dance,   270
So that the stranger can tell his friends back home
How superior we are in seamanship,
In fleetness of foot, in dancing, and in song.
Someone go get Demodocus his lyre,
Which is lying somewhere in the palace halls."   275

Thus godlike Alcinous, and the herald left
To get the hollow lyre from the king's palace.
Then up rose the officials, nine in all,
Who were in charge of the games. They marked out
A wide dancing ring and made the ground level.   280
The herald returned with the lyre, and Demodocus
Moved to the middle of the dancing ring,
Surrounded by boys in the bloom of youth,
Accomplished dancers all. Their feet struck the floor
Of the sacred ring, and as Odysseus watched   285
He marveled at how their feet flashed in the air.

Then Demodocus swept the strings of his lyre
And began his song. He sang of the passion
Between Ares and gold-crowned Aphrodite,
How they first made love in Hephaestus' house,   290
Sneaking around, and how the War God Ares
Showered her with gifts and shamed the bed
Of her husband, Hephaestus. But it wasn't long
Before Hephaestus found out. Helios told him
That he had seen them lying together in love.[3]   295
When Hephaestus heard this heart-wrenching news
He went to his forge, brooding on his wrongs,
And set the great anvil up on its block
And hammered out a set of unbreakable bonds,
Bonds that couldn't loosen, bonds meant to stay put.   300
When he had wrought this snare, furious with Ares,
He went to his bedroom and spread the bonds
All around the bedposts, and hung many also
From the high roofbeams, as fine as cobwebs,

3. Aphrodite, the goddess of sex, was married to the god Hephaestus, but had an affair with
Ares, god of war; Helios, the sun god, who sees whatever the sun sees, revealed the truth.

So fine not even the gods could see them.   305
When he had spread this cunning snare
All around the bed, he pretended to leave
On a trip to Lemnos, his favorite city.
Ares wasn't blind, and when he saw Hephaestus
On his way out, he headed for the house   310
Of the glorious smith, itching to make love
To the Cytherean goddess.[4] She had been visiting
Her father, Zeus, and was just sitting down
When Ares came in, took her hand, and said:

"Let's go to bed, my love, and lie down together.   315
Hephaestus has left town, off to Lemnos no doubt
To visit the barbarous Sintians."

This suggestion appealed to the goddess,
And they climbed into bed. They were settling in
When the chains Hephaestus had cunningly wrought   320
Fell all around them. They couldn't move an inch,
Couldn't lift a finger, and by the time it sank in
That there was no escape, there was Hephaestus,
Gimpy-legged and glorious, coming in the door.
He had turned back on his way to Lemnos   325
As soon as Helios, his spy, gave him the word.
He stood in the doorway, seething with anger,
And with an ear-splitting yell called to the gods:

"Father Zeus and all you blessed gods eternal,
Come see something that is as ridiculous   330
As it is unendurable, how Aphrodite,
Daughter of Zeus, scorns me for being lame
And loves that marauder Ares instead
Because he is handsome and well-knit, whereas I
Was born misshapen, which is no one's fault   335
But my parents', who should have never begotten me!
Come take a look at how these two
Have climbed into my bed to make love and lie
In each other's arms. It kills me to see it!
But I don't think they will want to lie like this   340
Much longer, no matter how loving they are.
No, they won't want to sleep together for long,
But they're staying put in my little snare
Until her father returns all of the gifts
I gave him to marry this bitch-faced girl,   345
His beautiful, yes, but faithless daughter."

Thus Hephaestus, and the gods gathered
At his bronze threshold.
                    Poseidon came,

4. Aphrodite.

The God of Earthquake, and Hermes the Guide,
And the Archer Apollo. The goddesses   350
All stayed home, out of modesty; but the gods
Stood in the doorway and laughed uncontrollably
When they saw Hephaestus' cunning and craft.
One of them would look at another and snigger:

"Crime doesn't pay."
                    "The slow catches the swift.   355
Slow as he is, old Gimpy caught Ares,
The fastest god on Olympus."
"Ares has to pay the fine for adultery."

That was the general drift of their jibes.
And then Apollo turned to Hermes and said: 360

"Tell me, Hermes, would you be willing
To be pinched in chains if it meant you could lie
Side by side with golden Aphrodite?"

And the quicksilver messenger shot back:

"I tell you what, Apollo. Tie me up   365
With three times as many unbreakable chains,
And get all the gods and goddesses, too,
To come here and look, if it means I can sleep
Side by side with golden Aphrodite."

The gods roared with laughter, except Poseidon   370
Who did not think it was funny. He kept
Pleading that Ares should be released,
And his words winged their way to Hephaestus:

"Let him go, and I will ensure he will pay you
Fair compensation before all the gods."   375

And the renowned god, lame in both legs:

"Do not ask me to do this, Poseidon.
Worthless is the surety assured for the worthless.
How could I ever hold you to your promise
If Ares slipped out of the bonds and the debt?"   380

Poseidon the Earthshaker did not back off:

"Hephaestus, if Ares gets free and disappears
Without paying the debt, I will pay it myself."

And the renowned god, lame in both legs:

"I cannot refuse you. It wouldn't be right."   385

And with that the strong smith undid the bonds,
And the two of them, free at last from their crimp,
Shot out of there, Ares to Thrace,
And Aphrodite, who loves laughter and smiles,
To Paphos on Cyprus, and her precinct there   390
With its smoking altar. There the Graces
Bathed her and rubbed her with the ambrosial oil
That glistens on the skin of the immortal gods.
And then they dressed her in beautiful clothes,
A wonder to see.

              This was the song   395
The renowned bard sang, and Odysseus
Was glad as he listened, as were the Phaeacians,
Men who are famed for their long-oared ships.

Then Alcinous had Halius and Laodamas
Dance alone, for no one could match them.   400
They picked up a beautiful iridescent ball,
The work of Polybus. One of them
Would lean backward and toss it high
Toward the shadowy clouds, and the other
Would leap and catch it and shoot it back up   405
Before his feet ever touched ground again.
When they had tried their skill with upward throws
They started to dance on the bounteous earth,
Tossing the ball constantly back and forth.
The others beat time as they stood on the field,   410
And thunderous applause rose from the crowd.

Then Odysseus said to Alcinous:

"Lord Alcinous, you said that your dancers
Are the best in the world, and your words
Have proved true. I am in awe before them."   415

So he spoke, and the sacred king was glad.
He turned to his sea-loving people and said:

"Hear me Phaeacian lords and counselors.
Our guest seems in my eyes to be a man
Of the highest discernment. Come, then,   420
Let us give him a gift that befits a guest.
Twelve honored kings are lords in Phaeacia,
And I myself am the thirteenth king.
Let each of you twelve bring here now
A fresh cloak and tunic and a bar of fine gold.   425
Let us get these all together at once,
So that our guest may have these gifts in hand
And be glad at heart when he goes to supper.
And let Euryalus apologize and give him a gift,
For what he said to our guest was in no way proper."   430

The lords all approved of what Alcinous said,
And each sent a herald to fetch the gifts.
Then Euryalus in turn answered Alcinous:

"Lord Alcinous, renowned above all men,
I will indeed apologize to our guest, as you bid.   435
And I will give him this sword, all bronze
And with a silver hilt. It comes with a scabbard
Of newly sawn ivory, and will be worth much to him."

And he put the silver-studded sword
Into Odysseus' hands and said to him: 440

"Revered stranger and guest, if any word
Has been harshly spoken, may the winds
Snatch it away. And may the gods grant
That you see your wife and come to your homeland,
For you have suffered long apart from your people."   445

And Odysseus, whose thoughts were many:

"And you, my friend, be well, and may the gods
Grant you happiness. And may you never miss
This sword you have given me to make amends."

He spoke, and slung the silver-studded sword   450
Around one shoulder.
                        The sun went down,
And the gifts were ready to be presented.
The heralds brought them into the palace
And Alcinous' sons set them down
Before their mother. They were beautiful gifts.   455
Alcinous, the sacred king, led the way
And the lords entered and sat on their thrones.
Then Alcinous in his might addressed Arete:

"Bring out the finest chest you have, my wife,
And place in it a newly washed cloak and tunic.   460
And heat water for our guest in a bronze cauldron,
So that when he has bathed and seen the gifts
The Phaeacians have brought all neatly stowed,
He will enjoy the feast and the words of the song.
And I will give him this beautiful cup,   465
Pure gold, to remember me by all of his days
As he pours wine to Zeus and to the other gods."

He spoke, and Arete signaled her women
To set a cauldron on the fire instantly.
They filled the cauldron with water for a bath,   470
Set kindling beneath it and lit the fire.
The flames licked the belly of the cauldron
And the water grew warm.
                        Arete meanwhile

Brought out a handsome chest for the stranger
And placed within it the beautiful gifts, 475
The clothes and the gold which the nobles gave.
And she herself placed in it a cloak
And beautiful tunic. And she said to Odysseus:

"There is the lid. Tie it down with a knot
As a precaution against someone robbing you 480
On your way back, when you are lying asleep
On your journey home in the swift, black ship."

When Odysseus, who had borne much, heard this,
He tied the lid down quickly with a cunning knot
He had learned from Circe. Then the housekeeper came 485
To tell him it was time to go and bathe. The warm bath
Was a welcome sight to Odysseus. He had not been
Cared for like this since leaving Calypso,
Who had treated him as if he were a god.

When the women had bathed him, rubbed him with oil, 490
And clothed him in a beautiful tunic and cloak,
Odysseus strode from the bath and was on his way
To join the men drinking wine.
                    Nausicaa,
Beautiful as only the gods could make her,
Stood by the doorpost of the great hall. 495
Her eyes went wide when she saw Odysseus,
And her words beat their way to him on wings:

"Farewell, stranger, and remember me
In your own native land. I saved your life."

And Odysseus, whose thoughts ran deep: 500

"Nausicaa, daughter of great Alcinous,
So may Zeus, Hera's thundering lord,
Grant that I see my homeland again.
There I will pray to you, as to a god,
All of my days. I owe you my life." 505

And he took his seat next to Lord Alcinous.
They were serving food and mixing the wine
When the herald came up leading the bard,
Honored Demodocus, and seated him on a chair
Propped against a tall pillar in the middle of the hall. 510
Odysseus, with great presence of mind,
Cut off part of a huge chine of roast pork
Glistening with fat, and said to the herald:

"Herald, take this cut of meat to Demodocus
For him to eat. And I will greet him 515
Despite my grief. Bards are revered

By all men upon earth, for the Muse
Loves them well and has taught them the songways."

The herald brought the cut of meat to Demodocus
And placed it in his hands, much to the bard's delight.   520
Then everyone reached out to the feast before them,
And when they had eaten and drunk to their hearts' content,
Odysseus spoke to Demodocus:

"I don't know whether it was the Muse
Who taught you, or Apollo himself,[5]   525
But I praise you to the skies, Demodocus.
When you sing about the fate of the Greeks
Who fought at Troy, you have it right,
All that they did and suffered, all they endured.
It's as if you had been there yourself,   530
Or heard a first-hand account. But now,
Switch to the building of the wooden horse
Which Epeius made with Athena's help,
The horse which Odysseus led up to Troy
As a trap, filled with men who would   535
Destroy great Ilion.[6] If you tell me this story
Just as it happened, I will tell the whole world
That some god must have opened his heart
And given to you the divine gift of song."

So he spoke, and the bard, moved by the god,   540
Began to sing. He made them see it happen,
How the Greeks set fire to their huts on the beach
And were sailing away, while Odysseus
And the picked men with him sat in the horse,
Which the Trojans had dragged into their city.   545
There the horse stood, and the Trojans sat around it
And could not decide what they should do.
There were three ways of thinking:
Hack open the timbers with pitiless bronze,
Or throw it from the heights to the rocks below,   550
Or let it stand as an offering to appease the gods.
The last was what would happen, for it was fated
That the city would perish once it enclosed
The great wooden horse, in which now sat
The Greek heroes who would spill Troy's blood.   555
The song went on. The Greeks poured out
Of their hollow ambush and sacked the city.
He sang how one hero here and another there
Ravaged tall Troy, but how Odysseus went,
Like the War God himself, with Menelaus   560
To the house of Deiphobus, and there, he said,
Odysseus fought his most daring battle
And won with the help of Pallas Athena.

5. God associated with poetry, who carried the lyre.
6. Troy.

This was his song. And Odysseus wept. Tears
Welled up in his eyes and flowed down his cheeks.   565

> *A woman wails as she throws herself upon*
> *Her husband's body. He has fallen in battle*
> *Before the town walls, fighting to the last*
> *To defend his city and protect his children.*
> *As she sees him dying and gasping for breath*   570
> *She clings to him and shrieks, while behind her*
> *Soldiers prod their spears into her shoulders and back,*
> *And as they lead her away into slavery*
> *Her tear-drenched face is a mask of pain.*

So too Odysseus, pitiful in his grief.   575
He managed to conceal his tears from everyone
Except Alcinous, who sat at his elbow
And could not help but hear his heavy sighs.
Alcinous acted quickly and said to his guests:

"Hear me, Phaeacian counselors and lords—   580
Demodocus should stop playing his lyre.
His song is not pleasing to everyone here.
Ever since dinner began and the divine bard
Rose up to sing, our guest has not ceased
From lamentation. He is overcome with grief.   585
Let the lyre stop. It is better if we all,
Host and guest alike, can enjoy the feast.
All that we are doing we are doing on behalf
Of the revered stranger, providing him
With passage home and gifts of friendship.   590
A stranger and suppliant is as dear as a brother
To anyone with even an ounce of good sense.
So there is no need, stranger, for you to withhold
What I am about to ask for, no need to be crafty
Or think of gain. Better to speak the plain truth.   595
Tell me your name, the one you were known by
To your mother and father and your people back home.
No one is nameless, rich man or poor.
Parents give names to all of their children
When they are born. And tell me your country,   600
Your city, and your land, so that our ships
May take you there, finding their way by their wits.
For Phaeacian ships do not have pilots,
Nor steering oars, as other ships have.
They know on their own their passengers' thoughts,   605
And know all the cities and rich fields in the world,
And they cross the great gulfs with the greatest speed,
Hidden in mist and fog, with never a fear
Of damage or shipwreck.   But I remember hearing
My father, Nausithous, say how Poseidon   610
Was angry with us because we always give
Safe passage to men. He said that one day

Poseidon would smite a Phaeacian ship
As it sailed back home over the misty sea,
And would encircle our city within a mountain.   615
The old man used to say that, and either the god
Will bring it to pass or not, as suits his pleasure.
But tell me this, and tell me the truth.
Where have you wandered, to what lands?
Tell me about the people and cities you saw,   620
Which ones are cruel and without right and wrong,
And which are godfearing and kind to strangers.
And tell me why you weep and grieve at heart
When you hear the fate of the Greeks and Trojans.
This was the gods' doing. They spun that fate   625
So that in later times it would turn into song.
Did some kinsman of yours die at Troy,
A good, loyal man, your daughter's husband
Or your wife's father, someone near and dear,
Or perhaps even a relative by blood?   630
Or was it a comrade, tried and true?
A friend like that is no less than a brother."

BOOK IX

And Odysseus, his great mind teeming:

"My Lord Alcinous, what could be finer
Than listening to a singer of tales
Such as Demodocus, with a voice like a god's?
Nothing we do is sweeter than this—   5
A cheerful gathering of all the people
Sitting side by side throughout the halls,
Feasting and listening to a singer of tales,
The tables filled with food and drink,
The server drawing wine from the bowl   10
And bringing it around to fill our cups.
For me, this is the finest thing in the world.
But you have a mind to draw out of me
My pain and sorrow, and make me feel it again.
Where should I begin, where end my story?   15
Heaven has sent me many tribulations.
I will tell you my name first, so that you, too,
Will know who I am, and when I escape
The day of my doom, I will always be
Your friend and host, though my home is far.   20
I am Odysseus, great Laertes' son,
Known for my cunning throughout the world,
And my fame reaches even to heaven.
My native land is Ithaca, a sunlit island
With a forested peak called Neriton,   25
Visible for miles. Many other islands
Lie close around her—Doulichion, Samê,
And wooded Zacynthus—off toward the sunrise,

But Ithaca lies low on the evening horizon,
A rugged place, a good nurse of men.   30
No sight is sweeter to me than Ithaca. Yes,
Calypso, the beautiful goddess, kept me
In her caverns, yearning to possess me;
And Circe, the witch of Aeaea, held me
In her halls and yearned to possess me;   35
But they could not persuade me or touch my heart.
Nothing is sweeter than your own country
And your own parents, not even living in a rich house—
Not if it's far from family and home.
But let me tell you of the hard journey homeward   40
Zeus sent me on when I sailed from Troy.

From Ilion the wind took me to the Cicones
In Ismaros. I pillaged the town and killed the men.
The women and treasure that we took out
I divided as fairly as I could among all hands   45
And then gave the command to pull out fast.
That was my order, but the fools wouldn't listen.
They drank a lot of wine and slaughtered
A lot of sheep and cattle on the shore.
Some of the town's survivors got away inland   50
And called their kinsmen. There were more of them,
And they were braver, too, men who knew how to fight
From chariots and on foot. They came on as thick
As leaves and flowers in spring, attacking
At dawn. We were out of luck, cursed by Zeus   55
To suffer heavy losses. The battle-lines formed
Along our beached ships, and bronze spears
Sliced through the air. As long as the day's heat
Climbed toward noon, we held our ground
Against superior numbers. But when the sun   60
Dipped down, the Cicones beat us down, too.
We lost six fighting men from each of our ships.
The rest of us cheated destiny and death.

We sailed on in shock, glad to get out alive
But grieving for our lost comrades.   65
I wouldn't let the ships get under way
Until someone had called out three times
For each mate who had fallen on the battlefield.
And then Zeus hit us with a norther,
A freak hurricane. The clouds blotted out   70
Land and sea, and night climbed up the sky.
The ships pitched ahead. When their sails
Began to shred in the gale-force winds,
We lowered them and stowed them aboard,
Fearing the worst, and rowed hard for the mainland.   75
We lay offshore two miserable days and nights.
When Dawn combed her hair in the third day's light,
We set up the masts, hoisted the white sails,

And took our seats. The wind and the helmsmen
Steered the ships, and I would have made it home   80
Unscathed, but as I was rounding Cape Malea
The waves, the current, and wind from the North
Drove me off course past Cythera Island.

Nine days of bad winds blew us across
The teeming seas. On the tenth day we came   85
To the land of the Lotus-Eaters.
                                    We went ashore,
And the crews lost no time in drawing water
And preparing a meal beside their ships.
After they had filled up on food and drink,
I sent out a team—two picked men and a herald—   90
To reconnoiter and sound out the locals.
They headed out and made contact with the Lotus-Eaters,
Who meant no harm but did give my men
Some lotus to eat. Whoever ate that sweet fruit
Lost the will to report back, preferring instead   95
To stay there, munching lotus, oblivious of home.
I hauled them back wailing to the ships,
Bound them under the benches, then ordered
All hands to board their ships on the double
Before anyone else tasted the lotus.   100
They were aboard in no time and at their benches,
Churning the sea white with their oars.

We sailed on, our morale sinking,
And we came to the land of the Cyclopes,
Lawless savages who leave everything   105
Up to the gods. These people neither plow nor plant,
But everything grows for them unsown:
Wheat, barley, and vines that bear
Clusters of grapes, watered by rain from Zeus.
They have no assemblies or laws but live   110
In high mountain caves, ruling their own
Children and wives and ignoring each other.

A fertile island slants across the harbor's mouth,
Neither very close nor far from the Cyclopes' shore.
It's well-wooded and populated with innumerable   115
Wild goats, uninhibited by human traffic.
Not even hunters go there, tramping through the woods
And roughing it on the mountainsides.
It pastures no flocks, has no tilled fields—
Unplowed, unsown, virgin forever, bereft   120
Of men, all it does is support those bleating goats.
The Cyclopes do not sail and have no craftsmen
To build them benched, red-prowed ships
That could supply all their wants, crossing the sea
To other cities, visiting each other as other men do.   125
These same craftsmen would have made this island

Into a good settlement. It's not a bad place at all
And would bear everything in season. Meadows
Lie by the seashore, lush and soft,
Where vines would thrive. It has level plowland   130
With deep, rich soil that would produce bumper crops
Season after season. The harbor's good, too,
No need for moorings, anchor-stones, or tying up.
Just beach your ship until the wind is right
And you're ready to sail. At the harbor's head   135
A spring flows clear and bright from a cave
Surrounded by poplars.
                              There we sailed in,
Some god guiding us through the murky night.
We couldn't see a thing. A thick fog
Enveloped the ships, and the moon   140
Wasn't shining in the cloud-covered sky.
None of us could see the island, or the long waves
Rolling toward the shore, until we ran our ships
Onto the sandy beach. Then we lowered sail,
Disembarked, and fell asleep on the sand.   145

Dawn came early, with palmettoes of rose,
And we explored the island, marveling at it.
The spirit-women, daughters of Zeus,
Roused the mountain goats so that my men
Could have a meal. We ran to the ships,   150
Got our javelins and bows, formed three groups
And started to shoot. The god let us bag our game,
Nine goats for each of the twelve ships,
Except for my ship, which got ten.

So all day long until the sun went down   155
We feasted on meat and sweet wine.
The ships had not yet run out of the dark red
Each crew had taken aboard in large jars
When we ransacked the Cicones' sacred city.
And we looked across at the Cyclopes' land.   160
We could see the smoke from their fires
And hear their voices, and their sheep and goats.
When the sun set, and darkness came on
We went to sleep on the shore of the sea.
As soon as dawn brightened in the rosy sky,   165
I assembled all the crews and spoke to them:

'The rest of you will stay here while I go
With my ship and crew on reconnaissance.
I want to find out what those men are like,
Wild savages with no sense of right or wrong   170
Or hospitable folk who fear the gods.'

With that, I boarded ship and ordered my crew
To get on deck and cast off. They took their places
And were soon whitening the sea with their oars.

As we pulled in over the short stretch of water,   175
There on the shoreline we saw a high cave
Overhung with laurels. It was a place
Where many sheep and goats were penned at night.
Around it was a yard fenced in by stones
Set deep in the earth, and by tall pines and crowned oaks.   180
This was the lair of a huge creature, a man
Who pastured his flocks off by himself,
And lived apart from others and knew no law.
He was a freak of nature, not like men who eat bread,
But like a lone wooded crag high in the mountains.   185

I ordered part of my crew to stay with the ship
And counted off the twelve best to go with me.
I took along a goatskin filled with red wine,
A sweet vintage I had gotten from Maron,
Apollo's priest on Ismaros, when I spared both him   190
And his wife and child out of respect for the god.
He lived in a grove of Phoebus Apollo
And gave me splendid gifts: seven bars of gold,
A solid-silver bowl, and twelve jars of wine,
Sweet and pure, a drink for the gods.   195
Hardly anyone in his house, none of the servants,
Knew about this wine—just Maron, his wife,
And a single housekeeper. Whenever he drank
This sweet dark red wine, he would fill one goblet
And pour it into twenty parts of water,   200
And the bouquet that spread from the mixing bowl
Was so fragrant no one could hold back from drinking.
I had a large skin of this wine, a sack
Of provisions—and a strong premonition
That we had a rendezvous with a man of great might,   205
A savage with no notion of right and wrong.

We got to the cave quickly. He was out,
Tending his flocks in the rich pastureland.
We went inside and had a good look around.
There were crates stuffed with cheese, and pens   210
Crammed with lambs and kids—firstlings,
Middlings, and newborns in separate sections.
The vessels he used for milking—pails and bowls
Of good workmanship—were brimming with whey.
My men thought we should make off with some cheese   215
And then come back for the lambs and kids,
Load them on board, and sail away on the sea.
But I wouldn't listen. It would have been far better
If I had! But I wanted to see him, and see
If he would give me a gift of hospitality.   220
When he did come he was not a welcome sight.

We lit a fire and offered sacrifice
And helped ourselves to some of the cheese.
Then we sat and waited in the cave

Until he came back, herding his flocks.   225
He carried a huge load of dry wood
To make a fire for his supper and heaved it down
With a crash inside the cave. We were terrified
And scurried back into a corner.
He drove his fat flocks into the wide cavern,   230
At least those that he milked, leaving the males—
The rams and the goats—outside in the yard.
Then he lifted up a great doorstone,
A huge slab of rock, and set it in place.
Two sturdy wagons—twenty sturdy wagons—   235
Couldn't pry it from the ground—that's how big
The stone was he set in the doorway. Then,
He sat down and milked the ewes and bleating goats,
All in good order, and put the sucklings
Beneath their mothers. Half of the white milk   240
He curdled and scooped into wicker baskets,
The other half he let stand in the pails
So he could drink it later for his supper.
He worked quickly to finish his chores,
And as he was lighting the fire he saw us and said: 245

'Who are you strangers? Sailing the seas, huh?
Where from, and what for? Pirates, probably,
Roaming around causing people trouble.'

He spoke, and it hit us like a punch in the gut—
His booming voice and the sheer size of the monster—   250
But even so I found the words to answer him:
'We are Greeks, blown off course by every wind
In the world on our way home from Troy, traveling
Sea routes we never meant to, by Zeus' will no doubt.
We are proud to be the men of Agamemnon,   255
Son of Atreus, the greatest name under heaven,
Conquerer of Troy, destroyer of armies.
Now we are here, suppliants at your knees,
Hoping you will be generous to us
And give us the gifts that are due to strangers.   260
Respect the gods, sir. We are your suppliants,
And Zeus avenges strangers and suppliants,
Zeus, god of strangers, who walks at their side.'

He answered me from his pitiless heart:

'You're dumb, stranger, or from far away,   265
If you ask me to fear the gods. Cyclopes
Don't care about Zeus or his aegis
Or the blessed gods, since we are much stronger.
I wouldn't spare you or your men
Out of fear of Zeus. I would spare them only   270
If I myself wanted to. But tell me,

Where did you leave your ship? Far
Down the coast, or close? I'd like to know.'

Nice try, but I knew all the tricks and said:

'My ship? Poseidon smashed it to pieces   275
Against the rocks at the border of your land.
He pushed her in close and the wind did the rest.
These men and I escaped by the skin of our teeth.'

This brought no response from his pitiless heart
But a sudden assault upon my men. His hands   280
Reached out, seized two of them, and smashed them
To the ground like puppies. Their brains spattered out
And oozed into the dirt. He tore them limb from limb
To make his supper, gulping them down
Like a mountain lion, leaving nothing behind—   285
Guts, flesh, or marrowy bones.
Crying out, we lifted our hands to Zeus
At this outrage, bewildered and helpless.
When the Cyclops had filled his huge belly
With human flesh, he washed it down with milk,   290
Then stretched out in his cave among his flocks.
I crept up close and was thinking about
Drawing my sharp sword and driving it home
Into his chest where the lungs hide the liver.
I was feeling for the spot when another thought   295
Checked my hand: we would die to a man in that cave,
Unable to budge the enormous stone
He had set in place to block the entrance. And so,
Groaning through the night, we waited for dawn.

As soon as dawn came, streaking the sky red,   300
He rekindled the fire and milked his flocks,
All in good order, placing the sucklings
Beneath their mothers. His chores done,
He seized two of my men and made his meal.
After he had fed he drove his flocks out,   305
Easily lifting the great stone, which he then set
Back in place as lightly as if he were setting
A lid upon a quiver. And then, with loud whistling,
The Cyclops turned his fat flocks toward the mountain,
And I was left there, brooding on how   310
I might make him pay and win glory from Athena.

This was the best plan I could come up with:
Beside one of the sheep pens lay a huge pole
Of green olive which the Cyclops had cut
To use as a walking stick when dry. Looking at it   315
We guessed it was about as large as the mast
Of a black ship, a twenty-oared, broad-beamed

Freighter that crosses the wide gulfs.
That's how long and thick it looked. I cut off
About a fathom's length from this pole   320
And handed it over to my men. They scraped it
And made it smooth, and I sharpened the tip
And took it over to the fire and hardened it.
Then I hid it, setting it carefully in the dung
That lay in piles all around the cave.   325
And I told my men to draw straws to decide
Which of them would have to share the risk with me—
Lift that stake and grind it in his eye
While he was asleep. They drew straws and came up with
The very men I myself would have chosen.   330
There were four of them, and I made five.

At evening he came, herding his fleecy sheep.
He drove them straight into the cave, drove in
All his flocks in fact. Maybe he had some
Foreboding, or maybe some god told him to.   335
Then he lifted the doorstone and set it in place,
And sat down to milk the goats and bleating ewes,
All in good order, setting the sucklings
Beneath their mothers. His chores done,
Again he seized two of my men and made his meal.   340
Then I went up to the Cyclops and spoke to him,
Holding an ivy-wood bowl filled with dark wine.

'Cyclops, have some wine, now that you have eaten
Your human flesh, so you can see what kind of drink
Was in our ship's hold. I was bringing it to you   345
As an offering, hoping you would pity me
And help me get home. But you are a raving
Maniac! How do you expect any other man
Ever to visit you after acting like this?'

He took the bowl and drank it off, relishing   350
Every last, sweet drop. And he asked me for more:

'Be a pal and give me another drink. And tell me
Your name, so I can give you a gift you'll like.
Wine grapes grow in the Cyclopes' land, too.
Rain from the sky makes them grow from the earth.   355
But this—this is straight ambrosia and nectar.'

So I gave him some more of the ruby-red wine.
Three times the fool drained the bowl dry,
And when the wine had begun to work on his mind,
I spoke these sweet words to him:

                                    'Cyclops,   360
You ask me my name, my glorious name,

And I will tell it to you. Remember now,
To give me the gift just as you promised.
Noman is my name. They call me Noman[7]—
My mother, my father, and all my friends, too.'   365

He answered me from his pitiless heart:

'Noman I will eat last after his friends.
Friends first, him last. That's my gift to you.'

He listed as he spoke and then fell flat on his back,
His thick neck bent sideways. He was sound asleep,   370
Belching out wine and bits of human flesh
In his drunken stupor. I swung into action,
Thrusting the stake deep in the embers,
Heating it up, and all the while talking to my men
To keep up their morale. When the olivewood stake   375
Was about to catch fire, green though it was,
And was really glowing, I took it out
And brought it right up to him. My men
Stood around me, and some god inspired us.
My men lifted up the olivewood stake   380
And drove the sharp point right into his eye,
While I, putting my weight behind it, spun it around
The way a man bores a ship's beam with a drill,
Leaning down on it while other men beneath him
Keep it spinning and spinning with a leather strap.   385
That's how we twirled the fiery-pointed stake
In the Cyclops' eye. The blood formed a whirlpool
Around its searing tip. His lids and brow
Were all singed by the heat from the burning eyeball
And its roots crackled in the fire and hissed   390
Like an axe-head or adze a smith dips into water
When he wants to temper the iron—that's how his eye
Sizzled and hissed around the olivewood stake.
He screamed, and the rock walls rang with his voice.
We shrank back in terror while he wrenched   395
The blood-grimed stake from his eye and flung it
Away from him, blundering about and shouting
To the other Cyclopes, who lived around him
In caverns among the windswept crags.
They heard his cry and gathered from all sides   400
Around his cave and asked him what ailed him:

'Polyphemus, why are you hollering so much
And keeping us up the whole blessed night?
Is some man stealing your flocks from you,
Or killing you, maybe, by some kind of trick?'   405

And Polyphemus shouted out to them:

---

7. In Greek, "Noman"—*oudeis*—sounds a little like *Odysseus*.

'Noman is killing me by some kind of trick!'

They sent their words winging back to him:

'If no man is hurting you, then your sickness
Comes from Zeus and can't be helped.   410
You should pray to your father, Lord Poseidon.'

They left then, and I laughed in my heart
At how my phony name had fooled them so well.
Cyclops meanwhile was groaning in agony.
Groping around, he removed the doorstone   415
And sat in the entrance with his hands spread out
To catch anyone who went out with the sheep—
As if I could be so stupid. I thought it over,
Trying to come up with the best plan I could
To get us all out from the jaws of death.   420
I wove all sorts of wiles, as a man will
When his life is on the line. My best idea
Had to do with the sheep that were there, big,
Thick-fleeced beauties with wool dark as violets.
Working silently, I bound them together   425
With willow branches the Cyclops slept on.
I bound them in threes. Each middle sheep
Carried a man underneath, protected by
The two on either side: three sheep to a man.
As for me, there was a ram, the best in the flock.   430
I grabbed his back and curled up beneath
His shaggy belly. There I lay, hands twined
Into the marvelous wool, hanging on for dear life.
And so, muffling our groans, we waited for dawn.

When the first streaks of red appeared in the sky,   435
The rams started to bolt toward the pasture.
The unmilked females were bleating in the pens,
Their udders bursting. Their master,
Worn out with pain, felt along the backs
Of all of the sheep as they walked by, the fool,   440
Unaware of the men under their fleecy chests.
The great ram headed for the entrance last,
Heavy with wool—and with me thinking hard.
Running his hands over the ram, Polyphemus said:

'My poor ram, why are you leaving the cave   445
Last of all? You've never lagged behind before.
You were always the first to reach the soft grass
With your big steps, first to reach the river,
First to want to go back to the yard
At evening. Now you're last of all. Are you sad   450
About your master's eye? A bad man blinded me,
Him and his nasty friends, getting me drunk,
Noman—but he's not out of trouble yet!

If only you understood and could talk,
You could tell me where he's hiding. I would   455
Smash him to bits and spatter his brains
All over the cave. Then I would find some relief
From the pain this no-good Noman has caused me.'

He spoke, and sent the ram off through the door.
When we had gone a little way from the cave,   460
I first untangled myself from the ram
And then untied my men. Then, moving quickly,
We drove those fat, long-shanked sheep
Down to the ship, keeping an eye on our rear.
We were a welcome sight to the rest of the crew,   465
But when they started to mourn the men we had lost
I forbade it with an upward nod of my head,
Signaling each man like that and ordering them
To get those fleecy sheep aboard instead,
On the double, and get the ship out to sea.   470
Before you knew it they were on their benches
Beating the sea to white froth with their oars.
When we were offshore but still within earshot,
I called out to the Cyclops, just to rub it in:

'So, Cyclops, it turns out it wasn't a coward   475
Whose men you murdered and ate in your cave,
You savage! But you got yours in the end,
Didn't you? You had the gall to eat the guests
In your own house, and Zeus made you pay for it.'

He was even angrier when he heard this.   480
Breaking off the peak of a huge crag
He threw it toward our ship, and it carried
To just in front of our dark prow. The sea
Billowed up where the rock came down,
And the backwash pushed us to the mainland again,   485
Like a flood tide setting us down at the shore.
I grabbed a long pole and shoved us off,
Nodding to the crew to fall on the oars
And get us out of there. They leaned into it,
And when we were twice as far out to sea as before   490
I called to the Cyclops again, with my men
Hanging all over me and begging me not to:

'Don't do it, man! The rock that hit the water
Pushed us in and we thought we were done for.
If he hears any sound from us, he'll heave   495
Half a cliff at us and crush the ship and our skulls
With one throw. You know he has the range.'

They tried, but didn't persuade my hero's heart—
I was really angry—and I called back to him:

'Cyclops, if anyone, any mortal man,   500
Asks you how you got your eye put out,
Tell him that Odysseus the marauder did it,
Son of Laertes, whose home is on Ithaca.'

He groaned, and had this to say in response:

'Oh no! Now it's coming to me, the old prophecy.   505
There was a seer here once, a tall handsome man,
Telemos Eurymides. He prophesied well
All his life to the Cyclopes. He told me
That all this would happen some day,
That I would lose my sight at Odysseus' hands.   510
I always expected a great hero
Would come here, strong as can be.
Now this puny, little, good-for-nothing runt
Has put my eye out—because he got me drunk.
But come here, Odysseus, so I can give you a gift,   515
And ask Poseidon to help you on your way.
I'm his son, you know. He claims he's my father.
He will heal me, if he wants. But none
Of the other gods will, and no mortal man will.'

He spoke, and I shouted back to him: 520

'I wish I were as sure of ripping out your lungs
And sending you to Hell as I am dead certain
That not even the Earthshaker will heal your eye.'

I had my say, and he prayed to Poseidon,
Stretching his arms out to starry heaven: 525

'Hear me, Poseidon, blue-maned Earth-Holder,
If you are the father you claim to be.
Grant that Odysseus, son of Laertes,
May never reach his home on Ithaca.
But if he is fated to see his family again,   530
And return to his home and own native land,
May he come late, having lost all companions,
In another's ship, and find trouble at home.'

He prayed, and the blue-maned sea-god heard him.
Then he broke off an even larger chunk of rock,   535
Pivoted, and threw it with incredible force.
It came down just behind our dark-hulled ship,
Barely missing the end of the rudder. The sea
Billowed up where the rock hit the water,
And the wave pushed us forward all the way   540
To the island where our other ships waited
Clustered on the shore, ringed by our comrades
Sitting on the sand, anxious for our return.

We beached the ship and unloaded the Cyclops' sheep,
Which I divided up as fairly as I could   545
Among all hands. The veterans gave me the great ram,
And I sacrificed it on the shore of the sea
To Zeus in the dark clouds, who rules over all.
I burnt the thigh pieces, but the god did not accept
My sacrifice, brooding over how to destroy   550
All my benched ships and my trusty crews.

So all the long day until the sun went down
We sat feasting on meat and drinking sweet wine.
When the sun set and darkness came on
We lay down and slept on the shore of the sea.   555
Early in the morning, when the sky was streaked red,
I roused my men and ordered the crews
To get on deck and cast off. They took their places
And were soon whitening the sea with their oars.

We sailed on in shock, glad to get away alive   560
But grieving for the comrades we had lost."

BOOK X

"We came next to the island of Aeolia,
Home of Aeolus, son of Hippotas,
Dear to the immortals. Aeolia
Is a floating island surrounded by a wall
Of indestructible bronze set on sheer stone.   5
Aeolus' twelve children live there with him,
Six daughters and six manly sons.
He married his daughters off to his boys,
And they all sit with their father and mother
Continually feasting on abundant good cheer   10
Spread out before them. Every day
The house is filled with steamy savor
And the courtyard resounds. Every night
The men sleep next to their high-born wives
On blankets strewn on their corded beds.   15
We came to their city and their fine palace,
And for a full month he entertained me.
He questioned me in great detail about Troy,
The Greek fleet, and the Greeks' return home.
I told him everything, from beginning to end.   20
And when I, in turn, asked if I might leave
And requested him to send me on my way,
He did not refuse, and this was his send-off:
He gave me a bag made of the hide of an ox
Nine years old, which he had skinned himself,   25
And in this bag he bound the wild winds' ways,
For Zeus had made him keeper of the winds,
To still or to rouse whichever he will.

He tied this bag down in the hold of my ship
With a bright silver cord, so that not a puff   30
Could escape. But he let the West Wind out
To blow my ships along and carry us home.
It was not to be. Our own folly undid us.

For nine days and nights we sailed on.
On the tenth day we raised land, our own   35
Native fields, and got so close we saw men
Tending their fires. Then sleep crept up on me,
Exhausted from minding the sail the whole time
By myself. I wouldn't let any of my crew
Spell me, because I wanted to make good time.   40
As soon as I fell asleep, the men started to talk,
Saying I was bringing home for myself
Silver and gold as gifts from great Aeolus.
You can imagine the sort of things they said:

'This guy gets everything wherever he goes.   45
First, he's freighting home his loot from Troy,
Beautiful stuff, while we, who made the same trip,
Are coming home empty-handed. And now
Aeolus has lavished these gifts upon him.
Let's have a quick look, and see what's here,   50
How much gold and silver is stuffed in this bag.'

All malicious nonsense, but it won out in the end,
And they opened the bag. The winds rushed out
And bore them far out to sea, weeping
As their native land faded on the horizon.   55
When I woke up and saw what had happened
I thought long and hard about whether I should
Just go over the side and end it all in the sea
Or endure in silence and remain among the living.
In the end I decided to bear it and live.   60
I wrapped my head in my cloak and lay down on the deck
While an evil wind carried the ships
Back to Aeolia. My comrades groaned.

We went ashore and drew water
And the men took a meal beside the swift ships.   65
When we had tasted food and drink
I took a herald and one man
And went to Aeolus' glorious palace.
I found him feasting with his wife and children,
And when we came in and sat on the threshold   70
They were amazed and questioned me:

'What happened, Odysseus? What evil spirit
Abused you? Surely we sent you off

With all you needed to get back home
Or anywhere else your heart desired.'   75

I answered them from the depths of my sorrow:

'My evil crew ruined me, that and stubborn sleep.
But make it right, friends, for you have the power.'

I made my voice soft and tried to persuade them,
But they were silent. And then their father said: 80

'Begone from this island instantly!
You are the most cursed of all living things.
It would go against all that is right
For me to help or send on his way
A man so despised by the blessed gods.   85
Begone! You are cursed by heaven!'

And with that he sent me from his house,
Groaning heavily. We sailed on from there
With grief in our hearts. Because of our folly
There was no breeze to push us along,   90
And our morale sank because the rowing was hard.
We sailed on for six solid days and nights,
And on the seventh we came to Lamus,
The lofty city of Telepylus
In the land of the Laestrygonians,   95
Where a herdsman driving in his flocks at dusk
Calls to another driving his out at dawn.
A man could earn a double wage there
If he never slept, one by herding cattle
And another by pasturing white sheep,   100
For night and day make one twilight there.
The harbor we came to is a glorious place,
Surrounded by sheer cliffs. Headlands
Jut out on either side to form a narrow mouth,
And there all the others steered in their ships   105
And moored them close together in the bay.
No wave, large or small, ever rocks a boat
In that silvery calm. I alone moored my black ship
Outside the harbor, tying her up
On the rocks that lie on the border of the land.   110
Then I climbed to a rugged lookout point
And surveyed the scene. There was no sign
Of plowed fields, only smoke rising up from the land.

I sent out a team—two picked men and a herald—
To reconnoiter and find out who lived there.   115
They went ashore and followed a smooth road
Used by wagons to bring wood from the mountains
Down to the city. In front of the city
They met a girl drawing water. Her father

Was named Antiphates, and she had come down   120
To the flowing spring Artacia,
From which they carried water to the town.
When my men came up to her and asked her
Who the people there were and who was their king,
She showed them her father's high-roofed house.   125
They entered the house and found his wife inside,
A woman, to their horror, as huge as a mountain top.
At once she called her husband, Antiphates,
Who meant business when he came. He seized
One of my men and made him into dinner.   130
The other two got out of there and back to the ships,
But Antiphates had raised a cry throughout the city,
And when they heard it, the Laestrygonians
Came up on all sides, thousands of them,
Not like men but like the Sons of the Earth,   135
The Giants.[8] They pelted us from the cliffs
With rocks too large for a man to lift.
The sounds that came from the ships were sickening,
Sounds of men dying and boats being crushed.
The Laestrygonians speared the bodies like fish,   140
And carried them back for their ghastly meal.
While this was happening I drew my sword
And cut the cables of my dark-prowed ship,
Barking out orders for the crew to start rowing
And get us out of there. They rowed for their lives,   145
Ripping the sea, and my ship sped joyfully
Out and away from the beetling rocks,
But all of the others were destroyed as they lay.

We sailed on in shock, glad to get out alive
But grieving for the comrades we'd lost.   150
And we came to Aeaea, the island that is home
To Circe, a dread goddess with richly coiled hair
And a human voice. She is the sister
Of dark-hearted Aeetes, and they are both sprung
From Helios and Perse, daughter of Ocean.[9]   155
Some god guided us into a harbor
And we put in to shore without a sound.
We disembarked and lay there for two days and two nights,
Eating our hearts out with weariness and grief.
But when Dawn combed her hair in the third day's light,   160
I took my sword and spear and went up
From the ship to open ground, hoping to see
Plowed fields, and to hear human voices.
So I climbed to a rugged lookout point
And surveyed the scene. What I saw was smoke   165

8. The Giants were children of Earth, fertilized
by the blood of Uranus after his castration.
9. Perse is one of the many daughters of Ocean;

Aeetes was the cruel king of Colchis, owner of
the Golden Fleece and father of Medea.

Rising up from Circe's house. It curled up high
Through the thick brush and woods, and I wondered
Whether I should go and have a closer look.
I decided it was better to go back to the ship
And give my crew their meal, and then   170
Send out a party to reconnoiter.
I was on my way back and close to the ship
When some god took pity on me,
Walking there alone, and sent a great antlered stag
Right into my path. He was on his way   175
Down to the river from his pasture in the woods,
Thirsty and hot from the sun beating down,
And as he came out I got him right on the spine
In the middle of his back. The bronze spear bored
All the way through, and he fell in the dust   180
With a groan, and his spirit flew away.
Planting my foot on him, I drew the bronze spear
Out of the wound and laid it down on the ground.
Then I pulled up a bunch of willow shoots
And twisted them together to make a rope   185
About a fathom long. I used this to tie
The stag's feet together so I could carry him
Across my back, leaning on my spear
As I went back to the ship. There was no way
An animal that large could be held on one shoulder.   190
I flung him down by the ship and roused my men,
Going up to each in turn and saying to them:

'We're not going down to Hades, my friends,
Before our time. As long as there is still
Food and drink in our ship, at least   195
We don't have to starve to death.'

When they heard this, they drew their cloaks
From their faces, and marveled at the size
Of the stag lying on the barren seashore.
When they had seen enough, they washed their hands   200
And prepared a glorious feast. So all day long
Until the sun went down we sat there feasting
On all that meat, washing it down with wine.
When the sun set and darkness came on,
We lay down to sleep on the shore of the sea.   205

When Dawn brushed the eastern sky with rose,
I called my men together and spoke to them:

'Listen to me, men. It's been hard going.
We don't know east from west right now,
But we have to see if we have any good ideas left.   210
We may not. I climbed up to a lookout point.
We're on an island, ringed by the endless sea.

The land lies low, and I was able to see
Smoke rising up through the brushy woods.'

This was too much for them. They remembered   215
What Antiphates, the Laestrygonian, had done,
And how the Cyclops had eaten their comrades.
They wailed and cried, but it did them no good.
I counted off the crew into two companies
And appointed a leader for each. Eurylochus   220
Headed up one group and I took the other,
And then we shook lots in a bronze helmet.
Out jumped the lot of Eurylochus, brave heart,
And so off he went, with twenty-two men,
All in tears, leaving us behind in no better mood.   225

They went through the woods and found Circe's house
In an upland clearing. It was built of polished stone
And surrounded by mountain lions and wolves,
Creatures Circe had drugged and bewitched.
These beasts did not attack my men, but stood   230
On their hind legs and wagged their long tails,
Like dogs fawning on their master who always brings
Treats for them when he comes home from a feast.
So these clawed beasts were fawning around my men,
Who were terrified all the same by the huge animals.   235
While they stood like this in the gateway
They could hear Circe inside, singing in a lovely voice
As she moved about weaving a great tapestry,
The unfading handiwork of an immortal goddess,
Finely woven, shimmering with grace and light.   240
Polites, a natural leader, and of all the crew
The one I loved and trusted most, spoke up then:

'Someone inside is weaving a great web,
And singing so beautifully the floor thrums with the sound.
Whether it's a goddess or a woman, let's call her out now.'   245

And so they called to her, and she came out
And flung open the bright doors and invited them in.
They all filed in naively behind her,
Except Eurylochus, who suspected a trap.
When she had led them in and seated them   250
She brewed up a potion of Pramnian wine
With cheese, barley, and pale honey stirred in,
And she laced this potion with insidious drugs
That would make them forget their own native land.
When they had eaten and drunk, she struck them   255
With her wand and herded them into the sties outside.
Grunting, their bodies covered with bristles,
They looked just like pigs, but their minds were intact.
Once in the pens, they squealed with dismay,

And Circe threw them acorns and berries—   260
The usual fare for wallowing swine.

Eurylochus at once came back to the ship
To tell us of our comrades' unseemly fate,
But, hard as he tried, he could not speak a word.
The man was in shock. His eyes welled with tears,   265
And his mind was filled with images of horror.
Finally, under our impatient questioning,
He told us how his men had been undone:

'We went through the woods, as you told us to,
Glorious Odysseus, and found a beautiful house   270
In an upland clearing, built of polished stone.
Someone inside was working a great loom
And singing in a high, clear voice, some goddess
Or a woman, and they called out to her,
And she came out and opened the bright doors   275
And invited them in, and they naively
Filed in behind her. But I stayed outside,
Suspecting a trap. And they all disappeared,
Not one came back. I sat and watched
For a long, long time, and not one came back.'   280

He spoke, and I threw my silver-studded sword
Around my shoulders, slung on my bow,
And ordered Eurylochus to retrace his steps
And lead me back there. But he grabbed me by the knees
And pleaded with me, wailing miserably: 285
'Don't force me to go back there. Leave me here,
Because I know that you will never come back yourself
Or bring back the others. Let's just get out of here
With those that are left. We might still make it.'

There were his words, and I answered him;   290

'All right, Eurylochus, you stay here by the ship.
Get yourself something to eat and drink.
I'm going, though. We're in a really tight spot.'

And so I went up from the ship and the sea
Into the sacred woods. I was closing in   295
On Circe's house, with all its bewitchment,
When I was met by Hermes. He had a golden wand
And looked like a young man, a hint of a moustache
Above his lip—youth at its most charming.
He clasped my hand and said to me: 300

'Where are you off to now, unlucky man,
Alone, and in rough, uncharted terrain?

Those men of yours are up in Circe's house,
Penned like pigs into crowded little sties.
And you've come to free them? I don't think so.   305
You'll never return; you'll have to stay there, too.
Oh well, I will keep you out of harm's way.
Take this herb with you when you go to Circe,
And it will protect you from her deadly tricks.
She'll mix a potion and spike it with drugs,   310
But she won't be able to cast her spell
Because you'll have a charm that works just as well—
The one I'll give you—and you'll be forewarned.
When Circe strikes you with her magic wand,
Draw your sharp sword from beside your thigh   315
And rush at her with murder in your eye.
She'll be afraid and invite you to bed.
Don't turn her down—that's how you'll get
Your comrades freed and yourself well loved.
But first make her swear by the gods above   320
She will not unsex you when you are nude,
Or drain you of your manly fortitude.'

So saying, Hermes gave me the herb,
Pulling it out of the ground, and showed it to me.
It was black at the root, with a milk-white flower.   325
Moly, the gods call it, hard for mortal men to dig up,
But the gods can do anything. Hermes rose
Through the wooded island and up to Olympus,
And I went on to Circe's house, brooding darkly
On many things. I stood at the gates   330
Of the beautiful goddess' house and gave a shout.
She heard me call and came out at once,
Opening the bright doors and inviting me in.
I followed her inside, my heart pounding.
She seated me on a beautiful chair   335
Of finely wrought silver, and prepared me a drink
In a golden cup, and with evil in her heart
She laced it with drugs. She gave me the cup
And I drank it off, but it did not bewitch me.
So she struck me with her wand and said: 340

'Off to the sty, with the rest of your friends.'

At this, I drew the sharp sword that hung by my thigh
And lunged at Circe as if I meant to kill her.
The goddess shrieked and, running beneath my blade,
Grabbed my knees and said to me wailing: 345

'Who are you, and where do you come from?
What is your city and who are your parents?
I am amazed that you drank this potion
And are not bewitched. No other man

Has ever resisted this drug once it's past his lips.   350
But you have a mind that cannot be beguiled.
You must be Odysseus, the man of many wiles,
Who Quicksilver Hermes always said would come here
In his swift black ship on his way home from Troy.
Well then, sheath your sword and let's   355
Climb into my bed and tangle in love there,
So we may come to trust each other.'

She spoke, and I answered her:

'Circe, how can you ask me to be gentle to you
After you've turned my men into swine?   360
And now you have me here and want to trick me
Into going to bed with you, so that you can
Unman me when I am naked. No, Goddess,
I'm not getting into any bed with you
Unless you agree first to swear a solemn oath   365
That you're not planning some new trouble for me.'

Those were my words, and she swore an oath at once
Not to do me any harm, and when she finished
I climbed into Circe's beautiful bed.

Meanwhile, her serving women were busy,   370
Four maidens who did all the housework,
Spirit women born of the springs and groves
And of the sacred rivers that flow to the sea.
One of them brought rugs with a purple sheen
And strewed them over chairs lined with fresh linen.   375
Another drew silver tables up to the chairs
And set golden baskets upon them. The third
Mixed honey-hearted wine in a silver bowl
And set out golden cups. The fourth
Filled a cauldron with water and lit a great fire   380
Beneath it, and when the water was boiling
In the glowing bronze, she set me in a tub
And bathed me, mixing in water from the cauldron
Until it was just how I liked it, and pouring it over
My head and shoulders until she washed from my limbs   385
The weariness that had consumed my soul.
When she had bathed me and rubbed me
With rich olive oil, and had thrown about me
A beautiful cloak and tunic, she led me to the hall
And had me sit on a silver-studded chair,   390
Richly wrought and with a matching footstool.
A maid poured water from a silver pitcher
Over a golden basin for me to wash my hands
And then set up a polished table nearby.
And the housekeeper, grave and dignified,   395
Set out bread and generous helpings

From all the dishes she had. She told me to eat,
But nothing appealed. I sat there with other thoughts
Occupying my mind, and my mood was dark.
When Circe noticed I was just sitting there,   400
Depressed, and not reaching out for food,
She came up to me and spoke winged words:

'Why are you just sitting there, Odysseus,
Eating your heart out and not touching your food?
Are you afraid of some other trick? You need not be.   405
I have already sworn I will do you no harm.'

So she spoke, and I answered her:

'Circe, how could anyone bring himself—
Any decent man—to taste food and drink
Before seeing his comrades free?   410
If you really want me to eat and drink,
Set my men free and let me see them.'

So I spoke, and Circe went outside
Holding her wand and opened the sty
And drove them out. They looked like swine   415
Nine or ten years old. They stood there before her
And she went through them and smeared each one
With another drug. The bristles they had grown
After Circe had given them the poisonous drug
All fell away, and they became men again,   420
Younger than before, taller and far handsomer.
They knew me, and they clung to my hands,
And the house rang with their passionate sobbing.
The goddess herself was moved to pity.

Then she came to my side and said: 425

'Son of Laertes in the line of Zeus,
My wily Odysseus, go to your ship now
Down by the sea and haul it ashore.
Then stow all the tackle and gear in caves
And come back here with the rest of your crew.'   430

So she spoke, and persuaded my heart.
I went to the shore and found my crew there
Wailing and crying beside our sailing ship.
When they saw me they were like farmyard calves
Around a herd of cows returning to the yard.   435
The calves bolt from their pens and run friskily
Around their mothers, lowing and mooing.
That's how my men thronged around me
When they saw me coming. It was as if
They had come home to their rugged Ithaca,   440
And wailing miserably they said so to me:

'With you back, Zeus-born, it is just as if
We had returned to our native Ithaca.
But tell us what happened to the rest of the crew.'

So they spoke, and I answered them gently: 445

'First let's haul our ship onto dry land
And then stow all the tackle and gear in caves.
Then I want all of you to come along with me
So you can see your shipmates in Circe's house,
Eating and drinking all they could ever want.'   450

They heard what I said and quickly agreed.
Eurylochus, though, tried to hold them back,
Speaking to them these winged words:

'Why do you want to do this to yourselves,
Go down to Circe's house? She will turn all of you   455
Into pigs, wolves, lions, and make you guard her house.
Remember what the Cyclops did when our shipmates
Went into his lair? It was this reckless Odysseus
Who led them there. It was his fault they died.'

When Eurylochus said that, I considered   460
Drawing my long sword from where it hung
By my thigh and lopping off his head,
Close kinsman though he was by marriage.
But my crew talked me out of it, saying things like:

'By your leave, let's station this man here   465
To guard the ship. As for the rest of us,
Lead us on to the sacred house of Circe.'

And so the whole crew went up from the sea,
And Eurylochus did not stay behind with the ship
But went with us, in mortal fear of my temper.   470

Meanwhile, back in Circe's house, the goddess
Had my men bathed, rubbed down with oil,
And clothed in tunics and fleecy cloaks.
We found them feasting well in her halls.
When they recognized each other, they wept openly   475
And their cries echoed throughout Circe's house.
Then the shining goddess stood near me and said:

'Lament no more. I myself know
All that you have suffered on the teeming sea
And the losses on land at your enemies' hands.   480
Now you must eat, drink wine, and restore the spirit
You had when you left your own native land,
Your rugged Ithaca. You are skin and bones now

And hollow inside. All you can think of
Is your hard wandering, no joy in your heart,   485
For you have, indeed, suffered many woes.'

She spoke, and I took her words to heart.
So we sat there day after day for a year,
Feasting on abundant meat and sweet wine.
But when a year had passed, and the seasons turned,   490
And the moons waned and the long days were done,
My trusty crew called me out and said:

'Good god, man, at long last remember your home,
If it is heaven's will for you to be saved
And return to your house and your own native land.'   495

They spoke, and I saw what they meant.
So all that long day until the sun went down
We sat feasting on meat and sweet red wine.
When the sun set and darkness came on,
My men lay down to sleep in the shadowy hall,   500
But I went up to Circe's beautiful bed
And touching her knees I beseeched the goddess:

'Circe, fulfill now the promise you made
To send me home. I am eager to be gone
And so are my men, who are wearing me out   505
Sitting around whining and complaining
Whenever you happen not to be present.'

So I spoke, and the shining goddess answered:

'Son of Laertes in the line of Zeus,
My wily Odysseus—you need not stay   510
Here in my house any longer than you wish.
But there is another journey you must make first—
To the house of Hades and dread Persephone,[1]
To consult the ghost of Theban Tiresias,
The blind prophet, whose mind is still strong.   515
To him alone Persephone has granted
Intelligence even after his death.
The rest of the dead are flitting shadows.'

This broke my spirit. I sat on the bed   *Suicide.*
And wept. I had no will to live, nor did I care   520
If I ever saw the sunlight again.
But when I had my fill of weeping and writhing,
I looked at the goddess and said:

1. Hades is god of the underworld. Persephone is his wife.

'And who will guide me on this journey, Circe?
No man has ever sailed his black ship to Hades.'   525

And the goddess, shining, answered at once:

'Son of Laertes in the line of Zeus,
My wily Odysseus—do not worry about
A pilot to guide your ship. Just set up the mast,
Spread the white sail, and sit yourself down.   530
The North Wind's breath will bear her onwards.
But when your ship crosses the stream of Ocean
You will see a shelving shore and Persephone's groves,
Tall poplars and willows that drop their fruit.
Beach your ship there by Ocean's deep eddies,   535
And go yourself to the dank house of Hades.
There into Acheron flow Pyriphlegethon
And Cocytus, a branch of the water of Styx.
And there is a rock where the two roaring rivers
Flow into one. At that spot, hero, gather yourself   540
And do as I say.
                     Dig an ell-square pit,
And around it pour libation to all the dead,
First with milk and honey, then with sweet wine,
And a third time with water. Then sprinkle barley
And pray to the looming, feeble death-heads,   545
Vowing sacrifice on Ithaca, a barren heifer,
The herd's finest, and rich gifts on the altar,
And to Tiresias alone a great black ram.
After these supplications to the spirits,
Slaughter a ram and a black ewe, turning their heads   550
Toward Erebus,² yourself turning backward
And leaning toward the streams of the river.
Then many ghosts of the dead will come forth.
Call to your men to flay the slaughtered sheep
And burn them as a sacrifice to the gods below,   555
To mighty Hades and dread Persephone.
You yourself draw your sharp sword and sit there,
Keeping the feeble death-heads from the blood
Until you have questioned Tiresias.
Then, and quickly, the great seer will come.   560
He will tell you the route and how long it will take
For you to reach home over the teeming deep.'

Dawn rose in gold as she finished speaking.
Circe gave me a cloak and tunic to wear
And the nymph slipped on a long silver robe   565
Shimmering in the light, cinched it at the waist
With a golden belt and put a veil on her head.
I went through the halls and roused my men,
Going up to each with words soft and sweet:

2. The underworld.

'Time to get up! No more sleeping late.   570
We're on our way. Lady Circe has told me all.'

So I spoke, and persuaded their heroes' hearts.
But not even from Circe's house could I lead my men
Unscathed. One of the crew, Elpenor, the youngest,
Not much of a warrior nor all that smart,   575
Had gone off to sleep apart from his shipmates,
Seeking the cool air on Circe's roof
Because he was heavy with wine.
He heard the noise of his shipmates moving around
And sprang up suddenly, forgetting to go   580
To the long ladder that led down from the roof.
He fell headfirst, his neck snapped at the spine,
And his soul went down to the house of Hades.

As my men were heading out I spoke to them:

'You think, no doubt, that you are going home,   585
But Circe has plotted another course for us,
To the house of Hades and dread Persephone,
To consult the ghost of Theban Tiresias.'

This broke their hearts. They sat down
Right where they were and wept and tore their hair,   590
But no good came of their lamentation.

While we were on our way to our swift ship
On the shore of the sea, weeping and crying,
Circe had gone ahead and tethered a ram and a black ewe
By our tarred ship. She had passed us by   595
Without our ever noticing. Who could see
A god on the move against the god's will?"

BOOK XI

"When we reached our black ship
We hauled her onto the bright saltwater,
Set up the mast and sail, loaded on
The sheep, and boarded her ourselves,
Heartsick and weeping openly by now.   5
The dark prow cut through the waves
And a following wind bellied the canvas,
A good sailing breeze sent by Circe,
The dread goddess with a human voice.
We lashed everything down and sat tight,   10
Leaving the ship to the wind and helmsman.
All day long she surged on with taut sail;
Then the sun set, and the sea grew dark.

The ship took us to the deep, outermost Ocean
And the land of the Cimmerians, a people   15

Shrouded in mist. The sun never shines there,
Never climbs the starry sky to beam down at them,
Nor bathes them in the glow of its last golden rays;
Their wretched sky is always racked with night's gloom.
We beached our ship there, unloaded the sheep,   20
And went along the stream of Ocean
Until we came to the place spoken of by Circe.

There Perimedes and Eurylochus held the victims
While I dug an ell-square pit with my sword,
And poured libation to all the dead,   25
First with milk and honey, then with sweet wine,
And a third time with water. Then I sprinkled
White barley and prayed to the looming dead,
Vowing sacrifice on Ithaca—a barren heifer,
The herd's finest, and rich gifts on the altar,   30
And to Tiresias alone a great black ram.
After these supplications to the spirits,
I cut the sheeps' throats over the pit,
And the dark blood pooled there.
                         Then out of Erebus
The souls of the dead gathered, the ghosts   35
Of brides and youths and worn-out old men
And soft young girls with hearts new to sorrow,
And many men wounded with bronze spears,
Killed in battle, bearing blood-stained arms.
They drifted up to the pit from all sides   40
With an eerie cry, and pale fear seized me.
I called to my men to flay the slaughtered sheep
And burn them as a sacrifice to the gods,
To mighty Hades and dread Persephone.
Myself, I drew my sharp sword and sat,   45
Keeping the feeble death-heads from the blood
Until I had questioned Tiresias.

First to come was the ghost of Elpenor,
Whose body still lay in Circe's hall,
Unmourned, unburied, since we'd been hard pressed.   50
I wept when I saw him, and with pity in my heart
Spoke to him these feathered words:

'Elpenor, how did you get to the undergloom
Before me, on foot, outstripping our black ship?'

I spoke, and he moaned in answer: 55

'Bad luck and too much wine undid me.
I fell asleep on Circe's roof. Coming down
I missed my step on the long ladder
And fell headfirst. My neck snapped
At the spine and my ghost went down to Hades.   60

Now I beg you—by those we left behind,
By your wife and the father who reared you,
And by Telemachus, your only son,
Whom you left alone in your halls—
When you put the gloom of Hades behind you   65
And beach your ship on the Isle of Aeaea,
As I know you will, remember me, my lord.
Do not leave me unburied, unmourned,
When you sail for home, or I might become
A cause of the gods' anger against you.   70
Burn me with my armor, such as I have,
Heap me a barrow on the grey sea's shore,
In memory of a man whose luck ran out.
Do this for me, and fix in the mound the oar
I rowed with my shipmates while I was alive.'   75

Thus Elpenor, and I answered him:

'Pitiful spirit, I will do this for you.'

Such were the sad words we exchanged
Sitting by the pit, I on one side holding my sword
Over the blood, my comrade's ghost on the other.   80

Then came the ghost of my dead mother,
Anticleia, daughter of the hero Autolycus.
She was alive when I left for sacred Ilion.
I wept when I saw her, and pitied her,
But even in my grief I would not allow her   85
To come near the blood until I had questioned Tiresias.

And then he came, the ghost of Theban Tiresias,
Bearing a golden staff. He knew me and said:

'Odysseus, son of Laertes, master of wiles,
Why have you come, leaving the sunlight   90
To see the dead and this joyless place?
Move off from the pit and take away your sword,
So I may drink the blood and speak truth to you.'

I drew back and slid my silver-studded sword
Into its sheath. After he had drunk the dark blood   95
The flawless seer rose and said to me:

'You seek a homecoming sweet as honey,
Shining Odysseus, but a god will make it bitter,
For I do not think you will elude the Earthshaker,
Who has laid up wrath in his heart against you,   100
Furious because you blinded his son. Still,
You just might get home, though not without pain,
You and your men, if you curb your own spirit,

And theirs, too, when you beach your ship
On Thrinacia. You will be marooned on that island 105
In the violet sea, and find there the cattle
Of Helios the Sun, and his sheep, too, grazing.
Leave these unharmed, keep your mind on your homecoming,
And you may still reach Ithaca, though not without pain.
But if you harm them, I foretell doom for you, 110
Your ship, and your crew. And even if you
Yourself escape, you will come home late
And badly, having lost all companions
And in another's ship. And you shall find
Trouble in your house, arrogant men 115
Devouring your wealth and courting your wife.
Yet vengeance will be yours, and when you have slain
The suitors in your hall, by ruse or by sword,
Then you must go off again, carrying a broad-bladed oar,
Until you come to men who know nothing of the sea, 120
Who eat their food unsalted, and have never seen
Red-prowed ships or oars that wing them along.
And I will tell you a sure sign that you have found them,
One you cannot miss. When you meet another traveler
Who thinks you are carrying a winnowing fan, 125
Then you must fix your oar in the earth
And offer sacrifice to Lord Poseidon,
A ram, a bull, and a boar in its prime.
Then return to your home and offer
Perfect sacrifice to the immortal gods 130
Who hold high heaven, to each in turn.
And death will come to you off the sea,
A death so gentle, and carry you off
When you are worn out in sleek old age,
Your people prosperous all around you. 135
All this will come true for you as I have told.'

Thus Tiresias. And I answered him:

'All that, Tiresias, is as the gods have spun it.
But tell me this: I see here the ghost
Of my dead mother, sitting in silence 140
Beside the blood, and she cannot bring herself
To look her son in the eye or speak to him.
How can she recognize me for who I am?'

And Tiresias, the Theban prophet:

'This is easy to tell you. Whoever of the dead 145
You let come to the blood will speak truly to you.
Whoever you deny will go back again.'

With that, the ghost of Lord Tiresias
Went back into Hades, his soothsaying done.

But I stayed where I was until my mother   150
Came up and drank the dark blood. At once
She knew me, and her words reached me on wings:

'My child, how did you come to the undergloom
While you are still alive? It is hard for the living
To reach these shores. There are many rivers to cross,   155
Great bodies of water, nightmarish streams,
And Ocean itself, which cannot be crossed on foot
But only in a well-built ship. Are you still wandering
On your way back from Troy, a long time at sea
With your ship and your men? Have you not yet come   160
To Ithaca, or seen your wife in your halls?'

So she spoke, and I answered her:

'Mother, I came here because I had to,
To consult the ghost of the prophet Tiresias.
I have not yet come to the coast of Achaea   165
Or set foot on my own land. I have had nothing
But hard travels from the day I set sail
With Lord Agamemnon to go to Ilion,
Famed for its horses, to fight the Trojans.
But tell me truly, how did you die?   170
Was it a long illness, or did Artemis
Shoot you suddenly with her gentle arrows?
And tell me about my father and my son,
Whom I left behind. Does the honor I had
Still remain with them, or has it passed   175
To some other man, and do they all say
I will never return? And what about my wife?
What has she decided, what does she think?
Is she still with my son, keeping things safe?
Or has someone already married her,   180
Whoever is now the best of the Achaeans?'[3]

So I spoke, and my mother answered at once:

'Oh, yes indeed, she remains in your halls,
Her heart enduring the bitter days and nights.
But the honor that was yours has not passed   185
To any man. Telemachus holds your lands
Unchallenged, and shares in the feasts
To which all men invite him as the island's lawgiver.
Your father, though, stays out in the fields
And does not come to the city. He has no bed   190
Piled with bright rugs and soft coverlets
But sleeps in the house where the slaves sleep,
In the ashes by the fire, and wears poor clothes.
In summer and autumn his vineyard's slope

3. Greeks.

Is strewn with beds of leaves on the ground, 195
Where he lies in his sorrow, nursing his grief,
Longing for your return. His old age is hard.
I died from the same grief. The keen-eyed goddess
Did not shoot me at home with her gentle shafts,
Nor did any long illness waste my body away. 200
No, it was longing for you, my glorious Odysseus,
For your gentle heart and your gentle ways,
That robbed me of my honey-sweet life.'

So she spoke, and my heart yearned
To embrace the ghost of my dead mother. 205
Three times I rushed forward to hug her,
And three times she drifted out of my arms
Like a shadow or a dream. The pain
That pierced my heart grew ever sharper,
And my words rose to my mother on wings: 210

'Mother, why do you slip away when I try
To embrace you? Even though we are in Hades,
Why can't we throw our arms around each other
And console ourselves with chill lamentation?
Are you a phantom sent by Persephone 215
To make me groan even more in my grief?'

And my mother answered me at once:

'O my child, most ill-fated of men,
It is not that Persephone is deceiving you.
This is the way it is with mortals. 220
When we die, the sinews no longer hold
Flesh and bones together. The fire destroys these
As soon as the spirit leaves the white bones,
And the ghost flutters off and is gone like a dream.
Hurry now to the light, and remember these things, 225
So that later you may tell them all to your wife.'

That was the drift of our talk.

                              Then the women came,
Sent by Persephone, all those who had been
The wives and daughters of the heroes of old.
They flocked together around the dark blood, 230
But I wanted to question them one at a time.
The best way I could think of to question them
Was to draw the sharp sword from beside my thigh,
And keep them from drinking the blood all at once.
They came up in procession then, and one by one 235
They declared their birth, and I questioned them all.
The first one I saw was highborn Tyro,
Who said she was born of flawless Salmoneus

And was wed to Cretheus, a son of Aeolus.
She fell in love with a river, divine Enipeus,   240
The most beautiful of all the rivers on earth,
And she used to play in his lovely streams.
But the Earthshaker took Enipeus' form
And lay with her in the swirling eddies
Near the river's mouth. And an indigo wave,   245
Towering like a mountain, arched over them
And hid the god and the mortal woman from view.
He unbound the sash that had kept her virgin
And shed sleep upon her. And when the god
Had finished his lovemaking, he took her hand   250
And called her name softly and said to her:

'Be happy in this love, woman. As the year turns
You will bear glorious children, for a god's embrace
Is never barren. Raise them and care for them.
Now go to your house and say nothing of this,   255
But I am Poseidon, who makes the earth tremble.'

With that he plunged into the surging sea.
And Tyro conceived and bore Pelias and Neleus,
Who served great Zeus as strong heroes both,
Pelias with his flocks in Iolcus' grasslands,   260
And Neleus down in sandy Pylos.
She bore other children to Cretheus: Aeson,
Pheres, and the charioteer Amythaon.

Then I saw Antiope, daughter of Asopus,
Who boasted she had slept in the arms of Zeus   265
And bore two sons, Amphion and Zethus,
Who founded seven-gated Thebes and built its walls,
Since they could not live in the wide land of Thebes
Without walls and towers, mighty though they were.

Next I saw Alcmene, Amphitryon's wife,   270
Who bore Heracles, the lionhearted battler,
After lying in Zeus' almighty embrace.
And I saw Megara, too, wife of Heracles,
The hero whose strength never wore out.

I saw Oedipus' mother, beautiful Epicaste,   275
Who unwittingly did a monstrous deed,
Marrying her son, who had killed his father.
The gods soon brought these things to light;
Yet, for all his misery, Oedipus still ruled
In lovely Thebes, by the gods' dark designs.   280
But Epicaste, overcome by her grief,
Hung a deadly noose from the ceiling rafters
And went down to implacable Hades' realm,

Leaving behind for her son all of the sorrows
A mother's avenging spirits can cause.[4]   285

And then I saw Chloris, the great beauty
Whom Neleus wedded after courting her
With myriad gifts. She was the youngest daughter
Of Amphion, king of Minyan Orchomenus.
As queen of Pylos, she bore glorious children,   290
Nestor, Chromius, and lordly Periclymenus,
And magnificent Pero, a wonder to men.
Everyone wanted to marry her, but Neleus
Would only give her to the man who could drive
The cattle of mighty Iphicles to Pylos,   295
Spiral-horned, broad-browed, stubborn cattle,
Difficult to drive. Only Melampus,
The flawless seer, rose to the challenge,
But he was shackled by Fate. Country herdsmen
Put him in chains, and months went by   300
And the seasons passed and the year turned
Before he was freed by mighty Iphicles,
After he had told him all of his oracles,
And so the will of Zeus was fulfilled.

I saw Leda also, wife of Tyndareus,   305
Who bore to him two stout-hearted sons,
Castor the horseman and the boxer Polydeuces.
They are under the teeming earth though alive,
And have honor from Zeus in the world below,
Living and dying on alternate days.   310
Such is the honor they have won from the gods.

After her I saw Iphimedeia,
Aloeus' wife. She made love to Poseidon
And bore two sons, who did not live long,
Godlike Otus and famed Ephialtes,   315
The tallest men ever reared upon earth
And the handsomest after gloried Orion.
At nine years old they measured nine cubits
Across the chest, and were nine fathoms tall.
They threatened to wage a furious war   320
Against the immortal Olympian gods,
And were bent on piling Ossa on Olympus,
And forested Pelion on top of Ossa
And so reach the sky. And they would have done it,
But the son of Zeus and fair-haired Leto   325
Destroyed them both before the down blossomed
Upon their cheeks and their beards had come in.

---

4. This passage gives a version of the myth different from that of Sophocles' play, in which
Oedipus's mother is called Jocasta.

And I saw Phaedra and Procnis
And lovely Ariadne, whom Theseus once
Tried to bring from Crete to sacred Athens   330
But had no joy of her. Artemis first
Shot her on Dia, the seagirt island,
After Dionysus told her he saw her there.[5]

And I saw Maera and Clymene
And hateful Eriphyle, who valued gold   335
More than her husband's life.[6]
                              But I could not tell you
All the wives and daughters of heroes I saw.
It would take all night. And it is time
To sleep now, either aboard ship with the crew
Or here in this house. My journey home   340
Is up to you, and to the immortal gods."

He paused, and they sat hushed in silence,
Spellbound throughout the shadowy hall.
And then white-armed Arete began to speak:

"Well, Phaeacians, does this man impress you   345
With his looks, stature, and well-balanced mind?
He is my guest, moreover, though each of you
Shares in that honor. Do not send him off, then,
Too hastily, and do not stint your gifts
To one in such need. You have many treasures   350
Stored in your halls by grace of the gods."

Then the old hero Echeneus spoke up:

"Friends, the words of our wise queen
Are not wide of the mark. Give them heed.
But upon Alcinous depend both word and deed."   355

And Alcinous answered:

"Arete's word will stand, as long as I live
And rule the Phaeacians who love the oar.
But let our guest, though he longs to go home,
Endure until tomorrow, until I have time   360
To make our gift complete. We all have a stake
In getting him home, but mine is greatest,
For mine is the power throughout the land."

And Odysseus, who missed nothing:

---

5. In other versions of the myth, Ariadne was abandoned by Theseus on the island of Naxos and rescued by Dionysus, god of wine.
6. Bribed with the necklace of Harmonia, she persuaded her husband, Amphrarus, to join the attack on Thebes, although she knew he would die.

"Lord Alcinous, most renowned of men,   365
You could ask me to stay for even a year
While you arranged a send-off with glorious gifts,
And I would assent. Better far to return
With a fuller hand to my own native land.
I would be more respected and loved by all   370
Who saw me come back to Ithaca."

Alcinous answered him:

"Odysseus, we do not take you
For the sort of liar and cheat the dark earth breeds
Among men everywhere, telling tall tales   375
No man could ever test for himself.
Your words have outward grace and wisdom within,
And you have told your tale with the skill of a bard—
All that the Greeks and you yourself have suffered.
But tell me this, as accurately as you can: 380
Did you see any of your godlike comrades
Who went with you to Troy and met their fate there?
The night is young—and magical. It is not yet time
To sleep in the hall. Tell me these wonders.
Sit in our hall and tell us of your woes   385
For as long as you can bear. I could listen until dawn."

And Odysseus, his mind teeming:

"Lord Alcinous, most glorious of men,
There is a time for words and a time for sleep.
But if you still yearn to listen, I will not refuse   390
To tell you of other things more pitiable still,
The woes of my comrades who died after the war,
Who escaped the Trojans and their battle-cry
But died on their return through a woman's evil.

When holy Persephone had scattered   395
The women's ghosts, there came the ghost
Of Agamemnon, son of Atreus,
Distraught with grief. Around him were gathered
Those who died with him in Aegisthus' house.
He knew me as soon as he drank the dark blood.   400
He cried out shrilly, tears welling in his eyes,
And he stretched out his hands, trying to touch me,
But he no longer had anything left of the strength
He had in the old days in those muscled limbs.
I wept when I saw him, and with pity in my heart   405
I spoke to him these winged words:

'Son of Atreus, king of men, most glorious
Agamemnon—what death laid you low?
Did Poseidon sink your fleet at sea,
After hitting you hard with hurricane winds?   410
Or were you killed by enemy forces on land,

As you raided their cattle and flocks of sheep
Or fought to capture their city and women?'

And Agamemnon answered at once:

'Son of Laertes in the line of Zeus,   415
My crafty Odysseus—No,
Poseidon did not sink my fleet at sea
After hitting us hard with hurricane winds,
Nor was I killed by enemy forces on land.
Aegisthus was the cause of my death.   420
He killed me with the help of my cursed wife
After inviting me to a feast in his house,
Slaughtered me like a bull at a manger.
So I died a most pitiable death,
And all around me my men were killed   425
Relentlessly, like white-tusked swine
For a wedding banquet or dinner party
In the house of a rich and powerful man.
You have seen many men cut down, both
In single combat and in the crush of battle,   430
But your heart would have grieved
As never before at the sight of us lying
Around the wine-bowl and the laden tables
In that great hall. The floor steamed with blood.
But the most piteous cry I ever heard   435
Came from Cassandra, Priam's daughter.[7]
She had her arms around me down on the floor
When Clytemnestra ran her through from behind.
I lifted my hands and beat the ground
As I lay dying with a sword in my chest,   440
But that bitch, my wife, turned her back on me
And would not shut my eyes or close my lips
As I was going down to Death. Nothing
Is more grim or more shameless than a woman
Who sets her mind on such an unspeakable act   445
As killing her own husband. I was sure
I would be welcomed home by my children
And all my household, but she, with her mind set
On stark horror, has shamed not only herself
But all women to come, even the rare good one.'   450

Thus Agamemnon, and I responded:

'Ah, how broad-browed Zeus has persecuted
The house of Atreus from the beginning,
Through the will of women. Many of us died
For Helen's sake, and Clytemnestra   455
Set a snare for you while you were far away.'[8]

---

7. Cassandra, who had the gift of prophecy   prize of war by Agamemnon.
from Apollo, was brought back from Troy as a   8. Helen and Clytemnestra were sisters.

And Agamemnon answered me at once:

'So don't go easy on your own wife either,
Or tell her everything you know.
Tell her some things, but keep some hidden.   460
But your wife will not bring about your death,
Odysseus. Icarius' daughter,
Your wise Penelope, is far too prudent.
She was newly wed when we went to war.
We left her with a baby boy still at the breast,   465
Who must by now be counted as a man,
And prosperous. His father will see him
When he comes, and he will embrace his father,
As is only right. But my wife did not let me
Even fill my eyes with the sight of my son.   470
She killed me before I could do even that.
But let me tell you something, Odysseus:
Beach your ship secretly when you come home.
Women just can't be trusted any more.
And one more thing. Tell me truthfully   475
If you've heard anything about my son
And where he is living, perhaps in Orchomenus,
Or in sandy Pylos, or with Menelaus in Sparta.
For Orestes has not yet perished from the earth.'

So he spoke, and I answered him: 480

'Son of Atreus, why ask me this?
I have no idea whether he is alive or dead,
And it is not good to speak words empty as wind.'

Such were the sad words we had for each other
As we stood there weeping, heavy with grief.   485

Then came the ghost of Achilles,[9] son of Peleus,
And those of Patroclus and peerless Antilochus
And Ajax,[1] who surpassed all the Danaans,
Except Achilles, in looks and build.
Aeacus' incomparable grandson, Achilles, knew me,   490
And when he spoke his words had wings:

'Son of Laertes in the line of Zeus,
Odysseus, you hard rover, not even you
Can ever top this, this bold foray
Into Hades, home of the witless dead   495
And the dim phantoms of men outworn.'

So he spoke, and I answered him:

---

9. Best of the Greek heroes, prominent character in the *Iliad*.

1. Strong Greek hero known for defensive fighting.

'Achilles, by far the mightiest of the Achaeans,
I have come here to consult Tiresias,
To see if he has any advice for me   500
On how I might get back to rugged Ithaca.
I've had nothing but trouble, and have not yet set foot
On my native land. But no man, Achilles,
Has ever been as blessed as you, or ever will be.
While you were alive the army honored you   505
Like a god, and now that you are here
You rule the dead with might. You should not
Lament your death at all, Achilles.'

I spoke, and he answered me at once:

'Don't try to sell me on death, Odysseus.   510
I'd rather be a hired hand back up on earth,
Slaving away for some poor dirt farmer,
Than lord it over all these withered dead.
But tell me about that boy of mine.
Did he come to the war and take his place   515
As one of the best? Or did he stay away?
And what about Peleus? What have you heard?
Is he still respected among the Myrmidons,
Or do they dishonor him in Phthia and Hellas,
Crippled by old age in hand and foot?   520
And I'm not there for him up in the sunlight
With the strength I had in wide Troy once
When I killed Ilion's best and saved the army.
Just let me come with that kind of strength
To my father's house, even for an hour,   525
And wrap my hands around his enemies' throats.
They would learn what it means to face my temper.'

Thus Achilles, and I answered him:

'I have heard nothing of flawless Peleus,
But as for your son, Neoptolemus,   530
I'll tell you all I know, just as you ask.
I brought him over from Scyros myself,
In a fine vessel, to join the Greek army
At Troy, and every time we held council there,
He was always the first to speak, and his words   535
Were never off the mark. Godlike Nestor and I
Alone surpassed him. And every time we fought
On Troy's plain, he never held back in the ranks
But charged ahead to the front, yielding
To no one, and he killed many in combat.   540
I could not begin to name them all,
All the men he killed when he fought for us,
But what a hero he dismantled in Telephus' son,

Eurypylus, dispatching him and a crowd
Of his Ceteian compatriots. Eurypylus   545
Came to Troy because Priam bribed his mother.
After Memnon, I've never seen a handsomer man.
And then, too, when all our best climbed
Into the wooden horse Epeius made,
And I was in command and controlled the trapdoor,   550
All the other Danaan leaders and counselors
Were wiping away tears from their eyes
And their legs shook beneath them, but I never saw
Neoptolemus blanch or wipe away a tear.
No, he just sat there handling his sword hilt   555
And heavy bronze spear, and all he wanted
Was to get out of there and give the Trojans hell.
And after we had sacked Priam's steep city,
He boarded his ship with his share of the loot
And more for valor. And not a scratch on him.   560
He never took a hit from a spear or sword
In close combat, where wounds are common.
When Ares rages anyone can be hit.'

So I spoke, and the ghost of swift-footed Achilles
Went off with huge strides through the fields of asphodel,   565
Filled with joy at his son's preeminence.

The other ghosts crowded around in sorrow,
And each asked about those who were dear to him.
Only the ghost of Telamonian Ajax
Stood apart, still furious with me   570
Because I had defeated him in the contest at Troy
To decide who would get Achilles' armor.
His goddess mother had put it up as a prize,
And the judges were the sons of the Trojans
And Pallas Athena. I wish I had never won.   575
That contest buried Ajax, that brave heart,
The best of the Danaans in looks and deeds,
After the incomparable son of Peleus.
I tried to win him over with words like these:

'Ajax, son of flawless Telamon,   580
Are you to be angry with me even in death
Over that accursed armor? The gods
Must have meant it to be the ruin of the Greeks.
We lost a tower of strength to that armor.
We mourn your loss as we mourn the loss   585
Of Achilles himself. Zeus alone
Is to blame. He persecuted the Greeks
Terribly, and he brought you to your doom.
No, come back, Lord Ajax, and listen!
Control your wrath and rein in your proud spirit.'   590

I spoke, but he said nothing. He went his way
To Erebus, to join the other souls of the dead.
He might yet have spoken to me there, or I
Might yet have spoken to him, but my heart
Yearned to see the other ghosts of the dead.   595

There I saw Minos,[2] Zeus' glorious son,
Scepter in hand, judging the dead
As he sat in the wide-gated house of Hades;
And the dead sat, too, and asked him for judgments.

And then Orion[3] loomed up before me,   600
Driving over the fields of asphodel
The beasts he had slain in the lonely hills,
In his hands a bronze club, forever unbroken.

And I saw Tityos, a son of glorious Earth,
Lying on the ground, stretched over nine acres,   605
And two vultures sat on either side of him
And tore at his liver, plunging their beaks
Deep into his guts, and he could not beat them off.
For Tityos had raped Leto, a consort of Zeus,
As she went to Pytho through lovely Panopeus.   610

And I saw Tantalus there in his agony,
Standing in a pool with water up to his chin.
He was mad with thirst, but unable to drink,
For every time the old man bent over
The water would drain away and vanish,   615
Dried up by some god, and only black mud
Would be left at his feet. Above him dangled
Treetop fruits, pears and pomegranates,
Shiny apples, sweet figs, and luscious olives.
But whenever Tantalus reached up for them,   620
The wind tossed them high to the shadowy clouds.

And I saw Sisyphus there in his agony,
Pushing a monstrous stone with his hands.
Digging in hard, he would manage to shove it
To the crest of a hill, but just as he was about   625
To heave it over the top, the shameless stone
Would teeter back and bound down to the plain.
Then he would strain every muscle to push it back up,
Sweat pouring from his limbs and dusty head.

And then mighty Heracles loomed up before me—   630
His phantom that is, for Heracles himself

2. Son of Zeus and Europa; he became judge   3. Famous hunter.
of the dead.

Feasts with the gods and has as his wife
Beautiful Hebe,[4] daughter of great Zeus
And gold-sandaled Hera. As he moved
A clamor arose from the dead around him,   635
As if they were birds flying off in terror.
He looked like midnight itself. He held his bow
With an arrow on the string, and he glared around him
As if he were always about to shoot. His belt,
A baldric of gold crossing his chest,   640
Was stark horror, a phantasmagoria
Of Bears, and wild Boars, and green-eyed Lions,
Of Battles, and Bloodshed, Murder and Mayhem.
May this be its maker's only masterpiece,
And may there never again be another like it.   645
Heracles recognized me at once,
And his words beat down on me like dark wings:

'Son of Laertes in the line of Zeus,
Crafty Odysseus—poor man, do you too
Drag out a wretched destiny   650
Such as I once bore under the rays of the sun?
I was a son of Zeus and grandson of Cronus,
But I had immeasurable suffering,
Enslaved to a man who was far less than I
And who laid upon me difficult labors.[5]   655
Once he even sent me here, to fetch
The Hound of Hell,[6] for he could devise
No harder task for me than this. That hound
I carried out of the house of Hades,
With Hermes and grey-eyed Athena as guides.'   660

And Heracles went back into the house of Hades.
But I stayed where I was, in case any more
Of the heroes of yesteryear might yet come forth.
And I would have seen some of them—
Heroes I longed to meet, Theseus and Peirithous,[7]   665
Glorious sons of the gods—but before I could,
The nations of the dead came thronging up
With an eerie cry, and I turned pale with fear
That Persephone would send from Hades' depths
The pale head of that monster, the Gorgon.[8]   670

---

4. Hebe means "youth."
5. Eurystheus, at the behest of the goddess Hera, laid the labors on Heracles, whom she resented as an illegitimate son of her husband, Zeus.
6. Cerberus, guard dog of the underworld.
7. A son of Poseidon, Theseus was a mythic king of Athens and killer of the Minotaur. Peirithous was his best friend, a son of Zeus; together they went to the underworld, hoping to abduct Persephone.
8. Female monster whose gaze turns onlookers to stone.

I went to the ship at once and called to my men
To get aboard and untie the stern cables.
They boarded quickly and sat at their benches.
The current bore the ship down the River Ocean.
We rowed at first, and then caught a good tailwind." 675

BOOK XII

"Our ship left the River Ocean
And came to the swell of the open sea
And the Island of Aeaea,
Where Dawn has her dancing grounds
And the Sun his risings. We beached our ship 5
On the sand, disembarked, and fell asleep
On the shore, waiting for daybreak.

Light blossomed like roses in the eastern sky,
And I sent some men to the house of Circe
To bring back the body of Elpenor. 10
We cut wood quickly, and on the headland's point
We held a funeral, shedding warm tears.
When the body was burned, and the armor with it,
We heaped up a mound, dragged a stone onto it,
And on the tomb's very top we planted his oar. 15

While we were busy with these things,
Circe, aware that we had come back
From the Underworld, put on her finest clothes
And came to see us. Her serving women
Brought meat, bread, and bright red wine, 20
And the goddess shone with light as she spoke:

'So you went down alive to Hades' house.
Most men die only once, but you twice.
Come, though, eat and drink wine
The whole day through. You sail at dawn. 25
I will tell you everything on your route,
So that you will not come to grief
In some web of evil on land or sea.'

She spoke, and our proud hearts consented.
All day long until the sun went down 30
We sat feasting on meat and good red wine.
When the sun set and darkness came on
My men went to sleep beside the ship's stern-cables.
But Circe took me by the hand and had me sit
Away from my men. And she lay down beside me 35
And asked me about everything. I told her all
Just as it happened, and then the goddess spoke:

'So all that is done. But now listen
To what I will tell you. One day a god

Will remind you of it. First, you will come 40
To the Sirens, who bewitch all men
Who come near. Anyone who approaches
Unaware and hears their voice will never again
Be welcomed home by wife and children
Dancing with joy at his return— 45
Not after the Sirens bewitch him with song.
They loll in a meadow, and around them are piled
The bones of shriveled and moldering bodies.
Row past them, first kneading sweet wax
And smearing it into the ears of your crew 50
So they cannot hear. But if you yourself
Have a mind to listen, have them bind you
Hand and foot upright in the mast-step
And tie the ends of the rope to the mast.
Then you can enjoy the song of the Sirens. 55
If you command your crew and plead with them
To release you, they should tie you up tighter.
After your men have rowed past the Sirens,
I will not prescribe which of two ways to go.
You yourself must decide. I will tell you both. 60

'One route takes you past beetling crags
Pounded by blue-eyed Amphitrítê's seas.
The blessed gods call these the Wandering Rocks.
Not even birds can wing their way through.
Even the doves that bring ambrosia to Zeus 65
Crash and perish on that slick stone,
And the Father has to replenish their numbers.
Ships never get through. Whenever one tries,
The sea is awash with timbers and bodies
Blasted by the waves and the fiery winds. 70
Only one ship has ever passed through,
The famous Argo as she sailed from Aeetes,
And even she would have been hurled onto those crags
Had not Hera loved Jason and sent his ship through.[9]

'On the other route there are two rocks. 75
One stabs its peak into the sky
And is ringed by a dark blue cloud. This cloud
Never melts, and the air is never clear
During summer or autumn. No mortal man
Could ever scale this rock, not even if he had 80
Twenty hands and feet. The stone is as smooth
As if it were polished. Halfway up the cliff
Is a misty cave facing the western gloom.
It is there you will sail your hollow ship

9. The Greek hero Jason went in the world's first ship, the *Argo*, to get the Golden Fleece from Aeetes, king of Colchis; the goddess Hera helped him get home.

If you listen to me, glorious Odysseus.   85
The strongest archer could not shoot an arrow
Up from his ship all the way to the cave,
Which is the lair of Scylla. She barks and yelps
Like a young puppy, but she is a monster,
An evil monster that not even a god   90
Would be glad to see. She has—listen to this—
Twelve gangly legs and six very long necks,
And on each neck is perched a bloodcurdling head,
Each with three rows of close-set teeth
Full of black death. Up to her middle   95
She is concealed in the cave, but her heads dangle
Into the abyss, and she fishes by the rock
For dolphins and seals or other large creatures
That the moaning sea breeds in multitudes.
No crew can boast to have sailed past Scylla   100
Unscathed. With each head she carries off a man,
Snatching him out of his dark-prowed vessel.

'The other rock, as you will see, Odysseus,
Lies lower—the two are close enough
That you could shoot an arrow across—   105
And on this rock is a large, leafy fig tree.
Beneath this tree the divine Charybdis
Sucks down the black water. Three times a day
She belches it out and three times a day
She sucks it down horribly. Don't be there   110
When she sucks it down. No one could save you,
Not even Poseidon, who makes the earth tremble.
No, stay close to Scylla's rock, and push hard.
Better to mourn six than the whole crew at once.'

Thus Circe. And I, in a panic: 115

'I beg you, goddess, tell me, is there
Any way I can escape from Charybdis
And still protect my men from the other?'

And the goddess, in a nimbus of light:

'There you go again, always the hero.   120
Won't you yield even to the immortals?
She's not mortal, she's an immortal evil,
Dread, dire, ferocious, unfightable.
There is no defense. It's flight, not fight.
If you pause so much as to put on a helmet   125
She'll attack again with just as many heads
And kill just as many men as before.

Just row past as hard as you can. And call upon
Crataiïs, the mother who bore her as a plague to men.
She will stop her from attacking a second time.   130

'Then you will come to Thrinacia,
An island that pastures the cattle of the Sun,
Seven herds of cattle and seven flocks of sheep,
Fifty in each. They are immortal.
They bear no young and they never die off,   135
And their shepherds are goddesses,
Nymphs with gorgeous hair, Phaethusa
And Lampetiê, whom gleaming Neaera
Bore to Helios, Hyperion the Sun.[1]
When she had borne them and reared them   140
She sent them to Thrinacia, to live far away
And keep their father's spiral-horned cattle.
If you leave these unharmed and keep your mind
On your journey, you might yet struggle home
To Ithaca. But if you harm them, I foretell   145
Disaster for your ship and crew, and even if you
Escape yourself, you shall come home late
And badly, having lost all your companions.'

Dawn rose in gold as she finished speaking,
And light played about her as she disappeared   150
Up the island.
                I went to the ship
And got my men going. They loosened
The stern cables and were soon in their benches,
Beating the water white with their oars.
A following wind rose in the wake   155
Of our dark-prowed ship, a sailor's breeze
Sent by Circe, that dread, beautiful goddess.
We tied down the tackling and sat tight,
Letting the wind and the helmsman take over.

Then I made a heavy-hearted speech to my men: 160

'Friends, it is not right that one or two alone
Should know what the goddess Circe foretold.
Better we should all know, live or die.
We may still beat death and get out of this alive.
First, she told us to avoid the eerie voices   165
Of the Sirens and sail past their soft meadows.
She ordered me alone to listen. Bind me
Hand and foot upright in the mast-step
And tie the ends of the rope to the mast.
If I command you and plead with you   170
To release me, just tie me up tighter.'

1. Helios and Hyperion are both sun gods, here confused.

Those were my instructions to the crew.

Meanwhile, our good ship was closing fast
On the Sirens' island, when the breeze we'd had
Tailed off, and we were becalmed—not a breath   175

Of wind left—some spirit lulled the waves.
My men got up and furled the sails,
Stowed them in the ship's hold, then sat down
At their oars and whitened the water with pine.
Myself, I got out a wheel of wax, cut it up   180
With my sharp knife, and kneaded the pieces
Until they were soft and warm, a quick job
With Lord Helios glaring down from above.
Then I went down the rows and smeared the wax
Into all my men's ears. They in turn bound me   185
Hand and foot upright to the mast,
Tied the ends of the rope to the mast, and then
Sat down and beat the sea white with their oars.
We were about as far away as a shout would carry,
Surging ahead, when the Sirens saw our ship   190
Looming closer, and their song pierced the air:

'Come hither, Odysseus,
    glory of the Achaeans,
Stop your ship
    so you can hear our voices.
No one has ever sailed
    his black ship past here
Without listening to the honeyed
    sound from our lips.   195
He journeys on delighted
    and knows more than before.
For we know everything
    that the Greeks and Trojans
Suffered in wide Troy
    by the will of the gods.
We know all that happens
    on the teeming earth.'

They made their beautiful voices carry,   200
And my heart yearned to listen. I ordered my men
To untie me, signaling with my brows,
But they just leaned on their oars and rowed on.
Perimedes and Eurylochus jumped up,
Looped more rope around me, and pulled tight.   205
When we had rowed past, and the Sirens' song
Had faded on the waves, only then did my crew
Take the wax from their ears and untie me.

We had no sooner left the island when I saw
The spray from an enormous wave   210
And heard its booming. The oars flew
From my men's frightened hands
And shirred in the waves, stopping the ship
Dead in the water. I went down the rows
And tried to boost the crew's morale: 215

'Come on, men, this isn't the first time
We've run into trouble. This can't be worse
Than when the Cyclops with his brute strength
Had us penned in his cave. We got out
By my courage and fast thinking. One day   220
We'll look back on this. Now let's do as I say,
Every man of you! Stay on your benches
And beat the deep surf with your oars!
Zeus may yet deliver us from death.
Helmsman, here's my command to you,   225
And make sure you remember it, since
You're steering this vessel: Keep the ship
Away from this heavy surf. Hug the cliff,
Or before you know it she'll swerve
To starboard and you'll send us all down.'   230

I spoke, they obeyed. But I didn't mention
Scylla. There was nothing we could do about that,
And I didn't want the crew to freeze up,
Stop rowing, and huddle together in the hold.
Then I forgot Circe's stern warning   235
Not to arm myself no matter what happened.
I strapped on my bronze, grabbed two long spears
And went to the foredeck, where I thought
Scylla would first show herself from the cliff.
But I couldn't see her anywhere, and my eyes   240
Grew weary scanning the misty rock face.

We sailed on up the narrow channel, wailing,
Scylla on one side, Charybdis on the other
Sucking down saltwater. When she belched it up
She seethed and bubbled like a boiling cauldron   245
And the spray would reach the tops of the cliffs.
When she sucked it down you could see her
Churning within, and the rock bellowed
And roared, and you could see the sea floor
Black with sand. My men were pale with fear.   250
While we looked at her, staring death in the eyes,
Scylla seized six of my men from our ship,
The six strongest hands aboard. Turning my eyes
To the deck and my crew, I saw above me

Their hands and feet as they were raised aloft.   255
They cried down to me, calling me by name
That one last time in their agony.
                           You know
How a fisherman on a jutting rock
Casts his bait with his long pole. The horned hook
Sinks into the sea, and when he catches a fish   260
He pulls it writhing and squirming out of the water.
Writhing like that my men were drawn up the cliff.
And Scylla devoured them at her door, as they shrieked
And stretched their hands down to me
In their awful struggle. Of all the things   265
That I have borne while I scoured the seas,
I have seen nothing more pitiable.

When we had fled Charybdis, the rocks,
And Scylla, we came to the perfect island
Of Hyperion the Sun, where his herds ranged   270
And his flocks browsed. While our black ship
Was still out at sea I could hear the bleating
Of the sheep and the lowing of the cattle
As they were being penned, and I remembered
The words of the blind seer, Theban Tiresias,   275
And of Circe, who gave me strict warnings
To shun the island of the warmth-giving Sun.
And so I spoke to my crew with heavy heart:

'Hear my words, men, for all your pain.
So I can tell you Tiresias' prophecies   280
And Circe's, too, who gave me strict warnings
To shun the island of the warmth-giving Sun,
For there she said was our gravest peril.
No, row our black ship clear of this island.'

This broke their spirits, and at once   285
Eurylochus answered me spitefully:

'You're a hard man, Odysseus, stronger
Than other men, and you never wear out,
A real iron-man, who won't allow his crew,
Dead tired from rowing and lack of sleep,   290
To set foot on shore, where we might make
A meal we could enjoy. No, you just order us
To wander on through the swift darkness
Over the misty deep, and be driven away
From the island. It is at night that winds rise   295
That wreck ships. How could we survive
If we were hit by a South Wind or a West,
Which sink ships no matter what the great gods want?
No, let's give in to black night now

And make our supper. We'll stay by the ship,   300
Board her in the morning, and put out to sea.'

Thus Eurylochus, and the others agreed.
I knew then that some god had it in for us,
And my words had wings:

          'Eurylochus,
It's all of you against me alone. All right,   305
But swear me a great oath, every last man:
If we find any cattle or sheep on this island,
No man will kill a single cow or sheep
In his recklessness, but will be content
To eat the food immortal Circe gave us.'   310

They swore they would do just as I said,
And when they had finished the words of the oath,
We moored our ship in a hollow harbor
Near a sweet-water spring. The crew disembarked
And skillfully prepared their supper.   315
When they had their fill of food and drink,
They fell to weeping, remembering how Scylla
Had snatched their shipmates and devoured them.
Sweet sleep came upon them as they wept.
Past midnight, when the stars had wheeled around,   320
Zeus gathered the clouds and roused a great wind
Against us, an ungodly tempest that shrouded
Land and sea and blotted out the night sky.
At the first blush of Dawn we hauled our ship up
And made her fast in a cave where you could see   325
The nymphs' beautiful seats and dancing places.
Then I called my men together and spoke to them:

'Friends, there is food and drink in the ship.
Let's play it safe and keep our hands
Off those cattle, which belong to Helios,   330
A dread god who hears and sees all.'

So I spoke, and their proud hearts consented.

Then for a full month the South Wind blew,
And no other wind but the East and the South.
As long as my men had grain and red wine   335
They didn't touch the cattle—life was still worth living.
But when all the rations from the ship were gone,
They had to roam around in search of game—
Hunting for birds and whatever they could catch
With fishing hooks. Hunger gnawed at their bellies.   340

I went off by myself up the island
To pray to the gods to show me the way.

When I had put some distance between myself
And the crew, and found a spot
Sheltered from the wind, I washed my hands   345
And prayed to the gods, but all they did
Was close my eyelids in sleep.

                    Meanwhile,
Eurylochus was giving bad advice to the crew:

'Listen to me, shipmates, despite your distress.
All forms of death are hateful, but to die   350
Of hunger is the most wretched way to go.
What are we waiting for? Let's drive off
The prime beef in that herd and offer sacrifice
To the gods of broad heaven. If we ever
Return to Ithaca, we will build a rich temple   355
To Hyperion the Sun, and deposit there
Many fine treasures. If he becomes angry
Over his cattle and gets the other gods' consent
To destroy our ship, well, I would rather
Gulp down saltwater and die once and for all   360
Than waste away slowly on a desert island.'

Thus Eurylochus, and the others agreed.
In no time they had driven off the best
Of Helios' cattle, pretty, spiral-horned cows
That were grazing close to our dark-prowed ship.   365
They surrounded these cows and offered prayers
To the gods, plucking off tender leaves
From a high-crowned oak in lieu of white barley,
Of which there was none aboard our benched ship.
They said their prayers, cut the cows' throats,   370
Flayed the animals and carved out the thigh joints,
Wrapped these in a double layer of fat
And laid all the raw bits upon them.
They had no wine to pour over the sacrifice
And so used water as they roasted the entrails.   375
When the thighs were burned and the innards tasted,
They carved up the rest and skewered it on spits.

That's when I awoke, bolting upright.
I started down to the shore, and as I got near the ship
The aroma of sizzling fat drifted up to me.   380
I groaned and cried out to the undying gods:

'Father Zeus, and you other immortals,
You lulled me to sleep—and to my ruin—
While my men committed this monstrous crime!'

Lampetiê rushed in her long robes to Helios   385
And told him that we had killed his cattle.
Furious, the Sun God addressed the immortals:

'Father Zeus, and you other gods eternal,
Punish Odysseus' companions, who have insolently
Killed the cattle I took delight in seeing   390
Whenever I ascended the starry heaven
And whenever I turned back from heaven to earth.
If they don't pay just atonement for the cows
I will sink into Hades and shine on the dead.'

And Zeus, who masses the clouds, said: 395

'Helios, you go on shining among the gods
And for mortal men on the grain-giving earth.
I will soon strike their ship with sterling lightning
And shatter it to bits on the wine-purple sea.'

All this I heard from rich-haired Calypso,   400
Who said she heard it from Hermes the Guide.

When I reached the ship I chewed out my men,
Giving each one an earful. But there was nothing
We could do. The cattle were already dead.
Then the gods showed some portents   405
Directed at my men. The hides crawled,
And the meat, both roasted and raw,
Mooed on the spits, like cattle lowing.

Each day for six days my men slaughtered oxen
From Helios' herd and gorged on the meat.   410
But when Zeus brought the seventh day,
The wind tailed off from gale force.
We boarded ship at once and put out to sea
As soon as we had rigged the mast and sail.
When we left the island behind, there was   415
No other land in sight, only sea and sky.
Then Zeus put a black cloud over our ship
And the sea grew dark beneath it. She ran on
A little while, and then the howling West Wind
Blew in with hurricane force. It snapped   420
Both forestays, and the mast fell backward
Into the bilge with all of its tackle.
On its way down the mast struck the helmsman
And crushed his skull. He fell from the stern
Like a diver, and his proud soul left his bones.   425
In the same instant, Zeus thundered
And struck the ship with a lightning bolt.
She shivered from stem to stern and was filled
With sulfurous smoke. My men went overboard,
Bobbing in the waves like sea crows   430
Around the black ship, their day of return
Snuffed out by the Sun God.
I kept pacing the deck until the sea surge
Tore the sides from the keel. The waves

Drove the bare keel on and snapped the mast   435
From its socket; the leather backstay
Was still attached, and I used this to lash
The keel to the mast. Perched on these timbers
I was swept along by deathly winds.

Then the West Wind died down,   440
And, to my horror, the South Wind rose.
All that way, back to the whirlpool,
I was swept along the whole night through
And at dawn reached Scylla's cliff
And dread Charybdis. She was sucking down   445
Seawater, and I leapt up
To the tall fig tree, grabbed hold of it
And hung on like a bat. I could not
Plant my feet or get myself set on the tree
Because its roots spread far below   450
And its branches were high overhead,
Long, thick limbs that shaded Charybdis.
I just grit my teeth and hung on
Until she spat out the mast and keel again.
It seemed like forever. Finally,   455
About the hour a man who has spent the day
Judging quarrels that young men bring to him
Rises from the marketplace and goes to dinner,
My ship's timbers surfaced again from Charybdis.
I let go with my hands and feet   460
And hit the water hard beyond the spars.
Once aboard, I rowed away with my hands.
As for Scylla, Zeus never let her see me,
Or I would have been wiped out completely.

I floated on for nine days. On the tenth night   465
The gods brought me to Ogygia
And to Calypso, the dread, beautiful goddess,
Who loved me and took care of me.
But I have told that tale only yesterday,
Here in your hall, to yourself and your wife,   470
And I wouldn't bore you by telling it again."

BOOK XIII

Odysseus finished his story,
And they were all spellbound, hushed
To silence throughout the shadowy hall,
Until Alcinous found his voice and said:

"Odysseus, now that you have come to my house,   5
High-roofed and founded on bronze, I do not think

You will be blown off course again
Before reaching home.
                              Hear now my command,
All who drink the glowing wine of Elders
Daily in my halls and hear the harper sing: 10
Clothes for our guest lie in a polished sea-chest,
Along with richly wrought gold and all the other gifts
The Phaeacian lords have brought to the palace.
But now each man of us gives him a cauldron, too.
We will recoup ourselves later with a general tax.   15
It is hard to make such generous gifts alone."

They were all pleased with what Alcinous said.
Each man went to his own house to sleep,
And when Dawn's rosy fingers appeared in the sky
They hurried to the ship with their gifts of bronze.   20
Alcinous, the sacred king himself, went on board
And stowed them away beneath the benches
Where they would not hinder the rowers' efforts.
Then they all went back to feast in the palace.

In their honor Alcinous sacrificed an ox   25
To Zeus, the Dark Cloud, who rules over all.
They roasted the haunches and feasted gloriously
While the godlike harper, honored Demodocus,
Sang in their midst.
                      But Odysseus
Kept turning his head toward the shining sun,   30
Urging it down the sky. He longed to set forth.

A man who has been in the fields all day
With his wooden plow and wine-faced oxen
Longs for supper and welcomes the sunset
That sends him homeward with weary knees.   35

So welcome to Odysseus was the evening sun.
As soon as it set he addressed the Phaeacians,
Alcinous especially, and his words had wings:

"Lord Alcinous, I bid you and your people
To pour libation and send me safely on my way.   40
And I bid you farewell. All is now here
That my heart has desired—passage home
And cherished gifts that the gods in heaven
Have blessed me with. When I reach home
May I find my wife and loved ones unharmed.   45

May you enjoy your wife and children here,
May the gods send you everything good,
And may harm never come to your island people."

They all cheered this speech, and demanded
That the stranger and guest be given passage home.   50
Alcinous then nodded to his herald:

"Pontonous, mix a bowl of wine and serve
Cups to all, that we may pray to Lord Zeus
And send our guest to his own native land."

Thus the King, and Pontonous mixed   55
The mellow-hearted wine and served it to all.
Still seated, they tipped their cups to the gods
Who possess wide heaven. Then Odysseus
Stood up and placed a two-handled cup
In Arete's hands, and his words rose on wings: 60

"Be well, my queen, all of your days, until age
And death come to you, as they come to all.
I am leaving now. But you, Lady—enjoy this house,
Your children, your people, and Lord Alcinous."

And godlike Odysseus stepped over the threshold.   65
Alcinous sent a herald along
To guide him to the shore and the swift ship there,
And Arete sent serving women with him,
One carrying a cloak and laundered shirt,
And another to bring the strong sea-chest.   70
A third brought along bread and red wine.
They came down to the sea, and the ship's crew
Stowed all these things away in the hold,
The food and drink, too. Then they spread out
A rug and a linen sheet on the stern deck   75
For Odysseus to sleep upon undisturbed.
He climbed on board and lay down in silence
While they took their places upon the benches
And untied the cable from the anchor stone.
As soon as they dipped their oars in the sea,   80
A deep sleep fell on his eyelids, a sleep
Sound, and sweet, and very much like death.

And as four yoked stallions spring all together
Beneath the lash, leaping high,
And then eat up the dusty road on the plain,   85

So lifted the keel of that ship, and in her wake
An indigo wave hissed and roiled

As she ran straight ahead. Not even a falcon,
Lord of the skies, could have matched her pace,
So light her course as she cut through the waves,   90
Bearing a man with a mind like the gods',
A man who had suffered deep in his heart,
Enduring men's wars and the bitter sea—
But now he slept, his sorrows forgotten.

      The sea turned silver   95
Under the star that precedes the dawn,
And the great ship pulled up to Ithaca.

Phorcys,[2] the Old Man of the Sea,
Has a harbor there. Two fingers of rock
Curl out from the island, steep to seaward   100
But sloping down to the bay they protect
From hurricane winds and high waves outside.
Inside, ships can ride without anchor
In the still water offshore.
At the harbor's head a slender-leaved olive   105
Stands near a cave glimmering through the mist
And sacred to the nymphs called Naiades.[3]
Inside are bowls and jars of stone
Where bees store honey, and long stone looms
Where the nymphs weave shrouds as dark as the sea.   110
Waters flow there forever, and there are two doors,
One toward the North Wind, by which humans
Go down, the other toward the South Wind,
A door for the gods. No men enter there:
It is the Way of Immortals.

      The Phaeacians   115
Had been here before. In they rowed,
And with such force that their ship was propelled
Half of its length onto the shelving shore.
The crew disembarked, lifting Odysseus
Out of the ship   sheet, carpet, and all   120
And laying him down, sound asleep, on the sand.
Then they hauled from the ship all of the goods
The Phaeacian lords had given him
As he was going home—all thanks to Athena.
They piled these together near the bole of the olive,   125
Away from the path, fearing that someone
Might come along before Odysseus awoke
And rob him blind.

      Then the Phaeacians went home.
But the Earthshaker did not forget the threats
He had leveled against Odysseus,   130
And he asked Zeus what he intended to do:

2. A sea god.   3. Sea nymphs.

"I lose face among the gods, Zeus,
When I'm not respected by mortal men—
The Phaeacians yet, my own flesh and blood!
I swore that Odysseus would have to suffer   135
Before getting home—I didn't say
He would never get home, because you had already
Agreed that he would—and now they've brought him
Over the sea while he napped on their ship,
And set him down in Ithaca, and given him   140
Gifts of bronze and clothing and gold,
More than he ever would have taken out of Troy
Had he come home safely with his share of the loot."

And Zeus, clouds scudding around him:

"What a thing for you to say—you, the Temblor!⁴   145
Dishonored by the gods? It would be hard for us
To sling insults at our eldest and best.
And if some over-confident hero fails
To pay you respect, you can always pay him back.
Do as you please, and as your heart desires."   150

And Poseidon, the Lord of Earthquake:

"I would do just that, Dark Cloud,
But I like to keep an eye on your temper.
I want to smash that beautiful Phaeacian ship
As it sails for home over the misty sea,   155
Smash it, so that they will stop this nonsense
Once and for all, giving men safe passage!
And I'll hem their city in with a mountain."

And Zeus, from out of his nimbus of cloud:

"Well, now, this is what I would do: 160
Wait until all of the people in the city see her
Pulling in to port, and then turn her to stone,
Stone shaped like a ship, a marvel for all men.
And then hem their city in with a mountain."

When he heard this, the Lord of Earthquake   165
Went to Schería, where the Phaeacians live,
And waited. The great seafaring ship
Was closing in fast when Poseidon slapped it
With the flat of his hand and turned it to stone
Rooted in the seafloor. Then the god was gone.   170

4. A "temblor" is an earth tremor.

The Phaeacians, men who understood the sea,
Kept turning to each other, saying things like:

"Who did that?"
                    "Stopped her dead in the water
When she was at top speed, pulling in home."

"She was in plain view, from stem to stern!"

                                    Winged words,   175
But they had no idea what had happened.

Then Alcinous spoke to his people:

"Alas for the prophecy of old that I heard
From my father. He said that Poseidon
Would be angry with us for giving safe passage   180
And that one day he would wreck a beautiful ship
As it sailed for home over the misty sea.
And he would hem our city in with a mountain.
What the old man said is all coming true.
Now hear what I have to say. Let us all agree   185
Never again to provide safe escort
To any man who comes to our city.
And we will sacrifice twelve chosen bulls
To Lord Poseidon, so may he pity us
And not enclose our town with a mountain."   190

Trembling with fear they prepared the bulls,
And soon all the Phaeacian leaders and lords
Were standing around Poseidon's altar
Saying their prayers.

                    Odysseus, meanwhile,
Awoke from sleep in his ancestral land—   195
And did not recognize it. He had been gone so long,
And Pallas Athena had spread haze all around.
The goddess wanted to explain things to him,
And to disguise him, so that his wife and dear ones
Would not know who he was until he had made   200
The arrogant suitors pay for their outrage.
So everything on Ithaca now looked different
To its lord—the winding trails, the harbors,
The towering rocks and the trees. Odysseus
Sprang to his feet and gazed at his homeland.   205
He groaned, smacked his thighs with his hands,
And in a voice choked with tears, said:

"What land have I come to now? Who knows
What kind of people live here—lawless savages,

Or godfearing men who take kindly to strangers?   210
Where am I going to take all these things? Where
Am I going to go myself? I should have stayed
With the Phaeacians until I could go on from there
To some other powerful king who would have
Entertained me and sent me off homeward bound.   215
Now I don't even know where to put this stuff.
I can't leave it here as easy pickings for a thief.
Those Phaeacian lords were not as wise
As they seemed, nor as just, bringing me here
To this strange land. They said they would bring me   220
To Ithaca's shore, but that's not what they've done.
May Zeus pay them back, Zeus, god of suppliants,
Who spots transgressors and punishes them.
Well, I'd better count my goods and go over them.
Those sailors may have made off with some in their ship."   225

And he set about counting the hammered tripods,
The cauldrons, the gold, the finely woven clothes.
Nothing was missing. It was his homeland he missed
As he paced along the whispering surf-line,
Utterly forlorn.
                    And then Athena was beside him   230
In the form of a young man out herding sheep.
She had the delicate features of a prince,
A fine-spun mantle folded over her shoulders,
Sandals on her glistening feet, a spear in her hand.
Odysseus' spirits soared when he saw her,   235
And he turned to her with these words on his lips:

"Friend—you are the first person I've met here—
I wish you well. Now don't turn on me.
Help me keep these things safe, and keep me safe,
I beg you at your knees as if you were a god.   240
And tell me this, so I will know:
What land is this, who are the people here?
Is this an island, or a rocky arm
Of the mainland shore stretching out to sea?"

Athena's eyes glinted with azure light: 245

"Where in the world do you come from, stranger,
That you have to ask what land this is?
It's not exactly nameless! Men from all over
Know this land, sailing in from the sunrise
And from far beyond the evening horizon.   250
It's got rough terrain, not for driving horses,
But it's not at all poor even without wide open spaces.
There's abundant grain here, and wine-grapes,
Good rainfalls, and rich, heavy dews.
Good pasture, too, for goats and for cattle,   255

And all sorts of timber, and year-round springs.
That's why Ithaca is a name heard even in Troy,
Which they say is far from any Greek land."

And Odysseus, who had borne much,
Felt joy at hearing his homeland described   260
By Pallas Athena, Zeus' own daughter.
His words flew out as if on wings—
But he did not speak the truth. He checked that impulse,
And, jockeying for an advantage, made up this story:

"I've heard of Ithaca, of course—even in Crete,   265
Far over the sea, and now I've just come ashore
With my belongings here. I left as much
To my sons back home. I've been on the run
Since killing a man, Orsilochus,
Idomeneus' son, the great sprinter.   270
No one in all Crete could match his speed.
He wanted to rob me of all of the loot
I took out of Troy—stuff I had sweated for
In hand-to-hand combat in the war overseas—
Because I wouldn't serve under his father at Troy   275
But led my own unit instead. I ambushed him
With one of my men, got him with a spear
As he came back from the fields. It was night,
Pitch-black. No one saw us, and I got away
With a clean kill with sharp bronze. Then,   280
I found a ship, Phoenician, and made it
Worth the crew's while to take me to Pylos,
Or Elis maybe, where the Epeans are in power.
Well, the wind pushed us back from those shores—
It wasn't their fault, they didn't want to cheat me—   285
And we were driven here in the middle of the night
And rowed like hell into the harbor. Didn't even
Think of chow, though we sure could have used some,
Just got off the boat and lay down, all of us.
I slept like a baby, dead to the world,   290
And they unloaded my stuff from the ship's hold
And set it down next to me where I lay on the sand.
Then off they went to Sidonia, the big city,
And I was left here, stranded, just aching inside."

Athena smiled at him, her eyes blue as the sea,   295
And her hand brushed his cheek. She was now
A tall, beautiful woman, with an exquisite touch
For handiwork, and her words had wings:

"Only a master thief, a real con artist,
Could match your tricks—even a god   300
Might come up short. You wily bastard,
You cunning, elusive, habitual liar!

Even in your own land you weren't about
To give up the stories and sly deceits
That are so much a part of you. 305
Never mind about that though. Here we are,
The two shrewdest minds in the universe,
You far and away the best man on earth
In plotting strategies, and I famed among gods
For my clever schemes. Not even you 310
Recognized Pallas Athena, Zeus' daughter,
I who stand by you in all your troubles
And who made you dear to all the Phaeacians.
And now I've come here, ready to weave
A plan with you, and to hide the goods 315
The Phaeacians gave you—which was my idea—
And to tell you what you still have to endure
In your own house. And you do have to endure,
And not tell anyone, man or woman,
That you have come home from your wanderings. 320
No, you must suffer in silence, and take a beating."

And Odysseus, his mind teeming:

"It would be hard for the most discerning man alive
To see through all your disguises, Goddess.
I know this, though: you were always kind to me 325
When the army fought at Troy.
But after we plundered Priam's steep city,
And boarded our ships, and a god scattered us,
I didn't see you then, didn't sense your presence
Aboard my ship or feel you there to help me. 330
No, and I suffered in my wanderings
Until the gods released me from my troubles.
It wasn't until I was on Phaeacia
That you comforted me—and led me to the city.
Now I beg you, by your Father—I don't believe 335
I've come to sunlit Ithaca, but to some other land.
I think you're just giving me a hard time,
And trying to put one over on me. Tell me
If I've really come to my own native land."

And Athena, her eyes glinting blue: 340

"Ah, that mind of yours! That's why
I can't leave you when you're down and out:
Because you're so intelligent and self-possessed.
Any other man come home from hard travels
Would rush to his house to see his children and wife. 345
But you don't even want to hear how they are
Until you test your wife, who,
As a matter of fact, just sits in the house,

Weeping away the lonely days and nights.
I never lost faith, though. I always knew in my heart   350
You'd make it home, all your companions lost,
But I couldn't bring myself to fight my uncle,
Poseidon, who had it in for you,
Angry because you blinded his son.[5]
And now, so you will believe, I will show you   355
Ithaca from the ground up: There is the harbor
Of Phorcys, the Old Man of the Sea, and here,
At its head, is the slender-leaved olive tree
Standing near a cave that glimmers in the mist
And is sacred to the nymphs called Naiades.   360
Under that cavern's arched roof you sacrificed
Many a perfect victim to the nymphs.
And there stands Mount Neriton, mantled in forest."

As she spoke, the goddess dispelled the mist.
The ground appeared, and Odysseus,   365
The godlike survivor, felt his mind soar
At the sight of his land. He kissed the good earth,
And with his palms to the sun, Odysseus prayed:

"Nymphs, Naiades, daughters of Zeus![6]
I never thought I would see you again.   370
Take pleasure in my whispered prayers
And we will give you gifts as before,
If Zeus' great daughter Athena
Allows me to live and my son to reach manhood."

And Athena, her eyes glinting blue: 375

"You don't have to worry about that.
Right now, let's stow these things in a nook
Of the enchanted cave, where they'll be safe for you.
Then we can talk about a happy ending."

With that, the goddess entered the shadowy cave   380
And searched out its recesses while Odysseus
Brought everything closer—the gold, the bronze,
The well-made clothes the Phaeacians had given him.
And Zeus' own daughter stored them away
And blocked the entrance to the cave with a stone.   385
Then, sitting at the base of the sacred olive,
The two plotted death for the insolent suitors.
Athena began their discussion this way:

5. Polyphemus the Cyclops.

6. The Naiades were sometimes presented as daughters of Poseidon.

"Son of Laertes in the line of Zeus,[7]
Odysseus, the master tactician—consider how   390
You're going to get your hands on the shameless suitors,
Who for three years now have taken over your house,
Proposing to your wife and giving her gifts.
She pines constantly for your return,
But she strings them along, makes little promises,   395
Sends messages—while her intentions are otherwise."

And Odysseus, his mind teeming:

"Ah, I'd be heading for the same pitiful death
That Agamemnon met in his house
If you hadn't told me all this, Goddess.   400
Weave a plan so I can pay them back!
And stand by me yourself, give me the spirit I had
When we ripped down Troy's shining towers!
With you at my side, your eyes glinting
And your mind fixed on battle—I would take on   405
Three hundred men if your power were with me."

And Athena, eyes reflecting the blue sea-light:

"Oh, I'll be there all right, and I'll keep my eye on you
When we get down to business. And I think
More than one of these suitors destroying your home   410
Will spatter the ground with their blood and brains.
Now let's see about disguising you. First,
I'll shrivel the skin on your gnarly limbs,
And wither that tawny hair. A piece of sail-cloth
Will make a nice, ugly cloak. Then   415
We'll make those beautiful eyes bleary and dim.
You'll look disgusting to all the suitors, as well as to
The wife and child you left behind in your halls.
But you should go first to your swineherd.
He may only tend your pigs, but he's devoted to you,   420
And he loves your son and Penelope.
You'll find him with the swine. They are feeding
By Raven's Rock and Arethusa's spring,
Gorging on acorns and drinking black water,
Which fattens swine up nicely. Stay with him,   425
Sit with him a while and ask him about everything,
While I go to Lacedaemon, land of lovely women,
To summon Telemachus. Your son, Odysseus,
Went to Menelaus' house in Sparta
Hoping for news that you are still alive."   430

And Odysseus, his mind teeming:

7. The word *diogenes*, "in the line of Zeus," is often used vaguely of monarchs, not necessarily implying genealogical descent.

"You knew. Why didn't you tell him?
So he could suffer too, roving barren seas
While my wife's suitors eat him out of house and home?"

Athena answered, her eyes glinting blue: 435

"You needn't worry too much about him.
I accompanied him in person. I wanted him
To make a name for himself by traveling there.
He's not exactly laboring as he takes his ease
In Menelaus' luxurious palace.   440
Sure, these young louts have laid an ambush for him
In a ship out at sea, meaning to kill him
Before he reaches home. But I don't think they will.
These suitors who have been destroying your home
Will be six feet under before that'll ever happen."   445

So saying, Athena touched him with a wand.
She shriveled the flesh on his gnarled limbs,
And withered his tawny hair. She wrinkled the skin
All over his body so he looked like an old man,
And she made his beautiful eyes bleary and dim.   450
Then she turned his clothes into tattered rags,
Dirty and smoke-grimed, and cast about him
A great deerskin cloak with the fur worn off.
And she gave him a staff and a ratty pouch
All full of holes, slung by a twisted cord.   455

Having laid their plans, they went their own ways,
The goddess off to Sparta to fetch Telemachus.

BOOK XIV

Odysseus went up from the harbor
Along a rough path until he reached a high,
Wooded area where Athena had told him
He would find the noble swineherd. This man
Cared for his master's property   5
Better than any other slave Odysseus had.

He found him sitting in front of his house,
Which had a high-fenced yard with a view all around.
It was a fine, spacious yard, built by the herdsman
For his absent master's swine. Neither Penelope   10
Nor old Laertes knew anything of it.
He had built it with huge stones coped with thorns
And wedged on the outside with close-set stakes
Of split, black heart-oak. Inside the yard
He had made twelve sties, one next to the other,   15
As beds for the swine, and in each were penned
Fifty wallowing swine—breeding females.

The boars slept outside, and were far scarcer,
Their numbers depleted by the godlike suitors
Who feasted on them. The swineherd was always   20
Sending the best of all the fatted hogs.
There were three hundred and sixty in all.

                                          Close by,
The dogs slept, four of them, wild as beasts,
Reared by the swineherd, who was a man
Who could have commanded a platoon in war.   25
At the moment, he was fitting sandals to his feet,
Cutting the tanned leather to size.
The other herdsman had gone off with the swine,
One here, one there, one to drive a boar to town
So that the insolent suitors could sacrifice it   30
And satisfy their hunger for meat.

                                     Suddenly,
The baying hounds caught sight of Odysseus
And rushed at him barking and snarling.
Odysseus, remembering his tricks, sat down
And let the staff fall from his hand. Even so,   35
He would have been mauled on his own farmstead,
But the swineherd was hot on the dogs' heels,
Dropping the leather as he ran through the gate
And calling aloud to the dogs. He scattered them
With a shower of stones, and then addressed   40
The man who was his master, saying:

"Another moment, old man, and the dogs
Would have ripped you open, and it's me
You would have blamed for it, as if the gods
Haven't given me enough grief already.   45
It's for my master, a man like a god, I grieve
As I stay out here raising fat hogs
For other men to eat, while he wanders hungry
In some foreign land, if he's still alive, that is,
And still sees the sunlight. But come with me.   50
Let's go to my hut, old man, so that you,
When you have had your fill of food and wine,
Can tell me your story—where you are from,
And all the suffering you have endured."

So the godlike swineherd led him into his hut.   55
Once inside, he had him sit down on a pile
Of thick brushwood over which he spread
The skin of a shaggy wild goat, a large, thick hide
On which he usually slept. Odysseus was glad
That he welcomed him like this, and said so: 60

"May Zeus and all the gods bless you, stranger,
For welcoming me with such an open heart."

And you answered him, Eumaeus, my swineherd:

"It would not be right for me to show less respect
Even to someone less worthy than you.   65
All strangers and beggars come from Zeus,
And our gifts to them are welcome though small,
Since this is how it is with slaves, always fearful
Of the masters over them, especially
Young masters. Yes, and the gods have blocked   70
The return of the master who would have treated me
With kindness, given me possessions of my own,
A house, some land, and a wife courted by many,
The things a kind master gives to his servant
Whose long, hard work a god has made prosper,   75
As the work I have done has come to prosper.
My master would have rewarded me richly for this,
Had he grown old here. But he's gone, perished—
As I wish Helen and all her clan had perished,
Since she has unstrung the knees of many heroes.   80
Yes, he too went to Ilion, land of fine horses,
To fight the Trojans on Agamemnon's account."

So saying, he tucked his tunic up in his belt
And went to the sties where the swine were penned.
He picked out two and slaughtered them both,   85
Singed them, butchered them, and put them on spits.
When he had roasted everything, he brought it out
Hot on the spits and served it to Odysseus,
Sprinkling the pork with white barley meal.
Then he mixed sweet wine in an ivy-wood bowl,   90
Sat down across from Odysseus, and said:

"Eat now, stranger, such food as slaves eat,
Young porkers. The fatted hogs the suitors eat,
Men who have no fear of the gods, and feel no pity.
The blessed ones do not love wickedness   95
But honor justice and repay righteousness!
Even men who wage war in a foreign land
And sail for home with their ships filled with loot—
Even men like that fear the wrath of the gods.
But these men here must know something,   100
Must have heard from a god that my master is dead,
Since they are so unwilling to conduct their courtship
In a way that is just, or to return to their homes.
They just lounge about squandering our goods,
Sparing nothing in their insolence.   105
Every day and night they slaughter our animals

Not just one or two, either—and waste our wine.
At least my master's holdings are huge. No hero,
Either on the dark mainland or Ithaca itself,
Has nearly as much. Twenty men together   110
Could not match his wealth. Let me count it for you.
Twelve herds of cattle over on the mainland,
And as many flocks of sheep, droves of swine,
And spreading herds of goats—all of them pastured
By his own herdsmen or hired foreigners.   115
And more herds of goats, eleven in all,
Range our island's coasts. Good men watch them,
And every day each of these men drives up
The best fatted goat in all of his flock
For the suitors to eat. Myself, I keep these swine,   120
And always pick out the best to send to them."

As he spoke, Odysseus was silently
Eating his pork and drinking wine—
And chewing on how to punish the suitors.
When he had satisfied his appetite for food,   125
The swineherd filled for him the drinking bowl
He ordinarily used himself and gave it to him
Brimming with wine. Odysseus gladly took it,
And his words flew on wings to the swineherd:

"Well, who was it, my friend, who bought you?   130
Who is this rich and powerful man?
You said he died fighting on Agamemnon's account.
Tell me his name. I might recognize it.
Zeus only knows who I might have met
And have some news of. I've wandered far."   135

And the swineherd, a leader of men:

"Old man, no wanderer who came with news of him
Could ever convince his wife and son. Besides,
All a needy vagabond ever does is tell lies.
He has no interest at all in telling the truth.   140
Whenever a wanderer comes to Ithaca,
He goes to my mistress with a cock and bull story.
She receives him kindly and questions him closely,
And tears fall from her eyes and she weeps and cries
The way a woman will whose husband dies abroad.   145
And you'd make up a story, too, old man,
In an instant, if you thought you could get
A cloak and tunic out of it.
                         But by now,
Dogs and birds have torn the flesh from his bones,
And his soul has crawled off. Or deep in the sea   150
Fish have picked his bones clean, and they now lie
On a shore somewhere, wrapped in deep sand.
No, he's dead and gone, and there is nothing left

For his dear ones but grief, and for me especially,
For never again will I find a master so mild,   155
However far I go, even if I go home again
To my mother and father, where I was born
And where they reared me. Yet,
As much as I miss them and miss my homeland,
I miss Odysseus more. There, I said his name.   160
I would rather not say his name when he is not here,
For he loved me greatly and cared for me. Instead,
I call him my brother, though he is not here."

Odysseus, who had borne much, replied:

"Well, my friend, since you refuse to believe,   165
And since you insist he will never come home,
I'll not just say it, but will solemnly swear
That Odysseus will come back. As for a reward
For bringing this news, give it to me
When he does return—a tunic and cloak—   170
And not a moment before. Until that man
Is actually here, I will accept nothing,
However great my need. I hate like hell
A man who caves in to his poverty
And tells a batch of lies.
                          I swear by Zeus,   175
Above all gods, and by this hospitable table,
And the hearth of flawless Odysseus himself—
That everything will happen just as I say:
Before this month is out Odysseus will come,
In the dark of the moon, before the new crescent.   180
He shall return, and take vengeance upon
All those who dishonor his wife and his son."

And you answered him, Eumaeus, my swineherd:

"I'll never be paying you any reward,
Nor will Odysseus ever come home.   185
Now let's just drink quietly and think about
Other things. Don't remind me of all this.
I feel such pain and grief in my heart
Whenever anyone mentions my master.
We'll just let your oath be. May Odysseus   190
Come back, as I desire, and as Penelope does,
And the old man Laertes, and godlike Telemachus,
Odysseus' son. And now he weighs on my mind,
Telemachus. The gods made him grow
Like a sapling, and I thought he would be a match   195
For his father, a splendid man to look at.
Then one of the immortals, or maybe a man,
Knocked the sense out of him, and he left
For sacred Pylos, trying to track down his father.

And now the suitors are ambushing him   200
As he sails for home, so that the line
Of godlike Arceisius may come to an end
On Ithaca, and leave no name behind.
But there's nothing we can do, whether he's caught
Or escapes with a helping hand from Zeus.   205
But tell me, old man, about your own troubles,
And tell me this, so that I can be sure of it.
Who are you, and where do you come from?
Where is your city, and where are your parents?
On what kind of ship did you come, and how   210
Did sailors bring you to Ithaca? Who were they?
I don't suppose you walked all the way here."

And Odysseus, his mind teeming:

"I will tell you all of this, down to the last detail.
If you and I could only have food and sweet wine   215
For the duration, feasting on and on quietly
Here in your hut, leaving the work to others—
It would easily take me a full year, and even then
I would not finish my heart's tale of sorrows,
All that I have endured by the will of the gods.   220
        I was born in Crete, son of a wealthy man
Who had many other sons born to his lawful wife.
My own mother was a concubine,
But my father, Castor, son of Hylax,
Treated me like one of his true-born sons.   225
He was honored as a god by the Cretans
For his wealth, prosperity, and glorious sons.
But death carried him away to Hades,
And his sons parceled out his estate
Among themselves, leaving me just a small share,   230
And a house to live in. But I was able to marry
A wife from a propertied family
Because of my real worth. I was no weakling,
And I held my own in battle. All that's gone now,
But I think you can judge the grain from the stubble.   235
I'm overwhelmed now with aches and pains,
But back then Athena and Ares
Gave me the power to crush men in war.
When I set an ambush, lying in wait
With hand-picked men to give the enemy hell,   240
I never got nervous, never saw death looming.
I was the first to jump out and kill whoever
Gave way before me and started to run.
I was good in war. But fieldwork
Was not to my taste, nor caring for a household   245
Where children are reared. Oared ships are what I liked,
And war, polished spears, and arrows,
All the grim things that make most people shudder.

I suppose I liked what a god put in my heart—
One man's meat is another man's poison. 250
Before the Greeks ever set foot in Troy,
I had already led nine expeditions,
Amphibious assaults against foreign cities.
I made a lot in those wars. I would cull
The loot I liked best and get even more 255
When the rest was divided later by lot.
So my house grew rich, and I became
One of the most feared and respected men in Crete.
　　　But when thundering Zeus opened the war
That unstrung the knees of many heroes, 260
I was urged to go with glorious Idomeneus
And lead our ships to Troy. I could not refuse.
The people's voice had to be heard. Nine years
We Greeks waged war, and in the tenth
We sacked Priam's city and sailed for home 265
In our ships, and a god scattered the fleet.
But Zeus had more trouble in store for me.
I stayed home for only a month, enjoying
My children, my wife, and all my possessions.
Then I felt an urge to voyage to Egypt 270
With my godlike companions. I fitted out
Nine ships with care. It didn't take long
For my men to gather, and when they had,
I feasted them for six days, giving them
All the animals they needed for sacrifice— 275
Enough for the gods and for their own banquets.
On the seventh day we set sail from Crete
Under a fresh North Wind and ran on as easily
As if we were in a current. My ships sailed
Without any mishap, free of disease, 280
Guided by the wind and the pilot's hand.
　　　On the fifth day I moored my ships
In the river Nile, and you can be sure I ordered
My trusty mates to stand by and guard them
While I sent out scouts to look around. 285
But the crews got restless and cocky
And started pillaging the Egyptian countryside,
Carrying off the women and children
And killing the men. The cry came to the city,
And at daybreak troops answered the call. 290
The whole plain was filled with infantry,
War chariots, and the glint of bronze.
Thundering Zeus threw my men into a panic,
And not one had the courage to stand and fight
Against odds like that. It was bad. 295
They killed many of us outright with bronze
And led the rest to their city to work as slaves.
But Zeus put an idea into my mind.
I'm sorry I took it. It would have been better

If I had died in Egypt, met my fate there—   300
So much more suffering was waiting for me.
I took off my helmet, dropped my shield,
Let the spear fall from my hands, and walked straight
To the king's chariot. I clasped his knees
And kissed them. It worked. He pitied me,   305
Took me in his chariot, and drove me weeping
To his own home, warding off all the spears
That were aimed at me by the angry mob,
For he respected Zeus, god of strangers,
Indignant and wrathful above all other gods.   310
        Seven years I stayed there, amassing wealth,
For all the Egyptians gave me gifts.
When the eighth year rolled around, there came
A man from Phoenicia, avaracious and sly,
And a general scoundrel. He persuaded me   315
To go off with him to his house in Phoenicia,
And I stayed with him there for one full year,
After which he took me in a seafaring ship
Bound for Libya, pretending we were taking
A cargo there, when his real intent   320
Was to sell me there for an enormous price.
I suspected treachery but had to go aboard.
The ship ran on under a fresh North Wind,
Staying above Crete in a mid-sea course.
Then Zeus devised the crew's utter destruction.   325
        When we left Crete behind, there was
No other land in sight, only sea and sky.
Then Zeus put a black cloud over our ship.
The sea grew dark beneath it, and Zeus thundered
And struck the ship with a lightning bolt.   330
She shivered from stem to stern and was filled
With sulfurous smoke. The men went overboard,
Bobbing in the waves like sea crows
Around the black ship, their day of return
Snuffed out by the god. As for me,   335
Zeus himself, in the midst of my distress,
Put into my hands the surging mast
Of the dark-prowed ship. That saved my life.
I clung to the mast as the terrible winds
Bore me along. I was out there nine days,   340
And on the tenth black night a great wave
Rolled me ashore in the Thesprotians' land.
The Thesprotian king, the hero Pheidon,
Took me in. There was no talk of ransom,
For his son had found me, overcome   345
With cold and fatigue, and raised me up
By the hand, and led me to his father's palace,
Where he gave me a tunic and cloak to wear.
        It was there I learned of Odysseus.
The king said he had been his guest there   350

On his way back to his native land. He showed me
All the treasure Odysseus had amassed,
Bronze, gold, and wrought iron, enough to feed
His children's children for ten generations,
All stored there for him in the halls of the king.   355
Odysseus, he said, had gone to Dodona
To consult the oak-tree oracle of Zeus[8]
And ask how he should return to Ithaca—
Openly or in secret—after being gone so long.
And he swore to me, as he poured libations   360
There in his house, that a ship was launched,
And a crew standing by, to take him home.
But he sent me off first, since a Thesprotian ship
Happened to be leaving for Dulichium,
Where I wanted to go. He told that crew   365
To escort me to King Acastus there.
Somehow the crew turned against me,
And I was destined for even more pain.
When the ship left land, it wasn't long before
They hatched a plot to sell me as a slave.   370
They stripped off my clothes, the tunic and cloak,
And made me wear the rags you see on me now.
At evening they reached the coast of Ithaca.
They tied me up in the ship and went ashore
And got busy with their supper there on the beach.   375
The gods themselves must have untied my bonds,
They came off so easily, and wrapping my head
In the rags I wore, I slid down the smooth plank
Into the sea. I started to swim a breast stroke
And was soon out of the water and away from them.   380
I went upland a ways and found a leafy thicket
And huddled up in it. They looked all over,
Moaning and groaning, but couldn't see any profit
In continuing their search, and so they went back aboard
Their hollow ship. The gods kept me under cover—   385
Easy for them—and guided me to the farmstead
Of a wise man. It seems I'm still destined to live."

And you answered him, Eumaeus, my swineherd:

"You poor, wandering wretch. You've wrung my heart
With all the particulars of your suffering.   390
But the part of your story about Odysseus
Just isn't right, and I'm not buying it.
Why should a man in such a fix as you are
Want to lie like that? I know all about
The return of my master—how the gods spited him   395
In not letting him die among the Trojans

8. Oracle in Epirus, in northwestern Greece. Here, priests and priestesses interpreted the rustling
of leaves, to determine the will of the gods.

Or in his friends' arms after he had wound up the war.
The entire Greek army would have buried him then,
And great honor would have passed on to his son.
As it is, the whirlwinds have snatched him away.   400
Myself, I live out here with the swine. I never go
Into the city, unless Penelope asks me to
When news comes to her from somewhere.
Then everyone sits around the visitor
And questions him, both those who miss   405
Their absent lord, and those who enjoy
Devouring his goods without recompense.
But I don't ask anything, not since the time
An Aetolian fooled me with his phony story.
He had killed a man and was wandering the earth.   410
He came to my house, and I welcomed him.
He said he had seen Odysseus in Crete
At Idomeneus' house, repairing some of his ships
That storms had battered. And he said he would be back
By summer or harvest, bringing with him   415
Piles of treasure and his godlike companions.
And now, you woeful old man, since some god
Has steered you my way, don't you try
To charm me or win me over with lies.
It's not for that I'll show you respect or kindness,   420
But for fear of Zeus, and out of pity for you."

And Odysseus, his mind teeming:

"You have a heart that just won't believe.
Not even my oath was enough to convince you.
Let's make a bet, with the gods on Olympus   425
As witnesses. If your master comes back,
You give me a cloak and tunic to wear
And get me to Dulichium, where I want to be.
But if he doesn't come back as I say he will,
Have your slaves jump me and throw me off a cliff,   430
So that the next beggar will think twice before lying."

And the noble, godlike swineherd answered:

"And that would earn me a fine reputation,
Now and forever, wouldn't it, stranger?
First I welcome you into my hut, and then   435
I take you outside and end your sweet life.
And afterwards I'll pray to Zeus, son of Cronus,
With a clear conscience!
                              It's time for supper.
I hope my men come back soon
So we can make a tasty meal here in the hut."   440

As they were speaking, the herders came up
Driving the swine. They put the sows in the sties

Where they always slept, and an amazing racket
Rose from the animals as they were being penned.
The swineherd called to the workers and said: 445

"Bring the best boar we have so I can slaughter him
For the stranger here, and for us, too.
We have worked long and hard with these tuskers
While others eat up our labor free of charge."

With that, he started to split wood with an axe   450
While they brought in a five-year-old fatted boar
And set him down by the hearth. The swineherd
Did not forget the immortals—he had a good mind for this—
Casting into the fire as a first offering
Bristles from the head of the white-tusked boar   455
And praying that Odysseus would return to his home.
Then he came down hard with a piece of split oak
And the boar's spirit left him. They cut his throat,
Singed him, and then butchered him quickly.
The swineherd cut off, as more first offerings,   460
Bits of raw flesh from each part of the animal,
Then wrapped them in fat, sprinkled them with barley,
And then threw them into the fire. The rest
They cut up and roasted with care on spits.
When it was done, they pulled the roast pork from the spits   465
And piled it on platters. The swineherd carved,
For he had a good sense of fairness,
And he divided the meat into seven portions.
He set aside one for the Nymphs and for Hermes,
Saying a prayer, and served the rest to the men,   470
Honoring Odysseus with the long chine
Of the white-tusked boar, and so pleasing his master.
And Odysseus, always thinking, said:

"Eumaeus, may you be as dear to Father Zeus
As you are to me, for so honoring a man like me."   475

And you answered him, Eumaeus, my swineherd:

"Eat, my strange guest, and enjoy what we have.
God gives us one thing and holds another back,
Just as he pleases, for he can do all things."

He spoke, and sacrificed the first offerings   480
To the eternal gods, and poured libations
Of sparkling wine. Then he handed the cup
To Odysseus, sacker of cities, and took his seat.
The bread was served by Mesaulius,
Whom the swineherd had bought all on his own   485
While his master was gone, without the help of his mistress
Or of old Laertes, buying him
From the Taphians with his own resources.

They reached for the good cheer spread before them,
And when they had enough of food and drink,   490
Mesaulius took away the leftovers, and they all
Longed for rest, their stomachs full of bread and meat.

The evening sky was foreboding and moonless,
And a damp West Wind was starting to blow.
It began to rain, and it would rain all night.   495
Odysseus spoke, testing the swineherd,
Seeing if he would take off his own cloak
And give it to him, or tell one of his men
To do so, since he cared for him deeply:

"Hear me now, Eumaeus, and the rest of you men,   500
While I boast a little. It must be the wine
Befuddling me, which gets even sensible men
Singing and laughing and up to dance,
And sometimes to say things better left unsaid.
But I've cut loose now and won't hide anything.   505
Oh, to be young again and with the strength I had
When we went out on ambush under Troy's wall.
Our leaders were Odysseus and Menelaus,
And I was third in command, at their request.
When we had come up close to the steep city wall,   510
We took our places on the perimeter
Down in the brush and reeds of the swampland,
Lying there crouched beneath our shields.
The North Wind swooped down, and night came on
Foul and bitter cold. Snow drifted down   515
And covered us like frost, and ice rimmed our shields.
Everyone else had on cloaks and tunics
And slept peacefully, their shields on their shoulders.
But I had stupidly left my cloak behind at camp,
Because I didn't think it would be cold that night,   520
And had come out with only my shield and belt.
During the third watch, when the stars had turned
In their wheeling course, I nudged Odysseus,
Who was lying next to me, and he heard me say,
'Son of Laertes in the line of Zeus,   525
Wily Odysseus—listen, I'm about dead over here;
This cold is killing me. I don't have a cloak.
Some god talked me into coming out here
With only a tunic, and now there's no going back.'
He put his mind to work and came up with a plan.   530
That's how he was; he could think up things
As well as he could fight. He whispered to me,
'Be quiet now, or one of our men will hear you.'
Then he propped his head up on an elbow and said,
'Listen, men. I had a dream from the gods.   535
We've come too far from the ships. We need someone
To request Agamemnon, commander-in-chief,

To send out more troops from our beach-head camp.'
He had no sooner spoken than Thoas
Was on his feet. He flung aside his purple cloak   540
And sprinted off to the ships, and wrapped in that cloak
I lay down gladly until Dawn shone with gold.
Oh, to be young again and still have my strength!
Then one of the swineherds would give me a cloak,
Both out of kindness and out of respect for a man.   545
But now they scorn me because I am dressed in rags."

And you answered him, Eumaeus, my swineherd:

"There's nothing wrong with your story, old man,
And nothing you've said is out of line
Or unprofitable. So you won't go without.   550
You'll have clothing, yes, and everything else
A suppliant in need ought to receive—
At least for tonight. But in the morning
You'll have to shake out those old rags of yours.
We don't have extra tunics or cloaks   555
Around here. Each man has only one.
But when Odysseus' son comes, he himself
Will give you a cloak and tunic to wear,
And will send you wherever your heart desires."

So saying, the swineherd sprang to his feet   560
And started to make up a bed for Odysseus
Near the fire, spreading it with goatskins and fleeces.
There Odysseus lay down, and Eumaeus
Threw over him a large, heavy cloak
That he kept as a spare for stormy weather.   565

So there Odysseus slept, with the young men
All around him. But not the swineherd.
He would not settle for a bed inside,
Away from the boars. He got himself ready
To go sleep outdoors, and Odysseus was glad   570
That he took such good care of the property
Of his absent master. First, Eumaeus
Slung his sharp sword over his sturdy shoulders
And put on a thick cloak to keep out the wind.
Then picking up the fleece of a large, fatted goat,   575
And grabbing a javelin to ward off dogs and men,
He went out to sleep with the white-tusked boars
Under a hollow rock, out of the cold North Wind.

BOOK XV

Pallas Athena now went to wide Lacedaemon
To tell Odysseus' son it was time to return.
She found Telemachus and Nestor's noble son

On the porch of Menelaus' palace.
Nestor's son was sleeping, but Telemachus   5
Had been lying awake all through the night
Thinking about his father. Athena,
Her eyes flashing in the dark, said to him:

"Telemachus, you've been away too long.
Think of the wealth you left behind at home   10
And all those insolent men ready to devour it.
Your journey will have been for nothing.
Hurry, now, and rouse Menelaus
To send you on your way, so you can find
Your blameless mother still at home.   15
Her father and brothers are pressuring her
To marry Eurymachus, because of all the suitors
He gives the best presents, and now has
Stepped up his wooing. You have to watch out
She doesn't carry off all your treasure.   20
You know what a woman's heart is like.
She wants to enrich the house of the one who weds her,
Never mind about her former children
And the husband she once loved. Once he's dead,
She doesn't give any of them a thought.   25
No, you go, and put all your possessions
In the keeping of the best maidservant in the house,
Until the gods show you your honored bride.
And one more thing for you to keep in mind.
The suitors' ringleaders have set up an ambush   30
In the strait between Ithaca and rocky Samos.
They mean to kill you before you make it home.
I don't think they will. Those mooching suitors
Will be in their graves before they can get at you.
But keep your ship out away from the islands,   35
And sail by night as well. One of the gods
Who watches over you will put a wind at your back.
When you make landfall on Ithaca,
Send your crew with the ship on to the city,
But you go first to the swineherd's hut;   40
He has a soft spot in his heart for you.
Spend the night there and tell him to go
Into the city and bring word to Penelope
That you are safe and have come back from Pylos."

And with that she was off to high Olympus.   45

Telemachus awoke and woke up Peisistratus
With a nudge of his heel, saying to him:

"Wake up, Peisistratus. Get your horses
And yoke them up so we can get on the road."

Nestor's son Peisistraus answered: 50

"Telemachus, there's no way we can drive
In the dark, no matter how eager we are
To get on the road. Besides, it'll be light soon,
And we should wait until Menelaus comes out
And sets gifts on the chariot and sends us off   55
With a farewell speech. A guest remembers
A host's hospitality for as long as he lives."

He spoke, and Dawn rose up splashed with gold.
Menelaus, who had just gotten out of bed
With Helen, was coming toward them,   60
And when Telemachus saw him
The young hero quickly threw on his silky tunic,
Flung a cloak on his shoulders, and went out,
The true son of godlike Odysseus.
When he reached Menelaus he said to him: 65

"Menelaus, son of Atreus in the line of Zeus,
Send me back home to my own native land,
For my heart is now eager to return to my home."

And Menelaus, famed for his war cry:

"Telemachus, far be it from me to detain you here   70
When you yearn to go home. I no more approve
Of a host who is too welcoming than of one
Who is too cold. Due measure in all things.
It is just as wrong to rush a guest's departure
When he doesn't want to go, as it is   75
To hold him back when he is ready to leave.
Make a guest welcome for as long as he stays
And send him off whenever he wants to go.
But do stay until I can bring some gifts out
And load them onto your chariot, fine gifts,   80
As you will see. And I will order the women
To prepare you a meal from our well-stocked larder.
It's a double honor, and sensible, too,
For the traveler to eat before setting forth
Over the boundless earth. And if you wish to go   85
All through Hellas and into the heart of Argos,
I myself will go with you. I'll yoke up horses
And give you a tour of the cities of men,
And no one will send us away empty-handed.
Everyone will give us at least one thing,   90
A fine bronze tripod or perhaps a cauldron,
A team of mules or a golden cup."

And Telemachus, in his cool-headed way:

"Menelaus, son of Atreus in the line of Zeus,
I would rather go straight home. I did not leave   95
Anyone behind to watch my possessions.
I'm afraid that in my search for my godlike father

I may perish myself, or that some precious thing
May be lost from my house while I am away."

When he heard this, Menelaus at once   100
Ordered his wife and her serving women
To prepare a meal from their well-stocked larder.
Then Eteoneus, just risen from bed,
Came up—his house was nearby—and Menelaus
Had him kindle a fire and roast some of the meat.   105
While he was doing this, Menelaus himself
Went down to his scented treasure chamber
Accompanied by Helen and Megapenthes.
When they came to where the treasure was stored
The son of Atreus took a two-handled cup   110
And had his son Megapenthes bring a mixing bowl
Of solid silver. But Helen went to the chests
That held her robes, the richly embroidered robes
She herself had made. And this beautiful woman,
Helen of Argos, lifted out the robe   115
That had the finest embroideries, an ample robe
That shone like starlight beneath all the rest.
Then they went back through the house and came
To Telemachus, to whom Menelaus said:

"Telemachus, may Zeus, Hera's thundering lord,   120
Bring you to your home, just as you desire.
Of all the gifts that lie stored in my house
I will give you the most beautiful—
And the most valuable—a well-wrought bowl,
Solid silver, with the lip finished in gold,   125
Made by Hephaestus. The hero Phaedimus,
King of the Sidonians, gave it to me
When I stayed at his house on my way home.
Now I want you to take it home with you."

And the son of Atreus placed the double-handled goblet   130
In Telemachus' hands. Then strong Megapenthes
Brought the gleaming silver mixing bowl over
And set it before him. And Helen, lovely in her bones,
Came up with the robe and said to him:

"I, too, give you a gift, dear child, this robe,   135
A memento from the hands of Helen,
For your bride to wear on your wedding day.
Until then let it lie in your mother's keeping.
And my wish for you is that you come with joy
To your native land and your ancestral home."   140

She put the robe in his hands, and he received it
With gratitude. Then Peisistratus put all of the gifts

Into the chariot's trunk and looked at them a while
With wonder in his heart.
                                     Menelaus now
Led them into the house, and the two sat down.   145
A maid poured water from a silver pitcher
Over a golden basin for them to wash their hands
And then set up a polished table nearby.
Another serving woman, grave and dignified,
Set out bread and generous helpings   150
From the other dishes she had. Boethus' son
Carved the meat nearby and divided it up,
And the son of Menelaus poured the wine.
They reached out to all the good cheer before them,
And when they had their fill of food and drink,   155
Telemachus and glorious Nestor's son
Yoked the horses, mounted the inlaid chariot,
And drove through the gate and echoing portico.
And the son of Atreus, red-haired Menelaus,
Went after them, holding in his right hand   160
A golden cup filled with honey-hearted wine
So they could pour libations before setting out.
He stood before the horses, lifted the cup, and said:

"Farewell, young men, and bring my greetings
To Nestor, the old commander. He was to me   165
Kind as a father when we Greeks fought at Troy."

And Telemachus, in his clear-headed way:

"We will tell him all these things, just as you say,
Zeus-born, when we come to his land,
As surely as I wish I would find Odysseus home,   170
So I could tell him how good you have been to me
During my visit with you, and tell him how
I come home myself with many a treasure."

As he spoke, a bird flew by on his right,
An eagle, clutching in his talons a silvery goose,   175
A large, tame fowl from the yard. Men and women
Ran after it shouting. The eagle got closer,
Then veered off to the right in front of the horses.
This lifted everyone's spirits. Nestor's son
Peisistratus was the first one to speak: 180

"Zeus-born Menelaus, what does this mean?
Is it a sign for us two, or for yourself?"

Menelaus, the warlord, was thinking this over,
Looking for the right way to interpret the sign,
When long-robed Helen took the words from his mouth: 185

"I will prophesy as the immortals prompt me
And as I see it myself. Just as this eagle
Came from the mountain, where he was born and bred,
And snatched up the goose bred in the house,
So shall Odysseus, after long, hard travels,   190
Return to his home, and take vengeance.
Or he is already at home and is even now
Sowing the seeds of the suitors' destruction."

And Telemachus, in his spirited way:

"May Hera's thundering lord[9] grant it,   195
And I will pray to you as to a god."

He flicked the lash and the horses took off
Through the city and out to the plain. All day long
They jostled the yoke that held them together.

As the sun set and the world grew dark,   200
They came to Pherae and pulled up at the house
Of Diocles, son of Ortilochus,
Himself a son of the river Alpheus.
There they spent the night, and Diocles
Gave them the hospitality due to guests.   205

When Dawn brushed the pale sky with rose,
They yoked the horses, stepped up into
The inlaid chariot and drove out through the gate
And echoing portico. Peisistratus
Flicked the lash and the horses took off.   210
Soon after they reached the high rock of Pylos,
And Telemachus had a word with Nestor's son:

"I wonder if you could do me a favor,
Peisistratus? You and I go back a long way
Because of our fathers' friendship. Moreover,   215
We're the same age, and this journey together
Will cement our friendship. This is what I want:
Do not drive me farther than my ship.
Drop me off there. I'm afraid the old man
Will keep me in his house against my will.   220
He means well, but I really have to get home."

Nestor's son thought it over, trying to decide
How he could rightfully do Telemachus this favor.
He made up his mind and turned off to the sea
And the ship there. He stowed the beautiful gifts   225
From Menelaus—the clothes and the gold—
In the ship's stern and urged his friend on,
Speaking to him words that had wings:

9. Zeus, husband of Hera, god of thunder.

"Get yourself and your crew aboard quickly,
Before I reach home and tell the old man.   230
If there's one thing I'm sure of it's this:
Once he has you in his house he won't let you go,
And he'll come here to get you himself
If he has to, and he won't go home empty-handed.
No matter what, he's going to be angry."   235

And he drove his horses back to the city
With their beautiful manes flowing in the wind
And quickly reached his father's palace.

Meanwhile, Telemachus was urging on his crew:

"Put all the gear in order on this black ship, men,   240
And let's go aboard and get under way."

They carried out his orders and were soon
All on board and sitting on their benches.

Telemachus was busy with all of this,
And was offering sacrifice to Athena   245
By the ship's stern, when there came up to him
A traveler from a distant land. He was in exile
From Argos, because he had killed a man,
And he was a seer. He traced his descent
From Melampus, who had lived in Pylos   250
In the old days as one of its wealthiest men
But left for other parts, fleeing great Neleus,
That most lordly man, who had seized his wealth
And kept it from him for one full year.
Melampus lay imprisoned in Phylacus' house   255
And suffered terribly because of Neleus' daughter
And the delusion which the goddess Erinys[1]
Had laid upon him. He escaped, however,
And drove off the lowing cattle from Phylace
To Pylos, and got even with godlike Neleus,   260
And brought Neleus' daughter home
To be his brother's wife. He himself then left
For the horse country of Argos, his destiny being
To live there and rule over many Argives.
There he took a wife and built a lofty house   265
And fathered two strong sons. These sons
Were Mantius and Antiphates, and one of them,
Antiphates, sired great-hearted Oicles,
And Oicles was the father of Amphiarus,
Whom Zeus and Apollo showered with love.   270
But he did not reach the threshold of old age,
Dying in Thebes because of a woman's gifts.
Melampus' other son, Mantius,

1. A Fury, divine spirit of vengeance, who could make her victims crazy.

Sired Polypheides and Clytius.
Clytius, because he was so beautiful,   275
Was snatched away by gold-stitched Dawn
To live with the immortals. And Apollo
Made Polypheides a seer, a high-hearted man
And the best of men after Amphiaraus was dead.
Eventually, he quarreled with his father   280
And moved to Hyperesia, and was the prophet there.

It was his son, Theoclymenus by name,
Who now came up to Telemachus
As he was pouring libations by his black ship
And spoke to him these winged words: 285

"Friend, since I find you making sacrifice here,
I implore you by your sacrifice and by your god,
Then by your own life and the lives of your crew—
Tell me truly what I ask and do not hide it.
Who are you, and where are you from?   290
Where is your city, and where do your parents live?"

Telemachus answered in his clear-headed way:

"Well then, stranger, I will tell you exactly.
I was born in Ithaca, and my father is Odysseus—
If he ever existed. But he has met a grim fate.   295
So I have taken my comrades and a black ship
In search of news of my long-absent father."

And godlike Theoclymenus answered:

"I, too, have left my country, because
I killed a man, one of my own clan.   300
He has many brothers and kinsmen left
In bluegrass Argos, powerful men,
And I am on the run to escape a black fate
At their hands. It seems I am doomed to be
A wanderer. Take me on your ship, please,   305
Since I have taken refuge with you now.
Don't let them kill me. I think they are coming."

And Telemachus, in his cool-headed way:

"I won't push you away if you want to come.
Welcome aboard, and share whatever we have."   310

With that he relieved him of his bronze spear
And slid it onto the deck of the ship.
They went aboard. Telemachus sat down
In the stern, Theoclymenus beside him.
The sailors untied the stern cables   315

And Telemachus called out orders to them
To take hold of the tackling. They fell to,
Raising the firwood mast and setting it
Into its socket. They made it fast with forestays
And hauled up the white sail with rawhide ropes.   320
And Athena, her eyes flashing with sea-light,
Gave them a tailwind that ripped through the sky,
Speeding the ship across the bright salt sea.
Krouni and Chalcis, with its beautiful streams,
Passed by quickly, and then the sun went down   325
And the seaways grew dark. The ship surged on
With Zeus' wind behind it, on to Pheae
And past limewhite Elis, where the Epeans rule.
Then Telemachus steered her out again
To the swiftly passing islands, wondering whether   330
He would dodge death or be caught by the suitors.

Meanwhile, Odysseus and the noble swineherd
Were having supper with the others in the hut.
When they had satisfied their appetite
For food and drink, Odysseus spoke among them,   335
Testing Eumaeus to see whether he would
Still take care of him there on the farmstead
Or send him off to the city:

"Listen now, Eumaeus, and you other men, too.
In the morning I'm off to beg in the city,   340
I don't want to eat you out of house and home.
So tell me what I need to know, and give me a guide
Who can lead me there. Once in the city
I can knock about on my own, as I must,
Hoping for a cup of water and a loaf of bread.   345
And I might go up to Odysseus' house
And bring some news to Penelope.
I might make the rounds of the insolent suitors
And see if they will give me some dinner
From all the good food they have. I might even   350
Start waiting on them, doing whatever they need.
I'll tell you something now. Thanks to Hermes,
The Guide, who lends grace and glory
To all that men do, when it comes to serving
No one can touch me, in splitting firewood,   355
Building a fire, roasting meat and carving it,
Or in pouring wine, or in any of the things
Lesser men do when they wait on nobles."

And the swineherd, greatly troubled, responded:

"Where did you get such a notion, stranger?   360
You must want to die, if you really intend
To go in there with that mob of suitors,

Whose arrogance reaches the iron heavens.
Their serving men are not at all like you.
They're young, well dressed in tunics and cloaks,   365
Handsome and sleek. The tables are polished
And piled high with bread, meat, and wine.
Stay here. You're not bothering anyone,
Not me nor any other man who is here.
But when Odysseus' son comes, he himself   370
Will give you a cloak and tunic to wear,
And will send you wherever your heart desires."

And the enduring, godlike Odysseus answered:

"Eumaeus, may you be as dear to father Zeus
As you are to me, for you have given me a rest   375
From wandering the world in grief and pain.
Nothing is harder on a man than homelessness.
But when it comes to feeding his belly, a man will endure
Whatever hardship and sorrows he must.
But now, since you are keeping me here   380
A while, and asking me to wait for Telemachus,
Tell me about noble Odysseus' mother,
And his father, whom he left behind
On the brink of old age when he went to Troy.
Are they still alive and under the sun,   385
Or are they dead now and in Hades' gloom?"

The noble swineherd made this response:

"I will tell you, stranger, since you ask.
Laertes is still alive, but prays constantly
That his life will dwindle away in his halls.   390
He grieves terribly for his missing son
And for his own lady, his wedded wife.
He took her death hard, and it delivered him
To an unripe old age. She herself died
Of grief for her son, a miserable death   395
That I would wish on no one dear to me.
For as long as she lived, hard as it was for her,
I always enjoyed seeing how she was,
Asking about her health, for she herself
Had brought me up with long-robed Ctimene,   400
Her youngest child. I was brought up with her,
Almost as if I were one of the family.
When we reached that lovely time of our youth,
They sent her to Samê, sent her off to be married,
And got themselves countless gifts in exchange.   405
As for me, my lady clothed me in a cloak and tunic,
Very fine ones, and gave me sandals for my feet,
And sent me off to the fields. But in her heart
She loved me more than that. I do without now,

But the blessed gods make my work prosper.   410
I stay busy with it, and it gives me enough
To eat and drink and give some to beggars.
From my mistress now I get nothing pleasant,
Word or deed. Trouble has come to the house—
These overbearing men. But servants still need   415
To speak to their mistress face to face,
Hear all the gossip, eat and drink,
And afterward take something back to the fields,
The sort of thing that warms a servant's heart."

Odysseus, his mind teeming, responded: 420

"You must have been awfully young, Eumaeus,
When you were forced to travel so far away
From your parents and home. How did it happen?
Did your parents live in a broad-wayed city
That was ransacked in war? Or were you alone   425
Out in the fields with your cattle and sheep
When raiders grabbed you and took you in their ship
And sold you for a good price to your master here?"

Then the swineherd Eumaeus told his story:

"Well, stranger, since you're curious about this,   430
Sit back and relax and drink your wine.
These nights are ungodly long. There's time to sleep
And to enjoy stories both. You shouldn't lie down
Too early. Too much sleep can leave a man tired.
If any of the rest of you would like,   435
You can go sleep outside. Just eat something
At daybreak and go out with our master's swine.
We two are going to stay here in the hut,
Eating and drinking and swapping stories
About each others' hard times. Past sorrows   440
Can comfort a man, especially one
Who has suffered much and wandered far.
But on to what you asked me about.
          There is an island called Syria—
You may have heard of it—above Ortygia   445
And off toward the setting of the summer sun.
It doesn't have many people, but it's good land,
Rich in flocks and herds, full of grapes and wheat.
There's never any famine, and no disease.
When folks grow old, Apollo and Artemis   450
Come to town with their silver bows
And shoot them dead with their gentle arrows.
There are two cities that take up the island,
And my father Ctesius, son of Ormenus,
Ruled over both, a man like a god.   455
          One day some Phoenician traders arrived,

Greedy men, with a shipload of baubles.
In my father's house was a Phoenician woman,
Tall and beautiful and skilled at crafts.
One of the craggy Phoenicians seduced her   460
As she was washing her clothes, lying with her
In their hollow ship—the sort of thing
That will gull the mind of any woman.
Afterward, he asked her who she was
And where she came from. She promptly pointed   465
To the high roof of my father's house:

'I am proud to say I am from bronze-rich Sidon
And am a daughter of Arybas, a wealthy man.
But Taphian pirates abducted me
As I came from the fields, and brought me here   470
And sold me to the master of that house over there,
Who paid a small fortune for me.'

"The man who had lain with her in secret said:

'Would you like to return with us to your home
And see your high-roofed house, and your parents, too?   475
They are still alive and said to be rich.'

"And the Phoenician woman responded:

'Perhaps, if you sailors will swear an oath
That you will bring me home without harming me.'

"When they had sworn the oath, the woman said: 480

'Be quiet now, and if any of you sees me
In the street or at the well, don't speak to me,
Or someone may tell the old king in the palace
And he might suspect something and lock me up
In painful bonds and sentence you to death.   485
Don't forget this. Just sell all your merchandise,
And as soon as your ship is laden with goods,
Send a messenger to me up in the palace.
I'll bring whatever gold I can lay my hands on.
And there's something else I can put up for my passage.   490
I'm the nurse of one of my master's children,
A clever boy who always tags along with me.
I'll bring him on board. He'll get a good price
In whatever foreign land you sell him off.'

"And with that she went off to the beautiful palace.   495
The Phoenicians stayed in our land for a full year
And filled their ship through all the trade they did.
When their ship was loaded for their voyage home,
They sent a messenger to tip off the woman.

A cunning man came to my father's house 500
With a golden necklace strung with amber.
While the women in the hall, and my noble mother,
Were looking it over and offering a price,
The man nodded to the woman in silence,
Nodded and went back to his hollow ship. 505
She took me by the hand and led me outside,
Stopping on the porch to scoop up three
Of the golden goblets left on the tables
By retainers of my father who had banqueted there
And then gone off to debate in the council. 510
She tucked these goblets into her bosom
And bore them off. I innocently followed.
The sun went down and the streets grew dark.
We hurried on to the glimmering harbor
Where the Phoenician ship was moored. 515
They had us board, and the ship set sail
Over the water with a following wind.
We sailed on for six solid days and nights,
But when Zeus put a seventh day in the sky,
Artemis came with her showering arrows 520
And shot the woman. She fell with a thud
Into the hold, like a tern plunging down.
They threw her overboard for the seals and fish,
And there I was, with a broken heart.
The wind and the waves bore the ship along 525
To Ithaca, where Laertes bought me.
And that was how I first saw this land."

Then Zeus-bred Odysseus said to him:

"Eumaeus, your story, with its tale
Of your painful ordeal, has touched my heart. 530
But in your case Zeus has set some good
Alongside the evil, since after all your suffering
You wound up at the house of a kindly man
Who gives you food and drink and treats you well.
You have a good life. But as for me, I came here 535
While wandering around from city to city."

They spoke to one another in this way
And then lay down to sleep, but not for long,
For Dawn soon rose in the blossoming sky.

Telemachus and his crew were now near to shore 540
And furling the sails in the early light.
They struck the mast quickly and rowed the ship
Up to her mooring. They threw out the anchor-stones,
Made the stern cables fast, and then disembarked
Onto the beach, where they prepared their meal 545
And mixed the glinting wine. After they had eaten,

Telemachus, clear-headed as ever, spoke to them:

"You men row the black ship to the town
While I go visit the fields and the herdsmen.
Around dusk, after I've looked over my lands,   550
I'll come to the city, and tomorrow morning
I'll set before you, as wages for your journey,
An excellent feast of meat and fine wine."

Then godlike Theoclymenus put in:

"And where shall I go, dear child? To whose house,   555
Of all those who are lords in rocky Ithaca?
Or should I go straight to yours and your mother's house?"

And Telemachus, in his clear-headed way:

"Ordinarily I would say go to our house,
For it has everything needed for hospitality.   560
But it wouldn't work out for you right now
Since I'll be away, and my mother won't see you.
She doesn't appear often before the suitors
But weaves at her loom in an upper chamber.
I'll tell you, though, whom you can go to: 565
Eurymachus, son of Polybus, whom now
The Ithacans look to as if he were a god.
He's the best man and is the most eager
To marry my mother and take over
My father's position. Only Olympian Zeus,   570
High in the air, knows if their doom will come
Crashing down on them before any wedding day."

As he spoke a bird flew by on the right,
A hawk, swift herald of Apollo, clutching
A dove in his talons, plucking her as he flew   575
And shedding her feathers down to the ground
Between the ship and Telemachus himself.
Theoclymenus called him aside
And, clasping his hand, said to him:

"Telemachus, that bird did not fly by on our right   580
Without a god sending it. I knew when I saw it
That it was a bird of omen. Your lineage
Is Ithaca's most royal. You will rule forever."

And Telemachus, clear-headed and calm:

"Would that what you say come true, stranger.   585
Then you would have from me such gifts
That whoever met you would call you blessed."

Then he said to Peiraeus, his trusted companion:

"Peiraeus, you have always come through for me,
And you went with me to Pylos. So now,   590
I ask you to show this stranger hospitality
In your house. Take good care of him until I come."

And Peiraeus, a spearman in his own right, said:

"Telemachus, no matter how long you stay out here,
I'll take care of him and give him my hospitality."   595

Then Peiraeus boarded the ship and gave the order
For the crew to board and untie the stern cables.
They were soon at their places. Telemachus, though,
Put on his fine sandals, took his bronze-tipped spear
From the ship's deck, and stood by as the crew   600
Untied the cables and shoved off.
                                    Then Odysseus' son
Stepped out with swift strides until he reached
The farmstead where his countless swine were kept
By a servant whose heart was loyal and true.

BOOK XVI

Meanwhile, in the hut, Odysseus
And the noble swineherd had kindled a fire
And were making breakfast in the early light.
They had already sent the herdsmen out
With the droves of swine.
                            The dogs fawned   5
Around Telemachus and did not bark at him
As he approached. Odysseus noticed
The dogs fawning and heard footsteps.
His words flew fast to Eumaeus:

"Eumaeus, one of your men must be coming,   10
Or at least someone you know. The dogs aren't barking
And are fawning around him. I can hear his footsteps."

His words weren't out when his own son
Stood in the doorway. Up jumped the swineherd
In amazement, and from his hands fell the vessels   15
He was using to mix the wine. He went
To greet his master, kissing his head
And his shining eyes and both his hands.

  And as a loving father embraces his own son
  Come back from a distant land after ten long years,   20
  His only son, greatly beloved and much sorrowed for—

So did the noble swineherd clasp Telemachus
And kiss him all over—he had escaped from death—
And sobbing he spoke to him these winged words:

"You have come, Telemachus, sweet light!   25
I thought I would never see you again
After you left in your ship for Pylos. But come in,
Dear child, let me feast my eyes on you
Here in my house, come back from abroad!
You don't visit the farm often, or us herdsmen,   30
But stay in town. It must do your heart good
To look at that weeviling crowd of suitors."

And Telemachus, in his clear-headed way:

"Have it your way, Papa. But it's for your sake I've come,
To see you with my own eyes, and to hear from you   35
Whether my mother is still in our house,
Or someone else has married her by now,
And Odysseus' bed, with no one to sleep in it,
Has become a nest of spider webs."

The swineherd answered him: 40

"Yes, she's in your house, waiting and waiting
With an enduring heart, poor soul,
Weeping away the lonely days and nights."

He spoke, and took the young man's spear.
Telemachus went in, and as he crossed   45
The stone threshold, Odysseus stood up
To offer him his seat, but Telemachus,
From across the room, checked him and said:

"Keep your seat, stranger. We'll find another one
Around the place. Eumaeus here can do that."   50

He spoke, and Odysseus sat down again.
The swineherd piled up some green brushwood
And covered it with a fleece, and upon this
The true son of Odysseus sat down.
Then the swineherd set out platters of roast meat—   55
Leftovers from yesterday's meal—
And hurried around heaping up bread in baskets
And mixing sweet wine in an ivy-wood bowl.
Then he sat down opposite godlike Odysseus,
And they helped themselves to the fare before them.   60
When they had enough to eat and drink,
Telemachus spoke to the godlike swineherd:

"Where did this stranger come from, Papa?
What kind of sailors brought him to Ithaca?
I don't suppose he walked to our island." 65

And you answered, Eumaeus, my swineherd:

"I'll tell you everything plainly, child.
He says he was born somewhere in Crete
And that it has been his lot to be a roamer
And wander from city to city. But now 70
He has run away from a Thesprotian ship
And come to my farmstead. I put him in your hands.
Do as you wish. He declares he is your suppliant."

And Telemachus, wise beyond his years:

"This makes my heart ache, Eumaeus. 75
How can I welcome this guest in my house?
I am still young, and I don't have the confidence
To defend myself if someone picks a fight.
As for my mother, her heart is torn.
She can't decide whether to stay here with me 80
And keep the house, honoring her husband's bed
And the voice of the people, or to go away
With whichever man among her suitors
Is the best of the Achaeans, and offers the most gifts.
But as to our guest—now that he's come to your house, 85
I will give him a tunic and cloak, fine clothes,
And a two-edged sword, and sandals for his feet,
And passage to wherever his heart desires.
Or keep him here if you wish, at your farmstead
And take care of him. I'll send the clothes 90
And all of his food, so it won't be a hardship
For you or your men. What I won't allow
Is for him to come up there among the suitors.
They are far too reckless and arrogant,
And I fear they will make fun of him, mock him, 95
And it would be hard for me to take that.
But what could I do? One man, however powerful,
Can't do much against superior numbers."

Then Odysseus, who had borne much, said:

"My friend—surely it is right for me to speak up— 100
It breaks my heart to hear you talk about
The suitors acting like this in your house
And going against the will of a man as great as you.
It is against your will, isn't it? What happened?
Do the people up and down the land all hate you? 105
Has a god turned them against you? Or do you blame

Your brothers, whom a man has to rely upon
In a fight, especially if a big fight comes up?
I wish I were as vigorous as I am angry,
Or were a son of flawless Odysseus, or Odysseus himself!   110
Then I would put my neck on the chopping block
If I did not give them hell when I came into
The halls of Odysseus, son of Laertes!
But if they overwhelmed me with superior numbers,
I would rather be dead, killed in my own halls,   115
Than have to keep watching these disgraceful deeds,
Strangers mistreated, men dragging the women
Through the beautiful halls, wine spilled,
Bread wasted, and all with no end in sight."

Telemachus answered in his clear-headed way: 120

"Well, stranger, I'll tell you the whole story.
It's not that the people have turned against me,
Nor do I have any brothers to blame. Zeus
Has made our family run in a single line.
Laertes was the only son of Arcesius,   125
And Laertes had only one son, Odysseus,
Who only had me, a son he never knew.
And so now our house is filled with enemies,
All of the nobles who rule the islands—
Dulichium, Samê, wooded Zacynthus—   130
And all of those with power on rocky Ithaca
Are courting my mother and ruining our house.
She neither refuses to make a marriage she hates
Or is able to stop it. They are eating us
Out of house and home, and will come after me soon.   135
But all of this rests on the knees of the gods.
Eumaeus, go tell Penelope right away
That I'm safe and back from Pylos.
I'll wait for you here. Tell only her
And don't let any of the suitors find out.   140
Many of them are plotting against me."

And you answered him, Eumaeus, my swineherd:

"I follow you, Telemachus, I understand.
But tell me this. Should I go the same way
To Laertes also, and tell him the news?   145
Poor man, for a while he still oversaw the fields,
Although he was grieving greatly for Odysseus,
And would eat and drink with the slaves in the house
Whenever he had a notion. But now, since the very day
You sailed to Pylos, they say he hasn't been   150
Eating or drinking as before, or overseeing the fields.
He just sits and groans, weeping his heart out,
And the flesh is wasting away from his bones."

And Telemachus, in his clear-headed way:

"That's hard, but we will let him be, despite our pain.   155
If mortals could have all their wishes granted,
We would choose first the day of my father's return.
No, just deliver your message and come back,
And don't go traipsing all through the countryside
Looking for Laertes. But tell my mother   160
To send the housekeeper as soon as she can,
Secretly. She could bring the old man the message."

So the swineherd got going. He tied on his sandals
And was off to the city.
                          The swineherd's departure
Was not unnoticed by Athena. She approached   165
The farmstead in the likeness of a woman,
Beautiful, tall, and accomplished in handiwork,
And stood in the doorway of Eumaeus' hut,
Showing herself to Odysseus. Telemachus
Did not see her before him or notice her presence,   170
For the gods are not visible to everyone.
But Odysseus saw her, and the dogs did, too,
And they did not bark, but slunk away whining
To the other side of the farmstead. The goddess
Lifted her brows, and Odysseus understood.   175
He went out of the hut, past the courtyard's great wall,
And stood before her. Athena said to him:

"Son of Laertes in the line of Zeus,
Tell your son now and do not keep him in the dark,
So that you two can plan the suitors' destruction   180
And then go into town. As for myself,
I will not be gone long. No, I am eager for battle."

With this, she touched him with her golden wand.
A fresh tunic and cloak replaced his rags,
And he was taller and younger, his skin tanned,   185
His jawline firm, and his beard glossy black.
Having worked her magic, the goddess left,
And Odysseus went back into the hut.
His son was astounded. Shaken and flustered,
He turned away his eyes for fear it was a god,   190
And words fell from his lips in nervous flurries:

"You look different, stranger, than you did before,
And your clothes are different, and your complexion.
You must be a god, one of the immortals
Who hold high heaven. Be gracious to us   195
So we can offer you acceptable sacrifice
And finely wrought gold. And spare us, please."

And godlike Odysseus, who had borne much:

"I am no god. Why liken me to the deathless ones?
No, I am your father, on whose account you have suffered   200
Many pains and endured the violence of men."

Saying this, he kissed his son, and let his tears
Fall to the ground. He had held them in until now.
But Telemachus could not believe
That this was his father, and he blurted out: 205

"You cannot be my father Odysseus.
You must be some spirit, enchanting me
Only to increase my grief and pain later.
No mortal man could figure out how to do this
All on his own. Only a god could so easily   210
Transform someone from old to young.
A while ago you were old and shabbily dressed,
And now you are like the gods who hold high heaven."

And Odysseus, from his mind's teeming depths:

"Telemachus, it does not become you to be so amazed   215
That your father is here in this house. You can be sure
That no other Odysseus will ever come.
But I am here, just as you see, home at last
After twenty years of suffering and wandering.
So you will know, this is Athena's doing.   220
She can make me look like whatever she wants:
A beggar sometimes, and sometimes a young man
Wearing fine clothes. It's easy for the gods
To glorify a man or to make him look poor."

He spoke, and sat down. And Telemachus   225
Threw his arms around his wonderful father
And wept. And a longing arose in both of them
To weep and lament, and their shrill cries
Crowded the air

      like the cries of birds—
Sea-eagles or taloned vultures—   230
Whose young chicks rough farmers have stolen
Out of their nests before they were fledged.

Their tears were that piteous. And the sun,
Its light fading, would have set on their weeping,
Had not Telemachus suddenly said to his father: 235

"What ship brought you here, Father,
And where did the crew say they were from?
I don't suppose you came here on foot."

And Odysseus, the godlike survivor:

"I'll tell you the truth about this, son.   240
The Phaeacians brought me, famed sailors
Who give passage to all who come their way.
They brought me over the sea as I slept
In their swift ship, and set me ashore on Ithaca
With donations of bronze and clothing and gold,   245
Splendid treasures that are now stored in caves
By grace of the gods. I have come here now
At Athena's suggestion. You and I must plan
How to kill our enemies. List them for me now
So I can know who they are, and how many,   250
And so I can weigh the odds and decide whether
You and I can go up against them alone
Or whether we have to enlist some allies."

Telemachus took a deep breath and said:

"Father, look now, I know your great reputation,   255
How you can handle a spear and what a strategist you are,
But this is too much for me. Two men
Simply cannot fight against such superior numbers
And superior force. There are not just ten suitors,
Or twice that, but many times more. Here's the count: 260
From Dulichium there are fifty-two—
The pick of their young men—and six attendants.
From Samê there are twenty-four,
From Zacynthus there are twenty,
And from Ithaca itself, twelve, all the noblest,   265
And with them are Medon the herald,
The divine bard, and two attendants who carve.
If we go up against all of them in the hall,
I fear your vengeance will be bitter indeed.
Please try to think of someone to help us,   270
Someone who would gladly be our ally."

And Ódysseus, who had borne much:

"I'll tell you who will help. Do you think
That Athena and her father, Zeus,
Would be help enough? Or should I think of more?"   275

Telemachus answered in his clear-headed way:

"You're talking about two excellent allies,
Although they do sit a little high in the clouds
And have to rule the whole world and the gods as well."

And Odysseus, who had borne much: 280

"Those two won't hold back from battle for long.
They'll be here, all right, when the fighting starts

Between the suitors and us in my high-roofed halls.
For now, go at daybreak up to the house,
And keep company with these insolent hangers-on.   285
The swineherd will lead me to the city later
Looking like an old, broken-down beggar.
If they treat me badly in the house,
Just endure it. Even if they drag me
Through the door by my feet, or throw things at me,   290
Just bear it patiently. Try to dissuade them,
Try to talk them out of their folly, sure,
But they won't listen to you at all,
Because their day of reckoning is near.
And here's something else for you to keep in mind: 295
When Athena in her wisdom prompts me,
I'll give you a signal. When you see me nod,
Take all the weapons that are in the hall
Into the lofted storeroom and stow them there.
When the suitors miss them and ask you   300
Where they are, set their minds at ease, saying:
'Oh, I have stored them out of the smoke.
They're nothing like they were when Odysseus
Went off to Troy, but are all grimed with soot.
Also, a god put this thought into my head,   305
That when you men are drinking, you might
Start quarreling and someone could get hurt,
Which would ruin your feasting and courting.
Steel has a way of drawing a man to it.'
But leave behind a couple of swords for us,   310
And two spears and oxhide shields—leave them
Where we can get to them in a hurry.
Pallas Athena and Zeus in his cunning
Will keep the suitors in a daze for a while.
        And one more thing before you go.   315
If you are really my son and have my blood
In your veins, don't let anyone know
That Odysseus is at home—not Laertes,
Not the swineherd, not anyone in the house,
Not even Penelope. You and I by ourselves   320
Will figure out which way the women are leaning.
We'll test more than one of the servants, too,
And see who respects us and fears us,
And who cares nothing about either one of us
And fails to honor you. You're a man now."   325

And Odysseus' resplendent son answered:

"You'll soon see what I'm made of, Father,
And I don't think you'll find me lacking.
But I'm not sure your plan will work
To our advantage. Think about it.   330
It'll take forever for you to make the rounds
Testing each man, while back in the house

The high-handed suitors are having a good time
Eating their way through everything we own.
I agree you should find out which of the women   335
Dishonor you, and which are innocent.
But as for testing the men in the fields,
Let's do that afterward, if indeed you know
Something from Zeus, who holds the aegis."

While these two were speaking to each other,   340
The sturdy ship that brought Telemachus
And his crew from Pylos was pulling in
To Ithaca. They sailed into the deep harbor
And hauled the black ship up onto the shore.
Porters in high spirits relieved them of their gear   345
And carried the beautiful gifts to Clytius' house.
They sent a herald ahead to Odysseus' palace
To tell Penelope that Telemachus
Was out in the country and had ordered the ship
To sail on to the city so that she, the queen,   350
Would not fall to weeping with worry.
So it happened that the swineherd and herald
Met while they were bringing the same message
To Odysseus' wife. When they reached the palace,
The herald spoke out in the women's presence: 355

"As of now, Lady, your son has returned."

But the swineherd went up to Penelope
And told her all that her son had asked him to.
His message delivered, he left the hall
And went through the courtyard and back to his swine.   360

This was bad news for the suitors.
They filed out of the hall and past the great wall
Of the courtyard and sat down before the gates.
Eurymachus, Polybus' son, was first to speak.

"Damn it! Telemachus has some nerve,   365
Pulling off this voyage. We never thought
We'd see it happen. Well, let's get a tarred ship
Out on the water, the best we have, and a crew
To man the oars and tell our men out at sea
To get back here as soon as they can."   370

He was still speaking when Amphinomus,
Turning around, saw a ship in the harbor,
Sails being furled, the crew with oars in their hands.
He chuckled softly and said to his companions:

"Well, so much for a message. Here they are.   375
Either some god told them, or they spotted
Telemachus' ship sailing by but couldn't catch her."

They trooped down to the shore and made quick work
Of hauling the black ship onto the beach.
Attendants relieved the crew of their gear,   380
And the whole company went off to the assembly.
They wouldn't allow anyone else, young or old,
To sit with them. Antinous rose to speak:

"Just look at how the gods have saved this man!
Day after day watchmen sat on the windy heights,   385
Relieving each other until the sun went down.
And we never spent the night on the shore
But were out at sea all night, waiting for dawn,
Waiting for Telemachus, out for his blood—
And now some god has delivered him home.   390
We'll have to find a way to do him in here.
We can't let him slip through our hands again.
As long as Telemachus is still alive
I don't like our odds in what we're trying to do.
He's shrewd and he's smart, and the people   395
Aren't on our side at all any more.
We have to act before he calls an assembly.
I don't think he's going to let things slide.
He's going to be angry, and he'll stand up
And tell everyone how we plotted his death   400
But could not catch him. They won't approve
When they hear of our crimes, and there's a danger
They'll do something to us, drive us out
Of our land, and we'll wind up in exile.
No, we have to beat him to it, jump him   405
Out in the fields away from the city,
Or on the road. We'll keep all his possessions,
Dividing them fairly among us. His house, though,
We'll give to his mother and whoever weds her.
But if you don't like this plan, if you'd rather   410
He stay alive and keep his ancestral wealth,
We shouldn't keep gathering here any more
And devouring all this pleasant fare.
Each man will have to court her from his own house,
Sending her gifts and trying to win her hand,   415
And she will marry the man who offers the most
And comes to her as her fated husband."

He spoke, and they all sat there in silence
Until Amphinomus stood up to speak.
Son of Nisus and grandson of Aretias,   420
He led the suitors who came from Dulichium,
With its grassy meadows and rich wheatfields.
Penelope liked him, for the way he spoke
And the good sense he showed, and now
He spoke to the suitors with good will to all: 425

"Friends, I would not willingly choose to kill
Telemachus. It is a serious matter to murder
Someone of royal stock. We should first consult
The will of the gods. If great Zeus ordains it,
I will kill him myself, and urge on others.   430
But if the gods are against it, I urge you to stop."

Amphinomus' speech carried the day. The suitors
Stood up and went back to Odysseus' house,
Entered and sat on their polished chairs.

Penelope now had a notion to come out   435
Among her overbearing, insolent suitors.
She had learned of the plot to kill her son
In his own house—the herald Medon told her
After he overheard the suitors talking—
And so the beautiful lady came   440
Into the hall with her serving women.
When she had come among the suitors
She stood shawled in light by a column
That supported the roof of the great house.
Hiding her cheeks behind her silken veils,   445
She spoke these harsh words to Antinous:

"Antinous, you are a haughty and evil man.
They say you are the best of your generation
In all of Ithaca in counsel and in speech,
But you don't measure up to your reputation.   450
You must be mad. Plotting Telemachus' death!
Don't you care at all that your father was once
A suppliant here? Zeus witnesses this,
And it is unholy for suppliants and hosts
To harm each other. Or haven't you heard   455
Of the time your father came to this house
As a fugitive? The people were angry with him
Because he had joined up with the Taphian pirates
And harassed our allies, the Thesprotians.
The citizens wanted to beat him to death   460
And gobble up his large and pleasant estate,
But they were held in check by Odysseus.
It is his house that you are now gobbling up
Without atonement, his wife you are wooing,
His son you are trying to kill—and as for me,   465
You are causing me unspeakable distress.
Stop it, I tell you, and tell the others to stop."

Then Eurymachus, son of Polybus, answered:

"Penelope, Icarius' wise daughter,
Cheer up. Don't be so upset by all this.   470

There's not a man alive, nor will there ever be,
Who will lay hands on your son, Telemachus,
While I still breathe and look upon this earth.
Anyone who tries, I give you my solemn assurance,
Will spill his black blood around the point of my spear.   475
No, I, too, often sat on Odysseus' knees,
And the great hero would put roast meat in my hands
And make me sip red wine. And so Telemachus
Is the dearest of all men to me, and I guarantee
He need have no fear of death—from the suitors,   480
That is. From the gods there is no avoiding it."

A heart-warming speech, but he was still planning
To kill her son.
                    Penelope went upstairs
To her softly lit rooms and wept for Odysseus,
Her beloved husband, until grey-eyed Athena   485
Cast sweet sleep upon the woman's eyelids.

Evening fell, and the swineherd came back
To Odysseus and his son, who had slaughtered
A yearling boar and were busy making supper.
Athena drew near to Odysseus and tapped him   490
With her wand, making him into an old man again,
Clothed in rags. She was afraid the swineherd
Would recognize him and, unable to keep the secret,
Go bring the news to Penelope.

Telemachus looked up and said to the swineherd: 495

"You're back, Eumaeus. What news from town?
Have the suitors returned from their ambush,
Or are they still looking for me to sail past?"

And you answered him, Eumaeus, my swineherd:

"It wasn't my business to nose around town   500
Asking about that, and I wanted to come back
As soon as I had delivered my message.
On the way in, though, I met up with a herald
Sent by your shipmates. He was fast
And got there first to tell your mother the news.   505
I know one more thing, for I saw it myself.
I was above the city, by the hill of Hermes,
On my way back, when I saw a sailing ship
Pull into our harbor. She had a large crew
And was loaded with shields and bladed spears.   510
I thought it was them, but I don't really know."

Telemachus smiled, feeling his ancestors' blood,
And glanced at Odysseus, avoiding the swineherd's eye.

When they had finished preparing the meal,
They fell to feasting. There was plenty for everyone,   515
And when they all had enough of food and drink,
Their minds turned toward rest, and they took the gift of sleep.

BOOK XVII

When Dawn brushed the early sky with rose
Odysseus' son bound on his beautiful sandals
And hefted his spear. He was in a hurry
To get to the city, and he said to his swineherd:

"I'm off to the town, Eumaeus. My mother   5
Won't stop crying until she sees me again,
In person. But this is what I want you to do.
Take this down-and-out stranger into the city
So that he can beg for food. Whoever wants to
Can give him some bread and a cup of water.   10
There's no way I can worry about everyone,
I have too much on my mind. If the stranger
Gets upset about this, it's just too bad.
I'm the sort of person who likes to talk straight."

And Odysseus, his mind teeming, said: 15

"Friend, don't think I'm eager myself
To be left behind here. For a beggar like me,
It's better to beg for food in the town
Than out in the fields, and whoever wants to
Can give me something. I'm past the age   20
Where I can stay on a farm and have to do
Everything some foreman tells me.
You go on. This man here will lead me to town
As soon as I have warmed myself by the fire
And the sun is higher. These clothes I'm wearing   25
Are not so good, and the morning frost
Might do me in. You say the city is pretty far."

Thus Odysseus, and Telemachus strode quickly
Out of the farmstead, sowing death for the suitors
With every step he took.
                        When he came to the house   30
He leaned his spear against a tall pillar
And went in over the stone threshold.
                                    Eurycleia
Spotted him first, as she was spreading fleeces
Over finely wrought chairs. She burst into tears
And ran straight over to him. The other maids   35
Of Odysseus' household gathered around
And kissed his head and shoulders in welcome.

Then from her bedroom came wise Penelope,
Looking like Artemis[2] or golden Aphrodite.
She burst into tears and threw her arms around him   40
And kissed his head and both his shining eyes,
And through her sobs spoke these winged words:

"You have come, Telemachus, sweet light!
I thought I would never see you again
After you left in your ship for Pylos—   45
Behind my back—for news of your father.
But tell me, what did you find out about him?"

Telemachus answered her coolly:

"Don't make me weep, mother, or get me
All worked up. I barely escaped with my life.   50
Now bathe yourself and put on clean clothes,
Then go to your bedroom upstairs with your maids
And vow formal sacrifice to the immortal gods
In the hope that Zeus will grant us vengeance.
I'm going to town so I can invite to our house   55
A stranger who came here with me from Pylos.
I sent him on ahead with some of my crew,
And I told Peiraeus to take him home
And show him hospitality until I arrived."

Penelope's response to this died on her lips.   60
She bathed, and dressed herself in clean clothes,
And vowed sacrifices to the immortal gods,
Praying that Zeus would grant them vengeance some day.

Telemachus went out through the hall
Holding a spear, two lean hounds at his side.   65
Athena shed a silver grace upon him,
And everyone marveled at him as he passed.
The haughty suitors crowded around him,
Fine words on their lips, and evil in their hearts.
Telemachus slipped away from the throng   70
And went to sit down over to one side
With Mentor, Antiphus, and Halitherses,
Old friends of his father. They wanted to know
Everything Telemachus had done. And then
Peiraeus came up, leading the stranger, Theoclymenus,   75
Up through the city to where the men were gathered.
Telemachus did not keep his back to him long
But went up to the stranger, who was his guest.
It was Peiraeus who spoke first, saying:

---

2. Artemis, goddess of hunting, was associated with chastity and the moon.

"Telemachus, get some women over to my house,   80
So I can send you the gifts Menelaus gave you."

And Telemachus, in his clear-headed way:

"Peiraeus, we don't know how things will turn out.
Should the suitors treacherously kill me at home
And divide among them my family's wealth,   85
I would rather that you keep all these gifts
And enjoy them, rather than any of that crowd.
But if I manage to sow the seeds of their death,
I'll be glad to have all of it back from you then."

Saying that, Telemachus led the stranger,   90
Who had endured much in life, to his house.
They went inside and laid their cloaks on chairs,
And then went into the polished tubs and bathed.
When the maids had bathed them and rubbed them
With oil, and flung upon them fleecy cloaks and tunics,   95
They came out of the baths and sat down on chairs.
A maid poured water from a golden pitcher
Into a silver basin for them to wash their hands
And then set up a polished table nearby.
Another serving woman, grave and dignified,   100
Set out bread and generous helpings
From the other dishes she had.
                    Penelope
Sat opposite her son by the doorpost of the hall,
Leaning back on a chair and spinning fine yarn.
The two men reached for the good cheer before them,   105
And when they had their fill of food and drink,
Penelope was the first to speak:

                    "Telemachus,
I think I will go now to my room upstairs
And lie down on my bed, which has become for me
A sorrowful bed, ever wet with my tears   110
Since the day Odysseus left for Troy
With the sons of Atreus. You do not have the heart
To tell me, before the suitors come in,
Whatever you have heard about your father's return."

And Telemachus, in his clear-headed way: 115

"Rest assured I will tell you now, mother.
We went to Pylos, and Nestor, the king there,
Took me into his house. He welcomed me
As a father might welcome his long-lost son,
And he put me up with his own glorious sons.   120
But he said he had heard nothing from anyone
About whether Odysseus was dead or alive.

He sent me in a chariot to visit Menelaus,
Atreus' son, and there I saw Helen,
For whose sake the Greek and Trojan armies   125
Suffered so much, by the will of the gods.
Then Menelaus asked me why I had come
To gleaming Lacedaemon. I told him why,
And this is exactly what he told me then:
'Those dogs! Those puny weaklings,   130
Wanting to sleep in the bed of a hero!
A doe might as well bed her suckling fawns
In the lair of a lion, leaving them there
In the bush and then going off over the hills
Looking for grassy fields. When the lion   135
Comes back, the fawns die an ugly death.
That's the kind of death these men will die
When Odysseus comes back. O Father Zeus,
And Athena and Apollo, bring Odysseus back
With the strength he showed in Lesbos once   140
When he wrestled a match with Philomeleides
And threw him hard, making all of us cheer—
That's the Odysseus I want the suitors to meet!
They'd get married all right—to bitter death.
But, as to what you ask me about,   145
I will not stray from the point or deceive you.
No, I will tell you all that the infallible
Old Man of the Sea told me, and hide nothing.
He said he saw him on an island, miserable,
In the halls of Calypso, who keeps him there   150
Against his will. He has no way to get home
To his native land. He has no ships left,
No crew to row him over the sea's broad back.'
Those were the words of Menelaus, Atreus' son,
The great spearman. When I finished up there,   155
I set out for home, and a fair wind from the gods
Brought me back quickly to my native land."

So he spoke, and his words wrung her heart.
Then Theoclymenus made his voice heard:

"Revered lady, wife of Laertes' son, Odysseus,   160
Menelaus is in the dark about all this, but now
Hear what I have to say, for I will prophesy
Unerringly to you and conceal nothing.
With Zeus above all gods as my witness,
I swear, by this table of hospitality,   165
And by Odysseus' hearth, to which I have come,
That this same Odysseus, mark my words,
Is at this moment in his own native land,
Sitting still or on the move, learning of this evil,
And he is sowing evil for all the suitors.   170
Such is the bird of omen I saw

From the ship, and I cried it out to Telemachus."

And Penelope, calm and circumspect:

"Ah, stranger, may your words come true.
Then you would know my kindness, and my gifts   175
Would make you blessed in all men's eyes."

While they spoke to each other in this way,
The suitors were entertaining themselves
In front of Odysseus' palace again,
Throwing the javelin and discus   180
On the level terrace, arrogant as ever.
When it was time for dinner, and the flocks
Were coming in from the fields, Medon,
Who was the suitors' favorite herald
And was always at their feasts, called out: 185

"Young men, now that you have enjoyed yourselves
On the field, come inside so we can prepare a feast.
Dinner at dinnertime is not a bad thing at all."

It didn't take much to persuade them. Up they rose
And filed into the stately house. They laid their cloaks   190
On the chairs, and some of them got busy
Slaughtering great sheep and plump goats,
Fattened hogs, too, and a heifer of the herd.

While they were making their dinner, Odysseus
And the noble swineherd were getting ready   195
To go up from the fields to the city.
The swineherd started off by saying:

"Well, stranger, since you're eager to go
To the city today, as my master ordered—
Although for my part I'd rather have you here   200
To mind the farm, but I do respect him
And fear him, and I certainly don't want
A tongue-lashing from him, which could go hard—
Anyway, we'd better get going. It's late
In the day, and it'll be colder toward evening."   205

And Odysseus, his mind teeming:

"No need to tell me that. I understand.
Let's go. You lead the way, all the way.
But, if you have one cut, give me a staff
To lean on. You said the trail was slippery."   210

He spoke, and threw around his shoulders
His ratty pouch, full of holes and slung
By a twisted cord. Eumaeus gave him a staff

That suited him, and the two of them set out.
The dogs and the herdsmen stayed behind   215
To guard the farmstead. And so the swineherd
Led his master to the city, looking like
An old, broken-down beggar, leaning
On a staff and dressed in miserable rags.

They were well along the rugged path   220
And near to the city when they came to a spring
Where the townspeople got their water.
This beautiful fountain had been made
By Ithacus, and Neritus, and Polyctor.
A grove of poplars encircled it   225
And the cold water flowed from the rock above,
On top of which was built an altar to the nymphs,
Where all wayfarers made offerings.
                                        There
Melanthius, son of Dolius, met them
As he was driving his she-goats, the best   230
In the herds, into town for the suitors' dinner.
Two herdsmen trailed along behind him.
When he saw Eumaeus and his companion,
He greeted them with language so ugly
It made Odysseus' blood boil to hear it: 235

"Well, look at this, trash dragging along trash.
Birds of a feather, as usual. Where
Are you taking this walking pile of shit,
You miserable hog-tender, this diseased beggar
Who will slobber all over our feasts?   240
How many doorposts has he rubbed with his shoulders,
Begging for scraps? You think he's ever gotten
A proper present, a cauldron or sword? Ha!
Give him to me and I'll have him sweep out the pens
And carry loads of shoots for the goats to eat,   245
Put some muscle on his thigh by drinking whey.
I'll bet he's never done a hard day's work in his life.
No, he prefers to beg his way through town
For food to stuff into his bottomless belly.
I'll tell you this, though, and you can count on it.   250
If he comes to the palace of godlike Odysseus,
He'll be pelted with footstools aimed at his head.
If he's lucky they'll only splinter on his ribs."

And as he passed Odysseus, the fool kicked him
On the hip, trying to shove him off the path.   255
Odysseus absorbed the blow without even quivering—
Only stood there and tried to decide whether
To jump the man and knock him dead with his staff
Or lift him by the ears and smash his head to the ground.
In the end, he controlled himself and just took it.   260

But the swineherd looked the man in the eye
And told him off, and lifted his hands in prayer:

"Nymphs of the spring, daughters of Zeus,
If Odysseus ever honored you by burning
Thigh bones of lambs and kids wrapped in rich fat,   265
Grant me this prayer:
               May my master come back,
May some god guide him back!
                  Then,
He would scatter all that puffery of yours,
All the airs you put on strutting around town
While bad herdsmen destroy all the flocks."   270

Melanthius, the goatherd, came back with this:

"Listen to the dog talk, with his big, bad notions.
I'm going to take him off in a black ship someday
Far from Ithaca, and sell him for a fortune.
You want my prayer? May Apollo with his silver bow   275
Strike Telemachus dead today in his halls,
Or may the suitors kill him, as surely as Odysseus
Is lost for good in some faraway land."

He left them with that. They walked on slowly,
While the goatherd pushed ahead and came quickly   280
To the palace. He went right in and sat down
Among the suitors, opposite Eurymachus,
Whom he liked best of all. The servers
Set out for him a helping of meat,
And the grave housekeeper brought him bread.   285

Odysseus and the swineherd came up to the house
And halted. The sound of the hollow lyre
Drifted out to them, for Phemius
Was sweeping the strings as he began his song,
Odysseus took the swineherd's hand and said: 290

"Eumaeus, this beautiful house must be Odysseus'.
It would stand out anywhere. Look at all the rooms
And stories, and the court built with wall and coping,
And the well-fenced double gates. No one could scorn it.
And I can tell there are many men feasting inside   295
From the savor of meat wafting out from it,
And the sound of the lyre, which rounds out a feast."

And you answered him, swineherd Eumaeus:

"You don't miss a thing, do you? Well,
Let's figure out what we should do here.   300
Either you go in first and mingle with the suitors,
While I wait here; or you wait here,

If you'd rather, and I'll go in before you.
But don't wait long, or someone might see you
And either throw something at you or smack you.   305
Think it over. What would you like to do?"

And Odysseus, the godlike survivor:

"I understand. You don't have to prompt me.
You go in before me, and I'll wait here.
I've had things thrown at me before,   310
And I have an enduring heart, Eumaeus.
God knows I've had my share of suffering
In war and at sea. I can take more if I have to.
But no one can hide a hungry belly.
It's our worst enemy. It's why we launch ships   315
To bring war to men across the barren sea."

And as they talked, a dog that was lying there
Lifted his head and pricked up his ears.
This was Argus, whom Odysseus himself
Had patiently bred—but never got to enjoy—   320
Before he left for Ilion. The young men
Used to set him after wild goats, deer, and hare.
Now, his master gone, he lay neglected
In the dung of mules and cattle outside the doors,
A deep pile where Odysseus' farmhands   325
Would go for manure to spread on his fields.
There lay the hound Argus, infested with lice.
And now, when he sensed Odysseus was near,
He wagged his tail and dropped both ears
But could not drag himself nearer his master.   330
Odysseus wiped away a tear, turning his head
So Eumaeus wouldn't notice, and asked him:

"Eumaeus, isn't it strange that this dog
Is lying in the dung? He's a beautiful animal,
But I wonder if he has speed to match his looks,   335
Or if he's like the table dogs men keep for show."

And you answered him, Eumaeus, my swineherd:

"Ah yes, this dog belonged to a man who has died
Far from home. He was quite an animal once.
If he were now as he was when Odysseus   340
Left for Troy, you would be amazed
At his speed and strength. There's nothing
In the deep woods that dog couldn't catch,
And what a nose he had for tracking!
But he's fallen on hard times, now his master   345
Has died abroad. These feckless women
Don't take care of him. Servants never do right

When their masters aren't on top of them.
Zeus takes away half a man's worth
The day he loses his freedom."

So saying,   350
Eumaeus entered the great house
And the hall filled with the insolent suitors.
But the shadow of death descended upon Argus,
Once he had seen Odysseus after twenty years.

Godlike Telemachus spotted the swineherd first   355
Striding through the hall, and with a nod of his head
Signaled him to join him. Eumaeus looked around
And took a stool that lay near, one that the carver
Ordinarily sat on when he sliced meat for the suitors
Dining in the hall. Eumaeus took this stool   360
And placed it at Telemachus' table, opposite him,
And sat down. A herald came and served him
A portion of meat, and bread from the basket.

Soon after, Odysseus came in, looking like
An old, broken-down beggar, leaning   365
On a staff and dressed in miserable rags.
He sat down on the ashwood threshold
Just inside the doors, leaning back
On the cypress doorpost, a post planed and trued
By some skillful carpenter in days gone by.   370
Telemachus called the swineherd over
And taking a whole loaf from the beautiful basket
And all the meat his hands could hold, said to him:

"Take this over to the stranger, and tell him
To go around and beg from each of the suitors.   375
Shame is no good companion for a man in need."

Thus Telemachus. The swineherd nodded,
And going over to Odysseus, said to him:

"Telemachus gives you this, and he tells you
To go around and beg from each of the suitors.   380
Shame, he says, is not good for a beggar."

And Odysseus, his mind teeming:

"Lord Zeus, may Telemachus be blessed among men
And may he have all that his heart desires."

And he took the food in both his hands   385
And set it down at his feet on his beggar's pouch.
Odysseus ate as long as the bard sang in the hall.
When the song came to an end, and the suitors

Began to be noisy and boisterous, Athena
Drew near to him and prompted him   390
To go among the suitors and beg for crusts
And so learn which of them were decent men
And which were scoundrels—not that the goddess had
The slightest intention of sparing any of them.

Odysseus made his rounds from right to left,   395
Stretching his hands out to every side,
As if he had been a beggar all his life.
They all pitied him and gave him something,
And they wondered out loud who he was
And where he had come from. To which questions   400
Melanthius, the goatherd, volunteered:

"Hear me, suitors of our noble queen.
As to this stranger, I have seen him before.
The swineherd brought him here, but who he is
I have no idea, or where he claims he was born."   405
At this, Antinous tore into the swineherd:

"Swineherd! Why did you bring this man to town?
Don't we have enough tramps around here without him,
This nuisance of a beggar who will foul our feast?
I suppose you don't care that these men are eating away   410
Your master's wealth, or you wouldn't have invited him."

The swineherd Eumaeus came back with this:

"You may be a fine gentleman, Antinous,
But that's an ugly thing to say. Who, indeed,
Ever goes out of his way to invite a stranger   415
From abroad, unless it's a prophet, or healer,
Or a builder, or a singer of tales—someone like that,
A master of his craft who benefits everyone.
Men like that get invited everywhere on earth.
But who would burden himself with a beggar?   420
You're just plain mean, the meanest of the suitors
To Odysseus' servants, and especially to me.
But I don't care, as long as my lady Penelope
Lives in the hall, and godlike Telemachus."

To which Telemachus responded coolly: 425

"Quiet! Don't waste your words on this man.
Antinous is nasty like that—provoking people
With harsh words and egging them on."

And then he had these fletched words for Antinous:

"Why, Antinous, you're just like a father to me,   430
Kindly advising me to kick this stranger out.

God forbid that should ever happen. No,
Go ahead and give him something. I want you to.
Don't worry about my mother or anyone else
In this house, when it comes to giving things away.   435
But the truth is that you're just being selfish
And would rather eat more yourself than give any away."

And Antinous answered him:

"What a high and mighty speech, Telemachus!
Look now, if only everyone gave him what I will,   440
It would be months before he darkened your door."

As he spoke he grabbed the stool upon which
He propped his shining feet whenever he dined
And brandished it beneath the table.
But all the rest gave the beggar something   445
And filled his pouch with bread and meat.
And Odysseus would have had his taste of the suitors
Free of charge, but on his way back to the threshold
He stopped by Antinous' place and said:

"Give me something, friend. You don't look like   450
You are the poorest man here—far from it—
But the most well off. You look like a king.
So you should give me more than the others.
If you did, I'd sing your praises all over the earth.
I, too, once had a house of my own, a rich man   455
In a wealthy house, and I gave freely and often
To any and everyone who wandered by.
I had slaves, too, more than I could count,
And everything I needed to live the good life.
But Zeus smashed it all to pieces one day—   460
Who knows why?—when he sent me out
With roving pirates all the way to Egypt
So I could meet my doom.
                        I moored my ships
In the river Nile, and you can be sure I ordered
My trusty mates to stand by and guard them   465
While I sent out scouts to look around.
Then the crews got cocky and overconfident
And started pillaging the Egyptian countryside,
Carrying off the women and children
And killing the men. The cry came to the city,   470
And at daybreak troops answered the call.
The whole plain was filled with infantry,
War chariots, and the glint of bronze.
Thundering Zeus threw my men into a panic,
And not one had the courage to stand and fight   475
Against odds like that. It was bad.
They killed many of us outright with bronze
And led the rest to their city to work as slaves.

But they gave me to a friend of theirs, from Cyprus,
To take me back there and give me to Dmetor,   480
Son of Iasus, who ruled Cyprus with an iron hand.
From there I came here, with all my hard luck."

Antinous had this to say in reply:

"What god has brought this plague in here?
Get off to the side, away from me,   485
Or I'll show you Egypt and Cyprus,
You pushy panhandler! You don't know your place.
You make your rounds and everyone
Hands things out recklessly. And why shouldn't they?
It's easy to be generous with someone else's wealth."   490

Odysseus took a step back and answered him:

"It's too bad your mind doesn't match your good looks.
You wouldn't give a suppliant even a pinch of salt
If you had to give it from your own cupboard.
Here you sit at another man's table   495
And you can't bear to give me a piece of bread
From the huge pile that's right by your hand."

This made Antinous even angrier,
And he shot back with a dark scowl:

"That does it. I'm not going to let you just   500
Breeze out of here if you're going to insult me."

As he spoke he grabbed the footstool and threw it,
Hitting Odysseus under his right shoulderblade.
Odysseus stood there as solid as a rock
And didn't even blink. He only shook his head   505
In silence, and brooded darkly.
Then he went back to the threshold and sat down
With his pouch bulging and spoke to the suitors:

"Hear me, suitors of our glorious queen,
So I can speak my mind. No one regrets   510
Being hit while fighting for his own possessions,
His cattle or sheep. But Antinous struck me
Because of my belly, that vile growling beast
That gives us so much trouble. If there are gods
For beggars, or avenging spirits,   515
May death come to Antinous before marriage does."

Antinous, son of Eupeithes, answered:

"Just sit still and eat, stranger—or get the hell out.
Keep talking like this and some of the young men here

Will haul you by the feet all through the house   520
And strip the skin right off your back."

Thus Antinous. But the other suitors
Turned on him, one of them saying:

"That was foul, Antinous, hitting a poor beggar.
You're done for if he turns out to be a god   525
Come down from heaven, the way they do,
Disguised as strangers from abroad or whatever,
Going around to different cities
And seeing who's lawless and who lives by the rules."

Antinous paid no attention to this.   530
Telemachus took it hard that his father was struck
But he kept it inside. Not a tear
Fell from his eye. He only shook his head
In silence, and brooded darkly.

When Penelope, sitting with her maids,   535
Heard the stranger had been struck, she said:

"So may you be struck by the Archer God."

And Eurynome, the housekeeper, said to her:

"If our prayers were answered, not one of these men
Would live to see Dawn take her seat in the sky."   540

Penelope answered in her circumspect way:

"They're all hateful, nurse, for their evil designs,
But Antinous is like black death itself.
Some poor stranger makes his rounds through the house
Begging alms from the men because he is in need,   545
And all the others fill his pouch with gifts,
But Antinous throws a footstool at him
And hits him in the back beneath his shoulder."

Thus Penelope, sitting with her women,
While noble Odysseus ate his dinner.   550
Then she called the swineherd to her and said:

"Noble Eumaeus, tell the stranger to come here
So that I can greet him and ask him if perhaps
He has heard anything about Odysseus
Or seen him with his own eyes. By his looks   555
He is a man who has wandered the world."

And you, my swineherd, answered her:

"I wish the men would keep quiet, Lady,
For his speech could charm your very soul.

Three nights I had him with me, and three days   560
I kept him in my hut, for it was to me he first came
When he jumped ship—but he still did not finish
The long story of all his hard times.
It was just as when men gaze at a bard
Who sings to them songs learned from the gods,   565
Bittersweet songs, and they could listen forever—
That's how he charmed me when he sat in my house.
He says he's an ancestral friend of Odysseus,
And that he comes from Crete, the land of Minos.[3]
It was from Crete he came here, on a hard journey   570
That gets ever harder as he wanders on
Like a rolling stone. He insists he has news
That Odysseus is near, over in Thesprotia,
Alive and well, and bringing many treasures home."

And Penelope, calm and circumspect: 575

"Go call him here, so he can tell me face to face.
As for these men, let them play their games outside
Or here in the house. They're in a good mood,
As well they might be, their own possessions
Lying safe at home, their bread and sweet wine   580
Feeding only their servants, while they themselves
Mob our house day after day, slaughtering
All our oxen, our sheep and fat goats,
Partying and recklessly drinking our wine,
Ruining everything. For there is no man here   585
Like Odysseus to protect this house.
But if Odysseus should ever come home,
He and his son would make them pay for this outrage."

Just as she finished, Telemachus sneezed,
A loud sneeze that rang through the halls.   590
Penelope laughed and said to Eumaeus:

"Go ahead and call the stranger for me!
Didn't you see my son sneeze at my words?
That means death will surely come to the suitors,
One and all. Not a single man will escape.   595
And one more thing—what do you think of this?
If I find that he speaks everything truly,
I'll clothe him in a handsome tunic and cloak."

The swineherd took this all in. He went over
To Odysseus, and his words flew fast: 600

"Penelope, Telemachus' mother,
Wants to see you. Her heart urges her,

3. Legendary king of Crete.

For all her pain, to ask you about her husband.
If she finds that you speak everything truly,
She will give you a handsome tunic and cloak,   605
Which you really do need. As for your belly,
You'll still have to fill it by public begging."

And Odysseus, who had borne much:

"Eumaeus, I will soon be telling the whole truth
To Penelope, Icarius' wise daughter.   610
For I know Odysseus very well,
And he and I have been through much the same grief.
But I'm leery of this mob of rough suitors,
Whose arrogance grates on the sky's iron dome.
Just now as I was making my way through the hall,   615
Not doing any harm to anyone, this man
Struck me—hard—and neither Telemachus
Nor anyone else did anything to stop him.
So please ask Penelope, for all her eagerness,
To wait in the hall until the sun goes down.   620
Then she can ask me about her husband's return.
And she can seat me nearer the fire. These clothes
I have on are not very good, as you should know,
For it was to you first I came as a suppliant."

When he heard this the swineherd went off,   625
And when he crossed the threshold Penelope said:

"You're not bringing him with you, Eumaeus.
What does he mean by this? Does he fear someone
More than he should, or is there something else here
That makes him hang back? A shy beggar's a poor one." 630

And you answered her, Eumaeus, my swineherd:

"What he says is right, as anyone would agree,
About avoiding the violence of arrogant men.
He asks you to wait until the sun goes down.
And it would be far seemlier for you too, Lady,   635
If you and the stranger had your talk in private."

Penelope answered in her circumspect way:

"Our guest is no fool. He sees what could happen.
These men are bent on senseless violence,
More than any mortal men I can imagine."   640

Thus Penelope, and the godlike swineherd,
Having said his piece to her, went off
Into the throng of suitors. He found Telemachus,
And with his head close to him so no one could hear,
He spoke to him these feathered words: 645

"I am going off now, dear Telemachus,
To guard the swine and all—
Your livelihood and mine. You take charge
Of everything here. Take care of yourself,
First and foremost, and be on the lookout   650
So you don't get hurt. Many of these men
Are up to no good. May Zeus destroy them
Utterly, before any harm can come to us."

And Telemachus, in his cool-headed way:

"Amen to that. Go after supper. But at dawn   655
Come back with your best boars for sacrifice.
Everything here is up to me, and the gods."

So the swineherd sat down again on a polished chair.
When he had eaten and drunk to his heart's content,
He went off to his swine, leaving the courts and hall   660
Full of banqueters. They were singing and dancing
And having a good time, for it was evening now.

BOOK XVIII

And now there came the town beggar
Making his rounds, known throughout Ithaca
For his greedy belly and endless bouts
Of eating and drinking. He had no real strength
Or fighting power—just plenty of bulk.   5
Arnaeus was the name his mother had given him,
But the young men all called him Irus
Because he was always running errands for someone.[4]
He had a mind to drive Odysseus out of his own house
And started in on him with words like this: 10

"Out of the doorway, geezer, before I throw you out
On your ear! Don't you see all these people
Winking at me to give you the bum's rush?
I wouldn't want to stoop so low, but if you don't
Get out now, I may have to lay hands on you."   15

Odysseus gave him a measured look and said:

"What's wrong with you? I'm not doing
Or saying anything to bother you. I don't mind
If someone gives you a handout, even a large one.
This doorway is big enough for both of us.   20
There's no need for you to be jealous of others.
Now look, you're a vagrant, just like I am.
Prosperity is up to the gods. But if I were you,

---

4. The name *Irus* recalls Iris, the messenger goddess who runs errands for the other gods.

I'd be careful about challenging me with your fists.
I might get angry, and old man though I am,   25
I just might haul off and bust you in the mouth.
I'd have more peace and quiet tomorrow.
I don't think you'd come back a second time
To the hall of Laertes' son, Odysseus."

This got Irus angry, and he answered: 30

"Listen to the mangy glutton run on,
Like an old kitchen woman! I'll fix him good—
Hit him with a left and then a right until
I knock his teeth out onto the ground,
The way we'd do a pig caught eating the crops.   35
Put 'em up, and everybody will see how we fight.
How are you going to stand up to a younger man?"

That's how they goaded each other on
There on the great polished threshold.
Antinous took this in and said with a laugh: 40

"How about this, friends? We haven't had
This much fun in a long time. Thank God
For a little entertainment! The stranger and Irus
Are getting into a fight. Let's have them square off!"

They all jumped up laughing and crowded around   45
The two tattered beggars. And Antinous said:

"Listen, proud suitors, to my proposal.
We've got these goat paunches on the fire,
Stuffed with fat and blood, ready for supper.
Whichever of the two wins and proves himself   50
The better man, gets the stuffed paunch of his choice.
Furthermore, he dines with us in perpetuity
And to the exclusion of all other beggars."

Everyone approved of Antinous' speech.
Then Odysseus, who knew all the moves, said: 55

"Friends, there's no way a broken-down old man
Can fight with a younger. Still, my belly,
That troublemaker, urges me on. So,
I'll just have to get beat up. But all of you,
Swear me an oath that no one, favoring Irus,   60
Will foul me and beat me for him."

They all swore that they wouldn't hit him,
And then Telemachus, feeling his power, said:

"Stranger, if you have the heart for this fight,
Don't worry about the onlookers. If anyone   65

Strikes you, he will have to fight us all.
I guarantee this as your host, and I am joined
By Antinous and Eurymachus,
Lords and men of discernment both."

Everyone praised this speech.
                                  Then Odysseus   70
Tied his rags around his waist, revealing
His sculpted thighs, his broad shoulders,
His muscular chest and arms. Athena
Stood near the hero, magnifying his build.
The suitors' jaws dropped open.   75
They looked at each other and said things like:

"Irus is history."
                    "Brought it on himself, too."
"Will you look at the thigh on that old man!"

So they spoke. Irus' heart was in his throat,
But some servants tucked up his clothes anyway   80
And dragged him out, his rolls of fat quivering.
Antinous laid into him, saying:

"You big slob. You'll be sorry
You were ever born, if you try to duck
This woebegone, broken-down old man.   85
I'm going to give it to you straight now.
If he gets the better of you and beats you,
I'm going to throw you on a black ship
And send you to the mainland to King Echetus,
The maimer,5 who will slice off your nose and ears   90
With cold bronze, and tear out your balls
And give them raw to the dogs to eat."

This made Irus tremble even more.
They shoved him out into the middle,
And both men put up their fists. Odysseus,   95
The wily veteran, thought it over.
Should he knock the man stone cold dead,
Or ease up on the punch and just lay him out flat?
Better to go easy and just flatten him, he thought,
So that the crowd won't get suspicious.   100
The fighters stood tall, circling each other,
And as Irus aimed a punch at his right shoulder,
Odysseus caught him just beneath the ear,
Crushing his jawbone. Blood ran from his mouth,
And he fell in the dust snorting like an ox   105
And gnashing his teeth, his heels kicking the ground.
The suitors lifted their hands and died

5. King in mainland Greece, with a reputation for cruelty.

With laughter. Odysseus took Irus by one fat foot
And dragged him out through the doorway
All the way to the court and the portico's gates.   110
He propped him up against the courtyard's wall,
Stuck his staff in his hand, and said to him:

"Sit there now and scare off the pigs and dogs,
And stop lording it over the other beggars,
You sorry bastard, or things could get worse."   115

And he slung his old pouch over one shoulder,
Walked back to the threshold, and sat down.
The suitors went inside, laughing and joking,
And one of them came up to Odysseus and said:

"May Zeus and the other gods grant you, stranger,   120
Whatever your heart most dearly desires,
Since you have ended this glutton's begging career.
We'll ship him off to Echetus the maimer!"

Odysseus took heart at these auspicious words.
Antinous set before him the huge paunch   125
Stuffed with fat and blood, and Amphinomus
Served him a couple of loaves from the basket,
Toasted him with a golden cup, and said:

"Hail to the revered stranger. May good fortune
Come to you, though you have only bad luck now."   130

And Odysseus, from his mind's teeming depths:

"Amphinomus, you come across as a sensible man,
Just as your father was. I have heard of him,
Nisus of Dulichium, a good man, and wealthy,
Known far and wide. They say you are his son,   135
And you seem soft-spoken, a good man yourself.
So I'll tell you something you should take to heart.
Of all the things that breathe and move upon it,
Earth nurtures nothing feebler than man.
While the gods favor him and his step is quick,   140
He thinks he will never have to suffer in life.
Then when the blessed ones bring evil his way,
He bears it in sorrow with an enduring heart.
Our outlook changes with the kind of day
Zeus our Father decides to give us.   145
I, too, once got used to prosperity,
And I did many foolish things in my pride,
Trusting my father and brothers would save me.
So I know a man should never be an outlaw,
But keep in peace the gifts heaven gives him.   150
Just look at what the suitors are doing now,
Wasting the wealth and dishonoring the wife

Of a man who, I tell you, will not be gone long
From his family and friends and his native land.
He's very close. Better for you if some god   155
Leads you away from here and takes you home
Before you meet him upon his return.
Once he's under this roof, I do not think
The suitors will escape without blood being spilled."

He spoke, poured a libation, drank the sweet wine,   160
And then gave the cup back to Amphinomus,
Who went away through the hall with his head bowed
And his heart heavy with a sense of foreboding.
He would not escape death, though. Pallas Athena
Had him pinned, and he would be killed outright   165
By a spear from the hand of Telemachus.

And now the Grey-eyed One put into the heart
Of Penelope, Icarius' wise daughter,
A notion to show herself to the suitors.
All of a sudden she wanted to make their blood pound—   170
And to make herself more worthy than ever
In the eyes of her son, and of her husband.
With a whimsical laugh she said to the housekeeper:

"Eurynome, my heart longs, though it never has before,
To show myself to the suitors, hateful as they are.   175
And I would like to say something to my son,
Something that might help him—he should not
Continually keep the company of the suitors,
Overbearing men who speak politely to his face
And plan all the while to hurt him later."   180

And the housekeeper Eurynome said:

"Yes indeed, child, everything you said is right.
Go on then, and speak your mind to your son
And don't hide anything—after you have bathed,
That is, and dabbed your cheeks with ointment.   185
Don't go like this, bleary-eyed from crying.
All this grieving only makes you look worse.
Your son is that age, you know. You prayed your heart out
For the gods to let you see him as a bearded man."

And Penelope, in her circumspect way: 190

"Eurynome, don't try, even though you love me,
To talk me into bathing and putting on makeup.
Any beauty I had the Olympian gods destroyed
On the day my husband left in the hollow ships.
But go tell Autonoë and Hippodameia   195
To come stand by my side when I enter the hall.
It would be shameful for me to go alone among men."

She spoke, and the old housekeeper went off
To tell the two women Penelope wanted them.

Athena's eyes glinted. She had another idea.   200
First, she made Penelope so sweetly drowsy
That she leaned back, her whole body limp,
And went to sleep right there on her couch.
Then the shimmering goddess went to work on her,
So that all the men would gape in wonder.   205
First she cleansed her lovely face, using
The pure, distilled Beauty that Aphrodite
Anoints herself with when she goes garlanded
Into the beguiling dance of the Graces.[6]
Then she made her look taller, and filled out her figure,   210
And made her skin whiter than polished ivory.
Her work done, the goddess glimmered away.
Just then, some of the women came by,
Talking noisily, and Penelope woke up.
She rubbed her cheeks with her hands and said: 215

"What a soft, sweet sleep! If only Artemis
Would send as soft a death to me at once
So I would no longer waste away in sorrow,
Longing for my dear husband's winning ways.
He was in all ways the very best of men."   220

She spoke. Light from the upper rooms
Flooded the stairs as Penelope came down,
Not alone, two maids trailed behind—
And when she had come among the suitors
She stood in her glory beside a column   225
That supported the roof of the great house,
Hiding her cheeks behind her silken veils,
Grave handmaidens standing on either side.
The suitors' knees grew weak when they saw her.
They were spellbound, in love, and each man prayed   230
That he would lie beside her in bed. But,

It was to her son, Telemachus, that she spoke:

"Telemachus, what can you be thinking of?
You were intelligent even as a child,
But now that you have reached manhood—   235
So handsome and tall that any stranger
Who happened to see you would be able to tell
You're a rich man's son—you're not thinking straight,
Not any more. Just look at what has happened
Here in these halls! How would you like it   240
If our guest, sitting as he is in our house,

---

6. Three goddesses, associated with beauty, joy, and good feelings.

Were to be treated roughly and come to harm?
It would be a disgrace, and the shame would be yours."

And Telemachus, in his clear-headed way:

"I don't blame you for being angry, Mother,   245
But I'm aware of all this myself. I know
Everything that is going on here, good and bad.
I used to think as a child, but not any more.
But I can't think clearly with all these men
Sitting around driving me to distraction.   250
They don't mean me any good, and I have
No one to help me. But I can tell you this,
That the fight between the stranger and Irus
Did not go the way the suitors wanted.
Our guest proved to be the better man.   255
O Father Zeus, and Athena and Apollo,
If only the suitors were beaten like that,
Their limbs unstrung, nodding their heads,
Some in the courtyard and some in the hall,
Just as Irus now sits by the gate,   260
Lolling his head as if he were drunk,
Unable to stand up or get himself home,
Wherever that is, because his limbs are like putty."

Thus mother and son. Then Eurymachus
Addressed Penelope, saying to her: 265

"Daughter of Icarius, wise Penelope,
If all the Greeks throughout the mainland
Could see you now, even more suitors
Would be here tomorrow, feasting in your hall,
For you are far and away the most beautiful   270
And most intelligent woman in the world."

And wise Penelope answered him:

"Eurymachus, the gods destroyed my beauty
On the day when the Argives sailed for Ilion
And with them went my husband, Odysseus.   275
If he were to come back and be part of my life,
My fame would be greater and more resplendent.
But now I grieve, so many sorrows
Has some spirit visited upon me.
And this much is true: when Odysseus left   280
He clasped my right hand in his and said to me:
'I do not think, my wife, that all the Greeks
Will return from Ilion safe and sound.
They say the Trojans are real warriors,
Spearmen and bowmen, and they drive chariots,   285
Which can turn the tide in any battle.
So I do not know whether the god of war

Will send me back or if I'll go down
There in Troy. So everything here is in your hands.
Take care of my father and of my mother   290
As you do now, or even more, when I am gone.
But when you see our son a bearded man,
Marry whom you will, and leave this house.'
So he spoke, and it's all coming true.
There will come a night when a hateful marriage   295
Will darken my bed, cursed as I am, my happiness
Destroyed by Zeus. And I have more heartache.
This isn't the way suitors usually behave
When men compete for the hand of a lady,
A woman of some worth, a rich man's daughter.   300
They bring cattle, and fat sheep,
To feast the bride's friends, and they give her
Glorious gifts. They do not devour
Another's livelihood without recompense."

She spoke, and Odysseus, the godlike survivor,   305
Smiled inwardly to see how she extracted gifts
From the suitors, weaving a spell upon them
With her words, while her mind was set elsewhere.

Then Antinous, Eupeithes' son, said to her:

"Daughter of Icarius, wise Penelope,   310
As far as gifts go, take whatever any man
Wishes to give. It's not good to refuse gifts.
But as for us, we're not going back to our lands
Or anywhere else until you marry
Whoever proves to be the best of the Achaeans."   315

Everyone approved of what Antinous said,
And each man sent a herald to fetch his gifts.
Antinous' man brought a beautiful robe,
All embroidered. It had twelve golden brooches,
Each of them fitted with hooked clasps.   320
Eurymachus' man came back right away
With an intricately crafted golden chain
Strung with amber and bright as the sun.
Eurydamas' attendants brought a pair of earrings,
Three elegant teardrops gleaming from each.   325
From the house of Peisander, Polyctor's son,
There came a necklace of exquisite beauty.
And so it went, each man bringing
One lovely gift after another.

                    And Penelope,
A moving silver grace, went up to her chamber,   330
Her women behind her bearing the beautiful gifts.

The suitors turned to amusing themselves
With dance and song until evening fell.
When twilight shaded their merrymaking
They set up three braziers in the great hall 335
To give them light. They stoked these with kindling,
Seasoned and dry and newly split with the axe.
They set torches between the braziers,
And the household women set about lighting them.
Zeus-bred Odysseus, always thinking, 340
Went up to these women and had a word with them:

"Maidservants of Odysseus, your long-absent lord,
Go off now to where your revered queen is sitting
And do your spinning, or card wool, by her side.
Sit with her and keep her company. Cheer her up. 345
I'll take care of keeping the torches lit
For these men. Even if they stay up until dawn
They won't outlast me. I can put up with a lot."

The women looked at each other and laughed.
Then Melantho, fair-cheeked and sassy, 350
Had some ugly words for him. This Melantho
Was born to Dolius, but Penelope
Had reared her as her very own child,
Spoiling her with toys and whatever she wanted.
Even so she had no feeling for Penelope 355
But loved Eurymachus and slept with him.
And now she lit into Odysseus:

"You must be out of your mind, you old wreck,
Unwilling to go to the blacksmith's to sleep
Or anywhere else. You just blabber on here, 360
Bold as can be, with all these real men around,
Feeling no fear. Are you drunk, or are you
Always like this, with all your blather?
Pleased with yourself, aren't you, because you beat that bum,
Irus? Someone a lot better than Irus 365
Might stand up to you soon and pound you
Bloody with his fists as he drives you outside."

Odysseus shot her a dark look and growled:

"Just let me tell Telemachus what you are saying,
You bitch. He'll cut you to ribbons on the spot." 370

His words scattered the women, sending them
Flying through the hall in terror, convinced
That he meant what he said.
                                Odysseus
Took his stand by the torches, keeping them lit

And watching all the men. But his heart seethed   375
With other business, soon to be finished.

Now Athena was not about to let the suitors
Abstain from insults. She wanted pain
To sink deeper into Odysseus' bones.
And so Eurymachus began to jeer   380
At him for his friends' entertainment:

"Hear me, suitors of our glorious queen,
While I speak my mind. It is not without
The will of the gods that this man has come
To Odysseus' palace. We get a nice glow   385
Of torchlight from him—from his head,
That is, since it doesn't have a hair on it!"

And then speaking directly to Odysseus,
Destroyer of cities, Eurymachus said:

"I wonder if you'd like to be a hired hand,   390
Stranger. Should I hire you to work
On one of my outlying farms gathering fieldstones
And planting tall trees? Oh, I'll pay you.
I'll keep you fed the year round out there,
Give you some clothes and sandals to wear.   395
But you've never done a hard day's work
In your life, preferring to beg your way through town
For food to stuff into your bottomless belly."

And Odysseus, his mind teeming:

"Eurymachus, I wish we could have a contest   400
Working in the fields during the summertime,
When the days are long, just you and I
Out in a hayfield with long, curved scythes,
And plenty of grass so we could test our work,
Fasting until late evening.
                          Or how about this?   405
We could each drive oxen, the best there are,
Big and tawny, both well fed with grass,
The same age, yoked the same way, tireless animals—
And each with four acres of rich soil to plow.
Then you'd see if I could cut a straight furrow   410
Clear to the end.
                  And it would be even better
If Zeus brought war upon us from somewhere,
Today, right now, and I had a shield, two spears,
And a bronze helmet that fit close to my temples.
Then you would see me out in the front ranks,   415
And you wouldn't stand here jeering at me
Because of my belly. But you are insufferable,

And you have a hard heart. No doubt you think
You are some great man, a tough guy,
Because you hang out with puny weaklings.   420
If Odysseus came back home, these doors,
Wide as they are, would be far too narrow
For you to squeeze through as you made for daylight."

This made Eurymachus all the more furious.
Scowling at Odysseus he said to him: 425

"You won't get away with this kind of talk,
Bold as can be with all these real men around,
Feeling no fear. Are you drunk, or are you
Always like this, with all your blather?
Are you all pumped up because you beat that bum, Irus?"   430

And he grabbed a footstool, but Odysseus,
Wary of the man, sat down at the knees
Of Amphinomus, the suitor from Dulichium,
And Eurymachus' missile struck a cupbearer
On the right hand. The wine jug he held   435
Clattered to the ground, and the man groaned
And fell backward into the dust.
                            The suitors
Were in an uproar throughout the shadowy hall.
One man would glance at his neighbor and say:

"Better if the stranger had never made it here;   440
Then he couldn't have brought us all this trouble.
Here we are, brawling about beggars. Our feasts
Will be ruined if we let things turn ugly."

Then Telemachus made his voice heard:

"You are all raving now. Your drunken guzzling   445
Is beginning to show, or some god
Is stirring you up. But now that you have feasted,
Go home and get some rest—whenever you're ready,
Of course. I'm not driving anyone away."

He spoke, and they all bit their lips and marveled   450
At Telemachus for speaking so boldly.
Then Amphinomus addressed the suitors:

"Friends, no man should be angry at a thing
Fairly spoken, or respond by arguing.
Do not mistreat this stranger any longer,   455
Or any of godlike Odysseus' household.
Now let the cupbearer start us off
So we can pour libation and go home to rest.
This stranger we will leave in Odysseus' halls—
Where he landed—and in Telemachus' keeping."   460

Amphinomus' words pleased everyone,
And a bowl was mixed by his herald, Mulius.
He served a cup to each man in turn,
And they poured libations to the blessed gods
And drank sweet wine to their hearts' content.   465
Then they all went home and took their rest.

BOOK XIX

So Odysseus was left alone in the hall,
Planning death for the suitors with Athena's aid.
He spoke winged words to Telemachus:

"Telemachus, get all the weapons out of the hall.
When the suitors miss them and ask you   5
Where they are, set their minds at ease, saying:
'Oh, I have stored them out of the smoke.
They're nothing like they were when Odysseus
Went off to Troy, but are all grimed with soot.
Also, a god put this thought into my head,   10
That when you men are drinking, you might
Start quarreling and someone could get hurt,
Which would ruin your feasting and courting.
Steel has a way of drawing a man to it."

Thus Odysseus. Telemachus nodded,   15
And calling Eurycleia he said to her:

"Nurse, shut the women inside their rooms
While I put my father's weapons away,
The beautiful weapons left out in the hall
And dulled by the smoke since he went off to war.   20
I was just a child then. But now I want
To store them away, safe from the smoke."

And Eurycleia, his old nurse, said:

"Yes, child, you are right
To care for the house and guard its wealth.   25
But who will fetch a light and carry it for you,
Since you won't let any of the women do it?"

Telemachus coolly answered her:

"This stranger here. I won't let anyone
Who gets rations be idle, even a traveler   30
From a distant land."

               Telemachus' words sank in,
And the nurse locked the doors of the great hall.
Odysseus and his illustrious son sprang up

And began storing away the helmets, bossed shields,
And honed spears. And before them Pallas Athena,   35
Bearing a golden lamp, made a beautiful light.
Telemachus suddenly blurted out to his father:

"Father, this is a miracle I'm seeing!
The walls of the house, the lovely panels,
The beams of fir, and the high columns   40
Are glowing like fire. Some god is inside,
One of the gods from the open sky."

Odysseus, his mind teeming, replied:

"Hush. Don't be too curious about this.
This is the way of the gods who hold high heaven.   45
Go get some rest. I'll remain behind here
And draw out the maids—and your mother,
Who in her grief will ask many questions."

And Telemachus went out through the hall
By the light of blazing torches. He came   50
To his room, lay down, and waited for dawn.
Odysseus again was alone in the hall,
Planning death for the suitors with Athena's aid.

Penelope, wary and thoughtful,
Now came from her bedroom, and she was like   55
Artemis or golden Aphrodite.
They set a chair for her by the fire
Where she always sat, a chair inlaid
With spiraling ivory and silver
Which the craftsman Icmalius had made long ago.   60
It had a footstool attached, covered now
With a thick fleece.
                    Penelope sat down,
Taking everything in. White-armed maids
Came out from the women's quarters
And started to take away all of the food,   65
Clearing the tables and picking up the cups
From which the men had been drinking.
They emptied the braziers, scattering the embers
Onto the floor, and then stocked them up
With loads of fresh wood for warmth and light.   70

Then Melantho started in on Odysseus again:

"Are we going to have to put up with you all night,
Roaming though the house and spying on the women?
Go on outside and be glad you had supper,
Or you'll soon stagger out struck with a torch."   75

And Odysseus answered from his teeming mind:

"What's wrong with you, woman? Are you mean to me
Because I'm dirty and dressed in rags
And beg through the land? I do it because I have to.
That's how it is with beggars and vagabonds.   80
You know, I too once lived in a house in a city,
A rich man in a wealthy house, and I often gave
Gifts to wanderers, whatever they needed.
I had servants, too, countless servants,
And plenty of everything else a man needs   85
To live the good life and be considered wealthy.
But Zeus crushed me. Who knows why?
So be careful, woman. Someday you may lose
That glowing beauty that makes you stand out now.
Or your mistress may become fed up with you.   90
Or Odysseus may come. We can still hope for that.
But even if, as seems likely, he is dead
And will never return, his son, Telemachus,
Is now very much like him, by Apollo's grace,
And if any of the women are behaving loosely   95
It won't get by him. He's no longer a child."

None of this was lost on Penelope,
And she scolded the maidservant, saying:

"Your outrageous conduct does not escape me,
Shameless whore that you are, and it will be   100
On your own head. You knew very well,
For you heard me say it, that I intended
To question the stranger here in my halls
About my husband; for I am sick with worry."

Then to Eurynome, the housekeeper, she said: 105

"Bring a chair here with a fleece upon it
So that the stranger can sit down and tell his tale
And listen to me. I have many questions for him."

So Eurynome brought up a polished chair
And threw a fleece over it, and upon it sat   110
Odysseus, patient and godlike.
Penelope, watchful, began with a question:

"First, stranger, let me ask you this:
Who are you and where are you from?"

Odysseus, his mind teeming, answered her: 115

"Lady, no one on earth could find fault with you,
For your fame reaches the heavens above,
Just like the fame of a blameless king,

A godfearing man who rules over thousands
Of valiant men, upholding justice. 120
His rich, black land bears barley and wheat,
The trees are laden with fruit, the flocks
Are always with young, and the sea teems with fish—
Because he rules well, and so his people prosper.
Ask me, therefore, about anything else, 125
But not about my birth or my native land.
That would fill my heart with painful memories.
I have many sorrows, and it wouldn't be right
To sit here weeping in another's house,
Nor is it good to be constantly grieving. 130
I don't want one of your maids, or you yourself,
To be upset with me and say I am awash with tears
Because the wine has gone to my head."

And Penelope, watching, answered him:

"Stranger, the gods destroyed my beauty 135
On the day when the Argives sailed for Ilion
And with them went my husband, Odysseus.
If he were to come back and be part of my life,
My fame would be greater and more resplendent so.
But now I ache, so many sorrows 140
Has some spirit showered upon me.
All of the nobles who rule the islands—
Dulichium, Samê, wooded Zacynthus—
And all those with power on rocky Ithaca
Are courting me and ruining this house. 145
So I pay no attention to strangers
Or to suppliants or public heralds. No,
I just waste away with longing for Odysseus.
My suitors press on, and I weave my wiles.
First some god breathed into me the thought 150
Of setting up a great loom in the main hall,
And I started weaving a vast fabric
With a very fine thread, and I said to them:

'Young men—my suitors, since Odysseus is dead—
Eager as you are to marry me, you must wait 155
Until I finish this robe—it would be a shame
To waste my spinning—a shroud for the hero
Laertes, when death's doom lays him low.
I fear the Achaean women would reproach me
If he should lie in death shroudless for all his wealth.' 160

"So I spoke, and their proud hearts consented.
Every day I would weave at the great loom,
And every night unweave the web by torchlight.
I fooled them for three years with my craft.
But in the fourth year, as the seasons rolled by, 165

And the moons waned, and the days dragged on,
My shameless and headstrong serving women
Betrayed me. The men barged in and caught me at it,
And a howl went up. So I was forced to finish the shroud.
Now I can't escape the marriage. I'm at my wit's end.   170
My parents are pressing me to marry,
And my son agonizes over the fact
That these men are devouring his inheritance.
He is a man now, and able to preside
Over a household to which Zeus grants honor.   175
But tell me of your birth, for you are not sprung,
As the saying goes, from stock or stone."

And Odysseus, from his mind's teeming depths:

"Honored wife of Laertes' son, Odysseus,
Will you never stop asking about my lineage?   180
All right, I will tell you, but bear in mind
You are only adding to the sorrows I have.
For so it is when a man has been away from home
As long as I have, wandering from city to city
And bearing hardships. Still, I will tell you.   185
          Crete is an island that lies in the middle
Of the wine-dark sea, a fine, rich land
With ninety cities swarming with people
Who speak many different languages.
There are Achaeans there, and native Cretans,   190
Cydonians, Pelasgians, and three tribes of Dorians.
One of the cities is great Cnossus,
Where Minos ruled and every nine years
Conversed with great Zeus. He was the father
Of my father, the great hero Deucalion.[7]   195
Deucalion had another son, Idomeneus,
Who sailed his beaked ships to Ilion
Following the sons of Atreus.[8] I was the younger,
And he the better man. My name is Aethon.
          It was in Crete that I saw Odysseus   200
And gave him gifts of hospitality.
He had been blown off course rounding Malea
On his way to Troy. He put in at Amnisus,
Where the cave of Eileithyia[9] is found.
That is a difficult harbor, and he barely escaped   205
The teeth of the storm. He went up to the city
And asked for Idomeneus, claiming to be
An old and honored friend. But Idomeneus' ships
Had left for Troy ten days before, so I
Took him in and entertained him well,   210

7. Every nine years, Minos, king of Crete, was   8. Agamemnon and Menelaus.
instructed on how to rule by his father, Zeus.   9. Goddess associated with childbirth.
Deucalion, his son, succeeded him as king.

Drawing on the ample supplies in the house.
I gathered his men and distributed to them
Barley meal, wine, and bulls for sacrifice
From the public supplies, to keep them happy.
They stayed for twelve days. A norther so strong   215
You could barely stand upright in it
Had them corraled—some evil spirit had roused it.
On the thirteenth day the wind dropped, and they left."

All lies, but he made them seem like the truth,
And as she listened, her face melted with tears.   220

> Snow deposited high in the mountains by the wild West Wind
> Slowly melts under the East Wind's breath,
> And as it melts the rivers rise in their channels.

So her lovely cheeks coursed with tears as she wept
For her husband, who was sitting before her.   225
Odysseus pitied her tears in his heart,
But his eyes were as steady between their lids
As if they were made of horn or iron
As he concealed his own tears through guile.
When Penelope had cried herself out,   230
She spoke to him again, saying:

"Now I feel I must test you, stranger,
To see if you really did entertain my husband
And his godlike companions, as you say you did.
Tell me what sort of clothes he wore, and tell me   235
What he was like, and what his men were like."

And Odysseus, from his mind's teeming depths:

"Lady, it is difficult for me to speak
After we've been apart for so long. It has been
Twenty years since he left my country.   240
But I have an image of him in my mind.
Odysseus wore a fleecy purple cloak,
Folded over, and it had a brooch
With a double clasp, fashioned of gold,
And on the front was an intricate design: 245
A hound holding in his forepaws a dappled fawn
That writhed to get free. Everyone marveled
At how, though it was all made of gold,
The hound had his eye fixed on the fawn
As he was strangling it, and the fawn   250
Twisted and struggled to get to its feet.
And I remember the tunic he wore,
Glistening like onionskin, soft and shiny
And with a sheen like sunlight. There were
Quite a few women who admired it.   255

But remember, now, I do not know
Whether Odysseus wore this at home,
Or whether one of his men gave it to him
When he boarded ship, or someone else,
For Odysseus was a man with many friends.   260
He had few equals among the Achaeans.
I, too, gave him gifts—a bronze sword,
A beautiful purple cloak, and a fringed tunic,
And I gave him a ceremonious send-off
In his benched ship. And one more thing: 265
He had a herald, a little older than he was,
And I will tell you what he looked like.
He was slope-shouldered, with dark skin
And curly hair. His name was Eurybates,
And Odysseus held him in higher esteem   270
Than his other men, because they thought alike."

These words stirred up Penelope's grief.
She recognized the unmistakeable tokens
Odysseus was giving her. She wept again,
And then composed herself and said to him: 275

"You may have been pitied before, stranger,
But now you will be loved and honored
Here in my halls. I gave him those clothes.
I folded them, brought them from the storeroom,
And pinned on the gleaming brooch,   280
To delight him. But I will never welcome him
Home again, and so the fates were dark
When Odysseus left in his hollow ship
For Ilion, that curse of a city."

And Odysseus, from his mind's teeming depths: 285

"Revered wife of Laertes' son, Odysseus,
Do not mar your fair skin with tears any more,
Or melt your heart with weeping for your husband.
Not that I blame you. Any woman weeps
When she has lost her husband, a man with whom   290
She has made love and whose children she has borne—
And the husband you've lost is Odysseus,
Who they say is like the immortal gods.
Stop weeping, though, and listen to my words,
For what I am about to tell you is true.   295
I have lately heard of Odysseus' return,
That he is near, in the rich land of Thesprotia,
Still alive. And he is bringing home treasures,
Seeking gifts, and getting them, throughout the land.
But he lost his trusty crew and his hollow ship   300
On the wine-dark sea. As he was sailing out
From the island of Thrinacia, Zeus and Helios

Hit him hard because his companions had killed
The cattle of the Sun. His men went under,
But he rode his ship's keel until the waves   305
Washed him ashore in the land of the Phaeacians,
Whose race is closely akin to the gods'.
They treated him as if he were a god,
Gave him many gifts, and were more than willing
To escort him home. And he would have been here   310
By now, but he thought it more profitable
To gather wealth by roaming the land.
No one is as good as Odysseus
At finding ways to gain an advantage.
I had all this from Pheidon, the Thesprotian king.   315
And he swore to me, as he poured libations
There in his house, that a ship was already launched,
And a crew standing by, to take him home.
He sent me off first, since a Thesprotian ship
Happened to be leaving for Dulichium,   320
But before I left, Pheidon showed me
All the treasure Odysseus had amassed,
Bronze, gold, and wrought iron, enough to feed
His children's children for ten generations,
All stored there for him in the halls of the king.   325
Odysseus, he said, had gone to Dodona
To consult the oak-tree oracle of Zeus
And ask how he should return to Ithaca—
Openly or in secret—after being gone so long.
So he is safe, and will come soon.   330
He is very near, and will not be away long
From his dear ones and his native land.
I will swear to this. Now Zeus on high
Be my witness, and this hospitable table,
And the hearth of flawless Odysseus himself—   335
That everything will happen just as I say:
Before this month is out Odysseus will come,
In the dark of the moon, before the new crescent."

And Penelope, watching him carefully:

"Ah, stranger, may your words come true.   340
Then you would know my kindness, and my gifts
Would make you blessed in all men's eyes.
But I know in my heart that Odysseus
Will never come home, and that you will never
Find passage elsewhere, since there is not now   345
Any master in the house like Odysseus—
If he ever existed—to send honored guests
Safely on their way, or to welcome them.
But still, wash our guest's feet, maidens,
And prepare a bed for him. Set up a frame   350
And cover it with cloaks and lustrous blankets

To keep him cozy and warm. When golden Dawn
Shows her first light, bathe him and anoint him,
So he can sit side by side with Telemachus
And share in the feast here in the hall.   355
And anyone who causes this man any pain
Will regret it sorely and will accomplish nothing
Here in this house, however angry he gets.
For how would you ever find out, stranger,
Whether or not I surpass all other women   360
In presence of mind, if you sit down to dinner
Squalid and disheveled here in my hall?
Our lives are short. A hard-hearted man
Is cursed while he lives and reviled in death.
But a good-hearted man has his fame spread   365
Far and wide by the guests he has honored,
And men speak well of him all over the earth."

And Odysseus, his mind teeming, answered her:

"Revered wife of Odysseus, Laertes' son,
I lost all interest in cloaks and blankets   370
On the day I left the snowy mountains of Crete
In my long-oared ship. I will lie down tonight,
As I have through many a sleepless night,
On a poor bed, waiting for golden-throned Dawn.
Nor do I have any taste for foot-baths,   375
And none of the serving women here in your hall
Will touch my feet, unless there is some old,
Trustworthy woman who has suffered as I have.
I would not mind if she touched my feet."

And Penelope, watching him carefully: 380

"Of all the travelers who have come to my house,
None, dear guest, have been as thoughtful as you
And none as welcome, so wise are your words.
I do have an old and trustworthy woman here,
Who nursed and raised my ill-starred husband,   385
Taking him in her arms the day he was born.
She will wash your feet, frail as she is.
Eurycleia, rise and wash your master's—that is,
Wash the feet of this man who is your master's age.
Odysseus' feet and hands are no doubt like his now,   390
For men age quickly when life is hard."

At this, the old woman hid her face in her hands.
Shedding warm tears, she spoke through her sobs:

"My lost child, I can do nothing for you.
Zeus must have hated you above all other men,   395

Zeus Joke

Although you were always godfearing. No one
Burned more offerings to the Lord of Lightning,
So many fat thighbones, bulls by the hundreds,
With prayers that you reach a sleek old age
And raise your glorious son. And now the god has   400
Deprived you alone of your day of return.
      And I suppose, stranger, women mocked him, too,
When he came to some man's gloried house
In a distant land, just as these cheeky bitches
All mock you here. It is to avoid their insults   405
That you will not allow them to wash your feet.
But Penelope, Icarius' wise daughter,
Has asked me to do it, and I will,
For her sake and for yours,
For my heart is throbbing with sorrow.   410
But listen now to what I have to say.
Many road-weary strangers have come here,
But I have never seen such a resemblance
As that between you and Odysseus,
In looks, voice—even the shape of your feet."   415

And Odysseus, from his mind's teeming depths:

"Oh, everyone who has seen us both says that,
Old woman, that we are very much alike,
Just as you yourself have noticed."

And the old woman took the shining basin   420
She used for washing feet, poured
Cold water into it, and then added the hot.
Odysseus, waiting, suddenly sat down at the hearth
And turned away toward the shadows. The scar!
It flashed through his mind that his old nurse   425
Would notice his scar as soon as she touched him,
And then everything would be out in the open.
She drew near and started to wash her master,
And knew at once the scar from the wound
He had gotten long ago from a boar's white tusk   430
When he had gone to Parnassus to visit Autolycus,
His mother's father, who was the best man on earth
At thieving and lying, skills he had learned
From Hermes.[1] He had won the god's favor
With choice burnt offerings of lambs and kids.   435

Autolycus had visited Ithaca once
When his grandson was still a newborn baby.
After he finished supper, Eurycleia
Put the child in his lap and said to him:

---

1. Trickster and messenger god.

"Autolycus, now name the child   440
Of your own dear child. He has been much prayed for."

Then Autolycus made this response:

"Daughter and son-in-law of mine,
Give this child the name I now tell you.
I come here as one who is odious,[2] yes,   445
Hateful to many for the pain I have caused
All over the land. Let this child, therefore,
Go by the name of Odysseus.
For my part, when he is grown up
And comes to the great house of his mother's kin   450
In Parnassus, where my possessions lie,
I will give him a share and send him home happy."

In due time, Odysseus came to get these gifts
From Autolycus. His grandfather
And his uncles all welcomed him warmly,   455
And Amphithea, his mother's mother,
Embraced Odysseus and kissed his head
And beautiful eyes. Autolycus told his sons
To prepare a meal, and they obeyed at once,
Leading in a bull, five years old,   460
Which they flayed, dressed, and butchered.
They skewered the meat, roasted it skillfully,
And then served out portions to everyone.
All day long until the sun went down
They feasted to their hearts' content.   465
But when the sun set and darkness came on
They went to bed and slept through the night.
When Dawn brushed the early sky with rose,
They went out to hunt—Autolycus' sons
Running their hounds—and with them went   470
Godlike Odysseus. They climbed the steep wooded slopes
Of Mount Parnassus and soon reached
The windy hollows. The sun was up now,
Rising from the damasked waters of Ocean
And just striking the fields, when the beaters came   475
Into a glade. The dogs were out front,
Tracking the scent, and behind the dogs
Came Autolycus' sons and noble Odysseus,
His brandished spear casting a long shadow.
Nearby, a great boar was lying in his lair,   480
A thicket that was proof against the wild wet wind
And could not be pierced by the rays of the sun,
So dense it was. Dead leaves lay deep
Upon the ground there. The sound of men and dogs

2. Again, the pun on Odysseus's name is in the Greek.

Pressing on through the leaves reached the boar's ears,   485
And he charged out from his lair, back bristling
And his eyes spitting fire. He stood at bay
Right before them, and Odysseus rushed him,
Holding his spear high, eager to thrust.
The boar was too quick. Slashing in,   490
He got Odysseus in the thigh, right above the knee,
His white tusk tearing a long gash in the muscle
Just shy of the bone. Even so, Odysseus
Did not miss his mark, angling his spear
Into the boar's right shoulder. The gleaming point   495
Went all the way through, and with a loud grunt
The boar went down and gasped out his life.
Autolycus' sons took care of the carcass
And tended the wound of the flawless Odysseus,
Skillfully binding it and staunching the blood   500
By chanting a spell. Then they quickly returned
To their father's house. When Odysseus
Had regained his strength, Autolycus and his sons
Gave him glorious gifts and sent him home happy,
Home to Ithaca. His mother and father   505
Rejoiced at his return and asked him all about
How he got his scar; and he told them the story
Of how a boar had gashed him with his white tusk
As he hunted on Parnassus with Autolycus' sons.

This was the scar the old woman recognized   510
When the palm of her hand ran over it
As she held his leg. She let the leg fall,
And his foot clanged against the bronze basin,
Tipping it over and spilling the water
All over the floor. Eurycleia's heart   515
Trembled with mingled joy and grief,
Tears filled her eyes, and her voice
Was choked as she reached out
And touched Odysseus' chin and said:

"You are Odysseus, dear child. I did not know you   520
Until I laid my hands on my master's body."

She spoke, and turned her eyes toward Penelope,
Wanting to show her that her husband was home.
But Penelope could not return her gaze
Or understand her meaning, for Athena   525
Had diverted her mind. Odysseus reached
For the old woman's throat, seized it in his right hand
And drawing her closer with his other, he said:

"Do you want to destroy me? You yourself
Nursed me at your own breast, and now   530
After twenty hard years I've come back home.

Now that some god has let you in on the secret,
You keep it to yourself, you hear? If you don't,
I'll tell you this, and I swear I'll do it:
If, with heaven's help, I subdue the suitors,   535
I will not spare you—even if you are my nurse—
When I kill the other women in the hall."

And Eurycleia, the wise old woman:

"How can you say that, my child? You know
What I'm made of. You know I won't break.   540
I'll be as steady as solid stone or iron.
And I'll tell you this, and you remember it:
If, with heaven's help, you subdue the proud suitors,
I'll list for you all the women in the house,
Those who dishonor you and those who are true."   545

And Odysseus, his mind teeming:

"Nurse, you don't have to tell me about them.
I'll keep an eye out and get to know each one.
Don't say a thing. Just leave it up to the gods."

At this, the old woman went off for more water   550
To wash his feet, since it had all been spilled.
When she had washed him and rubbed on oil,
Odysseus pulled his chair close to the fire again
To keep warm, and hid the scar with his rags.

Penelope now resumed their talk: 555

"There's one more thing I want to ask you about,
And then it will be time to get some sleep—
At least for those to whom sweet sleep comes
Despite their cares. But some god has given me
Immeasurable sorrow. By day   560
I console myself with lamentation
And see to my work and that of my women.
But at night, when sleep takes hold of others,
I lie in bed, smothered by my own anxiety,

Mourning restlessly, my heart racing.   565
Just as the daughter of Pandareus,
The pale nightingale, sings sweetly
In the greening of spring, perched in the leaves,
And trills out her song of lament for her son,
Her beloved Itylus, whom she killed unwittingly,   570
Itylus, the son of Zethus her lord[3]—

3. Zethus's wife envied her sister-in-law, Niobe, who had six sons to her one. She wanted to kill one of Niobe's children, but ended up killing her own son, Itylus, by mistake, in a fit of madness. Zeus changed her into a nightingale.

So too my heart is torn with dismay.
Should I stay here with my son
And keep everything safe and just as it is,
My goods, my slaves, my high-gabled house,   575
Honoring my husband's bed and public opinion—
Or should I go with whoever is best
Of all my suitors, and gives me gifts past counting?
And then there's my son. While he was young
And not yet mature, he kept me from leaving   580
My husband's house and marrying another.
But now that he's grown and come into manhood,
He begs me to leave, worried because
These Achaean men are devouring his goods.
     But listen now to a dream I had   585
And tell me what it means. In my dream
I have twenty geese at home. I love to watch them
Come out of the water and eat grains of wheat.
But a huge eagle with a hooked beak comes
Down from the mountain and breaks their necks,   590
Killing them all. They lie strewn through the hall
While he rides the wind up to the bright sky.
I weep and wail, still in my dream,
And Achaean ladies gather around me
As I grieve because the eagle killed my geese.   595
Then the eagle comes back and perches upon
A jutting roofbeam and speaks to me
In a human voice, telling me not to cry:

'Take heart, daughter of famed Icarius.
This is no dream, but a true vision   600
That you can trust. The geese are the suitors,
And I, who was once an eagle, am now
Your husband come back, and I will deal out doom,
A grisly death for all of the suitors.'

"So he spoke, and I woke up refreshed.   605
Looking around I saw the geese in the house,
Feeding on wheat by the trough, as before."

And Odysseus, his mind teeming:

"Lady, there is no way to give this dream
Another slant. Odysseus himself has shown you   610
How he will finish this business. The suitors' doom
Is clear. Not one will escape death's black birds."
And Penelope, in her circumspect way:

"Stranger, you should know that dreams
Are hard to interpret, and don't always come true.   615
There are two gates for dreams to drift through,
One made of horn and the other of ivory.

Dreams that pass through the gate of ivory
Are deceptive dreams and will not come true,
But when someone has a dream that has passed   620
Through the gate of polished horn, that dream
Will come true. My strange dream, though,
Did not come from there. If it had,
It would have been welcome to me and my child.
          One more thing, and, please, take it to heart.   625
Dawn is coming, the accursed dawn of the day
Which will sever me from the house of Odysseus.
I will announce a contest. Odysseus
Used to line up axes inside his hall,
Twelve of them, like the curved chocks   630
That prop up a ship when it is being built,
And he would stand far off and send an arrow
Whizzing through them all. I will propose   ← Test
This contest to my suitors, and whoever
Can bend that bow and slip the string on its notch   635
And shoot an arrow through all twelve axes,
With him will I go, leaving behind this house
I was married in, this beautiful, prosperous house,
Which I will remember always, even in my dreams."

And Odysseus, from the depths of his teeming mind: 640

"Revered wife of Laertes' son, Odysseus,
Do not put off this contest any longer,
For Odysseus will be here, with all his cunning,
Handling that polished bow, before these men
Could ever string it and shoot through the iron."   645

Then Penelope, still watching him:

"If you were willing, stranger, to sit here
Beside me in my halls and give me joy,
Sleep would never settle upon my eyes.
But we cannot always be sleepless,   650
For every thing there is a season, and a time
For all we do on the life-giving earth.
I will go now to my room upstairs
And lie on my bed, which has become
A sorrowful bed, wet with my tears   655
Since the day Odysseus left
For Ilion, that accursed city.
I will lie there, but you can lie here
In the hall. Spread some blankets on the floor,
Or have the maids make up a bed for you."   660

Saying this, Penelope went upstairs
To her softly lit room, not alone,
For her women went up with her.

Once in her room she wept for Odysseus,
Her beloved husband, wept until Athena   665
Let sweet sleep settle upon her eyelids.

BOOK XX

Odysseus lay down to sleep
On the outer porch. He spread out
An uncured oxhide, and on top of that
He layered fleeces from the many sheep
That were always being slaughtered
There in his house. Eurynome   5
Covered him with a cloak, and there he lay,
Sleepless, his mind racing with thoughts
Of how to punish the suitors.
                                And then the women
Came from the house, on their way,
As usual, to sleep with the suitors,   10
Laughing with each other and giggling.
Odysseus felt his chest tighten. He brooded
For a long time over what he should do—
Rush out and kill every last one of them,
Or let them sleep with the arrogant bastards   15
This one last time. He growled under his breath

   The way a dog standing over her pups growls
   When she sees a stranger and digs in to fight—

So Odysseus growled at their iniquity,
But he slapped his chest hard and scolded his heart: 20

"Endure, my heart. You endured worse than this
On that day when the invincible Cyclops
Ate our comrades. You bore it until your cunning
Got you out of the cave where you thought you would die."

In this way Odysseus scolded his heart,   25
And his heart in obedience beat steady and strong.
But the great hero himself tossed and turned.

   It was like a man roasting a paunch
   Stuffed with fat and blood over a fire.
   He can't wait for it to be done   30
   And so keeps turning it over and over—

Odysseus tossing and turning as he pondered how
To get his hands on the shameless suitors,
One man against many.
                        And then Athena came
Down from the sky, and stood above his head   35
In the form of a woman, and spoke to him:

"Why are you sleepless, most ill-fated of men?
This is your house, and in this house are your wife
And child, a son any father would hope for."

And Odysseus, his mind teeming: 40

"Yes, Goddess, all that you say is true,
But my heart is brooding over this—
How to get my hands on the shameless suitors,
Alone as I am, against the whole pack of them.
And worse, even if I were to kill them   45
By your will and the will of Zeus, how
Would I get out of it? Think about that."

And Athena, eyes flashing in the dark:

"Let it go, Odysseus. Some people trust
Their puny human friends more than you trust me.   50
And here I am, a goddess, protecting you
In all your trials. To put it plainly,
Even if there were fifty squadrons of armed men
All around us, doing their mortal best to kill us,
You would still be able to run off their cattle!   55
Now get some sleep. Staying up all night
Will only sap your strength. All your troubles,
Odysseus, will soon be over."
                                Athena spoke
And shed sleep on his eyelids, and then
She was off to Olympus, a being of light.   60

While Odysseus slept, his cares melting away
Under the spell of sleep, his wife awoke,
And she wept as she sat upon her soft bed.
When her heart had its fill of weeping,
The godlike woman prayed to Artemis: 65

"Artemis, mighty daughter of Zeus—please,
Shoot an arrow into my breast and take my life
This very moment. This is my wish,
Or that a storm wind snatch me away
And bear me off over the gloomy passes   70
And cast me down at the mouth of Ocean,
As winds once bore off Pandareus' daughters.
The gods had slain their parents, and they were left
Orphans in their halls. Aphrodite fed them
Cheese, sweet honey, and mellow wine;   75
Hera made them wise and beautiful
Beyond all women; holy Artemis made them tall;
And Athena taught them glorious handiwork.
But while Aphrodite was off to high Olympus
To arrange their marriages, on her way to Zeus,   80

Zeus heard the prayer

The high lord of thunder, who knows all,
All the good and bad fortune of mortal men—
The storm spirits snatched the girls away
And gave them as slaves to the hateful Furies.
So may the Olympians blot me out,   85
Or Artemis, in her tall headdress, shoot me,
That I may pass beneath the hateful earth
With Odysseus in my mind's eye, never
To gratify the heart of a lesser man.
Grief is endurable when one weeps by day   90
But can sleep at night. Sleep makes us forget
All things, both the good and the bad,
Once it enshrouds our eyelids. But some spirit
Keeps sending me bad dreams. This very night
There slept with me again someone who looked   95
Just like Odysseus when he left with the army,
And my heart was glad, because I did not think
It was a dream, but the waking truth at last."

She spoke, and Dawn came, seated on gold.
Odysseus heard Penelope's voice as she wept   100
And in that moment between sleep and waking
He felt in his heart that she knew him already
And was standing beside his head.
                                   He picked up
The cloak and fleeces on which he had slept
And put them on a chair in the hall. Then he took   105
The oxhide outside and set it down, and,
Lifting his palms to the sky, he prayed to Zeus:

"Father Zeus, if it was the gods' will
To bring me home over land and sea
After afflicting me, show me a sign.   110
Let someone of those stirring inside the house
Speak for me a word of good omen,
And send me a sign also from the open sky."

Zeus in his wisdom heard his prayer
And thundered from snow-capped Olympus   115
High above the clouds. Odysseus was glad.
And a woman uttered a word of omen
As she ground at a mill nearby in the house.
Twelve women in all worked the mills there,
Grinding barley and wheat into flour,   120
The marrow of men. The other women,
Their wheat ground, were sleeping now,
But she, the weakest of them, was still at it.
Stopping her mill, she spoke these words:

"Father Zeus, lord of gods and men.   125
That was a loud thunderclap out of a clear sky!
You must be showing someone a sign.

Will you answer an old woman's prayer?
Let this be the last and final day
The suitors feast in Odysseus' hall.   130
I've broken my back grinding their grain.
Let this meal be their last."

Odysseus smiled at this omen, and at the thunder
From Zeus. He would have his vengeance.

The other women were up now, huddled together   135
As they kindled the day's fire on the hearth.
Telemachus rose from bed, a godlike man,
And got dressed. He slung his sharp sword
Around one shoulder, tied fine leather sandals
Onto his supple feet, and, spear in hand,   140
Went to the threshold and spoke to Eurycleia:

"Dear nurse, have you looked after our guest;
Given him a bed and food, or is he lying uncared for?
That's my mother's style, wise as she is,
Honoring one man outrageously   145
And sending a better man away neglected."

And Eurycleia, with all her wits about her:

"Don't blame her, child, when she is blameless.
He sat and drank wine as long as he wanted,
But he said he wasn't hungry. She asked him.   150
When he got tired and wanted to sleep,
She told the women to make up a bed,
But he, like many who are down on their luck,
Wouldn't sleep on a bed, or under blankets.
He lay on an undressed oxhide and some fleeces   155
Out on the porch, and we threw a cloak over him."

Thus Eurycleia, and Telemachus went out,
Spear in hand and two hounds at his heels,
To join the other men in the public square.
Then Eurycleia, Peisenor's granddaughter,   160
A noble woman, called to her maids:

"Some of you get busy and sweep the hall
And sprinkle it, and put the purple coverlets
On the good chairs. And we'll need some others,
To sponge down the tables, and wash the bowls   165
And goblets. The rest of you go down
And fetch water from the spring, quickly.
The suitors will be here early today.
It's a feast day, a holiday for everyone."

She spoke, and they did as she said. Twenty   170
Went down to the spring with its dark water,
And the rest did their house work skillfully.

Then in came the town's serving men. They started
Splitting logs, doing a good job of it. The women
Came back from the spring, and behind them   175
Came the swineherd, driving three prime boars,
The herd's finest. He let them feed in the courtyard
And then turned to Odysseus with a pleasant manner:

"Stranger, are you getting any more respect yet,
Or are they still insulting you in the hall?"   180

And Odysseus, his mind teeming:

"Eumaeus, it is outrageous the way these men
Carry on in another man's house. May the gods
Punish them! They have no sense of shame."

After this exchange, Melanthius came up,   185
The goatherd, leading the best she-goats
From all the herds for the suitors' feast.
Two herdsmen followed him. He tethered the goats
In the echoing portico, and then taunted Odysseus:

"Are you still here, pestering everyone?   190
Why don't you get the hell outside?
You and I are going to have to settle this
With our fists. I don't like your way of begging.
There are other feasts you can go to, you know."

Odysseus made no response, but sat   195
Shaking his head and brooding darkly.

And then a third herdsman came, Philoetius,
Driving for the suitors a barren heifer
And fat she-goats. This livestock had been brought over,
Along with Philoetius, by ferrymen   200
Who ply the straits with all sorts of passengers.
He tethered the animals in the echoing portico
And then went up to the swineherd and asked:

"Who's the new arrival, swineherd?
Where does he say he comes from,   205
And who are his parents and kinsmen?
Poor guy! He looks like some kind of king,
But the gods can make it tough
For wanderers, even if they're royalty."

He spoke, then came up to Odysseus,   210
Stretched out his right hand, and said:

"Welcome, stranger, and may good luck
Come your way, hard as things are for you now.

Father Zeus, no god curses us worse than you!
You have no pity for men. You beget them,   215
Then plunge them into misery and pain.
Stranger, I broke into a sweat when I saw you,
And my eyes are full of tears. You remind me
Of Odysseus. He too is clothed in rags like this,
I suppose, and is a wanderer like you,   220
If he is still alive, that is, and still sees the sunlight.
But if he is already dead and has gone to Hades,
Then I weep for noble Odysseus.
He put me in charge of his cattle when I was a boy
In the land of the Cephallenians, and now   225
Those cattle are past counting. No breed
Ever flourished like that for any mortal man.
But now other men order me to drive them
So they can eat them, with no regard at all
For the son in the house, or the gods' wrath.   230
No, they're hot to divide among themselves
All the property of our long-absent master.
As for myself, I go around and around in my heart,
Trying to decide. It would be very bad of me,
While my master's son still lives, to go off   235
To some other place with my cattle,
To a foreign land. But it is worse still
To stay here and suffer, in charge of herds
Handed over to others. I would have fled
Long ago, believe me, to some powerful lord,   240
Because things here are no longer bearable,
Except that I still imagine, still have some hope
That my unfortunate master will someday return
And scatter the suitors out of this house."

And Odysseus, his great mind teeming: 245

"You're a good man, cowherd, and smart,
And I see that you understand things,
So I will say something and seal it with an oath.
With Zeus and all the gods above as witnesses,
And by Odysseus' hearth, and this table   250
Of hospitality to which I have come,
I swear that while you are here, Odysseus
Will come home, and you will see, if you wish,
The death of the suitors, who lord it over this hall."

To which the cowherd responded: 255

"May Zeus bring what you say to pass, stranger.
Then you would see what these hands can do."

And Eumaeus, too, prayed to all the gods
That wise Odysseus might return to his home.

So went their talk.
           The suitors, meanwhile,   260
Were laying plans for Telemachus' death,
But as they talked a bird appeared on their left,
A high-flying eagle with a dove in its talons.
This prompted Amphinomus to say to them:

"This plan of ours isn't going to work, friends—   265
Killing Telemachus. We might as well just eat."

The suitors all agreed with Amphinomus.
Going into the house of godlike Odysseus,
They laid their cloaks on chairs and got busy
Slaughtering big sheep and plump goats   270
And fatted swine, and the herd's prize heifer.
They roasted the entrails, served them, and mixed wine
In the bowls. The swineherd passed out the cups,
Philoetius handed out bread from a beautiful basket,
And Melanthius poured for them. They reached out   275
To all the tasty dishes spread before them.

Telemachus, pressing his advantage,
Showed Odysseus to a seat
Inside the great hall by the stone threshold,
Giving him a shabby stool beside a little table.   280
He served him a portion of the entrails
And a cup of wine, and he said to him:

"Sit here among these heroes and sip your wine.
I myself will protect you from their insults
And keep their hands from you. This house   285
Is not a public inn, but the palace of Odysseus,
Who inherited it to pass on to me.
So, all you suitors, control yourselves.
I don't want any fights breaking out here."

They bit their lips at this and wondered   290
At Telemachus. It had been a bold speech.
Then Antinous, Eupeithes' son, said:

"Hard as it is, we'd better listen to him, men.
Telemachus really means business now.
If Zeus had allowed it, we'd have shut his mouth   295
By now, here in these halls, fine speaker or not."

But Telemachus paid no attention to Antinous.

Meanwhile, down in the town, heralds
Were leading a sacrifice of one hundred bulls
Through the streets, and Achaean men,   300
Their long hair flowing, were gathering

In a shady grove sacred to Apollo,
The god whose arrows strike from afar.[4]

In Odysseus' palace they were now drawing
The roasted meat from the spits and dividing it up   305
For a glorious feast. The servers set out
A portion for Odysseus equal to the others,
This at the command of Telemachus,
Godlike Odysseus' own true son.

But Athena was not about to let the suitors   *why?*   310
Abstain from insults. She wanted the pain
To sink deeper into Odysseus' bones.
There was a particularly arrogant suitor
From the island of Samê—Ctessipus by name.
This man, relying on his enormous wealth,   315
Courted the wife of the long-absent Odysseus.
He spoke now among the insolent crowd:

"Hear me, suitors. I have something to say.
The stranger here has been served a portion
Equal to ours. This is all as it should be.   320
It would not be right to deprive any guest
Telemachus entertains here in these halls.
So I'd like to give him a gift myself,
A little gratuity he might want to pass on
To the bath woman or one of the other slaves   325
Who live in the house of godlike Odysseus."

So saying, he picked up an ox's hoof
From a basket and threw it hard. Odysseus
Snapped his head aside and dodged it,
Smiling to himself, a grim and bitter smile.   330
The ox's hoof crashed into the solid wall,

And Telemachus tore into Ctessipus:

"You're damned lucky you missed him,
Ctessipus—or rather that he dodged your throw—   *Telemachus
Or I would have rammed my spear into your gut,   stands firm*   335
And your father would have been busy
With your funeral instead of making plans for a wedding.
No more of this ugliness in my house—from anyone!
I understand now what's going on around here,
The good and the bad. I was a child before.   340
But we still have to put up with all this,
Seeing the sheep slaughtered, the wine drunk,
The bread—one man can't stop many.

4. Apollo carries a bow; his arrows can bring plague.

You don't have to be hostile to me,
But if you are determined to cut me down,   345
Well, I'd rather be killed in cold blood
Than have to watch this disgusting behavior—
Guests mistreated and men dragging the women
Shamefully through these beautiful halls."

Dead silence reigned in those beautiful halls   350
Until Agelaus, son of Damastor, said:

"Friends, no one should get angry at a speech
Justly spoken, or respond to it harshly.
We should stop mistreating the stranger
And all of the servants in Odysseus' house.   355
But I would like to offer to Telemachus,
And to his mother, some friendly advice,
And I hope that it gets through to both of them.
As long as you still held hope in your hearts
That Odysseus would find his way back home,   360
No one could blame you for waiting for him
And restraining the suitors—clearly the better course
Had he ever come back and returned to his home.
But now it is clear he will never return.
Sit down with your mother and tell her this.   365
Tell her to marry the best of her suitors,
Whoever that is, whoever gives her the most.
Then you can enjoy what your father has left you,
And she can keep another man's house."

Telemachus answered in his cool-headed way: 370

"I swear by Zeus and by my poor father,
Who has either perished far from Ithaca
Or is wandering still, that I do not, Agelaus,
Delay my mother's marriage. On the contrary,
I encourage her to marry the man of her choice,   375
And I offer her a dowry of gifts past counting.
But it would be shameful for me to order her to leave—
May the gods forbid it—against her own will."

Thus Telemachus. And Pallas Athena
Touched the suitors' minds with hysteria.   380
They couldn't stop laughing, and as they laughed
It seemed to them that their jaws were not theirs,
And the meat that they ate was dabbled with blood.
Tears filled their eyes, and their hearts raced.
Then the seer Theoclymenus spoke among them: 385

"Wretches, what wicked thing is this that you suffer?
You are shrouded in night from top to toe,
Lamentation flares, your cheeks melt with tears,

And the walls of the house are spattered with blood.
The porch and the court are crowded with ghosts   390
Streaming down to the undergloom. The sun is gone
From heaven, and an evil mist spreads over the land."

Thus the seer, and they just giggled at him.
Eurymachus was the first to actually speak:

"This newly arrived stranger has lost his mind!   395
Quick, get him outside, since he thinks it's night in here."

To which the seer Theoclymenus replied:

"I don't need any escorts, Eurymachus.
I have eyes, ears, and my own two feet,
And a mind in good working order.   400
I'll leave under my own power, for I can see
Evil coming upon you, inescapable evil
For every last one of you who in your blind pride
Do violence to the house of Odysseus."

And with that he left the great hall   405
And went to Peiraeus, who took him in gladly.
The suitors stood there smirking at each other
And tried to provoke Telemachus
By ridiculing his guests with comments like these:

"Hey, Telemachus, you don't have much luck   410
With the kind of guests you keep around.
You've got this filthy vagabond here
Who always wants a handout of bread and wine
And can't help out with anything, a useless load.
Then this other one posing as a prophet.   415
If you ask me we ought to throw them on a ship
And send them off to the Sicilians.
At least then you would turn a little profit."

So went their talk. But Telemachus ignored them,
Watching his father in silence, waiting for the moment   420
When he would lay his hands on the shameless suitors.

By now Penelope, Icarius' wise daughter,
Had set her chair across from the suitors
And heard the words of each man in the hall.
During all their laughter they had been busy   425
Preparing their dinner, a tasty meal
For which they had slaughtered many animals.
But no meal could be more graceless than the one
A goddess and a hero would serve to them soon.
After all, they started the whole ugly business.   430

BOOK XXI

[handwritten: Odysseus strings his bow]

Owl-eyed Athena now prompted Penelope
To set before the suitors Odysseus' bow
And the grey iron, implements of the contest
And of their death.
           Penelope climbed
The steep stairs to her bedroom and picked up   5
A beautiful bronze key with an ivory handle
And went with her maids to a remote storeroom
Where her husband's treasures lay—bronze, gold,
And wrought iron. And there lay the curved bow
And the quiver, still loaded with arrows,   10
Gifts which a friend of Odysseus had given him
When they met in Lacedaemon long ago.
This was Iphitus, Eurytus' son, a godlike man.
They had met in Messene, in the house of Ortilochus.
Odysseus had come to collect a debt   15
The Messenians owed him: three hundred sheep
They had taken from Ithaca in a sea raid,
And the shepherds with them. Odysseus
Had come to get them back, a long journey
For a young man, sent by his father and elders.   20
Iphitus had come to search for twelve mares
He had lost, along with the mules they were nursing.
These mares turned out to be the death of Iphitus
When he came to the house of Heracles,
Zeus' tough-hearted son, who killed him,   25
Guest though he was, without any regard
For the gods' wrath or the table they had shared—
Killed the man and kept the strong-hoofed mares.[5]
It was while looking for these mares that Iphitus
Met Odysseus and gave him the bow   30
Which old Eurytus had carried and left to his son.
Odysseus gave him a sword and spear
To mark the beginning of their friendship
But before they had a chance to entertain each other
Zeus' son killed Iphitus, son of Eurytus,   35
A man like the gods. Odysseus did not take
The bow with him on his black ship to Troy.
It lay at home as a memento of his friend,
And Odysseus carried it only on Ithaca.

Penelope came to the storeroom   40
And stepped onto the oak threshold
Which a carpenter in the old days had planed,
Leveled, and then fitted with doorposts
And polished doors. Lovely in the half-light,
She quickly loosened the thong from the hook,   45

---

5. Heracles killed Iphitus in a dispute over the mares of Iphitus's father, Eurytus.

Drove home the key and shot back the bolts.
The doors bellowed like a bull in a meadow
And flew open before her. Stepping through,
She climbed onto a high platform that held chests
Filled with fragrant clothes. She reached up   50
And took the bow, case and all, from its peg,
Then sat down and laid the gleaming case on her knees
Her eyes welling with tears. Then she opened the case
And took out her husband's bow. When she had her fill
Of weeping, she went back to the hall   55
And the lordly suitors, bearing in her hands
The curved bow and the quiver loaded
With whining arrows. Two maidservants
Walked beside her, carrying a wicker chest
Filled with the bronze and iron gear her husband   60
Once used for this contest. When the beautiful woman
Reached the crowded hall, she stood
In the doorway flanked by her maidservants.
Then, covering her face with her shining veil,
Penelope spoke to her suitors: 65

"Hear me, proud suitors. You have used this house   *ultimatum*
For an eternity now—to eat and drink
In its master's absence, nor could you offer
Any excuse except your lust to marry me.
Well, your prize is here, and this is the contest.   70
I set before you the great bow of godlike Odysseus.
Whoever bends this bow and slips the string on its notch
And shoots an arrow through all twelve axes,
With him will I go, leaving behind this house
I was married in, this beautiful, prosperous house,   75
Which I will remember always, even in my dreams."

Penelope said this, and then ordered Eumaeus
To set out for the suitors the bow and grey iron.
All in tears, Eumaeus took them and laid them down,
And the cowherd wept, too, when he saw   80
His master's bow. Antinous scoffed at them both:

"You stupid yokels! You can't see farther than your own noses.
What a pair! Disturbing the lady with your bawling.
She's sad enough already because she's lost her husband.
Either sit here in silence or go outside to weep,   85
And leave the bow behind for us suitors. This contest
Will separate the men from the boys. It won't be easy
To string that polished bow. There is no man here
Such as Odysseus was. I know. I saw him myself
And remember him well, though I was still a child."   90

So Antinous said, hoping in his heart
That he would string the bow first and shoot an arrow

Through the iron. But the only arrow
He would touch first would be the one shot
Into his throat from the hands of Odysseus,   95
The man he himself was dishonoring
While inciting his comrades to do the same.

And then Telemachus, with a sigh of disgust:

"Look at me! Zeus must have robbed me of my wits.
My dear mother declares, for all her good sense,   100
That she will marry another and abandon this house,
And all I do is laugh and think it is funny.
Well, come on, you suitors, here's your prize,
A woman the likes of whom does not exist
In all Achaea, or in sacred Pylos,   105
Nowhere in Argos or in Mycenae,
Or on Ithaca itself or on the dark mainland.
You all know this. Why should I praise my mother?
Let's get going. Don't start making excuses
To put off stringing the bow. We'll see what happens.   110
And I might give that bow a try myself.
If I string it and shoot an arrow through the axeheads,
It won't bother me so much that my honored mother
Is leaving this house and going off with another,
Because I would at least be left here as someone   115
Capable of matching his father's prowess."

With that he took off his scarlet cloak, stood up,
And unstrapped his sword from his shoulders.
Then he went to work setting up the axeheads,
First digging a long trench true to the line   120
To hold them in a row, and then tamping the earth
Around each one. Everyone was amazed
That he made such a neat job of it
When he had never seen it done before.
Then he went and took his stance on the threshold   125
And began to try the bow. Three times
He made it quiver as he strained to string it,
And three times he eased off, although in his heart
He yearned to draw that bow and shoot an arrow
Through the iron axeheads. And on his fourth try   130
He would have succeeded in muscling the string
Onto its notch, but Odysseus reined him in,
Signaling him to stop with an upward nod.
So Telemachus said for all to hear:

"I guess I'm going to be a weakling forever!   135
Or else I'm still too young and don't have the strength
To defend myself against an enemy.
But come on, all of you who are stronger than me—
Give the bow a try and let's settle this contest."

And he set the bow aside, propping it against   140
The polished, jointed door, and leaning the arrow
Against the beautiful latch. Then Telemachus
Sat down on the chair from which he had risen.

Antinous, Eupeithes' son, then said:

"All right. We go in order from left to right,   145
Starting from where the wine gets poured."

Everyone agreed with Antinous' idea.
First up was their soothsayer, Leodes,
Oenops' son. He always sat in the corner
By the wine-bowl, and he was the only one   150
Who loathed the way the suitors behaved.
He now carried the bow and the arrow
Onto the threshold, took his stance,
And tried to bend the bow and string it,
But his tender, unworn hands gave out,   155
And he said for all the suitors to hear:

"Friends, I'm not the man to string this bow.
Someone else can take it. I foresee it will rob
Many a young hero of the breath of life.
And that will be just as well, since it is far better   160
To die than live on and fall short of the goal
We gather here for, with high hopes day after day.
You might hope in your heart—you might yearn—
To marry Penelope, the wife of Odysseus,
But after you've tried this bow and seen what it's like,   165
Go woo some other Achaean woman
And try to win her with your gifts. And Penelope
Should just marry the highest bidder,
The man who is fated to be her husband."

And he set the bow aside, propping it against   170
The polished, jointed door, and leaning the arrow
Against the beautiful latch. Then
He sat down on the chair from which he had risen.
And Antinous heaped contempt upon him:

"What kind of thing is that to say, Leodes?   175
I'm not going to stand here and listen to this.
You think this bow is going rob some young heroes
Of life, just because you can't string it?
The truth is your mother didn't bear a son
Strong enough to shoot arrows from bows.   180
But there are others who will string it soon enough."

Then Antinous called to Melanthius, the goatherd:

"Get over here and start a fire, Melanthius,   *[handwritten: 2nd]*
And set by it a bench with a fleece over it,
And bring out a tub of lard from the pantry,   185
So we can grease the bow, and warm it up.
Then maybe we can finish this contest."

He spoke, and Melanthius quickly rekindled the fire
And placed by it a bench covered with a fleece
And brought out from the pantry a tub of lard   190
With which the young men limbered up the bow—
But they still didn't have the strength to string it.

Only Antinous and godlike Eurymachus,
The suitors' ringleaders—and their strongest—
Were still left in the contest.

                    Meanwhile,   195
Two other men had risen and left the hall—
The cowherd and swineherd—and Odysseus himself
Went out, too. When the three of them
Were outside the gates, Odysseus said softly:

"Cowherd and swineherd, I've been wondering   200
If I should tell you what I'm about to tell you now.
Let me ask you this. What would you do
If Odysseus suddenly showed up here
Out of the blue, just like that?
Would you side with the suitors or Odysseus?   205
Tell me how you stand."

And the cattle herder answered him:

"Father Zeus, if only this would come true!
Let him come back. Let some god guide him.
Then you would see what these hands could do."   210

And Eumaeus prayed likewise to all the gods
That Odysseus would return.

                    When Odysseus   *[handwritten: Odysseus exposes to his friend]*
Was sure of both these men, he spoke to them again:

"I am back, right here in front of you.
After twenty hard years I have returned to my home.   215
I know that only you two of all my slaves
Truly want me back. I have heard
None of the others pray for my return.
So this is my promise to you. If a god
Beats these proud suitors down for me,   220
I will give you each a wife, property,
And a house built near mine. You two shall be

Friends to me and brothers to Telemachus.
And look, so you can be sure of who I am,
Here's a clear sign, that scar from the wound   225
I got from a boar's tusk when I went long ago
To Parnassus with the sons of Autolycus."

And he pulled his rags aside from the scar.
When the two men had examined it carefully,
They threw their arms around Odysseus and wept,   230
And kept kissing his head and shoulders in welcome.
Odysseus kissed their heads and hands,
And the sun would have gone down on their weeping,
Had not Odysseus stopped them, saying:

"No more weeping and wailing now. Someone might come   235
Out of the hall and see us and tell those inside.
We'll go back in now—not together, one at a time.
I'll go first, and then you. And here's what to watch for.
None of the suitors will allow the bow and quiver
To be given to me. It'll be up to you, Eumaeus,   240
To bring the bow over and place it in my hands.
Then tell the women to lock the doors to their hall,
And if they hear the sound of men groaning
Or being struck, tell them not to rush out
But to sit still and do their work in silence.   245
Philoetius, I want you to bar the courtyard gate
And secure it quickly with a piece of rope."

With this, Odysseus entered his great hall
And sat down on the chair from which he had risen.
Then the two herdsmen entered separately.   250

Eurymachus was turning the bow
Over and over in his hands, warming it
On this side and that by the fire, but even so
He was unable to string it. His pride hurt,
Shoulders sagging, he groaned and then swore: 255

"Damn it! It's not just myself I'm sorry for,
But for all of us—and not for the marriage either.
That hurts, but there are plenty of other women,
Some here in Ithaca, some in other cities.
No, it's that we fall so short of Odysseus'   260
Godlike strength. We can't even string his bow!
We'll be laughed at for generations to come!"

Antinous, son of Eupeithes, answered him:

"That'll never happen, Eurymachus,
And you know it. Now look, today is a holiday   265
Throughout the land, a sacred feast

In honor of Apollo, the Archer God.
This is no time to be bending bows.
So just set it quietly aside for now.
As for the axes, why don't we leave them   270
Just as they are? No one is going to come
Into Odysseus' hall and steal those axes.
Now let's have the cupbearer start us off
So we can forget about the bow
And pour libations. Come morning,   275
We'll have Melanthius bring along
The best she-goats in all the herds,
So we can lay prime thigh-pieces
On the altar of Apollo, the Archer God,
And then finish this business with the bow."   280

Antinous' proposal carried the day.
The heralds poured water over everyone's hands,
And boys filled the mixing bowls up to the brim
And served out the wine, first pouring
A few drops into each cup for libation.   285
When they had poured out their libations
And drunk as much as they wanted, Odysseus
Spoke among them, his heart full of cunning:

"Hear me, suitors of the glorious queen—
And I address Eurymachus most of all,   290
And godlike Antinous, since his speech
Was right on the mark when he said that for now
You should stop the contest and leave everything
Up to the gods. Tomorrow the Archer God
Will give the victory to whomever he chooses.   295
But come, let me have the polished bow.
I want to see, here in this hall with you,
If my grip is still strong, and if I still have
Any power left in these gnarled arms of mine,
Or if my hard traveling has sapped all my strength."   300

They seethed with anger when they heard this,
Afraid that he would string the polished bow,
And Antinous addressed him contemptuously:

"You don't have an ounce of sense in you,
You miserable tramp. Isn't it enough   305
That we let you hang around with us,
Undisturbed, with a full share of the feast?
You even get to listen to what we say,
Which no other stranger, much less beggar, can do.
It's wine that's screwing you up, as it does   310
Anyone who guzzles it down. It was wine
That deluded the great centaur, Eurytion,
In the hall of Peirithous, the Lapith hero.

Eurytion got blind-drunk and in his madness
Did a terrible thing in Peirithous' house.   315
The enraged Lapiths sliced off his nose and ears
And dragged him outside, and Eurytion
Went off in a stupor, mutilated and muddled.
Men and centaurs have been at odds ever since.[6]
Eurytion hurt himself because he got drunk.   320
And you're going to get hurt, too, I predict,
Hurt badly, if you string the bow. No one
In all the land will show you any kindness.
We'll send you off in a black ship to Echetus,
Who maims them all. You'll never get out alive.   325
So just be quiet and keep on drinking,
And don't challenge men who are younger than you."

It was Penelope who answered Antinous:

"It is not good, or just, Antinous,
To cheat any of Telemachus' guests   330
Who come to this house. Do you think
That if this stranger proves strong enough
To string Odysseus' bow, he will then
Lead me to his home and make me his wife?
I can't imagine that he harbors this hope.   335
So do not ruin your feast on that account.
The very idea is preposterous."

Eurymachus responded to this:

"Daughter of Icarius, wise Penelope,
Of course it's preposterous that this man   340
Would marry you. That's not what we're worried about.
But we are embarrassed at what men—and women—will say:
'A bunch of weaklings were wooing the wife
Of a man they couldn't touch—they couldn't even string
His polished bow. Then along came a vagrant   345
Who strung it easily and shot through the iron.'
That's what they'll say, to our lasting shame."

And Penelope, her eyes narrowing:

"Eurymachus, men who gobble up
The house of a prince cannot expect   350
To have a good reputation anywhere.
So there isn't any point in bringing up honor.
This stranger is a very well-built man
And says he is the son of a noble father.
So give him the bow and let us see what happens.   355

6. The Lapiths were a legendary people of Thessaly; they fought with the Centaurs at the wedding
of Peirithous.

And here is my promise to all of you.
If Apollo gives this man the glory
And he strings the bow, I will clothe him
In a fine cloak and tunic, and give him
A javelin to ward off dogs and men,   360
And a double-edged sword, and sandals
For his feet, and I will give him passage
To wherever his heart desires."

This time it was Telemachus who answered:

"As for the bow, Mother, no man alive   365
Has a stronger claim than I do to give it
To whomever I want, or to deny it—
No, none of the lords on rocky Ithaca
Nor on the islands over toward Elis,
None of them could force his will upon me,   370
Not even if I wanted to give this bow
Outright, case and arrows and all,
As a gift to the stranger.
                    Go to your rooms,
Mother, and take care of your work,
Spinning and weaving, and have the maids do theirs.   375
This bow is men's business, and my business
Especially, since I am the master of this house."

Penelope was stunned and turned to go,
Her son's masterful words pressed to her heart.
She went up the stairs to her room with her women   380
And wept for Odysseus, her beloved husband,
Until grey-eyed Athena cast sleep on her eyelids.

Downstairs, the noble swineherd was carrying
The curved bow across the hall. The suitors
Were in an uproar, and one of them called out: 385

"Where do you think you're going with that bow,
You miserable swineherd? You're out of line.
Go back to your pigsties, where your own dogs
Will wolf you down—a nice, lonely death—
If Apollo and the other gods smile upon us."   390

Afraid, the swineherd stopped in his tracks
And set the bow down. Men were yelling at him
All through the hall, and now Telemachus weighed in:

"Keep going with the bow. You'll regret it
If you try to obey everyone. I may be   395
Younger than you, but I'll chase you back
Into the country with a shower of stones.
I am stronger than you. I wish I were as strong

When it came to the suitors. I'd throw more than one
Out of here in a sorry state. They're all up to no good."　　　　　400

This got the suitors laughing hilariously
At Telemachus. The tension in the room eased,
And the swineherd carried the bow
Across to Odysseus and put it in his hands.
Then he called Eurycleia aside and said:　　　　　405

"Telemachus says you should lock the doors to the hall,
And if the women hear the sound of men groaning
Or being struck, tell them not to rush out
But to sit still and do their work in silence."

Eumaeus' words sank in, and Eurycleia　　　　　410
Locked the doors to the crowded hall.

Meanwhile, Philoetius left without a word
And barred the gates to the fenced courtyard.
Beside the portico there lay a ship's hawser
Made of papyrus. Philoetius used this　　　　　415
To secure the gates, and then he went back in,
Sat down on the chair from which he had risen,
And kept his eyes on Odysseus.

He was handling the bow, turning it over and over
And testing its flex to make sure that worms　　　　　420
Had not eaten the horn in its master's absence.
The suitors glanced at each other
And started to make sarcastic remarks:

"Ha! A real connoisseur, an expert in bows!"

"He must have one just like it in a case at home."　　　　　425

"Or plans to make one just like it, to judge by the way
The masterful tramp keeps turning it in his hands."

"May he have as much success in life
As he'll have in trying to string that bow."

Thus the suitors, while Odysseus, deep in thought,　　　　　430
Was looking over his bow. And then, effortlessly,

　　Like a musician stretching a string
　　Over a new peg on his lyre, and making
　　The twisted sheep-gut fast at either end,

Odysseus strung the great bow. Lifting it up,　　　　　435
He plucked the string, and it sang beautifully
Under his touch, with a note like a swallow's.

The suitors were aghast. The color drained
From their faces, and Zeus thundered loud,
Showing his portents and cheering the heart   440
Of the long-enduring, godlike Odysseus.
One arrow lay bare on the table. The rest,
Which the suitors were about to taste,
Were still in the quiver. Odysseus picked up
The arrow from the table and laid it upon   445
The bridge of the bow, and, still in his chair,
Drew the bowstring and the notched arrow back.
He took aim and let fly, and the bronze-tipped arrow
Passed clean through the holes of all twelve axeheads
From first to last. And he said to Telemachus: 450

"Well, Telemachus, the guest in your hall
Has not disgraced you. I did not miss my target,
Nor did I take all day in stringing the bow.
I still have my strength, and I'm not as the suitors
Make me out to be in their taunts and jeers.   455
But now it is time to cook these men's supper,
While it is still light outside, and after that,
We'll need some entertainment—music and song—
The finishing touches for a perfect banquet."

He spoke, and lowered his brows. Telemachus,   460
The true son of godlike Odysseus, slung on
His sharp sword, seized his spear, and gleaming in bronze
Took his place by his father's side.

BOOK XXII

And now Odysseus' cunning was revealed.
He stripped off his rags and leapt with his bow
To the great threshold. Spreading the arrows
Out before his feet, he spoke to the suitors:

"Now that we've separated the men from the boys,   5
I'll see if I can hit a mark that no man
Has ever hit. Apollo grant me glory!"

As he spoke he took aim at Antinous,
Who at that moment was lifting to his lips
A golden cup—a fine, two-eared golden goblet—   10
And was just about to sip the wine. Bloodshed
Was the farthest thing from his mind.
They were at a banquet. Who would think
That one man, however strong, would take them all on
And so ensure his own death? Odysseus   15
Took dead aim at Antinous' throat and shot,
And the arrow punched all the way through
The soft neck tissue. Antinous fell to one side,

The cup dropped from his hands, and a jet
Of dark blood spurted from his nostrils.   20
He kicked the table as he went down,
Spilling the food on the floor, and the bread
And roast meat were fouled in the dust.
                                          The crowd
Burst into an uproar when they saw
Antinous go down. They jumped from their seats   25
And ran in a panic through the hall,
Scanning the walls for weapons—
A spear, a shield. But there were none to be had.
Odysseus listened to their angry jeers:

"You think you can shoot at men, you tramp?"   30

"That's your last contest—you're as good as dead!"

"You've killed the best young man in Ithaca!"

"Vultures will eat you on this very spot!"

They all assumed he had not shot to kill,
And had no idea how tightly the net   35
Had been drawn around them. Odysseus
Scowled at the whole lot of them, and said:

"You dogs! You thought I would never
Come home from Troy. So you wasted my house,
Forced the women to sleep with you,   40
And while I was still alive you courted my wife
Without any fear of the gods in high heaven
Or of any retribution from the world of men.
Now the net has been drawn tight around you."

At these words the color drained from their faces,   45
And they all looked around for a way to escape.
Only Eurymachus had anything to say:

"If you are really Odysseus of Ithaca,
Then what you say is just. The citizens
Have done many foolish things in this house   50
And many in the fields. But the man to blame   *death*
Lies here dead, <u>Antinous.</u> He started it all,
Not so much because he wanted a marriage
Or needed one, but for another purpose,
Which Zeus did not fulfill: he wanted to be king   55
In Ithaca, and to kill your son in ambush.
Now he's been killed, and he deserved it.
But spare your people. We will pay you back
For all we have eaten and drunk in your house.
We will make a collection; each man will put in   60

The worth of twenty oxen; we will make restitution
In bronze and gold until your heart is soothed.
Until then no one could blame you for being angry."

Odysseus fixed him with a stare and said:

"Eurymachus, not even if all of you   65
Gave me your entire family fortunes,
All that you have and ever will have,
Would I stay my hands from killing.
You courted my wife, and you will pay in full.
Your only choice now is to fight like men   70
Or run for it. Who knows, one or two of you
Might live to see another day. But I doubt it."

Their blood turned milky when they heard this.
Eurymachus now turned to them and said:

"Friends, this man is not going to stop at anything.   75
He's got his arrows and bow, and he'll shoot
From the threshold until he's killed us all.
We've got to fight back. Draw your swords
And use the tables as shields. If we charge him
In a mass and push him from the doorway   80
We can get reinforcements from town in no time.
Then this man will have shot his last shot."

With that, he drew his honed bronze sword
And charged Odysseus with an ear-splitting cry.
Odysseus in the same instant let loose an arrow   85
That entered his chest just beside the nipple
And spiked down to his liver. The sword fell   *dies*
From Eurymachus' hand. He spun around
And fell on a table, knocking off dishes and cups,
And rolled to the ground, his forehead banging   90
Up and down against it and his feet kicking a chair
In his death throes, until the world went dark.
Amphinomus went for Odysseus next,
Rushing at him with his sword drawn,
Hoping to drive him away from the door.   95
Telemachus got the jump on him, though,
Driving a bronze-tipped spear into his back
Square between his shoulder blades
And through to his chest. He fell with a thud,
His forehead hammering into the ground.   100
Telemachus sprang back, leaving the spear
Right where it was, stuck in Amphinomus,
Fearing that if he tried to pull it out
Someone would rush him and cut him down
As he bent over the corpse. So he ran over   105
To his father's side, and his words flew fast:

"I'll bring you a shield, Father, two spears
And a bronze helmet—I'll find one that fits.
When I come back I'll arm myself
And the cowherd and swineherd. Better armed than not."   110

And Odysseus, the great tactician:

"Bring me what you can while I still have arrows
Or these men might drive me away from the door."

And Telemachus was off to the room
Where the weapons were stored. He took   115
Four shields, eight spears, and four bronze helmets
With thick horsehair plumes and brought them
Quickly to his father. Telemachus armed himself,
The two servants did likewise, and the three of them
Took their stand alongside the cunning warrior,   120
Odysseus. As long as the arrows held out
He kept picking off the suitors one by one,
And they fell thick as flies. But when the master archer
Ran out of arrows, he leaned the bow
Against the doorpost of the entrance hall   125
And slung a four-ply shield over his shoulder,
Put on his head a well-wrought helmet
With a plume that made his every nod a threat,
And took two spears tipped with heavy bronze.

Built into the higher wall of the main hall   130
Was a back door reached by a short flight of stairs
And leading to a passage closed by double doors.
Odysseus posted the swineherd at this doorway,
Which could be attacked by only one man at a time.
It was just then that Agelaus called to the suitors: 135

"Let's one of us get up to the back door
And get word to the town. Act quickly
And this man will have shot his last."

But the goatherd Melanthius answered him:

"That won't work, Agelaus.   140
The door outside is too near the courtyard—
An easy shot from where he is standing—
And the passageway is dangerously narrow.
One good man could hold it against all of us.
Look, let me bring you weapons and armor   145
From the storeroom. That has to be where
Odysseus and his son have laid them away."

So saying, Melanthius clambered up
To Odysseus' storerooms. There he picked out

Twelve shields and as many spears and helmets 150
And brought them out quickly to give to the suitors.
Odysseus' heart sank, and his knees grew weak
When he saw the suitors putting on armor
And brandishing spears. This wasn't going to be easy.
His words flew out to Telemachus: 155

"One of the women in the halls must be
Waging war against us—unless it's Melanthius."

And Telemachus, cool-headed under fire:

"No, it's my fault, Father, and no one else's.
I must have left the storeroom door open, 160
And one of them spotted it.
                                  Eumaeus!
Go close the door to the storeroom,
And see whether one of the women is behind this,
Or Melanthius, son of Dolius, as I suspect."

As they were speaking, Melanthius the goatherd 165
Was making another trip to the storeroom
For more weapons. The swineherd spotted him
And was quick to point him out to Odysseus:

"There he goes, my lord Odysseus—
The sneak—just as we thought, on his way 170
To the storeroom! Tell me what to do.
Kill him if I prove to be the better man,
Or bring him to you, so he can pay in full
For all the wrongs he has done here in your house?"

Odysseus brought his mind to bear on this: 175

"Telemachus and I will keep the suitors busy
In the hall here. Don't worry about that.
Tie him up. Bend his arms and legs behind him
And lash them to a board strapped onto his back.
Then hoist him up to the rafters in the storeroom 180
And leave him there to twist in the wind."

This was just what Eumaeus and the cowherd
Wanted to hear. Off they went to the storeroom,
Unseen by Melanthius, who was inside
Rooting around for armor and weapons. 185
They lay in wait on either side of the door,
And when Melanthius crossed the threshold,
Carrying a beautiful helmet in one hand
And in the other a broad old shield,
Flecked with rust—a shield the hero Laertes 190
Had carried in his youth but that had long since

Been laid aside with its straps unstitched—
Eumaeus and the cowherd Philoetius
Jumped him and dragged him by the hair
Back into the storeroom. They threw him   195
Hard to the ground, knocking the wind out of him,
And tied his hands and feet behind his back,
Making it hurt, as Odysseus had ordered.
Then they attached a rope to his body
And hoisted him up along the tall pillar   200
Until he was up by the rafters, and you,
Swineherd Eumaeus, you mocked him:

"Now you'll really be on watch, Melanthius,
The whole night through, lying on a feather bed—
Just your style—and you're sure to see   205
The early dawn come up from Ocean's streams,
Couched in gold, at the hour when you drive your goats
Up to the hall to make a feast for the suitors."

So Melanthius was left there, racked with pain,
While Eumaeus and the cowherd put on their armor,   210
Closed the polished door, and rejoined Odysseus,
The cunning warrior. So they took their stand
There on the threshold, breathing fury,
Four of them against the many who stood in the hall.

And then Athena was with them, Zeus' daughter   215
Looking just like Mentor and assuming his voice.
Odysseus, glad to see her, spoke these words:

"Mentor, old friend, help me out here.
Remember all the favors I've done for you.
We go back a long way, you and I."   220

He figured it was Athena, the soldier's goddess.
On the other side, the suitors yelled and shouted,
Agelaus' voice rising to rebuke Athena:

"You there, Mentor, don't let Odysseus
Talk you into helping him and fighting us.   225
This is the way I see it turning out.
When we have killed these men, father and son,
We'll kill you next for what you mean to do
In this hall. You'll pay with your life.
And when we've taken care of all five of you,   230
We'll take everything you have, Mentor,
Everything in your house and in your fields,
And add it to Odysseus' property.
We won't let your sons stay in your house
Or let your daughters or even your wife   235
Go about freely in the town of Ithaca."

This made Athena all the more angry,
And she turned on Odysseus and snapped at him:

"I can't believe, Odysseus, that you,
Of all people, have lost the guts you had   240
When you fought the Trojans for nine long years
To get Helen back, killing so many in combat
And coming up with the plan that took wide Troy.[7]
How is it that now, when you've come home,
You get all teary-eyed about showing your strength   245
To this pack of suitors? Get over here
Next to me and see what I can do. I'll show you
What sort of man Mentor, son of Alcimus, is,
And how he repays favors in the heat of battle."

Athena spoke these words, but she did not yet   250
Give Odysseus the strength to turn the tide.
She was still testing him, and his glorious son,
To see what they were made of. As for herself,
The goddess flew up to the roofbeam
Of the smoky hall, just like a swallow.   255

The suitors were now rallied by Agelaus
And by Damastor, Eurynomus, and Amphimedon,
As well as by Demoptolemus and Peisander,
Son of Polyctor, and the warrior Polybus.
These were the best of the suitors lucky enough   260
To still be fighting for their lives. The rest
Had been laid low by the showers of arrows.
Agelaus now made this speech to them:

"He's had it now. Mentor's abandoned him
After all that hot air, and the four of them   265
Are left alone at the outer doors.
All right, now. Don't throw your spears all at once.
You six go first, and hope that Zeus allows
Odysseus to be hit and gives us the glory.
The others won't matter once he goes down."   270

They took his advice and gave it their best,
But Athena made their shots all come to nothing,
One man hitting the doorpost, another the door,
Another's bronze-tipped ash spear sticking
Into the wall. Odysseus and his men   275
Weren't even nicked, and the great hero said to them:

"It's our turn now. I say we throw our spears
Right into the crowd. These bastards mean to kill us
On top of everything else they've done to wrong me."

---

7. The Trojan Horse.

He spoke, and they all threw their sharp spears   280
With deadly aim. Odysseus hit Demoptolemus;
Telemachus got Euryades; the swineherd, Elatus;
And the cattle herder took out Peisander.
They all bit the dirt at the same moment,
And the suitors retreated to the back of the hall,   285
Allowing Odysseus and his men to run out
And pull their spears from the dead men's bodies.

The suitors rallied for another volley,
Throwing their sharp spears with all they had.
This time Athena made most of them miss,   290
One man hitting the doorpost, another the door,
Another's bronze-tipped ash spear sticking
Into the wall. But Amphimedon's spear
Grazed Telemachus' wrist, breaking the skin,
And Ctessipus' spear clipped Eumaeus' shoulder   295
As it sailed over his shield and kept on going
Until it hit the ground. Then Odysseus and his men
Got off another round into the throng,
Odysseus, sacker of cities, hitting Eurydamas;
Telemachus getting Amphimedon; the swineherd, Polybus;   300
And lastly the cattle herder striking Ctessipus
Square in the chest. And he crowed over him:

"Always picking a fight, just like your father.
Well, you can stop all your big talk now.
We'll let the gods have the last word this time.   305
Take this spear as your host's gift, fair exchange
For the hoof you threw at godlike Odysseus
When he made his rounds begging in the hall."

Thus the herder of the spiral-horned cattle.

Odysseus, meanwhile, had skewered Damastor's son   310
With a hard spear-thrust in hand-to-hand fighting,
And Telemachus killed Leocritus, Evenor's son,
Piercing him in the groin and driving his bronze spear
All the way through. Leocritus pitched forward,
His forehead slamming onto the ground.

                              Only then   315
Did Athena hold up her overpowering aegis
From her high perch, and the minds of the suitors
Shriveled with fear, and they fled through the hall

   Like a herd of cattle that an iridescent gadfly
   Goads along on a warm spring afternoon,   320

With Odysseus and his men after them

   Like vultures with crooked talons and hooked beaks
   Descending from the mountains upon a flock

Of smaller birds, who fly low under the clouds
And over the plain. The vultures swoop down   325
To pick them off; the smaller birds cannot escape,
And men thrill to see the chase in the sky.

Odysseus and his cohorts were clubbing the suitors
Right and left all through the hall; horrible groans
Rose from their lips as their heads were smashed in,   330
And the floor of the great hall smoked with blood.
It was then that Leodes, the soothsayer, rushed forward,
Clasped Odysseus' knees, and begged for his life:

"By your knees, Odysseus, respect me
And pity me. I swear I have never said or done   335
Anything wrong to any woman in your house.
I tried to stop the suitors when they did such things,
But they wouldn't listen, wouldn't keep their hands clean,
And now they've paid a cruel price for their sins.
And I, their soothsayer, who have done no wrong,   340
Will be laid low with them. That's the gratitude I get."

Odysseus scowled down at the man and said:

"If you are really their soothsayer, as you boast you are,
How many times must you have prayed in the halls
That my sweet homecoming would never come,   345
And that you would be the one my wife would go off with
And bear children to! You're a dead man."

As he spoke his strong hand reached for a sword
That lay nearby—a sword Agelaus had dropped
When he was killed. The soothsayer was struck   350
Full in the neck. His lips were still forming words
When his lopped head rolled in the dust.

All this while the bard, Phemius, was busy
Trying not to be killed. This man, Terpes' son,
Sang for the suitors under compulsion.   355
He stood now with his pure-toned lyre
Near the high back door, trying to decide
Whether he should slip out from the hall
And crouch at the altar of Zeus of the Courtyard—
The great altar on which Laertes and Odysseus   360
Had burned many an ox's thigh—
Or whether he should rush forward
And supplicate Odysseus by his knees.
Better to fall at the man's knees, he thought.
So he laid the hollow lyre on the ground   365
Between the wine-bowl and silver-studded chair
And ran up to Odysseus and clasped his knees.
His words flew up to Odysseus like birds:

"By your knees, Odysseus, respect me
And pity me. You will regret it someday   370
If you kill a bard—me—who sings for gods and men.
I am self-taught, and a god has planted in my heart
All sorts of songs and stories, and I can sing to you
As to a god. So don't be too eager
To slit my throat. Telemachus will tell you   375
That I didn't come to your house by choice
To entertain the suitors at their feasts.
There were too many of them; they made me come."

Telemachus heard him and said to his father: *spares his death*

"He's innocent; don't kill him.   380
And let's spare the herald, Medon,
Who used to take care of me when I was a child,
If Philoetius hasn't already killed him—
Or the swineherd—or if he didn't run into you
As you were charging through the house."   385

Medon heard what Telemachus said.
He was under a chair, wrapped in an oxhide,
Cowering from death. Now he jumped up,
Stripped off the oxhide, ran to Telemachus
And fell at his knees. His words rose on wings: 390

"I'm here, Telemachus! Hold back, and ask your father
To hold back too, or he might kill me with cold bronze,
Strong as he is and as mad as he is at the suitors,
Who ate away his house and paid you no honor."

Odysseus smiled at this and said to him: 395

"Don't worry, he's saved you. Now you know,
And you can tell the world, how much better
Good deeds are than evil. Go outside, now,
You and the singer, and sit in the yard
Away from the slaughter, until I finish   400
Everything I have to do inside the house."

So he spoke, and the two went out of the hall
And sat down by the altar of great Zeus,
Wide-eyed and expecting death at any moment.
Odysseus, too, had his eyes wide open,   405
Looking all through his house to see if anyone
Was still alive and hiding from death.
But everyone he saw lay in the blood and dust,
The whole lot of them,

like fish that fishermen
Have drawn up in nets from the grey sea   410

> *Onto the curved shore. They lie all in heaps*
> *On the sand beach, longing for the salt waves,*
> *And the blazing sun drains their life away.*

So too the suitors, lying in heaps.

Then Odysseus called to Telemachus: 415

"Go call the nurse Eurycleia for me.
I want to tell her something."

So Telemachus went
To Eurycleia's room, rattled the door, and called:

"Get up and come out here, old woman—you
Who are in charge of all our women servants. 420
Come on. My father has something to say to you."

Eurycleia's response died on her lips.
She opened the doors to the great hall,
Came out, and followed Telemachus
To where Odysseus, spattered with blood and grime
Stood among the bodies of the slain. 425

> *A lion that has just fed upon an ox in a field*
> *Has his chest and cheeks smeared with blood,*
> *And his face is terrible to look upon.*

So too Odysseus,
Smeared with gore from head to foot.

When Eurycleia 430
Saw all the corpses and the pools of blood,
She lifted her head to cry out in triumph—
But Odysseus stopped her cold,
Reining her in with these words:

"Rejoice in your heart, but do not cry aloud. 435
It is unholy to gloat over the slain. These men
Have been destroyed by divine destiny
And their own recklessness. They honored no one,
Rich or poor, high or low, who came to them.
And so by their folly they have brought upon themselves 440
An ugly fate.
Now tell me, which of the women
Dishonor me and which are innocent?"

And Eurycleia, the loyal nurse:

"Yes indeed, child, I will tell you all.
There are fifty women in your house, 445

Servants we have taught to do their work,
To card wool and bear all the drudgery.
Of these, twelve have shamed this house
And respect neither me nor Penelope herself.
Telemachus has only now become a man,   450
And his mother has not allowed him
To direct the women servants.
                                May I go now
To the upstairs room and tell your wife?
Some god has wrapped her up in sleep."

Odysseus, his mind teeming, answered her: 455

"Don't wake her yet. First bring those women
Who have acted so disgracefully."

While the old woman went out through the hall
To tell the women the news—and to summon twelve—
Odysseus called Telemachus and the two herdsmen   460
And spoke to them words fletched like arrows:

"Start carrying out the bodies,
And have the women help you.
                                Then sponge down
All of the beautiful tables and chairs.
When you have set the whole house in order,   465
Take the women outside between the round house
And the courtyard fence. Slash them with swords
Until they have forgotten their secret lovemaking
With the suitors. Then finish them off."

Thus Odysseus, and the women came in,   470
Huddled together and shedding salt tears.
First they carried out the dead bodies
And set them down under the courtyard's portico,
Propping them against each other. Odysseus himself
Kept them at it. Then he had them sponge down   475
All of the beautiful tables and chairs.
Telemachus, the swineherd, and the cowherd
Scraped the floor with hoes, and the women
Carried out the scrapings and threw them away.
When they had set the whole house in order,   480
They took the women out between the round house
And the courtyard fence, penning them in
With no way to escape. And Telemachus,
In his cool-headed way, said to the others:

"I won't allow a clean death for these women—   485
The suitors' sluts—who have heaped reproaches
Upon my own head and upon my mother's."

He spoke, and tied the cable of a dark-prowed ship
To a great pillar and pulled it about the round house,
Stretching it high so their feet couldn't touch the ground.   490

    Long-winged thrushes, or doves, making their way
    To their roosts, fall into a snare set in a thicket,
    And the bed that receives them is far from welcome.

So too these women, their heads hanging in a row,
The cable looped around each of their necks.   495
It was a most piteous death. Their feet fluttered
For a little while, but not for long.

Then they brought Melanthius outside,
And in their fury they sliced off
His nose and ears with cold bronze
And pulled his genitals out by the root—   500
Raw meat for the dogs—and chopped off
His hands and feet.

             This done,
They washed their own hands and feet
And went back into their master's great hall.   505

Then Odysseus said to Eurycleia:

"Bring me sulfur, old woman, and fire,
So that I can fumigate the hall.
And go tell Penelope to come down here,
And all of the women in the house as well."   510

And Eurycleia, the faithful nurse:

"As you say, child. But first let me bring you
A tunic and a cloak for you to put on.
You should not be standing here like this
With rags on your body. It's not right."   515

Odysseus, his mind teeming, answered her:

"First make a fire for me here in the hall."

He spoke, and Eurycleia did as she was told.
She brought fire and sulfur, and Odysseus
Purified his house, the halls and the courtyard.   520

Then the old nurse went through Odysseus'
Beautiful house, telling the women the news.
They came from their hall with torches in their hands
And thronged around Odysseus and embraced him.
And as they kissed his head and shoulders and hands   525
He felt a sudden, sweet urge to weep,
For in his heart he knew them all.

BOOK XXIII *23* *The Great Rooted Bed*

The old woman laughed as she went upstairs
To tell her mistress that her husband was home.
She ran up the steps, lifting her knees high,
And, bending over Penelope, she said:

"Wake up, dear child, so you can see for yourself   5
What you have yearned for day in and day out.
Odysseus has come home, after all this time,
And has killed those men who tried to marry you
And who ravaged your house and bullied your son."

And Penelope, alert now and wary: 10

Penelope doesn't believe

"Dear nurse, the gods have driven you crazy.
The gods can make even the wise mad,
Just as they often make the foolish wise.
Now they have wrecked your usually sound mind.
Why do you mock me and my sorrowful heart,   15
Waking me from sleep to tell me this nonsense—
And such a sweet sleep. It sealed my eyelids.
I haven't slept like that since the day Odysseus
Left for Ilion—that accursed city.
Now go back down to the hall.   20
If any of the others had told me this
And wakened me from sleep, I would have
Sent her back with something to be sorry about!
You can thank your old age for this at least."

And Eurycleia, the loyal nurse: 25

"I am not mocking you, child. Odysseus
Really is here. He's come home, just as I say.
He's the stranger they all insulted in the great hall.
Telemachus has known all along, but had
The self-control to hide his father's plans   30
Until he could pay the arrogant bastards back."

Penelope felt a sudden pang of joy. She leapt
From her bed and flung her arms around the old woman,
And with tears in her eyes she said to her:

"Dear nurse, if it is true, if he really has   35
Come back to his house, tell me how
He laid his hands on the shameless suitors,
One man alone against all of that mob."

Eurycleia answered her:

"I didn't see and didn't ask. I only heard the groaning   40
Of men being killed. We women sat
In the far corner of our quarters, trembling,

With the good solid doors bolted shut
Until your son came from the hall to call me,
Telemachus. His father had sent him to call me.   45
And there he was, Odysseus, standing
In a sea of dead bodies, all piled
On top of each other on the hard-packed floor.
It would have warmed your heart to see him,
Spattered with blood and filth like a lion.   50
And now the bodies are all gathered together
At the gates, and he is purifying the house
With sulfur, and has built a great fire,
And has sent me to call you. Come with me now
So that both your hearts can be happy again.   55
You have suffered so much, but now
Your long desire has been fulfilled.
He has come himself, alive, to his own hearth,
And has found you and his son in the hall.
As for the suitors, who did him wrong,   60
He's taken his revenge on every last man."

And Penelope, ever cautious:

"Dear nurse, don't gloat over them yet.
You know how welcome the sight of him
Would be to us all, and especially to me   65
And the son he and I bore. But this story
Can't be true, not the way you tell it.
One of the immortals must have killed the suitors,
Angry at their arrogance and evil deeds.
They respected no man, good or bad,   70
So their blind folly has killed them. But Odysseus
Is lost, lost to us here, and gone forever."

And Eurycleia, the faithful nurse:

"Child, how can you say this? Your husband
Is here at his own fireside, and yet you are sure   75
He will never come home! Always on guard!
But here's something else, clear proof:
The scar he got from the tusk of that boar.
I noticed it when I was washing his feet
And wanted to tell you, but he shrewdly clamped   80
His hand on my mouth and wouldn't let me speak.
Just come with me, and I will stake my life on it.
If I am lying you can torture me to death."

Still wary, Penelope replied:

"Dear nurse, it is hard for you to comprehend   85
The ways of the eternal gods, wise as you are.
Still, let us go to my son, so that I may see
The suitors dead and the man who killed them."

And Penelope descended the stairs, her heart
In turmoil. Should she hold back and question   90
Her husband? Or should she go up to him,
Embrace him, and kiss his hands and head?
She entered the hall, crossing the stone threshold,
And sat opposite Odysseus, in the firelight
Beside the farther wall. He sat by a column,   95
Looking down, waiting to see if his incomparable wife
Would say anything to him when she saw him.
She sat a long time in silence, wondering.
She would look at his face and see her husband,
But then fail to know him in his dirty rags.   100
Telemachus couldn't take it any more:

"Mother, how can you be so hard,
Holding back like that? Why don't you sit
Next to father and talk to him, ask him things?
No other woman would have the heart   105
To stand off from her husband who has come back
After twenty hard years to his country and home.
But your heart is always colder than stone."

And Penelope, cautious as ever:

"My child, I am lost in wonder   110
And unable to speak or ask a question
Or look him in the eyes. If he really is
Odysseus come home, the two of us
Will be sure of each other, very sure.
There are secrets between us no one else knows."   115

Odysseus, who had borne much, smiled,
And his words flew to his son on wings:

"Telemachus, let your mother test me
In our hall. She will soon see more clearly
Now, because I am dirty and wearing rags,   120
She is not ready to acknowledge who I am.
But you and I have to devise a plan.
When someone kills just one man,
Even a man who has few to avenge him,
He goes into exile, leaving country and kin.   125
Well, we have killed a city of young men,
The flower of Ithaca. Think about that."

And Telemachus, in his clear-headed way:

"You should think about it, Father. They say
No man alive can match you for cunning.   130
We'll follow you for all we are worth,
And I don't think we'll fail for lack of courage."

And Odysseus, the master strategist:

"Well, this is what I think we should do.
First, bathe yourselves and put on clean tunics   135
And tell the women to choose their clothes well.
Then have the singer pick up his lyre
And lead everyone in a lively dance tune,
Loud and clear. Anyone who hears the sound,
A passerby or neighbor, will think it's a wedding,   140
And so word of the suitors' killing won't spread
Down through the town before we can reach
Our woodland farm. Once there we'll see
What kind of luck the Olympian[8] gives us."

They did as he said. The men bathed   145
And put on tunics, and the women dressed up.
The godlike singer, sweeping his hollow lyre,
Put a song in their hearts and made their feet move,
And the great hall resounded under the tread
Of men and silken-waisted women dancing.   150
And people outside would hear it and say:

"Well, someone has finally married the queen,
Fickle woman. Couldn't bear to keep the house
For her true husband until he came back."

But they had no idea how things actually stood.   155

Odysseus, meanwhile, was being bathed
By the housekeeper, Eurynome. She
Rubbed him with olive oil and threw about him
A beautiful cloak and tunic. And Athena
Shed beauty upon him, and made him look   160
Taller and more muscled, and made his hair
Tumble down his head like hyacinth flowers.

    Imagine a craftsman overlaying silver
    With pure gold. He has learned his art
    From Pallas Athena and Lord Hephaestus,[9]   165
    And creates works of breathtaking beauty.

So Athena herself made his head and shoulders
Shimmer with grace. He came from the bath
Like a god, and sat down on the chair again
Opposite his wife, and spoke to her and said: 170

"You're a mysterious woman.
            The gods

8. Zeus.
9. Athena and Hephaestus are both associated with crafts.

Have given to you, more than to any
Other woman, an unyielding heart.
No other woman would be able to endure
Standing off from her husband, come back   175
After twenty hard years to his country and home.
Nurse, make up a bed for me so I can lie down
Alone, since her heart is a cold lump of iron."

And Penelope, cautious and wary:

"You're a mysterious man.
                    I am not being proud   180
Or scornful, nor am I bewildered—not at all.
I know very well what you looked like
When you left Ithaca on your long-oared ship.
Nurse, bring the bed out from the master bedroom,
The bedstead he made himself, and spread it for him   185
With fleeces and blankets and silky coverlets."

She was testing her husband.
                    Odysseus
Could bear no more, and he cried out to his wife:

"By God, woman, now you've cut deep.
Who moved my bed? It would be hard   190
For anyone, no matter how skilled, to move it.
A god could come down and move it easily,
But not a man alive, however young and strong,
Could ever pry it up. There's something telling
About how that bed's built, and no one else   195
Built it but me.
                    There was an olive tree
Growing on the site, long-leaved and full,
Its trunk thick as a post. I built my bedroom
Around that tree, and when I had finished
The masonry walls and done the roofing   200
And set in the jointed, close-fitting doors,
I lopped off all of the olive's branches,
Trimmed the trunk from the root on up,
And rounded it and trued it with an adze until
I had myself a bedpost. I bored it with an auger, 205
And starting from this I framed up the whole bed,
Inlaying it with gold and silver and ivory
And stretching across it oxhide thongs dyed purple.
So there's our secret. But I do not know, woman,
Whether my bed is still firmly in place, or if   210
Some other man has cut through the olive's trunk."

At this, Penelope finally let go.
Odysseus had shown he knew their old secret.

In tears, she ran straight to him, threw her arms
Around him, kissed his face, and said: 215

"Don't be angry with me, Odysseus. You,
Of all men, know how the world goes.
It is the gods who gave us sorrow, the gods
Who begrudged us a life together, enjoying
Our youth and arriving side by side   220
To the threshold of old age. Don't hold it against me
That when I first saw you I didn't welcome you
As I do now. My heart has been cold with fear
That an imposter would come and deceive me.
There are many who scheme for ill-gotten gains.   225
Not even Helen, daughter of Zeus,
Would have slept with a foreigner had she known
The Greeks would go to war to bring her back home.
It was a god who drove her to that dreadful act,
Or she never would have thought of doing what she did,   230
The horror that brought suffering to us as well.
But now, since you have confirmed the secret
Of our marriage bed, which no one has ever seen—
Only you and I and a single servant, Actor's daughter,
Whom my father gave me before I ever came here   235
And who kept the doors of our bridal chamber—
You have persuaded even my stubborn heart."

This brought tears from deep within him,
And as he wept he clung to his beloved wife.

    Land is a welcome sight to men swimming   240
    For their lives, after Poseidon has smashed their ship
    In heavy seas. Only a few of them escape
    And make it to shore. They come out
    Of the grey water crusted with brine, glad
    To be alive and set foot on dry land.   245

So welcome a sight was her husband to her.
She would not loosen her white arms from his neck,
And rose-fingered Dawn would have risen
On their weeping, had not Athena stepped in
And held back the long night at the end of its course   250
And stopped gold-stitched Dawn at Ocean's shores
From yoking the horses that bring light to men,
Lampus and Phaethon, the colts of Dawn.

Then Odysseus said to his wife:

"We have not yet come to the end of our trials.   255
There is still a long, hard task for me to complete,
As the spirit of Tiresias foretold to me
On the day I went down to the house of Hades

To ask him about my companions' return
And my own. But come to bed now,   260
And we'll close our eyes in the pleasure of sleep."

And Penelope calmly answered him:

"Your bed is ready for you whenever
You want it, now that the gods have brought you
Home to your family and native land.   265
But since you've brought it up, tell me
About this trial. I'll learn about it soon enough,
And it won't be any worse to hear it now."

And Odysseus, his mind teeming:

"You are a mystery to me. Why do you insist   270
I tell you now? Well, here's the whole story.   *tells of*
It's not a tale you will enjoy, and I have no joy   *trials*
In telling it.
            Tiresias told me that I must go
To city after city carrying a broad-bladed oar,
Until I come to men who know nothing of the sea,   275
Who eat their food unsalted, and have never seen
Red-prowed ships or the oars that wing them along.
And he told me that I would know I had found them
When I met another traveler who thought
The oar I was carrying was a winnowing fan.[1]   280
Then I must fix my oar in the earth
And offer sacrifice to Lord Poseidon,
A ram, a bull, and a boar in its prime.
Then at last I am to come home and offer
Grand sacrifice to the immortal gods   285
Who hold high heaven, to each in turn.
And death shall come to me from the sea,
As gentle as this touch, and take me off
When I am worn out in sleek old age,
With my people prosperous around me.   290
All this Tiresias said would come true."

Then Penelope, watching him, answered:

"If the gods are going to grant you a happy old age,
There is hope your troubles will someday be over."

While they spoke to one another,   295
Eurynome and the nurse made the bed
By torchlight, spreading it with soft coverlets.
Then the old nurse went to her room to lie down,
And Eurynome, who kept the bedroom,

1. I.e., the traveler will not recognize an oar, because he will never have seen the sea.

Led the couple to their bed, lighting the way.   300
When she had led them in, she withdrew,
And they went with joy to their bed
And to their rituals of old.

Telemachus and his men
Stopped dancing, stopped the women's dance,
And lay down to sleep in the shadowy halls.   305

After Odysseus and Penelope
Had made sweet love, they took turns
Telling stories to each other. She told him
All that she had to endure as the fair lady
In the palace, looking upon the loathsome throng   310
Of suitors, who used her as an excuse
To kill many cattle, whole flocks of sheep,
And to empty the cellar of much of its wine.
Odysseus told her of all the suffering
He had brought upon others, and of all the pain   315
He endured himself. She loved listening to him
And did not fall asleep until he had told the whole tale.

He began with how he overcame the Cicones
And then came to the land of the Lotus-Eaters,
And all that the Cyclops did, and how he   320
Paid him back for eating his comrades.
Then how he came to Aeolus,
Who welcomed him and sent him on his way,
But since it was not his destiny to return home then,
The stormwinds grabbed him and swept him off   325
Groaning deeply over the teeming saltwater.
Then how he came to the Laestrygonians,
Who destroyed his ships and all their crews,
Leaving him with only one black-tarred hull.
Then all of Circe's tricks and wiles,   330
And how he sailed to the dank house of Hades
To consult the spirit of Theban Tiresias
And saw his old comrades there
And his aged mother who nursed him as a child.
Then how he heard the Sirens' eternal song,   335
And came to the Clashing Rocks,
And dread Charybdis and Scylla,
Whom no man had ever escaped before.
Then how his crew killed the cattle of the Sun,
And how Zeus, the high lord of thunder,   340
Slivered his ship with lightning, and all his men
Went down, and he alone survived.
And he told her how he came to Ogygia,
The island of the nymph Calypso,
Who kept him there in her scalloped caves,   345
Yearning for him to be her husband,
And how she took care of him, and promised

To make him immortal and ageless all his days
But did not persuade the heart in his breast.
Then how he crawled out of the sea in Phaeacia,   350
And how the Phaeacians honored him like a god
And sent him on a ship to his own native land
With gifts of bronze and clothing and gold.

He told the story all the way through,
And then sleep, which slackens our bodies,   355
Fell upon him and released him from care.

The Grey-eyed One knew what to do next.
When she felt that Odysseus was satisfied
With sleep and with lying next to his wife,
She roused the slumbering, golden Dawn,   360
Who climbed from Ocean with light for the world.
Odysseus got up from his rose-shadowed bed
And turned to Penelope with these instructions:

"My wife, we've had our fill of trials now,
You here, weeping over all the troubles   365
My absence caused, and I, bound by Zeus
To suffer far from the home I yearned for.
Now that we have both come to the bed
We have long desired, you must take charge
Of all that is mine in the house, while I   370
See to replenishing the flocks and herds
The insolent suitors have depleted.
I'll get some back on raids, some as tribute,
Until the pens are full again. But now,
I want you to know I am going to our farm   375
To see my father, who has suffered terribly
On my account. You don't need me to tell you
That when the sun rises the news will spread
That I have killed the suitors in our hall. So,
Go upstairs with your women and sit quietly,   380
Don't look outside or speak to anyone."

Odysseus spoke and put on his beautiful armor.
He woke Telemachus, and the cowherd
And swineherd, and had them arm also.
They strapped on their bronze, opened the doors   385
And went out, Odysseus leading the way.
It was light by now, but Athena hid them
In darkness, and spirited them out of the city.

BOOK XXIV   *Peace*

Hermes, meanwhile, was calling forth
The ghosts of the suitors. He held the wand
He uses to charm mortal eyes to sleep
And make sleepers awake; and with this beautiful,

Golden wand he marshaled the ghosts,   5
Who followed along squeaking and gibbering.

   Bats deep inside an eerie cave
   Flit and gibber when one of them falls
   From the cluster clinging to the rock overhead.

So too these ghosts, as Hermes led them   10
Down the cold, dank ways, past
The streams of Ocean, past the White Rock,
Past the Gates of the Sun and the Land of Dreams,
Until they came to the Meadow of Asphodel,
Where the spirits of the dead dwell, phantoms   15
Of men outworn.

               Here was the ghost of Achilles,
And those of Patroclus, of flawless Antilochus,
And of Ajax, the best of the Achaeans
After Achilles, Peleus' incomparable son.
These ghosts gathered around Achilles   20
And were joined by the ghost of Agamemnon,
Son of Atreus, grieving, he himself surrounded
By the ghosts of those who had died with him
And met their fate in the house of Aegisthus.
The son of Peleus was the first to greet him: 25

"Son of Atreus, we believed that you of all heroes
Were dear to thundering Zeus your whole life through,
For you were the lord of the great army at Troy,
Where we Greeks endured a bitter campaign.
But you too had an early rendezvous with death,   30
Which no man can escape once he is born.
How much better to have died at Troy
With all the honor you commanded there!
The entire Greek army would have raised you a tomb,
And you would have won glory for your son as well.   35
As it was, you were doomed to a most pitiable death."

And the ghost of Agamemnon answered:

"Godlike Achilles, you did have the good fortune
To die in Troy, far from Argos. Around you fell
Some of the best Greeks and Trojans of their time,   40
Fighting for your body, as you lay there
In the howling dust of war, one of the great,
Your horsemanship forgotten. We fought all day
And would never have stopped, had not Zeus
Halted us with a great storm. Then we bore your body   45
Back to the ships and laid it on a bier, and cleansed
Your beautiful flesh with warm water and ointments,
And the men shed many hot tears and cut their hair.

Then your mother[2] heard, and she came from the sea
With her saltwater women, and an eerie cry   50
Rose over the deep. The troops panicked,
And they would have run for the ships, had not
A man who was wise in the old ways stopped them,
Nestor, whose counsel had prevailed before.
Full of concern, he called out to the troops: 55

'Argives and Achaeans, halt! This is no time to flee.
It is his mother, with her immortal nymphs,
Come from the sea to mourn her dead son.'

"When he said that the troops settled down.
Then the daughters of the Old Man of the Sea   60
Stood all around you and wailed piteously,
And they dressed you in immortal clothing.
And the Muses, all nine, chanted the dirge,
Singing responsively in beautiful voices.
You couldn't have seen a dry eye in the army,   65
So poignant was the song of the Muses.
For seventeen days we mourned you like that,
Men and gods together. On the eighteenth day
We gave you to the fire, slaughtering sheep
And horned cattle around you. You were burned   70
In the clothing of the gods, with rich unguents
And sweet honey, and many Greek heroes
Paraded in arms around your burning pyre,
Both infantry and charioteers,
And the sound of their marching rose to heaven.   75
When the fire had consumed you,
We gathered your white bones at dawn, Achilles,
And laid them in unmixed wine and unguents.
Your mother had given us a golden urn,
A gift of Dionysus, she said, made by Hephaestus.   80
In this urn lie your white bones, Achilles,
Mingled with those of the dead Patroclus,
Just apart lie the bones of Antilochus
Whom you honored most after Patroclus died.
Over them all we spearmen of the great army   85
Heaped an immense and perfect barrow
On a headland beside the broad Hellespont
So that it might be seen from far out at sea
By men now and men to come.
                              Your mother, Thetis,
Had collected beautiful prizes from the gods   90
And now set them down in the middle of the field
To honor the best of the Achaean athletes.
You have been to many heroes' funeral games
Where young men contend for prizes,

2. Thetis, a sea goddess.

6.40

But you would have marveled at the sight   95
Of the beautiful prizes silver-footed Thetis
Set out for you. You were very dear to the gods.
Not even in death have you lost your name,
Achilles, nor your honor among men.
But what did I get for winding up the war?   100
Zeus worked out for me a ghastly death
At the hands of Aegisthus and my murderous wife."

As these two heroes talked with each other,
Quicksilver Hermes was leading down
The ghosts of the suitors killed by Odysseus.   105
When Hermes and these ghosts drew near,
The two heroes were amazed and went up to see
Who they were. The ghost of Agamemnon
Recognized one of them, Amphimedon,
Who had been his host in Ithaca, and called out: 110

"Amphimedon! Why have you come down
Beneath the dark earth, you and your company,
All men of rank, all the same age? It's as if
Someone had hand-picked the city's best men.
Did Poseidon sink your ships and drown you   115
In the wind-whipped waves? Was it that, or
Did an enemy destroy you on land
As you cut off their cattle and flocks of sheep—
Or as they fought for their city and women?
Tell me. Remember who is asking—   120
An old friend of your house. I came there
With godlike Menelaus to urge Odysseus
To sail with the fleet to Ilion. A full month
That journey to Ithaca took us—hard work
Persuading Odysseus, destroyer of cities."   125

The ghost of Amphimedon responded:

"Son of Atreus, most glorious Agamemnon,
I remember all that, just as you tell it,
And I will tell you exactly what happened to us,
And how it ended in our bitter death.   130
We were courting the wife of Odysseus,
Long gone by then. She loathed the thought
Of remarrying, but she wouldn't give us a yes or no.
Her mind was bent on death and darkness for us.
Here is one of the tricks she dreamed up: 135
She set up a loom in the hall and started weaving—
A huge, fine-threaded piece—and then came out and said:

'Young men—my suitors, since Odysseus is dead—
Eager as you are to marry me, you must wait

Until I finish this robe—it would be a shame   140
To waste my spinning—a shroud for the hero
Laertes, when death's doom lays him low.
I fear the Achaean women would reproach me
If he should lie shroudless for all his wealth.'

"We went along with this appeal to our honor.   145
Every day she would weave at the great loom,
And every night she would unweave by torchlight.
She fooled us for three years with her craft.
But in the fourth year, as the seasons rolled by,
And the moons waned, and the days dragged on,   150
One of her women who knew all about it
Told us, and we caught her unweaving
The gloried shroud. Then we forced her to finish it.
When it was done she washed it and showed it to us,
And it shone like the sun or the moon.
                                        It was then   155
That some evil spirit brought Odysseus
From who knows where to the border of his land,
Where the swineherd lived. Odysseus' son
Put in from Pylos in his black ship and joined him.
These two, after they had plotted an ugly death   160
For the suitors, came up to the town, first Telemachus
And then later Odysseus, led by the swineherd,
Who brought his master wearing tattered clothes,
Looking for all the world like a miserable old beggar,
Leaning on a staff, his rags hanging off him.   165
None of us could know who he was, not even
The older men, when he showed up like that.
We threw things at him and gave him a hard time.
He just took it, pelted and taunted in his own house,
Until, prompted by Zeus, he and Telemachus   170
Removed all the weapons from the hall
And locked them away in a storeroom.
Then he showed all his cunning. He told his wife
To set before the suitors his bow and grey iron—
Implements for a contest, and for our ill-fated death.   175
None of us were able to string that bow.
We couldn't even come close. When it came
Around to Odysseus, we cried out and objected,
'Don't give the bow to that beggar,
No matter what he says!' Telemachus alone   180
Urged him on and encouraged him to take it.
And he did. The great Odysseus
Took the bow, strung it easily, and shot an arrow
Straight through the iron. Then he stood on the threshold,
Poured the arrows out, and glaring around him   185
He shot Lord Antinous. And then he shot others,
With perfect aim, and we fell thick and fast.
You could see that some god was helping them,

The way they raged through the hall, cutting us down
Right and left; and you could hear   190
The hideous groans of men as their heads
Were bashed in. The floor smoked with blood.
          That's how we died, Agamemnon. Our bodies
Still lie uncared for in Odysseus' halls.
Word has not yet reached our friends and family,   195
Who could wash the black blood from our wounds
And lay us out with wailing, as is due the dead."

And the ghost of Agamemnon responded:

"Well done, Odysseus, Laertes' wily son!
You won a wife of great character   200
In Icarius' daughter. What a mind she has,
A woman beyond reproach! How well Penelope
Kept in her heart her husband, Odysseus.
And so her virtue's fame will never perish,
And the gods will make among men on earth   205
A song of praise for steadfast Penelope.
But Tyndareus' daughter³ was evil to the core,
Killing her own husband, and her song will be
A song of scorn, bringing ill-repute
To all women, even the virtuous."   210

That was the drift of their talk as they stood
In the Dark Lord's halls deep under the earth.

Odysseus and the others went from the town
And made good time getting down to Laertes'
Well-kept fields. The old man had worked hard   215
Reclaiming the land from the wilderness.
His farmhouse was there with a row of huts around it
Where the field hands ate and rested and slept.
These were his slaves, and they did as he wished.
There was an old Sicilian woman, too,   220
Who took good care of the old man out in the country.

Odysseus had a word with the herdsmen and his son:

"Go into the farmhouse and make yourselves busy.
Sacrifice the best pig and roast it for dinner.
I am going to test my father. Will he recognize me?   225
Will he know who I am after all these years?"

He disarmed and gave his weapons to the herdsmen.
They hurried off indoors, leaving Odysseus
To search through the rows of fruit trees and vines.
He did not find Dolius, or any of his sons   230

---

3. Clytemnestra.

Anywhere in the orchard. Old Dolius had taken them
To gather fieldstones for a garden wall.
But he found his father, alone, on a well-banked plot,
Spading a plant. He had on an old, dirty shirt,
Mended and patched, and leather leggings   235
Pieced together as protection from scratches.
He wore gloves because of the bushes, and on his head
He had a goatskin cap, crowning his sorrow.
Odysseus, who had borne much, saw him like this,
Worn with age and a grieving heart,   240
And wept as he watched from a pear tree's shade.
He thought it over. Should he just throw his arms
Around his father, kiss him and tell him all he had done,
And how he'd returned to his homeland again—
Or should he question him and feel him out first?   245
Better that way, he thought, to feel him out first
With a few pointed remarks. With this in mind,
Godlike Odysseus walked up to his father,
Who kept his head down and went on digging.
His illustrious son stood close by him and said: 250

"Well, old-timer, you certainly know how to garden.
There's not a plant, a fig tree, a vine or an olive,
Not a pear tree or leek in this whole garden untended.
But if I may say so without getting you angry,
You don't take such good care of yourself. Old age   255
Is hard, yes. But unwashed, scruffy and dressed in rags?
It can't be that your lord is too lax to care for you,
And anyway there's nothing in your build or looks
To suggest you're a slave. You look more like a king,
The sort of man who after he has bathed and eaten   260
Sleeps on a soft bed, as is only right for elders.
Come on now and give me a straight answer.
Whose slave are you? Whose orchard is this?
And tell me this, too, so that I can be sure:
Is this really Ithaca I've come to, as I was told   265
By that man I ran into on my way over here?
He wasn't very polite, couldn't be bothered
To tell me what I wanted, or even to hear me out.
I've been trying to find out about an old friend
I entertained at my house once, whether he's still alive   270
Or is dead by now and gone down to Hades.
So I'll ask you, if you'll give me your attention.
I was host to a man once back in my own country,
A man who means more to me than anyone else
Who has ever visited my home from abroad.   275
He claimed his family was from Ithaca, and he said
His father was Laertes, son of Arcesius.
I took him into my home, and entertained him
In a style befitting the wealth in my house,
And gave him suitable gifts to seal our friendship: 280

Seven ingots of fine gold, a silver mixing bowl
Embossed with flowers, twelve cloaks, as many
Carpets, mantles and tunics, and his choice of four
Beautiful women superbly trained in handicrafts."

A tear wet his father's cheek as he answered: 285

"You've come to the land you're looking for, stranger,
But it's in the hands of haughty and violent men.
You've given all those generous gifts in vain.
If you were to find him alive here in Ithaca
He would send you off with the beautiful gifts   290
And fine hospitality you deserve as his friend.
But tell me this now, and tell me the truth:
How many years has it been since you hosted
Your ill-fated guest, my son—if I ever had a son?
Born for sorrow he was, and now far from home,   295
Far from his loved ones, his bones are picked clean
By fish undersea; or on some wild shore
His body is feeding the scavenging birds,
Unburied, unmourned by his mother and me,
Who brought him into this world. Nor has his wife,   300
Penelope, patient and wise, who brought him so much,
Lamented her husband on a funeral bier
Or closed his eyelids, as is due the dead.
And tell me this, too, so that I will know.
Who are you?   305
What city are you from? Who are your parents?
And where have you moored the sailing ship
That brought you and your crew of heroes here?
Or did you come as a passenger on another's ship
That put you ashore and went on its way?"   310

And Odysseus, his great mind teeming:

"I'll tell you everything point by point.
I come from Alybas and have my home there.
I'm the son of Apheidas and Polypemon's grandson.
My name is Eperitus. Some storm spirit drove me   315
Off course from Sicily and, as luck had it, here.
My ship stands off wild country far from the town.
As for Odysseus, it's been five years now
Since he left my land, ill-fated maybe,
But the birds were good when he sailed out—   320
On the right. This cheered me as I sent him off,
And he was cheered, too, our hearts full of hope
We would meet again and exchange splendid gifts."

A black mist of pain shrouded Laertes.
He scooped up fistfuls of shimmering dust   325
And groaned as he poured it upon his grey head.

This wrung Odysseus' heart, and bitter longing
Stung his nostrils as he watched his father.
With a bound he embraced him, kissed him and said:

"I'm the one that you miss, Father, right here,   330
Back in my homeland after twenty years.
But don't cry now. Hold back your tears.
I'm telling you, we really have to hurry.
I've killed the suitors in our house and avenged
All of the wrongs that have grieved your heart."   335

But Laertes' voice rang out in answer:

"If you are really Odysseus and my son come back,
Give me a sign, a clear sign I can trust."

And Odysseus, the master strategist:

"First, here's the scar I got on Parnassus   340
From that boar's bright tusk. Mother and you
Had sent me to my grandfather Autolycus
To collect some presents he had promised me
When he had visited us here. And let me count off
All of the trees in the orchard rows   345
You gave me one day when I was still a boy.
You gave me thirteen pear trees, ten apple trees,
Forty fig trees, and fifty vine rows
That ripened one by one as the season went on
With heavy clusters of all sorts of grapes."   350

He spoke, and the old man's knees went slack
As he recognized the signs Odysseus showed him.
He threw his arms around his beloved son
And gasped for breath. And godly Odysseus,
Who had borne much, embraced him.   355
When he had caught his breath and his spirit returned,
Laertes' voice rang out to the sky:

"Father Zeus, there are still gods on high Olympus,
If the suitors have really paid the price!
But now I have a terrible fear   360
That all of Ithaca will be upon us soon,
And word will have gone out to Cephallenia, too."

And Odysseus, his mind teeming:

"We don't have to worry about that right now.
Let's go to the cottage near the orchard.   365
I sent Telemachus there, and the cowherd
And swineherd, to prepare a meal for us."

And they went together to the house
With its comfortable rooms and found
Telemachus and the two herdsmen there   370
Carving huge roasts and mixing wine.
While they were busy with these tasks,
The old Sicilian woman bathed great Laertes
In his own house and rubbed him down
With olive oil and threw about his shoulders   375
A handsome cloak. And Athena came
And made the shepherd of the people
Taller than before and added muscle to his frame.
When he came from the bath, his son marveled
At his deathless, godlike appearance,   380
And his words rose to his father on wings:

"Father, surely one of the gods eternal
Has made you larger, and more handsome, too."

And Laertes, feeling the magic, answered him:

"I wish by Zeus and Athena and Apollo   385
That I could have stood at your side yesterday
In our house, armor on my shoulders,
As the man I was when I took Nericus,
The mainland town, commanding the Cephallenians!
I would have beaten the daylights out of them   390
There in our halls, and made your heart proud."

While they were talking, the others
Had finished preparing the meal.
They all sat down on benches and chairs
And were just serving themselves food   395
When old Dolius came in with his sons,
Weary from their work in the fields.
Their mother, the old Sicilian woman,
Had gone out to call them. It was she
Who made their meals and took care   400
Of Dolius, now that old age had set in.
When they saw Odysseus, and realized
Who he was, they stood there dumbfounded.
Odysseus spoke to them gently and said:

"Old man, sit down to dinner, and all of you,   405
You can stop being amazed. Hungry as we are,
We've been waiting a long time for you."

He spoke, and Dolius ran up to him
With arms outstretched, and clasped
Odysseus' hand and kissed him on the wrist.   410
Trembling with excitement, the old man said:

"My dear Odysseus, you have come back home.
We missed you so much but never hoped
To see you again. The gods themselves
Have brought you back. Welcome, welcome,   415
And may the gods grant you happiness.
But tell me this—I have to know—
Does Penelope know that you have returned,
Or should we send her a messenger?"

And Odysseus, his mind teeming: 420

"She knows, old man. You don't have to worry."

He spoke, and Dolius sat down in a polished chair.
His sons then gathered around glorious Odysseus
And greeted him and clasped his hands
And then sat down in order next to their father.   425

While they were busy with their meal,
Rumor, that swift messenger, flew
All through the city, telling everyone
About the grim fate the suitors had met.
Before long a crowd had gathered   430
Outside Odysseus' palace, and the sound
Of their lamentation hung in the air.
They carried their dead out of the hall
And buried them. Those from other cities
They put aboard ships to be brought home by sea.   435
Then they all went to the meeting place,
Sad at heart. When they were assembled,
Eupeithes rose and spoke among them,
Upon his heart an unbearable grief
For his son Antinous, the first man   440
Whom Odysseus killed. Weeping for him
He addressed the assembly and said:

"My friends, it is truly monstrous—
What this man has done to our city.
First, he sailed off with many of our finest men   445
And lost the ships and every man aboard.
Now he has come back and killed many others,
By far the best of the Cephallenians.
We must act now, before he runs off to Pylos
Or takes refuge with the Epean lords of Elis.   450
We will be disgraced forever if we don't avenge
Our sons' and brothers' deaths, and if we don't,
I see no point in living. I'd rather be dead.
Let's move now, before they cross the sea!"

He wept as he spoke, and they all pitied him.   455
Then up came Medon and the godlike bard

From Odysseus' halls. They had just woken up
From a long sleep and now stood in the midst
Of the wondering crowd. Medon had this to say:

"Hear me, men of Ithaca. It was not without the will   460
Of the deathless gods that Odysseus managed this.
I myself saw one of the immortals
Close to Odysseus. He looked just like Mentor
But was a god, now appearing in front of Odysseus,
Urging him on, then raging through the hall   465
Terrifying the suitors, who fell thick and fast."

He spoke, and they all turned pale with fear.
Then the old hero Halitherses, son of Mastor,
Rose to speak. He alone looked ahead and behind,
And spoke with the best of intentions to them: 470

"Now hear what I have to say, men of Ithaca.
You have only yourselves to blame, my friends,
For what has happened. You would not obey me
Nor Mentor, shepherd of the people, when we told you
To make your sons stop their foolishness.   475
It was what your sons did that was truly monstrous,
Wasting the wealth and dishonoring the wife
Of a great man, who they said would never return.
Now listen to me and keep your peace. Some of you
Are asking for trouble—and you just might find it."   480

Less than half of them took his advice
And stayed in their seats. Most of them
Jumped up with a whoop and went with Eupeithes.
They rushed to get weapons, and when the mob
Had armed themselves in glowing bronze,   485
They put the city behind them, following Eupeithes,
Who in his folly thought he would avenge
His son's death, but met his own fate instead.
Eupeithes would never return home again.

Athena, meanwhile, was having a word with Zeus: 490

"Father of us all, Son of Cronus most high,
Tell me what is hidden in that mind of yours.
Will you let this grim struggle go on?
Or will you establish peace on Ithaca?"

And Zeus in his thunderhead responded: 495

"Why question me, Daughter? Wasn't this
Your plan, to have Odysseus pay them back
With a vengeance? Do as you will,
But I will tell you what would be fitting.
Now that Odysseus has paid the suitors back,   500
Let all parties swear a solemn oath,

That he will be king on Ithaca all of his days.
We, for our part, will have them forget
The killing of their sons and brothers.
Let them live in friendship as before,   505
And let peace and prosperity abound."

This was all Athena needed to hear,
And she streaked down from Olympus' peaks.

The meal was over. Seeing that his company
Had satisfied their hunger, Odysseus said: 510

"Someone should go out to see if they're coming."

One of Dolius' sons went to the doorway,
Looked out, and saw the mob closing in.
His words flew fast to Odysseus:

"They're almost here. We'd better arm quickly."   515

They jumped up and put on their gear,
Odysseus and his three men and Dolius' six sons.
Laertes and Dolius armed themselves, too,
Warriors in a pinch despite their white hair.
When they had strapped on their bronze   520
They opened the doors and headed out
Behind Odysseus.

                    Athena joined them,
Looking for all the world like Mentor,
And Odysseus was glad to see her. He turned
To his son Telemachus and said: 525

"Telemachus, now you will see firsthand
What it means to distinguish yourself in war.
Don't shame your ancestors. We have been
Strong and brave in every generation."

And Telemachus coolly answered him: 530

"The way I feel now, I don't think you'll see me
Shaming my ancestors, as you put it, Father."

Laertes was delighted with this and exclaimed:

"What a day, dear gods! My son and grandson
Going head to head to see who is best."   535

The Grey-eyed One stood next to him and said:

"Son of Arcesius, my dearest comrade,
Say a prayer to Zeus and his grey-eyed daughter,
And then cast your long-shadowed spear."

Pallas Athena breathed great strength into him,   540
And with a prayer to Zeus' grey-eyed daughter,
Laertes cast his long-shadowed spear
And hit Eupeithes square in the helmet.
Bronze bored through bronze, and Eupeithes
Thudded to the ground, his armor clattering.   545
Odysseus and his glorious son
Charged the front lines, thrusting hard
With their swords and spears. They would have killed
Every last man—not one would have gone home—
Had not Athena, daughter of the Storm Cloud,   550
Given voice to a cry that stopped them all cold:

"ITHACANS!
            Lay down your arms now,
And go your ways with no more bloodshed."

Thus Athena, and they turned pale with fear.
The weapons dropped from their trembling hands   555
And fell to the ground as the goddess' voice
Sent shock waves through them. They turned
Back toward the city and ran for their lives.
With a roar, the great, long-suffering Odysseus
Gathered himself and swept after them   560

    Like a soaring raptor.

            At that moment
Zeus, Son of Cronus, hurled down
A flaming thunderbolt that landed at the feet
Of his owl-eyed daughter, who said:

"Son of Laertes in the line of Zeus,   565
Cunning Odysseus—restrain yourself.
End this quarrel and cease from fighting
Lest broad-browed Zeus frown upon you."

Thus Athena. The man obeyed and was glad,
And the goddess made both sides swear binding oaths—   570
Pallas Athena, daughter of the Storm Cloud,
Who looked like Mentor and spoke with his voice.

SAPPHO

born ca. 630 B.C.E.

Sappho is the only ancient Greek female author whose work survives at all. She was an enormously talented poet, much admired in antiquity; a later poet called her the tenth Muse. In the third century B.C.E., scholars at the great library in Alexandria arranged her poems in nine books, of which the first contained more than a thousand lines. But what we have now are pitiful remnants: one (or possibly two) complete short poems, and a collection of quotations from her work by ancient writers, supplemented by bits and pieces written on ancient scraps of papyrus found in excavations in Egypt. Yet these fragments fully justify the enthusiasm of the ancient critics; Sappho's poems (insofar as we can guess at their nature from the fragments) give us the most vivid evocation of the joys and sorrows of desire in all Greek literature.

About Sappho's life we know almost nothing. She was born about 630 B.C.E. on the fertile island of Lesbos, off the coast of Asia Minor, and spent most of her life there. Her poems suggest that she was married and had a daughter—although we should never assume that Sappho's "I" implies autobiography. It is difficult to find any evidence to answer the questions that we most want to ask. Were these poems performed for women only, or for mixed audiences? Was it common for women to compose poetry on ancient Lesbos? How did Sappho's work win acceptance in the male-dominated world of ancient Greece? We simply do not know. We also know frustratingly little about ancient attitudes toward female same-sex relationships. In the nineteenth century, Sappho's poems were the inspiration for the coinage of the modern term *lesbian*. But no equivalent term was used in the ancient world. Sappho's poems evoke a world in which girls lived an intense communal life of their own, enjoying activities and festivals in which only women took part, in which they were fully engaged with one another. Beyond the evidence of the poems themselves, however, little remains to put these works into historical context.

What we do know, and what we must always bear in mind while reading these poems, is that they were composed not to be read on papyrus or in a book but to be performed by a group of dancing, singing women and girls (a "chorus"), to the accompaniment of musical instruments. Other poets of the period composed in the choral genre, including Alcaeus, a male contemporary who was also from Lesbos. The ancient Greek equivalent of the short, nonnarrative literary form we refer to as lyric poetry was literally "lyric": it was sung to the lyre or kithara, ancestors of the modern guitar. It is not really poetry but the lyrics to songs, whose music is lost. These songs evoke many vivid actions, emotions, and images, which were presumably dramatized by the dancers, who might well, for example, have acted out the swift journey of Aphrodite's chariot in poem 1 ["Deathless Aphrodite of the spangled mind"], "whipping their wings down the sky."

Sappho's poems were produced almost two hundred years after the Homeric epics, and we can read them as offering a response, and perhaps a challenge, to the (mostly masculine) world of epic. The *Iliad* concentrates on the battlefield, where men fight and die, while the *Odyssey* shows us the struggles of a male warrior to rebuild his homeland in the aftermath of war. By contrast, Sappho's poems focus on women more than men, and on feelings more than actions. Like **Homer**, Sappho often refers to the physical world in vivid detail (the stars, the trees, the flowers, the sunlight), as well as to the Olympian gods, and to mythology. But she interprets these topics very differently. In poem 44, she uses the characters of the *Iliad* but concentrates on the marriage of Hector and Andromache rather than the war. Aphrodite, goddess of love and sex, seems more important to Sappho than Zeus, the father of the gods. Poem 16 offers another reinterpretation of the Trojan War, as a story not about men fighting but about a woman in love: "(Helen) / left her fine husband / behind and went sailing to Troy." Sappho emphasizes beauty and personal choices, and suggests that love matters more than armies, and more even than home, family, parents, or children.

But Sappho's vision of love is anything but sentimental. Many of these poems evoke intense negative emotions: alienation, jealousy, and rage. In poem 31, for example, the speaker describes her overwhelming feelings as she watches the woman she loves talking to a man: she trembles, her heart races, she feels close to death. The precise clinical detail of the narrator, as she observes herself, adds to the vividness of this account of emotional breakdown. Sappho is able to describe feelings both from the outside and from the inside, and painfully

evokes a sense of distance, from the beloved and from herself: "I don't know what to do / two states of mind in me," she says in a fragment (51). In the last poem included here, the speaker is suffering from a different kind of alienation: watching young girls dance and sing, she stands aside, unable to participate, and bitterly regrets the loss of her own youth.

Sappho repeatedly invokes the goddess associated with sexual desire: Aphrodite. It may be tempting to read Aphrodite as simply a personification of the speaker's own desires. But Sappho presents her as a real and terrifying force in the universe, who may afflict the speaker with all the "sweet-bitter" agony of love, and who may also be invoked—as in poem 1—to serve her rage and aggression, acting as Sappho's own military "ally" in her desire to inflict pain on the girl who has hurt her.

Some passages of Sappho, including the famous account of jealousy, poem 31, were preserved through quotation by other ancient writers. But many of these poems survived only on scraps of papyrus, mostly dug up from the trash-heaps of the ancient Egyptian city of Oxyrhynchus. It is exciting that we have even this much Sappho: much of our present text was discovered as late as the nineteenth century; the final poem in the selection here was found in 2004 in the papier-mâché-type wrapping used on an Egyptian mummy. Most of the papyrus finds are torn and crumpled, so that words and whole lines are often missing from the poems. Some of these gaps can be filled in from our knowledge of Sappho's dialect and the strict meter in which she wrote. In poem 16, for instance, at the end of the third stanza and the beginning of the fourth, the mutilated papyrus tells us that someone or something led Helen astray, and there are traces of a word that seems to have described Helen. The name *Cypris* (the "Cyprian One," the love goddess Aphrodite) and phrases that mean "against her will" or "as soon as she saw him [Paris]" would fit the spaces and the meter. Uncertain as these supplements are, they could help determine our understanding of the poem. Rather than give possibly misleading reconstructions here and in similar cases, the translator, Anne Carson, has marked gaps in the text with square brackets, so that the reader can decide what Sappho might have meant. As you read, also bear in mind that the translator determined the layout on the page, including line breaks and brackets. The final poem is translated by Martin West, in a somewhat different style.

Poem 1[1]

Deathless Aphrodite of the spangled mind,[2]
child of Zeus, who twists lures, I beg you
do not break with hard pains,
    O lady, my heart

but come here if ever before   5
you caught my voice far off
and listening left your father's
    golden house and came,

yoking your car. And fine birds brought you,
quick sparrows[3] over the black earth   10
whipping their wings down the sky
    through midair—

they arrived. But you, O blessed one,
smiled in your deathless face
and asked what (now again) I have suffered and why   15
    (now again) I am calling out

and what I want to happen most of all
in my crazy heart. Whom should I persuade (now again)
to lead you back into her love? Who, O
    Sappho, is wronging you?   20

1. All selections except the last are translated by Anne Carson.
2. Or "of the spangled throne"; the manuscripts preserve both readings (in the Greek there is a single letter's difference between them). The word translated here as "spangled" usually refers to a surface shimmering with bright contrasting colors. The reader should choose whether to imagine a goddess seated in splendor on a highly wrought throne or a love goddess whose mind is shifting and fickle.
3. Aphrodite's sacred birds.

For if she flees, soon she will pursue.
If she refuses gifts, rather will she give them.
If she does not love, soon she will love
      even unwilling.

Come to me now: loose me from hard   25
care and all my heart longs
to accomplish, accomplish. You
      be my ally.

Poem 16

Some men say an army of horse and some men say an army on foot
and some men say an army of ships is the most beautiful thing
on the black earth. But I say it is
      what you love.

Easy to make this understood by all.   5
For she who overcame everyone
in beauty (Helen)[4]
      left her fine husband

behind and went sailing to Troy.
Not for her children nor her dear parents   10
had she a thought, no—
      ][5] led her astray

      ] for
      ] lightly
      ] reminded me now of Anaktoria[6]   15
      who is gone.
I would rather see her lovely step
and the motion of light on her face
than chariots of Lydians[7] or ranks
      of footsoldiers in arms.[8]   20

4. Helen, wife of Menelaus, who left her husband for Paris of Troy—the start of the Trojan War.
5. Square brackets indicate where the papyrus on which the poem is preserved is torn and words or whole lines are missing.
6. Presumably a girlfriend; nothing is known about her. The name may connote "princess" (since *anax* means "leader" or "king"). "Anaktoria" was also the name for the city of Miletus, a powerful community in Asia Minor, which became incorporated into the Lydian Empire.

7. A wealthy and powerful non-Greek people in Asia Minor, with whom Sappho, living on Lesbos just off the coast, shows herself familiar. A generation or so later, the Lydians would be absorbed into the expanding Persian Empire, but in Sappho's time they were near the height of their prosperity.
8. The poem may have ended here. The papyrus preserves scraps of three more stanzas that may have belonged either to this or to a different poem.

Poem 31

He seems to me equal to gods that man
whoever he is who opposite you
sits and listens close
       to your sweet speaking

and lovely laughing—oh it   5
puts the heart in my chest on wings
for when I look at you, even a moment, no speaking
       is left in me

no: tongue breaks and thin
fire is racing under skin   10
and in eyes no sight and drumming
       fills ears

and cold sweat holds me and shaking
grips me all, greener than grass
I am and dead—or almost   15
       I seem to me.

But all is to be dared, because even a person of poverty[9]

Poem 44[1]

Kypros[2]
herald came
Idaos[3]   swift messenger
]
and of the rest of Asia   imperishable fame.   5
Hektor and his men are bringing a glancing girl
from holy Thebe and from onflowing Plakia[4]—
delicate Andromache on ships over the salt
sea. And many gold bracelets and purple
perfumed clothes, painted toys,   10
and silver cups innumerable and ivory.

9. The quotation that is our only source for this poem breaks off here, although this looks like the beginning of a new stanza.

1. This poem is our only surviving example of Sappho's narrative poetry. It tells the story of the wedding of Hector and Andromache, characters famous in myth who are featured in the *Iliad*. Some scholars believe that this poem may have been performed at a real wedding.

2. The island of Cyprus ("Kypros") was one of the most important cult centers for the goddess Aphrodite. It is not clear how the island fits into this poem, whose beginning is lost.

3. Herald in Troy.

4. Homeland of Andromache, in central Greece.

So he spoke. And at once the dear father rose up.
And news went through the wide town to friends.
Then sons of Ilos[5] led mules beneath
fine-running carts and up climbed a whole crowd   15
of women and maidens with tapering ankles,
but separately the daughters of Priam   [
And young men led horses under chariots   [
]in great style
]charioteers   20
]

                                    ]like to gods
                                    ]holy all together
set out   for Ilios[6]
and sweetflowing flute and kithara[7] were mingled
with the clip of castanets and piercingly then the maidens   25
sang a holy song and straight up the air went
amazing sound   [
and everywhere in the roads was [
bowls and cups   [
myrrh and cassia and frankincense were mingled.   30
And all the elder women shouted aloud
and all the men cried out a lovely song
calling on Paon[8] farshooting god of the lyre,
and they were singing a hymn for Hektor and Andromache
   like to gods.   35

Fragment 48

you came and I was crazy for you
and you cooled my mind that burned with longing

Fragment 51

I don't know what to do
                    two states of mind in me

Fragment 55[9]

Dead you will lie and never memory of you
will there be nor desire into the aftertime—for you do not

5. The "sons of Ilos" are Trojans, since Ilos was
the legendary founder of Troy (Ilium).
6. Troy.
7. A stringed instrument, similar to the lyre;
perhaps this poem itself was sung to the kithara.

8. Apollo.
9. This passage was part of a longer poem,
apparently addressed to a rich but untalented
woman; it survives only in quotation.

share in the roses
of Pieria,[1] but invisible too in Hades' house[2]
you will go your way among dim shapes. Having been breathed out.

Poem 94

I simply want to be dead.
Weeping she left me

with many tears and said this:
Oh how badly things have turned out for us.
Sappho, I swear, against my will I leave you.   5

And I answered her:
Rejoice, go and
remember me. For you know how we cherished you.

But if not, I want
to remind you   10
                    ]and beautiful times we had.

For many crowns of violets
and roses
            ]at my side you put on

and many woven garlands   15
made of flowers
around your soft throat.
And with sweet oil
costly
you anointed yourself   20

and on a soft bed
delicate
you would let loose your longing

and neither any[   ]nor any
holy place nor   25
was there from which we were absent

no grove[   ]no dance
                    ]no sound
            [

1. Pieria is the birthplace of the Muses,
according to Hesiod. Sappho suggests that
those who are blessed with poetic talent are
given the "roses / of Pieria."

2. Hades is the god of the dead.

Fragment 102

sweet mother I cannot work the loom
I am broken with longing for a boy by slender Aphrodite

Fragment 130

Eros[3] the melter of limbs (now again) stirs me—
sweetbitter unmanageable creature who steals in

Poem 168B[4]

Moon has set
and Pleiades:[5] middle
night, the hour goes by,
alone I lie.[6]

The New Sappho[7]

(You for) the fragrant-bosomed (Muses') lovely gifts
(be zealous,) girls, (and the) clear melodious lyre:
(but my once tender) body old age now
(has seized;) my hair's turned (white) instead of dark;
my heart's grown heavy, my knees will not support me,   5
that once on a time were fleet for the dance as fawns.
This state I oft bemoan; but what's to do?
Not to grow old, being human, there's no way.
Tithonus[8] once, the tale was, rose-armed Dawn,
love-smitten, carried off to the world's end,   10
handsome and young then, yet in time gray age
o'ertook him, husband of immortal wife.

3. God of love.
4. It is not certain that this fragment is by Sappho.
5. A cluster of seven stars; in Greek mythology, they were originally seven nymphs.
6. In the Greek, the form of the word for "alone" shows that the speaker is female.
7. Translated by Martin West. In this poem, the round brackets enclose words conjectured by the translator.
8. The goddess Dawn fell in love with a Trojan called Tithonus and carried him off. She could make him immortal, but not immune to old age. In some versions of the myth, he turned into a cicada, whom the Greeks imagined as eternally singing—a kind of insect poet.

ANCIENT
ATHENIAN DRAMA

Modern readers usually find Athenian drama easy to appreciate. Aristophanes' physical, earthy humor is still funny today, and his wild fantasies raise political and social questions that are still relevant in modern times. The tragedies of Aeschylus, **Sophocles,** and **Euripides** provide compelling stories about human relationships, whose absorbing, often violent or melodramatic plots invite us to think about profound issues, such as the nature of justice, the meaning of suffering, and clashes between family and state and between human and divine perspectives.

But the original performance contexts of Greek drama were radically different from anything modern readers and theatergoers have experienced. The city festivals of Athens, at which all new comedies and tragedies were first performed, involved a mixture of things we usually regard as wholly separate: politics, religion, music, poetry, serious drama, slapstick, open-air spectacles, and dance. For the combination of drama with song and dance, in a popular format performed for large audiences, our closest analogy might be the Broadway musical. Like Greek tragedy, shows such as *Beauty and the Beast* and *The Little Mermaid* update a traditional, mythic story for a contemporary audience. But Broadway shows usually take place indoors, and have no obvious connection to politics or religion. To get a sense of the strangeness of Athenian dramatic festivals, imagine a major public political event, like the inauguration of a new American president,

combine it with a major religious gathering like an evangelical rally, a papal audience, or the Hajj to Mecca, then add to the mix the Cannes Film festival, a Veterans Day march, a Thanksgiving Day parade (with all the floats), and a grand open-air musical event like Woodstock. The resulting hybrid would be a modern equivalent of the two major Athenian religious occasions that included major dramatic performances: the Great Dionysia and the Lernaea. Both festivals included tragedy and comedy, although tragedy was more central to the Dionysia, while comedy played a larger role at the Lernaea.

Both festivals were held in honor of the god Dionysus, who was associated with alcohol, and, more generally, with overturning the rules and conventions of the normal, everyday world. Dionysus was a wild figure: he rode a chariot pulled by leopards, dressed in strange, effeminate clothing and an ivy crown, and was accompanied by ecstatic, crazy women (the Maenads) and hairy, permanently erect half-goat men called Satyrs. The Athenians knew him as an exotic, foreign god who originated somewhere in Asia Minor before being incorporated in the Olympian pantheon. We should remember the subversive, outsider status of this god when reading Athenian drama.

We know very little about the origins of tragedy or comedy. The word *comedy* seems to come from *komos,* a Greek word denoting a drunken procession. Aristotle tells us that *tragedy* (*tragoidia* in Greek) means "goat song," and suggests that the genre originated as part of a ritual in which a goat was sacrificed or offered as a prize. Sometime in the late sixth century B.C.E., rural celebrations in honor of Dionysus became an official, annual part of the urban festival calendar. Originally, the main entertainment was probably choruses of dancers, who sang hymns and competed for prizes; later, some form of tragedy and, later still, comedy were added to the program. Thespis, from whose name we get the term *thespian*—a character about whom we know next to nothing—is traditionally said to have invented tragedy in the year 534 B.C.E. He "stepped out of the Chorus," creating a part for a single actor who could talk back to the chorus. The invention of the individual actor, distinct from the group, was enormously important: it paved the way for the whole subsequent history of Western drama.

Tragedy was something new in the late sixth century, but contests of poetry in performance had long been a part of Athenian culture. At the largest city festival, the Panathenaia ("All-Athenian," in honor of the city's goddess, Athena), performers called rhapsodes recited parts of **Homer's** **Iliad** and **Odyssey**; the best performers won prizes. The Homeric poems were an essential model for later drama. Aeschylus supposedly called his own work "slices from the feast of Homer." It was not merely the plots of Greek tragedy that were "Homeric," although like the *Iliad* and *Odyssey* many tragedies dealt with the heroes who fought in the Trojan War. Dramatists also learned from Homer how to create vivid dialogue and fast, exciting narrative, as well as sympathy for a range of different characters, Greek and foreigner alike.

Each year at the Great Dionysia, three tragic poets were chosen by the official city governor (the *archon*), to produce a tetralogy of plays for each day's entertainment. Performances began at dawn

This detail from the so-called Pronomos Vase, painted in the late fifth century B.C.E., depicts actors preparing for a satyr play.

and included three tragedies, which might or might not concentrate on a linked set of stories, followed by a lighter play featuring satyrs (a "satyr play"). A rich Athenian citizen put up the money to pay for the costs of each day's performance, including purchase of costumes and masks, and training of the chorus members and actors. These producers prided themselves on their participation, and gloated if the performance they had financed won the competition: at least one backer tried to rig the results by making a night raid to destroy the gold crowns and costumes that had been ordered for his rival's chorus to wear. Before the dramatic performances began, the tribute paid to the city of Athens by

A contemporary photograph of the remains of the theater of Dionysus in Athens.

her allies was heaped up in the theater for all to see, and the orphans of Athenian men killed in war in the previous year marched in front of the audience, wearing armor provided at the expense of the city. Athenian drama itself can be seen as a comparable display, a demonstration to foreigners and to the Athenians themselves of the city's artistic and intellectual riches, as well as a meditation on its vulnerability.

The only complete works of Greek drama that have survived are a small selection of the tragedies of Aeschylus, Sophocles, and Euripides, and a few comedies by Aristophanes. But of course far more people composed plays in this period, some of which were probably excellent; there were other poets—such as Agathon, the tragedian who appears in Plato's *Symposium*—who were awarded first prize in the competitions. We have just the names of most of these other dramatists, along with some titles and some tantalizing fragments.

Similarly, the scripts are all that survive of Greek drama, and wishful think-ing leads one to imagine that what we have is the most important part: we tend to think of these plays simply as "literature," words on a page. But the words must have formed only a small part of the total effect of the original performances. Those sitting in the upper areas of the theater may well not have been able to hear everything, despite the good acoustics of the theater. The music, gestures, costumes, props, and visual effects may well have had a larger impact on most audience members than any individual detail of phrasing. Writing the script was also a tiny part of the work of a dramatist. The poet was also the director, composer, and choreographer of the plays he created; in the earliest days of drama, the poets were probably also actors in their own work. The prizes were not awarded for writing, but for the work of coaching the actors and dancers: the usual phrase to describe what a dramatist does is "to teach a chorus." In 425, when Aristophanes wrote his first play but had it directed by somebody else,

A reconstruction of the Dionysus theater by the theater and architectural scholar Richard Leacroft. An actor stands in the *orchēstra*, while another stands on the roof of the *skēnē*.

the prize was awarded to the director, not the poet.

The theater of Dionysus, where the plays were performed, held at least 13,000 people, perhaps as many as 17,000—a number comparable to the seating available in Madison Square Garden. This figure represents a high proportion of the male citizen body, estimated to have been about forty or sixty thousand people—although the total population of Athens, including women, children, foreigners, and slaves may have been ten times that large.

It is possible that a few women came to the theater in the fifth century; women were almost certainly in attendance by the fourth century. We do not know whether slaves were present. In any case, the majority of the audience consisted of male citizens. In the participatory democracy of fifth-century Athens, the whole citizen body was eligible to participate in policy making, and citizens were accustomed to meet together in public to determine military and domestic policy, at least once a month and usually more often. The structure of the dramatic festival was reminiscent of other political assemblies, where citizens sat to hear speeches on several sides of a case and made their decisions between competing sides.

The theater was an open-air venue, with seating in the round. The central space, called the *orchēstra* (which means "dancing area"), lay at the lowest point of the valley; on the slopes of the hill, spectators sat on wooden benches, surrounding the performance area on three sides. At one end of the *orchēstra* was a wooden platform or stage, with a wooden building on it (the *skēnē*), which could be used to represent whatever interior space was necessary for the play: a palace, a house, a cave, or any other type of structure. There were thus three possible ways for actors to come on and off stage: to the left or right of the stage, or through the doors of the building. Entrances and exits tend to be particularly important in Greek drama, because they took a long time;

the audience would have been watching the characters make their way into the playing area before they actually reached the stage. When reading these plays, it is a good idea to pay particular attention to the moments when a new character comes on.

There were also two major structural devices that expanded the possibilities of the playing space. The *ekkuklēma* ("trolley" or "thing that rolls out") was a wooden platform on wheels, which could be trundled out from the central doors of the *skēnē*, and was conventionally used to represent the interior space. This was an essential device by which dramatists could bring the events from indoors before the eyes of the outdoor audience. The second device was the *mēchanē* ("machine" or "device"), a pulley system that allowed for the appearance and disappearance of actors in the air, above the *skēnē* building. Using the *mēchanē*, playwrights could make a god suddenly appear in the air above the palace, as a literal *deus ex māchinā* ("god from the machine"), to resolve the twists of the plot.

All the actors who performed in Athenian drama were men—including those playing female parts. All actors wore masks. Tragedy and comedy both used a tiny number of actors for the speaking parts. In the first few decades of the century, there were only two actors; later, three actors were used. This meant that the same actors had to play multiple roles, appearing in different masks as the play required. The use of masks, as well as the open-air space, must have necessitated a very different style of acting from that of modern cinema, television, or stage. Facial expressions would have been invisible behind the mask, and were therefore irrelevant; instead, actors must have relied on gestures, body language, and a strongly projected voice.

The dialogue sections of ancient Athenian plays usually show two—occasionally three—characters in confrontation or discussion with one another. Dialogue may be free-flowing and apparently natural. But dramatists made use of two important dialogue techniques. One is the *agon* ("contest" or "struggle"), in which one character makes a long, sometimes legalistic speech, arguing a particular case, and a second character replies with another speech, putting the case against. The other is *stichomythia* ("line-speech"), in which characters speak just a single line each—allowing for a fast-paced, usually argumentative exchange.

Greek drama was always composed in verse, but not in the epic meter of Homer, the hexameter (a line with a six-part pattern). The rhythm of the dialogue elements was iambic (based on a fairly flexible pattern of alternating short and long syllables), which was supposed to be the verse form closest to normal speech (like the iambic pentameter used by Shakespeare). The choral passages, by contrast, were composed in extremely complex meters, designed to be sung and accompanied by elaborate choreography. Athenian drama thus combined two very different theatrical experiences, interspersing plot-driven, character-heavy dialogue with music, poetry, and dance.

The chorus was composed of twelve—later, fifteen—masked dancers, of whom only one, the "leader," had a speaking role. This group is used in different ways by the different dramatists, and varies radically from play to play. In comedy, the choruses are often nonhuman: Aristophanes, whose plays are frequently named for the chorus, created groups of frogs, birds, wasps, and clouds. The choruses of tragedy are usually more naturalistic; a notable exception is the divine, snake-haired Furies who form the chorus of Aeschylus's *Eumenides*.

The chorus is often a group of inhabitants of the place where the action occurs: it can be used to represent the voice of the ordinary person or the word on the street—although it does not always express the voice of common sense, and it frequently fails to get things right. Sometimes the chorus listens sympathetically to the main characters, acting as an internal audience and allowing for the revelation of inner thoughts that might otherwise be hard for the dramatist to bring out. Sometimes, on the other hand, the chorus is either neutral or positively hostile toward the main characters. Choruses can be characters themselves, with their own biases and preoccupations.

The choral songs and dances can allow the dramatist to put the events of the play in a broader perspective: the chorus may take us back in time, looking to earlier events in the same myth, or tracing parallels between this story and others; or it may reflect on the ethical, theological, and metaphysical implications of the events at hand. The poet may also use the chorus to provide a break from the main narrative, a switch to an entirely different mood or perspective. Choral songs can increase the dramatic tension or surprise, as when a cheerful, optimistic song is followed by disaster.

Mutilation and violent death, by murder or suicide, accident, fate, or the gods, are frequent events in Greek tragedy. The threat of violence—which may or may not be averted—provides a strong element in the interest of these plays. But compared to modern television drama or action movies, there is little visible horror. Dead bodies are often displayed onstage, but the actual killing usually takes place offstage. The messenger speech is therefore one of the most important conventions of Athenian drama. Long, vivid, blow-by-blow accounts of offstage disasters allow the audience to imagine and visualize events that the dramatist cannot or will not bring onstage.

Comic poets made up their own plots from scratch, and were able to create stories that combined reality, fantasy, and myth however they chose. Comic poets could depict caricatures of real people—famous politicians, fellow poets like Euripides, or the philosopher Socrates—mixing with made-up characters, as well as with gods and heroes (like Dionysus and Heracles) and personifications (like "The People"). Comedy often made direct references to recent events, and parodied, satirized, or directly attacked the behavior of real contemporary people.

The plots of Greek tragedy, by contrast, focus on a few traditional story patterns, set in the distant past and in non-Athenian city-states: Argos, Thebes, or Troy. But though tragedians used preexisting stories, they felt free, within reason, to shape the myths in their own way; for instance, Aeschylus, Sophocles, and Euripides created very different plays focused on the story of Electra, daughter of the murdered Agamemnon. Tragedy was often relevant in some way to contemporary concerns, but its political and social perspectives are never as explicit as those of comedy.

Since Greek tragedy and comedy were always performed at a religious festival, we might expect these dramas to be more obviously "religious" than they seem at first blush. Comedians often bring gods on stage, but they are not treated in a markedly reverent way: for instance, Dionysus in Aristophanes' Frogs is a craven coward with a flatulence problem. The power of the gods is usually a more serious issue in tragedy; but even here, modern readers may be surprised at how cruel and unreliable the Greek gods often seem to be. It is perhaps helpful to remember that Athenians of the fifth century—unlike most believers in modern monotheistic religions—saw no necessary connection between religion and morality. Gods are, by definition, immortal and powerful; they need not also be nice. Athenian drama was an act of service to the gods in general, and to Dionysus in particular, because it overturned the everyday world and explored the power of the imagination, showing—in Euripides' words—"how god makes possible the unexpected." By serving the gods, displaying the strange and surprising ways that divine forces operate on human lives, Athenian dramatists were also serving their audiences, creating dramas that were gripping, profound, and unpredictable: qualities that readers still appreciate in these works today.

SOPHOCLES

ca. 496–406 B.C.E.

The seven surviving plays of Sophocles are often considered the most perfect achievement of ancient Athens. They show us people—presented with psychological depth and subtlety—who stand apart from others, on the edges of their social groups. Sophocles invites us to ask what it means to be part of a family, part of a city, part of a team or an army, or part of the human race. Can we choose to embrace or reject our family, friends, and society, or do we have to accept the place to which we were born? Is it a gesture of heroism or folly to be an outsider? What should we do if forced to choose between our family and a wider social group? These thought-provoking and compelling dramas explore themes that are just as relevant today as they were in the fifth century B.C.E., and they provide the classic treatments of mythic figures, such as Oedipus and Antigone, who have been central to later Western culture.

LIFE AND TIMES

Sophocles was a generation younger than Aeschylus, and had an unusually long, successful, productive, and apparently happy life. He was born at the start of the fifth century, around 496 B.C.E., in the village of Colonus, which was a short distance north of Athens. His family was probably fairly wealthy—his father may have owned a workshop producing armor, a particularly saleable product at this time of war—and Sophocles seems to have been well educated. An essential element in Greek boys' education at this time was studying the Homeric poems, and Sophocles obviously learned this lesson well; in later times, he was called the "most Homeric" of the three surviving Athenian tragedians. He was a good-looking, charming boy and a talented dancer. In 480, when he was about fifteen or sixteen, he was chosen to lead a group of naked boys who danced in the victory celebrations for Athens' defeat of the Persian navy at Salamis. The beginning of his public career thus coincided with his city's period of greatest glory and international prestige.

Athens became the major power in the Mediterranean world in the middle decades of the fifth century, a period known as the golden or classical age. The most important political figure in the newly dominant city-state was Pericles, a statesman who was also Sophocles' personal friend and who particularly encouraged the arts. Pericles seems to have instituted various legal measures to enable the theater to flourish: for instance, rich citizens were obliged to provide funding for theater productions, and the less wealthy may have had their theater tickets subsidized.

The prosperity of Sophocles' city took a sharp turn for the worse around 431 B.C.E., when the poet would have been in his mid-sixties. The Peloponnesian War, between Athens and Sparta, began at that time and would last until after Sophocles' death. Soon after the outbreak of war, Sophocles' friend Pericles died in a terrible plague that afflicted the whole city. In the last decades of the century, the city became increasingly impoverished and demoralized by war.

Sophocles worked in the Athenian theater all his life. He made some important technical changes in the theater, including the introduction of scene painting, and the increase of the chorus members from twelve to fifteen. His most important innovation was bringing in a third actor (a "tritagonist"). This allowed for three-way dialogues, and a drama that concentrates on the complex interactions and relationships of individuals with one another. The chorus in Sophocles' dramas became far less central to the plot than it had been in Aeschylus; this is part of the reason why Sophocles' plays may seem more modern to twenty-first century readers and audiences.

Another quality that makes Sophocles particularly accessible to modern readers is his interest in realistic characterization. Sophocles' most memorable characters are intense, passionate, and often larger than life, but always fully human. They frequently adopt positions that seem extreme, but for which they have the best of motives. Sophocles'

tragedies ask us to consider when and how it is right to compromise, and to measure the slim divide between concession and selling out. Clashes between stubborn heroism and the voice of moderation are found in all Sophocles' surviving plays.

Contemporaries gave Sophocles' talent its due. He won first prize at the Great Dionysia for the first time in 468, defeating his older rival, Aeschylus; he was still under thirty at the time. Sophocles would defeat Aeschylus several more times in the course of his career. His output was large: he composed over a hundred and twenty plays. The seven that survive include the three Theban plays, dealing with Oedipus and his family: *Oedipus the King*, *Antigone*, and *Oedipus at Colonus*. These were written at intervals of many years, and were never intended to be performed together. The other four surviving tragedies are: *Ajax*, about a strongman hero who is driven mad by Athena and about the consequences of his madness; *Trachiniae*, about Heracles' agonizing death at the hands of his jealous wife Deineira (who had thought the poison she gave him was a love potion); *Electra*, which focuses on the unending grief and rage of Agamemnon's daughter after her father's murder; and *Philoctetes*, about the Greek embassy to persuade an embittered, wounded hero to return to battle in Troy. The dating of most of these plays is uncertain, although we know *Philoctetes* is a late play, composed in 409 B.C.E. The judges at the Great Dionysia loved Sophocles' work: he won first prize over twenty times, and never came lower than second.

Sophocles seems to have been equally popular as a person, known for his mellow, easygoing temperament, his religious piety, and his appreciation for the beauty of adolescent boys. We are told that he had "so much charm of character that he was loved everywhere, by everyone." He was friendly with the prominent intellectuals of his day, including the world's first historian, Herodotus. He participated actively in the political activity of the city; he served under Pericles as a treasurer in 443 and 442, and was elected as a general under him in 441. After the Sicilian disaster in 413, in which Athens lost enormous numbers of men and ships, Sophocles—then in his eighties—was one of ten men elected to an emergency group formed for policy formation. Sophocles' participation in public life suggests that he was seen as a trustworthy and wise member of the community. Sophocles was married and had five sons, one of whom, Iophon, became a tragedian himself. He lived to advanced old age, and was over ninety when he died.

OEDIPUS THE KING

Many first-time readers of *Oedipus the King* will already know the shocking skeleton Oedipus eventually discovers: that he killed his father and married his mother, without knowing what he was doing. The mythical background to this play is familiar to readers today, and would have been well known, in its broad outlines, to Sophocles' original audience. This is a drama not of surprise, but of suspense: we watch Oedipus uncover the buried truth about himself and his parentage, of which he, unlike us, is ignorant. The mystery, which is gradually revealed to the spectators in the course of Sophocles' play, is not what the king has done, but how he will discover what he has done, and how he will respond to this terrible new knowledge.

The legend goes that Laios, son of Labdakos and king of Thebes, learned long ago from the Delphic oracle (sacred to Apollo) that his son would kill him. When Laius had a son, by his wife Jokasta, he gave the baby to a shepherd to be exposed on Mount Kithaeron.

Exposure, a fairly common practice in the ancient world, involved leaving a baby out in some wild place, presumably to die; it allowed parents to dispose of unwanted children without incurring blood guilt. Laios increased the odds against the child's survival by piercing and binding his feet, so there was no chance he could crawl away. But the shepherd felt sorry for the boy and saved him. He was adopted by the childless king and queen of Corinth (Korinth), Polybos and Merope, and grew up believing himself to be their son.

One day another oracle warned Oedipus that he would kill his father and marry his mother. Oedipus fled Corinth and ran away, in the direction of Thebes, to avoid this fate. At a place where three paths crossed, he encountered his real father, Laios, without knowing who he was; they quarreled, and Oedipus killed Laios. When he reached Thebes, he found the city oppressed by a dreadful female monster, a Sphinx—part human, part lion, often also depicted in Greek art with the wings of an eagle and the tail of a snake. The Sphinx refused to let anybody into the city unless they could answer her riddle: "What walks on four legs in the morning, two legs at noon, and three legs in the evening?" She strangled and devoured all travelers who failed to answer the riddle. But Oedipus gave the right answer: "Man," (Human beings crawl on all fours in infancy, walk on two feet in adulthood, and use a cane in old age.) The Sphinx was defeated, and Oedipus was welcomed into the city as a savior. He married the newly widowed queen, Jokasta, and took over the throne.

When Sophocles' play begins, Oedipus has been ruling Thebes successfully for many years, and has four children by Jokasta, two sons and two daughters. But a new trouble is now afflicting the city. Plague has come to Thebes, and the dying inhabitants are searching for the reason why the gods are angry with the city.

The city of Athens suffered a terrible plague in 429 B.C.E., and the play may well have been composed and performed soon afterward—although the dating is uncertain and disputed. Sophocles certainly seems to invite comparisons between the real Athens and the mythical Thebes. Oedipus himself can be seen as a typical fifth-century Athenian: he is optimistic, irascible, self-confident, both pious and skeptical in his attitudes toward religion, and a committed believer in the power of human reason.

In his *Poetics*, the philosopher Aristotle describes this play as the finest of all Greek tragedies. It includes two plot patterns that he thought were essential to good drama: a reversal of fortune (*peripeteia*), and a recognition (*anagnorisis*). Aristotle famously cites Oedipus as an example of someone whose fall into misfortune is the result not of bad deeds or evil character, but of some "mistake"—the Greek word is *hamartia*. Later critics applied the quite different concept of a "tragic flaw" to Oedipus, suggesting that we are supposed to see the disastrous events of the drama as somehow the king's own fault. An important consideration against this reading is that in *Oedipus at Colonus*, a later play about the last days of Oedipus, Sophocles makes his hero give a compelling self-defense: "How is my *nature* evil— / if all I did was to return a blow?" There is a clear distinction in Greek thought between moral culpability—which is attached to deliberate, conscious actions—and religious pollution, which may afflict even those who are morally innocent. Readers must decide for themselves how far they think Sophocles goes in presenting his Oedipus as a sympathetic or even admirable figure.

Another popular approach to the play has been to see it as a classic "tragedy of fate," in which a man is brought low by destiny or the gods. Here, we need to distinguish the myth—which can plausibly be seen as a story about the inevitable unfolding of divine will—from Sophocles' treatment of the myth in his play, which suggests a more complex relationship between destiny and human action. Before Sophocles, Aeschylus had produced a trilogy that dealt with the family of Laius and Oedipus. This does not survive, but it is likely that it showed the gradual fulfillment of an inherited curse. In Sophocles' play, our attention is focused less on the original events and their causes (the killing of Laios and the marriage to Jokasta) than on the process by which Oedipus uncovers what he has done.

Sophocles multiplies the number of oracles and messengers in the story, and Apollo—the god associated with prophecy, poetry, and interpretation, as well as with light and the sun—presides over the complex unfolding of the truth. Oracles are only one of many types of riddling, ambiguous, or ambivalent language used in the play, which is concerned with all kinds of interpretation. Moments of dramatic irony, when the audience hears a meaning of which the speaker is unaware, are another important reminder that words may have more than one sense. For instance, Oedipus says, "Laios / had no luck fathering children," and vows to fight for him "as I would for my own father"—speaking more truly than he knows. The interplay between literal and metaphorical meanings forms another essential technique in the play. Sophocles creates a relationship between literal and metaphorical blindness, between the light of the sun and the light of insight, between Oedipus as "father" of his people and as real father to his own siblings, and between sickness as a physical affliction and as a metaphor for pollution.

The riddle of the Sphinx defines humanity by the number of feet we use at different points in our lives. Sophocles seems to suggest that the name *Oedipus* is closely associated with feet: it can be read either as "Know-Foot" (from the verb *oida*, "to know," and *pous*, "foot"— an appropriate name for the man who guessed the Sphinx's riddle), or as "Swell-Foot" (from the verb *oidao*, to swell— a reminder of the baby Oedipus's wounded feet). The first interpretation of his name makes Oedipus seem like an Everyman figure, a representative of all humanity: he is the one who truly understands the human condition. The second reminds us of the ways in which Oedipus is not like us: his feet mark the fact that he was cast out by his parents, rejected from his city, and that he has, unwittingly, done things that seem to make it impossible for him to be part of any human community.

Sigmund Freud famously claimed that the Oedipus myth represents a universal psychological phenomenon, the "Oedipus Complex," which involves the (supposed) desire of all boys to kill their fathers and marry their mothers. But Sophocles' Oedipus does not suffer from Freud's complex: his terrible actions are committed in total ignorance, not through an unconscious desire for patricide or sex with his mother. Another way to think of Sophocles' Oedipus is as a hero who, like Odysseus, struggles to find his way back home after many wanderings and an encounter with terrible monsters—but finds himself in a perverted version of the homecoming story, in which the arrival is not the end but the beginning of a nightmare.

A play whose secret you already know might seem unlikely to be interesting. But it is impossible to be bored by *Oedipus the King*. The plot races to its terrible conclusion with the twisting, breakneck pace of a thrilling murder mystery, while the contradictory figure of Oedipus himself—the blind rationalist, the polluted king, the killer of his father, the son and husband of Jokasta, the hunter and the hunted, the stranger in his own home—is a commanding presence, who dominates the stage even when he can no longer see.

The translation printed here uses versions of the names and places that are closer to the Greek, rather than the more usual Latin forms—for instance, Korinth, not Corinth; Jokasta, not Jocasta; Bakkhos, not Bacchus, and so on.

Oedipus the King[1]

CHARACTERS

DELEGATION OF THEBANS, *mostly young (silent)*
OEDIPUS, *King of Thebes*
PRIEST OF ZEUS
KREON, *Jokasta's brother*
CHORUS *of older Theban men*
LEADER *(of the Chorus)*
TIRESIAS, *blind prophet of Apollo*
Boy to lead Tiresias *(silent)*
JOKASTA, *Oedipus' wife*
Attendants and maids *(silent)*

1. Translated by Robert Bagg.

MESSENGER *from Korinth*
HERDSMAN, *formerly of Laios' house*
SERVANT, *from Oedipus' house*
ANTIGONE *and* ISMENE, *Oedipus' daughters (silent)*

SCENE: *Before the Royal Palace in Thebes. The palace has an imposing central double door. Two altars stand near it; one is to Apollo. The delegation of Thebans enters carrying olive branches wound with wool strips. * * * Oedipus enters through the great doors.*[2]

OEDIPUS	My children—*you* are the fresh green life	
	old Kadmos[3] nurtures and protects.	
	But why are you surging at *me* like this—	
	with your wool-strung boughs[4]—while	
	the city is swollen with howls of pain,	5
	reeking incense, and prayers sung	
	to the Healing God?[5] To have others	
	tell me these things wouldn't be right,	
	my sons. So I've come out myself.	
	My name is Oedipus—the famous—	10
	as everyone calls me.	
	Tell me, old man,	
	yours is the natural voice for the rest,	
	what troubles you? You're terrified?	
	Looking for reassurance? Be certain	
	I'll give you all the help I can.	15
	I'd be a hard man if an approach	
	like yours failed to rouse my pity.	
PRIEST	You rule our land Oedipus! You can see	
	who comes to your altars—how varied	
	we are in years: children too weak-winged	20
	to fly far, others hunched with age,	
	a few priests—I am a priest of Zeus—	
	joined by the best of our young lads.	
	More of us wait with wool-strung boughs	
	in the markets, and at Athena's two temples.	25
	Some, at the river shrine, are watching	
	ashes for the glow of prophecy.[6]	
	You can see our city going under,	
	too feeble to lift its head clear	
	of the angry murderous waves.	30
	Plague blackens our flowering farmland,	
	sickens our cattle where they graze.	
	Our women in labor give birth to nothing.	

2. All stage directions (in italics), as well as the list of characters, are by the translator.
3. The mythical founder of the city of Thebes.
4. Representing their status as supplicants.

5. Apollo.
6. Divinators and priests told the future by looking at the burnt embers of sacrificed animals.

A burning god rakes his fire through our town; 35
he hates us with fever, he empties
the House of Kadmos, enriching
black Hades[7] with our groans and tears.
We haven't come to beg at your hearth
because we think you're the gods' equal. 40
We've come because you are the best man
at handling trouble or confronting gods.
You came to Thebes, you freed us
from the tax we paid with our lives
to that rasping Singer.[8] You did it with no 45
help from us. We had nothing to teach you.

People say—they believe!—you had a god's
help when you restored life to our city.
Oedipus, we need *now* the great power
men everywhere know you possess. 50
Find some way to protect us—learn it
from a god's whisper, or a man's.
This much I know: guidance
from men proven right in the past
will meet a crisis with the surest force. 55
Act as our greatest man! Act
as you did when you first seized fame!
We believe your nerve saved us then.
Don't let us look back on your rule and say,
He lifted us once, but then let us down. 60
Put us firmly back on our feet,
so Thebes will never fall again.

You were a bird from god, you brought good luck
the day you rescued us. Be that man now!
If you want to rule us, it's better
to rule the living than a barren waste; 65
walled cities and ships are worthless
when they've been emptied of people.

OEDIPUS I do pity you, children. Don't think I'm unaware.
I know what need brings you: this sickness
ravages all of you. Yet, sick as you are, 70
not one of you suffers a sickness like mine.
Yours is a private grief, you feel
only what touches you. But my heart grieves
for you, for myself, and for our city.

7. Land of the dead.
8. The Sphinx, the winged female monster that terrorized the city of Thebes until her riddle was finally answered by Oedipus. The riddle comes in various different versions and is never actually cited by Sophocles, but one common version goes, "What walks on four feet in the morning, two at noon, and three at night?" Oedipus answered, "Man," because humans crawl in infancy, walk on two feet as adults, and walk with a stick in old age.

	You've come to wake me to all this.	75

You've come to wake me to all this. 75
There was no need. I haven't been sleeping.
I have wept tears enough, for long enough;
my mind has raced down every twisting path.
And after careful thought, I've set in motion
the only cure I could find: I've sent Kreon, 80
my wife's brother, to Phoibos at Delphi,[9]
to hear what action or what word of mine
will save this town. Already, counting the days,
I'm worried: what is Kreon doing?
He takes too long, more time than he needs. 85
But when he comes, I'd be the criminal—*not*
to do everything god shows me to do.

PRIEST   Well-timed! The moment you spoke,
your men gave the sign: Kreon's arriving.

OEDIPUS   O Lord Apollo 90
may the luck he brings save us! Luck so bright
we can see it—just as we see him now.

(KREON *enters from the countryside, wearing a laurel crown
speckled with red.*[1])

PRIEST   He must bring pleasing news. If not, why would
he wear a laurel crown dense with berries?

OEDIPUS   We'll know very soon; he's within earshot. 95
Prince! Brother kinsman, son of Menoikeos!
What kind of answer have you brought from god?

KREON   A good one. No matter how dire, if troubles
turn out well—everything will be fine.

OEDIPUS   What did the god say? Nothing you've said 100
so far alarms or reassures me.

KREON   Do you want me to speak in front of these men?
If so, I will. If not, let's go inside.

OEDIPUS   Speak here, to all of us. I suffer
more for them than for my own life. 105

KREON   Then I'll report what I heard from Apollo.
He made his meaning very clear.
He commands we drive out what corrupts us,
what sickens our city. We now harbor
something incurable. He says: purge it. 110

OEDIPUS   Tell me the source of our trouble.
How do we cleanse ourselves?

KREON   By banishing a man or killing him. It's blood—
kin murder—that brings this storm on our city.

OEDIPUS   Who is the man god wants us to punish? 115

KREON   As you know, King, our city was ruled once
by Laios, before you came to take the helm.

OEDIPUS   I've heard as much. Though I never saw him.

9. Apollo, whose oracle was at Delphi.   1. A sign of good news.

KREON	Well, Laios was murdered. Now god tells you
	plainly: with your own hands punish 120
	the very men whose hands killed Laios.
OEDIPUS	Where do I find these men? How do I track
	vague footprints from a bygone crime? *talking to himself*
KREON	The god said: here, in our own land.
	What we look for we can capture; 125
	what we ignore goes free.
OEDIPUS	Was Laios killed at home? Or in the fields?
	Or did they murder him on foreign ground?
KREON	He told us his journey would take him
	close to god. But he never came back. 130
OEDIPUS	Did none of his troop see and report
	what happened? Isn't there anyone
	to question whose answers might help?
KREON	All killed but a single terrified
	survivor, able to tell us but one fact. 135
OEDIPUS	What was it? One fact might lead to many,
	if we had one small clue to give us hope.
KREON	They had the bad luck, he said, to meet bandits
	who struck them with a force many hands strong.
	This wasn't the violence of one man only. 140
OEDIPUS	What bandit would dare commit such a crime . . .
	unless somebody here had hired him?
KREON	That was our thought, but after Laios
	died, we were mired in new
	troubles—and no avenger came. 145
OEDIPUS	But here was your kingship murdered!
	What kind of trouble could have blocked your search?
KREON	The Sphinx's song. So wily, so baffling!
	She forced us to forget the dark past,
	to confront what lay at our feet. 150
OEDIPUS	Then I'll go back, start fresh,
	and light up that darkness.
	Apollo was exactly right, and so were you,
	to turn our minds back to the murdered man.
	It's time I joined your search for vengeance; 155
	our country and the god deserve no less.
	This won't be on behalf of distant kin—
	I'll banish this plague for my own sake.
	Laios' killer might one day come for me,
	exacting vengeance with that same hand. 160
	Defending the dead man serves *my* interest.
	Rise, children, quick, up from the altar,
	pick up those branches that appeal to god.
	Someone go call the people of Kadmos here—
	tell them I'm ready to do anything. 165
	With god's help our good luck
	is assured; without it we're doomed.

(*Exit* OEDIPUS, *into the palace.*)

PRIEST   Stand up, children. He has proclaimed
himself the cure we came to find.
May god Apollo, who sent the oracle,   170
be our savior and end this plague!

(*The Theban suppliants leave; the* CHORUS *enters.*)

CHORUS   What will you say to Thebes,
Voice from Zeus?[2] What sweet sounds
convey your will from golden Delphi
to our bright city?   175
We're at the breaking point,
our minds are wracked with dread.
Our wild cries reach out to you,
Healing God from Delos[3]—
in holy fear we ask: does your will   180
bring a new threat, or has an old doom
come round again as the years wheel by?
Say it, Great Voice,
you who answer us always,
speak as Hope's golden child.   185

  Athena, immortal daughter of Zeus,
your help is the first we ask;
then Artemis your sister
who guards our land, throned
in the heart of our city.   190
And Apollo, whose arrows
strike from far off![4] Our three
defenders against death: come now!
Once before, when ruin threatened,
you drove the flames of fever from our city.   195
Come to us now!
The troubles I suffer are endless.
The plague attacks our troops;
I can think of no weapon
that will keep a man safe.   200
Our rich earth shrivels what it grows;
women in labor scream, but no
children are born to ease their pain.
One life after another flies—
you see them pass—   205
like birds driving their strong wings
faster than flash-fire
to the death god's western shore.

2. Apollo was the son of Zeus, and spoke for
him.
3. Island of Apollo's birth.
4. Athena: warrior goddess, daughter of Zeus,
associated with wisdom and technology. Artemis:
sister of Apollo, a goddess associated with hunting, childbirth, and the moon, who protected the
weak. Apollo: god associated with sunlight,
poetry, prophecy, healing, and plague. His arrows
could cause disease.

Our city dies as its people die
these countless deaths, her children   210
rot in the streets, unmourned,
spreading more death.
Young wives and gray mothers
wash to our altars, their cries
carry from all sides, sobbing   215
for help, each lost in her pain.
A hymn rings out to the Healer;
an oboe answers,
keening in a courtyard.
Against all this, Goddess,   220
golden child of Zeus,[5]
send us the bright shining
face of courage.

Force that raging killer, the god Ares,[6]
to turn his back and run from our land.   225
He wields no weapons of war to kill us,
but burning with his fever,
we shout in the hot blast of his charge.
Blow Ares to the vast sea-room
of Amphitritê, banish him   230
under a booming wind
to jagged harbors in the roiling
seas off Thrace.[7] If night
doesn't finish the god's black work,
the day will finish it.   235
Lightning lurks
in your fiery will,
O Zeus, our Father. Blast it
into the god who kills us.
Apollo, lord of the morning light,   240
draw back your taut, gold-twined
bowstring, fire the sure arrows
that rake our attackers and keep them at bay.

Artemis, bring your radiance
into battle on bright quick feet   245
down through the morning hills.
I call on the god whose hair
is bound with gold,
the god who gave us our name,
Bakkhos!—the wine-flushed—who answers   250
the maenads' cries,[8] running

---

5. Athena. The Healer is Apollo.
6. God of war, not elsewhere associated with plague.
7. Thrace was a place in the northeast of

Greece, known for its savagery. Amphitrite is a sea goddess, consort of Poseidon.
8. Bakkhos is god of wine; the maenads (or bacchantes) are his female followers.

beside them! Bakkhos,
come here on fire,
pine-torch flaring.
Face with us the one god   255
all the gods hate: Ares!

(OEDIPUS *has entered while the* CHORUS *was singing.*)

OEDIPUS   I heard your prayer. It will be answered
if you trust and obey my words:
pull hard with me, bear down on the one cure
that will stop this plague. Help   260
will come, the evils will be gone.
I hereby outlaw the killer
myself, by my own words, though I'm a stranger
both to the crime and to accounts of it.

But unless I can mesh some clue I hold   265
with something known of the killer, I will
be tracking him alone, on a cold trail.
Since I've come late to your ranks, Thebans,
and the crime is past history,
there are some things that you,   270
the sons of Kadmos, must tell me.

If any one of you knows how Laios,
son of Labdakos, died, he must
tell me all that he knows.
He should not be afraid to name   275
himself the guilty one: I swear
he'll suffer nothing worse than exile.
Or if you know of someone else—
a foreigner—who struck the blow, speak up.
I will reward you now, I will thank you always.   280
But if you know the killer and don't speak—
out of fear—to shield kin or yourself,
listen to what that silence will cost you.
I order everyone in my land,
where I hold power and sit as king: 285

don't let that man under your roof,
don't speak with him, no matter who he is.
Don't pray or sacrifice with him,
don't pour purifying water for him.
I say this to all my people: 290
drive him from your houses.
He is our sickness. He poisons us.
This the Pythian god⁹ has shown me.

cries not for killer to be named

9. Apollo, whose priestess at Delphi was called the Pythia.

This knowledge makes me an ally—
of both the god and the dead king.   295
I pray god that the unseen killer,
whoever he is, and whether he killed
alone or had help, be cursed with a life
as evil as he is, a life
of utter human deprivation.   300
I pray this, too: if he's found at my hearth,
inside my house, and I know he's there,
may the curses I aimed at others punish me.
I charge you all—act on my words,
for my sake and the god's, for our dead land   305
stripped barren of its harvests,
abandoned by its gods.
Even if god had not forced the issue,
this crime should not have gone uncleansed.
You should have looked to it! The dead man   310
was not only noble, he was your king!
But as my luck would have it,
I have his power, his bed—a wife
who shares our seed. And had she borne
the children of us both, she might   315
have linked us closer still. But Laios
had no luck fathering children, and Fate
itself came down on his head.
These concerns make me fight for Laios
as I would for my own father.   320
I'll stop at nothing to trace his murder
back to the killer's hand.
I act in this for Labdakos and Polydoros,
for Kadmos and Agenor[1]—all our kings.
I warn those who would disobey me: 325
god make their fields harvest dust,
their women's bodies harvest death.
                                              O you gods,
let them die from the plague that kills
us now, or die from something worse.
As for the rest of us, who are   330
the loyal sons of Kadmos:
may justice go with us,
the gods be always at our side.

CHORUS   King, your curse forces me to speak.
None of us is the killer.   335
And none of us can point to him.
Apollo ordered us to search,
it's up to him to find the killer.

---

1. Kadmos, son of Agenor, was founder and first king of Thebes; Polydoros was his son, and
Labdakos, son of Polydoros, Laios's father, was his grandson.

OEDIPUS	So he must. But what man can force
	the gods to act against their will?
LEADER	May I suggest a second course of action?
OEDIPUS	Don't stop at two. Not if you have more.
LEADER	Tiresias[2] is the man whose power of seeing
	shows him most nearly what Apollo sees.
	If we put our questions to him, King,
	he could give us the clearest answers.
OEDIPUS	But I've seen to this already.
	At Kreon's urging I've sent for him—twice now.
	I find it strange that he still hasn't come.
LEADER	There were rumors—too faint and old to be much help.
OEDIPUS	What were they? I'll examine every word.
LEADER	They say Laios was killed by some travelers.
OEDIPUS	That's something even I have heard.
	But the man who did it—no one sees him.
LEADER	If fear has any hold on him
	he won't linger in Thebes, not after
	he hears threats of the kind you made.
OEDIPUS	If murder didn't scare him, my words won't.
LEADER	There's the man who will convict him:
	god's prophet, led here at last.
	God gave to him what he gave no one else:
	the truth—it's living in his mind.

(*Enter* TIRESIAS, *led by a* BOY.)

OEDIPUS	Tiresias, you are master of the hidden world.
	You can read earth and sky, you know
	what knowledge to reveal and what to hide.
	Though your eyes can't see it,
	your mind is well aware of the plague
	that afflicts us. Against it, we have no
	savior or defense but you, my Lord.
	If you haven't heard it from messengers,
	we now have Apollo's answer: to end
	this plague we must root out Laios' killers.
	Find them, then kill or banish them.
	Help us do this. Don't begrudge us
	what you divine from bird cries, show us
	everything prophecy has shown you.
	Save Thebes! Save yourself! Save me!
	Wipe out what defiles us, keep
	the poison of our king's murder
	from poisoning the rest of us.
	We're in your hands. The best use a man
	makes of his powers is to help others.
TIRESIAS	The most terrible knowledge is the kind
	it pays no wise man to possess.

2. Prophet of Thebes.

	I knew this, but I forgot it.	385
	I should never have come here.	
OEDIPUS	What? You've come, but with no stomach for this?	
TIRESIAS	Let me go home. Your life will then	
	be easier to bear—and so will mine.	
OEDIPUS	It's neither lawful nor humane	390
	to hold back god's crucial guidance	
	from the city that raised you.	
TIRESIAS	What you've said has made matters worse.	
	I won't let that happen to me.	
OEDIPUS	For god's sake, if you know something,	395
	don't turn your back on us! We're on our knees.	
TIRESIAS	You don't understand! If I spoke	
	of my grief, then it would be yours.	
OEDIPUS	What did you say? You know and won't help?	
	You would betray us all and destroy Thebes?	400
TIRESIAS	I'll cause no grief to you or me. Why ask	
	futile questions? You'll learn nothing.	
OEDIPUS	So the traitor won't answer.	
	You would enrage a rock.	

OEDIPUS   Still won't speak?
Are you so thick-skinned nothing touches you?   405

TIRESIAS	You blame your rage on *me*? When you	
	don't see how she embraces you,	
	this fury you live with?[3] No, you blame me.	
OEDIPUS	Who wouldn't be enraged? Your refusal	
	to speak dishonors the city.	410
TIRESIAS	It will happen. My silence can't stop it.	
OEDIPUS	If it must happen, you should tell me now.	
TIRESIAS	I'd rather not. Rage at that, if you like,	
	with all the savage fury in your heart.	
OEDIPUS	That's right. I *am* angry enough to speak	415
	my mind. I think you helped plot the murder.	
	Did everything but kill him with your own hands	
	Had you eyes, though, I would have said	
	you alone were the killer.	
TIRESIAS	That's your truth? Now hear mine:	420
	honor the curse your own mouth spoke.	
	From this day on, don't speak to me	
	or to your people here. You are the plague.	
	You poison your own land.	
OEDIPUS	So. The appalling charge has been at last	425
	flushed out, into the open. What makes you	
	think you'll escape?	

TIRESIAS   I have escaped.
I foster truth, and truth guards me.

---

3. "Rage" or "fury" is a feminine noun (*orge*) in the original, reinforcing the veiled reference to the female inhabitant of the palace, Jokasta.

OEDIPUS	Who taught you this truth? Not your prophet's trade.	
TIRESIAS	You did. By forcing me to speak.	430
OEDIPUS	Speak what? Repeat it so I understand.	
TIRESIAS	You missed what I said the first time? Are you provoking me to make it worse?	
OEDIPUS	I heard you. But you made no sense. Try again.	
TIRESIAS	You killed the man whose killer you now hunt.	435
OEDIPUS	The second time is even more outrageous. You'll wish you'd never said a word.	
TIRESIAS	Shall I feed your fury with more words?	
OEDIPUS	Use any words you like. They'll be wasted.	
TIRESIAS	I say: you have been living unaware in the most hideous intimacy with your nearest and most loving kin, immersed in evil that you cannot see.	440
OEDIPUS	You think you can blithely go on like this?	
TIRESIAS	I can, if truth has any strength.	445
OEDIPUS	Oh, truth has strength, but you have none. You have blind eyes, blind ears, and a blind brain.	
TIRESIAS	And you're a desperate fool—throwing taunts at me that these men, very soon, will throw at you.	
OEDIPUS	You survive in the grip of black unbroken night! You can't harm me or any man who can see the sunlight.	450
TIRESIAS	I'm not the one who will bring you down. Apollo will do that. You're his concern.	
OEDIPUS	Did you make up these lies? Or was it Kreon?	455
TIRESIAS	Kreon isn't your enemy. You are.	
OEDIPUS	Wealth and a king's power, the skill that wins every time— how much envy, what malice they provoke! To rob me of power—power I didn't ask for, but which this city thrust into my hands— my oldest friend here, loyal Kreon, worked quietly against me, aching to steal my throne. He hired for the purpose this fortuneteller— conniving bogus beggar-priest!—a man who knows what he wants but cannot seize it, being but a blind groper in his art. Tell us now, when or where did you ever prove you had the power of a seer? Why—when the Sphinx who barked black songs was hounding us—why didn't you speak up and free the city? Her riddle wasn't the sort just anyone who happened by could solve: prophetic skill was needed. But the kind you learned from birds or gods failed you. It took Oedipus, the know-nothing, to silence her. I needed no help from the birds;	460 465 470 475

I used my wits to find the answer.
I solved it—the same man for whom you plot
disgrace and exile, so you can   480
maneuver close to Kreon's throne.
But your scheme to rid Thebes of its plague
will destroy both you and the man who planned it.
Were you not so frail, I'd make you
suffer exactly what you planned for me.   485

LEADER   He spoke in anger, Oedipus—but so
did you, if you'll hear what we think.
We don't need angry words. We need insight—
how best to carry out the god's commands.

TIRESIAS   You may be king, but my right   490
to answer makes me your equal.
In this respect, I am as much
my own master as you are.
You do not own my life.
Apollo does. Nor am I   495
Kreon's man. Hear me out.
Since you have thrown my blindness at me
I will tell you what your eyes don't see:
what evil you are steeped in.
                    You don't see
where you live or who shares your house.   500
Do you know your parents?
                    You are their enemy
in this life and down there with the dead.
And soon their double curse—
your father's and your mother's—
will lash you out of Thebes   505
on terror-stricken feet.
Your eyes, which now see life,
will then see darkness.
Soon your shriek will burrow
in every cave, bellow   510
from every mountain outcrop on Kithairon,⁴
when what your marriage means strikes home,
when it shows you the house
that took you in. You sailed
a fair wind to a most foul harbor.   515
Evils you cannot guess
will bring you down to what you are.
To what your children are.
Go on, throw muck at Kreon,
and at the warning spoken through my mouth.   520
No man will ever be
ground into wretchedness as you will be.

---

4. Mountain range near Thebes, on which Oedipus was left to die as an infant.

OEDIPUS	Should I wait for him to attack me more?
	May you be damned. Go. Leave my house
	now! Turn your back and go. 525
TIRESIAS	I'm here only because you sent for me.
OEDIPUS	Had I known you would talk nonsense,
	I wouldn't have hurried to bring you here.
TIRESIAS	I seem a fool to you, but the parents
	who gave you birth thought I was wise. 530
OEDIPUS	What parents? Hold on. Who was my father?
TIRESIAS	Today you will be born. Into ruin.
OEDIPUS	You've always got a murky riddle in your mouth.
TIRESIAS	Don't you outsmart us all at solving riddles?
OEDIPUS	Go ahead, mock what made me great. 535
TIRESIAS	Your very luck is what destroyed you.
OEDIPUS	If I could save the city, I wouldn't care.
TIRESIAS	Then I'll leave you to that. Boy, guide me out.

OEDIPUS   Yes, let him lead you home. Here, underfoot,
          you're in the way. But when you're gone,   540
          you'll give us no more grief.

TIRESIAS I'll go. But first I must finish
          what you brought me to do—
          your scowl can't frighten me.
          The man you have been looking for,   545
          the one your curses threaten, the man
          you have condemned for Laios' death:
          I say that man is here.
                              You think he's an immigrant,
          but he will prove himself a Theban native,
          though he'll find no joy in that news.   550
          A blind man who still has eyes,
          a beggar who's now rich, he'll jab
          his stick, feeling the road to foreign lands.

          (OEDIPUS *enters the palace*.)[5]

          He'll soon be shown father and brother
          to his own children, son and husband   555
          to the mother who bore him—she took
          his father's seed and his seed,
          and he took his own father's life.
          You go inside. Think through
          everything I have said.   560
          If I have lied, say of me, then—
          I have failed as a prophet.

          (*Exit* TIRESIAS.)

---

5. Like all the stage directions, this one is added by the translator. If Oedipus is still within earshot, it is hard to understand how he could fail to make sense of Tiresias's words.

CHORUS   What man provokes
          the speaking rock of Delphi?
          This crime that sickens speech   565
          is the work of *his* bloody hands.
          Now his feet will need to outrace
          a storm of wild horses, for
          Apollo is running him down,
          armed with bolts of fire.   570
          He and the Fates close in,
          dread gods who never miss.

          From snowfields
          high on Parnassos
          the word blazes out to us all: 575
          track down the man no one can see.
          He takes cover in thick brush,
          he charges up the mountain
          bull-like to its rocks and caves,
          going his bleak, hunted way,   580
          struggling to escape the doom
          Earth spoke from her sacred mouth.[6]
          But that doom buzzes low,
          never far from his ear.

          Fear is what the man who reads birds[7]   585
          makes us feel, fear we can't fight.
          We can't accept what he says
          but have no power to challenge him.
          We thrash in doubt, we can't see
          even the present clearly,   590
          much less the future.
          And we've heard of no feud
          embittering the House
          of Oedipus in Korinth[8]
          against the House of Laios here,   595
          no past trouble and none now,
          no proof that would make us blacken
          our king's fame, as he seeks
          to avenge our royal house
          for this murder not yet solved.   600

          Zeus and Apollo make no mistakes
          when they predict what people do.

6. Delphi was supposed to be the center of Earth.
7. Ancient priests and seers tried to interpret
the will of the gods by observing the flight
patterns of birds.

8. The chorus still assumes that Oedipus comes
from the house of Korinth (more usually spelled
Corinth), the son of Polybos and Merope.

But there is no way to tell
whether an earthbound prophet sees
more of the future than we can—   605
though in knowledge and skill
one person may surpass another.
But never, not till I see the charges
proved against him,
will I give credence   610
to a man who blames Oedipus.
All of us saw his brilliance
prevail when the wingèd virgin
Sphinx came at him: he passed the test
that won the people's love.   615
My heart can't find him guilty.

(KREON *enters.*)

KREON   Citizens, I hear that King Oedipus
has made a fearful charge against me.
I'm here to prove it false.
If he thinks anything I've said or done   620
has made this crisis worse, or injured him,
then I have no more wish to live.
This is no minor charge.
It's the most deadly I could suffer,
if my city, my own people—you!—   625
believe I'm a traitor.

LEADER   He could have spoken in a flash
of ill-considered anger.

KREON   Did he say *I* persuaded the prophet to lie?

LEADER   That's what he said. What he meant wasn't clear.   630

KREON   When he announced my guilt—tell me,
how did his eyes look? Did he seem sane?

LEADER   I can't say. I don't question what my rulers do.
Here he comes, now, out of the palace.

(OEDIPUS *enters.*)

OEDIPUS   So? You come here? You have the nerve   635
to face me in my own house? When you're exposed
as its master's murderer?
Caught trying to steal my kingship?
In god's name, what weakness did you see
in me that led you to plot this?   640
Am I a coward or a fool?
Did you suppose I wouldn't notice
your subtle moves? Or not fight back?
Aren't you attempting something
downright stupid—to win absolute power   645
without partisans or even friends?
For that you'll need money—and a mob.

KREON	Now you listen to me.
	You've had your say, now hear mine.
	Don't judge until you've heard me out. 650
OEDIPUS	You speak shrewdly, but I'm a poor learner
	from someone I know is my enemy.
KREON	I'll prove you are mistaken to think that.
OEDIPUS	How can you prove you're not a traitor?
KREON	If you think mindless presumption 655
	is a virtue, then you're not thinking straight.
OEDIPUS	If you think attacking a kinsman
	will bring you no harm, you must be mad.
KREON	I'll grant that. Now, how have I attacked you?
OEDIPUS	Did you, or did you not, urge me 660
	to send for that venerated prophet?
KREON	And I would still give you the same advice.
OEDIPUS	How long ago did King Laios . . .
KREON	Laios? Did what? Why speak of him?
OEDIPUS	. . . die in that murderous attack? 665
KREON	That was far back in the past.
OEDIPUS	Did this seer practice his craft here, then?
KREON	With the same skill and respect he has now.
OEDIPUS	Back then, did he ever mention my name?
KREON	Not in my hearing. 670
OEDIPUS	Didn't you try to hunt down the killer?
KREON	Of course we did. We found out nothing.
OEDIPUS	Why didn't your expert seer accuse me then?
KREON	I don't know. So I'd rather not say.
OEDIPUS	There is one thing you can explain. 675
KREON	What's that? I'm holding nothing back.
OEDIPUS	Just this. If that seer hadn't conspired with you,
	he would never have called me Laios' killer.
KREON	If he said that, *you heard him*, I didn't.
	I think you owe me some answers. 680
OEDIPUS	Question me. I have no blood on my hands.
KREON	Did you marry my sister?
OEDIPUS	Do you expect me to deny that?
KREON	You both have equal power in this country?
OEDIPUS	I give her all she asks. 685
KREON	Do I share power with you both as an equal?
OEDIPUS	You shared our power and betrayed us with it.
KREON	You're wrong. Think it through rationally, as I have.
	Who would prefer the anxiety-filled
	life of a king to one that lets him sleep at night— 690
	if his share of power still equaled a king's?
	Nothing in my nature hungers for power—
	for me it's enough to enjoy a king's rights,
	enough for any prudent man. All I want,
	you give me—and it comes with no fear. 695

To be king would rob my life of its ease.
How could my share of power be more pleasant
than this painless pre-eminence, this ready
influence I have? I'm not so misguided
that I would crave honors that are burdens.   700
But as things stand, I'm greeted and wished well
on all sides. Those who want something from you
come to me, their best hope of gaining it.
Should I quit this good life for a worse one?
Treason never corrupts a healthy mind.   705
I have no love for such exploits.
Nor would I join someone who did.
Test me. Go to Delphi yourself.
Find out whether I brought back
the oracle's exact words. If you find   710
I plotted with that omen-reader, seize me
and kill me—not on your authority
alone, but on mine, for I'd vote my own death.
But don't convict me because of a wild thought
you can't prove, one that only you believe.   715
There's no justice in your reckless confusion
of bad men with good men, traitors with friends.
To cast off a true friend is like suicide—
killing what you love as much as your life.
Time will instruct you in these truths, for time   720
alone is the sure test of a just man—
but you can know a bad man in a day.

LEADER That's good advice, my lord—
for someone anxious not to fall.
Quick thinkers can stumble.   725

OEDIPUS When a conspirator moves
abruptly and in secret against me,
I must out-plot him and strike first.
If I pause and do nothing, he
will take charge, and I will have lost.   730

KREON What do you want? My banishment?

OEDIPUS No. It's your death I want.

KREON Then start by defining "betrayal" . . .

OEDIPUS You talk as though you don't believe me.

KREON How can I if you won't use reason?   735

OEDIPUS I reason in my own interest.

KREON You should reason in mine as well.

OEDIPUS In a traitor's interest?

KREON What if you're wrong?

OEDIPUS I still must rule.   740

KREON Not when you rule badly.

OEDIPUS Did you hear him, Thebes!

KREON Thebes isn't yours alone. It's mine as well!

LEADER   My Lords, stop this. Here's Jokasta
         leaving the palace—just in time   745
         to calm you both. With her help, end your feud.

         (*Enter* JOKASTA *from the palace.*)

JOKASTA Wretched men! Why are you out here
         so reckless, yelling at each other?
         Aren't you ashamed? With Thebes sick and dying
         you two fight out some personal grievance?   750
         Oedipus. Go inside. Kreon, go home.
         Don't make us all miserable over nothing.

KREON   Sister, it's worse than that. Oedipus
         your husband threatens either to drive me
         from my own country, or to have me killed.   755

OEDIPUS That's right. I caught him plotting to kill me,
         Lady. False prophecy was his weapon.

KREON   I ask the gods to sicken and destroy me
         if I did anything you charge me with.

JOKASTA Believe what he says, Oedipus.   760
         Accept the oath he just made to the gods.
         Do it for my sake too, and for these men.

LEADER   Give in to him, Lord, we beg you.
         With all your mind and will.

OEDIPUS What do you want me to do?   765

LEADER   Believe him. This man was never a fool.
         Now he backs himself up with a great oath.

OEDIPUS You realize what you're asking?

LEADER   I do.

OEDIPUS Then say it to me outright.   770

LEADER   Groundless rumor shouldn't be used by you
         to scorn a friend who swears his innocence.

OEDIPUS You know, when you ask this of me
         you ask for my exile—or my death.

LEADER   No! We ask neither. By the god   775
         outshining all others, the Sun—
         may I die the worst death possible, die
         godless and friendless, if I want those things.
         This dying land grinds pain into my soul—
         grinds it the more if the bitterness   780
         you two stir up adds to our misery.

OEDIPUS Then let him go, though it means my death
         or my exile from here in disgrace.
         What moves my pity are your words, not his.
         He will be hated wherever he goes.   785

KREON   You are as bitter when you yield
         as you are savage in your rage.
         But natures like your own
         punish themselves the most—
         which is the way it should be.   790

OEDIPUS   Leave me alone. Go.
KREON   I'll go. You can see nothing clearly.
          But these men see that I'm right.

          (KREON *goes off.*)

LEADER   Lady, why the delay? Take him inside.
JOKASTA   I will, when you tell me what happened.   795
LEADER   They had words. One drew a false
          conclusion; the other took offense.
JOKASTA   Both sides were at fault?
LEADER   Both sides.
JOKASTA   What did they say?   800
LEADER   Don't ask that. Our land needs no more trouble.
          No more trouble! Let it go.
OEDIPUS   I know you mean well when you try to calm me,
          but do you realize where it will lead?
LEADER   King, I have said this more than once.   805
          I would be mad, I would lose my good sense,
          if I lost faith in you—you
          who put our dear country
          back on course when you found her
          wandering, crazed with suffering.   810
          Steer us straight, once again,
          with all your inspired luck.
JOKASTA   In god's name, King, tell me, too.
          What makes your rage so relentless?
OEDIPUS   I'll tell you, for it's you I respect, not the men.   815
          Kreon brought on my rage by plotting against me.
JOKASTA   Go on. Explain what provoked the quarrel.
OEDIPUS   He says I murdered Laios.
JOKASTA   Does he know this himself? Or did someone tell him?
OEDIPUS   Neither. He sent that crooked seer to make the charge   820
          so he could keep his own mouth innocent.
JOKASTA   Then you can clear yourself of all his charges.
          Listen to me, for I can make you believe
          no man, ever, has mastered prophecy.
          This one incident will prove it.   825
          A long time back, an oracle reached Laios—
          I don't say Apollo himself sent it,
          but the priests who interpret him did.
          It said that Laios was destined to die
          at the hands of a son born to him and me.   830
          Yet, as rumor had it, foreign bandits
          killed Laios at a place where three roads meet.

          (OEDIPUS *reacts with sudden intensity to her words.*)

          But the child was barely three days old
          when Laios pinned its ankle joints together,
          then had it left, by someone else's hands,   835

high up a mountain far from any roads.
That time Apollo failed to make Laios die
the way he feared—at the hands of his own son.
Doesn't that tell you how much sense
prophetic voices make of our lives?   840
You can forget them. When god wants
something to happen, he makes it happen.
And has no trouble showing what he's done.

OEDIPUS   Just now, something you said made my heart race.
          Something . . . I remember . . . wakes up terrified.   845

JOKASTA   What fear made you turn toward me and say that?

OEDIPUS   I thought you said, Laios was struck down
          where three roads meet.

JOKASTA   That's the story they told. It hasn't changed.

OEDIPUS   Tell me, where did it happen?   850

JOKASTA   In a place called Phokis, at the junction
          where roads come in from Delphi and from Daulis.

OEDIPUS   How long ago was it? When it happened?

JOKASTA   We heard the news just before you came to power.

OEDIPUS   O Zeus! What did you will me to do?   855

JOKASTA   Oedipus, you look heartsick. What is it?

OEDIPUS   Don't ask me yet. Describe Laios to me.
          Was he a young man, almost in his prime?

JOKASTA   He was tall, with some gray salting his hair.
          He looked then not very different from you now.   860

OEDIPUS   Like me? I'm finished! It was aimed at me,
          that savage curse I hurled in ignorance.

JOKASTA   What did you say, my Lord? Your face scares me.

OEDIPUS   I'm desperately afraid the prophet sees.
          Tell me one more thing. Then I'll be sure.   865

JOKASTA   I'm so frightened I can hardly answer.

OEDIPUS   Did Laios go with just a few armed men,
          or the large troop one expects of a prince?

JOKASTA   There were five only, one was a herald.
          And there was a wagon, to carry Laios.   870

OEDIPUS   Ah! I see it now. Who told you this, Lady?

JOKASTA   Our slave. The one man who survived and came home.

OEDIPUS   Is he by chance on call here, in our house?

JOKASTA   No. When he returned and saw
          that you had all dead Laios' power,   875
          he touched my hand and begged me to send him
          out to our farmlands and sheepfolds,
          so he'd be far away and out of sight.
          I sent him. He was deserving—though a slave—
          of a much larger favor than he asked.   880

OEDIPUS   Can you send for him right away?

JOKASTA   Of course. But why do you need him?

OEDIPUS   I'm afraid, Lady, I've said too much.
          That's why I want to see him now.

JOKASTA	I'll have him come. But don't I have the right	885
	to know what so deeply disturbs you, Lord?	
OEDIPUS	So much of what I dreaded has come true.	
	I'll tell you everything I fear.	
	No one has more right than you do,	
	to know the risks to which I'm now exposed.	890
	Polybos of Korinth was my father.	
	My mother was Merope, a Dorian.	
	I was the leading citizen, when Chance	
	struck me a sudden blow.	
	Alarming as it was, I took it	895
	much too hard. At a banquet,	
	a man who had drunk too much wine	
	claimed I was not my father's son.	
	Seething, I said nothing. All that day	
	I barely held it in. But next morning	900
	I questioned mother and father. Furious,	
	they took their anger out on the man	
	who shot the insult. They reassured me.	
	But the rumor still rankled, it hounded me.	
	So with no word to my parents,	905
	I traveled to the Pythian oracle.	
	But the god would not honor me	
	with the knowledge I craved.	

Instead,
his words flashed other things—
horrible, wretched things—at me: 910
I would be my mother's lover,
I would show the world children
no one could bear to look at, I
would murder the father whose seed I am.
When I heard that, and ever after,   915
I traced the road back to Korinth
only by looking at the stars. I fled
to somewhere I'd never see outrages
like those the god promised, happen to me.
But my flight carried me to just the place   920
where, you tell me, the king was killed.
Oh, woman, here is the truth. As I approached
the place where three roads joined,
a herald, a colt-drawn wagon, and a man
like the one you describe, met me head on.   925
The man out front and the old man himself
began to crowd me off the road.
The driver, who's forcing me aside,
I smash in anger.

The old man watches me,
he measures my approach, then leans out   930
lunging with his two-spiked goad

dead at my skull. He's more than repaid:
I hit him so fast with the staff
this hand holds, he's knocked back
rolling off the cart. Where he lies, face up.   935
Then I kill them all.

But if this stranger and Laios . . . were the same blood,
whose triumph could be worse than mine?
Is there a man alive the gods hate more?
Nobody, no Theban, no foreigner,   940
can take me to his home.
No one can speak with me.
They all must drive me out.
I am the man—no one else—
who laid this curse on myself.   945
I make love to his wife with hands
repulsive from her husband's blood.
Can't you see that I'm evil,
my whole nature, utter filth?
Look, I must be banished. I must   950
never set eyes on my people, never
set foot in my homeland, because . . .
I'll marry my own mother, &
kill Polybos my father,
who brought me up and gave me birth.   955
If someone said things like these
must be the work of a savage god,
he'd be speaking the truth. O you
pure and majestic gods! Never,
never, let the day such things happen   960
arrive for me. Let me never see it.
Let me vanish from men's eyes
before that doom comes down on me.

LEADER   What you say terrifies us, Lord. But don't lose hope
          until you hear from the eyewitness.   965
OEDIPUS   That is the one hope I have left—to wait
          for this man to come in from the fields.
JOKASTA   When he comes, what do you hope to hear?
OEDIPUS   This: if his story matches yours,
          I will have escaped disaster.   970
JOKASTA   What did I say that would make such a difference?
OEDIPUS   He told you Laios was killed by bandits.
          If he still claims there were several,
          then I cannot be the killer. One man
          cannot be many. But if he says: one man,   975
          braving the road alone, did it,
          there's no more doubt.
          The evidence will drag me down.

JOKASTA   You can be sure that was the way
           he first told it. How can he take it back?   980
           The entire city heard him, not just me.
           Even if now he changes his story,
           Lord, he could never prove that Laios'
           murder happened as the god predicted.
                                                Apollo
           said plainly: my son would kill Laios.   985
           That poor doomed child had no chance
           to kill his father, for he was killed first.
           After that, no oracle ever
           made me look right, then left, in fear.
OEDIPUS   You've thought this out well. Still, you must   990
           send for that herdsman. Don't neglect this.
JOKASTA   I'll send for him now. But come inside.
           Would I do anything to displease you?

           (OEDIPUS and JOKASTA enter the palace.)

CHORUS   Let it be my good luck
           to win praise all my life
           for respecting the sky-walking laws   995
           born to stride
           through the light-filled heavens.
           Olympos
           alone was their father,   1000
           no human mind could conceive them;
           those laws
           neither sleep nor forget—
           a mighty god lives on in them
           who does not age.   1005
           A violent will[9]
           fathers the tyrant,
           and violence, drunk
           on wealth and power,
           does him no good;   1010
           he scales the heights—
           until he's thrown
           down to his doom,
           where quick feet are no use.
           But there's another fighting spirit   1015
           I ask god never to destroy—
           the kind that makes our city thrive.
           That god will protect us
           I will never cease to believe.

           But if a man   1020
           speaks and acts with contempt—

---

9. The Greek word here for "will" is *hubris*, which usually connotes "violence."

flouts the law, sneers
at the stone gods in their shrines—
let a harsh death punish
his doomed indulgence.   1025
Even as he wins he cheats,
he denies himself nothing,
his hand reaches for things
too sacred to be touched.
When crimes like these, which god hates,   1030
are not punished—but *honored*—
what good man will think his own life
safe from god's arrows piercing his soul?
Why should I dance[1] to *this* holy song?

If prophecies don't show the way   1035
to events all men can see,
I will no longer honor
the holy place untouchable:
Earth's navel at Delphi.[2]
I will not go to Olympia   1040
nor the temple at Abai.[3]
You, Zeus who hold power, if Zeus
lord of all is really who you are,
look at what's happening here:
prophecies made to Laios fade,   1045
men ignore them;
Apollo is nowhere
glorified with praise;
the gods lose force.

(JOKASTA *enters from the palace carrying a suppliant's branch and
some smoldering incense. She approaches the altar of Apollo near
the palace door.*)

JOKASTA   Lords of my country, this thought   1050
             came to me: to visit the gods' shrines
             with incense and a bough in my hands.
             Oedipus lets alarms of every kind
             inflame his mind. He won't let past
             experience calm his present fears,   1055
             as a man of sense would.
             He's at the mercy of everybody's
             terrifying words. Since he won't listen to me,
             Apollo—you're the nearest god—

(*Enter* MESSENGER *from the countryside.*)

---

1. The Greek verb here, *choreuein*, connotes
"dance in a chorus," linking the mythical drama
to the real theatrical performance.
2. Delphi had a sacred stone, supposed to be
the belly button of the earth.
3. Olympia was the site of a sanctuary of
Zeus; Abai is a city in central Greece.

	I come praying for your good will. Look,	1060
	here is my branch. Cleanse us, cure our sickness.	
	When we see Oedipus distraught, we all shake,	
	as though sailing with a fearful helmsman.	
MESSENGER	Can you point out to me, strangers,	
	the house where King Oedipus lives? Better	1065
	yet, tell me if you know where he is now.	
LEADER	That's the house where he lives, stranger. He's inside.	
	This woman is his wife and mother . . . of his children.	
MESSENGER	I wish her joy, and the family joy	
	that comes when a marriage bears fruit.	1070
JOKASTA	And joy to you, stranger, for those kind words.	
	What have you to tell us? Or to ask?	
MESSENGER	Great news, Lady, for you and your mate.	
JOKASTA	What news? Who sent you to us?	
MESSENGER	I come from Korinth.	1075
	You'll rejoice at my news, I'm sure—	
	but it may also make you grieve.	
JOKASTA	What? How can it possibly do both?	
MESSENGER	They're going to make him king. So say	
	the people who live on the isthmus.[4]	1080
JOKASTA	Isn't old Polybos still in power?	
MESSENGER	No longer. Death has laid him in the tomb.	
JOKASTA	You're saying, old man, Polybos has died?	
MESSENGER	Kill me if that's not the truth.	

(JOKASTA speaks to a servant girl, who then runs inside.)

JOKASTA	Girl, run to your master with the news.	1085
	You oracles of the gods! Where are you now?	
	The man Oedipus feared he would kill,	
	the man he ran from, that man's dead.	
	Chance killed him. Not Oedipus. Chance!	

(OEDIPUS enters quickly from the palace.)

OEDIPUS	Darling Jokasta, my loving wife,	1090
	why did you ask me to come out?	
JOKASTA	Listen to what this man has to say.	
	See what it does to god's proud oracle.	
OEDIPUS	Where's he from? What's his news?	
JOKASTA	From Korinth. Your father isn't . . .	1095
	Polybos . . . is no more . . . he's dead.	
OEDIPUS	Say it, old man. I want to hear it from your mouth.	
MESSENGER	If plain fact is what you want first,	
	have no doubt he is dead and gone.	
OEDIPUS	Was it treason, or did disease bring him down?	1100
MESSENGER	A slight push tips an old man into stillness.	
OEDIPUS	Then some sickness killed him?	
MESSENGER	That, and the long years he had lived.	

4. Korinth was built on an isthmus.

OEDIPUS	Oh, yes, wife! Why should we scour Pythian smoke
	or fear birds shrieking overhead? 1105
	If signs like these had been telling the truth
	I would have killed my father. But he's dead.
	He's safely in the ground. And here I am,
	who didn't lift a spear. Or did he
	die of longing for me? That might 1110
	have been what my killing him meant.
	This time, Polybos' death has dragged
	those worthless oracles with him to Hades.
JOKASTA	Didn't I tell you that before?
OEDIPUS	You did. But I was still driven by fear. 1115
JOKASTA	Don't let these things worry you anymore.
OEDIPUS	Not worry that I'll share my mother's bed?
JOKASTA	Why should a human being live in fear?
	Chance rules our lives!
	Who has any sure knowledge of the future? 1120
	It's best to take life as it comes.
	This marriage with your mother—don't fear it.
	In their very dreams, too, many men
	have slept with their mothers.
	Those who believe such things mean nothing 1125
	will have an easier time in life.
OEDIPUS	A brave speech! I would like to believe it.
	But how can I if my mother's still living?
	While she lives, I will live in fear,
	no matter how persuasive you are. 1130
JOKASTA	Your father's tomb shines a great light.
OEDIPUS	On him, yes! But I fear her. She's alive.
MESSENGER	What woman do you fear?
OEDIPUS	I dread that oracle from the god, stranger.
MESSENGER	Would it be wrong for someone else to know it? 1135
OEDIPUS	No, you may hear it. Apollo told me
	I would become my mother's lover, that I
	would have my father's blood on these hands.
	Because of that, I haven't gone near Korinth.
	So far, I've been very lucky—and yet, 1140
	there's no greater pleasure
	than to look our parents in the eyes!
MESSENGER	Did this oracle drive you into exile?
OEDIPUS	I didn't want to kill my father, old man.
MESSENGER	Then why haven't I put your fears to rest, 1145
	King? I came here hoping to be useful.
OEDIPUS	I would give anything to be free of fear.
MESSENGER	I confess I came partly for that reason—
	to be rewarded when you've come back home.
OEDIPUS	I will never live where my parents live. 1150
MESSENGER	My son, you can't possibly know what you're doing.
OEDIPUS	Why is that, old man? In god's name, tell me.

MESSENGER	Is it because of them you won't go home?
OEDIPUS	I am afraid Apollo spoke the truth.
MESSENGER	Afraid you'd do your parents unforgivable harm? 1155
OEDIPUS	Exactly that, old man. I am in constant fear.
MESSENGER	Your fear is groundless. Do you understand?
OEDIPUS	How can it be groundless if I'm their son?
MESSENGER	But Polybos was no relation to you.
OEDIPUS	What? Polybos was not my father? 1160
MESSENGER	No more than I am. Exactly the same.
OEDIPUS	How the same? He fathered me and you didn't.
MESSENGER	He didn't father you any more than I did.
OEDIPUS	Why did he say, then, that I was his son?
MESSENGER	He took you from my hands as a gift. 1165
OEDIPUS	He loved me so much—knowing I came from you?
MESSENGER	He had no children. That moved him to love you.
OEDIPUS	And you? Did you buy me? Or find me somewhere?
MESSENGER	I found you in the wooded hollows of Kithairon.
OEDIPUS	Why were you wandering way out there? 1170
MESSENGER	I had charge of the sheep grazing those slopes.
OEDIPUS	A migrant hired to work our flocks?
MESSENGER	I saved your life that day, my son.
OEDIPUS	When you picked me up, what was wrong with me?
MESSENGER	Your ankles know. Let them tell you. 1175
OEDIPUS	Ahh! Why do you bring up that ancient wound?
MESSENGER	Your ankles had been pinned. I set you free.
OEDIPUS	From birth I've carried the shame of those scars.
MESSENGER	That was the luck that named you, Oedipus.[5]
OEDIPUS	Did my mother or my father do this to me? 1180
	Speak the truth for god's sake.
MESSENGER	I don't know. The man who gave you to me
	will know.
OEDIPUS	You took me from someone?
	You didn't chance on me yourself?
MESSENGER	I took you from another shepherd. 1185
OEDIPUS	Who was he? Tell me as plainly as you can.
MESSENGER	He was known as someone who worked for Laios.
OEDIPUS	The same Laios who was once king *here*?
MESSENGER	The same. This man worked as his shepherd.
OEDIPUS	Is he alive? Can I see him? 1190
MESSENGER	Someone from here could answer that better.
OEDIPUS	Does anyone here know what has become
	of this shepherd? Has anyone seen him
	in town or in the fields? Speak up now.
	The time has come to make everything known. 1195
LEADER	I believe he means that same herdsman
	you've already sent for. Your wife
	would be the best one to ask.

5. In Greek the name *Oedipus* suggests "Swollen Foot."

OEDIPUS   Lady, do you
              recall the man we sent for?
              Is that the man he means?   1200
JOKASTA   Why ask about him? Don't listen to him.
              Ignore his words. Forget he said them.
OEDIPUS   With clues like these in my hands, how can I
              fail to solve the mystery of my birth?
JOKASTA   For god's sake, if you care about your life,   1205
              give up your search. Let my pain be enough!
OEDIPUS   You'll be fine! What if my mother was born
              from slaves—from three generations of slaves—
              how could that make you lowborn?
JOKASTA   Listen to me: I beg you. Don't do this.   1210
OEDIPUS   I cannot listen. I must have the truth.
JOKASTA   I'm thinking only of what's best for you.
OEDIPUS   *What's best for me* exasperates me now.
JOKASTA   You poor child! Never find out who you are.
OEDIPUS   Someone, bring me the herdsman. Let   1215
              that woman glory in her precious birth.
JOKASTA   Oh you poor doomed child! That is the only name
              I can call you now. None other, forever!

              (JOKASTA *runs into the palace.*)

LEADER   Why has she left like that, Oedipus,
              driven off by a savage grief? I'm afraid   1220
              something horrendous will break this silence.
OEDIPUS   Let it burst! My seed may well *be* common!
              Even so, I still must know who I am.
              The meanness of my birth may shame
              her womanly pride. But since, in my   1225
              own eyes, I am the child of Luck—
              she is the source of my well-being—
              never will I be dishonored.
              Luck is the mother who raised me; the months
              are my brothers, who've seen me through   1230
              the low times in my life and the high ones.
              Those are the powers that made me.
              I could never betray them *now*—
              by calling off the search
              for the secret of my birth!   1235
CHORUS   By the gods of Olympos, if I have
              a prophet's range of eye and mind—
              tomorrow's moonlight
              will shine on you, Kithairon.
              Oedipus will honor you—   1240
              his native mountain,
              his nurse, his mother. Nothing
              will keep us from dancing
              then, mountain joyful to our king!

We call out to Phoibos Apollo: 1245
be the cause of our joy!

(CHORUS *turns toward* OEDIPUS.)

My son, who was your mother?
Which nymph bore you to Pan,[6]
the mountain rover?
Was it Apollo's bride   1250
to whom you were born
in the grassy highlands?
Or did Hermes, Lord of Kyllene,
or Bakkhos of the mountain peaks,
take you—a sudden joy—   1255
from nymphs of Helikon,
whose games he often shares?[7]

OEDIPUS   Old men, if it's possible
to recognize a man I've never met,
I think I see the herdsman we've been waiting for.   1260
Our fellow would be old, like the stranger approaching.
Those leading him are my own men.
But I expect you'll know him better.
Some of you will know him by sight.

(*Enter* HERDSMAN, *led by Oedipus' servants.*)

LEADER   I do know him. He is from Laios' house,   1265
a trustworthy shepherd if he ever had one.

OEDIPUS   Korinthian, I'll ask you to speak first:
is this the man you mean?

MESSENGER   You're looking at him.

OEDIPUS   Now you, old man. Look at me.   1270
Answer every question I ask you.
Did you once come from Laios' house?

HERDSMAN   I did. I wasn't a bought slave,
I was born and raised in their house.

OEDIPUS   What was your job? How did you spend your time?   1275

HERDSMAN   My life I have spent tending sheep.

OEDIPUS   In what region did you normally work?

HERDSMAN   Mainly Kithairon, and the country thereabouts.

(OEDIPUS *gestures toward the* MESSENGER.)

OEDIPUS   That man. Do you recall ever seeing him?

HERDSMAN   Recall how? Doing what? Which man?   1280

(OEDIPUS *goes to the* MESSENGER *and puts
his hand on him.*)

OEDIPUS   This man right here. Have you ever seen him before?

---

6. Pan was a woodland god, patron of shepherds.   and mountains. Hermes was born on Mount
7. Dionysos (Bakkhos), god of wine, like Pan   Kyllene in Arcadia.
and Hermes, haunted the wild places, woods,

HERDSMAN	Not that I recognize—not right away.
MESSENGER	It's no wonder, master. His memory's faded,
	but I'll revive it for him. I'm sure he knows me.
	We worked the pastures on Kithairon together—	1285
	he with his two flocks, me with one—
	for three whole grazing seasons, from early spring
	until Arcturos[8] rose. When the weather turned cold
	I'd drive my flocks home to their winter pens,
	he'd drive his away to Laios' sheepfolds.	1290
	Do I describe what happened, old friend? Or don't I?
HERDSMAN	That's the truth, but it was so long ago.
MESSENGER	Do you remember giving me a boy
	I was to raise as my own son?
HERDSMAN	What? Why ask me that?	1295
MESSENGER	There, my friend, is the man who was that boy.

(*He nods toward* OEDIPUS.)

HERDSMAN	Damn you! Shut up and say nothing.
OEDIPUS	Don't attack him for his words, old man.
	Yours beg to be punished far more than his.
HERDSMAN	Tell me, royal master, what've I done wrong?	1300
OEDIPUS	You didn't answer him about the boy.
HERDSMAN	He's trying to make something out of nothing.
OEDIPUS	Speak of your own free will. Or under torture.
HERDSMAN	Dear god! I'm an old man. Don't hurt me.
OEDIPUS	One of you, bind his arms behind his back.	1305

(SERVANTS *approach the* HERDSMAN *and*
start to seize his arms.)

HERDSMAN	Why this, you doomed man? What else must you know?
OEDIPUS	Did you give him the child, as he claims you did?
HERDSMAN	I did. I wish that day I had died.
OEDIPUS	You will die if you don't speak the truth.
HERDSMAN	Answering you is what will get me killed.	1310
OEDIPUS	I think this man is deliberately stalling
HERDSMAN	No! I've said it once. I gave him the boy.
OEDIPUS	Was the boy from your house? Or someone else's?
HERDSMAN	Not from my house. Someone gave him to me.
OEDIPUS	The person! Name him! From what house?	1315
HERDSMAN	Don't ask me that, master. For god's sake, don't.
OEDIPUS	If I have to ask one more time, you'll die.
HERDSMAN	He was a child from the house of Laios.
OEDIPUS	A slave? Or a child born of Laios' blood?
HERDSMAN	Help me! I am about to speak terrible words.	1320
OEDIPUS	And I to hear them. But hear them I must!
HERDSMAN	The child was said to be Laios' own son.
	Your lady in the house would know that best.
OEDIPUS	*She* gave the child to you?

8. The main star in the constellation Boötes; its appearance in the sky, just before dawn, in September, signals the end of summer.

HERDSMAN	She gave him, King.
OEDIPUS	To do what?
HERDSMAN	I was to let it die.
OEDIPUS	Kill her own child?
HERDSMAN	She feared prophecies.
OEDIPUS	What prophecies?
HERDSMAN	That this child would kill his father.
OEDIPUS	Why, then, did you give him to this old man?

HERDSMAN   Out of pity, master. I hoped this man   1330
would take him back to his own land.
But that man saved him for this—
the worst grief of all. If the child
he speaks of is you, master, now you
know: your birth has doomed you.   1335

OEDIPUS   All! All! It all happened!
It was all true. O light! Let this
be the last time I look on you.
You see now what I am—
the child who must not be born!   1340
I loved where I must not love!
I killed where I must not kill!

(OEDIPUS *runs into the palace.*)

CHORUS   Men and women who live and die,
I set no value on your lives.
Which one of you ever, reaching   1345
for blessedness that lasts,
finds more than what *seems* blest?
You live in that seeming
a while, then it vanishes.
Your fate teaches me this, Oedipus,   1350
yours, you suffering man, the story
god spoke through you: never call
any man fortunate.

O Zeus, no man drew a bow like this man!
He shot his arrow home,   1355
winning power, pleasure, wealth;
he killed the virgin Sphinx,
who sang the god's dark oracles;
her claws were hooked and sharp.
He fought off death in our land;   1360
he towered against its threat.
Since those times I've called you my king,
honoring you mightily, my Oedipus,
who wielded the great might of Thebes.

But now—nobody's story   1365
has the sorrow of yours,

O my so famous Oedipus—
the same great harbor
welcomed you
first as child, then as father   1370
tumbling upon your bridal bed.
How could the furrows your father plowed, doomed
man, how could they suffer so long in silence?

Time, who sees all, caught you
living a life you never willed.   1375
Time damns this marriage that is
no marriage, where the fathered child
fathered children himself.
O son of Laios, I wish
I'd never seen you! I fill my lungs,   1380
I sing with all my power
the plain truth in my heart.
Once you gave me new breath,
O my Oedipus!—but now
you close my eyes in darkness.   1385

(*Enter* SERVANT *from the palace.*)

SERVANT   You've always been our land's most honored men.
If you still have a born Theban's love
for the House of Labdakos, you'll be crushed
by what you're about to see and hear.
No rivers could wash this house clean—   1390
not the Danube, not the Rion—
it hides so much evil that now
is coming to light. What happened here
was not involuntary evil, it was willed.
The griefs that punish us the most   1395
are those we've chosen for ourselves.
LEADER   We already knew more than enough
to make us grieve. Do you have more to tell?
SERVANT   It is the briefest news to say or hear.
Our royal lady Jokasta is dead.   1400
LEADER   That pitiable woman. How did she die?
SERVANT   She killed herself. You will be spared the worst—
since you weren't there to see it.
But you will hear, exactly as I can
recall it, what that wretched woman suffered.   1405
She came raging through the courtyard
straight for her marriage bed, the fists
of both her hands clenched in her hair.
Once in, she slammed the doors shut and called out
to Laios, so long dead; she remembered   1410
his living sperm of long ago, who killed Laios,
while she lived on to breed with her son

more ruined children.
                              She grieved for the bed
she had loved in, giving birth
to all those doubled lives—   1415
husband fathered by husband,
children sired by her child.
From this point on I don't know how she died—
Oedipus burst in shouting,
distracting us from her misery.   1420
We looked on, stunned, as he plowed through us
raging, asking us for a spear,
asking for the wife who was no wife
but the same furrowed twice-mothering earth
from whom he and his children sprang.   1425
He was frantic, yet some divine hand
drove him toward his wife—none of us near him did.
As though someone were guiding him, he lunged,
with a savage yell, at the double doors,
wrenching the bolts from their sockets.   1430
He burst into the room. We saw her there:
the woman above us, hanging by the neck,
swaying there in a noose of tangled cords.
He saw. And bellowing in anguish
he reached up, loosening the noose that held her.   1435
With the poor lifeless woman laid out on the ground
this, then, was the terror we saw: he pulled
the long pins of hammered gold clasping her gown,
held them up, and punched them into his eyes,
back through the sockets. He was screaming: 1440
"Eyes, now you will not, no, never
see the evil I suffered, the evil I caused.
You will see blackness—where once
were lives you should never have lived to see,
yearned-for faces you so long failed to know."   1445
While he howled out these tortured words—
not once, but many times—his raised hands
kept beating his eyes. The blood kept coming,
drenching his beard and cheeks. Not a few wet drops,
but a black storm of bloody hail lashing his face.   1450

What this man and this woman did
broke so much evil loose! That evil joins
the whole of both their lives in grief.
The happiness they once knew was real,
but now that happiness is in ruins—   1455
wailing, death, disgrace. Whatever misery
we have a name for, is here.
LEADER   Has his grief eased at all?

SERVANT   He shouts for someone to open the door bolts:
"Show this city its father-killer," he cries,   1460
"Show it its mother . . ." He said the word, I can't.
He wants to banish himself from the land,
not doom this house any longer
by living here, under his own curse.
He's so weak, though, he needs to be helped.   1465
No one could stand up under a sickness like his.
Look! The door bolts are sliding open.
You will witness a vision of such suffering
even those it revolts will pity.

(OEDIPUS *emerges from the slowly opening palace doors. He is blinded.*
* * * *He moves with the aid of a servant.*)

LEADER   Your pain is terrible to see,   1470
pure, helpless anguish,
more moving than anything
my eyes have ever touched.
                     O man of pain,
where did your madness come from?
What god would go   1475
to such inhuman lengths
to savage your defenseless life?

(*Moans.*)

I cannot look at you—
though there's so much
to ask you, so much to learn,   1480
so much that holds my eyes—
so strong are the shivers of awe
you send through me.

OEDIPUS   Ahhh! My life
screams in pain.   1485
Where is my misery
taking me?
How far does my voice fly,
fluttering out there
on the wind?   1490
O god, how far have you thrown me?

LEADER   To a hard place. Hard to watch, hard to hear.

OEDIPUS   Darkness buries me in her hate, takes me
in her black hold.
Unspeakable blackness.   1495
It can't be fought off,
it keeps coming,
wafting evil all over me.
Ahhh!
Those goads piercing my eyes,   1500
those crimes stabbing my mind,

	strike through me—one deep wound.
LEADER	It is no wonder you feel
	nothing but pain now,
	both in your mind and in your flesh.
OEDIPUS	Ah friend, you're still here,
	faithful to the blind man.
	I know you are near me. Even
	in my darkness I know your voice.
LEADER	You terrify us. How could you
	put out your eyes? What god drove you to it?
OEDIPUS	It was Apollo who did this.
	He made evil, consummate evil,
	out of my life.
	But the hand
	that struck these eyes
	was my hand.
	I in my wretchedness
	struck me, no one else did.
	What good was left for my eyes to see?
	Nothing in this world could I see now
	with a glad heart.
LEADER	That is so.
OEDIPUS	Whom could I look at? Or love?
	Whose greeting could I answer
	with fondness, friends?
	Take me quickly from this place.
	I am the most ruined, the most cursed,
	the most god-hated man who ever lived.
LEADER	You're broken by what happened, broken
	by what's happening in your own mind.
	I wish you'd never learned the truth.
OEDIPUS	May he die, the man
	who found me in the pasture,
	who unshackled my feet,
	who saved me from that death for a worse life,
	a life I cannot thank him for.
	Had I died then, I would have caused
	no great grief to my people and myself.
LEADER	I wish he had let you die.
OEDIPUS	I wouldn't have come home to kill my father,
	no one could call me lover
	of her from whose body I came.
	I have no god now.
	I'm son to a fouled mother,
	I fathered children in the bed
	where my father once gave me
	deadly life. If ever an evil
	rules all other evils

1505
1510
1515
1520
1525
1530
1535
1540
1545

	it is my evil, the life	1550
	god gave to Oedipus.	
LEADER	I wish I could say you acted wisely.	
	You would have been better off dead than blind.	
OEDIPUS	There was no better way than mine.	
	No more advice! If I had eyes, how could	1555

it is my evil, the life   1550
god gave to Oedipus.
LEADER   I wish I could say you acted wisely.
          You would have been better off dead than blind.
OEDIPUS   There was no better way than mine.
          No more advice! If I had eyes, how could   1555
          they bear to look at my father in Hades?
          Or at my devastated mother? Not even
          hanging could right the wrongs I did them both.
          You think I'd find the sight of my children
          delightful, born to the life mine must live?   1560
          Never, ever, delightful to my eyes!
          Nor this town, its wall, gates and towers;
          nor the sacred images of our gods.
          I severed myself from these joys when I
          banished the vile killer—myself!—   1565
          totally wretched now, though I was raised
          more splendidly than any Theban.
          But now the gods have proven me
          defiled, and of Laios' own blood.
          And once I've brought such disgrace on myself,   1570
          how could I look calmly on my people?
          I could not! If I could deafen my ears
          I would. I'd deaden my whole body,
          go blind and deaf to shut those evils out.
          The silence in my mind would be sweet.   1575
          O Kithairon, why did you take me in?
          Or once you had seized me, why didn't you
          kill me instantly, leaving no trace of my birth?
          O Polybos and Korinth, and that palace
          they called the ancient home of my fathers!   1580
          I was their glorious boy growing up,
          but under that fair skin
          festered a hideous disease.
          My vile self now shows its vile birth.
                                    You,
          three roads, and you, darkest ravine,   1585
          you, grove of oaks, you, narrow place
          where three paths drank blood from my hands,
          my fathering blood pouring into you:
          Do you remember what I did while you watched?
          And when I came here, what I did then?   1590
          O marriages! You marriages! You created us,
          we sprang to life, then from that same seed
          you burst fathers, brothers, sons,
          kinsmen shedding kinsmen's blood,
          brides and mothers and wives—the most loathsome   1595
          atrocities that strike mankind.

I must not name what should not be.
If you love the gods, hide me out there,
kill me, heave me into the sea,
anywhere you can't see me.   1600
Come, take me. Don't shy away. Touch
this human derelict. Don't fear me, trust me.
No other man, only myself,
can be afflicted with my sorrows.

LEADER   Here's Kreon. He's come when you need him,   1605
to take action or to give you advice.
He is the only ruler we have left
to guard Thebes in your place.

OEDIPUS   Can I say anything he'll listen to?
Why would he believe me?   1610
I wronged him so deeply.
I proved myself so false to him.

(KREON *enters.*)

KREON   I haven't come to mock you, Oedipus.
I won't dwell on the wrongs you did me.

(KREON *speaks to the attendants.*)

Men, even if you've no respect   1615
for a fellow human being, show some
for the life-giving flame of the Sun god:
don't leave this stark defilement out here.
The earth, the holy rain, the light, can't bear it.

Quickly, take him back to the palace.   1620
If these sorrows are shared
only among the family,
that will spare us further impiety.

OEDIPUS   Thank god! I feared much worse from you.
Since you've shown me, a most vile man,   1625
such noble kindness, I have one request.
For your sake, not for mine.

KREON   What is it? Why do you ask me like that?

OEDIPUS   Expel me quickly to some place
where no living person will find me.   1630

KREON   I would surely have done that. But first
I need to know what the god wants me to do.

OEDIPUS   He's given his command already.
I killed my father. I am unholy. I must die.

KREON   So the god said. But given   1635
the crisis we're in, we had better
be absolutely sure before we act.

OEDIPUS   You'd ask about a broken man like me?

KREON   Surely, by now, you're willing to trust god.

OEDIPUS   I am. But now I must ask for something   1640
within your power. I beg you! Bury her

who's lying inside—as you think proper.
Give her the rites due your kinswoman.
As for me, don't condemn my father's city
to house me while I'm still alive.   1645
Let me live out my life on Kithairon,
the very mountain—
the one I've made famous—
that my father and mother chose for my tomb.
Let me die there, as my parents decreed.   1650
And yet, I know this much:
no sickness can kill me. Nothing can.
I was saved from that death
to face an extraordinary evil.
Let my face take me now, where it will.   1655

My children, Kreon. My sons.
They're grown now. They won't need your help.

They'll find a way to live anywhere.
But my poor wretched girls, who never
ate anywhere but at my table;   1660
they've never lived apart from me.
I fed them with my own hands.
                                        Care for them.
If you're willing, let me touch them now,
let me give in to my grief.
Grant it Kreon, from your great heart.   1665
If I could touch them, I would
imagine them as my eyes once saw them.

(*The gentle sobbing of Oedipus' two daughters is
heard offstage. Soon two small girls enter.*)

What's this?
O gods, are these my children sobbing?
Has Kreon pitied me?   1670
Given me my own dear children?
Has he?
KREON   I have. I brought them to you
because I knew how much joy,
as always, you would take in them.   1675
OEDIPUS Bless this kindness of yours. Bless your luck.
May the gods guard you better than they did me.
Children, where are you? Come to me.
These are your brother's hands, hands
of the man who created you, hands that caused   1680
my once bright eyes to go dark.
He, children, saw nothing, knew nothing,
he fathered you where his own life began,
where his own seed grew. Though I can't

see you, I can weep for you . . . 1685

(OEDIPUS *takes his daughters in his arms.*)

when I think how bitter your lives will be.
I know the life that men will make you live.
What public gatherings, what festivals
could you attend? None! You would be sent home
in tears, without your share of holy joy. 1690
When the time comes to marry, my daughters,
what man will risk the revulsion—
the infamy!—that will wound you
just as it wounded your parents?
What evil is missing? Your father killed 1695
his father, he had children with the mother
who bore him, fathered you
at the source of his own life.

                Those are the insults
you will face. Who will marry you?
No one, my children. You will grow old 1700
unmarried, living a dried-up childless life.
Kreon, you're all the father they have now.
The parents who conceived them are both lost.
Keep these two girls from rootless wandering,
unmarried and helpless. They are your kin. 1705
Don't bring them down to what I am.
Pity them. They are so young, and but for you,
alone. Touch my hand, kind man,
make that touch your promise.

(KREON *touches him.*)

Children, had you been old enough 1710
to comprehend, I would have taught you more.
Now, all I can do is ask you to pray:
that you live only where you're welcomed;
that your lives be happier than mine was,
the father from whose seed you were born. 1715

KREON   Enough grief. Go inside now.
OEDIPUS   Bitter words, which I must obey.
KREON   Time runs out on all things.
OEDIPUS   Grant my request before I go.
KREON   Speak. 1720
OEDIPUS   Banish me from my homeland.
KREON   Ask god to do that, not me.
OEDIPUS   I am the man the gods hate most.
KREON   Then you will have your wish.
OEDIPUS   You consent? 1725
KREON   I never promise if I can't be sure.
OEDIPUS   Then lead me inside.
KREON   Come. Let go of your children now.

OEDIPUS	Don't take them from me.
KREON	Give up your power, too. 1730
	You won the power once, but you couldn't
	keep it to the end of your life.

(KREON *leads* OEDIPUS *into the palace*.)

CHORUS	Thebans, that man is the same Oedipus
	whose great mind solved the famous riddle.
	He was a most powerful man. 1735
	Which of us seeing his glory, his prestige,
	did not wish his luck could be ours?
	Now look at what wreckage the seas
	of savage trouble have made of his life.
	To know the truth of a man, wait 1740
	till you see his life end.
	On that day, look at him.
	Don't claim any man is god's friend
	until he has passed through life
	and crossed the border into death—
	never having been god's victim. 1746

(*All leave*.)

EURIPIDES

ca. 480–406 B.C.E.

LIFE AND TIMES

Euripides strikes many readers as the liveliest, funniest, and most provocative of the three great Athenian tragedians whose work survives. A younger contemporary of Aeschylus and **Sophocles**, Euripides lived through most of the cultural and political turmoil of the fifth century, and was seen as one of the most influential voices for the revolutionary new ideas that were developing in this period. Controversial in his own time for his use of colloquial language and his depictions of unheroic heroes, sexually promiscuous women, and cruel, violent gods, Euripides has lost none of his power to shock, provoke, amuse, and engage his audiences.

We know little of Euripides' personal life. He seems to have been married twice, and had three sons. He was a productive but only moderately successful tragedian: he wrote over ninety plays, but won first prize only four times. He specialized in unexpected plot twists and novel approaches to his mythological material: for instance, his play about Helen of Troy (*Helen*) makes her an entirely virtuous woman, who never ran off with Paris or committed adultery. There are many moments of humor in Euripides, far more so than in Aeschylus or Sophocles. At the same time, his vision is often very dark. His later plays about the Trojan War (such as *Hecuba* and *Trojan Women*) are easy to read as terrible indictments of the suffering caused to women, children, and families by the contemporary Peloponnesian War between Athens and Sparta.

He spent most of his life in Athens, but in his old age went to visit Macedon, where he died. It has often been suggested that he left Athens in outrage at the city's failure to appreciate him, but there is no evidence for this. Euripides was probably always popular with audiences, albeit less so with the judges of the dramatic competition, who perhaps felt an obligation to uphold civic ideals. Euripides continued to be widely read, quoted, and enjoyed for generations after his death.

Medea was first performed in the spring of 431 B.C.E., immediately before the outbreak of the Peloponnesian War. It was a time of prosperity for the city: the Greeks had defeated the Persians in the year of Euripides' birth, and now the Athenian Empire extended across the Mediterranean. Athens was full of pride in the political, artistic, and intellectual achievements of the citizens.

It was also a time of new, antitraditional ideas, brought by the Sophists, men from other societies who came to Athens to teach "cleverness" or "wisdom"—*sophia*. The Sophists were seen by some as a mark of Athens' progressive openness to new modes of thought, but by others as a dangerous influence, liable to corrupt the city's young men. The tragedies of Euripides were associated by the comic dramatist, Aristophanes, and probably many others, with the iconoclasm of the Sophists. The plays were clearly found shocking and controversial by contemporaries.

Euripides uses traditional myths, but shifts attention away from the deeds of heroes toward domestic wrangling, and shows up moral and psychological weaknesses. Euripides was seen as a cynical realist about human nature: Sophocles said that while he showed people as they ought to be, Euripides showed them as they are.

Euripides put male heroes onstage in humiliated positions: they are bedraggled and dressed in rags, or are presented as obvious cowards, liars, or brutes. Lower-class characters and slaves are prominent, and sympathetically portrayed. Euripides' outspoken, lustful or violent, though often sympathetic, women were found particularly outrageous by his contemporaries. In religious terms, too, his plays were challenging and controversial: his characters often question the old Greek myths about the gods, and the gods themselves often seem arbitrary or cruel in their dealings with humanity. Euripides also included vivid and realistic descriptions of violence, as in the messenger speech of the *Medea*, a horrifying account of how the princess Creusa's hair was burned up by her golden crown, while her poisoned dress corroded her skin and finally ripped the flesh from her bones.

THE WORK

Medea, like almost all Greek tragedies, is based on a traditional story. According to myth, the hero Jason was told by his uncle, Pelias, that he could not claim his rightful inheritance, the throne of Iolcus, unless he could perform a seemingly impossible quest: cross the Black Sea to the distant barbarian land of Colchis, ruled by the savage king Aeetes, and bring back to Greece the Golden Fleece, which was guarded by a dragon. Jason assembled a group of the finest Greek heroes, and built the world's first ship—the *Argo*—to take them to Colchis. Once they arrived, King Aeetes set Jason the task of ploughing a field with a team of fire-breathing bulls. Luckily, the king's daughter, Medea, fell in love with Jason. She was skilled in magic, and enabled him to plough the field, lull the dragon to sleep, steal the fleece, and escape back to Greece, killing her own brother to distract the attention of their enraged Colchian pursuers. When they arrived in Iolcus, Pelias tried to go back on his word, and hang onto power. Medea got back at him by persuading Pelias' daughters that they could make their father immortal by boiling him alive—which was, of course, untrue. After the scandal was discovered, Jason and Medea were forced into exile. The couple had children, and eventually moved to Corinth. There, Jason decided to divorce Medea and marry a native Corinthian princess instead. With that, the action of *Medea* begins.

The most well-known part of the myth was the story of the quest of the Argonauts (sailors in the *Argo*) for the Golden Fleece. But Euripides focuses not on this heroic narrative but on its squalid aftermath, and he seems to have invented certain key aspects of the story. In previous versions, the children were either murdered by Creon's family or, according to another story, accidentally killed by Medea, when she tried to use magic to make them immortal. The shocking events at the end of this play would not have been anticipated by Euripides' audience.

Euripides' concentration on the domestic troubles in Corinth, rather than the heroic quest, allows him to present Jason in a disturbingly unheroic light: as a cad who struggles to muster unconvincing strategic and rhetorical arguments to justify his shabby treatment of his first wife. Although Jason tries to talk like a Sophist, it is Medea who is the real possessor of *sophia* in the play. The term *sophia* has negative and positive connotations: it can suggest deep understanding, but it can also imply mere cleverness. The play invites us to consider which character is the smartest: Jason, with his dodges and evasions, or Medea, with her unpredictable, cruel stratagems.

Medea is strongly marked as an outsider in three crucial ways: as a woman in a male-dominated world; as a foreigner or "barbarian" in a Greek city; and as a smart person surrounded by fools. On all these grounds, the play initially seems to invite us to side with Medea. She is obviously the wronged party in her relationship with Jason; and yet, even as she expresses her devastation at the betrayal, she never presents herself as a victim. Rather, she is fierce, "like a wild lion," and highly articulate in her analysis of her situation. She claims even the male values of military honor for herself and for all women, suggesting in one famous passage that women who undergo the pain and danger of childbirth are far braver than men who fight in war: "I'd rather take my stand behind / a shield three times than go through childbirth once." It is tempting to read these lines as proto-feminist, and to see Euripides, the clever poet, as sympathetic to his clever heroine, and as a defender of the rights and dignity of women and foreigners, before an audience of Athenian male citizens.

But as the play goes on, our vision of Medea is likely to change. We may begin to see her, not as strong and brave, but as scarily violent; not as wise, but as too clever by half. This is a disturbing play, which forces readers to revise their feelings several times. Is Medea smart and sensible in her defense of her honor and her rights, or is she driven crazy by the gods of passion? Or should we see her as an agent of the gods, imposing divine justice on oath-breaking humans? Is Euripides challenging or confirming Greek male prejudices against foreigners and women? Is he recommending new forms of wisdom, or warning against the false cleverness of upstarts and outsiders? And what does it say about the city of Athens, that it is the Athenian king, Aegeus, who will welcome this terrifying figure into his community?

Thematically, the most important threads in the play include the opposition of order and chaos, and the idea of time, especially the reversal of time. The Nurse opens the play by wishing that history could be reversed: "I wish the Argo never had set sail," she declares: the play begins with a desire to undo the beginning. Medea is the granddaughter of a god, Helios, the Sun, which associates her closely with the regular passing of time, in the sun's rising and setting. Her violent revenge at the injustice done to her can be seen as an attempt to do the impossible: to undo, by violence, her life history ever since the sailing of the *Argo*, to regain her lost honor and go back to her old self, an unmarried princess. It can also be seen as an attempt at justice, a restoration of order out of chaos—but at a terrible cost, and in violation of all moderation and humanity.

Medea is an endlessly fascinating play that seems strikingly modern in its examination of family life, infidelity, failed sexual relationships, the experience of immigrants in a foreign land, and how it feels to be an oppressed or marginalized member of society. It also points to the fear, felt by many people both ancient and modern, that the apparently weaker members of a community, such as women and resident aliens, may be smarter than their masters, and may, if provoked enough, rise up to destroy their oppressors.

Medea[1]

CHARACTERS

NURSE, *of Medea*
TUTOR, *of Medea and Jason's children*
MEDEA
CHORUS, *women of Corinth*
CREON, *king of Corinth*

JASON
AEGEUS, *king of Athens*
MESSENGER
CHILDREN, *of Medea and Jason*

SCENE: *A normal house on a street in Corinth. The elderly* NURSE *steps out of its front door.*[2]

NURSE   I wish the *Argo*[3] never had set sail,
   had never flown to Colchis through the dark
   Clashing Rocks;[4] I wish the pines had never
   been felled along the hollows on the slopes
   of Pelion, to fit their hands with oars—   5
   those heroes who went off to seek the golden
   pelt for Pelias. My mistress then,
   Medea, never would have sailed away

1. Translated by Diane Arnson Svarlien.
2. The list of characters and all stage directions, in italics, are by Robin Mitchell-Boyask.
3. The first ship, constructed by Jason for his

quest for the Golden Fleece.
4. Colchis, home of Medea, lay on the other side of the Black Sea, past the rocks near the mouth of the Bosphorus.

to reach the towers of Iolcus' land;[5]
the sight of Jason never would have stunned   10
her spirit with desire. She would have never
persuaded Pelias' daughters to kill their father,[6]
never had to come to this land—Corinth.[7]
Here she's lived in exile with her husband
and children, and Medea's presence pleased   15
the citizens. For her part, she complied
with Jason in all things. There is no greater
security than this in all the world:
when a wife does not oppose her husband.
But now, there's only hatred. What should be   20
most loved has been contaminated, stricken
since Jason has betrayed them—his own children,
and my lady, for a royal bed.
He's married into power: Creon's daughter.[8]
Poor Medea, mournful and dishonored,   25
shrieks at his broken oaths, the promise sealed
with his right hand (the greatest pledge there is)—
she calls the gods to witness just how well
Jason has repaid her. She won't touch food;
surrendering to pain, she melts away   30
her days in tears, ever since she learned
of this injustice. She won't raise her face;
her eyes are glued to the ground. Friends talk to her,
try to give her good advice; she listens
the way a rock does, or an ocean wave.   35
At most, she'll turn her pale neck aside,
sobbing to herself for her dear father,
her land, her home, and all that she betrayed
for Jason, who now holds her in dishonor.
This disaster made her realize: 40
a fatherland is no small thing to lose.
She hates her children, feels no joy in seeing them.
I'm afraid she might be plotting something.
Her mind is fierce, and she will not endure
ill treatment. I know her. I'm petrified   45
to think what thoughts she might be having now:
a sharpened knife-blade thrust right through the liver—
she could even strike the royal family, murder
the bridegroom too, make this disaster worse.
She's a terror. There's no way to be   50
her enemy and come out as the victor.

5. Thessaly, in Greece.
6. Pelias, Jason's uncle, reneged on a promise to give Jason the throne of Iolchus if he brought back the Golden Fleece. In revenge, Medea persuaded Pelias's daughters to boil him alive, in the belief that they would make him young again.
7. After the scandal of Pelias's murder, Jason and Medea had to go into exile, to Corinth.
8. Creon, king of Corinth, is not the same as the Kreon of Thebes in Sophocles' Theban plays.

Here come the children, resting from their games,
with no idea of their mother's troubles.
A child's mind is seldom filled with pain.

    (*Enter the* TUTOR *from the house with the two children of* JASON *and* MEDEA.)

TUTOR   Timeworn stalwart of my mistress' household,   55
why do you stand here by the gates, alone,
crying out your sorrows to yourself?
You've left Medea alone. Doesn't she need you?
NURSE   Senior attendant to the sons of Jason,
decent servants feel their masters' griefs   60
in their own minds, when things fall out all wrong.
As for me, my pain was so intense
that a desire crept over me to come out here
and tell the earth and sky my mistress' troubles.
TUTOR   Poor thing. Is she not done with weeping yet?   65
NURSE   What blissful ignorance! She's barely started.
TUTOR   The fool—if one may say such things of masters—
she doesn't even know the latest outrage.
NURSE   What is it, old man? Don't begrudge me that.
TUTOR   Nothing. I'm sorry that I spoke at all.   70
NURSE   By your beard, don't hide this thing from *me*,
your fellow-servant. I can keep it quiet.
TUTOR   As I approached the place where the old men
sit and play dice, beside the sacred spring
Peirene,[9] I heard someone say—he didn't   75
notice I was listening—that Creon,
the ruler of this land, intends to drive
these children and their mother out of Corinth.
I don't know if it's true. I hope it isn't.
NURSE   Will Jason let his sons be so abused,   80
even if he's fighting with their mother?
TUTOR   He has a new bride; he's forgotten them.
He's no friend to this household anymore.
NURSE   We are destroyed, then. Before we've bailed our boat
from the first wave of sorrow, here's a new one.   85
TUTOR   But please, don't tell your mistress. Keep it quiet.
It's not the time for her to know of this.
NURSE   Children, do you hear the way your father
is treating you? I won't say, *May he die!*
—he is my master—but it's obvious   90
he's harming those whom he should love. He's guilty.
TUTOR   Who isn't? Are you just now learning this,
that each man loves himself more than his neighbor?
If their father doesn't cherish them, because
he's more preoccupied with his own bed—   95

---

9. Spring in Corinth.

NURSE   Go inside now, children. Everything
   will be all right.

>   (*The* TUTOR *turns the children toward the house.*)

>   And you, keep them away—
don't let them near their mother when she's like this.
I've seen her: she looks fiercer than a bull;
she's giving them the eye, as if she means   100
to do something. Her rage will not let up,
I know, until she lashes out at someone.
May it be enemies she strikes, and not her loved ones!

>   (*In the following passage,* MEDEA *sings and the* NURSE *chants.*)

MEDEA   (*From within the house, crying out in rage.*)

Aaaah!
Oh, horrible, horrible, all that I suffer,   105
my unhappy struggles. I wish I could die.

NURSE   You see, this is it. Dear children, your mother
   has stirred up her heart, she has stirred up her rage.
   Hurry up now and get yourselves inside the house—
   but don't get too close to her, don't let her see you:
   her ways are too wild, her nature is hateful,   110
   her mind is too willful.

>   Go in. Hurry up!

>   (*Exit the* TUTOR *and children into the house.*)

It's clear now, it's starting: a thunderhead rising,
swollen with groaning, and soon it will flash
as her spirit ignites it—then what will she do?
Her heart is so proud, there is no way to stop her;   115
her soul has been pierced by these sorrows.

MEDEA   *Aaaah!*
The pain that I've suffered, I've suffered so much,
worth oceans of weeping. O children, accursed,
may you die—with your father! Your mother is hateful.
Go to hell, the whole household! Every last one.   120

NURSE   Oh, lord. Here we go. What have *they* done—the children?
   Their father's done wrong—why should you hate *them?*
   Oh, children, my heart is so sore, I'm afraid
   you will come to some harm.

>   Rulers are fierce
   in their temperament; somehow, they will not be governed;   125
   they like to have power, always, over others.
   They're harsh, and they're stubborn. It's better to live
   as an equal with equals. I never would want
   to be grand and majestic—just let me grow old
   in simple security. Even the *word*   130

"moderation" sounds good when you say it. For mortals
the middle is safest, in word and in deed.
Too much is too much, and there's always a danger
a god may get angry and ruin your household.

(*Enter the* CHORUS *of Corinthian women from the right, singing.*)

CHORUS *I heard someone's voice, I heard someone shout:* 135
the woman from Colchis: poor thing, so unhappy.
Is her grief still unsoftened? Old woman, please tell us—
I heard her lament through the gates of my hall.
Believe me, old woman, I take no delight
when this house is in pain. I have pledged it my friendship. 140

NURSE This house? It no longer exists. It's all gone.
He's taken up with his new royal marriage.
She's in her bedroom, my mistress, she's melting
her life all away, and her mind can't be eased
by a single kind word from a single dear friend. 145

MEDEA *Aaaah!*
May a fire-bolt from heaven come shoot through my skull!
What do I gain by being alive?
Oh, god. How I long for the comfort of death.
I hate this life. How I wish I could leave it. 150

[Strophe]

CHORUS Do you hear, O Zeus, O sunlight and earth,
this terrible song, the cry
of this unhappy bride?
Poor fool, what a dreadful longing,
this craving for final darkness.
You'll hasten your death. Why do it? 155
Don't pray for this ending.
If your husband reveres a new bed, a new bride,
don't sharpen your mind against him.
You'll have Zeus himself supporting
your case. Don't dissolve in weeping 160
for the sake of your bedmate.

MEDEA *Great goddess Themis and Artemis, holy one:*[1]
do you see what I suffer, although I have bound
my detestable husband with every great oath?
May I see him, along with his bride and the palace 165
scraped down to nothing, crushed into splinters.
He started it. He was the one with the nerve

1. Themis, whose name means "Right" or "Lawfulness," is a female Titan associated with order and keeping promises. Artemis is a goddess who protects virgins and women in childbirth.

to commit this injustice. Oh father, oh city,
I left you in horror—I killed my own brother.[2]

NURSE   You hear what she says, and the gods that she prays to: 170
Themis, and Zeus, the enforcer of oaths?
There's no way my mistress's rage will die down
into anything small.

[Antistrophe]

CHORUS   How I wish she'd come outside, let us see
her face, let her hear our words   175
and the sound of our voice.
If only she'd drop her anger,
unburden her burning spirit,
let go of this weight of madness.
I'll stand by our friendship.   180
Hurry up, bring her here, get her out, go inside,
and bring her to us. Go tell her
that we are her friends. Please hurry!
She's raging—the ones inside may
feel the sting of her sorrow.   185
NURSE   I'll do as you ask, but I fear that my mistress
won't listen to me.
I will make the effort—what's one more attempt?
But her glare is as fierce as a bull's, let me tell you—
she's wild like a lion who's just given birth   190
whenever a servant tries telling her anything.

You wouldn't go wrong, you'd be right on the mark,
if you called them all half-wits, the people of old:
they made lovely songs for banquets and parties,
but no one took time to discover the music   195
that might do some good, the chords or the harmony
people could use to relieve all the hateful
pain and distress that leads to the downfall
of houses, the deaths and the dreadful misfortunes.
Let me tell you, there would be some gain in that—music   200
with the power to heal. When you're having a sumptuous
feast, what's the point of a voice raised in song?
Why bother with singing? The feast is enough
to make people happy. That's all that they need.

(*Exit the* NURSE *into the house.*)

CHORUS   *I heard a wail, a clear cry of pain;*   205
she rails at the betrayer of her bed,

---

2. After the theft of the Golden Fleece, Jason and Medea were pursued by the outraged Colchians. To slow them down, Medea killed her brother, Aspyrtus, and threw his body parts behind her.

the bitter bridegroom.
For the injustice she suffers, she calls on the gods:
Themis of Zeus, protectress of oaths,
who brought her to Hellas,[3] over the salt water dark as night,   210
through the waves of Pontus' forbidding gate.[4]

    (*Enter* MEDEA *from the house, attended by the* NURSE *and other female*
    servants. Here spoken dialogue resumes.)

MEDEA   Women of Corinth, I have stepped outside
  so you will not condemn me. Many people
  act superior—I'm well aware of this.
  Some keep it private; some are arrogant   215
  in public view. Yet there are other people
  who, just because they lead a quiet life,
  are thought to be aloof. There is no justice
  in human eyesight: people take one look
  and hate a man, before they know his heart,   220
  though no injustice has been done to them.
  A foreigner must adapt to a new city,
  certainly. Nor can I praise a citizen
  who's willful, and who treats his fellow townsmen
  harshly, out of narrow-mindedness.   225

  My case is different. Unexpected trouble
  has crushed my soul. It's over now; I take
  no joy in life. My friends, I want to die.
  My husband, who was everything to me—
  how well I know it—is the worst of men.   230

  Of all the living creatures with a soul
  and mind, we women are the most pathetic.
  First of all, we have to buy a husband:[5]
  spend vast amounts of money, just to get
  a master for our body—to add insult   235
  to injury. And the stakes could not be higher:
  will you get a decent husband, or a bad one?
  If a woman leaves her husband, then she loses
  her virtuous reputation. To refuse him
  is just not possible. When a girl leaves home   240
  and comes to live with new ways, different rules,
  she has to be a prophet—learn somehow
  the art of dealing smoothly with her bedmate.
  If we do well, and if our husbands bear
  the yoke without discomfort or complaint,   245
  our lives are admired. If not, it's best to die.

3. Greece.
4. Pontus is the Black Sea; the "gate" is the
Bosphorus.

5. In ancient Greece, the bride's family had to
pay a dowry to the husband.

A man, when he gets fed up with the people
at home, can go elsewhere to ease his heart
—he has friends, companions his own age.
We must rely on just one single soul.   250
They say that we lead safe, untroubled lives
at home while they do battle with the spear.
They're wrong. I'd rather take my stand behind
a shield three times than go through childbirth once.

Still, my account is quite distinct from yours.   255
This is your city. You have your fathers' homes,
your lives bring joy and profit. You have friends.
But I have been deserted and outraged—
left without a city by my husband,
who stole me as his plunder from the land   260
of the barbarians. Here I have no mother,
no brother, no blood relative to help
unmoor me from this terrible disaster.
So, I will need to ask you one small favor.
If I should find some way, some strategy   265
to pay my husband back, bring him to justice,
keep silent. Most of the time, I know, a woman
is filled with fear. She's worthless in a battle
and flinches at the sight of steel. But when
she's faced with an injustice in the bedroom,   270
there is no other mind more murderous.

CHORUS   I'll do as you ask. You're justified, Medea,
in paying your husband back. I'm not surprised
you grieve at your misfortunes.
                        Look! I see Creon,
the lord of this land, coming toward us now.   275
He has some new decision to announce.

        (*Enter* CREON *from the right, with attendants.*)

CREON   You with the grim face, fuming at your husband,
Medea, I hereby announce that you
must leave this land, an exile, taking with you
your two children. You must not delay.   280
This is my decision. I won't leave
until I've thrown you out, across the border.

MEDEA   Oh, god. I'm crushed; I'm utterly destroyed.
My enemies, their sails unfurled, attack me
and there's no land in sight, there's no escape   285
from ruin. Although I suffer, I must ask:
Creon, why do you send me from this land?

CREON   I'll speak plainly: I'm afraid of you.
You could hurt my daughter, even kill her.
Every indication points that way.   290
You're wise by nature, you know evil arts,

and you're upset because your husband's gone
away from your bedroom. I have heard reports
that you've made threats, that you've devised a plan
to harm the bride, her father, and the bridegroom.   295
I want to guard against that. I would rather
have you hate me, woman, here and now,
than treat you gently and regret it later.
MEDEA   Oh, god.
Creon, this is not the first time: often
I've been injured by my reputation.   300
Any man who's sensible by nature
will set a limit on his children's schooling
to make sure that they never grow too wise.
The wise are seen as lazy, and they're envied
and hated. If you offer some new wisdom   305
to half-wits, they will only think you're useless.
And those who are considered experts hate you
when the city thinks you're cleverer than they are.
I myself have met with this reaction.
Since I am wise, some people envy me,   310
some think I'm idle, some the opposite,
and some feel threatened. Yet I'm not all that wise.

And you're afraid of me. What do you fear?
Don't worry, Creon. I don't have it in me
to do wrong to a man with royal power.   315
What injustice have you done to me?
Your spirit moved you, and you gave your daughter
as you saw fit. My husband is the one
I hate. You acted well, with wise restraint.
And now, I don't begrudge your happiness.   320
My best to all of you—celebrate the wedding.
Just let me stay here. I know when I'm beaten.
I'll yield to this injustice. I'll submit
in silence to those greater than myself.
CREON   Your words are soothing, but I'm terrified   325
of what's in your mind. I trust you less than ever.
It's easier to guard against a woman
(or man, for that matter) with a fiery spirit
than one who's wise and silent. You must leave
at once—don't waste my time with talk. It's settled.   330
Since you are my enemy, and hate me,
no ruse of yours can keep you here among us.

    (MEDEA *kneels before* CREON *and grasps his hand and knees in supplication.*)⁶
MEDEA   No, by your knees! By your new-married daughter!
CREON   You're wasting words. There's no way you'll persuade me.

6. This was a conventional way of asking a favor.

| MEDEA | You'll drive me out, with no reverence for my prayers? | 335 |

MEDEA You'll drive me out, with no reverence for my prayers? 335
CREON I care more for my family than for you.
MEDEA How clearly I recall my fatherland.
CREON Yes, that's what *I* love most—after my children.
MEDEA Oh, god—the harm Desire does to mortals!
CREON Depending on one's fortunes, I suppose. 340
MEDEA Zeus, do not forget who caused these troubles.
CREON Just leave, you fool. I'm tired of struggling with you.
MEDEA Struggles. Yes. I've had enough myself.
CREON My guards will force you out in just a moment.
MEDEA Oh please, not that! Creon, I entreat you! 345
CREON You intend to make a scene, I gather.
MEDEA I'll leave, don't worry. That's not what I'm asking.
CREON Why are you forcing me? Let go of my hand!
MEDEA Please, let me stay just one more day, that's all.
    I need to make arrangements for my exile, 350
    find safe asylum for my children, since
    their father doesn't give them any thought.
    Take pity on them. You yourself have children.
    It's only right for you to treat them kindly.
    If we go into exile, I'm not worried 355
    about myself—I weep for their disaster.
CREON I haven't got a ruler's temperament;
    reverence has often led me into ruin.
    Woman, I realize this is all wrong,
    but you shall have your wish. I warn you, though: 360
    if the sun god's lamp should find you and your children
    still within our borders at first rising,
    it means your death. I've spoken; it's decided.
    Stay for one day only, if you must.
    You won't have time to do the things I fear. 365

(*Exit* CREON *and attendants to the right.* MEDEA *rises to her feet.*)

CHORUS Oh, god! This is horrible, unhappy woman,
    the grief that you suffer. Where will you turn?
    Where will you find shelter? What country, what home
    will save you from sorrow? A god has engulfed you,
    Medea—this wave is now breaking upon you, 370
    there is no way out.
MEDEA Yes, things are all amiss. Who could deny it?
    Believe me, though, that's not how it will end.
    The newlyweds have everything at stake,
    and struggles await the one who made this match. 375
    Do you think I ever could have fawned
    on him like that without some gain in mind,
    some ruse? I never would have spoken to him,
    or touched him with my hands. He's such an idiot.
    He could have thrown me out, destroyed my plans; 380

instead he's granted me a single day
to turn three enemies to three dead bodies:
the father, and the bride, and my own husband.
I know so many pathways to their deaths,
I don't know which to turn to first, my friends.   385
Shall I set the bridal home on fire,
creeping silently into their bedroom?

There's just one threat. If I am apprehended
entering the house, my ruse discovered,
I'll be put to death; my enemies   390
will laugh at me. The best way is the most
direct, to use the skills I have by nature
and poison them, destroy them with my drugs.

Ah, well.

All right, they die. What city will receive me?
What host will offer me immunity,   395
what land will take me in and give me refuge?
There's no one. I must wait just long enough
to see if any sheltering tower appears.
Then I will kill in silence, by deceit.
But if I have no recourse from disaster,   400
I'll take the sword and kill them, even if
it means my death. I have the utmost nerve.
Now, by the goddess whom I most revere,
Hecate,[7] whom I choose as my accomplice,
who dwells within my inmost hearth, I swear: 405
no one can hurt my heart and then fare well.
I'll turn their marriage bitter, desolate—
they'll regret the match, regret my exile.

And now, spare nothing that is in your knowledge,
Medea: make your plan, prepare your ruse.   410
Do this dreadful thing. There is so much
at stake. Display your courage. Do you see
how you are suffering? Do not allow
these Sisyphean snakes[8] to laugh at you
on Jason's wedding day. Your father is noble;   415
your grandfather is Helios. You have
the knowledge, not to mention woman's nature:
for any kind of noble deed, we're helpless;
for malice, though, our wisdom is unmatched.

---

7. Goddess associated with the moon and with witchcraft.
8. Sisyphus, an earlier king of Corinth, was notorious for his treachery; the "Sisyphean snakes" are the Corinthians.

CHORUS

[Strophe 1]

The streams of the holy rivers are flowing backward.   420
Everything runs in reverse—justice is upside down.
Men's minds are deceitful, and nothing is settled,
not even oaths that are sworn by the gods.
The tidings will change, and a virtuous reputation
will grace my name. The race of women will reap   425
honor, no longer the shame of disgraceful rumor.

[Antistrophe 1]

The songs of the poets of old will no longer linger
on my untrustworthiness. Women were never sent
the gift of divine inspiration by Phoebus
Apollo, lord of the elegant lyre,[9]   430
the master of music—or I could have sung my own song
against the race of men. The fullness of time
holds many tales: it can speak of both men and women.

[Strophe 2]

You sailed away from home and father,
driven insane in your heart; you traced a path   435
between the twin cliffs of Pontus.[1]
The land you live in is foreign.
Your bed is empty, your husband
gone. Poor woman, dishonored,
sent into exile.   440

[Antistrophe 2]

The Grace of oaths is gone, and Reverence
flies away into the sky, abandoning
great Hellas.[2] No father's dwelling
unmoors you now from this heartache.
Your bed now yields to another: 445
now a princess prevails,
greater than you are.

(*Enter* JASON *from the right.*)

JASON   This is not the first time—I have often
observed that a fierce temper is an evil
that leaves you no recourse. You could have stayed   450
here in this land, you could have kept your home
by simply acquiescing in the plans
of those who are greater. You are now an exile

---

9. Phoebus ("shining") Apollo is the god of
the sun and of poetry, usually depicted with
the lyre, a stringed instrument that was used

to accompany poetic performance.
1. The path between the cliffs is Bosphorus.
2. Greece.

because of your own foolish words. To me
it makes no difference. You can keep on calling   455
Jason the very worst of men. However,
the words you spoke against the royal family—
well, consider it a gain that nothing worse
than exile is your punishment. As for me,
I wanted you to stay. I always tried   460
to calm the king, to soothe his fuming rage.
But you, you idiot, would not let up
your words against the royal family. That's why
you are now an exile. All the same,
I won't let down my loved ones. I have come here   465
looking out for your best interests, woman,
so you won't be without the things you need
when you go into exile with the children.
You'll need money—banishment means hardship.
However much you hate me, I could never   470
wish you any harm.

MEDEA   You are the worst!
You're loathsome—that's the worst word I can utter.
You're not a man. You've come here—most detested
by the gods, by me, by all mankind.
That isn't courage, when you have the nerve   475
to harm your friends, then look them in the face.
No, that's the worst affliction known to man:
shamelessness.
                    And yet, I'm glad you've come.
Speaking ill to you will ease my soul,
and listening will cause you pain. I'll start   480
at the beginning. First, I saved your life—
as every single man who sailed from Hellas
aboard the *Argo* knows—when you were sent
to yoke the fire-breathing bulls, and sow
the deadly crop.[3] I killed the dragon, too: 485
the sleepless one, who kept the Golden Fleece
enfolded in his convoluted coils;[4]
I was your light, the beacon of your safety.
For my part, I betrayed my home, my father,
and went with you to Pelion's slopes, Iolcus[5]   490
with more good will than wisdom—and I killed
Pelias, in the cruelest possible way:
at his own children's hands. I ruined their household.

3. Jason was challenged by Medea's father, King Aeetes, to plough a field with a pair of fire-breathing bulls, and sow it with dragon's teeth, which would instantly grow into armed men. With Medea's help, he succeeded.

4. The Golden Fleece hung from a tree, round which coiled a fierce dragon; Medea succeeded in defeating the dragon.

5. Ancestral kingdom of Jason.

And you—you *are* the very worst of men—
betrayed me, after all of that. You wanted   495
a new bed, even though I'd borne you children.
If you had still been childless, anyone
could understand your lust for this new marriage.

All trust in oaths is gone. What puzzles me
is whether you believe those gods (the ones   500
who heard you swear) no longer are in power,
or that the old commandments have been changed?
You realize full well you broke your oath.

Ah, my right hand, which you took so often,
clinging to my knees.⁶ What was the point   505
of touching me? You are despicable.
My hopes have all gone wrong. Well, then! You're here:
I have a question for you, friend to friend.
(What good do I imagine it will do?
Still, I'll ask, since it makes you look worse.)   510
Where do I turn now? To my father's household
and fatherland, which I betrayed for you?
Or Pelias' poor daughters? Naturally
they'll welcome me—the one who killed their father!

Here is my situation. I've become   515
an enemy to my own family, those
whom I should love, and I have gone to war
with those whom I had no reason at all
to hurt, and all for your sake. In exchange,
you've made me the happiest girl in all of Hellas.   520
I have you, the perfect spouse, a marvel,
so trustworthy—though I must leave the country
friendless and deserted, taking with me
my friendless children! What a charming scandal
for a newlywed: your children roam   525
as beggars, with the one who saved your life.

Zeus! For brass disguised as gold, you sent us
reliable criteria to judge.
But when a man is base, how can we know?
Why is there no sign stamped upon his body?   530
CHORUS   This anger is a terror, hard to heal,
    when loved ones clash with loved ones in dispute.
JASON   It seems that I must have a way with words
    and, like a skillful captain, reef my sails

---

6. Touching a person's right hand and knees
was a way of asking for a favor, assuming the
position of a supplicant. Medea is implying
that Jason has failed to pay her back for the
favors she did him.

in order to escape this gale that blows   535
without a break—your endless, tired harangue.
The way I see it, woman (since you seem
to feel that I must owe you some huge favor),
it was Cypris,[7] no other god or mortal,
who saved me on my voyage. Yes, your mind   540
is subtle. But I must say—at the risk
of stirring up your envy and your grudges—
Eros[8] was the one who forced your hand:
his arrows, which are inescapable,[9]
compelled you to rescue me. But I won't put   545
too fine a point on that. You *did* support me.
You saved my life, in fact. However, you
received more than you gave, as I shall prove.
First of all, you live in Hellas now
instead of your barbarian land. With us,   550
you know what justice is, and civil law:
not mere brute force. And every single person
in Hellas knows that you are wise. You're famous.
You'd never have that kind of reputation
if you were living at the edge of nowhere.   555
As for me, I wouldn't wish for gold
or for a sweeter song than Orpheus'[1]
unless I had the fame to match my fortune.

Enough about my struggles—you're the one
who started this debate. As for my marriage   560
to the princess, which you hold against me,
I shall show you how I acted wisely
and with restraint, and with the greatest love
toward you and toward our children—Wait! Just listen!
When I moved here from Iolcus, bringing with me   565
disaster in abundance, with no recourse,
what more lucky windfall could I find
(exile that I was) than marrying
the king's own child? It's not that I despised
your bed—the thought that irritates you most—   570
nor was I mad with longing for a new bride,
or trying to compete with anyone—
to win the prize for having the most children.
I have enough—no reason to complain.
My motive was the best: so we'd live well   575
and not be poor. I know that everyone

7. Aphrodite, goddess of sex.
8. Cupid, god of sex—the son of Aphrodite.
9. Eros fires arrows that inspire desire.
1. Orpheus, son of the god Apollo and the muse
Calliope, was a poet-singer with semimagical

powers: even wild animals were fascinated by
his songs. Orpheus was famously devoted to his
wife, Eurydice; when she died, he traveled down
to the underworld to try to rescue her.

avoids a needy friend. I wanted to raise
sons in a style that fits my family background,
give brothers to the ones I had with you,
and treat them all as equals. This would strengthen   580
the family, and I'd be blessed with fortune.
What do *you* need children for? For me, though,
it's good if I can use my future children
to benefit my present ones. Is that
bad planning? If you weren't so irritated   585
about your bed, you'd never say it was.
But you're a woman—and you're all the same!
If everything goes well between the sheets
you think you have it all. But let there be
some setback or disaster in the bedroom   590
and suddenly you go to war against
the things that you should value most. I mean it—
men should really have some other method
for getting children. The whole female race
should not exist. It's nothing but a nuisance.   595
CHORUS   Jason, you've composed a lovely speech.
But I must say, though you may disagree:
you have betrayed your wife. You've been unjust.
MEDEA   Now, this is where I differ from most people.
In my view, someone who is both unjust   600
and has a gift for speaking—such a man
incurs the greatest penalty. He uses
his tongue to cover up his unjust actions,
and this gives him the nerve to stop at nothing
no matter how outrageous. Yet he's not   605
all that wise. Take your case, for example.

Spare me this display of cleverness;
a single word will pin you to the mat.
If you weren't in the wrong, you would have told me
your marriage plans, not kept us in the dark—   610
your loved ones, your own family!
JASON   Yes, of course
you would have been all for it! Even now
you can't control your rage against the marriage.
MEDEA   That's not what you were thinking. You imagined
that for an older man, a barbarian wife   615
was lacking in prestige.
JASON   No! Please believe me:
It wasn't for the woman's sake I married
into the king's family. As I have said,
I wanted to save you, and give our children
royal brothers, a safeguard for our household.   620
MEDEA   May I not have a life that's blessed with fortune
so painful, or prosperity so irritating.

JASON   Your prayer could be much wiser: don't consider
what's useful painful. When you have good fortune,
don't see it as a hardship.
MEDEA   Go ahead—   625
you have somewhere to turn!—commit this outrage.
I am deserted, exiled from this land.
JASON   You brought that on yourself. Don't blame another.
MEDEA   Did I remarry? How did I betray you?
JASON   You blasphemously cursed the royal family.   630
MEDEA   And I'm a curse to your family as well.
JASON   I won't discuss this with you any further.
If you'd like me to help you and the children
with money for your exile, then just say so.
I'm prepared to give with an open hand,   635
and make arrangements with my friends to show you
hospitality. They'll treat you well.
You'd be an idiot to refuse this offer.
You'll gain a lot by giving up your anger.
MEDEA   I wouldn't stay with your friends, and I would never   640
accept a thing from you. Don't even offer.
There is no profit in a bad man's gift.
JASON   All the same, I call the gods to witness:
I only want to help you and the children.
But you don't want what's good; you push away   645
your friends; you're willful. And you'll suffer for it.
MEDEA   Get out of here. A craving for your new bride
has overcome you—you've been away so long.
Go, celebrate your wedding. It may be
(the gods will tell) a marriage you'll regret.   650
        (*Exit* JASON *to the right.*)
CHORUS

[Strophe 1]

Desire, when it comes on too forcefully, never bestows
excellence, never makes anyone prestigious.
When she comes with just the right touch, there's no goddess
    more gracious
than Cypris.
Mistress, never release from your golden bow   655
an inescapable arrow, smeared with desire
and aimed at my heart.

[Antistrophe 1]

Please, let me be cherished by Wisdom, be loved by Restraint,
loveliest gift of the gods. May dreadful Cypris
never stun my spirit with love for the bed of another   660
and bring on
anger, battles of words, endless fighting, strife.

Let her be shrewd in her judgment; let her revere
the bedroom at peace.

[Strophe 2]

O fatherland, O home, never allow   665
me to be without a city:
a grief without recourse, life that's hard to live through,
most distressing of all fates.
May I go to my death, my death
before I endure that; I'd rather face   670
my final day. There's no worse heartache
than to be cut off from your fatherland.

[Antistrophe 2]

We've seen it for ourselves; nobody else
gave me this tale to consider.
No city, no friend will treat you with compassion   675
in your dreadful suffering.
May he die, the ungracious man
who won't honor friends, who will not unlock
his mind to clear, calm thoughts of kindness.
I will never call such a man my friend.   680

(*Enter* AEGEUS *from the left.*)[2]

AEGEUS[3]   Medea, I wish all the best to you.
There is no finer way to greet a friend.
MEDEA   All the best to you, Aegeus, son
of wise Pandion. Where are you traveling from?
AEGEUS   I've come from Phoebus' ancient oracle.[4]   685
MEDEA   What brought you to the earth's prophetic navel?[5]
AEGEUS   Seeking how I might beget a child.
MEDEA   By the gods, are you still childless?
AEGEUS   Still childless. Some god must be to blame.
MEDEA   Do you have a wife, or do you sleep alone?   690
AEGEUS   I'm married, and we share a marriage bed.
MEDEA   Well, what did Phoebus say concerning children?
AEGEUS   His words were too profound for human wisdom.
MEDEA   May I hear the oracle? Is it permitted?
AEGEUS   Yes, why not? This calls for a wise mind.   695
MEDEA   Then tell me, if indeed it is permitted.
AEGEUS   He said, "Don't loose the wineskin's hanging foot . . ."[6]

---

2. This stage direction is a modern guess, though presumably the direction of Aegeus' entrance must differ from those of all previous entrances in the play—underscoring the unexpectedness of his arrival.
3. The king of Athens.
4. Delphi.
5. At Delphi was a stone that was supposedly the navel of the Earth.
6. Wine was sometimes stored in animal skins, the leg being used as a spigot for dispensing drinks. The imagery suggests both "Don't get drunk" and "Don't have sex."

MEDEA   Before you do what thing? Or reach what place?
AEGEUS   Before returning to my paternal hearth.
MEDEA   And why have you sailed here? What do you need?   700
AEGEUS   There is a man named Pittheus, lord of Troezen . . .[7]
MEDEA   Pelops' son.[8] They say he's very pious.
AEGEUS   I want to bring this prophecy to him.
MEDEA   Yes. He's wise, and well-versed in such things.
AEGEUS   And most beloved of my war companions.   705
MEDEA   Good luck to you. May you get what you desire.
AEGEUS   But you—your eyes are melting. What's the matter?
MEDEA   My husband is the very worst of men.
AEGEUS   What are you saying? Why the low spirits? Tell me.
MEDEA   Jason treats me unjustly. I've done him no harm.   710
AEGEUS   What has he done? Explain to me more clearly.
MEDEA   He has another wife, who takes my place.
AEGEUS   No. He wouldn't dare. It's much too shameful.
MEDEA   It's true. His former loved ones are dishonored.
AEGEUS   Did he desire another? Or tire of you?   715
MEDEA   Oh yes, he felt desire. We cannot trust him.
AEGEUS   Let him go, if he's as bad as you say.
MEDEA   He desired a royal marriage-bond.
AEGEUS   Who's giving away the bride? Go on, continue.
MEDEA   Creon, the ruler of this land of Corinth.   720
AEGEUS   Woman, your pain is understandable.
MEDEA   I am destroyed. And that's not all—I'm exiled.
AEGEUS   By whom? This is new trouble on top of trouble.
MEDEA   By Creon. He is driving me from Corinth.
AEGEUS   And Jason is allowing it? Shame on him.   725
MEDEA   He claims to be against it, but he'll manage
to endure it somehow.

(MEDEA *again assumes the supplicant position.*)

                    Listen, I entreat you;
by your beard and by your knees, I beg you:
Have pity on me; pity my misfortune.
Don't let me go deserted into exile;   730
receive me in your home and at your hearth.
If you do it, may the gods grant your desire
for children; may you die a prosperous man.
You don't know what a windfall you have found!
I'll cure your childlessness, make you a father.   735
I know the drugs required for such things.
AEGEUS   For many reasons, woman, I am eager
to grant this favor to you: first, the gods;
and secondly, the children that you promise.
I'm at a total loss where that's concerned.   740

7. Pittheus will give his daughter Aethra to Aegeus, after getting him drunk; the Athenian hero Theseus will be conceived in this way.
8. Pelops, son of Tantalus, was served up as food to the gods by his father. The gods restored him to life, and he became the founder of the Peloponnese.

But this is how it is. When you arrive,
I'll treat you justly, try to shelter you.
However, you must know this in advance:
I'm not willing to escort you from this land.
If you can come to my house on your own,   745
I'll let you stay there—it will be your refuge.
I will not give you up to anyone.
But you must leave this land all by yourself.
My hosts here must have no complaint with me.

MEDEA   So be it. But if I had some assurance   750
that I could trust you, I'd have all I need.

AEGEUS   You don't believe me? Tell me, what's the problem?

MEDEA   Oh, I believe you. But I have enemies:
Creon, and the house of Pelias.
If they come for me, and you're not bound   755
by any oath, then you might let them take me.
A promise in words only, never sworn
by any gods, might not be strong enough
to keep you from befriending them, from yielding
to their delegations. I'm completely helpless;   760
they have prosperity and royal power.

AEGEUS   Your words show forethought. If you think it's best,
I'll do it without any hesitation.
In fact, this is the safest course for me:
I'll have a good excuse to turn away   765
your enemies. And things are settled well
for you, of course. I'll swear: just name the gods.

MEDEA   Swear by the Earth we stand on, and by Helios—
my father's father[9]—and the whole race of gods.

AEGEUS   To do or not do what? Just say the word.   770

MEDEA   Never to expel me from your land yourself,
and never, as long as you live, to give me up
willingly to any enemy.

AEGEUS   I swear by Earth, by Helios' sacred light,
by all the gods: I'll do just as you say.   775

MEDEA   Fine. And if you don't? What would you suffer?

AEGEUS   Whatever an unholy man deserves.

          (MEDEA rises.)

MEDEA   Fare well, then, on your voyage. This is good.
I'll find you in your city very soon,
once I've done my will, and had my way.   780

          (Exit AEGEUS to the left. The CHORUS address him as he leaves.)

CHORUS   May lord Hermes, the child of Maia,[1] escort you
and bring you back home. May you do as you please,
and have all you want. In my judgment, Aegeus,
you're a good, noble man.

9. Helios, the Sun, is father of Aeetes, king of
Colchis, Medea's father.

1. Hermes, the messenger god, was the child
of Zeus by the nymph Maia.

MEDEA O Zeus, and Zeus's Justice, and the light   785
of Helios, I now shall be the victor
over my enemies. My friends, I've set my foot
upon the path. My enemies will pay
what justice demands—I now have hope of this.
This man, when I was at my lowest point,   790
appeared, the perfect harbor for my plans.
When I reach Pallas' city,[2] I shall have
a steady place to tie my ship. And now
I'll tell you what my plans are. Hear my words;
they will not bring you pleasure. I will send   795
a servant to bring Jason here to see me.
When he comes, I'll soothe him with my words:
I'll say that I agree with him, that he
was right to marry into the royal family,
betraying me—well done, and well thought out!   800
"But let my children stay here!" I will plead—
not that I would leave them in this land
for my enemies to outrage—my own children.
No: this is my deceit, to kill the princess.
I'll send them to her, bearing gifts in hand   805
—a delicate robe, and a garland worked in gold.
If she takes these fine things and puts them on,
she, and anyone who touches her,
will die a painful death. Such are the drugs
with which I will smear them.
                          But enough of that.   810
Once that's done, the next thing I must do
chokes me with sorrow. I will kill the children—
my children. No one on this earth can save them.
I'll ruin Jason's household, then I'll leave
this land, I'll flee the slaughter of the children   815
I love so dearly. I will have the nerve
for this unholy deed. You see, my friends,
I will not let my enemies laugh at me.

Let it go. What do I gain by being alive?
I have no fatherland, no home, no place   820
to turn from troubles. The moment I went wrong
was when I left my father's house, persuaded
by the words of that Greek man. If the gods will help me,
he'll pay what justice demands. He'll never see
them alive again, the children that I bore him.   825
Nor will he ever father another child:
his new bride, evil woman, she must die
an evil death, extinguished by my drugs.
Let no one think that I'm a simpleton,

2. Athens, city of Athena (Pallas).

or weak, or idle—I am the opposite. 830
I treat my friends with kindness, and come down hard
on the heads of my enemies. This is the way to live,
the way to win a glorious reputation.
CHORUS   Since you have brought this plan to us, and since
I want to help you, and since I support 835
the laws of mankind, I ask you not to do this.
MEDEA   There is no other way. It's understandable
that you would say this—you're not the one who's suffered.
CHORUS   Will you have the nerve to kill your children?
MEDEA   Yes: to wound my husband the most deeply. 840
CHORUS   And to make yourself the most miserable of women.
MEDEA   Let it go. Let there be no more words
until it's done.

          (*To her attendant.*)

               You: go now, and bring Jason.
When I need to trust someone, I turn to you.
If you're a woman and mean well to your mistress, 845
do not speak of the things I have resolved.

          (*Exit the attendant to the right.*)

CHORUS

[Strophe 1]

The children of Erechtheus[3] have always prospered,
descended from blessèd gods.
They graze, in their sacred stronghold, on glorious
     wisdom,
with a delicate step through the clear and brilliant air. 850
They say that there
the nine Pierian Muses[4] once gave birth
to Harmony with golden hair.

[Antistrophe 1]

They sing that Cypris dipped her pitcher in the waters
of beautiful Cephisus;[5] 855
she sighed, and her breaths were fragrant
     and temperate breezes.
With a garland of sweet-smelling roses in her hair
she sends Desires
to take their places alongside Wisdom's throne
and nurture excellence with her. 860

---

3. Athenians. Erechtheus was a legendary king of Athens.
4. The Muses are the daughters of Zeus and Mnemosyne (Memory). They inspire poetic and musical creation, and their birthplace is Pieria.
5. River in Athens.

[Strophe 2]

How can this city
of holy rivers,
receiver of friends and loved ones,
receive you—when you've murdered your own children,
most unholy woman—among them?   865
Just think of this deathblow aimed at the helpless,
think of the slaughter you'll have on your hands.
Oh no, by your knees, we beg you,
we beg you, with every plea
we can plead: do not kill your children.   870

[Antistrophe 2]

Where will you find it,
the awful courage?
The terrible nerve—how can you?
How can your hand, your heart, your mind go through with
this slaughter? How will you be able   875
to look at your children, keep your eyes steady,
see them beseech you, and not fall apart?
Your tears will not let you kill them;
your spirit, your nerve will fail:
you will not soak your hands in their blood.   880

(*Enter* JASON *from the right.*)

JASON   I've come because you summoned me. Despite
the hate between us, I will hear you out.
What is it this time, woman? What do you want?
MEDEA   Jason, I beg you, please forgive the things
I said. Your heart should be prepared, receptive   885
like a seed bed. We used to love each other.
It's only right for you to excuse my anger.
I've thought it over, and I blame myself.
Pathetic! Really, I must have been insane
to stand opposed to those who plan so well,   890
to be an enemy to those in power
and to my husband, who's done so well by me:
marrying the royal princess, to beget
brothers for my children. Isn't it time
to drop my angry spirit, since the gods   895
have been so bountiful? What's wrong with me?
Don't I have children? Aren't we exiles? Don't we
need whatever friendship we can get?
That's what I said to myself. I realize
that I've been foolish, that there is no point   900
to all my fuming rage. I give you credit
for wise restraint, for making this connection,
this marriage that's in all our interests. Now
I understand that you deserve my praise.

I was such a moron. I should have supported 905
your plans, I should have made arrangements with you,
I should have stood beside the bridal bed,
rejoiced in taking care of your new bride.

We women—oh, I won't say that we're bad,
but we are what we are. You shouldn't sink 910
down to our level, trading childish insults.
I ask for your indulgence. I admit
I wasn't thinking straight, but now my plans
are much improved where these things are concerned.

(MEDEA *turns toward the house to call the children.*)

Oh, children! Come out of the house, come here, 915
come out and greet your father, speak to him.
Come set aside, together with your mother,
the hatred that we felt toward one we love.

(*The* CHILDREN *come out from the house, escorted
by the* TUTOR *and attendants.*)

We've made a treaty. My rage has gone away.
Take his right hand.
                          Oh, god, my mind is filled 920
with bad things, hidden things. Oh, children, look—
your lovely arms, the way you stretch them out.
Will you look this way your whole long lives?
I think I'm going to cry. I'm filled with fear.
After all this time, I'm making up 925
my quarrel with your father. This tender sight
is washed with tears; my eyes are overflowing.
CHORUS   In my eyes too fresh tears are welling up.
     May this evil not go any further.
JASON   Woman, I approve your new approach— 930
     not that I blame you for the way you felt.
     It's only right for a female to get angry
     if her husband smuggles in another wife.
     But this new change of heart is for the best.
     After all this time, you've recognized 935
     the winning plan. You're showing wise restraint.
     And as for you, my children, you will see
     your father is no fool. I have provided
     for your security, if the gods will help me.
     Yes, I believe that you will be the leaders 940
     here in Corinth, with your future brothers.
     Grow up strong and healthy. All the rest
     your father, with the favor of the gods,
     will take care of. I pray that I may see you
     grown up and thriving, holding sway above 945
     my enemies.

(JASON *turns to* MEDEA.)

> You! Why have you turned
your face away, so pale? Why are fresh tears
pouring from your eyes? Why aren't you happy
to hear what I have had to say?

MEDEA It's nothing.
I was only thinking of the children. 950

JASON Don't worry now. I'll take good care of them.

MEDEA I'll do as you ask. I'll trust in what you say.
I'm female, that's all. Tears are in my nature.

JASON So—why go on? Why moan over the children?

MEDEA They're mine. And when you prayed that they would live, 955
pity crept over me. I wondered: would they?
As for the things you came here to discuss,
we've covered one. I'll move on to the next.
Since the royal family has seen fit
to exile me (and yes, I realize 960
it's for the best—I wouldn't want to stay
to inconvenience you, or this land's rulers,
who see me as an enemy of the family),
I will leave this land, go into exile,
but you must raise your children with your own hand: 965
ask Creon that they be exempt from exile.

JASON Though I may not persuade him, I must try.

MEDEA And ask your wife to ask her father: please
let the children be exempt from exile.

JASON Certainly. I think I will persuade her. 970

MEDEA No doubt, if she's a woman like all others.
And for this work, I'll lend you my support.
I'll send her gifts, much lovelier, I know,
than any living person has laid eyes on:
a delicate robe, and a garland worked in gold. 975
The children will bear them. Now, this very minute,
let one of the servants bring these fine things here.

(An attendant goes into the house to carry out this request.
She, or another servant, returns with the finery.)

She will be blessed a thousandfold with fortune:
with you, an excellent man to share her bed,
and these possessions, these fine things that once 980
my father's father, Helios, passed down
to his descendants. Take these wedding gifts
in your arms, my children; go and give them
to the lucky bride, the royal princess.
These are gifts that no one could find fault with. 985

(The attendant puts the gifts in the children's arms.)

JASON You fool! Why let these things out of your hands?
Do you think the royal household needs more robes,
more gold? Hold onto these. Don't give them up.

If my wife thinks anything of me,
I'm sure that I mean more to her than wealth.   990
MEDEA Don't say that. Even the gods can be persuaded
by gifts. And gold is worth a thousand words.
She has the magic charm; the gods are helping
her right now: she's young, and she has power.
To save my children from exile, I'd give my life,   995
not merely gold. You, children, when you've entered
that wealthy house, must supplicate your father's
young wife, my mistress. You must plead with her
and ask her that you be exempt from exile.
Give her these fine things. That is essential: 1000
she must receive these gifts with her own hands.
Go quickly now, and bring back to your mother
the good news she desires—that you've succeeded.

    (*The children, bearing the gifts, leave with the* TUTOR *to the right.*)

CHORUS

[Strophe 1]

Now I no longer have hope that the children will live,
no longer. They walk to the slaughter already.   1005
The bride will receive the crown of gold;
she'll receive her horrible ruin.
Upon her golden hair, with her very own hands,
she'll place the fine circlet of Hades.[6]

[Antistrophe 1]

She'll be persuaded; the grace and the heavenly gleam   1010
will move her to try on the robe and the garland.
The bride will adorn herself for death,
for the shades below. She will fall
into this net; her death will be horrible. Ruin
will be inescapable, fated.   1015

[Strophe 2]

And you, poor thing, bitter bridegroom, in-law to
    royalty:
you don't know you're killing your children,
bringing hateful death to your bride.
How horrible: how unaware you are of your fate.

[Antistrophe 2]

I cry for your pain in turn, poor thing; you're a   1020
    mother, yet
you will slaughter them, your own children,

---

6. Death.

for the sake of your bridal bed,
the bed that your husband now shares with somebody else.

(*The* TUTOR *returns, at the right, from the palace with the children.*)

TUTOR   Mistress, your children are released from exile.
The princess happily received the gifts   1025
with her own hands. As far as she's concerned,
the children's case is settled; they're at peace.

Ah!
Why are you upset by your good fortune?
MEDEA   Oh, god.
TUTOR   Your cry is out of tune. This is good news!
MEDEA   Oh god, oh god.
TUTOR   Have I made some mistake?   1030
Is what I've said bad news, and I don't know it?
MEDEA   You've said what you have said. I don't blame you.
TUTOR   So—why are you crying? Why are your eyes cast down?
MEDEA   Old man, I am compelled. The gods and I
devised this strategy. What was I thinking?   1035
TUTOR   Don't worry now. Your children will bring you home.
MEDEA   I'll send others home before that day.
TUTOR   You're not the only woman who's lost her children.
We're mortals. We must bear disasters lightly.
MEDEA   I'll do as you ask. Now, go inside the house   1040
and see to the children's needs, as usual.

(*Exit* TUTOR *into the house.*)

Oh, children, children, you two have a city
and home, in which you'll live forever parted
from your mother. You'll leave poor me behind.
I'll travel to another land, an exile,   1045
before I ever have the joy of seeing
you blessed with fortune—before your wedding days,
before I prepare your beds and hold the torches.[7]
My willfulness has cost me all this grief.
I raised you, children, but it was no use;   1050
no use, the way I toiled, how much it hurt,
the pain of childbirth, piercing like a thorn.
And I had so much hope when you were born:
you'd tend to my old age, and when I died,
you'd wrap me in my shroud with your own hands: 1055
an admirable fate for anyone.
That sweet thought has now been crushed. I'll be parted
from both of you, and I will spend my years
in sorrow and in pain. Your eyes no longer
will look upon your mother. You'll move on   1060

7. Torches were an important feature of ancient weddings, which took place at night.

to a different life.
                    Oh god, your eyes, the way
you look at me. Why do you smile, my children,
your very last smile? Aah, what will I do?
The heart goes out of me, women, when I look
at my children's shining eyes. I couldn't do this.   1065
Farewell to the plans I had before.
I'll take my children with me when I leave.
Why should I, just to cause their father pain,
feel twice the pain myself by harming them?
I will not do it. Farewell to my plans.   1070
But wait—what's wrong with me? What do I want?
To allow my enemies to laugh at me?
To let them go unpunished?
                    What I need
is the nerve to do it. I was such a weakling,
to let a soothing word enter my mind.   1075
Children, go inside the house.

> (*The children start to go toward the house, but, as* MEDEA
> *continues to speak, they continue to watch and listen
> to her, delaying their entry inside.*)
                    Whoever
is not permitted to attend these rites,
my sacrifice, let that be his concern.
I won't hold back the force that's in my hand.

Aah!
Oh no, my spirit, please, not that! Don't do it.   1080
Spare the children. Leave them alone, poor thing.
They'll live with me there. They will bring you joy.

By the avenging ones[8] who live below
in Hades, no, I will not leave my children
at the mercy of my enemies' outrage.   1085
Anyway, the thing's already done.
She won't escape. The crown is on her head.
The royal bride's destroyed, wrapped in her robes.
I know it. Now, since I am setting foot
on a path that will break my heart, and sending them   1090
on one more heartbreaking still, I want to speak
to my children.

> (MEDEA *reaches toward her children; they come back to her.*)
                    Children, give me your right hands,
give them to your mother, let me kiss them.
Oh, how I love these hands, how I love these mouths,
the way the children stand, their noble faces!   1095

8. The Furies.

May fortune bless you—in the other place.
Your father's taken all that once was here.
Oh, your sweet embrace, your tender skin,
your lovely breath, oh children.
                                        Go now—go.

(*The children go inside.*)

I cannot look at them. Grief overwhelms me.   1100
I know that I am working up my nerve
for overwhelming evil, yet my spirit
is stronger than my mind's deliberations:
this is the source of mortals' deepest grief.
CHORUS   Quite often I've found myself venturing deeper   1105
    than women do normally into discussions
    and subtle distinctions, and I would suggest
    that we have our own Muse, who schools us in wisdom—
    not every woman, but there are a few,
    you'll find one among many, a woman who doesn't   1110
    stand entirely apart from the Muses.

    Here's my opinion: the childless among us,
    the ones who have never experienced parenthood,
    have greater good fortune than those who have children.
    They don't know—how could they?—if children   1115
        are pleasant
    or hard and distressing. Their lack of experience
    saves them from heartache.
    But those who have children, a household's sweet
        offshoot—
    I see them consumed their whole lives with concern.
    They fret from the start: are they raising them well?   1120
    And then: will they manage to leave them enough?
    Then finally: all of this toil and heartache,
    is it for children who'll turn out to be
    worthless or decent? That much is unclear.

    There's one final grief that I'll mention. Supposing   1125
    your children have grown up with plenty to live on,
    they're healthy, they're decent—if fortune decrees it,
    Death comes and spirits their bodies away
    down to the Underworld. What is the point, then,
    if the gods, adding on to the pains that we mortals   1130
    endure for the sake of our children, send death,
    most distressing of all? Tell me, where does that leave us?
MEDEA   My friends, I have been waiting for some time,
    keeping watch to see where this will lead.
    Look now: here comes one of Jason's men   1135
    breathing hard—he seems to be about
    to tell us of some new and dreadful act.

(*Enter the* MESSENGER *from the right.*)

MESSENGER   Medea, run away! Take any ship
   or wagon that will carry you. Leave now!
MEDEA   Why should I flee? What makes it necessary?   1140
MESSENGER   The royal princess and her father Creon
   have just now died—the victims of your poison.
MEDEA   This news is excellent. From this day forth
   I'll count you as a friend and benefactor.
MESSENGER   What are you saying? Are you sane at all,   1145
   or raving? You've attacked the royal hearth—
   how can you rejoice, and not be frightened?
MEDEA   I could tell my own side to this story.
   But calm down, friend, and please describe to me
   how they were destroyed. If you can say   1150
   that they died horribly, I'll feel twice the pleasure.
MESSENGER   When we saw that your two boys had come
   together with their father to the bride's house,
   all of us—we servants who have felt
   the pain of your misfortunes—were delighted;   1155
   the talk was that you'd settled your differences,
   you and your husband. We embraced the boys,
   kissing their hands, their golden hair. And I,
   overjoyed as I was, accompanied
   the children to the women's quarters. She—   1160
   the mistress we now honor in your place—
   before she caught sight of your pair of boys
   was gazing eagerly at Jason. Then
   she saw the children, and she covered up
   her eyes, as if the sight disgusted her,   1165
   and turned her pale cheek aside. Your husband
   tried to cool down the girl's bad temper,
   saying, "Don't be hateful toward your loved ones!
   Please, calm your spirit, turn your head this way,
   and love those whom your husband loves. Receive   1170
   these gifts, and ask your father, for my sake,
   not to send these children into exile."
   Well, when she saw the fine things, she gave in
   to everything the man said. They had barely
   set foot outside the door—your children and   1175
   their father—when she took the intricate
   embroidered robe and wrapped it round her body,
   and set the golden crown upon her curls,
   and smiled at her bright image—her lifeless double—
   in a mirror, as she arranged her hair.   1180
   She rose, and with a delicate step her lovely
   white feet traversed the quarters. She rejoiced
   beyond all measure in the gifts. Quite often
   she extended her ankle, admiring the effect.

   What happened next was terrible to see.   1185
   Her skin changed color, and her legs were shaking;

she reeled sideways, and she would have fallen
straight to the ground if she hadn't collapsed in
    her chair.
Then one of her servants, an old woman,
thinking that the girl must be possessed   1190
by Pan[9] or by some other god, cried out—
a shriek of awe and reverence—but when
she saw the white foam at her mouth, her eyes
popping out, the blood drained from her face,
she changed her cry to one of bitter mourning.   1195
A maid ran off to get the princess' father;
another went to tell the bride's new husband
of her disaster. Everywhere the sound
of running footsteps echoed through the house.
And then, in less time than it takes a sprinter   1200
to cover one leg of a stadium race,
the girl, whose eyes had been shut tight, awoke,
poor thing, and she let out a terrible groan,
for she was being assaulted on two fronts:
the golden garland resting on her head   1205
sent forth a marvelous stream of all-consuming
fire, and the delicate robe, the gift
your children brought, was starting to corrode
the white flesh of that most unfortunate girl.
She jumped up, with flames all over her,   1210
shaking her hair, tossing her head around,
trying to throw the crown off. But the gold
gripped tight, and every movement of her hair
caused the fire to blaze out twice as much.
Defeated by disaster, she fell down   1215
onto the ground, unrecognizable
to anyone but a father. She had lost
the look her eyes had once had, and her face
had lost its beauty. Blood was dripping down,
mixed with fire, from the top of her head   1220
and from her bones the flesh was peeling back
like resin, shorn by unseen jaws of poison,
terrible to see. We all were frightened
to touch the corpse. We'd seen what had just
    happened.
But her poor father took us by surprise: 1225
he ran into the room and threw himself—
not knowing any better—on her corpse.
He moaned, and wrapped her in his arms,
    and kissed her,
crying, "Oh, my poor unhappy child,
what god dishonors you? What god destroys you?   1230

9. Woodland or countryside god, usually represented with goat legs, associated with violent divine possession and fear ("panic").

Who has taken you away from me,
an old man who has one foot in the grave?
Let me die with you, child." When he was done
with his lament, he tried to straighten up
his aged body, but the delicate robe   1235
clung to him as ivy clings to laurel,
and then a terrible wrestling match began.
He tried to flex his knee; she pulled him back.
If he used force, he tore the aged flesh
off of his bones. He finally gave up,   1240
unlucky man; his soul slipped away
when he could fight no longer. There they lie,
two corpses, a daughter and her aged father,
side by side, a disaster that longs for tears.

About your situation, I am silent.   1245
You realize what penalty awaits you.
About our mortal lives, I feel the way
I've often felt before: we are mere shadows.
I wouldn't hesitate to say that those
who seem so wise, who deal in subtleties—   1250
they earn the prize for being the greatest fools.
For really, there is no man blessed with fortune.
One man might be luckier, more prosperous
than someone else, but no man's ever blessed.

(*Exit the* MESSENGER *to the right.*)

CHORUS   On this day fortune has bestowed on Jason   1255
much grief, it seems, as justice has demanded.
Poor thing, we pity you for this disaster,
daughter of Creon, you who have descended
to Hades' halls because of your marriage to Jason.
MEDEA   My friends, it is decided: as soon as possible   1260
I must kill my children and leave this land
before I give my enemies a chance
to slaughter them with a hand that's moved by
    hatred.
They must die anyway, and since they must,
I will kill them. I'm the one who bore them.   1265
Arm yourself, my heart. Why am I waiting
to do this terrible, necessary crime?
Unhappy hand, act now. Take up the sword,
just take it; approach the starting post of pain
to last a lifetime; do not weaken, don't   1270
remember that you love your children dearly,
that you gave them life. For one short day
forget your children. Afterward, you'll grieve.
For even if you kill them, they were yours;
you loved them. I'm a woman cursed by fortune.   1275

(MEDEA *enters the house.*)

CHORUS

[Strophe 1]

O Earth, O radiant beam
of Helios, look down and see her—
this woman, destroyer, before she can lay
her hand stained with blood,
her kin-killing hand   1280
upon her own children
descended from you
the gods' golden race;
for such blood to spill
at the hands of a mortal   1285
fills us with fear.
Light born from Zeus,
stop her, remove
this bloodstained Erinys;[1]
take her away   1290
from this house cursed with vengeance.

[Antistrophe 1]

Your toil has all been in vain,
in vain, all the heartache of raising
your children, your dearest, O sorrowful one
who once left behind   1295
the dark Clashing Rocks
most hostile to strangers.
What burden of rage
descended upon
your mind? Why does wild   1300
slaughter follow on slaughter?
Blood-spatter, stain,
slaughter of kin,
murder within
the family brings grief   1305
tuned to the crime
from the gods to the household.

CHILD   (*From within the house.*)
     Oh no!

CHORUS

[Strophe 2]

Do you hear the shouts, the shouts of her children?
Poor woman: she's cursed, undone by her fortune.   1310
CHILD 1   Oh, how can I escape my mother's hand?
CHILD 2   Dear brother, I don't know. We are destroyed.

1. Fury.

CHORUS   Shall I go inside?
  I ought to prevent this,
  the slaughter of children.
CHILD 1 Yes, come and stop her! That is what we need.   1315
CHILD 2 We're trapped; we're caught! The sword is at our throats.
CHORUS   Poor thing: after all
  you were rock, you were iron:
  to reap with your own hand
  the crop that you bore;   1320
  to cut down your kin
  with a fate-dealing hand.

[Antistrophe 2]

I've heard of just one, just one other woman
who dared to attack, to hurt her own children:

Ino, whom the gods once drove insane   1325
and Zeus's wife sent wandering from her home.[2]

The poor woman leapt
to sea with her children:
an unholy slaughter.

She stepped down from a steep crag's rocky edge   1330
and died with her two children in the waves.
What terrible deed
could surpass such an outrage?
O bed of their marriage,
O woman's desire: 1335
such harm have you done,
so much pain have you caused.
  (Enter JASON from the right.)
JASON   Women, you who stand here near the house—
  is she at home, Medea, the perpetrator
  of all these terrors, or has she gone away?   1340
  Oh yes, she'll have to hide beneath the earth
  or lift her body into the sky with wings
  to escape the royal family's cry for justice.
  Does she think she can murder this land's rulers
  then simply flee this house, with no requital?   1345
  I'm worried about the children more than her—
  the ones she's hurt will pay her back in kind.
  I've come to save my children, save their lives.
  The family might retaliate, might strike
  the children for their mother's unholy slaughter.   1350

2. Ino, a daughter of Cadmus, king of Thebes, was driven mad by Dionysos to participate—along with Cadmus's mother—in the dismemberment of her nephew, Pentheus. Later, she was married to King Athamas and, driven mad by Hera, she leapt into the sea with one or more of their sons.

CHORUS Poor man. Jason, if you realized
  how bad it was, you wouldn't have said that.
JASON What is it? Does she want to kill *me* now?
CHORUS Your children are dead, killed by their mother's hand.
JASON What are you saying, women? You have destroyed me.   1355
CHORUS Please understand: your children no longer exist.
JASON Where did she kill them? Inside the house, or outside?
CHORUS Open the gates; you'll see your children's slaughter.
JASON Servants, quick, open the door, unbar it;
  undo the bolts, and let me see this double   1360
  evil: their dead bodies, and the one
  whom I will bring to justice.

> (MEDEA *appears above the roof in a flying chariot,
> with the bodies of the children.*)[3]

MEDEA   Why are you trying
  to pry those gates? Is it their corpses you seek,
  and me, the perpetrator? Stop your struggle.
  If you need something, ask me. Speak your mind.   1365
  But you will never touch us with your hand.
  My father's father, Helios, gives me safety
  from hostile hands. This chariot protects me.
JASON You hateful thing, O woman most detested
  by the gods, by me, by all mankind—   1370
  you dared to strike your children with a sword,
  children you bore yourself. You have destroyed me,
  left me childless. And yet you live, you look
  upon the sun and earth, you who had the nerve
  to do this most unholy deed. I wish   1375
  you would die. I have more sense now than I had
  the day I took you from your barbarian land
  and brought you to a Greek home—you're a plague,
  betrayer of your father and the land
  that raised you. But the gods have sent the vengeance   1380
  that *you* deserve to crash down on *my* head.
  You killed your brother right at home, then climbed
  aboard the *Argo* with its lovely prow.
  That's how your career began. You married
  me, and bore me children. For the sake   1385
  of passion, of your bed, you have destroyed them.
  No Greek woman would have had the nerve
  to do this, but I married you instead:
  a hateful bond. You ruined me. You're not
  a woman; you're a lion, with a nature   1390
  more wild than Scylla's,[4] the Etruscan freak.
  I couldn't wound you with ten thousand insults;
  there's nothing you can't take. Get out of here,

---

3. The stage mechanism used in the original
production would have been the *mechane*, a
crane typically used for divine appearances in
Athenian tragedy.
4. Scylla is the sea monster who threatens
Odysseus and his men in the *Odyssey*.

you filth, you child-murderer. For me,
all that's left is tears for my misfortune.   1395
I'll never have the joy of my bride's bed,
nor will I ever again speak to my children,
my children, whom I raised. And now I've lost them.
MEDEA   I would have made a long speech in reply
to yours, if father Zeus were unaware   1400
of what I've done for you, and how you've acted.
You dishonored my bed. There was no way
you could go on to lead a pleasant life,
to laugh at me—not you, and not the princess;
nor could Creon, who arranged your marriage,   1405
exile me and walk away unpunished.
So go ahead, call me a lion, call me
a Scylla, skulking in her Etruscan cave.
I've done what I had to do. I've jabbed your heart.
JASON   You feel the pain yourself. This hurts you, too.   1410
MEDEA   The pain is good, as long as you're not laughing.
JASON   O children, you were cursed with an evil mother.
MEDEA   O sons, you were destroyed by your father's sickness.
JASON   *My* right hand is not the one that killed them.
MEDEA   Your outrage, and your newfound bride, destroyed them.   1415
JASON   The bedroom was enough to make you kill?
MEDEA   Does that pain mean so little to a woman?
JASON   Yes,
to one with wise restraint. To you, it's everything.
MEDEA   *They* exist no longer. That will sting you.
JASON   They exist. They live to avenge your crime.   1420
MEDEA   The gods know who was first to cause this pain.
JASON   Oh yes. They know your mind. They spit on it.
MEDEA   Go on and hate me. I detest your voice.
JASON   I feel the same. That makes it easy to leave you.
MEDEA   What shall I do, then? I'd like nothing better.   1425
JASON   Let me bury their bodies. Let me grieve.
MEDEA   Forget it. I will take them away myself
and bury them with this hand, in the precinct
sacred to Hera of the rocky heights.
No enemy will treat their graves with outrage.   1430
To this land of Sisyphus[5] I bequeath
a holy festival, a ritual
to expiate in times to come this most
unholy slaughter.[6] I myself will go
to live together with Pandion's son   1435
Aegeus, in Erechtheus's city.[7]

---

5. Corinth. Sisyphus was a notorious traitor, punished in the underworld for his deceitfulness by having to push a rock eternally up a hill, never managing to get it to the top without its rolling back down.
6. There really was a sacred cult to "Hera of the rocky heights" at Corinth.
7. Athens.

And you, an evil man, as you deserve,
will die an evil death, struck on the head
by a fragment of the *Argo*. You will see
how bitter was the outcome of my marriage.   1440

(*Here the meter changes from spoken dialogue to chanted anapests.*)[8]

JASON   May you be destroyed by the children's Erinys[9]
and bloodthirsty Justice!
MEDEA   What spirit, what god
listens to you, you liar, you breaker
of oaths, you deceiver of guests?
JASON   You are loathsome.
You murdered your children.
MEDEA   Get out of here, go—   1445
go bury your wife.
JASON   I'm leaving, bereft
of my sons.
MEDEA   Do you think that you're mourning them now?
Just wait till you're old.
JASON   Oh, dearest children.
MEDEA   To me, not to you.
JASON   And yet you still did this?
MEDEA   To make you feel pain.   1450
JASON   I wish I could hold them and kiss them, my children.
MEDEA   You long for them now and you want to embrace them,
but you are the one who pushed them away.
JASON   By the gods, let me touch the soft skin of my children.
MEDEA   No. What's the point? You are wasting your words.   1455

(*The chariot flies away with* MEDEA *and the bodies of the children.*)

JASON   Zeus, do you hear how I'm driven away,
do you see what I suffer at her loathsome hands,
this lion, this child-killer!
                    With all my strength
I mourn for them now and I call on the gods
and spirits to witness that you killed my children   1460
and now won't allow me to touch them or bury them.
I wish now that I'd never fathered them, only
to see them extinguished, to see what you've done.

(*Exit* JASON *to the right, accompanied by the* CHORUS.)

CHORUS   Zeus on Olympus enforces all things;
the gods can accomplish what no one would hope for.   1465
What we expect may not happen at all,
while the gods find a way, against all expectation,
to do what they want, however surprising.
And that is exactly how this case turned out.

8. This rhythm was often used for marching; it signals that the chorus and other characters will soon be leaving the theater.
9. Spirit of vengeance.

CATULLUS

ca. 84–ca. 54 B.C.E.

The poetry of Gaius Valerius Catullus conveys intense, and often conflicting, emotions. *Odi et amo*, he wrote: "I hate and love." These poems evoke the personal desires and enmities of a privileged but insecure and very young man: Catullus was only about thirty when he died. Reading Catullus, we feel in touch with raw feelings in a way that is rare in the literature of the ancient world. Catullus was also a technical master, who wrote in an impressive range of different verse patterns, and whose moods range from joy to grief, from vituperative obscenities to gentle teasing, and from self-pity to quiet nostalgia for lost and easier days. The pain, passion, lyricism, and humor in his poetry was a lasting inspiration for later love poets, both in ancient Rome and in modern times.

LIFE AND TIMES

Catullus was born in the northern Italian city of Verona, into a prominent aristocratic family (of the high social class called "equestrian"). He spent most of his life in Rome, making close friends and bitter enemies among his fellow Roman aristocrats. Perhaps he had an intense love affair (or several), which inspired the "Lesbia" poems. He does not seem to have married. Traditionally, Lesbia has been identified with Clodia Metella, an aristocratic, educated woman, whom Cicero cast as a sexual predator, a husband killer, and a drunk. But we have no contemporary evidence for the identification, and, of course, poets do not always base their love poems on real life. The name *Les-bia* is obviously designed to evoke literature as much as life: it alludes to the Greek poet **Sappho**, of Lesbos, who, like Catullus, wrote about the conflicting pains and pleasures of bittersweet love.

We know that in his late twenties, Catullus held a position in government that involved a trip to Bithynia, in Asia Minor; en route, he stopped at his brother's tomb, as he describes in a beautiful poem of quiet grief and farewell (poem 101). At some point after he returned to Rome, he died; we do not know the cause.

Catullus lived out his short life in the last century of the Roman Republic. It was a time of conflict, especially between populist and aristocratic factions in Rome. Catullus lived to see the rise of the populist general Julius Caesar, who won extensive victories in Britain and Gaul, although he died before Caesar was assassinated (44 B.C.E.). Catullus sometimes satirizes Caesar, and flaunts his lack of interest in Caesar's activities: "I've no great urge to find favor with you, Caesar," he declares (poem 93). Catullus can be read as a deliberately antipolitical writer, who forms a novel and personal interpretation of conventional Roman public virtues. Masculinity, for Catullus, is defined not by military exploits like Caesar's but by sexual prowess and emotional control; even duty (*pietas* in Latin) is redefined, applied to Catullus's love for his treacherous girlfriend. Catullus makes use of the values and norms of his society, but often turns them on their head.

POEMS

One hundred sixteen poems of Catullus survive, collected in a little book or pamphlet (*libellus*). We do not know whether the arrangement as we have it represents Catullus's own authorial wishes. The poems are arranged by meter, not by subject, so that, for instance, the Lesbia poems do not all appear together. They are richly varied, including imitations of Greek poets, long poems on Greek mythological themes, personal and often obscene attacks on contemporaries ("Up yours and sucks!" one begins), lyrical celebrations of places and seasons, comic verse, and original love poems—some addressed to a woman named Lesbia, and a few to other love objects, such as the boy Juventius ("Youth").

The Lesbia poems are the most famous of Catullus's work. These poems present all the phases of a love affair, and their tone ranges from joy to torment to the depths of self-pity and back. Their direct and simple language seems to give readers immediate access to the experience of desire and betrayal and the feelings it arouses. Yet these are not diary entries but complex literary artefacts: it is one of the remarkable characteristics of Catullus's poetry that strong emotion and technical sophistication are not at odds with each other. Poem 51, for example, powerfully describes the physical symptoms of love in the speaker; but it is also a translation into Latin of one of Sappho's most passionate Greek lyrics, which achieves the feat of also imitating Sappho's rhythms in Latin.

Catullus is a highly self-conscious poet who achieves a dynamic dialogue with his readers. The first poem of the collection asks, What kind of reader does Catullus want for his work? And will the reader be worthy of the poet's trust? How are we to interpret what we hear? Catullus often puts his readers in a tempting but awkward position, as if they were eavesdropping on a private conversation—either between Catullus and another person, or between Catullus and himself. In poem 83, for example, when Lesbia seems to abuse Catullus in the presence of her husband, the speaker interprets this as a sign of love for himself to which the husband is obtusely oblivious. But we may also wonder whether this is a wishful interpretation. Who really is the dupe? The reader never gets access to Lesbia's feelings; instead, the poems present the speaker himself constantly struggling to understand the mixed signals in their changing relationship. The poet subjects his own persona to deep and sometimes damaging analysis: we see his defensive constructions and deconstructions of his own masculine identity, and his unresolved tensions and self-deceptions. In the brilliant poem 8, for example, a dialogue the speaker has with himself at the time of a break-up, he resolves, over and over, to "hang tough," to be a man and get over his beloved; but the reader, overhearing, is aware of how far he is from the goal.

One of the major themes that runs through much of Catullus's work is the vast distance between one era and another, one moment and the next, as well as between one person and another, or even between the same person at different times. The Lesbia poems celebrate moments of connection, which can be violently ruptured by betrayal—like the flower brutally cut down in its prime by a plough that never notices its existence (poem 11). Even in the best of times, the joys of connectedness can be fragile, and may depend on delicate threads—a mortal sparrow, a finite number of kisses: the beautiful celebration of arrival and homecoming, poem 31, emphasizes that this place of relaxation and joy is a "near-island," almost cut off from the mainland. Spring, in the lovely poem 46, is a time of "lush green meadows," but also a time for friends to say goodbye. The longest poem included here, poem 64, is a celebration of the marriage of Thetis and Peleus, the parents of Achilles. On one level, the subject allows Catullus to challenge the writers of epic, to reinterpret the themes of the *Iliad* from an original angle: it is an "epyllion," a mini-epic. On another, the poem is a joyful and sometimes funny celebration of a magical wedding at sea. But this poem also has surprisingly dark elements: the story embroidered on the comforter to be used on the marriage bed depicts a scene of betrayal, of the Greek hero Theseus abandoning his bride, Ariadne, and leaving her crying alone on the island of Naxos. At a time when Rome was expanding into an enormous empire, but when internal factions threatened to destroy the city's stability, the poems of Catullus express a deep awareness of how quickly, and with what devastating consequences, everything can change.

Poems[1]

1

Who's the dedicatee of my new witty
booklet, all fresh-polished with abrasive?[2]
You, Cornelius: for you always used to
feel my trivia possessed some substance,
even when you dared—the lone Italian!—   5
that great three-decker treatment of past ages:[3]
scholarly stuff, my god, and *so* exhaustive!
So take this little booklet, this mere trifle,
whatever it may be worth—and Patron Virgin,[4]
let it outlast at least *one* generation!   10

2

Sparrow, precious darling of my sweetheart,
always her plaything, held fast in her bosom,

1. Translated by Peter Green. Note that the translator has tried to reproduce the meters of the Latin, such as Catullus's most characteristic meter, the hendecasyllable (an eleven-syllable line).
2. This "booklet" of poems would have been a papyrus scroll, its ends rubbed smooth with pumice stone.
3. Cornelius Nepos, a Roman biographical writer and a friend of Catullus, apparently wrote a three-volume history of the world, from the beginning of time to the present, called the *Chronica* ("Times"). He was the "lone Italian" to have done so, because up to that point Romans had only written more limited histories of particular periods.
4. The Muse.

whom she loves to provoke with outstretched finger
tempting the little pecker⁵ to nip harder
when *my* incandescent longing fancies   5
just a smidgin of fun and games and comfort
for the pain she's feeling (I believe it!),
something to lighten that too-heavy ardor—
how I wish I could sport with you as she does,
bring some relief to the spirit's black depression!   10

3

Mourn, Cupids all, every Venus,⁶ and whatever
company still exists of caring people:
Sparrow lies dead, my own true sweetheart's sparrow,
Sparrow, the pet and darling of my sweetheart,
loved by her more than she valued her own eyesight.   5
Sweet as honey he was, and knew his mistress
no less closely than a child her mother;
nor from her warm lap's safety would he ever
venture far, but hopping this and that way
came back, cheeping, always to his lady.   10
Now he's travelling on that dark-shroud journey
whence, they tell us, none of the departed
ever returns. The hell with you, you evil
blackness of Hell, devouring all that's lovely—
such a beautiful sparrow you've torn from me!   15
Oh wicked deed! Oh wretched little sparrow!
It's your fault that now my sweetheart's eyelids
are sore and swollen red from all her weeping.

5

Let's live, Lesbia⁷ mine, and love—and as for
scandal, all the gossip, old men's strictures,
value the lot at no more than a farthing!
Suns can rise and set ad infinitum—
for us, though, once our brief life's quenched, there's only   5
one unending night that's left to sleep through.
Give me a thousand kisses, then a hundred,
then a thousand more, a second hundred,
then yet another thousand then a hundred—
then when we've notched up all these many thousands,   10
shuffle the figures, lose count of the total,
so no maleficent enemy can hex us
knowing the final sum of all our kisses.

---

5. The translator's double entendre is deliberate; many scholars interpret the sparrow in
phallic terms.
6. Cupid (the Greek Eros, god of desire) and
his mother, Venus (the Greek Aphrodite, goddess of sex), usually exist only in the singular.
7. The name *Lesbia* alludes to the poet Sappho, who lived on the island of Lesbos.

7

You'd like to know how many of your kisses
would be enough and over, Lesbia, fór me?
Match them to every grain of Libyan sand in
silphium-rich[8] Cyrene, from the shrine of
torrid oracular Jupiter to the sacred   5
sepulchre of old Battus; reckon their total
equal to all those stars that in the silent
night look down on the stolen loves of mortals.
That's the number of times I need to kiss you,
That's what would satisfy your mad Catullus—   10
far too many for the curious to figure,
or for an evil tongue to work you mischief!

8

Wretched Catullus, stop this stupid tomfool stuff
and what you see has perished treat as lost for good.
Time was, every day for you the sun shone bright,
when you scurried off wherever *she* led *you*—
that girl you loved as no one shall again be loved.   5
There, when so many charming pleasures all went on,
things that *you* wanted, things *she* didn't quite turn down,
then for you truly every day the sun shone bright.
Now she's said *No*, so you too, feeble wretch, say *No*.
Don't chase reluctance, don't embrace a sad-sack life—   10
make up your mind, be stubborn, obdurate, hang tough!
So goodbye, sweetheart. Now Catullus *will* hang tough,
won't ask, "Where is she?" won't, since you've said *No*, beg, plead.
You'll soon be sorry, when you get these pleas no more—
bitch, wicked bitch, poor wretch, what life awaits *you* now?   15
Who'll now pursue you, still admire you for your looks?
Whom will you love now? Who will ever call you theirs?
Who'll get your kisses? Whose lips will you bite in play?
You, though, Catullus, keep your mind made up, *hang tough!*

11

Furius and Aurelius,[9] comrades of Catullus,
whether he'll penetrate the distant Indies[1]
where the shore's slammed by far-resounding Eastern
     thunderous breakers,

or make for Hyrcania, or the queening Arabs,   5
or the Sacae, or the Parthians with their quivers,

8. Silphium is an extinct plant known as giant fennel, which was used for cooking and medicine.
9. Marcus Furius Bibaculus was a poet, and Marcus Aurelius Cotta Maximus Messalinus was a politician; they seem to have been per-sonal enemies of Catullus, so "comrades" is ironic. They have apparently tried to tag along with Catullus on his travels, in the hope of personal profit by association with Caesar.
1. India. The poem goes on to list the most distant parts of the Roman Empire at the time.

or that flat delta to which the seven-channelled
    Nile gives its color,

or toil across high-towering Alpine passes
to visit the monuments of mighty Caesar,[2]
the Gaulish Rhine, those rude back-of-beyonders
    the woad-dyed Britons—

All this, or whatever the high gods in heaven
may bring, you're both ready to face together;
just find my girl, deliver her this short and
    blunt little message:

Long may she live and flourish with her gallants,
embracing all three hundred in one session,
loving none truly, yet cracking each one's loins
    over and over.

Let her no more, as once, look for my passion,
which through her fault lies fallen like some flower
at the field's edge, after the passing ploughshare's
    cut a path through it.

16

Up yours both, and sucks to the pair of you,[3]
Queen Aurelius, Furius the faggot,[4]
who dared judge *me* on the basis of my verses—
they mayn't be manly: does that make *me* indecent?
Squeaky-clean, that's what every proper poet's
person should be, but not his bloody squiblets,
which, in the last resort, lack salt and flavor
if *not* "unmanly" and rather less than decent,
just the ticket to work a furious itch up,
I won't say in boys, but in those hirsute
clods incapable of wiggling their hard haunches.
Just because you've read about my countless
thousand kisses, you think I'm less than virile?
Up yours both, and sucks to the pair of you!

51[5]

In my eyes he seems like a god's co-equal,
he, if I dare say so, eclipses godhead,

2. Julius Caesar, who campaigned in Gaul and Britain.
3. This is, if anything, a fairly restrained translation. The Latin literally means, "I will fuck your asses and fuck your faces."
4. The politician and poet who were addressed in poem 11.
5. This poem is a translation or adaptation of Sappho's poem 31. The last stanza corresponds to nothing in the original.

who now face to face, uninterrupted,
    watches and hears you

sweetly laughing—*that* sunders unhappy me from   5
all my senses: the instant I catch sight of
you now, Lesbia, dumbness grips my voice, it
    dies on my vocal

cords, my tongue goes torpid, and through my body
thin fire lances down, my ears are ringing   10
with their own thunder, while night curtains both my
    eyes into darkness.

Leisure, Catullus, is dangerous to you: leisure
urges you into extravagant behavior:
leisure in time gone by has ruined kings and   15
    prosperous cities.

70

My woman declares there's no one she'd sooner marry
    than me, not even were Jove himself to propose.
She declares—but a woman's words to her eager lover
    should be written on running water, on the wind.

72

You told me once, Lesbia, that Catullus alone understood you,
    That you wouldn't choose to clasp Jupiter rather than me.
I loved you then, not just as the common herd their women,
    but as a father loves his sons and sons-in-law.
Now, though, I *know* you. So yes, though I burn more fiercely,   5
    yet for me you're far cheaper, lighter. "How,"
you ask, "can that be?" It's because such injury forces
    a lover to love more, but to cherish less.

75

My mind has been brought so low by your conduct, Lesbia,
    and so undone itself through its own goodwill
that now if you were perfect it couldn't like you,
    nor cease to love you now, whatever you did.

83

Lesbia keeps insulting me in her husband's presence:
    this fills the fatuous idiot with delight.
Mule, you've no insight. If she shut up and ignored me
    that'd show healthy indifference; all these insults mean
is, she not only remembers, but—words of sharper import—   5
    feels angry. That is, the lady burns—and talks.

85

I hate and love. You wonder, perhaps, why I'd do that?
    I have no idea. I just feel it. I am crucified.

92

Lesbia's always bad-mouthing me, never stops talking of me.
    That means Lesbia loves me, or I'll be damned.
What proves it? I'm just the same still—praying nonstop
    to lose her. But *I* love *her* still. Or I'll be damned.

93

I've no great urge to find favor with you, Caesar, nor to
    discover whether, as man, you're black or white.

101

A journey across many seas and through many nations
    has brought me here, brother, for these poor obsequies,
to let me address, all in vain, your silent ashes,
    and render you the last service for the dead,
since fortune, alas, has bereft me of your person,   5
    my poor brother, so unjustly taken from me.
Still, here now I offer those gifts which by ancestral custom
    are presented, sad offerings, at such obsequies:
accept them, soaked as they are with a brother's weeping,
    and, brother, forever now hail and farewell.   10

107

If anything ever came through for one who so longingly
    yearned for it, yet without hope—that's balm for the soul.
So, there's balm for us too, than gold more precious,
    Lesbia, in this: that you've brought yourself back to me
and my yearning for you: yes, back to my hopeless yearning,   5
    to me, by your own choice. O brighter than white
day! Who lives happier than I do? Who can argue
    that life holds any more desirable bliss?

109

You're suggesting, my life, that this mutual love between us
    can be a delight—*and* in perpetuity?
Great gods, only let her promise be in earnest,
    let her be speaking truly, and from the heart,
so that we can maintain, for the rest of our life together,   5
    our hallowed friendship through this eternal pact!

VIRGIL

70–19 B.C.E.

Virgil's *Aeneid* is the greatest epic poem from ancient Rome. It has been one of the most profoundly influential works of all classical literature in the later Western cultural and literary tradition. The *Aeneid* can be described in ways that make it sound off-putting: as a work of nationalistic propaganda for a nation that no longer exists, or as a twelve-book poem about the importance of doing your duty. But such descriptions are entirely false to most readers' experience of this emotionally engaging and thought-provoking story. The *Aeneid* is an absorbing book, full of adventure, beauty, magic, dreams, love, loss, and violence. The characters make hard choices and have complex inner lives. The poem is also a profound meditation on the rights and wrongs of empire and colonialism that prompts us to ask whether civilizations, even the best of them, are ever founded without enormous personal and military cost.

LIFE AND TIMES

Virgil, whose full Roman name was Publius Vergilius Maro, was born near the peaceful northern Italian town of Mantua. His father probably owned land, and Virgil's poetry often shows a nostalgic appreciation for the quiet life of the Italian countryside. Before composing the *Aeneid*, Virgil wrote two books with a rural setting: the *Eclogues*, a set of ten poems featuring the songs and sorrows of fictional shepherds, and the *Georgics*, a four-book account of the struggles and triumphs of life on a farm. Ostensibly, neither of these texts has much to do with the subject of the *Aeneid*, which is about the quest to found an empire. But Virgil's poetic focus is surprisingly consistent throughout his career. Whether the setting is an empire or a village garden, he is interested in the value and pathos of the human struggle to build a home, even in hostile or near-impossible conditions. The farmer in the *Georgics*, whose hard work is washed away by a violent storm, is just as much a hero as the shipwrecked Trojans in the *Aeneid*.

When Virgil was young, the world beyond Mantua saw great political and military unrest. Rome had already, through its impressive military discipline, become the dominant power in the Mediterranean world; the city had defeated its main rival, the North African state of Carthage, some two generations before (in 146 B.C.E.). Now Rome was engaged in various further wars, struggling to expand the empire both eastward and westward. These wars generated greater glory for the nation, but also greater instability at home. In Virgil's childhood, Rome was still a Republic: no single man had control of the country; instead, government was divided among the people, the magistrates, and the Senate (an assembly of councilmen). But power was shifting away from the Senate and toward the military generals responsible for Rome's victories abroad. After a series of civil wars, Julius Caesar, one of these generals, became dictator of Rome. He was assassinated when Virgil was twenty-six (44 B.C.E.). More civil wars followed, and caused disruptions both at home and abroad: many country landowners—including some around Mantua, though apparently not Virgil's family—were forced to leave their homes, to make room for veterans returning from war. Finally, some twelve years after the assassination, Julius Caesar's adopted great-nephew Octavian defeated the joint forces of Antony and Cleopatra, and took control of Rome. In this volatile environment, Octavian was careful not to style himself "dictator," as Julius had done. Instead, he claimed to be restoring the old ways of the Republic. He named himself "Augustus" ("The Respected One"), the "Princeps" ("First Man") and "Emperor Caesar." Throughout his rule, Augustus was interested in controlling his public image: he knew that careful manipulation of information was essential if he were to avoid the fate of his great-uncle. In this context, it is not surprising that the emperor had a close personal relationship with the writers of Rome, who would, as Augustus knew, play an important part in his public image even after his death. Augustus hoped that Virgil would provide him with a great national epic, to justify, glorify, and immortalize Augustan Roman power.

We do not know how happy Augustus was with the poem that Virgil actually produced, although apparently the poet read parts of it aloud to the emperor and his sister, to great emotional effect: the sister fainted. It is possible that Augustus had hoped for a more direct account of his own glorious deeds. But perhaps he was smart enough to realize that direct propaganda never has much of a shelf life. We also do not know whether Virgil himself was satisfied with his creation. He was apparently a quiet man, moderate in his ways; thanks to Augustus's favor, he was given an expensive villa in Rome, but he seems to have preferred the quiet life of the country. He never married. As a poet, he was a perfectionist, willing to spend many hours editing his work. We are told that he compared himself to a mother bear who licks her cubs into shape. This process shows in the complex rhythms and careful patterns of Virgil's poetic style. He

died of a fever at the age of fifty-one, returning from a trip to Greece. The *Aeneid* was still incomplete, and apparently he gave orders from his deathbed for it to be burned. Fortunately for us, Augustus countermanded the orders, and saved the poem for posterity.

THE *AENEID*

Virgil's masterpiece is about Rome, but only indirectly. The story takes us back in time, to a period well before the foundation of the city. It tells of how one civilization mutates into another, finding the origins of Rome in the destruction of Troy. The poem follows the Trojan Aeneas as he escapes with his father, son, and a few companions from the smoking ruins of his home. On the journey to find a new home in the "western land," he has many adventures, including an affair with Dido, the beautiful queen of Carthage, and a trip down to the underworld, to meet his dead father. When he arrives in Italy, he struggles to establish a base in his new land—where some of the native inhabitants are far from welcoming.

The *Aeneid* deals with universal themes, including the basic human need to find, or create, a home. The story is accessible even to those who know nothing about ancient history. But readers will find it helpful to think carefully about how Virgil incorporates his own times into this mythical story. When Virgil was writing, Rome had only recently emerged from a long, terrifying period of civil war. Aeneas, like Augustus, must show strong leadership to a people traumatized by years of violence. Virgil's account of the sack of Troy, including the horrible slaughter of old king Priam before the eyes of his family, is vivid and harrowing—and many contemporary readers will have witnessed similar scenes with their own eyes. But the historical parallels in this poem are complex, and one cannot simply identify Aeneas with

Augustus. The affair between Aeneas and Dido looks further back in history, to the Roman wars with Carthage. This episode also invites comparison with events of the more recent past: like Augustus's military and political rival Antony, Aeneas falls in love with a beautiful Eastern queen; Dido, in this interpretation, foreshadows Cleopatra, who also ended up killing herself. Once Aeneas has arrived in Italy, there are further questions. Is Aeneas a foreign invader, pushing the boundaries of his empire into new lands—as Augustus did? Or are these battles between different Italian peoples more like a civil war? Virgil's evocation of historical parallels is rich and fascinating precisely because it is so hard to pin down. Moreover, temporal paradoxes are created by telling "history in the future tense": from the Roman reader's point of view, Carthage has already been defeated; but from Dido's perspective, her city has just begun to be built.

Virgil's use of literary antecedents is equally interesting. His poem combines the themes of the *Odyssey* (the wanderer in search of home) and the *Iliad* (the hero in battle). He borrows Homeric turns of phrase, similes, sentiments, and whole incidents; for instance, his Aeneas, like Odysseus, passes the land of the Cyclops, and descends alive to the world of the dead; like Achilles, he receives a new set of armor from his goddess mother, and kills in rage to avenge a dead friend. But Virgil is not playing a sterile game of copying **Homer**. Rather, Homeric parallels are part of how the poem generates meaning. Virgil often uses several Homeric allusions at the same time. For instance, Turnus—the Italian prince who is originally engaged to Lavinia, the woman who will become Aeneas's wife—is in some ways like one of the suitors in the *Odyssey*: the rival who must be defeated and killed. But on another level, Turnus is like Hector, the doomed Trojan hero of the *Iliad*, who dies defending his city and his people. From Turnus's perspective, Aeneas himself is more like the suitors of the *Odyssey*: he is a usurper in a place he does not belong.

The *Aeneid*'s approach to storytelling is very different from that of the Homeric poems. Virgil often tells the parts of the story Homer left untold: for example, it is in Virgil, not Homer, that we get the full story of the Trojan Horse. On a more profound level, Virgil's presentation of war, peace, and human nature is quite unlike Homer's—it is both broader and deeper. Virgil is interested in communities that extend beyond the tribe or clan to the nation or the empire, and he evokes time that goes beyond the generations of a single family to the broad sweep of history. The characters, especially Aeneas, are more introspective and prone to ambivalent feelings than those in Homer; Virgil explores conflicts not just between one person and another but within an individual, between duty and the longings of the heart. In this way, Aeneas is a different kind of hero from any in Greek literature. The first time his name is mentioned, he is risking death by shipwreck and is overwhelmed by despair, wishing he could have died with his friends at Troy: he holds his hands to the sky and cries, "Three, four times blest, my comrades / lucky to die . . . before their parents' eyes!" Aeneas feels not only physical fear but also despair at being a survivor, with no home to go to. We can contrast this sense of being totally lost with the first mention of Odysseus in the *Odyssey*: he longs for a home that still exists, whereas Aeneas's home has been destroyed. A little later, we see a different Aeneas, when he talks to his men and tries to calm their fears, giving no hint of his own: "Bear up," he tells them, "dismiss your grief and fear." From the start of the poem, Aeneas will be put in situations where he cannot allow himself to show, or act on, his deepest feelings.

Virgil also seems to question the values of the Homeric warrior code. Aeneas is

This detail from a black figure vase by the "Louvre Painter" (6th century B.C.E.) shows Aeneas carrying his father, Anchises, on his shoulders as they escape Troy.

not, like Achilles, a man fighting for his personal honor, against even the leaders of his own side; rather, he is, and must be, a consensus builder, a team player. Odysseus (Romanized as *Ulysses*) is presented in the *Aeneid* as a cruel brute, lacking in the mercy for the defeated that Aeneas's father, Anchises, characterizes as an essential feature of the true Roman ("to spare the defeated, break the proud in war"). Moreover, Ulysses' cleverness—epitomized by the invention of the Trojan Horse—seems in this poem to be more like wicked dishonesty. Truthfulness is an essential element in the Roman code of honor: this is partly why Dido's accusation that Aeneas has deceived and betrayed her cuts so deeply.

Aeneas is often seen as the prototype of the ideal Roman ruler, devoted above all to *pietas*—a word from which we get *pity* and *piety*, and which covers both senses, though it is often translated as "duty." But whereas *duty* may suggest adherence to a set of abstract moral principles, the Latin word connotes devotion to particular people and entities: to the gods above all, but also to one's country, leaders, community, and family, especially father and sons. An iconic moment of Aeneas's *pietas* comes as he leaves his burning city, carrying his lame old father on his shoulders, holding the images of his household gods, and leading his little son by the hand. This scene reminds us that Aeneas is struggling to hold on to a community and create continuity even from the ruins of his old home. The *pietas* that holds families and cities together is contrasted in this poem with *furor* ("rage," "fury"), the wild passion that inspires bloodlust, both in Troy and on Italian shores.

But being good is not easy, and Virgil shows that Aeneas's repression of his own feelings for the sake of devotion comes at an enormous cost. Moreover, the poem seems to suggest that duty can even be harmful to other people. Aeneas, on the instructions of the gods, abandons the great passion of his life, his love for Dido, who had convinced herself that their relationship was equivalent to marriage. In despair, she kills herself. Virgil makes us admire and sympathize with Dido, and in doing so, we are forced to question whether Aeneas's mission is worthwhile. The *Aeneid* is not merely a celebration of Roman power; it is also an analysis of the costs of empire, both to the conquered and the conquerors. Moreover, we may wonder whether Rome itself—a city famously built by Romulus, who killed his brother Remus, a city defined by foreign and civil wars—is truly a civilization in which *pietas* is the defining value. This moral ambiguity continues up to the last lines of the poem, which many first-time readers will find shocking. We are left to wonder whether moderation or violence will be the truly defining quality of the future Roman Empire.

A NOTE ON THE TRANSLATION

Translation of this complex poem often reflects the ideological biases of the translator. Some versions make Virgil sound whole-heartedly enthusiastic about imperialism, eliminating much of his ambivalence; others make him sound unrelentingly gloomy about everything. Virgil's Latin is dignified, not colloquial, and has a beautiful, musical rhythm; but trying to reproduce this effect in modern English risks sounding merely pompous.

Several excellent recent translations have steered clear of these dangers and given us readable, fast-paced versions of the *Aeneid*. We have chosen Robert Fagles's translation because it is particularly good at evoking the psychological depth of Virgil's characters, and it allows readers to experience the sheer narrative pleasure of reading the *Aeneid*.

From The Aeneid[1]

BOOK I

[*Safe Haven after Storm*]

Wars and a man I sing—an exile driven on by Fate,
he was the first to flee the coast of Troy,
destined to reach Lavinian[2] shores and Italian soil,
yet many blows he took on land and sea from the gods above—
thanks to cruel Juno's[3] relentless rage—and many losses   5
he bore in battle too, before he could found a city,
bring his gods to Latium, source of the Latin race,
the Alban lords and the high walls of Rome.[4]

                              Tell me,
Muse, how it all began. Why was Juno outraged?
What could wound the Queen of the Gods with all her power?   10
Why did she force a man, so famous for his devotion,[5]
to brave such rounds of hardship, bear such trials?
Can such rage inflame the immortals' hearts?

    There was an ancient city held by Tyrian settlers,[6]
Carthage, facing Italy and the Tiber River's mouth[7]   15
but far away—a rich city trained and fierce in war.
Juno loved it, they say, beyond all other lands
in the world, even beloved Samos,[8] second best.
Here she kept her armor, here her chariot too,
and Carthage would rule the nations of the earth   20
if only the Fates were willing. This was Juno's goal
from the start, and so she nursed her city's strength.
But she heard a race of men, sprung of Trojan blood,
would one day topple down her Tyrian stronghold,

1. Translated by Robert Fagles.
2. Lavinium is the city founded in Italy by Aeneas, near the later city of Rome. It is named after his Latin wife, Lavinia. "Lavinian" here means "Italian."
3. Juno is queen of the gods, wife of Jupiter.
4. According to legend, after Aeneas died, his son Ascanius moved from Latium and founded the city of Alba Longa; from there came Romulus and Remus, who built the walls of Rome.
5. The Latin word is *pietas*: "piety," "duty," "loyalty."
6. Tyre was the main city of the Phoenicians, an ancient seafaring merchant people.
7. The Tiber runs through Rome.
8. A Greek island famous for its cult of Hera.

breed an arrogant people ruling far and wide,   25
proud in battle, destined to plunder Libya.
So the Fates were spinning out the future . . . [9]
This was Juno's fear
and the goddess never forgot the old campaign
that she had waged at Troy for her beloved Argos.[1]   30
No, not even now would the causes of her rage,
her bitter sorrows drop from the goddess' mind.
They festered deep within her, galled her still:
the judgment of Paris, the unjust slight to her beauty,
the Trojan stock she loathed, the honors showered on Ganymede   35
ravished to the skies.[2] Her fury inflamed by all this,
the daughter of Saturn[3] drove over endless oceans
Trojans left by the Greeks and brute Achilles.[4]
Juno kept them far from Latium, forced by the Fates
to wander round the seas of the world, year in, year out.   40
Such a long hard labor it was to found the Roman people.

    Now, with the ridge of Sicily barely out of sight,
they spread sail for the open sea, their spirits buoyant,
their bronze beaks churning the waves to foam as Juno,
nursing deep in her heart the everlasting wound,   45
said to herself: "Defeated, am I? Give up the fight?
Powerless now to keep that Trojan king from Italy?
Ah but of course—the Fates bar my way.
And yet Minerva could burn the fleet to ash
and drown my Argive crews in the sea, and all for one,   50
one mad crime of a single man, Ajax, son of Oileus![5]
She hurled Jove's all-consuming bolt from the clouds,
she shattered a fleet and whipped the swells with gales.
And then as he gasped his last in flames from his riven chest
she swept him up in a cyclone, impaled the man on a crag.   55
But I who walk in majesty, I the Queen of the Gods,
the sister and wife of Jove—I must wage a war,
year after year, on just one race of men!
Who will revere the power of Juno after this—
lay gifts on my altar, lift his hands in prayer?"   60

9. Refers to the Punic Wars of the third and
second centuries B.C.E., in which Rome finally
defeated Carthage; "Libya" is used as a generic term for the North African coast.
1. Argos is the homeland of Agamemnon and
Menelaus; in the *Iliad*, Hera favors the Argives
as they fight the Trojans and try to win back
Helen, Menelaus's wife.
2. Paris, Prince of Troy, was asked to choose
one of three goddesses: Hera, Athena (Minerva in Roman mythology), or Aphrodite
(Venus to the Romans). He picked Aphrodite,
and was rewarded with Helen, whom he took
from her husband and led back to Troy. The
second insult from the Trojans against Hera is

that her husband, Zeus, once fell in love with
a Trojan boy, Ganymede, and brought him up
to heaven to be his cupbearer.
3. Saturn, the Roman god of agriculture, was
the father of both Jupiter and Juno.
4. The greatest Greek warrior. These survivors are the few Trojans whom Achilles has
not killed.
5. In the aftermath of the Greek victory at
Troy, one of the Greek soldiers, this Ajax (who
is not the same as the strong hero Telemonian
Ajax) raped the Trojan princess Cassandra in
the temple of Minerva. The goddess took
revenge by setting light to the Greek fleet, and
then overwhelming it with a storm.

With such anger seething inside her fiery heart
the goddess reached Aeolia, breeding-ground of storms,
their home swarming with raging gusts from the South.
Here in a vast cave King Aeolus[6] rules the winds,
brawling to break free, howling in full gale force   65
as he chains them down in their dungeon, shackled fast.
They bluster in protest, roaring round their prison bars
with a mountain above them all, booming with their rage.
But high in his stronghold Aeolus wields his scepter,
soothing their passions, tempering their fury.   70
Should he fail, surely they'd blow the world away,
hurling the land and sea and deep sky through space.
Fearing this, the almighty Father banished the winds
to that black cavern, piled above them a mountain mass
and imposed on all a king empowered, by binding pact,   75
to rein them back on command or let them gallop free.

　　Now Juno made this plea to the Lord of Winds:
"Aeolus, the Father of Gods and King of Men gave you
the power to calm the waves or rouse them with your gales.
A race I loathe is crossing the Tuscan Sea,[7] transporting   80
Troy to Italy, bearing their conquered household gods—
thrash your winds to fury, sink their warships, overwhelm them
or break them apart, scatter their crews, drown them all!
I happen to have some sea-nymphs, fourteen beauties,
Deiopea the finest of all by far . . .   85
I'll join you in lasting marriage, call her yours
and for all her years to come she will live with you
and make you the proud father of handsome children.
Such service earns such gifts."
　　　　　　　　　　　　Aeolus warmed
to Juno's offer: "Yours is the task, my queen,   90
to explore your heart's desires. Mine is the duty
to follow your commands. Yes, thanks to you
I rule this humble little kingdom of mine.
You won me the scepter, Jupiter's favors too,
and a couch to lounge on, set at the gods' feasts—   95
you made me Lord of the Stormwind, King of Cloudbursts."
With such thanks, swinging his spear around he strikes home
at the mountain's hollow flank and out charge the winds
through the breach he'd made, like armies on attack
in a blasting whirlwind tearing through the earth.   100
Down they crash on the sea, the Eastwind, Southwind,
all as one with the Southwest's squalls in hot pursuit,
heaving up from the ocean depths huge killer-breakers
rolling toward the beaches. The crews are shouting,
cables screeching—suddenly cloudbanks blotting out   105
the sky, the light of day from the Trojans' sight

---

6. Mythical king of the winds from the
Odyssey.

7. Just west of central Italy; the Trojans have
almost reached their destination.

as pitch-black night comes brooding down on the sea
with thunder crashing pole to pole, bolt on bolt
blazing across the heavens—death, everywhere
men facing instant death. 110
At once Aeneas, limbs limp in the chill of fear,
groans and lifting both his palms toward the stars
cries out: "Three, four times blest, my comrades
lucky to die beneath the soaring walls of Troy—
before their parents' eyes! If only I'd gone down 115
under your right hand—Diomedes, strongest Greek afield—
and poured out my life on the battle grounds of Troy![8]
Where raging Hector lies, pierced by Achilles' spear,
where mighty Sarpedon lies, where the Simois River
swallows down and churns beneath its tides so many 120
shields and helmets and corpses of the brave!"[9]
                                        Flinging cries
as a screaming gust of the Northwind pounds against his sail,
raising waves sky-high. The oars shatter, prow twists round,
taking the breakers broadside on and over Aeneas' decks
a mountain of water towers, massive, steep. 125
Some men hang on billowing crests, some as the sea
gapes, glimpse through the waves the bottom waiting,
a surge aswirl with sand.
                              Three ships the Southwind grips
and spins against those boulders lurking in mid-ocean—
rocks the Italians call the Altars, one great spine 130
breaking the surface—three the Eastwind sweeps
from open sea on the Syrtes' reefs, a grim sight,
girding them round with walls of sand.
                                        One ship
that carried the Lycian[1] units led by staunch Orontes—
before Aeneas' eyes a toppling summit of water 135
strikes the stern and hurls the helmsman overboard,
pitching him headfirst, twirling his ship three times,
right on the spot till the ravenous whirlpool gulps her down.
Here and there you can sight some sailors bobbing in heavy seas,
strewn in the welter now the weapons, men, stray spars 140
and treasures saved from Troy.
                                Now Ilioneus' sturdy ship,
now brave Achates', now the galley that carried Abas,
another, aged Aletes, yes, the storm routs them all,
down to the last craft the joints split, beams spring
and the lethal flood pours in.
                                All the while Neptune[2] 145

8. In the *Iliad*, Aeneas is wounded by the
Greek hero Diomedes, and is rescued by his
mother, Aphrodite.
9. Hector, the greatest Trojan hero, is killed
by Achilles in the *Iliad*. Sarpedon is another
fighter on the Trojan side, the favorite of Zeus,
who is killed by Achilles' friend Patroclus. The

Simois is the river at Troy, which in the *Iliad*
becomes thick with the blood and bodies of
those killed by Achilles.
1. Region in modern Turkey, allied with Troy
in the *Iliad*.
2. God of the sea.

sensed the furor above him, the roaring seas first and
the storm breaking next—his standing waters boiling up
from the sea-bed, churning back. And the mighty god,
stirred to his depths, lifts his head from the crests
and serene in power, gazing out over all his realm,   150
he sees Aeneas' squadrons scattered across the ocean,
Trojans overwhelmed by the surf and the wild crashing skies.
Nor did he miss his sister Juno's cunning wrath at work.
He summons the East- and Westwind, takes them to task:
"What insolence! Trusting so to your lofty birth?   155
You winds, you dare make heaven and earth a chaos,
raising such a riot of waves without my blessings.
You—what I won't do! But first I had better set
to rest the flood you ruffled so. Next time, trust me,
you will pay for your crimes with more than just a scolding.   160
Away with you, quick! And give your king this message:
Power over the sea and ruthless trident is mine,
not his—it's mine by lot, by destiny. His place,
Eastwind, is the rough rocks where you are all at home.
Let him bluster there and play the king in his court,   165
let Aeolus rule his bolted dungeon of the winds!"

   Quicker than his command he calms the heaving seas,
putting the clouds to rout and bringing back the sun.
Struggling shoulder-to-shoulder, Triton and Cymothoë[3]
hoist and heave the ships from the jagged rocks   170
as the god himself whisks them up with his trident,
clearing a channel through the deadly reefs, his chariot
skimming over the cresting waves on spinning wheels
to set the seas to rest. Just as, all too often,
some huge crowd is seized by a vast uprising,   175
the rabble runs amok, all slaves to passion,
rocks, firebrands flying. Rage finds them arms
but then, if they chance to see a man among them,
one whose devotion and public service lend him weight,
they stand there, stock-still with their ears alert as   180
he rules their furor with his words and calms their passion.
So the crash of the breakers all fell silent once their Father,
gazing over his realm under clear skies, flicks his horses,
giving them free rein, and his eager chariot flies.

   Now bone-weary, Aeneas' shipmates make a run   185
for the nearest landfall, wheeling prows around
they turn for Libya's coast. There is a haven shaped
by an island shielding the mouth of a long deep bay, its flanks
breaking the force of combers pounding in from the sea
while drawing them off into calm receding channels.   190
Both sides of the harbor, rock cliffs tower, crowned
by twin crags that menace the sky, overshadowing

3. Triton is a lesser sea god; Cymothoë is a sea nymph.

reaches of sheltered water, quiet and secure.
Over them as a backdrop looms a quivering wood,
above them rears a grove, bristling dark with shade,   195
and fronting the cliff, a cave under hanging rocks
with fresh water inside, seats cut in the native stone,
the home of nymphs. Never a need of cables here to moor
a weathered ship, no anchor with biting flukes to bind her fast.

    Aeneas puts in here with a bare seven warships   200
saved from his whole fleet. How keen their longing
for dry land underfoot as the Trojans disembark,
taking hold of the earth, their last best hope,
and fling their brine-wracked bodies on the sand.
Achates is first to strike a spark from flint,   205
then works to keep it alive in dry leaves,
cups it around with kindling, feeds it chips
and briskly fans the tinder into flame.
Then, spent as they were from all their toil,
they set out food, the bounty of Ceres,⁴ drenched   210
in sea-salt, Ceres' utensils too, her mills and troughs,
and bend to parch with fire the grain they had salvaged,
grind it fine on stones.
               While they see to their meal
Aeneas scales a crag, straining to scan the sea-reach
far and wide . . . is there any trace of Antheus now,   215
tossed by the gales, or his warships banked with oars?
Or Capys perhaps, or Caicus' stern adorned with shields?⁵
Not a ship in sight. But he does spot three stags
roaming the shore, an entire herd behind them
grazing down the glens in a long ranked line.   220
He halts, grasps his bow and his flying arrows,
the weapons his trusty aide Achates keeps at hand.
First the leaders, antlers branching over their high heads,
he brings them down, then turns on the herd, his shafts
stampeding the rest like rabble into the leafy groves.   225
Shaft on shaft, no stopping him till he stretches
seven hefty carcases on the ground—a triumph,
one for each of his ships—and makes for the cove,
divides the kill with his whole crew and then shares out
the wine that good Acestes,⁶ princely man, had brimmed   230
in their casks the day they left Sicilian shores.

    The commander's words relieve their stricken hearts:
"My comrades, hardly strangers to pain before now,
we all have weathered worse. Some god will grant us
an end to this as well. You've threaded the rocks   235
resounding with Scylla's howling rabid dogs,
and taken the brunt of the Cyclops' boulders, too.

---

4. Goddess of grain and harvest.
5. Names of lost Trojan leaders.

6. King in Sicily who gave the Trojans shelter
and extra supplies.

Call up your courage again. Dismiss your grief and fear.
A joy it will be one day, perhaps, to remember even this.
Through so many hard straits, so many twists and turns   240
our course holds firm for Latium.[7] There Fate holds out
a homeland, calm, at peace. There the gods decree
the kingdom of Troy will rise again. Bear up.
Save your strength for better times to come."
                                        Brave words.
Sick with mounting cares he assumes a look of hope   245
and keeps his anguish buried in his heart.
The men gird up for the game, the coming feast,
they skin the hide from the ribs, lay bare the meat.
Some cut it into quivering strips, impale it on skewers,
some set cauldrons along the beach and fire them to the boil.   250
Then they renew their strength with food, stretched out
on the beachgrass, fill themselves with seasoned wine
and venison rich and crisp. Their hunger sated,
the tables cleared away, they talk on for hours,
asking after their missing shipmates—wavering now   255
between hope and fear: what to believe about the rest?
Were the men still alive or just in the last throes,
forever lost to their comrades' farflung calls?
Aeneas most of all, devoted to his shipmates,
deep within himself he moans for the losses . . .   260
now for Orontes, hardy soldier, now for Amycus,
now for the brutal fate that Lycus may have met,
then Gyas and brave Cloanthus, hearts of oak.

    Their mourning was over now as Jove[8] from high heaven,
gazing down on the sea, the whitecaps winged with sails,   265
the lands outspread, the coasts, the nations of the earth,
paused at the zenith of the sky and set his sights
on Libya, that proud kingdom. All at once,
as he took to heart the struggles he beheld,
Venus[9] approached in rare sorrow, tears abrim   270
in her sparkling eyes, and begged: "Oh you who rule
the lives of men and gods with your everlasting laws
and your lightning bolt of terror, what crime could my Aeneas
commit against you, what dire harm could the Trojans do
that after bearing so many losses, this wide world   275
is shut to them now? And all because of Italy.
Surely from them the Romans would arise one day
as the years roll on, and leaders would as well,
descended from Teucer's blood brought back to life,
to rule all lands and seas with boundless power—   280
you promised! Father, what motive changed your mind?
With that, at least, I consoled myself for Troy's demise,
that heart-rending ruin—weighing fate against fate.

7. Region of central Italy, home of the Latin   8. Alternative name of Jupiter.
race.   9. Aeneas's mother; goddess of love and sex.

But now after all my Trojans suffered, still
the same disastrous fortune drives them on and on.   285
What end, great king, do you set to their ordeals?

"Antenor[1] could slip out from under the Greek siege,
then make his passage through the Illyrian gulfs and,
safe through the inlands where the Liburnians rule,
he struggled past the Timavus River's source.[2]   290
There, through its nine mouths as the mountain caves
roar back, the river bursts out into full flood,
a thundering surf that overpowers the fields.
Reaching Italy, he erected a city for his people,
a Trojan home called Padua—gave them a Trojan name,   295
hung up their Trojan arms and there, after long wars,
he lingers on in serene and settled peace.
                          "But we,
your own children, the ones you swore would hold
the battlements of heaven—now our ships are lost,
appalling! We are abandoned, thanks to the rage   300
of a single foe, cut off from Italy's shores.
Is this our reward for reverence,[3]
this the way you give us back our throne?"

   The Father of Men and Gods, smiling down on her
with the glance that clears the sky and calms the tempest,   305
lightly kissing his daughter on the lips, replied:
"Relieve yourself of fear, my lady of Cythera,[4]
the fate of your children stands unchanged, I swear.
You will see your promised city, see Lavinium's walls
and bear your great-hearted Aeneas up to the stars on high.   310
Nothing has changed my mind. No, your son, believe me—
since anguish is gnawing at you, I will tell you more,
unrolling the scroll of Fate
to reveal its darkest secrets. Aeneas will wage
a long, costly war in Italy, crush defiant tribes   315
and build high city walls for his people there
and found the rule of law. Only three summers
will see him govern Latium, three winters pass
in barracks after the Latins have been broken.
But his son Ascanius, now that he gains the name   320
of Iulus—Ilus he was, while Ilium ruled on high[5]—
will fill out with his own reign thirty sovereign years,
a giant cycle of months revolving round and round,
transferring his rule from its old Lavinian home
to raise up Alba Longa's mighty ramparts.   325

1. Trojan leader who escaped the city's sack and settled in northern Italy.
2. Illyrium was a district, the Liburnians a people, and Timavus a river on the coast of the northern Adriatic sea.
3. *Pietas.*
4. Greek island where there was a cult of Aphrodite.
5. *Ilium* is another name for Troy. The Julian family, which included Julius Caesar and Augustus, claimed descent from Iulus (Julus).

There, in turn, for a full three hundred years
the dynasty of Hector will hold sway till Ilia,
a royal priestess great with the brood of Mars,
will bear the god twin sons.[6] Then one, Romulus,
reveling in the tawny pelt of a wolf that nursed him,   330
will inherit the line and build the walls of Mars
and after his own name, call his people Romans.[7]
On them I set no limits, space or time:
I have granted them power, empire without end.
Even furious Juno, now plaguing the land and sea and sky   335
with terror: she will mend her ways and hold dear with me
these Romans, lords of the earth, the race arrayed in togas.
This is my pleasure, my decree. Indeed, an age will come,
as the long years slip by, when Assaracus' royal house
will quell Achilles' homeland, brilliant Mycenae too,   340
and enslave their people, rule defeated Argos.[8]
From that noble blood will arise a Trojan Caesar,
his empire bound by the Ocean, his glory by the stars:
Julius, a name passed down from Iulus, his great forebear.
And you, in years to come, will welcome him to the skies,   345
you rest assured—laden with plunder of the East,
and he with Aeneas will be invoked in prayer.[9]
Then will the violent centuries, battles set aside,
grow gentle, kind. Vesta[1] and silver-haired Good Faith
and Romulus flanked by brother Remus will make the laws.   350
The terrible Gates of War with their welded iron bars
will stand bolted shut,[2] and locked inside, the Frenzy
of civil strife will crouch down on his savage weapons,
hands pinioned behind his back with a hundred brazen shackles,
monstrously roaring out from his bloody jaws."
                              So   355

he decrees and speeds the son of Maia[3] down the sky
to make the lands and the new stronghold, Carthage,
open in welcome to the Trojans, not let Dido,
unaware of fate, expel them from her borders.
Down through the vast clear air flies Mercury,   360
rowing his wings like oars and in a moment
stands on Libya's shores, obeys commands
and the will of god is done.
The Carthaginians calm their fiery temper

---

6. Ilia, also known as Rhea Silvia, was a priestess sworn to religious celibacy. She was raped by Mars, the god of war, and gave birth to twins, Romulus and Remus. Her brother, jealous of his own power, ordered that the babies be killed; but instead, his servant abandoned them in the wild, to be rescued by a wolf, who suckled them and raised them.
7. Virgil omits the fact that Romulus killed his brother, Remus, to gain sole power over the city.
8. Assaracus was an early king of Troy.

9. The "Trojan Caesar" is either Julius Caesar, who made Rome an empire, or Augustus himself, who had plundered "the East" by defeating the Egyptian queen Cleopatra.
1. Vesta is the goddess of the hearth, representative of home life.
2. There were real Gates of War in the temple of Janus, which Augustus shut in 25 B.C.E.—the first time they had been shut since 235 B.C.E.
3. Mercury (Roman version of Hermes), the messenger god.

and Queen Dido, above all, takes to heart   365
a spirit of peace and warm good will to meet
the men of Troy.
            But Aeneas, duty-bound,
his mind restless with worries all that night,
reached a firm resolve as the fresh day broke.
Out he goes to explore the strange terrain . . .   370
what coast had the stormwinds brought him to?
Who lives here? All he sees is wild, untilled—
what men, or what creatures? Then report the news
to all his comrades. So, concealing his ships
in the sheltered woody narrows overarched by rocks   375
and screened around by trees and trembling shade,
Aeneas moves out, with only Achates at his side,
two steel-tipped javelins balanced in his grip.
Suddenly, in the heart of the woods, his mother
crossed his path. She looked like a young girl,   380
a Spartan girl decked out in dress and gear
or Thracian Harpalyce tiring out her mares,
outracing the Hebrus River's rapid tides.⁴
Hung from a shoulder, a bow that fit her grip,
a huntress for all the world, she'd let her curls   385
go streaming free in the wind, her knees were bare,
her flowing skirts hitched up with a tight knot.

  She speaks out first: "You there, young soldiers,
did you by any chance see one of my sisters?
Which way did she go? Roaming the woods,   390
a quiver slung from her belt,
wearing a spotted lynx-skin, or in full cry,
hot on the track of some great frothing boar?"
So Venus asked and the son of Venus answered:
"Not one of your sisters have I seen or heard . . .   395
but how should I greet a young girl like you?
Your face, your features—hardly a mortal's looks
and the tone of your voice is hardly human either.
Oh a goddess, without a doubt! What, are you
Apollo's sister? Or one of the breed of Nymphs?   400
Be kind, whoever you are, relieve our troubled hearts.
Under what skies and onto what coasts of the world
have we been driven? Tell us, please. Castaways,
we know nothing, not the people, not the place—
lost, hurled here by the gales and heavy seas.   405
Many a victim will fall before your altars,
we'll slaughter them for you!"

---

4. The goddess Venus is dressed like a Spartan, a famously athletic and militaristic Greek people, or Harpalyce, a girl who lived in the wilds and devoted herself to hunting. The Hebrus is a river in Thrace. In Greco-Roman tradition, hunting was considered antithetical to sex and marriage.

But Venus replied:
"Now there's an honor I really don't deserve.
It's just the style for Tyrian girls to sport
a quiver and high-laced hunting boots in crimson.   410
What you see is a Punic[5] kingdom, people of Tyre
and Agenor's town, but the border's held by Libyans
hard to break in war. Phoenician Dido is in command,
she sailed from Tyre, in flight from her own brother.
Oh it's a long tale of crime, long, twisting, dark,   415
but I'll try to trace the high points in their order . . .

   "Dido was married to Sychaeus, the richest man in Tyre,
and she, poor girl, was consumed with love for him.
Her father gave her away, wed for the first time,
a virgin still, and these her first solemn rites.   420
But her brother held power in Tyre—Pygmalion,
a monster, the vilest man alive.
A murderous feud broke out between both men.
Pygmalion, catching Sychaeus off guard at the altar,
slaughtered him in blood. That unholy man, so blind   425
in his lust for gold he ran him through with a sword,
then hid the crime for months, deaf to his sister's love,
her heartbreak. Still he mocked her with wicked lies,
with empty hopes. But she had a dream one night.
The true ghost of her husband, not yet buried,   430
came and lifting his face—ashen, awesome in death—
showed her the cruel altar, the wounds that pierced his chest
and exposed the secret horror that lurked within the house.
He urged her on: 'Take flight from our homeland, quick!'
And then he revealed an unknown ancient treasure,   435
an untold weight of silver and gold, a comrade
to speed her on her way.
                "Driven by all this,
Dido plans her escape, collects her followers
fired by savage hate of the tyrant or bitter fear.
They seize some galleys set to sail, load them with gold—   440
the wealth Pygmalion craved—and they bear it overseas
and a woman leads them all. Reaching this haven here,
where now you will see the steep ramparts rising,
the new city of Carthage—the Tyrians purchased land as
large as a bull's-hide could enclose but cut in strips for size   445
and called it Byrsa, the Hide, for the spread they'd bought.
But you, who are you? What shores do you come from?
Where are you headed now?"
                   He answered her questions,
drawing a labored sigh from deep within his chest:
"Goddess, if I'd retrace our story to its start,   450
if you had time to hear the saga of our ordeals,
before I finished the Evening Star would close
the gates of Olympus, put the day to sleep . . .

5. Carthaginian.

From old Troy we come—Troy it's called, perhaps
you've heard the name—sailing over the world's seas   455
until, by chance, some whim of the winds, some tempest
drove us onto Libyan shores. I am Aeneas, duty-bound.
I carry aboard my ships the gods of house and home
we seized from enemy hands. My fame goes past the skies.
I seek my homeland—Italy—born as I am from highest Jove.   460
I launched out on the Phrygian sea with twenty ships,
my goddess mother marking the way, and followed hard
on the course the Fates had charted. A mere seven,
battered by wind and wave, survived the worst.
I myself am a stranger, utterly at a loss,   465
trekking over this wild Libyan wasteland,
forced from Europe, Asia too, an exile—"

   Venus could bear no more of his laments
and broke in on his tale of endless hardship:
"Whoever you are, I scarcely think the Powers hate you: 470
you enjoy the breath of life, you've reached a Tyrian city.
So off you go now. Take this path to the queen's gates.
I have good news. Your friends are restored to you,
your fleet's reclaimed. The winds swerved from the North
and drove them safe to port. True, unless my parents   475
taught me to read the flight of birds for nothing.
Look at those dozen swans triumphant in formation!
The eagle of Jove[6] had just swooped down on them all
from heaven's heights and scattered them into open sky,
but now you can see them flying trim in their long ranks,   480
landing or looking down where their friends have landed—
home, cavorting on ruffling wings and wheeling round
the sky in convoy, trumpeting in their glory.
So homeward bound, your ships and hardy shipmates
anchor in port now or approach the harbor's mouth,   485
full sail ahead. Now off you go, move on,
wherever the path leads you, steer your steps."
                                              At that,
as she turned away her neck shone with a rosy glow,
her mane of hair gave off an ambrosial fragrance,
her skirt flowed loose, rippling down to her feet   490
and her stride alone revealed her as a goddess.
He knew her at once—his mother—
and called after her now as she sped away:
"Why, you too, cruel as the rest? So often
you ridicule your son with your disguises!   495
Why can't we clasp hands, embrace each other,
speak out, and tell the truth?"

   Reproving her so, he makes his way toward town
but Venus screens the travelers off with a dense mist,

6. The eagle, king of the birds, was associated with Jupiter.

pouring round them a cloak of clouds with all her power,   500
so no one could see them, no one reach and hold them,
cause them to linger now or ask why they had come.
But she herself, lifting into the air, wings her way
toward Paphos,[7] racing with joy to reach her home again
where her temples stand and a hundred altars steam   505
with Arabian incense, redolent with the scent
of fresh-cut wreaths.
              Meanwhile the two men
are hurrying on their way as the path leads,
now climbing a steep hill arching over the city,
looking down on the facing walls and high towers.   510
Aeneas marvels at its mass—once a cluster of huts—
he marvels at gates and bustling hum and cobbled streets.
The Tyrians press on with the work, some aligning the walls,
struggling to raise the citadel, trundling stones up slopes;
some picking the building sites and plowing out their boundaries,   515
others drafting laws, electing judges, a senate held in awe.
Here they're dredging a harbor, there they lay foundations
deep for a theater, quarrying out of rock great columns
to form a fitting scene for stages still to come.
As hard at their tasks as bees in early summer,   520
working the blooming meadows under the sun
escorting a new brood out, young adults now,
or pressing oozing honey into the combs, the nectar
brimming the bulging cells, or gathering up the plunder
workers haul back in, or closing ranks like an army,   525
driving the drones, that lazy crew, from home.
The hive seethes with life, exhaling the scent
of honey sweet with thyme.
              "How lucky they are,"
Aeneas cries, gazing up at the city's heights,
"their walls are rising now!" And on he goes,   530
cloaked in cloud—remarkable—right in their midst
he blends in with the crowds, and no one sees him.

   Now deep in the heart of Carthage stood a grove,
lavish with shade, where the Tyrians, making landfall,
still shaken by wind and breakers, first unearthed that sign: 535
Queen Juno had led their way to the fiery stallion's head
that signaled power in war and ease in life for ages.
Here Dido of Tyre was building Juno a mighty temple,
rich with gifts and the goddess' aura of power.
Bronze the threshold crowning a flight of stairs,   540
the doorposts sheathed in bronze, and the bronze doors
groaned deep on their hinges.
              Here in this grove
a strange sight met his eyes and calmed his fears
for the first time. Here, for the first time,

---

7. Greek island where there was a cult center of Aphrodite.

Aeneas dared to hope he had found some haven,   545
for all his hard straits, to trust in better days.
For awaiting the queen, beneath the great temple now,
exploring its features one by one, amazed at it all,
the city's splendor, the work of rival workers' hands
and the vast scale of their labors—all at once he sees,   550
spread out from first to last, the battles fought at Troy,
the fame of the Trojan War now known throughout the world,
Atreus' sons and Priam—Achilles, savage to both at once.[8]
Aeneas came to a halt and wept, and "Oh Achates,"
he cried, "is there anywhere, any place on earth   555
not filled with our ordeals? There's Priam, look!
Even here, merit will have its true reward . . .
even here, the world is a world of tears
and the burdens of mortality touch the heart.
Dismiss your fears. Trust me, this fame of ours   560
will offer us some haven."
                    So Aeneas says,
feeding his spirit on empty, lifeless pictures,
groaning low, the tears rivering down his face
as he sees once more the fighters circling Troy.
Here Greeks in flight, routed by Troy's young ranks,   565
there Trojans routed by plumed Achilles in his chariot.
Just in range are the snow-white canvas tents of Rhesus—
he knows them at once, and sobs—Rhesus' men betrayed
in their first slumber, droves of them slaughtered
by Diomedes splattered with their blood, lashing   570
back to the Greek camp their highstrung teams
before they could ever savor the grass of Troy
or drink at Xanthus' banks.[9]
                    Next Aeneas sees
Troilus[1] in flight, his weapons flung aside,
unlucky boy, no match for Achilles' onslaught—   575
horses haul him on, tangled behind an empty warcar,
flat on his back, clinging still to the reins, his neck
and hair dragging along the ground, the butt of his javelin
scrawling zigzags in the dust.
                    And here the Trojan women
are moving toward the temple of Pallas,[2] their deadly foe,   580
their hair unbound as they bear the robe, their offering,
suppliants grieving, palms beating their breasts
but Pallas turns away, staring at the ground.
                    And Hector—
three times Achilles has hauled him round the walls of Troy
and now he's selling his lifeless body off for gold.   585

8. That is, Achilles was angry with Greeks as well as Trojans.
9. Rhesus, king of Thrace, came to help the Trojans, but was slaughtered by Odysseus and Diomedes in a night raid. An oracle had proclaimed that if Rhesus's horses ate Trojan grass and drank from the river Xanthus, Troy would not fall.
1. Troilus was a young son of King Priam of Troy.
2. Athena, who was hostile to Troy.

Aeneas gives a groan, heaving up from his depths,
he sees the plundered armor, the car, the corpse
of his great friend, and Priam reaching out
with helpless hands . . . [3]
                          He even sees himself
swept up in the melee, clashing with Greek captains,   590
sees the troops of the dawn and swarthy Memnon's[4] arms.
And Penthesilea leading her Amazons bearing half-moon shields[5]—
she blazes with battle-fury out in front of her army,
cinching a golden breastband under her bared breast,
a girl, a warrior queen who dares to battle men.
                                          And now   595
as Trojan Aeneas, gazing in awe at all the scenes of Troy,
stood there, spellbound, eyes fixed on the war alone,
the queen aglow with beauty approached the temple,
Dido, with massed escorts marching in her wake.
Like Diana urging her dancing troupes along   600
the Eurotas' banks or up Mount Cynthus' ridge[6]
as a thousand mountain-nymphs crowd in behind her,
left and right—with quiver slung from her shoulder,
taller than any other goddess as she goes striding on
and silent Latona[7] thrills with joy too deep for words.   605
Like Dido now, striding triumphant among her people,
spurring on the work of their kingdom still to come.
And then by Juno's doors beneath the vaulted dome,
flanked by an honor guard beside her lofty seat,
the queen assumed her throne. Here as she handed down   610
decrees and laws to her people, sharing labors fairly,
some by lot, some with her sense of justice, Aeneas
suddenly sees his men approaching through the crowds,
Antheus, Sergestus, gallant Cloanthus, other Trojans
the black gales had battered over the seas   615
and swept to far-flung coasts.
                        Aeneas, Achates,
both were amazed, both struck with joy and fear.
They yearn to grasp their companions' hands in haste
but both men are unnerved by the mystery of it all.
So, cloaked in folds of mist, they hide their feelings,   620
waiting, hoping to see what luck their friends have found.
Where have they left their ships, what coast? Why have they come?
These picked men, still marching in from the whole armada,
pressing toward the temple amid the rising din
to plead for some good will.

---

3. Having killed Hector, Achilles dragged his corpse around the city behind his chariot, until Priam came to ransom his son's body.
4. Memnon was king of the Ethiopians, and fought on the Trojan side.
5. The Amazons were a race of warrior women who fought for Troy.

6. Diana (Artemis in Greek mythology) is the virgin goddess associated with hunting. She was born on Delos, the island location of Mount Cynthus; Eurotas was a river in Sparta where she was worshipped.
7. Leto, Diana's mother.

Once they had entered, 625
allowed to appeal before the queen—the eldest,
Prince Ilioneus, calm, composed, spoke out:
"Your majesty, empowered by Jove to found
your new city here and curb rebellious tribes
with your sense of justice—we poor Trojans, 630
castaways, tossed by storms over all the seas;
we beg you: keep the cursed fire off our ships!
Pity us, god-fearing men! Look on us kindly,
see the state we are in. We have not come
to put your Libyan gods and homes to the sword, 635
loot them and haul our plunder toward the beach.
No, such pride, such violence has no place
in the hearts of beaten men.
                    "There is a country—
the Greeks called it Hesperia, Land of the West,
an ancient land, mighty in war and rich in soil. 640
Oenotrians[8] settled it; now we hear their descendants
call their kingdom Italy, after their leader, Italus.
Italy-bound we were when, surging with sudden breakers
stormy Orion[9] drove us against blind shoals and from the South
came vicious gales to scatter us, whelmed by the sea, 645
across the murderous surf and rocky barrier reefs:
We few escaped and floated toward your coast.
What kind of men are these? What land is this,
that you can tolerate such barbaric ways?
We are denied the sailor's right to shore— 650
attacked, forbidden even a footing on your beach.
If you have no use for humankind and mortal armor,
at least respect the gods. They know right from wrong.
They don't forget.
                    "We once had a king, Aeneas . . .
none more just, none more devoted to duty, none 655
more brave in arms. If Fate has saved that man,
if he still draws strength from the air we breathe,
if he's not laid low, not yet with the heartless shades,
fear not, nor will you once regret the first step
you take to compete with him in kindness. 660
We have cities too, in the land of Sicily,
arms and a king, Acestes, born of Trojan blood.
Permit us to haul our storm-racked ships ashore,
trim new oars, hew timbers out of your woods, so that,
if we are fated to sail for Italy—king and crews restored— 665
to Italy, to Latium we will sail with buoyant hearts.
But if we have lost our haven there, if Libyan waters
hold you now, my captain, best of the men of Troy,
and all our hopes for Iulus have been dashed,
at least we can cross back over Sicilian seas, 670

8. An ancient Italic people.
9. This constellation marks the approach of winter.

the straits we came from, homes ready and waiting,
and seek out great Acestes for our king."

So Ilioneus closed. And with one accord
the Trojans murmured Yes.
                                    Her eyes lowered,
Dido replies with a few choice words of welcome: 675
"Cast fear to the winds, Trojans, free your minds.
Our kingdom is new. Our hard straits have forced me
to set defenses, station guards along our far frontiers.
Who has not heard of Aeneas' people, his city, Troy,
her men, her heroes, the flames of that horrendous war?   680
We are not so dull of mind, we Carthaginians here.
When he yokes his team, the Sun shines down on us as well.
Whatever you choose, great Hesperia—Saturn's fields—
or the shores of Eryx with Acestes as your king,[1]
I will provide safe passage, escorts and support   685
to speed you on your way. Or would you rather
settle here in my realm on equal terms with me?
This city I build—it's yours. Haul ships to shore.
Trojans, Tyrians: they will be all the same to me.
If only the storm that drove you drove your king   690
and Aeneas were here now! Indeed, I'll send out
trusty men to scour the coast of Libya far and wide.
Perhaps he's shipwrecked, lost in woods or towns."

Spirits lifting at Dido's welcome, brave Achates
and captain Aeneas had long chafed to break free   695
of the mist, and now Achates spurs Aeneas on:
"Son of Venus, what feelings are rising in you now?
You see the coast is clear, our ships and friends restored.
Just one is lost. We saw him drown at sea ourselves.
All else is just as your mother promised."   700

He'd barely ended when all at once the mist
around them parted, melting into the open air,
and there Aeneas stood, clear in the light of day,
his head, his shoulders, the man was like a god.
His own mother had breathed her beauty on her son,   705
a gloss on his flowing hair, and the ruddy glow of youth,
and radiant joy shone in his eyes. His beauty fine
as a craftsman's hand can add to ivory, or aglow
as silver or Parian marble[2] ringed in glinting gold.

Suddenly, surprising all, he tells the queen: 710
"Here I am before you, the man you are looking for,
Aeneas the Trojan, plucked from Libya's heavy seas.
You alone have pitied the long ordeals of Troy—unspeakable—

---

1. Hesperia is "the western land," that is, Italy. In Roman mythology, the Titan god Saturn, when driven out by Jupiter, fled to Italy and estab- lished the Golden Age. Eryx is a city in Sicily.
2. That is, marble from the island of Paros; famous for its whiteness.

and here you would share your city and your home with us,
this remnant left by the Greeks. We who have drunk deep   715
of each and every disaster land and sea can offer.
Stripped of everything, now it's past our power
to reward you gift for gift, Dido, theirs as well,
whoever may survive of the Dardan people still,
strewn over the wide world now. But may the gods,   720
if there are Powers who still respect the good and true,
if justice still exists on the face of the earth,
may they and their own sense of right and wrong
bring you your just rewards.
What age has been so blest to give you birth?   725
What noble parents produced so fine a daughter?
So long as rivers run to the sea, so long as shadows
travel the mountain slopes and the stars range the skies,
your honor, your name, your praise will live forever,
whatever lands may call me to their shores."
                                        With that,   730
he extends his right hand toward his friend Ilioneus,
greeting Serestus with his left, and then the others,
gallant Gyas, gallant Cloanthus.
                        Tyrian Dido marveled,
first at the sight of him, next at all he'd suffered,
then she said aloud: "Born of a goddess, even so   735
what destiny hunts you down through such ordeals?
What violence lands you on this frightful coast?
Are you that Aeneas whom loving Venus bore
to Dardan Anchises on the Simois' banks at Troy?
Well I remember . . . Teucer[3] came to Sidon once,   740
banished from native ground, searching for new realms,
and my father Belus helped him. Belus had sacked Cyprus,
plundered that rich island, ruled with a victor's hand.
From that day on I have known of Troy's disaster,
known your name, and all the kings of Greece.   745
Teucer, your enemy, often sang Troy's praises,
claiming his own descent from Teucer's ancient stock.
So come, young soldiers, welcome to our house.
My destiny, harrying me with trials hard as yours,
led me as well, at last, to anchor in this land.   750
Schooled in suffering, now I learn to comfort
those who suffer too."
                    With that greeting
she leads Aeneas into the royal halls, announcing
offerings in the gods' high temples as she goes.
Not forgetting to send his shipmates on the beaches   755
twenty bulls and a hundred huge, bristling razorbacks
and a hundred fatted lambs together with their mothers:
gifts to make this day a day of joy.

---

3. A warrior who fought at Troy and was later exiled; he founded a city on the island of Cyprus.

Within the palace
all is decked with adornments, lavish, regal splendor.
In the central hall they are setting out a banquet,   760
draping the gorgeous purple, intricately worked,
heaping the board with grand displays of silver
and gold engraved with her fathers' valiant deeds,
a long, unending series of captains and commands,
traced through a line of heroes since her country's birth.   765

Aeneas—a father's love would give the man no rest—
quickly sends Achates down to the ships to take
the news to Ascanius, bring him back to Carthage.
All his paternal care is focused on his son.
He tells Achates to fetch some gifts as well,   770
plucked from the ruins of Troy: a gown stiff
with figures stitched in gold, and a woven veil
with yellow sprays of acanthus round the border.
Helen's glory, gifts she carried out of Mycenae,
fleeing Argos for Troy to seal her wicked marriage—   775
the marvelous handiwork of Helen's mother, Leda.
Aeneas adds the scepter Ilione used to bear,
the eldest daughter of Priam; a necklace too,
strung with pearls, and a crown of double bands,
one studded with gems, the other, gold. Achates,   780
following orders, hurries toward the ships.

But now Venus is mulling over some new schemes,
new intrigues. Altered in face and figure, Cupid[4]
would go in place of the captivating Ascanius,
using his gifts to fire the queen to madness,   785
weaving a lover's ardor through her bones.
No doubt Venus fears that treacherous house
and the Tyrians' forked tongues,
and brutal Juno inflames her anguish too
and her cares keep coming back as night draws on.   790
So Venus makes an appeal to Love, her winged son:
"You, my son, are my strength, my greatest power—
you alone, my son, can scoff at the lightning bolts
the high and mighty Father hurled against Typhoeus.[5]
Help me, I beg you. I need all your immortal force.   795
Your brother Aeneas is tossed round every coast on earth,
thanks to Juno's ruthless hatred, as you well know,
and time and again you've grieved to see my grief.
But now Phoenician Dido has him in her clutches,
holding him back with smooth, seductive words,   800
and I fear the outcome of Juno's welcome here . . .
She won't sit tight while Fate is turning on its hinge.
So I plan to forestall her with ruses of my own

4. Cupid (whose name means "desire") is the   Typhoeus (Typhon), and finally trapped him
son of Venus and the god of sexual desire.   under Mount Etna.
5. Jupiter hurled thunderbolts at the monster

and besiege the queen with flames,
and no goddess will change her mood—she's mine,   805
my ally-in-arms in my great love for Aeneas.

    "Now how can you go about this? Hear my plan.
His dear father has just sent for the young prince—
he means the world to me—and he's bound for Carthage now,
bearing presents saved from the sea, the flames of Troy.   810
I'll lull him into a deep sleep and hide him far away
on Cythera's heights or high Idalium,[6] my shrines,
so he cannot learn of my trap or spring it open
while it's being set. And you with your cunning,
forge his appearance—just one night, no more—put on   815
the familiar features of the boy, boy that you are,
so when the wine flows free at the royal board
and Dido, lost in joy, cradles you in her lap,
caressing, kissing you gently, you can breathe
your secret fire into her, poison the queen   820
and she will never know."
                          Cupid leaps at once
to his loving mother's orders. Shedding his wings
he masquerades as Iulus, prancing with his stride.
But now Venus distils a deep, soothing sleep
into Iulus' limbs, and warming him in her breast   825
the goddess spirits him off to her high Idalian grove
where beds of marjoram breathe and embrace him with aromatic
flowers and rustling shade.
                          Now Cupid is on the move,
under her orders, bringing the Tyrians royal gifts,
his spirits high as Achates leads him on.   830
Arriving, he finds the queen already poised
on a golden throne beneath the sumptuous hangings,
commanding the very center of her palace. Now Aeneas,
the good captain, enters, then the Trojan soldiers,
taking their seats on couches draped in purple.   835
Servants pour them water to rinse their hands,
quickly serving them bread from baskets, spreading
their laps with linens, napkins clipped and smooth.
In the kitchens are fifty serving-maids assigned
to lay out foods in a long line, course by course,   840
and honor the household gods by building fires high.
A hundred other maids and a hundred men, all matched in age,
are spreading the feast on trestles, setting out the cups.
And Tyrians join them, bustling through the doors,
filling the hall with joy, to take invited seats   845
on brocaded couches. They admire Aeneas' gifts,
admire Iulus now—the glowing face of the god
and the god's dissembling words—and Helen's gown
and the veil adorned with a yellow acanthus border.

6. Another town with a temple of Venus, in Cyprus.

But above all, tragic Dido, doomed to a plague   850
about to strike, cannot feast her eyes enough,
thrilled both by the boy and gifts he brings
and the more she looks the more the fire grows.
But once he's embraced Aeneas, clung to his neck
to sate the deep love of his father, deluded father,   855
Cupid makes for the queen. Her gaze, her whole heart
is riveted on him now, and at times she even warms him
snugly in her breast, for how can she know, poor Dido,
what a mighty god is sinking into her, to her grief?
But he, recalling the wishes of his mother Venus,   860
blots out the memory of Sychaeus bit by bit,
trying to seize with a fresh, living love
a heart at rest for long—long numb to passion.
                                          Then,
with the first lull in the feast, the tables cleared away,
they set out massive bowls and crown the wine with wreaths.   865
A vast din swells in the palace, voices reverberating
through the echoing halls. They light the lamps,
hung from the coffered ceilings sheathed in gilt,
and blazing torches burn the night away.
The queen calls for a heavy golden bowl,   870
studded with jewels and brimmed with unmixed wine,
the bowl that Belus[7] and all of Belus' sons had brimmed,
and the hall falls hushed as Dido lifts a prayer:
"Jupiter, you, they say, are the god who grants
the laws of host and guest. May this day be one   875
of joy for Tyrians here and exiles come from Troy,
a day our sons will long remember. Bacchus,[8]
giver of bliss, and Juno, generous Juno,
bless us now. And come, my people, celebrate
with all good will this feast that makes us one!"   880

     With that prayer, she poured a libation to the gods,
tipping wine on the board, and tipping it, she was first
to take the bowl, brushing it lightly with her lips,
then gave it to Bitias—laughing, goading him on
and he took the plunge, draining the foaming bowl,   885
drenching himself in its brimming, overflowing gold,
and the other princes drank in turn. Then Iopas,
long-haired bard, strikes up his golden lyre
resounding through the halls. Giant Atlas[9]
had been his teacher once, and now he sings   890
the wandering moon and laboring sun eclipsed,
the roots of the human race and the wild beasts,
the source of storms and the lightning bolts on high,
Arcturus, the rainy Hyades and the Great and Little Bears,[1]

---

7. Dido's father.
8. God of wine (Dionysus in Greek mythology).
9. A Titan condemned for his defiance of

Jupiter to hold up the sky forever.
1. Constellations and stars.

and why the winter suns so rush to bathe themselves in the sea   895
and what slows down the nights to a long lingering crawl . . .
And time and again the Tyrians burst into applause
and the Trojans took their lead. So Dido, doomed,
was lengthening out the night by trading tales
as she drank long draughts of love—asking Aeneas   900
question on question, now about Priam, now Hector,
what armor Memnon, son of the Morning, wore at Troy,
how swift were the horses of Diomedes? How strong was Achilles?
"Wait, come, my guest," she urges, "tell us your own story,
start to finish—the ambush laid by the Greeks, the pain   905
your people suffered, the wanderings you have faced.
For now is the seventh summer that has borne you
wandering all the lands and seas on earth."

BOOK II

[The Final Hours of Troy]

Silence. All fell hushed, their eyes fixed on Aeneas now
as the founder of his people, high on a seat of honor,
set out on his story: "Sorrow, unspeakable sorrow,
my queen, you ask me to bring to life once more,
how the Greeks uprooted Troy in all her power,   5
our kingdom mourned forever. What horrors I saw,
a tragedy where I played a leading role myself.
Who could tell such things—not even a Myrmidon,
a Dolopian,² or comrade of iron-hearted Ulysses³—
and still refrain from tears? And now, too,   10
the dank night is sweeping down from the sky
and the setting stars incline our heads to sleep.
But if you long so deeply to know what we went through,
to hear, in brief, the last great agony of Troy,
much as I shudder at the memory of it all—   15
I shrank back in grief—I'll try to tell it now . . .

   "Ground down by the war and driven back by Fate,
the Greek captains had watched the years slip by
until, helped by Minerva's superhuman skill,
they built that mammoth horse, immense as a mountain,   20
lining its ribs with ship timbers hewn from pine.
An offering to secure safe passage home, or so
they pretend, and the story spreads through Troy.
But they pick by lot the best, most able-bodied men
and stealthily lock them into the horse's dark flanks   25
till the vast hold of the monster's womb is packed
with soldiers bristling weapons.
                            "Just in sight of Troy
an island rises, Tenedos, famed in the old songs,

2. Myrmidons and Dolopians are companions   3. Odysseus.
of Achilles.

powerful, rich, while Priam's realm stood fast.
Now it's only a bay, a treacherous cove for ships. 30
Well there they sail, hiding out on its lonely coast
while we thought—gone! Sped home on the winds to Greece.
So all Troy breathes free, relieved of her endless sorrow.
We fling open the gates and stream out, elated to see
the Greeks' abandoned camp, the deserted beachhead. 35
Here the Dolopians[4] formed ranks—
                              "Here savage Achilles
pitched his tents—
                    "Over there the armada moored
and here the familiar killing-fields of battle.
Some gaze wonderstruck at the gift for Pallas,
the virgin never wed[5]—transfixed by the horse, 40
its looming mass, our doom. Thymoetes leads the way.
'Drag it inside the walls,' he urges, 'plant it high
on the city heights!' Inspired by treachery now
or the fate of Troy was moving toward this end.
But Capys with other saner heads who take his side, 45
suspecting a trap in any gift the Greeks might offer,
tells us: 'Fling it into the sea or torch the thing to ash
or bore into the depths of its womb where men can hide!'
The common people are split into warring factions.

      "But now, out in the lead with a troop of comrades, 50
down Laocoön runs from the heights in full fury,
calling out from a distance: 'Poor doomed fools,
have you gone mad, you Trojans?
You really believe the enemy's sailed away?
Or any gift of the Greeks is free of guile? 55
Is that how well you know Ulysses? Trust me,
either the Greeks are hiding, shut inside those beams,
or the horse is a battle-engine geared to breach our walls,
spy on our homes, come down on our city, overwhelm us—
or some other deception's lurking deep inside it. 60
Trojans, never trust that horse. Whatever it is,
I fear the Greeks, especially bearing gifts.'
"In that spirit, with all his might he hurled
a huge spear straight into the monster's flanks,
the mortised timberwork of its swollen belly. 65
Quivering, there it stuck, and the stricken womb
came booming back from its depths with echoing groans.
If Fate and our own wits had not gone against us,
surely Laocoön would have driven us on, now,
to rip the Greek lair open with iron spears 70
and Troy would still be standing—
proud fortress of Priam, you would tower still!

---

4. From Dolopia, a region in Greece.   5. The goddess Athena was famously a virgin.

"Suddenly, in the thick of it all, a young soldier,
hands shackled behind his back, with much shouting
Trojan shepherds were haling him toward the king.   75
They'd come on the man by chance, a total stranger.
He'd given himself up, with one goal in mind:
to open Troy to the Greeks and lay her waste.
He trusted to courage, nerved for either end,
to weave his lies or face his certain death.   80
Young Trojan recruits, keen to have a look,
came scurrying up from all sides, crowding round,
outdoing each other to make a mockery of the captive.
Now, hear the treachery of the Greeks and learn
from a single crime the nature of the beast . . .   85
Haggard, helpless, there in our midst he stood,
all eyes riveted on him now, and turning a wary glance
at the lines of Trojan troops he groaned and spoke:
'Where can I find some refuge, where on land, on sea?
What's left for me now? A man of so much misery!   90
Nothing among the Greeks, no place at all. And worse,
I see my Trojan enemies crying for my blood.'
                                    "His groans
convince us, cutting all our show of violence short.
We press him: 'Tell us where you were born, your family.
What news do you bring? Tell us what you trust to,   95
such a willing captive.'
                        "'All of it, my king,
I'll tell you, come what may, the whole true story.
Greek I am, I don't deny it. No, that first.
Fortune may have made me a man of misery
but, wicked as she is,   100
she can't make Sinon a lying fraud as well.
                                    "'Now,
perhaps you've caught some rumor of Palamedes,[6]
Belus' son, and his shining fame that rings in song.
The Greeks charged him with treason, a trumped-up charge,
an innocent man, and just because he opposed the war   105
they put him to death, but once he's robbed of the light,
they mourn him sorely. Now I was his blood kin,
a youngster when my father, a poor man, sent me
off to the war at Troy as Palamedes' comrade.
Long as he kept his royal status, holding forth   110
in the councils of the kings, I had some standing too,
some pride of place. But once he left the land of the living,
thanks to the jealous, forked tongue of our Ulysses—
you're no stranger to *his* story—I was shattered,
I dragged out my life in the shadows, grieving,   115
seething alone, in silence . . .
outraged by my innocent friend's demise until

---

6. A Greek warrior who advised the Greeks to return home from Troy. Odysseus persuaded them that he was a traitor, and had him killed. He was descended from the Egyptian king Belus.

I burst out like a madman, swore if I ever returned
in triumph to our native Argos, ever got the chance
I'd take revenge, and my oath provoked a storm of hatred.   120
That was my first step on the slippery road to ruin.
From then on, Ulysses kept tormenting me, pressing
charge on charge; from then on, he bruited about
his two-edged rumors among the rank and file.
Driven by guilt, he looked for ways to kill me,   125
he never rested until, making Calchas[7] his henchman—
but why now? Why go over that unforgiving ground again?
Why waste words? If you think all Greeks are one,
if hearing the name *Greek* is enough for you,
it's high time you made me pay the price.   130
How that would please the man of Ithaca,[8]
how the sons of Atreus would repay you!'

                              "Now, of course,
we burn to question him, urge him to explain—
blind to how false the cunning Greeks could be.
All atremble, he carries on with his tale,   135
lying from the cockles of his heart:

                              "'Time and again
the Greeks had yearned to abandon Troy—bone-tired
from a long hard war—to put it far behind and
beat a clean retreat. Would to god they had.
But time and again, as they were setting sail,   140
the heavy seas would keep them confined to port
and the Southwind filled their hearts with dread
and worst of all, once this horse, this mass of timber
with locking planks, stood stationed here at last,
the thunderheads rumbled up and down the sky.   145
So, at our wit's end, we send Eurypylus off
to question Apollo's oracle now, and back
he comes from the god's shrine with these bleak words:
"With blood you appeased the winds, with a virgin's sacrifice
when you, you Greeks, first sought the shores of Troy.[9]   150
With blood you must seek fair winds to sail you home,
must sacrifice one more Greek life in return."

    "'As the word spread, the ranks were struck dumb
and icy fear sent shivers down their spines.
Whom did the god demand? Who'd meet his doom?   155
Just that moment the Ithacan haled the prophet,
Calchas, into our midst—he'd twist it out of him,
what was the gods' will? The army rose in uproar.
Even then our soldiers sensed that I was the one,
the target of that Ulysses' vicious schemes—   160
they saw it coming, still they held their tongues.

---

7. Greek prophet.
8. Ulysses.
9. Iphigenia was sacrificed by her father,
Agamemnon, to allow the winds to blow the
fleet to Troy.

For ten days the seer, silent, closed off in his tent,
refused to say a word or betray a man to death.
But at last, goaded on by Ulysses' mounting threats
but in fact conniving in their plot, he breaks his silence   165
and dooms me to the altar. And the army gave consent.
The death that each man dreaded turned to the fate
of one poor soul: a burden they could bear.

    "'The day of infamy soon came . . .
the sacred rites were all performed for the victim,   170
the salted meal strewn, the bands tied round my head.
But I broke free of death, I tell you, burst my shackles,
yes, and hid all night in the reeds of a marshy lake,
waiting for them to sail—if only they would sail!
Well, no hope now of seeing the land where I was born   175
or my sweet children, the father I longed for all these years.
Maybe they'll wring from *them* the price for my escape,
avenge my guilt with my loved ones' blood, poor things.
I beg you, king, by the Powers who know the truth,
by any trust still uncorrupt in the world of men,   180
pity a man whose torment knows no bounds.
Pity me in my pain.
I know in my soul I don't deserve to suffer.'

    "He wept and won his life—our pity, too.
Priam takes command, has him freed from the ropes   185
and chains that bind him fast, and hails him warmly:
'Whoever you are, from now on, now you've lost the Greeks,
put them out of your mind and you'll be one of us.
But answer my questions. Tell me the whole truth.
Why did they raise up this giant, monstrous horse?   190
Who conceived it? What's it for? its purpose?
A gift to the gods? A great engine of battle?'

    "He broke off. Sinon, adept at deceit,
with all his Greek cunning lifted his hands,
just freed from their fetters, up to the stars   195
and prayed: 'Bear witness, you eternal fires of the sky
and you inviolate will of the gods! Bear witness,
altar and those infernal knives that I escaped
and the sacred bands I wore myself: the victim.
It's right to break my sworn oath to the Greeks,   200
it's right to detest those men and bring to light
all they're hiding now. No laws of my native land
can bind me here. Just keep your promise, Troy,
and if I can save you, you must save me too—
if I reveal the truth and pay you back in full.   205

    "'All the hopes of the Greeks, their firm faith
in a war they'd launched themselves
had always hinged on Pallas Athena's help.

But from the moment that godless Diomedes,
flanked by Ulysses, the mastermind of crime, 210
attacked and tore the fateful image of Pallas[1]
out of her own hallowed shrine, and cut down
the sentries ringing your city heights and seized
that holy image and even dared touch the sacred bands
on the virgin goddess' head with hands reeking blood— 215
from that hour on, the high hopes of the Greeks
had trickled away like a slow, ebbing tide . . .
They were broken, beaten men,
the will of the goddess dead set against them.
Omens of this she gave in no uncertain terms. 220
They'd hardly stood her image up in the Greek camp
when flickering fire shot from its glaring eyes
and salt sweat ran glistening down its limbs
and three times the goddess herself—a marvel—
blazed forth from the ground, shield clashing, spear brandished. 225
The prophet spurs them at once to risk escape by sea:
"You cannot root out Troy with your Greek spears unless
you seek new omens in Greece and bring the god back here"—
the image they'd borne across the sea in their curved ships.
So now they've sailed away on the wind for home shores, 230
just to rearm, recruit their gods as allies yet again,
then measure back their course on the high seas and
back they'll come to attack you all off guard.

   "'So Calchas read the omens. At his command
they raised this horse, this effigy, all to atone 235
for the violated image of Pallas, her wounded pride,
her power—and expiate the outrage they had done.
But he made them do the work on a grand scale,
a tremendous mass of interlocking timbers towering
toward the sky, so the horse could not be trundled 240
through your gates or hauled inside your walls
or guard your people if they revered it well
in the old, ancient way. For if your hands
should violate this great offering to Minerva,
a total disaster—if only god would turn it 245
against the seer himself!—will wheel down
on Priam's empire, Troy, and all your futures.
But if your hands will rear it up, into your city,
then all Asia in arms can invade Greece, can launch
an all-out war right up to the walls of Pelops.[2] 250
That's the doom that awaits our sons' sons.'

   "Trapped by his craft, that cunning liar Sinon,
we believed his story. His tears, his treachery seized

1. An oracle stated that Troy could not be captured as long as the statue of Athena, the Palladium (after one of Athena's titles, Pallas), remained in place in her shrine.
2. Pelops was the grandfather of Agamemnon and Menelaus; his walls are the walls of Argos.

the men whom neither Tydeus' son[3] nor Achilles could defeat,
nor ten long years of war, nor all the thousand ships.   255

   "But a new portent strikes our doomed people
now—a greater omen, far more terrible, fatal,
shakes our senses, blind to what was coming.
Laocoön, the priest of Neptune picked by lot,
was sacrificing a massive bull at the holy altar   260
when—I cringe to recall it now—look there!
Over the calm deep straits off Tenedos swim
twin, giant serpents, rearing in coils, breasting
the sea-swell side by side, plunging toward the shore,
their heads, their blood-red crests surging over the waves,   265
their bodies thrashing, backs rolling in coil on mammoth coil
and the wake behind them churns in a roar of foaming spray,
and now, their eyes glittering, shot with blood and fire,
flickering tongues licking their hissing maws, yes, now
they're about to land. We blanch at the sight, we scatter.   270
Like troops on attack they're heading straight for Laocoön—
first each serpent seizes one of his small young sons,
constricting, twisting around him, sinks its fangs
in the tortured limbs, and gorges. Next Laocoön
rushing quick to the rescue, clutching his sword—   275
they trap him, bind him in huge muscular whorls,
their scaly backs lashing around his midriff twice
and twice around his throat—their heads, their flaring necks
mounting over their victim writhing still, his hands
frantic to wrench apart their knotted trunks,   280
his priestly bands splattered in filth, black venom
and all the while his horrible screaming fills the skies,
bellowing like some wounded bull struggling to shrug
loose from his neck an axe that's struck awry,
to lumber clear of the altar . . .   285
Only the twin snakes escape, sliding off and away
to the heights of Troy where the ruthless goddess
holds her shrine, and there at her feet they hide,
vanishing under Minerva's great round shield.
                                                 "At once,
I tell you, a stranger fear runs through the harrowed crowd.   290
Laocoön deserved to pay for his outrage, so they say,
he desecrated the sacred timbers of the horse,
he hurled his wicked lance at the beast's back.
'Haul Minerva's effigy up to her house,' we shout,
'Offer up our prayers to the power of the goddess!'   295
We breach our own ramparts, fling our defenses open,
all pitch into the work. Smooth running rollers
we wheel beneath its hoofs, and heavy hempen ropes
we bind around its neck, and teeming with men-at-arms
the huge deadly engine climbs our city walls . . .   300

3. Diomedes.

And round it boys and unwed girls sing hymns,
thrilled to lay a hand on the dangling ropes
as on and on it comes, gliding into the city,
looming high over the city's heart.
                                        "Oh my country!
Troy, home of the gods! You great walls of the Dardans[4]   305
long renowned in war!
                        "Four times it lurched to a halt
at the very brink of the gates—four times the armor
clashed out from its womb. But we, we forged ahead,
oblivious, blind, insane, we stationed the monster
fraught with doom on the hallowed heights of Troy.   310
Even now Cassandra[5] revealed the future, opening
lips the gods had ruled no Trojan would believe.
And we, poor fools—on this, our last day—we deck
the shrines of the gods with green holiday garlands
all throughout the city . . .
                                "But all the while   315
the skies keep wheeling on and night comes sweeping in
from the Ocean Stream, in its mammoth shadow swallowing up
the earth, and the Pole Star, and the treachery of the Greeks.
Dead quiet. The Trojans slept on, strewn throughout
their fortress, weary bodies embraced by slumber.   320
But the Greek armada was under way now, crossing
over from Tenedos, ships in battle formation
under the moon's quiet light, their silent ally,
homing in on the berths they know by heart—
when the king's flagship sends up a signal flare,   325
the cue for Sinon, saved by the Fates' unjust decree,
and stealthily loosing the pine bolts of the horse,
he unleashes the Greeks shut up inside its womb.
The horse stands open wide, fighters in high spirits
pouring out of its timbered cavern into the fresh air: 330
the chiefs, Thessandrus, Sthenelus, ruthless Ulysses
rappeling down a rope they dropped from its side,
and Acamas, Thoas, Neoptolemus, son of Achilles,
captain Machaon, Menelaus, Epeus himself,
the man who built that masterpiece of fraud.   335
They steal on a city buried deep in sleep and wine,
they butcher the guards, fling wide the gates and hug
their cohorts poised to combine forces. Plot complete.

    "This was the hour when rest, that gift of the gods
most heaven-sent, first comes to beleaguered mortals,   340
creeping over us now . . . when there, look,
I dreamed I saw Prince Hector before my eyes,
my comrade haggard with sorrow, streaming tears,

4. Dardanus founded the city of Dardania, just above Troy; hence the Dardans or Dardanians are the Trojans.
5. Daughter of King Priam. Apollo fell in love with her and gave her the gift of unerring prophecy; but when she refused him, he turned the gift into a curse, by ensuring that nobody would ever believe her predictions.

just as he once was, when dragged behind the chariot,
black with blood and grime, thongs piercing his swollen feet—   345
what a harrowing sight! What a far cry from the old Hector
home from battle, decked in Achilles' arms—his trophies—
or fresh from pitching Trojan fire at the Greek ships.
His beard matted now, his hair clotted with blood,
bearing the wounds, so many wounds he suffered   350
fighting round his native city's walls . . .
I dreamed I addressed him first, in tears myself
I forced my voice from the depths of all my grief:
'Oh light of the Trojans—last, best hope of Troy!
What's held you back so long? How long we've waited,   355
Hector, for you to come, and now from what far shores?
How glad we are to see you, we battle-weary men,
after so many deaths, your people dead and gone,
after your citizens, your city felt such pain.
But what outrage has mutilated your face   360
so clear and cloudless once? Why these wounds?'

    Wasting no words, no time on empty questions,
heaving a deep groan from his heart he calls out:
'Escape, son of the goddess, tear yourself from the flames!
The enemy holds our walls. Troy is toppling from her heights.   365
You have paid your debt to our king and native land.
If one strong arm could have saved Troy, my arm
would have saved the city. Now, into your hands
she entrusts her holy things, her household gods.
Take them with you as comrades in your fortunes.   370
Seek a city for them, once you have roved the seas,
erect great walls at last to house the gods of Troy!'

    Urging so, with his own hands he carries Vesta forth
from her inner shrine, her image clad in ribbons,
filled with her power, her everlasting fire.[6]
                                        "But now,   375
chaos—the city begins to reel with cries of grief,
louder, stronger, even though father's palace
stood well back, screened off by trees, but still
the clash of arms rings clearer, horror on the attack.
I shake off sleep and scrambling up to the pitched roof   380
I stand there, ears alert, and I hear a roar like fire
assaulting a wheatfield, whipped by a Southwind's fury,
or mountain torrent in full spate, flattening crops,
leveling all the happy, thriving labor of oxen,
dragging whole trees headlong down in its wake—   385
and a shepherd perched on a sheer rock outcrop
hears the roar, lost in amazement, struck dumb.
No doubting the good faith of the Greeks now,
their treachery plain as day.

6. In the temple of Vesta, the hearth goddess, was a fire that was never allowed to go out.

        "Already, there,
the grand house of Deiphobus[7] stormed by fire,   390
crashing in ruins—
            "Already his neighbor Ucalegon
up in flames—
            "The Sigean straits[8] shimmering back the blaze,
the shouting of fighters soars, the clashing blare of trumpets.
Out of my wits, I seize my arms—what reason for arms?
Just my spirit burning to muster troops for battle,   395
rush with comrades up to the city's heights,
fury and rage driving me breakneck on
as it races through my mind
what a noble thing it is to die in arms!
            "But now, look,
just slipped out from under the Greek barrage of spears,   400
Panthus, Othrys' son, a priest of Apollo's shrine
on the citadel—hands full of the holy things,
the images of our conquered gods—he's dragging along
his little grandson, making a wild dash for our doors.
'Panthus, where's our stronghold? our last stand?'—   405
words still on my lips as he groans in answer:
'The last *day* has come for the Trojan people,
no escaping this moment. Troy's no more.
Ilium, gone—our awesome Trojan glory.
Brutal Jupiter hands it all over to Greece,   410
Greeks are lording over our city up in flames.
The horse stands towering high in the heart of Troy,
disgorging its armed men, with Sinon in his glory,
gloating over us—Sinon fans the fires.
The immense double gates are flung wide open,   415
Greeks in their thousands mass there, all who ever
sailed from proud Mycenae. Others have choked
the cramped streets, weapons brandished now
in a battle line of naked, glinting steel
tense for the kill. Only the first guards   420
at the gates put up some show of resistance,
fighting blindly on.'

   "Spurred by Panthus' words and the gods' will,
into the blaze I dive, into the fray, wherever
the din of combat breaks and war cries fill the sky,   425
wherever the battle-fury drives me on and now
I'm joined by Rhipeus, Epytus mighty in armor,
rearing up in the moonlight—
Hypanis comes to my side, and Dymas too,
flanked by the young Coroebus, Mygdon's son.   430
Late in the day he'd chanced to come to Troy
incensed with a mad, burning love for Cassandra:
son-in-law to our king, *he* would rescue Troy. Poor man,
if only he'd marked his bride's inspired ravings!

---

7. A son of Priam.   8. Promontory leading into the Aegean Sea.

Seeing their close-packed ranks, hot for battle,   435
I spur them on their way: 'Men, brave hearts,
though bravery cannot save us—if you're bent on
following me and risking all to face the worst,
look around you, see how our chances stand.
The gods who shored our empire up have left us,   440
all have deserted their altars and their shrines.
You race to defend a city already lost in flames.
But let us die, go plunging into the thick of battle.
One hope saves the defeated: they know they can't be saved!'
That fired their hearts with the fury of despair.

                                  "Now   445
like a wolfpack out for blood on a foggy night,
driven blindly on by relentless, rabid hunger,
leaving cubs behind, waiting, jaws parched—
so through spears, through enemy ranks we plow
to certain death, striking into the city's heart,   450
the shielding wings of the darkness beating round us.
Who has words to capture that night's disaster,
tell that slaughter? What tears could match
our torments now? An ancient city is falling,
a power that ruled for ages, now in ruins.   455
Everywhere lie the motionless bodies of the dead,
strewn in her streets, her homes and the gods' shrines
we held in awe. And not only Trojans pay the price in blood—
at times the courage races back in their conquered hearts
and they cut their enemies down in all their triumph.   460
Everywhere, wrenching grief, everywhere, terror
and a thousand shapes of death.
                              "And the first Greek
to cross our path? Androgeos leading a horde of troops
and taking *us* for allies on the march, the fool,
he even gives us a warm salute and calls out: 465
'Hurry up, men. Why holding back, why now,
why drag your heels? Troy's up in flames,
the rest are looting, sacking the city heights.
But you, have you just come from the tall ships?'
Suddenly, getting no password he can trust,   470
he sensed he'd stumbled into enemy ranks!
Stunned, he recoiled, swallowing back his words
like a man who threads his way through prickly brambles,
pressing his full weight on the ground, and blindly treads
on a lurking snake and back he shrinks in instant fear   475
as it rears in anger, puffs its blue-black neck.
Just so Androgeos, seeing us, cringes with fear,
recoiling, struggling to flee but we attack,
flinging a ring of steel around his cohorts—
panic takes the Greeks unsure of their ground   480
and we cut them all to pieces.
Fortune fills our sails in that first clash
and Coroebus, flushed, fired with such success,
exults: 'Comrades, wherever Fortune points the way,

wherever the first road to safety leads, let's soldier on.   485
Exchange shields with the Greeks and wear their emblems.
Call it cunning or courage: who would ask in war?
Our enemies will arm us to the hilt.'
                              "With that he dons
Androgeos' crested helmet, his handsome blazoned shield
and straps a Greek sword to his hip, and comrades,   490
spirits rising, take his lead. Rhipeus, Dymas too
and our corps of young recruits—each fighter
arms himself in the loot that he just seized
and on we forge, blending in with the enemy,
battling time and again under strange gods,   495
fighting hand-to-hand in the blind dark
and many Greeks we send to the King of Death.
Some scatter back to their ships, making a run
for shore and safety. Others disgrace themselves,
so panicked they clamber back inside the monstrous horse,   500
burying into the womb they know so well.
                              "But, oh
how wrong to rely on gods dead set against you!
Watch: the virgin daughter of Priam, Cassandra,
torn from the sacred depths of Minerva's shrine,
dragged by the hair, raising her burning eyes   505
to the heavens, just her eyes, so helpless,
shackles kept her from raising her gentle hands.
Coroebus could not bear the sight of it—mad with rage
he flung himself at the Greek lines and met his death.
Closing ranks we charge after him, into the thick of battle   510
and face our first disaster. Down from the temple roof
come showers of lances hurled by our own comrades there,
duped by the look of our Greek arms, our Greek crests
that launched this grisly slaughter. And worse still,
the Greeks roaring with anger—we had saved Cassandra—   515
attack us from all sides! Ajax, fiercest of all and
Atreus' two sons and the whole Dolopian army,
wild as a rampaging whirlwind, gusts clashing,
the West and the South and Eastwind riding high
on the rushing horses of the dawn, and the woods howl   520
and Nereus[9] thrashing his savage trident, churns up
the sea exploding in foam from its rocky depths.
And those Greeks we had put to rout, our ruse
in the murky night stampeding them headlong on
throughout the city—back they come, the first   525
to see that our shields and spears are naked lies,
to mark the words on our lips that jar with theirs.
In a flash, superior numbers overwhelm us.
Coroebus is first to go,
cut down by Peneleus' right hand he sprawls   530

9. An old sea god.

at Minerva's shrine, the goddess, power of armies.[1]
Rhipeus falls too, the most righteous man in Troy,
the most devoted to justice, true, but the gods
had other plans.
        "Hypanis, Dymas die as well,
run through by their own men—
                "And you, Panthus,   535
not all your piety, all the sacred bands you wore
as Apollo's priest could save you as you fell.
Ashes of Ilium, last flames that engulfed my world—
I swear by you that in your last hour I never shrank
from the Greek spears, from any startling hazard of war—   540
if Fate had struck me down, my sword-arm earned it all.
Now we are swept away, Iphitus, Pelias with me,
one weighed down with age and the other slowed
by a wound Ulysses gave him—heading straight
for Priam's palace, driven there by the outcries.   545

    "And there, I tell you, a pitched battle flares!
You'd think no other battles could match its fury,
nowhere else in the city were people dying so.
Invincible Mars[2] rears up to meet us face-to-face
with waves of Greeks assaulting the roofs, we see them   550
choking the gateway, under a tortoise-shell of shields,[3]
and the scaling ladders cling to the steep ramparts—
just at the gates the raiders scramble up the rungs,
shields on their left arms thrust out for defense,
their right hands clutching the gables.   555
Over against them, Trojans ripping the tiles
and turrets from all their roofs—the end is near,
they can see it now, at the brink of death, desperate
for weapons, some defense, and these, these missiles they send
reeling down on the Greeks' heads—the gilded beams,   560
the inlaid glory of all our ancient fathers.
Comrades below, posted in close-packed ranks,
block the entries, swordpoints drawn and poised.
My courage renewed, I rush to relieve the palace,
brace the defenders, bring the defeated strength.   565

    There was a secret door, a hidden passage
linking the wings of Priam's house—remote,
far to the rear. Long as our realm still stood,
Andromache, poor woman, would often go this way,
unattended, to Hector's parents, taking the boy   570
Astyanax[4] by the hand to see grandfather Priam.
I slipped through the door, up to the jutting roof

1. Minerva was a warrior goddess, often depicted carrying weapons.
2. God of war.
3. Position adopted by Roman soldiers: packed tightly together, they put their shields above their heads, making the army look like a tortoise.
4. Hector and Andromache's son.

where the doomed Trojans were hurling futile spears.
There was a tower soaring high at the peak toward the sky,
our favorite vantage point for surveying all of Troy   575
and the Greek fleet and camp. We attacked that tower
with iron crowbars, just where the upper-story planks
showed loosening joints—we rocked it, wrenched it free
of its deep moorings and all at once we heaved it toppling
down with a crash, trailing its wake of ruin to grind   580
the massed Greeks assaulting left and right. But on
came Greek reserves, no letup, the hail of rocks,
the missiles of every kind would never cease.

   "There at the very edge of the front gates
springs Pyrrhus, son of Achilles, prancing in arms,   585
aflash in his shimmering brazen sheath like a snake
buried the whole winter long under frozen turf,
swollen to bursting, fed full on poisonous weeds
and now it springs into light, sloughing its old skin
to glisten sleek in its newfound youth, its back slithering, 590
coiling, its proud chest rearing high to the sun,
its triple tongue flickering through its fangs.
Backing him now comes Periphas, giant fighter,
Automedon too, Achilles' henchman, charioteer
who bore the great man's armor—backing Pyrrhus,   595
the young fighters from Scyros raid the palace,
hurling firebrands at the roofs. Out in the lead,
Pyrrhus seizes a double-axe and batters the rocky sill
and ripping the bronze posts out of their sockets,
hacking the rugged oaken planks of the doors,   600
makes a breach, a gaping maw, and there, exposed,
the heart of the house, the sweep of the colonnades,
the palace depths of the old kings and Priam lie exposed
and they see the armed sentries bracing at the portals.

   "But all in the house is turmoil, misery, groans,   605
the echoing chambers ring with cries of women,
wails of mourning hit the golden stars.
Mothers scatter in panic down the palace halls
and embrace the pillars, cling to them, kiss them hard.
But on he comes, Pyrrhus with all his father's force,   610
no bolts, not even the guards can hold him back—
under the ram's repeated blows the doors cave in,
the doorposts, prised from their sockets, crash flat.
Force makes a breach and the Greeks come storming through,
butcher the sentries, flood the entire place with men-at-arms. 615
No river so wild, so frothing in spate, bursting its banks
to overpower the dikes, anything in its way, its cresting
tides stampeding in fury down on the fields to sweep
the flocks and stalls across the open plain.
I saw him myself, Pyrrhus crazed with carnage   620
and Atreus' two sons just at the threshold—

"I saw
Hecuba with her hundred daughters and daughters-in-law,[5]
saw Priam fouling with blood the altar fires
he himself had blessed.
                    "Those fifty bridal-chambers
filled with the hope of children's children still to come,   625
the pillars proud with trophies, gilded with Eastern gold,
they all come tumbling down—
and the Greeks hold what the raging fire spares.

    "Perhaps you wonder how Priam met his end.
When he saw his city stormed and seized, his gates   630
wrenched apart, the enemy camped in his palace depths,
the old man dons his armor long unused, he clamps it
round his shoulders shaking with age and, all for nothing,
straps his useless sword to his hip, then makes
for the thick of battle, out to meet his death.   635
At the heart of the house an ample altar stood,
naked under the skies,
an ancient laurel bending over the shrine,
embracing our household gods within its shade.
Here, flocking the altar, Hecuba and her daughters   640
huddled, blown headlong down like doves by a black storm—
clutching, all for nothing, the figures of their gods.
Seeing Priam decked in the arms he'd worn as a young man,
'Are you insane?' she cries, 'Poor husband, what impels you
to strap that sword on now? Where are you rushing?   645
Too late for such defense, such help. Not even
my own Hector, if _he_ came to the rescue now . . .
Come to me, Priam. This altar will shield us all
or else you'll die with us.'
                    "With those words,
drawing him toward her there, she made a place   650
for the old man beside the holy shrine.
                            "Suddenly,
look, a son of Priam, Polites, just escaped
from slaughter at Pyrrhus' hands, comes racing in
through spears, through enemy fighters, fleeing down
the long arcades and deserted hallways—badly wounded,   655
Pyrrhus hot on his heels, a weapon poised for the kill,
about to seize him, about to run him through and pressing
home as Polites reached his parents and collapsed,
vomiting out his life blood before their eyes.
At that, Priam, trapped in the grip of death,   660
not holding back, not checking his words, his rage:
'You!' he cries, 'you and your vicious crimes!
If any power on high recoils at such an outrage,

---

5. Wife of Priam, king of Troy. He had fifty sons and fifty daughters—not all by Hecuba.

let the gods repay you for all your reckless work,
grant you the thanks, the rich reward you've earned.   665
You've made me see my son's death with my own eyes,
defiled a father's sight with a son's life blood.
You say you're Achilles' son? You lie! Achilles
never treated his enemy Priam so. No, he honored
a suppliant's rights, he blushed to betray my trust,   670
he restored my Hector's bloodless corpse for burial,
sent me safely home to the land I rule!'
                                        With that
and with all his might the old man flings his spear—
but too impotent now to pierce, it merely grazes
Pyrrhus' brazen shield that blocks its way   675
and clings there, dangling limp from the boss,
all for nothing. Pyrrhus shouts back: 'Well then,
down you go, a messenger to my father, Peleus' son![6]
Tell him about my vicious work, how Neoptolemus
degrades his father's name—don't you forget.   680
Now—die!'
            That said, he drags the old man
straight to the altar, quaking, slithering on through
slicks of his son's blood, and twisting Priam's hair
in his left hand, his right hand sweeping forth his sword—
a flash of steel—he buries it hilt-deep in the king's flank.   685

   "Such was the fate of Priam, his death, his lot on earth,
with Troy blazing before his eyes, her ramparts down,
the monarch who once had ruled in all his glory
the many lands of Asia, Asia's many tribes.
A powerful trunk is lying on the shore.[7]   690
The head wrenched from the shoulders.
A corpse without a name.
                        "Then, for the first time
the full horror came home to me at last. I froze.
The thought of my own dear father filled my mind
when I saw the old king gasping out his life   695
with that raw wound—both men were the same age—
and the thought of my Creusa, alone, abandoned,
our house plundered, our little Iulus' fate.[8]
I look back—what forces still stood by me?
None. Totally spent in war, they'd all deserted,   700
down from the roofs they'd flung themselves to earth
or hurled their broken bodies in the flames.

6. Achilles was the son of Peleus. He was already dead at this point, killed by Paris with an arrow to the heel.
7. The detail that the body is left "on the shore"—which makes no narrative sense, since Priam is killed in the center of the city—is an allusion to the assassination of Pompey the Great. In the civil war of 49–45 B.C.E., Pompey, representing the more aristocratic party, was defeated by the more populist Julius Caesar, and eventually assassinated; his body was famously abandoned on the beach of Egypt.
8. Creusa is Aeneas's wife; Iulus is his son.

["So,[9]
at just that moment I was the one man left
and then I saw her, clinging to Vesta's threshold,
hiding in silence, tucked away—Helen of Argos.
Glare of the fires lit my view as I looked down,   705
scanning the city left and right, and there she was . . .
terrified of the Trojans' hate, now Troy was overpowered,
terrified of the Greeks' revenge, her deserted husband's rage—
that universal Fury, a curse to Troy and her native land   710
and here she lurked, skulking, a thing of loathing
cowering at the altar: Helen. Out it flared,
the fire inside my soul, my rage ablaze to avenge
our fallen country—pay Helen back, crime for crime.

    "'So, this woman,' it struck me now, 'safe and sound   715
she'll look once more on Sparta, her native Greece?
She'll ride like a queen in triumph with her trophies?
Feast her eyes on her husband, parents, children too?
Her retinue fawning round her, Phrygian[1] ladies, slaves?
That—with Priam put to the sword? And Troy up in flames?   720
And time and again our Dardan shores have sweated blood?
Not for all the world. No fame, no memory to be won
for punishing a woman: such victory reaps no praise
but to stamp this abomination out as she deserves,
to punish her now, they'll sing my praise for *that*.   725
What joy, to glut my heart with the fires of vengeance,
bring some peace to the ashes of my people!'

    "Whirling words—I was swept away by fury now]
when all of a sudden there my loving mother[2] stood
before my eyes, but I had never seen her so clearly,   730
her pure radiance shining down upon me through the night,
the goddess in all her glory, just as the gods behold
her build, her awesome beauty. Grasping my hand
she held me back, adding this from her rose-red lips:
'My son, what grief could incite such blazing anger?   735
Why such fury? And the love you bore me once,
where has it all gone? Why don't you look first
where you left your father, Anchises, spent with age?
Do your wife, Creusa, and son Ascanius still survive?
The Greek battalions are swarming round them all,   740
and if my love had never rushed to the rescue,
flames would have swept them off by now or
enemy sword-blades would have drained their blood.
Think: it's not that beauty, Helen, you should hate,
not even Paris, the man that you should blame, no,   745
it's the gods, the ruthless gods who are tearing down
the wealth of Troy, her toppling crown of towers.

9. This passage is bracketed because many scholars believe it does not belong in the poem, since it is contradicted by a passage in book 6 (573–623). The contradiction may be a sign of the *Aeneid*'s unfinished status at Virgil's death.
1. That is, Trojan.
2. Venus.

Look around. I'll sweep it all away, the mist
so murky, dark, and swirling around you now,
it clouds your vision, dulls your mortal sight.   750
You are my son. Never fear my orders.
Never refuse to bow to my commands.
           " 'There,
yes, where you see the massive ramparts shattered,
blocks wrenched from blocks, the billowing smoke and ash—
it's Neptune himself,[3] prising loose with his giant trident 755
the foundation-stones of Troy, he's making the walls quake,
ripping up the entire city by her roots.
          " 'There's Juno,
cruelest in fury, first to commandeer the Scaean Gates,[4]
sword at her hip and mustering comrades, shock troops
streaming out of the ships.
          " 'Already up on the heights— 760
turn around and look—there's Pallas holding the fortress,
flaming out of the clouds, her savage Gorgon glaring.[5]
Even Father himself, he's filling the Greek hearts
with courage, stamina—Jove in person spurring the gods
to fight the Trojan armies!
         " 'Run for your life, my son. 765
Put an end to your labors. I will never leave you,
I will set you safe at your father's door.'

  "Parting words. She vanished into the dense night.
And now they all come looming up before me,
terrible shapes, the deadly foes of Troy,   770
the gods gigantic in power.
        "Then at last
I saw it all, all Ilium settling into her embers,
Neptune's Troy, toppling over now from her roots
like a proud, veteran ash on its mountain summit,
chopped by stroke after stroke of the iron axe as 775
woodsmen fight to bring it down, and over and
over it threatens to fall, its boughs shudder,
its leafy crown quakes and back and forth it sways
till overwhelmed by its wounds, with a long last groan
it goes—torn up from its heights it crashes down 780
in ruins from its ridge . . .
Venus leading, down from the roof I climb
and win my way through fires and massing foes.
The spears recede, the flames roll back before me.

  "At last, gaining the door of father's ancient house, 785
my first concern was to find the man, my first wish

---

3. The sea god (Poseidon in Greek mythology), who was hostile to the Trojans, since Laomedon, an early king of Troy, failed to repay him for helping to build the city walls.
4. The Scaean Gates are the main entrance to Troy.
5. Pallas Athena's shield displays the head of a Gorgon: the monster that turns those who look at it to stone.

to spirit him off, into the high mountain range,
but father, seeing Ilium razed from the earth,
refused to drag his life out now and suffer exile.
'You,' he argued, 'you in your prime, untouched by age,   790
your blood still coursing strong, you hearts of oak,
you are the ones to hurry your escape. Myself,
if the gods on high had wished me to live on,
they would have saved my palace for me here.
Enough—more than enough—that I have seen   795
one sack of my city, once survived its capture.[6]
Here I lie, here laid out for death. Come say
your parting salutes and leave my body so.
I will find my own death, sword in hand:
my enemies keen for spoils will be so kind.   800
Death without burial? A small price to pay.
For years now, I've lingered out my life,
despised by the gods, a dead weight to men,
ever since the Father of Gods and King of Mortals
stormed at me with his bolt and scorched me with its fire.'[7]   805

    "So he said, planted there. Nothing could shake him now.
But we dissolved in tears, my wife, Creusa, Ascanius,
the whole household, begging my father not to pull
our lives down with him, adding his own weight
to the fate that dragged us down.   810
He still refuses, holds to his resolve,
clings to the spot. And again I rush to arms,
desperate to die myself. Where could I turn?
What were our chances now, at this point?
'What!' I cried. 'Did you, my own father,   815
dream that I could run away and desert you here?
How could such an outrage slip from a father's lips?
If it please the gods that nothing of our great city
shall survive—if you are bent on adding your own death
to the deaths of Troy and of all your loved ones too,   820
the doors of the deaths you crave are spread wide open.
Pyrrhus will soon be here, bathed in Priam's blood,
Pyrrhus who butchers sons in their fathers' faces,
slaughters fathers at the altar. Was it for this,
my loving mother, you swept me clear of the weapons,   825
free of the flames? Just to see the enemy camped
in the very heart of our house, to see my son, Ascanius,
see my father, my wife, Creusa, with them, sacrificed,
massacred in each other's blood?

6. Troy had been sacked by Hercules, when
the previous king (Laomedon) cheated him.
7. When Anchises had his affair with Venus,
he was sworn to secrecy. He broke his word
and boasted about sleeping with the goddess,
so Jupiter hurled a thunderbolt at him as punishment, making him lame.

'Arms, my comrades,
bring me arms! The last light calls the defeated.   830
Send me back to the Greeks, let me go back
to fight new battles. Not all of us here
will die today without revenge.'
                        "Now buckling on
my sword again and working my left arm through
the shieldstrap, grasping it tightly, just as I   835
was rushing out, right at the doors my wife, Creusa,
look, flung herself at my feet and hugged my knees
and raised our little Iulus up to his father.
'If you are going off to die,' she begged,
'then take us with you too,   840
to face the worst together. But if your battles
teach you to hope in arms, the arms you buckle on,
your first duty should be to guard our house.
Desert us, leave us now—to whom? Whom?
Little Iulus, your father and your wife,   845
so I once was called.'
                    "So Creusa cries,
her wails of anguish echoing through the house
when out of the blue an omen strikes—a marvel!
Now as we held our son between our hands
and both our grieving faces, a tongue of fire,   850
watch, flares up from the crown of Iulus' head,
a subtle flame licking his downy hair, feeding
around the boy's brow, and though it never harmed him,
panicked, we rush to shake the flame from his curls
and smother the holy fire, damp it down with water.   855
But Father Anchises lifts his eyes to the stars in joy
and stretching his hands toward the sky, sings out:
'Almighty Jove! If any prayer can persuade you now,
look down on us—that's all I ask—if our devotion
has earned it, grant us another omen, Father,   860
seal this first clear sign.'
                        "No sooner said
than an instant peal of thunder crashes on the left
and down from the sky a shooting star comes gliding,
trailing a flaming torch to irradiate the night
as it comes sweeping down. We watch it sailing   865
over the topmost palace roofs to bury itself,
still burning bright, in the forests of Mount Ida,
blazing its path with light, leaving a broad furrow,
a fiery wake, and miles around the smoking sulfur fumes.
Won over at last, my father rises to his full height   870
and prays to the gods and reveres that holy star:
'No more delay, not now! You gods of my fathers,
now I follow wherever you lead me, I am with you.
Safeguard our house, safeguard my grandson Iulus!
This sign is yours: Troy rests in your power.   875

I give way, my son. No more refusals.
I will go with you, your comrade.'
                                        "So he yielded
but now the roar of flames grows louder all through Troy
and the seething floods of fire are rolling closer.
'So come, dear father, climb up onto my shoulders!   880
I will carry you on my back. This labor of love
will never wear me down. Whatever falls to us now,
we both will share one peril, one path to safety.
Little Iulus, walk beside me, and you, my wife,
follow me at a distance, in my footsteps.   885
Servants, listen closely . . .
Just past the city walls a gravemound lies
where an old shrine of forsaken Ceres stands
with an ancient cypress growing close beside it—
our fathers' reverence kept it green for years.   890
Coming by many routes, it's there we meet,
our rendezvous. And you, my father, carry
our hearthgods now, our fathers' sacred vessels.
I, just back from the war and fresh from slaughter,
I must not handle the holy things—it's wrong—   895
not till I cleanse myself in running springs.'
                                        "With that,
over my broad shoulders and round my neck I spread
a tawny lion's skin for a cloak, and bowing down,
I lift my burden up. Little Iulus, clutching
my right hand, keeps pace with tripping steps.   900
My wife trails on behind. And so we make our way
along the pitch-dark paths, and I who had never flinched
at the hurtling spears or swarming Greek assaults—
now every stir of wind, every whisper of sound
alarms me, anxious both for the child beside me   905
and burden on my back. And then, nearing the gates,
thinking we've all got safely through, I suddenly
seem to catch the steady tramp of marching feet
and father, peering out through the darkness, cries:
'Run for it now, my boy, you must. They're closing in,   910
I can see their glinting shields, their flashing bronze!'

     "Then in my panic something strange, some enemy power
robbed me of my senses. Lost, I was leaving behind
familiar paths, at a run down blind dead ends
when—
          "Oh dear god, my wife, Creusa—   915
torn from me by a brutal fate! What then,
did she stop in her tracks or lose her way?
Or exhausted, sink down to rest? Who knows?
I never set my eyes on her again.
I never looked back, she never crossed my mind—   920
Creusa, lost—not till we reached that barrow
sacred to ancient Ceres where, with all our people

rallied at last, she alone was missing. Lost
to her friends, her son, her husband—gone forever.
Raving, I blamed them all, the gods, the human race—   925
what crueler blow did I feel the night that Troy went down?
Ascanius, father Anchises, and all the gods of Troy,
entrusting them to my friends, I hide them well away
in a valley's shelter, don my burnished gear
and back I go to Troy . . .   930
my mind steeled to relive the whole disaster,
retrace my route through the whole city now
and put my life in danger one more time.
                                      "First then,
back to the looming walls, the shadowy rear gates
by which I'd left the city, back I go in my tracks,   935
retracing, straining to find my footsteps in the dark,
with terror at every turn, the very silence makes me cringe.
Then back to my house I go—if only, only she's gone there—
but the Greeks have flooded in, seized the entire place.
All over now. Devouring fire whipped by the winds   940
goes churning into the rooftops, flames surging
over them, scorching blasts raging up the sky.
On I go and again I see the palace of Priam
set on the heights, but there in colonnades
deserted now, in the sanctuary of Juno, there   945
stand the elite watchmen, Phoenix, ruthless Ulysses
guarding all their loot. All the treasures of Troy
hauled from the burning shrines—the sacramental tables,
bowls of solid gold and the holy robes they'd seized
from every quarter—Greeks, piling high the plunder.   950
Children and trembling mothers rounded up
in a long, endless line.
                                 "Why, I even dared fling
my voice through the dark, my shouts filled the streets
as time and again, overcome with grief I called out
'Creusa!' Nothing, no reply, and again 'Creusa!'   955
But then as I madly rushed from house to house,
no end in sight, abruptly, right before my eyes
I saw her stricken ghost, my own Creusa's shade.
But larger than life, the life I'd known so well.
I froze. My hackles bristled, voice choked in my throat,   960
and my wife spoke out to ease me of my anguish:
'My dear husband, why so eager to give yourself
to such mad flights of grief? It's not without
the will of the gods these things have come to pass.
But the gods forbid you to take Creusa with you,   965
bound from Troy together. The king of lofty Olympus[8]
won't allow it. A long exile is your fate . . .
the vast plains of the sea are yours to plow

8. Jupiter.

until you reach Hesperian land, where Lydian Tiber[9]
flows with its smooth march through rich and loamy fields,   970
a land of hardy people. There great joy and a kingdom
are yours to claim, and a queen to make your wife.
Dispel your tears for Creusa, whom you loved.
I will never behold the high and mighty pride
of their palaces, the Myrmidons, the Dolopians,   975
or go as a slave to some Greek matron, no, not I,
daughter of Dardanus that I am, the wife of Venus' son.
The Great Mother of Gods[1] detains me on these shores.
And now farewell. Hold dear the son we share,
we love together.'
                     "These were her parting words   980
and for all my tears—I longed to say so much—
dissolving into the empty air she left me now.
Three times I tried to fling my arms around her neck,
three times I embraced—nothing . . . her phantom
sifting through my fingers,   985
light as wind, quick as a dream in flight.
                                  "Gone—
and at last the night was over. Back I went to my people
and I was amazed to see what throngs of new companions
had poured in to swell our numbers, mothers, men,
our forces gathered for exile, grieving masses.   990
They had come together from every quarter,
belongings, spirits ready for me to lead them
over the sea to whatever lands I'd choose.
And now the morning star was mounting above
the high crests of Ida, leading on the day.   995
The Greeks had taken the city, blocked off every gate.
No hope of rescue now. So I gave way at last and
lifting my father, headed toward the mountains."

Summary of Book III   Aeneas and his fleet travel across the Mediterranean. On the
way, they meet the monstrous bird-women (Harpies) and visit Andromache, widow of Hector.
Anchises dies, and the storm carries the Trojans to Carthage.

BOOK IV

[The Tragic Queen of Carthage]

But the queen—too long she has suffered the pain of love,
hour by hour nursing the wound with her lifeblood,
consumed by the fire buried in her heart.
The man's courage, the sheer pride of his line,
they all come pressing home to her, over and over.   5
His looks, his words, they pierce her heart and cling—
no peace, no rest for her body, love will give her none.

9. "Hesperian" is literally "western." The Tiber   were thought to come from Lydia.
runs through Rome. "Lydian" is used as an   1. Cybele is the mother goddess.
alternative for "Etruscan," since the Etruscans

A new day's dawn was moving over the earth, Aurora's torch
cleansing the sky, burning away the dank shade of night
as the restless queen, beside herself, confides now   10
to the sister of her soul: "Dear Anna, the dreams
that haunt my quaking heart! Who is this stranger
just arrived to lodge in our house—our guest?
How noble his face, his courage, and what a soldier!
I'm sure—I know it's true—the man is born of the gods.   15
Fear exposes the lowborn man at once. But, oh, how tossed
he's been by the blows of fate. What a tale he's told,
what a bitter bowl of war he's drunk to the dregs.
If my heart had not been fixed, dead set against
embracing another man in the bonds of marriage—   20
ever since my first love deceived me, cheated me
by his death—if I were not as sick as I am
of the bridal bed and torch,[2] this, perhaps,
is my one lapse that might have brought me down.
I confess it, Anna, yes. Ever since my Sychaeus,   25
my poor husband met his fate, and my own brother
shed his blood and stained our household gods,
this is the only man who's roused me deeply,
swayed my wavering heart . . .
The signs of the old flame, I know them well.   30
I pray that the earth gape deep enough to take me down
or the almighty Father blast me with one bolt to the shades,
the pale, glimmering shades in hell, the pit of night,
before I dishonor you, my conscience, break your laws.
He's carried my love away, the man who wed me first—   35
may he hold it tight, safeguard it in his grave."

    She broke off, her voice choking with tears
that brimmed and wet her breast.
                    But Anna answered:
"Dear one, dearer than light to me, your sister,
would you waste away, grieving your youth away, alone,   40
never to know the joy of children, all the gifts of love?
Do you really believe that's what the dust desires,
the ghosts in their ashen tombs? Have it your way.
But granted that no one tempted you in the past,
not in your great grief,   45
no Libyan suitor, and none before in Tyre,
you scorned Iarbas and other lords of Africa,
sons bred by this fertile earth in all their triumph:
why resist it now, this love that stirs your heart?
Don't you recall whose lands you settled here,   50
the men who press around you? On one side
the Gaetulian cities, fighters matchless in battle,
unbridled Numidians—Syrtes, the treacherous Sandbanks.

2. Torches were used at weddings in antiquity.

On the other side an endless desert, parched earth
where the wild Barcan marauders[3] range at will.   55
Why mention the war that's boiling up in Tyre,
your brother's deadly threats? I think, in fact,
the favor of all the gods and Juno's backing drove
these Trojan ships on the winds that sailed them here.
Think what a city you will see, my sister, what a kingdom   60
rising high if you marry such a man! With a Trojan army
marching at our side, think how the glory of Carthage
will tower to the clouds! Just ask the gods for pardon,
win them with offerings. Treat your guests like kings.
Weave together some pretext for delay, while winter   65
spends its rage and drenching Orion whips the sea—
the ships still battered, weather still too wild."

These were the words that fanned her sister's fire,
turned her doubts to hopes and dissolved her sense of shame.
And first they visit the altars, make the rounds,   70
praying the gods for blessings, shrine by shrine.
They slaughter the pick of yearling sheep, the old way,
to Ceres, Giver of Laws, to Apollo, Bacchus who sets us free
and Juno above all, who guards the bonds of marriage.[4]
Dido aglow with beauty holds the bowl in her right hand,   75
pouring wine between the horns of a pure white cow
or gravely paces before the gods' fragrant altars,
under their statues' eyes refreshing her first gifts,
dawn to dusk. And when the victims' chests are splayed,
Dido, her lips parted, pores over their entrails,   80
throbbing still, for signs . . . [5]
But, oh, how little they know, the omniscient seers.
What good are prayers and shrines to a person mad with love?
The flame keeps gnawing into her tender marrow hour by hour
and deep in her heart the silent wound lives on.   85
Dido burns with love—the tragic queen.
She wanders in frenzy through her city streets
like a wounded doe caught all off guard by a hunter
stalking the woods of Crete, who strikes her from afar
and leaves his winging steel in her flesh, and he's unaware   90
but she veers in flight through Dicte's woody glades,
fixed in her side the shaft that takes her life.
                                               And now
Dido leads her guest through the heart of Carthage,
displaying Phoenician power, the city readied for him.
She'd speak her heart but her voice chokes, mid-word.   95

3. African groups living near Carthage.
4. Ceres: goddess of grain and agriculture.
Apollo: god of the sun, associated with civilization. Bacchus: god of wine. Juno: queen of the
gods, goddess of marriage. All were associated
with the foundation of cities.
5. It was Roman custom to inspect the entrails
of the sacrificial victim and interpret any unusual features as signs of the future.

Now at dusk she calls for the feast to start again,
madly begging to hear again the agony of Troy,
to hang on his lips again, savoring his story.
Then, with the guests gone, and the dimming moon
quenching its light in turn, and the setting stars   100
inclining heads to sleep—alone in the echoing hall,
distraught, she flings herself on the couch that he left empty.
Lost as he is, she's lost as well, she hears him, sees him
or she holds Ascanius back and dandles him on her lap,
bewitched by the boy's resemblance to his father,   105
trying to cheat the love she dare not tell.
The towers of Carthage, half built, rise no more,
and the young men quit their combat drills in arms.
The harbors, the battlements planned to block attack,
all work's suspended now, the huge, threatening walls   110
with the soaring cranes that sway across the sky.

    Now, no sooner had Jove's dear wife perceived
that Dido was in the grip of such a scourge—
no thought of pride could stem her passion now—
than Juno approaches Venus and sets a cunning trap: 115
"What a glittering prize, a triumph you carry home!
You and your boy there, you grand and glorious Powers.
Just look, one woman crushed by the craft of two gods!
I am not blind, you know. For years you've looked askance
at the homes of rising Carthage, feared our ramparts.   120
But where will it end? What good is all our strife?
Come, why don't we labor now to live in peace?
Eternal peace, sealed with the bonds of marriage.
You have it all, whatever your heart desires—
Dido's ablaze with love,   125
drawing the frenzy deep into her bones. So,
let us rule this people in common: joint command.
And let her marry her Phrygian lover, be his slave
and give her Tyrians over to your control,
her dowry in your hands!"
                        Perceiving at once   130
that this was all pretense, a ruse to shift
the kingdom of Italy onto Libyan shores,
Venus countered Juno: "Now who'd be so insane
as to shun your offer and strive with you in war?
If only Fortune crowns your proposal with success!   135
But swayed by the Fates, I have my doubts. Would Jove
want one city to hold the Tyrians and the Trojan exiles?
Would he sanction the mingling of their peoples,
bless their binding pacts? You are his wife,
with every right to probe him with your prayers.   140
You lead the way. I'll follow."
                        "The work is mine,"
imperious Juno carried on, "but how to begin
this pressing matter now and see it through?

I'll explain in a word or so. Listen closely.
Tomorrow Aeneas and lovesick Dido plan to hunt   145
the woods together, soon as the day's first light
climbs high and the Titan's rays lay bare the earth.
But while the beaters scramble to ring the glens with nets,
I'll shower down a cloudburst, hail, black driving rain—
I'll shatter the vaulting sky with claps of thunder.   150
The huntsmen will scatter, swallowed up in the dark,
and Dido and Troy's commander will make their way
to the same cave for shelter. And I'll be there,
if I can count on your own good will in this—
I'll bind them in lasting marriage, make them one.   155
Their wedding it will be!"
                    So Juno appealed
and Venus did not oppose her, nodding in assent
and smiling at all the guile she saw through . . .

      Meanwhile Dawn rose up and left her Ocean bed
and soon as her rays have lit the sky, an elite band   160
of young huntsmen streams out through the gates,
bearing the nets, wide-meshed or tight for traps
and their hunting spears with broad iron heads,
troops of Massylian horsemen galloping hard,
packs of powerful hounds, keen on the scent.   165
Yet the queen delays, lingering in her chamber
with Carthaginian chiefs expectant at her doors.
And there her proud, mettlesome charger prances
in gold and royal purple, pawing with thunder-hoofs,
champing a foam-flecked bit. At last she comes,   170
with a great retinue crowding round the queen
who wears a Tyrian cloak with rich embroidered fringe.
Her quiver is gold, her hair drawn up in a golden torque
and a golden buckle clasps her purple robe in folds.
Nor do her Trojan comrades tarry. Out they march,   175
young Iulus flushed with joy.
Aeneas in command, the handsomest of them all,
advancing as her companion joins his troop with hers.
So vivid. Think of Apollo leaving his Lycian haunts
and Xanthus in winter spate, he's out to visit Delos,   180
his mother's isle,[6] and strike up the dance again
while round the altars swirls a growing throng
of Cretans, Dryopians, Agathyrsians with tattoos,
and a drumming roar goes up as the god himself
strides the Cynthian ridge,[7] his streaming hair   185
braided with pliant laurel leaves entwined
in twists of gold, and arrows clash on his shoulders.

6. The sun god Apollo is imagined leaving Lycia   Delos, which was sacred to his mother, Leto.
when the river Xanthus floods, and going to   7. Mount Cynthus was on Delos.

So no less swiftly Aeneas strides forward now
and his face shines with a glory like the god's.

    Once the huntsmen have reached the trackless lairs   190
aloft in the foothills, suddenly, look, some wild goats
flushed from a ridge come scampering down the slopes
and lower down a herd of stags goes bounding across
the open country, ranks massed in a cloud of dust,
fleeing the high ground. But young Ascanius,   195
deep in the valley, rides his eager mount
and relishing every stride, outstrips them all,
now goats, now stags, but his heart is racing, praying—
if only they'd send among this feeble, easy game
some frothing wild boar or a lion stalking down   200
from the heights and tawny in the sun.
                                     Too late—
The skies have begun to rumble, peals of thunder first
and the storm breaking next, a cloudburst pelting hail
and the troops of hunters scatter up and down the plain,
Tyrian comrades, bands of Dardans, Venus' grandson Iulus   205
panicking, running for cover, quick, and down the mountain
gulleys erupt in torrents. Dido and Troy's commander
make their way to the same cave for shelter now.
Primordial Earth and Juno, Queen of Marriage,
give the signal and lightning torches flare   210
and the high sky bears witness to the wedding,
nymphs on the mountaintops wail out the wedding hymn.
This was the first day of her death, the first of grief,
the cause of it all. From now on, Dido cares no more
for appearances, nor for her reputation, either.   215
She no longer thinks to keep the affair a secret,
no, she calls it a marriage,
using the word to cloak her sense of guilt.

    Straightway Rumor flies through Libya's great cities,
Rumor, swiftest of all the evils in the world.   220
She thrives on speed, stronger for every stride,
slight with fear at first, soon soaring into the air
she treads the ground and hides her head in the clouds.
She is the last, they say, our Mother Earth produced.
Bursting in rage against the gods, she bore a sister   225
for Coeus and Enceladus:[8] Rumor, quicksilver afoot
and swift on the wing, a monster, horrific, huge
and under every feather on her body—what a marvel—
an eye that never sleeps and as many tongues as eyes
and as many raucous mouths and ears pricked up for news.   230
By night she flies aloft, between the earth and sky,

---

8. Titans, the first children of Earth.

whirring across the dark, never closing her lids
in soothing sleep. By day she keeps her watch,
crouched on a peaked roof or palace turret,
terrorizing the great cities, clinging as fast   235
to her twisted lies as she clings to words of truth.
Now Rumor is in her glory, filling Africa's ears
with tale on tale of intrigue, bruiting her song
of facts and falsehoods mingled . . .
"Here this Aeneas, born of Trojan blood,   240
has arrived in Carthage, and lovely Dido deigns
to join the man in wedlock. Even now they warm
the winter, long as it lasts, with obscene desire,
oblivious to their kingdoms, abject thralls of lust."

    Such talk the sordid goddess spreads on the lips of men,   245
then swerves in her course and heading straight for King Iarbas,
stokes his heart with hearsay, piling fuel on his fire.

    Iarbas—son of an African nymph whom Jove had raped—
raised the god a hundred splendid temples across
the king's wide realm, a hundred altars too,   250
consecrating the sacred fires
that never died, eternal sentinels of the gods.
The earth was rich with blood of slaughtered herds
and the temple doorways wreathed with riots of flowers.
This Iarbas, driven wild, set ablaze by the bitter rumor,   255
approached an altar, they say, as the gods hovered round,
and lifting a suppliant's hands, he poured out prayers to Jove:
"Almighty Jove! Now as the Moors adore you, feasting away
on their gaudy couches, tipping wine in your honor—
do you see this? Or are we all fools, Father,   260
to dread the bolts you hurl? All aimless then,
your fires high in the clouds that terrify us so?
All empty noise, your peals of grumbling thunder?
That woman, that vagrant! Here in my own land
she founded her paltry city for a pittance.   265
We tossed her some beach to plow—on my terms—
and then she spurns our offer of marriage, she
embraces Aeneas as lord and master in her realm.
And now this second Paris . . .
leading his troupe of eunuchs, his hair oozing oil,   270
a Phrygian bonnet tucked up under his chin, he revels
in all that he has filched, while we keep bearing gifts
to your temples—yes, yours—coddling your reputation,
all your hollow show!"
                    So King Iarbas appealed,
his hand clutching the altar, and Jove Almighty heard   275
and turned his gaze on the royal walls of Carthage
and the lovers oblivious now to their good name.

He summons Mercury,⁹ gives him marching orders:
"Quick, my son, away! Call up the Zephyrs,¹
glide on wings of the wind. Find the Dardan captain   280
who now malingers long in Tyrian Carthage, look,
and pays no heed to the cities Fate decrees are his.
Take my commands through the racing winds and tell him
this is not the man his mother, the lovely goddess, promised,
not for *this* did she save him twice from Greek attacks.   285
Never. He would be the one to master an Italy
rife with leaders, shrill with the cries of war,
to sire a people sprung from Teucer's noble blood²
and bring the entire world beneath the rule of law.
If such a glorious destiny cannot fire his spirit,   290
if he will not shoulder the task for his own fame,
does the father of Ascanius grudge his son
the walls of Rome? What is he plotting now?
What hope can make him loiter among his foes,
lose sight of Italian offspring still to come   295
and all the Lavinian fields?³ Let him set sail!
This is the sum of it. This must be our message."

    Jove had spoken. Mercury made ready at once
to obey the great commands of his almighty father.
First he fastens under his feet the golden sandals,   300
winged to sweep him over the waves and earth alike
with the rush of gusting winds. Then he seizes the wand
that calls the pallid spirits up from the Underworld
and ushers others down to the grim dark depths,
the wand that lends us sleep or sends it away,   305
that unseals our eyes in death.⁴ Equipped with this,
he spurs the winds and swims through billowing clouds
till in mid-flight he spies the summit and rugged flanks
of Atlas, whose long-enduring peak supports the skies.⁵
Atlas: his pine-covered crown is forever girded   310
round with black clouds, battered by wind and rain;
driving blizzards cloak his shoulders with snow,
torrents course down from the old Titan's chin
and shaggy beard that bristles stiff with ice.
Here the god of Cyllene⁶ landed first,   315
banking down to a stop on balanced wings.
From there, headlong down with his full weight
he plunged to the sea as a seahawk skims the waves,

9. The messenger god; Hermes in Greek mythology.
1. Personified winds. Zephyr is usually the gentle west wind.
2. Teucer was the first king of Troy.
3. Lavinium is the city Aeneas will found in Italy.

4. Mercury is the god who guides the dead to the underworld.
5. Atlas is a Titan who was condemned by Zeus to stand holding up the sky.
6. Mercury was born on Mount Cyllene, in Greece.

rounding the beaches, rounding cliffs to hunt for fish inshore.
So Mercury of Cyllene flew between the earth and sky   320
to gain the sandy coast of Libya, cutting the winds
that sweep down from his mother's father, Atlas.
                                                        Soon
as his winged feet touched down on the first huts in sight,
he spots Aeneas founding the city fortifications,
building homes in Carthage. And his sword-hilt   325
is studded with tawny jasper stars, a cloak
of glowing Tyrian purple drapes his shoulders,
a gift that the wealthy queen had made herself,
weaving into the weft a glinting mesh of gold.
Mercury lashes out at once: "You, so now you lay   330
foundation stones for the soaring walls of Carthage!
Building her gorgeous city, doting on your wife.
Blind to your own realm, oblivious to your fate!
The King of the Gods, whose power sways earth and sky—
he is the one who sends me down from brilliant Olympus,   335
bearing commands for you through the racing winds.
What are you plotting now?
Wasting time in Libya—what hope misleads you so?
If such a glorious destiny cannot fire your spirit,
[if you will not shoulder the task for your own fame,]⁷   340
at least remember Ascanius rising into his prime,
the hopes you lodge in Iulus, your only heir—
you owe him Italy's realm, the land of Rome!"
This order still on his lips, the god vanished
from sight into empty air.
                              Then Aeneas   345
was truly overwhelmed by the vision, stunned,
his hackles bristle with fear, his voice chokes in his throat.
He yearns to be gone, to desert this land he loves,
thunderstruck by the warnings, Jupiter's command . . .
But what can he do? What can he dare say now   350
to the queen in all her fury and win her over?
Where to begin, what opening? Thoughts racing,
here, there, probing his options, turning
to this plan, that plan—torn in two until,
at his wits' end, this answer seems the best.   355
He summons Mnestheus, Sergestus, staunch Serestus,
gives them orders: "Fit out the fleet, but not a word.
Muster the crews on shore, all tackle set to sail,
but the cause for our new course, you keep it secret."
Yet he himself, since Dido who means the world to him   360
knows nothing, never dreaming such a powerful love
could be uprooted—he will try to approach her,
find the moment to break the news gently,

---

7. Bracketed because some editors believe the line does not belong in the text.

a way to soften the blow that he must leave.
All shipmates snap to commands,   365
glad to do his orders.
                      True, but the queen—
who can delude a lover?—soon caught wind
of a plot afoot, the first to sense the Trojans
are on the move . . . She fears everything now,
even with all secure. Rumor, vicious as ever,   370
brings her word, already distraught, that Trojans
are rigging out their galleys, gearing to set sail.
She rages in helpless frenzy, blazing through
the entire city, raving like some Maenad[8]
driven wild when the women shake the sacred emblems,   375
when the cyclic orgy, shouts of "Bacchus!" fire her on
and Cithaeron echoes round with maddened midnight cries.

    At last she assails Aeneas, before he's said a word:
"So, you traitor, you really believed you'd keep
this a secret, this great outrage?—steal away   380
in silence from my shores? Can nothing hold you back?
Not our love? Not the pledge once sealed with our right hands?
Not even the thought of Dido doomed to a cruel death?
Why labor to rig your fleet when the winter's raw,
to risk the deep when the Northwind's closing in?   385
You cruel, heartless—Even if you were not
pursuing alien fields and unknown homes,
even if ancient Troy were standing, still,
who'd sail for Troy across such heaving seas?
You're running away—from me? Oh, I pray you   390
by these tears, by the faith in your right hand—
what else have I left myself in all my pain?—
by our wedding vows, the marriage we began,
if I deserve some decency from you now,
if anything mine has ever won your heart,   395
pity a great house about to fall, I pray you,
if prayers have any place—reject this scheme of yours!
Thanks to you, the African tribes, Numidian warlords
hate me, even my own Tyrians rise against me.
Thanks to you, my sense of honor is gone,   400
my one and only pathway to the stars,
the renown I once held dear. In whose hands,
my guest, do you leave me here to meet my death?
'Guest'—that's all that remains of 'husband' now.
But why do I linger on? Until my brother Pygmalion   405
batters down my walls? Or Iarbas drags me off, his slave?
If only you'd left a baby in my arms—our child—
before you deserted me! Some little Aeneas

8. The Maenads (Bacchae) were female worshippers of Bacchus, who ran wild on Mount Cithaeron in a ritual held every other year—as depicted in Euripides' *Bacchae*, in which one such god-frenzied woman kills her own son.

playing about our halls, whose features at least
would bring you back to me in spite of all,   410
I would not feel so totally devastated,
so destroyed."
                    The queen stopped but he,
warned by Jupiter now, his gaze held steady,
fought to master the torment in his heart. At last
he ventured a few words: "I . . . you have done me   415
so many kindnesses, and you could count them all.
I shall never deny what you deserve, my queen,
never regret my memories of Dido, not while I
can recall myself and draw the breath of life.
I'll state my case in a few words. I never dreamed   420
I'd keep my flight a secret. Don't imagine that.
Nor did I once extend a bridegroom's torch
or enter into a marriage pact with you.
If the Fates had left me free to live my life,
to arrange my own affairs of my own free will,   425
Troy is the city, first of all, that I'd safeguard,
Troy and all that's left of my people whom I cherish.
The grand palace of Priam would stand once more,
with my own hands I would fortify a second Troy
to house my Trojans in defeat. But not now.   430
Grynean Apollo's oracle says that I must seize
on Italy's noble land, his Lycian lots say 'Italy!'[9]
There lies my love, there lies my homeland now.
If you, a Phoenician, fix your eyes on Carthage,
a Libyan stronghold, tell me, why do you grudge   435
the Trojans their new homes on Italian soil?
What is the crime if *we* seek far-off kingdoms too?

        "My father, Anchises, whenever the darkness shrouds
the earth in its dank shadows, whenever the stars
go flaming up the sky, my father's anxious ghost   440
warns me in dreams and fills my heart with fear.
My son Ascanius . . . I feel the wrong I do
to one so dear, robbing him of his kingdom,
lands in the West, his fields decreed by Fate.
And now the messenger of the gods—I swear it,   445
by your life and mine—dispatched by Jove himself
has brought me firm commands through the racing winds.
With my own eyes I saw him, clear, in broad daylight,
moving through your gates. With my own ears I drank   450
his message in. Come, stop inflaming us both
with your appeals. I set sail for Italy—
all against my will."
                    Even from the start
of his declaration, she has glared at him askance,

9. Grynia was an Aeolian city sacred to Apollo. Lycia is another cult center of Apollo.

her eyes roving over him, head to foot, with a look
of stony silence . . . till abruptly she cries out   455
in a blaze of fury: "No goddess was your mother!
No Dardanus sired your line, you traitor, liar, no,
Mount Caucasus fathered you on its flinty, rugged flanks
and the tigers of Hyrcania gave you their dugs to suck![1]
Why hide it? Why hold back? To suffer greater blows?   460
Did *he* groan when *I* wept? Even look at me? Never!
Surrender a tear? Pity the one who loves him?
What can I say first? So much to say. Now—
neither mighty Juno nor Saturn's son, the Father,[2]
gazes down on this with just, impartial eyes.   465
There's no faith left on earth!
He was washed up on my shores, helpless, and I,
I took him in, like a maniac let him share my kingdom,
salvaged his lost fleet, plucked his crews from death.
Oh I am swept by the Furies, gales of fire![3] Now   470
it's Apollo the Prophet, Apollo's Lycian oracles:
they're his masters now, and now, to top it off,
the messenger of the gods, dispatched by Jove himself,
comes rushing down the winds with his grim-set commands.
Really! What work for the gods who live on high,   475
what a concern to ruffle their repose!
I won't hold you, I won't even refute you—go!—
strike out for Italy on the winds, your realm across the sea.
I hope, I pray, if the just gods still have any power,
wrecked on the rocks midsea you'll drink your bowl   480
of pain to the dregs, crying out the name of Dido
over and over, and worlds away I'll hound you then
with pitch-black flames, and when icy death has severed
my body from its breath, then my ghost will stalk you
through the world! You'll pay, you shameless, ruthless—   485
and I will hear of it, yes, the report will reach me
even among the deepest shades of Death!"
                              She breaks off
in the midst of outbursts, desperate, flinging herself
from the light of day, sweeping out of his sight,
leaving him numb with doubt, with much to fear   490
and much he means to say.
Catching her as she faints away, her women
bear her back to her marble bridal chamber
and lay her body down upon her bed.
                              But Aeneas
is driven by duty now. Strongly as he longs   495
to ease and allay her sorrow, speak to her,
turn away her anguish with reassurance, still,
moaning deeply, heart shattered by his great love,

1. Dardanus was the legendary founder of
Troy. The Caucasus mountains, between the
Black and Caspian Seas, and Hyrcania, south
of the Caspian, were notoriously wild, uncivi-
lized regions.
2. Jupiter was the son of Saturn.
3. The Furies are spirits of vengeance who
carry flaming torches.

in spite of all he obeys the gods' commands
and back he goes to his ships.   500
Then the Trojans throw themselves in the labor,
launching their tall vessels down along the beach
and the hull rubbed sleek with pitch floats high again.
So keen to be gone, the men drag down from the forest
untrimmed timbers and boughs still green for oars.   505
You can see them streaming out of the whole city,
men like ants that, wary of winter's onset, pillage
some huge pile of wheat to store away in their grange
and their army's long black line goes marching through the field,
trundling their spoils down some cramped, grassy track.   510
Some put shoulders to giant grains and thrust them on,
some dress the ranks, strictly marshal stragglers,
and the whole trail seethes with labor.

    What did you feel then, Dido, seeing this?
How deep were the groans you uttered, gazing now   515
from the city heights to watch the broad beaches
seething with action, the bay a chaos of outcries
right before your eyes?
               Love, you tyrant!
To what extremes won't you compel our hearts?
Again she resorts to tears, driven to move the man,   520
or try, with prayers—a suppliant kneeling, humbling
her pride to passion. So if die she must,
she'll leave no way untried.
           "Anna, you see
the hurly-burly all across the beach, the crews
swarming from every quarter? The wind cries for canvas,   525
the buoyant oarsmen crown their sterns with wreaths.
This terrible sorrow: since I saw it coming, Anna,
I can endure it now. But even so, my sister,
carry out for me one great favor in my pain.
To you alone he used to listen, the traitor,   530
to you confide his secret feelings. You alone
know how and when to approach him, soothe his moods.
Go, my sister! Plead with my imperious enemy.
Remind him I was never at Aulis, never swore a pact
with the Greeks to rout the Trojan people from the earth![4]   535
I sent no fleet to Troy, I never uprooted the ashes
of his father, Anchises, never stirred his shade.
Why does he shut his pitiless ears to my appeals?
Where's he rushing now? If only he would offer
one last gift to the wretched queen who loves him: 540
to wait for fair winds, smooth sailing for his flight!
I no longer beg for the long-lost marriage he betrayed,
nor would I ask him now to desert his kingdom, no,

---

4. The Greek forces mustered at Aulis before sailing to Troy. It was here that Agamemnon killed
his daughter to make the wind blow. Now again, a woman must die to release a fleet.

his lovely passion, Latium.[5] All I ask is time,
blank time: some rest from frenzy, breathing room   545
till my fate can teach my beaten spirit how to grieve.
I beg him—pity your sister, Anna—one last favor,
and if he grants it now, I'll pay him back,
with interest, when I die."
                                        So Dido pleads and
so her desolate sister takes him the tale of tears   550
again and again. But no tears move Aeneas now.
He is deaf to all appeals. He won't relent.
The Fates bar the way
and heaven blocks his gentle, human ears.
As firm as a sturdy oak grown tough with age   555
when the Northwinds blasting off the Alps compete,
fighting left and right, to wrench it from the earth,
and the winds scream, the trunk shudders, its leafy crest
showers across the ground but it clings firm to its rock,
its roots stretching as deep into the dark world below   560
as its crown goes towering toward the gales of heaven—
so firm the hero stands: buffeted left and right
by storms of appeals, he takes the full force
of love and suffering deep in his great heart.
His will stands unmoved. The falling tears are futile.[6]
                                                   Then,   565
terrified by her fate, tragic Dido prays for death,
sickened to see the vaulting sky above her.
And to steel her new resolve to leave the light,
she sees, laying gifts on the altars steaming incense—
shudder to hear it now—the holy water going black   570
and the wine she pours congeals in bloody filth.[7]
She told no one what she saw, not even her sister.
Worse, there was a marble temple in her palace,
a shrine built for her long-lost love, Sychaeus.
Holding it dear she tended it—marvelous devotion—   575
draping the snow-white fleece and festal boughs.
Now from its depths she seemed to catch his voice,
the words of her dead husband calling out her name
while night enclosed the earth in its dark shroud,
and over and over a lonely owl perched on the rooftops   580
drew out its low, throaty call to a long wailing dirge.
And worse yet, the grim predictions of ancient seers
keep terrifying her now with frightful warnings.
Aeneas the hunter, savage in all her nightmares,
drives her mad with panic. She always feels alone,   585
abandoned, always wandering down some endless road,
not a friend in sight, seeking her own Phoenicians
in some godforsaken land. As frantic as Pentheus

5. Region of central Italy, land of the Latins.   three.
6. In the Latin, as here, it is unclear who is   7. Dido is trying to pour libations—liquid
crying; it could be Anna, Dido, Aeneas, or all   offerings to the gods.

seeing battalions of Furies, twin suns ablaze
and double cities of Thebes before his eyes.[8]   590
Or Agamemnon's Orestes hounded off the stage,
fleeing his mother armed with torches, black snakes,
while blocking the doorway coil her Furies of Revenge.[9]

    So, driven by madness, beaten down by anguish,
Dido was fixed on dying, working out in her mind   595
the means, the moment. She approaches her grieving
sister, Anna—masking her plan with a brave face
aglow with hope, and says: "I've found a way,
dear heart—rejoice with your sister—either
to bring him back in love for me or free me   600
of love for him. Close to the bounds of Ocean,
west with the setting sun, lies Ethiopian land,
the end of the earth, where colossal Atlas turns
on his shoulder the heavens studded with flaming stars.
From there, I have heard, a Massylian priestess comes   605
who tended the temple held by Hesperian daughters.[1]
She'd safeguard the boughs in the sacred grove
and ply the dragon with morsels dripping loops
of oozing honey and poppies drowsy with slumber.
With her spells she vows to release the hearts   610
of those she likes, to inflict raw pain on others—
to stop the rivers in midstream, reverse the stars
in their courses, raise the souls of the dead at night
and make earth shudder and rumble underfoot—you'll see—
and send the ash trees marching down the mountains.   615
I swear by the gods, dear Anna, by your sweet life,
I arm myself with magic arts against my will.[2]
                                        "Now go,
build me a pyre in secret, deep inside our courtyard
under the open sky. Pile it high with his arms—
he left them hanging within our bridal chamber—   620
the traitor, so devoted then! and all his clothes
and crowning it all, the bridal bed that brought my doom.
I must obliterate every trace of the man, the curse,
and the priestess shows the way!"
                                        She says no more
and now as the queen falls silent, pallor sweeps her face.   625

8. Pentheus is the king of Thebes who, in Euripides' *Bacchae*, was driven mad so that he thought he saw two suns in the sky and was then killed by his own mother.
9. Agamemnon's son, Orestes, killed his mother in revenge for her killing his father. He was then driven mad by the Furies. The myth is the subject of Aeschylus's *Oresteia* and Euripides' *Orestes*.
1. The Massylians were a North African tribe. The daughters of Hesperus, the Evening Star, tended a garden containing the golden apples that belonged to Hera. A never-sleeping dragon with a hundred heads also guarded the apples.
2. These allusions to witchcraft make Dido sound like Medea, the princess of Colchis with magical powers, who helped Jason steal the Golden Fleece from her father and escape back to Greece. Later, after several years of marriage, Jason abandoned Medea; she then, according to Euripides' *Medea*, took revenge by killing their children.

Still, Anna cannot imagine these outlandish rites
would mask her sister's death. She can't conceive
of such a fiery passion. She fears nothing graver
than Dido's grief at the death of her Sychaeus.
So she does as she is told.
                    But now the queen,   630
as soon as the pyre was built beneath the open sky,
towering up with pitch-pine and cut logs of oak—
deep in the heart of her house—she drapes the court
with flowers, crowning the place with wreaths of death,
and to top it off she lays his arms and the sword he left   635
and an effigy of Aeneas, all on the bed they'd shared,
for well she knows the future. Altars ring the pyre.
Hair loose in the wind, the priestess thunders out
the names of her three hundred gods, Erebus, Chaos
and triple Hecate, Diana the three-faced virgin.[3]   640
She'd sprinkled water, simulating the springs of hell,
and gathered potent herbs, reaped with bronze sickles
under the moonlight, dripping their milky black poison,
and fetched a love-charm ripped from a foal's brow,
just born, before the mother could gnaw it off.   645
And Dido herself, standing before the altar,
holding the sacred grain in reverent hands—
with one foot free of its sandal, robes unbound[4]—
sworn now to die, she calls on the gods to witness,
calls on the stars who know her approaching fate.   650
And then to any Power above, mindful, evenhanded,
who watches over lovers bound by unequal passion,
Dido says her prayers.
                    The dead of night,
and weary living creatures throughout the world
are enjoying peaceful sleep. The woods and savage seas   655
are calm, at rest, and the circling stars are gliding on
in their midnight courses, all the fields lie hushed
and the flocks and gay and gorgeous birds that haunt
the deep clear pools and the thorny country thickets
all lie quiet now, under the silent night, asleep.   660
But not the tragic queen . . .
torn in spirit, Dido will not dissolve
into sleep—her eyes, her mind won't yield to night.
Her torments multiply, over and over her passion
surges back into heaving waves of rage—   665
she keeps on brooding, obsessions roil her heart:
"And now, what shall I do? Make a mockery of myself,
go back to my old suitors, tempt them to try again?
Beg the Numidians, grovel, plead for a husband—
though time and again I scorned to wed their likes?   670
What then? Trail the Trojan ships, bend to the Trojans'
every last demand? So pleased, are they, with all the help,

---

3. Erebus is Darkness, son of Chaos. Hecate,   goddess, was the goddess of witchcraft.
sometimes identified with Diana the moon   4. All magical practices.

the relief I lent them once? And memory of my service past
stands firm in grateful minds! And even if I were willing,
would the Trojans allow me to board their proud ships—   675
a woman they hate? Poor lost fool, can't you sense it,
grasp it yet—the treachery of Laomedon's breed?[5]
What now? Do I take flight alone, consorting
with crews of Trojan oarsmen in their triumph?
Or follow them out with all my troops of Tyrians   680
thronging the decks? Yes, hard as it was to uproot
them once from Tyre! How can I force them back to sea
once more, command them to spread their sails to the winds?
No, no, die!
        You deserve it—
                        end your pain with the sword!
You, my sister, you were the first, won over by my tears,   685
to pile these sorrows on my shoulders, mad as I was,
to throw me into my enemy's arms. If only I'd been free
to live my life, untested in marriage, free of guilt
as some wild beast untouched by pangs like these!
I broke the faith I swore to the ashes of Sychaeus."   690

    Such terrible grief kept breaking from her heart
as Aeneas slept in peace on his ship's high stern,
bent on departing now, all tackle set to sail.
And now in his dreams it came again—the god,
his phantom, the same features shining clear.   695
Like Mercury head to foot, the voice, the glow,
the golden hair, the bloom of youth on his limbs
and his voice rang out with warnings once again:
"Son of the goddess, how can you sleep so soundly
in such a crisis? Can't you see the dangers closing   700
around you now? Madman! Can't you hear the Westwind
ruffling to speed you on? That woman spawns her plots,
mulling over some desperate outrage in her heart,
lashing her surging rage, she's bent on death.
Why not flee headlong?   705
Flee headlong while you can! You'll soon see
the waves a chaos of ships, lethal torches flaring,
the whole coast ablaze, if now a new dawn breaks
and finds you still malingering on these shores.
Up with you now. Enough delay. Woman's a thing   710
that's always changing, shifting like the wind."
With that he vanished into the black night.

    Then, terrified by the sudden phantom,
Aeneas, wrenching himself from sleep, leaps up
and rouses his crews and spurs them headlong on: 715
"Quick! Up and at it, shipmates, man the thwarts!
Spread canvas fast! A god's come down from the sky

5. Laomedon, father of Priam and previous king of Troy, broke a promise to repay Apollo and Neptune for building his city walls.

once more—I've just seen him—urging us on
to sever our mooring cables, sail at once!
We follow you, blessed god, whoever you are—   720
glad at heart we obey your commands once more.
Now help us, stand beside us with all your kindness,
bring us favoring stars in the sky to blaze our way!"

    Tearing sword from sheath like a lightning flash,
he hacks the mooring lines with a naked blade.   725
Gripped by the same desire, all hands pitch in,
they hoist and haul. The shore's deserted now,
the water's hidden under the fleet—they bend to it,
churn the spray and sweep the clear blue sea.
                       By now
early Dawn had risen up from the saffron bed   730
of Tithonus,[6] scattering fresh light on the world.
But the queen from her high tower, catching sight
of the morning's white glare, the armada heading out
to sea with sails trimmed to the wind, and certain
the shore and port were empty, stripped of oarsmen—   735
three, four times over she beat her lovely breast,
she ripped at her golden hair and "Oh, by God,"
she cries, "will the stranger just sail off
and make a mockery of our realm? Will no one
rush to arms, come streaming out of the whole city,   740
hunt him down, race to the docks and launch the ships?
Go, quick—bring fire!
                Hand out weapons!
                         Bend to the oars!
What am I saying? Where am I? What insanity's this
that shifts my fixed resolve? Dido, oh poor fool,
is it only *now* your wicked work strikes home?   745
It should have then, when you offered him your scepter.
Look at his hand clasp, look at his good faith now—
that man who, they say, carries his fathers' gods,
who stooped to shoulder his father bent with age!
Couldn't I have seized him then, ripped him to pieces,   750
scattered them in the sea? Or slashed his men with steel,
butchered Ascanius, served him up as his father's feast?[7]
True, the luck of battle might have been at risk—
well, risk away! Whom did I have to fear?
I was about to die. I should have torched their camp   755
and flooded their decks with fire. The son, the father,
the whole Trojan line—I should have wiped them out,
then hurled myself on the pyre to crown it all!

6. The goddess Dawn had a human lover
named Tithonus, whom she had made immortal (though not ageless) and brought to live
with her.
7. These horrible possibilities have mythic
precedents. Medea, when she eloped with

Jason, ripped up her little brother's body and
scattered the pieces on the sea, to distract their
father as he tried to pursue the boat. Atreus,
father of Agamemnon and Menelaus, killed his
brother's children and served them up to him
at a feast.

"You, Sun, whose fires scan all works of the earth,[8]
and you, Juno, the witness, midwife to my agonies—   760
Hecate greeted by nightly shrieks at city crossroads—
and you, you avenging Furies and gods of dying Dido!
Hear me, turn your power my way, attend my sorrows—
I deserve your mercy—hear my prayers! If that curse
of the earth must reach his haven, labor on to landfall—   765
if Jove and the Fates command and the boundary stone is fixed,
still, let him be plagued in war by a nation proud in arms,
torn from his borders, wrenched from Iulus' embrace,
let him grovel for help and watch his people die
a shameful death! And then, once he has bowed down   770
to an unjust peace, may he never enjoy his realm
and the light he yearns for, never, let him die
before his day, unburied on some desolate beach!

"That is my prayer, my final cry—I pour it out
with my own lifeblood. And you, my Tyrians,   775
harry with hatred all his line, his race to come:
make that offering to my ashes, send it down below.
No love between our peoples, ever, no pacts of peace!
Come rising up from my bones, you avenger still unknown,
to stalk those Trojan settlers, hunt with fire and iron,   780
now or in time to come, whenever the power is yours.
Shore clash with shore, sea against sea and sword
against sword—this is my curse—war between all
our peoples, all their children, endless war!"

With that, her mind went veering back and forth—   785
what was the quickest way to break off from the light,
the life she loathed? And so with a few words
she turned to Barce, Sychaeus' old nurse—her own
was now black ashes deep in her homeland lost forever:
"Dear old nurse, send Anna my sister to me here.   790
Tell her to hurry, sprinkle herself with river water,
bring the victims marked for the sacrifice I must make.
So let her come. And wrap your brow with the holy bands.
These rites to Jove of the Styx that I have set in motion,
I yearn to consummate them, end the pain of love,   795
give that cursed Trojan's pyre to the flames."
The nurse bustled off with an old crone's zeal.
                                              But Dido,
trembling, desperate now with the monstrous thing afoot—
her bloodshot eyes rolling, quivering cheeks blotched
and pale with imminent death—goes bursting through   800
the doors to the inner courtyard, clambers in frenzy
up the soaring pyre and unsheathes a sword, a Trojan sword
she once sought as a gift, but not for such an end.
And next, catching sight of the Trojan's clothes
and the bed they knew by heart, delaying a moment   805
for tears, for memory's sake, the queen lay down

8. The sun (Helios) was sometimes personified as a god; he was the grandfather of Medea.

and spoke her final words: "Oh, dear relics,
dear as long as Fate and the gods allowed,
receive my spirit and set me free of pain.
I have lived a life. I've journeyed through 810
the course that Fortune charted for me. And now
I pass to the world below, my ghost in all its glory.
I have founded a noble city, seen my ramparts rise.
I have avenged my husband, punished my blood-brother,
our mortal foe. Happy, all too happy I would have been 815
if only the Trojan keels had never grazed our coast."
She presses her face in the bed and cries out:
"I shall die unavenged, but die I will! So—
so—I rejoice to make my way among the shades.
And may that heartless Dardan, far at sea, 820
drink down deep the sight of our fires here
and bear with him this omen of our death!"

    All at once, in the midst of her last words,
her women see her doubled over the sword, the blood
foaming over the blade, her hands splattered red. 825
A scream goes stabbing up to the high roofs,
Rumor raves like a Maenad through the shocked city—
sobs, and grief, and the wails of women ringing out
through homes, and the heavens echo back the keening din—
for all the world as if enemies stormed the walls 830
and all of Carthage or old Tyre were toppling down
and flames in their fury, wave on mounting wave
were billowing over the roofs of men and gods.

    Anna heard and, stunned, breathless with terror,
raced through the crowd, her nails clawing her face, 835
fists beating her breast, crying out to her sister now
at the edge of death: "Was it all for *this,* my sister?
You deceived me all along? Is this what your pyre
meant for me—this, your fires—this, your altars?
You deserted me   what shall I grieve for first? 840
Your friend, your sister, you scorn me now in death?
You should have called me on to the same fate.
The same agony, same sword, the one same hour
had borne us off together. Just to think I built
your pyre with my own hands, implored our fathers' gods 845
with my own voice, only to be cut off from you—
how very cruel—when you lay down to die . . .
You have destroyed your life, my sister, mine too,
your people, the lords of Sidon and your new city here.
Please, help me to bathe her wounds in water now, 850
and if any last, lingering breath still hovers,
let me catch it on my lips."
                        With those words
she had climbed the pyre's topmost steps and now,
clasping her dying sister to her breast, fondling her
she sobbed, stanching the dark blood with her own gown. 855
Dido, trying to raise her heavy eyes once more, failed—

deep in her heart the wound kept rasping, hissing on.
Three times she tried to struggle up on an elbow,
three times she fell back, writhing on her bed.
Her gaze wavering into the high skies, she looked   860
for a ray of light and when she glimpsed it, moaned.

    Then Juno in all her power, filled with pity
for Dido's agonizing death, her labor long and hard,
sped Iris[9] down from Olympus to release her spirit
wrestling now in a deathlock with her limbs.   865
Since she was dying a death not fated or deserved,
no, tormented, before her day, in a blaze of passion—
Proserpina had yet to pluck a golden lock from her head
and commit her life to the Styx and the dark world below.[1]
So Iris, glistening dew, comes skimming down from the sky   870
on gilded wings, trailing showers of iridescence shimmering
into the sun, and hovering over Dido's head, declares:
"So commanded, I take this lock as a sacred gift
to the God of Death, and I release you from your body."

    With that, she cut the lock with her hand and all at once   875
the warmth slipped away, the life dissolved in the winds.

Summary of Books V–XI   The Trojans sail back to Sicily, where they mark the death of
Anchises with funeral rites and games. They journey to Cumae, Italy, where Aeneas consults the
Sibyl, prophetess of Apollo, who helps him descend into the underworld. There, he meets his dead
father, who foretells the future history of Rome up to the time of Augustus. Back in the upper
world, Aeneas travels to the future site of Rome. He meets Latinus, king of the Latin race, who has
just one daughter, Lavinia. An oracle has foretold that she must marry a stranger, and the Latin
people welcome Aeneas as their future king. But Queen Amata, Latinus's wife, had hoped that her
daughter would marry Turnus, a leader of the rival Rutulian tribe. Juno, jealous at Trojan success,
rouses the people to war and leads the native Italians against the invading Trojans. Aeneas manages
to forge an alliance with another nearby tribe, the Arcadians, who are descended from Greeks and
led by a friendly king called Evander; they live in the future site of Rome. Aeneas combines his
forces both with the Arcadians and yet another tribe, the Etrurians. He also gets new armor from
his mother, Venus, forged by the god Vulcan, which includes a shield depicting scenes from the
future of Rome. Now Aeneas and his allies have a fighting chance against the forces led by Turnus.
But the war becomes bloody and violent. Jupiter orders a council of the gods, reminding them that
there was supposed to be peace between the Trojans and Italians, but he ends up renouncing
responsibility for what happens: "the Fates will find a way," he declares. Pallas, son of Evander,
enters the battle and is killed by Turnus. Aeneas longs to kill Turnus in revenge, but cannot find
him; Juno has spirited him away. Attempts at peace-making fail, and many are killed on both sides,
including a warrior princess named Camilla, who is an ally of Turnus. Turnus announces that the
time has come for him to fight Aeneas hand-to-hand. Aeneas promises that if Turnus wins, the
Trojans will leave Italy; if he himself wins, the Trojans will not enslave the native Italians, but will
join together to form a new nation. But the pact is broken when Turnus's sister, Juturna, intervenes,
and fighting breaks out again. Aeneas is wounded in the leg, but healed by his mother, Venus. The
Trojans begin to attack the city of the Latins directly, and Aeneas threatens to level it to the ground
unless the native Italians surrender. As we pick up the story, Turnus has become aware that his
people are in a desperate situation. He resolves to fight Aeneas, even if it means his death.

9. Iris is the goddess who sometimes acts as
messenger between heaven and earth; she
appears as a rainbow (hence "iridescence").
1. Proserpina, queen of the underworld, would

normally have taken a lock of Dido's hair to
release her life; since her death is premature,
Iris does it.

FROM **BOOK XII**

[*The Sword Decides All*]

* * *

Stunned by pictures
of these disasters blurring through his mind,
Turnus stood there, staring, speechless, churning
with mighty shame, with grief and madness all aswirl
in that one fighting heart: with love spurred by rage   775
and a sense of his own worth too. As soon as the shadows
were dispersed and the light restored to his mind,
he turned his fiery glance toward the ramparts,
glaring back from his chariot to the town.
                                        But now,
look, a whirlwind of fire goes rolling story to story,   780
billowing up the sky, and clings fast to a mobile tower,
a defense he built himself of wedged, rough-hewn beams,
fitting the wheels below it, gangways reared above.
"Now, now, my sister, the Fates are in command.
Don't hold me back. Where God and relentless   785
Fortune call us on, that's the way we go!
I'm set on fighting Aeneas hand-to-hand,
set, however bitter it is, to meet my death.
You'll never see me disgraced again—no more.
Insane as it is, I beg you, let me rage before I die!"   790

   He leapt from his chariot, hit the ground at a run
through enemies, Trojan spears, and left his sister
grieving as he went bursting through the lines.
Wild as a boulder plowing headlong down from a summit,
torn out by the tempests—whether the stormwinds washed it free   795
or the creeping years stole under it, worked it loose,
down the cliff it crashes, ruthless crag of rock
bounding over the ground with enormous impact,
churning up in its onrush woods and herds and men.
So Turnus bursts through the fractured ranks, charging   800
toward the walls where the earth runs red with blood
and the winds hiss with spears and, hand flung up,
he cries with a ringing voice: "Hold back now,
you Rutulians! Latins, keep your arms in check!
Whatever Fortune sends, it's mine. Better   805
for me alone to redeem the pact for you
and let my sword decide!"
                        All ranks scattered,
leaving a no-man's-land between them both.
                              But Aeneas,
the great commander, hearing the name of Turnus,
deserts the walls, deserts the citadel's heights   810
and breaks off all operations, jettisons all delay—
he springs in joy, drums his shield and it thunders terror.

As massive as Athos, massive as Eryx or even Father
Apennine himself, roaring out with his glistening oaks,
elated to raise his snow-capped brow to the winds.[2] And then,   815
for a fact, the Rutulians, Trojans, all the Italians,
those defending the high ramparts, those on attack
who batter the walls' foundations with their rams:
all armies strained to turn their glances round
and lifted their battle-armor off their shoulders.   820
Latinus himself is struck that these two giant men,
sprung from opposing ends of the earth, have met,
face-to-face, to let their swords decide.
                             But they,
as soon as the battlefield lay clear and level,
charge at speed, rifling their spears at long range,   825
then rush to battle with shields and clanging bronze.
The earth groans as stroke after stroke they land
with naked swords: fortune and fortitude mix
in one assault. Charging like two hostile bulls
fighting up on Sila's woods or Taburnus' ridges,   830
ramping in mortal combat, both brows bent for attack
and the herdsmen back away in fear and the whole herd
stands by, hushed, afraid, and the heifers wait and wonder,
who will lord it over the forest? who will lead the herd?—
while the bulls battle it out, horns butting, locking,   835
goring each other, necks and shoulders roped in blood
and the woods resound as they grunt and bellow out.
So they charge, Trojan Aeneas and Turnus, son of Daunus,
shields clang and the huge din makes the heavens ring.
Jove himself lifts up his scales, balanced, trued,   840
and in them he sets the opposing fates of both . . .
Whom would the labor of battle doom? Whose life
would weigh him down to death?
                         Suddenly Turnus
flashes forward, certain he's in the clear and
raising his sword high, rearing to full stretch   845
strikes—as Trojans and anxious Latins shout out,
with the gaze of both armies riveted on the fighters.
But his treacherous blade breaks off, it fails Turnus
in mid-stroke—enraged, his one recourse, retreat,
and swifter than Eastwinds, Turnus flies as soon   850
as he sees that unfamiliar hilt in his hand,
no defense at all. They say the captain, rushing
headlong on to harness his team and board his car
to begin the duel, left his father's sword behind
and hastily grabbed his charioteer Metiscus' blade.   855
Long as the Trojan stragglers took to their heels and ran,
the weapon did its work, but once it came up against
the immortal armor forged by the God of Fire, Vulcan,

---

2. Mount Athos is in Greece; Mount Eryx is in Sicily; the Apennine Mountains are a range
extending all the way down Italy.

the mortal sword burst at a stroke, brittle as ice,
and glinting splinters gleamed on the tawny sand.   860
So raging Turnus runs for it, scours the field,
now here, now there, weaving in tangled circles
as Trojans crowd him hard, a dense ring of them
shutting him in, with a wild swamp to the left
and steep walls to the right.   Nor does Aeneas flag,   865
though slowed down by his wound, his knees unsteady,
cutting his pace at times but he's still in full fury,
hot on his frantic quarry's tracks, stride for stride.
Alert as a hunting hound that lights on a trapped stag,
hemmed in by a river's bend or frightened back by the ropes   870
with blood-red feathers[3]—the hound barking, closing, fast
as the quarry, panicked by traps and the steep riverbanks,
runs off and back in a thousand ways but the Umbrian hound,[4]
keen for the kill, hangs on the trail, his jaws agape—
and now, now he's got him, thinks he's got him, yes   875
and his jaws clap shut, stymied, champing the empty air.
Then the shouts break loose, and the banks and rapids round
resound with the din, and the high sky thunders back. Turnus—
even in flight he rebukes his men as he races, calling
each by name, demanding his old familiar sword.   880
Aeneas, opposite, threatens death and doom at once
to anyone in his way, he threatens his harried foes
that he'll root their city out and, wounded as he is,
keeps closing for the kill. And five full circles
they run and reel as many back, around and back,   885
for it's no mean trophy they're sporting after now,
they race for the life and the lifeblood of Turnus.

       By chance a wild olive, green with its bitter leaves,
stood right here, sacred to Faunus,[5] revered by men
in the old days, sailors saved from shipwreck.   890
On it they always fixed their gifts to the local god
and they hung their votive clothes in thanks for rescue.
But the Trojans—no exceptions, hallowed tree that it was—
chopped down its trunk to clear the spot for combat.
Now here the spear of Aeneas had stuck, borne home   895
by its hurling force, and the tough roots held it fast.
He bent down over it, trying to wrench the iron loose and
track with a spear the kill he could not catch on foot.
Turnus, truly beside himself with terror—"Faunus!"
he cried, "I beg you, pity me! You, dear Earth,   900
hold fast to that spear! If I have always kept
your rites—a far cry from Aeneas' men
who stain your rites with war."

3. Hunters used ropes and nets decorated with feathers.
4. A dog breed known for its skill in hunting.
5. An old Roman god associated with the countryside and forest.

So he appealed,
calling out for the god's help, and not for nothing.
Aeneas struggled long, wasting time on the tough stump,   905
no power of *his* could loose the timber's stubborn bite.
As he bravely heaves and hauls, the goddess Juturna,
changing back again to the charioteer Metiscus,
rushes in and returns her brother's sword to Turnus.
But Venus, incensed that the nymph has had her brazen way,   910
steps up and plucks Aeneas' spear from the clinging root.
So standing tall, with their arms and fighting hearts refreshed—
one who trusted all to his sword, the other looming fiercely
with his spear—confronting each other, both men breathless,
brace for the war-god's fray.
           Now at the same moment   915
Jove, the king of mighty Olympus, turns to Juno,
gazing down on the war from her golden cloud, and says:
"Where will it end, my queen? What is left at the last?
Aeneas the hero, god of the land: you know yourself,
you confess you know that he is heaven bound,   920
his fate will raise Aeneas to the stars.
What are you plotting? What hope can make you
cling to the chilly clouds? So, was it right
for a mortal hand to wound, to mortify a god?
Right to restore that mislaid sword to Turnus—   925
for without your power what could Juturna do?—
and lend the defeated strength? Have done at last.
Bow to my appeals. Don't let your corrosive grief
devour you in silence, or let your dire concerns come
pouring from your sweet lips and plaguing me forever.   930
We have reached the limit. To harass the Trojans
over land and sea, to ignite an unspeakable war,
degrade a royal house and blend the wedding hymn
with the dirge of grief: all that lay in your power.
But go no further. I forbid you now."
               Jove said no more.   935
And so, with head bent low, Saturn's daughter replied:
"Because I have known your will so well, great Jove,
against my *own* I deserted Turnus and the earth.
Or else you would never see me now, alone
on a windswept throne enduring right and wrong.   940
No, wrapped in flames I would be up on the front lines,
dragging the Trojan into mortal combat. Juturna?
I was the one, I admit, who spurred her on
to help her embattled brother, true, and blessed
whatever greater daring it took to save his life,   945
but never to shower arrows, never tense the bow.
I swear by the unappeasable fountainhead of the Styx,[6]
the one dread oath decreed for the gods on high.

6. River in the underworld.

           "So,
now I yield, Juno yields, and I leave this war I loathe.
But this—and there is no law of Fate to stop it now—   950
this I beg for Latium, for the glory of your people.
When, soon, they join in their happy wedding-bonds—
and wedded let them be—in pacts of peace at last,
never command the Latins, here on native soil,
to exchange their age-old name,   955
to become Trojans, called the kin of Teucer,
alter their language, change their style of dress.
Let Latium endure. Let Alban kings hold sway for all time.
Let Roman stock grow strong with Italian strength.
Troy has fallen—and fallen let her stay—   960
with the very name of Troy!"
        Smiling down,
the creator of man and the wide world returned:
"Now there's my sister. Saturn's second child—
such tides of rage go churning through your heart.
Come, relax your anger. It started all for nothing.   965
I grant your wish. I surrender. Freely, gladly too.
Latium's sons will retain their fathers' words and ways.
Their name till now is the name that shall endure.
Mingling in stock alone, the Trojans will subside.
And I will add the rites and the forms of worship,   970
and make them Latins all, who speak one Latin tongue.
Mixed with Ausonian blood,[7] one race will spring from them,
and you will see them outstrip all men, outstrip all gods
in reverence. No nation on earth will match the honors
they shower down on you."
       Juno nodded assent to this,   975
her spirit reversed to joy. She departs the sky
and leaves her cloud behind.
       His task accomplished,
the Father turned his mind to another matter, set
to dismiss Juturna from her brother's battles.
They say there are twin Curses called the Furies . . .   980
Night had born them once in the dead of darkness,
one and the same spawn, and birthed infernal Megaera,
wreathing all their heads with coiled serpents,
fitting them out with wings that race the wind.
They hover at Jove's throne, crouch at his gates   985
to serve that savage king
and whet the fears of afflicted men whenever
the king of gods lets loose horrific deaths and plagues
or panics towns that deserve the scourge of war.
Jove sped one of them down the sky, commanding: 990
"Cross Juturna's path as a wicked omen!"

7. Ausonian: Italian.

Down she swoops, hurled to earth by a whirlwind,
swift as a darting arrow whipped from a bowstring
through the clouds, a shaft armed by a Parthian,[8]
tipped with deadly poison, shot by a Parthian   995
or a Cretan archer—well past any cure—
hissing on unseen through the rushing dark.
So raced this daughter of Night and sped to earth.
Soon as she spots the Trojan ranks and Turnus' lines
she quickly shrinks into that small bird that often,   1000
hunched at dusk on deserted tombs and rooftops, sings
its ominous song in shadows late at night. Shrunken so,
the demon flutters over and over again in Turnus' face,
screeching, drumming his shield with its whirring wings.
An eerie numbness unnerved him head to toe with dread,   1005
his hackles bristled in horror, voice choked in his throat.

Recognizing the Fury's ruffling wings at a distance,
wretched Juturna tears her hair, nails clawing her face,
fists beating her breast, and cries to her brother:
"How, Turnus, how can your sister help you now?   1010
What's left for me now, after all I have endured?
What skill do I have to lengthen out your life?
How can I fight against this dreadful omen?
At last, at last I leave the field of battle.
Afraid as I am, now frighten me no more,   1015
you obscene birds of night! Too well I know
the beat of your wings, the drumbeat of doom.
Nor do the proud commands of Jove escape me now,
our great, warm-hearted Jove. Are these his wages
for taking my virginity? Why did he grant me life   1020
eternal—rob me of our one privilege, death?
Then, for a fact, I now could end this agony,
keep my brother company down among the shades.
Doomed to live forever? Without you, my brother,
what do I have still mine that's sweet to taste?   1025
If only the earth gaped deep enough to take me down,
to plunge this goddess into the depths of hell!"
                                        With that,
shrouding her head with a gray-green veil and moaning low,
down to her own stream's bed the goddess sank away.

All hot pursuit, Aeneas brandishes high his spear,   1030
that tree of a spear, and shouts from a savage heart:
"More delay! Why now? Still in retreat, Turnus, why?
This is no foot-race. It's savagery, swordplay cut-and-thrust!
Change yourself into any shape you please, call up
whatever courage or skill you still have left.   1035
Pray to wing your way to the starry sky
or bury yourself in the earth's deep pits!"

8. Parthia (a region in modern Iran) was known for its skillful archers.

Turnus shakes his head: "I don't fear you,
you and your blazing threats, my fierce friend.
It's the gods that frighten me—Jove, my mortal foe." 1040

No more words. Glancing around he spots a huge rock,
huge, ages old, and lying out in the field by chance,
placed as a boundary stone to settle border wars.
A dozen picked men could barely shoulder it up, men
of such physique as the earth brings forth these days, 1045
but he wrenched it up, hands trembling, tried to heave it
right at Aeneas, Turnus stretching to full height, the hero
at speed, at peak strength. Yet he's losing touch with himself,
racing, hoisting that massive rock in his hands and hurling,
true, but his knees buckle, blood's like ice in his veins 1050
and the rock he flings through the air, plummeting under
its own weight, cannot cover the space between them,
cannot strike full force . . .
                              Just as in dreams
when the nightly spell of sleep falls heavy on our eyes
and we seem entranced by longing to keep on racing on, 1055
no use, in the midst of one last burst of speed
we sink down, consumed, our tongue won't work,
and tried and true, the power that filled our body
fails—we strain but the voice and words won't follow.
So with Turnus. Wherever he fought to force his way, 1060
no luck, the merciless Fury blocks his efforts.
A swirl of thoughts goes racing through his mind,
he glances toward his own Rutulians and their town,
he hangs back in dread, he quakes at death—it's here.
Where can he run? How can he strike out at the enemy? 1065
Where's his chariot? His charioteer, his sister? Vanished.

As he hangs back, the fatal spear of Aeneas streaks on—
spotting a lucky opening he had flung from a distance,
all his might and main. Rocks heaved by a catapult
pounding city ramparts never storm so loudly, never 1070
such a shattering bolt of thunder crashing forth.
Like a black whirlwind churning on, that spear
flies on with its weight of iron death to pierce
the breastplate's lower edge and the outmost rim
of the round shield with its seven plies and right 1075
at the thick of Turnus' thigh it whizzes through,
it strikes home and the blow drops great Turnus
down to the ground, battered down on his bent knees.
The Rutulians spring up with a groan and the hillsides
round groan back and the tall groves far and wide 1080
resound with the long-drawn moan.
                                  Turnus lowered
his eyes and reached with his right hand and begged,
a suppliant: "I deserve it all. No mercy, please,"
Turnus pleaded. "Seize your moment now. Or if
some care for a parent's grief can touch you still, 1085

I pray you—you had such a father, in old Anchises—
pity Daunus in his old age and send me back
to my own people, or if you would prefer,
send them my dead body stripped of life. Here,
the victor and vanquished, I stretch my hands to you,   1090
so the men of Latium have seen me in defeat.
Lavinia is your bride.
Go no further down the road of hatred."

    Aeneas, ferocious in armor, stood there, still,
shifting his gaze, and held his sword-arm back,   1095
holding himself back too as Turnus' words began
to sway him more and more . . . when all at once
he caught sight of the fateful sword-belt of Pallas,
swept over Turnus' shoulder, gleaming with shining studs
Aeneas knew by heart. Young Pallas, whom Turnus had overpowered,   1100
taken down with a wound, and now his shoulder flaunted
his enemy's battle-emblem like a trophy. Aeneas,
soon as his eyes drank in that plunder—keepsake
of his own savage grief—flaring up in fury,
terrible in his rage, he cries: "Decked in the spoils   1105
you stripped from one I loved—escape my clutches? Never—
Pallas strikes this blow, Pallas sacrifices you now,
makes you pay the price with your own guilty blood!"
In the same breath, blazing with wrath he plants
his iron sword hilt-deep in his enemy's heart.   1110
Turnus' limbs went limp in the chill of death.
His life breath fled with a groan of outrage
down to the shades below.[9]

9. The same lines are used in book 11 for the death of the woman warrior, Camilla.

OVID

43 B.C.E.–17 C.E.

Ovid (whose full name was Publius Ovidius Naso) was one of the smartest, most prolific, and most consistently entertaining of the Roman poets. During his long and productive career, he wrote funny, perceptive poems about sex and relationships in contemporary Rome, as well as vivid retellings of ancient myths. His way of telling stories remains extraordinary for its subtlety and its depth of psychological understanding. His work had a massive influence on the poets and artists of the Middle Ages, the Renaissance, and beyond, and it is one of our most important and accessible sources for the rich mythology of ancient Greece and Rome.

LIFE AND TIMES

Ovid was born into an aristocratic ("equestrian") family, in the provincial Roman town of Sulmo, east of Rome. His father wanted him to become a lawyer, and therefore had him trained in rhetoric. Ovid's writing shows the influence of rhetorical technique, in its polished, witty style. But Ovid had no real interest in the law. He was a natural poet, and at the age of twenty, to his father's disappointment and disapproval, he quit his legal training. He held various minor governmental posts, but eventually became a full-time poet, with the financial aid of a rich patron called Messalla. Ovid became part of the literary circles of Rome: he knew the poets Propertius and Horace, and met **Virgil**, who was some twenty-seven years older.

Ovid married three times; he had been divorced twice before the age of thirty. His third wife seems to have had a daughter by a previous husband, but Ovid had no children of his own. Beyond that, we know little of Ovid's personal life. He wrote a great deal about extramarital sex, but emphasized that his poetic persona should not be taken as autobiography, declaring, "My Muse is slutty, but my life is chaste."

Ovid's work included various collections of poems on mythological topics, such as the *Fasti* (never finished), on the Roman calendar, and a set of poetic letters, the *Heroides*, from mythical heroines like Helen of Troy to their boyfriends. But most notorious, in his own time and later, were his two books about sex and relationships: the *Amores* and the *Ars Amatoria*. These used the tradition of Roman love elegy, which had begun with **Catullus** and had been developed by Ovid's friend Propertius, who evoked the desperate, abject longing of a man for a beloved and unreliable girlfriend. Ovid's love poetry focuses less on feelings than on behavior, and less on love than on sex, which he treats in a light, knowing tone. He gives, for example, a titillating account of some hot afternoon sex; tells anecdotes about his girlfriend's bad experiences with hair dye and about her attempted abortion; and offers advice about the best places to go and best lines to use for picking up a date.

All this was guaranteed to irritate the more conservative members of Roman society, who included—unfortunately for Ovid—the emperor, Augustus. Having seized power after winning the battle of Actium (in 31 B.C.E.), at the end of a long civil war, Augustus was eager to impose order on the fragmented society of Rome. A key element in his domestic strategy was to reform the morals and increase the population of the Roman elite, by promoting marriage and traditional family structures. New laws were imposed in 19–18 B.C.E. to encourage married couples to have children, and to punish adultery with exile. In this context, Ovid's *Ars Amatoria* seems deliberately calculated to enrage the emperor. The poem points up the hypocrisy of Roman sexual mores and suggests that, in fact, having lots of extramarital sex is far more traditional than Augustan family values, since the Romans have been doing it ever since the foundation of the city: it was through the rape of the Sabine women that the male inhabitants of the new city acquired wives and were able to supply Rome with future citizens.

Ovid seems to have gotten himself into even worse trouble by what he calls a mistake. We do not know exactly what happened; Ovid suggests that he saw something he should not have seen, perhaps involving the emperor's daughter, Julia, who was having an adulterous affair. Combined with the *Ars Amatoria* and Ovid's generally provocative stance toward Augustus, this mistake was the last straw; in 8 C.E., the emperor—acting, unusually, on his own initiative, without input from the Senate—condemned Ovid to permanent exile from Rome to Tomis, a remote town on the Black Sea, in modern Romania. He lived out the remaining eight years of his life in grim isolation, far from family and friends, in a cold, bleak place where, he claims, nobody even spoke Latin. Ovid wrote a series of poems from exile, mostly letters bewailing his sufferings and pleading—to friends, family, acquaintances, the general public, and to the emperor himself—to be forgiven and to be allowed back home. All were unsuccessful; Ovid died in Tomis, alone and unforgiven.

METAMORPHOSES

At the time of his exile in 8 C.E., Ovid was finishing his greatest work, the *Metamorphoses* (Greek for "changes"). It is less obviously provocative than Ovid's love poetry, but it, too, provides a radical challenge both to Augustan moral and political values and to traditional poetic norms. Virgil had written what Augustus wanted to be the official epic of the new order. For all its innovations, the **Aeneid** focused on the deeds of a single hero, and it treated its culture's dominant values (such as duty, imperial power, and military honor) with respect. The *Metamorphoses* is recognizably epic; it is the only poem Ovid wrote in the epic meter, dactylic hexameter. But it can be seen as a critical response to Virgil, even an anti-*Aeneid*. Ovid produced a series of miniature stories strung together into a long narrative of fifteen books. The transitions between them, and the connections drawn by the narrator, are often transparently contrived—perhaps in mockery of the idea of narrative unity. There is no single hero, and no moral values are presented without irony. There is, however, an element common to these stories: change; and despite its leisurely and roundabout course, the narrative has a discernible direction—as Ovid says in his introduction, "from the world's beginning to the present day." Starting with the creation of the world, the transformation of matter into living bodies (the first great metamorphosis), Ovid tells of human beings changed into animals, flowers, and trees. He proceeds through Greek myth to stories of early Rome and so to his own time, culminating in the ascension of the murdered Julius Caesar to the heavens in the form of a star and the divine promise that Augustus too, far in the future, will become a god; it is tempting to speculate that Ovid hoped—vainly—to improve his relationship with the emperor by means of these few lines. The last change of all is that of Ovid himself, who will, he declares, be transformed from a mortal man into his own immortal poem.

Change underlies both the narrative style and the vision of the world the poem projects. Virgil also told of a transformation, the new (Roman) order arising from the ruins of the old (Troy). But once the transformation was completed by the Augustan order, there was to be stability, permanence. Ovid tells of a world ceaselessly coming to be in a process that never ends. Augustan Rome is not the culminating point of history here, as it was in the *Aeneid*; indeed, the whole idea of a historical end or goal seems, in the *Metamorphoses*, impossible and absurd. Ovid's epic without a hero presents shifting perspectives and offers the reader no single point of view from which to judge his complex narratives. Against the forced imposition of political and moral unity he sets change itself.

Change is also central to the narrative manner of the *Metamorphoses*. Ovid constantly shifts his point of view, telling a story first from one character's perspective, and then from another's. One story is embedded in another, so that one narrative voice is piled on top of another, as when Venus tells Adonis the story of Atalanta. This story is set within the tale of Venus's love for Adonis and of his death, which is one of a series of stories sung by Orpheus in the poem's main narrative. In such cases, the immediate and the larger contexts give the same story different shades of meaning. And there are thematic connections between stories, so that motifs and images also change their meaning from one story to another, or over the course of a single story. Daphne and Syrinx are turned into plants (the laurel and the reed) that are henceforth attributes of the gods who tried to rape them, a form of appropriation that substitutes for sexual violence.

A common element of many stories is the lust of male gods for female humans. On one level, the gods' desire is presented as ridiculous: when Jupiter turns himself into a bull, the narrator comments, "Majestic power and erotic love / do not get on together very well." But these stories are also focused on rape, and, at least some of the time, the narrator shows the terror and suffering of the human victim. These stories of rape may have political implications, for rape is the ultimate imposition of control. When powerful gods force themselves on defenseless women, the reader is invited to remember how easily authority can be abused.

Giovanni Bernini's seventeenth-century interpretation in marble of the rape of Proserpina, one of the stories told in the *Metamorphoses*.

But male gods are not the only sexual agents in the poem: women and goddesses, too, can be overwhelmed by desire, and can themselves become sexual predators. The stories selected here from book 10 of the *Metamorphoses* bring out the complexity of Ovid's presentation of gender and sexuality, showing various ways in which desire causes pain, distorts our perceptions, and ends in disaster. The tale of Pygmalion may seem an exception, but we should remember that it begins with the artist's hatred of women for their loose morals, and that the story as a whole, whatever it may say about the power of art, can also be read as a fable of man's fabrication of woman—her person and her functions—according to his desires. These stories are narrated by Orpheus, the archetypal poet, after his failure to bring Eurydice back from the underworld. The pathology of desire is fundamental to Ovid's poem, since the lover hopes to stop time, to achieve permanent possession of the beloved; but all these stories show us how impossible such a dream is. The girl is always running from the god; the boy is always running from the goddess; Orpheus's wife cannot be brought back from the land of the dead. Reaching for the body of another, the lover's own body is transformed. The closest any of these characters can get to permanence is to be transformed into a growing (living, changing) plant that will always represent their unfulfilled longings.

It was surely not only the fact that the *Metamorphoses* draws into itself most of the major classical myths (and a number of lesser-known stories as well) that has made the poem a source of subjects for artists and poets ever since but also the memorable ways these stories are told and their rich potential for meaning. The poem shows, again and again, the irresistible power of a well-told narrative to hold the attention and shape the imagination of those who read or listen to it.

From Metamorphoses[1]

FROM BOOK I

[*Proem*]

My mind leads me to speak now of forms changed
into new bodies: O gods above, inspire
this undertaking (which you've changed as well)
and guide my poem in its epic sweep
from the world's beginning to the present day.   5

[*The Creation*]

Before the seas and lands had been created,
before the sky that covers everything,
Nature displayed a single aspect only
throughout the cosmos; Chaos was its name,
a shapeless, unwrought mass of inert bulk   10

---

1. Translated by Charles Martin.

and nothing more, with the discordant seeds
of disconnected elements all heaped
together in anarchic disarray.
    The sun as yet did not light up the earth,
nor did the crescent moon renew her horns,   15
nor was the earth suspended in midair,
balanced by her own weight, nor did the ocean
extend her arms to the margins of the land.
    Although the land and sea and air were present,
land was unstable, the sea unfit for swimming,   20
and air lacked light; shapes shifted constantly,
and all things were at odds with one another,
for in a single mass cold strove with warm,
wet was opposed to dry and soft to hard,
and weightlessness to matter having weight.   25
    Some god (or kinder nature) settled this
dispute by separating earth from heaven,
and then by separating sea from earth
and fluid aether[2] from the denser air;
and after these were separated out   30
and liberated from the primal heap,
he bound the disentangled elements
each in its place and all in harmony.
    The fiery and weightless aether leapt
to heaven's vault and claimed its citadel;   35
the next in lightness to be placed was air;
the denser earth drew down gross elements
and was compressed by its own gravity;
encircling water lastly found its place,
encompassing the solid earth entire.[3]   40
    Now when that god (whichever one it was)
had given Chaos form, dividing it
in parts which he arranged, he molded earth
into the shape of an enormous globe,
so that it should be uniform throughout.   45
    And afterward he sent the waters streaming
in all directions, ordered waves to swell
under the sweeping winds, and sent the flood
to form new shores on the surrounded earth;
he added springs, great standing swamps and lakes,   50
as well as sloping rivers fixed between
their narrow banks, whose plunging waters (all
in varied places, each in its own channel)
are partly taken back into the earth

2. A region of refined air, fiery in nature, believed to be above the "denser air" that was closer to the earth and composed the breathable atmosphere.

3. From Homer on, the ancients conceived of Ocean as a stream that surrounded the earth.

and in part flow until they reach the sea,   55
when they—received into the larger field
of a freer flood—beat against shores, not banks.
He ordered open plains to spread themselves,
valleys to sink, the stony peaks to rise,
and forests to put on their coats of green.   60
    And as the vault of heaven is divided
by two zones on the right and two on the left,
with a central zone, much hotter, in between,
so, by the care of this creator god,
the mass that was enclosed now by the sky   65
was zoned in the same way, with the same lines
inscribed upon the surface of the earth.
Heat makes the middle zone unlivable,
and the two outer zones are deep in snow;
between these two extremes, he placed two others   70
of temperate climate, blending cold and warmth.[4]
    Air was suspended over all of this,
proportionately heavier than aether,
as earth is heavier than water is.
He ordered mists and clouds into position,   75
and thunder, to make test of our resolve,[5]
and winds creating thunderbolts and lightning.
    Nor did that world-creating god permit
the winds to roam ungoverned through the air;
for even now, with each of them in charge   80
of his own kingdom, and their blasts controlled,
they scarcely can be kept from shattering
the world, such is the discord between brothers.
    Eurus[6] went eastward, to the lands of Dawn,
the kingdoms of Arabia and Persia,   85
and to the mountain peaks that lie below
the morning's rays; and Zephyr took his place
on the western shores warmed by the setting sun.
The frozen north and Scythia were seized
by bristling Boreas; the lands opposite,   90
continually drenched by fog and rain,
are where the south wind, known as Auster, dwells.
Above these winds, he set the weightless aether,
a liquid free of every earthly toxin.
    No sooner had he separated all   95
within defining limits, when the stars,
which formerly had been concealed in darkness,

---

4. The sky, that is, is divided into five horizon-
tal zones, and therefore so is the earth beneath
it. On either side of the earth's uninhabitable
torrid region, over which the sun passes, lies a
temperate zone, and the northern one contains the inhabited, civilized lands on earth
(ancient writers were vague about what the
southern temperate zone contained). The two
outermost zones, farthest from the sun, were
too cold to live in.
5. Thunder was considered an omen.
6. The east wind. Zephyr, Boreas, and
Auster were the west, north, and south winds,
respectively.

began to blaze up all throughout the heavens;
and so that every region of the world
should have its own distinctive forms of life,   100
the constellations and the shapes of gods
occupied the lower part of heaven;
the seas gave shelter to the shining fishes,
earth received beasts, and flighty air, the birds.
  An animal more like the gods than these,   105
more intellectually capable
and able to control the other beasts,
had not as yet appeared: now man was born,
either because the framer of all things,
the fabricator of this better world,   110
created man out of his own divine
substance—or else because Prometheus[7]
took up a clod (so lately broken off
from lofty aether that it still contained
some elements in common with its kin),   115
and mixing it with water, molded it
into the shape of gods, who govern all.
  And even though all other animals
lean forward and look down toward the ground,
he gave to man a face that is uplifted,   120
and ordered him to stand erect and look
directly up into the vaulted heavens
and turn his countenance to meet the stars;
the earth, that was so lately rude and formless,
was changed by taking on the shapes of men.   125

* * *

[Apollo and Daphne]

Daphne,[8] the daughter of the river god
Peneus, was the first love of Apollo;
this happened not by chance, but by the cruel   630
outrage of Cupid, Phoebus, in the triumph
of his great victory against the Python,[9]
observed him bending back his bow and said,
  "What are *you* doing with such manly arms,
lascivious boy? That bow befits *our* brawn,[1]   635
wherewith we deal out wounds to savage beasts
and other mortal foes, unerringly:
just now with our innumerable arrows
we managed to lay low the mighty Python,

---

7. A god best known for stealing fire from the gods and giving it to mortals. In some stories he also created humans out of clay.
8. Literally, "Laurel" (Greek).

9. The enormous snake that Apollo (Phoebus) had to kill in order to found his oracle at Delphi. "Cupid": god of sexual desire.
1. The bow was one of Apollo's attributes.

whose pestilential belly covered acres!   640
Content yourself with kindling love affairs
with your wee torch—and don't claim *our* glory!"
    The son of Venus[2] answered him with this:
"Your arrow, Phoebus, may strike everything:
mine will strike you: as animals to gods,   645
your glory is so much the less than mine!"
    He spoke, and soaring upward through the air
on wings that thundered, in no time at all
had landed on Parnassus'[3] shaded height;
and from his quiver drew two arrows out   650
which operated at cross-purposes,
for one engendered flight, the other, love;
the latter has a polished tip of gold,
the former has a tip of dull, blunt lead;
with this one, Cupid struck Peneus' daughter,   655
while the other pierced Apollo to his marrow.
    One is in love now, and the other one
won't hear of it, for Daphne calls it joy
to roam within the forest's deep seclusion,
where she, in emulation of the chaste   660
goddess Phoebe,[4] devotes herself to hunting;
one ribbon only bound her straying tresses.
    Many men sought her, but she spurned her suitors,
loath to have anything to do with men,
and rambled through the wild and trackless groves   665
untroubled by a thought for love or marriage.
    Often her father said, "You owe it to me,
child, to provide me with a son-in-law
and grandchildren!"
                 "Let me remain a virgin,
father most dear," she said, "as once before   670
Diana's father, Jove, gave her that gift."
    Although Peneus yielded to you, Daphne,
your beauty kept your wish from coming true,
your comeliness conflicting with your vow:
at first sight, Phoebus loves her and desires   675
to sleep with her; desire turns to hope,
and his own prophecy deceives the god.
    Now just as in a field the harvest stubble
is all burned off, or as hedges are set ablaze
when, if by chance, some careless traveler   680
should brush one with his torch or toss away
the still-smoldering brand at break of day—
just so the smitten god went up in flames
until his heart was utterly afire,
and hope sustained his unrequited passion.   685
    He gazes on her hair without adornment:
"What if it were done up a bit?" he asks,

2. Goddess of love (Aphrodite in Greek).
3. Mountain in central Greece, near Delphi.

4. Diana (Artemis in Greek), Apollo's sister, virgin goddess of the hunt.

and gazes on her eyes, as bright as stars,
and on that darling little mouth of hers,
though sight is not enough to satisfy;   690
he praises everything that he can see—
her fingers, hands, and arms, bare to her shoulders—
and what is hidden prizes even more.
    She flees more swiftly than the lightest breeze,
nor will she halt when he calls out to her: 695
"Daughter of Peneus, I pray, hold still,
hold still! I'm not a foe in grim pursuit!
Thus lamb flees wolf, thus dove from eagle flies
on trembling wings, thus deer from lioness,
thus any creature flees its enemy,   700
but I am stalking you because of love!
    "Wretch that I am: I'm fearful that you'll fall,
brambles will tear your flesh because of me!
The ground you're racing over's very rocky,
slow down, I beg you, restrain yourself in flight,   705
and I will follow at a lesser speed.
    "Just ask yourself who finds you so attractive!
I'm not a caveman, not some shepherd boy,
no shaggy guardian of flocks and herds—
you've no idea, rash girl, you've no idea   710
whom you are fleeing, that is why you flee!
    "Delphi, Claros, Tenedos are all mine,
I'm worshiped in the city of Patara![5]
Jove is my father, I alone reveal
what was, what is, and what will come to be!   715
The plucked strings answer my demand with song!
    "Although my aim is sure, another's arrow
proved even more so, and my careless heart
was badly wounded—the art of medicine
is my invention, by the way, the source   720
of my worldwide fame as a practitioner
of healing through the natural strength of herbs.
    "Alas, there is no herbal remedy
for the love that I must suffer, and the arts
that heal all others cannot heal their lord—"   725
    He had much more to say to her, but Daphne
pursued her fearful course and left him speechless,
though no less lovely fleeing him; indeed,
disheveled by the wind that bared her limbs
and pressed the blown robes to her straining body   730
even as it whipped up her hair behind her,
the maiden was more beautiful in flight!
    But the young god had no further interest
in wasting his fine words on her; admonished
by his own passion, he accelerates,   735
and runs as swiftly as a Gallic hound[6]

---

5. All centers of Apollo's cult.   6. A hunting breed famous for speed.

chasing a rabbit through an open field;
the one seeks shelter and the other, prey—
he clings to her, is just about to spring,
with his long muzzle straining at her heels,   740
while she, not knowing whether she's been caught,
in one swift burst, eludes those snapping jaws,
no longer the anticipated feast;
so he in hope and she in terror race.
    But her pursuer, driven by his passion,   745
outspeeds the girl, giving her no pause,
one step behind her, breathing down her neck;
her strength is gone; she blanches at the thought
of the effort of her swift flight overcome,
but at the sight of Peneus, she cries,   750
"Help me, dear father! If your waters hold
divinity, transform me and destroy
that beauty by which I have too well pleased!"
    Her prayer was scarcely finished when she feels
a torpor take possession of her limbs—   755
her supple trunk is girdled with a thin
layer of fine bark over her smooth skin;
her hair turns into foliage, her arms
grow into branches, sluggish roots adhere
to feet that were so recently so swift,   760
her head becomes the summit of a tree;
all that remains of her is a warm glow.
    Loving her still, the god puts his right hand
against the trunk, and even now can feel
her heart as it beats under the new bark;   765
he hugs her limbs as if they were still human,
and then he puts his lips against the wood,
which, even now, is adverse to his kiss.
    "Although you cannot be my bride," he says,
"you will assuredly be my own tree,   770
O Laurel, and will always find yourself
girding my locks, my lyre, and my quiver too—
you will adorn great Roman generals
when every voice cries out in joyful triumph
along the route up to the Capitol;   775
you will protect the portals of Augustus,
guarding, on either side, his crown of oak;[7]
and as I am—perpetually youthful,
my flowing locks unknown to the barber's shears—
so you will be an evergreen forever   780
bearing your brilliant foliage with glory!"
    Phoebus concluded. Laurel shook her branches
and seemed to nod her summit in assent.

---

7. The laurel tree, sacred to Apollo, was the symbol of victory not only in athletic contests but also in war; victorious Roman generals honored with a triumphal procession through the city to the Capitol wore a laurel wreath. The oak was sacred to Jupiter.

[Jove and Io]

There is a grove in Thessaly,[8] enclosed
on every side by high and wooded hills: 785
they call it Tempe. The river Peneus,
which rises deep within the Pindus range,
pours its turbulent waters through this gorge
and over a cataract that deafens all
its neighbors far and near, creating clouds   790
that drive a fine, cool mist along, until
it drips down through the summits of the trees.
   Here is the house, the seat, the inner chambers
of the great river; here Peneus holds court
in his rocky cavern and lays down the law   795
to water nymphs and tributary streams.
   First to assemble were the native rivers,
uncertain whether to congratulate,
or to commiserate with Daphne's father:
the Sperchios, whose banks are lined with poplars,   800
the ancient Apidanus and the mild
Aeas and Amprysus; others came later—
rivers who, by whatever course they take,
eventually bring their flowing streams,
weary of their meandering, to sea.   805
   Inachus[9] was the only river absent,
concealed in the recesses of his cave:
he added to his volume with the tears
he grimly wept for his lost daughter Io,
not knowing whether she still lived or not;   810
but since he couldn't find her anywhere,
assumed that she was nowhere to be found—
and in his heart, he feared a fate far worse.
   For Jupiter had seen the girl returning
from her father's banks and had accosted her: 815
"O maiden worthy of almighty Jove
and destined to delight some lucky fellow
(I know not whom) upon your wedding night,
come find some shade," he said, "in these deep woods—"
(showing her where the woods were *very* shady)   820
"while the sun blazes high above the earth!
   "But if you're worried about entering
the haunts of savage beasts all by yourself,
why, under the protection of a god
you will be safe within the deepest woods—   825
and no plebeian god, for I am he
who bears the celestial scepter in his hand,
I am he who hurls the roaming thunderbolt—
don't run from me!"
                     But run she did, through Lerna

8. A region of central Greece.
9. A river near Argos in the northeast Peloponnesus.

and Lyrcea,[1] until the god concealed 830
the land entirely beneath a dense
dark mist and seized her and dishonored her.
　Juno,[2] however, happened to look down
on Argos, where she noticed something odd:
swift-flying clouds had turned day into night 835
long before nighttime. She realized
that neither falling mist nor rising fog
could be the cause of this phenomenon,
and looked about at once to find her husband,
as one too well aware of the connivings 840
of a mate so often taken in the act.
　When he could not be found above, she said,
"Either I'm mad—or I am being had."
She glided down to earth from heaven's summit
immediately and dispersed the clouds. 845
　Having intuited his wife's approach,
Jove had already metamorphosed Io
into a gleaming heifer—a beauty still,
even as a cow. Despite herself,
Juno gave this illusion her approval, 850
and feigning ignorance, asked him whose herd
this heifer had come out of, and where from;
Jove, lying to forestall all inquiries
as to her origin and pedigree,
replied that she was born out of the earth. 855
Then Juno asked him for her as a gift.
　What could he do? Here is his beloved:
to hand her over is unnatural,
but not to do so would arouse suspicion;
shame urged him onward while love held him back. 860
Love surely would have triumphed over shame,
except that to deny so slight a gift
to one who was his wife and sister both
would make it seem that this was no mere cow!
　Her rival given up to her at last, 865
Juno feared Jove had more such tricks in mind,
and couldn't feel entirely secure
until she'd placed this heifer in the care
of Argus, the watchman with a hundred eyes:
in strict rotation, his eyes slept in pairs, 870
while those that were not sleeping stayed on guard.
No matter where he stood, he looked at Io,
even when he had turned his back on her.
　He let her graze in daylight; when the sun
set far beneath the earth, he penned her in 875
and placed a collar on her indignant neck.

1. A mountain on the border between Argos　the territory of Argos, near the coast.
and Arcadia to the west. "Lerna": a marsh in　2. Wife of Jupiter (Hera in Greek).

She fed on leaves from trees and bitter grasses,
and had no bed to sleep on, the poor thing,
but lay upon the ground, not always grassy,
and drank the muddy waters from the streams.   880
    Having no arms, she could not stretch them out
in supplication to her warden, Argus;
and when she tried to utter a complaint
she only mooed—a sound which terrified her,
fearful as she now was of her own voice.   885
    Io at last came to the riverbank
where she had often played; when she beheld
her own slack jaws and newly sprouted horns
in the clear water, she fled, terrified!
    Neither her naiad sisters[3] nor her father   890
knew who this heifer was who followed them
and let herself be petted and admired.
Inachus fed her grasses from his hand;
she licked it and pressed kisses on his palm,
unable to restrain her flowing tears.   895
    If words would just have come, she would have spoken,
telling them who she was, how this had happened,
and begging their assistance in her case;
but with her hoof, she drew lines in the dust,
and letters of the words she could not speak   900
told the sad story of her transformation.
    "Oh, wretched me," cried Io's father, clinging
to the lowing calf's horns and snowy neck.
"Oh, wretched me!" he groaned. "Are you the child
for whom I searched the earth in every part?   905
Lost, you were less a grief than you are, found!
    "You make no answer, unable to respond
to our speech in language of your own,
but from your breast come resonant deep sighs
and—all that you can manage now—you *moo*!   910
    "But I—all unaware of this—was busy
arranging marriage for you, in the hopes
of having a son-in-law and grandchildren.
Now I must pick your husband from my herd,
and now must find your offspring there as well!   915
    "Nor can I end this suffering by death;
it is a hurtful thing to be a god,
for the gates of death are firmly closed against me,
and our sorrows must go on forever."
    And while the father mourned his daughter's loss,   920
Argus of the hundred eyes removed her
to pastures farther off and placed himself
high on a mountain peak, a vantage point
from which he could keep watch in all directions.
    The ruler of the heavens cannot bear   925

---

3. River nymphs.

the sufferings of Io any longer,
and calls his son, born of the Pleiades,[4]
and orders him to do away with Argus.
  Without delay, he takes his winged sandals,
his magic, sleep-inducing wand, and cap;   930
and so equipped, the son of father Jove
glides down from heaven's summit to the earth,
where he removes and leaves behind his cap
and winged sandals, but retains the wand;
and sets out as a shepherd, wandering   935
far from the beaten path, driving before him
a flock of goats he rounds up as he goes,
while playing tunes upon his pipe of reeds.
  The guardian of Juno is quite taken
by this new sound: "Whoever you might be,   940
why not come sit with me upon this rock,"
said Argus, "for that flock of yours will find
the grass is nowhere greener, and you see
that there is shade here suitable for shepherds."
  The grandson of great Atlas takes his seat   945
and whiles away the hours, chattering
of this and that—and playing on his pipes,
he tries to overcome the watchfulness
of Argus, struggling to stay awake;
even though Slumber closes down some eyes,   950
others stay vigilant. Argus inquired
how the reed pipes, so recently invented,
had come to be, and Mercury responded:
  "On the idyllic mountains of Arcadia,[5]
among the hamadryads[6] of Nonacris,   955
one was renowned, and Syrinx[7] was her name.
Often she fled—successfully—from Satyrs,[8]
and deities of every kind as well,
those of the shady wood and fruited plain.
  "In her pursuits and in virginity   960
Diana was her model, and she wore
her robe hitched up and girt above the knees
just as her goddess did; and if her bow
had been made out of gold, instead of horn,
anyone seeing her might well have thought   965
she *was* the goddess—as, indeed, some did.
  "Wearing his crown of sharp pine needles, Pan[9]
saw her returning once from Mount Lycaeus,[1]

---

4. Mercury (Hermes in Greek) was the son of
Maia, one of the Pleiades or daughters of Atlas.
They were changed into stars when the hunter
Orion was pursuing them along with their
mother Pleione, whom he wanted to rape.
5. The rustic central region of the Peloponnesus. Nonacris was a town in its northern part.
6. Tree nymphs.

7. The name means "shepherd's pipe," a
musical instrument made of reeds.
8. Woodland creatures—half man, half goat,
bald, bearded, and highly sexed.
9. A god of the wild mountain pastures and
woods, with goat's feet and horns. He was particularly associated with Arcadia.
1. A high mountain in Arcadia.

and began to say. . . ."

                  There remained to tell
of how the maiden, having spurned his pleas,   970
fled through the trackless wilds until she came
to where the gently flowing Ladon stopped
her in her flight; how she begged the water nymphs
to change her shape, and how the god, assuming
that he had captured Syrinx, grasped instead   975
a handful of marsh reeds! And while he sighed,
the reeds in his hands, stirred by his own breath,
gave forth a similar, low-pitched complaint!

    The god, much taken by the sweet new voice
of an unprecedented instrument,   980
said this to her: "At least we may converse
with one another—I can have that much."

    That pipe of reeds, unequal in their lengths,
and joined together one-on-one with wax,
took the girl's name, and bears it to this day.   985

    Now Mercury was ready to continue
until he saw that Argus had succumbed,
for all his eyes had been closed down by sleep.
He silences himself and waves his wand
above those languid orbs to fix the spell.   990

    Without delay he grasps the nodding head
and where it joins the neck, he severs it
with his curved blade and flings it bleeding down
the steep rock face, staining it with gore.
O Argus, you are fallen, and the light   995
in all your lamps is utterly put out:
one hundred eyes, one darkness all the same!

    But Saturn's daughter[2] rescued them and set
those eyes upon the feathers of her bird,[3]
filling his tail with constellated gems.   1000

    Her rage demanded satisfaction, *now*:
the goddess set a horrifying Fury
before the eyes and the imagination
of her Grecian rival; and in her heart
she fixed a prod that goaded Io on,   1005
driving her in terror through the world
until at last, O Nile, you let her rest
from endless labor; having reached your banks,
she went down awkwardly upon her knees,
and with her neck bent backward, raised her face   1010
as only she could do it, to the stars;
and with her groans and tears and mournful mooing,
entreated Jove, it seemed, to put an end
to her great suffering.

                  Jove threw his arms
around the neck of Juno in embrace,   1015

2. Juno.   3. The peacock.

imploring her to end this punishment:
"In future," he said, "put your fears aside:
never again will you have cause to worry—
about *this* one." And swore upon the Styx.[4]
    The goddess was now pacified, and Io   1020
at once began regaining her lost looks,
till she became what she had been before;
her body lost all of its bristling hair,
her horns shrank down, her eyes grew narrower,
her jaws contracted, arms and hands returned,   1025
and hooves divided themselves into nails;
nothing remained of her bovine nature,
unless it was the whiteness of her body.
She had some trouble getting her legs back,
and for a time feared speaking, lest she moo,   1030
and so quite timidly regained her speech.
    She is a celebrated goddess now,
and worshiped by the linen-clad Egyptians.[5]
Her son, Epaphus, is believed to be
sprung from the potent seed of mighty Jove,   1035
and temples may be found in every city
wherein the boy is honored with his parent.

*   *   *

FROM BOOK X[6]

[Pygmalion]

"Pygmalion observed how these women[7] lived lives of sordid
indecency, and, dismayed by the numerous defects
of character Nature had given the feminine spirit,
stayed as a bachelor, having no female companion.   315
    "During that time he created an ivory statue,
a work of most marvelous art, and gave it a figure
better than any living woman could boast of,
and promptly conceived a passion for his own creation.
You would have thought it alive, so like a real maiden   320
that only its natural modesty kept it from moving:
art concealed artfulness. Pygmalion gazed in amazement,
burning with love for what was in likeness a body.
    "Often he stretched forth a hand to touch his creation,
attempting to settle the issue: *was* it a body,   325
or was it—this he would not yet concede—a mere statue?
He gives it kisses, and they are returned, he imagines;

4. One of the rivers of the underworld; the gods swore solemn oaths by it.
5. Io was identified with Isis, at least by the Greeks and Romans.
6. This selection of stories is part of the song sung by Orpheus, the legendary singer, after he has failed to redeem his wife, Eurydice, from the underworld. His theme, announced in the prologue of his song, is "young boys whom the gods have desired, / and . . . girls seized by forbidden and blameworthy passions."
7. Orpheus has just told of the Propoetides of Cyprus, who, as punishment for having denied Venus's divinity, became the first women to prostitute themselves.

now he addresses and now he caresses it, feeling
his fingers sink into its warm, pliant flesh, and
fears he will leave blue bruises all over its body; 330
he seeks to win its affections with words and with presents
pleasing to girls, such as seashells and pebbles, tame birds,
armloads of flowers in thousands of different colors,
lilies, bright painted balls, curious insects in amber;
he dresses it up and puts diamond rings on its fingers, 335
gives it a necklace, a lacy brassiere and pearl earrings,
and even though all such adornments truly become her,
she does not seem to be any less beautiful naked.
He lays her down on a bed with a bright purple cover
and calls her his bedmate and slips a few soft, downy pillows 340
under her head as though she were able to feel them.
    "The holiday honoring Venus has come, and all Cyprus[8]
turns out to celebrate; heifers with gilded horns buckle
under the deathblow[9] and incense soars up in thick clouds;
having already brought his own gift to the altar, 345
Pygmalion stood by and offered this fainthearted prayer:
'If you in heaven are able to give us whatever
we ask for, then I would like as my wife—' and not daring
to say, '—my ivory maiden,' said, '—one like my statue!'
Since golden Venus was present there at her altar, 350
she knew what he wanted to ask for, and as a good omen,
three times the flames soared and leapt right up to the heavens.
    "Once home, he went straight to the replica of his sweetheart,
threw himself down on the couch and repeatedly kissed her;
she seemed to grow warm and so he repeated the action, 355
kissing her lips and exciting her breasts with both hands.
Aroused, the ivory softened and, losing its stiffness,
yielded, submitting to his caress as wax softens
when it is warmed by the sun, and handled by fingers,
takes on many forms, and by being used, becomes useful. 360
Amazed, he rejoices, then doubts, then fears he's mistaken,
while again and again he touches on what he has prayed for.
She is alive! And her veins leap under his fingers!
    "You can believe that Pygmalion offered the goddess
his thanks in a torrent of speech, once again kissing 365
those lips that were not untrue; that she felt his kisses,
and timidly blushing, she opened her eyes to the sunlight,
and at the same time, first looked on her lover and heaven!
The goddess attended the wedding since she had arranged it,
and before the ninth moon had come to its crescent, a daughter 370
was born to them—Paphos,[1] who gave her own name to the island.

    "She had a son named Cinyras, who would be regarded
as one of the blessèd, if he had only been childless.
I sing of dire events: depart from me, daughters,

8. Island in the eastern Mediterranean sacred
to Venus.
9. I.e., as they are sacrificed.

1. One of the cities of Cyprus, whose name is
often used for the island as a whole.

depart from me, fathers; or, if you find my poems charming,   375
believe that I lie, believe these events never happened;
or, if you believe that they did, then believe they were punished.
  "If Nature allows us to witness such impious misdeeds,
then I give my solemn thanks that the Thracian people
and the land itself are far away from those regions[2]   380
where evil like that was begotten: let fabled Panchaea[3]
be rich in balsam and cinnamon, costum and frankincense,
the sweat that drips down from the trees; let it bear incense
and flowers of every description: it also bears myrrh, and
too great a price was paid for that new creation.   385
  "Cupid himself denies that his darts ever harmed you,
Myrrha, and swears that his torches likewise are guiltless;
one of the three sisters,[4] bearing a venomous hydra
and waving a Stygian firebrand, must have inspired your passion.
Hating a parent is wicked, but even more wicked   390
than hatred is this kind of love. Princes elected
from far and wide desire you, Myrrha; all Asia
sends its young men to compete for your hand in marriage:
choose from so many just one of these men for your husband,
so long as a certain one is not the one chosen.   395
  "She understood and struggled against her perversion,
asking herself, 'What have I begun? Where will it take me?
May heaven and piety and the sacred rights of fathers
restrain these unspeakable thoughts and repel my misfortune,
if this indeed *is* misfortune; yet piety chooses   400
not to condemn this love outright: without distinctions
animals copulate; it is no crime for the heifer
to bear the weight of her father upon her own back;
daughters are suitable wives in the kingdom of horses;
the billy goats enter the flocks that they themselves sire,   405
and birds are inseminated by those who conceive them:
blessed, the ones for whom such love is permitted!
  "'Human morality gives us such stifling precepts,
and makes indecent what Nature freely allows us!
But people say there are nations where sons and their mothers,   410
where fathers and daughters, may marry each other, increasing
the bonds of piety by their redoubled affections.
Wretched am I, who hadn't the luck to be born there,
injured by nothing more than mischance of location!
  "'Why do I obsess? Begone, forbidden desires;   415
of course he is worthy of love—but love for a father!
So, then, if I were not the daughter of great Cinyras,
I would be able to have intercourse with Cinyras:
though he is mine, he is not mine, and our nearness
ruins me: I would be better off as a stranger.   420
  "'It would be good for me to go far away from my country,
as long as I could escape from my wicked desires,

2. A reminder that Orpheus is singing in
Thrace (the region stretching along the north
coast of the Aegean Sea).

3. An imaginary island near Arabia, rich in
spices.
4. The Furies.

for what holds me here is the passion that I have to see him,
to touch and speak to Cinyras and give him my kisses—
if nothing more is permitted. You impious maiden,   425
what more can you imagine will ever be granted?
Are you aware how you confuse all rights and relations?
Would you be your mother's rival? The whore of your father?
Would you be called your son's sister? Your brother's own mother?
Do you not shudder to think of the serpent-coiffed sisters[5]   430
thrusting their bloodthirsty torches into the faces
of the guilty wretches that those three appear to and torture?
     "'But you, while your body is undefiled, keep your mind chaste,
and do not break Nature's law with incestuous pairing.
Think what you ask for: the very act is forbidden.   435
and he is devout and mindful of moral behavior—
ah, how I wish that he had a similar madness!'
     "She spoke and Cinyras, whom an abundance of worthy
suitors had left undecided, consulted his daughter,
ran their names by her and asked whom she wished for a husband;   440
silent at first, she kept her eyes locked on her father,
seething until the hot tears spilled over her eyelids:
Cinyras, attributing this to the fears of a virgin,
bade her cease weeping, wiped off her cheeks, and kissed her;
Myrrha rejoiced overmuch at his gesture and answered   445
that she would marry a man 'just like you.' Misunderstanding
the words of his daughter, Cinyras approved them, replying,
'May you be this pious always.' Hearing that last word,
the virgin lowers her head, self-convicted of evil.
     "Midnight: now sleep dissolves all the cares of the body;   450
Cinyras' daughter, however, lies tossing, consumed by
the fires of passion, repeating her prayers in a frenzy;
now she despairs, now she'll attempt it; now she is shamefaced,
now eager: uncertain: *What should she do now?* She wavers,
just like a tree that the axe blade has girdled completely,   455
when only the last blow remains to be struck, and the woodsman
cannot predict the direction it's going to fall in,
she, after so many blows to her spirit, now totters,
now leaning in one, and now in the other, direction,
nor is she able to find any rest from her passion   460
save but in death. Death pleases her, and she gets up,
determined to hang herself from a beam with her girdle:
'Farewell, dear Cinyras: may you understand why I do this!'
she said, as she fitted the noose around her pale neck.
     "They say that, hearing her murmuring, her faithful old nurse   465
in the next chamber arose and entered her bedroom:
at sight of the grim preparations, she screams out, and striking
her breasts and tearing her garments, removes the noose from
around the girl's neck, and then, only then she collapses,
and weeping, embraces her, asking her why she would do it.   470
     "Myrrha remained silent, expressionless, with her eyes downcast,
sorrowing only because her attempt was detected.

---

5. Again, the Furies.

But the woman persists, baring her flat breasts and white hair,
and by the milk given when she was a babe in the cradle
beseeches her to entrust her old nurse with the cause of her sorrow.   475
The girl turns away with a groan; the nurse is determined
to learn her secret, and promises not just to keep it:
    "'Speak and allow me to aid you,' she says, 'for in my old age,
I am not utterly useless: if you are dying of passion,
my charms and herbs will restore you; if someone wishes you evil,   480
my rites will break whatever spell you are under;
is some god wrathful? A sacrifice placates his anger.
What else could it be? I can't think of anything—Fortune
favors your family, everything's going quite smoothly,
both of your parents are living, your mother, your father—'   485
Myrrha sighed deeply, hearing her father referred to,
but not even then did the nurse grasp the terrible evil
in the girl's heart, although she felt that her darling
suffered a passion of some kind for some kind of lover.
    "Nurse was unyielding and begged her to make known her secret.   490
whatever it was, pressing the tearful girl to her bosom;
and clasping her in an embrace that old age had enfeebled,
she said, 'You're in love—I am certain! I will be zealous
in aiding your cause, never you fear—and your father
will be none the wiser!'
                                    "Myrrha in frenzy leapt up   495
and threw herself onto the bed, pressing her face in the pillows:
'Leave me, I beg you,' she said. 'Avoid my wretched dishonor;
leave me or cease to ask me the cause of my sorrow:
what you attempt to uncover is sinful and wicked!'
    "The old woman shuddered: extending the hands that now trembled   500
with fear and old age, she fell at the feet of her darling,
a suppliant, coaxing her now, and now attempting to scare her;
threatening now to disclose her attempted self-murder,
but pledging to aid her if she confesses her passion.
    "She lifted her head with her eyes full of tears spilling over   505
onto the breast of her nurse and repeatedly tried to
speak out, but repeatedly stopped herself short of confession,
hiding her shame-colored face in the folds of her garments,
until she finally yielded, blurting her secret:
'O mother,' she cried, 'so fortunate you with your husband!'   510
and said no more but groaned.
                                    "The nurse, who now understood it,
felt a chill run through her veins, and her bones shook with tremor,
and her white hair stood up in stiff bristles. She said whatever
she could to dissuade the girl from her horrible passion,
and even though Myrrha knew the truth of her warning,   515
she had decided to die if she could not possess him.
'Live, then,' the other replied, 'and possess your—' Not daring
to use the word 'father,' she left her sentence unfinished,
but called upon heaven to stand by her earlier promise.
    "Now it was time for the annual feast days of Ceres;   520
the pious, and married women clad in white vestments,
thronged to the celebration, offering garlands

of wheat as firstfruits of the season; now for nine nights
the intimate touch of their men is considered forbidden.
Among these matrons was Cenchreïs, wife of Cinyras,   525
for her attendance during these rites was required.
And so, while the queen's place in his bed was left vacant,
the overly diligent nurse came to Cinyras,
finding him drunk, and spoke to him of a maiden
whose passion for him was real (although her name wasn't)   530
and praising her beauty; when asked the age of this virgin,
she said, 'the same age as Myrrha.' Commanded to fetch her,
nurse hastened home, and entering, cried to her darling,
'Rejoice, my dear, we have won!' The unlucky maiden
could not feel joy in her heart, but only grim sorrow,   535
yet still she rejoiced, so distorted were her emotions.
    "Now it is midnight, when all of creation is silent;
high in the heavens, between the two Bears, Boötes[6]
had turned his wagon so that its shaft pointed downward;
Myrrha approaches her crime, which is fled by chaste Luna,[7]   540
while under black clouds the stars hide their scandalized faces;
Night lacks its usual fires; you, Icarus,[8] covered
your face and were followed at once by Erigone,
whose pious love of her father merited heaven.
    "Thrice Myrrha stumbles and stops each time at the omen,   545
and thrice the funereal owl sings her his poem of endings;
nevertheless she continues, her shame lessened by shadows.
She holds the left hand of her nurse, and gropes with the other
blindly in darkness: now at the bedchamber's threshold,
and now she opens the door: and now she is led within,   550
where her knees fail her; she falters, nearly collapsing,
her color, her blood, her spirit all flee together.
    "As she approaches the crime, her horror increases;
regretting her boldness, she wishes to turn back, unnoticed,
but even as she holds back, the old woman leads her   555
by the hand to the high bed, where she delivers her, saying,
'Take her, Cinyras—she's yours,' and unites the doomed couple.
The father accepts his own offspring in his indecent
bed and attempts to dispel the girl's apprehensions,
encouraging her not to be frightened of him, and   560
addressing her, as it happened, with a name befitting
her years: he called her 'daughter' while she called him 'father,'
so the right names were attached to their impious actions.
    "Filled with the seed of her father, she left his bedchamber,
having already conceived, in a crime against nature   565
which she repeated the following night and thereafter,
until Cinyras, impatient to see his new lover

6. The Ox-herder, a constellation that was imagined as driving Ursa Major, the Great Bear.
7. The Moon, often associated with Diana, one of whose attributes was chastity.
8. More properly Icarius, a mythic Athenian. He received Dionysus into the city, and the god rewarded him with wine, which he shared with his countrymen. Feeling its effect, they thought they had been poisoned and killed him. His daughter Erigone hanged herself in grief, and both were changed into stars.

after so many encounters, brought a light in,
and in the same moment discovered his crime and his daughter;
grief left him speechless; he tore out his sword from the scabbard;   570
Myrrha sped off, and, thanks to night's shadowy darkness,
escaped from her death. She wandered the wide-open spaces,
leaving Arabia, so rich in palms, and Panchaea,
and after nine months, she came at last to Sabaea,[9]
where she found rest from the weariness that she suffered,   575
for she could scarcely carry her womb's heavy burden.
    "Uncertain of what she should wish for, tired of living
but frightened of dying, she summed up her state in this prayer:
'O gods, if there should be any who hear my confession,
I do not turn away from the terrible sentence   580
that my misbehavior deserves; but lest I should outrage
the living by my survival, or the dead by my dying,
drive me from both of these kingdoms, transform me
wholly, so that both life and death are denied me.'
    "Some god *did* hear her confession, and heaven answered   585
her final prayer, for, even as she was still speaking,
the earth rose up over her legs, and from her toes burst
roots that spread widely to hold the tall trunk in position;
her bones put forth wood, and even though they were still hollow,
they now ran with sap and not blood; her arms became branches,   590
and those were now twigs that used to be called her fingers,
while her skin turned to hard bark. The tree kept on growing,
over her swollen belly, wrapping it tightly,
and growing over her breast and up to her neck; she
could bear no further delay, and, as the wood rose,   595
plunged her face down into the bark and was swallowed.
    "Loss of her body has meant the loss of all feeling;
and yet she weeps, and the warm drops spill from her tree trunk;
those tears bring her honor: the distillate myrrh preserves and
will keep the name of its mistress down through the ages.   600
    "But under the bark, the infant conceived in such baseness
continued to grow and now sought a way out of Myrrha;
the pregnant trunk bulged in the middle and its weighty burden
pressed on the mother, who could not cry out in her sorrow
nor summon Lucina with charms to aid those in childbirth.   605
So, like a woman exerting herself to deliver,
the tree groaned and bent over double, wet from its weeping.
Gentle Lucina stood by the sorrowing branches,
laid her hands onto the bark and recited the charms that
aid in delivery; the bark split open; a fissure   610
ran down the trunk of the tree and its burden spilled out,
a bawling boychild, whom naiads placed in soft grasses
and bathed in the tears of its mother. Not even Envy
could have found fault with his beauty, for he resembled
one of the naked cherubs depicted by artists,   615
and would have been taken as one, if you had provided
him with a quiver or else removed one from those others.

9. Arabia Felix, the southern tip of the Arabian Peninsula.

[Venus and Adonis]

"Time swiftly glides by in secret, escaping our notice,
and nothing goes faster than years do: the son of his sister
by his grandfather, the one so recently hidden   620
within a tree, so recently born, a most beautiful infant,
now is an adolescent and now a young man
even more beautiful than he was as a baby,
pleasing now even to Venus and soon the avenger
of passionate fires that brought his mother to ruin.   625
    "For while her fond Cupid was giving a kiss to his mother,
he pricked her unwittingly, right in the breast, with an arrow
projecting out of his quiver; annoyed, the great goddess
swatted him off, but the wound had gone in more deeply
than it appeared to, and at the beginning deceived her.   630
    "Under the spell of this fellow's beauty, the goddess
no longer takes any interest now in Cythera,[1]
nor does she return to her haunts on the island of Paphos,
or to fish-wealthy Cnidus or to ore-bearing Amathus;[2]
she avoids heaven as well, now—preferring Adonis,   635
and clings to him, his constant companion, ignoring
her former mode of unstrenuous self-indulgence,
when she shunned natural light for the parlors of beauty;
now she goes roaming with him through woods and up mountains
and over the scrubby rocks with her garments hitched up   640
and girded around her waist like a nymph of Diana,[3]
urging the hounds to pursue unendangering species,
hoppety hares or stags with wide-branching antlers,
or terrified does; but she avoids the fierce wild boars and
rapacious wolves and bears armed with sharp claws,   645
and shuns the lions, sated with slaughter of cattle.
    "And she warns you also to fear the wild beasts, Adonis,
if only her warning were heeded. 'Be bold with the timid,'
she said, 'but against the daring, daring is reckless.
Spare me, dear boy, the risk involved in your courage;   650
don't rile the beasts that Nature has armed with sharp weapons,
lest I should find the glory you gain much too costly,
For lions and bristling boars and other fierce creatures
look with indifferent eyes and minds upon beauty
and youth and other qualities Venus is moved by;   655
pitiless boars deal out thunderbolts with their curved tusks,
and none may withstand the frenzied assault of the lions,
whom I despise altogether.'
                        "And when he asked why,
she said, 'I will tell you this story which will amaze you,
with its retribution delivered for ancient wrongdoing.   660
    "'But this unaccustomed labor has left me exhausted—

---

1. Island south of the Peloponnesus, and like
Cyprus sacred to Venus.
2. All three were important centers of Venus's
cult: Paphos and Amathus were cities on the
island of Cyprus, and Cnidus was a city in Asia
Minor.
3. As a virgin and huntress, the antithesis of
Venus.

look, though—a poplar entices with opportune shade, and
offers a soft bed of turf we may rest on together,
as I would like to.' And so she lay down on the grasses
and on her Adonis, and using his breast as a pillow, 665
she told this story, mixing her words with sweet kisses:

"'Perhaps you'll have heard of a maiden able to vanquish
the swiftest of men in a footrace; this wasn't a fiction,
for she overcame all contestants; nor could you say whether
she deserved praise more for her speed or her beauty. 670
She asked some god about husbands. "A husband," he answered,
"is not for you, Atalanta: flee from a husband!
But you will not flee—and losing yourself, will live on!"

"'Frightened by his grim prediction, she went to the forest
and lived there unmarried, escaping the large and persistent 675
throng of her suitors by setting out cruel conditions;
"You cannot have me," she said, "unless you outrun me;
come race against me! A bride and a bed for the winner,
death to the losers. Those are the rules of the contest."

"'Cruel? Indeed—but such was this young maiden's beauty 680
that a foolhardy throng of admirers took up the wager.
As a spectator, Hippomenes sat in the grandstand,
asking why anyone ever would risk such a danger,
just for a bride, and disparaging their headstrong passion.
However, as soon as he caught a glimpse of her beauty, 685
like mine or like yours would be if you were a woman,'
said Venus, 'her face and her body, both bared for the contest,
he threw up both hands and cried out, "I beg your pardons,
who only a moment ago disparaged your efforts,
but truly I had no idea of the trophy you strive for!" 690

"'Praises ignited the fires of passion and made him
hope that no young man proved to be faster than she was
and fear that one would be. Jealous, he asked himself why he
was leaving the outcome of this competition unventured:
"God helps those who improve their condition by daring," 695
he said, addressing himself as the maiden flew by him.
Though she seemed no less swift than a Scythian arrow,
nevertheless, he more greatly admired her beauty,
and the grace of her running made her seem even more lovely;
the breezes blew back the wings attached to her ankles 700
while her loose hair streamed over her ivory shoulders
and her brightly edged knee straps fluttered lightly; a russet
glow fanned out evenly over her pale, girlish body,
as when a purple awning covers a white marble surface,
staining its artless candor with counterfeit shadow. 705

"'She crossed the finish line while he was taking it in, and
Atalanta, victorious, was given a crown and the glory;
the groaning losers were taken off: end of *their* story.
But the youth, undeterred by what had become of the vanquished,
stood on the track and fixed his gaze on the maiden: 710
"Why seek such an easy victory over these sluggards?

Contend with me," he said, "and if Fortune makes me the winner,
you will at least have been beaten by one not unworthy:
I am the son of Megareus, grandson of Neptune,
my great-grandfather; my valor is no less impressive 715
than is my descent; if you should happen to triumph,
you would be famous for having beaten Hippomenes."
    "'And as he spoke, Atalanta's countenance softened:
she wondered whether she wished to win or to *be* won,
and asked herself which god, jealous of her suitor's beauty, 720
sought to destroy him by forcing him into this marriage:
"If *I* were judging, I wouldn't think I was worth it!
Nor am I moved by his beauty," she said, "though I could be,
but I *am* moved by his youth: his boyishness stirs me—
but what of his valor? His mind so utterly fearless? 725
What of his watery origins? His relation to Neptune?
What of the fact that he loves me and wishes to wed me,
and is willing to die if bitter Fortune denies him?
    "'"Oh, flee from a bed that still reeks with the gore of past victims,
while you are able to, stranger; marrying *me* is 730
certain destruction! No one would wish to reject you,
and you may be chosen by a much wiser young lady!
    "'"But why should I care for you—after so many have perished?
Now *he* will learn! Let him die then, since the great slaughter
of suitors has taught him nothing! He must be weary of living! 735
So—must he die then, because he wishes to wed me,
and is willing to pay the ultimate price for his passion?
He shouldn't have to! And even though it won't be *my* fault,
my victory surely will turn the people against me!
    "'"If only you would just give it up, or if only, 740
since you're obsessed with it, you were a little bit faster!
How very girlish is the boy's facial expression!
O poor Hippomenes! I wish you never had seen me!
You're worthy of life, and if only *my* life had been better,
or if the harsh Fates had not prevented my marriage, 745
you would have been the one I'd have chosen to marry!"
    "'She spoke, and, moved by desire that struck without warning,
loved without knowing what she was doing or feeling.
Her father and people were clamoring down at the racecourse,
when Neptune's descendent Hippomenes anxiously begged me: 750
"Cytherian Venus, I pray you preside at my venture,
aiding the fires that you yourself have ignited."
A well-meaning breeze brought me this prayer, so appealing
that, I confess, it aroused me and stirred me to action,
though I had scant time enough to bring off his rescue. 755
    "'There is a field upon Cyprus, known as Tamasus,
famed for its wealth; in olden days it was given
to me and provides an endowment now for my temples;
and there in this field is a tree; its leaves and its branches
glisten and shimmer, reflecting the gold they are made of; 760
now, as it happened, I'd just gotten back from a visit,
carrying three golden apples that I had selected:

and showing myself there to Hippomenes only,
approached him and showed him how to use them to advantage.
   "'Both of them crouched for the start; when horns gave the signal,   765
they took off together, their feet barely brushing the surface;
you would have thought they were able to keep their toes dry
while skimming over the waves, and could touch on the ripened
heads of wheat in the field without bending them under.
   "'Cries of support and encouragement cheered on the young man;   770
"Now is the time," they screamed, "go for it, go for it, hurry,
Hippomenes, give it everything that you've got now!
Don't hold back! Victory!" And I am uncertain whether
these words were more pleasing to him or to his Atalanta,
for often, when she could have very easily passed him,   775
she lingered beside, her gaze full of desperate longing,
until she reluctantly sped ahead of his features.
   "'And now Hippomenes, dry-mouthed, was breathlessly gasping,
the finish line far in the distance; he threw out an apple,
and the sight of that radiant fruit astounded the maiden,   780
who turned from her course and retrieved the glittering missile;
Hippomenes passed her: the crowd roared its approval.
   "'A burst of speed now and Atalanta makes up for lost time:
once more overtaking the lad, she puts him behind her!
A second apple: again she falls back, but recovers,   785
now she's beside him, now passing him, only the finish
remains: "Now, O goddess," he cries, "my inspiration, be with me!"
   "'With all the strength of his youth he flings the last apple
to the far side of the field: *this* will really delay her!
The maiden looked doubtful about its retrieval: I forced her   790
to get it and add on its weight to the burden she carried:
time lost and weight gained were equal obstructions: the maiden
(lest my account should prove longer than even the race was)
took second place: the trophy bride left with the victor.
   "'But really, Adonis, wasn't I worthy of being   795
thanked for my troubles? Offered a gift of sweet incense?
Heedless of all I had done, he offered me neither!
Immediate outrage was followed by keen indignation;
and firmly resolving not to be spurned in the future,
I guarded against it by making this pair an example.   800
   "'Now they were passing a temple deep in the forest,
built long ago by Echion to honor Cybele,[4]
Mother of Gods, and now the length of their journey
urged them to rest here, where unbridled desire
possessed Hippomenes, moved by the strength of my godhead.   805
There was a dim and cave-like recess near the temple,
hewn out of pumice, a shrine to the ancient religion,
wherein a priest of these old rites had set a great many
carved wooden idols. Hippomenes entered that place, and
by his forbidden behavior defiled it;[5] in horror,   810

---

4. A fertility goddess of Asia Minor known as
the Great Mother. She was often pictured
wearing a crown that resembled a city wall
with towers, and flanked by lions or riding in a
cart drawn by them.
5. It was considered sacrilege to have sexual
intercourse in the precinct of a temple.

the sacred images turned away from the act, and Cybele
prepared to plunge the guilty pair in Stygian waters,
but that seemed too easy; so now their elegant pale necks
are cloaked in tawny manes; curved claws are their fingers;
arms are now forelegs, and all the weight of their bodies   815
shifts to their torsos; and now their tails sweep the arena;
fierce now, their faces; growls supplant verbal expression;
the forest now is their bedroom; a terror to others,
meekly these lions champ at the bit of the harness
on either side of the yoke of Cybele's chariot.   820
    "'My darling, you must avoid these and all other wild beasts,
who will not turn tail, but show off their boldness in battle;
flee them or else your courage will prove our ruin!'

    "And after warning him, she went off on her journey,
carried aloft by her swans; but his courage resisted   825
her admonitions. It happened that as his dogs followed
a boar they were tracking, they roused it from where it was hidden,
and when it attempted to rush from the forest, Adonis
pierced it, but lightly, casting his spear from an angle;
with its long snout, it turned and knocked loose the weapon   830
stained with its own blood, then bore down upon our hero,
and, as he attempted to flee for his life in sheer terror,
it sank its tusks deep into the young fellow's privates,
and stretched him out on the yellow sands, where he lay dying.
    "Aloft in her light, swan-driven chariot, Venus   835
had not yet gotten to Cyprus; from a great distance
she recognized the dying groans of Adonis
and turned her birds back to him; when she saw from midair
his body lying there, lifeless, stained with its own blood,
she beat her breasts and tore at her hair and her garments,   840
and leapt from her chariot, raging, to argue with grim Fate:
    "'It will not be altogether as you would have it,'
she said. 'My grief for Adonis will be remembered
forever, and every year will see, reenacted
in ritual form, his death and my lamentation;   845
and the blood of the hero will be transformed to a flower.
Or were *you* not once allowed to change a young woman[6]
to fragrant mint, Persephone? Do you begrudge me
the transformation of my beloved Adonis?'
    "And as she spoke, she sprinkled his blood with sweet nectar, 850
which made it swell up, like a transparent bubble
that rises from muck; and in no more than an hour
a flower sprang out of that soil, blood red in its color,
just like the flesh that lies underneath the tough rind
of the seed-hiding pomegranate. Brief is its season,   855
for the winds from which it takes its name, the anemone,
shake off those petals so lightly clinging and fated to perish."

6. Mentha, Hades' mistress, trampled by the jealous Persephone and transformed into the mint (the meaning of her name).

II

Ancient India

The Indian subcontinent stretches from the borders of Iran and Afghanistan to those of Myanmar, and from the edges of Tibet and China to the Indian Ocean; also called South Asia, it covers an area as large as western Europe. From about the fifth century B.C.E. onward, the ancient Greeks knew this region as *Indos*, a term adapted from the Persians; after the seventh century C.E., Muslim societies came to refer to it as *al-Hind*. For much of its long history, the subcontinent has not been politically united, but it has been remarkably cohesive in its social and cultural practices: it has evolved as a distinct "cultural zone" within Asia, very different in language, religion, art, population, and ways of life from the comparable cultural zones of China and the Middle East.

THE PREHISTORIC ORIGINS OF INDIAN LITERATURE

The kinds of stories ancient Indian literature tells, the forms they take, and the themes they explore are connected to the subcontinent's past before the appearance of historical records. The earliest settled society in South Asia organized on a significant scale was that of the Indus Valley and Harappa

Kṛṣṇa battles the horse demon, Keshi. From a fifth-century C.E. terra-cotta carving.

677

(ca. 2600–1900 B.C.E.), which established a far-flung network of small towns and ports across what are now Pakistan and western India. This civilization had extensive contacts with Mesopotamia during the period in which the epic *Gilgamesh* was being composed in Sumerian. The Indus-Harappan people had a writing system of their own, but it remains undeciphered, even though we know a great deal about their material culture. Conquered or gradually displaced by the Indo-Aryans, or overcome by economic, political, or natural disasters, this population receded from the subcontinent's prehistory by about 1900 B.C.E., some segments perhaps surviving among the aboriginal and other ancient groups dispersed across the Indian peninsula down to modern times.

The Indo-Aryan people may have begun to arrive on the Indian subcontinent as early as 2000 B.C.E., and to create a new settled society over the next few centuries in what are now northern Pakistan and India. Originally a nomadic pastoral people who moved with vast herds of cattle in search of grazing land, the Indo-Aryans branched off from the Indo-Iranian people, who probably migrated from the Caucasus Mountains region (modern Chechnya) to the plateau of Iran late in the third millennium B.C.E. The Indo-Iranians were themselves one of the major groups of the Indo-European people, who spread in many stages from their Caucasian homeland westward into Europe and eastward into Asia. One western Indo-European group, roughly contemporaneous with the earliest Indo-Iranians and Indo-Aryans, migrated to the Mediterranean region also around 2000 B.C.E., initially establishing the Mycenaean civilization and subsequently emerging

An eighteenth-century watercolor depicting Kṛṣṇa protecting cowherds and cows during a fire.

in history as the ancient Greeks and Romans.

When the Indo-Aryans started settling in Punjab (now divided between India and Pakistan) in the second millennium B.C.E., they established an organized agrarian village society distinct from the urban society of their Indus-Harappan predecessors, who had focused on trade. This Indo-Aryan innovation, with its economic basis in agriculture (on small family farms) and animal husbandry (mainly of the domesticated cow), has proven to be the subcontinent's enduring social form of the past 3,500 years. In the mid-twentieth century, when it still had nearly 750,000 such villages, Mahatma Gandhi famously characterized India as a "land of villages"; and, in our own times, we still invoke the "holy cow"—an image that the Indo-Aryans created in their earliest poems on the subcontinent.

The Indo-Aryans brought with them the language that eventually became Sanskrit, the medium of the largest body of Indian literature, produced continuously from approximately 1200 B.C.E. to 1800 C.E. Sanskrit is intimately related to Greek and Latin: these languages share much of their grammar, use similar sentence structures, and draw on hundreds of common roots for their vocabularies. All three languages, along with ancient Persian, may therefore have evolved from a single source called proto-Indo-European, a language (lost since antiquity) presumably used by the ancestors of the Greeks, Romans, Indo-Iranians, and Indo-Aryans a few thousand years earlier.

But the connections among these scattered peoples are not merely linguistic. When they settled at the end of their respective migrations, they began to worship pantheons of gods, establish social hierarchies, practice rituals and customs, and adopt political models that strongly resembled one another. Most important, their songs, tales, and cycles of myths seemed to invoke a common stock of older memories, images, and narratives. By the first millennium B.C.E., Greek, Sanskrit, and Latin were highly differentiated from one another, and their emerging literatures—from, respectively, **Homer** (ca. eighth century B.C.E.); **Vālmīki** (ca. sixth century B.C.E.), the author of the original *Rāmāyaṇa*; and **Virgil** (first century B.C.E.) onward—developed along independent trajectories. But they still contained remarkable echoes of one another that we cannot fully explain.

ORALITY AND WRITING IN INDIA

The first works on the subcontinent were hymns and ritual formulas (*mantras*) composed in Sanskrit, which were gathered with commentary and other theological material in four large groupings of discourse called the Vedas; these gave rise to an extensive, interconnected body of philosophy and mystical speculation called the Upaniṣads, fifty-two of which are important. Developed between approximately 1200 and 700 B.C.E., much of this literature was classified as scripture (*śruti*, revelation that is heard) and revealed knowledge (*veda*). Although the Vedic hymns are in verse, and some of them are poetry of the highest order, and even though the visionaries (*ṛṣis*) who "received them from the gods" are called *kavis* (poets), the texts themselves are not classified as *kāvya* (poetry): from this perspective, *mantras* are of divine origin and hence sacred, whereas poetry—no matter how beautiful and profound—is made by human authors and hence always mundane. Since divine revelation and knowledge need to be explained to human audiences, the Vedas and the Upaniṣads engendered many works of authoritative and specialized commentary (*śāstras*) as well as numerous compendiums and rule books (*sūtras*), which, by the latter half of the first millennium B.C.E., became part of the canon of Vedic religion and, centuries later, of classical Hinduism, one of the most important cultural forces on the subcontinent.

Although some of the essential commentaries and rule books were prepared after a writing system became available, the Hindu canon as a whole was transmitted orally throughout the ancient period. In this method of oral transmission, which is still practiced in our times, specialist priests and scholars belonging to the *brāhmaṇa* caste are trained from early childhood to memorize an entire work in multiple forms: by phoneme (sound unit), word, verse, chapter, and book; by mnemonic summaries of the whole work, and by its "indexed" words; and even by the reverse order of its verses. Taught orally for a dozen years, a good Vedic priest who specializes in the *Ṛg-veda* (ca. 1000 B.C.E.), for example, can recite all 1,028 hymns in its ten books, can confirm their correct order, can reproduce any individual verse at will, and can orally list every occurrence of a given word in the text. Unlike a bard, a Vedic reciter communicates divine revelation, and hence is not free to invent, embellish, or err. In post-Vedic times (starting ca. 500 B.C.E.), this method was extended to other kinds of composition in Sanskrit. In the classical period (ca. 400–1100 C.E.), for instance, poets and literary scholars memorized entire bodies of *kāvya*, so that their literature was always at hand— a practice that also continued well into the twentieth century.

Knowledge of the early writing system of the Indus-Harappan people did not survive the end of their civilization, around 1900 B.C.E. A new system of indigenous writing most likely reappeared around 500 B.C.E., and acquired its canonical form some 250 years later. This was the Brahmi script system, in

This coin, from the late second-century B.C.E. kingdom of Satavahana, has a few characters of the Brahmī script on either side of the elephant.

which writing proceeds from left to right and uses alphabetical letters and diacritical marks to represent syllables (whole sounds), and hence is classified as an alpha-syllabary system, as distinct from the Greek and Latin scripts, which are strictly alphabetical. Brahmi migrated rapidly across South Asia after 250 B.C.E., spawning what would eventually become, over the next 1,500 years or so, the dozen distinct script systems in which most of the languages of the region are recorded. These include Sanskrit, Bengali, Hindi, Marathi, Kannada, and Tamil, among other languages, Urdu being among the few exceptions written in a modified Persian-Arabic script, which arrived from outside the subcontinent. During the same period, Brahmi also migrated out of India and became a transnational phenomenon of world importance: it engendered the scripts of Tibetan (Tibet), Burmese (Myanmar), Thai (Thailand), Javanese and Sumatran (Indonesia), Cham (Vietnam), and Tagalog (the Philippines), and hence launched literacy and literature across a wide swath of Asia.

By the beginning of the Common Era, professional scribes had begun to produce manuscripts with a metal stylus on prepared sheets of bark or palm leaves, tied together with string. Paper and ink first became common on the Indian subcontinent in the thirteenth century C.E.; until then, for more than a millennium, the principal form of a Sanskrit book was a palm-leaf manuscript: though highly perishable, it succeeded in recording an enormous quantity of literature, disseminating Indian epics, lyrics, stories, and plays all over the subcontinent, and well beyond its boundaries.

SOCIETY, POLITICS, AND RELIGION

The first Vedic hymns (ca. 1200 B.C.E.), and the first collection of hymns, the *Ṛg-veda saṃhitā* (ca. 1000 B.C.E.), were most likely composed in Punjab, "the land of five rivers" that are the tributaries of the Indus. Over the next few centuries, the Indo-Aryans pushed farther east, settling on the wider and equally fertile plains surrounding the Ganges river system, up to modern Bihar and Bengal. By the seventh century B.C.E., the expansion of agriculture and cattle breeding produced enough prosperity to support the first towns and cities across northern India, such as Banaras and Ayodhyā (which still flourish today). With this emerged the first recognizable political form in India: the small republic centered around an urban capital, not unlike a city-state, ruled by a lineage of hereditary monarchs. This became both the historical context and the narrative setting of the first Sanskrit epic, the *Rāmāyaṇa*, begun in the sixth century B.C.E. and composed on the central Gangetic plains.

A couple of centuries later, the small republics started to give way to bigger kingdoms that could garner sufficient surpluses from the land to maintain large armies, and control territories of several hundred square miles. Shortly after Alexander the Great invaded western and northern India, reaching Punjab in 327 B.C.E. and leaving behind a Greek colony in Gandhara (today's Peshawar and Swat Valley region, in Pakistan), the Maurya dynasty established the subcontinent's first empire—which stretched from Afghanistan to Bengal, and from the Himalayan foothills to the Deccan Plateau. Situated imaginatively in the transitional period between small republics and a vast empire, the other ancient Sanskrit epic, the *Mahābhārata* (ca. 400 B.C.E.– 400 C.E.), represents a world of powerful monarchies and many medium-sized kingdoms, from which the older republican ideal was beginning to fade.

This evolving world was shaped by the religion we now call Hinduism. As we see from the *Rāmāyaṇa* and the *Mahābhārata*, one of the most influential ideas in Hinduism is that the universe, as it exists, is fashioned in a vast process of self-generation, in which all the primordial substance out of which it is made is godhead itself. Godhead, or "the god beyond god," is the absolute and undifferentiated original matter of the universe, and it divides itself into everything that exists; it is eternal and indestructible, and hence has no beginning or end in time. God in this view is not a creator god, or an anthropomorphic father, or a wrathful or vengeful deity; godhead is unknowable, unimaginable, and indescribable. Since everything that exists is made out of godhead (and there is no other elemental matter in the universe), god is everywhere and in everything—a view that constitutes pantheism. In some Vedic hymns, this all-pervading godhead is called *Puruṣa*, "spirit" (in the masculine gender); in the Upaniṣads, it is renamed *Brahman* (not to be confused

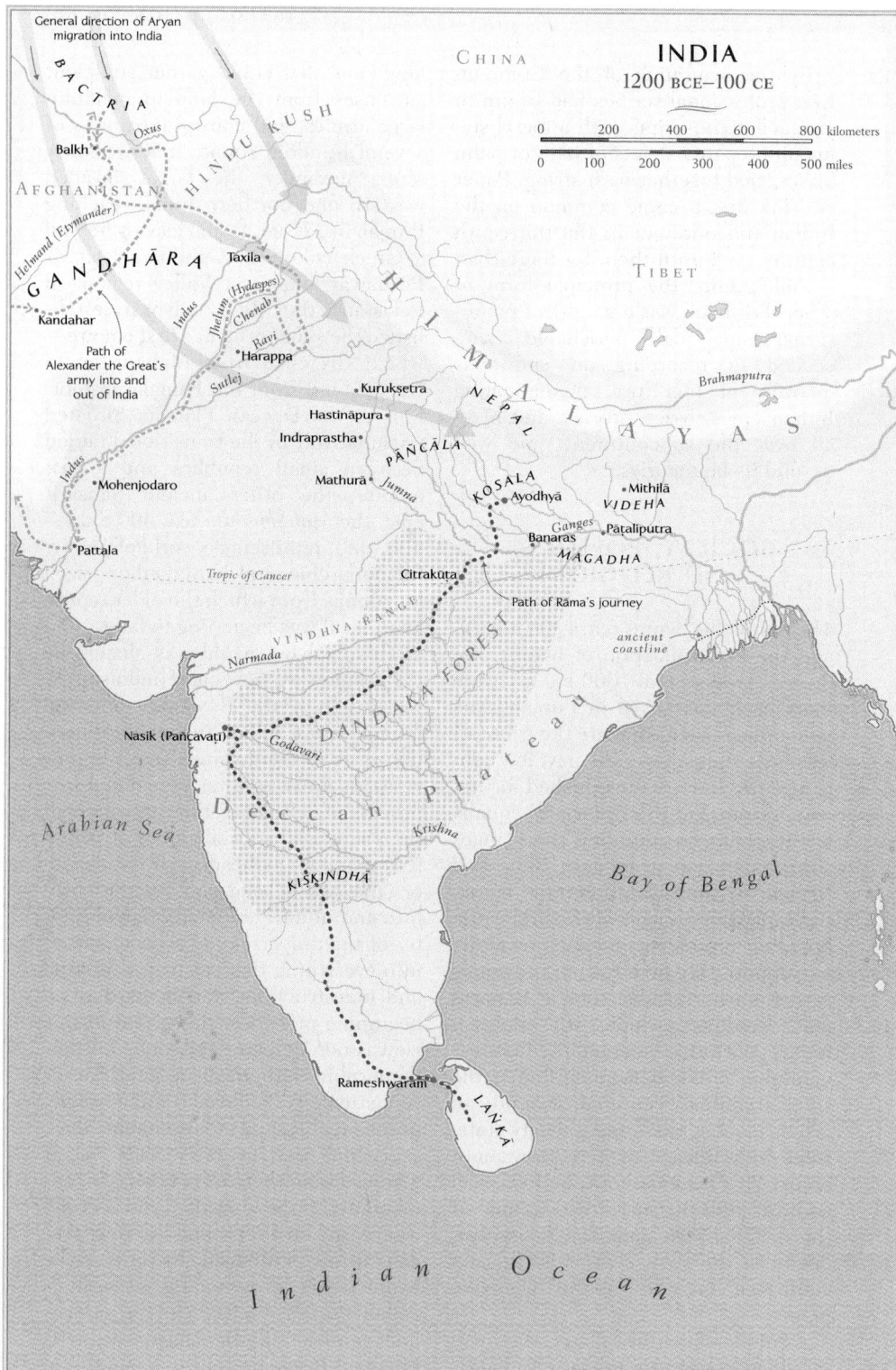

General direction of Aryan migration into India

CHINA

INDIA
1200 BCE–100 CE

| 0 | 200 | 400 | 600 | 800 kilometers |

| 0 | 100 | 200 | 300 | 400 | 500 miles |

BACTRIA

Oxus

Balkh

AFGHANISTAN

HINDU KUSH

GANDHĀRA

Helmand (Etymander)

Kandahar

Path of Alexander the Great's army into and out of India

Taxila

Indus

Jhelum (Hydaspes)

Chenab

Ravi

Harappa

Sutlej

Mohenjodaro

Indus

Pattala

Tropic of Cancer

TIBET

HIMALAYAS

Brahmaputra

Kurukṣetra

NEPAL

Hastināpura

Indraprastha

PĀÑCĀLA

Mathurā

Jumna

KOSALA

Ayodhyā

Mithilā

VIDEHA

Banaras

Ganges

Pāṭaliputra

MAGADHA

Citrakūṭa

Path of Rāma's journey

VINDHYA RANGE

Narmada

DANDAKA FOREST

ancient coastline

Deccan Plateau

Godavari

Nasik (Pañcavaṭī)

Krishna

Arabian Sea

KIṢKINDHĀ

Bay of Bengal

Rameshwaram

LANKĀ

Indian Ocean

with either *brāhmaṇa*, the priestly caste-group, or Brahmā, the later, anthropomorphic "god of creation"). The soul, spirit, or "self" (*ātman*) that animates every living creature is nothing but a piece of *Puruṣa* or *Brahman*, so it, too, is eternal and indestructible. The universe as we know it has a beginning in cosmic time, and therefore also comes to an end; since godhead cyclically differentiates itself into a particular universe, all its indestructible substance must return to it at the end of a cycle and be reintegrated into its primordial state. Any life-form's ultimate goal therefore is to be reunited with absolute godhead; for an individual soul or *ātman*, such a union with the elemental stuff of the universe is possible only if it can achieve *mokṣa*, or "liberation," from its differentiated existence.

Works such as the *Rāmāyaṇa* and the *Mahābhārata* further show us that many of Hinduism's characteristic doctrines follow from this theology of *Brahman* and *ātman*. Each of the popular gods in its pantheon becomes an aspect or a manifestation of godhead in an anthropomorphic or concrete form,

which is especially useful in making divinity accessible to humans. The great gods Viṣṇu and Śiva are manifestations of godhead in equal measure; though Viṣṇu is often characterized as the god of preservation, and Śiva is distinguished as the god of destruction, each performs all the functions of creation, preservation, and destruction that only pure godhead can perform. The same is true of the anthropomorphic Brahmā, usually called the god of creation; and, by extension—because Hinduism, in the final analysis, does not attribute gender to godhead—it is equally true of the goddesses Lakṣmī, Pārvatī, and Sarasvatī (the consorts of Viṣṇu, Śiva, and Brahmā, respectively), each of whom also is a complete embodiment of godhead. Since godhead can thus take on countless forms, there cannot be any one true representation of divinity; from its earliest phase, Hinduism therefore consistently commits itself to polytheism, the belief that there are many gods. As a result, from its very beginnings in agrarian Indo-Aryan society in northern India, Hinduism emerges as a fundamentally pluralistic religion,

A sandstone sculpture at the Temple of Śiva, Elephanta (ca. seventh–eighth centuries C.E.), depicting the "Trimurti" of Hinduism: Śiva, Viṣṇu, and Brahmā.

tolerant (in principle) of the worship of many different gods in many different ways, and of the pursuit of divergent ways of life, each of which has the potential to discover a path to *mokṣa* for an individual *ātman*.

THE RELIGIOUS CONTEXTS OF EPIC AND TALE

Within this broad matrix, India's early epics and narrative traditions develop along specific religious lines, but also in keeping with the social world shaped by Hinduism. Vālmīki's *Rāmāyaṇa*, composed and transmitted orally at the outset, is classified as the first poem in Sanskrit because it emphasizes imaginative and aesthetic excellence outside a religious context; but it also takes the mythology of Viṣṇu and the practices of Hindu society for granted. In this framework, Viṣṇu is the "supreme god" who manifests all aspects of godhead; and Vedic rituals are essential for pleasing various gods and ensuring that individuals can pursue *mokṣa*. At the same time, the epic depicts a hierarchical society divided into four main caste-groups by birth: *brāhmaṇas* (priests), *kṣatriyas* (warriors), *vaiśyas* (traders), and *śūdras* (servants and cultivators). Theologically, this separation of castes is part of the primary differentiation of godhead into distinct categories of existence, and hence is divinely ordained and immutable; in most circumstances, an individual therefore cannot migrate from one caste to another on the basis of, say, talent or accomplishment. This structure is maintained by a system of endogamous marriage, in which legitimate spouses must belong to the same caste-group, so that their children are also born into their social category; in such a world, marriage is irrevocable, and miscegenation and adultery across castes can deeply desta-

bilize not only the human order, but the cosmic moral order as well. The *Rāmāyaṇa* also depicts a society of villages and small republics, in which dynasties of kings do not yet pursue imperial ambitions: their role here is to preserve the divine order of things, in both the mundane world and the cosmos at large, which is populated by human beings, animal, plants, and inanimate things as well as demons, celestial beings, and gods.

In the *Mahābhārata*, composed a little later, village society coexists with a more complex urban world: the land is now divided into many sizable dynastic kingdoms on the verge of imperial formations. The four caste-groups (*varṇas*) have separated into five, with the addition of "untouchables" and foreigners (such as the Greeks left behind by Alexander's army); and each caste-group is differentiated into numerous specific castes (*jātīs*). While the *Rāmāyaṇa* upholds the ideal of monogamous marriage within caste boundaries, the *Mahābhārata* explores multiple marriages and reproductive relationships, overlaying polygamy with polyandry and complicating issues of legitimacy, illegitimacy, and legacy by birth. Whereas the earlier epic distinguishes sharply between good and evil, the later poem adopts more complex and varying views on how action (karma) can accord with divine law (*dharma*); as the laws revealed by the gods in the Vedas and explained in later authoritative discourse (such as the *śāstras* and *sūtras*) are intricate, many judgments regarding the rightness and wrongness of particular actions founder in uncertainty. The **Bhagavad-gītā**, which is part of the *Mahābhārata*, tackles the dilemmas of *karma* in the most difficult of situations: when is war just, how can violence and killing ever be justified, and under what circumstances can human beings even conceive of taking up arms against family and loved ones? The philosophical and theological arguments about the human and the divine, and about social and political organization, launched by the Indo-Aryans toward the end of the second millennium B.C.E., thus reach a poetic culmination in the encyclopedic structure of the *Mahābhārata* a thousand years later.

By the sixth century B.C.E.—the likely date of Vālmīki's original *Rāmāyaṇa*—several indigenous responses to the Hindu theology of *Brahman* and *ātman* had already found historical expression. The strongest criticism and rejection came from two near contemporaries of Vālmīki: Mahāvīra, the last of Jainism's founders, and Siddhartha-Gautama Buddha, who launched Buddhism. Adopting a severe form of philosophical skepticism and atheism, Buddhism argued that there is no god beyond god (as postulated in Hinduism), no creation by differentiation, and that the universe therefore has no substantial reality. If *Brahman* does not exist, then living creatures have no eternal and indestructible *ātmans*; our perception that we possess an enduring self is therefore an illusion, and the only end of life can be a "snuffing out" or extinction of illusory identity. Such a snuffing out—the literal meaning of *nirvāṇa*—is the exact opposite of what the Hindus call *mokṣa*, the liberation of a substantial *ātman* from a material body for reunification with the ultimate, primordial substance, *Brahman*.

And yet, perhaps paradoxically, Buddhism accepts the reality of karma and rebirth: even an illusory self is reborn numerous times, because it is deluded into believing that it has a persistent identity. This delusion ends only when the self reaches Enlightenment (the condition of being a Buddha), understands that it is not a substantial entity, and hence acquires the power to extinguish itself, attaining *nirvāṇa*.

As this historical overview suggests, for most of the ancient period the Indian subcontinent was not politically united. This pattern was to continue in the Common Era, down to modern times; since the end of British colonial rule (1757–1947), South Asia has come to be divided into seven nations, and its total population is now nearly 1.6 billion people, about three-fourths of whom live in contemporary India. The ancient period also witnessed internal religious division, with Jainism and Buddhism dissenting from Hinduism—a process that was repeated later with the arrival of other faiths, such as Zoroastrianism (ca. eleventh century) and Christianity, and the rise of Sikhism (both sixteenth century). Nevertheless, for the more than three millennia since the establishment of agrarian Indo-Aryan village society, the subcontinent has functioned as a cohesive cultural zone characterized by diversity and pluralism, which define the distinctive context of its early epics and tales.

THE RĀMĀYAṆA OF VĀLMĪKI

ca. 550 B.C.E.

The *Rāmāyaṇa* is many things to many people. It is a tale of adventure across a vast land, from palace to forest to sea; and a love story about an ideal prince and an ideal woman, whose relationship falters late in their marriage. It is a heroic epic about injustice and war, abduction and disinheritance, but also a wondrous tale involving gods, humans, animals, and demons with supernatural powers. It is a religious epic that explains the ways of the gods to human beings, and offers a model of justice and prosperity on earth. Moreover, it is great entertainment: like a roller coaster, it takes us up and down through many facets of human experience, from goodness, beauty, and romance to fear and tragedy.

CONTEXT

All we know about Vālmīki is the little he tells us about himself in his poem. He was an ascetic spiritual practitioner who had renounced normal life in human society, and lived in a small ashram, a hermit's enclave, on the banks of a river. One day he saw a pair of birds making love to each other, but a moment later a hunter shot and killed the male bird with an arrow. Incensed with this violent intrusion into a scene of great natural tenderness and beauty, Vālmīki pronounced an irrevocable curse on the hunter. Reflecting on what he had just uttered, the poet realized that he had spontaneously composed a *śloka*, an unrhymed metrical verse like a couplet, which fully expressed his compassionate grief for the slaughtered bird. Realizing that this verse form would be a perfect vehicle for story as well as song, Vālmīki set about using the *śloka* to compose the heroic and romantic tale of Rāma and Sītā, whose twin sons, Lava and Kuśa—by a twist of events—were then being raised in his ashram. Thus, the poet's life and character are fully integrated with the heroic world he creates and the tale he chooses to narrate. In the version of the epic we have inherited, and in the tradition since Vālmīki's time, he is celebrated as "the first poet," and his *Rāmāyaṇa* is known as "the inaugural poem" in Indian literature.

Vālmīki's epic tale—nearly one-and-a-half times the combined length of the **Iliad** and the **Odyssey**—was originally composed in Sanskrit around the sixth century B.C.E. By that time, a settled society had been in place in northern India for at least a thousand years. Agriculture had become the principal economic activity on the fertile plains around the Indus and Ganges rivers, and it supported a network of prosperous villages, towns, and cities. Society was organized by caste, with priests (*brāhmaṇas*), warriors (*kṣatriyas*), and traders (*vaiśyas*) comprising the three main groups, and the large populace that served them (*śūdras*) constituting the fourth category in the hierarchy. The caste structure was maintained primarily by a system of arranged marriage, in which, ideally, the bridegroom and the bride belonged to the same caste but not the same clan. Each caste-group had its own laws and moral codes (*dharma*), which defined its members' duties and obligations, but it also had to obey laws that applied to all of society. These laws were not made by human beings: they were given by the gods, and were contained in scripture.

Hinduism, which was central to upholding this social order, had been established in its early form several centuries before Vālmīki; its scriptural canon included ritual texts (the Vedas) as well as philosophy and theology (the Upaniṣads). In this system of beliefs, human beings could find "salvation" only if they accumulated "good karma" by propitiating the gods and following *dharma* precisely. But moral laws and codes of conduct are always complex and subtle, and hence easy to violate; numerous rituals are therefore necessary to keep the gods happy, maintain the moral and social orders, and make up for ethical lapses.

The world of the *Rāmāyaṇa* is structured in a similar way, but it also contains many gods, among whom three are the most important: Brahmā, primarily a benign and paternalistic god of creation; Śiva, chiefly an angry and retributive god who engenders cycles of creation and destruction; and Viṣṇu, mainly a benevolent god who preserves the moral balance of the universe. Much of the flux and dynamism of the universe is due to the perpetual struggle for supremacy between Śiva and Viṣṇu. Śiva intervenes in the human world directly, in his multifaceted anthropomorphic form; Viṣṇu, in contrast, "comes down on earth" in a series of distinct avatars or incarnations, living temporarily among mortal creatures each time for the purpose of destroying a particular source of evil. A vital feature of the *Rāmāyaṇa* is that it tells the story of Lord Viṣṇu's seventh incarnation, when he embodied himself as prince Rāma, in order to end the demonic king Rāvaṇa's reign of terror on earth and beyond.

The mundane world that Vālmīki's characters inhabit is also a deeply political one, where the two upper caste-groups, the *brāhmaṇas* (priests) and the *kṣatriyas* (warriors and rulers), dominate society. The land is divided into small, autonomous republics with prosperous cities for their capitals. The king belongs to a dynasty of warriors, but is not an absolute monarch; his power is mediated by court priests and scholarly *brāhmaṇas*. He is defined as a "protector of *dharma*," and his ideal role is to ensure that he and his subjects follow all laws. He is also fully answerable to his subjects; as their moral caretaker, he is obliged to pay attention to their needs, their voices of affirmation and protest. Moreover, the king is further constrained by life in his palace: he is usually polygamous, and has several queens; he is therefore the head of an extended family whose members participate actively in affairs of state. The warrior-dynasties in these republics follow the law of primogeniture, so that the eldest son ascends the throne in the next generation; but the inheritance of the kingdom can be complicated by the protodemocratic politics of the royal family as well as of public opinion, or by the inability of the king and his queens to beget a son. All these aspects of early Indian society, religion, and politics come into play in the dramatic narrative of the *Rāmāyaṇa*.

WORK

While Vālmīki probably composed his poem around 550 B.C.E., it was expanded and polished anonymously by others over the next five or six hundred years. Since writing systems did not exist in his society, he must have composed the epic orally, using a large repertoire of formulaic expressions. During its first few centuries, the *Rāmāyaṇa* must have been transmitted with the sophisticated methods of memorization, preservation, and reproduction already used for Hindu scripture. In its modern canonical form, the Sanskrit *Rāmāyaṇa* contains about 24,000 couplets (*ślokas*) and is divided into seven books (*kāṇḍas*), each subdivided into a large number of chapters (*sargas*), most of which contain between twenty and fifty couplets. The first and last books seem to have been added later; they explicitly interpret Rāma as an avatar of Viṣṇu, and provide a multilayered narrative frame for the five books in the middle.

The English version of the *Rāmāyaṇa* reproduced here is not a translation but an adaptation and retelling of Vālmīki's poem. For the most part, it condenses the narrative of each chapter in a style that appeals to modern readers; but, in select passages, especially with important pieces of dialogue, its rendering is closer to the original. Our selection consists of excerpts from books 2, 3, and 6 that capture the key moments of the tale.

To understand our selection, it is necessary to know what happens in book 1, *Bāla* ("Childhood"), which is not represented here. In that book, Rāvaṇa, the brilliant and highly accomplished king of Laṅkā (an island in the south, modern Sri Laṅkā), has become invincible, demonic, and evil. Lord Viṣṇu therefore has to descend to earth in a human form and destroy him, and so takes birth as Rāma, the eldest son of Daśaratha, king of Kosala, and his principal queen, Kausalyā. Daśaratha also has two other queens, who bear him sons (Rāma's half-brothers): Kaikeyī is the mother of Bharata, whereas Sumitrā has twins, Lakṣmaṇa and Śatrughna. All four boys are trained as warriors and future rulers; Rāma and Lakṣmaṇa, inseparable since childhood, become the pupils of the sage Viśvāmitra. As teenagers, they travel with Viśvāmitra to the neighboring Videha, where Rāma wins a suitors' contest for Sītā, the foster-daughter of that republic's king but actually a child of the goddess Earth.

Our selection begins with book 2, *Ayodhyā*, where Daśaratha follows the code of primogeniture and proclaims Rāma as heir apparent to Kosala's throne, and the republic's citizens celebrate the decision enthusiastically. But following an intrigue in the extended family, Daśaratha gives in to the demand that his second son, Bharata, be made king, and that Rāma be exiled for fourteen years. We then see how Rāma responds to this development, and what decisions he, Sītā, Lakṣmaṇa, and Bharata make under the circumstances. The chapters in this book are composed in a realistic style on the whole, and they give us vivid glimpses into the thoughts and feelings of the characters involved in the struggle for power.

The excerpts from the remaining books focus on Rāma, Sītā, and Lakṣmaṇa's fourteen-year exile together, and the narrative now has the atmosphere of fairy tale and fantasy. In book 3, *Āraṇya* ("The Forest"), the trio pushes deeper into the vast Daṇḍaka forest, south of the River Ganges, whose only inhabitants are animals, ascetics, and demons. We discover how they learn to survive under hostile conditions, and what kinds of dangers and temptations they encounter. While the three are living peacefully in the Pañcavaṭī woodlands (in central India), Rāma and Lakṣmaṇa unwittingly initiate a conflict with Śūrpaṇakhā and her brother Rāvaṇa, the demonic king of Laṅkā. Enraged by their provocation, Rāvaṇa decides to destroy Rāma by abducting Sītā; how he carries out his plan constitutes a pivotal moment in the epic. When Rāma realizes that Sītā is gone, he virtually goes mad with grief.

A "Mughal"-style illustration from the *Rāmāyaņa* dating from ca. 1600 C.E. shows Rāma chasing a golden deer.

Books 4 and 5 (not in the anthology) follow Rāma and Lakṣmaṇa as they search desperately for Sītā. In Book 4, Kiṣkindhā ("The Kingdom of the Monkeys"), they encounter a tribe of monkeys whose citadel is at Kiṣkindhā, in southern India. Intervening in the political quarrels among their factions, the princes persuade the monkeys, and one of their powerful leaders, Hanumāna, to help them look for her. In book 5, *Sundara* ("The Sundara Hill" [in Laṅkā]), Hanumāna spies on Rāvaṇa's capital, and discovers where Sītā is held captive. But she refuses to escape with Hanumāna for reasons that deepen the moral dimension of the story, and that leave him in a quandary. Hanumāna then sets fire to Rāvaṇa's city as a warning of impending war, and returns to apprise Rāma of the situation.

In book 6, *Yuddha* ("The War"), the monkeys build a bridge or causeway across the straits to Laṅkā with remarkable inventiveness. One of Rāvaṇa's brothers betrays him and joins the princes, helping them with their battle plans. After a lengthy conflict, in which Rāvaṇa's other brothers are killed and Lakṣmaṇa is wounded, Rāma finally confronts the demon king in single combat. When he recovers Sītā, however, he finds himself deeply troubled by the question of whether she has been faithful to him during her long captivity. Resolving his dilemma with a dramatic test of fidelity, Rāma returns to Ayodhyā with Sītā and Lakṣmaṇa, and is crowned king. His reign brings peace, prosperity, and justice to the republic of Kosala, and represents the ideal of kingship.

Our selection ends on this happy note, but the canonical version of Vālmīki's epic continues further. In book 7, *Uttara* ("The Final Book"), not included here, Rāma seems set to rule happily for the rest of his days; but people soon begin to gossip viciously about Sītā's probable infidelity with Rāvaṇa. In a misguided attempt to be morally answerable to his subjects, Rāma banishes Sītā, even though he knows that the rumors are false and that she is pregnant. Sītā takes refuge in the sage Vālmīki's ashram, where she gives birth to twin boys, Lava and Kuśa. Vālmīki composes a long poem about the life of Rāma; he trains the twins as bards, and teaches them to sing his epic beautifully. One day they sing the tale before the king, who does not know that they are his sons; when he recognizes them, he sends for his beloved queen. Overwhelmed by her suffering by then, however, Sītā asks her mother, the Earth, to take her back; the ground opens beneath her feet, and she disappears forever. Heartbroken, Rāma divides his kingdom between his sons, gives up his life on earth, and returns to heaven in his divine form as Viṣṇu, his task of destroying Rāvaṇa's evil accomplished.

Vālmīki's style in the original varies according to narrative mode. Many important events are narrated directly from an omniscient point of view; in contrast, when characters in the story tell a tale or engage in dialogue, the verse is adapted to capture their voices and personalities. In book 2, when the action is situated in the palace, the descriptions are frequently realistic; in book 3, when the action is set in the forest, the atmosphere and effect are often fantastic. Even in the forest scenes, however, dream-like passages can be interspersed with flashes of realism, indicating how carefully the text is crafted throughout.

Vālmīki's poem articulates a strong moral vision. It offers us the ideals of Rāma as a son, husband, and king who is serene, courageous, and circumspect; Sītā as a vibrant, thoughtful, and selfless wife and mother; Lakṣmaṇa as a brother and brother-in-law whose first thought is always for his extended family; and Hanumāna as a loyal devotee. All these characters are larger than life, but each of them is also flawed or suffers great injustice. Moreover, in a polygamous society, Vālmīki's epic proposes the norm of monogamous marriage based on mutual love between husband and wife; in a world of political conflict, it portrays republics that build alliances for peace, and rulers and subjects who live by the law, aiming for social harmony. It explicitly promotes justice, goodness, balance, and morality in forms that remain valid today, even though we may not always agree on the details from a modern perspective.

As a literary narrative with scripture-like religious authority, the story of Rāma is special because it is fully integrated into the annual Hindu calendar, the way the story of Christ and the rituals of Christmas, Good Friday, and Easter are woven into the Christian calendar. Every year, in the weeks following the autumnal equinox, the public festivals of Dusehrā and Dīvālī mark the anniversaries, respectively, of Rāma's victory over Rāvaṇa and Rāma's return to Ayodhyā. Over the nine nights preceding Dusehrā, thousands of local Hindu communities throughout India perform the Rāma-līlā, "the play of Rāma"; in each community, children, teenagers, and adults enact the full story of Rāma in nightly installments on an amateur stage, culminating in a ritual burning of gigantic effigies representing Rāvaṇa and his brothers. On the next night of the new moon (usually in late October), every Indian village, town, and city celebrates Dīvālī, the festival of lights, a symbolic affirmation of Rāma's coronation as king and the cyclical restoration of goodness and justice in the world.

During the past two millennia, Vālmīki's Rāmāyaṇa has spread astonishingly far. In India, hundreds of translations, imitations, adaptations, and retellings have appeared in the dozens of languages that gradually replaced Sanskrit after the first millennium C.E.

Many of these local and regional versions of the epic—such as Kamban's Īrāmavatāram (Tamil, twelfth century) and Tulsīdās's Rāmacaritamānasa (Avadhi/Hindi, sixteenth century)—have become literary and religious classics in their own right; and many of them are transmitted orally, in a form called the Rāma-kathā ("the story of Rāma"), in public readings and recitations by professional performers sponsored annually by local communities. Outside India, the Rāmāyaṇa has migrated to the Persian, Arabic, and Chinese worlds; the central character of the Monkey King in *Journey to the West*, one of the four major classical novels in Chinese, is modeled on Hanumāna. The epic has also reached every part of Southeast Asia, from Malaysia and Indonesia to the Philippines. Vālmīki's tale (originally a Hindu work) reappears with variations in the Thai Rāmakien (thirteenth century), the national epic of Thailand; in the relief sculptures at Angkor Wat, the Hindu temple complex in Cambodia (twelfth century onward); in Balinese classical and folk dance, dance drama, and pantomime; and in the spectacular puppet and shadow-puppet theaters of Malaysia and Indonesia (Muslim-majority societies) and Thailand and Cambodia (Buddhist-majority societies). The characters and stories of Rāma and Sītā, Lakṣmaṇa and Hanumāna and Rāvaṇa, are among the best known for almost half the world's population today.

The Rāmāyaṇa of Vālmīki[1]

From Book 2

Ayodhyā

AYODHYĀ 15–16

The brāhmaṇas[2] had got everything ready for the coronation ceremonies. Gold pots of holy water from all the sacred rivers, most of them gathered at their very source, were ready. All the paraphernalia like the umbrella, the chowries,[3] an elephant and a white horse, were ready, too.

But, the king did not emerge, though the sun had risen and the auspicious hour was fast approaching. The priests and the people wondered: "Who can awaken the king, and inform him that he had better hurry up!" At that moment, Sumantra[4] emerged from the palace. Seeing them, he told them: "Under the king's orders I am going to fetch Rāma." But, on second thought, knowing that the preceptors and the priests commanded even the king's respect, he returned to the king's presence to announce that they were awaiting him. Standing near the king, Sumantra sang: "Arise, O king! Night has flown. Arise and do what should be done." The weary king asked: "I ordered you to fetch Rāma, and I am not asleep. Why do you not do as you are told to do?" This time, Sumantra hurried out of the palace and sped to Rāma's palace.

Entering the palace and proceeding unobstructed through the gates and entrances of the palace, Sumantra beheld the divine Rāma, and said to him: "Rāma, the king who is in the company of queen Kaikeyī desires to see you at once." Immediately, Rāma turned to Sītā and announced: "Surely, the king and mother Kaikeyī wish to discuss with me some important details in connection with the coronation ceremony. I shall go and return soon." Sītā, for her part, offered a heartfelt prayer to the gods: "May I have the blessing of humbly serving you during the auspicious coronation ceremony!"

As Rāma emerged from his palace there was great cheer among the people who hailed and applauded him. Ascending his swift chariot he proceeded to the king's palace, followed by the regalia. Women standing at the windows of their houses and richly adorned to express their joy, showered flowers on Rāma. They praised Kausalyā, the mother of Rāma; they praised Sītā, Rāma's consort: "Obviously she must have done great penance to get him as her husband." The people rejoiced as if they themselves were being installed on the throne. They said to one another: "Rāma's coronation is truly a blessing to all the people. While he rules, and he will rule for a long time, no one will even have an unpleasant experience, or ever suffer." Rāma too was happy to see the huge crowds of people, the elephants and the horses—indicating that people had come to Ayodhyā from afar to witness the coronation.

---

1. Translated by Swami Venkatesananda.
2. Priests, members of the highest caste.
3. Yak-tail fans used to ward off flies; kings were attended by fan bearers.

4. King Daśaratha's charioteer and chief bard. The charioteer/bard (*sūta*) composed and narrated ancient epics and sagas.

AYODHYĀ 17–18

As Rāma proceeded in his radiant chariot towards his father's palace, the people were saying to one another: "We shall be supremely happy hereafter, now that Rāma will be king. But, who cares for all this happiness? When we behold Rāma on the throne, we shall attain eternal beatitude!" Rāma heard all this praise and the people's worshipful homage to him, with utter indifference as he drove along the royal road.[5] The chariot entered the first gate to the palace. From there on Rāma went on foot and respectfully entered the king's apartments. The people who had accompanied him eagerly waited outside.

Rushing eagerly and respectfully to his father's presence, Rāma bowed to the feet of his father and then devoutly touched the feet of his mother Kaikeyī, too. "O Rāma!" said the king: he could not say anything more, because he was choked with tears and grief. He could neither see nor speak to Rāma. Rāma sensed great danger: as if he had trodden on a most poisonous serpent. Turning to Kaikeyī, Rāma asked her: "How is it that today the king does not speak kindly to me? Have I offended him in any way? Is he not well? Have I offended prince Bharata or any of my mothers? Oh, it is agonizing: and incurring his displeasure I cannot live even for an hour. Kindly reveal the truth to me."

In a calm, measured and harsh tone, Kaikeyī now said to Rāma: "The king is neither sick nor angry with you. What he must tell you he does not wish to, for fear of displeasing you. He granted me two boons. When I named them, he recoiled. How can a truthful man, a righteous king, go back on his own word? Yet that is his predicament at the moment. I shall reveal the truth to you if you assure me that you will honor your father's promise." For the first time Rāma was distressed: "Ah, shame! Please do not say such things to me! For the sake of my father I can jump into fire. And, I assure you, Rāma does not indulge in double talk. Hence, tell me what the king wants to be done."

Kaikeyī lost no time. She said: "Long ago I rendered him a great service, and he granted me two boons. I claimed them now: and he promised. I asked for these boons: that Bharata should be crowned, and that you should go away to Daṇḍaka forest now. If you wish to establish that both you and your father are devoted to truth, let Bharata be crowned with the same paraphernalia that have been got ready for you, and go away to the forest for fourteen years. Do this, O best of men, for that is the word of your father; and thus would you redeem the king."

AYODHYĀ 19–20

Promptly and without the least sign of the slightest displeasure, Rāma said: "So be it! I shall immediately proceed to the forest, to dwell there clad in bark and animal skin.[6] But why does not the king speak to me, nor feel happy in my presence? Please do not misunderstand me; I shall go, and I myself will gladly give away to my brother Bharata the kingdom, wealth, Sītā and even my own life, and it is easier when all this is done in obedience to my father's command. Let

5. Rāma is an equanimous hero, one who is not affected by praise or blame.
6. Hermits and ascetics who lived in forests had to wear tree bark and animal skins. Queen Kaikeyī's demands included requiring Rāma to live the austere life of a hermit.

Bharata be immediately requested to come. But it breaks my heart to see that father does not say a word to me directly."

Kaikeyī said sternly: "I shall attend to all that, and send for Bharata. I think, however, that you should not delay your departure from Ayodhyā even for a moment. Even the consideration that the father does not say so himself, should not stop you. Till you leave this city, he will neither bathe nor eat." Hearing this, the king groaned, and wailed aloud: "Alas, alas!" and became unconscious again. Rāma decided to leave at once and he said to Kaikeyī: "I am not fond of wealth and pleasure: but even as the sages are, I am devoted to truth. Even if father had not commanded me, and you had asked me to go to the forest I would have done so! I shall presently let my mother and also Sītā know of the position and immediately leave for the forest."

Rāma was not affected at all by this sudden turn of events. As he emerged from the palace, with Lakṣmaṇa, the people tried to hold the royal umbrella over him: but he brushed them aside. Still talking pleasantly and sweetly with the people, he entered his mother's apartment. Delighted to see him, Kausalyā began to glorify and bless him and asked him to sit on a royal seat. Rāma did not, but calmly said to her: "Mother, the king has decided to crown Bharata as the yuvarājā[7] and I am to go to the forest and live there as a hermit for fourteen years." When she heard this, the queen fell down unconscious and grief-stricken. In a voice choked with grief, she said: "If I had been barren, I would have been unhappy; but I would not have had to endure this terrible agony. I have not known a happy day throughout my life. I have had to endure the taunts and the insults of the other wives of the king. Nay, even he did not treat me with kindness or consideration: I have always been treated with less affection and respect than Kaikeyī's servants were treated. I thought that after your birth, and after your coronation my luck would change. My hopes have been shattered. Even death seems to spurn me. Surely, my heart is hard as it does not break into pieces at this moment of the greatest misfortune and sorrow. Life is not worth living without you; so if you have to go to the forest, I shall follow you."

AYODHYĀ 21

Lakṣmaṇa said: "I think Rāma should not go to the forest. The king has lost his mind, overpowered as he is by senility and lust. Rāma is innocent. And, no righteous man in his senses would forsake his innocent son. A prince with the least knowledge of statesmanship should ignore the childish command of a king who has lost his senses." Turning to Rāma, he said: "Rāma, here I stand, devoted to you, dedicated to your cause. I am ready to kill anyone who would interfere with your coronation—even if it is the king! Let the coronation proceed without delay."

Kausalyā said: "You have heard Lakṣmaṇa's view. You cannot go to the forest because Kaikeyī wants you to. If, as you say, you are devoted to dharma, then it is your duty to stay here and serve me, your mother. I, as your mother, am as much worthy of your devotion and service as your father is: and I do not give you permission to go to the forest. If you disobey me in this, terrible will be

7. Crown prince.

your suffering in hell. I cannot live here without you. If you leave, I shall fast unto death."

Rāma, devoted as he was to dharma, spoke: "Among our ancestors were renowned kings who earned fame and heaven by doing their father's bidding. Mother, I am but following their noble example." To Lakṣmaṇa he said: "Lakṣmaṇa, I know your devotion to me, love for me, your prowess and your strength. The universe rests on truth: and I am devoted to truth. Mother has not understood my view of truth, and hence suffers. But I am unable to give up my resolve. Abandon your resolve based on the principle of might; resort to dharma;[8] let not your intellect become aggressive. Dharma, prosperity and pleasure are the pursuit of mankind here;[9] and prosperity and pleasure surely follow dharma: even as pleasure and the birth of a son follow a dutiful wife's service of her husband. One should turn away from that action or mode of life which does not ensure the attainment of all the three goals of life, particularly of dharma; for hate springs from wealth and the pursuit of pleasure is not praiseworthy. The commands of the guru, the king, and one's aged father, whether uttered in anger, cheerfully, or out of lust, should be obeyed by one who is not of despicable behavior, with a view to the promotion of dharma. Hence, I cannot swerve from the path of dharma which demands that I should implicitly obey our father. It is not right for you, mother, to abandon father and follow me to the forest, as if you are a widow. Therefore, bless me, mother, so that I may have a pleasant and successful term in the forest."

AYODHYĀ 22–23

Rāma addressed Lakṣmaṇa again: "Let there be no delay, Lakṣmaṇa. Get rid of these articles assembled for the coronation. And with equal expedition make preparations for my leaving the kingdom immediately. Only thus can we ensure that mother Kaikeyī attains peace of mind. Otherwise she might be worried that her wishes may not be fulfilled! Let father's promise be fulfilled. Yet, so long as the two objects of Kaikeyī's desire are not obtained, there is bound to be confusion in everyone's mind. I must immediately leave for the forest; then Kaikeyī will get Bharata here and have him installed on the throne. This is obviously the divine will and I must honor it without delay. My banishment from the kingdom as well as my return are all the fruits of my own doing (kṛtānta: end of action). Otherwise, how could such an unworthy thought enter the heart of noble Kaikeyī? I have never made any distinction between her and my mother; nor has she ever shown the least disaffection for me so far. The 'end' (reaction) of one's own action cannot be foreseen: and this which we call 'daiva' (providence or divine will) cannot be known and cannot be avoided by anyone. Pleasure, pain, fear, anger, gain, loss, life and death—all these are brought about by 'daiva.' Even sages and great ascetics are prompted by the divine will to give up their self-control and are subjected to lust and anger. It is

---

8. The religious and moral law, code of righteousness.
9. The phrase "dharma, prosperity and pleasure" refers to the first three goals of life for Hindu householders: "religious acts, wealth and public life, and sexual love and family life."

unforeseen and inviolable. Hence, let there be no hostility towards Kaikeyī; she is not to blame. All this is not her doing, but the will of the divine."

Lakṣmaṇa listened to all this with mixed feelings: anger at the turn events had taken, and admiration for Rāma's attitude. Yet, he could not reconcile himself to the situation as Rāma had done. In great fury, he burst forth: "Your sense of duty is misdirected, O Rāma. Even so is your estimation of the divine will. How is it, Rāma, that being a shrewd statesman, you do not see that there are self-righteous people who merely pretend to be good for achieving their selfish and fraudulent ends? If all these boons and promises be true, they could have been asked for and given long ago! Why did they have to wait for the eve of coronation to enact this farce? You ignore this aspect and bring in your argument of the divine will! Only cowards and weak people believe in an unseen divine will: heroes and those who are endowed with a strong mind do not believe in the divine will. Ah, people will see today how my determination and strong action set aside any decrees of the divine will which may be involved in this unrighteous plot. Whoever planned your exile will go into exile! And you will be crowned today. These arms, Rāma, are not handsome limbs, nor are these weapons worn by me ornaments: they are for your service."

AYODHYĀ 24–25

Kausalyā said again: "How can Rāma born of me and the mighty emperor Daśaratha live on food obtained by picking up grains and vegetables and fruits that have been discarded? He whose servants eat dainties and delicacies—how will he subsist on roots and fruits? Without you, Rāma, the fire of separation from you will soon burn me to death. Nay, take me with you, too, if you must go."

Rāma replied: "Mother, that would be extreme cruelty towards father. So long as father lives, please serve him: this is the eternal religion. To a woman her husband is verily god himself. I have no doubt that the noble Bharata will be very kind to you and serve you as I serve you. I am anxious that when I am gone, you should console the king so that he does not feel my separation at all. Even a pious woman who is otherwise righteous, if she does not serve her husband, is deemed to be sinner. On the other hand, she who serves her husband attains blessedness even if she does not worship the gods, perform the rituals or honor the holy men."

Seeing that Rāma was inflexible in his resolve, Kausalyā regained her composure and blessed him. "I shall eagerly await your return to Ayodhyā, after your fourteen years in the forest," said Kausalyā.

Quickly gathering the articles necessary, she performed a sacred rite to propitiate the deities and thus to ensure the health, safety, happy sojourn and quick return of Rāma. "May dharma which you have protected so zealously protect you always," said Kausalyā to Rāma. "May those to whom you bow along the roads and the shrines protect you! Even so, let the missiles which the sage Viśvāmitra[1] gave you ensure your safety. May all the birds and beasts of

---

1. "Missiles" (astra) are magical weapons bestowed on worthy heroes by gods and sages. The sage Viśvāmitra had presented the young Rāma and Lakṣmaṇa with such missiles when they protected his sacrificial rites in the forest from attacks by demons (Book 1, Bāla).

the forest, celestial beings and gods, the mountains and the oceans, and the deities presiding over the lunar mansions, natural phenomena and the seasons be propitious to you. May the same blessedness be with you that Indra enjoyed on the destruction of his enemy Vṛtra, that Vinatā bestowed upon her son Garuḍa, that Aditi pronounced upon her son Indra when he was fighting the demons, and that Viṣṇu enjoyed while he measured the heaven and earth.[2] May the sages, the oceans, the continents, the Vedas and the heavens be propitious to you."[3]

As Rāma bent low to touch her feet, Kausalyā fondly embraced him and kissed his forehead, and then respectfully went round him before giving him leave to go.

AYODHYĀ 26–27

Taking leave of his mother, Rāma sought the presence of his beloved wife, Sītā. For her part, Sītā who had observed all the injunctions and prohibitions connected with the eve of the coronation and was getting ready to witness the auspicious event itself, perceived her divine spouse enter the palace and with a heart swelling with joy and pride, went forward to receive him. His demeanor, however, puzzled her: his countenance reflected sorrow and anxiety. Shrewd as she was she realized that something was amiss, and hence asked Rāma: "The auspicious hour is at hand; and yet what do I see! Lord, why are you not accompanied by the regalia, by men holding the ceremonial umbrella, by the royal elephant and the horses, by priests chanting the Vedas, by bards singing your glories? How is it that your countenance is shadowed by sorrow?"

Without losing time and without mincing words, Rāma announced: "Sītā, the king has decided to install Bharata on the throne and to send me to the forest for fourteen years. I am actually on my way to the forest and have come to say good-bye to you. Now that Bharata is the yuvarājā, nay king, please behave appropriately towards him. Remember: people who are in power do not put up with those who sing others' glories in their presence: hence do not glorify me in the presence of Bharata. It is better not to sing my praises even in the presence of your companions. Be devoted to your religious observances and serve my father, my three mothers and my brothers. Bharata and Śatrughna should be treated as your own brothers or sons. Take great care to see that you do not give the least offense to Bharata, the king. Kings reject even their own sons if they are hostile, and are favorable to even strangers who may be friendly. This is my counsel."

Sītā feigned anger, though in fact she was amused. She replied to Rāma: "Your advice that I should stay here in the palace while you go to live in the forest is unworthy of a heroic prince like you, Lord. Whereas one's father,

2. The narrative of the heroic god Indra's victory over the dragonlike demon Vṛtra is an important myth in the Ṛg-veda, the oldest of the Hindu scriptures. Aditi is the mother of the gods. The eagle Garuḍa is the mount of Viṣṇu, the god of preservation. In the fifth of his ten incarnations, Viṣṇu took the form of a dwarf (Vāmana), who subsequently grew into the gigantic figure Trivikrama ("the god of three strides"), spanned earth and sky with two strides, then crushed the demon Bali with his third step.

3. The four Vedas are the ancient scriptures of the Hindus. The oceans, continents, and heavens of the Hindu universe are held to have sacred powers.

mother, brother, son and daughter-in-law enjoy their own good or misfortune, the wife alone shares the life of her husband. To a woman, neither father nor son nor mother nor friends but the husband alone is her sole refuge here in this world and in the other world, too. Hence I shall accompany you to the forest. I shall go ahead of you, clearing a path for you in the forest. Life with the husband is incomparably superior to life in a palace, or an aerial mansion, or a trip to heaven! I have had detailed instructions from my parents on how to conduct myself in Ayodhyā! But I shall not stay here. I assure you, I shall not be a burden, an impediment, to you in the forest. Nor will I regard life in the forest as exile or as suffering. With you it will be more than heaven to me. It will not be the least hardship to me; without you, even heaven is hell."

AYODHYĀ 28–29

Thinking of the great hardships they would have to endure in the forest, however, Rāma tried to dissuade Sītā in the following words: "Sītā, you come of a very wealthy family dedicated to righteousness. It is therefore proper that you should stay behind and serve my people here. Thus, by avoiding the hardships of the forest and by lovingly serving my people here, would you gladden my heart. The forest is not a place for a princess like you. It is full of great dangers. Lions dwell in the caves; and it is frightening to hear their roar. These wild beasts are not used to seeing human beings; the way they attack human beings is horrifying even to think about. Even the paths are thorny and it is hard to walk on them. The food is a few fruits which might have fallen on their own accord from the trees: living on them, one has to be contented all day. Our garments will be bark and animal skins: and the hair will have to be matted and gathered on the top of the head. Anger and greed have to be given up, the mind must be directed towards austerity and one should overcome fear even where it is natural. Totally exposed to the inclemencies of nature, surrounded by wild animals, serpents and so on, the forest is full of untold hardships. It is not a place for you, my dear."

This reiteration on the part of Rāma moved Sītā to tears. "Your gracious solicitude for my happiness only makes my love for you more ardent, and my determination to follow you more firm. You mentioned animals: they will never come anywhere near me while you are there. You mentioned the righteousness of serving your people: but, your father's command that you should go to the forest demands I should go, too; I am your half: and because of this, again I cannot live without you. In fact you have often declared that a righteous wife will not be able to live separated from her husband. And listen! This is not new to me: for even when I was in my father's house, long before we were married, wise astrologers had rightly predicted that I would live in a forest for some time. If you remember, I have been longing to spend some time in the forest, for I have trained myself for that eventuality. Lord, I feel actually delighted at the very thought that I shall at last go to the forest, to serve you constantly. Serving you, I shall not incur the sin of leaving your parents: thus have I heard from those who are well-versed in the Vedas and other scriptures, that a devoted wife remains united with her husband even after they leave this earth-plane. There is therefore no valid reason why you should wish to leave me here and go. If you still refuse to take me with you, I have no alternative but to lay down my life."

To the further persuasive talk of Rāma, Sītā responded with a show of annoyance, courage and firmness. She even taunted Rāma in the following words: "While choosing you as his son-in-law, did my father Janaka realize that you were a woman at heart with a male body? Why, then are you, full of valor and courage, afraid even on my account? If you do not take me with you I shall surely die; but instead of waiting for such an event, I prefer to die in your presence. If you do not change your mind now, I shall take poison and die." In sheer anguish, the pitch of her voice rose higher and higher, and her eyes released a torrent of hot tears.

Rāma folded her in his arms and spoke to her lovingly, with great delight: "Sītā, I could not fathom your mind and therefore I tried to dissuade you from coming with me. Come, follow me. Of course I cannot drop the idea of going to the forest, even for your sake. I cannot live having disregarded the command of my parents. Indeed, I wonder how one could adore the unmanifest god, if one were unwilling to obey the commands of his parents and his guru whom he can see here. No religious activity nor even moral excellence can equal service of one's parents in bestowing supreme felicity on one. Whatever one desires, and whatever region one desires to ascend to after leaving this earth-plane, all this is secured by the service of parents. Hence I shall do as commanded by father; and this is the eternal dharma. And you have rightly resolved, to follow me to the forest. Come, and get ready soon. Give away generous gifts to the brāhmaṇas and distribute the rest of your possessions to the servants and others."

Lakṣmaṇa now spoke to Rāma: "If you are determined to go, then I shall go ahead of you." Rāma, however, tried to dissuade him: "Indeed, I know that you are my precious and best companion. Yet, I am anxious that you should stay behind and look after our mothers. Kaikeyī may not treat them well. By thus serving our mothers, you will prove your devotion to me." But Lakṣmaṇa replied quickly: "I am confident, Rāma, that Bharata will look after all the mothers, inspired by your spirit of renunciation and your adherence to dharma. If this does not prove to be the case, I can exterminate all of them in no time. Indeed, Kausalyā is great and powerful enough to look after herself: she gave birth to you! My place is near you; my duty to serve you."

Delighted to hear this, Rāma said: "Then let us all go. Before leaving I wish to give away in charity all that I possess to the holy brāhmaṇas. Please get them all together. Take leave of your friends and get our weapons ready, too."

* * *

From Book 3

Āraṇya

ĀRAṆYA 14–15

Rāma, Lakṣmaṇa and Sītā were proceeding towards Pañcavaṭī.[4] On the way they saw a huge vulture. Rāma's first thought was that it was a demon in disguise. The vulture said: "I am your father's friend!" Trusting the vulture's words, Rāma asked for details of its birth and ancestry.

The vulture said: "You know that Dakṣa Prajāpati[5] had sixty daughters and the sage Kaśyapa married eight of them. One day Kaśyapa said to his wives: 'You will give birth to offspring who will be foremost in the three worlds.' Aditi, Diti, Danu and Kālaka listened attentively; the others were indifferent. As a result, the former four gave birth to powerful offspring who were superhuman. Aditi gave birth to thirty-three gods. Diti gave birth to demons. Danu gave birth to Aśvagrīva. And, Kālaka had Naraka and Kālikā. Of the others, men were born of Manu, and the sub-human species from the other wives of Kaśyapa. Tāmra's daughter was Śukī whose granddaughter was Vinatā who had two sons, Garuḍa and Aruṇa. My brother Sampāti and I are the sons of Aruṇa. I offer my services to you, O Rāma. If you will be pleased to accept them, I shall guard Sītā when you and Lakṣmaṇa may be away from your hermitage. As you have seen, this formidable forest is full of wild animals and demons, too."

Rāma accepted this new friendship. All of them now proceeded towards Pañcavaṭī in search of a suitable place for building a hermitage. Having arrived at Pañcavaṭī, identified by Rāma by the description which the sage Agastya had given, Rāma said to Lakṣmaṇa: "Pray, select a suitable place here for building the hermitage. It should have a charming forest, good water, firewood, flowers and holy grass." Lakṣmaṇa submitted: "Even if we live together for a hundred years, I shall continue to be your servant. Hence, Lord, you select the place and I shall do the needful." Rejoicing at Lakṣmaṇa's attitude, Rāma pointed to a suitable place, which satisfied all the requisites of a hermitage. Rāma said: "This is holy ground; this is charming; it is frequented by beasts and birds. We shall dwell here." Immediately Lakṣmaṇa set about building a hermitage for all of them to live in.

Rāma warmly embraced Lakṣmaṇa and said: "I am delighted by your good work and devoted service: and I embrace you in token of such admiration. Brother, you divine the wish of my heart, you are full of gratitude, you know dharma; with such a man as his son, father is not dead but is eternally alive."

Entering that hermitage, Rāma, Lakṣmaṇa and Sītā dwelt in it with great joy and happiness.

ĀRAṆYA 16

Time rolled on. One day Lakṣmaṇa sought the presence of Rāma early in the morning and described what he had seen outside the hermitage. He said: "Winter, the season which you love most, has arrived, O Rāma. There is dry

---

4. "Five banyan trees," a grove in western India, toward which Rāma has been directed by the sage Agastya.

5. A progenitor god in ancient Hindu mythology.

cold everywhere; the earth is covered with foodgrains. Water is uninviting; and fire is pleasant. The first fruits of the harvest have been brought in; and the agriculturists have duly offered some of it to the gods and the manes, and thus reaffirmed their indebtedness to them. The farmer who thus offers the first fruits to gods and manes is freed from sin.

"The sun moves in the southern hemisphere; and the north looks lusterless. Himālaya, the abode of snow, looks even more so! It is pleasant to take a walk even at noon. The shade of a tree which we loved in summer is unpleasant now. Early in the morning the earth, with its rich wheat and barley fields, is enveloped by mist. Even so, the rice crop. The sun, even when it rises, looks soft and cool like the moon. Even the elephants which approach the water, touch it with their trunk but pull the trunk quickly away on account of the coldness of the water.

"Rāma, my mind naturally thinks of our beloved brother Bharata. Even in this cold winter, he who could command the luxury of a king, prefers to sleep on the floor and live an ascetic life. Surely, he, too, would have got up early in the morning and has perhaps had a cold bath in the river Sarayū. What a noble man! I can even now picture him in front of me: with eyes like the petals of a lotus, dark brown in color, slim and without an abdomen, as it were. He knows what dharma is. He speaks the truth. He is modest and self-controlled, always speaks pleasantly, is sweet-natured, with long arms and with all his enemies fully subdued.[6] That noble Bharata has given up all his pleasures and is devoted to you. He has already won his place in heaven, Rāma. Though he lives in the city; yet, he has adopted the ascetic mode of life and follows you in spirit.

"We have heard it said that a son takes after his mother in nature: but in the case of Bharata this has proved false. I wonder how Kaikeyī, in spite of having our father as her husband, and Bharata as her son, has turned out to be so cruel."

When Lakṣmaṇa said this, Rāma stopped him, saying: "Do not speak ill of our mother Kaikeyī, Lakṣmaṇa. Talk only of our beloved Bharata. Even though I try not to think of Ayodhyā and our people there, when I think of Bharata, I wish to see him."

ĀRAṆYA 17—18

After their bath and morning prayers, Rāma, Lakṣmaṇa and Sītā returned to their hermitage. As they were seated in their hut, there arrived upon the scene a dreadful demoness. She looked at Rāma and immediately fell in love with him! He had a handsome face; she had an ugly face. He had a slender waist; she had a huge abdomen. He had lovely large eyes; she had hideous eyes. He had lovely soft hair; she had red hair. He had a lovable form; she had a terrible form. He had a sweet voice; hers resembled the barking of a dog. He was young; she was haughty. He was able; her speech was crooked. He was of noble conduct; she was of evil conduct. He was beloved; she had a forbidding appearance. Such a demoness spoke to Rāma: "Who are you, young men; and what are both of you doing in this forest, with this lady?"

---

6. A list of the conventional attributes of a handsome, brave, and virtuous warrior.

Rāma told her the whole truth about himself, Lakṣmaṇa and Sītā, about his banishment from the kingdom, etc. Then Rāma asked her: "O charming lady,[7] now tell me who you are." At once the demoness replied: "Ah, Rāma! I shall tell you all about myself immediately. I am Śūrpaṇakhā, the sister of Rāvaṇa. I am sure you have heard of him. He has two other brothers, Kumbhakarṇa and Vibhīṣaṇa.[8] Two other brothers Khara and Dūṣaṇa live in the neighborhood here. The moment I saw you, I fell in love with you. What have you to do with this ugly, emaciated Sītā? Marry me. Both of us shall roam about this forest. Do not worry about Sītā or Lakṣmaṇa: I shall swallow them in a moment." But, Rāma smilingly said to her: "You see I have my wife with me here. Why do you not propose to my brother Lakṣmaṇa who has no wife here?" Śūrpaṇakhā did not mind that suggestion. She turned to Lakṣmaṇa and said: "It is all right. You please marry me and we shall roam about happily." She was tormented by passion.

Lakṣmaṇa said in a teasing mood: "O lady, you see that I am only the slave of Rāma and Sītā. Why do you choose to be the wife of a slave? You will only become a servant-maid. Persuade Rāma to send away that ugly wife of his and marry you." Śūpaṇakhā turned to Rāma again. She said: "Unable to give up this wife of yours, Sītā, you turn down my offer. See, I shall at once swallow her. When she is gone you will marry me; and we shall roam about in this forest happily." So saying, she actually rushed towards Sītā. Rāma stopped her in time, and said to Lakṣmaṇa: "What are you doing, Lakṣmaṇa? It is not right to jest with cruel and unworthy people. Look at the plight of Sītā. She barely escaped with her life. Come, quickly deform this demoness and send her away."

Lakṣmaṇa drew his sword and quickly cut off the nose and the ears of Śūpaṇakhā. Weeping and bleeding she ran away. She went to her brother Khara and fell down in front of him.

* * *

Summary   Distraught and furious, Śūrpaṇakhā asks her brothers Khara and Dūṣaṇa, who live in nearby Janasthāna, to avenge her insult by killing Rāma and Lakṣmaṇa. However, Rāma and Lakṣmaṇa kill the brothers and all their troops.

ĀRAṆYA 32–33

Śūrpaṇakhā witnessed the wholesale destruction of the demons of Janasthāna,[9] including their supreme leader Khara. Stricken with terror, she ran to Laṅkā. There she saw her brother Rāvaṇa, the ruler of Laṅkā, seated with his ministers in a palace whose roof scraped the sky.[1] Rāvaṇa had twenty arms, ten heads, was broad chested and endowed with all the physical qualifications of a monarch. He had previously fought with the gods, even with their chief Indra. He was well versed in the science of warfare and knew the use of the celestial missiles in battle. He had been hit by the gods, even by the discus[2] of lord Viṣṇu,

7. This formulaic phrase used in addressing a lady is meant ironically here.
8. The names of the demons are suggestive: Śūrpaṇakhā means "woman with nails as large as winnowing baskets" and Kumbhakarṇa

means "pot ear." Vibhīṣaṇa means "terrifying."
9. A region near Pañcavaṭī.
1. A conventional description of a palace or mansion.
2. A wheel with sharp points, Viṣṇu's weapon.

but he did not die. For, he had performed breathtaking austerities for a period of ten thousand years, and offered his own heads in worship to Brahmā the creator and earned from him the boon that he would not be killed by any superhuman or subhuman agency (except by man). Emboldened by this boon, the demon had tormented the gods and particularly the sages.

Śūrpaṇakhā entered Rāvaṇa's presence, clearly displaying the physical deformity which Lakṣmaṇa had caused to her. She shouted at Rāvaṇa in open assembly: "Brother, you have become so thoroughly infatuated and addicted to sense-pleasure that you are unfit to be a king any longer. The people lose all respect for the king who is only interested in his own pleasure and neglects his royal duties. People turn away from the king who has no spies, who has lost touch with the people and whom they cannot see, and who is unable to do what is good for them. It is the employment of spies that makes the king 'far-sighted' for through these spies he sees quite far. You have failed to appoint proper spies to collect intelligence for you. Therefore, you do not know that fourteen thousand of your people have been slaughtered by a human being. Even Khara and Dūṣaṇa have been killed by Rāma. And, Rāma has assured the ascetics of Janasthāna which is your territory, that the demons shall not do them any harm. They are now protected by him. Yet, here you are; reveling in little pleasures!

"O brother, even a piece of wood, a clod of earth or just dust, has some use; but when a king falls from his position he is utterly useless. But that monarch who is vigilant, who has knowledge of everything, through his spies, who is self-controlled, who is full of gratitude and whose conduct is righteous—he rules for a long time. Wake up and act before you lose your sovereignty."

This made Rāvaṇa reflect.

ĀRAŅYA 34–35

And, Rāvaṇa's anger was roused. He asked Śūrpaṇakhā: "Tell me, who is it that disfigured you thus? What do you think of Rāma? Why has he come to Daṇḍaka forest?"

Śūrpaṇakhā gave an exact and colorful description of the physical appearance of Rāma. She said: "Rāma is equal in charm to Cupid himself. At the same time, he is a formidable warrior. When he was fighting the demons of Janasthāna, I could not see what he was doing; I only saw the demons falling dead on the field. You can easily understand when I tell you that within an hour and a half he had killed fourteen thousand demons. He spared me, perhaps because he did not want to kill a woman. He has a brother called Lakṣmaṇa who is equally powerful. He is Rāma's right hand man and alter ego; Rāma's own life-force moving outside his body. Oh, you must see Sītā, Rāma's wife. I have not seen even a celestial nymph who could match her in beauty. He who has her for his wife, whom she fondly embraces, he shall indeed be the ruler of gods. She is a fit bride for you; and you are indeed the most suitable suitor for her. In fact, I wanted to bring that beautiful Sītā here so that you could marry her: but Lakṣmaṇa intervened and cruelly mutilated my body. If you could only look at her for a moment, you would immediately fall in love with her. If this proposal appeals to you, take some action quickly and get her here."

Rāvaṇa was instantly tempted. Immediately he ordered his flying chariot to be got ready. This vehicle which was richly adorned with gold, could move freely wherever its owner willed. Its front part resembled mules with fiendish heads. Rāvaṇa took his seat in this vehicle and moved towards the seacoast. The coastline of Laṅkā was dotted with hermitages inhabited by sages and also celestial and semi-divine beings. It was also the pleasure resort of celestials and nymphs who went there to sport and to enjoy themselves. Driving at great speed through them, Rāvaṇa passed through caravan parks scattered with the chariots of the celestials. He also drove through dense forests of sandal trees, banana plantations and cocoanut palm groves. In those forests there were also spices and aromatic plants. Along the coast lay pearls and precious stones. He passed through cities which had an air of opulence.

Rāvaṇa crossed the ocean in his flying chariot and reached the hermitage where Mārīca[3] was living in ascetic garb, subsisting on a disciplined diet. Mārīca welcomed Rāvaṇa and questioned him about the purpose of his visit.

ĀRAṆYA 36–37

Rāvaṇa said to Mārīca: "Listen, Mārīca. You know that fourteen thousand demons, including my brother Khara and the great warrior Triśira have been mercilessly killed by Rāma and Lakṣmaṇa who have now promised their protection to the ascetics of Daṇḍaka forest, thus flouting our authority. Driven out of his country by his angry father, obviously for a disgraceful action, this unrighteous and hard-hearted prince Rāma has killed the demons without any justification. And, they have even dared to disfigure my beloved sister Śūrpaṇakhā. I must immediately take some action to avenge the death of my brother and to restore our prestige and our authority. I need your help; kindly do not refuse this time.

"Disguising yourself as a golden deer of great beauty, roam near the hermitage of Rāma. Sītā would surely be attracted, and she would ask Rāma and Lakṣmaṇa to capture you. When they go after you, leaving Sītā alone in the hermitage, I shall easily abduct Sītā." Even as Rāvaṇa was unfolding this plot, Mārīca's mouth became dry and parched with fear. Trembling with fear, Mārīca said to Rāvaṇa:

"O king, one can easily get in this world a counselor who tells you what is pleasing to you; but hard it is to find a wise counselor who tells you the unpleasant truth which is good for you—and harder it is to find one who heeds such advice. Surely, your intelligence machine is faulty and therefore you have no idea of the prowess of Rāma. Else, you would not talk of abducting Sītā. I wonder: perhaps Sītā has come into this world to end your life, or perhaps there is to be great sorrow on account of Sītā, or perhaps maddened by lust, you are going to destroy yourself and the demons and Laṅkā itself. Oh, no, you were wrong in your estimation of Rāma. He is not wicked; he is righteousness incarnate. He is not cruel hearted; he is generous to a fault. He has not been disgraced and exiled from the kingdom. He is here to honor the promise his father had given his mother Kaikeyī, after joyously renouncing his kingdom.

"O king, when you entertain ideas of abducting Sītā you are surely playing with fire. Please remember: when you stand facing Rāma, you are standing face to face with your own death. Sītā is the beloved wife of Rāma, who is

3. An uncle of Rāvaṇa, expert in sorcery.

extremely powerful. Nay, give up this foolish idea. What will you gain by thus gambling with your sovereignty over the demons, and with your life itself? Please consult the noble Vibhīṣaṇa and your virtuous ministers before embarking upon such unwise projects. They will surely advise you against them."

* * *

ĀRAṆYA 42

Rāvaṇa was determined, and Mārīca knew that there was no use arguing with him. Hence, after the last-minute attempt to avert the catastrophe, Mārīca said to Rāvaṇa: "What can I do when you are so wicked? I am ready to go to Rāma's āśrama.[4] God help you!" Not minding the taunt, Rāvaṇa expressed his unabashed delight at Mārīca's consent. He applauded Mārīca and said: "That is the spirit, my friend: you are now the same old Mārīca that I knew. I guess you had been possessed by some evil spirit a few minutes ago, on account of which you had begun to preach a different gospel. Let us swiftly get into this vehicle and proceed to our destination. As soon as you have accomplished the purpose, you are free to go and to do what you please!"

Both of them got into the flying chariot and quickly left the hermitage of Mārīca. Once again they passed forests, hills, rivers and cities: and soon they reached the neighborhood of the hermitage of Rāma. They got down from that chariot which had been embellished with gold. Holding Mārīca by the hand, Rāvaṇa said to him: "Over there is the hermitage of Rāma, surrounded by banana plantations. Well, now, get going with the work for which we have come here." Immediately Mārīca transformed himself into an attractive deer. It was extraordinary, totally unlike any deer that inhabited the forest. It was unique. It dazzled like a huge gem stone. Each part of its body had a different color. The colors had an unearthly brilliance and charm. Thus embellished by the colors of all the precious stones, the deer which was the demon Mārīca in disguise, roamed about near the hermitage of Rāma, nibbling at the grass now and then. At one time it came close to Sītā; then it ran away and joined the other deer grazing at a distance. It was very playful, jumping about and chasing its tail and spinning around. Sītā went out to gather flowers. She cast a glance at that extraordinary and unusual deer. As she did so, the deer too, sensing the accomplishment of the mission, came closer to her. Then it ran away, pretending to be afraid. Sītā marveled at the very appearance of this unusual deer the like of which she had not seen before and which had the hue of jewels.

ĀRAṆYA 43

From where she was gathering flowers, Sītā, filled with wonder to see that unusual deer, called out to Rāma: "Come quick and see, O Lord; come with your brother. Look at this extraordinary creature. I have never seen such a beautiful deer before." Rāma and Lakṣmaṇa looked at the deer, and Lakṣmaṇa's suspicions were aroused: "I am suspicious; I think it is the same demon Mārīca

4. Hermitage.

in disguise. I have heard that Mārīca could assume any form at will, and through such tricks he had brought death and destruction to many ascetics in this forest. Surely, this deer is not real: no one has heard of a deer with rainbow colors, each one of its limbs shining resplendent with the color of a different gem! That itself should enable us to understand that it is a demon, not an animal."

Sītā interrupted Lakṣmaṇa's talk, and said: "Never mind, one thing is certain; this deer has captivated my mind. It is such a dear. I have not seen such an animal near our hermitage! There are many types of deer which roam about near the hermitage; this is just an extraordinary and unusual deer. It is superlative in all respects: its color is lovely, its texture is lovely, and even its voice sounds delightful. It would be a wonderful feat if it could be caught alive. We could use it as a pet, to divert our minds. Later we could take it to Ayodhyā: and I am sure all your brothers and mothers would just adore it. If it is not possible to capture it alive, O Lord, then it can be killed, and I would love to have its skin. I know I am not behaving myself towards both of you: but I am helpless; I have lost my heart to that deer. I am terribly curious."

In fact, Rāma was curious, too! And so, he took Sītā's side and said to Lakṣmaṇa: "It is beautiful, Lakṣmaṇa. It is unusual. I have never seen a creature like this. And, princes do hunt animals and cherish their skins.[5] By sporting and hunting kings acquire great wealth! People say that that is real wealth which one pursues without premeditation. So, let us try to get the deer or its skin. If, as you say, it is a demon in disguise, then surely it ought to be killed by me, just as Vātāpi who was tormenting and destroying sages and ascetics was justly killed by the sage Agastya.[6] Vātāpi fooled the ascetics till he met the sage Agastya. This Mārīca, too, has fooled the ascetics so far: till coming to me today! The very beauty of his hide is his doom. And, you, Lakṣmaṇa, please guard Sītā with great vigilance, till I kill this deer with just one shot and bring the hide along with me."

ĀRAŅYA 44–45

Rāma took his weapons and went after the strange deer. As soon as the deer saw him pursuing it, it started to run away. Now it disappeared, now it appeared to be very near, now it ran fast, now it seemed confused—thus it led Rāma far away from his hermitage. Rāma was fatigued, and needed to rest. As he was standing under a tree, intrigued by the actions of the mysterious deer, it came along with other deer and began to graze not far from him. When Rāma once again went for it, it ran away. Not wishing to go farther nor to waste more time, Rāma took his weapon and fitted the missile of Brahmā[7] to it and fired. This missile pierced the illusory deer-mask and into the very heart of the demon.

5. Hermits are required to take a vow of non-violence, but Rāma, a warrior prince, is allowed to carry arms and to hunt.
6. The demon Vātāpi killed ascetics by tricking them. Disguising himself, he would invite innocent wayfarers to a meal. He would magically conceal himself in the food, thus entering his guests' bellies; he would then kill the men by splitting open their stomachs. The sage Agastya outwitted and killed Vātāpi by digesting his meal, and with it, the demon himself, before he could tear the sage's stomach open.
7. The creator god in the triad of Hindu great gods.

Mārīca uttered a loud cry, leapt high into the sky and then dropped dead onto the ground. As he fell, however, he remembered Rāvaṇa's instructions and assuming the voice of Rāma cried aloud: "Hey Sītā; Hey Lakṣmaṇa."

Rāma saw the dreadful body of the demon. He knew now that Lakṣmaṇa was right. And, he was even more puzzled by the way in which the demon wailed aloud before dying. He was full of apprehension. He hastened towards the hermitage.

In the hermitage, both Sītā and Lakṣmaṇa heard the cry. Sītā believed it was Rāma's voice. She was panic-stricken. She said to Lakṣmaṇa: "Go, go quickly: your brother is in danger. And, I cannot live without him. My breath and my heart are both violently disturbed." Lakṣmaṇa remembered Rāma's admonition that he should stay with Sītā and not leave her alone. He said to her: "Pray, be not worried." Sītā grew suspicious and furious. She said to him: "Ah, I see the plot now! You have a wicked eye on me and so have been waiting for this to happen. What a terrible enemy of Rāma you are, pretending to be his brother!" Distressed to hear these words, Lakṣmaṇa replied: "No one in the three worlds can overpower Rāma, blessed lady! It was not his voice at all. These demons in the forest are capable of simulating the voice of anyone. Having killed that demon disguised as a deer, Rāma will soon be here. Fear not." His calmness even more annoyed Sītā, who literally flew into a rage. She said again: "Surely, you are the worst enemy that Rāma could have had. I know now that you have been following us, cleverly pretending to be Rāma's brother and friend. I know now that your real motive for doing so is either to get me or you are Bharata's accomplice. Ah, but you will not succeed. Presently, I shall give up my life. For I cannot live without Rāma." Cut to the quick by these terrible words, Lakṣmaṇa said: "You are worshipful to me: hence I cannot answer back. It is not surprising that women should behave in this manner: for they are easily led away from dharma; they are fickle and sharp-tongued. I cannot endure what you said just now. I shall go. The gods are witness to what took place here. May those gods protect you. But I doubt if when Rāma and I return, we shall find you." Bowing to her, Lakṣmaṇa left.

ĀRAṆYA 46

Rāvaṇa was looking for this golden opportunity. He disguised himself as an ascetic, clad in ocher robes, carrying a shell water-pot, a staff and an umbrella, and approached Sītā who was still standing outside the cottage eagerly looking for Rāma's return. His very presence in that forest was inauspicious: and even the trees and the waters of the rivers were frightened of him, as it were. In a holy disguise, Rāvaṇa stood before Sītā: a deep well covered with grass; a death-trap.

Gazing at the noble Sītā, who had now withdrawn into the cottage and whose eyes were raining tears, Rāvaṇa came near her, and though his heart was filled with lust, he was chanting Vedic hymns. He said to Sītā in a soft, tender and affectionate tone: "O young lady! Pray, tell me, are you the goddess of fortune or the goddess of modesty, or the consort of Cupid himself?" Then Rāvaṇa described her incomparable beauty in utterly immodest terms, unworthy of an anchorite whose form he had assumed. He continued: "O charming lady! You have robbed me of my heart. I have not seen such a beautiful lady, neither a divine or a semi-divine being. Your extraordinary form and your youthfulness, and your living in this forest, all these together agitate my mind. It is not right that you should live in this forest. You should stay in palaces. In the forest monkeys, lions, tigers and other wild animals live. The forest is the natural habitat of demons who roam freely. You are living alone in this dreadful forest: are you not afraid, O fair lady? Pray, tell me, why are you living in this forest?"

Rāvana was in the disguise of a brāhmana. Therefore, Sītā offered him the worship and the hospitality that it was her duty to offer a brāhmana. She made him sit down; she gave him water to wash his feet and his hands. Then she placed food in front of him.

Whatever she did only aggravated his lust and his desire to abduct her and take her away to Lankā.

ĀRANYA 47–48

Sītā, then, proceeded to answer his enquiry concerning herself. He appeared to be a brāhmana; and if his enquiry was not answered, he might get angry and curse her.[8] Sītā said: "I am a daughter of the noble king Janaka; Sītā is my name. I am the beloved consort of Rāma. After our marriage, Rāma and I lived in the palace of Ayodhyā for twelve years." She then truthfully narrated all that took place just prior to Rāma's exile to the forest. She continued: "And so, when Rāma was twenty-five and I was eighteen, we left the palace and sought the forest-life.[9] And so the three of us dwell in this forest. My husband, Rāma, will soon return to the hermitage gathering various animals and also wild fruits. Pray, tell me who you are, O brāhmana, and what you are doing in this forest roaming all alone."

Rāvana lost no time in revealing his true identity. He said: "I am not a brāhmana, O Sītā: I am the lord of demons, Rāvana. My very name strikes terror in the hearts of gods and men. The moment I saw you, I lost my heart to you; and I derive no pleasure from the company of my wives. Come with me, and be my queen, O Sītā. You will love Lankā. Lankā is my capital, it is surrounded by the ocean and it is situated on the top of a hill. There we shall live together, and you will enjoy your life, and never even once think of this wretched forest-life."

Sītā was furious to hear this. She said: "O demon-king! I have firmly resolved to follow Rāma who is equal to the god of gods, who is mighty and charming, and who is devoted to righteousness.[1] If you entertain a desire for me, his wife, it is like tying yourself with a big stone and trying to swim across the ocean: you are doomed. Where are you and where is he: there is no comparison. You are like a jackal; he the lion.[2] You are like base metal; he gold."

8. Priestly *brāhmanas* and sages have the power to curse people as well as to bestow boons.
9. Rāma must have been thirteen and Sītā six years old when they were married. The practice of "child marriage" continued in India until very recently.

1. A special epithet of Rāma. "God of gods": an epithet used for warriors, kings, and heroes. It is a reference to Indra, king of heaven and all the gods.
2. King of animals, the lion represents regal majesty and courage, while the jackal is the embodiment of cunning and deceit.

But Rāvaṇa would not give up his desire. He repeated: "Even the gods dare not stand before me, O Sītā! For fear of me even Kubera the god of wealth abandoned his chariot and ran away to Kailāsa. If the gods, headed by Indra, even sense I am angry, they flee. Even the forces of nature obey me. Laṅkā is enclosed by a strong wall; the houses are built of gold with gates of precious stones. Forget this Rāma, who lives like an ascetic, and come with me. He is not as strong as my little finger!" Sītā was terribly angered: "Surely you seek the destruction of all the demons, by behaving like this, O Rāvaṇa. It cannot be otherwise since they have such an unworthy king with no self-control. You may live after abducting Indra's wife, but not after abducting me, Rāma's wife."

ĀRAṆYA 49–50

Rāvaṇa made his body enormously big and said to Sītā: "You do not realize what a mighty person I am. I can step out into space, and lift up the earth with my arms; I can drink up the waters of the oceans; and I can kill death itself. I can shoot a missile and bring the sun down. Look at the size of my body." As he expanded his form, Sītā turned her face away from him. He resumed his original form with ten heads and twenty arms. Again he spoke to Sītā: "Would you not like to be renowned in the three worlds? Then marry me. And, I promise I shall do nothing to displease you. Give up all thoughts of that mortal and unsuccessful Rāma."

Rāvaṇa did not wait for an answer. Seizing Sītā by her hair and lifting her up with his arm, he left the hermitage. Instantly the golden chariot appeared in front of him. He ascended it, along with Sītā. Sītā cried aloud: "O Rāma." As she was being carried away, she wailed aloud: "O Lakṣmaṇa, who is ever devoted to the elder brother, do you not know that I am being carried away by Rāvaṇa?" To Rāvaṇa, she said: "O vile demon, surely you will reap the fruits of your evil action: but they do not manifest immediately." She said as if to herself: "Surely, Kaikeyī would be happy today." She said to the trees, to the river Godāvarī, to the deities dwelling in the forest, to the animals and birds: "Pray, tell Rāma that I have been carried away by the wicked Rāvaṇa." She saw Jaṭāyu and cried aloud: "O Jaṭāyu! See, Rāvaṇa is carrying me away."

Hearing that cry, Jaṭāyu woke up. Jaṭāyu introduced himself to Rāvaṇa: "O Rāvaṇa, I am the king of vultures, Jaṭāyu. Pray, desist from this action unworthy of a king. Rāma, too, is a king; and his consort is worthy of our protection. A wise man should not indulge in such action as would disgrace him in the eyes of others. And, another's wife is as worthy of protection as one's own. The cultured and the common people often copy the behavior of the king. If the king himself is guilty of unworthy behavior what becomes of the people? If you persist in your wickedness, even the prosperity you enjoy will leave you soon.

"Therefore, let Sītā go. One should not get hold of a greater load than one can carry; one should not eat what he cannot digest. Who will indulge in an action which is painful and which does not promote righteousness, fame or permanent glory? I am sixty thousand years old and you are young. I warn you. If you do not give up Sītā, you will not be able to carry her away while I am alive and able to restrain you! I shall dash you down along with that chariot."

ĀRAŅYA 51

Rāvaņa could not brook this insult: he turned towards Jatāyu in great anger. Jatāyu hit the chariot and Rāvaņa; Rāvaņa hit Jatāyu back with terrible ferocity. This aerial combat between Rāvaņa and Jatāyu looked like the collision of two mountains endowed with wings. Rāvaņa used all the conventional missiles, the Nālikas, the Nārācas and the Vikarņis. The powerful eagle shrugged them off. Jatāyu tore open the canopy of the chariot and inflicted wounds on Rāvaņa himself.

In great anger, Jatāyu grabbed Rāvaņa's weapon (a cannon) and broke it with his claws. Rāvaņa took up a more formidable weapon which literally sent a shower of missiles. Against these Jatāyu used his own wings as an effective shield. Pouncing upon this weapon, too, Jatāyu destroyed it with his claws. Jatāyu also tore open Rāvaņa's armor. Nay, Jatāyu even damaged the gold-plated propellers of Rāvaņa's flying chariot, which had the appearance of demons, and thus crippled the craft which would take its occupant wherever he desired and which emitted fire. With his powerful beak, Jatāyu broke the neck of Rāvaņa's pilot.

With the chariot thus rendered temporarily useless, Rāvaņa jumped out of it, still holding Sītā with his powerful arm. While Rāvaņa was still above the ground, Jatāyu again challenged him: "O wicked one, even now you are unwilling to turn away from evil. Surely, you have resolved to bring about the destruction of the entire race of demons. Unknowingly or wantonly, you are swallowing poison which would certainly kill you and your relations. Rāma and Lakṣmaṇa will not tolerate this sinful act of yours: and you cannot stand before them on the battlefield. The manner in which you are doing this unworthy act is despicable: you are behaving like a thief not like a hero." Jatāyu swooped on Rāvaņa and violently tore at his body.

Then there ensued a hand-to-hand fight between the two. Rāvaņa hit Jatāyu with his fist; but Jatāyu tore Rāvaņa's arms away. However, new ones sprang up instantly. Rāvaņa hit Jatāyu and kicked him. After some time, Rāvaņa drew his sword and cut off the wings of Jatāyu. When the wings were thus cut, Jatāyu fell, dying. Looking at the fallen Jatāyu, Sītā ran towards him in great anguish, as she would to the side of a fallen relation. In inconsolable grief, Sītā began to wail aloud.

ĀRAŅYA 52–53

As Sītā was thus wailing near the body of Jatāyu, Rāvaņa came towards her. Looking at him with utter contempt, Sītā said: "I see dreadful omens, O Rāvaņa. Dreams as also the sight and the cries of birds and beasts are clear indicators of the shape of things to come.[3] But you do not notice them! Alas, here is Jatāyu, my father-in-law's friend who is dying on my account. O Rāma, O Lakṣmaṇa, save me, protect me!"

Once again Rāvaņa grabbed her and got into the chariot which had been made airworthy again. The Creator, the gods and the celestials who witnessed

---

3. Dreams and omens play a comparable role in the culture of the Greeks and Romans.

this, exclaimed: "Bravo, our purpose is surely accomplished."[4] Even the sages of the Daṇḍaka forest inwardly felt happy at the thought, "Now that Sītā has been touched by this wicked demon, the end of Rāvaṇa and all the demons is near." As she was carried away by Rāvaṇa, Sītā was wailing aloud: "O Rāma, O Lakṣmaṇa."

Placed on the lap of Rāvaṇa, Sītā was utterly miserable. Her countenance was full of sorrow and anguish. The petals of the flowers that dropped from her head fell and covered the body of Rāvaṇa for a while. She was of beautiful golden complexion; and he was of dark color. Her being seated on his lap looked like an elephant wearing a golden sash, or the moon shining in the midst of a dark cloud, or a streak of lightning seen in a dense dark cloud.

The chariot streaked through the sky as fast as a meteor would. On the earth below, trees shook as if to reassure Sītā: "Do not be afraid," the waterfalls looked as if mountains were shedding tears, and people said to one another, "Surely, dharma has come to an end, as Rāvaṇa is carrying Sītā away."

Once again Sītā rebuked Rāvaṇa: "You ought to feel ashamed of yourself, O Rāvaṇa. You boast of your prowess; but you are stealing me away! You have not won me in a duel, which would be considered heroic. Alas, for a long, long time to come, people will recount your ignominy, and this unworthy and unrighteous act of yours will be remembered by the people. You are taking me and flying at such speed: hence no one can do anything to stop you. If only you had the courage to stop for a few moments, you would find yourself dead. My lord Rāma and his brother Lakṣmaṇa will not spare you. Leave me alone, O demon! But, you are in no mood to listen to what is good for your own welfare. Even as, one who has reached death's door loves only harmful objects. Rāma will soon find out where I am and ere long you will be transported to the world of the dead."

Rāvaṇa flew along, though now and then he trembled in fear.

ĀRAṆYA 54–55

The chariot was flying over hills and forests and was approaching the ocean. At that time, Sītā beheld on the ground below, five strong vānaras[5] seated and watching the craft with curiosity. Quickly, Sītā took off the stole she had around her shoulders and, removing all her jewels and putting them in that stole, bundled them all up and threw the bundle into the midst of the vānaras, in the hope that should Rāma chance to come there they would give him a clue to her whereabouts.

Rāvaṇa did not notice this but flew on. And now the craft, which shot through space at great speed, was over the ocean; a little while after that, Rāvaṇa entered Laṅkā along with his captive Sītā. Entering his own apartments, Rāvaṇa placed Sītā in them, entrusting her care to some of his chief female attendants. He said to them: "Take great care of Sītā. Let no male approach these apartments without my express permission. And, take great care to let Sītā have whatever she wants and asks for. Any neglect on your part means instant death."

4. We are reminded here that Viṣṇu incarnated himself as Rāma at the request of the gods, who wished Rāvaṇa to be killed.
5. Some scholars have suggested that *vānaras*, usually translated as "monkeys" or "apes," refers to tribal people or apelike human beings. This translator has left the word untranslated.

Rāvaṇa was returning to his own apartments: on the way he was still considering what more could be done to ensure the fulfilment of his ambition. He sent for eight of the most ferocious demons and instructed them thus: "Proceed at once to Janasthāna. It was ruled by my brother Khara; but it has now been devastated by Rāma. I am filled with rage to think that a mere human being could thus kill Khara, Dūṣaṇa and all their forces. Never mind: I shall put an end to Rāma soon. Keep an eye on him and keep me informed of his movements. You are free to bring about the destruction of Rāma." And, the demons immediately left.

Rāvaṇa returned to where Sītā was and compelled her to inspect the apartments. The palace stood on pillars of ivory, gold, crystal and silver and was studded with diamonds. The floor, the walls, the stairways—everything was made of gold and diamonds. Then again he said to Sītā: "Here at this place there are over a thousand demons ever ready to do my bidding. Their services and the entire Laṅkā I place at your feet. My life I offer to you; you are to me more valuable than my life. You will have under your command even the many good women whom I have married. Be my wife. Laṅkā is surrounded by the ocean, eight hundred miles on all sides. It is unapproachable to anybody; least of all to Rāma. Forget the weakling Rāma. Do not worry about the scriptural definitions of righteousness: we shall also get married in accordance with demoniacal wedding procedure. Youth is fleeting. Let us get married soon and enjoy life."

ĀRAṆYA 56

Placing a blade of grass between Rāvaṇa and herself,[6] Sītā said: "O demon! Rāma, the son of king Daśaratha, is my lord, the only one I adore. He and his brother Lakṣmaṇa will surely put an end to your life. If they had seen you lay your hands on me, they would have killed you on the spot, even as they laid Khara to eternal rest. It may be that you cannot be killed by demons and gods; but you cannot escape being killed at the hands of Rāma and Lakṣmaṇa. Rāvaṇa, you are doomed, beyond doubt. You have already lost your life, your good fortune, your very soul and your senses, and on account of your evil deeds Laṅkā has attained widowhood.[7] Though you do not perceive this, death is knocking at your door, O Rāvaṇa. O sinner, you cannot under any circumstances lay your hands on me. You may bind this body, or you may destroy it: it is after all insentient matter, and I do not consider it worth preserving, nor even life worth living—not in order to live a life which will earn disrepute for me."

Rāvaṇa found himself helpless. Hence, he resorted to threat. He said: "I warn you, Sītā. I give you twelve months in which to make up your mind to accept me as your husband. If within that time you do not so decide, my cooks will cut you up easily for my breakfast." He had nothing more to say to her. He turned to the female attendants surrounding her and ordered them: "Take this Sītā away to the Aśoka grove. Keep her there. Use every method of persuasion that you know of to make her yield to my desire. Guard her vigilantly. Take her and break her will as you would tame a wild elephant."

6. The magical power of Sītā's virtue allows her to use even a blade of grass as an effective barrier between herself and her abductor.

7. The ancient Indian king was considered to be the husband of the land he ruled, and kingdoms were often personified as a goddess.

The demonesses thereupon took Sītā away and confined her to the Aśoka grove, over which they themselves mounted guard day and night. Sītā did not find any peace of mind there, and stricken with fear and grief, she constantly thought of Rāma and Lakṣmaṇa.

It is said that at the same time, the creator Brahmā felt perturbed at the plight of Sītā. He spoke to Indra, the chief of gods: "Sītā is in the Aśoka grove. Pining for her husband, she may kill herself. Hence, go reassure her, and give her the celestial food to sustain herself till Rāma arrives in Laṅkā." Indra, thereupon, appeared before Sītā. In order to assure her of his identity he showed that his feet did not touch the ground and his eyes did not wink.[8] He gave her the celestial food, saying: "Eat this, and you will never feel hunger or thirst, nor will fatigue overpower you." While Indra was thus talking to Sītā, the goddess of sleep (Nidrā) had overpowered the demonesses.

ĀRAṆYA 57–58

Mārīca, the demon who had disguised himself as a unique deer, had been slain. But Rāma was intrigued and puzzled by the way in which Mārīca died, after crying: "O Sītā, O Lakṣmaṇa." Rāma sensed a deep and vicious plot. Hence he made haste to return to his hermitage. At the same time, he saw many evil omens. This aggravated his anxiety. He thought: "If Lakṣmaṇa heard that voice, he might rush to my aid, leaving Sītā alone. The demons surely wish to harm Sītā; and this might well have been a plot to achieve that purpose."

As he was thus brooding and proceeding towards his hermitage, he saw Lakṣmaṇa coming towards him. The distressed Rāma met the distressed Lakṣmaṇa; the sorrowing Rāma saw the sorrowful Lakṣmaṇa. Rāma caught hold of Lakṣmaṇa's arm and asked him, in an urgent tone: "O Lakṣmaṇa, why have you left Sītā alone and come? My mind is full of anxiety and terrible apprehension. When I see all these evil omens around us, I fear that something terrible has happened to Sītā. Surely Sītā has been stolen, killed or abducted."

Lakṣmaṇa's silence and grief-stricken countenance added fuel to the fire of anxiety in Rāma's heart. He asked again: "Is all well with Sītā? Where is my Sītā, the life of my life, without whom I cannot live even for an hour? Oh, what has happened to her? Alas, Kaikeyī's desire has been fulfilled today. If I am deprived of Sītā, I shall surely die. What more could Kaikeyī wish for? If, when I enter my hermitage, I do not find Sītā alive, how shall I live? Tell me, Lakṣmaṇa; speak. Surely, when that demon cried: 'O Lakṣmaṇa' in my voice, you were afraid that something had happened to me. Surely, Sītā also heard that cry and in a state of terrible mental agony, sent you to me. It is a painful thing that thus Sītā has been left alone; the demons who were waiting for an opportunity to hit back have been given that opportunity. The demons were sore distressed by my killing of the demon Khara. I am sure that they have done some great harm to Sītā, in the absence of both of us. What can I do now? How can I face this terrible calamity?"

Still, Lakṣmaṇa could not utter a word concerning what had happened. Both of them arrived near their hermitage. Everything that they saw reminded them of Sītā.

8. Attributes of the immortals.

ĀRAṆYA 59–60

And, once again before actually reaching the hermitage, and full of apprehension on account of Sītā, Rāma said to Lakṣmaṇa: "Lakṣmaṇa, you should not have come away like this, leaving Sītā alone in the hermitage. I had entrusted her to your care." When Rāma said this again and again, Lakṣmaṇa replied: "I have not come to you, leaving Sītā alone, just because I heard the demon Mārīca cry: 'O Lakṣmaṇa, O Sītā in your voice. I did so only upon being literally driven by Sītā to do so. When she heard the cry, she immediately felt distressed and asked me to go to your help. I tried to calm her saying: 'It is not Rāma's voice; it is unthinkable that Rāma, who is capable of protecting even the gods, would utter the words, 'save me.' She, however, misunderstood my attitude. She said something very harsh, something very strange, something which I hate even to repeat. She said: 'Either you are an agent of Bharata or you have unworthy intentions towards me and therefore you are happy that Rāma is in distress and do not rush to his help.' It is only then that I had to leave."

In his anxiety for Sītā, Rāma was unimpressed by this argument. He said to Lakṣmaṇa: "Swayed by an angry woman's words, you failed to carry out my words; I am not highly pleased with what you have done, O Lakṣmaṇa."

Rāma rushed into their hermitage. But he could find no trace of Sītā in it. Confused and distressed beyond measure, Rāma said to himself, as he continued to search for Sītā: "Where is Sītā? Alas, she could have been eaten by the demons. Or, taken away by someone. Or, she is hidden somewhere. Or, she has gone to the forest." The search was fruitless. His anguish broke its bounds. Not finding her, he was completely overcome by grief and he began to behave as if he were mad.[9]

Unable to restrain himself, he asked the trees and the birds and the animals of the forest; "Where is my beloved Sītā?" The eyes of the deer, the trunk of the elephant, the boughs of trees, the flowers—all these reminded Rāma of Sītā. "Surely, you know where my beloved Sītā is. Surely, you have a message from her. Won't you tell me? Won't you assuage the pain in my heart?" Thus Rāma wailed. He thought he saw Sītā at a distance and going up to 'her,' he said: "My beloved, do not run away. Why are you hiding yourself behind those trees? Will you not speak to me?" Then he said to himself: "Surely it was not Sītā. Ah, she has been eaten by the demons. Did I leave her alone in the hermitage only to be eaten by the demons?" Thus lamenting, Rāma roamed awhile and ran around awhile.

ĀRAṆYA 61–62

Again Rāma returned to the hermitage, and, seeing it empty, gave way to grief again. He asked Lakṣmaṇa: "Where has my beloved Sītā gone, O Lakṣmaṇa? Or, has she actually been carried away by someone?" Again, imagining that it

---

9. The description of the lover maddened by grief, searching for his beloved, is a theme in many literary traditions: examples include the Greek myth of Orpheus's search for Eurydice and the Persian story of Majnun ("the mad lover"), who wanders in the wilderness looking for Laila.

was all fun and a big joke which Sītā was playing, he said: "Enough of this fun, Sītā; come out. See, even the deer are stricken with grief because they do not see you." Turning to Lakṣmaṇa again, he said: "Lakṣmaṇa, I cannot live without my Sītā. I shall soon join my father in the other world. But, he may be annoyed with me and say: 'I told you to live in the forest for fourteen years; how have you come here before that period?' Ah Sītā, do not forsake me."

Lakṣmaṇa tried to console him: "Grieve not, O Rāma. Surely, you know that Sītā is fond of the forest and the caves on the mountainside. She must have gone to these caves. Let us look for her in the forest. That is the proper thing to do; not to grieve."

These brave words took Rāma's grief away. Filled with zeal and eagerness, Rāma along with Lakṣmaṇa, began to comb the forest. Rāma was distressed: "Lakṣmaṇa, this is strange; I do not find Sītā anywhere." But Lakṣmaṇa continued to console Rāma: "Fear not, brother; you will surely recover the noble Sītā soon."

But this time, these words were less meaningful to Rāma. He was overcome by grief, and he lamented: "Where shall we find Sītā, O Lakṣmaṇa, and when? We have looked for her everywhere in the forest and on the hills, but we do not find her." Lamenting thus, stricken with grief, with his intelligence and his heart robbed by the loss of Sītā, Rāma frequently sighed in anguish, muttering: "Ah my beloved."

Suddenly, he thought he saw her, hiding herself behind the banana trees, and now behind the karnikara trees. And, he said to 'her': "My beloved, I see you behind the banana trees! Ah, now I see you behind the karnikara tree: my dear, enough, enough of this play: for your fun aggravates my anguish. I know you are fond of such play; but pray, stop this and come to me now."

When Rāma realized that it was only his hallucination, he turned to Lakṣmaṇa once more and lamented: "I am certain now that some demon has killed my beloved Sītā. How can I return to Ayodhyā without Sītā? How can I face Janaka, her father? Oh, no: Lakṣmaṇa, even heaven is useless without Sītā; I shall continue to stay in the forest; you can return to Ayodhyā. And you can tell Bharata that he should continue to rule the country."

ĀRAŅYA 63–64

Rāma was inconsolable and even infected the brave Lakṣmaṇa. Shedding tears profusely, Rāma continued to speak to Lakṣmaṇa who had also fallen a prey to grief by this time: "No one in this whole world is guilty of as many misdeeds as I am, O Lakṣmaṇa: and that is why I am being visited by sorrow upon sorrow, grief upon grief, breaking my heart and dementing me. I lost my kingdom, and I was torn away from my relations and friends. I got reconciled to this misfortune. But then I lost my father. I was separated from my mother. Coming to this hermitage, I was getting reconciled to that misfortune. But I could not remain at peace with myself for long. Now this terrible misfortune, the worst of all, has visited me.

"Alas, how bitterly Sītā would have cried while she was carried away by some demon. May be she was injured; may be her lovely body was covered with blood. Why is it that when she was subjected to such suffering, my body did not split into pieces? I fear that the demon must have cut open Sītā's neck and drunk her blood. How terribly she must have suffered when she was dragged by the demons.

"Lakṣmaṇa, this river Godāvarī was her favorite resort. Do you remember how she used to come and sitting on this slab of stone talk to us and laugh? Probably she came to the river Godāvarī in order to gather lotuses? But, no: she would never go alone to these places.

"O sun! You know what people do and what people do not do. You know what is true and what is false. You are a witness to all these. Pray, tell me, where has my beloved Sītā gone. For, I have been robbed of everything by this grief. O wind! You know everything in this world, for you are everywhere. Pray, tell me, in which direction did Sītā go?"

Rāma said: "See, Lakṣmaṇa, if Sītā is somewhere near the river Godāvarī." Lakṣmaṇa came back and reported that he could not find her. Rāma himself went to the river and asked the river: "O Godāvarī, pray tell me, where has my beloved Sītā gone?" But the river did not reply. It was as if, afraid of the anger of Rāvaṇa, Godāvarī kept silent.

Rāma was disappointed. He asked the deer and the other animals of the forest: "Where is Sītā? Pray, tell me in which direction has Sītā been taken away." He then observed the deer and the animals; all of them turned southwards and some of them even moved southwards. Rāma then said to Lakṣmaṇa: "O Lakṣmaṇa, see, they are all indicating that Sītā has been taken in a southerly direction."

ĀRAṆYA 64

Lakṣmaṇa, too, saw the animals' behavior as sure signs indicating that Sītā had been borne away in a southerly direction, and suggested to Rāma that they should also proceed in that direction. As they were thus proceeding, they saw petals of flowers fallen on the ground. Rāma recognized them and said to Lakṣmaṇa: "Look here, Lakṣmaṇa, these are petals from the flowers that I had given to Sītā. Surely, in their eagerness to please me, the sun, the wind and the earth, have contrived to keep these flowers fresh."

They walked further on. Rāma saw footprints on the ground. Two of them he immediately recognized as those of Sītā. The other two were big—obviously the footprints of a demon. Bits and pieces of gold were strewn on the ground. Lo and behold, Rāma also saw blood which he concluded was Sītā's blood: he wailed again: "Alas, at this spot, the demon killed Sītā to eat her flesh." He also saw evidence of a fight: and he said: "Perhaps there were two demons fighting for the flesh of Sītā."

Rāma saw on the ground pieces of a broken weapon, an armor of gold, a broken canopy, and the propellers and other parts of a flying chariot. He also saw lying dead, one who had the appearance of the pilot of the craft. From these he concluded that two demons had fought for the flesh of Sītā, before one carried her away. He said to Lakṣmaṇa: "The demons have earned my unquenchable hate and wrath. I shall destroy all of them. Nay, I shall destroy all the powers that be who refuse to return Sītā to me. Look at the irony of fate, Lakṣmaṇa: we adhere to dharma, but dharma could not protect Sītā who has been abducted in this forest! When these powers that govern the universe witness Sītā being eaten by the demons, without doing anything to stop it, who is there to do what is pleasing to us? I think our meekness is misunderstood to be weakness. We are full of self-control, compassion and devoted to the welfare of all beings: and yet these virtues have become as good as vices in us now. I shall set aside all these virtues and the universe shall witness my supreme glory which will bring about the destruction of all creatures, including the demons. If Sītā is not immediately brought back to me, I shall destroy the three worlds—the gods, the demons and other creatures will perish, becoming targets of my most powerful missiles. When I take up my weapon in anger, O Lakṣmaṇa, no one can confront me, even as no one can evade old age and death."

ĀRAŅYA 65–66

Seeing the world-destroying mood of Rāma, Lakṣmaṇa endeavored to console him. He said to Rāma:

"Rāma, pray, do not go against your nature. Charm in the moon, brilliance in the sun, motion in the air, and endurance in the earth—these are their essential nature: in you all these are found and in addition, eternal glory. Your nature cannot desert you; even the sun, the moon and the earth cannot abandon their nature! Moreover, being king, you cannot punish all the created beings for the sin of one person. Gentle and peaceful monarchs match punishment to crime: and, over and above this, you are the refuge of all beings and their goal. I shall without fail find out the real criminal who has abducted Sītā; I shall find out whose armor and weapons these are. And you shall mete out just punishment to the sinner. Oh, no, no god will seek to displease you, O Rāma: Nor these trees, mountains and rivers. I am sure they will all eagerly aid us in our search for Sītā. Of course, if Sītā cannot be recovered through peaceful means, we shall consider other means.

"Whom does not misfortune visit in this world, O Rāma? And, misfortune departs from man as quickly as it visits him. Hence, pray, regain your composure. If you who are endowed with divine intelligence betray lack of endurance in the face of this misfortune, what will others do in similar circumstances?

"King Nahuṣa, who was as powerful as Indra, was beset with misfortune.[1] The sage Vasiṣṭha, our family preceptor, had a hundred sons and lost all of them on one day! Earth is tormented by volcanic eruptions, and earthquakes. The sun and the moon are afflicted by eclipses. Misfortune strikes the great ones and even the gods.

"For, in this world people perform actions whose results are not obvious; and these actions which may be good or evil, bear their own fruits. Of course, these fruits are evanescent. People who are endowed with enlightened intelligence know what is good and what is not good. People like you do not grieve over misfortunes and do not get deluded by them.

"Why am I telling you all this, O Rāma? Who in this world is wiser than you? However, since, as is natural, grief seems to veil wisdom, I am saying all this. All this I learnt only from you: I am only repeating what you yourself taught me earlier. Therefore, O Rāma, know your enemy and fight him."

1. King Nahuṣa, an ancestor of Rāma, became so powerful that he claimed the throne of Indra, king of gods, but an arrogant act soon effected his fall from his exalted position.

ĀRAṆYA 67–68

Rāma then asked Lakṣmaṇa: "O Lakṣmaṇa, tell me, what should we do now?" Lakṣmaṇa replied: "Surely, we should search this forest for Sītā."

This advice appealed to Rāma. Immediately he fixed the bayonet to his weapon and with a look of anger on his face, set out to search for Sītā. Within a very short time and distance, both Rāma and Lakṣmaṇa chanced upon Jaṭāyu, seriously and mortally wounded and heavily bleeding. Seeing that enormous vulture lying on the ground, Rāma's first thought was: "Surely, this is the one that has swallowed Sītā." He rushed forward with fixed bayonet.

Looking at Rāma thus rushing towards him, and rightly inferring Rāma's mood, Jaṭāyu said in a feeble voice: "Sītā has been taken away by Rāvaṇa. I tried to intervene. I battled with the mighty Rāvaṇa. I broke his armor, his canopy, the propellers and some parts of his chariot. I killed his pilot. I even inflicted injuries on his person. But he cut off my wings and thus grounded me." When Rāma heard that the vulture had news of Sītā, he threw his weapon away and kneeling down near the vulture embraced it.

Rāma said to Lakṣmaṇa: "An additional calamity to endure, O Lakṣmaṇa. Is there really no end to my misfortune? My misfortune plagues even this noble creature, a friend of my father's." Rāma requested more information from Jaṭāyu concerning Sītā, and also concerning Rāvaṇa. Jaṭāyu replied: "Taking Sītā with him, the demon flew away in his craft, leaving a mysterious storm and cloud behind him. I was mortally wounded by him. Ah, my senses are growing dim. I feel life ebbing away, Rāma. Yet, I assure you, you will recover Sītā." Soon Jaṭāyu lay lifeless. Nay, it was his body, for he himself ascended to heaven. Grief-stricken afresh, Rāma said to Lakṣmaṇa: "Jaṭāyu lived a very long life; and yet has had to lay down his life today. Death, no one in this world can escape. And what a noble end! What a great service this noble vulture has rendered to me! Pious and noble souls are found even amongst subhuman creatures, O Lakṣmaṇa. Today I have forgotten all my previous misfortunes: I am extremely tormented by the loss of this dear friend who has sacrificed his life for my sake. I shall myself cremate it, so that it may reach the highest realms."

Rāma himself performed the funeral rites, reciting those Vedic mantras[2] which one recites during the cremation of one's own close relations. After this, Rāma and Lakṣmaṇa proceeded on their journey in search of Sītā.

* * *

Summary   While searching desperately for Sītā, Rāma and Lakṣmana encounter a tribe of monkeys, whose citadel is at Kiṣkindhā in southern India. Intervening in the political quarrels among their factions, the princes persuade the monkeys, and one of their powerful leaders, Hanumāna, to help them look for her. Hanumāna eventually discovers where Sītā is held captive, after spying on Rāvaṇa's capital. Sītā refuses to escape with Hanumāna, insisting instead that Rāma himself must free her from captivity. Hanumāna sets fire to Rāvaṇa's city as a warning of impending war, and returns to apprise Rāma of the situation. The monkey hordes build a bridge across the straits to Laṅkā, giving the princes and their army a passage to Laṅkā, where they begin to wage battle. One of Rāvaṇa's brothers betrays him and joins Rāma and Lakṣmana against Rāvaṇa. After a lengthy conflict, in which Rāvaṇa's other brothers are killed and Lakṣmana is wounded, Rāma finally confronts the demon king in single combat.

2. Sacred chants, usually from the scriptures.

From Book 6

Yuddha

YUDDHA 109, 110, 111

When Rāma and Rāvaṇa began to fight, their armies stood stupefied, watching them! Rāma was determined to win; Rāvaṇa was sure he would die: knowing this, they fought with all their might. Rāvaṇa attacked the standard on Rāma's car: and Rāma similarly shot the standard on Rāvaṇa's car. While Rāvaṇa's standard fell; Rāma's did not. Rāvaṇa next aimed at the "horses" of Rāma's car: even though he attacked them with all his might, they remained unaffected.

Both of them discharged thousands of missiles: these illumined the skies and created a new heaven, as it were! They were accurate in their aim and their missiles unfailingly hit the target. With unflagging zeal they fought each other, without the least trace of fatigue. What one did the other did in retaliation.

Rāvaṇa shot at Mātali[3] who remained unaffected by it. Then Rāvaṇa sent a shower of maces and mallets at Rāma. Their very sound agitated the oceans and tormented the aquatic creatures. The celestials and the holy brāhmaṇas witnessing the scene prayed: "May auspiciousness attend to all the living beings, and may the worlds endure forever. May Rāma conquer Rāvaṇa." Astounded at the way in which Rāma and Rāvaṇa fought with each other, the sages said to one another: "Sky is like sky, ocean is like ocean; the fight between Rāma and Rāvaṇa is like Rāma and Rāvaṇa—incomparable."

Taking up a powerful missile, Rāma correctly aimed at the head of Rāvaṇa; it fell. But another head appeared in its place. Every time Rāma cut off Rāvaṇa's head, another appeared! Rāma was puzzled. Mātali, Rāma's driver, said to Rāma: "Why do you fight like an ordinary warrior, O Rāma? Use the Brahmā-missile; the hour of the demon's death is at hand."

Rāma remembered the Brahmā-missile which the sage Agastya had given him. It had the power of the wind-god for its "feathers"; the power of fire and sun at its head; the whole space was its body; and it had the weight of a mountain. It shone like the sun or the fire of nemesis. As Rāma took it in his hands, the earth shook and all living beings were terrified. Infallible in its destructive power, this ultimate weapon of destruction shattered the chest of Rāvaṇa, and entered deep into the earth.

Rāvaṇa fell dead. And the surviving demons fled, pursued by the vānaras. The vānaras shouted in great jubilation. The air resounded with the drums of the celestials. The gods praised Rāma. The earth became steady, the wind blew softly and the sun was resplendent as before. Rāma was surrounded by mighty heroes and gods who were all joyously felicitating him on the victory.

YUDDHA 112, 113

Seeing Rāvaṇa lying dead on the battlefield, Vibhīṣaṇa burst into tears. Overcome by brotherly affection, he lamented thus: "Alas, what I had predicted has come true: and my advice was not relished by you, overcome as you were by

3. Indra, king of the gods, has sent his own charioteer, Mātali, to drive Rāma's chariot in battle.

lust and delusion. Now that you have departed, the glory of Laṅkā has departed. You were like a tree firmly established in heroism with asceticism for its strength, spreading out firmness in all aspects of your life: yet you have been cut down. You were like an elephant with splendor, noble ancestry, indignation, and pleasant nature for parts: yet you have been killed. You, who were like blazing fire have been extinguished by Rāma."

Rāma approached the grief-stricken Vibhīṣaṇa and gently and lovingly said to him: "It is not right that you should thus grieve, O Vibhīṣaṇa, for a mighty warrior fallen on the battlefield. Victory is the monopoly of none: a hero is either slain in battle or he kills his opponent. Hence our ancients decreed that the warrior who is killed in combat should not be mourned. Get up and consider what should be done next."

Vibhīṣaṇa regained his composure and said to Rāma: "This Rāvaṇa used to give a lot in charity to ascetics; he enjoyed life; he maintained his servants well; he shared his wealth with his friends, and he destroyed his enemies. He was regular in his religious observances; learned he was in the scriptures. By your grace, O Rāma, I wish to perform his funeral in accordance with the scriptures, for his welfare in the other world." Rāma was delighted and said to Vibhīṣaṇa: "Hostility ends at death. Take steps for the due performance of the funeral rites. He is your brother as he is mine, too."

The womenfolk of Rāvaṇa's court, and his wives, hearing of his end, rushed out of the palace, and, arriving at the battlefield, rolled on the ground in sheer anguish. Overcome by grief they gave vent to their feelings in diverse heart-rending ways. They wailed: "Alas, he who could not be killed by the gods and demons, has been killed in battle by a man standing on earth. Our beloved lord! Surely when you abducted Sītā and brought her to Laṅkā, you invited your own death! Surely it was because death was close at hand that you did not listen to the wise counsel of your own brother Vibhīṣaṇa, and you ill-treated him and exiled him. Even later if you had restored Sītā to Rāma, this evil fate would not have overtaken you. However, it is surely not because you did what you liked, because you were driven by lust, that you lie dead now: God's will makes people do diverse deeds. He who is killed by the divine will dies. No one can flout the divine will, and no one can buy the divine will nor bribe it."

* * *

YUDDHA 115, 116

Rāma returned to the camp where the vānara troops had been stationed. He turned to Lakṣmaṇa and said: "O Lakṣmaṇa, install Vibhīṣaṇa on the throne of Laṅkā and consecrate him as the king of Laṅkā. He has rendered invaluable service to me and I wish to behold him on the throne of Laṅkā at once."

Without the least loss of time, Lakṣmaṇa made the necessary preparations and with the waters of the ocean consecrated Vibhīṣaṇa as king of Laṅkā, in strict accordance with scriptural ordinance. Rāma, Lakṣmaṇa and the others were delighted. The demon-leaders brought their tributes and offered them to Vibhīṣaṇa who in turn placed them all at Rāma's feet.

Rāma said to Hanumān: "Please go, with the permission of king Vibhīṣaṇa, to Sītā and inform her of the death of Rāvaṇa and the welfare of both myself and Lakṣmaṇa." Immediately Hanumān left for the Aśoka-grove. The grief-stricken Sītā was happy to behold him. With joined palms Hanumān submitted Rāma's message and added: "Rāma desires me to inform you that you can shed fear, for you are in your own home as it were, now that Vibhīṣaṇa is king of Lankā." Sītā was speechless for a moment and then said: "I am delighted by the message you have brought, O Hanumān; and I am rendered speechless by it. I only regret that I have nothing now with which to reward you; nor is any gift equal in value to the most joyous tidings you have brought me." Hanumān submitted: "O lady, the very words you have uttered are more precious than all the jewels of the world! I consider myself supremely blessed to have witnessed Rāma's victory and Rāvaṇa's destruction." Sītā was even more delighted: she said, "Only you can utter such sweet words, O Hanumān, endowed as you are with manifold excellences. Truly you are an abode of virtues."

Hanumān said: "Pray, give me leave to kill all these demonesses who have been tormenting you so long." Sītā replied: "Nay, Hanumān, they are not responsible for their actions, for they were but obeying their master's commands. And, surely, it was my own evil destiny that made me suffer at their hands. Hence, I forgive them. A noble man does not recognize the harm done to him by others: and he never retaliates, for he is the embodiment of goodness. One should be compassionate towards all, the good and the wicked, nay even towards those who are fit to be killed: who is free from sin?" Hanumān was thrilled to hear these words of Sītā, and said: "Indeed you are the noble consort of Rāma and his peer in virtue and nobility. Pray, give me a message to take back to Rāma." Sītā replied: "Please tell him that I am eager to behold his face." Assuring Sītā that she would see Rāma that very day, Hanumān returned to Rāma.

YUDDHA 117, 118, 119

Hanumān conveyed Sītā's message to Rāma who turned to king Vibhīṣaṇa and said: "Please bring Sītā to me soon, after she has had a bath and has adorned herself." Immediately Vibhīṣaṇa went to Sītā and compelled her to proceed seated in a palanquin, to where Rāma was. Vānaras and demons had gathered around her, eager to look at Sītā. And Vibhīṣaṇa, in accordance with the tradition, wished to ensure that Sītā was not seen by these and rebuked them to go away. Restraining him, Rāma said: "Why do you rebuke them, O Vibhīṣaṇa? Neither houses nor clothes nor walls constitute a veil for a woman; her character alone is her veil. Let her descend from the palanquin and walk up to me." So she did.

Rāma said sternly: "My purpose has been accomplished, O Sītā. My prowess has been witnessed by all. I have fulfilled my pledge. Rāvaṇa's wickedness has been punished. The extraordinary feat performed by Hanumān in crossing the ocean and burning Lankā[4] has borne fruit. Vibhīṣaṇa's devotion has been rewarded." Rāma's heart was in a state of conflict, afraid as he was of public ridicule. Hence, he continued: "I wish to let you know that all this was done not for your sake, but for the sake of preserving my honor. Your conduct is

---

4. When Hanumān destroys the groves of Lankā, Rāvaṇa's henchmen capture him and set his tail on fire. Hanumān sets fire to Lankā's mansions with his fiery tail and himself escapes unhurt.

open to suspicion, hence even your sight is displeasing to me. Your body was touched by Rāvaṇa: how then can I, claiming to belong to a noble family, accept you? Hence I permit you to go where you like and live with whom you like—either Lakṣmaṇa, Bharata, Śatrughna, Sugrīva or even Vibhīṣaṇa. It is difficult for me to believe that Rāvaṇa, who was so fond of you, would have been able to keep away from you for such a long time."

Sītā was shocked. Rāma's words wounded her heart. Tears streamed down her face. Wiping them, she replied: "O Rāma, you are speaking to me in the language of a common and vulgar man speaking to a common woman. That which was under my control, my heart, has always been yours; how could I prevent my body from being touched when I was helpless and under another person's control? Ah, if only you had conveyed your suspicion through Hanumān when he came to meet me, I would have killed myself then and saved you all this trouble and the risk involved in the war." Turning to Lakṣmaṇa, she said: "Kindle the fire, O Lakṣmaṇa: that is the only remedy. I shall not live to endure this false calumny." Lakṣmaṇa looked at Rāma and with his approval kindled the fire. Sītā prayed: "Even as my heart is ever devoted to Rāma, may the fire protect me. If I have been faithful to Rāma in thought, word or deed, may the fire protect me. The sun, the moon, the wind, earth and others are witness to my purity; may the fire protect me." Then she entered into the fire, even as an oblation poured into the fire would. Gods and sages witnessed this. The women who saw this screamed.

YUDDHA 120, 121

Rāma was moved to tears by the heart-rending cries of all those women who witnessed the self-immolation of Sītā. At the same time, all the gods, including the trinity—the Creator, the Preserver, and the Redeemer (or Transformer)[5]— arrived upon the scene in their personal forms. Saluting Rāma, they said: "You are the foremost among the gods, and yet you treat Sītā as if you were a common human being!"

Rāma replied to these divinities: "I consider myself a human being, Rāma the son of Daśaratha. Who I am, and whence I am, may you tell me!"

Brahmā the creator said: "You are verily lord Nārāyaṇa.[6] You are the imperishable cosmic being. You are the truth. You are eternal. You are the supreme dharma of the worlds. You are the father even of the chief of the gods, Indra. You are the sole refuge of perfected beings and holy men. You are the Om,[7] and you are the spirit of sacrifice. You are that cosmic being with infinite heads, hands and eyes.[8] You are the support of the whole universe. The whole universe is your body. Sītā is Lakṣmī[9] and you are lord Viṣṇu, who is of a dark hue, and who is the creator of all beings. For the sake of the destruction of Rāvaṇa you entered into a human body. This mission of ours has been fully accomplished by you. Blessed it is to be in your presence; blessed it is to sing

---

5. The triad of the three great gods, Brahmā (Creator), Viṣṇu (Preserver), and Śiva (Redeemer or Transformer).
6. Viṣṇu in his primeval cosmic form.
7. A sacred chant (mantra) of the Vedas.
8. The cosmic being described here is Puruṣa,

or "Man," a primeval being with innumerable heads, arms, and eyes who was offered as the sacrificial victim by the gods and sages in the first sacrifice, described in a hymn of the Ṛg-veda.
9. Goddess-consort of Viṣṇu.

your glories; they are truly blessed who are devoted to you, for their life will be attended with success."

As soon as Brahmā finished saying this, the god of fire emerged from the fire in his personal form, holding up Sītā in his hands. Sītā shone in all her radiance. The god of fire who is the witness of everything that takes place in the world, said to Rāma: "Here is your Sītā, Rāma. I find no fault in her. She has not erred in thought, word or deed. Even during the long period of her detention in the abode of Rāvaṇa, she did not even think of him, as her heart was set on you. Accept her: and I command you not to treat her harshly."

Rāma was highly pleased at this turn of events. He said: "Indeed, I was fully aware of Sītā's purity. Even the mighty and wicked Rāvaṇa could not lay his hands upon her with evil intention. Yet, this baptism by fire was necessary, to avoid public calumny and ridicule, for though she was pure, she lived in Laṅkā for a long time. I knew, too, that Sītā would never be unfaithful to me: for we are non-different from each other even as the sun and its rays are. It is therefore impossible for me to renounce her."

After saying so, Rāma was joyously reunited with Sītā.

YUDDHA 122, 123

Lord Śiva then said to Rāma: "You have fulfilled a most difficult task. Now behold your father, the illustrious king Daśaratha who appears in the firmament to bless you and to greet you."

Rāma along with Lakṣmaṇa saw that great monarch, their father clad in a raiment of purity and shining by his own luster. Still seated in his celestial vehicle, Daśaratha lifted up Rāma and placing him on his lap, warmly embraced him and said: "Neither heaven nor even the homage of the gods is as pleasing to me as to behold you, Rāma. I am delighted to see that you have successfully completed the period of your exile and that you have destroyed all your enemies. Even now the cruel words of Kaikeyī haunt my heart; but seeing you and embracing you, I am rid of that sorrow, O Rāma. You have redeemed my word and thus I have been saved by you. It is only now that I recognize you to be the supreme person incarnated as a human being in this world in order to kill Rāvaṇa."

Rāma said: "You remember that you said to Kaikeyī, 'I renounce you and your son'? Pray, take back that curse and may it not afflict Kaikeyī and Bharata." Daśaratha agreed to it and then said to Lakṣmaṇa: "I am pleased with you, my son, and you have earned great merit by the faithful service you have rendered to Rāma."

Lastly, king Daśaratha said to Sītā: "My dear daughter, do not take to heart the fire ordeal that Rāma forced you to undergo: it was necessary to reveal to the world your absolute purity. By your conduct you have exalted yourself above all women." Having thus spoken to them, Daśaratha ascended to heaven.

Before taking leave of Rāma, Indra prayed: "Our visit to you should not be fruitless, O Rāma. Command me, what may I do for you?" Rāma replied: "If you are really pleased with me, then I pray that all those vānaras who laid down their lives for my sake may come back to life. I wish to see them hale and hearty as before. I also wish to see the whole world fruitful and prosperous." Indra replied: "This indeed is an extremely difficult task. Yet, I do not go back on my word, hence I grant it. All the vānaras will come back to life and be restored to their original form, with all their wounds healed. Even as you had asked, the world will be fruitful and prosperous."

Instantly, all the vānaras arose from the dead and bowed to Rāma. The others who witnessed this marveled and the gods beheld Rāma who had all his wishes fulfilled. The gods returned to their abodes.

*   *   *

Summary   After crowning Vibhīsana king of Laṅkā, Rāma, Laksmana and Sītā fly to Ayodhyā in Rāvana's flying chariot, accompanied by Vibhīsana, Sugrīva, Hanumān, and the monkey hordes.

YUDDHA 130

Bharata immediately made the reception arrangements. He instructed Śatrughna: "Let prayers be offered to the gods in all temples and houses of worship with fragrant flowers and musical instruments."

Śatrughna immediately gave orders that the roads along which the royal procession would wend its way to the palace should be leveled and sprinkled with water, and kept clear by hundreds of policemen cordoning them. Soon all the ministers, and thousands of elephants and men on horse-back and in cars went out to greet Rāma. The royal reception party, seated in palanquins,[1] was led by the queen-mother Kausalyā herself; Kaikeyī and the other members of the royal household followed—and all of them reached Nandigrāma.[2]

From there Bharata headed the procession with the sandals of Rāma placed on his head, with the white royal umbrella and the other regalia.[3] Bharata was the very picture of an ascetic though he radiated the joy that filled his heart at the very thought of Rāma's return to the kingdom.

Bharata anxiously looked around but saw no signs of Rāma's return! But, Hanumān reassured him: "Listen, O Bharata, you can see the cloud of dust raised by the vānaras rushing towards Ayodhyā. You can now hear the roar of the Puspaka flying chariot."

"Rāma has come!"—these words were uttered by thousands of people at the same time. Even before the Puspaka landed, Bharata humbly saluted Rāma who was standing on the front side of the chariot. The Puspaka landed. As Bharata approached it, Rāma lifted him up and placed him on his lap. Bharata bowed down to Rāma and also to Sītā and greeted Laksmana. And he embraced Sugrīva, Jāmbavān, Aṅgada, Vibhīsana and others. He said to Sugrīva: "We are four brothers, and with you we are five. Good deeds promote friendship, and evil is a sign of enmity."

Rāma bowed to his mother who had become emaciated through sorrow, and brought great joy to her heart. Then he also bowed to Sumitrā and Kaikeyī. All the people thereupon said to Rāma: "Welcome, welcome back, O Lord."

Bharata placed the sandals in front of Rāma, and said: "Rāma here is your kingdom which I held in trust for you during your absence. I consider myself

---

1. Litters in which people were carried by bearers.
2. The village outside the city of Ayodhyā, from which Bharata ruled the kingdom on behalf of Rāma.

3. By carrying Rāma's sandals on his head, Bharata indicates his subservience to and reverence for Rāma as his sovereign, elder brother, and teacher.

supremely blessed in being able to behold your return to Ayodhyā. By your grace, the treasury has been enriched tenfold by me, as also the storehouses and the strength of the nation." Rāma felt delighted. When the entire party had disembarked, he instructed that the Puṣpaka be returned to its original owner, Kubera.[4]

YUDDHA 131

The coronation proceedings were immediately initiated by Bharata. Skilled barbers removed the matted locks of Rāma. He had a ceremonial bath and he was dressed in magnificent robes and royal jewels. Kausalyā herself helped the vānara ladies to dress themselves in royal robes; all the queens dressed Sītā appropriately for the occasion. The royal chariot was brought; duly ascending it, Rāma, Lakṣmaṇa and Sītā, went in a procession to Ayodhyā, Bharata himself driving the chariot. When he had reached the court, Rāma gave his ministers and counselors a brief account of the events during his exile, particularly the alliance with the vānara chief Sugrīva, and the exploits of Hanumān. He also informed them of his alliance with Vibhīṣaṇa.

At Bharata's request, Sugrīva despatched the best of the vānaras to fetch water from the four oceans, and all the sacred rivers of the world. The aged sage Vasiṣṭha thereupon commenced the ceremony in connection with the coronation of Rāma. Rāma and Sītā were seated on a seat made entirely of precious stones. The foremost among the sages thereupon consecrated Rāma with the appropriate Vedic chants. First the brāhmaṇas, then the virgins, then the ministers and warriors, and later the businessmen poured the holy waters on Rāma.[5] After that the sage Vasiṣṭha placed Rāma on the throne made of gold and studded with precious stones, and placed on his head the dazzling crown which had been made by Brahmā the creator himself. The gods and others paid their homage to Rāma by bestowing gifts upon him. Rāma also gave away rich presents to the brāhmaṇas and others, including the vānara chiefs like Sugrīva. Rāma then gave to Sītā a necklace of pearls and said: "You may give it to whom you like, Sītā." And, immediately Sītā bestowed that gift upon Hanumān.

After witnessing the coronation of Rāma, the vānaras returned to Kiṣkindhā. So did Vibhīṣaṇa return to Laṅkā. Rāma looked fondly at Lakṣmaṇa and expressed the wish that he should reign as the prince regent. Lakṣmaṇa did not reply: he did not want it. Rāma appointed Bharata as prince regent. Rāma thereafter ruled the earth for a very long time.

During the period of Rāma's reign, there was no poverty, no crime, no fear, and no unrighteousness in the kingdom. All the people constantly spoke of Rāma; the whole world had been transformed into Rāma. Everyone was devoted to dharma. And Rāma was highly devoted to dharma, too. He ruled for eleven thousand years.

YUDDHA 131

Rāma's rule of the kingdom was characterized by the effortless and spontaneous prevalence of dharma. People were free from fear of any sort. There were no widows in the land: people were not molested by beasts and snakes,

---

4. God of wealth.
5. The *brāhmaṇas*, ministers and warriors, and businessmen represent the three highest caste-groups in Hindu society.

nor did they suffer from diseases. There was no theft, no robbery nor any violence. Young people did not die making older people perform funeral services for them. Everyone was happy and everyone was devoted to dharma; beholding Rāma alone, no one harmed another. People lived long and had many children. They were healthy and they were free from sorrow. Everywhere people were speaking all the time about Rāma; the entire world appeared to be the form of Rāma. The trees were endowed with undying roots, and they were in fruition all the time and they flowered throughout the year. Rain fell whenever it was needed. There was a pleasant breeze always. The brāhmaṇas (priests), the warriors, the farmers and businessmen, as also the members of the servant class, were entirely free from greed, and were joyously devoted to their own dharma and functions in society. There was no falsehood in the life of the people who were all righteous. People were endowed with all auspicious characteristics and all of them had dharma as their guiding light. Thus did Rāma rule the world for eleven thousand years, surrounded by his brothers.

This holy epic Rāmāyaṇa composed by the sage Vālmīki, promotes dharma, fame, long life and in the case of a king, victory. He who listens to it always is freed from all sins. He who desires sons gets them, and he who desires wealth becomes wealthy, by listening to the story of the coronation of Rāma. The king conquers the whole world, after overcoming his enemies. Women who listen to this story will be blessed with children like Rāma and his brothers. And they, too, will be blessed with long life, after listening to the Rāmāyaṇa. He who listens to or reads this Rāmāyaṇa propitiates Rāma by this; Rāma is pleased with him; and he indeed is the eternal lord Viṣṇu.

LAVA AND KUŚA said: Such is the glorious epic, Rāmāyaṇa. May all recite it and thus augment the glory of dharma, of lord Viṣṇu. Righteous men should regularly listen to this story of Rāma, which increases health, long-life, love, wisdom and vitality.

THE BHAGAVAD-GĪTĀ

ca. fourth century B.C.E.–fourth century C.E.

The *Bhagavad-gītā* asks the most difficult of questions. What is a just war, and when can the use of armed conflict to resolve a political stalemate be justified? Under what circumstances is it possible to engage in a violent conflict with family members, clansmen, teachers, and friends—the very people who have nurtured us since infancy— and claim a victory that is morally right? What is such a victory worth if, in the name of life, wealth, or truth, it destroys what we love? As a philosophical poem, the *Bhagavad-gītā* does not provide simple answers but offers explanations that are appropriately difficult because they involve dilemmas that cannot be resolved once and for all.

During the past two centuries, it has become commonplace to treat the *Bhagavad-gītā* as an independent poem, which can be read and understood by itself for its philosophical message as a meditation on universal issues. But the work is actually an integral part of the *Mahābhārata*, and was originally composed as the sixty-third minor book of that epic, and included in its sixth major book, *Bhīṣma*. Since it is a poem within a poem, the *Bhagavad-gītā* is best interpreted in relation to the epic's larger narrative, setting, and background.

The *Mahābhārata* is attributed to a single poet or compiler named Kṛṣṇa Dvaipāyana, but it was composed collaboratively by many generations of poets in Sanskrit between about 400 B.C.E. and 400 C.E. Its main story concerns a protracted conflict between two branches of a royal dynasty in northern India, over the inheritance of a kingdom and the succession to its throne. The embattled groups are the Kauravas and the Pāṇḍavas, who are paternal cousins; the Kauravas are one hundred brothers, led by their eldest, Duryodhana, whereas the Pāṇḍavas are five half brothers, the three eldest being Yudhiṣṭhira, Bhīma, and Arjuna. Both branches have strong and legitimate claims to the kingdom, and one possible settlement is a division of the dominion, so that each set of cousins can rule its own territory without conflict. But Duryodhana and his brothers, the Kauravas, resist such a solution; using a variety of strategies, they deny the Pāṇḍavas' claim, and send the five brothers and their shared wife (in a polyandrous marriage) into a thirteen-year exile, with the promise to restore their share of territory if they meet several conditions. The Pāṇḍavas complete their exile as required, but when they return to Duryodhana's court, he refuses to honor his word.

At this point in the main narrative, Lord Kṛṣṇa—a human avatar of Viṣṇu, the god who primarily preserves the moral order of the universe—intervenes on behalf of the Pāṇḍavas. In the course of his life in human form, Kṛṣṇa became a close friend of the third Pāṇḍava, Arjuna, in his youth; now, many years later, when Arjuna and his half brothers find themselves in an impossible situation with their cousins, Kṛṣṇa agrees to serve as their ambassador to Duryodhana. Even though Kṛṣṇa (whose divinity is evident to the other characters in the epic) offers the Kauravas a peaceable solution in accordance with *dharma* (law, morality, duty, obligation), Duryodhana refuses to give the Pāṇḍavas even five small villages as their share of the kingdom. In consultation with Kṛṣṇa, the Pāṇḍavas decide that the only way in which they can now assert their legitimate claim to the kingdom is by going to war with the Kauravas. This is a just war because their claim is based strictly on the *dharma* of succession and inheritance; and it is a justifiable war because they have exhausted every possibility of a peaceful resolution of the stalemate with the Kauravas.

The Kauravas and Pāṇḍavas then prepare for armed conflict, and their respective armies gather on the battlefield of Kurukṣetra (about sixty-five miles north of modern Delhi). Arjuna, the most skilled and feared archer of his times, enters the battlefield on a chariot, with Kṛṣṇa serving as his charioteer. But in the moments just before the battle begins, Arjuna looks at the forces arrayed on the enemy side, and sees in their midst all his cousins as well as many people he grew up with—teachers, friends, and members of his clan, people he has known and loved much of his life. Faced with the prospect of shedding their blood, he throws down his weapons and refuses to fight: he cannot imagine how any such war could possibly be good or right. But, in doing so, he immediately places himself in moral jeopardy as a warrior, because *dharma* requires that a *kṣatriya* be prepared to wage war whenever necessary, and in this case his cause is just. Caught between his fundamental duty as a warrior and his equally powerful obligation to preserve the lives of those he loves, Arjuna turns to Kṛṣṇa— his friend, aide, and counselor—and asks for his divine advice under the circumstances. The *Bhagavad-gītā* is the poetic record of that moment of crisis in Arjuna's mind, and of the conversation he has with God on the brink of war.

WORK

The *Bhagavad-gītā* is divided into eighteen chapters or cantos composed in verse, and its total length runs to seven hundred couplets. In the translation from which our selection of passages is drawn, each canto is called a "chapter"; it contains, in part, Kṛṣṇa's instruction to Arjuna about what is involved in war, violence, duty, courage, life, and death (among other things), and why it is essential to fight a just war, even if it means destroying precious lives.

The structure of the *Bhagavad-gītā* as a whole has two layers of interspersed dialogue: one between Sañjaya and Dhṛtarāṣṭra, which defines the outer frame of the book, and the other between Arjuna and Kṛṣṇa, which occurs in an inner frame. Dhṛtarāṣṭra is the father of the Kauravas and the current head of the dynasty; he is blind and old, and cannot participate in or even observe the battle. He sits in his chariot on the edge of the battlefield with his charioteer, a youth named Sañjaya; on the eve of the war, Dvaipāyana, the original author of the *Mahābhārata*, grants Sañjaya "celestial vision," so that he can omnisciently observe everything in the past, present, and future, and everything that happens on the battlefield, in public and in private; throughout the eighteen days of the war, Sanjaya tells the blind Dhṛtarāṣṭra what happens in the war, and we, the readers, also witness the entire conflict through Sañjaya's "visionary eye." Our excerpts here mostly omit the dialogue between Sañjaya and Dhṛtarāṣṭra in the various cantos; the main exception is the passage from Chapter Eleven, which ends with a portion of Sañjaya's narrative.

In the excerpt from Chapter One we hear Arjuna's voice, explaining to Kṛṣṇa at length why he is unable to take up arms against his blood relatives, mentors, and friends. In the segments from Chapter Two, Kṛṣṇa begins his response to Arjuna's dilemma by explaining the nature of the imperishable self or soul embodied in every human being. In the portions reproduced from Chapter Three, Arjuna raises fresh questions about human action in relation to the inner self and to evil, and Kṛṣṇa teaches him the yoga or discipline of action, especially as it should be practiced by a warrior. In the next excerpt, which jumps ahead to Chapter Six, Kṛṣṇa then explains what self-discipline in general is, and what a man who establishes complete control over himself can accomplish. In the final passage, drawn from Chapter Eleven, Arjuna achieves a comprehensive, new understanding of his task as a warrior, and asks Kṛṣṇa to reveal his full divine form; Kṛṣṇa does so, but the vision is so intense that a merely human eye cannot experience it. The narrator Sañjaya, talking to King Dhṛtarāṣṭra, therefore intercedes with his extraordinary visual capacity, and reports, in part, what Kṛṣṇa reveals to Arjuna.

The passages from the *Bhagavad-gītā* reproduced here cover only a small portion of Lord Kṛṣṇa's advice to Arjuna on the battlefield of Kurukṣetra. In the course of the eighteen cantos of the book, Kṛṣṇa constructs a long argument, containing many strands, about the justification for violence in the context of a war that is morally right and in complete accordance with all applicable aspects of *dharma*. Especially when encountered in excerpts, this argument can be, and often has been, easily misunderstood. Kṛṣṇa emphatically does *not* offer a general justification for violence under all circumstances; the use of violence to settle a major dispute can be justified only when every possible option for a peaceful resolution has been explored within the full scope of the law, and all such options have failed. Moreover, in a just war, only the thoroughly trained and disciplined warrior can use violence, and even he can do so only when he is in complete control of himself, and selflessly pursues his duty as defined by *dharma*.

Arjuna's distress and refusal to fight

From The Bhagavad-gītā[1]

CHAPTER ONE[2]

* * *

20   "Now Monkey-Bannered Arjuna,[3]
seeing his foes drawn up for war,
raised his bow, that Son of Pandu,
as the weapons began to clash.

21   "Then he said these words to Krishna:[4]
'Lord of the Earth, Unshaken One,
bring my chariot to a halt
between the two adverse armies,

22   'so I may see these men, arrayed
here for the battle they desire,
whom I am soon to undertake
a warrior's delight in fighting!

23   'I see those who have assembled,
the warriors prepared to fight,
eager to perform in battle
for Dhritarashtra's evil son!'[5]

24   "When Arjuna had spoken so
to Krishna, O Bharata,[6]
he, having brought their chariot
to a halt between the armies,

1. Translated by Gavin Flood and Charles Martin. Verse numbers run to the left of the text.
2. Most of the *Bhagavad-gītā* is narrated by Sañjaya; the double quotation marks throughout these excerpts represent Sanjaya's direct speech, addressed to Dhṛtarāṣtra. For an explanation of these two characters, who define the outer narrative frame of the poem, see the "Work" section of the headnote. The single quotation marks represent the dialogue between Arjuna and Kṛṣṇa,
which takes place within Sanjaya's narrative.
3. The third of the five sons of Pāṇḍu.
4. An incarnation of Viṣṇu, the preserver god.
5. Duryodhana, the leader of the Kauravas, who is the eldest son of Dhṛtarāṣtra.
6. An alternate name or epithet for Dhṛtarāṣtra, who, like his brother Pāṇḍu and their respective sons, is a descendant of Bhārata, the founder of their dynasty of kings.

25   "in the face of Bhishma, Drona,[7]
    and the other Lords of the Earth,[8]
    said, 'Behold, O Son of Pritha,[9]
    how these Kurus[1] have assembled!'

26   "And there the son of Pritha saw
    rows of grandfathers and grandsons;
    sons and fathers, uncles, in-laws;
    teachers, brothers and companions,

27   "all relatives and friends of his
    in both of the assembled armies.
    And seeing them arrayed for war,
    Arjuna, the Son of Kunti,

28   "felt for them a great compassion,
    as well as great despair, and said,
    'O Krishna, now that I have seen
    my relatives so keen for war,

29   'I am unstrung: my limbs collapse
    beneath me, and my mouth is dry,
    there is a trembling in my body,
    and my hair rises, bristling;

30   'Gandiva, my immortal bow,[2]
    drops from my hand and my skin burns,
    I cannot stand upon my feet,
    my mind rambles in confusion—

31   'All inauspicious are the signs
    that I see, O Handsome-Haired One![3]
    I foresee no good resulting
    from slaughtering my kin in war!

32   'I have no wish for victory,
    nor for kingship and its pleasures!
    O Krishna, what good is kingship?
    What good even life and pleasure?

33   'Those for whose sake we desire
    kingship, pleasures and enjoyments,
    are now drawn up in battle lines,
    their lives and riches now abandoned:

7. Droṇa was the teacher or guru of both the Kauravas and the Pāṇḍavas; Bhīṣma is the granduncle of both these branches of the family.
8. "Lord of the earth" is a common epithet for a king in epic Sanskrit.
9. Another name for Kuṅtī, the mother of Arjuna and the Pāṇḍavas.
1. Another name for the Kauravas.
2. A powerful celestial bow of great antiquity and renown that Arjuna won from the fire god, Agni.
3. Kṛṣṇa is often depicted with long, flowing hair.

34 'fathers, grandfathers; sons, grandsons;
my mother's brothers and the men
who taught me in my youth; brothers-
and fathers-in-law: kinsmen all!

35 'Though they are prepared to slay us,
I do not wish to murder them,
not even to rule the three worlds—
how much less one earthly kingdom?

36 'What joy for us in murdering
Dhritarashtra's sons, O Krishna?
for if we killed these murderers,
evil like theirs would cling to us!

37 'So we cannot in justice slay
our kinsmen, Dhritarashtra's sons,
for, having killed our people, how
could we be pleased, O Madhava?[4]

38 'Even if they, mastered by greed,
are blind to the consequences
of the family's destruction,
of friendships lost to treachery,

39 'how are we not to comprehend
that we must turn back from evil?
The wrong done by this destruction
is evident, O Shaker of Men.

40 'For with the family destroyed,
its eternal laws must perish;
and when they perish, lawlessness
overwhelms the whole family.

41 'Whelmed by lawlessness, the women
of the family are corrupted;
from corrupted women comes
the intermingling of classes.[5]

42 'Such intermingling sends to hell
the family and its destroyers:
their ancestors fall then, deprived
of rice and water offerings.[6]

---

4. One of Viṣṇu's 1,008 names in Hindu ritual and mythology, meaning "the one sweet as honey."
5. "Intermingling" here refers to miscegenation, and "classes" to caste-groups. The caste system is based on endogamy, or marriage within a caste-group (varṇa) or caste (jātī); only if both partners come from the same social category can that category be reproduced in the next generation. Here Kṛṣṇa affirms that if two spouses belong to different social categories (varṇa or jātī), then their children do not belong to the same category as their parents, and hence undermine the "laws of caste."
6. Hindus are required to make these ritual offerings to their ancestors.

43 'Those who destroy the family,
who institute class-mingling,
cause the laws of the family
and laws of caste to be abolished.

44 'Men whose familial laws have been
obliterated, O Krishna,
are damned to dwell eternally
in hell, as we have often heard.

45 'It grieves me that as we intend
to murder our relatives
in our greed for pleasures, kingdoms,
we are fixed on doing evil!

46 'If the sons of Dhritarashtra,
armed as they are, should murder me
weaponless and unresisting,
I would know greater happiness!'

47 "And having spoken, Arjuna
collapsed into his chariot,
his bow and arrows clattering,
and his mind overcome with grief."

CHAPTER TWO

* * *

"The Lord[7] said:

11 'Although you seem to speak wisely,
you have mourned those not to be mourned:
the wise do not grieve for those gone
or for those who are not yet gone.

12 'There was no time when I was not,
nor you, nor these lords around us,
and there will never be a time
henceforth when we shall not exist.

13 'The embodied one passes through
childhood, youth, and then old age,
then attains another body;
in this the wise are undeceived.[8]

7. Lord Kṛṣṇa, who now addresses Arjuna.
8. Here Kṛṣṇa explains the process of reincarnation, emphasizing the identity of the seemingly finite embodied soul (*ātman*) with the infinite and imperishable universal spirit or godhead (*Brahman*).

Karma Yoga

14   'Contacts with matter by which we
      feel heat and cold, pleasure and pain,
      are transitory, come and go:
      these you must manage to endure.

15   'Such contacts do not agitate
      a wise man, O Bull among Men,
      to whom pleasure and pain are one.
      He is fit for immortality.

16   'Non-being cannot come to be,
      nor can what is come to be not.
      The certainty of these sayings
      is known by seers of the truth.

17   'Know it as indestructible,
      that by which all is pervaded;
      no one may cause the destruction
      of the imperishable one.

18   'Bodies of the embodied one,
      eternal, boundless, all-enduring,
      are said to die; the one cannot:
      therefore, take arms, O Bharata!

19   'This man believes the one may kill;
      That man believes it may be killed;
      both of them lack understanding:
      it can neither kill nor be killed.

20   'It is not born, nor is it ever mortal,
      and having been, will not pass from existence;
      ancient, unborn, eternally existing,
      it does not die when the body perishes.

21   'How can a man who knows the one
      to be eternal (both unborn
      and without end) murder or cause
      another to? Whom does he kill?

22   'Someone who has abandoned worn-out garments
      sets out to clothe himself in brand new raiment;
      just so, when it has cast off worn-out bodies,
      the embodied one will encounter others.

23   'This may not be pierced by weapons,
      nor can this be consumed by flames;
      flowing waters cannot drench this,
      nor blowing winds desiccate this.

24 'Not to be pierced, not to be burned,
neither drenched nor desiccated—
eternal, all-pervading, firm,
unmoving, everlasting this!

25 'This has been called unmanifest,
unthinkable and unchanging;
therefore, because you know this now,
you should not lament, Arjuna.

26 'But even if you think that this
is born and dies time after time,
forever, O great warrior,
not even then should you mourn this.

27 'Death is assured to all those born,
and birth assured to all the dead;
you should not mourn what is merely
inevitable consequence.

28 'Beginnings are unmanifest,
but manifest the middle-state,
and ends unmanifest again;
so what is your complaint about?

29 'Somebody looks upon this as a marvel,
and likewise someone tells about this marvel,
and yet another hears about this marvel,
but even having heard it, no one knows it.

30 'The one cannot ever perish
in a body it inhabits,
O Descendent of Bharata;
and so no being should be mourned.

31 'Nor should you tremble to perceive
your duty as a warrior;
for him there is nothing better
than a battle that is righteous.

32 'And if by chance they will have gained
the wide open gate of heaven,
O Son of Pritha, warriors
rejoice in fighting such as that!

33 'If you turn from righteous warfare,
your behavior will be evil,
for you will have abandoned both
your duty and your honored name.

34 'People will speak of your disgrace
forever, and an honored man

who falls from honor into shame
suffers a fate much worse than death.

*   *   *

47 "'Your concern should be with action, *act itself however*
never with an action's fruits; *But not the reward*
these should never motivate you, *or penalty*
nor attachment to inaction.

48 'Established in this practice, act
without attachment, Arjuna,
unmoved by failure or success!
Equanimity is yoga. *alignment of God*

49 'Action is far inferior
to the practice of higher mind;
seek refuge there, for pitiful
are those moved by fruit of action!

50 'One disciplined by higher mind
here casts off good and bad actions;
therefore, be yoked to discipline;
discipline is skill in actions.

51 'Having left the fruit of action,
the wise ones yoked to higher mind
are freed from the bonds of rebirth,
and go where no corruption is.

52 'When your higher mind has crossed
over the thicket of delusion,
you will become disenchanted
with what is heard in the Vedas.[9]

53 'When, unvexed by revelation,
your higher mind is motionless
and stands fixed in meditation,
then you will attain discipline.'

"Arjuna asked,

54 'Tell me, Krishna, how may I know
the man steady in his wisdom,
who abides in meditation?
How should that one sit, speak and move?'

"The Blessed Lord replied,

---

9. Kṛṣṇa suggests here that the older ritualistic knowledge embodied in the Vedas is useless for the liberation of the individual self or soul from the bondage of karma.

55 'When he renounces all desires
    entering his mind, Arjuna,
    and his self rests within the Self,[1]
    then his wisdom is called steady.

56 'He who is not agitated
    by suffering or by desires,
    freed from anger, fear and passions,
    is called a sage of steady mind.

57 'Who is wholly unimpassioned,
    not rejoicing in the pleasant,
    nor rejecting the unpleasant,
    is established in his wisdom.

58 'And when this one wholly withdraws
    all his senses from their objects,
    as a tortoise draws in its limbs,
    his wisdom is well-established.'"

* * *

CHAPTER THREE

"Arjuna said:

1 'If you regard the intellect
    as superior to action,
    why urge me, O Handsome-Haired One,
    into actions so appalling?

2 'By your equivocating speech,
    my mind is, as it were, confused.
    Tell me this one thing, and clearly:
    By what means may I reach the best?'

"The Blessed Lord said:

3 'As I have previously taught,
    there are two paths, O Blameless One:
    there is the discipline of knowledge
    and the discipline of action.

4 'Not by not acting in this world
    does one become free from action,
    nor does one approach perfection
    by renunciation only.

---

1. This is a play on the word *ātman*, which means both "the self" (soul) and "oneself." Kṛṣṇa now begins to describe the techniques for and effects of "withdrawing" one's senses from interaction with the external world and focusing them instead on the interior self.

loka Sangraha
Welfare of the
world

5 'Not even for a moment does
someone exist without acting.
Even against one's will, one acts
by the nature-born qualities.[2]

6 'He who has restrained his senses,
but sits and summons back to mind
the sense-objects, is said to be
a self-deluding hypocrite.

7 'But he whose mind controls his senses,
who undertakes the discipline
of action by the action-organs,
without attachment, is renowned.

8 'You must act as bid, for action
is better than non-action is:
not even functions of the body
could be sustained by non-action.

9 'This world is bound by action, save
for action which is sacrifice;
therefore, O Son of Kunti, act
without attachment to your deeds.

10 'When Prajapati brought forth life,
he brought forth sacrifice as well,
saying, "By this may you produce,
may this be your wish-fulfilling cow."[3]

11 'Nourish the gods with sacrifice,
and they will nourish you as well.
By nourishing each other, you
will realize the highest good.

12 'Nourished by sacrifice, the gods
will give the pleasures you desire.
One who enjoys such gifts without
repaying them is just a thief.

13 'The good, who eat of the remains
from sacrifice, rise up faultless.
But the wicked, who cook only
for their own sakes, eat their own filth.

2. There are three such primary qualities: *sattva* (purity, light), *rajas* (passion, heat), and *tamas* (inertia, darkness).
3. In Vedic religion, Prajapati is the god (creator) of all mortal creatures. In Hindu mythology generally, *kāmadhenu* is a celestial cow who has the power to fulfill the wishes of any-one who worships her. Here Prajāpatī suggests that the act of sacrificing is itself like a wish-granting *kāmadhenu*. In the Vedic worldview, the preservation of the universe depends on the sacrifices made to the gods, and such ritual was at the center of the religion.

14 'Beings come to exist by food,
which emanates from the rain god,
who comes to be by sacrifice,
which arises out of action.

15 'Know that action comes from Brahman,
Brahman comes from the eternal;
so the all-pervading Brahman
is based in sacrifice forever.

16 'One who in this world does not turn
the wheel, thus setting it in motion,
lives uselessly, O Son of Pritha,
a sensual, malicious life.

17 'But the man whose only pleasure
and satisfaction is the self,
which is his sole contentment too,
has no task he must accomplish.

18 'That man finds no significance
in what has, or has not, been done;
moreover, he does not depend
on any being whatsoever.

19 'Therefore, act without attachment
in whatever situation,
for by the practice of detached
action, one attains the highest.

20 'Only by action Janaka[4]
and the others reached perfection.
In order to maintain the world,
your obligation is to act.

21 'Whatever the best leader does
the rank and file will also do;
everyone will fall in behind
the standard such a leader sets.

22 'O Son of Pritha, there is nought
that I need do in the three worlds,[5]
nor anything I might attain;
and yet I take part in action.

23 'For if I were not always to
engage in action ceaselessly,

---

4. Celebrated character in the dialogues of
the Bṛhadāraṇyaka Upaniṣad; an exemplar of
the warrior-king who is also a man of discipline (a yogi).
5. Heaven, earth, and the underworld.

men everywhere would soon follow
in my path, O Son of Pritha.

24 'Should I not engage in action,
these worlds would perish, utterly;
I would cause a great confusion,
and destroy all living beings.

25 'The unwise are attached to action
even as they act, Arjuna;
so, for the welfare of the world,
the wise should act with detachment.'"

* * *

"Arjuna said:

36 'Say what impels a man to do
such evil, Krishna, what great force
urges him, forces him into it,
even if he is unwilling?'

"The Blessed Lord said:

37 'Know that the enemy is this:
desire, anger, whose origins
are in the quality of passion,
all consuming, greatly harmful.

38 'As fire is obscured by smoke,
or by dust, a mirror's surface,
or an embryo by its membrane,
so this is covered up by that.

39 'Knowledge is constantly obscured
by this enemy of the wise,
by this insatiable fire
whose form, Arjuna, is desire.

40 'The senses, mind, and intellect
are its abode, as it is said.
Having obscured knowledge with these,
it deludes the embodied one.

41 'When you have subdued your senses,
then, O Bull of the Bharatas,
kill this demon, the destroyer
of all knowledge and discernment.

42 'Senses are said to be important,
but mind is higher than they are,
and intellect is above mind;
but Self is greater than all these.

43   'So knowing it to be supreme,
       and sustaining the self with Self,
       slay the foe whose form is desire,
       so hard to conquer, Arjuna.'"

CHAPTER SIX

* * *

10   "'The yogi should be self-subdued
       always, and stand in solitude,
       alone, controlled in thought and self,
       without desires or possessions.

controlling the mind and fixing it on the divine who is Krishna

11   'Having established for himself
       a steady seat in a pure place,
       neither too high nor yet too low,
       covered with grass, deer hide and cloth,

12   'with his mind sharpened to one point,
       with thought and senses both subdued,
       there he should sit, doing yoga
       so as to purify the self,

13   'keeping his head, neck and body
       aligned, erect and motionless,
       gaze fixed on the tip of his nose,
       not looking off distractedly,

14   'now fearless and with tranquil self,
       firm in avowed celibacy,
       with his thought focused on myself,
       he should sit, devoted to me.

15   'Thus always chastening himself
       the yogi's mind, subdued, knows peace,
       whose farthest point is cessation;
       thereafter, he abides in me.

16   'Yoga is not for the greedy,
       nor yet for the abstemious;
       not for one too used to sleeping,
       nor for the sleepless, Arjuna.

17   'Yoga destroys the pain of one
       temperate in his behavior,
       in his food and recreation,
       and in his sleep and waking too.

18   'After his thought has been subdued,
       and abides only in the Self,
       free from all longing and desire,
       then he is said to be steadfast.

19 '"Like a lamp in a windless place
unflickering," is the likeness
of the yogi subdued in thought,
performing yoga of the Self.

20 'Where all thought comes to cease, restrained
by the discipline of yoga,
where, by the self, the Self is seen,
one is satisfied in the Self.

21 'When he knows that eternal joy
grasped only by the intellect,
beyond the senses where he dwells,
he does not deviate from truth;

22 'having attained it, he believes
there is no gain superior;
abiding there, he is unmoved
even by profound suffering.

23 'Let him know that the dissolving
of the union with suffering
is called yoga, to be practiced
with persistence, mind undaunted.

24 'Having abandoned all desires
born to satisfy intentions,
and having utterly restrained
the many senses by the mind,

25 'Gradually let him find rest,
his intellect under control,
his mind established in the Self,
not thinking about anything.

26 'Having subdued the unsteady
mind in motion, he should lead it
back from wherever it strays to,
into the domain of the Self.

27 'Supreme joy comes to the yogi
of calm mind and tranquil passion,
who has become one with Brahman
and is wholly free of evil.

28 'Constantly controlling himself,
the yogi, freed from evil now,
swiftly attains perpetual
joy of contact here with Brahman.

29 'He whose self is yoked by yoga
and who perceives sameness always,
will see the Self in all beings
and see all beings in the Self.

30 'I am not lost for someone who
perceives my presence everywhere,
and everything perceives in me,
nor is that person lost for me.

31 'The yogi firmly set in oneness
who worships me in all beings,
whatever the path that he takes,
will nonetheless abide in me.

32 'The yogi who sees all the same
analogous to his own Self
in happiness or suffering
is thought supreme, O Arjuna.'"

Summary   In Chapters Seven through Ten, Krishna explains diverse aspects of the nature
of the infinite spirit, gradually unveiling the mystery of his own identity as the highest manifestation of that universal spirit and thus leading up to the revelation of his cosmic form in Chapter Eleven.

CHAPTER ELEVEN

"Arjuna said,

1 'As a result of your kindness
in speaking of that greatest secret
recognized as the Supreme Self,
I have been left undeluded.

2 'I have, in detail, heard you speak
Of creatures' origins and ends,
and of your eternal greatness,
O One of Lotus-Petal-Eyes.

3 'This is just as you have spoken
about yourself, O Supreme Lord.
I desire to behold your
lordly form, O Supreme Spirit.

4 'If you think it is possible
for me to see this, then, O God,
O Lord of Yoga, allow me
to behold your eternal Self!'

"The Blessed Lord said,

5 'O Son of Pritha, look upon
my hundredfold, no, thousandfold
forms various and celestial,
forms of diverse shapes and colors!

6 'Behold the Adityas and Vasus,
the Rudras, Ashvins and Maruts,[6]
many unseen previously!
Behold these wonders, Arjuna!

7 'Here behold all the universe,
beings moving and motionless,
standing as one in my body,
and all else that you wish to see!

8 'Because you are unable to
behold me with your mortal eye,
I give you one that is divine:
Behold my majestic power!'"

Sanjaya[7] said,

9 "And after saying this, O King,
Vishnu, the great Lord of Yoga,
revealed his supreme, majestic
form to him, the Son of Pritha.

10 "That form has many eyes and mouths,
and many wonders visible,
with many sacred ornaments,
and many sacred weapons raised.

11 "Clothed in sacred wreaths and garments,
with many sacred fragrances,
and comprising every wonder,
the infinite, omniscient god!

12 "If in the sky a thousand suns
should have risen all together,
the brilliance of it would be like
the brilliance of that Great-Souled One.

13 "And then the Son of Pandu saw
the universe standing as one,
divided up in diverse ways,
embodied in the god of gods."

* * *

"Arjuna said:

43 'Father of all the world, the still and moving,
you are what it worships and its teacher;
with none your match, how could there be one greater
in the three worlds, O Power-Without-Equal?

6. Groups of Hindu deities: Adityas are sun gods; Vasus are elemental deities; Rudras are wind gods; the Ashvins are twin gods of sunrise and sunset; and the Maruts are storm gods.
7. The bard who is narrating the events of the battle to King Dhṛtarāṣṭra.

44 'Making obeisance, lying in prostration,
I beg your indulgence, praiseworthy ruler;
as father to son, as one friend to another,
as lover to beloved, show your mercy!

45 'I am pleased to have seen what never has been
seen before, yet my mind quakes in its terror:
show me, O God, your human form; have mercy,
O Lord of Gods, abode of all the cosmos!

46 'I wish to see you even as I did once,
wearing a diadem, with mace and discus;
assume that form now wherein you have four arms,
O thousand-armed, of every form the master!'

"The Blessed Lord said,

47 'For you, Arjuna, by my grace and favor,
this highest form is brought forth by my power,
of splendor made, universal, endless, primal,
and never seen before by any other.

48 'Not Vedic sacrifice nor recitation,
gifts, rituals, strenuous austerities,
will let this form of mine be seen by any
mortal but you, O Hero of the Kurus!

49 'You should not tremble, nor dwell in confusion
at seeing such a terrible appearance.
With your fears banished and your mind now cheerful,
look once again upon my form, Arjuna.'

Sanjaya said,

50 "So Krishna, having spoken to Arjuna,
stood before him once more in his own aspect;
having resumed again a gentle body,
the Great Soul calmed the one who had been frightened.

"Arjuna said,

51 'Seeing once again your gentle,
human form now, I am composed,
O Agitator of Mankind;
my mind is restored to normal.'

"The Blessed Lord said,

52 'It is difficult to see this
aspect of me that you have seen;
even the gods are forever
desirous of seeing it.

53 'Not by studying the Vedas,
    nor even by austerities,
    and not by gifts or sacrifice,
    may I be seen as you saw me;

54 'but by devotion undisturbed
    can I be truly seen and known,
    and entered into, Arjuna,
    O Scorcher of the Enemy!

55 'Who acts for me, depends on me,
    devoutly, without attachment
    or hatred for another being,
    comes to me, O Son of Pandu!'"

III

Early Chinese Literature and Thought

M any great civilizations have perished with little consequence. What we know of them comes from the imaginative recon-structions of scholars, from inscriptions, and from the accounts of early travelers. Civilizations like those of ancient Egypt and Mesopotamia left exten-sive written records that were swept aside by other civilizations; the very names by which we refer to them—Egypt and Mesopotamia—are Greek. This is not the case with China, the oldest surviving civi-lization, whose literary tradition stretches over more than three thousand years. Its earliest literature set patterns and posed questions that shaped the actions and values of the Chinese people for thou-sands of years, serving as the connective tissue that gave its civilization a sense of unity and continuity.

Throughout China's long history, its territories, ruling classes, capitals, religions, and customs kept changing with the rise and fall of ruling dynasties; and its peoples have spoken a great number of widely divergent Chinese dialects as well as many non-Chinese languages from the Turkic, Mongo-lian, and even Indo-European language families. Thus, China might easily have become fragmented by regional interests and linguistic differences like

A contemporary rubbing made from a Han Dynasty (206 B.C.E.–220 C.E.) earthenware tile that depicts scenes of hunting and harvesting.

Europe after the fall of the Roman Empire. But whereas Rome was truly a conquest empire, a political center that ruled over many peoples, each with its own sense of distinct ethnic identity, traditional China was an idea tied to cultural values and the power of the written word. Certainly, Chinese emperors did at certain times in history conquer territories as remote as Korea, Vietnam, Tibet, and Taiwan. But China could survive periods of turmoil and even rule by non-Chinese conquerors such as the Mongols and the Manchus because peoples on the margins of the ancient heartland had for centuries been adopting China's writing, cultural values, and institutions, and had thus become "Chinese." Many times in China's history, regional identity has become subordinate to a belief in cultural and political unity.

BEGINNINGS: EARLY SAGE RULERS

Although China has always been in contact with western parts of the Eurasian landmass, it developed independently from the earlier Mesopotamian, Egyptian, and Indus Valley city civilizations. By the third millennium B.C.E. at least a dozen Neolithic (New Stone Age) cultures flourished along the Yellow River in the north and the Yangzi River in the south. By the second millennium B.C.E. most settlements had defensive walls made of rammed earth, a sign of the increasing influence of military elites, who defended the populace against other rising city-states. Later Chinese historians placed into this early period a lineage of sage rulers who laid the foundations for Chinese civilization. Fu Xi reputedly taught people how to raise silkworms. He also invented the eight trigrams, symbols consisting of three broken or unbroken (Yin and Yang) lines each,

which became the basis for China's canonical divination text, the *Classic of Changes (Yijing)*. Shennong invented the plow and instructed people in the use of medicinal herbs. Huangdi, the "Yellow Emperor," was a patron of medicine and agriculture. His scribe, Cang Jie, invented writing by creating graphs that imitated the articulate tracks of birds, realizing that the new technology "could regulate the various professions and keep under scrutiny the various kinds of people." Among three later sage rulers, Yao disinherited his inept son and chose a commoner to succeed him on the throne, thus establishing the principle of virtue and merit over blood lineage. This commoner, Shun, was an ideal ruler and a model of filial piety (he remained true to his parents despite their repeated attempts to kill him). His successor, the Great Yu, showed exemplary dedication to the welfare of his people and invented irrigation, constructing channels to tame the Great Flood that occurred during his reign.

Encapsulated in this lineage of legendary rulers are fundamental values of Chinese civilization: the importance of writing and divination; an economy based on intensive agriculture and silk production; a political philosophy of virtue that emphasizes fixed social roles; and practices of self-cultivation and herbal medicine.

EARLIEST DYNASTIES: CHINA DURING THE BRONZE AGE AND THE BEGINNING OF WRITING

China's Bronze Age began around 2000 B.C.E. By 1200 B.C.E., cultures in several regions of China made ample use of bronze for the molding of more effective weapons, for the new technology of spoke-wheel chariots, and for the production of ritual bronze ves-

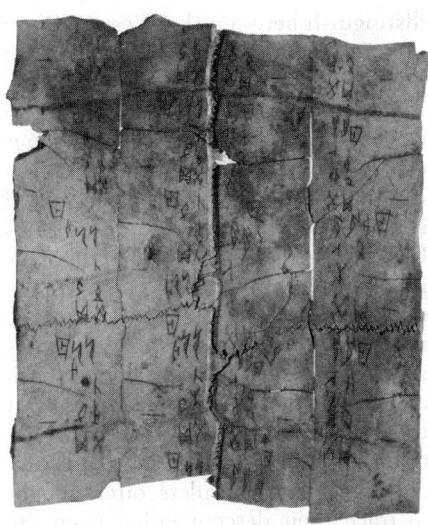

This tortoiseshell, inscribed with writing dating from ca. 1200 B.C.E., was used for ceremonial divination.

sels used in ceremonies for gods and ancestors. A small area in the Yellow River basin of north-central China is the best known of these Bronze Age cultures: thanks to the groundbreaking archeological discovery of inscriptions on tortoiseshells and cattle bones in 1898, this area could be identified as the so-called second dynasty—the Shang (ca. 1500–1045 B.C.E.). The first dynasty is traditionally identified as the Xia, whose name and list of kings are recorded in later texts, but whose existence hasn't been linked conclusively to any of the known Bronze Age archeological sites.

The Shang was a loose confederation of city-states with a complex state system, large settlements, and, most important, a common writing system. Although it remains unclear when the Chinese script began to be developed, it appeared as a fully functional writing system during the later period of the Shang dynasty. To date, more than 48,000 fragments of inscribed shells and bones have been found. These so-called oracle bone inscriptions are usu-

ally short records of divination rituals. Ritual specialists and the Shang kings would apply heat to the bones and use the resulting cracks to interpret or predict events: determining weather, harvest, floods, or tribute payments; divining the outcome of imminent war or the birth of male offspring; or even finding the causes for the toothache of a royal family member. Thus, writing was part of ritual practices that guided political decision making and harmonized the relation between human beings and the world of unpredictable spiritual forces in the cosmos. Its use was a prerogative of the Shang king and his elites.

From the inscriptions we can see that the Shang kings paid meticulous attention to the veneration of their dead ancestors and various gods, including the highest god, *Di*, who also commanded rain and thunder. They used war captives as slaves and sacrificial victims and employed conscript workers for monumental labor projects. For example, the sumptuous grave

Among the many objects fashioned out of bronze during the Shang Dynasty were "fangding," ritual vessels for cooking and presenting food. This fangding is the only extant example that is decorated with a human face.

site of Lady Hao, one of the prominent Shang king Wu Ding's many wives, contained hundreds of bronze objects.

THE ZHOU CONQUEST AND THE "MANDATE OF HEAVEN"

Around 1045 B.C.E. the Zhou people overthrew the Shang. The Zhou were an agrarian people and former allies of the Shang. Their justification of the conquest set the model for subsequent dynastic shifts in Chinese history. Texts recorded during the first centuries of Zhou rule claimed that a new power, "Heaven," transferred the political mandate to the Zhou, because the moral worth of the Shang had declined and the last Shang rulers were decadent tyrants without regard for the people. In turn, the first rulers of the Zhou, King Wen (the "cultured" or "civilized" king) and his son King Wu (the "martial" king), who completed the conquest, were praised as paragons of virtue and "sons of Heaven" deserving of the mandate. After the Zhou conquest, the claim to power in China depended on the claim to virtuous rule, which in large measure meant holding to the statutes and models of the earliest sage rulers and the virtuous early Zhou kings.

THE DECLINE OF THE EASTERN ZHOU AND THE AGE OF CHINA'S PHILOSOPHICAL MASTERS

After their conquest, the early Zhou kings rewarded their allies with gifts of land. But initially strong personal ties between the Zhou kings and their allies weakened over the centuries, and in 771 B.C.E. some vassals joined forces with nomadic tribesmen and killed the king. The Zhou court fled and moved the capital to the east. Historians thus distinguish between the Western Zhou (1045–771 B.C.E.) and the Eastern Zhou (770–256 B.C.E.) periods. The Zhou kings never regained full control over their vassals. Although its kings continued to rule for another five centuries, the Eastern Zhou Dynasty lacked strong central authority, allowing its former vassals to build up their domains into belligerent independent states. On the southern and western borders of the old Zhou domain, powerful new states arose: Chu, Wu, and Yue in the south and Qin in the west. Although many of these new kingdoms had their distinct traditions, they gradually absorbed Zhou culture, and their rulers often sought to trace their descent either from the Zhou royal house or from more ancient, northern Chinese ancestors. Just before the defeat of the Western Zhou, there were around two hundred lords with domains of varying size, all under the titular rule of the Zhou king. By the third century B.C.E., only seven powerful states were left in the struggle over supremacy, and in 256 B.C.E. the last Zhou king was killed.

The Eastern Zhou Period was one of the most formative periods in Chinese history. The Eastern Zhou rulers built new institutions, and among its vassal states a lively interstate diplomacy unfolded; new military technology revolutionized warfare, and the old aristocracy was gradually dismantled and replaced by a new class of advisers and strategists. During the earlier part of the Eastern Zhou Period, the so-called Spring and Autumn Annals Period (722–481 B.C.E., named after the court chronicle of Confucius's home state of Lu in eastern China), the old aristocracy in their chariots were still central to combat, and an honor code of military conduct was respected. Battles started with an agreement on both sides, states that were in mourning for their rulers were not attacked, and, if a state was defeated, the conqueror respectfully continued the ancestral sacrifices for the vanquished ruling lineage. This changed dramatically during the latter half of the Eastern Zhou, the so-called Warring States Period (403–221 B.C.E., named after a collection of stories about political intrigues between the Zhou states): mass infantry armies built on coercive drafts replaced the old aristocracy; raw power politics and strategic deception became the norm; the newly invented crossbow allowed soldiers to kill their enemies at greater distance, not in noble close combat; and rulers of the larger Zhou states started to call themselves kings, indicating that they not only defied the authority of the Zhou king but also intended to replace him as ruler over all of China.

It was in this climate that **Confucius**, and the philosophical masters who followed in his wake, formulated visions of how to live and govern well in a corrupt world. Chinese call this the period when "a hundred schools of thought bloomed." The Eastern Zhou Period coincides with the period when the religions and philosophies of ancient India, Greece, Persia, and Israel took shape, and scholars have compared the social and political conditions facilitating this flourishing in these different civilizations. In China, rulers of the feudal states employed able advisers, or "masters," to help them gain more resources, territory, and power, and the Chinese masters often moved between states in search for employment and patronage.

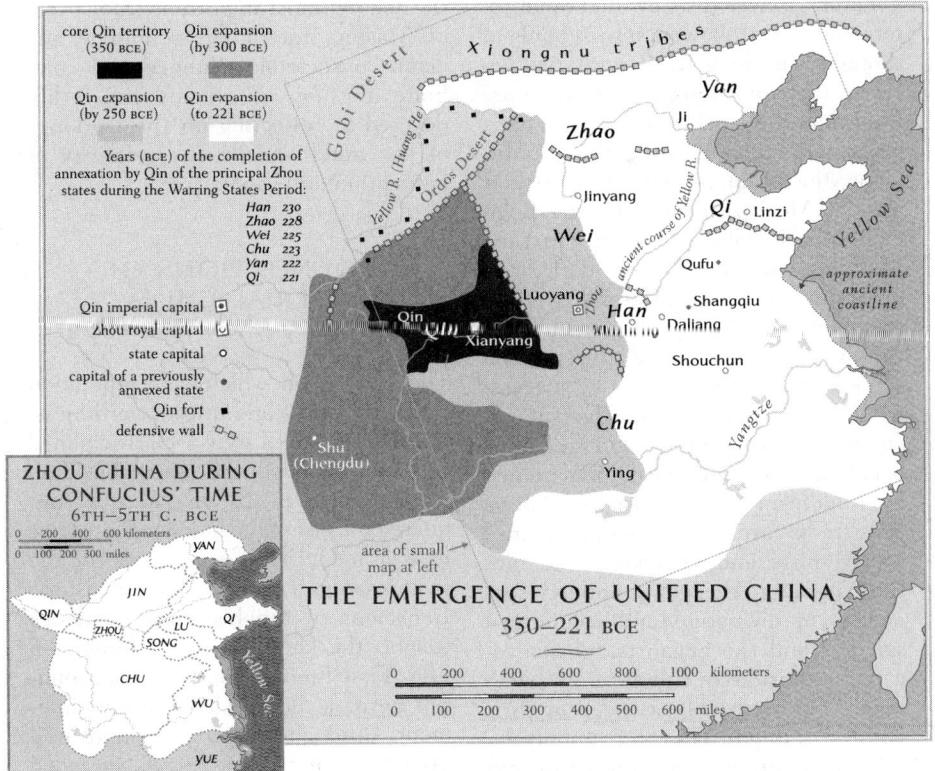

Chinese call the texts written by masters or compiled by their disciples "Masters Literature." This name derives from texts that show a charismatic master in vivid conversation with disciples, rulers, or other contemporaries. Masters Literature flourished from the time of Confucius through the Han Dynasty (206 B.C.E.–220 C.E.). This rich corpus of texts, represented in this anthology by selections from the *Analects*, and from *Laozi* and *Zhuangzi*, reveals the broad spectrum of opinions on fundamental questions: How can we create social order in a society that is incessantly at war? How can we become exemplary, fulfilled human beings in a less-than-ideal society? How can we make use of history and existing precedents to create a better future? How should we use words, and what impact can words and ideas have on social reality?

Later Chinese texts divided the masters and their followers into schools of thought, although the boundaries between their positions were often more fluid than the labels suggest. The most prominent schools were the Confucians, the Mohists (named after their master, Mozi), the Daoists, the Logicians, the Legalists, and the Yin-Yang Masters, each advocating their own programs, adopting different styles of argument, and engaging the rival camps in polemical disputes. The schools had varied degrees of success: while Confucianism and Daoism became the intellectual and religious backbone of traditional China (joined by Buddhism after it reached China from India around the Common Era), the Mohists and Logicians died out, the Yin-Yang Masters produced specialists in divination and calendrical science, and the Legalists, who advocated authoritarian rule through harsh laws, became the black sheep of early Chinese thought. They were openly decried as tyrannical and inhuman, but

many of their ideas and methods were used by the architects of the imperial bureaucracy throughout the centuries.

Confucius, the first and most exemplary master whose sayings are preserved in the *Analects*, believed that a return to the values of the virtuous early Zhou kings, a respect for social hierarchies, self-cultivation through proper ritual behavior, and the study of ancient texts could bring order. The most radical opponents of Confucius and his followers were thinkers who advocated passivity and following of the natural "way," or *dao*. The Daoists had a deep mistrust of human-made things: conscious effort, artifice, and words. *Laozi*, a collection of poems and the foundational text of Daoism, proposed passivity as a means of ultimately prevailing over one's opponents and gaining spiritual and political control. By contrast, many passages in *Zhuangzi*, the second most important Daoist text of Masters Literature, renounce any claim to societal influence and celebrate the joy of an unharmed life devoted to reflecting on the workings of the mind and on the relativity of perception and values.

FOUNDATIONS OF IMPERIAL CHINA: THE QIN AND THE HAN

The state of Qin, which had a reputation for ruthlessness and untrustworthiness, but whose armies were well disciplined and well supplied, destroyed the Zhou royal domain in 256 B.C.E. and conquered the last of the independent states in 221 B.C.E. That year is one of the most important dates in Chinese history. Conscious of the historical moment's weight, the king of Qin conferred the title "First Emperor of Qin" upon himself to mark the novelty of his achievement. Although the Qin was a short-lived dynasty, many of its measures—designed to create a new type of state with a strong centralized bureaucracy—were adopted and adapted by the rulers of the subsequent Han Dynasty (206 B.C.E.–220 C.E.). With the Qin unification, China was finally an empire. Imperial China, with its upheavals, dynastic shifts, and momentous changes, would last another 2,100 years—until the Republican Revolution of 1911.

Some scholars credit the Qin Dynasty's policy reforms with the success of the Chinese empire. Since the fourth century B.C.E. ministers associated with the Legalist school advised the kings of Qin to reduce the power of the old nobility and to base governance on a direct connection between ruler and bureaucrats controlled by the strict rule of written law codes and policies. In the decades before the Qin unification, the Legalist thinker Han Feizi (d. ca. 233 B.C.E.) had found particular favor with the king of Qin. Although Han Feizi was ultimately forced into

suicide by the slander of suspicious colleagues, his vision of governance was adopted for the new empire.

The First Emperor's megalomania became legendary in later Chinese history, exerting as much fascination as horror. Though much of his statecraft was subtle, many of his most famous policies had a chilling simplicity. Some, such as unifying the currency, the various scripts, and the weights and measures used in different states, deserve credit. But his solution to intellectual disagreement was the suppression of scholars and the burning of all books except for practical manuals of medicine, agriculture, and divination and for the historical records of Qin. The "Qin Burning of the Books," of 213 B.C.E., was one of the most traumatic events in Chinese history.

After the death of the First Emperor, rebellions broke out. Many of the rebels tried to restore the old pre-Qin states, but the final winner, a simple

Perhaps the most illustrative symbol of the First Emperor's megalomania and imperial ambitions is the vast terra-cotta army, unearthed in 1974, that the emperor had buried with him. Over 7,000 life-size sculptures fill the burial site.

commoner named Liu Bang, became the first emperor of the Han Dynasty and continued the centralized government strategy of the Qin, while eliminating its unpopular features, loosening some particularly cruel laws, cutting taxes, and refraining from the constant labor mobilizations that the Qin emperor had forced on his people.

The Han Dynasty lasted more than four hundred years and was a crucial phase of imperial consolidation that set patterns for future Chinese dynasties. During this period China expanded its boundaries into Central Asia and parts of modern Korea and Vietnam. Han emperors learned to deal with the challenging threat of northern frontier tribes, developing strategies that proved effective for subsequent empires: fight them, pay them off, or appease them

with marriage alliances, offering Chinese princesses as brides to the tribal chieftains.

The most influential Han ruler was Emperor Wu, whose long reign lasted from 141 to 87 B.C.E. He undertook costly campaigns to expand the empire and established government monopolies on the production of iron, salt, and liquor to finance them. He was a generous patron of the arts, of music, and of scholarship. Although he was intrigued by immortality techniques, portents, and the occult, he was the first emperor to privilege Confucian scholars, founding a state academy for the education of government officials and setting up positions for professors to teach the so-called Five Classics: the *Classic of Changes*, used for divination; the *Classic of Documents*, a collection of proclamations by early

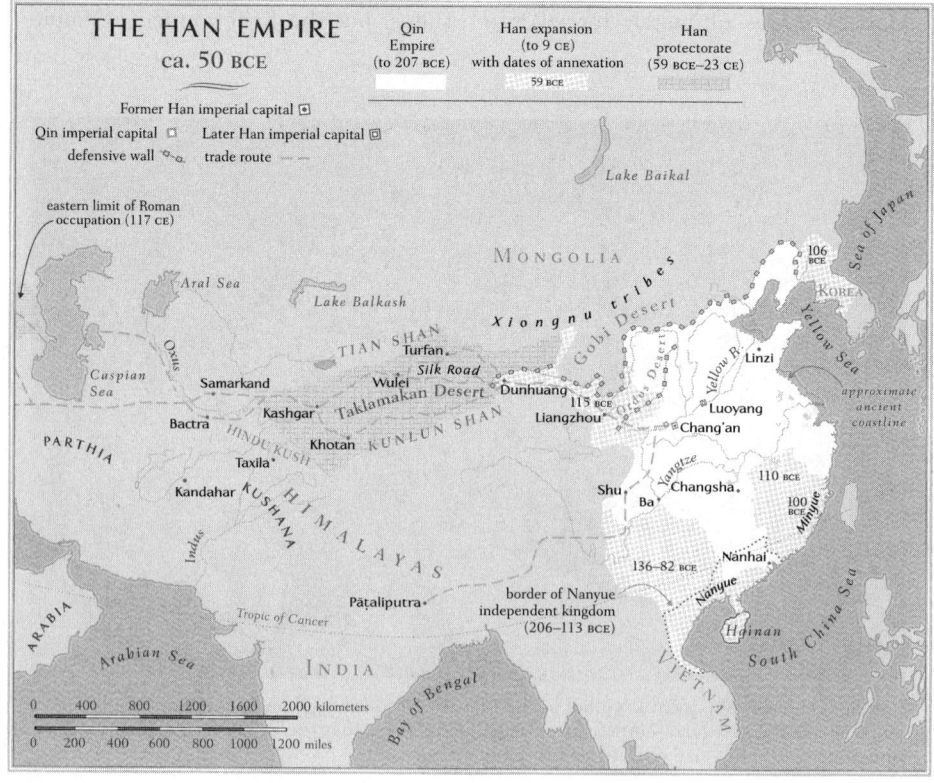

sage kings and ministers; the **Classic of Poetry**, a collection of poetry including hymns to the Zhou ancestors and ballads recounting the history of the Zhou; the *Spring and Autumn Annals*, a historical chronicle, and the *Record of Rites*, the most important of several works on ritual. During Emperor Wu's reign the first comprehensive history of China was written, by a court historian and his son, Sima Qian (ca. 145–86 B.C.E.), who suffered the punishment of castration for a minor disagreement with Emperor Wu but persisted in finishing his monumental history, which became the model for subsequent dynastic histories of China into the twentieth century.

Early China was a groundbreaking period of enduring influence on all subsequent periods of Chinese history. These first 1,500 years of Chinese history, from the Shang Dynasty to the end of the Han Dynasty, saw the emergence of enduring political institutions and ideologies, of moral standards and social manners. The literature produced during this period encapsulates these values and formative patterns and is still the canonical foundation of Chinese civilization.

CLASSIC OF POETRY

ca. 1000–600 B.C.E.

Standing at the beginning of China's three-millennia-long literary tradition, the *Classic of Poetry* (also *Book of Songs* or *Book of Odes*) is the oldest poetry collection of East Asia. Its poems reflect the breadth of early Chinese society. Some poems convey the history and values of the earlier part of the Zhou Dynasty (ca. 1045–256 B.C.E.), whose founding kings set a standard of ideal governance for later generations. Others treat themes familiar from folk ballads: courtship, marriage and love, birth and death, and the stages of the agricultural cycle such as planting and harvesting. Filled with images of nature and the plain life of an agricultural society, the *Classic of Poetry* offers a distinctive, fresh simplicity. Because of the collection's canonical status, centuries of commentary and interpretation have accrued around it, adding to its meaning and significance and endowing the simple scenes in the poems with moral or political purpose. The anthology has had a profound impact on the literatures of Korea, Japan, and Vietnam and was an important element of the traditional curriculum throughout East Asia until the beginning of the twentieth century.

THE ANTHOLOGY AND ITS SIGNIFICANCE

While other ancient literary traditions were founded on epics about gods and heroes, or sprawling legends about the origins of the cosmos, the *Classic of Poetry* provided a different sort of foundation for Chinese literature, made up of the compact and evocative form of lyric poetry. Because Chinese literature originated with the *Classic of Poetry*, short verse gained a degree of political, social, and pedagogical importance in East Asia that it has hardly enjoyed anywhere else in the world.

The *Classic of Poetry* contains 305 poems and consists of three parts, the "Airs of the Domains" (*Guofeng*, 160 poems), the "Odes/Elegances" (*Ya*, 105 poems), and the "Hymns" (*Song*, 40 poems). The "Hymns" are the oldest part and contain songs used in ritual performances to celebrate the Zhou royal house. Next are the "Odes," narrative ballads about memorable historical events. The youngest poems are the "Airs of the Domains," based on folk ballads from some fifteen domains of the Zhou kingdom. (The early Zhou kings gave lands to their loyal vassals and gradually built a multistate system of "domains" extending from modern-day Beijing far beyond the Yangtze River in the south.) Tradition credited **Confucius**, the most important of the early philosophical masters, with the compilation of the *Classic of Poetry*. He allegedly selected the poems in the collection from three thousand poems he found in the archives of the Zhou kingdom. Therefore, the choice and arrangement of the poems were seen as an expression of Confucius's philosophy. Confucius believed that political order depended on the ability of individuals in society to cultivate their moral virtue and thus contribute to social order. We know from the *Analects*, a collection containing Confucius's sayings, that Confucius thought highly of the

Classic of Poetry. He advised his own son to study the *Classic of Poetry* to enhance his ability to express his opinions, he praised disciples who quoted passages from the *Classic of Poetry* to make a particular point, and he saw a comprehensive educational program in the anthology: "The *Classic of Poetry* can provide you with stimulation and with observation, with a capacity for communion, and with a vehicle for grief. At home, they [the poems] enable you to serve your father, and abroad, to serve your lord. Also, you will learn there the names of many birds, animals, plants, and trees." Confucius's high opinion of the *Classic of Poetry* led to its inclusion in the canon of "Confucian Classics," which became the curriculum of the state academy that Emperor Wu of the Han Dynasty founded in 124 B.C.E.

As a further sign of the *Classic of Poetry's* canonization during the Han Dynasty, a "Great Preface" written for the anthology became the single most fundamental statement about the nature and function of poetry in East Asia. Written more than half a millennium after the anthology's compilation, the "Great Preface" claimed that there were "six principles" (*liu yi*) of poetry: the three categories in which the poems were placed ("Airs of the Domains," "Odes," and "Hymns") and the three rhetorical devices of "enumeration" (*fu*), "comparison" (*bi*), and "evocative image" (*xing*). Scholars and poets have debated the usefulness and precise meaning of these principles for the last two millennia, but on a basic level the principles illuminate rhetorical patterns that distinguish the *Classic of Poetry* and even later Chinese poetry. The concept of *feng* is a good case in point: it refers to the "Airs of the Domains" section of the anthology, but it also contains a rich web of associations that grew up around its literal meaning, "wind": Like wind that causes grass to sway, the ruler can

"influence" (*feng*) his people and instill virtuous behavior in them through poetry. For their part, his subjects can express their dissatisfaction with their ruler through "criticism" (*feng*). In reality, most poems in the anthology contain at best indirect criticism. But the idea that poetry and song can bridge the gulf between social classes, that they can serve as a tool for mutual "influence" and "criticism" and give the people a voice, helping them keep bad rulers in check, was central to the Confucian understanding of poetry and society. Poetry made room for social critique and created the institution of "remonstration," the duty of officials in the bureaucracy to speak out against abuses of power.

THE POEMS

Our selections come from the "Odes" section ("She Bore the Folk") and the "Airs" section (all other poems). Although almost all poems in the *Classic of Poetry* are anonymous, they give voice to many different players in Zhou society, such as kings, aristocrats and peasants, men and women in love, and, collectively, to communities as they celebrate harvest or worship their ancestors. Poems put into the mouths of peasants or soldiers show considerable literary skill, which suggests that a member of the educated elite at the courts of the Zhou domains must have given them their final shape.

The constraints imposed by society and the conflict between individual desire and social expectations are important themes in the "Airs" section. Marriage is often praised as a sanctioned form of sexual relation, but some poems also celebrate the pleasures of transgression. "Boat of Cypress" is a remarkable outcry of a heart that refuses to bend to society's wishes. Unlike the virtuous Zhou Dynasty, the domain of Zheng and its music were associated with sensual pleasures: "Zhen and Wei," for example, depicts a festival scene along two rivers. Although its frolicking man and woman do not go beyond politely exchanging flowers as courtship gifts, the scene is highly charged with eroticism.

The protagonists in the romantic plots that appear in the poems of the "Airs of the Domains" could be from any culture past or present, but the extensive tradition of commentaries endowed these poems with specific moral and historical significance. According to the canonical "Mao commentary," "Fishhawk," the first poem of the Classic of Poetry, in which a young man is tormented by his desire for a girl, is not a simple romantic folk song. Instead, the commentary claims that the poem praises the consort of King Wen for being free from jealousy when her husband takes a new consort, a typical situation in traditional Chinese society, where men could have several wives. This counterintuitive reading of the poem established "Fishhawk" as a model of exemplary female behavior for all times and embedded it in the history of the early Zhou kings.

The central stylistic device of the Classic of Poetry is repetition with variation. Many of the poems consist of three rhyming stanzas of four or six lines with four syllables each. The stanza format encourages line repetitions, which give the poems melodic rhythm and, with the introduction of small variations, additional meaning. In "Plums Are Falling," the fruits become fewer with each repetition until the woman has finally decided whom among her suitors she wants to marry. In "Peach Tree Soft and Tender," the peach tree goes through the natural cycle of bearing blossoms, fruits, and leaves while a new bride, who it is hoped will bear many descendants for the family line, is introduced into the household. Far from being a simplistic rhetorical device, repetition with variation gives compelling shape to a suitor's

intrusive desire and his lover's fear of scandal in "Zhongzi, Please." As the insolent Zhongzi systematically advances stanza by stanza from the village wall to the family's fence and through the garden towards his lover's bedchamber, the helpless woman, fearing her parents' and brothers' reproach and society's disapproval, fends her lover off by promising to keep him in her thoughts.

Among the rhetorical devices listed in the "Great Preface" to the Classic of Poetry, "enumeration" and "evocative image" are particularly interesting. Enumeration, the telling of sequences of events in straightforward narrative fashion, structures longer odes like "She Bore the Folk," a poem on the miraculous birth of Lord Millet, the inventor of agriculture and legendary ancestor of the Zhou people. Lord Millet's birth by a resourceful mother who steps into a god's footprint and his subsequent development into the Zhou's ancestor and cultural hero are recounted through vivid enumeration. Enumeration also lists the order of the ritual acts that the Zhou people perform to celebrate the harvest and commemorate their ancestor. Poems from the "Airs" section, by contrast, mostly employ "comparisons" and "evocative images." Comparisons are like similes: "Huge Rat" compares an exploitative lord directly to a voracious rodent. Evocative images are much more elusive and do not easily translate into any rhetorical trope in the Western tradition. Xing, the term rendered as "evocative image," literally means "stimulus" or "excitement." Xing brings natural images into suggestive resonance with human situations, stimulating the imagination and pushing perception beyond a simple comparison of one thing to another. Often, the animals or plants used to evoke human situations appear in the same scene with the human protagonists, but the relation between the animals or plants and the humans is mysterious. For example, in "Dead Roe Deer" the reader sees a landscape in which a girl, a "maiden white as marble," who has just been seduced by a man, hovers next to a dead deer "wrapped in white rushes."

The resonant, elusive imagery of the *Classic of Poetry* has enticed readers through the ages. The poet and critic Ezra Pound (1885–1972), attracted to and inspired by the use of imagery in Chinese poetry, spearheaded the new movement of "imagism" in the 1910s, experimenting with the poetic power that sparse juxtaposition of images whose relation remains obscure can produce. His adoption of such poetic techniques in turn profoundly influenced modernist writers such as T. S. Eliot and James Joyce. Although Pound did not know Chinese, he eventually produced a poetic rendering of the *Classic of Poetry* in collaboration with the Harvard sinologist Achilles Fang. Because of their divergence from the wording of the originals, Pound's versions might better be conceived as English poems in their own right than translations. Yet they can come close to the Chinese originals in other ways. In Pound's version, the second stanza of "Dead Roe Deer" reads, "Where the scrub elm skirts the wood, be it not in white mat bound, as a jewel flawless found, dead as doe is maidenhood." Death hovers ominously over the deer, the woman, and her maidenhood. Here we see the drama of the distinctive Chinese trope of *xing* in full play, transposed into the English language.

The *Classic of Poetry* has left deep traces in the literary cultures of East Asia into the modern period. Because its compilation was attributed to Confucius and its traditional interpretations emphasized Confucian values, it was part and parcel of the education of political elites. Yet, despite the dominant moralizing interpretations, the poems of the *Classic of Poetry* have retained their pristine simplicity and have lost nothing of their evocative power to voice fundamental human emotions and challenges.

Classic of Poetry[1]

I. Fishhawk

The fishhawks sing *guan guan*
on sandbars of the stream.
Gentle maiden, pure and fair,
fit pair for a prince.

Watercress grows here and there,   5
right and left we gather it.
Gentle maiden, pure and fair,
wanted waking and asleep.

Wanting, sought her, had her not,
waking, sleeping, thought of her,   10

1. Translated by Stephen Owen.

on and on he thought of her,
he tossed from one side to another.

Watercress grows here and there,
right and left we pull it.
Gentle maiden, pure and fair,   15
with harps we bring her company.

Watercress grows here and there,
right and left we pick it out.
Gentle maiden, pure and fair,
with bells and drums do her delight.   20

VI. Peach Tree Soft and Tender

Peach tree soft and tender,
how your blossoms glow!
The bride is going to her home,
she well befits this house.

Peach tree soft and tender,   5
plump, the ripening fruit.
The bride is going to her home,
she well befits this house.

Peach tree soft and tender,
its leaves spread thick and full.   10
The bride is going to her home,
she well befits these folk.

XX. Plums Are Falling

Plums are falling,
seven are the fruits;
many men want me,
let me have a fine one.

Plums are falling,   5
three are the fruits;
many men want me,
let me have a steady one.

Plums are falling,
catch them in the basket;   10
many men want me,
let me be bride of one.

XXIII. Dead Roe Deer

A roe deer dead in the meadow,
all wrapped in white rushes.
The maiden's heart was filled with spring;
a gentleman led her astray.

Undergrowth in forest,   5
dead deer in the meadow,
all wound with white rushes,
a maiden white as marble.

Softly now, and gently, gently,
do not touch my apron, sir,   10
and don't set the cur to barking.

XXVI. Boat of Cypress

That boat of cypress drifts along,
it drifts upon the stream.
Restless am I, I cannot sleep,
as though in torment and troubled.
Nor am I lacking wine   5
to ease my mind and let me roam.

This heart of mine is no mirror,
it cannot take in all.
Yes, I do have brothers,
but brothers will not be my stay.   10
I went and told them of my grief
and met only with their rage.

This heart of mine is no stone;
you cannot turn it where you will.
This heart of mine is no mat;   15
I cannot roll it up within.
I have behaved with dignity,
in this no man can fault me.

My heart is uneasy and restless,
I am reproached by little men.   20
Many are the woes I've met,
and taken slights more than a few.
I think on it in the quiet,
and waking pound my breast.

Oh Sun! and you Moon!   25
Why do you each grow dim in turn?
These troubles of the heart

are like unwashed clothes.
I think on it in the quiet,
I cannot spread wings to fly away.   30

XLII. Gentle Girl

A gentle girl and fair
awaits by the crook of the wall;
in shadows I don't see her;
I pace and scratch my hair.

A gentle girl and comely   5
gave me a scarlet pipe;
scarlet pipe that gleams—
in your beauty I find delight.

Then she brought me a reed from the pastures,
it was truly beautiful and rare.
Reed—the beauty is not yours—   10
you are but beauty's gift.

LXIV. Quince

She cast a quince to me,
a costly garnet I returned;
it was no equal return,
but by this love will last.

She cast a peach to me,   5
costly opal I returned;
it was no equal return,
but by this love will last.

She cast a plum to me,
a costly ruby I returned;   10
it was no equal return,
but by this love will last.

LXXVI. Zhongzi, Please

Zhongzi, please
don't cross my village wall,
don't break the willows planted there.
It's not that I care so much for them,

but I dread my father and mother;   5
Zhongzi may be in my thoughts,
but what my father and mother said—
that too may be held in dread.

Zhongzi, please
don't cross my fence,   10
don't break the mulberries planted there.
It's not that I care so much for them,
but I dread my brothers;
Zhongzi may be in my thoughts,
but what my brothers said—   15
that too may be held in dread.

Zhongzi, please
don't cross into my garden,
don't break the sandalwood planted there.
It's not that I care so much for them,   20
but I dread others will talk much;
Zhongzi may be in my thoughts,
but when people talk too much—
that too may be held in dread.

XCV. Zhen and Wei

O Zhen and Wei together,
swollen now they flow.
Men and maids together,
chrysanthemums in hand.
The maid says, "Have you looked?"   5
The man says, "I have gone."
"Let's go then look across the Wei,
it is truly a place for our pleasure."
Man and maid together
each frolicked with the other   10
and gave as gift the peony.

O Zhen and Wei together,
flowing deep and clear.
Men and maids together,
teeming everywhere.   15
The maid says, "Have you looked?"
The man says, "I have gone."
"Let's go then look across the Wei,
it is truly a place for our pleasure."
Man and maid together   20
each will frolic with the other
and give as gift the peony.

CXIII. Huge Rat

Huge rat, huge rat,
eat my millet no more,
for three years I've fed you,
yet you pay me no heed.

I swear that I will leave you 5
and go to a happier land.
A happy land, a happy land,
and there I will find my place.

Huge rat, huge rat,
eat my wheat no more, 10
for three years I've fed you
and you show no gratitude.

I swear that I will leave you
and go to a happier realm.
A happy realm, a happy realm, 15
there I will find what I deserve.

Huge rat, huge rat,
eat my sprouts no more,
for three years I have fed you,
and you won't reward my toil. 20

I swear that I will leave you
and go to happy meadows.
Happy meadows, happy meadows
where none need wail and cry.

CCXLV. She Bore the Folk

She who first bore the folk—
Jiang it was, First Parent.
How was it she bore the folk?—
she knew the rite and sacrifice.
To rid herself of sonlessness 5
she trod the god's toeprint
    and she was glad.
She was made great, on her luck settled,
the seed stirred, it was quick.
She gave birth, she gave suck, 10
and this was Lord Millet.

When her months had come to term,
her firstborn sprang up.
Not splitting, not rending,

working no hurt, no harm.   15
He showed his godhead glorious,
the high god was greatly soothed.
He took great joy in those rites
and easily she bore her son.

She set him in a narrow lane,   20
but sheep and cattle warded him.
She set him in the wooded plain,
he met with those who logged the plain.
She set him on cold ice,
birds sheltered him with wings.   25
Then the birds left him
and Lord Millet wailed.
This was long and this was loud;
his voice was a mighty one.

And then he crept and crawled,   30
he stood upright, he stood straight.
He sought to feed his mouth,
and planted there the great beans.
The great beans' leaves were fluttering,
the rows of grain were bristling.   35
Hemp and barley dense and dark,
the melons, plump and round.

Lord Millet in his farming
had a way to help things grow:
He rid the land of thick grass,   40
he planted there a glorious growth.
It was in squares, it was leafy,
it was planted, it grew tall.
It came forth, it formed ears,
it was hard, it was good.   45
Its tassels bent, it was full,
he had his household there in Dai.

He passed us down these wondrous grains:
our black millets, of one and two kernels,
Millets whose leaves sprout red or white,   50
he spread the whole land with black millet,
And reaped it and counted the acres,
spread it with millet sprouting red or white,
hefted on shoulders, loaded on backs,
he took it home and began this rite.   55

And how goes this rite we have?—
at times we hull, at times we scoop,
at times we winnow, at times we stomp,
we hear it slosh as we wash it,
we hear it puff as we steam it.   60

Then we reckon, then we consider,
take artemisia, offer fat.
We take a ram for the flaying,
then we roast it, then we sear it,
to rouse up the following year.   65

We heap the wooden trenchers full,
wooden trenchers, earthenware platters.
And as the scent first rises
the high god is peaceful and glad.
This great odor is good indeed,   70
for Lord Millet began the rite,
and hopefully free from failing or fault,
it has lasted until now.

CONFUCIUS

551–479 B.C.E.

To this day there is virtually no aspect of East Asia on which Confucius and his ideas have not had some impact. When Confucius died in 479 B.C.E., he was a relatively little-known figure, having failed to find a ruler willing to implement his philosophical vision. Although he had attracted quite a few followers and had even established a school toward the end of his life, nobody could have anticipated then how this man's legacy would shape the destiny of China, East Asia, and the world. About 350 years later, Confucian values were not only widely known and revered but had also become the basis for official Chinese state ideology during the Han Dynasty (206 B.C.E.–220 C.E.). Twenty-five hundred years later, Confucius is a national icon for China's venerable past, although Confucianism, the system of beliefs and practices that developed on the basis of Confucius's ideas, took a severe beating in mainland China during much of the twentieth century.

LIFE AND TIMES

Confucius was born in the northeastern state of Lu in today's Shandong Province. Confucius came from the lower ranks of hereditary nobility. Like other masters during the fifth to the third centuries B.C.E., a period of heated intellectual debates comparable to the contemporary flourishing of Greek philosophy, he was eager to put his talents at the disposal of an able ruler who would implement his ideas. But the rulers of Lu were often at the mercy of powerful clans whose arrogance scandalized Confucius. For example, Confucius took offence when one of the great local clans in Lu used eight rows of dancers for the ceremonies at their ancestral temple, a lavish number that only the Zhou king had the prerogative to use. In Confucius's mind, this was not a simple breach of superficial protocol but a blatant symptom of the rottenness of the political system. Disgusted with the situation in his home state, Confucius left Lu and spent many years wandering from court to court, in search of a ruler who would appreciate his talents and political vision. He finally returned to Lu and lived out his life as a teacher, gathering a considerable following.

THE ZHOU HERITAGE AND CONFUCIUS'S INNOVATION

Confucius's philosophical vision brims with admiration for the values of the early Zhou rulers. The Zhou Dynasty (ca. 1045–256 B.C.E.), by Confucius's time already five centuries old, began with two exemplary rulers, King Wen and King Wu. King Wu had destroyed the last remnants of the supposedly decadent Shang Dynasty in the eleventh century B.C.E., and instituted a new government that took pride in showing concern for the people and enforcing wise policies. After King Wu's death his brother, the Duke of Zhou, conducted government affairs for the duke's young nephew, King Cheng, who was still a child. Besides King Wen, the Duke of Zhou had particular importance for Confucius, not just because he was the ancestor of the ducal family of Confucius's home state. The Duke of Zhou also protected his nephew from rebellions and challenges to the newly founded dynasty and was an exemplary regent, with an eye on the welfare of the dynasty, not on his personal ambitions. But the splendor of the dynastic founders vanished over the next half millennium, as the Zhou kings increasingly lost control over the feudal lords, who had started out as their allies in the war against the Shang. By Confucius's time the Zhou kings had only nominal power and China consisted of rival states, whose local rulers competed for territory and power. In the *Analects* Confucius often sharply criticizes the irreverent behavior of the feudal lords toward the Zhou king and

This rubbing on paper, copied from an engraved stone slab, shows how later ages imagined Confucius. It is from Qufu, Shandong Province, Confucius's birthplace.

showcases their corruption to explain his vision of proper government.

Although Confucius claims in the *Analects* that he is merely the "transmitter" of Zhou values and not an "innovator," he actually built a new tradition. Confucius's conviction that the political chaos he perceived around him could be avoided by returning to the moral values of the venerable founders of the Zhou Dynasty, Kings Wu and Wen and the Duke of Zhou, paid homage to tradition but was also visionary, even revolutionary. His emphasis on the importance of social roles and rituals could reinforce existing hierarchies, but at the same time it allowed individuals to develop their inner potential and find a meaningful place in society. His pedagogical program, which promoted the reading of a group of texts, later called "Confucian Classics," and their application to life's challenges, could lead to mindless memorization designed merely for career advancement, but it also enabled people to better understand and take control of their lives by following the moral models, historical precedents, and words of wisdom contained in these canonical texts.

DIVERSITY AND CORE VALUES
IN THE *ANALECTS*

Confucius's vision has been extraordinarily influential over the past two and a half millennia and has profoundly shaped the societies not just of China but also of Korea, Japan, and Vietnam. The *Analects*, best translated as "Collected Sayings," convey the power of Confucius's vision. A collection of brief quotations, conversations, and anecdotes from the life of Confucius, the *Analects* were not written by the master himself, but compiled by later generations of disciples. They probably reached their current form only during the second century B.C.E., when Confucius's ideas were gaining influence and it became necessary to create a representative collection of his sayings out of the vast body of Confucius lore that circulated in various other books. Later it became the key text to understanding the great master's character and ideas. The *Analects* throw light on people, concrete situations, and above all the exemplary model of Confucius himself, instead of supplying systematic expositions of his ideas or abstract definitions of moral philosophy. When commenting on central concepts such as "goodness" or "humanity" (*ren*), "ritual"

(*li*), and "respect for one's parents" (*xiao*), Confucius might utter different, even contradictory maxims: sometimes he claims that anybody who wants to can become "humane" in a moment, but at other times he turns the concept into a distant ideal. He also explains that his answers sometimes differ, because an overeager disciple needs to be held back, while a timid one needs to be encouraged. Another explanation for the widely divergent pieces of advice to be found in the *Analects* is that it was compiled over several centuries and thus includes the changing opinions of the compilers.

RITUAL

Despite the diversity of views expounded in the *Analects*, it is possible to identify a core set of values. First, there is Confucius's emphasis on ritual. Everything we do in life is a ritual, whether we greet each other with a handshake or mark life's important moments, such as birth and death, with special observances. Although Confucius briefly refers to earlier notions of the powers of Heaven and declares that he respects the gods and spirits, his concern is with our world, the world of human society. Rituals are thus used not to communicate with divine powers, but instead to make social life meaningful. One learns and perfects these rituals in one's community through continuous practice and self-cultivation. The person who has perfected himself in this manner is the *junzi*—the "superior person," or "gentleman." The word referred originally to a prince of aristocratic birth, but Confucius boldly applies it to moral, not hereditary, superiority. Although Confucius at times denies having reached the stage of *junzi* himself, he makes clear that anybody can become a *junzi*, and that everyone should strive to reach that ideal. The *Analects* also idealize historical figures whom Confucius considers models of exemplary moral conduct. Even before the sage rulers of the Zhou, there were the sage emperors of highest antiquity, including Emperor Shun, whose moral charisma was so overwhelming that it sufficed for him to sit in proper ritual position on his throne to induce spontaneous order in his empire. In Confucianism, models of proper ritual behavior are crucial to guiding one's moral self-cultivation, and book 10 of the *Analects* enshrines the master himself as such a model actor: it is the only book in which the master does not speak, but is simply shown in silent ritual action. That the compilers of the *Analects* placed this book at the heart of the *Analects'* twenty books shows that they admired Confucius not just for what he said, but for his exemplary conduct throughout his life.

SOCIAL ROLES

A second recurrent concern in the *Analects* is Confucius's attention to social roles. In his words humans owe each other "goodness" or "humanity" (*ren*)— that is, empathy and reciprocal concern, mutual respect and obligation. Some later Confucians, such as Mencius (ca. 372–289 B.C.E.), believed that this natural ability for empathy was even more important than ritual. The natural and spontaneous basis for respect is the relation between child and parent. From this experience, respect is extended to other figures, such as elder siblings, seniors, and rulers.

Although Confucius endorses social hierarchies, he abhorred any form of force and coercion. Because Confucianism and its canonical texts became the basis for the recruitment of bureaucrats and part of the ideology of government in imperial China, it is sometimes portrayed as a philosophy that, in contrast to Daoism, puts social duty over natural desires. Yet the stance of Confucius in the *Analects* is much more complex. He often navigates between the instincts of inborn nature and the need for cultivation, the power of spontaneous action and the importance of patient learning, the pleasures of a life in harmony with one's wishes and the duties of a life devoted to political service. In book 18 we see Confucius attracted to recluses, dropouts who reject life in society; another time Confucius praises the view of a disciple who values ritual celebration and joyful singing with friends over petty state service. At yet another point Confucius recommends avoiding government service unless a virtuous ruler is on the throne.

EFFICIENT ACTION

Goodness, ritual, and attention to social roles create order in society; efficient action, another major Confucian concern, helps to maintain it and to effect change in the world. One of Confucius's most attractive ideas is his promise that it is possible to harmonize one's natural impulses with social norms and thus become an efficient, harmonious agent in society. He himself apparently reached this balance only in old age: "At seventy I followed my heart's desire without overstepping the line." Throughout the *Analects*, Confucius is fascinated with various kinds of efficiency. Emperor Shun, facing south on his throne and thereby creating order in the world, is the prime incarnation of minimalist action put to great effect. The notion that the moral charisma of a sage ruler can be so powerful that there is no need to resort to lowly means of war and violence became the basis of the traditional Chinese view of rulership. Confucius's admiration for efficient thinking is best exemplified by his praise of his favorite disciple Yan Hui: "When he is told one thing he understands ten." The master of efficient speech, Confucius himself seems always to know more than he says: his utterances can be so short that they verge on the obscure. Sometimes he even speaks of his desire to reject language altogether.

THE IMPORTANCE OF CANONICAL TEXTS IN CONFUCIANISM

Confucius and his followers, called *Ru*, or "traditionalist scholars," considered the study of the ancient texts that contained the legacy of the Zhou as paramount to self-cultivation. Confucius is traditionally associated with the composition of the *Classic of Poetry, Classic of History, Record of Ritual, Spring and Autumn Annals*, and *Classic of Changes*, which were later called the "Confucian Classics." Today hardly anybody believes that they were written or compiled by Confucius. These books became the curriculum in the first Chinese state university, founded in 124 B.C.E. by Emperor Wu of the Han Dynasty. Later the Confucian Classics and other canonical Confucian texts such as the *Analects* formed the basis for the all-important civil service examination system, which allowed hundreds of thousands of individuals to attain office in the expansive bureaucracy of the Chinese empire. For more than two millennia these texts were the backbone of the training of political and cultural elites throughout East Asia and Confucius was venerated in temples as "the foremost teacher," a deity of moral perfection and learning.

Throughout its long history, Confucianism has served many political,

social, and religious causes, and it has therefore also met with strident criticism. Already in the late fifth century B.C.E., Mozi, the first forceful critic of Confucius, wrote a devastating piece, "Against the Confucians," in which he parodied Confucians as "beggars, greedy hamsters, and staring he-goats who puff themselves up like wild boars." Their clothes, cries Mozi, are hopelessly old-fashioned, and they cling to the importance of ritual only because they hope to get a good meal out of the sacrificial food prepared for the occasion.

In the twentieth century, Chinese intellectuals and the Communist Party waged mass campaigns against Confucianism, considering it the utmost evil and blaming it for everything that supposedly went wrong with China's modernization. Yet many public intellectuals in Taiwan and the United States have been propagating "Neo-Confucianism" and are convinced that it can help renew humanistic values in today's harsh and cynical world. Since the 1990s the Confucius temples in mainland China have been rebuilt. Confucius is now discussed on television talk shows, and the Chinese government uses his name to represent China in the world. References to Confucius hovered over the Beijing Olympics of 2008, and in the first decade of the twenty-first century the government founded several hundred "Confucius Institutes" around the world and thus uses the old sage as an icon for the propagation of Chinese language and culture. The future of Confucius's legacy is as bright as ever.

From Analects[1]

From *Book I*

1.1. The Master said: "To learn something and then to put it into practice at the right time: is this not a joy? To have friends coming from afar: is this not a delight? Not to be upset when one's merits are ignored: is this not the mark of a gentleman?"

---

1. Translated by Simon Leys.

1.4. Master Zeng said: "I examine myself three times a day. When dealing on behalf of others, have I been trustworthy? In intercourse with my friends, have I been faithful? Have I practiced what I was taught?"

1.11. The Master said: "When the father is alive, watch the son's aspirations. When the father is dead, watch the son's actions. If three years later, the son has not veered from the father's way, he may be called a dutiful son indeed."

From *Book II*

2.1. The Master said: "He who rules by virtue is like the polestar, which remains unmoving in its mansion while all the other stars revolve respectfully around it."

2.2. The Master said: "The three hundred *Poems*[2] are summed up in one single phrase: 'Think no evil.'"

2.4. The Master said: "At fifteen, I set my mind upon learning. At thirty, I took my stand. At forty, I had no doubts. At fifty, I knew the will of Heaven. At sixty, my ear was attuned. At seventy, I follow all the desires of my heart without breaking any rule."

2.7. Ziyou asked about filial piety. The Master said: "Nowadays people think they are dutiful sons when they feed their parents. Yet they also feed their dogs and horses. Unless there is respect, where is the difference?"

2.11. The Master said: "He who by revising the old knows the new, is fit to be a teacher."

2.19. Duke Ai[3] asked: "What should I do to win the hearts of the people?" Confucius replied: "Raise the straight and set them above the crooked, and you will win the hearts of the people. If you raise the crooked and set them above the straight, the people will deny you their support."

From *Book III*

3.5. The Master said: "Barbarians who have rulers are inferior to the various nations of China who are without."

3.21. Duke Ai asked Zai Yu which wood should be used for the local totem. Zai Yu replied: "The men of Xia used pine; the men of Yin used cypress; the men of Zhou used *fir*, for (they said) the people should *fear*."[4]

The Master heard of this; he said: "What is done is done, it is all past; there would be no point in arguing."

---

2. Another name for the *Classic of Poetry*.
3. Ruler of the dukedom of Lu, Confucius's home state.
4. Zai Yu, one of Confucius's disciples, replies to the duke with a pun: in the original text the chestnut tree (*li*), translated here as "fir," puns on "fear" (*li*).

3.24. The officer in charge of the border at Yi requested an interview with Confucius. He said: "Whenever a gentleman comes to these parts, I always ask to see him." The disciples arranged an interview. When it was over, the officer said to them: "Gentlemen, do not worry about his dismissal. The world has been without the Way for a long while. Heaven is going to use your master to ring the tocsin."

From *Book IV*

4.8. The Master said: "In the morning hear the Way; in the evening die content."

4.15. The Master said: "Shen, my doctrine has one single thread running through it." Master Zeng Shen replied: "Indeed."

The Master left. The other disciples asked: "What did he mean?" Master Zeng said: "The doctrine of the Master is: Loyalty and reciprocity, and that's all."

From *Book V*

5.9. The Master asked Zigong: "Which is the better, you or Yan Hui?"[5]— "How could I compare myself with Yan Hui? From one thing he learns, he deduces ten; from one thing I learn, I only deduce two." The Master said: "Indeed, you are not his equal, and neither am I."

5.10. Zai Yu was sleeping during the day. The Master said: "Rotten wood cannot be carved; dung walls cannot be troweled. What is the use of scolding him?"

The Master said: "There was a time when I used to listen to what people said and trusted that they would act accordingly, but now I listen to what they say and watch what they do. It is Zai Yu who made me change."

5.20. Lord Ji Wen[6] always thought thrice before acting. Hearing this, the Master said: "Twice is enough."

5.26. Yan Hui and Zilu were in attendance. The Master said: "How about telling me your private wishes?"

Zilu said: "I wish I could share my carriages, horses, clothes, and furs with my friends without being upset when they damage them."

Yan Hui said: "I wish I would never boast of my good qualities or call attention to my good deeds."

Zilu said: "May we ask what are our Master's private wishes?"

The Master said: "I wish the old may enjoy peace, friends may enjoy trust, and the young may enjoy affection."

---

5. Confucius's most beloved disciple.

6. Grand officer of the state of Lu, who lived before Confucius's time.

From *Book VI*

6.3. Duke Ai asked: "Which of the disciples has a love of learning?" Confucius replied: "There was Yan Hui who loved learning; he never vented his frustrations upon others; he never made the same mistake twice. Alas, his allotted span of life was short; he is dead. Now, for all I know, there is no one with such a love of learning."

6.12. Ran Qiu said: "It is not that I do not enjoy the Master's way, but I do not have the strength to follow it." The Master said: "He who does not have the strength can always give up halfway. But you have given up before starting."

6.13. The Master said to Zixia: "Be a noble scholar, not a vulgar pedant."

6.18. The Master said: "When nature prevails over culture, you get a savage; when culture prevails over nature, you get a pedant. When nature and culture are in balance, you get a gentleman."

6.20. The Master said: "To know something is not as good as loving it; to love something is not as good as rejoicing in it."

6.22. Fan Chi asked about wisdom. The Master said: "Secure the rights of the people; respect ghosts and gods, but keep them at a distance—this is wisdom indeed."

Fan Chi asked about goodness. The Master said: "A good man's trials bear fruit—this is goodness indeed."

6.23. The Master said: "The wise find joy on the water, the good find joy in the mountains. The wise are active, the good are quiet. The wise are joyful, the good live long."

From *Book VII*

7.1. The Master said: "I transmit, I invent nothing. I trust and love the past. In this, I dare to compare myself to our venerable Peng."[7]

7.3. The Master said: "Failure to cultivate moral power, failure to explore what I have learned, incapacity to stand by what I know to be right, incapacity to reform what is not good—these are my worries."

7.5. The Master said: "I am getting dreadfully old. It has been a long time since I last saw in a dream the Duke of Zhou."[8]

---

7. Identifications of this figure vary, but venerable Peng might have been a virtuous official of the Shang Dynasty (ca. 1500–1045 B.C.E.).
8. Son of King Wen, who together with King Wu founded the Zhou Dynasty (1045–256 B.C.E.). He laid the groundwork for basic institutions of the Zhou Dynasty and is the founding ancestor of the state of Lu, Confucius's home state.

7.16. The Master said: "Even though you have only coarse grain for food, water for drink, and your bent arm for a pillow, you may still be happy. Riches and honors without justice are to me as fleeting clouds."

7.21. The Master never talked of: miracles; violence; disorders; spirits.

From *Book VIII*

8.5. Master Zeng said: "Competent, yet willing to listen to the incompetent; talented, yet willing to listen to the talentless; having, yet seeming not to have; full, yet seeming empty; swallowing insults without taking offense—long ago, I had a friend who practiced these things."

8.8. The Master said: "Draw inspiration from the *Poems*; steady your course with the ritual; find your fulfillment in music."

8.13. The Master said: "Uphold the faith, love learning, defend the good Way with your life. Enter not a country that is unstable: dwell not in a country that is in turmoil. Shine in a world that follows the Way; hide when the world loses the Way. In a country where the Way prevails, it is shameful to remain poor and obscure; in a country which has lost the Way, it is shameful to become rich and honored."

8.17. The Master said: "Learning is like a chase in which, as you fail to catch up, you fear to lose what you have already gained."

From *Book IX*

9.5. The Master was trapped in Kuang. He said: "King Wen is dead: is civilization not resting now on me? If Heaven intends civilization to be destroyed, why was it vested in me? If Heaven does not intend civilization to be destroyed, what should I fear from the people of Kuang?"[9]

9.6. The Grand Chamberlain asked Zigong: "Is your Master not a saint? But then, why should he also possess so many particular aptitudes?" Zigong replied: "Heaven indeed made him a saint; but he also happens to have many aptitudes."

Hearing of this, the Master said: "The Grand Chamberlain truly knows me. In my youth, I was poor; therefore, I had to become adept at a variety of lowly skills. Does such versatility befit a gentleman? No, it does not."

9.12. The Master was very ill. Zilu organized the disciples in a retinue, as if they were the retainers of a lord. During a remission of his illness, the Master said: "Zilu, this farce has lasted long enough. Whom can I deceive with these sham retainers? Can I deceive Heaven? Rather than die amidst retainers,

---

9. Kuang was a border town where Confucius nearly fell into the hands of a lynch mob who mistook him for an adventurer who had ransacked the region. Confucius uses a pun in making his point: the name of King Wen, the founder of the Zhou Dynasty, also means "civilization" (*wen*).

I prefer to die in the arms of my disciples. I may not receive a state funeral, but still I shall not die by the wayside."

9.14. The Master wanted to settle among the nine barbarian tribes of the East. Someone said: "It is wild in those parts. How would you cope?" The Master said: "How could it be wild, once a gentleman has settled there?"

9.17. The Master stood by a river and said: "Everything flows like this, without ceasing, day and night."

9.23. The Master said: "One should regard the young with awe: how do you know that the next generation will not equal the present one? If, however, by the age of forty or fifty, a man has not made a name for himself, he no longer deserves to be taken seriously."

From *Book X*

10.2. At court, when conversing with the under ministers, he was affable; when conversing with the upper ministers, he was respectful. In front of the ruler, he was humble yet composed.

10.4. When entering the gate of the Duke's palace, he walked in discreetly. He never stood in the middle of the passage, nor did he tread on the threshold.

When he passed in front of the throne, he adopted an expression of gravity, hastened his step, and became as if speechless. When ascending the steps of the audience hall, he lifted up the hem of his gown and bowed, as if short of breath; on coming out, after descending the first step, he expressed relief and contentment.

At the bottom of the steps, he moved swiftly, as if on wings. On regaining his place, he resumed his humble countenance.

From *Book XI*

11.9. Yan Hui died. The Master said: "Alas! Heaven is destroying me, Heaven is destroying me!"

11.10. Yan Hui died. The Master wailed wildly. His followers said: "Master, such grief is not proper." The Master said: "In mourning such a man, what sort of grief would be proper?"

11.26. Zilu, Zeng Dian, Ran Qiu, and Gongxi Chi were sitting with the Master. The Master said: "Forget for one moment that I am your elder. You often say: 'The world does not recognize our merits.' But, given the opportunity, what would you wish to do?"

Zilu rushed to reply first: "Give me a country not too small,[1] but squeezed between powerful neighbors; it is under attack and in the grip of a famine. Put

---

1. Literally "a country of a thousand chariots."

me in charge: within three years, I would revive the spirits of the people and set them back on their feet."

The Master smiled. "Ran Qiu, what about you?"

The other replied: "Give me a domain of sixty to seventy—or, say, fifty to sixty leagues; within three years I would secure the prosperity of its people. As regards their spiritual well-being, however, this would naturally have to wait for the intervention of a true gentleman."

"Gongxi Chi, what about you?"

"I don't say that I would be able to do this, but I would like to learn: in the ceremonies of the Ancestral Temple, such as a diplomatic conference for instance, wearing chasuble and cap, I would like to play the part of a junior assistant."

"And what about you, Zeng Dian?"

Zeng Dian, who had been softly playing his zithern, plucked one last chord and pushed his instrument aside. He replied: "I am afraid my wish is not up to those of my three companions." The Master said: "There is no harm in that! After all, each is simply confiding his personal aspirations."

"In late spring, after the making of the spring clothes has been completed, together with five or six companions and six or seven boys, I would like to bathe in the River Yi, and then enjoy the breeze on the Rain Dance Terrace, and go home singing." The Master heaved a deep sigh and said: "I am with Dian!"

The three others left; Zeng Dian remained behind and said: "What did you think of their wishes?" The Master said: "Each simply confided his personal aspirations."

"Why did you smile at Zilu?"

"One should govern a state through ritual restraint; yet his words were full of swagger."

"As for Ran Qiu, wasn't he in fact talking about a full-fledged state?"

"Indeed; have you ever heard of 'a domain of sixty to seventy, or fifty to sixty leagues'?"

"And Gongxi Chi? Wasn't he also talking about a state?"

"A diplomatic conference in the Ancestral Temple! What could it be, if not an international gathering? And if Gongxi Chi were there merely to play the part of a junior assistant, who would qualify for the main role?"

From *Book XII*

12.2. Ran Yong asked about humanity. The Master said: "When abroad, behave as if in front of an important guest. Lead the people as if performing a great ceremony. What you do not wish for yourself, do not impose upon others. Let no resentment enter public affairs; let no resentment enter private affairs."

Ran Yong said: "I may not be clever, but with your permission I shall endeavor to do as you have said."

12.5. Sima Niu was grieving: "All men have brothers; I alone have none." Zixia said: "I have heard this: life and death are decreed by fate, riches and honors are allotted by Heaven. Since a gentleman behaves with reverence and diligence, treating people with deference and courtesy, all within the Four Seas are his brothers. How could a gentleman ever complain that he has no brothers?"

12.7. Zigong asked about government. The Master said: "Sufficient food, sufficient weapons, and the trust of the people." Zigong said: "If you had to do without one of these three, which would you give up?—"Weapons."—"If you had to do without one of the remaining two, which would you give up?"—"Food; after all, everyone has to die eventually. But without the trust of the people, no government can stand."

12.11. Duke Jing of Qi asked Confucius about government. Confucius replied: "Let the lord be a lord; the subject a subject; the father a father; the son a son." The Duke said: "Excellent! If indeed the lord is not a lord, the subject not a subject, the father not a father, the son not a son, I could be sure of nothing anymore—not even of my daily food."

12.18. Lord Ji Kang was troubled by burglars. He consulted with Confucius. Confucius replied: "If you yourself were not covetous, they would not rob you, even if you paid them to."

12.19. Lord Ji Kang asked Confucius about government, saying: "Suppose I were to kill the bad to help the good: how about that?" Confucius replied: "You are here to govern, what need is there to kill? If you desire what is good, the people will be good. The moral power of the gentleman is wind, the moral power of the common man is grass. Under the wind, the grass must bend."

From *Book XIII*

13.1. Zilu asked about government. The Master said: "Guide them. Encourage them." Zilu asked him to develop these precepts. The Master said: "Untiringly."

13.3. Zilu asked: "If the ruler of Wei were to entrust you with the government of the country, what would be your first initiative?" The Master said: "It would certainly be to rectify the names." Zilu said: "Really? Isn't this a little farfetched? What is this rectification for?" The Master said: "How boorish can you get! Whereupon a gentleman is incompetent, thereupon he should remain silent. If the names are not correct, language is without an object. When language is without an object, no affair can be effected. When no affair can be effected, rites and music wither. When rites and music wither, punishments and penalties miss their target. When punishments and penalties miss their target, the people do not know where they stand. Therefore, whatever a gentleman conceives of, he must be able to say; and whatever he says, he must be able to do. In the matter of language, a gentleman leaves nothing to chance."

13.10. The Master said: "If a ruler could employ me, in one year I would make things work, and in three years the results would show."

13.11. The Master said: " 'When good men have been running the country for a hundred years, cruelty can be overcome, and murder extirpated.' How true is this saying!"

13.12. The Master said: "Even with a true king, it would certainly take one generation for humanity to prevail."

13.20. Zigong asked: "How does one deserve to be called a gentleman?" The Master said: "He who behaves with honor, and, being sent on a mission to the four corners of the world, does not bring disgrace to his lord, deserves to be called a gentleman."

"And next to that, if I may ask?"

"His relatives praise his filial piety and the people of his village praise the way he respects the elders."

"And next to that, if I may ask?"

"His word can be trusted; whatever he undertakes, he brings to completion. In this, he may merely show the obstinacy of a vulgar man; still, he should probably qualify as a gentleman of lower category."

"In this respect, how would you rate our present politicians?"

"Alas! These puny creatures are not even worth mentioning!"

From *Book XIV*

14.24. The Master said: "In the old days, people studied to improve themselves. Now they study in order to impress others."

14.35. The Master said: "No one understands me!" Zigong said: "Why is it that no one understands you?" The Master said: "I do not accuse Heaven, nor do I blame men; here below I am learning, and there above I am being heard. If I am understood, it must be by Heaven."

14.38. Zilu stayed for the night at the Stone Gate. The gatekeeper said: "Where are you from?" Zilu said: "I am from Confucius's household."—"Oh, is that the one who keeps pursuing what he knows is impossible?"

14.43. Yuan Rang sat waiting, with his legs spread wide. The Master said: "A youth who does not respect his elders will achieve nothing when he grows up, and will even try to shirk death when he reaches old age: he is a parasite." And he struck him across the shin with his stick.

From *Book XV*

15.3. The Master said: "Zigong, do you think that I am someone who learns a lot of things and then stores them all up?"—"Indeed; is it not so?" The Master said: "No. I have one single thread on which to string them all."

15.5. The Master said: "Shun[2] was certainly one of those who knew how to govern by inactivity. How did he do it? He sat reverently on the throne, facing south—and that was all."

15.7. The Master said: "How straight Shi Yu was! Under a good government, he was straight as an arrow: under a bad government, he was straight as an arrow. What a gentleman was Qu Boyu![3] Under a good government, he displayed his talents. Under a bad government, he folded them up in his heart."

---

2. Emperor of high antiquity known for his exemplary virtue. The throne usually faced south.
3. Shi Yu and Qu Boyu were both high officials in the state of Wei. Confucius was once hosted by Qu Boyu.

15.31. The Master said: "In an attempt to meditate, I once spent a whole day without food and a whole night without sleep: it was no use. It is better to study."

From *Book XVII*

17.4. The Master went to Wucheng, where Ziyou was governor. He heard the sound of stringed instruments and hymns. He was amused and said with a smile: "Why use an ox-cleaver to kill a chicken?" Ziyou replied: "Master, in the past I have heard you say: 'The gentleman who cultivates the Way loves all men; the small people who cultivate the Way are easy to govern.'" The Master said: "My friends, Ziyou is right. I was just joking."

17.9. The Master said: "Little ones, why don't you study the *Poems*? The *Poems* can provide you with stimulation and with observation, with a capacity for communion, and with a vehicle for grief. At home, they enable you to serve your father, and abroad, to serve your lord. Also, you will learn there the names of many birds, animals, plants, and trees."

17.19. The Master said: "I wish to speak no more." Zigong said: "Master, if you do not speak, how would little ones like us still be able to hand down any teachings?" The Master said: "Does Heaven speak? Yet the four seasons follow their course and the hundred creatures continue to be born. Does Heaven speak?"

17.21. Zai Yu asked: "Three years mourning for one's parents—this is quite long. If a gentleman stops all ritual practices for three years, the practices will decay; if he stops all musical performances for three years, music will be lost. As the old crop is consumed, a new crop grows up, and for lighting the fire, a new lighter is used with each season. One year of mourning should be enough." The Master said: "If after only one year, you were again to eat white rice and to wear silk, would you feel at ease?"—"Absolutely."—"In that case, go ahead! The reason a gentleman prolongs his mourning is simply that, since fine food seems tasteless to him, and music offers him no enjoyment, and the comfort of his house makes him uneasy, he prefers to do without all these pleasures. But now, if you can enjoy them, go ahead!"

Zai Yu left. The Master said: "Zai Yu is devoid of humanity. After a child is born, for the first three years of his life, he does not leave his parents' bosom. Three years mourning is a custom that is observed everywhere in the world. Did Zai Yu never enjoy the love of his parents, even for three years?"

From *Book XVIII*

18.5. Jieyu, the Madman of Chu, went past Confucius, singing:

> Phoenix, oh Phoenix!
> The past cannot be retrieved,
> But the future still holds a chance
> Give up, give up!
> The days of those in office are numbered!

Confucius stopped his chariot, for he wanted to speak with him, but the other hurried away and disappeared. Confucius did not succeed in speaking to him.

18.6. Changju and Jieni were ploughing together. Confucius, who was passing by, sent Zilu to ask where the ford was. Changju said: "Who is in the chariot?" Zilu said: "It is Confucius." "The Confucius from Lu?" "Himself."—"Then he already knows where the ford is."

Zilu then asked Jieni, who replied: "Who are you?"—"I am Zilu."—"The disciple of Confucius, from Lu?"—"Yes."—"The whole universe is swept along by the same flood; who can reverse its flow? Instead of following a gentleman who keeps running from one patron to the next, would it not be better to follow a gentleman who has forsaken the world?" All the while he kept on tilling his field.

Zilu came back and reported to Confucius. Rapt in thought, the Master sighed: "One cannot associate with birds and beasts. With whom should I keep company, if not with my own kind? If the world were following the Way, I would not have to reform it."

DAODEJING / LAOZI

sixth–third centuries B.C.E.

Attributed to a master called Laozi, the *Daodejing* ("The Classic of the Way and Its Virtue") is the most often translated early Chinese text. It is also the most paradoxical, because it uses logical contradictions to articulate its vision. The *Daodejing* exhorts its readers in pithy, simple language to return to the natural way of things, to reject the corruptions of human civilization, and to adopt a productive passiveness, a stance of "nonaction," that promises unexpected success. It claims that those who understand it will preserve their lives in a dangerous world, reach their goals, and gain political power. The *Daodejing* declares at one point that its message is easy to understand, but the fact that more than seven hundred commentaries have been written on the *Daodejing* over the past 2,200 years

shows that it is hardly self-explanatory. The lack of agreement among readers about the *Daodejing*'s message has only increased its popularity. It has become familiar to readers around the world thanks to the great number of translations, which sometimes differ so considerably that readers wonder whether they are all reading the same source text.

The *Daodejing* contains eighty-one short chapters written in rhythmic verse. It is divided into two main parts: one part on the "Way" (*dao*) and one part on "Virtue" (*de*). The Way refers to a natural, uncorrupted way of being that pervades everything in heaven and earth, from all beings in the cosmos to humans. Virtue is the power inherent in each thing in its natural state and the force that allows humans to reach their full potential. Both concepts were central to the intense philosophical debates initiated by **Confucius** (551–479 B.C.E.), and they remained important during the so-called Warring States Period (403–221 B.C.E.), when China was divided into small rival states. During this time thinkers traveled from state to state to offer political advice to rulers hungry for territory and power. The rich corpus of so-called Masters Literature, philosophical texts centered around charismatic master figures, allows us to follow these masters' arguments in great detail. Much of the debate focused on how rulers should govern their states, and how individuals can live the best possible life. Although the thinkers of the Warring States Period did not agree about the meaning of the Way and of Virtue, they all considered these concepts important, and they discussed and debated them at length. Yet the *Daodejing* placed so much emphasis on the concept of *dao* that, together with **Zhuangzi**, it became the foundational text of Daoism, the "School of the Way." Recent excavations that produced copies of the *Daodejing* from a tomb datable to around 300 B.C.E. confirm that the text existed by that time in its more or less finished form, though the order of chapters differs.

Many Masters Texts argue for good government and a good life by referring to memorable historical events and people. But the *Daodejing* boldly projects its message beyond any specific time and place. Instead, it evokes cosmic categories such as the Way and relies on the power not of history but of universal natural imagery: the "uncarved block," the "spirit of the valley," the "gateway of the manifold secrets," or "the mysterious female." The text has no identifiable speaker, except for an indefinite "I" that delivers words of wisdom as if talking from the "cosmic void." Claiming that the Way cannot be named or explained, many chapters define it negatively. They criticize conventional wisdom and elevate the values that contradict it. The *Daodejing* teaches that weakness, softness, and passivity, not force, rigidity, and assertive action, are key qualities for surviving in a dangerous world. It preaches that emptiness, not fullness; the female, not the male principle; and counterintuitive, not conventional wisdom are needed to succeed. Unlike most early Chinese texts that hurl their attacks directly against their opponents, the *Daodejing* cleverly abstains from naming rival schools of thought and thus places itself above the heated intellectual strife that surrounds it. It does not mention Confucius by name, but its polemical attack on Confucian values such as moral virtue, positive action, and refinement through education, which leads away from the state of nature, leaves no doubt that the *Daodejing* was partly written as a refutation of Confucius and his followers.

Despite its praise of weakness and nonaction, the *Daodejing* contains a powerful political philosophy and provides recipes of how to "win the empire" and how to succeed in a world of political competition and intrigue. This aspect of its message is addressed to those aspiring to become both sages and rulers: they should preserve their power by keeping the populace ignorant and manipulating them imperceptibly from above, giving the impression of not interfering but ultimately exercising absolute power.

In traditional China, the *Daodejing* was attractive because it provided a radical alternative to the Confucian vision of human morality and cultivation and was couched in poignant paradoxical formulations. Instead of arguing against the Confucian vision, it built an alternative universe that seemed to transcend the intellectual disputes of the centuries during which it was written. Although its political teachings appear abstract to the point of becoming impractical, the *Daodejing* has lost nothing of its influence. It is present in ever new editions on bookshelves around the world and variously praised as a manual of self-actualization, professional success, and leadership training in a postindustrial world.

Daodejing[1]

I

The way that can be spoken of
Is not the constant way;
The name that can be named
Is not the constant name.
The nameless was the beginning of heaven
    and earth;   5
The named was the mother of the myriad creatures.
Hence always rid yourself of desires in order to
    observe its secrets;
But always allow yourself to have desires in order
    to observe its manifestations.
These two are the same
But diverge in name as they issue forth.   10
Being the same they are called mysteries,
Mystery upon mystery—
The gateway of the manifold secrets.

II

The whole world recognizes the beautiful as the beautiful, yet this is
    only the ugly; the whole world recognizes the good as the good,
    yet this is only the bad.
Thus Something and Nothing produce each other;
The difficult and the easy complement each other;
The long and the short off-set each other;
The high and the low incline towards each other;   5
Note and sound harmonize with each other;
Before and after follow each other.
Therefore the sage keeps to the deed that consists in taking no action
    and practises the teaching that uses no words.
The myriad creatures rise from it yet it claims no authority;   10
It gives them life yet claims no possession;
It benefits them yet exacts no gratitude;
It accomplishes its task yet lays claim to no merit.
It is because it lays claim to no merit
That its merit never deserts it.   15

1. Translated by D. C. Lau.

III

Not to honor men of worth will keep the people from contention; not to value goods which are hard to come by will keep them from theft; not to display what is desirable will keep them from being unsettled of mind.

Therefore in governing the people, the sage empties their minds but fills their bellies, weakens their wills but strengthens their bones. He always keeps them innocent of knowledge and free from desire, and ensures that the clever never dare to act.

Do that which consists in taking no action, and order will prevail.

IV

The way is empty, yet use will not drain it.
Deep, it is like the ancestor of the myriad creatures.
Blunt the sharpness;
Untangle the knots;
Soften the glare;   5
Let your wheels move only along old ruts.
Darkly visible, it only seems as if it were there.
I know not whose son it is.
It images the forefather of God.

V

Heaven and earth are ruthless, and treat the myriad creatures as straw
dogs;[2] the sage is ruthless, and treats the people as straw dogs.
Is not the space between heaven and earth like a bellows?
It is empty without being exhausted:
The more it works the more comes out.
Much speech leads inevitably to silence.   5
Better to hold fast to the void

VI

The spirit of the valley never dies.
This is called the mysterious female.
The gateway of the mysterious female
Is called the root of heaven and earth.
Dimly visible, it seems as if it were there,   5
Yet use will never drain it.

2. Straw dogs were sometimes used in rituals. They were treated with great respect during the ceremony, only to be trampled on and discarded afterward.

VII

Heaven and earth are enduring. The reason why heaven and earth can be
    enduring is that they do not give themselves life. Hence they are able
    to be long-lived.
Therefore the sage puts his person last and it comes first,
Treats it as extraneous to himself and it is preserved.
Is it not because he is without thought of self that he is able to accomplish
    his private ends?

VIII

Highest good is like water. Because water excels in benefiting the myriad
    creatures without contending with them and settles where none would
    like to be, it comes close to the way.
In a home it is the site that matters;
In quality of mind it is depth that matters;
In an ally it is benevolence that matters;
In speech it is good faith that matters;
In government it is order that matters;   5
In affairs it is ability that matters;
In action it is timeliness that matters.
It is because it does not contend that it is never at fault.

XI

Thirty spokes
Share one hub.
Adapt the nothing therein to the purpose in hand, and you will have the
    use of the cart. Knead clay in order to make a vessel. Adapt the
    nothing therein to the purpose in hand, and you will have the use of
    the vessel. Cut out doors and windows in order to make a room. Adapt
    the nothing[3] therein to the purpose in hand, and you will have the use
    of the room.
Thus what we gain is Something, yet it is by virtue of Nothing that this can
    be put to use.

XII

The five colors make man's eyes blind;
The five notes make his ears deaf;
The five tastes injure his palate;
Riding and hunting

---

3. "Nothing" in these instances refers to the empty spaces of wheels, vessels, and rooms.

Make his mind go wild with excitement;   5
Goods hard to come by
Serve to hinder his progress.
Hence the sage is
For the belly
Not for the eye.   10
Therefore he discards the one and takes the other.

XVI

I do my utmost to attain emptiness;
I hold firmly to stillness.
The myriad creatures all rise together
And I watch their return.
The teaming creatures   5
All return to their separate roots.
Returning to one's roots is known as stillness.
This is what is meant by returning to one's destiny.
Returning to one's destiny is known as the constant.
Knowledge of the constant is known as discernment.   10
Woe to him who wilfully innovates
While ignorant of the constant,
But should one act from knowledge of the constant
One's action will lead to impartiality,
Impartiality to kingliness,   15
Kingliness to heaven,
Heaven to the way,
The way to perpetuity,
And to the end of one's days one will meet with no danger.

XVII

The best of all rulers is but a shadowy presence to his subjects.
Next comes the ruler they love and praise;
Next comes one they fear;
Next comes one with whom they take liberties.
When there is not enough faith, there is lack of good faith.   5
Hesitant, he does not utter words lightly.
When his task is accomplished and his work done
The people all say, 'It happened to us naturally.'

XVIII

When the great way falls into disuse
There are benevolence and rectitude;
When cleverness emerges

There is great hypocrisy;
When the six relations[4] are at variance   5
There are filial children;
When the state is benighted
There are loyal ministers.

XIX

Exterminate the sage, discard the wise,
And the people will benefit a hundredfold;
Exterminate benevolence, discard rectitude,
And the people will again be filial;
Exterminate ingenuity, discard profit,   5
And there will be no more thieves and bandits.
These three, being false adornments, are not enough
And the people must have something to which they
        can attach themselves:
Exhibit the unadorned and embrace the uncarved
        block,
Have little thought of self and as few desires as
        possible.   10

XX

Exterminate learning and there will no longer be worries.
Between yea and nay
How much difference is there?
Between good and evil
How great is the distance?   5
What others fear
One must also fear.
And wax without having reached the limit.
The multitude are joyous
As if partaking of the *tai lao*[5] offering   10
Or going up to a terrace in spring.
I alone am inactive and reveal no signs,
Like a baby that has not yet learned to smile,
Listless as though with no home to go back to.
The multitude all have more than enough.   15
I alone seem to be in want.
My mind is that of a fool—how blank!
Vulgar people are clear.

4. One commentator takes them as the relation between father and son, elder and younger
brother, and husband and wife.

5. A ritual feast, where three kinds of animals—
ox, sheep, and pig—were sacrificed.

I alone am drowsy.
Vulgar people are alert.   20
I alone am muddled.
Calm like the sea:
Like a high wind that never ceases.
The multitude all have a purpose.
I alone am foolish and uncouth.   25
I alone am different from others
And value being fed by the mother.

XXV

There is a thing confusedly formed,
Born before heaven and earth.
Silent and void
It stands alone and does not change,
Goes round and does not weary.   5
It is capable of being the mother of the world.
I know not its name
So I style it 'the way'.
I give it the makeshift name of 'the great'.
Being great, it is further described as receding,   10
Receding, it is described as far away,
Being far away, it is described as turning back.
Hence the way is great; heaven is great; earth is great; and the king is also
    great. Within the realm there are four things that are great, and the
    king counts as one.
Man models himself on earth,
Earth on heaven,   15
Heaven on the way,
And the way on that which is naturally so.

XXVIII

Know the male
But keep to the role of the female
And be a ravine to the empire.
If you are a ravine to the empire,
Then the constant virtue will not desert you   5
And you will again return to being a babe.
Know the white
But keep to the role of the black
And be a model to the empire.
If you are a model to the empire,   10
Then the constant virtue will not be wanting
And you will return to the infinite.
Know honor

But keep to the role of the disgraced
And be a valley to the empire.   15
If you are a valley to the empire,
Then the constant virtue will be sufficient
And you will return to being the uncarved block.
When the uncarved block shatters it becomes vessels.
The sage makes use of these and becomes the lord   20
over the officials.
Hence the greatest cutting
Does not sever.

XXXVII

The way never acts yet nothing is left undone.
Should lords and princes be able to hold fast to it,
The myriad creatures will be transformed of their
    own accord.
After they are transformed, should desire raise its
    head,
I shall press it down with the weight of the nameless
    uncarved block.   5
The nameless uncarved block
Is but freedom from desire,
And if I cease to desire and remain still,
The empire will be at peace of its own accord.

XXXVIII

A man of the highest virtue does not keep to virtue and that is why he has
    virtue. A man of the lowest virtue never strays from virtue and that is
    why he is without virtue. The former never acts yet leaves nothing
    undone. The latter acts but there are things left undone. A man of the
    highest benevolence acts, but from no ulterior motive. A man of the
    highest rectitude acts, but from ulterior motive. A man most
    conversant in the rites acts, but when no one responds rolls up his
    sleeves and resorts to persuasion by force.
Hence when the way was lost there was virtue; when virtue was lost there
    was benevolence; when benevolence was lost there was rectitude;
    when rectitude was lost there were the rites.
The rites are the wearing thin of loyalty and good faith
And the beginning of disorder;
Foreknowledge is the flowery embellishment of the way   5
And the beginning of folly.
Hence the man of large mind abides in the thick not in the thin, in the fruit
    not in the flower.
Therefore he discards the one and takes the other.

XLII

The way begets one; one begets two; two begets three; three begets the
  myriad creatures.
The myriad creatures carry on their backs the *yin* and embrace in their
  arms the *yang* and are the blending of the generative forces of the two.
There are no words which men detest more than 'solitary', 'desolate', and
  'hapless', yet lords and princes use these to refer to themselves.
Thus a thing is sometimes added to by being diminished and diminished by
  being added to.
What others teach I also teach. 'The violent will not come to a natural end.'
  I shall take this as my precept.

XLVIII

In the pursuit of learning one knows more every day; in the pursuit of the
  way one does less every day. One does less and less until one does
  nothing at all, and when one does nothing at all there is nothing that is
  undone.
It is always through not meddling that the empire is won. Should you
  meddle, then you are not equal to the task of winning the empire.

LXIV

It is easy to maintain a situation while it is still
    secure;
It is easy to deal with a situation before symptoms
    develop;
It is easy to break a thing when it is yet brittle;
It is easy to dissolve a thing when it is yet minute.
Deal with a thing while it is still nothing;   5
Keep a thing in order before disorder sets in.
A tree that can fill the span of a man's arms
Grows from a downy tip;
A terrace nine storeys high
Rises from hodfuls of earth;   10
A journey of a thousand miles
Starts from beneath one's feet.
Whoever does anything to it will ruin it; whoever lays hold of it will lose it.
Therefore the sage, because he does nothing, never ruins anything; and,
    because he does not lay hold of anything, loses nothing.
In their enterprises the people   15
Always ruin them when on the verge of success.
Be as careful at the end as at the beginning
And there will be no ruined enterprises.
Therefore the sage desires not to desire
And does not value goods which are hard to come by;   20

Learns to be without learning
And makes good the mistakes of the multitude
In order to help the myriad creatures to be natural
    and to refrain from daring to act.

LXX

My words are very easy to understand and very easy to put into practice, yet no
    one in the world can understand them or put them into practice.
Words have an ancestor and affairs have a sovereign. It is because people are
    ignorant that they fail to understand me.
Those who understand me are few;
Those who imitate me are honoured.
Therefore the sage, while clad in homespun, conceals on his person a
    priceless piece of jade.   5

LXXVI

A man is supple and weak when living, but hard and stiff when dead. Grass and
    trees are pliant and fragile when living, but dried and shrivelled when dead.
    Thus the hard and the strong are the comrades of death; the supple and
    the weak are the comrades of life.
Therefore a weapon that is strong will not vanquish;
A tree that is strong will suffer the axe.
The strong and big takes the lower position,
The supple and weak takes the higher position.   5

LXXXI

Truthful words are not beautiful; beautiful words are not truthful. Good words
    are not persuasive; persuasive words are not good. He who knows has no
    wide learning; he who has wide learning does not know.
The sage does not hoard.
Having bestowed all he has on others, he has yet more;
Having given all he has to others, he is richer still.
The way of heaven benefits and does not harm; the way of the sage is bountiful
    and does not contend.   5

ZHUANGZI

fourth–second centuries B.C.E

The *Zhuangzi*, a text attributed to a figure called Zhuangzi (ca. 369–286 B.C.E), is the most iridescent example of early Chinese Masters Literature. Conveying wisdom about how to live a good life in a world filled with violence and conceit, the rich philosophical genre of Masters Literature flourished for half a millennium, beginning at the time of **Confucius** (551–479 B.C.E). Next to the *Daodejing* ("The Classic of the Way and Its Virtue," attributed to a master called **Laozi**), the *Zhuangzi* is considered the second most foundational text of Daoist philosophy. For Zhuangzi the good life was one of freedom from societal bounds, spent far away from political obligation, in blissful accordance with the *dao*, the "natural Way." As Zhuangzi claims at one point, he preferred happily "dragging his tail in the mud" like a giant tortoise to getting involved in current affairs. *Zhuangzi*'s wit and literary versatility is playful, while always giving his readers the sense that something fundamental is being said, and this has made the *Zhuangzi* fresh and thought provoking for generations of readers.

Little is known about the philosopher Zhuangzi beyond what we hear about him in *Zhuangzi*. Many masters of his time traveled from state to state and offered political advice to rulers during the contentious Warring States Period (fourth–third centuries B.C.E), which preceded the unification of China under the Qin Dynasty (221 B.C.E.). They relied on the patronage of these fickle rulers in return. Zhuangzi did not seek patronage or office, but seemed content to tell his stories and write. He did, however, gather admirers: only the first seven of the *Zhuangzi*'s thirty-three chapters are attributed to him, while the remaining chapters were probably written over several centuries by later followers.

The *Zhuangzi* is written in a prose of constantly changing styles, with embedded verse passages. It moves from wise jokes and funny parables to moments of passionate seriousness, to tight philosophical arguments that turn imperceptibly into parodies. It hovers between hilarious anecdotes and complex philosophical treatises, between deriding and celebrating the power of language, between humiliating proponents of clever logic and brilliantly mobilizing their tools against them, and between rhetorical pyrotechnics and gestures toward some grand truth. This grand truth is often conveyed by fantastic creatures, such as monstrous birds, ocean spirits, or remarkable trees, which populate a gigantic universe that dwarfs our human world and teaches—and laughs at—the ultimate relativity of our perspective.

For Zhuangzi the greatest sources of misunderstanding are words. Words acquire meaning through human convention and are therefore limited to a human scale and human problems. In chapter 2, our selection below, he moves into a logical argument on the relativity of the terms *this* and *that* as well as *right* and *wrong*. The argument is intricate and stylized, and at some point readers begin to suspect that they are reading the parody of an argument, a suspicion confirmed when Zhuangzi's grand summation culminates in a joke. But then again, this is perhaps the only proper conclusion for an argument against the absolute validity of arguments and of the meaning of words.

Alongside the *Daodejing*, the *Zhuangzi* is one of the foundational texts of Daoist philosophy. While these two texts share a general outlook—a rejection of conventional wisdom, a pleasure in paradox, a call to return to a natural Way, and a polemical stance against Confucianism—their visions diverge on crucial points. Zhuangzi's happy abstention from any will to rule is foreign to the *Daodejing*'s advice on how to gain power and become a successful ruler. His joyful embrace of death contrasts with the notion in the *Daodejing* that death is a state of alienation and rigidity, and runs completely counter to the pursuit of immortality through bodily practices and drugs in later Daoism. Most important, while the *Daodejing* repeats its pithy paradoxes in short verse over and over again, Zhuangzi revels in the pleasure of storytelling, sometimes adding narrative flesh to the abstract cosmic arguments of the *Daodejing*, and sometimes varying or contradicting them.

In the intellectual world of China and beyond, the *Zhuangzi* is unique: its anecdotes and parables shimmer with comic playfulness and wear their weighty philosophical themes with unbearable lightness. The uncertainty of whether Zhuangzi is the butterfly or the butterfly is Zhuangzi does not create the intellectual pessimism or existential angst of a radical skeptic who solemnly doubts everything in the world. Rather, there is an exuberant joy in being part of the "great transformation of things." With this philosophical style, his sophisticated reflection on language, and his whiff of iconoclasm, Zhuangzi has been popular with ancients and moderns alike: Oscar Wilde, the famous Irish wit, was attracted to the text and reviewed one of its early translations into English in 1889. For all his readers, nobody can quite pin Zhuangzi down. As his earliest followers said: "Above he wandered with the Creator, below he made friends with those who had gone beyond life and death. . . . So veiled and arcane! He has never been completely comprehended."

CHAPTER 2[1]

Discussion on Making All Things Equal

Ziqi of south wall sat leaning on his armrest, staring up at the sky and breathing—vacant and far away, as though he'd lost his companion.[2] Yan Cheng Ziyou, who was standing by his side in attendance, said, "What is this? Can you really make the body like a withered tree and the mind like dead ashes? The man leaning on the armrest now is not the one who leaned on it before!"

Ziqi said, "You do well to ask the question, Yan. Now I have lost myself. Do you understand that? You hear the piping of men, but you haven't heard the piping of earth. Or if you've heard the piping of earth, you haven't heard the piping of Heaven!"

Ziyou said, "May I venture to ask what this means?"

Ziqi said, "The Great Clod[3] belches out breath and its name is wind. So long as it doesn't come forth, nothing happens. But when it does, then ten thousand

---

1. Translated by Burton Watson.
2. Interpreted variously to mean his associates, his wife, or his own body.

3. The earth.

hollows begin crying wildly. Can't you hear them, long drawn out? In the mountain forests that lash and sway, there are huge trees a hundred spans around with hollows and openings like noses, like mouths, like ears, like jugs, like cups, like mortars, like rifts, like ruts. They roar like waves, whistle like arrows, screech, gasp, cry, wail, moan, and howl, those in the lead calling out *yeee!*, those behind calling out *yuuu!* In a gentle breeze they answer faintly, but in a full gale the chorus is gigantic. And when the fierce wind has passed on, then all the hollows are empty again. Have you never seen the tossing and trembling that goes on?"

Ziyou said, "By the piping of earth, then, you mean simply [the sound of] these hollows, and by the piping of man [the sound of] flutes and whistles. But may I ask about the piping of Heaven?"

Ziqi said, "Blowing on the ten thousand things in a different way, so that each can be itself—all take what they want for themselves, but who does the sounding?"

Great understanding is broad and unhurried; little understanding is cramped and busy. Great words are clear and limpid; little words are shrill and quarrelsome. In sleep, men's spirits go visiting; in waking hours, their bodies hustle. With everything they meet they become entangled. Day after day they use their minds in strife, sometimes grandiose, sometimes sly, sometimes petty. Their little fears are mean and trembly; their great fears are stunned and overwhelming. They bound off like an arrow or a crossbow pellet, certain that they are the arbiters of right and wrong. They cling to their position as though they had sworn before the gods, sure that they are holding on to victory. They fade like fall and winter—such is the way they dwindle day by day. They drown in what they do—you cannot make them turn back. They grow dark, as though sealed with seals—such are the excesses of their old age. And when their minds draw near to death, nothing can restore them to the light.

Joy, anger, grief, delight, worry, regret, fickleness, inflexibility, modesty, will-fulness, candor, insolence—music from empty holes, mushrooms springing up in dampness, day and night replacing each other before us, and no one knows where they sprout from. Let it be! Let it be! [It is enough that] morning and evening we have them, and they are the means by which we live. Without them we would not exist; without us they would have nothing to take hold of. This comes close to the matter. But I do not know what makes them the way they are. It would seem as though they have some True Master, and yet I find no trace of him. He can act—that is certain. Yet I cannot see his form. He has identity but no form.

The hundred joints, the nine openings, the six organs, all come together and exist here [as my body]. But which part should I feel closest to? I should delight in all parts, you say? But there must be one I ought to favor more. If not, are they all of them mere servants? But if they are all servants, then how can they keep order among themselves? Or do they take turns being lord and servant? It would seem as though there must be some True Lord among them. But whether I succeed in discovering his identity or not, it neither adds to nor detracts from his Truth.

Once a man receives this fixed bodily form, he holds on to it, waiting for the end. Sometimes clashing with things, sometimes bending before them, he runs his course like a galloping steed, and nothing can stop him. Is he not pathetic?

Sweating and laboring to the end of his days and never seeing his accomplishment, utterly exhausting himself and never knowing where to look for rest—can you help pitying him? I'm not dead yet! he says, but what good is that? His body decays, his mind follows it—can you deny that this is a great sorrow? Man's life has always been a muddle like this. How could I be the only muddled one, and other men not muddled?

If a man follows the mind given him and makes it his teacher, then who can be without a teacher? Why must you comprehend the process of change and form your mind on that basis before you can have a teacher? Even an idiot has his teacher. But to fail to abide by this mind and still insist upon your rights and wrongs—this is like saying that you set off for Yue today and got there yesterday.⁴ This is to claim that what doesn't exist exists. If you claim that what doesn't exist exists, then even the holy sage Yu couldn't understand you, much less a person like me!

Words are not just wind. Words have something to say. But if what they have to say is not fixed, then do they really say something? Or do they say nothing? People suppose that words are different from the peeps of baby birds, but is there any difference, or isn't there? What does the Way rely upon, that we have true and false? What do words rely upon, that we have right and wrong? How can the Way go away and not exist? How can words exist and not be acceptable? When the Way relies on little accomplishments and words rely on vain show, then we have the rights and wrongs of the Confucians and the Mo-ists.⁵ What one calls right the other calls wrong; what one calls wrong the other calls right. But if we want to right their wrongs and wrong their rights, then the best thing to use is clarity.

Everything has its "that," everything has its "this." From the point of view of "that" you cannot see it, but through understanding you can know it. So I say, "that" comes out of "this" and "this" depends on "that"—which is to say that "this" and "that" give birth to each other. But where there is birth there must be death; where there is death there must be birth. Where there is acceptability there must be unacceptability; where there is unacceptability there must be acceptability. Where there is recognition of right there must be recognition of wrong; where there is recognition of wrong there must be recognition of right. Therefore the sage does not proceed in such a way, but illuminates all in the light of Heaven.⁶ He too recognizes a "this," but a "this" which is also "that," a "that" which is also "this." His "that" has both a right and a wrong in it; his "this" too has both a right and a wrong in it. So, in fact, does he still have a "this" and "that"? Or does he in fact no longer have a "this" and "that"? A state in which "this" and "that" no longer find their opposites is called the hinge of the Way. When the hinge is fitted into the socket, it can respond endlessly. Its right then is a single endlessness and its wrong too is a single endlessness. So, I say, the best thing to use is clarity.

To use an attribute to show that attributes are not attributes is not as good as using a nonattribute to show that attributes are not attributes. To use a horse to show that a horse is not a horse is not as good as using a non-horse to show

---

4. A typical paradox of the logician Huizi.
5. Followers of a utilitarian philosophical school who opposed the traditional ceremo-nies that the Confucians saw as essential to a good society.
6. Nature or the Way.

that a horse is not a horse,[7] Heaven and earth are one attribute; the ten thousand things are one horse.

What is acceptable we call acceptable; what is unacceptable we call unacceptable. A road is made by people walking on it; things are so because they are called so. What makes them so? Making them so makes them so. What makes them not so? Making them not so makes them not so. Things all must have that which is so; things all must have that which is acceptable. There is nothing that is not so, nothing that is not acceptable.

For this reason, whether you point to a little stalk or a great pillar, a leper or the beautiful Xishi, things ribald and shady or things grotesque and strange, the Way makes them all into one. Their dividedness is their completeness; their completeness is their impairment. No thing is either complete or impaired, but all are made into one again. Only the man of far-reaching vision knows how to make them into one. So he has no use [for categories], but relegates all to the constant. The constant is the useful; the useful is the passable; the passable is the successful; and with success, all is accomplished. He relies upon this alone, relies upon it and does not know he is doing so. This is called the Way.

But to wear out your brain trying to make things into one without realizing that they are all the same—this is called "three in the morning." What do I mean by "three in the morning"? When the monkey trainer was handing out acorns, he said, "You get three in the morning and four at night." This made all the monkeys furious. "Well, then," he said, "you get four in the morning and three at night." The monkeys were all delighted. There was no change in the reality behind the words, and yet the monkeys responded with joy and anger. Let them, if they want to. So the sage harmonizes with both right and wrong and rests in Heaven the Equalizer. This is called walking two roads.

The understanding of the men of ancient times went a long way. How far did it go? To the point where some of them believed that things have never existed—so far, to the end, where nothing can be added. Those at the next stage thought that things exist but recognized no boundaries among them. Those at the next stage thought there were boundaries but recognized no right and wrong. Because right and wrong appeared, the Way was injured, and because the Way was injured, love became complete. But do such things as completion and injury really exist, or do they not?

There is such a thing as completion and injury—Mr. Zhao playing the lute is an example. There is such a thing as no completion and no injury—Mr. Zhao not playing the lute is an example.[8] Zhao Wen played the lute; Music Master Kuang waved his baton; Huizi leaned on his desk. The knowledge of these three was close to perfection. All were masters, and therefore their names have been handed down to later ages. Only in their likes they were different from him [the true sage]. What they liked, they tried to make clear. What he is not

---

7. Zhuangzi pokes fun at the logician Gongsun Long and his treatises "A White Horse Is Not a Horse" and "Attributes Are Not Attributes in and of Themselves."

8. Zhao Wen was a famous lute (*qin*) player. But the best music he could play (i.e., complete) was only a pale and partial reflection of the ideal music, which was thereby injured and impaired, just as the unity of the Way was injured by the appearance of love—i.e., someone's likes and dislikes. Hence, when Mr. Zhao refrained from playing the lute, there was neither completion nor injury.

clear about, they tried to make clear, and so they ended in the foolishness of "hard" and "white."[9] Their sons, too, devoted all their lives to their fathers' theories, but till their death never reached any completion. Can these men be said to have attained completion? If so, then so have all the rest of us. Or can they not be said to have attained completion? If so, then neither we nor anything else have ever attained it.

The torch of chaos and doubt—this is what the sage steers by. So he does not use things but relegates all to the constant. This is what it means to use clarity.

Now I am going to make a statement here. I don't know whether it fits into the category of other people's statements or not. But whether it fits into their category or whether it doesn't, it obviously fits into some category. So in that respect it is no different from their statements. However, let me try making my statement.

There is a beginning. There is not yet beginning to be a beginning. There is a not yet beginning to be a not yet beginning to be a beginning. There is being. There is nonbeing. There is a not yet beginning to be nonbeing. There is a not yet beginning to be a not yet beginning to be nonbeing. Suddenly there is nonbeing. But I do not know, when it comes to nonbeing, which is really being and which is nonbeing. Now I have just said something. But I don't know whether what I have said has really said something or whether it hasn't said something.

There is nothing in the world bigger than the tip of an autumn hair,[1] and Mount Tai is tiny. No one has lived longer than a dead child, and Pengzu died young. Heaven and earth were born at the same time I was, and the ten thousand things are one with me.

We have already become one, so how can I say anything? But I have just *said* that we are one, so how can I not be saying something? The one and what I said about it make two, and two and the original one make three. If we go on this way, then even the cleverest mathematician can't tell where we'll end, much less an ordinary man. If by moving from nonbeing to being we get to three, how far will we get if we move from being to being? Better not to move, but to let things be!

The Way has never known boundaries; speech has no constancy. But because of [the recognition of a] "this," there came to be boundaries. Let me tell you what the boundaries are. There is left, there is right, there are theories, there are debates, there are divisions, there are discriminations, there are emulations, and there are contentions. These are called the Eight Virtues. As to what is beyond the Six Realms,[2] the sage admits its existence but does not theorize. As to what is within the Six Realms, he theorizes but does not debate. In the case of the *Spring and Autumn*,[3] the record of the former kings of past ages,

9. The logicians Huizi and Gongsun Long spent much time discussing paradoxes involving the relation between attributes such as "hard" and "white" and the things to which they pertain.
1. Figure for something extremely tiny. The strands of animal fur were believed to grow

particularly fine in autumn.
2. The universe: heaven, earth, and the four directions.
3. Probably a reference to the *Spring and Autumn Annals*, a history of the state of Lu said to have been compiled by Confucius.

the sage debates but does not discriminate. So [I say,] those who divide fail to divide; those who discriminate fail to discriminate. What does this mean, you ask? The sage embraces things. Ordinary men discriminate among them and parade their discriminations before others. So I say, those who discriminate fail to see.

The Great Way is not named; Great Discriminations are not spoken; Great Benevolence is not benevolent; Great Modesty is not humble; Great Daring does not attack. If the Way is made clear, it is not the Way. If discriminations are put into words, they do not suffice. If benevolence has a constant object, it cannot be universal. If modesty is fastidious, it cannot be trusted. If daring attacks, it cannot be complete. These five are all round, but they tend toward the square.[4]

Therefore understanding that rests in what it does not understand is the finest. Who can understand discriminations that are not spoken, the Way that is not a way? If he can understand this, he may be called the Reservoir of Heaven. Pour into it and it is never full, dip from it and it never runs dry, and yet it does not know where the supply comes from. This is called the Shaded Light.

So it is that long ago Yao said to Shun, "I want to attack the rulers of Zong Kuai and Xu'ao. Even as I sit on my throne, this thought nags at me. Why is this?"

Shun replied, "These three rulers are only little dwellers in the weeds and brush. Why this nagging desire? Long ago, ten suns came out all at once and the ten thousand things were all lighted up. And how much greater is virtue than these suns!"[5]

Nie Que asked Wang Ni, "Do you know what all things agree in calling right?"

"How would I know that?" said Wang Ni.

"Do you know that you don't know it?"

"How would I know that?"

"Then do things know nothing?"

"How would I know that? However, suppose I try saying something. What way do I have of knowing that if I say I know something I don't really not know it? Or what way do I have of knowing that if I say I don't know something I don't really in fact know it? Now let me ask *you* some questions. If a man sleeps in a damp place, his back aches and he ends up half paralyzed, but is this true of a loach? If he lives in a tree, he is terrified and shakes with fright, but is this true of a monkey? Of these three creatures, then, which one knows the proper place to live? Men eat the flesh of grass-fed and grain-fed animals, deer eat grass, centipedes find snakes tasty, and hawks and falcons relish mice. Of these four, which knows how food ought to taste? Monkeys pair with monkeys, deer go out with deer, and fish play around with fish. Men claim that Mao-qiang and Lady Li were beautiful, but if fish saw them they would dive to the bottom of the stream, if birds saw them they would fly away, and if deer saw

---

4. All are originally perfect, but may become "squared"—i.e., impaired by the misuses mentioned.

5. Here virtue is to be understood in a positive sense, as the power of the Way.

them they would break into a run. Of these four, which knows how to fix the standard of beauty for the world? The way I see it, the rules of benevolence and righteousness and the paths of right and wrong are all hopelessly snarled and jumbled. How could I know anything about such discriminations?"

Nie Que said, "If you don't know what is profitable or harmful, then does the Perfect Man likewise know nothing of such things?"

Wang Ni replied, "The Perfect Man is godlike. Though the great swamps blaze, they cannot burn him; though the great rivers freeze, they cannot chill him; though swift lightning splits the hills and howling gales shake the sea, they cannot frighten him. A man like this rides the clouds and mist, straddles the sun and moon, and wanders beyond the four seas. Even life and death have no effect on him, much less the rules of profit and loss!"

Ju Quezi said to Zhang Wuzi, "I have heard Confucius say that the sage does not work at anything, does not pursue profit, does not dodge harm, does not enjoy being sought after, does not follow the Way, says nothing yet says something, says something yet says nothing, and wanders beyond the dust and grime. Confucius himself regarded these as wild and flippant words, though I believe they describe the working of the mysterious Way. What do you think of them?"

Zhang Wuzi said, "Even the Yellow Emperor would be confused if he heard such words, so how could you expect Confucius to understand them? What's more, you're too hasty in your own appraisal. You see an egg and demand a crowing cock, see a crossbow pellet and demand a roast dove. I'm going to try speaking some reckless words and I want you to listen to them recklessly. How will that be? The sage leans on the sun and moon, tucks the universe under his arm, merges himself with things, leaves the confusion and muddle as it is, and looks on slaves as exalted. Ordinary men strain and struggle; the sage is stupid and blockish. He takes part in ten thousand ages and achieves simplicity in oneness. For him, all the ten thousand things are what they are, and thus they enfold each other.

"How do I know that loving life is not a delusion? How do I know that in hating death I am not like a man who, having left home in his youth, has forgotten the way back?

"Lady Li was the daughter of the border guard of Ai.[6] When she was first taken captive and brought to the state of Jin, she wept until her tears drenched the collar of her robe. But later, when she went to live in the palace of the ruler, shared his couch with him, and ate the delicious meats of his table, she wondered why she had ever wept. How do I know that the dead do not wonder why they ever longed for life?

"He who dreams of drinking wine may weep when morning comes; he who dreams of weeping may in the morning go off to hunt. While he is dreaming he does not know it is a dream, and in his dream he may even try to interpret a dream. Only after he wakes does he know it was a dream. And someday there will be a great awakening when we know that this is all a great dream. Yet the stupid believe they are awake, busily and brightly assuming they understand

6. She was taken captive by Duke Xian of Jin in 671 B.C.E., and later became his consort.

things, calling this man ruler, that one herdsman—how dense! Confucius and you are both dreaming! And when I say you are dreaming, I am dreaming, too. Words like these will be labeled the Supreme Swindle. Yet, after ten thousand generations, a great sage may appear who will know their meaning, and it will still be as though he appeared with astonishing speed.

"Suppose you and I have had an argument. If you have beaten me instead of my beating you, then are you necessarily right and am I necessarily wrong? If I have beaten you instead of your beating me, then am I necessarily right and are you necessarily wrong? Is one of us right and the other wrong? Are both of us right or are both of us wrong? If you and I don't know the answer, then other people are bound to be even more in the dark. Whom shall we get to decide what is right? Shall we get someone who agrees with you to decide? But if he already agrees with you, how can he decide fairly? Shall we get someone who agrees with me? But if he already agrees with me, how can he decide? Shall we get someone who disagrees with both of us? But if he already disagrees with both of us, how can he decide? Obviously, then, neither you nor I nor anyone else can decide for each other. Shall we wait for still another person?

"But waiting for one shifting voice [to pass judgment on] another is the same as waiting for none of them. Harmonize them all with the Heavenly Equality, leave them to their endless changes, and so live out your years. What do I mean by harmonizing them with the Heavenly Equality? Right is not right; so is not so. If right were really right, it would differ so clearly from not right that there would be no need for argument. If so were really so, it would differ so clearly from not so that there would be no need for argument. Forget the years; forget distinctions. Leap into the boundless and make it your home!"

Penumbra said to Shadow, "A little while ago you were walking and now you're standing still; a little while ago you were sitting and now you're standing up. Why this lack of independent action?"

Shadow said, "Do I have to wait for something before I can be like this? Does what I wait for also have to wait for something before it can be like this? Am I waiting for the scales of a snake or the wings of a cicada? How do I know why it is so? How do I know why it isn't so?"

Once Zhuang Zhou dreamt he was a butterfly, a butterfly flitting and fluttering around, happy with himself and doing as he pleased. He didn't know he was Zhuang Zhou. Suddenly he woke up and there he was, solid and unmistakable Zhuang Zhou. But he didn't know if he was Zhuang Zhou who had dreamt he was a butterfly, or a butterfly dreaming he was Zhuang Zhou. Between Zhuang Zhou and a butterfly there must be *some* distinction! This is called the Transformation of Things.

IV

Circling the Mediterranean: Europe and the Islamic World

The word "Mediterranean" comes from Latin, meaning "in the middle of the lands." From antiquity through the Middle Ages, the centrally located Mediterranean Sea—also called by those who lived along its shores *Mare nostrum,* or "our sea"—facilitated trade and exchange. Not only commodities but also stories and songs continually circulated from place to place, crisscrossing the water to link nations in Europe, North Africa, and the Near and Middle East. Port cities all around the Mediterranean were sites of particularly intense cultural and economic interaction, collectively making up a single complex web that knit together distant lands.

While earlier generations of historians have tended to see the diverse cultures of the Mediterranean region in monolithic terms, conceiving of an Islamic world and a Christian world that were fundamentally opposed, more recent research has unearthed the intimate links between the various cultures of the region. There was both a great deal of interaction *between* the cultural spheres conventionally marked as "Europe" and "the Islamic world" and, on the other hand, a great deal of diversity *within* each one of these apparently undifferentiated units. "Europe," as a multinational concept, almost never appeared during the Middle Ages; people referred to themselves as

A fourteenth-century image of the Venetian trader Marco Polo, embarking from Venice.

"English," "Franks," "Normans," and "Lombards," not as "Europeans." "The Islamic world" was similarly divided by rival efforts to lead the Muslim community in the caliphates of Damascus, Baghdad, and Cairo, as well as by the Mongol invasions of the thirteenth century. The opposition of "the Islamic world" and "Europe" is a modern invention: it was not the way medieval people described themselves or the world they lived in.

The false division between Europe and the Islamic world enabled a misleading view of history in which Christian Europe was seen as the sole heir to a rich legacy of Greco-Roman philosophy and literature, uncontaminated by Arabic or Persian influences—an uninterrupted cultural bloodline, so to speak, reaching back from Aquinas to Aristotle, from **Dante** to **Virgil**. Nothing could be further from the truth. The Arabic translations of ancient Greek philoso-

phy and science that made the work of Plato, Aristotle, and Ptolemy available to Europeans as they slowly emerged from a long period of intellectual dormancy were not just passive vessels that transmitted ancient knowledge to an awakening Europe on the cusp of the Renaissance: on the contrary, the cultural ferment of the Islamic world was an essential element in the emergence of the early modern West. The story of premodern history and literature is, therefore, above all a story of connections, interaction, and mutual influence.

CHRISTIANITY AND PLATONISM

By the year 100, broad changes were under way in the lands circling the Mediterranean Sea. The Roman Empire, which had reached its pinnacle of cultural and military supremacy during the

This image, from an illuminated thirteenth-century Arabic manuscript, depicts the Greek philosopher Socrates discoursing with his students.

reign of Augustus Caesar, had expanded to the point that unrest in the eastern provinces was a perpetual worry. In the Roman-ruled province of Judea (roughly, modern Israel), the suppression by the civil authorities of a loosely organized rebellion culminated in the destruction of Jerusalem and scattering (or "diaspora") of the Jewish community in 70 C.E. Those exiled from the region included the Jewish followers of James and John who had embraced the message of the gospel, as well as those mixed Jewish and Gentile communities that took up the intensely hellenized brand of Christianity developed by Paul and his followers, which drew on the philosophy of Plato as well as of mystical Neoplatonists such as Plotinus and Porphyry. Not until about three centuries later would this heterogeneous collection of new religious orientations become codified as a single Christian doctrine, encapsulated in Jerome's production of the Latin (or "Vulgate") **Bible** and in **Augustine**'s masterful synthesis of Christian doctrine and Greek philosophy.

Augustine's autobiography, the **Confessions**, pays tribute to the theologian's engagement with the philosophy and literature of the Roman world: he paraphrases Seneca and Cicero, and movingly describes the tears he shed while reading Virgil's account of Dido in the *Aeneid*. These moments illustrate the imaginative pull of classical literature, which persisted during the period of Christianity's emergence. The values of Rome, its celebration of the arts and worldly pleasures, were very much at odds with a Christian ethic that demanded a rejection of the things of this world. Music, art, and poetry were to be avoided, unless they were explicitly in the service of God: liturgical music, as part of the act of communal worship, along with painted images of the crucified Christ, the Virgin Mary, and apostles, became increasingly important in early Christianity, while the classical principles of poetic composi-

tion were applied to new types of writing such as religious hymns and saints' lives. Writers found that poetry could be made to serve Christ, in the same way that figurative parables could disseminate the eternal truths of scripture. Jesus had told illustrative anecdotes, such as the parable of the Sower or the parable of the Wise and Foolish Virgins: preachers therefore believed that they too were authorized to use fictions, as long as the effort was wholly in the service of the Lord and not intended to seduce the soul with bodily pleasures.

The yearning for a mystical faith that would provide a sense of purpose was ubiquitous in the late Roman Empire. Christianity was just one of a number of religious cults that had fashioned a kind of cultural compromise with the philosophical orientation of the period; but it thrived as no other religion did, ultimately becoming the state religion of the Roman Empire under the rule of Constantine in the fourth century. While the Italian city of Rome remained the seat of imperial power in the West, the capital city of Byzantium (modern Istanbul, in Turkey) represented Rome in the East. Renamed "Constantinople" (Constantine's city) by the Christian emperor of Rome, the city would be simply known as "al-Rum" (Rome) to speakers of Arabic and Persian. An empire stretched so widely that it had two capitals, one in the West and one in the East, was ripe for dissolution: sooner or later in the history of every empire, things fall apart. The waves of invasion of Italy by Germanic tribes came to a head in the fifth century, when Rome endured a series of weak rulers. The eastern Roman capital of Constantinople, by contrast, remained intact until the end of the Middle Ages, though during that time its character had changed very substantially from what it had been in the age of the Caesars. Both Augustine and Boethius, writing in the fifth and sixth centuries, bear witness to the decay of

This Byzantine mosaic in the monastery church in Hosios Loukas, Greece, depicts Christ saving Adam, Eve, King David, and King Solomon, who had been confined in limbo.

Rome—and to the birth of something entirely new, as a Christian culture, various and diffuse, rose out of the ashes of empire.

The diaspora—literally, "scattering" (Greek)—of Jews from Jerusalem in 70 C.E. not only facilitated the spread of Christianity throughout the Roman Empire but also created a new cultural environment that would lead to the development of rabbinic Judaism. The simultaneous emergence of rabbinic Judaism and Christianity can be described as a kind of twin birth, both of them formed in the crucible of Roman aggression in the first century. Beyond the physical experience of exile, the figurative concept of diaspora—like the ancient paradigm of the mass movement of people described in Exodus, which recounts the migration of the Jewish na-

tion from Egypt to the promised land after many years of exile—provided an enormously powerful model for thinking about the movement of peoples in the early Middle Ages. Whereas the Jewish people were thought to be consigned to a permanent state of diaspora, endlessly wandering in the desert of the wide world, other communities sometimes claimed for themselves the role of the "true Israel": for medieval Christians, thinking of themselves as the true Israel meant identifying themselves as a chosen people. But their promised land was not to be found on the earth—it was the Heavenly Jerusalem, whose pleasures would be enjoyed only in the afterlife. National histories, too, made the history of the Jewish people into a template for their own myths of origin: this can be seen in medieval chronicles that liken accounts of the Trojans, who fled the ruins of Troy to found the great city of Rome, to accounts of the Jews in the diaspora.

THE SPREAD OF ISLAM

Like the emergence of Christianity in the wake of the Jewish diaspora, the dissemination of the **Qur'an** by Muhammad and his followers in the seventh century and the subsequent formation of an Islamic community had a dramatic effect on the development of Mediterranean culture. In his account of Muhammad's life, the early biographer Ibn Ishaq describes a community struggling to form itself not only in accord with the explicit dictates found in its holy book, the Qur'an, but also in conformity with the exemplary life led by its prophet, Muhammad. These two models, the revealed book and the life perfectly led, were the religious guidelines of an empire that grew almost overnight to dominate large swathes of the Middle East and North Africa: in 750, little more than a century after Muhammad began delivering the Qur'an in 610, Islamic rule extended westward through Spain into southern France and eastward through Persia (modern Iran) into India. The spread of Islam took place not only through cultural and religious means but also through direct military conquest, such as the assault on the Byzantine Christian empire that culminated in the Battle of Yarmūk in 636: after that time, the southern regions of Anatolia (modern Turkey) and virtually the whole of the Levant (modern Near East) were under the control of the armies of Islam. In spite of its military successes and dynamic expansion, this new empire was far from monolithic: after the fall of the Umayyad caliphate (literally, "headship") that had been based in Damascus, the Abbasid caliphate was established at Baghdad, where it endured for more than five hundred years until the Mongol invasions from Central Asia in the mid-thirteenth century. Even after their fall from power in the East, however, the Umayyads retained control in the West, where they continued to rule the Spanish provinces they had named "al-Andalus."

In addition to the political divisions centered on the caliphates, religious divisions also cut across the nations gathered under Islamic rule. The most important of these is the division of Sunni from Shi'a Islam: the former centers on a strict conformity to the exemplary life of the Prophet Muhammad and a literal reading of the Holy Book; the latter instead prescribes a special veneration of the family of the Prophet, especially his daughter Fatima, her husband (who was also the Prophet's cousin) Ali, and their sons Hasan and Hussain. The highly emotional, affective quality of Shi'a Islam is expressed in devotional stories and plays chronicling the martyrdom of the members of the Prophet's family, as well as in the later medieval emergence of Sufi mysticism; the mystics used figurative poetic language to convey the soul's experience of the divine. Both Shi'a veneration of the family of the Prophet and Sufi poetic expressions of religious devotion were regarded with suspicion wherever Sunni practice was the norm; the literature of Shi'a and Sufi piety, however, has continued to be widely popular not only in the Arabic and Persian-speaking populations of the Near and Middle East but also—in translation—throughout the world.

Divisions, both political and religious, persisted throughout the lands of medieval Islam: in response to the alienation of the Shi'a community by the Abbasids who ruled from Baghdad, a separate Fatimid caliphate that was Shi'a in orientation arose in Cairo. Internal squabbling finally gave way to utter chaos with the invasion of the

EUROPE, NORTH AFRICA, ARABIA, ASIA MINOR & WESTERN CENTRAL ASIA

ca. 750–1200

| 0 | 200 | 400 | 600 | 800 kilometers |

| 0 | 100 | 200 | 300 | 400 | 500 miles |

Limits of the Byzantine Empire
as of 750

Seljuk Empire in 1100

Sunni Muslim state
between 900–1200

Shiite Muslim state
between 900–1200

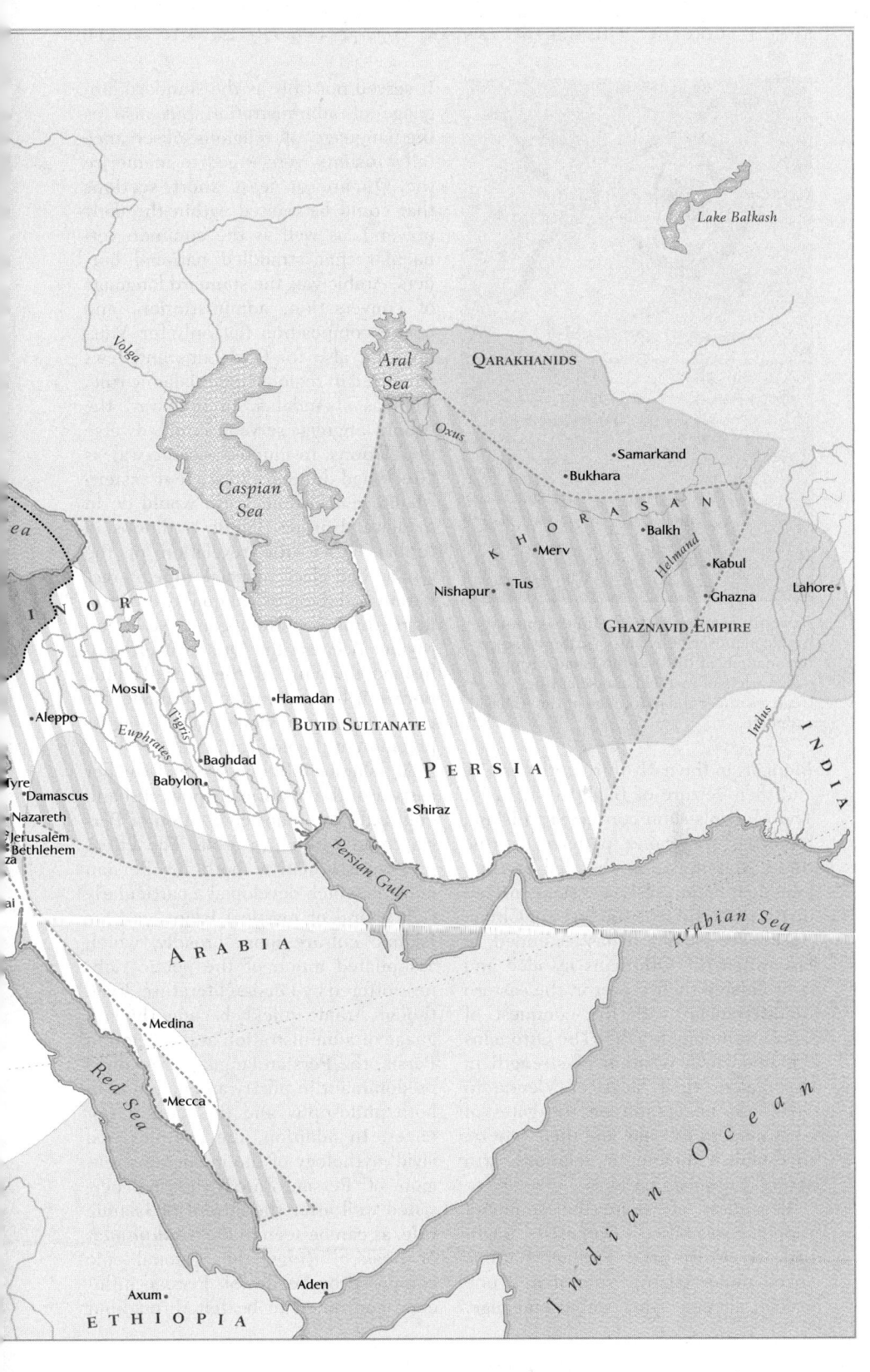

Lake Balkash

Volga

Aral
Sea

QARAKHANIDS

Oxus

•Samarkand

•Bukhara

Caspian
Sea

K H O R A S A N

•Balkh

•Merv

Nishapur• •Tus

Helmand

•Kabul

•Ghazna

Lahore•

GHAZNAVID EMPIRE

I N O R

ea

Mosul•

•Hamadan

•Aleppo

Tigris

BUYID SULTANATE

Euphrates

P E R S I A

•Baghdad

Babylon•

Indus

I N D I A

INDIA

Tyre

•Damascus

Nazareth

•Jerusalem
•Bethlehem

za

ai

•Shiraz

Persian Gulf

Arabian Sea

A R A B I A

Medina•

Red Sea

•Mecca

I n d i a n   O c e a n

Axum•

Aden•

ETHIOPIA

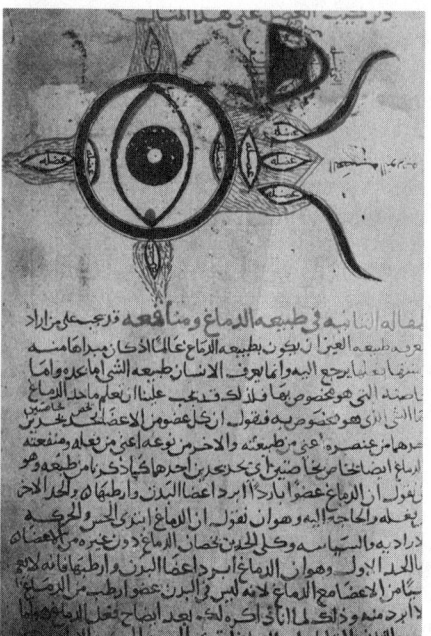

A twelfth-century copy of a ninth-century Arabic manuscript by Hunayn Ibn Ishaq on the anatomy of the eye. Ibn Ishaq wrote a wide variety of medical and scientific treatises under the patronage of the Abbasid caliphate.

Mongols in the early thirteenth century and their seizure of Baghdad in 1258. The Mongols soon converted to Islam, following the same pattern of rule through assimilation that led to their long domination of East Asia, centered on the powerful regional force of China. Successive Islamic dynasties ended, at last, when the Ottomans invaded and consolidated their power in the eastern Mediterranean with the conquest of Constantinople in 1453. The Ottomans remained in a position of strength in the region: their siege of Vienna in 1683 was an assault on the gates of early modern Europe, and they went on to establish diplomatic relations with several European nations.

Regardless of where the dominant caliphate was based—Damascus, Baghdad, or Cairo—the various nations yoked under Islamic rule shared one crucial element: the Arabic language.

It served not only as the standard language of administration but also as the language of religious observance (all Muslims were urged to memorize the Qur'an, at least short sections that could be recited within the daily prayers), as well as the common vernacular that straddled national borders. Arabic was the standard language of conversation, administration, and poetic composition not only for Muslims but also for Christians and Jews who lived in regions under Islamic rule, such as al-Andalus. In this way, the Arabic language served to unify diverse populations, in much the same way as Greek had done in the ancient eastern Mediterranean and Latin would do in medieval Europe. Poetic traditions in Arabia before the revelation of the Qur'an had placed special value on recitation and the musical quality of verse, its rhythmic repetitions and use of end rhyme. Because the Qur'an itself conformed to many of these pre-Islamic norms, it became a standard model for poetic excellence while maintaining its preeminent theological value.

As Islamic influence spread further eastward, the historically powerful and culturally dominant civilization of Persia came within its orbit. The effect was transformative, both for Persian culture, which developed a particularly rich strand of mystical Islam, and for Islamic culture more broadly, which assimilated much of the poetic richness offered by Persian literature. Even though Arabic quickly became the language of administration and religion in Persia, the Persian language remained predominant in poetry and common in both philosophy and the natural sciences. In addition, the complex and vivid mythology of the indigenous religion of Persia, Zoroastrianism, persisted well after the advent of Islamic rule, as can be seen in the **Shahnameh** or *Book of Kings*, the national epic composed by **Ferdowsi**. Persian influence continued to be felt throughout the Islamic world, especially after the Mongol invasions and the establishment of Ottoman rule at Constantinople (renamed Istanbul). The Ottomans held Persian language, art, and poetics in high esteem, and imported painters as well as writers to serve their imperial court. Finally, the marriage of religious devotion and an exquisite poetic sensibility, so finely expressed in the lyrics of Attar, Rumi, and Hafez, would come to be a crucial part of the literary legacy of Islam, widely disseminated not only among the community of Muslim readers but also among the diverse modern audiences of world literature.

In addition to the intersection of poetics and theology, an extraordinarily productive feature of medieval culture was the intersection of poetics and philosophy, in the Latin Christian realm as well as in the Islamic world. Just as Augustine integrated Christian doctrine with Platonic philosophy in his theological writings, so too the Persian philosopher-poet Avicenna integrated the Islamic narrative of miraculous ascent into the heavens with a Platonic vision of the cosmos and its relationship to the individual soul in his *Mi'raj-nameh*. In these strikingly parallel cases, Platonic philosophy supplied the means to express a religious worldview that focuses particularly—whether in Christian or in Islamic terms—on how the individual soul can come to experience the divine presence. Versions of the *mi'raj*, or miraculous night journey, of the Prophet Muhammad first appeared in conservative, highly traditional Sunni accounts of the early history of Islam. Later versions of the mi'raj, such as that attributed to Avicenna, began to interpret the literal journey metaphorically or even mystically, understanding the singular ascent of the Prophet as a model for the journey that every soul must make toward God. By the thirteenth century, versions of the mi'raj had been produced in al-Andalus, including one translated into Castilian at the

order of the Spanish ruler Alfonso the Wise. This text, known as the *Libro della Scala* (or *Book of the Ladder*) was widely disseminated, providing a vision of the layered heavens that would inspire European Christian writers, including Dante.

The influence of Islamic literature was felt not only through the exalted union of philosophy and theology with poetics but also on a more mundane, vernacular level. The vibrant tradition of frame-tale narratives, in which an outer layer organizes a series of nested narratives that are contained within the frame like the layers of an onion, had a long history in the Mediterranean region: writers as early as **Ovid** and Apuleius, in the first and second centuries, had relied on nested narratives. But with the arrival of more elaborate frame-tale models—especially *Kalila wa Dimna*, a series of animal fables based on the Indian *Pañcatantra*—the genre took off in Persian and Arabic literatures. Perhaps the best known example of the frame tale, **The Thousand and One Nights**, survives in its earliest versions in the Persian language; these were soon supplemented by a range of retellings in Arabic. The *Nights* circulated about the Mediterranean, with bits and pieces of it finding its way into other collections and its frame-tale form serving as the inspiration for many European manifestations of the genre, including Boccaccio's *Decameron* and **Chaucer's *Canterbury Tales***.

THE INVENTION OF THE WEST

For writers in the Islamic world, "the West" (*al-maghrib*) was the northern coast of Africa and al-Andalus, a region that was recognized as at once part of the Islamic sphere of influence and yet culturally and regionally distinctive. The idea of the West as a synonym for Christian Europe—which seems so

EUROPE
ca. 1300

FINNS

ESTONIANS

Baltic Sea

Novgorod

LETTS

(3)

TEUTONIC ORDER

RUSSIANS

LITHUANIANS

0   200   400   600   800 kilometers

0   100   200   300   400   500 miles

General directions of the expansion of Latin Christendom
from the 7th to the 15th centuries—

(1) through the Spanish Reconquista
(2) through the Norman conquest of Sicily
(3) through migration and conquest in eastern and northern Europe
(4) through the Crusades

POLES

Vistula

Kiev

(3)

SLOVAKS

Dneister

Approximate line of
division between Roman
Catholics and Orthodox
Christians in the 14th century

Dneiper

Prut

Approximate line of division
between Christendom and
the Muslim world in 1300

Volga

AGYARS

CARPATHIAN MOUNTAINS

Danube

Black Sea

BULGARS

Trebizond

BYZANTINE EMPIRE

Constantinople

SELJUK   STATES

ASIA MINOR

MESOPOTAMIA

Chios

Smyrna (Izmir)

CAPPADOCIA

Tigris

Chiarenza

Athens

Aegean Sea

Morea

Aegina

TAURUS MOUNTAINS

Aleppo

Euphrates

Antioch

Rhodes

Paphos

Cyprus

Damascus

Sea

Crete

(4)

Syrian Desert

CRUSADER STATES

Jerusalem

Alexandria

MUMLAKS

The so-called Hereford Mappamundi, ca. 1300. Jerusalem sits at the center of this medieval map; Asia occupies most of the top half; and Europe is in the lower-left quadrant.

natural and familiar to modern readers— did not even begin to emerge until the late Middle Ages. Medieval inhabitants of Europe instead categorized them- selves in different ways: in terms of their ethnic origin or "nation," in terms of their primary language, and—above all—in terms of their religion. Unlike in the areas under Islamic rule, where Jews and Christians were tolerated albeit subject to special taxation and restrictions (so-called *dhimmi* rule), in Christian Europe Jews were only spo- radically tolerated, and Muslims were virtually unknown. We can thus infer that Europe exhibited much more reli- gious homogeneity, at least until the first glimmerings of early Protestant reform impulses in the late fourteenth century. Uniformity of religion was further strengthened by uniformity of language, as Latin was used not only for all religious but also all political and administrative purposes, just as Arabic was in the Islamic world. Indeed, Lat- in's cultural hold was stronger: medi- eval Christians used it exclusively to compose their philosophical and scien- tific works, while both Arabic and Per- sian functioned as languages of literature

and learning for Muslims. Beginning in the ninth century, however, and with increasing frequency from the twelfth century onward, vernacular languages such as English, French, German, Ital- ian, and Spanish became more com- mon vehicles for poetic composition.

Medieval people defined themselves first of all by their religious orientation and next by ethnic origin, relying not at all on the categories familiar to modern readers. This perspective on the place of the self in the world is well illustrated on the medieval world maps, or *mappae- mundi*, that were used not as practical guides to navigation but rather as abstract overviews of both the literal shape of the world and its metaphorical meaning. Accordingly, such maps conventionally place Jerusalem at the exact center, marking the site of Christ's crucifixion as the fixed point about which the whole world revolves. The mappamundi itself is almost always oriented toward the east (Latin *oriens*), rather than toward the north as on modern maps, so that its easternmost point, the Gar- den of Eden, appears—appropriately—as both the beginning of space and the beginning of time. Asia, Europe, and

A detail from a page of the Luttrell Psalter (ca. 1300) depicts Richard I and Saladin jousting during the Third Crusade. Saladin is drawn with a grotesque blue face—a rendering that makes it all the easier for the psalter's Christian readers to see the conflict as a clearly defined battle between good and evil.

Africa, the three known continents, are depicted symmetrically on the map. Asia takes up twice as much space as the other two, dominating the top half of the world sphere; Europe is tucked away at the lower left; and "the West" (Latin *occidens*) lies, rather forlornly, at the bottom.

The medieval map, with its deeply religious imaginative geography and central focus on Jerusalem, illuminates the ways in which the repeated cycles of European warfare around the Mediterranean and into the Middle East—called "Crusades," after the cross (Latin *crux*) sewn by the warriors onto their garments—functioned not just as actual military campaigns but also as symbolic assaults designed to reclaim control of the spiritual homeland of the medieval Christian. The First Crusade, launched in 1095, included a violent assault on Jerusalem that ended with the slaughter of most of the city's inhabitants and the establishment of the "Latin Kingdom of Jerusalem": a significant outpost of Europeans occupying Jerusalem itself together with additional European fortifications in adjoining towns along the coast (most importantly Acre, which remained in European hands until 1291). Although expeditions continued to be launched intermittently until the end of the Middle Ages—including the dramatic

Third Crusade, which united the English army of Richard the Lion-Hearted with the armies of Philip of France and Frederick Barbarossa of Germany—no later military successes matched those of the First Crusade that began them all. The Crusades functioned mainly as opportunities for economic development and international cooperation among the nations of Europe, helping to unify these disparate Christian nations through their shared opposition to the Muslim enemy. The passions stirred by this effort to stimulate political unity through religious fervor came at a high price: with each successive call to crusade, violent attacks were made on the only locally available non-Christian populations within the cities of Europe—that is, the Jews. Anti-Muslim violence in the form of crusade was therefore closely linked with the persecution of Jews and the early emergence of anti-Semitism.

The opposition of Christian and non-Christian, so fundamental to the ideology of crusade, permeates the epic literature of the Middle Ages. It is especially visible in the poetry of the eleventh century, such as the **Song of Roland**, which is often described as the national epic of France: "Christian" and "pagan" are set against one another throughout the work, as the conflict is cast as white versus black, right versus wrong. The ultimate triumph of the Christian forces of

Charlemagne over the Muslims at Saragossa literally takes place in medieval Spain; metaphorically, however, the victory of Christian over pagan is presented as a template for all holy war—including the First Crusade, which was being launched at the very moment that *Roland* (originally an oral poem) was committed to the page.

The epic genre began to emerge, originally in oral form and subsequently in written texts, by the ninth century. Like the Persian *Shahnameh* of Ferdowsi, the Anglo-Saxon **Beowulf** describes a shadowy era in which myth and history are intertwined; both works also have a similar complicated relationship to the religions that had become obligatory in their cultures but were anachronisms in the mythic worlds that they evoked. For Ferdowsi, Islam was an overlay that covered over but did not obscure the indigenous Persian myth that animates the epic of kings; for the anonymous author of *Beowulf*, Christianity is likewise an innovation applied as a veneer, here on a pagan Germanic past. The Germanic notion of *wyrd* or fate is aligned, by the *Beowulf*-poet, with Christian notions of divine providence, but it remains clear that the two concepts are far from identical. Epic, whether in England or in Persia, thus creates a sense of national identity by evoking a common historical origin, but it also grafts upon the rootstock of native myth new forms of identity—especially religious forms imported from outside the borders of the nation.

Epic is often opposed to romance: the former is portrayed as a masculine genre dedicated to the deeds of knights and the matter of war, the latter as a feminine genre that focuses on the relations of the lady and her lover, confined to the domestic sphere of the court. However, both genres, which rose to prominence in the twelfth century, share the idealized image of the knight: if he expresses his chivalry on the field of battle, the work is epic, but if his prowess is displayed in the private space of the bedchamber, the work is romance. The romances of Chrétien de Troyes, like the shorter romance works or *lais* of his predecessor, **Marie de France**, highlight this idealized role of the knight, which is also seen in the later medieval English, German, and Italian romances that were adapted from French originals. The French origins of the romance genre are also closely tied to the emergence of French as a literary language. Latin was unquestionably the primary language of scholarly learning, whether theological, philosophical, or scientific, but vernacular or spoken languages increasingly came to be the first choice for poetic composition. In the twelfth century, French was the first of the European languages to be elevated in this way; by the fourteenth century, other vernaculars had also begun to be widely used. Explicitly, in his treatise on languages (*De vulgari eloquentia*), and implicitly, in his **Divine Comedy**, Dante Alighieri stakes a claim for the local Florentine dialect of Italian as the "most illustrious vernacular," while Chaucer will make similar claims for English in his *Canterbury Tales*.

In spite of this ongoing shift, Latin experienced an important revival in the fourteenth century. Paradoxically at just the moment when literature in the vernacular was reaching new levels of sophistication with works such as Boccaccio's *Decameron* and Chaucer's *Canterbury Tales*, classical forms of Latin were being championed in humanistic circles under the guiding hand of **Petrarch**. Ambivalence about the competing claims of a revived classical Latin, on the one hand, and the potent spontaneity of the vernacular, on the other hand, is evident in the work of Petrarch himself: the author of several Latin treatises and a powerful advocate for classical scholarship, his exquisite lyrics in Italian would exert a powerful influence on the rise of Renaissance lyric not only in Italy but also in France and England. This paradox is reflected in modern scholarship, which tends to label Petrarch, who wrote in the early fourteenth century, as a "Renaissance" poet and his friend and disciple Boccaccio, who wrote in the mid-fourteenth century, as a "medieval" writer. The example of these two contemporaries illustrates the ways in which period divisions, like geographical divisions, sometimes obscure the profound continuities that underlie literary history.

Though Boccaccio wrote his masterwork, the *Decameron*, in Italian, he also composed (at the encouragement of Petrarch) several treatises in Latin. Chaucer did not write in Latin, but he shared Boccaccio's consciousness of the importance of the legacy of Roman antiquity and Latin literature; he produced several English translations of Latin works, including Boethius's *Consolation of Philosophy*. In late medieval French circles too, as illustrated in the mythographic works of Christine de Pizan written under the influence of Boccaccio, the Greco-Roman past loomed large. In all three of these major writers, the yearning for a revival of classical antiquity reveals the extent to which the wholehearted embrace of the ancient past that we tend to associate exclusively with the Renaissance was foreshadowed in the work of at least some late medieval authors, especially those whose perspective was particularly cosmopolitan, rooted in the experience of the city as a cultural, economic, linguistic, and—above all—literary crossroads.

THE CHRISTIAN BIBLE
THE NEW TESTAMENT GOSPELS
ca. first century C.E.

For some readers, the Bible is to be read as sacred history and divine revelation, as a book whose truth is grounded by religious faith. For others, it is a rich trove of cultural history, sometimes supported by archaeology and other corroborating evidence, sometimes not. Beginning in the nineteenth century, however, readers started to also think of the Bible as a work of literature, analyzing it in terms of genre and poetics and comparing it to other literary works written around the same time. The Gospels of Matthew, Mark, and Luke, for instance, all of which retell the life of Jesus, can be read as examples of Greco-Roman biography as practiced around the Mediterranean during the first century C.E. The metaphorical language of the Gospel of John reflects the strong influence of Platonic philosophy on Jewish communities within the Roman Empire. This literary approach to the Bible has inspired recent generations of modern intellectuals, writers, and artists— sometimes from a devout perspective, sometimes not. Yet it is crucial to realize that considering the Christian Bible as literature is not a modern novelty: over the past two thousand years, poets have constantly quoted and paraphrased the Gospels in order to enrich their own work with the resonant, messianic tone and powerful turns of phrase that appear in what is arguably the single most influential text of world literature.

CHRISTIAN CULTURE IN THE ROMAN EMPIRE

Jesus was born in the town of Bethlehem, a town located in the province of Judea in the eastern part of the Roman Empire. While Latin was the language mainly used in Rome itself, in far-off Judea the language of administration was Greek. For most local inhabitants, however, the vernacular was Aramaic, a language related to Hebrew but sufficiently different from it that Aramaic speakers would not necessarily have understood Hebrew. The polyglot nature of the region was mirrored in the wide range of ethnicities and religious orientations found there. Judea and the surrounding lands had formerly been part of the vast empire established by Alexander the Great, under whose influence the local Jewish population— especially the more affluent and educated classes—had embraced Greek literature and philosophy. This religious and cultural ferment gave rise to a variety of religious groups; some became marginalized and died out, but others (including Christianity and rabbinic Judaism) would live on.

From Roman administrative records, we know that there was a historical Jesus, a disruptive rabble-rouser who attracted the attention of the local authorities and was ultimately executed. Yet the Jesus of the gospel accounts is something far more complex, more a phenomenon than a man. It is clear that the events of his life rapidly led to the establishment of not just a single community but a number of communities organized around the symbolic significance that could be assigned to this man, his words, and his deeds. These included both Jewish communities, for whom Jesus was to be identified with the long-awaited Messiah, and non-Jewish (or "Gentile") communities around the Mediterranean Sea. The dating system we use today reflects the fundamental break in time that early Christians believed had taken place. Dates in the Roman Empire were ordinarily based on the number of the year in the reign of the individual ruler, but Christians viewed Jesus as a divine lord whose authority surmounted that of any earthly kingdom or empire. Consequently, they began to number the years "A.D."— that is, *Anno Domini*, or "In the year of the Lord." Today, we more often use the more inclusive abbreviation c.e. for the Common Era, but we continue to number years from the birth of Jesus—a practice that reflects the early Christians' profound sense of a temporal rupture, the belief that a new age had dawned.

WORK

Together with the Gospel of Mark, the three books of the Bible excerpted here—the Gospels of Matthew, Luke, and John—form the core of the collection of twenty-seven books that Christians call the New Testament. This label, taken with the "Old Testament," encapsulates the Christian perspective on the relationship of Jesus' mission to the history of the Jewish people recounted in the **Hebrew Bible**, comprising the Pentateuch (the first five books, or Torah), the books of prophets and history, and the poetic books. For Christians, the old covenant established by God with Abraham and, after the flood, reestablished with Noah was merely a prefiguration, the first stage of a process that would be fulfilled only with the advent of Jesus and subsequent rise of Christianity. In some ways, this perspective honors and elevates the role of the Jewish people; in other ways, it denigrates Judaism, relegating it to a subordinate position in the divine plan for humanity.

Although the Gospels present themselves as eyewitness testimony to events in the life of Jesus, they were actually committed to written form decades after his death. The earliest of them, the Gospel of Mark, probably dates to about 70 c.e.; the latest, the Gospel of John, dates to about 100 c.e. The sequence of four gospels was established relatively early on, as was the authoritativeness of their testimony. The second-century theologian Irenaeus of Lyons declared that there are only four gospels, just as there are only four corners of the earth, and four winds in the heavens. This declaration served to exclude the many alternative accounts of the life of Jesus that were also in circulation, and to give a more specific structure to the teachings of Jesus and his authorized followers; the final result was a codified form of the New Testament and, ultimately, Christian theology. The Gospels of Matthew, Mark, and Luke are called the Synoptic Gospels, because they give a panorama or overview (synopsis) of the life of Jesus, all telling the same story but from rather distinctive perspectives. The Gospel of John also recounts the life of Jesus, but with a very different narrative line and a deep concern to integrate Platonic philosophy and mysticism into the expression of divinity in the person of Jesus Christ, identified as the Word of God.

The Synoptic Gospels have a number of episodes in common, of which the most important are the Sermon on the Mount, the Last Supper, and the crucifixion and resurrection of Jesus. Yet each of the three gospels also has its own individual character: Luke tells us the most about the childhood and parentage of Jesus, and his work is closely related to the noncanonical tradition of "infancy gospels"—stories about the life of Jesus as a child that survive in Arabic as well as in Greek and Syriac versions. Mark provides the tightest and most focused account, placing special emphasis on the death of Jesus and recounting his biography in simpler, more primitive language. Mark appears to be addressing a Gentile audience, and his gospel is sometimes associated with the early foundation of Christian communities in Rome or, at least, in the regions of the Roman Empire lying to the west of Judea. Matthew, conversely, clearly directs his biography at an audience that is quite familiar with the Hebrew Bible: he gives a very detailed account of Jesus' preaching mission and his role as the long-awaited Messiah. Matthew exhibits a special interest in the ways in which Jewish history is fulfilled in the coming of Jesus Christ, and in the ways in which the old covenant established between God and man is renewed in and superseded by the new covenant established with the sacrifice of Christ in the crucifixion.

Matthew also displays a central concern with the ways in which Jesus preached, especially his use of parables: little stories that reveal profound spiritual truths through metaphorical, even allegorical language. The excerpts presented here include parables of Jesus as recounted both by Matthew and by Luke, passages of the Gospels that are among those with the most profound literary influence on writers throughout the Middle Ages. The figurative, philosophical language of the Gospel of John would also go on to be highly influential, disseminated through a wide range of poetic evocations of the divine nature. John's account of the birth of Christ, excerpted here, seemingly describes the same transformative event narrated in the infancy chapters of Luke. Yet the two accounts could not be more different, as they represent two totally different perspectives on the nature of Jesus Christ, understood as that deepest of all paradoxes, the being who is at once both God and man. For John, Christ is the Word through which God creates all things, a mediator between matter and spirit, the temporal and the eternal. For Luke, he is Jesus of Nazareth, whose divine nature smoothly coexists with his human status, rooted in the cultural norms and social structures of first-century Judea.

The Gospels as we have them today reflect a complex and intertwined linguistic history: Jesus and his apostles would have spoken Aramaic, which we hear when Jesus cries out on the crucifix, "Eli, eli, lama sabachthani?" ("My God, my God, why have you forsaken me?" [Matthew 27.46]). However, the Gospels were written down in koine Greek, the vernacular that was the lingua franca of the eastern Mediterranean. This was a language meant to travel, and so the Gospels did: they were swiftly passed on in both oral and written form across the Mediterranean Sea, through Asia, Europe, and northern Africa. Latin translations of the Gospels soon began to be produced, and in 382 Pope Damasus asked the theologian Jerome to prepare a full, authorized translation into Latin. This version, known as the Vulgate, would become the standard version of the Bible read for more than a thousand years in the West, until new versions of the sacred text began to be produced at the dawn of the Reformation. Over the five hundred years since then, translations of the Bible have multiplied exponentially, as every spoken language has produced its own version of holy scripture. Most recently, modern writers and artists have moved the Bible into new formats such as the graphic novel, used by devout Christians to educate their children and enjoyed by a wide range of nonreligious readers.

THE BIBLE: THE NEW TESTAMENT GOSPELS[1]

Luke 2

[The Birth and Youth of Jesus]

It happened in those days that a decree went forth from Augustus Caesar[2] that all the world should be enrolled in a census. This was the first census, when Quirinius was governor of Syria. And all went to be enrolled, each to his own city. And Joseph also went up from Galilee,[3] from the city of Nazareth, to Judaea, to the city of David[4] which is called Bethlehem, because he was of the house and family of David; to be enrolled with Mary his promised wife, who was pregnant. And it happened that while they were there her time was completed, and she bore a son, her first-born, and she wrapped him in swaddling clothes and laid him in a manger, because there was no room for them in the inn. And there were shepherds in that region, camping out at night and keeping guard over their flock. And an angel of the Lord stood before them, and the glory of the Lord shone about them, and they were afraid with a great fear. The angel said to them: Do not be afraid; behold, I tell you good news, great joy which shall be for all the people; because this day there has been born for you in the city of David a savior who is Christ the Lord. And here is a sign for you; you will find a baby wrapped in swaddling clothes and lying in a manger. And suddenly with the angel there was a multitude of the heavenly host, praising God and saying: Glory to God in the highest and peace on earth among men of good will. And it happened that after the angels had gone off from them into the sky, the shepherds began saying to each other: Let us go to Bethlehem and see this thing which has happened, which the Lord made known to us; and they went, hastening, and found Mary and Joseph, and the baby lying in the manger; and when they had seen, they spread the news about what had been told them concerning this baby. And all who heard wondered at what had been told them by the shepherds; and Mary kept in mind all these sayings as she pondered them in her heart. And the shepherds returned, glorifying and praising God over all they had heard and seen, as it had been told them.

And when eight days were past, for his circumcision, his name was called Jesus, as it was named by the angel before he was conceived in the womb.

And when the days for their purification[5] according to the Law of Moses had been completed, they took him up to Jerusalem to set him before the Lord, as it has been written in the Law of the Lord: Every male child who opens the womb shall be called sacred to the Lord; and to give sacrifice as it is stated in the Law of the Lord, a pair of turtle doves or two young pigeons. And behold, there was a man in Jerusalem whose name was Simeon, and this man was righteous and virtuous and looked forward to the consolation of Israel, and the Holy Spirit was upon him; and it had been prophesied to him by the Holy Spirit that he should not look upon his death until he had looked on the Lord's Anointed. And in the

1. Translated by Richmond Lattimore.
2. Gaius Julius Caesar (63 B.C.E.–14 C.E.), who took the title Augustus as the first Roman emperor.
3. The region surrounding the Sea of Galilee, in the Roman province of Judea (modern Israel).

4. Second king of Israel, according to the Hebrew Bible; he was anointed king in Bethlehem, his traditional birthplace.
5. The ritual cleansing following childbirth (prescribed in Leviticus 12).

spirit he went into the temple; and as his parents brought in the child Jesus so that they could do for him what was customary according to the law, Simeon himself took him in his arms and blessed God and said: Now, Lord, you release your slave, in peace, according to your word; because my eyes have looked on your salvation, what you made ready in the presence of all the peoples; a light for the revelation to the Gentiles, and the glory of your people, Israel. And his father and his mother were in wonder at what was being said about him. And Simeon blessed them and said to Mary his mother: Behold, he is appointed for the fall and the rise of many in Israel; and as a sign which is disputed; and through your soul also will pass the sword; so that the reasonings of many hearts may be revealed. And there was Anna, a prophetess, the daughter of Phanuel, of the tribe of Asher. And she was well advanced in years, having lived with her husband seven years from the time of her maidenhood, and now she was eighty-four years a widow. And she did not leave the temple, serving night and day with fastings and prayers. And at this same time she came near and gave thanks to God and spoke of the child to those who looked forward to the deliverance of Jerusalem.

And when they had done everything according to the Law of the Lord, they went back to Galilee, to their own city, Nazareth.

And the child grew in stature and strength as he was filled with wisdom, and the grace of God was upon him.

Now his parents used to journey every year to Jerusalem for the feast of the Passover.[6] And when he was twelve years old, when they went up according to their custom for the festival and had completed their days there, on their return the boy Jesus stayed behind in Jerusalem, and his parents did not know it. And supposing that he was in their company they went a day's journey and then looked for him among their relatives and friends, and when they did not find him they turned back to Jerusalem in search of him. And it happened that after three days they found him in the temple sitting in the midst of the masters, listening to them and asking them questions. And all who heard him were amazed at his intelligence and his answers. And they were astonished at seeing him, and his mother said to him: Child, why did you do this to us? See, your father and I have been looking for you, in distress. He said to them: But why were you looking for me? Did you not know that I must be in my father's house? And they did not understand what he had said to them. And he returned with them and came to Nazareth, and was in their charge. And his mother kept all his sayings in her heart. And Jesus advanced in wisdom and stature, and in the favor of God and men.

---

6. The holiday (Heb. *Pesach*) commemorating the liberation of the people of Israel, led by Moses, from bondage in Egypt.

Matthew 5–7

[*The Sermon on the Mount*]

And seeing the multitudes he went up onto the mountain, and when he was seated, his disciples came to him, and he opened his mouth and taught them, saying:

Blessed are the poor in spirit, because theirs is the Kingdom of Heaven.

Blessed are they who sorrow, because they shall be comforted.

Blessed are the gentle, because they shall inherit the earth.

Blessed are they who are hungry and thirsty for righteousness, because they shall be fed.

Blessed are they who have pity, because they shall be pitied.

Blessed are the pure in heart, because they shall see God.

Blessed are the peacemakers, because they shall be called the sons of God.

Blessed are they who are persecuted for their righteousness, because theirs is the Kingdom of Heaven.

Blessed are you when they shall revile you and persecute you and speak every evil thing of you, lying, because of me. Rejoice and be glad, because your reward in heaven is great; for thus did they persecute the prophets before you.

You are the salt of the earth; but if the salt loses its power, with what shall it be salted? It is good for nothing but to be thrown away and trampled by men. You are the light of the world. A city cannot be hidden when it is set on top of a hill. Nor do men light a lamp and set it under a basket, but they set it on a stand, and it gives its light to all in the house. So let your light shine before men, so that they may see your good works and glorify your father in heaven.

Do not think that I have come to destroy the law[1] and the prophets. I have not come to destroy but to complete. Indeed, I say to you, until the sky and the earth are gone, not one iota or one end of a letter must go from the law, until all is done. He who breaks one of the least of these commandments and teaches men accordingly shall be called the least in the Kingdom of Heaven; he who performs and teaches these commandments shall be called great in the Kingdom of Heaven. For I tell you, if your righteousness is not more abundant than that of the scribes and the Pharisees,[2] you may not enter the Kingdom of Heaven.

You have heard that it was said to the ancients. You shall not murder. He who murders shall be liable to judgment. I say to you that any man who is angry with his brother shall be liable to judgment; and he who says to his brother, fool, shall be liable before the council; and he who says to his brother, sinner, shall be liable to Gehenna.[3] If then you bring your gift to the altar, and there remember that your brother has some grievance against you, leave your gift before the altar, and go first and be reconciled with your brother, and then go and offer your gift. Be quick to be conciliatory with your adversary at law when you are in the street with him, for fear your adversary may turn you over to the judge, and the judge to the officer, and you be thrown into prison. Truly I tell you, you cannot come out of there until you pay the last penny.

1. That is, the Torah, the five books of the law that begin the Hebrew Bible.
2. A major Jewish sect that emphasized strict observance of Jewish law; they were instrumental in the development of rabbinic Judaism.
3. Hell (Heb. *gehinnom*); figurative use of the name of a valley outside Jerusalem where children were sacrificed to pagan gods.

ive heard that it has been said: You shall not commit adultery. I tell you
/ man who looks at a woman so as to desire her has already committed
y with her in his heart. If your right eye makes you go amiss, take it out and
cast it from you; it is better that one part of you should be lost instead of your
whole body being cast into Gehenna. And if your right hand makes you go amiss,
cut it off and cast it from you; it is better that one part of you should be lost instead
of your whole body going to Gehenna. It has been said: If a man puts away his
wife, let him give her a contract of divorce. I tell you that any man who puts away
his wife, except for the reason of harlotry, is making her the victim of adultery; and
any man who marries a wife who has been divorced is committing adultery. Again,
you have heard that it has been said to the ancients: You shall not swear falsely,
but you shall make good your oaths to the Lord. I tell you not to swear at all: not
by heaven, because it is the throne of God; not by the earth, because it is the footstool for his feet; not by Jerusalem, because it is the city of the great king; not by
your own head, because you cannot make one hair of it white or black. Let your
speech be yes yes, no no; more than that comes from the evil one.

    You have heard that it has been said: An eye for an eye and a tooth for a
tooth. I tell you not to resist the wicked man; but if one strikes you on the right
cheek, turn the other one to him also; and if a man wishes to go to law with you
and take your tunic, give him your cloak also, and if one makes you his porter
for a mile, go with him for two. Give to him who asks, and do not turn away
one who wishes to borrow from you. You have heard that it has been said: You
shall love your neighbor and hate your enemy. I tell you, love your enemies and
pray for those who persecute you, so that you may be sons of your father who
is in heaven, because he makes his sun rise on the evil and the good, and rains
on the just and the unjust. For if you love those who love you, what reward do
you have? Do not even the tax collectors do the same? And if you greet only
your brothers, what do you do that is more than others do? Do not even the
pagans do the same? Be perfect as your father in heaven is perfect.

Take care not to practice your righteousness publicly before men so as to be
seen by them; if you do, you shall have no recompense from your father in
heaven. Then when you do charity, do not have a trumpet blown before you, as
the hypocrites do in the synagogues and the streets, so that men may think well
of them. Truly I tell you, they have their due reward. But when you do charity,
let your left hand not know what your right hand is doing, so that your charity
may be in secret; and your father, who sees what is secret, will reward you. And
when you pray, you must not be like the hypocrites, who love to stand up in the
synagogues and the corners of the squares to pray, so that they may be seen by
men. Truly I tell you, they have their due reward. But when you pray, go into
your inner room and close the door and pray to your father, who is in secret;
and your father, who sees what is secret, will reward you. When you pray, do
not babble as the pagans do; for they think that by saying much they will be
heard. Do not then be like them; for your father knows what you need before
you ask him. Pray thus, then:[4] Our father in heaven, may your name be hallowed, may your kingdom come, may your will be done, as in heaven, so upon

---

4. The following verses, commonly known as the Lord's Prayer, are central to Christian religious
practice.

earth. Give us today our sufficient bread, and forgive us our debts, as we also have forgiven our debtors. And do not bring us into temptation, but deliver us from evil. For if you forgive men their offenses, your heavenly father will forgive you; but if you do not forgive men, neither will your father forgive you your offenses. And when you fast, do not scowl like the hypocrites; for they make ugly faces so that men can see that they are fasting. Truly I tell you, they have their due reward. But when you fast, anoint your head and wash your face, so that you may not show as fasting to men, but to your father, in secret; and your father, who sees what is secret, will reward you.

Do not store up your treasures on earth, where the moth and rust destroy them, and where burglars dig through and steal them; but store up your treasures in heaven, where neither moth nor rust destroys them, and where burglars do not dig through or steal; for where your treasure is, there also will be your heart. The lamp of the body is the eye. Thus if your eye is clear, your whole body is full of light; but if your eye is soiled, your whole body is dark. If the light in you is darkness, how dark it is. No man can serve two masters. For either he will hate the one and love the other, or he will cling to one and despise the other; you cannot serve God and mammon.[5] Therefore I tell you, do not take thought for your life, what you will eat, or for your body, what you will wear. Is not your life more than its food and your body more than its clothing? Consider the birds of the sky, that they do not sow or harvest or collect for their granaries, and your heavenly father feeds them. Are you not preferred above them? Which of you by taking thought can add one cubit to his growth? And why do you take thought about clothing? Study the lilies in the field, how they grow. They do not toil or spin; yet I tell you, not even Solomon[6] in all his glory was clothed like one of these. But if God so clothes the grass of the field, which grows today and tomorrow is thrown in the oven, will he not much more clothe you, you men of little faith? Do not then worry and say: What shall we eat? Or: What shall we drink? Or: What shall we wear? For all this the Gentiles study. Your father in heaven knows that you need all these things. But seek out first his kingdom and his justice, and all these things shall be given to you. Do not then take thought of tomorrow; tomorrow will take care of itself, sufficient to the day is its own evil.

Do not judge, so you may not be judged. You shall be judged by that judgment by which you judge, and your measure will be made by the measure by which you measure. Why do you look at the straw which is in the eye of your brother, and not see the log which is in your eye? Or how will you say to your brother: Let me take the straw out of your eye, and behold, the log is in your eye. You hypocrite, first take the log out of your eye, and then you will see to take the straw out of the eye of your brother. Do not give what is sacred to the dogs, and do not cast your pearls before swine, lest they trample them under their feet and turn and rend you. Ask, and it shall be given you; seek, and you shall find; knock, and the door will be opened for you. Everyone who asks receives, and he who seeks finds, and for him who knocks the door will be opened. Or what man is there among you, whose son shall ask him for bread, that will give him a stone?

5. Wealth (an Aramaic word transliterated into Greek); the personification of Mammon as a god became a common trope in later Christian literature.

6. King of Israel and son of David, famed for his wisdom and for building the First Temple in Jerusalem.

Or ask him for fish, that will give him a snake? If then you, who are corrupt, know how to give good gifts to your children, by how much more your father who is in heaven will give good things to those who ask him. Whatever you wish men to do to you, so do to them. For this is the law and the prophets.

Go in through the narrow gate; because wide and spacious is the road that leads to destruction, and there are many who go in through it; because narrow is the gate and cramped the road that leads to life, and few are they who find it. Beware of the false prophets, who come to you in sheep's clothing, but inside they are ravening wolves. From their fruits you will know them. Do men gather grapes from thorns or figs from thistles? Thus every good tree produces good fruits, but the rotten tree produces bad fruits. A good tree cannot bear bad fruits, and a rotten tree cannot bear good fruits. Every tree that does not produce good fruit is cut out and thrown in the fire. So from their fruits you will know them. Not everyone who says to me Lord Lord will come into the Kingdom of Heaven, but he who does the will of my father in heaven. Many will say to me on that day: Lord, Lord, did we not prophesy in your name, and in your name did we not cast out demons, and in your name did we not assume great powers? And then I shall admit to them: I never knew you. Go from me, for you do what is against the law.

Every man who hears what I say and does what I say shall be like the prudent man who built his house upon the rock. And the rain fell and the rivers came and the winds blew and dashed against that house, and it did not fall, for it was founded upon the rock. And every man who hears what I say and does not do what I say will be like the reckless man who built his house on the sand. And the rain fell and the rivers came and the winds blew and battered that house, and it fell, and that was a great fall.

And it happened that when Jesus had ended these words, the multitudes were astonished at his teaching, for he taught them as one who has authority, and not like their own scribes.

Luke 15

[Parables]

All the tax collectors and the sinners kept coming around him, to listen to him. And the Pharisees and the scribes muttered, saying: This man receives sinners and eats with them. But he told them this parable, saying: Which man among you who has a hundred sheep and has lost one of them will not leave the ninety-nine in the wilds and go after the lost one until he finds it? And when he does find it, he sets it on his shoulders, rejoicing, and goes to his house and invites in his friends and his neighbors, saying to them: Rejoice with me, because I found my sheep which was lost. I tell you that thus there will be joy in heaven over one sinner who repents, rather than over ninety-nine righteous ones who have no need of repentance. Or what woman who has ten drachmas,[1] if she loses one drachma, does not light the lamp and sweep the house and search diligently until she finds it? And finding it she invites in her friends

1. Greek silver coins, each roughly equivalent in value to a manual laborer's wages for one day.

and neighbors, saying: Rejoice with me, because I found the drachma I lost. Such, I tell you, is the joy among the angels of God over one sinner who repents.

And he said: There was a man who had two sons. And the younger of them said to his father: Father, give me my appropriate share of the property. And the father divided his substance between them. And not many days afterward the younger son gathered everything together and left the country for a distant land, and there he squandered his substance in riotous living. And after he had spent everything, there was a severe famine in that country, and he began to be in need. And he went and attached himself to one of the citizens of that country, who sent him out into the fields to feed the pigs. And he longed to be nourished on the nuts that the pigs ate, and no one would give to him. And he went and said to himself: How many hired servants of my father have plenty of bread while I am dying of hunger here. I will rise up and go to my father and say to him: Father, I have sinned against heaven and in your sight, I am no longer worthy to be called your son. Make me like one of your hired servants. And he rose up and went to his father. And when he was still a long way off, his father saw him and was moved and ran and fell on his neck and kissed him. The son said to him: Father, I have sinned against heaven and in your sight, I am no longer worthy to be called your son. But his father said to his slaves: Quick, bring the best clothing and put it on him, and have a ring for his hand and shoes for his feet, and bring the fatted calf, slaughter him, and let us eat and make merry because this man, my son, was a dead man and came to life, he was lost and he has been found. And they began to make merry. His older son was out on the estate, and as he came nearer to the house he heard music and dancing, and he called over one of the servants and asked what was going on. He told him: Your brother is here, and your father slaughtered the fatted calf, because he got him back in good health. He was angry and did not want to go in. But his father came out and entreated him. But he answered and said to his father: Look, all these years I have been your slave and never neglected an order of yours, but you never gave me a kid so that I could make merry with my friends. But when this son of yours comes back, the one who ate up your livelihood in the company of whores, you slaughtered the fatted calf for him. But he said to him: My child, you are always with me, and all that is mine is yours; but we had to make merry and rejoice, because your brother was a dead man and came to life, he was lost and has been found.

From Matthew 13

[Why Jesus Teaches in Parables]

On that day Jesus went out of the house and sat beside the sea; and a great multitude gathered before him, so that he went aboard a ship and sat there, and all the multitude stood on the shore. And he talked to them, speaking mostly in parables: Behold, a sower went out to sow. And as he sowed, some of the grain fell beside the way, and birds came and ate it. Some fell on stony ground where there was not much soil, and it shot up quickly because there was no depth of soil, but when the sun came up it was parched, and because it had no roots it dried away. Some fell among thorns, and the thorns grew up and stifled it. But some fell upon the good soil and bore fruit, some a hundred-fold, some sixtyfold, some thirtyfold. He who has ears, let him hear. Then his disciples came to him and said: Why do you talk to them in parables? He answered them and said: Because it is given to you to understand the secrets of the Kingdom of Heaven, but to them it is not given. When a man has, he shall be given, and it will be more than he needs; but when he has not, even what he has shall be taken away from him. Therefore I talk to them in parables, because they have sight but do not see, and hearing but do not hear or understand. And for them is fulfilled the prophecy of Isaiah,[1] saying: With your hearing you shall hear and not understand, and you shall use your sight and look but not see. For the heart of this people is stiffened, and they hear with difficulty, and they have closed their eyes; so that they may never see with their eyes, or hear with their ears and with their hearts understand and turn back, so that I can heal them.

Blessed are your eyes because they see, and your ears because they hear. Truly I tell you that many prophets and good men have longed to see what you see, and not seen it, and to hear what you hear, and not heard it. Hear, then, the parable of the sower. To every man who hears the word of the Kingdom and does not understand it, the evil one comes and seizes what has been sown in his heart. This is the seed sown by the way. The seed sown on the stony ground is the man who hears the word and immediately accepts it with joy; but he has no root in himself, and he is a man of the moment, and when there comes affliction and persecution, because of the word, he does not stand fast. The seed sown among thorns is the man who hears the word, and concern for the world and the beguilement of riches stifle the word, and he bears no fruit. And the seed sown on the good soil is the man who hears the word and understands it, who bears fruit and makes it, one a hundredfold, one sixtyfold, and one thirtyfold.

He set before them another parable, saying: The Kingdom of Heaven is like a man who sowed good seed in his field. And while the people were asleep, his enemy came and sowed darnel in with the grain, and went away. When the plants grew and produced a crop, the darnel was seen. Then the slaves of the master came to him and said: Master, did you not sow good grain in your field? Where does the darnel come from? He said to them: A man who is my enemy did it. His slaves said: Do you wish us to go out and gather it? But he said: No, for fear that when you gather the darnel you may pull up the grain with it. Let them both grow until harvest time, and in the time of harvest I shall say to the harvesters: First gather the darnel, and bind it in sheaves for burning, but store the grain in my granary.

He set before them another parable, saying: The Kingdom of Heaven is like a grain of mustard, which a man took and sowed in his field; which is the smallest of all seeds, but when it grows, it is the largest of the greens and grows into a tree, so that the birds of the air come and nest in its branches.

He told them another parable: The Kingdom of Heaven is like leaven, which a woman took and buried in three measures of dough, so that it all rose.

All this Jesus told the multitudes in parables, and he did not talk to them except in parables; so as to fulfill the word spoken by the prophet, saying: I will open my mouth in parables, and pour out what has been hidden since the creation. Then he sent away the multitudes and went to the house. And his

1. See Isaiah 6.9–10.

disciples came to him and said: Make plain to us the parable of the darnel in the field. He answered them and said: The sower of the good seed is the son of man; the field is the world; the good seed is the sons of the Kingdom; the darnel is the sons of the evil one, and the enemy who sowed it is the devil; the harvest time is the end of the world, and the harvesters are angels. Then as the darnel is gathered and burned in the fire, so it is at the end of the world. The son of man will send out his angels, and they will gather from his Kingdom all that misleads, and the people who do what is not lawful, and cast them in the furnace of fire; and there will be weeping and gnashing of teeth. Then the righteous men will shine forth like the sun in the Kingdom of their father. He who has ears, let him hear. The Kingdom of Heaven is like a treasure hidden in the field, which a man found and hid, and for joy of it he goes and sells all he has and buys that field. Again, the Kingdom of Heaven is like a trader looking for fine pearls; he found one of great value, and went and sold all he had and bought it. Again, the Kingdom of Heaven is like a dragnet cast into the sea and netting every kind of fish; and when it is full they draw it out and sit on the beach and gather the good ones in baskets, but the bad they throw away. So will it be at the end of the world. The angels will go out and separate the bad from the midst of the righteous, and cast them in the furnace of fire; and there will be weeping and gnashing of teeth. Do you understand all this? They said to him: Yes. And he said to them: Therefore every scribe who is learned in the Kingdom of Heaven is like a man who is master of a house, who issues from his storehouse what is new and what is old.

Matthew 27–28

[*Crucifixion and Resurrection*]

When morning came, all the high priests and elders of the people held a meeting against Jesus, to have him killed. And they bound him and took him away and gave him over to Pilate the governor.[1]

Then when Judas, who had betrayed him, saw that he had been condemned, he repented and proffered the thirty pieces of silver back to the high priests and the elders, saying: I did wrong to betray innocent blood. They said: What is that to us? You look to it. And he threw down the silver pieces in the temple and went away, and when he was alone he hanged himself. The high priests took up the silver pieces and said: We cannot put them in the treasury, since it is blood money. Then they took counsel together and with the money they bought the potter's field[2] to bury strangers in. Therefore that field has been called the Field of Blood, to this day. Then was fulfilled the word spoken by Jeremiah the prophet,[3] saying: I took the thirty pieces of silver, the price of him on whom a price was set, whom they priced from among the sons of Israel, and I gave the money for the field of the potter, as my Lord commanded me.

---

1. Pontius Pilate, imperial adminstrator of the Roman province of Judea (26–36 C.E.).
2. A place where clay was dug to make pottery; after the Gospels, a common term for a burying place for the poor.

3. Alluding perhaps to the purchase of a field in Jeremiah 32, or to the potter of Jeremiah 18–19 (though the citation is to Zechariah 11.13).

Now Jesus stood before the governor; and the governor questioned him, saying: Are you the King of the Jews? Jesus answered: It is you who say it. And while he was being accused by the high priests and the elders he made no answer. Then Pilate said to him: Do you not hear all their testimony against you? And he made no answer to a single word, so that the governor was greatly amazed.

For the festival, the governor was accustomed to release one prisoner for the multitude, whichever one they wished. And they had at that time a notorious man, who was called Barabbas.[4] Now as they were assembled Pilate said to them: Which one do you wish me to release for you, Barabbas, or Jesus, who is called Christ? For he knew that it was through malice that they had turned him over. Now as he was sitting on the platform, his wife sent him a message, saying: Let there be nothing between you and this just man; for I have suffered much today because of a dream about him. But the high priests and the elders persuaded the crowd to ask for Barabbas and destroy Jesus. Then the governor spoke forth and said to them: Which of the two shall I give you? They answered: Barabbas. Pilate said to them: What then shall I do with Jesus, who is called Christ? They all said: Let him be crucified. But Pilate said: Why? What harm has he done? But they screamed all the more, saying: Let him be crucified. And Pilate, seeing that he was doing no good and that the disorder was growing, took water and washed his hands before the crowd, saying: I am innocent of the blood of this man. You see to it. And all the people answered and said: His blood is upon us and upon our children. Then Pilate gave them Barabbas, but he had Jesus flogged, and gave him over to be crucified.

Then the soldiers of the governor took Jesus to the residence, and drew up all their battalion around him. And they stripped him and put a red mantle about him, and wove a wreath of thorns and put it on his head, and put a reed in his right hand, and knelt before him and mocked him, saying: Hail, King of the Jews. And they spat upon him and took the reed and beat him on the head. And after they had mocked him, they took off the mantle and put his own clothes on him, and led him away to be crucified. And as they went out they found a man of Cyrene, named Simon. They impressed him for carrying the cross.

Then they came to a place called Golgotha, which means the place of the skull, and gave him wine mixed with gall to drink. When he tasted it he would not drink it. Then they crucified him, and divided up his clothes, casting lots, and sat there and watched him. Over his head they put the label giving the charge against him, where it was written: This is Jesus, the King of the Jews. Then there were crucified with him two robbers, one on his right and one on his left. And those who passed by blasphemed against him, wagging their heads, and saying: You who tear down the temple and rebuild it in three days, save yourself, and come down from the cross, if you are the son of God. So too the high priests, mocking him along with the scribes and the elders, said: He saved others, he cannot save himself. He is King of Israel, let him come down from the cross and we will believe in him. He trusted in God, let him save him now, if he will; for he said: I am the son of God. And the robbers who were crucified with him spoke abusively to him in the same way.

4. Bar-Abbas, meaning "son of Abbas" (literally, "son of the Father"). John 18.40 calls Barabbas a "bandit" (*lēstēs*), a term often applied to the Jewish revolutionaries who defied Roman rule (Mark 15.7 refers to his involvement in "sedition").

But from the sixth hour there was darkness over all the earth until the ninth hour. But about the ninth hour Jesus cried out in a great voice, saying: *Elei elei lema sabachthanei?*[5] Which is: My God, my God, why have you forsaken me? But some of those who were standing there heard and said: This man calls to Elijah.[6] And at once one of them ran and took a sponge, soaked it in vinegar and put it on the end of a reed, and gave it to him to drink. But the rest said: Let us see if Elijah comes to save him.

Then Jesus cried out again in a great voice, and gave up his life. And behold, the veil of the temple[7] was split in two from top to bottom, and the earth was shaken, and the rocks were split, and the tombs opened and many bodies of the holy sleepers rose up; and after his resurrection they came out of their tombs and went into the holy city, and were seen by many. But the company commander and those with him who kept guard over Jesus, when they saw the earthquake and the things that happened, were greatly afraid, saying: In truth this was the son of God. And there were many women watching from a distance there, who had followed Jesus from Galilee, waiting on him. Among them were Mary the Magdalene, and Mary the mother of James and Joseph, and the mother of the sons of Zebedee.

When it was evening, there came a rich man of Arimathaea, Joseph by name, who also had been a disciple of Jesus. This man went to Pilate and asked for the body of Jesus. Then Pilate ordered that it be given up to him. And Joseph took the body and wrapped it in clean linen, and laid it in his new tomb, which he had cut in the rock, and rolled a great stone before the door of the tomb, and went away. But Mary the Magdalene and the other Mary were there, sitting before the tomb. On the next day, which is the day after the Day of Preparation, the high priests and the Pharisees gathered in the presence of Pilate, and said: Lord, we have remembered how that impostor said while he was still alive: After three days I shall rise up. Give orders, then, that the tomb be secured until after the third day, for fear his disciples may come and steal him away and say to the people: He rose from the dead. And that will be the ultimate deception, worse than the former one. Pilate said to them: You have a guard. Go and secure it as best you can. And they went and secured the tomb, sealing it with the help of the guard.

Late on the sabbath, as the light grew toward the first day after the sabbath, Mary the Magdalene and the other Mary came to visit the tomb. And behold, there was a great earthquake, for the angel of the Lord came down from heaven and approached the stone and rolled it away and was sitting on it. His look was like lightning, and his clothing white as snow. And those who were on guard were shaken with fear of him and became like dead men. But the angel spoke forth and said to the women: Do not you fear; for I know that you look for Jesus, who was crucified. He is not here. For he rose up, as he said. Come here, and look at the place where he lay. Then go quickly and tell his disciples that he has risen from the dead, and behold, he goes before you into Galilee. There you will see him. See; I have told you. And quickly leaving the tomb, in fear and great

---

5. These words are in Aramaic, a Semitic language commonly spoken in the region (closely related to Hebrew and Syriac); the rest of the gospel is in vernacular Greek.
6. The prophet who was bodily taken up to heaven in a chariot of fire (2 Kings 2.8–11);

his return was prophesied to herald the coming of the Messiah (Malachi 3.1; 4.5).
7. The veil covering the door of the inner sanctuary of the Temple (Exodus 26.31–34), where God was said to appear (Leviticus 16.2).

joy, they ran to tell the news to his disciples. And behold, Jesus met them, saying: I give you greeting. They came up to him and took his feet and worshipped him. Then Jesus said to them: Do not fear. Go and tell my brothers to go into Galilee, and there they will see me. And as they went on their way, behold, some of the guards went into the city and reported to the high priests all that had happened. And they met with the elders and took counsel together, and gave the soldiers a quantity of money, saying: Say that the disciples came in the night and stole him away while we were sleeping. And if this is heard in the house of the governor, we shall reason with him, and make it so that you have nothing to fear. And they took the money and did as they were instructed. And this is the story that has been spread about among the Jews, to this day.

Then the eleven disciples went on into Galilee, to the mountain where Jesus had given them instructions to go; and when they saw him, they worshipped him; but some doubted. And Jesus came up to them and talked with them, saying: All authority has been given to me, in heaven and on earth. Go out, therefore, and instruct all the nations, baptizing them in the name of the Father and the Son and the Holy Spirit, teaching them to observe all that I have taught you. And behold, I am with you, all the days until the end of the world.

John 1

[The Word]

In the beginning was the word, and the word was with God, and the word was God. He was in the beginning, with God. Everything came about through him, and without him not one thing came about. What came about in him was life, and the life was the light of mankind; and the light shines in the darkness, and the darkness did not understand it.

There was a man sent from God; his name was John. This man came for testimony, to testify concerning the light, so that all should believe through him. He was not the light, but was to testify concerning the light. The light was the true light, which illuminates every person who comes into the world. He was in the world, and the world came about through him, and the world did not know him. He went to his own and his own people did not accept him. Those who accepted him, he gave them power to become children of God, to those who believed in his name, who were born not from blood or from the will of the flesh or from the will of man, but from God.

And the word became flesh and lived among us, and we have seen his glory, glory as of a single son from his father, full of grace and truth. John bears witness concerning him, and he cried out, saying (for it was he who was speaking): He who is coming after me was before me, because he was there before I was; because we have all received from his fullness, and grace for grace. Because the law was given through Moses; the grace and the truth came through Jesus Christ. No one has ever seen God; the only-born God who is in the bosom of his father, it is he who told of him.

And this is the testimony of John, when the Jews sent priests and Levites[1] from Jerusalem to ask him: Who are you? And he confessed, and made no

---

1. Members of the tribe of Levi (one of the sons of Jacob), who formed a hereditary subordinate priesthood (see Numbers 18.1–6).

denial, but confessed: I am not the Christ. And they asked him: What then? Are you Elijah? And he said: I am not. Are you the prophet? And he answered: No. Then they said to him: Who are you? So that we can give an answer to those who sent us. What do you say about yourself? He said: I am the voice of one crying in the desert: Make straight the way of the Lord; as Isaiah the prophet said. Now they had been sent by the Pharisees. And they questioned him and said to him: Why then do you baptize, if you are not the Christ, or Elijah or the prophet? John answered them saying: I baptize with water; but in your midst stands one whom you do not know, who is coming after me, and I am not fit to untie the fastening of his shoe. All this happened in Bethany beyond the Jordan,[2] where John was baptizing.

The next day he saw Jesus coming toward him and said: See, the lamb of God who takes away the sinfulness of the world. This is the one of whom I said: A man is coming after me who was before me, because he was there before I was. And I did not know him. But so that he might be made known to Israel, this was why I came baptizing with water. And John bore witness, saying: I have seen the Spirit descending like a dove from the sky, and it remained upon him; and I did not know him, but the one who sent me to baptize with water was the one who said to me: That one, on whom you see the Spirit descending and remaining upon him, is the one who baptizes with the Holy Spirit. And I have seen, and I have borne witness that this is the son of God.

The next day John was standing with two of his disciples, and he saw Jesus walking about and said: See, the lamb of God. His two disciples heard what he said and followed Jesus. Jesus turned about and saw them following him and said: What are you seeking? They said to him: Rabbi (which translated means master), where are you staying? He said to them: Come and see. So they came, and saw where he was staying, and stayed with him for that day. It was about the tenth hour. Andrew, one of the two who heard Jesus and followed him, was the brother of Simon Peter. He went first and found his brother Simon and said to him: We have found the Messiah (which is, translated, the Christ). He took him to Jesus. Jesus looked at him and said: You are Simon, the son of John. You shall be called Cephas[3] (which means Peter).

The next day Jesus wished to go out to Galilee. And he found Philip and said to him: Follow me. Philip was from Bethsaida, the city of Andrew and Peter. Philip found Nathanael and said to him. We have found the one of whom Moses wrote in the law, and the prophets: Jesus the son of Joseph, from Nazareth. And Nathanael said to him: Can anything good come from Nazareth? Philip said to him: Come and see. Jesus saw Nathanael coming toward him and said of him: See, a true son of Israel, in whom there is no guile. Nathanael said to him: How is it that you know me? Jesus answered and said to him: I saw you when you were under the fig tree, before Philip called you. Nathanael answered: Master, you are the son of God, you are the King of Israel. Jesus answered and said to him: Because I told you I saw you under the fig tree, you believe? You will see greater things than that. And he said to him: Truly truly I tell you, you will see the heaven open and the angels of God ascending and descending to the son of man.[4]

2. The river that forms the border between modern Israel and, to the east, Jordan and Syria.
3. Kêfâ (Aramaic), meaning "rock" or "stone" (Greek petros).
4. Compare Jacob's vision of the ladder at Bethel (Genesis 28.10–17).

AUGUSTINE
354–430

When Augustine lay dying in August of 430, Vandal armies were besieging the African city of Hippo (modern Annaba, Algeria), where Augustine was the spiritual leader of a vibrant community of Christians living under the rule of the Roman Empire. Within weeks, Hippo would fall; the great city of Rome itself would be captured within thirty years. Born into the culture of antiquity but laying the foundations for the medieval millennium that was just about to begin, Augustine stands with one foot in each world. His monumental autobiography, the *Confessions*, constantly draws on the rich literature of the Roman orators and prose writers, especially Cicero. Yet it also reaches forward, innovatively exploring the ways in which the reader—like Augustine himself—might find that the Word of God has all along been lodged within his innermost soul.

LIFE AND TIMES

Augustine was a native of the northern African regions that were part of the Roman Empire. Yet the empire was in a gradual state of collapse throughout Augustine's lifetime: strong military leaders were running the government in all but name from 395 onward, and the final Roman emperor would be deposed by rebellious mercenary troops in 476. It was a transitional period—a time of great instability and, simultaneously, cultural and religious ferment. Mystery and cult religions were particularly popular, as witnessed by Augustine's account of his years with the Manichaeans. Despite the instability and uncertainty of the period, the administrative and economic structures of the empire were still healthy enough to ease travel between its various parts, allowing Augustine to journey throughout northern Africa and Italy.

Augustine spent his early years in Africa, where there were several provincial cities of substantial size. Born at Thagaste (modern Souk-Ahras, Algeria), he had his first schooling at the nearby town of Madaurus and, later, at the sophisticated cultural capital of Carthage. There, Augustine became intrigued by Manichaeanism, a dualistic religion that resembled early Christianity in emphasizing the life of the mind and the drive toward increasing spiritual purity, though the two religions differed very significantly in their views of the nature of God. Augustine quickly rose to the top of his profession as an educator and public speaker, teaching grammar at his birthplace of Thagaste and, later, rhetoric at Carthage. These provincial successes impelled him to Rome, where he established a school of rhetoric; he was then invited to come to Milan, which had become a capital of the Western Roman Empire, to take on the chair of rhetoric and such duties as writing honorific speeches to be presented at court. At Milan, Augustine entered into a very sophisticated intellectual community, where he became deeply involved in Neoplatonism both as a philosophy and as a quasi-religious form of mysticism. He also came to know Ambrose, the bishop of Milan. At the time, Augustine says, he told himself that he was attending Ambrose's sermons simply to judge his excellence as a public speaker. In fact, Augustine was becoming increasingly drawn to Christianity, a religion to which his mother, Monica, had vainly tried to introduce him since he was a young child.

The bond between Augustine and Ambrose was strengthened enormously by Monica, who had followed her son to Milan and become close to Ambrose; the bishop reciprocated, constantly telling his friend Augustine what a treasure he had in his faithful and devout mother. The *Confessions* shows that Monica played a major role in her son's spiritual growth, which culminated in Augustine's conversion and baptism on Easter 386, at age thirty-two. This was a moment of complete change for Augustine, not just spiritually but also practically: he gave up his chair in rhetoric at the imperial court of Milan, withdrew from his engagement to marry, and went with his mother to the port of Ostia to return to Africa. But before they could sail from Italy, Monica died, as did Augustine's son, Adeodatus, who had been born in Carthage to Augustine's longtime mistress, traveled to Italy with Augustine, and undergone baptism alongside his father. Alone back in Thagaste, Augustine surrounded himself with spiritual brothers—members of the growing Christian community in the region—and transformed his family home into a monastery. When he paid a visit to a friend at Hippo in 391, Augustine found that his reputation as a spiritual leader had preceded him. The community at Hippo begged Augustine to remain with them, and he was ordained a priest at their request. By 396, he was bishop of Hippo, a position he held until his death.

WORK

Augustine probably began work on the *Confessions* in 397, when he was forty-three years old. He seems to have been suffering from a terrible case of writer's block, with several half-finished pieces of work on hand. The experience of writing the *Confessions* apparently cured it, for almost immediately after completing it Augustine went on to produce an extraordinarily large number of works. The *Confessions* is, as the name suggests, autobiographical, the story of one man's life in his own words. But it is also confessional in the sense of being a full account of one's sins; a story addressed first of all to God, the hearer who is able to forgive the transgressions that Augustine recounts. At the same time, the *Confessions* has a secondary addressee, as Augustine himself acknowledges: other would-be Christians who might be able to trace the path of their own spiritual journey as a result of having read about the struggles of another. Of the thirteen books of the *Confessions*, only the first nine are autobiographical, covering the period from Augustine's early childhood memories to his stay in Ostia in 387, as he waits for the boat that would take him home. The autobiographical genre, almost without precedent in this period, is perhaps Augustine's greatest literary legacy. We hear nothing from Augustine about his later years in Africa; instead, the final books of the *Confessions* are an analysis of the account of creation in Genesis, along with a sustained meditation on the nature of time and memory. The overall effect of the *Confessions* is to turn the reader inward, away from the individual journey of Augustine and toward the collective journey of humanity toward the divine.

Surprisingly for a book dedicated to the relationship of the soul to God, the most moving parts of the *Confessions* focus on Augustine's relationship to other human beings—not just his mother, Monica, who was so instrumental to Augustine's conversion to Christianity, but also his beloved son, Adeodatus, and the unnamed mistress who was Augustine's companion from age seventeen (when he first went to Carthage) until his mother persuaded him to enter into an arranged marriage in 385, shortly before his conversion. This woman, whom Augustine simply calls "the One," faithfully followed him on his journeys, first to Rome and then to Milan. When Augustine finally renounced his relationship with her, she returned to Africa, "swearing that she would never know another man." All of these human relationships, however passionate, are in the end subsumed within Augustine's all-consuming relationship with God. He addresses God familiarly throughout the *Confessions*, as if he were an intimate friend who knew all Augustine's secrets, but who also had the terrifying capacity to destroy, inspiring both adoration and fear.

Augustine writes frankly about his self-fashioning within the various communities to which he belonged, from his involvement in a gang of undisciplined youths to his immersion in the Manichaean community at Carthage, his time among the Neoplatonists in Milan, and his final place of rest among the Christian community at Hippo. His journey is, at a deep level, a search for the self, which he comes to find only after long struggle, and only through the companionship of others. Augustine comes home first spiritually, with a con-version inspired by the supernatural voice of a child, and then physically, sailing from Ostia to Thagaste, where he will make a new spiritual home filled with Christian believers among the bricks and mortar of his childhood house. Desire and longing structure the narrative of the *Confessions*, from Augustine's heady days in Carthage, at the theater by day and in the arms of his mistress by night, to his patient vigil at the port of Ostia, consumed at once by sorrow for the death of Monica and joy in his discovery of Christ. Caught between his love for human beings and his longing for the divine, Augustine is never more present to us than when, shortly before his conversion, he cries out to God, "Make me chaste—but not yet." Augustine's painstaking examination of his innermost self, racked with contradictions and unexplained desires, had a profound influence not only on the medieval Christians who sought, like Augustine, to purge their souls of sin but also on the secular self-examination of early modern writers such as **Montaigne** and **Rousseau**.

From Confessions[1]

FROM BOOK I

[*Childhood*]

What have I to say to Thee, God, save that I know not where I came from, when I came into this life-in-death—or should I call it death-in-life? I do not know. I only know that the gifts Your mercy had provided sustained me from the first moment: not that I remember it but so I have heard from the parents of my flesh, the father from whom, and the mother in whom, You fashioned me in time.

Thus for my sustenance and my delight I had woman's milk: yet it was not my mother or my nurses who stored their breasts for me: it was Yourself, using them to give me the food of my infancy, according to Your ordinance and the riches set by You at every level of creation. It was by Your gift that I desired what You gave and no more, by Your gift that those who suckled me willed to give me what You had given them: for it was by the love implanted in them by You that they gave so willingly that milk which by Your gift flowed in the

1. Translated by F. J. Sheed.

breasts. It was a good for them that I received good from them, though I received it not *from* them but only through them: since all good things are from You, O God, and *from God is all my health*.[2] But this I have learnt since: You have made it abundantly clear by all that I have seen You give, within me and about me. For at that time I knew how to suck, to lie quiet when I was content, to cry when I was in pain: and that was all I knew.

Later I added smiling to the things I could do, first in sleep, then awake. This again I have on the word of others, for naturally I do not remember; in any event, I believe it, for I have seen other infants do the same. And gradually I began to notice where I was, and the will grew in me to make my wants known to those who might satisfy them; but I could not, for my wants were within me and those others were outside: nor had they any faculty enabling them to enter into my mind. So I would fling my arms and legs about and utter sounds, making the few gestures in my power—these being as apt to express my wishes as I could make them: but they were not very apt. And when I did not get what I wanted, either because my wishes were not clear or the things not good for me, I was in a rage—with my parents as though I had a right to their submission, with free human beings as though they had been bound to serve me; and I took my revenge in screams. That infants are like this, I have learnt from watching other infants; and that I was like it myself I have learnt more clearly from these other infants, who did not know me, than from my nurses who did.

* * *

From infancy I came to boyhood, or rather it came to me, taking the place of infancy. Yet infancy did not go: for where was it to go to? Simply it was no longer there. For now I was not an infant, without speech, but a boy, speaking. This I remember; and I have since discovered by observation how I learned to speak. I did not learn by elders teaching me words in any systematic way, as I was soon after taught to read and write. But of my own motion, using the mind which You, my God, gave me, I strove with cries and various sounds and much moving of my limbs to utter the feelings of my heart—all this in order to get my own way. Now I did not always manage to express the right meanings to the right people. So I began to reflect [I observed that][3] my elders would make some particular sound, and as they made it would point at or move towards some particular thing: and from this I came to realize that the thing was called by the sound they made when they wished to draw my attention to it. That they intended this was clear from the motions of their body, by a kind of natural language common to all races which consists in facial expressions, glances of the eye, gestures, and the tones by which the voice expresses the mind's state—for example whether things are to be sought, kept, thrown away, or avoided. So, as I heard the same words again and again properly used in different phrases, I came gradually to grasp what things they signified; and forcing my mouth to the same sounds, I began to use them to express my own wishes. Thus I learnt to convey what I meant to those about me; and so took another long step along the stormy way of human life in society, while I was still subject to the authority of my parents and at the beck and call of my elders.

2. Throughout the *Confessions* Augustine quotes liberally from the Bible; the quotations are set off in italics. When a quotation bears on Augustine's situation, it is annotated.
3. Words in brackets are the translator's.

O God, my God, what emptiness and mockeries did I now experience: for it was impressed upon me as right and proper in a boy to obey those who taught me, that I might get on in the world and excel in the handling of words[4] to gain honor among men and deceitful riches. I, poor wretch, could not see the use of the things I was sent to school to learn; but if I proved idle in learning, I was soundly beaten. For this procedure seemed wise to our ancestors: and many, passing the same way in days past, had built a sorrowful road by which we too must go, with multiplication of grief and toil upon the sons of Adam.

Yet, Lord, I observed men praying to You: and I learnt to do likewise, thinking of You (to the best of my understanding) as some great being who, though unseen, could hear and help me. As a boy I fell into the way of calling upon You, my Help and my Refuge; and in those prayers I broke the strings of my tongue—praying to You, small as I was but with no small energy, that I might not be beaten at school.[5] And when You did not hear me (*not as giving me over to folly*), my elders and even my parents, who certainly wished me no harm, treated my stripes as a huge joke, which they were very far from being to me. Surely, Lord, there is no one so steeled in mind or cleaving to You so close—or even so insensitive, for that might have the same effect—as to make light of the racks and hooks and other torture instruments[6] (from which in all lands men pray so fervently to be saved) while truly loving those who are in such bitter fear of them. Yet my parents seemed to be amused at the torments inflicted upon me as a boy by my masters, though I was no less afraid of my punishments or zealous in my prayers to You for deliverance. But in spite of my terrors I still did wrong, by writing or reading or studying less than my set tasks. It was not, Lord, that I lacked mind or memory, for You had given me as much of these as my age required; but the one thing I revelled in was play; and for this I was punished by men who after all were doing exactly the same things themselves. But the idling of men is called business; the idling of boys, though exactly like, is punished by those same men: and no one pities either boys or men. Perhaps an unbiased observer would hold that I was rightly punished as a boy for playing with a ball: because this hindered my progress in studies—studies which would give me the opportunity as a man to play at things more degraded. And what difference was there between me and the master who flogged me? For if on some trifling point he had the worst of the argument with some fellow-master, he was more torn with angry vanity than I when I was beaten in a game of ball.

* * *

But to continue with my boyhood, which was in less peril of sin than my adolescence. I disliked learning and hated to be forced to it. But I *was* forced to it, so that good was done to me though it was not my doing. Short of being driven to it, I certainly would not have learned. But no one does well against his will, even if the thing he does is a good thing to do. Nor did those who forced me do well: it was by You, O God, that well was done. Those others had no deeper vision of the use to which I might put all they forced me to learn, but to sate the insatiable desire of man for wealth that is but penury and glory that is but shame.

But You, Lord, *by Whom the very hairs of our head are numbered,*[7] used for my good the error of those who urged me to study; but my own error, in that I had no will to learn, you used for my punishment—a punishment richly deserved by one so small a boy and so great a sinner. Thus, You brought good for me out of those who did ill, and justly punished me for the ill I did myself. So You have ordained and so it is: that every disorder of the soul is its own punishment.

To this day I do not quite see why I so hated the Greek tongue[8] that I was made to learn as a small boy. For I really liked Latin—not the rudiments that we got from our first teachers but the literature that we came to be taught later. For the rudiments—reading and writing and figuring—I found as hard and hateful as Greek. Yet this too could come only from sin and the vanity of life, because *I was flesh, and a wind that goes away and returns not.* For those first lessons were the surer. I acquired the power I still have to read what I find written and to write what I want to express; whereas in the studies that came later I was forced to memorize the wanderings of Aeneas[9]—whoever he was— while forgetting my own wanderings; and to weep for the death of Dido[1] who killed herself for love, while bearing dry-eyed my own pitiful state, in that among these studies I was becoming dead to You, O God, my life.

Nothing could be more pitiful than a pitiable creature who does not see to pity himself, and weeps for the death that Dido suffered through love of Aeneas and not for the death he suffers himself through not loving You, O God, Light of my heart, Bread of my soul, Power wedded to my mind and the depths of my thought. I did not love You and I went away from You in fornication:[2] and all around me in my fornication echoed applauding cries "Well done! Well done!" *For the friendship of this world is fornication against Thee:* and the world cries "Well done" so loudly that one is ashamed of unmanliness not to do it. And for this I did not grieve; but I grieved for Dido, slain as she sought by the sword an end to her woe,[3] while I too followed after the lowest of Your creatures, forsaking You, earth going unto earth. And if I were kept from reading, I grieved at not reading the tales that caused me such grief. This sort of folly is held nobler and richer than the studies by which we learn to read and write!

But now let my God cry aloud in my soul, and let Your truth assure me that it is not so: the earlier study is the better. I would more willingly forget the wanderings of Aeneas and all such things than how to write and read. Over the entrance of these grammar schools hangs a curtain:[4] but this should be seen not as lending honor to the mysteries, but as a cloak to the errors taught within. Let not those masters—who have now lost their terrors for me—cry out against me, because I confess to You, my God, the desire of my soul, and find soul's rest in blaming my evil ways that I may love Your holy ways. Let not the buyers or sellers

---

7. Who knows and attends to the smallest detail of each life (compare Matthew 10.30).
8. Important not only for gaining knowledge of Greek literature but also because it was the official language of the Eastern Roman Empire. Augustine never really mastered Greek, though his remark elsewhere that he had acquired so little Greek that it amounted to practically none is overmodest.
9. Virgil's *Aeneid* 3.
1. Queen of Carthage whose unrequited love for the Trojan warrior Aeneas ended in her

untimely death; Aeneas was obliged to pursue his destiny to be the founding father of Rome (Virgil, *Aeneid*, esp. book 4).
2. Here, metaphorically.
3. Virgil, *Aeneid* 6.457.
4. In Augustine's time, school entrances were covered by veils with an attendant standing by to make sure that only those who paid tution were admitted; the veil was also a symbol of the hidden knowledge that lay across the threshold.

of book-learning cry out against me. If I ask them whether it is true, as the poet says, that Aeneas ever went to Carthage, the more ignorant will have to answer that they do not know, the more scholarly that he certainly did not. But if I ask with what letters the name Aeneas is spelt, all whose schooling has gone so far will answer correctly, according to the convention men have agreed upon for the use of letters. Or again, were I to ask which loss would be more damaging to human life—the loss from men's memory of reading and writing or the loss of these poetic imaginings—there can be no question what anyone would answer who had not lost his own memory. Therefore as a boy I did wrong in liking the empty studies more than the useful—or rather in loving the empty and hating the useful. For one and one make two, two and two make four, I found a loathsome refrain; but such empty unrealities as the Wooden Horse with its armed men, and Troy on fire, and Creusa's Ghost, were sheer delight.[5]

* * *

Give me leave, O my God, to speak of my mind, Your gift, and of the follies in which I wasted it. It chanced that a task was set me, a task which I did not like but had to do. There was the promise of glory if I won, the fear of ignominy, and a flogging as well, if I lost. It was to declaim the words uttered by Juno in her rage and grief when she could not keep the Trojan prince from coming to Italy.[6] I had learnt that Juno had never said these words, but we were compelled to err in the footsteps of the poet who had invented them: and it was our duty to paraphrase in prose what he had said in verse. In this exercise that boy won most applause in whom the passions of grief and rage were expressed most powerfully and in the language most adequate to the majesty of the personage represented.

What could all this mean to me, O My true Life, My God? Why was there more applause for the performance I gave than for so many classmates of my own age? Was not the whole business so much smoke and wind? Surely some other matter could have been found to exercise mind and tongue. Thy praises, Lord, might have upheld the fresh young shoot of my heart, so that it might not have been whirled away by empty trifles, defiled, a prey to the spirits of the air. For there is more than one way of sacrificing to the fallen angels. * * *

FROM BOOK II

[The Pear Tree]

I propose now to set down my past wickedness and the carnal corruptions of my soul, not for love of them but that I may love Thee, O my God. I do it for love of Thy love, passing again in the bitterness of remembrance over my most evil ways that Thou mayest thereby grow ever lovelier to me, O Loveliness that dost not deceive, Loveliness happy and abiding: and I collect my self out of

5. While at a feast held in his honor by Dido, Aeneas tells the story of the fall of Troy and his escape from the burning city, during which he lost his wife, Creusa (Virgil, *Aeneid*, book 2, esp. 2.772).
6. Augustine was assigned the task of delivering a prose paraphrase of Juno's angry speech in *Aeneid* 1. In it she complains that her ene-mies, the Trojans under Aeneas, are on their way to their destined goal in Italy in spite of her resolution to prevent them. Rhetorical exercises such as this were common in the schools, because they served the double purpose of teaching both literature and rhetorical composition.

that broken state in which my very being was torn asunder because I was turned away from Thee, the One, and wasted myself upon the many.

Arrived now at adolescence I burned for all the satisfactions of hell, and I sank to the animal in a succession of dark lusts: *my beauty consumed away,* and I stank in Thine eyes, yet was pleasing in my own and anxious to please the eyes of men.

My one delight was to love and to be loved. But in this I did not keep the measure of mind to mind, which is the luminous line of friendship; but from the muddy concupiscence of the flesh and the hot imagination of puberty mists steamed up to becloud and darken my heart so that I could not distinguish the white light of love from the fog of lust. Both love and lust boiled within me, and swept my youthful immaturity over the precipice of evil desires to leave me half drowned in a whirlpool of abominable sins. Your wrath had grown mighty against me and I knew it not. I had grown deaf from the clanking of the chain of my mortality, the punishment for the pride of my soul: and I departed further from You, and You left me to myself: and I was tossed about and wasted and poured out and boiling over in my fornications: and You were silent, O my late-won Joy. You were silent, and I, arrogant and depressed, weary and restless, wandered further and further from You into more and more sins which could bear no fruit save sorrows.

* * *

Where then was I, and how far from the delights of Your house, in that sixteenth year of my life in this world, when the madness of lust—needing no licence from human shamelessness, receiving no licence from Your laws—took complete control of me, and I surrendered wholly to it? My family took no care to save me from this moral destruction by marriage: their only concern was that I should learn to make as fine and persuasive speeches as possible.

* * *

Your law, O Lord, punishes theft; and this law is so written in the hearts of men that not even the breaking of it blots it out: for no thief bears calmly being stolen from—not even if he is rich and the other steals through want. Yet I chose to steal, and not because want drove me to it—unless a want of justice and contempt for it and an excess for iniquity. For I stole things which I already had in plenty and of better quality. Nor had I any desire to enjoy the things I stole, but only the stealing of them and the sin. There was a pear tree near our vineyard, heavy with fruit, but fruit that was not particularly tempting either to look at or to taste. A group of young blackguards, and I among them, went out to knock down the pears and carry them off late one night, for it was our bad habit to carry on our games in the streets till very late. We carried off an immense load of pears, not to eat—for we barely tasted them before throwing them to the hogs. Our only pleasure in doing it was that it was forbidden. Such was my heart, O God, such was my heart: yet in the depth of the abyss You had pity on it. Let that heart now tell You what it sought when I was thus evil for no object, having no cause for wrongdoing save my wrongness. The malice of the act was base and I loved it—that is to say I loved my own undoing, I loved the evil in me—not the thing for which I did the evil, simply the evil: my soul was depraved, and hurled itself down from security in You into utter destruction, seeking no profit from wickedness but only to be wicked.

There is an appeal to the eye in beautiful things, in gold and silver and all such; the sense of touch has its own powerful pleasures; and the other senses find qualities in things suited to them. Worldly success has its glory, and the power to command and to overcome: and from this springs the thirst for revenge. But in our quest of all these things, we must not depart from You, Lord, or deviate from Your Law. This life we live here below has its own attractiveness, grounded in the measure of beauty it has and its harmony with the beauty of all lesser things. The bond of human friendship is admirable, holding many souls as one. Yet in the enjoyment of all such things we commit sin if through immoderate inclination to them—for though they are good, they are of the lowest order of good—things higher and better are forgotten, even You, O Lord our God, and Your Truth and Your Law. These lower things have their delights but not such as my God has, for He made them all: *and in Him doth the righteous delight, and He is the joy of the upright of heart.*

Now when we ask why this or that particular evil act was done, it is normal to assume that it could not have been done save through the desire of gaining or the fear of losing some one of these lower goods. For they have their own charm and their own beauty, though compared with the higher values of heaven they are poor and mean enough. Such a man has committed a murder. Why? He wanted the other man's wife or his property; or he had chosen robbery as a means of livelihood; or he feared to lose this or that through his victim's act; or he had been wronged and was aflame for vengeance. Would any man commit a murder for no cause, for the sheer delight of murdering? The thing would be incredible. There is of course the case of the man [Catiline] who was said[7] to be so stupidly and savagely cruel that he practised cruelty and evil even when he had nothing to gain by them. But even there a cause was stated—he did it, he said, lest through idleness his hand or his resolution should grow slack. And why did he want to prevent that? So that one day by the multiplication of his crimes the city should be his, and he would have gained honors and authority and riches, and would no longer be in fear of the law or in the difficulties that want of money and the awareness of his crimes had brought him. So that not even Catiline loved his crimes as crimes: he loved some other thing which was his reason for committing them.

What was it then that in my wretched folly I loved in you, O theft of mine, deed wrought in that dark night when I was sixteen? For you were not lovely: you were a theft. Or are you anything at all, that I should talk with you? The pears that we stole were beautiful for they were created by Thee, Thou most Beautiful of all, Creator of all, Thou good God, my Sovereign and true Good. The pears were beautiful but it was not pears that my empty soul desired. For I had any number of better pears of my own, and plucked those only that I might steal. For once I had gathered them I threw them away, tasting only my own sin and savouring that with delight; for if I took so much as a bite of any one of those pears, it was the sin that sweetened it. And now, Lord my God, I ask what was it that attracted me in that theft, for there was no beauty in it to attract. I do not mean merely that it lacked the beauty that there is in justice and prudence, or in the mind of man or his senses and vegetative life: or even so much as the beauty and glory of the stars in the heavens, or of earth and sea

---

7. By the Roman historian Sallust (*Catiline 16*). Cataline was a Roman politician whose conspiracy against the state was foiled by the consul Cicero in 63 B.C.E.

with their oncoming of new life to replace the generations that pass. It had not even that false show or shadow of beauty by which sin tempts us.

[For there *is* a certain show of beauty in sin.] Thus pride wears the mask of loftiness of spirit, although You alone, O God, are high over all. Ambition seeks honor and glory, although You alone are to be honored before all and glorious forever. By cruelty the great seek to be feared, yet who is to be feared but God alone: from His power what can be wrested away, or when or where or how or by whom? The caresses by which the lustful seduce are a seeking for love: but nothing is more caressing than Your charity, nor is anything more healthfully loved than Your supremely lovely, supremely luminous Truth. Curiosity may be regarded as a desire for knowledge, whereas You supremely know all things. Ignorance and sheer stupidity hide under the names of simplicity and innocence: yet no being has simplicity like to Yours: and none is more innocent than You, for it is their own deeds that harm the wicked. Sloth pretends that it wants quietude: but what sure rest is there save the Lord? Luxuriousness would be called abundance and completeness; but You are the fullness and inexhaustible abundance of incorruptible delight. Wastefulness is a parody of generosity: but You are the infinitely generous giver of all good. Avarice wants to possess overmuch: but You possess all. Enviousness claims that it strives to excel: but what can excel before You? Anger clamors for just vengeance: but whose vengeance is so just as Yours? Fear is the recoil from a new and sudden threat to something one holds dear, and a cautious regard for one's own safety: but nothing new or sudden can happen to You, nothing can threaten Your hold upon things loved, and where is safety secure save in You? Grief pines at the loss of things in which desire delighted: for it wills to be like to You from whom nothing can be taken away.

Thus the soul is guilty of fornication when she turns from You and seeks from any other source what she will nowhere find pure and without taint unless she returns to You. Thus even those who go from You and stand up against You are still perversely imitating You. But by the mere fact of their imitation, they declare that You are the creator of all that is, and that there is nowhere for them to go where You are not.

So once again what did I enjoy in that theft of mine? Of what excellence of my Lord was I making perverse and vicious imitation? Perhaps it was the thrill of acting against Your law—at least in appearance, since I had no power to do so in fact, the delight a prisoner might have in making some small gesture of liberty—getting a deceptive sense of omnipotence from doing something forbidden without immediate punishment. I was that slave, who fled from his Lord and pursued his Lord's shadow. O rottenness, O monstrousness of life and abyss of death! Could you find pleasure only in what was forbidden, and only because it was forbidden? * * *

FROM BOOK III

[Student at Carthage]

I came to Carthage[8] where a cauldron of illicit loves leapt and boiled about me. I was not yet in love, but I was in love with love, and from the very depth of my need hated myself for not more keenly feeling the need. I sought some object

---

8. The capital city of the province, where Augustine went to study rhetoric.

to love, since I was thus in love with loving; and I hated security and a life with no snares for my feet. For within I was hungry, all for the want of that spiritual food which is Thyself, my God; yet [though I was hungry for want of it] I did not hunger for it: I had no desire whatever for incorruptible food, not because I had it in abundance but the emptier I was, the more I hated the thought of it. Because of all this my soul was sick, and broke out in sores, whose itch I agonized to scratch with the rub of carnal things—carnal, yet if there were no soul in them, they would not be objects of love. My longing then was to love and to be loved, but most when I obtained the enjoyment of the body of the person who loved me.

Thus I polluted the stream of friendship with the filth of unclean desire and sullied its limpidity with the hell of lust. And vile and unclean as I was, so great was my vanity that I was bent upon passing for clean and courtly. And I did fall in love, simply from wanting to. O my God, my Mercy, with how much bitterness didst Thou in Thy goodness sprinkle the delights of that time! I was loved, and our love came to the bond of consummation: I wore my chains with bliss but with torment too, for I was scourged with the red hot rods of jealousy, with suspicions and fears and tempers and quarrels.

I developed a passion for stage plays, with the mirror they held up to my own miseries and the fuel they poured on my flame. How is it that a man wants to be made sad by the sight of tragic sufferings that he could not bear in his own person? Yet the spectator does want to feel sorrow, and it is actually his feeling of sorrow that he enjoys. Surely this is the most wretched lunacy? For the more a man feels such sufferings in himself, the more he is moved by the sight of them on the stage. Now when a man suffers himself, it is called misery; when he suffers in the suffering of another, it is called pity. But how can the unreal sufferings of the stage possibly move pity? The spectator is not moved to aid the sufferer but merely to be sorry for him; and the more the author of these fictions makes the audience grieve, the better they like him. If the tragic sorrows of the characters—whether historical or entirely fictitious—be so poorly represented that the spectator is not moved to tears, he leaves the theatre unsatisfied and full of complaints; if he is moved to tears, he stays to the end, fascinated and revelling in it. So that tears and sorrow, it would seem, are things to be sought. Yet surely every man prefers to be joyful. May it be that whereas no one wants to be miserable, there is real pleasure in pitying others—and we love their sorrows because without them we should have nothing to pity?

* * *

Those of my occupations at that time which were held as reputable[9] were directed towards the study of the law, in which I meant to excel—and the less honest I was, the more famous I should be. The very limit of human blindness is to glory in being blind. By this time I was a leader in the School of Rhetoric and I enjoyed this high station and was arrogant and swollen with importance: though You know, O Lord, that I was far quieter in my behavior and had no share in the riotousness of the *eversores*—the Overturners[1]—for this blackguardly

9. That is, his rhetorical studies.
1. *Eversores* is the Latin word that means "overturners": a group of students who prided

themselves on their wild actions and lack of discipline.

diabolical name they wore as the very badge of sophistication. Yet I was much in their company and much ashamed of the sense of shame that kept me from being like them. I was with them and I did for the most part enjoy their companionship, though I abominated the acts that were their specialty—as when they made a butt of some hapless newcomer, assailing him with really cruel mockery for no reason whatever, save the malicious pleasure they got from it. There was something very like the action of devils in their behavior. They were rightly called Overturners, since they had themselves been first overturned and perverted, tricked by those same devils who were secretly mocking them in the very acts by which they amused themselves in mocking and making fools of others.

With these men as companions of my immaturity, I was studying the books of eloquence; for in eloquence it was my ambition to shine, all from a damnable vaingloriousness and for the satisfaction of human vanity. Following the normal order of study I had come to a book of one Cicero,[2] whose tongue[3] practically everyone admires, though not his heart. That particular book is called *Hortensius*[4] and contains an exhortation to philosophy. Quite definitely it changed the direction of my mind, altered my prayers to You, O Lord, and gave me a new purpose and ambition. Suddenly all the vanity I had hoped in I saw as worthless, and with an incredible intensity of desire I longed after immortal wisdom. I had begun that journey upwards by which I was to return to You. My father was now dead two years; I was eighteen and was receiving money from my mother for the continuance of my study of eloquence. But I used that book not for the sharpening of my tongue; what won me in it was what it said, not the excellence of its phrasing.

* * *

So I resolved to make some study of the Sacred Scriptures and find what kind of books they were. But what I came upon was something not grasped by the proud, not revealed either to children, something utterly humble in the hearing but sublime in the doing, and shrouded deep in mystery. And I was not of the nature to enter into it or bend my neck to follow it. When I first read those Scriptures, I did not feel in the least what I have just said; they seemed to me unworthy to be compared with the majesty of Cicero. My conceit was repelled by their simplicity, and I had not the mind to penetrate into their depths. They were indeed of a nature to grow in Your little ones.[5] But I could not bear to be a little one; I was only swollen with pride, but to myself I seemed a very big man. * * *

2. Marcus Tullius Cicero (106–43 B.C.E.), Roman philosopher, politican, and lawyer. Augustine's admiration of Cicero is obvious; calling him "a certain Cicero" is a rhetorical convention; Augustine uses the same phrase to refer to the Apostle Paul.
3. Style.
4. Cicero's *Hortensius*, written in 45 B.C.E. and

now lost, was an analysis of the sources of happiness, which Cicero concluded lay in the pursuit of wisdom.
5. Refers not only to the rhetorical simplicity of Jesus' teachings but also to his interest in teaching children; compare Matthew 19.14: "For of such is the kingdom of heaven."

[Augustine Leaves Carthage for Rome]

It was by Your action upon me that I was moved to go to Rome and teach there what I had taught in Carthage. How I was persuaded to this, I shall not omit to confess to you, because therein Your most profound depths and Your mercy ever present towards us are to be meditated upon and uttered forth. My reason for going to Rome was not the greater earnings and higher dignity promised by the friends who urged me to go—though at that time, these considerations certainly influenced my mind: the principal and practically conclusive reason, was that I had heard that youths there pursued their studies more quietly and were kept within a stricter limit of discipline. For instance, they were not allowed to come rushing insolently and at will into the school of one who was not their own master, nor indeed to enter it at all unless he permitted.

At Carthage the licence of the students is gross and beyond all measure. They break in impudently and like a pack of madmen play havoc with the order which the master has established for the good of his pupils. They commit many outrages, extraordinarily stupid acts, deserving the punishment of the law if custom did not protect them. Their state is the more hopeless because what they do is supposed to be sanctioned, though by Your eternal law it could never be sanctioned; and they think they do these things unpunished, when the very blindness in which they do them is their punishment, so that they suffer things incomparably worse than they do. When I was a student I would not have such habits in myself, but when I became a teacher I had to endure them in others; and so I decided to go to a place where, as I had been told by all who knew, such things were not done. But You, O my Hope and my Portion in the land of the living, forced me to change countries for my soul's salvation: You pricked me with such goads at Carthage as drove me out of it, and You set before me certain attractions by which I might be drawn to Rome—in either case using men who loved this life of death, one set doing lunatic things, the other promising vain things: and to reform my ways You secretly used their perversity and my own. For those who had disturbed my peace were blind in the frenzy of their viciousness, and those who urged me to go elsewhere savoured of earth. While I, detesting my real misery in the one place, hoped for an unreal happiness in the other.

Why I left the one country and went to the other, You Knew, O God, but You did not tell either me or my mother. She indeed was in dreadful grief at my going and followed me right to the seacoast.[6] There she clung to me passionately, determined that I should either go back home with her or take her to Rome with me, but I deceived her with the pretence that I had a friend whom I did not want to leave until he had sailed off with a fair wind. Thus I lied to my mother, and such a mother; and so got away from her. But this also You have mercifully forgiven me, bringing me from the waters of that sea, filled as I was with execrable uncleanness, unto the water of Your grace; so that when I was washed clean,[7] the floods that poured from my mother's eyes, the tears with

6. Here, Monica and Augustine are in the roles of Dido and Aeneas; see Virgil, *Aeneid*, book 4.
7. Ritual of immersion in water to signify the cleansing of the soul from sin; in Augustine's day, baptism was often put off until death was near, even by relatively observant Christians.

which daily she watered the ground towards which she bent her face in prayer for me, should cease to flow. She would not return home without me, but I managed with some difficulty to persuade her to spend the night in a place near the ship where there was an oratory in memory of St. Cyprian.[8] That night I stole away without her: she remained praying and weeping. And what was she praying for, O my God, with all those tears but that You should not allow me to sail! But You saw deeper and granted the essential of her prayer: You did not do what she was at that moment asking, that You might do the thing she was always asking. The wind blew and filled our sails and the shore dropped from our sight. And the next morning she was frantic with grief and filled Your ears with her moaning and complaints because You seemed to treat her tears so lightly, when in fact You were using my own desires to snatch me away for the healing of those desires, and were justly punishing her own too earthly affection for me with the scourge of grief. For she loved to have me with her, as is the way of mothers but far more than most mothers; and she did not realize what joys you would bring her from my going away. She did not realize it, and so she wept and lamented, and by the torments she suffered showed the heritage of Eve in her, seeking with sorrow what in sorrow she had brought forth. But when she had poured out all her accusation at my cruel deception, she turned once more to prayer to You for me. She went home and I to Rome. * * *

FROM BOOK VI

[Earthly Love]

By this time my mother had come to me, following me over sea and land with the courage of piety and relying upon You in all perils. For they were in danger from a storm, and she reassured even the sailors—by whom travelers newly ventured upon the deep are ordinarily reassured—promising them safe arrival because thus You had promised her in a vision. She found me in a perilous state through my deep despair of ever discovering the truth. But even when I told her that if I was not yet a Catholic Christian, I was no longer a Manichean,[9] she was not greatly exultant as at some unlooked-for good news, because she had already received assurance upon that part of my misery; she bewailed me as one dead certainly, but certainly to be raised again by You, offering me in her mind as one stretched out dead, that You might say to the widow's son: "Young man, I say to thee arise":[1] and he should sit up and begin to speak and You should give him to his mother.

* * *

Great effort was made to get me married. I proposed, the girl was promised me. My mother played a great part in the matter for she wanted to have me married

8. Bishop of Carthage, local martyr, and saint who was especially popular among North African Christians.
9. Augustine had for nine years been a member of this religious sect, which followed the teaching of the Babylonian mystic Mani (216–277). The Manicheans believed that the world was a battleground for the forces of good and evil; redemption in a future life would come to the elect, who renounced worldly occupations and possessions and practiced a severe asceticism (including abstention from meat). Augustine's mother, Monica, was a Christian, and lamented her son's Manichean beliefs.
1. Luke 7.14, recounting one of Christ's miracles.

and then cleansed with the saving waters of baptism,[2] rejoicing to see me grow every day more fitted for baptism and feeling that her prayers and Your promises were to be fulfilled in my faith. By my request and her own desire she begged You daily with the uttermost intensity of her heart to show her in a vision something of my future marriage, but You would never do it. She did indeed see certain vain fantasies, under the pressure of her mind's preoccupation with the matter; and she told them to me, not, however, with the confidence she always had when You had shown things to her, but as if she set small store by them; for she said that there was a certain unanalyzable savor, not to be expressed in words, by which she could distinguish between what You revealed and the dreams of her own spirit. Still she pushed on with the matter of my marriage, and the girl was asked for. She was still two years short of the age for marriage but I liked her and agreed to wait.[3]

There was a group of us friends who had much serious discussion together, concerning the cares and troubles of human life which we found so hard to endure. We had almost decided to seek a life of peace, away from the throng of men. This peace we hoped to attain by putting together whatever we could manage to get, and making one common household for all of us: so that in the clear trust of friendship, things should not belong to this or that individual, but one thing should be made of all our possessions, and belong wholly to each one of us, and everybody own everything. It seemed that there might be perhaps ten men in this fellowship. Among us there were some very rich men, especially Romanianus, our fellow townsman, who had been a close friend of mine from childhood and had been brought to the court in Milan by the press of some very urgent business. He was strongest of all for the idea and he had considerable influence in persuasion because his wealth was much greater than anyone else's. We agreed that two officers should be chosen every year to handle the details of our life together, leaving the rest undisturbed. But then we began to wonder whether our wives would agree, for some of us already had wives and I meant to have one. So the whole plan, which we had built up so neatly, fell to pieces in our hands and was simply dropped. We returned to our old sighing and groaning and treading of this world's broad and beaten ways:[4] for many thoughts were in our hearts, but *Thy counsel standeth forever.* And out of Thy counsel didst Thou deride ours and didst prepare Thine own things for us, meaning to *give us meat in due season and to open Thy hands and fill our souls with Thy blessing.*

Meanwhile my sins were multiplied. She with whom I had lived so long was torn from my side as a hindrance to my forthcoming marriage.[5] My heart

---

2. He could not be baptized while living in sin with his mistress, a liaison that resulted in the birth of a son, Adeodatus, who later accompanied Augustine to Italy.
3. Under Roman law, the minimum age for marriage was twelve, so the girl that Monica arranged for Augustine to marry must have been about ten. Augustine was in his early

thirties at the time.
4. Compare Matthew 7.13: "Broad is the way that leadeth to destruction," that is, to damnation.
5. This woman had been Augustine's companion since he was seventeen and had accompanied him from Carthage to Rome.

which had held her very dear was broken and wounded and shed blood. She went back to Africa, swearing that she would never know another man, and left with me the natural son I had had of her. But I in my unhappiness could not, for all my manhood, imitate her resolve. I was unable to bear the delay of two years which must pass before I was to get the girl I had asked for in marriage. In fact it was not really marriage that I wanted. I was simply a slave to lust. So I took another woman, not of course as a wife; and thus my soul's disease was nourished and kept alive as vigorously as ever, indeed worse than ever, that it might reach the realm of matrimony in the company of its ancient habit. Nor was the wound healed that had been made by the cutting off of my former mistress. For there was first burning and bitter grief; and after that it festered, and as the pain grew duller it only grew more hopeless. * * *

FROM BOOK VIII

[Conversion]

* * * Thus I was sick at heart and in torment, accusing myself with a new intensity of bitterness, twisting and turning in my chain in the hope that it might be utterly broken, for what held me was so small a thing! But it still held me. And You stood in the secret places of my soul, O Lord, in the harshness of Your mercy redoubling the scourges of fear[6] and shame lest I should give way again and that small slight tie which remained should not be broken but should grow again to full strength and bind me closer even than before. For I kept saying within myself: "Let it be now, let it be now," and by the mere words I had begun to move toward the resolution. I almost made it, yet I did not quite make it. But I did not fall back into my original state, but as it were stood near to get my breath. And I tried again and I was almost there, and now I could all but touch it and hold it: yet I was not quite there, I did not touch it or hold it. I still shrank from dying unto death and living unto life. The lower condition which had grown habitual was more powerful than the better condition which I had not tried. The nearer the point of time came in which I was to become different, the more it struck me with horror; but it did not force me utterly back nor turn me utterly away, but held me there between the two.

Those trifles of all trifles, and vanities of vanities, my one-time mistresses, held me back, plucking at my garment of flesh and murmuring softly: "Are you sending us away?" And "From this moment shall we not be with you, now or forever?" And "From this moment shall this or that not be allowed you, now or forever?" What were they suggesting to me in the phrase I have written "this or that," what were they suggesting to me, O my God? Do you in your mercy keep from the soul of Your servant the vileness and uncleanness they were suggesting. And now I began to hear them not half so loud; they no longer stood against me face to face, but were softly muttering behind my back and, as I tried to depart, plucking stealthily at me to make me look behind. Yet even that was enough, so hesitating was I, to keep me from snatching myself free,

---

6. Virgil, *Aeneid* 5.547.

from shaking them off and leaping upwards on the way I was called: for the strong force of habit said to me: "Do you think you can live without them?"

But by this time its voice was growing fainter. In the direction toward which I had turned my face and was quivering in fear of going, I could see the austere beauty of Continence,[7] serene and indeed joyous but not evilly, honorably soliciting me to come to her and not linger, stretching forth loving hands to receive and embrace me, hands full of multitudes of good examples. With her I saw such hosts of young men and maidens, a multitude of youth and of every age, gray widows and women grown old in virginity, and in them all Continence herself, not barren but the fruitful mother of children, her joys, by You, Lord, her Spouse. And she smiled upon me and her smile gave courage as if she were saying: "Can you not do what these men have done, what these women have done? Or could men or women have done such in themselves, and not in the Lord their God? The Lord their God gave me to them. Why do you stand upon yourself and so not stand at all? Cast yourself upon Him and be not afraid; He will not draw away and let you fall. Cast yourself without fear, He will receive you and heal you."

Yet I was still ashamed, for I could still hear the murmuring of those vanities, and I still hung hesitant. And again it was as if she said: "Stop your ears against your unclean members, that they may be mortified. They tell you of delights, but not of such delights as the law of the Lord your God tells." This was the controversy raging in my heart, a controversy about myself against myself. And Alypius[8] stayed by my side and awaited in silence the issue of such agitation as he had never seen in me.

When my most searching scrutiny had drawn up all my vileness from the secret depths of my soul and heaped it in my heart's sight, a mighty storm arose in me, bringing a mighty rain of tears. That I might give way to my tears and lamentations, I rose from Alypius: for it struck me that solitude was more suited to the business of weeping. I went far enough from him to prevent his presence from being an embarrassment to me. So I felt, and he realized it. I suppose I had said something and the sound of my voice was heavy with tears. I arose, but he remained where we had been sitting, still in utter amazement. I flung myself down somehow under a certain fig tree and no longer tried to check my tears, which poured forth from my eyes in a flood, *an acceptable sacrifice to Thee*. And much I said not in these words but to this effect: *"And Thou, O Lord, how long? How long, Lord; wilt Thou be angry forever? Remember not our former iniquities."*[9] For I felt that I was still bound by them. And I continued my miserable complaining: "How long, how long shall I go on saying tomorrow and again tomorrow? Why not now, why not have an end to my uncleanness this very hour?"

---

7. Self-control or abstinence, especially with regard to sexuality; here personified as a woman.
8. A student of Augustine's at Carthage; he had joined the Manichees with Augustine, followed him to Rome and Milan, and now shared his desires and doubts. Alypius finally became a bishop in North Africa in 394.
9. Compare Psalm 79.5–8; Augustine compares his spiritual despair with that of captive and subjected Israel.

Such things I said, weeping in the most bitter sorrow of my heart. And suddenly I heard a voice from some nearby house, a boy's voice or a girl's voice, I do not know: but it was a sort of singsong, repeated again and again. "Take and read, take and read." I ceased weeping and immediately began to search my mind most carefully as to whether children were accustomed to chant these words in any kind of game, and I could not remember that I had ever heard any such thing. Damming back the flood of my tears I arose, interpreting the incident as quite certainly a divine command to open my book of Scripture and read the passage at which I should open. For it was part of what I had been told about Anthony,[1] that from the Gospel which he happened to be reading he had felt that he was being admonished as though what he read was spoken directly to himself: *Go, sell what thou hast and give to the poor and thou shalt have treasure in heaven; and come follow Me.*[2] By this experience he had been in that instant converted to You. So I was moved to return to the place where Alypius was sitting, for I had put down the Apostle's[3] book there when I arose. I snatched it up, opened it and in silence read the passage upon which my eyes first fell: *Not in rioting and drunkenness, not in chambering and impurities, not in contention and envy, but put ye on the Lord Jesus Christ and make not provision for the flesh in its concupiscences.* [Romans 13.13.] I had no wish to read further, and no need. For in that instant, with the very ending of the sentence, it was as though a light of utter confidence shone in all my heart, and all the darkness of uncertainty vanished away. Then leaving my finger in the place or marking it by some other sign, I closed the book and in complete calm told the whole thing to Alypius and he similarly told me what had been going on in himself, of which I knew nothing. He asked to see what I had read. I showed him, and he looked further than I had read. I had not known what followed. And this is what followed: *"Now him that is weak in faith, take unto you."* He applied this to himself and told me so. And he was confirmed by this message, and with no troubled wavering gave himself to God's goodwill and purpose—a purpose indeed most suited to his character, for in these matters he had been immeasurably better than I.

Then we went in to my mother and told her, to her great joy. We related how it had come about: she was filled with triumphant exultation, and praised You who are mighty beyond what we ask or conceive: for she saw that You had given her more than with all her pitiful weeping she had ever asked. For You converted me to Yourself so that I no longer sought a wife nor any of this world's promises, but stood upon that same rule of faith in which You had shown me to her so many years before.[4] Thus You changed her mourning into

---

1. St. Anthony the Great, also called Anthony of the Desert (ca. 251–356), a Coptic Christian saint whose biography by Athanasius of Alexandria was widely circulated throughout the Mediterranean and was credited with many conversions.
2. Luke 18.22.

3. The Apostle Paul; Augustine is reading his letter to the Romans.
4. At Carthage, when Augustine was still a Manichee, Monica had dreamed that she was standing on a wooden ruler weeping for her son and then saw that he was standing on the same ruler as herself.

joy, a joy far richer than she had thought to wish, a joy much dearer and purer than she had thought to find in grandchildren of my flesh.

FROM BOOK IX

[Death of His Mother]

We kept together, meaning to live together in our devout purpose. We thought deeply as to the place in which we might serve You most usefully. As a result we started back for Africa. And when we had come as far as Ostia[5] on the Tiber, my mother died. I pass over many things, for I must make haste. Do You, O my God, accept my confessions and my gratitude for countless things of which I say nothing. But I will not omit anything my mind brings forth concerning her, Your servant, who brought me forth—brought me forth in the flesh to this temporal light, and in her heart to light eternal. Not of her gifts do I speak but of Your gifts in her. For she did not bring herself into the world or educate herself in the world: it was You who created her, nor did her father or mother know what kind of being was to come forth from them. It was the scepter of Your Christ, the discipline of your Only-Begotten, that brought her up in holy fear, in a Catholic family which was a worthy member of Your church. Yet it was not the devotion of her mother in her upbringing that she talked most of, but of a certain aged servant, who had indeed carried my mother's father on her back when he was a baby, as little ones are accustomed to be carried on the backs of older girls. Because of this, because also of her age and her admirable character, she was very much respected by her master and mistress in their Christian household. As a result she was given charge of her master's daughters. This charge she fulfilled most conscientiously, checking them sharply when necessary with holy severity and teaching them soberly and prudently. Thus, except at the times when they ate—and that most temperately—at their parents' table, she would not let them even drink water, no matter how tormenting their thirst. By this she prevented the forming of a bad habit, and she used to remark very sensibly: "Now you drink water because you are not allowed to have wine: but when you are married, and thus mistresses of food-stores and wine-cellars, you will despise water, but the habit of drinking will still remain." By this kind of teaching and the authority of her commands she moderated the greediness that goes with childhood and brought the little girls' thirst to such a control that they no longer wanted what they ought not to have.

Yet, as Your servant told me, her son, there did steal upon my mother an inclination to wine. For when, in the usual way, she was sent by her parents, as a well-behaved child, to draw wine from the barrel, she would dip the cup in, but before pouring the wine from the cup into the flagon, she would sip a little with the very tip of her lips, only a little because she did not yet like the taste sufficiently to take more. Indeed she did it not out of any craving for wine, but rather from the excess of childhood's high spirits, which tend to boil over in absurdities, and are usually kept in check by the authority of elders. And so, adding to that daily drop a little more from day to day—for he that despises small things, falls little by little—she fell into the habit, so that she would drink

---

5. On the southwest coast of Italy; it was the port of Rome and the point of departure for Africa.

off greedily cups almost full of wine. Where then was that wise old woman with her forceful prohibitions? Could anything avail against the evil in us, unless Your healing, O Lord, watched over us? When our father and mother and nurses are absent, You are present, who created us, who call us, who can use those placed over us for some good unto the salvation of our souls. What did You do then, O my God? How did You cure her, and bring her to health? From another soul you drew a harsh and cutting sarcasm, as though bringing forth a surgeon's knife from Your secret store, and with one blow amputated that sore place. A maidservant with whom she was accustomed to go to the cellar, one day fell into a quarrel with her small mistress when no one else chanced to be about, and hurled at her the most biting insult possible, calling her a drunkard. My mother was pierced to the quick, saw her fault in its true wickedness, and instantly condemned it and gave it up. Just as the flattery of a friend can pervert, so the insult of an enemy can sometimes correct. Nor do You, O God, reward men according to what You do by means of them, but according to what they themselves intended. For the girl being in a temper wanted to enrage her young mistress, not to amend her, for she did it when no one else was there, either because the time and place happened to be thus when the quarrel arose, or because she was afraid that elders[6] would be angry because she had not told it sooner. But You, O Lord, Ruler of heavenly things and earthly, who turn to Your own purposes the very depths of rivers as they run and order the turbulence of the flow of time, did by the folly of one mind bring sanity to another; thus reminding us not to attribute it to our own power if another is amended by our word, even if we meant to amend him.

My mother, then, was modestly and soberly brought up, being rather made obedient to her parents by You than to You by her parents. When she reached the age for marriage, and was bestowed upon a husband, she served him as her lord. She used all her effort to win him to You, preaching You to him by her character, by which You made her beautiful to her husband, respected and loved by him and admirable in his sight. For she bore his acts of unfaithfulness quietly, and never had any jealous scene with her husband about them. She awaited Your mercy upon him, that he might grow chaste through faith in You. And as a matter of fact, though generous beyond measure, he had a very hot temper. But she knew that a woman must not resist a husband in anger, by deed or even by word. Only, when she saw him calm again and quiet, she would take the opportunity to give him an explanation of her actions, if it happened that he had been roused to anger unreasonably. The result was that whereas many matrons with much milder husbands carried the marks of blows to disfigure their faces, and would all get together to complain of the way their husbands behaved, my mother—talking lightly but meaning it seriously—advised them against their tongues: saying that from the day they heard the matrimonial contract read to them they should regard it as an instrument by which they became servants; and from that time they should be mindful of their condition and not set themselves up against their masters. And they often expressed amazement—for they knew how violent a husband she had to live with—that it had never been heard, and there was no mark to show, that Patricius[7] had beaten his wife or that there had been any family quarrel

6. Leaders of the church.   7. Augustine's father.

between them for so much as a single day. And when her friends asked her the reason, she taught them her rule, which was as I have just said. Those who followed it, found it good and thanked her; those who did not, went on being bullied and beaten.

Her mother-in-law began by being angry with her because of the whispers of malicious servants. But my mother won her completely by the respect she showed, and her unfailing patience and mildness. She ended by going to her son, telling him of the tales the servants had bandied about to the destruction of peace in the family between herself and her daughter-in-law, and asking him to punish them for it. So he, out of obedience to his mother and in the interests of order in the household and peace among his womenfolk, had the servants beaten whose names he had been given, as she had asked when giving them. To which she added the promise that anyone must expect a similar reward from her own hands who should think to please her by speaking ill of her daughter-in-law. And as no one had the courage to do so, they lived together with the most notable degree of kindness and harmony.

This great gift also, O my God, my Mercy, You gave to Your good servant, in whose womb You created me, that she showed herself, wherever possible, a peacemaker between people quarreling and minds at discord. For swelling and undigested discord often belches forth bitter words when in the venom of intimate conversation with a present friend hatred at its rawest is breathed out upon an absent enemy. But when my mother heard bitter things said by each of the other, she never said anything to either about the other save what would help to reconcile them. This might seem a small virtue, if I had not had the sorrow of seeing for myself so many people who—as if by some horrible widespreading infection of sin—not only tell angry people the things their enemies said in anger, but even add things that were never said at all. Whereas, on the contrary, ordinary humanity would seem to require not merely that we refrain from exciting or increasing wrath among men by evil speaking, but that we study to extinguish wrath by kind speaking. Such a one was she: and You were the master who taught her most secretly in the school of her heart.

The upshot was that toward the very end of his life she won her husband to You; and once he was a Christian she no longer had to complain of the things she had had to bear with before he was a Christian. Further, she was a servant of Your servants. Such of them as knew her praised and honored and loved You, O God, in her; for they felt Your presence in her heart, showing itself in the fruit of her holy conversation. She had been *the wife of one husband, had requited her parents, had governed her house* piously, *was well reported of for good works. She had brought up her children,*[8] being in labor of them as often as she saw them swerving away from You. Finally of all of us Your servants, O Lord—since by Your gift You suffer us to speak—who before her death were living together[9] after receiving the grace of baptism, she took as much care as if she had been the mother of us all, and served us as if she had been the daughter of us all.

When the day was approaching on which she was to depart this life—a day that You knew though we did not—it came about, as I believe by Your secret

8. Augustine is paraphrasing Paul's description of the duties of a widow, given in 1 Timothy 5.　　9. Augustine and his fellow converts.

arrangement, that she and I stood alone leaning in a window, which looked inwards to the garden within the house where we were staying, at Ostia on the Tiber; for there we were away from everybody, resting for the sea voyage from the weariness of our long journey by land. There we talked together, she and I alone, in deep joy; and *forgetting the things that were behind and looking forward to those that were before,* we were discussing in the presence of Truth, which You are, what the eternal life of the saints could be like, *which eye has not seen nor ear heard, nor has it entered into the heart of man.* But with the mouth of our heart we panted for the high waters of Your fountain, the fountain of the life which is with You: that being sprinkled from that fountain according to our capacity, we might in some sense meditate upon so great a matter.

And our conversation had brought us to this point, that any pleasure whatsoever of the bodily senses, in any brightness whatsoever of corporeal light, seemed to us not worthy of comparison with the pleasure of that eternal Light, not worthy even of mention. Rising as our love flamed upward towards that Selfsame,[1] we passed in review the various levels of bodily things, up to the heavens themselves, whence sun and moon and stars shine upon this earth. And higher still we soared, thinking in our minds and speaking and marveling at Your works: and so we came to our own souls, and went beyond them to come at last to that region of richness unending, where You feed Israel forever with the food of truth:[2] and there life is that Wisdom by which all things are made, both the things that have been and the things that are yet to be. But this Wisdom itself is not made: it is as it has ever been, and so it shall be forever: indeed "has ever been" and "shall be forever" have no place in it, but it simply is, for it is eternal: whereas "to have been" and "to be going to be" are not eternal. And while we were thus talking of His Wisdom and panting for it, with all the effort of our heart we did for one instant attain to touch it; then sighing, and leaving the first fruits of our spirit bound to it, we returned to the sound of our own tongue, in which a word has both beginning and ending. For what is like to your Word, Our Lord, who abides in Himself forever, yet grows not old and makes all things new!

So we said: If to any man the tumult of the flesh grew silent, silent the images of earth and sea and air: and if the heavens grew silent, and the very soul grew silent to herself and by not thinking of self mounted beyond self: if all dreams and imagined visions grew silent, and every tongue and every sign and whatsoever is transient—for indeed if any man could hear them, he should hear them saying with one voice: We did not make ourselves, but He made us who abides forever: but if, having uttered this and so set us to listening to Him who made them, they all grew silent, and in their silence He alone spoke to us, not by them but by Himself: so that we should hear His word, not by any tongue of flesh nor the voice of an angel nor the sound of thunder nor in the darkness of a parable,[3] but that we should hear Himself whom in all these things we love, should hear Himself and not them: just as we two had but now

---

1. Reality, the divine principle. This ecstasy of Augustine and Monica is throughout described in philosophical terms, in which God is Wisdom.

2. Reference to the manna that fed the Israelites in the desert during their flight from Egypt; see Exodus 16.11–35.

3. Compare Luke 8.10: "Unto you it is given to know the mysteries of the kingdom of God: but to others in parables; that seeing they might not see, and hearing they might not understand."

reached forth and in a flash of the mind attained to touch the eternal Wisdom which abides over all: and if this could continue, and all other visions so different be quite taken away, and this one should so ravish and absorb and wrap the beholder in inward joys that his life should eternally be such as that one moment of understanding for which we had been sighing—would not this be: *Enter Thou into the joy of Thy Lord?* But when shall it be? Shall it be when *we shall all rise again* and *shall not all be changed?*[4]

Such thoughts I uttered, though not in that order or in those actual words; but You know, O Lord, that on that day when we talked of these things the world with all its delights seemed cheap to us in comparison with what we talked of. And my mother said: "Son, for my own part I no longer find joy in anything in this world. What I am still to do here and why I am here I know not, now that I no longer hope for anything from this world. One thing there was, for which I desired to remain still a little longer in this life, that I should see you a Catholic Christian before I died. This God has granted me in superabundance, in that I now see you His servant to the contempt of all worldly happiness. What then am I doing here?"

What answer I made, I do not clearly remember; within five days or not much longer she fell into a fever. And in her sickness, she one day fainted away and for the moment lost consciousness. We ran to her but she quickly returned to consciousness, and seeing my brother and me standing by her she said as one wondering: "Where was I?" Then looking closely upon us as we stood wordless in our grief, she said: "Here you will bury your mother." I stayed silent and checked my weeping. But my brother said something to the effect that he would be happier if she were to die in her own land and not in a strange country. But as she heard this she looked at him anxiously, restraining him with her eye because he savored of earthly things, and then she looked at me and said: "See the way he talks." And then she said to us both: "Lay this body wherever it may be. Let no care of it disturb you: this only I ask of you that you should remember me at the altar of the Lord wherever you may be." And when she had uttered this wish in such words as she could manage, she fell silent as her sickness took hold of her more strongly.

But as I considered Your gifts, O unseen God, which You send into the hearts of Your faithful to the springing up of such wonderful fruits, I was glad and gave thanks to You, remembering what I had previously known of the care as to her burial which had always troubled her: for she had arranged to be buried by the body of her husband. Because they had lived together in such harmony, she had wished—so little is the human mind capable of rising to the divine—that it should be granted her, as an addition to her happiness and as something to be spoken of among men, that after her pilgrimage beyond the sea the earthly part of man and wife should lie together under the same earth. Just when this vain desire had begun to vanish from her heart through the fullness of Your goodness, I did not know; but I was pleased and surprised that it had now so clearly vanished: though indeed in the conversation we had had together at the window, when she said: "What am I still doing here?" there had appeared no desire to die in her own land. Further I heard afterwards that in the time we were at

---

4. Compare 1 Corinthians 15.52: "the trumpet shall sound, and the dead shall be raised incorruptible, and we shall be changed," referring to the Last Judgment.

Ostia, she had talked one day to some of my friends, as a mother talking to her children, of the contempt of this life and of the attraction of death. I was not there at the time. They marveled at such courage in a woman—but it was You who had given it to her—and asked if she was not afraid to leave her body so far from her own city. But she said: "Nothing is far from God, and I have no fear that He will not know at the end of the world from what place He is to raise me up." And so on the ninth day of her illness, in the fifty-sixth year of her life and the thirty-third of mine, that devout and holy soul was released from the body.

I closed her eyes; and an immeasurable sorrow flowed into my heart and would have overflowed in tears. But my eyes under the mind's strong constraint held back their flow and I stood dry-eyed. In that struggle it went very ill with me. As she breathed her last, the child Adeodatus[5] broke out into lamentation and we all checked him and brought him to silence. But in this very fact the childish element in me, which was breaking out into tears, was checked and brought to silence by the manlier voice of my mind. For we felt that it was not fitting that her funeral should be solemnized with moaning and weeping and lamentation, for so it is normal to weep when death is seen as sheer misery or as complete extinction. But she had not died miserably, nor did she wholly die. Of the one thing we were sure by reason of her character, of the other by the reality of our faith.

What then was it that grieved my heart so deeply? Only the newness of the wound, in finding the custom I had so loved of living with her suddenly snapped short. It was a joy to me to have this one testimony from her: when her illness was close to its end, meeting with expressions of endearment such services as I rendered, she called me a dutiful loving son, and said in the great affection of her love that she had never heard from my mouth any harsh or reproachful word addressed to herself. But what possible comparison was there, O my God who made us, between the honor I showed her and the service she had rendered me?

Because I had now lost the great comfort of her, my soul was wounded and my very life torn asunder, for it had been one life made of hers and mine together. When the boy had been quieted and ceased weeping, Evodius took up the psalter and began to chant—with the whole house making the responses— the psalm *Mercy and judgment I will sing to Thee, O Lord.*[6] And when they heard what was being done, many of the brethren and religious women came to us; those whose office it was were making arrangement for the burial, while, in another part of the house where it could properly be done I discoursed, with friends who did not wish to leave me by myself, upon matters suitable for that time. Thus I used truth as a kind of fomentation[7] to bring relief to my torment, a torment known to You, but not known to those others: so that listening closely to me they thought that I lacked all feeling of grief. But in Your ears, where none of them could hear, I accused the emotion in me as weakness; and I held in the flood of my grief. It was for the moment a little diminished, but returned with fresh violence, not with any pouring of tears or change of countenance: but I knew what I was crushing down in my heart. I was very much ashamed that these human emotions could have such power over me—though

5. Augustine's son, Monica's grandson, then about fifteen or sixteen years old.

6. Compare Psalm 101.1.

7. Soothing dressing for a wound.

it belongs to the due order and the lot of our earthly condition that they should come to us—and I felt a new grief at my grief and so was afflicted with a two-fold sorrow.

When the body was taken to burial, I went and returned without tears. During the prayers which we poured forth to you when the sacrifice of our redemption[8] was offered for her—while the body, as the custom there is, lay by the grave before it was actually buried—during those prayers I did not weep. Yet all that day I was heavy with grief within and in the trouble of my mind I begged of You in my own fashion to heal my pain; but You would not—I imagine because You meant to impress upon my memory by this proof how strongly the bond of habit holds the mind even when it no longer feeds upon deception. The idea came to me to go and bathe, for I had heard that the bath—which the Greeks call βαλανεῖον[9]—is so called because it drives anxiety from the mind. And this also I acknowledge to Your mercy, O Father of orphans, that I bathed and was the same man after as before. The bitterness of grief had not sweated out of my heart. Then I fell asleep, and woke again to find my grief not a little relieved. And as I was in bed and no one about, I said over those true verses that Your servant Ambrose[1] wrote of You:

> God, the creator of all things
> and ruler of the heavens
> you who clothe the day with the glory of light,
> and the night with the gift of sleep,
>
> so that rest may relax the limbs
> and restore them for the day's work
> relieve the fatigue of the mind
> and dispel anxiety and grief (Latin).

And then little by little I began to recover my former feeling about Your handmaid, remembering how loving and devout was her conversation with You, how pleasant and considerate her conversation with me, of which I was thus suddenly deprived. And I found solace in weeping in Your sight both about her and for her, about myself and for myself. I no longer tried to check my tears, but let them flow as they would, making them a pillow for my heart: and it rested upon them, for it was Your ears that heard my weeping, and not the ears of a man, who would have misunderstood my tears and despised them. But now, O Lord, I confess it to You in writing, let him read it who will and interpret it as he will: and if he sees it as sin that for so small a portion of an hour I wept for my mother, now dead and departed from my sight, who had wept so many years for me that I should live ever in Your sight—let him not scorn me but rather, if he is a man of great charity, let him weep for my sins to You, the Father of all the brethren of Your Christ.

Now that my heart is healed of that wound, in which there was perhaps too much of earthly affection, I pour forth to You, O our God, tears of a very different sort for Your handmaid—tears that flow from a spirit shaken by the

---

8. Perhaps a communion service.
9. Augustine evidently derives *balaneion* ("bath") from the words *ballō* ("cast away") and *ania* ("sorrow").

1. Ambrose (ca. 337–397), bishop of Milan and mentor to Augustine, was the author of many theological works as well as poetic hymns.

thought of the perils there are for every soul that dies in Adam.[2] For though she had been made alive in Christ, and while still in the body had so lived that Your name was glorified in her faith and her character, yet I dare not say that from the moment of her regeneration in baptism no word issued from her mouth contrary to Your Command. Your Son, who is Truth, has said: *Whosoever shall say to his brother, Thou fool, shall be in danger of hell fire;*[3] and it would go ill with the most praiseworthy life lived by men, if You were to examine it with Your mercy laid aside! But because You do not enquire too fiercely into our sins, we have hope and confidence of a place with You. Yet if a man reckons up before You the merits he truly has, what is he reckoning except Your own gifts? If only men would know themselves to be but men, so that he that glories would glory in the Lord!

Thus, my Glory and my Life, God of my heart, leaving aside for this time her good deeds, for which I give thanks to Thee in joy, I now pray to Thee for my mother's sins. Grant my prayer through the true Medicine of our wounds,[4] who hung upon the cross and who now sitting at Thy right hand makes intercession for us. I know that she dealt mercifully, and from her heart forgave those who trespassed against her: do Thou also forgive such trespasses as she may have been guilty of in all the years since her baptism, forgive them, Lord, forgive them, I beseech Thee: enter not into judgment with her. Let Thy mercy be exalted above Thy justice for Thy words are true and Thou hast promised that the merciful shall obtain mercy. That they should be merciful is Thy gift who *hast mercy on whom Thou wilt, and wilt have compassion on whom Thou wilt.*

And I believe that Thou hast already done what I am now asking; but be not offended, Lord, at the things my mouth would utter. For on that day when her death was so close, she was not concerned that her body should be sumptuously wrapped or embalmed with spices, nor with any thought of choosing a monument or even for burial in her own country. Of such things she gave us no command, but only desired to be remembered at Thy altar, which she had served without ever missing so much as a day, on which she knew that the holy Victim was offered; *by whom the handwriting is blotted out of the decree that was contrary to us,*[5] by which offering too the enemy was overcome who, reckoning our sins and seeking what may be laid to our charge, found nothing in Him, in whom we are conquerors. Who shall restore to Him his innocent blood? Who shall give Him back the price by which He purchased us and so take us from Him? To this sacrament of our redemption Thy handmaid had bound her soul by the bond of faith. Let none wrest her from Thy protection; let neither the lion nor the dragon[6] bar her way by force or craft. For she will not answer that she owes nothing, lest she should be contradicted and confuted by that cunning accuser: but she will answer that her debts have been remitted by Him, to whom no one can hand back the price which He paid for us, though He owed it not.

2. That is, with the curse of Adam not nullified through baptism in Jesus Christ and conformity with his teachings.
3. From Matthew 5.22, Jesus' Sermon on the Mount. He is preaching a more severe moral code than the traditional one that whoever kills shall be liable to judgment.
4. Jesus.

5. An allusion to Christ's redemption of humanity from the curse of Adam through the Crucifixion.
6. Compare Psalm 91.13: "Thou shalt tread upon the lion and the adder: the young lion and the dragon shalt thou trample under feet," which invokes God's protection of the godly."

So let her rest in peace, together with her husband, for she had no other before nor after him, but served him, in patience bringing forth fruit for Thee, and winning him likewise for Thee. And inspire, O my Lord my God, inspire Thy servants my brethren, Thy sons my masters, whom I serve with heart and voice and pen, that as many of them as read this may remember at Thy altar Thy servant Monica, with Patricius, her husband, by whose bodies Thou didst bring me into this life, though how I know not.[7] May they with loving mind remember these who were my parents in this transitory light, my brethren who serve Thee as our Father in our Catholic mother, and those who are to be fellow citizens with me in the eternal Jerusalem,[8] which Thy people sigh for in their pilgrimage from birth until they come there: so that what my mother at her end asked of me may be fulfilled more richly in the prayers of so many gained for her by my Confessions than by my prayers alone.

* * *

7. Augustine does not understand the seemingly miraculous process by which the fetus grows in the womb.
8. That is, heaven.

THE QUR'AN
610–632

The word *qur'an* literally means "the recitation." For Muslims, the Qur'an is not so much a book as a living and vibrant act of speech that has been passed down through an unbroken chain of human beings from the time of Muhammad, who with his companions in seventh-century Arabia formed the first community of Muslims. At the same time, the Qur'an is also conceived of as a book: not a literal object on the shelf but a divine work that exists only in the heavenly realm of paradise. Any physical copy of the Arabic text is thought of as a pale reflection of that ideal book, a tool to enable the reader to memorize and then recite the Qur'anic text. As divine speech, moreover, the Qur'an can never be rendered perfectly in the medium of the human voice, a deficiency that testifies to its fundamental inimitability, or *i'jaz*.

In accord with this view of the nature of the Qur'an, no translation into any other language is thought of as actually being the holy book itself. The most that any translation can be, for the believer, is an aid to understanding the original.

The Qur'an presents itself as the last of a sequence of revealed holy books, including the Torah (in Arabic, Tawrat), the Psalms (Zabur), and the Gospels (Injil). Similarly, Muhammad is presented as one in a lineage of prophets (that is, those who have received communications directly from God) that begins with the first man, Adam. Earlier holy books each have an associated prophet: for the Torah, Moses; for the Psalms, David; and for the Gospels, Jesus and also Mary—who, despite being female, is also recognized as part of the prophetic lineage. Indeed, a minority of classical Muslim scholars, including Ibn Hazm (d. 1065), considered her to be a prophet outright. Stories and characters from Jewish and Christian scripture reappear in the Qur'an, as seen in the chapters (or suras) on Jonah, Joseph, and Mary. When hearing these verses, the earliest converts to Islam, drawn from the local Christian and Jewish communities located in Arabia, would have marveled at the different perspective brought to bear on familiar stories by this new revelation. The Qur'an recognizes the followers of other monotheistic religions, such as Jews and Christians, as "people of the Book"—those who follow the word of God as revealed by his prophets. From the point of view of Islam, the people of the Book who lived before the revelation of the Qur'an were also followers of *islam*, in the literal sense of "submission" to God's will. Those who continued to reverence their own, pre-Islamic holy books, such as Jews and Christians, could be tolerated within the Muslim community, but this inclusiveness of monotheism had its limits. Muslims generally viewed their Prophet as the last of his kind, "the seal of prophets," and the Qur'an as the last holy book that would ever be revealed to humanity. The Torah and the Gospels, while divine in their inspiration, had become corrupt over time. Only through submission to the divine will as revealed in the Qur'an, Muslims believed, could the faithful be sure they would enter into paradise and avoid the punishments of hell.

Only from the nineteenth century on has the **Bible** begun to be read as a work of literature as well as a divinely inspired text, and so too this dual focus on the Qur'an has been recent. From the Middle Ages to the twenty-first century, Western readers of the Qur'an have all too often condemned what they saw as its theological deviance and narrative incoherence. As a result, Muslims have hesitated to offer up the Qur'an for study within the framework of literary history

or to allow it to move beyond the conservative framework of faith-based perspectives. This attitude has begun to change, however, because of innovative approaches to Qur'anic interpretation on the part of Muslim communities and an increasing willingness to place the Qur'an into dialogue with other sacred scriptures. The Qur'an itself invites comparison with other literary traditions—most explicitly, the rich traditions of oral poetry found in pre-Islamic Arabia. In that context, it appears as a marvel of literature whose divine inspiration is manifest in the form of lyrical chant and resonant verse. Reading the Qur'an on the page, in translation, weakly conveys its virtue, which can be appreciated only in the musical oral recitation (*tajwid*) that reveals the rhythmic quality of the verse and the haunting repetition of syllables at the ends of successive lines. It is possible to get a sense of this music in the repeated refrain of the sura "The Lord of Mercy" ("Ar Rahman"), translated below.

The Qur'an is divided into 144 suras, some of which are quite short; others are very long, resembling a biblical book in form. Each sura is made up of a number of verses (*ayat*; singular *aya*). The Qur'an is also conventionally divided up into thirty sections (*ajza'*; singular *juz'*) of roughly equal length to facilitate recitation of the entire work over the period of one month. Because of the emphasis placed on its oral recitation, which must be performed as part of the five daily prayers, Muslims begin to memorize the Qur'an at a young age; they start with the introductory sura, "The Opening" ("Al Fatiha"), and continue on with the short Meccan suras that are concentrated near the end of the Qur'an, including "Purity" ("Al Ikhlas"). Instead of being arranged in the order that Muhammad received them, the suras are arranged as Muhammad said he had been instructed by God. Some of the suras were revealed at Mecca, when the Muslim community was starting to develop, and others at Medina, where the persecuted community took refuge; the two types tend to differ not only in length but also in subject matter and in tone. Instead of being carefully separated, however, the Meccan and Medinan suras are intermingled, and many of the Meccan suras dating from early in Muhammad's prophetic mission appear near the end of the text. The effect is one of fragments arranged in a mosaic—yet that mosaic has a very clearly defined form, delineated by strands running throughout. The repetition of phrases and motifs across suras, often from different periods, creates a pattern as intricate as a woven tapestry.

With the exception of "The Feast" and "The Lord of Mercy," which were revealed at Medina, the excerpts reproduced here are Meccan suras, which tend to be relatively short. Our aim was to provide entire chapters rather than abbreviated selections, so that the highly structured nature of the suras could be grasped. The tightly ordered form illustrated on the level of the individual sura is also evident more generally in the Qur'an, in which the parts all contribute to make up the whole, but each part can also stand for the whole. Several of the suras are known by another name, reflecting this part–whole relationship: "The Opening," which is the first sura, is also known as "The Mother of the Book," while sura "Yasin" is sometimes called "The Heart of the Qur'an." One of the last suras, "Purity," was described by Muhammad himself as being "one-third of the Qur'an," because its highly condensed verses on the unity of God encapsulate the very core of Islamic theology. Other suras, such as "Jonah," "Joseph," and "Mary," illuminate the extent to which the Qur'an is intertwined with Jewish and Christian faith traditions. These connections can also be seen in one of the Medinan suras excerpted here, "The Feast," which begins with a description of allowed and prohibited foods that recalls the intricate rules laid down in Leviticus, thus elaborating one important area of common practice shared by Judaism and Islam. Yet the table, an image that is central to "The Feast," represents more than just a literal piece of furniture. It is also the figurative table shared by the people of the Book, given form in the table spread with food that Jesus presides over at the Last Supper. In the latter part of the sura, Jesus thanks God for what he has already given and asks for something more for the table: "Send down to us a feast from heaven. . . . Provide for us: You are the best provider." God replies, "I will send it down to you." This final gift for the table is understood as being the Prophet Muhammad, or even the Qur'an itself.

The Qur'an was received by Muhammad through the mediation of the angel Gabriel (Jibreel) over a period of about twenty-three years, beginning when he was forty years old and ending with his death in 632. During that time, the Qur'an existed as an oral recitation, repeated both by Muhammad himself and by the growing community of Muslims. After Muhammad's death, the community recognized the need to record the oral text to ensure that errors not creep into the recitation. The closest companions of Muhammad, under the supervision of the first caliph (or ruler) of the Muslim community, Abu Bakr, assembled the Qur'an in written form. The third caliph, Uthman, supervised the finalized version of the text, which was completed in 651, and then ordered all imperfect copies to be destroyed. It is this version of the Qur'an that we read today. Translations began to be produced almost immediately, beginning with a rendering of "The Opening" into the Persian language by Salman, one of the companions of the Prophet Muhammad. A full Persian translation of the Qur'an was made in the ninth century, attesting to the rapid embrace of Islam by the inhabitants of Persia (modern Iran). As is the case today, these translations were not made with the purpose of substituting Qur'anic verses in the local vernacular for the Arabic originals during prayer; instead, they were aids to understanding intended to enable fuller assimilation of the Arabic scripture within a new culture. Western audiences started to read the Qur'an in the Middle Ages, beginning with Robert of Ketton's Latin translation in 1143. The Qur'an is never accompanied by pictorial illustrations, in keeping with the Islamic practice of iconoclasm (the prohibition of any representation of living things, thereby avoiding the temptation of idolatry). It is, however, often rendered in elaborate calligraphy, a style of writing so ornate that it becomes art, fusing word with image in the aural masterpiece that is the Qur'an.

FROM THE QUR'AN[1]

1. The Opening

In the name of God, the Lord of Mercy, the Giver of Mercy! Praise belongs to God, Lord of the Worlds, the Lord of Mercy, the Giver of Mercy, Master of the Day of Judgement. It is You we worship; it is You we ask for help. Guide us to the straight path: the path of those You have blessed, those who incur no anger and who have not gone astray.

5. The Feast

In the name of God, the Lord of Mercy, the Giver of Mercy

You who believe, fulfil your obligations. Livestock animals are lawful as food for you, with the exception of what is about to be announced to you. You are forbidden to kill game while you are on pilgrimage—God commands what He will, so, you who believe, do not violate the sanctity of God's rites, the Sacred Month, the offerings, their garlands, nor those going to the Sacred House[2] to seek the bounty and pleasure of their Lord—but when you have completed the rites of pilgrimage you may hunt. Do not let your hatred for the people who barred you from the Sacred Mosque induce you to break the law: help one another to do what is right and good; do not help one another towards sin and hostility. Be mindful of God, for His punishment is severe.

You are forbidden to eat carrion; blood; pig's meat; any animal over which any name other than God's has been invoked; any animal strangled, or victim of a violent blow or a fall, or gored or savaged by a beast of prey, unless you still slaughter it [in the correct manner]; or anything sacrificed on idolatrous altars. You are also forbidden to allot shares [of meat] by drawing marked arrows[3]—a

1. Translated by M. A. S. Abdel Haleem; the bracketed material in the text is his.
2. The Ka'aba, central point of the pilgrimage to Mecca that takes place during "the Sacred Month" of the hajj. According to the Qur'an it was originally established by Abraham as a place to worship the one true God, and Muslims always face it when they pray.
3. That is, casting lots by a method commonly used in pre-Islamic Arabia to make decisions or select an individual.

heinous practice—today the disbelievers have lost all hope that you will give up your religion. Do not fear them: fear Me. Today I have perfected your religion for you, completed My blessing upon you, and chosen as your religion *islam*: [total devotion to God]; but if any of you is forced by hunger to eat forbidden food, with no intention of doing wrong, then God is most forgiving and merciful.

They ask you, Prophet, what is lawful for them. Say, 'All good things are lawful for you.' [This includes] what you have taught your birds and beasts of prey to catch, teaching them as God has taught you, so eat what they catch for you, but first pronounce God's name over it. Be mindful of God: He is swift to take account. Today all good things have been made lawful for you. The food of the People of the Book[4] is lawful for you as your food is lawful for them. So are chaste, believing, women as well as chaste women of the people who were given the Scripture before you, as long as you have given them their bride-gifts and married them, not taking them as lovers or secret mistresses. The deeds of anyone who rejects faith will come to nothing, and in the Hereafter he will be one of the losers.

You who believe, when you are about to pray, wash your faces and your hands up to the elbows, wipe your heads, wash your feet up to the ankles and, if required,[5] wash your whole body. If any of you is sick or on a journey, or has just relieved himself, or had intimate contact with a woman, and can find no water, then take some clean sand and wipe your face and hands with it. God does not wish to place any burden on you: He only wishes to cleanse you and perfect His blessing on you, so that you may be thankful. Remember God's blessing on you and the pledge with which you were bound when you said, 'We hear and we obey.' Be mindful of God: God has full knowledge of the secrets of the heart.

You who believe, be steadfast in your devotion to God and bear witness impartially: do not let hatred of others lead you away from justice, but adhere to justice, for that is closer to awareness of God. Be mindful of God: God is well aware of all that you do. God has promised forgiveness and a rich reward to those who have faith and do good works; those who reject faith and deny Our revelations will inhabit the blazing Fire.

You who believe, remember God's blessing on you when a certain people were about to raise their hands against you and He restrained them. Be mindful of God: let the believers put their trust in Him.

 God took a pledge from the Children of Israel. We made twelve leaders arise among them, and God said, 'I am with you: if you keep up the prayer, pay the prescribed alms, believe in My messengers and support them, and lend God a good loan, I will wipe out your sins and admit you into Gardens[6] graced with flowing streams. Any of you who now ignore this [pledge] will be far from the right path.' But they broke their pledge, so We distanced them [from Us] and hardened their hearts. They distort the meaning of [revealed] words and have forgotten some of what they were told to remember: you [Prophet] will always find treachery in all but a few of them. Overlook this and pardon them: God loves those who do good. We also took a pledge from those who say, 'We are

---

4. The Jews.
5. For example, if unclean from sexual intercourse or menstruation.

6. The heavenly paradise, depicted in the Qur'an as a garden.

Christians,' but they too forgot some of what they were told to remember, so We stirred up enmity and hatred among them until the Day of Resurrection, when God will tell them what they have done.

People of the Book,[7] Our Messenger has come to make clear to you much of what you have kept hidden of the Scripture, and to overlook much [you have done]. A light has now come to you from God, and a Scripture making things clear, with which God guides to the ways of peace those who follow what pleases Him, bringing them from darkness out into light, by His will, and guiding them to a straight path. Those who say, 'God is the Messiah,[8] the son of Mary,' are defying the truth. Say, 'If it had been God's will, could anyone have prevented Him from destroying the Messiah, son of Mary, together with his mother and everyone else on earth? Control of the heavens and earth and all that is between them belongs to God: He creates whatever He will. God has power over everything.' The Jews and the Christians say, 'We are the children of God and His beloved ones.' Say, 'Then why does He punish you for your sins? You are merely human beings, part of His creation: He forgives whoever He will and punishes whoever He will. Control of the heavens and earth and all that is between them belongs to Him: all journeys lead to Him.' People of the Book, Our Messenger comes to you now, after a break in the sequence of messengers, to make things clear for you in case you should say, 'No one has come to give us good news or to warn us.' So someone has come to you, to give you good news and warn you: God has the power to do all things.

Moses said to his people, 'My people, remember God's blessing on you: how He raised prophets among you and appointed kings for you and gave you what he had not given to any other people. My people, go into the holy land which God has ordained for you—do not turn back or you will be the losers.' They said, 'Moses, there is a fearsome people in this land. We will not go there until they leave. If they leave, then we will enter.' Yet two men whom God had blessed among those who were afraid said, 'Go in to them through the gate and when you go in you will overcome them. If you are true believers, put your trust in God.' They said, 'Moses, we will never enter while they are still there, so you and your Lord go in and fight, and we will stay here.' He said, 'Lord, I have authority over no one except myself and my brother: judge between the two of us and these disobedient people.' God said, 'The land is forbidden to them for forty years: they will wander the earth aimlessly. Do not grieve over those who disobey.'[9]

[Prophet], tell them the truth about the story of Adam's two sons:[1] each of them offered a sacrifice, and it was accepted from one and not the other. One said, 'I will kill you,' but the other said, 'God only accepts the sacrifice of those who are mindful of Him. If you raise your hand to kill me, I will not raise mine to kill you. I fear God, the Lord of all worlds, and I would rather you were burdened with my sins as well as yours and became an inhabitant of the Fire: such is the evildoers' reward.' But his soul prompted him to kill his brother: he killed him and became one of the losers. God sent a raven to scratch up the ground and show him how to cover his brother's corpse and he said, 'Woe is me! Could

---

7. Here, the Jews and the Christians.
8. In Jewish belief, the promised redeemer who will come at the end of time; in Christian belief,
that redeemer is identified with Jesus Christ.
9. Compare Numbers 13.1–14.35.
1. Cain and Abel; see Genesis 4.1–15.

murder

I not have been like this raven and covered up my brother's body?' He became remorseful. On account of [his deed], We decreed to the Children of Israel that if anyone kills a person—unless in retribution for murder or spreading corruption in the land—it is as if he kills all mankind, while if any saves a life it is as if he saves the lives of all mankind. Our messengers came to them with clear signs, but many of them continued to commit excesses in the land. Those who wage war against God and His Messenger and strive to spread corruption in the land should be punished by death, crucifixion, the amputation of an alternate hand and foot, or banishment from the land: a disgrace for them in this world, and then a terrible punishment in the Hereafter, unless they repent before you overpower them—in that case bear in mind that God is forgiving and merciful.

You who believe, be mindful of God, seek ways to come closer to Him and strive for His cause, so that you may prosper. If the disbelievers possessed all that is in the earth and twice as much again and offered it to ransom themselves from torment on the Day of Resurrection, it would not be accepted from them—they will have a painful torment. They will wish to come out of the Fire but they will be unable to do so: theirs will be a lasting torment.

Cut off the hands of thieves, whether they are man or woman, as punishment for what they have done—a deterrent from God: God is almighty and wise. But if anyone repents after his wrongdoing and makes amends, God will accept his repentance: God is most forgiving, most merciful. Do you [Prophet] not know that control of the heavens and earth belongs solely to God? He punishes whoever He will and forgives whoever He will: God has power over everything.

Messenger, do not be grieved by those who race to surpass one another in disbelief—those who say with their mouths, 'We believe,' but have no faith in their hearts, and the Jews who listen eagerly to lies and to those who have not even met you, who distort the meanings of [revealed] words and say [to each other], 'If you are given this ruling, accept it, but if you are not, then beware!'—if God intends some people to be so misguided, you will be powerless against God on their behalf. These are the ones whose hearts God does not intend to cleanse—a disgrace for them in this world, and then a heavy punishment in the Hereafter—they listen eagerly to lies and consume what is unlawful. If they come to you [Prophet] for judgement, you can either judge between them, or decline—if you decline, they will not harm you in any way, but if you do judge between them, judge justly: God loves the just—but why do they come to you for judgement when they have the Torah[2] with God's judgement, and even then still turn away? These are not believers. We revealed the Torah with guidance and light, and the prophets, who had submitted to God, judged according to it for the Jews. So did the rabbis and the scholars in accordance with that part of God's Scripture which they were entrusted to preserve, and to which they were witnesses. So [rabbis and scholars] do not fear people, fear Me; do not barter away My messages for a small price; those who do not judge according to what God has sent down are rejecting [God's teachings]. In the Torah We prescribed for them a life for a life, an eye for an eye, a nose for a nose, an ear for an ear, a tooth for a tooth, an equal wound for a wound:[3] if anyone for-

2. The first five books of the Hebrew Bible (literally, "law" [Heb.]), traditionally ascribed to Moses.

3. See Leviticus 24.19–21; Deuteronomy 19.21.

Jesus

goes this out of charity, it will serve as atonement for his bad deeds. Those who do not judge according to what God has revealed are doing grave wrong.

We sent Jesus, son of Mary, in their footsteps, to confirm the Torah that had been sent before him: We gave him the Gospel with guidance, light, and confirmation of the Torah already revealed—a guide and lesson for those who take heed of God. So let the followers of the Gospel judge according to what God has sent down in it. Those who do not judge according to what God has revealed are lawbreakers.

We sent to you [Muhammad] the Scripture with the truth, confirming the Scriptures that came before it, and with final authority over them: so judge between them according to what God has sent down. Do not follow their whims, which deviate from the truth that has come to you. We have assigned a law and a path to each of you. If God had so willed, He would have made you one community, but He wanted to test you through that which He has given you, so race to do good, you will all return to God and He will make clear to you the matters you differed about. So [Prophet] judge between them according to what God has sent down. Do not follow their whims, and take good care that they do not tempt you away from any of what God has sent down to you. If they turn away, remember that God intends to punish them for some of the sins they have committed, a great many people are lawbreakers. Do they want judgement according to the time of pagan ignorance? Is there any better judge than God for those of firm faith?

You who believe, do not take the Jews and Christians as allies, they are allies only to each other. Anyone who takes them as an ally becomes one of them— God does not guide such wrongdoers—yet you [Prophet] will see the perverse at heart rushing to them for protection, saying, 'We are afraid fortune may turn against us.' But God may well bring about a triumph or some other event of His own making: then they will rue the secrets they harboured in their hearts, and the believers will say, 'Are these the men who swore by God using their strongest oaths that they were with you?' All they did was in vain: they have lost everything.

You who believe, if any of you go back on your faith, God will soon replace you with people He loves and who love Him, people who are humble towards the believers, hard on the disbelievers, and who strive in God's way without fearing anyone's reproach. Such is God's favour. He grants it to whoever He will. God has endless bounty and knowledge. Your true allies are God, His Messenger, and the believers—those who keep up the prayer, pay the prescribed alms, and bow down in worship. Those who turn for protection to God, His Messenger, and the believers [are God's party]: God's party is sure to triumph.

You who believe, do not take as allies those who ridicule your religion and make fun of it—whether people who were given the Scripture before you, or disbelievers—and be mindful of God if you are true believers. When you make the call to prayer, they ridicule it and make fun of it: this is because they are people who do not reason. Say [Prophet], 'People of the Book, do you resent us for any reason other than the fact that we believe in God, in what has been sent down to us, and in what was sent before us, while most of you are disobedient?' Say, 'Shall I tell you who deserves a worse punishment from God than [the one you wish upon] us? Those God distanced from Himself, was angry with, and condemned as apes and pigs, and those who worship idols: they are worse in rank and have strayed further from the right path.

When they come to you [believers], they say, 'We believe,' but they come disbelieving and leave disbelieving—God knows best what they are hiding. You [Prophet] see many of them rushing into sin and hostility and consuming what is unlawful. How evil their practices are! Why do their rabbis and scholars not forbid them to speak sinfully and consume what is unlawful? How evil their deeds are! The Jews have said, 'God is tight-fisted,' but it is they who are tight-fisted, and they are rejected for what they have said. Truly, God's hands are open wide: He gives as He pleases. What has been sent down to you from your Lord is sure to increase insolence and defiance in many of them. We have sown enmity and hatred amongst them till the Day of Resurrection. Whenever they kindle the fire of war, God will put it out. They try to spread corruption in the land, but God does not love those who corrupt. If only the People of the Book would believe and be mindful of God, We would take away their sins and bring them into the Gardens of Delight. If they had upheld the Torah and the Gospel and what was sent down to them from their Lord, they would have been given abundance from above and from below: some of them are on the right course, but many of them do evil.

Messenger, proclaim everything that has been sent down to you from your Lord—if you do not, then you will not have communicated His message—and God will protect you from people. God does not guide those who defy Him. Say, 'People of the Book, you have no true basis [for your religion] unless you uphold the Torah, the Gospel, and that which has been sent down to you from your Lord,' but what has been sent down to you [Prophet] from your Lord is sure to increase many of them in their insolence and defiance: do not worry about those who defy [God]. For the [Muslim] believers, the Jews, the Sabians,[4] and the Christians—those who believe in God and the Last Day and do good deeds—there is no fear: they will not grieve.

We took a pledge from the Children of Israel, and sent messengers to them. Whenever a messenger brought them anything they did not like, they accused some of lying and put others to death; they thought no harm could come to them and so became blind and deaf [to God]. God turned to them in mercy but many of them again became blind and deaf: God is fully aware of their actions. Those who say, 'God is the Messiah, son of Mary,' have defied God. The Messiah himself said, 'Children of Israel, worship God, my Lord and your Lord.' If anyone associates others with God, God will forbid him from the Garden, and Hell will be his home. No one will help such evildoers.

Those people who say that God is the third of three are defying [the truth]: there is only One God. If they persist in what they are saying, a painful punishment will afflict those of them who persist. Why do they not turn to God and ask His forgiveness, when God is most forgiving, most merciful? The Messiah, son of Mary, was only a messenger; other messengers had come and gone before him; his mother was a virtuous woman; both ate food [like other mortals]. See how clear We make these signs for them; see how deluded they are. Say, 'How can you worship something other than God, that has no power to do

---

4. Apparently a monotheistic group in Iraq who especially venerated the Psalms; they, too, were people of the Book.

you harm or good? God alone is the All Hearing and All Knowing.' Say, 'People of the Book, do not overstep the bounds of truth in your religion and do not follow the whims of those who went astray before you—they led many others astray and themselves continue to stray from the even path.'

Those Children of Israel who defied [God] were rejected through the words of David,[5] and Jesus, son of Mary, because they disobeyed, they persistently overstepped the limits, they did not forbid each other to do wrong. How vile their deeds were! You [Prophet] see many of them allying themselves with the disbelievers. How terrible is what their souls have stored up for them: God is angry with them and they will remain tormented. If they had believed in God, in the Prophet, and in what was sent down to him, they would never have allied themselves with the disbelievers, but most of them are rebels.

You [Prophet] are sure to find that the most hostile to the believers are the Jews and those who associate other deities with God; you are sure to find that the closest in affection towards the believers are those who say, 'We are Christians,' for there are among them people devoted to learning and ascetics. These people are not given to arrogance, and when they listen to what has been sent down to the Messenger, you will see their eyes overflowing with tears because they recognize the Truth [in it]. They say, 'Our Lord, we believe, so count us amongst the witnesses. Why should we not believe in God and in the Truth that has come down to us, when we long for our Lord to include us in the company of the righteous?' For saying this, God has rewarded them with Gardens graced with flowing streams, and there they will stay: that is the reward of those who do good. Those who reject the truth and deny Our messages will be the inhabitants of Hellfire.

You who believe, do not forbid the good things God has made lawful to you—do not exceed the limits: God does not love those who exceed the limits—but eat the lawful and good things that God provides for you. Be mindful of God, in whom you believe. God does not take you [to task] for what is thoughtless in your oaths, only for your binding oaths: the atonement for breaking an oath is to feed ten poor people with food equivalent to what you would normally give your own families, or to clothe them, or to set free a slave—if a person cannot find the means, he should fast for three days. This is the atonement for breaking your oaths—keep your oaths. In this way God makes clear His revelations to you, so that you may be thankful.

You who believe, intoxicants and gambling, idolatrous practices, and [divining with] arrows are repugnant acts—Satan's doing—shun them so that you may prosper. With intoxicants and gambling, Satan seeks only to incite enmity and hatred among you, and to stop you remembering God and prayer. Will you not give them up? Obey God, obey the Messenger, and always be on your guard: if you pay no heed, bear in mind that the sole duty of Our Messenger is to deliver the message clearly. Those who believe and do good deeds will not be blamed for what they may have consumed [in the past] as long as they are mindful of God, believe and do good deeds, then are mindful of God and believe, then are mindful of God and do good deeds: God loves those who do good deeds.

<hr>

5. Second king of Israel, according to the Hebrew Bible (see Samuel, 1 Kings, and 1 Chronicles); the model for later monarchs, despite his moral lapses, he is traditionally credited with authorship of the Psalms.

You who believe, God is sure to test you with game within reach of your hands and spears, to find out who fears Him even though they cannot see Him: from now on, anyone who transgresses will have a painful punishment. You who believe, do not kill game while you are in the state of consecration [for pilgrimage]. If someone does so intentionally the penalty is an offering of a domestic animal brought to the Ka'ba[6] equivalent—as judged by two just men among you—to the one he has killed; alternatively, he may atone by feeding the needy or by fasting an equivalent number of days, so that he may taste the full gravity of his deed. God forgives what is past, but if anyone re-offends, God will exact the penalty from him: God is mighty, and capable of exacting the penalty. It is permitted for you to catch and eat seafood—an enjoyment for you and the traveller—but hunting game is forbidden while you are in the state of consecration [for pilgrimage]. Be mindful of God to whom you will be gathered.

God has made the Ka'ba—the Sacred House—a means of support for people, and the Sacred Months, the animals for sacrifice and their garlands: all this. Know that God has knowledge of all that is in the heavens and earth and that He is fully aware of all things. Know too that God is severe in punishment yet most forgiving and merciful. The Messenger's duty is only to deliver the message: God knows what you reveal and what you conceal.

Say [Prophet], 'Bad cannot be likened to good, though you may be dazzled by how abundant the bad is. Be mindful of God, people of understanding, so that you may prosper.' You who believe, do not ask about matters which, if made known to you, might make things difficult for you—if you ask about them while the Qur'an is being revealed, they will be made known to you—for God has kept silent about them: God is most forgiving and forbearing. Before you, some people asked about things, then ignored [the answers]. God did not institute the dedication of such things as bahira, sa'iba, wasila, or ham[7] to idols; but the disbelievers invent lies about God. Most of them do not use reason: when it is said to them, 'Come to what God has sent down, and to the Messenger,' they say, 'What we inherited from our forefathers is good enough for us,' even though their forefathers knew nothing and were not guided. You who believe, you are responsible for your own souls; if anyone else goes astray it will not harm you so long as you follow the guidance; you will all return to God, and He will make you realize what you have done.

You who believe, when death approaches any of you, let two just men from among you act as witnesses to the making of a bequest, or two men from another people if you are journeying in the land when death approaches. Keep the two witnesses back after prayer, if you have any doubts, and make them both swear by God, 'We will not sell our testimony for any price, even if a close relative is involved. We will not hide God's testimony, for then we should be doing wrong.' If it is discovered that these two are guilty [of perjury], two of those whose rights have been usurped have a better right to bear witness in their place. Let them swear by God, 'Our testimony is truer than theirs. We have said nothing but the truth, for that would make us wrongdoers': that will make it more likely they will give true and proper testimony, or fear that their oaths might be refuted by others afterwards. Be mindful of God and listen; God does not guide those who break His laws.

6. Also "Ka'aba"; see p. 861, n. 2.
7. Different classes of animals consecrated to idols in pre-Islamic Arabia.

On the Day when God assembles all the messengers and asks, 'What response did you receive?' they will say, 'We do not have that knowledge: You alone know things that cannot be seen,' Then God will say, 'Jesus, son of Mary! Remember My favour to you and to your mother: how I strengthened you with the holy spirit, so that you spoke to people in your infancy and as a grown man; how I taught you the Scripture and wisdom, the Torah and the Gospel; how, by My leave, you fashioned the shape of a bird out of clay, breathed into it, and it became, by My leave, a bird; how, by My leave, you healed the blind person and the leper; how, by My leave, you brought the dead back to life; how I restrained the Children of Israel from [harming] you when you brought them clear signs, and those of them who disbelieved said, "This is clearly nothing but sorcery";[8] and how I inspired the disciples to believe in Me and My messengers—they said, "We believe and bear witness that we devote ourselves [to God]."'

When the disciples said, 'Jesus, son of Mary, can your Lord send down a feast to us from heaven?' he said, 'Beware of God if you are true believers.' They said, 'We wish to eat from it; to have our hearts reassured; to know that you have told us the truth; and to be witnesses of it.' Jesus, son of Mary, said, 'Lord, send down to us a feast from heaven so that we can have a festival—the first and last of us—and a sign from You. Provide for us: You are the best provider.' God said, 'I will send it down to you, but anyone who disbelieves after this will be punished with a punishment that I will not inflict on anyone else in the world.'

When God says, 'Jesus, son of Mary, did you say to people, "Take me and my mother as two gods alongside God"?' he will say, 'May You be exalted! I would never say what I had no right to say—if I had said such a thing You would have known it: You know all that is within me, though I do not know what is within You, You alone have full knowledge of things unseen—I told them only what You commanded me to: "Worship God, my Lord and your Lord." I was a witness over them during my time among them. Ever since You took my soul, You alone have been the watcher over them: You are witness to all things and if You punish them, they are Your servants; if You forgive them, You are the Almighty, the Wise.' God will say, 'This is a Day when the truthful will benefit from their truthfulness. They will have Gardens graced with flowing streams, there to remain for ever. God is pleased with them and they with Him: that is the supreme triumph.' Control of the heavens and earth and everything in them belongs to God: He has power over all things.

10. Jonah

In the name of God, the Lord of Mercy, the Giver of Mercy

Alif Lam Ra[1]

These are the verses of the wise Book. Is it so surprising to people that We have revealed to a man from among them that he should warn people, and give

---

8. This account of Jesus' miracles is similar to that found in apocryphal Christian accounts of his childhood (the so-called infancy gospels).

1. Letters of the Arabic alphabet; their meaning in this context is unclear.

glad news to those who believe, that they are on a sure footing with their Lord? [Yet] those who disbelieve say, 'This man is clearly a sorcerer.'

Your Lord is God who created the heavens and earth in six Days, then established Himself on the Throne, governing everything; there is no one that can intercede with Him, unless He has first given permission: this is God your Lord so worship Him. How can you not take heed? It is to Him you shall all return—that is a true promise from God. It was He who created [you] in the first place, and He will do so again, so that He may justly reward those who believe and do good deeds. But the disbelievers will have a drink of scalding water, and agonizing torment, because they persistently disbelieved.

It is He who made the sun a shining radiance and the moon a light, determining phases for it so that you might know the number of years and how to calculate time. God did not create all these without a true purpose; He explains His signs to those who understand. In the succession of night and day, and in what God created in the heavens and earth, there truly are signs for those who are aware of Him. Those who do not expect to meet Us and are pleased with the life of this world, contenting themselves with it and paying no heed to Our signs, shall have the Fire for their home because of what they used to do. But as for those who believe and do good deeds, their Lord will guide them because of their faith. Streams will flow at their feet in the Gardens of Bliss. Their prayer in them will be, 'Glory be to You, God!' their greeting, 'Peace,' and the last part of their prayer, 'Praise be to God, Lord of the Worlds.'[2]

If God were to hasten on for people the harm [they have earned] as they wish to hasten on the good, their time would already be up. But We leave those who do not expect to meet Us to wander blindly in their excesses. When trouble befalls man he cries out to Us, whether lying on his side, sitting, or standing, but as soon as We relieve him of his trouble he goes on his way as if he had never cried out to Us to remove his trouble. In this way the deeds of such heedless people are made attractive to them. Before you people, We destroyed whole generations when they did evil—their messengers brought them clear signs but they refused to believe. This is how We repay the guilty. Later We made you their successors in the land, to see how you would behave.

When Our clear revelations are recited to them, those who do not expect to meet with Us say, 'Bring [us] a different Qur'an, or change it.' [Prophet], say, 'It is not for me to change it of my own accord; I only follow what is revealed to me, for I fear the torment of an awesome Day, if I were to disobey my Lord.' Say, 'If God had so willed, I would not have recited it to you, not would He have made it known to you. I lived a whole lifetime among you before it came to me. How can you not use your reason?'

Who could be more wicked than someone who invents lies against God or denies His revelations? The guilty will never prosper. They worship alongside God things that can neither harm not benefit them, and say, 'These are our intercessors with God.' Say, 'Do you think you can tell God about something He knows not to exist in the heavens or earth? Glory be to Him! He is far above the partner-gods they associate with Him! All people were originally one single community, but later they differed. If it had not been for a word from your Lord, the

---

2. This phrase, taken from "The Opening," is repeated several times in each one of the five prescribed daily prayers.

preordained judgement would already have been passed between them regarding their differences. They say, 'Why has no miraculous sign been sent down to him from his Lord?' Say [Prophet], 'Only God knows the unseen, so wait—I too am waiting.' No sooner do We let people taste some mercy after some hardship has afflicted them, than they begin to scheme against Our revelations. Say, 'God schemes even faster.' Our messengers[3] record all your scheming.

It is He who enables you to travel on land and sea until, when you are sailing on ships and rejoicing in the favouring wind, a storm arrives: waves come at those on board from all sides and they feel there is no escape. Then they pray to God, professing sincere devotion to Him, 'If You save us from this we shall be truly thankful.' Yet no sooner does He save them than, back on land, they behave outrageously against all that is right. People! Your outrageous behaviour only works against yourselves. Take your little enjoyment in this present life; in the end you will return to Us and We shall confront you with everything you have done.

The life of this world is like this: rain that We send down from the sky is absorbed by the plants of the earth, from which humans and animals eat. But when the earth has taken on its finest appearance, and adorns itself, and its people think they have power over it, then the fate We commanded comes to it, by night or by day, and We reduce it to stubble, as if it had not flourished just the day before. This is the way We explain the revelations for those who reflect.

But God invites [everyone] to the Home of Peace, and guides whoever He will to a straight path. Those who did well will have the best reward and more besides. Neither darkness nor shame will cover their faces: these are the companions in Paradise, and there they will remain. As for those who did evil, each evil deed will be requited by its equal and humiliation will cover them—no one will protect them against God—as though their faces were covered with veils cut from the darkness of the night. These are the inmates of the Fire, and there they shall remain.

On the Day We gather them all together, We shall say to those who associate partners with God, 'Stay in your place, you and your partner-gods.' Then We shall separate them, and their partner-gods will say, 'It was not us you worshipped—God is witness enough between us and you—we had no idea that you worshipped us.' Every soul will realize, then and there, what it did in the past. They will be returned to God, their rightful Lord, and their invented [gods] will desert them.

Say [Prophet], 'Who provides for you from the sky and the earth? Who controls hearing and sight? Who brings forth the living from the dead and the dead from the living, and who governs everything?' They are sure to say, 'God.' Then say, 'So why do you not take heed of Him? That is God, your Lord, the Truth. Apart from the Truth, what is there except error? So how is it that you are dissuaded?' In this way, your Lord's word about those who defy [the Truth] has been proved—they do not believe. Ask them, 'Can any of your partner-gods originate creation, then bring it back to life again in the end?' Say, 'It is God that originates creation, and then brings it back to life, so how can you be misled?' Say, 'Can any of your partner-gods show the way to the Truth?' Say, 'God shows the way to the Truth. Is someone who shows the way to the Truth more

3. That is, angels (in Greek, *angeloi*).

worthy to be followed, or someone who cannot find the way unless he himself is shown? What is the matter with you? How do you judge?' Most of them follow nothing but assumptions, but assumptions can be of no value at all against the Truth: God is well aware of what they do.

Nor could this Qur'an have been devised by anyone other than God. It is a confirmation of what was revealed before it and an explanation of the Scripture— let there be no doubt about it—it is from the Lord of the Worlds. Or do they say, 'He has devised it'? Say, 'Then produce a sura like it, and call on anyone you can beside God if you are telling the truth.'[4] But they are denying what they cannot comprehend—its prophecy has yet to be fulfilled for them. In the same way, those before them refused to believe—see what was the end of those evildoers!

Some of them believe in it, and some do not: your Lord knows best those who cause corruption. If they do not believe you, [Prophet], say, 'I act for myself, and you for yourselves. You are not responsible for my actions nor am I responsible for yours.' Some of them do listen to you: but can you make the deaf hear if they will not use their minds? Some of them look at you: but can you guide the blind if they will not see? God does not wrong people at all—it is they who wrong themselves.

On the Day He gathers them together, it will be as if they have stayed [in the world] no longer than a single hour, and they will recognize one another. Those who denied the meeting with God will be the losers, for they did not follow the right guidance. Whether We let you [Prophet] see some of the punishment We have threatened them with, or cause you to die [first], they will return to Us: God is witness to what they do. Every community is sent a messenger, and when their messenger comes, they will be judged justly; they will not be wronged. They ask, 'When will this promise be fulfilled, if what you say is true?' Say [Prophet], 'I cannot control any harm or benefit that comes to me, except as God wills. There is an appointed term for every community, and when it is reached they can neither delay not hasten it, even for a moment.' Say, 'Think: if His punishment were to come to you, during the night or day, what part of it would the guilty wish to hasten? Will you believe in it, when it actually happens?' It will be said, 'Now [you believe], when [before] you sought to hasten it?' It will be said to the evildoers, 'Taste lasting punishment. Why should you be rewarded for anything but what you did?'

They ask you [Prophet], 'Is it true?' Say, 'Yes, by my Lord, it is true, and you cannot escape it.' Every soul that has done evil, if it possessed all that is on the earth, would gladly offer it as ransom. When they see the punishment, they will repent in secret, but they will be judged with justice and will not be wronged. It is to God that everything in the heavens and the earth truly belongs: God's promise is true, but most people do not realize it. It is He who gives life and takes it, and you will all be returned to Him.

People, a teaching from your Lord has come to you, a healing for what is in [your] hearts, and guidance and mercy for the believers. Say [Prophet], 'In God's grace and mercy let them rejoice: these are better than all they accumulate.' Say, 'Think about the provision God has sent down for you, some of

---

4. This challenge is based on literary merit: the Qur'an dares any poet to match the eloquence of a single sura.

which you have made unlawful and some lawful.' Say, 'Has God given you permission [to do this], or are you inventing lies about God?' What will those people who invent lies about Him think on the Day of Resurrection? God is bountiful towards people, but most of them do not give thanks.

In whatever matter you [Prophet] may be engaged and whatever part of the Qur'an you are reciting, whatever work you [people] are doing, we witness you when you are engaged in it. Not even the weight of a speck of dust in the earth or sky escapes your Lord, nor anything lesser or greater: it is all written in a clear record. But for those who are on God's side there is no fear, nor shall they grieve. For those who believe and are conscious of God, for them there is good news in this life and in the Hereafter—there is no changing the promises of God—that is truly the supreme triumph. Do not let their words grieve you [Prophet]. Power belongs entirely to God; He hears all and knows all; indeed, all who are in the heavens and on the earth belong to Him. Those who call upon others beside God are not really following partner-gods; they are only following assumptions and telling lies. It is He who made the night so that you can rest in it and the daylight so that you can see—there truly are signs in this for those who hear.

They say, 'God has children!' May He be exalted! He is the Self-Sufficient One; everything in the heavens and the earth belongs to Him. You have no authority to say this. How dare you say things about God without any knowledge? Say [Prophet], 'Those who invent lies about God will not prosper.' They may have a little enjoyment in this world, but then they will return to Us. Then We shall make them taste severe punishment for persisting in blasphemy.

Tell them the story of Noah.[5] He said to his people, 'My people, if my presence among you and my reminding you of God's signs is too much for you, then I put my trust in God. Agree on your course of action, you and your partner-gods—do not be hesitant or secretive about it—then carry out your decision on me and give me no respite. But if you turn away, I have asked no reward from you; my reward is with God alone, and I am commanded to be one of those who devote themselves to Him.' But they rejected him. We saved him and those with him on the Ark and let them survive; and We drowned those who denied Our revelations—see what was the end of those who were forewarned!

Then, after him, We sent messengers to their peoples bringing them clear signs. But they would not believe in anything they had already rejected: in this way We seal the hearts of those who are full of hostility. After them We sent Moses and Aaron with Our signs to Pharaoh[6] and his leading supporters, but they acted arrogantly—they were wicked people. When the truth came to them from Us, they said, 'This is blatant sorcery.' Moses said, 'Is this what you say about the Truth when it comes to you? Is this sorcery? Sorcerers never prosper.' They said, 'Have you come to turn us away from the faith we found our fathers following, so that you and your brother can gain greatness in this land? We will never believe in you.' And Pharaoh said, 'Bring me every learned sorcerer.' When the sorcerers came, Moses said to them, 'Throw down whatever you have.' When they did so, Moses said, 'Everything you have brought is sorcery and God will show it to be false. God does not make the work of mischief-makers right; He will uphold the Truth with His words, even if the evildoers

---

5. Compare Genesis 5.28–9.29.   **6.** Compare Exodus 6.26–14.31.

hate it.' But no one believed in Moses except a few of his own people, for fear that Pharaoh and their leaders would persecute them: Pharaoh was domineering in the land and prone to excess.

Moses said, 'My people, if you have faith in God and are devoted to Him, put your trust in Him.' They said, 'We have put our trust in God. Lord! Do not make us an object of persecution for the oppressors. Save us, in Your mercy, from those who reject [Your message].' We revealed to Moses and his brother: 'House your people in Egypt and make these houses places of worship; keep up the prayer; give good news to the believers!' And Moses said, 'Our Lord, You have given Pharaoh and his chiefs splendour and wealth in this present life and here they are, Lord, leading others astray from Your path. Our Lord, obliterate their wealth and harden their hearts so that they do not believe until they see the agonizing torment.' God said, 'Your prayers are answered, so stay on the right course, and do not follow the path of those who do not know.'

We took the Children of Israel across the sea. Pharaoh and his troops pursued them in arrogance and aggression. But as he was drowning he cried, 'I believe there is no God except the one the Children of Israel believe in. I submit to Him.' 'Now? When you had always been a rebel, and a troublemaker! Today We shall save only your corpse as a sign to all posterity. A great many people fail to heed Our signs.' We settled the Children of Israel in a good place and provided good things as sustenance for them. It was only after knowledge had come to them that they began to differ among themselves. Your Lord will judge between them on the Day of Resurrection regarding their differences.

So if you [Prophet] are in doubt about what We have revealed to you, ask those who have been reading the scriptures before you. The Truth has come to you from your Lord, so be in no doubt and do not deny God's signs—then you would become one of the losers. Those against whom your Lord's sentence is passed will not believe, even if every sign comes to them, until they see the agonizing torment. If only a single town had believed and benefited from its belief! Only Jonah's people did so, and when they believed, We relieved them of the punishment of disgrace in the life of this world, and let them enjoy life for a time. Had your Lord willed, all the people on earth would have believed. So can you [Prophet] compel people to believe? No soul can believe except by God's will, and He brings disgrace on those who do not use their reason. Say, 'Look at what is in the heavens and on the earth.' But what use are signs and warnings to people who will not believe? What are they waiting for but the punishment that came to those before them? Say, 'Wait then, I am waiting too.' In the end We shall save Our messengers and the believers. We take it upon Ourself to save the believers.

[Prophet] say, 'People, even if you are in doubt about my religion, I do not worship those you worship other than God, but I worship God who will cause you to die, and I am commanded to be a believer.' [Prophet], set your face towards religion as a man of pure faith. Do not be one of those who join partners with God; do not pray to any other [god] that can neither benefit nor harm you: if you do, you will be one of the evildoers. If God inflicts harm on you, no one can remove it but Him, and if He intends good for you, no one can turn His bounty away; He grants His bounty to any of His servants He will. He is the Most Forgiving, the Most Merciful. Say, 'People, the Truth has come to you from your Lord. Whoever follows the right path follows it for his own good, and whoever strays does so to his own loss: I am not your guardian.' [Prophet], follow what is being revealed to you, and be steadfast until God gives His judgement, for He is the Best of Judges.

12. Joseph

In the name of God, the Lord of Mercy, the Giver of Mercy

Alif Lam Ra

These are the verses of the Scripture that makes things clear—We have sent it down as an Arabic Qur'an so that you [people] may understand.

We tell you [Prophet] the best of stories in revealing this Qur'an to you. Before this you were one of those who knew nothing about them. Joseph said to his father,[1] 'Father, I dreamed of eleven stars and the sun and the moon: I saw them all bow down before me,' and he replied, 'My son, tell your brothers nothing of this dream, or they may plot to harm you—Satan is man's sworn enemy. This is about how your Lord will choose you, teach you to interpret dreams, and perfect His blessing on you and the House of Jacob, just as He perfected it earlier on your forefathers Abraham and Isaac:[2] your Lord is all knowing and wise.'

There are lessons in the story of Joseph and his brothers for all who seek them. The brothers said [to each other], 'Although we are many, Joseph and his brother are dearer to our father than we are—our father is clearly in the wrong.' [One of them said], 'Kill Joseph or banish him to another land, and your father's attention will be free to turn to you. After that you can be righteous.' [Another of them] said, 'Do not kill Joseph, but, if you must, throw him into the hidden depths of a well where some caravan may pick him up.'

They said to their father, 'Why do you not trust us with Joseph? We wish him well. Send him with us tomorrow and he will enjoy himself and play—we will take good care of him.' He replied, 'The thought of you taking him away with you worries me: I am afraid a wolf may eat him when you are not paying attention.' They said, 'If a wolf were to eat him when there are so many of us, we would truly be losers!'

Then they took him away with them, resolved upon throwing him into the hidden depths of a well—We inspired him, saying, 'You will tell them of all this [at a time] when they do not realize [who you are]!'—and at nightfall they returned to their father weeping. They said, 'We went off racing one another, leaving Joseph behind with our things, and a wolf ate him. You will not believe us, though we are telling the truth!' and they showed him his shirt, deceptively stained with blood. He cried, 'No! Your souls have prompted you to do wrong! But it is best to be patient: from God alone I seek help to bear what you are saying.'

Some travellers came by. They sent someone to draw water and he let down his bucket. 'Good news!' he exclaimed. 'Here is a boy!' They hid him like a piece of merchandise—God was well aware of what they did—and then sold him for a small price, for a few pieces of silver: so little did they value him.

---

1. Compare Genesis 37.9–11.
2. Isaac is Jacob's father, and Abraham is his grandfather; all three are recognized as prophets in Islam.

The Egyptian who bought him said to his wife, 'Look after him well! He may be useful to us, or we may adopt him as a son.' In this way We settled Joseph in that land and later taught him how to interpret dreams: God always prevails in His purpose, though most people do not realize it.

When he reached maturity, We gave him judgement and knowledge: this is how We reward those who do good. The woman in whose house he was living tried to seduce him:[3] she bolted the doors and said, 'Come to me,' and he replied, 'God forbid! My master has been good to me; wrongdoers never prosper.' She made for him, and he would have succumbed to her if he had not seen evidence of his Lord—We did this in order to keep evil and indecency away from him, for he was truly one of Our chosen servants. They raced for the door—she tore his shirt from behind—and at the door they met her husband. She said, 'What, other than prison or painful punishment, should be the reward of someone who tried to dishonour your wife?' but he said, 'She tried to seduce me.' A member of her household suggested, 'If his shirt is torn at the front, then it is she who is telling the truth and he who is lying, but if it is torn at the back, then she is lying and he is telling the truth.' When the husband saw that the shirt was torn at the back, he said, 'This is another instance of women's treachery: your treachery is truly great. Joseph, overlook this; but you [wife], ask forgiveness for your sin—you have done wrong.'

Some women of the city said, 'The governor's wife is trying to seduce her slave! Love for him consumes her heart! It is clear to us that she has gone astray.' When she heard their malicious talk, she prepared a banquet and sent for them, giving each of them a knife. She said to Joseph, 'Come out and show yourself to them!' and when the women saw him, they were stunned by his beauty, and cut their hands, exclaiming, 'Great God! He cannot be mortal! He must be a precious angel!' She said, 'This is the one you blamed me for. I tried to seduce him and he wanted to remain chaste, but if he does not do what I command now, he will be put in prison and degraded.' Joseph said, 'My Lord! I would prefer prison to what these women are calling me to do. If You do not protect me from their treachery, I shall yield to them and do wrong,' and his Lord answered his prayer and protected him from their treachery—He is the All Hearing, the All Knowing.

In the end they thought it best, after seeing all the signs of his innocence, that they should imprison him for a while. Two young men went into prison alongside him. One of them said, 'I dreamed that I was pressing grapes'; the other said, 'I dreamed that I was carrying bread on my head and that the birds were eating it.' [They said], 'Tell us what this means—we can see that you are a knowledgeable man.'

He said, 'I can tell you what this means before any meal arrives: this is part of what my Lord has taught me. I reject the faith of those who disbelieve in God and deny the life to come, and I follow the faith of my forefathers Abraham, Isaac, and Jacob. Because of God's grace to us and to all mankind, we would never worship anything beside God, but most people are ungrateful. Fellow prisoners, would many diverse gods be better than God the One, the All Powerful? [No indeed!] All those you worship instead of Him are mere names you and your forefathers have invented, names for which God has sent

3. Compare Genesis 39.7–41.45.

down no sanction. Authority belongs to God alone, and He orders you to worship none but Him: this is the true faith, though most people do not realize it. Fellow prisoners, one of you will serve his master with wine; the other will be crucified and the birds will peck at his head. That is the end of the matter on which you asked my opinion.' Joseph said to the one he knew would be saved, 'Mention me to your master,' but Satan made him forget to do this, and so Joseph remained in prison for a number of years.

The king said, 'I dreamed about seven fat cows being eaten by seven lean ones; seven green ears of corn and [seven] others withered. Counsellors, if you can interpret dreams, tell me the meaning of my dream.' They said, 'These are confusing dreams and we are not skilled at dream-interpretation,' but the prisoner who had been freed at last remembered [Joseph] and said, 'I shall tell you what this means. Give me leave to go.'

'Truthful Joseph! Tell us the meaning of seven fat cows being eaten by seven lean ones, seven green ears of corn and [seven] others withered, then I can return to the people to inform them.' Joseph said, 'You will sow for seven consecutive years as usual. Store all that you reap, left in the ear, apart from the little you eat. After that will come seven years of hardship which will consume all but a little of what you stored up for them; after that will come a year when the people will have abundant rain and will press grapes.'

The king said, 'Bring him to me,' but when the messenger came to fetch Joseph, he said, 'Go back to your master and ask him about what happened to those women who cut their hands—my Lord knows all about their treachery.' The king asked the women, 'What happened when you tried to seduce Joseph?' They said, 'God forbid! We know nothing bad of him!' and the governor's wife said, 'Now the truth is out: it was I who tried to seduce him—he is an honest man.' [Joseph said, 'This was] for my master to know that I did not betray him behind his back: God does not guide the mischief of the treacherous. I do not pretend to be blameless, for man's very soul incites him to evil unless my Lord shows mercy: He is most forgiving, most merciful.'

The king said, 'Bring him to me: I will have him serve me personally,' and then, once he had spoken with him, 'From now on you will have our trust and favour.' Joseph said, 'Put me in charge of the nation's storehouses: I shall manage them prudently and carefully.' In this way We settled Joseph in that land to live wherever he wished: We grant Our mercy to whoever We will and do not fail to reward those who do good. The reward of the Hereafter is best for those who believe and are mindful of God.

Joseph's brothers came[4] and presented themselves before him. He recognized them—though they did not recognize him—and once he had given them their provisions, he said, 'Bring me the brother [you left with] your father![5] Have you not seen me giving generous measure and being the best of hosts? You will have no more corn from me if you do not bring him to me, and you will not be permitted to approach me.' They said, 'We shall do all we can to persuade his father to send him with us, indeed we shall.' Joseph said to his servants, 'Put their [traded] goods back into their saddlebags, so that they may recognize them when they go back to their family, and [be eager to] return.'

4. Compare Genesis 42.3–46.7.
5. Benjamin, Joseph's full brother; his other brothers had different mothers.

When they returned to their father, they said, 'Father, we have been denied any more corn, but send our brother back with us and we shall be given another measure. We shall guard him carefully.' He said, 'Am I to entrust him to you as I did his brother before? God is the best guardian and the Most Merciful of the merciful.' Then, when they opened their packs, they discovered that their goods had been returned to them and they said, 'Father! We need no more [goods to barter]: look, our goods have been returned to us. We shall get corn for our household; we shall keep our brother safe; we shall be entitled to another camel-load of grain—an extra measure so easily achieved!' He said, 'I will never send him with you, not unless you swear by God that you will bring him back to me if that is humanly possible.' Then, when they had given him their pledge, he said, 'Our words are entrusted to God.' He said, 'My sons, do not enter all by one gate—use different gates. But I cannot help you against the will of God: all power is in God's hands. I trust in Him; let everyone put their trust in Him,' and, when they entered as their father had told them, it did not help them against the will of God, it merely satisfied a wish of Jacob's. He knew well what We had taught him, though most people do not.

Then, when they presented themselves before Joseph, he drew his brother apart and said, 'I am your brother, so do not be saddened by their past actions,' and, once he had given them their provisions, he placed the drinking-cup in his brother's pack. A man called out, 'People of the caravan! You are thieves!' and they turned and said, 'What have you lost?' They replied, 'The king's drinking-cup is missing,' and, 'Whoever returns it will get a camel-load [of grain],' and, 'I give you my word.' They said, 'By God! You must know that we did not come to make mischief in your land: we are no thieves.' They asked them, 'And if we find that you are lying, what penalty shall we apply to you?' and they answered, 'The penalty will be [the enslavement of] the person in whose bag the cup is found: this is how we punish wrongdoers.' [Joseph] began by searching their bags, then his brother's, and he pulled it out from his brother's bag.

In this way We devised a plan for Joseph—if God had not willed it so, he could not have detained his brother as a penalty under the king's law—We raise the rank of whoever We will. Above everyone who has knowledge there is the One who is all knowing.

[His brothers] said, 'If he is a thief then his brother was a thief before him,' but Joseph kept his secrets and did not reveal anything to them. He said, 'You are in a far worse situation. God knows best the truth of what you claim.' They said, 'Mighty governor, he has an elderly father. Take one of us in his place. We can see that you are a very good man.' He replied, 'God forbid that we should take anyone other than the person on whom we found our property: that would be unjust of us.' When they lost hope of [persuading] him, they withdrew to confer with each other: the eldest of them said, 'Do you not remember that your father took a solemn pledge from you in the name of God and before that you failed in your duty with regard to Joseph? I will not leave this land until my father gives me leave or God decides for me—He is the best decider—so go back to your father and say, "Your son stole. We can only tell you what we saw. How could we guard against the unforeseen? Ask in the town where we have been; ask the people of the caravan we travelled with: we are telling the truth."'

Their father said, 'No! Your souls have prompted you to do wrong! But it is best to be patient: may God bring all of them back to me—He alone is the All Knowing, the All Wise,' and he turned away from them, saying, 'Alas for Joseph!' His eyes went white with grief and he was filled with sorrow. They said, 'By God! You will ruin your health if you do not stop thinking of Joseph, or even die.' He said, 'I plead my grief and sorrow before God. I have knowledge from God that you do not have. My sons, go and seek news of Joseph and his brother and do not despair of God's mercy—only disbelievers despair of God's mercy.'

Then, when they presented themselves before Joseph, they said, 'Mighty governor, misfortune has afflicted us and our family. We have brought only a little merchandise, but give us full measure. Be charitable to us: God rewards the charitable.' He said, 'Do you now realize what you did to Joseph and his brother when you were ignorant?' and they cried, 'Could it be that you are Joseph?' He said, 'I am Joseph. This is my brother. God has been gracious to us: God does not deny anyone who is mindful of God and steadfast in adversity the rewards of those who do good.' They said, 'By God! God really did favour you over all of us and we were in the wrong!' but he said, 'You will hear no reproaches today. May God forgive you: He is the Most Merciful of the merciful. Take my shirt and lay it over my father's face: he will recover his sight. Then bring your whole family back to me.'

Later, when the caravan departed, their father said, 'You may think I am senile but I can smell Joseph,' but [people] said, 'By God! You are still lost in that old illusion of yours!' Then, when the bearer of good news came and placed the shirt on to Jacob's face, his eyesight returned and he said, 'Did I not tell you that I have knowledge from God that you do not have?' The [brothers] said, 'Father, ask God to forgive our sins—we were truly in the wrong.' He replied, 'I shall ask my Lord to forgive you: He is the Most Forgiving, the Most Merciful.'

Later, when they presented themselves before Joseph, he drew his parents to him—he said, 'Welcome to Egypt: you will all be safe here, God willing'—and took them up to [his] throne. They all bowed down before him and he said, 'Father, this is the fulfilment of that dream I had long ago. My Lord has made it come true and has been gracious to me—He released me from prison and He brought you here from the desert—after Satan sowed discord between me and my brothers. My Lord is most subtle in achieving what He will, He is the All Knowing, the Truly Wise. My Lord! You have given me authority; You have taught me something about the interpretation of dreams; Creator of the heavens and the earth, You are my protector in this world and in the Hereafter. Let me die in true devotion to You. Join me with the righteous.'

This account is part of what was beyond your knowledge [Muhammad]. We revealed it to you: you were not present with Joseph's brothers when they made their treacherous plans. However eagerly you may want them to, most men will not believe. You ask no reward from them for this: it is a reminder for all people and there are many signs in the heavens and the earth that they pass by and give no heed to—most of them will only believe in God while also joining others with Him. Are they so sure that an overwhelming punishment from God will not fall on them, or that the Last Hour will not come upon them suddenly when they least expect it? Say, 'This is my way: based on clear evidence, I, and all who follow me, call [people] to God—glory be to God!—I do not join others with Him.'

All the messengers We sent before you [Muhammad] were men to whom We made revelations, men chosen from the people of their towns. Have the [disbelievers] not travelled through the land and seen the end of those who went before them? For those who are mindful of God, the Home in the Hereafter is better. Do you [people] not use your reason? When the messengers lost all hope and realized that they had been dismissed as liars, Our help came to them: We saved whoever We pleased, but Our punishment will not be turned away from guilty people. There is a lesson in the stories of such people for those who understand. This revelation is no fabrication: it is a confirmation of the truth of what was sent before it; an explanation of everything; a guide and a blessing for those who believe.

19. Mary

In the name of God, the Lord of Mercy, the Giver of Mercy

Kaf Ha Ya 'Ayn Sad

This is an account of your Lord's grace towards His servant, Zachariah,[1] when he called to his Lord secretly, saying, 'Lord, my bones have weakened and my hair is ashen grey, but never, Lord, have I ever prayed to You in vain: I fear [what] my kinsmen [will do] when I am gone, for my wife is barren, so grant me a successor—a gift from You—to be my heir and the heir of the family of Jacob. Lord, make him well pleasing [to You].' 'Zachariah, We bring you good news of a son whose name will be John—We have chosen this name for no one before him.' He said, 'Lord, how can I have a son when my wife is barren, and I am old and frail?' He said, 'This is what your Lord has said: "It is easy for Me: I created you, though you were nothing before."'

He said, 'Give me a sign, Lord.' He said, 'Your sign is that you will not [be able to] speak to anyone for three full [days and] nights.' He went out of the sanctuary to his people and signalled to them to praise God morning and evening.

[We said], 'John, hold on to the Scripture firmly.' While he was still a boy, We granted him wisdom, tenderness from Us, and purity. He was devout, kind to his parents, not domineering or rebellious. Peace was on him the day he was born, the day he died, and it will be on him the day he is raised to life again.

Mention in the Qur'an the story of Mary. She withdrew from her family to a place to the east and secluded herself away; We sent Our Spirit to appear before her in the form of a perfected man. She said, 'I seek the Lord of Mercy's protection against you: if you have any fear of Him [do not approach]!' but he said, 'I am but a Messenger from your Lord, [come] to announce to you the gift of a pure son.' She said, 'How can I have a son when no man has touched me? I have not been unchaste,' and he said, 'This is what your Lord said: "It is easy for Me—We shall make him a sign to all people, a blessing from Us."' And so it was ordained: she conceived him. She withdrew to a distant place and, when the pains of childbirth drove her to [cling to] the trunk of a palm tree, she exclaimed, 'I wish I had been dead and forgotten long before all this!' but a voice cried to her from below,

1. Compare Luke 1.5–64.

'Do not worry: your Lord has provided a stream at your feet and, if you shake the trunk of the palm tree towards you, it will deliver fresh ripe dates for you, so eat, drink, be glad, and say to anyone you may see: "I have vowed to the Lord of Mercy to abstain from conversation, and I will not talk to anyone today."'

She went back to her people carrying the child, and they said, 'Mary! You have done something terrible! Sister of Aaron! Your father was not an evil man; your mother was not unchaste!' She pointed at him. They said, 'How can we converse with an infant?' [But] he said: 'I am a servant of God. He has granted me the Scripture; made me a prophet; made me blessed wherever I may be. He commanded me to pray, to give alms as long as I live, to cherish my mother. He did not make me domineering or graceless. Peace was on me the day I was born, and will be on me the day I die and the day I am raised to life again.' Such was Jesus, son of Mary.

[This is] a statement of the Truth about which they are in doubt: it would not befit God to have a child. He is far above that: when He decrees something, He says only, 'Be,' and it is. 'God is my Lord and your Lord, so serve Him: that is a straight path.' But factions have differed among themselves. What suffering will come to those who obscure the truth when a dreadful Day arrives! How sharp of hearing, how sharp of sight they will be when they come to Us, although now they are clearly off course! Warn them [Muhammad] of the Day of Remorse when the matter will be decided, for they are heedless and do not believe. It is We who will inherit the earth and all who are on it: they will all be returned to Us.

Mention too, in the Qur'an, the story of Abraham. He was a man of truth, a prophet. He said to his father, 'Father, why do you worship something that can neither hear nor see nor benefit you in any way? Father, knowledge that has not reached you has come to me, so follow me: I will guide you to an even path. Father, do not worship Satan—Satan has rebelled against the Lord of Mercy. Father, I fear that a punishment from the Lord of Mercy may afflict you and that you may become Satan's companion [in Hell].' His father answered, 'Abraham, do you reject my gods? I will stone you if you do not stop this. Keep out of my way!' Abraham said, 'Peace be with you: I will beg my Lord to forgive you—He is always gracious to me—but for now I will leave you, and the idols you all pray to, and I will pray to my Lord and trust that my prayer will not be in vain.' When he left his people and those they served beside God, We granted him Isaac and Jacob and made them both prophets: We granted Our grace to all of them, and gave them a noble reputation.

Mention too, in the Qur'an, the story of Moses. He was specially chosen, a messenger and a prophet: We called to him from the right-hand side of the mountain and brought him close to Us in secret communion; out of Our grace We granted him his brother Aaron as a prophet. Mention too, in the Qur'an, the story of Ishmael.[2] He was true to his promise, a messenger and a prophet. He commanded his household to pray and give alms, and his Lord was well pleased with him. Mention too, in the Qur'an, the story of Idris.[3] He was a man of truth, a prophet. We raised him to a high position.

2. The first son of Abraham, the older half-brother of Isaac.
3. Unlike the earlier prophets mentioned,

Idris appears in neither the Hebrew Bible nor the Gospels.

These were the prophets God blessed—from the seed of Adam, of those We carried in the Ark with Noah, from the seed of Abraham and Israel—and those We guided and chose. When the revelations of the Lord of Mercy were recited to them, they fell to their knees and wept, but there came after them generations who neglected prayer and were driven by their own desires. These will come face to face with their evil, but those who repent, who believe, who do righteous deeds, will enter Paradise. They will not be wronged in the least: they will enter the Gardens of Lasting Bliss, promised by the Lord of Mercy to His servants—it is not yet seen but truly His promise will be fulfilled. There they will hear only peaceful talk, nothing bad; there they will be given provision morning and evening. That is the Garden We shall give as their own to those of Our servants who were devout.

[Gabriel[4] said], 'We only descend [with revelation] at your Lord's command—everything before us, everything behind us, everything in between, all belongs to Him—your Lord is never forgetful. He is Lord of the heavens and earth and everything in between so worship Him: be steadfast in worshipping Him. Do you know of anyone equal to Him?'

Man says, 'What? Once I am dead, will I be brought back to life?' but does man not remember that We created him when he was nothing before? By your Lord [Prophet] We shall gather them and the devils together and set them on their knees around Hell; We shall seize out of each group those who were most disobedient towards the Lord of Mercy—We know best who most deserves to burn in Hell—but every single one of you will approach it, a decree from your Lord which must be fulfilled. We shall save the devout and leave the evildoers there on their knees.

When Our revelations are recited to them in all their clarity, [all that] the disbelievers say to the believers [is], 'Which side is better situated? Which side has the better following?' We have destroyed many a generation before them who surpassed them in riches and outward glitter! Say [Prophet], 'The Lord of Mercy lengthens [the lives] of the misguided, until, when they are confronted with what they have been warned about—either the punishment [in this life] or the Hour [of Judgement]—they realize who is worse situated and who has the weakest forces.' But God gives more guidance to those who are guided, and good deeds of lasting merit are best and most rewarding in your Lord's sight. Have you considered the man who rejects Our revelation, who says, 'I will certainly be given wealth and children'? Has he penetrated the unknown or received a pledge to that effect from the Lord of Mercy? No! We shall certainly record what he says and prolong his punishment: We shall inherit from him all that he speaks of and he will come to Us all alone.

They have taken other gods beside God to give them strength, but these gods will reject their worship and will even turn against them. Have you [Prophet] not seen how We send devils to incite the disbelievers to sin? There is no need for you to be impatient concerning them: We are counting down their [allotted] time. On the Day We gather the righteous as an honoured company before the Lord of Mercy and drive the sinful like a thirsty herd into Hell, no one will have power to intercede except for those who have permission from the Lord of Mercy.

4. In Christian tradition, an angel important as the messenger who came to Mary to announce that she would give birth to Jesus (Luke 1.26; cf. 1.19); in Islamic tradition, the messenger who delivers the Qur'an to Muhammad.

The disbelievers say, 'The Lord of Mercy has offspring.'[5] How terrible is this thing you assert: it almost causes the heavens to be torn apart, the earth to split asunder, the mountains to crumble to pieces, that they attribute offspring to the Lord of Mercy. It does not befit the Lord of Mercy [to have offspring]: there is no one in the heavens or earth who will not come to the Lord of Mercy as a servant—He has counted them all: He has numbered them exactly—and they will each return to Him on the Day of Resurrection all alone.

But the Lord of Mercy will give love to those who believe and do righteous deeds: We have made it easy, in your own language [Prophet], so that you may bring glad news to the righteous and warnings to a stubborn people. How many generations We have destroyed before them! Do you perceive a single one of them now, or hear as much as a whisper?

55. The Lord of Mercy

In the name of God, the Lord of Mercy, the Giver of Mercy

It is the Lord of Mercy who taught the Qur'an. He created man and taught him to communicate. The sun and the moon follow their calculated courses; the plants and the trees submit[1] to His designs; He has raised up the sky. He has set the balance so that you may not exceed in the balance: weigh with justice and do not fall short in the balance. He set down the Earth for His creatures, with its fruits, its palm trees with sheathed clusters, its husked grain, its fragrant plants. Which, then, of your Lord's blessings do you both deny?[2]

He created mankind out of dried clay, like pottery, the jinn out of smokeless fire. Which, then, of your Lord's blessings do you both deny?

He is Lord of the two risings and Lord of the two settings.[3] Which, then, of your Lord's blessings do you both deny?

He released the two bodies of [fresh and salt] water. They meet, yet there is a barrier between them they do not cross. Which, then, of your Lord's blessings do you both deny?

Pearls come forth from them: large ones, and small, brilliant ones. Which, then, of your Lord's blessings do you both deny?

His are the moving ships that float, high as mountains, on the sea. Which, then, of your Lord's blessings do you both deny?

Everyone on earth perishes; all that remains is the Face of your Lord, full of majesty, bestowing honour. Which, then, of your Lord's blessings do you both deny?

Everyone in heaven and earth entreats Him; every day He is at work. Which, then, of your Lord's blessings do you both deny?

We shall attend to you two huge armies [of jinn and mankind]. Which, then, of your Lord's blessings do you both deny?

---

5. A reference not to the Christian belief that Jesus is the Son of God—a view criticized elsewhere in the Qur'an—but to the belief in pre-Islamic Arabia that the angels were the daughters of God.
1. Literally, to bow down or submit (*sajada*).
2. "Both" is usually interpreted as humans and jinn (supernatural creatures also constrained by divine law).
3. The rising of the sun and the moon, or perhaps the farthest points of sunrise and sunset in summer and winter; an image of opposition and symmetry.

Jinn and mankind, if you can pass beyond the regions of heaven and earth, then do so: you will not pass without Our authority. Which, then, of your Lord's blessings do you both deny?

A flash of fire and smoke will be released upon you and no one will come to your aid. Which, then, of your Lord's blessings do you both deny?

When the sky is torn apart and turns crimson, like red hide. Which, then, of your Lord's blessings do you both deny?

On that Day neither mankind nor jinn will be asked about their sins. Which, then, of your Lord's blessings do you both deny?

The guilty will be known by their mark and will be seized by their foreheads and their feet. Which, then, of your Lord's blessings do you both deny?

This is the Hell the guilty deny, but they will go round between its flames and scalding water. Which, then, of your Lord's blessings do you both deny?

For those who fear [the time when they will] stand before their Lord there are two gardens. Which, then, of your Lord's blessings do you both deny?

With shading branches. Which, then, of your Lord's blessings do you both deny?

With a pair of flowing springs. Which, then, of your Lord's blessings do you both deny?

With every kind of fruit in pairs. Which, then, of your Lord's blessings do you both deny?

They will sit on couches upholstered with brocade, the fruit of both gardens within easy reach. Which, then, of your Lord's blessings do you both deny?

There will be maidens restraining their glances, untouched beforehand by man or jinn. Which, then, of your Lord's blessings do you both deny?

Like rubies and brilliant pearls. Which, then, of your Lord's blessings do you both deny?

Shall the reward of good be anything but good? Which, then, of your Lord's blessings do you both deny?

There are two other gardens below these two.[4] Which, then, of your Lord's blessings do you both deny?

Both of deepest green. Which, then, of your Lord's blessings do you both deny?

With a pair of gushing springs. Which, then, of your Lord's blessings do you both deny?

With fruits—date palms and pomegranate trees. Which, then, of your Lord's blessings do you both deny?

There are good-natured, beautiful maidens. Which, then, of your Lord's blessings do you both deny?

Dark-eyed, sheltered in pavilions. Which, then, of your Lord's blessings do you both deny?

Untouched beforehand by man or jinn. Which, then, of your Lord's blessings do you both deny?

They will all sit on green cushions and fine carpets. Which, then, of your Lord's blessings do you both deny? Blessed is the name of your Lord, full of majesty, bestowing honour.

---

4. The Islamic paradise has several ranks or levels, into which believers are to be placed after death according to their degree of merit; compare Dante's *Paradiso* for an adaptation of the structure of the Islamic paradise within a Christian framework.

112. Purity [of Faith]

In the name of God, the Lord of Mercy, the Giver of Mercy

Say, 'He is God the One, God the eternal.[1] He begot no one nor was He begotten. No one is comparable to Him.'

---

1. The word here translated as "eternal" (*samad*) is sometimes rendered "self-sufficient" or "self-contained."

BEOWULF
ninth century

Surviving in a single tattered manuscript, its edges burned by fire, *Beowulf* provides a startlingly vivid glimpse into the early medieval past. Written in Old English, with a vocabulary that would have seemed old-fashioned even to its very first audience, the poem recalls a heroic age in which monsters stalked men by night, dragons guarded hoards of precious gems and heirloom swords, and heroes carried out great deeds of warfare that would later be commemorated by song and feasting. The bonds of family and clan give shape to the world of Beowulf and his companions, leading sometimes to the formation of new alliances, sometimes to the violent conflict of blood feud that lasted for generations. Like much Old English poetry, the poem is fundamentally elegiac, celebrating the beauty and mourning the disappearance of a culture that, by the year 1000, had already become part of the past.

The sole surviving copy of *Beowulf* can be dated with some certainty to the years around 1000, a time of rich flowering of Anglo-Saxon literature and learning, expressed in both Old English and Anglo-Latin poetry. Yet this time was also the end of an era, just a few generations before English society would be completely transformed by the Norman Conquest of 1066. The poem thus sums up a particular form of English culture that would very soon vanish. Among the other works included in the manuscript containing *Beowulf* are saints' lives and exotic tales of the Orient: despite their varied genres, all are unified by a common theme of monsters and heroes. The three monsters of *Beowulf*—Grendel, Grendel's mother, and the dragon—and the superhuman hero who fights against them appear beside other examples of nonhuman nature, from the so-called monstrous races encountered by Alexander the Great in the extreme reaches of India to the dog-headed (or "cynocephalic") Saint Christopher. Read in this context, the poem sheds light on the nature of medieval English culture, especially on its ability to integrate pagan Germanic history within the framework of the Christian Middle Ages.

While we can date the manuscript of *Beowulf* to the years around 1000, the poem itself is almost certainly much older—a judgment based on the poem's old-fashioned vocabulary and certain genealogical allusions as well as the manuscript itself, whose copying errors suggest that a long history of transmission lies behind it. Yet the poem in its oral form is even older, drawing on a rich stock of myth and legend that was surely familiar among the northern Germanic peoples who inhabited the regions now known as Scandinavia, the Low Countries, and the British Isles. Those who read *Beowulf* or heard it recited in the eleventh century would have likely recognized allusions to ancient blood feuds and tribal clashes that are only dimly comprehensible to modern readers. The poem appears to be set in the sixth century (in particular, we can date the death of Beowulf's lord, Hygelac, to around 520), and so the story would already have seemed like ancient history to the poem's earliest hearers. To the eleventh-century reader, the events of the poem are thus doubly removed into the past. Like **Homer's** *Iliad*, whose written text codifies a much older oral form of the poem, *Beowulf* emerges as a written work of literature only at the end of generations of transmission as song.

Although we are accustomed to thinking of *Beowulf* as an "English" poem, its subject matter is not English people at all: Beowulf himself is a member of the tribe of the Geats, who live in the south of what is now Sweden, and he goes to serve in the court of Hrothgar, king of the Danes. In the period that the poem is set, England was only beginning to be settled by Germanic tribes, which had first invaded the island around 450. For the medieval English person reading the poem around 1000, therefore, the subject matter of the poem would have been at once strange and familiar—made up of persons and places that were remote in space and time from current-day England, but connected to the poem's audience by lines of heritage and descent. This simultaneous sense of strangeness and familiarity would have been heightened by *Beowulf*'s

treatment of religion. While the readers and hearers of the poem, beginning in the ninth century and almost certainly earlier, would have brought a Christian perspective to the poem, the characters clearly belong to a pre-Christian world where *wyrd* (fate) governs the events that unfold in the lives of man. Yet the text is careful to maintain ambiguity regarding the role of Christianity in the world of the poem: the monstrous Grendel is said to be one of "Cain's clan," and is thus identified as an outcast from humanity in specifically biblical terms.

Grendel is only the first of three monsters that the hero Beowulf must confront. The initial single combat against this man-beast is quickly succeeded by a similar battle—this time carried out in the watery deeps of a distant wasteland—against Grendel's mother, an even more loathsome creature. After these successes, Beowulf's heroism is acclaimed, he is richly rewarded, and he returns to his own Geatish homeland to eventually become ruler of his people. Only decades later, in that homeland, does the third episode of combat take place, which pits Beowulf against a fierce dragon guarding a buried hoard of gems and shining weapons. Once again he enters battle alone, but before the struggle ends he is aided by his kinsman and companion Wiglaf. These clashes are among the most gripping scenes of the poem. First the hero wrestles with a dreadful monster who bites through his victim's bones, drinks his blood, and swallows his flesh in great chunks, consuming him "hand and foot." The horror of the confrontation with Grendel's vengeful mother is still greater: she is a "swamp-thing from hell." In Beowulf's final monstrous encounter, the dragon "billowed and spewed" venomous fire, at once burning and poisoning his victim.

Yet Beowulf's horrific enemies are more complex than they might first appear: Grendel is both monster and man, one of the family of Cain. Like Cain himself, he is said to be "God-cursed," and his status as an outcast, cut off from the community of men, makes him seem curiously forlorn, "spurned and joyless." Although he is undoubtedly a monster, Grendel shows human emotions; he is whipped into a blind and jealous fury against those able to enjoy the bonds of family and tribe, who sleep blissfully in the communal space of Heorot's great hall. Similarly, Grendel's mother is driven not just by her monstrous nature but also by a maternal desire to avenge the death of her son—and according to the codes of Germanic tribal society, revenge was an entirely appropriate motive. Even the fight with the dragon is not cast in simple terms: when Beowulf enters his cavernous lair, it is the hero—not the monster—who is identified as the invader, and the dragon is called the "hordweard," or guardian of the hoard. Although one is a man and one is a beast, both are said to be clad in armor, the hero bearing his shield and helm, the dragon his "enameled scales." As the line that separates human from nonhuman is blurred, every violent clash, whether man against man or man against monster, is couched in terms of equivalence and balance.

As vivid as these encounters are, the poem also has an important second level, concerned with the interpersonal ties of kinship and tribe, as well as the voluntary relationship of lord and warrior. We see Beowulf take on a series of roles within this social system. He begins among the Geats as a strong fighter of somewhat marginal status as a nephew of the king, Hygelac; he then is adopted with great honor into the household of Hrothgar, king of the Danes, after defeating Grendel and his mother; and finally Beowulf becomes ruler of the Geats, when Hygelac dies without a male heir. Beowulf appears first as a warrior in the service of his lord, and later as himself a lord—in

the language of the poem, a "giver of rings" as well as one who receives them. The relationship of king and warrior is reciprocal, as the warrior provides service while his lord offers protection and distributes wealth, often in the form of armbands or neck torques ("rings"). Yet perhaps the most valuable gift that the lord grants is entrance into the community itself: in *Beowulf*, as in Old English poetry more generally, no burden is heavier than involuntary solitude. The warm bonds of fellowship nurture the warrior, and to be cut off from them is unimaginably bitter. Such isolation afflicts Grendel, as we have seen, and is memorably evoked in the poem's description of how the dragon's golden hoard came into being. It was the accumulated treasure of a long-ago people, the poet says, buried for safekeeping by the last of their line: "Death had come / and taken them all," leaving just one man "deserted and alone, lamenting his unhappiness / day and night." For the despairing survivor, there is "No trembling harp, / no tuned timber, no tumbling hawk / swerving through the hall." Bereft of the joys of the hall, the only man left alive can do little more than mourn as he waits for death.

The hall offers both the most secure and stable environment that a warrior can possibly inhabit and the culture's greatest point of vulnerability. Beowulf is given the opportunity to display his heroic nature in combat with Grendel because of the need to defend Heorot, the great hall of Hrothgar: the accursed monster has been sneaking into the hall by night, seizing and devouring warriors one by one. The threat is not simply to the lives of Hrothgar's men but to the very basis of the community, as the Danish warriors are reduced to fearful individuals, each concerned for his own life. The great hall of Heorot is a place of communal gathering and feasting, of goodwill and social bonds, where oaths of loyalty are sworn and golden rings are distributed, where heroic deeds are sung and the genealogies of kings recounted. Yet this idyllic space, representing the unity of the king and his people, is only temporary, for the danger posed to Heorot is not erased by the death of Grendel: other threats are darkly foreshadowed in the poem through allusions to the fate of the Danes after Hrothgar's reign ended. For the poem's medieval audiences, these passing references brought to mind the full story of the tragic downfall of Hrothgar's house and the burning of Heorot.

Swords and other weaponry appear throughout the poem, not just as tools of the warfare that punctuates the narrative at regular intervals but as a kind of social glue that links the community of warriors both in the present and across time and space. As treasures are shared, kings disburse weapons along with golden rings, items that are as precious for their ability to create interpersonal connections as for their physical material. Hrothgar's queen, Wealhtheow, rewards Beowulf with a golden collar that marks a new bond of affinity between the Geatish hero and the ruling house of the Danes, accompanying the sumptuous gift with the request that Beowulf do his best to support her young son in the future. The ring thus carries both material and social value, marking a bond of loyalty between persons and groups. Similarly, Hrothgar later rewards Beowulf with magnificent armor, which Beowulf goes on to deliver to his own Geatish lord, Hygelac, just as he also gives to Hygelac's queen, Hygd, the neck ring bestowed on him by Wealhtheow. Beowulf's gifts unite the Danes and the Geats and thereby redouble his own honor. And the connections formed by heirloom weapons can extend far into the past. As Beowulf prepares to battle Grendel's mother, the Danish warrior Unferth lends him "a rare and ancient sword," and he in turn leaves his own weapon, a "sharp-honed, wave-sheened wonder-blade," with the Dane, who may keep it if he fails to return. In the muddy pool where Beowulf defeats Grendel's mother, he finds another blade, whose gold hilt is inscribed with "rune-markings" telling the name of the one "for whom the sword had first been made." This sword, "from the days of the giants," passes through time, wielded by men and by monsters, until it finally comes into the hands of Beowulf, who in turn delivers its remnants to the Danish king Hrothgar. The chain of descent confers glory on the hero, and unites the community of warriors across the ages.

Each of these three ancient swords is described as an heirloom or "ealde lafe": literally, an "old thing that is left," a remainder of past glory. The weapon is thus an instrument of warfare and a symbol of continuity, linking past, present, and future as successive men bear it. Such work of commemoration suffuses the poem, perhaps nowhere more movingly than in the songs of heroes that punctuate the communal celebrations and feasting held in Heorot. Like the "ealde lafe," the heroic song recalls figures of the past and makes them live again as the warriors listen and join in the imagined community of the tribal nation and the symbolic space of the hall. After the defeat of Grendel, Hrothgar's minstrel sings a song of the Frisian king Finn and his Danish wife Hildeburh. The story is tragic, telling of the feud that destroyed their family, but the shared experience of the minstrel's music and tale brings Hrothgar's court together—a sense of community reawakened, perhaps, for the medieval audiences who heard *Beowulf* performed for them.

The translation here, by Seamus Heaney, seeks to reproduce the rhythmic quality of the Old English line—made up of two half-lines, each containing two beats. Coupled with the alliteration (repeated initial consonant sounds) that is prevalent in Old English poetry, the line produces a strong sense of rhythm, a recurrent thrumming sound that gives the poem its songlike quality, impossible to ignore even in written form. To give a clearer sense of the sound of the original work, reproduced below are the closing lines (2262–69) of the lament of the last survivor, who long ago buried the hoard of treasure guarded by the dragon that is Beowulf's last and most dangerous enemy. Below these lines is a very literal, rhythmic translation that conveys the lines' aural quality more emphatically than does Heaney's version.

BEOWULF, LINES 2262–69

gomen gleobeames,
geond sæl swingeð,
burhstede beateð.
fela feorhcynna
Swa giomormod
an æfter eallum,
dæges ond nihtes,
hran æt heortan.

"Næs hearpan wyn,
ne god hafoc
ne se swifta mearh
Bealocwealm hafað
forð onsended."
giohtho mænde,
unbliðe hwearf
oððæt deades wylm

that joyful singing wood,
shoot through the hall,
beat his feet in the yard.
sent out of this world
So, sad in spirit,
one left after all were gone,
through both day and night,
touched his heart.

"There is no delight in the harp,
nor does the fine hawk
nor does the swift steed
Baleful death has
too many of our kind."
he lamented his loss,
unhappily went on
until death's wave

(trans. Suzanne Akbari)

TRIBES AND GENEALOGIES

1. The Danes (Bright-, Half-, Ring-, Spear-, North-, East-, South-, West-Danes; Shieldings, Honor-, Victor-, War-Shieldings: Ing's friends).

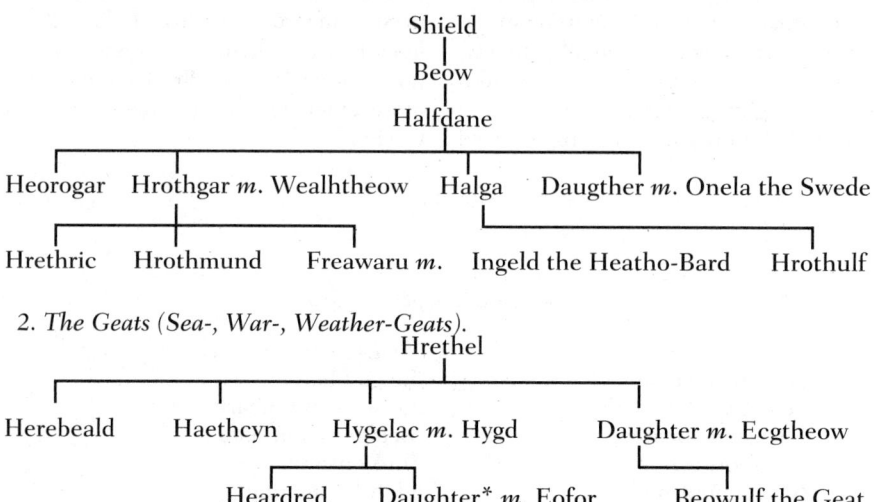

2. The Geats (Sea-, War-, Weather-Geats).

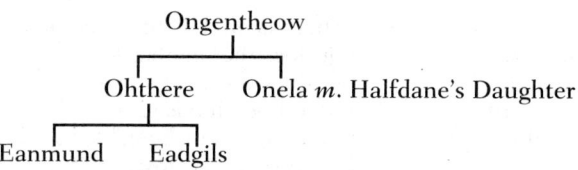

3. The Swedes

Ongentheow

Ohthere   Onela *m.* Halfdane's Daughter

Eanmund   Eadgils

*The daughter of Hygelac who was given to Eofor may have been born to him by a former wife, older than Hygd.

4. Miscellaneous.

A. The Half-Danes (also called Shieldings) involved in the fight at Finnsburg may represent a different tribe from the Danes described above. Their king Hoc had a son, Hnaef, who succeeded him, and a daughter Hildeburh, who married Finn, king of the Jutes.

B. The Jutes, or Frisians, are represented as enemies of the Danes in the fight at Finnsburg and as allies of the Franks at the time Hygelac the Geat made the attack in which he lost his life and from which Beowulf swam home. Also allied with the Franks at this time were the Hetware.

C. The Heatho-Bards (i.e., "Battle-Bards") are represented as inveterate enemies of the Danes. Their king Froda had been killed in an attack on the Danes, and Hrothgar's attempt to make peace with them by marrying his daughter Freawaru to Froda's son Ingeld failed when the latter attacked Heorot. The attack was repulsed, although Heorot was burned.

Beowulf[1]

[Prologue: The Rise of the Danish Nation]

So. The Spear-Danes in days gone by
and the kings who ruled them had courage and greatness.
We have heard of those princes' heroic campaigns.

There was Shield Sheafson,[2] scourge of many tribes,
a wrecker of mead-benches, rampaging among foes.   5
This terror of the hall-troops had come far.
A foundling to start with, he would flourish later on
as his powers waxed and his worth was proved.
In the end each clan on the outlying coasts
beyond the whale-road had to yield to him   10
and begin to pay tribute. That was one good king.

Afterward a boy-child was born to Shield,
a cub in the yard, a comfort sent
by God to that nation. He knew what they had tholed,[3]
the long times and troubles they'd come through   15
without a leader; so the Lord of Life,
the glorious Almighty, made this man renowned.
Shield had fathered a famous son:
Beow's name was known through the north.
And a young prince must be prudent like that,   20
giving freely while his father lives
so that afterward in age when fighting starts
steadfast companions will stand by him
and hold the line. Behavior that's admired
is the path to power among people everywhere.   25

Shield was still thriving when his time came
and he crossed over into the Lord's keeping.
His warrior band did what he bade them
when he laid down the law among the Danes:
they shouldered him out to the sea's flood,   30
the chief they revered who had long ruled them.
A ring-whorled prow rode in the harbor,
ice-clad, outbound, a craft for a prince.
They stretched their beloved lord in his boat,
laid out by the mast, amidships,   35
the great ring-giver. Far-fetched treasures
were piled upon him, and precious gear.
I never heard before of a ship so well furbished
with battle-tackle, bladed weapons
and coats of mail. The massed treasure   40
was loaded on top of him: it would travel far
on out into the ocean's sway.
They decked his body no less bountifully

---

1. Translated by Seamus Heaney.
2. Translates *Scyld Scefing*, which probably means "son of Sheaf." Scyld's origins are mysterious.
3. An Anglo-Saxon word that means "suf-
fered, endured" and that survives in the trans-
lator's native land of Northern Ireland. In using this word, he maintains an alliterative pattern similar to the original ("that . . . they . . . tholed").

with offerings than those first ones did
who cast him away when he was a child   45
and launched him alone out over the waves.[4]
And they set a gold standard up
high above his head and let him drift
to wind and tide, bewailing him
and mourning their loss. No man can tell,   50
no wise man in hall or weathered veteran
knows for certain who salvaged that load.
    Then it fell to Beow to keep the forts.
He was well regarded and ruled the Danes
for a long time after his father took leave   55
of his life on earth. And then his heir,
the great Halfdane, held sway
for as long as he lived, their elder and warlord.
He was four times a father, this fighter prince:
one by one they entered the world,   60
Heorogar, Hrothgar, the good Halga,
and a daughter,[5] I have heard, who was Onela's queen,
a balm in bed to the battle-scarred Swede.
    The fortunes of war favored Hrothgar.
Friends and kinsmen flocked to his ranks,   65
young followers, a force that grew
to be a mighty army. So his mind turned
to hall-building: he handed down orders
for men to work on a great mead-hall
meant to be a wonder of the world forever;   70
it would be his throne-room and there he would dispense
his God-given goods to young and old—
but not the common land or people's lives.[6]
Far and wide through the world, I have heard,
orders for work to adorn that wallstead   75
were sent to many peoples. And soon it stood there
finished and ready, in full view,
the hall of halls. Heorot[7] was the name
he had settled on it, whose utterance was law.
Nor did he renege, but doled out rings   80
and torques[8] at the table. The hall towered,
its gables wide and high and awaiting
a barbarous burning.[9] That doom abided,
but in time it would come: the killer instinct
unleashed among in-laws, the blood-lust rampant.   85

---

4. Since Shield arrived with nothing, this sentence is a litotes or understatement, a characteristic of the laconic style of old Germanic poetry.
5. The text is faulty here, and the name of Halfdane's daughter has been lost. Halfdane: according to another source, Halfdane's mother was Swedish; hence his name.
6. Apparently, slaves, along with pastureland used by all, were not in the king's power to give away.
7. That is, "hart," a symbol of royalty.
8. Golden bands worn around the neck.
9. The destruction by fire of Heorot—when the Heatho-Bard Ingeld attacked his father-in-law, Hrothgar—occurred at a later time than that of the poem's action. For a more detailed account of this feud and of Hrothgar's hope that it could be settled by the marriage of his daughter to Ingeld, see lines 2020–69.

[Heorot Is Attacked]

Then a powerful demon, a prowler through the dark,
nursed a hard grievance. It harrowed him
to hear the din of the loud banquet
every day in the hall, the harp being struck
and the clear song of a skilled poet   90
telling with mastery of man's beginnings,
how the Almighty had made the earth
a gleaming plain girdled with waters;
in His splendor He set the sun and the moon
to be earth's lamplight, lanterns for men,   95
and filled the broad lap of the world
with branches and leaves; and quickened life
in every other thing that moved.
    So times were pleasant for the people there
until finally one, a fiend out of hell,   100
began to work his evil in the world.
Grendel was the name of this grim demon
haunting the marches, marauding round the heath
and the desolate fens; he had dwelt for a time
in misery among the banished monsters,   105
Cain's clan, whom the Creator had outlawed
and condemned as outcasts.[1] For the killing of Abel
the Eternal Lord had exacted a price:
Cain got no good from committing that murder
because the Almighty made him anathema   110
and out of the curse of his exile there sprang
ogres and elves and evil phantoms
and the giants too who strove with God
time and again until He gave them their reward.[2]
    So, after nightfall, Grendel set out   115
for the lofty house, to see how the Ring-Danes
were settling into it after their drink,
and there he came upon them, a company of the best
asleep from their feasting, insensible to pain
and human sorrow. Suddenly then   120
the God-cursed brute was creating havoc:
greedy and grim, he grabbed thirty men
from their resting places and rushed to his lair,
flushed up and inflamed from the raid,
blundering back with the butchered corpses.   125
    Then as dawn brightened and the day broke,
Grendel's powers of destruction were plain:
their wassail was over, they wept to heaven
and mourned under morning. Their mighty prince,
the storied leader, sat stricken and helpless,   130
humiliated by the loss of his guard,

1. Genesis 4.9–12.
2. The poet is thinking here of Genesis 6.2–8, where the Latin Bible in use at the time refers to giants mating with women who were understood to be the descendants of Cain and thereby creating the wicked race that God destroyed with the flood.

bewildered and stunned, staring aghast
at the demon's trail, in deep distress.
He was numb with grief, but got no respite — *Bjou olf* 135
for one night later merciless Grendel
struck again with more gruesome murders.
Malignant by nature, he never showed remorse.
It was easy then to meet with a man
shifting himself to a safer distance
to bed in the bothies,³ for who could be blind 140
to the evidence of his eyes, the obviousness
of the hall-watcher's hate? Whoever escaped
kept a weather-eye open and moved away.
　So Grendel ruled in defiance of right,
one against all, until the greatest house 145
in the world stood empty, a deserted wallstead.
For twelve winters, seasons of woe,
the lord of the Shieldings⁴ suffered under
his load of sorrow; and so, before long,
the news was known over the whole world. 150
Sad lays were sung about the beset king,
the vicious raids and ravages of Grendel,
his long and unrelenting feud,
nothing but war; how he would never
parley or make peace with any Dane 155
nor stop his death-dealing nor pay the death-price.⁵
No counselor could ever expect
fair reparation from those rabid hands.
All were endangered; young and old
were hunted down by that dark death-shadow 160
who lurked and swooped in the long nights
on the misty moors; nobody knows
where these reavers from hell roam on their errands.
　So Grendel waged his lonely war,
inflicting constant cruelties on the people, 165
atrocious hurt. He took over Heorot,
haunted the glittering hall after dark,
but the throne itself, the treasure-seat,
he was kept from approaching; he was the Lord's outcast.
　These were hard times, heartbreaking 170
for the prince of the Shieldings; powerful counselors,
the highest in the land, would lend advice,
plotting how best the bold defenders
might resist and beat off sudden attacks.
Sometimes at pagan shrines they vowed 175
offerings to idols, swore oaths
that the killer of souls might come to their aid

---

3. Outlying buildings; the word is current in Northern Ireland.
4. Hrothgar; as descendants of Shield, the Danes are called Shieldings.

5. According to Germanic law, a slayer could achieve peace with his victim's kinsmen only by paying them *wergild* ("man-price") as compensation for the slain man.

and save the people.[6] That was their way,
their heathenish hope; deep in their hearts
they remembered hell. The Almighty Judge   180
of good deeds and bad, the Lord God,
Head of the Heavens and High King of the World,
was unknown to them. Oh, cursed is he
who in time of trouble has to thrust his soul
in the fire's embrace, forfeiting help;   185
he has nowhere to turn. But blessed is he
who after death can approach the Lord
and find friendship in the Father's embrace.

[The Hero Comes to Heorot]

So that troubled time continued, woe
that never stopped, steady affliction   190
for Halfdane's son, too hard an ordeal.
There was panic after dark, people endured
raids in the night, riven by the terror.
    When he heard about Grendel, Hygelac's thane
was on home ground, over in Geatland.   195
There was no one else like him alive.
In his day, he was the mightiest man on earth,
highborn and powerful. He ordered a boat
that would ply the waves. He announced his plan:
to sail the swan's road[7] and seek out that king,   200
the famous prince who needed defenders.
Nobody tried to keep him from going,
no elder denied him, dear as he was to them.
Instead, they inspected omens and spurred
his ambition to go, whilst he moved about   205
like the leader he was, enlisting men,
the best he could find; with fourteen others
the warrior boarded the boat as captain,
a canny pilot along coast and currents.
    Time went by, the boat was on water,   210
in close under the cliffs.
Men climbed eagerly up the gangplank,
sand churned in surf, warriors loaded
a cargo of weapons, shining war-gear
in the vessel's hold, then heaved out,   215
away with a will in their wood-wreathed ship.
Over the waves, with the wind behind her
and foam at her neck, she flew like a bird
until her curved prow had covered the distance,

---

6. The poet interprets the heathen gods to whom the Danes make offerings as different incarnations of Satan. Naturally, the pagan Danes do not think of their gods in these biblical terms, but as the poet makes clear in the following lines, they have no other recourse.
7. That is, the sea. This is an example of a "kenning," a metaphoric phrase that is used to describe a common object. These kennings are very common throughout Anglo-Saxon poetry. See, for another instance, line 258, where the poet describes a man's capacity for speech as his "word-hoard."

and on the following day, at the due hour,   220
those seafarers sighted land,
sunlit cliffs, sheer crags
and looming headlands, the landfall they sought.
It was the end of their voyage and the Geats vaulted
over the side, out on to the sand,   225
and moored their ship. There was a clash of mail
and a thresh of gear. They thanked God
for that easy crossing on a calm sea.
    When the watchman on the wall, the Shieldings' lookout
whose job it was to guard the sea-cliffs,   230
saw shields glittering on the gangplank
and battle-equipment being unloaded
he had to find out who and what
the arrivals were. So he rode to the shore,
this horseman of Hrothgar's, and challenged them   235
in formal terms, flourishing his spear:
"What kind of men are you who arrive
rigged out for combat in your coats of mail,
sailing here over the sea-lanes
in your steep-hulled boat? I have been stationed   240
as lookout on this coast for a long time.
My job is to watch the waves for raiders,
any danger to the Danish shore.
Never before has a force under arms
disembarked so openly—not bothering to ask   245
if the sentries allowed them safe passage
or the clan had consented. Nor have I seen
a mightier man-at-arms on this earth
than the one standing here: unless I am mistaken,
he is truly noble. This is no mere   250
hanger-on in a hero's armor.
So now, before you fare inland
as interlopers, I have to be informed
about who you are and where you hail from.
Outsiders from across the water,   255
I say it again: the sooner you tell
where you come from and why, the better."
    The leader of the troop unlocked his word-hoard;
the distinguished one delivered this answer:
"We belong by birth to the Geat people   260
and owe allegiance to Lord Hygelac.
In his day, my father was a famous man,
a noble warrior-lord named Ecgtheow.
He outlasted many a long winter
and went on his way. All over the world   265
men wise in counsel continue to remember him.
We come in good faith to find your lord
and nation's shield, the son of Halfdane.
Give us the right advice and direction.
We have arrived here on a great errand   270
to the lord of the Danes, and I believe therefore

there should be nothing hidden or withheld between us.
So tell us if what we have heard is true
about this threat, whatever it is,
this danger abroad in the dark nights,   275
this corpse-maker mongering death
in the Shieldings' country. I come to proffer
my wholehearted help and counsel.
I can show the wise Hrothgar a way
to defeat his enemy and find respite—   280
if any respite is to reach him, ever.
I can calm the turmoil and terror in his mind.
Otherwise, he must endure woes
and live with grief for as long as his hall
stands at the horizon on its high ground."   285
    Undaunted, sitting astride his horse,
the coast-guard answered: "Anyone with gumption
and a sharp mind will take the measure
of two things: what's said and what's done.
I believe what you have told me, that you are a troop   290
loyal to our king. So come ahead
with your arms and your gear, and I will guide you.
What's more, I'll order my own comrades
on their word of honor to watch your boat
down there on the strand—keep her safe   295
in her fresh tar, until the time comes
for her curved prow to preen on the waves
and bear this hero back to Geatland.
May one so valiant and venturesome
come unharmed through the clash of battle."   300
    So they went on their way. The ship rode the water,
broad-beamed, bound by its hawser
and anchored fast. Boar-shapes[8] flashed
above their cheek-guards, the brightly forged
work of goldsmiths, watching over   305
those stern-faced men. They marched in step,
hurrying on till the timbered hall
rose before them, radiant with gold.
Nobody on earth knew of another
building like it. Majesty lodged there,   310
its light shone over many lands.
So their gallant escort guided them
to that dazzling stronghold and indicated
the shortest way to it; then the noble warrior
wheeled on his horse and spoke these words: 315
"It is time for me to go. May the Almighty
Father keep you and in His kindness
watch over your exploits. I'm away to the sea,
back on alert against enemy raiders."
    It was a paved track, a path that kept them   320

---

8. Images of boars—a cult animal among the Germanic tribes and sacred to the god Freyr—were fixed atop helmets in the belief that they would provide protection from enemy blows.

in marching order. Their mail-shirts glinted,
hard and hand-linked; the high-gloss iron
of their armor rang. So they duly arrived
in their grim war-graith⁹ and gear at the hall,
and, weary from the sea, stacked wide shields   325
of the toughest hardwood against the wall,
then collapsed on the benches; battle-dress
and weapons clashed. They collected their spears
in a seafarers' stook,¹ a stand of grayish
tapering ash. And the troops themselves   330
were as good as their weapons.
                            Then a proud warrior
questioned the men concerning their origins:
"Where do you come from, carrying these
decorated shields and shirts of mail,
these cheek-hinged helmets and javelins?   335
I am Hrothgar's herald and officer.
I have never seen so impressive or large
an assembly of strangers. Stoutness of heart,
bravery not banishment, must have brought you to Hrothgar."
    The man whose name was known for courage,   340
the Geat leader, resolute in his helmet,
answered in return: "We are retainers
from Hygelac's band. Beowulf is my name.
If your lord and master, the most renowned
son of Halfdane, will hear me out   345
and graciously allow me to greet him in person,
I am ready and willing to report my errand."
    Wulfgar replied, a Wendel² chief
renowned as a warrior, well known for his wisdom
and the temper of his mind: "I will take this message,   350
in accordance with your wish, to our noble king,
our dear lord, friend of the Danes,
the giver of rings. I will go and ask him
about your coming here, then hurry back
with whatever reply it pleases him to give."   355
    With that he turned to where Hrothgar sat,
an old man among retainers;
the valiant follower stood foursquare
in front of his king: he knew the courtesies.
Wulfgar addressed his dear lord: 360
"People from Geatland have put ashore.
They have sailed far over the wide sea.
They call the chief in charge of their band
by the name of Beowulf. They beg, my lord,
an audience with you, exchange of words   365
and formal greeting. Most gracious Hrothgar,

---

9. "Graith" is an archaic word for equipment
or armor.
1. An archaic word for a pile or mass.
2. The Wendels or Vandals are another Ger-

manic nation; it is not unusual for people to
be members of nations different from the ones
in which they reside. Hence Beowulf himself
is both a Geat and a Waegmunding.

do not refuse them, but grant them a reply.
From their arms and appointment, they appear well born
and worthy of respect, especially the one
who has led them this far: he is formidable indeed." 370
    Hrothgar, protector of Shieldings, replied:
"I used to know him when he was a young boy.
His father before him was called Ecgtheow.
Hrethel the Geat³ gave Ecgtheow
his daughter in marriage. This man is their son, 375
here to follow up an old friendship.
A crew of seamen who sailed for me once
with a gift-cargo across to Geatland
returned with marvelous tales about him:
a thane,⁴ they declared, with the strength of thirty 380
in the grip of each hand. Now Holy God
has, in His goodness, guided him here
to the West-Danes, to defend us from Grendel.
This is my hope; and for his heroism
I will recompense him with a rich treasure. 385
Go immediately, bid him and the Geats
he has in attendance to assemble and enter.
Say, moreover, when you speak to them,
they are welcome to Denmark."
                        At the door of the hall,
Wulfgar duly delivered the message: 390
"My lord, the conquering king of the Danes,
bids me announce that he knows your ancestry;
also that he welcomes you here to Heorot
and salutes your arrival from across the sea.
You are free now to move forward 395
to meet Hrothgar in helmets and armor,
but shields must stay here and spears be stacked
until the outcome of the audience is clear."
    The hero arose, surrounded closely
by his powerful thanes. A party remained 400
under orders to keep watch on the arms:
the rest proceeded, led by their prince
under Heorot's roof. And standing on the hearth
in webbed links that the smith had woven,
the fine-forged mesh of his gleaming mail-shirt, 405
resolute in his helmet, Beowulf spoke:
"Greetings to Hrothgar. I am Hygelac's kinsman,
one of his hall-troop. When I was younger,
I had great triumphs. Then news of Grendel,
hard to ignore, reached me at home: 410
sailors brought stories of the plight you suffer
in this legendary hall, how it lies deserted,

---

3. The leader of the Geats prior to his son Hygelac, who is the current leader. Note that Ecgtheow's marriage to Hrethel's daughter makes

Beowulf part of the royal line.
4. That is, a warrior in the service of a lord
like Hrethel or Hrothgar himself.

empty and useless once the evening light
hides itself under heaven's dome.
So every elder and experienced councilman   415
among my people supported my resolve
to come here to you, King Hrothgar,
because all knew of my awesome strength.
They had seen me boltered[5] in the blood of enemies
when I battled and bound five beasts,   420
raided a troll-nest and in the night-sea
slaughtered sea-brutes. I have suffered extremes
and avenged the Geats (their enemies brought it
upon themselves; I devastated them).
Now I mean to be a match for Grendel,   425
settle the outcome in single combat.
And so, my request, O king of Bright-Danes,
dear prince of the Shieldings, friend of the people
and their ring of defense, my one request
is that you won't refuse me, who have come this far,   430
the privilege of purifying Heorot,
with my own men to help me, and nobody else.
I have heard moreover that the monster scorns
in his reckless way to use weapons;
therefore, to heighten Hygelac's fame   435
and gladden his heart, I hereby renounce
sword and the shelter of the broad shield,
the heavy war-board: hand-to-hand
is how it will be, a life-and-death
fight with the fiend. Whichever one death fells   440
must deem it a just judgment by God.
If Grendel wins, it will be a gruesome day;
he will glut himself on the Geats in the war-hall,
swoop without fear on that flower of manhood
as on others before. Then my face won't be there   445
to be covered in death: he will carry me away
as he goes to ground, gorged and bloodied;
he will run gloating with my raw corpse
and feed on it alone, in a cruel frenzy
fouling his moor-nest. No need then   450
to lament for long or lay out my body:
if the battle takes me, send back
this breast-webbing that Weland[6] fashioned
and Hrethel gave me, to Lord Hygelac.
Fate goes ever as fate must."   455
   Hrothgar, the helmet of Shieldings, spoke:
"Beowulf, my friend, you have traveled here
to favor us with help and to fight for us.
There was a feud one time, begun by your father.
With his own hands he had killed Heatholaf   460
who was a Wulfing;[7] so war was looming

---

5. Clotted, sticky—a Northern Irish term.   7. The Wulfings are another Germanic nation.
6. The blacksmith of the Norse gods.

and his people, in fear of it, forced him to leave.
He came away then over rolling waves
to the South-Danes here, the sons of honor.
I was then in the first flush of kingship,   465
establishing my sway over the rich strongholds
of this heroic land. Heorogar,
my older brother and the better man,
also a son of Halfdane's, had died.
Finally I healed the feud by paying: 470
I shipped a treasure-trove to the Wulfings,
and Ecgtheow acknowledged me with oaths of allegiance.

    "It bothers me to have to burden anyone
with all the grief that Grendel has caused
and the havoc he has wreaked upon us in Heorot,   475
our humiliations. My household-guard
are on the wane, fate sweeps them away
into Grendel's clutches—but God can easily
halt these raids and harrowing attacks!

    "Time and again, when the goblets passed   480
and seasoned fighters got flushed with beer
they would pledge themselves to protect Heorot
and wait for Grendel with their whetted swords.
But when dawn broke and day crept in
over each empty, blood-spattered bench,   485
the floor of the mead-hall where they had feasted
would be slick with slaughter. And so they died,
faithful retainers, and my following dwindled.
Now take your place at the table, relish
the triumph of heroes to your heart's content."   490

[Feast at Heorot]

    Then a bench was cleared in that banquet hall
so the Geats could have room to be together
and the party sat, proud in their bearing,
strong and stalwart. An attendant stood by
with a decorated pitcher, pouring bright   495
helpings of mead. And the minstrel sang,
filling Heorot with his head-clearing voice,
gladdening that great rally of Geats and Danes.

    From where he crouched at the king's feet,
Unferth, a son of Ecglaf's, spoke   500
contrary words.[8] Beowulf's coming,
his sea-braving, made him sick with envy:
he could not brook or abide the fact
that anyone else alive under heaven
might enjoy greater regard than he did: 505
"Are you the Beowulf who took on Breca

8. Unferth is Hrothgar's *thyle*, a kind of
licensed spokesman who here engages Beowulf
in a traditional "flytting" or verbal combat; see
the note to line 1457. Ecglaf appears in the
poem only as the father of Unferth.

in a swimming match[9] on the open sea,
risking the water just to prove that you could win?
It was sheer vanity made you venture out
on the main deep. And no matter who tried,   510
friend or foe, to deflect the pair of you,
neither would back down: the sea-test obsessed you.
You waded in, embracing water,
taking its measure, mastering currents,
riding on the swell. The ocean swayed,   515
winter went wild in the waves, but you vied
for seven nights; and then he outswam you,
came ashore the stronger contender.
He was cast up safe and sound one morning
among the Heatho-Reams,[1] then made his way   520
to where he belonged in Bronding[2] country,
home again, sure of his ground
in strongroom and bawn.[3] So Breca made good
his boast upon you and was proved right.
No matter, therefore, how you may have fared   525
in every bout and battle until now,
this time you'll be worsted; no one has ever
outlasted an entire night against Grendel."
    Beowulf, Ecgtheow's son, replied:
"Well, friend Unferth, you have had your say   530
about Breca and me. But it was mostly beer
that was doing the talking. The truth is this:
when the going was heavy in those high waves,
I was the strongest swimmer of all.
We'd been children together and we grew up   535
daring ourselves to outdo each other,
boasting and urging each other to risk
our lives on the sea. And so it turned out.
Each of us swam holding a sword,
a naked, hard-proofed blade for protection   540
against the whale-beasts. But Breca could never
move out farther or faster from me
than I could manage to move from him.
Shoulder to shoulder, we struggled on
for five nights, until the long flow   545
and pitch of the waves, the perishing cold,
night falling and winds from the north
drove us apart. The deep boiled up
and its wallowing sent the sea-brutes wild.
My armor helped me to hold out;   550
my hard-ringed chain-mail, hand-forged and linked,
a fine, close-fitting filigree of gold,

---

9. The original Anglo-Saxon describing this contest can be interpreted in such a way that Breca and Beowulf are competing not in swimming but in rowing, which is more plausible.
1. A people of southern Norway.
2. The Brondings are the nation to which Breca belonged, but nothing is known of their territory.
3. Fortified outwork of a court or castle. The word was used by English planters in Ulster to describe fortified dwellings they erected on lands confiscated from the Irish [translator's note].

kept me safe when some ocean creature
pulled me to the bottom. Pinioned fast
and swathed in its grip, I was granted one   555
final chance: my sword plunged
and the ordeal was over. Through my own hands,
the fury of battle had finished off the sea-beast.
    "Time and again, foul things attacked me,
lurking and stalking, but I lashed out,   560
gave as good as I got with my sword.
My flesh was not for feasting on,
there would be no monsters gnawing and gloating
over their banquet at the bottom of the sea.
Instead, in the morning, mangled and sleeping   565
the sleep of the sword, they slopped and floated
like the ocean's leavings. From now on
sailors would be safe, the deep-sea raids
were over for good. Light came from the east,
bright guarantee of God, and the waves   570
went quiet; I could see headlands
and buffeted cliffs. Often, for undaunted courage,
fate spares the man it has not already marked.
However it occurred, my sword had killed
nine sea-monsters. Such night dangers   575
and hard ordeals I have never heard of
nor of a man more desolate in surging waves.
But worn out as I was, I survived,
came through with my life. The ocean lifted
and laid me ashore, I landed safe   580
on the coast of Finland.
                         Now I cannot recall
any fight you entered, Unferth,
that bears comparison. I don't boast when I say
that neither you nor Breca were ever much
celebrated for swordsmanship   585
or for facing danger on the field of battle.
You killed your own kith and kin,
so for all your cleverness and quick tongue,
you will suffer damnation in the depths of hell.[4]
The fact is, Unferth, if you were truly   590
as keen or courageous as you claim to be
Grendel would never have got away with
such unchecked atrocity, attacks on your king,
havoc in Heorot and horrors everywhere.
But he knows he need never be in dread   595
of your blade making a mizzle[5] of his blood
or of vengeance arriving ever from this quarter—
from the Victory-Shieldings, the shoulderers of the spear.
He knows he can trample down you Danes
to his heart's content, humiliate and murder   600

4. The manuscript is damaged here, and the   translation of the line.
word "hell" may well be "hall": "You will suffer   5. That is, drizzle.
condemnation in the hall" is an acceptable

without fear of reprisal. But he will find me different.
I will show him how Geats shape to kill
in the heat of battle. Then whoever wants to
may go bravely to mead,[6] when the morning light
scarfed in sun-dazzle, shines forth from th   605
and brings another daybreak to
    Then the gray-haired
far-famed in battle,
and keeper of his pe
on the warrior's stead   610
So the laughter started
and the crowd was hap
Hrothgar's queen, obse
Adorned in her gold, she
the men in the hall, then
first to Hrothgar, their ho
urging him to drink deep a
because he was dear to the
like the warlord he was, with
So the Helming woman went
queenly and dignified, decked
offering the goblet to all ranks,
treating the household and the
until it was Beowulf's turn to ta
With measured words she welco   625
and thanked God for granting her
that a deliverer she could believe in would arrive
to ease their afflictions. He accepted the cup,
a daunting man, dangerous in action
and eager for it always. He addressed Wealhtheow;   630
Beowulf, son of Ecgtheow, said:
"I had a fixed purpose when I put to sea.
As I sat in the boat with my band of men,
I meant to perform to the uttermost
what your people wanted or perish in the attempt,   635
in the fiend's clutches. And I shall fulfill that purpose,
prove myself with a proud deed
or meet my death here in the mead-hall."
This formal boast by Beowulf the Geat
pleased the lady well and she went to sit   640
by Hrothgar, regal and arrayed with gold.
    Then it was like old times in the echoing hall,
proud talk and the people happy,
loud and excited; until soon enough
Halfdane's heir had to be away   645
to his night's rest. He realized
that the demon was going to descend on the hall,
that he had plotted all day, from dawn-light

6. An alcoholic drink made by fermenting honey and adding water.

until darkness gathered again over the world
and stealthy night-shapes came stealing forth   650
under the cloud-murk. The company stood
as the two leaders took leave of each other:
Hrothgar wished Beowulf health and good luck,
named him hall-warden and announced as follows:
"Never, since my hand could hold a shield   655
have I entrusted or given control
of the Danes' hall to anyone but you.
Ward and guard it, for it is the greatest of houses.
Be on your mettle now, keep in mind your fame,
beware of the enemy. There's nothing you wish for   660
that won't be yours if you win through alive."

[The Fight with Grendel]

    Hrothgar departed then with his house-guard.
The lord of the Shieldings, their shelter in war,
left the mead-hall to lie with Wealhtheow,
his queen and bedmate. The King of Glory   665
(as people learned) had posted a lookout
who was a match for Grendel, a guard against monsters,
special protection to the Danish prince.
And the Geat placed complete trust
in his strength of limb and the Lord's favor.   670
    He began to remove his iron breast-mail,
took off the helmet and handed his attendant
the patterned sword, a smith's masterpiece,
ordering him to keep the equipment guarded.
And before he bedded down, Beowulf,   675
that prince of goodness, proudly asserted:
"When it comes to fighting, I count myself
as dangerous any day as Grendel.
So it won't be a cutting edge I'll wield
to mow him down, easily as I might.   680
He has no idea of the arts of war,
of shield or sword-play, although he does possess
a wild strength. No weapons, therefore,
for either this night: unarmed he shall face me
if face me he dares. And may the Divine Lord   685
in His wisdom grant the glory of victory
to whichever side He sees fit."
    Then down the brave man lay with his bolster
under his head and his whole company
of sea-rovers at rest beside him.   690
None of them expected he would ever see
his homeland again or get back
to his native place and the people who reared him.
They knew too well the way it was before,
how often the Danes had fallen prey   695
to death in the mead-hall. But the Lord was weaving

a victory on His war-loom for the Weather-Geats.
Through the strength of one they all prevailed;
they would crush their enemy and come through
in triumph and gladness. The truth is clear: 700
Almighty God rules over mankind
and always has.
               Then out of the night
came the shadow-stalker, stealthy and swift.
The hall-guards were slack, asleep at their posts,
all except one; it was widely understood   705
that as long as God disallowed it,
the fiend could not bear them to his shadow-bourne.
One man, however, was in fighting mood,
awake and on edge, spoiling for action.
    In off the moors, down through the mist-bands   710
God-cursed Grendel came greedily loping.
The bane of the race of men roamed forth,
hunting for a prey in the high hall.
Under the cloud-murk he moved toward it
until it shone above him, a sheer keep   715
of fortified gold. Nor was that the first time
he had scouted the grounds of Hrothgar's dwelling—
although never in his life, before or since,
did he find harder fortune or hall-defenders.
Spurned and joyless, he journeyed on ahead   720
and arrived at the bawn. The iron-braced door
turned on its hinge when his hands touched it.
Then his rage boiled over, he ripped open
the mouth of the building, maddening for blood,
pacing the length of the patterned floor   725
with his loathsome tread, while a baleful light,
flame more than light, flared from his eyes.
He saw many men in the mansion, sleeping,
a ranked company of kinsmen and warriors
quartered together. And his glee was demonic,   730
picturing the mayhem: before morning
he would rip life from limb and devour them,
feed on their flesh; but his fate that night
was due to change, his days of ravening
had come to an end.   735
              Mighty and canny,
Hygelac's kinsman was keenly watching
for the first move the monster would make.
Nor did the creature keep him waiting
but struck suddenly and started in;
he grabbed and mauled a man on his bench,   740
bit into his bone-lappings,[7] bolted down his blood
and gorged on him in lumps, leaving the body

---

7. That is, joints.

utterly lifeless, eaten up
hand and foot. Venturing closer,
his talon was raised to attack Beowulf   745
where he lay on the bed, he was bearing in
with open claw when the alert hero's
comeback and armlock forestalled him utterly.
The captain of evil discovered himself
in a handgrip harder than anything   750
he had ever encountered in any man
on the face of the earth. Every bone in his body
quailed and recoiled, but he could not escape.
He was desperate to flee to his den and hide
with the devil's litter, for in all his days   755
he had never been clamped or cornered like this.
Then Hygelac's trusty retainer recalled
his bedtime speech, sprang to his feet
and got a firm hold. Fingers were bursting,
the monster back-tracking, the man overpowering.   760
The dread of the land was desperate to escape,
to take a roundabout road and flee
to his lair in the fens. The latching power
in his fingers weakened; it was the worst trip
the terror-monger had taken to Heorot.   765
And now the timbers trembled and sang,
a hall-session[8] that harrowed every Dane
inside the stockade: stumbling in fury,
the two contenders crashed through the building.
The hall clattered and hammered, but somehow   770
survived the onslaught and kept standing:
it was handsomely structured, a sturdy frame
braced with the best of blacksmith's work
inside and out. The story goes
that as the pair struggled, mead-benches were smashed   775
and sprung off the floor, gold fittings and all.
Before then, no Shielding elder would believe
there was any power or person upon earth
capable of wrecking their horn-rigged hall
unless the burning embrace of a fire   780
engulf it in flame. Then an extraordinary
wail arose, and bewildering fear
came over the Danes. Everyone felt it
who heard that cry as it echoed off the wall,
a God-cursed scream and strain of catastrophe,   785
the howl of the loser, the lament of the hell-serf
keening his wound. He was overwhelmed,

8. In Hiberno-English the word "session" (*seissiún* in Irish) can mean a gathering where musicians and singers perform for their own enjoyment [translator's note]. In other words, the poet is making a laconic joke, since the main function of the hall is celebration and singing.

manacled tight by the man who of all men
was foremost and strongest in the days of this life.
    But the earl-troop's leader was not inclined   790
to allow his caller to depart alive:
he did not consider that life of much account
to anyone anywhere. Time and again,
Beowulf's warriors worked to defend
their lord's life, laying about them   795
as best they could, with their ancestral blades.
Stalwart in action, they kept striking out
on every side, seeking to cut
straight to the soul. When they joined the struggle
there was something they could not have known at the time,   800
that no blade on earth, no blacksmith's art
could ever damage their demon opponent.
He had conjured the harm from the cutting edge
of every weapon.[9] But his going away
out of this world and the days of his life   805
would be agony to him, and his alien spirit
would travel far into fiends' keeping.
    Then he who had harrowed the hearts of men
with pain and affliction in former times
and had given offense also to God   810
found that his bodily powers failed him.
Hygelac's kinsman kept him helplessly
locked in a handgrip. As long as either lived,
he was hateful to the other. The monster's whole
body was in pain; a tremendous wound   815
appeared on his shoulder. Sinews split
and the bone-lappings burst. Beowulf was granted
the glory of winning; Grendel was driven
under the fen-banks, fatally hurt,
to his desolate lair. His days were numbered,   820
the end of his life was coming over him,
he knew it for certain; and one bloody clash
had fulfilled the dearest wishes of the Danes.
The man who had lately landed among them,
proud and sure, had purged the hall,   825
kept it from harm; he was happy with his nightwork
and the courage he had shown. The Geat captain
had boldly fulfilled his boast to the Danes:
he had healed and relieved a huge distress,
unremitting humiliations,   830
the hard fate they'd been forced to undergo,
no small affliction. Clear proof of this
could be seen in the hand the hero displayed
high up near the roof: the whole of Grendel's
shoulder and arm, his awesome grasp.   835

9. Grendel is magically protected from weapons.

[Celebration at Heorot]

Then morning came and many a warrior
gathered, as I've heard, around the gift-hall,
clan-chiefs flocking from far and near
down wide-ranging roads, wondering greatly
at the monster's footprints. His fatal departure   840
was regretted by no one who witnessed his trail,
the ignominious marks of his flight
where he'd skulked away, exhausted in spirit
and beaten in battle, bloodying the path,
hauling his doom to the demons' mere.[1]   845
The bloodshot water wallowed and surged,
there were loathsome upthrows and overturnings
of waves and gore and wound-slurry.
With his death upon him, he had dived deep
into his marsh-den, drowned out his life   850
and his heathen soul: hell claimed him there.

  Then away they rode, the old retainers
with many a young man following after,
a troop on horseback, in high spirits
on their bay steeds. Beowulf's doings   855
were praised over and over again.
Nowhere, they said, north or south
between the two seas or under the tall sky
on the broad earth was there anyone better
to raise a shield or to rule a kingdom.   860
Yet there was no laying of blame on their lord,
the noble Hrothgar; he was a good king.

  At times the war-band broke into a gallop,
letting their chestnut horses race
wherever they found the going good   865
on those well-known tracks. Meanwhile, a thane
of the king's household, a carrier of tales,
a traditional singer deeply schooled
in the lore of the past, linked a new theme
to a strict meter.[2] The man started   870
to recite with skill, rehearsing Beowulf's
triumphs and feats in well-fashioned lines,
entwining his words.
                      He told what he'd heard
repeated in songs about Sigemund's exploits,[3]
all of those many feats and marvels,   875
the struggles and wanderings of Waels's son,
things unknown to anyone

---

1. A lake or pool.
2. The singer or *scop* composes extemporaneously in alliterative verse.
3. According to Norse legend, Sigemund, the son of Waels (or Volsung, as he is known in Norse), slept with his sister Sigurth, who bore a son named Fitela; Fitela was thus also

Sigemund's nephew, as he is described here. The singer here contrasts Sigemund's bravery in killing a dragon with the defeat of the Danish king Heremod, who could not protect his people. For more on Heremod as a bad king, see lines 1709–22.

except to Fitela, feuds and foul doings
confided by uncle to nephew when he felt
the urge to speak of them: always they had been 880
partners in the fight, friends in need.
They killed giants, their conquering swords
had brought them down.

After his death
Sigemund's glory   grew and grew
because of his courage   when he killed the dragon, 885
the guardian of the hoard.   Under gray stone
he had dared to enter   all by himself
to face the worst   without Fitela.
But it came to pass   that his sword plunged
right through   those radiant scales 890
and drove into the wall.   The dragon died of it.
His daring had given him   total possession
of the treasure-hoard,   his to dispose of
however he liked.   He loaded a boat:
Waels's son   weighted her hold 895
with dazzling spoils.   The hot dragon melted.
  Sigemund's name   was known everywhere.
He was utterly valiant   and venturesome,
a fence round his fighters   and flourished therefore
after King Heremod's   prowess declined 900
and his campaigns slowed down.   The king was betrayed,
ambushed in Jutland,   overpowered
and done away with.   The waves of his grief
had beaten him down,   made him a burden,
a source of anxiety   to his own nobles: 905
that expedition   was often condemned
in those earlier times   by experienced men,
men who relied   on his lordship for redress,
who presumed that the part   of a prince was to thrive
on his father's throne   and defend the nation, 910
the Shielding land   where they lived and belonged,
its holdings and strongholds.   Such was Beowulf
in the affection of his friends   and of everyone alive.
But evil entered   into Heremod.
  Meanwhile, the Danes kept racing their mounts 915
down sandy lanes. The light of day
broke and kept brightening. Bands of retainers
galloped in excitement to the gabled hall
to see the marvel; and the king himself,
guardian of the ring-hoard, goodness in person, 920
walked in majesty from the women's quarters
with a numerous train, attended by his queen
and her crowd of maidens, across to the mead-hall.
  When Hrothgar arrived at the hall, he spoke,
standing on the steps, under the steep eaves, 925
gazing toward the roofwork and Grendel's talon:
"First and foremost, let the Almighty Father

be thanked for this sight. I suffered a long
harrowing by Grendel. But the Heavenly Shepherd
can work His wonders always and everywhere.   930
Not long since, it seemed I would never
be granted the slightest solace or relief
from any of my burdens: the best of houses
glittered and reeked and ran with blood.
This one worry outweighed all others—   935
a constant distress to counselors entrusted
with defending the people's forts from assault
by monsters and demons. But now a man,
with the Lord's assistance, has accomplished something
none of us could manage before now   940
for all our efforts. Whoever she was
who brought forth this flower of manhood,
if she is still alive, that woman can say
that in her labor the Lord of Ages
bestowed a grace on her. So now, Beowulf,   945
I adopt you in my heart as a dear son.
Nourish and maintain this new connection,
you noblest of men; there'll be nothing you'll want for,
no worldly goods that won't be yours.
I have often honored smaller achievements,   950
recognized warriors not nearly as worthy,
lavished rewards on the less deserving.
But you have made yourself immortal
by your glorious action. May the God of Ages
continue to keep and requite you well."   955
    Beowulf, son of Ecgtheow, spoke:
"We have gone through with a glorious endeavor
and been much favored in this fight we dared
against the unknown. Nevertheless,
if you could have seen the monster himself   960
where he lay beaten, I would have been better pleased.
My plan was to pounce, pin him down
in a tight grip and grapple him to death—
have him panting for life, powerless and clasped
in my bare hands, his body in thrall.   965
But I couldn't stop him from slipping my hold.
The Lord allowed it, my lock on him
wasn't strong enough; he struggled fiercely
and broke and ran. Yet he bought his freedom
at a high price, for he left his hand   970
and arm and shoulder to show he had been here,
a cold comfort for having come among us.
And now he won't be long for this world.
He has done his worst but the wound will end him.
He is hasped and hooped and hirpling⁴ with pain,   975

---

4. That is, limping.

limping and looped in it. Like a man outlawed
for wickedness, he must await
the mighty judgment of God in majesty."

There was less tampering and big talk then
from Unferth the boaster, less of his blather   980
as the hall-thanes eyed the awful proof
of the hero's prowess, the splayed hand
up under the eaves. Every nail,
claw-scale and spur, every spike
and welt on the hand of that heathen brute   985
was like barbed steel. Everybody said
there was no honed iron hard enough
to pierce him through, no time-proofed blade
that could cut his brutal, blood-caked claw.

Then the order was given for all hands   990
to help to refurbish Heorot immediately:
men and women thronging the wine-hall,
getting it ready. Gold thread shone
in the wall-hangings, woven scenes
that attracted and held the eye's attention.   995
But iron-braced as the inside of it had been,
that bright room lay in ruins now.
The very doors had been dragged from their hinges.
Only the roof remained unscathed
by the time the guilt-fouled fiend turned tail   1000
in despair of his life. But death is not easily
escaped from by anyone:
all of us with souls, earth-dwellers
and children of men, must make our way
to a destination already ordained   1005
where the body, after the banqueting,
sleeps on its deathbed.
                                 Then the due time arrived
for Halfdane's son to proceed to the hall.
The king himself would sit down to feast.
No group ever gathered in greater numbers   1010
or better order around their ring-giver.
The benches filled with famous men
who fell to with relish; round upon round
of mead was passed; those powerful kinsmen,
Hrothgar and Hrothulf, were in high spirits   1015
in the raftered hall. Inside Heorot
there was nothing but friendship. The Shielding nation
was not yet familiar with feud and betrayal.[5]

Then Halfdane's son presented Beowulf

---

5. The poet here refers to the later history of
the Danes, when after Hrothgar's death his
nephew Hrothulf drove his son Hrethric from
the throne. For Wealhtheow's fear that this
betrayal will indeed come to pass, see lines
1168–90.

with a gold standard as a victory gift,   1020
an embroidered banner; also breast-mail
and a helmet; and a sword carried high,
that was both precious object and token of honor.
So Beowulf drank his drink, at ease;
it was hardly a shame to be showered with such gifts   1025
in front of the hall-troops. There haven't been many
moments, I am sure, when men exchanged
four such treasures at so friendly a sitting.
An embossed ridge, a band lapped with wire
arched over the helmet: head-protection   1030
to keep the keen-ground cutting edge
from damaging it when danger threatened
and the man was battling behind his shield.
Next the king ordered eight horses
with gold bridles to be brought through the yard   1035
into the hall. The harness of one
included a saddle of sumptuous design,
the battle-seat where the son of Halfdane
rode when he wished to join the sword-play:
wherever the killing and carnage were the worst,   1040
he would be to the fore, fighting hard.
Then the Danish prince, descendant of Ing,[6]
handed over both the arms and the horses,
urging Beowulf to use them well.
And so their leader, the lord and guard   1045
of coffer and strongroom, with customary grace
bestowed upon Beowulf both sets of gifts.
A fair witness can see how well each one behaved.
   The chieftain went on to reward the others:
each man on the bench who had sailed with Beowulf   1050
and risked the voyage received a bounty,
some treasured possession. And compensation,
a price in gold, was settled for the Geat
Grendel had cruelly killed earlier—
as he would have killed more, had not mindful God   1055
and one man's daring prevented that doom
Past and present, God's will prevails.
Hence, understanding is always best
and a prudent mind. Whoever remains
for long here in this earthly life   1060
will enjoy and endure more than enough.
   They sang then and played to please the hero,
words and music for their warrior prince,
harp tunes and tales of adventure:
there were high times on the hall benches,   1065
and the king's poet performed his part
with the saga of Finn and his sons, unfolding

6. A Germanic deity and the protector of the Danes.

the tale of the fierce attack in Friesland
where Hnaef, king of the Danes, met death.[7]

Hildeburh
            had little cause 1070
to credit the Jutes:
            son and brother,
she lost them both
            on the battlefield.
She, bereft
            and blameless, they
foredoomed, cut down
            and spear-gored. She,
the woman in shock,
            waylaid by grief, 1075
Hoc's daughter—
            how could she not
lament her fate
            when morning came
and the light broke
            on her murdered dears?
And so farewell
            delight on earth,
war carried away
            Finn's troop of thanes 1080
all but a few.
            How then could Finn
hold the line
            or fight on
to the end with Hengest,
            how save
the rump of his force
            from that enemy chief?
So a truce was offered
            as follows: first 1085
separate quarters
            to be cleared for the Danes,
hall and throne
            to be shared with the Frisians.
Then, second:
            every day
at the dole-out of gifts
            Finn, son of Focwald,

---

7. This song recounts the fight at Finnsburg between the Dane Hengest and the Jute (or Frisian) Finn. The poet begins with the bereft Hildeburh, daughter of the Danish king Hoc and wife of the Jute Finn, whose unnamed son and brother Hnaef have already been killed in the first battle with Finn. He then tells how Hengest, the new leader of the Danes, is offered a truce by the weakened Finn, how together they cremate their dead, following which Hengest and the remaining Danes spend the winter with Finn and the Jutes. But with the coming of spring, the feud breaks out again and Finn and the Jutes are slaughtered by Hengest with the help of two other Danes, Guthlaf and Oslaf.

should honor the Danes,
                bestow with an even   1090
hand to Hengest
                and Hengest's men
the wrought-gold rings,
                bounty to match
the measure he gave
                his own Frisians—
to keep morale
                in the beer-hall high.
Both sides then
                sealed their agreement.   1095
With oaths to Hengest
                Finn swore
openly, solemnly,
                that the battle survivors
would be guaranteed
                honor and status.
No infringement
                by word or deed,
no provocation
                would be permitted.   1100
Their own ring-giver
                after all
was dead and gone,
                they were leaderless,
in forced allegiance
                to his murderer.
So if any Frisian
                stirred up bad blood
with insinuations
                or taunts about this,   1105
the blade of the sword
                would arbitrate it.
A funeral pyre
                was then prepared,
effulgent gold
                brought out from the hoard.
The pride and prince
                of the Shieldings lay
awaiting the flame.
                Everywhere   1110
there were blood-plastered
                coats of mail.
The pyre was heaped
                with boar-shaped helmets
forged in gold,
                with the gashed corpses
of wellborn Danes—
                many had fallen.
Then Hildeburh

     ordered her own   1115
son's body
      be burnt with Hnaef's
the flesh on his bones
       to sputter and blaze
beside his uncle's.
     The woman wailed
and sang keens,
     the warrior went up.[8]
Carcass flame
     swirled and fumed,   1120
they stood round the burial
       mound and howled
as heads melted,
     crusted gashes
spattered and ran
     bloody matter.
The glutton element
      flamed and consumed
the dead of both sides.
      Their great days were gone.   1125
Warriors scattered
     to homes and forts
all over Friesland,
     fewer now, feeling
loss of friends.
     Hengest stayed,
lived out that whole
     resentful, blood-sullen
winter with Finn,
     homesick and helpless.   1130
No ring-whorled prow
     could up then
and away on the sea.
     Wind and water
raged with storms,
     wave and shingle
were shackled in ice
     until another year
appeared in the yard
     as it does to this day,   1135
the seasons constant,
     the wonder of light
coming over us.
     Then winter was gone,
earth's lap grew lovely,
     longing woke
in the cooped-up exile

---

8. The warrior (Hildeburh's son) either goes up on the pyre or goes up in smoke. "Keens": an Irish word for funeral laments.

    for a voyage home—
but more for vengeance,
     some way of bringing   1140
things to a head:
    his sword arm hankered
to greet the Jutes.
    So he did not balk
*once Hunlafing*⁹
    placed on his lap
Dazzle-the-Duel,
    the best sword of all,
whose edges Jutes
    knew only too well.   1145
Thus blood was spilled,
    the gallant Finn
slain in his home
    *after Guthlaf and Oslaf*¹
back from their voyage
    made old accusation:
the brutal ambush,
    the fate they had suffered,
all blamed on Finn.
    The wildness in them   1150
had to brim over.
    The hall ran red
with blood of enemies.
    Finn was cut down,
the queen brought away
    and everything
the Shieldings could find
    inside Finn's walls—
the Frisian king's
    gold collars and gemstones—   1155
swept off to the ship.
    Over sea-lanes then
back to Daneland
    the warrior troop
bore that lady home.

The poem was over,
the poet had performed, a pleasant murmur
started on the benches, stewards did the rounds   1160
with wine in splendid jugs, and Wealhtheow came to sit
in her gold crown between two good men,
uncle and nephew, each one of whom
still trusted the other;² and the forthright Unferth,

---

9. A Danish follower of Hengest.
1. Danes who seem to have gone home in order to bring reinforcements to Hengest. But it is possible that these two have been with Hengest all along and that "their voyage" is an unrelated journey.
2. See p. 912, n. 5.

admired by all for his mind and courage   1165
although under a cloud for killing his brothers,
reclined near the king.
                        The queen spoke:
"Enjoy this drink, my most generous lord;
raise up your goblet, entertain the Geats
duly and gently, discourse with them,   1170
be open-handed, happy and fond.
Relish their company, but recollect as well
all of the boons that have been bestowed on you.
The bright court of Heorot has been cleansed
and now the word is that you want to adopt   1175
this warrior as a son. So, while you may,
bask in your fortune, and then bequeath
kingdom and nation to your kith and kin,
before your decease. I am certain of Hrothulf.
He is noble and will use the young ones well.   1180
He will not let you down. Should you die before him,
he will treat our children truly and fairly.
He will honor, I am sure, our two sons,
repay them in kind, when he recollects
all the good things we gave him once,   1185
the favor and respect he found in his childhood."
She turned then to the bench where her boys sat,
Hrethric and Hrothmund, with other nobles' sons,
all the youth together; and that good man,
Beowulf the Geat, sat between the brothers.   1190
    The cup was carried to him, kind words
spoken in welcome and a wealth of wrought gold
graciously bestowed: two arm bangles,
a mail-shirt and rings, and the most resplendent
torque of gold I ever heard tell of   1195
anywhere on earth or under heaven.
There was no hoard like it since Hama snatched
the Brosings' neck-chain and bore it away
with its gems and settings to his shining fort,
away from Eormenric's wiles and hatred,   1200
and thereby ensured his eternal reward.³
Hygelac the Geat, grandson of Swerting,
wore this neck-ring on his last raid;⁴
at bay under his banner, he defended the booty,
treasure he had won. Fate swept him away   1205
because of his proud need to provoke
a feud with the Frisians. He fell beneath his shield,
in the same gem-crusted, kingly gear

3. The legend alluded to here seems to be that Hama stole the golden necklace of the Brosings from Eormenric (a historical figure, the king of the Ostrogoths, who died ca. 375), and then gave it to the goddess Freya.

4. The poet here refers to the death of Hygelac while raiding the Frisian territory of the Franks. This raid and Hygelac's death are recorded by the historian Gregory of Tours (d. 594) as having taken place about 520.

he had worn when he crossed the frothing wave-vat.
So the dead king fell into Frankish hands.   1210
They took his breast-mail, also his neck-torque,
and punier warriors plundered the slain
when the carnage ended; Geat corpses
covered the field.
                    Applause filled the hall.
Then Wealhtheow pronounced in the presence of the company: 1215
"Take delight in this torque, dear Beowulf,
wear it for luck and wear also this mail
from our people's armory: may you prosper in them!
Be acclaimed for strength, for kindly guidance
to these two boys, and your bounty will be sure.   1220
You have won renown: you are known to all men
far and near, now and forever.
Your sway is wide as the wind's home,
as the sea around cliffs. And so, my prince,
I wish you a lifetime's luck and blessings   1225
to enjoy this treasure. Treat my sons
with tender care, be strong and kind.
Here each comrade is true to the other,
loyal to lord, loving in spirit.
The thanes have one purpose, the people are ready: 1230
having drunk and pledged, the ranks do as I bid."
   She moved then to her place. Men were drinking wine
at that rare feast; how could they know fate,
the grim shape of things to come,
the threat looming over many thanes   1235
as night approached and King Hrothgar prepared
to retire to his quarters? Retainers in great numbers
were posted on guard as so often in the past.
Benches were pushed back, bedding gear and bolsters
spread across the floor, and one man   1240
lay down to his rest, already marked for death.
At their heads they placed their polished timber
battle-shields; and on the bench above them,
each man's kit was kept to hand:
a towering war-helmet, webbed mail-shirt   1245
and great-shafted spear. It was their habit
always and everywhere to be ready for action,
at home or in the camp, in whatever case
and at whatever time the need arose
to rally round their lord. They were a right people.   1250

[Another Attack]

   They went to sleep. And one paid dearly
for his night's ease, as had happened to them often,
ever since Grendel occupied the gold-hall,
committing evil until the end came,
death after his crimes. Then it became clear,   1255

obvious to everyone once the fight was over,
that an avenger lurked and was still alive,
grimly biding time. Grendel's mother,
monstrous hell-bride, brooded on her wrongs.
She had been forced down into fearful waters,   1260
the cold depths, after Cain had killed
his father's son, felled his own
brother with a sword. Branded an outlaw,
marked by having murdered, he moved into the wilds,
shunned company and joy. And from Cain there sprang   1265
misbegotten spirits, among them Grendel,
the banished and accursed, due to come to grips
with that watcher in Heorot waiting to do battle.
The monster wrenched and wrestled with him,
but Beowulf was mindful of his mighty strength,   1270
the wondrous gifts God had showered on him:
he relied for help on the Lord of All,
on His care and favor. So he overcame the foe,
brought down the hell-brute. Broken and bowed,
outcast from all sweetness, the enemy of mankind   1275
made for his death-den. But now his mother
had sallied forth on a savage journey,
grief-racked and ravenous, desperate for revenge.
    She came to Heorot. There, inside the hall,
Danes lay asleep, earls who would soon endure   1280
a great reversal, once Grendel's mother
attacked and entered. Her onslaught was less
only by as much as an amazon warrior's
strength is less than an armed man's
when the hefted sword, its hammered edge   1285
and gleaming blade slathered in blood,
razes the sturdy boar-ridge off a helmet.
Then in the hall, hard-honed swords
were grabbed from the bench, many a broad shield
lifted and braced; there was little thought of helmets   1290
or woven mail when they woke in terror.
    The hell-dam was in panic, desperate to get out,
in mortal terror the moment she was found.
She had pounced and taken one of the retainers
in a tight hold, then headed for the fen.   1295
To Hrothgar, this man was the most beloved
of the friends he trusted between the two seas.
She had done away with a great warrior,
ambushed him at rest.
                          Beowulf was elsewhere.
Earlier, after the award of the treasure,   1300
the Geat had been given another lodging.
    There was uproar in Heorot. She had snatched their trophy,
Grendel's bloodied hand. It was a fresh blow
to the afflicted bawn. The bargain was hard,

both parties having to pay   1305
with the lives of friends. And the old lord,
the gray-haired warrior, was heartsore and weary
when he heard the news: his highest-placed adviser,
his dearest companion, was dead and gone.
    Beowulf was quickly brought to the chamber: 1310
the winner of fights, the arch-warrior,
came first-footing in with his fellow troops
to where the king in his wisdom waited,
still wondering whether Almighty God
would ever turn the tide of his misfortunes.   1315
So Beowulf entered with his band in attendance
and the wooden floorboards banged and rang
as he advanced, hurrying to address
the prince of the Ingwins,[5] asking if he'd rested
since the urgent summons had come as a surprise.   1320
    Then Hrothgar, the Shieldings' helmet, spoke:
"Rest? What is rest? Sorrow has returned.
Alas for the Danes! Aeschere is dead.
He was Yrmenlaf's elder brother
and a soul-mate to me, a true mentor,   1325
my right-hand man when the ranks clashed
and our boar-crests had to take a battering
in the line of action. Aeschere was everything
the world admires in a wise man and a friend.
Then this roaming killer came in a fury   1330
and slaughtered him in Heorot. Where she is hiding,
glutting on the corpse and glorying in her escape,
I cannot tell; she has taken up the feud
because of last night, when you killed Grendel,
wrestled and racked him in ruinous combat   1335
since for too long he had terrorized us
with his depredations. He died in battle,
paid with his life; and now this powerful
other one arrives, this force for evil
driven to avenge her kinsman's death.   1340
Or so it seems to thanes in their grief,
in the anguish every thane endures
at the loss of a ring-giver, now that the hand
that bestowed so richly has been stilled in death.
    "I have heard it said by my people in hall,   1345
counselors who live in the upland country,
that they have seen two such creatures
prowling the moors, huge marauders
from some other world. One of these things,
as far as anyone ever can discern,   1350
looks like a woman; the other, warped
in the shape of a man, moves beyond the pale

5. The friends of the god Ing—that is, the Danes. See p. 913, n. 6.

bigger than any man, an unnatural birth
called Grendel by the country people
in former days. They are fatherless creatures, 1355
and their whole ancestry is hidden in a past
of demons and ghosts.[6] They dwell apart
among wolves on the hills, on windswept crags
and treacherous keshes, where cold streams
pour down the mountain and disappear 1360
under mist and moorland.

                A few miles from here
a frost-stiffened wood waits and keeps watch
above a mere; the overhanging bank
is a maze of tree-roots mirrored in its surface.
At night there, something uncanny happens: 1365
the water burns. And the mere bottom
has never been sounded by the sons of men.
On its bank, the heather-stepper halts:
the hart in flight from pursuing hounds
will turn to face them with firm-set horns 1370
and die in the wood rather than dive
beneath its surface. That is no good place.
When wind blows up and stormy weather
makes clouds scud and the skies weep,
out of its depths a dirty surge 1375
is pitched toward the heavens. Now help depends
again on you and on you alone.
The gap of danger where the demon waits
is still unknown to you. Seek it if you dare.
I will compensate you for settling the feud 1380
as I did the last time with lavish wealth,
coffers of coiled gold, if you come back."

[Beowulf Fights Grendel's Mother]

Beowulf, son of Ecgtheow, spoke:
"Wise sir, do not grieve. It is always better
to avenge dear ones than to indulge in mourning. 1385
For every one of us, living in this world
means waiting for our end. Let whoever can
win glory before death. When a warrior is gone,
that will be his best and only bulwark.
So arise, my lord, and let us immediately 1390
set forth on the trail of this troll-dam.
I guarantee you: she will not get away,
not to dens under ground nor upland groves
nor the ocean floor. She'll have nowhere to flee to.
Endure your troubles today. Bear up 1395
and be the man I expect you to be."

6. Note that Hrothgar doesn't know of the biblical genealogy of Grendel and his mother that the
poet has given us in lines 102–14.

With that the old lord sprang to his feet
and praised God for Beowulf's pledge.
Then a bit and halter were brought for his horse
with the plaited mane. The wise king mounted   1400
the royal saddle and rode out in style
with a force of shield-bearers. The forest paths
were marked all over with the monster's tracks,
her trail on the ground wherever she had gone
across the dark moors, dragging away   1405
the body of that thane, Hrothgar's best
counselor and overseer of the country.
So the noble prince proceeded undismayed
up fells and screes, along narrow footpaths
and ways where they were forced into single file,   1410
ledges on cliffs above lairs of water-monsters.
He went in front with a few men,
good judges of the lie of the land,
and suddenly discovered the dismal wood,
mountain trees growing out at an angle   1415
above gray stones: the bloodshot water
surged underneath. It was a sore blow
to all of the Danes, friends of the Shieldings,
a hurt to each and every one
of that noble company when they came upon   1420
Aeschere's head at the foot of the cliff.
   Everybody gazed as the hot gore
kept wallowing up and an urgent war-horn
repeated its notes: the whole party
sat down to watch. The water was infested   1425
with all kinds of reptiles. There were writhing sea-dragons
and monsters slouching on slopes by the cliff,
serpents and wild things such as those that often
surface at dawn to roam the sail-road
and doom the voyage. Down they plunged,   1430
lashing in anger at the loud call
of the battle-bugle. An arrow from the bow
of the Geat chief got one of them
as he surged to the surface: the seasoned shaft
stuck deep in his flank and his freedom in the water   1435
got less and less. It was his last swim.
He was swiftly overwhelmed in the shallows,
prodded by barbed boar-spears,
cornered, beaten, pulled up on the bank,
a strange lake-birth, a loathsome catch   1440
men gazed at in awe.
                    Beowulf got ready,
donned his war-gear, indifferent to death;
his mighty, hand-forged, fine-webbed mail
would soon meet with the menace underwater.
It would keep the bone-cage of his body safe: 1445

no enemy's clasp could crush him in it,
no vicious armlock choke his life out.
To guard his head he had a glittering helmet
that was due to be muddied on the mere bottom
and blurred in the upswirl. It was of beaten gold,   1450
princely headgear hooped and hasped
by a weapon-smith who had worked wonders
in days gone by and adorned it with boar-shapes;
since then it had resisted every sword.
And another item lent by Unferth   1455
at that moment of need was of no small importance:
the brehon[7] handed him a hilted weapon,
a rare and ancient sword named Hrunting.
The iron blade with its ill-boding patterns
had been tempered in blood. It had never failed   1460
the hand of anyone who hefted it in battle,
anyone who had fought and faced the worst
in the gap of danger. This was not the first time
it had been called to perform heroic feats.
    When he lent that blade to the better swordsman,   1465
Unferth, the strong-built son of Ecglaf,
could hardly have remembered the ranting speech
he had made in his cups. He was not man enough
to face the turmoil of a fight under water
and the risk to his life. So there he lost   1470
fame and repute. It was different for the other
rigged out in his gear, ready to do battle.
    Beowulf, son of Ecgtheow, spoke:
"Wisest of kings, now that I have come
to the point of action, I ask you to recall   1475
what we said earlier: that you, son of Halfdane
and gold-friend to retainers, that you, if I should fall
and suffer death while serving your cause,
would act like a father to me afterward.
If this combat kills me, take care   1480
of my young company, my comrades in arms.
And be sure also, my beloved Hrothgar,
to send Hygelac the treasures I received.
Let the lord of the Geats gaze on that gold,
let Hrethel's son take note of it and see   1485
that I found a ring-giver of rare magnificence
and enjoyed the good of his generosity.
And Unferth is to have what I inherited:
to that far-famed man I bequeath my own
sharp-honed, wave-sheened wonder-blade.   1490
With Hrunting I shall gain glory or die."
    After these words, the prince of the Weather-Geats

7. One of an ancient class of lawyers in Ireland [translator's note]. The word is used to translate
the Anglo-Saxon *thyle*.

was impatient to be away and plunged suddenly:
without more ado, he dived into the heaving
depths of the lake. It was the best part of a day   *swims to Bottom*   1495
before he could see the solid bottom.
   Quickly the one who haunted those waters,
who had scavenged and gone her gluttonous rounds
for a hundred seasons, sensed a human
observing her outlandish lair from above.   1500
So she lunged and clutched and managed to catch him
in her brutal grip; but his body, for all that,
remained unscathed: the mesh of the chain-mail
saved him on the outside. Her savage talons
failed to rip the web of his war-shirt.   1505
Then once she touched bottom, that wolfish swimmer
carried the ring-mailed prince to her court
so that for all his courage he could never use
the weapons he carried; and a bewildering horde
came at him from the depths, droves of sea-beasts   1510
who attacked with tusks and tore at his chain-mail
in a ghastly onslaught. The gallant man
could see he had entered some hellish turn-hole
and yet the water there did not work against him
because the hall-roofing held off   1515
the force of the current; then he saw firelight,
a gleam and flare-up, a glimmer of brightness.
   The hero observed that swamp-thing from hell,
the tarn-hag[8] in all her terrible strength,
then heaved his war-sword and swung his arm: 1520
the decorated blade came down ringing
and singing on her head. But he soon found
his battle-torch extinguished; the shining blade
refused to bite. It spared her and failed
the man in his need. It had gone through many   1525
a hand-to-hand fight, had hewed the armor
and helmets of the doomed, but here at last
the fabulous powers of that heirloom failed.
   Hygelac's kinsman kept thinking about
his name and fame: he never lost heart.   1530
Then, in a fury, he flung his sword away.
The keen, inlaid, worm-loop-patterned steel
was hurled to the ground: he would have to rely
on the might of his arm. So must a man do
who intends to gain enduring glory   1535
in a combat. Life doesn't cost him a thought.
Then the prince of War-Geats, warming to this fight
with Grendel's mother, gripped her shoulder
and laid about him in a battle frenzy:
he pitched his killer opponent to the floor   1540

8. A "tarn" is a small lake.

but she rose quickly and retaliated,
grappled him tightly in her grim embrace.
The sure-footed fighter felt daunted,
the strongest of warriors stumbled and fell.
So she pounced upon him and pulled out   1545
a broad, whetted knife: now she would avenge
her only child. But the mesh of chain-mail
on Beowulf's shoulder shielded his life,
turned the edge and tip of the blade.
The son of Ecgtheow would have surely perished   1550
and the Geats lost their warrior under the wide earth
had the strong links and locks of his war-gear
not helped to save him: holy God
decided the victory. It was easy for the Lord,
the Ruler of Heaven, to redress the balance   1555
once Beowulf got back up on his feet.
          Then he saw a blade that boded well,
a sword in her armory, an ancient heirloom
from the days of the giants, an ideal weapon,
one that any warrior would envy,   1560
but so huge and heavy of itself
only Beowulf could wield it in a battle.
So the Shieldings' hero hard-pressed and enraged,
took a firm hold of the hilt and swung
the blade in an arc, a resolute blow   1565
that bit deep into her neck-bone
and severed it entirely, toppling the doomed
house of her flesh; she fell to the floor.
The sword dripped blood, the swordsman was elated.
    A light appeared and the place brightened   1570
the way the sky does when heaven's candle
is shining clearly. He inspected the vault:
with sword held high, its hilt raised
to guard and threaten, Hygelac's thane
scouted by the wall in Grendel's wake.   1575
Now the weapon was to prove its worth.
The warrior determined to take revenge
for every gross act Grendel had committed—
and not only for that one occasion
when he'd come to slaughter the sleeping troops,   1580
fifteen of Hrothgar's house-guards
surprised on their benches and ruthlessly devoured,
and as many again carried away,
a brutal plunder. Beowulf in his fury
now settled that score: he saw the monster   1585
in his resting place, war-weary and wrecked,
a lifeless corpse, a casualty
of the battle in Heorot. The body gaped
at the stroke dealt to it after death:
Beowulf cut the corpse's head off.   1590
    Immediately the counselors keeping a lookout
with Hrothgar, watching the lake water,

saw a heave-up and surge of waves
and blood in the backwash. They bowed gray heads,
spoke in their sage, experienced way   1595
about the good warrior, how they never again
expected to see that prince returning
in triumph to their king. It was clear to many
that the wolf of the deep had destroyed him forever.
    The ninth hour of the day arrived.   1600
The brave Shieldings abandoned the cliff-top
and the king went home; but sick at heart,
staring at the mere, the strangers held on.
They wished, without hope, to behold their lord,
Beowulf himself.
                    Meanwhile, the sword   1605
began to wilt into gory icicles
to slather and thaw. It was a wonderful thing,
the way it all melted as ice melts
when the Father eases the fetters off the frost
and unravels the water-ropes, He who wields power   1610
over time and tide: He is the true Lord.
    The Geat captain saw treasure in abundance
but carried no spoils from those quarters
except for the head and the inlaid hilt
embossed with jewels; its blade had melted   1615
and the scrollwork on it burned, so scalding was the blood
of the poisonous fiend who had perished there.
Then away he swam, the one who had survived
the fall of his enemies, flailing to the surface.
The wide water, the waves and pools,   1620
were no longer infested once the wandering fiend
let go of her life and this unreliable world.
    The seafarers' leader made for land,
resolutely swimming, delighted with his prize,
the mighty load he was lugging to the surface.   1625
His thanes advanced in a troop to meet him,
thanking God and taking great delight
in seeing their prince back safe and sound.
Quickly the hero's helmet and mail-shirt
were loosed and unlaced. The lake settled,   1630
clouds darkened above the bloodshot depths.
    With high hearts they headed away
along footpaths and trails through the fields,
roads that they knew, each of them wrestling
with the head they were carrying from the lakeside cliff,   1635
men kingly in their courage and capable
of difficult work. It was a task for four
to hoist Grendel's head on a spear
and bear it under strain to the bright hall.
But soon enough they neared the place,   1640
fourteen Geats in fine fettle,
striding across the outlying ground
in a delighted throng around their leader.

In he came then, the thanes' commander,
the arch-warrior, to address Hrothgar: 1645
his courage was proven, his glory was secure.
Grendel's head was hauled by the hair,
dragged across the floor where the people were drinking,
a horror for both queen and company to behold.
They stared in awe. It was an astonishing sight.   1650

[Another Celebration at Heorot]

Beowulf, son of Ecgtheow, spoke:
"So, son of Halfdane, prince of the Shieldings,
we are glad to bring this booty from the lake.
It is a token of triumph and we tender it to you.
I barely survived the battle under water.   1655
It was hard-fought, a desperate affair
that could have gone badly; if God had not helped me,
the outcome would have been quick and fatal.
Although Hrunting is hard-edged,
I could never bring it to bear in battle.   1660
But the Lord of Men allowed me to behold—
for He often helps the unbefriended—
an ancient sword shining on the wall,
a weapon made for giants, there for the wielding.
Then my moment came in the combat and I struck   1665
the dwellers in that den. Next thing the damascened[9]
sword blade melted; it bloated and it burned
in their rushing blood. I have wrested the hilt
from the enemies' hand, avenged the evil
done to the Danes; it is what was due.   1670
And this I pledge, O prince of the Shieldings:
you can sleep secure with your company of troops
in Heorot Hall. Never need you fear
for a single thane of your sept[1] or nation,
young warriors or old, that laying waste of life   1675
that you and your people endured of yore."
    Then the gold hilt was handed over
to the old lord, a relic from long ago
for the venerable ruler. That rare smithwork
was passed on to the prince of the Danes   1680
when those devils perished; once death removed
that murdering, guilt-steeped, God-cursed fiend,
eliminating his unholy life
and his mother's as well, it was willed to that king
who of all the lavish gift-lords of the north   1685
was the best regarded between the two seas.
    Hrothgar spoke; he examined the hilt,
that relic of old times. It was engraved all over

---

9. Ornamented with inlaid designs.   1. An Irish term meaning a clan or division of a
                                                   tribe.

and showed how war first came into the world
and the flood destroyed the tribe of giants.   1690
They suffered a terrible severance from the Lord;
the Almighty made the waters rise,
drowned them in the deluge for retribution.
In pure gold inlay on the sword-guards
there were rune-markings correctly incised,   1695
stating and recording for whom the sword
had been first made and ornamented
with its scrollworked hilt. Then everyone hushed
as the son of Halfdane spoke this wisdom:
"A protector of his people, pledged to uphold   1700
truth and justice and to respect tradition,
is entitled to affirm that this man
was born to distinction. Beowulf, my friend,
your fame has gone far and wide,
you are known everywhere. In all things you are even-tempered,   1705
prudent and resolute. So I stand firm by the promise of friendship
we exchanged before. Forever you will be
your people's mainstay and your own warriors'
helping hand.
             Heremod was different,
the way he behaved to Ecgwela's sons.[2]   1710
His rise in the world brought little joy
to the Danish people, only death and destruction.
He vented his rage on men he caroused with,
killed his own comrades, a pariah king
who cut himself off from his own kind,   1715
even though Almighty God had made him
eminent and powerful and marked him from the start
for a happy life. But a change happened,
he grew bloodthirsty, gave no more rings
to honor the Danes. He suffered in the end   1720
for having plagued his people for so long:
his life lost happiness.
                So learn from this
and understand true values. I who tell you
have wintered into wisdom.
                It is a great wonder
how Almighty God in His magnificence   1725
favors our race with rank and scope
and the gift of wisdom; His sway is wide.
Sometimes He allows the mind of a man
of distinguished birth to follow its bent,
grants him fulfillment and felicity on earth   1730
and forts to command in his own country.
He permits him to lord it in many lands
until the man in his unthinkingness

---

2. That is, the Danes. Ecgwela was evidently a former king of the Danes.

forgets that it will ever end for him.
He indulges his desires; illness and old age   1735
mean nothing to him; his mind is untroubled
by envy or malice or the thought of enemies
with their hate-honed swords. The whole world
conforms to his will, he is kept from the worst
until an element of overweening   1740
enters him and takes hold
while the soul's guard, its sentry, drowses,
grown too distracted. A killer stalks him,
an archer who draws a deadly bow.
And then the man is hit in the heart,   1745
the arrow flies beneath his defenses,
the devious promptings of the demon start.
His old possessions seem paltry to him now.
He covets and resents; dishonors custom
and bestows no gold; and because of good things   1750
that the Heavenly Powers gave him in the past
he ignores the shape of things to come.
Then finally the end arrives
when the body he was lent collapses and falls
prey to its death; ancestral possessions   1755
and the goods he hoarded are inherited by another
who lets them go with a liberal hand.
    "O flower of warriors, beware of that trap.
Choose, dear Beowulf, the better part,
eternal rewards. Do not give way to pride.   1760
For a brief while your strength is in bloom
but it fades quickly; and soon there will follow
illness or the sword to lay you low,
or a sudden fire or surge of water
or jabbing blade or javelin from the air   1765
or repellent age. Your piercing eye
will dim and darken; and death will arrive,
dear warrior, to sweep you away.
    "Just so I ruled the Ring-Danes' country
for fifty years, defended them in wartime   1770
with spear and sword against constant assaults
by many tribes: I came to believe
my enemies had faded from the face of the earth.
Still, what happened was a hard reversal
from bliss to grief. Grendel struck   1775
after lying in wait. He laid waste to the land
and from that moment my mind was in dread
of his depredations. So I praise God
in His heavenly glory that I lived to behold
this head dripping blood and that after such harrowing   1780
I can look upon it in triumph at last.
Take your place, then, with pride and pleasure,
and move to the feast. Tomorrow morning
our treasure will be shared and showered upon you."

The Geat was elated and gladly obeyed   1785
the old man's bidding; he sat on the bench.
And soon all was restored, the same as before.
Happiness came back, the hall was thronged,
and a banquet set forth; black night fell
and covered them in darkness.
                              Then the company rose   1790
for the old campaigner: the gray-haired prince
was ready for bed. And a need for rest
came over the brave shield-bearing Geat.
He was a weary seafarer, far from home,
so immediately a house-guard guided him out,   1795
one whose office entailed looking after
whatever a thane on the road in those days
might need or require. It was noble courtesy.

[Beowulf Returns Home]

That great heart rested. The hall towered,
gold-shingled and gabled, and the guest slept in it   1800
until the black raven with raucous glee
announced heaven's joy, and a hurry of brightness
overran the shadows. Warriors rose quickly,
impatient to be off: their own country
was beckoning the nobles; and the bold voyager   1805
longed to be aboard his distant boat.
Then that stalwart fighter ordered Hrunting
to be brought to Unferth, and bade Unferth
take the sword and thanked him for lending it.
He said he had found it a friend in battle   1810
and a powerful help; he put no blame
on the blade's cutting edge. He was a considerate man.
    And there the warriors stood in their war-gear,
eager to go, while their honored lord
approached the platform where the other sat.   1815
The undaunted hero addressed Hrothgar.
Beowulf, son of Ecgtheow, spoke:
"Now we who crossed the wide sea
have to inform you that we feel a desire
to return to Hygelac. Here we have been welcomed   1820
and thoroughly entertained. You have treated us well.
If there is any favor on earth I can perform
beyond deeds of arms I have done already,
anything that would merit your affections more,
I shall act, my lord, with alacrity.   1825
If ever I hear from across the ocean
that people on your borders are threatening battle
as attackers have done from time to time,
I shall land with a thousand thanes at my back
to help your cause. Hygelac may be young   1830

to rule a nation, but this much I know
about the king of the Geats: he will come to my aid
and want to support me by word and action
in your hour of need, when honor dictates
that I raise a hedge of spears around you.   1835
Then if Hrethric should think about traveling
as a king's son to the court of the Geats,
he will find many friends. Foreign places
yield more to one who is himself worth meeting."
    Hrothgar spoke and answered him: 1840
"The Lord in his wisdom sent you those words
and they came from the heart. I have never heard
so young a man make truer observations.
You are strong in body and mature in mind,
impressive in speech. If it should come to pass   1845
that Hrethel's descendant dies beneath a spear,
if deadly battle or the sword blade or disease
fells the prince who guards your people
and you are still alive, then I firmly believe
the seafaring Geats won't find a man   1850
worthier of acclaim as their king and defender
than you, if only you would undertake
the lordship of your homeland. My liking for you
deepens with time, dear Beowulf.
What you have done is to draw two peoples,   1855
the Geat nation and us neighboring Danes,
into shared peace and a pact of friendship
in spite of hatreds we have harbored in the past.
For as long as I rule this far-flung land
treasures will change hands and each side will treat   1860
the other with gifts; across the gannet's bath,
over the broad sea, whorled prows will bring
presents and tokens. I know your people
are beyond reproach in every respect,
steadfast in the old way with friend or foe."   1865
    Then the earls' defender furnished the hero
with twelve treasures and told him to set out,
sail with those gifts safely home
to the people he loved, but to return promptly.
And so the good and gray-haired Dane,   1870
that highborn king, kissed Beowulf
and embraced his neck, then broke down
in sudden tears. Two forebodings
disturbed him in his wisdom, but one was stronger:[3]
nevermore would they meet each other   1875
face to face. And such was his affection
that he could not help being overcome:
his fondness for the man was so deep-founded,

---

3. We are not told what the other foreboding is, but it is probably the old man's awareness of the imminence of his own death.

it warmed his heart and wound the heartstrings
tight in his breast.   The embrace ended   1880
and Beowulf, glorious in his gold regalia,
stepped the green earth. Straining at anchor
and ready for boarding, his boat awaited him.
So they went on their journey, and Hrothgar's generosity
was praised repeatedly. He was a peerless king   1885
until old age sapped his strength and did him
mortal harm, as it has done so many.
     Down to the waves then, dressed in the web
of their chain-mail and war-shirts the young men marched
in high spirits. The coast-guard spied them,   1890
thanes setting forth, the same as before.
His salute this time from the top of the cliff
was far from unmannerly; he galloped to meet them
and as they took ship in their shining gear,
he said how welcome they would be in Geatland.   1895
Then the broad hull was beached on the sand
to be cargoed with treasure, horses and war-gear.
The curved prow motioned; the mast stood high
above Hrothgar's riches in the loaded hold.
     The guard who had watched the boat was given   1900
a sword with gold fittings, and in future days
that present would make him a respected man
at his place on the mead-bench.   Then the keel plunged
and shook in the sea; and they sailed from Denmark.
     Right away the mast was rigged with its sea-shawl;   1905
sail-ropes were tightened, timbers drummed
and stiff winds kept the wave-crosser
skimming ahead; as she heaved forward,
her foamy neck was fleet and buoyant,
a lapped prow loping over currents,   1910
until finally the Geats caught sight of coastline
and familiar cliffs. The keel reared up,
wind lifted it home, it hit on the land.
     The harbor guard came hurrying out
to the rolling water: he had watched the offing   1915
long and hard, on the lookout for those friends.
With the anchor cables, he moored their craft
right where it had beached, in case a backwash
might catch the hull and carry it away.
Then he ordered the prince's treasure-trove   1920
to be carried ashore. It was a short step
from there to where Hrethel's son and heir,
Hygelac the gold-giver, makes his home
on a secure cliff, in the company of retainers.
     The building was magnificent, the king majestic,   1925
ensconced in his hall; and although Hygd, his queen,
was young, a few short years at court,

her mind was thoughtful and her manners sure.
Haereth's daughter[4] behaved generously
and stinted nothing when she distributed   1930
bounty to the Geats.
                        Great Queen Modthryth
perpetrated terrible wrongs.[5]
If any retainer ever made bold
to look her in the face, if an eye not her lord's[6]
stared at her directly during daylight,   1935
the outcome was sealed: he was kept bound,
in hand-tightened shackles, racked, tortured
until doom was pronounced—death by the sword,
slash of blade, blood-gush, and death-qualms
in an evil display. Even a queen   1940
outstanding in beauty must not overstep like that.
A queen should weave peace, not punish the innocent
with loss of life for imagined insults.
But Hemming's kinsman put a halt to her ways
and drinkers round the table had another tale: 1945
she was less of a bane to people's lives,
less cruel-minded, after she was married
to the brave Offa,[7] a bride arrayed
in her gold finery, given away
by a caring father, ferried to her young prince   1950
over dim seas. In days to come
she would grace the throne and grow famous
for her good deeds and conduct of life,
her high devotion to the hero king
who was the best king, it has been said,   1955
between the two seas or anywhere else
on the face of the earth. Offa was honored
far and wide for his generous ways,
his fighting spirit and his farseeing
defense of his homeland; from him there sprang Eomer,   1960
Garmund's grandson, kinsman of Hemming,[8]
his warriors' mainstay and master of the field.
    Heroic Beowulf and his band of men
crossed the wide strand, striding along
the sandy foreshore; the sun shone,   1965
the world's candle warmed them from the south
as they hastened to where, as they had heard,
the young king, Ongentheow's killer[9]

4. That is, Hygd.
5. A Danish queen whose wickedness is being used as a foil to Hygd.
6. Probably her father, although the Anglo-Saxon word can also refer to a husband.
7. A legendary king of the Angles, one of the Germanic peoples who invaded England and established a kingdom named Mercia in the north of the country prior to the composition of *Beowulf*. Hemming is evidently a forebear of the Angles.
8. Garmund is Offa's father, Eomer his son.
9. Hygelac, king of the Geats; he led the attack against the Swedes, although a Geat named Eofor actually killed Ongentheow. This is the first reference to the feud between the Geats and the Swedes (or Shylfings); see below, lines 2379–96, 2468–89, 2922–98.

and his people's protector, was dispensing rings
inside his bawn. Beowulf's return   1970
was reported to Hygelac as soon as possible,
news that the captain was now in the enclosure,
his battle-brother back from the fray
alive and well, walking to the hall.
Room was quickly made, on the king's orders,   1975
and the troops filed across the cleared floor.
　　After Hygelac had offered greetings
to his loyal thane in a lofty speech,
he and his kinsman, that hale survivor,
sat face to face. Haereth's daughter[1]   1980
moved about with the mead-jug in her hand,
taking care of the company, filling the cups
that warriors held out. Then Hygelac began
to put courteous questions to his old comrade
in the high hall. He hankered to know   1985
every tale the Sea-Geats had to tell:
"How did you fare on your foreign voyage,
dear Beowulf, when you abruptly decided
to sail away across the salt water
and fight at Heorot? Did you help Hrothgar   1990
much in the end? Could you ease the prince
of his well-known troubles? Your undertaking
cast my spirits down, I dreaded the outcome
of your expedition and pleaded with you
long and hard to leave the killer be,   1995
let the South-Danes settle their own
blood-feud with Grendel. So God be thanked
I am granted this sight of you, safe and sound."
　　Beowulf, son of Ecgtheow, spoke:
"What happened, Lord Hygelac, is hardly a secret   2000
any more among men in this world—
myself and Grendel coming to grips
on the very spot where he visited destruction
on the Victory-Shieldings and violated
life and limb, losses I avenged   2005
so no earthly offspring of Grendel's
need ever boast of that bout before dawn,
no matter how long the last of his evil
family survives.
　　　　　　　When I first landed
I hastened to the ring-hall and saluted Hrothgar.   2010
Once he discovered why I had come,
the son of Halfdane sent me immediately
to sit with his own sons on the bench.
It was a happy gathering. In my whole life
I have never seen mead enjoyed more   2015
in any hall on earth. Sometimes the queen

1. That is, Hygd.

herself appeared, peace-pledge between nations,[2]
to hearten the young ones and hand out
a torque to a warrior, then take her place.
Sometimes Hrothgar's daughter distributed   2020
ale to older ranks, in order on the benches:
I heard the company call her Freawaru
as she made her rounds, presenting men
with the gem-studded bowl, young bride-to-be
to the gracious Ingeld,[3] in her gold-trimmed attire.   2025
The friend of the Shieldings favors her betrothal:
the guardian of the kingdom sees good in it
and hopes this woman will heal old wounds
and grievous feuds.
          But generally the spear
is prompt to retaliate when a prince is killed,   2030
no matter how admirable the bride may be.
   "Think how the Heatho-Bards are bound to feel,
their lord, Ingeld, and his loyal thanes,
when he walks in with that woman to the feast:
Danes are at the table, being entertained,   2035
honored guests in glittering regalia,
burnished ring-mail that was their hosts' birthright,
looted when the Heatho-Bards could no longer wield
their weapons in the shield-clash, when they went down
with their beloved comrades and forfeited their lives.   2040
Then an old spearman will speak while they are drinking,
having glimpsed some heirloom that brings alive
memories of the massacre; his mood will darken
and heart-stricken, in the stress of his emotion,
he will begin to test a young man's temper   2045
and stir up trouble, starting like this:
'Now, my friend, don't you recognize
your father's sword, his favorite weapon,
the one he wore when he went out in his war-mask
to face the Danes on that final day?   2050
After Withergeld[4] died and his men were doomed,
the Shieldings quickly claimed the field;
and now here's a son of one or other
of those same killers coming through our hall
overbearing us, mouthing boasts,   2055
and rigged in armor that by right is yours.'
And so he keeps on, recalling and accusing,
working things up with bitter words
until one of the lady's retainers lies

2. Wealhtheow, Hrothgar's queen, is called a "peace-pledge between nations" because kings attempted to end feuds by marrying their daughters to the sons of the kings of enemy nations. But as we have already seen in the case of the marriage of the Dane Hildeburh to the Jute Finn, and as we shall shortly learn again, such a strategy seems rarely to have worked.

3. King of the Heatho-Bards, whose father, Froda, was killed by the Danes.

4. A Heatho-Bard warrior.

spattered in blood, split open   2060
on his father's account.[5] The killer knows
the lie of the land and escapes with his life.
Then on both sides the oath-bound lords
will break the peace, a passionate hate
will build up in Ingeld, and love for his bride   2065
will falter in him as the feud rankles.
I therefore suspect the good faith of the Heatho-Bards,
the truth of their friendship and the trustworthiness
of their alliance with the Danes.
                                    But now, my lord,
I shall carry on with my account of Grendel,   2070
the whole story of everything that happened
in the hand-to-hand fight.
                              After heaven's gem
had gone mildly to earth, that maddened spirit,
the terror of those twilights, came to attack us
where we stood guard, still safe inside the hall.   2075
There deadly violence came down on Hondscio[6]
and he fell as fate ordained, the first to perish,
rigged out for the combat. A comrade from our ranks
had come to grief in Grendel's maw:
he ate up the entire body.   2080
There was blood on his teeth, he was bloated and dangerous,
all roused up, yet still unready
to leave the hall empty-handed;
renowned for his might, he matched himself against me,
wildly reaching. He had this roomy pouch,[7]   2085
a strange accoutrement, intricately strung
and hung at the ready, a rare patchwork
of devilishly fitted dragon-skins.
I had done him no wrong, yet the raging demon
wanted to cram me and many another   2090
into this bag—but it was not to be
once I got to my feet in a blind fury.
It would take too long to tell how I repaid
the terror of the land for every life he took
and so won credit for you, my king,   2095
and for all your people. And although he got away
to enjoy life's sweetness for a while longer,
his right hand stayed behind him in Heorot,
evidence of his miserable overthrow
as he dived into murk on the mere bottom.   2100
    "I got lavish rewards from the lord of the Danes
for my part in the battle, beaten gold
and much else, once morning came

---

5. A Danish attendant to Freawaru, whose   6. A Geat who was accompanying Beowulf;
father killed a Heatho-Bard in the original   his name means "glove."
battle; this action is envisioned as taking place 7. The Anglo-Saxon word translated as
at Ingeld's court after the marriage.   "pouch" literally means "glove."

and we took our places at the banquet table.
There was singing and excitement: an old reciter,   2105
a carrier of stories, recalled the early days.
At times some hero made the timbered harp
tremble with sweetness, or related true
and tragic happenings; at times the king
gave the proper turn to some fantastic tale,   2110
or a battle-scarred veteran, bowed with age,
would begin to remember the martial deeds
of his youth and prime and be overcome
as the past welled up in his wintry heart.
    "We were happy there the whole day long   2115
and enjoyed our time until another night
descended upon us. Then suddenly
the vehement mother avenged her son
and wreaked destruction. Death had robbed her,
Geats had slain Grendel, so his ghastly dam   2120
struck back and with bare-faced defiance
laid a man low. Thus life departed
from the sage Aeschere, an elder wise in counsel.
But afterward, on the morning following,
the Danes could not burn the dead body   2125
nor lay the remains of the man they loved
on his funeral pyre. She had fled with the corpse
and taken refuge beneath torrents on the mountain.
It was a hard blow for Hrothgar to bear,
harder than any he had undergone before.   2130
And so the heartsore king beseeched me
in your royal name to take my chances
underwater, to win glory
and prove my worth. He promised me rewards.
Hence, as is well known, I went to my encounter   2135
with the terror-monger at the bottom of the tarn.
For a while it was hand-to-hand between us,
then blood went curling along the currents
and I beheaded Grendel's mother in the hall
with a mighty sword. I barely managed   2140
to escape with my life; my time had not yet come.
But Halfdane's heir, the shelter of those earls,
again endowed me with gifts in abundance.
    "Thus the king acted with due custom.
I was paid and recompensed completely,   2145
given full measure and the freedom to choose
from Hrothgar's treasures by Hrothgar himself.
These, King Hygelac, I am happy to present
to you as gifts. It is still upon your grace
that all favor depends. I have few kinsmen   2150
who are close, my king, except for your kind self."
Then he ordered the boar-framed standard to be brought,
the battle-topping helmet, the mail-shirt gray as hoar-frost,
and the precious war-sword; and proceeded with his speech:

"When Hrothgar presented this war-gear to me   2155
he instructed me, my lord, to give you some account
of why it signifies his special favor.
He said it had belonged to his older brother,
King Heorogar, who had long kept it,
but that Heorogar had never bequeathed it   2160
to his son Heoroward, that worthy scion,
loyal as he was.
                    Enjoy it well."
    I heard four horses were handed over next.
Beowulf bestowed four bay steeds
to go with the armor, swift gallopers,   2165
all alike. So ought a kinsman act,
instead of plotting and planning in secret
to bring people to grief, or conspiring to arrange
the death of comrades. The warrior king
was uncle to Beowulf and honored by his nephew: 2170
each was concerned for the other's good.
    I heard he presented Hygd with a gorget,
the priceless torque that the prince's daughter,
Wealhtheow, had given him; and three horses,
supple creatures brilliantly saddled.   2175
The bright necklace would be luminous on Hygd's breast.
    Thus Beowulf bore himself with valor;
he was formidable in battle yet behaved with honor
and took no advantage; never cut down
a comrade who was drunk, kept his temper   2180
and, warrior that he was, watched and controlled
his God-sent strength and his outstanding
natural powers. He had been poorly regarded
for a long time, was taken by the Geats
for less than he was worth: and their lord too   2185
had never much esteemed him in the mead-hall.
They firmly believed that he lacked force,
that the prince was a weakling; but presently
every affront to his deserving was reversed.
    The battle-famed king, bulwark of his earls,   2190
ordered a gold-chased heirloom of Hrethel's[8]
to be brought in; it was the best example
of a gem-studded sword in the Geat treasury.
This he laid on Beowulf's lap
and then rewarded him with land as well,   2195
seven thousand hides;[9] and a hall and a throne.
Both owned land by birth in that country,
ancestral grounds; but the greater right
and sway were inherited by the higher born.

---

8. Hygelac's father and, through his daughter, Beowulf's grandfather.
9. A "hide" varied in size, but was considered

to be sufficient land to support a peasant and
his family.

[*The Dragon Wakes*]

A lot was to happen in later days   2200
in the fury of battle. Hygelac fell
and the shelter of Heardred's shield proved useless
against the fierce aggression of the Shylfings:[1]
ruthless swordsmen, seasoned campaigners,
they came against him and his conquering nation,   2205
and with cruel force cut him down
so that afterwards
      the wide kingdom
reverted to Beowulf. He ruled it well
for fifty winters, grew old and wise
as warden of the land
      until one began   2210
to dominate the dark, a dragon on the prowl
from the steep vaults of a stone-roofed barrow[2]
where he guarded a hoard; there was a hidden passage,
unknown to men, but someone managed[3]
to enter by it and interfere   2215
with the heathen trove. He had handled and removed
a gem-studded goblet; it gained him nothing,
though with a thief's wiles he had outwitted
the sleeping dragon. That drove him into rage,
as the people of that country would soon discover.   2220
  The intruder who broached the dragon's treasure
and moved him to wrath had never meant to.
It was desperation on the part of a slave
fleeing the heavy hand of some master,
guilt-ridden and on the run,   2225
going to ground. But he soon began
to shake with terror; . . . . . . in shock
the wretch . . . .
  . . . . panicked and ran
away with the precious   2230
metalwork. There were many other
heirlooms heaped inside the earth-house,
because long ago, with deliberate care,
somebody now forgotten
had buried the riches of a highborn race   2235
in this ancient cache. Death had come
and taken them all in times gone by
and the only one left to tell their tale,
the last of their line, could look forward to nothing
but the same fate for himself: he foresaw that his joy   2240
in the treasure would be brief.

---

1. Hygelac died in the raid against the Franks (see p. 918, n. 4); Heardred died in the long feud against the Swedes or Shylfings (see p. 934, n. 9).
2. A burial mound.

3. In the single manuscript of *Beowulf*, the page containing lines 2215–31 is badly damaged, and the translation is therefore conjectural. The ellipses of lines 2227–30 indicate lines that cannot be reconstructed at all.

                 A newly constructed
barrow stood waiting, on a wide headland
close to the waves, its entryway secured.
Into it the keeper of the hoard had carried
all the goods and golden ware   2245
worth preserving. His words were few:
"Now, earth, hold what earls once held
and heroes can no more; it was mined from you first
by honorable men. My own people
have been ruined in war; one by one   2250
they went down to death, looked their last
on sweet life in the hall. I am left with nobody
to bear a sword or to burnish plated goblets,
put a sheen on the cup. The companies have departed.
The hard helmet, hasped with gold,   2255
will be stripped of its hoops; and the helmet-shiner
who should polish the metal of the war-mask sleeps;
the coat of mail that came through all fights,
through shield-collapse and cut of sword,
decays with the warrior. Nor may webbed mail   2260
range far and wide on the warlord's back
beside his mustered troops. No trembling harp,
no tuned timber, no tumbling hawk
swerving through the hall, no swift horse
pawing the courtyard. Pillage and slaughter   2265
have emptied the earth of entire peoples."
And so he mourned as he moved about the world,
deserted and alone, lamenting his unhappiness
day and night, until death's flood
brimmed up in his heart.
                Then an old harrower of the dark   2270
happened to find the hoard open,
the burning one who hunts out barrows,
the slick-skinned dragon, threatening the night sky
with streamers of fire. People on the farms
are in dread of him. He is driven to hunt out   2275
hoards under ground, to guard heathen gold
through age-long vigils, though to little avail.
For three centuries, this scourge of the people
had stood guard on that stoutly protected
underground treasury, until the intruder   2280
unleashed its fury; he hurried to his lord
with the gold-plated cup and made his plea
to be reinstated. Then the vault was rifled,
the ring-hoard robbed, and the wretched man
had his request granted. His master gazed   2285
on that find from the past for the first time.
    When the dragon awoke, trouble flared again.
He rippled down the rock, writhing with anger
when he saw the footprints of the prowler who had stolen
too close to his dreaming head.   2290

So may a man not marked by fate
easily escape exile and woe
by the grace of God.
           The hoard-guardian
scorched the ground as he scoured and hunted
for the trespasser who had troubled his sleep.   2295
Hot and savage, he kept circling and circling
the outside of the mound. No man appeared
in that desert waste, but he worked himself up
by imagining battle; then back in he'd go
in search of the cup, only to discover   2300
signs that someone had stumbled upon
the golden treasures. So the guardian of the mound,
the hoard-watcher, waited for the gloaming
with fierce impatience; his pent-up fury
at the loss of the vessel made him long to hit back   2305
and lash out in flames. Then, to his delight,
the day waned and he could wait no longer
behind the wall, but hurtled forth
in a fiery blaze. The first to suffer
were the people on the land, but before long   2310
it was their treasure-giver who would come to grief.
    The dragon began to belch out flames
and burn bright homesteads; there was a hot glow
that scared everyone, for the vile sky-winger
would leave nothing alive in his wake.   2315
Everywhere the havoc he wrought was in evidence.
Far and near, the Geat nation
bore the brunt of his brutal assaults
and virulent hate. Then back to the hoard
he would dart before daybreak, to hide in his den.   2320
He had swinged[4] the land, swathed it in flame,
in fire and burning, and now he felt secure
in the vaults of his barrow; but his trust was unavailing.
    Then Beowulf was given bad news,
the hard truth: his own home,   2325
the best of buildings, had been burned to a cinder,
the throne-room of the Geats. It threw the hero
into deep anguish and darkened his mood:
the wise man thought he must have thwarted
ancient ordinance of the eternal Lord,   2330
broken His commandment. His mind was in turmoil,
unaccustomed anxiety and gloom
confused his brain; the fire-dragon
had razed the coastal region and reduced
forts and earthworks to dust and ashes,   2335
so the war-king planned and plotted his revenge.
The warriors' protector, prince of the hall-troop,

---

4. That is, singed, scorched.

ordered a marvelous all-iron shield
from his smithy works. He well knew
that linden boards would let him down   2340
and timber burn. After many trials,
he was destined to face the end of his days,
in this mortal world, as was the dragon,
for all his long leasehold on the treasure.
    Yet the prince of the rings was too proud   2345
to line up with a large army
against the sky-plague. He had scant regard
for the dragon as a threat, no dread at all
of its courage or strength, for he had kept going
often in the past, through perils and ordeals   2350
of every sort, after he had purged
Hrothgar's hall, triumphed in Heorot
and beaten Grendel. He outgrappled the monster
and his evil kin.
            One of his cruelest
hand-to-hand encounters had happened   2355
when Hygelac, king of the Geats, was killed
in Friesland: the people's friend and lord,
Hrethel's son, slaked a sword blade's
thirst for blood. But Beowulf's prodigious
gifts as a swimmer guaranteed his safety: 2360
he arrived at the shore, shouldering thirty
battle-dresses, the booty he had won.
There was little for the Hetware[5] to be happy about
as they shielded their faces and fighting on the ground
began in earnest. With Beowulf against them,   2365
few could hope to return home.
    Across the wide sea, desolate and alone,
the son of Ecgtheow swam back to his people.
There Hygd offered him throne and authority
as lord of the ring-hoard: with Hygelac dead,   2370
she had no belief in her son's ability
to defend their homeland against foreign invaders.
Yet there was no way the weakened nation
could get Beowulf to give in and agree
to be elevated over Heardred as his lord   2375
or to undertake the office of kingship.
But he did provide support for the prince,
honored and minded him until he matured
as the ruler of Geatland.
             Then over sea-roads
exiles arrived, sons of Ohthere.[6]   2380

---

5. A Frankish tribe.
6. King of the Swedes or Shylfings; after his death his sons, Eanmund and Eadgils, were driven out by their uncle Onela. They were taken in by Heardred, Hygelac's son, who was then king of the Geats, who was then in turn attacked and killed (along with Eanmund) by Onela. At this point Beowulf became king of the Geats and supported Eadgils in his successful attack on Onela.

They had rebelled against the best of all
the sea-kings in Sweden, the one who held sway
in the Shylfing nation, their renowned prince,
lord of the mead-hall. That marked the end
for Hygelac's son: his hospitality   2385
was mortally rewarded with wounds from a sword.
Heardred lay slaughtered and Onela returned
to the land of Sweden, leaving Beowulf
to ascend the throne, to sit in majesty
and rule over the Geats. He was a good king.   2390
    In days to come, he contrived to avenge
the fall of his prince; he befriended Eadgils
when Eadgils was friendless, aiding his cause
with weapons and warriors over the wide sea,
sending him men. The feud was settled   2395
on a comfortless campaign when he killed Onela.
    And so the son of Ecgtheow had survived
every extreme, excelling himself
in daring and in danger, until the day arrived
when he had to come face to face with the dragon.   2400
The lord of the Geats took eleven comrades
and went in a rage to reconnoiter.
By then he had discovered the cause of the affliction
being visited on the people. The precious cup
had come to him from the hand of the finder,   2405
the one who had started all this strife
and was now added as a thirteenth to their number.
They press-ganged and compelled this poor creature
to be their guide. Against his will
he led them to the earth-vault he alone knew,   2410
an underground barrow near the sea-billows
and heaving waves, heaped inside
with exquisite metalwork. The one who stood guard
was dangerous and watchful, warden of the trove
buried under earth: no easy bargain   2415
would be made in that place by any man.
    The veteran king sat down on the cliff-top.
He wished good luck to the Geats who had shared
his hearth and his gold. He was sad at heart,
unsettled yet ready, sensing his death.   2420
His fate hovered near, unknowable but certain:
it would soon claim his coffered soul,
part life from limb. Before long
the prince's spirit would spin free from his body.
    Beowulf, son of Ecgtheow, spoke: 2425
"Many a skirmish I survived when I was young
and many times of war: I remember them well.
At seven, I was fostered out by my father,
left in the charge of my people's lord.
King Hrethel kept me and took care of me,   2430
was openhanded, behaved like a kinsman.
While I was his ward, he treated me no worse

as a wean[7] about the place than one of his own boys,
Herebeald and Haethcyn, or my own Hygelac.
For the eldest, Herebeald, an unexpected   2435
deathbed was laid out, through a brother's doing,
when Haethcyn bent his horn-tipped bow
and loosed the arrow that destroyed his life.
He shot wide and buried a shaft
in the flesh and blood of his own brother.   2440
That offense was beyond redress, a wrongfooting
of the heart's affections; for who could avenge
the prince's life or pay his death-price?
It was like the misery felt by an old man
who has lived to see his son's body   2445
swing on the gallows. He begins to keen
and weep for his boy, watching the raven
gloat where he hangs: he can be of no help.
The wisdom of age is worthless to him.
Morning after morning, he wakes to remember   2450
that his child is gone; he has no interest
in living on until another heir
is born in the hall, now that his first-born
has entered death's dominion forever.
He gazes sorrowfully at his son's dwelling,   2455
the banquet hall bereft of all delight,
the windswept hearthstone; the horsemen are sleeping,
the warriors under ground; what was is no more.
No tunes from the harp, no cheer raised in the yard.
Alone with his longing, he lies down on his bed   2460
and sings a lament; everything seems too large,
the steadings and the fields.
                         Such was the feeling
of loss endured by the lord of the Geats
after Herebeald's death. He was helplessly placed
to set to rights the wrong committed,   2465
could not punish the killer in accordance with the law
of the blood-feud, although he felt no love for him.
Heartsore, wearied, he turned away
from life's joys, chose God's light
and departed, leaving buildings and lands   2470
to his sons, as a man of substance will.
    "Then over the wide sea Swedes and Geats
battled and feuded and fought without quarter.
Hostilities broke out when Hrethel died.
Ongentheow's sons[8] were unrelenting,   2475
refusing to make peace, campaigning violently

7. A young child [translator's note]; a Northern Irish word.
8. Ohthere and Onela, who attacked the Geats and killed Haethcyn; Haethcyn was then avenged by his brother Hygelac, whose attack on the Swedes resulted in the death of Ongentheow at the hands of the Geat Eofor (described below in lines 2922–98). These events took place before those of lines 2379–96, which describe the Geats' role in the struggle between Onela and Ohthere's two sons after Ongentheow's death.

from coast to coast, constantly setting up
terrible ambushes around Hreosnahill.[9]
My own kith and kin avenged
these evil events, as everybody knows, 2480
but the price was high: one of them paid
with his life. Haethcyn, lord of the Geats,
met his fate there and fell in the battle.
Then, as I have heard, Hygelac's sword
was raised in the morning against Ongentheow, 2485
his brother's killer. When Eofor cleft
the old Swede's helmet, halved it open,
he fell, death-pale: his feud-calloused hand
could not stave off the fatal stroke.
    "The treasures that Hygelac lavished on me 2490
I paid for when I fought, as fortune allowed me,
with my glittering sword. He gave me land
and the security land brings, so he had no call
to go looking for some lesser champion,
some mercenary from among the Gifthas[1] 2495
or the Spear-Danes or the men of Sweden.
I marched ahead of him, always there
at the front of the line; and I shall fight like that
for as long as I live, as long as this sword
shall last, which has stood me in good stead 2500
late and soon, ever since I killed
Dayraven the Frank in front of the two armies.
He brought back no looted breastplate
to the Frisian king but fell in battle,
their standard-bearer, highborn and brave. 2505
No sword blade sent him to his death:
my bare hands stilled his heartbeats
and wrecked the bone-house. Now blade and hand,
sword and sword-stroke, will assay the hoard."

[Beowulf Attacks the Dragon]

    Beowulf spoke, made a formal boast 2510
for the last time: "I risked my life
often when I was young. Now I am old,
but as king of the people I shall pursue this fight
for the glory of winning, if the evil one will only
abandon his earth-fort and face me in the open." 2515
    Then he addressed each dear companion
one final time, those fighters in their helmets,
resolute and highborn: "I would rather not
use a weapon if I knew another way
to grapple with the dragon and make good my boast 2520
as I did against Grendel in days gone by.

---

9. The place of the battle can be translated as   1. A tribe related to the Goths.
Sorrow Hill.

But I shall be meeting molten venom
in the fire he breathes, so I go forth
in mail-shirt and shield. I won't shift a foot
when I meet the cave-guard: what occurs on the wall 2525
between the two of us will turn out as fate,
overseer of men, decides. I am resolved.
I scorn further words against this sky-borne foe.
        "Men-at-arms, remain here on the barrow,
safe in your armor, to see which one of us 2530
is better in the end at bearing wounds
in a deadly fray. This fight is not yours,
nor is it up to any man except me
to measure his strength against the monster
or to prove his worth. I shall win the gold 2535
by my courage, or else mortal combat,
doom of battle, will bear your lord away."
        Then he drew himself up beside his shield.
The fabled warrior in his war-shirt and helmet
trusted in his own strength entirely 2540
and went under the crag. No coward path.
        Hard by the rock-face that hale veteran,
a good man who had gone repeatedly
into combat and danger and come through,
saw a stone arch and a gushing stream 2545
that burst from the barrow, blazing and wafting
a deadly heat. It would be hard to survive
unscathed near the hoard, to hold firm
against the dragon in those flaming depths.
Then he gave a shout. The lord of the Geats 2550
unburdened his breast and broke out
in a storm of anger. Under gray stone
his voice challenged and resounded clearly.
Hate was ignited. The hoard-guard recognized
a human voice, the time was over 2555
for peace and parleying. Pouring forth
in a hot battle-fume, the breath of the monster
burst from the rock. There was a rumble under ground.
Down there in the barrow, Beowulf the warrior
lifted his shield: the outlandish thing 2560
writhed and convulsed and viciously
turned on the king, whose keen-edged sword,
an heirloom inherited by ancient right,
was already in his hand. Roused to a fury,
each antagonist struck terror in the other. 2565
Unyielding, the lord of his people loomed
by his tall shield, sure of his ground,
while the serpent looped and unleashed itself.
Swaddled in flames, it came gliding and flexing
and racing toward its fate. Yet his shield defended 2570
the renowned leader's life and limb
for a shorter time than he meant it to:

that final day was the first time
when Beowulf fought and fate denied him
glory in battle. So the king of the Geats 2575
raised his hand and struck hard
at the enameled scales, but scarcely cut through:
the blade flashed and slashed yet the blow
was far less powerful than the hard-pressed king
had need of at that moment. The mound-keeper 2580
went into a spasm and spouted deadly flames:
when he felt the stroke, battle-fire
billowed and spewed. Beowulf was foiled
of a glorious victory. The glittering sword,
infallible before that day, 2585
failed when he unsheathed it, as it never should have.
For the son of Ecgtheow, it was no easy thing
to have to give ground like that and go
unwillingly to inhabit another home
in a place beyond; so every man must yield 2590
the leasehold of his days.
             Before long
the fierce contenders clashed again.
The hoard-guard took heart, inhaled and swelled up
and got a new wind; he who had once ruled
was furled in fire and had to face the worst. 2595
No help or backing was to be had then
from his highborn comrades; that hand-picked troop
broke ranks and ran for their lives
to the safety of the wood. But within one heart
sorrow welled up: in a man of worth 2600
the claims of kinship cannot be denied.
   His name was Wiglaf, a son of Weohstan's,
a well-regarded Shylfing warrior
related to Aelfhere.[2] When he saw his lord
tormented by the heat of his scalding helmet, 2605
he remembered the bountiful gifts bestowed on him,
how well he lived among the Waegmundings,
the freehold he inherited from his father[3] before him.
He could not hold back: one hand brandished
the yellow-timbered shield, the other drew his sword— 2610
an ancient blade that was said to have belonged
to Eanmund, the son of Ohthere, the one
Weohstan had slain when he was an exile without friends.
He carried the arms to the victim's kinfolk,
the burnished helmet, the webbed chain-mail 2615

2. Wiglaf is, like Beowulf, a member of the clan of the Waegmundings (see lines 2813–14), although both consider themselves Geats as well. See p. 898, n. 2. Nothing is known of Aelfhere.
3. Wiglaf's father is Weohstan, who, as we learn shortly, was the man who killed Eanmund, Ohthere's son, when he had taken refuge among the Geats (lines 2379–84). How Wiglaf then became a Geat is not clear, although it may have been when Beowulf helped Eanmund's brother Eadgils avenge himself on Onela, who had usurped the throne of the Swedes; Eadgils then became king.

and that relic of the giants. But Onela returned
the weapons to him, rewarded Weohstan
with Eanmund's war-gear. He ignored the blood-feud,
the fact that Eanmund was his brother's son.[4]
Weohstan kept that war-gear for a lifetime,   2620
the sword and the mail-shirt, until it was the son's turn
to follow his father and perform his part.
Then, in old age, at the end of his days
among the Weather-Geats, he bequeathed to Wiglaf
innumerable weapons.
                        And now the youth   2625
was to enter the line of battle with his lord,
his first time to be tested as a fighter.
His spirit did not break and the ancestral blade
would keep its edge, as the dragon discovered
as soon as they came together in the combat.   2630
    Sad at heart, addressing his companions,
Wiglaf spoke wise and fluent words:
"I remember that time when mead was flowing,
how we pledged loyalty to our lord in the hall,
promised our ring-giver we would be worth our price,   2635
make good the gift of the war-gear,
those swords and helmets, as and when
his need required it. He picked us out
from the army deliberately, honored us and judged us
fit for this action, made me these lavish gifts—   2640
and all because he considered us the best
of his arms-bearing thanes. And now, although
he wanted this challenge to be one he'd face
by himself alone—the shepherd of our land,
a man unequaled in the quest for glory   2645
and a name for daring—now the day has come
when this lord we serve needs sound men
to give him their support. Let us go to him,
help our leader through the hot flame
and dread of the fire. As God is my witness,   2650
I would rather my body were robed in the same
burning blaze as my gold-giver's body
than go back home bearing arms.
That is unthinkable, unless we have first
slain the foe and defended the life   2655
of the prince of the Weather-Geats. I well know
the things he has done for us deserve better.
Should he alone be left exposed
to fall in battle? We must bond together,
shield and helmet, mail-shirt and sword."   2660
Then he waded the dangerous reek and went
under arms to his lord, saying only:

---

4. That is, Onela ignored the fact that Weohstan had killed his nephew Eanmund since he in
fact wanted Eanmund dead.

"Go on, dear Beowulf, do everything
you said you would when you were still young
and vowed you would never let your name and fame 2665
be dimmed while you lived. Your deeds are famous,
so stay resolute, my lord, defend your life now
with the whole of your strength. I shall stand by you."
    After those words, a wildness rose
in the dragon again and drove it to attack, 2670
heaving up fire, hunting for enemies,
the humans it loathed. Flames lapped the shield,
charred it to the boss, and the body armor
on the young warrior was useless to him.
But Wiglaf did well under the wide rim 2675
Beowulf shared with him once his own had shattered
in sparks and ashes.   Inspired again
by the thought of glory, the war-king threw
his whole strength behind a sword stroke
and connected with the skull. And Naegling snapped. 2680
Beowulf's ancient iron-gray sword
let him down in the fight. It was never his fortune
to be helped in combat by the cutting edge
of weapons made of iron. When he wielded a sword,
no matter how blooded and hard-edged the blade, 2685
his hand was too strong, the stroke he dealt
(I have heard) would ruin it. He could reap no advantage.
    Then the bane of that people, the fire-breathing dragon,
was mad to attack for a third time.
When a chance came, he caught the hero 2690
in a rush of flame and clamped sharp fangs
into his neck. Beowulf's body
ran wet with his life-blood: it came welling out.
    Next thing, they say, the noble son of Weohstan
saw the king in danger at his side 2695
and displayed his inborn bravery and strength.
He left the head alone,[5] but his fighting hand
was burned when he came to his kinsman's aid.
He lunged at the enemy lower down
so that his decorated sword sank into its belly 2700
and the flames grew weaker.
                Once again the king
gathered his strength and drew a stabbing knife
he carried on his belt, sharpened for battle.
He stuck it deep in the dragon's flank.
Beowulf dealt it a deadly wound. 2705
They had killed the enemy, courage quelled his life;
that pair of kinsmen, partners in nobility,
had destroyed the foe. So every man should act,
be at hand when needed; but now, for the king,

_____

5. That is, the dragon's flame-breathing head.

this would be the last of his many labors   2710
and triumphs in the world.
                                        Then the wound
dealt by the ground-burner earlier began
to scald and swell; Beowulf discovered
deadly poison suppurating inside him,
surges of nausea, and so, in his wisdom,   2715
the prince realized his state and struggled
toward a seat on the rampart. He steadied his gaze
on those gigantic stones, saw how the earthwork
was braced with arches built over columns.
And now that thane unequaled for goodness   2720
with his own hands washed his lord's wounds,
swabbed the weary prince with water,
bathed him clean, unbuckled his helmet.
    Beowulf spoke: in spite of his wounds,
mortal wounds, he still spoke   2725
for he well knew his days in the world
had been lived out to the end—his allotted time
was drawing to a close, death was very near.
    "Now is the time when I would have wanted
to bestow this armor on my own son,   2730
had it been my fortune to have fathered an heir
and live on in his flesh. For fifty years
I ruled this nation. No king
of any neighboring clan would dare
face me with troops, none had the power   2735
to intimidate me. I took what came,
cared for and stood by things in my keeping,
never fomented quarrels, never
swore to a lie. All this consoles me,
doomed as I am and sickening for death;   2740
because of my right ways, the Ruler of mankind
need never blame me when the breath leaves my body
for murder of kinsmen. Go now quickly,
dearest Wiglaf, under the gray stone
where the dragon is laid out, lost to his treasure;   2745
hurry to feast your eyes on the hoard.
Away you go: I want to examine
that ancient gold, gaze my fill
on those garnered jewels; my going will be easier
for having seen the treasure, a less troubled letting-go   2750
of the life and lordship I have long maintained."
    And so, I have heard, the son of Weohstan
quickly obeyed the command of his languishing
war-weary lord; he went in his chain-mail
under the rock-piled roof of the barrow,   2755
exulting in his triumph, and saw beyond the seat
a treasure-trove of astonishing richness,
wall-hangings that were a wonder to behold,
glittering gold spread across the ground,
the old dawn-scorching serpent's den   2760

packed with goblets and vessels from the past,
tarnished and corroding. Rusty helmets
all eaten away. Armbands everywhere,
artfully wrought. How easily treasure
buried in the ground, gold hidden   2765
however skillfully, can escape from any man!
    And he saw too a standard, entirely of gold,
hanging high over the hoard,
a masterpiece of filigree; it glowed with light
so he could make out the ground at his feet   2770
and inspect the valuables. Of the dragon there was no
remaining sign: the sword had dispatched him.
Then, the story goes, a certain man[6]
plundered the hoard in that immemorial howe,[7]
filled his arms with flagons and plates,   2775
anything he wanted; and took the standard also,
most brilliant of banners.
                              Already the blade
of the old king's sharp killing-sword
had done its worst: the one who had for long
minded the hoard, hovering over gold,   2780
unleashing fire, surging forth
midnight after midnight, had been mown down.
    Wiglaf went quickly, keen to get back,
excited by the treasure. Anxiety weighed
on his brave heart—he was hoping he would find   2785
the leader of the Geats alive where he had left him
helpless, earlier, on the open ground.
    So he came to the place, carrying the treasure
and found his lord bleeding profusely,
his life at an end; again he began   2790
to swab his body. The beginnings of an utterance
broke out from the king's breast-cage.
The old lord gazed sadly at the gold.
    "To the everlasting Lord of all,
to the King of Glory, I give thanks   2795
that I behold this treasure here in front of me,
that I have been allowed to leave my people
so well endowed on the day I die.
Now that I have bartered my last breath
to own this fortune, it is up to you   2800
to look after their needs. I can hold out no longer.
Order my troop to construct a barrow
on a headland on the coast, after my pyre has cooled.
It will loom on the horizon at Hronesness[8]
and be a reminder among my people—   2805
so that in coming times crews under sail
will call it Beowulf's Barrow, as they steer
ships across the wide and shrouded waters."

6. That is, Wiglaf.   8. The name means "Whaleness."
7. An Irish word for dwelling.

Then the king in his great-heartedness unclasped
the collar of gold from his neck and gave it   2810
to the young thane, telling him to use
it and the war-shirt and gilded helmet well.
"You are the last of us, the only one left
of the Waegmundings. Fate swept us away,
sent my whole brave highborn clan   2815
to their final doom. Now I must follow them."
     That was the warrior's last word.
He had no more to confide. The furious heat
of the pyre would assail him. His soul fled from his breast
to its destined place among the steadfast ones.   2820

[Beowulf's Funeral]

     It was hard then on the young hero,
having to watch the one he held so dear
there on the ground, going through
his death agony. The dragon from underearth,
his nightmarish destroyer, lay destroyed as well,   2825
utterly without life. No longer would his snakefolds
ply themselves to safeguard hidden gold.
Hard-edged blades, hammered out
and keenly filed, had finished him
so that the sky-roamer lay there rigid,   2830
brought low beside the treasure-lodge.
     Never again would he glitter and glide
and show himself off in midnight air,
exulting in his riches: he fell to earth
through the battle-strength in Beowulf's arm.   2835
There were few, indeed, as far as I have heard,
big and brave as they may have been,
few who would have held out if they had had to face
the outpourings of that poison-breather
or gone foraging on the ring-hall floor   2840
and found the deep barrow-dweller
on guard and awake.
                              The treasure had been won,
bought and paid for by Beowulf's death.
Both had reached the end of the road
through the life they had been lent.
                                   Before long   2845
the battle-dodgers abandoned the wood,
the ones who had let down their lord earlier,
the tail-turners, ten of them together.
When he needed them most, they had made off.
Now they were ashamed and came behind shields,   2850
in their battle-outfits, to where the old man lay.
They watched Wiglaf, sitting worn out,
a comrade shoulder to shoulder with his lord,
trying in vain to bring him round with water.

Much as he wanted to, there was no way   2855
he could preserve his lord's life on earth
or alter in the least the Almighty's will.
What God judged right would rule what happened
to every man, as it does to this day.
    Then a stern rebuke was bound to come   2860
from the young warrior to the ones who had been cowards.
Wiglaf, son of Weohstan, spoke
disdainfully and in disappointment:
"Anyone ready to admit the truth
will surely realize that the lord of men   2865
who showered you with gifts and gave you the armor
you are standing in—when he would distribute
helmets and mail-shirts to men on the mead-benches,
a prince treating his thanes in hall
to the best he could find, far or near—   2870
was throwing weapons uselessly away.
It would be a sad waste when the war broke out.
Beowulf had little cause to brag
about his armed guard; yet God who ordains
who wins or loses allowed him to strike   2875
with his own blade when bravery was needed.
There was little I could do to protect his life
in the heat of the fray, but I found new strength
welling up when I went to help him.
Then my sword connected and the deadly assaults   2880
of our foe grew weaker, the fire coursed
less strongly from his head. But when the worst happened
too few rallied around the prince.
    "So it is good-bye now to all you know and love
on your home ground, the open-handedness,   2885
the giving of war-swords. Every one of you
with freeholds of land, our whole nation,
will be dispossessed, once princes from beyond
get tidings of how you turned and fled
and disgraced yourselves. A warrior will sooner   2890
die than live a life of shame."
    Then he ordered the outcome of the fight to be reported
to those camped on the ridge, that crowd of retainers
who had sat all morning, sad at heart,
shield-bearers wondering about   2895
the man they loved: would this day be his last
or would he return? He told the truth
and did not balk, the rider who bore
news to the cliff-top. He addressed them all:
"Now the people's pride and love,   2900
the lord of the Geats, is laid on his deathbed,
brought down by the dragon's attack.
Beside him lies the bane of his life,
dead from knife-wounds. There was no way
Beowulf could manage to get the better   2905
of the monster with his sword. Wiglaf sits

at Beowulf's side, the son of Weohstan,
the living warrior watching by the dead,
keeping weary vigil, holding a wake
for the loved and the loathed.
                    Now war is looming   2910
over our nation, soon it will be known
to Franks and Frisians, far and wide,
that the king is gone. Hostility has been great
among the Franks since Hygelac sailed forth
at the head of a war-fleet into Friesland: 2915
there the Hetware harried and attacked
and overwhelmed him with great odds.
The leader in his war-gear was laid low,
fell among followers: that lord did not favor
his company with spoils. The Merovingian king   2920
has been an enemy to us ever since.
   "Nor do I expect peace or pact-keeping
of any sort from the Swedes. Remember:
at Ravenswood, Ongentheow
slaughtered Haethcyn, Hrethel's son,   2925
when the Geat people in their arrogance
first attacked the fierce Shylfings.
The return blow was quickly struck
by Ohthere's father.[9] Old and terrible,
he felled the sea-king and saved his own   2930
aged wife, the mother of Onela
and of Ohthere, bereft of her gold rings.
Then he kept hard on the heels of the foe
and drove them, leaderless, lucky to get away
in a desperate rout into Ravenswood.   2935
His army surrounded the weary remnant
where they nursed their wounds; all through the night
he howled threats at those huddled survivors,
promised to axe their bodies open
when dawn broke, dangle them from gallows   2940
to feed the birds. But at first light
when their spirits were lowest, relief arrived.
They heard the sound of Hygelac's horn,
his trumpet calling as he came to find them,
the hero in pursuit, at hand with troops.   2945
   "The bloody swathe that Swedes and Geats
cut through each other was everywhere.
No one could miss their murderous feuding.
Then the old man made his move,
pulled back, barred his people in: 2950
Ongentheow withdrew to higher ground.
Hygelac's pride and prowess as a fighter
were known to the earl; he had no confidence
that he could hold out against that horde of seamen,
defend his wife and the ones he loved   2955

9. Ongentheow.

from the shock of the attack. He retreated for shelter
behind the earthwall. Then Hygelac swooped
on the Swedes at bay, his banners swarmed
into their refuge, his Geat forces
drove forward to destroy the camp.   2960
There in his gray hairs, Ongentheow
was cornered, ringed around with swords.
And it came to pass that the king's fate
was in Eofor's hands,[1] and in his alone.
Wulf, son of Wonred, went for him in anger,   2965
split him open so that blood came spurting
from under his hair. The old hero
still did not flinch, but parried fast,
hit back with a harder stroke:
the king turned and took him on.   2970
Then Wonred's son, the brave Wulf,
could land no blow against the aged lord.
Ongentheow divided his helmet
so that he buckled and bowed his bloodied head
and dropped to the ground. But his doom held off.   2975
Though he was cut deep, he recovered again.
    "With his brother down, the undaunted Eofor,
Hygelac's thane, hefted his sword
and smashed murderously at the massive helmet
past the lifted shield. And the king collapsed,   2980
the shepherd of people was sheared of life.
Many then hurried to help Wulf,
bandaged and lifted him, now that they were left
masters of the blood-soaked battle-ground.
One warrior stripped the other,   2985
looted Ongentheow's iron mail-coat,
his hard sword-hilt, his helmet too,
and carried the graith[2] to King Hygelac,
he accepted the prize, promised fairly
that reward would come, and kept his word.   2990
For their bravery in action, when they arrived home,
Eofor and Wulf were overloaded
by Hrethel's son, Hygelac the Geat,
with gifts of land and linked rings
that were worth a fortune. They had won glory,   2995
so there was no gainsaying his generosity.
And he gave Eofor his only daughter
to bide at home with him, an honor and a bond.
    "So this bad blood between us and the Swedes,
this vicious feud, I am convinced,   3000
is bound to revive; they will cross our borders
and attack in force when they find out
that Beowulf is dead. In days gone by
when our warriors fell and we were undefended,
he kept our coffers and our kingdom safe.   3005

1. The killing of Ongentheow by Eofor is   2. Armor.
described in lines 2486–89.

He worked for the people, but as well as that
he behaved like a hero.
           We must hurry now
to take a last look at the king
and launch him, lord and lavisher of rings,
on the funeral road. His royal pyre   3010
will melt no small amount of gold:
heaped there in a hoard, it was bought at heavy cost,
and that pile of rings he paid for at the end
with his own life will go up with the flame,
be furled in fire: treasure no follower   3015
will wear in his memory, nor lovely woman
link and attach as a torque around her neck—
but often, repeatedly, in the path of exile
they shall walk bereft, bowed under woe,
now that their leader's laugh is silenced,   3020
high spirits quenched. Many a spear
dawn-cold to the touch will be taken down
and waved on high; the swept harp
won't waken warriors, but the raven winging
darkly over the doomed will have news,   3025
tidings for the eagle of how he hoked[3] and ate,
how the wolf and he made short work of the dead."
   Such was the drift of the dire report
that gallant man delivered. He got little wrong
in what he told and predicted.
                The whole troop   3030
rose in tears, then took their way
to the uncanny scene under Earnaness.[4]
There, on the sand, where his soul had left him,
they found him at rest, their ring-giver
from days gone by. The great man   3035
had breathed his last. Beowulf the king
had indeed met with a marvelous death.
   But what they saw first was far stranger:
the serpent on the ground, gruesome and vile,
lying facing him. The fire-dragon   3040
was scaresomely burned, scorched all colors.
From head to tail, his entire length
was fifty feet. He had shimmered forth
on the night air once, then winged back
down to his den; but death owned him now,   3045
he would never enter his earth-gallery again.
Beside him stood pitchers and piled-up dishes,
silent flagons, precious swords
eaten through with rust, ranged as they had been
while they waited their thousand winters under ground.   3050
That huge cache, gold inherited
from an ancient race, was under a spell—
which meant no one was ever permitted

3. Rooted about, a Northern Irish word [adapted from translator's note].

4. The place where Beowulf fought the dragon; it means "Eagleness."

to enter the ring-hall unless God Himself,
mankind's Keeper, True King of Triumphs,   3055
allowed some person pleasing to Him—
and in His eyes worthy—to open the hoard.
    What came about brought to nothing
the hopes of the one who had wrongly hidden
riches under the rock-face. First the dragon slew   3060
that man among men, who in turn made fierce amends
and settled the feud. Famous for his deeds
a warrior may be, but it remains a mystery
where his life will end, when he may no longer
dwell in the mead-hall among his own.   3065
So it was with Beowulf, when he faced the cruelty
and cunning of the mound-guard. He himself was ignorant
of how his departure from the world would happen.
The highborn chiefs who had buried the treasure
declared it until doomsday so accursed   3070
that whoever robbed it would be guilty of wrong
and grimly punished for their transgression,
hasped in hell-bonds in heathen shrines.
Yet Beowulf's gaze at the gold treasure
when he first saw it had not been selfish.   3075
    Wiglaf, son of Weohstan, spoke:
"Often when one man follows his own will
many are hurt. This happened to us.
Nothing we advised could ever convince
the prince we loved, our land's guardian,   3080
not to vex the custodian of the gold,
let him lie where he was long accustomed,
lurk there under earth until the end of the world.
He held to his high destiny. The hoard is laid bare,
but at a grave cost; it was too cruel a fate   3085
that forced the king to that encounter.
I have been inside and seen everything
amassed in the vault. I managed to enter
although no great welcome awaited me
under the earthwall. I quickly gathered up   3090
a huge pile of the priceless treasures
handpicked from the hoard and carried them here
where the king could see them. He was still himself,
alive, aware, and in spite of his weakness
he had many requests. He wanted me to greet you   3095
and order the building of a barrow that would crown
the site of his pyre, serve as his memorial,
in a commanding position, since of all men
to have lived and thrived and lorded it on earth
his worth and due as a warrior were the greatest.   3100
Now let us again go quickly
and feast our eyes on that amazing fortune
heaped under the wall. I will show the way
and take you close to those coffers packed with rings

and bars of gold. Let a bier be made 3105
and got ready quickly when we come out
and then let us bring the body of our lord,
the man we loved, to where he will lodge
for a long time in the care of the Almighty."
    Then Weohstan's son, stalwart to the end, 3110
had orders given to owners of dwellings,
many people of importance in the land,
to fetch wood from far and wide
for the good man's pyre:
                  "Now shall flame consume
our leader in battle, the blaze darken 3115
round him who stood his ground in the steel-hail,
when the arrow-storm shot from bowstrings
pelted the shield-wall. The shaft hit home.
Feather-fledged, it finned the barb in flight."
    Next the wise son of Weohstan 3120
called from among the king's thanes
a group of seven: he selected the best
and entered with them, the eighth of their number,
under the God-cursed roof; one raised
a lighted torch and led the way. 3125
No lots were cast for who should loot the hoard
for it was obvious to them that every bit of it
lay unprotected within the vault,
there for the taking. It was no trouble
to hurry to work and haul out 3130
the priceless store. They pitched the dragon
over the cliff-top, let tide's flow
and backwash take the treasure-minder.
Then coiled gold was loaded on a cart
in great abundance, and the gray-haired leader, 3135
the prince on his bier, borne to Hronesness.
    The Geat people built a pyre for Beowulf,
stacked and decked it until it stood foursquare,
hung with helmets, heavy war-shields
and shining armor, just as he had ordered. 3140
Then his warriors laid him in the middle of it,
mourning a lord far-famed and beloved.
On a height they kindled the hugest of all
funeral fires; fumes of woodsmoke
billowed darkly up, the blaze roared 3145
and drowned out their weeping, wind died down
and flames wrought havoc in the hot bone-house,
burning it to the core. They were disconsolate
and wailed aloud for their lord's decease.
A Geat woman too sang out in grief; 3150
with hair bound up, she unburdened herself
of her worst fears, a wild litany
of nightmare and lament: her nation invaded,
enemies on the rampage, bodies in piles,
slavery and abasement. Heaven swallowed the smoke. 3155

Then the Geat people began to construct
a mound on a headland, high and imposing,
a marker that sailors could see from far away,
and in ten days they had done the work.
It was their hero's memorial; what remained from the fire   3160
they housed inside it, behind a wall
as worthy of him as their workmanship could make it.
And they buried torques in the barrow, and jewels
and a trove of such things as trespassing men
had once dared to drag from the hoard.   3165
They let the ground keep that ancestral treasure,
gold under gravel, gone to earth,
as useless to men now as it ever was.
Then twelve warriors rode around the tomb,
chieftains' sons, champions in battle,   3170
all of them distraught, chanting in dirges,
mourning his loss as a man and a king.
They extolled his heroic nature and exploits
and gave thanks for his greatness; which was the proper thing,
for a man should praise a prince whom he holds dear   3175
and cherish his memory when that moment comes
when he has to be convoyed from his bodily home.
So the Geat people, his hearth-companions,
sorrowed for the lord who had been laid low.
They said that of all the kings upon earth   3180
he was the man most gracious and fair-minded,
kindest to his people and keenest to win fame.

ABOLQASEM FERDOWSI

940–1020

The *Shahnameh*, literally "book of kings," is sometimes called Persia's national epic. It is what the *Iliad* is to the Greeks, the *Aeneid* to the Romans, *Beowulf* to the English, or the *Song of Roland* to the French. But the label "epic" only begins to capture the scope and ambitions of Ferdowsi's capacious text, which opens with the creation of the world and ends with the lineage of medieval Persian kings; along the way, it includes fairies and jinns, flying horses and giant birds. Standing on the threshold of the fall of his Persian patrons to invading Turkish armies, Ferdowsi was writing with one eye on the glories of the past and one eye on the turbulent court politics of his own day.

Abolqasem Ferdowsi was born in Khorasan, a region encompassing what is now northeastern Iran and the adjoining regions of Afghanistan, Turkmenistan, and Uzbekistan, in a village near the city of Tus. He wrote his major work, the *Shahnameh*, under the patronage of the Iranian Samanid rulers of Khorasan (819–1005), who were eager to revive Persian literature and culture after a long period of dormancy following the Arab Islamic invasions of Persia that began in 633. The Samanid ruler Nuh ibn Mansur ordered that a prose compendium be produced of all the Persian literature that had been suppressed over the past centuries, drawing on oral and written sources of Persian mythology and the native monotheistic religion of Zoroastrianism. Ferdowsi tells us that the first poet told to turn this (now lost) prose account into an epic poem, Daqiqi-e Balkhi, died suddenly before he could finish more than a thousand lines. Ferdowsi claims to have incorporated Daqiqi's verses into his own *Shahnameh*—but because he ascribes to Daqiqi the most un-Islamic part of the poem, centering on the life of the prophet Zoroaster and the religion he founded, it is possible that the attribution is not so much fact as a clever tactic aimed at self-preservation. While Ferdowsi was at work on the *Shahnameh*, his Samanid patron fell from power. Though the rulers of this new regime, the Ghaznavid Turks, were ethnically distinct from and more rigorously Islamic than the Persian Samanids, they valued Persian culture highly. Ferdowsi therefore continued his work on the poem, sending selections to Mahmoud, the new Ghaznavid ruler, along with short poems praising his generosity.

Although the *Shahnameh* is an epic, it encompasses other genres as well. It begins with the creation of the world, the creation of the first human beings, and an account of their lineage, and thus resembles texts like **Gilgamesh** or **Genesis**. It is national in its evocation of the great mythic heroes of the Persian past, juxtaposed with a historical account of Persian rulers up through the Middle Ages. Beyond myth and history, the *Shahnameh* also contains elements of romance, star-crossed lovers and tragic scenes of misrecognition, fantastical creatures and supernatural events. Further complicating all these diverse elements is their presentation, as the stories are told in intricately rhymed verse. In addition, the *Shahnameh* functions as a "mirror for princes"—that is, a guidebook for rulers: the exemplary kings appear as models to be emulated, while the deeds of bad rulers to be avoided. This aspect of the *Shahnameh* is most evident in the story of Alexander (Sekandar) but is woven throughout the text, especially in the repeated stories of father–son relationships that have gone tragically wrong.

The *Shahnameh* can be divided into three parts: a relatively brief opening section focusing on origin myths, a long second section on the heroes of Persian antiquity, and a third section on the history of the kings. The material becomes steadily more grounded in historical fact as the text goes on; heroic kings who live for several hundred years dominate the middle section, which makes up the bulk of the work, but rulers of normal life spans appear in the later ages. The figure of Alexander the Great, whose life story is excerpted here, is placed at the crucial junction linking the age of heroes with the history of the kings. Alexander appears as a transitional figure, as more than a man yet an integral part of the history of Persian rule. The description of the end of his reign is followed by an extremely brief overview of the dissolution of his empire into a number of small principalities before the rise of the Sassanid dynasty, whose royal lineage makes up the rest of the *Shahnameh*. The poem ends not in Ferdowsi's own times but instead with the last Sassanid ruler, Yazdgerd III, who was forced off his throne by the invading Arab Islamic armies in 651. This poetic celebration of the Persian mythic and historical heritage thus draws a discreet curtain over the period when the advent of Islam threatened to overwhelm the native culture. Moreover, the *Shahnameh* provides a powerful counternarrative to the history of conquest, a counternarrative that depends a great deal on the figure of Alexander the Great. For Persians, it is an article of faith that their nation has never been conquered, even though at times it may have adopted new customs, new religions, and new rulers. In keeping with this perspective, the figure of Alexander is presented in the *Shahnameh* not as a Macedonian invader but as a Persian prince. Instead of being the alien enemy of the Persian ruler, he is Darius's brother and rival.

The legends of Alexander the Great, who emerged from Macedonia to build an empire that stretched from Spain to India, were widely disseminated all around the Mediterranean Sea, reaching throughout Europe and much of Asia. The basic outline of the Alexander story as presented in the *Shahnameh* will be familiar to anyone who has read any one of the many versions of his legend, including the war against Darius (Dara), ruler of Persia; the battles against Porus (Foor), king of India; and the letters describing the marvels of the East exchanged by Alexander with his old teacher, the Greek philosopher Aristotle (Arestalis). Yet Ferdowsi faced a particular challenge in describing Alexander's journeys of conquest into the remotest reaches of the Orient, where he ultimately met his doom. For European readers, Alexander's adventures in Babylon were set in the exotic Orient; for Ferdowsi's readers, Babylon was just down the road. Ferdowsi therefore constructs an even more oriental Orient for his hero, sending Alexander as far as China in search of marvels. At the same time, Ferdowsi's Alexander is also made familiar to Persian readers, drawn into the fold of the lineage of Persian kings. The rivalry between Alexander and his brother ends in the death of Darius, who gives his kingdom to Alexander on the condition that Alexander marry his daughter and uphold the local religion of Zoroastrianism. Here, conquest is transformed into cultural assimilation, and the heroic age moves smoothly into the lists of Persian kings. Implicitly, the transition ushered in by Alexander foreshadows the greater transition that informs the last lines of the *Shahnameh*, which recount the rule of the Sassanid Yazdgerd III. He would be the last native ruler of Persia until the rise of the Samanid rulers of Khorasan—Ferdowsi's patrons—in 819.

The celebration of Persian identity so poetically expressed in the *Shahnameh* continues to be enormously popular not only within modern Iran but also in communities of Iranians throughout the world. Along with the lyric poetry of Hafez, Ferdowsi's narrative poetry is widely quoted and used for inscriptions. Unlike the delicate ghazals of Hafez, however, the *Shahnameh* has also been rendered as a popular series of graphic novels. The endurance of the *Shahnameh* is partly due to how little the Persian language (Farsi) has changed over the thousand years since Ferdowsi completed his epic work. Modern speakers of Persian can read Ferdowsi without difficulty, much as we might read Shakespeare's English. For them, Ferdowsi's Persian is a living language, as resonant in the present moment as at any time in the past millennium.

A NOTE ON TRANSLATION

The *Shahnameh* has repeatedly been translated into European languages, usually in the form of an excerpt taken from the tragic story of the hero Rostam and his doomed son Sohrab; one of the best-known examples is Matthew Arnold's poem "Sohrab and Rustum" (1853). This narrative appealed to nineteenth-century

European readers not just because of its emotional power and beauty but also because the story line of a father destroying his son corresponded well with an Orientalist view of the decadent East. The translation by Dick Davis reproduced here, by contrast, makes a real effort to bring the Persian text to readers of English on its own terms. Davis's versions of Persian narrative and lyric poetry have been particularly popular among diasporic Iranians, who are eager to rediscover their national literature within new cultural environments. Davis, himself a poet, renders Ferdowsi's heroic couplets in a lyrical, rhythmic prose punctuated by short passages in verse that mark moments of great emotional tension.

From Shahnameh[1]

The Birth of Sekandar

One night this lovely moon,[2] arrayed in jewels and scents, lay sleeping beside the king. Suddenly she sighed deeply, and the king[3] turned his head away, offended by the smell of her breath. This bad odor sickened him, and he frowned, wondering what could be done about it. He sent knowledgeable doctors to her; one who was especially expert was able to find a remedy. There is an herb that burns the palate, which they call "Sekandar" in Greece, and he rubbed this against the roof of her mouth. She wept a few tears and her face turned as red as brocade, because it burned her mouth, but the ugly smell was gone. But although this beautiful woman's breath was now as sweet as musk, the king no longer felt any love for her. His heart had grown cold toward his bride, and he sent her back to Filqus. The princess grieved, because she was pregnant, but she told no one of this.

When nine months had gone by she gave birth to a boy as splendid as the sun. Because of his stature and splendor, and the sweet smell that his flesh exhaled, she named him Sekandar, after the herb that had cured her of her malady. Her father the king told everyone that the boy was his and made no mention of Darab, because he was ashamed to tell people that Darab had rejected his daughter. The same night that Sekandar was born, a cream-colored mare in the royal stables, a huge warlike horse, gave birth to a gray foal with a lion-like chest and short pasterns.[4] Filqus took this as a good omen, raising his hands to the heavens in gratitude. At dawn the next day he had both the newborn child and the mare and her foal brought to him and passed his hands over the foal's eyes and chest, because he was exactly the same age as Sekandar.

So the heavens turned and the years passed. Sekandar grew to have a princely heart, and his speech was that of a warrior. Filqus treated him even more attentively than a son and loved to dress him as a champion. In a little while the boy gained in wisdom; he became adroit, intelligent, grave in his manner, and knowledgeable. He was made the kingdom's crown prince, and Filqus delighted in his presence. Sekandar learned the arts of kingship from

1. Translated by Dick Davis.
2. Nahid, daughter of Filqus (Philip), King of Macedon, sent to marry Darab, King of Persia. In Persian poetry, the moon often symbolizes feminine beauty.

3. Darab (Darius), King of Persia.
4. Bucephalus, who is featured prominently in classical Greek biographies of Alexander the Great.

his teachers, and it seemed he was born to administer justice, to occupy a throne, and to found an empire.

In Persia, after Nahid had returned to her father, Darab took another wife. She gave birth to a fine, princely son who was a year younger than Sekandar. On the day he was born he was named Dara, and it was hoped that his good fortune would be greater than his father's. Then, after twelve years, Darab's star declined: he grew sick and wasted away and knew he would be called to another place. He summoned his nobles and counselors and spoke to them at length about the business of government and kingship. Then he added: "Dara, my son, will guide you well. Listen to him and obey him, and may your souls know peace in obedience to his commands. This royal throne is no one's for long, and in the midst of pleasure we are called away. Strive to be kind and just, and rejoice when you remember me." Having said this he heaved a sigh from the depths of his being, and the rosy pomegranate petal turned as pale as fenugreek.[5]

* * *

Dara's Dying Words to Sekandar

Dara's counselors made their way to Sekandar and said, "Wise and victorious lord, we have killed your enemy: his days as king are over." When Sekandar heard Janushyar's words, he said to him and to Mahyar,[6] "Where is this enemy of mine whom you've cast aside in this way? Take me to him." The two led Sekandar, whose heart was bursting with rage, to where Dara lay with his chest covered in gore, and his face as pale as fenugreek. Sekandar gave orders that no one else should approach, and that Dara's two counselors be detained. Quick as the wind he dismounted and laid the wounded man's head on his thigh. He rubbed both his hands against Dara's face until he began to revive and speak. Then Sekandar removed the royal diadem from Dara's head and loosened his armor. No doctor was nearby, and when he saw Dara's wounds, a few tears dropped from Sekandar's eyes. "May this pass easily from you," he said, "and may the hearts of those who wish you ill tremble in terror! Get up, and let me lay you in a golden litter, or if you have the strength, sit yourself in the saddle. I will bring doctors from India and Greece, and I shall weep tears of blood for your pain. I shall restore your kingdom to you, and when you have recovered, we shall swear friendship. This instant I shall hang from a gibbet those who have injured you. When I heard last night what had happened, my heart filled with sorrow, my soul with anger. We are from the same stock, the same root, the same people: why should we destroy one another for ambition's sake?"

When he heard Sekandar, Dara said, "May wisdom always be your companion! I think that you will find the reward for what you have said from God himself. You said that Iran is mine, and that the crown and the throne of the brave are mine; but death is closer to me than the throne. The throne is over for me, and my luck has run out. So the high heavens revolve; their turning is toward sorrow, and their profit is pain. Look at me before you say 'I am exalted above all this great company of heroes.' Know that evil and good both come from God, and see that you remain grateful to him for as long as you live. My

5. A light green herb.
6. Janushyar and Mahyar, Zoroastrians serving in the royal retinue, have fatally wounded

Dara, Sekandar's half-brother and rival for the crown of Persia.

own state shows you the truth of what I say. Look how I, who had such sovereignty and glory and wealth, am now despised by everyone. I who never injured anyone, who had such armor and such armies, such splendid horses, such crowns and thrones, who had such sons and relatives, and so many allies whose hearts bore my brand. Earth and time were my slaves, and remained so while my luck held. But now I am separated from good fortune, and have fallen into the hands of murderers. I despair of my sons and family; the earth has turned dark for me, and my eyes are white like the eyes of a blind man. Our own people cannot help us; my one hope is in God the Creator. I lie here wounded on the earth, fallen into the trap of death, but this is the way of the heavens whether we are kings or heroes. Greatness too must pass: it is the prey, and its hunter is death."

Sekandar's pity made his face turn pale, and he wept for the wounded king, lying there stretched out on the earth. Dara said to him, "Do not weep, there is no profit in it. My part in the fires of life is now merely smoke. This was my fate from him who apportions our fates. This is the goal toward which the splendor of my earthly days has led me. Listen to the advice I shall give you, accept it into your heart, and remember it." Sekandar said, "It is for you to order me: I give you my word." Then Dara spoke quickly, going over his wishes and omitting nothing. He began by saying, "You have achieved fame, but see that you fear the world's Creator, who has made the heavens and the earth and time, and the strong and the weak. Look after my children and my family, and my veiled wise women. Ask for my daughter's hand in marriage, and keep her gently and in comfort in the court. Her mother named her Roshanak and saw that the world was always a place of happiness and delight for her. Do not despise my daughter, or let malevolent men speak badly of her. She has been brought up as a princess, and at our feasts she has always been the loveliest person present. It may be that you shall have a son with her, and that the name of Esfandyar[7] will be renewed in him, that he will preserve the fires of Zoroastrianism and live by the Zend-Avesta,[8] keeping the Feasts of Sadeh and No-Ruz[9] and preserving our fire temples. Such a son will honor Hormozd[1] and the sun and moon, and wash his soul and face in the waters of wisdom; he will renew the ways of Lohrasp and Goshtasp,[2] treating men according to their station whether it be high or low; he will make our faith flourish and his days will be fortunate."

Sekandar answered him, "Your heart is pure and your words are wise, O king. I accept all that you have said, and I shall not stray from your words while I am within the borders of your kingdom. I shall accomplish the good deeds you recommend, and your wisdom will be my guide." The master of the world grasped Sekandar's hand and began to weep bitterly.

---

7. A legendary Iranian hero, son of King Goshtasp; his battle with the mighty Rostam is recounted earlier in the *Shahnameh*.

8. The sacred scripture of Zoroastrianism: a collection of hymns and liturgical texts, together with their theological interpretations. The religion was founded by the prophet Zoroaster in Iran in the 6th century B.C.E. and was the state religion at the time of Alexander's conquest and from the 3rd century C.E. until shortly before the adoption of Islam.

9. The Persian New Year, which takes place on the spring equinox (March 20 or 21); Sadeh is a midwinter festival held fifty days earlier. Both festivals involve the celebration of light, especially fire.

1. An early Iranian god (also called Ahura Mazda), who was proclaimed the single uncreated God by Zoroaster and is the highest deity in Zoroastrianism.

2. Legendary Iranian kings.

He kissed Sekandar's palm and said, "I pray
That God will keep and guide you on your way.
I give my flesh to dust, to God my spirit,
My sovereignty is yours now to inherit."

He spoke, and his soul rose up from his body. All those gathered nearby began to weep, and Sekandar rent his clothes and poured dust on the royal diadem. Sekandar made a splendid tomb for him according to local custom and, now that the time for Dara's eternal sleep had come, the blood was washed from his body with clear rosewater. His body was wrapped in brocade woven with gold and sewn with jewels; it was then covered with camphor, even his face, so that no one could see it. As Dara's corpse was placed within its golden coffin the bystanders wept, and then it was carried in procession, passed hand to hand by the mourners, with Sekandar leading the cortege on foot, and as he approached the tomb, it seemed as if his skin would split with sorrow. The king's coffin was placed within the tomb according to the ancient royal rites, and the huge doors of the building were sealed. Then Sekandar had two gibbets built, one bearing the name Janushyar and the other Mahyar, and the two regicides were strung up on them. The soldiers who were there took rocks in their fists and stoned them to death, as a warning to those who would kill a king. When the Persians saw how Sekandar honored Dara and mourned for him, they offered the young king their homage and loyalty.

* * *

Sekandar's Letter to Foor

Having hidden his treasure in this way,[3] Sekandar led his army out from Milad and bore down on Qanuj like the wind. He wrote a threatening, bellicose letter, "From Sekandar, the son of Filqus, who lights the flames of prosperity and adversity, to Foor, the lord of India, favored by the heavens, commander of the armies of Sind."[4] The letter opened with praise of God the Creator who is eternal, saying that those to whom he gives victory never want for countries, crowns, and thrones, while those from whom he turns away become wretched, and the sun never shines on them. "You will have heard how God has given me *farr*,[5] victory, good fortune, crowns, thrones, and sovereignty over this dark earth. But none of this will last, and my days draw on; another will come after me to enjoy my conquests. My only ambition is to leave a good name and no disgrace behind me on this sublunar earth. When they bring this letter to you, free your dark soul from sorrow; descend from your throne, do not consult with your priests or advisors, but mount your horse and come to me asking for my protection. Those who try to trick me only prolong matters, and if for one moment you disobey me by choosing arrogance and warfare, I shall descend on your country like a fire, bringing an army of picked warriors, and once you see my cavalry you will regret your delay in submitting to me." The letter was sealed with Sekandar's mark, and a soldier who was eager for fame was chosen to take it. The messenger arrived at the court, and when Foor was told of his arrival he was summoned into the royal presence.

3. A concealment just described in a passage not included here.
4. China. "Foor": the Persian form of the Greek Porus.
5. God-given glory.

When Foor read Sekandar's letter he started up in rage and immediately wrote a furious reply, planting a tree in the garden of vengeance. "We should fear God, and not use such presumptuous language, because a boastful man will find himself friendless and with no resources. Have you no shame that you summon me like this? Isn't your wisdom disturbed by this kind of talk? If it were Filqus writing thus to Foor, that would be something, but you? You dare to stir up trouble in this way? Your victory over Dara has gone to your head, but the heavens had had enough of him, and fate deals in this way with people who won't listen to good advice. And you found your quarrel with Kayd[6] was like a feast, so now you think all kings are your prey to hunt down. The ancient kings of Iran never addressed us in this way. I am Foor, descended from the family of Foor, and we have never paid any attention to Caesars[7] from the west. When Dara asked for my help, I sent him war elephants to buy time, although I saw that neither his heart nor his fortune were as they should be. When he was murdered by a slave, good fortune deserted the Persians. If evil came to him from an evil counselor, is that any reason for you to lose your good sense? Don't be so eager for battle and so disrespectful toward me; soon enough you'll see my war elephants and armies crowding the way before you. All you think of is your own glory, but inside you are the color of Ahriman.[8] Don't sow these seeds of strife throughout the world; fear misfortune and the harm that will come to you. I mean well by this letter, and may it gratify your heart."

Sekandar Leads His Army Against Foor

After reading this letter, Sekandar immediately selected chieftains from his army, men who were worthy of command: old in their understanding but young in years. Then he led his men against Foor, and they were so numerous that the earth was like a heaving sea. They traveled by every pathway, so that there seemed to be no track that they didn't take, over mountains, along the seashores, and through the most difficult terrain. The army grew weary of harsh traveling and fierce battles, and one evening when they pitched camp, a group of them came before the king. They said,

> "Sovereign of Greece and of all Asia too,
> Earth cannot hold the massive armies you
> Lead out against the world: Foor will not fight,
> And China's emperor quails before your might.
> Why should your army's valiant soldiers die
> For worthless lands beneath an alien sky?
> In all our ranks we cannot find one horse
> That's fit for war; if we reverse our course
> The infantry and cavalry will stray
> By unfamiliar paths and lose their way.
> Before, we fought and gained our victories
> Against the strength of human enemies,

---

6. An Indian king.
7. That is, emperors.

8. In Zoroastrian theology, the god of evil and darkness, fundamentally opposed to Hormozd.

> But none of us desires to die in wars
> With mountains and the sea's infertile shores;
> Men do not fight with rocks and ocean tides,
> With barren plains and rugged mountain sides.
> Do not convert the glory of our fame
> To ignominious and ignoble shame."

Sekandar was angered by their words, and he made short work of their complaints. He said, "In the war with the Persians, no Greek soldier was injured; Dara was killed by his own slaves, and none of you suffered. I shall continue on my way without you, and place my foot on the dragon's heart alone. You will see that the wretched Foor will have no desire for either battles or banquets when I have dealt with him. My help comes from God and the Persian army, and I have no need of Greek goodwill." Frightened by his anger, the army begged him to pardon them and said, "We are all our Caesar's slaves, and we tread the earth only as he wills us to. We shall go on, and when there are no horses left, we shall fight on foot. If the earth becomes a sea with our blood, and the low places become hills of corpses, even if the heavens rain down mountainous rocks, no enemy will ever see our backs in battle. We are your slaves, here for you to command, and how could you suffer any injury from us?"

Sekandar then formed a new battle plan. He chose thirty thousand Persian warriors headed by experienced, well-armored chieftains. Behind them he placed forty thousand Greek cavalry, and behind them his warlike Egyptian cavalry, who fought with swords. Forty thousand of Dara's troops and men from the Persian royal family accompanied them. Sekandar picked out twelve thousand Greek and Egyptian cavalry to bring up the rear and scour the plains and valleys. With his army Sekandar had sixty astrologers and sages to advise him on the most auspicious days for combat.

When Foor became aware of the enemy's approach, he chose a place suitable for battle, and his troops crowded the plain for four miles, with elephants in the van and his warriors behind them. Meanwhile Sekandar's spies told him of the war elephants in Foor's army, and how with their overpowering trunks (that were under the protection of Saturn) they could destroy two miles of cavalry, who would be unable either to defeat them or to get back to their own ranks. The spies drew a picture of an elephant on a piece of paper and showed it to the king, who had a model of the animal made from wax. Then he turned to his advisors and said, "Who can think of some way to defeat this?" The wise men of his court pondered the problem and then gathered together, from Greece, Egypt, and Persia, a group of more than forty times thirty blacksmiths, all of whom were expert at their trade. They made a horse of iron, with an iron saddle and an iron rider; its joints were held together with nails and solder, and then they polished both the rider and his steed. It was mounted on wheels and filled with black oil. They pushed it in front of Sekandar, who was pleased by the device and saw that it would be very useful. He ordered that more than a thousand of these iron horses and riders be made. What king had ever seen an army of dappled, gray, bay, and black horses, all of them made of iron? The devices went forward on wheels, and looked exactly like cavalry prepared for war.

Sekandar's Battle Against the Indian Troops; He Kills Foor

As Sekandar approached Foor's forces, the two armies caught sight of each other; amid clouds of dust a great cry went up from each side, and the warriors advanced on each other eager for battle. Then Sekandar's men set fire to oil in the iron horses and routed Foor's forces. Flames flared out from the iron steeds, and as soon as the elephants saw this they plunged precipitately this way and that. Foor's army was in turmoil, and when the elephants wrapped their trunks around the burning horses, they were maddened by their wounds, and their mahouts were bewildered as to what to do. The whole Indian army, including its mighty elephants, began to flee, and Sekandar pursued his malicious enemies like the wind. As the air darkened at nightfall there was nowhere left for the army to fight. Sekandar and the Greeks halted at a place between two mountains and sent out scouts to keep their camp safe from the enemy.

When the sun rose like a gold ingot, making the world as bright as clear crystal, the din of trumpets, bugles, and fifes rang out, and the two armies, thrusting their lances into the heavens, prepared to fight again. Clutching his Greek sword, Sekandar came between the hosts and sent a horseman to shout from a distance to Foor,

> "Sekandar stands before his troops and seeks
> To talk with Foor, and hear the words he speaks."

When Foor heard this he hurried to the head of his troops. Sekandar said,

> "Two armies have been shattered on these plains
> Where feral scavengers eat human brains,
> And horses tread on bones. We're brave and young,
> Each of us is a noble champion—
> Our warriors have been killed, or they have fled:
> Why should they flee, or be left here for dead?
> Why should two countries fight when combat can
> Decide who is the victor, man to man?
> Prepare to face me, one of us alone
> Will live to claim these armies and this throne."

Foor agreed to his proposal, thinking that his own body was like a lion's and that his horse was the equal of any fierce dragon, while Sekandar was as thin as a reed, wore light armor, and rode an exhausted mount. He said,

> "This is a noble custom: hand to hand
> We will decide who's ruler of this land."

Grasping their swords, they advanced on one another in the space between the two hosts. When Sekandar saw his massive opponent, his fearsome sword in hand and mounted on a huge horse, he was astonished and almost despaired of his life. Nevertheless he went forward, and as he did so Foor was distracted by a cry that went up from the rear of his army and turned toward it. Like the wind then Sekandar bore down on him, and struck the lion-like warrior with a mighty sword blow. The blade sliced through Foor's neck and trunk, and he fell from his horse to the earth.

The Greek commander was overjoyed and his warriors rushed forward; the earth and clouds re-echoed with the thunder of a lion-skin drum, and the blare of trumpets. The Indian warriors looked on Sekandar with fury and were ready to fight, but a voice rang out from the Greek ranks: "Foor's head lies here in the dust, his mammoth body is hacked and torn, who is it you wish to fight for, who will benefit from more sword blows and destruction? Sekandar has become to you as Foor was; it is he you must look to now for battles and banquets." With a roar the Indian warriors called out their agreement, and they came forward to gaze at Foor's hacked and bloody body. A wail of sorrow went up from their ranks, and they threw down their weapons. Fearfully they went before Sekandar, groaning and heaping dust on their heads, but Sekandar returned their weapons, and his words were welcoming: "One Indian has died here, but you should not grieve. I shall cherish you more than he did and try to drive sorrow from your lives. I will distribute his wealth among you, and make the Indians powerful with crowns and throne." Then he mounted Foor's throne; on the one side there was mourning and on the other feasting. But this is the way of the passing world, which brings sorrow to those who dwell in it.

For two months Sekandar sat on the Indian throne, distributing wealth to the army; then he placed there as his regent an Indian nobleman called Savorg, saying to him, "Don't hide your gold away. Distribute and consume whatever comes to you, and put no faith in this passing world, which sometimes favors Sekandar, sometimes Foor, and sometimes gives us pain and rage, sometimes joy and feasting." Savorg too distributed gold and silver to the Indian warriors.

* * *

Sekandar Leads His Army to Egypt

When he returned from his pilgrimage he bestowed gold on Nasr,[9] enriching those who had been poor and obliged to find food by their own labors. Then he led his army to Jeddah, where he didn't stay long. The soldiers were set to work making ships and a number of boats, in which the world conqueror and his army set off for Egypt. The Egyptian king at that time was named Qaytun, and he possessed an unimaginably large army; when he heard that a victorious world conqueror was coming with a following wind from the shrine at Mecca, he set out with a large company of soldiers to welcome him and took coins, slaves, and crowns as presents. Sekandar was pleased to see him and stayed in Egypt for a year, until he and his troops were well rested.

Andalusia[1] was ruled over by a woman; she was wise, had innumerable troops at her disposal, and ruled in prosperity and happiness. The name of this generous and ambitious woman was Qaydafeh.[2] She sought out a painter from the

9. An Arab descendant of Ishmael (the older son of Abraham and the legendary forefather of the Arab people); he welcomes Sekandar to the Hijaz (modern Arabia) and Yemen. While there, Sekandar makes a pilgrimage to the Ka'aba at Mecca (a site of worship even before the rise of Islam).
1. Andalusia (or, more accurately, al-Andalus)

became the name of modern Spain during the period of Islamic rule, which began about a thousand years after Alexander died and extended well past Ferdowsi's own time.
2. Queen of Andalusia; she corresponds to Candace, queen of the White Ethiopians, in Greek, Latin, and European versions of the Alexander story.

ranks of her soldiers, someone who could make an accurate likeness, and said to him, "Go to Sekandar, and see that you make no mention of my country or of me. Look carefully at him, see what his complexion is, examine his face and stature, and then paint me a full-length portrait of him." The painter heard her and immediately mounted his horse, ready to carry out his sovereign's orders. As quick as a royal courier he made his way from Andalusia to Egypt and into the presence of Sekandar. He observed him when he gave audience and when he was in the saddle; then he took paper and Chinese ink,[3] drew his portrait exactly as he was in real life, and returned to Andalusia. Qaydafeh was moved when she saw Sekandar's face and sighed to herself, then hid the portrait away.

Sekandar asked Qaytun, "Who is Qaydafeh's equal in the world?"

> And King Qaytun replied, "In all the earth
> There's no one of her glory and her worth;
> Unless he were to read the muster rolls
> No one could count the soldiers she controls.
> You won't find anyone in any land
> Who has the wealth she's able to command,
> Who has her dignity, her eloquence,
> Her wisdom, goodness, and magnificence.
> She's built from stone a wide and wondrous town
> So strong no leopard's claws could tear it down—
> Four parasangs in length, no man can measure
> Its endless width. And if you ask for treasure,
> Hers is uncountable; for years there's been
> Talk in the world of this exalted queen."

Sekandar's Letter to Qaydafeh

Sekandar summoned a scribe and had a letter written on silk, from Sekandar, the slayer of lions and conqueror of cities, to Qaydafeh the wise, whose name is unequalled in glory. The letter opened by invoking God, who is generous and just and who bestows prosperity on those who merit it, and continued: "I have not rushed into war with you; rather, I have been weighing the reports of the splendor of your court. When they bring you this letter, may it enlighten your dark soul. Send tribute to me, and understand that you do not have the strength to oppose me. You are wise, so act with foresight, as a powerful and religious sovereign should. If you attempt any kind of trick against me, you will see nothing but adverse fortune come your way. You don't have to look far to learn this lesson: consider what happened to Dara and Foor." As soon as the ink had dried the letter was sealed with musk.

A quick messenger took the letter at Sekandar's command, and when Qaydafeh read it she was astonished at its language. Her answer was as follows: "Praise be to him who created the earth, who has made you victorious over Foor of India, over Dara, and over the nobles of Sind. Your victory over these warriors has made you willful. You have crowned yourself in victory, but how can you put me on their level? I am far greater than they were, in *farr* and

---

3. Very high quality ink.

in glory, in my armies, and in my royal wealth. How can I submit to a Greek overlord, and how can you expect me to tremble with fear because of your threats? My armies number more than a thousand thousand men, and princes command every one of those armies. Who are you that you should boast in this way? Your defeat of Dara has made you the prince of braggarts!" She placed her gold seal on the letter and dispatched the messenger, who rode like the wind.

The Greeks Capture Qaydafeh's Son

Sekandar read her letter and then he had the trumpets sounded and his army led out. They marched for a month until they reached the borders of Qaydafeh's lands. A king called Faryan reigned there, a man possessed of an army and wealth, and successful in his life. His city was built to withstand war, and its walls were so high that cranes could not overfly them. He and his army occupied this fortress, and Sekandar ordered that balistas and catapults be brought up to batter the walls. After a week of fighting his army entered the town, and the victor gave orders that no blood was to be spilled.

One of Qaydafeh's sons, named Qaydrus, was married to Faryan's daughter, and was in the city, as his father-in-law delighted in his company. Qaydrus and his wife, however, had been captured by a man named Shahrgir; Sekandar knew of this and looked for some way to free them. He summoned his vizier, a wise and reasonable man named Bitqun, and showed him his crown and throne, saying, "Qaydrus and his bride will come before you, and I shall call you Sekandar, the son of Filqus. You will be seated on the throne here like a king, and I will stand ready to serve you. You will give orders that Qaydrus's head is to be severed from his shoulders by the executioner. I will humble myself before you and plead for them; you will clear the audience hall of courtiers, and when I redouble my pleas, you will grant my request." The vizier was very troubled by all this, as he was unsure what it meant. Sekandar continued, "This business must remain secret. Call me in as an envoy and talk a little about Qaydafeh; then cordially send me off to her with ten horsemen, saying, 'Hurry and take this letter and bring me the answer.'" Bitqun replied, "I will do it: I'll carry out this deception according to your orders."

Dawn came, the sun drew its glittering dagger, and night fled away in fear. Bitqun sat on the royal throne, but there was shame in his face and anxiety in his heart. Sekandar stood before him as a servant: he had closed the doors to the court and opened the doors to deception. When Shahrgir led in Qaydafeh's weeping son as a captive, together with his young and beautiful wife, who was wringing her hands in grief, Bitqun quickly said, "Who is this man, who has cause to weep so much?" The young man answered, "Come to your senses! I am Qaydrus, Qaydafeh's son, and this is Faryan's daughter, my sole wife. I wish to take her home and cherish her like my own soul, but I am a prisoner in Shahrgir's hands, my soul wounded by the stars, my body by arrows." When Bitqun heard him he was distressed and angry. He started up and said to the executioner, "These two must be buried beneath the dust! Cut off their heads with your Indian sword: now, just as they are, in chains here."

Sekandar came forward and kissed the ground, and said, "Great king of royal lineage, if you will free them for my sake, I shall be able to hold my head up in any company. Why should you vengefully cut off the heads of innocent people? The world's Creator will not look well on us for this." Wise Bitqun answered him, "You have freed these two from death," and to Qaydrus he added, "You've kept your head, which was already leaving your shoulders! Now I shall send you and this man who has interceded for you to your mother, and he can explain what has happened. It would be good if she would then send us tribute: this would mean that no one will lose his skin in this quarrel. Look after this vizier of mine, who will offer your mother war with me or prosperity; act well toward him as he has done toward you, since a noble man's heart is moved to repay kindness. When he has received the queen's answer, send him safely back to me." Qaydrus replied,

> "I will not take my heart or ears or eyes
> From him: how could I treat him otherwise
> Since he has here restored to me my wife,
> My soul, the living sweetness of my life?"

Sekandar Goes as an Envoy to Qaydafeh

Sekandar selected ten suitable companions from among the Greeks: they were all privy to his identity and willing to keep his secret. He said to them, "On this journey address me as Bitqun." Qaydrus led the group, and Sekandar watched him and listened to him attentively. Their splendid horses galloped forward like fire, until the travelers came to a mountain made all of crystal, yet with fruit trees and many plants growing on its slopes. They continued into the queen's realm, and when Qaydafeh heard that her son, about whom she had been anxiously seeking news, was approaching, she went out to welcome him with a large escort of nobles. As soon as Qaydrus saw his mother he dismounted and made his obeisance before her. She told him to remount, and as they rode on together, she grasped his hand in hers. Qaydrus told her all that he had seen and heard, and he turned pale as he described his sufferings in Faryan's city, and how he was now bereft of his crown, throne, army, and wealth. And he added, "This man who has come with us saved my and my bride's lives; if he hadn't intervened, Sekandar would have ordered that my head be cut off and my body burned. Treat him well, and don't hold back with excuses that would make me break my promise to him."

Hearing her son's words, Qaydafeh was distraught with grief. She had the messenger summoned from her palace where he had been installed and motioned him to a fine throne. She questioned him closely and made much of him and saw that a special residence was set aside for his stay. There she sent fine foods, clothes, and carpets.

At dawn the next morning Sekandar made his way to the court to talk with the queen. Servants drew the curtain aside and let his horse enter. He stared in wonder at Qaydafeh on her ivory throne, with her crown studded with rubies and turquoise, wearing a Chinese cloak woven with gold, her many serving girls with their necklaces and earrings standing around her, her face shining like the sun, her throne supported on crystal columns, her gold dress woven with jewels and clasped with a precious black and white Yemeni stone. Under his breath he called on God repeatedly. He saw that her throne alone surpassed anything that Greece or Persia could provide. He came forward and kissed the ground, like a man anxious to make a good impression. Qaydafeh encouraged him by asking a number of questions; then, like the sun passing from the dome of the sky she declared that the audience for strangers was over, and summoned a meal, wine, and musicians. Tables made of teak and inlaid with gold on an ivory ground were brought in; various kinds of food were served, and wine was set out for when they had finished eating. Gold and silver trays were put before them; first they drank to Qaydafeh herself, and then, as she drank more deeply, the queen began to look closely at Sekandar. She said to her steward, "Bring me that shining silk with the charming face painted on it; bring it quickly, just as it is. Don't stand there wringing your hands, go!"

The steward brought the cloth and laid it before her. She stared at it for a long time and then looked at Sekandar's face: she saw no difference between them. Qaydafeh knew that her guest was the Greek king and the commander of his armies, that he had made himself his own messenger and bravely come into her presence. She said to him, "You seem a man well favored by fortune. Tell me, what message did Sekandar give to you?" And he replied, "The world's king spoke to me in the presence of our nobles. He said to tell the pure-hearted Qaydafeh, 'Pursue only honesty, pay attention to what I say, and do not turn your head aside from my orders. If your heart harbors any rebellion, I shall bring an army against you that will break it in pieces. I have found evidence of your greatness, and I have not hurried to declare war on you. Wisdom and modesty are yours, and your subtle policies maintain the world in safety. If you willingly pay me tribute, you need have no fear of me; if you refuse to go the way of rebellion and disaster, you will see from me nothing but kindness and righteousness.'"

Qaydafeh was infuriated when she heard this, but she thought that silence was the best policy. She said, "Go to your quarters now, and rest with your companions. When you come to me tomorrow, I shall give you my answer and some good advice for your return journey." Sekandar went to the building that had been assigned to him and spent the night considering what he should do. When the world's lamp appeared above the mountaintops, and the plains and foothills took on the appearance of glittering brocade, Sekandar made his way back to Qaydafeh's court; his lips were full of smiles, his heart of grief and anxiety. The chancellor recognized him as the foreign envoy and, after questioning him, led him into the queen's presence. The audience hall was full of strangers. The queen's throne was crystal patterned with agates and emeralds surrounding gems of royal worth; its base was sandal and aloes wood and it rested on pillars studded with turquoise. Sekandar was astonished at the splendor and glory he saw, and he thought, "This is indeed a throne room, and no God-fearing man ever saw its like." He came forward to the queen and was directed to a subsidiary golden throne. Qaydafeh said to him, "Well, Bitqun, why are you staring in this way? Is it that Greece can't produce the like of what you see here, in my humble country?"

Sekandar replied, "Your majesty, you should not speak contemptuously of this palace. It is far more glorious than the palaces of other kings and seems like a mine of precious stones." Qaydafeh laughed at his reaction, and she felt delight in her heart that she was able to tease him in this way. Then she cleared the court and motioned the envoy to come closer to her. She said to him,

"Filqus's son, I see you're fashioned for
Battles and royal banquets, peace and war!"

Sekandar turned pale at her words, and then blushed violently; his soul was filled with distress. He said, "Wise queen, such words are not worthy of you. I am Bitqun, don't say that I am a son of Filqus. I give thanks to God that there is no one of noble lineage here, because if he reported what you have said to my king my soul would soon be separated from my body." Qaydafeh replied,

"Enough excuses! If with your own eyes
You see yourself, then you must recognize
The truth of what I say, and don't attempt
Either to lie or treat me with contempt."

Then she produced the silk with the charming face painted upon it and laid it before him; if the painted face had moved at all you would have said that it was Sekandar himself. Sekandar saw it and he nervously chewed his lower lip; the day had suddenly turned as dark as night for him. He said, "A man should never go out in the world without a hidden dagger!" Qaydafeh answered, "If you had your sword belt on and stood before me with a dagger, you'd have neither the strength nor an adequate sword nor a place to fight nor a means of escape." Sekandar said, "A noble and ambitious man should not flinch at danger; a low-minded person will never rise in the world. If I had my arms and armor here, all your palace would be a sea of blood; I'd have killed you, or ripped open my own belly in front of those who hate me!"

Qaydafeh Gives Sekandar Some Advice

Qaydafeh laughed at his blustering manliness and his angry words. She said, "O lion-like king, don't let yourself be led astray by your male pride! The Indian king Foor wasn't killed because of your glory, and neither were Dara and the heroes of Sind. Their good fortune was at an end, and yours was in the ascendant; and now you're so full of your manly valor because you've become the greatest man on earth at the moment. But you should know that all good things come from God, and while you live you should be grateful to him. You say the world is yours because of your knowledge, but what you say does not seem true to me. What will knowledge avail you when you go into the maw of the dragon death? Acting as your own envoy is sewing your shroud while you are still young. I am not in the habit of shedding blood, nor of attacking rulers. When a monarch has power and is merciful and just, that is when he becomes knowledgeable. Know that whoever spills a king's blood will see nothing but fire as his reward. Be assured of your safety, and leave here with joy. But when you have gone change your habits: don't go acting as your own messenger again, because even the dust knows that you are Sekandar. And I'm not aware of any great hero whose portrait I don't possess, stored away with a reliable courtier. While you remain here I will call you Bitqun and seat you at court accordingly, so that no one will guess your secret or hear your name. I will send you on your way in safety, but you, my lord, must be reasonable and swear that you will never plot against my son, my country, or any of my people or allies, and that you will refer to me only as your equal, as the ruler of my own country."

Freed from the threat of being killed, Sekandar rejoiced to hear her words. He swore by the just God, by the Christian faith, and by the dust of battle that he would act only kindly and righteously toward her land, her son, and her noble allies, and that he would never plot their destruction. When she had heard his oath, Qaydafeh said, "There is one other piece of advice that should not be kept from you: know then that my son Taynush has little sense and pays scant attention to my knowledge and advice. He is Foor's son-in-law and he must not in any way suspect that you and Sekandar occupy the same skin, or even that you are friends. He is eager to avenge Foor, and to confound the earth and sky in war. Now, go joyfully and safely to your own quarters, and have no fear of the world's sorrows."

* * *

Sekandar Sees a Corpse in the Palace of Topazes

The king and his army marched onward for a month and were sorely tried by their journey. They came to a mountain, where they saw no sign of either wild or domestic animals. The mountain's crest was of lapis lazuli, and a palace stood there, made of topazes. It was filled with crystal chandeliers, and in its midst was a fountain of salt water. Next to this fountain was a throne for two people, on which was stretched a wretched corpse. He had a man's body, but his head was like that of a boar; there was a pillow of camphor beneath his head, and a brocade covering had been drawn up over his body. Instead of a lamp a brilliant red jewel shone there, illuminating the whole area; its rays twinkled like stars in the water, and all the chamber glowed as if in sunlight. Whoever went there to take something, or even simply set foot within the palace, found himself rooted to the spot; his whole body began to tremble, and he started to waste away.

A cry came from the salt water, saying, "O king, still filled with longing and desire, don't play the fool much longer! You have seen many things that no man ever saw, but now it's time to draw rein. Your life has shortened now, and the royal throne is without its king." Sekandar was afraid and hurried back to his camp as fast as wind-blown smoke. Quickly he led his army away, weeping and calling on God's name. From that mountain he headed toward the desert, afflicted with sorrow and concerned for his soul. And so he went forward, at the head of his troops, weeping and in pain.

Sekandar Sees the Speaking Tree

The desert road led to a city, and Sekandar was relieved when he heard human voices there. The whole area was one of gardens and fine buildings and was a place to delight any man. The city's noblemen welcomed him, calling out greetings and showering him with gold and jewels. "It is wonderful that you have come to visit us," they said. "No army has ever entered this town, and no one in it has ever heard the name of 'king.' Now that you have come our souls are yours, and may you live with bodily health and spiritual serenity." Sekandar was pleased by their welcome and rested from the journey across the desert. He said to them, "What is there here that's astonishing, that should be inquired into?" A guide said to him, "Victorious king, there is a marvel here, a tree that has two separate trunks together, one of which is female and the other male, and these splendid tree limbs can speak. At night the female trunk becomes sweet smelling and speaks, and when the daylight comes, the male speaks." Sekandar and his Greek cavalry, with the nobles of the town gathered around, listened and said, "When is it you say that the tree speaks in a loud voice?" The translator replied, "A little after day has disappeared one of the trunks begins to speak, and a lucky man will hear its voice; in the dark night the female speaks, and its leaves then smell like musk."

Sekandar answered, "When we go beyond the tree, what wonders are there on the other side?" The reply was, "When you pass the tree there is little argument about which way to take, as there is no place beyond there; guides say it is the world's end. A dark desert lies ahead of you, but no man is so weary of his own soul as to go there. None of us have ever seen or heard that there are any animals there, or that birds fly there." Sekandar and his troops went forward, and when they came near the speaking tree the ground throbbed with heat and the soil there was covered with the pelts of wild beasts. He asked his guide what the pelts were, and who it was that had skinned so many animals in this way. The man answered, "The tree has many worshippers, and when they come here to worship, they feed on the flesh of wild animals."

When the sun reached its zenith Sekandar heard a voice above him, coming from the leaves of the tree; it was a voice to strike terror and foreboding in a man. He was afraid and said to the interpreter, "You are wise and mean well, tell me what the leaves are saying, which makes my heart dissolve within me." "O king, favored by fortune, the leaves say, 'However much Sekandar wanders in the world, he has already seen his share of blessings: when he has reigned for fourteen years, he must quit the royal throne.'" At the guide's words Sekandar's heart filled with pain, and he wept bitterly. He was sad and silent then, speaking to no one, until midnight. Then the leaves of the other trunk began to speak, and Sekandar again asked the interpreter what they said. He replied, "The female tree says, 'Do not puff yourself up with greed; why torment your soul in this way? Greed makes you wander the wide world, harass mankind, and kill kings. But you are not long for this earth now; do not darken and deaden your days like this.'" Then the king said to the interpreter, "Pure of heart and noble as you are, ask them one question: Will this fateful day come in Greece; will my mother see me alive again, before someone covers my face in death?"

The speaking tree replied, "Few days remain;
You must prepare your final baggage train.
Neither your mother, nor your family,
Nor the veiled women of your land will see
Your face again. Death will come soon: you'll die
In a strange land, with strangers standing by.
The stars and crown and throne and worldly glory
Are sated with Sekandar and his story."

Sekandar left the tree, his heart wounded as if by a sword. When he returned to his camp, his chieftains went into the town to collect the gifts from the town's nobility. Among these was a cuirass that shone like the waters of the Nile and was as huge as an elephant skin: it had two long tusks attached to it and was so heavy it was hard to lift. There was other armor, as well as fine brocade, a hundred golden eggs each weighing sixty *man*,[4] and a rhinoceros made of gold and jewels. Sekandar accepted the gifts and led off his army, weeping bitter tears as he went.

Sekandar Visits the Emperor of China

Now Sekandar led his army toward China. For forty days they traveled, until they reached the sea. There the army made camp and the king pitched his brocade pavilion. He summoned a scribe to write a letter to the Chinese emperor from Sekandar, the seizer of cities. The message was filled with promises and threats, and when it was completed Sekandar himself went as the envoy, taking with him an intelligent companion who was one with him in heart and speech and who could advise him as to what to do and what not to do. He entrusted his troops to the army's commander and chose five Greeks as his escort.

When news reached the Chinese emperor that an envoy was approaching his country, he sent troops out to meet him. Sekandar reached the court and the emperor came forward in welcome, but his heart was filled with suspicious thoughts. Sekandar ran forward and made his obeisance to him, and then was seated in the palace for a long while. The emperor questioned him and made much of him and assigned him noble sleeping quarters. As the sun rose over the mountains, dying their summits gold, the envoy was summoned to court. Sekandar spoke at length, saying what was appropriate, and then handed over the letter. It was addressed from the king of Greece, possessor of the world, lord of every country, on whom other kings call down God's blessings. It continued, "My orders for China are that she remain prosperous, and that she should not prepare for war against me; it was war against me that destroyed Foor, and Dara, who was the lord of the world, and Faryan the Arab, and other sovereigns. From the east to the west no one ignores my commands, the heavens themselves do not know the number of my troops, and Venus[5] and the sun could not count them. If you disobey any command of mine you will bring distress on yourself and your country. When you read my letter, bring me tribute; do not trouble yourself about this, or look for evil allies to make war on me. If you come you will see me in the midst of my troops, and when I see that you are honest and mean well I shall confirm you in the possession of your crown and throne, and no misfortune will come to you. If, however, you are reluctant to come before your king, send me things that are peculiar to China—your country's gold work, horses, swords, seal rings, clothes, cloth, ivory thrones, fine brocade, necklaces, crowns—that is, if you have no wish to be harmed by me. Send my soldiers back to me, and rest assured that your wealth, throne, and crown are safe."

When the emperor of China saw what was in the letter, he started up in fury, but then chose silence as a better course. He laughed and said to the envoy, "May your king be a partner to the heavens! Tell me what you know about him. Tell me about his conversation, his height and appearance, and what kind of a man he is." The envoy said, "Great lord of China, you should understand that

---

4. A Persian unit of weight, usually equivalent to about 9 lbs.

5. The morning and the evening star, as well as the Roman goddess of love.

there is no one else in the world like Sekandar. In his manliness, policy, good fortune, and wisdom he surpasses all that anyone could imagine. He is as tall as a cypress tree, has an elephant's strength, and is as generous as the waters of the Nile; his tongue can be as cutting as a sword, but he can charm an eagle down from the clouds." When he heard all this, the emperor changed his mind. He ordered that wine and a banquet be laid out in the palace gardens. He drank till evening brought darkness to the world, and the company became tipsy. Then he said to the envoy, "May your king be Jupiter's[6] partner. At first light I'll compose an answer to his letter, and what I write will make the day seem splendid to your eyes." Sekandar was half drunk, and he staggered from the garden to his quarters with an orange in his hand.

When the sun rose in Leo[7] and the heavens dispelled the darkness, Sekandar went to the emperor, and all suspicious thoughts were far from his heart. The emperor asked him, "How did you spend the night? When you left you were quite overcome with wine." Then he summoned a scribe, who brought paper, musk, and ambergris, and dictated a letter. He began with praise of God, the lord of chivalry, justice, and ability, of cultivated behavior, abstinence, and piety, and called down his blessings on the Greek king. Then he continued, "Your eloquent envoy has arrived, bringing the king's letter. I have read through the royal words and discussed its contents with my nobles. As for your claims concerning the wars against Dara, Faryan, and Foor, in which you were victorious, so that you became a shepherd whose flock consists of kings, you should not consider what comes about through the will of the Lord of the Sun and Moon as the result of your own valor and the might of your army. When a great man's days are numbered, what difference does it make whether he dies in battle or at a banquet? If they died in battle with you this is because their fate was fixed for that day, and fate is not to be hurried or delayed. You should not pride yourself so much on your victories over them, because even if you are made of iron there is no doubt that you too will die. Where now are Feraydun, Zahhak, and Jamshid,[8] who came like the wind and left like a breath? I am not afraid of you and I will not make war against you, neither shall I puff myself up with pride as you are doing. It is not my habit to shed blood, and besides it would be unworthy of my faith for me to do evil in this way. You summon me, but to no purpose; I serve God, not kings. I send with this more riches than you have dreamed of, so that there shall be no doubting my munificence."

These words were an arrow in Sekandar's vital organs, and he blushed with shame. In his heart he said, "Never again shall I go somewhere disguised as my own envoy." He returned to his quarters and prepared to leave the Chinese court.

The proud emperor opened his treasuries' doors, since he was not a man who found generosity difficult. First he ordered that fifty crowns and ten ivory thrones encrusted with jewels be brought; then a thousand camel loads of gold and silver goods, and a thousand more of Chinese brocades and silks, of camphor, musk, perfumes, and ambergris. He had little regard for wealth, and it eased his heart to be bountiful in this way. He had ten thousand each of the pelts of gray

6. In Roman mythology, the king of the gods.
7. Sekandar's birth sign (the sun rises in Leo in midsummer), viewed in astrology as fiery

and masculine.
8. Legendary Persian heroic rulers whose stories appear earlier in the *Shahnameh*.

squirrel, ermine, and sable brought, and as many carpets and crystal goblets, and his wise treasurer saw to their being loaded on pack animals. Then he added three hundred silver saddles and fifty golden ones, together with three hundred red-haired camels loaded with Chinese rarities. He chose as envoy an eloquent and dignified Chinese sage and told him to take his message to the Greek king with all goodwill and splendor, and to say that Sekandar would be warmly welcomed at the Chinese court for as long as he wished to stay there.

The envoy traveled with Sekandar, unaware that he was the Greek king. But when Sekandar's regent came forward and the king told him of his adventures, and the army congratulated him on his safe return and bowed to the ground before him, the envoy realized that he was indeed the Greek king and dismounted in consternation. Sekandar said to him, "There is no need for apologies, but do not tell your emperor of this!" They rested for a night, and the next morning Sekandar sat on the royal throne. He gave gifts to the envoy and said to him, "Go to your emperor and tell him that I say 'You have found honor and respect with me. If you wish to stay where you are, all China is yours, and if you wish to go elsewhere, that too is open to you. I shall rest here for a while, because such a large army as mine cannot be mobilized quickly.'" The envoy returned like the wind, and gave Sekandar's message to the emperor.

Sekandar Leads His Army to Babylon

Sekandar camped there for a month, and then led his army toward Babylon, and the air was darkened with the dust of their march. They pressed on for a month, and no one had any rest during this time. They came to a mountain range so high that its summit was hidden by dark clouds, as if it reached to Saturn. The king and his army could see no way forward but over the mountains and so with difficulty they climbed up toward the crest. The climb exhausted them, but once there they saw a deep lake lying below them. Joyfully and praising God, they began their descent; there was game of all kinds on every side, and for a while the soldiers lived off what they hunted.

Then in the distance a wild man appeared. He was covered in hair, and his body beneath the hair was a dark blue color, and he had huge ears, as big as an elephant's. The soldiers captured him and dragged him to Sekandar, who called on God in his astonishment at being confronted by such a creature. He said, "What kind of a man are you? What is your name? What can you find to live off in this lake, and what do you want from life?" The man replied, "O king, my mother and father call me Pillow-Ears." Then the king asked what it was that he could see in the middle of the lake, over toward where the sun rises. The man answered, "O king, and may you always be renowned in the world, that's a town that is like heaven; you'd say that earth had no part in its making. You won't see a single building there that isn't covered with fish skins and fish bones. On the walls they've painted the face of Afrasyah,[9] and he looks more splendid than the sun itself; and warlike Khosrow's[1] face is there too, and you can see his greatness and generosity by looking at it. They're painted on bones; you won't see

---

9. King of Turan, the archenemy of Iran; a powerful warrior, he was the agent of the evil god Ahriman.

1. One of the greatest of the Persian kings (531–579), famous for military conquests, cultural achievements, and major building projects.

one bit of soil in the whole city! The people eat fish there; that's the only thing they have to nourish them. If the king orders me to, I'll go there, but without any of your soldiers." Sekandar said to the man with huge ears, "Go, and bring back someone from the town, so that we can see something new."

Pillow-Ears hurried off to the town and soon came back with some of its inhabitants. Seventy men crossed the water with him; some were young and some old, and they were dressed in various kinds of silks. The older, more dignified men each carried a golden goblet filled with pearls, and the young ones each carried a crown; they came before Sekandar with their heads reverently bowed. They made their obeisance to him, and he talked with them for a long time. The army stayed there that night, and at cockcrow next morning the din of drums rang out from the king's pavilion. Sekandar continued the march to Babylon, and the air was dark with the dust sent up by his soldiers.

Sekandar's Letter to Arestalis[2] and Arestalis's Reply

The king knew that death was close, and that his days were darkening, and he decided that no one of royal lineage should be left alive in the world: he wanted to ensure that no man would be able to lead an army against Greece. With his mind fixed on this arrogant scheme, he wrote a letter to Arestalis, saying he would invite everyone of royal lineage to his court, where they were to come unsuspecting of what was in store for them. When this letter was delivered to the Greek sage, his heart seemed to break in two. Immediately he wrote a reply, weeping as if his ink were tears. "The king of the world's missive arrived, and he should give up this evil design of his. As for the evil you have already done, think no more of it but distribute goods to the poor. For the future, abstain from evil and give your soul to God; sow nothing but seeds of goodness in the world. From birth we are all marked for death, and we have no choice but to submit. No one who dies takes his sovereignty with him; he leaves, and hands on his greatness to another. Live within limits and do not shed the blood of the great families, which will make you cursed until the resurrection. And if there is no army or king in Persia, armies will sweep in from Turkestan, India, Scythia, and China, and it would be no surprise if whoever took Persia then marched on the west. The descendants of the Persian kings should not be harmed so much as by a breath of wind. Summon them to your court, but be generous to them, feast them, and consult with them. Treat each according to his rank and see that their names are listed in your pension rolls, since it is from them that you took the world, paying nothing for it. Do not give any of them power over another, or refer to any of them as king of the world, but make these royal nobles a shield to protect the west against foreign invasion."

Sekandar changed his mind when he read this letter. He summoned the world's nobly born, all who were chivalrous by nature, to his court, and assigned them suitable places there. He wrote a charter, which designated the portion of each, with the stipulation that none was to encroach on another's power: these nobles he called "kings of the peoples."

2. The Greek philosopher Aristotle (384– 322 B.C.E.), who tutored Alexander the Great. A fictional exchange of letters between Alexander and Aristotle (sometimes called *Wonders of the East*) circulated widely in Europe and the Islamic world throughout the Middle Ages.

That night Sekandar reached Babylon, where he was joyfully greeted by the local nobility. During the same night a woman gave birth to an astonishing child that had a lion's head, a human chest and human shoulders, a cow's tail, and hooves. The baby was stillborn, and it would have been better if the woman had had no offspring at all rather than such a monster. Immediately they brought the child to Sekandar, who took it as an omen, and ordered that it be buried. He told his astrologers of the child, who grew pensive and silent. He demanded their opinion, saying, "If you keep anything back from me I'll cut your heads from your bodies this minute, and your shroud will be a lion's maw." When the king stormed in this way, they said:

> "First then, as scribes have written, at your birth
> The lion's emblem, Leo, ruled the earth.
> You saw the dead child had a lion's head,
> Which means your majesty will soon be dead.
> The world will be a place of strife until
> A new king bends its peoples to his will."
> The king grew pensive, then replied, "I see
> Death comes, for which there is no remedy.
> I'm not long for this world, I know, but I
> Refuse to brood on this until I die.
> Death comes to us on the appointed day—
> We cannot make fate hurry, or delay."

Sekandar's Letter to His Mother

That day, in Babylon, he fell sick, and he knew that his end was approaching. He summoned an experienced scribe and dictated what was in his heart, in a letter to his mother. He said, "The signs of death cannot be hidden; I have lived the life allotted to me in this world, and we cannot hurry or delay our fate. Do not grieve at my death, for this is not a new thing in the world: all who are born must die, be they kings or paupers. I shall tell our chieftains that when they return from this land to Greece they must obey you alone. I have established those Persians who fought against our armies as lords over their realm, so that they shall have no desire to attack Greece; our country will be secure and at peace. See that my body is buried in Egypt, and that you fulfill all that I say here. Every year distribute ten thousand gold coins of my wealth to the peasantry. If Roshanak[3] bears a son, then my name will surely survive; no one but he must become king of Greece, and he will renew the country's prosperity. But if, when her labor pains come to her, she bears a daughter, marry the child to one of Filqus's sons and call him my son, not my son-in-law, so that my name shall be remembered in the world. As for Kayd's innocent daughter, send her back to her father in India, together with the crowns and silver and gold and all the dowry she brought. Now I have completed my affairs and have no choice but to prepare my heart for death. First, see that my coffin is of gold and that my body's shroud is worthy of me; let it be of Chinese silk impregnated with sweet scents, and see that no one neglects the offices due to me. The joints of my coffin should be sealed with pitch, as well as camphor, musk, and ambergris. Honey should be poured into the coffin, then a layer of brocade

---

3. Sekandar's wife, the daughter of Darab.

placed there, on which my body is to be laid; when my face has been covered there is no more to be said. When I have gone, wise mother, remember my words. As for the things that I have sent from India, China, Turan, Iran, and Makran, keep what you need and distribute the surplus. Dear mother, my desire is that you be sensible and serene in your soul; do not torment yourself on my behalf, since no one who lives in the world lives forever. When your days too draw to a close, my soul shall surely see yours again; patience is a greater virtue than love, and a person blown hither and thither by emotion is contemptible. For months and years you lovingly cared for my body; now pray to God for my soul; with these prayers you will still care for me. And consider, who is there in all the world whose soul is not cast down by death?"

He sealed the letter and ordered that it be taken with all speed from Babylon to Greece, to give news there that the imperial glory had been eclipsed.

Sekandar Dies in Babylon

When the army learned of the king's illness, the world grew dark before them. Their eyes turned toward the throne, and the world was filled with rumors. Knowing that he had few days left to live and hearing of his army's concern, Sekandar gave orders that his sickbed be taken from the palace out to the open plain. His saddened troops saw his face devoid of color, and the plain rang from end to end with lamentations, as if the soldiers were burning in flames; they cried, "It is an evil day when the Greeks lose their king: misfortune triumphs, and now our country will be destroyed. Our enemies have reached their hearts' desire, while for us the world has turned bitter, and we shall mourn publicly and in secret."

> Then in a failing voice their king replied,
> "Live humbly, fearfully, when I have died,
> And if you'd grow and prosper see that you
> Keep my advice henceforth, in all you do.
> This is your duty to me when I'm gone
> Lest time undo the work that I have done."
> He spoke, and then his soul rose from his breast:
> The king who'd shattered armies was at rest.

An earsplitting wail went up from his troops as they heaped dust on their heads and wept bitter tears. They set fire to the royal pavilion, and the very earth seemed to cry out in sorrow. They cut the tails of a thousand horses and set their saddles on them back to front, as a sign of mourning. As they brought the golden coffin their cries resounded in the heavens; a bishop washed the corpse in clear rosewater and scattered pure camphor over it. They shrouded their king in golden brocade, lamenting as they did so, then placed him beneath a covering of Chinese silk, his body soaked from head to toe in honey. The coffin lid was fastened, and the noble tree whose shade had spread so widely was no more.

They passed the coffin from hand to hand across the plain, and as they went forward, two opinions began to be heard. The Persians said, "He should not be buried anywhere but here: this is the land of emperors, what are they doing carrying the coffin about the world like this?" But a Greek guide said, "It would not be right to bury him here; if you hear my view you'll see that I'm right. Sekandar should be buried in the soil that nourished him." A Persian interrupted, "No matter how much you continue this conversation it won't get to the root of the matter. I'll show you a meadow near here that's been preserved since the time of our ancient kings: old folk call it Jorm. There is a wooded area there, and a lake; if you ask it a question, an answer will come from the mountain nearby. Take an old man there, together with the coffin, and ask your question; if the mountain answers, it will give you the best advice." As quickly as mountain sheep they made their way to the thicket called Jorm. And when they asked their question, the answer came, "What are you doing with this royal coffin? The dust of Sekandar belongs in Alexandria, the town he founded while he was alive." As soon as they heard this, the soldiers hurried from the area.

The Mourning for Sekandar

When Sekandar's body reached Alexandria the world was beset with new disputes. The coffin was set down on the plain, and the land was filled with rumor and gossip. As many as a hundred thousand children, men, and women flocked there. The philosopher Arestalis was there, his eyes filled with bitter tears; the world watched as he stretched out his hand to the coffin and said, "Where are your intelligence, knowledge, and foresight, now that a narrow coffin is your resting place? Why in the days of your youth did you choose the earth as your couch?"

The Greek sages crowded round, each speaking in turn, lamenting Sekandar's death. And then his mother came running, and placed her face on his chest, and said,

> "O noble king, world-conqueror, whose state
> Was princely, and whose stars were fortunate,
> You're far away from me and seem so near,
> Far from your kin, far from your soldiers here.
> Would that my soul were your soul's slave, that I
> Might see the hearts of those who hate you die."
> Then Roshanak ran grieving to his side,
> Crying, "Where are those kings now, and their pride?
> Where's Dara, who once ruled the world? Where's Foor?
> Where's Ashk? Faryan? The sovereign of Sharzoor,
> And all those other lords who put their trust
> In battle and were dragged down to the dust?
> You seemed a storm cloud charged with hail: I said
> That you could never die, that you had shed
> So much blood, fought so many wars, that there
> Must be some secret you would not declare,
> Some talisman that fate had given you
> To keep you safe whatever you might do.
> You cleared the world of petty kings, brought down
> Into the dirt an empire's ancient crown,
> And when the tree you'd planted was to bear
> Its fruits you died, and left me in despair."

When the sky's golden shield descended, the nobles were exhausted by their grief, and they placed the coffin in the ground. There is nothing in the world so terrible and fearful as the fact that one comes like the wind and departs as a breath, and that neither justice nor oppression are apparent in this. Whether you are a king or a pauper you will discover no rhyme or reason to it. But one must act well, with valor and chivalry, and one must eat well and rejoice: I see no other fate for you, whether you are a subject or a prince. This is the way of the ancient world: Sekandar departed, and what remains of him now is the words we say about him. He killed thirty-six kings, but look how much of the world remained in his grasp when he died. He founded ten prosperous cities, and those cities are now reed beds. He sought things that no man has ever sought, and what remains of him within the circle of the horizon is words, nothing more. Words are the better portion since they do not decay as an old building decays in the snow and rain. I have finished with Sekandar now, and with the barrier that he built may our days be fortunate and prosperous.

SONG OF ROLAND
eleventh century

"Pagans are wrong and Christians are right." This poetic refrain, dividing the world into right and wrong, good and bad, white and black, Christian and non-Christian, expresses the fundamental outlook of the *Song of Roland*, which tells the story of how the heroic rearguard of Charlemagne's army was wiped out in an ambush at the mountain pass of Roncesvalles following their military victories in northern Spain. Yet this dualism goes beyond the metaphorical white hats and black hats of the Christian warriors and their "Saracen" (Muslim) opponents: from the first words of the poem, which identify Charlemagne as being at once "king" of the French people and "emperor" of the entire Christian world, the poem continuously defines things and persons from two points of view. The poetic rhythms of the text reaffirm this dualism as well, both within individual lines and in the doubling of stanzas (or *laisses*), when a heroic encounter on the battlefield is recounted first in simple terms, and a second time more elaborately. Yet the work never feels slow or repetitive: instead, the sequence of double stanzas heightens the reader's sense of anticipation, as the epic battle moves inexorably toward its bloody climax.

LIFE AND TIMES

At the very end of the earliest surviving copy of the *Song of Roland*, the so-called Oxford manuscript, the writer names himself: "Ci falt la geste que Turoldus declinet" ("here ends the story that Turoldus tells"). His name, a Latinized version of the Norman name "Turold" (Old Norse "Thorvaldr"), along with the French dialect of the poem, suggests that the poet who wrote and the courtly audiences who read—or, more likely, listened to—the *Song of Roland* were members of the new Anglo-Norman elite who dominated England following the Norman Conquest of 1066. These were the descendents of those same knights who, according to the twelfth-century chronicles of William of Malmesbury and Wace, had marched on the Anglo-Saxon armies of Harold, the last English claimant to the throne, while listening to their minstrel Taillefer "sing a song of Roland." This advancing Norman army would not be the last to find inspiration in the narrative of Charlemagne's heroic knight: in modern times, the *Song of Roland* has come to be seen as the foundational national epic of the French nation and, during the early twentieth century, was even used as a form of political propaganda.

THE SONG OF ROLAND

Although the Oxford manuscript dates to the mid-twelfth century, we know from Latin sources that the *Song of Roland* must have circulated much earlier in a variety of different forms, all of which were likely sung or recited. There may have been earlier manuscripts, now lost, but the text presented here is undoubtedly among the first versions of the song to be written down and thus fixed in its permanent form. Its oral origins persist, however, in the enigmatic "AOI" refrain, which appears at the close of several of the long *laisses* and may reflect a sung musical phrase or a chord played on the harp to note moments of particular drama. In the *Song of Roland*, we see one of the first manifestations of the rise of the vernacular into the realm of literature; before that time, written texts were almost exclusively in Latin, and the language spoken in daily life was thought to be simply a convenient medium for conversation, or for the evening entertainments of songs and recited tales as performed by jongleurs or minstrels. But by the time of the Oxford *Roland*, such works were entering into the poetic mainstream, begin-

ning to take their place alongside the epic tradition of **Virgil's** *Aeneid* and the histories of Alexander the Great. Known as the *chansons de geste*, or "songs of great deeds," these popular epics would gradually develop into the romances of the later Middle Ages, such as *Sir Gawain and the Green Knight*.

In keeping with the thematic dualism that underlies the *Song of Roland*—its division of the world into "pagan" wrong and "Christian" right—the setting of time and place as recounted in the Oxford manuscript is likewise double. The poem explicitly tells the story of the aftermath of the Frankish campaign in Spain, when in the late summer of 778 the victorious army of Charlemagne was ambushed by a band of local inhabitants at the pass of Roncesvalles. But by describing the attackers as an overwhelmingly large "Saracen" force instead of scattered Basque guerrillas, the poem reinvents eighth-century history in terms of the eleventh-century present. The result was a story of Christian battle against Muslim armies, inseparable—for the medieval reader—from the waves of crusades then being launched by European nations in an effort to conquer the Holy City of Jerusalem. The *Song of Roland* thus simultaneously looks backward to an idealized past, when the mighty king and emperor Charlemagne built his Holy Roman Empire, and forward to an anticipated period of unified European Christian rule over Jerusalem and, by extension, the whole world.

The poem opens with Charlemagne contemplating his seven long years of armed assault on Spain and deciding to return to his kingdom north of the Pyrenees, to "the sweet land of France." His army has conquered all the cities of Spain with the exception of Zaragoza, but Charlemagne, weary of battle, decides that rather than attacking the city he will accept a pledge of loyalty from its Saracen king, Marsilion. This decision precipitates the two parallel plots of the *Song of Roland*, one centering on the conflict between Christian and Saracen armies and the other centering on dissension within Charlemagne's own retinue of noble knights—his *douzepers*, or company of "twelve peers." These two plots are linked by the shared theme of treachery, in the form both of the deceitful behavior of the Saracen Marsilion, who lies to Charlemagne and attacks his men as soon as the French army begins its retreat from Spain, and of the betrayal carried out by Ganelon, the noble knight appointed by Charlemagne (at the suggestion of Roland, Ganelon's stepson and rival) to serve as messenger to Marsilion. While the first plot is acted out on the grand scale of armies, nations, and religions, the second plot is carried out on a more intimate stage, as something of a family feud. Because Ganelon is married to Charlemagne's sister, Roland is Charlemagne's nephew; and though that position brings him honor, it also obliges him to avoid the appearance of favoritism and to constantly prove his bravery and loyalty—even if doing so requires the rashest of deeds.

Roland is the exemplar of the ethical code of knighthood that is repeatedly praised in the poem, a code that entails not just exhibiting the conventional chivalric virtues of truthfulness, bravery, and loyalty but also balancing their competing claims—a more complex task. Roland's death results precisely from his extreme expression of the knightly virtues: when the rearguard is suddenly ambushed, he refuses to sound the alarm that would call back the main forces of Charlemagne's army, because he believes that asking for aid would cause him shame and prefers death to disgrace. That Roland is excessive, almost reckless, in his bravery is highlighted by the contrast with

Oliver, his closest companion and the brother of his fiancée, Aude. As the poet puts it while praising the shared excellence of the two knights, who are among the brightest lights in Charlemagne's retinue, "Roland is good [*proz*—literally, 'brave'], and Oliver is wise." Oliver's wisdom casts a shadow on Roland's more impetuous behavior: bravery is admirable, but taken to an extreme it leads not only to Roland's death but to the extermination of the entire rearguard. At the same time, it is important to stress that these deaths were not in vain, for it is the tragic fate of the rearguard that ultimately spurs Charlemagne to gather his forces and strike decisively at the Saracen armies of Spain. In this light, Roland's death appears as a necessary sacrifice, the loss that sets the stage for the greater victory.

The conflict of Muslim Spain and Christian France that erupts fully after Roland's death is initially played out between the armies of Marsilion and Charlemagne; after Marsilion is mortally wounded, however, the leadership of the Saracens shifts to Baligant, their "emir" (ruler), who suddenly appears in the poem. This thousand-line section of the text, about a quarter of the whole, is almost certainly a twelfth-century addition to the basic narrative of the *Song of Roland*. It gives the sense of the perpetual, ongoing nature of the "pagan" threat to Christendom, as another leader springs up almost immediately to replace his fallen predecessor. Yet in spite of the fundamental opposition of Christian and pagan, right and wrong, the code of knightly behavior informs the behavior of warriors on both sides. When Charlemagne's knights meet the Saracen Baligant on the field (as described in a passage not included below), they are struck not by his difference from them but by the ways in which he seems to belong to their own kind: "God, what a noble lord," they exclaim, "if only he were made a Christian." Indeed, religious conversion, held out as a possible means of bridging the gap separating pagan and Christian on the battlefield, is achieved after the final conquest of Zaragoza by the armies of Charlemagne. The French offer the choice of conversion or death to all the inhabitants, with one significant exception: the Saracen queen Bramimunde, widow of King Marsilion. Charlemagne insists that she be converted *pur amur*, that is, "through love." For the writer of the Oxford *Song of Roland*, this phrase appears to imply a sincere religious conversion, suggesting that Bramimunde—now renamed "Juliana"—embraces Christianity out of love for Jesus Christ. Other versions of this story feature a Saracen queen whose motivation is more personal: namely, erotic love for one of the Christian knights. Such fantasies encouraged medieval readers to believe that their victory in the ongoing series of Crusades was inevitable, not just because of European military might but because of the Christian West's innate desirability.

In keeping with the double plot of the *Song of Roland*, with its grand narrative of battling armies and its intimate story of interpersonal conflict within Charlemagne's company, the poem has two separate climactic scenes of narrative closure. After the mass conversion and slaughter in Zaragoza, resolving the first level of the plot, Charlemagne and his men turn to the second level of the plot: the trial of Ganelon. The emperor finds that the peers are divided regarding the degree of Ganelon's culpability: on the one hand, his behavior can be understood as treachery; on the other hand, it is arguably an appropriate expression of independence on the part of a powerful noble within the conventional obligations of a feudal relationship. In the end, after a trial by combat in which his champion is slain, Ganelon is condemned, his efforts at autonomy denounced as treason, and his punishment decreed: he is to be torn to pieces by four horses. Ganelon's broken body symbolizes the bonds of community shattered by the act of treason. The kinsmen who had stood with Ganelon and bound themselves as hostages before the trial are also condemned to death, by hanging; as the poet blandly puts it, "A traitor brings death, on himself and on others."

Despite these repeated scenes of closure, from the conversion and slaughter at Zaragoza to the punishment carried out after Ganelon's trial, the last lines of the *Song of Roland* insist on the essentially open-ended nature of the Christian mission. The poem ends with Charlemagne, exhausted and sorrowful after his years in Spain and the loss of his beloved nephew Roland, in the grip of a visionary dream in which the angel Gabriel commands him to embark upon a new campaign, renewing the unending cycle of battle between Christian and pagan. The king weeps bitterly, crying out, "God! . . . the pains, the labors of my life!"; nonetheless, he obeys the call.

For medieval readers, the *Song of Roland* was not an isolated, singular text but rather one episode within a whole cluster of stories about Charlemagne and his men, a cluster that was itself one among several comparable "cycles" of epic poetry. In the twelfth century, these *chansons de geste* were heroic models of the distant past that helped both inspire and perpetuate the ongoing warfare carried out by Crusaders in their repeated attempts to seize Jerusalem. In the twenty-first century, they are vivid reminders of an age in which warfare was the highest expression of human virtue, when the will of God was the compass that determined the actions of mankind.

From Song of Roland[1]

1

Charles the King, our Emperor, the Great,
has been in Spain for seven full years,
has conquered the high land down to the sea.
There is no castle that stands against him now,
no wall, no citadel left to break down— 5
except Saragossa, high on a mountain.[2]
King Marsilion holds it, who does not love God,
who serves Mahumet and prays to Apollin.[3]
He cannot save himself: his ruin will find him there. AOI.[4]

2

King Marsilion was in Saragossa. 10
He has gone forth into a grove, beneath its shade,
and he lies down on a block of blue marble,
twenty thousand men, and more, all around him.
He calls aloud to his dukes and his counts:
"Listen, my lords, to the troubles we have. 15
The Emperor Charles of the sweet land of France
has come into this country to destroy us.
I have no army able to give him battle,
I do not have the force to break his force.
Now act like my wise men: give me counsel, 20
save me, save me from death, save me from shame!"
No pagan there has one word to say to him
except Blancandrin, of the castle of Valfunde.

3

One of the wisest pagans was Blancandrin,
brave and loyal, a great mounted warrior, 25
a useful man, the man to aid his lord;
said to the King: "Do not give way to panic.
Do this: send Charles, that wild, terrible man,
tokens of loyal service and great friendship: 30
you will give him bears and lions and dogs,
seven hundred camels, a thousand molted hawks,
four hundred mules weighed down with gold and silver,
and fifty carts, to cart it all away:
he'll have good wages for his men who fight for pay.
Say he's made war long enough in this land: 35
let him go home, to France, to Aix, at last—

---

1. Translated by Frederick Goldin. Many of Goldin's notes have been adapted for use here.
2. Saragossa, in northeastern Spain, is not actually on a mountaintop. The poet's geography is not always accurate.
3. The Greek god Apollo; but the poet is mistaken, for these people worship only one god,

Allah. "Mahumet": Muhammad (ca. 570–632), founder of the Islamic religion.
4. These three mysterious letters appear at certain moments throughout the text, 180 times in all. No one has ever adequately explained them, though every reader feels their effect.

come Michaelmas[5] you will follow him there,
say you will take their faith, become a Christian,
and be his man with honor, with all you have.
If he wants hostages, why, you'll send them,   40
ten, or twenty, to give him security.
Let us send him the sons our wives have borne.
I'll send my son with all the others named to die.
It is better that they should lose their heads[6]
than that we, Lord, should lose our dignity   45
and our honors—and be turned into beggars!" AOI.

4

Said Blancandrin: "By this right hand of mine
and by this beard that flutters on my chest,
you will soon see the French army disband,
the Franks will go to their own land, to France.   50
When each of them is in his dearest home,
King Charles will be in Aix, in his chapel.
At Michaelmas he will hold a great feast—
that day will come, and then our time runs out,
he'll hear no news, he'll get no word from us.   55
This King is wild, the heart in him is cruel:
he'll take the heads of the hostages we gave.
It is better, Lord, that they lose their heads
than that we lose our bright, our beautiful Spain—
and nothing more for us but misery and pain!"   60
The pagans say: "It may be as he says."

* * *

6

Marsilion brought his council to an end,
said to his men: "Lords, you will go on now,
and remember: olive branches in your hands;   80
and in my name tell Charlemagne the King
for his god's sake to have pity on me—
he will not see a month from this day pass
before I come with a thousand faithful;
say I will take that Christian religion   85
and be his man in love and loyalty.
If he wants hostages, why, he'll have them."
Said Blancandrin: "Now you will get good terms." AOI.

5. The feast of St. Michael, September 29. *Aix:* Aix-la-Chapelle, or Aachen, was the capital of Charlemagne's empire.
6. The speaker expects that the hostages will be killed by the French when the deception becomes clear. Sometime before, hostages sent by the French had been similarly slain (see lines 207–09).

7

King Marsilion had ten white mules led out,
sent to him once by the King of Suatilie,[7]   90
with golden bits and saddles wrought with silver.
The men are mounted, the men who brought the message,
and in their hands they carry olive branches.
They came to Charles, who has France in his keeping.
He cannot prevent it: they will fool him. AOI.   95

8

The Emperor is secure and jubilant:
he has taken Cordres, broken the walls,
knocked down the towers with his catapults.
And what tremendous spoils his knights have won—
gold and silver, precious arms, equipment.   100
In the city not one pagan remained
who is not killed or turned into a Christian.
The Emperor is in an ample grove,
Roland and Oliver are with him there,
Samson the Duke and Ansëis the fierce,   105
Geoffrey d'Anjou, the King's own standard-bearer;
and Gerin and Gerer, these two together always,
and the others, the simple knights, in force:
fifteen thousand from the sweet land of France.
The warriors sit on bright brocaded silk;   110
they are playing at tables to pass the time,
the old and the wisest men sitting at chess,
the young light-footed men fencing with swords.
Beneath a pine, beside a wild sweet-briar,
there was a throne, every inch of pure gold.   115
There sits the King, who rules over sweet France.
His beard is white, his hair flowering white.
That lordly body! the proud fierce look of him!—
If someone should come here asking for him,
there'd be no need to point out the King of France.
The messengers dismounted, and on their feet   120
they greeted him in all love and good faith.

9

Blancandrin spoke, he was the first to speak,
said to the King: "Greetings, and God save you,
that glorious God whom we all must adore.
Here is the word of the great king Marsilion: 125
he has looked into this law of salvation,
wants to give you a great part of his wealth,
bears and lions and hunting dogs on chains,

7. A subordinate king, owing allegiance to Marsilion.

seven hundred camels, a thousand molted hawks,
four hundred mules packed tight with gold and silver,   130
and fifty carts, to cart it all away;
and there will be so many fine gold bezants,[8]
you'll have good wages for the men in your pay.
You have stayed long—long enough!—in this land,
it is time to go home, to France, to Aix.   135
My master swears he will follow you there."
The Emperor holds out his hands toward God,
bows down his head, begins to meditate. AOI.

                              10
The Emperor held his head bowed down;
never was he too hasty with his words: 140
his custom is to speak in his good time.
When his head rises, how fierce the look of him;
he said to them: "You have spoken quite well.
King Marsilion is my great enemy.
Now all these words that you have spoken here—   145
how far can I trust them? How can I be sure?"
The Saracen: "He wants to give you hostages.
How many will you want? ten? fifteen? twenty?
I'll put my son with the others named to die.[9]
You will get some, I think, still better born.   150
When you are at home in your high royal palace,
at the great feast of Saint Michael-in-Peril,[1]
the lord who nurtures me will follow you,
and in those baths[2]—the baths God made for you—
my lord will come and want to be made Christian."   155
King Charles replies: "He may yet save his soul." AOI.

                              11
Late in the day it was fair, the sun was bright.
Charles has them put the ten mules into stables.
The King commands a tent pitched in the broad grove,
and there he has the ten messengers lodged;   160
twelve serving men took splendid care of them.
There they remained that night till the bright day.
The Emperor rose early in the morning,
the King of France, and heard the mass and matins.
And then the King went forth beneath a pine,   165
calls for his barons to complete his council:
he will proceed only with the men of France. AOI.

                        * * *

8. Gold coins; the name is derived from
Byzantium.
9. That is, if the promise is broken. "Saracen": the usual term for the enemy.
1. The epithet "in peril of the sea" was applied
to the famous sanctuary Mont-St.-Michel off
the Normandy coast because it could be reached
on foot only at low tide, and pilgrims were
endangered by the incoming tide. Eventually,
the phrase was applied to the saint himself.
2. Famous healing springs at Aix-la-Chapelle.

13

"Barons, my lords," said Charles the Emperor,   180
"King Marsilion has sent me messengers,
wants to give me a great mass of his wealth,
bears and lions and hunting dogs on chains,
seven hundred camels, a thousand molting hawks,
four hundred mules packed with gold of Araby,   185
and with all that, more than fifty great carts;
but also asks that I go back to France:
he'll follow me to Aix, my residence,
and take our faith, the one redeeming faith,
become a Christian, hold his march[3] lands from me.   190
But what lies in his heart? I do not know."
And the French say: "We must be on our guard!" AOI.

14

The Emperor has told them what was proposed.
Roland the Count will never assent to that,
gets to his feet, comes forth to speak against it;   195
says to the King: "Trust Marsilion—and suffer!
We came to Spain seven long years ago,
I won Noples for you, I won Commibles,
I took Valterne and all the land of Pine,
and Balaguer and Tudela and Seville.   200
And then this king, Marsilion, played the traitor:
he sent you men, fifteen of his pagans—
and sure enough, each held an olive branch;
and they recited just these same words to you.
You took counsel with all your men of France;   205
they counseled you to a bit of madness:
you sent two Counts across to the Pagans,
one was Basan, the other was Basile.
On the hills below Haltille, he took their heads.
They were your men. Fight the war you came to fight!   210
Lead the army you summoned on to Saragossa!
Lay siege to it all the rest of your life!
Avenge the men that this criminal murdered!" AOI.

15

The Emperor held his head bowed down with this,
and stroked his beard, and smoothed his mustache down,   215
and speaks no word, good or bad, to his nephew.
The French keep still, all except Ganelon:
he gets to his feet and, come before King Charles,
how fierce he is as he begins his speech;
said to the King: "Believe a fool—me or   220
another—and suffer! Protect your interest!
When Marsilion the King sends you his word

---

3. A frontier province or territory.

that he will join his hands⁴ and be your man,
and hold all Spain as a gift from your hands
and then receive the faith that we uphold—   225
whoever urges that we refuse this peace,
that man does not care, Lord, what death we die.
That wild man's counsel must not win the day here—
let us leave fools, let us hold with wise men!" AOI.

16

And after that there came Naimon the Duke—   230
no greater vassal in that court than Naimon—
said to the King: "You've heard it clearly now,
Count Ganelon has given you your answer:
let it be heeded, there is wisdom in it.
King Marsilion is beaten in this war,   235
you have taken every one of his castles,
broken his walls with your catapults,
burnt his cities and defeated his men.
Now when he sends to ask you to have mercy,
it would be a sin to do still more to him.   240
Since he'll give you hostages as guarantee,
this great war must not go on, it is not right."
And the French say: "The Duke has spoken well." AOI.

* * *

[**Summary**   Charlemagne asks for a volunteer to serve as a messenger to Marsilion;
Roland immediately offers to go, followed by Turpin, but Charlemagne refuses both.]

20

"My noble knights," said the Emperor Charles,
"choose me one man: a baron from my march,   275
to bring my message to King Marsilion."
And Roland said: "Ganelon, my stepfather."
The French respond: "Why, that's the very man!
pass this man by and you won't send a wiser."
And hearing this Count Ganelon began to choke,   280
pulls from his neck the great furs of marten
and stands there now, in his silken tunic,
eyes full of lights, the look on him of fury,
he has the body, the great chest of a lord;
stood there so fair, all his peers gazed on him;   285
said to Roland: "Madman, what makes you rave?
Every man knows I am your stepfather,
yet you named me to go to Marsilion.
Now if God grants that I come back from there,
you will have trouble: I'll start a feud with you,   290
it will go on till the end of your life."

---

4. Part of the gesture of homage; the lord enclosed the joined hands of his vassal with his own.

Roland replies: "What wild words—all that blustering!
Every man knows that threats don't worry me.
But we need a wise man to bring the message:
if the King wills, I'll gladly go in your place."   295

21

Ganelon answers: "You will not go for me. AOI.
You're not my man, and I am not your lord.
Charles commands me to perform this service:
I'll go to Marsilion in Saragossa.
And I tell you, I'll play a few wild tricks   300
before I cool the anger in me now."
When he heard that, Roland began to laugh. AOI.

* * *

[**Summary**   Furious at Roland's ridicule, Ganelon reluctantly agrees to serve as messenger, but openly declares his hatred for Roland.]

25

The Emperor offers him his right glove.
But Ganelon would have liked not to be there.
When he had to take it, it fell to the ground.
"God!" say the French, "What's that going to mean?
What disaster will this message bring us!"   335
Said Ganelon: "Lords, you'll be hearing news."

26

Said Ganelon: "Lord, give me leave to go,
since go I must, there's no reason to linger."
And the King said: "In Jesus' name and mine,"
absolved him and blessed him with his right hand.   340
Then he gave him the letter and the staff.

27

Count Ganelon goes away to his camp.
He chooses, with great care, his battle-gear,
picks the most precious arms that he can find.
The spurs he fastened on were golden spurs;   345
he girds his sword, Murgleis, upon his side;
he has mounted Tachebrun, his battle horse,
his uncle, Guinemer, held the stirrup.
And there you would have seen brave men in tears,
his men, who say: "Baron, what bad luck for you!   350
All your long years in the court of the King,
always proclaimed a great and noble vassal!
Whoever it was doomed you to go down there—
Charlemagne himself will not protect that man.
Roland the Count should not have thought of this—   355
and you the living issue of a mighty line!"
And then they say: "Lord, take us there with you!"

Ganelon answers: "May the Lord God forbid!
It is better that I alone should die
    than so many good men and noble knights.
You will be going back, Lords, to sweet France: 360
go to my wife and greet her in my name,
and Pinabel, my dear friend and peer,
and Baldewin, my son, whom you all know:
give him your aid, and hold him as your lord."
And he starts down the road; he is on his way. AOI.   365

28

Ganelon rides to a tall olive tree,
there he has joined the pagan messengers.
And here is Blancandrin, who slows down for him:
and what great art they speak to one another.
Said Blancandrin: "An amazing man, Charles!   370
conquered Apulia, conquered all of Calabria,
crossed the salt sea on his way into England,
won its tribute,[5] got Peter's pence[6] for Rome:
what does he want from us here in our march?"
Ganelon answers: "That is the heart in him.   375
There'll never be a man the like of him." AOI.

29

Said Blancandrin: "The Franks are a great people.
Now what great harm all those dukes and counts do
to their own lord when they give him such counsel:
they torment him, they'll destroy him, and others."   380
Ganelon answers: "Well, now, I know no such man
except Roland, who'll suffer for it yet.
One day the Emperor was sitting in the shade:
his nephew came, still wearing his hauberk,
he had gone plundering near Carcassonne;   385
and in his hand he held a bright red apple:
'Dear Lord, here, take,' said Roland to his uncle;
'I offer you the crowns of all earth's kings.'
Yes, Lord, that pride of his will destroy him,
for every day he goes riding at death.   390
And *should* someone kill him, we would have peace." AOI.

30

Said Blancandrin: "A wild man, this Roland!
wants to make every nation beg for his mercy
and claims a right to every land on earth!
But what men support him, if that is his aim?"   395
Ganelon answers: "Why, Lord, the men of France.

---

5. Although begun perhaps as early as the 8th
century, the tribute was not the result of any
effort of Charlemagne, who did not in fact
visit England.
6. A tribute of one penny per house "for the use
of Saint Peter," that is, for the pope in Rome.

They love him so, they will never fail him.
He gives them gifts, masses of gold and silver,
mules, battle horses, brocaded silks, supplies.
And it is all as the Emperor desires: 400
he'll win the lands from here to the Orient." AOI.

                                    31
Ganelon and Blancandrin rode on until
each pledged his faith to the other and swore
they'd find a way to have Count Roland killed.
They rode along the paths and ways until,   405
in Saragossa, they dismount beneath a yew.
There was a throne in the shade of a pine,
covered with silk from Alexandria.
There sat the king who held the land of Spain,
and around him twenty thousand Saracens.   410
There is no man who speaks or breathes a word,
poised for the news that all would like to hear.
Now here they are: Ganelon and Blancandrin.

                                    32
Blancandrin came before Marsilion,
his hand around the fist of Ganelon,   415
said to the King: "May Mahumet save you,
and Apollin, whose sacred laws we keep!
We delivered your message to Charlemagne:
when we finished, he raised up both his hands
and praised his god. He made no other answer.   420
Here he sends you one of his noble barons,
a man of France, and very powerful.
You'll learn from him whether or not you'll have peace."
"Let him speak, we shall hear him," Marsilion answers. AOI.

                                    33
But Ganelon had it all well thought out.   425
With what great art he commences his speech,
a man who knows his way about these things;
said to the King: "May the Lord God save you,
that glorious God, whom we must all adore.
Here is the word of Charlemagne the King: 430
you are to take the holy Christian faith;
he will give you one half of Spain in fief.
If you refuse, if you reject this peace,
you will be taken by force, put into chains,
and then led forth to the King's seat at Aix;   435
you will be tried; you will be put to death:
you will die there, in shame, vilely, degraded."
King Marsilion, hearing this, was much shaken.
In his hand was a spear, with golden feathers.
He would have struck, had they not held him back. AOI.   440

* * *

36

Now Ganelon drew closer to the King
and said to him: "You are wrong to get angry,
for Charles, who rules all France, sends you this word: 470
you are to take the Christian people's faith;
he will give you one half of Spain in fief,
the other half goes to his nephew: Roland—
quite a partner you will be getting there!
If you refuse, if you reject this peace,   475
he will come and lay siege to Saragossa;
you will be taken by force, put into chains,
and brought straight on to Aix, the capital.
No saddle horse, no war horse for you then,
no he-mule, no she-mule for you to ride: 480
you will be thrown on some miserable dray;
you will be tried, and you will lose your head.
Our Emperor sends you this letter."
He put the letter in the pagan's right fist.

* * *

[**Summary**   Enraged by Charlemagne's letter, Marsilion reaffirms his secret agreement
with Ganelon and presents him with gifts of furs and gold. Marsilion asks Ganelon to tell him
more about the French king and his knights.]

42

Said the pagan: "Truly, how I must marvel   550
at Charlemagne, who is so gray and white—
over two hundred years, from what I hear;
gone through so many lands a conqueror,
and borne so many blows from strong sharp spears,
killed and conquered so many mighty kings: 555
when will he lose the heart for making war?"
"Never," said Ganelon, "while one man lives: Roland!
no man like him from here to the Orient!
There's his companion, Oliver, a brave man.
And the Twelve Peers, whom Charles holds very dear,   560
form the vanguard, with twenty thousand Franks.
Charles is secure, he fears no man alive." AOI.

43

"Dear Lord Ganelon," said Marsilion the King,
"I have my army, you won't find one more handsome:
I can muster four hundred thousand knights!   565
With this host, now, can I fight Charles and the French?"
Ganelon answers: "No, no, don't try that now,
you'd take a loss: thousands of your pagans!
Forget such foolishness, listen to wisdom:
send the Emperor so many gifts   570
there'll be no Frenchman there who does not marvel.
For twenty hostages—those you'll be sending—
he will go home: home again to sweet France!

And he will leave his rear-guard behind him.
There will be Roland, I do believe, his nephew,   575
and Oliver, brave man, born to the court.
These Counts are dead, if anyone trusts me.
Then Charles will see that great pride of his go down,
he'll have no heart to make war on you again." AOI.

44

"Dear Lord Ganelon," said Marsilion the King,   580
"What must I do to kill Roland the Count?"
Ganelon answers: "Now I can tell you that.
The King will be at Cize,[7] in the great passes,
he will have placed his rear-guard at his back:
there'll be his nephew, Count Roland, that great man,   585
and Oliver, in whom he puts such faith,
and twenty thousand Franks in their company.
Now send one hundred thousand of your pagans
against the French—let them give the first battle.
The French army will be hit hard and shaken.   590
I must tell you: your men will be martyred.
Give them a second battle, then, like the first.
One will get him, Roland will not escape.
Then you'll have done a deed, a noble deed,
and no more war for the rest of your life!" AOI.   595

45

"If someone can bring about the death of Roland,
then Charles would lose the right arm of his body,
that marvelous army would disappear—
never again could Charles gather such forces.
Then peace at last for the Land of Fathers!"[8]   600
When Marsilion heard that, he kissed his neck.
Then he begins to open up his treasures. AOI.

* * *

47

There stood a throne made all of ivory.
Marsilion commands them bring forth a book: 610
it was the law of Mahum and Tervagant.[9]
This is the vow sworn by the Saracen of Spain:
if he shall find Roland in the rear-guard,
he shall fight him, all his men shall fight him,
and once he finds Roland, Roland will die.   615
Says Ganelon: "May it be as you will." AOI.

* * *

7. The pass through the Pyrenees.
8. "Tere Majur," in the original; it can mean either "the great land" or "the land of fathers, ancestors." It always refers to France.
9. Or Termagant, a fictitious deity whom medieval Christians believed to be worshipped by Muslims.

[*Summary*   Marsilion and his knights present Ganelon with personal presents, including weapons and gold, while the pagan queen Bramimunde provides jewels for Ganelon's wife. Marsilion also provides official presents for Charlemagne and his court.]

52

Marsilion took Ganelon by the shoulder
and said to him: "You're a brave man, a wise man.
Now by that faith you think will save your soul,
take care you do not turn your heart from us.   650
I will give you a great mass of my wealth,
ten mules weighed down with fine Arabian gold;
and come each year, I'll do the same again.
Now you take these, the keys to this vast city:
present King Charles with all of its great treasure;   655
then get me Roland picked for the rear-guard.
Let me find him in some defile or pass,
I will fight him, a battle to the death."
Ganelon answers: "It's high time that I go."
Now he is mounted, and he is on his way. AOI.   660

* * *

54

The Emperor rose early in the morning,
the King of France, and has heard mass and matins.   670
On the green grass he stood before his tent.
Roland was there, and Oliver, brave man,
Naimon the Duke, and many other knights.
Ganelon came, the traitor, the foresworn.
With what great cunning he commences his speech;   675
said to the King: "May the Lord God save you!
Here I bring you the keys to Saragossa.
And I bring you great treasure from that city,
and twenty hostages, have them well guarded.
And good King Marsilion sends you this word: 680
Do not blame him concerning the Algalife:
I saw it all myself, with my own eyes:
    four hundred thousand men, and all in arms,
their hauberks on, some with their helms laced on,
swords on their belts, the hilts enameled gold,
who went with him to the edge of the sea.   685
They are in flight: it is the Christian faith—
they do not want it, they will not keep its law.
They had not sailed four full leagues out to sea
when a high wind, a tempest swept them up.
They were all drowned; you will never see them;   690
if he were still alive, I'd have brought him.
As for the pagan King, Lord, believe this:
before you see one month from this day pass,
he'll follow you to the Kingdom of France

and take the faith—he will take your faith, Lord,   695
and join his hands and become your vassal.
He will hold Spain as a fief from your hand."
Then the King said: "May God be thanked for this.
You have done well, you will be well rewarded."
Throughout the host they sound a thousand trumpets.   700
The French break camp, strap their gear on their pack-horses.
They take the road to the sweet land of France. AOI.

55

King Charlemagne laid waste the land of Spain,
stormed its castles, ravaged its citadels.
The King declares his war is at an end.   705
The Emperor rides toward the land of sweet France.
Roland the Count affixed the gonfanon,[1]
raised it toward heaven on the height of a hill;
the men of France make camp across that country.
Pagans are riding up through these great valleys,   710
their hauberks on, their tunics of double mail,
their helms laced on, their swords fixed on their belts,
shields on their necks, lances trimmed with their banners.
In a forest high in the hills they gathered:
four hundred thousand men waiting for dawn.   715
God, the pity of it! the French do not know! AOI.

* * *

[**Summary**   Charlemagne has a prophetic dream including three wild beasts: a boar,
a leopard, and a ferocious hound.]

58

The day goes by, and the bright dawn arises.
Throughout that host. . . .[2]
The Emperor rides forth with such fierce pride.
"Barons, my lords," said the Emperor Charles,   740
"look at those passes, at those narrow defiles—
pick me a man to command the rear-guard."
Ganelon answers: "Roland, here, my stepson.
You have no baron as great and brave as Roland."
When he hears that, the King stares at him in fury;   745
and said to him: "You are the living devil,
a mad dog—the murderous rage in you!
And who will precede me, in the vanguard?"
Ganelon answers, "Why, Ogier of Denmark,
you have no baron who could lead it so well."   750

1. Pennant.
2. The rest of the line is unintelligible in the manuscript.

59

Roland the Count, when he heard himself named,
knew what to say, and spoke as a knight must speak:
"Lord Stepfather, I have to cherish you!
You have had the rear-guard assigned to me.
Charles will not lose, this great King who rules France,   755
I swear it now, one palfrey, one war horse—
while I'm alive and know what's happening—
one he-mule, one she-mule that he might ride,
Charles will not lose one sumpter, not one pack horse
that has not first been bought and paid for with swords."
Ganelon answers: "You speak the truth, I know." AOI.   760

60

When Roland hears he will lead the rear-guard,
he spoke in great fury to his stepfather:
"Hah! you nobody, you base-born little fellow,
and did you think the glove would fall from my hands
as the staff fell[3] from yours before King Charles?" AOI.   765

61

"Just Emperor," said Roland, that great man,
"give me the bow that you hold in your hand.
And no man here, I think, will say in reproach
I let it drop, as Ganelon let the staff drop[4]
from his right hand, when he should have taken it."   770
The Emperor bowed down his head with this,
he pulled his beard, he twisted his mustache,
cannot hold back, tears fill his eyes, he weeps.

62

And after that there came Naimon the Duke,
no greater vassal in the court than Naimon,   775
said to the King: "You've heard it clearly now:
it is Count Roland. How furious he is.
He is the one to whom the rear-guard falls,
no baron here can ever change that now.
Give him the bow that you have stretched and bent,   780
and then find him good men to stand with him."
The King gives him the bow; Roland has it now.

63

The Emperor calls forth Roland the Count:
"My lord, my dear nephew, of course you know
I will give you half my men, they are yours.   785

---

3. Ganelon had let fall a glove, not a staff (line
333). For this and other less objective reasons,
some editors have questioned the authenticity of
this *laisse* (stanza).

4. In this *laisse* a reviser tried to make the text
more consistent by adding the reference to the
staff.

Let them serve you, it is your salvation."
"None of that!" said the Count. "May God strike me
if I discredit the history of my line.
I'll keep twenty thousand Franks—they are good men.
Go your way through the passes, you will be safe.   790
You must not fear any man while I live."

* * *

68

King Charles the Great cannot keep from weeping.
A hundred thousand Franks feel pity for him;
and for Roland, an amazing fear.
Ganelon the criminal has betrayed him;
got gifts for it from the pagan king,   845
gold and silver, cloths of silk, gold brocade,
mules and horses and camels and lions.
Marsilion sends for the barons of Spain,
counts and viscounts and dukes and almaçurs,
and the emirs,[5] and the sons of great lords: 850
four hundred thousand assembled in three days.
In Saragossa he has them beat the drums,
they raise Mahumet upon the highest tower:
no pagan now who does not worship him
and adore him. Then they ride, racing each other,   855
search through the land, the valleys, the mountains;
and then they saw the banners of the French.
The rear-guard of the Twelve Companions
will not fail now, they'll give the pagans battle.

* * *

79

* * *

The day was fair, the sun was shining bright,
all their armor was aflame with the light;
a thousand trumpets blow: that was to make it finer.
That made a great noise, and the men of France heard.   1005
Said Oliver: "Companion, I believe
we may yet have a battle with the pagans."
Roland replies: "Now may God grant us that.
We know our duty: to stand here for our King.
A man must bear some hardships for his lord,   1010
stand everything, the great heat, the great cold,
lose the hide and hair on him for his good lord.
Now let each man make sure to strike hard here:
let them not sing a bad song about us!
Pagans are wrong and Christians are right!   1015
They'll make no bad example of me this day!" AOI.

5. All lords of high rank.

80

Oliver climbs to the top of a hill,
looks to his right, across a grassy vale,
sees the pagan army on its way there;
and called down to Roland, his companion: 1020
"That way, toward Spain: the uproar I see coming!
All their hauberks, all blazing, helmets like flames!
It will be a bitter thing for our French.
Ganelon knew, that criminal, that traitor,
when he marked us out before the Emperor."   1025
"Be still, Oliver," Roland the Count replies.
"He is my stepfather—my stepfather.
I won't have you speak one word against him."

* * *

82

Said Oliver: "I saw the Saracens,
no man on earth ever saw more of them—   1040
one hundred thousand, with their shields, up in front,
helmets laced on, hauberks blazing on them,
the shafts straight up, the iron heads like flames—
you'll get a battle, nothing like it before.
My lords, my French, may God give you the strength.   1045
Hold your ground now! Let them not defeat us!"
And the French say: "God hate the man who runs!
We may die here, but no man will fail you." AOI.

83

Said Oliver: "The pagan force is great;
from what I see, our French here are too few.   1050
Roland, my companion, sound your horn then,
Charles will hear it, the army will come back."
Roland replies: "I'd be a fool to do it.
I would lose my good name all through sweet France.
I will strike now, I'll strike with Durendal,   1055
the blade will be bloody to the gold from striking!
These pagan traitors came to these passes doomed!
I promise you, they are marked men, they'll die." AOI.

* * *

86

Said Oliver: "I see no blame in it—
I watched the Saracens coming from Spain,
the valleys and mountains covered with them,
every hillside and every plain all covered,   1085
hosts and hosts everywhere of those strange men—
and here we have a little company."
Roland replies: "That whets my appetite.
May it not please God and his angels and saints
to let France lose its glory because of me—   1090

let me not end in shame, let me die first.
The Emperor loves us when we fight well."

87

Roland is good, and Oliver is wise,
both these vassals men of amazing courage:
once they are armed and mounted on their horses,   1095
they will not run, though they die for it, from battle.
Good men, these Counts, and their words full of spirit.
Traitor pagans are riding up in fury.
Said Oliver: "Roland, look—the first ones,
on top of us—and Charles is far away.   1100
You did not think it right to sound your olifant:
if the King were here, we'd come out without losses.
Now look up there, toward the passes of Aspre—
you can see the rear-guard: it will suffer.
No man in that detail will be in another."   1105
Roland replies: "Don't speak such foolishness—
shame on the heart gone coward in the chest.
We'll hold our ground, we'll stand firm—we're the ones!
We'll fight with spears, we'll fight them hand to hand!" AOI.

88

When Roland sees that there will be a battle,   1110
it makes him fiercer than a lion or leopard;
shouts to the French, calls out to Oliver:
"Lord, companion: friend, do not say such things.
The Emperor, who left us these good French,
had set apart these twenty thousand men: 1115
he knew there was no coward in their ranks.
A man must meet great troubles for his lord,
stand up to the great heat and the great cold,
give up some flesh and blood—it is his duty.
Strike with the lance, I'll strike with Durendal—   1120
it was the King who gave me this good sword!
If I die here, the man who gets it can say:
it was a noble's, a vassal's, a good man's sword."

89

And now there comes the Archbishop Turpin.
He spurs his horse, goes up into a mountain,   1125
summons the French; and he preached them a sermon:
"Barons, my lords, Charles left us in this place.
We know our duty: to die like good men for our King.
Fight to defend the holy Christian faith.
Now you will have a battle, you know it now,   1130
you see the Saracens with your own eyes.
Confess your sins, pray to the Lord for mercy.
I will absolve you all, to save your souls.
If you die here, you will stand up holy martyrs,

you will have seats in highest Paradise."   1135
The French dismount, cast themselves on the ground;
the Archbishop blesses them in God's name.
He commands them to do one penance: strike.

                                    90
The French arise, stand on their feet again;
they are absolved, released from all their sins: 1140
the Archbishop has blessed them in God's name.
Now they are mounted on their swift battle horses,
bearing their arms like faithful warriors;
and every man stands ready for the battle.
Roland the Count calls out to Oliver: 1145
"Lord, Companion, you knew it, you were right,
Ganelon watched for his chance to betray us,
got gold for it, got goods for it, and money.
The Emperor will have to avenge us now.
King Marsilion made a bargain for our lives,   1150
but still must pay, and that must be with swords." AOI.

                              * * *

                                    92
Said Oliver: "I will waste no more words.   1170
You did not think it right to sound your olifant,
there'll be no Charles coming to your aid now.
He knows nothing, brave man, he's done no wrong;
those men down there—they have no blame in this.
Well, then, ride now, and ride with all your might!   1175
Lords, you brave men, stand your ground, hold the field!
Make up your minds, I beg you in God's name,
to strike some blows, take them and give them back!
Here we must not forget Charlemagne's war cry."
And with that word the men of France cried out.   1180
A man who heard that shout: Munjoie! Munjoie![6]
would always remember what manhood is.
Then they ride, God! Look at their pride and spirit!
and they spur hard, to ride with all their speed,
come on to strike—what else would these men do?   1185
The Saracens kept coming, never fearing them.
Franks and pagans, here they are, at each other.

                                    93
Marsilion's nephew is named Aëlroth.
He rides in front, at the head of the army,
comes on shouting insults against our French: 1190
"French criminals, today you fight our men.
One man should have saved you: he betrayed you.

6. Charlemagne's war cry is derived from the name of his sword, Joiuse.

A fool, your King, to leave you in these passes.
This is the day sweet France will lose its name,
and Charlemagne the right arm of his body."   1195
When he hears that—God!—Roland is outraged!
He spurs his horse, gives Veillantif its head.
The Count comes on to strike with all his might,
smashes his shield, breaks his hauberk apart,
and drives: rips through his chest, shatters the bones,   1200
knocks the whole backbone out of his back,
casts out the soul of Aëlroth with his lance;
which he thrusts deep, makes the whole body shake,
throws him down dead, lance straight out,[7] from his horse;
he has broken his neck; broken it in two.   1205
There is something, he says, he must tell him:
"Clown! Nobody! Now you know Charles is no fool,
he never was the man to love treason.
It took his valor to leave us in these passes!
France will not lose its name, sweet France! today.   1210
Brave men of France, strike hard! The first blow is ours!
We're in the right, and these swine in the wrong!" AOI.

94

A duke is there whose name is Falsaron,
he was the brother of King Marsilion,
held the wild land of Dathan and Abiram;[8]   1215
under heaven, no criminal more vile;
a tremendous forehead between his eyes—
a good half-foot long, if you had measured it.
His pain is bitter to see his nephew dead;
rides out alone, baits the foe with his body,   1220
and riding shouts the war cry of the pagans,
full of hate and insults against the French:
"This is the day sweet France will lose its honor!"
Oliver hears, and it fills him with fury,
digs with his golden spurs into his horse,   1225
comes on to strike the blow a baron strikes,
smashes his shield, breaks his hauberk apart,
thrusts into him the long streamers of his gonfalon,
knocks him down, dead, lance straight out, from the saddle;
looks to the ground and sees the swine stretched out,   1230
and spoke these words—proud words, terrible words:
"You nobody, what are your threats to me!
Men of France, strike! Strike and we will beat them!"
Munjoie! he shouts—the war cry of King Charles. AOI.

* * *

---

7. The lance is held, not thrown, and used to knock the enemy from his horse. To throw one's weapons is savage and ignoble. See *laisses* 154 and 160 and the outlandish names of the things the pagans throw at Roland, Gautier, and Turpin.
8. See Numbers 16.1–35.

104

The battle is fearful and wonderful   1320
and everywhere. Roland never spares himself,
strikes with his lance as long as the wood lasts:
the fifteenth blow he struck, it broke, was lost.
Then he draws Durendal, his good sword, bare,
and spurs his horse, comes on to strike Chernuble,   1325
smashes his helmet, carbuncles shed their light,
cuts through the coif, through the hair on his head,
cut through his eyes, through his face, through that look,
the bright, shining hauberk with its fine rings,
down through the trunk to the fork of his legs,   1330
through the saddle, adorned with beaten gold,
into the horse; and the sword came to rest:
cut through the spine, never felt for the joint;
knocks him down, dead, on the rich grass of the meadow;
then said to him: "You were doomed when you started,   1335
Clown! Nobody! Let Mahum help you now.
No pagan swine will win this field today."

105

Roland the Count comes riding through the field,
holds Durendal, that sword! it carves its way!
and brings terrible slaughter down on the pagans.   1340
To have seen him cast one man dead on another,
the bright red blood pouring out on the ground,
his hauberk, his two arms, running with blood,
his good horse—neck and shoulders running with blood!
And Oliver does not linger, he strikes!   1345
and the Twelve Peers, no man could reproach them;
and the brave French, they fight with lance and sword.
The pagans die, some simply faint away!
Said the Archbishop: "Bless our band of brave men!"
Munjoie! he shouts—the war cry of King Charles. AOI.   1350

106

Oliver rides into that battle-storm,
his lance is broken, he holds only the stump;
comes on to strike a pagan, Malsarun;
and he smashes his shield, all flowers and gold,
sends his two eyes flying out of his head,   1355
and his brains come pouring down to his feet;
casts him down, dead, with seven hundred others.
Now he has killed Turgis and Esturguz,
and the shaft bursts, shivers down to his fists.
Count Roland said: "Companion, what are you doing?   1360
Why bother with a stick in such a battle?
Iron and steel will do much better work!
Where is your sword, your Halteclere—that name!
Where is that crystal hilt, that golden guard?"

"Haven't had any time to draw it out,   1365
been so busy fighting," said Oliver. AOI.

107

Lord Oliver has drawn out his good sword—
that sword his companion had longed to see—
and showed him how a good man uses it:
strikes a pagan, Justin of Val Ferrée,   1370
and comes down through his head, cuts through the center,
through his body, his hauberk sewn with brass,
the good saddle beset with gems in gold,
into the horse, the backbone cut in two;
knocks him down, dead, before him on the meadow.   1375
Count Roland said: "Now I know it's you, Brother.
The Emperor loves us for blows like that."
Munjoie! that cry! goes up on every side. AOI.

* * *

109

In the meantime, the fighting grew bitter.
Franks and pagans, the fearful blows they strike—
those who attack, those who defend themselves;
so many lances broken, running with blood,
the gonfanons in shreds, the ensigns torn,   1400
so many good French fallen, their young lives lost:
they will not see their mothers or wives again,
or the men of France who wait for them at the passes. AOI.
Charlemagne waits and weeps and wails for them.
What does that matter? They'll get no help from him.   1405
Ganelon served him ill that day he sold,
in Saragossa, the barons of his house.
He lost his life and limbs for what he did:
was doomed to hang in the great trial at Aix,
and thirty of his kin were doomed with him,   1410
who never expected to die that death. AOI.

110

The battle is fearful and full of grief.
Oliver and Roland strike like good men,
the Archbishop, more than a thousand blows,
and the Twelve Peers do not hang back, they strike!   1415
the French fight side by side, all as one man.
The pagans die by hundreds, by thousands:
whoever does not flee finds no refuge from death,
like it or not, there he ends all his days.
And there the men of France lose their greatest arms;   1420
they will not see their fathers, their kin again,
or Charlemagne, who looks for them in the passes.
Tremendous torment now comes forth in France,

a mighty whirlwind, tempests of wind and thunder,
rains and hailstones, great and immeasurable,   1425
bolts of lightning hurtling and hurtling down:
it is, in truth, a trembling of the earth.
From Saint Michael-in-Peril to the Saints,
from Besançon to the port of Wissant,
there is no house whose veil of walls does not crumble.   1430
A great darkness at noon[9] falls on the land,
there is no light but when the heavens crack.
No man sees this who is not terrified,
and many say: "The Last Day! Judgment Day!
The end! The end of the world is upon us!"   1435
They do not know, they do not speak the truth:
it is the worldwide grief for the death of Roland.

111

The French have fought with all their hearts and strength,
pagans are dead by the thousands, in droves:
of one hundred thousand, not two are saved.   1440
Said the Archbishop: "Our men! What valiant fighters!
No king under heaven could have better.
It is written in the Gesta Francorum:[1]
our Emperor's vassals were all good men."
They walk over the field to seek their dead,   1445
they weep, tears fill their eyes, in grief and pity
for their kindred, with love, with all their hearts.
Marsilion the King, with all his men
in that great host, rises up before them. AOI.

112

King Marsilion comes along a valley
with all his men, the great host he assembled: 1450
twenty divisions, formed and numbered by the King,
helmets ablaze with gems beset in gold,
and those bright shields, those hauberks sewn with brass.
Seven thousand clarions sound the pursuit,
and the great noise resounds across that country.   1455
Said Roland then: "Oliver, Companion, Brother,
that traitor Ganelon has sworn our deaths:
it is treason, it cannot stay hidden,
the Emperor will take his terrible revenge.
We have this battle now, it will be bitter,   1460
no man has ever seen the like of it.
I will fight here with Durendal, this sword,
and you, my companion, with Halteclere—

9. As during the crucifixion of Jesus, according to the gospel accounts (Matthew 27.45,
Mark 15.33, Luke 23.44).

1. The Deeds of the French (Latin), title of an
account of these events that has not survived.

we've fought with them before, in many lands!
how many battles have we won with these two! 1465
Let no one sing a bad song of our swords." AOI.

* * *

125

Marsilion sees his people's martyrdom.
He commands them: sound his horns and trumpets;
and he rides now with the great host he has gathered. 1630
At their head rides the Saracen Abisme:
no worse criminal rides in that company,
stained with the marks of his crimes and great treasons,
lacking the faith in God, Saint Mary's son.
And he is black, as black as melted pitch, 1635
a man who loves murder and treason more
than all the gold of rich Galicia,
no living man ever saw him play or laugh;
a great fighter, a wild man, mad with pride,
and therefore dear to that criminal king; 1640
holds high his dragon,[2] where all his people gather.
The Archbishop will never love that man,
no sooner saw than wanted to strike him;
considered quietly, said to himself:
"That Saracen—a heretic, I'll wager. 1645
Now let me die if I do not kill him—
I never loved cowards or cowards' ways." AOI.

126

Turpin the Archbishop begins the battle.
He rides the horse that he took from Grossaille,
who was a king this priest once killed in Denmark. 1650
Now this war horse is quick and spirited,
his hooves high-arched, the quick legs long and flat,
short in the thigh, wide in the rump, long in the flanks,
and the backbone so high, a battle horse!
and that white tail, the yellow mane on him, 1655
the little ears on him, the tawny head!
No beast on earth could ever run with him.
The Archbishop—that valiant man!—spurs hard,
he will attack Abisme, he will not falter,
strikes on his shield, a miraculous blow: 1660
a shield of stones, of amethysts, topazes,
esterminals,[3] carbuncles all on fire—
a gift from a devil, in Val Metas,
sent on to him by the Amiral Galafre.
There Turpin strikes, he does not treat it gently— 1665

---

2. Banner.   3. Precious ornaments.

after that blow, I'd not give one cent for it;
cut through his body, from one side to the other,
and casts him down dead in a barren place.
And the French say: "A fighter, that Archbishop!
Look at him there, saving souls with that crozier!"   1670

127

Roland the Count calls out to Oliver:
"Lord, Companion, now you have to agree
the Archbishop is a good man on horse,
there's none better on earth or under heaven,
he knows his way with a lance and a spear."   1675
The Count replies: "Right! Let us help him then."
And with these words the Franks began anew,
the blows strike hard, and the fighting is bitter;
there is a painful loss of Christian men.
To have seen them, Roland and Oliver,   1680
these fighting men, striking down with their swords,
the Archbishop with them, striking with his lance!
One can recount the number these three killed:
it is written—in charters, in documents;
the Geste tells it: it was more than four thousand.   1685
Through four assaults all went well with our men;
then comes the fifth, and that one crushes them.
They are all killed, all these warriors of France,
all but sixty, whom the Lord God has spared:
they will die too, but first sell themselves dear. AOI.   1690

128

Count Roland sees the great loss of his men,
calls on his companion, on Oliver:
"Lord, Companion, in God's name, what would you do?
All these good men you see stretched on the ground.
We can mourn for sweet France, fair land of France!   1695
a desert now, stripped of such great vassals.
Oh King, and friend, if only you were here!
Oliver, Brother, how shall we manage it?
What shall we do to get word to the King?"
Said Oliver: "I don't see any way.   1700
I would rather die now than hear us shamed." AOI.

129

And Roland said: "I'll sound the olifant,
Charles will hear it, drawing through the passes,
I promise you, the Franks will return at once."
Said Oliver: "That would be a great disgrace,   1705
a dishonor and reproach to all your kin,
the shame of it would last them all their lives.
When I urged it, you would not hear of it;
you will not do it now with my consent.
It is not acting bravely to sound it now—   1710

look at your arms, they are covered with blood."
The Count replies: "I've fought here like a lord."[4] AOI.

130

And Roland says: "We are in a rough battle.
I'll sound the olifant, Charles will hear it."
Said Oliver: "No good vassal would do it.   1715
When I urged it, friend, you did not think it right.
If Charles were here, we'd come out with no losses.
Those men down there—no blame can fall on them."
Oliver said: "Now by this beard of mine,
If I can see my noble sister, Aude,   1720
once more, you will never lie in her arms!"[5] AOI.

131

And Roland said: "Why are you angry at me?"
Oliver answers: "Companion, it is your doing.
I will tell you what makes a vassal good:
it is judgment, it is never madness;
restraint is worth more than the raw nerve of a fool.   1725
Frenchmen are dead because of your wildness.
And what service will Charles ever have from us?
If you had trusted me, my lord would be here,
we would have fought this battle through to the end,
Marsilion would be dead, or our prisoner.   1730
Roland, your prowess—had we never seen it!
And now, dear friend, we've seen the last of it.
No more aid from us now for Charlemagne,
a man without equal till Judgment Day,
you will die here, and your death will shame France.
We kept faith, you and I, we were companions;
and everything we were will end today.   1735
We part before evening, and it will be hard." AOI.

132

Turpin the Archbishop hears their bitter words,
digs hard into his horse with golden spurs
and rides to them; begins to set them right:
"You, Lord Roland, and you, Lord Oliver,   1740
I beg you in God's name do not quarrel.
To sound the horn could not help us now, true,
but still it is far better that you do it:
let the King come, he can avenge us then—
these men of Spain must not go home exulting!   1745
Our French will come, they'll get down on their feet,

---

4. Some have found lines 1710–12 difficult. Oliver means, "We have fought this far—look at the enemy's blood on your arms: It is too late, it would be a disgrace to summon help when there is no longer any chance of being saved." But Roland thinks that that is the one time when it is not a disgrace.
5. Aude had been betrothed to Roland.

and find us here—we'll be dead, cut to pieces.
They will lift us into coffins on the backs of mules,
and weep for us, in rage and pain and grief,
and bury us in the courts of churches;   1750
and we will not be eaten by wolves or pigs or dogs."
Roland replies, "Lord, you have spoken well." AOI.

* * *

134
And now the mighty effort of Roland the Count:
he sounds his olifant; his pain is great,
and from his mouth the bright blood comes leaping out,
and the temple bursts in his forehead.
That horn, in Roland's hands, has a mighty voice: 1765
King Charles hears it drawing through the passes.
Naimon heard it, the Franks listen to it.
And the King said: "I hear Count Roland's horn;
he'd never sound it unless he had a battle."
Says Ganelon: "Now no more talk of battles!   1770
You are old now, your hair is white as snow,
the things you say make you sound like a child.
You know Roland and that wild pride of his—
what a wonder God has suffered it so long!
Remember? he took Noples without your command: 1775
the Saracens rode out, to break the siege;
they fought with him, the great vassal Roland.
Afterwards he used the streams to wash the blood
from the meadows: so that nothing would show.
He blasts his horn all day to catch a rabbit,   1780
he's strutting now before his peers and bragging—
who under heaven would dare meet him on the field?
So now: ride on! Why do you keep on stopping?
The Land of Fathers lies far ahead of us." AOI.

135
The blood leaping from Count Roland's mouth,   1785
the temple broken with effort in his forehead,
he sounds his horn in great travail and pain.
King Charles heard it, and his French listen hard.
And the King said: "That horn has a long breath!"
Naimon answers: "It is a baron's breath.   1790
There is a battle there, I know there is.
He betrayed him! and now asks you to fail him!
Put on your armor! Lord, shout your battle cry,
and save the noble barons of your house!
You hear Roland's call. He is in trouble."   1795

136
The Emperor commanded the horns to sound,
the French dismount, and they put on their armor:

their hauberks, their helmets, their gold-dressed swords,
their handsome shields; and take up their great lances,
the gonfalons of white and red and blue. 1800
The barons of that host mount their war horses
and spur them hard the whole length of the pass;
and every man of them says to the other:
"If only we find Roland before he's killed,
we'll stand with him, and then we'll do some fighting!" 1805
What does it matter what they say? They are too late.

137

It is the end of day, and full of light,
arms and armor are ablaze in the sun,
and fire flashes from hauberks and helmets,
and from those shields, painted fair with flowers, 1810
and from those lances, those gold-dressed gonfanons.
The Emperor rides on in rage and sorrow,
the men of France indignant and full of grief.
There is no man of them who does not weep,
they are in fear for the life of Roland. 1815
The King commands: seize Ganelon the Count!
and gave him over to the cooks of his house;
summons the master cook, their chief, Besgun:
"Guard him for me like the traitor he is:
he has betrayed the barons of my house." 1820
Besgun takes him, sets his kitchen comrades,
a hundred men, the best, the worst, on him;
and they tear out his beard and his mustache,
each one strikes him four good blows with his fist;
and they lay into him with cudgels and sticks, 1825
put an iron collar around his neck
and chain him up, as they would chain a bear;
dumped him, in dishonor, on a packhorse,
and guard him well till they give him back to Charles.

* * *

139

King Charles the Great rides on, a man in wrath,
his great white beard spread out upon his hauberk.[6]
All the barons of France ride spurring hard,
there is no man who does not wail, furious 1845
not to be with Roland, the captain count,
who stands and fights the Saracens of Spain,
so set upon, I cannot think his soul abides.
God! those sixty men who stand with him, what men!
No king, no captain ever stood with better. AOI. 1850

---

6. A gesture of defiance toward the enemy.

140

Roland looks up on the mountains and slopes,
sees the French dead, so many good men fallen,
and weeps for them, as a great warrior weeps:
"Barons, my lords, may God give you his grace,
may he grant Paradise to all your souls,   1855
make them lie down among the holy flowers.
I never saw better vassals than you.
All the years you've served me, and all the times,
the mighty lands you conquered for Charles our King!
The Emperor raised you for this terrible hour!   1860
Land of France, how sweet you are, native land,
laid waste this day, ravaged, made a desert.
Barons of France, I see you die for me,
and I, your lord—I cannot protect you.
May *God* come to your aid, that God who never failed.   1865
Oliver, brother, now I will not fail *you.*
I will die here—of grief, if no man kills me.
Lord, Companion, let us return and fight."

* * *

142

When a man knows there'll be no prisoners,
what will that man not do to defend himself!
And so the Franks fight with the fury of lions.
Now Marsilion, the image of a baron,
mounted on that war horse he calls Gaignun,   1890
digs in his spurs, comes on to strike Bevon,
who was the lord of Beaune and of Dijon;
smashes his shield, rips apart his hauberk,
knocks him down, dead, no need to wound him more.
And then he killed Yvorie and Yvon,   1895
and more: he killed Gerard of Rousillon.
Roland the Count is not far away now,
said to the pagan: "The Lord God's curse on you!
You kill my companions, how you wrong me!
You'll feel the pain of it before we part,   1900
you will learn my sword's name by heart today";
comes on to strike—the image of a baron.
He has cut off Marsilion's right fist;
now takes the head of Jurfaleu the blond—
the head of Jurfaleu! Marsilion's son.   1905
The pagans cry: "Help, Mahumet! Help us!
Vengeance, our gods, on Charles! the man who set
these criminals on us in our own land,
they will not quit the field, they'll stand and die!"
And one said to the other: "Let *us* run then."   1910
And with that word, some hundred thousand flee.
Now try to call them back: they won't return. AOI.

143

What does it matter? If Marsilion has fled,
his uncle has remained: the Algalife,[7]
who holds Carthage, Alfrere, and Garmalie,   1915
and Ethiopia: a land accursed;
holds its immense black race under his power,
the huge noses, the enormous ears on them;
and they number more than fifty thousand.
These are the men who come riding in fury,   1920
and now they shout that pagan battle cry.
And Roland said: "Here comes our martyrdom;
I see it now: we have not long to live.
But let the world call any man a traitor
        who does not make them pay before he dies!
My lords, attack! Use those bright shining swords!   1925
Fight a good fight for your deaths and your lives,
let no shame touch sweet France because of us!
When Charles my lord comes to this battlefield
and sees how well we punished these Saracens,
finds fifteen of their dead for one of ours,   1930
I'll tell you what he will do: he will bless us." AOI.

* * *

145

The Saracens, when they saw these few French,   1940
looked at each other, took courage, and presumed,
telling themselves: "The Emperor is wrong!"
The Algalife rides a great sorrel horse,
digs into it with his spurs of fine gold,
strikes Oliver, from behind, in the back,   1945
shattered the white hauberk upon his flesh,
drove his spear through the middle of his chest;
and speaks to him: "Now you feel you've been struck!
Your great Charles doomed you when he left you in this pass.
That man wronged us, he must not boast of it.   1950
I've avenged all our dead in you alone!"

146

Oliver feels: he has been struck to death;
grips Halteclere, that steel blade shining, strikes
on the gold-dressed pointed helm of the Algalife,
sends jewels and flowers crackling down to the earth,   1955
into the head, into the little teeth;
draws up his flashing sword, casts him down, dead,
and then he says: "Pagan, a curse on you!
If only I could say Charles has lost nothing—

---

7. The Caliph, Marsilion's uncle, whom Ganelon lied about to Charlemagne (see lines 680–91).

but no woman, no lady you ever knew
will hear you boast, in the land you came from,
that you could take one thing worth a cent from me,
or do me harm, or do any man harm";
then cries out to Roland to come to his aid. AOI.

1960

147

Oliver feels he is wounded to death,
will never have his fill of vengeance, strikes,
as a baron strikes, where they are thickest,
cuts through their lances, cuts through those buckled shields,
through feet, through fists, through saddles, and through flanks.
Had you seen him, cutting the pagans limb
from limb, casting one corpse down on another,
you would remember a brave man keeping faith.
Never would he forget Charles' battle-cry,
Munjoie! he shouts, that mighty voice ringing;
calls to Roland, to his friend and his peer:
"Lord, Companion, come stand beside me now.
We must part from each other in pain today." AOI.

1965

1970

1975

148

Roland looks hard into Oliver's face,
it is ashen, all its color is gone,
the bright red blood streams down upon his body,
Oliver's blood spattering on the earth.
"God!" said the Count, "I don't know what to do,
Lord, Companion, your fight is finished now.
There'll never be a man the like of you.
Sweet land of France, today you will be stripped
of good vassals, laid low, a fallen land!
The Emperor will suffer the great loss";
faints with that word, mounted upon his horse. AOI.

1980

1985

149

Here is Roland, lords, fainted on his horse,
and Oliver the Count, wounded to death:
he has lost so much blood, his eyes are darkened—
he cannot see, near or far, well enough
to recognize a friend or enemy:
struck when he came upon his companion,
strikes on his helm, adorned with gems in gold,
cuts down straight through, from the point to the nasal,[8]
but never harmed him, he never touched his head.
Under this blow, Count Roland looked at him;
and gently, softly now, he asks of him:
"Lord, Companion, do you mean to do this?
It is Roland, who always loved you greatly.
You never declared that we were enemies."

1990

1995

2000

---

8. The nosepiece protruding down from the cone-shaped helmet.

Said Oliver: "Now I hear it is you—
I don't see you, may the Lord God see you.
Was it you that I struck? Forgive me then."   2005
Roland replies: "I am not harmed, not harmed,
I forgive you, Friend, here and before God."
And with that word, each bowed to the other.
And this is the love, lords, in which they parted.

* * *

151

Roland the Count, when he sees his friend dead,
lying stretched out, his face against the earth,   2025
softly, gently, begins to speak the regret:[9]
"Lord, Companion, you were brave and died for it.
We have stood side by side through days and years,
you never caused me harm, I never wronged you;
when you are dead, to be alive pains me."   2030
And with that word the lord of marches faints
upon his horse, which he calls Veillantif.
He is held firm by his spurs of fine gold,
whichever way he leans, he cannot fall.

152

Before Roland could recover his senses   2035
and come out of his faint, and be aware,
a great disaster had come forth before him:
the French are dead, he has lost every man
except the Archbishop, and Gautier de l'Hum,
who has come back, down from that high mountain: 2040
he has fought well, he fought those men of Spain.
His men are dead, the pagans finished them;
flees now down to these valleys, he has no choice,
and calls on Count Roland to come to his aid:
"My noble Count, my brave lord, where are you?   2045
I never feared whenever you were there
It is Walter: I conquered Maëlgut,
my uncle is Droün, old and gray: your Walter
and always dear to you for the way I fought;
and I have fought this time: my lance is shattered,   2050
my good shield pierced, my hauberk's meshes broken;
and I am wounded, a lance struck through my body.
I will die soon, but I sold myself dear."
And with that word, Count Roland has heard him,
he spurs his horse, rides spurring to his man. AOI.   2055

153

Roland in pain, maddened with grief and rage:
rushes where they are thickest and strikes again,
strikes twenty men of Spain, strikes twenty dead,

---

9. What follows is a formal and customary lament for the dead.

and Walter six, and the Archbishop five.
The pagans say: "Look at those criminals!   2060
Now take care, Lords, they don't get out alive,
only a traitor will not attack them now!
Only a coward will let them save their skins!"
And then they raise their hue and cry once more,
rush in on them, once more, from every side. AOI.   2065

154

Count Roland was always a noble warrior,
Gautier de l'Hum is a fine mounted man,
the Archbishop, a good man tried and proved:
not one of them will ever leave the others;
strike, where they are thickest, at the pagans.   2070
A thousand Saracens get down on foot,
and forty thousand more are on their mounts:
and I tell you, not one will dare come close,
they throw, and from afar, lances and spears,
wigars and darts, mizraks, javelins, pikes.   2075
With the first blows they killed Gautier de l'Hum
and struck Turpin of Reims, pierced through his shield,
broke the helmet on him, wounded his head;
ripped his hauberk, shattered its rings of mail,
and pierced him with four spears in his body,   2080
the war horse killed under him; and now there comes
great pain and rage when the Archbishop falls. AOI.

155

Turpin of Reims, when he feels he is unhorsed,
struck to the earth with four spears in his body,
quickly, brave man, leaps to his feet again;   2085
his eyes find Roland now, he runs to him
and says one word: "See! I'm not finished yet!
What good vassal ever gives up alive!";
and draws Almace, his sword, that shining steel!
and strikes, where they are thickest, a thousand blows, and more.   2090
Later, Charles said: Turpin had spared no one;
he found four hundred men prostrate around him,
some of them wounded, some pierced from front to back,
some with their heads hacked off. So says the Geste,
and so says one who was there, on that field,   2095
the baron Saint Gilles,[1] for whom God performs miracles,
who made the charter setting forth these great things
in the Church of Laon. Now any man
who does not know this much understands nothing.

---

1. St. Gilles of Provence. These lines explain how the story of Rencesvals could be told after all
who had fought there died.

156

Roland the Count fights well and with great skill,
but he is hot, his body soaked with sweat;   2100
has a great wound in his head, and much pain,
his temple broken because he blew the horn.
But he must know whether King Charles will come;
draws out the olifant, sounds it, so feebly.
The Emperor drew to a halt, listened.   2105
"Seigneurs," he said, "it goes badly for us—
My nephew Roland falls from our ranks today.
I hear it in the horn's voice: he hasn't long.
Let every man who wants to be with Roland
ride fast! Sound trumpets! Every trumpet in this host!"   2110
Sixty thousand, on these words, sound, so high
the mountains sound, and the valleys resound.
The pagans hear: it is no joke to them;
cry to each other: "We're getting Charles on us!"

157

The pagans say: "The Emperor is coming, AOI.   2115
listen to their trumpets—it is the French!
If Charles comes back, it's all over for us,
if Roland lives, this war begins again
and we have lost our land, we have lost Spain."
Some four hundred, helmets laced on, assemble,   2120
some of the best, as they think, on that field.
They storm Roland, in one fierce, bitter attack.
And now Count Roland has some work on his hands. AOI.

158

Roland the Count, when he sees them coming,
how strong and fierce and alert he becomes!   2125
He will not yield to them, not while he lives.
He rides the horse they call Veillantif, spurs,
digs into it with his spurs of fine gold,
and rushes at them all where they are thickest,
the Archbishop—that Turpin!—at his side.   2130
Said one man to the other: "Go at it, friend.
The horns we heard were the horns of the French,
King Charles is coming back with all his strength."[2]

159

Roland the Count never loved a coward,
a blusterer, an evil-natured man,   2135
a man on horse who was not a good vassal.
And now he called to Archbishop Turpin:
"You are on foot, Lord, and here I am mounted,

---

2. The lines could be spoken either by Roland and the archbishop or by the pagans.

and so, here I take my stand: for love of you.
We'll take whatever comes, the good and bad,   2140
together, Lord: no one can make me leave you.
They will learn our swords' names today in battle,
the name of Almace, the name of Durendal!"
Said the Archbishop: "Let us strike or be shamed!
Charles is returning, and he brings our revenge."   2145

160

Say the pagans: "We were all born unlucky!
The evil day that dawned for us today!
We have lost our lords and peers, and now comes Charles—
that Charlemagne!—with his great host. Those trumpets!
that shrill sound on us—the trumpets of the French!   2150
And the loud roar of that Munjoie! This Roland
is a wild man, he is too great a fighter—
What man of flesh and blood can ever hope
to bring him down? Let us cast at him, and leave him there."
And so they did: arrows, wigars, darts,   2155
lances and spears, javelots[3] dressed with feathers;
struck Roland's shield, pierced it, broke it to pieces,
ripped his hauberk, shattered its rings of mail,
but never touched his body, never his flesh.
They wounded Veillantif in thirty places,   2160
struck him dead, from afar, under the Count.
The pagans flee, they leave the field to him.
Roland the Count stood alone, on his feet. AOI.

161

The pagans flee, in bitterness and rage,
strain every nerve running headlong toward Spain,   2165
and Count Roland has no way to chase them,
he has lost Veillantif, his battle horse;
he has no choice, left alone there on foot.
He went to the aid of Archbishop Turpin,
unlaced the gold-dressed helmet, raised it from his head,   2170
lifted away his bright, light coat of mail,
cut his under tunic into some lengths,
stilled his great wounds with thrusting on the strips;
then held him in his arms, against his chest,
and laid him down, gently, on the green grass;   2175
and softly now Roland entreated him:
"My noble lord, I beg you, give me leave:
our companions, whom we have loved so dearly,
are all dead now, we must not abandon them.
I want to look for them, know them once more,   2180
and set them in ranks, side by side, before you."
Said the Archbishop: "Go then, go and come back.
The field is ours, thanks be to God, yours and mine."

---

3. Small spears or javelins.

162

So Roland leaves him, walks the field all alone,
seeks in the valleys, and seeks in the mountains.   2185
He found Gerin, and Gerer his companion,
and then he found Berenger and Otun,
Anseïs and Sansun, and on that field
he found Gerard the old of Roussillon;
and carried them, brave man, all, one by one,   2190
came back to the Archbishop with these French dead,
and set them down in ranks before his knees.
The Archbishop cannot keep from weeping,
raises his hand and makes his benediction;
and said: "Lords, Lords, it was your terrible hour.   2195
May the Glorious God set all your souls
among the holy flowers of Paradise!
Here is my own death, Lords, pressing on me,
I shall not see our mighty Emperor."

163

And Roland leaves, seeks in the field again;   2200
he has found Oliver, his companion,
held him tight in his arms against his chest;
came back to the Archbishop, laid Oliver
down on a shield among the other dead.
The Archbishop absolved him, signed him with the Cross.   2205
And pity now and rage and grief increase;
and Roland says: "Oliver, dear companion,
you were the son of the great duke Renier,
who held the march of the vale of Runers.
Lord, for shattering lances, for breaking shields,   2210
for making men great with presumption weak with fright,
for giving life and counsel to good men,
for striking fear in that unbelieving race,
no warrior on earth surpasses you."

164

Roland the Count, when he sees his peers dead,   2215
and Oliver, whom he had good cause to love,
felt such grief and pity, he begins to weep;
and his face lost its color with what he felt:
a pain so great he cannot keep on standing,
he has no choice, falls fainting to the ground.   2220
Said the Archbishop: "Baron, what grief for you."

165

The Archbishop, when he saw Roland faint,
felt such pain then as he had never felt;
stretched out his hand and grasped the olifant.
At Rencesvals there is a running stream: 2225
he will go there and fetch some water for Roland;

and turns that way, with small steps, staggering;
he is too weak, he cannot go ahead,
he has no strength: all the blood he has lost.
In less time than a man takes to cross a little field   2230
that great heart fails, he falls forward, falls down;
and Turpin's death comes crushing down on him.

166

Roland the Count recovers from his faint,
gets to his feet, but stands with pain and grief;
looks down the valley, looks up the mountain, sees: 2235
on the green grass, beyond his companions,
that great and noble man down on the ground,
the Archbishop, whom God sent in His name;
who confesses his sins, lifts up his eyes,
holds up his hands joined together to heaven,   2240
and prays to God: grant him that Paradise.
Turpin is dead, King Charles' good warrior.
In great battles, in beautiful sermons
he was ever a champion against the pagans.
Now God grant Turpin's soul His holy blessing. AOI.   2245

167

Roland the Count sees the Archbishop down,
sees the bowels fallen out of his body,
and the brain boiling down from his forehead.
Turpin has crossed his hands upon his chest
beneath the collarbone, those fine white hands.   2250
Roland speaks the lament, after the custom
followed in his land: aloud, with all his heart:
"My noble lord, you great and well-born warrior,
I commend you today to the God of Glory,
whom none will ever serve with a sweeter will.   2255
Since the Apostles no prophet the like of you[4]
arose to keep the faith and draw men to it.
May your soul know no suffering or want,
and behold the gate open to Paradise."

168

Now Roland feels that death is very near.   2260
His brain comes spilling out through his two ears;
prays to God for his peers: let them be called;
and for himself, to the angel Gabriel;
took the olifant: there must be no reproach!
took Durendal his sword in his other hand,   2265
and farther than a crossbow's farthest shot
he walks toward Spain, into a fallow land,
and climbs a hill: there beneath two fine trees

---

4. Cf. Deuteronomy 34.10, on the death of Moses: "And there arose not a prophet since in
Israel like unto Moses, whom the Lord knew face to face."

stand four great blocks of stone, all are of marble;
and he fell back, to earth, on the green grass,   2270
has fainted there, for death is very near.

169

High are the hills, and high, high are the trees;
there stand four blocks of stone, gleaming of marble.
Count Roland falls fainting on the green grass,
and is watched, all this time, by a Saracen: 2275
who has feigned death and lies now with the others,
has smeared blood on his face and on his body;
and quickly now gets to his feet and runs—
a handsome man, strong, brave, and so crazed with pride
that he does something mad and dies for it: 2280
laid hands on Roland, and on the arms of Roland,
and cried: "Conquered! Charles's nephew conquered!
I'll carry this sword home to Arabia!"
As he draws it, the Count begins to come round.

170

Now Roland feels: *someone taking his sword!*   2285
opened his eyes, and had one word for him:
"I don't know you, you aren't one of ours";
grasps that olifant that he will never lose,
strikes on the helm beset with gems in gold,
shatters the steel, and the head, and the bones,   2290
sent his two eyes flying out of his head,
dumped him over stretched out at his feet dead;
and said: "You nobody! how could you dare
lay hands on me—rightly or wrongly: how?
Who'll hear of this and not call you a fool?   2295
Ah! the bell-mouth of the olifant is smashed,
the crystal and the gold fallen away."

171

Now Roland the Count feels: his sight is gone;
gets on his feet, draws on his final strength,
the color on his face lost now for good.   2300
Before him stands a rock; and on that dark rock
in rage and bitterness he strikes ten blows:
the steel blade grates, it will not break, it stands unmarked.
"Ah!" said the Count, "Blessed Mary, your help!
Ah Durendal, good sword, your unlucky day,   2305
for I am lost and cannot keep you in my care.
The battles I have won, fighting with you,
the mighty lands that holding you I conquered,
that Charles rules now, our King, whose beard is white!
Now you fall to another: it must not be
a man who'd run before another man!   2310
For a long while a good vassal held you:
there'll never be the like in France's holy land."

172

Roland strikes down on that rock of Cerritania:
the steel blade grates, will not break, stands unmarked.
Now when he sees he can never break that sword,   2315
Roland speaks the lament, in his own presence:
"Ah Durendal, how beautiful and bright!
so full of light, all on fire in the sun!
King Charles was in the vales of Moriane
when God sent his angel and commanded him,   2320
from heaven, to give you to a captain count.
That great and noble King girded it on me.
And with this sword I won Anjou and Brittany,
I won Poitou, I won Le Maine for Charles,
and Normandy, that land where men are free,   2325
I won Provence and Aquitaine with this,
and Lombardy, and every field of Romagna,
I won Bavaria, and all of Flanders,
all of Poland, and Bulgaria, for Charles,
Constantinople, which pledged him loyalty,   2330
and Saxony, where he does as he wills;
and with this sword I won Scotland and Ireland,
and England, his chamber, his own domain—
the lands, the nations I conquered with this sword,
for Charles, who rules them now, whose beard is white!   2335
Now, for this sword, I am pained with grief and rage:
Let it not fall to pagans! Let me die first!
Our Father God, save France from that dishonor."

173

Roland the Count strikes down on a dark rock,
and the rock breaks, breaks more than I can tell,   2340
and the blade grates, but Durendal will not break,
the sword leaped up, rebounded toward the sky.
The Count, when he sees that sword will not be broken,
softly, in his own presence, speaks the lament:
"Ah Durendal, beautiful, and most sacred,   2345
the holy relics in this golden pommel!
Saint Peter's tooth and blood of Saint Basile,
a lock of hair of my lord Saint Denis,
and a fragment of blessed Mary's robe:
your power must not fall to the pagans,   2350
you must be served by Christian warriors.
May no coward ever come to hold you!
It was with you I conquered those great lands
that Charles has in his keeping, whose beard is white,
the Emperor's lands, that make him rich and strong."   2355

174

Now Roland feels: death coming over him,
death descending from his temples to his heart.
He came running underneath a pine tree
and there stretched out, face down, on the green grass,

lays beneath him his sword and the olifant.　　　　　　　2360
He turned his head toward the Saracen hosts,
and this is why: with all his heart he wants
King Charles the Great and all his men to say,
he died, that noble Count, a conqueror;
makes confession, beats his breast often, so feebly,　　2365
offers his glove, for all his sins, to God. AOI.

175

Now Roland feels that his time has run out;
he lies on a steep hill, his face toward Spain;
and with one of his hands he beat his breast:
"Almighty God, *mea culpa* in thy sight,[5]　　　　　　2370
forgive my sins, both the great and the small,
sins I committed from the hour I was born
until this day, in which I lie struck down."
And then he held his right glove out to God.
Angels descend from heaven and stand by him. AOI.　　2375

176

Count Roland lay stretched out beneath a pine;
he turned his face toward the land of Spain,
began to remember many things now:
how many lands, brave man, he had conquered;
and he remembered: sweet France, the men of his line,　2380
remembered Charles, his lord, who fostered him:
cannot keep, remembering, from weeping, sighing;
but would not be unmindful of himself:
he confesses his sins, prays God for mercy:
"Loyal Father, you who never failed us,　　　　　　　2385
who resurrected Saint Lazarus from the dead,
and saved your servant Daniel from the lions:[6]
now save the soul of me from every peril
for the sins I committed while I still lived."
Then he held out his right glove to his Lord:　　　　　2390
Saint Gabriel took the glove from his hand.
He held his head bowed down upon his arm,
he is gone, his two hands joined, to his end.
Then God sent him his angel Cherubin[7]
and Saint Michael, angel of the sea's Peril;　　　　　2395
and with these two there came Saint Gabriel:
they bear Count Roland's soul to Paradise.

* * *

[**Summary**　　Following the defeat and death of Marsilion, Charlemagne faces the renewed pagan army headed by Baligant, emir of Cairo and Marsilion's overload; he defeats the pagans and returns to his capital at Aix. Shocked at the news of Roland's death, his fiancée, Aude, collapses and dies; Charlemagne now turns to punish the treason of Ganelon.]

5. See Psalm 51.4: "Against thee, thee only, have I sinned, and done this evil in thy sight." 6. See Daniel 6.12–23. For the raising of Lazarus, see John 11.1–44.

7. The poet seems to have regarded this as the name of a single angel, though "cherubim" is the plural of "cherub."

288

Now Charlemagne summons his counts and dukes:
"What is your counsel regarding those I have held?
They came to court to stand for Ganelon,   3950
bound themselves hostages for Pinabel."
The Franks reply: "Not one of them must live."
The King commands his officer, Basbrun:
"Go, hang them all on the accursed tree,
and by this beard, by the white hairs in this beard,   3955
if one escapes, you are lost, a dead man."
Basbrun replies: "What should I do but hang them?";
leads them, by force, with a hundred sergeants.
They are thirty men, and thirty men are hanged.
A traitor brings death, on himself and on others. AOI.   3960

289

Bavarians and Alemans returned,
and Poitevins, and Bretons, and Normans,
and all agreed, the Franks before the others,
Ganelon must die, and in amazing pain.
Four war horses are led out and brought forward;   3965
then they attach his two feet, his two hands.
These battle horses are swift and spirited,
four sergeants come and drive them on ahead
toward a river in the midst of a field.
Ganelon is brought to terrible perdition,   3970
all his mighty sinews are pulled to pieces,
and the limbs of his body burst apart;
on the green grass flows that bright and famous blood.
Ganelon died a traitor's and recreant's death.
Now when one man betrays another,
it is not right that he should live to boast of it.   3975

290

When the Emperor had taken his revenge,
he called to him his bishops of France,
Bavaria, Germany: "In my household
there is a noble captive, and she has heard,
for so long now, such sermons and examples,   3980
she longs for faith in God, the Christian faith.
Baptize this Queen, that God may have her soul."
And they reply: "Let her be baptized now
by godmothers, ladies of noble birth."
At the baths of Aix there is a great crowd gathered,   3985
there they baptized the noble Queen of Spain,
and they found her the name Juliana;
she is Christian, by knowledge of the Truth.

291

When the Emperor had brought his justice to pass
and peace comes now to that great wrath of his,   3990

he put the Christian faith in Bramimunde;
the day passes, the soft night has gathered,
the King lay down in his vaulted chamber.
Saint Gabriel! come in God's name to say:
"Charles, gather the great hosts of your Empire!   3995
Go to the land of Bire, with all your force,
you must relieve King Vivien at Imphe,
the citadel, pagans have besieged it:
Christians are calling you, they cry your name!"
The Emperor would have wished not to go.   4000
"God!" said the King, "the pains, the labors of my life!";
weeps from his eyes, pulls his white beard.

Here ends the song	that Turold composes, paraphrases, amplifies,[8] 4003
	that Turold completes, relates,
Here ends the tale	that Turold declaims, recounts, narrates,
	that Turold copies, transcribes,
Here ends the geste	for Turold grows weak, grows weary, declines,
Here ends the written history,	
Here ends the source	that Turold turns into poetry.

8. The last line of the poem reads "Ci falt la geste que Turoldus declinet." The meaning of the words *geste* and *declinet* and the syntax of *que* have never been finally settled, and no line in the poem contains so many possible meanings as the last one. Some of the interpretations that have been proposed are given here, and every one is plausible.

MARIE DE FRANCE
1150?–1200?

"Marie ai num, si sui de France" (Marie is my name, and I am from France). With these words, the author of the *Lais* tells us her name and her homeland. Yet Marie was an English writer, composing in the Anglo-Norman dialect that had become the mother tongue of the English ruling classes following the Norman Conquest a century before. Her short, intense stories of love and loss reflect the complex cultural encounter of Celtic folktale, Anglo-French court setting, and English landscape, and they set the stage for the flowering of the romance genre in the last decades of the twelfth century.

We know little about Marie beyond what she herself tells us in the Prologue to her *Lais*, which is reprinted here, and in the closing lines of her collection of animal fables. She is likely to have been a nun—possibly an abbess in a position of authority within her community; in offering her collection of twelve *Lais* as a gift to Henry II, King of England and Duke of Normandy, she uses terms that presume some degree of familiarity, perhaps even a family relationship. It was not uncommon in twelfth-century Europe for the illegitimate female offspring of noble or royal figures to enter convents, less because these women were pious than because it was expedient to prevent them from marrying political rivals and bearing children who might complicate the smooth order of future succession. Marie's place in the world, attached at once to the cloister and to the court, may reflect some such family history.

In addition to her *Fables*, which she claims to have translated from a now-lost text by the Anglo-Saxon king Alfred, Marie's other surviving works include the mysterious journey to the afterlife recounted in *Saint Patrick's Purgatory* (adapted from a Latin original) and an account of the life and works of the English saint Audrey. Her poems stand at the intersection of oral and written forms of literature, as well as at the crossroads of cultures—not just English and French, but Welsh or Breton as well. Celtic cultures had survived the warfare of English and French barons, both in the mountains of Wales and in Cornwall, to the north of the English Channel, and in the upper regions of Normandy and Brittany, to the south. In her Prologue, Marie describes her desire to preserve these Breton songs: having heard them sung, she writes, "I don't want to neglect or forget them." She expresses a similar sentiment in the epilogue to her *Fables*, in which she tells the reader her own name "pur remembrance," "for remembrance." Through the *Lais*, Marie has ensured that both she and the ancient songs she has written down will live on in memory.

The two lais included here, "Lanval" and "Laüstic," represent two very different types: the first, more elaborate, offers a very fully developed psychology of the main characters, and the second, shorter and jewel-like, crystallizes an essential truth about the nature of love in poetic form. In "Lanval," we encounter the now-familiar world of Arthurian romance, with its tales of Arthur and Guenevere, Yvain and Gawain, and the hidden realm of Avalon. Yet Marie was the first to bring this oral Breton material into the mainstream of European literature, a move that was amplified by her French successor, Chrétien de Troyes (in his various Arthurian romances), and, later, by the anonymous English poet who wrote *Sir Gawain and the Green Knight* and by Thomas Malory in his *Morte d'Arthur*. In "Lanval," the realistic, practical world of the Arthurian court is suddenly punctured by the intrusion of the mysterious Otherworld when the knight's enigmatic lady appears to rescue her lover from the accusations of a false and potentially adulterous queen, and takes him home with her to Avalon.

"Laüstic" similarly recounts love's triumph, although here in a darker and more sorrowful vein. The affair of a woman and her husband's friend comes to a brutal end when the beautiful nightingale, whose nighttime song fuels the dreams of lovers, is killed by the jealous husband. The body of the bird becomes a token of their forbidden passion, first wrapped in an embroidered shroud by the lady, and then preserved in a begemmed reliquary by her lover. The miniature lai, like the miniature sarcophagus, remains as a potent reminder of the power of love.

From Lais[1]

Prologue

Whoever has received knowledge
and eloquence in speech from God
should not be silent or secretive
but demonstrate it willingly.
When a great good is widely heard of,   5
then, and only then, does it bloom,
and when that good is praised by many,
it has spread its blossoms.
The custom among the ancients—
as Priscian[2] testifies—   10
was to speak quite obscurely
in the books they wrote,
so that those who were to come after
and study them
might gloss the letter   15
and supply its significance from their own wisdom.
Philosophers knew this,
they understood among themselves
that the more time they spent,
the more subtle their minds would become   20
and the better they would know how to keep themselves
from whatever was to be avoided.
He who would guard himself from vice
should study and understand
and begin a weighty work   25
by which he might keep vice at a distance,
and free himself from great sorrow.
That's why I began to think
about composing some good stories
and translating from Latin to Romance;   30
but that was not to bring me fame:
too many others have done it.
Then I thought of the *lais* I'd heard.
I did not doubt, indeed I knew well,
that those who first began them   35
and sent them forth
composed them in order to preserve
adventures they had heard.
I have heard many told;
and I don't want to neglect or forget them.   40
To put them into word and rhyme
I've often stayed awake.

1. Translated from the French by Robert Hanning and Joan Ferrante.   2. Latin grammarian (early 6th century C.E.), widely read in the Middle Ages.

In your honor, noble King,[3]
who are so brave and courteous,
repository of all joys   45
in whose heart all goodness takes root,
I undertook to assemble these *lais*
to compose and recount them in rhyme.
In my heart I thought and determined,
sire, that I would present them to you.   50
If it pleases you to receive them,
you will give me great joy;
I shall be happy forever.
Do not think me presumptuous
if I dare present them to you.   55
Now hear how they begin.

Lanval

I shall tell you the adventure of another *lai,*
just as it happened:
it was composed about a very noble vassal;
in Breton,[4] they call him Lanval.

Arthur, the brave and the courtly king,   5
was staying at Cardoel,[5]
because the Scots and the Picts
were destroying the land.
They invaded Logres[6]
and laid it waste.   10
At Pentecost,[7] in summer,
the king stayed there.
He gave out many rich gifts:
to counts and barons,
members of the Round Table[8]—   15
such a company had no equal in all the world—
he distributed wives and lands,
to all but one who had served him.
That was Lanval; Arthur forgot him,
and none of his men favored him either.   20
For his valor, for his generosity,
his beauty and his bravery,
most men envied him;
some feigned the appearance of love
who, if something unpleasant happened to him,   25

3. Henry II, King of England, who also held
substantial properties in France.
4. A Celtic language spoken in Brittany (a
region of modern northern France), closely
related to Welsh.
5. Carlisle, an English city on the border of
modern Scotland.

6. That is, England (a name often used in
tales of King Arthur).
7. A Christian feast day, observed seven Sundays after Easter.
8. King Arthur's legendary table, whose shape
symbolized the equality of every knight seated
at it.

would not have been at all disturbed.
He was the son of a king of high degree
but he was far from his heritage.
He was of the king's household
but he had spent all his wealth,   30
for the king gave him nothing
nor did Lanval ask.
Now Lanval was in difficulty,
depressed and very worried.
My lords, don't be surprised: 35
a strange man, without friends,
is very sad in another land,
when he doesn't know where to look for help.
The knight of whom I speak,
who had served the king so long,   40
one day mounted his horse
and went off to amuse himself.
He left the city
and came, all alone, to a field;
he dismounted by a running stream   45
but his horse trembled badly.
He removed the saddle and went off,
leaving the horse to roll around in the meadow.
He folded his cloak beneath his head
and lay down.   50
He worried about his difficulty,
he could see nothing that pleased him.
As he lay there
he looked down along the bank
and saw two girls approaching;   55
he had never seen any lovelier.
They were richly dressed,
tightly laced,
in tunics of dark purple;
their faces were very lovely.   60
The older one carried basins,
golden, well made, and fine;
I shall tell you the truth about it, without fail.
The other carried a towel.
They went straight   65
to where the knight was lying.
Lanval, who was very well bred,
got up to meet them.
They greeted him first
and gave him their message: 70
"Sir Lanval, my lady,
who is worthy and wise and beautiful,
sent us for you.
Come with us now.
We shall guide you there safely.   75
See, her pavilion is nearby!"

The knight went with them;
giving no thought to his horse
who was feeding before him in the meadow.
They led him up to the tent,   80
which was quite beautiful and well placed.
Queen Semiramis,[9]
however much more wealth,
power, or knowledge she had,
or the emperor Octavian[1]   85
could not have paid for one of the flaps.
There was a golden eagle on top of it,
whose value I could not tell,
nor could I judge the value of the cords or the poles
that held up the sides of the tent;   90
there is no king on earth who could buy it,
no matter what wealth he offered.
The girl was inside the tent:
the lily and the young rose
when they appear in the summer   95
are surpassed by her beauty.
She lay on a beautiful bed—
the bedclothes were worth a castle—
dressed only in her shift.
Her body was well shaped and elegant;   100
for the heat, she had thrown over herself,
a precious cloak of white ermine,
covered with purple alexandrine,[2]
but her whole side was uncovered,
her face, her neck and her bosom;   105
she was whiter than the hawthorn flower.
The knight went forward
and the girl addressed him.
He sat before the bed.
"Lanval," she said, "sweet love,   110
because of you I have come from my land;
I came to seek you from far away.
If you are brave and courtly,
no emperor or count or king
will ever have known such joy or good;   115
for I love you more than anything."
He looked at her and saw that she was beautiful;
Love stung him with a spark
that burned and set fire to his heart.
He answered her in a suitable way.   120
"Lovely one," he said, "if it pleased you,
if such joy might be mine

9. Legendary queen of Assyria (medieval Babylon), renowned for her extravagance and her
lust.
1. Augustus Caesar (63 B.C.E.–14 C.E.), the

first Roman emperor.
2. Sumptuous silk fabric imported from Alexandria, Egypt; because of its expense, purple dye
(like ermine fur) was associated with royalty.

that you would love me,
there is nothing you might command,
within my power, that I would not do, 125
whether foolish or wise.
I shall obey your command;
for you, I shall abandon everyone.
I want never to leave you.
That is what I most desire." 130
When the girl heard the words
of the man who could love her so,
she granted him her love and her body.
Now Lanval was on the right road!
Afterward, she gave him a gift: 135
he would never again want anything,
he would receive as he desired;
however generously he might give and spend,
she would provide what he needed.
Now Lanval is well cared for. 140
The more lavishly he spends,
the more gold and silver he will have.
"Love," she said, "I admonish you now,
I command and beg you,
do not let any man know about this. 145
I shall tell you why:
you would lose me for good
if this love were known;
you would never see me again
or possess my body." 150
He answered that he would do
exactly as she commanded.
He lay beside her on the bed;
now Lanval is well cared for.
He remained with her 155
that afternoon, until evening
and would have stayed longer, if he could,
and if his love had consented.
"Love," she said, "get up.
You cannot stay any longer. 160
Go away now; I shall remain
but I will tell you one thing:
when you want to talk to me
there is no place you can think of
where a man might have his mistress 165
without reproach or shame,
that I shall not be there with you
to satisfy all your desires.
No man but you will see me
or hear my words." 170
When he heard her, he was very happy,
he kissed her, and then got up.
The girls who had brought him to the tent

dressed him in rich clothes;
when he was dressed anew,   175
there wasn't a more handsome youth in all the world;
he was no fool, no boor.
They gave him water for his hands
and a towel to dry them,
and they brought him food.   180
He took supper with his love;
it was not to be refused.
He was served with great courtesy,
he received it with great joy.
There was an entremet[3]   185
that vastly pleased the knight
for he kissed his lady often
and held her close.
When they finished dinner,
his horse was brought to him.   190
The horse had been well saddled;
Lanval was very richly served.
The knight took his leave, mounted,
and rode toward the city,
often looking behind him.   195
Lanval was very disturbed;
he wondered about his adventure
and was doubtful in his heart;
he was amazed, not knowing what to believe;
he didn't expect ever to see her again.   200
He came to his lodging
and found his men well dressed.
That night, his accommodations were rich
but no one knew where it came from.
There was no knight in the city   205
who really needed a place to stay
whom he didn't invite to join him
to be well and richly served.
Lanval gave rich gifts,
Lanval released prisoners,   210
Lanval dressed jongleurs [performers],
Lanval offered great honors.
There was no stranger or friend
to whom Lanval didn't give.
Lanval's joy and pleasure were intense;   215
in the daytime or at night,
he could see his love often;
she was completely at his command.

In that same year, it seems to me,
after the feast of St. John,[4]   220

---

3. Dish served between courses at a banquet.   4. John the Baptist; his feast day is June 24.

about thirty knights
were amusing themselves
in an orchard beneath the tower
where the queen was staying.
Gawain was with them   225
and his cousin, the handsome Yvain;
Gawain, the noble, the brave,
who was so loved by all, said:
"By God, my lords, we wronged
our companion Lanval,   230
who is so generous and courtly,
and whose father is a rich king,
when we didn't bring him with us."
They immediately turned back,
went to his lodging   235
and prevailed on Lanval to come along with them.
At a sculpted window
the queen was looking out;
she had three ladies with her.
She saw the king's retinue,   240
recognized Lanval and looked at him.
Then she told one of her ladies
to send for her maidens,
the loveliest and the most refined;
together they went to amuse themselves   245
in the orchard where the others were.
She brought thirty or more with her;
they descended the steps.
The knights came to meet them,
because they were delighted to see them.   250
The knights took them by the hand;
their conversation was in no way vulgar.
Lanval went off to one side,
far from the others; he was impatient
to hold his love,   255
to kiss and embrace and touch her;
he thought little of others' joys
if he could not have his pleasure.
When the queen saw him alone,
she went straight to the knight.   260
She sat beside him and spoke,
revealing her whole heart:
"Lanval, I have shown you much honor,
I have cherished you, and loved you.
You may have all my love;   265
just tell me your desire.
I promise you my affection.
You should be very happy with me."
"My lady," he said, "let me be!
I have no desire to love you.   270
I've served the king a long time;

I don't want to betray my faith to him.
Never, for you or for your love,
will I do anything to harm my lord."
The queen got angry;   275
in her wrath, she insulted him:
"Lanval," she said, "I am sure
you don't care for such pleasure;
people have often told me
that you have no interest in women.   280
You have fine-looking boys
with whom you enjoy yourself.
Base coward, lousy cripple,
my lord made a bad mistake
when he let you stay with him.   285
For all I know, he'll lose God because of it."
When Lanval heard her, he was quite disturbed;
he was not slow to answer.
He said something out of spite
that he would later regret.   290
"Lady," he said, "of that activity
I know nothing,
but I love and I am loved
by one who should have the prize
over all the women I know.   295
And I shall tell you one thing;
you might as well know all:
any one of those who serve her,
the poorest girl of all,
is better than you, my lady queen,   300
in body, face, and beauty,
in breeding and in goodness."
The queen left him
and went, weeping, to her chamber.
She was upset and angry   305
because he had insulted her.
She went to bed sick;
never, she said, would she get up
unless the king gave her satisfaction
for the offense against her.   310
The king returned from the woods,
he'd had a very good day.
He entered the queen's chambers.
When she saw him, she began to complain.
She fell at his feet, asked his mercy,   315
saying that Lanval had dishonored her;
he had asked for her love,
and because she refused him
he insulted and offended her:
he boasted of a love   320
who was so refined and noble and proud
that her chambermaid,

the poorest one who served her,
was better than the queen.
The king got very angry;   325
he swore an oath:
if Lanval could not defend himself in court
he would have him burned or hanged.
The king left her chamber
and called for three of his barons;   330
he sent them for Lanval
who was feeling great sorrow and distress.
He had come back to his dwelling,
knowing very well
that he'd lost his love,   335
he had betrayed their affair.
He was all alone in a room,
disturbed and troubled;
he called on his love, again and again,
but it did him no good.   340
He complained and sighed,
from time to time he fainted;
then he cried a hundred times for her to have mercy
and speak to her love.
He cursed his heart and his mouth;   345
it's wonder he didn't kill himself.
No matter how much he cried and shouted,
ranted and raged,
she would not have mercy on him,
not even let him see her.   350
How will he ever contain himself?
The men the king sent
arrived and told him
to appear in court without delay:
the king had summoned him   355
because the queen had accused him.
Lanval went with his great sorrow;
they could have killed him, for all he cared.
He came before the king;
he was very sad, thoughtful, silent;   360
his face revealed great suffering.
In anger the king told him:
"Vassal, you have done me a great wrong!
This was a base undertaking,
to shame and disgrace me   365
and to insult the queen.
You have made a foolish boast:
your love is much too noble
if her maid is more beautiful,
more worthy, than the queen."   370
Lanval denied that he'd dishonored
or shamed his lord,
word for word, as the king spoke:

he had not made advances to the queen;
but of what he had said, 375
he acknowledged the truth,
about the love he had boasted of,
that now made him sad because he'd lost her.
About that he said he would do
whatever the court decided. 380
The king was very angry with him;
he sent for all his men
to determine exactly what he ought to do
so that no one could find fault with his decision.
They did as he commanded, 385
whether they liked it or not.
They assembled,
judged, and decided,
than Lanval should have his day;
but he must find pledges for his lord 390
to guarantee that he would await the judgment,
return, and be present at it.
Then the court would be increased,
for now there were none but the king's household.
The barons came back to the king 395
and announced their decision.
The king demanded pledges.
Lanval was alone and forlorn,
he had no relative, no friend.
Gawain went and pledged himself for him, 400
and all his companions followed.
The king addressed them: "I release him to you
on forfeit of whatever you hold from me,
lands and fiefs, each one for himself."
When Lanval was pledged, there was nothing else to do. 405
He returned to his lodging.
The knights accompanied him,
they reproached and admonished him
that he give up his great sorrow;
they cursed his foolish love. 410
Each day they went to see him,
because they wanted to know
whether he was drinking and eating;
they were afraid that he'd kill himself.
On the day that they had named, 415
the barons assembled.
The king and the queen were there
and the pledges brought Lanval back.
They were all very sad for him:
I think there were a hundred 420
who would have done all they could
to set him free without a trial
where he would be wrongly accused.
The king demanded a verdict

according to the charge and rebuttal.   425
Now it all fell to the barons.
They went to the judgment,
worried and distressed
for the noble man from another land
who'd gotten into such trouble in their midst.   430
Many wanted to condemn him
in order to satisfy their lord.
The Duke of Cornwall[5] said:
"No one can blame us;
whether it makes you weep or sing   435
justice must be carried out.
The king spoke against his vassal
whom I have heard named Lanval;
he accused him of felony,
charged him with a misdeed—   440
a love that he had boasted of,
which made the queen angry.
No one but the king accused him:
by the faith I owe you,
if one were to speak the truth,   445
there should have been no need for defense,
except that a man owes his lord honor
in every circumstance.
He will be bound by his oath,
and the king will forgive us our pledges   450
if he can produce proof;
if his love would come forward,
if what he said,
what upset the queen, is true,
then he will be acquitted,   455
because he did not say it out of malice.
But if he cannot get his proof,
we must make it clear to him
that he will forfeit his service to the king;
he must take his leave."   460
They sent to the knight,
told and announced to him
that he should have his love come
to defend and stand surety for him.
He told them that he could not do it: 465
he would never receive help from her.
They went back to the judges,
not expecting any help from Lanval.
The king pressed them hard
because of the queen who was waiting.   470
When they were ready to give their verdict
they saw two girls approaching,

---

5. Extreme southwestern part of England, a Celtic region that was the seat of Arthurian legend.

riding handsome palfreys.[6]
They were very attractive,
dressed in purple taffeta,   475
over their bare skin.
The men looked at them with pleasure.
Gawain, taking three knights with him,
went to Lanval and told him;
he pointed out the two girls.   480
Gawain was extremely happy, and begged him
to tell if his love were one of them.
Lanval said he didn't know who they were,
where they came from or where they were going.
The girls proceeded   485
still on horseback;
they dismounted before the high table
at which Arthur, the king, sat.
They were of great beauty,
and spoke in a courtly manner: 490
"King, clear your chambers,
have them hung with silk
where my lady may dismount;
she wishes to take shelter with you."
He promised it willingly   495
and called two knights
to guide them up to the chambers.
On that subject no more was said.
The king asked his barons
for their judgment and decision;   500
he said they had angered him very much
with their long delay.
"Sire," they said, "we have decided.
Because of the ladies we have just seen
we have made no judgment.   505
Let us reconvene the trial."
Then they assembled, everyone was worried;
there was much noise and strife.
While they were in that confusion,
two girls in noble array,   510
dressed in Phrygian[7] silks
and riding Spanish mules,
were seen coming down the street.
This gave the vassals great joy;
to each other they said that now   515
Lanval, the brave and bold, was saved.
Gawain went up to him,
bringing his companions along.
"Sire," he said, "take heart.

6. Saddle horses, especially those used by   7. That is, Eastern.
ladies (as opposed to warhorses).

For the love of God, speak to us.   520
Here come two maidens,
well adorned and very beautiful;
one must certainly be your love."
Lanval answered quickly
that he did not recognize them,   525
he didn't know them or love them.
Meanwhile they'd arrived,
and dismounted before the king.
Most of those who saw them praised them
for their bodies, their faces, their coloring;   530
each was more impressive
than the queen had ever been.
The older one was courtly and wise,
she spoke her message fittingly:
"King, have chambers prepared for us   535
to lodge my lady according to her need;
she is coming here to speak with you."
He ordered them to be taken
to the others who had preceded them.
There was no problem with the mules.   540
When he had seen to the girls,
he summoned all his barons
to render their judgment;
it had already dragged out too much.
The queen was getting angry   545
because she had fasted so long.
They were about to give their judgment
when through the city came riding
a girl on horseback:
there was none more beautiful in the world.   550
She rode a white palfrey,
who carried her handsomely and smoothly:
he was well apportioned in the neck and head,
no finer beast in the world.
The palfrey's trappings were rich;   555
under heaven there was no count or king
who could have afforded them all
without selling or mortgaging lands.
She was dressed in this fashion:
in a white linen shift   560
that revealed both her sides
since the lacing was along the side.
Her body was elegant, her hips slim,
her neck whiter than snow on a branch,
her eyes bright, her face white,   565
a beautiful mouth, a well-set nose,
dark eyebrows and an elegant forehead,
her hair curly and rather blond;
golden wire does not shine
like her hair in the light.   570

Her cloak, which she had wrapped around her,
was dark purple.
On her wrist she held a sparrow hawk,
a greyhound followed her.[8]
In the town, no one, small or big, 575
old man or child,
failed to come look.
As they watched her pass,
there was no joking about her beauty.
She proceeded at a slow pace. 580
The judges who saw her
marveled at the sight;
no one who looked at her
was not warmed with joy.
Those who loved the knight 585
came to him and told him
of the girl who was approaching,
if God pleased, to rescue him.
"Sir companion, here comes one
neither tawny nor dark; 590
this is, of all who exist,
the most beautiful woman in the world."
Lanval heard them and lifted his head;
he recognized her and sighed.
The blood rose to his face; 595
he was quick to speak.
"By my faith," he said, "that is my love.
Now I don't care if I am killed,
if only she forgives me.
For I am restored, now that I see her." 600
The lady entered the palace;
no one so beautiful had ever been there.
She dismounted before the king
so that she was well seen by all.
And she let her cloak fall 605
so they could see her better.
The king, who was well bred,
rose and went to meet her;
all the others honored her
and offered to serve her. 610
When they had looked at her well,
when they had greatly praised her beauty,
she spoke in this way,
she didn't want to wait:
"I have loved one of your vassals: 615
you see him before you—Lanval.
He has been accused in your court—
I don't want him to suffer
for what he said; you should know
that the queen was in the wrong. 620

8. Both animals were used in hunting.

He never made advances to her.
And for the boast that he made,
if he can be acquitted through me,
let him be set free by your barons."
Whatever the barons judged by law   625
the king promised would prevail.
To the last man they agreed
that Lanval had successfully answered the charge.
He was set free by their decision
and the girl departed.   630
The king could not detain her,
though there were enough people to serve her.
Outside the hall stood
a great stone of dark marble
where heavy men mounted   635
when they left the king's court;
Lanval climbed on it.
When the girl came through the gate
Lanval leapt, in one bound,
onto the palfrey, behind her.   640
With her he went to Avalun,[9]
so the Bretons tell us,
to a very beautiful island;
there the youth was carried off.
No man heard of him again,   645
and I have no more to tell.

Laüstic (The Nightingale)

I shall tell you an adventure
about which the Bretons made a *lai*.
Laüstic was the name, I think,
they gave it in their land.
In French it is *rossignol*,   5
and *nightingale* in proper English.
At Saint-Malo,[1] in that country,
there was a famous city.
Two knights lived there,
they both had strong houses.   10
From the goodness of the two barons
the city acquired a good name.
One had married a woman
wise, courtly, and handsome;
she set a wonderfully high value on herself,   15
within the bounds of custom and usage.
The other was a bachelor,
well known among his peers
for bravery and great valor;
he delighted in living well.   20

9. Avalon, in Celtic mythology the abode of the blessed dead; in Arthurian legend, the island where Arthur goes after he is mortally wounded.

1. A seaport in northwest France, in Brittany.

He jousted often, spent widely
and gave out what he had.
He also loved his neighbor's wife;
he asked her, begged her so persistently,
and there was such good in him,   25
that she loved him more than anything,
as much for the good that she heard of him
as because he was close by.
They loved each other discreetly and well,
concealed themselves and took care   30
that they weren't seen
or disturbed or suspected.
And they could do this well enough
since their dwellings were close,
their houses were next door,   35
and so were their rooms and their towers;
there was no barrier or boundary
except a high wall of dark stone.
From the rooms where the lady slept,
if she went to the window   40
she could talk to her love
on the other side, and he to her,
and they could exchange their possessions,
by tossing and throwing them.
There was scarcely anything to disturb them,   45
they were both quite at ease;
except that they couldn't come together
completely for their pleasure,
for the lady was closely guarded
when her husband was in the country.   50
Yet they always managed,
whether at night or in the day,
to be able to talk together;
no one could prevent
their coming to the window   55
and seeing each other there.
For a long time they loved each other,
until one summer
when the woods and meadows were green
and the orchards blooming.   60
The little birds, with great sweetness,
were voicing their joy above the flowers.
It is no wonder if he understands them,
he who has love to his desire.
I'll tell you the truth about the knight: 65
he listened to them intently
and to the lady on the other side,
both with words and looks.
At night, when the moon shone
when her lord was in bed,   70
she often rose from his side

and wrapped herself in a cloak.
She went to the window
because of her lover, who, she knew,
was leading the same life,   75
awake most of the night.
Each took pleasure in the other's sight
since they could have nothing more;
but she got up and stood there so often
that her lord grew angry   80
and began to question her, to ask
why she got up and where she went.
"My lord," the lady answered him,
"there is no joy in this world
like hearing the nightingale sing.   85
That's why I stand there.
It sounds so sweet at night
that it gives me great pleasure;
it delights me so and I so desire it
that I cannot close my eyes."   90
When her lord heard what she said
he laughed in anger and ill will.
He set his mind on one thing:
to trap the nightingale.
There was no valet in his house   95
that he didn't set to making traps, nets, or snares,
which he then had placed in the orchard;
there was no hazel tree or chestnut
where they did not place a snare or lime
until they trapped and captured him.   100
When they had caught the nightingale,
they brought it, still alive, to the lord.
He was very happy when he had it;
he came to the lady's chambers.
"Lady," he said, "where are you?   105
Come here! Speak to us!
I have trapped the nightingale
that kept you awake so much.
From now on you can lie in peace:
he will never again awaken you."   110
When the lady heard him,
she was sad and angry.
She asked her lord for the bird
but he killed it out of spite,
he broke its neck in his hands—   115
too vicious an act—
and threw the body on the lady;
her shift was stained with blood,
a little, on her breast.
Then he left the room.   120
The lady took the little body;
she wept hard and cursed

those who betrayed the nightingale,
who made the traps and snares,
for they took great joy from her. 125
"Alas," she said, "now I must suffer.
I won't be able to get up at night
or go and stand in the window
where I used to see my love.
I know one thing for certain: 130
he'd think I was pretending.
I must decide what to do about this.
I shall send him the nightingale
and relate the adventure."
In a piece of samite, 135
embroidered in gold and writing,
she wrapped the little bird.
She called one of her servants,
charged him with her message,
and sent him to her love. 140
He came to the knight,
greeted him in the name of the lady,
related the whole message to him,
and presented the nightingale.

When everything had been told and revealed to the knight, 145
after he had listened well,
he was very sad about the adventure,
but he wasn't mean or hesitant.
He had a small vessel fashioned,
with no iron or steel in it; 150
it was all pure gold and good stones,
very precious and very dear;
the cover was very carefully attached.
He placed the nightingale inside
and then he had the casket sealed— 155
he carried it with him always.

This adventure was told,
it could not be concealed for long.
The Bretons made a *lai* about it
which men call *The Nightingale*. 160

DANTE ALIGHIERI

1265–1321

"Midway along the journey of our life / I woke to find myself in a dark wood, / for I had wandered off from the straight path." With these opening words, Dante compels his reader to inhabit the point of view of a narrator who, halfway through not "my" but "our" lifetime, suddenly realizes that he is lost. His life is thus our life, and the ethical or righteous "straight path" that the narrator hopes to rediscover also comes to be the reader's own goal. Yet this identification of reader and narrator is countered, again and again in *The Divine Comedy*, by an insistence on the specific circumstances of Dante's own life: traveling into the underworld and into the other realms of the afterlife, we meet his old teacher, Brunetto Latini; the father of his close friend Guido Cavalcanti; his great-great-grandfather, Cacciaguida; and, most importantly, the beautiful Beatrice Portinari, whom Dante has loved (he tells us) since they were both children. In spite of the particularity of the details of this afterlife—or, perhaps, because of them—the reader constantly identifies with the narrator experiencing the painful turns of the journey as well as the joyful expectation of heavenly bliss at the road's end.

LIFE AND TIMES

Dante Alighieri was born and raised in Florence, a northern Italian city that was at once central to his sense of identity and—as depicted in *The Divine Comedy*—a place that he loathed and despised, a degenerate community rife with corruption and discord. During the years around 1300, Florence, like other cities in northern Italy, was caught up in a large-scale confrontation between forces favoring the power of the church and those favoring the independence of city-states. Dante quickly became deeply involved with these issues, both as a member of the political governing body within the city of Florence and in his role as envoy from the city to the seat of the papal government in Rome. Dante's own view—expressed most explicitly in his *Monarchia* (1318), a political treatise that in some ways anticipates **Machiavelli's *The Prince***—was that secular rule and ecclesiastical rule should be clearly divided. Dante argued that a strong ruler in the person of an idealized emperor was necessary for the church to appropriately exercise its moral and religious authority. Because it sought to place limitations on the exercise of political power by the church, *The Monarchia* was immediately condemned; it remained on the list (or "Index") of books that Catholics are forbidden to read until 1881.

Florence had taken a leading role in the disputes concerning secular and ecclesiastical power, split first into the factions of the Guelphs (who supported the pope) and the Ghibellines (who supported the Holy Roman Emperor). By the time Dante became involved in Florentine politics, the Guelphs had become dominant within the city, but an internal fracture soon developed between the Black Guelphs, who continued to support Boniface VIII, and the White Guelphs, who had come to oppose his despotism. Dante was allied with the latter, and when he was in Rome on a diplomatic mission, the Black Guelphs seized control of the city. Dante was consequently forbidden from ever reentering the city of his birth, under penalty of death by burning at the stake. Even worse, the split into the White and Black parties divided his family, as the Black Guelphs were led by the Donatis—relatives of his wife, Gemma Donati—and his wife and their four children remained in Florence.

Deeply embittered by the experience of exile, Dante spent the next twenty years wandering from city to city, all the while continuing with his political writing as well as his poetic efforts. The scandal arising from the *Monarchia* undoubtedly hampered Dante's efforts to return to Florence. In his *Divine Comedy*, he movingly recalls "the bitter taste of others' bread, how salty it is," and laments "how hard a path it is to go ascending and descending others' stairs." Dante never saw his sentence of exile lifted; indeed, Florence's city council finally revoked it only in 2008. That the vote was not unanimous—the motion passed 19 to 5—suggests that the city's political divisions may have lingered for seven hundred years.

WORK

Dante himself called his monumental poem simply the *Commedia*, or "comedy"; the adjective "divine" was added later by Giovanni Boccaccio, author of *The Decameron*, the other great work of medieval Italian literature. Boccaccio thereby signaled not just the subject matter of the work—that is, the realm of the afterlife, including the domains of hell, purgatory, and heaven—but also the elevated style in which it was written. The claim of direct inspiration by God, which Dante makes explicitly throughout the work, was taken at face value by the first generations of commentators, who accepted the work as the faithful poetic record of a real visionary experience. The theological content of the *Comedy* is both dense and elaborate: perhaps the most ambitious aspect of the poem's theology

centers on purgatory, a place where souls are able to do penance for their sins even after death, to which Dante devotes the second of the three parts of his work. Purgatory would not become official Christian doctrine until well after the *Comedy* was completed, but Dante was responding to contemporary popular beliefs in the ability of the prayers of the living to affect the condition of the souls of the dead. He also reflects contemporary theological views of the persistence of the union of body and soul even after death, especially in the way that the shades that populate the afterworld of *The Divine Comedy* retain their individual bodily features though their flesh has been replaced by empty form. For modern readers, the term "comedy" might seem peculiar, conditioned as we are to associate comedy with laughter, just as we associate tragedy with tears. For medieval readers, however, following classical notions of genre, a comedy was simply a story that ended on a high note, with joy and—in the case of *The Divine Comedy*—with the narrator literally being lifted up into the heavens.

The Divine Comedy is divided into three books; each charts a different realm of the afterlife, from the depths of Hell in the *Inferno*, up the mountain of Purgatory in the *Purgatorio*, and finally through the ever-higher spheres of Heaven in the *Paradiso*. The three parts form a single path, as the narrator traverses a rugged landscape marked by hills, ravines, treacherous pathways, and difficult stairways, relying throughout on the help of a guide. For the journey through Hell and Purgatory, he follows in the footsteps of **Virgil**. The Roman poet is more than the literal guide of the wanderer within the fiction of the poem, for his *Aeneid*, the epic account of the fall of Troy and the foundation of Rome by Aeneas, is the constant poetic underpinning of Dante's own epic enterprise. But Virgil, as a pagan, cannot accompany him

This painted limestone statue, discovered in Saqqara, Egypt, in 1850, depicts a scribe writing on a tablet. It dates from the third millennium B.C.E. Scribes were highly respected members of court in ancient literate societies; their work is the primary reason we have any sense of life in deep antiquity.

Clay tablets (right and top) and envelope (left) from central Turkey, dating from
ca. 1850 B.C.E. These objects contain a letter, written in cuneiform, from someone named
"Ashur-malik" to his brother "Ashur-idi" in which the former complains that his family
has been left in Ashur without food, fuel, or clothing over the winter. The letter writer
ran out of room on the large tablet and so had to continue his complaint on the little
supplemental tablet.

An "oracle bone," dating from the Shang Dynasty (2nd millennium B.C.E.) in China. Oracle
bones were often made of ox scapula (shoulder blades) or tortoise belly-shells and were
inscribed with divinations using a bronze pin or other carving implement. These bones
represent the earliest significant gathering of Chinese writing.

Ancient Egyptians of aristocratic status were often buried with a specially commissioned papyrus manuscript of the *Book of the Dead* that pictured them making their way to the afterlife. The manuscript here, written in hieroglyphic script and with an image of the departed at the center, is the *Book of the Dead* for an Egyptian noble of Nubian origin named Maiherperi. It dates from the reign of the pharaoh Thutmose IV, ca. fourteenth century B.C.E.

One form of writing that was a basic part of citizenship in Athens during its classical period (the fifth and fourth centuries B.C.E.) was ballot-casting. The most common medium for casting votes was broken earthenware, on which citizens would write their selection. These shards, called *ostraka*, often record a vote on the question of whether or not to banish or exile someone. This term is the source of the English word *ostracism*.

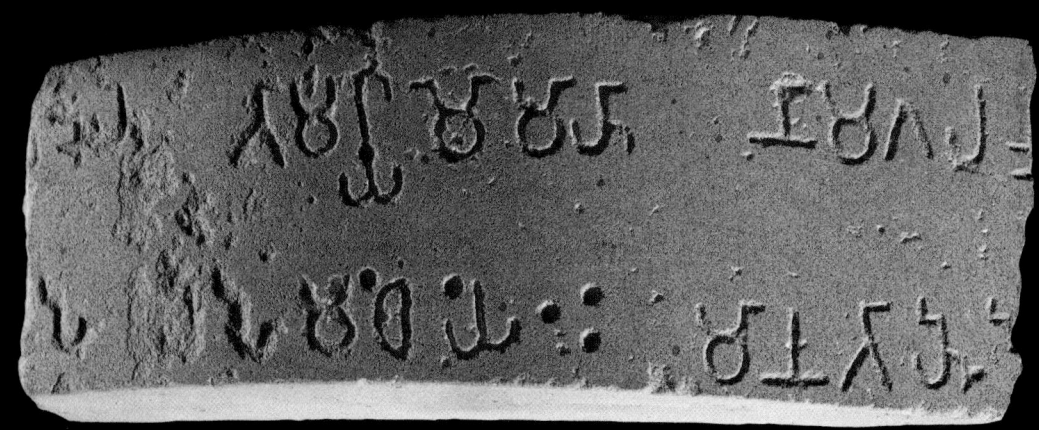

This fragment, part of the 'sixth pillar edict' of King Aśoka (third century B.C.E.), shows the Brahmi script used during the Mauryan Dynasty in northern India. The Brahmi script is the ancestral source of all modern Indian scripts.

This Roman fresco painting, from a house in Pompeii whose details were preserved because of the eruption of Mount Vesuvius in 79 c.e., depicts a young woman holding a stylus and a wax tablet. Writing on wax tablets was a common means of taking notes and recording other ephemera in classical antiquity. The surface could be reused by warming and smoothing the wax to remove prior markings.

Beginning in Roman antiquity and continuing into medieval times, one of the highest-quality portable writing mediums was vellum. Made from the skin of domesticated mammals (calf, sheep, and goat skins were most common), vellum was smooth and durable and was generally reserved for special texts. Pictured here is a vellum manuscript of Homer's *Iliad* (called the *Ambrosian Iliad* or *Ilia Picta*) dating from the fifth century C.E. It is the only illustrated copy of Homer from classical antiquity to have survived.

CODICIBVS SACRIS HOSTILI CLADE PERVSTIS
ESDRA DO FERVENS HOC REPARAVIT OPVS

This page from the Codex Amiatinus (ca. 8th century C.E.), the earliest surviving manuscript of the Latin Vulgate Bible, depicts the Jewish scribe Ezra. Ezra is traditionally credited with

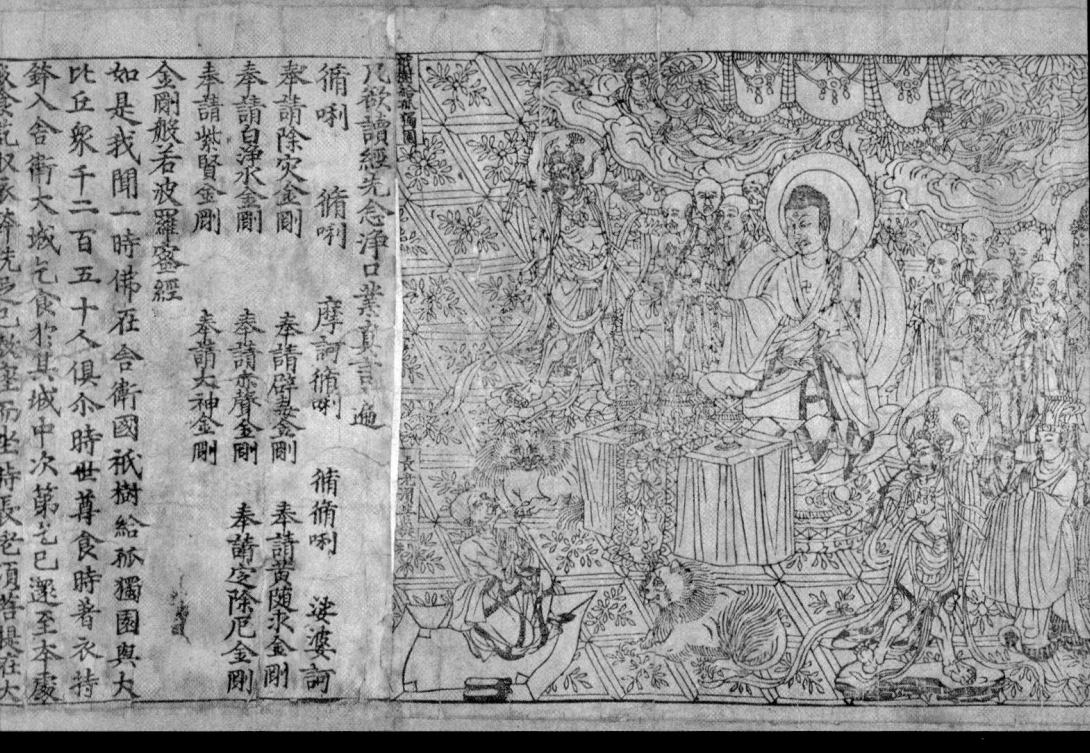

Frontispiece from the world's earliest dated printed book: a Chinese translation of the Buddhist *Diamond Sūtra*. This translation, consisting of a series of woodblock prints on a sixteen-foot scroll, was printed in 868 C.E.

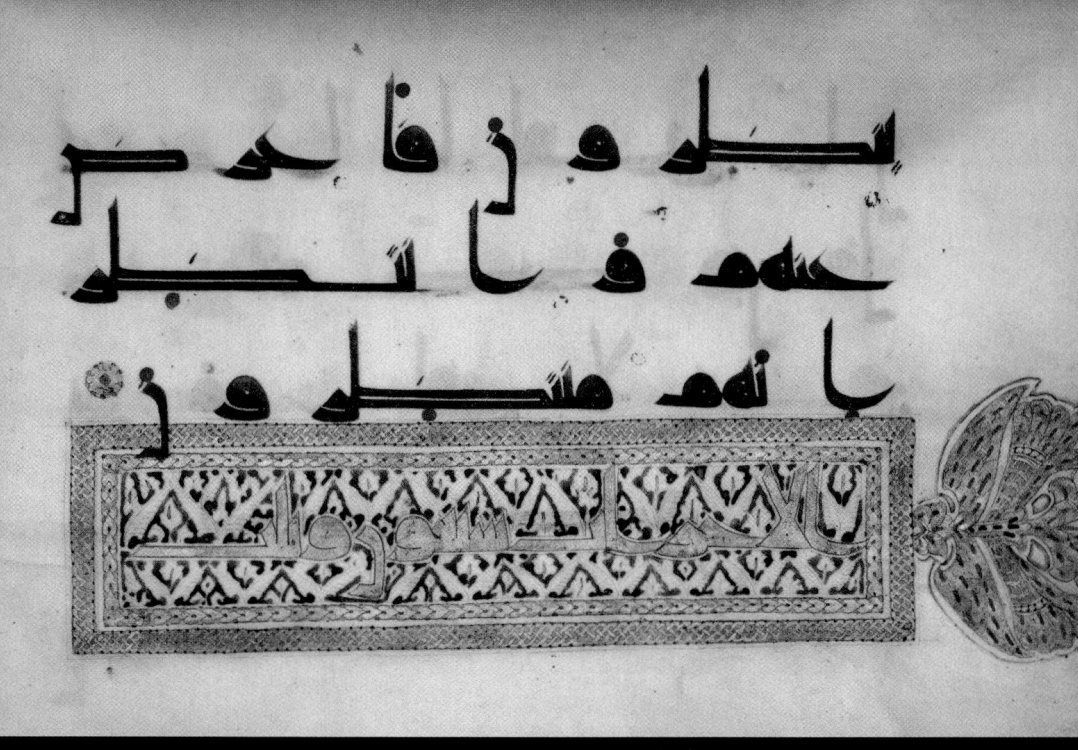

A fragment of the Qur'an (specifically, the beginning of sura 33) written in Kufic script, the oldest calligraphic form of Arabic script. This parchment manuscript, decorated with designs in black and red ink and gold leaf, dates from the ninth or tenth century C.E.

The Old English poem *Beowulf* survives in only one manuscript copy, a page of which is pictured here. Though the poem is set in sixth-century Scandinavia, the date of its composition isn't known. This manuscript was copied sometime in the early eleventh century.

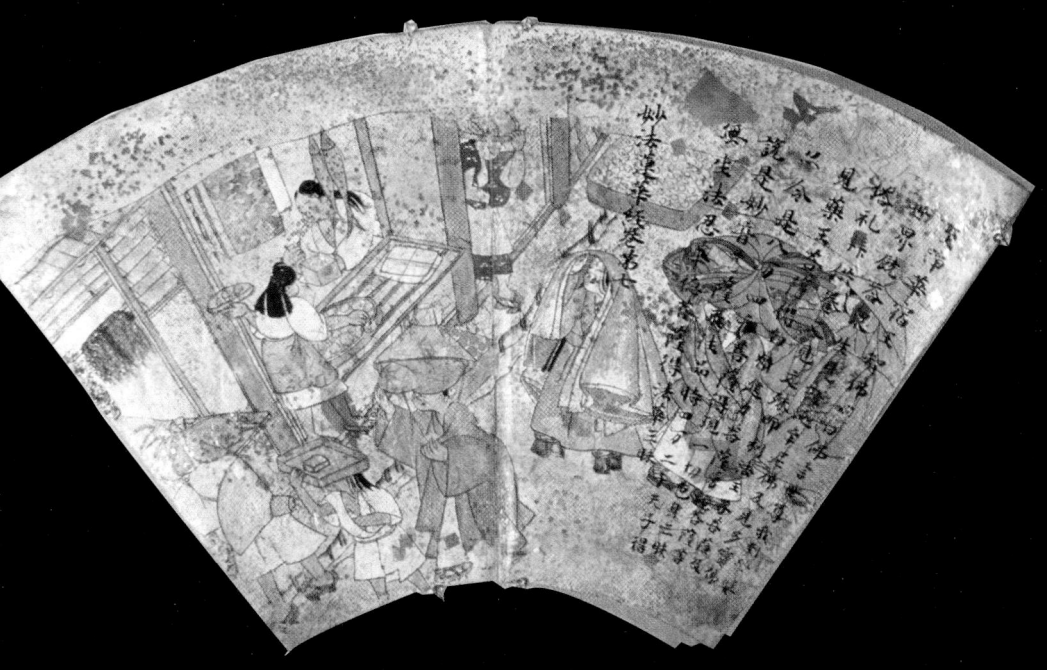

A single leaf from a fan-shaped album of excerpts from the Buddhist *Lotus Sūtra* that was produced near the end of the Heian Period in Japan (i.e., sometime during the late twelfth century). In addition to the calligraphic excerpt on the right, this page features a genre painting of servants performing their duties. The illustrations in these fan-shaped albums were typically unrelated to the quoted sutra.

Typographus. Der Buchdrucker.

ARte mea reliquas illustro Typographus artes,
  Imprimo dum varios ære micante libros.
Quæ prius aucta situ, quæ puluere plena iacebant,
  Vidimus obscura nocte sepulta premi.

Hæc veterum renouo neglecta volumina Patrum
  Atq scolis curo publica facta legi.
Artem prima nouam reperisse Moguntia fertur,
  Vrbs grauis, & multis ingeniosa modis.
Qua nihil vtilius videt, aut preciosius orbis,
  Vix melius quicquam secla futura dabunt.

C 3   Char-

A woodcut print from Jost Amman's *The Book of Trades* (1568), a short
guide to the various ranks of European society, illustrates the operation of
a printer's workshop. Though this book was published over a century after
Johannes Gutenberg's revolutionary innovations in movable-type printing,
the technology pictured here is quite similar to that used by Gutenberg

A page from an illuminated manuscript of the Persian epic *Shahnameh*. This version is attributed to Muzaffar Ali, a famous Persian miniaturist who thrived during the reign of Shah Tahmasp (1525–76).

A detail from the Codex Féjervàry-Mayer, a pre-Hispanic Aztec manuscript on deerskin parchment, believed to have originated in Veracruz. Pictured is an Aztec origin myth: the Nahuatl god Tezcatlipoca uses his foot as bait to lure the Earth Monster to the surface. After she swallows his foot, she is unable to sink back to her lair, and thus the surface of

Als nw die werlt durch das gepew göttlicher weißheit der sechs tag: volēdet vn̄ himel vn̄ erde beschaffē geordnet gezieret vn̄ zu letst volbracht wordē sind. do hat der glori wirdig got sein werck erfüllet vn̄ am sybendē tag von den werckē seiner hendt geruet. nach dē er die gantzē werlt vnd alle ding die dar in sind beschaf fen het do hat er auffgehört. nit als zewürckē müede. sunder zemachen ein newe creatur d' materi oder gleichnus nit vergangē wer dan̄ er hort nit auff zewürckē das werck der geperungen. vnd der herr hat dē selbē tag gebe nedeyet vn̄ geheiligt vnd ine geheyssē sabathū. das nach hebreyscher züge ein rüe bedeüttet darūmb das er an dē selben tag ruet vō allem werck das er gemacht het. do vō auch die iuden an dem tag vō aigner arbait zefeiren er̄ kant werdē. Dē selbē tag habē auch etlich haidemische völker vor dem gesetz feirlich gehaltē. vnd also sein wir zu end der göttlichen werck komē. darūmb so söllen wir dē in dem alle sichtliche vnd vnsichtliche ding sind för̄ chten. liebhaben vnd eren. vnd von dem herren des himels. von dem herren aller gütter. dem gewalt gegebē ist in himel vnd erden. die gegenwürtigen güter. souer die gut sind. vnd auch die waren seligkait des ewigen lebēs suchen.

Hartmann Schedel's 1493 book, *World Chronicle* (in German, *Weltchronik*), an illustrated world history, was one of the first printed books to bring maps and illustrations to a wide readership. This page depicts the universe as it was understood at the time: with the earth at the center and other celestial bodies surrounding it. Fifty years later, the Renaissance astronomer Nicolaus Copernicus (1473–1543) would overturn this model, placing the sun at the center.

Dedicatory page from Antoine du Four's *The Lives of Famous Women* (ca. 1505). The author, on bended knee, offers the book to Queen Anne of Brittany (1477–1514), who commissioned the work and for whom du Four served as confessor. The book chronicles the lives of famous women from Eve to Joan of Arc.

A page from the *Kitab-i Bahriye (Book of Navigation)* by Piri Reis (ca. 1465–1555), an Ottoman military commander, geographer, and cartographer. Published in 1521, the *Kitab-i Bahriye* is one of the most famous books of navigation from early modernity. It provided a comprehensive and detailed overview of the known world of the time, including the recently explored shorelines of the African and American continents. Pictured here is the port city of Venice.

The Reader. A Persian miniature from an unidentified manuscript, ca. sixteenth century.

An illustration from the north Indian poetry anthology *Rasik Priya* (1591), by the Sanskrit scholar and Hindi poet Keśavdās (1555–1617). This manuscript dates from the early seventeenth century, after Keśavdās's death.

To the Reader.

This Figure, that thou here seest put,
    It was for gentle Shakespeare cut;
Wherein the Grauer had a strife
    with Nature, to out-doo the life :
O, could he but haue drawne his wit
    As well in brasse, as he hath hit
His face ; the Print would then surpasse
    All, that vvas euer vvrit in brasse.
But, since he cannot, Reader, looke
    Not on his Picture, but his Booke.

B. I.

Mr. WILLIAM
SHAKESPEARES
COMEDIES,
HISTORIES, &
TRAGEDIES.

Published according to the True Originall Copies.

LONDON
Printed by Isaac Iaggard, and Ed. Blount. 1623.

Frontispiece and title page of one of the most famous books of the Renaissance: the 1623 "First Folio" of the plays of William Shakespeare. The portrait by Martin Droeshout was not made from life, and yet it has fixed the public's sense of Shakespeare's appearance. The poem on the facing page, by Ben Jonson, urges readers to "looke / Not on his Picture, but his Booke."

This 1645 portrait of the court jester Don Diego de Acedo is by the Spanish master Diego Velázquez (1599–1660). Intending to convey his status and his intelligence (while also acknowledging his deformity), Velázquez poses de Acedo with a book (a traditional signal in court portraiture of gentlemanly status), notebook, stylus, and inkwell.

in Paradise: there Dante is led by Beatrice Portinari, his idealized love since childhood, who died in 1290. Both of these guides, as well as others who aid Dante along his way (such as Saint Lucy, who appears in the form of a golden eagle), are sent by a benefactor whom Dante only gradually comes to know: the *donna gentil* or "gracious lady" of Heaven, the Virgin Mary.

However important the theological message of *The Divine Comedy*, it never overshadows the essential realism and tangibility of the world Dante describes. From the horrible landscape of the ruined City of Dis seen in Hell to the brilliant light of the planets in Paradise, the reader's senses are continually stimulated. This stimulation is especially acute in the *Inferno*, where the vividness of the landscape is mirrored in the emotional affect of the narrator: he is moved to tears of pity by the sight of Paolo and Francesca, whose crime was to have given themselves over to the experience of love, but shows contempt for the traitor Bocca degli Abati, kicking him and pulling out tufts of his hair. In keeping with Christian doctrine, the souls in this underworld have no material bodies, yet their shades retain the appearance of the bodies they had in life, and the punishments they suffer in Hell leave marks on their flesh. In the circle of schismatics, whose sin is that they have divided the community of the faithful, Dante finds Muhammad, the Prophet of Islam, his body "split from the chin" down through his entrails. In this wound, as in the quartered body of Ganelon in the *Song of Roland*, the wrongful division of society, whether the body politic or the religious community, is made manifest on the canvas of the human body.

The structure of Hell, like that of Purgatory and Heaven, is highly symmetrical and full of numerical significance. *The Divine Comedy* is made up of one hundred chapters that Dante calls *cantos* (literally, "songs"), divided into three groups of thirty-three; the extra is added to the *Inferno*, which opens with an introductory canto. The numerological structure of the poem is also revealed in the landscape of each part. Hell is divided into nine circles, each containing a different category of sinners receiving their own proper form of punishment. The mountain of Purgatory is divided into nine parts as well, its seven main terraces (corresponding to the Seven Deadly Sins) surrounded by the entranceway of Ante-Purgatory and capped, at its summit, by the Earthly Paradise of Eden. Finally, the seven spheres of Heaven that lie above the mountain are brought to nine by the addition of those of the Fixed Stars and of the Primum Mobile—the first mover that imparts motion to all the other heavenly spheres. Beyond these nine are found only God and his angels. The constant play on the number three and its cube, three times three, highlights the Trinitarian theology that underlies the spiritual world of *The Divine Comedy*. Christian revelation places the earth at the center of the universe, surrounded by the spheres of the planets and of the stars and itself wounded by the cavernous pit of hell. At the base of the infernal pit, at the very center of the earth, Satan appears not wrapped in flames but rather frozen in a lake of ice. In Dante's memorable phrase, Satan is "the hairy worm . . . that pierces the earth's core" as if it were a rotten apple.

Climbing over the hairy body of Satan and twisting through a narrow passageway, Dante and his guide emerge from the bowels of the earth to the base of the mountain of Purgatory. A new mood infuses the work from this point on, as the hopefulness of the narrator reflects the very different circumstances of those who suffer pain in Purgatory. Here, unlike in Hell, suffering has a purpose, gradually redeeming the inhabitants from their former state

Dante's Hell

cantos

Dark Wood

1–2

Ante-Inferno — Neutrals — 3

Acheron

CIRCLE I — Virtuous Pagans — 4

Minos

CIRCLE II — Lustful — 5

Cerberus

CIRCLE III — Gluttons — 6

Plutus

CIRCLE IV — Prodigal and Miserly — 7

CIRCLE V — Wrathful — 8

Styx

CIRCLE VI — Arch-Heretics — 9–10

City of Dis

INCONTINENT (wolf)

Minotaur

CIRCLE VII — Violent—

—against neighbors — 12

Phlegethon

—against self — 13

Wood of Suicides

—against God — 14–16

Burning Plain

Geryon — 17

Great Barrier

VIOLENT (lion)

CIRCLE VIII

i. Panderers and Seducers — 18

ii. Flatterers

iii. Simonists — 19

iv. Soothsayers — 20

v. Grafters — 21–22

vi. Hypocrites — 23

vii. Thieves — 24–25

viii. Deceivers — 26–27

ix. Sowers of Discord — 28

x. Falsifiers — 29–30

FRAUDULENT (leopard)

Antaeus

CIRCLE IX

Treacherous—

—to kindred: Caina — 32

—to country: Antenora — 33

—to guests: Tolomea — 34

—to benefactors: Judecca — 34

Satan

of sin and enabling their souls to rise upward. At the summit of the mountain, Dante enters the Earthly Paradise of Eden, now hidden away in Purgatory to keep it from fallen humans. Here his wonder at a magnificent procession climaxes in a moment of staggering recognition: as he puts it, "I recognize signs of the ancient flame." Here Dante is met by Beatrice, his first love and the soul who will lead him the rest of the way on his upward journey.

Moving through the spheres of Paradise entails progressive dematerialization: instead of the rugged landscape of Hell, we find instead a sequence of spheres—each of which eclipses the last, each adorned with a symbolic form. In the sphere of the Crusaders, we see a mighty eagle; in the exalted spheres of the Empyrean, a celestial rose, studded with saintly souls. One of the very last of these symbolic forms is the great book "bound . . . by love," whose "scattered leaves" make up the universe. In this vivid image, the unity of divine revelation and of the written text of *The Divine Comedy* is complete. The love that binds the book reappears in the poem's last lines, as the narrator describes the endless motion of the heavens, turned by "the Love that moves the sun and the other stars." This earth-centered image of the cosmos would soon give way to a new worldview, with the sun at its center and with humanity placed in a very different relationship to its Creator.

From The Divine Comedy[1]

Inferno

CANTO I

Halfway through his life, Dante the Pilgrim wakes to find himself lost in a dark wood. Terrified at being alone in so dismal a valley, he wanders until he comes to a hill bathed in sunlight, and his fear begins to leave him. But when he starts to climb the hill his path is blocked by three fierce beasts: first a Leopard, then a Lion, and finally a She-Wolf. They fill him with fear and drive him back down to the sunless wood. At that moment the figure of a man appears before him; it is the shade of Virgil, and the Pilgrim begs for help. Virgil tells him that he cannot overcome the beasts which obstruct his path; they must remain until a "Greyhound" comes who will drive them back to Hell. Rather by another path will the Pilgrim reach the sunlight, and Virgil promises to guide him on that path through Hell and Purgatory, after which another spirit, more fit than Virgil, will lead him to Paradise. The Pilgrim begs Virgil to lead on, and the Guide starts ahead. The Pilgrim follows.

Midway along the journey of our life[2]
  I woke to find myself in a dark wood,
    for I had wandered off from the straight path.[3]   3
How hard it is to tell what it was like,
  this wood of wilderness, savage and stubborn

---

1. Translated from the Italian by Mark Musa.
2. Born in 1265, Dante was 35 in 1300, the fictional date of the poem. The biblical span of human life is 70 (see Psalms 90.10 and Isaiah 23.15).
3. See Proverbs 2.13–14 and 4.18–19, and also 2 Peter 2.15.

(the thought of it brings back all my old fears),   6
a bitter place! Death could scarce be bitterer.
   But if I would show the good that came of it
   I must talk about things other than the good.   9
How I entered there I cannot truly say,
   I had become so sleepy⁴ at the moment
   when I first strayed, leaving the path of truth;⁵   12
but when I found myself at the foot of a hill,
   at the edge of the wood's beginning, down in the valley,
   where I first felt my heart plunged deep in fear,   15
I raised my head and saw the hilltop shawled
   in morning rays of light sent from the planet
   that leads men straight ahead on every road.⁶   18
And then only did terror start subsiding,
   in my heart's lake,⁷ which rose to heights of fear
   that night I spent in deepest desperation.   21
Just as a swimmer, still with panting breath,
   now safe upon the shore, out of the deep,
   might turn for one last look at the dangerous waters,   24
so I, although my mind was turned to flee,
   turned round to gaze once more upon the pass
   that never let a living soul escape.⁸   27
I rested my tired body there awhile
   and then began to climb the barren slope
   (I dragged my stronger foot and limped along).⁹   30
Beyond the point the slope begins to rise
   sprang up a leopard, trim and very swift!
   It was covered by a pelt of many spots.   33
And, everywhere I looked, the beast was there
   blocking my way, so time and time again
   I was about to turn and go back down.   36
The hour was early in the morning then,
   the sun was climbing up with those same stars
   that had accompanied it on the world's first day,   39
the day Divine Love set their beauty turning;¹
   so the hour and sweet season of creation
   encouraged me to think I could get past   42
that gaudy beast, wild in its spotted pelt,
   but then good hope gave way and fear returned
   when the figure of a lion loomed up before me,   45
and he was coming straight toward me, it seemed,

---

4. See Romans 13.11–12.
5. See Psalms 23.3.
6. The sun, which in the astronomical system of Dante's time was a planet thought to revolve around the earth.
7. This phrase refers to the inner chamber of the heart, a cavity that in the physiology of Dante's time was the location of fear. Not coincidentally, Dante's last stop in the *Inferno* ends at the lake of Cocytus (see 31.123).
8. This simile of Dante as the survivor of a passage through the sea invokes the story of the escape of the Israelites from Egypt through the Red Sea, a central metaphor throughout the *Comedy*: see Exodus 14. There is also probably an allusion to the opening of the *Aeneid*, where Aeneas and his men survive a storm.
9. The pilgrim is limping because he suffers from the injury of original sin.
1. In the Middle Ages it was thought that the world was created in spring, when the sun is in the constellation Aries.

with head raised high, and furious with hunger—
   the air around him seemed to fear his presence.   48
And now a she-wolf came, that in her leanness
   seemed racked with every kind of greediness
   (how many people she has brought to grief!).   51
This last beast brought my spirit down so low
   with fear that seized me at the sight of her,
   I lost all hope of going up the hill.²   54
As a man who, rejoicing in his gains,
   suddenly seeing his gain turn into loss,
   will grieve as he compares his then and now,   57
so she made me do, that relentless beast;
   coming toward me, slowly, step by step,
   she forced me back to where the sun is mute.   60
While I was rushing down to that low place,
   my eyes made out a figure coming toward me
   of one grown faint, perhaps from too much silence.³   63
And when I saw him standing in this wasteland,
   "Have pity on my soul," I cried to him,
   "whichever you are, shade or living man!"   66
"No longer living man, though once I was,"
   he said, "and my parents were from Lombardy,
   both of them were Mantuans by birth.⁴   69
I was born, though somewhat late, *sub Julio*,⁵
   and lived in Rome when good Augustus reigned,
   when still the false and lying gods were worshipped.   72
I was a poet and sang of that just man,
   son of Anchises, who sailed off from Troy
   after the burning of proud Ilium.⁶   75
But why retreat to so much misery?
   Why not climb up this blissful mountain here,
   the beginning and the source of all man's joy?"   78
"Are you then Virgil, are you then that fount
   from which pours forth so rich a stream of words?"
   I said to him, bowing my head modestly.   81
"O light and honor of the other poets,
   may my long years of study, and that deep love
   that made me search your verses, help me now!   84
You are my teacher, the first of all my authors,
   and you alone the one from whom I took
   the noble style that was to bring me honor.   87

2. The meaning of the leopard, lion, and she-wolf is open to a number of interpretations, the most plausible being that they represent the three major forms of sin found in Hell, respectively fraud, violence, and incontinence or immoderation (see 11.79 ff.). The structure of Hell indicates that the last is the least seriously morally, but its role in this canto shows that it is the most difficult to overcome psychologically. Dante probably took the identities of these three beasts from a passage in Jeremiah 5.6.

3. The Roman poet Virgil's voice has not been heard since he died in 19 B.C.E.

4. Lombardy is the most northern area of Italy; Mantua is located to the east of Milan.

5. Virgil (70–19 B.C.E.) was born *sub Julio*, during the reign of Julius Caesar (assassinated in 44 B.C.E.), who was regarded by Dante as the founder of the Roman Empire.

6. Aeneas, the hero of Virgil's *Aeneid*.

You see the beast that forced me to retreat;
   save me from her, I beg you, famous sage,
   she makes me tremble, the blood throbs in my veins."   90
"But you must journey down another road,"
   he answered, when he saw me lost in tears,
   "if ever you hope to leave this wilderness;   93
this beast, the one you cry about in fear,
   allows no soul to succeed along her path,
   she blocks his way and puts an end to him.   96
She is by nature so perverse and vicious,
   her craving belly is never satisfied,
   still hungering for food the more she eats.   99
She mates with many creatures, and will go on
   mating with more until the greyhound comes
   and tracks her down to make her die in anguish.[7]   102
He will not feed on either land or money:
   his wisdom, love, and virtue shall sustain him;
   he will be born between Feltro and Feltro.[8]   105
He comes to save that fallen Italy
   for which the maid Camilla gave her life
   and Turnus, Nisus, Euryalus died of wounds.[9]   108
And he will hunt for her through every city
   until he drives her back to Hell once more,
   whence Envy first unleashed her on mankind.   111
And so, I think it best you follow me
   for your own good, and I shall be your guide
   and lead you out through an eternal place   114
where you will hear desperate cries, and see
   tormented shades, some old as Hell itself,
   and know what second death is, from their screams.[1]   117
And later you will see those who rejoice
   while they are burning, for they have hope of coming,
   whenever it may be, to join the blessèd[2]—   120
to whom, if you too wish to make the climb,
   a spirit, worthier than I, must take you;[3]
   I shall go back, leaving you in her care,   123
because that Emperor dwelling on high
   will not let me lead any to His city,
   since I in life rebelled against His law.[4]   126
Everywhere He reigns, and there He rules;
   there is His city, there is His high throne.
   Oh, happy the one He makes His citizen!"   129

---

7. Dante's prediction of a modern political redeemer is so enigmatic that there can be no certainty of his identity. Most commentators think it is Cangrande (i.e., the great dog) della Scala of Verona, Dante's benefactor after his exile from Florence.
8. Feltre and Montefeltro are towns that roughly mark the limits of Cangrande's domains. But other interpretations are possible.

9. Characters in the *Aeneid* who die during Aeneas's conquest of Italy.
1. The second death is damnation; see Revelation 21.8.
2. The souls in Purgatory; the blessed are the saved in Paradise.
3. Beatrice.
4. Virgil "rebelled" against God because he was not a Christian.

And I to him: "Poet, I beg of you,
   in the name of God, that God you never knew,
   save me from this evil place and worse.   132
lead me there to the place you spoke about
   that I may see the gate Saint Peter guards
   and those whose anguish you have told me of."   135
Then he moved on, and I moved close behind him.

CANTO II

*But the Pilgrim begins to waver, he expresses to Virgil his misgivings about his abil-
ity to undertake the journey proposed by Virgil. His predecessors have been Aeneas
and Saint Paul, and he feels unworthy to take his place in their company. But Virgil rebukes his cowardice, and relates the chain of events that led him to come to
Dante. The Virgin Mary took pity on the Pilgrim in his despair and instructed Saint
Lucia to aid him. The Saint turned to Beatrice because of Dante's great love for her,
and Beatrice in turn went down to Hell, into Limbo, and asked Virgil to guide her
friend until that time when she herself would become his guide. The Pilgrim takes
heart at Virgil's explanation and agrees to follow him.*

The day was fading and the darkening air
   was releasing all the creatures on our earth
   from their daily tasks, and I, one man alone,   3
was making ready to endure the battle
   of the journey, and of the pity it involved,
   which my memory, unerring, shall now retrace.   6
O Muses! O high genius! Help me now!
   O memory that wrote down what I saw,
   here your true excellence shall be revealed!   9
Then I began: "O poet come to guide me,
   tell me if you think my worth sufficient
   before you trust me to this arduous road.   12
You wrote about young Sylvius's father,[5]
   who went beyond, with flesh corruptible,
   with all his senses, to the immortal realm;   15
but if the Adversary of all evil
   was kind to him, considering who he was,
   and the consequence that was to come from him,   18
this cannot seem, to thoughtful men, unfitting,
   for in the highest heaven he was chosen
   father of glorious Rome and of her empire,   21
and both the city and her lands, in truth,
   were established as the place of holiness
   where the successors of great Peter sit.[6]   24
And from this journey you celebrate in verse,
   Aeneas learned those things that were to bring
   victory for him, and for Rome, the Papal seat;   27

5. Aeneas, who visited the underworld in
Aeneid 6.

6. The Apostle Peter is considered by the
Catholic Church to be the first pope.

then later the Chosen Vessel, Paul, ascended
　　to bring back confirmation of that faith
　　which is the first step on salvation's road.[7]　　　　　30
But why am I to go? Who allows me to?
　　I am not Aeneas, I am not Paul,
　　neither I nor any man would think me worthy;　　　　33
and so, if I should undertake the journey,
　　I fear it might turn out an act of folly—
　　you are wise, you see more than my words express."　　36
As one who unwills what he willed, will change
　　his purpose with some new second thought,
　　completely quitting what he first had started,　　　　39
so I did, standing there on that dark slope,
　　thinking, ending the beginning of that venture
　　I was so quick to take up at the start.　　　　　　42
"If I have truly understood your words,"
　　that shade of magnanimity replied,
　　"your soul is burdened with that cowardice　　　　45
which often weighs so heavily on man,
　　it turns him from a noble enterprise
　　like a frightened beast that shies at its own shadow.　　48
To free you from this fear, let me explain
　　the reason I came here, the words I heard
　　that first time I felt pity for your soul:　　　　　51
I was among those dead who are suspended,[8]
　　when a lady summoned me. She was so blessed
　　and beautiful, I implored her to command me.[9]　　54
With eyes of light more bright than any star,
　　in low, soft tones she started to address me
　　in her own language, with an angel's voice:　　　　57
'O noble soul, courteous Mantuan,
　　whose fame the world continues to preserve
　　and will preserve as long as world there is,　　　　60
my friend, who is no friend of Fortune's, strays
　　on a desert slope; so many obstacles
　　have crossed his path, his fright has turned him back　　63
I fear he may have gone so far astray,
　　from what report has come to me in Heaven,
　　that I may have started to his aid too late.　　　　66
Now go, and with your elegance of speech,
　　with whatever may be needed for his freedom,
　　give him your help, and thereby bring me solace.　　69
I am Beatrice, who urges you to go;
　　I come from the place I am longing to return to;[1]
　　love moved me, as it moves me now to speak.　　　72
When I return to stand before my Lord,
　　often I shall sing your praises to Him.'
　　And then she spoke no more. And I began,　　　　75

---

7. St. Paul; see 2 Corinthians 12.2–4.
8. In Limbo, where the souls experience "neither joy nor sorrow" (4.84).

9. As we soon learn, the lady is Beatrice.
1. Paradise.

'O Lady of Grace, through whom alone mankind
   may go beyond all worldy things contained
   within the sphere that makes the smallest round,[2]   78
your plea fills me with happy eagerness—
   to have obeyed already would still seem late!
   You needed only to express your wish.   81
But tell me how you dared to make this journey
   all the way down to this point of spacelessness,
   away from your spacious home that calls you back.'   84
'Because your question searches for deep meaning,
   I shall explain in simple words,' she said,
   'just why I have no fear of coming here.   87
A man must stand in fear of just those things
   that truly have the power to do us harm,
   of nothing else, for nothing else is fearsome.   90
God gave me such a nature through His Grace,
   the torments you must bear cannot affect me,
   nor are the fires of Hell a threat to me.   93
A gracious lady[3] sits in Heaven grieving
   for what happened to the one I send you to,
   and her compassion breaks Heaven's stern decree.   96
She called Lucia[4] and making her request,
   she said, "Your faithful one is now in need
   of you, and to you I now commend his soul."   99
Lucia, the enemy of cruelty,
   hastened to make her way to where I was,
   sitting by the side of ancient Rachel,[5]   102
and said to me: "Beatrice, God's true praise,
   will you not help the one whose love was such
   it made him leave the vulgar crowd for you?   105
Do you not hear the pity of his weeping,
   do you not see what death it is that threatens him
   along that river the sea shall never conquer?"[6]   108
There never was a worldly person living
   more anxious to promote his selfish gains
   than I was at the sound of words like these—   111
to leave my holy seat and come down here
   and place my trust in you, in your noble speech
   that honors you and all those who have heard it!'   114
When she had finished reasoning, she turned
   her shining eyes away, and there were tears
   How eager then I was to come to you!   117
And I have come to you just as she wished,
   and I have freed you from the beast that stood
   blocking the quick way up the mount of bliss.   120
So what is wrong? Why, why do you delay?
   Why are you such a coward in your heart,
   why aren't you bold and free of all your fear,   123

2. The sphere of the moon.
3. The Virgin Mary.
4. St. Lucy, a 3rd-century martyr and the patron saint of those afflicted with poor or damaged sight.
5. Rachel signifies the contemplative life: see Genesis 29.16–17.
6. These are the metaphoric waters of 1.22–24.

when three such gracious ladies, who are blessed,
    watch out for you up there in Heaven's court,
    and my words, too, bring promise of such good?"   126
As little flowers from the frosty night
    are closed and limp, and when the sun shines down
    on them, they rise to open on their stem,   129
my wilted strength began to bloom within me,
    and such warm courage flowed into my heart
    that I spoke like a man set free of fear.   132
"O she, compassionate, who moved to help me!
    And you, all kindness, in obeying quick
    those words of truth she brought with her for you—   135
you and the words you spoke have moved my heart
    with such desire to continue onward
    that now I have returned to my first purpose.   138
Let us start, for both our wills, joined now, are one.
    You are my guide, you are my lord and teacher."
    These were my words to him and, when he moved,   141
I entered on that deep and rugged road.

CANTO III

As the two poets enter the vestibule that leads to Hell itself, Dante sees the inscription above the gate, and he hears the screams of anguish from the damned souls. Rejected by God and not accepted by the powers of Hell, the first group of souls are "nowhere," because of their cowardly refusal to make a choice in life. Their punishment is to follow a banner at a furious pace forever, and to be tormented by flies and hornets. The Pilgrim recognizes several of these shades but mentions none by name. Next they come to the River Acheron, where they are greeted by the infernal boatman, Charon. Among those doomed souls who are to be ferried across the river, Charon sees the living man and challenges him, but Virgil lets it be known that his companion must pass. Then across the landscape rushes a howling wind, which blasts the Pilgrim out of his senses, and he falls to the ground.

I AM THE WAY INTO THE DOLEFUL CITY,
    I AM THE WAY INTO ETERNAL GRIEF,
    I AM THE WAY TO A FORSAKEN RACE.   3
JUSTICE IT WAS THAT MOVED MY GREAT CREATOR;
    DIVINE OMNIPOTENCE CREATED ME,
    AND HIGHEST WISDOM JOINED WITH PRIMAL LOVE.[7]   6
BEFORE ME NOTHING BUT ETERNAL THINGS
    WERE MADE, AND I SHALL LAST ETERNALLY.
    ABANDON EVERY HOPE, ALL YOU WHO ENTER.   9
I saw these words spelled out in somber colors
    inscribed along the ledge above a gate;
    "Master," I said, "these words I see are cruel."   12
He answered me, speaking with experience:
    "Now here you must leave all distrust behind;
    let all your cowardice die on this spot.   15

7. God as Father, Son, and Holy Ghost.

We are at the place where earlier I said
  you could expect to see the suffering race
  of souls who lost the good of intellect."[8]   18
Placing his hand on mine, smiling at me
  in such a way that I was reassured,
  he led me in, into those mysteries.   21
Here sighs and cries and shrieks of lamentation
  echoed throughout the starless air of Hell;
  at first these sounds resounding made me weep: 24
tongues confused, a language strained in anguish
  with cadences of anger, shrill outcries
  and raucous groans that joined with sounds of hands,   27
raising a whirling storm that turns itself
  forever through that air of endless black,
  like grains of sand swirling when a whirlwind blows.   30
And I, in the midst of all this circling horror,
  began, "Teacher, what are these sounds I hear?
  What souls are these so overwhelmed by grief?"   33
And he to me: "This wretched state of being
  is the fate of those sad souls who lived a life
  but lived it with no blame and with no praise.   36
They are mixed with that repulsive choir of angels
  neither faithful nor unfaithful to their God,
  who undecided stood but for themselves.[9]   39
Heaven, to keep its beauty, cast them out,
  but even Hell itself would not receive them,
  to fear the damned might glory over them."   42
And I: "Master, what torments do they suffer
  that force them to lament so bitterly?"
  He answered: "I will tell you in few words: 45
these wretches have no hope of truly dying,
  and this blind life they lead is so abject
  it makes them envy every other fate.   48
The world will not record their having been there;
  Heaven's mercy and its justice turn from them.
  Let's not discuss them; look and pass them by."   51
And so I looked and saw a kind of banner
  rushing ahead, whirling with aimless speed
  as though it would not ever take a stand;   54
behind it an interminable train
  of souls pressed on, so many that I wondered
  how death could have undone so great a number.   57
When I had recognized a few of them,
  I saw the shade of the one who must have been
  the coward who had made the great refusal.[1]   60
At once I understood, and I was sure
  this was that sect of evil souls who were
  hateful to God and to His enemies.   63

8. "The good of intellect": i.e., God.
9. The "neutral angels," not mentioned in the
Bible but discussed by theologians throughout
the Middle Ages, were those who declined to
choose either side when Satan rebelled against
God.
1. This is Pope Celestine V, who was elected
in July 1294 but resigned five months later.

These wretches, who had never truly lived,
   went naked, and were stung and stung again
   by the hornets and the wasps that circled them   66
and made their faces run with blood in streaks;
   their blood, mixed with their tears, dripped to their feet,
   and disgusting maggots collected in the pus.   69
And when I looked beyond this crowd I saw
   a throng upon the shore of a wide river,
   which made me ask, "Master, I would like to know: 72
who are these people, and what law is this
   that makes those souls so eager for the crossing—
   as I can see, even in this dim light?"   75
And he: "All this will be made plain to you
   as soon as we shall come to stop awhile
   upon the sorrowful shore of Acheron."[2]   78
And I, with eyes cast down in shame, for fear
   that I perhaps had spoken out of turn,
   said nothing more until we reached the river.   81
And suddenly, coming toward us in a boat,
   a man of years[3] whose ancient hair was white
   shouted at us, "Woe to you, perverted souls!   84
Give up all hope of ever seeing Heaven:
   I come to lead you to the other shore,
   into eternal darkness, ice, and fire.   87
And you, the living soul, you over there,
   get away from all these people who are dead."
   But when he saw I did not move aside,   90
he said, "Another way, by other ports,
   not here, shall you pass to reach the other shore;
   a lighter skiff than this must carry you."[4]   93
And my guide, "Charon, this is no time for anger!
   It is so willed, there where the power is
   for what is willed; that's all you need to know."   96
These words brought silence to the woolly cheeks
   of the ancient steersman of the livid marsh,
   whose eyes were set in glowing wheels of fire.   99
But all those souls there, naked, in despair,
   changed color and their teeth began to chatter
   at the sound of his announcement of their doom.   102
They were cursing God, cursing their own parents,
   the human race, the time, the place, the seed
   of their beginning, and their day of birth.   105
Then all together, weeping bitterly,
   they packed themselves along the wicked shore
   that waits for every man who fears not God.   108

2. The first of the four rivers of Hell.
3. Charon; see *Aeneid* 6.
4. Charon knows that after death Dante will be taken not to Hell but to Purgatory in a "swift and light" vessel piloted by an angel; the arrival of the souls in Purgatory is described in *Purgatorio* 2.22–48. This is the first of several places in the *Commedia* where Dante predicts his own salvation.

The devil, Charon, with eyes of glowing coals,
    summons them all together with a signal,
    and with an oar he strikes the laggard sinner.   111
As in autumn when the leaves begin to fall,
    one after the other (until the branch
    is witness to the spoils spread on the ground),   114
so did the evil seed of Adam's Fall
    drop from that shore to the boat, one at a time,
    at the signal, like the falcon to its lure.⁵   117
Away they go across the darkened waters,
    and before they reach the other side to land,
    a new throng starts collecting on this side.   120
"My son," the gentle master said to me,
    "all those who perish in the wrath of God
    assemble here from all parts of the earth;   123
they want to cross the river, they are eager;
    it is Divine Justice that spurs them on,
    turning the fear they have into desire.   126
A good soul never comes to make this crossing,
    so, if Charon grumbles at the sight of you,
    you see now what his words are really saying."   129
He finished speaking, and the grim terrain
    shook violently; and the fright it gave me
    even now in recollection makes me sweat.   132
Out of the tear-drenched land a wind arose
    which blasted forth into a reddish light,
    knocking my senses out of me completely,   135
and I fell as one falls tired into sleep.⁶

CANTO IV

*Waking from his swoon, the Pilgrim is led by Virgil to the First Circle of Hell, known
as Limbo, where the sad shades of the virtuous non-Christians dwell. The souls here,
including Virgil, suffer no physical torment, but they must live, in desire, without hope
of seeing God. Virgil tells about Christ's descent into Hell and His salvation of several
Old Testament figures. The poets see a light glowing in the darkness, and as they proceed toward it, they are met by the four greatest (other than Virgil) pagan poets:
Homer, Horace, Ovid, and Lucan, who take the Pilgrim into their group. As they come
closer to the light, the Pilgrim perceives a splendid castle, where the greatest non-
Christian thinkers dwell together with other famous historical figures. Once within the
castle, the Pilgrim sees, among others, Electra, Aeneas, Caesar, Saladin, Aristotle,
Plato, Orpheus, Cicero, Avicenna, and Averroës. But soon they must leave; and the
poets move from the radiance of the castle toward the fearful encompassing darkness.*

A heavy clap of thunder! I awoke
    from the deep sleep that drugged my mind—startled,
    the way one is when shaken out of sleep.   3

---

5. These similes are drawn from *Aeneid*
6.56–60 (all line references are to the edition
in this anthology).
6. Dante is describing an earthquake, which

medieval science understood as the escape of
vapors from within the earth; it is while he is
unconscious that he crosses Acheron into Hell
proper.

I turned my rested eyes from side to side,
　already on my feet and, staring hard,
　I tried my best to find out where I was, 6
and this is what I saw: I found myself
　upon the brink of grief's abysmal valley
　that collects the thunderings of endless cries. 9
So dark and deep and nebulous it was,
　try as I might to force my sight below,
　I could not see the shape of anything. 12
"Let us descend into the sightless world,"
　began the poet (his face was deathly pale):
　"I will go first, and you will follow me." 15
And I, aware of his changed color, said:
　"But how can I go on if you are frightened?
　You are my constant strength when I lose heart." 18
And he to me: "The anguish of the souls
　that are down here paints my face with pity—
　which you have wrongly taken to be fear. 21
Let us go, the long road urges us."
　He entered then, leading the way for me
　down to the first circle of the abyss. 24
Down there, to judge only by what I heard,
　there were no wails but just the sounds of sighs
　rising and trembling through the timeless air, 27
the sounds of sighs of untormented grief
　burdening these groups, diverse and teeming,
　made up of men and women and of infants. 30
Then the good master said, "You do not ask
　what sort of souls are these you see around you.
　Now you should know before we go on farther, 33
they have not sinned. But their great worth alone
　was not enough, for they did not know Baptism,
　which is the gateway to the faith you follow, 36
and if they came before the birth of Christ,
　they did not worship God the way one should;
　I myself am a member of this group. 39
For this defect, and for no other guilt,
　we here are lost. In this alone we suffer:
　cut off from hope, we live on in desire." 42
The words I heard weighed heavy on my heart;
　to think that souls as virtuous as these
　were suspended in that limbo, and forever! 45
"Tell me, my teacher, tell me, O my master,"
　I began (wishing to have confirmed by him
　the teachings of unerring Christian doctrine), 48
"did any ever leave here, through his merit
　or with another's help, and go to bliss?"
　And he, who understood my hidden question,[7] 51

7. Dante's question is about the Harrowing of Hell, when according to Christian doctrine, Christ descended into Hell after the crucifix- ion and rescued the souls of the righteous of Israel; see also 12.44.

answered: "I was a novice in this place
   when I saw a mighty lord descend to us
   who wore the sign of victory as his crown.   54
He took from us the shade of our first parent,[8]
   of Abel, his good son, of Noah, too,
   and of obedient Moses, who made the laws;   57
Abram, the Patriarch, David the King,
   Israel with his father and his children,
   with Rachel, whom he worked so hard to win;   60
and many more he chose for blessedness;
   and you should know, before these souls were taken,
   no human soul had ever reached salvation."   63
We did not stop our journey while he spoke,
   but continued on our way along the woods—
   I say the woods, for souls were thick as trees.   66
We had not gone too far from where I woke
   when I made out a fire up ahead,
   a hemisphere of light that lit the dark.   69
We were still at some distance from that place,
   but close enough for me vaguely to see
   that honorable souls possessed that spot.   72
"O glory of the sciences and arts,
   who are these souls enjoying special honor,
   dwelling apart from all the others here?"   75
And he to me: "The honored name they bear
   that still resounds above in your own world
   wins Heaven's favor for them in this place."[9]   78
And as he spoke I heard a voice announce:
   "Now let us honor our illustrious poet,
   his shade that left is now returned to us."   81
And when the voice was silent and all was quiet
   I saw four mighty shades approaching us,
   their faces showing neither joy nor sorrow.   84
Then my good master started to explain:
   "Observe the one who comes with sword in hand,
   leading the three as if he were their master.   87
It is the shade of Homer, sovereign poet,
   and coming second, Horace, the satirist;
   Ovid is the third, and last comes Lucan.[1]   90
Since they all share one name with me, the name
   you heard resounding in that single voice,
   they honor me and do well doing so."   93
So I saw gathered there the noble school
   of the master singer of sublimest verse,
   who soars above all others like the eagle.   96
And after they had talked awhile together,
   they turned and with a gesture welcomed me,
   and at that sign I saw my master smile.   99

8. Adam.
9. The "honored name" is "poet."

1. Horace, Ovid, and Lucan are famous
Roman poets.

Greater honor still they deigned to grant me:
    they welcomed me as one of their own group,
    so that I numbered sixth among such minds.   102
We walked together toward the shining light,
    discussing things that here are best kept silent,
    as there they were most fitting for discussion.   105
We reached the boundaries of a splendid castle
    that seven times was circled by high walls
    defended by a sweetly flowing stream.[2]   108
We walked right over it as on hard ground;
    through seven gates I passed with those wise spirits,
    and then we reached a meadow fresh in bloom.[3]   111
There people were whose eyes were calm and grave,
    whose bearing told of great authority;
    seldom they spoke and always quietly.   114
Then moving to one side we reached a place
    spread out and luminous, higher than before,
    allowing us to view all who were there.   117
And right before us on the lustrous green
    the mighty shades were pointed out to me
    (my heart felt glory when I looked at them).   120
There was Electra standing with a group,
    among whom I saw Hector and Aeneas,
    and Caesar, falcon-eyed and fully armed.[4]   123
I saw Camilla and Penthesilea;
    across the way I saw the Latian King,
    with Lavinia, his daughter, by his side.[5]   126
I saw the Brutus who drove out the Tarquin;
    Lucretia, Julia, Marcia, and Cornelia;
    off, by himself, I noticed Saladin,[6]   129
and when I raised my eyes a little higher
    I saw the master sage of those who know,[7]
    sitting with his philosophic family.   132
All gaze at him, all pay their homage to him;
    and there I saw both Socrates and Plato,
    each closer to his side than any other;   135
Democritus, who said the world was chance,
    Diogenes, Thales, Anaxagoras,
    Empedocles, Zeno, and Heraclitus;   138

2. Commentators have suggested that this is a Castle of Fame, its seven walls symbolizing the seven liberal arts, a system of knowledge developed in the classical period.

3. A locale reminiscent of the classical Elysian fields as described in *Aeneid* 6.468–73.

4. Julius Caesar. "Electra": the mother of Dardanus, the founder of Troy. "Hector": the leading warrior of the Trojans in the *Iliad*. "Aeneas": the hero of the *Aeneid*.

5. Heiress to King Latinus who ruled the area of Italy where Rome was later located and who married Aeneas. "Camilla": a female warrior in the *Aeneid*, where she is compared to Penthe-silea, who fought for the Trojans against the Greeks.

6. Admired for his chivalry in fighting against the Crusaders, he was sultan of Egypt and Syria and died in 1193. "Brutus": not the Brutus who killed Julius Caesar, but an earlier Roman who drove out the tyrant Tarquin. All four of the women mentioned were virtuous Roman matrons.

7. Aristotle (384–322 B.C.E.), Greek philosopher. The men mentioned in lines 132–38 are Greek philosophers of the 7th through the 4th centuries B.C.E.

I saw the one who classified our herbs:
   Dioscorides I mean. And I saw Orpheus,
   Tully, Linus, Seneca the moralist,[8]   141
Euclid the geometer, and Ptolemy,
   Hippocrates, Galen, Avicenna,
   and Averroës, who made the Commentary.[9]   144
I cannot tell about them all in full;
   my theme is long and urges me ahead,
   often I must omit things I have seen.   147
The company of six becomes just two;
   my wise guide leads me by another way
   out of the quiet into tempestuous air.   150
I come into a place where no light is.

CANTO V

From Limbo Virgil leads his ward down to the threshold of the Second Circle of Hell, where for the first time he will see the damned in Hell being punished for their sins. There, barring their way, is the hideous figure of Minòs, the bestial judge of Dante's underworld; but after strong words from Virgil, the poets are allowed to pass into the dark space of this circle, where can be heard the wailing voices of the Lustful, whose punishment consists in being forever whirled about in a dark, stormy wind. After seeing a thousand or more famous lovers—including Semiramis, Dido, Helen, Achilles, and Paris—the Pilgrim asks to speak to two figures he sees together. They are Francesca da Rimini and her lover, Paolo, and the scene in which they appear is probably the most famous episode of the Inferno. At the end of the scene, the Pilgrim, who has been overcome by pity for the lovers, faints to the ground.

This way I went, descending from the first
   into the second round, that holds less space
   but much more pain—stinging the soul to wailing.   3
There stands Minòs grotesquely, and he snarls,
   examining the guilty at the entrance;
   he judges and dispatches, tail in coils.[1]   6
By this I mean that when the evil soul
   appears before him, it confesses all,
   and he, who is the expert judge of sins,   9
knows to what place in Hell the soul belongs;
   the times he wraps his tail around himself
   tell just how far the sinner must go down.   12

8. Roman philosopher and dramatist, killed by Nero in 65 C.E. "Dioscorides": Greek physician (1st century C.E.). "Orpheus": mythical Greek poet. "Tully": Cicero (d. 43 B.C.E.), Roman orator.
9. Avicenna (d. 1037) and Averroës (d. 1198) were Islamic philosophers who wrote commentaries on Aristotle's works that were highly influential in Christian Europe. "Euclid": Greek mathematician (4th century B.C.E.).

"Ptolemy": Greek astronomer and geographer (1st century C.E.) credited with devising the cosmological system that was accepted until the time of Copernicus in the 16th century (hence the term *Ptolemaic universe*). "Hippocrates and Galen": Greek physicians (4th and 2nd centuries B.C.E., respectively).
1. In *Aeneid* 6.207–11 Minos is described as judge of the underworld.

The damned keep crowding up in front of him:
   they pass along to judgment one by one;
   they speak, they hear, and then are hurled below.   15
"O you who come to the place where pain is host,"
   Minòs spoke out when he caught sight of me,
   putting aside the duties of his office,   18
"be careful how you enter and whom you trust
   it's easy to get in, but don't be fooled!"
   And my guide said to him: "Why keep on shouting?   21
Do not attempt to stop his fated journey;
   it is so willed there where the power is
   for what is willed,[2] that's all you need to know."   24
And now the notes of anguish start to play
   upon my ears; and now I find myself
   where sounds on sounds of weeping pound at me.   27
I came to a place where no light shone at all,
   bellowing like the sea racked by a tempest,
   when warring winds attack it from both sides.   30
The infernal storm, eternal in its rage,
   sweeps and drives the spirits with its blast:
   it whirls them, lashing them with punishment.   33
When they are swept back past their place of judgment,
   then come the shrieks, laments, and anguished cries;
   there they blaspheme God's almighty power.   36
I learned that to this place of punishment
   all those who sin in lust have been condemned,
   those who make reason slave to appetite;   39
and as the wings of starlings in the winter
   bear them along in wide-spread, crowded flocks,
   so does that wind propel the evil spirits: 42
now here, then there, and up and down, it drives them
   with never any hope to comfort them—
   hope not of rest but even of suffering less.   45
And just like cranes in flight, chanting their lays,
   stretching an endless line in their formation,
   I saw approaching, crying their laments,   48
spirits carried along by the battling winds,
   And so I asked, "Teacher, tell me, what souls
   are these punished in the sweep of the black wind?"   51
"The first of those whose story you should know,"
   my master wasted no time answering,
   "was empress over lands of many tongues;   54
her vicious tastes had so corrupted her
   she licensed every form of lust with laws
   to cleanse the stain of scandal she had spread;   57
she is Semiramis,[3] who, legend says,
   was Ninus' wife as well as his successor;
   she governed all the land the Sultan rules.   60

2. It is willed in Heaven by God, who has the power to accomplish whatever he wills.
3. Renowned for licentiousness, a mythical queen of Assyria and wife of Ninus, the legendary founder of Ninevah. Because both the capital of Assyria and Old Cairo were known as Babylon, her land is here confused with that ruled by the sultan of Egypt.

The next is she who killed herself for love
   and broke faith with the ashes of Sichaeus;[4]
   and there is Cleopatra, who loved men's lusting.   63
See Helen there, the root of evil woe
   lasting long years, and see the great Achilles,
   who lost his life to love, in final combat;[5]   66
see Paris, Tristan"[6]—then, more than a thousand
   he pointed out to me, and named them all,
   those shades whom love cut off from life on earth.   69
After I heard my teacher call the names
   of all these knights and ladies of ancient times,
   pity confused my senses, and I was dazed.   72
I began: "Poet, I would like, with all my heart,
   to speak to those two there who move together
   and seem to be so light upon the winds."[7]   75
And he: "You'll see when they are closer to us;
   if you entreat them by that love of theirs
   that carries them along, they'll come to you."   78
When the winds bent their course in our direction
   I raised my voice to them, "O wearied souls,
   come speak with us if it be not forbidden."   81
As doves, called by desire to return
   to their sweet nest, with wings raised high and poised,
   float downward through the air, guided by will,   84
so these two left the flock where Dido is
   and came toward us through the malignant air,
   such was the tender power of my call.   87
"O living creature, gracious and so kind,
   who makes your way here through this dingy air
   to visit us who stained the world with blood,   90
if we could claim as friend the King of Kings,
   we would beseech him that he grant you peace,
   you who show pity for our atrocious plight.   93
Whatever pleases you to hear or speak
   we will hear and we will speak about with you
   as long as the wind, here where we are, is silent.   96
The place where I was born lies on the shore
   where the river Po with its attendant streams
   descends to seek its final resting place.[8]   99
Love, quick to kindle in the gentle heart,
   seized this one for the beauty of my body,
   torn from me, (How it happened still offends me!)   102
Love, that excuses no one loved from loving,
   seized me so strongly with delight in him
   that, as you see, he never leaves my side.   105

4. Dido, whose suicide for love of Aeneas is described in *Aeneid* 4.542–942, was the widow of Sichaeus. Cleopatra killed herself after the death of her lover, Mark Antony, in 30 B.C.E.
5. The medieval version of the Troy story described Achilles as enamored of a Trojan princess, Polyxena, and killed in an ambush set by Paris when he went to meet her. Helen's seduction by Paris (see line 67) was the cause of the Trojan War.
6. The lover of Iseult, wife of his lord King Mark.
7. Francesca da Rimini and her brother-in-law Paolo Malatesta.
8. The Po is a river in northern Italy that empties into the Adriatic sea at Ravenna.

Love led us straight to sudden death together.
　　Caïna awaits the one who quenched our lives."[9]
　　These were the words that came from them to us. 108
When those offended souls had told their story,
　　I bowed my head and kept it bowed until
　　the poet said, "What are you thinking of?" 111
When finally I spoke, I sighed, "Alas,
　　all those sweet thoughts, and oh, how much desiring
　　brought these two down into this agony." 114
And then I turned to them and tried to speak;
　　I said, "Francesca, the torment that you suffer
　　brings painful tears of pity to my eyes. 117
But tell me, in that time of your sweet sighing
　　how, and by what signs, did love allow you
　　to recognize your dubious desires?" 120
And she to me: "There is no greater pain
　　than to remember, in our present grief,
　　past happiness (as well your teacher knows)! 123
But if your great desire is to learn
　　the very root of such a love as ours,
　　I shall tell you, but in words of flowing tears. 126
One day we read, to pass the time away,
　　of Lancelot,[1] of how he fell in love;
　　we were alone, innocent of suspicion. 129
Time and again our eyes were brought together
　　by the book we read; our faces flushed and paled.
　　To the moment of one line alone we yielded: 132
it was when we read about those longed-for lips
　　now being kissed by such a famous lover,
　　that this one (who shall never leave my side) 135
then kissed my mouth, and trembled as he did.
　　Our Galehot[2] was that book and he who wrote it.
　　That day we read no further."[3] And all the while 138
the one of the two spirits spoke these words,
　　the other wept, in such a way that pity
　　blurred my senses; I swooned as though to die, 141
and fell to Hell's floor as a body, dead, falls.

CANTO VI

On recovering consciousness the Pilgrim finds himself with Virgil in the Third Circle, where the Gluttons are punished. These shades are mired in filthy muck and are eternally battered by cold and dirty hail, rain, and snow. Soon the travelers come upon Cerberus, the three-headed, doglike beast who guards the Gluttons, but Virgil

9. Caïna is the circle of Cain (described in canto 32), where those who killed their kin are punished; the lovers were killed by Gianciotto Malatesta, Francesca's husband and Paolo's brother.
1. In Arthurian legend, the lover of Arthur's wife, Guinevere.

2. The knight who, in the French romance being read by the lovers, acted as a go-between for Lancelot and Guinevere.
3. Compare this line to Augustine's account in *Confessions* of his conversion by reading a passage in Paul's Epistle to the Romans.

pacifies him with fistfuls of slime and the two poets pass on. One of the shades
recognizes Dante the Pilgrim and hails him. It is Ciacco, a Florentine who, before
they leave, makes a prophecy concerning the political future of Florence. As the
poets move away, the Pilgrim questions Virgil about the Last Judgment and other
matters until the two arrive at the next circle.

Regaining now my senses, which had fainted
   at the sight of these two who were kinsmen lovers,
   a piteous sight confusing me to tears,   3
new suffering and new sinners suffering
   appeared to me, no matter where I moved
   or turned my eyes, no matter where I gazed.   6
I am in the third circle, in the round of rain
   eternal, cursed, cold, and falling heavy,
   unchanging beat, unchanging quality.   9
Thick hail and dirty water mixed with snow
   come down in torrents through the murky air,
   and the earth is stinking from this soaking rain.   12
Cerberus,[4] a ruthless and fantastic beast,
   with all three throats howls out his doglike sounds
   above the drowning sinners of this place.   15
His eyes are red, his beard is slobbered black,
   his belly swollen, and he has claws for hands;
   he rips the spirits, flays and mangles them.   18
Under the rain they howl like dogs, lying
   now on one side with the other as a screen,
   now on the other turning, these wretched sinners.   21
When the slimy Cerberus caught sight of us,
   he opened up his mouths and showed his fangs;
   his body was one mass of twitching muscles.   24
My master stooped and, spreading wide his fingers,
   he grabbed up heaping fistfuls of the mud
   and flung it down into those greedy gullets.   27
As a howling cur, hungering to get fed,
   quiets down with the first mouthful of his food,
   busy with eating, wrestling with that alone,   30
so it was with all three filthy heads
   of the demon Cerberus, used to barking thunder
   on these dead souls, who wished that they were deaf.   33
We walked across this marsh of shades beaten
   down by the heavy rain, our feet pressing
   on their emptiness that looked like human form.   36
Each sinner there was stretched out on the ground
   except for one[5] who quickly sat up straight,
   the moment that he saw us pass him by.   39
"O you there being led through this inferno,"
   he said, "try to remember who I am,

---

4. For this creature as one of the guardians of Hell, see *Aeneid* 6.190–97.   5. A Florentine named Ciacco, known only through his appearance here.

for you had life before I gave up mine."[6]   42
I said: "The pain you suffer here perhaps
   disfigures you beyond all recognition:
   I can't remember seeing you before.   45
But tell me who you are, assigned to grieve
   in this sad place, afflicted by such torture
   that—worse there well may be, but none more foul."   48
"Your own city," he said, "so filled with envy
   its cup already overflows the brim,
   once held me in the brighter life above.   51
You citizens gave me the name of Ciacco;
   and for my sin of gluttony I am damned,
   as you can see, to rain that beats me weak.   54
And my sad sunken soul is not alone,
   for all these sinners here share in my pain
   and in my sin." And that was his last word.   57
"Ciacco," I said to him, "your grievous state
   weighs down on me, it makes me want to weep;
   but tell me what will happen, if you know,   60
to the citizens of that divided state?
   And are there any honest men among them?
   And tell me, why is it so plagued with strife?"   63
And he replied:[7] "After much contention
   they will come to bloodshed; the rustic party
   will drive the other out by brutal means.   66
Then it will come to pass, this side will fall
   within three suns, and the other rise to power
   with the help of one now listing toward both sides.   69
For a long time they will keep their heads raised high,
   holding the others down with crushing weight,
   no matter how these weep or squirm for shame.   72
Two just men there are,[8] but no one listens,
   for pride, envy, avarice are the three sparks
   that kindle in men's hearts and set them burning."   75
With this his mournful words came to an end.
   But I spoke back: "There's more I want to know;
   I beg you to provide me with more facts: 78
Farinata and Tegghiaio, who were so worthy,
   Jacopo Rusticucci, Arrigo, Mosca,
   and all the rest so bent on doing good,[9]   81
where are they? Tell me what's become of them;
   one great desire tortures me: to know
   whether they taste Heaven's sweetness or Hell's gall."   84

6. "You were born before I died."
7. The enigmatic "prophecy" that follows
refers first to the triumph of the Whites, or
"the rustic party" (to which Dante was allied),
in 1300 and then their defeat by the Blacks,
aided by Pope Boniface ("one now listing
toward both sides"), in 1302, at which time
Dante was exiled.
8. The identity of these two is unknown.
9. Dante asks about famous Florentines; he
will find Farinata in canto 10, Tegghiaio and
Rusticucci in canto 16, and Mosca in canto
28. Arrigo does not appear.

"They lie below with blacker souls," he said,
  "by different sins pushed down to different depths;
  if you keep going you may see them all.   87
But when you are once more in the sweet world
  I beg you to remind our friends of me.
  I speak no more; no more I answer you."   90
He twisted his straight gaze into a squint
  and stared awhile at me, then bent his head,
  falling to join his other sightless peers.   93
My guide then said to me: "He'll wake no more
  until the day the angel's trumpet blows,
  when the unfriendly Judge shall come down here;   96
each soul shall find again his wretched tomb,
  assume his flesh and take his human shape,
  and hear his fate resound eternally."[1]   99
And so we made our way through the filthy mess
  of muddy shades and slush, moving slowly,
  talking a little about the afterlife.   102
I said, "Master, will these torments he increased,
  or lessened, on the final Judgment Day,
  or will the pain be just the same as now?"   105
And he: "Remember your philosophy:
  the closer a thing comes to its perfection,
  more keen will be its pleasure or its pain.   108
Although this cursèd race of punished souls
  shall never know the joy of true perfection,
  more perfect will their pain be then than now."[2]   111
We circled round that curving road while talking
  of more than I shall mention at this time,
  and came to where the ledge begins descending;   114
there we found Plutus, mankind's arch-enemy.[3]

CANTO VII

At the boundary of the Fourth Circle the two travelers confront clucking Plutus, the god of wealth, who collapses into emptiness at a word from Virgil. Descending farther, the Pilgrim sees two groups of angry, shouting souls who clash huge rolling weights against each other with their chests. They are the Prodigal and the Miserly. Their earthly concern with material goods prompts the Pilgrim to question Virgil about Fortune and her distribution of the worldly goods of men. After Virgil's explanation, they descend to the banks of the swamplike river Styx, which serves as the Fifth Circle. Mired in the bog are the Wrathful, who constantly tear and mangle each other. Beneath the slime of the Styx, Virgil explains, are the Slothful; the bubbles on the muddy surface indicate their presence beneath. The poets walk around the swampy area and soon come to the foot of a high tower.

1. Virgil refers to the Last Judgment, when the dead will regain their bodies.
2. They will be more perfect because body and soul will be reunited (a principle derived from Aristotelian science), which will only increase their pain.
3. Dante combines Pluto, the classical god of the underworld, with Plutus, the classical god of wealth.

"Pape Satàn, pape Satàn aleppe!"[4]
    the voice of Plutus clucked these words at us,
    and that kind sage, to whom all things were known,   3
said reassuringly: "Do not let fear
    defeat you, for whatever be his power,
    he cannot stop our journey down this rock."   6
Then he turned toward that swollen face of rage,
    crying, "Be quiet, cursèd wolf of Hell:
    feed on the burning bile that rots your guts.   9
This journey to the depths does have a reason,
    for it is willed on high, where Michael wrought
    a just revenge for the bold assault on God."[5]   12
As sails swollen by wind, when the ship's mast breaks,
    collapse, deflated, tangled in a heap,
    just so the savage beast fell to the ground.   15
And then we started down a fourth abyss,
    making our way along the dismal slope
    where all the evil of the world is dumped.   18
Ah, God's avenging justice! Who could heap up
    suffering and pain as strange as I saw here?
    How can we let our guilt bring us to this?   21
As every wave Charybdis[6] whirls to sea
    comes crashing against its counter-current wave,
    so these folks here must dance their roundelay.   24
More shades were here than anywhere above,
    and from both sides, to the sound of their own screams,
    straining their chests, they rolled enormous weights.   27
And when they met and clashed against each other
    they turned to push the other way, one side
    screaming, "Why hoard?," the other side, "Why waste?"   30
And so they moved back round the gloomy circle,
    returning on both sides to opposite poles
    to scream their shameful tune another time;   33
again they came to clash and turn and roll
    forever in their semicircle joust.
    And I, my heart pierced through by such a sight,   36
spoke out, "My Master, please explain to me
    who are these people here? Were they all priests,
    these tonsured[7] souls I see there to our left?"   39
He said, "In their first life all you see here
    had such myopic minds they could not judge
    with moderation when it came to spending;   42
their barking voices make this clear enough,

---

4. Virgil apparently understands this mysterious outburst regarding Satan, but commentators have remained baffled.
5. A reference to the battle in heaven between the Archangel Michael and Satan in the form of a dragon: see Revelation 12.7–9.
6. A famous whirlpool in the Straits of Messina, between Sicily and Italy, described in *Aeneid* 3.
7. The tonsure—a shaving of part of the head—was a mark of clerical status.

when they arrive at the two points on the circle
    where opposing guilts divide them into two.   45
The ones who have the bald spot on their heads
    were priests and popes and cardinals, in whom
    avarice is most likely to prevail."   48
And I: "Master, in such a group as this
    I should be able to recognize a few
    who dirtied themselves by such crimes as these."   51
And he replied, "Yours is an empty hope:
    their undistinguished life that made them foul
    now makes it harder to distinguish them.   54
Eternally the two will come to blows;
    then from the tomb they will be resurrected:
    these with tight fists, those without any hair.   57
It was squandering and hoarding that have robbed them
    of the lovely world, and got them in this brawl:
    I will not waste choice words describing it!   60
You see, my son, the short-lived mockery
    of all the wealth that is in Fortune's keep,
    over which the human race is bickering;   63
for all the gold that is or ever was
    beneath the moon won't buy a moment's rest
    for even one among these weary souls."   66
"Master, now tell me what this Fortune is
    you touched upon before. What is she like
    who holds all worldly wealth within her fists?"   69
And he to me, "O foolish race of man,
    how overwhelming is your ignorance!
    Now listen while I tell you what she means:[8]   72
that One, whose wisdom knows infinity,
    made all the heavens and gave each one a guide,
    and each sphere shining shines on all the others,   75
so light is spread with equal distribution:
    for worldly splendors He decreed the same
    and ordained a guide and general ministress   78
who would at her discretion shift the world's
    vain wealth from nation to nation, house to house,
    with no chance of interference from mankind;   81
so while one nation rules, another falls,
    according to whatever she decrees
    (her sentence hidden like a snake in grass).   84
Your knowledge has no influence on her;
    for she foresees, she judges, and she rules
    her kingdom as the other gods do theirs.   87
Her changing changes never take a rest;
    necessity keeps her in constant motion,
    as men come and go to take their turn with her.   90

8. Virgil now explains that each area of life is presided over by a "guide," a kind of angel, under the ultimate authority of God. The classical goddess Fortune—the "ministress" of line 78—who was thought to distribute the world's goods capriciously is here described as acting according to God's supervision.

And this is she so crucified and cursed;
   even those in luck, who should be praising her,
   instead revile her and condemn her acts.   93
But she is blest and in her bliss hears nothing;
   with all God's joyful first-created creatures
   she turns her sphere and, blest, turns it with joy.   96
Now let's move down to greater wretchedness;
   the stars that rose when I set out for you
   are going down—we cannot stay too long."9   99
We crossed the circle to its other bank,
   passing a spring that boils and overflows
   into a ditch the spring itself cut out.   102
The water was a deeper dark than perse,
   and we, with its gray waves for company,
   made our way down along a rough, strange path.   105
This dingy little stream, when it has reached
   the bottom of the gray malignant slopes,
   becomes a swamp that has the name of Styx.1   108
And I, intent on looking as we passed,
   saw muddy people moving in that marsh,
   all naked, with their faces scarred by rage.   111
They fought each other, not with hands alone,
   but struck with head and chest and feet as well,
   with teeth they tore each other limb from limb.   114
And the good teacher said: "My son, now see
   the souls of those that anger overcame;
   and I ask you to believe me when I say,   117
beneath the slimy top are sighing souls
   who make these waters bubble at the surface;
   your eyes will tell you this—just look around.   120
Bogged in this slime they say, 'Sluggish we were
   in the sweet air made happy by the sun,
   and the smoke of sloth was smoldering in our hearts;   123
now we lie sluggish here in this black muck!'
   This is the hymn they gurgle in their throats
   but cannot sing in words that truly sound."   126
Then making a wide arc, we walked around
   the pond between the dry bank and the slime,
   our eyes still fixed on those who gobbled mud.   129
We came, in time, to the foot of a high tower.2

CANTO VIII

*But before they had reached the foot of the tower, the Pilgrim had noticed two signal
flames at the tower's top, and another flame answering from a distance; soon he realizes that the flames are signals to and from Phlegyas, the boatman of the Styx, who*

9. The stars that were rising at the start of the
journey (1.37–40) are now setting: Good Friday
has passed, and the time is now the early hours
of Holy Saturday.
1. The second river of Hell.

2. This watchtower guards the entrance to
lower Hell or the city of Dis—another name
for Pluto, the classical god of the underworld,
that is throughout the *Inferno* applied to Satan
(see 11.65 and 34.20).

*suddenly appears in a small boat speeding across the river. Wrathful and irritated
though he is, the steersman must grant the poets passage, but during the crossing an
angry shade rises from the slime to question the Pilgrim. After a brief exchange of
words, scornful on the part of the Pilgrim, who has recognized this sinner, the spirit
grabs hold of the boat. Virgil pushes him away, praising his ward for his just scorn,
while a group of the wrathful attack the wretched soul, whose name is Filippo Argenti.
At the far shore the poets debark and find themselves before the gates of the infernal
City of Dis, where howling figures threaten them from the walls. Virgil speaks with
them privately, but they slam the gate shut in his face. His ward is terrified, and Virgil
too is shaken, but he insists that help from Heaven is already on the way.*

I must explain, however, that before
    we finally reached the foot of that high tower,
    our eyes had been attracted to its summit   3
by two small flames we saw flare up just there;
    and, so far off the eye could hardly see,
    another burning torch flashed back a sign.   6
I turned to that vast sea of human knowledge:
    "What signal is this? And the other flame,
    what does it answer? And who's doing this?"   9
And he replied: "You should already see
    across the filthy waves what has been summoned,
    unless the marsh's vapors hide it from you."   12
A bowstring never shot an arrow off
    that cut the thin air any faster than
    a little boat I saw that very second   15
skimming along the water in our direction,
    with a solitary steersman, who was shouting,
    "Aha, I've got you now, you wretched soul!"   18
"Phlegyas, Phlegyas,[3] this time you shout in vain,"
    my lord responded, "you will have us with you
    no longer than it takes to cross the muck."   21
As one who learns of some incredible trick
    just played on him flares up resentfully—
    so, Phlegyas there was seething in his anger.   24
My leader calmly stepped into the skiff
    and when he was inside, he had me enter,
    and only then it seemed to carry weight.   27
Soon as my guide and I were in the boat
    the ancient prow began to plough the water,
    more deeply, now, than any time before.[4]   30
And as we sailed the course of this dead channel,
    before me there rose up a slimy shape
    that said: "Who are you, who come before your time?"   33
And I spoke back, "Though I come, I do not stay;
    but who are you, in all your ugliness?"
    "You see that I am one who weeps," he answered.   36

---

3. A mythological figure condemned to Hell
for setting fire to the temple of Apollo in
revenge for the god's seduction of his daughter: Dante found him in *Aeneid* 6.444–47.
4. Because of the weight of the living Dante.

And then I said to him: "May you weep and wail,
　　stuck here in this place forever, you damned soul,
　　for, filthy as you are, I recognize you."　　　　　　　　　　　39
With that he stretched both hands out toward the boat
　　but, on his guard, my teacher pushed him back:
　　"Away, get down there with the other curs!"　　　　　　　　42
And then he put his arms around my neck
　　and kissed my face and said, "Indignant soul,
　　blessèd is she in whose womb you were conceived.[5]　　　　45
In the world this man was filled with arrogance,
　　and nothing good about him decks his memory;
　　for this, his shade is filled with fury here.　　　　　　　　48
Many in life esteem themselves great men
　　who then will wallow here like pigs in mud,
　　leaving behind them their repulsive fame."　　　　　　　　51
"Master, it certainly would make me happy
　　to see him dunked deep in this slop just once
　　before we leave this lake—it truly would."　　　　　　　　54
And he to me, "Before the other shore
　　comes into sight, you will be satisfied:
　　a wish like that is worthy of fulfillment."　　　　　　　　57
Soon afterward, I saw the wretch so mangled
　　by a gang of muddy souls that, to this day,
　　I thank my Lord and praise Him for that sight:　　　　　　60
"Get Filippo Argenti!"[6] they all cried.
　　And at those shouts the Florentine, gone mad,
　　turned on himself and bit his body fiercely.　　　　　　　63
We left him there, I'll say no more about him.
　　A wailing noise began to pound my ears
　　and made me strain my eyes to see ahead.　　　　　　　　66
"And now, my son," the gentle teacher said,
　　"coming closer is the city we call Dis,
　　with its great walls and its fierce citizens."　　　　　　　69
And I, "Master, already I can see
　　the clear glow of its mosques above the valley,
　　burning bright red, as though just forged, and left　　　　72
to smolder." And he to me: "Eternal fire
　　burns within, giving off the reddish glow
　　you see diffused throughout this lower Hell."　　　　　　　75
And then at last we entered those deep moats
　　that circled all of this unhappy city
　　whose walls, it seemed to me, were made of iron.　　　　78
For quite a while we sailed around, until
　　we reached a place and heard our boatsman shout
　　with all his might, "Get out! Here is the entrance."　　　81
I saw more than a thousand fiendish angels[7]

---

5. See Luke 11.27, where these words are applied to Jesus.
6. A Florentine contemporary of Dante.

7. The rebel angels, cast out of Heaven; see Luke 10.18 and Revelation 12.9.

perching above the gates enraged, screaming:
    "Who is the one approaching? Who, without death,   84
dares walk into the kingdom of the dead?"
    And my wise teacher made some kind of signal
    announcing he would speak to them in secret.   87
They managed to suppress their great resentment
    enough to say: "You come, but he must go
    who thought to walk so boldly through this realm.   90
Let him retrace his foolish way alone,
    just let him try. And you who led him here
    through this dark land, you'll stay right where you are."   93
And now, my reader, consider how I felt
    when those foreboding words came to my ears!
    I thought I'd never see our world again!   96
"O my dear guide, who more than seven times
    restored my confidence, and rescued me
    from the many dangers that blocked my going on,   99
don't leave me, please," I cried in my distress,
    "and if the journey onward is denied us
    let's turn our footsteps back together quickly."   102
Then that lord who had brought me all this way
    said, "Do not fear, the journey we are making
    none can prevent: such power did decree it.   105
Wait here for me and feed your weary spirit
    with comfort and good hope; you can be sure
    I will not leave you in this underworld."   108
With this he walks away. He leaves me here,
    that gentle father, and I stay, doubting,
    and battling with my thoughts of "yes"—but "no."   111
I could not hear what he proposed to them,
    but they did not remain with him for long;
    I saw them race each other back for home.   114
Our adversaries slammed the heavy gates
    in my lord's face, and he stood there outside,
    then turned toward me and walked back very slowly   117
with eyes downcast, all self-assurance now
    erased from his forehead—sighing, "Who are these
    to forbid my entrance to the halls of grief!"   120
He spoke to me: "You need not be disturbed
    by my vexation, for I shall win the contest,
    no matter how they plot to keep us out!   123
This insolence of theirs is nothing new;
    they used it once at a less secret gate,[8]
    which is, and will forever be, unlocked;   126
you saw the deadly words inscribed above it;
    and now, already past it, and descending,
    across the circles, down the slope, alone,   129
comes one by whom the city will be opened."

8. A reference to Christ's descent into Hell after the crucifixion for the "harrowing": see above, canto 4.53.

CANTO IX

The help from Heaven has not yet arrived; the Pilgrim is afraid and Virgil is obviously worried. He reassures his ward by telling him that, soon after his own death, he was forced by the Sorceress Erichtho to resume mortal shape and go to the very bottom of Hell in order to bring up the soul of a traitor; thus Virgil knows the way well. But no sooner is the Pilgrim comforted than the Three Furies appear before him, on top of the tower, shrieking and tearing their breasts with their nails. They call for Medusa, whose horrible face has the power of turning anyone who looks on her to stone. Virgil turns his ward around and covers his eyes. After an "address to the reader" calling attention to the coming allegory, a strident blast splits the air, and the poets perceive an Angel coming through the murky darkness to open the gates of the City for them. Then the angel returns on the path whence he had come, and the two travelers enter the gate. Within are great open burning sarcophagi, from which groans of torment issue. Virgil explains that these are Arch-Heretics and their lesser counterparts.

The color of the coward on my face,
   when I realized my guide was turning back,
   made him quickly change the color of his own.   3
He stood alert, like one who strains to hear;
   his eyes could not see far enough ahead
   to cut the heavy fog of that black air.   6
"But surely we were meant to win this fight,"
   he said, "or else . . . but no, such help was promised!
   Oh, how much time it's taking him to come!"   9
I saw too well how quickly he amended
   his opening words with what he added on!
   They were different from the ones he first pronounced;   12
but nonetheless his words made me afraid,
   perhaps because the phrase he left unfinished
   I finished with worse meaning than he meant.   15
"Has anyone before ever descended
   to this sad hollow's depths from that first circle
   whose pain is all in having hope cut off?"[9]   18
I put this question to him. He replied,
   "It is not usual for one of us
   to make the journey I am making now.   21
But it happens I was down here once before,
   conjured by that heartless witch, Erichtho[1]
   (who could recall the spirit to its body).   24
Soon after I had left my flesh in death
   she sent me through these walls, and down as far
   as the pit of Judas to bring a spirit out;   27
and that place is the lowest and the darkest

9. "Has anyone from Limbo ever descended into lower Hell before?"
1. A legendary sorceress. The story of Virgil's prior descent into Hell is apparently Dante's own invention, although in the Middle Ages Virgil had the reputation of being a magician.

and the farthest from the sphere that circles all;[2]
    I know the road, and well, you can be sure.   30
This swamp that breathes with a prodigious stink
    lies in a circle round the doleful city
    that now we cannot enter without strife."   33
And he said other things, but I forget them,
    for suddenly my eyes were drawn above,
    up to the fiery top of that high tower   36
where in no time at all and all at once
    sprang up three hellish Furies[3] stained with blood,
    their bodies and their gestures those of females;   39
their waists were bound in cords of wild green hydras,
    horned snakes and little serpents grew as hair,
    and twined themselves around the savage temples.   42
And he who had occasion to know well
    the handmaids of the queen of timeless woe[4]
    cried out to me "Look there! The fierce Erinyes!   45
That is Megaera, the one there to the left,
    and that one raving on the right, Alecto,
    Tisiphone, in the middle." He said no more.   48
With flailing palms the three would beat their breasts,
    then tear them with their nails, shrieking so loud,
    I drew close to the poet, confused with fear.   51
"Medusa,[5] come, we'll turn him into stone,"
    they shouted all together glaring down,
    "how wrong we were to let off Theseus[6] lightly!"   54
"Now turn your back and cover up your eyes,
    for if the Gorgon comes and you should see her,
    there would be no returning to the world!"   57
These were my master's words. He turned me round
    and did not trust my hands to hide my eyes
    but placed his own on mine and kept them covered.   60
O all of you whose intellects are sound,
    look now and see the meaning that is hidden
    beneath the veil that covers my strange verses:[7]   63
and then, above the filthy swell, approaching,
    a blast of sound, shot through with fear, exploded,
    making both shores of Hell begin to tremble;   66
it sounded like one of those violent winds,
    born from the clash of counter-temperatures,
    that tear through forests; raging on unchecked,   69

2. Judecca, the last subdivision of the last circle of Hell, where Judas is punished.
3. Three mythological monsters who represent the spirit of vengeance, known in Greek as the Erinyes (see below, line 45, and line 46–48 for their individual names); they figure prominently in the *Aeneid* and other Latin poetry.
4. In classical mythology the queen of Hell is Hecate, or Proserpina, the wife of Pluto.

5. A mythological figure known as a Gorgon (line 56), so frightful in appearance that she turned those who gazed on her into stone.
6. Theseus, a legendary Athenian hero, descended into the underworld in order to try to rescue Proserpina, whom Pluto had abducted, and was rescued by Hercules.
7. Dante here reminds us of the need to interpret his poetry, although the lesson of this particular episode is far from self-evident.

it splits and rips and carries off the branches
   and proudly whips the dust up in its path
   and makes the beasts and shepherds flee its course!   72
He freed my eyes and said, "Now turn around
   and set your sight along the ancient scum,
   there where the marsh's mist is hovering thickest."   75
As frogs before their enemy, the snake,
   all scatter through the pond and then dive down
   until each one is squatting on the bottom,   78
so I saw more than a thousand fear-shocked souls
   in flight, clearing the path of one who came
   walking the Styx, his feet dry on the water.[8]   81
From time to time with his left hand he fanned
   his face to push the putrid air away,
   and this was all that seemed to weary him.   84
I was certain now that he was sent from Heaven.
   I turned to my guide, but he made me a sign
   to keep my silence and bow low to this one.   87
Ah, the scorn that filled his holy presence!
   He reached the gate and touched it with a wand;
   it opened without resistance from inside.   90
"O Heaven's outcasts, despicable souls,"
   he started, standing on the dreadful threshold,
   "what insolence is this that breeds in you?   93
Why do you stubbornly resist that will
   whose end can never be denied and which,
   more than one time, increased your suffering?   96
What do you gain by locking horns with fate?
   If you remember well, your Cerberus
   still bears his chin and throat peeled clean for that!"[9] 99
He turned then and retraced the squalid path,
   without one word to us, and on his face
   the look of one concerned and spurred by things   102
that were not those he found surrounding him.
   And then we started moving toward the city
   in the safety of the holy words pronounced.   105
We entered there, and with no opposition.
   And I, so anxious to investigate
   the state of souls locked up in such a fortress,   108
once in the place, allowed my eyes to wander,
   and saw, in all directions spreading out,
   a countryside of pain and ugly anguish.   111
As at Arles where the Rhône turns to stagnant waters
   or as at Pola near Quarnero's Gulf
   that closes Italy and bathes her confines,   114
the sepulchers make all the land uneven,

8. This is an angel, although described in a way reminiscent of Mercury, the classical messenger of the gods.

9. According to classical mythology, Hercules dragged Cerberus into the daylight.

so they did here, strewn in all directions,
   except the graves here served a crueler purpose:[1]   117
for scattered everywhere among the tombs
   were flames that kept them glowing far more hot
   than any iron an artisan might use.   120
Each tomb had its lid loose, pushed to one side,
   and from within came forth such fierce laments
   that I was sure inside were tortured souls.   123
I asked, "Master, what kind of shades are these
   lying down here, buried in the graves of stone,
   speaking their presence in such dolorous sighs?"   126
And he replied: "There lie arch-heretics
   of every sect, with all of their disciples;
   more than you think are packed within these tombs.   129
Like heretics lie buried with their like
   and the graves burn more, or less, accordingly."
   Then turning to the right, we moved ahead   132
between the torments there and those high walls.

CANTO X

They come to the tombs containing the Epicurean heretics, and as they are walking by them, a shade suddenly rises to full height in one tomb, having recognized the Pilgrim's Tuscan dialect. It is the proud Farinata, who, in life, opposed Dante's party; while he and the Pilgrim are conversing, another figure suddenly rises out of the same tomb. It is the shade of Cavalcante de Cavalcanti, who interrupts the conversation with questions about his son Guido. Misinterpreting the Pilgrim's confused silence as evidence of his son's death, Cavalcante falls back into his sepulcher and Farinata resumes the conversation exactly where it had been broken off. He defends his political actions in regard to Florence and prophesies that Dante, like himself, will soon know the pain of exile. But the Pilgrim is also interested to know how it is that the damned can see the future but not the present. When his curiosity is satisfied, he asks Farinata to tell Cavalcante that his son is still alive, and that his silence was caused only by his confusion about the shade's inability to know the present.

Now onward down a narrow path, between
   the city's ramparts and the suffering,
   my master walks, I following close behind.   3
"O lofty power who through these impious gyres[2]
   lead me around as you see fit," I said,
   "I want to know, I want to understand: 6
the people buried there in sepulchers,
   can they be seen? I mean, since all the lids
   are off the tombs and no one stands on guard."   9
And he: "They will forever be locked up,

1. Arles, located on the Rhone River in southern France, and Pola, located on the bay of Quarnero in what is now Yugoslavia, were sites of Roman cemeteries.
2. Circular turns.

when they return here from Jehoshaphat
    with the bodies that they left up in the world.[3]   12
The private cemetery on this side
    serves Epicurus[4] and his followers,
    who make the soul die when the body dies.   15
As for the question you just put to me,
    it will be answered soon, while we are here;
    and the wish you are keeping from me will be granted."[5]   18
And I: "O my good guide, I do not hide
    my heart; I'm trying not to talk too much,
    as you have told me more than once to do."   21
"O Tuscan walking through our flaming city,
    alive, and speaking with such elegance,
    be kind enough to stop here for a while.   24
Your mode of speech identifies you clearly
    as one whose birthplace is that noble city
    with which in my time, perhaps, I was too harsh."   27
One of the vaults resounded suddenly
    with these clear words, and I, intimidated,
    drew up a little closer to my guide,   30
who said, "What are you doing? Turn around
    and look at Farinata,[6] who has risen,
    you will see him from the waist up standing straight."   33
I already had my eyes fixed on his face,
    and there he stood out tall, with his chest and brow
    proclaiming his disdain for all this Hell.   36
My guide, with a gentle push, encouraged me
    to move among the sepulchers toward him:
    "Be sure you choose your words with care," he said.   39
And when I reached the margin of his tomb
    he looked at me, and half-contemptuously
    he asked, "And *who* would *your* ancestors be?"   42
And I who wanted only to oblige him
    held nothing back but told him everything.
    At this he lifted up his brows a little,   45
then said, "Bitter enemies of mine they were
    and of my ancestors and of my party;
    I had to scatter them not once but twice."[7]   48
"They were expelled, but only to return
    from everywhere," I said, "not once but twice—
    an art your men, however, never mastered!"[8]   51
Just then along that same tomb's open ledge
    a shade appeared, but just down to his chin,

3. According to the Bible, the Last Judgment when the dead will again receive their bodies will take place in the Valley of Jehosaphat: see Joel 3.2 and 3.12, and Matthew 25.31–32.
4. Greek philosopher (d. 270 B.C.E.) who rejected the idea of the immortality of the soul.
5. Presumably Dante's desire to see the Florentines who inhabit this circle.

6. Farinata degli Uberti (d. 1264), a leader of the Ghibelline faction in Florence.
7. Dante's family were Guelphs, who were driven out of Florence twice, in 1248 and 1260.
8. The Ghibellines were exiled in 1280, never to return.

beside this other; I think he got up kneeling.[9]   54
He looked around as though he hoped to see
  if someone else, perhaps, had come with me
  and, when his expectation was deceived,   57
he started weeping: "If it be great genius
  that carries you along through this blind jail,
  where is my son? Why is he not with you?"   60
"I do not come alone," I said to him,
  "that one waiting over there guides me through here,
  the one, perhaps, your Guido held in scorn."[1]   63
(The place of pain assigned him, and what he asked,
  already had revealed his name to me
  and made my pointed answer possible.)   66
Instantly, he sprang to his full height and cried,
  "What did you say? He *held*? Is he not living?
  The day's sweet light no longer strikes his eyes?"[2]   69
And when he heard the silence of my delay
  responding to his question, he collapsed
  into his tomb, not to be seen again.   72
That other stately shade, at whose request
  I had first stopped to talk, showed no concern
  nor moved his head nor turned to see what happened;   75
he merely picked up where we had left off:
  "If that art they did not master," he went on,
  "that gives me greater pain than does this bed.   78
But the face of the queen who reigns down here[3] will glow
  not more than fifty times before you learn
  how hard it is to master such an art;[4]   81
and as I hope that you may once more know
  the sweet world, tell me, why should your party be
  so harsh to my clan in every law they make?"   84
I answered: "The massacre and butchery
  that stained the waters of the Arbia red[5]
  now cause such laws to issue from our councils."   87
He sighed, shaking his head. "It was not I
  alone took part," he said, "not certainly
  would I have joined the rest without good cause.   90
But I alone stood up when all of them

9. This is Cavalcante de Cavalcanti, father of Dante's friend and fellow poet Guido. A Guelph, Guido married the daughter of Farinata in an unsuccessful attempt to heal the feud. In June 1300—after the fictional date of this conversation—Guido was exiled to a part of Italy where he caught the malaria from which he died in August. Dante was at that time a member of the governing body that made the decision to exile Guido.
1. The passage is ambiguous in the original Italian: as translated here, the "one" refers to Virgil; but the Italian word can also be translated to refer to Beatrice, so that these two lines would then read: "that one waiting over there guides me through here, / to her whom your Guido perhaps held in scorn."
2. In line 61 Dante used a verbal form known in Italian as the remote past, which leads Cavalcante to believe, wrongly, that now, in April 1300, Guido is dead—although, ironically, in about four months he will indeed die, as Dante knew when he was writing this canto.
3. Proserpina, who is also the goddess of the moon.
4. Farinata here predicts Dante's own exile.
5. A stream near the hill of Montaperti, where the Ghibellines defeated the Guelphs in 1260.

were ready to have Florence razed. It was *I*
  who openly stood up in her defense."   93
"And now, as I would have your seed find peace,"
  I said, "I beg you to resolve a problem
  that has kept my reason tangled in a knot: 96
if I have heard correctly, all of you
  can see ahead to what the future holds
  but your knowledge of the present is not clear."   99
"Down here we see like those with faulty vision
  who only see," he said, "what's at a distance;
  this much the sovereign lord grants us here.   102
When events are close to us, or when they happen,
  our mind is blank, and were it not for others
  we would know nothing of your living state.   105
Thus you can understand how all our knowledge
  will be completely dead at that time when
  the door to future things is closed forever."[6]   108
Then I, moved by regret for what I'd done[7]
  said, "Now, will you please tell the fallen one
  his son is still on earth among the living;   111
and if, when he asked, silence was my answer,
  tell him: while he was speaking, all my thoughts
  were struggling with that point you solved for me."   114
My teacher had begun to call me back,
  so I quickly asked that spirit to reveal
  the names of those who shared the tomb with him.   117
He said, "More than a thousand lie with me,
  the Second Frederick[8] is here and the Cardinal[9]
  is with us. And the rest I shall not mention."   120
His figure disappeared. I made my way
  to the ancient poet, reflecting on
  those words which were prophetic enemies.[1]   123
He moved, and as we went along he said,
  "What troubles you? Why are you so distraught?"
  And I told him all the thoughts that filled my mind.   126
"Be sure your mind retains," the sage commanded,
  "those words you heard pronounced against yourself,
  and listen carefully now." He raised a finger: 129
"When at last you stand in the glow of her sweet ray,[2]
  the one whose splendid eyes see everything,
  from her you'll learn your life's itinerary."   132
Then to the left he turned. Leaving the walls,
  he headed toward the center by a path
  that strikes into a vale, whose stench arose,   135
disgusting us as high up as we were.

6. The damned can see the future but not the
present; after the Last Judgment, when human
time is abolished, they will know nothing.
7. See n. 2 to line 69 above.
8. Frederick II, Holy Roman Emperor from
1215 until his death in 1250; he reputedly

denied that there was life after death.
9. Ottaviano degli Ubaldini (d. 1273), who is
reputed to have said, "If I have a soul, I have
lost it for the Ghibellines."
1. That is, Farinata's prediction of his exile.
2. Beatrice's.

CANTO XI

Continuing their way within the Sixth Circle, where the heretics are punished, the poets are assailed by a stench rising from the abyss ahead of them which is so strong that they must stop in order to accustom themselves to the odor. They pause beside a tomb whose inscription declares that within is Pope Anastasius. When the Pilgrim expresses his desire to pass the time of waiting profitably, Virgil proceeds to instruct him about the plan of punishments in Hell. Then, seeing that dawn is only two hours away, he urges the Pilgrim on.

We reached the curving brink of a steep bank
   constructed of enormous broken rocks;
   below us was a crueler den of pain.   3
And the disgusting overflow of stench
   the deep abyss was vomiting forced us
   back from the edge. Crouched underneath the lid   6
of some great tomb, I saw it was inscribed:
   "Within lies Anastasius, the pope
   Photinus lured away from the straight path."[3]   9
"Our descent will have to be delayed somewhat
   so that our sense of smell may grow accustomed
   to these vile fumes; then we will not mind them,"   12
my master said. And I: "You will have to find
   some way to keep our time from being wasted."
   "That is precisely what I had in mind,"   15
he said, and then began the lesson:[4] "My son,
   within these boulders' bounds are three more circles,
   concentrically arranged like those above,   18
all tightly packed with souls; and so that, later,
   the sight of them alone will be enough,
   I'll tell you how and why they are imprisoned.   21
All malice has injustice as its end,
   an end achieved by violence or by fraud;
   while both are sins that earn the hate of Heaven,   24
since fraud belongs exclusively to man,
   God hates it more and, therefore, far below,
   the fraudulent are placed and suffer most.   27
In the first of the circles below are all the violent;
   since violence can be used against three persons,
   into three concentric rounds it is divided: 30
violence can be done to God, to self,
   or to one's neighbor—to him or to his goods,
   as my reasoned explanation will make clear.   33
By violent means a man can kill his neighbor

3. Pope Anastasius (d. 498) was thought, wrongly, to have accepted a heresy promoted by the 5th-century theologian Photinus that Christ was not divine but only human.

4. Virgil now describes the three remaining circles of Hell, the seventh, eighth, and ninth. The seventh is for the violent and is divided into three parts; the eighth and ninth are for the fraudulent, the eighth for those who deceive generally, the ninth for those who betray those who love them. For the scheme of Hell as a whole, see the diagram on p. 1052.

or wound him grievously; his goods may suffer
    violence by arson, theft, and devastation;   36
so, homicides and those who strike with malice,
    those who destroy and plunder, are all punished
    in the first round, but all in different groups.   39
Man can raise violent hands against himself
    and his own goods; so in the second round,
    paying the debt that never can be paid,   42
are suicides, self-robbers of your world,
    or those who gamble all their wealth away
    and weep up there when they should have rejoiced.   45
One can use violence against the deity
    by heartfelt disbelief and cursing Him,
    or by despising Nature and God's bounty;   48
therefore, the smallest round stamps with its seal
    both Sodom and Cahors[5] and all those souls
    who hate God in their hearts and curse His name.   51
Fraud, that gnaws the conscience of its servants,
    can be used on one who puts his trust in you
    or else on one who has no trust invested.   54
This latter sort seems only to destroy
    the bond of love that Nature gives to man;
    so in the second circle there are nests   57
of hypocrites, flatterers, dabblers in sorcery,
    falsifiers, thieves, and simonists,[6]
    panders, seducers, grafters, and like filth.   60
The former kind of fraud both disregards
    the love Nature enjoys and that extra bond
    between men which creates a special trust;   63
thus, it is in the smallest of the circles,
    at the earth's center, around the throne of Dis,[7]
    that traitors suffer their eternal pain."   66
And I, "Master, your reasoning runs smooth,
    and your explanation certainly makes clear
    the nature of this pit and of its inmates,   69
but what about those in the slimy swamp,
    those driven by the wind, those beat by rain,
    and those who come to blows with harsh refrains?   72
Why are they, too, not punished here inside
    the city of flame, if they have earned God's wrath?
    If they have not, why are they suffering?"   75

---

5. In the Middle Ages the names of Sodom (see Genesis 18.20–19.29) and Cahors, a city in southern France, became synonymous with sodomites and userers, respectively. Usury, forbidden by the medieval church, is charging interest on loans; the logic of this prohibition—based on the argument that usury, like sodomy, is unnatural—is explained in lines 97–111 below.

6. Simony is the sin of selling a spiritual good, such as a church office or a sacrament like confession, for material gain. It is named after Simon Magus, a magician who sought to buy from the Apostles the power of baptism in Acts 8.9–24.

7. Dis is Satan, who is found at the bottom of Hell (see canto 34).

And he to me, "Why do you let your thoughts
    stray from the path they are accustomed to?
    Or have I missed the point you have in mind?   78
Have you forgotten how your *Ethics*[8] reads,
    those terms it explicates in such detail:
    the three conditions that the heavens hate,   81
incontinence, malice, and bestiality?
    Do you not remember how incontinence
    offends God least, and merits the least blame?   84
If you will reconsider well this doctrine
    and then recall to mind who those souls were
    suffering pain above, outside the walls,   87
you will clearly see why they are separated
    from these malicious ones, and why God's vengeance
    beats down upon their souls less heavily."   90
"O sun that shines to clear a misty vision,
    such joy is mine when you resolve my doubts
    that doubting pleases me no less than knowing!   93
Go back a little bit once more," I said,
    "to where you say that usury offends
    God's goodness, and untie that knot for me."   96
"Philosophy," he said, "and more than once,
    points out to one who reads with understanding
    how Nature takes her course from the Divine   99
Intellect, from its artistic workmanship,[9]
    and if you have your *Physics*[1] well in mind
    you will find, not many pages from the start,   102
how your art too, as best it can, imitates
    Nature, the way an apprentice does his master;
    so your art may be said to be God's grandchild.   105
From Art and Nature man was meant to take
    his daily bread to live—if you recall
    the book of Genesis near the beginning,[2]   108
but the usurer, adopting other means,
    scorns Nature in herself and in her pupil,
    Art—he invests his hope in something else.[3]   111
Now follow me, we should be getting on;
    the Fish are shimmering over the horizon,
    the Wain is now exactly over Caurus,[4]   114
and the passage down the bank is farther on."

---

8. Aristotle's *Nicomachean Ethics*.
9. The laws of nature are determined by God.
1. Aristotle's *Physics*, which argues that human art should follow natural laws.
2. In Genesis 3.17–19, God decrees that because of the Fall people must toil, supporting themselves by the sweat of their brows.
3. The usurer makes money not from labor but from money itself, which is an unnatural and therefore illicit art.
4. The position of stars shows that it is now about 4 A.M. on Holy Saturday.

CANTO XII

They descend the steep slope into the Seventh Circle by means of a great landslide,
which was caused when Christ descended into Hell. At the edge of the abyss is the
Minotaur, who presides over the circle of the Violent and whose own bestial rage
sends him into such a paroxysm of violence that the two travelers are able to run
past him without his interference. At the base of the precipice, they see a river of
boiling blood, which contains those who have inflicted violence upon others. But
before they can reach the river they are intercepted by three fierce Centaurs, whose
task it is to keep those who are in the river at their proper depth by shooting arrows
at them if they attempt to rise. Virgil explains to one of the centaurs (Chiron) that
this journey of the Pilgrim and himself is ordained by God; and he requests him to
assign someone to guide the two of them to the ford in the river and carry the Pil-
grim across it to the other bank. Chiron gives the task to Nessus, one of the centaurs,
who, as he leads them to the river's ford, points out many of the sinners there in the
boiling blood.

Not only was that place, where we had come
   to descend, craggy, but there was something there
   that made the scene appalling to the eye.   3
Like the ruins this side of Trent left by the landslide
   (an earthquake or erosion must have caused it)
   that hit the Adige on its left bank,[5]   6
when, from the mountain's top where the slide began
   to the plain below, the shattered rocks slipped down,
   shaping a path for a difficult descent—   9
so was the slope of our ravine's formation.
   And at the edge, along the shattered chasm,
   there lay stretched out the infamy of Crete:[6]   12
the son conceived in the pretended cow.
   When he saw us he bit into his flesh,
   gone crazy with the fever of his rage.   15
My wise guide cried to him: "Perhaps you think
   you see the Duke of Athens come again,
   who came once in the world to bring your death?[7]   18
Begone, you beast, for this one is not led
   down here by means of clues your sister[8] gave him;
   he comes here only to observe your torments."   21
The way a bull breaks loose the very moment
   he knows he has been dealt the mortal blow,
   and cannot run but jumps and twists and turns,   24
just so I saw the Minotaur perform,

5. A famous landslide on a mountain on the
Adige River near Trent, a city in northern
Italy.
6. The Minotaur, half man and half bull, was
conceived when Pasiphaë, the wife of King
Minos of Crete, had a wooden cow built within
which she placed herself so as to have intercourse with a bull. The story of the Minotaur

is told by Ovid, *Metamorphoses* 8.
7. Virgil is referring to Theseus, who killed
the Minotaur in the labyrinth in which it was
imprisoned.
8. Ariadne, daughter of Minos and Pasiphaë,
who taught Theseus how to escape from the
labyrinth within which the Minotaur was
imprisoned.

and my guide, alert, cried out: "Run to the pass!
   While he still writhes with rage, get started down."   27
And so we made our way down through the ruins
   of rocks, which often I felt shift and tilt
   beneath my feet from weight they were not used to.   30
I was deep in thought when he began: "Are you,
   perhaps, thinking about these ruins protected
   by the furious beast I quenched in its own rage?   33
Now let me tell you that the other time
   I came down to the lower part of Hell,
   this rock had not then fallen into ruins;   36
but certainly, if I remember well,
   it was just before the coming of that One
   who took from Hell's first circle the great spoil,   39
that this abyss of stench, from top to bottom
   began to shake,[9] so I thought the universe
   felt love—whereby, some have maintained, the world   42
has more than once renewed itself in chaos.[1]
   That was the moment when this ancient rock
   was split this way—here, and in other places.   45
But now look down the valley. Coming closer
   you will see the river of blood that boils the souls
   of those who through their violence injured others."   48
(Oh, blind cupidity[2] and insane wrath,
   spurring us on through our short life on earth
   to steep us then forever in such misery!)   51
I saw a river—wide, curved like a bow—
   that stretched embracing all the flatland there,
   just as my guide had told me to expect.   54
Between the river and the steep came centaurs,[3]
   galloping in single file, equipped with arrows,
   off hunting as they used to in the world;   57
then, seeing us descend, they all stopped short
   and three of them departed from the ranks
   with bows and arrows ready from their quivers.   60
One of them cried from his distant post: "You there,
   on your way down here, what torture are you seeking?
   Speak where you stand, if not, I draw my bow."   63
And then my master shouted back: "Our answer
   we will give to Chiron[4] when we're at his side;
   as for you, I see you are as rash as ever!"   66

9. Because of the earthquake that accompanied Christ's death, which occurred just before his descent to Hell and the "harrowing," Christ's rescue from the First Circle of the virtuous Israelites (see above, canto 4.52–63).
1. A reference to a theory of the Greek philosopher Empedocles that the universe is held together by alternating forces of love and hate, and that if either one predominates the result is chaos. This classical theory is not consistent with the Christian belief that the universe is created and organized by God's love.
2. Desire for wealth.
3. Mythological creatures that are half man and half horse.
4. A centaur renowned for wisdom who educated many legendary Greek heroes, including Achilles.

He nudged me, saying: "That one there is Nessus,[5]
  who died from loving lovely Dejanira,
  and made of himself, of his blood, his own revenge.   69
The middle one, who contemplates his chest,
  is great Chiron, who reared and taught Achilles;
  the last is Pholus,[6] known for his drunken wrath.   72
They gallop by the thousands round the ditch,
  shooting at any daring soul emerging
  above the bloody level of his guilt."   75
When we came closer to those agile beasts,
  Chiron drew an arrow, and with its notch
  he parted his beard to both sides of his jaws,   78
and when he had uncovered his great mouth
  he spoke to his companions: "Have you noticed,
  how the one behind moves everything he touches?   81
This is not what a dead man's feet would do!"
  And my good guide, now standing by the torso
  at the point the beast's two natures joined,[7] replied: 84
"He is indeed alive, and so alone
  that I must show him through this dismal valley;
  he travels by necessity, not pleasure.   87
A spirit[8] came, from singing Alleluia,
  to give me this extraordinary mission;
  he is no rogue nor I a criminal spirit.[9]   90
Now, in the name of that power by which I move
  my steps along so difficult a road,
  give us one of your troop to be our guide: 93
to lead us to the ford and, once we are there,
  to carry this one over on his back,
  for he is not a spirit who can fly."   96
Chiron looked over his right breast and said
  to Nessus, "You go, guide them as they ask,
  and if another troop protests, disperse them!"   99
So with this trusted escort we moved on
  along the boiling crimson river's bank,[1]
  where piercing shrieks rose from the boiling souls.   102
There I saw people sunken to their eyelids,
  and the huge centaur explained, "These are the tyrants
  who dealt in bloodshed and plundered wealth.   105
Their tears are paying for their heartless crimes:
  here stand Alexander and fierce Dionysius,
  who weighed down Sicily with years of pain;[2]   108

5. Nessus fell in love with Deianira, wife of Hercules, who killed him; while dying, Nessus poisoned with his own blood a robe that killed Hercules when he put it on.
6. Another centaur, killed by Hercules, whose rage is typical of the race.
7. When standing, Virgil reaches to the centaur's chest where his human and animal natures join.
8. Beatrice.
9. Virgil is answering the question of lines 61–62, which assumes that they are condemned spirits.
1. A river of blood, which we later learn is named Phlegethon (see 14.116).
2. Alexander the Great (d. 323 B.C.E.) and Dionysius of Syracuse in Sicily (d. 367 B.C.E.).

and there, that forehead smeared with coal-black hair,
   is Azzolino;[3] the other one, the blond,
   Opizzo d'Esti, who, and this is true,   111
was killed by his own stepson in your world."[4]
   With that I looked to Virgil, but he said
   "Let him instruct you now, don't look to me."   114
A little farther on, the centaur stopped
   above some people peering from the blood
   that came up to their throats. He pointed out   117
a shade off to one side, alone, and said:
   "There stands the one who, in God's keep, murdered
   the heart still dripping blood above the Thames."[5]   120
Then I saw other souls stuck in the river
   who had their heads and chests above the blood,
   and I knew the names of many who were there.   123
The river's blood began decreasing slowly
   until it cooked the feet and nothing more,
   and here we found the ford where we could cross.   126
"Just as you see the boiling river here
   on this side getting shallow gradually,"
   the centaur said, "I would also have you know   129
that on the other side the riverbed
   sinks deeper more and more until it reaches
   the deepest meeting place where tyrants moan: 132
it is there that Heaven's justice strikes its blow
   against Attila,[6] known as the scourge of earth,
   against Pyrrhus and Sextus,[7] and forever   135
extracts the tears the scalding blood produces.
   from Rinier da Corneto and Rinier Pazzo,[8]
   whose battlefields were highways where they robbed." 138
Then he turned round and crossed the ford again.

CANTO XIII

No sooner are the poets across the Phlegethon than they encounter a dense forest, from which come wails and moans, and which is presided over by the hideous harpies—half-woman, half-beast, bird-like creatures. Virgil tells his ward to break off a branch of one of the trees; when he does, the tree weeps blood and speaks. In life he was Pier della Vigna, chief counselor of Frederick II of Sicily; but he fell out of

3. Azzolino III (d. 1259), a brutal ruler in northern Italy.
4. Opizzo II d'Este (d. 1293), another cruel northern Italian tyrant, reputedly murdered by his son; he is called "stepson" either because of the unnaturalness of the crime or because Opizzo suspected his wife of adultery.
5. Guy de Montfort (d. 1298), who killed his cousin Prince Henry of Cornwall during a church service ("in God's keep") in the Italian city of Viterbo. Nessus's image of the blood

dripping from the victim's heart indicates his focus on the fact that the murder is still unavenged.
6. Attila the Hun (d. 453).
7. Sextus, the son of the Roman consul Pompey, became a pirate (1st century B.C.E.); Pyrrhus, Achilles' son, killed the aged Priam at the fall of Troy, as described in *Aeneid* 2.595–704.
8. Both Riniers were bandits of Dante's day; they are now weeping from pain, whereas in life they never wept for their sins.

favor, was accused unjustly of treachery, and was imprisoned, whereupon he killed himself. The Pilgrim is overwhelmed by pity. The sinner also explains how the souls of the suicides come to this punishment and what will happen to them after the Last Judgment. Suddenly they are interrupted by the wild sounds of the hunt, and two naked figures, Lano of Siena and Giacomo da Sant' Andrea, dash across the landscape, shouting at each other, until one of them hides himself in a thorny bush; immediately a pack of fierce, black dogs rush in, pounce on the hidden sinner, and rip his body, carrying away mouthfuls of flesh. The bush, which has been torn in the process, begins to lament. The two learn that the cries are those of a Florentine who had hanged himself in his own home.

Not yet had Nessus reached the other side
   when we were on our way into a forest
   that was not marked by any path at all.   3
No green leaves, but rather black in color,
   no smooth branches, but twisted and entangled,
   no fruit, but thorns of poison bloomed instead.   6
No thick, rough, scrubby home like this exists—
   not even between Cecina and Corneto[9]—
   for those wild beasts that hate the run of farmlands.   9
Here the repulsive Harpies[1] twine their nests,
   who drove the Trojans from the Strophades
   with filthy forecasts of their close disaster.   12
Wide-winged they are, with human necks and faces,
   their feet are clawed, their bellies fat and feathered;
   perched in the trees they shriek their strange laments.   15
"Before we go on farther," my guide began,
   "remember, you are in the second round
   and shall be till we reach the dreadful sand,[2]   18
now look around you carefully and see
   with your own eyes what I will not describe,
   for if I did, you wouldn't believe my words."   21
Around me wails of grief were echoing,
   and I saw no one there to make those sounds;
   bewildered by all this, I had to stop.   24
I think perhaps he thought I might be thinking
   that all the voices coming from those stumps
   belonged to people hiding there from us,   27
and so my teacher said, "If you break off
   a little branch of any of these plants,
   what you are thinking now will break off too."[3]   30
Then slowly raising up my hand a bit

9. Two towns that mark the limits of the Maremma, a desolate area in Tuscany.
1. Birds with the faces of women and clawed hands; in *Aeneid* 3 they drive the wandering Trojans from their refuge in the Strophades Islands and predict their future suffering.

2. The "dreadful sand" is in the third ring or "round" of the seventh circle, described in the next canto.
3. Your thoughts that the moans come from people concealed among the trees will cease or "break off."

I snapped the tiny branch of a great thornbush,
  and its trunk cried: "Why are you tearing me?"[4]   33
And when its blood turned dark around the wound,
  it started saying more: "Why do you rip me?
  Have you no sense of pity whatsoever?   36
Men were we once, now we are changed to scrub;
  but even if we had been souls of serpents,
  your hand should have shown more pity than it did."   39
Like a green log burning at one end only,
  sputtering at the other, oozing sap,
  and hissing with the air it forces out,   42
so from that splintered trunk a mixture poured
  of words and blood. I let the branch I held
  fall from my hand and stood there stiff with fear.   45
"O wounded soul," my sage replied to him,
  "if he had only let himself believe
  what he had read in verses I once wrote,[5]   48
he never would have raised his hand against you,
  but the truth itself was so incredible,
  I urged him on to do the thing that grieves me.   51
But tell him who you were; he can make amends,
  and will, by making bloom again your fame
  in the world above, where his return is sure."   54
And the trunk: "So appealing are your lovely words,
  I must reply. Be not displeased if I
  am lured into a little conversation.[6]   57
I am that one who held both of the keys
  that fitted Frederick's heart; I turned them both,
  locking and unlocking, with such finesse   60
that I let few into his confidence.
  I was so faithful to my glorious office,
  I lost not only sleep but life itself.   63
That courtesan who constantly surveyed
  Caesar's household with her adulterous eyes,
  mankind's undoing, the special vice of courts,[7]   66
inflamed the hearts of everyone against me,
  and these, inflamed, inflamed in turn Augustus,
  and my happy honors turned to sad laments.   69
My mind, moved by scornful satisfaction,

---

4. This episode derives from *Aeneid* 3, where Aeneas and his Trojan companions, stopping in their search for a new home, discover Polydorus transformed into a bush. Sent out by Priam during the war to solicit aid from the Thracians, Polydorus had been murdered by his hosts, and the javelins with which his body had been pierced had grown into the bush from which Aeneas breaks off a branch that bleeds. See also Ovid, *Metamorphoses* 2.
5. Had Dante been able to believe the story of Polydorus recounted in the *Aeneid*.

6. This is the soul of Pier della Vigna (ca. 1190–1249), who had risen to become minister to the Emperor Frederick II (on whom see n. 9 on 10.119); Frederick is referred to here as "Caesar" and "Augustus" because he sought to imitate the imperial court of Rome. Pier's name means Peter of the Vine, probably because his father had been a simple worker in a vineyard.
7. Pier means Envy, on whom he blames his fall from favor.

believing death would free me from all scorn,
  made me unjust to me, who was all just.[8]
By these strange roots of my own tree I swear
  to you that never once did I break faith
  with my lord, who was so worthy of all honor.   75
If one of you should go back to the world,
  restore the memory of me, who here
  remain cut down by the blow that Envy gave."   78
My poet paused awhile, then said to me,
  "Since he is silent now, don't lose your chance,
  ask him, if there is more you wish to know."   81
"Why don't you keep on questioning," I said,
  "and ask him, for my part, what I would ask,
  for I cannot, such pity chokes my heart."   84
He began again: "That this man may fulfill
  generously what your words cry out for,
  imprisoned soul, may it please you to continue   87
by telling us just how a soul gets bound
  into these knots, and tell us, if you know,
  whether any soul might someday leave his branches."   90
At that the trunk breathed heavily, and then
  the breath changed to a voice that spoke these words:
  "Your question will be answered very briefly.   93
The moment that the violent soul departs
  the body it has torn itself away from,
  Minòs sends it down to the seventh hole;   96
it drops to the wood, not in a place allotted,
  but anywhere that fortune tosses it.
There, like a grain of spelt,[9] it germinates,   99
  soon springs into a sapling, then a wild tree;
  at last the Harpies, feasting on its leaves,
  create its pain, and for the pain an outlet.   102
Like the rest, we shall return to claim our bodies,[1]
  but never again to wear them—wrong it is
  for a man to have again what he once cast off.   105
We shall drag them here and, all along the mournful
  forest, our bodies shall hang forever more,
  each one on a thorn of its own alien shade."   108
We were standing still attentive to the trunk,
  thinking perhaps it might have more to say,
  when we were startled by a rushing sound,   111
such as the hunter hears from where he stands:
  first the boar, then all the chase approaching,
  the crash of hunting dogs and branches smashing,   114
then, to the left of us appeared two shapes[2]

---

8. I unjustly committed suicide even though
I was innocent of the accusations brought
against me.
9. Wheat.
1. At the Last Judgment.

2. Lano of Siena and Giacomo da Sant' Andrea
of Padua, two Italians of a generation earlier
than Dante's; both were reputed to be spendthrifts.

naked and gashed, fleeing with such rough speed
  they tore away with them the bushes' branches.   117
The one ahead: "Come on, come quickly, Death!"
  The other, who could not keep up the pace,
  screamed, "Lano, your legs were not so nimble   120
when you jousted in the tournament of Toppo!"³
  And then, from lack of breath perhaps, he slipped
  into a bush and wrapped himself in thorns.   123
Behind these two the wood was overrun
  by packs of black bitches ravenous and ready,
  like hunting dogs just broken from their chains;   126
they sank their fangs in that poor wretch who hid,
  they ripped him open piece by piece, and then
  ran off with mouthfuls of his wretched limbs.   129
Quickly my escort took me by the hand
  and led me over to the bush that wept
  its vain laments from every bleeding sore.⁴   132
"O Giacomo da Sant' Andrea," it said,
  "what good was it for you to hide in me?
  What fault have I if you led an evil life?"   135
My master, standing over it, inquired:
  "Who were you once that now through many wounds
  breathes a grieving sermon with your blood?"   138
He answered us: "O souls who have just come
  in time to see this unjust mutilation
  that has separated me from all my leaves,   141
gather them round the foot of this sad bush.
  I was from the city that took the Baptist
  in exchange for her first patron,⁵ who, for this,   144
swears by his art she will have endless sorrow;
  and were it not that on the Arno's⁶ bridge
  some vestige of his image still remains,   147
those citizens who built anew the city
  on the ashes that Attila left behind
  would have accomplished such a task in vain;⁷   150
I turned my home into my hanging place."

CANTO XIV

They come to the edge of the Wood of the Suicides, where they see before them a stretch of burning sand upon which flames rain eternally and through which a stream of boiling blood is carried in a raised channel formed of rock. There, many groups of tortured souls are on the burning sand; Virgil explains that those lying supine on the ground are the Blasphemers, those crouching are the Usurers, and

3. Lano was killed at a battle on the river Toppo in 1287.
4. Nothing is known about this suicide, who hanged himself from his own house.
5. Florence; when the Florentines converted to Christianity, John the Baptist replaced Mars

as patron of the city, and therefore Mars will forever persecute the city with civil war.
6. The river that runs through Florence.
7. According to legend, Attila the Hun destroyed Florence when he invaded Italy in the 5th century.

those wandering aimlessly, never stopping, are the Sodomites. Representative of the
blasphemers is Capaneus, who died cursing his god. The Pilgrim questions his guide
about the source of the river of boiling blood; Virgil's reply contains the most elabo-
rate symbol in the Inferno, that of the Old Man of Crete, whose tears are the source
of all the rivers in Hell.

The love we both shared for our native city
   moved me to gather up the scattered leaves
   and give them back to the voice that now had faded.   3
We reached the confines of the woods that separate
   the second from the third round.[8] There I saw
   God's justice in its dreadful operation.   6
Now to picture clearly these unheard-of things:
   we arrived to face an open stretch of flatland
   whose soil refused the roots of any plant;   9
the grieving forest made a wreath around it,
   as the sad river of blood enclosed the woods.
   We stopped right here, right at the border line.   12
This wasteland was a dry expanse of sand,
   thick, burning sand, no different from the kind
   that Cato's[9] feet packed down in other times.   15
O just revenge of God! how awesomely
   you should be feared by everyone who reads
   these truths that were revealed to my own eyes!   18
Many separate herds of naked souls I saw,
   all weeping desperately; it seemed each group
   had been assigned a different penalty: 21
some souls were stretched out flat upon their backs,
   others were crouching there all tightly hunched,
   some wandered, never stopping, round and round.   24
Far more there were of those who roamed the sand
   and fewer were the souls stretched out to suffer,
   but their tongues were looser, for the pain was greater.   27
And over all that sandland, a fall of slowly
   raining broad flakes of fire showered steadily
   (a mountain snowstorm on a windless day),   30
like those that Alexander saw descending
   on his troops while crossing India's torrid lands:
   flames falling, floating solid to the ground,   33
and he with all his men began to tread
   the sand so that the burning flames might be
   extinguished one by one before they joined.[1]   36
Here too a never-ending blaze descended,
   kindling the sand like tinder under flint-sparks,
   and in this way the torment there was doubled.   39

8. The third ring of the seventh circle is surrounded by the second ring of the woods through
which Dante has just passed and the first ring of
the river of blood described in canto 12.
9. Roman general (1st century B.C.E.) who

campaigned in Libya.
1. Dante is here following an account by the
philosopher Albertus Magnus (d. 1280) of a
legendary adventure that befell Alexander the
Great in his conquest of India.

Without a moment's rest the rhythmic dance
  of wretched hands went on, this side, that side,
  brushing away the freshly fallen flames.   42
And I: "My master, you who overcome
  all opposition (except for those tough demons
  who came to meet us at the gate of Dis),   45
who is that mighty one that seems unbothered
  by burning, stretched sullen and disdainful there,
  looking as if the rainfall could not tame him?"[2]   48
And that very one, who was quick to notice me
  inquiring of my guide about him, answered:
  "What I was once, alive, I still am, dead!   51
Let Jupiter wear out his smith,[3] from whom
  he seized in anger that sharp thunderbolt
  he hurled, to strike me down, my final day;   54
let him wear out those others, one by one,
  who work the soot-black forge of Mongibello[4]
  (as he shouts, 'Help me, good Vulcan, I need your help,'   57
the way he cried that time at Phlegra's battle),[5]
  and with all his force let him hurl his bolts at me,
  no joy of satisfaction would I give him!"   60
My guide spoke back at him with cutting force,
  (I never heard his voice so strong before):
  "O Capaneus, since your blustering pride   63
will not be stilled, you are made to suffer more:
  no torment other than your rage itself
  could punish your gnawing pride more perfectly."   66
And then he turned a calmer face to me,
  saying, "That was a king, one of the seven
  besieging Thebes; he scorned, and would seem still   69
to go on scorning God and treat him lightly,
  but, as I said to him, he decks his chest
  with ornaments of lavish words that prick him.   72
Now follow me and also pay attention
  not to put your feet upon the burning sand,
  but to keep them well within the wooded line."   75
Without exchanging words we reached a place
  where a narrow stream came gushing from the woods
  (its reddish water still runs fear through me!);   78
like the one that issues from the Bulicame,[6]
  whose waters are shared by prostitutes downstream,
  it wore its way across the desert sand.   81
This river's bed and banks were made of stone,

---

2. Capaneus, one of the seven legendary kings
who beseiged Thebes as described in the *Thebaid* by Statius (d. 95 C.E.). He was struck
with a thunderbolt when he boasted that not
even Jupiter could stop him.
3. Vulcan.
4. The Sicilian name for Mt. Etna, thought to

be Vulcan's furnace. "Those others" are the
Cyclopes, Vulcan's helpers.
5. Jove defeated the rebellious Titans at the
battle of Phlegra (see 31.44).
6. A hot sulphurous spring that supplied
water to brothels in an area of northern Italy.

so were the tops on both its sides; and then
    I understood this was our way across.   84
"Among the other marvels I have shown you,
    from the time we made our entrance through the gate
    whose threshold welcomes every evil soul,   87
your eyes have not discovered anything
    as remarkable as this stream you see here
    extinguishing the flames above its path."   90
These were my master's words, and I at once
    implored him to provide me with the food
    for which he had given me the appetite.   93
"In the middle of the sea there lies a wasteland,"
    he immediately began, "that is known as Crete,
    under whose king the world knew innocence.[7]   96
There is a mountain there that was called Ida;
    then happy in its verdure and its streams,
    now deserted like an old, discarded thing;   99
Rhea chose it once as a safe cradle
    for her son, and, to conceal his presence better,
    she had her servants scream loud when he cried.[8]   102
In the mountain's core an ancient man stands tall;
    he has his shoulders turned toward Damietta[9]
    and faces Rome as though it were his mirror.   105
His head is fashioned of the finest gold;
    pure silver are his arms and hands and chest;
    from there to where his legs spread, he is brass;   108
the rest of him is all of chosen iron,
    except his right foot which is terra cotta;
    he puts more weight on this foot than the other.[1]   111
Every part of him, except the gold, is broken
    by a fissure dripping tears down to his feet,
    where they collect to erode the cavern's rock;   114
from stone to stone they drain down here, becoming
    rivers: the Acheron, Styx, and Phlegethon,
    then overflow down through this tight canal   117
until they fall to where all falling ends:
    they form Cocytus.[2] What that pool is like
    I need not tell you. You will see, yourself."   120
And I to him: "If this small stream beside us
    has its source, as you have told me, in our world,
    why have we seen it only on this ledge?"   123
And he to me: "You know this place is round,

---

7. Saturn, mythical king of Crete during the golden age.
8. Jupiter was hidden by his mother, Rhea, from his father, Saturn, who tried to devour all his children to thwart a prophecy that he would be dethroned by one of them. So that Saturn would not hear the infant's cries, Rhea had her servants cry out and beat their shields with their swords.

9. A city in Egypt. The Old Man has been interpreted as an emblem of the decline of human history.
1. The four metals and the clay represent the degeneration of history; Dante took them from Daniel 2.31–35.
2. The frozen lake at the bottom of Hell: see 32.22–30 and 34.52.

and though your journey has been long, circling
    toward the bottom, turning only to the left,   126
you still have not completed a full circle;
    so you should never look surprised, as now,
    if you see something you have not seen before."   129
And I again: "Where, Master, shall we find
    Lethe and Phlegethon? You omit the first
    and say the other forms from the rain of tears."   132
"I am very happy when you question me,"
    he said, "but that the blood-red water boiled
    should answer certainly one of your questions.³   135
And Lethe you shall see, but beyond this valley,
    at a place where souls collect to wash themselves
    when penitence has freed them of their guilt.⁴   138
Now it is time to leave this edge of woods,"
    he added. "Be sure you follow close behind me:
    the margins are our road, they do not burn,   141
and all the flames above them are extinguished."

CANTO XV

*They move out across the plain of burning sand, walking along the ditchlike edge of
the conduit through which the Phlegethon flows, and after they have come some
distance from the wood they see a group of souls running toward them. One, Brunetto Latini, a famous Florentine intellectual and Dante's former teacher, recognizes the Pilgrim and leaves his band to walk and talk with him. Brunetto learns the
reason for the Pilgrim's journey and offers him a prophecy of the troubles lying in
wait for him—an echo of Ciacco's words in Canto VI. Brunetto names some of the
others being punished with him (Priscian, Francesco d'Accorso, Andrea de' Mozzi);
but soon, in the distance, he sees a cloud of smoke approaching, which presages a
new group, and because he must not associate with them, like a foot-racer Brunetto
speeds away to catch up with his own band.*

Now one of those stone margins bears us on
    and the river's vapors hover like a shade,
    sheltering the banks and the water from the flames.   3
As the Flemings, living with the constant threat
    of flood tides rushing in between Wissant
    and Bruges,⁵ build their dikes to force the sea back;   6
as the Paduans build theirs on the shores of Brenta⁶
    to protect their town and homes before warm weather
    turns Chiarentana's snow to rushing water—   9
so were these walls we walked upon constructed,
    though the engineer, whoever he may have been,
    did not make them as high or thick as those.   12

3. See n. 1 to 12.101.
4. Lethe is crossed when Dante passes into
the Earthly Paradise on the top of Mount Purgatory.
5. Cities that, for Dante, mark the two ends of

the dike that protects Flanders from the sea.
6. A river that flows through Padua, fed by
the melting snows in the mountains of the
province of Chiarentana (modern Carinthia in
Austria).

We had left the wood behind (so far behind,
   by now, that if I had stopped to turn around,
   I am sure it could no longer have been seen)   15
when we saw a troop of souls come hurrying
   toward us beside the bank, and each of them
   looked us up and down, as some men look   18
at other men, at night, when the moon is new.
   They strained their eyebrows, squinting hard at us,
   as an old tailor might at his needle's eye.   21
Eyed in such a way by this strange crew,
   I was recognized by one of them, who grabbed
   my garment's hem and shouted: "How marvelous!"   24
And I, when he reached out his arm toward me,
   straining my eyes, saw through his face's crust,
   through his burned features that could not prevent   27
my memory from bringing back his name;
   and bending my face down to meet with his,
   I said: "Is this really you, here, Ser Brunetto?"[7]   30
And he: "O my son, may it not displease you
   if Brunetto Latini lets his troop file on
   while he walks at your side for a little while."   33
And I: "With all my heart I beg you to,
   and if you wish me to sit here with you,
   I will, if my companion does not mind."   36
"My son," he said, "a member of this herd
   who stops one moment lies one hundred years
   unable to brush off the wounding flames,   39
so, move on; I shall follow at your hem
   and then rejoin my family that moves
   along, lamenting their eternal pain."   42
I did not dare step off the margin-path
   to walk at his own level but, with head
   bent low in reverence, I moved along.   45
He began: "What fortune or what destiny
   leads you down here before your final hour?
   And who is this one showing you the way?"   48
"Up there above in the bright living life
   before I reached the end of all my years,
   I lost myself in a valley," I replied;   51
"just yesterday at dawn I turned from it.
   This spirit here appeared as I turned back,
   and by this road he guides me home again."   54
He said to me: "Follow your constellation
   and you cannot fail to reach your port of glory,
   not if I saw clearly in the happy life;   57
and if I had not died just when I did,

---

7. Brunetto Latini (ca. 1220–1294), active in Florentine politics and the author of—among other works—two books: a prose encyclopedia in French called the *Trésor*, which emphasizes the qualities needed for civic duty, and a shorter allegorical poem in Italian called the *Tesoretto*, which combines autobiography with philosophy.

I would have cheered you on in all your work,
    seeing how favorable Heaven was to you.   60
But that ungrateful and malignant race
    which descended from the Fiesole[8] of old,
    and still have rock and mountain in their blood,   63
will become, for your good deeds, your enemy—
    and right they are: among the bitter berries
    there's no fit place for the sweet fig to bloom.[9]   66
They have always had the fame of being blind,
    an envious race, proud and avaricious;
    you must not let their ways contaminate you.   69
Your destiny reserves such honors for you:
    both parties shall be hungry to devour you,
    but the grass will not be growing where the goat is.[1] 72
Let the wild beasts of Fiesole make fodder
    of each other, and let them leave the plant untouched
    (so rare it is that one grows in their dung-heap)   75
in which there lives again the holy seed
    of those remaining Romans who survived there
    when this new nest of malice was constructed."   78
"Oh, if all I wished for had been granted,"
    I answered him, "you certainly would not,
    not yet, be banished from our life on earth;   81
my mind is etched (and now my heart is pierced)
    with your kind image, loving and paternal,
    when, living in the world, hour after hour   84
you taught me how man makes himself eternal.[2]
    And while I live my tongue shall always speak
    of my debt to you, and of my gratitude.   87
I will write down what you tell me of my future
    and save it, with another text, to show
    a lady who can interpret, if I can reach her.[3]   90
This much, at least, let me make clear to you:
    if my conscience continues not to blame me,
    I am ready for whatever Fortune wants.   93
This prophecy is not new to my ears,
    and so let Fortune turn her wheel, spinning it
    as she pleases, and the peasant turn his spade."[4]   96
My master, hearing this, looked to the right,
    then, turning round and facing me, he said:
    "He listens well who notes well what he hears."   99
But I did not answer him; I went on talking,

8. A hill town north of Florence whose rustic inhabitants were supposed to have joined with noble Romans in the founding of Florence, creating an unstable mixture.
9. The "bitter berries" are the Florentines descended from Fiesole; the "sweet fig" is Brunetto's term for the aristocratic Dante.
1. Either both parties will ask you to join them or both parties will want to devour you—
but keep yourself apart.
2. In the *Trésor* Brunetto says that earthly glory gives man a second life through an enduring reputation.
3. Beatrice.
4. The traditional image of Fortune and her wheel is here compared to the rustic image of the peasant turning the soil with his hoe.

walking with Ser Brunetto, asking him
  who of his company were most distinguished. 102
And he: "It might be good to know who some are,
  about the rest I feel I should be silent,
  for the time would be too short, there are so many. 105
In brief, let me tell you, all here were clerics
  and respected men of letters of great fame,
  all befouled in the world by one same sin:[5] 108
Priscian is traveling with that wretched crowd
  and Francesco d'Accorso too,[6] and also there,
  if you could have stomached such repugnancy, 111
you might have seen the one the Servant of Servants
  transferred to the Bacchiglione from the Arno
  where his sinfully erected nerves were buried.[7] 114
I would say more, but my walk and conversation
  with you cannot go on, for over there
  I see a new smoke rising from the sand: 117
people approach with whom I must not mingle.
  Remember my *Trésor*, where I live on,
  this is the only thing I ask of you." 120
Then he turned back, and he seemed like one of those
  who run Verona's race across its fields
  to win the green cloth prize;[8] and he was like 123
the winner of the group, not the last one in.

CANTO XVI

Continuing through the third round of the Circle of Violence, the Pilgrim hears the distant roar of a waterfall, which grows louder as he and his guide proceed. Suddenly three shades, having recognized him as a Florentine, break from their company and converse with him, all the while circling like a turning wheel. Their spokesman, Jacopo Rusticucci, identifies himself and his companions (Guido Guerra and Tegghiaio Aldobrandi) as well-known and honored citizens of Florence, and begs for news of their native city. The three ask to be remembered in the world and then rush off. By this time the sound of the waterfall is so deafening that it almost drowns out speech, and when the poets reach the edge of the precipice, Virgil takes a cord which had been bound around his pupil's waist and tosses it into the abyss. It is a signal, and in response a monstrous form looms up from below, swimming through the air. On this note of suspense, the canto ends.

5. Sodomy, condemned in the Middle Ages as unnatural.
6. Priscian was a Greek grammarian (6th century C.E.), Francesco d'Accorso a Florentine law professor (d. 1293).
7. Andrea de' Mozzi, bishop of Florence (1287–95), transferred by Pope Boniface (designated here by an official title for the pope,

"the Servant of [Christ's] Servants") from Florence to Vicenza; the Arno runs through Florence, the Bacchiglione through Vicenza.
8. A footrace run at Verona on the first Sunday in Lent, the prize being a piece of green cloth. For the race to be run by the Christian, see 1 Corinthians 9.24–25.

Already we were where I could hear the rumbling
   of the water plunging down to the next circle,
   something like the sound of beehives humming,   3
when three shades with one impulse broke away,
   running, from a group of spirits passing us
   beneath the rain of bitter suffering.   6
They were coming toward us shouting with one voice:
   "O you there, stop! From the clothes you wear, you seem
   to be a man from our perverted city."⁹   9
Ah, the wounds I saw covering their limbs,
   some old, some freshly branded by the flames!
   Even now, when I think hack to them, I grieve.   12
Their shouts caught the attention of my guide,
   and then he turned to face me, saying, "Wait,
   for these are shades that merit your respect.   15
And were it not the nature of this place
   to rain with piercing flames, I would suggest
   you run toward *them*, for it would be more fitting."¹   18
When we stopped, they resumed their normal pace
   and when they reached us, then they started circling;
   the three together formed a turning wheel,   21
just like professional wrestlers stripped and oiled,
   eyeing one another for the first, best grip
   before the actual blows and thrusts begin.²   24
And circling in this way each kept his face
   pointed up at me, so that their necks and feet
   moved constantly in opposite directions.   27
"And if the misery along these sterile sands,"
   one of them said, "and our charred and peeling flesh
   make us, and what we ask, repulsive to you,   30
let our great wordly fame persuade your heart
   to tell us who you are, how you can walk
   safely with living feet through Hell itself.   33
This one in front, whose footsteps I am treading,
   even though he runs his round naked and skinned,
   was of noble station, more than you may think: 36
he was the grandson of the good Gualdrada;
   his name was Guido Guerra,³ and in his life
   he accomplished much with counsel and with sword.   39
This other one, who pounds the sand behind me,
   is Tegghiaio Aldobrandi,⁴ whose wise voice
   the world would have done well to listen to.   42
And I, who share this post of pain with them,

---

9. Florence.
1. To hurry was considered undignified.
2. The three naked Florentines form a circle and are compared to oiled wrestlers (a sport practiced in Dante's time).
3. A leading participant in the civil strife in Florence (d. 1272).
4. An ally of Guido (see 6.79).

was Jacopo Rusticucci[5] and for sure
my reluctant wife first drove me to my sin."   45
If I could have been sheltered from the fire,
I would have thrown myself below with them,
and I think my guide would have allowed me to;   48
but, as I knew I would be burned and seared,
my fear won over my first good intention
that made me want to put my arms around them.   51
And then I spoke: "Repulsion, no, but grief
for your condition spread throughout my heart
(and years will pass before it fades away),   54
as soon as my lord here began to speak
in terms that led me to believe a group
of such men as yourselves might be approaching.   57
I am from your city, and your honored names
and your accomplishments I have always heard
rehearsed, and have rehearsed, myself, with fondness.   60
I leave the bitter gall, and journey toward
those sweet fruits promised me by my true guide,[6]
but first I must go down to the very center."   63
"So may your soul remain to guide your body
for years to come," that same one spoke again,
"and your fame's light shine after you are gone,   66
tell us if courtesy and valor dwell
within our city as they used to do,
or have they both been banished from the place?   69
Guglielmo Borsiere,[7] who joined our painful ranks
of late, and travels there with our companions,
has given us reports that make us grieve."[8]   72
"A new breed of people with their sudden wealth
have stimulated pride and unrestraint
in you, O Florence, made to weep so soon."   75
These words I shouted with my head strained high,
and the three below took this to be my answer
and looked, as if on truth, at one another.   78
"If you always answer questions with such ease,"
they all spoke up at once, "O happy you,
to have this gift of ready, open speech;   81
therefore, if you survive these unlit regions
and return to gaze upon the lovely stars,
when it pleases you to say 'I was down there,'   84
do not fail to speak of us to living men."
They broke their man-made wheel and ran away,
their nimble legs were more like wings in flight.   87

5. An ally of Tegghiaio who blames his wife
for his sodomy (see 6.80).
6. Leave Hell and head for Paradise.
7. An elegant member of Florentine society.

8. An account of the recent dissension within
the city, to which Dante himself was soon to
fall victim.

"Amen" could not have been pronounced as quick
   as they were off, and vanished from our sight;
   and then my teacher thought it time to leave.   90
I followed him, and we had not gone far
   before the sound of water was so close
   that if we spoke we hardly heard each other.   93
As that river on the Apennines' left slope,[9]
   first springing from its source at Monte Veso,
   then flowing eastward holding its own course   96
(called Acquacheta at its start above
   before descending to its lower bed
   where, at Forli, it has another name),   99
reverberates there near San Benedetto
   dell'Alpe (plunging in a single bound),
   where at least a thousand vassals could be housed,   102
so down a single rocky precipice
   we found the tainted waters falling, roaring
   sound loud enough to deafen us in seconds.   105
I wore a cord that fastened round my waist,[1]
   with which I once had thought I might be able
   to catch the leopard with the gaudy skin.[2]   108
As soon as I removed it from my body
   just as my guide commanded me to do,
   I gave it to him looped into a coil.   111
Then taking it and turning to the right,
   he flung it quite a distance past the bank
   and down into the deepness of the pit.   114
"Now surely something strange is going to happen,"
   I thought to myself, "to answer the strange signal
   whose course my master follows with his eyes."   117
How cautious a man must be in company
   with one who can not only see his actions
   but read his mind and understand his thoughts![3]   120
He spoke: "Soon will rise up what I expect;
   and what you are trying to imagine now
   soon must reveal itself before your eyes."   123
It is always better to hold one's tongue than speak
   a truth that seems a bold-faced lie when uttered,
   since to tell this truth could be embarrassing;   126
but I shall not keep quiet; and by the verses
   of my *Comedy*—so may they be received
   with lasting favor, Reader—I swear to you   129
I saw a figure coming, it was swimming

9. Dante compares the roar of Phlegethon to the Montone River in northern Italy, whose course he traces in the next nine lines.
1. While commentators disagree, it seems likely that this cord is a reference both to Job 41.1, where God says he can draw Leviathan up with a hook and bind his tongue with a cord, and to Francis of Assisi, who wore a cord as a sign of humility and obedience. As a layman, Dante may have had a connection with the Franciscan friars, a common circumstance at the time.
2. The leopard of canto I, representing fraud.
3. Dante now realizes that Virgil can read his thoughts.

through the thick and murky air, up to the top
    (a thing to startle even stalwart hearts),   132
like one returning who has swum below
    to free the anchor that has caught its hooks
    on a reef or something else the sea conceals,   135
spreading out his arms, and doubling up his legs.

CANTO XVII

*The beast that had been seen approaching at the end of the last canto is the horrible
monster Geryon; his face is appealing like that of an honest man, but his body ends
in a scorpionlike stinger. He perches on the edge of the abyss and Virgil advises his
ward, who has noticed new groups of sinners squatting on the fiery sand, to learn
who they are, while he makes arrangements with Geryon for the descent. The sinners are the Usurers, unrecognizable except by the crests on the moneybags hanging
about their necks, which identify them as members of the Gianfigliazzi, Ubriachi,
and Scrovegni families. The Pilgrim listens to one of them briefly but soon returns
to find his master sitting on Geryon's back. After he conquers his fear and mounts,
too, the monster begins the slow, spiraling descent into the Eighth Circle.*

"And now, behold the beast with pointed tail
    that passes mountains, annulling walls and weapons,
    behold the one that makes the whole world stink!"[4]   3
These were the words I heard my master say
    as he signaled for the beast to come ashore,
    up close to where the rocky levee ends.   6
And that repulsive spectacle of fraud
    floated close, maneuvering head and chest
    on to the shore, but his tail he let hang free.   9
His face was the face of any honest man,
    it shone with such a look of benediction;
    and all the rest of him was serpentine;   12
his two clawed paws were hairy to the armpits,
    his back and all his belly and both flanks
    were painted arabesques and curlicues: 15
the Turks and Tartars never made a fabric
    with richer colors intricately woven,
    nor were such complex webs spun by Arachne.[5]   18
As sometimes fishing boats are seen ashore,
    part fixed in sand, and part still in the water;
    and as the beaver,[6] living in the land   21
of drunken Germans,[7] squats to catch his prey,
    just so that beast, the worst of beasts, hung waiting
    on the bank that bounds the stretch of sand in stone. 24

4. Geryon, the embodiment of fraud. For this figure Dante drew upon classical literature, where he had not three natures—human, reptilian, and bestial—combined into one, as here, but three bodies and three heads.
5. A woman in classical literature famous for weaving, turned into a spider: see Ovid, *Metamorphoses* 6.
6. Which was thought to catch fish by putting its tail into the water.
7. Accusing Germans of drunkenness was a tradition going back to the Romans.

In the void beyond he exercised his tail,
   twitching and twisting-up the venomed fork
   that armed its tip just like a scorpion's stinger.   27
My leader said: "Now we must turn aside
   a little from our path, in the direction
   of that malignant beast that lies in wait."   30
Then we stepped off our path down to the right
   and moved ten paces straight across the brink
   to keep the sand and flames at a safe distance.   33
And when we stood by Geryon's side, I noticed,
   a little farther on, some people crouched
   in the sand quite close to the edge of emptiness.   36
Just then my master spoke: "So you may have
   a knowledge of this round that is complete,"
   he said, "go and see their torment for yourself.   39
But let your conversation there be brief;
   while you are gone I shall speak to this one
   and ask him for the loan of his strong back."   42
So I continued walking, all alone,
   along the seventh circle's outer edge
   to where the group of sufferers were sitting.   45
The pain was bursting from their eyes; their hands
   went scurrying up and down to give protection
   here from the flames, there from the burning sands.   48
They were, in fact, like a dog in summertime
   busy, now with his paw, now with his snout,
   tormented by the fleas and flies that bite him.   51
I carefully examined several faces
   among this group caught in the raining flames
   and did not know a soul, but I observed   54
that around each sinner's neck a pouch was hung,
   each of a different color, with a coat of arms,
   and fixed on these they seemed to feast their eyes.[8]   57
And while I looked about among the crowd,
   I saw something in blue on a yellow purse
   that had the face and bearing of a lion;   60
and while my eyes continued their inspection
   I saw another purse as red as blood
   exhibiting a goose more white than butter.   63
And one who had a blue sow, pregnant-looking,
   stamped on the whiteness of his moneybag
   asked me: "What are you doing in this pit?   66
Get out of here! And since you're still alive,
   I'll tell you that my neighbor Vitaliano
   will come to take his seat on my left side.[9]   69
Among these Florentines I sit, one Paduan:

8. These are usurers, men who lent money for interest, which was forbidden by the church in the Middle Ages (although often practiced). Each has a coat of arms on his purse by which he can be identified; all are Italians.

9. The speaker is from Padua and here maliciously identifies another Paduan who will soon be joining him.

time after time they fill my ears with blasts
  of shouting: 'Send us down the sovereign knight[1]
who will come bearing three goats on his pouch.'"
    As final comment he stuck out his tongue—
  as far out as an ox licking its nose.
And I, afraid my staying there much longer
  might anger the one who warned me to be brief,
  turned my back on these frustrated sinners.
I found my guide already sitting high
  upon the back of that fierce animal;
  he said: "And now, take courage and be strong.
From now on we descend by stairs like these.
  Get on up front. I want to ride behind,
  to be between you and the dangerous tail."[2]
A man who feels the shivers of a fever
  coming on, his nails already dead of color,
  will tremble at the mere sight of cool shade;
I was that man when I had heard his words.
  But then I felt those stabs of shame that make
  a servant brave before his valorous master.
As I squirmed around on those enormous shoulders,
  I wanted to cry out, "Hold on to me,"
  but I had no voice to second my desire.
Then he who once before had helped me out
  when I was threatened put his arms around me
  as soon as I was settled, and held me tight;
and then he cried: "Now Geryon, start moving,
  descend with gentle motion, circling wide:
  remember you are carrying living weight."
Just as a boat slips back away from shore,
  back slowly, more and more, he left that pier;
  and when he felt himself all clear in space,
to where his breast had been he swung his tail
  and stretched it undulating like an eel,
  as with his paws he gathered in the air.
I doubt if Phaëthon[3] feared more—that time
  he dropped the sun-reins of his father's chariot
  and burned the streak of sky we see today—
or if poor Icarus[4] did—feeling his sides
  unfeathering as the wax began to melt,
  his father shouting: "Wrong, your course is wrong"—
than I had when I felt myself in air
  and saw on every side nothing but air;
  only the beast I sat upon was there.
He moves along slowly, and swimming slowly,

72

75

78

81

84

87

90

93

96

99

102

105

108

111

114

---

1. A prominent Florentine banker.
2. Virgil protects Dante from Geryon's scorpion's tail.
3. Son of Apollo, Phaëthon tried to drive the chariot of the sun, but when it got out of control

it scorched both Earth and the heavens, creating the Milky Way (Ovid, *Metamorphoses* 2).
4. Flying with wings made of wax and feathers, Icarus went too near the sun and fell (Ovid, *Metamorphoses* 8).

descends a spiral path—but I know this
  only from a breeze ahead and one below;   117
I hear now on my right the whirlpool roar
  with hideous sound beneath us on the ground;
  at this I stretch my neck to look below,   120
but leaning out soon made me more afraid,
  for I heard moaning there and saw the flames;
  trembling, I cowered back, tightening my legs,   123
and I saw then what I had not before:
  the spiral path of our descent to torment
  closing in on us, it seemed, from every side.   126
As the falcon on the wing for many hours,
  having found no prey, and having seen no signal
  (so that his falconer sighs: "Oh, he falls already"),   129
descends, worn out, circling a hundred times
  (instead of swooping down), settling at some distance
  from his master, perched in anger and disdain,[5]   132
so Geryon brought us down to the bottom
  at the foot of the jagged cliff, almost against it,
  and once he got our bodies off his back,   135
he shot off like a shaft shot from a bowstring.

CANTO XVIII

The Pilgrim describes the view he had of the Eighth Circle of Hell while descending through the air on Geryon's back. It consists of ten stone ravines called Malebolge *(Evil Pockets), and across each* bolgia *is an arching bridge. When the poets find themselves on the edge of the first ravine they see two lines of naked sinners, walking in opposite directions. In one are the Pimps or Panderers, and among them the Pilgrim recognizes Venedico Caccianemico; in the other are the Seducers, among whom Virgil points out Jason. As the two move toward the next* bolgia, *they are assailed by a terrible stench; for here the Flatterers are immersed in excrement. Among them are Alessio Interminei and Thaïs the whore.*

There is a place in Hell called Malebolge,
  cut out of stone the color of iron ore,
  just like the circling cliff that walls it in.   3
Right at the center of this evil plain
  there yawns a very wide, deep well, whose structure
  I will talk of when the place itself is reached.[6]   6
That belt of land remaining, then, runs round
  between the well and cliff, and all this space
  is divided into ten descending valleys,   9
just like a ground-plan for successive moats
  that in concentric circles bind their center
  and serve to protect the ramparts of the castle.   12
This was the surface image they presented;

---

5. Unless it sights prey or is called back with a lure by its master, a trained falcon will continue flying until exhaustion compels it to descend.

6. The last, or ninth, circle of Hell, described in cantos 31–34.

and as bridges from a castle's portal stretch
   from moat to moat to reach the farthest bank,   15
so, from the great cliff's base, just spokes of rock,
   crossing from bank to bank, intersecting ditches
   until the pit's hub cuts them off from meeting.   18
This is the place in which we found ourselves,
   once shaken from the back of Geryon.
   The poet turned to the left, I walked behind him.   21
There, on our right, I saw new suffering souls,
   new means of torture, and new torturers,
   crammed into the depths of the first ditch.   24
Two files of naked souls walked on the bottom,
   the ones on our side faced us as they passed,
   the others moved as we did but more quickly.   27
The Romans, too, in the year of the Jubilee[7]
   took measures to accommodate the throngs
   that had to come and go across their bridge: 30
they fixed it so on one side all were looking
   at the castle, and were walking to St. Peter's;
   on the other, they were moving toward the mount.   33
On both sides, up along the deadly rock,
   I saw horned devils with enormous whips
   lashing the backs of shades with cruel delight.   36
Ah, how they made them skip and lift their heels
   at the very first crack of the whip! Not one of them
   dared pause to take a second or a third!   39
As I walked on my eyes met with the glance
   of one down there; I murmured to myself:
   "I know this face from somewhere, I am sure."[8]   42
And so I stopped to study him more closely;
   my leader also stopped, and was so kind
   as to allow me to retrace my steps;   45
and that whipped soul thought he would hide from me
   by lowering his face—which did no good.
   I said, "O you, there, with your head bent low,   48
if the features of your shade do not deceive me,
   you are Venedico Caccianemico, I'm sure.
   How did you get yourself in such a pickle?"   51
"I'm not so keen on answering," he said,
   "but I feel I must; your plain talk is compelling,
   it makes me think of old times in the world.   54
I was the one who coaxed Ghisolabella
   to serve the lusty wishes of the Marquis,
   no matter how the sordid tale is told;   57
I'm not the only Bolognese who weeps here—

7. The year 1300 was a Jubilee Year, and Dante here describes the crowd control on the bridge that ran between the Castle of St. Angelo and St. Peter's.

8. This is Venedico Caccianemico, a man from Bologna who was reputed to have turned his sister Ghisolabella over to the Marquis of Este.

hardly! This place is packed with us; in fact,
   there are more of us here than there are living tongues,   60
between Savena and Reno, saying 'Sipa';[9]
   I call on your own memory as witness:
   remember we have avaricious hearts."   63
Just at that point a devil let him have
   the feel of his tailed whip and cried: "Move on,
   you pimp, you can't cash in on women here!"   66
I turned and hurried to rejoin my guide;
   we walked a few more steps and then we reached
   the rocky bridge that juts out from the bank.   69
We had no difficulty climbing up,
   and turning right, along the jagged ridge,
   we left those shades to their eternal circlings.   72
When we were where the ditch yawned wide below
   the ridge, to make a passage for the scourged,
   my guide said: "Stop and stand where you can see   75
these other misbegotten souls, whose faces
   you could not see before, for they were moving
   in the same direction we were, over there."   78
So from the ancient bridge we viewed the train
   that hurried toward us along the other tract—
   kept moving, like the first, by stinging whips.   81
And the good master, without my asking him,
   said, "Look at that imposing one approaching,
   who does not shed a single tear of pain: 84
what majesty he still maintains down there!
   He is Jason,[1] who by courage and sharp wits,
   fleeced the Colchians of their golden ram.   87
He later journeyed through the isle of Lemnos,
   whose bold and heartless females, earlier,
   had slaughtered every male upon the island;   90
there with his words of love, and loving looks,
   he succeeded in deceiving young Hypsipyle,
   who had in turn deceived the other women.   93
He left her there, with child, and all alone;
   such sin condemns him to such punishment,
   and Medea, too, gets her revenge on him.   96
With him go all deceivers of this type,
   and let this be enough to know concerning
   the first valley and the souls locked in its jaws."   99
We were already where the narrow ridge
   begins to cross the second bank, to make it
   an abutment for another ditch's arch.   102

9. *Sipa* is a word for "yes" in the dialect spoken in the territory between the rivers Savena and Reno, which comprise the boundaries of Bologna.

1. Jason led the Argonauts on the voyage to the island of Colchis, where they stole the golden fleece. He seduced and abandoned Hypsipyle, who had hidden her father when the other women of Lemnos were killing all the males. He also abandoned Medea, the daughter of the King of Colchis. For his story, see Ovid, *Metamorphoses* 7.

Now we could hear the shades in the next pouch
  whimpering, making snorting grunting sounds
  and sounds of blows, slapping with open palms.   105
From a steaming stench below, the banks were coated
  with a slimy mold that stuck to them like glue,
  disgusting to behold and worse to smell.   108
The bottom was so hollowed out of sight,
  we saw it only when we climbed the arch
  and looked down from the bridge's highest point: 111
there we were, and from where I stood I saw
  souls in the ditch plunged into excrement
  that might well have been flushed from our latrines;   114
my eyes were searching hard along the bottom,
  and I saw somebody's head so smirched with shit,
  you could not tell if he were priest or layman.   117
He shouted up: "Why do you feast your eyes
  on me more than these other dirty beasts?"
  And I replied: "Because, remembering well,   120
I've seen you with your hair dry once or twice.
  You are Alessio Interminei from Lucca,[2]
  that's why I stare at you more than the rest."   123
He beat his slimy forehead as he answered:
  "I am stuck down here by all those flatteries
  that rolled unceasing off my tongue up there."   126
He finished speaking, and my guide began:
  "Lean out a little more, look hard down there
  so you can get a good look at the face   129
of that repulsive and disheveled tramp
  scratching herself with shitty fingernails,
  spreading her legs while squatting up and down: 132
it is Thaïs the whore,[3] who gave this answer
  to her lover when he asked: 'Am I very worthy
  of your thanks?': 'Very? Nay, incredibly so!'   135
I think our eyes have had their fill of this."

CANTO XIX

From the bridge above the Third Bolgia can be seen a rocky landscape below filled with holes, from each of which protrude a sinner's legs and feet; flames dance across their soles. When the Pilgrim expresses curiosity about a particular pair of twitching legs, Virgil carries him down into the bolgia so that the Pilgrim himself may question the sinner. The legs belong to Pope Nicholas III, who astounds the Pilgrim by mistaking him for Boniface VIII, the next pope, who, as soon as he dies, will fall to the same hole, thereby pushing Nicholas farther down. He predicts that soon after Boniface, Pope Clement V will come, stuffing both himself and Boniface still deeper. To Nicholas's rather rhetoric-filled speech the Pilgrim responds with equally high language, inveighing against the Simonists, the evil churchmen who are

2. A prominent citizen of Lucca, in northern
Italy.

3. A character in a play by the Roman writer
Terence (186 or 185–159? B.C.E.).

punished here. Virgil is much pleased with his pupil and, lifting him in an affectionate embrace, he carries him to the top of the arch above the next bolgia.

O Simon Magus![4] O scum that followed him!
  Those things of God that rightly should be wed
  to holiness, you, rapacious creatures,
for the price of gold and silver, prostitute.   3
  Now, in your honor, I must sound my trumpet
  for here in the third pouch is where you dwell.   6
We had already climbed to see this tomb,
  and were standing high above it on the bridge,
  exactly at the mid-point of the ditch.   9
O Highest Wisdom, how you demonstrate
  your art in Heaven, on earth, and here in Hell!
  How justly does your power make awards![5]   12
I saw along the sides and on the bottom
  the livid-colored rock all full of holes;
  all were the same in size, and each was round.   15
To me they seemed no wider and no deeper
  than those inside my lovely San Giovanni,[6]
  in which the priest would stand or baptize from;   18
and one of these, not many years ago,
  I smashed for someone who was drowning in it:
  let this be mankind's picture of the truth!   21
From the mouth of every hole were sticking out
  a single sinner's feet, and then the legs
  up to the calf—the rest was stuffed inside.   24
The soles of every sinner's feet were flaming;
  their naked legs were twitching frenziedly—
  they would have broken any chain or rope.   27
Just as a flame will only move along
  an object's oily outer peel, so here
  the fire slid from heel to toe and back.   30
"Who is that one, Master, that angry wretch,
  who is writhing more than any of his comrades,"
  I asked, "the one licked by a redder flame?"[7]   33
And he to me, "If you want to be carried down
  along that lower bank to where he is,
  you can ask him who he is and why he's here."   36
And I, "My pleasure is what pleases you:

4. Because in the Bible Simon Magus tried to buy spiritual power from the apostles (Acts 8.9–24), the selling of any spiritual good for material gain was known in the Middle Ages as simony. The most common form of simony was the selling of church offices.
5. Dante is here applauding the artfulness of divine justice because the simoniacs, who cared most for their purses, are here stuffed into fiery purses hewn into the rock; see line 72 below.

6. The baptistery in Florence where Dante was baptized. The subsequent personal reference has never been satisfactorily explained.
7. Pope Nicholas III (pope 1277–80). He mistakenly believes that one of his successors, Boniface VIII, has come to be squeezed into the hole (line 53). Like all damned souls, Nicholas has foreknowledge, and because Boniface did not die until 1303 Nicholas is surprised at what he thinks is his appearance in 1300.

you are my lord, you know that from your will
  I would not swerve. You even know my thoughts."   39
When we reached the fourth bank, we began to turn
  and, keeping to the left, made our way down
  to the bottom of the holed and narrow ditch.   42
The good guide did not drop me from his side
  until he brought me to the broken rock
  of that one who was fretting with his shanks.   45
"Whatever you are, holding your upside down,
  O wretched soul, stuck like a stake in ground,
  make a sound or something," I said, "if you can."   48
I stood there like a priest who is confessing
  some vile assassin who, fixed in his ditch,
  has called him back again to put off dying.[8]   51
He cried: "Is that *you*, here, already, upright?
  Is that you here already upright, Boniface?
  By many years the book has lied to me!   54
Are you fed up so soon with all that wealth
  for which you did not fear to take by guile
  the Lovely Lady,[9] then tear her asunder?"   57
I stood there like a person just made fun of,
  dumbfounded by a question for an answer,
  not knowing how to answer the reply.   60
Then Virgil said: "Quick, hurry up and tell him:
  'I'm not the one, I'm not the one you think!'"
  And I answered just the way he told me to.   63
The spirit heard, and twisted both his feet,
  then, sighing with a grieving, tearful voice,
  he said: "Well then, what do you want of me?   66
If it concerns you so to learn my name
  that for this reason you came down the bank,
  know that I once was dressed in the great mantle.   69
But actually I was the she-bear's son,[1]
  so greedy to advance my cubs, that wealth
  I pocketed in life, and here, myself.   72
Beneath my head are pushed down all the others
  who came, sinning in simony, before me,
  squeezed tightly in the fissures of the rock.   75
I, in my turn, shall join the rest below
  as soon as *he* comes, the one I thought you were
  when, all too quick, I put my question to you.   78
But already my feet have baked a longer time
  (and I have been stuck upside-down like this)
  than he will stay here planted with feet aflame: 81
soon after him shall come one from the West,[2]

8. Hired murderers were occasionally executed by being placed head-down in a ditch and then buried alive.
9. The church.
1. The arms of Nicholas's family (the Orsini) included a "she-hear."
2. Clement V, who became pope in 1305 after agreeing with the French king to remove the papacy to Avignon in France. He is "from the West" because he was born in western France.

a lawless shepherd, one whose fouler deeds
    make him a fitting cover for us both.   84
He shall be another Jason,[3] like the one
    in Maccabees: just as his king was pliant,
    so France's king shall soften to this priest."   87
I do not know, perhaps I was too bold here,
    but I answered him in tune with his own words:
    "Well, tell me now: what was the sum of money   90
that holy Peter had to pay our Lord
    before He gave the keys into his keeping?
    Certainly He asked no more than 'Follow me.'[4]   93
Nor did Peter or the rest extort gold coins
    or silver from Matthias when he was picked
    to fill the place the evil one had lost.[5]   96
So stay stuck there, for you are rightly punished,
    and guard with care the money wrongly gained
    that made you stand courageous against Charles.[6] 99
And were it not for the reverence I have
    for those highest of all keys that you once held
    in the happy life—if this did not restrain me, 102
I would use even harsher words than these,
    for your avarice brings grief upon the world,
    crushing the good, exalting the depraved.   105
You shepherds it was the Evangelist[7] had in mind
    when the vision came to him of her who sits
    upon the waters playing whore with kings: 108
that one who with the seven heads was born
    and from her ten horns managed to draw strength
    so long as virtue was her bridegroom's joy.   111
You have built yourselves a God of gold and silver!
    How do you differ from the idolator,
    except he worships one, you worship hundreds? 114
O Constantine,[8] what evil did you sire,
    not by your conversion, but by the dower
    that the first wealthy Father got from you!"   117
And while I sang these very notes to him,

---

3. Jason became high priest of the Jews by bribing the king: see 2 Maccabees 4.7–9.
4. See Matthew 16.18–19: the keys are the church's power to bind (condemn) and to loose (absolve). For "follow me," see Matthew 4.18–19.
5. Matthias was chosen by lot to fill the place of Judas (Acts 1.23–26).
6. Nicholas was supposed to be involved in a plot against Charles of Anjou (1226–1285), ruler of Naples and Sicily.
7. John, author of Revelation, who in the Middle Ages was identified with the author of the Gospel according to John: for this passage, which was originally interpreted as referring to pagan Rome but which Dante applies to the corrupt church, see Revelation 17.1–18. The "seven heads" are the seven Sacraments; the "ten horns," the Ten Commandments; the "bridegroom," God.
8. Roman emperor (d. 337) who was the supposed author of a document—known as the Donation of Constantine—in which he granted temporal power and the right to acquire wealth to Pope Sylvester I, "the first wealthy Father" of this passage. The document was proved to be a forgery in the 15th century.

his big flat feet kicked fiercely out of anger,
   —or perhaps it was his conscience gnawing him.   120
I think my master liked what I was saying,
   for all the while he smiled and was intent
   on hearing the ring of truly spoken words.   123
Then he took hold of me with both his arms,
   and when he had me firm against his breast,
   he climbed back up the path he had come down.   126
He did not tire of the weight clasped tight to him,
   but brought me to the top of the bridge's arch,
   the one that joins the fourth bank to the fifth.   129
And here he gently set his burden down—
   gently, for the ridge, so steep and rugged,
   would have been hard even for goats to cross.   132
From there another valley opened to me.

CANTO XX

In the Fourth Bolgia they see a group of shades weeping as they walk slowly along the valley; they are the Soothsayers and their heads are twisted completely around so that their hair flows down their fronts and their tears flow down to their buttocks. Virgil points out many of them, including Amphiaraus, Tiresias, Aruns, and Manto. It was Manto who first inhabited the site of Virgil's home city of Mantua, and the poet gives a long description of the city's founding, after which he names more of the condemned soothsayers: Eurypylus, Michael Scot, Guido Bonatti, and Asdente.

Now I must turn strange torments into verse
   to form the matter of the twentieth canto
   of the first chant, the one about the damned.   3
Already I was where I could look down
   into the depths of the ditch: I saw its floor
   was wet with anguished tears shed by the sinners,   6
and I saw people in the valley's circle,
   silent, weeping, walking at a litany pace
   the way processions push along in our world.⁹   9
And when my gaze moved down below their faces,
   I saw all were incredibly distorted,
   the chin was not above the chest, the neck   12
was twisted—their faces looked down on their backs;
   they had to move ahead by moving backward,
   for they never saw what was ahead of them.   15
Perhaps there was a case of someone once
   in a palsy fit becoming so distorted,
   but none that I know of! I doubt there could be!   18
So may God grant you, Reader, benefit
   from reading of my poem, just ask yourself
   how I could keep my eyes dry when, close by,   21
I saw the image of our human form

9. A "litany" is a form of public prayer, often recited during stately "processions" in the church.

so twisted—the tears their eyes were shedding
    streamed down to wet their buttocks at the cleft.   24
Indeed I did weep, as I leaned my body
    against a jut of rugged rock. My guide:
    "So you are still like all the other fools?   27
In this place piety lives when pity is dead,
    for who could he more wicked than that man
    who tries to bend divine will to his own!¹   30
Lift your head up, lift it, see him for whom
    the earth split wide before the Thebans's eyes,
    while they all shouted, 'Where are you rushing off to,   33
Amphiaraus?² Why do you quit the war?'
    He kept on rushing downward through the gap
    until Minòs, who gets them all, got him.   36
You see how he has made his back his chest:
    because he wished to see too far ahead,
    he sees behind and walks a backward track.   39
Behold Tiresias,³ who changed his looks:
    from a man he turned himself into a woman,
    transforming all his body, part for part;   42
then later on he had to take the wand
    and strike once more those two snakes making love
    before he could get back his virile parts.   45
Backing up to this one's chest comes Aruns,⁴
    who, in the hills of Luni, worked by peasants
    of Carrara dwelling in the valley's plain,   48
lived in white marble cut into a cave,
    and from this site, where nothing blocked his view,
    he could observe the sea and stars with ease.   51
And that one, with her hair loose, flowing back
    to cover both her breasts you cannot see,
    and with her hairy parts in front behind her,   54
was Manto,⁵ who had searched through many lands
    before she came to dwell where I was born;
    now let me tell you something of her story.   57
When her father had departed from the living,
    and Bacchus' sacred city⁶ fell enslaved,
    she wandered through the world for many years.   60
High in fair Italy there spreads a lake,
    beneath the mountains bounding Germany
    beyond the Tyrol, known as Lake Benaco;⁷   63

1. This is a rebuke to Dante, who errs by showing sympathy for the damned.

2. A priest swallowed up by the Earth in a battle against the Thebans as described in Statius's *Thebaid* (see n. 2 to 14.48). For Minos, see 5.4.

3. A soothsayer of Thebes, he struck two coupling serpents with his rod and was transformed into a woman. Seven years later he repeated the action and was changed back into a man. See Ovid, *Metamorphoses* 3.

4. An Etruscan soothsayer from the city of Luni, in the area of Carrera where marble is quarried, is described by the Roman poet Lucan (d. 65 C.E.) in his *Pharsalia*.

5. Another Theban soothsayer described by Roman poets.

6. Thebes.

7. The present-day Lake Garda in northern Italy, located in terms of an island where the boundaries of the three dioceses of Trent, Brescia, and Verona meet.

by a thousand streams and more, I think, the Alps
   are bathed from Garda to the Val Camonica[8]
   with the waters flowing down into that lake;   66
at its center is a place where all three bishops
   of Trent and Brescia and Verona could,
   if they would ever visit there, say Mass;   69
Peschiera[9] sits, a handsome well-built fortress,
   to ward off Brescians and the Bergamese,
   along the lowest point of that lake's shore,   72
where all the water that Benaco's basin
   cannot hold must overflow to make a stream
   that winds its way through countrysides of green;   75
but when the water starts to flow, its name
   is not Benaco, but Mencio, all the way
   to Governol,[1] where it falls into the Po;   78
but before its course is run it strikes a lowland,
   on which it spreads and turns into a marsh
   that can become unbearable in summer.   81
Passing this place one day the savage virgin
   saw land that lay in the center of the mire,
   untilled and empty of inhabitants.   84
There, to escape all human intercourse,
   she stopped to practice magic with her servants;
   there she lived, and there she left her corpse.   87
Later on, the men who lived around there gathered
   on that very spot, for it was well protected
   by the bog that girded it on every side.   90
They built a city over her dead bones,
   and for her, the first to choose that place, they named it
   Mantua,[2] without recourse to sorcery.   93
Once, there were far more people living there,
   before the foolish Casalodi listened
   to the fraudulent advice of Pinamonte.[3]   96
And so, I warn you, should you ever hear
   my city's origin told otherwise,
   let no false tales adulterate the truth."[4]   99
And I replied: "Master, your explanations
   are truth for me, winning my faith entirely;
   any others would be just like burned-out coals.   102
But speak to me of these shades passing by,
   if you see anyone that is worth noting;
   for now my mind is set on only that."   105

---

8. Garda is a town by the lake and Val Camonica a valley below it.
9. Peschiera is a town on the south shore of the lake; the Brescians and the Bergamese are inhabitants of two towns to the northwest of Peschiera.
1. A town some 30 miles south of Peschiera. Presumably Virgil provides this detailed geography to illustrate that he is a native of this region.

2. Virgil's native city.
3. A reference to the internal intrigues of the rulers of Mantua in the 13th century.
4. Dante's Virgil contradicts the account of Mantua's founding in *Aeneid* 10.198–200. It is not clear why Dante has Virgil contradict his own poem unless he is trying to clear Virgil of any taint of himself being a magician (see n. 1 to 9.23).

He said: "That one, whose beard flows from his cheeks
  and settles on his back and makes it dark,
    was (when the war stripped Greece of all its males,   108
so that the few there were still rocked in cradles)
  an augur who, with Calchas,[5] called the moment
    to cut the first ship's cable free at Aulis: 111
he is Eurypylus. I sang his story
  this way, somewhere in my high tragedy:
    you should know where—you know it, every line.   114
That other one, whose thighs are scarcely fleshed,
  was Michael Scot,[6] who most assuredly
    knew every trick of magic fraudulence.   117
See there Guido Bonatti; see Asdente,[7]
  who wishes now he had been more devoted
    to making shoes—too late now for repentance.   120
And see those wretched hags[8] who traded in
  needle, spindle, shuttle, for fortune-telling,
    and cast their spells with image-dolls and potions.   123
Now come along. Cain[9] with his thorn-bush straddles
  the confines of both hemispheres already
    and dips into the waves below Seville;   126
and the moon last night already was at full;
  and you should well remember that at times
    when you were lost in the dark wood she helped you."   129
And we were moving all the time he spoke.

CANTO XXI

When the two reach the summit of the arch over the Fifth Bolgia, *they see in the ditch below the bubbling of boiling pitch. Virgil's sudden warning of danger frightens the Pilgrim even before he sees a black devil rushing toward them, with a sinner slung over his shoulder. From the bridge the devil flings the sinner into the pitch, where he is poked at and tormented by the family of Malebranche devils. Virgil, advising his ward to hide behind a rock, crosses the bridge to face the devils alone. They threaten him with their pitchforks, but when he announces to their leader, Malacoda, that Heaven has willed that he lead another through Hell, the devil's arrogance collapses. Virgil calls the Pilgrim back to him. Scarmiglione, who tries to take a poke at him, is rebuked by his leader, who tells the travelers that the sixth arch is broken here but farther on they will find another bridge to cross. He chooses a squad of his devils to escort them there: Alichino, Calcabrina, Cagnazzo, Barbariccia,*

---

5. Calchas and Eurypylus were prophets (or augurs) involved in the Trojan War; here Virgil says that they determined when the Greeks were to set out for the war from the island of Aulis, although *Aeneid* 2 gives a different account.
6. A famous scientist, philosopher, and astrologer from Scotland, Scot spent many years at the court of Frederick II (10.119) in Palermo and died in 1235.
7. A shoemaker famous as a soothsayer in 13th-century Italy. Guido Bonatti: an astrologer at the court of Guido da Montefeltro (see canto 27).
8. Common soothsayers and potion makers.
9. Popular belief held that God placed Cain in the moon after the murder of Abel; "Cain with his thorn-bush" means the moon with its spots, which is now setting at the western edge of the Northern Hemisphere. Overhead, in Jerusalem, it is the dawn of Holy Saturday.

Libicocco, Draghignazzo, Ciriatto, Graffiacane, Farfarello, and Rubicante. The Pilgrim's suspicion about their unsavory escorts is brushed aside by his guide, and the squad starts off, giving an obscene salute to their captain, who returns their salute with a fart.

From this bridge to the next we walked and talked
   of things my Comedy does not care to tell;
   and when we reached the summit of the arch,   3
we stopped to see the next fosse¹ of Malebolge
   and to hear more lamentation voiced in vain:
   I saw that it was very strangely dark!   6
In the vast and busy shipyard of the Venetians²
   there boils all winter long a tough, thick pitch
   that is used to caulk the ribs of unsound ships.   9
Since winter will not let them sail, they toil:
   some build new ships, others repair the old ones,
   plugging the planks come loose from many sailings;   12
some hammer at the bow, some at the stern,
   one carves the oars while others twine the ropes,
   one mends the jib, one patches up the mainsail;   15
here, too, but heated by God's art, not fire,
   a sticky tar was boiling in the ditch
   that smeared the banks with viscous residue.   18
I saw it there, but I saw nothing in it,
   except the rising of the boiling bubbles
   breathing in air to burst and sink again.   21
I stood intently gazing there below,
   my guide, shouting to me: "Watch out, watch out!"
   took hold of me and drew me to his side.   24
I turned my head like one who can't resist
   looking to see what makes him run away
   (his body's strength draining with sudden fear),   27
but, looking back, does not delay his flight;
   and I saw coming right behind our backs,
   rushing along the ridge, a devil, black!   30
His face, his look, how frightening it was!
   With outstretched wings he skimmed along the rock,
   and every single move he made was cruel;   33
on one of his high-hunched and pointed shoulders
   he had a sinner slung by both his thighs,
   held tightly clawed at the tendons of his heels.   36
He shouted from our bridge: "Hey, Malebranche,³
   here's one of Santa Zita's elders for you!
   You stick him under—I'll go back for more;   39
I've got that city stocked with the likes of him,

---

1. Ditch or pouch.
2. The huge shipyard at Venice was called the Arsenal.
3. "Malebranche" (Evil-Claws) is the generic name for the devils in this ditch, and each has a proper name as well (lines 76, 105, 118–23). The elders of Saint Zita in Lucca (a town near Florence) were ten citizens who ran the government.

they're all a bunch of grafters, save Bonturo![4]
   You can change a 'no' to 'yes' for cash in Lucca."   42
He flung him in, then from the flinty cliff
   sprang off. No hound unleashed to chase a thief
   could have taken off with greater speed than he.   45
That sinner plunged, then floated up stretched out,
   and the devils underneath the bridge all shouted:
   "You shouldn't imitate the Holy Face!   48
The swimming's different here from in the Serchio![5]
   We have our grappling-hooks along with us—
   don't show yourself above the pitch, or else!"   51
With a hundred prongs or more they pricked him, shrieking:
   "You've got to do your squirming under cover,
   try learning how to cheat beneath the surface."   54
They were like cooks who make their scullery boys
   poke down into the caldron with their forks
   to keep the meat from floating to the top.   57
My master said: "We'd best not let them know
   that you are here with me; crouch down behind
   some jutting rock so that they cannot see you;   60
whatever insults they may hurl at me,
   you must not fear, I know how things are run here;
   I have been caught in as bad a fix before."[6]   63
He crossed the bridge and walked on past the end;
   as soon as he set foot on the sixth bank
   he forced himself to look as bold as possible.   66
With all the sound and fury that breaks loose
   when dogs rush out at some poor begging tramp,
   making him stop and beg from where he stands,   69
the ones who hid beneath the bridge sprang out
   and blocked him with a flourish of their pitchforks,
   but he shouted: "All of you behave yourselves!   72
Before you start to jab me with your forks,
   let one of you step forth to hear me out,
   and then decide if you still care to grapple."   75
They all cried out: "Let Malacoda[7] go!"
   One stepped forward—the others stood their ground—
   and moving, said, "What good will this do him?"   78
"Do you think, Malacoda," said my master,
   "that you would see me here, come all this way,
   against all opposition, and still safe,   81
without propitious fate and God's permission?
   Now let us pass, for it is willed in Heaven
   that I lead another by this savage path."   84
With this the devil's arrogance collapsed,

4. A current official in Lucca, Bonturo Datí
was in fact known as the most corrupt of all;
the devil is being ironic.
5. The Serchio is a river near Lucca. The
Holy Face of Lucca was a venerated icon.

6. Virgil may be referring to his difficulties
with the devils in 8.82–130, when he and
Dante tried to enter the city of Dis.
7. Evil-Tail.

his pitchfork, too, dropped right down to his feet,
    as he announced to all: "Don't touch this man!"   87
"You, hiding over there," my guide called me,
    "behind the bridge's rocks, curled up and quiet,
    come back to me, you may return in safety."   90
At his words I rose and then I ran to him
    and all the devils made a movement forward;
    I feared they would not really keep their pact.   93
(I remember seeing soldiers under truce,
    as they left the castle of Caprona, frightened
    to be passing in the midst of such an enemy.)⁸   96
I drew up close to him, as close as possible,
    and did not take my eyes from all those faces
    that certainly had nothing good about them.   99
Their prongs were aimed at me, and one was saying:
    "Now do I let him have it in the rump?"
    They answered all for one: "Sure, stick him good!"   102
But the devil who had spoken with my guide
    was quick to spin around and scream an order:
    "At ease there, take it easy, Scarmiglione!"   105
Then he said to us: "You cannot travel straight
    across this string of bridges, for the sixth arch
    lies broken at the bottom of its ditch;⁹   108
if you have made your mind up to proceed,
    you must continue on along this ridge;
    not far, you'll find a bridge that crosses it.¹   111
Five hours more and it will be one thousand,
    two hundred sixty-six years and a day
    since the bridge-way here fell crumbling to the ground.²   114
I plan to send a squad of mine that way
    to see that no one airs himself down there;
    go along with them, they will not misbehave.   117
Front and center, Alichino, Calcabrina,"
    he shouted his commands, "you too, Cagnazzo;
    Barbariccia, you be captain of the squad.   120
Take Libicocco with you and Draghignazzo,
    toothy Ciriatto and Graffiacane,
    Farfarello and our crazy Rubicante.³   123
Now tour the ditch, inspect the boiling tar;
    these two shall have safe passage to the bridge
    connecting den to den without a break."   126

8. A battle outside Florence in 1289, in which
Dante may have taken part.
9. The bridge across the fifth ditch was
smashed, as Malacoda explains, by the earthquake that occurred at the time of the crucifixion.
1. As the travelers discover, this is a lie.
2. According to medieval tradition, Christ's
death on the cross occurred on Good Friday at
noon, in his thirty-third year, which would be

34 C.E.; the time at which Dante and Virgil are
in this fifth ditch of Malebolge is 7 A.M. of
Holy Saturday, 1300, which is 1266 years plus
one day, less five hours later.
3. These names—like Scarmiglione in line
105—imply raffish irreverence in general,
although some do have specific if ignoble
meanings: Cagnazzo = "Big Dog," Barbariccia =
"Curly Beard," Graffiacane = "Dog-Scratcher."

"O master, I don't like the looks of this,"
   I said, "let's go, just you and me, no escort,
   you know the way. I want no part of them!   129
If you're observant, as you usually are,
   why is it you don't see them grind their teeth
   and wink at one another?—we're in danger!"   132
And he to me: "I will not have you frightened;
   let them do all the grinding that they want,
   they do it for the boiling souls, not us."   135
Before they turned left-face along the bank
   each one gave their good captain a salute
   with farting tongue pressed tightly to his teeth,   138
and he blew back with his bugle of an ass-hole.

CANTO XXII

The note of grotesque comedy in the bolgia of the Malebranche *continues, with a comparison between Malacoda's salute to his soldiers and different kinds of military signals the Pilgrim has witnessed in his lifetime. He sees many Grafters squatting in the pitch, but as soon as the Malebranche draw near, they dive below the surface. One unidentified Navarrese, however, fails to escape and is hoisted up on Graffiacane's hooks; Rubicante and the other Malebranche start to tear into him, but Virgil, at his ward's request, manages to question him between torments. The sinner briefly tells his story, and then relates that he has left below in the pitch an Italian, Fra Gomita, a particularly adept grafter, who spends his time talking to Michel Zanche.*

   The Navarrese sinner promises to lure some of his colleagues to the surface for the devils' amusement, if the tormentors will hide themselves for a moment. Cagnazzo is skeptical but Alichino agrees, and no sooner do the Malebranche turn away than the crafty grafter dives below the pitch. Alichino flies after him, but too late; now Calcabrina rushes after Alichino and both struggle above the boiling pitch, and then fall in. Barbariccia directs the rescue operation as the two poets steal away.

I have seen troops of horsemen breaking camp,
   opening the attack, or passing in review,
   I have even seen them fleeing for their lives;   3
I have seen scouts ride, exploring your terrain,
   O Aretines,[4] and I have seen raiding-parties
   and the clash of tournaments, the run of jousts—   6
to the tune of trumpets, to the ring of clanging bells,
   to the roll of drums, to the flash of flares on ramparts,
   to the accompaniment of every known device;   9
but I never saw cavalry or infantry
   or ships that sail by landmarks or by stars
   signaled to set off by such strange bugling!   12
So, on our way we went with those ten fiends.
   What savage company! But—in church, with saints—
   with rowdy good-for-nothings, in the tavern![5]   15

4. The people of Arezzo, a city south of Florence.   **5.** A popular proverb.

My attention now was fixed upon the pitch
   to see the operations of this *bolgia*,
   and how the cooking souls got on down there.   18
Much like the dolphins that are said to surface
   with their backs arched to warn all men at sea
   to rig their ships for stormy seas ahead,[6]   21
so now and then a sinner's back would surface
   in order to alleviate his pain,
   then dive to hide as quick as lightning strikes.   24
Like squatting frogs along the ditch's edge,
   with just their muzzles sticking out of water,
   their legs and all the rest concealed below,   27
these sinners squatted all around their pond;
   but as soon as Barbariccia would approach
   they quickly ducked beneath the boiling pitch.   30
I saw (my heart still shudders at the thought)
   one lingering behind[7]—as it sometimes happens
   one frog remains while all the rest dive down—   33
and Graffiacane, standing in front of him,
   hooked and twirled him by his pitchy hair
   and hoisted him. He looked just like an otter!   36
By then I knew the names of all the fiends:
   I had listened carefully when they were chosen,
   each of them stepping forth to match his name.   39
"Hey, Rubicante, dig your claws down deep
   into his back and peel the skin off him,"
   this fiendish chorus egged him on with screams.   42
I said: "Master, will you, if you can, find out
   the name of that poor wretch who has just fallen
   into the cruel hands of his adversaries?"   45
My guide walked right up to the sinner's side
   and asked where he was from, and he replied:
   "I was born and bred in the kingdom of Navarre;   48
my mother gave me to a lord to serve,
   for she had me by some dishonest spendthrift
   who ran through all he owned and killed himself.   51
Then I became a servant in the household
   of good King Thibault. There I learned my graft,
   and now I pay my bill by boiling here."   54
Ciriatto, who had two tusks sticking out
   on both sides of his mouth, just like a boar's,
   let him feel how just one tusk could rip him open.   57
The mouse had fallen prey to evil cats,
   but Barbariccia locked him with his arms,
   shouting: "Get back while I've got hold of him!"   60
Then toward my guide he turned his face and said:

6. A common medieval belief.
7. The identity of this sinner is not known, but he was employed in the household of Thibaut II of Champagne, a man renowned for his honesty who was also king of Navarre, the area of Spain that is now Basque country.

"If you want more from him, keep questioning
   before he's torn to pieces by the others."   63
My guide went on: "Then tell me, do you know
   of some Italian stuck among these sinners
   beneath the pitch?" And he, "A second ago   66
I was with one who lived around those parts.
   Oh, I wish I were undercover with him now!
   I wouldn't have these hooks or claws to fear."   69
Libicocco cried: "We've waited long enough,"
   then with his fork he hooked the sinner's arm
   and, tearing at it, he pulled out a piece.   72
Draghignazzo, too, was anxious for some fun;
   he tried the wretch's leg, but their captain quickly
   spun around and gave them all a dirty look.   75
As soon as they calmed down a bit, my master
   began again to interrogate the wretch,
   who still was contemplating his new wound: 78
"Who was it, you were saying, that unluckily
   you left behind you when you came ashore?"
   "Gomita," he said, "the friar from Gallura,[8]   81
receptacle for every kind of fraud:
   when his lord's enemies were in his hands,
   the treatment they received delighted them: 84
he took their cash, and as he says, hushed up
   the case and let them off; none of his acts
   was petty grafting, all were of sovereign order.   87
He spends his time with don Michele Zanche
   of Logodoro, talking on and on
   about Sardinia—their tongues no worse for wear![9]   90
Oh, but look how that one grins and grinds his teeth;
   I could tell you so much more, but I am afraid
   he is going to grate my scabby hide for me."   93
But their master-sergeant turned to Farfarello,
   whose wild eyes warned he was about to strike,
   shouting, "Get away, you filthy bird of prey."   96
"If you would like to see Tuscans or Lombards,"
   the frightened shade took up where he left off,
   "and have a talk with them, I'll bring some here;   99
but the Malebranche must back up a bit,
   or else those shades won't risk a surfacing;
   I, by myself, will bring you up a catch   102
of seven, without moving from this spot,
   just by whistling—that's our signal to the rest
   when one peers out and sees the coast is clear."   105
Cagnazzo raised his snout at such a story,
   then shook his head and said: "Listen to the trick
   he's cooked up to get off the hook by jumping!"   108

8. A friar who was chancellor of the Gallura district on the island of Sardinia. He was hanged by his master, a lord of Pisa, when it was discovered that he had sold prisoners their freedom.
9. Little is known of this sinner, except that he too was a Sardinian.

And he, full of the tricks his trade had taught him,
   said: "Tricky, I surely am, especially
   when it comes to getting friends into worse trouble."   111
But Alichin could not resist the challenge,
   and in spite of what the others thought, cried out:
   "If you jump, I won't come galloping for you,   114
I've got my wings to beat you to the pitch.
   We'll clear this ledge and wait behind that slope.
   Let's see if one of you can outmatch us!"   117
Now listen, Reader, here's a game that's strange:
   they all turned toward the slope, and first to turn
   was the fiend who from the start opposed the game.   120
The Navarrese had perfect sense of timing:
   feet planted on the ground, in a flash he jumped,
   the devil's plan was foiled, and he was free.   123
The squad was stung with shame but most of all
   the one who brought this blunder to perfection;[1]
   he swooped down, howling, "Now I've got you caught!"   126
Little good it did, for wings could not outstrip
   the flight of terror: down the sinner dived
   and up the fiend was forced to strain his chest   129
like a falcon swooping down on a wild duck:
   the duck dives quickly out of sight, the falcon
   must fly back up dejected and defeated.   132
In the meantime, Calcabrina, furious,
   also took off, hoping the shade would make it,
   so he could pick a fight with his companion.   135
And when he saw the grafter hit the pitch,
   he turned his claws to grapple with his brother,
   and they tangled in mid-air above the ditch;   138
but the other was a full-fledged hawk as well
   and used his claws on him, and both of them
   went plunging straight into the boiling pond.   141
The heat was quick to make them separate,
   but there seemed no way of getting out of there;
   their wings were clogged and could not lift them up.   144
Barbariccia, no less peeved than all his men,
   sent four fiends flying to the other shore
   with their equipment at top speed; instantly,   147
some here, some there, they took the posts assigned them.
   They stretched their hooks to reach the pitch-dipped pair,
   who were by now deep-fried within their crusts.   150
And there we left them, all messed up that way.

CANTO XXIII

The antics of Ciampolo, the Navarrese, and the Malebranche *bring to the Pilgrim's mind the fable of the frog, the mouse, and the hawk—and that in turn reminds him of the immediate danger he and Virgil are in from the angry* Malebranche. *Virgil*

---

1. Alichin.

senses the danger too, and grabbing his ward as a mother would her child, he dashes
to the edge of the bank and slides down the rocky slope into the Sixth Bolgia—*not a*
moment too soon, for at the top of the slope they see the angry Malebranche. *When*
the Pilgrim looks around him he sees weeping shades slowly marching in single file,
each one covered from head to foot with a golden cloak lined with lead, which
weights them down. These are the Hypocrites. Two in this group identify themselves
as Catalano de' Malavolti and Loderingo degli Andalò, two Jovial Friars. The Pil-
grim is about to address them when he sees the shade of Caiaphas (the evil coun-
selor who advised Pontius Pilate to crucify Christ), crucified and transfixed by three
stakes to the ground. Virgil discovers from the two friars that in order to leave this
bolgia they must climb up a rockslide; he also learns that this is the only bolgia *over*
which the bridge is broken. Virgil is angry with himself for having believed Mala-
coda's lie about the bridge over the Sixth Bolgia (*Canto XXI, iii*).

In silence, all alone, without an escort,
   we moved along, one behind the other,
   like minor friars[2] bent upon a journey.   3
I was thinking over one of Aesop's fables[3]
   that this recent skirmish had brought back to mind,
   where he tells the story of the frog and mouse;   6
for "yon" and "there" could not be more alike
   than the fable and the fact, if one compares
   the start and finish of both incidents.   9
As from one thought another often rises,
   so this thought gave quick birth to still another,
   and then the fear I first had felt was doubled.   12
I was thinking: "Since these fiends, on our account,
   were tricked and mortified by mockery,
   they certainly will be more than resentful;   15
with rage now added to their evil instincts,
   they will hunt us down with all the savagery
   of dogs about to pounce upon the hare."   18
I felt my body's skin begin to tighten—
   I was so frightened!—and I kept looking back:
   "O master," I said, "if you do not hide   21
both of us, and very quick, I am afraid
   of the Malebranche—right now they're on our trail—
   I feel they're there, I think I hear them now."   24
And he replied: "Even if I were a mirror
   I could not reflect your outward image faster
   than your inner thoughts transmit themselves to me.   27
In fact, just now they joined themselves with mine,
   and since they were alike in birth and form,
   I decided to unite them toward one goal: 30
if the right-hand bank should slope in such a way
   as to allow us to descend to the next *bolgia*,
   we could escape that chase we have imagined."   33

2. Franciscan friars, who were known as "minor"
or "lesser" friars because Francis of Assisi, the
founder of the order, insisted upon humility.
3. The fable that Dante seems to be referring

to tells how a frog offers to ferry a mouse
across a river, then halfway over tries to drown
him, only to be seized by a kite (a hawklike
bird) while the mouse escapes.

He had hardly finished telling me his plan
   when I saw them coming with their wings wide open
   not too far off, and now they meant to get us!   36
My guide instinctively caught hold of me,
   like a mother waking to some warning sound,
   who sees the rising flames are getting close   39
and grabs her son and runs—she does not wait
   the short time it would take to put on something;
   she cares not for herself, only for him.   42
And over the edge, then down the stony bank
   he slid, on his back, along the sloping rock
   that walls the higher side of the next *bolgia*.   45
Water that turns a mill wheel never ran
   the narrow sluice at greater speed, not even
   at the point before it hits the paddle-blades,[4]   48
than down that sloping border my guide slid,
   bearing me with him, clasping me to his chest
   as though I were his child, not his companion.   51
His feet had hardly touched rock bottom, when
   there they were, the ten of them, above us
   on the height; but now there was no need to fear: 54
High Providence that willed for them to be
   the ministers in charge of the fifth ditch
   also willed them powerless to leave their realm.   57
And now, down there, we found a painted people,
   slow-motioned; step by step, they walked their round
   in tears, and seeming wasted by fatigue.   60
All were wearing cloaks with hoods pulled low
   covering the eyes (the style was much the same
   as those the Benedictines wear at Cluny),[5]   63
dazzling, gilded cloaks outside, but inside
   they were lined with lead, so heavy that the capes
   King Frederick used, compared to these, were straw.[6]   66
O cloak of everlasting weariness!
   We turned again, as usual, to the left
   and moved with them, those souls lost in their mourning;   69
but with their weight that tired-out race of shades
   paced on so slowly that we found ourselves
   in new company with every step we took;   72
and so I asked my guide: "Please look around
   and see, as we keep walking, if you find
   someone whose name or deeds are known to me."   75
And one who overheard me speaking Tuscan
   cried out somewhere behind us: "Not so fast,
   you there, rushing ahead through this heavy air,   78

---

4. A mill built on the land while the water of
the river turns its wheel.
5. One of the largest monasteries in Europe,
located in Burgundy in France; the Benedictines are monks who follow the Rule of
St. Benedict (d. 587), one of the founders of
monasticism.
6. Frederick II (see n. 8 to 10.119) was reported
to have punished traitors by encasing them in
lead and throwing them into heated cauldrons.

perhaps from me you can obtain an answer."
 At this my guide turned toward me saying, "Stop,
 and wait for him, then match your pace with his."   81
I paused and saw two shades with straining faces
 revealing their mind's haste to join my side,
 but the weight they bore and the crowded road delayed them.   84
When they arrived, they looked at me sideways
 and for some time, without exchanging words;
 then they turned to one another and were saying: 87
"He seems alive, the way his throat is moving,
 and if both are dead, what privilege allows them
 to walk uncovered by the heavy cloak?"   90
Then they spoke to me: "O Tuscan who has come
 to visit the college of the sullen hypocrites,
 do not disdain to tell us who you are."   93
I answered them: "I was born and I grew up
 in the great city on the lovely Arno's shore,
 and I have the body I have always had.   96
But who are you, distilling tears of grief,
 so many I see running down your cheeks?
 And what kind of pain is this that it can glitter?"   99
One of them answered: "The orange-gilded cloaks
 are thick with lead so heavy that it makes us,
 who are the scales it hangs on, creak as we walk.   102
Jovial Friars we were, both from Bologna.
 My name was Catalano, his, Loderingo,
 and both of us were chosen by your city,   105
that usually would choose one man alone,
 to keep the peace. Evidence of what we were
 may still be seen around Gardingo's parts."[7]   108
I began: "O Friars, all your wretchedness . . ."
 but said no more; I couldn't, for I saw
 one crucified with three stakes on the ground.[8]   111
And when he saw me all his body writhed,
 and through his beard he heaved out sighs of pain;
 then Friar Catalano, who watched the scene,   114
remarked: "That impaled figure you see there
 advised the Pharisees it was expedient
 to sacrifice one man for all the people.   117
Naked he lies stretched out across the road,
 as you can see, and he must feel the load
 of every weight that steps on him to cross.   120
His father-in-law[9] and the other council members,

7. Gardingo: a district in Florence, was destroyed by a civil war incited by their meddling in Florentine affairs. Jovial Friars: a military and religious order in Bologna called the Knights of the Blessed Virgin Mary, or popularly the Jovial Friars because of the laxity of its rules. The members were meant to fight only in order to protect the weak and enforce peace. Catalano and Loderingo were two citizens of Bologna who were involved in founding the Jovial Friars in 1261.
8. This is Caiaphas, the high priest under Pontius Pilate who advised that Christ be crucified (John 11.45–52).
9. Annas: see John 18.13.

who were the seed of evil for all Jews,
   are racked the same way all along this ditch."   123
And I saw Virgil staring down amazed
   at this body stretching out in crucifixion,
   so vilely punished in the eternal exile.   126
Then he looked up and asked one of the friars:
   "Could you please tell us, if your rule permits:
   is there a passage-way on the right, somewhere,   129
by which the two of us may leave this place
   without summoning one of those black angels
   to come down here and raise us from this pit?"   132
He answered: "Closer than you might expect,
   a ridge jutting out from the base of the great circle
   extends, and bridges every hideous ditch   135
except this one, whose arch is totally smashed
   and crosses nowhere; but you can climb up
   its massive ruins that slope against this bank."   138
My guide stood there awhile, his head bent low,
   then said: "He told a lie about this business,
   that one who hooks the sinners over there."[1]   141
And the friar: "Once, in Bologna, I heard discussed
   the devil's many vices; one of them is
   that he tells lies and is father of all lies."[2]   144
In haste, taking great strides, my guide walked off,
   his face revealing traces of his anger.
   I turned and left the heavy-weighted souls   147
to make my way behind those cherished footprints.

CANTO XXIV

*After an elaborate simile describing Virgil's anger and the return of his composure,
the two begin the difficult, steep ascent up the rocks of the fallen bridge. The Pilgrim can barely make it to the top even with Virgil's help, and after the climb he sits
down to catch his breath; but his guide urges him on, and they make their way back
to the bridge over the Seventh Bolgia. From the bridge confused sounds can be
heard rising from the darkness below. Virgil agrees to take his pupil down to the
edge of the eighth encircling bank, and once they are there, the scene reveals a terrible confusion of serpents, and Thieves madly running.*

*Suddenly a snake darts out and strikes a sinner's neck, whereupon he flares up,
turning into a heap of crumbling ashes; then the ashes gather together into the
shape of a man. The metamorphosed sinner reveals himself to be Vanni Fucci, a
Pistoiese condemned for stealing the treasure of the sacristy of the church of San
Zeno at Pistoia. He makes a prophecy about the coming strife in Florence.*

In the season of the newborn year, when the sun
   renews its rays beneath Aquarius[3]
   and nights begin to last as long as days,   3

1. See 21.111.   3. January 21–February 21.
2. For this description of the devil, see John
8.44.

at the time the hoarfrost paints upon the ground
    the outward semblance of his snow-white sister[4]
    (but the color from his brush soon fades away),   6
the peasant wakes, gets up, goes out and sees
    the fields all white. No fodder for his sheep!
    He smites his thighs in anger and goes back   9
into his shack and, pacing up and down,
    complains, poor wretch, not knowing what to do;
    once more he goes outdoors, and hope fills him   12
again when he sees the world has changed its face
    in so little time, and he picks up his crook
    and out to pasture drives his sheep to graze—   15
just so I felt myself lose heart to see
    my master's face wearing a troubled look,
    and as quickly came the salve to heal my sore: 18
for when we reached the shattered heap of bridge,
    my leader turned to me with that sweet look
    of warmth I first saw at the mountain's foot.   21
He opened up his arms (but not before
    he had carefully studied how the ruins lay
    and found some sort of plan) to pick me up.   24
Like one who works and thinks things out ahead,
    always ready for the next move he will make,
    so, while he raised me up toward one great rock,   27
he had already singled out another,
    saying, "Now get a grip on that rock there,
    but test it first to see it holds your weight."   30
It was no road for one who wore a cloak!
    Even though I had his help and he weighed nothing,
    we could hardly lift ourselves from crag to crag.   33
And had it not been that the bank we climbed
    was lower than the one we had slid down[5]—
    I cannot speak for him—but I for one   36
surely would have quit. But since the Evil Pits
    slope toward the yawning well that is the lowest,
    each valley is laid out in such a way   39
that one bank rises higher than the next.
    We somehow finally reached the point above
    where the last of all that rock was shaken loose.   42
My lungs were so pumped out of breath by the time
    I reached the top, I could not go on farther,
    and instantly I sat down where I was.   45
"Come on, shake off the covers of this sloth,"
    the master said, "for sitting softly cushioned,
    or tucked in bed, is no way to win fame;   48
and without it man must waste his life away,
    leaving such traces of what he was on earth
    as smoke in wind and foam upon the water.   51

---

4. I.e., snow.
5. Because the whole of the eighth circle is tilted downward, the downside wall of each ditch is lower than that on the upside.

Stand up! Dominate this weariness of yours
 with the strength of soul that wins in every battle
 if it does not sink beneath the body's weight.   54
Much steeper stairs than these we'll have to climb;[6]
 we have not seen enough of sinners yet!
 If you understand me, act, learn from my words." 57
At this I stood up straight and made it seem
 I had more breath than I began to breathe,
 and said: "Move on, for I am strong and ready." 60
We climbed and made our way along the bridge,
 which was jagged, tight and difficult to cross,
 and steep—far more than any we had climbed. 63
Not to seem faint, I spoke while I was climbing;
 then came a voice from the depths of the next chasm,
 a voice unable to articulate.   66
I don't know what it said, even though I stood
 at the very top of the arch that crosses there;
 to me it seemed whoever spoke, spoke running. 69
I was bending over, but no living eyes
 could penetrate the bottom of that darkness;
 therefore I said: "Master, why not go down 72
this bridge onto the next encircling bank,[7]
 for I hear sounds I cannot understand,
 and I look down but cannot see a thing." 75
"No other answer," he replied, "I give you
 than doing what you ask, for a fit request
 is answered best in silence and in deed." 78
From the bridge's height we came down to the point
 where it ends and joins the edge of the eighth bank,
 and then the *bolgia* opened up to me:[8] 81
down there I saw a terrible confusion
 of serpents, all of such a monstrous kind
 the thought of them still makes my blood run cold.[9] 84
Let all the sands of Libya boast no longer,
 for though she breeds chelydri and jaculi,
 phareans, cenchres, and head-tailed amphisbenes, 87
she never bred so great a plague of venom,
 not even if combined with Ethiopia
 or all the sands that lie by the Red Sea. 90
Within this cruel and bitterest abundance
 people ran terrified and naked, hopeless
 of finding hiding-holes or heliotrope.[1] 93
Their hands were tied behind their backs with serpents,
 which pushed their tails and heads around the loins
 and coiled themselves in knots around the front. 96

6. Both the climb from the pit of Hell back to Earth and the climb up Mount Purgatory.
7. Of the seventh ditch.
8. They cross the bridge over the seventh ditch and then climb down the wall between the seventh and eighth ditches.
9. The following list of exotic serpents derives from a description by the Roman poet Lucan (39–65 C.E.) of the plagues of Libya.
1. A fictitious stone that was supposed to make the bearer invisible.

And then—at a sinner running by our bank
    a snake shot out and, striking, hit his mark:
    right where the neck attaches to the shoulder.   99
No *o* or *i* was ever quicker put
    by pen to paper than he flared up and burned,
    and turned into a heap of crumbled ash;   102
and then, these ashes scattered on the ground
    began to come together on their own
    and quickly take the form they had before: 105
precisely so, philosophers declare,
    the phoenix dies to be reborn again
    as she approaches her five-hundredth year;[2]   108
alive, she does not feed on herbs or grain,
    but on teardrops of frankincense and balm,
    and wraps herself to die in nard and myrrh.   111
As a man in a fit will fall, not knowing why
    (perhaps some hidden demon pulls him down,
    or some oppilation chokes his vital spirits),   114
then, struggling to his feet, will look around,
    confused and overwhelmed by the great anguish
    he has suffered, moaning as he stares about—   117
so did this sinner when he finally rose.
    Oh, how harsh the power of the Lord can be,
    raining in its vengeance blows like these!   120
My guide asked him to tell us who he was,
    and he replied: "It's not too long ago
    I rained from Tuscany to this fierce gullet.   123
I loved the bestial life more than the human,
    like the bastard that I was; I'm Vanni Fucci,
    the beast! Pistoia was my fitting den."[3]   126
I told my guide: "Tell him not to run away;
    ask him what sin has driven him down here,
    for I knew him as a man of bloody rage."   129
The sinner heard and did not try to feign;
    directing straight at me his mind and face,
    he reddened with a look of ugly shame,   132
and said: "That you have caught me by surprise
    here in this wretched *bolgia*, makes me grieve
    more than the day I lost my other life.   135
Now I am forced to answer what you ask:
    I am stuck so far down here because of theft:
    I stole the treasure of the sacristy—   138
a crime falsely attributed to another.

2. The "phoenix" is a mythical bird that is supposed to burn to death in its own nest every five
hundred years, after which either itself or its
son is reborn from the ashes; for these details,
including its diet of exotic herbs and its funeral
preparations (lines 110–11), see Ovid, *Metamorphoses* 15. In medieval mythography the
phoenix was often taken as a symbol of Christ.
3. The illegitimate son of a noble father of
Pistoia, a town just north of Florence: known
as "the beast" because of the extravagance of
his misbehavior. He reputedly robbed a church
in Pistoia, a crime for which a similarly named
man was wrongly hanged.

I don't want you to rejoice at having seen me,
  if ever you escape from these dark pits,   141
so open your ears and hear my prophecy:[4]
  Pistoia first shall be stripped of all its Blacks,
  and Florence then shall change its men and laws;   144
from Valdimagra Mars shall thrust a bolt
  of lightning wrapped in thick, foreboding clouds,
  then bolt and clouds will battle bitterly   147
in a violent storm above Piceno's fields,
  where rapidly the bolt will burst the cloud,
  and no White will escape without his wounds.   150
And I have told you this so you will suffer!"

CANTO XXV

*The wrathful Vanni Fucci directs an obscene gesture to God, whereupon he is
attacked by several snakes, which coil about him, tying him so tight that he cannot
move a muscle. As soon as he flees, the centaur Cacus gallops by with a fire-breathing
dragon on his back, and following close behind are three shades, concerned because
they cannot find Cianfa—who soon appears as a snake and attacks Agnèl; the two
merge into one hideous monster, which then steals off. Next, Guercio, in the form of
a snake, strikes Buoso, and the two exchange shapes. Only Puccio Sciancato is left
unchanged.*

When he had finished saying this, the thief
  shaped his fists into figs[5] and raised them high
  and cried: "Here, God, I've shaped them just for you!"   3
From then on all those snakes became my friends,
  for one of them at once coiled round his neck
  as if to say, "That's all you're going to say,"   6
while another twisted round his arms in front;
  it tied itself into so tight a knot,
  between the two he could not move a muscle.   9
Pistoia, ah, Pistoia! why not resolve
  to burn yourself to ashes, ending all,
  since you have done more evil than your founders?[6]   12
Throughout the circles of this dark inferno
  I saw no shade so haughty toward his God,
  not even he who fell from Thebes' high walls.[7]   15
Without another word he fled, and then
  I saw a raging centaur gallop up
  roaring: "Where is he, where is that untamed beast?"   18
I think that all Maremma[8] does not have

4. Vanni Fucci now prophesies, in the enigmatic terms appropriate to the genre, that the party of the Blacks (of which he was a member) will first be expelled from Pistoia by the Whites, but that then the Whites of Florence (Dante's party) will be defeated. The prophecy refers to events that occurred in either 1302 or 1306.
5. An obscene gesture made by thrusting a protruding thumb between the first and second fingers of a closed fist.
6. The most important founder of Pistoia was Catiline, who was a traitor against the Roman Republic in the 1st century B.C.E.
7. Capaneus (see 14.46–75).
8. A region infested with snakes; see 13.8.

as many snakes as he had on his back,
  right up to where his human form begins.   21
Upon his shoulders, just behind the nape,
  a dragon with its wings spread wide was crouching
  and spitting fire at whoever came its way.   24
My master said to me: "That one is Cacus,[9]
  who more than once in the grotto far beneath
  Mount Aventine spilled blood to fill a lake.   27
He does not go the same road as his brothers
  because of the cunning way he committed theft
  when he stole his neighbor's famous cattle-herd;   30
and then his evil deeds came to an end
  beneath the club of Hercules, who struck
  a hundred blows, and he, perhaps, felt ten."   33
While he was speaking Cacus galloped off;
  at the same time three shades appeared below us;
  my guide and I would not have seen them there   36
if they had not cried out: "Who are you two?"
  At this we cut our conversation short
  to give our full attention to these three.   39
I didn't know who they were, but then it happened,
  as often it will happen just by chance,
  that one of them was forced to name another: 42
"Where did Cianfa[1] go off to?" he asked. And then,
  to keep my guide from saying anything,
  I put my finger tight against my lips.   45
Now if, my reader, you should hesitate
  to believe what I shall say, there's little wonder,
  for I, the witness, scarcely can believe it.   48
While I was watching them, all of a sudden
  a serpent—and it had six feet—shot up
  and hooked one of these wretches with all six.   51
With the middle feet it hugged the sinner's stomach
  and, with the front ones, grabbed him by the arms,
  and bit him first through one cheek, then the other;   54
the serpent spread its hind feet round both thighs,
  then stuck its tail between the sinner's legs,
  and up against his back the tail slid stiff.   57
No ivy ever grew to any tree
  so tight entwined, as the way that hideous beast
  had woven in and out its limbs with his;   60
and then both started melting like hot wax
  and, fusing, they began to mix their colors
  (so neither one seemed what he was before),   63
just as a brownish tint, ahead of flame,
  creeps up a burning page that is not black
  completely, even though the white is dying.   66

9. A monster who lived in a cave on Mount Aventine in Rome and was killed by Hercules, from whom he stole cattle; see *Aeneid* 8.
1. A noble Florentine, reputedly a thief.

The other two who watched began to shout:
  "O Agnèl![2] If you could see how you are changing!
  You're not yourself, and you're not both of you!"   69
The two heads had already fused to one
  and features from each flowed and blended into
  one face where two were lost in one another;   72
two arms of each were four blurred strips of flesh;
  and thighs with legs, then stomach and the chest
  sprouted limbs that human eyes have never seen.   75
Each former likeness now was blotted out:
  both, and neither one it seemed—this picture
  of deformity. And then it sneaked off slowly.   78
Just as a lizard darting from hedge to hedge,
  under the stinging lash of the dog-days' heat,
  zips across the road, like a flash of lightning,   81
so, rushing toward the two remaining thieves,
  aiming at their guts, a little serpent,
  fiery with rage and black as pepper-corn,   84
shot up and sank its teeth in one of them,
  right where the embryo receives its food,
  then back it fell and lay stretched out before him.   87
The wounded thief stared speechless at the beast,
  and standing motionless began to yawn
  as though he needed sleep, or had a fever.   90
The snake and he were staring at each other;
  one from his wound, the other from its mouth
  fumed violently, and smoke with smoke was mingling.   93
Let Lucan from this moment on be silent,
  who tells of poor Nasidius and Sabellus,[3]
  and wait to hear what I still have in store;   96
and Ovid, too, with his Cadmus and Arethusa[4]—
  though he metamorphosed one into a snake,
  the other to a fountain, I feel no envy,   99
for never did he interchange two beings
  face to face so that both forms were ready
  to exchange their substance, each one for the other's,   102
an interchange of perfect symmetry:
  the serpent split its tail into a fork,
  and the wounded sinner drew his feet together;   105
the legs, with both the thighs, closed in to join
  and in a short time fused, so that the juncture
  didn't show signs of ever having been there,   108
the while the cloven tail assumed the features
  that the other one was losing, and its skin
  was growing soft, the other's getting scaly;   111
I saw his arms retreating to the armpits,
  and the reptile's two front feet, that had been short,
  began to stretch the length the man's had shortened;   114
the beast's hind feet then twisted round each other

---

2. Another noble Florentine thief.   *Pharsalia.*
3. Two soldiers bitten by serpents in Lucan's   4. See *Metamorphoses* 4.

and turned into the member man conceals,
  while from the wretch's member grew two legs.   117
The smoke from each was swirling round the other,
  exchanging colors, bringing out the hair
  where there was none, and stripping off the other's.   120
The one rose up, the other sank, but neither
  dissolved the bond between their evil stares,
  fixed eye to eye, exchanging face for face;   123
the standing creature's face began receding
  toward the temples; from the excess stuff pulled back,
  the ears were growing out of flattened cheeks,   126
while from the excess flesh that did not flee
  the front, a nose was fashioned for the face,
  and lips puffed out to just the normal size.   129
The prostrate creature strains his face out long
  and makes his ears withdraw into his head,
  the way a snail pulls in its horns. The tongue,   132
that once had been one piece and capable
  of forming words, divides into a fork,
  while the other's fork heals up. The smoke subsides.   135
The soul that had been changed into a beast
  went hissing off along the valley's floor,
  the other close behind him, spitting words.   138
Then he turned his new-formed back on him and said
  to the shade left standing there: "Let Buoso run
  the valley on all fours, the way I did."[5]   141
Thus I saw the cargo of the seventh hold
  exchange and interchange; and let the strangeness
  of it all excuse me, if my pen has failed.   144
And though this spectacle confused my eyes
  and stunned my mind, the two thieves could not flee
  so secretly I did not recognize   147
that one was certainly Puccio Sciancato[6]
  (and he alone, of that company of three
  that first appeared, did not change to something else),   150
the other, he who made you mourn, Gaville.[7]

CANTO XXVI

*From the ridge high above the Eighth Bolgia can be perceived a myriad of flames
flickering far below, and Virgil explains that within each flame is the suffering soul
of a Deceiver. One flame, divided at the top, catches the Pilgrim's eye and he is told
that within it are jointly punished Ulysses and Diomed. Virgil questions the pair for
the benefit of the Pilgrim. Ulysses responds with the famous narrative of his last voyage, during which he passed the Pillars of Hercules and sailed the forbidden sea
until he saw a mountain shape, from which came suddenly a whirlwind that spun
his ship around three times and sank it.*

5. The identity of this Buoso is uncertain.
6. This third thief is also a noble Florentine.
7. The "little serpent" of line 83 above is now
identified as Francesco de Cavalcanti, a
Florentine nobleman who lived in Gaville: a
town south of Florence. When he was murdered by his townsmen, his kinsmen took brutal revenge.

Be joyful, Florence, since you are so great
  that your outstretched wings beat over land and sea,
  and your name is spread throughout the realm of Hell!   3
I was ashamed to find among the thieves
  five of your most eminent citizens,[8]
  a fact which does you very little honor.   6
But if early morning dreams have any truth,
  you will have the fate, in not too long a time,
  that Prato and the others crave for you.[9]   9
And were this the day, it would not be too soon!
  Would it had come to pass, since pass it must!
  The longer the delay, the more my grief.   12
We started climbing up the stairs of boulders
  that had brought us to the place from where we watched;
  my guide went first and pulled me up behind him.   15
We went along our solitary way
  among the rocks, among the ridge's crags,
  where the foot could not advance without the hand.   18
I know that I grieved then, and now again
  I grieve when I remember what I saw,
  and more than ever I restrain my talent   21
lest it run a course that virtue has not set;
  for if a lucky star or something better
  has given me this good, I must not misuse it.   24
As many fireflies (in the season when
  the one who lights the world hides his face least,
  in the hour when the flies yield to mosquitoes)   27
as the peasant on the hillside at his ease
  sees, flickering in the valley down below,
  where perhaps he gathers grapes or tills the soil—   30
with just so many flames all the eighth *bolgia*
  shone brilliantly, as I became aware
  when at last I stood where the depths were visible.   33
As he[1] who was avenged by bears beheld
  Elijah's chariot at its departure,
  when the rearing horses took to flight toward Heaven,   36
and though he tried to follow with his eyes,
  he could not see more than the flame alone
  like a small cloud once it had risen high—   39
so each flame moves itself along the throat
  of the abyss, none showing what it steals
  but each one stealing nonetheless a sinner.   42
I was on the bridge, leaning far over—so far
  that if I had not grabbed some jut of rock
  I could easily have fallen to the bottom.   45

8. Cianfa (25.43), Agnello (25.68), Francesco (25.82, 149), Buoso (25.140), and Puccio (25.148) are all Florentines.
9. A town just north of Florence, on the way to Pistoia. The reason for this threat is unclear.

1. Elisha, an Old Testament prophet, was mocked by children, who were then attacked by bears. He saw the ascent to heaven of the prophet Elijah in his chariot and continued Elijah's mission: 2 Kings 2.1–25.

And my guide, who saw me so absorbed, explained:
  "There are souls concealed within these moving fires,
  each one swathed in his burning punishment." 48
"O master," I replied, "from what you say
  I know now I was right; I had guessed already
  it might be so, and I was about to ask you: 51
Who's in that flame with its tip split in two,
  like that one which once sprang up from the pyre
  where Eteocles was placed beside his brother?"[2] 54
He said: "Within, Ulysses and Diomed[3]
  are suffering in anger with each other,
  just vengeance makes them march together now. 57
And they lament inside one flame the ambush
  of the horse become the gateway that allowed
  the Romans' noble seed[4] to issue forth. 60
Therein they mourn the trick that caused the grief
  of Deïdamia,[5] who still weeps for Achilles;
  and there they pay for the Palladium." 63
"If it is possible for them to speak
  from within those flames," I said, "master, I pray
  and repray you—let my prayer be like a thousand— 66
that you do not forbid me to remain
  until the two-horned flame comes close to us;
  you see how I bend toward it with desire!" 69
"Your prayer indeed is worthy of highest praise,"
  he said to me, "and therefore I shall grant it;
  but see to it your tongue refrains from speaking. 72
Leave it to me to speak, for I know well
  what you would ask; perhaps, since they were Greeks,
  they might not pay attention to your words."[6] 75
So when the flame had reached us, and my guide
  decided that the time and place were right,
  he addressed them and I listened to him speaking: 78
"O you who are two souls within one fire,
  if I have deserved from you when I was living,
  if I have deserved from you much praise or little, 81
when in the world I wrote my lofty verses,
  do not move on; let one of you tell where
  he lost himself through his own fault, and died." 84
The greater of the ancient flame's two horns

---

2. Eteocles and his brother, Polynices, were the sons of Oedipus; cursed by their father for their imprisonment of him, they engaged in a civil war over Thebes, killed each other, and were cremated on the same pyre, the flame of which divided into two as a sign of their enmity.
3. Two of the Greek leaders in the Trojan War. They devised the trick of the Trojan horse and stole the Palladium, a statue of Pallas Athena that protected the city. Their vil-

lainy is described by Aeneas in *Aeneid* 2.
4. The Trojan survivors, who founded Rome.
5. Achilles' lover, who tried to prevent him from going to the Trojan War but was thwarted by Ulysses.
6. Virgil may assume that Greeks would disdain anyone who, like Dante, did not know Greek (and was therefore a "barbarian"); or that because he derives from the classical world he is the more appropriate interlocutor.

began to sway and quiver, murmuring
   just like a flame that strains against the wind;   87
then, while its tip was moving back and forth,
   as if it were the tongue itself that spoke,
   the flame took on a voice and said: "When I   90
set sail from Circe,[7] who, more than a year,
   had kept me occupied close to Gaëta
   (before Aeneas called it by that name),[8]   93
not sweetness of a son, not reverence
   for an aging father, not the debt of love
   I owed Penelope[9] to make her happy,   96
could quench deep in myself the burning wish
   to know the world and have experience
   of all man's vices, of all human worth.   99
So I set out on the deep and open sea
   with just one ship and with that group of men,
   not many, who had not deserted me.   102
I saw as far as Spain, far as Morocco,
   both shores; I had left behind Sardinia,
   and the other islands which that sea encloses.   105
I and my mates were old and tired men.
   Then finally we reached the narrow neck
   where Hercules put up his signal-pillars   108
to warn men not to go beyond that point.[1]
   On my right I saw Seville, and passed beyond;
   on my left, Ceüta had already sunk behind me.   111
'Brothers,' I said, 'who through a hundred thousand
   perils have made your way to reach the West,
   during this so brief vigil of our senses   114
that is still reserved for us, do not deny
   yourself experience of what there is beyond,
   behind the sun, in the world they call unpeopled.[2] 117
Consider what you came from: you are Greeks!
   You were not born to live like mindless brutes
   but to follow paths of excellence and knowledge.' 120
With this brief exhortation I made my crew
   so anxious for the way that lay ahead,
   that then I hardly could have held them back; 123
and with our stern turned toward the morning light,
   we made our oars our wings for that mad flight,
   gaining distance, always sailing to the left. 126
The night already had surveyed the stars

7. Dante places Circe's home near Gaëta, on the coast of Italy north of Naples; she was a sorceress who transformed men into beasts.
8. Aeneas named it after his nurse Caieta, who died there: *Aeneid* 7.
9. Ulysses' faithful wife.
1. The straits of Gibraltar, with Seville on the European side and Ceüta on the African. According to myth, Hercules separated a single mountain into two to mark the point beyond which human beings should not venture.
2. According to the geography of Dante's day, the Southern Hemisphere was made up entirely of water, with the only land being Mount Purgatory. To go "behind the sun" means to follow a westward course.

the other pole contains; it saw ours so low
  it did not show above the ocean floor.[3]   129
Five times we saw the splendor of the moon
  grow full and five times wane away again
  since we had entered through the narrow pass—   132
when there appeared a mountain shape, darkened
  by distance, that arose to endless heights.
  I had never seen another mountain like it.[4]   135
Our celebrations soon turned into grief:
  from the new land there rose a whirling wind
  that beat against the forepart of the ship   138
and whirled us round three times in churning waters;
  the fourth blast raised the stern up high, and sent
  the bow down deep, as pleased Another's will.   141
And then the sea was closed again, above us."

CANTO XXVII

As soon as Ulysses has finished his narrative, another flame—its soul within having recognized Virgil's Lombard accent—comes forward asking the travelers to pause and answer questions about the state of affairs in the region of Italy from which he came. The Pilgrim responds by outlining the strife in Romagna and ends by asking the flame who he is. The flame, although he insists he does not want his story to be known among the living, answers because he is supposedly convinced that the Pilgrim will never return to earth. He is another famous deceiver, Guido da Montefeltro, a soldier who became a friar in his old age; but he was untrue to his vows when, at the urging of Pope Boniface VIII, he counseled the use of fraud in the pope's campaign against the Colonna family. He was damned to Hell because he failed to repent his sins, trusting instead in the pope's fraudulent absolution.

By now the flame was standing straight and still,
  it said no more and had already turned
  from us, with sanction of the gentle poet,   3
when another, coming right behind it,
  attracted our attention to its tip,
  where a roaring of confusing sounds had started.   6
As the Sicilian bull—that bellowed first
  with cries of that one (and it served him right)
  who with his file had fashioned such a beast[5]—   9
would bellow with the victim's voice inside,
  so that, although the bull was only brass,
  the effigy itself seemed pierced with pain: 12
so, lacking any outlet to escape
  from the burning soul that was inside the flame,
  the suffering words became the fire's language.   15

3. They had crossed the equator and could see only the stars of the Southern Hemisphere.
4. This is Mount Purgatory.
5. According to classical legend, Phalaris, the tyrant of Agrigentum in Sicily, had an artisan build a brazen bull in which he roasted his victims alive, their shrieks emerging as the sounds of a bull's bellowing. His first victim was the artisan himself, Perillus.

But after they had made their journey upward
  to reach the tip, giving it that same quiver
  the sinner's tongue inside had given them,   18
we heard the words:[6] "O you to whom I point
  my voice, who spoke just now in Lombard,[7] saying:
  'you may move on, I won't ask more of you.'   21
although I have been slow in coming to you,
  be willing, please, to pause and speak with me.
  You see how willing I am—and I burn!   24
If you have just now fallen to this world
  of blindness, from that sweet Italian land
  where I took on the burden of my guilt,   27
tell me, are the Romagnols[8] at war or peace?
  For I come from the hills between Urbino
  and the mountain chain that lets the Tiber loose."   30
I was still bending forward listening
  when my master touched my side and said to me:
  "*You* speak to him; *this* one is Italian."   33
And I, who was prepared to answer him,
  began without delaying my response:
  "O soul who stands concealed from me down there, 36
your Romagna is not now and never was
  without war in her tyrants' hearts, although
  there was no open warfare when I came here.   39
Ravenna's[9] situation has not changed:
  the eagle of Polenta broods up there,
  covering all of Cervia with its pinions;   42
the land[1] that stood the test of long endurance
  and left the French piled in a bloody heap
  is once again beneath the verdant claws.   45
Verrucchio's Old Mastiff and its New One,[2]
  who both were bad custodians of Montagna,
  still sink their fangs into their people's flesh;   48
the cities by Lamone and Santerno[3]
  are governed by the Lion of the White Lair,
  who changes parties every change of season.   51

---

6. The speaker is Guido da Montefeltro (d. 1298), a nobleman deeply involved in the constant warfare of 13th-century Italy but who became a friar two years before his death (see line 67).

7. The dialect of northern Italy. Dante believed that since Virgil came from Mantua, his spoken language would be not Latin but this dialect.

8. The people of Romagna, an area northeast of Florence and bordering the Adriatic Sea; the city of Urbino marks its southern limit, the Apennine mountains its northern. The subsequent passage describes the political conditions in the cities of Romagna.

9. The major city of Romagna, ruled at the time by the Polenta family, who also controlled the small city of Cervia.

1. Forlì, which defeated French invaders but then fell under the control of the tyrannical Ordelaffi family, which had green paws on its coat of arms.

2. Malatesta de Verrucchio and his son Malatestino were tyrants of Rimini who killed their enemy Montagna.

3. The cities of Faenza and Imola, on the Lamone and Santerno Rivers respectively, governed by an unreliable ruler who had a lion on a white ground on his coat of arms.

As for the town⁴ whose side the Savio bathes:
　　just as it lies between the hills and plains,
　　it lives between freedom and tyranny.　　　　　　　　　　54
And now I beg you tell us who you are—
　　grant me my wish as yours was granted you—
　　so that your fame may hold its own on earth."　　　　　57
And when the fire, in its own way, had roared
　　awhile, the flame's sharp tip began to sway
　　to and fro, then released a blow of words:　　　　　　60
"If I thought that I were speaking to a soul
　　who someday might return to see the world,
　　most certainly this flame would cease to flicker;　　63
but since no one, if I have heard the truth,
　　ever returns alive from this deep pit,
　　with no fear of dishonor I answer you:　　　　　　　66
I was a man of arms and then a friar,
　　believing with the cord to make amends;
　　and surely my belief would have come true　　　　　69
were it not for that High Priest⁵ (his soul be damned!)
　　who put me back among my early sins;
　　I want to tell you why and how it happened.　　　　72
While I still had the form of the bones and flesh
　　my mother gave me, all my actions were
　　not those of a lion, but those of a fox;　　　　　　75
the wiles and covert paths, I knew them all,
　　and so employed my art that rumor of me
　　spread to the farthest limits of the earth.　　　　78
When I saw that the time of life had come
　　for me, as it must come for every man,
　　to lower the sails and gather in the lines,　　　　81
things I once found pleasure in then grieved me;
　　repentant and confessed, I took the vows
　　a monk takes. And, oh, to think it could have worked!　84
And then the Prince of the New Pharisees
　　chose to wage war upon the Lateran
　　instead of fighting Saracens or Jews,⁶　　　　　　87
for all his enemies were Christian souls
　　(none among the ones who conquered Acri,⁷
　　none a trader in the Sultan's kingdom).　　　　　90
His lofty papal seat, his sacred vows
　　were no concern to him, nor was the cord
　　I wore (that once made those it girded leaner).⁸　　93
As Constantine once had Silvestro brought

---

4. Cesena, located on the Savio River, was a free municipality although its politics were dominated by a single family.
5. Pope Boniface VIII.
6. Boniface was struggling to retain the papacy against the challenge of another Roman family, the Colonnas.

7. City in the Holy Land, captured by the Crusaders and then recaptured by the Saracens.
8. Guido refers to the rough cord worn as a belt by Franciscan friars, a symbol of both obedience and poverty (hence it would make the wearer "leaner"); for another reference to this cord, see 16.106.

from Mount Soracte to cure his leprosy,[9]
  so this one sought me out as his physician   96
to cure his burning fever caused by pride.
  He asked me to advise him. I was silent,
  for his words were drunken. Then he spoke again: 99
'Fear not, I tell you: the sin you will commit,
  it is forgiven. Now you will teach me how
  I can level Palestrina[1] to the ground.   102
Mine is the power, as you cannot deny,
  to lock and unlock Heaven. Two keys I have,
  those keys my predecessor did not cherish."[2] 105
And when his weighty arguments had forced me
  to the point that silence seemed the poorer choice,
  I said: 'Father, since you grant me absolution 108
for the sin I find I must fall into now:
  ample promise with a scant fulfillment
  will bring you triumph on your lofty throne.' 111
Saint Francis[3] came to get me when I died,
  but one of the black Cherubim cried out:
  'Don't touch him, don't cheat me of what is mine! 114
He must come down to join my other servants
  for the false counsel he gave. From then to now
  I have been ready at his hair, because 117
one cannot be absolved unless repentant,
  nor can one both repent and will a thing
  at once—the one is canceled by the other!"[4] 120
O wretched me! How I shook when he took me,
  saying: 'Perhaps you never stopped to think
  that I might be somewhat of a logician!'[5] 123
He took me down to Minòs,[6] who eight times
  twisted his tail around his hardened back,
  then in his rage he bit it, and announced: 126
'He goes with those the thievish fire burns.'
  And here you see me now, lost, wrapped this way,
  moving, as I do, with my resentment." 129
When he had brought his story to a close,
  the flame, in grievous pain, departed from us
  gnarling and flickering its pointed horn. 132
My guide and I moved farther on; we climbed
  the ridge until we stood on the next arch
  that spans the fosse where penalties are paid 135
by those who, sowing discord, earned Hell's wages.

9. According to legend, the Emperor Constantine (d. 337) was cured of his leprosy by Pope Sylvester, who was hiding on Mount Soracte, some 20 miles north of Rome; see 19.115.
1. The fortress of the Colonnas.
2. The keys are those of damnation and absolution, given by Christ to Peter; see 19.92. Boniface's "predecessor" was Celestine V, who resigned after five months; see 3.59–60.

3. Francis of Assisi (1181/82–1226), founder of the order of friars joined by Guido.
4. Guido wanted forgiveness for his sin of guile at the same time as he was committing it; in willing the sin he showed that he was not truly repentant, the precondition for forgiveness.
5. The devil is referring to the logical law of noncontradiction.
6. For Minos, see 5.4.

CANTO XXVIII

In the Ninth Bolgia *the Pilgrim is overwhelmed by the sight of mutilated, bloody shades, many of whom are ripped open, with entrails spilling out. They are the Sowers of Scandal and Schism, and among them are Mahomet, Ali, Pier da Medicina, Gaius Scribonius Curio, Mosca de' Lamberti, and Bertran de Born. All bemoan their painful lot, and Mahomet and Pier da Medicina relay warnings through the Pilgrim to certain living Italians who are soon to meet terrible ends. Bertran de Born, who comes carrying his head in his hand like a lantern, is a particularly arresting example of a Dantean* contrapasso.

Who could, even in the simplest kind of prose
   describe in full the scene of blood and wounds
   that I saw now—no matter how he tried!   3
Certainly any tongue would have to fail:
   man's memory and man's vocabulary
   are not enough to comprehend such pain.   6
If one could bring together all the wounded
   who once upon the fateful soil of Puglia
   grieved for their life's blood spilled by the Romans,[7]   9
and spilled again in the long years of the war
   that ended in great spoils of golden rings
   (as Livy's history tells, that does not err),[8]   12
and pile them with the ones who felt the blows
   when they stood up against great Robert Guiscard,[9]
   and with those others whose bones are still in heaps   15
at Ceprano[1] (there where every Puglian
   turned traitor), and add those from Tagliacozzo,[2]
   where old Alardo conquered, weaponless—   18
if all these maimed with limbs lopped off or pierced
   were brought together, the scene would be nothing
   to compare with the foul ninth *bolgia*'s bloody sight.   21
No wine cask with its stave or cant-bar sprung
   was ever split the way I saw someone
   ripped open from his chin to where we fart.   24
Between his legs his guts spilled out, with the heart
   and other vital parts, and the dirty sack
   that turns to shit whatever the mouth gulps down.   27
While I stood staring into his misery,
   he looked at me and with both hands he opened
   his chest and said: "See how I tear myself!   30

7. Puglia is in southern Italy, and Dante refers here to those killed when the Trojans conquered it in the *Aeneid* 7–12.
8. Livy is a Roman historian (d. 17 C.E.) and the "war" he chronicled is the Second Punic War (218–201 B.C.E.) between Rome and Carthage under Hannibal. After the Battle of Cannae (216) the victorious Carthaginians displayed rings taken from fallen Romans.
9. A Norman conqueror (1015–1085) who fought the Greeks and Saracens for control of Sicily and southern Italy in the 11th century.
1. A town that the barons of Puglia were pledged to defend for Manfred, the natural son of Frederick II (10.119), but whom they betrayed; he was then killed at the battle of Benevento in 1266.
2. A town where in 1268 Manfred's nephew Conradin was defeated by the strategy rather than the brute force of Alardo de Valery.

See how Mahomet[3] is deformed and torn!
  In front of me, and weeping, Ali walks,
  his face cleft from his chin up to the crown.   33
The souls that you see passing in this ditch
  were all sowers of scandal and schism in life,
  and so in death you see them torn asunder.   36
A devil stands back there who trims us all
  in this cruel way, and each one of this mob
  receives anew the blade of the devil's sword   39
each time we make one round of this sad road,
  because the wounds have all healed up again
  by the time each one presents himself once more.   42
But who are you there, gawking from the bridge
  and trying to put off, perhaps, fulfillment
  of the sentence passed on you when you confessed?"   45
"Death does not have him yet, he is not here
  to suffer for his guilt," my master answered;
  "but that he may have full experience,   48
I, who am dead, must lead him through this Hell
  from round to round, down to the very bottom,
  and this is as true as my presence speaking here."   51
More than a hundred in that ditch stopped short
  to look at me when they had heard his words,
  forgetting in their stupor what they suffered.   54
"And you, who will behold the sun, perhaps
  quite soon, tell Fra Dolcino[4] that unless
  he wants to follow me here quick, he'd better   57
stock up on food, or else the binding snows
  will give the Novarese their victory,
  a conquest not won easily otherwise."   60
With the heel of one foot raised to take a step,
  Mahomet said these words to me, and then
  stretched out and down his foot and moved away.   63
Another, with his throat slit, and his nose
  cut off as far as where the eyebrows start
  (and he only had a single ear to show),   66
who had stopped like all the rest to stare in wonder,
  stepped out from the group and opened up his throat,
  which ran with red from all sides of his wound,   69
and spoke: "O you whom guilt does not condemn,
  whom I have seen in Italy up there,
  unless I am deceived by similarity,   72
recall to mind Pier da Medicina,[5]

3. Muhammad, founder of Islam (570–632), regarded by some medieval Christians as a renegade Christian and a creator of religious disunity. Ali was his nephew and son-in-law, and his disputed claim to the rulership (or caliphate) divided Islam into Sunni and Shi'a sects.
4. In 1300 Fra Dolcino was head of a reformist order known as the Apostolic Brothers that was condemned as heretical by the pope. He and his followers escaped to the hills near the town of Novara, but starvation forced them out and many were executed.
5. The town of Medicina lies in the Po Valley between Vercelli and Marcabò. Nothing certain is known of Pier de Medicina.

should you return to see the gentle plain
　　declining from Vercelli to Marcabò,　　　　　　　　　　75
and inform the two best citizens of Fano[6]—
　　tell Messer Guido and tell Angiolello—
　　that, if our foresight here is no deception,　　　　　　78
from their ship they shall be hurled bound in a sack
　　to drown in the water near Cattolica,
　　the victims of a tyrant's treachery;　　　　　　　　　81
between the isles of Cyprus and Mallorca
　　so great a crime Neptune never witnessed
　　among the deeds of pirates or the Argives.[7]　　　　84
That traitor, who sees only with one eye
　　and rules the land that someone with me here
　　wishes he'd never fed his eyes upon,[8]　　　　　　　87
will have them come to join him in a parley,
　　then see to it they do not waste their breath
　　on vows or prayers to escape Focara's wind."　　　90
And I to him: "If you want me to bring back
　　to those on earth your message—who is the one
　　sated with the bitter sight? Show him to me."　　　93
At once he grabbed the jaws of a companion[9]
　　standing near by, and squeezed his mouth half open,
　　announcing, "Here he is, and he is mute.　　　　　96
This man, in exile, drowned all Caesar's doubts
　　and helped him cast the die, when he insisted:
　　'A man prepared, who hesitates, is lost.'"　　　　　99
How helpless and bewildered he appeared,
　　his tongue hacked off as far down as the throat,
　　this Curio, once so bold and quick to speak!　　　102
And one[1] who had both arms but had no hands,
　　raising the gory stumps in the filthy air
　　so that the blood dripped down and smeared his face,　　105
cried: "You, no doubt, also remember Mosca,
　　who said, alas, 'What's done is over with,'
　　and sowed the seed of discord for the Tuscans."　　　108
"And of death for all your clan," I quickly said,
　　and he, this fresh wound added to his wound,
　　turned and went off like one gone mad from pain.　　111
But I remained to watch the multitude,

6. A town on the Adriatic coast of Italy; its
two leaders—named in the next line—were
drowned in 1312 by the one-eyed tyrant Malatestino of Rimini (27.46) near the promontory
of Focara (see line 90) after he had invited
them to the town of La Cattolica for a parley.
7. Cyprus and Majorca are islands at the
western and eastern ends of the Mediterranean. Neptune is the classical god of the sea
and Argives is another name for Greeks.
8. This "someone" is Caius Curio, whose story
is told in lines 94–102.

9. Caius Curio, a Roman of the 1st century
B.C.E., was bribed by Julius Caesar to betray
his friends; he urged Caesar to cross the Rubi-
con and invade the Roman Republic, starting
a civil war.
1. A Florentine noble, who in 1215 started
the civil strife that tore the city apart by advising a father to avenge the slight to his daughter by killing the man who had broken his
engagement to her. Mosca's own family was a
victim of the strife some 60 years later.

and saw a thing that I would be afraid
  to tell about without more evidence,
were I not reassured by my own conscience—   114
  that good companion enheartening a man
  beneath the breastplate of its purity.
I saw it, I'm sure, and I seem to see it still: 117
  a body with no head that moved along,
  moving no differently from all the rest;
he held his severed head up by its hair,   120
  swinging it in one hand just like a lantern,
  and as it looked at us it said: "Alas!"
Of his own self he made himself a light   123
  and they were two in one and one in two.
  How could this be? He who ordained it knows.
And when he had arrived below our bridge,   126
  he raised the arm that held the head up high
  to let it speak to us at closer range.
It spoke:[2] "Now see the monstrous punishment,   129
  you there still breathing, looking at the dead,
  see if you find suffering to equal mine!
And that you may report on me up there,   132
  know that I am Bertran de Born, the one
  who evilly encouraged the young king.
Father and son I set against each other: 135
  Achitophel with his wicked instigations
  did not do more with Absalom and David.
Because I cut the bonds of those so joined,   138
  I bear my head cut off from its life-source,
  which is back there, alas, within its trunk.
In me you see the perfect *contrapasso*!"[3]   141

CANTO XXIX

When the Pilgrim is rebuked by his mentor for his inappropriate interest in these wretched shades, he replies that he was looking for someone. Virgil tells the Pilgrim that he saw the person he was looking for, Geri del Bello, pointing a finger at him. They discuss Geri until they reach the edge of the next bolgía, *where all types of Falsifiers are punished. There miserable, shrieking shades are afflicted with diseases of various kinds and are arranged in various positions. Sitting back to back, madly scratching their leprous sores, are the shades of Griffolino da Arezzo and one Capocchio, who talk to the Pilgrim, the latter shade making wisecracks about the Sienese.*

The crowds, the countless, different mutilations,
  had stunned my eyes and left them so confused
  they wanted to keep looking and to weep,   3
but Virgil said: "What are you staring at?

---

2. This is Bertran de Born, a Provençal noble-man and poet, who reputedly advised the son of Henry II of England to rebel against his father. For Achitophel's similar scheming between David and his son Absalom, see 2 Sam-uel 15–17.

3. Literally, "counter penalty": in Dante's hell, the sinner is punished by having to commit his sin for all of eternity.

Why do your eyes insist on drowning there
   below, among those wretched, broken shades?   6
You did not act this way in other *bolge*.
   If you hope to count them one by one, remember
   the valley winds some twenty-two miles around;[4]   9
and already the moon is underneath our feet;
   the time remaining to us now is short[5]—
   and there is more to see than you see here."   12
"If you had taken time to find out what
   I was looking for," I started telling him,
   "perhaps you would have let me stay there longer."   15
My guide was moving on, with me behind him,
   answering as I did while we went on,
   and adding: "Somewhere down along this ditch   18
that I was staring at a while ago,
   I think there is a spirit of my family
   mourning the guilt that's paid so dear down there."   21
And then my master said: "From this time on
   you should not waste another thought on him;
   think on ahead, and let him stay behind,   24
for I saw him standing underneath the bridge
   pointing at you, and threatening with his gesture,
   and I heard his name called out: Geri del Bello.[6]   27
That was the moment you were so absorbed
   with him who was the lord of Altaforte[7]
   that you did not look his way before he left."   30
"Alas, my guide," I answered him, "his death
   by violence, which has not yet been avenged
   by anyone who shares in his disgrace,   33
made him resentful, and I suppose for this
   he went away without a word to me,
   and because he did I feel great piety."   36
We spoke of this until we reached the start
   of the bridge across the next *bolgia*, from which
   the bottom, with more light, might have been seen.   39
Having come to stand above the final cloister
   of Malebolge, we saw it spreading out,
   revealing to our eyes its congregation.   42
Weird shrieks of lamentation pierced through me
   like arrow-shafts whose tips are barbed with pity,
   so that my hands were covering my ears.   45
Imagine all the sick in the hospitals
   of Maremma, Valdichiana, and Sardinia
   between the months of July and September,[8]   48

---

4. The reason for this exact measurement is not known. At 30.86 we are told that the circumference of the ninth circle is 11 miles, showing that Hell is shaped like a funnel.
5. This means that the sun (which they cannot see) is over their heads, and the time is about 2 P.M. The journey to the center of Hell lasts 24 hours, so only 4 hours are left.

6. First cousin to Dante's father; his death at the hands of a member of another Florentine family initiated a feud between the two families that lasted some 50 years.
7. Bertran de Born (see 28.134).
8. The region of Maremma, the river valley of Val di Chiana, and the island of Sardinia were all plagued by malaria.

crammed all together rotting in one ditch—
   such was the misery here; and such a stench
   was pouring out as comes from flesh decaying.   51
Still keeping to our left, we made our way
   down the long bridge onto the final bank,
   and now my sight was clear enough to find   54
the bottom where the High Lord's ministress,
   Justice infallible, metes out her punishment
   to falsifiers she registers on earth.   57
I doubt if all those dying in Aegina[9]
   when the air was blowing sick with pestilence
   and the animals, down to the smallest worm,   60
all perished (later on this ancient race,
   according to what the poets tell as true,
   was born again from families of ants)   63
offered a scene of greater agony
   than was the sight spread out in that dark valley
   of heaped-up spirits languishing in clumps.   66
Some sprawled out on others' bellies, some
   on others' backs, and some, on hands and knees,
   dragged themselves along that squalid alley.   69
Slowly, in silence, slowly we moved along,
   looking, listening to the words of all those sick,
   who had no strength to raise their bodies up.   72
I saw two sitting, leaning against each other
   like pans propped back to back against a fire,[1]
   and they were blotched from head to foot with scabs.   75
I never saw a curry-comb[2] applied
   by a stable-boy who is harried by his master,
   or simply wants to finish and go to bed,   78
the way those two applied their nails and dug
   and dug into their flesh, crazy to ease
   the itching that can never find relief.   81
They worked their nails down, scraping off the scabs
   the way one works a knife to scale a bream[3]
   or some other fish with larger, tougher scales.   84
"O you there scraping off your scabs of mail
   and even making pincers of your fingers,"
   my guide began to speak to one of them,   87
"so may your fingernails eternally
   suffice their task, tell us: among the many
   packed in this place is anyone Italian?"   90
"Both of us whom you see disfigured here,"
   one answered through his tears, "we are Italians.
   But you, who ask about us, who are you?"   93
"I am one accompanying this living man

---

9. A mythical island that was infected by Juno with a pestilence that killed all its inhabitants and was then repopulated when Jupiter turned ants into men: see Ovid, *Metamorphoses* 7.
1. The image is of pans leaned against one another before a kitchen fireplace.
2. A "curry-comb" is a bristled brush used to groom horses.
3. A "bream" is a large fish like a carp.

descending bank from bank," my leader said,
   "and I intend to show him all of Hell."   96
With that each lost the other back's support
   and each one, shaky, turned to look at me,
   as others did who overheard these words.   99
My gentle master came up close to me
   and said: "Now ask them what you want to know,"
   and since he wanted me to speak, I started: 102
"So may the memory of you not fade
   from the minds of men up there in the first world,
   but rather live on under many suns,   105
tell me your names and where it was you lived;
   do not let your dreadful, loathsome punishment
   discourage you from speaking openly."   108
"I'm from Arezzo," one of them replied,
   "and Albert of Siena had me burned,
   but I'm not here for what I died for there;[4]   111
it's true I told him, jokingly, of course:
   'I know the trick of flying through the air,'
   and he, eager to learn and not too bright,   114
asked me to demonstrate my art; and only
   just because I didn't make him Daedalus,
   he had me burned by one whose child he was.   117
But here, to the last *bolgia* of the ten,
   for the alchemy[5] I practiced in the world
   I was condemned by Minòs, who cannot err."   120
I said to my poet: "Have you ever known
   people as silly as the Sienese?
   Even the French cannot compare with them!"   123
With that the other leper[6] who was listening
   feigned exception to my quip: "Excluding,
   of course, Stricca, who lived so frugally,   126
and Niccolo, the first to introduce
   the luxury of the clove for condiment
   into that choice garden where the seed took root, 129
and surely not that fashionable club
   where Caccia squandered all his woods and vineyards
   and Abbagliato flaunted his great wit!   132
That you may know who this is backing you
   against the Sienese, look sharply at me
   so that my face will give you its own answer,   135

4. Griffolino of Arezzo cheated Albero of Siena by promising to teach him the art of Daedalus—flying. The bishop of Siena, father of the illegitimate Albero, had Griffolino burned as a heretic.
5. A practice that sought to turn base metals like lead into gold.
6. The speaker is Capocchio, a Florentine burned in 1293 for alchemy, which he here admits was mere counterfeiting. The people he lists were rich young noblemen of Siena who joined a "Spendthrifts' Club"—the "fashionable club" of line 130—and sought to outdo each other in profligacy. For another member of this club, Lano of Siena, see 13.115.

and you will recognize Capocchio's shade,
    betrayer of metals with his alchemy;
    you'll surely recall—if you're the one I think—   138
how fine an ape of nature[7] I once was."

CANTO XXX

Capocchio's remarks are interrupted by two mad, naked shades who dash up, and one of them sinks his teeth into Capocchio's neck and drags him off; he is Gianni Schicchi and the other is Myrrha of Cyprus. When they have gone, the Pilgrim sees the ill-proportioned and immobile shade of Master Adamo, a counterfeiter, who explains how members of the Guidi family had persuaded him to practice his evil art in Romena. He points out the fever-stricken shades of two infamous liars, Potiphar's Wife and Sinon the Greek, whereupon the latter engages Master Adamo in a verbal battle. Virgil rebukes the Pilgrim for his absorption in such futile wrangling, but his immediate shame wins Virgil's immediate forgiveness.

In ancient times when Juno was enraged
    against the Thebans because of Semele[8]
    (she showed her wrath on more than one occasion),   3
she made King Athamas go raving mad:
    so mad that one day when he saw his wife
    coming with his two sons in either arm,   6
he cried: "Let's spread the nets, so I can catch
    the lioness with her lion cubs at the pass!"
    Then he spread out his insane hands, like talons,   9
and, seizing one of his two sons, Learchus,
    he whirled him round and smashed him on a rock.
    She drowned herself with the other in her arms.   12
And when the wheel of Fortune brought down low
    the immeasurable haughtiness of Trojans,[9]
    destroying in their downfall king and kingdom,   15
Hecuba sad, in misery, a slave
    (after she saw Polyxena lie slain,
    after this grieving mother found her son   18
Polydorus left unburied on the shore),
    now gone quite mad, went barking like a dog—
    it was the weight of grief that snapped her mind.   21
But never in Thebes or Troy were madmen seen
    driven to acts of such ferocity
    against their victims, animal or human,   24
as two shades I saw, white with rage and naked,

7. By "ape of nature" Capocchio means that he merely imitated change in his alchemical displays rather than actually accomplishing it.
8. Daughter of the king of Thebes, Semele was loved by Jupiter and therefore incited the wrath of Juno, who drove her brother-in-law Athamas insane. While mad, Athamas thought his wife, Ino, and his two sons, Learchus and Melicertes, were a lioness and two cubs: he killed Learchus, and Ino drowned herself and Melicertes. See Ovid, *Metamorphoses* 4.
9. Parallel to the fate of Thebes is that of Troy, which is here represented by the madness into which Queen Hecuba fell when she saw her daughter Polyxena sacrificed on Achilles' tomb and the unburied body of her betrayed son Polydorus. See Ovid, *Metamorphoses* 13.

running, snapping crazily at things in sight,
    like pigs, directionless, broken from their pen.   27
One, landing on Capocchio, sank his teeth
    into his neck, and started dragging him
    along, scraping his belly on the rocky ground.   30
The Aretine[1] spoke, shaking where he sat:
    "You see that batty shade? He's Gianni Schicchi![2]
    He's rabid and he treats us all that way."   33
"Oh," I answered, "so may that other shade
    never sink its teeth in you—if you don't mind,
    please tell me who it is before it's gone."   36
And he to me: "That is the ancient shade
    of Myrrha,[3] the depraved one, who became,
    against love's laws, too much her father's friend.   39
She went to him, and there she sinned in love,
    pretending that her body was another's—
    just as the other there fleeing in the distance,   42
contrived to make his own the 'queen of studs,'
    pretending that he was Buoso Donati,
    making his will and giving it due form."   45
Now that the rabid pair had come and gone
    (from whom I never took my eyes away),
    I turned to watch the other evil shades.   48
And there I saw a soul shaped like a lute,
    if only he'd been cut off from his legs
    below the belly, where they divide in two.   51
The bloating dropsy,[4] disproportioning
    the body's parts with unconverted humors,
    so that the face, matched with the paunch, was puny,   54
forced him to keep his parched lips wide apart,
    as a man who suffers thirst from raging fever
    has one lip curling up, the other sagging.   57
"O you who bear no punishment at all
    (I can't think why) within this world of sorrow,"
    he said to us, "pause here and look upon   60
the misery of one Master Adamo:[5]
    in life I had all that I could desire,
    and now, alas, I crave a drop of water.   63
The little streams that flow from the green hills
    of Casentino, descending to the Arno,
    keeping their banks so cool and soft with moisture,   66

1. Griffolino (see 29.111).
2. A Florentine who impersonated Buoso Donati (line 44), who had just died, and dictated a new will that gave him Buoso's best beast ("the queen of studs" of line 43).
3. Myrrha impersonated another woman in order to sleep with her father: see Ovid, *Metamorphoses* 10.
4. A disease in which fluid ("humors" of line

53) gathers in the cells and the affected part becomes grotesquely swollen.
5. A counterfeiter, burned in 1281, who made coins stamped with the image of John the Baptist, the patron saint of Florence, that contained 21 rather than 24 carats of gold (see line 90); he worked for a noble family of Romena (individual members are mentioned in line 77), a town in the Florentine district of Casentino.

forever flow before me, haunting me;
   and the image of them leaves me far more parched
   than the sickness that has dried my shriveled face.   69
Relentless Justice, tantalizing me,
   exploits the countryside that knew my sin,
   to draw from me ever new sighs of pain: 72
I still can see Romena, where I learned
   to falsify the coin stamped with the Baptist,
   for which I paid with my burned body there;   75
but if I could see down here the wretched souls
   of Guido or Alexander or their brother,
   I would not exchange the sight for Branda's fountain.[6]   78
One is here already, if those maniacs
   running around this place have told the truth,
   but what good is it, with my useless legs?   81
If only I were lighter, just enough
   to move one inch in every hundred years,
   I would have started on my way by now   84
to find him somewhere in this gruesome lot,
   although this ditch winds round eleven miles
   and is at least a half a mile across.   87
It's their fault I am here with this choice family:
   they encouraged me to turn out florins
   whose gold contained three carats' worth of alloy."   90
And I to him: "Who are those two poor souls
   lying to the right, close to your body's boundary,
   steaming like wet hands in wintertime?"   93
"When I poured into this ditch, I found them here,"
   he answered, "and they haven't budged since then,
   and I doubt they'll move through all eternity.   96
One is the false accuser of young Joseph;
   the other is false Sinon, the Greek in Troy:[7]
   it's their burning fever makes them smell so bad."   99
And one of them, perhaps somewhat offended
   at the kind of introduction he received,
   with his fist struck out at the distended belly,   102
which responded like a drum reverberating;
   and Master Adam struck him in the face
   with an arm as strong as the fist he had received,   105
and he said to him: "Although I am not free
   to move around, with swollen legs like these,
   I have a ready arm for such occasions."   108
"*But* it was *not* as free and ready, was it,"
   the other answered, "when you went to the stake?
   Of course, when you were coining, it was readier!"   111
And he with the dropsy: "*Now* you tell the truth,

6. A fountain near Romena.
7. The "false accuser" is Potiphar's wife, who
falsely accused Joseph of trying to lie with her

(Genesis 39.6–20); Sinon is the Greek priest
who persuaded the Trojans to accept the
wooden horse (*Aeneid* 2).

but you were not as full of truth that time
    when you were asked to tell the truth at Troy!"   114
"My words were false—so were the coins you made,"
    said Sinon, "and I am here for one false act
    but *you* for more than any fiend in hell!"   117
"The horse, recall the horse, you falsifier,"
    the bloated paunch was quick to answer back,
    "may it burn your guts that all the world remembers!"   120
"May your guts burn with thirst that cracks your tongue,"
    the Greek said, "may they burn with rotting humors
    that swell your hedge of a paunch to block your eyes!"   123
And then the money-man: "So there you go,
    your evil mouth pours out its filth as usual;
    for if *I* thirst, and humors swell me up,   126
you burn more, and your head is fit to split,
    and it wouldn't take much coaxing to convince you
    to lap the mirror of Narcissus dry!"[8]   129
I was listening, all absorbed in this debate,
    when the master said to me: "Keep right on looking,
    a little more, and I shall lose my patience."   132
I heard the note of anger in his voice
    and turned to him; I was so full of shame
    that it still haunts my memory today.   135
Like one asleep who dreams himself in trouble
    and in his dream he wishes he were dreaming,
    longing for that which is, as if it were not,   138
just so I found myself: unable to speak,
    longing to beg for pardon and already
    begging for pardon, not knowing that I did.   141
"Less shame than yours would wash away a fault
    greater than yours has been," my master said,
    "and so forget about it, do not be sad.   144
If ever again you should meet up with men
    engaging in this kind of futile wrangling,
    remember I am always at your side;   147
to have a taste for talk like this is vulgar!"

CANTO XXXI

Through the murky air they move, up across the bank that separates the Malebolge
from the pit of Hell, the Ninth (and last) Circle of the Inferno. *From a distance is
heard the blast of a mighty horn, which turns out to have been that of the giant Nimrod. He and other giants, including Ephialtes, are fixed eternally in the pit of Hell;
all are chained except Antaeus, who, at Virgil's request, lifts the two poets in his
monstrous hand and deposits them below him, on the lake of ice known as Cocytus.*

The very tongue that first spoke—stinging me,
    making the blood rush up to both my cheeks—
    then gave the remedy to ease the pain,   3

8. Narcissus saw his reflection in a pool of water, referred to here as a "mirror" (Ovid, *Metamorphoses* 3).

just as, so I have heard, Achilles' lance,
   belonging to his father, was the source
   of pain, and then of balm, to him it struck.[9]   6
Turning our backs on that trench of misery
   gaining the bank again that walls it in,
   we cut across, walking in dead silence.   9
Here it was less than night and less than day,
   so that my eyes could not see far ahead;
   but then I heard the blast of some high horn   12
which would have made a thunder-clap sound dim;
   it drew my eyes directly to one place,
   as they retraced the sound's path to its source.   15
After the tragic rout when Charlemagne[1]
   lost all his faithful, holy paladins,
   the sound of Roland's horn was not as ominous.   18
Keeping my eyes still turned that way, I soon
   made out what seemed to be high, clustered towers.
   "Master," I said, "what city lies ahead?"   21
"Because you try to penetrate the shadows,"
   he said to me, "from much too far away,
   you confuse the truth with your imagination.   24
You will see clearly when you reach that place
   how much the eyes may be deceived by distance,
   and so, just push ahead a little more."   27
Then lovingly he took me by the hand
   and said: "But now, before we go on farther,
   to prepare you for the truth that could seem strange,   30
I'll tell you these aren't towers, they are giants;
   they're standing in the well around the bank—
   all of them hidden from their navels down."   33
As, when the fog begins to thin and clear,
   the sight can slowly make out more and more
   what is hidden in the mist that clogs the air,   36
so, as I pierced the thick and murky air,
   approaching slowly, closer to the well,
   confusion cleared and my fear took on more shape.   39
For just as Montereggion[2] is crowned with towers
   soaring high above its curving ramparts,
   so, on the bank that runs around the well,   42
towering with only half their bodies out,
   stood the terrible giants,[3] forever threatened
   by Jupiter in the heavens when he thunders.   45
And now I could make out one of the faces,

9. Achilles' father, Peleus, gave him a lance that would heal any wound it inflicted.
1. In *The Song of Roland*. Roland blows his horn to alert Charlemagne to the fact that the rear guard Roland commands has been slaughtered. Paladins are the twelve peers or great warriors of Charlemagne's court.
2. A castle surrounded by towers, built to protect Siena from attack by Florence.
3. These "giants" are the mythological Titans, monsters born of the Earth who assaulted Olympus and were defeated and imprisoned by Jupiter.

the shoulders, the chest and a good part of the belly
    and, down along the sides, the two great arms.[4]   48
Nature, when she cast away the mold
    for shaping beasts like these, without a doubt
    did well, depriving Mars of more such agents.   51
And if she never did repent of whales
    and elephants, we must consider her,
    on sober thought, all the more just and wary: 54
for when the faculty of intellect
    is joined with brute force and with evil will,
    no man can win against such an alliance.   57
His face, it seemed to me, was about as long
    and just as wide as St. Peter's cone in Rome,[5]
    and all his body's bones were in proportion,   60
so that the bank which served to cover him
    from his waist down showed so much height above
    that three tall Frisians[6] on each other's shoulders   63
could never boast of stretching to his hair,
    for downward from the place men clasp their cloaks
    I saw a generous thirty hand-spans of him.[7]   66
"Raphel may a mech zabi almi!"[8]
    He played these sputtering notes with prideful lips
    for which no sweeter psalm was suitable.   69
My guide called up to him: "Blathering idiot,
    stick to your horn[9] and take it out on that
    when you feel a fit of anger coming on;   72
search round your neck and you will find the strap
    it's tied to, you poor muddle-headed soul,
    and there's the horn so pretty on your chest."   75
And then he turned to me: "His words accuse him.
    He is Nimrod, through whose infamous device
    the world no longer speaks a common language.   78
But let's leave him alone and not waste breath,
    for he can no more understand our words
    than anyone can understand his language."   81
We had to walk still farther than before,
    continuing to the left, a full bow's-shot,
    to find another giant,[1] huger and more fierce.   84
What engineer it took to bind this brute
    I cannot say, but there he was, one arm
    pinned to his back, the other locked in front,   87

4. This is Nimrod, described in Genesis as "a mighty hunter before the Lord" (10.9) and understood by medieval commentators to be a giant. He ruled over Babylon, where the tower of Babel was built (11.1–9).
5. This bronze pine cone, over 12 feet high, stood outside St. Peter's Cathedral in Dante's time; today it can be seen in the papal gardens in the Vatican.
6. Inhabitants of the northernmost province of what is now the Netherlands, considered the tallest men of the time.
7. About 15 feet.
8. Appropriately for the builder of Babel, he speaks an incomprehensible language.
9. Nimrod has a "horn" because in the Bible he is described as a hunter (Genesis 10.9).
1. This is Ephialtes, a Titan who with his twin brother Otus tried to attack Olympus by piling Mount Ossa on Mount Pelion; see Virgil, Aeneid 6.

with a giant chain winding around him tight,
  which, starting from his neck, made five great coils—
  and that was counting only to his waist.   90
"This beast of pride decided he would try
  to pit his strength against almighty Jove,"
  my leader said, "and he has won this prize.   93
He's Ephialtes, who made his great attempt
  when the giants arose to fill the Gods with panic;
  the arms he lifted then, he moves no more."   96
And I to him: "If it were possible,
  I would really like to have the chance to see
  the fantastic figure of Briareus."[2]   99
His answer was: "Not far from here you'll see
  Antaeus,[3] who can speak and is not chained;
  he will set us down in the very pit of sin.   102
The one you want to see is farther off;
  he too is bound and looks just like this one,
  except for his expression, which is fiercer."   105
No earthquake of the most outrageous force
  ever shook a tower with such violence
  as, suddenly, Ephialtes shook himself.   108
I never feared to die as much as then,
  and my fear might have been enough to kill me,
  if I had not already seen those chains.   111
We left him and continued moving on
  and came to where Antaeus stood, extending
  from the well a good five ells up to his head.[4]   114
"O you who in the celebrated valley[5]
  (that saw Scipio become the heir of glory,
  when Hannibal with all his men retreated)   117
once captured a thousand lions as your quarry
  (and with whose aid, had you chosen to take part
  in the great war with your brothers, the sons of earth   120
would, as many still think, have been the victors),
  do not disdain this modest wish: take us,
  and put us down where ice locks in Cocytus.[6]   123
Don't make us go to Tityus or Typhon;[7]
  this man can give you what all long for here,
  and so bend down, and do not scowl at us.   126
He still can spread your legend in the world,
  for he yet lives, and long life lies before him,
  unless Grace summons him before his time."   129
Thus spoke my master, and the giant in haste
  stretched out the hands whose formidable grip

2. Another Titan.
3. A Titan born too late to participate in the rebellion against Jupiter and therefore not chained; he was known for eating lions (line 118) and was defeated by Hercules in a wrestling match (line 132).
4. About 15 feet.

5. The "valley" of the Bagradas River in Tunisia, where the Roman Scipio defeated the Carthaginian Hannibal in 202 B.C.E.
6. The frozen lake of Cocytus is in the ninth and last circle of Hell.
7. Two more Titans.

great Hercules once felt, and took my guide.   132
And Virgil, when he felt the grasping hands,
   called out: "Now come and I'll take hold of you."
   Clasped together, we made a single burden.   135
As the Garisenda[8] looks from underneath
   its leaning side, at the moment when a cloud
   comes drifting over against the tower's slant,   138
just so the bending giant Antaeus seemed
   as I looked up, expecting him to topple.
   I wished then I had gone another way.   141
But he, most carefully, handed us down
   to the pit that swallows Lucifer with Judas.[9]
   And then, the leaning giant immediately   144
drew himself up as tall as a ship's mast.

CANTO XXXII

They descend farther down into the darkness of the immense plain of ice in which shades of Traitors are frozen. In the outer region of the ice-lake, Caïna, are those who betrayed their kin in murder; among them, locked in a frozen embrace, are Napoleone and Alessandro of Mangona, and others are Mordred, Focaccia, Sassol Mascheroni, and Camicion de' Pazzi. Then the two travelers enter the area of ice called Antenora, and suddenly the Pilgrim kicks one of the faces sticking out of the ice. He tries to force the sinner to reveal his name by pulling out his hair, and when another shade identifies him as Bocca degli Abati, the Pilgrim's fury mounts still higher. Bocca, himself furious, names several other sinners in Antenora, including Buoso da Duera, Tesauro dei Beccheria, Gianni de' Soldanier, Ganelou, and Tibbald. Going farther on, the Pilgrim sees two heads frozen in one hole, the mouth of one gnawing at the brain of the other.

If I had words grating and crude enough
   that really could describe this horrid hole
   supporting the converging weight of Hell,   3
I could squeeze out the juice of my memories
   to the last drop. But I don't have these words,
   and so I am reluctant to begin.   6
To talk about the bottom of the universe
   the way it truly is, is no child's play,
   no task for tongues that gurgle baby-talk.   9
But may those heavenly ladies[1] aid my verse
   who aided Amphion to wall-in Thebes,
   that my words may tell exactly what I saw.   12
O misbegotten rabble of all rabble,
   who crowd this realm, hard even to describe,
   it were better you had lived as sheep or goats!   15
When we reached a point of darkness in the well
   below the giant's feet, farther down the slope,

8. A leaning tower of Bologna: when a cloud passes over it, moving opposite to the tower's slant, it appears to be falling away from the sky.

9. Two of the inhabitants of Cocytus.
1. The Muses who helped the legendary musician Amphion raise the walls of Thebes with the music of his lyre.

and I was gazing still at the high wall,   18
I heard somebody say: "Watch where you step!
    Be careful that you do not kick the heads
    of this brotherhood of miserable souls."   21
At that I turned around and saw before me
    a lake of ice stretching beneath my feet,
    more like a sheet of glass than frozen water.[2]   24
In the depths of Austria's wintertime, the Danube
    never in all its course showed ice so thick,
    nor did the Don beneath its frigid sky,   27
as this crust here; for if Mount Tambernic[3]
    or Pietrapana would crash down upon it,
    not even at its edges would a crack creak.   30
The way the frogs (in the season when the harvest
    will often haunt the dreams of the peasant girl)
    sit croaking with their muzzles out of water,   33
so these frigid, livid shades were stuck in ice
    up to where a person's shame appears;
    their teeth clicked notes like storks' beaks snapping shut.[4]   36
And each one kept his face bowed toward the ice:
    the mouth bore testimony to the cold,
    the eyes, to sadness welling in the heart.   39
I gazed around awhile and then looked down,
    and by my feet I saw two figures clasped
    so tight that one's hair could have been the other's.   42
"Tell me, you two, pressing your chests together,"
    I asked them, "who are you?"[5] Both stretched their necks
    and when they had their faces raised toward me,   45
their eyes, which had before been only glazed,
    dripped tears down to their lips, and the cold froze
    the tears between them, locking the pair more tightly.   48
Wood to wood with iron was never clamped
    so firm! And the two of them like billy-goats
    were butting at each other, mad with anger.   51
Another one with both ears frozen off,
    and head still bowed over his icy mirror,
    cried out: "What makes you look at us so hard?   54
If you're interested to know who these two are:
    the valley where Bisenzio's waters[6] flow
    belonged to them and to their father, Albert;   57
the same womb bore them both, and if you scour
    all of Caïna,[7] you will not turn up one
    who's more deserving of this frozen aspic—   60

2. The water for this lake derives from the crack in the Old Man of Crete (14.103).
3. Probably Mount Tambura, close to Mount Pietrapana in the Italian Alps.
4. A harsh, clacking sound. "Where a person's shame appears" is the face because of blushing.
5. These are the two sons of Count Alberto degli Alberti of Florence; when he died (ca. 1280), they killed each other over politics and their inheritance.
6. Bisenzio is a river north of Florence.
7. Named after Cain: this first of the four subdivisions of Cocytus is where those who betrayed their kin are imprisoned.

not him who had his breast and shadow pierced
 with one thrust of the lance from Arthur's hand;[8]
 not Focaccia, not even this one here,   63
whose head gets in my way and blocks my view,
 known in the world as Sassol Mascheroni,[9]
 and if you're Tuscan you must know who he was.   66
To save me from your asking for more news:
 I was Camicion de' Pazzi,[1] and I await
 Carlin,[2] whose guilt will make my own seem less."   69
Farther on I saw a thousand doglike faces,
 purple from the cold. That's why I shudder,
 and always will, when I see a frozen pond.   72
While we were getting closer to the center
 of the universe,[3] where all weights must converge,
 and I was shivering in the eternal chill—   75
by fate or chance or willfully perhaps,
 I do not know—but stepping among the heads,
 my foot kicked hard against one of those faces.   78
Weeping, he screamed: "Why are you kicking me?[4]
 You have not come to take revenge on me
 for Montaperti, have you? Why bother me?"   81
And I: "My master, please wait here for me,
 let me clear up a doubt concerning this one,
 then I shall be as rapid as you wish."   84
My leader stopped, and to that wretch, who still
 had not let up in his barrage of curses,
 I said: "Who are you, insulting other people?"   87
"And you, who are *you* who march through Antenora[5]
 kicking other people in their faces?
 No living man could kick as hard!" he answered.   90
"I am a living man," was my reply,
 "and it might serve you well, if you seek fame,
 for me to put your name down in my notes."   93
And he said: "That's the last thing I would want!
 That's not the way to flatter in these lowlands!
 Stop pestering me like this—get out of here!"   96
At that I grabbed him by his hair in back[6]

8. "Not him . . . hand": This is Mordred, Arthur's nephew and son; when Arthur pierced him with a sword, he created a wound so large that the sun shone through, thus creating a hole in Mordred's shadow. Focaccia in the next line is a nobleman of Pistoia who killed his cousin.
9. A Florentine nobleman who murdered a relative.
1. A Florentine who killed his kinsman.
2. A Florentine who betrayed a castle belonging to his party. When he dies he will therefore be sent to the next subdivision, Antenora, for those who committed treachery against their country, city, or party—a harsher pun-

ishment, which Camicion says "will make my own [guilt] seem less."
3. The "center of the universe" is where gravity is most strong and to which all material things are drawn.
4. Bocca degli Abati (his name is betrayed by one of the fellow damned in line 106); Bocca betrayed his party at the battle of Montaperti in 1260.
5. Dante and Virgil have moved into the second subdivision of Caïna, which is named after Antenor, a Trojan who betrayed the city to the Greeks; it is the location of those who betrayed their country.
6. The hair at the nape of the neck.

and said: "You'd better tell me who you are
   or else I'll not leave one hair on your head."   99
And he to me: "Go on and strip me bald
   and pound and stamp my head a thousand times,
   you'll never hear my name or see my face."   102
I had my fingers twisted in his hair
   and already I'd pulled out more than one fistful,
   while he yelped like a cur with eyes shut tight,   105
when someone else[7] yelled: "What's the matter, Bocca?
   It's bad enough to hear your shivering teeth;
   now you bark! What the devil's wrong with you?"   108
"There's no need now for you to speak," I said,
   "you vicious traitor! Now I know your name
   and I'll bring back the shameful truth about you."   111
"Go away!" he answered. "Tell them what you want;
   but if you do get out of here, be sure
   you also tell about that blabbermouth,   114
who's paying here what the French silver cost him:
   'I saw,' you can tell the world, 'the one from Duera
   stuck in with all the sinners keeping cool.'   117
And if you should be asked: 'Who else was there?'
   Right by your side is the one from Beccheria[8]
   whose head was chopped off by the Florentines.   120
As for Gianni Soldanier,[9] I think you'll find him
   farther along with Ganelon and Tibbald,
   who opened up Faenza while it slept."   123
Soon after leaving him I saw two souls
   frozen together in a single hole,
   so that one head used the other for a cap.   126
As a man with hungry teeth tears into bread,
   the soul with capping head had sunk his teeth
   into the other's neck, just beneath the skull.   129
Tydeus[1] in his fury did not gnaw
   the head of Menalippus with more relish
   than this one chewed that head of meat and bones.   132
"O you who show with every bestial bite
   your hatred for the head you are devouring,"
   I said, "tell me your reason, and I promise,   135
if you are justified in your revenge,
   once I know who you are and this one's sin,
   I'll repay your confidence in the world above   138
unless my tongue dry up before I die."

---

7. This is Buoso da Duera, who betrayed Manfred, the ruler of Naples, to his enemy Charles of Anjou in 1265.

8. Tesauro de' Beccheria, a churchman executed for treason in Florence in 1258.

9. Gianni Soldanier was a Florentine nobleman who switched political parties; Ganelon (line 122) is the betrayer of Roland in the *Song of Roland*; Tibbald (line 122) was the citizen of Faenza (a town east of Florence) who betrayed it to its enemies.

1. In the war against Thebes, Tydeus was mortally wounded by Menalippus, whom he killed and whose skull he gnawed in fury while dying.

CANTO XXXIII

Count Ugolino is the shade gnawing at the brain of his onetime associate Archbishop
Ruggieri, and Ugolino interrupts his gruesome meal long enough to tell the story of his
imprisonment and cruel death, which his innocent offspring shared with him. Moving
farther into the area of Cocytus known as Tolomea, where those who betrayed their
guests and associates are condemned, the Pilgrim sees sinners with their faces raised
high above the ice, whose tears freeze and lock their eyes. One of the shades agrees to
identify himself on condition that the ice be removed from his eyes. The Pilgrim agrees,
and learns that this sinner is Friar Alberigo and that his soul is dead and damned even
though his body is still alive on earth, inhabited by a devil. Alberigo also names a fellow
sinner with him in the ice, Branca d'Oria, whose body is still functioning up on earth.
But the Pilgrim does not honor his promise to break the ice from Alberigo's eyes.

Lifting his mouth from his horrendous meal,
　　this sinner² first wiped off his messy lips
　　in the hair remaining on the chewed-up skull,　　　　　　　　　3
then spoke: "You want me to renew a grief
　　so desperate that just the thought of it,
　　much less the telling, grips my heart with pain;　　　　　　　　6
but if my words can be the seed to bear
　　the fruit of infamy for this betrayer,
　　who feeds my hunger, then I shall speak—in tears.　　　　　　9
I do not know your name, nor do I know
　　how you have come down here, but Florentine
　　you surely seem to be, to hear you speak.　　　　　　　　　12
First you should know I was Count Ugolino
　　and my neighbor here, Ruggieri the Archbishop;
　　now I'll tell you why I'm so unneighborly.　　　　　　　　　15
That I, trusting in him, was put in prison
　　through his evil machinations, where I died,
　　this much I surely do not have to tell you.　　　　　　　　　18
What you could not have known, however, is
　　the inhuman circumstances of my death.
　　Now listen, then decide if he has wronged me!　　　　　　　21
Through a narrow slit of window high in that mew³
　　(which is called the tower of hunger, after me,
　　and I'll not be the last to know that place)　　　　　　　　　24
I had watched moon after moon after moon go by,
　　when finally I dreamed the evil dream
　　which ripped away the veil that hid my future.　　　　　　27
I dreamed of this one here as lord and huntsman,
　　pursuing the wolf and the wolf cubs up the mountain⁴
　　(which blocks the sight of Lucca from the Pisans)　　　　　30

2. Ugolino, a governor of Pisa who was
betrayed by his enemy Archbishop Ruggieri in
1288. His own crime is obliquely explained by
his narrative.
3. A cage for birds; the prison in Pisa where
Ugolino and his relatives were confined
became known as the Torre de Fame or Tower
of Hunger.

4. Mount San Giuliano lies between Pisa and
Lucca. "The wolf and the wolf cubs": Ugolino
and his four sons, each of whom are named in
subsequent lines (50, 68, 89). In fact, Ugolino
was imprisoned with two sons (who were
grown men) and two adolescent grandsons.

with skinny bitches, well trained and obedient;
   he had out front as leaders of the pack
   Gualandi with Sismondi and Lanfranchi.[5]   33
A short run, and the father with his sons
   seemed to grow tired, and then I thought I saw
   long fangs sunk deep into their sides, ripped open.   36
When I awoke before the light of dawn,
   I heard my children sobbing in their sleep
   (you see they, too, were there), asking for bread.   39
If the thought of what my heart was telling me
   does not fill you with grief, how cruel you are!
   If you are not weeping now—do you ever weep?   42
And then they awoke. It was around the time
   they usually brought our food to us. But now
   each one of us was full of dread from dreaming;   45
then from below I heard them driving nails
   into the dreadful tower's door; with that,
   I stared in silence at my flesh and blood.   48
I did not weep, I turned to stone inside;
   they wept, and my little Anselmuccio spoke:
   'What is it, father? Why do you look that way?'   51
For them I held my tears back, saying nothing,
   all of that day, and then all of that night,
   until another sun shone on the world.   54
A meager ray of sunlight found its way
   to the misery of our cell, and I could see
   myself reflected four times in their faces;   57
I bit my hands in anguish. And my children,
   who thought that hunger made me bite my hands,
   were quick to draw up closer to me, saying: 60
'O father, you would make us suffer less,
   if you would feed on us: you were the one
   who gave us this sad flesh; you take it from us!'[6]   63
I calmed myself to make them less unhappy.
   That day we sat in silence, and the next day.
   O pitiless earth! You should have swallowed us!   66
The fourth day came, and it was on that day
   my Gaddo fell prostrate before my feet,
   crying: 'Why don't you help me? Why, my father?'[7]   69
There he died. Just as you see me here,
   I saw the other three fall one by one,
   as the fifth day and the sixth day passed. And I,   72
by then gone blind, groped over their dead bodies.
   Though they were dead, two days I called their names.
   Then hunger proved more powerful than grief."   75
He spoke these words; then, glaring down in rage,
   attacked again the wretched skull with his teeth

5. Pisan families of the political party opposed to that of Ugolino.
6. See Job 1.21.
7. See Matthew 27.46.

sharp as a dog's, and as fit for grinding bones.   78
O Pisa, blot of shame upon the people
    of that fair land where the sound of "sì" is heard![8]
Since your neighbors hesitate to punish you,   81
let Capraia and Gorgona[9] move and join,
    damming up the River Arno at its mouth,
    and let every Pisan perish in its flood!   84
For if Count Ugolino was accused
    of turning traitor, trading-in your castles,[1]
    you had no right to make his children suffer.   87
Their newborn years (O newborn Thebes!)[2] made them
    all innocents: Brigata, Uguiccione,
    and the other two soft names my canto sings.   90
We moved ahead to where the frozen water
    wraps in harsh wrinkles another sinful race,
    with faces not turned down but looking up.[3]   93
Here, the weeping puts an end to weeping,
    and the grief that finds no outlet from the eyes
    turns inward to intensify the anguish: 96
for the tears they first wept knotted in a cluster
    and like a visor made for them in crystal,
    filled all the hollow part around their eyes.   99
Although the bitter coldness of the dark
    had driven all sensation from my face,
    as though it were not tender skin but callous,   102
I thought I felt the air begin to blow,
    and I: "What causes such a wind, my master?
    I thought no heat could reach into these depths."[4]   105
And he to me: "Before long you will be
    where your own eyes can answer for themselves,
    when they will see what keeps this wind in motion."   108
And one of the wretches with the frozen crust
    screamed out at us: "O wicked souls, so wicked
    that you have been assigned the ultimate post,   111
break off these hard veils covering my eyes
    and give relief from the pain that swells my heart —
    at least until the new tears freeze again."   114
I answered him: "If this is what you want,
    tell me your name; and if I do not help you,
    may I be forced to drop beneath this ice!"   117

8. I.e., Italy, where *si* means "yes."
9. Islands belonging to Pisa that lie close to the mouth of the Arno, which flows through Pisa.
1. In 1285 Ugolino conveyed three Pisan castles to Lucca and Florence.
2. In classical mythology, Thebes was notorious for its internecine violence, such as the story of Oedipus, his father, Laius, and his sons, Eteocles and Polynices (see 26.54).
3. Virgil and Dante pass into the third subdivision of Cocytus, called Tolomea (line 124) after Ptolemy, governor of Jericho, who killed his father-in-law, Simon, and two of his sons while they were dining with him (I Maccabees 16.11–17). In Tolomea those who have betrayed their guests are punished.
4. Since the sun's heat was thought to cause wind, Dante wonders why he feels wind in this cold place. The answer will be given in 34.46–52.

He answered then: "I am Friar Alberigo,[5]
  I am he who offered fruit from the evil orchard:
  here dates are served me for the figs I gave."   120
"Oh, then!" I said. "Are you already dead?"
  And he to me: "Just how my body is
  in the world above, I have no way of knowing.   123
This zone of Tolomea is very special,
  for it often happens that a soul falls here
  before the time that Atropos[6] should send it.   126
And that you may more willingly scrape off
  my cluster of glass tears, let me tell you:
  whenever a soul betrays the way I did,   129
a demon takes possession of the body,
  controlling its maneuvers from then on,
  for all the years it has to live up there,   132
while the soul falls straight into this cistern here;
  and the shade in winter quarters just behind me
  may well have left his body up on earth.   135
But you should know, if you've just come from there:
  he is Ser Branca d'Oria;[7] and many years
  have passed since he first joined us here, icebound."   138
"I think you're telling me a lie," I said,
  "for Branca d'Oria is not dead at all;
  he eats and drinks, he sleeps and wears out clothes."   141
"The ditch the Malebranche watch above,"
  he said, "the ditch of clinging, boiling pitch,
  had not yet caught the soul of Michel Zanche,   144
when Branca left a devil in his body
  to take his place, and so did his close kinsman,
  his accomplice in this act of treachery.   147
But now, at last, give me the hand you promised.
  Open my eyes." I did not open them.
  To be mean to him was a generous reward.   150
O all you Genovese, you men estranged
  from every good, at home with every vice,
  why can't the world be wiped clean of your race?   153
For in company with Romagna's rankest soul[8]
  I found one of your men, whose deeds were such
  that his soul bathes already in Cocytus   156
but his body seems alive and walks among you.

---

5. A member of the Jovial Friars (see 23.103), he killed two of his relatives during a banquet at his house, signaling the assassins with an order to bring the fruit. In saying that he is now being served dates instead of figs, he is ironically complimenting God for his generosity, since a date would be more valuable than a fig.
6. One of the mythological figures known as the Fates; she is the one who cuts the thread of life.
7. A nobleman of Genoa (a "Genovese" in line 151), who with a "close kinsman" (line 146) killed his father-in-law, Michel Zanche (line 144), at a banquet in 1275 or 1290.
8. That is, Friar Alberigo (line 118); Romagna is the part of Italy from which he and Branca come.

CANTO XXXIV

Far across the frozen ice can be seen the gigantic figure of Lucifer, who appears from this distance like a windmill seen through fog; and as the two travelers walk on toward that terrifying sight, they see the shades of sinners totally buried in the frozen water. At the center of the earth Lucifer stands frozen from the chest downward, and his horrible ugliness (he has three faces) is made more fearful by the fact that in each of his three mouths he chews on one of the three worst sinners of all mankind, the worst of those who betrayed their benefactors: Judas Iscariot, Brutus, and Cassius. Virgil, with the Pilgrim on his back, begins the descent down the shaggy body of Lucifer. They climb down through a crack in the ice, and when they reach the Evil One's thighs, Virgil turns and begins to struggle upward (because they have passed the center of the earth), still holding on to the hairy body of Lucifer, until they reach a cavern, where they stop for a short rest. Then a winding path brings them eventually to the earth's surface, where they see the stars.

"Vexilla regis prodeunt Inferni,"⁹
   my master said, "closer to us, so now
   look ahead and see if you can make him out."   3
A far-off windmill turning its huge sails
   when a thick fog begins to settle in,
   or when the light of day begins to fade,   6
that is what I thought I saw appearing.
   And the gusts of wind it stirred made me shrink back
   behind my guide, my only means of cover.   9
Down here,¹ I stood on souls fixed under ice
   (I tremble as I put this into verse);
   to me they looked like straws worked into glass.   12
Some lying flat, some perpendicular,
   either with their heads up or their feet,
   and some bent head to foot, shaped like a bow.   15
When we had moved far enough along the way
   that my master thought the time had come to show me
   the creature who was once so beautiful,²   18
he stepped aside, and stopping me, announced:
   "This is he, this is Dis;³ this is the place
   that calls for all the courage you have in you."   21
How chilled and nerveless, Reader, I felt then;
   do not ask me—I cannot write about it—
   there are no words to tell you how I felt.   24
I did not die—I was not living either!
   Try to imagine, if you can imagine,
   me there, deprived of life and death at once.   27

9. The first three words—"the banners of the king advance"—are the opening lines of a 6th-century Latin hymn traditionally sung during Holy Week to celebrate Christ's Passion. Dante has added the last word, *Inferni*—"the banners of the king of Hell advance"—in order to apply the words to Satan.
1. This is the last and lowest subdivision of Caïna, known as Judecca after Judas; the sinners here are those who betrayed their benefactors.
2. Lucifer, the "light-bearer," was the most beautiful of angels before he rebelled and was renamed Satan.
3. A classical name for Pluto, here applied to Satan (see also 11.65).

The king of the vast kingdom of all grief
　　stuck out with half his chest above the ice;
　　my height is closer to the height of giants　　　　　　30
than theirs is to the length of his great arms;
　　consider now how large all of him was:
　　this body in proportion to his arms.　　　　　　33
If once he was as fair as now he's foul
　　and dared to raise his brows against his Maker,
　　it is fitting that all grief should spring from him.　　　　36
Oh, how amazed I was when I looked up
　　and saw a head—one head wearing three faces![4]
　　One was in front (and that was a bright red),　　　　　　39
the other two attached themselves to this one
　　just above the middle of each shoulder,
　　and at the crown all three were joined in one:　　　　42
The right face was a blend of white and yellow,
　　the left the color of those people's skin
　　who live along the river Nile's descent.[5]　　　　　　45
Beneath each face two mighty wings stretched out,
　　the size you might expect of this huge bird
　　(I never saw a ship with larger sails):　　　　　　48
not feathered wings but rather like the ones
　　a bat would have. He flapped them constantly,
　　keeping three winds continuously in motion　　　　51
to lock Cocytus eternally in ice.
　　He wept from his six eyes, and down three chins
　　were dripping tears all mixed with bloody slaver.　　　　54
In each of his three mouths he crunched a sinner,
　　with teeth like those that rake the hemp and flax,
　　keeping three sinners constantly in pain;　　　　57
the one in front—the biting he endured
　　was nothing like the clawing that he took:
　　sometimes his back was raked clean of its skin.　　　　60
"That soul up there who suffers most of all,"
　　my guide explained, "is Judas Iscariot:
　　the one with head inside and legs out kicking.　　　63
As for the other two whose heads stick out,
　　the one who hangs from that black face is Brutus[6]—
　　see how he squirms in silent desperation;　　　　66
the other one is Cassius,[7] he still looks sturdy.
　　But soon it will be night. Now is the time
　　to leave this place, for we have seen it all."　　　69
I held on to his neck, as he told me to.
　　while he watched and waited for the time and place,
　　and when the wings were stretched out just enough,　　72

4. Satan's three faces (and much else) make him an infernal parody of the Trinity.
5. I.e., Ethiopians. The significance of these three colors is not certain; it has been suggested that they represent hatred, impotence, and ignorance as the opposites of the divine attributes of love, omnipotence, and wisdom (see 3.5–6).
6. The murderer of Julius Caesar in 44 B.C.E. and thus for Dante a betrayer of the empire.
7. The other murderer of Caesar.

he grabbed on to the shaggy sides of Satan;
    then downward, tuft by tuft, he made his way
    between the tangled hair and frozen crust.   75
When we had reached the point exactly where
    the thigh begins, right at the haunch's curve,
    my guide, with strain and force of every muscle,   78
turned his head toward the shaggy shanks of Dis
    and grabbed the hair as if about to climb—
    I thought that we were heading back to Hell.[8]   81
"Hold tight, there is no other way," he said,
    panting, exhausted, "only by these stairs
    can we leave behind the evil we have seen."   84
When he had got me through the rocky crevice,
    he raised me to its edge and set me down,
    then carefully he climbed and joined me there.   87
I raised my eyes, expecting I would see
    the half of Lucifer I saw before.
    Instead I saw his two legs stretching upward.   90
If at that sight I found myself confused,
    so will those simple-minded folk who still
    don't see what point it was I must have passed.   93
"Get up," my master said, "get to your feet,
    the way is long, the road a rough climb up,
    already the sun approaches middle tierce!"[9]   96
It was no palace promenade we came to,
    but rather like some dungeon Nature built:
    it was paved with broken stone and poorly lit.   99
"Before we start to struggle out of here,
    O master," I said when I was on my feet,
    "I wish you would explain some things to me.   102
Where is the ice? And how can he be lodged
    upside-down? And how, in so little time,
    could the sun go all the way from night to day?"   105
"You think you're still on the center's other side,"
    he said, "where I first grabbed the hairy worm
    of rottenness that pierces the earth's core;   108
and you *were* there as long as I moved downward
    but, when I turned myself, you passed the point
    to which all weight from every part is drawn.[1]   111

8. Virgil's reversal marks the point at which the two travelers pass from the Northern to the Southern Hemisphere. They began by climbing down Satan's body, but now reverse directions and climb up from the Earth's center (hence when they have passed through the center Dante sees Satan's legs sticking up [line 90]). Note that the travelers pass through the glassy ice, a passage that probably echoes I Corinthians 13.12: "For now we see through a glass, darkly; but then face to face."

9. About 7:30 A.M. on Holy Saturday. Dante has added 12 hours to his scheme so that the travelers will emerge from the Earth and arrive at the shore of Mount Purgatory just before sunrise on the next day, Easter Sunday. 1. The center of the earth, which is for Dante the center of the universe, and therefore the place where gravity is the strongest. Being furthest from Heaven, it is also the place which is most material and least spiritual.

Now you are standing beneath the hemisphere[2]
   which is opposite the side covered by land,
   where at the central point was sacrificed   114
the Man whose birth and life were free of sin.
   You have both feet upon a little sphere
   whose other side Judecca occupies;   117
when it is morning here, there it is evening.[3]
   And he whose hairs were stairs for our descent
   has not changed his position since his fall.   120
When he fell from the heavens on this side,[4]
   all of the land that once was spread out here,
   alarmed by his plunge, took cover beneath the sea   123
and moved to our hemisphere; with equal fear
   the mountain-land, piled up on this side, fled
   and made this cavern here when it rushed upward.   126
Below somewhere there is a space, as far
   from Beelzebub[5] as the limit of his tomb,
   known not by sight but only by the sound   129
of a little stream[6] that makes its way down here
   through the hollow of a rock that it has worn,
   gently winding in gradual descent."   132
My guide and I entered that hidden road
   to make our way back up to the bright world.
   We never thought of resting while we climbed.   135
We climbed, he first and I behind, until,
   through a small round opening ahead of us
   I saw the lovely things the heavens hold,   138
and we came out to see once more the stars.[7]

2. I.e., under the Southern Hemisphere, exactly opposite Jerusalem where Christ ("the Man whose birth and life were free of sin") was crucified. Jerusalem is the center of the Northern Hemisphere (see Ezekiel 5.5) and is located directly over the cavity of Hell.
3. The "little sphere" upon which they stand is the other side of Judecca, which is a hollow. The sun is now over the Southern Hemisphere, and therefore it is night in the Northern, where Hell is located.
4. The land that was in the Southern Hemisphere before Satan fell fled to the Northern to avoid him; hence the Southern Hemisphere is composed of water. The exception is that when Satan plunged into the center of the world, the earth close to his body in the Northern Hemisphere moved "with equal fear" (line 124) to the Southern Hemisphere and became "mountain-land" (line 125), which is Mount Purgatory. "This cavern" (line 126) refers to Hell: Mount Purgatory is thus comprised of the land displaced by Satan in his fall. This elaborate explanation for medieval geography is Dante's own poetic scheme.
5. Satan.
6. This stream must flow down from Purgatory, perhaps from Lethe. It finds its source in "a space" (line 127) on Mount Purgatory; thus it is "as far from Beelzebub as the limit of his tomb"—that is, it is located on the surface of the Southern Hemisphere, which since Satan is at the center of the earth is the same distance from him as Hell (his "tomb") is deep. When Dante has Virgil say that it is "below" (line 127) he must be writing from the perspective of the Northern Hemisphere, since Mount Purgatory is at this moment above the travelers.
7. Each of the three parts of the *Divine Comedy* end with the word "stars" as an affirmation of God's benevolent order.

THE THOUSAND AND ONE NIGHTS
(ALF LAYLA WA-LAYLA)
fourteenth century

A text built from many texts, *The Thousand and One Nights* is an extraordinarily flexible and capacious storytelling machine, one that has absorbed stories from a range of cultures across Asia and North Africa and then cast them back out again into the world in many new forms, including theater, opera, film, cartoons, video games, fashion, children's toys, and, of course, other texts. Considered in the work's many manifestations, the "nights" are not "one thousand and one"—they are innumerable.

THE TEXT IN CONTEXT

The Thousand and One Nights was written by many unknown authors, scattered over many centuries and countries of the Middle East. The first document bearing any physical evidence of *The Thousand and One Nights* was a single piece of very rare old Syrian paper that dates from 879 C.E. Discovered in 1948 by a scholar studying in a Cairo archive, the page contained, among various other scrawls and jottings, a signature, a date, and a few words from the opening lines of the *Nights*. The next trace of the *Nights* appears in the tenth century, when Ibn al-Nadim, a book dealer in Baghdad, mentions in his catalogue a number of story collections; among them is a book of tales concerning "Shahrazad," which, he notes, is adapted from a Persian original called *Hazar Afsan*, or *Thousand Tales*. Another tenth-century writer, al-Mas'udi, also mentions Shahrazad and the now-lost Persian *Hazar Afsan*, and adds the title of the Arabic version of the work: *Alf Layla*, or *Thousand Nights*. The title that comes down to us in the earliest complete manuscript, a Syrian text dating from the fourteenth century, is the familiar *Alf Layla wa-Layla*, or *Thousand and One Nights*. The number—one thousand and one—seems precise, and in fact the first generation of Western readers took it literally, assuming that the manuscript, which contained far fewer than one thousand stories, must be incomplete. But its sense is instead symbolic: adding one more to a thousand implies an unending abundance. There is always one more tale to be told.

The Thousand and One Nights is an Arabic text, but one derived from a Persian source (reflected in the Persian names of the characters of the frame story—Shahrazad and her sister Dunyazad, King Shahrayar and his brother Shahzaman). Behind both the Arabic and the Persian texts may lie a Sanskrit original, but this original, if it exists, has never been discovered. Whatever its early sources, the *Nights* quickly swelled with new stories from Arab traditions as its influence spread. One cluster of stories centers on Baghdad and its early ninth-century ruler, Harun al-Rashid, and his vizier Ja'far al-Barmaki. Other groups of stories, which entered the collection at a later date, reflect the culture of medieval Cairo; still others allude to the itinerant heritage of the Bedouin of the Arabian Peninsula. The text of the *Nights*—if we can call such a flexible and changeable organism a "text"—was above all an inspiration for sharing stories, and was thus subject to change with each new telling.

Though the content of the *Nights* is unique, its literary form—the frame tale—is common in Eastern and Western traditions. The frame tale is an open-ended genre, in which an outer story or "frame" provides a structure within which other, shorter stories can be told. Frame tales are among the most popular of literary forms, surviving in the major works of Boccaccio and **Chaucer, Marie de France**, and many others. The genre most likely has its origins in India. The *Pañcatantra*, a Sanskrit collection of animal stories, is among the world's best-known and oldest frame tales, and it was the inspiration for the Arabic *Kalila and Dimna*, which was quickly disseminated throughout medieval Europe. While *Kalila and Dimna* was popular in the West because of the didactic and edifying quality of the tales (they each conclude, as do Aesop's Fables, with a moral), *The Thousand and One Nights* were avidly read by Europeans for less noble reasons: they believed the *Nights* could offer insights into the duplicitous and irrational character of "the Oriental," and they found pleasure in the tales' sensuous details and often unrestrained sexuality. The long history of "Orientalist" approaches to *The Thousand and One Nights* in the West takes nothing away from our own enjoyment of the tales, but it is certainly a reminder of the dangers of interpreting any text as somehow embodying the culture in which it originated.

WORK

The overall frame of *The Thousand and One Nights* centers on a good king who has become a tyrant. After discovering the secret promiscuity of his wife, King Shahrayar decides that he will avoid the deception of women forever by taking a new bride every night and putting her to death in the morning. The deaths rapidly mount, the kingdom is filled with mourning parents—and to the horror and despair of the king's loyal vizier, his daughter, Shahrazad, volunteers to marry the king. He tries to dissuade her, but Shahrazad has a plan. By telling a story to the king every night, each one more marvelous and entrancing than the last, Shahrazad will continually defer the doom that awaits his bride. Yet she also has another goal, beyond self-preservation or even the salvation of her countrywomen. By telling stories that repeatedly address the problems of rule—both the rule of oneself and the rule of others—she will teach the king how to restore order in his own realm, as well as in his own soul.

Even among frame tales, *The Thousand and One Nights* is unique for its enchantingly intricate nested structure. Very often, a character in a tale will pause to tell yet another tale, with one story inside the next inside the next, like Russian nested dolls. In "The Story of the Merchant and the Demon," for example, three old men tell stories, each more fantastic than the last, to the dangerous jinn in their sucessful effort to purchase the merchant's freedom. This structure makes *The Thousand and One Nights* an unusually playful text, seemingly spontaneous and improvisational even on the page, and wonderfully suited to public entertainment and oral performance.

Perhaps the *Nights* is most extraordinary for the persistence of its fertile, regenerative quality even after being taken up by Western readers and rendered in a host of European and, later, American translations and adaptations. This process began in 1704, with the publication in French (by Antoine Galland) of a selection of tales from the earliest surviving complete manuscript. Readers were immediately captivated by the work: an unauthorized English translation of the French version appeared in 1706, and Galland himself quickly produced additional volumes for publication. When he ran out of tales to translate from the Syrian manuscript (which, like all the early collections, contains only about 280), Galland turned to other sets of Arabic tales, including the famous stories of Aladdin and Ali Baba. As he sought to reach the target number of one thousand and one, Galland even added some tales for which there were no written Arabic sources but only oral versions picked up from Arab visitors to Paris. The tremendous European appetite for *The Thousand and One Nights* led to the production of composite Arabic story collections in Cairo during the eighteenth and nineteenth centuries, and subsequently these versions were published in Arabic editions and translated. We can thus think of two separate lineages for the modern reception of the *Nights*: one can be traced back to the earliest complete text, the fourteenth-century Syrian manuscript translated by Galland, and the other to the later composite texts assembled in eighteenth- and nineteenth-century Cairo. The selections reproduced here come from the Syrian manuscript, but it would be wrong to think of these as the "authentic" tales and to dismiss those in the Cairo versions as unimportant innovations. Instead, the Syrian manuscript can best be thought of as a snapshot, an image captured of the *Nights* at a certain moment in time, in a certain cultural location. The Cairo manuscripts also represent a specific time and place in the life of the *Nights*—one intimately connected with the history

of French and, later, British rule in Egypt.

Western reception of *The Thousand and One Nights* has been uniformly enthusiastic, and yet wildly heterogeneous—a good example of the changing fortunes in the relations between Europe and the Middle East. This heterogeneity can be seen, for example, in the nineteenth-century English translations of the *Nights*, all of which were based on the enlarged Cairo compilations. The earliest of these was by Edward Lane, an Englishman living in Cairo; it tries to conjure up an entire way of life through the medium of the *Nights*. For Lane, the stories are not so much an end in themselves as a way for him to re-create the daily experiences of a nineteenth-century Egyptian who might have listened to such stories as they were performed in the coffeehouse. The translation of the philologist John Payne, published for a very limited audience of specialists, sought to use the *Nights* to construct an ethnographic portrait of Egyptian society, while the sexually explicit, extensively footnoted, and deliberately archaic translation by the extraordinary explorer Sir Richard Burton is in a category by itself. The variety of these encounters with the *Nights*, all so different yet all produced in the same language over the span of a few decades, was wittily summed up by a nineteenth-century commentator in the *Edinburgh Review* who states that each version has "its proper destination: Galland for the nursery, Lane for the library, Payne for the study, and Burton for the sewers."

The influence of *The Thousand and One Nights* continued to spread out across the globe. Thus late nineteenth-century portrait photography in Japan shows a fascination with the "Arabian Nights" theme, which had become fashionable in stage costume and dress styles, theater and opera, music and ballet. Today, reflections of the *Nights* are visible in children's cartoons, adult film, graphic novels, and coloring books. In the modern Middle East, however, attitudes toward *The Thousand and One Nights* are more ambivalent; they have even at times led to censorship, whether because of the text's graphic language or, more likely, because of the complicated history of the *Nights* in shaping European fantasies about the Orient.

While Eastern studies of the *Nights* have tended to consider the work in the context of folklore and oral storytelling, Western scholars are often preoccupied with the effort to nail down the work's point of origin. They want to know: Which is the original version? When was it composed? Is *The Thousand and One Nights* an Arab text? a Persian text? Indian? These questions ultimately slip away, because what the text *is* turns out to be much less interesting than what it *does. The Thousand and One Nights* has its life in transit—always becoming something new, leaving its reader in a perpetual state of anticipation. It is less a collection of stories than a machine that makes stories possible.

From The Thousand and One Nights[1]

Prologue

[*The Story of King Shahrayar and Shahrazad, His Vizier's[2] Daughter*]

It is related—but God knows and sees best what lies hidden in the old accounts of bygone peoples and times—that long ago, during the time of the Sasanid dynasty,[3] in the peninsulas of India and Indochina, there lived two kings who were brothers. The older brother was named Shahrayar, the younger Shahzaman. The older, Shahrayar, was a towering knight and a daring champion, invincible, energetic, and implacable. His power reached the remotest corners of the land and its people, so that the country was loyal to him, and his subjects obeyed him. Shahrayar himself lived and ruled in India and Indochina, while to his brother he gave the land of Samarkand[4] to rule as king.

Ten years went by, when one day Shahrayar felt a longing for his brother the king, summoned his vizier (who had two daughters, one called Shahrazad, the other Dinarzad) and bade him go to his brother. Having made preparations, the vizier journeyed day and night until he reached Samarkand. When Shahzaman heard of the vizier's arrival, he went out with his retainers to meet him. He dismounted, embraced him, and asked him for news from his older brother,

---

1. All selections translated from the Arabic by Husain Haddawy except for "The Third Old Man's Tale," translated from the Arabic by Jerome W. Clinton.
2. Literally, "one who bears burdens": the

highest state official or administrator under a caliph or shah.
3. The last pre-Islamic dynasty (226–652).
4. A city and province in central Asia, now in Uzbekistan.

Shahrayar. The vizier replied that he was well, and that he had sent him to request his brother to visit him. Shahzaman complied with his brother's request and proceeded to make preparations for the journey. In the meantime, he had the vizier camp on the outskirts of the city, and took care of his needs. He sent him what he required of food and fodder, slaughtered many sheep in his honor, and provided him with money and supplies, as well as many horses and camels.

For ten full days he prepared himself for the journey; then he appointed a chamberlain in his place, and left the city to spend the night in his tent, near the vizier. At midnight he returned to his palace in the city, to bid his wife good-bye. But when he entered the palace, he found his wife lying in the arms of one of the kitchen boys. When he saw them, the world turned dark before his eyes and, shaking his head, he said to himself, "I am still here, and this is what she has done when I was barely outside the city. How will it be and what will happen behind my back when I go to visit my brother in India? No. Women are not to be trusted." He got exceedingly angry, adding, "By God, I am king and sovereign in Samarkand, yet my wife has betrayed me and has inflicted this on me." As his anger boiled, he drew his sword and struck both his wife and the cook. Then he dragged them by the heels and threw them from the top of the palace to the trench below. He then left the city and going to the vizier ordered that they depart that very hour. The drum was struck, and they set out on their journey, while Shahzaman's heart was on fire because of what his wife had done to him and how she had betrayed him with some cook, some kitchen boy. They journeyed hurriedly, day and night, through deserts and wilds, until they reached the land of King Shahrayar, who had gone out to receive them.

When Shahrayar met them, he embraced his brother, showed him favors, and treated him generously. He offered him quarters in a palace adjoining his own, for King Shahrayar had built two beautiful towering palaces in his garden, one for the guests, the other for the women and members of his household. He gave the guest house to his brother, Shahzaman, after the attendants had gone to scrub it, dry it, furnish it, and open its windows, which overlooked the garden. Thereafter, Shahzaman would spend the whole day at his brother's, return at night to sleep at the palace, then go back to his brother the next morning. But whenever he found himself alone and thought of his ordeal with his wife, he would sigh deeply, then stifle his grief, and say, "Alas, that this great misfortune should have happened to one in my position!" Then he would fret with anxiety, his spirit would sag, and he would say, "None has seen what I have seen." In his depression, he ate less and less, grew pale, and his health deteriorated. He neglected everything, wasted away, and looked ill.

When King Shahrayar looked at his brother and saw how day after day he lost weight and grew thin, pale, ashen, and sickly, he thought that this was because of his expatriation and homesickness for his country and his family, and he said to himself, "My brother is not happy here. I should prepare a goodly gift for him and send him home." For a month he gathered gifts for his brother; then he invited him to see him and said, "Brother, I would like you to know that I intend to go hunting and pursue the roaming deer, for ten days. Then I shall return to prepare you for your journey home. Would you like to go hunting with me?" Shahzaman replied, "Brother, I feel distracted and depressed. Leave me here and go with God's blessing and help." When Shahrayar heard his brother, he thought that his dejection was because of his homesickness for his country. Not wishing to coerce him, he left him behind, and set out with his retainers and men. When they entered the wilderness, he deployed his men in a circle to begin trapping and hunting.

After his brother's departure, Shahzaman stayed in the palace and, from the window overlooking the garden, watched the birds and trees as he thought of his wife and what she had done to him, and sighed in sorrow. While he agonized over his misfortune, gazing at the heavens and turning a distracted eye on the garden, the private gate of his brother's palace opened, and there emerged, strutting like a dark-eyed deer, the lady, his brother's wife, with twenty slave-girls, ten white and ten black. While Shahzaman looked at them, without being seen, they continued to walk until they stopped below his window, without looking in his direction, thinking that he had gone to the hunt with his brother. Then they sat down, took off their clothes, and suddenly there were ten slave-girls and ten black slaves dressed in the same clothes as the girls. Then the ten black slaves mounted the ten girls, while the lady called, "Mas'ud, Mas'ud!" and a black slave jumped from the tree to the ground, rushed to her, and, raising her legs, went between her thighs and made love to her. Mas'ud topped the lady, while the ten slaves topped the ten girls, and they carried on till noon. When they were done with their business, they got up and washed themselves. Then the ten slaves put on the same clothes again, mingled with the girls, and once more there appeared to be twenty slave-girls. Mas'ud himself jumped over the garden wall and disappeared, while the slave-girls and the lady sauntered to the private gate, went in and, locking the gate behind them, went their way.

All of this happened under King Shahzaman's eyes. When he saw this spectacle of the wife and the women of his brother the great king—how ten slaves put on women's clothes and slept with his brother's paramours and concubines and what Mas'ud did with his brother's wife, in his very palace—and pondered over this calamity and great misfortune, his care and sorrow left him and he said to himself, "This is our common lot. Even though my brother is king and master of the whole world, he cannot protect what is his, his wife and his concubines, and suffers misfortune in his very home. What happened to me is little by comparison. I used to think that I was the only one who has suffered, but from what I have seen, everyone suffers. By God, my misfortune is lighter than that of my brother." He kept marveling and blaming life, whose trials none can escape, and he began to find consolation in his own affliction and forget his grief. When supper came, he ate and drank with relish and zest and, feeling better, kept eating and drinking, enjoying himself and feeling happy. He thought to himself, "I am no longer alone in my misery; I am well."

For ten days, he continued to enjoy his food and drink, and when his brother, King Shahrayar, came back from the hunt, he met him happily, treated him attentively, and greeted him cheerfully. His brother, King Shahrayar, who had missed him, said, "By God, brother, I missed you on this trip and wished you were with me." Shahzaman thanked him and sat down to carouse with him, and when night fell, and food was brought before them, the two ate and drank, and again Shahzaman ate and drank with zest. As time went by, he continued to eat and drink with appetite, and became lighthearted and carefree. His face regained color and became ruddy, and his body gained weight, as his blood circulated and he regained his energy; he was himself again, or even better.

King Shahrayar noticed his brother's condition, how he used to be and how he had improved, but kept it to himself until he took him aside one day and said, "My brother Shahzaman, I would like you to do something for me, to satisfy a wish, to answer a question truthfully." Shahzaman asked, "What is it, brother?" He replied, "When you first came to stay with me, I noticed that you kept losing weight, day after day, until your looks changed, your health deteriorated, and your energy sagged. As you continued like this, I thought that what ailed you was your homesickness for your family and your country, but even though I kept noticing that you were wasting away and looking ill, I refrained from questioning you and hid my feelings from you. Then I went hunting, and when I came back, I found that you had recovered and had regained your health. Now I want you to tell me everything and to explain the cause of your deterioration and the cause of your subsequent recovery, without hiding anything from me." When Shahzaman heard what King Shahrayar said, he bowed his head, then said, "As for the cause of my recovery, that I cannot tell you, and I wish that you would excuse me from telling you." The king was greatly astonished at his brother's reply and, burning with curiosity, said, "You must tell me. For now, at least, explain the first cause."

Then Shahzaman related to his brother what happened to him with his own wife, on the night of his departure, from beginning to end, and concluded, "Thus all the while I was with you, great King, whenever I thought of the event and the misfortune that had befallen me, I felt troubled, careworn, and unhappy, and my health deteriorated. This then is the cause." Then he grew silent. When King Shahrayar heard his brother's explanation, he shook his head, greatly amazed at the deceit of women, and prayed to God to protect him from their wickedness, saying, "Brother, you were fortunate in killing your wife and her lover, who gave you good reason to feel troubled, careworn, and ill. In my opinion, what happened to you has never happened to anyone else. By God, had I been in your place, I would have killed at least a hundred or even a thousand women. I would have been furious; I would have gone mad. Now praise be to God who has delivered you from sorrow and distress. But tell me what has caused you to forget your sorrow and regain your health?" Shahzaman replied, "King, I wish that for God's sake you would excuse me from telling you." Shahrayar said, "You must." Shahzaman replied, "I fear that you will feel even more troubled and careworn than I." Shahrayar asked, "How could that be, brother? I insist on hearing your explanation."

Shahzaman then told him about what he had seen from the palace window and the calamity in his very home—how ten slaves, dressed like women, were sleeping with his women and concubines, day and night. He told him everything from beginning to end (but there is no point in repeating that). Then he concluded, "When I saw your own misfortune, I felt better—and said to myself, 'My brother is king of the world, yet such a misfortune has happened to him, and in his very home.' As a result I forgot my care and sorrow, relaxed, and began to eat and drink. This is the cause of my cheer and good spirits."

When King Shahrayar heard what his brother said and found out what had happened to him, he was furious and his blood boiled. He said, "Brother, I can't believe what you say unless I see it with my own eyes." When Shahzaman saw that his brother was in a rage, he said to him, "If you do not believe me, unless you see your misfortune with your own eyes, announce that you plan to go hunting. Then you and I shall set out with your troops, and when we get outside the city, we shall leave our tents and camp with the men behind, enter the city secretly, and go together to your palace. Then the next morning you can see with your own eyes."

King Shahrayar realized that his brother had a good plan and ordered his army to prepare for the trip. He spent the night with his brother, and when God's morning broke, the two rode out of the city with their army, preceded by the camp attendants, who had gone to drive the poles and pitch the tents where the king and his army were to camp. At nightfall King Shahrayar summoned his chief chamberlain and bade him take his place. He entrusted him with the army and ordered that for three days no one was to enter the city. Then he and his brother disguised themselves and entered the city in the dark. They went directly to the palace where Shahzaman resided and slept there till the morning. When they awoke, they sat at the palace window, watching the garden and chatting, until the light broke, the day dawned, and the sun rose. As they watched, the private gate opened, and there emerged as usual the wife of King Shahrayar, walking among twenty slave-girls. They made their way under the trees until they stood below the palace window where the two kings sat. Then they took off their women's clothes, and suddenly there were ten slaves, who mounted the ten girls and made love to them. As for the lady, she called, "Mas'ud, Mas'ud," and a black slave jumped from the tree to the ground, came to her, and said, "What do you want, you slut? Here is Sa'ad al-Din Mas'ud." She laughed and fell on her back, while the slave mounted her and like the others did his business with her. Then the black slaves got up, washed themselves, and, putting on the same clothes, mingled with the girls. Then they walked away, entered the palace, and locked the gate behind them. As for Mas'ud, he jumped over the fence to the road and went on his way.

When King Shahrayar saw the spectacle of his wife and the slave-girls, he went out of his mind, and when he and his brother came down from upstairs, he said, "No one is safe in this world. Such doings are going on in my kingdom, and in my very palace. Perish the world and perish life! This is a great calamity, indeed." Then he turned to his brother and asked, "Would you like to follow me in what I shall do?" Shahzaman answered, "Yes. I will." Shahrayar said, "Let us leave our royal state and roam the world for the love of the Supreme Lord. If we should find one whose misfortune is greater than ours, we shall return. Otherwise, we shall continue to journey through the land, without need for the trappings of royalty." Shahzaman replied, "This is an excellent idea. I shall follow you."

Then they left by the private gate, took a side road, and departed, journeying till nightfall. They slept over their sorrows, and in the morning resumed their day journey until they came to a meadow by the seashore. While they sat in the meadow amid the thick plants and trees, discussing their misfortunes and the recent events, they suddenly heard a shout and a great cry coming from the middle of the sea. They trembled with fear, thinking that the sky had fallen on the earth. Then the sea parted, and there emerged a black pillar that, as it swayed forward, got taller and taller, until it touched the clouds. Shahrayar and Shahzaman were petrified; then they ran in terror and, climbing a very tall tree, sat hiding in its foliage. When they looked again, they saw that the black pillar was cleaving the sea, wading in the water toward the green meadow, until it touched the shore. When they looked again, they saw that it was a black demon, carrying on his head a large glass chest with four steel locks. He came out, walked into the meadow, and where should he stop but under the very tree where the two kings were hiding. The demon sat down and placed the glass chest on the ground. He took out four keys and, opening the locks of the chest, pulled out a full-grown woman. She had a beautiful figure, and a face like the full moon, and a lovely smile. He took her out, laid her under the tree, and looked at her, saying, "Mistress of all noble women, you whom I carried away on your wedding night, I would like to sleep a little." Then he placed his head on the young woman's lap, stretched his legs to the sea, sank into sleep, and began to snore.

Meanwhile, the woman looked up at the tree and, turning her head by chance, saw King Shahrayar and King Shahzaman. She lifted the demon's head from her lap and placed it on the ground. Then she came and stood under the tree and motioned to them with her hand, as if to say, "Come down slowly to me." When they realized that she had seen them, they were frightened, and they begged her and implored her, in the name of the Creator of the heavens, to excuse them from climbing down. She replied, "You must come down to me." They motioned to her, saying, "This sleeping demon is the enemy of mankind. For God's sake, leave us alone." She replied, "You must come down, and if you don't, I shall wake the demon and have him kill you." She kept gesturing and pressing, until they climbed down very slowly and stood before her. Then she lay on her back, raised her legs, and said, "Make love to me and satisfy my need, or else I shall wake the demon, and he will kill you." They replied, "For God's sake, mistress, don't do this to us, for at this moment we feel nothing but dismay and fear of this demon. Please, excuse us." She replied, "You must," and insisted, swearing, "By God who created the heavens, if you don't do it, I shall wake my husband the demon and ask him to kill you and throw you into the sea." As she persisted, they could no longer resist and they made love to her, first the older brother, then the younger. When they were done and withdrew from her, she said to them, "Give me your rings," and, pulling out from the folds of her dress a small purse, opened it, and shook out ninety-eight rings of different fashions and colors. Then she asked them, "Do you know what these rings are?" They answered, "No." She said, "All the owners of these rings slept with me, for whenever one of them made love to me, I took a ring from him. Since you two have slept with me, give me your rings, so that I may add them to the rest, and make a full hundred. A hundred men have known me under the very horns of this filthy, monstrous cuckold, who has imprisoned me in this chest, locked it with four locks, and kept me in the middle of this raging, roaring sea. He has guarded me and tried to keep me pure and chaste, not realizing that nothing can prevent or alter what is predestined and that when a woman desires something, no one can stop her." When Shahrayar and Shahzaman heard what the young woman said, they were greatly amazed, danced with joy, and said, "O God, O God! There is no power and no strength, save in God the Almighty, the Magnificent. Great is women's cunning." Then each of them took off his ring and handed it to her. She took them and put them with the rest in the purse. Then sitting again by the demon, she lifted his head, placed it back on her lap, and motioned to them, "Go on your way, or else I shall wake him."

They turned their backs and took to the road. Then Shahrayar turned to his brother and said, "My brother Shahzaman, look at this sorry plight. By God, it is worse than ours. This is no less than a demon who has carried a young woman away on her wedding night, imprisoned her in a glass chest, locked her up with four locks, and kept her in the middle of the sea, thinking that he could guard her from what God had foreordained, and you saw how she has managed to sleep with ninety-eight men, and added the two of us to make a hundred. Brother, let us go back to our kingdoms and our cities, never to marry a woman again. As for myself, I shall show you what I will do."

Then the two brothers headed home and journeyed till nightfall. On the morning of the third day, they reached their camp and men, entered their tent, and sat on their thrones. The chamberlains, deputies, princes, and viziers came to attend King Shahrayar, while he gave orders and bestowed robes of honor, as well as other gifts. Then at his command everyone returned to the city, and he went to his own palace and ordered his chief vizier, the father of the two girls Shahrazad and Dinarzad, who will be mentioned below, and said to him, "Take that wife of mine and put her to death." Then Shahrayar went to her himself, bound her, and handed her over to the vizier, who took her out and put her to death. Then King Shahrayar grabbed his sword, brandished it, and, entering the palace chambers, killed every one of his slave-girls and replaced them with others. He then swore to marry for one night only and kill the woman the next morning, in order to save himself from the wickedness and cunning of women, saying, "There is not a single chaste woman anywhere on the entire face of the earth." Shortly thereafter he provided his brother Shahzaman with supplies for his journey and sent him back to his own country with gifts, rarities, and money. The brother bade him good-bye and set out for home.

Shahrayar sat on his throne and ordered his vizier, the father of the two girls, to find him a wife from among the princes' daughters. The vizier found him one, and he slept with her and was done with her, and the next morning he ordered the vizier to put her to death. That very night he took one of his army officers' daughters, slept with her, and the next morning ordered the vizier to put her to death. The vizier, who could not disobey him, put her to death. The third night he took one of the merchants' daughters, slept with her till the morning, then ordered his vizier to put her to death, and the vizier did so. It became King Shahrayar's custom to take every night the daughter of a merchant or a commoner, spend the night with her, then have her put to death the next morning. He continued to do this until all the girls perished, their mothers mourned, and there arose a clamor among the fathers and mothers, who called the plague upon his head, complained to the Creator of the heavens, and called for help on Him who hears and answers prayers.

Now, as mentioned earlier, the vizier, who put the girls to death, had an older daughter called Shahrazad and a younger one called Dinarzad. The older daughter, Shahrazad, had read the books of literature, philosophy, and medicine. She knew poetry by heart, had studied historical reports, and was acquainted with the sayings of men and the maxims of sages and kings. She was intelligent, knowledgeable, wise, and refined. She had read and learned. One day she said to her father, "Father, I will tell you what is in my mind." He asked, "What is it?" She answered, "I would like you to marry me to King Shahrayar, so that I may either succeed in saving the people or perish and die like the rest." When the vizier heard what his daughter Shahrazad said, he got angry and said to her, "Foolish one, don't you know that King Shahrayar has sworn to spend but one night with a girl and have her put to death the next morning? If I give you to him, he will sleep with you for one night and will ask me to put you to death the next morning, and I shall have to do it, since I cannot disobey him." She said, "Father, you must give me to him, even if he kills me." He asked, "What has possessed you that you wish to imperil yourself?" She replied, "Father, you must give me to him. This is absolute and final." Her father the vizier became furious and said to her, "Daughter, 'He who misbehaves, ends up in trouble,' and 'He who considers not the end, the world is not his friend.' As the popular saying goes, 'I would be sitting pretty, but for my curiosity.' I am afraid that what happened to the donkey and the ox with the merchant will happen to you." She asked, "Father, what happened to the donkey, the ox, and the merchant?" He said:

[The Tale of the Ox and the Donkey]

There was a prosperous and wealthy merchant who lived in the countryside and labored on a farm. He owned many camels and herds of cattle and employed many men, and he had a wife and many grown-up as well as little children. This merchant was taught the language of the beasts, on condition that if he revealed his secret to anyone, he would die; therefore, even though he knew the language of every kind of animal, he did not let anyone know, for fear of death. One day, as he sat, with his wife beside him and his children playing before him, he glanced at an ox and a donkey he kept at the farmhouse, tied to adjacent troughs, and heard the ox say to the donkey, "Watchful one, I hope that you are enjoying the comfort and the service you are getting. Your ground is swept and watered, and they serve you, feed you sifted barley, and offer you clear, cool water to drink. I, on the contrary, am taken out to plow in the middle of the night. They clamp on my neck something they call yoke and plow, push me all day under the whip to plow the field, and drive me beyond my endurance until my sides are lacerated, and my neck is flayed. They work me from nighttime to nighttime, take me back in the dark, offer me beans soiled with mud and hay mixed with chaff, and let me spend the night lying in urine and dung. Meanwhile you rest on well-swept, watered, and smoothed ground, with a clean trough full of hay. You stand in comfort, save for the rare occasion when our master the merchant rides you to do a brief errand and returns. You are comfortable, while I am weary; you sleep, while I keep awake."

When the ox finished, the donkey turned to him and said, "Greenhorn, they were right in calling you ox, for you ox harbor no deceit, malice, or meanness. Being sincere, you exert and exhaust yourself to comfort others. Have you not heard the saying 'Out of bad luck, they hastened on the road'? You go into the field from early morning to endure your torture at the plow to the point of exhaustion. When the plowman takes you back and ties you to the trough, you go on butting and beating with your horns, kicking with your hoofs, and bellowing for the beans, until they toss them to you; then you begin to eat. Next time, when they bring them to you, don't eat or even touch them, but smell them, then draw back and lie down on the hay and straw. If you do this, life will be better and kinder to you, and you will find relief."

As the ox listened, he was sure that the donkey had given him good advice. He thanked him, commended him to God, and invoked His blessing on him, and said, "May you stay safe from harm, watchful one." All of this conversation took place, daughter, while the merchant listened and understood. On the following day, the plowman came to the merchant's house and, taking the ox, placed the yoke upon his neck and worked him at the plow, but the ox lagged behind. The plowman hit him, but following the donkey's advice, the ox, dissembling, fell on his belly, and the plowman hit him again. Thus the ox kept getting up and falling until nightfall, when the plowman took him home and tied him to the trough. But this time the ox did not bellow or kick the ground with his hoofs. Instead, he withdrew, away from the trough. Astonished, the plowman brought him his beans and fodder, but the ox only smelled the fodder and pulled back and lay down at a distance with the hay and straw, complaining till the morning. When the plowman arrived, he found the trough as he had left it, full of beans and fodder, and saw the ox lying on his back, hardly breathing, his belly puffed, and his legs raised in the air. The plowman felt sorry for him and said to himself, "By God, he did seem weak and unable to work." Then he went to the merchant and said, "Master, last night, the ox refused to eat or touch his fodder."

The merchant, who knew what was going on, said to the plowman, "Go to the wily donkey, put him to the plow, and work him hard until he finishes the ox's task." The plowman left, took the donkey, and placed the yoke upon his neck. Then he took him out to the field and drove him with blows until he finished the ox's work, all the while driving him with blows and beating him until his sides were lacerated and his neck was flayed. At nightfall he took him home, barely able to drag his legs under his tired body and his drooping ears. Meanwhile the ox spent his day resting. He ate all his food, drank his water, and lay quietly, chewing his cud in comfort. All day long he kept praising the donkey's advice and invoking God's blessing on him. When the donkey came back at night, the ox stood up to greet him saying, "Good evening, watchful one! You have done me a favor beyond description, for I have been sitting in comfort. God bless you for my sake." Seething with anger, the donkey did not reply, but said to himself, "All this happened to me because of my miscalculation. 'I would be sitting pretty, but for my curiosity.' If I don't find a way to return this ox to his former situation, I will perish." Then he went to his trough and lay down, while the ox continued to chew his cud and invoke God's blessing on him.

"You, my daughter, will likewise perish because of your miscalculation. Desist, sit quietly, and don't expose yourself to peril. I advise you out of compassion for you." She replied, "Father, I must go to the king, and you must give me to him." He said, "Don't do it." She insisted, "I must." He replied, "If you don't desist, I will do to you what the merchant did to his wife." She asked, "Father, what did the merchant do to his wife?" He said:

[The Tale of the Merchant and His Wife]

After what had happened to the donkey and the ox, the merchant and his wife went out in the moonlight to the stable, and he heard the donkey ask the ox in his own language, "Listen, ox, what are you going to do tomorrow morning, and what will you do when the plowman brings you your fodder?" The ox replied, "What shall I do but follow your advice and stick to it? If he brings me my fodder, I will pretend to be ill, lie down, and puff my belly." The donkey shook his head, and said, "Don't do it. Do you know what I heard our master the merchant say to the plowman?" The ox asked, "What?" The donkey replied, "He said that if the ox failed to get up and eat his fodder, he would call the butcher to slaughter him and skin him and would distribute the meat for alms and use the skin for a mat. I am afraid for you, but good advice is a matter of faith; therefore, if he brings you your fodder, eat it and look alert lest they cut your throat and skin you." The ox farted and bellowed.

The merchant got up and laughed loudly at the conversation between the donkey and the ox, and his wife asked him, "What are you laughing at? Are you making fun of me?" He said, "No." She said, "Tell me what made you laugh." He replied, "I cannot tell you. I am afraid to disclose the secret conversation of the animals." She asked, "And what prevents you from telling me?" He answered, "The fear of death." His wife said, "By God, you are lying. This is nothing but an excuse. I swear by God, the Lord of heaven, that if you don't tell me and explain the cause of your laughter, I will leave you. You must tell me." Then she went back to the house crying, and she continued to cry till the morning. The merchant said, "Damn it! Tell me why you are crying. Ask for God's forgiveness, and stop questioning and leave me in peace." She said, "I insist and will not desist." Amazed at her, he replied, "You insist! If I tell you what the donkey said to the ox, which made me laugh, I shall die." She said, "Yes, I insist, even if you have to die." He replied, "Then call your family," and she called their two daughters, her parents and relatives, and some neighbors. The merchant told them that he was about to die, and everyone, young and old, his children, the farmhands, and the servants began to cry until the house became a place of mourning. Then he summoned legal witnesses, wrote a will, leaving his wife and children their due portions, freed his slave-girls, and bid his family good-bye, while everybody, even the witnesses, wept. Then the wife's parents approached her and said, "Desist, for if your husband had not known for certain that he would die if he revealed his secret, he wouldn't have gone through all this." She replied, "I will not change my mind," and everybody cried and prepared to mourn his death.

Well, my daughter Shahrazad, it happened that the farmer kept fifty hens and a rooster at home, and while he felt sad to depart this world and leave his children and relatives behind, pondering and about to reveal and utter his secret, he overheard a dog of his say something in dog language to the rooster, who, beating and clapping his wings, had jumped on a hen and, finishing with her, jumped down and jumped on another. The merchant heard and understood what the dog said in his own language to the rooster, "Shameless, no-good rooster. Aren't you ashamed to do such a thing on a day like this?" The rooster asked, "What is special about this day?" The dog replied, "Don't you know that our master and friend is in mourning today? His wife is demanding that he disclose his secret, and when he discloses it, he will surely die. He is in this predicament, about to interpret to her the language of the animals, and all of us are mourning for him, while you clap your wings and get off one hen and jump on another. Aren't you ashamed?" The merchant heard the rooster reply, "You fool, you lunatic! Our master and friend claims to be wise, but he is foolish, for he has only one wife, yet he does not know how to manage her." The dog asked, "What should he do with her?"

The rooster replied, "He should take an oak branch, push her into a room, lock the door, and fall on her with the stick, beating her mercilessly until he breaks her arms and legs and she cries out, 'I no longer want you to tell me or explain anything.' He should go on beating her until he cures her for life, and she will never oppose him in anything. If he does this, he will live, and live in peace, and there will be no more grief, but he does not know how to manage." Well, my daughter Shahrazad, when the merchant heard the conversation between the dog and the rooster, he jumped up and, taking an oak branch, pushed his wife into a room, got in with her, and locked the door. Then he began to beat her mercilessly on her chest and shoulders and kept beating her until she cried for mercy, screaming, "No, no, I don't want to know anything. Leave me alone, leave me alone. I don't want to know anything," until he got tired of hitting her and opened the door. The wife emerged penitent, the husband learned good management, and everybody was happy, and the mourning turned into a celebration.

"If you don't relent, I shall do to you what the merchant did to his wife." She said, "Such tales don't deter me from my request. If you wish, I can tell you many such tales. In the end, if you don't take me to King Shahrayar, I shall go to him by myself behind your back and tell him that you have refused to give me to one like him and that you have begrudged your master one like me." The vizier asked, "Must you really do this?" She replied, "Yes, I must."

Tired and exhausted, the vizier went to King Shahrayar and, kissing the ground before him, told him about his daughter, adding that he would give her to him that very night. The king was astonished and said to him, "Vizier, how is it that you have found it possible to give me your daughter, knowing that I will, by God, the Creator of heaven, ask you to put her to death the next morning and that if you refuse, I will have you put to death too?" He replied, "My King and Lord, I have told her everything and explained all this to her, but she refuses and insists on being with you tonight." The king was delighted and said, "Go to her, prepare her, and bring her to me early in the evening."

The vizier went down, repeated the king's message to his daughter, and said, "May God not deprive me of you." She was very happy and, after preparing herself and packing what she needed, went to her younger sister, Dinarzad, and said, "Sister, listen well to what I am telling you. When I go to the king, I will send for you, and when you come and see that the king has finished with me, say, 'Sister, if you are not sleepy, tell us a story.' Then I will begin to tell a story, and it will cause the king to stop his practice, save myself, and deliver the people." Dinarzad replied, "Very well."

At nightfall the vizier took Shahrazad and went with her to the great King Shahrayar. But when Shahrayar took her to bed and began to fondle her, she wept, and when he asked her, "Why are you crying?" she replied, "I have a sister, and I wish to bid her good-bye before daybreak." Then the king sent for the sister, who came and went to sleep under the bed. When the night wore on, she woke up and waited until the king had satisfied himself with her sister Shahrazad and they were by now all fully awake. Then Dinarzad cleared her throat and said, "Sister, if you are not sleepy, tell us one of your lovely little tales to while away the night, before I bid you good-bye at daybreak, for I don't know what will happen to you tomorrow." Shahrazad turned to King Shahrayar and said, "May I have your permission to tell a story?" He replied, "Yes," and Shahrazad was very happy and said, "Listen":

[The Story of the Merchant and the Demon]

THE FIRST NIGHT

It is said, O wise and happy King, that once there was a prosperous merchant who had abundant wealth and investments and commitments in every country. He had many women and children and kept many servants and slaves. One day, having resolved to visit another country, he took provisions, filling his saddlebag with loaves of bread and with dates, mounted his horse, and set out on his journey. For many days and nights, he journeyed under God's care until he reached his destination. When he finished his business, he turned back to his home and family. He journeyed for three days, and on the fourth day, chancing to come to an orchard, went in to avoid the heat and shade himself from the sun of the open country. He came to a spring under a walnut tree and, tying his horse, sat by the spring, pulled out from the saddlebag some loaves of bread and a handful of dates, and began to eat, throwing the date pits right and left until he had had enough. Then he got up, performed his ablutions, and performed his prayers.

But hardly had he finished when he saw an old demon, with sword in hand, standing with his feet on the ground and his head in the clouds. The demon approached until he stood before him and screamed, saying, "Get up, so that I may kill you with this sword, just as you have killed my son." When the merchant saw and heard the demon, he was terrified and awestricken. He asked, "Master, for what crime do you wish to kill me?" The demon replied, "I wish to kill you because you have killed my son." The merchant asked, "Who has killed your son?" The demon replied, "You have killed my son." The merchant said, "By God, I did not kill your son. When and how could that have been?" The demon said, "Didn't you sit down, take out some dates from your saddlebag, and eat, throwing the pits right and left?" The merchant replied, "Yes, I did." The demon said, "You killed my son, for as you were throwing the stones right and left, my son happened to be walking by and was struck and killed by one of them, and I must now kill you." The merchant said, "O my lord, please don't kill me." The demon replied, "I must kill you as you killed him—blood for blood." The merchant said, "To God we belong and to God we turn. There is no power or strength, save in God the Almighty, the Magnificent. If I killed him, I did it by mistake. Please forgive me." The demon replied, "By God, I must kill you, as you killed my son." Then he seized him, and throwing him to the ground, raised the sword to strike him. The merchant began to weep and mourn his family and his wife and children. Again, the demon raised his sword to strike, while the merchant cried until he was drenched with tears, saying, "There is no power or strength, save in God the Almighty, the Magnificent." Then he began to recite the following verses:

> Life has two days: one peace, one wariness,
> And has two sides: worry and happiness.

Ask him who taunts us with adversity,
"Does fate, save those worthy of note, oppress?
Don't you see that the blowing, raging storms   5
Only the tallest of the trees beset,
And of earth's many green and barren lots,
Only the ones with fruits with stones are hit,
And of the countless stars in heaven's vault
None is eclipsed except the moon and sun?   10
You thought well of the days, when they were good,
Oblivious to the ills destined for one.
You were deluded by the peaceful nights,
Yet in the peace of night does sorrow stun."

When the merchant finished and stopped weeping, the demon said, "By God, I must kill you, as you killed my son, even if you weep blood." The merchant asked, "Must you?" The demon replied, "I must," and raised his sword to strike.

But morning overtook Shahrazad, and she lapsed into silence, leaving King Shahrayar burning with curiosity to hear the rest of the story. Then Dinarzad said to her sister Shahrazad, "What a strange and lovely story!" Shahrazad replied, "What is this compared with what I shall tell you tomorrow night if the king spares me and lets me live? It will be even better and more entertaining." The king thought to himself, "I will spare her until I hear the rest of the story; then I will have her put to death the next day." When morning broke, the day dawned, and the sun rose; the king left to attend to the affairs of the kingdom, and the vizier, Shahrazad's father, was amazed and delighted. King Shahrayar governed all day and returned home at night to his quarters and got into bed with Shahrazad. Then Dinarzad said to her sister Shahrazad, "Please, sister, if you are not sleepy, tell us one of your lovely little tales to while away the night." The king added, "Let it be the conclusion of the story of the demon and the merchant, for I would like to hear it." Shahrazad replied, "With the greatest pleasure, dear, happy King":

THE SECOND NIGHT

It is related, O wise and happy King, that when the demon raised his sword, the merchant asked the demon again, "Must you kill me?" and the demon replied, "Yes." Then the merchant said, "Please give me time to say good-bye to my family and my wife and children, divide my property among them, and appoint guardians. Then I shall come back, so that you may kill me." The demon replied, "I am afraid that if I release you and grant you time, you will go and do what you wish, but will not come back." The merchant said, "I swear to keep my pledge to come back, as the God of Heaven and earth is my witness." The demon asked, "How much time do you need?" The merchant replied, "One year, so that I may see enough of my children, bid my wife good-bye, discharge my obligations to people, and come back on New Year's Day." The demon asked, "Do you swear to God that if I let you go, you will come back on New Year's Day?" The merchant replied, "Yes, I swear to God."

After the merchant swore, the demon released him, and he mounted his horse sadly and went on his way. He journeyed until he reached his home and came to his wife and children. When he saw them, he wept bitterly, and when his family saw his sorrow and grief, they began to reproach him for his behavior, and his wife said, "Husband, what is the matter with you? Why do you mourn, when we are happy, celebrating your return?" He replied, "Why not mourn when I have only one year to live?" Then he told her of his encounter with the demon and informed her that he had sworn to return on New Year's Day, so that the demon might kill him.

When they heard what he said, everyone began to cry. His wife struck her face in lamentation and cut her hair, his daughters wailed, and his little children cried. It was a day of mourning, as all the children gathered around their father to weep and exchange good-byes. The next day he wrote his will, dividing his property, discharged his obligations to people, left bequests and gifts, distributed alms, and engaged reciters to read portions of the Quran in his house. Then he summoned legal witnesses and in their presence freed his slaves and slave-girls, divided among his elder children their shares of the property, appointed guardians for his little ones, and gave his wife her share, according to her marriage contract. He spent the rest of the time with his family, and when the year came to an end, save for the time needed for the journey, he performed his ablutions, performed his prayers, and, carrying his burial shroud, began to bid his family good-bye. His sons hung around his neck, his daughters wept, and his wife wailed. Their mourning scared him, and he began to weep, as he embraced and kissed his children good-bye. He said to them, "Children, this is God's will and decree, for man was created to die." Then he turned away and, mounting his horse, journeyed day and night until he reached the orchard on New Year's Day.

He sat at the place where he had eaten the dates, waiting for the demon, with a heavy heart and tearful eyes. As he waited, an old man, leading a deer on a leash, approached and greeted him, and he returned the greeting. The old man inquired, "Friend, why do you sit here in this place of demons and devils? For in this haunted orchard none come to good." The merchant replied by telling him what had happened to him and the demon, from beginning to end. The old man was amazed at the merchant's fidelity and said, "Yours is a magnificent pledge," adding, "By God, I shall not leave until I see what will happen to you with the demon." Then he sat down beside him and chatted with him. As they talked . . .

But morning overtook Shahrazad, and she lapsed into silence. As the day dawned, and it was light, her sister Dinarzad said, "What a strange and wonderful story!" Shahrazad replied, "Tomorrow night I shall tell something even stranger and more wonderful than this."

THE THIRD NIGHT

When it was night and Shahrazad was in bed with the king, Dinarzad said to her sister Shahrazad, "Please, if you are not sleepy, tell us one of your lovely little tales to while away the night." The king added, "Let it be the conclusion of the merchant's story." Shahrazad replied, "As you wish":

I heard, O happy King, that as the merchant and the man with the deer sat talking, another old man approached, with two black hounds, and when he reached them, he greeted them, and they returned his greeting. Then he asked them about themselves, and the man with the deer told him the story of the merchant and the demon, how the merchant had sworn to return on New Year's Day, and how the demon was waiting to kill him. He added that when he himself heard the story, he swore never to leave until he saw what would happen between the merchant and the demon. When the man with the two dogs heard the story, he was amazed, and he too swore never to leave them until he saw what would happen between them. Then he questioned the merchant, and the merchant repeated to him what had happened to him with the demon.

While they were engaged in conversation, a third old man approached and greeted them, and they returned his greeting. He asked, "Why do I see the two of you sitting here, with this merchant between you, looking abject, sad, and dejected?" They told him the merchant's story and explained that they were sitting and waiting to see what would happen to him with the demon. When he heard the story, he sat down with them, saying, "By God, I too like you will not leave, until I see what happens to this man with the demon." As they sat, conversing with one another, they suddenly saw the dust rising from the open country, and when it cleared, they saw the demon approaching, with a drawn steel sword in his hand. He stood before them without greeting them, yanked the merchant with his left hand, and, holding him fast before him, said, "Get ready to die." The merchant and the three old men began to weep and wail.

But dawn broke and morning overtook Shahrazad, and she lapsed into silence. Then Dinarzad said, "Sister, what a lovely story!" Shahrazad replied, "What is this compared with what I shall tell you tomorrow night? It will be even better; it will be more wonderful, delightful, entertaining, and delectable if the king spares me and lets me live." The king was all curiosity to hear the rest of the story and said to himself, "By God, I will not have her put to death until I hear the rest of the story and find out what happened to the merchant with the demon. Then I will have her put to death the next morning, as I did with the others." Then he went out to attend to the affairs of his kingdom, and when he saw Shahrazad's father, he treated him kindly and showed him favors, and the vizier was amazed. When night came, the king went home, and when he was in bed with Shahrazad, Dinarzad said, "Sister, if you are not sleepy, tell us one of your lovely little tales to while away the night." Shahrazad replied, "With the greatest pleasure":

THE FOURTH NIGHT

It is related, O happy King, that the first old man with the deer approached the demon and, kissing his hands and feet, said, "Fiend and King of the demon kings, if I tell you what happened to me and that deer, and you find it strange and amazing, indeed stranger and more amazing than what happened to you and the merchant, will you grant me a third of your claim on him for his crime and guilt?" The demon replied, "I will." The old man said:

[The First Old Man's Tale]

Demon, this deer is my cousin, my flesh and blood. I married her when I was very young, and she a girl of twelve, who reached womanhood only afterward. For thirty years we lived together, but I was not blessed with children, for she bore neither boy nor girl. Yet I continued to be kind to her, to care for her, and to treat her generously. Then I took a mistress, and she bore me a son, who grew up to look like a slice of the moon.[5] Meanwhile, my wife grew jealous of my mistress and my son. One day, when he was ten, I had to go on a journey. I entrusted my wife, this one here, with my mistress and son, bade her take good care of them, and was gone for a whole year. In my absence my wife, this cousin of mine, learned soothsaying and magic and cast a spell on my son and turned him into a young bull. Then she summoned my shepherd, gave my son to him, and said, "Tend this bull with the rest of the cattle." The shepherd took him and tended him for a while. Then she cast a spell on the mother, turning her into a cow, and gave her also to the shepherd.

When I came back, after all this was done, and inquired about my mistress and my son, she answered, "Your mistress died, and your son ran away two months ago, and I have had no news from him ever since." When I heard her, I grieved for my mistress, and with an anguished heart I mourned for my son for nearly a year. When the Great Feast of the Immolation[6] drew near, I summoned the shepherd and ordered him to bring me a fat cow for the sacrifice. The cow he brought me was in reality my enchanted mistress. When I bound her and pressed against her to cut her throat, she wept and cried, as if saying, "My son, my son," and her tears coursed down her cheeks. Astonished and seized with pity, I turned away and asked the shepherd to bring me a different cow. But my wife shouted, "Go on. Butcher her, for he has none better or fatter. Let us enjoy her meat at feast time." I approached the cow to cut her throat, and again she cried, as if saying, "My son, my son." Then I turned away from her and said to the shepherd, "Butcher her for me." The shepherd butchered her, and when he skinned her, he found neither meat nor fat but only skin and bone. I regretted having her butchered and said to the shepherd, "Take her all for yourself, or give her as alms to whomever you wish, and find me a fat young bull from among the flock." The shepherd took her away and disappeared, and I never knew what he did with her.

Then he brought me my son, my heartblood, in the guise of a fat young bull. Then my son saw me, he shook his head loose from the rope, ran toward me, and, throwing himself at my feet, kept rubbing his head against me. I was astonished and touched with sympathy, pity, and mercy, for the blood hearkened to the blood and the divine bond, and my heart throbbed within me when I saw the tears coursing over the cheeks of my son the young bull, as he dug the earth with his hoofs. I turned away and said to the shepherd, "Let him go with the rest of the flock, and be kind to him, for I have decided to spare him. Bring me another one instead of him." My wife, this very deer, shouted, "You shall sacrifice none but this bull." I got angry and replied, "I listened to you and butchered the cow uselessly. I will not listen to you and kill this bull, for I have decided to spare him." But she pressed me, saying, "You must butcher this bull," and I bound him and took the knife . . .

5. The moon is a symbol of beauty for men and women.
6. The Feast of Sacrifice, celebrated throughout the Muslim world at the end of the pilgrimage to Mecca; to commemorate Abraham, who was willing to sacrifice his son Isaac when commanded by God but was allowed to offer a ram instead, Muslims sacrifice animals to God.

But dawn broke, and morning overtook Shahrazad, and she lapsed into silence, leaving the king all curiosity for the rest of the story. Then her sister Dinarzad said, "What an entertaining story!" Shahrazad replied. "Tomorrow night I shall tell you something even stranger, more wonderful, and more entertaining if the king spares me and lets me live."

THE FIFTH NIGHT

The following night, Dinarzad said to her sister Shahrazad, "Please, sister, if you are not sleepy, tell us one of your little tales." Shahrazad replied, "With the greatest pleasure":

I heard, dear King, that the old man with the deer said to the demon and to his companions:

I took the knife and as I turned to slaughter my son, he wept, bellowed, rolled at my feet, and motioned toward me with his tongue. I suspected something, began to waver with trepidation and pity, and finally released him, saying to my wife, "I have decided to spare him, and I commit him to your care." Then I tried to appease and please my wife, this very deer, by slaughtering another bull, promising her to slaughter this one next season. We slept that night, and when God's dawn broke, the shepherd came to me without letting my wife know, and said, "Give me credit for bringing you good news." I replied, "Tell me, and the credit is yours." He said, "Master, I have a daughter who is fond of soothsaying and magic and who is adept at the art of oaths and spells. Yesterday I took home with me the bull you had spared, to let him graze with the cattle, and when my daughter saw him, she laughed and cried at the same time. When I asked her why she laughed and cried, she answered that she laughed because the bull was in reality the son of our master the cattle owner, put under a spell by his stepmother, and that she cried because his father had slaughtered the son's mother. I could hardly wait till daybreak to bring you the good news about your son."

Demon, when I heard that, I uttered a cry and fainted, and when I came to myself, I accompanied the shepherd to his home, went to my son, and threw myself at him, kissing him and crying. He turned his head toward me, his tears coursing over his cheeks, and dangled his tongue, as if to say, "Look at my plight." Then I turned to the shepherd's daughter and asked, "Can you release him from the spell? If you do, I will give you all my cattle and all my possessions." She smiled and replied, "Master, I have no desire for your wealth, cattle, or possessions. I will deliver him, but on two conditions: first, that you let me marry him; second, that you let me cast a spell on her who had cast a spell on him, in order to control her and guard against her evil power." I replied, "Do whatever you wish and more. My possessions are for you and my son. As for my wife, who has done this to my son and made me slaughter his mother, her life is forfeit to you." She said, "No, but I will let her taste what she has inflicted on others." Then the shepherd's daughter filled a bowl of water, uttered an incantation and an oath, and said to my son, "Bull, if you have been created in this image by the All-Conquering, Almighty Lord, stay as you are, but if you have been treacherously put under a spell, change back to your human form, by the will of God, Creator of the wide world." Then she sprinkled him with the water, and he shook himself and changed from a bull back to his human form.

As I rushed to him, I fainted, and when I came to myself, he told me what my wife, this very deer, had done to him and to his mother. I said to him, "Son, God has sent us someone who will pay her back for what you and your mother and I have suffered at her hands." Then, O demon, I gave my son in marriage to the shepherd's daughter, who turned my wife into this very deer, saying to me, "To me this is a pretty form, for she will be with us day and night, and it is better to turn her into a pretty deer than to suffer her sinister looks." Thus she stayed with us, while the days and nights followed one another, and the months and years went by. Then one day the shepherd's daughter died, and my son went to the country of this very man with whom you have had your encounter. Some time later I took my wife, this very deer, with me, set out to find out what had happened to my son, and chanced to stop here. This is my story, my strange and amazing story.

The demon assented, saying, "I grant you one-third of this man's life."

Then, O King Shahrayar, the second old man with the two black dogs approached the demon and said, "I too shall tell you what happened to me and to these two dogs, and if I tell it to you and you find it stranger and more amazing than this man's story will you grant me one-third of this man's life?" The demon replied, "I will." Then the old man began to tell his story, saying . . .

But dawn broke, and morning overtook Shahrazad, and she lapsed into silence. Then Dinarzad said, "This is an amazing story," and Shahrazad replied, "What is this compared with what I shall tell you tomorrow night if the king spares me and lets me live!" The king said to himself, "By God, I will not have her put to death until I find out what happened to the man with the two black dogs. Then I will have her put to death, God the Almighty willing."

THE SIXTH NIGHT

When the following night arrived and Shahrazad was in bed with King Shahrayar, her sister Dinarzad said, "Sister, if you are not sleepy, tell us a little tale. Finish the one you started." Shahrazad replied, "With the greatest pleasure":

I heard, O happy King, that the second old man with the two dogs said:

[The Second Old Man's Tale]

Demon, as for my story, these are the details. These two dogs are my brothers. When our father died, he left behind three sons, and left us three thousand dinars,[7] with which each of us opened a shop and became a shopkeeper. Soon my older brother, one of these very dogs, went and sold the contents of his shop for a thousand dinars, bought trading goods, and, having prepared himself for his trading trip, left us. A full year went by, when one day, as I sat in my

---

7. Gold coins; the basic Muslim money units [translator's note].

shop, a beggar stopped by to beg. When I refused him, he tearfully asked, "Don't you recognize me?" and when I looked at him closely, I recognized my brother. I embraced him and took him into the shop, and when I asked him about his plight, he replied, "The money is gone, and the situation is bad." Then I took him to the public bath, clothed him in one of my robes, and took him home with me. Then I examined my books and checked my balance, and found out that I had made a thousand dinars and that my net worth was two thousand dinars. I divided the amount between my brother and myself, and said to him, "Think as if you have never been away." He gladly took the money and opened another shop.

Soon afterward my second brother, this other dog, went and sold his merchandise and collected his money, intending to go on a trading trip. We tried to dissuade him, but he did not listen. Instead, he bought merchandise and trading goods, joined a group of travelers, and was gone for a full year. Then he came back, just like his older brother. I said to him, "Brother, didn't I advise you not to go?" He replied tearfully, "Brother, it was foreordained. Now I am poor and penniless, without even a shirt on my back." Demon, I took him to the public bath, clothed him in one of my new robes, and took him back to the shop. After we had something to eat, I said to him, "Brother, I shall do my business accounts, calculate my net worth for the year, and after subtracting the capital, whatever the profit happens to be, I shall divide it equally between you and myself. When I examined my books and subtracted the capital, I found out that my profit was two thousand dinars, and I thanked God and felt very happy. Then I divided the money, giving him a thousand dinars and keeping a thousand for myself. With that money he opened another shop, and the three of us stayed together for a while. Then my two brothers asked me to go on a trading journey with them, but I refused, saying, "What did you gain from your ventures that I can gain?"

They dropped the matter, and for six years we worked in our stores, buying and selling. Yet every year they asked me to go on a trading journey with them, but I refused, until I finally gave in. I said, "Brothers, I am ready to go with you. How much money do you have?" I found out that they had eaten and drunk and squandered everything they had, but I said nothing to them and did not reproach them. Then I took inventory, gathered all I had together, and sold everything. I was pleased to discover that the sale netted six thousand dinars. Then I divided the money into two parts, and said to my brothers, "The sum of three thousand dinars is for you and myself to use on our trading journey. The other three thousand I shall bury in the ground, in case what happened to you happens to me, so that when we return, we will find three thousand dinars to reopen our shops." They replied, "This is an excellent idea." Then, demon, I divided my money and buried three thousand dinars. Of the remaining three I gave each of my brothers a thousand and kept a thousand for myself. After I closed my shop, we bought merchandise and trading goods, rented a large seafaring boat, and after loading it with our goods and provisions, sailed day and night, for a month.

But morning overtook Shahrazad, and she lapsed into silence. Then her sister Dinarzad said, "Sister, what a lovely story!" Shahrazad replied, "Tomorrow night I shall tell you something even lovelier, stranger, and more wonderful if I live, the Almighty God willing."

THE SEVENTH NIGHT

The following night Dinarzad said to her sister Shahrazad, "For God's sake, sister, if you are not sleepy, tell us a little tale." The king added, "Let it be the completion of the story of the merchant and the demon." Shahrazad replied, "With the greatest pleasure":

I heard, O happy King, that the second old man said to the demon:

For a month my brothers, these very dogs, and I sailed the salty sea, until we came to a port city. We entered the city and sold our goods, earning ten dinars for every dinar. Then we bought other goods, and when we got to the seashore to embark, I met a girl who was dressed in tatters. She kissed my hands and said, "O my lord, be charitable and do me a favor, and I believe that I shall be able to reward you for it." I replied, "I am willing to do you a favor regardless of any reward." She said, "O my lord, marry me, clothe me, and take me home with you on this boat, as your wife, for I wish to give myself to you. I, in turn, will reward you for your kindness and charity, the Almighty God willing. Don't be misled by my poverty and present condition." When I heard her words, I felt pity for her, and guided by what God the Most High had intended for me, I consented. I clothed her with an expensive dress and married her. Then I took her to the boat, spread the bed for her, and consummated our marriage. We sailed many days and nights, and I, feeling love for her, stayed with her day and night, neglecting my brothers. In the meantime they, these very dogs, grew jealous of me, envied me for my increasing merchandise and wealth, and coveted all our possessions. At last they decided to betray me and, tempted by the Devil, plotted to kill me. One night they waited until I was asleep beside my wife; then they carried the two of us and threw us into the sea.

When we awoke, my wife turned into a she-demon and carried me out of the sea to an island. When it was morning, she said, "Husband, I have rewarded you by saving you from drowning, for I am one of the demons who believe in God.[8] When I saw you by the seashore, I felt love for you and came to you in the guise in which you saw me, and when I expressed my love for you, you accepted me. Now I must kill your brothers." When I heard what she said, I was amazed and I thanked her and said, "As for destroying my brothers, this I do not wish, for I will not behave like them." Then I related to her what had happened to me and them, from beginning to end. When she heard my story, she got very angry at them, and said, "I shall fly to them now, drown their boat, and let them all perish." I entreated her, saying, "For God's sake, don't. The proverb advises 'Be kind to those who hurt you.' No matter what, they are my brothers after all." In this manner, I entreated her and pacified her. Afterward, she took me and flew away with me until she brought me home and put me down on the roof of my house. I climbed down, threw the doors open, and dug up the money I had buried. Then I went out and, greeting the people in the market, reopened my shop. When I came home in the evening, I found these two dogs tied up, and when they saw me, they came to

---

8. According to the Qur'an, God created both humans and demons (jinns), some of whom accepted Islam.

me, wept, and rubbed themselves against me. I started, when I suddenly heard my wife say, "O my lord, these are your brothers." I asked, "Who has done this to them?" She replied, "I sent to my sister and asked her to do it. They will stay in this condition for ten years, after which they may be delivered." Then she told me where to find her and departed. The ten years have passed, and I was with my brothers on my way to her to have the spell lifted, when I met this man, together with this old man with the deer. When I asked him about himself, he told me about his encounter with you, and I resolved not to leave until I found out what would happen between you and him. This is my story. Isn't it amazing?

The demon replied, "By God, it is strange and amazing. I grant you one-third of my claim on him for his crime."

Then the third old man said, "Demon, don't disappoint me. If I told you a story that is stranger and more amazing than the first two would you grant me one-third of your claim on him for his crime?" The demon replied, "I will." Then the old man said, "Demon, listen":

But morning overlook Shahrazad, and she lapsed into silence. Then her sister said, "What an amazing story!" Shahrazad replied, "The rest is even more amazing." The king said to himself, "I will not have her put to death until I hear what happened to the old man and the demon; then I will have her put to death, as is my custom with the others."

THE EIGHTH NIGHT

The following night Dinarzad said to her sister Shahrazad, "For God's sake, sister, if you are not sleepy, tell us one of your lovely little tales to while away the night." Shahrazad replied, "With the greatest pleasure":

[The Third Old Man's Tale][9]

The demon said, "This is a wonderful story, and I grant you a third of my claim on the merchant's life."

The third sheikh approached and said to the demon, "I will tell you a story more wonderful than these two if you will grant me a third of your claim on his life, O demon!"

To which the demon agreed.

So the sheikh began:

O sultan and chief of the demons, this mule was my wife. I had gone off on a journey and was absent from her for a whole year. At last I came to the end of my journey and returned home late one night. When I entered the house I saw a black slave lying in bed with her. They were chatting and dallying and laughing and kissing and quarreling together. When she saw me my wife leaped out of bed, ran to the water jug, recited a spell over it, then splashed me with some of the water and said, "Leave this form for the form of a dog."

9. Translated by Jerome W. Clinton. Because the earliest manuscript does not include a story for the third sheikh, later narrators sup- plied one. This brief anecdote comes from a manuscript found in the library of the Royal Academy in Madrid.

Immediately I became a dog and she chased me out of the house. I ran out of the gate and didn't stop running until I reached a butcher's shop. I entered it and fell to eating the bones lying about. When the owner of the shop saw me, he grabbed me and carried me into his house. When his daughter saw me, she hid her face and said, "Why are you bringing this strange man in with you?"

"What man?" her father asked.

"This dog is a man whose wife has put a spell on him," she said, "but I can set him free again." She took a jug of water, recited a spell over it, then splashed a little water from it on me, and said, "Leave this shape for your original one."

And I became myself again. I kissed her hand and said, "I want to cast a spell on my wife as she did on me. Please give me a little of that water."

"Gladly," she said, "if you find her asleep, sprinkle a few drops on her and she will become whatever you wish."

Well, I did find her asleep, and I sprinkled some water on her and said, "Leave this shape for the shape of a she mule." She at once became the very mule you see here, oh sultan and chief of the demons."

The demon then turned to him and asked, "Is this really true?"

"Yes," he answered, nodding his head vigorously, "it's all true."

When the sheikh had finished his story, the demon shook with laughter and granted him a third of his claim on the merchant's blood.

Then the demon released the merchant and departed. The merchant turned to the three old men and thanked them, and they congratulated him on his deliverance and bade him good-bye. Then they separated, and each of them went on his way. The merchant himself went back home to his family, his wife, and his children, and he lived with them until the day he died. But this story is not as strange or as amazing as the story of the fisherman.

Dinarzad asked, "Please, sister, what is the story of the fisherman?" Shahrazad said: . . .

GEOFFREY CHAUCER
1340?–1400

While there was plenty of literature in English before Chaucer, later generations of writers would identify his *Canterbury Tales* as the foundation of the English poetic tradition. Chaucer was the first to conceive of poetry in English not as the product of an isolated, provincial nation located in an obscure corner of Europe but as a vital agent in the fourteenth-century emergence of the vernacular as a literary language. For this reason, Chaucer's models and rivals were not so much the English authors of **Beowulf** and *Sir Gawain and the Green Knight* as the Europeans **Dante, Petrarch,** and Boccaccio. Queen Elizabeth's tutor, Roger Ascham, recognized

Chaucer's foundational role by calling him "our English **Homer**." The sentiment was reiterated by Dryden, who translated several of the tales alongside selections from **Ovid**'s *Metamorphoses*, declaring "I hold him in the same degree of veneration as the Grecians held Homer or the Romans **Virgil**." In his *Faerie Queene*, Spenser calls Chaucer the "well of English undefiled," a stream of poetic influence still visible in the opening lines of T. S. Eliot's *The Waste Land*. For these writers, Chaucer's vivid, naturalistic English was the firm ground on which they could anchor a national literature.

LIFE

Chaucer's family origins were solidly middle class. His father and grandfather had been wine merchants, and by placing the youthful Chaucer as a servant at the royal court they set in motion a social transition that would ultimately lead to the family's participation in the upper classes of English society. Chaucer's granddaughter, Alice de la Pole, married a duke, and her grandson was named as the heir to his uncle, Richard III (though he never reached the throne). Chaucer's own family history is an example of the increasing social fluidity of late medieval English culture, in which status could change dramatically over just a few generations. Unlike many premodern poets who were supported by wealthy patrons, Chaucer was obliged to hold a mundane day job for most of his career. He had the time-consuming and tedious position of record keeper at the customs authority in London, and later supervised a number of building projects in his role as clerk of public works. In his *House of Fame*, Chaucer describes poring over his financial ledgers all day, and his books of poetry and fiction all night.

Chaucer's entry into the bureaucracy of English government followed from his early placement in a series of households within the royal family, beginning as a page in the retinue of the Countess of Ulster, daughter-in-law of King Edward III. In fact, the very first documentation of the poet's existence appears in a record of clothes purchased for the then-teenage Chaucer when he was attached to the countess's household. Later in his career, Chaucer was directly rewarded for his work for the court by Edward's grandson, King Richard II, and had the support of Edward's son John of Gaunt, the Duke of Lancaster (who, through a late third marriage, also became Chaucer's brother-in-law). Chaucer had a genius for keeping on the right side of power in a difficult and competitive era, a time characterized by civil unrest, international war, and, ultimately, seizure of the throne in 1399 by John of Gaunt's son and Richard II's cousin, Henry IV. Chaucer appears to have seamlessly transferred his loyalty from Richard to the new king, addressing one of his final lyrics, "A Complaint to His Purse," to the "conqueror of Brutus's Albion, who by lineage and free election is the true king." His subtle and politically astute poetry is as much the product of social and economic turmoil as is Dante's *Divine Comedy*: unlike Dante, however, who ended his days in exile, Chaucer knew how to play all sides against each other in order to protect himself.

As a soldier in the Hundred Years' War and, later, a diplomatic envoy for the English government, Chaucer traveled repeatedly to France, Spain, and—most importantly—Italy; there he encountered the work of Dante, Petrarch, and Boccaccio, which became central to his own writing. French literature had already had a strong impact on English writers of the period, but Italian literature was something new and exciting: through Chaucer, the humanist tradition championed by Petrarch began to be felt in England, along with the high allegorical mode of Dante and the story collections of Boccaccio. While the exact chronology of Chaucer's works is uncertain, they are often divided roughly into three periods: the so-called French phase, which includes the *Book of the Duchess*, an elegiac dream vision that owes much to the *Romance of the Rose* and the poetry of Machaut and Froissart; the Italian phase, which features the *Parliament of Fowls* and the *House of Fame*, both of which refer explicitly to Dante's *Divine Comedy*; and the English phase, during which Chaucer composed his *Canterbury Tales*. This sequence has many faults—most seriously, it tends to privilege the final, culminating period of the poet's career as specifically "English." Yet despite simplifying, it provides a useful way to contextualize a series of major works, each of which represents a significant innovation beyond what had come before.

In addition to the literature of his French and Italian contemporaries, Chaucer was deeply indebted to the major classical authors, especially Ovid and Virgil. A more particular influence, however, was the late antique philosophical poem of Boethius, the *Consolation of Philosophy*. Chaucer was a penetrating reader of the *Consolation*, which he translated into English, and he repeatedly turned to Boethian themes such as the competing roles of Fortune and Providence, the place of free will in the human soul, and the role of love as source of both chaos and order. In his dream visions and *Troilus and Criseyde*, Chaucer ostentatiously displays his classical learning and makes continual reference to the poems of his French and Italian contemporaries. But in the *Canterbury Tales*, Chaucer suddenly begins to wear his learning much more lightly: allusions become indirect and often parodic, and the focus of the poetry shifts instead to the landscape

of society and, especially, to the relationship between the nature of a storyteller and the story he or she tells.

TIMES

Chaucer's England was the crucible of Reformation: the last years of the fourteenth century witnessed the emergence of religiously unorthodox communities loosely grouped under the term "Lollardy," an originally derogatory term used to identify such would-be reformers as dangerous heretics who sowed discord in the church. Lollard preachers argued that the Bible should be available in the vernacular language so that each person could know scripture at first hand, that images were really idols leading away from rather than toward God, and that pilgrimages were nothing more than social gatherings thinly disguised as devotional practice. In Chaucer's day, such unorthodox views were regarded with suspicion but were not yet as energetically suppressed as they would be just a few years after his death, when those suspected of Lollardy might be burned in the public square along with their unauthorized translations. Chaucer's Parson, who recounts a penitential treatise as the concluding story of the *Canterbury Tales*, is mocked by the Host, who exclaims, "I smell a Lollard in the wind." This kind of mockery, still just barely playful in the last decade of the fourteenth century, would soon evolve into denunciation and persecution. After this violent suppression, the aims of the Lollards would reemerge more successfully in the sixteenth century.

The same impulse that led medieval English men and women to want to read the Bible in English also led to other expressions of religious piety, including the tremendously popular stories of the lives of saints (two of which appear in the *Canterbury Tales*, in the Prioress's Tale and the Second Nun's Tale) and autobiographies of devout women such as Julian of Norwich and Margery Kempe. Chaucer's Wife of Bath is far less focused on heavenly goals than were these women: for her, pilgrimage is less about retracing the pathway to God than about "wandering by the way." Like Margery Kempe, however, the Wife of Bath is a strong female representative of the emerging bourgeois class whose wealth was built on local industries such as brewing (Margery Kempe) and weaving (the Wife of Bath), and whose independence was expressed physically through the act of travel both within England and abroad. Chaucer's pilgrims exemplify the late medieval English eagerness to find the right path to God, whether through the unmediated experience of scripture, as advocated by the Lollards, or through the highly overdetermined mediation of pardons (certificates from Rome that guaranteed the devout buyer a shorter stay in purgatory).

The same instability that had come to threaten the church's control of the Christian flock in England, through the rise of Lollardy, also affected the smooth working of government. The reign of Richard II, who had ascended the throne as a child in 1377 following the death of his grandfather Edward III, was marked by capricious rule, discord between the king's advisers and the major lords of the realm, and repeated heavy taxation necessitated by the ongoing war between England and France. Discord within the capital city of London itself was particularly intense, as the burghers of the city became increasingly involved in the disputes between Parliament and the king. The greatest disruption took place in 1381, as a popular uprising broke out in the countryside in response to the imposition of yet another heavy tax. The Peasants' Revolt, as it was later called, moved rapidly through the towns and fields outside London, entering the city with violence. When the archbishop of Canterbury confronted the mob, urging the peasants to return to their homes, he was decapitated and his head impaled on a pike on London Bridge. The peasants rampaged through the streets, sacking and burning the palace of the king's uncle and chief adviser, John of Gaunt. Gaunt was connected to Chaucer both as his main patron and through family ties, but the revolt struck still closer to home for Chaucer: the mob slaughtered a group of Flemish immigrant workers in a London street where Chaucer had lived as a boy, and it entered the city through a major gate— Aldgate—above which Chaucer had his lodgings. Although Chaucer must have witnessed this violence at first hand, his allusions to social unrest are always oblique and, above all, cautious.

WORK

The Canterbury Tales is a frame-tale poem; like ***The Thousand and One Nights*** and Boccaccio's *Decameron*, it has a beginning and ending within which a series of tales are related. Unlike *The Thousand and One Nights*, which has (for the most part) a single storyteller, and the *Decameron*, which has a relatively homogenous company of noble young narrators, *The Canterbury Tales* revels in the extraordinary range of possible tales and possible tale-tellers. From the humble Miller to the chivalric Knight, from the bossy Wife of Bath to the effete Pardoner, Chaucer's diverse pilgrims span the range of medieval English life. The pilgrims are, in a way, types or ideals of each manner of life available to the individual: the company includes a nun, a lawyer, a squire, a sailor, and so on. But each teller is also an individual, characterized as such not only in the prefatory prologues that introduce each tale but also in the manner in which the tale itself is told. Petty rivalries, as between the Miller and the Reeve or between the Friar and the Summoner, are played out during the interludes between tales; tale-tellers pay back or "quite" one another by telling stories that indirectly comment on their fellows, causing sometimes argument and discord, sometimes laughter, or sometimes—as at the end of the Pardoner's Tale—both.

Chaucer's Wife of Bath is endowed with a vivid personality and a complex inner life that she herself tells us all about. In her Prologue, she sets her female experience against the misogynist stereotypes of women as lawless, sexually voracious, and manipulative creatures, a view promoted by certain traditions of medieval religious thought. Yet the reader is forced to ask if the Wife's frank celebration of her own sexuality, and her account of the torment she has inflicted on her three old husbands, does not in fact confirm those stereotypes. An answer is suggested by the Wife's claim that she is only playing: indeed, at one point she speaks as if she were showing her almost exclusively male audience how she would conduct a kind of school for wives. She seems, in other words, to be putting on a performance, pretending to reveal to her fascinated audience the secrets that women share among themselves and thereby letting men witness the intimate life of a woman. Yet as the Prologue proceeds we feel that her playful dramatics give way to a more serious, more authentic self-revelation. We learn that not only have her husbands suffered in marriage but that she has too, that she is unavoidably (if cheerfully) aware of her advancing years, and that what she seems to value most is neither money nor the sex she

so aggressively celebrates but the companionship and love she comes finally to share with her fifth husband. In the same way, her tale gradually reveals itself to be more than simply a nostalgic wish fulfillment for the return of youth and beauty. When the criminal knight tries to learn what women most desire, he is offered a series of misogynist answers; but when forced to marry he discovers, through the moral lecture his old wife delivers, that she possesses a wisdom that he himself lacks. This is why he leaves the final decision about what form she will assume up to her, and in granting her mastery he is rewarded not merely with youth and beauty but with a marriage of mutual affection. It is through this experience, then, rather than by relying on the authority of time-honored opinions, that the knight comes to learn about the true nature of women.

CHAUCER'S LANGUAGE

Chaucer's Middle English strikes the present-day reader as both familiar and strange, separated from Modern English by peculiarities of pronunciation and word order, but recognizable as its ancestor through names and terms that have remained essentially unchanged. Unlike the Old English of *Beowulf*, which must be learned as though it were a foreign language, Middle English is usually approached as if it were a dialect or an idiom— close to home, but still uncannily strange. We reproduce below the first eighteen lines of the General Prologue to the *Tales*, not only to illustrate the gap between English of the fourteenth century and the twenty-first, and to provide a frame of reference for the modern English translation that follows, but also to give a taste of the unfamiliar familiar tongue of the father of English poetry.

Whan that Aprill with his shoures soote
The droghte of March hath perced to the roote,
And bathed every veyne in swich licour
Of which vertu engendred is the flour;
Whan Zephirus eek with his sweete breeth
Inspired hath in every holt and heeth
The tender croppes, and the yonge sonne
Hath in the Ram his halve cours yronne,
And smale foweles maken melodye,
That slepen al the nyght with open ye
(So priketh hem nature in hir corages);
Thanne longen folk to goon on pilgrimages,
And palmeres for to seken straunge strondes,
To ferne halwes, kowthe in sondry londes;
And specially from every shires ende
Of Engelond to Caunterbury they wende,
The hooly blissful martir for to seke,
That hem hath holpen whan that they were seeke.

From The Canterbury Tales[1]

The General Prologue

Here begins the Book of the Tales of Canterbury.

When April comes and with its showers sweet
Has, to the root, pierced March's drought complete,
And then bathed every vein in such elixir
That, by its strength, engendered is the flower;
When Zephirus[2] with his sweet breath   5
Inspires life anew, through grove and heath,
In tender shoots, and when the spring's young sun
Has, in the Ram,[3] full half its course now run,
And when small birds begin to harmonize
That sleep throughout the night with open eyes   10
(So nature, stirring them, pricks up their courage),
Then folks, too, long to go on pilgrimage,
And palmers hope to seek there, on strange strands,[4]
Those far-off shrines well known in many lands;
And especially, from every shire's end   15
Of England, to Canterbury they wend;
The holy, blessed martyr[5] they all seek,

---

1. Translated from Middle English by Sheila Fisher.
2. Zephyr, the west wind.
3. Aries, the first sign of the zodiac in the solar year (March 21–April 20).
4. Shores, beaches. "Palmers": pilgrims who had returned from the Holy Land (they carried palm fronds in imitation of Jesus and his apostles during their entry into Jerusalem).
5. St. Thomas Becket (ca. 1118–1170), killed by assailants loyal to King Henry II of England as he stood before the altar of his church at Canterbury; until the Reformation, the site was something of a national center of religious devotion.

Who has helped them when they were sick and weak.

    It happened, in that season, on a day
In Southwark,[6] at the Tabard as I lay   *singular*   20
Ready to start out on my pilgrimage
To Canterbury, with true, devoted courage,
At night, there came into that hostelry,[7]
Fully nine-and-twenty in a company   *29 guests*
Of sundry folks, as chance would have them fall   25
In fellowship, and pilgrims were they all,
Who, toward Canterbury, wished to ride.
The chambers and the stables were all wide,
And we were put at ease with all the best.   *plural*
And, shortly, when the sun went to its rest,   30
I had so spoken with them, every one,
That I was in their fellowship anon,
And to rise early I gave them my vow,
To make our way, as I will tell you now.   *audience*

    But, nonetheless, while I have time and space,   35
Before much further in this tale I pace,
It seems quite right and proper to relate
To you the full condition and the state   *audience*
Of each of them, just as they seemed to me,
And what they were, and of what degree,   40
And also of the clothes they were dressed in,
And with a knight, then, I will first begin.

    A KNIGHT there was, and that, a worthy man,
Who, from the time when he first began
To ride to war, he loved most chivalry,   45
Truth and honor, largesse and courtesy.
Full worthy he, to fight in his lord's war,
No other man had ridden half so far,
As much in Christian as in heathen lands,
And all honor his worthiness commands;   50

    At Alexandria[8] he was, when it was won.
At banquets, he was many times the one
Seated with honor above all knights in Prussia;
In Lithuania, he'd raided, and in Russia,
Unrivalled among knightly Christian men.   55
In Granada, at the siege, he'd also been
Of Algeciras; he rode at Belmarin.
At Ayas and at Adalia had he been
When they fell; and then in the Great Sea[9]
At fine armed conquests, he fought worthily.   60
In fifteen mortal battles had he been,

6. A suburb of London, south of the Thames, where theaters, brothels, and other businesses of dubious repute set up shop beyond the reach of the city's laws.
7. I.e., the Tabard.
8. A city in northern Egypt, sacked by Peter I of Cyprus in 1365. The following places named, ranging from eastern Europe to the Muslim-held regions in southern Spain and North Africa, demonstrate both the large number and the wide variety of the Knight's campaigns.
9. The Mediterranean.

And thrice he fought for God at Tlemcen
Alone in lists, and always slew his foe.
And this same worthy knight had been also
At one time fighting alongside Balat's lord   65
Against another Turkish heathen horde;
And always was his fame a sovereign prize.
Not only was he was worthy, he was wise;
And in his bearing, meek as is a maid.
In all his life, no rude word had he said   70
To any man, however much his might.
He was a true and perfect gentle knight.
But now to tell you about his array,
His horse was good, but his dress was not gay.
His tunic was of fustian, coarse and plain,   75
Which by his rusty mailcoat was all stained,
For just lately he'd come from his voyage,
And now he went to make his pilgrimage.
    With him there was his son, a young SQUIRE,
A lover and in arms, a bachelor,   80
His locks waved like they'd seen a curling press.
About twenty years of age he was, I guess.
In his stature, he was of average length,
And wonderfully deft, and of great strength.
He'd ridden sometimes with the cavalry   85
In Flanders, in Artois, and Picardy,[1]
And fared quite well, within small time and space,
In hope of standing in his lady's grace.
Embroidered was he, as if he were a bed
All full of fresh spring flowers, white and red.   90
Singing he was, or fluting, all the day;
He was as fresh as is the month of May.
Short was his gown, its sleeves hung long and wide.
Well could he sit his horse, and nicely ride.
And also he wrote songs, both verse and note,   95
He jousted and he danced, he drew and wrote.
So hotly loved he that when nighttime came,
The nightingale and he slept both the same.[2]
Courteous and meek, to serve, quite able,
He carved before his father at the table.[3]   100
    A YEOMAN[4] had he—no servants beside,
For at this time, that's how he chose to ride,
And he was clad in coat and hood of green.
A sheaf of peacock arrows, bright and keen,
Under his belt, he bore quite properly   105
(For he could tend his gear quite yeomanly;

1. Regions in modern Belgium and northern France.
2. That is, not at all. In Persian, Arabic, Occitan, and French poetry, the nightingale was a symbol of erotic love.
3. One of the duties of a squire, and also a sign of obedience and loyalty.
4. A superior grade of servant in a noble household.

His arrows did not droop with feathers low),
And in his hand he bore a mighty bow.
A close-cropped head had he, a face well browned.
No man more skilled in woodcraft might be found.　　110
Upon his arm he wore a gay wrist guard,
And by his side a small shield and a sword,
By his other side, a bright, gay dagger fell,
As sharp as a spear's point, and sheathed up well;
On his breast, a silver Christopher[5] was seen.　　115
He bore a horn, its baldric was of green;
A forester, he was, truly, as I guess.
　　　　There was also a Nun, a PRIORESS,
Who in her smiling was simple and gracious;
Her greatest oath was "by Saint Eligius";[6]　　120
And she was known as Madame Eglentine.[7]
Quite well she sang the liturgy divine,
Intoning it in her nose quite properly;
And French she spoke quite well and elegantly,
After the school of Stratford-at-the-Bow,[8]　　125
Because Parisian French she did not know.
In dining, she was well taught overall;
She let no morsel down from her lips fall,
Nor wet her fingers in her sauce so deep;
Deftly she could lift up a bite, and keep　　130
A single drop from falling on her breast.
In courtesy, she found what pleased her best.
Her upper lip she wiped so nice and clean
That in her cup no single speck was seen
Of grease, because she drank her drink so neat.　　135
Quite daintily, she reached out for her meat.
And truthfully, she was so very pleasant,
And amiable, her manners excellent;
She pained herself to imitate the ways
Of court, and to be stately all her days,　　140
And to be held worthy of reverence.
But, now, to speak about her conscience,
She was so full of pity and charity,
That she'd cry for a mouse that she might see
Caught in a trap, if it bled or was dead.　　145
With her, she had her small hounds, which she fed
With roasted flesh, or milk and pure white bread.[9]
Sorely she wept if one of them were dead,
Or if men smote it so hard it would smart;
With her, all was conscience and tender heart.　　150

5. A medal bearing the image of the patron saint of travelers.
6. The patron saint of goldsmiths, said to have been a remarkably attractive man.
7. The name of a kind of wild rose (more appropriate to a romance heroine than a nun).
8. A village 2 miles from London.
9. A diet enjoyed only by the wealthy; in this period, most ate black or brown bread, with little meat.

Quite properly, her pleated wimple draped,
Her eyes blue gray as glass, her nose well-shaped,
Her mouth quite small, and also soft and red.
But, certainly, she had a fair forehead;
It was almost a span[1] in breadth, I own;   155
For, truth to tell, she was not undergrown.
Quite elegant, her cloak, I was aware.
Made of small corals on her arm she'd bear,
A rosary, set off with beads of green,
And thereon hung a broach of golden sheen,   160
On which the letter "A," inscribed and crowned
With "Amor vincit omnia"[2] was found.
        Another NUN riding with her had she,
Who was her secretary, and priests three.
        A MONK there was, the handsomest to see,   165
An outrider, who most loved venery,[3]
A manly man, to be an abbot able.
Many a striking horse had he in stable,
And when he rode, men might his bridle hear
Jingling in a whistling wind as clear   170
And just as loud as tolls the chapel bell
Of the house where he was keeper of the cell.
The rule of Saints Maurus and Benedict,[4]
Because it was so old and somewhat strict—
This same Monk let the old things pass away   175
And chose the new ways of the present day.
For that text he'd not give you one plucked hen
That said that hunters are not holy men,
Or that a monk who disobeys his order
Is likened to a fish out of the water—   180
That is to say, a monk out of the cloister.
But that text, he held not worth an oyster.
And I said his opinion was good.
What! Should he study, and make himself mad should
He, always poring over books in cloister,   185
Or should he work with his hands and labor
As Augustine bids?[5] How shall the world be served?
For Augustine, let this work be reserved!
A fine hard-pricking spursman he, all right;
He had greyhounds as swift as birds in flight;   190
In pricking and in hunting for the hare,
Lay all his lust; for no cost would he spare.
I saw his sleeves were fur lined at the hand
With rich, gray squirrel, the finest in the land;

1. A handspan (a wide forehead was a sign of beauty).
2. "Love conquers all" (Latin).
3. Hunting; also, sexual pleasure (Latin, *veneria*). "Outrider": here, the monk whose duty was to look after the lands belonging to the monastery.
4. The founder (d. 547) of the Benedictine order; Maurus (d. 584), his disciple, founded an abbey in France.
5. The rule of St. Augustine of Hippo (354–430), author of the *Confessions*, requires that monks engage in manual labor.

And to fasten his hood beneath his chin,   195
He had, all wrought from gold, a fancy pin;
A love knot on the larger end was cast.
His head was bald, and it shone just like glass,
His face shone, too, as though he'd been anointed.
He was a lord full fat and well appointed;   200
His eyes rolled in his head and shone as bright
As fires under furnace pots, cast light;
His boots were supple, his horses strong and fit;
Now, certainly, he was a fair prelate;
He was not pale like a tormented ghost.   205
A fat swan[6] loved he best of any roast.
His palfrey was as brown as is a berry.
     A FRIAR there was, a wanton one, and merry,
A limitor,[7] quite an important man.
In all four orders[8] is no one who can   210
Talk quite so smoothly, with such winning speech.
Many marriages made he in the breach
For young women and at his own expense.
In him, his order found a fine defense.
Quite well beloved and on close terms was he   215
With the franklins[9] all throughout his country,
And with all the town's most worthy women,
For he had the right to hear confession,
As he said, more than a curate surely,
For, by his order, he was licensed fully.   220
So, quite sweetly, would he hear confession,
And quite pleasant was his absolution:
He was an easy man in giving penance,
Where he knew he'd get more than a pittance.
If to a poor order one has given,   225
It's a sure sign that one's been well shriven;
If a man gave, he knew well what it meant:
He dared boast that this person would repent.
For many a man is just so hard of heart,
He may not weep, though he may sorely smart,   230
Therefore, instead of giving tears and prayers,
Men must yield up their silver to poor friars.
His hood's tip always was stuffed full of knives
And pins, for him to give out to fair wives.
Certainly his merry voice was pleasing: 235
And he could play the fiddle well and sing;
For ballads, he took first prize utterly.
His neck was white as is the fleur-de-lis.[1]
A strong champion was he in a brawl.
The taverns in each town, he knew them all;   240

6. An expensive and rare delicacy; ordinarily, monks abstained from eating meat.
7. A friar licensed to beg in a specific territory.
8. In the 14th century, Franciscans, Augustinians, Carmelites, and Dominicans. Friars, unlike monks, circulated among the people.
9. Upper-middle-class landowners, ranked below the gentry.
1. A lily (in heraldry, the royal arms of France).

Each innkeeper and every barmaid, too,
More than lepers[2] or beggar girls, he knew,
Because, for such a worthy man as he,
It would not do, with his ability,
With sick lepers to have an acquaintance.   245
It is not right; it hardly can advance
Him if he has to waste time with the poor,
Just with the rich and victualers, for sure.
And over all, where profit should arise,
Polite was he, and served in humble guise.   250
No man was so effective anywhere:
He was, in his house, the best beggar there.
For private begging turf, he laid out rent;
None of his brothers came there where he went;
And although one were a shoeless widow,   255
So charming was his "In principio,"[3]
A farthing he would get before he went.
His income was much higher than his rent.
And he could rage just like a little whelp.
On love-days,[4] like a judge, well could he help,   260
For there, he was not like a cloisterer
In a threadbare cloak, like a poor scholar,
But like a master or the pope as well.
Of double worsted, rounded as a bell
Fresh from the casting, was his short, rich cloak.   265
With affectation, he lisped when he spoke,
To make his English sweet upon his tongue;
In his harping, whenever he had sung,
His eyes would twinkle in his head as bright
As do the stars upon a frosty night.   270
This worthy limitor was named Huberd.
    A MERCHANT was there, too, with a forked beard,
In mixed-hued clothes; high on his horse he sat;
Upon his head, a Flemish beaver hat,
And his fair boots were fastened stylishly.   275
He uttered his ideas quite solemnly,
Sounding always increase in his winning.
He wished the sea safe, more than anything,
Between the ports of Middleburgh and Orwell.[5]
Well could he in exchange his florins sell.[6]   280
This worthy man quite deftly used his wit:
Were he in debt, no one would know of it,
So stately was he in his management
Of borrowing, buying, selling where he went.

2. Shunned through antiquity and the Middle
Ages, but healed by Jesus (see Mark 1.40–45;
Luke 17.11–19).
3. "In the beginning" (Latin), the opening
words of the Vulgate translation of the Gospel
of John, whose first fourteen verses were used
by friars in devotions and in greetings.

4. Days when disputes were judged out of
court.
5. Cities in the Netherlands and England,
respectively.
6. I.e., he also profited in currency exchange.
Florins were gold coins minted in Florence,
Italy.

Surely, he was a worthy man, in all, 285
But, truth to say, I don't know what he's called.
    A CLERK from Oxford[7] was with us also,
Whose work in logic started long ago.
As skinny was his horse as is a rake,
And he was not so fat, I undertake; 290
He looked hollow, and thus, grave and remote.
Quite threadbare was his outermost short coat;
He had as yet no clerical appointment,
And wasn't made for secular employment.
For he would rather have, at his bed's head, 295
Twenty books, all well bound in black or red,
Of Aristotle[8] and his philosophy
Than rich robes, or fiddle, or gay psaltery.
But, for all that he was a philosopher,
He had but little gold piled in his coffer;[9] 300
For, anything that his friends to him lent,
On books and on his learning, it got spent.
Busily, for the souls of them he prayed
Who, so that he could go to school, had paid.
Of his studies, he took most care and heed. 305
Not one word spoke he more than he had need,
And that was said with dignity and respect,
And short, and quick, and full of intellect;
Resounding in moral virtue was his speech,
And gladly would he learn, and gladly teach. 310
    A SERGEANT OF THE LAW,[1] wary and wise,
Who often in Saint Paul's court[2] did advise,
There was also, quite rich in excellence.
Dignified and judicious in each sense—
Or he seemed such, his words were all so wise. 315
He was often a judge at the assize,[3]
With full commission—and through royal consent.
For all his learning and his fame's extent,
Fees and robes, he did have, many a one.
So great a land buyer elsewhere was none; 320
He would directly buy up the estate;
His purchase, no one could invalidate.
Nowhere was such a busy man as he;
He seemed than he was, actually.
Busier he knew the precedents for everything 325
The law had done since William was the king.[4]
Fine legal texts, thus could he draft and draw

In which no one could find a single flaw;
Every statute, he could recite by rote.
He rode there in a simple mixed-hued coat.　　　　　　330
A striped silk belt around his waist he wore;
About his dress, I won't tell any more.
　　　A FRANKLIN rode there in his company,
And his beard was as white as is the daisy;
His mood was sanguine,[5] his face rosy red.　　　　　　335
Well loved he, in the morning, wine-soaked bread;
To live in sheer delight was his one care,
For he was Epicurus's[6] own heir,
Who thought to lead life in all its pleasure
Was true perfect bliss beyond all measure.　　　　　　340
A householder, and a full great one, was he;
A Saint Julian[7] he was, in his country.
His bread, his ale, were always very fine;
No other man had better stocks of wine.
His house was never lacking in baked meat,　　　　　　345
Or fish or flesh, in plenty so complete
That it snowed, in his house, with food and drink,
With any dainties of which men could think.
According to the seasons of the year,
New dishes on his table would appear.　　　　　　350
Fat partridges in coops, when he did like;
He kept his fish pond stocked with bream and pike.
And woe unto his cook if he'd not got
His gear set and the sauce, spicy and hot.
Covered and ready did his table stay　　　　　　355
Set up for meals within the hall all day.
At county courts, he was the lord and sire;
And went to Parliament to serve his shire.
A two-edged dagger and a purse of silk
Hung from his girdle, white as morning's milk.　　　　　　360
A sheriff had he been, an auditor,[8]
And nowhere such a worthy landholder.
　　　A HABERDASHER and a CARPENTER,
A WEAVER, DYER, and a TAPESTRY MAKER—
They were all clothed in the same livery　　　　　　365
Of one great parish guild fraternity.[9]
All fresh and newly furbished was their gear;
On their knives no brass mountings were found here,
But only silver; fashioned just as fit,
Their girdles and their purses, every bit.　　　　　　370
Each of them seemed such a worthy burgess[1]
He might sit in the guildhall on the dais.
And each, with all the wisdom that he can,

---

5. In medieval physiology, the dominance of blood (one of the four bodily humors), indicated by his red face, was believed to explain a cheerful disposition.
6. Greek philosopher (340–270 B.C.E.), viewed in the Middle Ages as a proponent of hedonism.
7. The legendary patron saint of innkeepers.
8. An official responsible for verifying accounts.
9. A trade group whose purposes were social, religious, and economic.
1. Propertied citizen.

Was suited to be made an alderman.
Income had they enough, and property, 375
To this their wives would certainly agree;
Or else, quite surely, they would all be blamed.
It is quite nice "My Lady" to be named,
At feasts and vigils, to march first in line,
And have, borne royally, a mantel² fine. 380
    For this trip, a Cook rode with them then
To boil the marrowbones up with the hens,
Along with spices tart and galingale.³
Well did he know a draught of London ale.
He could both roast and simmer, boil and fry, 385
Make stews and hash and also bake a pie.
But it was a real shame, it seemed to me,
That on his shin, a pus-filled sore had he.
A milky pudding made he with the best.
    A Shipman was there, who lived in the west; 390
He came from Dartmouth,⁴ for all that I guessed.
To ride a packhorse he did try his best,
In a gown of coarse wool cloth cut to the knee.
A dagger hanging on a strap had he
Around his neck, under his arm coming down. 395
The hot summer had turned his skin all brown.
And certainly, he was a good fellow.
So many draughts of fine wine from Bordeaux⁵
Had he drawn, while the merchants were asleep.
In a good conscience, small stock did he keep. 400
If, when he fought, he had the upper hand,
He sent them all, by water, back to land.
But in the art of reckoning the tides,
The currents and all perils near, besides,
The moon and piloting and anchorage, 405
No one was so skilled from Hull to Carthage.⁶
Hardy and wise in what was undertaken,
With many tempests had his beard been shaken.
He knew well all the harbors that there were,
Stretching from Gotland to Cape Finisterre,⁷ 410
And each inlet from Brittany to Spain;
His sailing ship was called the "Magdalene."⁸
    With us was a Doctor of Medicine;
No one was like him, all the world within,
To speak of medicine and surgery, 415
For he was schooled well in astrology.
Through natural magic,⁹ he gave patients hope

---

2. I.e., a mantle (Chaucer's spelling, now obsolete).
3. Aromatic root, also used as a powder.
4. Port on the southwest coast of England.
5. A center of the wine trade, in southwest France.
6. I.e., from northern England to North Africa (Carthage) or Spain (Cartagena; Chaucer has "Cartage"); the Shipman is widely traveled.

7. From an island off the coast of Sweden to the west coast of Spain.
8. Named after Mary Magdalen, Jesus' disciple; according to a French tradition, she, her brother Lazarus, and some companions came to the port city of Marseille in the south of France and converted all of Provence.
9. As opposed to black magic.

By keeping close watch on their horoscope.
He could divine when planets were ascendant
To aid the star signs governing his patient.   420
Of every malady, he knew the source
In humors hot, cold, moist, or dry, of course,
And where they were engendered, from which humor.[1]
He was a perfect, true practitioner.
The cause and root known of the malady,   425
At once he gave the sick their remedy.
Quite ready had he his apothecaries
To send him their drugs and electuaries,[2]
For each made profit for the other one—
Their friendship had not recently begun.   430
Well knew he his old Aesculapius,[3]
Dioscorides, and also Rufus,
Old Hippocrates, Hali, and Galen,
Rhazes, Avicenna, Serapion,
Averroës, Damascien, Constantinus,   435
Bernard, Gaddesden, Gilbertus Anglicus.
Of his own diet, moderate was he,
For it contained no superfluity,
But was nourishing and digestible.
His study was but little on the Bible.   440
In blood red and in blue he was all clad,
A lining of two kinds of silk he had.
Yet he was quite cautious with expenses;
He saved what he earned in pestilences.
In medicine, gold[4] works well for the heart,   445
Therefore, he'd loved gold from the very start.
       A good WIFE was there from nearby to BATH;
It was a pity she was deaf by half.
In cloth-making she had such a talent
She far passed those from Ypres and from Ghent.[5]   450
And throughout all her parish, there was no
Wife who might first to the offering go
Before her; if one did, so mad was she
That she lost any sense of charity.
Her coverchiefs of fine linen were found;   455
I dare swear that they weighed a full ten pounds,
The ones that, Sundays, sat upon her head.
Her stockings were all fine and scarlet red,
Quite tightly laced, her shoes quite soft and new.[6]
Bold was her face, and fair, and red of hue.   460
Worthy she was as any woman alive,

1. According to humoral physiology, illness was caused by imbalance in the four humors—the different combinations of the four qualities (hot, cold, moist, dry).
2. Medicinal pastes.
3. Greek god of healing. The list that follows names medical authors from ancient Greece, the Arabic world (including Avicenna), and medieval England (John of Gaddesden [d. 1348/49] and Gilbert the Englishman [d. ca. 1250]).
4. Used as a medicine in the Middle Ages.
5. Two cities in Flanders (modern Belgium) renowned for cloth production.
6. I.e., of good quality, supple leather.

Husbands at the church door, she had had five,
Not counting other company in youth—
No need to speak of that now, to tell the truth.
And thrice she had been to Jerusalem;[7]   465
Many a foreign sea, she'd covered them;
At Rome she'd been, and also at Boulogne,
At Saint James in Galicia and Cologne.
She knew much of wandering by the way.
Gap toothed[8] she was, it is the truth to say.   470
On her ambling horse, quite easily she sat,
Wearing a wimpled headdress and a hat
Like a buckler or a shield as broad and round;
A foot-mantle about her large hips wound,
And on her feet a pair of sharp spurs poked.   475
In fellowship, quite well she laughed and joked.
The remedies of love she knew by heart,
For of that old dance, she knew all the art.
        A good man was there of religion,
Of a town, he served as the poor PARSON.   480
But he was rich in holy thought and work.
He was also a learned man, a clerk,
And Christ's gospel truthfully he would preach;
His parishioners devoutly he would teach.
Gracious he was, a wonder of diligence,   485
And in adversity, he had such patience,
And in this, he had often tested been.
For tithes, he found it loathsome to curse men,
But he would rather give, there is no doubt,
To his poor parishioners, round about,   490
From Mass offerings and his own pay, too.
With little, he could easily make do.
Wide was his parish, the houses far asunder,
But he would not leave them, for rain or thunder,
If sickness or if trouble should befall   495
The farthest in his parish, great or small,
He'd go on foot, his staff in hand he'd keep.
This noble example he gave to his sheep:
That first he wrought, and afterward, he taught.
Out of the Gospels, those words he had caught,   500
And his own metaphor he added, too:
If gold should rust, then what will iron do?
For if a priest is foul, in whom we trust,
No wonder that a foolish man should rust;
And it's a shame, if care he does not keep—   505
A shepherd to be shitty with clean sheep.
Well should a priest a good example give,
By his own cleanness, how his sheep should live.

---

7. The major pilgrimage site for medieval Christians; lesser popular pilgrimage sites—in Italy, France, Spain, and Germany, respectively—follow.

8. According to medieval lore, a sign of a tendency to wander, associated especially with sexual excess.

His parish, he would not put out for hire
And leave his sheep encumbered in the mire 510
To run to London to Saint Paul's[9] to switch
And be a chantry priest[1] just for the rich,
Nor by guild brothers would he be detained;[2]
But he stayed home and with his flock remained,
So that the wolf would not make it miscarry; 515
He was a shepherd, not a mercenary.
And though he holy was, and virtuous,
To sinners, he was not contemptuous,
Nor haughty nor aloof was he in speech,
With courtesy and kindness would he teach. 520
To draw folks up to heaven with his fairness,
By good example: this was all his business.
But if there were a person who was stubborn,
Whoever he was, high or low rank born,
Then he would scold him sharply, at the least. 525
There is nowhere, I know, a better priest.
He expected no pomp or reverence;
For him, no finicky, affected conscience,
But the words of Christ and his apostles twelve
He taught: but first, he followed them himself. 530
     With him, his brother who was a PLOWMAN rode;
Of dung, this man had hauled out many a load;
A true laborer, and a good one was he,
Living in peace and perfect charity.
God loved he best with all of his whole heart 535
At all times, though it caused him joy or smart,
And next, his neighbor, just as he loved himself.
He would thresh, dig ditches, and also delve,
For Christ's sake and the sake of each poor man,
And without pay, he'd do all that he can. 540
His tithes, with all due fairness, he'd not shirk,
But paid from what he owned and with his work.
In a workman's smock, he rode on a mare.
     A REEVE and a MILLER were also there,
A SUMMONER and then a PARDONER, 545
A MAN and myself—that's all there were.
     The MILLER was a stout churl, it is true;
Quite big he was in brawn, and in bones, too.
That stood him in good stead; for where he came,
He'd win the ram[3] in every wrestling game. 550
He was short necked and broad, a thick-thewed thug;
There was no door around he couldn't lug
Right off its hinges, or break with his head.

---

9. The largest cathedral in medieval England.
1. A priest supported by an endowment to say daily mass for the souls of particular individuals (usually wealthy men or their family members).

2. I.e., he would not take the lucrative position of priest for a guild.
3. I.e., the prize for the winner of a village wrestling contest.

His beard, just like a sow or fox, was red,[4]
And also broad, as though it was a spade.   555
Right up atop his nose's ridge was laid
A wart; on it, a tuft of hairs grew now,
Red as the bristles in ears of a sow;
His nostrils were quite black, and also wide.
A sword and buckler bore he by his side.   560
His mouth was as great as a great cauldron.
A jangling goliard, he was quite the one—
Of sin and harlotries, he most would tell.
He made three times his pay and stole corn well;
And yet, he had a thumb of gold, all right.[5]   565
A blue hood wore he, and a coat of white.
A bagpipe he knew how to blow and play.
And sounding it, he led us on our way.
    A good MANCIPLE[6] did business for a law school;
All food buyers could follow well his rule   570
For prudent buying; it would earn them merit;
For, whether he paid straight or took on credit,
In buying, he watched carefully and waited,
So he was in good shape and well ahead.
Now, is it not from God a sign of grace   575
That this unlearned man's wit can outpace
The wisdom of a heap of learned men?
Of his masters, he had more than thrice ten,
Who were quite skilled and expert in the law,
And in that house, a full dozen one saw   580
Worthy to be stewards of rents and land
For any lord who dwells now in England,
To make him live within the means he had
In debtless honor (unless he were mad),
Or as frugally as he could desire,   585
And able thus to help out all the shire
In any circumstance that may befall:
And yet this Manciple hoodwinked them all.
    The REEVE was a slender, choleric[7] man.
He shaved his beard as closely as one can;   590
His hair, short and up by his ears, he'd crop,
And, like a priest's, he'd dock it on the top.
Quite long his legs were; they were also lean,
And just like sticks; no calf was to be seen.
He could well guard the granary and bin;   595
No auditor around could with him win.

---

4. His coloration, together with the description of his nostrils and mouth, would suggest to medieval readers a temperament given to strong displays of temper or rage.
5. "An honest miller has a golden thumb" was a proverb expressing the general belief that all millers were dishonest (either because no such miller existed or because millers cheated their customers with a heavy thumb on the scale).
6. Agent responsible for buying supplies and paying bills, especially for a college or monastery.
7. Dominated by choler, the humor associated with irascibility. "Reeve": farm or estate manager.

He knew well, by the drought and by the rain,
The yieldings of his seed and of his grain.
His lord's sheep, his cattle, and his dairy,
His swine and horses, his livestock and poultry   600
Were wholly under this Reeve's governing,
And by his contract, he gave reckoning,
Because his lord, in age, was twenty years.
No man alive could bring him in arrears.[8]
No bailiff, herdsman, worker there might be   605
But he knew all their tricks and treachery;
As they feared death, of him they were all scared.
His dwelling place upon a heath was fair;
All shaded with green trees on every hand.
He could, much better than his lord, buy land.   610
Quite richly had he stocked up, privately.
And he could please his lord so cleverly
That he'd lend to him from his lord's own goods,
And have his thanks, then, plus a coat and hood.
When he was young, he had learned a fine trade,   615
A good wright, a skilled carpenter he made.
The Reeve on his stout farm horse sat that day,
Which was called Scot and was a dapple gray.
His overcoat was long, of darkish blue,
And by his side, a rusty blade hung, too.   620
From Norfolk[9] was this Reeve, of whom I tell,
From near a town that men call Baldeswell.
Like a friar's, he tucked his coat up fast.
In our company, he always rode the last.
     A SUMMONER[1] was with us in that place,   625
Who had a fiery-red cherubic face,
Pimply was he, with eyes swollen and narrow.
Hot he was and lecherous as a sparrow,[2]
With scabbed black brows; his beard had lost some hair.
And of his visage, children were quite scared.   630
Not lead monoxide, mercury, or sulphur,
Not borax, white lead, or cream of tartar—
No single ointment that would cleanse or bite—
Could help him to remove those pustules white,
Nor cure the pimples sitting on his cheeks.   635
Well loved he garlic, onions, also leeks,[3]
And drinking blood red wine, strongly fermented;
Then he would speak and cry as though demented.
And when of this good wine he'd drunk his fill,
No words but Latin from his mouth would spill.   640
A few such terms he knew, like two or three,
That he had learned by hearing some decree—

8. I.e., convict him of having unpaid debts.
9. County northeast of London.
1. An officer of the ecclesiastical courts who served summonses to individuals charged with offenses against canon law.
2. A proverbially lecherous bird; this behavior is a manifestation of the Summoner's "hot" temperament.
3. These foods, according to medieval medicine, would increase the heat of the body and thus also cause lust, outbursts of fury, and outbreaks of the skin.

It's no wonder, for he heard it all day;
And thus you know full well how any jay[4]
Can call out "Walter" as well as the pope.   645
But whoever might on other matters grope,
Then his philosophy was spent thereby;
Always, "Questio quid iuris,"[5] cry would he.
He was a noble rascal in his kind;
A better fellow men would never find.   650
And he would suffer, for a quart of wine,
A good fellow to have his concubine
A full year, and excuse him thus completely;
For he himself could pluck a finch[6] discreetly.
If he found a good fellow anywhere,   655
Then he would quickly teach to him that there
Was no need to fear archdeacons' curses,[7]
Unless men's souls were found in their purses;
For in their purses, they will punished be.
"The purse is the archdeacon's hell," said he.   660
He downright lied, I know, in what he said;
Excommunication guilty men should dread.
Absolving saves, but cursing slays indeed;
Of Significavit,[8] men should well take heed.
Under his thumb, he had, as it did please   665
Him, the young girls there of the diocese;
He counseled all who told him things in secret.
A garland he had fashioned and then set,
Big as an ale-house sign, upon his head.
He'd made a buckler from a loaf of bread.   670
    With him, there rode a gentle PARDONER
Of Roncevalles,[9] and good, close friends they were.
He'd come straight from the papal court at Rome,
And loudly sang, "Come hither, love, to me!"
With a stiff bass, the Summoner sang along;   675
No trumpet's sound was ever half so strong.
This Pardoner had hair yellow as wax,
But smooth it hung as does a hank of flax;
In skinny strands, the locks hung from his head,
And with them, he his shoulders overspread;   680
But thin it lay; its strands hung one by one.
For stylishness, a hood he would wear none,
Since it was trussed up within his wallet.
He thought he wore the latest fashions yet;
With loose hair, his head save for his cap, was bare.   685
Such staring eyes he had, just like a hare.

---

4. A popinjay, or parrot.
5. "The question [is], what [point] of law [applies]" (Latin); a phrase familiar to the Summoner from the ecclesiastical courts.
6. To trick or blackmail; to have sexual relations.
7. I.e., excommunication.

8. Literally, "he has signified" (Latin): the writ issued for the arrest of an excommunicated person.
9. A church-affiliated hospital in London, supported in part by the sale of pardons—papal indulgences purchased to shorten the time spent by souls in purgatory.

A veronica[1] he'd sewn on his cap.
His wallet lay before him in his lap,
With pardons hot from Rome stuffed to the brim.
A voice high as a goat's came out of him.   690
No beard had he, nor should he wait for one;
His face smooth like his shaving'd just been done.
I think he was a gelding or a mare.
But, in his craft, from Berwick down to Ware,[2]
No pardoner like him in all the land.   695
In his bag was a pillowcase on hand,
And he declared it was Our Lady's[3] veil;
He said he had a big piece of the sail
Saint Peter used upon his boat when he,
Before Christ took him, had gone out to sea.   700
He had a fake gold cross bedecked with stones,
A glass he had that carried some pig bones.[4]
But with these relics, whenever he spied
A poor parson out in the countryside,
On that day, much more money would he make   705
Than, in two months, the poor parson might take;
And thus, with his feigned flattery and japes,
He made the parson and people his apes.
But to tell the whole truth, now, finally,
In church, a noble ecclesiastic, he.   710
Well could he read a lesson or a story,
But best of all, he sang the offertory;
For well he knew, when that song had been sung,
Then he must preach and smoothly file his tongue
To win his silver, as quite well could he;   715
Therefore, he sang quite loud and merrily.
      Now, I have told you truly, in a clause,
The rank, the dress, the number, and the cause
That brought together all this company
In Southwark, at this noble hostelry   720
That's called the Tabard, next door to the Bell.
But now it's time that to you I should tell
How that we all behaved on that same night
When we should in that hostelry alight;
Afterward, I will tell of our voyage   725
And all the rest about our pilgrimage.
But first I pray you, by your courtesy,
That you not blame my own vulgarity,
Although I might speak plainly in this matter,
When I tell you their words and their demeanor,   730
Or if I speak their words, exact and true.

---

1. A reproduction of Jesus' features, as were
said to have been miraculously impressed on
the cloth offered to him by St. Veronica on
his way to his crucifixion. The veronica was
also a key point of reference for medieval artists who wished to claim a divine origin for
their craft.

2. I.e., from northernmost England to the
south.
3. The Virgin Mary.
4. The Pardoner has a variety of false saints'
relics; such relies were believed to possess the
saints' spiritual power and thus found eager
buyers.

For this you all know just as well as I do:
Whoever tells a tale after a man,
He must repeat, as closely as he can,
Every last word, if that is his duty,   735
Even if he has to speak quite rudely,
Or otherwise, he makes his tale untrue,
Or makes things up, or finds words that are new.
He may not spare, though that man were his brother;
He might as well say one word as another.   740
Christ himself plainly spoke in Holy Writ;
You know no vulgarity is in it.
And Plato says, whoever can him read,
That words must be the cousin to the deed.[5]
Also, I pray you that you will forgive me   745
Although I've not ranked folks by their degree
Here in this tale, the way that they should stand.
My wit is short, you may well understand.
    Our Host put us at ease with his great cheer;
At once, he set up supper for us here.   750
He served us all with victuals that were fine;
It pleased us well to drink his good, strong wine.
An impressive man our HOST was, all in all;
He could have been a marshal in a hall.
A large man he, with eyes both bright and wide—   755
No fairer burgess anywhere in Cheapside[6]—
Bold in his speech, and wise, and quite well taught.
And in his manhood, he did lack for naught.
Moreover, he was quite a merry man;
After supper, to amuse us, he began,   760
And spoke of pleasure, among other things,
When we had settled up our reckonings.
He then said thus: "Now, my good lords, truly,
To me, you are quite welcome, heartily;
For, by my word, if that I shall not lie,   765
So merry a company, this whole year, I
Have not seen in this inn, as I see now
I'd gladly make you happy, knew I how.
I've just thought what would be entertaining;
It'd please you, and it wouldn't cost a thing.   770
    You go to Canterbury—bless the Lord,
May the blissful martyr pay you your reward!
I know well, as you travel by the way,
You all intend to tell tales and to play;
For truly, comfort and mirth both have flown   775
If you ride on the way dumb as a stone;
Now, I know a way I can divert you,
As I have said, and give you comfort, too.
And if it pleases you to give assent
So you all agree to trust my judgment,   780

5. Apparently an allusion to Plato's *Timaeus* 29B, borrowed by Chaucer from Boethius's *Consolation of Philosophy* (ca. 525 C.E.) or from the *Roman de la Rose* (ca. 1275).
6. A major business district in London.

And to do according to what I say,
Tomorrow, when you all ride by the way,
Now, by the soul of my father who is dead,
Unless you're merry, I'll give you my head!
Hold up your hands, now, without further speech."   785
       All our assent took not long to beseech.
It did not seem worthwhile to make a fuss,
For we did not need more time to discuss,
And we told him to give his verdict then.
"My lords," said he, "this plan is best. Now, listen.   790
But take it not, I pray you, with disdain.
This is the point, to speak now, short and plain:
Each one of you, to help shorten our way,
Along this journey, two tales you will say,
Toward Canterbury, as I mean you to,   795
And homeward, you'll tell us another two,
Of adventures that in old times did befall.
The one who bears himself the best of all—
That is to say, the one of you who might
Tell tales that have most meaning and delight—   800
Shall have a supper paid for by us all,
Sitting right near this post here in this hall,
When we all come again from Canterbury.
And to make you all even more merry,
I will myself quite gladly with you ride,   805
Right at my own expense, and be your guide.
Whoever will my judgment now gainsay
Shall pay for all we spend along the way.
If it be so, and all of you agree,
Without more words, at once, now you tell me,   810
And I'll make myself ready long before."
       This thing was granted, and our oaths we swore
With quite glad hearts, and we prayed him also
That he fully would agree to do so,
And that he would become our governor,   815
And of our tales, the judge and record keeper,
And set the supper at a certain price,
And we would all be ruled by his advice
In all respects; and thus, with one assent
We were all accorded with his judgment.   820
And thereupon, the wine was fetched in fast;
We drank, and to our rest we went at last,
Without us any longer tarrying.
       In the morning, as day began to spring,
Up rose our Host, and was, for us, the cock,   825
And gathered us together in a flock;
With slow gait, we started on our riding,
Till we came to Saint Thomas's Watering;[7]
And there, our Host began to stop his horse
And said, "My lords, listen—if you please, of course.   830
Let me remind you that you gave your word.

7. A spring dedicated to St. Thomas (not far from the inn).

If evening-song and morning-song accord,[8]
Let see now who shall tell us the first tale.
As ever may I drink of wine or ale,
Whoso now rebels against my judgment   835
Shall pay for all that by the way is spent.
Now let's draw straws, and then we shall depart;
Whoever has the shortest straw will start.
Sir Knight, my master and my lord," he said,
"Now you draw first, for thus I have decided.   840
Come near," said he, "my lady Prioress.
And you, sir Clerk, leave off your bashfulness.
Don't study now. Lay hands to, every man!"
At once, to draw straws, everyone began;
To quickly tell the way it did advance,   845
Were it by fortune or by luck or chance,
The truth is this: the draw fell to the Knight,
For which we were quite glad, as it was right;
By agreement and arrangement, now he must
Tell us his tale, as it was only just,   850
As you have heard; what more words need be spent?
And when this good man saw the way it went,
Because he wise was, and obedient
To keep the word he gave by free assent,
He said, "Now, since I shall begin the game,   855
What, welcome is this straw, in the Lord's name!
Now, let us ride, and hearken what I say."
And with that word, we rode forth on our way,
And he began with then a merry cheer
His tale at once, and said as you may hear.   860

The Wife of Bath's Prologue and Tale

The Wife of Bath's Prologue

"Experience, though no authority
Were in this world, is right enough for me
To speak of the woe that is in marriage;
For, my lords, since I was twelve years of age,[1]
Thanks be to God, eternally alive,   5
Husbands at the church door, I have had five—
If quite so often I might wedded be—
And all were worthy men in their degree.
But it was told me not so long ago,[2]
That since just once our Christ did ever go   10
To a wedding, in Cana in Galilea,[3]
That by that same example, he taught me

---

8. I.e., if your intention at night matches what
you promised in the morning.
1. The minimum age of marriage, in canon
law.
2. Many of the biblical sources cited by the

Wife of Bath in the argument that follows can
be found in St. Jerome's *Adversus Jovinianum*
(392 C.E.), a polemical diatribe that is highly
critical of both women and marriage.
3. See John 2.2.

That only one time I should wedded be.
Lo, listen, what a sharp word then spoke he,
Beside a well when Jesus, God and man,   15
Spoke in reproof of the Samaritan:[4]
"Thou hast had five husbands,' then said he,
'And that same man here who now hath thee
Is not thy husband,' said he by the well.
But what he meant thereby, I cannot tell;   20
Except I ask, why is it the fifth man
Was not husband to the Samaritan?
How many might she have in marriage?
Yet I've never heard tell, in all my age,
About this, any number definite.   25
Up and down, men gloss[5] and guess about it,
But well I know, expressly, it's no lie,
That God bade us to wax and multiply;[6]
This gentle text, I can well understand.
Also, well I know, he said my husband   30
Should leave mother and father and cleave to me.[7]
But of no number a mention made he,
Of bigamy, or of octogamy;[8]
Why then should men speak of it villainy?
      Lo, here is the wise king, Don[9] Solomon;   35
I think he had some wives, well more than one.
Now would to God it lawful were for me
To be refreshed here half so much as he!
A gift from God had he with all his wives!
No man has such a gift who's now alive.   40
This noble king, God knows, as I would judge it,
That first night had many a merry fit
With each of them, so well was he alive.
Blessèd be God that I have wedded five!
Of whom I have picked out the very best,   45
For both their nether purse[1] and money chest.
Different schools can turn out perfect clerks,
And different practices in sundry works
Make the workman perfect, it's no lie;
From my five husbands, studying am I.   50
Welcome the sixth, when he shall come along.
In truth, I won't keep chaste for very long.
And when my husband from this world has passed,
Another Christian man will wed me fast;
Then the apostle[2] says that I am free   55
To wed, by God, where it most pleases me.
He says to be wedded is not sinning;

4. A woman from Samaria (see John 4.7–18).
5. Interpret.
6. Genesis 1.28.
7. Genesis 2.24.
8. Marriage to two or to eight. Usually, *bigamy* involves concurrent marriages (as below, in references to biblical figures), but the Wife of Bath often instead means consecutive marriages.
9. Master. The biblical king Solomon was proverbially renowned for his great wisdom and for his hundreds of wives and concubines (see 1 Kings 11.3).
1. I.e., scrotum.
2. St. Paul; see 1. Corinthians 7.39, 9.

Better to be wedded than be burning.
What do I care if folks speak villainy
About accursed Lamech's bigamy?[3]   60
Abraham was a holy man, I know;
And as I understand it, Jacob also;
And each of them had wives now, more than one,
As many other holy men have done.
Where, can you say, in any kind of age,   65
That our high God has forbidden marriage
Expressly, in a word? I pray, tell me.
Or where did he command virginity?
I know as well as you, or else you should,
The apostle, when he speaks of maidenhood,   70
Said that a precept for it he had none.[4]
Men may counsel a woman to be one,
But counseling does not make a commandment.
All of it left to our own judgment;
For if our God commanded maidenhood,   75
Then wedding with the deed, he'd damn for good.
And surely, if no seed were ever sown,
From what, then, would virginity be grown?
And at the least, Paul never dared demand
Something his own Master won't command.   80
The prize is set up for virginity;
Catch it who may; who runs the best, let's see.
        To everyone, this word does not apply,
But only where God's might wants it to lie.
I know the apostle was a virgin;   85
Nonetheless, although he wrote and said then
He wished that everyone was such as he,
This is but counsel to virginity.[5]
He gave me leave to be a wife, all the same,
With his permission, so it is no shame,   90
If my mate dies, to go then and wed me,
Without objections about bigamy.
Though it may be good not to touch women[6]—
In his bed or on his couch, he meant then—
Fire and flax together make peril so—   95
What this example resembles, you all know.
The sum is this: he held virginity
More perfect than to wed from frailty.
Frailty I call it, unless he and she
Wished to lead all their lives in chastity.   100
        I grant it well that I have no envy,
Though maidenhood's preferred to bigamy.
To be clean pleases them, body and spirit;
Of my state, I make no boast about it,

---

3. See Genesis 4.19. Lamech (cursed as a murderer) is the first man in the Bible said to have had more than one wife (or a wife and a concubine) at the same time, but he was hardly the last, as the Wife of Bath points out.
4. 1 Corinthians 7.25.
5. 1 Corinthians 7.8.
6. 1 Corinthians 7.1.

For you well know, a lord in his household, 105
He has not every vessel made of gold;⁷
Some come from wood, and serve their lord withal.
In sundry ways, folks to him God does call,
Each has God's special gift while he must live,
Some this, some that, it pleases God to give.⁸ 110
　　　Virginity thus is great perfection,
And also continence spurred by devotion,
But Christ, who of perfection is the well,
Bade not that every person should go sell
All that he has and give it to the poor, 115
And follow in his footsteps thus, for sure.
He spoke to those who would live perfectly,⁹
And my lords, by your leave, that is not me.
I will bestow the flower of my life
In married acts and fruits, and be a wife. 120
　　　Tell me, for what purpose and conclusion
Were the members¹ made for generation,
And by so perfectly wise a maker wrought?
Trust it well now: they were not made for nought.
Say what you will, or hedge it by glossing, 125
That they were made simply for the purging
Of urine; and both our small things also
Were made so male from female we could know,
And for no other cause—do you say no?
Experience well knows it is not so. 130
So the clerks will not be angry at me,
They were made for both: I say this truly.
That is, to do our business and for ease
In engendering, where God we don't displease.
Why should men otherwise in their books set 135
It down that man should yield his wife her debt?²
Now how to her should he make his payment,
Unless he'd used his silly³ instrument?
Thus, they were bestowed upon a creature
To purge urine, and so we could engender. 140
　　　But I don't say that each one's obligated,
Who has the harness that I've just related,
To go and use it for engendering.
Then for chastity, men wouldn't care a thing.
Christ was a maiden and shaped like a man, 145
And many saints, since first the world began;
They lived forever in perfect chastity.
I won't envy any virginity.
Let them be bread of wheat that's been refined,
As barley bread, let us wives be defined; 150
And yet, with barley bread, as Mark can tell,

7. See 2 Timothy 2.20.
8. See 1 Corinthians 7.7.
9. See Matthew 19.21.
1. I.e., sexual organs.

2. The marital debt, mutually owed; see 1 Corinthians 7.3–4.
3. Innocent.

Our Lord has refreshed many men quite well.[4]
In whatever rank God's called to us,
I'll persevere; I'm not fastidious.
In wifehood, I will use my instrument   155
As freely as my Maker has it sent.
If I'm aloof, then God send me dismay!
My husband can well have it, night and day,
When it pleases him to come and pay his debt.
A husband I will have—I won't stop yet—   160
Who shall be both my debtor and my slave,
With tribulation, unless he behaves,
Upon his flesh while I may be his wife.
I have the power, during all my life
Over his own body, and not he.   165
Thus the Apostle has told this to me,
And bade our husbands they should love us well.[5]
This meaning, I like more than I can tell"—
      Up the Pardoner starts, immediately;
"Now, Madame, by God and Saint John," said he,   170
"You are a noble preacher on this strife.
Alas! I was about to wed a wife.
Why on my flesh now pay a price so dear?
I'd rather not wed any wife this year!"
      "Just wait! My tale is not begun," said she.   175
"No, you'll drink from another cask, you'll see,
Before I go, that will taste worse than ale.
And when I will have told you all my tale
Of the tribulation that's in marriage—
About which I'm an expert in my age—   180
That is to say that I have been the whip—
Then you can choose if you might want to sip
Out of the cask that I will open here.
Beware of it, before you come too near;
For I shall give examples, more than ten.   185
'Whoever won't be warned by other men,
By him will other men corrected be.'
Those same words were written by Ptolemy;[6]
Read his *Almageste,* and there you'll find it still."
      "Madame, I pray you, if it be your will,"   190
Said this Pardoner, "now as you began,
Tell forth your tale, and don't spare any man;
Teach us young men all about your practice."
      "Gladly," said she, "since you might well like this;
But yet I pray to all this company,   195
If I speak after my own fantasy,
Do not be aggrieved by what I say,
For my intent is only now to play.

4. See not Mark but John 6.9–13.
5. Ephesians 5.25.
6. Greek astronomer and mathematician (2nd century C.E.); his textbook, the *Almagest,* dominated astronomy for more than a thousand years; a preface containing proverbial wisdom attributed to Ptolemy was later added to the text.

And now, sir, now I'll tell on with my tale.
As ever I might drink of wine or ale,   200
I'll tell the truth; those husbands that I had,
Some three of them were good, and two were bad.
The three who were good men were rich and old;
And so they barely could the statute hold
Through which they all had bound themselves to me.   205
By God, you know what I mean, certainly!
So help me God, I laugh to remember
How pitifully at night I made them labor!
In faith, I set no store by their pleasure.
To me, they had given land and treasure;   210
No longer need I use my diligence
To win their love or do them reverence.
They loved me so well that, by God above,
I set no value then upon their love!
A wise woman will be the busy one   215
To get herself love, yes, where she has none.
But since I had them wholly in my hand,
And since to me they'd given all their land,
Why should I take care that I should them please
Unless it were for my profit and my ease?   220
I set them so to hard work, by my lights,
That they sung "Wey-la-way!" on many nights.
I don't think the bacon was meant for them now
That some men win in Essex at Dunmow.[7]
I governed them so well, after my law,   225
That each of them was eager, as I saw,
To bring me home some gay things from the fair.
They were glad when my speech to them was fair;
I scolded them, as God knows, spitefully.
    Now, listen how I acted properly,   230
You wise wives, who can so well understand.
Thus should you accuse falsely, out of hand.
For half so boldly knows no living man
How to swear and lie just as a woman can.
This statement about wise wives, I don't make—   235
Unless it be when they've made some mistake.
A wise wife, who knows what's good for her,
Will swear the tattling crow is mad for sure,[8]
And make sure that her maid has assented
As her witness. But hear now what I said: 240
    'Sir old dotard, is this your array?
Why is it that my neighbor's wife's so gay?
She is honored everywhere she goes;
I sit at home; I have no decent clothes.
What do you do at my neighbor's house there?   245

7. A village ca. 35 miles northeast of London. In the 13th century, the custom began of awarding a side of bacon to the couple who swore not to have quarreled or regretted their marriage during the first year after their wedding.

8. The talking bird who reveals a wife's infidelity by repeating words it has heard is a common motif in folktales.

Are you so amorous? Is she so fair?
What do you whisper to our maid? Bless me!
Sir old lecher, now let your jokes be!
If, without guilt, I have a chum or friend,
Just like a fiend, you scold me without end   250
If I should play or walk down to his house!
But you come home as drunken as a mouse,
And then preach from your bench, no proof from you!
And it's great mischief, as you tell me too,
A poor woman to wed, for the expense;   255
If she's rich and born to lofty parents,
Then you say that a torment it will be
To bear her pride and sullen melancholy.
And if she should be fair, you horrid cur,
You say every lecher soon will have her;   260
For she can't long in chastity abide,
Who is always assailed on every side.
    You say some folk want us for our richness,
Some for our figure, and some for our fairness,
Some because she can either dance or sing,   265
Some for gentility and socializing;
And some because their hands and arms are small;
By your lights, to the devil thus goes all.
You say men cannot defend a castle wall
When it's so long assailed by large and small.   270
    And if she should be ugly, you say she
Will covet every man that she may see,
For like a spaniel, she will on him leap
Until she finds a man to buy her cheap.
No goose goes out there on the lake so gray   275
That she will be without a mate, you say.
You say it's hard for men to have controlled
A thing that no man willingly would hold.
Thus you say, scoundrel, when you go to bed,
That no wise man has any need to wed,   280
Nor one who toward heaven would aspire.
With wild thunder claps and lightning's fire
May your old withered neck break right in two!
    You say that leaky houses, and smoke too,
And scolding wives all cause a man to flee   285
Out of his own house; ah now, God bless me!
What can ail such an old man, who must chide?
You say that we wives will our vices hide
Till we're hitched, and then we show them to you—
Well may that be the proverb of a shrew!   290
    You say horses, hounds, asses, and oxen
At different times can be tried out by men;
Wash bowls and basins, spoons and stools, you say,
All household things men try before they pay;
The same thing goes for clothes and gear and pots;   295
But to try out a wife, a man may not

Till they are wedded—you old dotard shrew!—
And then we show our vices, so say you.
    You say also that it displeases me
Unless you will always praise my beauty, 300
Or else always pour over my face,
And call me "Fair Madame" in every place.
Unless you make a feast upon the day
That I was born, and dress me fresh and gay;
Unless to my nurse, you do all honor, 305
And to the chambermaid within my bower,[9]
And to my father's folk and kin all day—
Old barrelful of lies, all this you say!
    Yet of Jenkin, who is our apprentice,
Whose curly hair shines just like gold—for this, 310
And because he will squire me around,
A cause for false suspicions, you have found.
I don't want him, though you should die tomorrow!
    Tell me: why do you hide, to my sorrow,
The keys now of your chest[1] away from me? 315
They are my goods as well as yours, bless me!
Will you make an idiot of your dame?
Now, by that good lord who is called Saint James,
You will not, though it might make you crazy,
Be master of both my goods and body; 320
One of them you'll forgo, to spite your eyes.
What good is it to ask around and spy?
I think you want to lock me in your chest!
You should say, 'Wife, go where you think is best;
Enjoy yourself; I'll believe no tales of this. 325
I know you for my own true wife, Dame Alice.'
We love no man who will take heed or charge
Of where we go; we want to be at large.
    And of all men, quite blessèd must he be,
That wise astrologer, Don Ptolemy, 330
Who says this proverb in his *Almageste,*
'Of all men, his wisdom is the highest
Who never cares who holds the world in hand.'
By this proverb, you should well understand,
If you have enough, why then should you care 335
How merrily some other folks might fare?
For certainly, old dotard, by your leave,
You'll have some quaint things sure enough come eve.
He is too great a niggard who would spurn
A man to light a candle at his lantern; 340
By God, from that, he doesn't have less light.
If you've enough, complaining isn't right.
    You also say if we make ourselves gay
With our clothing and with precious array,
That it is peril to our chastity; 345

9. Bedroom.   1. Strongbox.

Woe to you—you then enforce it for me,
And say these words in the Apostle's name:
'In clothing made from chastity and shame
You women all should dress yourselves,' said he,
'Not with well-coifed hair and with gay jewelry,   350
Not with rich clothes, with pearls, or else with gold.'[2]
With your text and your rubric,[3] I don't hold,
Or follow them as much as would a gnat.
        You said this: that I was just like a cat;
Whoever wanted to singe a cat's skin   355
He could be sure the cat would then stay in;
And if the cat's skin were so sleek and gay,
She'd not stay in the house for half a day;
Forth she'd go, before the day was dawning,
To show her skin and to go caterwauling.   360
That is to say, if I am gay, sir shrew,
I'll run to put my poor old clothes on view.
        Sir old fool, what help is it if you spy?
Though you prayed Argus[4] with his hundred eyes
To be my bodyguard, as he'd know best,   365
He'd not guard me till I let him, I'll be blessed.
I'd hoodwink him, as I am prospering!
        Yet you also say that there are three things,
And that these same things trouble all this earth,
And that no man might yet endure the fourth.[5]   370
Oh, dear sir shrew, Jesus shorten your life!
Yet you will preach and say a hateful wife
Is one of these misfortunes that you reckon.
Aren't there other kinds of comparison
That, for all your parables, you could use,   375
Unless a poor wife were the one you'd choose?
        You liken, too, a woman's love to hell,
To barren land where water may not dwell.
You liken it also to a wild fire;
The more it burns, the more it has desire   380
To consume everything that burned will be.
You say that just as worms destroy a tree,
A wife destroys her husband, you have found;
This, they well know who to wives have been bound.'
        My lords, right thus, as you can understand,   385
I stiffly[6] kept my old husbands in hand
And swore they said thus in their drunkenness;
And all was false; except I took witness
On Jenkin there, and on my niece, also.
Oh Lord! The pain I did them and the woe.   390
And, by God's sweet pain, they were not guilty!
For, like a horse, I could bite and whinny.

2. See I Timothy 2.9–10.
3. Direction written in red.
4. In classical myth, a monster used by
Hera/Juno, queen of the gods, to watch over
one of her husband's paramours.
5. See Proverbs 30.21–23.
6. Firmly.

I knew how to complain well even when
I had the guilt, or I'd been ruined then.
Whoever comes first to the mill, first grinds;   395
Complaining first, our war stopped, I did find.
They were glad to excuse themselves quite quickly
For things of which they never had been guilty.
Of wenches, I'd accuse them out of hand
When, in their sickness, they could hardly stand.   400
    Yet it tickled his heart, because then he
Thought that I had for him such great fancy!
I swore that all my walking out at night
Was to spy on wenches he was holding tight;
Using that cover, I enjoyed much mirth.   405
For all such wit is given us at birth;
Deceit, weeping, and spinning God did give
To women by nature, all the time they live.
And thus of one thing, I can surely boast:
In the end, I'm the one who won the most   410
By tricks or force or by some other thing
As much as constant grumbling and grousing.
Namely, then, they would have bad luck in bed:
I did them no pleasure, and I chided;
I would no longer in the bed abide,   415
If I felt his arm come over my side,
Till he had paid his ransom down to me;
Then I'd suffer him to do his foolery.
Therefore, to every man this tale I tell:
Win whoso may, for all is there to sell;   420
With empty hands men may no hawks then lure.
For profit, I would all their lust endure,
And I would fake it with feigned appetite;
And yet in bacon,[7] I had no delight.
That was the reason I would always chide them,   425
For though the pope were sitting right beside them,
At their own table, I would never spare.
In truth, I repaid them word for word there.
So help me, oh true God omnipotent,
If now I made my will and testament,   430
There was not one unpaid word I did owe.
By my own wit, I brought it all about so
That they must give it up, and for the best,
Or otherwise, we never would have rest;
Though he looked as crazy as a lion,   435
He would fail at gaining his conclusion.
    Then I would say to him, 'sweetheart, take heed—
See how meek our sheep Willie looks, indeed!
Come near, my spouse, and let me kiss your cheek!
Truly you should be all patient and meek,   440
And have, too, a carefully spiced conscience,

---

7. I.e., preserved (old) meat; or perhaps a reference to the prize at Dunmow.

Since you always preach about Job's patience.[8]
Suffer always, since you can so well preach;
Unless you do, for sure we shall you teach
That it's nice to have a wife in peace now.   445
Doubtless, one of the two of us must bow,
And so, since man is more reasonable
Than woman, to suffer you are able.
What ails you now that thus you grouse and groan?
Do you just want my quaint thing[9] for your own?   450
Why, take it all! Lo, have it through and through!
You love it well, by Peter,[1] curse on you;
For if I wanted to sell my *belle chose*,[2]
Then I could walk as fresh as is a rose;
But I will keep it just for your own tooth.   455
You are to blame, by God! I tell the truth.'
These are the kinds of words I had on hand.
And now I will speak of my fourth husband.
    My fourth husband was a reveler—
That is to say, he had a paramour—   460
And young and full of wantonness was I,
Stubborn, strong and jolly as a magpie.
How I'd danced when the small harp was playing;
Like a nightingale's was all my singing,
When I had drunk my draught of fine sweet wine!   465
Metellius, the foul churl, the swine,
Who, with a staff, bereft his wife of life,
Because she drank wine;[3] if I were his wife,
He wouldn't frighten me away from drink!
And after wine, on Venus[4] I must think,   470
For just as sure as cold engenders hail,
A lecherous mouth must have lecherous tail.
In wine-drunk women, there is no defence—
This, lechers know from their experience.
    But—Lord Christ!—when memories come back to me,   475
About my youth and all my jollity,
It tickles me right down to my heart's root.
To this day, it does my heart good, to boot,
That I have had my world right in my time.
But age, alas, that poisons what is prime,   480
Has bereft me of my beauty and my pith.[5]
Let it go. Farewell! The devil go therewith!
The flower's gone; there is no more to tell;
The bran, as I best can, now must I sell;
But yet to be right merry I have planned.   485
And now I will tell of my fourth husband.
    I say, I had in my heart a great spite

8. Proverbial; see the book of Job.
9. Genitals.
1. St. Peter.
2. Pretty thing (French).
3. One of the historical anecdotes compiled

in the rhetorical handbook by Valerius Maximus
(1st century C.E.), which presents Metellius's
act as justified.
4. Roman goddess of love.
5. Energy.

That he in any other took delight.
By God and Saint Judocus,[6] he's repaid!
Of the same wood, a cross for him I made;   490
Not in a foul manner with my body,
But I made folks such cheer that certainly
I made him fry enough in his own grease
Because his jealous anger would not cease.
By God, on earth I was his purgatory,   495
For which, I hope his soul will be in glory.
God knows, he often sat and sang "Alack"
When his shoe so bitterly pinched him back.
There was no man who knew, save God and he,
In what ways I twisted him so sorely.   500
When I came from Jerusalem, he died;
Buried beneath the cross's beam,[7] he lies.
His tomb is not fancy or curious
As was the sepulcher of Darius,
Which Appelles had formed so skillfully;[8]   505
A waste to bury him expensively.
Let him fare well. God rest his soul, I ask it!
He is now in his grave and in his casket.
    Now of my fifth husband I will tell.
May God let his soul never go to hell!   510
Yet to me he was the biggest scoundrel;
On my whole row of ribs, I feel it still,
And ever shall until my dying day.
But in our bed, he was so fresh and gay,
And he knew so well just how to gloss me   515
When he wanted my *belle chose,* as you'll see;
Although he'd beaten me on every bone,
Quickly he'd win back my love for his own.
I believe that I loved him best since he
Could be standoffish with his love for me.   520
We women have, and no lie this will be,
In this matter, our own quaint[9] fantasy:
Whatever thing won't lightly come our way,
Then after it we'll cry and crave all day.
Forbid us something, and that desire we;   525
Press on us fast, and then we're sure to flee.
With standoffishness, we spread out all our wares;
Great crowds at market make the goods dear there,
Too great a bargain isn't thought a prize;
And this knows every woman who is wise.   530

6. St. Judoc or Josse, a 7th-century Breton saint (never canonized) whose emblem was the pilgrim's staff.
7. I.e., in a place of honor within the church itself.
8. According to the (fictional) account in Walter of Châtillon's 12th-century Latin epic, *Alexandreis,* the famous painter Apelles (4th c. B.C.E.) decorated the tomb of the Persian king Darius (d. 486 B.C.E.).
9. "Queynt," meaning "quaint" in the modern English sense and also a pun on the slang word for the female sex organ; the pun is especially likely coming a few lines after the last reference to Wife's *"belle chose"* (510).

My fifth husband—now God his soul should bless—
Whom I took for love and not for richness,
Formerly, he was a clerk at Oxford,
And had left school, and went back home to board
With my close friend who in our town did dwell. 535
God save her! Her name's Alison, as well.
She knew both my heart and my privacy
More than our parish priest did, so help me!
With her, I shared my secrets one and all.
For had my husband pissed upon a wall, 540
Or done a thing that should have cost his life,
To her and to another worthy wife,
And to my niece, whom I did love so well,
All of his secrets I'd be sure to tell.
God knows too that I did this quite often 545
So I made his face both red and hot then
From shame itself. He blamed himself that he
Had ever shared with me his privacy.
        And so it happened that one time in Lent—
For often times to my close friend I went, 550
Because I always did love being gay,
And to walk out in March, April, and May,
From house to house, and sundry tales to hear—
Jenkin the clerk, Alison, my friend dear,
And I myself, into the fields all went. 555
My husband was at London all that Lent;
More leisure for my playing, I then had,
To see and to be seen (and I was glad)
By lusty folks. Did I know where good grace
Was destined to find me, or in what place? 560
Therefore, I made all my visitations
To vigils and also to processions,
To preachings and to these pilgrimages,
To miracle plays[1] and to marriages,
And always wore my gowns of scarlet bright. 565
Neither the worms nor moths nor any mites,
On my soul's peril, had my gowns abused.
Do you know why? Because they were well used.
        Now I'll tell you what happened then to me.
I say that out into the fields walked we, 570
Till truly, we had such a flirtation,
This clerk and I, that I made due provision
And spoke to him, and said to him how he,
Were I a widow, should be wed to me.
For certainly—and I'm not boasting here— 575
I have not ever lacked provisions clear
For marriage, or for such things, so to speak.
I hold a mouse's heart not worth a leek

---

1. Medieval dramas focused on the lives and acts of the saints or on events from the Bible (also called "mystery plays"); performed in the vernacular, they were extremely popular.

Who's only got one hole where it can run,
And if that fails, then everything is done.   580
    I made him think he had enchanted me—
My mother taught me all that subtlety—
And said I had dreamed this of him all night:
As I lay on my back he'd slain me quite,
And I dreamed full of blood then was my bed;   585
'But yet I hope you'll do me good,' I said,
'For blood betokens gold, as was taught me.'
And all was false; I had no dream, you see,
But I always followed my mother's lore,
In this as well as other things before.   590
    But now, sirs, let's see what I shall say then.
Aha! By God, I've got my tale again.
    When my fourth husband lay up on his bier,
I wept quite long and made a sorry cheer,
As wives must, for it is common usage.   595
With my coverchief, I hid my visage,
But since I was provided with my next mate,
I didn't weep much—this to you I'll state.
    To church was my husband borne next morning
With the neighbors, who for him were mourning;   600
And there Jenkin, our clerk, was one of those.
So help me God, when I saw how he goes
Behind the bier, I thought he had a pair
Of legs and feet that were so clean and fair,
I gave him all my heart for him to hold.   605
He was, I think, just twenty winters old,
And I was forty, if I tell the truth;
But yet I always had a coltish tooth[2]
Gap toothed was I, and that became me well;
With Venus's seal[3] I'm printed, I can tell.   610
So help me God, I was a lusty one,
And fair and rich and young and well begun,
And truly, as my husbands all told me,
I had the best *quoniam*[4] there might be.
For certainly, I'm all Venerian   615
In feeling, and my heart is Martian.[5]
Venus gave me my love and lecherousness,
And Mars gave me my sturdy hardiness;
My ascendant's sign's Taurus,[6] with Mars therein.
Alas! Alas! That ever love was sin!   620
I always followed my inclination
By virtue of my stars' constellation;
Thus I could not withdraw—I was made so—
My chamber of Venus from a good fellow.

---

2. I.e., youthful appetites.
3. An alluring birthmark.
4. Literally, "whereas" (Latin): another slang form for female genitals.

5. Belonging to Mars, the Roman god of war.
6. Sign of the zodiac (April 21–May 20) in which Venus is dominant.

Yet I have Mars's mark[7] upon my face,   625
And also in another private place.
For as God so wise is my salvation,
I have never loved in moderation,
But I always followed my appetite,
Should he be long or short or black or white;   630
I took no heed, so long as he liked me,
Of how poor he was, or of what degree.
     What should I say, but at the month's end, he,
This pretty clerk, this Jenkin, so handy,[8]
Has wedded me with great solemnity,   635
And I gave him all land and property
That ever had been given me before.
But after, I was made to rue that sore;
My desires he would not suffer to hear.
By God, he hit me once upon the ear,   640
Because, out of his book, a leaf I rent,
And from that stroke, my ear all deaf then went.
But, like a lionness, I was stubborn,
And with my tongue, I was a jangler[9] born,
And I would walk around, as I once did,   645
From house to house, although he did forbid;
Because of this, quite often he would preach,
And from old Roman stories, he would teach;
How one Simplicius Gallus[1] left his wife,
And her forsook for the rest of his life,   650
Because one day, and for no reason more,
Bareheaded she was looking out the door.
     Another Roman he told me by name,
Who, since his wife was at a summer's game
Without his knowledge, he then her forsook.   655
And then he would into his Bible look
For the proverb of Ecclesiasticus[2]
Where he commands, and he does forbid thus:
That man shall not suffer wife to roam about.
Then would he say right thus, without a doubt;   660
    'Whoever builds his house up all from willow
And pricks his blind horse over fields so fallow,
And lets his wife go seeking shrines so hallowed,
Is worthy to be hanging on the gallows!'
But all for nought: I didn't give a straw   665
For all his old proverbs or his saws,
Nor by him would I then corrected be.
I hate him who my vices tells to me,
And so do more of us, God knows, than me.
This drove him mad about me, utterly;   670
For I wouldn't bear with any of this.

7. Probably a red birthmark.
8. Clever; courteous.
9. Chatterer.
1. This story and the next (lines 647–49) are
found in Valerius Maximus.
2. See Ecclesiasticus 25.25–26.

I'll tell you the truth now, by Saint Thomas,[3]
Why once out of his book a leaf I rent,
For which he hit me so that deaf I went.
    He had a book that, gladly, night and day,   675
For his pleasure, he would be reading always;[4]
It's called Valerius and Theophrastus;
He always laughed as he read it to us.
And also there was once a clerk at Rome,
A cardinal, who was called Saint Jerome,   680
Who made a book against Jovinian;
In which book was also Tertullian,
Crisippus, Trotula, and Heloise,
An abbess near to Paris, if you please,
And too the Parables of Solomon,   685
Ovid's *Ars,* and more books, many a one,
And all of these in one volume were bound,
And every night and day, some time he found
When he had some leisure and vacation
From his other worldly occupation,   690
To read then in this book of wicked wives.
He knew of them more legends and more lives
Then there are of good wives in the Bible.
For trust it well, it is impossible
For any clerk to speak some good of wives,   695
Unless he speaks about holy saints' lives:
This for no other women will he do.
Now who painted the lion, tell me who?[5]
By God, if women had written stories,
Like clerks do within their oratories,   700
They would have written of men more wickedness
Than all the mark of Adam could redress.
The children of Venus and Mercury[6]
In their actions, are always contrary;
Mercury loves both wisdom and science;   705
Venus, revelry and extravagance.
Because of their different dispositions,
Each falls in the other sign's exaltation.
And thus, God knows, Mercury's despondent
In Pisces,[7] when Venus is ascendant,   710

3. Thomas Becket, to whose shrine the pilgrims are traveling.
4. This single anthology contains a number of works, all hostile or cast as hostile to women: *Letter of Valerius Concerning Not Marrying,* by Walter Map (12th century); *Against Jovinian* (a 4th-century monk), by the Church Father Jerome (d. 420), which mentions a lost *Golden Book of Marriage* by the Greek philosopher Theophrastus (d. 285 B.C.E.) and writings by the Church Father Tertullian (d. ca. 220) and Crisippus (otherwise unknown); Trotula, a legendary 11th-century Italian female doctor;

Heloise (d. 1164), a participant in a scandalous love affair who wrote that philosophers should never marry; the biblical book of Proverbs; and the *Art of Love* by Ovid (43 B.C.E.– 17 C.E.), a how-to book on seduction.
5. In one of Aesop's fables, a lion argues that the representation of a man killing a lion did not prove the man's superiority: if a lion could create an artwork, it would depict the opposite.
6. Winged messenger of the Roman gods, the god of commerce and trickery.
7. Sign of the zodiac (February 20–March 20).

And Venus falls where Mercury is raised.
Therefore, no woman by a clerk is praised.
The clerk, when he is old and may not do
Of Venus's work what's worth his old shoe,
Then he sits down and writes in his dotage   715
That women cannot keep up their marriage!
        But now to my purpose, why I told you
That I was beaten for a book, it's true!
One night Jenkin, who was our lord and sire,
Read in this book, as he sat by the fire,   720
Of Eve first: because of her wickedness,
All mankind was brought into wretchedness,
And thus Jesus Christ himself was slain then,
Who bought us with his own heart's blood again.
Lo, here, expressly, of woman you find   725
That woman was the loss of all mankind.
        He read to me how Samson lost his hair:
His lover cut it while he did sleep there;
And through this treason, he lost both his eyes.[8]
        And then he read to me, if I don't lie,   730
About Dianyra and Hercules;[9]
She made him set himself on fire, if you please.
        Nor forgot he the woe throughout his life
That Socrates[1] endured from his two wives,
How Xantippa cast piss upon his head.   735
This foolish man sat still like he were dead;
He wiped his head and no more dared say plain,
But 'Before thunder stops, there comes the rain!'
        Of Pasiphaë, who was the queen of Crete,
From evilness, the tale seemed to him sweet;   740
Fie! Speak no more—it is a grisly thing—
Of her lust and horrible desiring.[2]
        Of Clytemnestra, who, from lechery,
Falsely made her husband die,[3] you see,
He read out that tale with great devotion.   745
        He told me also on what occasion
Amphiaraus at Thebes had lost his life.[4]
My husband had a legend of his wife,
Eriphyle, who, for a brooch of gold
Has privately unto the Greeks then told   750
Where her husband had kept his hiding place,

8. See Judges 13–16 for the story of Delilah and Samson, whose superhuman strength lay in his hair.
9. The greatest hero of classical mythology, who died because his wife unwittingly gave him a poisoned cloak. (Many of the following exempla are drawn from myth.)
1. The Greek philosopher (469–399 B.C.E.) immortalized in the dialogues of his pupil Plato; Xantippa is protrayed as a shrew in ancient biographies.
2. The union of Pasiphaë with a bull produced the Minotaur.
3. Conspiring with her lover, the queen of Mycenae murdered her husband, Agamemnon, when he returned from leading the Greeks in the Trojan War.
4. He was forced to join the war against Thebes, whose disastrous outcome he foresaw, by his wife, who had been bribed.

And thus at Thebes he suffered sorry grace.
    Of Livia and Lucia,[5] then heard I:
How both of them had made their husbands die,
The one for love, the other one for hate.   755
This Livia, for sure, one evening late,
Poisoned her husband for she was his foe;
Lecherous Lucia loved her husband so
That, to make sure he'd always on her think,
She gave to him such a kind of love-drink   760
He was dead before it was tomorrow;
And thus, always, husbands have had sorrow.
    Then he told me how one Latumius
Complained once to his fellow Arrius
That in his garden there grew such a tree   765
On which, he said, that all of his wives three
Hung themselves with spite, one then another.
Said this Arrius, 'Beloved brother,
Give me a shoot from off that blessèd tree,
And in my garden, planted it will be.'[6]   770
    And later on, about wives he has read,
And some had slain their husbands in their bed,
And let their lechers hump them all the night,
While on the floor the corpses lay upright.
And some have driven nails into the brain,   775
While they did sleep, and thus they had them slain.
And some did give them poison in their drink.
He spoke more slander than the heart can think,
And on top of it, he knew more proverbs
Than in this world there can grow grass and herbs.   780
'Better,' he said, 'that your habitation
Be either with a lion or foul dragon,
Than with a woman who is used to chide.
Better,' said he, 'high on the roof abide,
Than down in the house with an angry wife;[7]   785
They're so wicked and contrary all their lives,
That they hate what their husbands love always.'
He said, 'A woman casts her shame away,
When she casts off her shift.' He spoke more so:
'A fair woman, unless she's chaste also,   790
Is just like a gold ring in a sow's nose.'[8]
Who would imagine, or who would suppose
The woe that in my heart was, and the pain?
    And when I saw he never would refrain
From reading on this cursed book all night,   795
Then suddenly, three leaves I have ripped right
Out of his book, as he read, and also

5. According to Jerome, Livia, who had a lover, deliberately poisoned her husband, Drusus (d. 23 C.E.), whose father later became the Roman emperor Tiberius, and Lucia (Lucilla) accidentally poisoned her husband, the poet Lucretius (d. 55 B.C.E.), with a love potion.
6. A story told in the *Letter of Valerius*.
7. Proverbs 21.9.
8. Proverbs 11.22.

With my fist, I took him on the cheek so
That backward in our fire, right down fell he.
He starts up like a lion who's gone crazy,
And with his fist, he hit me on the head
So on the floor I lay like I were dead.   800
And when he saw how still it was I lay,
He was aghast, and would have fled away,
Till, at last, out of my swoon I awoke.
'Oh! Hast thou slain me, false thief?' then I spoke,
'And for my land, hast thou now murdered me?   805
Before I'm dead, yet will I still kiss thee.'
    And fairly he kneeled down when he came near,
And he said, 'Alison, my sister dear,
Never more will I hit you, in God's name!   810
If I've done so, you are yourself to blame.
I pray you, your forgiveness now I seek.'
And right away, I hit him on the cheek,
And said, 'thief, now this much avenged am I;   815
I may no longer speak, now I will die.'
But then, at last, after much woe and care,
We two fell into an agreement there,
He gave me all the bridle in my hand
To have the governing of house and land,   820
And of his tongue, and of his hands, then, too;
I made him burn his book without ado.
And when I had then gotten back for me,
By mastery, all the sovereignty,
And when he said to me, 'My own true wife,   825
Do as you like the rest of all your life;
Keep your honor, and keep my rank and state'—
After that day, we never had debate.
God help me so, there's no wife you would find
From Denmark to India who was so kind,   830
And also true, and so was he to me.
I pray to God, who sits in majesty,
To bless his soul with all his mercy dear,
Now will I tell my tale, if you will hear."

Behold the words between the Summoner and the Friar.

    The Friar laughed, when he had heard all this;   835
"Madame," said he, "so have I joy or bliss,
This is a long preamble to a tale!"
The Summoner had heard his windy gale,
"By God's two arms," the Summoner said, "lo!
Always will a friar interfere so.   840
Lo, good men, a fly and then a friar
Will both fall in every dish and matter.
Of preambulation, what's to say of it?
What! Amble, trot, keep still, or just go sit!
You're hindering our sport in this manner."   845

"You say so, sir Summoner?" said the Friar;
"Now, by my faith, I shall, before I go,
Tell a tale of a summoner, you know,
That all the folks will laugh at in this place."
 "Now, elsewise, Friar, I do curse your face," 850
Said this Summoner. "And I curse myself, too,
Unless I tell some tales, at least a few,
Of friars before I come to Sittingbourne[9]
So that, be sure, I will make your heart mourn.
I know full well that you're out of patience." 855
 Our Host cried out, "Peace now! And that at once!"
And he said, "Let the woman tell her tale.
You act like folks who are all drunk on ale.
Do, madame, tell your tale, and all the rest."
 "All ready, sir," said she, "as you think best, 860
If I have license of this worthy Friar."
 "Yes, madame," said he, "tell on. I will hear."

Here the Wife of Bath ends her Prologue.

The Wife of Bath's Tale

Here begins the Tale of the Wife of Bath.

 In the olden days of good King Arthur,
Of whom Britons still speak with great honor,
This whole land was all filled up with fairies. 865
The elf queen, with her pretty company,
Went dancing then through many a green mead.
I think this was the old belief, indeed;
I speak of many hundred years ago.
But now no one sees elves and fairies go, 870
For now all the charity and prayers
Of limitors[1] and other holy friars,
Who haunt through every land and every stream
As thick as motes floating in a sun beam,
Blessing halls and chambers, kitchens, bowers, 875
Cities, boroughs, castles, and high towers,
Barns and villages, cowsheds and dairies—
This is the reason why there are no fairies.
For there where once was wont to walk an elf,
Now there the begging friar walks himself 880
In the afternoons and in the mornings,
He says his matins[2] and his holy things
As he walks all throughout his begging grounds.
Now women may go safely all around.
In every bush and under every tree, 885

9. A town on the road to Canterbury, 40 miles from London.

1. Friars licensed to beg in a specific territory.
2. I.e., morning prayers.

There is no other incubus[3] but he,
And he'll do them no harm but dishonor.
    So it happened that this good King Arthur
Once had a lusty knight, a bachelor,
Who, one day, came riding from the river,   890
And it chanced that, as he was born, alone,
He saw a maiden walking on her own,
From which maid, then, no matter what she said,
By very force, he took her maidenhead;
This oppressive violence caused such clamor,   895
And such a suit for justice to King Arthur
That soon this knight was sentenced to be dead,
By the course of law, and should have lost his head—
By chance that was the law back long ago—
Except the queen and other ladies also   900
So long had then prayed to the king for grace
Till he had granted his life in that place,
And gave him to the queen, to do her will,
To choose whether she would him save or kill.
    The queen then thanked the king with all her might,   905
And after this, thus spoke she to the knight,
When, on a day, she saw that it was time.
"You stand," she said, "in this state for your crime:
That of your life, you've no security.
I grant you life, if you can tell to me   910
What thing it is that women most desire.
Keep your neck-bone from the ax now, sire!
And if, at once, the answer you don't know,
Still, I will give you leave so you can go
A twelvemonth and a day, to search and learn   915
Sufficient answer before you return;
Before you leave, I'll have security
That here you'll surrender up your body."
    Woe was this knight, and he sighs sorrowfully;
But what! He can't do all he likes completely.   920
And at last, he decided that he'd wend
His way and come back home at the year's end,
With such an answer as God would convey;
He takes his leave and goes forth on his way.
    He seeks in every house and every place   925
Where he has hopes that he'll find some good grace
To learn the thing that women love the most,
But he could not arrive on any coast
Where he might find out about this matter,
Two creatures who agreed on it together.   930
    Some said that all women best loved richness,
Some said honor, and some said jolliness,
Some, rich array, and some said lust in bed,
And often times to be widowed and wed.

3. An evil spirit believed to have sex with women as they sleep.

Some said that our hearts were most often eased   935
When we could be both flattered and well pleased.
He got quite near the truth, it seems to me.
A man shall win us best with flattery,
Solicitude, and eager busyness.
Thus we are captured, both the more and less.   940
    And some said that the best of all love we
To do what pleases us, and to be free,
And that no man reproves us for our folly,
But says that we are wise and never silly.
For truly, there is not one of us all,   945
If any one will claw us where it galls,
That we won't kick when what he says is true.
Try, and he'll find it so who will so do;
For, be we ever so vicious within,
We want to be held wise and clean of sin.   950
    And some say that we find it very sweet
Dependable to be thought, and discreet,
And in one purpose steadfastly to dwell,
And not betray a thing that men us tell.
A rake handle isn't worth that story.   955
We women can't keep secrets, by God's glory;
See Midas—will you hear the tale withal?[4]
    Once Ovid, among some other things small,
Said Midas covered up with his long hair,
On his head two ass's ears that grew there,   960
And this flaw he did hide as best he might
Quite cleverly from every mortal's sight,
So that, save for his wife, no one did know.
He loved her most, and trusted her also;
He prayed her that to no other creature   965
She would tell how he was so disfigured.
    She swore to him, "No"; all this world to win,
She would not do that villainy or sin,
To make her husband have so foul a name.
She wouldn't tell because of her own shame.   970
But, nonetheless, it seemed to her she died
Because so long she must that secret hide;
She thought it swelled so sorely near her heart
That some word from her must, by needs, depart;
Since she dared not tell it to any man,   975
Down to the marsh that was nearby, she ran—
Until she got there, her heart was on fire—
And as a bittern[5] bellows in the mire,
Down by the water, she did her mouth lay:
"Thou water, with your sound do not betray: 980
To thee I tell, and no one else," she said;
"My husband has long ass ears on his head!

---

4. See Ovid, *Metamorphoses* 11.172–93 (where Midas's secret is discovered by a servant, not by his wife).

5. A wading bird with a deep, booming call.

Now is my heart all whole; now is it out.
I could no longer keep it, without doubt."
Here you see, if a time we might abide,   985
Yet it must out; we can no secret hide.
If of this tale you want to hear the rest,
Read Ovid, and there you will learn it best.
    This knight, about whom my tale is concerned,
Seeing that the answer he'd not learned—   990
That is to say, what women love the best—
Sorrowful was the spirit in his breast.
But home he goes; no more might he sojourn;
The day had come when homeward he must turn.
And on his way, it happened he did ride,   995
With all his cares, near to a forest's side,
Where he saw come together for a dance,
Some four and twenty ladies there by chance;
Toward which dance he eagerly did turn,
In hopes some wisdom from them he might learn.   1000
But truly, before he had arrived there,
The dancing ladies vanished—who knew where.
No creature saw he left there who bore life,
Save on the green, he saw sitting a wife[6]—
A fouler creature, none imagine might.   1005
This old wife then arose to meet the knight.
"Sir knight, there's no road out of here," said she.
"What you are seeking, by your faith, tell me.
Perhaps, then, you'll be better prospering."
She said, "These old folks can know many things."   1010
    "Beloved mother," said this knight, "it's fate
That I am dead unless I can relate
What thing it is that women most desire.
Could you tell me, I'd well repay your hire."
    "Pledge me your troth," said she, "here in my hand,   1015
And swear to me the next thing I demand,
You shall do it if it lies in your might,
And I'll tell you the answer before night."
    "I grant," he said, "you have this pledge from me."
    "Then, Sire, I dare well boast to you," said she,   1020
"Your life is safe, and I will stand thereby;
Upon my life, the queen will say as I.
Let see who is the proudest of them yet
Who wears either a coverchief or hair-net
Who dares say 'Nay' to what I will you teach.   1025
Let us go forth without a longer speech."
Then she whispered a message in his ear,
And bade him to be glad, and have no fear.
    When they came to the court, this knight did say
That, as he'd pledged, he had held to his day,   1030

6. A woman.

And he said his answer was ready then.
Many noble wives and many maidens
And many widows, because wise are they,
With the queen sitting as the judge that day,
Were all assembled, his answer to hear;   1035
And then this knight was told he should appear.
     It was commanded that there should be silence
And that the knight should tell in audience
The thing that worldly women love the best.
The knight did not stand like a beast at rest;   1040
At once to his question then he answered
With manly voice, so all the court it heard:
     "My liege lady, generally," said he,
"Women desire to have sovereignty
As well over their husbands as their loves,   1045
And to be in mastery them above.
This is your greatest desire, though me you kill.
Do as you like; I am here at your will."
In all the court, there was no wife or maiden
Nor widow who denied what he had said then,   1050
But they said he was worthy of his life.
And with that word, then, up jumps the old wife,
Whom the knight had seen sitting on the green:
"Mercy," said she, "my sovereign lady queen!
Before your court departs, by me do right.   1055
I taught this very answer to this knight;
For which he pledged to me his troth and hire,
So that the first thing I'd of him require,
This he would do, if it lay in his might.
Before the court, then I pray you, sir knight,"   1060
Said she, "that you now take me for your wife,
For well you know that I have saved your life.
Upon my faith, if I say false, say 'nay.'"
     This knight answered, "Alas, and well away!
I know that was my promise, I'll be blessed.   1065
But for God's love now, choose a new request!
Take all my goods, and let my body go."
     "Oh no," said she, "I curse us both then so!
For though I may be foul and poor and old,
I'd not want all the metal, ore, or gold   1070
That's buried in the earth or lies above,
Unless I were your lady and your love."
     "My love?" said he, "oh, no, my damnation!
Alas, that one of my birth and station
Ever should so foully disparaged be!"   1075
But all for naught; the end is this, that he
Constrained was here; by needs, he must her wed,
And take his old wife, and go off to bed.
     Now here some men would want to say perhaps
That I take no care—so it is a lapse—   1080
To tell you all the joy and the array

That at the wedding feast was on that day:
To which, my answer here is short and small:
I say there was no joy or feast at all.
Only sorrow and heaviness, I say.   1085
For privately he wedded her next day,
And all day after, he hid like an owl,
For woe was he that his wife looked so foul.
    Great was the woe the knight had in his thoughts,
When he was with his wife to their bed brought;   1090
He wallows and he writhes there, to and fro.
His old wife just lay smiling, even so,
And said, "Oh husband dear, God save my life!
Like you, does every knight fare with his wife?
Is this the law here in the house of Arthur?   1095
Is each knight to his wife aloof with her?
I am your own love, and I am your wife;
And I am she who has just saved your life.
Surely, toward you I have done only right;
Why fare you thus with me on this first night?   1100
You're faring like a man who's lost his wits,
What's my guilt? For love of God, now tell it,
And it will be amended if I may."
    "Amended?" said this knight, "Alas! No way!
It will not be amended, this I know.   1105
You are so loathly, and so old also,
And come from such low lineage, no doubt,
Small wonder that I wallow and writhe about.
I would to God my heart burst in my breast!"
    "Is this," said she, "the cause of your unrest?"   1110
    "Yes," said he, "no wonder is, that's certain."
    "Sir," said she, "I could mend this again,
If I liked, before there'd passed days three,
If you might now behave well toward me.
    But since you speak now of such gentleness[7]   1115
As descends to you down from old richness,
So that, because of it, you're gentle men,
Such arrogance is just not worth a hen.
See who is most virtuous all their lives,
In private and in public, and most strives   1120
To always do what gentle deeds he can:
Now take him for the greatest gentle men.
Christ wills we claim from him our gentleness,
Not from our elders and from their old richness.
Though they leave us their worldly heritage,   1125
And we claim that we're from high lineage,
Yet they may not bequeath a single thing
To us here of their virtuous living,
Which is what made them be called gentle men;

7. Gentility; nobility.

This is the path they bade us follow then.   1130
    Well can he, the wise poet of Florence,
Who's named Dante,[8] speak forth with this sentence.
Lo, Dante's tale is in this kind of rhyme:
'Seldom up his family tree's branches climbs
A man's prowess, for God, in his goodness,   1135
Wills that from him we claim our gentleness';
For, from our elders, we may no thing claim
But temporal things that may hurt us and maim.
    And every man knows this as well as me,
If gentleness were planted naturally   1140
In a certain lineage down the line, yet
They'd not cease in public or in private,
From gentleness, to do their fair duty;
They might not then do vice or villainy.
    Take fire and bring it in the darkest house,   1145
From here to mountains of the Caucasus,[9]
And let men shut the doors and go return;
Yet still the fire will lie as fair and burn
Like twenty thousand men might it behold;
Its natural duty it will always hold,   1150
On my life, till extinguished it may be.
    Here, may you well see how gentility
Is not connected to one's possessions,
Since folks don't follow its operation
Always, as does the fire, lo, in its kind.   1155
For, God knows it, men may well often find
That a lord's son does shame and villainy;
And he who wants praise for his gentility,
Since a gentle house he was born into,
And had elders full of noble virtue,   1160
And who will not himself do gentle deeds,
And dead gentle ancestors hardly heeds,
He is not gentle, be he duke or earl;
A villain's sinful deeds do make a churl.
For such gentleness is only fame   1165
From your elders' high goodness and their name,
Which is a thing your person does not own.
Your gentleness must come from God alone.
Thus our true gentleness must come from grace;
It's not a thing bequeathed us with our place.   1170
    Think how noble, as says Valerius,
Was this one Tullius Hostillius,[1]

---

8. Dante Alighieri (1265–1321), Florentine poet whose *Divine Comedy* had a significant influence on Chaucer; the following lines echo *Purgatorio* 7.121–23.
9. The mountain range on the southwest bor-

der of Russia, between the Black and Caspian Seas.
1. Third king of Rome (7th century B.C.E.); according to legend, he began life as a herdsman.

Nobility did poverty succeed.
Read Seneca, and Boethius[2] read;
There you shall see expressly that, indeed,   1175
The man is gentle who does gentle deeds.
And therefore, my dear husband, I conclude:
Though my ancestors were humble and rude,
Yet may the high God, and for this I pray,
Grant me grace to live virtuously each day.   1180
I am gentle, whenever I begin,
To live virtuously and to waive sin.
    You reproach me for poverty, indeed,
High God above, on whom we base our creed,
In willing poverty did live his life.   1185
And certainly each man, maiden, or wife
May understand that Jesus, heaven's king,
Would not choose a vicious way of living.
Glad poverty's an honest thing, it's true;
Thus Seneca and other clerks say, too.   1190
He who sees he's well paid by poverty,
Though he had no shirt, he seems rich to me.
He is a poor man who can only covet,
For he wants what he lacks power to get;
He who has naught, and does not covet, too,   1195
Is rich, though he a peasant seems to you.
True poverty, it sings out properly;
Now Juvenal[3] says of it merrily:
'The poor man, when he should go by the way,
Before the thieves, this man can sing and play.'   1200
Poverty is a hateful good, I guess,
A great encouragement to busyness;
Great improver of wisdom and good sense
For him who can suffer it with patience.
Poverty, though miserable seems its name,   1205
Is a possession no one else will claim.
Poverty often, when a man is low,
Can make him both his God and himself know.
Poverty's an eyeglass, it seems to me,
Through which he might his good and true friends see.   1210
And sire, now, if I don't grieve you, therefore
For poverty don't blame me anymore.
    Now, sire, with old age you have reproached me;
And truly, sire, though no authority
Were in books, you gentlemen of honor   1215
Say folks to an old man should show favor

2. Christian Roman philosopher (d. 474), whose *Consolation of Philosophy*, written in prison before his execution, was translated from Latin by Chaucer. Seneca the Younger (d. 65 C.E.), Roman Stoic moralist and drama-tist who committed suicide by order of the emperor Nero.
3. Roman poet (d. ca. 120 C.E.); the quota-tion is from *Satire* 10.22.

And call him father, in your gentleness;
And I shall find authorities, I guess.
  Now, since you say that I am foul and old,
You don't have to fear to be a cuckold;   1220
For filth and age, so far as I can see,
Are great wardens upon one's chastity.
But, nonetheless, since I know your delight,
I shall fulfill your worldly appetite.
  Choose now," said she, "of these things, one of two: 1225
Till I die, to have me foul and old, too,
And be to you a true and humble wife,
And never displease you in all my life,
Or else you can have now a fair, young thing,
And take your chances with the visiting   1230
That happens at your house because of me,
Or in some other place, as well may be.
Choose yourself whichever one will please you."
  This knight now ponders and sighs sorely, too,
But finally, he said in this way here: 1235
"My lady and my love and wife so dear,
I put myself in your wise governing;
Choose yourself which one may be most pleasing
And most honor to both you and me too.
I do not care now which one of the two;   1240
What pleases you suffices now for me."
  "Then have I got mastery from you," said she,
"Since I may choose and govern all the rest?"
  "Yes, truly, wife," said he, "I think it best."
  "Kiss me," said she, "we are no longer angry,   1245
For, by my troth,[4] to you I will both be—
Yes, now both fair and good, as will be plain.
I pray to God that I might die insane,
Unless to you I'm also good and true
As any wife's been, since the world was new.   1250
Unless tomorrow I'm as fair to see
As any queen or empress or lady,
Who is between the east and then the west,
Do with my life and death as you think best.
Cast up the curtain; how it is, now see."   1255
  And when the knight saw all this verily,
That she now was so fair and so young, too,
For joy he seized her within his arms two,
His heart was all bathed in a bath of bliss.
A thousand times in a row, he did her kiss,   1260
And she obeyed him then in everything
That was to his pleasure or his liking.
  And thus they both lived until their lives' end
In perfect joy; and Jesus Christ us send,

---

4. I.e., "I swear."

Husbands meek and young and fresh in bed,   1265
And the grace to outlive those whom we wed;
I pray that Jesus may shorten the lives
Of those who won't be governed by their wives;
And old and stingy niggards who won't spend,
To them may God a pestilence soon send!   1270

V

India's Classical Age

During the ancient period (ca. 1200 B.C.E.–400 C.E.), society on the Indian subcontinent evolved in several distinct stages. Beginning from agrarian villages, it developed a caste system and a religion centered on Vedic scripture and ritual; as the rural economy increasingly supported the growth of towns and cities, the first subcontinent-wide empires arose. The caste system grew more intricate, with five main categories that included so-called untouchables as well as numerous specific castes, even as the coexistence of monogamy, polygamy, and polyandry complicated the rules of social classification. The Vedic canon of scripture, commentaries, and code books came to articulate the concepts of *Brahman*, or undifferentiated godhead, and *ātman*, enduring individual self or soul; *mokṣa*, the soul's liberation from mundane existence, so that it can be reunited with godhead; and karma, or action and its consequences, as well as *dharma*, law and duty as defined by the gods. Vedic ritual, designed to please many deities and to increase its performer's chances of attaining *mokṣa*, was complemented by sophisticated debates about the nature of good and evil, morality and power, and ethics and justice, thereby laying the

This detail from a seventh-century Buddhist wall painting depicts the Hindu deity Indra kneeling in veneration before the Buddha.

foundation for Hinduism in the classical period. By the start of the Common Era, India was well-defined as a distinct cultural zone within Asia, characterized by its acceptance of pantheism and polytheism, its religious pluralism and tolerance, and its accommodation of social and cultural diversity.

THE TRANSITION TO THE CLASSICAL PERIOD

In the closing centuries of the ancient period, the subcontinent underwent several far-reaching changes that were part of a lengthy transition to the classical period (ca. 400–1100 C.E.). One major shift was a transformation of its political organization, which became evident under the Maurya dynasty (ca. 321–180 B.C.E.). Established immediately after Alexander the Great's invasion of India (327 B.C.E.), the Mauryan empire unified most of the country—then inhabited by about 50 million people—under a centralized administration and a single system of laws. The new empire interconnected its districts with highways, easing the movement of goods and people; and it established diplomatic and trade links with Greece, Rome, Egypt, Syria, and Central Asia. The visionary Mauryan emperor Aśoka (ruled 269–232 B.C.E.), in particular, influenced subsequent Indian and Asian history on a significant scale. He institutionalized the idea that a king "turns the wheel of *dharma*" on earth, and hence is fully responsible for his people's well-being under cosmic or universal law. His royal chancery standardized the Brahmi script system, which was used in his famous rock inscriptions, paving the way for the subcontinent's future literacy and the spread of writing throughout Southeast Asia. The standardization also emphasized multilingual pluralism, as Brahmi writing was simultaneously transcribed into the Greek and Kharosṭhī scripts (the latter a variant of the Aramaic), which were used widely along the ancient Silk Road linking Asia to Europe.

Equally important, Aśoka personally converted to Buddhism, patronized the Third Buddhist Council, and sent Buddhist embassies to various parts of Asia. Because of his adoption of *ahiṃsā* (nonviolence) as a state policy, as well as his unusual balance between Buddhist proselytizing and the official tolerance of many religions (Hinduism, Jainism, and Greek polytheism, among others), he became the first figure of transnational importance in the history of Buddhism; he is portrayed in the canon of Theravada Buddhism as second in importance only to Gautama Buddha. Aśoka's conception and practice of imperial rule became a multifaceted model for Indian empires and kingdoms in the classical period and later.

Another change during the transitional centuries was the consolidation of royal patronage for the arts, architecture and construction, and public works. Aśoka built many of the oldest, most venerated monuments of Buddhism, and he invested in hospitals, libraries, monasteries, and institutions of learning; his support initiated the growth and spread of Buddhist art and architecture across Asia over many centuries. A successor of the Mauryan state, the Kuṣāṇa empire (first–third century C.E.), particularly under Kaniṣka (ruled ca. 100 C.E.), sponsored the Indo-Greek sculpture and architecture of Gandhara and Mathura, which displayed the influence of the Greek colony Alexander established near Peshawar, Pakistan. After he, like Aśoka, converted to Buddhism, Kaniṣka hosted the Fourth Buddhist Council in Kashmir, which launched Mahāyāna Buddhism and its subsequent momentous spread to China and Japan. He patronized painters, musicians, and poets, including the poet-dramatist Aśvaghoṣa, whose *Buddhacarita* (*The Life of the Buddha,* second century C.E.) invented the style of Sanskrit *kāvya,* or poetry, that was to dominate the classical period.

SOCIAL AND POLITICAL CONTEXTS OF CLASSICAL LITERATURE

The "classical" phase—during which Indian literature achieved an exceptional degree of aesthetic balance, stylistic refinement, intellectual sophistication, and originality—began in the second century C.E.; it came to maturity during the Gupta empire (ca. 320–550), specifically under Candragupta Vikramāditya (ruled ca. 375–415). Despite turbulence in its latter half, the classical period lasted until the end of the eleventh century, after which Islam, having arrived from the Middle East, irreversibly transformed the subcontinent's politics, society, and economy.

Stretching across the whole of northern India, and building alliances with lesser powers to its south, the Gupta empire achieved a remarkable expansion and stabilization of the Indian economy. Agriculture and dairy farming yielded an array of grains, fresh produce, and milk products, at the same time, weaving and spinning guilds, salt and mineral mines, metalworks, jewelers' workshops, and specialized castes of artisans produced a wide range of luxury goods and items for everyday consumption. An efficient bureaucracy, regulated coinage, and banking led to an increase in travel and pilgrimage and the growth of shipping, ports, inland cities, and overland and maritime commerce. While trade with the Roman Empire declined, that with China and Southeast Asia—especially the Indonesian archipelago—flourished, creating prosperity across the countryside as well as in urban areas. The economic improvements of the Gupta empire continued, on a smaller scale, in the successor kingdoms of Harṣavardhana of Kannauj (seventh century, near Delhi) and of dynasties in central and eastern India (eighth–eleventh centuries).

The Gupta empire's prosperity and political stability had broad ramifications for the subcontinent's arts, religions, and literature. Like the Mauryas and Kuśānas before them, the Guptas had a pluralistic policy of supporting Hinduism, Jainism, and Buddhism, though more lavishly; but they themselves were Hindus, and their patronage powerfully aided the consolidation of what we now call classical Hinduism. Mainly because of their stimulus, Hinduism shifted from an elite focus on Vedic ritual and sacrifice to a more populist form of engagement, centered on pilgrimages to holy river sites and public worship in temples. It devalued many of the Vedic gods, who resembled the gods in the Greek and Roman pantheons, and elevated Viṣṇu (the god of preservation) and Śiva (the god of destruction) to the status of major deities. Moreover, it produced a vast new canon of theological and mythological works, called Purāṇas, focused on these gods; eventually, they significantly displaced the Vedas (ca. 1200–900 B.C.E.), the original revealed scripture, in the popular imagination. The Guptas aided this shift by financing temple architecture and construction on a grand scale; these edifices later served as models for temple complexes not only in India but also in Borobudur (Indonesia) and Angkor Wat (Cambodia). They also championed major advances in classical Indian stone and metal sculpture—examples are now widely represented in major museums around the world—which influenced the plastic arts throughout Asia.

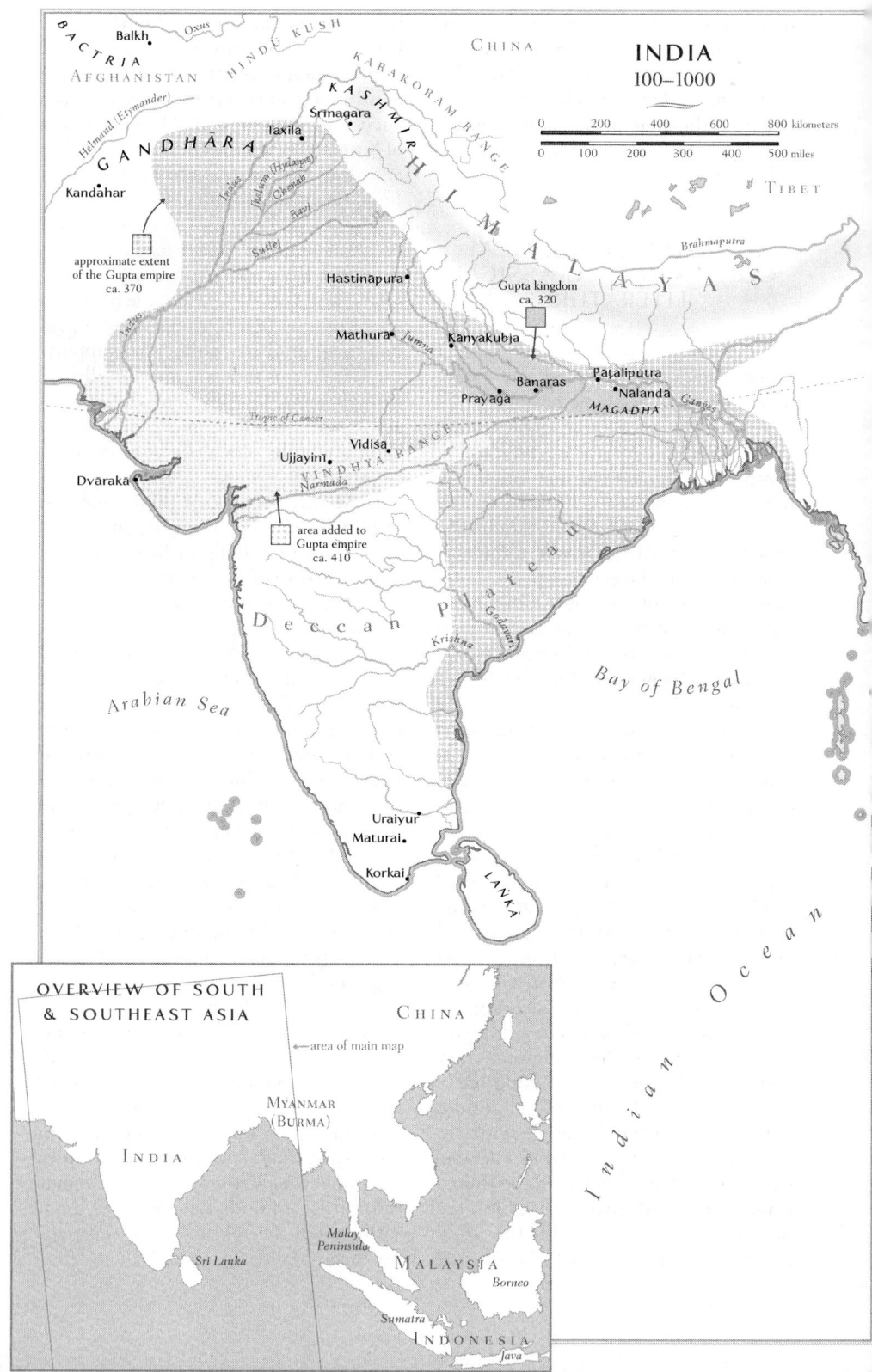

INDIA
100–1000

The Dashavatar temple, dedicated to Viṣṇu, in Deogarh, India—characteristic of temple architecture during the height of the Gupta dynasty in the fifth century.

The Gupta dynasty extended patronage at their court to writers, scholars, and artists as well; they appointed a *rāja-kavi*, or poet laureate; and they maintained royal libraries. They initiated the tradition of underwriting the preparation and conservation of manuscripts by professional scribes, and the production of dramas and other entertainments. Kālidāsa's plays were written for and staged at the Gupta court; centuries later, the courtier-poet Rājasekhara (one of the writers in our anthology) could draw on this tradition as he hosted play productions at his home. The Guptas also reinforced the older Mauryan and Kuṣāṇa practice of patronizing the writing and collection of manuscripts at monasteries and temples of various faiths.

The Guptas' paradigm of royal patronage spread literacy and literature beyond the networks of the *brāhmaṇa* (priestly) caste, which had largely monopolized writing and scholarship in earlier Hindu society. Now, the caste groups of *kṣatriyas* (warriors) and *vaiśyas* (traders) were able to develop their own literate cultures, and the Buddhists and Jains—who had broken away around the sixth century B.C.E.—were able to extend and refine theirs. By the end of the Gupta empire, the Jains in particular had defined a cultural role for themselves that has proved central to Indian history: drawing on royal patronage from across the subcontinent, they became its informal "librarians," collecting and preserving manuscripts in virtually every language and period.

CLASSICAL GENRES AND THE CLASSICAL POET

The classical period witnessed an expansion in how literature and the figure of the writer were understood. Sanskrit prose had appeared early in the ancient period, but during the first millennium B.C.E. its purposes were solely theological and practical. In the classical period, as prose became a medium with aesthetic qualities, it was used to compose fictional narratives in the genre of *kathā* (tale) or nonfictional narratives in the genre of *ākhyāyikā* (history, biography).

In the ancient period, the *Rāmāyana* and the *Mahābhārata* described themselves as *kāvyas*—that is, as epics in verse. The classical period, in both theory and practice, expanded the term's application to the full range of literary composition in verse, prose, and mixtures of verse and prose, whether oral or written. The category thus came to include drama, epics, tales, and lyrics, as well as didactic and nonfictional composition—but it contained only those works that displayed aesthetic qualities appropriate to their form and genre. Within classical *kāvya*, major forms, such as long poems in interwoven cantos, had equal footing with minor forms, such as topical satires, prayers, benedictions, and epigrams, which could be as short as a single verse. By the end of the first millennium C.E., Sanskrit literature had burgeoned, abandoning its original, narrow definition to refashion itself into a vast storehouse of texts in several dozen genres.

Whereas the *kavi* (poet) of the ancient period dealt primarily with oral transmission, the classical Indian author inhabited a more complex literary world permeated with orality, performance, and writing. His social life was also busy: as we know from the *Kāmasūtra* (fourth century) and other texts, the classical intellectual was a connoisseur of the arts and a man about town, with a taste for life's tangible pleasures. As a poet, he had to be trained in grammar, poetics, and philosophy; moreover, he had to command not just his mother tongue but also a regional lingua franca and Sanskrit. So that he could produce and interpret allusions, it was essential that *kāvya* as well as religious discourse and mythology (especially Hindu and Buddhist) be a part of his repertoire. A poet could not be original unless he knew what had been done in the past, and he could not be inventive unless he had mastered all the tools of his trade.

While classical society valued learning and versatility, these qualities were not sufficient to ensure greatness: an author had to display imagination and brilliance of conception (*pratibhā*) as well as urbane decorum (*aucitya*). And as the classical period progressed, he increasingly had to display his individuality. Among the writers we have selected, **Bhartṛhari** from the fifth century is a shadowy figure; **Murāri**, **Rājaśekhara**, and **Somadeva**, several centuries later, have constructed more individuated literary personae. In the classical period, literature (*sāhitya*) by definition produced "mutual benefit" for the author and audience; a poet therefore had to employ his learning and skill to create something of moral or spiritual value for himself and for his readers and listeners. Most important, a classical *kavi* had to use all his resources to reach through and speak directly to his reader, a connoisseur who ideally was in sympathy with him—his true "companion at heart" (*sahṛdaya*). In a famous verse included in this anthology, the seventh-century poet-dramatist Bhavabhūtī memorably describes his search for the ideal reader:

> The people in this world who
>   scorn me
> no doubt have a special wisdom,
> so I don't write for them:
>
> instead, I write with the thought
> that since the world is wide and
>   time is endless,
> one day someone will be born
>
> whose nature is the same as mine.
>
> (trans. Vinay Dharwadker)

THE ROLE OF POETICS IN THE CLASSICAL PERIOD

One aspect of the new literary culture of the classical period was a fresh interest in theoretical reflection on the nature of beauty. Probably the result of imperial patronage of intellectual activity, poetics had a double relation to literature and the arts in classical India: it laid out both the ideals to which artistic practitioners should aspire, based on general considerations, and broad aesthetic rules, derived from the actual practice of past writers. Classical works of poetics and aesthetics therefore functioned simultaneously as philosophical expositions and as practical guides or manuals.

The earliest of these, and the broadest in its influence, was Bharata's *Nāṭyaśāstra* (*The Discipline of the Performing Arts*, second century B.C.E.–second century C.E.), which may have been composed during Kuṣāṇa imperial rule.

A treatise on drama, stagecraft, dance, and music, it comprehensively charts their varieties, materials, techniques, and goals. It also provides guidelines for the training of performers, covering topics from acting, directing, set design, costume, and makeup to song and instrumental music. Within this framework, the *Nāṭyaśāstra* discusses ten main forms of drama, including the play in multiple acts; dramatic structure and language as well as types of character; and diction, versification, and meter.

According to Bharata, the overall goal of a literary work is to lead its audience to experience a *rasa*. *Rasa* is literally the taste, essence, or flavor of a human emotion, but it can be captured only via representation—that is,

This tenth-century sculpture of Śiva and his consort, Pārvatī, depicts the gods in a particular gesture and attitude that has a long history in Indian art and a specific name: "Uma Maheshvara."

in works of art: the raw emotion of real life (called *bhāva*) is something quite different. A writer extracts the universal essence of an ordinary, specific *bhāva*; an actor or dancer on stage does the same, but instead of using words alone he selects and combines all the elements of his craft, including song, gesture, movement, and melody. Through *rasa*, the audience experiences an emotion in its pure, sublime form, without the messiness that accompanies it in everyday life; such an experience refines the audience's aesthetic and moral sensibilities, thereby achieving the primary goal of "culture" or self-cultivation. A poet's aim therefore should be to take any one or more of the nine emotional states fundamental to human experience—love, joy, pity, anger, valor, terror, disgust, wonder, and peace—and transform them into the best words in the best order for a sublime effect on his readers or listeners. Bharata's analysis of the performing arts became the dominant poetic theory of the classical period, and its influence ultimately spread throughout Southeast Asia, from Java and Bali to Thailand and Cambodia. Its greatest adherent in India was Kālidāsa.

The second major aesthetic theory appeared in Daṇḍin's *Kāvayādarśa* (*The Ideal of Poetry,* or *The Mirror of Literature,* sixth–seventh century), which limited itself to imaginative writing. A poet and theorist from the Tamil region in southern India, Daṇḍin asked a simple question: what makes a poem poetic? His answer, in effect, was that the poetic quality of poetry or the literariness of literature lies in a distinctive handling of language—in deviation from everyday speech and practical communication by the use of *alaṃkāra,* "embellishment." To achieve this deflection from the "normal," authors rely on a large repertoire of devices, falling broadly into the categories of figures of speech (such as alliteration, onomato-

poeia, and rhyme) and figures of thought (such as metonymy, or association, and metaphor). Among the poets in our anthology, Bhavabhūtī and Murārī especially are masters of *alaṃkāra* in the Daṇḍin tradition, inventing superb metaphors with effortless skill. The first Indian work of poetics devoted exclusively to literature, Daṇḍin's exposition was widely celebrated in its time; within a few decades, it found its way to China, where, in translation, it became a theoretical template for T'ang and later Chinese poetry.

The third major aesthetic system of the classical period was articulated in Ānandavardhana's *Dhvanyāloka* (*The Radiance of Suggestion,* ninth century), a work produced in Kashmir. According to followers of this school of thought, the aesthetic effects of an artwork can largely be explained by how it conveys its meanings to an audience: they view such a conclusion as logical, since meaningless discourse (babble) fails to create beauty. In the perspective that Ānandavardhana adopts, meaning is grounded in language, and each word signifies at three levels: denotation, which supplies the word's literal or conventional meaning; connotation, which includes one or more secondary associative meanings; and suggestion, which produces a broader range of meanings evoked by the word's placement in a particular larger structure, such as a sentence, verse, or prose passage. For example, the word "village" by itself denotes "a small group of houses in a rural area"; it connotes life on a farm, a world with barnyard animals, a close-knit community, and a lack of urban amenities. In a phrase like "the village on the banks of the Ganges," however, the word suggests other, unexpected meanings: an exotic landscape, the coolness and serenity of a river, timelessness and simplicity, peace and holiness. This last method of signification, called *dhvani,* is the principal device of poetry.

Persuaded by Ānandavardhana, many poets and readers of the late classical period and after came to believe that the beauty of poetry lies primarily in its power to create new meanings through the subtle use of suggestion. *Dhvanyāloka*, of course, also describes the technique of poetic suggestion as practiced by earlier writers; Bhartṛhari and Dharmakīrti are among the poets who exemplify the use of suggestion early in the classical period. But whichever theory or combination of theories they followed—*rasa, alaṃkāra*, or *dhvani*—classical authors and audiences alike found themselves engaged in unprecedented ways not only with the practice of literature but also with larger questions about its nature, function, and value.

Over a thousand years, between the transition from the ancient period and the arrival of Islam as a political power on the subcontinent, the varieties of literature in India gradually multiplied into an unprecedented diversity of texts and genres. Besides a voluminous body of *kāvya* in Sanskrit, the rich literary culture encompassed writing in regional Prakrits—languages such as Mahāraṣṭrī, Magadhī, and Śaurasenī—as well as the remarkable, completely different canon of *caṅkam* poetry in classical Tamil. A vital achievement of the period was the establishment of a reciprocal relation between literary theory and practice, which defined the materials, means, sources, and ends of poetry afresh and encouraged both authors and audiences to engage in sophisticated debates about the function and value of literature. Classical India thus radically altered the literary landscape it had inherited from the ancient period.

BHARTṚHARI

Bhartṛhari (fifth century) was a court poet whose skill in composing short poems in various genres made him a model for subsequent generations. Collected soon after his lifetime, his poetry is preserved in the *Śatakatryam* (*The Three Centuries*, or *Three Hundred Poems*); it is celebrated most for its chiseled images, its melancholy tone, and its biting criticism of the ways of the world. The poems, complete in themselves (rather than excerpts from longer works), are grouped into three thematic sections or "centuries." In the original book, the poems in the first section deal with ethical and moral issues that arise in worldly affairs, those in the second focus on love and desire, while those in the third express disillusionment with the world and explore the complexities of renunciation. "I haven't been the cloud," for example, gives us unprecedented insight into a child's moral debt to its mother. "When she is out of sight" paints a small but exact picture of sexual attraction. And "For a moment he's a child" contemplates life's stages with the detachment of old age—foreshadowing **Shakespeare's** image of "the seven ages of man" more than a thousand years later.

[I haven't been the cloud]¹

I haven't been the cloud
   that brings a rain of riches
to fields parched by lack of money;

I haven't been the powerful storm
   that devastates   5
a mountain-range of enemies;

I haven't even been the bee
   that buzzes around the lotus-faces
of sweet-eyed young women—

I've only been the axe   10
   that cut my mother's youth in two.

[When she's out of sight]

When she's out of sight,
   we desire to see her;
when we behold her,
   we want to hold her in a sweet embrace;
when this long-eyed beauty   5
   is in our arms,
we wish our separate bodies
   to be one at once—
without difference.

[When I knew little]

When I knew little,
I was like an elephant, blind in rut—
I know everything, I said,
   and proudly thought my mind was omniscient.

But when I kept the company   5
of wise people, little by little
I learned that *I'm a fool*—
   and the madness left me, like a fever.

To His Patron

You're the master of wealth,
of infinite means.

---

1. Translated by Vinay Dharwadker. The poems are drawn from Bhartṛhari's *Śatakatryam*.

I'm a master, too—
of words and their infinite meanings.
You're a great warrior—   5
    I'm a debater
    with limitless skill in the art
    of crushing my opponents' pride.
Those who serve you
are blinded by riches—   10
    but they also wish to hear me,
    to purify their minds.
You disregard me,
so I disregard you more—
    I'm gone, O king,   15
and greater than your presence at court
    is my absence from it.

[A human being]

A human being
is allotted a span
    of a hundred years.
Half of it
passes at night;   5
half of the other half
is consumed by childhood,
    old age;
the rest is spent
in serving others—   10
with illness, separation, grief
    for companions.
What's happiness, then,
for living things,
in a life that's like   15
    the bubbles in the froth
    on ocean waves?

[As the sun rises and sets]

As the sun rises and sets,
comes and goes,
life is whittled away
    day by day.
Engrossed in business,   5
weighed down by many tasks,
we don't know
    how time passes.
We witness birth, old age,

misfortune, death—
but they leave us
    unshaken.   10
The world has taken leave of its senses,
drunk on the heady wine
of worldliness   15
    and the gratification
    of the senses.

[For a moment he's a child]

For a moment he's a child—
for a moment, too, a youth—
a connoisseur of love and desire.

For a moment he's a beggar—
and—also for a moment—   5
a master of all wealth, all luxury.

At the end of his active life,
a man—his limbs wizened by age—
like an actor—his face painted with wrinkles—

retires behind the curtain of death.   10

THREE WOMEN POETS

VIKAṬANITAMBĀ

As is the case for the other women poets in classical Sanskrit and ancient Indian literature, we know practically nothing about Vikaṭanitambā beyond what we can infer from the few poetic pieces attributed to her. Her name indicates that she may have belonged to southern India; brief references by later poets and scholars provide evidence that she lived sometime between the fifth and seventh centuries. She treats erotic themes candidly, skillfully using images to show rather than tell and preferring the technique of suggestion over graphic description. In "As he came to bed," for example, she heightens the moment of passion by hinting at the act of love rather than providing distracting details.

572[1]

As he came to bed the knot fell open of itself,
the dress held only somehow to my hips
by the strands of the loosened girdle.
So much I know, my dear;
but when within his arms, I can't remember who he was   5
or who I was, or what we did or how.

1. Translated by D. H. H. Ingalls. The number refers to the poem's position in Vidyākara's *Subhāṣitaratnakośa*.

BHĀVAKADEVĪ

Like Vikaṭanitambā, Bhāvakadevī probably belonged to the middle of the classical period of Sanskrit poetry, but we can surmise even less about her life or personality. Her literary name indicates that she was prized by her contemporaries and successors for her emotional sensitivity. In "At first our bodies knew," Bhāvakadevī memorably evokes her bitterness in marriage by referring only indirectly to its source in her husband's unfaithfulness.

646[2]

At first our bodies knew a perfect oneness,
but then grew two with you as lover
and I, unhappy I, the loved.
Now you are husband, I the wife,
what's left except of this my life,   5
too hard to break, to reap the bitter fruit,
your broken faith.

2. Translated by D. H. H. Ingalls. The number refers to the poem's position in Vidyākara's *Subhāṣitaratnakośa*.

VIDYĀ

Like Vikaṭanitambā and Bhāvakadevī, Vidyā is among the most frequently quoted women poets in classical Sanskrit, but only a few fragments of her poetry have survived. It is likely that she, too, lived between the fifth and the seventh centuries, but later than the other two women. Also like them, she is celebrated for her finely crafted love poems; they are explicitly set in the countryside, suggesting that she was more familiar with village life than with life at a royal court in a city. Her poem here is very oblique in its use of the technique of *dhvani*, or suggestion: a village housewife requests a neighbor to keep an eye on her hut while she goes out, ostensibly to fetch water from the river; but her expectation that she will return with visible scratches on her body indicates that she is really headed for a tryst with a lover on the riverbank.

807[3]

Good neighbor wife, I beg you
keep your eye upon my house a moment;
the baby's father hates to drink
the tasteless water from the well.
Better I go then, though alone, to the river bank   5
dark with *tamāla* trees and thick with canes,[4]
which with their sharp and broken stems
may scratch my breast.

---

3. Translated by D. H. H. Ingalls. The number refers to the poem's position in Vidyākara's *Subhāṣitaratnakośa*.
4. Vegetation characteristic of central India. In classical Sanskrit and later Indian lyric poetry, the riverbank—with shade and ground cover, not far from a village—is the favorite site for lovers' trysts, both before and after marriage.

DHARMAKĪRTI

The poet Dharmakīrti (early seventh century) was a Buddhist; probably a monk in a monastery sponsored by a royal patron, he may have been the same person as the famous logician and philosopher of that name and time. His lyric pieces, which express specifically Buddhist values, stand out for their uncompromising wit, epigrammatic quality, and philosophical depth. "Never to ask the wicked," for instance, is a perfect poetic expression of Buddhism's principles of moral firmness, mindfulness, and pursuit of the Middle Way, a path that avoids all extremes. But whether Hindu or Buddhist, the poet in classical India uses a short poem to create a specific mood, an aesthetic representation of a heightened emotional state. Thus, Dharmakīrti's "Your union with your lover" projects the mood of someone falling in love, highlighting the state of infatuation that occurs early in the process.

477[1]

Your union with your lover will be very brief,
like a dream or a magical illusion,
    and it will end in distaste:

I reflect on these truths a hundred times,
but my heart can't forget that girl   5
    with the eyes of a gazelle.

1213

Never to ask the wicked
for favors;
never to borrow
from a friend of meager means;

to be kind and loving in disposition,   5
just in action;
not to play foul
even at the hour of death;

to stand upright
in misfortune;   10
to follow in the footsteps
of the great:[2]

it's hard to do this—
as hard as it is to walk
on a sword's edge—   15

but good folks
don't need a sermon
about it.

1. Translated by Vinay Dharwadker. The   ṣitaratnakośa.
numbers assigned to Dharmakīrti's poems   2. Several core principles of Buddhism.
refer to their position in Vidyākara's *Subhā-*

BHAVABHŪTĪ

Bhavabhūtī, a Hindu *brāhmaṇa*, was the best-known dramatist of the classical period after Kālidāsa. Most of the lyric verse with which he is represented in Sanskrit anthologies is taken from his two major poetic plays, *Mālatīmādhava* (*Mālatī and Mādhava*) and *Uttararāmacarita* (*King Rāma's Final Act*). He is celebrated for his individualism and experimentalism, for pushing his verse techniques and themes to an extreme, but he is especially renowned for his love poetry. "My love is married to me," which translates a single verse in Sanskrit, is a perfect example of Bhavabhūtī's originality and technical virtuosity: it projects the emotional state of a lover in a torrent of words and images resembling a modernist-style interior monologue, even as its content reminds us of a central theme in **Shakespeare's** sonnets—a lover's desire for a complete and enduring "marriage of true minds" with his beloved. In thematic contrast, "The people in this world who scorn me" (one of the most frequently quoted lyrics in all of Sanskrit literature) gives us a unique image of a poet alienated from his own time and place who dreams of finding his ideal reader in posterity—a dream that this verse makes a reality for Bhavabhūtī himself. Many classical readers consider his "And as we talked together softly, secretly" to be the single most beautiful verse about love in Sanskrit poetry.

598[1]

And as we talked together softly, secretly,
cheek closely pressed to cheek
while our arms were busied in their tight embrace,
the night was gone without our knowing
the hours as they passed.   5

783[2]

My love is married to me
as though she had melted into my mind

or was reflected in it or painted on it or sculpted in it
or set in it like a gem or cemented to it or engraved upon it

or as if she were nailed to it   5
by the five arrows of the god of love

or finely woven into the threads
of the very fabric of its thought

1731[3]

The people in this world who scorn me
no doubt have a special wisdom,
so I don't write for them:

1. The numbers assigned to Bhavabhūtī's poems refer to their positions in Vidyākara's *Subhāṣitaratnakośa*. This poem is translated by D. H. H. Ingalls.
2. Translated by Vinay Dharwadker.
3. Translated by Vinay Dharwadker.

instead, I write with the thought
that since the world is wide and time is endless,   5
one day someone will be born

whose nature is the same as mine.

YOGEŚVARA

Yogeśvara (ninth century) was a poet patronized by a king in eastern India in the late classical period. Probably from Bengal, he became the most celebrated lyric poet of "village and field"—of all aspects of country life—in Sanskrit. He captures the intangible qualities of village life and the countryside in several poems through a series of descriptions; but even when he seems to merely depict physical scenes in human and natural landscapes from a bird's-eye view, he succeeds in evoking powerful moods and emotions. Yogeśvara's range of emotions and situations is wider than we might expect: in "Now may one prize the peasant houses," we experience the sheer joy of harvest time; in "The warmth of their straw borne off by icy winds" we shiver with the peasants in the cold of incoming winter after threshing time; and in "When the rain pours down on the decrepit house" we feel deeply for the harried village wife struggling to survive in poverty.

291[1]

The days are sweet with ripening of sugar cane;
the autumn rice is high;
and brahmins, being overfed at feasts
to which the leading families invite them,
find that the heat grows hard to bear.[2]   5

314

Now may one prize the peasant houses
happy in the first harvest of the winter rice
and sweet with perfume from the jars of new-stored grain;

1. Translated by D. H. H. Ingalls. The numbers assigned to Yogeśvara's poems refer to their position in Vidyākara's *Subhāṣitaratnakośa*.

2. A satirical representation of the "parasitical" priestly caste. The poet is more sympathetic to the poor peasants in the countryside.

where the farmgirls take the pounder,
raise and shake and smoothly drop it,   5
their bracelets jingling as they raise their arms.

318

The warmth of their straw borne off by icy winds,
time and again the peasants wake the fire
whose flame dies ever back, stirring with their sticks.
From the smoking bank of mustard chaff,
noisy with the crackling of the husks,   5
a penetrating odor spreads
to every corner of the threshing floor.

1163

The cat has humped her back;
mouth raised and tail curling,
she keeps one eye in fear upon the inside of the house;
her ears are motionless.
The dog, his mouthful of great teeth wide open   5
to the back of his spittle-covered jaws,
swells at the neck with held-in breath
until he jumps her.

1312

When the rain pours down on the decrepit house
she dries the flooded barley grits
and quiets the yelling children;
she bails out water with a potsherd
and saves the bedding straw.   5
With a broken winnowing basket on her head
the poor man's wife is busy everywhere.

MURĀRĪ

Like **Yogeśvara** before him, Murārī
(mid-ninth century) was also a poet
patronized by a king in eastern India.
He may have belonged to Odisha or
Orissa (the coastal region south of
Bengal); without question he was a
learned *brāhmaṇa* courtier, often
praised for his highly elegant language,

intricate craftsmanship, and wide-ranging literary allusions. His only surviving play is a dramatization of the *Rāmāyaṇa*, but his lyric poetry has also been preserved in quotations by later writers. Murārī's verses are dense and compact, full of surprising images and metaphors: in his two poems on moonlight, for example, he refers to "a group of carpenters" polishing "the tree of heaven," and to the power of a magnet to attract iron filings; in "My limbs are frail," he conjures up the idea that an aging man is "an actor in a farce," who is forced to wear "white hair / for makeup."

913[1]

Is the moonlight
   nothing but the powder
of the cleansing nut
   with which this sea of darkness
has been scrubbed bright,   5
   and its residue
precipitated to the bottom
   as shadows?
Or could the moon's rays
   be a group of carpenters   10
who polish the tree of heaven
   by planing it clean,
leaving its fallen bark
   for shadows?

958

As the moon ages,
   darkness covers the sky,
as if it were the smoke
   of opals about to burst into flames;
and though the sun   5
   hasn't released its light as yet,
it draws out the bees
   imprisoned in the lotuses[2]
as a magnet attracts
   iron filings.   10

1. Translated by Vinay Dharwadker. The numbers assigned to Murāri's poems refer to their position in Vidyākara's *Subhāṣitaratnakoṣa*.
2. The lotus is photosensitive: its petals open at sunrise and close at sunset. The suggestion here is that if a bee happens to be feeding on a lotus at sundown, it may be "imprisoned" in the flower overnight when its petals close.

1019

O pearl free of flaws,
publish yourself—
   go furnish a house
or a king's necklace
   with your splendor,   5
bring your own virtues
   to fruit.
Why waste your life
   shut up in an oyster shell?
The ocean is enormous—   10
   who in this hole
can even calculate
   your worth?

1526

My limbs are frail,
my voice is weak,
   I suck up to the powerful—
I've been reduced
   to an actor in a farce.   5
I don't know
   in what new play
old age will cast me
   to play my part—
with this white hair   10
   for makeup.

RĀJAŚEKHARA

Rājaśekhara (late ninth–early tenth century) was probably the son of a powerful court official in the Gurjara-Pratihara kingdom of north-central India. He was a poet and playwright composing in Sanskrit and in literary Prakrits, a theorist of literature, and a much-loved patron and friend of poets. He is especially famous because he publicly acknowledged his wife, Avantisundarī, as his equal in learning and taste, crediting her for his own literary success (the first

Indian author to do so); he wrote his most famous play to please her, and she most likely hosted its first performance at their home. Rājaśekhara's short poems are verses taken from his plays; the best of them give us memorable images of the beauty of women and of the joys and intricacies of love. In "When people see her face," he pushes the technique of suggestion to an extreme with a clever inversion: he hints at a girl's extraordinary beauty by enumerating things to which her face, skin, eyes, eyebrows, and smile cannot be compared.

457[1]

When people see her face
    they stop talking about the moon;
when they see her skin,
    there's no more talk of gold.
Waterlilies lose the contest   5
    against her eyes;
what's the nectar of moonlight
    when compared to her smile?
And the love god's bow is nothing
    when held up to her eyebrows.   10
But why say more—
    the truth is too well known,
that in the order of Creation
    the Creator shuns repetition.

336[2]

Youthfulness inscribes all her parts,
but is especially skillful in her eye's maturity,

for her gaze gathers all the expressions
of whichever man she chooses to look at,

and then conveys back to him   5
all that he feels as the one who looks at her,

whom she has found worthy of her gaze.

---

1. The numbers assigned to Rājaśekhara's poems refer to their position in Vidyākara's *Subhāṣitaratnakośa*. This poem is translated by Vinay Dharwadker.
2. Translated by Vinay Dharwadker.

SOMADEVA
eleventh century

How many different stories—truly different stories—have human beings invented? If we could read every story in the world and strip it down to its bare bones, how many distinct narrative cores would we find? Somadeva, a master storyteller from eleventh-century India, suggests that stories flow out of their tellers in streams and that all the streams, broadening into rivers, flow into an ocean of narrative that is potentially infinite.

LIFE

Somadeva was a brāhmaṇa scholar and courtier whose patron was Queen Sūryamati of Kashmir, an unusual woman with a strong interest in learning and the arts. In his prologue, he tells us that he compiled and composed the *Kathāsaritsāgara* to entertain the queen "when her mind had been wearied by the continuous study of the sciences." Trained in the traditional Indian disciplines of grammar, poetics and rhetoric, and philosophy (considered essential for any writer), he was exceptionally skilled in the crafts of both versification and narrative in the genre and style of Sanskrit *kāvya*.

Somadeva lived toward the end of the classical period of Indian literature, which stretched from about the fourth to the eleventh century. This period began with the establishment of the Gupta empire (320–550 C.E.) in northern India, and smaller imperial formations and kingdoms then emerged elsewhere on the subcontinent. The expansion of agriculture, mining and metallurgy, textile and handicraft production, and especially trade and commerce under the Gupta dynasty led to the rise of a wealthy and powerful merchant class and inaugurated several centuries of prosperity. Merchants became prominent citizens in busy port towns and cosmopolitan inland cities, investing in architecture and shipping; they crisscrossed the land on business and traveled widely overseas. Although they patronized pilgrimage sites and endowed temples and monasteries, their values were often secular and materialistic, focused on the acquisition and uses of wealth.

WORK

The large body of stories that Somadeva gathered in his *Kathāsaritsāgara* in the eleventh century reflected these developments. In contrast to earlier literature, which mostly emphasized frugality and otherworldliness in poorer economic conditions, the popular new tales of the classical period depicted a crowded world of traders, bankers, shopkeepers, con men, and thieves. Although the heroes and villains of these narratives are colorful characters, and their intrigues and wild schemes are often crooked, the stories themselves are concerned with more than the crass pursuit of wealth. Their recurrent concerns include the ancient Hindu themes of karma and rebirth, the memory of past lives and the power of curses, and *mokṣa*, the quest for liberation from worldly attachments. They also celebrate love and beauty in all their aspects, as well as the art of storytelling itself.

Somadeva brought together about 350 well-known stories, most of them transmitted from an earlier collection called *The Great Story* by Guṇāḍhya, which by the seventh century had been lost. Somadeva retold the tales in elegant Sanskrit couplets, in a heightened and distinctive style of verse narrative. The title, *Kathāsaritsāgara*, identifies the book as "the ocean into which the streams of narrative flow"; the work is thus intended to be, and has been received by generations of readers as, a large repository of all kinds of memorable stories. All the tales in the work are contained inside a main frame story, which recounts the adventures of Prince Naravāhanadatta, who becomes the king of the Vidyādharas (aerial spirits); the dominant themes of this narrative are the prince's acquisition of wealth and magical powers and his amorous relationships with several princesses and other beautiful women— including his great love, a courtesan he idealized. The nested short tales are told by various characters in the outer frame to amuse their friends, lovers, and spouses, in imitation of the stories that the great god Śiva is believed to tell his consort, Pārvatī, for her entertainment.

"The Red Lotus of Chastity," the story selected here, is a lively and entertaining example of the stories typically found in Somadeva's work and in classical literature in Sanskrit, as distinct from that language's earlier epic and religious narrative traditions. Though written much later, the story is set in the Gupta period of Indian history (probably in the fifth century); many of its characters belong to the wealthy merchant class of that time, and its action takes place in mainland India and on the islands of Indonesia. Its central theme is the value of fidelity in a marriage based on love, as it details the lengths to which a husband and a wife can go in order to remain faithful to each other.

The setup of the plot is unusual. A rich merchant of Bengal sails with his marriageable son to Indonesia to find a suitable bride for the young man in the community of wealthy Indian traders settled there. When they find a good match, however, the girl's father demurs because he does not want his beloved daughter to live far away, in India. But the girl has fallen completely in love and decides to marry the young man against her parents' wishes. Years later, after inheriting his father's trade in precious stones, the young husband decides to travel to another island in Indonesia; his wife, however, fears that he will be unfaithful to her during his long business trip abroad. To resolve their mutual anxieties, the couple appeals to the god Śiva, who gives them each a magical red lotus; if either of them commits adultery, then the lotus in the other's possession will wilt immediately.

What follows from this initial situation is a rollicking comedy of romantic love, sexual intrigue, and crafty worldliness. We encounter vivid characters— among them, the spoiled sons of a rich merchant, a corrupt Buddhist nun and her equally amoral protégée, and a wise and just king in a foreign land. The atmosphere is like that of a fairy tale, in which extraordinary events transform the destinies of ordinary people. But the characters themselves are realistically delineated and belong to social types that became standard figures both in India and abroad: Yogakaraṇḍikā and Siddhīkarī in "The Red Lotus of Chastity" are forerunners of the errant monks and nuns in later writing (such as **Chaucer's** *Canterbury Tales*), and Yogakaraṇḍikā, who makes a career of procuring women for men, also foreshadows the bawd in European Renaissance literature. The story's heroine, Devasmitā, bravely disguises herself as a man and undertakes a perilous journey overseas to foil an evil plot, to prove her own fidelity, and to test the love of her husband, Guhasena. She reminds us of many other cross-dressing women in both Indian and Western literature.

Like the earlier Buddhist *Jātaka* tales and Hindu animal fables of the *Pañcatantra,* the more secular and entertaining stories of the *Kathāsaritsā-gara* migrated from India to the Middle East and later to Europe. Besides the examples mentioned above, characters, situations, and plots from Somadeva's narratives turn up in works ranging from Boccaccio's *Decameron* in the fifteenth century and **Shakespeare** at the end of the sixteenth century to Salman Rushdie's *Haroun and the Sea of Stories* (1990), which explicitly acknowledges its debt to the original "ocean of stories." Somadeva's eleventh-century work is especially famous as a model for ***The Thousand and One Nights.***

From Kathāsaritsāgara[1]

The Red Lotus of Chastity

In this world is a famous port, Tāmraliptī,[2] and there lived a rich merchant whose name was Dhanadatta. He had no sons, so he assembled many brahmins, prostrated himself before them, and requested: "See to it that I get a son!"

"That is not at all difficult," said the priests, "for the brahmins can bring about everything on earth by means of the scriptural sacrifices.[3]

"For example," they continued, "long ago there was a king who had no sons, though he had one hundred and five women in his seraglio. He caused a special sacrifice for a son to be performed, and a son was born to him. The boy's name was Jantu, and in the eyes of all the king's wives he was the rising new moon. Once when he was crawling about on all fours, an ant bit him on the thigh, and the frightened child cried out. The incident caused a terrific disturbance in the seraglio, and the king himself lamented—'My son! O my son!'—like a commoner. After a while, when the ant had been removed and the child comforted, the king blamed his own anxiety on the fact that he had only one son.

" 'There must be a way to have more sons,' he thought, and in his grief he consulted the brahmins. They replied: 'Indeed, Your Majesty, there is one way by which you can have more sons. Kill the son you have and sacrifice all his flesh in the sacred fire. When the royal wives smell the burning flesh, they will all bear sons.' The king had everything done as they said and got as many sons as he had wives.

"Thus with the help of a sacrifice," concluded the brahmins, "we can bring you, too, a son."

So at the advice of the brahmins, merchant Dhanadatta settled on a stipend for their sacerdotal services, and the priests performed the sacrifice for him. Subsequently a son was born to the merchant. The boy, who was given the name Guhasena, grew up in due time, and his father Dhanadatta was seeking a wife for him.

1. Translated by J. A. B. van Buitenen.
2. During the Gupta era, an important port on the Bay of Bengal, a center for north India's trade
with south India and Southeast Asia.
3. That is, those described in the Vedas.

And the merchant voyaged with his son to the Archipelago[4] to find a bride, though he pretended that it was just a business expedition. In the Archipelago he asked the daughter of a prominent merchant, Dharmagupta, a girl named Devasmitā, On-Whom-the-Gods-Have-Smiled, in marriage for his son Guhasena. Dharmagupta, however, did not favor the alliance, for he loved his daughter very much and thought that Tāmraliptī was too far away. But Devasmitā herself, as soon as she had set eyes on Guhasena, was so carried away by his qualities that she decided to desert her parents. Through a companion of hers she arranged a meeting with the man she loved and sailed off from the island at night with him and his father. On their arrival in Tāmraliptī they were married; and the hearts of husband and wife were caught in the noose of love.

Then father Dhanadatta died, and, urged by his relatives to continue his father's business, Guhasena made plans for a voyage to the island of Cathay.[5] Devasmitā, however, did not approve of his going, for she was a jealous wife and naturally suspected that he would love another woman. So with his relatives urging him on and his wife opposing, Guhasena was caught in the middle and could not get on with his business.

Thereupon he went to a temple and took a vow of fasting. "Let God in this temple show me a way out," he thought. Devasmitā came along, and she took the same vow. God Śiva[6] appeared to both of them in a dream. He gave them two red lotuses and spoke: "Each of you must keep this lotus in his hand. If one of you commits adultery while the other is far away, the lotus in the other's hand will wither away. So be it!" The couple woke up, and each saw in the other's hand the red lotus which was an image of the lover's heart.

So, carrying his lotus, Guhasena departed, and Devasmitā stayed home watching hers. Presently Guhasena reached Cathay and went about his business, trading in precious stones. But the lotus he carried around in his hands aroused the curiosity of four merchant's sons who noticed that the flower never seemed to fade. They tricked him into accompanying them home and gave him quantities of mead to drink: when he was drunk, they asked him about the lotus, and he told them. Calculating that the merchant's trade in precious stones would take a long time to be completed, the mischievous merchant's sons plotted together, and, their curiosity aroused, all four set sail at once for Tāmraliptī, without telling anybody, to see if they could not undo the chastity of Guhasena's wife. Reconnoitering in Tāmraliptī, they sought out a wandering nun,[7] Yogakarandikā, who lived in a Buddhist monastery. They ingratiated themselves with her and proposed, "Reverend Madam, if you can bring about what we wish, we shall reward you richly."

"Of course, you boys want some girl in town," said the nun. "Tell me. I shall see to it. I have no desire for money, because I have a clever pupil named Siddhīkarī,[8] and thanks to her I have amassed a great fortune."

"How is that? You have acquired great wealth through the favor of your pupil?" the merchant's sons asked.

"If you are curious to hear the story, my sons," said the nun, "I shall tell you. Listen.

4. Islands of Southeast Asia and Indonesia.
5. Not China but an island in Southeast Asia or Indonesia.
6. The destroyer god (Śiva), one of the two great gods of Hinduism.

7. Buddhist monks and nuns must have no possessions and are required to live on alms, which they collect by wandering.
8. She Who Can Accomplish What One Desires.

"Some time ago a merchant came to town from the North. While he was stay-ing here, my pupil, in disguise, contrived to get herself employed in his house as a maid of all work; and as soon as the merchant had come to trust her, she stole all the gold he had in his house and sneaked away at dawn. A drummer[9] saw her leave town and, his suspicions aroused by her fast pace, started with his drum in his hand to pursue and rob her in turn. Siddhīkarī had reached the foot of a ban-yan tree when she saw the drummer approach, and the cunning girl called out to him in a miserable voice: 'I have quarreled with my husband, and now I have run away from home to kill myself. Could you fasten the noose for me, my friend?'

" 'If she is going to hang herself, then why should I kill the woman?' thought the drummer, and he tied a noose to the tree. He stepped on his drum, put his head through the noose, and said, 'This is the way to do it.' The same instant Siddhīkarī kicked the drum to pieces—and the drummer himself perished in the noose. But at that moment the merchant came looking for her, and from a dis-tance he discerned the maid who had stolen his entire fortune. She saw him come, however, and immediately climbed up the tree and hid among the leaves. When the merchant came to the tree with his servants, he saw only the drummer dangling from the tree, for Siddhīkarī was nowhere in sight.

" 'Can she have climbed up the tree?' the merchant questioned, and immedi-ately one of the servants went up.

" 'I have always loved you, and here you are, with me in a tree!' whispered Siddhīkarī. 'Darling, all the money is yours. Take me!' And she embraced him and kissed him on the mouth and bit the fool's tongue off with her teeth. Overcome with pain the servant tumbled out of the tree, spitting blood, and cried something unintelligible that sounded like 'la-la-la.' When he saw him, the merchant thought that the man was possessed by a ghost, and in terror he fled home with his ser-vants. No less terrified, Siddhīkarī, my pupil, climbed down from the top of the tree and went home with all the money."

The nun's pupil entered just as her mistress finished, and the nun presented her to the merchant's sons.

"But now tell me the truth," resumed the nun, "which woman do you want? I shall prepare her for you at once!"

"Her name is Devasmitā," they replied, "Guhasena's wife. Bring her to bed with us!" The nun promised to do so and gave the young men lodging in her house.

The wandering nun ingratiated herself with the servants at Guhasena's house by giving them delicacies and so on, and thus she gained entrance to the house with her pupil. But when she came to the door of Devasmitā's chambers, a dog which was kept on a chain at the door barked at her, though never before had the bitch been known to bark. Then Devasmitā saw her, and wondering who the woman was that had come, she sent a servant girl to inquire and then herself conducted the nun into her chamber. When she was inside, the nun gave Devas-mitā her blessing, and after courteous amenities for which she found a pretext, the wicked woman said to the chaste wife: "I have always had a desire to see you, and today I saw you in a dream.[1] That is why I have come to visit you. I see that

---

9. A *domba*, an executioner or low-caste func-tionary in cemeteries.

1. Holy persons are thought to have super-

natural gifts, such as the ability to dream true events and interpret them.

you are separated from your husband, and my heart suffers for you; if youth and beauty are deprived of love's pleasures, they are fruitless."

With such talk the nun gained Devasmitā's confidence, and after having chatted awhile she returned to her own home. The next day the nun took a piece of meat covered with sneezing powder and went to Devasmitā's house. She gave the meat to the dog at the door, and the animal at once swallowed it. The sneezing powder caused the dog's eyes to run, and the animal sneezed incessantly. Then the nun entered Devasmitā's apartment, and once she had settled down to her hostess' hospitality, the shrew began to weep. Pressed by Devasmitā she said, as if with great reluctance; "Oh, my daughter, go and look outside at your dog; she is crying. Just now she recognized me from a former life[2] when we knew each other, and she burst out in tears. Pity moved me to weep with her."

Devasmitā looked outside the door and saw the dog which seemed to be weeping. "What miracle is this?" she wondered for the space of a moment. Then the nun said: "Daughter, in a former life both she and I were the wives of a brahmin. Our husband had to travel everywhere at the king's orders as his envoy, and while he was gone, I carried on with other men as I pleased, to avoid frustrating the senses and the element. Our highest duty, you know, is to yield to the demands of sense and element. That is why I in this present life have the privilege of remembering past existences. But she in her ignorance guarded her chastity, and so she has been reborn a bitch, though she does remember her other life."

"What kind of moral duty is that?" thought Devasmitā, who was clever enough. "This nun has some crooked scheme afoot!" Then she said: "Reverend Madam, how long I have been ignorant of my real duty! You must introduce me to some handsome man!"

"There are some merchant's sons from the Archipelago who are staying in town," said the nun. "I shall bring them to you if you want."

Overjoyed the nun went home. And Devasmitā said secretly to her servant girls: "I am sure that some merchant's sons have seen the never-fading lotus which my husband carries in his hand, and out of curiosity they have asked him about it when he was drinking. Now the scoundrels have come here from their island to seduce me and have engaged that depraved nun as their go-between. Fetch me immediately some liquor loaded with Datura[3] drug and go and have a dog's-paw branding iron made." The maids did as their mistress told them, and one of them, at Devasmitā's instructions, dressed up as her mistress.

Meanwhile the nun selected one of the four merchant's sons, who each commanded to be taken first, and brought him, disguised as her own pupil, to Devasmitā's house. There she bade him go inside and went away unobserved. The maid who posed as Devasmitā gave the young merchant with all due courtesies the drugged liquor to drink, and the drink (as though it were his own depravity) robbed him of his senses. Then the girls stripped him of everything he wore and robed him monastically in air.[4] Thereupon they branded the dog's-paw iron on his forehead, dragged him outside, and threw him in a cesspool. In the last hours of night he came to his senses and found himself sunk in the cesspool—the very

2. The memory of past lives is a gift, enabling the rememberer to make amends for evil deeds of such lives.
3. A narcotic plant.

4. The Digambaras ("clad in air"), a major sect of Jaina monks, wander naked.

image of the Avīcī hell[5] which his own wickedness had brought on! He got up, bathed, and, fingering the mark on his forehead, he returned naked to the nun's house.

"I won't be the only ridiculous one!" he thought, and so he told his brothers in the morning that he had been robbed on his way back. Pretending a headache from his long night and deep drinking, he kept his marked forehead wrapped in a turban's cloth.

The second merchant's son who went to Devasmitā's house that night was manhandled in the same way. He too came home naked and said that, despite leaving his jewelry at home, he had been stripped by robbers as he came back. And the next morning he too kept his head bandaged, supposedly because of a headache, to conceal the brand on his forehead. All four of them, though they dissimulated everything, were castigated, branded, plundered, and put to shame in the same fashion. Without disclosing to the nun how they had been maltreated ("Let the same thing happen to her!"), they departed.

The next day the nun, who thought that her plan had succeeded, went with her pupil to Devasmitā's house. With a show of gratitude Devasmitā courteously poured them drinks with Datura, and when the nun and her pupil had passed out, the chaste wife cut off their noses and ears[6] and tossed them outside in a sewage pit.

But then Devasmitā began to worry. "Might those merchant's sons now kill my husband in revenge?" She went to her mother-in-law and told her everything that had happened.

"Daughter," said her mother-in-law, "you have done well. But something bad may now happen to my son."

"Then I shall save him as Śaktimatī once saved her husband with her presence of mind!"

"And how did she save her husband?" asked her mother-in-law. "Tell me, my daughter."

"In my country," Devasmitā began, "we have a great Yakṣa[7] who is famous under the name of Maṇibhadra. He is very powerful, and our ancestors have built him a temple in our town. My countrymen come to this temple, each with his own presents, to offer them to Maṇibhadra in order to gain whatever it is they wish. There is a custom that any man who is found in this temple at night with another man's wife is kept with the woman in the sanctum of Maṇibhadra for the rest of the night, and the next morning they are brought to court, where they will confess to their behavior and be thrown in jail.

"One night a merchant named Samudradatta was caught in the act with another man's wife by one of the temple guards. The guard led the merchant away with the woman and threw them into the sanctum of the temple where they were securely chained. After a while the merchant's faithful wife, Śaktimatī, who was very ingenious, got to know what had happened. Immediately she took an offering for pūjā worship[8] and, disguised, went out into the night to the temple, full of self-confidence and chaperoned by her confidantes. When she came to the temple, the pūjā priest, greedy for the stipend she offered him, opened the gates

---

5. One of the many hells described in Hindu and Buddhist mythology.
6. In Hindu law a punishment for women who commit adultery.

7. A type of demigod common to Hindu, Buddhist, and Jaina mythologies.
8. The rite of worshipping holy or noble persons, guests, and images of gods and goddesses.

for her, after informing the captain of the guard. Inside the temple she found her husband who was caught with the woman. She dressed the woman up to pass for herself and told her to get out. The woman went out into the night in her disguise, and Śaktimatī herself stayed in the sanctum with her husband. When in the morning the king's magistrates came to examine them, they all saw that the merchant had only his wife with him. The king, on learning the fact, punished the captain of the guard and released the merchant from the temple as from the yawning mouth of death.

"So did Śaktimatī save her husband that time with her wits," concluded Devasmitā, and the virtuous wife added in confidence to her mother-in-law, "I shall go and save my husband with a trick, as she did."

Then Devasmitā and her maids disguised themselves as merchants,[9] boarded a ship on the pretext of business, and departed for Cathay where her husband was staying. And on her arrival she saw her husband Guhasena—reassurance incarnate!—in the midst of traders. Guhasena saw her too, from a distance, and drank deep of the male image of his beloved wife. He wondered what such a delicate person could have to do with the merchant's profession.

Devasmitā went to the local king and announced: "I have a message. Assemble all your people." Curious, the king summoned all citizens and asked Devasmitā, who still wore her merchant's disguise, "What is your message?"

"Among these people here," said Devasmitā, "are four runaway slaves of mine. May it please Your Majesty to surrender them."

"All the people of this town are assembled here," replied the king. "Look them over, and when you recognize your slaves, take them back."

Thereupon she arrested on their own threshold the four merchant's sons, whom she had manhandled before. They still wore her mark on their foreheads.

"But these are the sons of a caravan trader," protested the merchants who were present. "How can they be your slaves?"

"If you do not believe me," she retorted, "have a look at their foreheads. I have branded them with a dog's paw."

"So we shall," they said. They unwound the turbans of the four men, and they all saw the dog's paw on their foreheads. The merchants' guild was ashamed, and the king surprised.

"What is behind this?" the king asked, questioning Devasmitā in person, and she told the story, and they all burst out laughing.

"By rights they are your slaves, my lady," said the king, whereupon the other merchants paid the king a fine and the virtuous woman a large ransom to free the four from bondage. Honored by all upright people, Devasmitā, with the ransom she had received and the husband she had rejoined, returned to their city Tāmraliptī and never again was she separated from the husband she loved.

---

9. The motif of a woman disguising herself as a man, especially to perform a daring feat, is common in folk literature. Devasmitā bears a striking resemblance to more than one of Shakespeare's heroines.

VI

Medieval Chinese Literature

The "Middle" in the European "Middle Ages" signifies the time between the Roman Empire and the Renaissance, a transitional period that has often been seen as a time of relative intellectual and cultural stagnation. In the case of China the situation is quite the reverse. If we use Western period terms, the *middle* of a Chinese "Middle Age" would mean "central." It is a period when Chinese thought and literature reached what many regard as their highest forms. During the medieval Period of Disunion (third through sixth centuries), a notoriously tumultuous age of political division, Buddhism, which had spread from India to China, took deep root in Chinese society, stimulating renewed interest in Daoist philosophy and the rise of religious Daoism. During the following two great medieval Chinese dynasties, the Tang and the Song (seventh through thirteenth centuries), classical Chinese poetry and prose reached unprecedented heights to which later ages would look back with awe and a sense that the achievements of its greatest writers could never be matched.

A Southern Song Dynasty hand scroll, "Streams and Mountains Under Fresh Snow," attributed to Liu Songnian, twelfth century.

CHINA'S PERIOD OF DISUNION (220-589)

In the second century the Han Empire (206 B.C.E.–220 C.E.) was crumbling. Natural disasters, bad labor conditions, and political intrigues in the central government all helped weaken it. In 184 C.E. the leader of a Daoist religious cult called "Way of Great Peace" staged a major insurrection, gathering hundreds of thousands of followers who attacked local government offices throughout the country. Although the rebellion was suppressed by local armies initially encouraged by the Han government, it ultimately fostered the rise of warlords, often former Han generals, and eventually led to the division of China into three kingdoms: Shu in the west, Wu in the south, and Wei in the northern heartland under the Cao family. The battles of the "Three Kingdoms Period" (220–280) caught the Chinese imagination, and their heroes have lived on in poetry, prose romances, and, recently, epic film series. The empire was briefly reunified by the short-lived Western Jin Dynasty, but in 316 non-Chinese invaders raided the north and the great aristocratic clans fled to the area around Nanjing, where a new government was set up by a prince of the royal house. For the first time in Chinese history non-Chinese rulers took control of China's traditional northern heartland—around the old capitals of Chang'an and Luoyang—forcing the Chinese court aristocracy to flee to the southeastern hinterland. The émigrés from the north, which had been the center of Chinese civilization for more than fifteen hundred years, found themselves suddenly in the rustic southeastern provinces, while their ancestral graves and estates were taken over by northern "barbarians." In exile of sorts, the Chinese aristocracy developed a strong cultural pride and sense of "Chineseness." Cultural legitimacy came to be defined not by the occupation of a place (the North China plain) but by the possession of a portable tradition. Although the northern ruling houses were "barbarian" in the eyes of the former Chinese aristocracy, they were no wild nomads. Their subjects were a largely Chinese population and some, like the Northern Wei Dynasty (386–534) of the Xianbei people, very astutely mixed tribal traditions with Chinese customs. China remained divided partly under foreign rule for centuries: China's north was split among various non-Chinese states and dynasties, while the south was ruled by a succession of short-lived Chinese dynasties.

NEW RELIGIONS OF SALVATION

The non-Chinese rulers of the north also understood that they needed a political tool to legitimate their governance over an ethnically mixed populace and to create harmony among peoples of various social and ethnic backgrounds—a tool that, ideally, was foreign like them: Buddhism. Buddhism originated in India around 500 B.C.E. when a prince of the Shakya clan in a small state in what today is south Nepal turned away in disgust from his privileged palace life, subjected himself to ascetic hardships, and eventually gained enlightenment. For the rest of his life he wandered and spread his teachings. In his first sermon he preached the "Four Noble Truths," central to all of the numerous schools of Buddhism that developed over time. He claimed that (1) pain, suffering, and anxiety are inevitable parts of human life; (2) they are caused by human desires and attachments; (3) it is possible for humans to overcome these attachments; and (4) humans can triumph over them by following the simple trajectory of the

"Eightfold Path," a regime of psychological and physical self-control that enables individuals to leave the cycle of constant rebirths and reach "buddhahood," the passing into nirvana (nothingness), like the historical Buddha himself.

The extraordinary success of Buddhism in China and, spreading from there, throughout East Asia is one of the great surprises of Asian history. China became Buddhist even though there were no forced conversions imposed by missionaries and traditional Chinese Confucian values and Buddhist practices were often at odds. Becoming a Buddhist monk meant betraying on the personal and political levels the duties of Confucian filial piety: you gave up the chances to continue the family line, and by shaving your head you mutilated the body that you had received from your parents and that you needed to return to your ancestors unharmed when leaving the world; even worse, as a follower of the Buddha you could claim to be no longer subordinate to state power, the paternal authority of the political world.

Buddhism radically altered the face of China. Brought by merchants active in the east–west trade along the so-called Silk Road, Buddhism was a religion for the masses. Like Christianity, which was gaining believers around the same time at the other end of Eurasia, it promised personal salvation and escape from a world of suffering, and its soothing ethics of compassion and mercy included people of all social classes, men and women alike. Chinese cities became home to large temple complexes that hosted religious services and addressed the needs of education and charity; the countryside was suddenly dotted with monasteries and colossal Buddha statues carved in stone (images of deities in human form had not existed in China, and the Chinese found the innovation so strange that

The Giant Wild Goose Pagoda in a Buddhist temple complex in Chang'an (modern-day Xi'an), China, was built during the Tang Dynasty. This is where the Chinese monk Xuanzang, whose adventure-filled trip to India is described in the novel *Journey to the West* (included in Vol. 2), deposited the Buddhist scriptures he had acquired in the homeland of Buddhism.

they called the new religion "the teaching of images"). Buddhism mobilized people as pilgrims set out on travels in search of holy places of Buddhism, scriptures, devotional objects, and wise teachers in China and even India.· The new faith was welcomed by the people and patronized by rulers. Monasteries were not taxed, and monks and nuns were not required to perform labor service or military duty.

While Buddhism clashed with Confucian values, it resonated with Daoism in its promise of personal salvation from a corrupt world. Daoism was indigenous to China and took various forms before the arrival of Buddhism. Its intellectual foundations rested on two early Chinese

"Master Texts," **Laozi** and **Zhuangzi**. But Daoism also included a variety of practices, such as methods to promote longevity, certain breathing and sexual techniques, gymnastics, herbal medicine, and alchemy; and the leaders of some popular movements mobilized the underprivileged and poor for their own purposes under the banner of Daoist prophecies. The arrival of Buddhism in China transformed Daoism from an amorphous phenomenon into an organized religion and institution. Daoism now acquired a set of canonical texts (recorded from revelations), temples and monasteries with a celibate clergy, and a vast pantheon of Daoist gods, all on the model of the Buddhist canon of scriptures, the Buddhist monasteries, and the large pantheon of bodhisattvas (Buddhas who returned to the human world in order to help others attain buddhahood). Buddhism and Daoism were in fierce competition over patronage and audiences in part because their teachings were so similar. The closeness of Buddhist and Daoist ideas and teachings is evident from the frequency with which the earliest Chinese translations of Buddhist sutras—sermons of the Buddha recorded in Sanskrit and other Indian languages—used Daoist terminology to express new Buddhist concepts. This appropriation of Buddhism as a form of Daoism took a sudden turn in the fourth century when the brilliant Buddhist scholar and monk Kumārajīva (350–413), born of an Indian father and a Central Asian mother, was abducted by a Chinese ruler and set to work on translating Buddhist texts into Chinese; his abduction marked the beginning of large state-sponsored workshops that translated countless scriptures into Chinese. Kumārajīva rejected the earlier Daoist terminology, creating new words for the foreign Buddhist concepts out of transcriptions of the Sanskrit words into Chinese. Buddhism had become an independent cultural force in China.

The arrival of Buddhism and the emergence of the Daoist church led to a veneration of the ideal of the "recluse." Some recluses were true hermits, living far away from civilization; others cultivated a form of libertine resistance to social norms; still others, such as the poet-recluse **Tao Qian**, decided to live on his family farm and not serve in government.

THE NEW COSMOPOLITAN EMPIRES OF THE SUI AND TANG (589–907)

In the long run it was a northern dynasty, the Sui (589–618), that reunified China; these rulers were quickly supplanted by another northern dynasty, the Tang (618–907). The two dynasties forged a new culture that combined northern and southern traditions. The Sui emperors razed the old southern capital near Nanjing and forced the southern aristocracy to relocate to the old northern capital of Chang'an. Between the Yangzi and the Yellow River they built a canal that became a crucial means to transport goods and people between the north and south, reconnecting territory that had been divided for more than three centuries. But its attempt to recover the possessions of the Han Empire, in particular repeated unsuccessful campaigns against Korea, brought down the dynasty. The Sui Dynasty was overthrown by a provincial governor who founded his own dynasty, the Tang.

The long Tang Dynasty was an age of cultural confidence and, initially, of expansion, as Tang armies pushed outward at every frontier. Particularly important was the expansion to the northwest and control of the trade routes to the west. Chang'an, an old capital now clothed in new splendor, mirrored the cosmopolitan empire it controlled. It was laid out on a grid pattern, with a mighty walled palace city at its north and two bustling markets to the south. The city teemed with foreigners, who came to the Chinese capital by the Central Asian land routes or the South Asian maritime trade routes as merchants, diplomatic envoys, pilgrims, monks, or adventurers. Nestorian Christians, Zoroastrians, Jews, and Arab merchants mingled with Japanese monks and Persian doctors. The people of Chang'an quickly adopted new hairstyles, new games such as polo, and new musical instruments, and were enthralled by exotic melodies and dances from China's Central Asian "west."

The Tang was an age of innovation. Tea became a major commercial crop, and its consumption spread from China to East Asia via monks who used it to stay awake during long hours of meditation and sutra recitation. New Buddhist schools appeared, such as Chan (better known in its Japanese form, "Zen"), an iconoclastic form of Buddhism that espoused mind-to-mind transmission of truth, claiming that the study of scriptures was of no use.

The most influential invention during the Tang Dynasty was printing. A printed copy of the Buddhist Diamond Sutra, dated 868, is considered the world's oldest printed book. Sealed in a cave in remote Dunhuang, a Silk Road oasis in northwest China some 1100 miles from Chang'an, it was discovered by archaeologists in the early twentieth century.

The Tang period is most famous for its poetry. The civil service examination used by the Tang in recruiting its elites for government service came to require the composition of poetry, and it also became an integral part of social life—a medium of social exchange. In few other places in the world has lyric poetry ever enjoyed such centrality, and a number of major poets emerged whose works have made them renowned in China to this day. A great poem might deal with large philosophical issues, but it was just as likely to describe a meeting with an old friend. Poetry was seen as a way to record both an individual's personality and a country's historic moments. The writings of **Wang Wei, Li Bo,** and **Du Fu** came to exemplify poetic perfection, in different styles. The Tang was also the first period to witness the flowering of prose tales, such as **Yuan Zhen's "The Story**

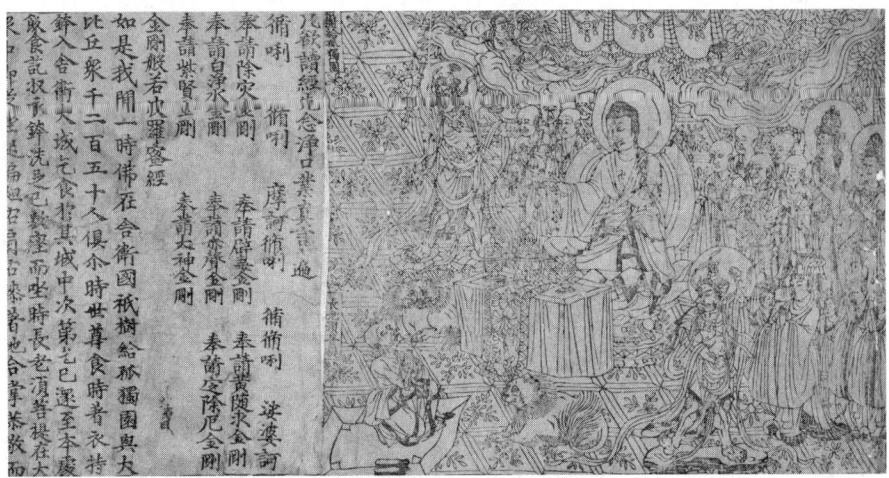

A copy of the Diamond Sūtra, printed in 868 C.E. It is considered the world's oldest printed book.

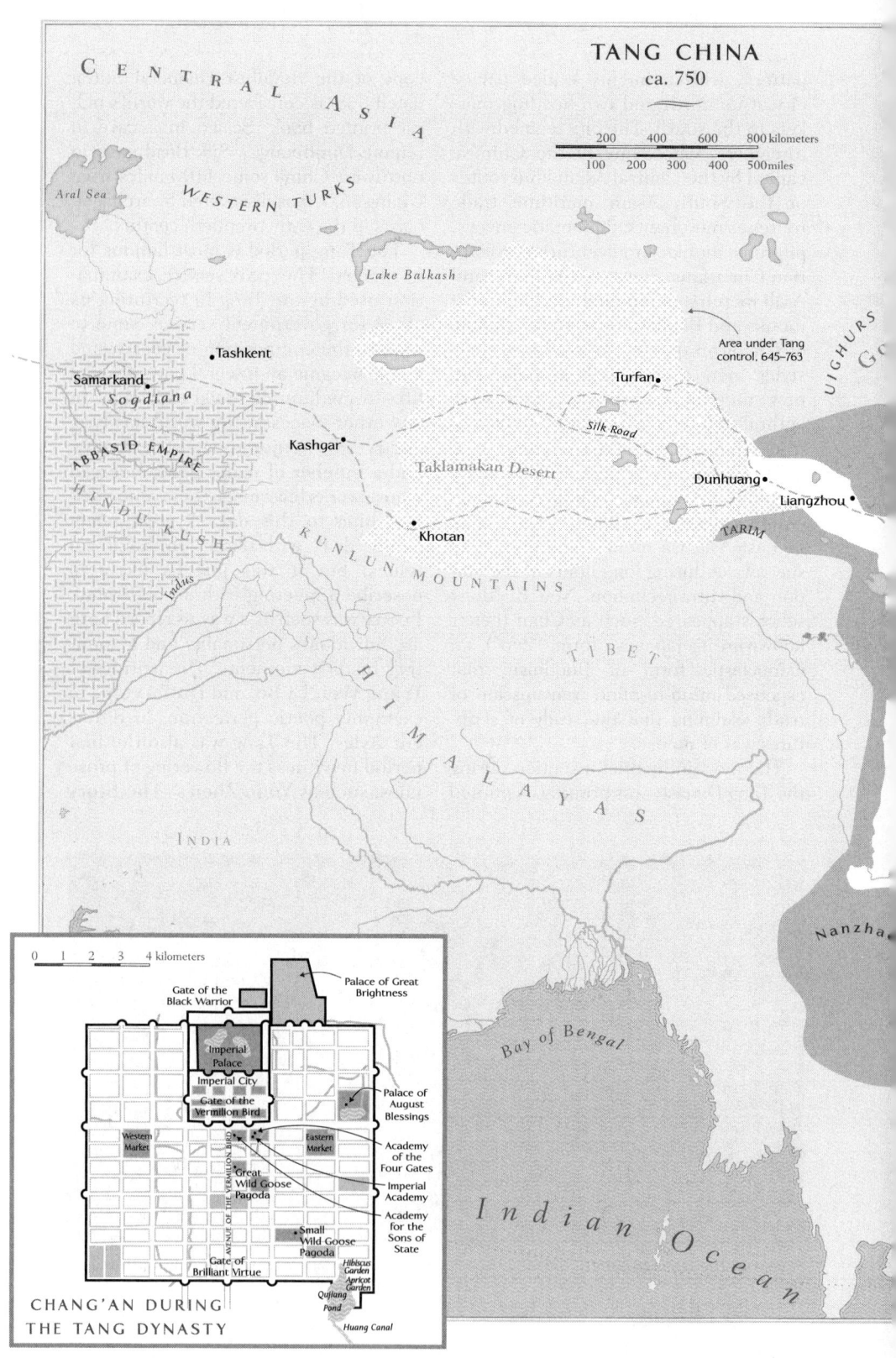

TANG CHINA
ca. 750

200   400   600   800 kilometers

100   200   300   400   500 miles

CENTRAL ASIA

WESTERN TURKS

Aral Sea

Lake Balkash

UIGHURS

Go

Area under Tang
control, 645–763

•Tashkent

Turfan•

Samarkand•

Sogdiana

Silk Road

Kashgar•

Taklamakan Desert

Dunhuang•

Liangzhou•

ABBASID EMPIRE

Khotan•

HINDU KUSH

Indus

KUNLUN MOUNTAINS

TARIM

HIMALAYAS

TIBET

INDIA

Nanzha

Bay of Bengal

Indian Ocean

CHANG'AN DURING THE TANG DYNASTY

0 1 2 3 4 kilometers

Palace of Great
Brightness

Gate of the
Black Warrior

Imperial
Palace

Imperial City

Gate of the
Vermilion Bird

Palace of
August
Blessings

Western
Market

Eastern
Market

Academy
of the
Four Gates

Great
Wild Goose
Pagoda

Imperial
Academy

AVENUE OF THE VERMILION BIRD

Academy
for the
Sons of
State

Small
Wild Goose
Pagoda

Gate of
Brilliant Virtue

Hibiscus
Garden
Apricot
Garden

Qujiang
Pond

Huang Canal

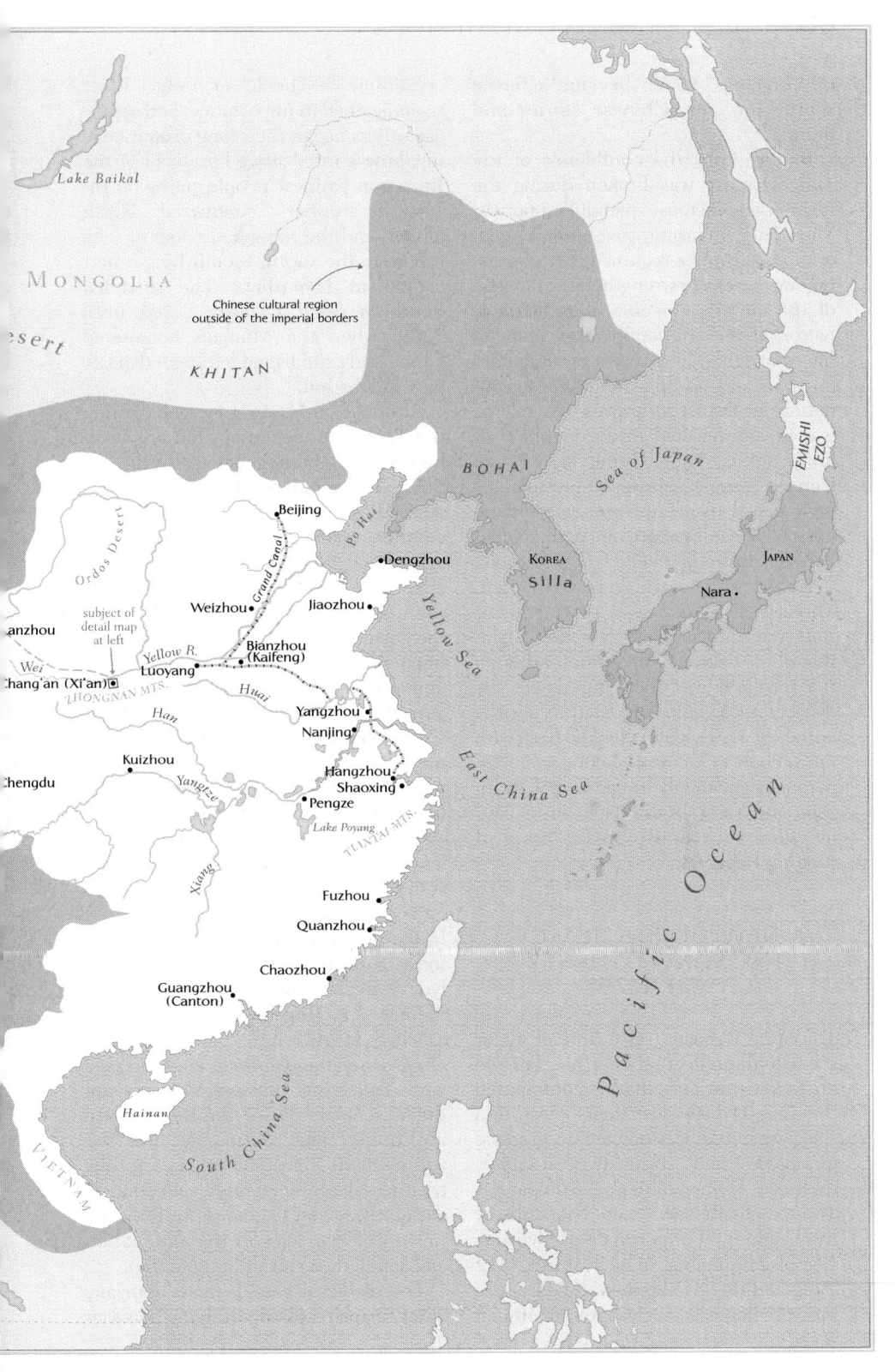

Lake Baikal

MONGOLIA

Desert

KHITAN

Chinese cultural region
outside of the imperial borders

BOHAI

Sea of Japan

EMISHI
EZO

•Beijing

Po Hai

•Dengzhou

KOREA
Silla

JAPAN

Nara •

Weizhou

Grand Canal

Jiaozhou•

Yellow Sea

Ordos Desert

subject of
detail map
at left

anzhou

Yellow R.

Bianzhou
(Kaifeng)

Wei

hang'an (Xi'an)

Luoyang

ZHONGNAN MTS.

Huai

Han

Yangzhou•

Nanjing•

East China Sea

Pacific Ocean

Kuizhou

hengdu

Yangtze

Hangzhou•

Shaoxing•

•Pengze

Lake Poyang

TIANTAI MTS.

Xiang

Fuzhou•

Quanzhou•

Chaozhou•

Guangzhou
(Canton)

Hainan

South China Sea

VIETNAM

of Yingying," which became a fertile source for later Chinese stories and drama.

In the 750s, the confidence of the Tang Dynasty was broken during the reign of one its most splendid emperors, Xuanzong. Xuanzong gave military governors in frontier regions great powers, hoping thereby to strengthen the defense of the empire. An able administrator, patron of the arts, and even scholar in his own right—he wrote a commentary on *Laozi* and set up a school for examinations in Daoist scriptures—Xuanzong was greatly devoted to a concubine of lower status, Yang Guifei (or "Prized Consort Yang"), whose family increasingly began to occupy strategic official positions. An Lushan, an associate of Yang's kinsmen, rebelled in 755, took Chang'an, and put the emperor to flight. Threatened by his own armies, Xuanzong was forced to witness the execution of his beloved concubine. Although the rebellion was soon put down, the dynasty never quite regained its former authority. Later writers looked back with melancholy to Xuanzong's long and prosperous reign, and the tragic love of Xuanzong and Yang Guifei lived on in later literature such as **Bo Juyi's "Song of Lasting Regret."**

A NEW DOMESTIC AGE: THE SONG DYNASTY (960–1279)

The Song Dynasty was a time of major social and intellectual changes. The old aristocratic families that had dominated the Tang Dynasty lost their power, and the government was opened up to social groups that had previously been largely excluded from political participation. Their inclusion was made possible by the heightened importance of civil service examinations, which during the Tang had merely supplemented hereditary privilege as a channel to official

appointment. The lower Yangzi River region gained in importance, and southeasterners began their long prominence in Chinese intellectual life. In 1127 the Jin, a non-Chinese people on the northeastern frontier, conquered North China, and the Song court had to seek refuge in the south, establishing a new capital in Hangzhou. The so-called Southern Song Dynasty lasted until 1279, when the Mongols conquered China and established a foreign dynasty on Chinese soil.

Although printing emerged during the Tang, the technology did not revolutionize Chinese society until the Song. The rapid development of commercial printing during the eleventh century enabled literary works and scholarship to reach a far wider audience than ever before. As in Europe, the dissemination of learning through the printed book had a significant impact on all aspects of culture. A reexamination of the Confucian classics gave rise to a movement known as Neo-Confucianism, which came to dominate intellectual life.

Meanwhile, Song Dynasty classical literature continued the forms of the Tang period, but with a difference—a less intense, more reflective and introverted tone that for later ages seemed to embody the personality of the dynasty. In the urban centers of the south a new form of poetry developed; these "song lyrics" treated lighter, more domestic themes. **Li Qingzhao**, a female poet, excelled in this new mode; she was also a scholar and connoisseur obsessed with collecting ancient objects—not unlike scholars during the Renaissance in Europe. The riveting account she wrote about how she unsuccessfully tried to salvage her family collection of antiquities when fleeing south from the Jin in 1127 testifies to the antiquarian and scholarly tastes of Song literati.

The medieval period, more than any other, shaped traditional China. Between the third and the thirteenth centuries China became a thoroughly Buddhist empire, with a powerful Daoist church and a political system predicated on the recruitment of bureaucrats through the Confucian civil service examinations. Tang poetry defined the standards for the later Chinese literary tradition. Chinese institutions, law codes, religions, literature, art, architecture, and material culture spread throughout East Asia, as younger emerging cultures on the Korean Peninsula and the Japanese archipelago were eager to adapt the newest technologies, ideologies, and art forms of Chinese civilization to their own domestic purposes. China's medieval period was thus the defining moment when East Asia emerged as a cultural sphere under Chinese influence.

TAO QIAN

365–427

"Whenever I have been involved in official life I was mortgaging myself to my mouth and belly." Thus Tao Qian (also known as Tao Yuanming) explains his decision to leave public office and return to his family farm. No Chinese poet before or after him captures with more immediate emotion the simple pleasures of country life, the value of being true to one's inner nature, and the necessity to make and unmake choices in life. He is one of the most beloved figures in the Chinese poetic tradition. Generations of readers have been enticed by Tao Qian's candor and his pursuit of personal integrity. Yet his poetry gains its depth and appeal from its roots in the tensions of his humble circumstances, reflecting the fear of failure and mortality.

Although Tao Qian talks much about himself in his poems and became the stuff of legend in later ages, very little is known about his life. His great-grandfather was a noted official and general, and initially Tao Qian followed in his footsteps, serving for thirteen years in several undistinguished official posts. But in 405, when he was magistrate of Pengze, a county seat some thirty miles from his hometown, he suddenly resigned. He had occupied the position for only about eighty days. Instead of living off the grain paid to government officials as their salary, he returned to his family farm to produce his own; self-sufficiency became the principle that would allow him to pursue his true inclinations and live out the last two decades of his life in peace and tranquillity.

Tao Qian lived during the so-called Period of Disunion, the four hundred years between two great empires, the Han (206 B.C.E.–220 C.E.) and the Tang (618–907). This was a time of unprecedented uncertainty, when a series of dynasties followed each other in quick succession. In 316, half a century before Tao Qian was born, non-Chinese tribes invaded northern China. In the ensuing turmoil many of the great aristocratic families and their retainers emigrated to the region south of the Yangzi River. For the first time in Chinese history, "China" no longer meant the territory of the traditional northern heartland; it was now a shared cultural heritage held dear and claimed by the émigrés in the new south. For Tao Qian's generation, the climate, food, and landscape of the south must still have been novelties, enticing people to seek the simple life in the countryside and capture it in poetry.

Also, during the Period of Disunion Buddhism spread to all classes of Chinese society, and the Daoist church (an institution whose founders based their claims to religious leadership on earlier Daoist philosophical texts) gained many supporters. Both Buddhism and Daoism sanctioned the retreat from public life; Confucianism, in contrast, valued active service in the state bureaucracy above all else and accepted withdrawal only in times of incompetent government. Even though Tao Qian described his decision to leave public life as a personal choice, he lived in an age in which political turmoil and new religions encouraged such a choice.

Tao Qian's poetry celebrates the pleasures of wine, friendship, and gardening; the joys of composing poetry, reading books, and playing the zither; and the desire for liberation from social strictures to pursue one's own inclinations. Poverty, hunger, and destitution do not call into doubt but rather throw into relief Tao Qian's decision to renounce public office. One grand theme of his poetry is the return to one's natural self, but it is unclear quite how far Tao Qian is willing to push this idea. To be sure, he renounces the pursuit of fame and official recognition and enjoys instead his wine and his garden. But he is also proud of his family line and seems deeply disappointed with his sons' lack of accomplishment. By the same token, writing and reading poetry was an exclusive domain of the educated elite, but the peasants in Tao Qian's poetry, his new neighbors, are apparently literate and he portrays them as sharing his literary interests.

Tao Qian despised worldly ambition, but no poet before him wrote so much about himself. "Substance, Shadow, and Spirit" dramatizes some of his inner tensions by staging a mock debate between three characters, each of whom proposes a different solution to how best to live life: to enjoy wine and forget mortality, as suggested by Substance; to strive to do good and precisely not to forget oneself, as endorsed by Shadow; or, as suggested by the conciliatory Spirit, to forget about both bodily pleasures and moral achievements and simply give oneself over "to the waves of the Great Change." "Biography of Master Five Willows" has been read as a self-portrait of Tao Qian, although he makes no direct reference to himself. In "Elegy" he seems to be coming back from the grave to imagine the scene of his own death and burial, an unprecedented use of a genre reserved for addressing the dead. Even "Peach Blossom Spring" is an autobiography of sorts, a tale about escape from oppressive rule (here from the First Emperor of the Qin Dynasty [221–206 B.C.E.], known in history for his extraordinary cruelty) to a land of self-sufficient happiness. It is also a parable of the impossibility of simply willing things to happen: the fisherman, an ambivalent figure who lives both in tune with nature and in contact with society, stumbles by chance upon the hidden cave while idly exploring an impressive grove of peach trees. After returning, the fisherman reports to the magistrate his spectacular discovery of a cave inhabited by a utopian society that managed to escape the vicissitudes of political turmoil. But to the official who sets out under orders to find the cave, the blissful cave of Peach Blossom Spring is forever beyond reach.

At first Tao Qian was admired as a recluse and man of principle, not as a poet. His straightforward style and simple diction contrast with the ornate imagery and sophisticated allusions in the poetry of his contemporaries. But a renewed interest in simplicity of expression during the Tang Dynasty propelled him to literary fame and has secured him a prominent position in the canon of Chinese poetry ever since. A sixth-century editor of Tao Qian's poetry praises him thus: "An extraordinary person rising above the crowd, Tao Qian followed his natural impulses and was content with his choices." An icon of self-fulfillment, whose poetry convinced people that reaching a state of contentment of sorts is possible, Tao Qian has timeless appeal.

The Peach Blossom Spring[1]

During the Taiyuan period of the Jin dynasty[2] a fisherman of Wuling once rowed upstream, unmindful of the distance he had gone, when he suddenly came to a grove of peach trees in bloom. For several hundred paces on both banks of the stream there was no other kind of tree. The wild flowers growing under them were fresh and lovely, and fallen petals covered the ground—it made a great impression on the fisherman. He went on for a way with the idea of finding out how far the grove extended. It came to an end at the foot of a mountain whence issued the spring that supplied the stream. There was a small opening in the mountain and it seemed as though light was coming through it. The fisherman left his boat and entered the cave, which at first was extremely narrow, barely admitting his body; after a few dozen steps it suddenly opened out onto a broad and level plain where well-built houses were surrounded by rich fields and pretty ponds. Mulberry, bamboo and other trees and plants grew there, and criss-cross paths skirted the fields. The sounds of cocks crowing and dogs barking could be heard from one courtyard to the next. Men and women were coming and going about their work in the fields. The clothes they wore were like those of ordinary people. Old men and boys were carefree and happy.

When they caught sight of the fisherman, they asked in surprise how he had got there. The fisherman told the whole story, and was invited to go to their house, where he was served wine while they killed a chicken for a feast. When the other villagers heard about the fisherman's arrival they all came to pay him a visit. They told him that their ancestors had fled the disorders of Qin times[3] and, having taken refuge here with wives and children and neighbors, had never ventured out again; consequently they had lost all contact with the outside world. They asked what the present ruling dynasty was, for they had never heard of the Han, let alone the Wei and the Jin.[4] They sighed unhappily as the fisherman enumerated the dynasties one by one and recounted the vicissitudes of each. The visitors all asked him to come to their houses in turn, and at every house he had wine and food. He stayed several days. As he was about to go away, the people said, "There's no need to mention our existence to outsiders."

After the fisherman had gone out and recovered his boat, he carefully marked the route. On reaching the city, he reported what he had found to the magistrate, who at once sent a man to follow him back to the place. They proceeded according to the marks he had made, but went astray and were unable to find the cave again.

A high-minded gentleman of Nanyang named Lui Ziji heard the story and happily made preparations to go there, but before he could leave he fell sick and died. Since then there has been no one interested in trying to find such a place.

---

1. All selections translated by James Robert Hightower except "Biography of Master Five Willows."
2. From 376 to 396 C.E.
3. During the first short-lived Chinese imperial dynasty (221–206 B.C.E.); the First Emperor was known for his megalomania and cruelty.
4. The dynasties that followed the Qin. The inhabitants did not know about anything that happened in the outside world between the third century B.C.E. up to the fourth century C.E.

The Ying clan[5] disrupted Heaven's ordinance
And good men withdrew from such a world.
Huang and Qi[6] went off to Shang Mountain
And these people too fled into hiding.
Little by little their tracks were obliterated   5
The paths they followed overgrown at last.
By agreement they set about farming the land
When the sun went down each rested from his toil.
Bamboo and mulberry provided shade enough.
They planted beans and millet, each in season.   10
From spring silkworms came the long silk thread
On the fall harvest no king's tax was paid.
No sign of traffic on overgrown roads,
Cockcrow and dogsbark within each other's earshot.
Their ritual vessels were of old design,   15
And no new fashions in the clothes they wore.
Children wandered about singing songs,
Graybeards went paying one another calls.
When grass grew thick they saw the time was mild,
As trees went bare they knew the wind was sharp.   20
Although they had no calendar to tell,
The four seasons still filled out a year.
Joyous in their ample happiness
They had no need of clever contrivance.
Five hundred years this rare deed stayed hid,   25
Then one fine day the fay retreat was found.
The pure and the shallow belong to separate worlds:
In a little while they were hidden again.
Let me ask you who are convention-bound,
Can you fathom those outside the dirt and noise?   30
I want to tread upon the thin thin air
And rise up high to find my own kind.

The Return

I was poor, and what I got from farming was not enough to support my family.
The house was full of children, the rice-jar was empty, and I could not see any
way to supply the necessities of life. Friends and relatives kept urging me to
become a magistrate, and I had at last come to think I should do it, but there
was no way for me to get such a position. At the time I happened to have business abroad and made a good impression on the grandees as a conciliatory and
humane sort of person. Because of my poverty an uncle offered me a job in a
small town, but the region was still unquiet and I trembled at the thought of
going away from home. However, Pengze was only thirty miles from my native

---

5. That is, the clan of the First Emperor of Qin.
6. Virtuous men who went into reclusion in

the mountains to protest the tyranny of the
Qin emperor.

place, and the yield of the fields assigned the magistrate was sufficient to keep me in wine, so I applied for the office. Before many days had passed, I longed to give it up and go back home. Why, you may ask. Because my instinct is all for freedom, and will not brook discipline or restraint. Hunger and cold may be sharp, but this going against myself really sickens me. Whenever I have been involved in official life I was mortgaging myself to my mouth and belly, and the realization of this greatly upset me. I was deeply ashamed that I had so compromised my principles, but I was still going to wait out the year, after which I might pack up my clothes and slip away at night. Then my sister who had married into the Cheng family died in Wuchang, and my only desire was to go there as quickly as possible. I gave up my office and left of my own accord. From mid-autumn to winter I was altogether some eighty days in office, when events made it possible for me to do what I wished. I have entitled my piece 'The Return'; my preface is dated the eleventh moon of the year *yisi*.[1]

To get out of this and go back home!
My fields and garden will be overgrown with weeds—I must go back.
It was my own doing that made my mind my body's slave
Why should I go on in melancholy and lonely grief?
I realize that there's no remedying the past   5
But I know that there's hope in the future.
After all I have not gone far on the wrong road
And I am aware that what I do today is right, yesterday wrong.
My boat rocks in the gentle breeze
Flap, flap, the wind blows my gown;   10
I ask a passerby about the road ahead,
Grudging the dimness of the light at dawn.
Then I catch sight of my cottage—
    Filled with joy I run.
The servant boy comes to welcome me   15
    My little son waits at the door.
The three paths are almost obliterated
    But pines and chrysanthemums are still here.
Leading the children by the hand I enter my house
    Where there is a bottle filled with wine.   20
I draw the bottle to me and pour myself a cup;
Seeing the trees in the courtyard brings joy to my face.
I lean on the south window and let my pride expand,
I consider how easy it is to be content with a little space.
Every day I stroll in the garden for pleasure,   25
There is a gate there, but it is always shut.
Cane in hand I walk and rest
Occasionally raising my head to gaze into the distance.
The clouds aimlessly rise from the peaks,
The birds, weary of flying, know it is time to come home.   30
As the sun's rays grow dim and disappear from view
I walk around a lonely pine tree, stroking it.

1. A year in the Chinese sixty-year cycle; eleventh month in this lunar calendar corresponds approximately to December.

Back home again!
May my friendships be broken off and my wanderings come to an end.
The world and I shall have nothing more to do with one another.   35
If I were again to go abroad, what should I seek?
Here I enjoy honest conversation with my family
And take pleasure in books and zither to dispel my worries.
The farmers tell me that now spring is here
There will be work to do in the west fields.   40
Sometimes I call for a covered cart
Sometimes I row a lonely boat
Following a deep gully through the still water
Or crossing the hill on a rugged path.
The trees put forth luxuriant foliage,   45
The spring begins to flow in a trickle.
I admire the seasonableness of nature
And am moved to think that my life will come to its close.
    It is all over—
So little time are we granted human form in the world!   50
Let us then follow the inclinations of the heart:
Where would we go that we are so agitated?
I have no desire for riches
And no expectation of Heaven.
Rather on some fine morning to walk alone   55
Now planting my staff to take up a hoe,
Or climbing the east hill and whistling long
Or composing verses beside the clear stream:
So I manage to accept my lot until the ultimate homecoming.
Rejoicing in Heaven's command, what is there to doubt?   60

Biography of Master Five Willows[1]

We don't know what age the master lived in, and we aren't certain about his real name. Beside his cottage were five willow trees, so he took his name from them. He lived in perfect peace, a man of few words, with no desire for glory or gain. He liked to read but didn't try too hard to understand. Yet whenever there was something that caught his fancy, he would be so happy he would forget to eat. He had a wine-loving nature, but his household was so poor he couldn't always obtain wine. His friends, knowing how he was, would invite him to drink. And whenever he drank, he finished what he had right away, hoping to get very drunk. When drunk, he would withdraw, not really caring whether he went or stayed. His dwelling was a shambles, providing no protection against wind and sun. His coarse clothes were full of holes and patches; his plate and pitcher always empty; he was at peace. He forgot all about gain and loss and in this way lived out his life.

Qianlou's[2] wife once said, "Feel no anxiety about loss or low station; don't be too eager for wealth and honor." When we reflect on her words, we suspect that

1. Translated by Stephen Owen. "Master Five Willows" is Tao Qian's playful name for himself.

2. A figure of antiquity who preferred a life of poverty to serving in office.

Five Willows may have been such a man—swigging wine and writing poems to satisfy his inclinations. Was he a person of the age of Lord No-Cares? Was he a person of the age of Getian?[3]

Substance, Shadow, and Spirit

Noble or base, wise or stupid, none but cling tenaciously to life. This is a great delusion. I have put in the strongest terms the complaints of Substance and Shadow and then, to resolve the matter, have made Spirit the spokesman for naturalness. Those who share my tastes will all get what I am driving at.

I

Substance to Shadow

Earth and heaven endure forever,
Streams and mountains never change.
Plants observe a constant rhythm,
Withered by frost, by dew restored.
But man, most sentient being of all,   5
In this is not their equal.
He is present here in the world today,
Then leaves abruptly, to return no more.
No one marks there's one man less—
Not even friends and family think of him;   10
The things that he once used are all that's left
To catch their eye and move them to grief.
I have no way to transcend change,
That it must be, I no longer doubt.
I hope you will take my advice: 15
When wine is offered, don't refuse.

II

Shadow to Substance

No use discussing immortality
When just to keep alive is hard enough.
Of course I want to roam in paradise,
But it's a long way there and the road is lost.
In all the time since I met up with you   5
We never differed in our grief and joy.
In shade we may have parted for a time,
But sunshine always brings us close again.
Still this union cannot last forever—
Together we will vanish into darkness.   10

3. Two legendary rulers of a golden age, before there were troubles in the world.

The body goes; that fame should also end
Is a thought that makes me burn inside.
Do good, and your love will outlive you;
Surely this is worth your every effort.
While it is true, wine may dissolve care   15
That is not so good a way as this.

III

Spirit's Solution

The Great Potter[1] cannot intervene—
All creation thrives of itself.
That Man ranks with Earth and Heaven
Is it not because of me?
Though we belong to different orders,   5
Being alive, I am joined to you.
Bound together for good or ill
I cannot refuse to tell you what I know:
The Three August Ones[2] were great saints
But where are they living today?   10
Though Pengzu[3] lasted a long time
He still had to go before he was ready.
Die old or die young, the death is the same,
Wise or stupid, there is no difference.
Drunk every day you may forget,   15
But won't it shorten your life span?
Doing good is always a joyous thing
But no one has to praise you for it.
Too much thinking harms my life;
Just surrender to the cycle of things,   20
Give yourself to the waves of the Great Change
Neither happy nor yet afraid.
And when it is time to go, then simply go
Without any unnecessary fuss.

Returning to the Farm to Dwell

I

From early days I have been at odds with the world;
My instinctive love is hills and mountains.
By mischance I fell into the dusty net
And was thirteen years away from home.

1. The personified force of creation and change in the cosmos.
2. Sage kings of antiquity, believed to have lived to a fabulous old age.
3. A legendary figure who supposedly lived eight hundred years.

The migrant bird longs for its native grove.   5
The fish in the pond recalls the former depths.
Now I have cleared some land to the south of town,
Simplicity intact, I have returned to farm.
The land I own amounts to a couple of acres
The thatched-roof house has four or five rooms.   10
Elms and willows shade the eaves in back,
Peach and plum stretch out before the hall.
Distant villages are lost in haze,
Above the houses smoke hangs in the air.
A dog is barking somewhere in a hidden lane,   15
A cock crows from the top of a mulberry tree.
My home remains unsoiled by worldly dust
Within bare rooms I have my peace of mind.
For long I was a prisoner in a cage
And now I have my freedom back again.   20

II

Here in the country human contacts are few
On this narrow lane carriages seldom come.
In broad daylight I keep my rustic gate closed,
From the bare rooms all dusty thoughts are banned.
From time to time through the tall grass   5
Like me, village farmers come and go;
When we meet we talk of nothing else
Than how the hemp and mulberry are growing.
Hemp and mulberry grow longer every day
Every day the fields I have plowed are wider;   10
My constant worry is that frost may come
And my crops will wither with the weeds.

Begging for Food

Hunger came and drove me out
To go I had no notion where.
I walked until I reached this town,
Knocked at a door and fumbled for words
The owner guessed what I was after   5
And gave it, but not just the gift alone.
We talked together all day long,
And drained our cups as the bottle passed.
Happy in our new acquaintance
We sang old songs and wrote new poems.   10
You are as kind as the washerwoman,
But to my shame I lack Han's talent.[1]

---

1. Han Xin, eventually a general of Liu Bang, the founder of the Han Dynasty (206 B.C.E.–220 C.E.), was able to repay the kindness he received from the washerwoman who had given him food when he was a poor youth.

I have no way to show my thanks
And must repay you from the grave.[2]

On Moving House

I

For long I yearned to live in Southtown—
Not that a diviner told me to—
Where many simple-hearted people live
With whom I would rejoice to pass my days.
This I have had in mind for several years   5
And now at last have carried out my plan.
A modest cottage does not need be large
To give us shelter where we sit and sleep.
From time to time my neighbors come
And we discuss affairs of long ago.   10
A good poem excites our admiration
Together we expound the doubtful points.

II

In spring and fall are many perfect days
For climbing high to write new poetry.
As we pass the doors, we hail each other,
And anyone with wine will pour us some.
When the farm work is done, we all go home   5
And then have time to think of one another—
So thinking, we at once throw on a coat
And visit, never tired of talk and jokes.
There is no better way of life than this,
No need to be in a hurry to go away.   10
Since food and clothing have to be provided,
If I do the plowing, it will not cheat me.

In the Sixth Month of 408, Fire

I built my thatched hut in a narrow lane,
Glad to renounce the carriages of the great.
In midsummer, while the wind blew long and sharp,
Of a sudden grove and house caught fire and burned.
In all the place not a roof was left to us   5
And we took shelter in the boat by the gate.

---

2. An allusion to the story of a ghost who repaid a debt of gratitude to Lord Huan of Wei by tripping his enemy.

Space is vast this early autumn evening,
The moon, nearly full, rides high above.
The vegetables begin to grow again
But the frightened birds still have not returned.　　　　10
Tonight I stand a long time lost in thought;
A glance encompasses the Nine Heavens.[1]
Since youth I've held my solitary course
Until all at once forty years have passed.
My outward form follows the way of change　　　　15
But my heart remains untrammelled still.
Firm and true, it keeps its constant nature,
No jadestone is as strong, adamantine.
I think back to the time when East-Gate[2] ruled
When there was grain left out in the fields　　　　20
And people, free of care, drummed full bellies,
Rising mornings and coming home to sleep.
Since I was not born in such a time,
Let me just go on watering my garden.

From Twenty Poems After Drinking Wine

Preface

Living in retirement here I have few pleasures, and now the nights are growing longer; so, as I happen to have some excellent wine, not an evening passes without a drink. All alone with my shadow I empty a bottle until suddenly I find myself drunk. And once I am drunk I write a few verses for my own amusement. In the course of time the pages have multiplied, but there is no particular sequence in what I have written. I have had a friend make a copy, with no more in mind than to provide a diversion.

V

I built my hut beside a traveled road
Yet here no noise of passing carts and horses.
You would like to know how it is done?
With the mind detached, one's place becomes remote.
Picking chrysanthemums by the eastern hedge　　　　5
I catch sight of the distant southern hills:
The mountain air is lovely as the sun sets
And flocks of flying birds return together.
In these things is a fundamental truth
I would like to tell, but lack the words.　　　　10

---

1. That is, the entire sky; heaven was imagined as having nine layers.

2. A legendary ruler in the golden age, a time of such plenty that no one bothered to steal.

IX

I heard a knock this morning at my door
In haste I pulled my gown on wrongside out
And went to ask the caller, Who is there?
It was a well-intentioned farmer, come
With a jug of wine to pay a distant call.   5
Suspecting me to be at odds with the times:
'Dressed in rags beneath a roof of thatch
Is not the way a gentleman should live.
All the world agrees on what to do—
I hope that you will join the muddy game.'   10
'My sincere thanks for your advice, old man.
It's my nature keeps me out of tune.
Though one can learn of course to pull the reins,
To go against oneself is a real mistake.
So let's just have a drink of this together—   15
There's no turning back my carriage now.'[1]

X

Once I made a distant trip
Right to the shore of the Eastern Sea
The road I went was long and far,
The way beset by wind and waves.
Who was it made me take this trip?   5
It seems that I was forced by hunger.
I gave my all to eat my fill
When just a bit was more than enough.
Since this was not a famous plan
I stopped my cart and came back home.   10

Elegy

The year is *dingmao* of the cycle, the season that of the tone *wuyi*,[1] when days are cold and the nights long, when the wind blows mournfully as the wild fowl migrate, and leaves turn yellow and fall. Master Tao is about to depart from this lodging house to return for all time to his own home. Old friends are grieved and mourn for him: this evening they give him a farewell banquet, offering a sacrificial food, pouring libations of clear wine. They look, and his face is dim; listening, they no longer hear the sound of his voice.

Alas, alas, this vast clod, earth, that illimitable high firmament, together produce all things, even me who am a man. But from the time I attained human estate, my lot has been poverty. Rice-bin and wine-gourd have often been empty, and I have faced winters in thin clothes. Still I have gone happily to draw water

---

1. That is, he has decided on the course of his life.

1. Winter. *"Dingmao"*: a cyclical date name (427 C.E.).

from the brook and have sung as I walked under a load of firewood, going about my daily affairs in the obscurity of my cottage. As springs gave way to autumn, I have busied myself in my garden, hoeing, cultivating, planting or tending. I have rejoiced in my books and have been soothed by my zither. Winters I have warmed myself in the sun, summers I have bathed in the brook. There was little enough reward for my labor, but my mind enjoyed a constant leisure. Content with Heaven and accepting my lot, I have lived out the years of my life.

Men fear to waste their lives, concerned that they may fail to succeed. They cling to the days and lament passing time. During their life they are honored by the world, and after their death they still are mourned. But I have gone my own way, which is not their way. I take no glory in their esteem, nor do I feel defamed by their slander. I have lived alone in my poor house, drinking wine and writing poetry.

Aware of my destined end, of which one cannot be ignorant, I find no cause for regret in this present transformation. I have lived out my lifespan, and all my life I have desired quiet retirement. Now that I am dying, an old man, what have I left to wish for?

Hot and cold hasten on, one after the other.[2] The dead have nothing in common with the survivors. Relatives come in the morning, friends arrive in the evening, to bury me in the meadow and give comfort to my soul. Dark is my journey, desolate the grave. It is shameful to be buried extravagantly as was Huan Tui (whose stone coffin was three years a-making), and ridiculous to be parsimonious like Yang Wangsun (who was buried naked), for after death there is nothing. Raise me no mound, plant me no grove; time will pass with the revolving sun and moon. I never cared for praise in my lifetime, and it matters not at all what eulogies are sung after my death. Man's life is hard enough in truth; and death is not to be avoided.

2. That is, the second pass.

TANG POETRY

The poetry of the Tang Dynasty (618–907) is generally considered the high point of China's three-millennia-old history of poetry. Much compelling verse was written after the period, not least because the poetic giants of the Tang inspired later poets to write with self-conscious sophistication and skill. But later poets generally agreed that **Du Fu, Li Bo**, and their contemporaries had set a standard that could not be surpassed. For many centuries the elegant urgency and technical virtuosity with which these poets captured the world, as well as the scope of their poetic visions and themes, formed the basis for later poetic training and inspiration. The primacy of Tang poetry in the Chinese poetic canon continued until the early twentieth century, when Chinese intellectuals launched a revolutionary movement to replace the classical written idiom with vernacular spoken language. Today traditional poetry is popular once again, and the accomplishments of the Tang poets remain the high-water mark of what poetry can do.

POETRY AND TANG SOCIETY

Every educated Chinese during the Tang Dynasty was expected to be able to spontaneously dash off a poem with grace, or at least technical competence. Poetry was a form of social communication, not an arcane and highbrow art. The sheer mass of Tang poems still extant—close to 50,000, by some 2,200 authors—clearly indicates how common poetry was in everyday life. Many of those whose poems survived spent their lives in some official government position, after taking the civil service examination that qualified them for office. Whenever these scholar-officials were sent to a new post in the vast territory of the Tang Empire they would take leave from their colleagues and friends with a "farewell" poem and expect a poetic gift in return. In their new province, they would make friends by going on pleasure excursions or visiting temples and invariably writing poems about their journeys. They could also write poems to praise the imperial court or to criticize its policies. Poetry thus was a cultural custom, a craft that taught people how to pay attention to and share the significant moments in their lives—to find something lovely in a scene; to convey feelings about separation and friendship, painful and pleasurable events; to thank a host for a splendid evening party; or simply to express what would otherwise be awkward or impossible to say. Though the practice of writing poetry was general, only some thirty or forty truly talented poets achieved renown as artists of the highest caliber. Yet some otherwise undistinguished writers produced a remarkable number of fine poems that would be read and memorized for the next thousand years.

THE ORIGIN OF TANG POETRY

Chinese literature began with the folk songs and ritual ballads about historical events preserved in the *Classic of Poetry* (ca. 600 B.C.E.). Most of the poems in that collection have stanzas of four to six lines containing four to six characters each, with end rhymes for every couplet. During the Han Dynasty (206 B.C.E.–220 C.E.), about half a millennium after the compilation of the *Classic of Poetry*, a new genre of poetry emerged. Written in lines of five or seven characters and displaying a much more melodious and flexible rhythm, it became the basis for Tang poetry. During the century preceding the Tang Dynasty, poets began to experiment with introducing tonal patterns into their poems. Although variations in tone are common in many languages, including English, they are usually associated with sentence patterns. Chinese differs in attaching tones to individual syllables. Poets started to arrange the tones of each syllable of the poem—in modern Mandarin Chinese, a syllable can be pronounced in one of four different tones—in symmetrical patterns. This innovation led to the birth of so-called "regulated poetry," a verse form that requires syllables to alternate "level" and "deflected" tones and demands training to master. The spread of Buddhism in the first half of the first millennium may have helped spark the development of regulated poetry. Chinese monks translating Sanskrit texts into Chinese must have been struck by the absence of tones in Sanskrit, and this new awareness of a defining feature of their own language perhaps inspired the introduction of rules mandating the alternation of tones in poetry. Whatever the reason, the emergence of regulated poetry (also called "recent-style" poetry, as earlier poetic forms such as those used by **Tao Qian** came to be called "old-style" poetry) radically changed the reading and writing of poetry. By imposing more rules on the game of poetry, it enabled readers to judge poetic craftsmanship more objectively.

Both the prominent place of poetry in social communication and everyday life and these new technical demands gave poetry an unprecedented status in Tang society. Poetry was introduced into the prestigious civil service examination; successful aspirants were awarded the "presented scholar" degree (*jinshi*), a prerequisite for a career as a government official. Although there were debates about whether the inclusion of poetry composition was appropriate for such exams, and was later abolished, the tight formal requirements of the regulated poem made it easier to judge and compare the candidates' relative worth. Also, the candidates were forced to learn how to compose succinctly and eloquently. This skill would be useful in their later careers in government service, as they drafted many complex official documents.

REGULATED POETRY OF THE TANG

The two basic forms of regulated poetry are in four lines (*jueju*) and eight lines (*lüshi*), although longer poems composed of several stanzas were also common. Regulated poetry placed a new emphasis on the couplet, a unit of two lines. For the ambitious Tang poet, couplets presented an opportunity to display virtuosity, as they provided a showcase for the parallelism required of the regulated poem. Consider **Du Fu's "Spring Prospect,"** which describes the fall of the Tang capital to rebels in 755 and the destruction of the great Tang Empire against the backdrop of innocent spring:

The nation shattered, mountains and rivers remain;
city in spring, grass and trees burgeoning.
Feeling the times, blossoms draw tears;
hating separation, birds alarm the heart.
Beacon fires three months in succession,

a letter from home worth ten thousand in gold.
White hairs, fewer for the scratching,
soon too few to hold a hairpin up.

Let us examine how this five-syllable regulated poem reads in classical Chinese. Some of the rhymes and tones are hardly recognizable in the modern Mandarin pronunciation of the characters given here, but they did rhyme and tonally harmonize during the Tang Dynasty. "Level tones" are marked with a hyphen (–); "deflected tones," with a straight line (|):

FIRST COUPLET

國	破	山	河	在	
guó	pò	shān	hé	zài	(modern Mandarin pronunciation)
			–	–		(tonal pattern)
nation	shattered	mountain	river	remain	(word-for-word translation)

(Chinese characters)

城	春	草	木	深	
chéng	chūn	cǎo	mù	shēn^(rhyme word)	
–	–				–
city	spring	grass	tree	grow thick	

SECOND COUPLET

感	時	花	濺	淚	
gǎn	shí	huā	jiàn	lèi	
(|)	–	–				
feel	time	blossom	shed	tear	

恨	別	鳥	驚	心	
hèn	bié	niǎo	jīng	xīn^(rhyme word)	
				–	
hate	separation	bird	alarm	heart	

THIRD COUPLET

烽	火	連	三	月	
fēng	huǒ	lián	sān	yuè	
(–)			–	–		
beacon	fire	in succession	3	months	

家	書	抵	萬	金
jiā	shū	dǐ	wàn	jīn(rhyme word)
–	–	|	|	–
home	letter	worth	10,000	gold

白	頭	搔	更	短	FOURTH COUPLET
bái	tóu	sāo	gèng	duǎn	
(|)	–	–	|	|	
white	head	scratch	even	shorter	

渾	欲	不	勝	簪
hùn	yù	bú	shèng	zān(rhyme word)
|	|	|	(–)	–
simply	want	not	hold	hairpin

The poem consistently relies on parallelism as it poignantly contrasts the stability of the natural cycle with the abrupt changes brought about by the rebellion. In the first couplet the capital Chang'an is taken by rebel forces, the emperor has fled to Sichuan Province and abdicated, and the "nation is shattered," yet, perversely, we see the "city in spring," untouched by the disaster of historic proportion. In the second couplet, even blossoms and birds appear startled by the human tragedy. The third couplet shows the economic costs of the rebellion: the rebels have cordoned off the capital so tightly that letters have become almost priceless, smuggled in and out only at risk of one's life. The last couplet lacks precise parallelisms but ends with thematic resonances and shows the poet in despair: the hairpin no longer secures his official cap to his head, because he has become too old for service and the dynasty he wanted to serve has fallen on hard times.

Parallelism in Tang poetry functioned on many levels beyond the grammatical, including thematic parallelism and contrast between lines or in the poem as a whole. Thus Tang writings on poetry distinguish many types. The parallel couplet was the central device of regulated poetry, and during the Tang people would write out their favorite couplets in lavish calligraphy on little hanging scrolls, which they could carry when traveling. Indeed, Tang poets compiled entire anthologies containing only beautiful couplets excerpted from famous poems. The emphasis on fashioning beautiful couplets created a huge market for practical manuals that explained how to avoid violating the tonal rules and how to come up with an impressive parallel. This approach later drew criticism from poets who saw artistic ambition and inspiration, rather than craft and training, as the keys to good poetry. But the attraction of Tang poetry lies precisely in the felicitous match of craft with inspiration. It was solid training in the rules of regulated poetry that enabled Tang poets to capture their experience of the world in memorable words. The ultimate art of Tang poetry is that it often hides its artfulness under the serene surface of natural imagery.

WANG WEI

ca. 699–761

One of the most prominent poets of his time, Wang Wei was also a well-respected painter and musician. He confesses in one poem that he was a poet only "by mistake" and that he must have been a painter in an earlier life.

Wang Wei was born into an aristocratic family and passed the civil service examination at the age of twenty. He rose steadily in the ranks of the official bureaucracy but his career was interrupted in 755, when the frontier general An Lushan rebelled against the Tang—leading to the siege that occasioned **Du Fu**'s "**Spring Prospect**." Although the emperor and his immediate entourage fled, many officials were captured by the rebels and forced to work for An Lushan's military government. When the revolt was put down, Wang Wei escaped charges of collaboration only thanks to the intervention of his brother, a high-ranking government official. Once rehabilitated, he served in office until his death.

The An Lushan Rebellion was the most catastrophic event in three centuries of Tang Dynasty rule (618–907). That a simple frontier general of Central Asian origin could bring down an empire that was at the time the largest and most efficiently administered in the world came as a profound shock to the Chinese and their East Asian neighbors; and it became a defining moment for Wang Wei's generation. Yet unlike many of his contemporaries, such as Du Fu, Wang Wei wrote almost nothing about it. The poem "While I Was Imprisoned in Puti Monastery" is unusual in this regard. Written when Wang Wei was held captive by An Lushan's rebels, it describes efforts of the former Tang court musicians to resist the rebel government's request to perform at its victory banquet. The poem was circulated after the rebellion as proof of Wang Wei's resistance to the rebel government, thereby aiding his rehabilitation.

Although he could write in an ornate style on public court occasions, Wang Wei is known mainly for his ability to evoke tranquil scenes of rural retreat and convey a sense of dispassionate detachment from the world. His vignettes of reclusive life combine simplicity and deliberate craft. He bought a retreat in the Zhongnan Mountains and later the "Wang River" estate outside the capital, which he and his friend Pei Di celebrated in a series of poems.

Wang Wei also painted the various scenic spots he mentions in his poetry. None of his original paintings are preserved, but the survival of many imitations suggests that they were very popular. Wang Wei is considered a pioneer of Chinese landscape art, known particularly for his monochrome painting, which uses black ink-wash on white paper; this technique allows the painter to depict landscapes dominated by white. His interest in snow scenes is also evident in "White Rock Rapids," in which he paints—in poetry—families washing white silk under bright moonlight, with white rocks and dark rushes implicit in the background.

Wang Wei's poetry echoes his friendship with Buddhist monks and recluses and his commitment to Buddhism. Whereas other poets celebrated the landscape as it appears to the senses, Wang Wei often represents an insubstantiality that corresponds to the notion of the "emptiness" of things—the fundamental Buddhist conviction that all we perceive is illusion.

Zhongnan Retreat[1]

In middle years I am rather fond of the Tao;
My late home is at the foot of Southern Mountain.
When the feeling comes, each time I go there alone.
That splendid things are empty, of course, I know.
I walk to the place where the water ends   5
And sit and watch the time when clouds rise.
Meeting by chance an old man of the forest,
I chat and laugh without a date to return.

In Response to Vice-Magistrate Zhang

In late years I care for tranquility alone—
A myriad affairs do not concern my heart.
A glance at myself: there are no long-range plans.
I only know to return to the old forest.
Pine winds blow, loosening my belt;   5
The mountain moon shines as I pluck my zither.
You ask about reasons for success and failure:
A fisherman's song enters the shore's deeps.

From Wang River Collection

Preface: My retreat is in the Wang River mountain valley. The places to walk
to include: Meng Wall Cove, Huazi Hill, Grained Apricot Lodge, Clear Bamboo
Range, Deer Enclosure, Magnolia Enclosure, Dogwood Bank, Sophora Path,
Lakeside Pavilion, Southern Hillock, Lake Yi, Willow Waves, Luan Family Shallows, Gold Powder Spring, White Rock Rapids, Northern Hillock, Bamboo Lodge,
Magnolia Bank, Lacquer Tree Garden, and Pepper Tree Garden. When Pei Di[2]
and I were at leisure, we each composed the following quatrains.

*   *   *

Deer Enclosure

Empty mountain, no man is seen.
Only heard are echoes of men's talk.
Reflected light enters the deep wood
And shines again on blue-green moss.

Lake Yi

Blowing flutes cross to the distant shore.
At day's dusk I bid farewell to you.
On the lake with one turn of the head:
Mountain green rolls into white clouds.

1. All selections translated by and with notes
adapted from Pauline Yu.

2. A fellow poet and minor official (b. 716),
one of Wang Wei's closest friends.

Gold Powder Spring

Drink each day at Gold Powder Spring
And you should have a thousand years or more:
To soar on an azure phoenix with striped dragons,
And with plumes and tassels attend the Jade Emperor's court.[3]

White Rock Rapids

Clear and shallow, White Rock Rapids.
Green rushes once could be grasped.
Families live east and west of the water,
Washing silk beneath the bright moon.

Written on Crossing the Yellow River to Quinghe

A boat sailing on the great river—
The gathered waters reach to the end of the sky.
Sky and waves suddenly split asunder:
A commandery city—a thousand, ten thousand homes.
Farther on I see a city market again;   5
There seems to be some mulberry and hemp.
Looking back at my old home country:
The water's expanse joins the clouds and mist.

While I Was Imprisoned in Puti Monastery, Pei Di Came to See Me. He Spoke of How the Rebels Ordered Music Played at Frozen Emerald Pond; after the Court Musicians Began to Play, Their Tears Fell. I Secretly Recited and Presented This to Pei Di[4]

From ten thousand homes of grieving hearts arises wild smoke.
The hundred officials—when will they again attend court?
Autumn sophora leaves fall within the empty palace.
Next to Frozen Emerald Pond, music from pipes and strings.

Farewell

Dismounting I give you wine to drink,
And inquire where you are going.
You say you did not achieve your wishes
And return to rest at the foot of Southern Mountain.
But go—do not ask again: 5
White clouds have no ending time.

---

3. Daoists often engaged in alchemical experiments, believing that gold could confer immortality. Both the Queen Mother of the West, who rode on a phoenix chariot pulled by striped dragons, and the Jade Emperor, supreme deity in the Daoist pantheon, are associated with immortality.

4. Probably Wang Wei's only expression of political protest, written when he was imprisoned during the An Lushan rebellion in 756. After An Lushan and his soldiers entered the capital Chang'an, they forced members of the imperial conservatory to perform at a victory banquet for the rebels.

LI BO
701–762

Although Li Bo (also known as Li Po and Li Bai) was raised in Sichuan in western China, speculations about his Turkic family background have enhanced his image as an exotic eccentric. Li Bo never attempted to take the civil service examination, which was the primary but not sole venue for advancement. Thanks to his connection with an influential Daoist at court, Li Bo gained a post at the eminent Hanlin Academy, an institution founded by Emperor Xuanzong to support unconventional intellectuals and literary talents. But Li Bo's drinking habits and unusual personality led to his dismissal only two years later. During the An Lushan Rebellion he joined the cause of a prince who attempted to establish an independent regime in southeast China, and after the rebellion was suppressed he was arrested for treason. Sentenced to exile, he was pardoned before he reached his remote destination; he died a few years later.

There are many legends about Li Bo's life, encouraged by the nonchalant poses projected in his poetry: according to one such legend, he drowned while trying to embrace the moon's reflection on the water. For someone who claimed in his poetry to converse and drink with the moon such an end was not implausible, though overindulgence in alcohol and Daoist longevity elixirs, which often contained mercury, might have played a role.

Much Tang poetry tends to treat the world at hand; Li Bo supplies an additional dimension by describing Daoist worlds beyond the world, evoking moments of history and legend, and even transforming everyday occasions into something miraculous. Because of his flair and capacity to see the world with fresh eyes, his contemporaries called him "the banished immortal"—an ethereal heaven-dwelling being exiled for a lifetime in the world of mortals as punishment for some extravagant misdemeanor. Li Bo cultivated this reputation by writing poems that tell of encounters with immortals and of cloud-climbing excursions through the heavens.

Of the thousand-some poems by Li Bo that survive, many are written in the old verse form popular before the rise of regulated poetry during the Tang. Li Bo particularly liked to imitate folk songs and infuse his poetry with colloquial and bold language. In this way he could sometimes give voice to the common people's hardships: in "South of the Walls We Fought," for example, he echoes an older anonymous lament of soldiers fallen in battle, turning it into bitter criticism of the constant warfare of his time on the northern and northwestern frontier of Tang China against peoples such as the Tibetans.

Li Bo and **Du Fu** are considered the most important Tang poets, and readers and critics over the past millennium have devoted considerable effort to debating their relative merits and shortcomings. Quite apart from the greatness of their poetry, they made a particularly fitting couple, because they embody the two poles of poetic creativity that have been of greatest concern in the Chinese literary tradition: while Du Fu became the poet who captured, chronicled, and criticized reality within its limits, Li Bo came to stand for the poet who dedicated himself to breaking free from social convention and from the limits imposed by reality.

The Sun Rises and Sets[1]

The sun comes up from its nook in the east,
Seems to rise from beneath the earth,
Passes on through Heaven,
   sets once again in the western sea,
And where, oh, where, can its team of six dragons   5
   ever find any rest?
Its daily beginnings and endings,
   since ancient times never resting.
And man is not made of its Primal Stuff—
   how can he linger beside it long?   10
Plants feel no thanks for their flowering in spring's wind,
Nor do trees hate losing their leaves
   under autumn skies:
Who wields the whip that drives along
   four seasons of changes—   15
The rise and the ending of all things
   is just the way things are.

Xihe! Xihe![2]
Why must you always drown yourself
   in those wild and reckless waves?   20
What power had Luyang[3]
That he halted your course by shaking his spear?
This perverts the Path of things,
   errs from Heaven's will—
So many lies and deceits!   25
I'll wrap this Mighty Mudball of a world
   all up in a bag
And be wild and free like Chaos itself!

South of the Walls We Fought[4]

We fought last year at the Sanggan's source,
this year we fight on the Cong River road.
We washed weapons in the surf of Tiaozhi,
grazed horses on grass in Sky Mountain's snow.[5]

---

1. Translated by Stephen Owen.
2. Goddess who drove the sun's carriage.
3. According to legend, the lord of Luyang stopped the sun so that he could continue to

fight in combat.
4. Translated by Stephen Owen.
5. Four locations of Tang campaigns in the north and northwest.

Thousands of miles ever marching and fighting: 5
until all the Grand Army grows frail and old.

The Xiongnu[6] treat slaughter as farmers treat plowing;
since bygone days only white bones are seen
   in their fields of yellow sand.
The House of Qin built the wall   10
   to guard against the Turk;
for the House of Han the beacon fires
   were blazing still.

Beacon fires blaze without ceasing,
the marching and battle never end.   15
They died in fighting on the steppes,
their vanquished horses neigh,
   mourning to the sky.
Kites and ravens peck men's guts,
fly with them dangling from their beaks   20
   and hang them high
      on boughs of barren trees.
The troops lie mud-smeared in grasses,
and the general acted all in vain.
Now I truly see that weapons   25
   are evil's tools:
the Sage will use them only
   when he cannot do otherwise.

Bring in the Wine[7]

Look there!
   The waters of the Yellow River,
   coming down from Heaven,
   rush in their flow to the sea,
   never turn back again   5
Look there!
   Bright in the mirrors of mighty halls
   a grieving for white hair,
   this morning blue-black strands of silk,
   now turned to snow with evening.   10
For satisfaction in this life
   taste pleasure to the limit,
And never let a goblet of gold
   face the bright moon empty.
Heaven bred in me talents,   15
   and they must be put to use.

6. Formidable enemies of the Han Empire   7. Translated by Stephen Owen.
(206 B.C.E.–220 C.E.).

I toss away a thousand in gold,
    it comes right back to me.
So boil a sheep,
    butcher an ox,
        make merry for a while,   20
And when you sit yourself to drink, always
    down three hundred cups.
    Hey, Master Cen,
    Ho, Danqiu,[8]   25
    Bring in the wine!
    Keep the cups coming!
And I, I'll sing you a song,
You bend me your ears and listen—
The bells and the drums, the tastiest morsels,   30
    it's not these that I love—
All I want is to stay dead drunk
    and never sober up.
The sages and worthies of ancient days
    now lie silent forever,   35
And only the greatest drinkers
    have a fame that lingers on!
Once long ago
    the prince of Chen
        held a party at Pingle Lodge.[9]   40
A gallon of wine cost ten thousand cash,
    all the joy and laughter they pleased.
        So you, my host,
How can you tell me you're short on cash?
Go right out!   45
    Buy us some wine!
        And I'll do the pouring for you!
Then take my dappled horse,
    Take my furs worth a fortune,
Just call the boy to get them,   50
    and trade them for lovely wine,
And here together we'll melt the sorrows
    of all eternity!

Question and Answer in the Mountains[1]

They ask me why I live in the green mountains.
I smile and don't reply; my heart's at ease.
Peach blossoms flow downstream, leaving no trace—
And there are other earths and skies than these.

---

8. Two friends of Li Bo.
9. The scene of merry parties described by the poet Cao Zhi (192–232), the brother of Cao Pi, the author of "A Discourse on Literature."
1. Translated by Vikram Seth.

Summer Day in the Mountains[2]

Lazily waving a fan of white feathers,
Stripped naked here in the green woods,
I take off my headband, hang it on a cliff,
My bare head splattered by wind through pines.

Drinking Alone with the Moon[3]

A pot of wine among the flowers.
I drink alone, no friend with me.
I raise my cup to invite the moon.
He and my shadow and I make three.

The moon does not know how to drink;   5
My shadow mimes my capering;
But I'll make merry with them both—
And soon enough it will be Spring.

I sing—the moon moves to and fro.
I dance—my shadow leaps and sways.   10
Still sober, we exchange our joys.
Drunk—and we'll go our separate ways.

Let's pledge—beyond human ties—to be friends,
And meet where the Silver River ends.

In the Quiet Night[4]

The floor before my bed is bright:
Moonlight—like hoarfrost—in my room.
I lift my head and watch the moon.
I drop my head and think of home.

Sitting Alone by Jingting Mountain[5]

The flocks of birds have flown high and away,
A solitary cloud goes off calmly alone.
We look at each other and never get bored—
Just me and Jingting Mountain.

2. Translated by Stephen Owen.
3. Translated by Vikram Seth.
4. Translated by Vikram Seth.
5. Translated by Stephen Owen.

DU FU

712-770

Du Fu failed in his political ambitions, and his poetry was not widely read during his lifetime. But during the Song Dynasty (960–1279) he rose to the top of the poetic canon because of his versatility and ability to capture the dramatic historical events and spirit of his age. Ever since that time, Du Fu, together with **Li Bo**, has maintained the reputation as the greatest of Chinese poets.

Du Fu was the grandson of a prominent court poet. Although he dreamed of an official career, that dream was dashed after he twice failed the civil service examination. When An Lushan rebelled in 755, the imperial court escaped but Du Fu was left behind in the capital. Eventually he slipped through the enemy lines and made his way to the court of the new emperor in exile. There he briefly held one of the court positions he had so much desired; but following the recapture of the capital, he was exiled to a minor provincial post. He soon quit in disgust and embarked on a lifetime of travels. He first went to seek the help of relatives in northwest China, and then took up residence in Chengdu in Sichuan Province. In his later years Du Fu moved to Kuizhou, where he produced his most admired poetry sequence, the "Autumn Meditations."

Du Fu is considered the "poet-historian" of Chinese literature, carrying out the Confucian duty to chronicle and criticize the events of his time. Prophetically, he grasped that the An Lushan Rebellion was an event of major historical proportions. But it was his ability to capture the rebellion's impact on his life and on the lives of the people around him that gave depth to his voice. In "Moonlight Night" Du Fu imagines his wife, whom he had managed to send to safety while he remained trapped in the occupied capital, watching the moon and worrying about him; "Qiang Village" conveys the riveting scene of reunion, after Du Fu has finally escaped from the capital and is reunited with his family. But the effects of the rebellion linger on even after it is quashed: a decade later, he devotes "Ballad of the Firewood Vendors" to the local working women in his new home in Kuizhou who despair that the loss of life has destroyed the marriage prospects of an entire generation.

The greatness of Du Fu's poetry lies in its extraordinary range of themes, styles, and observations. His poetic mastery is particularly visible in his preferred verse form, the regulated poem, in which he can be not just witty but also prophetic and visionary. Even when he is sober and humble, his everyday observations can reach cosmic proportions and take the unsuspecting reader by surprise.

Painted Hawk[1]

Wind-blown frost rises from plain white silk,
a gray falcon—paintwork's wonder.

Body strains, its thoughts on the cunning hare,
its eyes turn sidelong like a Turk in despair.

You could pinch the rays glinting on tie-ring,
its stance, to be called to the column's rail.

When will it strike the common birds?—
bloody feathers strewing the weed-covered plain.

Moonlight Night[2]

From her room in Fuzhou tonight,
all alone she watches the moon.

Far away, I grieve that her children
can't understand why she thinks of Chang'an.

Fragrant mist in her cloud hair damp,
clear lucence on her jade arms cold—

when will we lean by chamber curtains
and let it light the two of us, our tear stains dried?

Spring Prospect[3]

The nation shattered, mountains and rivers remain;
city in spring, grass and trees burgeoning.

Fooling the times, blossoms draw tears;
hating separation, birds alarm the heart.

Beacon fires three months in succession,
a letter from home worth ten thousand in gold.

White hairs, fewer for the scratching,
soon too few to hold a hairpin up.[4]

1. Translated by Stephen Owen.
2. Translated by Burton Watson. This poem was written in 756, when Du Fu was held captive in the fallen capital of Chang'an during the An Lushan Rebellion and his wife and family had fled to safety in Fuzhou in the north.
3. Translated by Burton Watson. This poem was written when Du Fu was still a captive in Chang'an.
4. Officials used hairpins to keep their caps in place.

Qiang Village I[5]

Lofted and lifted, west of the clouds of red,
The trek of the sun descends to the level earth.
By the brushwood gate songbirds and sparrows chaffer,
And the homebound stranger from a thousand *li*[6] arrives.
Wife and children marvel that I am here: 5
When the shock wears off, still they wipe away tears.
In the disorders of the age was I tossed and flung;
That I return alive is a happening of chance.
Neighbors swarm up to the tops of the walls,
Touched and sighing, even they sob and weep.   10
The night wastes on, and still we hold the candle,
Across from another, as if asleep and in a dream.

My Thatched Roof Is Ruined by the Autumn Wind[7]

In the high autumn skies of September
    the wind cried out in rage,
Tearing off in whirls from my rooftop
    three plies of thatch.
The thatch flew across the river,   5
    was strewn on the floodplain,
The high stalks tangled in tips
    of tall forest trees,
The low ones swirled in gusts across ground
    and sank into mud puddles.   10
The children from the village to the south
    made a fool of me, impotent with age,
Without compunction plundered what was mine
    before my very eyes,
Brazenly took armfuls of thatch,   15
    ran off into the bamboo,
And I screamed lips dry and throat raw,
    but no use.
Then I made my way home, leaning on staff,
    sighing to myself.   20
A moment later the wind calmed down,
    clouds turned dark as ink,
The autumn sky rolling and overcast,
    blacker towards sunset,
And our cotton quilts were years old   25
    and cold as iron,
My little boy slept poorly,
    kicked rips in them.

5. Translated by Paul Kroll. This poem was written in 757, when Du Fu finally rejoined his family after their separation during the tur- moil of the An Lushan Rebellion.
6. About 250 miles.
7. Translated by Stephen Owen.

Above the bed the roof leaked,
  no place was dry,   30
And the raindrops ran down like strings,
  without a break.
I have lived through upheavals and ruin
  and have seldom slept very well,
But have no idea how I shall pass   35
  this night of soaking.
Oh, to own a mighty mansion
  of a hundred thousand rooms,
A great roof for the poorest gentlemen
  of all this world,   40
  a place to make them smile,
A building unshaken by wind or rain,
  as solid as a mountain,
Oh, when shall I see before my eyes
  a towering roof such as this?   45
Then I'd accept the ruin of my own little hut
  and death by freezing.

I Stand Alone[8]

A single bird of prey beyond the sky,
a pair of white gulls between riverbanks.

Hovering wind-tossed, ready to strike;
the pair, at their ease, roaming to and fro.

And the dew is also full on the grasses,   5
spiders' filaments still not drawn in.

Instigations in nature approach men's affairs—
I stand alone in thousands of sources of worry.

Spending the Night in a Tower by the River[9]

A visible darkness grows up mountain paths,
I lodge by river gate high in a study,

Frail cloud on cliff edge passing the night,
The lonely moon topples amid the waves.

Steady, one after another, a line of cranes in flight;   5
Howling over the kill, wild dogs and wolves.

No sleep for me. I worry over battles.
I have no strength to right the universe.

8. Translated by Stephen Owen.   9. Translated by Stephen Owen.

Thoughts while Travelling at Night[1]

Light breeze on the fine grass.
I stand alone at the mast.

Stars lean on the vast wild plain.
Moon bobs in the Great River's spate.

Letters have brought no fame.   5
Office? Too old to obtain.

Drifting, what am I like?
A gull between earth and sky.

Ballad of the Firewood Vendors[2]

Kuizhou women, hair half gray,
forty, fifty, and still no husbands;
since the ravages of rebellion, harder than ever
      to marry—
a whole life steeped in bitterness and long sighs.   5
Local custom decrees that men sit, women stand;
men mind the house door, women go out and work,
at eighteen, nineteen, off peddling firewood,
with money they get from firewood, making
      ends meet.   10
Till they're old, hair in two buns dangling to the neck,
stuck with wild flowers, a mountain leaf, a silver pin,
they struggle up the steep paths, flock to the market gate,
risk their lives for extra gain by dipping from salt wells.   15
Faces powdered, heads adorned, sometimes a trace
      of tears,
cramped fields, thin clothing, the weariness of
      stony slopes—
But if you say all are ugly as the women of Witch's   20
      Mountain,
how to account for Zhaojun,[3] born in a village to
      the north?

---

1. Translated by Vikram Seth.
2. Translated by Burton Watson. This poem, written in 766, describes local customs in Kuizhou, set on steep hillsides along the Yangzi River, where Du Fu had settled.
3. Wang Zhaojun, a stunningly beautiful court lady of the Han Dynasty (206 B.C.E.–220 C.E.) who embodied the suffering of exile, because she was married off to a tribal chief of the fierce Xiongnu tribes as part of Han diplomacy on the unruly northern frontier. "Witch's Mountain": Wushan, near Kuizhou.

Autumn Meditations IV[4]

I've heard them say, Chang'an's like a chessboard;
sad beyond bearing, the happenings of these
    hundred years!
Mansions of peers and princes, all with new
    owners now;   5
in civil or martial cap and garb, not the same as before.
Over mountain passes, due north, gongs and
    drums resound;
wagons and horses pressing west speed the
    feather-decked dispatches.[5]   10
Fish and dragons sunk in sleep, autumn rivers cold;
old homeland, those peaceful times, forever in
    my thoughts!

---

4. Translated by Burton Watson. This poem
comes from Du Fu's most famous poetic cycle,
"Autumn Meditations."
5. Feathers attached to military dispatches

marked the message as urgent; Uighurs were
threatening from the north and Tibetans from
the west.

BO JUYI
772–846

With more than 2,800 poems, Bo Juyi (or Bai Juyi) stands out as the most prolific Tang poet. Like no writer before him Bo Juyi recorded his daily life in poetry, considering such matters as his taste for fresh bamboo shoots, prices on the flower market, or the purchase of his beloved estate outside the capital. Seeking to write poetry as autobiography, he was also a highly self-conscious poet.

Bo Juyi came from a modest scholar-official family, passed the civil service examination in his late twenties, and then embarked on a succession of government appointments, interrupted by several years in exile after he incurred the emperor's displeasure. While serving in powerful positions in the provinces away from the capital he became increasingly drawn to Buddhism and the joys of reclusive life.

Bo Juyi wrote in many styles and guises, but his "New Music Bureau Poetry," which drew attention to corrupt political practices and social abuses, was especially important to him. During the earlier Han Dynasty

(206 B.C.E.–220 C.E.) the imperial Music Bureau was founded to collect songs from the people and provide musical performances. Its mission reflected the Confucian conviction that rulers should adjust their policies to the needs of their subjects and that song and poetry were particularly effective means of communicating the complaints of the people to the emperor and the ruling class. Bo Juyi revived this method of conveying grievances.

Though Bo Juyi sternly castigated the abuse of power for private gains, he sympathized with a different kind of abuse of power that would have fatal consequences: the infatuation of Emperor Xuanzong (685–762) with "Prized Consort Yang" (Yang Guifei). The emperor's love for the consort enabled her clan to advance into positions of power at court on the eve of the An Lushan Rebellion. Although their connection with the rebellion is unclear, people held her and her clan responsible; and when the capital was overrun by rebels and Emperor Xuanzong tried to escape, the military demanded Yang Guifei's execution—so she was strangled before the emperor's eyes. Yang's taste for luxury and the exclusive attention the emperor lavished on her both fascinated and repelled people. This tale of fateful conflict between duty and love inspired many later poems,

novels, and plays, but Bo Juyi's "Song of Lasting Regret," composed half a century after the rebellion, became its most influential early treatment; his friend Chen Hong added a prose account to it. Though Bo Juyi and Chen Hong treat the same set of events, they differ markedly in how they structure the story, what significant details they choose to dramatize it, and how they judge the lovers. These differences go beyond a personal disagreement of opinion between two friends, also showing that poetry and prose had its distinct narrative logic and moral values regarding love affairs.

Bo Juyi achieved great fame during his lifetime. Copies of his poetry collection spread outside China to other East Asian countries, including Japan, where he became one of the most popular Chinese poets. His poetry was included in Japanese anthologies, his "New Music Bureau Poetry" became a basic primer for male and female students alike, and his song about the tragic love of Emperor Xuanzong and Yang Guifei was taken as the archetypal expression of impossible and tragic love; as such, it was frequently alluded to in the central masterpiece of Japanese literature, the eleventh-century *Tale of Genji* by the court lady **Murasaki Shikibu**.

The Song of Lasting Regret[1]

Monarch of Han, he doted on beauty, yearned for a bewitching temptress;
Through the dominions of his sway, for many years he sought but did
    not find her.
There was in the family of Yang a maiden just then reaching fullness,[2]
Raised in the women's quarters protected, unacquainted yet with others.   4

1. Translated by and with notes adapted from Paul Kroll. The asterisks in this selection mark divisions, not excerptions.

2. The future Yang Guifei, the Emperor Xuanzong's "prized consort."

Heaven had given her a ravishing form, impossible for her to hide,
And one morning she was chosen for placement at the side of the
    sovereign king.
When she glanced behind with a single smile, a hundred seductions
    were quickened;
All the powdered and painted ones in the Six Palaces[3] now seemed   8
    without beauty of face.
In the coolness of springtime, she was permitted to bathe in the
    Huaqing pools,[4]
Where the slickening waters of the hot springs washed over her firm flesh.
Supported as she rose by a waiting-maid, she was so delicate, listless:
This was the moment when first she acceded to His favor   12
    and beneficence.

Cloud-swept tresses, flowery features, quivering hair-pendants of gold,
And behind the warmth of lotus-bloom drapings, they passed the
    springtime nights—
Springtime nights so grievously brief, as the sun rose again high!
From this time onward the sovereign king no longer held early court.   16

Taken with pleasure, she attended on the feasts, continuing without let;
Springtime followed springtime outing, evening after evening
    she controlled.

Of the comely beauties of the rear palace,[5] there were three thousand
    persons,
And preferments and affection for all three thousand were placed on   20
    her alone.
In her golden room, with makeup perfect, the Delicate One serves for
    the night;
In a tower of jade, with the feast concluded, drunkenness befits love in
    spring.

Her sisters and brothers, older or younger, all were enfeoffed[6] with land;
The most enviable brilliance and glory quickened their doorways and   24
    gates.
Then it came to pass, throughout the empire, that the hearts of fathers
    and mothers
No longer valued the birth of a son but valued the birth of daughters.

The high sites of Mount Li's palace reached into clouds in the blue,
And transcendent music, wafted on the wind, was heard there   28
    everywhere.

Measured songs, languorous dancing merged with sound of strings and
    bamboo,
As the sovereign king looked on all day long, never getting enough . . .

3. Residences of the imperial concubines.   5. The women's quarters.
4. Famous hot springs some fifteen miles out-   6. Deeded.
side of the Tang capital of Chang'an.

Until, out of Yuyang, horse-borne war-drums came, shaking the earth,
To dismay and smash the melody of "Rainbow Skirts and Feathered   32
    Vestments."[7]

* * *

By the nine-layered walls and watchtowers, dust and smoke arose,
And a thousand chariots, ten thousand riders moved off to the southwest.[8]

The halcyon-plumed banners jounced and joggled along, moving and
    stopping again,
As they went forth westward from the metropolis' gates, something   36
    more than a hundred miles.
And then the Six Armies would go no farther—there was no other recourse,
But the fluently curved moth-eyebrows[9] must die before the horses.

Floriform filigrees were strewn on the ground, to be retrieved by no one,
Halcyon tailfeathers, an aigrette of gold, and hairpins made of jade.   40
The sovereign king covered his face—he could not save her;
When he looked back, it was with tears of blood that mingled in
    their flow.

* * *

Yellowish grit spreads and scatters, as the wind blows drear and doleful;
Cloudy walkways turn and twist, climbing Saber Gallery's[1] heights.   44
Below Mount Emei there are very few men who pass by;
Lightless now are the pennons and flags in the sun's dimmer aura.

Waters of Shu's[2] streams deepest blue, the mountains of Shu are green—
For the Paragon, the Ruler, dawn to dawn, night upon night, his   48
    feelings:
Seeing the moon from his transient palace—a sight that tears at his heart;
Hearing small bells in the evening rain—a sound that stabs his insides.

* * *

Heaven revolves, the days roll on, and the dragon carriage was turned
    around;[3]
Having reached the spot, faltering he halted, unable to leave it again.   52
But amidst that muddy earth, below Mawei Slope,[4]
Her jade countenance was not to be seen—just a place of empty death.

7. An exotic Central Asian dance melody;
Emperor Xuanzong rescored it, and Lady Yang
danced to it costumed as a moon maiden.
"Yuyang": the headquarters of the rebel An
Lushan, east of modern Beijing.
8. The emperor and his retinue, fleeing from
An Lushan's rebel army.

9. That is, Lady Yang.
1. A sacred mountain in the southwestern
province of Sichuan.
2. An ancient name for the region.
3. That is, the emperor returned to the capital.
4. The site of Lady Yang's execution.

Sovereign and servants beheld each other, cloaks wet from weeping;
And, looking east, to the metropolis' gates, let their horses take them   56
    homeward.

*   *   *

Returned home now, and the ponds, the pools, all were as before—
The lotuses of Grand Ichor Pool, the willows by the Night-is-Young Palace.

The lotus blossoms resemble her face, the willow branches her eyebrows;
Confronted with this, would it be possible that his tears should not fall?   60
From the day that peach and plum flowers open, in the springtime breezes,
Until the leaves of the "we-together"⁵ tree are shed in the autumn rain. . . .

The West Palace and the Southern Interior were rife with autumn grasses,
And fallen leaves covered the steps, their red not swept away.   64
The artistes, once young, of the Pear Garden have hair gone newly white;
The Pepper Room attendants and their budding nymphs are become
    aged now.

Fireflies flit through the hall-room at dusk, as he yearns in desolation;
When all the wick of his lone lamp is used, sleep still fails to come.   68
Ever later, more dilatory, sound the watch-drum and bell in the
    lengthening nights;
Fitfully sparkling, the River of Stars⁶ streams onward to the dawn-
    flushed sky.

The roof-tiles, paired as love-ducks, grow chilled, and flowers of frost
    grow thick;
The halcyon-plumed coverlet is cold—whom would he share it with?   72
Dim-distanced, far-faded, are the living from the dead, parted more
    than a year ago;
Neither her soul nor her spirit have ever yet come into his dreams.

*   *   *

A Daoist adept from Linqiong, a visitor to the Hongdu Gate,⁷
Could use the perfection of his essential being to contact souls and   76
    spirits.
Because of his broodings the sovereign king, tossing and turning,
    still yearned;
So he set to task this adept of formulas, to search for her sedulously.

Cleaving the clouds, driving the ethers, fleeting as a lightning-flash,
Ascending the heavens, entering into the earth, he sought her out   80
    everywhere.

5. A tree whose name sounds like the phrase   6. The Milky Way.
"we together." The falling of the leaves reminds   7. An ancient name for the capital's gates.
the emperor of his lost love.

On high he traversed the sky's cyan drop-off, and below to the Yellow Springs;[8]
In both places, to the limits of vision, she was nowhere to be seen.

Of a sudden he heard rumor then of a transcendent mountain in the sea,
A mountain resting in void and nullity, amidst the vaporous seemings.   84

High buildings and galleries shimmer there brightly, and five-colored
    clouds mount up;
In the midst of this, relaxed and unhurried, were hosts of tender sylphs.
And in *their* midst was one, known as Greatest Perfection,[9]
Whose snow-white skin and flower-like features appeared to resemble   88
    hers.

In the western wing of the gatehouse of gold, he knocked at the jade bolting,
In turn setting in motion Little Jade who made report to Doubly Completed.[1]
When word was told of the Son of Heaven's envoy, from the House of Han,
Then, within the nine-flowered drapings, her dreaming spirit startled.   92

She searched for her cloak, pushed pillow aside, arose, walked forth
    distractedly;
Door-screens of pearl, partitions of silver, she opened out one after another.
With her cloud-chignon half-mussed to one side, newly awakened from sleep,
With flowered cap set awry, down she came to the ceremonial hall.   96

Her sylphine sleeves, puffed by a breeze, were lifted, flared and fluttering,
Just the same as in the dance of "Rainbow Skirts and Feathered Vestments."
But her jade countenance looked bleak, forlorn, crisscrossed with tears—
A single branch of pear blossom, in springtime laden with rain.   100

Restraining her feelings, focusing her gaze, she asked her sovereign king's
    indulgence:
"Once we were parted, both voice and face were lost to limitless vagueness.
There, within Zhaoyang Basilica, affection and favor were cut short,
While here in Penglai's[2] palaces, the days and months have   104
    lengthened.

"Turning my head and looking down to the sites of the mortal sphere,
I can no longer see Chang'an,[3] what I see is dust and fog.
Let me take up these familiar old objects to attest to my deep love:
The filigree case, the two-pronged hairpin of gold, I entrust to you to   108
    take back.

---

8. A traditional name for the Chinese under-world. "Sky's cyan drop-off": the sky's blue reaches; also a Daoist technical term for a specific region in the "Heaven of Nascent Azure."
9. The religious name (Taizhen) adopted by Lady Yang when she briefly took orders as a Daoist priestess, before receiving a title as the emperor's consort.
1. Two of Lady Yang's servants. "Doubly Completed" was the servant of a central Daoist goddess, the "Queen Mother of the West."
2. A Daoist island of the immortals in the eastern ocean (during Bo Juyi's time, sometimes associated with Japan).
3. The Tang capital.

"Of the hairpin but one leg remains, and one leaf-fold of the case;
The hairpin is broken in its yellow gold, and the case's filigree halved.
But if only his heart is as enduring as the filigree and the gold,
Above in heaven, or amidst men, we shall surely see each other."   112

As the envoy was to depart, she entrusted poignantly to him words as well,
Words in which there was a vow that only two hearts would know:
"On the seventh day of the seventh month,[4] in the Hall of Protracted Life,
At the night's mid-point, when we spoke alone, with no one else around—   116
'In heaven, would that we might become birds of coupled wings!
On earth, would that we might be trees of intertwining limbs! . . .'"
Heaven is lasting, earth long-standing, but there is a season for their end;
This regret stretches on and farther, with no ending time.   120

Chen Hong, *An Account to Go with the "Song of Lasting Regret"*[5]

During the Kaiyuan Reign,[6] the omens of the Stair Stars showed a world at
peace, and there were no problems throughout all the land within the four
circling seas. Xuanzong, having been long on the throne, grew weary of having
to dine late and dress while it was still dark for the dawn audience; and he
began to turn over all questions of government, both large and small, to the
Assistant Director of the Right, Li Linfu, while the Emperor himself tended
either to stay deep in the palace or go out to banquets, finding his pleasure in
all the sensual delights of ear and eye. Previously the Empress Yuanxian and
the Consort Wuhui had both enjoyed His Majesty's favor, but each in turn had
departed this world; and even though there were in the palace over a thousand
daughters of good families, none of them really caught his fancy. His Majesty
was fretful and displeased.

In those days every year in December the imperial entourage would journey
to Huaqing Palace. The titled women, both from the inner palace and from
without, would follow him like luminous shadows. And he would grant them
baths in the warm waters there, in the very waves that had bathed the imperial
sun. Holy fluids in a springlike breeze went rippling through those places. It
was then that His Majesty's heart was smitten: for he had truly come upon the
one woman, and all the fair flesh that surrounded him seemed to him like dirt.
He summoned Gao Lishi to make a secret search for this woman in the palaces
of the princes; and there, in the establishment of the Prince of Shou, he found
the daughter of Yang Xuanyan. She had already become a mature woman. Her
hair and tresses were glossy and well arranged; neither slender nor plump, she
was exactly of the middle measure; and there was a sensuous allure in her
every motion, just like the Lady Li of Emperor Wu of the Han. He ordered a
special channel of the warm springs cut for her and commanded that it be

4. According to popular legend, the only day
when the constellation the Oxherd could cross
the Milky Way to meet with his lover, the
Weaver Maid; Lady Yang and the emperor had
exchanged a love oath on that auspicious

night. The festival is still celebrated today in
East Asia as a Valentine's Day of sorts.
5. Translated by Stephen Owen.
6. The golden years of Emperor Xuanzong's
reign, from 713 to 741.

offered to her gleaming fineness. When she came out of the water, her body seemed frail and her force spent, as if she could not even bear the weight of lace and gauze; yet she shed such radiance that it shone on all around her. His Majesty was most pleased. On the day he had her brought to meet him, he ordered the melody "Coats of Feathers, Rainbow Skirts" played to precede her. And on the eve when their love was consummated, he gave her, as proofs of his love, a golden hairpin and an inlaid box. He also commanded that she wear golden earrings and a hair-pick that swayed to her pace. The following year he had her officially listed as Guifei, Prized Consort, entitled to half the provision as an empress. From this point on she assumed a seductively coy manner and spoke wittily, suiting herself to His Majesty's wishes by thousands of fetching ways. And His Majesty came to dote on her ever more deeply.

At this time the Emperor made a tour of his nine domains and offered the gold-sealed tablets in ceremonies on the Five Sacred Peaks. On Mount Li during snowy nights and in Shangyang Palace on spring mornings she would ride in the same palanquin as the Emperor and spend the night in the same apartments; she was the main figure of feasts and had his bedchambers all to herself when he retired. There were three Great Ladies, nine Royal Spouses, twenty-seven Brides of the Age, eighty-one Imperial Wives, Handmaidens of the Rear Palace, Women Performers of the Music Bureau—and on none of these was the Son of Heaven the least inclined to look. And from that time on, no one from the Six Palaces was ever again brought forward to the royal bed. This was not only because of her sensual allure and great physical charms, but also because she was clever and smart, artful at flattery and making herself agreeable, anticipating His Majesty's wishes—so much so that it cannot be described. Her father, her uncle, and her brothers were all given high honorary offices and were raised to ranks of Nobility Equal to the Royal House. Her sisters were enfeoffed as Ladies of Domains. Their wealth matched that of the royal house; and their carriages, clothes, and mansions were on a par with the Emperor's aunt, Princess Taichang. Yet in power and the benefits of imperial favor, they surpassed her. They went in and out of the royal palace unquestioned, and the senior officers of the capital would turn their eyes away from them. There were doggerel rhymes in those days that went:

> If you have a girl, don't feel sad;
> if you have a boy, don't feel glad.

and:

> The boy won't be a noble,
>   but the daughter may be queen;
> so look on your daughters now
>   as the glory of the clan.

To such a degree were they envied by people.

At the end of the Tianbao Reign,[7] her uncle Yang Guozhong stole the position of Chancellor and abused the power he held. When An Lushan led his troops in an attack on the imperial palace, he used punishing Yang Guozhong as his pre-

---

7. Emperor Xuanzong's last reign period, from 742 to 756, leading up to the An Lushan Rebellion.

text. Tong Pass was left undefended, and the Kingfisher Paraphernalia of the imperial entourage had to set out southward.[8] After leaving Xianyang, their path came to Mawei Pavilion. There the Grand Army hesitated, holding their pikes in battle positions and refusing to go forward. Attendant officers, gentlemen of the court, and underlings bowed down before His Majesty's horse and asked that this current Chao Cuo[9] be executed to appease the world. Yang Guozhong then received the yak-hair hat ribbons and the pan of water, by which a great officer of the court presents himself to the Emperor for punishment, and he died there by the edge of the road. Yet the will of those who were with the Emperor was still not satisfied. When His Majesty asked what the problem was, those who dared speak out asked that the Prized Consort also be sacrificed to allay the wrath of the world. His Majesty knew that it could not be avoided, and yet he could not bear to see her die, so he turned his sleeve to cover his face as the envoys dragged her off. She struggled and threw herself back and forth in panic, but at last she came to death under the strangling cord.

Afterward, Xuanzong came to Chengdu on his Imperial Tour, and Suzong accepted the succession at Lingwu.[1] In the following year the Monster himself [An Lushan] forfeited his head, and the imperial carriage returned to the capital. Xuanzong was honored as His Former Majesty and given a separate establishment in the Southern Palace, then transferred to the western sector of the Imperial Compound. As time and events passed, all joy had gone from him and only sadness came. Every day of spring or night of winter, when the lotuses in the ponds opened in summer or when the palace ash trees shed their leaves in autumn, the performers of the Pear Garden Academy would produce notes on their jade flageolets; and if he heard one note of "Coats of Feathers, Rainbow Skirts," His Majesty's face would lose its cheer, and all those around him would sob and sigh. For three years there was this one thing on his mind, and his longing never subsided. His soul sought her out in dream, but she was so far away he could not reach her.

It happened then that a wizard came from Shu; and knowing that His Majesty was brooding so much on Yang the Prized Consort, he said that he possessed the skills of Li the Young Lord, the wizard who had summoned the soul of Lady Li for Emperor Wu of the Han. Xuanzong was very pleased, and ordered him to bring her spirit. The wizard then used all his skills to find her, but could not. He was also able to send his spirit on journeys by riding vapors; he went up into the precincts of Heaven and sank down into the vaults of the Earth looking for her; but he did not meet her. And then again he went to the margins and the encircling wastelands, high and low, to the easternmost extreme of Heaven and the Ocean, where he strode across Fanghu.

He saw there the highest of the mountains of the Undying, with many mansions and towers; at the end of the western verandah there was a deepest doorway facing east; the gate was shut, and there was written "The Garden of Taizhen, Jade Consort." The wizard pulled out a hatpin and rapped on the door, at which a young maiden with her hair done up in a double coil came out

---

8. That is, the emperor fled west to Sichuan.
9. A Han Dynasty official, executed in 155 B.C.E. because he was blamed for helping to incite a rebellion.

1. Emperor Xuanzong abdicated to his successor, Emperor Suzong.

to answer the door. The wizard was so flustered he couldn't manage to get a word out, so the maiden went back in. In a moment another servant girl in a green dress came out and asked where he was from. The wizard then identified himself as an envoy of the Tang Son of Heaven and conveyed the command he had been given. The servant said, "The Jade Consort has just gone to bed; please wait a while for her." Thereupon he was swallowed up in a sea of clouds with the dawn sun breaking through them as down a tunnel to the heavens; then the jasper door closed again and all was still and without a sound.

The wizard held his breath and did not move his feet, waiting at the gate with folded hands. After a long time, the servant invited him to come in and said, "The Jade Consort is coming out." Then he saw a person with a bonnet of golden lotuses, wearing lavender chiffon, with pendants of red jade hanging from her sash and phoenix slippers, and seven or eight persons in attendance on her. She greeted the wizard and asked, "Is the Emperor well?" Then she asked what had happened since the fourteenth year of the Tianbao Reign. When he finished speaking, she grew wistful and gestured to her servant to get a golden hairpin and inlaid box, each of which she broke in parts. She gave one part of each to the envoy, saying, "Express my gratitude to the Emperor and present him these objects as mementos of our former love."

The wizard received her words and these objects of surety; he was ready to go, but one could see in his face that something was troubling him. The Jade Consort insisted that he tell her what was the matter. Then he knelt down before her and said, "Please tell me something that happened back then, something of which no one else knew, so that I can offer to His Majesty as proof. Otherwise I am afraid that with the inlaid box and the golden hairpin I will be accused of the same kind of trickery that Xin Yuanping practiced on Emperor Wen of the Han."[2] The Jade Consort drew back lost in thought, as if there were something she were recalling with fondness. Then very slowly she said, "Back in the tenth year of the Tianbao Reign, I was attending on His Majesty, who had gone to the palace on Mount Li to escape the heat. It was autumn, in the seventh month, the evening when the Oxherd and the Weaver Star meet.[3] It was the custom of the people of Qin on that night to spread out embroidery and brocade, to put out food and drink, to set up flowers and melons, and to burn incense in the yard—they call this 'begging for deftness.' Those of the inner palace hold this custom in particularly high regard. It was almost midnight; and the guards and attendants in the eastern and western cloisters had been dismissed. I was waiting on His Majesty alone. His Majesty stood there, leaning on his shoulder, then looked up at the heavens and was touched by the legend of the Oxherd and Weaver Star. We then made a secret vow to one another, a wish that we could be husband and wife in every lifetime. When we stopped speaking, we held hands, and each of us was sobbing. Only the Emperor knows of this."

Then she said sadly, "Because of this one thought so much in my mind, I will be able to live on here no longer. I will descend again to the world below and our future destiny will take shape. Whether in Heaven or in the world of mortal

2. Xin Yuanping gained the favor of Emperor Wen of the Han Dynasty by producing fake omens, such as the miraculous appearance of a jade cup with an auspicious inscription. When his frauds were discovered, he was executed.

3. See p. 1327, n. 4.

men, it is certain that we will meet again and form our bond of love as before." Then she said, "His Former Majesty will not be long in the world of men. I hope that he will find some peace of mind and not cause himself suffering."

The envoy returned and presented this to His Former Majesty, and the Emperor's heart was shaken and much afflicted with grief. For days on end he could find no cheer. In the summer of that year, in the fourth month, His Majesty passed on.

In winter of the first year of the Yuanhe Reign, the twelfth month (February 807), Bo Juyi of Taiyuan left his position as Diarist in the Imperial Library to be the sheriff of Chou County. I, Chen Hong, and Wang Zhifu of Langya had our homes in this town; and on our days off we would go together visiting sites of the Undying and Buddhist temples. Our discussion touched on this story, and we were all moved to sighs. Zhifu lifted his winecup to Bo Juyi and said, "Unless such an event finds an extraordinary talent who can adorn it with colors, even something so rare will fade away with time and no longer be known in the world. Bo Juyi is deeply familiar with poetry and has strong sentiments. Why doesn't he write a song on the topic." At this Bo Juyi made the "Song of Lasting Regret." It is my supposition that he was not only moved by the event, but he also wanted to offer warning about such creatures that can so enthrall a man, to block the phases by which troubles come, and to leave this for the future. When the song was finished, he had me write a prose account for it. Of those things not known to the general public, I, not being a survivor of the Kaiyuan, have no way to know. For those things known to the general public, the "Annals of the Reign of Xuanzong" are extant. This is merely an account for the "Song of Lasting Regret."

YUAN ZHEN
779–831

The most important development in prose literature during the Tang was the emergence of the genre of so-called "classical tales" (*chuanqi*, literally "records of marvels"). Long fiction emerged late in Chinese literature; before the Tang Dynasty short anecdotes and parables were common. As tales became more popular, writers crafted longer narratives telling unusual stories of love and heroism, which sometimes included supernatural elements. Yuan Zhen's "The Story of Yingying" is the most famous and most enthralling example of this new genre.

Yuan Zhen's official career was a series of official appointments, followed by periods of exile caused by party politics, but he eventually rose to high office at court. He was the closest friend of **Bo Juyi,** with whom he exchanged many poems and shared, among much else, a fascination with tragic love affairs.

"The Story of Yingying," Yuan Zhen's only tale, may have been written while he was taking the civil service examination. It was intended as a "warming scroll"—a piece of writing that candidates circulated informally in the hope of getting the attention of potential patrons. It sets out as a typical "talented scholar meets beautiful woman" tale, a popular theme. "The Story of Yingying" describes the seduction and rejection of the heroine Yingying by her distant cousin, an aspiring exam candidate. In this scenario, marriage would have been the obvious outcome. Yet the lovers, each in their own way, thwart the possibility of legitimate marriage and instead contribute to a story of heartbreak. One might see this as a thinly disguised account of the author's personal experiences. If it is indeed autobiographical, he is portraying himself in a most unflattering light. Is Yuan Zhen trying to justify the outrageous behavior of the faithless scholar? Might he have tried to absolve his guilt over a shabby deed by writing a confessionary tale about it? Does he bitterly mock the naiveté of the formulaic plot popular during his time, attempting to show that happy endings are rare in real life?

Not least because of its uncertain intent, "The Story of Yingying" became very popular, and it went through some drastic transformations in subsequent adaptations. The most famous later version was the thirteenth-century play *Romance of the Western Chamber*. Here all the troubling aspects of the work are smoothed over. The remarkably willful and cultivated Yingying is transformed into an ordinary, docile heroine, and the lovers are ultimately reunited to live happily ever after.

The Story of Yingying[1]

During the Zhenyuan period[2] there lived a young man named Zhang. He was agreeable and refined, and good looking, but firm and self-contained, and capable of no improper act. When his companions included him in one of their parties, the others could all be brawling as though they would never get enough, but Zhang would just watch tolerantly without ever taking part. In this way he had gotten to be twenty-three years old without ever having had relations with a woman. When asked by his friends, he explained, "Deng Tuzi[3] was no lover, but a lecher. I am the true lover—I just never happened to meet the right girl. How do I know that? It's because things of outstanding beauty never fail to make a permanent impression on me. That shows I am not without feelings." His friends took note of what he said.

Not long afterward Zhang was traveling in Pu,[4] where he lodged some ten *li*[5] east of the city in a monastery called the Temple of Universal Salvation. It happened that a widowed Mrs. Cui had also stopped there on her way back to Chang'an. She had been born a Zheng; Zhang's mother had been a Zheng, and when they worked out their common ancestry, this Mrs. Cui turned out to be a rather distant cousin once removed on his mother's side.

This year Hun Zhen[6] died in Pu, and the eunuch Ding Wenya proved unpopular with the troops, who took advantage of the mourning period to mutiny. They plundered the citizens of Pu, and Mrs. Cui, in a strange place with all her wealth and servants, was terrified, having no one to turn to. Before the mutiny Zhang had made friends with some of the officers in Pu, and now he requested

---

1. Translated by and with notes adapted from James Robert Hightower.
2. From 785 to 804.
3. An archetypal lecher.

4. Puzhou, a province northeast of Chang'an.
5. About 2½ miles.
6. The regional commander of Jiangzhou; he died in 799.

a detachment of soldiers to protect the Cui family. As a result all escaped harm. In about ten days the imperial commissioner of inquiry, Du Que, came with full power from the throne and restored order among the troops.

Out of gratitude to Zhang for the favor he had done them, Mrs. Cui invited him to a banquet in the central hall. She addressed him: "Your widowed aunt with her helpless children would never have been able to escape alive from these rioting soldiers. It is no ordinary favor you have done us; it is rather as though you had given my son and daughter their lives, and I want to introduce them to you as their elder brother so that they can express their thanks." She summoned her son Huanlang, a very attractive child of ten or so. Then she called her daughter: "Come out and pay your respects to your brother, who saved your life." There was a delay; then word was brought that she was indisposed and asked to be excused. Her mother exclaimed in anger, "Your brother Zhang saved your life. You would have been abducted if it were not for him—how can you give yourself airs?"

After a while she appeared, wearing an everyday dress and no makeup on her smooth face, except for a remaining spot of rouge. Her hair coils straggled down to touch her eyebrows. Her beauty was extraordinary, so radiant it took the breath away. Startled, Zhang made her a deep bow as she sat down beside her mother. Because she had been forced to come out against her will, she looked angrily straight ahead, as though unable to endure the company. Zhang asked her age. Mrs. Cui said, "From the seventh month of the fifth year of the reigning emperor to the present twenty-first year, it is just seventeen years."

Zhang tried to make conversation with her, but she would not respond, and he had to leave after the meal was over. From this time on Zhang was infatuated but had no way to make his feelings known to her. She had a maid named Hongniang with whom Zhang had managed to exchange greetings several times, and finally he took the occasion to tell her how he felt. Not surprisingly, the maid was alarmed and fled in embarrassment. Zhang was sorry he had said anything, and when she returned the next day he made shamefaced apologies without repeating his request. The maid said, "Sir, what you said is something I would not dare repeat to my mistress or let anyone else know about. But you know very well who Miss Cui's relatives are; why don't you ask for her hand in marriage, as you are entitled to do because of the favor you did them?"

"From my earliest years I have never been one to make any improper connections," Zhang said, "Whenever I have found myself in the company of young women, I would not even look at them, and it never occurred to me that I would be trapped in any such way. But the other day at the dinner I was hardly able to control myself, and in the days since, I walk without knowing where I am going and eat without hunger—I am afraid I cannot last another day. If I were to go through a regular matchmaker, taking three months and more for the exchange of betrothal presents and names and birthdates[7]—you might just as well look for me among the dried fish in the shop.[8] Can't you tell me what to do?"

"Miss Cui is so very strict that not even her elders could suggest anything improper to her," the maid replied. "It would be hard for someone in my position

7. In order to determine an auspicious date for a wedding.
8. An allusion to the parable of help that comes too late, found in the early Chinese master text *Zhuangzi*.

to say such a thing. But I have noticed she writes a lot. She is always reciting poetry to herself and is moved by it for a long time after. You might see if you can seduce her with a love poem. That is the only way I can think of."

Zhang was delighted and on the spot composed two stanzas of spring verses which he handed over to her. That evening Hongniang came back with a note on colored paper for him, saying, "By Miss Cui's instructions."

The title of her poem was "Bright Moon on the Night of the Fifteenth":

> *I await the moon in the western chamber*
> *Where the breeze comes through the half-opened door.*
> *Sweeping the wall the flower shadows move:*
> *I imagine it is my lover who comes.*

Zhang understood the message: that day was the fourteenth of the second month, and an apricot tree was next to the wall east of the Cuis' courtyard. It would be possible to climb it.

On the night of the fifteenth Zhang used the tree as a ladder to get over the wall. When he came to the western chamber, the door was ajar. Inside, Hongniang was asleep on a bed. He awakened her, and she asked, frightened, "How did you get here?"

"Miss Cui's letter told me to come," he said, not quite accurately. "You go tell her I am here."

In a minute Hongniang was back. "She's coming! She's coming!"

Zhang was both happy and nervous, convinced that success was his. Then Miss Cui appeared in formal dress, with a serious face, and began to upbraid him: "You did us a great kindness when you saved our lives, and that is why my mother entrusted my young brother and myself to you. Why then did you get my silly maid to bring me that filthy poem? You began by doing a good deed in preserving me from the hands of ravishers, and you end by seeking to ravish me. You substitute seduction for rape—is there any great difference? My first impulse was to keep quiet about it, but that would have been to condone your wrongdoing, and not right. If I told my mother, it would amount to ingratitude, and the consequences would be unfortunate. I thought of having a servant convey my disapproval, but feared she would not get it right. Then I thought of writing a short message to state my case, but was afraid it would only put you on your guard. So finally I composed those vulgar lines to make sure you would come here. It was an improper thing to do, and of course I feel ashamed. But I hope that you will keep within the bounds of decency and commit no outrage."

As she finished speaking, she turned on her heel and left him. For some time Zhang stood, dumbfounded. Then he went back over the wall to his quarters, all hope gone.

A few nights later Zhang was sleeping alone by the veranda when someone shook him awake. Startled, he rose up, to see Hongniang standing there, a coverlet and pillow in her arms. She patted him and said, "She is coming! She is coming! Why are you sleeping?" And she spread the quilt and put the pillow beside his. As she left, Zhang sat up straight and rubbed his eyes. For some time it seemed as though he were still dreaming, but nonetheless he waited dutifully. Then there was Hongniang again, with Miss Cui leaning on her arm. She was shy and yielding, and appeared almost not to have the strength to move her limbs. The contrast with her stiff formality at their last encounter was complete.

This evening was the night of the eighteenth, and the slanting rays of the moon cast a soft light over half the bed. Zhang felt a kind of floating lightness and wondered whether this was an immortal who visited him, not someone from the world of men. After a while the temple bell sounded. Daybreak was near. As Hongniang urged her to leave, she wept softly and clung to him. Hongniang helped her up, and they left. The whole time she had not spoken a single word. With the first light of dawn Zhang got up, wondering, was it a dream? But the perfume still lingered, and as it got lighter he could see on his arm traces of her makeup and the teardrops sparkling still on the mat.

For some ten days afterward there was no word from her. Zhang composed a poem of sixty lines on "An Encounter with an Immortal" which he had not yet completed when Hongniang happened by, and he gave it to her for her mistress. After that she let him see her again, and for nearly a month he would join her in what her poem called the "western chamber," slipping out at dawn and returning stealthily at night. Zhang once asked what her mother thought about the situation. She said, "She knows there is nothing she can do about it, and so she hopes you will regularize things."

Before long Zhang was about to go to Chang'an, and he let her know his intentions in a poem. Miss Cui made no objections at all, but the look of pain on her face was very touching. On the eve of his departure he was unable to see her again. Then Zhang went off to the west. A few months later he again made a trip to Pu and stayed several months with Miss Cui.

She was a very good calligrapher and wrote poetry, but for all that he kept begging to see her work, she would never show it. Zhang wrote poems for her, challenging her to match them, but she paid them little attention. The thing that made her unusual was that, while she excelled in the arts, she always acted as though she were ignorant, and although she was quick and clever in speaking, she would seldom indulge in repartee. She loved Zhang very much, but would never say so in words. At the time she was subject to moods of profound melancholy, but she never let on. She seldom showed on her face the emotions she felt. On one occasion she was playing her zither alone at night. She did not know Zhang was listening, and the music was full of sadness. As soon as he spoke, she stopped and would play no more. This made him all the more infatuated with her.

Some time later Zhang had to go west again for the scheduled examinations. It was the eve of his departure, and though he had said nothing about what it involved, he sat sighing unhappily at her side. Miss Cui had guessed that he was going to leave for good. Her manner was respectful, but she spoke deliberately and in a low voice. "To seduce someone and then abandon her is perfectly natural, and it would be presumptuous of me to resent it. It would be an act of charity on your part if, having first seduced me, you were to go through with it and fulfill your oath of lifelong devotion. But in either case, what is there to be so upset about in this trip? However, I see you are not happy and I have no way to cheer you up. You have praised my zither playing, and in the past I have been embarrassed to play for you. Now that you are going away, I shall do what you so often requested."

She had them prepare her zither and started to play the prelude to the "Rainbow Robe and Feather Skirt."[9] After a few notes, her playing grew wild with grief until the piece was no longer recognizable. Everyone was reduced to tears, and Miss Cui abruptly stopped playing, put down the zither, and ran back to her mother's room with tears streaming down her face. She did not come back.

The next morning Zhang went away. The following year he stayed on in the capital, having failed the examinations. He wrote a letter to Miss Cui to reassure her, and her reply read roughly as follows:

> I have read your letter with its message of consolation, and it filled my childish heart with mingled grief and joy. In addition you sent me a box of ornaments to adorn my hair and a stick of pomade to make my lips smooth. It was most kind of you; but for whom am I to make myself attractive? As I look at these presents my breast is filled with sorrow.
>
> Your letter said that you will stay on in the capital to pursue your studies, and of course you need quiet and the facilities there to make progress. Still it is hard on the person left alone in this far-off place. But such is my fate, and I should not complain. Since last fall I have been listless and without hope. In company I can force myself to talk and smile, but come evening I always shed tears in the solitude of my own room. Even in my sleep I often sob, yearning for the absent one. Or I am in your arms for a moment as it used to be, but before the secret meeting is done I am awake and heartbroken. The bed seems still warm beside me, but the one I love is far away.
>
> Since you said good-bye the new year has come. Chang'an is a city of pleasure with chances for love everywhere. I am truly fortunate that you have not forgotten me and that your affection is not worn out. Loving you as I do, I have no way of repaying you, except to be true to our vow of lifelong fidelity.
>
> Our first meeting was at the banquet, as cousins. Then you persuaded my maid to inform me of your love; and I was unable to keep my childish heart firm. You made advances, like that other poet, Sima Xiangru.[1] I failed to repulse them as the girl did who threw her shuttle.[2] When I offered myself in your bed, you treated me with the greatest kindness, and I supposed, in my innocence, that I could always depend on you. How could I have foreseen that our encounter could not possibly lead to something definite, that having disgraced myself by coming to you, there was no further chance of serving you openly as a wife? To the end of my days this will be a lasting regret—I must hide my sighs and be silent. If you, out of kindness, would condescend to fulfill my selfish wish, though it came on my dying day it would seem to be a new lease on life. But if, as a man of the world, you curtail your feelings, sacrificing the lesser to the more important, and look on this connection as shameful, so that your solemn vow can be dispensed with, still my true love will not vanish though my bones decay

---

9. An exotic Central Asian dance melody mentioned in Bo Juyi's famous "Song of Lasting Regret" (see p. 1324, n. 7).
1. A bohemian poet (179–117 B.C.E.) who with his zither playing enticed the young widow Zhuo Wenjun to elope.
2. A neighbor girl repulsed the advances of Xie Kun (280–322) by throwing her shuttle in his face, knocking out two of his teeth.

and my frame dissolve; in wind and dew it will seek out the ground you walk on. My love in life and death is told in this. I weep as I write, for feelings I cannot express. Take care of yourself; a thousand times over, take care of your dear self.

This bracelet of jade is something I wore as a child; I send it to serve as a gentleman's belt pendant. Like jade may you be invariably firm and tender; like a bracelet may there be no break between what came before and what is to follow. Here are also a skein of multicolored thread and a tea roller of mottled bamboo. These things have no intrinsic value, but they are to signify that I want you to be true as jade, and your love to endure unbroken as a bracelet. The spots on the bamboo are like the marks of my tears,[3] and my unhappy thoughts are as tangled as the thread: these objects are symbols of my feelings and tokens for all time of my love. Our hearts are close, though our bodies are far apart and there is no time I can expect to see you. But where the hidden desires are strong enough, there will be a meeting of spirits. Take care of yourself, a thousand times over. The springtime wind is often chill; eat well for your health's sake. Be circumspect and careful, and do not think too often of my unworthy person.

Zhang showed her letter to his friends, and in this way word of the affair got around. One of them, Yang Juyuan, a skillful poet, wrote a quatrain on "Young Miss Cui":

> For clear purity jade cannot equal his complexion;
> On the iris in the inner court snow begins to melt.
> A romantic young man filled with thoughts of love.
> A letter from the Xiao girl,[4] brokenhearted.

Yuan Zhen[5] of Henan wrote a continuation of Zhang's poem "Encounter with an Immortal," also in thirty couplets:

> Faint moonbeams pierce the curtained window;
> Fireflies glimmer across the blue sky.
> The far horizon begins now to pale;
> Dwarf trees gradually turn darker green.
> A dragon song crosses the court bamboo;   5
> A phoenix air brushes the wellside tree.
> The silken robe trails through the thin mist;
> The pendant circles tinkle in the light breeze.
> The accredited envoy accompanies Xi wangmu;[6]
> From the cloud's center comes Jade Boy.[7]   10
> Late at night everyone is quiet;
> At daybreak the rain drizzles.

---

3. An allusion to the legend of the two wives of the sage ruler Shun, who stained the bamboo with their tears when he died.
4. A term for any young woman (here, Yingying).
5. That is, the author.
6. The Queen Mother of the West, a central goddess in the Daoist pantheon; she dwells in the Kunlun Mountains in China's far west, in a huge palace inhabited by other immortals. Within its precincts grow the magic peach trees that bear the fruits of immortality once every three thousand years. This might be an allusion to Yingying's mother.
7. Perhaps an allusion to Yingying's brother.

Pearl radiance shines on her decorated sandals;
Flower glow shows off the embroidered skirt.
Jasper hairpin: a walking colored phoenix;   15
Gauze shawl: embracing vermilion rainbow.
She says she comes from Jasper Flower Bank
And is going to pay court at Green Jade Palace.
On an outing north of Luoyang's[8] wall,
By chance he came to the house east of Song Yu.[9]   20
His dalliance she rejects a bit at first,
But her yielding love already is disclosed.
Lowered locks put in motion cicada shadows;
Returning steps raise jade dust.
Her face turns to let flow flower snow   25
As she climbs into bed, silk covers in her arms.
Love birds in a neck-entwining dance;
Kingfishers in a conjugal cage.
Eyebrows, out of shyness, contracted;
Lip rouge, from the warmth, melted.   30
Her breath is pure: fragrance of orchid buds;
Her skin is smooth: richness of jade flesh.
No strength, too limp to lift a wrist;
Many charms, she likes to draw herself together.
Sweat runs: pearls drop by drop;   35
Hair in disorder: black luxuriance.
Just as they rejoice in the meeting of a lifetime
They suddenly hear the night is over.
There is no time for lingering;
It is hard to give up the wish to embrace.   40
Her comely face shows the sorrow she feels;
With fragrant words they swear eternal love.
She gives him a bracelet to plight their troth;
He ties a lovers' knot as sign their hearts are one.
Tear-borne powder runs before the clear mirror;   45
Around the flickering lamp are nighttime insects.
Moonlight is still softly shining
As the rising sun gradually dawns.
Riding on a wild goose she returns to the Luo River.
Blowing a flute he ascends Mount Song.   50
His clothes are fragrant still with musk perfume;
The pillow is slippery yet with red traces.
Thick, thick, the grass grows on the dyke;
Floating, floating, the tumbleweed yearns for the isle.
Her plain zither plays the "Resentful Crane Song";   55
In the clear Milky Way she looks for the returning wild goose.[1]
The sea is broad and truly hard to cross;

---

8. Possibly a reference to the goddess of the
Luo River, near the eastern capital of Luoyang.
9. In "The Lechery of Deng Tuzi," the courtier
Song Yu tells of the beautiful girl next door
who climbed up on the wall to flirt with him.
1. A goose might be carrying a message.

The sky is high and not easy to traverse.
The moving cloud is nowhere to be found—
Xiao Shi[2] stays in his chamber.   60

All of Zhang's friends who heard of the affair marveled at it, but Zhang had determined on his own course of action. Yuan Zhen was especially close to him and so was in a position to ask him for an explanation. Zhang said, "It is a general rule that those women endowed by Heaven with great beauty invariably either destroy themselves or destroy someone else. If this Cui woman were to meet someone with wealth and position, she would use the favor her charms gain her to be cloud and rain or dragon or monster—I can't imagine what she might turn into. Of old, King Xin of the Shang and King You of the Zhou[3] were brought low by women, in spite of the size of their kingdoms and the extent of their power; their armies were scattered, their persons butchered, and down to the present day their names are objects of ridicule. I have no inner strength to withstand this evil influence. That is why I have resolutely suppressed my love."

At this statement everyone present sighed deeply.

Over a year later Cui was married, and Zhang for his part had taken a wife. Happening to pass through the town where she was living, he asked permission of her husband to see her, as a cousin. The husband spoke to her, but Cui refused to appear. Zhang's feelings of hurt showed on his face, and she was told about it. She secretly sent him a poem:

Emaciated, I have lost my looks,
Tossing and turning, too weary to leave my bed.
It's not because of others I am ashamed to rise;
For you I am haggard and before you ashamed.

She never did appear. Some days later when Zhang was about to leave, she sent another poem of farewell:

Cast off and abandoned, what can I say now,
Whom you loved so briefly long ago?
Any love you had then for me
Will do for the one you have now.

After this he never heard any more about her. His contemporaries for the most part conceded that Zhang had done well to rectify his mistake. I have often mentioned this among friends so that, forewarned, they might avoid doing such a thing, or if they did, that they might not be led astray by it. In the ninth month of a year in the Zhenyuan period, when an official, Li Gongchui, was passing the night in my house at the Pacification Quarter, the conversation touched on the subject. He found it most extraordinary and composed a "Song of Yingying" to commemorate the affair. Cui's child-name was Yingying, and Gongchui used it for his poem.

---

2. A well-known legendary flute player of early China.
3. Two ancient rulers whose infatuation with wicked concubines supposedly led to the end of their dynasties.

LI QINGZHAO

1084–ca. 1151

Li Qingzhao is one of the finest writers of Chinese song lyric (*ci*) and one of the most celebrated women poets of traditional China. Song lyric, a new poetic form that came to the fore during the Song Dynasty (960–1279), had begun as songs performed in the pleasure quarters of the bustling urban centers, but the genre eventually developed into a refined literary vehicle for delicately sketching mood and emotion. Li Qingzhao used the form with great virtuosity to capture her states of mind, displaying an effortless freshness that belies the precision of her poetic craftsmanship and her poems' emotional depth. She was also a true connoisseur of painting and antiquities in an age when the literary elite, like their European counterparts during the Renaissance, started to collect ancient artwork with great enthusiasm.

Born in northeastern China, in what is now Shandong Province, Li Qingzhao came from a distinguished literary family. Her father belonged to the literary circle of Su Shi, one of the greatest writers of the Song Dynasty, and after his appointment to the national academy in the capital, the family moved to Kaifeng. Her mother was also a poet, and Li Qingzhao was recognized as a promising poetic talent when still in her teens. In 1101, at age seventeen, she was married to Zhao Mingcheng, a student at the prestigious Hanlin Academy and son of a powerful official. Sharing an obsessive passion for books and learning, they began to amass a large collection of books, paintings, rubbings, and antiquities.

But the life they knew abruptly ended as the Song Dynasty lost its capital, the northern territories, and its emperor (himself an avid collector) to the invading Jin Tartars in 1126 and 1127. Li Qingzhao and her husband hastily fled south with part of their collection, but the pieces were gradually scattered and lost. Her husband left her due to an imperial summons and he soon fell ill and died. Li Qingzhao was now without a place of refuge and in constant flight from local rebellions. Finally she and the court settled in Hangzhou in the south in 1132. There has been much speculation as to whether Li Qingzhao married a second time in her late forties, then filed for divorce within a hundred days; a letter survives that accuses her second husband of greed and corruption, but many scholars deny its authenticity. Not much is known about her subsequent life, and even her year of death—1151 at the latest—is uncertain.

The relatively few surviving song lyrics by Li Qingzhao, some of which are included here, are among the finest examples of the form. The ties between poetry and song in traditional China were old and complex. The works of poets were often set to music and were sometimes modified to answer musical needs. During the Tang period, however, an entirely new kind of music became popular: stanza-like melodies with musical lines of unequal length. In a language in which the pitch of a word (or "tone") is essential to understanding its meaning, Chinese song lyrics had to pay careful attention to the requirements of a particular melody—to be comprehensible, the pitch of the word had to match the pitch of the music. Tang poets began the practice of composing lyrics for these popular irregular melodies, and this new poetic form came to be known as *ci*. These "song lyrics," which often concerned love, were frequently performed in the entertainment quarters of the great cities and at parties. By the early Song Dynasty the song lyric had evolved into a verse form whose character differed morkedly from that of classical poetry. Primarily associated with delicate sensibility, it sought to evoke the passing mood.

In the lyrics to the melody "Note After Note" Li Qingzhao takes up the essential concerns of the form and one of the oldest questions in the Chinese tradition: the adequacy of language to express what occurs in the mind and heart. The lyric, which attempts to capture the essence of a particular moment, closes by wondering how the complex emotion she has evoked can be named by the simple word *sorrow*. Li Qingzhao had a genius for presenting scenes that could evoke feeling, as in the lyrics to "Southern Song," in which she describes changing from light summer clothes to a warmer autumn dress, decorated with scenes of a lotus pond. But the dress is old and its gilt lotus leaves are flaking off, giving the appearance of dying vegetation—a change she takes as both physical evidence and symbol of her own aging. It is at such moments that she answers in her own way the ancient question of how words can express the feeling of the moment, showing herself a true master not just of a particular poetic form but of verbal art generally.

SONG LYRICS[1]

To "Southern Song"

Up in heaven the star-river turns,
in man's world below
   curtains are drawn.
A chill comes to pallet and pillow,
   damp with tracks of tears.   5
I rise to take off my gossamer dress
and just happen to ask, "How late is it now?"

The tiny lotus pods,
   kingfisher feathers sewn on;
as the gilt flecks away   10
   the lotus leaves grow few.
Same weather as in times before,
   the same old dress—
only the feelings in the heart
are not as they were before.   15

To "Free-Spirited Fisherman"

Billowing clouds touch sky and reach
   the early morning fog,

1. All selections translated by Stephen Owen.

    the river of stars is ready to set,
       a thousand sails dance.
    My dreaming soul moves in a daze   5
       to where the high god dwells—
    I hear Heaven speak,
    asking me with urgent concern
       where I am going now.

    And I reply that my road is long,   10
       and, alas, twilight draws on;
    I worked at my poems and for nothing have
       bold lines that cause surprise.
    Into strong winds ninety thousand miles
       upward the Peng[2] now flies.   15
    Let that wind never stop,
    let it blow this tiny boat away
       to the Three Immortal Isles.[3]

To "Like a Dream"

I will always recall that day at dusk,
    the pavilion by the creek,
and I was so drunk I couldn't tell
    the way home. My mood left me,
it was late when I turned back in my boat   5
and I strayed deep among lotuses—
how to get through?
how to get through?
and I startled to flight a whole shoal
    of egrets and gulls.   10

To "Drunk in the Shadow of Flowering Trees"

    Pale fog, then dense clouds—
       gloomy all day long;
    in the animal-shaped censer
       incense burns away.
    Once again it is that autumn holiday: 5
    to my jade pillow behind the gauze screen
    at midnight the cold first comes.

    By the eastern hedge I took wine in hand
       after twilight fell.
    A fragrance filled my sleeves unseen.   10
    Don't tell me this does not break your heart—

2. A huge mythical bird described in the ancient Masters Text *Zhuangzi* (see Page 791). Here it appears as a figure of greatness that smaller creatures cannot comprehend.
3. In the eastern sea, believed to be inhabited by immortals.

the west wind blowing up the curtains
and the person,
    as gaunt as the chrysanthemums.

To "Spring in Wuling"

The wind dies down, the fragrance in dirt,
    the flowers now are gone;
late afternoon, too weary to comb my hair.
Everything in the world is right; I am wrong;
    all that will happen is done;   5
before I can say it, tears come.

Yet I've heard it said that at Double Creek
    the spring is lovely still,
and I think I'll go boating there.
But then I fear   10
    those little boats of Double Creek
won't budge if they are made to bear
    this much melancholy.

To "Note After Note"

Searching and searching, seeking and seeking,
so chill, so clear,
dreary,
    and dismal,
        and forlorn.   5
That time of year
    when it's suddenly warm,
        then cold again,
now it's hardest of all to take care.
Two or three cups of weak wine—   10
how can they resist the biting wind
    that comes with evening?
The wild geese pass by—
that's what hurts the most—
and yet they're old acquaintances.   15

In piles chrysanthemums fill the ground,
looking all wasted, damaged—
who could pick them, as they are now?
I stay by the window,
how can I wait alone until blackness comes?   20
The beech tree,
    on top of that
        the fine rain,
on until dusk,
the dripping drop after drop.   25
In a situation like this
how can that one word "sorrow" grasp it?

VII

Japan's Classical Age

Although Japan consists of the four main islands of Hokkaidō, Honshū, Shikoku, and Kyūshū and about a thousand smaller islets, its contacts with the continent have always been close. In fact, much of what makes Japanese culture distinctive stems from the creative ways in which the Japanese adapted Chinese and Korean culture to their own circumstances. For example, the Japanese imported the Chinese writing system, but used it to produce their own distinct literature. They produced literature in two literary languages, one vernacular and the other Chinese-style, which differed strikingly in themes, rhetoric, and the gender of their authors. Some of the greatest works of Japanese literature were written by women in the vernacular language.

Much like the Romans confronting the older and more established civilization of the Greeks, early Japanese writers faced the challenging task of building their own literature on the sophisticated precedents of their mother culture while asserting their own originality. In addition to literature, Japan adopted crucial institutions and cultural practices from

Illustrated Biography of Prince Shōtoku, painted in 1069 by Hata no Chitei. This is part of a series of ten panels that depict the life of Prince Shōtoku (574–622), founder of Buddhism in Japan and considered the first author in Japanese history.

China, such as the concept of a state headed by a divine monarch, a government system based on administrative statutes and laws, Buddhism used as a state religion protecting the people's welfare, city planning, temple architecture, sacred sculpture, religious rituals, court music and elegant dances, imperial excursions, medicine, the culture of painting, calligraphy, and tea. But whereas Rome had conquered Greece and had its young elite educated by Greek slaves, early Japanese had relatively little actual contact with China and knew it mostly from books, thus feeling less self-conscious about their cultural identity. They believed in the numinous power of their language and their gods and were proud of the pristine simplicity of their earliest literature. Unlike parts of Korea and Vietnam, which at certain points in their history were conquered by China, Japan was never directly colonized by China; its inhabitants could admire their old neighbor at a safe distance.

CONTINENTAL CULTURE AND BI-LITERACY

The cultural dialogue with China resulted in one of the world's most complex literary traditions. Writing was invented in China some eighteen centuries before the Japanese learned how to read and write. Unlike Koreans and Vietnamese, who almost exclusively used Chinese-style writing for centuries, the Japanese used the Chinese writing system to produce texts in two literary languages: vernacular Japanese and Chinese-style writing (also called "Sino-Japanese," *kanbun*, or simply "Literary Chinese"). Chinese-style writing was transnational, enabling the Japanese court to participate in the diplomatic and cultural exchange with China and other states in the Chinese sphere of influence such as Korea and Vietnam;

playing a role similar to that of Latin in medieval Europe, it became the official language of the imperial administration and the Buddhist clergy, and was thus associated with high status, serious purpose, and male authorship. Although vernacular literature, in particular poetry, could serve similarly prestigious purposes at court, it became the preferred medium for emotional intimacy, romance, psychological sophistication, and fiction, all of which were associated with female sensibility.

Because the Chinese and Japanese languages belong to radically different language families, adopting Chinese characters to write Japanese required complex adjustments. Chinese is a noninflected language, with a "subject–predicate–object" word order; and literary Chinese is largely monosyllabic, meaning that most words consist of one or at most two syllables. Japanese, in contrast, is agglutinative, meaning that it strings short semantic elements together into long, complex words. It has highly inflected verbs and adjectives, which can carry a number of suffixes; these qualify such things as the mood, probability, or duration of an action or the social status of the speaker or the people she speaks about. Moreover, Japanese has a "subject–object–predicate" word order and is polysyllabic—indeed, one word can sometimes fill an entire line of poetry. Chinese-style writing was written according to the Chinese word order and used the Chinese characters "logographically" for their meaning, each character representing a word. When Chinese-style writing was read out loud, the Japanese reader would perform a translation of sorts, adjusting the Chinese-style phrase to Japanese word order and adding inflections as needed. In contrast, vernacular Japanese writing mixed characters used for meaning with characters used "phonographically," for their sound value only. These characters functioned basically like a syllabic alphabet. As a result, in phonographic writing one word could require many Chinese characters.

Despite this complexity, Japan was not a bilingual culture; very few people learned spoken Chinese in addition to their native tongue. Japanese readers voiced Chinese texts in Japanese pronunciation. Their East Asian neighbors would be able to read the same text but would pronounce it in their languages and dialects. This led to a fascinating communicative paradox that can occur only in cultures with nonalphabetic writing systems. The Japanese ambassadors who visited China in order to present tribute gifts and bring home the newest law codes, Buddhist texts, musical instruments, and poetry collections could usually not ask for directions or the simplest things. Yet they could write sophisticated Chinese-style poetry for their Chinese hosts and communicate through so-called "brush talk": conversations through written messages in the shared Chinese script.

THE LITERATURE OF THE NARA COURT (710–784)

In early Chinese histories, the Japanese islands appear as a fabled realm of multiple polities, one of which—the Yamato clan—was ruled by a female monarch. During the fourth and fifth centuries the chieftains of the Yamato clan, based in western Japan south of modern-day Kyoto, managed to assert their local power over a broader territory. They sent tribute missions to China, benefiting in turn from the authority they gained from the titles and gifts that the Chinese emperors bestowed on them. By the eighth century the Yamato clan had established hegemony over most of Japan in the Nara Basin south of modern-day Kyoto. With the help of scribal specialists who

had previously emigrated from Korea, the Yamato clan turned the medium of writing into a political tool that helped them enforce central control over an increasingly large territory. Rulers also realized that legitimate political authority required historical precedent. The two earliest longer texts produced in Japan were therefore historical chronicles that traced Yamato rule back to the age of the gods and their creation of the Japanese islands. *Records of Ancient Matters* (712), written in the vernacular, connected the Yamato clan to Amaterasu, the sun goddess, who is still worshipped today in the shrines at Ise as the ancestor of the reigning emperor. *Chronicles of Japan* (720), written in Chinese-style, also used Chinese yinyang cosmology to explain the emergence of the Japanese archipelago.

In the process of state formation, Japan's early rulers relied on the beliefs and practices of the "Way of the Gods," the Buddhist law, and Confucian political ethics. The Way of the Gods, called Shintō in Japanese, is rooted in early Japanese folk religion and is concerned with the veneration of sacred sites in nature (such as mountains and rivers), the exorcism of evil-doing spirits, and the purification from polluting forces such as illness and death; it found expression in *Records of Ancient Matters* and thus also legitimated the rule of Amaterasu's descendants over Japan. Buddhism, which originated in India with the teachings of Buddha Shakyamuni and reached Japan via China and Korea, was adopted by Yamato rulers in the sixth century C.E. as a means to promote the welfare of the state. Buddhism promised above all the salvation of human beings from the suffering that comes with desires and attachments to the impermanent things of this world. But already in China it had turned into an instrument of statecraft, through which a sovereign could claim universal legitimacy and ask for protection of his or her realm. Buddhism also provided an important cultural link to Korea and China, as Japanese monks went to study the most recent Buddhist debates and schools on the continent. Confucianism, too, had broad appeal for the individual and the state. **Confucius** had propagated an ethics of benevolent behavior and self-cultivation. He emphasized the importance of social hierarchies and the value of filial devotion toward one's parents, a value that also applied to the head of state. Early Japanese rulers adopted the Chinese model of elite education and founded a state academy for the study of the Confucian Classics. Although in Japan the examination system was never used as a tool for government recruitment as in China, Japanese education until the modern period was based on the canonical Chinese texts. They have left their traces in the entire corpus of Japanese literature up until the twentieth century.

State building on the Chinese model and increasing literacy resulted in the first great period of Japanese literature during the late seventh and the eighth centuries. In 710 Nara became the first stable capital. Previously, capitals had often moved for each new reign, because people feared that the death of the ruler polluted the site. Nara was a radiant city, modeled on Chinese capitals with their quadrangular grid of broad avenues and streets, a large palace complex to the north, and markets of various kinds. Its rulers commissioned the compilation of the earliest chronicles and of local gazettes. The Chinese-style poetry of Japan's earliest extant poetry anthology, *Florilegium of Cherished Airs* (751), describes imperial excursions, poetry banquets, and receptions for foreign diplomats who were entertained in the proud new capital and celebrated in verse. Slightly later, the earliest vernacular poetry anthology, **The Man'yōshū (***Collection of Myriad Leaves***)**, was compiled. Its prominent poets, including **Kakinomoto no Hitomaro, Ōtomo no Tabito**, and **Yamanoue no Okura**, developed a stunning breadth of themes and styles, ranging from ritual evocations of the

The Tōdaiji Temple complex in Nara, Japan, was built in the eighth century and has been frequently repaired and reconstructed over the centuries. The building here, the "Great Buddha Hall," is today one of the largest wooden buildings in the world.

divine imperial lineage to shattering death laments, from lighthearted praises of the powers of wine to desperate calls of support for the poor and oppressed. The literature of the Nara Period pulses with excitement over the new possibilities of technologies, such as writing and literature, and of active participation in the larger world of East Asia. Japan's new profile as an emerging state that had outgrown its tribal past did not go unnoticed among its neighbors. In the early eighth century it gained the new name "Nippon" ("at sun's root"), which signaled that Japan had been accepted as the eastern border of the Chinese sphere of influence.

HEIAN COURT CULTURE (794–1185)

As the result of struggles between the imperial court and the Buddhist clergy, the court moved to a new capital in 794: Heian-kyō ("the Capital of Peace"), modern-day Kyoto. Despite centuries of warrior rule and occasional civil wars, Kyoto would remain the seat of the imperial court until 1868. The four centuries of the Heian Period, when Kyoto was the sole political and cultural center of Japan, became in retrospect a golden age, viewed by subsequent ages as the pinnacle of culture. The literature produced by Kyoto's court aristocracy defined all later standards of taste and embodied a refinement of sensibilities that had timeless appeal.

Heian literature was mostly produced by and for the capital elite. There are descriptions of travel in the provinces, such as Ki no Tsurayuki's *Tosa Diary*, but Heian aristocrats found the countryside at best rustic and charming, at worst embarrassing and primitive. The capital was the center of all ambitions and hopes: aristocrats eagerly awaited the promotion ceremonies that could secure them a higher rank and better post in the extensive court bureaucracy. In their court diaries, written in Chinese-style, they meticulously recorded the daily court routine. These diaries show mostly the official side of Heian life. For a picture of Heian after nightfall, we need to look at vernacular tales and women's diaries. Here we learn that men often had several wives and carried on several romantic affairs at once. They visited their lovers in the women's homes, plying them with allusive poetry or the tasteful calligraphy of a "morning-after note," written on a paper of just the right shade and adorned with just the right twig or blossom in season.

We get a remarkable close-up of the everyday lives, pleasures, and anxieties of Heian aristocratic women from works such as **Murasaki Shikibu's *The Tale of Genji*** and Sei Shōnagon's *The Pillow Book*. Heian women were dressed in a dozen layers of clothing whose shades carefully matched the season and occasion. They were hidden from view, spending their days in the dimly lit interiors of their residences waiting for welcome distractions: the banter of servants, an occasional outside caller with whom to exchange the latest gossip (if it was a man, the lady hid behind a screen as they talked), a love letter, or, even better, festivals or pilgrimages to nearby temples that broke the daily routine. Aristocratic women usually received a thorough education in *waka* poetry (classical Japanese verse composed in the set pattern of 5-7-5-7-7 syllables). They were also trained in music, dance, and often even the Chinese Classics, although Chinese scholarship was traditionally a male domain. Heian elite women had ample time to read and write and developed a subtle sense of propriety and distinction in social relations, clothing decorum, the delicate psychology of romantic affairs, and poetry exchanges.

By the tenth century, *waka* poetry was enshrined as the canonical court genre. *Waka* was both a way to parade one's literary sophistication and a simple

This detail from a twelfth-century illustrated hand scroll of Lady Murasaki's diary gives us a glimpse of the dress and domestic situation of women at the Heian court.

form of everyday communication between men and women, who spent most of their time apart. A century earlier, two emperors with particularly Sinophile tastes had commissioned the compilation of Chinese-style poetry anthologies, which celebrated the cultural achievements of the court and its poets. But by the late ninth century the short and intimate *waka* form became popular: *waka* contests entertained the aristocracy and poets wrote *waka* on screen paintings in the imperial palace. Emperor Daigo's sponsorship of the first imperial *waka* anthology, *The Kokinshū* (*Collection of Ancient and Modern Poems*), in 905, first established the high status of *waka* at court. Between the tenth and fifteenth centuries Japanese emperors commissioned a total of twenty-one *waka* anthologies. Having one's name included in one of these anthologies was the highest aspiration for generations of poets.

Waka relied heavily on a vast, but well-defined, vocabulary of seasonal phenomena and romantic love. Poets used this metaphorical and allusive imagery on public occasions in order to commemorate court events, praise the emperor, or participate in poetry contests. But they also used *waka* for more intimate purposes—to rekindle a love affair, to convey travel experiences, or to express feelings of longing, loneliness, or existential frustration with the impermanence of the world. Ki no Tsurayuki, the author of the **"Japanese Preface"** (or **Kana Preface**) to *The Kokinshū*, boldly claimed that *waka* originated in the age of the gods out of the universal human impulse to burst out in "song" in response to the outside world. Tsurayuki's preface became the foundational statement on the nature, history, and function of poetry and had a profound impact not just on literature but also on other traditional arts.

In addition to the establishment of *waka* at court, the ninth century saw the invention of the kana syllabary, which profoundly changed Japanese literature. Although the invention of the kana syllabary did not fundamentally alter how Japanese wrote, it introduced a script that became specifically associated with women: it was called "women's hand." Before the tenth century, both Chinese-style and vernacular texts were written in Chinese characters. In the new kana system, the characters used phonographically, for sound value, were replaced with a letter standing for a syllable: the curvier *hiragana* script was used for inflections and grammatical particles, while the square-shaped *katakana* script transcribed foreign loanwords such as Sanskrit terms and Buddhist vocabulary (and Western-language words in the modern period). The invention of these two kana scripts expanded Japan's rich vernacular prose literature, adding to the literary spectrum fictional tales, autobiographical diaries, and other genres that were associated with female sensibility, if not outright female authorship.

Of the world's prominent premodern literary traditions, Japan's is the only one in which women dominated certain areas. An important element in the flourishing of women's literature was the rise of the Fujiwara clan. The Fujiwara managed to gain a position of great influence by inserting themselves as regents between the emperor and the court administration. Fujiwara regents married their daughters into the imperial family, hoping that their grandsons would become future emperors. To that end, Fujiwara regents often lavished attention on their daughters, securing for them an education of the highest distinction and providing them with the most talented ladies-in-waiting. Because the emperor usually had several consorts and other lower-ranking women at his disposal, such polish was a way to attract the emperor's attention and gain a competitive advantage over rivals. Some of the greatest works of Japanese literature

were written by prestigious ladies-in-waiting: Murasaki Shikibu and Sei Shōnagon served in the rival households of two Fujiwara daughters, empresses to Emperor Ichijō. The ambitions of the Fujiwara family to dominate the court and the imperial lineage created an environment in which female literary talent was instrumental in the success of the male members of the clan.

The political power of the Fujiwara clan also touched other aristocratic clans. Sugawara no Michizane, Japan's most celebrated Chinese-style poet, came from a prominent family of academy scholars. When he quickly rose in the ranks to one of the most prestigious court positions, a Fujiwara rival managed to have him demoted and exiled to distant Kyūshū, where he died in bitterness and misery. Despite these political maneuverings, the Heian Period was later considered a high point of cultural confidence and imperial rule.

MEDIEVAL JAPAN AND WARRIOR RULE

In the latter half of the twelfth century, the Heian world fell apart. The trigger was a protracted civil war between two warrior clans—the Heike and the Genji—vying for control over court and capital, a war that ultimately resulted in the establishment of a military government in Kamakura, southeast of today's Tokyo. Although the clans and the cities from where they ruled kept changing and a number of emperors attempted to reassert their imperial authority, Japan was dominated by military clans until 1868. Whereas the emperor—a symbolic figure of authority, often enjoying little actual power—remained in Kyoto with his court, military rulers, the so-called shoguns, in fact ruled the country through a feudal system of domain lords and their samurai. The civil war, which ushered

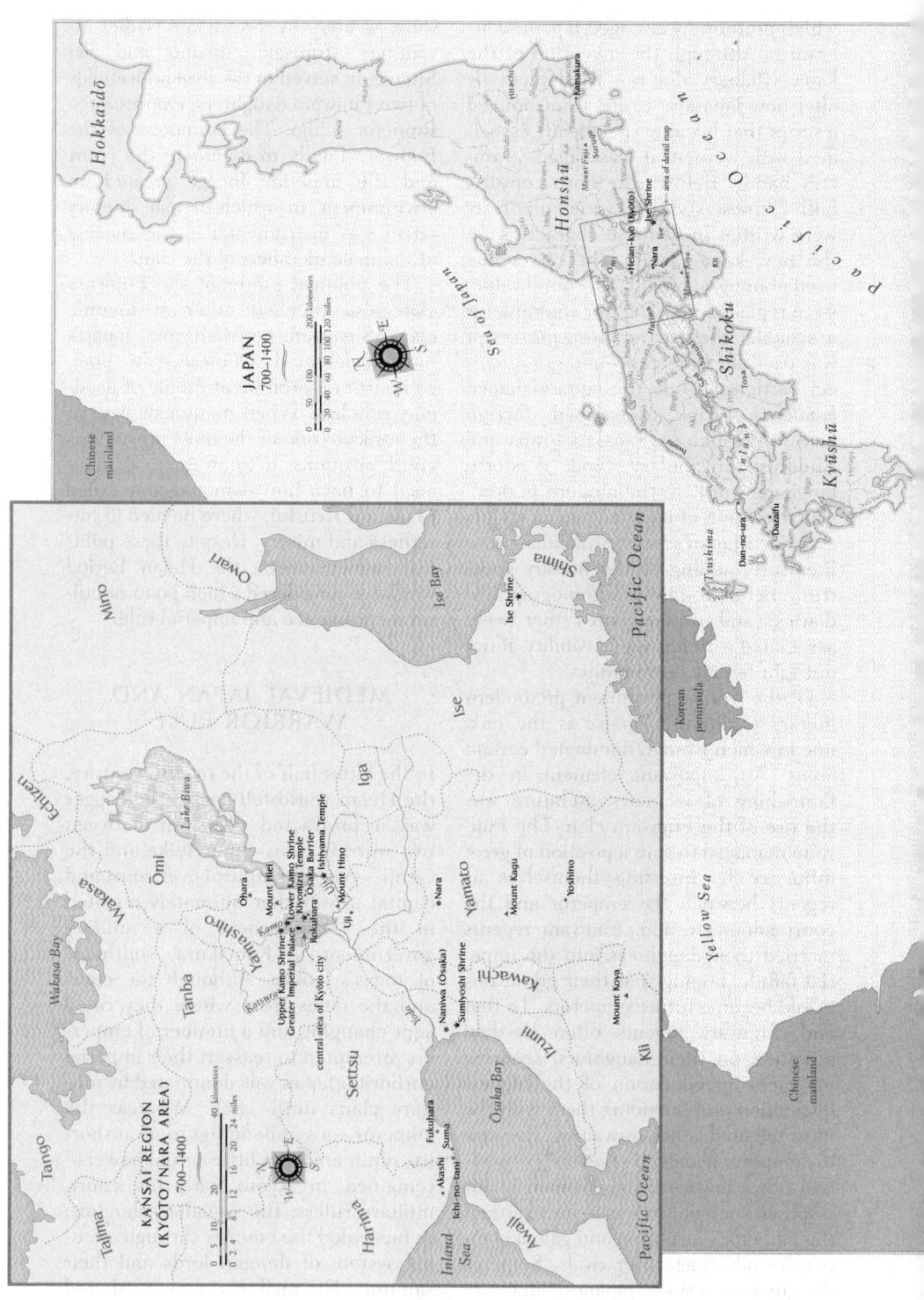

This is traditionally considered a portrait of Minamoto no Yorito (twelfth century), the founder of the Kamakura shogunate, although some scholars have argued that it represents the fourteenth-century shogun Ashikaga Tadayoshi.

own cultural validation, became generous patrons of the arts, enabling cultural and literary production to flourish in new sites beyond the imperial court. They sponsored Zen monasteries, which became centers of Chinese scholarship and a new type of Chinese-style poetry. The shoguns also patronized theater performances and Noh playwrights, including **Zeami Motokiyo**, the most important Noh dramatist, who wrote pieces that appealed to the warrior class such as *Atsumori*, a play based on the tragic death of a Heike noble.

Warrior rule also brought significant shifts in education and public values. Compared to the aristocratic Heian Period, now more people had access to basic education, and the austere warrior ethic valued honor, self-sacrifice, prowess, and loyalty to one's lord. Rather than depending largely on hereditary status within the administration of the imperial court, active involvement in government was now more haphazard and uncertain. Some responded by retreating from public life: they took Buddhist vows and settled outside the cities in the belief that Buddhist faith or artistic pursuits can address the uncertainties of life and the desire for salvation.

Although the medieval world remained attached to the values encapsulated in the works of the Heian Period, it produced a literature more strongly influenced by the warrior ethos and the needs of a broader spectrum of society. Despite the profound differences between these two periods, both classical and medieval Japan created works that laid the foundation for the Japanese literary tradition and can thus together be considered the formative age of Japanese culture.

in the medieval age in Japan, was so cataclysmic that Buddhist minstrels sang of the valiant deeds of the refined and courtly Heike—the eventual losers— and their wild and uncouth opponents from the east: the victorious Genji. Their chants were subsequently recorded in *The Tales of the Heike*. They infused what in reality had been a series of bloody wars with the Buddhist message that all power, splendor, and pride of this world must eventually fall before the law of impermanence. They endowed the Heike warriors with the elegance of the bygone Heian court to which medieval Japanese now looked back with nostalgia.

The medieval world was startlingly different from its Heian predecessor. Local shoguns, perhaps seeking their

THE MAN'YŌSHŪ
(COLLECTION OF MYRIAD LEAVES)
ca. 759

As one of Japan's two oldest extant poetry anthologies, *The Man'yōshū* stands at the beginning of Japan's literary tradition. So influential on later traditions was this collection that its title was adopted as a name for Japan's earliest period of cultural flourishing during the late seventh and eighth centuries: the "Man'yō Age." Containing more than 4,500 poems, *The Man'yōshū* is a monumental compendium of poetic knowledge. Many of its poems give expression to the most elemental human experiences: love, separation, and mourning. Others celebrate public occasions at court and are designed to inspire and entertain. Some poems describe the political order and praise the gods and the imperial institution, while others deplore the injustices of the world. The poems frequently refer to myths and legends about the origin of names, human institutions, and customs, but they also include an encyclopedic array of plant and animal names and references to the natural world. Because Japan adopted the Chinese writing system and imported the rich store of Chinese literature, the earliest Japanese poets also rested on the shoulders of some nineteen centuries of China's literate tradition. But part of the fascination of *The Man'yōshū* lies in its having taken shape during a time of bold experimentation, when Chinese and native traditions were blended—a time that also saw the first flowering of Chinese-style poetry composition in Japan.

THE MAN'YŌ AGE

During the two centuries preceding the compilation of *The Man'yōshū*, the Japanese archipelago underwent changes more profound than any others it would experience before the modern period. Within this brief span, a loose confederation of competing clans, whose wealth was drawn from the cultivation of rice and whose principal cultural accomplishment was the erection of enormous burial mounds, had remade itself into a society with a national identity, a ruling imperial family, an elaborate government administration, a complex system of religious beliefs, and a command of letters and literature. The introduction of Buddhism from Korea in the mid-sixth century changed the face of Japan, bringing along with it a culture of writing and literature, temple architecture, sophisticated art and religious sculpture, and a religious model for the protection of the state based on the imperial patronage of Buddhism. By the mid-seventh century, the future Emperor Tenji (626–671) enhanced the power of the Yamato rulers by doing away with powerful rival lineages and instituting an incisive set of reforms designed to centralize power. Tenji is said to have established a state academy for Chinese learning; the earliest Chinese-style poetry was composed during banquets at his court.

Literature depended on court culture, and until the eighth century the location of the court changed with each sovereign to avoid the pollution believed to be caused by the previous ruler's death. Tenji attempted to move away from the heartland of Yamato, where earlier capitals had been, to the north, near Lake Biwa. But after only four years the new capital of Ōmi was abandoned by his brother and successor Emperor Tenmu, who moved his court back to Yamato. Empress Jitō (r. 687–96), his wife and successor, had court poets like the Man'yōshū poet Kakinomoto no Hitomaro sing her praises, and she built the first Chinese-style capital, with a spacious gridlock pattern centered on the palace complex—the residence of the newly important "heavenly sovereign" (tennō), as the former Yamato tribal chieftain was now called.

How could Japan catch up so swiftly with contemporary developments in China? From the seventh through ninth centuries, Japan sent about twenty diplomatic missions to the Chinese court. From the Chinese perspective, Japan was paying homage and tribute to China, like many other states in the Chinese influence sphere. On its part, the young and fledgling state of Japan looked to the venerable civilization of China with great admiration. The envoys and monks who had visited China came home with a rich harvest of experience—and a treasure trove of texts. They made recommendations to the Japanese emperor on how to adapt the most recent Chinese law codes, ritual manuals, Buddhist scriptures, medicinal literature, or poetry collections to the political, religious, and aesthetic needs of the Japanese court. During this period Kyūshū, the southernmost of the four main Japanese islands, served as the gateway to China and Korea. Despite its peripheral location, the flourishing government quarters at Dazaifu frequently hosted embassies going back and forth between Japan, Korea, and China, and it was therefore nicknamed "the distant capital." The officials who served in Dazaifu were in particularly close contact with new developments, and some of the greatest Man'yōshū poets owed their inspiration to mix indigenous and Chinese traditions to the time they spent there.

THE ANTHOLOGY

The Man'yōshū was slowly aggregated over the course of the eighth century. It is an anthology of anthologies, made up of parts of earlier poetry collections that have not survived. Portions of its twenty volumes were already completed in the early eighth century, and its last poem dates from 759, but the entire collection probably reached its current form only in 785, when its final compiler, Ōtomo no Yakamochi, died. Most poems were composed between the mid-seventh and mid-eighth centuries. The poems are divided into three topical categories: "miscellaneous poems," composed during imperial excursions or on seasonal topics; "exchange poetry," songs exchanged between lovers, relatives, or friends; and "mourning poems" performed at the burial sites of sovereigns and princes or composed more generally on the subject of death, a particularly prominent topic in early Japanese poetry.

The Man'yōshū was compiled during the period when the new technology of writing was for the first time being used to produce longer texts. The anthology shows the ingenuity of early Japanese scribes in adapting the Chinese writing system to record the Japanese language. In the writing of the poems in The Man'yōshū, Chinese characters were used in three different ways: for their meaning, for their sound when read in Chinese, and for their sound when read in Japanese. The Chinese graph denoting "person," for instance, could naturally be used for its semantic value when the poet wanted to write the word "person." But it could also be used to approximate the sound of its Chinese pronunciation, which Japanese rendered jin, or nin (in modern Mandarin it is read ren). Or it could be used to represent the Japanese sound of its meaning: hito, the Japanese word for "person." For example, Hitomaro, the name of the first of the poets in the selections printed here, came to be written with the "person" character standing for the phonetic element "Hito." This system, which relied on thousands of Chinese characters working on three different levels, is daunting to master. But it allowed for a playfulness that still charms readers today and that is impossible in any language that, like English, relies solely on a phonetic alphabet.

The Man'yōshū also shows the variety of Japanese verse forms. In fact, it laid the groundwork for all later forms of poetry until haiku poetry, which came to the fore in the seventeenth century. Whereas the artistry of Chinese poetry is rooted in the dexterous use of rhyme and the tonal qualities of each syllable, the Japanese language has neither tones nor significant rhymes. Because the sound system of Japanese employs no stress accent, each syllable is pronounced with virtually equal emphasis; as a result the forms of meter based on stress that are familiar in English poetry are nonexistent in Japanese poetry. Moreover, because most Japanese syllables consist of a single vowel or consonants followed by a vowel, with only five vowel sounds, rhymes are so ubiquitous that they become meaningless to the ear. Instead, Japanese poetry depends on the rhythm created by alternating phrases of long and short syllable counts. Japan's most archaic songs employ this pattern, which originally varied from combinations of phrases with four syllables paired with those of six to alternations of five- and three-syllable phrases. By the mid-seventh century the accepted pattern became an alternation of five and seven syllables, establishing a rhythm that would prevail in Japanese poetry up to the present.

There are two main forms. The chōka, or long poem, consists of an indeterminate number of lines of alternating five- and seven-syllable phrases, culminating in a couplet of two seven-syllable phrases. The tanka, or short poem, is identical in form to the last five lines of a chōka: that is, it is a thirty-one-syllable poem arranged in lines whose syllable counts are 5, 7, 5, 7, 7. Approximately 4,200 of the 4,516 poems in the collection are tanka. Even most of the chōka have satellite tanka known as "envoys" that serve to sum up or expand on the theme of the original chōka. Although many of the chōka are the most memorable poems in the anthology, the form largely disappeared after the age of The Man'yōshū in favor of the thirty-one-syllable short verse, which became the dominant form of classical Japanese poetry.

The Man'yōshū was compiled at the imperial court and its prominent poets were literate and erudite, yet this earliest Japanese poetry anthology contains the voices of many people far from court, including simple peasants, soldiers guarding the eastern frontier against hostile tribes, and mothers seeing off their sons as they embark on dangerous missions to China. The collection transmits oral song traditions that were recorded owing to the new technology of writing, and almost two thousand poems of the collection are anonymous.

SELECTED POETS OF
THE MAN'YŌSHŪ

Attributed to Emperor Jomei (r. 629–41), a sovereign who ruled over a still largely preliterary realm, the second poem of the anthology (and the first poem included below) gives a vivid sense of the power of language that many poems in The Man'yōshū celebrate. The emperor gazes in satisfaction over his land, possibly performing the ritual of "land viewing," in which emperors would grace their territory symbolically with an imperial blessing while also asserting imperial control over it. The act of gazing draws its power from the act of naming parts of the divine landscape that the emperor sees from Mount Kagu, one of the three mountains of Yamato.

The poem by Princess Nukata (ca. 638–690s) leads us into the increasingly more literate world of Emperor Tenji's court. We know little about Nukata beyond her royal descent; she was one of those highly educated women in early Japan who distinguished themselves as poets, was at some point involved with the later Emperor Tenmu (r. 672–86), but then served his brother Emperor Tenji (r. 668–71). The occasion for the poem is courtly—an elegant competition to frame the better argument for the rival beauties of spring and autumn. Presenting a strong opinion on the topic, the poem is a famous example of the Chinese rhetoric of parallel couplets being put to new use in a Japanese vernacular poem.

Kakinomoto no Hitmaro (flourished ca. 680–700) is considered the foremost poet in *The Man'yōshū*. By the tenth century he was referred to as the "sage of poetry" and became a figure of religious veneration. He served Empress Jitō (r. 687–96), whom he accompanied on imperial excursions. He is the earliest poet whose poems have been preserved in large numbers on a wide range of topics. We know that there was a "Hitomaro poetry collection," which is now lost. Hitomaro could employ potent language of monumental simplicity: the *chōka* written at Yoshino, a numinous place situated in the mountains east of Yamato that since earliest times was associated with imperial visits, celebrates the power of the empress by comparing her to the pristine landscape. How he dealt with more ambivalent and risky topics can be seen in a poem he wrote on passing the ruins of Ōmi. Around 689 Hitomaro was in the retinue of Empress Jitō when passing

the capital where Emperor Tenji had ruled three decades earlier. Because Emperor Tenmu, Jitō's predecessor and husband, had violently deposed Tenji's son from his rule at Ōmi, the site was problematic for the Jitō court. In this poem the constancy of the place stands in ironic contrast to the disappearance of the ancient capital. The place-names express Hitomaro's ambivalence through the rhetorical device of poetic epithets (*makura kotoba*; literally, "pillow words"). These formulaic epithets, a feature of the Japanese poetic tradition, were attached to numinous place-names or the names of palaces and gods: Yamato, for example, is "sky-seen," while Tenji's cursed Ōmi is "far from heaven." Hitomaro's poetry expresses loss and transience with unique and poignant imagery. This power is especially evident in Hitomaro's many poems on death, represented in our selections by poems on the death of one of his wives and the death of a stranger, as well as Hitomaro's own deathbed poem.

The poetry of Ōtomo no Tabito (665–731) and Yamanoue no Okura (ca. 660–733) brings us into yet another world, when missions to the Chinese court had resumed after a hiatus of three decades, bringing a new wave of Chinese culture to Japan. Tabito held an official post in Dazaifu, on the southernmost island of Kyūshū, and his "Thirteen poems in praise of wine" pay homage to famous Chinese drinkers such as the bohemian "Seven Sages of the Bamboo Grove" and the recluse poet **Tao Qian**. The ironical verve with which the poet argues for the blessings of drunkenness is a poetic mode that was entirely new in Japanese poetry. Okura, possibly of Korean descent, spent several years in China as a member of a diplomatic mission. He infuses his poetry with novel themes such as reflections on moral and religious questions. A declaration of love to his children is couched as a playful jibe at the Buddha and his teaching that one should give up all worldly attachments. Using poetry to unmask injustices and failings in society was a tradition that ultimately went back to the Chinese *Classic of Poetry* (ca. 600 B.C.E.), and in his "Dialogue on Poverty" Okura puts this tradition to startling use: a plaint of a poor man is followed by one from a much poorer man, and in the end, although this "destitute man" has nothing left in his unused rice pot but spiderwebs, the village chief, whip in hand, appears to recruit him for forced government labor. The critical thrust of this poem—which might even be self-critical, given that Okura was himself a government official—is unique in early Japanese poetry.

As often happens with periods that bear the weight of representing the origins of a culture, the Man'yō Age came to be associated with notions of emotional immediacy and sincerity—with innocence, vigor, and a seeming artlessness that stood in marked contrast to the controlled, more self-conscious polish that would define Japanese poetry throughout the subsequent classical era. And yet, a careful reading of *The Man'yōshū* reveals a work of great variety and considerable complexity, in which new confidence in the artistic effects of language and the new technology of writing begin to take the place of preliterate beliefs in the incantatory power of words.

FROM THE MAN'YŌSHŪ[1] (COLLECTION OF MYRIAD LEAVES)

Emperor Jomei

A poem composed by the Emperor when he ascended Mount Kagu and viewed the land

> In Yamato
> There are crowds of mountains,
>   But our rampart
> Is Heavenly Mount Kagu:[2]
>   When I climb it   5
> And look out across the land,
>   Over the land-plain
> Smoke rises and rises;
>   Over the sea-plain
> Seagulls rise and rise.   10
>   A fair land it is,
>   Dragonfly Island,
> The land of Yamato.

---

1. All selections translated by Edwin Cranston, with the exception of Ōtomo Tabito's "Thirteen poems in praise of wine."
2. Mount Kagu was said to have descended from Heaven and settled among the hills in Yamato Province, the location of Jomei's court near the later capital of Nara. Yamato, like "Dragonfly Island," was also an ancient name for Japan.

Princess Nukata

When the Emperor [Tenji] commanded the Palace Minister, Fujiwara no Kama-tari, to match the radiance of the myriad blossoms of the spring mountains against the colors of the thousand leaves of the autumn mountains, Princess Nukata decided the question with this poem:

> When spring comes forth
> That lay in hiding all the winter through,
> The birds that did not sing
> Come back and sing to us once more;
> The flowers that did not bloom   5
> Have blossomed everywhere again.
> Yet so rife the hills
> We cannot make our way to pick,
> And so deep the grass
> We cannot pluck the flowers to see.   10
> But when on autumn hills
> We gaze upon the leaves of trees,
> It is the yellow ones
> We pluck and marvel for sheer joy.
> And the ones still green,   15
> Sighing, leave upon the boughs—
> Those are the ones I hate to lose.
> For me, it is the autumn hills.

Kakinomoto no Hitomaro

Poem composed by Kakinomoto no Hitomaro when the Sovereign went on an excursion to the palace at Yoshino[1]

> Where our Sovereign reigns,
> Ruling the earth in all tranquility,
> Under the heaven
> Of this realm she holds in sway,
> Many are the lands,   5
> But of their multitude,
> Seeing the clear pools
> That form along this mountain stream,
> She gave her heart
> To the fair land of Yoshino,   10
> And where blossoms fall
> Forever on the fields of Akizu
> She planted firm
> The mighty pillars of her palace halls.
> Now the courtiers,   15

1. A famous mountainous area that was known for its pristine and sacred beauty. Empress Jitō had a palace there, not far from the Yamato capitals, and Hitomaro visited it several times in her retinue.

Men of the palace of the hundred stones,
  Line up their boats
To row across the morning stream,
  Vie in their boats
To race upon the evening stream;   20
  And like the stream
This place shall last forever,
  Like these mountains
Ever loftier shall rise
  Beside the plunging waters   25
Of the torrent her august abode:
Long though I gaze, my eyes will never tire.

ENVOY

Long though I gaze,
Never shall I tire of Yoshino,
  Within whose stream   30
The water-moss grows smooth forever,
As I shall come to view these sights anew.

Poem composed by Kakinomoto no Hitomaro, sorely grieving with tears of blood, after his wife died

On the Karu Road,
Karu of the wing-filled sky,
  Was the village
Where she lived, my own dear wife,
  And to look at her   5
Was all I wanted in my heart:
  But had I always gone,
There were many eyes of men;
  Had I gone frequently
Others surely would have known.   10
  So, like branching vines,
After parting we would meet again,
  I thought, as confident
As one who rides in a great ship,
  And though ever yearning,   15
Kept our love secret, deep and still
  As a pool walled round with rock,
Gleaming softly like a glinting gem.
  But as the coursing sun
Goes down the sky to darkness,   20
  Or the radiant moon
Is lost to view within the clouds,
  So she who lay with me
As yielding as the seaweed to the wave
  Passed and was gone,   25

As leaves of autumn pass and are no more:
　　It was a messenger,
Azusa-wood staff in hand, who brought the news.
　　His words buzzed in my ears
Like a distant sound of *azusa*-wood bows:[1]　　30
　　Wordless, helpless,
Ignorant of all device,
　　I could not bear to stand
Listening to the mere bruit of it,
　　And so, imagining　　35
Even the thousandth portion
　　Of my longing
Might somehow be assuaged,
　　I went where she
Had always gone to look about,　　40
　　To the market of Karu,
And there I lingered listening.
　　On the hilltop
Of Unebi, called the Jewel-sash Mount,
　　The birds were singing,　　45
But I could not hear the voice I knew;
　　Nor were there any
Passing on the jewel-spear road,
　　Not even one,
Resembling her, of those that traveled there:　　50
　　In my helplessness
Crying my beloved's name,
I waved my useless sleeves.[2]

TWO TANKA

　　On the autumn hills
The trees are dense with yellow leaves—　　55
　　She has lost her way,
And I must go and search for her,
But do not know the mountain path.

　　Now that yellow leaves
Are scattering from the boughs,　　60
　　I see the messenger
With his *azusa*-wood staff,
And days with her return to mind.

1. The twanging of these bows was believed to summon spirits from the world beyond. Also, messengers were said to carry staffs of *azusa* (catalpa) wood.
2. The waving of sleeves was associated with rituals to call back the spirits of the dead.

Ōtomo no Tabito[1]

Thirteen poems in praise of wine by Lord Ōtomo Tabito, the Commander of the Dazaifu[2]

Rather than engaging
in useless worries,
it's better to down a cup
of raw wine.

Great sages of the past   5
gave the name of "sage"[3] to wine.
How well they spoke!

What the Seven Wise Men[4]
    of ancient times
wanted, it seems,   10
    was wine.
Rather than making pronouncements
    with an air of wisdom,
it's better to down the wine   15
and sob drunken tears.

What is most noble,
    beyond all words
    and beyond all deeds,
is wine.

Rather than be half-heartedly human,   20
I wish I could be a jug of wine
and be soaked in it!

How ugly!
    those men who,
        with airs of wisdom,   25
            refuse to drink wine.
Take a good look,
and they resemble apes.

How could even
a priceless treasure   30

---

1. Translated by Ian Hideo Levy.
2. Government headquarters in Kyūshū, southernmost of the main islands of Japan, an important outpost for regulating contacts with China and Korea. In Tabito's time the city was nicknamed "the distant capital."
3. So called by those who drank it secretly during a short period of prohibition in China.

4. The so-called Seven Sages of the Bamboo Grove, Daoist-inspired intellectuals in 3rd-century China who stayed aloof from the unstable political establishment by writing poetry, drinking, philosophizing, and offending common taste. Some of their poems are included in the "Hermits, Buddhists, and Daoists" cluster in this volume.

be better than a cup
    of raw wine?

How could even a gem
that glitters in the night
be as good as drinking wine   35
and cleansing the heart?

Here in this life,
on these roads of pleasure,
it is fun to sob drunken tears.

As long as I have fun   40
    in this life,
let me be an insect or a bird
    in the next.[5]

Since all who live
must finally die,   45
let's have fun
while we're still alive.

Smug and silent airs of wisdom
are still not as good
as downing a cup of wine   50
and sobbing drunken tears.

Yamanoue no Okura

Dialogue on Poverty

(THE POOR MAN)

On sodden nights
When rain comes gusting on the wind,
    On freezing nights
When snow falls mingled with the rain,
    Shivering helplessly   5
In the all-pervading cold,
    I take a lump
Of hardened salt and nibble on it
    While I sip diluted
Lees of *sake* from my cup.   10
    Clearing my throat,
Sniffling as my nose begins to run,
    Stroking the few hairs

---

5. According to Buddhism, bad actions in this life can result in rebirth into a lower state in the next.

Of my meager, scraggly beard,
   I puff myself up: 15
"What do people matter anyway,
   Aside from me?"
But still I'm cold, and so I take
   My hempen quilt
And pull it up around my shoulders. 20
   I put on every
Sleeveless homespun frock I own,
   Layer upon layer,
But the night is cold. And he,
   The man more destitute 25
Than even I, on such a night
   His father and mother
Must be starving, bodies chill and numb;
   His wife and children
Moaning softly in the dark: 30
   Yes, you—at times like these
How do you manage to go on,
How do you get through your life?

(THE DESTITUTE MAN)

Although men say
That heaven and earth are vast,
   Have they not dwindled 35
To a narrow frame for me?
   Although men say
That the sun and moon are bright,
   Have they not refused 40
To grant their shining unto me?
   Are all men thus,
   Or am I alone deprived?
   Though by rare chance
I was born into the world of men, 45
   And as any man
I toil to make my living on the land,
   Yet must I throw rags
About my shoulders, mere rotten
   Shreds of a sleeveless 50
Frock, hemp with no padding,
   Dangling like branches
Of sea pine over my bones;
   And in this crazy hut,
This flimsy, tumbling hovel, 55
   Flat on the ground
I spread my bedding of loose straw.
   By my pillowside
My father and my mother crouch,
   And at my feet 60

My wife and children; thus am I
   Surrounded by grief
And hungry, piteous cries.
   But on the hearth
No kettle sends up clouds of steam,   65
   And in our pot
A spider spins its web.
   We have forgotten
The very way of cooking rice;
   Then where we huddle,   70
Faintly whimpering like *nue* birds,[1]
   Deliberately,
As the saying goes, to cut
   The end of what
Was short enough before,   75
   There comes the voice
Of the village chief with his whip,
   Standing, shouting for me,
There outside the place we sleep.
   Does it come to this—   80
Is it such a helpless thing,
The path of man in this world?

Though we may think
Our lives are mean and frustrate
   In this world of men,   85
We cannot fly into the air,
It being so we are not birds.

Respectfully presented with deep obeisance by Yamanoue no Okura

A poem of longing for his children; with preface

Shaka Nyorai preached truly with his golden mouth that he had equal compassion for all beings, even as for Rāhula.[1] He also preached that there is no love surpassing that for a child. The greatest sage still had the feeling of love for his child. Who then of the green grass of the world would not love his children?

      When I eat melons
     My children come to my mind;
      When I eat chestnuts
     The longing is even worse.
     Where do they come from,   5

1. Ominous birds associated with loneliness and melancholy.
1. Shaka Nyorai is the Japanese name for the Buddha; Rāhula was the son he fathered while still an Indian prince, before becoming an ascetic and gaining enlightenment. Parental love is generally considered an attachment that prevents us from gaining enlightenment.

Flickering before my eyes,
    Making me helpless
Incessantly night after night,
Not letting me sleep in peace?

ENVOY

What are they to me,   10
Silver, or gold, or jewels?
    How could they ever
Equal the greater treasure
That is a child?

THE KOKINSHŪ

ca. 905

The age of *The Kokinshū*, the period around 900, was a turning point in Japanese history. Vernacular poetry gained public stature, and vernacular prose genres such as tales and diaries, which would culminate in *The Tale of Genji* and *The Pillow Book*, started to emerge. The flourishing of vernacular literature went hand in hand with the development of a new script—the kana syllabic alphabet, also called "women's hand"—which complemented the hitherto exclusive use of Chinese characters in writing Japanese. Politically, members of the Fujiwara family, which would dominate the court for the rest of the Heian Period, increasingly inserted themselves as powerful regents to the emperor, marrying their daughters into the imperial family.

Japan's earliest imperial poetry anthologies date from the early ninth century, when Emperor Saga, who was thoroughly trained in Chinese Classics and an avid poet himself, commissioned three anthologies of Chinese-style poetry.

Following this tradition, Emperor Daigo commissioned *The Kokinshū* (a short form of *Kokinwakashū*, "Collection of Ancient and Modern Waka Poems"), the first anthology of vernacular *waka* poetry. The success of this collection helped enshrine the thirty-one-syllable *waka* poem (composed in a 5-7-5-7-7 pattern) as the dominant form, intended to represent the splendor of the reigning court.

Compiled by a team headed by Ki no Tsurayuki (ca. 868–945), a leading figure of the emerging vernacular literature, *The Kokinshū* contains more than one thousand poems, complete with a vernacular Japanese and a Chinese-style preface, and is arranged by topical categories in twenty books. The books on the four seasons and on "love" dominate the collection, but there are also books on topics such as "parting," "travel," "mourning," and "puns and wordplay."

The anthology and its books are arranged according to principles of association and progression into an overarching narrative that far exceeds the meaning of the individual poems. Sequences of poems with subtle variations on the same topic are the building blocks that make the anthology into a coherent text of its own. For example, the books on the seasons and on love lend themselves to a natural cycle of beginning, high point, and end or the familiar pattern of first glimpse of the beloved, courtship, passion, marriage (or liaison), disillusion, separation, loneliness, and despair. The compilers' ability to fashion a narrative out of poems composed by many different authors on different occasions is often stunning and would be much imitated. Though the principles of association and progression invented by the compilers of *The Kokinshū* would become increasingly sophisticated in later poetry anthologies, these structural devices are already fully realized in the first imperial anthology, demonstrating that one of the world's most compressed genres can transcend the apparent limitations of its form.

In contrast to collections such as *The Man'yōshū*—Japan's earliest poetry anthology, with its tones of archaic grandeur and simplicity best exemplified by **Hitomaro**'s writings—*The Kokinshū* values poetic elegance, intellectual twists, and erudite refinement. The contradiction between empirical evidence and conventional knowledge generates many of the clever conceits of *Kokinshū* poetry: a typical strategy is "elegant confusion," as when early plum blossoms at the beginning of spring are mistakenly interpreted as late snowflakes, or vice versa, and the discovery of the error—or the uncertainty about the real nature of white stuff on plum

tree branches—becomes the main point of the poem. In addition to daring visual metaphor, the *waka* poetry in *The Kokinshū* relies on a variety of rhetorical figures that drastically condense poetic expression: "poetic pillows" (*utamakura*) are poetically evocative place-names, which in the space of a few syllables summon up a host of associations. An entire poetic geography of the Japanese archipelago developed that was based on these resonant names. "Pivot words" (*kakekotoba*) are phonetic puns, in which a sequence of syllables has two different meanings. Aided by the new phonetic kana syllabary, plays on double meaning apparently increased greatly during the Kokinshū age, showing a heightened awareness of the disjunction between phonetic sound and written character.

At least as influential as its poetry was Ki no Tsurayuki's "Japanese Preface" to *The Kokinshū* (also called "Kana Preface," because it used the vernacular syllabary). It is the canonical statement on the principles of *waka* poetry, grounding it in a universal instinct for song. Although Ki no Tsurayuki's vision of poetry ultimately relied on the Chinese *Classic of Poetry*, he argued against the traditions of arduous training and sophisticated craftsmanship that characterized traditional Chinese-style poetry, favoring instead a spontaneous expression of human imagination. Originally conceived fairly narrowly as a polemic against the high status of Chinese-style poetry and an attempt to elevate vernacular *waka* poetry to a courtly art, Tsurayuki's statement became so influential in Japanese culture that it came to inform broad assumptions about how humans are moved to create works of art.

THE KOKINSHŪ

From The Japanese Preface[1]

by Ki no Tsurayuki

The seeds of Japanese poetry lie in the human heart and grow into leaves of ten thousand words. Many things happen to the people of this world, and all that they think and feel is given expression in description of things they see and hear. When we hear the warbling of the mountain thrush in the blossoms or the voice of the frog in the water, we know every living being has its song.

It is poetry which, without effort, moves heaven and earth, stirs the feelings of the invisible gods and spirits, smooths the relations of men and women, and calms the hearts of fierce warriors.

Such songs came into being when heaven and earth first appeared. However, legend has it that in the broad heavens they began with Princess Shitateru, and on earth with the song of Susano-o no mikoto.[2]

In the age of the awesome gods, songs did not have a fixed number of syllables and were difficult to understand because the poets expressed themselves directly, without polish. By the time of the age of humans, beginning with Susano-o no mikoto, poems of thirty-one syllables were composed.[3] Since then many poems have been composed when people were attracted by the blossoms or admired the birds, when they were moved by the haze or regretted the swift passage of the dew, and both inspiration and forms of expression have become diverse. As a long journey to distant places begins with one step and is completed after many months and years, and as a high mountain is created by the accumulation of dust and mire at its skirts and gradually reaches the trailing clouds of the heavens, so too has poetry been.

* * *

Nowadays because people are concerned with gorgeous appearances and their hearts admire ostentation, insipid poems, short-lived poems have appeared. Poetry has become a sunken log submerged unknown to others in the homes of lovers. Poems are not things to bring out in public places as openly as the opening blossoms of the pampas grass.

Japanese poetry ought not to be thus. Consider its origins: Whenever there were blossoms at dawn in spring or moonlit autumn nights, the generations of sovereigns of old summoned their attendants to compose poetry inspired by these beauties. Sometimes the poet wandered through untraveled places to use the image of the blossoms; sometimes he went to dark unknown wilderness lands to write of the moon. The sovereigns surely read these and distinguished the wise from the foolish.

* * *

1. Translated by Laurel Rasplica Rodd.
2. The naughty younger brother of Amaterasu, the sun goddess who is the ancestor of the Japanese emperors. "Princess Shitateru": an earthly deity who composed a dirge after her husband was killed.

3. The earliest historical chronicles of Japan credit the god Susano-o with the composition of the first *waka* poem ("poems of thirty-one syllables"), in praise of a new palace he had constructed for his wife.

This poetry has been handed down since days of old, but it is especially since the Nara period that it has spread far and wide. In that era the sovereign must truly have appreciated poetry, and during his reign Kakinomoto no Hitomaro of the Senior Third Rank was a sage of poetry.[4] Thus ruler and subjects must have been one.

On an autumn evening the crimson leaves floating on the Tatsuta River looked like brocade to the sovereign, and on a spring morning the cherry blossoms on Yoshino Mountain reminded Hitomaro of clouds.[5] There was also a man named Yamabe no Akahito. He was an outstanding and superior poet. Hitomaro cannot be ranked above Akahito, nor Akahito ranked below Hitomaro.

Aside from these, other great poets were heard, as generations succeeded each other like the segments of the black bamboo in a line unbroken as a twisted thread. Earlier poems were gathered in a collection called the *Man'yōshū*.

After that there were one or two poets who knew the ancient songs and understood the heart of poetry. However, each had strengths and weaknesses. Since that time more than one hundred years and ten generations have gone by. Of those who composed during this century, few have known the ancient songs and understood poetry. I would like to give some examples, but I will exclude those of poets of high rank and office, whom I cannot criticize lightly.

Among the others, one of the best known of recent times[6] was Archbishop Henjō, whose style is good but who lacks sincerity. His poetry is like a painting of a woman which stirs one's heart in vain.

> along slender threads
> of delicate twisted green
> translucent dewdrops
> strung as small fragile jewels—
> new willow webs in spring

* * *

Ariwara no Narihira has too much feeling, too few words. His poems are like withered flowers, faded but with a lingering fragrance.

> is this not that moon—
> is this spring not that spring we
> shared so long ago—
> it seems that I alone am
> unaltered from what was then

* * *

4. Hitomaro (flourished ca. 680–700) is one of the most famous poets in *The Man'yōshū* (*Collection of Myriad Leaves*), an 8th-century compilation of this earliest flourishing of poetry.
5. The Tatsuta River was associated in poetry with colorful autumn foliage; Yoshino was famous for its scenic beauty and its cherry blossoms.
6. This section offers judgments of the so-called Six Poetry Immortals, six famous poets who lived closer to Ki no Tsurayuki's time.

Fun'ya no Yashuhide used words skillfully but the expression does not suit the contents. His poetry is like a tradesman attired in elegant robes.

> as soon as the gales
> begin to rage   the trees and
>   field grass bend before
> them   no wonder they call this
> wind from the mountains Tempest

* * *

The poetry of Priest Kisen of Mount Uji is vague, and the logic does not run smoothly from beginning to end. Reading his poems is like looking at the autumn moon only to have it obscured by the clouds of dawn. Since few of his poems are known, we cannot make comparisons and come to understand them.

> this is how I live
> in my retreat southwest of
>   the capital   though
> men call Uji Mountain[7] a
> reminder of worldly sorrow

Ono no Komachi is a modern Princess Sotōri.[8] She is full of sentiment but weak. Her poetry is like a noble lady who is suffering from a sickness, but the weakness is natural to a woman's poetry.

* * *

> I have sunk to the
> bottom   and like the rootless
>   shifting water weeds
> should the currents summon me
> I too would drift away

* * *

Ōtomo no Kuronushi's songs are rustic in form; they are like a mountaineer with a bundle of firewood on his back resting in the shade of the blossoms.

* * *

> well now   I'll go to
> Mirror Mountain   gaze upon
>   it and then travel
> on   for I wonder if I've
> aged in all these years I've lived

---

7. The name puns on "grief"; the mountain is generally associated with gloom.
8. The consort of a 5th-century emperor. Ono no Komachi is the best woman poet in *The Kokinshū*.

There are others as well who are known, as numerous as the leaves of the trees of the forest, as widespread as the ivy which crawls in the fields, but they think anything they compose is poetry and do not know what poems are.

In the reign of the present sovereign[9] the four seasons have unfolded nine times. The boundless waves of his benevolence flow beyond the boundaries of the Eight Islands;[1] his broad compassion provides a deeper shade than Mount Tsukuba. During his moments of leisure from the multifarious affairs of state, he does not neglect other matters: mindful of the past and desiring to revive the ancient ways, he wishes to examine them and to pass them on to future generations. On the eighteenth day of the Fourth Month of Engi 5 (905), he commanded Ki no Tomonori, Senior Secretary of the Ministry of Private Affairs, Ki no Tsurayuki, Chief of the Documents Division, Ōshikōchi no Mitsune, Former Junior Clerk of Kai Province, and Mibu no Tadamine, functionary in the Headquarters of the Palace Guards, Right Division, to present to him old poems not included in the *Man'yōshū* as well as our own. We have chosen poems on wearing garlands of plum blossoms, poems on hearing the nightingale, on breaking off branches of autumn leaves, on seeing the snow.[2] We have also chosen poems on wishing one's lord the lifespan of the crane and tortoise, on congratulating someone, on yearning for one's wife when one sees the autumn bush clover or the grasses of summer, on offering prayer strips on Ōsaka Hill, on seeing someone off on a journey, and on miscellaneous topics that cannot be categorized by season. These thousand poems in twenty books are called the *Kokinwakashū*. These collected poems will last as long as the waters flowing at the foot of the mountains; they are numerous as the grains of sand on the shore. There will be no complaints that they are like the shallows of the Asuka River;[3] they will give pleasure until the pebbles grow into boulders.

Now then, our poems have not the fragrance of spring blossoms, but a vain reputation lingers, long as the endless autumn night. Thus we fear the ear of the world and lack confidence in the heart of our poetry, but, whether going or staying like the trailing clouds, whether sleeping or rising like the belling deer, we rejoice that we were born in this generation and that we were able to live in the era when this event occurred.

Hitomaro is dead, but poetry is still with us. Times may change, joy and sorrow come and go, but the words of these poems are eternal, endless as the green willow threads, unchanging as the needles of the pine, long as the trailing vines, permanent as birds' tracks.[4] Those who know poetry and who understand the heart of things will look up to the old and admire the new as they look up to and admire the moon in the broad sky.

9. Emperor Daigo (r. 897–930).
1. The major islands of Japan.
2. The preface here alludes to the different books of *The Kokinshū*, starting with the books on the four seasons.

3. A river famous for its shallowness (often used as an image of shallow love).
4. Or "handwriting," referring to the physical manuscript of *The Kokinshū*.

From Book 1. Spring

1[1]

Composed on a day when spring arrived within the old year

Spring has come
before the year's turning:
should I speak now
of the old year
or call this the new year?[2]

Ariwara no Motokata

2

Composed on "the first day of spring"

Waters I cupped my
hands to drink, wetting
my sleeves, still frozen:
might this first day of
spring's wind thaw them?

Ki no Tsurayuki

3

Topic unknown

Where are the promised
mists of spring?
In Yoshino,[3] fair hills
of Yoshino, snow
falling still.

Anonymous

---

1. Poems 1–259 are translated by Lewis Cook; poems 495–500 and 553–554 are translated by Edwin Cranston.
2. This poem, which opens *The Kokinshū* and its six books of poetry on the seasons (two books each for spring and autumn, one book each for summer and winter), plays on the discrepancy between the official lunar and the unofficial solar calendars. According to the solar calendar, the first day of spring always occurs in early February; in the lunar calendar, the new year begins in January or February. Thus the (lunar) first day of spring sometimes preceded (solar) New Year's Day. Some commentators see this poem as alluding to the "old and new" poetry announced in the title of *The Kokinshū.*
3. A poetic place-name (*utamakura*), which by the time of *The Kokinshū* had become associated with heavy snowfall, cherry blossoms, and reclusion. Hitomaro, the leading *Man'yōshū* poet, had praised its beauties and imperial landscape when visiting in the retinue of an empress (see p. 1359).

From Book 2. Spring

69

Topic unknown

On hills where mists of spring
trail, glowing faintly,
do the flowers' fading
colors foretell
their fall?[4]

                    Anonymous

70

Topic unknown

If saying "stay!"
would stop their
falling, could I hold
these blossoms
more dear?

                    Anonymous

71

Topic unknown

It's their falling without regret
I admire—
Cherry blossoms:
a world of sadness
if they'd stayed.

                    Anonymous

---

4. This poem opens the second book of spring, marking the middle of the season. It is the first of a sequence of twenty-one poems on the topic "falling cherry blossoms."

72

Topic unknown

I seem bound to sleep
in this village tonight:
led astray by falling
blossoms, I've forgotten
my way home.

Anonymous

73

Topic unknown

Are they not like
this fleeting world?[5]
Cherry blossoms:
no sooner do they flower
than they fall.

Anonymous

From Book 6. Autumn

256

On seeing autumn leaves on Otowa Mountain while visiting Ishiyama

From that first day
the winds of autumn sounded,
the tips of trees on
Otowa Mountain's[6] peak
were turning color.

Ki no Tsurayuki

257

Composed for a poetry contest at the house of Prince Koresada

White dew
all of a single color:
how then does it dye

---

5. Literally, "world of a cicada's discarded shell."
6. A pun on *oto*, "sound," exemplifying the rhetorical device of "pivot words" (*kakekotoba*), or puns, which abound in *The Kokinshū*. The following four poems are from a 19-poem sequence on "autumn leaves."

the leaves of autumn
a thousand different shades?[7]

> Fujiwara no Toshiyuki

258

Composed for a poetry contest at the house of Prince Koresada

As the dew of autumn's night
settles in place,
will the falling tears
of wild geese
dye the fields yet deeper?

> Mibu no Tadamine

259

Topic unknown

Surely the autumn dew
must have its varied ways
to turn the mountain's leaves
so many shades
of color.

> Anonymous

From Book 11. Love

495

Topic unknown

Memories revive
As on evergreen mountains
  Wild azalea flares:
Unspoken love burns stronger
For the silence where it dwells.

> Anonymous

---

7. The assumption here and in 258 and 259 is that dew causes the leaves to change color.

496

Topic unknown

Loving secretly
Is too hard for me to bear:
    I shall let my heart
Reveal to him its color,
The blush of the safflower.

Anonymous

497

Topic unknown

On the autumn fields,
Mingled with the plumegrass,
    Blossoming flowers—
Colors flaunted openly, I'll love;
If not, there is no way to meet.

Anonymous

498

Topic unknown

The warbler[8] singing
On the very topmost branch
    Of my garden plum:
Even such a cry as that
Will break forth from my yearning!

Anonymous

499

Topic unknown

Can the young cuckoo[9]
Singing in the footsore hills
    Be as sad as I,
Yearning for you all night long,
Unable to sleep a wink?

Anonymous

---

8. A spring bird.

9. A bird associated with early summer.

500

Topic unknown

The mosquito flares,[1]
Sputtering, fill the house with smoke,
    Now that summer's here—
How long must they still smolder on,
These fires in my stifled heart?

                              Anonymous

553

Topic unknown

Once I fell asleep
In a momentary doze, and saw
    Him for whom I long,
Since when I have begun to place
My trust in the things called dreams.

                              Ono no Komachi

554

Topic unknown

When pressed with longing
Fiercely through desire's hour
    In the bead-black dark,
I slip off the robe of night
To lie with it inside out.[2]

                              Ono no Komachi

1. One of the few annoying items of everyday life accepted in the refined vocabulary of the courtly *waka* tradition.

2. Wearing nightclothes inside out was believed to bring a desired dream. "Bead-black": a poetic epithet (*makurakotoba*) for night.

MURASAKI SHIKIBU

ca. 978–ca. 1014

The Tale of Genji is the undisputed masterpiece of Japanese prose and often considered the first great novel in the history of world literature. That it was written by an eleventh-century court lady is even more extraordinary. Virginia Woolf, who reviewed its first complete English translation—the masterful rendering by Arthur Waley—in 1925, responded to Murasaki Shikibu with the lonely empathy of an early twentieth-century woman author: "There was Sappho and a little group of women all writing poetry on a Greek island six hundred years before the birth of Christ. They fall silent. Then about the year 1000 we find a certain court lady, the Lady Murasaki, writing a very long and beautiful novel in Japan." Although originally written for a narrow circle of court aristocrats in Kyoto, *The Tale of Genji* had unparalleled success in engaging generations of passionate readers and it is now uniquely representative of Japanese literature. Vast in scale and peopled by hundreds of characters, this thousand-page tale depicts the lives and loves of a former prince—Genji—who dies two-thirds through the book, and the lives and loves of his descendants. On a deeper level, *The Tale of Genji* is about the human ability to be touched by other people and by the outside world, about the tantalizing line between love and lust, and about the vulnerability of women in a male-dominated world. It celebrates the power of poetry, music, and dance to shape society and give depth to human life. Revered for its psychological insight, it captures a world that, however remote from our own, has always retained the sharp authenticity of real life. At its most basic, it chronicles the struggle with the most fundamental of human experiences: love, art, and death.

LIFE AND TIMES

The actual name of the author of *The Tale of Genji* is unknown. It was common at the time to name women after the office held by a male relative. "Shikibu" refers to the appointment her father held at the "Ministry of Ceremonial." The nickname "Murasaki" ("lavender," "purple") is based either on the heroine Murasaki in *The Tale of Genji* or on the color of wisteria, the emblematic flower of her clan. Murasaki Shikibu's ancestors had belonged to a branch of the Fujiwara ("wisteria fields") clan, which had managed since the tenth century to dominate the throne by ruling as regents on behalf of young emperors and marrying their daughters into the imperial family. Despite Murasaki's distinguished ancestry, her family eventually declined to the level of provincial governors. Her father had a mediocre career in the court administration, although he was known as a poet and scholar of Chinese literature. Through him Murasaki got a glimpse of life outside the Heian capital of Kyoto, when in her teens she accompanied him for a couple of years on one of his appointments in the provinces. After returning to the capital, Murasaki was briefly married to the much older Fujiwara no Nobutaka, a middle-ranking aristocrat. When he died in 1001, Murasaki was in her early twenties, now a widow with a two-year-old daughter. Murasaki probably started writing *The Tale of Genji* after the death of her husband. These early chapters won her a growing reputation and led to an invitation from Empress Shōshi around 1006 to serve as lady-in-waiting at the imperial court, where she remained until her death around 1014.

The flourishing of female literature during this time was in no small part a result of the efforts of the Fujiwara regents to fill the ranks of their daughters' entourage with the most talented and educated women. Shōshi was one of the consorts of Emperor Ichijō, and she was far more successful than her rival, Empress Teishi, whom Sei Shōnagon, the author of *The Pillow Book*, served. She bore Ichijō two emperors and her fortunes reflected the power of her father, the regent Fujiwara no Michinaga. Employment as ladies-in-waiting gave Heian women writers the financial support and leisure to produce literature that commanded the attention of society in the capital.

Murasaki had broad learning in vernacular literature—*waka* poetry, women's diaries, and tales—but also acquired a profound understanding of the Chinese Classics and Chinese poetry. While aristocratic women at the time were often knowledgeable in Chinese literature, they did not produce Chinese-style texts in the authoritative idiom of the male court bureaucracy and the Buddhist clergy, writing instead in the vernacular language. In her diary Murasaki confesses.

> When my brother, the Secretary at the Ministry of Ceremonial, was young and studied the Chinese classics, I used to listen to him and became unusually good at understanding those passages which he found too difficult to grasp. My father, a most learned man, was always lamenting this fact: "Just my luck!" he would say. "What a pity that she was not born a man!"

A father's admiration for his daughter's academic brilliance cannot conceal the fact that in Heian society, Chinese learning was truly valuable only for men.

In Heian Japan men and women were strictly segregated and women's lives were extremely circumscribed. The role of a lady was to marry and bear children; and if she came from a suitably good family, she was apt to find herself a pawn in the marriage politics of the imperial court. A noblewoman's days were spent behind curtains and screens, hidden from the world (or from the male world). A man's first marriage often took place when he was still a boy of twelve or thirteen; women were even a year or two younger. Because of the ages of the spouses and the likelihood of the first marriage in particular being a political and economic arrangement, both husband and wife tended eventually to seek love elsewhere, although only men could have multiple marriage partners. The purpose of marriage was procreation, continuation of the family line, and the creation of advantageous alliances with other families. Ordinarily a man's several wives lived in different establishments. His first wife would typically remain in her parents' house. Initially, the young husband might take up residence there or merely visit. Sometimes her parents would furnish the newlyweds with a house of their own, though doing so was less common when the couple married at a young age and the maternal grandparents would be expected to assume many of the child-rearing duties. If in time a man took a second or third wife, he would usually live with his first (and main) wife and commute between the separate residences. It was in this world of gender asymmetries that Heian women's literature thrived. At the same time, Heian women used the status they had as female authors to voice how women suffered from their dependence on their husbands, lovers, and patrons.

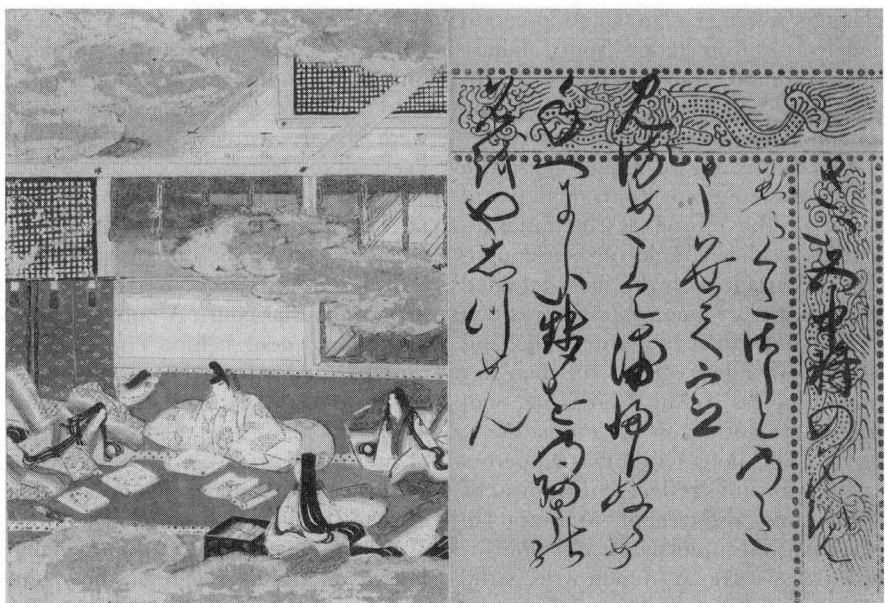

An early sixteenth-century illustrated calligraphic excerpt from chapter 17, "The picture contest," of *The Tale of Genji*. The artwork is attributed to Reizei Tamehiro.

THE TALE OF GENJI

Although Genji's women play an important role in the tale, it is named after its male protagonist. He is the son of the reigning emperor and his beloved but low-ranking consort, Kiritsubo ("Paulownia Pavilion"). Her favor with the emperor makes her a target of vicious rivalry among the emperor's higher-ranking women, such as the Kokiden Consort, his principal wife. Genji's mother dies in despair when he is in his third year, and his father is eventually forced to remove him from the imperial line to protect him from the ill will of his other consorts. He makes the boy a commoner, bestowing the family name "Genji" on him. As Genji grows up his brilliance elicits sighs of admiration wherever he appears, and he is soon being called "the Radiant Prince." The emperor dotes on his remarkable son, who reminds him all the more painfully of his former favorite consort. He eventually finds solace in the young Fujitsubo, daughter of a previous emperor, who resembles Kiritsubo but is of highest rank.

With even more determination than his father, Genji embarks on a search for women who can replace the mother he barely remembers. His fatal attraction to Fujitsubo leads to one of his greatest transgressions. Fujitsubo gives birth to a son who later becomes emperor and whom everybody believes to be the son of Genji's father. Later, Fujitsubo's niece Murasaki becomes Genji's great love. Sometimes Genji's escapades with women of very high rank lead to disaster: after his affair with Oborozukiyo, who is the younger sister of his father's principal wife, the Kokiden consort (and thus his mortal enemy), he is forced into exile to the rustic countryside. Sometimes lack of attention, rather than sexual transgression, brings about disaster: Genji's failure to respond to the jealous passion of the lady at Rokujō, widow of a former crown prince, leads inexorably to the death of some of the most important women in his life.

Genji is charismatic, irresistible, and tantalizingly flawed. Charming and handsome, brilliant and ardent, rakish but faithful in his own way (unlike other men, he never abandons any woman he has loved), he is an extraordinary literary figure. Readers may hate Genji or adore him, but we can hardly deny that his creator has fashioned a character who is both larger than life and believably human.

The fifty-four-chapter tale falls broadly into three parts. The first thirty-three chapters describe Genji's career from his birth through his exile and his eventual glorious return to the capital. They focus on the various women with whom he becomes involved in his younger years. Chapters 34 through 41 treat the darker years of Genji's life, concluding with the death of Murasaki and Genji's own death. The remaining thirteen chapters, not featured here, move away from the elegant capital to the countryside. Lacking the radiance of Genji's presence, the world is populated with compromised protagonists and darker entanglements with life's sufferings.

Though *The Tale of Genji* is a coherent whole, it can also be appreciated as a collection of interrelated episodes revolving around Genji, his women, and their descendants, in part because of how the work was composed. Since Murasaki wrote it over a span of a dozen years, probably starting with what eventually became chapter 5 ("Little Purple Gromwell," included here), the tale developed in thematic sequences. It first circulated in various shorter installments—single chapters or sequences—among Kyoto's court aristocracy. The sequences show how Murasaki's protagonists, interests, and narrative techniques evolved over time. The "Broom Cypress Sequence," for

example, which includes chapters 2, 4, 6, and sequels in chapters 15 and 16, was apparently inserted later. Whereas the core chapters of the tale's first part show Genji dangerously in love with high-ranking women who were close to the emperor, in the "Broom Cypress Sequence" he pursues women of the middle and lower aristocracy. The key prelude to Genji's later conquests occurs in chapter 2 ("Broom Cypress," included here), when the seventeen-year-old Genji and his friends while away a rainy night in his quarters at the palace debating what makes the perfect woman. In the process, the young men trade stories of their experiences with women. Although Genji dozes off now and then, he takes away the lessons from that night and applies them to his pursuit of women in the following chapters of the sequence.

In *The Tale of Genji* Murasaki sometimes relied on conventions from earlier tales, so-called *monogatari*. A typical plot element was an illustrious aristocrat's discovery of a heroine in humble circumstances. This describes the situation of Genji's mother, and also many of Genji's exploits. Liaisons between high-ranking men and humble women were far more popular in literary romances than in Heian reality. A real-life Genji would probably never have married somebody like the character Murasaki, orphaned and without appropriate family background. But in romantic tales, the total infatuation of an aristocrat with a lower-ranking woman was an expression of passion and emotional depth; for female readers it perhaps even inspired hope that they might find salvation and social mobility through the power of romantic love. Because of the social gap between Genji and his lovers, the tale's low-ranking heroines spend considerable energy agonizing about their lowly position and trying to cope with social marginalization. Another typical plot element of earlier tales is the pursuit of love in unexpected or forbidden places. There is no lack of such episodes in Genji's career; he strongly resembles the real-life Ariwara no Narihira (825–880), the epitome of a romantic lover and hero of the earlier *monogatari The Tales of Ise*.

The Tale of Genji displays the remarkable blend of Murasaki's talents. She was a gifted poet, inserting several hundred poems in the tale. Where modern readers might expect Genji and his lovers to exchange love letters in prose, Murasaki has them communicate through elaborate poems. Indeed, most of the protagonists are named after imagery from those poems, and until the early modern period readers studied *The Tale of Genji* to enhance their skills in poetry composition. Also, Murasaki was a perceptive reader of women's confessional diaries and a masterful prose stylist, relying on the nuanced expression of interiority developed by women diarists before her time for the intimate psychological portrayal of *The Tale of Genji*'s fictional protagonists. Lastly, her expertise in Chinese literature inspired her to enrich recurring motifs with resonant references to Chinese poetry. In the first chapter she evokes "**The Song of Lasting Regret**" by the Tang poet **Bo Juyi**, which tells of the tragic love between a Chinese emperor and a low-ranking concubine, as a poignant analogy to the fate of Genji's mother; like a motif in music, Bo Juyi's gripping ballad keeps reappearing throughout the novel in various guises.

In its day *The Tale of Genji* was just another vernacular tale that, in the estimation of the learned elite, stood far below the Chinese-style writing by Heian men. Chinese learning—a cov-

eted quality for a male aristocrat—was a dubious asset for a court lady. In her diary Murasaki tells how angry she was when somebody teased her for her Chinese learning and gave her the nickname "Our Lady of the Chronicles." But in truth this title should have pleased her: in "Fireflies" (chapter 25, included here) Genji discusses the worth of romantic tales with Tamakazura, his best friend's daughter, and she inspires him to argue that fiction is in some way more truthful than official Chinese-style histories such as the venerable *Chronicles of Japan*: vernacular tales tell the real stories that are left out of the Chinese-style histories.

Whether meant as a playful jibe or a serious polemical claim, Murasaki's bold comparison of popular vernacular tales to canonical Chinese-style histories facilitated the canonization of *The Tale of Genji* in later ages. *The Tale of Genji* became the subject of erudite scholastic commentaries; it inspired screen paintings and illustrated hand scrolls, Noh and puppet plays, poetry handbooks, parodies, and, more recently, woodblock prints, films, and manga (comic book) versions. This "Genji cult" is in part a result of the late nineteenth-century promotion of *The Tale of Genji* from the status of a brilliant masterpiece to that of a modern national classic said to encapsulate Japanese sensibility. But leaving politics aside, one of the many reasons for *The Tale of Genji*'s timeless appeal is that it is a grand meditation on the emotional and psychological dynamics of love. It seduces the reader with its extensive depictions of courtship and passion, but its ultimate theme is the deeper longing to find a common language through which to connect with another person.

Main Characters in *The Tale of Genji*

AKASHI LADY, *daughter of the Akashi Novice; meets Genji during his exile and bears him a daughter who eventually becomes empress*

AKASHI NOVITIATE, *former governor of Harima, father of the Akashi Lady*

ASSISTANT HANDMAID, *Genji's aged and coquettish admirer*

BISHOP, *Murasaki's great-uncle, a distinguished Buddhist cleric*

EMPEROR SUZAKU, *Genji's elder half brother, son of the Kokiden Consort; succeeds the Kiritsubo Emperor on the throne*

EMPEROR REIZEI, *son of Genji and Fujitsubo, but believed to be the son of Genji's father; succeeds Suzaku as emperor*

FUJITSUBO, *daughter of an earlier emperor; Genji's father's empress with whom Genji has a son, the later Emperor Reizei*

GENJI'S WIFE, *daughter of the Minister of the Left; marries Genji at age 16, when Genji is 12*

KIRITSUBO EMPEROR, *Genji's father*

KOKIDEN CONSORT, *daughter of the Minister of the Right; mother of Emperor Suzaku and archenemy of Genji*

KOREMITSU, *Genji's foster brother and confidant*

LADY AT ROKUJŌ, *daughter of a Minister and widow of a deceased Heir Apparent; Genji's neglect of her has fatal consequences*

MINISTER OF THE LEFT, *father of Genji's wife and of Tō no Chūjō, Genji's friend*

MINISTER OF THE RIGHT, *father of the Kokiden Consort and Oborozukiyo*

MURASAKI, *unrecognized daughter of Prince Hyōbu and niece of Fujitsubo; raised by Genji, who later marries her*

OBOROZUKIYO, *daughter of the Minister of the Right and younger sister of Kokiden; enters the service of Suzaku; Genji's affair with her leads to his exile*

PRINCE HYŌBU, *Fujitsubo's elder brother, Murasaki's father*

TAMAKAZURA, *daughter of Tō no Chūjō by a low-ranking mistress; discovered by Genji, who installs her into his mansion and passes her off as his own daughter*

TŌ NO CHŪJŌ, *son of the Minister of the Left and brother of Aoi; his name is the title of a post he occupies*

From The Tale of Genji[1]

FROM CHAPTER I

Kiritsubo

The Lady of the Paulownia-Courtyard Chambers

In whose reign was it that a woman of rather undistinguished lineage captured the heart of the Emperor and enjoyed his favor above all the other imperial wives and concubines? From the very moment she began serving His Majesty certain ladies at the court whose high noble status gave them a sense of vain entitlement despised and reviled her as an unworthy upstart. The situation was

1. Translated by Dennis Washburn. Except as indicated, all notes are his. Murasaki Shikibu often alludes directly to works of poetry (both Chinese and Japanese), fiction, history, and court records. Most of these allusions are to Japanese poems compiled in imperial anthologies during the 10th and early 11th centuries. Notes throughout this selection cite the source of only some of these allusions.

even more vexing for ladies of lower rank, since they knew His Majesty would never bestow such affectionate attention on them. As a result, the mere presence of the woman at morning rites or evening ceremonies seemed to provoke hostile reactions among her rivals; and the anxiety she suffered as a consequence of these ever-increasing displays of jealousy was such a heavy burden that gradually her health began to fail.

His Majesty could see how forlorn she was, how often she returned to her family home. He felt sorry for her and wanted to help; and though he could scarcely afford to ignore the admonitions of his advisers, his behavior eventually became the subject of palace gossip. Ranking courtiers and attendants found it difficult to stand by and observe the troubling situation, which they viewed as deplorable. They were fully aware that a similarly ill-fated romance had thrown the Chinese state into chaos.[2] Feelings of concern and consternation gradually spread through the court, since it appeared that nothing could be done. Many considered the relationship scandalous, so much so that some openly referred to the example of the Prized Consort Yang. The only thing that made it possible for the woman to continue to serve was the Emperor's gracious devotion.

The woman's father had risen to the third rank as a Major Counselor before he died. Her mother, the principal wife of her father, was a woman of old-fashioned upbringing and character who was well trained in the customs and rituals of the court. Thus, the reputation of her family was in no way inferior and did not suffer by comparison with the brilliance of the highest nobility. Unfortunately, her family had no patrons who could provide political support, and after her father's death she had no one she could trust. She thus found herself at the mercy of events and with uncertain prospects.

Was she not, then, bound to the Emperor by some deep love from a previous life? For in spite of her travails, she eventually bore him a prince—a pure radiant gem like nothing of this world. Following the child's birth His Majesty had to wait impatiently, wondering when he would finally be allowed to see the boy. As soon as it could be ritually sanctioned, he had the infant brought from the home of the woman's mother, where the birth had taken place,[3] and the instant he gazed on the child's countenance he recognized a rare beauty.

Now as it so happened the Crown Prince[4] had been born three years earlier to the Kokiden Consort, who was the daughter of the Minister of the Right. As the unquestioned heir to the throne the boy had many supporters and the courtiers all treated him with the utmost respect and deference. He was, however, no match for the radiant beauty of the newborn prince; and even though the Emperor was bound to acknowledge the higher status of his older son and to favor him in public, in private he could not resist treating the younger prince as his favorite and lavishing attention upon him.

2. The courtiers are referring to "Song of Lasting Regret" by the Tang Dynasty poet Bai [Bo] Juyi (722–846). The poem recounts the infatuation of the Emperor Xuanzong (685–762) with Yang Guifei, which caused him to neglect affairs of state. Due to a rebellion he was forced to execute his lover.

3. It was customary for births to take place outside the palace in order to avoid defilement. A period of confinement for ritual purification usually followed a birth, which is why the Emperor has to wait to see his son.

4. Genji's half brother Suzaku [editors' note].

The mother of the newborn prince did not come from a family of the highest rank, but neither was she of such low status that she should have been constantly by the Emperor's side like a common servant. Certainly her reputation was flawless, and she comported herself with noble dignity; but because His Majesty obsessively kept her near him, willfully demanding that they not be separated, she had to be in attendance at all formal court performances or elegant entertainments. There were times when she would spend the night with him, and then be obliged to continue in service the following day. Consequently, as one might expect, other courtiers came to look down on her not only as a person of no significance, but also as a woman who lacked any sense of propriety. Moreover, because the Emperor treated her with special regard following the birth of his second son, the Kokiden Consort and her supporters grew anxious; they worried about the effect of such an infatuation on the prospects of the Crown Prince and wondered if the younger prince might not surpass his half brother in favor and usurp his position. The Kokiden Consort had been the Emperor's first wife. She had arrived at the palace before all the other women, and so His Majesty's feelings of affection for her were in no way ordinary. He considered her protests troubling, but he also had to acknowledge that she was deserving of sympathy, since she had given him two imperial princesses in addition to the Crown Prince.

Even though the mother of the newborn prince relied on the Emperor's benevolence for protection, many of the ladies at court scorned her. She grew physically weak, and because she felt powerless and had no one to turn to for help, she suffered greatly because of his love.

Her chambers at the palace were in the Kiritsubo—named for its courtyard, which was graced with paulownia trees. Because the Kiritsubo was in the northeast corner of the palace, and thus separated from the Emperor's quarters in the Seiryōden, he would have to pass by the chambers of many of the other court ladies on his frequent visits to her. Their resentment of these displays was not at all unreasonable, and so it was decided that the woman herself would have to go more often to the Seiryōden. The more she went, however, the more her rivals would strew the covered passageways connecting the various parts of the palace with filth. It was an absolutely intolerable situation, for the hems of the robes of the accompanying attendants would be soiled. On other occasions, when the woman could not avoid taking the interior hallways, her rivals would arrange for the doors at both ends to be closed off so that she could neither proceed forward nor turn back, trapping her inside and making her feel utterly wretched. As the number of these cruel incidents mounted, His Majesty felt sorry that his beloved should have to suffer so and ordered that she be installed in the chambers of the Kōrōden, a hall next to the Seiryōden. To do so, however, he had to move the lady who had resided there from the very beginning of her service at court to other quarters, causing her to nurse a deep resentment that proved impossible to placate.

When the young prince turned three, the court observed the ceremony of the donning of his first trousers. Employing all the treasures from the Imperial Storehouse and the Treasury, the event was every bit as lavish as the ceremony for the Crown Prince. Numerous objections were raised as a consequence of this ostentatious display, and everyone censured the ceremony as a breach of protocol. Fortunately, as the young prince grew his graceful appearance and matchless temperament became a source of wonder to all, and it was impossible for anyone to entirely resent him. Discerning courtiers who possessed the most refined sensibility could only gaze in amazement that such a child should have been born into this world.

During the summer of the year when the young prince turned three, his mother's health began to fail. She asked for permission to leave the court and return to her family home, but the Emperor would not hear of it and refused to let her go. She had been sickly and frail for some time, and so His Majesty had grown accustomed to seeing her in such a condition. "Wait a little while," he simply told her, "and let's see how you feel later." Whereupon, over the course of the next five or six days, she became seriously ill. The woman made a tearful entreaty, and at last she received permission to leave the palace. Even under these dire circumstances she was very careful to avoid any behavior that could be criticized as untoward or inappropriate. She decided to retire from the court in secret, leaving her young son behind.

Resigned to the fact that the life of his true love was approaching its end, and mindful of the taboo against defiling the palace with death, His Majesty was nonetheless grief-stricken beyond words that the dictates of protocol prevented him from seeing her off. The woman's face, with its lambent beauty conveying that air of grace so precious to him, was now thin and wasted. She had tasted the sorrows of the world to the full, but as she slipped in and out of consciousness, she could not convey to him even those feelings that might have been put into words. The Emperor, who now realized that his beloved was on the verge of death, lost control and made all sorts of tearful vows to her, no longer able to distinguish past from future. She, however, could not respond to him. The expression of weariness in her eyes made her all the more alluringly vulnerable as she lay there in a semiconscious state. The Emperor was beside himself and had no idea what he should do. He had granted her the honor of leaving in a carriage drawn by servants, but when he returned to her chambers again, he simply could not bring himself to let her go.

"Didn't we swear an oath to journey together on the road to death? No matter what, I cannot let you abandon me," he said.

She was deeply moved by his display of sorrowful devotion. Though breathing with great difficulty, she still managed to compose a verse for him.

> Now in deepest sorrow as I contemplate
> Our diverging roads, this fork where we must part
> How I long to walk the path of the living

"Had I known that things would turn out like this . . . " She evidently wanted to say more to him, but her breathing was labored. She was so weak and in such pain the Emperor longed to keep her at the palace and see it through to the end, come what may. But when he received an urgent message informing him that the most skilled of priests had been called to her family home to chant the requisite prayers of healing for her that evening, His Majesty at last agreed that his beloved should leave the palace, unbearable as it was for him to make that decision.

His heart was full and he could not sleep as he impatiently waited for the short summer night to end. Even though his messenger had barely had time to get to the woman's home and return with news of her condition, a dark foreboding

Kiritsubomon
death
Genji
man

assailed him. As it turned out, when the messenger arrived at the woman's residence, he had found the family distraught and weeping. "She passed away after
midnight," they informed him. The messenger returned to the palace in a state
of shock. The Emperor, stunned and shaken by the news, was so upset that he
shut himself away from the rest of the court.

His Majesty desperately wanted to see the young prince his beloved had left
behind at the palace, but there was no precedent for permitting anyone to
serve at court while having to wear robes of mourning. So it was decided that
the boy should be sent from the palace to his mother's residence. Too young to
fully comprehend what was going on, he knew from the way people around
him were behaving, and from the Emperor's ceaseless tears, that something
was terribly wrong. The death of loved ones is always a source of grief, but the
little boy's puzzled expression only added to the unspeakable sadness of it all.

* * *

The days passed in a meaningless blur for the Emperor, who dutifully observed
each of the seven-day ceremonies leading up to the forty-ninth day after the
funeral. Despite the passage of time, His Majesty was so lost in grief he could
find no comfort. He was indifferent to the consorts and ladies-in-waiting who
attended him in the evenings and instead passed his days and nights distracted
and disconsolate. For all who observed his grief it was truly an autumn drenched
by a dew of tears.

Over in the chambers of the Kokiden the mother of the Crown Prince and
her faction remained implacably unforgiving. "Is he still so in love with her,"
she complained, "that even after her death he doesn't consider the feelings of
others?" And indeed it was true that whenever the Emperor looked at the
Crown Prince, his thoughts would inevitably drift in yearning to the younger
prince, and he would then dispatch his most trusted ladies-in-waiting or nurses
to the family home of his late beloved to inquire after the boy.

* * *

The soughing of the wind, the chirring of insects . . . these brought only sadness
to him. The quarters of the Kokiden Consort were close by on the north side of
his private chambers in the Seiryōden. It had been a long time since she last
came to serve him here, and on this particular evening, with the moon in full
splendor, he could hear her indulging in musical entertainment to pass the
night. The Emperor was appalled and found it quite unpleasant. The courtiers
and ladies-in-waiting who observed his countenance at that moment listened
uneasily as well. The Kokiden Consort was a proud and haughty woman who
behaved as though she couldn't care less about His Majesty's grief.

* * *

The days and months passed, and the young prince finally came back to the
palace. He had grown even more splendid and handsome—to the point where
he did not seem to belong to this mortal world. His worried father, knowing
that the beautiful die young, took the boy's good looks as an unlucky omen.

In the spring of the following year the time came for the Emperor to formally
designate the heir apparent. He was seized by a desire to pass over the presumed Crown Prince, his son by the Kokiden Consort, and appoint his favored

he would rather to lead tract
new son cerny
But

younger son instead, but he knew that the little prince had no supporters and that the court would never accept such a move, which might prove dangerous to the boy. So in the end he went against his personal wishes and confirmed the Crown Prince as his heir apparent—all the while keeping his true feelings concealed. The courtiers remarked among themselves that no matter how much His Majesty preferred the younger son, he knew there were limits to his affection. When the Kokiden Consort caught wind of these rumors, she felt both relief and satisfaction.

The grandmother of the young prince had long been sunk in a deep depression and, finding no means to console herself, she finally passed away. Was her death the answer to her prayers to be allowed to go to her daughter? The Emperor was once more plunged into grief beyond the measure of ordinary mortals. By this time the young prince was almost six and was old enough now to understand what was happening. Deeply attached to his grandmother, he wept inconsolably. As she neared her death, she recognized how accustomed her grandson had grown to being with her through the years, and she repeated over and over how sad she was to leave him alone in the world.

With both his mother and grandmother gone, the young prince moved back to the palace for good. When he turned seven he underwent the ceremony of the First Reading, which initiated him into the study of the Chinese classics. The court had never known a child so precociously intelligent, and His Majesty, knowing how others felt and believing that talent and beauty die young, could not help but view such abilities with alarm. "How could anyone possibly resent him now," the Emperor declared. "Because he has lost his mother, I want him treated with affection." Eventually even the Kokiden Consort and her attendants were won over, and whenever the young prince accompanied his father to the Kokiden chambers, he would be permitted entry behind the curtains where the ladies-in-waiting were serving His Majesty. The fiercest warriors and most implacable enemies would have smiled had they seen him, and the ladies of the court were reluctant to let him out of their sight. The Kokiden Consort had given the Emperor two princesses as well, but neither of them could compare in beauty to this boy. The other consorts and ladies felt no inhibitions around him—indeed, they allowed him to catch glimpses of their faces—and his own appearance was so elegant that they would experience an embarrassed excitement whenever they saw him. All the courtiers considered him exceptionally splendid, a playmate to be treated with special deference.

His formal training included instruction on the koto and flute, and word of his talents echoed throughout the palace—though if I were to go into all the details about his abilities my account would seem exaggerated and he would come across as too good to be true.

The Emperor learned that among the members of a mission from the Korean kingdom of Koryō was a diviner skilled at the art of physiognomy. An old edict by the Emperor Uda had forbidden the presence of foreigners within the palace, so His Majesty discreetly arranged to have the young prince meet with this man at the Kōrōkan, the residence provided for foreign missions. The Major Controller of the Right assumed the role of guardian and accompanied the boy to the mission under the pretense that he was the father of the child. The diviner was both puzzled and astounded. Tilting his head back and forth in disbelief that this child could really be the Major Controller's son, he said,

"The young man's features tell me he is destined to be ruler of this country, perhaps even attaining the supreme position of emperor. Yet if that is what fate has in store for him, I foresee chaos and great sorrow for the court. On the other hand, if his destiny is to ascend to a position such as Chancellor and act as a guardian of imperial rule, then it appears he will be a great benefactor to the state. Still, I must say that judging by his features alone the path leading to the Chancellorship seems less likely."

The Major Controller was himself a scholar of considerable learning and discernment, and his conversations with the men of the Korean mission were deeply engaging. The party composed and exchanged verses in Chinese; and because the mission planned to leave for home in a day or two, one of the diviner's poems expressed the joy at having met such a remarkable boy face-to-face and the sorrow of having to part from him so soon. In response to the heartfelt expression of this poem the young prince composed an accomplished verse of his own. The diviner praised his effort as auspicious and bestowed lavish gifts on him. In return, the diviner received splendid presents from the imperial household. Naturally, news of this encounter spread through the court. His Majesty did not let on that he knew anything about it, but the grandfather of the Crown Prince, who happened to be the Minister of the Right, caught wind of the gossip and, not knowing quite what to make of it, grew suspicious.

The Emperor in his wisdom had earlier sought out the opinion of a Japanese diviner, whose reading of the boy's physiognomy accorded with his own thinking at the time. His Majesty had been holding back on installing the young prince in the line of succession, and was thus impressed by the perspicacity of the Korean diviner, who recognized the boy's imperial lineage. Even so, he could not be sure how long his own reign would last, and he hesitated to appoint his son prince-without-rank. He anxiously wondered whether the boy, who lacked support from his mother's family, would not end up precariously adrift once he was no longer in the line of succession. For that reason he determined that the boy's prospects might be better if he were made to serve as a loyal subject of the imperial court, and so he had his son tutored accordingly in the arts and in various fields of learning. The boy was so exceptionally bright it seemed a shame to demote him to commoner status, but the Emperor knew that if he made the boy a prince of the blood his son would suffer the calumny and scorn of the court. He consulted yet another diviner who was wise in the ways of Indic astrology; and when this reading proved to be in line with the others and with His Majesty's own thoughts on the matter, it was decided to confer on the boy the clan name of Minamoto—Genji[5]—thereby making him a commoner.

Months and years passed, but there was never a moment when the Emperor forgot his love for the lady who had resided in the chambers looking out on the paulownia courtyard. Thinking he might find someone who could assuage his grief, he had women of appropriate breeding and talents brought before him. But it was all in vain, for where in the world could he expect to find her equal? Just when he had reached the point where he found everything tiresome and was contemplating retiring from the world, an Assistant Handmaid informed him of a young woman, the fourth princess of the previous emperor, whose beauty was matchless, whose reputation at court was beyond reproof, and

---

5. The name "Genji" is the reading of the characters for Minamoto (*gen*) and "family name" (*ji*).

whose mother had raised her with extraordinary care and devotion. Since this Assistant Handmaid had once served at the court of the previous emperor, she was familiar with the mother of this young woman and accustomed to waiting on her. In the course of her service she had been able to observe the fourth princess as she grew from childhood, and even now would occasionally see her. "I have served at court for three successive reigns," she told the Emperor, "and I have never before seen anyone who even closely resembles the late lady of the Kiritsubo. The daughter of the former empress, however, definitely puts me in mind of her. She is a woman of exquisite refinement and beauty." *Could this really be true?* His Majesty, who could barely contain himself, began to make some discreet inquiries.

The mother of the fourth princess warned her daughter about the situation at the palace. "The Kokiden Consort is a vindictive woman. Just look at the unfortunate example of the lady in the Kiritsubo. The treatment she suffered was truly appalling." She was still struggling with the Emperor's request, unable to decide if she should allow her daughter to go to him, when she passed away. Thinking that the princess was now helpless and alone, His Majesty again approached her, saying "I will think of you as an equal to my own daughters." Her ladies-in-waiting, her supporters from her mother's family, and her older brother, Prince Hyōbu, who served in the Ministry of War, were all of the opinion that attending the Emperor would bring solace to her and would be preferable to living in her current wretched condition. So it was that she was sent to the palace and installed in the Higyōsha, which was also called the Fujitsubo because its chambers looked out onto a courtyard graced with wisteria. The young woman was thereafter referred to as Fujitsubo, and truly in face and figure she bore an uncanny resemblance to the deceased lady of the Kiritsubo. Fujitsubo, however, was of undeniably higher birth, and that status protected her from criticism, since the courtiers were predisposed to judge her a superior woman. Since she lacked no qualifications, the Emperor did not feel constrained in his relationship with her. The court had never accepted His Majesty's love for the lady of the Kiritsubo, and so his affection for her was viewed as inappropriate and inopportune. The Emperor never wavered in his undying love for the lady of the paulownia-courtyard chambers, but it is a poignant fact of human nature that feelings change over time. Inevitably his attention shifted toward Fujitsubo, who, it seems, brought comfort to his heart.

Because the young Genji was always at his father's side, he was constantly in the presence of the women who attended His Majesty most frequently. These women grew familiar with the boy and gradually came to feel that they did not have to be reserved around him. Of course, none of the consorts considered herself inferior to the others, but even though each one was very attractive in her own individual way, there was no denying that they all had passed, or were on the verge of passing, the peak of their charms . . . all but Fujitsubo, that is. She still possessed the loveliness of youthful beauty, and try as she might to keep herself hidden away behind her screens, Genji, who was always nearby, would catch glimpses of her figure. He had no memory of his mother, and when he heard the head of the imperial household staff say that Fujitsubo looked just like her, his young heart ached with wistful longing—if only he could always be close to his father's new consort!

Genji and Fujitsubo were the two most precious people to the Emperor. "Do not be shy around the boy," His Majesty told Fujitsubo. "It may seem strange and curious, but I feel as though it is fitting for him to think of you as his mother. Do not think him discourteous, but cherish him for my sake. His face and expressions are so like his mother's—and since you resemble her, you can't blame him for thinking of you the way he does." After the Emperor made his request, Genji, in his boyish emotions, would try everything, even references to the transient blossoms of spring or the blazing leaves of autumn, to get Fujitsubo to recognize his yearning affection for her. When the Kokiden Consort learned of the unprecedented favoritism His Majesty was displaying toward these two, she once more grew cold and distant toward Fujitsubo and her retinue. Moreover, her earlier ominous dislike of Genji and his mother flared up again, and she found the boy repellent. Her son, the Crown Prince, was considered flawlessly handsome, and his reputation was above reproach. Nonetheless, he was no match for the lustrous beauty of Genji, who possessed an aura that prompted the courtiers to call him the Radiant Prince. Because Fujitsubo was his equal in looks and in the affections of the Emperor, she came to be referred to as the Princess of the Radiant Sun.

It pained the Emperor that his son would eventually grow out of his youthful good looks, but when Genji turned twelve preparations were made for the coming-of-age ceremony in which his hair would be done up and his clothes and cap worn in the style of an adult. His Majesty personally tended to every little detail of the ceremony, adding touches that went beyond custom and set a new standard. The ceremony that had initiated the Crown Prince into manhood had been a spectacular affair held in the Shishinden, the great ceremonial hall of the palace. The Emperor wanted Genji's ceremony to be just as majestic and proper. He had various offices, including the Treasury and the Imperial Granaries, make formal preparations for the many banquets and celebrations that would follow the ceremony, and he left special instructions that no expense should be spared and that his directives should be carried out so as to make the occasion one of utmost splendor.

His Majesty was seated facing east under the eastern eaves of his residence in the Seiryōden, and the seats for Genji and the minister who would bestow the cap were located in front of him. Genji appeared before the Emperor at around four in the afternoon, during the Hour of the Monkey.[6] The lambent glow of his face, which was still framed on either side by the twin loops of his boyish hairdo, made his father feel all the more regretful about the change in appearance that was about to take place. The honor of trimming back Genji's hair fell to the Minister of the Treasury, whose face betrayed the pain he felt the moment he cut Genji's beautiful locks. The Emperor had a hard time keeping his emotions in check. *If only his mother were here to see this ceremony*, he thought, struggling to maintain his composure.

The capping ritual followed, and when that was finished, Genji withdrew to an antechamber to rest and change into the formal attire of an adult—an outer

6. In premodern Japan the hours of the day, like the months, were designated by the signs of the Chinese zodiac. The Hour of the Monkey was ca. 3–5 P.M. [editors' note].

robe with the underarm vents sewn up. Stepping down into the garden east of the Seiryōden, he faced his father and performed obeisance, placing his ceremonial wand on the ground, rising and bowing left, right and left again, then sitting and repeating his actions to show his gratitude. He cut such a magnificent figure that all in attendance were moved to tears. As might be expected, the Emperor found it harder than the others to hide his feelings. At that moment the sad events of the past, which he normally kept himself from dwelling on, came flooding back. Since Genji was still at a tender age, His Majesty had fretted that cutting his locks and putting his hair up in the style of an adult man would spoil his looks. To his amazement the ceremony only added to Genji's aura of masculine beauty.

The Minister of the Left, who performed the capping ritual, had taken the younger sister of the Emperor as his principal wife. She gave him a daughter, whom he doted upon, raising her with the utmost care. The Minister was troubled when he learned that the Crown Prince evidently desired his daughter, because he was secretly planning to arrange a match for her with Genji. And so in the days leading up to the ceremony, he approached the Emperor with his proposal. His Majesty replied, "I see. Well . . . given that the boy seems to have no patrons for his coming-of-age ceremony, and since we have to select an aristocratic young woman to sleep with him on the night of his initiation, let's choose your daughter." Thus encouraged, the Minister followed through with his plans.

After the ceremony, Genji withdrew into the attendant's antechamber. As the party was making a celebratory toast in his honor, the Emperor gave permission for Genji, who had no rank, to sit at a place below the imperial princes, but above the ministers. The Minister of the Left, who was seated next to him, casually dropped a few hints about his daughter, but Genji, who was still at an age when he felt diffident and embarrassed about such matters, did not respond.

An attendant from the imperial household staff brought a message from the Emperor to the Minister, requesting his presence. The Minister went to the imperial quarters where a senior lady-in-waiting presented him with the appropriate gifts that custom demanded—a white oversized woman's robe made especially for this presentation, along with a set of three robes. His Majesty vented his pent-up emotions, presenting a cup of rice wine to the Minister and reminding him of his responsibilities toward Genji.

> When you with purple cords first bound his hair
> Did you not also bind your heart and swear
> Eternal vows to give him your daughter

The Minister composed this reply.

> So long as the deep purple cords that bind our hearts
> As firmly as they bind this youth's hair never fade
> So our mutual vow will retain its deep hue

He stepped down from the long bridge that connected the imperial residence in the Seiryōden and the Ceremonial Court in the Shishinden, and performed obeisance in the east garden. There he received a horse from the Left Division of the imperial stables and a falcon caged in a mew from the Office of the Chamberlain. Princes and nobles lined up along the foot of the stairs leading down from the Seiryōden into the east garden and each received gifts appropriate to their rank.

Decorative boxes of thin cypress wood filled with delicacies and baskets of
fruit were among the items prepared for the Emperor that day. The Major
Controller of the Right, who had acted earlier as Genji's guardian, had been
put in charge of the presentations. The garden overflowed with trays stacked
with rice cakes flavored with various fillings, and with four-legged chests of
Chinese-style lacquer stuffed with presents for the lower ranking attendants—
so many that their numbers surpassed even the presentations made at the
coming-of-age ceremony held for the Crown Prince. Indeed, it was an incomparably magnificent affair.

That evening Genji departed for the residence of the Minister of the Left,
which was located on Sanjō avenue. The ceremony welcoming Genji as groom
and solemnizing his wedding was conducted with unprecedented attention to
proper form. Feeling a touch of dread, the Minister was captivated by the masculine beauty of Genji, who still looked quite boyish. In contrast his daughter,
who at sixteen was four years older than her new husband, was put off by
Genji's youthfulness and considered their match inappropriate.

The Minister enjoyed the full confidence of the Emperor. After all, his principal wife, the mother of the bride, was His Majesty's full sister. Thus, the
bride came from a distinguished line on both sides of her family. Moreover, the
addition of Genji to the Minister's family diminished the prestige of his rival
the Minister of the Right, who as grandfather of the Crown Prince would eventually assume power as Chancellor. The Minister of the Left had numerous
children by several wives. His principal wife had given him, in addition to
Genji's bride, a son who was now Middle Captain in the Inner Palace Guard.
This young man, Tō no Chūjō,[7] was exceptionally handsome, and the Minister
of the Right could hardly ignore such a promising prospect, even though he
was not on good terms with the Minister of the Left, his main rival for power.
He therefore arranged to marry the young Tō no Chūjō to his fourth daughter,
who was his greatest treasure in the world. His regard for his son-in-law was
every bit as strong as that given to Genji by the Minister of the Left. For their
part, the two young men forged an ideal friendship.

Because the Emperor was always summoning him, Genji found it difficult to
live at his wife's residence.[8] In his heart, he was obsessed with the matchless
beauty of the Fujitsubo Consort, who seemed to be exactly the kind of woman
he wanted to take as his wife. *Was there no one else like her*, he wondered. He
found his bride to be a woman of great charm and proper training, but he was
not really attracted to her. He had been drawn to Fujitsubo when he was a
child, and the torment caused by his feelings for her was excruciating. Now
that he was an adult, he was no longer permitted behind the curtains of the

7. I am following custom and using this name
for Genji's close friend, brother-in-law, and
rival. The name "Tō no Chūjō" refers to his positions as Middle Captain in the Inner Palace
Guard (Chūjō) and in the Office of the Chamberlain. Like most of the male characters, he is
identified by his position at court throughout
the narrative, but since his positions and ranks
change over time, it is easier to refer to him
throughout by this initial appellation.

8. Uxorilocal marriage arrangements were
widespread in the Heian period, and thus it
was common for a young nobleman to make
his father-in-law's residence his primary abode
[editors' note].

consorts. Whenever there was a musical entertainment, he would play the flute in accompaniment to Fujitsubo's koto, his notes subtly conveying his true feelings for her. The sound of her soft voice was a comfort to him, and the only times he felt happy was when he was at the palace. He would serve there for five or six days in succession, occasionally spending a mere two or three days at his wife's residence. His father-in-law attributed Genji's behavior to his youth and did not fault him for it, but continued to do all he could to offer support at court. He chose only the most exceptional ladies-in-waiting to serve his son-in-law and daughter, and he went out of his way to put on the musical entertainments that Genji so enjoyed and to show him every favor.

When Genji stayed at the palace he took up residence in the Kiritsubo. The women who had once served his mother had not been dismissed and scattered, and so they were now assigned to wait on him. Orders were sent down to the Office of Palace Repairs and to the Bureau of Skilled Artisans to rebuild and expand the former residence of Genji's mother, a villa on Nijō avenue. The project was to be carried out so splendidly that there would be no other villa like it. The setting of the surrounding woods and hills was already unparalleled; and when the garden pond was enlarged the result was so eye-catching that it created a stir. Genji thought wistfully that such a villa would be the perfect residence for a wife who had all the qualities of his ideal woman, Fujitsubo.

It is said that it was the Korean diviner who, in his admiration, first bestowed on Genji the sobriquet, Radiant Prince.

FROM CHAPTER II

Hahakigi

Broom Cypress

The Radiant Prince—a splendid, if somewhat bombastic, title. In fact, his failings were so numerous that such a lofty sobriquet was perhaps misleading. He engaged in all sorts of flings and dalliances, but he sought to keep them secret out of fear he would end up as fodder for those gossips who delighted in passing along stories about him and thereby leave behind for later generations a reputation as a careless, frivolous man. Genji was keen to avoid the censure of the court, and, thus constrained, went about with a serious and sincere demeanor for a time, abstaining from all elegantly seductive or charming affairs. No doubt the Lieutenant of Katano, that legendary lover, would have been amused.[9]

Genji was serving as Middle Captain in the Palace Guard at the time, and in fact he preferred being stationed there. Consequently, his visits to his wife, who resided at the estate of her father, the Minister of the Left, all but ceased. Although people expressed their suspicions about him, wondering if his heart wasn't in wild turmoil over a secret lover, Genji was not the sort who carried on common affairs impulsively or brazenly. There were rare occasions, however, when he strayed from his professed path of moderation; and he had the unfortunate tendency to become obsessed with relationships that brought him stress and pain, giving himself over entirely to behavior that could hardly be called proper.

9. The tale of the amorous Lieutenant of Katano referred to here has not survived.

During a stretch in the rainy season when there was no break in the clouds, a directional taboo[1] forced Genji to stay on and attend the Emperor for a longer than normal period. The members of the household of the Minister of the Left grew anxious and resentful at Genji's neglect of his wife, but they continued to arrange every detail of his wardrobe so that he would cut a remarkable figure at court. Moreover, the sons of the Minister, Genji's brothers-in-law, would spend all their free time in Genji's palace quarters when they happened to be in service. One of these sons, Tō no Chūjō, was a Middle Captain who also served in the Office of the Chamberlain. He was a full sibling to Genji's wife—he and his sister had both been born to Princess Ōmiya—and of all the Minister's children he was closest to Genji and could behave in a more intimate and relaxed manner in his friend's presence at entertainments and amusements. Tō no Chūjō preferred the company of Genji because the residence that his own father-in-law, the Minister of the Right, had painstakingly provided and maintained for him was a dreary, uninspiring place. It must be added that he was fond of having affairs with other women.

Tō no Chūjō also had dazzlingly furnished quarters at his father's residence at Sanjō, but he was always accompanying Genji on his comings and goings. They were constantly together, day and night, pursuing the same interests and diversions, and he in no way lagged behind the Radiant Prince in his accomplishments. Because they were inseparable, it was natural that they did not stand on ceremony with one another. They never kept their innermost feelings hidden, but displayed an easygoing harmony whenever they spoke.

They had spent a particularly tedious day doing nothing at all on account of the interminable rain; and because there was hardly a sign of anyone in the palace during the tedious hours of the early evening, Genji's quarters there took on a more relaxed atmosphere than usual. Drawing an oil lamp beside him, Genji perused some Chinese classics. Tō no Chūjō pulled out some letters written on paper of various hues from a small cabinet near him and was seized by the desire to read them. Genji would not allow that, but he did say, "I'll let you look at a few of the more appropriate ones . . . there are several I'd be ashamed for you to read." Tō no Chūjō protested, feeling a little resentful. "But it's just those letters you don't feel free to share with me that I'm most curious about. I've exchanged many letters of the most common variety with ladies of all ranks, and at the time we were corresponding I couldn't wait to read them. Yet when I go back over them, the only ones really worth looking at were written when the women were being petulant or impatient from waiting." Tō no Chūjō knew, of course, that Genji would never keep letters from high-ranking ladies—letters he had to keep absolutely secret—lying scattered about in a commonplace cabinet like this where anyone could see them. Genji would certainly hide his most intriguing letters in a secret location, and would be comfortable sharing only those from easygoing ladies of decidedly second-rate backgrounds. "Well, you certainly have a lot of them, don't you," said Tō no

---

1. A directional taboo, or prohibition, required a person to avoid traveling in a certain direction so as not to disturb gods whose movements over time were predictable (based on Chinese zodiacal and calendrical practices) and could be charted by the Bureau of Divination. Such prohibitions were often used as a convenient excuse for a gentleman to avoid meeting his wife or lover [editors' note].

Chūjō, who went on to interrogate Genji about the author of each of the missives. He found it amusing that his suppositions and guesses about the letters were sometimes right on the money, and other times wildly off the mark. Still, Genji gave very little away, and, by leading his friend on, he managed to disguise the identities of the letter writers.

"You must have a great number of letters at your place," said Genji. "I'd really like to take a peek at them. If you let me, I'll gladly open this cabinet to you." Tō no Chūjō answered, "I have very few worth looking at. You see, I've come to the realization that as far as women are concerned there aren't many who are flawless enough to make you think *she's the one*. I've come across many who have passable skills in the arts, who can write flowing characters that create an impression of a superficial elegance, who show a kind of facile understanding of how to respond in verse on certain occasions . . . and yet even if you choose a woman on the basis of such accomplishments, she almost always fails to live up to the expectations created by her talents and disappoints in the end. She'll swell with pride, going on and on about her own accomplishments, looking down on others and, all in all, behaving rather foolishly. Her parents are always waiting on her, spoiling her with affection and lavishing attention, keeping their precious little princess hidden away in the recesses of their estates until some man hears about her extraordinary gifts and gets all worked up. Beautiful, young, and carefree, with little to distract her, she'll follow the lead of others, dedicate herself to some trivial diversion, and as a result acquire and perfect some skill. Naturally those who look after her keep silent about her flaws, keeping up appearances and spreading plausible-sounding rumors that make her seem better than she really is. Since such rumors are all a man has to go on, can he really afford to assume the worst about her without actually meeting her? So a man goes about, wondering if she's the genuine article, and when they finally meet . . . well, it's rare that a woman actually lives up to her reputation."

Listening to Tō no Chūjō's lament, which gave the impression of a world-weary man who had experienced the shame of such disappointments, Genji smiled wryly. Although he knew that his friend's account of women was hardly the whole of the matter, he had had a few affairs that matched Tō no Chūjō's experiences. "Can there really be women," Genji asked, "who lack even the most trivial merits?"

"I'm not saying that," Tō no Chūjō responded. "Who would be foolish enough to be drawn to a woman with absolutely no talent? A woman who has nothing to recommend her is as rare as one who is perfect in every way. My point is that a woman who is born into the nobility is raised with the greatest care, which includes concealing her many faults. So of course she's going to look superior to other women. A woman born into a family of middling rank will reveal her sensibility and habits of mind with a style and personality all her own, and so you would expect to discover various things that distinguish her from others. As for women of the lowest class . . . well, I'm not especially interested in learning anything about them."

Genji's curiosity was piqued by the worldly posture his friend had assumed. "I wonder about your standards. Can you really classify all women on the basis of just three levels? How do you discriminate between a woman born of a noble family . . . say rank three or above . . . whose social position has been ruined and whose rank has fallen so that it is indistinguishable from others, and a woman of less distinguished background . . . say rank four or lower . . . whose family has so prospered at court that they can now lavishly furnish her residence and adopt a smug attitude that proclaims their daughter inferior to no one?" Just as Genji posed his question, the Warden of the Left Mounted Guard and the Junior Secretary from the Ministry of Rites showed up, explaining that directional prohibitions for that day were keeping them confined to the palace. They both had reputations as elegant lovers, and since they were also eloquent speakers—fluent, logical, and precise—Tō no Chūjō was eager to detain them and get their opinions on his idea of classifying women according to three levels. Their subsequent conversation touched upon topics of a highly questionable and even slightly disreputable nature.

The Warden addressed the matter straight away. "A woman who is a parvenu will likely be judged by court society as inferior despite her rise in status, especially if her pedigree is not appropriate to her rank. On the other hand, a woman who may have a distinguished pedigree, but who lacks the means to make her way at court will see her fortunes and position diminish over time, and her prospects and reputation crumble away until she cannot maintain her status in spite of her pride. Events will then conspire to make her situation more and more untenable. Looking at each of these types of women, I'm afraid we have to relegate them both to your middle category. Provincial governors toil away, tied up with petty people and affairs; but even among that lot, consigned to a middling station in life, there are various gradations that distinguish them. We live in an age when we sometimes find governors who are really not at all inferior, even though they come from the middle ranks. Actually, there are some of the fourth rank who are qualified to serve as a counselor, who have unsullied reputations and comfortable fortunes and prospects, and who are easier to take than some inexperienced or immature nobility of higher rank. There are many instances of such men who maintain splendid households where their daughters are nurtured with the utmost care. Nothing is lacking, nothing held back, no expense spared to raise them in the most dazzling manner . . . and as a result they grow into excellent young ladies who are beyond reproach. These women go into court service and many of them find unexpected good fortune, marrying above their station."

Genji smiled at that. "I guess that when all is said and done, the key is finding a girl from a rich family."

Tō no Chūjō responded petulantly. "Now you're talking nonsense. Such a remark is not worthy of you."

The Warden continued his disquisition. "The highborn lady who brings together both pedigree and public reputation, yet who in private lacks personal breeding and manners, is eccentric and not worth discussing. She's the type who makes you wonder in disappointment how she could have been brought up like that. Of course, it strikes one as perfectly natural when a woman's pedigree and reputation are in harmony and her character is flawless. So you assume that's the way things ought to be and aren't surprised by her, even though such a woman is a rarity. But perhaps I should set aside any discussion of the highest-ranking ladies, for someone as lowly as I could never be on their level. Beyond these types, you sometimes unexpectedly come across an adorable, defenseless girl whose existence is unknown to court society. She lives in a lonely, sublimely dilapidated residence shut away from the world behind a gate overgrown with weeds, and so of course you think of her as an exceptionally rare find. You're mysteriously drawn to her, your imagination stimulated by the things that make her different, and you wonder how she could have ended up in a place like that. Her father is likely to be some pathetic, overweight old man, her brothers probably all have unpleasant faces, and there in the women's quarters in the inner recesses of the residence . . . which, no matter how you try to imagine it, is nothing out of the ordinary . . . is a fiercely proud lady with all the refined demeanor of one who has somehow managed to acquire some accomplishments, even if she is not of the first rank and thus not all that much to talk about. And yet because you would never expect to find a woman like that in such a place, how could you not find her alluring? Of course, you can't compare the discovery of a woman like that to opting for a flawless woman of superior rank, but by the same token it is difficult to simply toss her aside."

The Warden here glanced knowingly at the Junior Secretary, who, interpreting the expression as a subtle reference to the flawless reputation of his own sister, kept his counsel on the matter. Genji seemed lost in thought: *I wonder about all this. Are there really women like that out in the world? After all, when I consider my wife, there don't seem to be any perfect women among the highest classes.* Genji was dressed in an intentionally casual manner in an informal robe, minus trousers, over soft white under robes. He had neglected to tie up the cords of his outer robes, and as he half-reclined amidst his books and papers in the dim shadows cast by the lamp, he cut such an attractive figure that the other men felt a desire to see him as a woman. He was so beautiful that pairing him with the very finest of the ladies at the court would fail to do him justice.

During the course of the young men's discussion of various types of women, the Warden remarked, "There are women who are flawless enough for a commonplace affair, but when the time comes to take a wife, you find it impossible to decide even if you have a large number of women to choose from. The same is true of men who serve at court and are expected to be rock-solid pillars of society. It proves quite difficult to produce a man of true worth and ability, and so no matter how gifted or clever he may be, in the end there will never be more than one or two who are fit to govern. That's why superior people command their inferiors, and inferiors follow their superiors, mutually accommodating each other to carry out public affairs. Now then, just consider the person who is to take charge of the private affairs of your household. It wouldn't do at all if she doesn't have the proper qualifications. That being the case, a man is naturally going to look around because he knows that a woman may possess some good qualities while lacking others. After all, it is rare to find one who, though maybe not perfect, is at least acceptable . . . and even a man who is not inclined to compare the appearance of this woman to that one is going to take great care in making his decision, since the one he chooses will be his mate for life. All things being equal, he will take someone whose tastes match his own and who does not have the kind of flaws he must spend all his time correcting and setting in order. Well, this is all very hard, and a woman is not necessarily going to fulfill all a man's expectations. That's why a man who does not allow his affections to stray, who focuses his attention on one woman and does not discard the karmic bonds of his first marriage vows, will always be seen as sincere, honest and loyal. And a woman who is able to keep her husband from straying is the one we take to be refined and attractive.

"Given all that . . . how should I put this . . . having observed all sorts of relationships in society, I can't help having doubts as to whether there is any woman who is perfectly elegant, or who can live up to the ideals in a man's heart. In the case of your lordships, what kind of woman could ever be worthy enough to meet your exalted standards? No doubt she would have to be young and beautiful and beyond reproach in every way. She would be well versed in composition, but her choice of words would be modest and her brushstrokes light and delicate, leaving you a little agitated and longing for a more revealing response. You are forced to wait, feeling unbearably impatient until that moment when you can get close enough to her to make your advances and exchange a few words. But she will say very little, speaking under her breath in a faint voice that shows how adept she is at concealing her flaws. Just when you think she is most pliant and feminine, she starts to fret about whether or not you really love her. And then when you humor her, she becomes flirtatious. This has to be the worst fault in women.

"Above all, a wife must never neglect her duty to assist her husband. A husband can get along well enough if a woman is not too emotionally demanding, does not make a big fuss over niceties, and doesn't give herself over to fashion. Of course, a man doesn't want a wife who is too serious, who busies herself with supporting her husband and managing the household to the extent that she keeps her hair swept back all the time, exposing her ears and making herself unattractive. A man who goes to work in the morning and returns home in the evening doesn't want to have to go to the trouble of talking with a stranger about the odd behavior of people he has encountered in public and private, or about the good and bad things he has seen and heard. If he has a wife who is close to him and will listen to his stories and understand him, then doesn't he assume he should be able to discuss such matters with her? Maybe he suddenly recalls something and smiles, or perhaps tears come to his eyes, or maybe he relives some feeling of righteous indignation at something that occurred to someone. Or he might have feelings that he just cannot keep to himself, and thinks he might share them with her and ask her opinion. But if she is unattractive or too preoccupied to understand, he ends up turning away in disillusionment. Remembering something he has kept inside, a thought that makes him laugh or let out an audible sigh, he will mention it, almost as if speaking to himself, and all she will do is look up with a blank expression and reply, 'Did you just say something?' What man wouldn't regret marrying someone like that?

"When all is said and done, we men really should consider picking a completely childlike, compliant woman . . . a woman we can mold into an acceptable and flawless wife. Even when she gives you some cause for concern, you still have the feeling that there is some value in disciplining her. When you are with such a woman face-to-face, she is truly vulnerable and precious to you, and you are compelled to view her faults through forgiving eyes. Even so, there will be occasions when you have to be apart, and you tell her about something important that must be done, or give her some task, trivial or practical, that must be carried out to the letter. It will turn out that she cannot act on her own and is unable to do things as you instructed. This is really quite annoying and her unreliability will cause you no end of trouble. Why does it always seem that it's the cold, distant, slightly unpleasant woman who, depending on the occasion, is able to perform well in front of others and bring honor to your house?" The Warden had tried to cover all aspects of the subject, but was unable to come to any firm conclusions. Instead, he finished his analysis by heaving a great sigh.

"Considering all of this," the Warden continued, "you can't choose a wife solely on the basis of her family background, and certainly not on the basis of her looks alone. If you can find a woman who is not so strange or demure as to make you regret your choice, if she is serious through and through and has a quiet personality, then you ought to consider her dependable. Should she have any talents beyond these basic qualifications, or be sweet-tempered, you should count yourself lucky. Even if she is deficient in certain respects, you shouldn't make unreasonable demands for her to improve. So long as she is morally upright and not fretful or jealous, then she will over time acquire an outward grace. Her comportment will be modest, she will protect her honor, and she will endure things she has a right to complain about, hiding her resentment behind feigned ignorance or pretending to be nonchalant. Unfortunately, there are cases where a woman can no longer suppress the emotions that have been building up inside her heart, and she will leave behind some fierce words that chill your soul, or compose a moving poem to which she has attached a memento that will remind you of her, then hide herself away in some village deep in the mountains or on a deserted strand along the shore. When I was a child I would hear stories like that, which the ladies-in-waiting would read aloud, and I found them so touching I was moved to tears. Now, when I think back on it, their tales seem frivolous and overly dramatic. A woman who casts aside a man who has deep feelings for her and runs off to hide in utter disregard of the husband's feelings, even when she has just cause for being upset, will stir anxieties that last a lifetime. The whole affair is extremely tiresome. Some people will praise her actions, saying how exquisitely profound her emotions are; and as a result her feelings of sad regret will accumulate to the point where she decides to become a nun. Having made up her mind, her heart seems pure and serene and she can no longer even consider returning to her former life. Her acquaintances come to call on her, telling her how melancholy it is that things should have come to this. When her husband hears of this he weeps, and the messenger and older ladies-in-waiting tell her what a shame it is and how sad that her husband has such deep feelings. The woman, who still has lingering affection for him, will then realize she had no reason to throw away his love. She will gather together the hair she had clipped from her forehead when she took vows as a nun and, feeling forlorn and helpless now that there is no turning back, will break down and cry. Though she had kept her emotions in check up to that moment, once she gives in to her feelings she is no longer able to hold back her tears whenever she considers her situation. Because she now seems to have so many regrets, the Buddha himself must look at her as one whose heart is tainted by base attachments. Half-hearted devotion to the Buddha is an even more certain path to Hell than being mired in the five evils of earthly existence.[2] Even if the marital bond was deep enough

2. In Buddhism the five evils are lust, wrath, greed, worldly attachment, and pride (ego).

that the husband takes her back before she renounces the world, is there any couple that would not harbor at least some resentment upon recalling such an incident? For better or worse they live together as husband and wife, and their relationship is based on a deep karmic bond and shared emotions that can weather almost anything that might happen. Yet whenever a wife runs away, can any couple ever completely put aside their feelings of mutual reproach?

"It is folly for a wife to resent her husband, display her anger, and quarrel obsessively over some little affair he has had on the side. A man's affections may stray, but so long as he is still capable of the kind of feelings he had for her when they were first married, then she has good reason to think that their relationship has strong emotional bonds. If she makes a big fuss over his dalliances, however, those bonds may be cut for good.

"In general, then, a woman should be modest in all things. She should give a gentle hint when she knows something is going on that justifies her resentment. Or she should imply, without being spiteful, that there have been some occasions that have bothered her. If she behaves in such a way, her husband's regard for her will surely increase. Most of the time a man's wandering heart can be calmed by the guidance of his wife. A woman who is too lenient and turns a blind eye to her husband's behavior may in contrast seem easygoing and lovable, but in the end will be dismissed as frivolous. As Bai Juyi put it, 'Who can tell where an unmoored ship will drift?'[3] Isn't that the truth?"

Tō no Chūjō nodded and replied, "Staying on the same subject, it's a serious matter when a person you like for her charm and sensitivity gives you cause to wonder if they can be trusted. Although people may choose to put up with their partner's wayward behavior and even fool themselves into believing they see some improvement, that doesn't mean that the wayward partner has reformed. In any case, when an indiscretion brings discord to a marriage, there is probably no better recourse than to calmly ignore it." His remarks described perfectly the situation of his own sister, which was no doubt his intention, and so it irritated him that her husband, Genji, was not joining in the discussion, but was pretending to nod off instead.

The Warden, who now found himself regarded as the expert on such matters, whinnied on and on. Tō no Chūjō, who wanted to hear what he had to say, assumed the role of disciple and listened eagerly.

"Compare women to artisans, if you will," the Warden continued. "For example, a woodworker may indulge his imagination and create all sorts of items . . . toys meant for a moment's diversion, objects not based on any model or pattern. These things look fashionable and amaze you with the cleverness of their construction, and insofar as they are new and different and in keeping with the times, they attract attention as modern and up-to-date, and so have a certain charm. Yet to have something of true beauty made properly . . . formal furnishings, say, or some decorative object for your residence that has a conventional form . . . the distinction between a maker of novelties and a master craftsman is plain for all to see. To take another example, there are many skilled painters at the palace, but when you have to pick one to do basic sketching for a work, it is hard to tell at a glance which ones are the truly skilled artists. Paintings that present startling scenes of the mountains on the isle of

3. A reference to a poem on marriage included in the collected writings of [Bo] Juyi.

Hōrai where the immortals dwell, or that show the stern visages of beasts from exotic lands or the faces of demons no man has ever seen all give play to the imagination and astonish our eyes, since they bear no resemblance to the real world. Such works are fine, given what they are, and any painter will do. But when it comes to realistically depicting scenes in the everyday world . . . mountain vistas, flowing streams, the familiar look of our dwellings . . . the attention to detail and the technical execution of the master painter in serenely presenting familiar objects or in depicting the steep, rugged landscape of the mountains or in piling layer upon layer of thick foliage to create the impression that one is far removed from society or in placing a garden enclosed by a bamboo fence in the foreground . . . all require a special power and grace that are far beyond the skills of an ordinary artist.

"Or take calligraphy. Even a person with no real knowledge of the art can add a flourish here and there to create the impression . . . at least at a cursory glance . . . that he has great talent, while a person who can in fact write with true skill and care may appear to lack the ability of a master. But when you compare the works of such people side by side, you can see that the latter is closer to the genuine thing. So it is with all trivial matters of art and pleasure. I know that when it comes to human emotions it is even more the case that you cannot trust the affected elegance a woman puts on as a show for a particular occasion. Shall I tell you how I came by this knowledge, though I may have to speak indiscreetly about an affair?" He shifted a little closer, and Genji woke up. Tō no Chūjō was sitting across from him, his chin cupped in his hands, listening in earnest anticipation. It made for a charming tableau, resembling a scene in which a learned priest expounds on the ways of the world. It was the kind of moment, however, when young men find it hard to keep their relationships secret.

"Some time ago," the Warden resumed, "when I was still a very low-ranking official, I was quite taken with a young woman. But, as I presumed to mention to your highnesses earlier, she was not exceptionally beautiful, and so I decided in my youthful, fickle heart that I would not take her as my main wife. Though I thought of her as someone I could always turn to and rely on, there was something lacking, and I was sure I could do better. So I played around and cheated on her, and when she became distressingly jealous she lost favor with me. I kept hoping that she would not be like that, and wanted her to be a little less sensitive. While I found it irksome that she was so unforgiving and suspicious, I was also puzzled that she had lost patience with a man of such a low rank as I. At the same time, I couldn't understand why she still had feelings for me. I often felt sorry for her, and so I eventually brought my tendency to stray under control.

"Her temperament was such that somehow or another she contrived to do her best for me, even in matters for which she had no innate ability. She prodded herself, ashamed of faults she didn't want others to see, and she earnestly supported me in every way, trying her best never to go against my wishes in even the slightest matter. At the beginning I had thought of her as a strong-willed woman, but in the end she was yielding and accommodating. She worried that she might put me off if she did not make herself attractive, and whenever she allowed herself to be seen by someone not close to her, she would fret about it, feeling that perhaps she had shamed her husband. She did her utmost to maintain her wifely virtue, and as we grew accustomed to living as husband and wife, I was not at all ill disposed toward her except for that one detestable flaw . . . her jealousy, which she could not control.

"At the time she seemed so absurdly obedient and fearful, and I thought I should teach her a lesson . . . you know, shake her up a little so she would stop being jealous and mend her ways. So I pretended I was truly fed up and that we should break off our relationship. Since she had previously shown only a submissive attitude to me, I thought for sure I could teach her a lesson, and intentionally treated her with wretched callousness. When, as usual, she got angry, I told her that if she were going to be so willful and disagreeable, then I would put an end to our marriage and not meet her again despite the deep bond we shared as husband and wife. I said, 'If you really want us to separate, just keep harboring your baseless suspicions. But if you want us to have a long future together, then you have to accept that there will be hardships and try to not let things bother you. Rid yourself of your twisted disposition, and I will find you endearing. As soon as I work my way up at court and achieve respectable status, no other woman will ever compete with you for my devotion.' I thought I was being so clever in straightening her out with such assertive words, but she just smiled vaguely and replied, 'It doesn't bother or worry me that you are in a period in your life when you have neither status nor distinction, nor am I waiting impatiently for you to achieve success. But I find it painfully unbearable to have to always hide my feeling of wretchedness and rely on the uncertain hope that as the months and years go by the day will finally arrive when you reform your behavior. So the time has come when we must go our separate ways.' Her spiteful words made me very angry and I said a number of hateful things to her. At that point the woman, unable to control her passions, grabbed my hand and bit one of my fingers. I put on a show of outrage and, holding out my crooked finger, stalked out. 'Now that you've disfigured me like this,' I threatened, 'how can I possibly show myself at court? You yourself said I'm of no consequence, so now that you've done this how do you expect me to get ahead? If this is how things are, then it looks like we really are through from now on.' I composed a poem.

> As I bend my wounded fingers counting
> The times I called on you, your flaws it seems
> Are not confined to jealousy alone

'You won't have me to resent anymore,' I said, and as expected she burst into tears and shot back.

> Having counted in my heart the times
> I showed restraint at your behavior
> Now I have to take my hand from yours

She challenged me in this manner, and even though I did not believe our relationship would really change, I drifted about seeing women here and there and let many days pass without once communicating with her. Then one night, near the end of the eleventh month, I was detained at the palace in order to rehearse music and dance for the Rinji festival at the Kamo Shrine. A miserable sleet was falling that night, and as I was saying good-bye to my companions, who were going their separate ways, it occurred to me that I had no other place to go but hers. Sleeping at the palace seemed a dreary prospect, and the thought of visiting some woman who puts on an air of refined elegance chilled me to the bone. And so, all the while wondering what she thought about me, I went to peek in on her and see how she was faring. As I brushed the snow off myself, I felt constrained by feelings of embarrassment; and yet I hoped that perhaps tonight her icy resentment had thawed. The lamps had been dimmed and turned toward the walls, and softly padded robes had been plumped up and hung over a large filigree basket to be warmed and perfumed. The blinds were raised just as they were supposed to be, and the room gave the appearance that she had been waiting for me to return that very evening. Since everything was prepared just to my liking, I felt a swelling pride until I noticed she was nowhere to be found. Only the women who served her were there, as I had expected, and they told me she had gone to her parents' residence for the evening. She had left no elegant poem to rouse my interest, no word at all that she was anxious to see me. She had simply left and locked herself away, showing no consideration for me. I was quite let down and couldn't help wondering if her unyielding spitefulness wasn't implicitly signaling to me that I should go ahead and hate her if I wanted. The rooms gave no indication she was having an affair . . . was her aim to make me angry and suspicious of her? Yet the hues and stitching of the robes she had laid out for me were prepared with more than normal care, just as I would have wished. Clearly she was taking care to look after me even though she now assumed I had abandoned her.

"Things being the way they were, I figured she would never cut me off completely, and so I tried to downplay our spat and make up with her. And though she did not defy me by hiding herself away and making me run around looking for her, or by replying in a way that would cause me embarrassment, still she told me, 'I cannot continue putting up with you the way you are now. If you reform and develop a more steady disposition, then maybe we can see each other.' Even though she spoke to me like that, I was convinced she could never leave me, and so I thought I'd let her stew a while longer to punish her. 'All right, then, let's do as you suggest,' I told her, showing her just how stubborn I could be. She suffered so much during that time that at last she died. I knew then that I should never have made light of her, and I can't help thinking now that it's good enough for a man if his wife is someone who is wholly dependable. It was always worthwhile talking to her, regardless of whether we were discussing some trivial, passing matter or an important issue. She was so skilled at dyeing cloth that it's no exaggeration to compare her to the goddess of fall foliage, Princess Tatsuta herself. And when it came to weaving, she was as skillful as the Celestial Weaver Maid we celebrate at Tanabata.[4] Gifted in such ways, she was an exceptional wife." The Warden felt a keen sorrow at the memory. Tō no Chūjō tried to console him, saying "Her weaving may have been unsurpassed, but her real virtue was following the example of the Celestial Weaver Maid, who faithfully keeps her vow of love with the Celestial Oxherd. The fact is, you cannot expect to find someone again whose weaving

4. Tanabata is a festival on the seventh day of the seventh lunar month that celebrates the annual meeting of the young lovers Orihime (the celestial weaver maid, i.e., the star Vega) and Hikoboshi (the celestial oxherd, i.e., the star Altair). Because their love distracted them from their heavenly responsibilities, they were separated by the Milky Way and are allowed to meet only once a year, crossing on a bridge formed by the wings of a flock of magpies. Princess Tatsuta (Tatsuta-hime) is the goddess of fall who weaves the brocade of autumn foliage on Mount Tatsuta. She is thus the patron goddess of weaving and dyeing.

compares with that of Princess Tatsuta. When the passing flowers or autumn foliage are not in harmony with the hues of the season, they do not stand out as brightly, and their beauty dissipates. Women are just like that . . . their beauty passing out of season. That's why it's so difficult in this hard life to decide upon a wife." His words were an encouragement to continue talking.

The Warden once more resumed his discussion. "After she died, I started calling on a woman whose family lineage was peerless and who seemed to have an exquisitely refined temperament. She wrote poetry in a flowing hand, was well trained in the plucking style of the koto, and sang like a master. I couldn't find any flaws in anything I saw or heard of her. She was also passably good-looking, and so even while I continued to be on familiar terms with the woman who bit my finger, I was also secretly visiting this other woman, and eventually grew very attracted to her. After the death of my wife, while I was grieving and wondering what I should do, I came to the realization that nothing could be done for those who have died and started visiting the other woman more frequently. After I became familiar with her, I began to notice that she was somewhat ostentatious . . . and flirtatious. Since she did not seem to be the sort of woman I could trust, I began to keep my distance a little, and when I did so she started meeting another man in secret.

"It was an autumn evening during the tenth month. The moon was bright and seductive, and as I set out from the palace I encountered a certain high-ranking courtier. We got into my carriage together, and though I was intending to stay the night at the home of my father, who was a Major Counselor at the time, this courtier told me he was quite eager to stop by a certain place where a woman was waiting for him. Because the house he mentioned happened to be on the way to my father's house, I caught a glimpse of its garden through the fence and saw the moon shimmering on the surface of the pond. Finding it hard to pass by a dwelling where even the moon seemed to have taken up residence, I dismounted the carriage with the man. He apparently had had this sort of rendezvous before, and seemed very excited when he sat down on the widely spaced boards of an open veranda near the inner gate. He struck a dashing pose as he gazed up at the moon. Chrysanthemums, their colors faded by the autumn frost, were arrayed gorgeously, and the scarlet profusion of scattered maple leaves rustling in the breeze looked magnificent. The man took out a flute from the breast fold of his robe and began to play various popular *saibara* such as "The shade is good."[5] He also sang a few verses: "Let us tarry awhile at the well of Asuka, the shade is good, the waters cool, the grasses inviting . . . " The woman inside accompanied him skillfully, having apparently readied her six-string koto. Her instrument reverberated clearly, and she played it flawlessly, softly, having tuned it to a folksy minor key, and the sound that wafted from the other side of the bamboo blinds seemed quite fashionably modern, a perfect accompaniment to the pure autumn moon. The man was charmed and impressed, and moved closer to the blind. Alluding to a poem about visiting the abode of a beautiful woman, he tried to get a response from her, saying 'I see no trace of anyone having disturbed the fallen leaves in your garden.' He picked some chrysanthemums and composed a poem.

5. The genre of music referred to here, the *saibara*, was a popular form in which the lyrics of folk songs (usually) were set to Chinese music. Lines from various *saibara* appear throughout the narrative.

> How lovely are the peerless moon
> And music here . . . yet do they draw
> Aught but coldhearted men to you

'I hear you have spoken ill of me. But never mind. Let me have one more song. When a person you want to encourage to listen is present, you should put all your skills on display.' The woman replied to his brazen bantering, affecting a disinterested voice.

> A leaf can never hope to stay the autumn breeze
> Any more than words or music could make tarry
> This flutist who accompanies the bitter wind

She responded seductively, unaware that I was witness to her distasteful forwardness. She then switched to a larger thirteen-string koto tuned to the *banshiki* mode,[6] darker in tone and thus appropriate for the season. Her style of plucking was lively and contemporary, and yet, even though her playing sparkled, listening to her left me feeling unsettled and embarrassed. When a lady you are seeing intimately from time to time goes out of her way to be fashionably elegant, she is certainly very alluring, at least on those infrequent occasions when you actually meet. But if on one of your rare visits a woman you are considering as a possible mate behaves too voluptuously, then you begin to grow wary and worry she might not be reliable after all. On the basis of what I observed that evening, I decided to end my affair with that lady.

"Though I was young and inexperienced at the time, when I look back and compare those two women, their capriciousness made them seem inscrutable and unreliable to me. And from now on I will likely be even more inclined to feel that way about women. Your lordships may take delight only in the pleasures of those fragile and fleeting charms of a young lady who poets would liken to the dew on bush clover that scatters when you pluck the flower, or to sleet on leaves of dwarf bamboo that melts away at your touch. But though you may feel that way now, just wait another seven years, and when you reach my age you will think the same way I do. Please take my poor, humble advice and be careful with women who lead you on. They'll cheat on you and make you look foolish in the eyes of others." And so he advised them.

Tō no Chūjō continued nodding. Genji smiled faintly, apparently agreeing with the Warden, and remarked, "It seems in both cases your romantic escapades were awkward and unlucky." They all had a good laugh.

Tō no Chūjō spoke up next. "I'd like to tell you about a foolish woman I knew. I started seeing her in secret, and because it looked as though I would have to keep seeing her on the sly, I didn't think our affair would last. But as we grew intimate I came to have deeper feelings for her, and even though I could not meet her very often, I simply couldn't get her out of my mind. Eventually our relationship reached the stage where I could see she trusted me, and many times I honestly thought if she depends on me so much, then there must be things I do that upset her. If there were, however, she never let on about them. Even when I did not visit her for long stretches, she did not jealously resent me or think me inconsiderate. Instead, she kept up appearances morn-

6. A musical mode particularly suitable for winter [editors' note].

ing and night, as if she expected me every day. She was so meek and docile that I was moved to pity and assured her that she could always rely on me.

"She had no parents and was quite lonely and helpless. That's why I found it touching that she apparently thought of me as her provider. She was so quiet and unassuming that I was unconcerned and let my guard down . . . but then, during one of those long stretches when I did not call on her, she received some rather deplorable messages from my wife's household . . . messages that implied threats against her. Unfortunately I heard about that only much later.

"I was unaware there had been such unpleasantness, and even though I had not forgotten her, we went so long without exchanging a word that she grew despondent. She was so wretched worrying over the baby girl I had fathered by her that she sent me a wild pink, suggesting, I suppose, that the child was like the flower, hidden from sight and easy to overlook." Tears welled up in Tō no Chūjō's eyes.

"And the letter that accompanied the flower?" asked Genji.

"Nothing special, really," he replied. "She sent this poem.

> The hedge around the hut of the mountain peasant
> Grows untended now . . . let fall your tender mercy
> Let it fall like dew and settle on this wild pink[7]

"With her verse fresh in my mind, I went to see her. She was as faithful and uncomplaining as ever, but her face was worn with care. It was autumn, and as she gazed out from her dilapidated house at the overgrown garden drenched in dew, her tearful expression seemed to vie in sadness with the melancholy chirring of the bell crickets. I felt as though I were in some old romance.

> I cannot judge which of these flowers is fairest
> Their colors mingling in never-ending summer
> But there is none dearer than my little wild pink

"I turned my attention from the child and comforted the lady by reminding her of the old poem in which a lover promises to visit always, so that dust never settles on their bed.[8] She replied with this.

> Autumn arrives and rough winds shake
> Dew from wild pinks and tears from sleeves
> That wipe dust from my lonely bed

7. The word translated as "wild pink" is *nadeshiko*. In the two poems that follow immediately below, the word for "wild pink" is *tokonatsu*. Although the two names refer to the same flower, Murasaki Shikibu uses both in this sequence of poems to distinguish between mother and child. In the first poem, *nadeshiko* refers to Tō no Chūjō's child by his lover, while in the second and third poems *tokonatsu* refers to the woman. Both *nadeshiko* and *tokonatsu* may be identified as other flowers (e.g., a carnation or a gillyflower), but both are generic names for "pinks." I have chosen to use the name "wild pink" to suggest the well-worn theme in the tradition of Japanese literature that Murasaki Shikibu drew on of a beautiful lover who is discovered by a man in an out-of-the-way place, like a wild flower growing in a hidden spot. The two poems below also play on the word *tokonatsu*, which is a homophone for "never-ending summer," and which has an element, *toko*, that is a homophone for "bed." [The mother appears in chapter 4 (*Yūgao*) as Genji's lover, the lady of the Evening Faces. The little girl is the future Tamakazura, who will later be taken in by Genji. In chapter 25, included in the selections below, she discusses with Genji the virtue and vices of romantic tales—editors' note.]

8. Poem from *The Kokinshū* by Ōshikōchi no Mitsune: "I long to stop even a mote of dust from settling on this bed of pinks that have come into bloom since first you and I lay on our bed."

"She spoke casually, giving no hint that she harbored any serious resentment. Even when she wept, she seemed ashamed and awkward and tried to hide her face from me. It was painful to her that I might see she felt I had been cruel, and so I was reassured about our relationship and did not visit her again for a long time. During that interval she ran off somewhere, disappearing without a trace.

"She may still be alive somewhere, but her situation must be precarious and uncertain. If only she had given some indication of how strongly attached to me she was at that moment when I was so moved by her plight, then she would never have had to run away like that. I would never have neglected her as I did, but would have treated her properly, just like any other woman I called on, and looked after her forever. I cherished that little wild pink, and so assumed I would always be able to visit her. But now I am unable to track her whereabouts. Certainly this woman belongs to the category of the unreliable type you mentioned earlier. She appeared so unruffled, never letting on that she found my treatment of her cruel, but in the end my feelings for her, which had never waned, turned out to be nothing more than a futile, one-sided love. Now, even as I'm slowly getting her out of my heart, I sometimes think about her, imagining that she has not forgotten me altogether . . . that there are evenings when she realizes she cannot blame anyone else for her predicament and her heart smolders with regret. She is certainly the type of woman you cannot rely on or hold to for very long.

"Although a difficult woman is memorable, and thus hard to get out of your mind, when things do not go well and you find it troublesome to continue seeing her . . . as you found with the woman who bit your finger . . . you tire of the relationship. And a talented woman like your koto player is almost certain to be burdened by the sin of infidelity. As for the woman I spoke of, she was so utterly lacking in character that I have doubts about her as well. So I have reached the point where I find it impossible to choose which type of woman is best. It has proven difficult to compare each respective relationship between men and women in this manner. Where is the woman who could combine the virtues of the three women we discussed without inevitably bringing with her all their unmanageable flaws? Set your sights on the beautiful goddess of fortune, Kichijōten,[9] and not only will her holiness bore you stiff, but you'll end up reeking of incense to boot!" The young men all laughed at that.

"But come now," Tō no Chūjō prodded the Junior Secretary from the Ministry of Rites, "there must be a few unusual affairs going on around your place. Tell us a little about them."

"Do you honestly think anything worth discussing happens in a place as lowly as mine?" the young man said. But Tō no Chūjō pressed him, insisting that he was waiting for a response, and so the Junior Secretary wracked his brain to come up with some tale.

"When I was still a student of letters at the academy in the Ministry of Ceremonials,[1] I happened to be calling on a clever young woman. Like the woman

9. Images of Kichijōten were common in Buddhist temples, and it was said that monks often fell in love with her [editors' note].
1. This official academy or university was loosely based on Chinese bureaucratic models and used to train young men for positions in the government. The course of study largely emphasized the Confucian Canon and focused on the fields of Chinese Classics, law, ethics, and letters (primarily history and poetry). It also provided instruction in practical fields such as mathematics and yin-yang studies [i.e., divination].

the Warden mentioned, she was a good companion. I could discuss official matters with her, and she was also deeply prudent when it came to the conduct of household affairs. Her brilliance would put an unprepared scholar to shame, and so it was hard to hold my own with her in any conversation we had.

"I began to attend an academy to study Chinese with a certain scholar who just happened to have many daughters. As things turned out, I became intimate with one of them, and when her father found out he brought out some ceremonial sake cups and spoke to me in an overly suggestive tone, reciting a line from Bai Juyi's poem in praise of marriage: 'Listen while I recite a poem about the two paths of life.' You know the poem . . . the one that extols the virtues of a wife who comes from an impoverished home and urges the husband to cherish her. I hadn't actually fallen head over heels for the woman or anything like that, but I was mindful of her father's feelings. In any case I was beholden to him, and she was a kind and considerate support to me. Even during our pillow talk she would impart her knowledge of Chinese, teaching many crucial things I would need for my official position. Her own writing was clear, almost mannish. She employed a precise, rational diction and never mixed the more feminine kana script with her Chinese characters. Naturally I couldn't break off the relationship, because with her as my teacher I was able to learn how to write halting verses in Chinese. Even now I can't forget the debt I owe her . . . but then again for a man like me who has no intellectual talents at all to have to rely on a woman I was intimate with and have her witness my pathetic performances . . . well, it was too shameful. Your lordships, of course, would never need such an efficient and rigorous helpmate. As for me, even though our relationship strikes me as trivial and regrettable now, at the same time she was someone I was drawn to, perhaps as a result of a karmic bond from a former life. It seems that men are really the feckless ones." The moment he finished, both Genji and Tō no Chūjō cajoled him, saying "Well, well, a most intriguing lady indeed" in order to get him to finish up his story. Knowing he was being led on, the Junior Secretary feigned distaste, a comical sneer crinkling his nose as he continued.

"Now then, I did not go to see her for the longest time, and when I finally dropped in on some errand, she was not at all the relaxed, familiar woman she had once been, but instead stayed behind a bothersome screen when we met. It seemed to me she was being peevish, which was foolish behavior, and so I thought this might be the perfect opportunity to break up with her. Yet I knew that such an intelligent woman would never hold a grudge for a frivolous reason. She understood the ways of the world and would not be resentful. She spoke in a voice that sounded rushed and breathy. 'These past few months I have been indisposed by a severe malady and prescribed a regimen of herbal tonic concocted mainly of garlic. This has rendered me extremely malodorous and incapable of meeting you tête-à-tête. Though we cannot meet directly, I would be pleased to undertake any miscellaneous tasks you might request of me.' Her words were so admirably learned, and so . . . manly. When I got up to leave she was perhaps feeling anxious and restless, for she added in a screechy voice, 'Please do come by when this odor has dissipated!' I felt very sorry to leave without responding to her, but there was no reason to hang around and, to tell the truth, the odor was getting to me. So I had no choice but to cast an imploring look at her as if to excuse myself. I sent this poem.

> On an evening when a spider's busy spinning
> Announces I will soon be here, why should I be told
> To wait until the smell of garlic passes from you

"'What sort of excuse are you giving me,' I asked. The words had barely left my lips, and I was on the verge of making my escape, when her reply came chasing me down.

> If my love could bring you every night,
> Why then should the daytime be so blinding
> Or this smell of garlic so offensive[2]

"You have to admit that she was certainly quick." He spoke so calmly that the young nobles found the whole account implausibly sordid. "A complete fabrication," they said, laughing. "Where could anyone ever find a woman like that? You might just as easily have gone off to meet a demon. The whole thing is creepy and weird." Flicking their thumbs with the nail of their index finger to show their disapproval, they chided the Junior Secretary and pressured him to tell them something better than that. But the young man just sat there and replied, "How can I serve you up anything stranger that that?"

The Warden interceded. "Generally speaking, it is really pathetic how people of no importance, men or women, think they have to show off every last little thing they have learned. A woman who acquires knowledge of Chinese and has read the Three Histories or the Five Classics lacks all feminine charm . . . but then again, why should we assume that a woman, just because she is a woman, would go through life without acquiring any knowledge at all of public and private affairs? Though she may not receive any formal education, a woman who has even a modicum of intelligence will retain many things she sees and hears. Through such knowledge she may learn to write cursive Chinese characters, and the next thing you know she's sending stiffly written letters half-filled with Chinese script to other ladies who don't have a clue what to do with them. When you see such a woman you're filled with chagrin, wondering why she couldn't be a bit more soft-spoken and ladylike. She may not have intended to show off her learning in the letter, but of course as it is being read aloud in a halting, strained voice the whole thing seems calculated. There are many examples of this sort of behavior among the upper ranks of court ladies.

"A woman with aspirations to being a poet will become so obsessed with the art of composition that she'll insert allusions to felicitous old phrases even in the opening lines of her correspondence. She'll send off a poem at the most inopportune moments, which can be quite off-putting. If the man doesn't reply, he's inconsiderate, and if he can't come up with an equally learned allusion, he looks ridiculous. For instance, at some seasonal festival, when a man is really busy . . . let's say on the morning of the Sweet Flag Festival in the fifth month when you don't have a moment to think calmly about anything . . . she whips out a poem with some fabulous allusion playing on the words 'sweet flag' and 'sweet eyes,' or some such nonsense. Or maybe it's the Chrysanthemum Festival, when you have no time at all to wrack your brains to come up with

---

2. The poem plays on the word *hiru*, meaning either "daytime" or "garlic." This wordplay explains the Junior Secretary's admiration of her quick wit.

some difficult poem in Chinese as the occasion demands, and here she is sending you a lamentation that strains to play on the words 'chrysanthemum' and 'dew.'[3] The poem is not only unsuitable to the time and place, but also a downright nuisance. What otherwise might have seemed a charming or moving poem at a subsequent reading ends up being totally inappropriate and not worth a second glance because of the manner in which it was sent. Composing a poem with no forethought is not very tactful.

"It is far easier to deal with a woman who has no talent for discerning the proper moment or season to compose, who does not put on airs and try to act refined in a way that leaves you wondering why she did what she did. In all cases a woman should pretend to be ignorant, even if she has a little learning. And when she has something to say, she should just focus on a couple of points and skip the rest."

While the Warden was droning on Genji was preoccupied with thoughts of one woman in particular . . . Fujitsubo. Comparing her to the women he had heard about this evening, he was moved to an even greater admiration, since she seemed to be that rare type who was neither extravagant nor lacking in any way.

There was no conclusion to their discussion; and in the end as daybreak neared their ramblings came to include some rather queer and disreputable stories.

* * *

FROM CHAPTER V

Wakamurasaki

Little Purple Gromwell

* * *

With no one to talk to, and with idle time to kill after the healing rites were completed, Genji stepped out under cover of the heavy evening mist and set out toward the fence he had seen earlier. He had already sent his attendants back to their homes and was peeking through the fence with Koremitsu. In a nearby room, which was facing west toward Amida's Pure Land,[4] they saw a nun performing religious devotions before her own personal image of Amida Buddha. The blinds were raised a little, and she was apparently making an offering of flowers. Leaning against one of the central pillars, she had placed a sutra scroll on top of an armrest and was struggling to read the scripture—but she did not look like an ordinary woman. She was probably over forty, her complexion quite fair and graceful, and though she was thin, her cheeks were plump, and the strands of her hair, which had been cut attractively to neatly

---

3. The Sweet Flag Festival, which fell on the fifth day of the Fifth Month, was celebrated at the court with equestrian and archery competitions. The Chrysanthemum Festival was observed on the ninth of the Ninth Month; chrysanthemums were thought to possess properties that ensured a long life, and so on that day, the flowers were wrapped in thin cot-ton cloths that, once dampened with dew, were rubbed over the body to take advantage of chrysanthemums' supposed life-prolonging properties [editors' note].

4. Devotees of Pure Land Buddhism believe that they will be reborn in the "Western Paradise" of the Buddha Amitabha [editors' note].

frame the area around her eyes, struck Genji as more distinctively fashionable than the long hair that was the common style. Watching her, he was touched by her appearance.

Two pretty adult attendants, also neatly turned out, were with her, and some young girls were playing there, running in and out of the room. One of them, who must have been about ten years old, was wearing a white singlet under a soft, crinkled outer robe dyed the rich yellow of mountain rose and lined with a yellow fabric. She didn't look like the other girls at all; her features were so attractive that Genji could tell at once that she would grow up to be a woman of surpassing beauty. Her hair flowed out behind her, spreading open in the shape of a fan as she stood there, her face red from brushing tears away.

"What happened?" the nun asked her. "Did you get into a quarrel with the other girls?" When the nun looked up to speak, Genji could see the resemblance in their faces and assumed that they must be mother and daughter.

"Inuki let my baby sparrow out of the cage and it flew away." The girl was pouting.

One of the young women sitting there said, "Careless as usual. Inuki's in for a real scolding this time. What a nuisance she is! So where did the sparrow go? It's such a darling little thing, it would be horrid if the crows get to it." She stood up and went out, her hair quite long and luxuriant. She was quite easy on the eyes, Genji thought. Apparently her name was Shōnagon, and she was the nurse who looked after the little girl.

"How childish!" the nun said. "Really, this whole thing is just too petty. You pay no heed to me, even though I could pass away any day now, and instead go running about chasing after sparrows. How many times have I told you it's a sin in the sight of Buddha to capture living creatures. It's deplorable. Come over here!"

The girl knelt down beside her. Her face was remarkably sweet, her unplucked eyebrows had the most charming air about them, and the cut of her hair and the look of her forehead, with those bangs swept up so innocently, were unbearably cute. Genji couldn't stop gazing at her. *I'd really love to see her when she's grown up.* It occurred to him that his desire to see her grown up was kindled by her uncanny resemblance to Fujitsubo, the woman to whom his heart was eternally devoted. It was thus natural that his gaze would be drawn to the girl, and tears came to his eyes.

Stroking the child's hair, the nun told her, "You may not be fond of combing your hair, but it's so lovely. You are such a silly girl, and your childishness weighs heavily on my mind. Other children your age don't act like this. Even though your mother was only ten when her father passed away, she still understood everything going on around her. It won't be long before I die and you'll be left completely alone in the world. How will you ever manage to get by?"

Seeing the nun weep so bitterly, Genji felt a pang of sympathetic sorrow. The girl, with her childish emotions, stared at her grandmother, then hung her head and stared at the floor. Her hair came cascading down around her face. It was splendidly lustrous.

Just then the nun composed a verse.

> The evanescent dewdrop tarries, reluctant
> To disappear into the sky and abandon
> The tender shoot of grass to its uncertain fate

The other young woman, who was still sitting in the room, was now crying. "How true!" she said, and composed this reply.

> How could the dewdrop disappear
> Without knowing the destiny
> Of the shoot of grass it clings to

Just then the bishop entered. "What are you doing? You're clearly visible from the outside. Why, today of all days, are you out on the veranda? I just found out from the ascetic who lives up the mountain that his lordship, Captain Genji, has arrived to receive treatment for his fever. He arrived in such secrecy that I knew nothing about it. I've been here all this time and didn't pay my respects to him."

"How awful," the nun said, lowering the blinds. "Has anyone seen us like this? We're not at all presentable."

"Don't you want to take this opportunity," asked the bishop, "to catch a glimpse of the Radiant Genji? After all, he has such a noble reputation at the court. His looks are enough to make even the heart of a monk who has renounced society forget the sorrows of life and desire to live on in this world. I shall send him a letter."

Upon hearing the bishop stand up to leave, Genji also retired, delighted at the thought that he had discovered such a gorgeous child under these circumstances. His amorous companions were always going out, and so they were skilled at finding the kind of unusual woman that one rarely meets at court. Genji, however, could only go out occasionally, and so he was even more delighted to have the unexpected good fortune to stumble across a girl like this. She was certainly lovely, but her beauty made him curious. Who was she? She resembled Fujitsubo so closely that he was completely taken with the notion that he might be able to make her a replacement for the woman he loved, keeping the girl by him mornings and evenings as a comfort to his heart.

Genji had withdrawn and was lying down and resting when a disciple of the bishop called out for Koremitsu. They were close by, so Genji could hear everything they said. The disciple was apparently reading the bishop's message: "I just now learned that his lordship has passed by my residence, and though I was caught by surprise, I still should have called on you. However, as you know, I have secluded myself in this temple, and so I regret that you have traveled here in secret, for I could have made my abode, rough and humble though it is, ready for you. I feel this is truly unfortunate, for it was in no way my intention to slight you."

Genji sent back a reply: "Starting around the tenth of this month I began suffering repeated bouts of ague. The attacks were so frequent I found them hard to bear, and so on the advice of others I came discreetly to see the ascetic here. I chose to keep my journey a strict secret, because if the ascetic's spells were ineffective for me, it would certainly damage his reputation. It would be a much greater pity if such a venerable ascetic were to fail than it would be if the healer were some ordinary priest, and so I wanted to exercise some caution. I shall go to your residence presently."

The bishop himself appeared soon after. Even though he was a priest, he had a reputation at court as a man of flawless breeding and dignity, and his bearing was enough to put people to shame. Genji, who was dressed in humble fashion, felt awkward before him. The bishop spoke of the time he had spent in seclusion here, and then insisted repeatedly that Genji pay him a visit. "My house is a rustic hut, not much different from this abode here, but you can at least get a view of a cool stream there." Genji felt embarrassed as he recalled the fawning manner in which the bishop had described his radiant looks to the women, who had never seen him. Still, he was eager to learn more about the lovely little girl, and so he went with the bishop.

Just as the bishop said, the garden at his residence exuded an air of elegance. The trees and grasses, which were familiar varieties, had been cultivated with special care. Because it was the night of the new moon, cressets had been set along the banks of the stream, the light from their fires reflecting in the water, and oil lamps were hung beneath the eaves. The room facing south at the front of the house had been cleaned and neatly prepared. The refined scent of incense wafted out from the interior and mingled with the scent of the ritual incense offered to the Buddha, suffusing the entire area around the residence. Genji's perfumed robes carried their own special scent, which the people in the house could not help but notice.

The reverend bishop instructed Genji on the evanescence of this world and on the worlds to come. Genji, with some trepidation, was forced to acknowledge to himself the gravity of his sin of loving Fujitsubo, and it was torment knowing he could do nothing about the one thing preoccupying his heart. It seemed that he was doomed to suffer obsessively on account of his sin for the rest of this life; and what made it worse for him was always imagining the kinds of terrible retribution that awaited him in future lives. He thought he would like to leave the base temptations of this world and retreat to a humble abode like this . . . but then he found it hard to concentrate on the bishop's lesson, since the alluring vision of that young girl he had spied on during the day lingered in his heart alongside the image of the woman, Fujitsubo, the girl so resembled.

"Who lives here?" Genji asked. "On arriving today, I was reminded of a dream I wanted to ask you about."

The bishop smiled. "So you want to suddenly change the subject to your dreams, do you? Well, you can ask, but I'm afraid I'll disappoint you. You probably didn't know the former Major Counselor, since he passed away some time ago, but his primary wife was my younger sister. After he died she took religious vows and left her household to become a nun. She has been suffering from a variety of ailments recently, and since I no longer go back to the capital she decided to seclude herself by taking my residence for her haven."

Genji said, "I've heard that the Major Counselor had a daughter. My motive in asking about her, by the way, is quite sincere. It is not frivolous curiosity."

"He did indeed. One daughter. Let's see . . . it's been more than ten years now since she died. The late Counselor intended to send her into service at the court, and so he raised her with the greatest care. When he passed away before he could realize his hopes and dreams, my sister ended up raising her daughter by herself. When the girl reached womanhood Prince Hyōbu, who was Minister of War at the time,[5] was able to conduct a clandestine affair with her, using one of her scheming ladies-in-waiting as his go-between. Prince Hyōbu's pri-

---

5. The name Prince Hyōbu is taken from the Ministry of War (Hyōbushō). Since this prince is identified by his position, I continue to use this name as a matter of convenience.

mary wife, however, was a woman of impeccable birth, and as a result my niece suffered various insults that brought worry and grief. She grew increasingly despondent day by day, until at last she died. I have witnessed with my own eyes how sick from worry a person can get."

Genji gathered from the bishop's story that the little girl he had seen was the granddaughter of the nun. The prince in question was the older brother of Fujitsubo, which explained the resemblance between the woman Genji loved and the little girl. Now he felt an even stronger desire to see the girl and make the child his own. She was possessed of both a noble lineage and extraordinary beauty, but she also had an obedient temperament, and was not impudent or forward. He wanted to get close to her, raise and train her in accordance with his own desires and tastes, and then make her his wife.

"A sad tale, indeed," Genji remarked. "Did your niece leave any children behind to remember her by?" He wanted to find out for sure what had become of the little girl he had seen earlier.

The bishop told him, "A child was born just before my niece died . . . a girl. The child is the cause of terrible worry for my sister, who as death approaches fears she will leave her granddaughter in an unsettled situation."

So she's the one I was looking at.

"I know this will sound like a bizarre request, but would you do me the kindness of asking the girl's grandmother to consider allowing me to take charge of the child? I have good reasons for this request. I do call upon my primary wife from time to time, but we really don't get along so well, and I live alone for the most part. You may not consider her the proper age for such an arrangement, and you may think I am motivated by some common, base desire. But if you do, you are being unkind and dishonoring my intentions."

"Such a proposition would normally be met with great joy, but the girl is still so innocent it would be difficult, would it not, to take her as a wife . . . even if the whole thing was done in jest? A woman becomes an adult when a husband looks after her, and so it is not my place to deal with the details concerning such a matter. If I may, I will consult with her grandmother and try to obtain an answer for you."

The bishop was so forbiddingly sincere and stiffly formal in his manner of speech that it made Genji's youthful spirit feel small, and he was unable to come up with a clever response.

"It's time," continued the bishop, "to perform my devotions before the shrine of Amida Buddha in the prayer hall. I have not finished early evening services yet, but I will call on you again when they are over."

The bishop left and Genji was feeling ill. It had started to rain, bringing a cooling breeze. To top it off, the water in the pool of a nearby waterfall had risen with the spring runoff, and the roar was clearly audible. He could just barely make out the sound of sleepy voices reciting sutras, a sound that sent chills through him. The atmosphere of the place would have affected even the most insensitive of people, and, coupled with his preoccupation with both Fujitsubo and the girl, it prevented him from getting any sleep at all. The bishop had told him that he was off to early evening devotions, but it was already late at night. Genji could clearly sense that the women who resided in the interior of the house were not asleep, and though they were trying to be quiet he could make out the clicking of rosary beads rubbing against an armrest and the elegant, inviting rustle of robes. Because they were near him, he slid open ever so slightly the center panels of the screens that had been set up outside his room and lightly tapped the palm of his hand with a fan in order to draw their attention. Apparently they thought it unlikely that anyone would be there, but at the same time they couldn't very well ignore his summons, and so he heard one of the women moving over toward him. Confused, she then retreated a bit and said, "That's odd. I thought I heard something. I must be deluded."

Genji spoke up. "They say the guiding voice of the Buddha will never delude you or lead you astray, even in the darkest places." The voice was so youthful and aristocratic that her own voice sounded hesitant and embarrassed when she asked, "Guiding to where? I'm not sure I understand you."

"You probably think something is amiss, which is reasonable, since I called out so suddenly. Please present the following to your mistress."

> Glimpsing that sweet child, so like a shoot of spring grass,
> The sleeves of my traveling robes never dry out
> Damp as they are from dew and my own endless tears

The woman responded, "You surely know there is no one here who would accept that kind of message. To whom should I give it?"

"It so happens," Genji explained, "that I have reasons for my request, and so I ask for your understanding."

The woman retreated back into the interior of the house and spoke with the nun, who was confused by the request. It was, after all, shocking in so many respects.

"Really, these young people and their modern ways!" she grumbled. "Apparently this lord is under the misapprehension that the girl is old enough to understand the relationship between men and women. And how did he come to hear about our poems that referred to her as 'young grass'?"

She was confused, but realized she was being rude by taking such an inordinately long time to respond. So she sent the following.

> Are you comparing the dew-soaked pillow
> Of a single night's journey to these sleeves
> Covered by the moss of ancient mountains

"My robes, it seems, will never dry."

"I'm not very experienced at communicating this way through a messenger," Genji answered. "Please forgive me, but I would be grateful if you would allow me a moment to speak with you about a serious matter."

The nun turned to her attendants. "I'm afraid he's mistakenly heard that the girl is older than she is. He seems to be such a high-ranking lord, I feel humbled before him. How should I respond?"

"You must answer him," one of her women advised. "It would be a pity if you made him feel awkward."

"Yes, I suppose you're right," the nun relented. "But if I were still a young woman, I'd find it rather improper to meet him. His words are so earnest they make me feel unworthy." She rose and moved nearer to him.

"I realize that this is all quite sudden for you, and under these circumstances you must think my request rash and immoderate. But I assure you, I have no base desires in my heart, and swear to you that the Amida Buddha himself understands the depths of my feelings, which you seem to find incomprehensible." Genji spoke in a very respectful manner, since he was himself feeling awkward about raising the subject so directly in the presence of her quiet dignity.

"I must admit I never imagined that we would meet," the nun responded, "but that doesn't mean I consider the karmic bond between us to be shallow. Why should I, since we are speaking to one another like this?"

"I was moved when I heard about the painful struggles the girl has endured," Genji continued, "and wondered if you would consider me a substitute for the mother who has passed away. I was at a very tender age myself when I lost my mother and grandmother, the ones who should have cared most closely for me. As the months and years have passed I feel I have been living in a peculiar, drifting state. The girl's situation is so similar to my own that I sincerely ask permission to be her companion. Because I am concerned about how you will interpret my request, I feel constrained in bringing this up to you. However, I will have very few opportunities to approach you."

"I know I should be overjoyed by your request, but I am very reluctant to grant it. I don't know what you've heard about the girl, but isn't it possible that you are misinformed about how old she is? Insignificant though I am, the girl who lives here is completely dependent on me for support, and she's so young, I couldn't possibly agree to your request."

"I know all about her." Genji pressed his case. "If you will just consider the depths of my feelings, which are anything but common, you will put your reservations aside."

In spite of his insistent pleadings, the nun was convinced Genji was unaware of the inappropriateness of the request and would not give her assent. When the bishop returned, Genji at once closed up the folding screen. *Well, at least I've made the request. At least I can feel relieved about that.*

With the arrival of dawn the sound of monks confessing their sins in the hall where they devotedly chanted the Lotus Sutra came drifting down the mountainside. Their voices mingled nobly with the roar of the waterfall.

Genji sent a verse to the bishop.

> Voices of atonement waft down the mountain . . .
> As I awake from dreams and earthly desires
> The sound of falling waters calls forth my tears

The bishop replied.

> Purified in these mountain waters
> My own heart is unmoved by the sound
> Calling forth the tears that soak your sleeves

"I wonder if my ears have grown accustomed to the falling waters?"

The sky brightened to reveal an overcast day. The continuous crying of mountain birds mingled together, so that Genji could not tell from which direction they were coming. The various blossoms on the trees and grasses, whose names he did not know, were scattering in wild profusion, making it look as though someone had spread a brocade cloth over the landscape. He looked on in wonder at the deer ambling about, pausing here and there as they moved along. The scene was a diversion from his illness.

Normally, the old healer wasn't able to get out and about very easily, but somehow he managed to make his way to the bishop's residence and performed a protective spell. His voice was hoarse, and he was missing so many teeth his pronunciation was a little off, but he read the *dharani*[6] in a voice that possessed the august quality appropriate to a priest of great distinction and merit.

The party that would escort Genji back to the capital arrived and, after offering their congratulations on his cure, presented him with a message conveying best wishes from the Emperor. The bishop busily prepared delicacies not normally served at court, offering unusual types of fruits and nuts that had been harvested from various places, including the deep valley below.

"I have made a solemn vow to remain here for the year," the bishop told Genji, offering him some rice wine, "and so I will not be able to see you off. Ironically, my vow is now making me regret having to part with you."

"The waters of this mountain will remain in my heart. I have been undeservedly blessed by a gracious message from His Majesty, who is anxiously awaiting my return. However, I shall return here again before the season of spring blossoms has passed."

> Returning to court, I shall tell them
> You must go see the mountain cherries
> Before the breeze scatters their petals

Genji's manner of speaking and the tenor of his voice were dazzling. The bishop replied.

> The udumbara blooms once in three thousand years
> When a perfect lord appears[7] . . . having looked on you
> I no longer have eyes for those mountain cherries

Genji smiled and sagely remarked, "The Lotus Sutra teaches that the flower of the udumbara blooms only once and in its proper time, which is quite rare. You flatter me."

The healer received the wine cup and looked at Genji in tearful reverence.

> The pine door waiting deep in the mountains
> Has now been opened so that I can see
> The face of a flower ne'er glimpsed before

As a memento of their meeting, he presented Genji a *tokko*.[8] The metal rod, with its diamond-shaped points at both ends, was one of the implements he used in his esoteric rituals to symbolize the strength and wisdom needed to break free of earthly desires.

The bishop also presented several appropriate gifts. One was a rosary made of embossed seeds from the fruit of the bodhi tree that the famed Prince Shōtoku had acquired from the Korean kingdom of Paekche. The rosary had been placed in a Chinese style box that was wrapped up in a gauze pouch and attached to a

6. Dharani are spells or incantations used for meditation, healing or protection. They consist of a phrase or line originally in Sanskrit that encapsulates a central teaching of a sacred text in Buddhism. Dharani were used as an aid in meditation and, in this case, as a protective spell.

7. A Buddhist belief (the udumbara is a variety of fig) [editors' note].

8. This is an abbreviation of *tokkosho* (Sanskrit, *vajra*), a Buddhist ritual implement [editors' note].

branch of five-needle pine. Another gift was a set of medicine jars made of lapis lazuli, which were filled with medicines and attached to branches of wisteria and cherry.

Genji had arranged to have gifts and offerings brought from the capital for the healer and for the monks who had chanted sutras for him. He presented the required gifts to everyone there, even the woodcutters who lived in the vicinity, and after making an offering for continued sutra readings, he prepared to leave.

The bishop went inside with Genji's message and conveyed it directly to the nun. She replied to him, "No matter what he says, I couldn't possibly give him an answer now. If his heart is really set on the girl, then maybe we can consider it in four or five years."

The bishop agreed with her and told Genji how matters stood. Genji was deeply dissatisfied that the nun had thwarted his desires and responded by having one of the pages serving at the bishop's residence take a note to her.

> Making my way back through morning mists
> Having seen the flower's hues at dusk
> How painful to have to leave them now

Though the nun dashed off her reply, the brushstrokes were elegant and her characters truly graceful.

> It may be hard for the mist to leave the flower
> But gazing at the sky obscured by morning haze
> I can judge neither what it portends . . . nor your aims

Just as Genji was about to board his carriage, a crowd of people, including his brothers-in-law, arrived from the palace to greet him.

"You left without bothering to tell any of us where you were going!" Tō no Chūjō and his brothers had wanted to follow Genji, and so they vented their grievances to him. "We would have loved to join you on your excursion here, but you heedlessly abandoned us. It would be a shame to return to the capital without resting for a while in the shade of these stunningly beautiful blossoms."

They all sat down on the moss in the shade of some craggy outcroppings and passed around the wine cups. The cascading waterfall behind them made an elegant backdrop.

Tō no Chūjō pulled a flute from the breastfold of his robe and began to play clear, dulcet notes. Sachūben kept time by tapping a fan on the palm of his left hand and sang the line "West of the temple at Toyora" from the *saibara* "Kazuraki." The men in the party were all extraordinarily handsome, but Genji, still listless from his fever and leaning against a boulder, was incomparable. His looks were so awesomely superior that no one could take their eyes off him. Tō no Chūjō was gifted at playing the flute, so he had made certain to bring with him attendants who could accompany him on the double-reed *hichiriki* and the seventeen-pipe *sho*.[9] The bishop brought out his own seven-string koto and insisted that Genji play it. "Please, just one song for us. I'd like to give the birds in the mountains a surprise."

---

9. The *hichiriki* is a type of flageolet. The *sho* is a mouth organ, similar to panpipes, made of bamboo.

Genji demurred. "I'm still not feeling all that strong," he said. But then before they all set off he managed to pluck out a not uncharming tune.

Even the humblest monks and pages wept in regret that Genji was leaving so soon. Within the bishop's residence some of the older nuns, having never before seen a man of such extraordinary appearance, remarked, "He surely cannot be a person of this world." The bishop wiped away a tear and said, "Ahh, I am so deeply saddened when I consider what karmic bond should have determined that a man so impressively handsome would be born during the final period of the Dharma in this troubled realm of the rising sun."[1]

To the little girl's innocent heart, Genji seemed a paragon of beauty. "He is even more splendid than my father, the Captain of the Guards."

"If that's how you feel," said one of the female attendants, "then why don't you become his child?"

The girl nodded, thinking how wonderful it would be if only she could. Subsequently, whenever she played with her Hina dolls[2] or drew pictures of the court, she pretended that the lord was the Radiant Genji, and she would dress him in the finest attire and treat him most solicitously.

Genji first went straight to the palace to inform his father of all that had happened in recent days. The Emperor thought his son looked thin and haggard, and he was worried that it might be something serious. He asked Genji about the effectiveness of the venerable healer, and, on hearing the details, remarked graciously, "We must promote him to a more senior rank as a priest. He has apparently accumulated much merit through years of austerities, so why have we never heard of him before?"

The Minister of the Left arrived at the palace as well and spoke to his son-in-law. "I thought about coming to meet you, but since you had gone off in secret I hesitated, not knowing what you were doing. Why don't you come and spend a leisurely day or two at my residence? I can escort you there right away."

Genji did not feel much like going with him, and left the palace reluctantly. The Minister had his own carriage brought around, and then humbled himself by getting in second. His deferential gesture was a polite way of showing the care and solicitude with which he was treating his son-in-law, but it made Genji feel uncomfortable.

Once they arrived at the Minister's residence Genji could see that they had made preparations for his visit. It had been a long time since they had last seen him, and in the interim they had refurbished everything, adding decorations so that the place shone like a burnished jewel. As usual, Genji's wife stayed in her quarters and did not come out to meet him. She finally appeared only after her father had coaxed her repeatedly. Genji watched as she sat there stiffly, not moving a muscle, so prim and proper, arranged like some fairy-tale princess in a painting. *I doubt if it would do any good to tell her what's in my heart or to speak about my trip to the mountains, but it would be wonderful if she would just respond to me in a pleasant manner. Still, the plain truth is that she remains cold and remote in my presence, and we're becoming increasingly distant and estranged as the years go by.* He found the whole situation unfair and intolerable.

1. This is a reference to the doctrine of *mappō*, the last of the Three Ages of Buddhism, when the Law or Dharma is corrupted. This doctrine was extremely influential during the Heian Period in Japan.
2. Dolls dressed as highborn men and women [editors' note].

"Just once in a while I'd like to see you acting like a normal wife. I've been quite ill recently, but you couldn't be bothered to even ask how I was. I know that such callous behavior isn't rare for you, but I resent it all the same."

She paused for a moment, then responded, "Yes, I know how you feel. As the poet put it, 'How hurtful it is to be ignored.'" She cast a sidelong glance at him—an expression that gave her face an air of extreme reticence and an affect of grace and beauty.

"You so rarely speak to me," Genji shot back, "so why is it that when you do, you have to say such strange and unpleasant things? You cite the line 'How hurtful it is to be ignored,' but that poem referred to lovers having an affair, not to married couples. What a deplorable thing to say! You're always doing things to put me off, to make me feel awkward. And all the while I've tried various things hoping that the time will come when your attitude toward me changes. But now I see that you have grown even more distant. All right then, perhaps some day, in some life to come . . ."

He withdrew to their bedchamber for the night, but she did not follow after him. He couldn't bring himself to call for her, and so he sighed and lay down. He pretended to fall asleep, even though he was thoroughly disgruntled, his mind troubled by all the difficulties that may arise in relationships between men and women.

He couldn't get the girl out of his mind, and he was curious to see what that little shoot of grass would look like when she was fully grown. The nun, acting as the girl's grandmother, had not been at all unreasonable thinking that the child was not an appropriate age for him. It would thus be difficult to make any hurried advances at this stage. So how could he contrive to bring her with him and always have her as a comfort and joy? The girl's father, Prince Hyōbu, was certainly a refined and graceful man, but his looks did not possess her lambent sheen. So how could it be that the girl bore such a striking family resemblance to Fujitsubo? Was it because the girl's father and aunt were both born to the same imperial consort? Mulling over these points, the family connections made him feel closer to her, and somehow his desires became more urgent.

The day after returning from his mountain retreat, Genji sent letters to the house in Kitayama. His letter to the bishop merely implied what his intentions were. In the letter to the nun he wrote: "Awed and constrained by your august countenance, I was unable to express my thoughts clearly and openly to you, I would be overjoyed if you could at least understand that my decision to address you in this manner is evidence of the depth of my feelings and the sincerity of my motives." He enclosed a letter to the girl as well, which he had folded up in a knot.

> The vision of the mountain cherry
> Continues lingering inside me
> Though I left my feelings there with you

"As Prince Motoyoshi put it, 'I fear the wind that blows in the night.' I too worry that the wind might scatter the blossoms so that I may no longer view them."[3]

---

3. See the following *waka* poem: "Anxious that the wind during the night may have scattered the blossoms of plum, I rise early to view them."

The handwriting was of course magnificent, and even though the letter had been wrapped casually, to the eyes of the older people there it was startlingly beautiful. They were troubled about how to respond, perplexed by the situation.

The nun sent a reply. "I did not give your proposition any serious consideration after you left, and now, even though you have so graciously written to us, I have no idea how to respond. She is not even capable of writing the *Naniwazu*[4] in kana yet, and so even though she now has your letter, it really does no good.

> You left your heart just before
> The mountain blossoms scatter
> Short-lived, like your devotion

"I am now all the more concerned."

The bishop's reply was essentially the same, and Genji was frustrated. After a few days he sent Koremitsu off as a messenger. "There should be a person there, a nurse named Shōnagon. Meet her and find out what you can." *It's his nature I suppose*, Koremitsu thought. *He can never let anything go.* Koremitsu had caught only the briefest glimpse of the girl—and thought she looked very young—but it was pleasant to recall the moment he had seen her.

Receiving yet another letter of proposal from Genji, the bishop thanked Koremitsu, who then met with Shōnagon and conveyed Genji's wishes. He spoke in detail about Genji's feelings and told her about his status and circumstances. He was a smooth, glib talker, and was able to put together quite a convincing case for his lord. For all that, the girl was absurdly young to be married off, and everyone there felt that the request was somehow ominous, even distasteful, and they wondered what Genji had in mind.

Genji had poured his soul into his letter, which was written with deep sincerity, and as he had done before, he included a folded note for the little girl: "I long to see those unconnected characters as you practice writing 'My love for you is not shallow like the reflection of Mount Asaka you see when you peek into the mountain spring.'"[5]

> What does shallow Mount Asaka have to do
> With these deep feelings . . . why is the reflection
> Of your face in the mountain spring so distant

The nun replied for the girl.

> They say one feels regret after drawing water
> From a mountain spring . . . so how could you see the face
> Of a lover in a spring as shallow as this

Koremitsu carried the general sense of her rejection back to Genji. The nurse, Shōnagon, had told him, "Once we have spent some time here and my

4. The *Naniwazu* refers to a poem in the Kana Preface to *The Kokinshū* included in this volume that children in particular used, along with the poem on Mount Asaka that appears below, as a text to practice writing the kana syllabary: "The flowers blooming on the trees in Naniwazu tell us winter is over, the spring is here. Flowers blooming on the trees!"

5. The place-name Asaka plays on the homophone *asa*, meaning shallow. The poem Genji cites that the girl would have practiced writing is from the *Man'yōshū*. The poems that follow make variations on similar lines in the *Kokin rokujō*, a *waka* anthology.

young lady's grandmother is feeling better, we will travel to the capital and definitely be in touch with you then." Genji was irritated and dissatisfied.

Fujitsubo was ill and had withdrawn from the palace to her home. Genji could see his father's anxious, grieving expression, which aroused great feelings of pity. Yet he also considered it an opportunity, and was soon lost in a reverie, as if his spirit had drifted out of his body. He stopped calling on his various women and instead idled away the days at the palace or at his own villa, dreamily gazing out until evening, when he would then pester one of Fujitsubo's ladies-in-waiting, Ōmyōbu, to intercede on his behalf. It is not clear how she managed to arrange a tryst, but after some truly outrageous and exhausting machinations she pulled it off and Genji was able at last to be with the woman he considered perfect. His meetings with her were so brief, however, they merely intensified the pain of his lonely yearnings. Were these trysts real, or were they a dream? He could no longer tell.

Her Highness was in a state of constant distraction, for she was all too aware that her unimaginable affair with Genji was genuinely shocking. She was determined to put an end to their relationship, since she found the prospect of continuing to meet him extremely unpleasant and depressing, and her appearance betrayed just how difficult it was for her to cope with the situation. Still, she somehow managed to maintain a sweet and familiar attitude toward Genji, and her dignified demeanor and discretion put him to shame. Her behavior only made him realize that there was no one like her in the world, that he could find no flaws in her—and that realization gave rise to a wistful anguish as he was left to wonder why it was that the woman who turned out to be his ideal was forbidden to him.

How could he possibly tell her all the things he wanted to say? He wished he might reside in obscurity in the perpetual darkness of the Kurabu Mountains. Unfortunately, his nights were short, and brought him nothing but sorrow and pain.

> Though I am with you here and now
> So rare are nights like this I long
> To lose myself inside this dream

He was sobbing now. Feeling pity for him, she replied.

> Will we not be forever the stuff of gossip . . .
> No one has ever suffered the anguish I feel
> Trapped in a dream from which I never awaken

Fujitsubo's turmoil was understandable, and he felt ashamed before her. Ōmyōbu gathered up his robes and brought them to him.

Genji returned to his residence and spent a tearful day in bed. When he was told that Fujitsubo would no longer accept his messages, even though he knew she had always refused to read them anyway, he was hurt and could not focus his thoughts. He did not appear at court, but locked himself away for two or three days. His Majesty was worried by his son's absence and wondered if something was wrong, if he had fallen ill again. In the face of what Genji had done with Fujitsubo, he was terrified by his father's concern.

Fujitsubo was distressed by her plight, and her illness, which had prompted her to withdraw from the palace in the first place, worsened. Messengers arrived one after another urging her to return to the palace, but she refused. There could be no doubt that she was not feeling normal, but no one knew what was wrong with her. As it turned out, she had already secretly surmised her condition, and the shock of realizing that she was expecting a child upset her. She was now panicked and confused. *What will become of me?* More and more, as the summer progressed, she refused to get up. She was now in her third month, and her condition was obvious. Her ladies-in-waiting observed this and grew worried and suspicious. She lamented that she should have to suffer such a strange and unhappy fate.

Because no one guessed what had actually happened, Fujitsubo's attendants were surprised to learn that their lady had said nothing to His Majesty until now. Only Fujitsubo knew, in her heart of hearts, what had happened. Her closest attendants, Ōmyōbu and Ben, the daughter of Fujitsubo's nurse, tended to her intimately in the bath, and so they had clearly seen her condition and recognized what was happening. They were troubled, because they knew they did not dare discuss the situation between themselves. Ōmyōbu in particular felt sad that her lady's inescapable karmic destiny had brought her to this pass. In order to explain the delay in reporting the pregnancy, they had no choice but to tell the Emperor that they had been beguiled by a spirit and had not recognized their mistress's condition right away. The women who served Fujitsubo all assumed that that was indeed the case, and the Emperor, overwhelmed with even more feelings of pity and concern, was constantly sending messengers to ask how she was doing. Their visits, however, only kept her in a constant state of dread and depression.

Genji had a weird and terrifying dream. He summoned a diviner to interpret it and was told it signified that he would be the father of an emperor. This was shocking and unthinkable. The diviner added, "Your dream also means that your fortunes are crossed and that you must exercise caution and good behavior."

Genji felt awkward, and so he told the diviner, "This isn't my dream. I have merely relayed to you what someone of very high rank told me. So until the dream actually comes true, don't say anything to anyone about it." Genji was trying to make sense of things in his own mind, but when he heard that Fujitsubo was pregnant he realized that her child might be what his dream portended. He sent increasingly desperate messages to Fujitsubo, but Ōmyōbu was now having second thoughts. Communicating like this was extremely risky and difficult, and she found she could no longer act as a go-between for Genji. Even her brief one-line replies, which had always been infrequent at best, stopped altogether.

Fujitsubo returned to the palace in the seventh month. Because he had not seen her for so long, His Majesty's desire had only grown stronger, and he lavished his gracious affection on her. She was now a little plump, and her face had grown thin and careworn, but her appearance was truly, incomparably lovely. As he had done before, the Emperor would spend the whole day in her chambers. The early autumn sky told them it was the appropriate season for musical diversions, and so His Majesty was constantly calling for Genji, who had a talent for performance, to come and play various pieces on the koto or the flute. Genji had to struggle to keep his emotions in check on these occasions, though there were moments when his expression betrayed the feelings he found so hard to suppress. For her part, Fujitsubo would obsess over things she wished had turned out differently.

The health of the nun who had been staying at the mountain temple in Kitayama improved, and she finally returned to her residence in the capital. Genji inquired after her and sent her letters from time to time. It did not surprise him that in her replies she continued to refuse his proposition, but it didn't bother him that much because he was preoccupied by his concern with Fujitsubo and had little time to think much about other matters.

By the ninth month, as the end of autumn was approaching, Genji was lonely and depressed. A gorgeous moonlit evening inspired him at last to go to the place of a woman he had been secretly visiting. But then the weather changed—it turned stormy and a chill evening rain began to fall. The lady lived in the vicinity of Rokujō and Kyōgoku, and as he left the palace her place began to seem a little far off to him. On the way he saw a weather-beaten house standing in the gloomy shade of an ancient grove of trees.

Koremitsu was accompanying Genji as usual. "That used to be the house of the late Major Counselor. I guess you should know that I visited it recently and learned that the nun has taken a turn for the worse. They have no idea what to do for her."

"What a pity," Genji replied. "I must pay her a visit. Why didn't you tell me about this earlier? Have a message taken to her."

Koremitsu sent one of the attendants in with instructions to say that Genji had arrived with the express purpose of calling on the nun. The messenger entered and announced his lord's visit. The women were caught off guard, and one of them said, "This is most awkward. Our lady has been feeling much worse these last few days and couldn't possibly meet your lord." Still, it would have been rude and uncouth to send him away, so they prepared a space on the veranda under the eaves on the south side of the house and invited Genji in.

"Frightfully untidy, I'm afraid," one of the women said to him, "but my lady wanted to show some gratitude for your visit. Your arrival was so unexpected, however, that you caught us unprepared. So please forgive the dark and gloomy atmosphere of this chamber."

The place did strike Genji as quite odd, but he answered, "I have been meaning to visit you all this time, but I refrained from doing so because I have been treated in such a way as to make me believe nothing would come of it. I am anxious about you, having just learned that your illness has taken a turn for the worse."

"My ailments are no worse than usual, though I do sense now that I am nearing my end," the nun told him. "You have been gracious enough to call on me, but I'm not able to greet you directly. With regards to your proposal, the girl is still at an innocent age and lacks judgment, but once she is a little more mature, by all means think of her as you would any other woman and take her as one of your own. I'm so worried about leaving her behind in this world, isolated and helpless, that my anxiety creates a burden of attachment for me that will surely be a hindrance on the path to the salvation I pray for."

Because she was in a room close by, Genji could catch fragments of her weary voice. "We are not worthy of this, and should be grateful for his attentions," he heard her continue. "If only the girl were old enough to be able to thank him properly."

Genji was keenly moved. "If my feelings for the girl were truly shallow, then why would I embarrass myself by coming here and possibly looking lecherous?

The moment I recognized there was some kind of karmic bond between us, I was deeply attracted to the girl and convinced to an almost mystical degree that our bond was not something that belonged to this world." He turned to one of the attendants and continued. "My visit here may have been in vain, but may I ask for a word with the girl herself?"

"Oh, I don't know about that," one of the nun's attendants interjected. "She has been kept in the dark about all of this, and is now fast asleep." Just as the woman said these words, the girl's voice could be heard inside. "Grandmama, Lord Genji is here . . . you know, the man who visited us at the temple? So why haven't you gone out to meet him?" The women were all mortified and tried to hush the girl. But she protested, "But didn't Grandmama say that the sight of him was always a comfort to her?" She spoke as if she were informing them of something that would benefit her grandmother. Genji was utterly charmed, but he had to be considerate of the bruised feelings of the flustered women there, and so he pretended he hadn't heard a thing. After politely bidding farewell and leaving his best wishes for them, he made his way home. *She may be a little girl*, he thought, *but I can't wait to see her after she's been properly trained.*

The next day Genji sent a most solicitous letter inquiring after the health of the nun. As always, he included a small folded letter for the girl.

> Hearing a young crane cry I long to go to it
> But my boat tangled among the reeds is hindered
> And I cannot leave this inlet to tend its needs

"As the poet put it, 'I always yearn to go back to the same person.'"[6] Genji deliberately composed his note in a childish hand that was so delightful the women told the girl to imitate it in her copybook.

Shōnagon replied, "Our lady may not make it through the day, and we are preparing to take her back to the temple in Kitayama. She may not be able to express in this world her gratitude for your visit and your expressions of concern." Genji felt very sad when he heard this.

One autumn evening, when he was more preoccupied than ever with his longing for Fujitsubo, the woman who constantly tormented his heart, he felt his seemingly perverse desire to possess her little niece growing even stronger. He remembered a line from the nun's poem—"The evanescent dewdrop tarries, reluctant to disappear into the sky"—and thought lovingly of the girl. At the same time he was anxious and unsure, thinking that she might not live up to his expectations. The image of a *murasaki*[7]—a little purple gromwell—popped into his head.

---

6. *Kokinshū* 732 (Anonymous): "I always yearn to go back to the same person, like a little boat that has made its way through the channel and comes rowing home."
7. The Japanese species of gromwell is a small plant that produces white flowers in the summer. Its purple roots were used to make dye for clothing. As in other cultures, purple was associated with royalty, and so I have translated *murasaki* as "purple gromwell" to indicate both the rustic image of the word and its imperial associations. The Japanese name for wisteria is *fuji*, alluding to the girl's aunt, Fujitsubo, and suggesting through the color purple shared by the two plants the nature of their relationship. Since *murasaki* (or *wakamurasaki*) is the smaller, more rustic plant, Genji's poem acknowledges a difference in their relative status. His poem alludes to *Kokinshū* 867 (Anonymous): "Because of this one purple gromwell, I look on all the grasses in Musashino with tender feelings."

> How I yearn to quickly pluck up and make my own
> That little purple gromwell sprouting in the wild
> With roots that share their color with wisteria

During the tenth month His Majesty decided to plan a visit to the Suzaku Palace. The dancers for the day of departure were to be selected from among sons of aristocratic families, high-ranking officials, and courtiers who had talents suitable for the occasion. From princes and ministers on down, each and everyone practiced their skills. It was a hectic, busy time.

Because of all the preparations, it occurred to Genji that he had not contacted the nun in her mountain temple for some time. When at last he sent a messenger there, he received the following reply from the bishop: "I am sorry to report that she passed away on the twentieth of last month. I know it is the reality of this world that we must all die, but still I cannot help mourning her."

After reading this, Genji experienced the poignant sorrow of the evanescent world and wondered what would become of the girl who had been the source of such worry for the nun. The girl was so young, she must be yearning for her grandmother. Genji had vague memories of being left behind by his own mother, and so he sent his deepest condolences. Shōnagon composed a sympathetic reply.

Genji learned that after the twenty-day period of mourning and confinement was over, the girl came back to the capital and was now at the late nun's residence. He waited until a seemly period of time passed, then went to call on her one evening when he had some free time. The place was run-down and desolate and there were few people about—the kind of place that would surely frighten a child. Genji was shown to the same space on the south side of the residence that they had used on his previous visit. He was moved to tears by Shōnagon's heartbreaking account of her mistress's final days.

"There is talk that the girl's father would have her come to his villa," Shōnagon told him. "But the nun was quite concerned about that prospect. After all, her own daughter, this child's late mother, found the place unbearably cruel and depressing. The girl is now at that in-between stage, no longer a child, but not old enough to really understand the motives of other people. And with all the other children at her father's residence, she is not likely to be welcomed with open arms, but will instead be belittled and treated as a stepchild. With so many indications that the girl will be badly served there, we are grateful for your passing words of kind consideration. Still, we cannot fathom your future intentions, and even though we should feel happy on occasions like this when you visit us, we remain extremely hesitant about your proposal . . . after all, the girl is simply not appropriate for you. Her character is immature and undeveloped, even for someone her age."

"Why do you continue to waver when I have repeatedly opened up to you like this? I know in my heart that my feelings of longing and pity, which her innocence stirs in me, are signs of a special bond between us from a former life. If I may, I would like to speak with her directly and tell her how I feel."

> Seeing the young tangled seaweed struggle to grow
> Amid reeds in the bay of Wakanoura
> Can the wave, once it has drawn near, recede again

"It would be too hateful for the wave to have to withdraw now," Genji concluded.

Shōnagon answered, "You are truly gracious, my lord, but . . . "

If the algae at Wakanoura yielded
Without knowing the true intentions of the wave
Would it not be set adrift upon the shallows[8]

"It just isn't reasonable." The polished manner of her verse made it almost possible for Genji to forgive her refusal. He murmured, "Why does the day when we may finally meet never come?"[9] The younger women in the house shivered in delight and admiration.

The little girl had been lying down, crying and grieving for her grandmother, but then her playmates told her, "A lord dressed in court robes has arrived. Perhaps it is the prince, your father!" She got up and went out to see for herself.

"Shōnagon!" she called out. "Where is the nobleman in court robes? Is my father here?" Her voice sounded achingly sweet as she approached.

"I'm not your father," said Genji, "but that doesn't mean you should treat me as a stranger. Come over here."

The girl immediately recognized his voice and realized this was the splendid lord who had called on them before, and she was embarrassed that she had spoken improperly. She went over to her nurse and said, "I want to go now. I'm sleepy."

"Why do you want to hide from me? Please come over here and rest at my knees. Please, come closer."

"As you can see," said Shōnagon, pushing the girl toward him, "she really knows very little about the world."

The girl sat innocently on the other side of the blinds from Genji, who put his hand through to search around for her. Her lustrous hair was draped over soft, rumpled robes, and even though he did not have a clear view of her, when he touched the rich thickness of the strands he imagined how attractive she must really be. When he tried to hold her hand she was put off that a stranger should have come so close to her and pulled away in fright. "I told you I was sleepy," she said to Shōnagon. At that moment Genji slipped inside the curtains and told her, "You must think of me now as the one you will rely upon. So please don't be distant or afraid."

His actions were upsetting to Shōnagon. "What are you thinking, my lord?" she exclaimed. "Impetuously barging in here like this during a period of mourning . . . it's outrageous. You can talk to her all you like, but it won't do you any good. She's just too young to understand."

"You may be right," Genji answered, "but just what do you think I'm going to do with someone so young? Carefully observe the sincerity of my feelings, the purity of my heart, and you will realize that they are peerless, that you will find nothing like them in this world."

The wind was blowing violently and hail began to fall. It was a lonely, terrifying night. "Why," Genji asked, tears in his eyes, "should she have to spend any more time in this isolated, deserted house?" He couldn't stand the idea of

8. Both poems play on the homophone *waka*, meaning "youthful."
9. Compare this *waka* poem by Fujiwara no Koremasa: "Though I keep my impatience a secret, as the years go by, why is it so hard to pass beyond the barrier gate of Ōsaka, the slope where we may finally meet?"

going home and abandoning them here. "Lower the shutters. It looks like it will be a frightful evening," he ordered. "I shall stand guard for you tonight. Please, everyone, gather closer to me."

With a remarkable air of familiarity about him, he went inside the curtained area where the girl slept. The women found his behavior shockingly abnormal, but they did not know what to do and did not even try to move from where they were sitting. Shōnagon couldn't stand it. She was beside herself, but she couldn't very well offer vehement objections, or make a scene; and so she stayed put as well, sighing in lament.

The girl, not knowing what was going on, was truly scared and trembling. Genji felt sorry for her, thinking that her beautiful figure was shivering because of the cold, and he had a singlet brought in and wrapped around her. Genji knew perfectly well that his behavior was not normal, and so he spoke sensitively to the girl.

"You really must come with me. There are many gorgeous paintings at my residence . . . and Hina court dolls to play with." His manner was kind and intimate as he spoke of things he was sure would appeal to her childish heart and allay her fears. Nonetheless, she still found it hard to sleep, and spent the night tossing and turning.

As the night wore on the wind continued to gust and the women whispered among themselves. "How forlorn we would have been had he not come here. If only they were a little closer in age, it would be so wonderful." Shōnagon, worried about her charge, hovered just outside the curtains the whole time. When the wind began to die down a little, Genji got ready to go home. It was still dark, and he had a knowing look on his face, as if he were leaving some romantic tryst.

"Now that I've witnessed her circumstances with my own eyes," Genji said, "it seems too pathetic and I will now, more than ever, be anxious about her. She should be moved to my residence, where I spend my days and nights in solitary reverie. How can she remain here like this? It's a wonder she isn't in a constant state of terror."

Shōnagan replied, "Prince Hyōbu has hinted that he would come for her, but that won't happen until after the forty-nine-day period of purification is complete."

"He is the one who really ought to look after her," Genji agreed, "but they have grown accustomed to living apart and the girl most likely regards him as much a stranger to her as I am. I may have only just met her today, but my feelings and motives are not shallow . . . indeed, they are far more worthy than her father's." Genji stroked the girl's hair, then glanced back repeatedly at her as he made his way out.

* * *

Genji experienced a swirl of conflicting emotions. There would be gossip about what was going on,[1] and he would undoubtedly gain a reputation as a lecher. If the girl were of an age when she could understand these matters and consent to the relationship, then people would understand and it would all seem normal. But she was not of that age, and if her father were to come

1. That is, Genji's intentions to take away the girl [editors' note].

searching for her, then Genji's own actions would be seen as wild and rash. Yet in spite of all this, if he were to let this opportunity slip away, he would have bitter regrets. And so he left while it was still dark. His wife remained her usual sullen and distant self. "I just remembered some pressing matters I have to attend to," Genji told her. "I shall return shortly." After going to his own quarters in the house at Sanjō and changing his robes, he set off alone with Koremitsu, who was riding alongside the carriage on his horse. He left before the women attendants even realized he was gone.

He knocked on the gate and someone who had been apprised of the situation opened it. Genji had his carriage drawn inside quietly. Koremitsu tapped at the double doors in the corner of the main hall, then coughed as a signal. On hearing this, Shōnagon knew who was there and came out. "My lord has arrived," Koremitsu announced.

"The girl is resting inside," Shōnagon told him. "Why have you come out so late at night?" She assumed they were stopping by on the way back from their previous rendezvous at the palace.

Genji spoke up. "I have something I must tell her before she is moved to her father's residence."

"Whatever would that be? And how could she possibly give you a clear answer?" Shōnagon laughed and began to withdraw.

Genji suddenly barged in, and Shōnagon was completely taken aback. "The older women are in there . . . they are absolutely unpresentable!"

"She's not awake yet, is she?" Genji said. "Well, then, I suppose I shall have to get her up. How can she remain asleep, oblivious to this lovely morning mist?" He went straight on in to the girl's sleeping quarters. Shōnagon was so flabbergasted that neither she nor her women could utter a peep in protest.

Genji picked up the girl, who was sleeping innocently, and woke her in his arms. She was still half asleep, and so she thought her father had come for her. Stroking her tangled hair, Genji said to her, "Come with me. I'm acting as a messenger for your father."

When she saw that it wasn't her father holding her, she was startled and fearful. "Come now, is that any way to act? I am just the same as your father." As he was carrying the girl out, Koremitsu, Shōnagon and the others all asked him what was happening.

"I told you I was worried about not being able to come here very often, and so I want to move her to my residence, which is much safer and more comfortable. If cruelly she were moved to her father's villa, it would be that much more difficult for me to communicate with her. One of you may accompany me if you wish."

Shōnagon, who was now frantic, replied, "But today is the worst possible time you could have chosen. What should I say when her father comes for her? If it is, as you say, truly fated for her to be your wife, then surely that is how things will turn out later on. As it is now, she is just too young, and you have given us no time to think about things, which is putting all of the attendants in an awkward position."

"Very well, then," Genji responded, "some of you may follow her later." He had his carriage brought around, and everyone there was stunned and at a loss what to do. The girl, not knowing what was happening, was frightened and started to cry.

With no way to stop him, Shōnagon brought out the clothes she had been sewing the previous night and, changing into a not altogether unattractive robe herself, got into the carriage with him.

Genji's residence in Nijō was close by, and so they arrived before the first light. The carriage was drawn up to the west hall and Genji alighted. He easily swept the girl up in his arms and brought her out. Shōnagon wavered. "This is all like a dream. What should I be doing?"

"That's entirely up to you. Now that I've brought the young lady here you may return if you wish. I'll be happy to have someone escort you back." Shōnagon smiled bitterly at his words, for she had no choice but to resign herself to the situation. She got out of the carriage. This had all been so sudden and outrageous that nothing could be done about it. She could not calm her heart. *What will her father say? And what about my young mistress? What will become of her? To have been left behind by all the people who loved her . . . it's just too much to bear . . .* She could hardly hold back her tears, but she knew that this was a momentous occasion and that to shed tears now would be an omen of bad luck. So she restrained herself.

The west hall was not usually inhabited, and there were no curtains or furnishings. Genji summoned Koremitsu and ordered him to have curtains, screens, and the like placed here and there where he indicated. He had the silk blinds hanging between the pillars around the inner chamber removed, and he had his attendants straighten up the room. When they were finished, he sent for robes and bedding from the east hall, then went in to rest. The girl now found the scene genuinely creepy, and, uncertain about Genji's intentions, she began to tremble. Still, she managed not to cry out loud.

"I want to sleep with Shōnagon," she whimpered in a girlish voice.

"You must no longer sleep with her," Genji instructed, whereupon the girl fell prostrate, weeping and feeling completely forlorn. Her nurse couldn't sleep either and stayed up all night lost in her thoughts.

As the dawn broke they looked around. The residence and furnishings gave off a resplendent air—even the sand in the garden looked as though someone had scattered jewels all around them. Shōnagon remained hesitant, but it appeared that there were no other women serving in this hall. It was a pavilion where Genji would receive less intimate guests who called infrequently. There were male servants just outside the bamboo blinds, and one of the men, who had heard that his lord had brought a woman here, was whispering to the others. "I wonder who she is? She must be someone extraordinary."

Cooked rice and water for washing up were brought in, and the sun was already high when they finally got up. Genji said, "This won't do at all . . . we have no one in service here. Choose those women at your former residence you would like to have as attendants for your young lady and I will send for them this evening." Genji next summoned some page girls from the east hall, then told his servants, "Have these pages select several younger girls to serve over here." Presently four captivating little girls appeared. The young lady was still asleep, her robes wrapped around her. Genji made her get up.

"This pouting and cold behavior will not do!" Genji scolded. "Would a man who is wild at heart have done all this for you? A woman must be kindhearted and obedient." And with those words, from that moment, her training began.

Her features were even more beautiful than when he had seen her from a distance. He spoke warmly to her, telling her stories and showing her all sorts of delightful pictures and playthings, which he had brought in for her, and did everything he could to soothe her feelings. Eventually she got up and inspected her quarters. She was wearing her dark mourning robes, soft and rumpled, and looked so adorable as she sat there with her innocent smile that Genji couldn't help smiling himself as he watched her.

Genji left for the east hall, and the young lady went over to the edge of the veranda and peeked out at the pond and the trees in the garden. She was fascinated by the grasses, which had been withered by the frost so that they looked like something out of a painting. A crowd of male courtiers of the fourth or fifth rank, none of whom she knew, bustled in and out, making her feel that she had come to some splendid place. She examined the captivating pictures on the folding screens and door panels, and with her childish disposition she was able to quickly comfort herself.

Genji did not go to the palace for two or three days so that he could spend time talking with the girl and making her feel at ease in her new surroundings. He wrote poems and drew pictures, presenting them to her with the thought that they might serve as a model for her own practice. He put them together to make a very charming collection. One of the poems, which he copied on purple-colored paper, was taken from *Kokin rokujō*.

> I've never been there, but lament my fate
> Each time I hear the name "Musashino"...
> The place where little *murasaki* grows

The girl took up the sheet of paper and studied the unusual, exquisite brush-strokes. In smaller characters Genji had added his own verse.

> Unable to cross the dewy plains of Musashino
> I have yet to see the purple roots of the gromwell there . . .
> How I long for you little kin of the wisteria

"Why don't you try writing something?" Genji encouraged her . . . though Fujitsubo was still obviously on his mind.

"But I can't write well," she protested, looking up at him. She was so lovely he couldn't help but smile.

"Even if you can't write well, you must at least try. You won't get better if you don't write anything. Let me show you."

He found it charming the way she held her brush and how she turned away from him when she wrote . . . and he thought it strange that he should have such feelings. "I've made a mistake," she said, trying to keep him from seeing what she wrote. But he made her show it to him anyway.

> I worry, unsure why you grieve . . .
> Tell me again which plant is it
> The one I am related to

Her writing was quite immature, but he could see at once that she had the talent to be accomplished in composition. The lines of her brush strokes were rich and gentle, and they resembled the hand of her late grandmother. If she practiced more modern models, he knew that she would be able to write very well.

He had court dolls and dollhouses made especially for her, and as they passed the time together he was able to distract himself from his painful longing for Fujitsubo.

The women who had remained behind at the girl's former residence were flustered and embarrassed when Prince Hyōbu came back and asked for his daughter, for they did not know what they should say to him. Genji had told them not to let anyone know what had happened . . . at least not for a while. Because Shōnagon was in agreement and told them it was best to keep quiet, all they could tell the father was "Shōnagon took your daughter into hiding, but she didn't tell us where." Prince Hyōbu assumed nothing could be done and resigned himself to the situation. *Her grandmother was opposed to sending the girl to my residence, and so Shōnagon was moved to carry out her wishes, even if it meant going to this extreme. But why couldn't she just gently tell me that it would be too unbearable to move the girl, rather than willfully spiriting her away?*

When he left the house he said tearfully, "Let me know if you hear any news of her." This troubled the women.

He sent an inquiry to the bishop as well, but the bishop had no clue as to her whereabouts. Prince Hyōbu suffered feelings of longing and regret about the child's beauty, which would now go to waste. The enmity his primary wife had harbored toward the girl's mother had abated, and even she regretted that she would not be able to raise the girl as she had hoped.

Gradually her attendants arrived and gathered in her quarters. Genji and the girl, whom he called his little Murasaki, possessed a rare, modern look as a couple. The youngest attendants and the little girls who were her playmates passed the time together without a care. Although there were lonely evenings when Genji was away and she cried out of yearning for her grandmother, she gave no thought at all to her father. From the beginning she had grown accustomed to not having him around, and she was now exceedingly close to the man who was her new father. Whenever he returned, she would be the first to go out to greet him. They would talk together lovingly, and she never felt distant or embarrassed when he held her to his bosom. Insofar as they looked like a father and a daughter, their behavior was quite endearing.

If a woman has a calculating heart and a troublesome disposition that makes an issue of everything, then a man has to take care that he not allow her emotions to lead her astray and keep her from fulfilling his desires. She will tend to be jealous and resentful, and difficulties he never imagined, such as a separation, will naturally arise. Murasaki, however, was an absolutely captivating companion for Genji. A real daughter, when she had reached this age, would not have been able to behave so intimately, to have gone to sleep or risen in such close proximity to him. Genji came to feel that his young Murasaki was a rare hidden treasure, his precious plaything.

* * *

FROM CHAPTER VII

Momiji no ga

An Imperial Celebration of Autumn Foliage

The procession to the Suzaku Palace was set to take place sometime after the tenth day of the tenth month. Because it promised to be an unusually lavish event, the imperial consorts and ladies, who were not permitted to leave the palace, complained bitterly that they would not be able to see it. His Majesty was also disappointed that Fujitsubo would not be able to view the procession, and so he had the musicians and dancers perform a dress rehearsal in front of his living quarters in the Seiryōden.

Genji, a Captain in the Palace Guard, performed a dance titled "Waves of the Blue Sea." His partner was Tō no Chūjō, who, as son of the Minister of the Left, was unquestionably superior to other men in terms of his looks and training. Performing next to Genji, however, he seemed like some nondescript tree deep in the mountains growing beside a cherry in full bloom. As the bright slanting rays of the setting sun shone down on them, the music swelled and the performance reached its climax. Genji was carefully following the prescribed form of the dance, but his movements and expressiveness were without peer. The music paused and he recited the accompanying verse in Chinese by Ono no Takamura in a voice as sweet and ethereal as the cry of the Buddha's heavenly Kalavínka bird.[2] The Emperor was so moved by the performance that he brushed away a tear, while all the upper-ranking courtiers and princes were weeping. At the conclusion of Genji's recitation the lively music, which had paused for him, started up again. Genji had twirled the sleeves of his robe around his arms at the very end of the verse, and he was now readjusting them, his face flushed, looking even more radiant than usual.

As auspiciously splendid as Genji's dance had been, the Kokiden Consort found it strangely disturbing and remarked, "His looks are enough to captivate the gods in the heavens. It seems weirdly unpleasant." The younger women deplored her unkind words.

Fujitsubo might have enjoyed viewing the dance more had it not been for the terrible guilt she felt at having received the Emperor's gracious gift of ordering this rehearsal for her benefit. To make matters worse, she had to watch a dance performed by the very man with whom she had conducted her outrageous affair. The whole thing seemed like a dream to her. That evening she was in service to the Emperor in his chambers.

"Waves of the Blue Sea" had swept everything before it at the rehearsal that day. "What did you think of it?" His Majesty asked Fujitsubo. She struggled to answer, but managed to stammer out, "It was certainly a special performance."

"Genji's partner did not look bad either," the Emperor continued. "When it comes to form and gesture, good breeding will out. Professional dancers, those who have some reputation, are no doubt skillful, but they cannot display the same natural, unaffected beauty and grace that we saw today. They performed so magnificently, I have to admit I'm worried that when they dance under the

2. A bird mentioned in Buddhist sutras for its surpassingly beautiful voice, to which the Buddha's voice is often compared [editors' note].

autumn foliage on the day of the procession, it might be a bit of a letdown. But never mind . . . I so wanted you to see the performance that I had them prepare for it."

The following morning Genji sent a note to Fujitsubo. "How did I look yesterday? As I danced, my heart was being torn apart by an unrequited love such as the world has never known."

I should never have danced in your presence
With thoughts so troubled . . . did you understand
When in wild abandon I twirled my sleeves

"I feel uncertain before your grace."

Unable to shake the captivating sight of his face and elegant dancing figure, Fujitsubo could not very well pretend she had not seen his note, and so she replied.

Chinese dancers conceived the "Waves of the Blue Sea"
Twirling their sleeves so long ago and far away
But your every gesture touched me here and now

"My heart is overflowing."

Genji had not expected a reply, and so he was ecstatic. Smiling, he thought that her words, which displayed knowledge of ancient dance and foreign courts, showed she had already acquired the dignity expected of a future empress. He unrolled the letter and pored over it as if it were some treasured sutra.

On the day of the procession the princes of the blood and all members of the court participated. Genji's older half brother, the Crown Prince, accompanied the Emperor, and as was customary two boats were rowed around the lake at the site of the performance. One boat, adorned with the head of a dragon, held performers playing Chinese court music, while the other boat, adorned with the head of a blue heron,[3] carried performers playing Korean court music. There were many varieties of Chinese and Korean dance, and the sound of musical instruments and drums reverberated in all directions. Genji had looked so spectacular at the rehearsal the previous evening that the Emperor's old fears that his son might be fated to die young were revived, and he had sutras read for Genji at various temples here and there to ward off evil. Members of the court who heard about this were sympathetic and thought it a reasonable precaution, but the Kokiden Consort, mother of the Crown Prince, spitefully remarked, "Isn't this really taking things a bit too far?"

The Emperor had gathered and selected the most distinguished players from among courtiers of both high and low rank to serve as the flutists and drummers who would accompany "Waves of the Blue Sea." He had the performers divided into sides—those playing Chinese music on the left, those playing Korean music on the right. He then chose two Consultants from the Council of State, men who also served as the directors of the Left and Right Gate Guards, to conduct the Chinese and Korean music respectively. Prior to this performance each aristocratic house had sought out the most skilled dance instructors and secluded themselves away to practice under their tutelage.

---

3. The term for these boats is *ryōtōgekisu* (dragon head, blue heron head). In China it referred to a single boat with a carving of a dragon's head at the prow and one of a blue heron's head at the stern, but in Japan it referred to a pair of boats.

The intermittent soughing of the wind in the pines mingled with the indescribably polished sound of forty musicians playing in the shade of tall trees in autumn foliage. Truly it sounded like a breeze blowing down from the deepest mountains, and amidst the multihued leaves that had fallen all around, the dazzling performance of "Waves of the Blue Sea" was sublime. The autumn leaves that had adorned Genji's headdress at the outset had dropped off as the dance proceeded. Having lost a little of its luster, the headdress was now suffering in comparison with Genji's lambent face. So the Consultant who was conducting the musicians of the Left plucked some of the chrysanthemums that had been placed in front of the Emperor and inserted them into the headdress. As the day drew to a close, a chill evening drizzle began to fall, as if the scene had moved the very sky itself. The color of the chrysanthemums now adorning Genji's spectacular figure had faded slightly with the frost, and their beauty was beyond the power of words to describe. Genji himself was putting all his skill into his performance, dancing in a way that would never be equaled again. As he executed the final movements, retracing his steps just before he exited with a flourish, it seemed that an unearthly chill coursed through all of the spectators. Lower-class people were also watching from beneath the trees, or from the shade of craggy rocks, or from beneath the fallen leaves of the mountain trees, and though one would hardly have imagined that they had the sensitivity to appreciate the performance, they were able to dimly recognize the sadness of transient beauty and wept accordingly.

The fourth prince, the Emperor's son by the Shōkyōden Consort, was still a boy. Nonetheless, his performance of "Dance of the Autumn Wind" proved to be the most spectacular event after Genji's dance. Because those two performances were so dazzling, everything that followed seemed bland by comparison, which put a damper on the whole affair.

That evening both Genji and Tō no Chūjō were promoted—Genji to the senior third rank, which was rather an extraordinary rise given his previous status; Tō no Chūjō to the lower division of the senior fourth rank, which was also an unusual rise. Other high-ranking courtiers had reason to rejoice as well, since those who deserved promotions received them. Since they had all benefited from Genji's success—his own rise having helped pull everyone up with him—it makes one curious to know just what virtue from a previous life now endowed him with the qualities that drew everyone's admiring eyes and caused hearts to be joyful.

At around the time of the procession Fujitsubo left the court and withdrew to her own residence. As always, Genji sought out every opportunity to see her, and consequently, complaints from the Minister of the Left's household to the effect that he was never around reached his ears. Moreover, he learned that his wife was more distressed than usual, because one of her attendants had reported to her that Genji had plucked a certain "wild grass"—meaning Murasaki—and that "he was keeping her in his villa at Nijō." *It's natural she would feel upset,* Genji thought, *since she knows nothing at all about the situation or how young Murasaki is. Even so, why can't she just tell me how she feels and vent her resentments like a normal woman. I could then speak without reserve, tell her all the things I feel in my heart and put her mind at ease. But no, she has to be so damnably suspicious all the time. It's no wonder I find myself conducting these illicit affairs.* Still, he had to admit that there were no flaws in his wife's appearance or manners that made him feel dissatisfied. And even though she did not understand his feelings for her, she was the first woman he had known, and so he could not help but regard her with special tenderness. He was sure that over time her attitude toward him would change and she would come to understand. After all, he had faith that, given her gentle and serious nature, she would naturally come around to him. The feelings he had for her were special and different from those he had for other women.

Murasaki was now comfortable with Genji. Possessed of both a virtuous character and attractive looks, she would innocently follow after Genji, clinging to him. For the moment, he was inclined not to give the people in his residence too much information about her, and he kept her in a separate wing of the villa, which he had done up in a lavish manner. He would visit her mornings and evenings, instructing her in all manner of things, copying out books for her to emulate in her writing practice. It made him feel as though he had taken in a daughter from some aristocratic household. He gave special care to setting up the household office and choosing the staff to serve her, so that she would never have cause for worry or complaint. Apart from Koremitsu, Genji kept everyone else in the dark about this woman he was treating so solicitously. Her father, Prince Hyōbu, had been unable to discover what had happened to her. Murasaki would often reflect on the past, and she missed her grandmother terribly. For that reason Genji would try to divert her whenever he was at Nijō, and he even spent the night with her on occasion. Yet he was busy going here and there, visiting his many other women and going out during the evening, and so there were times when she would call after him and tell him how she ached to be with him. He found her unbearably sweet at those moments. Whenever he returned from two or three days of service at the palace, or from a visit with his wife at Sanjō, she would always look depressed. He found this distressing, and because he sometimes felt as though he were caring for a motherless child, he was no longer comfortable going out on his nighttime escapades. Upon hearing how well Genji was caring for the girl, the bishop at Kitayama was relieved and happy, even though he still considered the arrangement abnormal. Each time he conducted a memorial service for his sister, the late nun, Genji never failed to provide solemn, elaborate offerings.

Genji very much wanted to find out how Fujitsubo was doing. She had withdrawn to her own villa on Sanjō avenue, and so he called on her there. He was met by several of her ladies-in-waiting—Ōmyōbu, Chūnagon, and Nakatsukasa—and it bothered him that they acted so formally, clearly treating him as if he were a stranger. He stayed calm, keeping his feelings to himself as he exchanged pleasantries and court gossip with the women. Just then the Minister of War, Prince Hyōbu, arrived. When he learned that Genji was there as well, he granted him an audience. The Prince's elegant looks and bearing bespoke of his high breeding, and Genji found his softly erotic, seductive manner so appealing that he imagined that the Prince would be a very alluring partner were he a woman. What's more, because the Prince was the older brother of Fujitsubo and the father of Murasaki, Genji felt a surge of intimacy with the man, speaking to him in a relaxed, warmly familiar way. Noticing that Genji was kindly opening up to him more than usual, the Prince found him quite enchanting. Unaware that Genji was now his son-in-law, he had a similar erotic fantasy, imagining what Genji would be like as a woman.

Being Fujitsubo's older brother, he had the right to go in behind her curtains to speak to her when evening came. Genji was jealous of him, recalling the times when, as a little boy, he would be permitted to accompany his father behind Fujitsubo's curtains and address her face-to-face with no intermediaries. When he thought of the pain their separation caused him, he could hardly stand it.

"Though I should visit you more often," Genji said, "I normally don't have any reason to come here, so naturally I have neglected to stay in touch. Still, it would make me happy if you would send word should you ever need me to take care of something." His manner was serious and he made no pretense of showing the usual charming warmth as he left Fujitsubo's residence. Ōmyōbu had been useless to Genji in arranging a meeting with Fujitsubo, and it was clear that Fujitsubo now regretted more than ever the karmic destiny that had brought them together. In the face of her mistress's coldhearted attitude, Ōmyōbu felt so ashamed, so at a loss, that as the days went by she found she was no longer able to help Genji in any way. Mutually lost in their unending torment, Fujitsubo and Genji realized how evanescent their bond had been.

Murasaki's nurse, Shōnagon, observed the wonderful though completely unexpected rapport that had developed between Genji and her young mistress and was convinced that their relationship was a blessing from the Buddha, to whom the old nun had constantly prayed and made hopeful offerings. Yet Shōnagon continued to be assailed with doubts about Murasaki's future. *Genji's wife is a woman of unquestionably high status and breeding, and he is involved with a number of other women as well. Surely when the girl came of age someone would cause problems for her, would they not?* It was only because Genji seemed so devoted to Murasaki that Shōnagon felt she could trust him.

Murasaki was told that three months was an appropriately long period to wear robes of mourning for her grandmother, and so she put them away at the end of the twelfth month, just in time for the New Year. Having known no parent other than her grandmother, she was influenced by the old nun's tastes and continued to wear modest robes of plain crimson, purple, or yellow. In spite of these preferences, she was lovely, and even cut a rather modern, fashionable figure.

On the morning of the first day of the New Year, Genji peeked in on Murasaki's quarters on his way to court to attend the ceremony offering congratulations to the Emperor.

"Your change of attire makes you look more grown up than usual," he laughed, exuding a dazzlingly gentle and affectionate appeal. Before he knew it, Murasaki was absorbed in arranging her Hina court dolls, setting out various accessories on a series of three-foot-long shelves and spreading the little dollhouses that had been made for her all around the room until it was overflowing with her playthings.

"That Inuki!" Murasaki grumbled. "Last night during the demon-purification ritual, she was following the exorcist and got so excited by his mask and lance that she broke this. I've been trying to fix it." Clearly she regarded this as a major crisis.

"She really is inconsiderate, isn't she?" Genji responded. "I'll have it repaired for you. You just remember that there is no crying or pouting today . . . it would bring bad luck."

His dashing looks, together with the grand size of his retinue, made his departure for court seem so ceremonious that the women attendants at his residence came out onto the veranda to see him off. Murasaki also stepped outside to watch him leave, then went back inside and dressed up her Genji doll to match the attire he was wearing to the palace.

"I hope you'll start acting a little more mature this year," Shōnagon scolded her charge. "Here you are, already past your tenth birthday and you're still playing with these dolls. It just won't do. You have a husband now, and you really must start behaving more like a proper wife, and looking more like a lady for him. You still can't stand for me to fix up your hair."

Shōnagon scolded Murasaki in order to shame the girl for always being so absorbed in her playthings. But the effect of her admonition was to make Murasaki finally understand her circumstances for the first time. *So he's my husband, is he? The attendants here all have husbands . . . but they're really ugly. Mine, on the other hand, is a dashing, handsome young man.* It may have been true that she was still attached to her playthings, but her newfound awareness of her relationship with Genji signaled that she was now a year older. The people who served at Genji's mansion had found her childish behavior, which could be quite pronounced at times, awkward and inappropriate; and yet they had no idea that she was in fact a wife in name only, for Genji had not had sex with her even though they slept together.

Following the ceremony at the palace, Genji went to the Minister of the Left's residence on Sanjō. His wife, as always, presented an icy, beautiful perfection that emitted not the slightest hint of demure attitude or endearing warmth. He felt uncomfortable in her presence. "How happy it would make me if this year at least you could exhibit a new attitude so that we might have a little more normal relationship as husband and wife." She, however, was in no mood for reconciliation. Having heard that he had set up another woman at his villa and that he was giving her special attention as someone of great value to him, she could not help feeling depressed and awkward around him. She struggled to act nonchalant, pretending that she knew nothing about what was going on; and she found it hard, whenever he was intimate and unreserved, to remain stubborn and refuse to open up to him. Indeed, the gentle way she always responded was a special quality that set her apart from other women. Four years older than her husband, she was, at the age of twenty-two, now in her prime; and this was a problem for Genji because her flawless beauty and manners made him lose confidence when he was in her presence. There was nothing lacking in her, no flaws that he could detect anyway, and when he reflected on his own behavior he had to admit that her resentment was justifiable, since it was caused by those inexcusable affairs his fickle heart led him to pursue. After all, she was the only daughter of the Minister of the Left—a man who of all the nobles of similar rank had the weightiest reputation at court— and Princess Ōmiya, who was the younger sister of the Emperor. The greatest care had been lavished on his wife's upbringing, which meant that her sense of pride was exceptionally strong and that she would take even the most trivial slight or indiscretion as a serious and unpleasant injustice. This in turn made Genji resentful, wondering why it was that he was the one who always had to humor her pride. And so their hearts remained distant and unreconciled.

The Minister of the Left was disturbed by his son-in-law's fickleness, and yet whenever he saw Genji he would always forget his resentments, treat him deferentially, and do everything in his power to look after him. The following morning, as Genji was dressing and preparing to leave for court, the Minister dropped by to look in on him. Now that Genji had been promoted to the third rank, his father-in-law had ordered the servants to bring in a famous obi made of lacquered leather studded with gemstones that would show at the back of his robe and indicate his new status. He also had his servants straighten up the back of Genji's robes, and was so particular about the choice of shoes it was almost as if he were putting them on Genji's feet himself. His solicitous behavior was somehow both touching and a little pathetic.

"Should I wear this on official occasions?" Genji asked. "The privy banquet will be held soon, on the Day of the Rat . . . is it the 21st or the 23rd this year? Either way, I have to practice my Chinese verse for the event."

"I have better obi for events like that," the Minister sniffed. "This one just struck me as rather unusual looking. That's all." He pressed Genji to put it on, being almost religiously devoted to looking after him any way he could. Genji's appearances at Sanjō were certainly infrequent, but just to see this remarkable young man coming and going from his residence was a source of great joy and pride for the Minister.

Genji set off to make his New Year's round of visits. He did not have all that many places to call on—he paid his respects to the Emperor, to the Crown Prince, and to Fujitsubo's father, the former emperor. He also dropped by Fujitsubo's villa on Sanjō.

"He looks even more remarkable today. It makes one shudder to think that he just gets better looking the older he is." Fujitsubo's women were praising him up and down, and so she could not resist peeking through the gaps between her curtains to steal a glimpse. Immediately she was lost in her own troubled thoughts.

Her pregnancy was a source of considerable anxiety. Would she survive it? She was supposed to have given birth during the twelfth month, but here it was, the New Year already. Her attendants were in a state of anticipation, thinking that surely their mistress would give birth sometime this month. Even His Majesty was having preparations made at court. But the first month passed with no indication that the birth was imminent, and rumors were now flying around court society. Was this delay the fault of some malign spirit? Such gossip made Fujitsubo feel even more miserable, for just as she was frightened by the possibility that she might die in childbirth, she was just as deathly afraid that the secret of her affair with Genji would be exposed. Her mental anguish eventually made her physically ill.

It was now increasingly clear to Genji that he was the father, and so to ward off evil spirits he discreetly ordered esoteric rites to be performed at various temples around the capital. He fully understood the evanescent nature of the world, but he could not help torturing himself with the thought that his relationship with Fujitsubo would end too soon and come to naught. Then, sometime after the tenth of the second month, Fujitsubo gave birth to a prince. The Emperor and all the people at Fujitsubo's residence in Sanjō were relieved and excited by this auspicious event, even if Genji and Fujitsubo were not. His Majesty had been praying for her to live a long life, yet now the thought of a long life was a burden to Fujitsubo, given all her cares. When rumors reached her that the Kokiden Consort had tried to curse her by praying for an unlucky birth, she realized that news of her death would have served as a source of amusement to some at the court. She drew strength and determination from that thought, and gradually her health and spirits improved.

The Emperor's desire to see the child as quickly as possible was boundless. Genji, who was keeping his feelings to himself, was also extremely anxious to see the child . . . to confirm whether or not he was the father. Choosing a time when he knew there would be no one else around, he paid a visit to Fujitsubo.

"My father is eagerly waiting to see the child," Genji told her. "I thought I might take a look at the baby and then report to the Emperor."

"That's out of the question . . . the baby was just born and is not presentable in his present condition." Fujitsubo quite reasonably refused, for there was no denying that the baby bore a shocking, almost otherwordly resemblance to Genji—a living reproduction. Suffering from the demon of guilty conscience, Fujitsubo was convinced that anyone who saw the baby would instantly understand the sin she had committed with Genji. Since sanctimonious people were always eager to discover and condemn even the most minor of faults, what would they say about this . . . what would happen to her reputation? Dwelling on such possibilities, Fujitsubo was deeply distressed, body and soul.

Genji would meet with Ōmyōbu once in a while, doing his utmost through her to plead his case with Fujitsubo. Not surprisingly, his pleas fell on deaf ears. He continually pestered her about the young prince until finally Ōmyōbu told him, "Why must you insist on seeing him? You'll have your chance in due time." Even though she tried to reassure him, she seemed as troubled at heart as he.

Constrained by his surroundings, Genji could not speak frankly with Ōmyōbu. "Will there ever be a time or conditions when I can speak directly to Fujitsubo, without having to rely on an intermediary?" It was heartbreaking to see him on the verge of tears.

> What bond from a previous life
> Should have joined us, then determined
> That now we must be kept apart

"I cannot understand these things," he lamented.

Having witnessed the torments her lady was experiencing, Omyōbu found it impossible, in the face of Genji's sadness, to curtly refuse him. She recalled the poem by Fujiwara no Kanesuke that evoked the "hearts of parents lost in darkness," and replied.

> One looks upon the child and suffers regret
> One cannot see the child and suffers in grief
> Through such darkness do parents wander this world

"How sad that the birth of this child should keep your hearts from finding peace," she murmured. With no means of communicating with Fujitsubo, Genji returned to his residence. Troubled by the possibility of idle chatter at the court, Fujitsubo told Ōmyōbu that she could no longer tolerate her leading Genji here . . . that was how she really felt. Wary that Ōmyōbu might bring Genji to her, she was no longer able to trust her lady-in-waiting as she had in the past, and stopped treating her as a confidante. She continued to treat

Ōmyōbu kindly, so that no one would suspect anything was amiss, but there were times now when she appeared displeased by Ōmyōbu's conduct. Aware that she was estranged from Fujitsubo, Ōmyōbu felt sad that things had not turned out as she had expected.

The baby was taken to the palace during the fourth month. Larger than usual for a baby that age, the boy was already able to turn himself over. His face bore a striking resemblance to Genji's, but it never occured to the Emperor that Genji might be the child's true father. Rather, he assumed that people who shared unparalleled good looks would naturally resemble one another. His affection and care for the baby were boundless. His affection for Genji also knew no limits, but the lack of recognition and support for Genji among the high-ranking courtiers had made it impossible for him to install Genji in the line of succession. He constantly regretted his decision, and it was a source of pain for him to now look on his son's mature bearing and features and have to think what a waste it was to have removed Genji from the imperial line. It was thus a source of consolation for him that Fujitsubo, the fourth daughter of the previous emperor, and thus a woman of unimpeachable status, had given him a son who possessed the same radiant beauty as Genji. He considered the child a flawless jewel and lavished the greatest care on him—attention that, for Fujitsubo, merely added to the guilt and anxiety filling her heart.

One day, when Genji decided, as was his wont, to pass the time performing music in Fujitsubo's quarters at the palace, His Majesty joined them. He was carrying the infant prince in his arms. "I have many, many children," he remarked to Genji, "but you were the only one I was able to be with all day from the time you were this one's age. Maybe it's because this little one brings those days back to me that I think he looks so much like you. I wonder if all children look the same when they are very young?" It was obvious that the Emperor found the child adorable.

Genji felt himself blanch. Fear, shame, elation, pity . . . all these emotions overwhelmed him to the point that he felt he was going to cry. The baby prattled and smiled, and looked almost preternaturally cute. Was it all that unreasonable or vain of Genji to think—assuming he really did resemble this child during his own infancy—that he himself must indeed have been incredibly precious. Fujitsubo could hardly stand to be there—she was so mortified that she began to perspire. At the same time Genji, who had been so eager to see the child, was unnerved in his presence, and the turmoil in his heart forced him to withdraw from Fujitsubo's quarters.

Genji returned to his Nijō villa and, after resting for a while to calm his nerves, he decided that he should pay a visit to his wife. Pinks were brightly blooming amidst the vibrant green of the plantings that seemed to cover the entire front garden, so he had one of them picked and sent to Ōmyōbu. There were so many things he had to write to Fujitsubo.

> Though I see you in him, the one so like this little pink,
> Because I cannot tell you so, my heart knows no comfort
> My tears heavier than the dew on this flower's petals

"No matter how much I long to see the little one bloom, because our relationship was not meant to last in this vain world . . ."

His note must have been delivered at an opportune moment. Ōmyōbu showed it to Fujitsubo and encouraged her lady to write back: "You really should answer him, even if, as Ōshikōchi no Mitsune put it, your response in no more than a mote of dust on the petal of a pink."[4] Fujitsubo was deeply moved and sent back a simple poem written in the faintest of hands. Her characters looked as though she had pulled the brush away before finishing each stroke.

> Though I may consider it the source
> Of the heavy dew that soaks my sleeves
> How could I discard this precious pink

Ōmyōbu was overjoyed that her lady had responded, and she promptly delivered the poem to Genji. At that moment Genji was lying languidly, absently lost in pensive thoughts, sure that his poem had been in vain and that no reply would be coming back to him. But as soon as he saw Ōmyōbu, his heart beat wildly and he was so happy he wept.

Feeling that it was not good for him to just lie around and mope, absorbed in his cares, he decided he should go to the west hall to see the one person who was his solace. His hair was mussed, he had carelessly tossed on a loose robe, and he was playing a sweetly nostalgic air on his flute when he looked in on Murasaki. She was reclining on an armrest, her elegant appearance calling to mind the image of pinks drenched in dew—perfectly lovely and cute. As enchanting as she looked, it turned out that she was nursing a new grudge against Genji. This was unusual for her, but there she was, sitting with her back toward him, annoyed that he had not come to see her sooner even though he had been in his quarters for some time. Genji moved over to the veranda at the edge of the room and knelt there.

"Come over here," Genji coaxed her, but she ignored him and continued to sulk. She expressed her resentment toward him by murmuring lines from the *Man'yōshū*: "Is he like seaweed on the shore at high tide, which I long for so much, but see so seldom?" She covered her mouth with the sleeve of her robe, apparently embarrassed at her own precociousness. It made her all the more sweetly charming.

"Ahh, that's unfortunate . . . you've already learned how to complain just like an adult. Well, then, let me remind you of this poem: "Were I to see you morning and night, just as often as the divers at Ise see the seaweed, would I not grow weary of you?"[5]

He summoned a servant and had her bring in a thirteen-string koto for Murasaki to play. "This instrument is difficult because the second string closest to you is thin and easily broken," Genji told her. He then tuned the instrument to a lower key to reduce the tension on the strings. He played a few short songs to test the tuning, and then pushed the koto over in front of her. Murasaki found it impossible to continue sulking, and she played beautifully. She was still so small that she had to raise herself up and stretch to reach the strings, but he found the movements of her left hand, as she pressed the strings to make the instrument reverberate, delightfully refined. He instructed her by accompanying her on the flute. She had a quick memory and could pick up even the difficult keys in just one try. Clever, possessed of a charming disposition . . . she was everything he had long hoped for in a woman. The court song "Hosoroguseri" may have had a peculiar sounding title, but as Genji focused on playing it in his

---

4. Poem from *The Kokinshū* (see p. 1407, n. 8).   **5.** Anonymous poem from *The Kokinshū*.

fascinating style, Murasaki accompanied him, skillfully keeping time to the rhythm even though she was so young.

Oil lamps were brought in and they looked at paintings together. He had mentioned earlier to his retinue that he intended to go out, and so a member of his escort began to cough to signal it was time to go. "It looks like it might rain . . ." one of his guards remarked, and Murasaki at once became sullen and depressed, as she always did when Genji was about to leave. She stopped looking at the paintings and lay face down. Genji found her so endearing that he began to stroke her hair, which was spilling abundantly over her shoulders. "I suppose you miss me when I'm away?" he asked her. She nodded.

"I hate going even a single day without seeing you." Genji was trying to comfort her. "But since you are still a child, I have to ask you to be patient a little while longer and to not worry so. I have such fond feelings for you, but I must also consider the feelings of others and not offend those who may be jealous and resentful. Those women are troublesome, and that's why, for the present at least, I have to visit them as I do. When you are grown up I won't have to go out anymore, but for now I want to avoid the harm that might arise as a result of the jealousy of other women so that we might live a long life and be together as much as we desire."

Murasaki felt embarrassed to hear Genji speak about their relationship in such detail, and so she did not answer him. She drew herself up onto Genji's lap and went to sleep. Genji felt terribly sorry for her and told his attendants, "I'll not be going out this evening." They all rose and withdrew, and he had his dinner, which he normally ate in his own rooms, brought to her quarters instead. He woke Murasaki and told her, "I'm not going out after all." Her mood at once improved and she got up. They ate together, but Murasaki was still anxious about his plans and merely picked at her food. "If you're not going out," she suggested, "then why not sleep here tonight?" *If it is so difficult for us to part at a moment like this*, Genji mused, *then how much more difficult will it be when we have to part on the inevitable road of death?*

* * *

FROM **CHAPTER IX**

Aoi

Leaves of Wild Ginger

The court changed when the Emperor abdicated and the Crown Prince took the throne as Emperor Suzaku. The Kokiden faction, headed by the Minister of the Right, was now in ascendance, and Genji began to feel that everything was more difficult for him. Just before His Majesty stepped down he had promoted his favored son to Major Captain of the Right—a rise in status that required the Radiant Prince, in keeping with the dignity of his new position, to begin showing more restraint in pursuing his frivolous nightly adventures. The result was that his many lovers began to complain more and more of his heartlessness. Was it in retribution for causing all these lamentations that Genji suffered from what he saw as the unending cruelty of Fujitsubo, who kept her distance from him? Now, more than ever, she served at the side of the Retired Emperor—almost as if she were some low-ranking attendant. This did not sit well with the Kokiden Consort, but she was now Imperial Mother and had to serve exclusively at the palace—an arrangement that was a source of considerable relief to Fujitsubo.

Depending on the occasion, the Retired Emperor would sponsor musical entertainments so lavish and spectacular they became the talk of court society. He seemed more content now than when he had held power. The only thing lacking for him was Fujitsubo's little son, the new Crown Prince. He yearned to see the boy, who could not be by his side. Having long worried that Fujitsubo's son had no supporters at court, he asked Genji to look after the boy's affairs—a request that was of course awkward for Genji, but one that also made him happy.

At this point I must bring up another, entirely separate matter. At the time Emperor Suzaku ascended the throne, an imperial princess was appointed as the new High Priestess for the Imperial Shrine at Ise. The mother of this princess was the lady at Rokujō—the woman Genji had long been visiting discreetly—while the father was an imperial prince who had actually been ahead of Suzaku in the line of succession, but who had died before he could take the throne. Because the princess was appointed High Priestess under these circumstances, the lady at Rokujō, who no longer had any confidence in the reliability of Genji's feelings, was greatly worried about her daughter's future. The girl was, after all, only thirteen and would be alone in Ise. Thus, the lady at Rokujō had for some time been giving serious consideration to leaving the capital herself and accompanying her daughter to the Imperial Shrine. When the Retired Emperor heard about her plans to leave, he was extremely upset and spoke sharply to Genji about the matter.

"Do I need to remind you," he scolded, "that she was the first wife of my late brother, and would have been an Imperial Consort? He had special affection for her, but now I hear rumors about how carelessly you treat her, as if she were some ordinary woman. It's pathetic. I look on her daughter, the High Priestess, as one of my own, and so you must put an end to this frivolous behavior . . . not just for her sake, but for mine as well. If you persist in playing these irresponsible little games, then don't be surprised when your reputation is in ruins."

Genji could not deny that his father was speaking the truth. Thoroughly chastened, he refrained from answering, whereupon the Retired Emperor added, his tone a little softer, "Never do anything to dishonor or shame a woman. Treat them all gently and give them no cause to resent you." With that admonition ringing in his ears, Genji humbly withdrew from his father's presence terrified at the thought that a day might come when his father learned the truth about Genji's wildly reckless affair with Fujitsubo.

If his father was lecturing him about it, it was obvious gossip about his affair with the lady at Rokujō had spread through the court, and that his promiscuity had damaged her honor and his reputation. He could just imagine how terribly she must be suffering, but there was simply no way he could formally acknowledge their relationship. For one thing, the lady herself was embarrassed that at the age of twenty-nine she was having an affair with a man seven years younger. Moreover, she always tried to appear distant and aloof, and so Genji had grown more reserved with her. Now, however, everyone at court, even the Retired Emperor, knew what was going on, and she lamented that Genji's feelings for her were so shallow.

Genji had long been pursuing the daughter of Prince Shikibu—a lady he knew as Asagao, Princess of the Bellflowers. His efforts had so far proven futile, however, and when Princess Asagao heard rumors of his affair, she resolved never to end up like the lady at Rokujō and refused to give even the most perfunctory of replies to his vain entreaties. Even so, she showed a proper attitude and conducted herself in a way that would give no offense to Genji, and so he continued to consider her a woman of superior qualities.

Needless to say, the household of the Minister of the Left was not amused by Genji's restless disposition; but then again, since he showed no qualms about carrying on so openly, it would have been useless to have complained to him about it. His wife, for one, did not harbor any deep resentment toward him, not least because she was now pregnant and suffering most pitifully not only from morning sickness, but also from anxiety over the dangers posed by the coming birth. Genji thought the pregnancy remarkable, and for the first time felt sympathy for his wife. Because everyone was so overjoyed for her, there was a concern that such happiness could invite bad fortune, and so various prayers and rituals of abstinence[6] were commissioned in order to ensure safe delivery for mother and child. With all these things going on, Genji had less and less time to even consider the feelings of his other women. He was especially mindful of the feelings of the lady at Rokujō, but despite his best intentions not to neglect her, his visits practically ceased altogether.

The High Priestess of the Kamo Shrine stepped down at about that time, and her successor was the third daughter of the Retired Emperor by the Kokiden Consort. This girl was a special favorite of both parents, and it bothered them that unlike her siblings she would have to live isolated from court life. Unfortunately, there were no other princesses appropriate for the position. Although the rituals of investiture were austere, as was customary with Shinto shrines, they would nonetheless be solemn and grand. The Festival of the Kamo Shrine, which was held in the fourth month, was always a major event in the capital; those who accompanied the High Priestess's procession would decorate their carriages and headdresses with heart-shaped leaves of wild ginger.[7] Because this year marked the new Priestess's inaugural procession, many attractions would be added to the public events already scheduled, and the Festival, in keeping with the special status of the High Priestess, would be an especially glorious one.

A few days before the start of the Kamo Festival twelve high-ranking officials were required to attend the Priestess during the procession to her ritual of purification, which took place on the banks of the Kamo River. Given the auspicious nature of the event, only men with honorable prospects and good looks were chosen for this task, and every detail of their appearance was carefully considered—from the color of the trains on their robes and the pattern of their trousers, to the choice of horses and saddles. By special order of Emperor Suzaku, Genji was chosen to participate, and when those who planned to view

---

6. That is, periods of seclusion [editors' note].

7. *Aoi,* the Japanese word for "wild ginger," is also a homophone for the words *au hi,* which mean "the day we will meet." The combination of the heart-shaped leaves of the plant, which is an evergreen, and the romantic implications

of its name is played on later in this chapter in an exchange of poems between Genji and an older lady, Naishi, who appears earlier in the tale. Because much of this chapter centers on Genji's wife, she has been identified traditionally as Aoi.

the procession heard about this decision, they gave extra thought in advance to preparing and positioning their carriages along the route.

The thoroughfare of Ichijō was crammed with carriages and bustling with people. Viewing platforms had been erected at various sites and decorated with great care. Those decorations, together with the sleeves of the court ladies' robes, which trailed out from beneath the blinds set up on the platforms, created their own splendid spectacle.

Genji's wife rarely left her father's residence to go view events like this. Moreover, she had given no thought at all of going to view this particular procession, since she was feeling ill and nervous. Her younger attendants, however, all complained to her.

"What is my lady thinking? How could we ever hope to enjoy the beauty of the procession if we have to sneak off just to take a peak?"

"Ordinary folk, even the lowest woodcutters and hunters who have no connection with anyone in the procession, will be there to take in the sights. They'll especially want to catch a glimpse of your husband."

"People from distant provinces will bring their wives and children to take a look. So it's just not fair that we have to miss it!"

Princess Ōmiya, who, as the younger sister of the Retired Emperor, truly understood the importance of such matters, heard these complaints and urged her daughter to go. "You've been feeling better recently, and your attendants will feel left out and dissatisfied if you don't." And with that, all the women were suddenly informed, to their joy, that their lady would be going out after all.

Because the sun was already well up, they left without formally preparing the carriages in a manner befitting the status of the Minister's household. By the time they arrived, Ichijō avenue was already packed with carriages lining both sides of the street, and it was difficult finding a place to park the imposing and dignified vehicles, unhitch the oxen, and set the shafts on their supports. Many noblewomen already had their carriages positioned there, and the male guards escorting Genji's wife decided to clear a space by pushing aside those that had no guardsmen protecting them.

Among the carriages that had been lined up in that space, two of them exuded a special air of refinement—informal in style, with roofs and blinds made of *hinoki*[8] wicker, slightly worn, but adorned with silk curtains. The women inside had obviously intended to remain inconspicuous. The fresh, vibrant colors of the cuffs of their sleeves, the hems of their skirts, and the ends of their singlets all peeked out coyly from beneath the blinds. The guards escorting Genji's wife were explicity told not to touch these two carriages and warned, "This is not a carriage you can just push aside as you wish!" Unfortunately, the young men in both parties had been drinking too much, and in the end there was no way to prevent the situation from getting out of control. The older retainers from the Minister's household commanded the young men to desist, but they were unable to stop a fight from breaking out.

The lady at Rokujō, whose daughter would soon go off to serve as the Ise Priestess, had been thinking she might find relief from her tormented feelings about Genji by coming discreetly to view the procession for the Purification Ritual. Her attendants, aware of her desire to remain incognito, did not reveal

8. A Japanese evergreen used for various building purposes [editors' note].

her identity, but it was obvious to the men accompanying Genji's wife whose carriages they were moving.

"Don't let them talk to us like that," several of the men shouted. "They must think they can still rely on Lord Genji!"

Several of Genji's attendants had been assigned to accompany his wife's party. They all regarded this incident as most regrettable, but it would have been extremely awkward for them to intervene, and so they looked the other way. In the end, the carriages of Genji's wife and her attendants were positioned in the spaces that had been cleared away, and the carriages of the lady at Rokujō had been relegated to a place behind them, where she could neither see nor be seen. She was in an agony of anger and indignation; and now that her identity had been revealed, after having gone to such great lengths to conceal it out of concern that her shameful feelings for Genji might be exposed, there was no limit to the feelings of chagrin and remorse she suffered. Because the stands for her carriage shafts had been broken in the melee, they had to be propped up on the wheel hubs of some unknown carriages next to hers. It must have looked unsightly, and she was mortified, wondering vainly why she had ever decided to come here.

She no longer wanted to view the procession and wished instead to go home, but there was no space to move her carriage. Just then cries rang out from the crowd, "They're on their way!" Her resolve weakened, and now she wanted to wait until her cruel lover had passed. She recalled an ancient poem in which the Goddess of Ise asks a man to stop his horse at Sasanokuma to let it drink from the Hinokuma River—all so that she might have the chance to gaze upon him.[9] Anxious, she wondered if Genji would stop to acknowledge her . . . but no, he continued on, coldly passing by without so much as a glance in her direction. The turmoil in her heart was greater than ever. Genji feigned disinterest in the many carriages that lined the way, even though they were more splendidly decorated than usual, with the hems of robes spilling out from beneath the blinds as though the occupants were in competition with one another. Still, he did occasionally smile and give a sly, sidelong glance at certain carriages, and when he recognized the carriages of his father-in-law, he assumed a solemn expression as he passed. The men in his escort silently bowed to show their deep respect for Genji's wife. The Rokujō lady, overwhelmed by this display, which clearly demonstrated the inferiority of her status, could not have felt more wretched.

> How cruel this river of purification . . . it grants
> The merest glimpse of your reflection in its chill waters
> Reminding me all the more of how wretched my fate is

She knew it would be disgraceful to weep in front of her women, so she comforted herself with the thought that she would have regretted passing up the opportunity to witness the radiance of his appearance and the beauty of his countenance on such a dazzling occasion.

The high-ranking nobles who accompanied the Kamo Priestess on the procession were superbly decked out, each in keeping with his status at court, and attended by magnificent-looking escorts. The appearance of those of the high-

---

9. A sacred song for the Sun Goddess from *The Kokinshū*.

est rank was especially breathtaking; and yet, as remarkable as they were, they seemed to pale in comparison with Genji's radiance. One of the eight men in his retinue, which had been assembled just for this event, was a man of the sixth rank, a lieutenant in the Right Imperial Guard. It was most unusual to assign someone of his status to this kind of duty, but he was so remarkably good-looking that he was chosen anyway. The other men in Genji's escort were also dazzlingly resplendent; and Genji's appearance, which was always esteemed by the court, was so awe-inspiring that the very trees and grasses seemed to bow before him. Normally, it would be considered improper and unsightly for ladies of rank who, for the sake of modesty, wore veils beneath their deep-brimmed hats, or for nuns who had renounced the world to literally fall over one another in an effort to catch a glimpse of him. Today, however, was different, and no one reproved them. Women of the lower classes—their mouths drawn in where they were missing teeth, their hair tucked modestly inside their robes—jostled each other and made fools of themselves, clasping their hands to their foreheads in supplication to Genji. Vulgar men were grinning stupidly from ear to ear, unaware of how ridiculous their faces looked. Daughters of minor provincial officials, who Genji would never so much as glance at, had arrived in their lavishly decorated carriages, hopelessly preening and posturing because they knew Genji would be passing by. So many amusing things to observe—including the many women who, having been favored by a covert visit from Genji, were now lamenting to themselves that they no longer belonged among the blessed few he favored.

Prince Shikibu, the Minister of Ceremonials, was viewing the procession from one of the platforms, and when he saw Genji, ominous thoughts came to him. *He has matured so, and his appearance is truly spectacular. Surely he will attract the attention of gods and demons.* His daughter, Princess Asagao, had exchanged many letters with Genji over several years and so she knew his sensibilities were anything but ordinary. Now that she was seeing his beauty for the first time, her heart was deeply moved. *A woman can be touched by a man's sincerity, even if he is rather ordinary looking. How much more appealing, then, is the sincerity of a man whose looks are as stunning as his?* Despite these sentiments, she was not inclined to allow her relationship with Genji to become any more familiar or intimate. Her younger attendants were all praising him so much they sounded uncouth, and she found it irritating to listen to them.

When the Kamo Festival proper was held a few days later, no one from the Minister of the Left's residence came out to view it. Genji had been informed of the quarrel between the carriages, and he felt sorry for the lady at Rokujō. He was also offended by his wife's conduct. "It's a shame," he remarked, "that such a dignified person should show so little sympathy or kindness toward others. She probably never intended for such a thing to happen, and yet her temperament prevents her from even considering the possibility that women who share the kind of relationship she and the lady do should be mutually affectionate and supportive. No wonder her subordinates, who lack judgment and status, acted as outrageously as they did. As for the lady who suffered this insult, she has such a superior upbringing and is so sensitive to any slight that the whole sordid incident must have been terribly unpleasant for her."

Genji felt such pity that he went to Rokujō to visit the lady. She, however, was reluctant to see him. Her daughter, after all, was still living in the residence while undergoing the rites of purification that would prepare her to serve as the High Priestess at Ise. Branches of the sacred *sakaki* tree[1] had been placed at all the corners and gates, and thus the lady did not feel comfortable letting Genji in to see her, since that would run the risk of defilement. Genji thought her precaution perfectly reasonable, but he still muttered to himself, "Why must things always be like this? Why do women have to flash their horns and quarrel?"

Genji retreated to his own residence at Nijō. On the day of the Kamo Festival he went with Murasaki to view the festivities. After ordering Koremitsu to prepare their carriages, he went over to the west hall.

"Will all your little ladies be going as well?" he teasingly asked, referring to Murasaki's playmates. Observing her outfit and makeup, which exuded an exceptionally graceful air, he couldn't help smiling. "Very well, then, shall we be going? Let's view the festival together." He stroked her hair, which looked even more lustrous than usual, and added, "It's been a while since you've had the ends trimmed. Today would be an auspicious time to do it." He summoned a scholar from the Bureau of Divination and asked him which hours that day would be lucky or unlucky for trimming hair. He then told Murasaki, "Have your little ladies come forth." He looked them over and found their childish figures delightfully charming. Their hair had been trimmed gorgeously and hung down in sharp relief over the outer trousers of their festive robes . . . altogether adorable. "I'll cut your hair," Genji said to Murasaki. "It's really thick, isn't it? What would become of it if you just let it grow out." He found trimming her hair a little difficult. "Ladies with very long hair tend to cut the side locks that frame their foreheads a little shorter than the rest. I don't think you would look as attractive without short locks." When he finished with the trimming, Genji offered the obligatory benediction, expressing the hope that her hair might grow "a thousand fathoms."

Murasaki's nurse, Shōnagon, had been watching them, her heart filled with gratitude. Genji composed and recited a verse.

> I shall protect you, watching your hair grow
> Like strands of rippling seaweed stretching up
> From the thousand-fathomed depths of the sea

Murasaki chose to write out her reply.

> You claim your love is as deep as the thousand-fathomed sea
> Yet how am I to know that's true, since you wander so much
> Coming in and going out like uncertain, restless tides

Such clever wit, and such youthful beauty. She's perfect, Genji thought.

So many sightseeing carriages had arrived for the Kamo Festival that there were no spaces anywhere this day as well. They had trouble finding a place to stop and pulled up near the parade grounds and pavilion where the Mounted Guard held their archery competition during the fifth month of each year. "So many high-ranking officials have brought their carriages here, the area is really

---

1. *Sakaki* is a flowering evergreen tree native to Japan. It is sacred in the Shinto religion and branches of *sakaki,* decorated with slips or streamers of paper, are used for ritual offerings and purifications.

bustling," Genji said, sounding a little confounded and irritable. He had his carriage pause for a moment next to a lady's carriage that was not at all inelegant. The lady's carriage was filled with occupants, and a fan was thrust out beckoning him over to them. "Would you like to set your carriage here?" a woman asked. "We could make some space for you." Genji was somewhat taken aback, wondering what kind of woman could be so coquettish. This spot, however, was an excellent place from which to view the Festival parade, and so he decided to accept the invitation. "How did you manage to come by this space?" he asked. "It's good enough to make people resent you, so I'll take you up on your offer." The lady in the carriage then broke off a section of her stylish folding fan and wrote out the following.

> The wild ginger, with its heart-shaped leaves, adorns another
> Though its name, *aoi*, promises the day when we'll meet . . .
> In vain I waited for the Kamo god to bless this day

"I cannot pass beyond the ropes marking off that sacred space."

Genji recognized the handwriting. It was the old Assistant Handmaid, Naishi no Suke. He found it shocking that someone her age should be flirting like a young woman. He was genuinely displeased and sent back a curt reply.

> The feelings of one adorned with those heart-shaped leaves
> Are certainly fickle, since she can "meet this day"
> Any man she wants from among the eighty clans

Naishi was filled with bitter thoughts at Genji's cruelty.

> A bitter adornment, this wild ginger
> With its empty promise of meeting you . . .
> Mere leaves signifying vain and false hopes

Many women, not just Naishi, experienced pangs of jealousy as they tried to guess the identity of the lady riding with Genji. They resented that for her sake he chose to keep his blinds down, because it denied them an opportunity to catch a glimpse of him. The women gossiped among themselves.

"He was so splendid-looking the day of the procession."

"Yes, but today he's going about rather informally, don't you think?"

"Who is that riding with him, I wonder? She must be a special woman."

Genji remained disgruntled. *What a complete waste of time, exchanging verses that play on a subject like leaves of wild ginger.* Anyone not as impudent as Naishi would certainly have refrained from sending a note out of respect for the lady riding with him.

For her part, the lady at Rokujō had never in all her life experienced the kind of torment brought on recently by her dark, obsessive thoughts. She had, it is true, resigned herself to Genji's cruel neglect, but the thought of leaving him behind in order to go with her daughter to Ise brought an agonizing sense of loneliness. She was also fully aware that she would be an object of derision at the court. Whenever she thought, wistfully, that perhaps she ought to stay behind in the capital, she would become anxious, for she knew that if she stayed she would expose herself to even more extreme levels of ridicule. Her days and nights were so filled with troubled thoughts that she couldn't help but recall the *Kokinshū* poem: "Am I a float on the line of the fisherman of Ise that my heart should be adrift like this, bobbing on the waves?"[2] Finding no relief from her obsessive, insecure state of mind, she fell ill.

Genji wasn't in the least concerned about her stated desire to accompany her daughter to Ise, and he never once tried to dissuade her by telling her that it was out of the question. Instead he remarked, rather sarcastically, "I understand. It's perfectly reasonable for you to find repugnant the prospect of continuing a relationship with a man as worthless as I. Yet no matter how unpleasant it may be for you now, if you were to stay with me to the end, that would indicate you're a woman of no shallow sensibility, would it not?" On hearing such hateful words, the lady withdrew even deeper into her dark thoughts. Distressed and depressed, she had decided to go see the procession only because she had wanted some relief from her insecurity and indecisiveness. And then, when she did go, she found herself buffeted about, as if she were adrift on the violent rapids of the river of lustration.

While all of this was taking place, a malignant spirit was causing concern for everyone at the Minister of the Left's Sanjō residence. Genji's wife was suffering terribly, and under the circumstances it was not appropriate for him to be going around visiting his other women. Indeed, during this period he only rarely went to his own residence in Nijō. True, he had never warmed to his wife much, but he did consider her someone of special importance to him. He was wracked with grief that she should now be suffering so much as a consequence of her remarkable pregnancy, and he had prayers and rites performed for her in his own quarters at his father-in-law's residence.

Many souls of the deceased and spirits of living persons were exorcised and forced to reveal their names. One particular spirit, however, resisted all attempts to move it into the body of a medium and persisted in clinging fast to Genji's wife. It did no real harm, but it would not leave her body, even for a few moments. The deeply obsessive nature of this spirit, which would not obey even the holiest of exorcists, made it clear that this was no commonplace possession. The attendants considered the various women Genji called on and whispered among themselves, "Only the ladies at Rokujō and Nijō have a special place in his heart . . . perhaps their resentment is especially strong." Diviners were brought in to confirm these suspicions, but they failed to do so. Whenever they questioned the spirits they learned nothing that would suggest any of them was driven by revenge or hatred. There was the spirit of a former nurse and spirits that had haunted the families of the Minister and Princess Ōmiya for generations; but these had appeared simply because their daughter was in a fragile condition. None of them were really malicious, but seemed to have shown up at random. Why, then, was Genji's wife constantly shouting out and weeping? She was always nauseous or had choking sensations, and she would writhe around as if in unbearable agony. Genji and her parents were frightened and upset, wondering how this would all turn out and worrying that she might die.

Because the Retired Emperor repeatedly sent messages of concern and graciously ordered prayers and rituals, her death would be all the more lamentable. Upon hearing that everyone at the court was worried, the lady at Rokujō was afflicted with the troubling thought that she was being diminished as sympathy for her rival grew. She had always had a jealous, competitive streak, but until

---

2. Anonymous poem from *The Kokinshū*.

that absurd quarrel over the carriages had unsettled her heart, it had never been as pronounced as it was now, and she felt a degree of resentment that no one at the Minister's household could have ever imagined.

The lady knew, as a result of her confused emotions, that her condition was not normal, and so she decided to undergo esoteric Buddhist healing rites. However, she had to move out of her residence and have the rites performed elsewhere in order to avoid defiling her daughter, who was still preparing to be the High Priestess of Ise. Genji heard about her plans and, moved to pity as he wondered how she was feeling, went to call on her. Because she was not at her usual residence in Rokujō, he had to be exceptionally discreet when he visited. He repeatedly asked her to overlook the way he had neglected her recently, pointing out that it was due to circumstances beyond his control. He even tried to elicit her sympathy by describing the terrible suffering of his wife.

"I'm not all that concerned about her myself," he said, "but I do feel sorry for her parents, who are upset and making rather too much of a fuss about it. So while she is in this condition, I really should stay close by her. If you could take all of these things into account, I would be very grateful." Genji pleaded with her, but he could see from the expression on her face that she was suffering even more than usual, and he felt terribly sorry for her.

The lady had been moody and withdrawn that night, but when, in the welter of her yearnings and resentments, she saw how ravishing he looked as he prepared to leave at the crack of dawn, she was tempted to reconsider her decision to leave the capital with her daughter. At the same time, she was realistic enough to know that Genji, who already held his wife in high esteem, would feel even greater affection and lavish his attentions solely on *that woman* once the child was born. And when that happened, *she* would be left waiting, fretting impatiently over whether Genji would ever show up and knowing that whenever he did come to see her, it would be out of some lukewarm sense of duty or pity. Her tangled emotions opened her eyes afresh to the reality of her situation. After waiting all day for his "morning-after" letter, it finally arrived that evening—a short, curt note with no poem attached: "Her condition had been improving recently, but now she has suffered a relapse, and I really must stay here."

She read the note and thought it was just another of his typical excuses. Even so, she sent a response.

> Intimate with the path of love, where dew has soaked my sleeves,
> My sad fate is to have followed that path too far and end
> With robes soaked in mud, like a peasant cultivating fields

"Perhaps it is fitting to remind you of the old poem about the water of the mountain well. The poet, having tried to draw water from a well so shallow, regrets that she too gets nothing but damp sleeves."[3]

Genji pored over her response, marveling at the beauty of her script, which was so superior to everyone else's, and wondered why the world had to be so damnably complicated. He felt painfully torn—on the one hand, he couldn't simply abandon a woman of her sensibility and looks, and, on the other, there was no way he could settle on just one woman. He sent his reply well after dark.

3. Anonymous poem from an earlier *waka* anthology, the *Kokin waka rokujō*.

"What do you mean that only your sleeves are damp? Your feelings for me must not be very deep."

> How shallow the path of love you follow
> That you merely dampen your sleeves with dew
> While I drench myself where the mud is deep

He added, among other things, "Do you imagine that my feelings for you are insincere, that I would not reply to you in person were my wife's condition not truly serious?"

At the Minister's residence the obsessive spirit was appearing more persistently and causing Genji's wife great distress. The lady at Rokujō then heard gossip to the effect that it was either her own living spirit or that of her late father. She gave the rumors careful consideration. Even though she had never wished ill fortune to befall others, she had often lamented her own bad luck, and she was aware that the living spirit of a person who is preoccupied with personal desires and attachments might wander from the body. She had lived for so many years convinced that she had suffered as much grief and anxiety as it was possible for one person to suffer, and now it was as if her soul had been torn asunder. That day when the foolish incident with the carriages occurred, she had been treated disdainfully, and *that woman*, Genji's wife, had in effect ignored her as though she were beneath contempt. After the procession to the Purification Ritual was over, her heart and mind lost their moorings and drifted, all on account of that one incident, and she found it truly difficult to calm her nerves.

Lately, whenever she dozed off, she began having a recurring dream. She would find herself in the beautifully appointed, luxurious quarters of some woman—Genji's wife, she assumed—and would then watch in horror as her living spirit, so completely different from her waking self, would move around the woman, pulling and tugging at her, and then, driven by menacingly obsessive emotions, violently striking and shaking her. Because of this recurring dream, the lady had many moments when she believed she was losing her grip on reality. *Ah, how horrible this is! What they say is true after all. A person's living spirit really can leave the body and wander about.*[4] *And even if it isn't true in my case, people at the court prefer to speak ill of others, and this situation will provide fodder to those who relish spreading malicious gossip.* Fearing that she would be notorious, the lady made a resolution to herself. *They say it's common for people to leave behind their obsessive attachments and resentments when they die. I've always considered such a thing deeply sinful and ominous, even when it has happened to people with whom I have no connections. But now there are rumors that it's my living spirit that's acting in such a grotesque, unearthly way. It must be retribution for the sins of a former life. I must never give another thought to that cruel man.* She resolved over and over to put him out of her mind, but, resolve as she might, to so resolve was just another way to think about *him*.

As part of a series of purification rites in preparation for her departure for Ise, the daughter of the lady at Rokujō was to have moved during the previous year into a detached residence at the palace called the Shosai-in, which served

---

4. Poem from *The Kokinshū* by Ōshikōchi Mitsune: "It must have wandered off, abandoning my body . . . this heart of mine that goes its own way, doing things I do not intend."

as the pavilion of the First Lustration. However, there had been a number of complications, and so it was decided that she would not move into the pavilion until the autumn. Thereafter, in the ninth month, the Ise Priestess would move again, undergoing the Second Lustration at a temporary shrine built for this purpose on the plains of Sagano, famous for its lovely autumn vistas. The attendants in the residence at Rokujō thus had to make preparations for two purification rites, one right after the other. Their mistress, alas, was distracted and depressed and lying prone in her suffering, unable to rouse herself. This was no trivial matter for the ladies-in-waiting to the Priestess, since her mother's illness could be defiling; and so they commissioned prayers and rites. In truth, the lady didn't really seem all that sick, and as the days and months passed no one was sure exactly what was wrong or how serious it was. Genji was constantly inquiring after the lady's health, but because his wife, who was far more important to him, was suffering so much, he was burdened with seemingly endless concerns.

Because they assumed it was not yet time for Genji's wife to give birth, everyone at the Sanjō residence was caught off guard when she went into labor and appeared to be on the verge of delivering the child. More and more malignant spirits were drawn to her as the moment of the birth neared, and the number and intensity of the prayers and rites meant to assure a safe childbirth increased. Still, that one stubborn, obsessive spirit remained more intransigent than ever. Even the most venerable of the priests found this spirit abnormal, and they were unable to exorcise it. As they tried to make the spirit show itself, their prayers finally forced it to speak to them through Genji's wife. The spirit, in a weeping voice wracked with pain, pleaded with the priests. "Please stop for a moment. I have something I must say to Lord Genji." The attendants at once whispered among themselves, "Just as we thought . . . there's some reason for this after all."

Genji was shown in where his wife was lying behind her curtains. Because she seemed to be near death, her parents withdrew a short distance away in case their daughter had some last words for her husband. The priests ceased their prayers and lowered their voices as they chanted the Kannon chapter of the Lotus Sutra. Their murmuring created an atmosphere at once uncanny and sublime. Genji lifted the curtains and looked in on his wife. There was something alluringly attractive about her as she lay there, her belly large and distended. Even someone with whom she had no connection at all would have been distracted gazing at her, so it was natural for Genji to feel overwhelmed with regret and sorrow. Her long, luxuriant black hair, which had been pulled back and tied up, stood out in a vivid contrast to the white of her maternity robes. She was always so prim and proper that Genji had never found her special elegance all that attractive. Now, for the first time, as she lay there in her vulnerable, helpless condition, she struck him as not just precious, but voluptuous.

He took her hand. "How terrible this is. Must you cause me to grieve so?" He began to cry and could speak no further. She weakly raised her head and gazed at him with that expression that had hitherto always made him feel uncertain and inadequate in her presence. Tears filled her eyes, and when he gazed back at her—a woman who now seemed so accessible to him—how could he not be deeply touched?

Because she was crying so intensely, Genji assumed she was thinking of her poor, anxious parents and, on seeing him here like this, regretting that they would soon part.

"You mustn't brood so much about everything," Genji comforted her. "You don't feel well now, but you'll get better. And even if death should separate us, remember that husbands and wives are destined to meet in the next world. You have a deep bond with your father and mother, and no matter how many times you are reborn, that bond is never-ending. I am sure there will be a time when you will see them again."

"No, no, that's not why I'm crying. I'm crying because the exorcists' prayers hurt me so. I asked for you to come here so that I might have a moment of relief from them. I never imagined that I would come here in this form, but now I know the truth. The spirit of a person lost in obsessive longing will actually wander from the body." The voice that came from his wife's lips had a gentle, seductive familiarity. "Just as they did in ancient times . . ."

> Bind the hems of my robes
> To keep my grieving soul
> From wandering the skies

As he was listening to the voice, his wife's appearance changed and she no longer looked like herself. Genji was trying to comprehend this inexplicable, eerie phenomenon when he suddenly realized he was gazing on the countenance of the lady at Rokujō. He was horrified. He had dismissed out of hand the rumors claiming the spirit possessing his wife was the lady's, considering them nothing more than the idle gossip of vulgar, insensitive people. But he was witnessing the possession with his own eyes and understood now that such things did happen in this world. It was uncanny. *How wretched*, he thought, and then answered her, saying, "You sound like someone I know, but I'm not certain. Tell me who you are." The spirit replied in a way that left no doubt it was *she*. To say that he was shocked would not do justice to the sense of horror he experienced. At the same time, the presence of the attendants made him feel awkward and embarrassed, since they might recognize that the spirit was the lady's.

When the voice grew a little more subdued, Genji's mother-in-law, thinking that her daughter was feeling more comfortable, brought in a hot medicinal infusion. The attendants raised his wife from behind and supported her in a squatting posture, and she gave birth to a boy. The joy everyone felt was boundless, though the malign spirits that had been forced into mediums raised a tremendous fuss, since they resented the safe delivery. There was still the afterbirth to worry about, but thanks to the numerous prayers and supplications to the Buddha, it was a normal birth. The abbot of the Enryakuji temple on Mt. Hiei and the other distinguished priests quickly withdrew, wiping the sweat from their proud, satisfied faces. All the women in the household were finally able to relax a little after so many days of worry and devoted service. They were sure that the worst was over; and even though new prayers and rites for the mother were ordered, for the moment the baby became the center of attention. Everyone let their guard down as they were absorbed in helping out with the remarkable child. The Retired Emperor, princes of the blood, and the highest ranking officials all attended, without fail, the traditional banquets held on the third, fifth, seventh and ninth nights following the birth to joyously celebrate. They brought with them exquisite and remarkable gifts of food and clothing, and because the child was a boy, the celebrations were all the more lively and auspicious.

When the lady at Rokujō learned about all of this, she grew agitated. She had heard that Genji's wife had been in a precarious state, but now, apparently, everything was fine, and she felt both jealous and disappointed. She continued to feel weird, as though she were not herself, and her robes reeked of the smell of poppy seeds exorcists burn to drive out a lingering spirit. Strangely, the smell would not dissipate, but continued to permeate her body no matter how often she tried washing her hair and changing her robes. She was disgusted at herself, and worried what others might say or think. She couldn't very well discuss this with anyone, so she was forced to suffer in isolation, which only made her emotional turmoil worse. Genji was feeling somewhat calmer, but whenever he recalled the unpleasant moment when the lady's spirit had addressed him unbidden in that weird and shocking manner, he was reminded of the pain she was experiencing because he had not called on her in such a long time. He vacillated, thinking that perhaps he should visit her in person. But then every time he considered the idea of a visit, he couldn't help worrying that he might be appalled, wondering how she could have fallen to such a state. After considering all the options, he decided it would be best for her if he just sent a message.

Everyone was worried about the prognosis for Genji's wife, who had suffered so grievously, and kept a vigilant watch over her. Naturally, Genji stopped going out on his nightly amorous excursions, even though his wife was still quite sick and unable to see her husband in the customary manner. The baby boy was exceptionally handsome, and because there were worries that his looks might attract the resentful attention of malignant spirits, every effort was made from the moment of his birth to protect him and bring him up with the greatest care. Genji's father-in-law was tremendously pleased, since things had worked out as he had hoped; and though he continued to show concern over his daughter, who had not yet fully recovered, he assumed that her condition was simply the aftereffect of having been so ill, and that there was no reason to be unduly alarmed.

On seeing the beauty of the eyes and features of the baby, who bore a striking resemblance to Fujitsubo's child, Genji thought lovingly of his other, unacknowledged son, the new Crown Prince, and was seized with an unbearable desire to go to the palace to visit him.

"I've not been to the palace for some time, and that concerns me. Since my confinement ends today, I had better go there." He then added, with some resentment, "I wonder if I might speak to my wife directly, without a curtain between us? Why do we always have to be so formal with one another, especially now?"

"As you wish, my lord," one of the women responded. "Your relationship with my lady need not be so formal and distant. Though she is terribly weakened by her ordeal, there is no need to separate the two of you with screens or curtains."

The attendants brought in a cushion for him and placed it close to where his wife was lying. He went in, sat down, and began speaking to her. She answered from time to time, but she still seemed very weak. He remembered the state she had been in at the time he was certain she was about to die, and now felt as if it had all been a dream. He spoke of the period when she had been in mortal danger, and it made his heart ache to think that she had been on the point of death, and to recall how she had stopped breathing, but then recovered and spoke to him so urgently.

"There is so much I want to tell you, but they say you are too weak and not up to it, so I'll let it go for now," he said. He reminded her to drink her medicine, and showed her consideration in other ways as well. Her attendants were deeply impressed by his ministrations, amazed that he had learned such things.

Her appearance as she lay there was heartbreakingly adorable, so weak and pale that he could hardly tell if she were dead or alive. Her abundant hair was properly done up, and the strands that were lying across the pillow were incomparably elegant. He gazed possessively at her, feeling strange that in all this time he should ever have found her deficient in any way.

"I must go visit my father, but I shall return quickly," Genji told her. "How happy it would make me if I could always gaze on you as I am doing now. But your mother is constantly nearby, and so out of deference to her I have refrained from seeing you directly, lest I be considered rash. You must do all you can to get well, then move back to your own chambers. One reason you are not improving may be that you have become too childishly dependent on others."

With these words he took his leave, put on splendid robes and went out. In the past she rarely saw him off, but this time she lay there watching him in rapt attention.

The Autumn Ceremonial for Court Promotions was scheduled for that evening, and because the Minister of the Left had to preside over the event, he too left his daughter at his Sanjō residence and headed for the palace. Each of his sons was hoping to receive a promotion, and since they didn't want to be separated from their father on this particular day, they all left with him.

As a result, there were very few people at the Minister's residence that evening, and while the villa was deserted a malignant spirit suddenly assaulted Genji's wife. The choking sensation she experienced made breathing difficult, and she was in great distress. She stopped breathing before there was time to inform those who had gone to the ceremony. On hearing the news, everyone was stunned, and they left the palace not knowing where their feet were taking them. Though it was the evening of the Autumn Ceremonial, in the face of such a tragedy it would not have been appropriate to continue the event. The crisis had arisen in the middle of the night, and so they were unable to call for the abbot at Mt. Hiei, or even for a distinguished priest. They had all relaxed and let their guard down, assuming that the worst was over, and because her death was so unexpected, the attendants at the Minister's residence were in a panic—confused, stumbling about, bumping into things. Messengers bearing condolences from various noble houses crowded into the residence at Sanjō, but there was no one to take their messages, and the whole house was shaking from the uproar. It was frightening to see how upset everyone was. Because so many malignant spirits had possessed her, they followed prescribed custom and left her body lying there. They didn't disturb her or move the position of her pillow, lest her soul fail to find its way back should it try to return. They kept watch over her for two or three days, but when her appearance began to change, they realized they had reached the end, that she was indeed gone, and were overwhelmed by grief.

With his wife's tragic death coming on the heels of his shocking encounter with the living spirit of the lady at Rokujō, Genji was preoccupied with thoughts of the tiresome nature of this world, and as a result he felt put off by the words of condolences he received from people—even from women with whom he had a special relationship. Genji's father-in-law, the Minister of the Left, was deeply honored to receive condolences directly from the Retired Emperor. It was an honor that brought a moment of relief to his unremitting sorrow, and it left him crying tears of both joy and grief. On the advice of others, the Minister spared no expense or effort in commissioning mystery rites intended to revive his daughter; and though it was evident for all to see that her body was decaying away, in his distracted state he vainly persisted until there was nothing more to be done. When at last they took his daughter's body to be cremated on the plains of Toribeno, many heartrending moments occurred along the way.

* * *

At the Nijō villa his men and women were preparing for his arrival, cleaning and polishing. The senior attendants all appeared before him, and they vied to outdo one another in the splendor of their clothing and makeup. Genji couldn't help but be touched by the lively scene before him, which contrasted so starkly with the lonely, melancholy scene he had left behind at the Sanjō residence. He changed out of his mourning robes and went over to Murasaki's quarters in the west hall. The clothing and furnishings there had been changed with the advent of winter, and the rooms had a bright, fresh look to them. The outfits of the pretty women and girls there were pleasing to his eyes, and Murasaki's nurse, Shōnagon, had made sure that all the preparations had been carried out to his complete satisfaction. Indeed, everything looked wonderful to him.

Murasaki was sweetly done up . . . really lovely. "It's been a long time," Genji began. "You've become quite the young lady." He raised the lower half of the curtains to peek in on her, and when he did so she shyly turned away from him. Even so, he could see that her beauty was perfection itself. Glimpsing her profile in the lamplight, he could tell from her eyes and face that she looked exactly like Fujitsubo, the woman who had so possessed his heart, and he was overjoyed. He moved closer to her and spoke of all the things that had happened, and of how anxious he had been, wondering how she had fared during his period of mourning. "I want to talk to you at leisure, tell you stories of all that took place while I was away. For the time being, however, I'll sleep in the east hall. Having just come out of mourning, it might be bad luck for me to stay here just now. But soon we will have all the time in the world to be together . . . so much so that you may come to regard me as a nuisance."

Shōnagon, who was listening in on them, was delighted by his words, but then she immediately began having anxious thoughts about the precarious position of her young charge. After all, there were many highborn ladies Genji visited discreetly; and it was also possible that he would be drawn to some new lady who might appear on the scene and take the place of his late wife. Shōnagon's suspicious nature was an unattractive trait, but her doubts were understandable, since her primary responsibility was to look after Murasaki.

Genji returned to his own chambers. One of his female attendants, Chūjō no kimi, massaged his legs, and he was finally able to relax and fall asleep. The next morning he sent a letter to his little son at Sanjō. The melancholy reply, obviously written for him by the boy's grandmother, filled him with inexhaustible grief.

With little to occupy him, Genji would lose himself in reveries of longing. Yet because he was reluctant to wander about on some random nocturnal adventure, he could not rouse himself to go out. His little Murasaki was now grown up and ideal in all respects. She looked spectacular, and he felt that now was the appropriate time to consummate their relationship. From time to time he would casually drop hints about their marriage, but she seemed to have no idea what he was talking about.

They whiled away the hours, relieving their tedium by playing Go or word games like *hentsugi*, writing down radicals or parts of a Chinese character and trying to guess which one it was. Murasaki had a clever and engaging personality, and she would demonstrate endearing talents in even the most trivial of pastimes. For several years he had driven all thoughts of taking her as a wife out of his mind, dismissing her talents as nothing more than the accomplishments of a precocious child. Now he could no longer control his passion—though he did feel pangs of guilt, since he was painfully aware of how innocent she was.

Her attendants assumed he would consummate their relationship at some point, but because he had always slept with her, there was simply no way for them to know when that moment would come. One morning Genji rose early, but Murasaki refused to get up. Her behavior worried her attendants. "What's wrong?" they whispered. "She seems unusually out of sorts today." Right before Genji returned to his own quarters, he placed just inside her curtains a box filled with inkstones, brushes, and paper, which she was to use for the customary morning-after letter.[5] When there was no one else around, Murasaki finally lifted her head and found his betrothal note folded in a love knot at her pillow. Still in a daze, she opened the letter.

> How strange that we have stayed apart so long
> Though we slept together night after night
> With only the robes we wore between us

The poem was written in a playful, spontaneous manner, as if he had allowed his emotions to carry him along. It had never crossed her mind that he might be the kind of man who harbored such thoughts about her, and she burned with shame when she recalled their sordid first night. *How could I have been so naïve? How could I have ever trusted a man with such base intentions?*

Genji returned to her quarters at midday, peeking in through her curtains. "Something seems to be bothering you . . . are you not well? It would be quite tedious for me if we weren't able to play Go today." Murasaki was still lying face down. She pulled the bedding up over her face so that she would not have to look at him. When her attendants withdrew, Genji went over to her. "Why are you acting so despondent? Are you displeased with me? I never imagined that you could be so cold. Your women must think this is all very queer." He tugged her bedding away. She was bathed in perspiration, and tears had soaked the hair framing her forehead. "Now this won't do at all!" Genji was put out.

---

5. After a couple's first night together the man was supposed to leave the woman a poem, to which she should respond [editors' note].

"Tears on the first day of your marriage? It's ominous . . . very inauspicious." He tried all sorts of things to cheer her up, but she thought him truly horrid and refused to speak. "All right, then, have it your way," he told her spitefully. "I won't come here anymore if you insist on putting me to shame!" He opened the box with the writing implements and checked inside. There was no reply note. *She's still a child after all*, he thought ruefully. He now felt sorry for her and decided to stay with her inside the curtains for the rest of the day. He passed the whole time trying to comfort her, but this proved difficult. Her refusal to warm up to him, however, merely made her look all the more precious to him.

It was the First Day of the Boar in the tenth month, when the moon rose in the north-northwest. The custom was to serve cakes made of pounded rice on this day, so as evening wore on and they reached the hour of the Boar a little after 9:00, Genji had rice cakes shaped to look like baby pigs brought in to him and Murasaki. The Boar was a symbol of fertility, but the First Day of the Boar was not an auspicious time for marriage. Moreover, Genji was still in mourning, and so he made sure their celebration was subdued, serving the rice cakes in Murasaki's quarters only. Looking at the various colors of the rice cakes, which were flavored with beans, or chestnuts, or poppy, among other things, and nestled in cypress boxes, Genji remembered that he had to have white rice cakes prepared for tomorrow evening, the Third Night of their marriage. He stepped out and summoned Koremitsu. "Have rice cakes brought here tomorrow," he ordered, "though not as many as today. This was not an auspicious day for rice cakes."

Seeing Genji's wry smile, Koremitsu caught on immediately. He did not press his lord on the matter, but simply replied with a perfectly serious expression on his face. "Of course, my lord. It is most reasonable of you to choose an auspicious day to serve rice cakes." He then added, rather drolly, "Let's see . . . tomorrow is the Day of the Rat. Shall I tell them you're having rice cakes in the shape of baby mice to celebrate the event? And just how many will you need?"

"I suppose a third as many as we had today . . . that should be enough," Genji told him. And with that Koremitsu, who knew just what to do, withdrew. *He's certainly an experienced hand*, thought Genji. Koremitsu spoke of this to no one else, and had the rice cakes prepared at his own residence, without telling anyone why he needed them. He was so discreet, in fact, it was almost as if he had made them himself.

Genji was finding it so difficult to comfort Murasaki that he was at a loss. At the same time he was delighted when it occurred to him that, for the first time in her life, she must have felt like a stolen bride. With that realization came another. *She has been precious to me for many years, but my feelings for her during all that time were nothing compared to what I feel for her now. The heart is a peculiar thing. Now I find it impossible to be apart from her, even for a single night.*

Koremitsu stealthily brought a box filled with the rice cakes Genji had ordered late the previous night. Deeply considerate and sensitive to the situation, Koremitsu thought it might be embarrassing for Murasaki if he asked her nurse, Shōnagon, to take the box into her chambers. So instead he summoned Shōnagon's daughter, Ben. "Take this to your young mistress, and don't let anyone see you." He handed her an incense jar, inside of which he had hidden the box of rice cakes. "Now listen to me. This is a gift to celebrate an auspicious event, so you must set it beside her pillow. Be very careful. You must carry out my instructions to the letter." Ben thought that this request was suspicious, but she took the jar anyway. "I have never," she insisted, "been unfaithful in serving my lady." He cut her short. "Don't use the word *unfaithful*. The very uttering of it on an occasion like this is bad luck." Ben considered the whole affair very odd, but she was young and really had no idea what Koremitsu was talking about. She placed the jar inside her lady's curtains next to her pillow. Genji, as he always did, explained the significance of the rice cakes to Murasaki.

Murasaki's attendants had known nothing about this. It wasn't until the next morning, when Genji had the box of rice cakes taken away, that they finally realized their lord had formally taken their young mistress as his wife. When could all of the dishes have been brought in? The stands on which the plates rested looked fabulous, their legs intricately carved in the shape of flowers. Various kinds of rice cakes had been specially prepared, and everything used for the Third Night celebration—the silver plates, silver chopsticks, silver chopstick rests—had been exquisitely arranged. Shōnagon wondered, *Has he actually gone so far as to recognize her as his wife?* And when she saw it was true, she was profoundly grateful and wept at this proof of Genji's honorable intentions. The other women were disappointed that they had not been let in on the secret, and they grumbled among themselves. "Of course it's wonderful that things have turned out like this, but why did our lord have to keep it secret? And that Koremitsu . . . whatever could he have been thinking?"

Following his marriage to Murasaki, Genji would feel so anxious about her whenever he went to the palace or called on the Retired Emperor, even for a short visit, that a vision of her would come to him and he would see her face. He found his own attraction to her mysterious. He received resentful letters from his other women enticing him to visit, and their notes did make him feel bad for them. But the very thought that such visits would be hard on his new bride troubled him. He recalled a line from an old *Man'yōshū* poem: "How can I endure a single night apart from you?"[6] He simply could not bring himself to go out on his nocturnal forays, but instead pretended he wasn't feeling well and was indisposed. He passed the time sending replies to his ladies along the lines of "I've been preoccupied of late with thoughts of the sad evanescence of this world. Once this mood of mine has passed, we shall, I assure you, meet again."

Oborozukiyo, the lady Genji associated with that evening of the misty moon, could not get him out of her mind. Her older sister, the Kokiden Consort, who was now the Imperial Mother, was extremely displeased to learn about this infatuation, and was further annoyed when her own father, the Minister of the Right, dismissed her concerns. "Why should I be bothered about this?" he said. "If she realizes her heart's desire and becomes one of Genji's wives, I won't complain. After all, the woman who was most significant to him has apparently died." The Kokiden Consort replied, "And what's wrong with her entering service in the Women's Quarters?" She seemed to have her heart firmly set on sending her younger sister to court to serve her son, Emperor Suzaku.

6. Poem from *The Man'yōshū*: "Now that we are betrothed, sharing a pillow of new grasses, how can I endure a single night apart from you?"

For his part, Genji did not consider Oborozukiyo just another woman, and he thought it a shame that she should be sent into service at the palace. At the present moment, however, he was not inclined to divide his attention among his women. He wanted to focus on Murasaki alone. *I'd better let it be,* he thought. *Murasaki is good enough. Life is brief, and so I should just settle down with her. I must never again stir resentment in a woman.*

This train of thought brought back the incident with the lady at Rokujō. He had learned a fearful lesson. He was sorry for her, but now he could never feel comfortable recognizing her formally as a wife. If she could be satisfied with continuing to meet as they had over the years, if she could go on being his companion, a woman who could talk with him on those occasions when it was natural and proper to do so, if they could just be a comfort to one another . . . as he mulled over their relationship he knew that no matter how difficult it was, she was a woman he could not easily abandon.

* * *

FROM **CHAPTER XII**

Suma

Exile to Suma

* * *

Oborozukiyo[7] returned to court service in the seventh month. Suzaku had a strong lingering affection for her, and so he kept her near him as he had always done, acting as though he knew nothing of the imprecations directed at her by certain courtiers. He would on occasion reproach her for one reason or another while also offering tender vows of love. In both looks and bearing Suzaku possessed a youthful grace and elegance, and Oborozukiyo was certainly grateful for, and embarrassed by, his show of noblesse oblige. Yet her heart had room only for her memories of Genji. On one occasion, during a musical performance, Suzaku remarked, "It's at times like this that I miss Genji the most. I venture to say that there are many here who miss him even more than I. It seems as if the light has gone out of everything." He then added, "I have acted contrary to my father's wishes. I shall come to regret my sin." Tears welled up in his eyes, and at that moment Oborozukiyo could no longer restrain her own. "I have learned from experience that the world is a tiresome place," he continued, "and no longer feel that I want to remain in it much longer. If I were no longer here, how would you feel about it? It makes me bitter to think that my death would not affect you nearly as much as the absence of one who still lives nearby. The poet who wrote the line 'while I am in this world'[8] did not express noble sentiments." His manner was so gentle, and his words suffused with such profound emotion, that tears began to stream down Oborozukiyo's cheeks. "For whom do you weep?" Suzaku asked. "It makes me sad that you have yet to give me a child . . . it's as if something were missing in my life. I have considered

7. Genji's affair with her, described in pages not included here, forced him to leave the capital and go into exile to rustic Suma [editors' note].
8. *Waka* poem by Ōtomo no Momoyo: "What

good would it do to die of longing? I want to be with my love for those days I am alive." The line *ikeru hi* ("those days I am alive") is misquoted in the text as *ikeru yo* (literally, "the world I live in").

adopting the Crown Prince as my father instructed me, but given the enmity between my mother and the Fujitsubo Consort it would cause too much trouble to do so." Certain people were conducting affairs of state in a manner contrary to his wishes, but he was too young and weak-willed to resist, even though he was disappointed and bothered by many things, including Genji's exile, that had been carried out in his name.

At Suma the winds of autumn, the "season of anxious grief,"[9] were intensifying; and though his villa was some distance from the shore, each night the waves, which Middle Counselor Yukihira observed were stirred by winds blowing through the barrier pass,[1] sounded as if they were breaking quite close. Genji had never experienced anything as affecting as the autumn in this place.

He had only a few attendants with him, and because they were all asleep he was lying awake by himself, his head propped up on his pillow, listening to the winds howling from every direction. Feeling as though the waves were crashing near his residence, tears welled up instinctively . . . so many that it seemed his pillow might float away. He tried playing his seven-string koto a little, but the music just made him feel even more frightened and alone, and so he abruptly stopped and murmured the following poem.

> Does the wind blow from where my loved ones mourn
> For I seem to hear in the sound of waves
> Voices crying in pain from loneliness

Hearing his poem, his attendants were startled awake. Seeing how splendid Genji looked, they were overcome by emotion, and as they arose unsteadily they were quietly wiping their noses to disguise their tears. Genji wondered, *How must my attendants feel? For my sake alone they have come wandering with me to this sorry existence, having left behind their comfortable, familiar homes and parted with parents and siblings from whom even the briefest absence would be hard to bear.* Such musings made him miserable, but then he realized that it must make his attendants feel forlorn to see him so downhearted like this. And so, during the days that followed, he diverted them with playful banter, and in moments of idle leisure he would make scrolls by gluing together pieces of paper of various hues and practice writing poems. He also drew remarkable-looking sketches and paintings on rare Chinese silk of patterned weave and used them to decorate the front panels of folding screens. Before he came to Suma he had heard about the views of the sea and mountains here, and he had imagined from afar what they looked like. Now that they were right before his own eyes, he depicted those rocky shores, whose incomparable beauty truly surpassed anything he had imagined, in charcoal sketches of unrivalled skill. A member of his escort remarked with impatient frustration, "If only we could summon the great masters Chieda and Tsunenori[2] and have them color in your sketches . . ." Genji's gentle, familiar behavior and splendid bearing helped his

---

9. Anonymous poem from *The Kokinshū*: "Looking upon the light of the moon filtering through the trees, I see that autumn, season of anxious grief, has arrived."

1. Poem from *The Kokinshū* by Ariwara no Yukihira: "How mournful, the winds that blow through the barrier pass onto the strands at Suma to chill a traveler's sleeves." The allusion here is not a perfect match, and Murasaki Shikibu may have cited the wrong poem.

2. Tsunenori flourished during the reign of Emperor Murakami (r. 946–67). Not much is known about Chieda.

attendants forget the cares of the world. Four or five were in constant attendance, and they were overjoyed to be able to serve him so intimately.

One pleasant evening, when the garden flowers near the veranda were a riot of colors, Genji stepped out into a passageway that framed a view of the sea. As he stood there motionless for a few moments, he didn't look like an earthly being, given the odd juxtaposition of his beauty and the setting, and so the divine splendor of his appearance was eerily unsettling. His loose purple trousers, cinched at the ankles, were lined with a pale green; his robe was a soft white silk twill. His dark blue cloak was loosely tied, giving him a casual air as he began reciting in hushed tones the opening lines of his ritual devotions: "I, a disciple of Shakyamuni Buddha . . ." He slowly chanted a sutra in a voice so sonorous that it too seemed like nothing of this world. From boats in the offing came voices of fishermen singing as they rowed over the waves. Viewed from a distance, the vague outlines of the boats resembled little birds floating on the sea, creating a lonesome effect. Just then a line of migrating geese flew overhead, their cries like the creaking of the oars, and Genji gazed out at the scene in rapt silence, his hands, white and lambent in contrast to the dark beads of his rosary, moving slightly to brush away the tears running down his cheeks. His magnificent appearance gave comfort to his retainers, all of whom were yearning for their loved ones back home. Genji composed a verse.

> Is it because these wild geese, the first of autumn
> Were with the loved ones I miss in the capital
> That their cries echo mournfully across the skies

Yoshikiyo responded.

> Though not companions of mine from the past
> These geese crying out still stir memories
> One after another of my old life

Koremitsu also responded.

> Am I to consider these geese as companions
> On my exile when they willfully chose to leave
> Familiar homes for distant realms beyond the clouds

The Lesser Captain of the Right Palace Guard—the young man whose loyalty cost him a promising career—composed yet another poem.

> Even wild geese who leave familiar homes
> To migrate through distant skies find comfort
> So long as they are with their companions

"What would become of me if I were to lose sight of my companions?" Although the Lesser Captain's father, who had once been Vice Governor of Iyo, had recently been appointed Vice Governor of Hitachi, the young man had decided not to accompany him, but went into exile with Genji instead. The choice must have caused him great distress, but he put on a brave front and pretended that nothing bothered him.

The full moon rose vivid and bright, bringing back memories to Genji. "That's right . . . tonight is the fifteenth." Staring up at the face of the moon, he lovingly imagined the music that would be playing on a night like this at the palace, with all the ladies gazing out at the night sky. When he murmured a line from Bai

Juyi—"Feelings for acquaintances of old, now two thousand leagues distant"[3]—
his attendants could not restrain their tears. With indescribable yearning he
recalled the poem Fujitsubo sent him complaining about how the "ninefold
mists" kept her from the palace. As memories of this and other moments came
to him, he wept aloud. He heard someone say "The hour is late." However, he
could not bring himself to retire.

> As I gaze at the moon I am at peace
> Even if only briefly, for it shines
> On the distant palace I long to see

He had warm recollections of a certain night when he had talked intimately
with Emperor Suzaku about times past. *How closely he resembles our late
father!* Genji whispered a line from a poem in Chinese by the exiled Sugawara
no Michizane: "The robe bestowed on me by the emperor is now with me
here."[4] Truly the robe never left his sight, but was always near him.

> My sleeves both right and left are wet with tears
> Tears of bitter resentment on the one
> Tears of longing for you on the other

* * *

As the days and months passed there were many occasions back in the capital when the courtiers, Emperor Suzaku first among them, experienced pangs
of wistful longing for Genji. The Crown Prince in particular constantly shed
tears whenever he thought of him, so that his nurses, especially Myōbu, looked
on with pity.

Fujitsubo, who had always been fearful about her son's position, was beside
herself with anxiety now that Genji was not there to look after his interests. At
the beginning of his exile the princes who were his half brothers and other high-
ranking noblemen who had been close to him would send sympathetic notes
inquiring how he was faring. Many at the court deemed these exchanges of
heartfelt correspondence, which included poetry in Chinese, extraordinarily
felicitous. When the Kokiden Consort learned about these letters, however, she
harshly disparaged them. "One might expect a man who has incurred official
censure to find it a daily struggle just to savor the taste of food as he would
like . . . but not Genji. He resides in an attractive villa, writing letters critical of
the court, and like that traitorous official in the Qin Dynasty, gets his syco-
phants to go along with everything he says. Why, they'd call a deer a horse if he
told them to!" When word spread of what she said and the asperity with which
she spoke, people at the court were afraid, and no one wrote to Genji anymore.

The passage of time brought no comfort to Murasaki. When the women
who had been serving Genji in the east hall moved to her quarters in the west
hall, they had been skeptical of her, wondering why their lord would have
brought such a young lady to his villa. But after they got to know her—her
charming, endearing looks, her steady, sincere personality, her kindness and

3. The poem by [Bo] Juyi from which this line
is taken was written on the moon festival in
autumn.
4. A line from a Chinese-style poem which
Sugawara no Michizane wrote in exile when

he looked at a robe he had received from the
emperor while still at court. The poetry of
famous Chinese and Japanese exiles, such as
[Bo] Juyi and Michizane, keeps Genji company
during his own time in exile [editors' note].

deep sensitivity—not one of them chose to leave. Those ladies-in-waiting of higher status and greater discernment were able once in a while to catch a glimpse of her behind her screens, and when they did they saw that their lord's preference for her over his other ladies was perfectly justified.

The longer Genji stayed at Suma, the more living apart from Murasaki became intolerable for him. Despite his torment, he rejected the idea of having her come to live with him in a place completely unsuitable for her. *How could I have her live in a place I myself consider retribution for past sins?* Everything in this province was so different from the capital. He had never before been exposed to the sight of lower class people, who had no inkling of who he was, and they were a shock to his sensibilities—naturally he found them uncouth and beneath him. From time to time smoke would rise quite near his villa, and at first he imagined it was from the fires the fishermen used to extract salt. Later he learned it was smoke from smoldering brush that had been cleared on the mountain behind the villa. It was all such a marvel to him that he composed a poem.

> Like brush burning at the huts of rustics
> My heart smolders with my constant yearnings
> For tidings from my loved one back at home

*   *   *

Just when life was feeling most tiresome, Tō no Chūjō suddenly paid a visit. He may have been the son of the Minister of the Left, but he was also the husband of the younger sister of the Kokiden Consort and so his career had not suffered. He was a man of sterling character and, having been promoted to Consultant at the third rank, he now possessed an impeccable reputation. Despite his good fortune, however, the palace was a dreary place for him with Genji gone, and at every event he found himself longing for his old friend. It finally reached the point where he no longer cared that he might become the subject of malicious gossip and censure, and he decided to venture to Suma. The moment he laid eyes on Genji he experienced a joy, mingled with a few tears, he had not savored in a long time.

In Tō no Chūjō's eyes the villa at Suma had a vaguely Chinese style about it. The setting was like something out of a painting, and the effect created by the fence of bamboo wattle, the stone steps, the pine pillars, all as rustic and simple as Bai Juyi's hut, was peculiarly charming.[5] Eschewing royal colors, Genji was dressed without ostentation, wearing dark bluish gray hunting cloak and trousers, cinched at the ankles, over a humble light red robe, creating the impression that he was a mountain peasant. Though Genji was intentionally dressed like a provincial, his looks were so dazzling that Tō no Chūjō couldn't help smiling. The personal effects he kept close at hand were simple and humble-looking, and his sitting room was completely exposed to view from the outside. The boards for Go and backgammon, the furnishings, and the pieces used for playing *tagi*[6] had all been fashioned intentionally to have an appropriately countrified look to them, while the implements used for the Buddhist

5. This resembles the description of the hut [Bo] Juyi gives in one of his poems.
6. A game that is similar to tiddlywinks, except that the object is to flip stones onto a board instead of into a cup.

rituals he practiced showed signs of his wholehearted devotion. Even the meal provided was prepared in an intriguing way in harmony with the setting.

Tō no Chūjō, spotting some fishermen carrying shellfish they had just harvested, summoned them over and asked them what it was like to live for so many years on these shores. They told him about the various hardships and worries they had experienced, and though their babbling speech was in a rough dialect he found hard to follow, he was nonetheless moved as he observed them, since they made him realize that all people, no matter what their status, experienced similar emotions and were not that different. As a reward for the shellfish, he adorned them with robes and other gifts, and the honor he bestowed on them made them think, if only for a moment, that the world was their oyster.

Genji's horses were stabled close by, and Tō no Chūjō watched in amazement as someone brought rice stalks from a strange-looking storehouse in the distance—apparently some kind of granary—to feed them. The scene reminded him of a line from the *saibara* "Asukai," and he sang the words "the grasses are inviting."[7] He then told Genji all that had happened during the months he had been away, alternately crying and laughing. "My father," he said, "is always fretting over your son, and it makes him feel sad that the little one should be so innocent about what is happening in the world." Genji could hardly bear to think about the boy. There is no way for me to record all that was said between them, and I can't even do justice to a small part of their conversation. They did not sleep that night, but passed the time composing Chinese poetry until dawn. Still, even Tō no Chūjō had to be mindful of the consequences of rumors at the court, and so he hurried back to the capital at daybreak. Such haste made his departure all the harder for Genji to take. They took up their cups of wine and toasted one another, reciting together a line of verse composed by Bai Juyi to bid farewell to his friend, Yuan Zhen, who had visited the poet in exile: "Into the wine cup in spring, Pour tears of drunken sorrow." All their companions wept with them, apparently in bitter regret that the two friends should have to part after so short a time together.

A formation of wild geese flew across the dimly lit sky. Genji composed the following.

> In what spring will I be allowed at last
> To go and view the capital again . . .
> How I envy these geese returning home

Tō no Chūjō could hardly bring himself to leave.

> Will not the wild geese that leave unsated
> From this enchanting abode lose their way
> On the road to the capital in bloom

The gifts from the capital were elegant and in good taste. In seeing off his guests, Genji showed his appreciation for them by making a present of a black horse. "You may think it inauspicious to receive a memento from someone in exile," he said, "but like me, this horse misses home, for he tends to neigh whenever he feels a breeze coming from the direction of the capital."[8] It was an exceptionally fine-looking steed.

---

7. "Let us tarry awhile at the well of Asuka, the shade is good, the waters cool, the grasses inviting . . ."

8. Allusion to a Chinese poem.

"Keep these in remembrance of us," Tō no Chūjō replied, presenting Genji with several items, including a remarkable flute that had a reputation at court for its fine tonal qualities. All the same, he was careful not to give presents that might invite censure. By now the sun was rising, and because it was already late to be starting off, he hurried away, flustered, glancing back over and over. How forlorn Genji looked as he saw the party off. "When will I see you again? Surely this exile won't last much longer."

Genji replied with a poem.

> Oh crane, you who can soar so near the clouds
> Above the palace . . . look on one whose life
> Is pure and spotless as a day in spring

"While I fully expect to return, it is difficult for people who suffer the misfortune of exile, even the wisest sages of the past, to mingle again successfully in court society, and so . . . well, I don't feel as though I want to see the capital again."

Tō no Chūjō answered with a verse of his own.

> Longing for the companion who flew beside him
> Wing-to-wing, the solitary crane, with no guide
> To help cries out among the clouds . . . and the palace

"Your absence is so painful, I now regret the good fortune of being your close friend." They had not had time to converse at their leisure, and his departure left such a void that Genji spent the rest of the day sunk in melancholy reverie.

On the Day of the Serpent, which fell during the first ten days of the third month, one of Genji's attendants, a person who took pride in his knowledge of such things, told him, "This is a day when a person who has the sort of cares that trouble you should perform rites of purification." And so Genji, who had wanted to go view the shore in any case, headed down to the sea. He had some simple soft blinds erected to create a temporary enclosure for himself, then summoned a diviner, a master of the way of yin-yang who traveled back and forth between the capital and this province. As part of the purification ritual, a large doll to which all defilements and malign spirits had been transferred was placed in a boat and set adrift on the waves. Watching it float away, Genji was reminded of his own fate.

> Like a ritual doll drifting out
> Into an unknown expanse of sea
> I am overwhelmed by my sorrow

Sitting in the midst of a bright, cheerful setting, he looked indescribably handsome. The surface of the sea was serenely calm and gave no sign which way the currents were flowing, but as he pondered the flow of his own life, his past and his future, he composed another poem.

> Surely the myriad deities
> Must take pity on me . . . after all
> Is what I have done truly a crime

The wind suddenly picked up and the skies darkened. People began bustling to get ready to leave, even though the purification ritual was not finished. Rain fell suddenly and violently, and his attendants were so flustered they were unable to raise the parasols as they made their way back to the residence. The party had not prepared for this kind of storm; the wind, unlike anything they had seen before, blew away everything around them, and the waves broke with terrifying power, forcing everyone to flee before their fury. With each flash of lightning and crash of thunder, the surface of the sea shimmered like a silk quilt spread out before them. While the party struggled, barely managing to make it back, they feared they might be struck by lightning at any moment.

"I've never gone through anything like this!" said one of the attendants.

"Usually you see some signs that the wind is going to pick up. This is a shockingly rare occurrence," replied another.

Even as they spoke, stunned and dismayed, the thunder continued unabated, and the torrential rain fell so hard it seemed as though it would pierce through whatever it struck. *Is the world coming to an end*, they all wondered, feeling forlorn and confounded. All the while Genji was calmly reciting a sutra. The thunder lessened somewhat when darkness fell, but the wind howled on throughout the night.

When it seemed that the storm was subsiding, one of the attendants remarked, "Surely this is a sign of the power of all the prayers I've been offering."

"If it had gone on much longer," his companion added, "we would have been swallowed up by the waves for sure."

"I've heard that a tsunami can kill a person in an instant," someone else chimed in, "but I never knew anything like this could happen."

When dawn approached everyone was finally able to fall asleep. Genji was also able to rest a little, but as he dozed off, someone—a person whose features he could not make out very clearly—approached him in a dream. "You have been summoned to the palace," the figure demanded, "so why have you not made an appearance?" The figure was walking about, apparently searching for him. Seeing this, Genji was startled awake. The Dragon King in the sea was known to be a connoisseur of genuine beauty, and so Genji realized he must have caught the deity's eye. The dream gave him such a horrifying, uncanny sensation that he could no longer stand residing in this abode by the sea.

FROM CHAPTER XIII

Akashi

The Lady at Akashi

Several days passed, but the rain and wind did not let up, and the thunder did not abate. These endless hardships made Genji increasingly lonely and miserable, and under such circumstances, facing a dark past and bleak future, he could no longer put on a brave front. *What should I do?* he asked himself as he pondered his situation. *If this storm drives me back to the capital before I receive a pardon, I'll be a laughingstock. Perhaps it would be best to leave here and seek out some abode deep in the mountains, leaving no trace of myself in the world.* But then he had second thoughts. *Even if I were to leave for the mountains, people would still gossip about me, saying that I retreated in a panic, driven off by the wind and waves. Later generations would consider me utterly contemptible.* These thoughts weren't the only thing troubling him. The dream he had a few nights earlier, during which he had seen that foreboding figure, kept recurring.

Day after day went by without a break in the clouds, and he grew increasingly anxious, fretting about what was happening in the capital and thinking abjectly that if things continued like this he would be cast utterly adrift. Yet because it was too stormy to even poke one's head outside, no one arrived from the capital to see him.

At last a messenger arrived from his Nijō villa. The man, who had rashly braved the weather, was soaked to the point of looking weird and unearthly. He was also of very humble station—had Genji passed such a person on the road at an earlier point in his life, he would not have recognized him as human, and would have had his servants brush him aside. The fact that Genji now felt a deep kinship with such a man brought home just how far he had come down in the world and how much his self-esteem had collapsed.

The man carried a letter from Murasaki: "This terrible, tedious storm goes on without end, making me feel as though the skies were closing me off from you even more than before, for now I cannot even gaze in your direction."

> How fiercely must the winds blow across those strands
> During this time when endless waves drench the sleeves
> Of one who is longing for you from afar

The account she gave of her anguish affected him greatly, and after opening her letter his mood turned to dark despair and he felt like the poet whose river of tears "overflowed its banks."[9]

"Even in the capital," the messenger informed him, "people are viewing this storm as an eerie omen, and I've heard they plan to hold a ritual congregation of the Sutra for Benevolent Rulers to protect against a disaster.[1] High-ranking officials who usually attend the palace to conduct affairs of state cannot do so because the roads are all blocked." The messenger's manner of talking was stiff and unclear, but because Genji was curious about court matters, he was eager to learn more. He summoned the man to appear before him and questioned him further.

"Day after day the rain falls with no let up and the winds continue to gust," the messenger said. "Everyone is alarmed and amazed by this extraordinary weather. Of course, we haven't seen anything like what you've had here at Suma, what with hail falling so hard it drills into the ground and with this constant rumbling of thunder." The expression on the man's face, which told of his surprise and fear of the terrible conditions at Suma, sharpened all the more the sense of isolation felt by Genji's attendants.

As the storm raged on and on, Genji began to wonder if this might not be the end of the world . . . but then, the following morning, the wind picked up with even greater intensity, the tide surged, and waves broke violently on the shore, looking as if they might sweep away even the rocky crags and hills. No words could describe the booming thunder or the flashing lightning, which seemed to be crashing down right on top of them. Everyone was frightened out of his wits.

---

9. Poem from Ki no Tsurayuki's *Tosa Diary*, included in this volume: "The river of tears has overflowed its banks and further dampens the sleeves of both the one who goes and the one who stays behind."

1. This congregation, called Ninnōe, was held in the palace in the fall and spring, or in times of emergency, to protect the realm.

"What misdeed did we commit," bemoaned one attendant, "that we should suffer this tragic destiny? Must we die without seeing our parents again, without looking on the beloved faces of our wives and children?"

Genji regained his composure, resolute in the conviction that having committed no great crime his life would not end on these shores. Still, his attendants were in such a state of panic that he had an offering of multicolored strips of cloth made to the gods of the sea. He also made numerous supplications. "Oh deity of Sumiyoshi,"[2] he intoned, "you who calm and protect these nearby shores, if truly you are the manifestation of the Buddha taken form as the guardian divinity of this region, then deliver us from harm!" His attendants were deeply distressed by the prospect that not only they themselves but their lord as well would be swept into the sea and perish in this unheard-of fashion. A few of them gathered their courage as best they could and, regaining a sense of propriety, joined their voices in praying to the Buddha and the gods, each offering his own life in exchange for the safety of their lord. Turning in the direction of the Sumiyoshi Shrine, they made their supplications.

"Our lord was reared in the bosom of the Emperor's palace, and had every sort of pleasure lavished upon him. Yet has not his profound compassion spread throughout this great realm of eight islands, lifting up and saving many who were mired in sin and impiety? What crime has he committed that he must now suffer retribution by drowning here amidst these foul, unjust waves and wind? You gods of heaven and of earth, show us clearly that you discern right from wrong! Though guiltless, he has been charged with crimes, stripped of office and rank, separated from home, driven into exile. Grieving anxiously morning and night, he has suffered this tragic fate . . . is he about to lose his life as well because of some sin in a former life, or some crime committed in this one? Gods and Buddha, if you are just, then put an end to our lordship's suffering!"

Genji once more offered prayers to the Dragon King and to the myriad gods of the sea, but the thunder only crashed all the more loudly, and lightning struck the gallery connecting Genji's quarters to the rest of the villa. Flames leapt up and the passageway caught on fire, throwing everyone into a state of panic. No one had enough wits about him to be able to deal with the situation, and so they had their lord move to the rear of the residence, to a room that, from the looks of it, must have been the kitchen. Everyone, irrespective of rank, crowded into the space, and the thunder could barely be heard above the tumultuous din of the crying and shouting there. As the day ended, the sky was black as an ink stone.

Finally the winds gradually subsided, the rain tapered off, and sparkling stars were visible. Genji's attendants felt embarrassed for their lord, thinking it was an affront to his dignity to remain in a place as strange and disreputable as this, and so they wanted to try to move him back to the main hall. They hesitated, however, discussing what they should do. One of them declared, "Even the quarters that escaped the fire have an ominous air about them. The people over there are in a state of shock, noisily stomping about, and the blinds have all been blown away." Another attendant replied, "In that case, let's wait until morning."

All the while Genji was meditating and softly invoking the name of the Buddha. Feeling unsettled and restless, he mulled over all that had happened.

2. A Shinto shrine near Osaka [editors' note].

After the moon rose he could make out clearly just how close to the villa the tide had surged. Pushing open a door of rough wattle and glancing outside, he gazed off toward the shore at the roiling surf left in the wake of the storm. No one in the immediate vicinity possessed the qualifications—sensitivity, proper judgment, ability to divine past and future—needed to make sense of all this and reliably sort things out. Instead, the only people to make their way to the villa were those strange, lowly fisher folk, who gathered at a residence where they had heard a nobleman resides, babbling away in an unfamiliar dialect; but even though Genji considered them exceedingly bizarre, he couldn't very well have them chased away. One of his attendants remarked, "If the wind hadn't subsided for a while, the high tide would have left nothing behind. The mercy of the gods is boundless!" Feeling forlorn, he composed a verse.

> Had the gods of the sea shown no mercy
> Then the tide surging from all directions
> Would surely have swept me into the deep

Genji had maintained his composure throughout the tumult of the storm, but it had been terribly nerve-wracking and exhausting and he began to doze off in spite of himself. The room he was using as a temporary shelter was so crude and rough that he could not lie down, so he slept while propping himself up against a pillar. As he did so, his late father came to him in a dream and stood before him, looking just as he did when he was alive. "Why do you remain in such a strange, unseemly place as this?" His father took his hand and, pulling Genji to his feet, exhorted him. "Hurry now! Board a boat and leave these shores, following wherever the deity of Sumiyoshi may lead you!"

Genji felt overjoyed. "From the moment I was separated from your august presence," he said, "I have been beset with all manner of sorrows, so that now I feel I ought to end my life on this shore."

"Such rash thoughts simply will not do! All these trials are a mere trifle . . . retribution for some minor misdeeds. Though I committed no serious breach of conduct during my reign, I was unknowingly guilty of some misdeeds and have spent all my time after death atoning for them[3] without once giving any thought to matters of this world. But then I saw how deeply mired you are in your troubles here, and I could not bear it. I entered the sea and rose up to these shores; and though I am now utterly exhausted, I must take this opportunity and hurry on to the capital, where I will speak to Suzaku on your behalf." With that he rose to leave.

Genji was upset his father was going away so soon, and because he wanted to accompany him, he began to weep. He looked up, but there was no one there—only the shining face of the moon. It had all felt so real, it hadn't felt like a dream at all. The lingering presence of his father remained, so palpable that Genji was profoundly moved by the sight of the wispy lines of clouds trailing across the night sky like traces of his father's ghostly presence. He had not seen his father's figure for many years, not even in his dreams; and now, even though he had glimpsed for only a few fleeting moments the face he had been longing so impatiently to see, the image continued to linger, hovering before

---

3. This statement by Genji's father is an apparent reference to a vision by the monk Nichizō, who saw the historical Emperor Daigo suffering the torments of hell.

his mind's eye. The poignant sense of gratitude he felt toward his father, who had flown to aid him when his life had reached its nadir and he was in despair and contemplating the end of his life, also made him look at the storm in a different, more positive light. The after-effect of his dream was a boundless sense of happiness and relief that someone was looking out for him. His heart was full of conflicting emotions, and even though he had seen his father only in a dream, the turmoil in his heart distracted him from the sorrows of the waking world. He wanted to go back to sleep in hopes of seeing his father again, but the irritation he felt at himself for not responding to his father in more detail kept him from being able to close his eyes, and he stayed awake until dawn.

A small boat approached the shore and several men came toward the exile's abode. When one of Genji's retainers asked them to identify themselves, they answered, "The former governor of Harima province, a novitiate who has recently taken his vows, had this boat readied and we journeyed here from the bay at Akashi. If Yoshikiyo, the Minamoto Lesser Counselor, is here, our lord would like to meet and discuss some matters at length."

Yoshikiyo was startled by their arrival and seemed not to know what to make of it. "I was familiar with the man before he was a novitiate and still governor of Harima, and had opportunities to converse with him over the course of several years. However, we had a mutual falling out over some trifling matter, so it has been a long time since we exchanged any correspondence of a particularly personal nature. What business would bring him here over such rough seas?"

Genji's dream, especially his father's exhortation, was still vivid in his mind, and he told Yoshikiyo to hurry up and meet with the novitiate. So Yoshikiyo went down to the boat, scarcely believing that it had set out during the storm amidst such violent waves and wind.

"Earlier this month," the novitiate explained, "a remarkable-looking figure came to me in a dream and told me something incredible. 'On the thirteenth of this month,' he announced, 'I will give you a clear sign, so have a boat prepared and no matter what happens, make for Suma when the wind and waves subside.' Because he had informed me in advance, I did as instructed and had a boat ready. Then I waited as long as I could, until the ferocity of the rain and wind and thunder alarmed me and made me worry for the safety of your lord. Then it hit me that there have been many examples, even in other lands, where a person who acted on his belief in a dream saved the state. Though your lord may have no use for my message, I could not let the appointed day spoken of in my dream pass without reporting these tidings to him. So I set out in the boat, and a miraculously favorable wind blew it along until we arrived at this strand. Truly this can only be a sign of divine favor. Is it possible that some sign was given to your lord here as well? If so, then please convey my words to him, ashamed though I am to beg your indulgence."

Yoshikiyo discreetly reported what he had heard. Genji mulled over the information, turning over in his mind all things past and future—disturbing things he had seen in both his dreams and his waking life—that might be taken as signs from the gods. *If I hesitate out of fear that gossips will ruin my reputation by criticizing me for following after some eccentric novitiate, I could end up rejecting what might be genuine divine assistance. If that happened, I'd be an even greater laughingstock. It is hard enough to turn away from the advice of men . . . how much harder, then, to defy the gods. It's proper that I should be deferential, even in minor matters, and yield to the views of those higher in rank who are older, respected and trustworthy. A sage of old once advised that 'One cannot be censured for following.' In truth, I failed to heed those words, and as a result I've had to undergo many bitter, unprecedented hardships, including this life-threatening storm. In the face of all that, salvaging my reputation for posterity no longer seems so important. What's more, my father did admonish me in my dream, so why should I have any doubts about the novitiate's story?*

After deliberating in this way, Genji sent his reply: "Though I have encountered unheard-of difficulties in this unfamiliar province, no one from the capital has inquired after me. I have gazed after the sun and moon coursing through the sky to who knows where, and thought of them as my only companions from home . . . but now to my great joy a fisherman's boat arrives.[4] Is there a retreat on the shores of Akashi, some place where I might withdraw in peace?" The novitiate's delight knew no bounds, and he expressed his deep gratitude. "This is all fine and well," said a member of Genji's escort, "but our lord should go aboard before dawn so that he will not be seen."

Genji boarded the boat accompanied by the usual retinue of four or five of his most trusted attendants. The miraculous breeze that had brought the boat here picked up again, and they arrived at Akashi so quickly it was as if they had flown there. The shores of Suma and Akashi were separated by only a few miles, and so the journey would have been short in any case. Even so, the willfulness of the breeze seemed uncanny all the same.

What Yoshikiyo had told him years earlier was true—the scenery on the shores of Akashi was truly spectacular. For Genji, who was hoping for a peaceful sanctuary, the only thing that detracted from the place was the large number of people bustling about. The novitiate's estate extended from the waterfront up into the recesses of the hills, and he had brought together on his land all sorts of attractive buildings constructed with an eye to how well they suited the seasons and the topography—a thatched-roof cottage near the shore that would intensify the pleasures of viewing the four seasons, a magnificent meditation hall standing beside a stream flowing down out of the hills on a site perfect for performing ritual devotions and focusing one's thoughts on the next world, a row of granaries, built to provide for the needs of this world and filled with the bountiful harvests of autumn in order to sustain the novitiate throughout his remaining years of life. Fearful of the recent tidal surges, the novitiate had moved his daughter and her entourage to a residence at the foot of the hills, allowing Genji to occupy comfortably the villa near the sea.

The sun was gradually rising just as Genji was moving from the boat to a carriage. As soon as the novitiate caught a glimpse of him in the dim early morning light, he immediately forgot about his own advancing years and felt as though his life had been extended. Beaming with a joyous smile, he at once offered a prayer to the deity of Sumiyoshi. It seemed to him that he had been allowed to grasp the light of the sun and the moon in his hands, and so it seemed perfectly natural that he should busy himself tending to Genji's needs.

To capture the scene in a painting—not just the beauty of the setting, which goes without saying, but also the elegance of the buildings, the indescribable

---

4. Poem by Ki no Tsurayuki: "To my great joy a fisherman's boat arrives, borne by a breeze that blows on one who has been soaked by waves."

appearance of the grove of trees surrounding them, the rocks and plants in the gardens, the waters of the inlet—seemed impossible for anyone but the most inspired of artists. The residence here was much brighter and more cheerful than the villa at Suma Genji had occupied these many months, and the utterly charming furnishings brought back fond memories. The novitiate's lifestyle was, as Yoshikiyo had reported, no different from that enjoyed at the most distinguished aristocratic houses in the capital; indeed, the blinding brilliance of his lifestyle appeared, if anything, to be superior.

* * *

It was now the fourth month, and with the change of the seasons Genji was provided with superb new robes and silk curtains to hang around the dais in his sleeping quarters. He found the tendency of his host, the novitiate, to obsess over every last detail when serving him somewhat pathetic and overdone, but at the same time he observed that the old man's proud dignity revealed a nobility of character, and so he allowed the novitiate to have his way in such matters.

Murasaki continued to send messages as frequently as ever. One quiet, calm moonlit evening, when a cloudless sky spread far into the distance over the sea, the scene brought to mind the water in the garden pond at his Nijō villa, and he was filled with an ineffable yearning—a yearning for what or for whom he could not articulate. Before his eyes, off in the distance, was the island of Awaji. "Ah, how far away it seemed . . ."[5] he murmured.

> This moon illuminates the poignant beauty
> Of Awaji island . . . ah, how far it seems
> Bringing painful longings for my distant home

He took his seven-string koto from its cover and plucked a few notes. He had not touched it for some time, and the sight of him aroused restless emotions in his attendants, who found their lord troublingly sad and beautiful.

Genji performed a tune titled "Kōryō,"[6] utilizing all his skills to produce an immaculate rendition. The music mingled with the rustling of the pines and the rippling sound of the waves and wafted toward the lady's residence at the foot of the hill, sending shivers of delight through the refined young ladies-in-waiting there. The rustic denizens of that shore, who certainly were unable to recognize the song, walked along the beach exhilarated, even though they ran the risk of catching cold in the sea breeze. Unable to restrain himself, the novitiate relaxed his devotions and hurried over to Genji's residence.

"It would seem I am still driven by memories to return to the world I supposedly left behind when I took my vows," he said, tears welling up. "The atmosphere conjured by your music, which draws me here this evening, is surely a harbinger of the Pure Land paradise I pray for in the coming life."

Memories came flooding back to Genji's heart as well—the musical entertainments to celebrate the various seasons at court, with this person on koto, that person on the flute, the sound of voices singing in chorus, the way people so often praised him lavishly for his skills, how it felt to be honored and

---

5. Poem by Ōshikōchi no Mitsune: "Ah, how far away it seemed . . . the moon I viewed at Awaji. Is it the special atmosphere of the setting here this evening that makes it look so near?"

6. A "secret" song composed by the legendary musician Linglin for the Yellow Emperor, China's fabled first emperor.

respected by everyone from the Emperor on down, not to mention the circumstances of those he loved and his own status back then. He felt like he was in a dream, and the overtones his koto produced as he played in that trancelike state conveyed an unearthly, frightening loneliness.

The novitiate could not help feeling maudlin, and he sent for a *biwa* lute[7] and a thirteen-string koto from the villa at the base of the hill. Playing the role of an itinerant priest performing on the lute, he played a couple of very charming, unusual tunes. He presented the thirteen-string koto to Genji, who played a little on the instrument. The novitiate marveled at how brilliantly talented he was in a variety of arts. Even an instrument that does not produce an especially distinct timbre may, depending on the occasion, sound quite superior. As the music drifted across the waters stretching interminably into the distance, the stirring cry of a water rail, so like the rapping of some paramour at the gate of his beloved, rang out amidst the shadows of trees in rampant foliage more vivid and fresh than even the blossoms of spring or the leaves of autumn at their peak.

Genji was impressed by the novitiate's koto, which produced such unique tones, and by his host's own sweetly charming skills. "The thirteen-string koto is most delightful when played in a relaxed, informal style by a woman who exudes a gentle and intimate grace." Genji was referring to women in general, but the old novitiate, misinterpreting his intent, smiled and replied, "I'm not sure that any woman, no matter how gentle or graceful, could play better than my lord. I myself learned to play under the tutelage of a disciple of the Engi-period emperor, Daigo,[8] but as you can see I'm not especially gifted, and so I've cast aside the things of this world. Still, whenever I was depressed I would play a little, and as a result there is someone here who learned the instrument by imitating me, and so her style naturally resembles Emperor Daigo's. Of course, I am just a humble mountain rustic, hard of hearing, and it may be that I am so used to the sound of the wind rustling in the pines that I can no longer tell the difference between it and the sound of the koto. Even so, would you permit me to arrange for you to hear her in private?" His voice was tremulous, and he seemed to be on the verge of breaking down in tears.

"I should have known that in a place such as this, where people are accustomed to the superior music of nature, my performance would not sound like a koto. All very regrettable . . ." Genji pushed the instrument away. "It's odd, really, but since ancient times the thirteen-string koto has been considered a woman's instrument. Emperor Saga[9] passed down the techniques, and it is said that his daughter, the fifth princess, was the most skillful virtuoso of her age, though no one remains in her lineage to pass along that style of performance. Nowadays, for the most part, those who have achieved a reputation as master of the koto choose to approach this instrument superficially, as a pleasant diversion and no more. Thus it is fascinating that an older style of performance should have survived, hidden away in a place like this. How will I manage to hear this person you spoke of?"

"There is nothing to prevent you from listening to her," the novitiate said. "You could even summon her. After all, if I may point to the story handed

7. A four-stringed pear-shaped Japanese lute [editors' note].

8. Daigo (885–930) ruled from 897 to 930 C.E.;

the Engi period was 901–23 [editors' note].

9. Ruled 809–23 C.E. [editors' note].

down by Bai Juyi, there was a woman, the wife of a merchant, who won praise for her talent with the lute . . . and what you said of the koto is true of the lute as well. In ancient times there were very few people who could calmly strum that instrument and reveal its true nature, but the lady I mentioned can play it exceptionally well, with a gentle charm and few hesitations. I'm not sure how she managed to learn the lute as well, but when I hear her music mingling with the sound of the waves it sometimes brings on feelings of melancholy, and other times provides a respite from my accumulating sorrows."

Delighted that the old man was a true connoisseur, Genji swapped instruments with him, exchanging the thirteen-string koto for the lute. As expected, the novitiate's skill on the koto was well above average. He played tunes in a style no longer heard in the modern world. His spectacular fingering showed a touch of continental flair, and the vibrato he produced with his left hand was deep and clear. Though they were not at Ise, Genji had one of his men, who had a fine voice, sing the line "Shall we pick up shells along the pristine shore?" from the *saibara* "The Sea at Ise," while he himself kept rhythm by using flat wooden clappers. From time to time he joined in the singing, and the novitiate would often pause to praise him. As the night wore on the old man had unusual delicacies brought out and pressed wine upon everyone so that they would naturally forget the cares of the world.

The late night breeze off the shore was chilly and the light of the setting moon seemed intensely clear. As the world grew quiet the novitiate opened up to Genji, telling him, through one small anecdote after another, all that had happened in his life—the burdens he had when he first moved to Akashi, and how he had devoted himself single-mindedly to his religious practice with the next life in mind. He even brought up, without prompting, his daughter's situation. Genji was amused by this show of paternal devotion, but at the same time he was also touched by the young lady's predicament.

"I hesitate to mention it," the old man continued, "but I wonder if your move to a strange province such as this, temporary though it may be, isn't the work of the gods and the Buddha who, by troubling your heart for a brief period, are showing kindness and pity toward an old priest like me who has prayed to them for so long. I say this because it has been eighteen years since I first placed my faith in the deity of Sumiyoshi. From the time my daughter was a little girl I had ambitions for her, and so each spring and autumn, without fail, I go to pray at the Sumiyoshi Shrine. I practice my devotions day and night at each of the six prescribed times, but rather than concentrating my prayers on the wish to be reborn on a lotus in the Pure Land, I ask that my ambitions for my daughter be fulfilled and that she be granted a noble position at court. Regrettably, sins from a previous life have brought me misfortune in this one, and I have become the miserable mountain peasant you see before you. My father was able to rise in status as a minister of state, but I have ended up a rustic provincial. It grieves me to imagine what might become of my descendants, how low they might sink should my family's decline continue; and that is why from the moment my daughter was born, I have invested all my hopes and expectations in her. As a consequence of my deep resolve to present her by any means possible to a high-ranking nobleman in the capital, I have rejected many suitors who wished to take her as a wife. Some of those suitors were men whose status was higher than mine, and I have suffered harsh treatment on account of their resentment of me. However, I don't consider that a hardship, and I admonish my daughter by reminding her that as long as I'm alive I'll look after her, even though, as you can see from the narrow cut of my sleeves, I don't have much wealth to give her. And I've told her that if I die while she is still young and unmarried, she should throw herself into the sea." He broke down sobbing. He said so many other things besides, it is impossible to relate them all here. Genji was listening to all this during a period in his own life when he had been beset constantly with various problems, and so the old man's story invited tears of sympathy.

"Accused without basis and cast adrift in an unfamiliar land," Genji responded, "I have wracked my brain trying vainly to identify the misdeed I supposedly committed. But now, on hearing your tale this evening and reconsidering the matter, I am deeply moved by the realization that we truly share a bond from a previous life that is anything but shallow. Why did you not tell me earlier that you knew all this? Once I had departed the capital I lost my attachments and came to find the fickleness of the world insipid and tiresome; and while passing the days and months pursuing only religious austerities, I grew disconsolate and melancholy. I heard faint reports about your daughter, but because it seemed likely that you would reject as inauspicious the suit of an exile without status, I had no confidence to even try. Now it appears that you are beckoning me to her quarters. To have her share my lonely bed would be a comfort."

The young lady's father was thrilled beyond measure at these words.

> Do you know as well what it means to sleep alone . . .
> Then perhaps you understand the boredom she feels
> Waiting for the dawn on Akashi's lonely strand

"You may well appreciate," he added, "how much greater my own sense of melancholy has been, wearied as I am from years of concern over her." Now that he had finally spoken of his daughter, his body was trembling in agitation—though he did not lose his air of refinement and dignity.

"That may be," Genji replied, "but those who are accustomed to living on this bay may not appreciate how lonely it is for someone like me . . ."

> In lonely travel robes, on a pillow of grass
> I wait in sleepless grief for dawn at Akashi
> Unable to weave a dream and join my lover[1]

Genji was in dishabille, and there is simply no way to describe how charming he looked at that moment.

The novitiate talked on and on at length about all sorts of things, but it would be annoying to record them all here. However, because I have not written down

---

1. This poem, like the one it answers, plays primarily on the word *akashi*—referring to the place-name and to dawn breaking. Lovers would share robes as part of their bedding, and it was believed this act ensured that they would meet in their dreams. Travel robes convey an image of sleeping alone, thus making it impossible to meet one's lover in a dream and intensifying the sense of loneliness.

everything exactly as it happened or was spoken, I may have accentuated some of the man's more eccentric and stubborn characteristics.

With things going more or less as he had hoped, the novitiate felt as though a burden had been lifted from him. At around noon the following day Genji sent a letter to the lady's residence at the base of the hill. He had given careful attention to the letter, thinking that the lady seemed on the one hand like someone of dauntingly superior talent who would be hard to approach, and, on the other, like an unexpected find hidden away in this obscure location. He prepared the letter with exquisite care, writing on light brown Korean paper.

> Gazing sadly at the sky, is it near or far . . .
> How I want to pay a visit to those treetops
> At the abode obscured by mist and faint rumor

"My longing for you has overwhelmed my secret love."[2] Was that the full extent of his letter?

The novitiate had already arrived at his daughter's residence and was waiting with secret anticipation. Things were working out as expected, and by the time the letter arrived he had already arranged for refreshments for the messenger, plying him with wine until the man was embarrassingly drunk.

The lady took a long time to compose her reply. Her father entered her quarters and pressed her to answer, but she refused to listen to him. Intimidated by the brilliant wit of Genji's letter, she felt inadequate and ashamed to set her own hand to paper, which would expose the truth about her. Comparing his status to hers, it was obvious that the gulf separating them was enormous. She withdrew to lie down, telling her father that she wasn't feeling well. Unable to persuade his daughter, and his patience now exhausted, the novitiate wrote the reply for her: "For a woman whose sleeves have about them the rustic air of the provinces, your graciousness brings a surfeit of happiness that is too much for her to bear. She is too overwhelmed even to read your letter, but observing her . . ."

> Lost in lonely thoughts, gazing sadly
> At the same sky you are viewing now
> Are not her feelings the same as yours

"Is my view of her perhaps too romantic?" The note was written on Michinokuni paper, which lent it an old-fashioned aura, but Genji was a little surprised, shocked even, at the seductive allure of the calligraphy, which was embellished with refined flourishes. The novitiate had presented Genji's messenger with, among other things, an exceptionally fine set of women's robes.

The following day Genji sent another note: "I've never seen a letter by proxy before."[3]

> How wretched my uncertain heart
> Knowing there is no one who asks
> "Do tell me, how are things with you"

---

2. Anonymous poem from *The Kokinshū*: "Though I never wanted to let the colors of my love show, my longing for you has overwhelmed my secret."

3. The word Genji uses, *senjigaki*, refers to a letter dictated by the emperor or by an aristocrat.

"The difficulty of speaking of my feelings to one I have not yet seen . . ." This time he used an extremely soft, thin paper, and his calligraphy was exquisite. Only a young lady who was excessively shy and introverted would have failed to appreciate it, and indeed when the Akashi lady saw it she was amazed. Still, she remained convinced that the immeasurable difference in status between them made any relationship hopelessly unsustainable, and it made her cry to know he was courting her even though she was of such inferior rank. She remained outwardly impassive, but this time she did as she was told and replied to him. Writing on heavily perfumed paper of light purple hue, her brush-strokes were thick and bold in some places, thin and wispy in others—a technique she employed to disguise any flaws in her hand.

> How could you ever declare such feelings
> To me, a person you have never met . . .
> Can rumors really trouble you so much

Her calligraphy and phrasing had an aristocratic flair not at all inferior to those of the most distinguished ladies.

Remembering all the exchanges he had engaged in with women back in the capital, Genji regarded the lady's letter with delight. Of course, he was mindful of prying eyes and of the censure he would surely suffer if he wrote too often, so he would let two or three days lapse between letters, and even then he corresponded only when he guessed that she might be experiencing emotions similar to his own—on an early evening passed in the quiet diversion of solitary idleness, for example, or a dawn that provided a scene of poignant beauty. Her replies on these occasions were always appropriate, and after thinking about her responses he concluded that she was a lady of discretion and noble character, and thus someone he very much wanted to meet. He asked Yoshikiyo to describe her and reacted with some distaste at the look on the young man's face as he did so—a look that seemed to say *she belongs to me*—and he felt a twinge of pity that his retainer's aspirations to win the lady for himself, which he had harbored for many years, would be thwarted right before his eyes. Genji believed, however, that he could justify his actions so long as the lady encouraged him to pursue a relationship. The problem was that she was proving even more aloof and proud than most highborn women. Genji found this kind of behavior damnably irritating, and so as time passed they began to engage in a contest of wills.

After crossing the barrier pass at Suma his anxiety about Murasaki back in the capital only grew worse, and many times his resolve weakened as he wondered what to do—after all, being apart made it difficult to "bear this foolish game."[4] Should he have her come in secret to Akashi? Each time he asked himself this question, he ended up thinking better of it. No matter what happened, he believed that he would not spend many more years like this in exile, and so if he brought her here now, he would be criticized.

That same year the court witnessed many uncanny omens and disturbing incidents. On the evening of the thirteenth day of the third month—that is, the very day of the storm at Suma—thunder and lightning crashed and wind and

---

4. Anonymous poem from *The Kokinshū*: "When I try to stay away and not meet you, just to see what will happen, my yearning is so great I can no longer bear this foolish game."

rain raged at the palace as well. During the night Emperor Suzaku dreamed that his father, the late Emperor, appeared below the steps leading out to the garden on the east side of the imperial quarters in the Seiryōden. His father was glaring at him, obviously in a foul mood, and so Suzaku sat up in a formal posture to show his respect. His father told him many things, and so must have said something about Genji. Suzaku was extremely frightened, but he was also moved to pity at the realization that his father's spirit had not yet been reborn in the Pure Land. Later, when he discussed his dream with his mother, the Kokiden Consort, she told him, "On nights when it rains and storms it's natural for you to dream of things that preoccupy your mind. A sovereign mustn't allow such trivial matters to upset him."

For some reason—perhaps because he had looked directly into his father's furious gaze—Suzaku began to have trouble with his eyes. His suffering was beyond endurance, and purification rites and exorcisms were performed constantly at both the palace and the residence of the Kokiden Consort.

Other incidents also brought grief to the palace. Suzaku's grandfather, the Minister of the Right who served as his Chancellor, suddenly died. Being advanced in years, his death was not unexpected or strange, but it was still a shock all the same, coming as it did after everything else that had happened. Then, on top of all this, the Kokiden Consort began to suffer from an unknown malady, and she grew weaker over time.

Occasionally Suzaku would give voice to his concerns, telling his mother, "If Genji has been exiled without just cause, then there is no escaping the conclusion that all these problems are the result of karmic retribution. I think the time has come to restore him to his former rank."

The Kokiden Consort brushed aside his concerns and strongly admonished her son. "If you do that you'll be criticized for lacking substance and lose respect. If you permit a man who has been expelled from the capital to return after less than three years, what will people say?" Her words made Suzaku waver, but as the days and months continued to go by, the afflictions he and his mother suffered grew ever more severe.

With the coming of autumn to Akashi the sea breezes began to blow, stirring melancholy thoughts that were especially poignant. Genji was still sleeping in his solitary bed, but his loneliness was unbearable. He often spoke to the novitiate, telling the old man, "One way or another you will have to devise some pretext to have your daughter come here." Genji was convinced that it would be improper for him to go to her, and in any case the lady had shown no indication that she was inclined to meet him. *Only a provincial woman whose circumstances were utterly wretched,* she thought, *would frivolously exchange vows as my father has encouraged me to do on the basis of some flimsy, seductive flattery from a man of the capital who has come here for a brief stay. He would never respect me or consider me one of his wives, and if I were to yield to him it would only add to my misery and woe, would it not? During this period of my life, while I remain a young, unmarried woman, my parents, who harbor these unattainable ambitions for me, seem to have placed their extravagant expectations for the future on very uncertain supports. And even if he did take me as a wife, wouldn't that merely add to their worries? So long as Genji remains at Akashi the happiness I feel just exchanging letters with him is fortune enough for me. For many years I heard reports about him, and now I'm able to catch brief, indirect signs of his presence at a place where I never imagined I might meet such a man. I was told that his skill on the koto was peerless, and when I hear the notes from his instrument wafting to me on the breeze, I can guess what he is doing during the day. Now he has gone so far as to recognize my existence by courting me like this, and that is too great an honor, much more than someone like me, someone whose circumstances have been reduced to the status of the fisher folk here, could ever deserve.* As these thoughts raced through her mind, she felt more and more ashamed, and could not bring herself to even contemplate the possibility that she might have an intimate relationship with Genji.

Although the lady's parents were confident that the prayers they had offered over so many years would surely be answered, they also began to have ominous misgivings as they imagined how much sorrow they would experience if, having thoughtlessly rushed to give their daughter to Genji, there came a time when he no longer cared for her or counted her among his wives. They had heard how great and magnanimous he was, and yet how bitter would be their misery were he to abandon her! Relying upon the unseen Buddha and gods with no sign or proof of their blessing, knowing nothing of Genji's intentions or of their own daughter's karmic destiny, they tortured themselves with their obsessive worrying.

Genji was constantly pressing the novitiate. "If only I could hear the sound of her koto mingling with the sound of the autumn waves . . . what a waste, not to be able to listen to her play in this perfect season."

The novitiate ignored his wife's concerns and, without a word to his servants, secretly chose a propitious day to arrange a tryst. He went about busily sprucing up his daughter's quarters so that her rooms looked resplendent, and then, on the thirteenth day of the eighth month, with a nearly full moon shining gloriously, he sent a message to Genji that consisted of nothing more than a single line of verse: "On an evening too precious to waste."[5] Though Genji considered the wily old man a rather elegant pander, that didn't stop him from donning an informal cloak and setting out very late that night. A stylish carriage had been provided for him, but he thought it was too ostentatious for an occasion such as this and set out on horseback instead. His escort, which included only Koremitsu and a few attendants, was modest. He realized for the first time that the villa at the foot of the hill was farther away than he thought. From the road he could see all around the shore, and the moonlight reflecting off the inlets brought to mind an old verse describing such a scene as one to be viewed with "dear companions."[6] The words "dear companions" at once brought his beloved Murasaki to mind, and he immediately felt the urge to ride on past the villa and continue on to the capital. Instinctively, he muttered a poem to himself.

> Take flight, my stallion, with autumn moon reflecting
> Off your lustrous coat . . . carry me through cloudy skies
> So I may meet my love, if but for a moment

The villa of the Akashi lady, a stylish structure with many admirable touches, was set deep in a grove of trees. Whereas the residence near the shore that

5. Poem by Minamoto no Saneakira: "On an evening too precious to waste, if only I could show the moon and the blossoms to one who understands, as I do, true beauty."

6. The source is not clear. An early commentary cites the following poem: "Shall we go to view it, dear companions, the moon's visage in the depths of the inlets at Tamatsushima?"

Genji was using was grand and attractive, the villa here was the kind of place where a person would lead a forlorn, solitary existence. Genji experienced a sweet, sublime sorrow at the thought that living here would allow him to contemplate to the full the sadness of life. The novitiate's handbell sounded a note of profound melancholy as it reverberated faintly from the meditation hall nearby and mingled with the soughing of the pines. The roots of the pine trees growing on the craggy rocks created a tasteful backdrop, and the chirruping of insects filled the garden. Genji glanced about, surveying the scene. The lady's quarters had been burnished with special care, and the door, made of exceptional wood, had been left open a crack so that the moonlight could stream in.

Genji stood uncertainly, hesitating before finally saying a few words of courtship. The lady, however, had been determined not to allow her relationship with him to become as intimate as this, and so she grew sullen and depressed, displaying a cold disposition that signaled she would not permit him to have his way.

She's getting above herself with these superior airs. Genji was irritated and resentful. *When a courtship has gone as far as ours, it is customary for the woman, even one whose high status makes her difficult to approach, to set aside her stubborn willfulness and yield. Could it be that she is belittling me for my loss of status? It would hardly be appropriate under the circumstances to force myself on her, but to lose a battle of wills with her would make me look pathetic.* If only his handsome figure, confused and resentful, could have been displayed to a woman who was truly sensitive to beauty!

A curtain close by rustled and one of the silk streamers decorating it brushed lightly across the strings of a koto. The faint notes conjured in Genji's mind a pleasant image of the lady plucking the instrument, looking relaxed and unguarded. "Is this the koto I've heard so much about?" He asked her this and many other things besides, all trying to persuade her to play.

> If there were someone I could talk to
> Intimately, would I awaken
> From the dream that is this world of woe

She replied.

> Wandering just as I am, lost in the darkness
> Of a night without end, how could I speak to you
> Not knowing what is dream, what is reality

The dignified bearing of her figure, which he could barely make out in the dim light, put him very much in mind of the lady at Rokujō, who was now in Ise with her daughter.

Apparently the Akashi lady had not been prepared for his visit and, unaware of her father's machinations, had been caught off guard. It had never occurred to her that he might make such outrageous advances like this, and so she was quite flustered and upset. Moving into a room just off her private chambers, she somehow managed to securely latch the sliding door from the inside. Genji had no intention, it seemed, of trying to force the door open, but then again, how could he simply leave things as they were? The lady was aristocratic and tall, and her sense of propriety and dignity made Genji feel embarrassed and uncertain. Thinking about how their relationship had been destined by these strange circumstances, he was moved by the depth of the bond ordained by their karma. Surely his love for her would grow stronger the more intimate they became with one another.

He had come to loathe the long nights of autumn, which dragged on tediously for him in his solitary bed; but this night seemed to be rushing toward dawn, and so, mindful as ever that prying eyes might catch sight of his visit, he hurriedly left her, murmuring sweetly gentle words to her.

He very discreetly dispatched the customary morning-after letter. His secrecy makes one wonder, was he bothered by a guilty conscience? The Akashi lady, worried about gossip, was equally careful to keep their affair secret, even from the others at her villa at the foot of the hill, and so she did not show the messenger bearing Genji's letter any special treatment or give him any lavish gifts. Her father deplored her aloof behavior.

Following this initial tryst, Genji would from time to time call on the lady in strictest secrecy. Their residences were separated by some distance, and there were nights when he was reluctant to venture out, concerned that he might encounter some of the local fishermen, who were by nature loquacious and prone to gossip. On those nights when he did not visit, the lady would be upset, taking his absence as proof that just as she had imagined all along his feelings for her were not sincere. Her father, seeing his daughter suffer and knowing she had good reason for feeling the way she did, worried about how it would all turn out. He forgot about his devotions and his prayers for rebirth in paradise, unable to focus on anything besides waiting and listening for indications that Genji was calling on his daughter. It was truly pathetic that the heart of a man who had ostensibly taken vows could be so troubled by worldly affairs.

* * *

FROM CHAPTER XXV

Hotaru

Fireflies

* * *

The rainy season continued for longer than usual this year, and the women at Rokujō were bored and had no way to brighten either the skies or their mood. So they passed the days and nights amusing themselves with illustrated tales. The Akashi lady prepared some stylish and interesting works of that type and sent them over to the quarters of her daughter, the Akashi Princess.

Meanwhile, the lady in the west hall, Tamakazura, was more intrigued than the others by these stories, which she found fascinating and strange, perhaps because she had come from the provinces. Whatever the reason, she was utterly absorbed in reading them day and night. Quite a few of the young women who had been assigned to her quarters were proficient at reading and copying, and so she was able to collect quite a few texts, many of which described the personal circumstances of a variety of remarkable characters. She couldn't tell if those stories were true or mere fiction, and, moreover, she couldn't find a single character whose circumstances were similar to her own. It appeared as though the heroine princess in *The Tale of Sumiyoshi*[7] experienced many remarkable incidents considered unusual not only in her own day,

---

7. A well-known tale in the author's time [editors' note].

but also in the present generation; and she compared the heroine's narrow escape from a forced marriage to the Chief Auditor to her own experience with the loathsome Taifu no Gen.

Genji couldn't avoid seeing these illustrated tales, which were left scattered all around Tamakazura's quarters. "Ahh . . . how tedious," he chided. "Women are by nature blithely content to allow others to deceive them. You know full well these tales have only the slightest connection to reality, yet you let your heart be moved by trivial words and get so caught up in the plots that you copy them out without giving a thought to the tangled mess your hair has become in this humid weather."

Genji smiled. "Of course, if we didn't have these old tales to read," he continued, "we'd have nothing to divert us in our idle hours. What's more, we can find even among this mass of falsehoods some stories that are properly written and exhibit enough sensitivity that we are moved to imagine that perhaps the events they relate really took place. On the one hand, we may know that it's all silly, but we're still fascinated and affected by the fiction. When we read about some lovely princess lost in troubled thoughts, we are drawn to her story . . . or when we encounter a tale that makes us wonder uncertainly if what it describes is really plausible or proper, we are nonetheless surprised and amazed that it can be told with such marvelous exaggeration. Of course later on, when we come back to the same tale again in a calmer state of mind, we might dislike it or think it inappropriate . . . yet even then there may be aspects of the story that seem as charming to us as when we first read it. Recently, whenever I overhear one of the ladies-in-waiting reading to my little daughter,[8] I have been struck by the realization that there are without doubt skilled storytellers in this world . . . that such tales must come from the mouths of people accustomed to spinning lies . . . but perhaps that is not the case?"

As soon as he spoke those words, Tamakazura shot back, "There is certainly no doubt that someone practiced at lying would be inclined to draw such a conclusion . . . for all sorts of reasons. I remain convinced, however, that these stories are quite truthful." She pushed her inkstone away, and when she did Genji responded, "Have I been speaking rudely of your stories? Tales have provided a record of events in the world since the age of the gods, but histories of Japan like the *Nihongi*[9] give only partial accounts of the facts. The type of tales you are reading provides detailed descriptions that make more sense and follow the way of history."

Genji smiled again before continuing. "A story may not relate things exactly as they happened out of consideration for the circumstances of its characters. Yet at those moments when one wants to pass on to later generations the appearance and condition of people living in the present . . . both the good and the bad, which are the things you never tire of reading about no matter how many times you've heard them . . . it is difficult to keep them shut away in your heart. And so you begin to tell stories about them. If you want to be upright and proper, then you will select only the good details to relate. Or if you want to play to people's baser interests, then you will compile the strange and won-

8. His daughter by the Akashi lady; she is being raised by Tamakazura [editors' note].
9. *Chronicles of Japan*. One of the two 8th-century chronicles of Japan, written in Sino-

Japanese and modeled on the Chinese official histories, that told the history of the Japanese islands from the Age of the Gods to recent times [editors' note].

drous details of bad behavior. But in either case you will always be speaking about things of this world. Styles of storytelling may differ in other lands, and even in Japan tales from the past certainly differ from those of the present . . . and of course there are distinctions between deep and shallow topics and themes. For that reason the narrow-minded conclusion that all tales are false-hoods misses the heart of the matter. Even the Dharma, which was explicated for us through Sakyamuni's[1] splendidly pure heart, contains *hōben*, those par-ables he told to illustrate the truth of the Law. There are many contradictory parts in the sutras that raise doubts in the mind of an unenlightened person. However, if you carefully consider the matter, you realize that all the sutras have a single aim. The distinction between enlightenment and suffering is really no different from the distinction between the good and the bad in tales such as these. In the end the correct view of the matter is that nothing is worthless." Genji was now claiming that tales were beneficial.

"So tell me," he concluded, "have you found any stories of piously foolish men like me among all your old scrolls? There couldn't possibly be any fictional prin-cesses in this world who are as extremely aloof and coldly heartless as you . . . who pretend not to notice anything. So how about it . . . shall we make a story unlike any other that has ever been told and pass it on to later generations?"

Genji sidled over next to her. Tamakazura turned away from him, hiding her face in her collar, and said "Even if we don't make a story together, the rela-tionship we do have is so bizarre and unbelievable it will likely never become the subject of court gossip."

"You think it's bizarre? Truly there has never been a daughter as cruel as you." He had moved close to her and was being much too forward.

> Having a surfeit of cares and longings
> I seek answers for them in tales of old
> But find there no child as unfilial

"Even the teachings of Buddha admonish unfilial children," he added. When she refused to show her face, he began stroking her hair. As he did so, her resentment led her to reply.

> Though I have searched through all these ancient tales
> Truly I find no models in this world
> For parental feelings resembling yours[2]

He felt ashamed when he heard her poem, and so went no farther than strok-ing her hair. Given her situation, whatever would become of her?

Murasaki was also reading illustrated tales, under the pretext that the Akashi Princess had requested them, and was finding it hard to put them down. Look-ing at an illustration from *Tales of Kumano*,[3] she remarked, "This is quite skill-fully rendered." She gazed at the little girl, who was innocently taking a nap, and remembered when she was that age.

Genji studied the illustration. "How precocious children were back then. I was quite reserved by comparison when I was their age . . . a model of behavior,

---

1. The Buddha (lit., "Sage of the Sakyas") [edi-tors' note].
2. Genji has taken Tamakazura in as his daughter, but is also attracted to her. His ear-lier advances have been a constant source of pain and consternation for Tamakazura [edi-tors' note].
3. This tale has been lost.

really." In truth, he was fond of being the model for all sorts of unheard-of behavior.

"You shouldn't be reading love stories in front of her," he continued. "She may not be all that intrigued by some young girl holding a secret love in her heart, but she is destined to be empress, and it would be most unfortunate if she grew to accept the idea that it was normal for such affairs to actually take place." Had Tamakazura heard what he just said, she certainly would have taken umbrage at the difference in the way he treated his daughter and the way he treated her.

"People with shallow minds may imitate the behavior they read about in these stories, but they look rather pathetic when they do," Murasaki replied. "In the *Tale of the Hollow Tree* the young Fujiwara princess, Atemiya, is a dignified woman of probity, and she never goes astray, but because her manner is so stiff and unyielding she lacks feminine grace, and her story ends up being just as bad an influence."

"People in real life seem to be the same," Genji said. "Everyone has their own way of doing things, but it is hard to strike a proper balance. A woman who has been brought up with the greatest care by parents who are not without breeding may grow up to be innocent and childlike, but the fact that she may also have many flaws will, sad to say, lead people to wonder what her parents were up to and how they went about raising their daughter. On the other hand, when you see a young woman who in appearance and behavior is exactly what she should be for someone of her status, clearly her parents' efforts have paid off and she brings honor to their house. If a young lady's nurses or attendants praise her to an absurd degree, then when her actions or words don't match her puffed-up reputation she will not seem as attractive. Parents should never let people who lack taste and judgment go about praising their daughters." He was determined to do everything in his power to ensure his own daughter would avoid criticism.

Many of the tales depicted mean, vindictive stepmothers. He worried that the Akashi Princess might get the idea that all stepmothers were like those she read about, so he took extra precaution in the selection of stories, and had clean copies and illustrations made for her.

* * *

FROM CHAPTER XL

Minori

The Rites

* * *

The following day Murasaki was in pain and unable to get up, perhaps because she had overexerted herself by staying up throughout the dedication ceremony. At every event like this she had ever attended over the years, she would always wonder if *this day* would be the last time she would see the faces and figures of those who had gathered, the last time she would see them display their various talents or hear them play the koto or the flute. On such occasions she would be moved even by the sight of faces normally beneath her notice. Her feelings were of course even stronger whenever she observed the other ladies at

Rokujō—women with whom she naturally shared a gentle rivalry, especially when they appeared together at some concert or diversion held in the summer or winter, and a mutual affection. Although no one can expect to remain for very long in this world, the thought that she would soon leave the other ladies behind, going forth all alone to an unknown destination, brought home to Murasaki the poignant sorrow of the evanescence of life.

When the dedication ceremony ended and each of the guests had begun to make his or her way home, she felt a twinge of regret that this would likely be the last time she saw any of them. She sent a poem to Hanachirusato.[4]

> While my life, like these rites, must soon come to an end
> We may rely on the truth of the sacred law
> That karma will bind us through all the worlds to come[5]

Hanachirusato replied.

> Even had these rites not been this magnificent,
> They would still have forged a lasting bond between us . . .
> Undeserving though I am, with little time left

Immediately after the dedication ceremony, other solemn rites such as the continuous reading of the Lotus Sutra and the ritual of confession and penance were attentively performed. Because the esoteric healing rites that had been carried out every day over a long period showed no signs of helping Murasaki recover, Genji commissioned additional services at various holy sites and temples known for the efficaciousness of their prayers.

When summer arrived, Murasaki's fainting spells increased even though the weather was no hotter than usual. There were no alarming symptoms that one could point to as the source of her malaise. She was simply growing weaker, without ever suffering the sort of pain that caused others distress. Worried about what was to become of their mistress if she continued to weaken, her attendants observed her condition with regret and sorrow, and fell into dark despair.

Because Murasaki's health was slowly failing, the Akashi Empress[6] withdrew from the palace and went to the Nijō villa. She was to take up residence in the east hall, and so Murasaki waited there to receive her. The ceremony greeting Her Majesty's arrival was nothing out of the ordinary, but Murasaki found everything about it moving, since she knew she would never witness it again. She listened attentively as the name of each nobleman who had escorted the Akashi Empress—a very large group of senior officials indeed—was read out.

Since the two women had not seen each other for a long time, they seized this moment as a rare opportunity to speak intimately and at length. Genji arrived. "I feel like a bird evicted from its own nest. It's obvious that I'm of absolutely no use this evening, so I'll take my leave and retire for the night." He

4. One of Genji's ladies, also living in his Rokujō mansion [editors' note].
5. This poetic exchange gives the chapter its title. The word *minori*, which clearly means "rites" here, also refers to the Law (the Dharma), that is, the Buddha's teachings.

6. Genji's daughter, the Akashi Princess who becomes the Kiritsubo Consort, has been elevated to the title of empress. From this point on I will identify Genji's daughter as the Akashi Empress.

went back to his quarters feeling quite happy to see Murasaki up and about—it was, however, only a brief moment of comfort for him.

"Since we will be staying in separate quarters," Murasaki said, "I would be deeply honored to have Your Majesty come to see me in the west hall. I know it is presumptuous of me to make such a request, but it is a considerable strain on me to leave my residence to visit you here." Murasaki said. She stayed a while longer, and when the Akashi lady joined them they continued their quiet, heartfelt conversation.

Murasaki had many things on her mind, but wisely she did not broach the subject of what would happen after her death. She calmly made a few passing references to the ephemeral nature of life, but the serious manner in which she talked made it clearer than any words she might have spoken just how sad and forlorn she felt. When she saw all the children of the Akashi Empress, tears welled up[7] and her face blushed with a most lovely glow. "I had so wanted to see each of them grow up . . . it would seem my heart regrets having so little time left."

Her Majesty wept as well and wondered why Murasaki had to be so fixated on death? The subject of their conversation shifted, providing Murasaki the chance to speak about the ladies-in-waiting who had served her closely over the years. She did her best to avoid saying anything inauspicious, as if she were making last requests, but she felt sorry for her attendants, who would have nowhere else to turn once she was gone. "When I am no longer around," she remarked, "please remember to look after them." Because a sutra reading[8] was about to begin, Murasaki retired to her own quarters in the west hall.

Niou, the Third Prince, had the most charming appearance of all Her Majesty's many children as he walked around the villa. During those intervals when Murasaki was feeling a little better, she would have him sit next to her and, when no one was around, ask him, "Would you remember me if I were not here?"

"I would miss you very much, Grandmama. You are much more important to me than father or mother! If you weren't here, I'd feel awful!" The way he rubbed his eyes to hide his tears was so adorable she had to smile despite her sadness.

"When you are all grown up, you are to live here, and when the red plum and the cherry tree that grow in front of the west hall are in bloom in their respective seasons you must not forget to view and enjoy them. And at the appropriate times you must make offerings of their branches to the Buddha in my memory."

The little boy nodded solemnly, then stared into Murasaki's face. Just as he was about to cry, he stood up and scampered off. She had raised him and the Third Princess with special consideration, and it filled her with pity and regret to know she would not be able to help raise them to adulthood.

The heat of summer was so oppressive she couldn't wait for autumn to arrive; and when it did, and the weather turned cooler, her spirits revived a

7. Because Murasaki had raised the Akashi Empress, she has a close connection to these children [editors' note].
8. This reading may be the *Sutra of Great Wisdom* (Daihannyakyō), which an empress would normally have performed during the second and eighth months (though the reading could be held on special occasions as well). However, the timing does not seem right here, and it is likely that the sutra reading is part of the healing rites for Murasaki.

little. Still, this was but a temporary respite, for even though the chill autumn winds were not yet blowing—winds that cut through one, bringing only sorrows[9]—she was already spending her days in dewy tears.

The Akashi Empress was preparing to return to the palace. Murasaki wanted to ask her to stay on a little longer, even though such a request would overstep the bounds of propriety. It would also have been awkward, since His Majesty was now sending one messenger after another urging her to return. In the end she didn't ask, and because she was so weak, she was unable to go to the east hall to see Her Majesty off. That was when the Empress took the extraordinary step of calling on her in the west hall. Murasaki was humbled and shamed that the Empress would deign to visit her, but she thought it would have been truly senseless not to meet, and so she had special seating and furnishings prepared to receive her exalted guest.

Despite the fact that she was terribly emaciated, Murasaki still looked remarkable; the loss of weight had, if anything, distilled her beauty, which now possessed a boundless nobility and grace. Once, in the glorious flowering of her prime, her looks exuded to an almost excessive degree a lambent glow like the bright fragrance of blossoms. Now her infinitely cherished appearance, which brought to mind the transient nature of the mortal world, possessed a deeper loveliness, one that evoked incomparable feelings of compassion and sweet sorrow.

At dusk, as a terrible, chilling wind began to blow, she propped herself up on an armrest thinking she would gaze out at her garden when she saw Genji arrive.

"How good that you're able to get up today! Her Majesty's visit has apparently cheered you, has it not?"

She felt bad for him—he looked so happy whenever she was briefly feeling better that it moved her to imagine how devastated he would be when the end came.

> How brief the moment when you see me sitting up . . .
> As brief as the time that dew clings to bush clover
> Before being blown off and scattered by the wind[1]

It was an apt comparison, for the dew clung precariously to the stems of bush clover in her garden that bent and sprang back with each gust of wind. Genji gazed out at the scene, and the feelings of melancholy desolation that accompanied this season were unbearable.

> Our lives are like fragile dewdrops vying
> To disappear . . . would that no time elapse
> Between the first one to go and the last

He could not brush all the tears from his eyes.

The Akashi Empress replied.

> Who can look at this world, so like the dewdrops
> That cannot resist the blasts of autumn winds
> And think only the drops on the top leaves fade

9. Poem by Izumi Shikibu: "What sort of wind is it, this wind that blows in autumn . . . how it cuts through one, bringing only sorrow."

1. Murasaki's poem plays on two senses of the word *oku*—"to be up/sit up" and "to settle."

As they exchanged poems, Genji treasured the sight of these two women, ideal beauties both; and though he wished he could go on gazing at them like this for a thousand years, he knew that such a dream could never be fulfilled, and his heart ached, for he had no way to keep his beloved from dying.

"You should leave now. I'm feeling very ill," Murasaki said. "It's terribly rude of me to say I'm too ill to do anything for you." She pulled a standing curtain over and lay down so that they would not have to see her suffering. This time it did not appear she would recover.

"What's wrong?" The Akashi Empress took Murasaki's hand and watched her tearfully. She really did look every bit like a dewdrop fading away, and so they hurriedly sent off countless messengers to commission more sutra readings. There had been episodes like this in the past, and she had always recovered, but Genji suspected that the malignant spirit of the Rokujō lady might still be at work, and so he did everything he could to protect Murasaki, ordering prayers and services to be held throughout the night. His efforts were in vain, however, for just as dawn approached, she passed away.

The Akashi Empress thought it a sign of the boundless karmic bond she shared with her surrogate mother that she had not returned to the palace and was with Murasaki until the very end. Neither she nor Genji could accept that her death was part of the natural order of things, that such partings were common to all. To them her death was singular and overwhelming, and so of course they felt as if they were wandering lost in the sort of dream one has in that twilight time between night and the dawn. No one there could make a rational judgment about anything. The attendants and other servants were completely stunned.

Genji suffered the most, and because he was upset and not thinking clearly, he summoned his son,[2] who was in attendance nearby, and had him move over in front of Murasaki's curtain. "It appears this is the end," he said. "It would be a great shame to go against her wishes at this point and not carry out what she had desired for so many years. The holy men who performed the healing rites and the priests reading scripture have all gone silent and have probably left, but some of them may still be here, so tell one of them to cut her hair like a nun's. It won't do any good for her in this life, but if she shows a mark of her devotion to the Buddha, then at least she may rely on his mercy to comfort her on the dark path she is to follow. Is there some priest suitable for the task?" From the expression he wore as he spoke, it seemed that Genji was trying to be strong, but the color had drained from his face and, unable to bear his loss, he could not stop his tears. His son looked on in sympathy, thinking his father's grief was perfectly understandable.

"Sometimes a malignant spirit will do this kind of thing just to torment the bereaved ones . . . what I mean is, the spirit may be making it appear that she is not breathing . . . that may be what's happening here. If that's the case," Genji's son offered, "then it would be best to do what she wanted in any case, since according to the Contemplation Sutra,[3] making vows to uphold the pre-

---

2. Genji's oldest child from his first marriage. Long ago this son once caught an enthralling glimpse of his stepmother Murasaki, but has had no chance since to satisfy his yearning to see her again [editors' note].

3. One of the three major scriptures of Pure Land Buddhism along with the *Sutra of Infinite Life*, which is also known as the *Larger Pure Land Sutra*, and the *Amida Sutra*.

cepts for even one day and night will lead to rebirth in Amida's Pure Land. Of course, if she *is* dead, simply cutting her hair at this point would have little benefit . . . it won't provide a light to guide her in the next world, and would make the grief of those who look at her even worse. So I wonder if it's for the best?" He wanted to do all he could to make arrangements for the funeral and period of confinement, and so he summoned several priests from among those who had not yet withdrawn and were willing to serve during the weeks ahead. He also saw to all other necessary preparations.

Although he had longed for Murasaki for years after catching a glimpse of her on the morning after the autumn tempest, Genji's son had never harbored any improper or presumptuous fantasies about her. *In what world to come will I ever see her again as I did on that morning long ago? I never did hear her speak . . . not even a faint whisper.* Not a day had gone by since when she hadn't been on his mind. *As it turns out, I will never hear her voice . . . and if I'm ever to satisfy my hope of seeing her again, the only time to do so is right now, even if it means gazing at her lifeless form.* He had been trying to control himself, since it would look odd if he exhibited excessive grief, but these thoughts brought him to tears. The attendants were loudly weeping and wailing, and Genji's son, in an effort to control his own emotions, scolded them. "Really now, be still for a while!" As he spoke, he lifted one of the panels of Murasaki's standing curtain and peered inside. Because it was still difficult to make things out in the dim light of early dawn, Genji had placed a lamp near Murasaki's bed and was gazing at her. He so regretted that such a lovely face would soon be no more—a face infinitely dear to him, one possessing such noble grace—it seemed he no longer had the will to even try to hide his beloved from the gaze of his son, who was peeking in on this scene.

"Here she is, her face looking the same as ever . . . and yet it's clear she's no longer with us." Genji covered his face with his sleeves. His son, blinded by tears, could not see very well. To clear his vision he closed his eyes tight and then opened them so he could look at her, and when he did he was overcome by a feeling of sadness unlike anything he had ever known. He feared he would lose his composure completely. Her hair was stretched out beside her, left just as it was when she died, incomparably lustrous and beautiful with not one strand of those thick, cascading tresses out of place. In the bright glare of the lamplight her complexion had an alabaster glow, and as she lay there passively, no longer concerned that she was exposed to his gaze, her face, needless to say, looked more pure and spotless than when she was alive, since she had always avoided being seen and concealed her real appearance under makeup. Gazing on her unique, extraordinary beauty, he wished her soul, which had already departed, would soon return to her body—though he knew such a wish was unreasonable.

The women who had been her closest attendants were too overcome by grief to be able to think clearly, and so Genji forced himself to calm down, regain his composure, and set about making arrangements for the funeral. Although he had witnessed many sorrowful events in the past, he had no experience handling such matters directly himself. Undertaking this sad responsibility was like nothing else he had ever done in the past or would do in the future.

* * *

ZEAMI MOTOKIYO

ca. 1363–1443

Imagine a theater without sets and with virtually no props, with no interest in depicting character development or dramatic conflict, a music-drama at the hypnotic pace of solemn ritual. This is Noh, the oldest dramatic form of Japan and one of the world's oldest living professional theater traditions.

Zeami Motokiyo, arguably Noh's foremost practitioner and theorist, did as much as anyone to establish the traditions and aesthetics of this sophisticated art form, which has fascinated modern dramatists in the West and which is practiced to this day.

THE BASICS OF NOH

The word *noh* may be translated as "talent," "skill," or "accomplishment." Like many traditional Japanese arts, Noh is hereditary: actors and musicians learn from their parents or masters and undergo strenuous training from early childhood on. True mastery is said to come only with advanced age.

Noh is the most stylized of Japan's dramatic genres; it also includes *kyōgen* ("wild words"), comical intermissions performed between Noh acts. Although Noh emerged in the fourteenth century, its basic elements of dance, music and recitation have older roots. It adapted elements from Buddhist chanting, from the music and dances of the Japanese imperial court (which were imported from China and Korea and are still practiced today) and from "monkey/comic music" (*sarugaku* or *sangaku*), variety entertainment that included acrobatics and mime. Out of these and other performance traditions Noh emerged, and the playwrights Kan'ami (1333–1384) and

his son Zeami gave the genre its defining shape.

Noh plays contain a limited number of actors: the "leading actor" and the opposite, though not antagonistic "supporting actor," with their companions. There is also a chorus, stage attendants, and occasional child actors. Although women played an important role in the development of Japanese dramatic arts, professional actors are traditionally all male. The current repertoire of some 240 plays is divided into five groups depending on their central protagonist: plays about gods, warriors, women, and demons, and miscellaneous plays. Most plays extract particular moments from famous literary works. They explore strong, obsessive emotions—grief, despair, anguish, love, devotion. Although today some plays are written on contemporary themes—a Noh play on heart transplants premiered in 1991—traditionally Noh plays are based on old stories and are studded with famous phrases from classical literature.

Noh is performed on an austere, undecorated stage of polished cypress wood, and consists of a main stage and a bridgeway, on which the actors enter the stage. Except for child actors and actors playing living adult characters, actors impersonating ghosts, gods, or demons wear masks. Because most masks have enigmatic expressions they are open to various interpretations. The actors mostly move at an extremely slow pace, and their performance is accompanied by a flutist and three drummers playing a hip, shoulder, and stick drum. The musicians sit along the back of the stage under the lone pine tree painted on the wall, the single and unvarying decoration for all Noh plays.

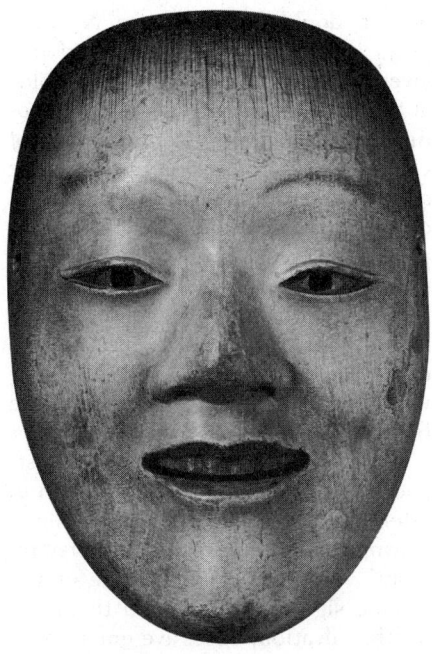

sometimes function as character, opponent, and narrator at the same time, as in a famous scene from Zeami's play *Tadanori*, where the protagonist at the crucial final moment plays both Tadanori and the warrior who kills him. The disjunction among actor, character, and voice gives the text an enthralling autonomy from the action on stage.

NOH PATRONAGE

Zeami was born to a father who was a gifted playwright and headed a *sarugaku* troupe. He attracted the attention of Ashikaga Yoshimitsu (1358–1408), the third shogun of the Muromachi military regime (1338–1573), when performing in his father's troupe as a beautiful boy actor. Although a later shogun shifted his patronage away from Zeami and even exiled him in 1435, Zeami's earlier favor with the shoguns gave a decisive turn to the fate of Noh: it was to become a sophisticated art sponsored by the military rulers for their domain lords and retainers to enjoy. In 1868, when Emperor Meiji abolished the shogunate, Noh lost its greatest patron. That Noh survived this watershed moment was partly thanks to the symbolic power of foreign relations. Mindful of Western opera which was presented to Japanese diplomats during their visits to the West, the Japanese government entertained the American president Ulysses Grant with a Noh performance when he visited Japan in 1879. From an obsolete tradition it became a national art: nowadays the Japanese government sponsors Noh and grants exquisite actors stipends and the honorary title of "Living National Treasures."

Stylization is central to Noh. Noh is like a slowly moving tapestry of emotions framed into fixed performance patterns, and every move on stage is precisely choreographed. For example, the act of weeping is suggested by the actor's slow raising of his hand to eye height, followed by an equally poised lowering. It is the vocabulary and grammar of these stylized moves that Noh actors need to master through tireless training not unlike a Western musician practicing typical cadences or trill patterns. The fixity of form and gesture in Noh is enhanced by the fluidity of space, time, and narration: the absence of a set leaves spatial boundaries and distances unclear; the key events belong to the murky realm of memories and dreams, where the boundaries between past and present merge; and narration is fluid because characters do not necessarily speak their own lines and thoughts. For example the chorus does not comment on the action as in Greek plays, but can take the place of a narrator or recite the words or thoughts of a character. In turn, actors can

THE WARRIOR PLAY *ATSUMORI*

Atsumori is an example of how Zeami gave the grisly subject matter of battle action and tormented warrior ghosts a new, cultivated form that appealed to the increasingly sophisticated warrior elite. It focuses on the death of the young Heike warrior Atsumori, a famous episode from *Tales of the Heike*. During the battle at Ichi-no-tani, a decisive moment in the civil wars between the Genji and Heike clans in the 1180s that resulted in the defeat of the Heike, the Genji supporter Naozane catches sight of a Heike warrior alone on the seashore. When Naozane realizes that the soldier, Atsumori, is only a boy the age of his own son, he takes pity, but is in the end forced to kill the boy when fellow Genji warriors suddenly approach the scene. The flute that Naozane finds under the dead boy's armor testifies to his courtly elegance. Plagued by remorse, Naozane soon becomes a monk to pray for Atsumori's salvation.

The Noh play revisits the final encounter between Atsumori, now a ghost, and Naozane, now a monk named Renshō. In the first act, Renshō meets Atsumori's ghost, who is disguised as a reaper. In the second act, the ghost appears in its true form and remembers the pleasures of a banquet held the night before his death. The play ends with a double salvation, as Naozane prays for Atsumori and Atsumori forgives him. Because the episode unfolds at Suma Bay, where Genji, the protagonist of the eleventh-century *Tale of Genji*, was exiled, *Atsumori* frequently alludes to Murasaki Shikibu's tale and draws an analogy between its central protagonist Genji and the young Atsumori. (Allusions in Noh plays could be powerful enough to bend history: a later puppet-play version of *Atsumori* claimed that the historical Atsumori was the son of an emperor, just like the fictional Genji.)

In an age of action movies and fast-paced entertainment, what has Noh to offer? Can we appreciate its ceremonial slowness and minimalist understatement? Measured on the scale of the cosmic significance of Noh themes— death, salvation, obsessive emotions— Noh performances have an eerie power to transform our perception of time, space, and significance. Although the artistry of Noh is fully realized only on stage, reading the rich and allusive text does give an indication of its graceful power.

Atsumori[1]

Persons in order of appearance

> The monk RENSHŌ, *formerly the Minamoto warrior Kumagai*
> A YOUTH (*no mask*)
> Two or three COMPANIONS *to the* YOUTH
> A VILLAGER
> The phantom of the Taira warrior ATSUMORI
> (Atsumori *or* Jūroku *mask*)

ACT I

Enter RENSHŌ, *carrying a rosary. He stands in base square,[2] facing rear of stage.*

RENSHŌ   The world is all a dream, and he who wakes
the world is all a dream, and he who wakes,
casting it from him, may yet know the real.
He turns to the audience.

---

1. Translated by Royall Tyler.   2. Back left corner of the stage.

You have before you one who in his time was Kumagai no Jirō Naozane, a warrior from Musashi province. Now I have renounced the world, and Renshō is my name. It was I, you understand, who struck Atsumori down; and the great sorrow of this deed moved me to become the monk you see. Now I am setting out for Ichi-no-tani, to comfort Atsumori and guide his spirit towards enlightenment.

> The wandering moon,
> issuing from among the Ninefold Clouds[3]
> issuing from among the Ninefold Clouds,
> swings southward by Yodo and Yamazaki,
> past Koya Pond and the Ikuta River,   *Mimes walking.*
> and Suma shore, loud with pounding waves,
> to Ichi-no-tani, where I have arrived
> to Ichi-no-tani, where I have arrived.

Having come so swiftly, I have reached Ichi-no-tani in the province of Tsu. Ah, the past returns to mind as though it were before me now. But what is this? I hear a flute from that upper field. I will wait for the player to come by and question him about what happened here.

Enter the YOUTH *and* COMPANIONS. *Each carries a split bamboo pole with a bunch of mowed grass secured in the cleft. They face each other at front.*

YOUTH *and* COMPANIONS

> The sweet music of the mower's flute
> the sweet music of the mower's flute
> floats, windborne, far across the fields.

YOUTH

> Those who gather grass on yonder hill
> now start for home, for twilight is at hand.

YOUTH *and* COMPANIONS

> They too head back to Suma, by the sea,
> and their way, like mine, is hardly long.
> Back and forth I ply, from hill to shore,
> heart heavy with the cares of thankless toil.
> Yes, should one perchance ask after me,
> my reply would speak of lonely grief.[4]
> On Suma shore
> the salty drops fall fast, though were I known
> the salty drops fall fast, though were I known,
> I myself might hope to have a friend.
> Yet, having sunk so low, I am forlorn,
> and those whom I once loved are strangers now.

While singing, YOUTH *goes to stand in base square,* COMPANIONS *before Chorus.*

> But I resign myself to what life brings,
> and accept what griefs are mine to bear   RENSHŌ *rises.*
> and accept what griefs are mine to bear.

RENSHŌ   Excuse me, mowers, but I have a question for you.

---

3. Reference to the capital. The moon suggests Renshō himself, wandering from Kyoto to the Suma shore, the site of the battle of Ichi-no-tani, where Atsumori was killed.

4. These and the following three lines allude to a poem by Ariwara no Yukihira (818–893 C.E.), who was also exiled to Suma.

YOUTH   For us, reverend sir? What is it, then?

RENSHŌ   Was it one of you I just heard playing the flute?

YOUTH   Yes, it was one of us.

RENSHŌ   How touching! For people such as you, that is a remarkably elegant thing to do![5] Oh yes, it is very touching.

YOUTH   It is a remarkably elegant thing, you say, for people like us to do? The proverb puts the matter well: 'Envy none above you, despise none below.' Besides,

> the woodman's songs and the mower's flute

YOUTH *and* COMPANIONS

> are called 'sylvan lays' and 'pastoral airs':[6]
> they nourish, too, many a poet's work,
> and ring out very bravely through the world.
> You need not wonder, then, to hear me play.

RENSHŌ

> I do not doubt that what you say is right.
> Then, 'sylvan lays' or 'pastoral airs'

YOUTH   mean the mower's flute,

RENSHŌ   the woodman's songs:

YOUTH   music to ease all the sad trials of life,

RENSHŌ   singing,

YOUTH   dancing,

RENSHŌ   fluting—

YOUTH   all these pleasures

Below, YOUTH *begins to move and gesture in consonance with the text.*

CHORUS

> are pastimes not unworthy of those
> who care to seek out beauty: for bamboo,
> who care to seek out beauty: for bamboo,
> washed up by the sea, yields Little Branch,
> Cicada Wing, and other famous flutes;
> while this one, that the mower blows,
> could be Greenleaf, as you will agree.
> Perhaps upon the beach at Sumiyoshi,
> one might expect instead a Koma flute;[7]
> but this is Suma. Imagine, if you will,
> a flute of wood left from saltmakers' fires
> a flute of wood left from saltmakers' fires.

Exeunt COMPANIONS. YOUTH, *in base square, turns to* RENSHŌ.

RENSHŌ   How strange! While the other mowers have gone home, you have stayed on, alone. Why is this?

YOUTH   You ask why have I stayed behind? A voice called me here, chanting the Name.[8] O be kind and grant me the Ten Invocations![9]

RENSHŌ   Very gladly. I will give you the Ten Invocations, as you ask. But then tell me who you are.

---

5. Flute playing is associated with the aristocracy.

6. Atsumori and his companions refer here to an elegant line from a Heian poetry collection.

7. Presumably bamboo washed up by the sea yielded particularly fine flutes. "Greenleaf": a legendary flute. "Little Branch": Atsumori's own flute, mentioned in this list of famous flutes. "Sumiyoshi": where ships from Koma (Korea) once used to put in, thus "Koma flute."

8. That of Amida, the "Buddha of Infinite Light." Invoking his name (*Namu Amida Bu*) saved the believer and was a typical practice of the Pure Land school of Buddhism.

9. Ten callings of the Name for the benefit of another were often requested of holy persons.

YOUTH   In truth, I am someone with a tie to Atsumori.

RENSHŌ   One with a tie to Atsumori?
Ah, the name recalls such memories!
Presses his palms together in prayer over his rosary.
'Namu Amida Bu,' I chant in prayer:
YOUTH *goes down on one knee and presses his palms together.*

YOUTH *and* RENSHŌ   'If I at last become a Buddha,
then all sentient beings who call my Name
in all the worlds, in the ten directions,
will find welcome in Me, for I abandon none.'[1]

CHORUS   Then, O monk, do not abandon me!
One calling of the Name should be enough,
but you have comforted me by night and day—
a most precious gift! As to my name,
no silence I might keep could quite conceal
the one you pray for always, dawn and dusk: YOUTH *rises.*
that name is my own. And, having spoken,
he fades away and is lost to view
he fades away and is lost to view.   *Exit* YOUTH.

INTERLUDE

VILLAGER *entered discreetly and sat at villager position.*
He now comes forward to base square.

VILLAGER   You see before you one who lives here at Suma, on the shore.
Today I will go down to the beach and pass the time watching the ships
sail by. [*Sees* RENSHŌ.] Well! There's a monk I've not seen before. May I ask
you, reverend sir, where you are from?

RENSHŌ   I came from Miyako. Do you live nearby?

VILLAGER   Yes, I do.

RENSHŌ   Then would you please come nearer? I have something to ask of you.

VILLAGER   Very well, reverend sir. [*Sits at centre, facing* RENSHŌ.] Now, what
is it?

RENSHŌ   Something rather unexpected, perhaps. I hear this is where the
Minamoto and the Taira fought, and where the young Taira noble,
Atsumori, died. Would you tell me all you know of the way he met his
end?

VILLAGER   That certainly is an unexpected request, reverend sir. I do live
here, it is true, but I really know very little about such things. Still, it
would be too bad of me, the very first time we meet, to claim I know
nothing at all. So I will tell you the story as I myself have heard it told.

RENSHŌ   That is very kind of you.

VILLAGER   [*Turns to audience.*] It came to pass that in the autumn of the
second year of Juei, Minamoto no Yoshinaka drove the Taira clan out of
Miyako.[2] This is where they came. Then the Minamoto, bent on destroying
the Taira for ever, split their army—sixty thousand and more mounted
warriors — into two wings and attacked without mercy. The Taira fled.

1. The canonical vow made by Amida, before
he became a Buddha, to save all beings by his
grace.
2. Yoshinaka, a Genji warrior who was later

killed by his own clan because of his ambitions
for power, conquered Kyoto, the "Miyako," in
1183 during the Genpei Wars (1180–85)
recounted in the *Tales of the Heike.*

Now one among them, a young gentleman of the fifth rank named Atsumori, was the son of Tsunemori, the Director of Palace Repairs. Atsumori was on his way down to the sea, meaning to board the imperial barge,[3] when he realized that back in the camp he had forgotten his flute, Little Branch. He prized this flute very highly and hated to leave it behind for the enemy's taking. So he turned back, fetched the flute, and again went down to the beach. But by this time, the imperial barge and the rest of the fleet had sailed. Just as he was riding into the sea, hoping to swim his horse out to the ships, Kumagai no Jirō Naozane, a warrior from Musashi province, spread his war fan and challenged him to fight.

Atsumori wheeled his horse and closed fiercely with Kumagai. The two crashed to the ground between their mounts. But Kumagai was a very powerful man. He instantly got Atsumori under him and ripped off his helmet, meaning to take his head. He saw a youth of fifteen or sixteen, with powdered face and blackened teeth—a young man of high rank, there was no doubt about that.[4] Kumagai wanted to spare him. Then he glanced behind him and saw Doi and Kajiwara riding up.[5] A good seven or eight other warriors were with them. 'I do not wish to kill you,' said Kumagai, 'but as you can see, there are many men from my own side behind me. I will take your head myself, then, and afterwards pray with all my heart for the peace of your spirit.' So he cut off Atsumori's head. On examining the body, he found a flute in a brocade bag attached to the waist. When he showed the flute to his commander, all present wet the sleeves of their armour with tears. To think that he had been carrying a flute at a time like that! Even among all those gentlemen from the court, he must have been an especially gentle youth! Eventually, Kumagai found out that his victim had been Atsumori.

I wonder whether it's true, as they say, that Kumagai made himself into a monk to pray for Atsumori. If he was that sort of man, though, he wouldn't have killed Atsumori in the first place. But he did kill him, so the story must be wrong. I'd like to see that Kumagai here now! I'd kill him myself, just to make Atsumori feel better.

Well, that is the way I have heard it told. But why did you ask? I am a bit puzzled.

RENSHŌ Thank you very much for your kind account. Perhaps there is no harm in my telling you who I am. In my time I was Kumagai no Jirō Naozane, but now I am a monk and my name is Renshō. I came here, you see, to give Atsumori's spirit comfort and guidance.

VILLAGER *You* are Kumagai, who fought in the battle here? Why, I had no idea! Please excuse all the silly things I said. They say the man mighty in good is mighty, too, in evil. I'm sure it's just as true the other way round. Anyway, do go on comforting Atsumori's spirit.

RENSHŌ I assure you, I am not in the least offended. Since I came here to comfort Atsumori, I will stay on a while and continue chanting the precious Sutra[6] for him.

3. The Taira (or Heike) fled Kyoto with the child emperor Antoku, whose mother belonged to the Taira.
4. Courtiers of both sexes wore white powder and blackened their teeth. Teeth in their natural state (certainly Kumagai's) were considered unsightly by the aristocracy.
5. Warriors, like Renshō, on the Genji side.
6. The Lotus Sutra, a central text in certain schools of Buddhism.

VILLAGER   If that is your intention, then please accept lodging at my house.
RENSHŌ   I will do so gratefully.
VILLAGER   Very well.

[*Exit.*]

ACT 2

RENSHŌ   Then it is well: to guide and comfort him
           then it is well: to guide and comfort him,
           I shall do holy rites, and through the night
           call aloud the Name for Atsumori,
           praying that he reach enlightenment
           praying that he reach enlightenment.

Enter ATSUMORI, *in the costume of a warrior. He stops in base square.*

ATSUMORI   Across to Awaji the plovers fly,
           while the Suma barrier guard sleeps on;
           yet one, I see, keeps nightlong vigil here.
           O keeper of the pass, tell me your name.[7]
           Behold, Renshō: I am Atsumori.
RENSHŌ   Strange! As I chant aloud the Name,
           beating out the rhythm on this gong,
           and wakeful as ever in broad day,
           I see Atsumori come before me.
           The sight can only be a dream.
ATSUMORI   Why need you take it for a dream?
           For I have come so far to be with you
           in order to clear karma that is real.
RENSHŌ   I do not understand you: for the Name
           has power to clear away all trace of sin.
           Call once upon the name of Amida
           and your countless sins will be no more:
           so the sutra promises. As for me,
           I have always called the Name for you.
           How could sinful karma afflict you still?
ATSUMORI   Deep as the sea it runs. O lift me up,
RENSHŌ   that I too may come to Buddhahood!
ATSUMORI   Let each assure the other's life to come,
RENSHŌ   for we, once enemies,
ATSUMORI   are now become,
RENSHŌ   in very truth,
ATSUMORI   fast friends in the Law.

Below, ATSUMORI *moves and gestures in consonance with the text.*

CHORUS   Now I understand!
           'Leave the company of an evil friend,
           cleave to the foe you judge a good man':
           and that good man is you! O I am grateful!

---

7. The barrier on the pass through the hills behind Suma was well known in poetry, which often features its nameless guard, an older man seen at night. Atsumori's words, "O keeper of the pass, tell me your name," are from a 12th-century poem.

How can I thank you as you deserve?
Then I will make confession of my tale,
and pass the night recounting it to you
and pass the night recounting it to you.

ATSUMORI *sits on a stool at centre, facing audience.*

The flowers of spring rise up and deck the trees
to urge all upwards to illumination;
the autumn moon plumbs the waters' depths
to show grace from on high saving all beings.

ATSUMORI Rows of Taira mansions lined the streets:
we were the leafy branches on the trees.
Like the rose of Sharon, we flowered one day;

CHORUS but as the Teaching that enjoins the Good
is seldom found,[8] birth in the human realm
quickly ends, like a spark from a flint.
This we never knew, nor understood
that vigour is followed by decline.

ATSUMORI Lords of the land, we were, but caused much grief;
CHORUS blinded by wealth, we never knew our pride.

ATSUMORI *rises now, and dances through the passage below.*

Yes, the house of Taira ruled the world
twenty years and more: a generation
that passed by as swiftly as a dream.
Then came the Juei years, and one sad fall,
when storms stripped the trees of all their leaves
and scattered them to the four directions,
we took to our fragile, leaflike ships,
and tossed in restless sleep upon the waves.
Our very dreams foretold no return.
We were like caged birds that miss the clouds,
or homing geese that have lost their way.
We never lingered long under one sky,
but travelled on for days, and months, and years,
till at last spring came round again,
and we camped here, at Ichi-no-tani.
So we stayed on, hard by Suma shore,

ATSUMORI while winds swept down upon us off the hills.
CHORUS The fields were bitterly cold. At the sea's edge
our ships huddled close, while day and night
the plovers cried, and our own poor sleeves
wilted in the spray that drenched the beach.
Together in the seafolk's huts we slept,
till we ourselves joined these villagers,
bent to their life like the wind-bent pines.
The evening smoke rose from our cooking fires
while we sat about on heaps of sticks
piled upon the beach, and thought and thought

8. It is only by great good fortune that a sentient being gets to hear the Buddha's teaching, and it is only as a human being that one has the potential to reach enlightenment.

of how we were at Suma, in the wilds,
and we ourselves belonged to Suma now,
even as we wept for all our clan.

ATSUMORI *stands before drums.*

ATSUMORI Then came the sixth night of the second month.
My father, Tsunemori, summoned us
to play and dance, and sing *imayō*.[9]

RENSHŌ Why, that was the music I remember!
A flute was playing so sweetly in their camp!
We, the attackers, heard it well enough.

ATSUMORI It was Atsumori's flute, you see:
the one I took with me to my death

RENSHŌ and that you wished to play this final time,

ATSUMORI while from every throat

CHORUS rose songs and poems
sung in chorus to a lively beat.

ATSUMORI *performs a lively dance, ending in base square. Below, be
continues dancing and miming in consonance with the text.*

ATSUMORI Then, in time, His Majesty's ship sailed,

CHORUS with the whole clan behind him in their own.
Anxious to be aboard, I sought the shore,
but all the warships and the imperial barge
stood already far, far out to sea.

ATSUMORI I was stranded. Reining in my horse,
I halted, at a loss for what to do.

CHORUS There came then, galloping behind me,
Kumagai no Jirō Naozane,
shouting, 'You will not escape my arm!'
At this Atsumori wheeled his mount
and swiftly, all undaunted, drew his sword.
We first exchanged a few rapid blows,
then, still on horseback, closed to grapple, fell,
and wrestled on, upon the wave-washed strand.
But you had bested me, and I was slain.
Now karma brings us face to face again.
'You are my foe!' Atsumori shouts, *Brandishes sword.*
lifting his sword to strike; but Kumagai *Drops to one knee.*
with kindness has repaid old enmity, *Rises, retreats.*
calling the Name to give the spirit peace.
They at last shall be reborn together
upon one lotus throne in paradise.
Renshō, you were no enemy of mine.

He drops his sword and, in base square, turns to RENSHŌ *with palms pressed together.*

Pray for me, O pray for my release!
Pray for me, O pray for my release!

Facing side from base square, stamps the final beat.

9. Popular songs much appreciated at court in the late 12th century.

VIII

Encounters
with
Islam

The Prophet Muhammed and the emergence of Islam united disparate Arab tribes over the course of the seventh century, turning them into a potent cultural and political force. Islam initially spread as the religion of a dynamic Arab state that took advantage of the weakness of the Byzantine and Persian Empires in the Middle East, and soon extended its political boundaries even further, to Spain, Central Asia, and Afghanistan. Once conquests slowed down and political boundaries were consolidated, traders carried the religion even further, to West Africa and China, as well as South and Southeast Asia. Arab traders established an increasingly far-flung network of cities and trading posts, facilitating an extraordinary exchange of goods. In Cordoba, the center of Muslim Spain, one had access to goods coming from Delhi, the Sultanate in northern India, and from what is now Bulgaria in eastern Europe to Sudan. Along with commodities, what traveled along these trade routes were armies. Islam became the religion of the ruling classes in the different empires. However, unlike Christianity, Islam did not seek

An illustration of the Ottoman fleet blockading the port of Marseille, from a sixteenth-century Ottoman manuscript that recounts the military campaigns of Süleyman the Magnificent.

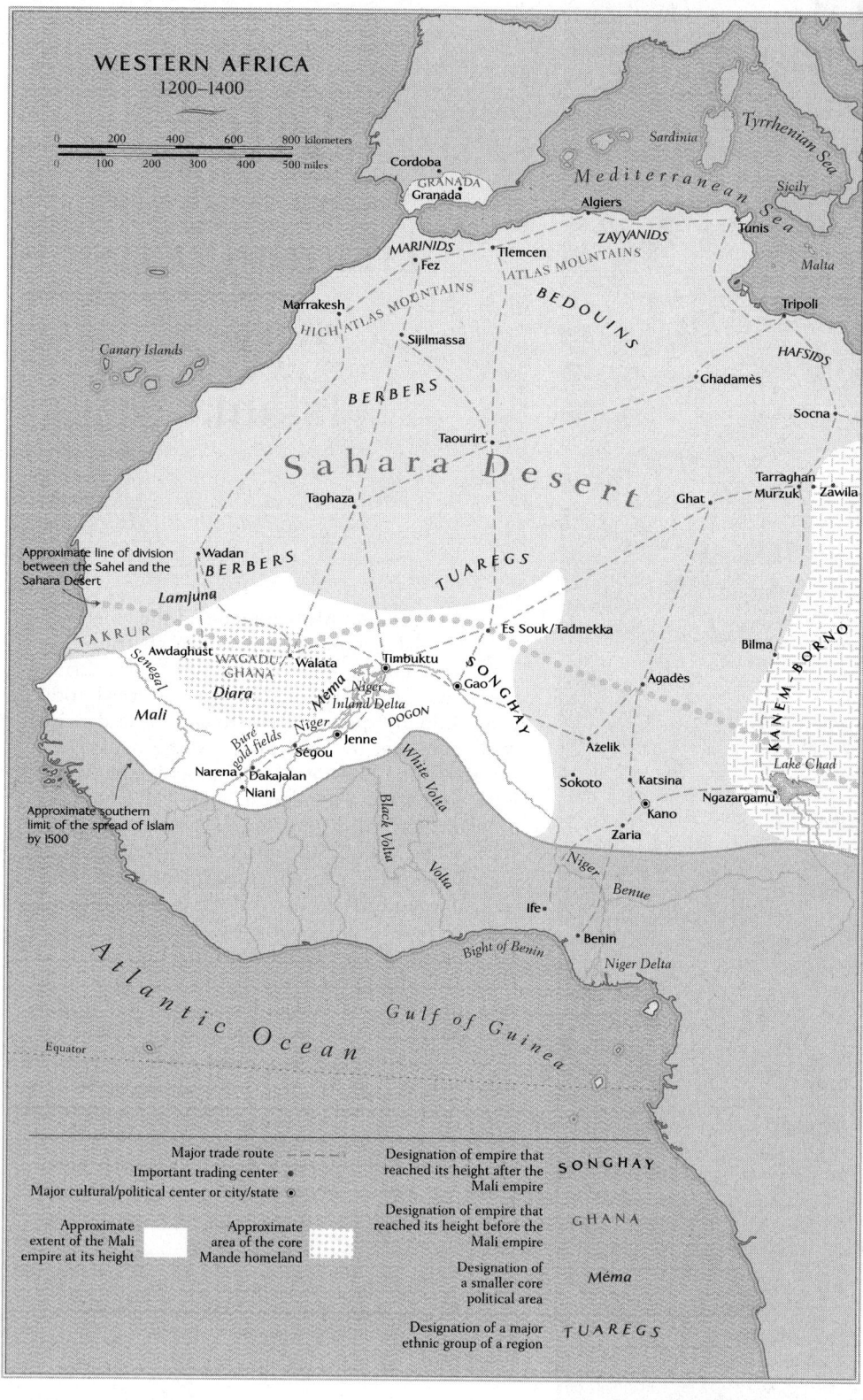

WESTERN AFRICA
1200–1400

0	200	400	600	800 kilometers
0	100	200	300	400	500 miles

Tyrrhenian Sea

Mediterranean Sea

Sardinia

Sicily

Malta

Cordoba
GRANADA
Granada

Algiers

Tunis

Tripoli

MARINIDS

Tlemcen

ZAYYANIDS

Fez

ATLAS MOUNTAINS

Marrakesh

BEDOUINS

HIGH ATLAS MOUNTAINS

Sijilmassa

HAFSIDS

Ghadamès

Socna

Canary Islands

BERBERS

Taourirt

Tarraghan

Murzuk

Zawila

Sahara Desert

Taghaza

Ghat

Approximate line of division
between the Sahel and the
Sahara Desert

Wadan

BERBERS

Lamjuna

TUAREGS

Es Souk/Tadmekka

Bilma

Senegal

TAKRUR

Awdaghust

WAGADU
GHANA

Walata

Timbuktu

SONGHAY

Gao

KANEM-BORNO

Agadès

Diara

Mêma

Mali

Niger Inland Delta

DOGON

Azelik

Lake Chad

Buré gold fields

Niger

Jenne

Ségou

Sokoto

Katsina

Approximate southern
limit of the spread of Islam
by 1500

Narena

Dakajalan

Ngazargamu

Niani

White Volta

Kano

Zaria

Black Volta

Volta

Niger

Benue

Ife

Atlantic Ocean

Benin

Bight of Benin

Niger Delta

Gulf of Guinea

Equator

Legend

Major trade route

• Important trading center

◉ Major cultural/political center or city/state

Approximate extent of the Mali empire at its height

Approximate area of the core Mande homeland

Designation of empire that reached its height after the Mali empire — **SONGHAY**

Designation of empire that reached its height before the Mali empire — GHANA

Designation of a smaller core political area — *Mêma*

Designation of a major ethnic group of a region — TUAREGS

converts, which meant that it often allowed local religious practices to exist alongside Islam, thus creating multicultural societies in which different religions existed side by side. The Ottoman Empire and the Mughal rule in India, for all the tensions that existed between different groups, set a standard for religious tolerance.

The same pattern held true of culture. Far from seeking to export a homogeneous notion of culture, the various Islamic empires were places of vibrant cultural exchange, in which art and ideas traveled as freely as goods and armies. Writing was especially enriched by the interchange; new literary forms that blended imported styles with existing local ones emerged throughout the Islamic world. Oral literature, such as the ones that fed into the Turkish epic *Dede Korkut* or the Mali epic **Sunjata**, continued to flourish, while incorporating Islamic elements, much as the pre-Christian epic **Beowulf** had received a late Christian layer or veneer to make the traditional story compatible with the new dominant religion. The result was a fascinating encounter of cultures and religions, whose products are presented here.

ISLAM AND PRE-ISLAMIC CULTURE IN NORTH AFRICA

Between 640 and 700 C.E., North Africa was occupied by Arab invaders seeking to expand the growing sphere of influence of an Arab world increasingly united by Islam. One far-reaching result of the Arab conquest was that it led to an economic revolution by combining the faltering economy of late Roman North Africa with the desert and savannah lands of West Africa into a vast commercial network that extended from the Atlantic to East Asia and from the equator throughout northern Europe. By the latter half of the eighth century,

most of the native Berber peoples of the Maghreb (Northwest Africa) had been converted to Islam. Owing to increasingly dynamic market forces to the north of the desert and the spread of camel-herding in the desert itself, Muslim Berber merchants became engaged in the systematic development of trans-Saharan trade.

The ninth-century Arab occupation of southern Morocco gave rise to a string of oasis cities south of the High Atlas Mountains. These included the bustling market town of Sijilmasa, which became the northern counterpart of the commercial centers of Tadmekka and Awdaghust on the southern edge of the Sahara. By the end of the tenth century, the southern trading centers had been colonized by Muslim (mostly Berber) immigrants from the north. They were merchants eager to trade with the markets of desert-edge kingdoms like Ghana, Takrur, and Gao, and especially to extract wealth from parts of the western Sudan described by Arab travelers as "the land of gold."

Thus, Islam arrived in West Africa via Muslim traders, and by 1068 the respected Arab geographer Al-Bakri was writing that there were significant Muslim populations occupying towns of the Mande peoples, which included the Maninka of the Upper Niger region who became founders of the Mali Empire in the thirteenth century.

But Islam was not only an economic force; it also reshaped the cultural landscape. By the thirteenth century Islam had become a common, though not universal, aspect of Mande culture. Far from imposing onto North Africa, including the Mali Empire, its own conception of art, Islam was gradually integrated into Mande culture, with Mande bards (*jeliw*) assimilating elements of Islamic tradition. Some of the stories told by Muslim clerics and by pilgrims returning from Mecca were adapted to local narrative repertoires.

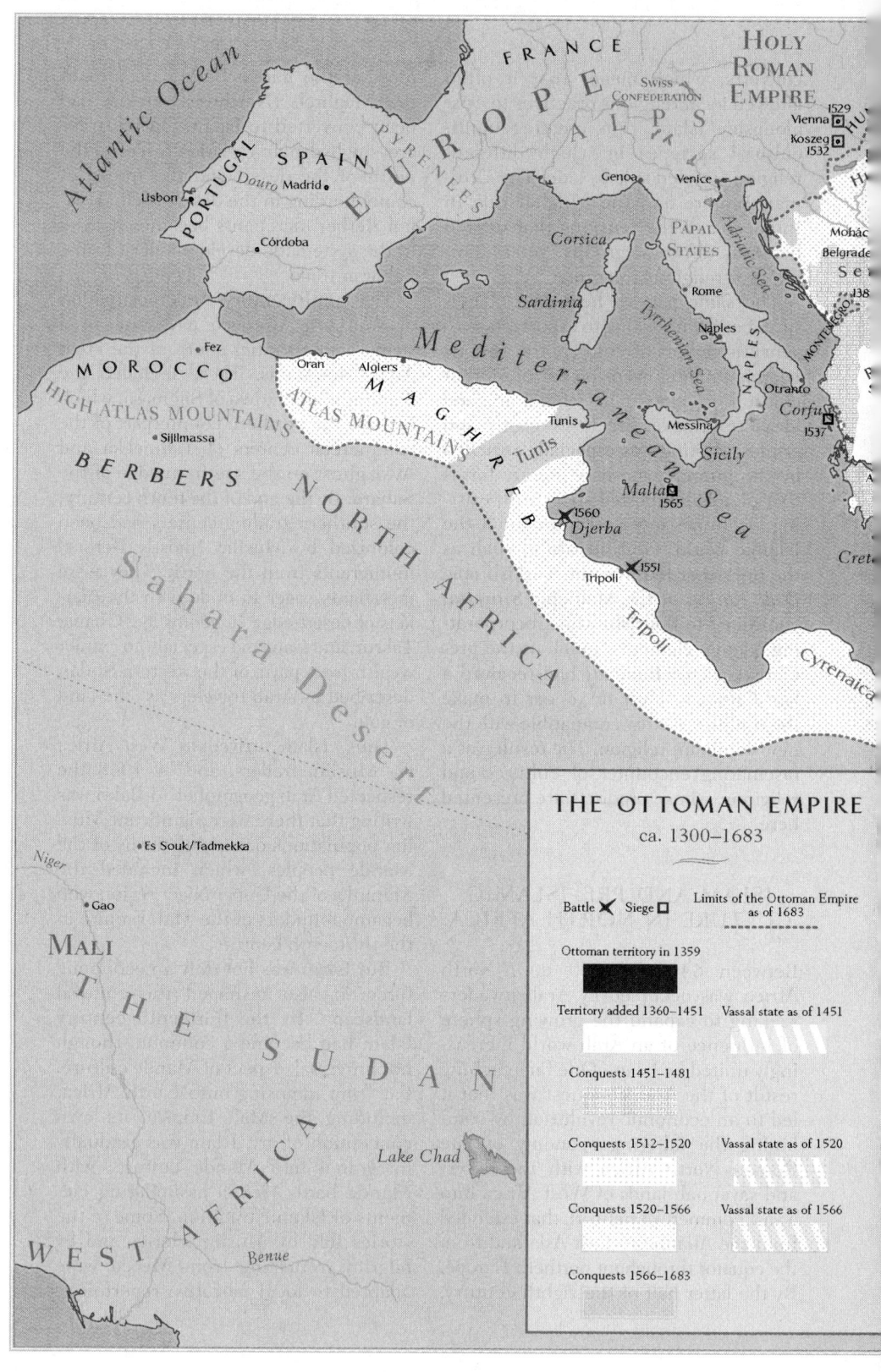

THE OTTOMAN EMPIRE

ca. 1300–1683

Battle ✖ Siege ◻ Limits of the Ottoman Empire
as of 1683
- - - - - - - - - -

Ottoman territory in 1359

Territory added 1360–1451   Vassal state as of 1451

Conquests 1451–1481

Conquests 1512–1520   Vassal state as of 1520

Conquests 1520–1566   Vassal state as of 1566

Conquests 1566–1683

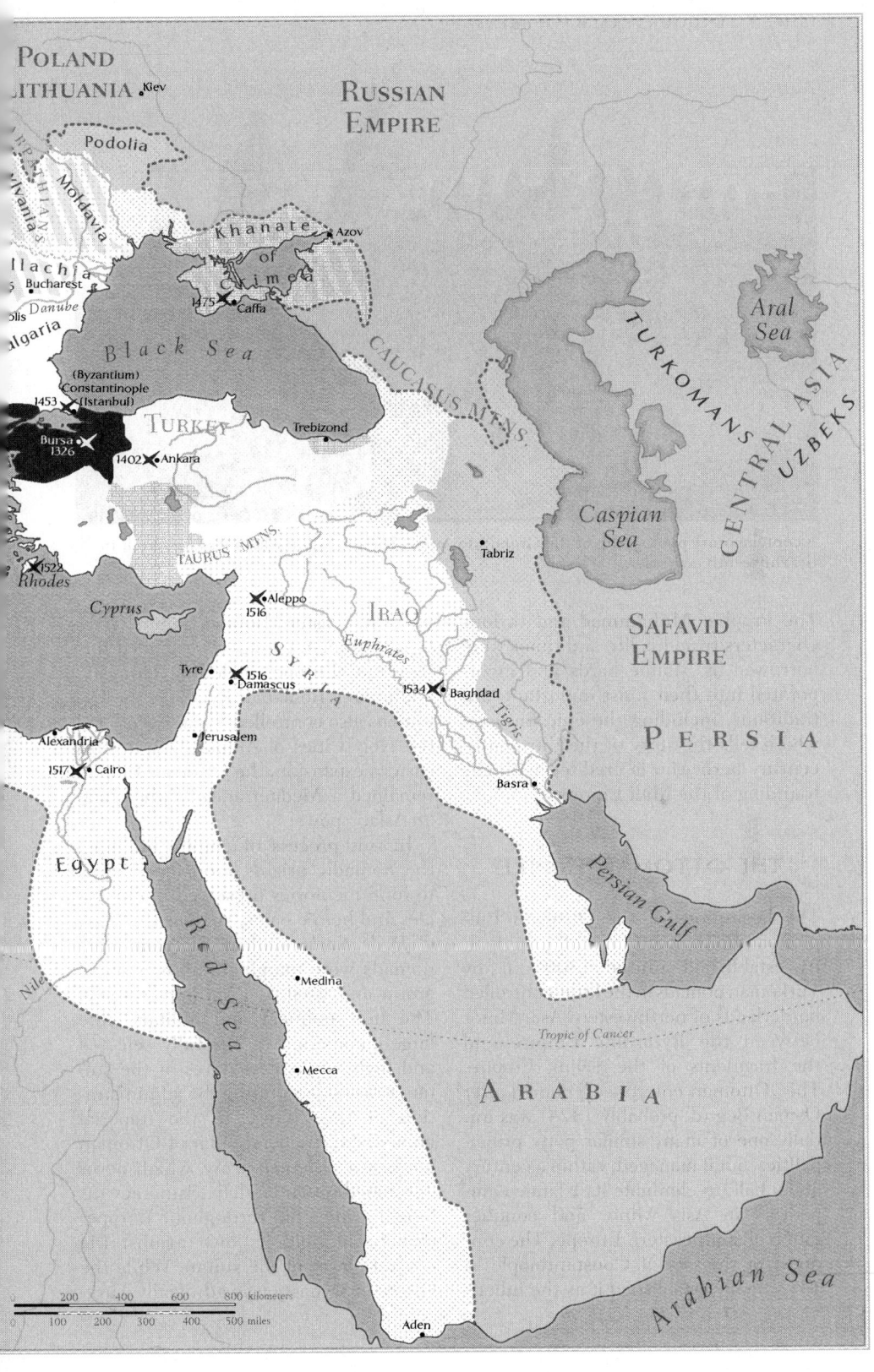

POLAND
LITHUANIA •Kiev

RUSSIAN
EMPIRE

Podolia

Moldavia

CARPATHIANS

TRANSYLVANIA

Wallachia
•Bucharest

Bulgaria

Danube

Khanate
of
Crimea •Azov

1475✗ •Caffa

Black Sea

CAUCASUS MTNS.

TURKOMANS

CENTRAL ASIA

UZBEKS

Aral
Sea

(Byzantium)
Constantinople
1453✗ (Istanbul)

TURKEY

•Trebizond

Bursa ✗
1326

1402✗ Ankara

Tabriz

Caspian
Sea

SAFAVID
EMPIRE

TAURUS MTNS.

1522✗
Rhodes

Cyprus

Syria

✗ Aleppo
1516

IRAQ

Euphrates

PERSIA

Tyre•

✗ 1516
Damascus

1534✗ •Baghdad

Tigris

•Alexandria

•Jerusalem

1517✗• Cairo

•Basra

Egypt

Red Sea

Nile

Persian Gulf

•Medina

Tropic of Cancer

•Mecca

ARABIA

Arabian Sea

•Aden

200   400   600   800 kilometers
100   200   300   400   500 miles

A contemporary photograph of the Grand Mosque at Djenne, Mali, which was first built in the thirteenth century.

The Prophet Muhammad and various characters from his life and times were borrowed by Mande bards and incorporated into their most important oral traditions, including the epic *Sunjata*, which tells the story of the thirteenth-century hero who is credited with the founding of the Mali Empire.

THE OTTOMAN EMPIRE

The beginnings of the Ottoman Empire can be traced to a small principality established around 1300 C.E. by Turkoman nomads in the little-controlled borderlands of northwestern Asia Minor between the Byzantine Empire and the fragments of the Seljuk Empire. The "Ottoman enterprise," named after Osman Beg (d. probably 1324) was initially one of many similar petty principalities, but it managed, within a century and a half, to eliminate its Islamic competitors in Asia Minor and conquer much of southeastern Europe. The conquest of the city of Constantinople in 1453 finally established it as the inheri-

tor of the eastern Roman Empire. Over time, Ottoman conquests extended further into Europe, including Hungary, and today's Romania. By 1517, the Ottomans also controlled Syria, Egypt, and the Holy Cities of Arabia. Despite this eastern expansion, the Ottoman Empire remained a Mediterranean rather than an Asiatic power.

In this process of empire building, the nomadic origins soon faded away to fond memories preserved in chronicles and heroic epics, such as the *Book of Dede Korkut*, while the remaining nomads were marginalized as a social group and used as a military reserve. The new political and military elite largely consisted of carefully selected and highly educated slaves of the sultan, thus concentrating the administration of the empire in the imperial household. A second pillar of Ottoman power was a feudal army, which never developed into a landed aristocracy (as feudal armies did throughout Europe) that could hold its own against the central power of the sultan. While the Ottoman Dynasty was ethnically Turkish, and the administrative language was Turkish as well, this elite was mostly recruited from Christian subjects, who were converted to Islam and culturally socialized into Ottoman-Turkish elite culture.

This elite culture found its classical expression in art, architecture, and literature between the late fifteenth and the beginning of the seventeenth century. Ottoman literature used a language that is Turkish in principle, but had come to incorporate so many Arabic and Persian words, phrases, and even syntactic constructions that it is sometimes difficult to tell whether a poem is Turkish or Persian. This literary Ottoman Turkish was worlds apart from the Turkish spoken on the street, the reserve of its erudite connoisseurs, who were all expected to be fluent in the "Three Languages"—Arabic, Persian, and Turkish—and their rich literary traditions. Evliya Çelebi's *Book of Travels* is a powerful late homage to these ideals of classical Ottoman culture.

Strictly speaking, the term Ottoman should be used only for the members of the imperial household and everybody else who shared this culturally defined identity, but more generally it has come to include the numerous subcultures that were allowed to thrive alongside it. Within this multilingual and multi-religious empire, place and social status, as well as affiliation with religious and social institutions were more important than ethnic background or language. Lacking a concept of "Ottoman citizenship," the Ottoman state with its small elite had neither an interest nor the means to impose any kind of cultural or religious identity on its subjects, and did not interfere in the internal communal affairs of its populations. This policy has often been praised as Ottoman tolerance, but it is important to realize that tolerance did not mean equality: different religious groups were taxed differently and did not have the same access to power. Yet the sheer diversity of the Ottoman Empire continues to command respect and elicit fascination.

ISLAM AND HINDUISM IN SOUTH ASIA

Muslim armies from Iraq entered South Asia early in the eighth century, initially conquering what are now the southern and western regions of Pakistan. Over the next three hundred years or so, immigrants from various parts of the Muslim world, together with local converts to Islam, gradually established distinctive settlements for themselves in the western and northwestern parts of the Indian subcontinent, from Sind and Gujarat to Punjab and Kashmir. During the eleventh and twelfth centuries, Muslim armies from Afghanistan and Central Asia (which included Turkish slave-warriors) carried out a succession of raids, or short-lived invasions, on towns and cities in northern India. In 1206, a Turkish slave-warrior proclaimed himself the Sultan of Delhi, laying the foundation for a Muslim empire in northern India that lasted more than three centuries, and was ruled by five different dynasties of Turkish-Afghan descent.

In the early sixteenth century, the Delhi Sultanate, which controlled the greater portion of western, northern, eastern, and central India by then, lost power to the Mughals, a dynasty with origins in today's Uzbekistan. The Mughals ruled most of South Asia from 1526 to 1857, creating a vast empire that, especially in the second half of the sixteenth century and in the seventeenth century, was the richest and most powerful political formation in Asia. Over a period of more than six centuries, the Delhi Sultanate and the Mughal empire, between them, provided a complex framework for the emergence of a

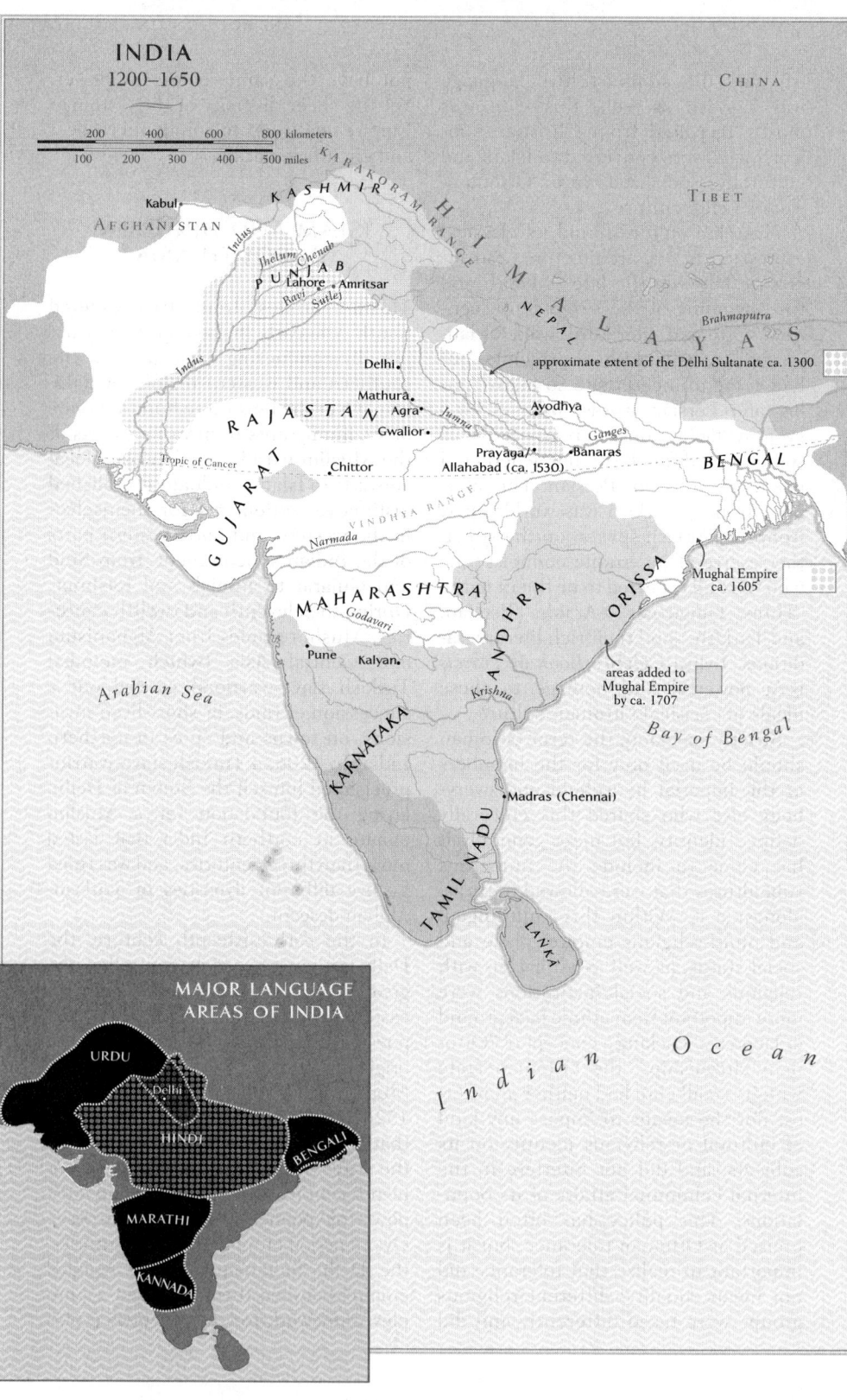

INDIA
1200–1650

200 400 600 800 kilometers
100 200 300 400 500 miles

CHINA

Kabul

AFGHANISTAN

KASHMIR

KARAKORAM RANGE

H I M A L A Y A S

TIBET

PUNJAB

Lahore Amritsar

Indus

Jhelum Chenab Ravi Sutlej

NEPAL

Brahmaputra

Delhi

approximate extent of the Delhi Sultanate ca. 1300

R A J A S T A N

Mathura
Agra
Gwalior

Jumna

Ayodhya

Ganges

Banaras

BENGAL

Tropic of Cancer

Chittor

Prayaga
Allahabad (ca. 1530)

G U J A R A T

VINDHYA RANGE

Narmada

Mughal Empire
ca. 1605

M A H A R A S H T R A

Godavari

A N D H R A

O R I S S A

areas added to
Mughal Empire
by ca. 1707

Pune Kalyan

Krishna

Bay of Bengal

Arabian Sea

K A R N A T A K A

Madras (Chennai)

T A M I L   N A D U

LANKA

Indian Ocean

MAJOR LANGUAGE
AREAS OF INDIA

URDU

Delhi

HINDI

BENGALI

MARATHI

KANNADA

unique Indo-Islamic civilization, which continues to shape the cultural life of South Asia to this day.

Before the arrival of Islam, the Indian subcontinent was predominantly Hindu in religion and culture, with Buddhism and Jainism practiced only by small minorities of the population. For much of the first millennium of the Common Era, Hinduism in its classical form involved polytheism (belief in the existence of many gods), worship in temples officiated by priests (belonging to the Brahmin caste), the worship of idols and the performance of numerous and intricate rituals (in accordance with elaborate scriptures, law books, and codes), and pilgrimages to designated holy places.

When Islam settled into South Asia, it challenged many of these ideas and practices in Hinduism. Islam's uncompromising monotheism (belief in a single, all-powerful God), as well as its attacks on idol-worship, compelled many Hindus to reconsider their polytheism and their worship in temples (which is centered around idols, often representing gods in anthropomorphic forms). Likewise, Islam's emphasis on social equality and a universal fraternity persuaded Hindus to question the caste hierarchy and its practice of discrimination on the basis of birth. Moreover, Sufism—a mystical form of Islam centered on the cultivation of music, dance, poetry, the visual arts, and techniques of ecstasy—offered forms of spiritualism that resonated with some Hindu conceptions of "union with God." The poets collected here, from different regions and religions of South Asia, all work through this productive tension between Islam and Hinduism, testifying to the fact that cross-cultural encounters are sometimes violent, but can also lead to artworks of stunning beauty.

SUNJATA: A WEST AFRICAN EPIC OF THE MANDE PEOPLES

late thirteenth–early fourteenth century

The West African epic named after its central hero, Sunjata, is an essential part of Mande culture. The heartland of Mande territory is located in what is now northeastern Guinea and southern Mali, but the Mande peoples are found in a much larger portion of sub-Saharan West Africa, speaking various related languages and dialects. The Mande, who include the Bamana of Mali and the Maninka of Guinea, are heirs to a vibrant historical legacy, the high point of which was the Mali Empire that flourished from the mid-thirteenth to the early fifteenth century. The epic narrative of Sunjata and his contemporaries illustrates the Mande peoples' own view of this glorious past both before and after Islam began to influence their culture, and it rightfully credits their ancestors with establishing one of the great empires of the medieval world.

In Mande culture, oral tradition is the domain of bards popularly known as griots, but as *jeliw* or *jelilu* (sing. *jeli*) to their own people. They are the hereditary oral artists responsible for relating the alleged deeds of the early ancestors, keeping them and their exploits alive in the community's memory. For many centuries the *jeliw* have served as genealogists, musicians, praise-singers, spokespersons and diplomats. As the principal narrators of oral tradition, the bards have been responsible for preserving narratives that express what peoples of the Mande cultural heartland believe to have happened in the distant past. For centuries, stories of the ancestors have passed from one generation of *jeliw* to the next, and the principal Mande clans frame their identities in terms of descent from the ancestors described in epic tradition.

As specialists in maintaining the oral traditions of their culture, *jeliw* are known to their people as guardians of "The Word." In early times they served as the spokespersons of chiefs (*dugutigiw*) and kings (*mansaw*), and were thus responsible for their patrons' reputations in the community. Generations of *jeli* families were permanently attached to leading households and ruling dynasties, who supported the bards in exchange for their services in the oral arts. The *jeliw* encouraged their patrons to achieve high goals by reminding them of the examples set by their heroic ancestors, as described in the epic narratives. They pointed out mistakes through the use of proverbs, and admonished their patrons when they threatened to fail in their duties. At the same time, the bards' own security depended on their rulers' political power and social prestige, so the stories they told tended to be biased in favor of their own patrons' ancestors.

In Mande societies all matters involving family, clan, and ethnic kinship are of supreme importance. People are identified by their *jamu*, which is the family name or patronymic associated with famous ancestors remembered for important deeds alleged to have occurred around the beginning of the thirteenth century. Thanks to regular exposure to live or locally taped performances by *jeliw* that are played

Three contemporary *jeliw* of Mali with instruments used to accompany the performance of oral narrative and song: *top*, the *bala* (indigenous xylophone) at Makandiana in 2007; *middle*, the *nkoni* (a small lute) at Kolokani in 1975; *bottom*, the *kora* (a twenty-one-string calabash harp) at Bamako in 1975. (All photos courtesy of David C. Conrad.)

privately or heard regularly on local radio broadcasts, general awareness of the heroes and heroines of ancient times, like those in *Sunjata*, enters the people's consciousness in childhood and remains there throughout their lives. Memories of the ancestors are constantly evoked in praise songs and narrative episodes that are sung or recited by the bards on virtually any occasion that calls for entertainment. When elders meet in village council, the ancestral spirits are felt to be present because, according to tradition, it was they who established the relative status of everyone present, as well as the administrative protocols to be followed and the values underpinning every decision. The ancestors who are described in *kuma koro* or "ancient speech" define the identity of virtually everyone of Mande origin.

The performance of *Sunjata* would often be accompanied by musical instruments: a small lute (*nkoni*), a twenty-one-string calabash harp (*kora*), or a *bala* (native xylophone). Even without music, Mande oral poetry incorporates a kind of call-and-response rhythm through the repeated assent of the "*naamu-sayer*" (responding person) to each line sung by the *jeli*. The *naamus* of this secondary performer might be translated as "yes" or "We hear you"; they are preserved here in the original to give a flavor of the repetitive, almost incantatory quality of the response. The variant spellings of "naamu" reflect different pronunciations used for emphasis. Common interjections include *tinye* ("it's true") in the indigenous language, as well as terms borrowed from Arabic and reflecting the influence of Islam, such as *walahi* ("I swear") and *amina* ("amen"). In all cases, the community hears not only the poem but an enthusiastic, repeated approbation of it. The *jeli*'s own language when narrating the stories of the ancestors is also distinct from everyday speech, as he turns to *kuma koro*

("ancient speech") for the performance. Even the most central names in the story may vary according to the pronunciation of the individual *jeliw* and to regional differences, so that Sunjata, for example, may appear as Son-Jara, So'olon Jara, or Sunjara.

Oral literature that has been passed down from generation to generation is difficult to date. The epic material feeding this version of the *Sunjata* epic was narrated and recorded only in the late twentieth century, although it retells stories that go back centuries. Djanka Tassey Condé, the *jeli* who narrated this version, lived his entire life in the small village of Fadama near the Niandan River in northeastern Guinea. Nominally a Muslim like most people in today's Mande society, Tassey was descended from a lineage of Condé bards who trace their ancestry to forebears who lived before the arrival of Islam, in the land of Dò ni Kiri as it is described in the Mande epic. Even among other bardic families of Manden, the Condé of Fadama are respected for their vast knowledge of Mande epic tradition. In the 1970s and 1980s, Tassey's brother Mamadi Condé was *belentigi* (chief bard) of Fadama, and one of the best-known orators in Manden, distinguished for his depth of knowledge. When Mamadi died in 1994, his brother Tassey became the *belentigi*. Several months later, David C. Conrad, who edited this version of *Sunjata*, began a collaborative relationship with Tassey Condé that lasted until that great bard's death in 1997.

The passages collected here are from the rendering by Tassey Condé of this communal, epic story. The narrative is episodic and often disjunct, full of magic (*dalilu*) and humor, as the *jeli* gives his own version of a story familiar to his listeners. The epic tells of the great expectation surrounding the birth of Sunjata, whose heroism has long been foretold. Foreigners come to defeat a wild buffalo that has been dec-imating Mande lands, and their first achievement is to recognize the buffalo woman Dò Kamissa as the culprit. They tame her with kindness, claiming that she resembles their mother, until she relents and offers them her wis-dom. Urging them to look beyond appearances, she commends to them the deformed Sogolon, who will be the mother of Sunjata. When Sunjata is finally born, into a world full of sorcery and treachery, he barely escapes the many plots against him, and is eventu-ally driven into exile by the jealousy of his stepbrother. His greatest achieve-ment comes with the defeat of the tyr-annous Sumaworo to liberate Manden, which the text recognizes as a founda-tional imperial gesture. Sunjata also emphasizes, however, that the hero's exalted stature comes at a great cost to the community: while Sumaworo furi-ously seeks the man who is fated to succeed him, we are told, the Mande people suffer his violent attacks.

Like most epics, Sunjata is a relation of the hero's many trials, which he sur-mounts through his courage, tenacity, and piety. Yet the singular hero is also deeply ensconced in his community: in order to lead he must find allies, culti-vate friends, and honor his family. Part of the charm of Sunjata lies in its atten-tion to detail, and its fresh humor as it relates the interactions of legendary heroes with the very concrete world around them. This is a poem about the power struggles that can lead to war, certainly, but it is also about people's relationship to a place and a landscape. Land takes on a concrete quality beyond its political significance as Sunjata pleads for a plot in which to bury his mother when she dies in exile. In its vivid re-creation of the hero's experi-ence, Sunjata knits together the mythic and the everyday, the ancestral and the contemporary, providing for its Mande listeners a recognizable, living history, and for everyone else rich insight into the culture of a once-glorious empire.

Sunjata: A West African Epic of the Mande Peoples[1]

The Search for a Wife of Destiny

	You say you want to know about Manden.	(Naamu)
	For us to give you many details about Manden,	(Naamu)
	With which part of Manden will we start?	(Naamu)
	Wo will start with Sunjata's father,	(Naamu)
5	Who is Farako Manko Farakonken.	(Naamu)
	The name of Sunjata's father is,	(Naamu)
	Manko Farakonken of Konfara.	(Naamu)
	Do you know where Konfara is?	(Naamu)
	It is on the frontier between Guinea and Mali,	
10	At a place now known as Kourémalé.	(Naamu)
	The swampy area,	
	Where the Kourémalé people dig their gold mines,	
	Is known as Konfara.	(Naamu)
	The father of Simbon was named after that,[2]	(Naamu)
15	But his real name is Maghan.	(Naamu)
	He is Maghan Konfara.	

1. Translated from the Maninka by David C. Conrad with Djobba Kamara and Lansana Magassouba.

2. A title of honor carrying the sense of "Mas-ter Hunter," which the bard applies to both Sunjata and his father.

That land of Konfara was acquired from us, the Condé.	(Naamu)
This Maghan Konfara of whom I speak,	(Naamu)
His son's name is Sunjata,	
20 The last *mansa* of Manden[3]	(Naamu)
When Manden was put in the care of Maghan Konfara,	(Naamu)
He had the power,	(Naamu)
He had the wealth,	(Naamu)
He was popular,	(Naamu)
25 He had *dalilu*,[4]	(Naamu)
But he had no child.	(Naamu)
Simbon, Sunjata's father, had no child.	(Naamu)
He craved a child.	(Naamu)
His friends had begun to have children,	(Naamu)
30 But no child was had by Maghan Konfara.	(Naamu)
Maghan Konfara was frustrated.	(Naamu)
All of Manden became frustrated.	(Naamu)
It is hard to give birth to a child who will be famous.	(Naamu)

[*In an omitted passage the narrator describes the Moroccan background of two brothers, Abdu Karimi and Abdu Kassimu, who will eventually become known as Danmansa Wulanni and Danmansa Wulanba. They travel to the land of Dò ni Kiri to hunt a buffalo that is devastating the countryside.*]

Two Hunters Arrive in Manden

Abdu Karimi and Abdu Kassimu came to Manden.	(Na-amu)
35 From Morocco they walked through the night.	(Naamu)
They bypassed Dò ni Kiri and went straight to Manden.	(Naamu)
The Mande people asked them, "Where did you come from?"	
The Arab *kamalenw*[5] said, "We come from Morocco."	(Ná-amuuu)
The Mande people asked them, "What is your family?"	(Naamu)
40 "We are Sharifu."	(Na-amu)
The Mande people saluted them, "You Haidara."	(Naamu)
The *kamalenw* replied, "Marahaba."[6]	(Naamu)
The Mande people said, "The honor is yours,	
The honor is Simbon's."	(Na-amu)
45 The *kamalenw* explained, "We have heard that the Condé are suffering,	(Naamu)
That they are quarreling with their sister,	
She has transformed herself into a buffalo.	

3. There were many kings (*mansaw*) after Sunjata. By this, the narrator means "the greatest of them all." The name "Sunjata" derives from the practice of identifying a male child by his mother's name, in this case "Sogolon." So'olon Jara (Sogolon's Lion) evolved to various forms including Son-Jara and Sunjata.
4. Magic, occult, or secret power; in everyday use, any means used to achieve a goal.

5. Worthy, able young men in their prime. The suffix "w" indicates the plural.
6. A standard response to a greeting honoring one's ancestors. "Sharifu": from the Arabic Shurafa' (sing. Sharif), a lineage claiming descent from the family of the Prophet Muhammad. "Haidara": a prestigious Muslim family name in Manden, here used in greeting as the equivalent of Sharifu.

Every morning in the twelve towns of Dò,   (Naamu)
The four towns of Kiri,   (Naamu)
50   And the six towns across the river,   (Naamu)
The buffalo has been killing people in all of them."   (Na-amuuu)
They said, "That is why we have come.   (Naamu)
We want to go to Dò ni Kiri.   (Naamu)
We want to go and help the Condé with their trouble."   (Na-amu)
55   As the hunters were leaving,   (Naamu)
Maghan Konfara said, "You Sharifu,"   (Na-amu)
He said, "The Condé foresee that anybody who
        kills this buffalo,   (Naamu)
That they will present three sets of girls to that person. (Na-amu)
Any one you choose will be your wife.   (Naamu)
60   When you go, you will kill the buffalo.   (Naamu)
When they bring the young girls to you,   (Naamu)
You should present me with a wife."   (Naamuuu)
They departed.   (Naamu)

Dò Kamissa the Buffalo Woman

When they had passed through the land of Konfara,   (Na-amu)
65   When they crossed into the land of the Condé,   (Naamu)
When they heard the pounding of the mortars and
        pestles[7] of Dò ni Kiri,   (Naamu)
They met Dò Kamissa herself.   (Na-amu)
She carried a hoe on her shoulder,   (Naamu)
A walking staff served as her third leg.   (Na-amu)
70   When they said, "Greetings mother,"   (Naamu)
Heeeh! She cursed their father.   (Naamu)
After that, she cursed their grandfather.   (Na-amu)
Then she cursed their mother.   (Naamu)
"You are calling me mother?   (Naamu)
75   Was I the one who gave birth to your father or
        your mother?"   (Na-amu)
She said every bad word to them.   (Naamu)
Abdu Karimi said, "Big brother,   (Naaaam')
Don't you think this lady resembles our mother?"   (Naamu)
Abdu Kassimu replied, "Heeh, this lady does resemble
        our mother.   (Na-amu)
80   Everything she is doing to us seems familiar."   (Naamu)
Abdu Karimi said, "The manner in which our own
        mother abuses us,   (Naamu)
That is the same way she abuses us.   (Na-amu)
Hey! Look at the way she walks,
As if she were our mother."   (Naamu)
85   Abdu Kassimu said, "Ma, where are you going?"   (Naamu)
She said, "Do I have to explain anything to you?   (Na-amu)

---

7. Women pound grain in large wooden receptacles with a heavy wooden club-shaped pestle that can be as long as five feet.

I am going to look for termites to feed my chickens." (Naamu)
Abdu Karimi said, "Ah, big brother, hold my bag." (Naamu)
He reached out to take the hoe from the old woman. (Naamu)
90 He said, "Give me your hoe,
I will dig termites for your chickens." (Naamu)
She replied, "When I look for termites,
Are you the one who always feeds my chickens? (Na-amu)
If you don't leave my hoe alone, (Naamu)
95 What you are looking for from me, you will get soon." (Na-amu)
They scuffled over the hoe until he took it from the
    old lady. (Naamu)
When he got the hoe from her he dug for termites, (Naamu)
Put them in a bag and loaded them on his head. (Naamu)
He said, "Let us go." (Naamu)

100 When they got some distance ahead of the woman, (Naamu)
Abdu Karimi said, "Big brother. (Naamuuu)
The thing that the female genie told us. (Na-amu)
Let us be careful because she said this is the buffalo. (Naamu)
The way the old woman looks. (Naamu)
105 Let us watch her carefully. (Naamu)
Let us walk briskly. (Na-amu)
If we leave her behind, (Naamu)
It will mean that the person we are looking for is still
    ahead of us. (Naamu)
If we do not leave her behind, (Naamu)
110 Then we can believe that this is the buffalo we were
    told about." (Naamu)
The two men walked very briskly. (Naamu)
The old woman was still behind them. (Na-amu)
As they walked, chu, chu, chu!
They would look back and see the old woman
    behind them. (Naamu)
115 The younger brother said, "Didn't I tell you she is
    the one?" (Na-amu)

When they reached the road to Dò ni Kiri, (Naamu)
The road leading to her hamlet branched off to
    the right. (Naamu)
The road to Dò ni Kiri branched off to the left. (Naamu)
When they started to take the big road to Dò ni Kiri, (Naamu)
120 She said, "Where are you going with my termites?" (Naamuuu)
Then they knew for sure. (Naamu)
She said, "Don't you know what happened,
Between me and the men of Dò ni Kiri? (Na-amu)
So why did you take my hoe from me? (Naamu)
125 If the termites belong to me, why are you taking
    that road? (Naamu)
Don't you see my road?" (Naamuuu)
They went on that road.

When they arrived there,
God caused Ma Sogolon's sister Dò Kamissa to
    soften toward them. (Naamu)
130 They were now in Dò ni Kiri. (Na-amu)
Everybody who had come to kill the buffalo was dead. (Naamu)
Every hunter who came. (Naamu)
A bird that was near the swamp, (Naamu)
Would call, *tumè-tumè*. (Naamu)
135 That was the buffalo woman's spy. (Naamuuu)
Even up to tomorrow, it is still acting as her spy. (Na-amu)
Even if you go into the swamp in the middle
    of the night,
You will hear it saying, "Someone is here." (Naamu)
As soon as the bird called *tumè-tumè*,
140 The buffalo would go out and kill them. (Naamu)

Many wild creatures were on her side. (Naamu)
She had a wild cat. (Naamu)
The wild cat and the tree squirrel, (Na-amu)
They were stealing the Condé's chickens. (Naamu)
145 The leopard and the hyena, (Na-amu)
They were stealing the Condé's cattle. (Naamu)
They attacked all of their livestock. (Na-amu)
The quarrel had now reached a critical stage. (Naaaam')
Dò Kamissa and the genies were also attacking the
    people of Dò ni Kiri. (Naamuuu)
150 This buffalo had now made widows of many women. (Naamu)
This buffalo had now caused many men to
    lose their wives. (Naamu)
This buffalo had caused many family heads to
    lose their children. (Na-amu)
This buffalo had killed all the sisters. (Na-amu)
While that was happening, the Arab *kamalenw* arrived. (Naamu)
155 After they greeted our ancestor Donsamogo Diarra, (Naamu)
He asked them, "How did you get here?" (Na-amu)
They said, "Thanks to God." (Naamu)
"Ah!" He said, "Where did you come from?" (Na-amu)
"We come from Morocco." (Naamu)
160 Donsamogo Diarra asked them, "What is your
    family name?" (Naamu)
The *kamalenw* replied, "We are Sharifu." (Na-amu)
Donsamogo Diarra saluted them, "You Haidara." (Naamu)
They replied, "Marahaba." (Naamu)
Donsamogo Diarra said, "Why have you come here? (Na-amu)
165 Have you not heard about the trouble here?" (Naamu)
He said, "Have you not heard that my sister
    Dò Kamissa has killed my people? (Naamu)
Should it be said that Sharifu wasted their
    blood in the land of the Condé? (Na-amu)
Huh! You Sharifu,

	I am not pleased with you coming here."	(Naaaam')
170	They said, "Allah!"	(Naamu)
	Donsamogo Diarra said, "Very well,	
	If it is God who has sent you,	(Naamu)
	Do not go into the bush.	(Naamu)
	Stay in town and I will assemble my children.	(Naamu)
175	I will give them to you so you can teach them.	(Na-amuuu)
	Do not go into the bush.	(Naamu)
	I do not want this country cursed because a	
	Sharif dies on my land.	(Na-amu)
	Dò ni Kiri must not be cursed."[8]	(Naamu)
	The Arab kamalenw said, "Very well."	(Na-amu)
180	They were given lodgings in a house.	(Naamu)

	The buffalo woman was somewhere else,	(Na-amu)
	Praise be to God.	(Naamu)
	After the kamalenw were settled in a house,	(Naamu)
	After one day, two days, their hosts killed a	
	chicken for them.	(Naamu)
185	When the chicken was killed for them,	(Na-amu)
	They put the sauce on the rice.	(Naamu)
	They took a thigh of the chicken,	(Naamu)
	And the backbone,	(Naamu)
	And put that in the saucepan.	(Naamu)
190	They went out the back door and took them to	
	the bad old lady in the bush.	(Naamu)
	She was the buffalo.	(Na-amu)
	When they got there they said, "Ma,	(Naamu)
	Did we not both tell you that you resemble our mother?"	(Na-amu)
	They said, "For God's sake,	
195	We cannot contradict ourselves,	
	You do resemble our mother.	(Naamu)
	Heh, when we separated from you, we didn't want to.	(Naamu)
	We came to town and your brother killed a chicken	
	for us.	(Naamu)
	When we are in Morocco and kill a chicken,	(Naamu)
200	What we give to our mother is the back.	(Naamu)
	What goes to our father is the thigh.	(Naamuuu)
	Our mother, our father,	(Naamu)
	You are all.	(Na-amu)
	What goes to our father,	(Naamu)
205	What goes to our mother,	(Naamu)
	It is all yours."	(Naamuuu)
	She reached out her hand and took that and the sauce,	(Naamu)
	And then she threw it at them.	(Naamu)
	She said, "For what reason did you bring the termites?	(Na-amu)
210	When you brought the termites, was it not for	
	the chickens?	(Naamu)

8. As descendants of the Prophet Muhammad, the Sharifu are Muslim elite, so he wants them to stay out of danger and give his children Koranic lessons.

When you left, did I tell you I had a craving for
    chicken meat?   (Na-amu)

Sharifu, stop trying to get what you want from me.   (Naamu)

You are being stubborn.   (Na-amu)

What you are doing to me now,   (Naamu)

215 If it had not been for the relations between the
    Sharifu and the Condé,   (Naamu)

What I have done to the others, I would have done
    to you.   (Naamu)

Won't you leave me alone?   (Na-amuuu)

I am talking to you."   (Naamuuu)

The *kamalenw* took the sauce and returned to town.   (Naamu)

220 One day, two days,   (Naamu)

Another chicken was killed for them.   (Naamu)

They did the same thing as before and took the
    pieces to her.   (Naamu)

She took them and gave them to the dogs,   (Na-amu)

And repeated the same words that she said before.   (Naamu)

225 They went back to town.   (Na-amu)

One day, two days,   (Naamu)

The Condé killed another chicken.   (Naamu)

The *kamalenw* repeated the deed.   (Naamu)

When they came and met her,   (Naamuuu)

230 She took the chicken pieces and put them on the shelf. (Na-amu)

She spoke to them the words that were in her mouth. (Naamu)

Dò Kamissa the buffalo woman said,
    "You have outdone me.   (Na-amu)

No one can get the better of people like you."   (Naamu)

She said, "You are polite.   (Na-amu)

235 You were brought up well.   (Naamu)

Eh! Despite everything you were told,   (Naamu)

You were not discouraged   (Na-amu)

You favor me?   (Naamu)

Now I will cooperate with you."   (Naamu)

240 She said, "Had it not been for that,

We would have wiped out Dò ni Kiri.   (Naamu)

My brother Donsamogo Diarra,   (Na-amu)

I was the first born of my father's children.   (Naamu)

After I was born, when I reached puberty,   (Naamu)

245 I said, 'My Lord God,   (Naamu)

If my father sires a son,   (Naamu)

When anyone tells me that my father has sired a son, (Naamu)

The two gold earrings that are on my ears,   (Naamu)

I will give the largest of them to the person
    who brings me the news.   (Naamu)

250 My Lord God, if my father sires a son,   (Naamu)

The first person who brings the news to me,   (Naamu)

Of the two wrappers I am wearing,   (Naamu)

I will give the beautiful outer one to that person.'   (Na-amu)
I was the first to offer a sacrifice for my brother.   (Naamu)
255 Therefore, should he tell me that women do
     not receive property?   (Naamuuu)
Huh!   (Na-amu)
I would have wiped out their lineage.   (Naamu)
But you Sharifu,   (Naamu)
You have outdone me.   (Naaaam')
260 I will cooperate with you,   (Naamu)
I will give you my life.   (Na-amu)
For I know that if you kill me,   (Naamu)
You will bury me.   (Na-amu)
If you kill me,   (Naamu)
265 My body will not go to God as a bad body."   (Naamuuu)

She said, "Before I give myself up to you,   (Na-amu)
I will tell you three things.   (Naamu)
If you agree to those three things,   (Na-amu)
Then I will cooperate with you.   (Naamu)
270 If you do not agree to those three things,   (Naamu)
I will keep after you until you do agree to those things." (Na-amu)
The *kamalenw* said, "Ma, tell us the three things."   (Naamu)
She said, "The first of those things,   (Na-amuuu)
When you kill the buffalo,   (Naamu)
275 Do not go to town immediately.   (Na-amu)
Come to this hamlet.   (Naamu)
You will come and find me dead.   (Naamu)
My brother must not see my corpse,   (Na-amu)
Because I am the only one who knows what I have done.   (Naaaam')
280 Come to this hamlet where you will find me dead.   (Naamu)
You will come and see that I have poured water on
     the fire.   (Naamu)
There will be a hoe,   (Naamu)
There will also be an axe.   (Naamu)
Take the axe and cut down a *toro* tree.   (Naamu)
285 Take the hoe and dig the grave.   (Naamu)
After you have laid me in it, fire the musket.[9]   (Naamu)
My brother must never see my body.   (Na-amu)
They must not carry my body to Dò ni Kiri.   (Naaaamuu)
He is my father's son.   (Na-amuuu)
290 I have not been doing good to them.   (Naaaam')
I have wiped out their children,   (Naamu)
I have wiped out their wives.   (Naamu)
There are many widows there today.   (Na-amu)
I am responsible for that."   (Naamu)

9. The first firearms did not arrive in West Africa until the 16th century, but the *jeliw* (bards) frequently speak of muskets in the 13th-century time of Sunjata. Linear chronology matters less than the imagery of a formidable weapon and a hero's power to repel any iron projectile.

295 "That is the first thing. (Naamu)
The second thing, is that they had promised, (Na-amu)
That anyone who kills me, (Naamu)
They said they will present three sets of girls
    from Dò ni Kiri, (Naamu)
And that the one chosen by that person will
    become his wife. (Naamu)
300 My second thing is, (Na-amu)
When they bring out their fine young daughters, (Naamu)
Do not accept any of them. (Naamuuu)
Refuse all of them, (Na-amuuu)
Because my father's last-born is still in the house. (Naamu)
305 Five age sets[1] of girls have gone to their husbands, (Naamu)
But she has not married. (Naamu)
If you do not marry her,
She will never be married. (Naamuuu)
Anyone who marries her,
310 Something special will be at her breast. (Naamu)
You must marry her, you the Sharifu. (Naamu)
She is very ugly. (Naamu)
Have you not heared that Sogolon is short? (Naamuuu)
The 'Short Sogolon' that you have heard about, (Na-amu)
315 Have you not heard that Sogolon is ugly? (Naamu)
The ugliness of Sogolon that you keep hearing about, (Naamu)
She is very ugly. (Naamuuu)
The duct in her eye is injured and the tears run down, (Naamu)
And I am responsible for that. (Naamu)
320 Her head is bald. (Na-amu)
She has a humped back. (Naamu)
I, Dò Kamissa, did that. (Na-amu)
Her feet are twisted. (Naamu)
When she walks she limps this way and that, (Naamu)
325 And I am the cause of that. (Na-amu)

How was I the cause? (Naamuuu)
If you see her damaged tear-duct, (Na-amu)
Her bald head, (Naamu)
A hump on her back, (Naamu)
330 I put my far-seeing mask[2] on her face, (Naamu)
Because of my love for her, (Na-amu)
Before she was old enough to wear it. (Naamu)
That is what cut her tear-duct. (Na-amu)
That is why her hair fell out. (Naamu)
335 That is what put a hump on her back. (Naamu)
I am responsible. (Na-amu)

---

1. Children born within the same span of about three–five years grow up together, going through the various initiation rituals into adulthood.
2. A magic object allowing the wearer to see unimaginable distances. The concept might have entered oral tradition when Europeans were observed using telescopes and binoculars, but there also could have been an indigenous mask imbued with such power.

If she does not get married,   (Naamu)
It will be my curse."   (Naamuuu)
She said, "If you see that her feet are twisted,   (Na-amu)
340 And she is knock-kneed,   (Naamu)
I was the cause of that.   (Naamu)
I set her on my sorcery horse,   (Naamu)
When she was too young.   (Naamu)
That is what caused her tendons to be stretched,   (Na-amu)
345 And her feet to be twisted.   (Naamu)
If she does not get married,   (Naamu)
It will be my curse."   (Na-amu)
She said, "I was the cause of all that.   (Naamu)
If my sister does not get married,
350 I take the blame for it.   (Na-amu)
Therefore, when you Sharifu come,   (Naamu)
And they bring those beautiful Condé women to you,   (Na-amu)
Do not accept any of them.   (Naamu)
Choose my father's last-born.   (Na-amu)
355 The name of that last-born is Sogolon Wulen Condé.   (Naamu)
Some call her Humpbacked Sogolon.   (Naamu)
Some call her Ugly Sogolon.   (Naamu)
Everybody used to call her whatever they felt like.   (Na-amu)
But her real name is Sogolon Wulen Condé."   (Naamuuu)
360 (That is who will be the mother of Sunjata.)   (Na-amu)
She said, "If you choose her,
There will be something special at her breast,
Because it will have all the *dalilu*.   (Naamu)
The beautiful daughters that they are talking about,   (Na-amu)
365 If you take her and are not satisfied with the way
    she looks,   (Naamu)
When you kill the buffalo, cut off its tail.   (Naamu)
It is laden with gold and silver,   (Naamu)
Because for every woman of Dò ni Kiri that I killed,   (Na-amu)
If they had gold on their ears,   (Naamu)
370 I would take out the gold earrings,
And attach them to the hair of my tail.   (Naamuuu)
For every woman of Dò ni Kiri that I killed,   (Na-amu)
Those who had silver rings in their ears,   (Naamu)
I would take out the silver ear-rings,
375 And attach them to the hair of my tail.   (Naamu)
I have a lot of tail hair and it is laden with gold,   (Na-amuuu)
The ear jewelry of Dò ni Kiri women.   (Naaaam')
Exchange some of that gold,   (Naamu)
So you can go and marry a beautiful woman
    somewhere else.   (Naamu)
380 You can add her to Sogolon Condé,
But do not refuse to take her.   (Na-amu)
That will be no problem.   (Naamu)
Will you accept that, or not?"   (Naamu)
The Sharifu said, "We agree to that."   (Na-amu)

385 She said, "That is the second thing. (Naamu)
The third one! (Na-amu)
When you kill the buffalo, (Naamu)
The buffalo's carcass must not be taken to the town." (Na-amu)
They said, "Eh, Condé woman! (Naamuuu)
390 We have agreed to the other ones, (Naamu)
But the one that you just said, (Na-amu)
We may not be able to convince your people about that. (Naamu)
We have no power to fight them off, (Naamu)
To take the carcass from them. (Naamu)
395 What if they force us? (Na-amu)
We might not be able to convince them." (Naamuuu)
The Condé woman said, "Oh,
You will do your best to heed what I have said. (Na-amu)
If you can do the other things, (Naamu)
400 Leave that one. (Naamuuu)
But the other two things, (Naamu)
You must respect them." (Na-amu)
They said, "Very well." (Naamu)

As they were about to leave, (Na-amu)
405 She said to them, "Sit down." (Naamu)
When they took their seats, (Naamu)
She said, "I control my own life. (Naamu)
The weapons you brought, (Na-amu)
They will not do anything to me. (Naamu)
410 The arrows and quivers you brought, (Naamu)
Those will not do anything. (Naamu)
I am in control of my own life." (Naamu)
She put her hand in her basket of cleaned cotton. (Naamu)
She pulled out the spindle and handed it to them. (Naamu)
415 She put her hand in the storage basket, (Naamu)
She took out the small distaff, (Naamu)
She took out the small staff that usually holds
the thread. (Naamu)
She took it and gave it to them. (Naamu)
She said, "When you go and find the buffalo, (Naamu)
420 Put this in your bow and shoot the buffalo with it. (Naamu)
That will stop the buffalo. (Na-amuuu)
If you do not shoot the buffalo with that, (Naamu)
If you shoot at it with your big arrow, (Naamu)
The buffalo will kill you." (Naamuuu)

Death of the Buffalo

425 They left the town and went to the bush, past the
lake of Dò ni Kiri. (Na-amu)
The buffalo was there. (Naamu)
The younger brother said to the elder brother, (Naamu)
Abdu Karimi told Abdu Kassimu, (Na-amu)

He said, "Big brother!

430 You take the magic dart and shoot it at the buffalo, (Na-amu)

Because the killing of this buffalo will make history. (Naamu)

The person who kills this one, (Naamu)

Up to the time when the trumpet is blown on
    Judgement Day, (Naamu)

This will be told in all the histories of future
    generations." (Na-amu)

435 He said, "You kill the buffalo." (Naamu)

Abu Kassimu said, "Little brother, (Na-amu)

When somebody knows something, let him do it." (Naamu)

He said, "I was the first to be born,

But I know what *dalilu* you have, (Naamu)

440 And I know you must kill the buffalo." (Na-amuuu)

He handed the magic dart to his younger brother. (Naamu)

Abdu Karimi told his elder brother to go on ahead. (Na-amu)

He lay down in the grass and began to crawl. (Naamu)

He went ever closer to the buffalo,

445 Remembering what the old woman had told him, (Naamu)

That he should not try to kill the buffalo until he
    was in its shadow. (Na-amu)

She had said, "Do not miss me! (Naamu)

If you miss the buffalo, I will kill you." (Naamu)

The younger brother crawled until he reached the
    buffalo's shadow. (Naamuu)

450 He took out the distaff and put it on the spindle. (Naamu)

He pulled it back and back, (Naamu)

He pulled it still harder, (Naamu)

And he could feel that he had something very
    powerful in his hand. (Naamuuu)

When he had pulled it until his hand was back
    to his shoulder, (Naamu)

455 He let it go, *paa*! (Naamu)

It went and pierced the buffalo here, it went into
    the chest. (Naamuuu)

When the thing pierced its chest the buffalo was
    shaken. (Naamuu)

When the buffalo shook, it raised its head and saw him. (Naamu)

It bellowed, *hrrr*! (Naamu)

460 Even while he was still right beside the buffalo, (Naamu)

He told his elder brother, "Keep going!" (Na-amuu)

The buffalo had been pierced and the struggle
    between them had begun. (Naaaam')

A source of greatness will not be acquired without
    hardship. (Na-amuu)

Before peace could return to Manden, (Naamu)

465 The hardship that it experienced up to the time
    that was born, (Naamu)

That is what we are narrating. (Naamuuu)

If this had not taken place,
would not have been born.   (Na-amu)
If had not been born,
470 Manden would not have been sweet.   (Naamu)
If Manden had not been sweet,
The Mande people would not have known themselves.   (Na-amuu)

The buffalo began to chase the *kamalenw*.   (Naamu)
Before Abdu Karimi could catch up with his elder
   brother,
475 The buffalo came closer.   (Na-amu)
When the buffalo caught up to them and bellowed,   (Naamu)
He dropped the bamboo stick,
Which instantly sprouted into a grove of bamboo.   (Naamu)
Before the buffalo could get through it,
480 The *kamalenw* had run far ahead.   (Na-amu)
When the buffalo passed the first obstacle,
It began chasing them again.   (Naamu)
When it caught up with them again and bellowed,   (Naamuu)
They dropped the hot charcoal.   (Naamu)
485 In those days the Mande bush had been there
        a long time.   (Naamu)
It had never been burned, so the bush caught on fire.   (Naamu)
When the buffalo tried to get through,
It was stopped by the fire.   (Naamu)
It was forced to go back while they were dashing
        through the grass.   (Naamu)
490 When the fire subsided,
The buffalo jumped into the ashes and chased
        them again.   (Naamuu)
When it got close to them again,
They were already at the lake of Dò ni Kiri.   (Na-amu)
By the time it arrived at the lake and began to bellow,   (Mmmm)
495 Abdu Karimi dropped the egg, which turned the
        ground into deep mud.   (Naamu)
The buffalo got stuck in the mud.   (Naamu)
That is what is referred to in the Condé song,
"Dala Kombo Kamba":   (Naamu)
"Condé drinker of big lake water,   (Naamu)
500 Those who drank the big lake water,   (Naamu)
They did not stop to clean it.   (Naamu)
Those who clean the big lake,   (Naamu)
They did not drink its big water."   (Naamuuu)
It was Danmansa Wulanba and Danmansa Wulanni,[3]
505 Who cleaned the water of the big lake.   (Naamu)
By the time they finished with that,   (Na-amu)

---

3. Only after the buffalo is mortally wounded
does Tassey Condé begin to use the names by
which the hunters are usually known, which
originated as praise names based on the brothers' exploits.

Water had penetrated the spindle wounds into the
  buffalo's intestines.   (Naamu)
When the buffalo got to that place it fell down.   (Na-amu)
When the buffalo fell, Danmansa Wulanni said to his
  elder brother,   (Naamu)
510 He said, "Big brother, look behind you!   (Naamu)
The buffalo has fallen."   (Naamuuu)

After they finished killing the buffalo,   (Naamu)
They saw that the tail was laden with gold and silver.   (Na-amu)
That was when they first started cutting off the
  tails of dead game.   (Naamu)
When you hear that a young hunter kills an animal and
515   cuts off its tail,   (Naamu)
This was the beginning of that custom.   (Na-amu)
Cutting off the buffalo's tail accomplished two
  things for them.   (Naamuu)
It was laden with gold and silver in its tail hairs.   (Naamu)
The second thing was that anybody who would deny
  that they killed it,   (Naamu)
520 Since it was a buffalo,
They knew that the tail could not be cut from a live one.   (Naamu)
As soon as they showed the tail,
People would know that the business was finished.   (Naamu)
Ahuh!
525 Because they knew that Dò Kamissa's buffalo wraith,   (Naamu)
Could only have its tail cut off if it had been finished.   (Na-amu)
That proved to Dò ni Kiri that the *kamalenw* had really
  killed the buffalo.   (Naamuu)

[*In an omitted passage, Danmansa Wulanba and Danmansa Wulanni try to
respect Dò Kamissa's wish that her wraith be buried in the bush, but the townspeople insist on retrieving the buffalo carcass and dragging it into town to be
desecrated.*]

Sogolon Wulen Condé of Dò ni Kiri

After finishing with the buffalo, the ceremonial drum
  was beaten.   (Naamu)
The twelve towns of Dò,   (Naamu)
530 The four towns of Kiri,   (Naamu)
The six towns across the river,   (Naamuu)
All of the people were expected to attend.   (Na-amu)
They all came.   (Naamu)
When the twenty-two towns were all present they said,
535 "What did we say?   (Naamuu)
We said any hunter who kills this one,   (Naamu)
We will bring out three age sets of girls,   (Naamu)
And any girl they choose from among them will
  become his wife."   (Naamu)

They said, "Bring your daughters forward."   (Naamuu)
540 Huh!
If you bring out three age sets of daughters from
    twenty-two towns,   (Na-amu)
Bring the older set first,   (Naamu)
Then the next one to those,   (Naamu)
Then the youngest set.   (Naamuu)
545 They brought out the beautiful Condé girls who
    formed three circles.   (Naamuu)
They told the boys to choose.   (Na-amu)
They said, "Even if you choose ten, they are your wives.   (Naamu)
Even if you choose twenty, they are your wives.   (Naamu)
Even if you choose only one, that is your wife.   (Naamu)
550 You have delivered us from disaster.   (Na-amu)
It is the wish of everyone to have their daughter
    married to these two."   (Naamu)
When the girls were brought out,   (Na-amu)
They said to them, "You the Sharifu,   (Naamu)
We do not go back on our promise.   (Naamu)
555 Take a look at these people.
Any one that pleases you, take her."   (Naamu)
The two men followed one another.   (Naamu)
They went around the circle,   (Naamu)
They went around the circle,   (Naamu)
560 They went around the circle.   (Naamu)
They came back to where they had started and said,
"Where are the rest of the girls?"   (Naamuu)
The Condé ancestor said, "You young men search
    every house,   (Naamuu)
So that no one can hide his daughter."   (Naamu)
565 They searched through the town and no one
    was found.   (Naamu)
Everybody was wishing for them to marry their
    daughter   (Naamuu)

When the searchers returned they said,
    "There is nobody left."   (Naamuu)
A bystander said, "What about the bad old woman
    who was just killed?   (Naamu)
She has her father's last-born still in the house."   (Naamu)
570 Somebody said, "Eeh, man!   (Naamu)
Heeeye, can we show that one to the strangers?"   (Na-amu)
Danmansa Wulanni said, "The exact one you are
    talking about,   (Naamu)
Go and get her.   (Na-amu)
Has she been married to another man?"
575 They said, "No."   (Naamu)
"Has she been married before?"
They said, "No."   (Naamu)
The brothers said, "If she is unmarried, go and get her."   (Naamu)

The people said, "Five age sets of girls have found
    husbands,
580 But she has remained unmarried." (Naamu)
They said, "Go and get her if she is an unmarried girl." (Naamu)
Ma Dò Kamissa had told them that when they went
    to choose her, (Naamu)
The door of her father's house was the one facing the
    town's meeting ground. (Naamuu)
She had told them, "When she is coming from
    my father's house, (Naamu)
585 To go into the town meeting ground, (Naamu)
A little black cat will come from behind her and
    pass in front of her, (Naamu)
The little black cat will go from in front of her and
    pass behind her. (Naamu)
If you see that happening to anyone,
That is the girl I am talking about." (Naamu)

590 When she was sent for, (Naamu)
As she was being brought out of the house, (Naamu)
When she got to the edge of the town meeting ground, (Naamu)
A black cat came from behind her and passed in
    front of her, (Naamu)
It went from in front of her and passed behind her. (Naamu)
595 As soon as the brothers saw her, they said,
"This is the one we have been talking about." (Naamu)
They heard people go, "Wooo!"
They were asked, "Is this the one you were
    talking about?" (Naamu)
The brothers said, "Yes, this is the one we have been
    talking about." (Na-amu)
600 She is the one who was taken and given to them, (Naamu)
The mother of Simbon. (Na-amu)
The birth of Simbon and the organizing of Manden, (Naamu)
The person about whom it was foretold, (Naamu)
Is the one who organized them all, (Naamu)
605 United them into one and called the place Manden, (Naamu)
The person who did it was Sunjata. (Naamu)
This is how his mother was married.

When night fell and they went to bed, (Naamu)
As men normally approach their brides, (Naamu)
610 When the elder brother, Danmansa Wulanba, got close
    to her, (Naamu)
She ejected two porcupine quills from her chest and
    they stuck in him. (Naamu)
He jumped up and fell on the ground. (Naamuu)
He spent the rest of the night sleeping on the opposite
    side of the room, (Naamuu)
Because of her sorcery. (Na-amu)

615 Ancestor Donsamogo Diarra had said to them, (Naamu)
He said, "You the Sharifu, (Naamu)
Is this the one you want?" (Naamu)
They replied, "This is the one we want." (Naamu)
"Are you sure this is the one you want?" (Naamu)
620 They said, "This is the one we want." (Naamu)
He said, "My sister whom you killed, (Naamu)
All the *dalilu* that she had, (Naamu)
This one's is even more powerful. (Naamuu)
But if you say that you want her, I am giving her to you. (Naamu)
625 Take her with you. (Na-amu)
If you are not compatible, (Naamu)
Bring her back so I can put her where you took her from, (Naamu)
And I will give you another one. (Naamuu)
She has powerful *dalilu*. (Na-amuu)
630 I don't want to contradict myself, but take a look at
    this group of girls. (Naamu)
These people will wait for you up to three months. (Naamuu)
If you are not compatible with my sister, (Naamu)
Come back and I will give you one of these. (Naamu)
I will put her back where she came from." (Naamuu)
635 They said, "Very well." (Na-amu)
She did not accept Danmansa Wulanba's advances. (Naamu)

In the morning when Danmansa Wulanni came to him, (Naamu)
He said, "Little brother, (Naamu)
Was I not the one who told you yesterday that you
    should kill the buffalo?" (Naamu)
640 He said, "Uh huuh." (Naamu)
"Did I not say that you are more knowledgeable than I? (Naamu)
Ahuh, you should marry this woman yourself. (Na-amu)
You should accept that. (Naamu)
The God who made it possible for you to kill
    the buffalo, (Naamu)
645 Has made me unable to take this woman. (Na-amu)
When we leave from here we will exchange this
    gold and silver, (Naamu)
We will marry another woman that I will keep.
Do not say anything to the Condé, (Na-amu)
So they cannot say 'wooo' to us the way they did
    yesterday. (Naamu)
650 Therefore, you take her without letting anybody
    here know about it." (Naamu)
When night fell,
Danmansa Wulanba was in a hurry for them to finish
    eating supper. (Naamu)
He took his blanket and went out to spend the
    night with his friends. (Naamu)
By then Danmansa Wulanni and Sogolon
    Condé were in the house. (Na-amu)

655 When they went to bed,
That was the one she really did something to, (Naamu)
Something she did not do to the elder brother. (Na-amu)
Danmansa Wulanba had spent the night on the other
    side of the room, (Naamu)
But Danmansa Wulanni slept outside. (Na-amu)

660 The next morning,
As soon as he saw Danmansa Wulanba coming,
    he said, *pah!* (Naamu)
He said, "Big brother! (Naamu)
I am not going to tell you anything. (Naamu)
Let us beg to take our leave. (Naamu)
665 There is no way that we can explain this. (Na-amu)
We rejected all those beautiful Condé women. (Naamu)
Eh! The old woman has really caused problems for us. (Naamu)
Eh! That old woman! (Na-amu)
She killed the men of Manden, but she sent us
    straight into decay. (Naamuu)
670 If we don't get another wife here, (Na-amu)
They will say we are too proud, that we look too high. (Naamu)
We were given a group of women to choose from.
We declined them, but the one we took, (Naamu)
We cannot keep her. (Naamu)
675 Let us beg to take our leave. (Na-amu)
We should not say that we don't want her. (Naamuu)
When we have gone, (Naamu)
When we see a river in flood, (Naamu)
When we get to it, we will leave her there. (Na-amu)
680 We will cross the river and go on. (Naamu)
If she waits there long enough,
She will go back because she will not be able to cross." (Naamu)
When the boys arrived at the river, the water
    was in flood. (Naamuu)

Danmansa Wulanni said, "Sister-in-law," (Naamu)
685 He said, "Wait here for us. (Na-amu)
You can see the water yourself. (Naamuu)
We want to go upstream. (Na-amu)
If we see any tree that has fallen across the river, (Naamu)
We will come to get you so we can cross together." (Naamu)
690 She said, "All right." (Na-amu)
She waited for them there with her baggage. (Naamu)
Everything was in her bundle. (Naamuu)
When they went upstream, they went farther
    and farther, (Naamu)
They went until they saw a *sèbè* tree that had fallen
    across the river. (Naamuu)
695 Aah, the Sharifu now had their way. (Na-amu)
They went across on it. (Naamu)

As they were crossing the river they said,
"Eh heh, we have done the right thing. (Na-amu)
Don't you see, she has attached herself to us. (Naamu)
700 She has slowed us down. (Na-amu)
Who would want to take her along? (Naamu)
Hey! Look at my chest." (Naamuu)
The elder brother said, "You don't even know what
    you're talking about. (Na-amu)
I won't even show you mine. (Naamu)
705 Sorceress! (Na-amu)
Who would want to take a sorceress and bring her to
    his father's house?" (Naamu)
While they were chatting, they arrived at Konfara. (Naamu)
At the outskirts of Konfara, (Na-amu)
They met the Condé woman sitting and waiting
    ahead of them. (Naamuu)
710 She said to them, "You the Sharifu, (Naamu)
Is this how you behave?" (Naamu)
They said, "Ah, Ma, please forgive." (Na-amu)

A New Sorceress Wife for the Mansa of Konfara

When they arrived in the town, (Naamu)
They went straight to Simbon's house. (Naamu)
715 They had arrived in Konfara. (Naamu)
It was in Konfara that Sunjata was born. (Naamu)
We should tell you that. (Na-amu)
At the place of Maghan Konfara in Konfara. (Naamu)
When they arrived there in Konfara,
720 Danmansa Wulanba began to speak. (Naamu)
He said, "I swear to God, you are a real king of diviners. (Na-amuu)
What you told us is what happened to us. (Naamu)
We went to Dò ni Kiri, (Naamu)
We killed the buffalo, (Naamu)
725 The people of Dò ni Kiri honored us, (Naamuu)
And the woman they gave us, (Na-amu)
Because of the way you foresaw things, (Naamu)
And because of your forthrightness, (Naamu)
And because of the way you help travelers, (Naamu)
730 We did not accept any other woman. (Naamu)
That is the one we have brought to you." (Naamu)

Simbon laughed. (Naamu)
"Aheh, where is the woman in question?" (Naamu)
They said, "She is outside." (Na-amu)
735 Simbon got up, took his elephant tail fly whisk,[4]
    and looked around. (Naamu)

4. Mande sorcerers do not perform public functions without carrying a fly whisk usually made of a horse tail. Signifying his stature as a powerful legendary sorcerer, Simbon carries a fly whisk from the larger animal, as does Suma-woro.

	He went and saw the sorceress sitting beside her bundle.	(Naamu)
	When he saw her beside it,	(Na-amu)
	When he looked at her he said, "Heeee,	
	Sharifulu, oh father!	(Naamu)
740	Take this one back.	(Naamu)
	I am not refusing her, I still want her.	(Naamu)
	But take her out of the town and let me prepare myself.	(Naamu)
	If you bring her to my house right now,	
	She will take my house from me.	(Na-amu)
745	But you brought me a gift that I want to keep."	(Naamu)
	"Go back outside the town."	(Naamu)
	They took her out of the town and waited there.	(Naamuu)

	When the co-wives were told, "You have your wife,"[5]	(Naamu)
	They took their places behind the bride.	(Naamu)
750	They said, "Sister-in-law, get up and let us go home."	(Na-amu)
	When they lifted her up she had a twisted foot.	(Na-amu)
	Her feet were twisted and she could not walk without	
	raising dust.	(Na-amu)
	When they lifted her up then,	(Naamu)
	The dust went this way,	(Na-amu)
755	The dust went that way.	(Naamu)
	The first song for welcoming brides in Manden was	
	sung then.	(Naamu)
	How did they sing this first bride-escorting song?	(Na-amu)
	The sisters sang:	
	"Walk well,	(Naamu)
760	Bride of my brother,	(Na-amu)
	Walk well.	(Naamu)
	Do not put us in the dust."	(Na-amuu)
	That became the first bride-escorting song of Manden.	(Naamu)
	They saw that her walk could not improve,	(Naamu)
765	That it was beyond her power.	(Naamu)
	The sisters said, "Let us carry her."	(Na-amu)
	That is how carrying the bride originated.	(Naamu)
	If you see that when the bride arrives at the outskirts	
	of the town,	(Naamu)
	The women pick up the bride and run with her,	(Naamu)
770	That was done because of the condition of Sogolon	
	Condé's feet.	(Na-amu)
	The sisters said, "Let us carry her."	(Naamu)
	While they were running,	
	Ma Sogolon Condé's headscarf fell off,	(Naamu)
	And her bald head was exposed.	(Naamu)
775	The co-wives made a new song.	(Na-amu)
	What did they say in this song of the co-wives?	(Na-amu)

5. The bride is thought of as the collective possession of the family and the village into which she marries.

They had not known that her head was bald.	(Naamu)
What did they sing?	(Naamu)
They sang:	
780 "The heron-head oooh.	(Naamu)
Our heron-head has come this year,	
Heron-head.	(Naamu)
The woman's heron-head has come this year with	
her crest."	(Naamu)
This offended Sogolon Condé.	(Na-amu)
785 She looked back at the women of Manden,	(Naamu)
And said, "Are you calling me a heron-head?	(Naamu)
Am I the one you are calling heron-head?	(Naamu)
Well, I have arrived."	(Na-amu)
Feeling angry, she was carried to her husband's door.	(Naamu)
790 The husband had been sitting in his lounge chair at	
the back of his room.	(Na-amu)
He had prepared himself with his own *dabali*.⁶	(Naamu)
He had taken out his sorcerer's whip and laid it at	
his side,	(Naamu)
Because he knew that what was coming to him would	
show him her *dalilu*.	(Na-amu)
If you see that when a Mande bride arrives at the door,	(Naamu)
795 The sisters will put their heads inside and then pull	
them back out,	(Naamu)
Put their heads inside and pull them back out,	(Naamu)
The third time, they send the bride into her husband.	(Na-amu)
That's how it all started.	(Naamu)
The first time they held the back of Sogolon's head,	
800 To push her inside to her husband,	(Naamu)
She ejected a sorcerer's dart from her eye,	
And tried to pierce her husband's eye.	(Na-amu)
It went *srrrrrr*!	(Naamuu)
Maghan Konfara caught it.	(Naamu)
805 He said, "Condé woman, you have brought me	
a present.	(Na-amu)
This is my seventh year,	(Naamu)
That I have had the meat of Mande sorcery in my teeth.	(Naamu)
An ordinary piece of straw will not be able to pick it	
from my teeth,	(Naamu)
Only a sorcerer's dart will do that.	(Naamu)
810 You have brought me a dart for a toothpick."	(Naamu)
He caught it and laid it beside him.	(Naamu)
He took his sorcerer's whip and lashed her on the head.	(Naamu)
She pulled back for the first time,	(Naamu)
And when she put her head in again,	(Naamuu)

6. Scheme.

815	She shot out her scalding breast milk,	(Naamu)
	Trying to splash it on Simbon to blister his skin,	(Naamu)
	To let him know that a real woman was coming.	(Naamu)
	Simbon repelled it.	
	He said, "Condé woman, you have really brought me a gift.	(Naamu)
820	Ordinary Mande water does not clean our faces as well as warm breast milk.	(Na-amu)
	You have brought me face-washing water."	(Naamu)
	He washed his face with that and again picked up his sorcerer's whip.	(Naamu)
	He lashed her on the head, *cho!*	(Naamu)
	She pulled back her head a second time.	(Naamuu)
825	The third time when the women tried to push her in,	(Naamu)
	If you see old men of Manden carrying a staff,	
	One with a small metal point on the end,	(Naamu)
	It was Sogolon Condé who brought it from Dò ni Kiri.	
	It belongs to the Condé.	(Naamu)
830	It was this staff that Sogolon Condé now took out,	(Naamu)
	Trying to spear Simbon in the chest,	(Naamuu)
	Because she could see that she was up against a real man.	(Naamu)
	She had sent two things and both were repelled.	(Naamu)
	But if this one went, it would pierce his chest.	(Naamuu)
835	When this was thrown, Simbon caught it.	(Naamu)
	He merely praised it.	(Naamu)
	He said, "We use the ebony walking stick with nothing on it,	(Naamu)
	But the Condé have sent us a walking stick wearing a hat."[7]	(Naamu)
	That is the staff in question.	(Na-amu)
840	It was not an ordinary spear.	(Naamu)
	It was your new bride's spear.	(Naamu)
	Simbon said, "We have received a protective spear."	(Naamu)
	He laid it beside him and picked up his sorcerer's whip,	(Naamu)
	And lashed her, *cho!*	(Naamu)
845	Sogolon had used up her sorcery.	(Naamu)
	They pushed her into him.	(Naamuu)
	When she was pushed inside to him,	(Na-amu)
	She reached for her bundle and took out her drinking ladle.	(Naamu)
	The ten kola nuts that are given to the women,	(Na-amu)
850	It was Sogolon Condé who first put them into water.	(Naamu)
	It is the woman who is supposed to put the kola in water,	
	And then hand it to her husband.	(Naamuu)
	Instead of handing them to her husband,	(Naamu)
	Sogolon Condé put them in her cup.	(Naamu)

7. The staff's metal tip.

855   She went and knelt in front of Maghan Konfara.   (Naamu)
  She said, "If you were not among the husbands
      of the world,   (Naamu)
  I would have gone to the other world unmarried.   (Naamu)
  I have now come to my husband.   (Na-amu)
  He is my married husband,
860   My husband who will take care of me,
  My husband by whom I will give birth.   (Naamu)
  I have gotten my husband.   (Na-amu)
  It is the crocodile of the stream that leads one to the
      crocodile of the river.   (Nam-naamu)
  I have come to Simbon.   (Naamu)
865   Drink."   (Naamuu)
  Simbon drank.   (Naamu)
  He accepted the ten kola nuts and set them down.   (Naamu)
  Alone, she went and sat on her husband's bed.   (Naamuu)
  If they had not finished with the sorcery,   (Naamu)
870   That is why when a new bride is brought,   (Naamu)
  If you see her sitting in a chair,   (Naamu)
  If she does not sit on her husband's bed she has
      something on her mind.   (Naamuu)
  She does not want to marry this man,
  She has another man's name to confess.   (Naamu)

  When Sogolon came to Maghan Konfara, she was
875   still a virgin.   (Naamuu)
  After three days her bloody virgin cloth was taken out.   (Naamu)
  The following month, she became pregnant with Sunjata.   (Na-amu)
  That is how Sunjata was conceived.   (Naamu)
  The co-wives said, "We will not be able to do anything
      against this woman."   (Naamuu)
880   She had gone to her husband almost at the end of the
      lunar month.   (Naamu)
  For the rest of that month she did not see the other moon.   (Naamu)
  She had conceived.   (Naamu)
  When the women of Manden heard this,   (Na-amu)
  They went outside the town and held a meeting under
      a baobab tree.   (Naamu)
885   They said, "Getting pregnant is one thing, delivering is
      another."   (Na-amu)
  They said, "Make miscarriage medicine,   (Naamu)
  Anything that will spoil the belly once it touches it.   (Na . . .)
  Everyone must prepare her own."   (Naamu)
  Sogolon Condé also had very powerful *dalilu*.   (Na-amu)
890   When the belly wanted to expand,   (Naamu)
  They would come and say, "Younger sister."   (Naamu)
  They would say, "This is the medicine for pregnant
      women here in Manden.   (Naamu)
  Aah, we wanted to get a child.   (Naamu)

With all of us women here,	(Naamu)
895 But we have not had any children.	(Naamu)
Therefore, if one person should bring luck to our husband,	(Naamu)
Heh, you are the one bearing it, but it is a child for all of us.	(Naamu)
Heh, M'ma, dilute this medicine in water and drink it."	(Naamu)
Heh, the Condé woman would dilute that medicine in water and drink it.	(Na-amu)
900 She would drink it.	(Naamu)
After drinking it, the belly would shrink.	(Naamu)
It would shrink away, jè!	(Na-amu)
This went on for seven years.	(Na-amu)
When the seventh year arrived,	(Naamu)
905 Sogolon Condé left the town.	(Naamu)
She prayed to God.	(Na-amu)
She said, "M'mari!	(Naamu)
That is enough!	(Naamuu)
The Mande people have done enough.	(Na-amu)
910 But I have come to you, God.	(Naamu)
I am only a stranger here.	(Naaaam')
Those who brought me,	(Na-amu)
This is beyond their power to help."	(Naamu)

The Childhood of Sunjata

That Sunjata,	(Naamu)
915 God made him into a person,	(Naamu)
Made him into a human fetus and he was born.	(Naamu)
After this son was born,	(Naamu)
When the Mande women were told about it,	(Naamu)
They gathered together again under the Mande baobab tree.	(Naamu)
920 They said, "It is one thing to give birth to a son,	(Naamu)
And another thing for him to survive."	(Naamuu)
What did they do again?	(Naamu)
Through sorcery they stretched the tendons of his two feet.	(Naamu)
They confined him to the ground.	(Na-amu)
925 His lameness forced him to remain on the ground.	(Na-amu)
One year!	(Naamu)
Two years!	(Na-amu)
Three years!	(Naamu)
Four years!	(Naamu)
930 Five years!	(Naamu)
Six years!	(Naamu)
The seventh year!	(Naamu)
The co-wives provoked Sogolon to anger.	(Naamuu)
In the seventh year there came a day,	(Na-amu)

935	When Maramajan Tarawelé went and picked some	
	baobab leaves,	(Naamu)
	While on her way back, Ma Sogolon Wulen Condé said,	(Naamu)
	She said, "Big sister Maramajan Tarawelé,	(Na-amu)
	Won't you give me a few of your baobab leaves?"	(Naamu)
	The house in which Sunjata was lodged,	(Na-amu)
940	This was said under its eaves.	(Naamu)
	Maramajan Tarawelé said, "Ah!"	(Na-amu)
	She said, "Younger sister,	(Naamu)
	You who are the owner of sons,	(Naamu)
	If you ask us for baobab leaves, what are we supposed	
	to do?	(Na-amu)
945	Your lame son is sitting right there inside the house.	(Naamu)
	You are alone in your search for baobab leaves.	
	Why don't you tell your son to get up and walk?"	(Na-amu)
	Sogolon Wulen Condé said, "Ah, that is not what I meant.	(Naamu)
	I thought I could depend on sisterhood.	(Naamu)
950	But I did not know you were upset because I had	
	this child."	(Naamuu)
	They didn't know Sunjata was listening to them.	(Na-amu)
	After that was said,	(Naamu)
	When Ma Sogolon Condé was passing by,	(Naamu)
	Sunjata said, "Mother!	(Naamuu)
955	Mother!"	(Na-amu)
	She did not answer because she knew he had overheard	
	them.	(Na-amu)
	He said, "Mother, what are they saying?"	(Naamu)
	She said, "Ah, forget about that talk."	(Naamu)
	He said, "Ah, how can I ignore that?"	
960	He said, "Mother, I will walk today."	(Na-amu)
	He said, "What they are talking about,	(Naamu)
	That you have a lame person in the house,	(Na-amu)
	That you should beg them for a baobab leaf."	(Naamu)
	He said, "I will walk today."	(Na-amu)
965	He said, "Go and get my father's ebony staff,	(Naamu)
	And bring it to me."	(Naamuu)
	He said, "I will walk today."	(Na-amu)
	Ma Sogolon Condé went and got the *sunsun* staff.[8]	(Na-amu)
	She brought it to Simbon.	(Na-amu)
970	When the ebony staff was thrust firmly into the ground,	(Naamu)
	When he attempted to stand holding the staff,	(Na-amu)
	The ebony staff broke.	(Naamuu)
	He said to her, "Ah, mother.	(Naamu)
	Go and bring my father's iron staff."	(Naamu)
975	He said, "They say you have a lame son in the house,	(Na-amu)

8. An extremely hard wood called "false ebony."

	But you gave birth to a real son.	(Naaaam')
	Nothing happens before its time.	(Naamu)
	Go and bring my father's iron staff."	(Na-amu)
	She went for the iron staff, but he also broke that.	(Naamu)
980	He said, "Go and tell my father's blacksmith,	(Naamu)
	Let him forge an iron staff so I can walk."	(Na-amu)
	The blacksmith carried one load of iron to the bellows,	(Naamu)
	Forged it and made it into an iron staff.	(Naamu)
	When it was thrust into the ground,	(Naamu)
985	When he attempted to stand, the staff bent.	(Naamuu)
	Where is that iron staff today?	(Na-amu)
	It is in Narena,	(Naaaam')
	The staff of Sunjata,	(Na-amu)
	He broke both of his father's staffs.	(Naamu)
990	The one that was forged for him is in Narena.	(Naamu)
	The one that was bent became a bow.	(Na-amu)
	Therefore, when he stood,	(Naamu)
	He lifted one foot,	(Na-amu)
	Then he lifted the other foot,	(Naamu)
995	Then the other foot.	(Naamu)
	Then his mother said, "Simbon has walked."	(Na-amu)
	It was rivalry that caused Sunjata to walk,	(Naamu)
	Because of the humiliation to his mother.	(Naamu)
	The father is everybody's, the mother is personal.	(Naamu)
1000	When you stand in the crowd,	(Na-amu)
	People do not talk about your father,	(Naamu)
	It is your mother they will talk about.	(Na-amu)
	After that, God gave him feet.	(Naamu)
	He went into the house and took his bow.	(Naamu)
1005	Some people say he made the iron staff into his bow,	(Naamu)
	He took the quiver and bow and went out of the town.	(Na-amu)
	When he got there, he embraced a baobab tree.	(Naamu)
	He shook it,	(Naamu)
	He shook it,	(Naamu)
1010	He uprooted it,	(Naamu)
	And then he put it on his shoulder.	(Naamuu)
	He brought it into his mother's yard.	(Na-amu)
	He said, "Now everyone will come here for baobab leaves."	(Naamu)
	Then when the Mande women came, they said,	(Naamu)
1015	"Aah, Sogolon Condé!	(Na-amu)
	We knew this would happen for you.	(Naamuu)
	The sacrifice that was made by everybody,	(Naamu)
	It has been answered through you."	(Na-amu)
	That was what they said as they picked the baobab leaves.	(Naamu)
1020	Before the time that Sunjata could walk,	(Naamuu)
	His younger brother Jamori had been born.	(Naamuu)
	While Sunjata was still on the ground,	(Naamu)
	Manden Bori was born.	(Naamu)
	After Sunjata walked,	(Naamu)

| 1025 | Kolonkan was born. | (Naamu) |
| | Sogolon stopped after four births. | (Na-amu) |

Step-Brother Rivalry and Nine Sorceresses of Manden

	Sunjata's ally among the nine sorceresses,	(Naamu)
	Was Jelimusoni Diawara.	(Naamu)
	In the middle of the night she went and told Simbon.	(Naamu)
1030	She said, "Sunjata, we will kill you the day after tomorrow,	(Naamu)
	If God agrees.	(Na-amu)
	You had better do something.	(Naamu)
	The big bull from your father's legacy,	(Na-amu)
	Your brother Dankaran Tuman has said that we should	
	kill you.	(Na-amu)
1035	If we kill you, he will give us that bull.	(Na-amu)
	Between sorcery and the craving for meat,	(Naamu)
	We have agreed to it.	(Na-amu)
	Watch out for yourself.	(Naamu)
	If you don't do something about it,	(Naamu)
1040	If you don't speak to them about this,	(Naamu)
	And make them an attractive offer,	(Naamu)
	The day after tomorrow,	(Naamu)
	Hunting in the bush is very important to you,	(Naamu)
	But if you go out we will kill you.	(Naamu)
1045	You are no match for us."	(Na-amu)

	Sunjata took her hand and said, "You have told me	
	the truth."	(Naamuu)
	He said, "Very well, go and tell them,	(Naamu)
	That I am the son of a Condé woman,	(Na-amu)
	They must spare me.	(Na-amuu)
1050	You should tell them that one bull,	(Naamu)
	Is not bigger than three male antelope.	(Naamuu)
	"Tell them that if they spare me,	(Naamu)
	And if God is willing,	(Naamu)
	I will give them three male antelope for the one bull.	(Naamu)
1055	Tell them to spare me,	
	They should not do what my brother asks."	(Naamu, you are right!)
	When she went and told them,	(Na-amu)
	The sorceresses said, "All we want is meat.	(Naamuu)
	Tell him if he does what he has said,	(Naamu)
1060	He will have no problem."	(Naamuu)

	When the following night had passed,	(Naamu)
	When the *sigbé* bird chirped at dawn,	(Naamu)
	Simbon took his hammock,	(Naamu)
	Put on his crocodile hat,	(Naamu)
1065	Hung his hunter's whistle on his chest,	(Na-amu)
	Took his quiver and bow,	(Naamu)
	And left the town.	(Naamu)

When he got one kilometer away from the town,	(Naamu)
He saw an antelope.	(Naamuu)
1070 He shot at it and knocked it down.	(Naamu)
He shot another arrow,	(Naamu)
Hit another antelope and knocked it down.	(Naamuu)
Again he shot an arrow,	(Naamu)
The sun did not get white before he had killed all three.	(Naamuu)
1075 God is with the just.	(Na-amu)
Everybody does what he wants,	(Naamu)
But God makes the final decision.	(Naamuu)
The chick destined to be a rooster will eventually crow,	(Naamu)
No matter what is laid in its path.	(Na-amu)
1080 It will overcome.	(Naamu)
After he killed them,	(Na-amu)
He carried the three antelope to the edge of town.	(Na-amu)
Then he went into the town.	(Naamu)
He told Jelimusoni Diawara,	(Naamu)
1085 That she should go and tell the nine sorceresses,	(Naamu)
That their meat was at the edge of town.	(Naaaam')
When they were told this, they set out.	(Naamu)
They went and found the game.	(Naamu)
They butchered them,	(Naamu)
1090 They roasted some of it,	(Naamu)
They boiled some of it.	(Naamu)
They said, "Sunjata,"	(Naamu)
They said, "Even a female genie will not harm you,	
Much less a human female."	(Na-amuu)
1095 What saved him?	(Naamu)
His hands.	(Na-amu)
When you are popular you must have an open hand.	(Naamu)
It is a man's generosity that will save him.	(Na-amu)
Nothing saved Sunjata but his hands.	(Naamu)
1100 They blessed him.	(Na-amu)
They said, "We are with you to the death.	(Naamu)
Even a female ant will never sting you.	(Na-amu)
No female genie will ever even chase you.	(Naamu)
No female wild animal will ever harm you."	(Na-amu)
1105 They spared him.	(Naamu)

Mistaken Murder and the Question of Exile

[*In an omitted passage, Dankaran Tuman and his mother conspire to have Sunjata murdered in his sleep. Meanwhile, Sunjata spends a rainy day playing the hunter's harp while he waits for the weather to change so he can go hunting.*]

Because of the rain, Sunjata was impatient to go to the bush.	(Naamu)
The hunter's calabash harp,	(Na-am . . .)

	The six-stringed harp,	(Naamu)
	He knew how to play it himself.	(Naamu)
1110	Sunjata took a hunter's harp,	(Naamu)
	He sat in his hammock,	
	And started singing to himself.	(Na-amu)
	As he sang in a low voice, some passing youths heard it.	(Naamu)
	They could not continue on their way,	(Naamu)
1115	They stood by the door.	(Naamu)
	One of them was also an apprentice hunter.	(Naamu)
	He said, "Until the rain stops, I will listen to Sunjata."	(Naamuu)
	As he stood at the door, Sunjata took snuff.	(Naamu)
	He had put some in his mouth.	(Naamu)
1120	When the snuff was wet,	(Naamu)
	He stopped playing the harp so he could spit.	(Na-amu)
	As he went to spit, he saw the young man by the door.	(Naamuu)
	He said, "Who is it?"	(Na-amu)
	The youth said, "Brother Sunjata, it is me."	(Naamu)
1125	"Ah," said Sunjata, "What are you doing here?"	(Naamu)
	He said, "Your brother sent a message,	(Naamu)
	That we should bring him some food supplies.	(Naamu)
	That's what I did, but it is raining.	(Naamu)
	A slave with wet clothes does not enter the house of	
	a noble.	(Naamuu)
1130	I am an apprentice hunter at the farm.	(Naamu)
	I heard your music, so I am standing here under the eaves.	(Naamu)
	Let me keep listening to you until the rain stops."	(Na-amuu)
	(The musket of conspiracy was being loaded in town.)	(Naamu)
	Sunjata said to him, "Come into the house."	(Naamu)
1135	The young man entered the house and sat on the edge of	
	the bed.	(Naamu)
	Simbon was playing the harp.	(Naamu)
	When he played certain parts, the young man would tap	
	his feet,	(Naamu)
	Because the harp music was so sweet.	(Na-amu)
	But he was tired.	(Naamu)
1140	The warm room felt good to him.	(Naamu)
	He became sleepy and started to nod.	(Naamu)
	Sunjata told him, "Lie on the bed."	(Naamu)
	When he lay on the bed,	(Na-amu)
	Simbon stood up and brought down his blanket and	
	covered the young man.	(Naamu)
1145	The young man slept.	(Na-amu)
	The young man was still asleep when the rain stopped.	(Naamu)
	When the rain stopped,	(Naamu)
	Sunjata forgot about the young man there.	(Na-amu)
	Simbon stood up,	(Naamu)
1150	Took his hunter's hammock,	(Naamu)
	Took his quiver and bow,	

	Took his fly whisk,	(Naamu)
	Put on his crocodile hat.	(Naamuu)
	He shut the front door and went out the back door.	(Naamu)
1155	He took a deep breath and went into the bush.	(Naamu)
	While the young man was still sleeping,	(Na-amu)
	The musket of conspiracy was loaded in the town.	(Naamu)
	While Simbon was in the bush,	(Naamu)
	Dankaran Tuman came and stood under the eaves and listened.	(Na-amu)
1160	He heard the young man snoring.	(Naamu)
	They did not know that Sunjata had left the house.	(Naamuu)
	Dankaran Tuman went and told the seven young men,	(Naamu)
	"Didn't I tell you?	(Na-amu)
	That any time it rains into the evening he sleeps?"	(Naamu)
1165	He said, "Go and get your clubs, he is asleep."	(Naamu)
	Those men got their clubs.	(Naamu)
	The seven young men came to the door,	(Naamu)
	But they were afraid of Simbon.	(Na-amu)
	They said, "Man, don't you know who Sunjata is?	(Naamu)
1170	One man cannot outdo him,	(Naamu)
	Two men cannot outdo him,	(Naamu)
	Even the seven of us cannot outdo him."	(Naamuu)
	They said, "When we go in,	(Naamu)
	Let us listen carefully.	(Naamu)
1175	The place where we hear the sound of his breathing,	(Naamu)
	Let us raise the clubs and hit him on the head.	(Naamu)
	If we only hit him on the back, he will capture us."	(Na-amu)
	They went in and surrounded the young man.	(Naamu)
	At the place where they could hear him breathing,	(Naamu)
1180	They raised the clubs and hit him on the head.	(Naamu)
	They beat him until he cooled off.	(Naamuu)
	When he was cooled off,	(Na-amu)
	They went out and told Dankaran Tuman,	(Naamu)
	That the work he had given them was finished.	(Naamu)
1185	Dankaran Tuman told his mother,	(Naamu)
	"Ahah," he said, "Mother.	(Naamu)
	The bad thing is now off our necks."	(Na-amu)
	(No matter how good one is,	(Naamu)
	You always do something bad to your enemy.)	(Naaaam')
1190	He said, "He is dead."	(Na-amu)
	"Eh! Dankaran Tuman," she said,	(Naamu)
	"Has he died?"	(Naamu)
	"Ah!" He said, "The son of the Condé woman has died today!"	(Na-amu)
	"Ah, my son!	(Naamu)
1195	I did not become the failure in my husband's home.	(Naamu)
	Now my heart is cool.	(Na-amu)

If you have killed Sunjata, *aagba*! (Naamu)
Manden Bori cannot stand up to you, (Naamu)
Jamori cannot stand up to you. (Naamu)
1200 The only one I was worried about is the one who has
  been killed." (Na-amuu)
Ma Sansun Bereté did not go back to bed. (Naamu)
Dankaran Tuman did not go back to bed. (Naamu)
Sansun Bereté said, "Heee, (Na-amu)
Just wait until Sogolon Condé knows this." (Naamu)

1205 They spent the night like that. (Na-amu)
When day broke, (Naamu)
As soon as they washed, they went to spy on Sunjata's
  mother. (Naamuu)
"Huh!" They whispered, "Don't say anything! (Naamu)
Leave it like that! (Naamu)
1210 When he stays a long time without waking up, (Naamu)
His mother will go and open the door on him." (Na-amuu)
Sansun Bereté said, "You should not say anything, (Naamu)
So it does not appear that you did it." (Naamu)
While they were there, as the soft morning sun was rising, (Naamu)
1215 They saw Sunjata coming. (Naamuu)
He was carrying three dead animals. (Naamu)
They saw the son of the Condé woman coming with three
  dead animals. (Naamuu)
One was hanging over his left shoulder, (Na-amu)
One was hanging over his right shoulder, (Naamu)
1220 One was on his head. (Naamu)
When he got there, (Na-amu)
Sansun Bereté said, "Dankaran Tuman! (Na-amu)
Didn't you say that Sunjata was dead?" (Naamu)
He said, "Mother, we really killed him." (Naamuu)
1225 She said, "Then who is this coming?" (Na-amuu)
She said, "Who is coming?" (Naamu)
He said, "It is Sunjata who is coming." (Na-amu)
When they saw that it really was Sunjata,
Dankaran Tuman urinated in his trousers. (Naamuu)
1230 When Sunjata got there, (Na-amu)
He said to Sansun Bereté, "Big mother,
Here is some wild game for you." (Naamu)
He laid another animal before his step-brother and said,
  "Big brother,
Here is one for you." (Naamu)
1235 There was no way for them to respond. (Naamuu)

He carried the last animal to his mother's place. (Na-amu)
He said, "Mother, here is your animal." (Naamu)
His mother said, "Ah, my son, thank you." (Naamuu)
He returned to his own house. (Na-amu)

1240   When he reached the door and pushed it open,   (Naamu)
Flies were all over the body, *wooooo*!   (Naaaam')
Sunjata shouted, "Mother, Mother!"   (Naamu)
He said, "Come here!"   (Naamuu)
He said, "I will kill today.   (Na-amu)
1245   From the time that I, Sunjata, was born,   (Naamuu)
I have never done anything bad.   (Na-amu)
This is the act of my brother.   (Naaaam', it's true)
I will take revenge."   (Naamu)
Ma Sogolon Condé came and opened the door.   (Naamu)
1250   Sunjata said, "The one you see lying here,   (Naamu)
I went to the bush and forgot about him.   (Naamu)
My brother's men beat him to death with their clubs."   (Naamuu)
He said, "You see this?   (Na-amu)
I will kill for this young man.   (Naamu)
1255   I know this is Dankaran Tuman's boy,   (Naamu)
But he died my death.   (Naamu)
I will prove to them that I am not the one who died."   (Na-amu)

Ma Sogolon Condé knew that when Sunjata spoke of
    revenge,   (Naamu)
Konfara would be destroyed,   (Naamuu)
1260   Because anyone known as a supporter of Dankaran
    Tuman would be killed.   (Na-amu)
Sunjata dashed out of the house.   (Naamu)
When he reached for his iron staff,   (Naamu)
His mother ran and called Jelimusoni Diawara.   (Naamu)
She said, "If you don't go right now,
1265   Your man will kill someone immediately."   (Na-amuu)
Jelimusoni Diawara went and took hold of Simbon.   (Naamu)
She said, "Simbon,   (Na-amu)
Won't you think about your mother?   (Naamu)
Simbon!   (Naamu)
1270   Won't you think of me?   (Na-amu)
Won't you leave this to God?   (Naamu, it's true, naamu)
Don't you realize that the finger has poked
    out its own eye?"   (Na-amu)
He tried to break away, but she would not let go.   (Naamu)
He struggled to get away, but she would not let go.   (Naamu)
1275   Ha! She was able to hold him.   (Naamuu)
That was what led to them going into exile.   (Naamuu)
Then Ma Sogolon Condé said,   (Naamu)
"My son Sunjata, you have no problem except for your
    popularity.   (Na-amu)
If they have started murdering people over you,   (Naamu)
1280   Should we not go away?"   (Na-amu)
(One never sells his father's homeland,   (Naamu)
But it can be pawned.)   (Na-amu)

Departure for Exile

[*In an omitted passage, Sunjata repeats his refusal to flee from his step-brother, but Sogolon argues that neither he nor Dankaran Tuman can understand the special circumstances of her background in Dò ni Kiri and how she was brought to their father because of Sunjata's special destiny. She convinces Sunjata that even if they go away, he will eventually take over the leadership of Manden.*]

	Ma Sogolon Condé then set out,	(Na-amu)
	And went to the Somono⁹ boatmen's ancestor,	
	Sansamba Sagado,	(Naamu)
1285	The Sansamba Sagado you have always heard about in the history of Manden.	(Naamu)
	The chief of the Somono was from Manden.	(Naamu)
	Sogolon went secretly to Sansamba Sagado.	(Naamuu)
	She said, "Sansamba Sagado."	(Na-amu)
	She removed her silver bracelet,	(Naamu)
1290	And handed it to the Somono ancestor Sansamba Sagado,	(Naamu)
	As the price for crossing the river at a future time.	(Na-amu)
	She removed her ankle bracelet,	(Naamu)
	And gave it to the Somono ancestor Sansamba Sagado,	(Naamu)
	As the price for crossing the river on a future date.	(Naamu)
1295	Any time that her children might go out in the middle of the night,	(Naamu)
	And ask him to take them across the river,	(Naamu)
	He would take them without anybody in Manden knowing about it.	(Naaaam')
	During the time of the organization of Manden,	(Naamu)
	Sansamba Sagado was involved with that.	(Na-amu)
1300	The Somono villages that you find,	(Naamu)
	Those towns along the bank of the river,	(Naamu)
	Those are populated by descendants of Sansamba Sagado.	(Naaaam')
	They are Mande people.	(Naamuu)
	If you talk about Manden without talking about Sansamba Sagado,	(Naamu)
1305	You have not covered the subject of Manden.	(Na-amu)
	Those days passed, and one day at three o'clock in the morning,	(Na-amu)
	Sogolon woke up her children.	(Naamu)
	She said, "The time has come for what we talked about."	(Na-amu)
	They left together.	(Naamu)
1310	When they came to the riverbank,	(Naamu)
	She took the path to go and wake Sansamba Sagado.	(Na-amu)
	She told him, "The day we talked about is today."	(Naamu)
	He was not a man to break his promise.	(Na-amu)
	He took his bamboo pole,	(Naamu)

9. An occupational term, referring to professional boatmen, canoemen, fishermen, ferry operators, etc., of Mande society.

1315 He took his paddle.	(Naamuu)
They came and met her children in the bushes on the	
bank of the river.	(Naamu)
The water had risen to the leaves on the bushes.	(Naamuu)
He went and unfastened his canoe that was attached to	
a *npeku* tree,	(Naamu)
And brought it to them, saying, "Get in!"	(Naamuu)
1320 Ma Sogolon Condé got into the canoe.	(Naamu)
Her daughter Kolonkan got in,	(Naamu)
Manden Bori got in,	(Naamu)
So'olon Jamori got in.	(Naamu)
They told Sunjata to get in, but he refused.	(Na-amu)
1325 Ma Sogolon Condé said, "Ah, Sunjata!	(Naamuu)
Do you want to cause me suffering?"	(Na-amu)
He said, "Mother,	(Naamu)
If I have told you that I will go,	(Naamu)
Take the canoe and I will join you later.	(Naamu)
1330 I will go."	(Na-amuu)
They crossed the river in the canoe.	(Naamu)
Before they could reach the other side, they saw Sunjata	
sitting on the bank.	(Naamuuu)
He had brought his *dalilu* with him.	(Na-amu)

A Visit to Soso

[*In an omitted passage, Sogolon decides to stop in Sumaworo's Soso. Meanwhile, Sumaworo's personal oracle informs him that the man who will eventually take Soso and Manden away from him not only has been born, but has grown up into a hunter and will be identifiable as the one who violates Sumaworo's taboo.*]

They were now in Soso.	(Naamuu)
1335 Sogolon Condé arrived and said, "Eh, Soso Mansa.	(Naamu)
These are the children of your former master,	
Maghan Konfara.	(Na-amu)
Their relationship with their brother Dankaran Tuman	
is strained.	(Naamu)
I have brought Sunjata and his younger siblings,	(Na-amu)
To come and put them under your protection.	(Naamuu)
1340 You should train them to be hunters,	
People who can kill their own game."	(Na-amuu)
(Oh! A message had been sent there,	
Dankaran Tuman asking them to kill Sunjata.)	(Naamu)
Sumaworo said, "Condé woman, that pleases me.	(Naamu)
1345 I agree to take them under my protection,	
So long as they do not interfere with my sacred taboo.	(Naamu)
I agree to care for them."	(Naamuu)
She said, "If God agrees, they will never spoil your taboo."	(Naamu)
He said, "Ho, if they do not interfere with my taboo."	(Naamu)
1350 He said, "I agree to protect them."	(Na-amu)
They spent that day there.	(Naamu)

That night in the evening,	(Naamu)
Ma Sogolon Condé said,	(Naamu)
That the children of Soso should go and collect a pile	
of dried cow dung,	(Na-amu)
1355 That she had brought a small amount of cotton,	(Naamu)
That she would like to spin at night,	(Na-amu)
So that she could light her lantern of conversation.	(Naamu)
They brought the cow dung to light the lantern of	
conversation.	(Na-amu)

Sumaworo took out his lute,	(Naamu)
1360 Came and sat down by people who were conversing.	(Na-amu)
Ma Sogolon Condé was content.	(Naamu)
Sunjata and the others came and sat down.	(Na-amu)
Ma Sogolon Condé said, "Wait.	(Naamu)
I will sing three songs."	(Naamu)
1365 They said, "Very well."	(Na-amu)
When anybody sang,	
Sumaworo would accompany them on the lute.	(Naamu)
For Ma Sogolon Condé's first song, she sang:	(Na-amuu)
"Big ram,	(Naamu)
1370 The pen where the rams are kept,	(Na-amu)
The leopard must not enter,	(Naamu)
Big ram.	(Naamu)
The pen where the rams are kept,	(Naamu)
The leopard must not enter."	(Na-amu)
1375 Sumaworo's lute was in harmony with her song.	(Naamu)
After that, what else did she sing?	(Naamu)
She sang: "Pit-water,	(Na-amu)
Don't compare yourself with clear water flowing over rocks,	(Naamu)
The pure white rocks.	(Naamu)
1380 Pit-water,	(Naamu)
Don't compare yourself with clear water flowing over rocks,	(Naamu)
The pure white rocks."	(Naamu)
Sumaworo's lute was in harmony with her song.	(Naamuu)
The third song she sang was:	
1385 "Big vicious dog,	(Naamu)
If you kill your vicious dog,	(Naamu)
Somebody else's will bite you,	(Naamu)
Vicious dog.	(Naamu)
If you kill your vicious dog,	(Naamu)
1390 Somebody else's will bite you."	(Naamu)
Sumaworo's lute was in harmony with her song.	(Naamuu)
The gathering then broke up.	(Naamu)

[*In omitted passages, Sumaworo performs a ritual to identify his rival for power, learns that it is Sunjata, and resolves to kill him. Sunjata intentionally violates a taboo by sitting in Sumaworo's sacred hammock, confirming that he is the rival described by the oracle.*]

Sumaworo's Tyranny over Manden

	When Sogolon and her children were in Nema,	(Naamu)
	When they were with ancestor Faran Tunkara	
	at Kuntunya,	(Naamuu)
1395	He would send Sunjata between himself and where	
	the sun sets.	(Naamu)
	Whenever war broke out, they would send for him.	(Naamu)
	Then Sunjata would come and join the army of Kuntunya.	(Naamu)
	They would march.	(Naamu)
	Whenever he captured three prisoners,	(Naamu)
1400	One captive would be for him.	(Naamu)
	Whenever he captured five prisoners,	(Naamu)
	Two captives would be for him.	(Naamu)
	Whenever he captured ten prisoners,	(Naamu)
	His share would be four captives.	(Naamu)
1405	The Kuntunya *mansa* would take six of the captives.	(Naamu)
	This is how Sunjata collected his own band of men.	(Naamu)
	He stayed there for twenty-seven years.	(Naamuu)
	Mhmm, before the end of the twenty-seventh year,	(Naamu)
	Heh! Things were very bad in Manden.	(Naaaam')
1410	Things were terrible in Manden!	(Naamu)
	Sumaworo had sent his warriors.	(Naamu)
	He was looking for Sunjata.	(Na-amu)
	He did not know where he was.	(Naamu)
	Whenever he consulted Nènèba, his oracle,	(Naamu)
1415	It would say, "Your successor has grown."	(Naamuu)
	Whenever he consulted Nènèba,	(Na-amu)
	Three age sets of young men used to fetch wood,	(Naamu)
	And pile it under the cauldron of Nènèba,	(Naaaam')
	Morning and evening.	(Naamu)
1420	That same oracle said, "Fire, fire, fire, fire, fire, fire."	(Naaaam')
	Whenever he went to it,	(Na-amu)
	He would bathe in the cauldron's medicines.	(Naamu)
	Whenever they would set out for war,	(Naamu)
	It was that Nènèba that would tell them what to sacrifice	
	for the war.	(Naamuu)
1425	Each time he woke up in the morning,	(Naamu)
	It would tell him, "Sumaworo,	(Naamuu)
	Only God knows the day.	(Na-amu)
	Your successor has grown up."	(Naamu)
	Sumaworo would question some Mande people,	(Naamu)
1430	Saying, "Has Sunjata returned to Manden?"	(Naamu)
	Meanwhile, he laid waste to Manden nine times.	(Naamu)
	As he searched for Sunjata,	(Naamu)
	The Mande people struggled,	(Naamu)
	And rebuilt it nine times.	(Naamuu)
1435	He failed to find Sunjata.	(Na-amu)

	When Sumaworo would kill,	(Naamu)
	He would tell his people to search among the bodies,	(Naamu)
	To find out if the Condé woman's son was among them.	(Na-amu)
	When Sumaworo's people would go and look,	(Naamu)
1440	They would say, "The Mande people do not know,	
	The whereabouts of the Condé woman's son."	(Naamuu)
	What he did then, was send a message to Manden,	(Naamu)
	That he wanted to see all of them at Kukuba.	(Naamu)
	He summoned all of them.	(Naamu)
1445	The leaders at that meeting were,	(Naamu)
	Turama'an,	(Naamu)
	Kankejan,	(Naamu)
	And Fakoli.	(Naamuu)
	Sunjata and his brothers were not there.	(Na-amu)
1450	When those men came,	(Naamu)
	All the men who came at that time,	(Naamu)
	Sumaworo killed them all.	(Naaaam')

	The people of Manden mourned.	(Naamu)
	He killed all the men,	(Na-amu)
1455	Except for Turama'an and Kankejan, who could disappear	
	in broad daylight,	(Naamuu)
	And Fakoli who could stand and vanish instantly.	(Naamuu)
	The people who had that kind of *dalilu*,	(Na-amu)
	Were the only ones he did not kill.	(Naamu)
	He killed all the other men who went.	(Naamu)
1460	The people of Manden wept.	(Naaaam')
	After another month had passed,	(Naamu)
	He summoned them to Bantamba,	(Naamuu)
	Saying, "I have to finish them off.	(Naamuu)
	If I continue doing that,	(Naamu)
1465	I will get my successor.	(Na-amu)
	If I continue killing human beings,	
	My successor will be among them."	(Naamu)
	He called them to Bantamba.	(Naamu)
	When they arrived at Bantamba,	(Na-amu)
1470	After the meeting he looked at the Mande people, *rrrr*,	
	And said, "Kill them all."	(Naamu)
	Only those who had the power to disappear in broad	
	daylight escaped.	(Na-amu)
	Again Manden wept.	(Naamuu)

	He summoned them to Nyèmi-Nyèmi.	(Naamu)
1475	Manden also wept for that.	(Na-amu)
	Every time Mande people were summoned,	(Naamu)
	Manden would be in mourning.	(Naamu)
	Sumaworo was killing the people of Manden.	(Naamuu)
	He would search among the bodies, hoping to identify	
	his successor.	(Naamu)

1480	Every time he killed like that,	(Naamu)
	He would go and consult his Nènèba.	(Naamu)
	The Nènèba would say, "Sumaworo, uh heh."	(Naamu)
	It would say,	
	"Up to now you have still not found him."	(Naamuu)
1485	It would say,	
	"Of all those who have been killed, he is not among them."	(Na-amu)
	He asked, "What should I do?"	(Naamu)
	It said, "Search for him."	(Naamu)
	It said, "He has reached maturity."	(Naamuu)

The Expedition to Find Sunjata and Return Him to Manden

[*In an omitted passage, the assembled elders summon diviners to learn who will be the liberator of Manden, and where he can be found. It is determined that Sunjata is the one who was foreseen, and that a special delegation must be sent to find Sogolon and her children. Volunteering are the Muslim diviners Manjan Bereté and Siriman Touré, as well as the female bard Jelimusoni Diawara and the female slave Jonmusoni Manyan. They plan to visit distant markets with food products that can be found only in Manden, as a way of finding the people they seek.*]

1490	They took the road to Kuntunya.	(Naamuu)
	When they arrived at Kuntunya,	(Naamu)
	The Kuntunya market was held on Friday.	(Naamu)
	They arrived there on Thursday evening.	(Naamuu)
	They slept outside the town.	(Naamu)
1495	At a house in that same town,	
	Ma Sogolon Condé said to her daughter Kolonkan,	(Naamu)
	She said, "Kolonkan, *aaaoy*!	(Naamu)
	My stomach is hurting me.	(Na-amu)
	Since I came from Manden,	(Naamu)
1500	This is the twenty-seventh year that I have not had *dado*.[1]	(Na-amu)
	Tomorrow morning,	(Naamu)
	Do not wash the dishes,	(Naamu)
	Do not scrub the pots,	(Naamu)
	Be the first one into the market, my child,	(Naamu)
1505	So I can have some *dado* to eat."	(Naamuu)
	When an eater of *dado* goes a long time without any,	
	the stomach hurts.	(Na-amu)
	All night she was complaining of that to her daughter.	(Naamu)
	The Mande people had brought *dado*,	
	But they spent the night outside of town.	(Naamu)
1510	As soon as the sun started to show its face,	(Naamu)
	Manjan Bereté said, "Take the things into the market."	(Naamu)
	The two women went and sat outside the covered part	
	of the market.	(Naamu)

---

1. Dried hibiscus blossoms used in food and drink preparation.

The two women had *dado* there,   (Naamu)
They set it out on display.   (Naamu)
1515 Ma So'olon Wulen Condé said to Kolonkan,   (Naamu)
"Go early to the market so you can get what you want."   (Naamu)

When Kolonkan arrived at one place,   (Naamu)
She saw two women standing there with *dado*.   (Naamu)
She clapped her hands.   (Na-amu)
1520 She said, "My mother has *dalilu*.   (Naamu)
From the time we came from Manden,   (Naamu)
She has not said anything about *dado*.   (Naamu)
It was only yesterday that she suddenly spoke of *dado*,   (Naamu)
And here it is.   (Naamu)
1525 Heh! My mother has *dalilu*."   (Naamu)
When she reached the *dado*,   (Naamu)
She did not even stop to greet the *dado* seller.   (Naamu)
She immediately reached for the *dado* and put some
      in her mouth.   (Naamu)
Jelimusoni Diawara said,   (Naamu)
1530 "Eh! You, girl, are impolite!   (Na-amu)
If you don't greet us first,
Don't touch our merchandise without asking us."   (Na-amu)
"Eeeh," said the girl, "I was so surprised!   (Naamu)
My mother told me to come to the market today to see
      if I could find *dado*.   (Na-amu)
1535 She said she has gone so long without eating the old things
      of Manden,
That her stomach hurts.   (Naamu)
Since we arrived here, we have not seen *dado*,
We have not seen anyone who sells it.   (Naamu)
I have just seen it and tasted it,   (Naamu)
1540 Because it is something we always used to have."   (Naamu)
Tunku Manyan Diawara said, "Who are you?"   (Naamu)
She asked, "Where do you come from?"   (Naamu)
"Ah, mother," replied Kolonkan,
"We come from Manden."   (Na-amu)
1545 "Who is with you here?"   (Naamu)
Kolonkan said, "I am here with my mother Sogolon
      Wulen Condé,   (Na-amu)
With my elder brother Sunjata."   (Naamu)
"Aaah! You are the people we have come for!   (Na-amu)
Our road has been good,   (Na-amu)
1550 Let us go to your house."   (Na-amu)

[*In an omitted passage, Kolonkan conducts the Mande delegation to her house
for a joyful reunion with Sogolon. The delegates announce that they have been
sent to ask Sogolon to return to Manden because Sunjata is needed there. Sogolon explains that her sons are hunting in the bush and concerns herself with
providing the customary hospitality to the guests.*]

Kolonkan Finds Meat for Guests from Manden

When they had given lodgings to the visitors from Manden, (Naamu)
Sogolon called Kolonkan. (Naamu)
She said, "Kolonkan, come here." (Naamu)
She said, "Go and look on the meat-drying rack. (Naamu)
1555 See if there is any meat, (Naamu)
Because these people who came from Manden are hungry." (Naamu)
Kolonkan went and looked. (Naamu)
She came back and said, "Mother!" (Naamu)
She said, "There is no fresh meat." (Naamu)
1560 "Eh," said Sogolon, "It will take a long time for the dried
    meat to cook." (Naamu)
Kolonkan was very happy. (Naamu)
She had long since reached the age of marriage, (Naamu)
And she knew that, (Naamu)
These people would not leave her behind. (Naamu)
1565 When she arrived in Manden, (Naamu)
She would be married. (Naamu)
She was feeling happy. (Naamu)
She told her mother, "Just let things be for now." (Naamu)
Kolonkan went out of the town. (Naamu)
1570 She sniffed over here, (Naamu)
But she did not smell her brothers in that direction. (Naamu)
She sniffed over there, (Naamu)
She did not smell her brothers in that direction either. (Naamu)
When she sniffed in the direction of the sunset, (Naamu)
1575 She smelled her brothers there. (Naamu)
She went into her *dalilu, shuwe!* (Naamu)

She went after her brothers. (Naamu)
When she went after them she found, (Naamu)
That they had killed a bushbuck that day. (Naamu)
1580 They had also killed a roan antelope. (Naamu)
She opened the animals, (Naamu)
She removed some internal pieces. (Naamu)
She took them out of there, (Naamu)
And went home with them, (Naamu)
1585 Without making any exterior cuts on the animal carcasses. (Naamu)
Kolonkan brought home the meat. (Naamu)
She said, "Mother!" (Naamu)
She said, "I went after my brothers, (Naamu)
And I have brought back some fresh meat." (Naamu)
1590 Her mother said, "Did you see them?" (Naamu)
"Oh," she said, "I saw the work they did." (Naamu)
Her mother said, "Did you not tell them that they should
    meet you in town?" (Naamu)
Kolonkan replied, "I thought you only wanted fresh meat." (Naamu)
Sogolon said, "Go and cut the meat into pieces, (Naamu)

1595 Cook some and put it over rice,	(Naamu)
And serve it to our guests."	(Naamu)
Kolonkan did that.	(Naamu)
After saying that,	(Naaam)
Ma So'olon Wulen Condé herself went out of the town.	(Naamu)
1600 She had agreed on a way of signaling Sunjata,	(Naamu)
And she went to do that	(Naamu)
Sunjata heard her and said to his younger siblings,	(Naamu)
"Let us butcher the game."	(Naamu)
He said, "Mother has called me.	(Naamu)
1605 Let us go home."	(Naaaa')
The game they had killed,	(Naamu)
They went to butcher the roan antelope.	(Naamu)
They found that its internal organs were missing.	(Naamu)
They went to butcher the bushbuck.	(Naamu)
1610 They found that its internal organs were missing.	(Naamu)
Sunjata said, "Manden Bori,	(Naamu)
Can God create an animal without internal organs?"	(Naaaa')
Manden Bori said, "Brother, that is not possible."	(Naamu)
He said, "Any animal created by God,	(Naamu)
1615 They all have internal organs.	(Naamu)
Let us butcher what remains of the animals."	(Naamu)
He said, "This was done by our little sister, Kolonkan."	(Naamu)
He said, "I will not spare her,	
She will soon know that I am wearing trousers.	(Naamu)
1620 Eh! Kolonkan came from town,	(Naamu)
Came and took the internal organs of the animals we killed,	(Naamu)
Without making any external cuts.	(Naamu)
Does she have to prove her female powers to us?	(Naamu)
We will not fail to see her in town."	(Naamu)
1625 Everyone has his own *dalilu*.	(Naamu)
That is why it is good for children of the same mother	
to be in harmony.	(Naaaa')

Manden Bori's Anger and Kolonkan's Curse

When the hunters returned,	(Naamu)
When Kolonkan and Manden Bori made eye contact,	(Naamu)
Eyes that often watch one another do not forget.	(Naamu)
1630 Kolonkan ducked behind her mother.	(Naamu)
Manden Bori paid no attention to the strangers,	(Naamu)
He was ready to pounce.	(Naamu)
Manden Bori stood his musket against the wall.	(Naamu)
He passed through the gathering of people.	(Naamu)
1635 He started to run after Kolonkan,	(Naamu)
Chased her into the main house.	
They did not stop there,	(Naamu)
They ran into a cooking hut.	(Naamu)

They did not stop there.	(Naamu)
1640 On their way back,	(Naamu)
He tripped her and threw her down.	(Naamu)
Her wrapper came loose.	(Naamuu)
Ma Sogolon Condé said, "Eh!	
Manden Bori, you are envious."	(Naamu)
1645 Kolonkan stood up.	(Naamu)
She said, "You have shamed me in front of the	
Mande people.	(Naamu)
I am the one who has been shamed.	(Na-amu)
Could you not overlook this when I was acting in your	
own interest?"	(Naamu)
Because of the power of Manden Bori's sorcery,	(Na-amu)
1650 The meat that had been fried and saved for them,	(Naamu)
When he touched it, fresh blood began to flow from it.	(Naamuu)
Kolonkan said, "Are you still trying to embarrass me?	(Naamu)
I was protecting your reputation.	(Na-amu)
The Mande people came to you on the question of kingship.	(Naamu)
1655 Because you have done this to me,	(Naamu)
The kingship will eventually be passed to	
your descendants,	(Naamu)
But they will never agree on one ruler until the trumpet	
is blown."	(Naamu)

[*Sogolon subsequently dies, and Sunjata tells Manden Bori to request a plot of land for her burial.*]

The Burial of Sogolon and Departure from Nema

Manden Bori took the path to town.	(Na-amu)
He met with Faran Tunkara, the *mansa* of Nema.	(Naamu)
1660 He said "Mansa."	(Na-amu)
He said, "My brother says that I should come and tell you,	(Naamu)
That my mother is dead.	(Naaaam')
If you agree,	(Naamu)
You should give him land,	(Naamu)
1665 So he can bury his mother."	(Na-amu)
Faran Tunkara had been unhappy to see the messengers	
come from Manden.	(Na-amu)
Because from the time Sunjata arrived, up to that day,	(Naamu)
He did not engage in any battle that was lost by the people	
of Kuntunya.	(Na-amu)
Every campaign he went on, he returned with slaves.	(Naamu)
1670 But he could not detain Sunjata, because he came by his	
own choice.	(Na-amu)
He wanted to start a quarrel so he could detain Sunjata.	(Naamu)
Nema Faran Tunkara said, "Manden Bori,	(Na-amu)

Go and tell your brother,	(Naamu)
That I, Nema Faran Tunkara, say,	(Na-amu)
1675 That you did not bring a piece of land with you	
from Manden,	(Naamuu)
That I am the owner of this place,	(Na-amu)
That you should take your corpse,	
Load it on your head, and go to Manden.	(Naamu)
Carry her back the same way you brought her.	(Naamu)
1680 Tell him that if you bury her in my land,	(Naamu)
I will force her removal with gunpowder."	(Naamu)

He said, "Go and tell your brother that."	(Naamu)
When Manden Bori was told this,	(Na-amu)
He took the path back to report to Sunjata.	(Naamu)
1685 Manjan Bereté said, "What kind of man is this?"	(Naamu)
He said, "Simbon, let me go and give him the message."	(Na-amu)
"Eee," said Sunjata, "Leave it like that.	(Naamu)
Huh, he will provide the land.	(Na-amu)
Ah! I have spent twenty-seven years here.	(Naamu)
1690 I am in his army.	(Na-amu)
And he says I should carry my mother's body back	
to Manden?	(Naamu)
He will soon provide the land."	(Na-amu)
He said to Manden Bori, "Go back and tell him,	(Naamu)
That I, the son of the Condé woman say,	(Naamu)
1695 That he should give me land,	(Naamu)
So my mother can be buried there.	(Naamuu)
Tell him it is I who say so."	(Na-amu)
When Tunkara was told this,	(Naaaam')
He said to Manden Bori,	(Naamu)
1700 "I do not want ever to see you here again."	(Na-amu)
He said, "I have known from the time you first came here,	
That you are a hot-headed man.	(Naamu)
Go and tell your brother,	(Na-amu)
That I do not go back on what I said twice.	(Naamu)
1705 Tell him I have no land for him here."	(Naamu)

Manden Bori went and told this to Sunjata.	(Naamu)
Sunjata said, "He will soon provide the land."	(Naamu)
He took the path that went behind the house.	(Naamu)
He picked up a fragment of old clay pot,	(Naamu)
1710 He picked up a piece of old calabash,	(Na-amu)
He picked up the feather of a guinea fowl.	(Naamu)
He picked up a partridge feather.	(Na-amu)
He added a stick of bamboo to these.	(Naamu)
He put the things together, gave them to Manden	
Bori, and said,	
1715 "Tell him that I say he should give me land to	
bury my mother in.	(Naamu, his land price)

If he needs a price for his land, this is his
    land price. (Naamu)
Let him agree for me to lay my mother in the ground." (Na-amu)
When Faran Tunkara was given these things, (Naamu)
Manden Bori said, "My brother says this is your
    land price,
1720 That you should agree to give him land." (Naamu)
Faran Tunkara said, "Is this what you pay for land
    in your country? (Na-amu)
Huh, Manden Bori? (Naamuu)
I do not ever want to see you here again. (Na-amu)
Take these things and go away." (Naamu)

1725 His *jeli* man was sitting there beside him. (Naamu)
He said, "He should not take those things away from here. (Na-amu)
Heh! This is an important message that has been sent
    to you." (Naaaam')
The *jeli* said, "Mba, when these people came, (Naamu)
Did I not tell you that you should kill him? (Naamuu)
1730 Did you not say he had come to place himself in your care, (Na-amu)
And that you must not do anything to him? (Naamu)
Ahuh! He has said something to you. (Naamu)
There is a message in these things that were sent. (Naamu)
If you do not understand it, I will tell you the meaning." (N . . .)
1735 Faran Tunkara said, "All right, tell me the meaning." (Na-amu)
The *jeli* said, "This piece of bamboo means, (Naamu)
That you should give him land so he can bury his
    mother in it. (Naamu)
If you do not give him land, (Naamu)
The Mande people will come and take it. (Naamu)
1740 If they came and called him for the kingship, (Na-amu)
After he finishes fighting that war for Manden, (Naamu)
He will take the army of Manden, (Naamu)
He will bring it here to Nema. (Naamu)
He will break Nema like an old clay pot. (Naamu)
1745 He will break Nema like a calabash. (Naamu)
This is the old calabash. (Naamu)
The guinea fowls and the partridges will take dust
    baths in the ruins of Nema. (Naamu)
These are the feathers of those guinea fowls and partridges. (Naamu)
You will not see anything growing here but weeds. (Naamu)
1750 This piece of bamboo stick is from the ruins." (Naamuu)

Mansa Tunkara was a good debater. (Naamu)
All arguments went in his favor. (Na-amu)
Faran Tunkara said, "I am right." (Naamu)
The *jeli* said, "How can you be right in this?" (Na-amu)
1755 Faran Tunkara said, "The reason I am right," (Naamu)
He said, "Since these people arrived here, (Naamu)

	This is their twenty-seventh year.	(Naamu)
	Those three men are in my army.	(Naamu)
	During that time I lost no battles.	(Naamu)
1760	They never cheated me,	(Naamu)
	They were never disobedient to me,	(Naamu)
	I never had to discipline them for women trouble.	(Naamu)
	But since their mother has died,	(Naamu)
	Are they going to say the corpse is mine,	
1765	Or will they just demand that I give them land?"	(Naamu)
	Everyone agreed that they should have observed the custom of saying,	
	"This is your corpse."	(Naamu)
	Faran Tunkara said, "Ah! This is why I refused."	(Naamu)
	Faran Tunkara said, "Eh! If they are children,	(Naamu)
1770	A child that is well-mannered,	(Naamu)
	They should have said that God has made this my opportunity,	(Naamu)
	That this is my corpse.	(Naamuu)
	Should they look for land to lay their mother in?	(Na-amu)
	Did they show me any respect?"	(Naamu)
1775	Everybody said, "You are right!"	(Naamu)
	Manjan Bereté himself came and said, "You are right."	(Naamu)
	"Very well," he said, "If I am right,	(Naamu)
	Give her to me and I will do the funeral."	(Na-amu)
	The woman's funeral was conducted as if she were a man.	(Naamu)
1780	Cows were killed,	(Naamu)
	Muskets were fired,	(Naamu)
	The special drum was beaten.	(Naamu)
	This all started with Ma So'olon Wulen Condé.	(Na-amu)
	Then they took the body to the town of Kuntunya.	(Naamu)
1785	On Thursday,	(Naamu)
	They did the burial.	(Naamu)
	When they were finished with the burial,	(Naamu)
	Simbon asked permission to take his leave.	(Na-amu)
	He said, "I will leave tomorrow."	(Naamu)
1790	When it was said, "I will go tomorrow,"	(Na-amu)
	There was no problem of debt between them.	(Naamu)
	Faran Tunkara said, "Go with my blessing."	(Naamuu)
	He said, "I give you the road."	(Naamu)
	Sunjata took the road toward home.	(Naamu)
1795	But Manden suffered while he was away.	(Na-amuu)
	It was Sumaworo who did it.	(Naamu)
	The only people left here were those with *dalilu*.	(Na-amu)
	Those who had *dalilu*,	(Na-amu)
	Sumaworo had caused even them to suffer.	(Naamu)
1800	The people said,	(Naamu)
	"You should take the legacy,	(Na-amuu)

So that Manden can be helped.	(Naamuu)
You have been called to take the legacy."	(Naamu)
"Take your legacy," *ko ila kè ta,* came to be spoken	
as "Keita."[2]	(Na-amu)

[*In an omitted passage Sunjata accepts the leadership of Manden, and an elaborate series of sacrifices is performed in preparation for war against Soso.*]

Fakoli Reveals His Power

1805	While they were in a meeting,	(Naamu)
	A message from Sumaworo arrived,	(Naamu)
	Saying that the Mande people must be told,	(Na-amu)
	That he has been expecting them for a long time.	(Mmmm)
	He said it had been a long time since their *mansa* arrived.	(Na-amu)
1810	He said he had not seen any messenger.	(Naamu)
	He said that since Sunjata was now there,	(Naamu)
	He wanted to see those people,	(Naamu)
	On the fourteenth of the new month at Dakajalan.	(Na-amu)
	The battle had now been set.	(Naamu)
1815	After that, Sunjata responded.	(Na-amuu)
	As soon as he heard that message,	
	He had them beat the signal drum.	(Naamu)
	Everybody went to the council hall.	(Na-amu)
	On their way to the council hall,	(Naamu)
1820	Fakoli was thinking, *frrrru!*	(Na-amuu)
	They were going to march against Soso.	(Naamu)
	But his mother and Sumaworo had suckled at the	
	same breast.	(Na-amu)
	He was wondering if he and the Mande people should	
	attack Sumaworo.	(Naamu)
	Fakoli's mind was on that.	(Na-amu)
1825	Fakoli thought, "As soon as I get to the council hall,	(Naamu)
	I will ask the Mande people,	(Na-amu)
	If they will give me leave so I can go to Soso.	(Na-amu)
	Let Manden come and fight both me and my uncle."	(Na-amu)
	When he got to the council hall,	(Naamu)
1830	That is what he told them.	(Naamu)
	But before he entered,	(Naamu)
	Manden Bori ridiculed him.	(Na-amu)
	When he was laughed at by Manden Bori,	(Naamu)
	Fakoli became angry.	(Na-amu)
1835	Whenever he entered the council hall,	(Naamu)
	Manden Bori would laugh at him.	(Naamu)
	That is why Fakoli said, "Turama'an,	(Na-amu)
	Let me say this to you.	(Naamu)

2. The alleged origin of Sunjata's family name, Keita.

	Tell this to Simbon:	(Na-amu)
1840	Let him ask his younger brother why he laughs at me.	(Naaaam')
	Everyone enters the council hall,	(Naamu)
	But whenever I enter, Manden Bori laughs at me.	(Na-amu)
	Why does he laugh at me?	(Naamu)
	What have I done to him?"	(Naamuu)
1845	When Sunjata was told this,	(Na-amu)
	Sunjata said, "Stop laughing at him.	
	Did you not hear Fakoli saying that you are ridiculing him?"	(Naamu)
	He said, "Why are you laughing at him?"	(Naamu)
	"Ah," Manden Bori said, "Big brother,	(Naamu)
1850	Whenever the tall men enter the council hall,	(Na-amu)
	They must duck their heads.	(Naamu)
	Fakoli is only one and a half arm-spans tall,	(Naamu)
	But when he enters, he also ducks his head.	
	That is what makes me laugh.	(Na-amu)
1855	Aaah, Fakoli, heh, heh."	(Naamu)
	Fakoli said, "Turama'an, tell Simbon,	(Naamu)
	That he should tell his younger brother,	(Naamu)
	That short Mande people can do things that tall Mande people cannot do."	(Na-amu)
	He said, "Let him believe that."	(Naamuu)
1860	When Manden Bori was told this,	(Na-amu)
	He said, "I will not believe that until I see it.	(Naamu)
	Do you believe that?	
	I do not believe that."	(Naamu)
	Fakoli picked up his goatskin rug.	(Naamu)
1865	He laid it in the center of the council hall.	(Na-amu)
	He sat down on the rug.	(Naamu)
	He waved his hand,	(Naamu)
	He grunted,	(Naamu)
	He grunted.	(Naamu)
1870	He raised the roof from the house.	
	The sun shone in on everybody.	(Na-amuu)
	He said, "Manden Bori, what about that?"	(Naamu)
	Manden Bori said, "You spoke the truth."	(Naamu)
	They were fair about crediting one another with the truth,	(Na-amu)
1875	They were always in search of more *dalilu*.	(Naamuu)
	They asked Fakoli to replace the roof where it belonged.	(Naamu)
	They said, "No tall man of Manden has done such a thing."	(Na-amu)
	Then Fakoli placed his hand in the middle of the council hall floor.	(Naamu)
	He crouched there and wrinkled his face,	(Naamu)
1880	Wrinkled his face!	(Naamu)
	Wrinkled his face!	(Naamu)
	He squeezed everyone against the wall.	(Na-amu)
	That was the beginning of the song "Nyari Gbasa."[3]	(Naamu)

3. A *fasa* or praise song referring to this episode of the Fakoli legend.

	They sang: "Fakoli, our arms will break,	(Na-amu)
1885	Fakoli, our heads will burst,	(Naamu)
	Fakoli, our stomachs will rupture."	(Na-amu)
	That song belongs to the Koroma family.	(Naamu)
	They said, "Stop that!"	(Na-amu)
	They said, "No tall man of Manden has done such a thing."	(Naamu)

Fakoli Explains His Dilemma and Takes His Leave from Manden

1890	After Fakoli did that, he spoke to the assembled elders.	(Naamu)
	He said, "Turama'an, I say to you,	
	I say to Simbon,	(Naamu)
	I say to everyone in the council hall,	(Na-amu)
	Sumaworo has sent a message,	(Naamu)
1895	That we should meet at Dakajalan.	(Naamu)
	My mother and Sumaworo,	(Naamu)
	They are children of three Touré women.	(Na-amu)
	For me to participate in Manden's attack on my uncle,	(Naamu)
	I would be shamed by that.	(Na-amu)
1900	If you will permit me,	(Naamu)
	Give me leave and let me go to Soso.	(Naamu)
	Let them come and attack me and my uncle.	(Naamu)
	Let them fight me and my uncle."	(Na-amuuu)
	Manden Bori refused to repeat this to Sunjata,	
1905	But Sunjata heard about it anyway.	
	He said, "Manden Bori, have I not told you?	(Na-amu)
	Fakoli is right.	(Naamu)
	You and I have uncles whose home is Dò ni Kiri.	(Naamu)
	What if it were said that Dò ni Kiri would be attacked?	(Na-amu)
1910	Would you and I stay here?"	(Naamu)
	Manden Bori said, "Would anyone dare to do that?"	(Naamu)
	"Oh," said Sunjata, "There you are.	
	If Fakoli says he is going to help his mother's kinsman,	(Na-amu)
	Leave him alone and let him go."	(Naamu)
1915	"But," said Sunjata, "Fakoli,	(Na-amu)
	You have done well for Manden.	(Naaaam')
	The nine invasions of Manden that are talked about,	(Na-amu)
	And the nine efforts to rebuild it,	(Naamu)
	You did well in all of that.	(Na-amu)
1920	Therefore, if you should say that,	(Naamu)
	You are going to help your uncle,	(Naamu)
	But if we meet during the battle,	(Naamu)
	There is no brotherhood,	(Naamu, true, naamu)
	There is no friendship.	(Na-amu)
1925	It must not be said that so-and-so is ungrateful.	(Naamu)
	When the shooting starts, that is not in the gunsmoke.	(Naaaam')
	That is all I have to say."	(Na-amu)
	Fakoli said, "Bisimillahi."[4]	(Naamu)

4. "With God's blessing."

Fakoli returned to his house for the night.   (Naamu)
1930 In the morning he bathed in the water of his seven
         medicine pots.   (Naamu)
      He took his battleaxe and hung it on his shoulder.   (Naamu)
      He brought out his horse and mounted it.   (Na-amu)
      His wife Keleya Konkon,   (Naamu)
      He lifted her up and sat her behind him.   (Na-amu)
1935 He took the ends of his scarf and tied them together.   (Naamu)
      He said, "Because I know the kind of man my uncle is,   (Naamu)
      He might wait for me on the road."   (Naamuu)
      While Fakoli was getting ready to leave,   (Naamu)
      Another message came from Sumaworo,   (Na-amu)
1940 That Fakoli should be told,   (Naamu)
      That Sumaworo had been informed of Fakoli's plan to go
         and help him,   (Naamu)
      And that he must not go to Soso.   (Na-amu)

      Sumaworo said he had been informed that if Fakoli went
         to Soso,
      And if the Mande people should succeed in
         conquering him,   (Naamu)
1945 That they would replace Sumaworo with Fakoli.   (Na-amu)
      He said that if Fakoli went to Soso,   (Naamu)
      His feet would bring his head.   (Naaaam')
      The Mande people said if Fakoli went,   (Naamu)
      They would cut off his head.   (Na-amu)
1950 The Soso people said if he went,   (Naamu)
      His feet would bring his head.   (Na-amu)
      Fakoli laughed,   (Naamu)
      "I will not die for Sunjata,
      I will not die for Sumaworo."   (Na-amu)
1955 Even up to tomorrow, that expression is often quoted.   (Naamu)
      He said, "Go and tell my uncle that I will soon be there.   (Na-amu)
      If I really plan to do what he said,   (Naamu)
      Then he will succeed with what he threatens to do to me.   (Na-amu)
      But if that is not my intention,   (Naamu)
1960 I will go to Soso today.   (Naamu)
      Tell him to get ready."   (Na-amuu)

Fakoli Finds Trouble in Soso

      When Sumaworo was told that Fakoli came alone,   (Naamu)
      With only him, his wife, and his slave,   (Naamu)
      Sumaworo told Bala Fasali, "Take the bala[5] and welcome
         my nephew."   (Naamu)
1965 He took the bala,   (Naamu)

---

5. Also known as *balafon*, the indigenous xylophone. "Bala Fasali": an unusual pronunciation of this famous bard's name, which is usually given as Bala Fasaké, or a variant thereof.

	And that was the beginning of the heroes' song "Janjon":[6]	(Na-amu)
	"Eh, Fakoli!	(Naamu)
	You became a son.	(Na-amu)
	If death is inevitable,	(Naamu)
1970	A formidable child should be born.	(Na-amu)
	The Mande people said,	(Naamu)
	That if you come, they will wait for you on the road.	(Naamu)
	The people of Soso said,	(Naamu)
	That if you come, your feet will bring your head.	(Na-amu)
1975	Knowing that, you still had no fear.	(Naamu)
	If death is inevitable,	(Naamu)
	A formidable child should be born."	(Na-amu)
	"Janjon" belonged to the Koroma family.	(Naamu, it's true)

	Sumaworo stood up and raised his elephant tail in salute.	(Naamu)
1980	He was welcoming Fakoli.	(Na-amu)
	Fakoli came and sat down.	(Naamu)
	He explained why he had come.	(Naamu)
	He said, "Bala Fasali, you take part in this.	(Na-amu)
	Let Sumaworo be a part of this.	(Naamu)
1985	If you see that I have come,	(Naamu)
	Sumaworo has done many things.	(Na-amu)
	If you see that I was invisible,	(Naamu)
	I came in good faith.	(Na-amu)
	The three Touré women gave birth to two of you,	
1990	My mother and Sumaworo.	(Naamu)
	Since a war has been declared,	(Na-amu)
	I have thought about my mother.	(Naamu)
	If my mother had been a man,	(Naamu)
	The war would have come to her as well as to Sumaworo.	(Naamu)
1995	That is why I decided to be here in place of my mother.	(Na-amu)
	That is the reason I came.	(Naaaam')
	I have come to him through the will of God.	(Naamu)
	Let us unite.	(Naamu)
	The war that is coming,	(Naamu)
2000	Let us fight it together."	(Na-amu)
	Sumaworo was pleased.	(Naaaam')
	Sumaworo said, "Bala Fasali, I say this to you,	
	I say this to Fakoli.	(Naamu)
	Tell him that I appreciate his words.	(Na-amu)
2005	I am well pleased,	(Naamu)
	I am glad."	(Naamu)

	Fakoli came and met Sumaworo's wives.	(Naamu)
	Three hundred wives, thirty wives, and three wives.	(Naamuu)

6. One of the oldest and most famous songs of Manden, said to have been originally composed for Fakoli but in later times played to honor any distinguished personage.

Fakoli's only wife was Keleya Konkon. (Na-amu)

2010 What did Sumaworo say then? (Naamu)

He said, "Fakoli has come at the time when, (Naamu)

The oracle Nènèba says that I am going to fight a war, (Na-amu)

That the sacrifice for that is, (Naamu)

Three hundred dishes, thirty dishes, and three dishes. (Na-amu)

2015 That is what I want to be prepared the day after tomorrow,
  on Friday. (Naaaam')

If we are allies, let Fakoli be told about that." (Na-amu)

Then Fakoli said, "That is a good thing. (Naamu)

Since I have come to take the place of my mother, (Na-amu)

The one bowl that my mother would have provided, (Naamu)

2020 My wife will cook that." (Naamu)

When they heard that, the Soso women said, *paki*! (Na-amu)

They said, "The Soso women and the Mande woman,

We will soon see how they cook." (Naamu)

That was insulting to Keleya Konkon. (Na-amu)

2025 Keleya Konkon said, "I have said that I would build my
  fire near theirs. (Naamu)

Go and look for a pot and bring it to me. (Na-amu)

Since they have said that, (Naamu)

They will learn that Manden also has kitchens." (Naamu)

She told her husband to find a cooking pot. (Na-amu)

2030 Her husband found a cooking pot and gave it to her. (Naamu)

Sumaworo's three hundred dishes and thirty dishes and
  three dishes, (Naamu)

Among them were beans, (Naamu)

Among them was rice, (Naamu)

Among them was fonio,[7] (Na-amu)

2035 Among them was cereal paste, (Naamu)

Among them was millet wafers, (Naamu)

Among them was wheat meal, (Na-amu)

Among them was cassava,[8] (Naamu)

Among them was porridge, (Naamu)

2040 All of those were among the three hundred dishes. (Na-amu)

Fakoli's wife said, "Look for a cooking pot. (Naamu)

Bring rice, (Na-amu)

Bring pounded cassava, (Naamu)

Bring fonio. (Naamu)

2045 If God agrees, (Naamu)

Whatever the consequences, (Naamu)

The bards will bear witness to this." (Na-amu)

She set her one pot on the fire. (Naamu)

Those who were cooking rice, (Naamu)

2050 When they were putting rice in their pots, (Naamu)

---

7. A variety of millet.

8. Also called yuca or manioc, a starchy tuberous root.

	She would put rice in her one pot,	(Naamu)
	Then she would sit down.	(Na-amu)
	Those who were cooking the fonio,	(Naamu)
	When they were putting fonio in their pots,	(Naamu)
2055	She would put the fonio in her one pot,	(Naamu)
	Then she would sit down.	(Naamu)
	Everything the Soso women put in their individual pots,	(Naamu)
	She put all the same things in her one pot.	(Naamu)
	When the women started dishing out rice,	(Naamu)
2060	She would take her rice bowl,	(Naamu)
	She would dish out her rice.	(Naamu)
	When the women started dishing out the fonio,	(Naamu)
	She would take her fonio bowl,	(Naamu)
	She would dish out her fonio from the same pot,	(Naamu)
2065	And put it into the fonio bowl.	(Naamu)
	Three hundred things,	(Naamu)
	And thirty things,	(Naamu)
	Were produced by Sumaworo's wives.	(Naamu)
	Three hundred things,	(Naamu)
2070	Thirty things,	(Naamu)
	And three things,	(Naamu)
	Were produced by Fakoli's wife in one pot,	(Naamuu)
	So the scandalmongers would not get the best of her.	(Na-amuu)
	The scandalmongers went and told Sumaworo,	(Na-amu)
2075	"Did we not tell you,	(Naaaam')
	That Fakoli came to take your place?	(Na-amu)
	You have three hundred wives and thirty wives and three wives.	(Naamu)
	You have produced three hundred dishes, thirty dishes and three dishes.	(Naamu)
	Your nephew has only one wife,	(Naamu)
2080	But he has also prepared three hundred dishes, thirty dishes and three dishes.	(Naamu)
	In fact his dishes are bigger than yours.	(Na-amu)
	Everything that you produced, he also produced.	(Naamu)
	He came to take your place.	(Naamuu)
	If you think this Fakoli business is not serious,	(Na-amu)
2085	He will take Soso away from you even before you go to war."	(Naamu)
	Sumaworo said, "Huh?"	(Na-amu)
	He said, "Oho."	(Naamu)
	He assembled his people.	(Naamu)
	The scandalmonger who brought the gossip to him,	(Na-amu)
2090	Sumaworo told him,	(Naamu)
	That he should go and call Fakoli.	(Naamu)
	The scandalmonger went and stood on the road.	(Na-amu)
	He did not go to where Fakoli was,	(Naamu)

	Then he went back to Sumaworo.	(Naamu)
2095	He came and said, "I have called him,"	
	But he had not gone to Fakoli.	(Na-amu)
	Much time passed without Fakoli coming to see Sumaworo.	(Naamu)
	When Sumaworo called someone,	(Naamu)
	He expected the person to arrive one minute after the messenger returned.	(Na-amu)
2100	"Ah!" He said,	
	"Did you not see my nephew?"	(Naamu)
	The scandalmonger said, "I saw him."	(Na-amu)
	"Ah, did you not call him?"	(Naamu)
	"I called him."	(Naamu)
2105	"All right, go and tell him I am waiting for him."	(Naamu)
	The scandalmonger went again and stood on the road.	(Naamu)
	He came back and told Sumaworo,	(Naamu)
	He said, "I have called him."	(Naamu)
	Much time passed and Fakoli did not appear.	(Naamu)
2110	Sumaworo sent another person.	(Naamu)
	He said, "You go and tell Fakoli,	(Naamu)
	That I am waiting for him."	(Naamu)
	Sumaworo was very angry.	(Naamu)
	The messenger went to Fakoli and said,	(Naamu)
2115	"Fakoli, This is the third time you have been called,	(Naamu)
	But you did not come.	
	Who do you think you are?"	(Naamu)
	Fakoli said, "Me?	(Naamuu)
	Was I called three times?"	(Na-amu)
2120	"Yes, the message came and came again."	
	Fakoli said, "Me?"	(Naamu)
	He said, "Mba, I refuse."	(Naamu)
	That messenger ran back to tell Sumaworo,	(Naamu)
	"Your nephew refuses to come."	(Na-amu)
2125	Sumaworo said, "I have heard it.	(Naamu)
	You tell me, Sumaworo, 'I refuse'?"	(Na-amu)
	When the last messenger had returned from Fakoli's place,	(Naamu)
	Fakoli put on his hat with three hundred bird's heads.	(Naamu)
	He put his axe on his shoulder,	(Naamu)
2130	He tied his headband around his head,	(Naamu)
	Because he knew there was going to be a falling-out.	(Na-amu)
	When Fakoli was on his way,	(Naamu)
	When they saw Fakoli coming,	(Na-amu)
	Sumaworo stood up from his royal seat.	(Naamu)
2135	He said, "Fakoli, am I the one to whom you said, 'I refuse'?"	(Naamu)
	Fakoli said, "I refuse."	(Naamu)
	Fakoli believed that to explain himself to Sumaworo would be cowardly.	(Na-amu)
	Sumaworo said, "Am I the one to whom you said, 'I refuse'?"	(Naamu)
	Fakoli said, "I refuse."	(Na-amu)
2140	He said, "Why?"	(Naamuu)

He said, "I refuse."   (Na-amu)
"Ah, very well."   (Naamu)
Sumaworo said, "What they told me is the truth."   (Na-amu)
He said, "You claim that you came to help me.
2145 You have not come to help me."   (Naamu)
He said, "You know what you came for.   (Na-amu)
I have three hundred wives, thirty wives, and three wives. (Naamu)
I have prepared three hundred dishes, thirty dishes, and
   three dishes.   (Na-amu)
You have only one wife.   (Naamu)
2150 You also produced three hundred dishes, thirty dishes,
   and three dishes.   (Naamu)
Did you come to help me?   (Na-amu)
Were you told that your head and my head
   are equal?   (Naamu, true, naamu)
But your wife with whom you are boasting,   (Na-amu)
I am taking her back."   (Naamu)

2155 Fakoli said, "Ah!   (Naamu)
Uncle, have things come down to that level?   (Naamu)
Has the dispute between us come to the point of
   taking back a wife?   (Na-amu)
Oooh, in fact I do not even want her now,   (Naamu)
Until after the battle smoke has settled.   (Na-amu)
2160 Since you have sent a message to the Mande people,
That we must meet at Dakajalan,   (Naamu)
I do not want to keep Keleya Konkon now."   (Na-amu)
He brought out his blanket and tore off a strip, *prrrr*!   (Naamu)
He threw it to Keleya Konkon and told her to use it for
   a mourning veil.   (Na-amu)
2165 He said, "I will not marry you again until I marry you
   in gunsmoke.   (Na . . . naamu)
I am returning to Manden."   (Na-amu)
He turned his back on Keleya Konkon.   (Naamu)
He took the road to Manden.   (Naamuu)
The diviners were still praying to God.   (Na-amu)

2170 When Fakoli got back to Manden,   (Naamu)
He went and stood at the door of the council hall.   (Naamu)
He said, "Simbon, my uncle and I have quarreled.
He has taken my wife from me.   (Na-amu)
I will not take back Keleya Konkon until I do it in
   gunsmoke."   (Naamu)
2175 "Huh," Sunjata laughed,   (Na-amu)
Manjan Bereté laughed,   (Naamu)
Siriman Kanda Touré laughed.   (Naamu)
They said, "Manden is now complete."   (Na-amu)

[*In omitted passages the army of Manden is divided into companies of men who possess occult powers, companies of those who have no magic, and one unit made up of famous ancestral figures with the power to become invisible. In a secret meeting Sunjata learns the elaborate strategy he must adopt to defeat Sumaworo.*]

Trading Insults and Swearing Oaths

	Manden had mourned after every battle against	
	Sumaworo.	(Naamu, it's true.)
2180	He made all the women widows.	(Na-amuu)
	He sewed shirts of human skin,	(Naamu)
	With the skins of Mande and Soso people.	(Naamu)
	He sewed trousers of human skin,	(Naamu)
	With the skins of Mande and Soso people.	(Na-amu)
2185	He sewed a hat of human skin.	(Naamu)
	After that, he sewed shoes of human skin.	(Naamu)
	He summoned the Mande people,	(Naamu)
	To come and give his shoes a name.	(Naamu)
	Anyone who came,	(Na-amu)
2190	If the person said, "Finfirinya Shoes,"	(Naamu)
	He would say, "That is not the name."	(Naamu)
	If somebody said, "Dulubiri,"[9]	(Naamu)
	He would say, "That is not the name."	(Naamu)
	They asked him,	(Naamu)
2195	"All right, Sumaworo,	(Naamu)
	What are your shoes called?"	(Na-amu)
	He said, "My shoes are called,	(Naamu)
	'Take the Air,	(Naamu)
	Take the Ground from the Chief.'	(Naamu)
2200	People must always be around me, Sumaworo.	(Naamu)
	I will always keep Manden in my power.	(Na-amu)
	That is the name of my human-skin shoes."	(Naamu)
	After they had made their preparations, the war began.	(Na-amu)
	To shorten this narrative,	(Naaaam')
2205	When the war began,	(Naamu)
	The three Mande divisions arrived.	(Na-amu)
	Those who could become invisible in the daytime,	(Naamu)
	The five *mori*[1] diviners,	(Na-amu)
	Simbon was over here,	(Naamu)
2210	Simbon was placed like this.	(Na-amu)
	They placed Manjan Bereté in front of him.	(Naamu)
	The head of his horse was touching the tail of the	
	horse in front.	(Na-amu)
	Sanbari Cissé and Siriman Touré were there,	(Naamu)

9. The exact meanings of "Finfirinya" and "Dulubiri" are unclear, but Sumaworo is indicating that these terms are unworthy of describing shoes that contribute to his legendary ability to be in more than one place at a time and to see everything happening in his kingdom.

1. Generally, a Muslim cleric (in French *marabout*), but in oral tradition often refers to a seer who draws on both the indigenous system of belief and Islam.

Kòn Mara and Djané were there,	(Na-amu)
2215 Manden Bori,	(Naamu)
And Tombonon Diawara,	(Na-amu)
And Turama'an,	(Naamu)
And Kankejan,	(Naamu)
And Fakoli.	(Naamu)
2220 They were placed out here,	(Naamu)
Like when ants are marching,	(Na-amu)
Back and forth,	(Naamu)
Back and forth.	(Na-amu)
Sunjata said they should maintain those positions on the battlefield.	(Naamu)
2225 Simbon was in the middle!	(Naamu, true, naamu)
When they marched and arrived at the battlefield,	(Naaaam')
Sunjata said, "You Mande people wait here."	(Na-amu)
He left the Mande troops there.	(Naamu)
He and the masked flag bearers,	(Naamu)
2230 He crossed the field with those men.	(Na-amuu)
As they crossed the field,	(Naaaam')
They approached Sumaworo's position.	(Naamu)
Sumaworo's troops were also there.	(Naamu)
They were waiting in position.	(Na-amu)
2235 Sumaworo was astride his horse,	(Naamu)
He was surrounded by his corps of guards.	(Naamu)
Sunjata drew nearer to Sumaworo.	(Na-amu)
As soon as Sunjata drew near,	(Naamu)
He said, "Father Sumaworo, good morning."	(Naamu)
2240 (True manhood is revealed by the mouth.)	(Na-amu)
Sumaworo said, "Marahaba, good morning."	(Naamu)
He said, "Where are the Mande troops?"	(Na-amu)
"Ah, Father Sumaworo, they are over on the Mande side."	(Naamu)
"Ah, is that your usual way of doing it?"	(Na-amuu)
2245 Sunjata said, "Ah, I have been away."	(Naaaam')
He said, "This is our first encounter in battle.	(Naamu)
If I bring them,	(Naamu)
I cannot allow them to mingle with your troops.	
We would not be able to tell them apart.	(Na-amu)
2250 You can see them standing over there on the Mande side."	(Naamu)
"Ah, Sunjata, this is not the usual procedure."	(Na-amu)
Sunjata said, "Well, there was nobody else available to do this."	(Naaaam')
He was very bold in his speech.	(Na-amuu)
Sumaworo said, "I say to you, Bala Fasali,	
2255 I say to Simbon,	(Naamu)
It was I who issued the challenge.	(Na-amu)
I have been told,	(Naamu)
That the Mande people sent for their battle commander.	(Na-amuu)
They did not inform him of anything that happened in his absence.	(Naamu)

2260 That is why I have challenged him, (Na-amu)
To come and meet in the field. (Naamu)
I will tell him what I have to say, (Naamu)
And let him tell me what is on his mind. (Naamu)
Then I will do to him what I planned to do. (Naamu)
2265 Or, he can try to do to me what he wants to do. (Na-amuu)
That is why I challenged him to come here." (Naamu)
Simbon said, "I appreciate that. (Na-amu)
Ah! You are my respected elder." (Naamu)

He said, "But, father Sumaworo, (Naamu)
2270 People may refuse peanuts, (Naamu)
But not ones that have been placed right in front of them. (Na-amu)
Let me say this to you." (Naamu)
Sumaworo said, "Mba, give me some snuff from Manden." (Naamuu)
Simbon said, (Na-amu)
2275 "Ah! Father Sumaworo," (Naamu)
He said, "It is appropriate for the master to give snuff to
        his apprentice,
Rather than for the apprentice to give snuff to his master." (Na-amu)
He said, "Give me some snuff from Soso, (Naamu)
So that I will know I have seen my father." (Naamu)
2280 Sumaworo took out his snuffbox, (Naamu)
And handed it to him. (Na-amu)
Simbon put some in his palm, (Naamu)
Took a pinch and snorted it, (Naamu)
Took another pinch and snorted it, (Naamu)
2285 And put some in his mouth. (Naamu)
He closed the snuffbox and gave it back to Sumaworo. (Naamu)
It did not even make his tongue quiver. (Naamu)
Sumaworo was surprised. (Na-amu)
Anybody who took that snuff would immediately fall over. (Naamu)
2290 It was poison!

Sunjata sucked on the snuff. (Naamu)
He did not even cough. (Naamu)
He spit the snuff on the ground. (Naamu)
Sumaworo said, "Give me some Mande snuff." (Na-amu)
2295 Simbon reached in his pocket, (Naamu)
And took out his snuffbox and handed it to him. (Naamu)
Sumaworo put some in his palm. (Naamu)
He took a pinch and snorted it, (Naamu)
Took some more and snorted it, (Naamu)
2300 And put the rest in his mouth. (Naamu)
That was specially prepared snuff, (Naamu)
But it did not do anything to him. (Naamuu)
Sumaworo said to him, (Na-amu)
He said, "I summoned you,
2305 Since the Mande people brought back their *mansa*. (Naamu)
You would not be here without *dalilu*. (Naamu)

	The *dalilu* you brought,	(Naamu)
	I told you when you passed through Soso,	(Naamu)
	That if they sent you against me,	(Naamu)
2310	That you should refuse.	(Naamu)
	I said that because,	(Naamu)
	As you have now learned,	(Naamu)
	I have become hot ashes surrounding Manden and Soso,	(Naamu)
	And if a toddler walks in it,	(Naamu)
2315	I will burn him,	(Naamu)
	Up to his thighs.	(Naamu)
	But here you are."	(Naamuu)
	"Ah, father Sumaworo, I also told you,	(Naamu)
	This is my father's home that you came to.	(Na-amu)
2320	You are not a son of this place.	(Naaaam')
	Your grandfather came from Folonengbe,	(Naamuu)
	He came to us.	(Na-amu)
	It was not your grandfather, it was your father who came.	(Naamu)
	You are the second generation since your people arrived.	(Na-amu)
2325	Since we have been here,	(Naamu)
	I am the eighth generation.	(Naamu)
	You only came yesterday.	(Naamu)
	Huh!" Sunjata continued,	(Na-amu)
	"And you say that I have just arrived?	(Naaaam')
2330	You are my respected elder.	
	I will not be the first to make a move.	
	You who summoned me,	(Naamu)
	Saying that your child is growing disrespectful,	(Naamu)
	You go ahead and show what you have."	(Naamuu)
2335	Sumaworo said, "Bisimillahi."	(Na-amu)

The Battle of Dakajalan and Fakoli's Revenge

	When something is filled to the brim,	(Naamu)
	It will overflow.	(Naaaam')
	Sumaworo took his sword and struck at Sunjata.	(Naamu)
	The sword-blade flexed like a whip.	(Naamu)
2340	Sunjata also struck with his sword.	(Naamu)
	The blade of his sword also bent.	(Naamu)
	Sumaworo raised his musket and fired at him.	(Naamu)
	Nothing touched Sunjata.	(Na-amu)
	Sunjata then fired his musket at Sumaworo.	(Naamu)
2345	It did not pierce Sumaworo.	(Na-amu)
	The *dalilu* was finished.	(Naamu)
	They were just standing there.	(Na-amu)
	Sumaworo reached into his saddlebag,	(Naamu)
	And took his whip.	(Naamu)
2350	As he raised his hand like this,	(Naamu)
	Sunjata seized his reins like this,	(Naamu)
	Clap! He dashed away.	(Na-amu)

The two armies were waiting.	(Naamu)
Soso waited on one side,	(Naamu)
2355 Manden waited on the other side.	(Naamu)
Everybody was watching the commanders on the	
battlefield.	(Na-amu)
Fakoli was off to one side of Sunjata.	(Naamu)
Turama'an was on his other side.	(Naamu)
Sumaworo's men were flanking him.	(Na-amu)
2360 *Blu, blu!*	(Naamuu)
They dashed across the field,	(Naamu)
They started up the hill.	(Na-amu)
As they began to climb,	(Naamu)
They disappeared from sight.	(Na-amu)
2365 Even their dust faded from sight.	(Naamu)
They reached the edge of a ravine.	(Naamu)
It was a very deep ravine!	(Naamu)
When they got there,	(Naamu)
Sunjata's sorcery mare approached the	
deep ravine.	(Naamu) (Naamu)
2370 The horse gathered itself to spring.	(Naamu)
It jumped and landed on the other side.	(Naamu)
Sumaworo approached the ravine.	(Naamu)
When his horse tried to jump,	(Naamu)
It tumbled into the ravine.	(Naamu)
2375 Fakoli's horse jumped and landed on the other side	
of the ravine.	(Naamu)
Turama'an's horse also jumped to the other side.	(Naamu)
They turned their horses and went to the edge of the ravine.	(N . . .)
Sumaworo was wearing the human-skin trousers.	(Naamuu)
Sunjata said, "Sumaworo, what is the matter?"	(Naamu)
2380 He replied, "Sunjata, kill me here,	
Do not carry me to the town.	(Na-amu)
Do not bring such shame to me,"	(Naamu)
Sumaworo said, "God controls all time.	(Na-amu)
Do not take me back."	(Naamu)
2385 Sumaworo removed his *dalilu*,	(Na-amu)
He released his horsewhip.	(Naamu)
He dropped everything and took off his human-skin shirt.	(Naamu)
He stripped his body.	(Na-amu)
Sunjata said, "I am not going to finish you off.	(Naamu)
2390 From where you are, nobody can climb out."	(Na-amuu)
He said, "I do not want your shirt of human skin,	(Naamu)
Because it is the skin of my father's relatives.	(Na-amu)
I do not want it."	(Naamu)
Sunjata would not take it.	(Naamu)
2395 When they said, "Come, let us go home,"	(Na-amu)
They had gone some distance,	
When Fakoli made a decision, turned and went back.	(Naamu)

When he got back to Sumaworo,	(Na-amu)
He said, "Sumaworo, what did I say to you?	(Naamu)
2400 When you took my wife back, what did I say?"	(Na-amu)
He took his axe from his shoulder,	(Naamu)
And struck Sumaworo on the head, *poh!*	(Naamu)
He said, "This will be sung about in Sunjata's praise song."	(Naamu)
They sang, "Head-breaking Mari Jata."[2]	(Na-amu)
2405 It was Fakoli who broke it.	(Naamuu)
When Fakoli started to leave there,	(Naamu)
He was still angry, so he went back again.	(Naamu)
He went back and struck Sumaworo on a leg, *gbao!*	(Naamu)
He broke his leg.	(Naamu)
2410 He said, "This will be sung in Sunjata's praise song."	(Naamu)
That is why it was sung, "Leg-breaking Mari Jata."	(Naamu)
It was Fakoli who did that.	(Naamuu)
He went back again and took his axe,	(Na-amu)
He swung it and broke Sumaworo's arm.	(Naamu)
2415 He said, "This will be sung in Sunjata's praise song."	(Naamu)
It was sung, "Arm-breaking Mari Jata."	(Naamu)
Aheh! It was not Jata who broke it!	(Naamu)
It was Fakoli who broke it.[3]	(Na-amuu)
After they did that,	(Naamu)
2420 They returned home.	(Na-amuu)
Laughter came to Manden.	(Naamu)
Soso became part of it.	(Naamu)

[*In omitted passages, the narrator describes how, following the defeat of Suma-woro, the people of Soso dispersed and eventually settled in various communities along the Atlantic coast. Meanwhile, Sunjata begins to initiate reforms and orga-nize the newly unified Mali Empire.*]

2. Based on the praise-name "Lion of Mali" (Mali Jara), one of several honorifics by which *jeliw* refer to Sunjata.

3. It is unusual for a *jeli* to describe the death of Sumaworo, as Tassey Condé does here. In many versions Sumaworo flees to the mountain at Koulikoro, where he disappears. The bards are usually careful not to say that Suma-woro was slain by anyone. Such things are taken seriously in modern times, because Maninka and Bamana identify with the ancestors whose names they carry. This was recorded in a private performance in the narrator's own house, but in a public perform-ance, giving details of a humiliating defeat (even one alleged to have occurred more than seven centuries ago) risks embarrassing any people in the audience who regard themselves as descendants of the defeated ancestor.

EVLIYA ÇELEBI
1611–ca. 1683

Evliya Çelebi's detailed descriptions of the far-flung corners of the Ottoman Empire, collected in his ten-volume *Book of Travels*, represent a high-water mark of travel literature. *The Book of Travels'* sheer scale and sweep, spanning more than forty years and the entire expanse of the empire, from Sudan to Vienna, the literary quality of its abundant anecdotes and other narratives, and the intertwining of observation and imagination make it an indispensable and immensely compelling window onto lost times, places, and people.

LIFE

Evliya's father was a goldsmith who worked for the Ottoman sultans. His mother was related to Grand Vizier Melek Ahmed Pasha, later Evliya's most important patron. His title "çelebi" marks him as educated and sets him apart from the career lines in Ottoman officialdom and in the military. Evliya distinguished himself early on by his beautiful voice, acting as müezzin (the caller to prayer) and reciter of the Qur'an. His seemingly effortless eloquence and wit, coupled with his impressive erudition (the product of a vast traditional education), made him an ideal boon companion first for Sultan Murad IV, then for Melek Ahmed Pasha and other members of the elite. Evliya accompanied these dignitaries to posts in every corner of the empire, serving them in a number of occasional tasks, like envoy, inspector, and müezzin. Remunerations and profits from such tasks, together with a modest fortune from his family, allowed him to live an independent life, and no marriage hindered his mobility. In 1671 he went on the pilgrimage to Mecca, and then settled in Cairo. Throughout his travels, Evliya gathered impressions and material; the anecdotal style and rich language of his narrative suggests that he may have told much of it orally first, during evening conversations in the social gatherings of his patrons and other members of the Ottoman elite. What sets him apart from many other entertaining travelers in a highly mobile elite was that, late in life, he wrote his impressions down in ten large volumes. Although complete, the book is missing the final touches, which suggests that he worked on it until his death. The date of his death, however, is a matter of speculation, because outside of his *Book of Travels*, there is barely any record of Evliya.

THE BOOK OF TRAVELS

Widely acclaimed today as the single most important work of Ottoman literature, *The Book of Travels* languished in obscurity for a long time after Evliya's death. Very few manuscript copies were made, and the scarce references by later authors dismiss Evliya as a storyteller and a liar. In the nineteenth century western orientalists began to draw attention to *The Book of Travels*, which was printed for the first time in the twentieth century, but only in the last few decades has appreciation of this text as a literary monument truly begun.

Bracketed by descriptions of the two most important Ottoman cities, Istanbul, where Evliya was born, and Cairo, where he spent his later years writing,

The Book of Travels is many things. It is a factual account, perceived with the eye of an administrator, of provinces, cities, villages, fiefs and other sources of revenue, roads, and waystations. It is also a repository for innumerable factoids and narratives—legends, histories, local lore, personal adventures, and tall tales—that the passionate storyteller inserted in order to make his work as entertaining as it was informative. Taken altogether, *The Book of Travels* is a carefully crafted, monumental mirror that Evliya presents to his Ottoman audience to show them who they are or ought to be.

Evliya wrote in a sophisticated and often playful style, afforded by Ottoman Turkish with its rich vocabulary of Persian and Arabic, that moved through every register between crude colloquialism and artistic rhymed prose. As the American Turcologist Robert Dankoff has observed, two discourses alternate, often unpredictably, in *The Book of Travels*: "one of persuasion, in which it was important that [Evliya's] listeners give credence to what he was saying; and one of diversion, in which it was more important to arouse their wonder and delight." Evliya measured cities and listed tax revenues, he recorded ancient legends of kings and saints, and he provided samples of all the languages he encountered, often in amazing accuracy. But he also noted the sensational and fantastical, such as the case of the girl who gave birth to a baby elephant, and the seemingly mundane, such as the typical names of the male and female slaves of Diyarbakir, a town in southeastern Turkey. His own adventures feature prominently, sometimes casting him in a heroic light, as when he faced down a notorious bandit in the Balkans, but they can also be farcical, as when an infidel fighter surprised him relieving himself not far from the battlefield. Everything goes, as long as it yields a good story, and it does not have to be true: Evliya's readers will certainly have known that the prophet Kaffah, whom he narrates in much detail, never existed, and might have recognized that some stories are patterned on ancient lore.

Serious or joking, however, Evliya remained a true Ottoman, committed to its elite ideals of cosmopolitan, multilingual erudition. His attention to the sacred spaces of mosques, dervish lodges, and tombs of saints betray a profound Islamic piety, lightened by the awareness of human fallibility and the wisdom which characterize the mystical form of Islam, Sufism. His rhetoric abounds with references to holy warfare (*ghaza*) and the ideal of Ottoman world domination, yet, in his work it is tinged with a kind of romantic nostalgia for an ideal of the past. Instead of religious fanaticism, his account is imbued with a deep spirit of humanism, which allowed him to acknowledge and overcome difference.

These various ingredients are especially visible in one of the rare instances of Evliya's travel leading beyond Ottoman boundaries—his visit to Vienna in 1665 (which is represented in the excerpt below). Evliya came to Vienna with the delegation of Kara Mehmed Pasha to negotiate a peace agreement after an Ottoman campaign had been halted at St. Gotthard in western Hungary. His description makes the Habsburg capital another part of the mirror, in which the Ottoman audience recognized itself, in positive or negative terms. Although not an official representative, Evliya writes with a keen awareness of Ottoman state interests, as he observes the symbolic jousting of the two diplomatic delegations in their encounter at the border. He explores every corner of Vienna with a natural curiosity, and is not shy to socialize with the locals, without losing his cultural superiority. As he mocks the Catholic ritual, he implicitly extols the somber practices of Islam; as he praises Austrian achievements in the arts, sciences, and technology, he criticizes his fellow countrymen for neglecting them. His truly Ottoman appreciation of beauty and the good life extends to the pretty youth and the lush gardens of infidel Austria.

Most importantly, however, Vienna for Evliya was a place charged with history and meaning. Vienna was identified with the "Golden Apple" of the old Turkish myth that promised eternal conquest to the Ottomans and that also held a prominent place in Ottoman political ritual. The memory of the first Ottoman siege of Vienna in 1529 under Süleyman I (1520–66), the idealized sultan of a "Golden Age," remained with Evliya throughout his visit. In Ottoman legendary lore on which Evliya draws, Süleyman's *ghazis* (warriors of faith) left numerous tokens throughout the city, such as the golden sphere on the bell tower of St. Stephen,

that promised, even as they were retreating, future conquest of the city. Yet at the time of his writing, Evliya had probably heard the news of the disastrous defeat that the Ottomans had suffered at the gates of Vienna in 1683, a defeat that forever tipped the balance of power in southeastern Europe toward the West.

The mixing of the factual and the legendary in Evliya's account of Vienna has puzzled readers to the point that historians long doubted that he was even there. Only the discovery in the 1970s of Evliya's name on a roster of the Ottoman delegation in the Austrian archives has ended these doubts. As a traveler records his impressions of foreign places and peoples, he gives them meaning in dialogue with his domestic audience and according to their cultural horizon. Evliya Çelebi's *Book of Travels* is a particularly rich and complex product of this process.

From The Book of Travels[1]

[*In 1665, Evliya Çelebi accompanied a diplomatic delegation under Kara Mehmed Pasha to Vienna to exchange the ratification of the peace treaty. In our first excerpt, delegations from the Habsburgs and the Ottomans have arrived at the border between the two empires to conclude the peace arrangement previously negotiated. Evliya describes the complicated ritual of the encounter at the border posts as a symbolic tournament of the two states, of course taking sides with his patron, the Ottoman ambassador.*]

The description of the border posts

These things they call border posts: when the deceased Sultan Süleyman took Esztergom and Székesfehérvár from the hands of the German Emperor he had a hillock thrown up about twelve hours from both of these cities, on the Danube river near Komárom.[2] On top there is plenty of space, enough to form a

1. These sections have been translated from the Turkish by Gottfried Hagan with guidance of the German translation by Richard Kreutel and Erich Prokosch: *Im Reiche des Goldenen Apfels. Des türkischen Weltenbummlers Evliyâ Çelebi denkwürdige Reise in das Giaurenland und in die Stadt und Festung Wien anno 1665*, Osmanische Geschichtssch-

reiber. Graz, Wien, Köln: Verlag Styria, 1985.
2. Sultan Süleyman (r. 1520–66) conquered Hungary for the Ottoman Empire and led a campaign against Vienna in 1529, the farthest point of Ottoman expansion into Europe. His reign is idealized by Evliya as the Golden Age of the Ottoman Empire.

circle. The hillock is round and extends from east to west; on our side as well as on the side of the infidels a wooden pole is erected, more than five times the height of a man. Exactly in the middle between the two poles there is a third, which demarcates the border. This is what they call border post.

* * *

The two ambassadors climbed the border mound erected by Sultan Süleyman, and from both sides the dragomans started to go back and forth, but the ambassadors themselves stood near their respective poles, each surrounded by fifty elders and experienced advisors. Our pasha, too, halted with his neat sword-bearers and footmen with their tassels and embroidered quivers and belts and sashes, and his lackeys in full armor, and his flask-bearers and his neatly dressed attendants, and was only talking to Hacı Mustafa Pasha of Székesfehérvár and İskender Pasha of Esztergom, and some elders and dragomans.[3] Occasionally, stewards and dragomans went to and fro, working to bring the two ambassadors to the middle pole so that they should shake hands and conclude the peace. The distance from one ambassador to the other was one hundred steps, and they were both fifty steps away from the middle pole.

* * *

Now the ambassador of the infidels got up from the foot of the pole on their side, and in the most circumspect way came towards our Pasha, dragging his feet all the while. When our ambassador saw this, he also got up from his stool, and very slowly walked towards their ambassador and drew nearer until the soldiers were only separated by the poles; the ambassadors were moving at a snail's pace.[4] In those situations ambassadors need to have the most considerate, circumspect, reasonable men around them, because according to the truthful hadith, "he who makes peace between two parties deserves the same reward as the martyr," one needs men who can improve the relations between the two emperors, so that the peace is not violated, because previously here there had been two months of fighting instead of peace.[5]

* * *

Finally, the infidel ambassador walked with hundred thousand pauses, so slowly as if he did not want to step on a single ant, and ours also came, until they joined hands at the middle pole, and greeted each other with greatest respect. They sat down at the middle pole on stools, and after a thousand excuses he accepted all the peace agreements, consisting of twenty-two articles from either party, for twenty-two years, according to the felicitous decree of our felicitous sultan.

3. Translators in the Ottoman service. "Pasha": title for the governors and military leaders, here of the border provinces next to the Habsburg dominions. Other denominations of ranks here refer to the personal service of Kara Mehmed Pasha, the ambassador.

4. To arrive at the border post *before* the other ambassador would have been interpreted as a sign of weakness.
5. The reward for the martyr, who dies for the sake of Islam, is paradise.

Description of Schwechat (Peşpihil)

[Shortly before arriving in Vienna, the Ottoman delegation passes through the town of Schwechat, where they observe local customs, and also mingle with the locals.]

These were the ignoble Ayanta holidays of the infidels.[6] Ten thousand monks and seventy or eighty thousand faithless infidels came to this large monastery with their crucifixes and flags and banners and organs and trumpets to conduct their worthless rituals. Afterward, they indulged in such wickedness and debauchery, jollity and drinking in the gardens of Schwechat that it is beyond description. Several thousand infidels and priests, burning incense and aloe and amber in gold and silver censers, paraded through the streets playing the trumpets, and returned to their monasteries.

The domes of every monastery are idolatrous temples covered with tin, tinfoil, yellow brass, and lead. In each of them are idols and chandeliers each worth the annual tribute of Egypt,[7] and on every dome and tower are golden crosses as tall as a man, which are sparkling all across the city. Their clock towers, too, are covered with tinned sheet metal, and the sound of the bells carries as far as one day's travel.

The river * * * passes through the middle of the town. It is just a little creek but [as sweet as] the water of life. It comes from the Little German [Mountains], flows through hamlets, villages, and small towns, waters the vineyards and gardens of this city, and then empties into the Danube below it. On both sides of the city there are innumerable vineyards and gardens with fruit trees and roses, and in paradisiac gardens like the garden of Aspuzu,[8] with tall castles, and enclosures decorated with water basins and fountains, remarkable pleasure grounds according to the taste of the Franks. In each garden a perfect master has erected an artful castle like the castle of Khavarnaq,[9] and in each there are colorful paintings by Frank painters like Mani with his Erjeng,[1] done in such remarkable, indeed magic art that anybody who understands painting puts the finger of astonishment to his lips full of admiration.[2]

All the notable and noble infidels from Vienna enjoy themselves for weeks and months in this city and its gardens, and their young boys and pretty girls swim in the river which runs through it, and, embracing each other in the heat of the joy of wine and liquor, amuse themselves in a quiet corner. Due to the mild climate [the beauty of] their boys and girls is famous far and wide.

Their men and women do not avoid each other; even when their wives sat together with us Ottomans in jollity and drinking, the husbands did not say

---

6. The delegation stayed in Schwechat during the holiday of Corpus Christi. How Evliya came up with the word Ayanta is not clear.
7. Egypt being the wealthiest Ottoman province, this is Evliya's hyperbolic way of saying "a lot of money."
8. The urbanites of Malatya in southeastern Anatolia used to have their summer residences in Aspuzu, which was famous for its orchards and vineyards.
9. The pre-Islamic palace of Khavarnaq in

Iraq was frequently cited by the ancient Arabian poets as one of the wonders of the world.
1. In the Islamic world Mani (ca. 216–276 c.e.), the founder of Manicheism, is remembered as the most accomplished painter of all times; Erjeng is the book in which his paintings were collected.
2. Putting one index finger to the lip was a common gesture of admiration, frequently seen in Islamic miniature paintings.

anything. They go out freely, which is not sinful, because in this entire land of the infidels it is the women who rule, which is their evil custom since the days of Virgin Mary.

Evliya's strange adventure in Vienna

About a most marvelous and bewildering spectacle: One day when I, your humble servant full of faults, strolled through the inner city, I came to the market of doctors which has about one hundred shops. In front of some of the shops I saw captives from the nation of Muhammad[3] sitting on stools, with white turbans, and Bosnian fur hats, and felt caps from Tekke and Hamid,[4] or with Tatar features and in Tatar garb, hands and feet of all of them in iron chains, some of them black negroes, and others young heroes, and others white-bearded feeble old men. Their necks bowed in grief, they sat on their stools grinding nutmeg, cinnamon, pepper, cardamom, ginger, and other spices in huge bronze mortars, working hard as if someone was holding a sword to their necks, in order to make them work faster. But the old ones worked agonizingly slow, their eyes rolling right and left with exhaustion.

I your humble servant felt my vein of compassion swelling, and reached for my wallet to give these old men a few silver coins. But my companion, fiefholder Boshnaq 'Ali from Esztergom prevented my good deed, saying: Hold on for now, give it to them when we come along again towards the evening. Now the owners of these captives are around, and would just take away what you give them. I your humble servant found this reasonable and put my wallet back into my pocket. We continued to stroll through markets, business streets, residential neighborhoods and other monuments we had not seen before, and around nightfall returned to the place of the captives. As we stood and watched they started to close the shops, and some infidels came and loosened the Muslim captives' belts, and took off their turbans and fur hats and felt caps, and took all their clothes. Then they stuck a key like one for a clock mechanism in the armpit of each of them and turned it around, and immediately these Muslim captives' hands and heads and eyes and eyebrows stopped moving. Now as their turbans had been taken off their heads and their clothes from their bodies I realized that these were all clock mechanisms made of bronze in the shape of humans, and moved like clock mechanisms if wound up. I was flabbergasted, and my companion 'Ali Agha mocked to me: For God's sake, Evliya Çelebi, give those poor captives a few silver coins. This was a marvelous and wonderful adventure indeed!

[*Evliya visits St. Stephen's Cathedral in Vienna, marveling at the various paintings and frescoes, and admiring the sound of the organ and the boys' choir. He also discovers a magnificent library*]

In the walls there are niches for the Gospels, the Thora, the Psalms, and the Quran, and their walls are all plastered with raw ambergris.[5] As many nations of different languages as there are, of all their authors and writers in their lan-

---

3. I.e., Islam.
4. Two Ottoman provinces in Asia Minor.

5. All these texts are considered valid revelations in Islam.

guages there are many times a hundred thousand books here, and specially employed priests look after them. It is a magnificent library well worth seeing.

Such a collection of precious books does not exist in any other country. There are God knows how many books in the mosques of Sultan Barqūq and Sultan Faraj[6] in Cairo, and in the mosques of [Sultan Meḥmed] The Conqueror and Sultan Süleymān and Sultan Bāyezīd and the New Mosque,[7] but in this St. Stephen's Monastery in Vienna there are even more, since there are, in the scripts of every language of the infidels, so many illustrated books, theological commentaries, the Atlas and the Atlas Minor, geography books, astronomy books called Mappa mundi; we do not have any of those because images are forbidden. This is why this monastery in Vienna has so many books. I, your humble servant, entered this library with the permission of the chief priest, and was stunned when I walked through it while the scents of musk and ambergris wafted through my brains.

Thus, my friend, the result and outcome of what I am saying is this: Despite all their infidelity these infidels, considering that they are God's own word, have all these books dusted off once a week, and have seventy or eighty servants for that purpose. Whereas we do in fact have the [mosque called] Jami' al-'Attarin in Alexandria which has so many shops and hostels and baths and stores and works of beneficence [to generate income for its maintenance], and yet is wrecked and in ruins, and in its library because of the rain of mercy several thousand volumes containing the precious word of glory written by the noble hands of Yāqūt al-Musta'simī and 'Abdallah al-Qirīmī and Shamsaddīn Ghumrawī and Sheykh Jūshī are rotting in the rain.[8] All the Muslims who come to the Friday prayer to this mosque once a week can hear the noises of the moths and worms and mice eating away at these books, but none of this nation of Muhammad ever thinks of saying: There are so many books of God perishing here, let us do something about it. [That is] because they do not love God's scripture as much as the infidels do. If only they could reconstruct that mosque like this church, and if only its servants and scholars would look at that poor mosque with the eye of mercy.

Description of the golden sphere on the steeple of St. Stephen

A strange adventure: In the city of Vienna there are 360 cathedrals and churches, each has one or two clock towers, with a total of 470. At noon first that big clock at St. Stephen's strikes once, and then, before its harmony has fully developed, all the other clock towers in the fortress of Vienna strike at one time. They have found a marvelous way of synchronizing those clocks. If a fellow in Rum has two clocks, one will definitively be one degree and two minutes ahead or behind the other, but the clocks of Vienna all strike at the same moment—so skillfully are their clocks made. That steeple of St. Stephen's

---

6. "Barqūq": Mamluk sultan of Egypt (r. 1382–99); "Faraj": Barqūq's son and successor, (r. 1399–1412).
7. The mosque of Aḥmed I (r. 1603–17), today known as the Blue Mosque. Meḥmed II

(r. 1451–81), Bāyezīd II (r. 1481–1512), Süleyman I (r. 1520–66), Ottoman sultans, all of whom erected mosques in Istanbul.
8. Four famous calligraphers, the most important being Yāqūt al-Musta'simī (1221–1298).

cathedral is higher than all the others, and its stair has 770 stone steps, and it has 360 large and small cells for the monks. On its highest tip there is a golden sphere, made from 150 oqqa of pure gold, big enough to hold ten shinik[9] of wheat. When Sultan Süleyman besieged Vienna in the year 936 [1529 C.E.] he could not bring himself to fire his cannons at this steeple, thinking that ultimately this would be a minaret for the call to Muslim prayer at a Muslim temple. [He thought to himself:] So this steeple should carry my sign. Thus he had that golden sphere made out there and sent it into the fortress to the king, and that erring king put the sphere up on the highest tip of that steeple in the very same night. That is why the fortress of Vienna is called the Golden Apple of Germany and Hungary because of this golden sphere. When Sultan Süleyman lifted the siege without victory and left, King Ferdinand[1] put a golden crescent and a silver sun on top of Süleyman Khan's sphere. When Sultan Süleyman heard that the infidels had dared to put some stuff on top of his own sphere, he warned them: Watch out, I am going to wage war against you. He went on his German campaign, conquered 176 fortresses within one year, and laid his country and provinces to waste. Finally King Ferdinand took the crescent and sun down from Sultan Süleyman's sphere and made peace with him. In the course of time Sultan Murad [IV] conquered Baghdad, the paradisical city, in 1048 [1638 C.E.], but after his return to Constantinople he took to drinking, and died soon thereafter. When Sultan Ibrahim succeeded him on the throne, the German emperor and evildoing king * * * violated the peace of Sultan Süleyman with the foolish act of putting a sort of fork shaped like a golden cross on top of the sphere. When he was asked: Why did you put this cross-shaped thing on Sultan Süleyman's Golden Apple?, he responded: We put this weather vane in the form of a cross up there so that no bird should perch up there. And indeed, it is a kind of weather vane in the shape of a cross on which no bird can perch when it whirls around in the wind like a top. Surely there will be a powerful sultan like Süleyman one day who takes this down from the sphere!

* * *

May God Almighty make it a minaret and grant that the call for the Muhammadan prayer is sounded from it—peace upon you.

---

9. A unit of volume, used for grain, ca., a quarter of a bushel. "Oqqa": a unit of weight, standardized at 1,283 gr (45.26 oz.).
1. Ferdinand I of Habsburg, King of Bohemia and Hungary since 1526, Holy Roman Emperor (r. 1558–64). In fact, the steeple had carried a crescent and star (a universal symbol that had nothing to do with Islam) in the 16th century.

INDIAN POETRY AFTER ISLAM
twelfth–seventeenth centuries

The mutual engagement of Islam and Hinduism in South Asia began as a "clash of civilizations" in the eighth century, and has continued to generate fresh political, economic, social, and ideological conflicts ever since. As faiths and as ways of life, they are each other's contraries, mainly because Islam is a religion of the Book whereas Hinduism (like Buddhism and Jainism) is not. Nevertheless, especially in literature, art, and modern popular culture, they have converged in unexpected ways in India to create a cultural synthesis that is rare in world history.

One prominent example of the encounter of Islam and Hinduism was the *bhakti* movement, which began on a smaller scale in southern India before the end of the first millennium C.E. *Bhakti* ("devotion"), which emphasized intense commitment and service to one chosen god out of many in the Hindu pantheon, was as much a theological, social, and political phenomenon as it was a literary and artistic one. It started as a movement to reform classical Hinduism and the caste system, rejecting temples, pollution, endogamy, hierarchy, and ritual. After the arrival of Islam, *bhakti* increasingly engaged with monotheism, iconoclasm, and abstract divinity (as contrasted to idols), as well as egalitarianism and community. In this apparent synthesis, however, *bhakti* did not completely overturn the central concepts of Hinduism. It retained the logic of karma and *mokṣa*,

so that union with God and liberation from reincarnation remained principal goals; it preserved the classical mythologies of Śiva and Viṣṇu; and it continued with earlier Hindu pantheism, in which godhead ("the God beyond God") pervades the universe, and hence can be found everywhere.

This cluster offers selections of poetry by three major figures in the *bhakti* movement from across the subcontinent. **Kabir** comes from the Hindi heartland in northern India in the fifteenth century, and articulates an early synthesis of Hindu and Muslim ideas, focusing on "the God beyond God" and seeking to mediate the conflicts between the two religions. **Mīrabāī** (a woman poet), from the western edge of the Hindi-speaking region in the sixteenth century, embodies a subsequent blend of Hindu and Sufi traditions of erotic mysticism, but also a reaction to Islam. **Tukaram**, who belongs to the Marathi-speaking region along the western edge of the Indian peninsula in the seventeenth century, represents a late phase in which *bhakti* responds to Islam's dominance in the public realm by revitalizing its own roots in Hinduism within local communities. These three poets represent about half a millennium in the literary history of India, a period in which, despite violent conflicts, Islam and Hinduism interacted with each other in remarkably creative ways, creating a unique amalgam of cultures.

KABIR

ca. 1398–1448

Kabir, whose name is of Arabic origin, was probably born a Muslim; he is said to have lived most of his life in Banaras (Varanasi) in northern India, the oldest and holiest city of Hinduism, and was a handloom weaver by occupation. Though poor and illiterate, he became a poet in the oral tradition, composing songs (*padas*) as well as proverb-like couplets (*dohās*), besides witty and stringent satires (classified as *sākhīs*, "poems of witness"). He is likely to have been persecuted equally by orthodox Hindus, conservative Muslims, and political authorities for his outspoken criticism of society and organized religion.

Kabir probably acquired an extensive reputation in his own lifetime; in the centuries following his death, a large and varied body of poetry was recorded in his name. More than 500 poems bearing his signature line were included in the *Ādi Grantha* (1604), the original scripture of Sikhism composed in Punjab, in which he is classified as the principal *bhagat* (a variant of *bhakta*, devotee of God) who preceded the Gurus, the canonized teachers of the new faith. Between the sixteenth and early nineteenth centuries, two other major repositories of Kabir's verse emerged in Rajasthan and Banaras, defining a legacy of nearly 6,000 short poems preserved in a mixture of scripts, languages, and dialects. A large number of songs, satires, and aphorisms ascribed to Kabir also circulated in oral and musical forms during this period, making him the best-known and most frequently quoted poet across northern India in the past half a millennium.

In the *bhakti* tradition, in Sikhism, among Hindus and Muslims, and among modern secular audiences, Kabir is celebrated mainly for his belief in "the God beyond God," or godhead in its absolute, undifferentiated form. In our selection, this theological position is expressed in "The Final State," where both godhead and the union of the self or soul with it prove to be indescribable in human terms. In a parable such as "Ant," the God beyond God hides like grains of sugar amid grains of sand, so that only someone as industrious and adept as an ant (in contrast to a clumsy elephant) can find Him or It.

In keeping with this view, Kabir's poems also criticize organized religion for promoting anthropomorphic representations of God, which falsify the nature of divinity; and for instituting pointless rituals that distract human worshipers from the true goal of life, which is union with godhead. "Mosque with Ten Doors" and "Purity" therefore satirize some of the ritual practices of Islam and Hinduism, respectively; whereas "The Simple State" attacks superstition and hypocrisy among various kinds of self-aggrandizing men of religion who exploit only the business potential of piety. Offering alternatives to such practices, "Don't Stay" points toward stoical forbearance in the face of the world's transitoriness and of the pain and suffering that afflict human life.

The Final State[1]

The ineffable tale
   of that final simple state:

it's utterly different.

It can't be weighed on a scale,
   can't be whittled down.   5
It doesn't feel heavy
   and doesn't feel light.

It has no rain, no sea,
   no sun or shade.
It doesn't contain   10
   creation or destruction.

No life, no death exist in it,
   no grief, no joy.
Both solitude and blissful union
   are absent from it.   15

It has no up or down,
   no high or low.
It doesn't contain
   either night or day.

There's no water, no air,   20
   no fire that flares again and again.
The True Master permeates
   everything there.

The Eternal One remains
   unmoving, imperceptible, unknowable.   25
You can attain Him
   with the Guru's grace [2]

     Kabir says, sacrifice yourself
       to the Guru,
     and remain ensconced   30
       in the true community.

---

1. This and the following poems by Kabir were translated by Vinay Dharwadker. This poem seeks to describe "the final state" into which the enduring human self or soul must enter when it "reunites" with godhead. It is a "simple" state because it is elemental or primordial; and, as the poem's successive verses argue, it lacks any physical or "normal" attributes. In fact, it is indescribable in human terms; and it is identical to the "state" of godhead itself. In older Hindu terms, "the final state" is the state of the soul's *mokṣa*, liberation from karma and rebirth.
2. The words and phrases "It," "the True Master," "the Eternal One," "Him," and "Guru" all refer to godhead, "the God beyond God." So the human soul can find or attain godhead or *mokṣa* only by "God's grace."

Ant

Beware of the world,
　　brothers,
　　be alert—
you're being robbed
　　while wide awake.   5
Beware of the Vedas,[3]
　　brothers,
　　be vigilant—
Death will carry you away
while the guard   10
　　looks on.

The neem tree[4]
becomes the mango tree,
　　the mango tree becomes
　　the neem.   15
The banana plant
spreads into a bush—
　　the fruit on the coconut palm
ripens into a berry
right under your noses,   20
　　you dumb and foolish
　　rustics!

Hari[5] becomes sugar
　　and scatters Himself
　　in the sand.   25
No elephant can sift
the crystals from the grains.
　　Kabir says, renounce
　　all family, caste, and clan.
Turn into an ant   30
　　instead—
pick the sugar from the sand
　　and eat.

Mosque with Ten Doors

Broadcast, O mullāh,[6]
your merciful call to prayer—
　　you yourself are a mosque
　　with ten doors.[7]

3. Here the Vedas represent institutional Hinduism, which is organized by human beings; hence, in Kabir's radically subversive perspective, Hindu scripture is not divine revelation but a manmade text.
4. The margosa tree, very common across South Asia.
5. An ancient Hindu epithet for God, most

often used for Viṣṇu; here a name for God in his most transcendent form.
6. A priest and theologian in Sunni Islam.
7. Kabir here imagines the Muslim priest's body as the "true mosque" of his religion, as contrasted with the physical mosque built with stone. "Ten doors" refers figuratively to the natural orifices of the human body.

Make your mind your Mecca,   5
your body, the Ka'aba[8]—
    your Self itself
is the Supreme Master.

In the name of Allāh,[9] sacrifice
your anger, error, impurity—   10
    chew up your senses,
become a patient man.

The lord of the Hindus and Turks[1]
is one and the same—
    why become a mullāh,   15
why become a sheikh?[2]

Kabir says, brother,
I've gone crazy—
    quietly, quietly, like a thief,
my mind has slipped into the simple state.   20

Purity

Tell me, O pandit,[3]
    what place is pure—
where I can sit
    and eat my meal?

Mother was impure,   5
    father was impure—
the fruits they bore
    were also impure.
They arrived impure,
    they left impure—   10
unlucky folks,
    they died impure.

---

8. Mecca is Islam's holiest city. The Ka'aba is the large black cubical structure in the Masjid al-Haram in Mecca; it marks Islam's most sacred site. At prayer-time anywhere in the world, a Muslim must face in the direction of the Ka'aba from his or her location.
9. God's principal name in the Qur'an, the scripture of Islam.
1. Since the early 13th century, Indians have commonly referred to Muslims as "Turks," mainly because armies made up of Turkish slaves were the successful conquerors of northern India, and the first to establish Muslim rule on the subcontinent.

2. Alludes to the title usually given to Sufi masters.
3. Common title of a learned priest of the *brāhmaṇa* caste group, which dominates the Hindu caste system. This poem attacks the system's insistence on ritual purity (which is very different from hygiene or cleanliness), and its discrimination against pollution; the higher castes maintain their superiority by claiming that they are "purer" than the "polluted" low castes. Kabir's strategy is to show that many supposedly pure things are manifestly impure; and that the supposed purity or impurity of many things leads to logical contradictions.

My tongue's impure,
    my words are impure,
my ears, my eyes,   15
    they're all impure—
you brahmins,
    you've stolen the fire,
but you can't burn off
    the impurity of the senses!   20

The fire, too, is impure,
    the water's impure—
so even the kitchen's
    nothing but impure.
The ladle's impure   25
    that serves a meal,
and they're impure
    who sit and eat their fill.

Cowdung's impure,
    the bathing-square's impure—   30
its very curbs
    are nothing but impure.
Kabir says,
    only they are pure
who've completely cleansed   35
    their thinking.

Debate

If you love your followers, Rāma,
    settle this quarrel, once and for all.[4]

Is Brahmā greater, or where He came from?
    Is the Veda greater, or its origin?

Is this mind greater, or what it believes in?   5
    Is Rāma greater, or the one who knows Him?

Kabir says, I'm in despair. Which is greater?
    The pilgrim-station, or Hari's devoted slave?

---

4. The quarrel Kabir asks God to settle is over a series of intellectual puzzles, which take two basic forms with enormous consequences for religious belief. When we have a cause and an effect (or a source and an outcome), which of the two is greater? And when we have a knower and an object of knowledge, which is greater? The poem's tantalizing suggestion is that an effect can be greater than its cause, and that a person who knows may logically be greater than what he knows.

Moth

Joy is brief.
Sorrow and grief are endless.
The mind's an elephant,
    mad, amnesiac.

Air and flame burn as one,   5
just as when the moth, its eye enchanted by light,
flies straight into the lamp,
    and wing and fire flare together.[5]

Who hasn't found
restful peace in a moment of pleasure?   10
So you brush aside the truth,
    and chase the lies you hold so dear.

At the end of your days
you feel the temptation, you covet joy,
even though old age and death   15
    are close at hand.

The world's embroiled in illusion, error:
this is the process always in motion.
Man attains a human birth:
    why does he waste and destroy it?   20

The Simple State

Listen,
you saints—
I see that the world
is crazy.

When I tell the truth,   5
people run
to beat me up—
when I tell lies,
they believe me.

I've seen   10
the pious ones,
the ritual-mongers—
they bathe at dawn.[6]

---

5. This poem centers on a popular image in Sufism (a mystical branch of Islam): the moth is so attracted to the flame of an oil lamp that it flies straight to its death in the flame.

6. This verse refers to Hindu *brāhmaṇas*, who bathe to ritually cleanse themselves of all "pollution."

They kill the true Self
and worship rocks[7]—   15
they know nothing.

I've seen
many masters and teachers—
they read their Book,
their Qur'ān.   20

They teach many students
their business tricks—
that's all they know.

They sit at home
in pretentious poses—   25
their minds are full
of vanity.

They begin to worship
brass and stone—
they're so proud   30
of their pilgrimages,
they forget the real thing.

They wear caps and beads,
they paint their brows
with the cosmetics   35
of holiness.[8]

They forget the true words
and the songs of witness
the moment they've sung them—
they haven't heard   40
the news of the Self.

The Hindu says
Rāma's dear to him,
the Muslim says it's Rahīm.

They go to war   45
and kill each other—
no one knows
the secret of things.

They do their rounds
from door to door,   50
selling their magical formulas—
they're vain
about their reputations.

7. Idols made of stone.
8. Practitioners of many faiths in India wear
"signs" of their religious identity or status;
these include various types of caps or headgear, beads (like rosaries), and distinctive cos-
metic marks painted on the body.

All the students
will drown with their teachers—   55
at the last moment
they'll repent.

Kabir says,
listen,
you saintly men,   60
forget all this vanity.

I've said it so many times
but nobody listens—
you must merge into
the simple state[9]   65
simply.

Don't Stay

Don't stay—
    the land's a wilderness.

This world's a paltry paper packet—
    a spot of rain
    will wash it away.   5

This world's a garden of thorns—
    snarled and snared,
    we'll perish in pain.

This world's all tree and tinder—
    kindled, it will roast us   10
    like sacrificial victims.

Kabir says, listen, my good men,
    the True Master's name[1]
    is our lasting abode—

    our station, our destination.   15

Aphorisms

3

Don't be vain, Kabir:
    you're just a wrapping of skin on bone.

Even those who ride on horses, under parasols,
    are buried quickly in the mud.

9. The self or soul's union with the godhead; the same as "the final state" described in the first poem in this selection.
1. God's "name," which mystics in Kabir's tra-dition are supposed to repeat constantly as a magical formula (*mantra*) for liberation from karma and rebirth.

9

Kabir, sow such a seed
　　that its tree will flourish perennially:

cool shade, abundant fruit,
　　foliage full of birds at play.

12

Even if you were to transform
　　the seven oceans into ink,

the world's trees into pens, the whole earth into paper,
　　you couldn't write down the list of God's excellences.

20

The man with a truthful heart is best:
　　there's no happiness without the truth,

no matter how many millions of times
　　one tries to find it by other means.

31

Knowledge ahead, knowledge behind,
　　knowledge to the left and right.

The knowledge that knows what knowledge is:
　　that's the knowledge that's mine.

37

Accomplish one thing and you accomplish all.
　　Seek to do all and you lose the one vital thing.

When you water the root of a plant,
　　it flowers and bears fruit to satisfaction.

MĪRABĀĪ

sixteenth century

We know nothing for certain about Mīrabāī, except that she was from Rajasthan, northern India's westernmost state. Legends claim that she was a princess from a Rajput clan (an ethnic group of the warrior caste); as a young married woman, she developed an interest in *bhakti*, and probably broke many social codes to keep company with itinerant ascetics, yogis, Sufis, and other "dubious" spiritual practitioners. Her husband, father, or father-in-law perhaps tried to poison her for nonconformity, and she gave up her life of privilege to become a homeless wanderer searching for union with God.

For Mīra (as she is commonly known), the god of choice was Kṛṣṇa, an avatar of Viṣṇu, part of the story of whose incarnation on earth is narrated in the ancient Sanskrit epic, the **Mahābhārata**. But she devoted herself to the aspect of Kṛṣṇa in which he is a young erotic god, in whom women of all ages and from every social class are said to find the fulfillment of their desires and destinies. The poetry attributed to Mīra—preserved in several varieties of Hindi—is a candid, ongoing, lyrical conversation with and about God as a divine lover.

Though few, if any, of Mīra's compositions have survived verifiably in their original forms, the several hundred *pada*s (short songs in metrical, rhymed couplets) preserved in her name represent Kṛṣṇa as "the dark one" and as "the cowherd" who moves, carries, or lifts "mountains"—phrases that evoke the erotic god's classical mythology, physical attractions, superhuman strength, and miracles. As our selection indicates, most of Mīra's poems represent the devotee in a state of painful separation from her divine beloved; she is lonely and wretched, anxious and desperate, full of emotional longing and physical desire. In "My sleep's rotten, my friend," she is like a "stranded fish thrashing for water," whereas in "Darling, come visit me," she is lovesick, with "No hunger by day, no sleep by night." She is also alienated from normal human society, being constantly persecuted: in "The cowherd who carries mountains," the chieftain sends her a cup of poison, and she leaves her relatives and companions and loses her "honor in the world."

The only woman poet in the *bhakti* movement in northern India between the fourteenth and eighteenth centuries, Mīra has been promoted in modern times by Mahatma Gandhi and others as a historical ideal of Indian womanhood: sensitive, bold, determined, rebellious, and spiritually self-reliant. This image has found wide appeal in India's popular culture today, from music, dance, and visual art to film, television, and other mass media.

[My sleep's rotten, my friend][1]

My sleep's rotten, my friend,
   my sleep's rotten.

I've spent my nights staring at the path
   my lover will take
when he comes to me.[2]   5

My friends, concerned,
   decided to intervene—
but my heart accepted nothing they said.

If I don't see him, there's no tomorrow—
   but I'm determined   10
not to be sore with him.

My body's lean with anxious waiting—
   My love, my love,
the only words locked upon my lips.

This separation, an agony inside me—   15
   no one else
can understand this pain.

Just like the thirsty bird
   obsessed with rain-clouds—
just like the stranded fish thrashing for water.   20

Being a woman
   wracked by separation,
Mīra has lost her wits.

1. This and the following poems by Mīrabāī were translated by Vinay Dharwadker.
2. Mīra's poetry of devotion to God is explicitly erotic. She consistently projects God—in his anthropomorphic forms as Viṣṇu, and as Viṣṇu's avatar, Kṛṣṇa—as her lover or husband. As a woman in the human world, she lives in a state of separation from her divine paramour, who exists "beyond" this world; as his metaphorical wife, she perpetually waits for him to come to her.

[The cowherd who carries mountains]

The cowherd who carries mountains[3]
   is the one for me—
I want no one else.

I've looked and looked
   all over the world—
I have no other savior.

I've left my brothers,
   left my bondsmen,
left my blood relations.

I've been hanging out
   with the likes of roaming holy men—
I've lost my honor in the world.[4]

I'm delighted to see
   my fellow devotees,
but I weep and weep when I see the world.

I've sown love's vine—
   I water it
with my flowing tears.

I've garnered the butter
   from the curds,
and thrown away the whey.[5]

3. This phrase, considered as one of Mīra's poetic signatures, refers to one part of the composite mythology of Kṛṣṇa, in which he is born as a cowherd in the Braj region of northern India (around Mathura, between modern Delhi and Agra). In this part of his human life, Kṛṣṇa is a young erotic god, with whom all the women of the region—young and old, married and unmarried—seek union; the women's longing for him is a "personification" of the soul's desire for union with God, for permanent liberation from earthly existence. In one episode, Kṛṣṇa saves the people of Braj from a deluge by uprooting and lifting an entire mountain, and holding it up with his superhuman strength like an enormous parasol or cover against the rain. He is thus their "ultimate savior."

4. In the settled society of Indian householders, wandering holy men are often regarded with distrust and suspicion; and it is especially dishonorable for women, whether unmarried or married (as Mīra is said to have been), to keep their company.

5. For at least 3,500 years, yogurt has been an essential part of Indian cuisine. When yogurt is churned to make buttermilk, the creamy portion of the suspension rises to the surface, and can be skimmed off to make butter. The solids that remain in the buttermilk can then be separated as "curds" from the liquid, which is called "whey." The butter is considered the most—and the whey, the least—nutritious and valuable portion of the suspension.

The chieftain sent me a poison cup[6]—
  lost in love,
I gulped it down, straight.

Mīra, you've found   25
  your true attachments[7]—
whatever happens now,

O let it happen as it will.

[I'm steeped]

I'm steeped,
  steeped
in the dark one's color.[8]

I dressed up in my finery,
  put on my dancing anklets,   5
abandoned all shame, and danced in public.[9]

Gave up reason, went crazy,
  kept the company of holy men,
found the true form of a devotee.

Sang and sang the praises   10
  of Hari's virtues,[1] night and day—
so saved myself from the serpent of mortality.[2]

Without my lord, the whole world's brackish—
  merely a mouthful of salt.
Apart from him, everything's disposable.   15

---

6. The most popular legend associated with Mīra says that she was a princess in a Rajput clan in Rajasthan (now a western Indian state), and that she married a chieftain or into a chieftain's family in the region. When she became a devoted worshipper (*bhakta*) of Kṛṣṇa, either her husband or father or father-in-law tried to poison her; the legend claims that she swallowed the poison, but her love of God was so great that she remained unharmed.

7. In contrast to her "false" attachments to her fellow human beings and to worldly things, her attachments to Kṛṣṇa and his divine love are "true."

8. In Hindu mythology, Viṣṇu in his anthropomorphic form is dark-complexioned, and so is his avatar Kṛṣṇa. Here Mīra suggests that she is "steeped" in Kṛṣṇa's dark skin color.

9. In conservative 16th-century Hindu society— probable historical context of Mīra's life— women did not dance in public.

1. Hari is one of Viṣṇu's, and hence also Kṛṣṇa's, most common alternative names; "virtues" here refers to Kṛṣṇa's divine qualities.

2. In *bhakti* poetry, the serpent usually represents the poisonous nature either of the world or of mortal human life.

Mīra asks her lord who lifts mountains[3]
   to give her the kind of devotion
that seeps with sweetness—that's luscious, flavorful.[4]

[Darling, come visit me]

Darling, come visit me,
   give me a vision of yourself—
I can't live without you.

A lotus without water, a night without the moon.
   That's what you look like   5
without your beloved—me.

Distressed, distraught,
   I wander night and day,
our separation gnawing at my heart.

No hunger by day, no sleep by night—   10
   and, when I speak,
no words from my mouth.

What shall I say? What's said is no use.
   Come visit me—
quench my body heat.[5]   15

You pervade my self, control my moods—
   why torment me with yearning?
Have mercy, my master—come visit me.

Your lifelong slave, in life after life,[6]
   Mīra   20
falls at your feet.

---

3. An allusion to the episode in Kṛṣṇa's mythology, in which he lifted up a mountain to save people from a deluge.
4. The sweetness and flavor of devotion invoke the idea that *bhakti* has its own special *rasa* or poetic emotion; here *rasa* explicitly refers to classical Indian aesthetics.

5. Here Mīra boldly invites her divine lover to a physical encounter with her in human sexual terms.
6. In this verse, Mīra claims that she has voluntarily enslaved herself to God in all her reincarnations.

[My lord who lifts mountains]

My lord who lifts mountains—
   I'm off to his home.

He's my one true love.
   The moment I see his form,
I'm entranced.   5

When night falls, I get up and go to him—
   when day breaks,
I get up and return.[7]

Night and day, I play with him.
   I keep him happy   10
any which way I can.

I wear whatever he asks me to wear—
   I eat whatever
he gives me to eat.

Our love's an ancient love.   15
   I can't survive
a single moment without him.

I sit wherever he tells me to sit—
   if he were ever to sell me,
I'd be willing to be sold.[8]   20

Mīra's master is the lord
   who lifts mountains—
again and again, she sacrifices herself to him.

---

7. The extended metaphor in this verse suggests that Mīra spends her days in the human world but her nights in Kṛṣṇa's divine realm.
8. Her voluntary obedience of and enslavement to God is so complete that even if he were to choose to "sell" her in the marketplace (like a callous slaveowner), she would accept his decision.

TUKARAM
1608–1649

Tukaram (1608–1649) is associated with Dehu, a village near the city of Pune in Maharashtra state, India. He was a peasant by birth and hence a *śūdra* by caste; he probably earned a meager living as a grocer. He was married twice early, first to an invalid and then to a shrewish woman; his parents died when he was seventeen, which made him the head of an impoverished household that included several siblings. During a severe drought and famine across western India in 1629–31, he turned to poetry as a means of spiritual survival; for the rest of his life, he was a devoted worshiper of the god Viṭṭhala, popularly believed to be a local manifestation of Viṣṇu.

Over two decades or more, Tukaram composed a large number of short poems in Marathi in the *abhanga* form (a lyric in metrical quatrains); the canon of his poetry contains about 4,600 *abhanga*s. The poems are designed to be sung, and hence are set to music and performed with a one-string drone, castanets, and a drum. Since the midseventeenth century, they have been sung in temples in Dehu and around Maharashtra, and during large pilgrimages; they are prominent in the folk as well as classical musical traditions of western India. Tukaram's poetry has been disseminated widely in oral, musical, written, and printed forms, and is a vital presence in both literary and popular culture in Marathi. The majority of Maharashtrians regard him as their community's most important poetic and spiritual "voice."

As our selection shows, Tukaram plays this role because, beyond his particular religious affiliation, he is a poet of the general human condition. He often speaks directly and without intrusive artifice as an ordinary man engaged in everyday domestic and community life; he refers to his personal feelings and circumstances humbly and honestly, without embarrassment. He is therefore able to explore moods, states of mind, and psychological and existential crises—from inadequacy and failure to guilt and despair—in remarkably modern and even secular ways. "Begging for God's Compassion," for example, is a frankly confessional poem: the poet is inextricably trapped by his own deeds and feels "completely powerless." Nevertheless, Tukaram is also a fearless social poet and critic; "The Rich Farmer" attacks the wealthy for their selfishness, greed, and moral double-standards, whereas "The Harvest" celebrates the unstinting labor and essential goodness of the common farmer. His prayers, such as "Viṭṭhala," are addressed to a Hindu god, but they contain universal expressions of frailty and desire in a hostile world, which resonate with people of many faiths in different times and places.

The Rich Farmer[1]

He has vowed undying devotion
to a god of stone,
but he won't let his wife go
listen to a holy recitation.

He has built a crematorium   5
with his hoarded wealth,
but he thinks it wrong to grow
holy basil at his door.

Thieves plunder his home
and bring him much grief,   10
but he won't give a coin
to a poor brahman.

He treats his son-in-law
like a guest of honor,
but he turns his back upon   15
his real guests.

Tukā says, curse him,
may he burn.
He's only a burden
and drains the earth.   20

The Harvest[2]

The field has ripened:
watch its four corners.
The grain is ready for harvest,
but you mustn't stop working.

Guard it, guard it!   5
Don't fall asleep,
don't take it easy:
the crop's still standing on the ground.

---

1. This and the following poems by Tukaram were translated by Vinay Dharwadker. Like other *bhakti* poems, this *abhanga* by Tukaram adopts the persona of a poor man—in a country village, in this case—to forthrightly criticize the wealthy for their hypocritical piety, greed, stinginess, incivility, and lack of compassion.

2. A parable about the spiritual worth of labor on the land, this poem treats the various activities involved in farming as "good karma" that results in salvation. Incessant, selfless, and vigilant labor is thus its own reward, because it yields a harvest that embodies justice and happiness for all.

Put a stone in your sling:
the force of your shot,   10
your shouting and shooing
will scatter all the flocks of birds.

Light a fire, keep awake,
keep changing places:
when your head rolls,   15
you won't have your strength, your wits.

Give generously from the threshing floor,
make the world happy.
When the grain's piled up,
pay your taxes, give everyone his share.   20

Tukā says that's the moment
when there's nothing left to be done.
What's ours is in our hands,
and the chaff and husks have been thrown away.

The Waterwheel

How long must you endure
the whirlwind of death, of time?
It's at your back
all the while.

Free yourself   5
from your eighty-four hundred thousand births.[3]
enter the shelter
of Pāṇḍuranga.[4]

The seed that sprouts to life
brings death with it,   10
and when it dies
it's quickly born again.

Tukā says one's lives
are strung like pots on a waterwheel:
a pot frees itself   15
only when the cord is broken.[5]

3. The traditional number of successive life-times for which a human self or soul is reborn in the world due to the consequences of karma.
4. Pāṇḍuranga ("the one who is white in color") is one of the forms or aspects of Viṭṭhala, an autochthonous god of the Maharashtra region, now a state in western peninsular India. Viṭṭhala is identified with—but is not an avatar of—Viṣṇu, the god of preservation in classical Hinduism. Viṭṭhala-Pāṇḍuranga is the god that Tukaram, as a *bhakta*, chooses to worship.
5. The waterwheel is a multifaceted metaphor for the cycle of rebirth under the effects of karma; the breaking of the cord on which the pots on the wheel are strung signifies the breaking of the bondage of karma, and hence the attainment of *mokṣa* or final liberation from earthly existence.

Begging for God's Compassion

The world has bothered me no end.
I've lain in the womb in my mother's belly.
I've become the beggar who begs at the doors
of eighty-four hundred thousand yonis.[6]

I live like a slave in someone else's hands.   5
I'm caught and whirled in the powerful snare
of all my deeds, done now and in earlier births,
whose fruits stick to me, to ripen now and later.

My belly's empty and there's no rest.
No destination, no resting place, no home town.   10
Lord, don't spin me like this, I've lost my strength.
My soul sputters in torment, like a rice grain on a hot griddle.

So many times have gone by like this,
and I don't know how many more lie ahead of me.
They come around again and again without a break.   15
Maybe the string will snap only when the world ends.

Who will take away such anguish from me?
On whom can I press my burden?
Your name ferries us across the world's ocean,
but you hide in a hole, waiting in ambush.   20

Strike me now, run me over, O Nārāyaṇa.[7]
Do this for me, impoverished wretch that I am.
Don't ask a man without goodness for good things.
Tukā begs for your compassion.

Viṭṭhala[8]

His name is good, his form lovely.
They cool my eye and drive away my fever.
Viṭṭhala, Viṭṭhala is my rosary.
So short and sweet, so easy, and always there.

---

6. The number of rebirths that an individual self undergoes, if it cannot break the chain of action and its consequences; and hence also the number of mothers' "wombs" or *yonis* through which it must "pass" before being liberated.
7. Like Hari, one of the ancient Indian names of God in his most general form; often used for Viṣṇu in his universal aspect.
8. A local god associated with the region of Maharashtra in western India, who is identified with Viṣṇu.

This name is a weapon, the arrow of nirvāṇa,[9]   5
a means for the moment when death is near.
What's the use of preparing for a funeral?
Nārāyaṇa[1] breaks up your pain if you fix your sights on him.

This is the very best of all that's known.
Because it frees you from the world, and frees you forever,   10
you must go and seek out the Lord's protection.
It's all you need to do, and it's enough.

That's why I'm angry with the world,
this gleaming, poisonous serpent.[2]
It keeps us apart, me and you, my giver,   15
with its sharp and hostile stratagems.

It has made me taste the fruit of this world,
it has fixed the wrong verses in my mind.
I've grown fat and heavy with my many sojourns.
I've grown bald with the mockery heaped on me.   20

I've had the punishment for what I've done.
I've eaten what's eaten in many castes and births.
I must break it up now, put an end to it.
Lord, Tūka lays himself down at your feet.

9. Buddhist term for liberation from karma and rebirth by means of "extinguishing" the self, but used in many Hindu and *bhakti* texts as a broad synonym for *mokṣa*, liberation from karma when the self reunites with God or godhead.

1. A name for Viṣṇu in his universal aspect, here used as an epithet for Viṭṭhala, Tukaram's chosen local god.
2. A personification of the world's deceptiveness and viciousness.

IX

Europe and the New World

" All the world's a stage, / And all the men and women merely players." **Shakespeare**'s famous comparison of human beings to actors playing their various roles in the great theater of the world conjures up the exhilarating liberty and mobility we associate with the memorable characters of Renaissance literature. Because "merely" meant, in Shakespeare's day, "wholly" and "entirely," the line evokes a lively sense of the men and women of that world performing their roles with the gusto of actors. Their social roles as princes, clowns, thieves, or housewives appear, from one angle, as exciting opportunities for the characters to explore. Yet such roles are also clearly confining: Renaissance men and women were born into societies that strictly regulated their actions and even their clothing—only actors had the right to vary their garb and dress above their station. Whether Renaissance subjects relished the pleasures of playing or resented the constraints of their social roles is a subject often taken up in the literature of the day.

The most memorable characters of Renaissance literature enjoy greater autonomy and more fully realized personalities, and are much more prone to introspection than their medieval predecessors. Characters like **Cervantes**' idealistic but mad Don

A detail from Hans Holbein's 1533 painting, commonly called *The Ambassadors*.

Quixote and Shakespeare's hesitant Hamlet are frequently presented in acts of thought, fantasy, planning, doubt, and internal debate. Deliberating with others and themselves about what to do seems at least as important to these characters as putting their plans into action.

One reason for this shift toward internal, mental, and psychological portraiture is that Renaissance authors, like the characters they invent, inhabited a world of such widespread revolutionary change that they could not passively receive the traditional wisdom of previous ages. The stage on which they played was transformed and expanded by both the scientific and the geographical advances of the age. When Nicolaus Copernicus (1473–1543) discovered that the earth moves around the sun and when Galileo Galilei (1564–1642) turned his telescope up to the heavens, the nature of the universe and creation had to be reconceived. When **Christopher Columbus** (1451–1506) sailed to what he thought were the Indies, he introduced a New World to Europe, which began for the first time to think of itself as the Old World. Around the time that Columbus was sailing to America, humanist thinkers in Italy began to use new scholarly methods that gave them fuller access to the cultural legacy of ancient Greece and Rome as well as a new sense of their own place in history. On scientific, geographical, and scholarly fronts, the world of Renaissance Europe was undergoing revolutionary change.

After Johannes Gutenberg's invention of the printing press in 1439, the new ideas and controversies of the age reached a broader audience than ever before. Texts of all sorts were printed widely, and the spread of the printing press across Europe meant that writers could often avoid local censorship by having texts printed elsewhere, as

A portrait of Nicolaus Copernicus, from the front matter of the first edition of his *De Revolutionibus Orbium Coelestium* (On the Revolutions of the Heavenly Spheres), published in 1543.

occurred with Protestant bibles in local languages that circulated widely despite Catholic prohibitions. Despite censorship, the average person's access to information increased dramatically.

The new discoveries, rapidly circulating, were avidly resisted in some quarters, as when the Inquisition forced Galileo to repudiate the Copernican theory that the earth rotates around the sun. At the same time, they led to an unprecedented sense of possibility. In his dialogue *The City of the Sun* (1602) Galileo's friend and supporter Tommasso Campanella (1568–1639) optimistically asserted that the three great inventions of his day—the compass, the printing press, and the gun—were "signs of the union of the entire world."

As the two great powers of the age, Habsburg Spain and the Ottoman Empire, grew ever more dominant, this "union of the world" could also seem threatening. With the defeat of the Muslim stronghold of Granada in 1492, and the expulsion of the Jews in the same year, Spain emerged as a centralized, militantly Christian state. Spain's modernized army effectively replaced older chivalric forms of combat with new troops armed with guns and cannons, making great inroads into Italy and France. Charles, King of Spain, was crowned Holy Roman Emperor in 1519, consolidating many of the great dynastic houses of Europe. Soon the Habsburg domains extended across the globe, from Europe to the New World in the west to Asia, in an empire without precedent.

ENCOUNTERING THE NEW WORLD

As emperor, Charles V took for his emblem the pillars of Hercules, which for the ancients had signaled the end of the known world at the Straits of Gibraltar. But Charles reversed the motto that accompanied the emblem, from the forbidding "Ne Plus Ultra" (*no further*, [Latin]) to the endlessly ambitious "Plus Ultra," which encouraged going *ever further*. So the Spanish did across the globe, all while battling the Ottomans' own expansion into the Mediterranean and North Africa.

The new discoveries challenged European centrality in the world and in creation. Contact with New World peoples forced Europeans to consider as never before what counted as culture, civilization, and even humanity, casting into doubt the authority of the classics that scholars had recently embraced with a new fervor. In an ironic exchange on Prospero's island in Shakespeare's *The Tempest*, Miranda exclaims, "Oh brave new world, that has such people in it," only to suffer her father's devastating correction: "Tis new to thee." Although Columbus considered the New World a *tabula rasa*—a clean slate ready to be

imprinted with Christianity and European ways—by the time the conquerors **Hernán Cortés** (1485–1547) and Francisco Pizarro (1478–1541) encountered the great civilizations of the Aztecs and the Incas in the 1520s and 1530s, Europe was forced to grapple with other versions of what culture could mean.

As the explorers contemplated complex societies that had been completely unknown to the Old World, the arbitrariness of European social arrangements became visible to many thoughtful observers. Thomas More (1478–1535) was inspired by reports of new social arrangements to imagine his own island of *Utopia*, a wry fantasy nonetheless full of hope for reform. In one of his skeptical, probing *essais* (called "On Cannibals") **Michel de Montaigne** (1533–1592) elaborated on recent ethnographies of the Tupinamba Indians in Brazil, to ask larger questions about European society, whose peculiarities proved as unintelligible to the "cannibals" as Tupinamba society was to Europeans.

Europeans assumed that the New World existed for their profit and delectation—an idea expressed in the famous engraving by Jan van der Straet that depicted America as a seductive woman welcoming the explorer Amerigo Vespucci with open arms. Yet this assumption was quickly challenged in the New World, both by an impregnable landscape and by the continued resistance of the native population. The massive **Florentine Codex** gathers traditional narratives and oratory as well as indigenous accounts of the Spaniards' arrival in what is now Mexico, and contrasts markedly with European accounts of those events. As the New World yielded untold mineral wealth, Spain set up an elaborate political structure to control it, while other European nations mounted their own expeditions or turned to piracy in efforts to rival Spanish successes. Meanwhile,

North Pole

North Pacific Ocean

NORTH AMERICA

Greenland

Spitsbergen

Hudson (1609)

Iceland

Hudson (1610)

Newfoundland

Cabot (1497)

Bristol London

Corte-Real (1500)

North Atlantic Ocean

EUROPE

Gulf of Mexico

Cuba

Azores Is. ● Velho (1431)

Venice
Genoa

Columbus (1: 1492)

Lisbon
Spain

Vivaldi (1291)

Palos
Sanlúcar
Cádiz

Hispaniola

Columbus (2: 1493)

Madeira
Canary Is.

Columbus (4: 1502)

Columbus (3: 1498)

Cape Verde Is.

AFRICA

Cão (1482)

SOUTH AMERICA

del Cano returns (1522)

Equator

da Gama (1497)

Dias (1487)

South Pacific Ocean

Cape of
Good
Hope

South Atlantic Ocean

Cape
Horn

MAJOR EUROPEAN
EXPLORATIONS BY SEA
1291–1610

Magellan/del Cano (1519)

Vespucci (1501)

From Jan van der Straet, *Vespucci Discovering America*, 1589. The fertility of the New World is represented as a sexualized female body.

the tremendous influx of wealth from the New World had a destabilizing effect across Europe, leading to persistent inflation and new possibilities of social mobility.

CONFLICTS IN EUROPE

If the New World proved difficult to control from across the ocean, Europe was no less riven by conflict. Not even the threat of "the Turk," as the Europeans referred to the Ottoman expansion, could paper over the serious rifts that divided the continent. The Protestant Reformation, which initially targeted the abuses and corruption of the Catholic Church, quickly became a political as well as a religious crisis. Movements originally intended to reform the Church—such as those led by Martin Luther (1483–1546) and John Calvin (1509–1564)—were rapidly adopted by Renaissance princes bridling under papal authority. The reformers' attacks on the Pope, who wielded enormous political and military as well as spiritual power, provided an opportunity for rulers across Europe to increase their own sway. Henry VIII of England famously broke with the Catholic Church and declared himself head of the Church of England, and the pattern of contesting or breaking with papal authority was repeated throughout Europe. By nationalizing religious authority, monarchs claimed for themselves more and more rights that traditionally had belonged to the Pope or that had been shared by parliaments. Securing these rights from these other institutions brought monarchs closer to the absolutist rule that they craved. Yet, the Protestant Reformation had so emboldened subjects to challenge religious and political authority that the advantage enjoyed by European monarchs in the later sixteenth

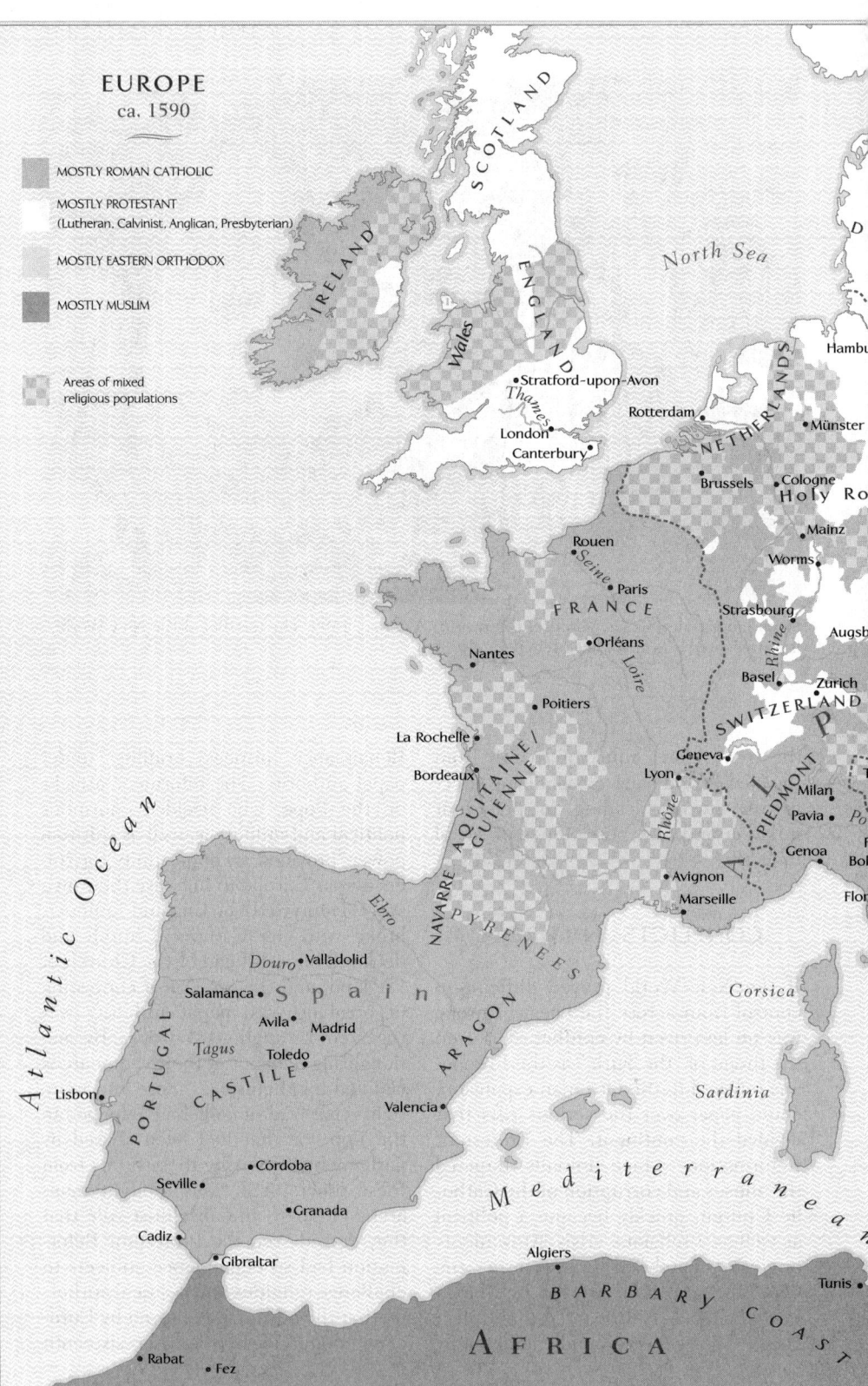

EUROPE
ca. 1590

MOSTLY ROMAN CATHOLIC

MOSTLY PROTESTANT
(Lutheran, Calvinist, Anglican, Presbyterian)

MOSTLY EASTERN ORTHODOX

MOSTLY MUSLIM

Areas of mixed
religious populations

SCOTLAND

IRELAND

ENGLAND

Wales

North Sea

Stratford-upon-Avon

Thames

Rotterdam

NETHERLANDS

Münster

London

Canterbury

Brussels

Cologne

Holy Ro

Mainz

Rouen

Worms

Seine

Paris

FRANCE

Strasbourg

Orléans

Augsbu

Loire

Basel

Zurich

Rhine

SWITZERLAND

Nantes

Poitiers

La Rochelle

Geneva

Lyon

PIEDMONT

Milan

Tr

Bordeaux

AQUITAINE/
GUIENNE

Rhône

Po

Pavia

Fe

Genoa

Bolo

NAVARRE

Avignon

Marseille

Flore

PYRENEES

Ebro

Atlantic Ocean

Douro

Valladolid

Corsica

Salamanca

S p a i n

ARAGON

Avila

Madrid

Tagus

Toledo

CASTILE

Sardinia

PORTUGAL

Valencia

Lisbon

Córdoba

Seville

Mediterranean

Granada

Cadiz

Gibraltar

Algiers

BARBARY COAST

Tunis

Rabat

Fez

AFRICA

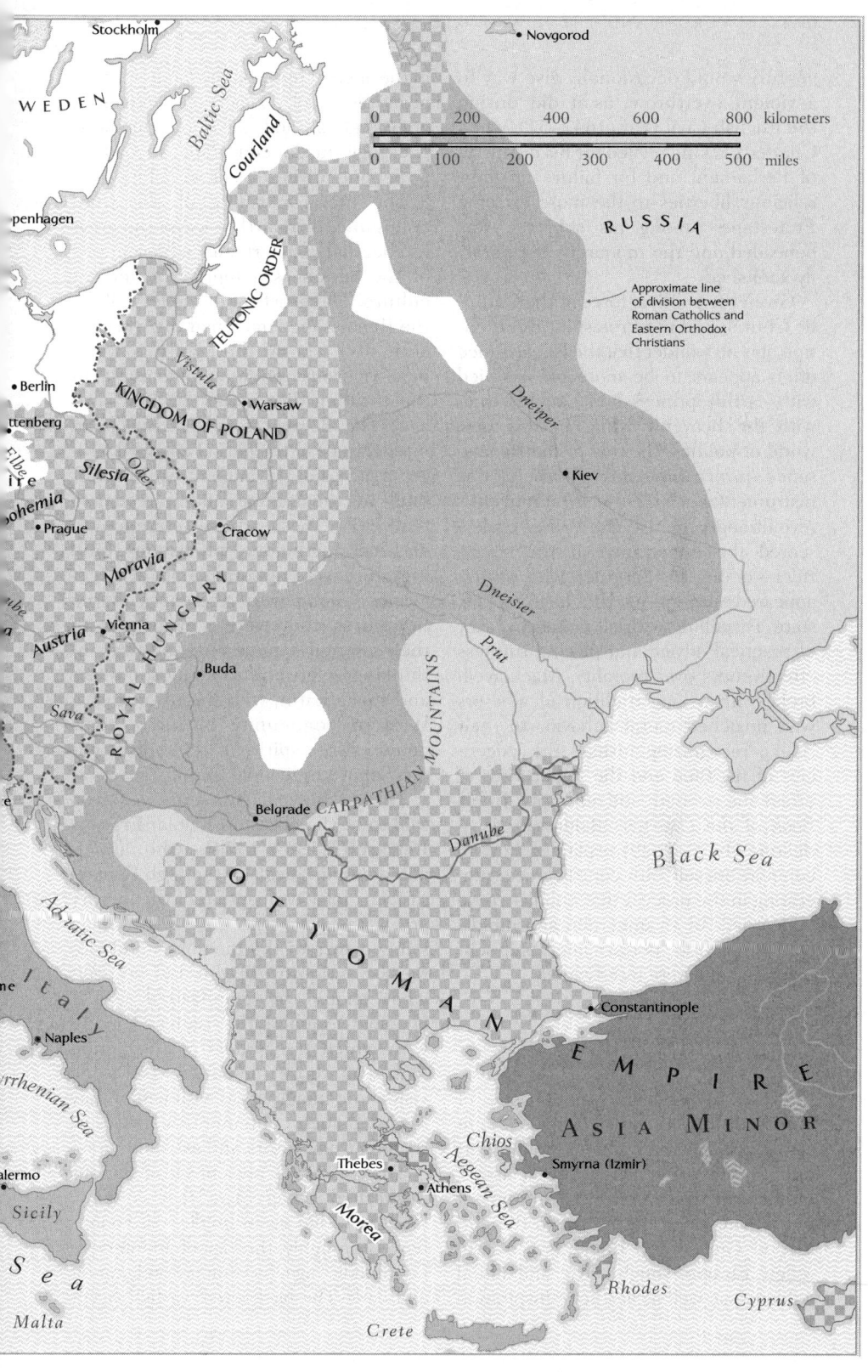

Stockholm

Novgorod

SWEDEN

Baltic Sea

Courland

0   200   400   600   800   kilometers
0   100   200   300   400   500   miles

penhagen

RUSSIA

TEUTONIC ORDER

Approximate line
of division between
Roman Catholics and
Eastern Orthodox
Christians

Berlin

Vistula

Warsaw

KINGDOM OF POLAND

Dnieper

ttenberg

Elbe

Silesia

Oder

Cracow

Kiev

ire

Bohemia

Prague

Moravia

Dneister

ube

Austria

Vienna

ROYAL HUNGARY

Prut

Buda

CARPATHIAN MOUNTAINS

Sava

Belgrade

Danube

Black Sea

Adriatic Sea

O T T O M A N

Italy

Naples

E M P I R E

Constantinople

yrrhenian Sea

ASIA MINOR

Chios

alermo

Thebes

Aegean Sea

Smyrna (Izmir)

Athens

Sicily

Morea

Sea

Rhodes

Cyprus

Malta

Crete

century would occasionally give way to a violent overthrow, as it did during the English Civil War (1642–51), when Charles I, a king reviled for his dismissal of Parliament and for failure to grant religious liberties to the more extreme Protestants among his subjects, was beheaded and the monarchy temporarily abolished.

Given the political force of the Catholic Church and the Protestant Reformation, it is no wonder that the Renaissance often appears to be more preoccupied with earthly princes and empires than with the heavenly King. In this new world of politics, the role of the Renaissance prince and his courtiers is instrumental. **Niccolò Machiavelli's** revolutionary treatise *The Prince* underscored the importance of the strong ruler—or at least a ruler who always appeared strong—as the head of his state. Dispelling with all pieties in favor of practical advice and placing ruthless effectiveness over morality, Machiavelli broke with a long tradition of advisors who preached moral behavior to their rulers, recognizing instead the exigencies of his time and the importance of projecting strength and authority. In his *Book of the Courtier*, Baldassare Castiglione (1478–1529) explained how to comport oneself with courtly grace, suggesting in the process that nobility could be learned. In an uncertain and rapidly changing world, performance and self-improvement were intertwined.

HUMANISM

The new Renaissance consciousness of how individuals could fashion themselves through their actions was in part due to the influence of the classics. Humanism, the intellectual movement that championed the return to the culture of Greece and Rome as a way to renew Europe, sought civic and moral guidance as well as aesthetic inspiration

in the ancient texts. As the modern European rulers took on cadres of secretaries, ambassadors, and advisors, humanist pedagogy made education a road to power and privilege as never before.

The literal meaning of the word *renaissance*—"rebirth"—casts the great intellectual and artistic achievements of the period as a reprise of ancient culture. The artists and intellectuals of the Renaissance imagined the world of antiquity "reborn" through their work, in a vigorous renewal comparable to the thrilling discoveries of their own age. The degree to which European intellectuals of the period engaged with the writings of the ancient world is difficult for the average modern reader to realize. For these writers, references to classical mythology, philosophy, and literature were not ornaments or affectations. Along with references to the Scriptures, they were a major part of their mental equipment and way of thinking. Every cultivated person wrote and spoke Latin, with the result that a Western community of intellectuals could exist, a spiritual "republic of letters" above individual nations.

The archetypal humanist is often said to be the poet and scholar **Francis Petrarch** (1304–1374), who anticipated certain ideals of the high Renaissance: a lofty conception of the literary art, a taste for the good life, and a strong sense of the memories and glories of antiquity. In this last respect, what should be emphasized is the imaginative quality, the visionary impulse with which the writers of the period looked at those memories—the same vision and imagination with which they regarded such contemporary heroes as the great navigators and astronomers.

The vision of an ancient age of glorious intellectual achievement that is "now" brought to life again implies, of course, however roughly, the idea of an intervening "middle" age, by comparison ignorant and dark. The hackneyed, vastly inaccurate notion that the "light" of the Renaissance broke through a long "night" of the Middle Ages was not devised by subsequent centuries; it was held by the humanist scholars of the Renaissance themselves. Petrarch imagined himself living in "sad times": "It were better to be born either earlier or much later, for there was once and perhaps will be again a happier age. In the middle, you see, in our time, squalor and baseness have flowed together." Addressing his book, Petrarch expresses his longing for a new age: "But if you, as is my wish and ardent hope, shall live on after me, a more propitious age will come again: this Lethean stupor surely can't endure forever. Our posterity, perchance, when the shadows have lifted, may enjoy once more the radiance the ancients knew." The combination of self-deprecation, aspiration, and arrogance aptly characterizes the period's sense of its own superiority over the recent past.

Despite the fractured political and religious landscape of Europe, especially in the sixteenth century, the great intellectual innovations of the Renaissance expanded across all boundaries. The movement had its inception in Italy with Petrarch, and developed most remarkably in the visual arts, made its way across Europe to Spain, France, and England, where its main achievements were in literature, particularly the drama. The intellectual fervor of humanism, like the poetic conventions of Petrarchism, gradually expanded into multiple languages and national traditions. Their dissemination led to new genres and to playful recombinations of older ones, inaugurating a period of great innovation in all forms of literature.

Definitions of the Renaissance must take account of the period's preoccupation with this life rather than with the life beyond. Though an oversimplification, one might say that an ideal medieval man or woman, whose mode of action is basically oriented toward the thought of the afterlife (and who

therefore conceives of life on earth as transient and preparatory) contrasts with an ideal Renaissance man or woman, whose enthusiasm for earthly interests is actually enhanced by the knowledge that one's time on earth is fleeting. Once again, Petrarch provides the best example: the *Rime Sparse* (Scattered Rhymes), the extensive sequence of love poems for which he is best known, are full of renunciation, as the poet searches in vain for religious consolation for the travails of earthly desire. Yet in the process of charting the futility of earthly love, the poems paint an incredibly detailed portrait of the poet-lover in all his earthly variations, rendering his interior life both immediate and engrossing.

THE WELL-LIVED LIFE

The emphasis on the immediate and tangible is reflected in the earthly, amoral, and aesthetic character of what we may call the Renaissance code of behavior. Human action is judged not in terms of right and wrong, of good and evil (as it is judged when life is viewed as a moral "test," with reward or punishment in the afterlife), but in terms of its present concrete validity and effectiveness, of the delight it affords, of its memorability and its beauty. Much of what is typical of the Renaissance, then, from architecture to poetry, from sculpture to rhetoric, may be related to a taste for the harmonious and the memorable, for the spectacular effect, for the successful striking of a pose. Individual human action, seeking in itself its own reward, finds justification in its formal appropriateness; in its being a well-rounded achievement, perfect of its kind; in the zest and gusto with which it is, here and now, performed; and, finally, in its proving worthy of remaining as a testimony to the performer's power on earth. In this sense, the purpose of life is the unrestrained and self-sufficient practice of one's "virtue," the competent and delighted exercise of one's skill.

The leaders of the period saw in a work of art the clearest instance of beautiful, harmonious, and self-justified performance. To create such a work became the valuable occupation par excellence, the most satisfactory display of virtue. The Renaissance view of antiquity exemplifies this attitude. The artists and intellectuals of the period not only drew on antiquity for certain practices and forms but also found there a recognition of the place of the arts among outstanding modes of human action. In this way, the concepts of "fame" and "glory" became particularly associated with the art of poetry because the Renaissance drew from antiquity the idea of the poet as celebrator of high deeds, the "dispenser of glory."

At the same time, there is no reason to forget that such virtues and skills are God's gift. Renaissance intellectuals, artists, aristocrats, and princes did not lack in abiding religious faith or fervor. Machiavelli, Rabelais, and Cervantes take for granted the presence of God in their own and in their heroes' lives. For many, the Protestant Reformation and the growth of mysticism within the Catholic Church led to a more intimate and individualized relationship with the divine. Much about the religious temper of the age is expressed in its art, particularly in Italian painting, where Renaissance Madonnas celebrate earthly beauty even as they inspire thoughts of the divine.

Madonna and Child, ca. 1465, by Fra Filippo Lippi. The object of the painting's devotions is somewhat unclear: is our eye focused on the baby Jesus, or on the beauty of Mary's face?

creation of works of art—the Renaissance assumption is that there are things here on earth that are highly worth doing, and that by doing them, humanity proves its privileged position in creation and therefore incidentally follows God's intent. The often-cited phrase "the dignity of man" describes this positive, strongly affirmed awareness of the intellectual and physical "virtues" of the human being, and of the individual's place in creation. And yet, alongside the delight of earthly achievement, there lurked in many Renaissance minds nagging doubts: What is the purpose or ultimate worth of all this activity? What meaningful relation does it bear to any all-inclusive, cosmic pattern? The Renaissance coincided with, and perhaps to some extent occasioned, a loss of firm belief in the final unity and the final intelligibility of the universe. In the wake of the geographic and scientific discov-

SKEPTICISM AND MELANCHOLY

Especially where there is a close association between the practical and the intellectual—as in the exercise of political power, the act of scientific discovery, the

Young Man Holding a Skull, 1519, by Lucas van Leyden. This young nobleman, a paragon of Renaissance fashion, points to a skull that he cradles in his left arm, reminding the viewer of the inevitable fate that even the best-dressed courtier will face.

eries, thinkers such as Montaigne and Descartes became skeptics, doubting and questioning received knowledge.

For some Renaissance writers and artists, the sense of uncertainty became so strong as to paralyze their aspiration to power or thirst for knowledge or delight in beauty. The resulting attitude we may call Renaissance melancholy. It was sometimes openly expressed (as by some characters in Elizabethan drama) and other times merely provided an undercurrent of sadness or wise resignation to a work (as in More's *Utopia* or Montaigne's *Essays*). Thus while on one, and perhaps the better-known, side of the picture, human intellect in Renaissance literature enthusiastically illuminates the realms of knowledge and unveils the mysteries of the universe, on the other it is beset by puzzling doubts and a profound mistrust of its own powers.

Doubts about the value of human action within the scheme of eternity did not, however, diminish the outpouring of ideas about the ideal ordering of this world. Renaissance poets and intellectuals tested ideas about the ideal prince, courtier, councilor, and humble subject as well as the ideal court and society. More's *Utopia* imagines a perfectly ordered society, as improbable as it is optimistic, while Machiavelli proposes his amoral ideas about the effective (rather than ideal) prince. Shakespeare's *Hamlet* gives us a prince far from ideal, confronting the effects of private violations on the public realm. In all the major works of the Renaissance, writers can be seen tirelessly examining the nature of their own world, the problem of power, and the vexed relations between the absolute authority of the prince and the rights and liberties of the people. Its zeal for defining the social contract partly explains why the Renaissance is often viewed as the "early modern" period; the "rebirth" and flourishing of antiquity also heralded ideas that we associate with the modern political world.

The joining of philosophical and imaginative thinking in literary expression is characteristic of the Renaissance, which cultivated the idea of "serious play." Throughout the literature of the period, we see the creative and restless mind of the Renaissance intellectual "freely ranging," as Sir Philip Sidney put it, "only in the zodiac of his own wit," creating fictional characters and worlds that might, if the poet is sufficiently persuasive, be put into practice and change the nature of the real world.

FRANCIS PETRARCH

1304–1374

Although Petrarch, a contemporary of **Dante** and Boccaccio, lived and died in the Middle Ages, he did everything in his power to distinguish himself and his scholarship from the period he dismissed as the "Dark Ages." Petrarch dedicated himself to the recovery of classical learning in a spirit commonly associated with a later period, in which humanist scholars zealously pursued the rebirth of antiquity. Yet Petrarch's status as a precursor of the Renaissance is primarily due to an aspect of his work that neither he nor his contemporaries regarded as a lasting contribution: his 366 lyric poems in the vernacular, mostly dedicated to his frustrated desire for an elusive woman named Laura. Petrarch's experience of love and sense of his own fragmented and fluid self set the standard for the lyric expression of subjective and erotic experience in the Renaissance. His efforts to scrutinize himself intently and at times unflatteringly and to capture his own elusive inner workings in verse inspired a poetic tradition that has influenced lyric sequences from **Shakespeare**'s sonnets to Walt Whitman's *Leaves of Grass* to contemporary pop lyrics.

Francis Petrarch was born in Arezzo on July 20, 1304, three years after his father and Dante Alighieri were exiled from Florence. In 1314, Petrarch's father moved his family to Avignon, the new seat of the papacy (1309–77), where he became prosperous in the legal profession. Petrarch himself initially trained as a law student, but chose instead to pursue the study of classical culture and literature. He soon came to the attention of the powerful Colonna family, whose patronage launched his career as a diplomat-scholar and allowed him to travel widely and move in the intimate circles of European princes and scholars. He refused the offices of bishop and papal secretary, preferring instead to ground his growing prestige in his humanistic scholarship. Imaginative conversation with the ancients, like imitation of their poetry, brought him into contact with the past: his research into classical history and arts profoundly influenced his sense of himself and his own cultural moment. He died in 1374 near Padua, his head resting on a volume of his beloved **Virgil**.

Petrarch's most famous work, the *Rime Sparse* (Scattered Rhymes) or *Rerum Fragmenta Vulgarium* (Fragments in the Vernacular), is a collection of 366 songs and sonnets (based on the calendar year associated with the liturgy) of extraordinary technical virtuosity and variety. Written in Italian and woven into a highly introspective narrative, the lyric collection takes the poet himself as its object of study. The poems painstakingly record how his thoughts and identity are scattered and transformed by the experience of love for a beautiful, unattainable woman named Laura. Even some of his friends suspected that Laura was merely the theme and emblem of his lyric poetry and not a historical woman; she appears to have been both. On the flyleaf of his magnificent copy of Virgil, Petrarch inscribed a note on her life:

> Laura, illustrious through her own virtues, and long famed through my

verses, first appeared to my eyes in my youth, in the year of our Lord 1327, on the sixth day of April, in the church of St. Clare in Avignon, at matins; and in the same city, also on the sixth day of April, at the same first hour, but in the year 1348, the light of her life was withdrawn from the light of day, while I, as it chanced, was in Verona, unaware of my fate. * * * Her chaste and lovely form was laid to rest at vesper time, on the same day on which she died in the burial place of the Brothers Minor. I am persuaded that her soul returned to the heaven from which it came, as Seneca says of Africanus. I have thought to write this, in bitter memory, yet with a certain bitter sweetness, here in this place that is often before my eyes, so that I may be admonished, by the sight of these words and by the consideration of the swift flight of time, that there is nothing in this life in which I should find pleasure; and that it is time, now that the strongest tie is broken, to flee from Babylon; and this, by the prevenient grace of God, should be easy for me, if I meditate deeply and manfully on the futile cares, the empty hopes, and the unforeseen events of my past years.

(Translated by E. H. Wilkins)

Petrarch's note illuminates the powerful role that Laura plays in his personal struggles between spiritual aspirations and earthly attachments. Thoughts of Laura return him to the problem of his own will, torn between spiritual and sensual desires, always delaying worldly renunciation. Even when he expresses disgust with earthly rewards and pleasures, it is conditional: he will choose the right course of action, Petrarch writes, *if* he meditates "deeply and manfully" on the disappointments and failures of his past and denies memory's seductively bittersweet pleasures.

In the *Rime Sparse*, Laura's ambiguous position between divine guide and earthly temptress contrasts sharply with the role that Beatrice played in Dante's spiritual pilgrimage, the *Divine Comedy*. Whereas Dante's love finally leads him to paradise, it is never clear to Petrarch whether he is pursuing heavenly or earthly delights and whether he will safely reach any destination or "port" (in the nautical image of sonnet 189). When Dante looks into Beatrice's eyes on Mount Purgatory, he sees a reflection of the heavens; when Petrarch gazes into Laura's eyes, he sees himself. Not even his use of the liturgical year (especially the anniversaries of Christ's death and resurrection) to structure his account of their relationship guarantees that a spiritual conversion will follow Petrarch's self-analysis or "confession" of his life. In a contrary and skeptical mood at the end of one of his most philosophical poems (song 264), Petrarch asserts, "I see the better, but choose the worse."

The lyric collection's first sonnet, in which Petrarch solicits compassion as well as pardon from his readers, establishes the *Rime Sparse*'s close relationship to confessional narrative. Its themes of conversion, memory, and forgetfulness (of God and oneself) evoke the model of **St. Augustine** and raise the question of whether Petrarch will follow suit: will he ultimately transcend his attachment to a woman's physical beauty, his love of language and poetic figures, and his narcissistic preoccupation with himself? In dramatic opposition to the transcendent model of Augustine is **Ovid** of the *Metamorphoses*, the classical counter-epic that artfully uses fragmentation, fluid change, and scattering to describe the effects of power—divine, political, or erotic—on bodies and on minds. Petrarch refers to a variety of Ovidian figures in the *Rime Sparse*, including Narcissus and Echo, Actaeon and Diana, Medusa, and Pygmalion. His chief

Ovidian model, however, is the story of Apollo, the god who "invents" the genre of lyric during his amorous chase of the nymph Daphne. While running, Apollo describes her various beauties—eyes, figure, and hair—and imaginatively embellishes what he sees. When Daphne eludes him through her transformation into the laurel, Apollo claims her as his tree, if not his lover, and declares that the laurel will be the sign of triumph in letters and warfare. The prominence of this tale in the *Rime Sparse* suggests that if Laura had not lived, Petrarch would have had to invent her. Her name interweaves key attributes of Petrarch's poetic imagination: *lauro* and *alloro* ("laurel"), *oro* ("gold," for her tresses and value), *l'aura* ("breeze" and "inspiration," which etymologically relates to "breath"), *laus* or *lauda* ("praise"). Such wordplay suggests the selective, even obsessive character of Petrarch's poetic style. Like Apollo, Petrarch also "translates" his beloved's elusive body into the more tangible figures of rhetoric.

Petrarch's great legacy to Renaissance European literature is the *Rime Sparse's* language of self-description, which starts from the conventional hyperbole, antithesis, and oxymoron (rhetorical exaggeration and opposition) that characterized troubadour songs, provençal lyric, and classical love elegy: *I freeze and burn, love is bitter and sweet, my sighs are tempests and my tears are floods, I am in ecstasy and agony, I am possessed by memories of her and I am in exile from myself*. Petrarch transformed such rhetorical figures or tropes of love into a powerful language of introspection and self-fashioning that swept through European literature. Although

it soon became so popular that writers endlessly repeated and even trivialized it, Petrarchism had serious dimensions that helped articulate growing questions about the self: is it determined by God or flexible and in the shaping hands of humankind? Do culture, history, and force of will compose and transform it?

Petrarchism offered rich formal possibilities as well: although Petrarch often wrote in other meters, the *sonnet* became in his hands an extraordinarily supple metrical form. A *Petrarchan sonnet*, as the form is now known, is a fourteen-line poem with a break after line eight. The *octet* is usually broken into two stanzas of four lines each, with a rhyme scheme of *a-b-b-a*, and the *sestet* is made up of two three-line stanzas, rhyming *c-d-c*. The sonnet proved remarkably flexible, allowing poets to express themselves in a compact and striking manner. The sestet and the octet may contrast formally or semantically, as may the stanzas within a section of the sonnet, while its rhyme can reinforce or contradict meaning. The possibilities are virtually endless, as Petrarch's many imitators were to demonstrate.

Across sixteenth- and seventeenth-century Europe, writers turned to Petrarch as a beacon of Italian humanism who offered a powerful intellectual and formal toolkit for introspection. Through their own poems, they made Petrarchism into an international language, adapting it to various national traditions and rehearsing it in countless iterations. Petrarch did not invent the idea of a divided, tormented lover, but his authoritative self-portrait defined an infinitely rich poetic tradition of erotic longing.

SONNETS

1[1]

You who hear in scattered rhymes the sound of those sighs with
which I nourished my heart during my first youthful error,[2] when
I was in part another man from what I am now:

for the varied style in which I weep and speak between vain
hopes and vain sorrow, where there is anyone who understands   5
love through experience, I hope to find pity, not only pardon.

But now I see well how for a long time I was the talk of the
crowd, for which often I am ashamed of myself within;[3]

and of my raving, shame is the fruit, and repentance, and the
clear knowledge that whatever pleases in the world is a brief   10
dream.

3[4]

It was the day when the sun's rays turned pale with grief for his
Maker[5] when I was taken, and I did not defend myself against it,
for your lovely eyes, Lady, bound me.

It did not seem to me a time for being on guard against Love's
blows; therefore I went confident and without fear, and so my   5
misfortunes began in the midst of the universal woe.[6]

Love found me altogether disarmed, and the way open through
my eyes to my heart, my eyes which are now the portal and
passageway of tears.

I therefore, as it seems to me, it got him no honor to strike me   10
with an arrow in that state,[7] and not even to show his bow to
you, who were armed.

---

1. Translated by Robert M. Durling.
2. Mental and physical "wandering" as well as a
moral "mistake." "Scattered rhymes": reference
to the sonnet collection's title, *Rime Sparse*.
3. The Italian, *di me medesmo meco mi ver-
gogno*, suggests intense self-consciousness.
4. Translated by Robert M. Durling.

5. The anniversary of Christ's crucifixion.
Elsewhere (sonnet 211 and a note in Petrarch's
copy of Virgil) given as April 6, 1327.
6. The communal Christian grief that contrasts with Petrarch's private woes.
7. State of grief over the crucifixion.

34[8]

Apollo, if the sweet desire is still alive that inflamed you beside
the Thessalian waves,[9] and if you have not forgotten, with the
turning of the years, those beloved blond locks;

against the slow frost and the harsh and cruel time that lasts as
long as your face is hidden, now defend the honored and holy   5
leaves where you first and then I were limed;

and by the power of the amorous hope that sustained you in
your bitter life, disencumber the air of these impressions.[1]

Thus we shall then together see a marvel[2]—our lady sitting on the
grass and with her arms making a shade for herself.   10

62[3]

Father in heaven, after each lost day,
Each night spent raving with that fierce desire
Which in my heart has kindled into fire
Seeing your acts adorned for my dismay;

Grant henceforth that I turn, within your light[4]   5
To another life and deeds more truly fair,
So having spread to no avail the snare
My bitter foe[5] might hold it in despite.

The eleventh year,[6] my Lord, has now come round
Since I was yoked beneath the heavy trace   10
That on the meekest weighs most cruelly.

Pity the abject plight where I am found;
Return my straying thoughts to a nobler place;
Show them this day you were on Calvary.

8. Translated by Robert M. Durling.
9. Petrarch links his love of Laura to the love
of Apollo for Daphne in Ovid's *Metamorphoses*. Daphne, daughter of the god of the Peneus
River in Thessaly, was pursued by Apollo, the
god of poetry. She begged her father to change
her form, which had "given too much pleasure," and was transformed into the laurel
tree. Apollo, whom Petrarch associates with
the sun god, claimed the laurel as his personal
emblem.
1. Grief, cloudy weather, and aging.
2. Supernatural and highly meaningful
spectacle.
3. Translated by Bernard Bergonzi.
4. Of grace.
5. Satan.
6. I.e., 1338.

126[7]

Clear, fresh, sweet waters,[8] where she who alone seems lady
to me rested her lovely body,
   gentle branch where it pleased her (with sighing I remember)
to make a column for her lovely side,
   grass and flowers that her rich garment covered along with   5
her angelic breast, sacred bright air where Love opened my heart
with her lovely eyes: listen all together to my sorrowful dying
words.

   If it is indeed my destiny and Heaven exerts itself that Love
close these eyes while they are still weeping,   10
   let some grace bury my poor body among you and let my soul
return naked to this its own dwelling;
   death will be less harsh if I bear this hope to the fearful pass,
for my weary spirit could never in a more restful port or a more
tranquil grave flee my laboring flesh and my bones.   15

   There will come a time perhaps when to her accustomed
sojourn the lovely, gentle wild one will return
   and, seeking me, turn her desirous and happy eyes toward
where she saw me on that blessed day,
   and oh the pity! seeing me already dust amid the stones,   20
Love will inspire her to sigh so sweetly that she will win mercy
for me and force Heaven, drying her eyes with her lovely veil.

   From the lovely branches was descending (sweet in
memory) a rain of flowers over her bosom,
   and she was sitting humble in such a glory,[9] already covered   25
with the loving cloud;
   this flower was falling on her skirt, this one on her blond
braids, which were burnished gold and pearls to see that day;
this one was coming to rest on the ground, this one on the water,
this one, with a lovely wandering, turning about seemed to say: 30
"Here reigns Love."[1]

   How many times did I say to myself then, full of awe: "She was
surely born in Paradise!"
   Her divine bearing and her face and her words and her sweet
smile had so laden me with forgetfulness   35
   and so divided me from the true image, that I was sighing:
"How did I come here and when?" thinking I was in Heaven, not
there where I was. From then on this grass has pleased me so that
elsewhere I have no peace.

   If you had as many beauties as you have desire, you could   40
boldly leave the wood and go among people.[2]

7. Translated by Robert M. Durling.
8. Of the river Sorgue.
9. An image associated with the Virgin Mary.
1. Amor (Cupid) or Christ. The floral and
bejeweled images associate Laura's body with
the bride of the Song of Songs, whose erotic
chastity is celebrated as an "enclosed garden"
and "fountain sealed."
2. The last two lines are addressed to the
poem.

189³

My ship laden with forgetfulness passes through a harsh sea, at
midnight, in winter, between Scylla and Charybdis, and at the
tiller sits my lord, rather my enemy;⁴

each oar is manned by a ready, cruel thought that seems to scorn
the tempest and the end; a wet, changeless wind of sighs, hopes,   5
and desires breaks the sail;

a rain of weeping, a mist of disdain wet and loosen the already
weary ropes, made of error twisted up with ignorance.

My two usual sweet stars⁵ are hidden; dead among the waves are
reason and skill; so that I begin to despair of the port.   10

333⁶

Go, grieving rimes of mine, to that hard stone
Whereunder lies my darling, lies my dear,
And cry to her to speak from heaven's sphere.
Her mortal part with grass is overgrown.

Tell her, I'm sick of living; that I'm blown   5
By winds of grief from the course I ought to steer,
That praise of her is all my purpose here
And all my business; that of her alone

Do I go telling, that how she lived and died
And lives again in immortality,   10
All men may know, and love my Laura's grace.

Oh, may she deign to stand at my bedside
When I come to die; and may she call to me
And draw me to her in the blessèd place!

---

3. Translated by Robert M. Durling.
4. Love. Scylla and Charybdis are the twinned
oceanic dangers through which Odysseus, in
Homer's *Odyssey*, and Aeneas, in Virgil's *Aeneid*, must chart a middle course. Forgetfulness
of oneself and of God is sinful in Augustinian
terms. The ship, captained by Reason, is a
traditional figure for the embodied soul.
5. Laura's eyes.
6. Translated by Morris Bishop.

NICCOLÒ MACHIAVELLI

1469–1527

Widely vilified and secretly admired, Niccolò Machiavelli attempted to teach the rulers of his time how to get power and hold on to it. Machiavelli transformed our conception of political power with his mix of clear-eyed, pragmatic observation and humanist idealism. Sharply contrasting traditional morality to the pragmatic necessities of ruling, Machiavelli tried to address the painful fragmentation and constant warfare of the many states that then made up what is today Italy. His solution—a strong, effective prince unconstrained by moral pieties—struck his contemporaries as a terrifying prescription for the use of force and deception, even though Machiavelli always stressed the ruler's need for popular support. Seeking to discuss the conduct of political affairs from a new rational basis, Machiavelli has been credited with having turned politics into a science.

LIFE AND TIMES

The son of a lawyer, Machiavelli was born to a well-connected but not wealthy family in the city-state of Florence, ruled by the beloved Lorenzo di Medici. He received a modest education, and was introduced to the scholarly circles around the ruler. Machiavelli's adult life was closely bound up with the political fortunes of his city-state. Renaissance Italy was a fractured collection of polities, constantly overrun by the armies of France, Spain, and the Holy Roman Empire, all of which took advantage of Italian fragmentation to expand their territorial claims. When Machiavelli was a young man, Florence experienced

its own profound political upheavals: after Lorenzo's death in 1492, the Medici were expelled from power and Florence was ruled by the Dominican preacher Savonarola. When Savonarola's regime collapsed, the city returned to republican government, and Machiavelli embarked on a distinguished career of public service, serving a city-state whose government was the most widely representative of its time. From 1498 to 1512, Machiavelli was secretary to the Second Chancery, charged with internal and war affairs. He also served as a diplomatic envoy (his low rank meant he could not be an ambassador), and, during the conflict between Florence and Pisa, dealt with military problems firsthand. His many missions to some of the most powerful rulers of his time— King Louis XII of France, Cesare Borgia, Pope Julius II, the Emperor Maximilian—allowed him to observe up close their methods for gaining and maintaining political power, and led to two books or *Portraits* of the affairs of their territories, written in 1508 and 1510. Machiavelli noted what made for effective conquest and rule, and contrasted the ruthlessness of a figure like Borgia to the slow deliberations of the consensus-based government in his own city. The constant threats and emergencies faced by Florence and other Italian states made the hardheaded, strong prince seem an appealing figure as a possible savior against foreign invasions.

As a student of politics and an acute observer of historical events, Machiavelli tried to apply his experience of other states to strengthening his own. He noted that one weakness of the Italian city-states was their reliance on mercenary soldiers, who were ever ready to change sides for higher pay. Instead, following Cesare Borgia's example, he set out in 1505 to establish an army of Florentine citizens, animated by their love for their country, which achieved some surprising victories. Yet the republican forces were not enough to fend off all attackers, and, in 1512, in a moment of military weakness, the Medici faction regained power. With the end of the Republic, Machiavelli lost his post. The Medici accused him unjustly of conspiracy, and had him imprisoned and tortured. Once released, he retreated from the city to his family's farm, with his wife, Marietta Corsini, and their five children. There, in a study where he imagined himself in conversation with the classical writers he most admired (as detailed in the "Letter to Francesco Vettori"), Machiavelli produced his major works: a study of republican government, the *Discourses on the First Ten Books of Livy* (1513–21), and one on princedoms, *The Prince*, written in 1513 with the hope that the Medici would ultimately grant him a public office. As his exile grew longer, he also wrote a number of literary works, including the much-applauded comedy *La mandragola* (The Mandrake), first performed in 1520. That same year Machiavelli was commissioned to write a history of Florence, which he presented in 1525 to Pope Clement VII (Giulio de' Medici).

After a reconciliation of sorts with the ruling Medicis, Machiavelli was entrusted with the upkeep of military fortifications in Florence. Here, too, he served the city well, presenting a strong enough defense that when the Holy Roman Empire invaded Italy in 1527, Florence avoided being attacked. Instead, the imperial forces sacked Rome with incredible violence. For Florence, which had long benefited from the strength of a series of Medici popes in Rome, the result was the collapse of Medici domination and, once more, the return of republican government. Despite Machiavelli's long history of service to the Republic, however, he was now regarded as a Medici sympathizer and passed over for public office. This last disappointment may have accelerated his end. He died on June 22, 1527, and was buried in the church of Santa Croce.

THE PRINCE

Although he wrote widely across many genres, Machiavelli's reputation—and his notoriety—is based on *The Prince*. This "handbook" on how to obtain and keep political power consists of twenty-six chapters. The first eleven deal with different types of dominions and how they are acquired and preserved—the early title of the whole book, in Latin, was *De principatibus* (Of Princedoms)— while the twelfth to fourteenth chapters focus on problems of military power. The book's astounding fame, however, is based on the final part (from chapter fifteen to the end), which deals primarily with the attributes and "virtues" of the prince himself.

Traditional manuals for rulers—a genre often referred to as the "mirror of princes"—couched their advice in the language of Christian morality. Their point was to remind the ruler to remain virtuous as they educated him and gave him advice. Erasmus's roughly contemporary *The Education of a Christian Prince* (1516), for example, which he presented to the future Charles V and also to Henry VIII, held that what the prince most needed was "the best possible understanding of Christ." Machiavelli's point, by stark contrast, is to make the ruler effective, by giving him advice on how to stay in power. For Machiavelli, the end of political stability justifies the means, even if those means include deception and violent force.

The view of humanity in Machiavelli is not cheerful. Indeed, the pessimistic notion that humanity is evil is not so much Machiavelli's conclusion about human nature as his premise, the point of departure for the course a ruler should follow: "A prudent ruler . . . cannot and should not observe faith when such observance is to his disadvantage and the causes that made him give his promise have vanished. If men were all good, this advice would not be good, but since men are wicked and do not keep their promises to you, you likewise do not have to keep yours to them." The idealism of Christian morality is checked by realism, by the facts on the ground. Machiavelli sees humanity as it is, not as it should be, and indicates the rules of the game as his experience shows it must, under the circumstances, be played. This kind of bald assessment did not sit well with European Christians invested in moral absolutes, and in the idea that it was God who bestowed power to rulers.

Yet despite his emphasis on ruthlessly preserving power, Machiavelli stresses over and over again the importance for a ruler of capturing the goodwill of his subjects. In Machiavelli's view, a ruthless leader such as Cesare Borgia would at least avoid the weakness of lords who "plundered their subjects rather than governed them" and allowed "thefts, brawls, and every sort of excess." It is better for a prince to be thought stingy, he explains, than for him to grow poor through lavishness and then be forced to rob his subjects.

Machiavelli's pragmatism, his emphasis on fact, on how the real world works, rather than on lofty ideals, contrasts with his own idealization of the strong ruler. His picture of the perfectly efficient ruler shows the Renaissance tendency toward "perfected" form. In this, he is closer than one might suspect to that more obvious treatise of political idealism, Thomas More's *Utopia* (1516), in which the desires and venality of humankind are curbed by a strong ruler and the rules he bequeaths to society. Machiavelli abandons complex reality in favor of an ideal vision most clearly at the end of the book, where he offers the conclusion to his many lessons: the ideal ruler, now technically equipped by Machiavelli's lessons, is to undertake a mission—the liberation of Italy. The realistic method described throughout now appears directed toward an ideal task. Instead of technical political considerations (choice of the opportune moment, evaluation of military power), Machiavelli invokes religious and ancient precedents, calling for a new Moses to lead Italy out of bondage: "Everything is now fully disposed for the work . . . if only your House adopts the methods of those I have set forth as examples. Moreover, we have before our eyes extraordinary and unexampled means prepared by God. The sea has been divided. A cloud has guided you on your way. The rock has given forth water. Manna has fallen."

Although *The Prince* did not succeed in winning Machiavelli the favor of the Medici, or, for that matter, in achieving the unification of Italy, it was hugely influential throughout Europe. The work circulated widely in manuscript before being published in 1532, and the response to it was unmitigated outrage. Whatever truths readers recognized in Machiavelli's little book, it was tempting to accuse him of provoking the amorality (or immorality) that in some cases he simply described. "Machiavellian" became an insult denoting amorality in the service of *Realpolitik*, and the complexities of Machiavelli's study of political power were overlooked. A careful reading of *The Prince* offers a very different impression, as the acute realism of the political observer gives way to the humanist dreaming of ancient glories.

Letter to Francesco Vettori[1]

["That Food Which Alone Is Mine"]

I am living on my farm, and since my last troubles[2] I have not been in Florence twenty days, putting them all together. Up to now I have been setting snares for thrushes with my own hands; I get up before daylight, prepare my birdlime, and go out with a bundle of cages on my back, so that I look like Geta when he came back from the harbor with the books of Amphitryo,[3] and catch at the least two thrushes and at the most six. So I did all of September; then this trifling diversion, despicable and strange as it is, to my regret failed. What my life is now I shall tell you.

In the morning I get up with the sun and go out into a grove that I am having cut; there I remain a couple of hours to look over the work of the past day and kill some time with the woodmen, who always have on hand some dispute either among themselves or among their neighbors. . . .

When I leave the grove, I go to a spring, and from there into my aviary. I have a book in my pocket, either Dante or Petrarch or one of the minor poets, as Tibullus,[4] Ovid, and the like. I read about their tender passions and their loves, remember mine, and take pleasure for a while in thinking about them. Then I go along the road to the inn, talk with those who pass by, ask the news of their villages, learn various things, and note the varied tastes and different fancies of men. It gets to be dinner time, and with my troop I eat what food my poor farm and my little property permit. After dinner, I return to the inn; there I usually find the host, a butcher, a miller, and two furnace-tenders. With these fellows I sink into vulgarity for the rest of the day, playing at *cricca* and *tricche-trach*;[5] from these games come a thousand quarrels and numberless offensive and insulting words; we often dispute over a penny, and all the same are heard shouting as far as San Casciano.[6] So, involved in these trifles, I keep my brain from getting mouldy, and express the perversity of Fate, for I am willing to have her drive me along this path, to see if she will be ashamed of it.

In the evening, I return to my house, and go into my study. At the door I take off the clothes I have worn all day, mud spotted and dirty, and put on regal and courtly garments. Thus appropriately clothed, I enter into the ancient courts of ancient men,[7] where, being lovingly received, I feed on that food which alone is mine, and which I was born for; I am not ashamed to speak with them and to

1. Translated by Allan H. Gilbert. From a letter dated December 10, 1513, to Vettori, ambassador in Rome.
2. Machiavelli had been suspected of participation in a conspiracy led by two young friends of his and had been imprisoned and subjected to torture before his innocence was recognized.
3. Allusion to a popular tale in which Amphitryo, returning to Thebes after having studied at Athens, sends forward from the harbor his servant Geta to announce his arrival to

his wife, Alemene, and loads him with his books.
4. Albius Tibullus (1st century B.C.E.), Roman elegiac poet.
5. Two popular games, the first played with cards, the second with dice thrown to regulate the movements of pawns on a chessboard.
6. Nearby village, in the region around Florence.
7. Machiavelli here refers figuratively to his study of ancient history.

ask the reasons for their actions, and they courteously answer me. For four hours I feel no boredom and forget every worry; I do not fear poverty, and death does not terrify me. I give myself completely over to the ancients. And because Dante says that there is no knowledge unless one retains what one has read,[8] I have written down the profit I have gained from their conversation, and composed a little book *De principatibus*,[9] in which I go as deep as I can into reflections on this subject, debating what a principate is, what the species are, how they are gained, how they are kept, and why they are lost. If ever any of my trifles can please you, this one should not displease you; and to a prince, and especially a new prince, it ought to be welcome.

FROM THE PRINCE[1]

[New Princedoms Gained with Other Men's Forces and through Fortune]

From CHAPTER 7

* * *

[Cesare Borgia][2]

Cesare Borgia, called by the people Duke Valentino, gained his position through his father's Fortune and through her lost it, notwithstanding that he made use of every means and action possible to a prudent and vigorous man for putting down his roots in those states that another man's arms and Fortune bestowed on him. As I say above, he who does not lay his foundations before-hand can perhaps through great wisdom and energy lay them afterward, though he does so with trouble for the architect and danger to the building. So on examining all the steps taken by the Duke, we see that he himself laid mighty foundations for future power. To discuss these steps is not superfluous; indeed I for my part do not see what better precepts I can give a new prince than the example of Duke Valentino's actions. If his arrangements did not bring him success, the fault was not his, because his failure resulted from an unusual and utterly malicious stroke of Fortune.[3]

[Pope Alexander VI Attempts to Make Cesare a Prince]

Alexander VI,[4] in his attempt to give high position to the Duke his son, had before him many difficulties, present and future. First, he saw no way in which he could make him lord of any state that was not a state of the Church, yet if

---

8. *Paradiso* 5.41–42: "For knowledge none can vaunt / Who retains not, although he have understood."
9. Of princedoms.
1. Translated by Allan H. Gilbert.
2. Son of Pope Alexander VI and duke of Valentinois and Romagna. His skillful and merciless

subjugation of the local lords of Romagna occurred between 1499 and 1502.
3. Ill health.
4. Rodrigo Borgia (ca. 1431–1503), pope (1492–1503), father of Cesare and Lucrezia Borgia.

the Pope tried to take such a state from the Church, he knew that the Duke of Milan and the Venetians[5] would not allow it because both Faenza and Rimini were already under Venetian protection. He saw, besides, that the weapons of Italy, especially those of which he could make use, were in the hands of men who had reason to fear the Pope's greatness; therefore he could not rely on them, since they were all among the Orsini and the Colonnesi[6] and their allies. He therefore was under the necessity of disturbing the situation and embroiling the states of Italy so that he could safely master part of them. This he found easy since, luckily for him, the Venetians, influenced by other reasons, had set out to get the French to come again into Italy. He not merely did not oppose their coming; he made it easier by dissolving the early marriage of King Louis.[7] The King then marched into Italy with the Venetians' aid and Alexander's consent; and he was no sooner in Milan than the Pope got soldiers from him for an attempt on Romagna; these the King granted for the sake of his own reputation.[8]

[Borgia Determines to Depend on Himself]

Having taken Romagna, then, and suppressed the Colonnesi, the Duke, in attempting to keep the province and to go further, was hindered by two things: one, his own forces, which he thought disloyal; the other, France's intention. That is, he feared that the Orsini forces which he had been using would fail him and not merely would hinder his gaining but would take from him what he had gained, and that the King would treat him in the same way. With the Orsini, he had experience of this when after the capture of Faenza he attacked Bologna, for he saw that they turned cold over that attack. And as to the King's purpose, the Duke learned it when, after taking the dukedom of Urbino, he invaded Tuscany—an expedition that the King made him abandon. As a result, he determined not to depend further on another man's armies and Fortune.

[The Duke Destroys His Disloyal Generals]

The Duke's first act to that end was to weaken the Orsini and Colonnesi parties in Rome by winning over to himself all their adherents who were men of rank, making them his own men of rank and giving them large subsidies; and he honored them, according to their stations, with military and civil offices, so that within a few months their hearts were emptied of all affection for the Roman parties, and it was wholly transferred to the Duke. After this, he waited for a good chance to wipe out the Orsini leaders, having scattered those of the Colonna family; such a chance came to him well and he used it better. When the Orsini found out, though late, that the Duke's and the Church's greatness was their ruin, they held a meeting at Magione, in Perugian territory. From that resulted the rebellion of Urbino, the insurrections in Romagna, and

---

5. The Venetian Republic opposed the expansion of the papal states. "Duke of Milan": Ludovico Il Moro, the flamboyant duke of the Sforza family.

6. Powerful Roman families.
7. Louis XII, king of France (d. 1515).
8. According to his agreement with Pope Alexander VI.

countless dangers for the Duke, all of which he overcame with the aid of the French. Thus having got back his reputation, but not trusting France or other outside forces, in order not to have to put them to a test, he turned to trickery. And he knew so well how to falsify his purpose that the Orsini themselves, by means of Lord Paulo,[9] were reconciled with him (as to Paulo the Duke did not omit any sort of gracious act to assure him, giving him money, clothing and horses) so completely that their folly took them to Sinigaglia into his hands. Having wiped out these leaders, then, and changed their partisans into his friends, the Duke had laid very good foundations for his power, holding all the Romagna along with the dukedom of Urbino, especially since he believed he had made the Romagna his friend and gained the support of all those people, through their getting a taste of well-being.

[Peace in Romagna; Remirro de Orco]

Because this matter is worthy of notice and of being copied by others, I shall not omit it. After the Duke had seized the Romagna and found it controlled by weak lords who had plundered their subjects rather than governed them, and had given them reason for disunion, not for union, so that the whole province was full of thefts, brawls, and every sort of excess, he judged that if he intended to make it peaceful and obedient to the ruler's arm, he must of necessity give it good government. Hence he put in charge there Messer[1] Remirro de Orco, a man cruel and ready, to whom he gave the most complete authority. This man in a short time rendered the province peaceful and united, gaining enormous prestige. Then the Duke decided there was no further need for such boundless power, because he feared it would become a cause for hatred; so he set up a civil court in the midst of the province, with a distinguished presiding judge, where every city had its lawyer. And because he knew that past severities had made some men hate him, he determined to purge such men's minds and win them over entirely by showing that any cruelty which had gone on did not originate with himself but with the harsh nature of his agent. So getting an opportunity for it, one morning at Cesena he had Messer Remirro laid in two pieces in the public square with a block of wood and a bloody sword near him. The ferocity of this spectacle left those people at the same time gratified and awe-struck.

[Princely Virtues]

From CHAPTER 15

On the Things for Which Men, and Especially Princes, Are Praised or Censured

* * * Because I know that many have written on this topic, I fear that when I too write I shall be thought presumptuous, because, in discussing it, I break away completely from the principles laid down by my predecessors. But since it is my purpose to write something useful to an attentive reader,

9. Member of the Orsini.   1. My lord.

I think it more effective to go back to the practical truth of the subject than to depend on my fancies about it. And many have imagined republics and principalities that never have been seen or known to exist in reality. For there is such a difference between the way men live and the way they ought to live, that anybody who abandons what is for what ought to be will learn something that will ruin rather than preserve him, because anyone who determines to act in all circumstances the part of a good man must come to ruin among so many who are not good. Hence, if a prince wishes to maintain himself, he must learn how to be not good, and to use that ability or not as is required.

Leaving out of account, then, things about an imaginary prince, and considering things that are true, I say that all men, when they are spoken of, and especially princes, because they are set higher, are marked with some of the qualities that bring them either blame or praise. To wit, one man is thought liberal, another stingy (using a Tuscan word, because *avaricious* in our language is still applied to one who desires to get things through violence, but *stingy* we apply to him who refrains too much from using his own property); one is thought open-handed, another grasping; one cruel, the other compassionate; one is a breaker of faith, the other reliable; one is effeminate and cowardly, the other vigorous and spirited; one is philanthropic, the other egotistic; one is lascivious, the other chaste; one is straight-forward, the other crafty; one hard, the other easy to deal with; one is firm, the other unsettled; one is religious, the other unbelieving; and so on.

And I know that everybody will admit that it would be very praiseworthy for a prince to possess all of the above-mentioned qualities that are considered good. But since he is not able to have them or to observe them completely, because human conditions do not allow him to, it is necessary that he be prudent enough to understand how to avoid getting a bad name because he is given to those vices that will deprive him of his position. He should also, if he can, guard himself from those vices that will not take his place away from him, but if he cannot do it, he can with less anxiety let them go. Moreover, he should not be troubled if he gets a bad name because of vices without which it will be difficult for him to preserve his position. I say this because, if everything is considered, it will be seen that some things seem to be virtuous, but if they are put into practice will be ruinous to him; other things seem to be vices, yet if put into practice will bring the prince security and well-being.

["Fortune is a woman"]

From CHAPTER 25

The Power of Fortune in Human Affairs, and to What Extent She Should Be Relied On

It is not unknown to me that many have been and still are of the opinion that the affairs of this world are so under the direction of Fortune and of God that man's prudence cannot control them; in fact, that man has no resource against them. For this reason many think there is no use in sweating much over such matters, but that one might as well let Chance take control. This opinion has been the more accepted in our times, because of the great changes in the state of the world that have been and now are seen every day, beyond all human surmise. And I myself, when thinking on these things, have now and then in some measure inclined to their view. Nevertheless, because the freedom of the will should not be wholly annulled, I think it may be true that Fortune is arbiter of half of our actions, but that she still leaves the control of the other half, or about that, to us.

I liken her to one of those raging streams that, when they go mad, flood the plains, ruin the trees and the buildings, and take away the fields from one bank and put them down on the other. Everybody flees before them; everybody yields to their onrush without being able to resist anywhere. And though this is their nature, it does not cease to be true that, in calm weather, men can make some provisions against them with walls and dykes, so that, when the streams swell, their waters will go off through a canal, or their currents will not be so wild and do so much damage. The same is true of Fortune. She shows her power where there is no wise preparation for resisting her, and turns her fury where she knows that no walls and dykes have been made to hold her in. And if you consider Italy—the place where these variations occur and the cause that has set them in motion—you will see that she is a country without dykes and without any wall of defence. If, like Germany, Spain, and France, she had had a sufficient bulwark of military vigor, this flood would not have made the great changes it has, or would not have come at all.

And this, I think, is all I need to say on opposing oneself to Fortune, in general. But limiting myself more to particulars, I say that a prince may be seen prospering today and falling in ruin tomorrow, though it does not appear that he has changed in his nature or any of his qualities. I believe this comes, in the first place, from the causes that have been discussed at length in preceding chapters. That is, if a prince bases himself entirely on Fortune, he will fall when she varies. I also believe that a ruler will be successful who adapts his mode of procedure to the quality of the times, and likewise that he will be unsuccessful if the times are out of accord with his procedure. Because it may be seen that in things leading to the end each has before him, namely glory and riches, men proceed differently. One acts with caution, another rashly; one with violence, another with skill; one with patience, another with its opposite; yet with these different methods each one attains his end. Still further, two cautious men will be seen, of whom one comes to his goal, the other does not. Likewise you will see two who succeed with two different methods, one of them being cautious and the other rash. These results are caused by nothing else than the nature of the times, which is or is not in harmony with the procedure of men. It also accounts for what I have mentioned, namely, that two persons, working differently, chance to arrive at the same result; and that of two who work in the same way, one attains his end, but the other does not.

On the nature of the times also depends the variability of the best method. If a man conducts himself with caution and patience, times and affairs may come around in such a way that his procedure is good, and he goes on successfully. But if times and circumstances change, he is ruined, because he does not change his method of action. There is no man so prudent as to understand how to fit himself to this condition, either because he is unable to deviate from the course to which nature inclines him, or because, having always prospered by walking in one path, he cannot persuade himself to leave it. So the cautious man, when the time comes to go at a reckless pace, does not know how to do it. Hence he comes to ruin. Yet if he could change his nature with the times and with circumstances, his fortune would not be altered.

Pope Julius II proceeded rashly in all his actions, and found the times and circumstances so harmonious with his mode of procedure that he was always so lucky as to succeed. Consider the first enterprise he engaged in, that of Bologna, while Messer Giovanni Bentivogli[2] was still alive. The Venetians were not pleased with it; the King of Spain felt the same way; the Pope was debating such an enterprise with the King of France. Nevertheless, in his courage and rashness Julius personally undertook that expedition. This movement made the King of Spain and the Venetians stand irresolute and motionless, the latter for fear, and the King because of his wish to recover the entire kingdom of Naples. On the other side, the King of France was dragged behind Julius, because the King, seeing that the Pope had moved and wishing to make him a friend in order to put down the Venetians, judged he could not refuse him soldiers without doing him open injury. Julius, then, with his rash movement, attained what no other pontiff, with the utmost human prudence, would have attained. If he had waited to leave Rome until the agreements were fixed and everything arranged, as any other pontiff would have done, he would never have succeeded, for the King of France would have had a thousand excuses, and the others would have raised a thousand fears. I wish to omit his other acts, which are all of the same sort, and all succeeded perfectly. The brevity of his life did not allow him to know anything different. Yet if times had come in which it was necessary to act with caution, they would have ruined him, for he would never have deviated from the methods to which nature inclined him.

I conclude, then, that since Fortune is variable and men are set in their ways, they are successful when they are in harmony with Fortune and unsuccessful when they disagree with her. Yet I am of the opinion that it is better to be rash than over-cautious, because Fortune is a woman and, if you wish to keep her down, you must beat her and pound her. It is evident that she allows herself to be overcome by men who treat her in that way rather than by those who proceed coldly. For that reason, like a woman, she is always the friend of young men, because they are less cautious, and more courageous, and command her with more boldness.

[The Roman Dream]

From CHAPTER 26

An Exhortation to Take Hold of Italy and Restore Her to Liberty from the Barbarians

Having considered all the things discussed above, I have been turning over in my own mind whether at present in Italy the time is ripe for a new prince to win prestige, and whether conditions there give a wise and vigorous ruler occasion to introduce methods that will do him honor, and bring good to the mass of the people of the land. It appears to me that so many things unite for the

2. Of the ruling family Bentivogli. The pope undertook to dislodge him from Bologna in 1506.

advantage of a new prince, that I do not know of any time that has ever been more suited for this. And, as I said, if it was necessary to make clear the ability of Moses that the people of Israel should be enslaved in Egypt, and to reveal Cyrus's greatness of mind that the Persians should be oppressed by the Medes, and to demonstrate the excellence of Theseus that the Athenians should be scattered, so at the present time, in order to make known the greatness of an Italian soul, Italy had to be brought down to her present position, to be more a slave than the Hebrews, more a servant than the Persians, more scattered than the Athenians; without head, without government; defeated, plundered, torn asunder, overrun; subject to every sort of disaster.

And though before this, certain persons[3] have showed signs from which it could be inferred that they were chosen by God for the redemption of Italy, nevertheless it has afterwards been seen that in the full current of action they have been cast off by Fortune. So Italy remains without life and awaits the man, whoever he may be, who is to heal her wounds, put an end to the plundering of Lombardy and the tribute laid on Tuscany and the kingdom of Naples, and cure her of those sores that have long been suppurating. She may be seen praying God to send some one to redeem her from these cruel and barbarous insults. She is evidently ready and willing to follow a banner, if only some one will raise it. Nor is there at present anyone to be seen in whom she can put more hope than in your illustrious House, because its fortune and vigor, and the favor of God and of the Church, which it now governs,[4] enable it to be the leader in such a redemption. This will not be very difficult, as you will see if you will bring to mind the actions and lives of those I have named above. And though these men were striking exceptions, yet they were men, and each of them had less opportunity than the present gives; their enterprises were not more just than this, nor easier, nor was God their friend more than he is yours. Here justice is complete. "A way is just to those to whom it is necessary, and arms are holy to him who has no hope save in arms."[5] Everything is now fully disposed for the work, and when that is true an undertaking cannot be difficult, if only your House adopts the methods of those I have set forth as examples. Moreover, we have before our eyes extraordinary and unexampled means prepared by God. The sea has been divided. A cloud has guided you on your way. The rock has given forth water. Manna has fallen.[6] Everything has united to make you great. The rest is for you to do. God does not intend to do everything, lest he deprive us of our free will and the share of glory that belongs to us.

It is no wonder if no one of the above-named Italians[7] has been able to do what we hope your illustrious House can. Nor is it strange if in the many revolutions and military enterprises of Italy, the martial vigor of the land always appears to be exhausted. This is because the old military customs were not good, and there has been nobody able to find new ones. Yet nothing brings so

---

3. Possibly Cesare Borgia and Francesco Sforza, who were discussed earlier in the book.
4. Pope Leo X (1475–1521) was a Medici (Giovanni de' Medici). "House": of Medici. *The Prince* was first meant for Giuliano de'

Medici. After Giuliano's death it was dedicated to his nephew Lorenzo, later duke of Urbino.
5. Livy's *History* 9.1, para. 10.
6. Another allusion to Moses.
7. Perhaps another reference to Borgia and Sforza.

much honor to a man who rises to new power, as the new laws and new methods he discovers. These things, when they are well founded and have greatness in them, make him revered and worthy of admiration. And in Italy matter is not lacking on which to impress forms of every sort. There is great vigor in the limbs if only it is not lacking in the heads. You may see that in duels and combats between small numbers, the Italians have been much superior in force, skill, and intelligence. But when it is a matter of armies, Italians cannot be compared with foreigners. All this comes from the weakness of the heads, because those who know are not obeyed, and each man thinks he knows. Nor up to this time has there been a man able to raise himself so high, through both ability and fortune, that the others would yield to him. The result is that for the past twenty years, in all the wars that have been fought when there has been an army entirely Italian, it has always made a bad showing. Proof of this was given first at the Taro, and then at Alessandria, Capua, Genoa, Vailà, Bologna, and Mestri.[8]

If your illustrious House, then, wishes to imitate those excellent men who redeemed their countries, it is necessary, before everything else, to furnish yourself with your own army, as the true foundation of every enterprise. You cannot have more faithful, nor truer, nor better soldiers. And though every individual of these may be good, they become better as a body when they see that they are commanded by their prince, and honored and trusted by him. It is necessary, therefore, that your House should be prepared with such forces, in order that it may be able to defend itself against the foreigners with Italian courage.

And though the Swiss and the Spanish infantry are properly estimated as terribly effective, yet both have defects. Hence a third type would be able not merely to oppose them but to feel sure of overcoming them. The fact is that the Spaniards are not able to resist cavalry, and the Swiss have reason to fear infantry, when they meet any as determined in battle as themselves. For this reason it has been seen and will be seen in experience that the Spaniards are unable to resist the French cavalry, and the Swiss are overthrown by Spanish infantry. And though of this last a clear instance has not been observed, yet an approach to it appeared in the battle of Ravenna,[9] when the Spanish infantry met the German battalions, who use the same methods as the Swiss. There the Spanish, through their ability and the assistance given by their shields, got within the points of the spears from below, and slew their enemies in security, while the Germans could find no means of resistance. If the cavalry had not charged the Spanish, they would have annihilated the Germans. It is possible, then, for one who realizes the defects of these two types, to equip infantry in a new manner, so that it can resist cavalry and not be afraid of foot-soldiers; but to gain this end they must have weapons of the right sorts, and adopt varied methods of combat. These are some of the things which, when they are put into service as novelties, give reputation and greatness to a new ruler.[1]

8. Sites of battles occurring between the end of the century and 1513.
9. Between Spain and France in April 1512.

1. Machiavelli was subsequently the author of the treatise Art of War (1521).

This opportunity, then, should not be allowed to pass, in order that after so long a time Italy may see her redeemer. I am unable to express with what love he would be received in all the provinces that have suffered from these foreign deluges; with what thirst for vengeance, what firm faith, what piety, what tears! What gates would be shut against him? what peoples would deny him obedience? what envy would oppose itself to him? what Italian would refuse to follow him? This barbarian rule stinks in every nostril. May your illustrious House, then, undertake this charge with the spirit and the hope with which all just enterprises are taken up, in order that, beneath its ensign, our native land may be ennobled, and, under its auspices, that saying of Petrarch may come true: "Manhood[2] will take arms against fury, and the combat will be short, because in Italian hearts the ancient valor is not yet dead."

2. An etymological translation of the original *virtù* (from the Latin *vir*, "man"). The quotation is from the canzone "My Italy."

MARGUERITE DE NAVARRE
1492–1549

The French "discovered" Italy in the latter part of the fifteenth century, both through travel and, starting in 1494, through military invasions. Eager to imitate more sophisticated Italian city-states, French rulers and aristocrats adapted Italian artistic, literary, and social values to their own culture. Marguerite de Navarre, one of the most influential members of French courtly society, played a significant part in bringing about this transformation. As a writer and a patron of artists, she also responded seriously to the spiritual and intellectual challenge to Christian faith brought about by the Reformation. Her lively collection of stories modeled on **Boccaccio**, the *Heptameron*, gives voice to characters whose different positions afford them starkly different views of the world.

LIFE AND TIMES

Marguerite was born in 1492 into the French royal family. Her brother, the future King Francis I, was born two years later. From her earliest years, Marguerite received an exceptionally good education, including instruction in Latin, Italian, Spanish, and German; later in life she also studied Greek and Hebrew. At seventeen she was married to Charles, duke of Alençon, a feudal lord who was intellectually not her match. When her brother succeeded Louis XII to the French throne in 1515, Marguerite became one of the most influential women at the royal court, where she advised the king and received dignitaries and ambassadors as well as eminent men of letters. Under Francis I, the French court flourished culturally, hiring Italian artists as famous as Leonardo da Vinci (1452–1519) and Benvenuto Cellini (1500–1571).

Francis I continued the Italian wars, the complicated conflicts fought on Italian soil between his forces and those of the Holy Roman Emperor, Charles V. His defeat in the crucial battle of Pavia in 1525 was a double blow for Marguerite: her brother was taken to Madrid as a prisoner and her husband died of battle wounds. Marguerite went to Madrid to assist her sick brother and helped negotiate with Charles V for his release.

The year following her husband's death, Marguerite became "queen of Navarre" when she married Henri d'Albret, the king of Navarre in title only, since most of that domain had been annexed by Spain in 1516. Eleven years younger than Marguerite, Henri d'Albret was a dashing, flighty, and intellectually disappointing husband— and is thought to be the prototype for the philandering and misogynistic character of Hircan in the *Heptameron*. Their only daughter, Jeanne, born in 1527, was the mother of the future King Henry IV of France.

Marguerite continued to be involved in her royal brother's activities, participating in diplomacy and peace talks. Her interest, however, was increasingly focused on intellectual and literary pursuits and on religious meditation and debate. Erasmus, John Calvin, and Pope Paul III were among her numerous correspondents. Throughout her life she was a protector of writers and thinkers accused or suspected of Protestant leanings. Her first published work, *The Mirror of the Sinful Soul* (1531), was found by the theologians of the Sorbonne to contain elements of Protestant "heresy"; the edition of 1533, containing an additional "Dialogue in the Form of a Night Vision" on the theological problem of salva-

tion, was condemned. The king had to intervene on behalf of his sister and her chaplain. Later it became more difficult for Francis I to manage the rivalry between Catholics and Protestants, which was a political and military matter as much as it was a religious dispute. Protestants and their sympathizers were persecuted, and several prominent intellectuals went into prudent exile or were burned at the stake. Marguerite, who had an intellectual and mystical faith, appears never to have abandoned Catholicism but to have hoped for internal reform.

After the death of her brother in 1547, she published her *Marguerite de la Marguerite des Princesses* (with a play on the word *marguerite*, which in French means both "pearl" and "daisy"), a collection including long devotional poems and theatrical pieces ranging from allegory to farce. In 1549 she retired to Navarre and died in the castle of Odos on December 21.

THE *HEPTAMERON*

Marguerite's greatest literary achievement is the *Heptameron*, which was not published until 1559, a decade after her death. A collection of seventy stories told over seven days, it is framed by a larger narrative that reveals the storytellers' characters and relationships with each other. We do not know the exact circumstances of its production, and there are doubts that Marguerite herself authored all of its parts. Some scholars have concluded that Marguerite collected or commissioned tales for the narrative, and perhaps composed only the frame narrative—in many ways the work's most compelling feature. In the prologue, five men and five women, all nobles, are brought together in the Pyrenees when natural and criminal forces—including a flood, bandits, a bear, and murderers—prevent them from returning home. They arrive independently at an abbey, where, at the suggestion of Parlamente, thought to represent Marguerite herself, they agree to tell stories each day until they are able to return home. The stories deal above all with the antagonism between the sexes, particularly concerning issues of marital fidelity and the status of women. The *Heptameron* pays considerable attention to ideas of masculinity and to ideals and stereotypes about women. Class tensions are somewhat more muted, although the stories often pit powerful lords and husbands against those whose only weapon is their cleverness. The courtly men and women who narrate and hear the stories are, to say the least, unafraid to disagree with each other about the tales' significances, both in the frame and through their stories, which implicitly debate such issues as the just desserts for the philandering husband or the clever wife.

The *Heptameron* belongs to a tradition of framed storytelling that includes the ***Thousand and One Nights***, Chaucer's *Canterbury Tales*, and Boccaccio's *Decameron*. In the prologue, Parlamente overtly ties the storytelling game to the *Decameron* and a recent translation into French (commissioned by Marguerite) that drew, she says, the admiration of the French court. In writing a French *Decameron*, however, the group proposed, "they should not write any story that was not truthful." The relationship between language and truth therefore becomes a dominant theme. Unable to devote themselves entirely to religious pursuits, the characters choose "truthful" stories as a worthwhile pastime.

By truthfulness, Marguerite means stories that are honest about social tensions. When the characters comment— in the frame and in their own stories—on each others' tales, they reveal how social factors influence their view of the world. Divine "truth" gives way to individual and social perspective: age, gender, social standing, education, marital status, and religious disposition form the grounds for rivalry and dispute among the group members.

The "amusing and virtuous" pastime of a privileged group of storytellers forced into reclusion becomes in these pages a lively debate on gender roles, true virtue, and the force of society's disapproval. Balanced between the court and broader social concerns, between older certainties and new challenges, the *Heptameron* presents a lively and complex portrait of Marguerite de Navarre's changing world. At the same time, it offers an enduring account of the gendered division of experience, exploring how men and women manage and mismanage their desires.

From The Heptameron[1]

From *Prologue*

* * *

Parlamente, the wife of Hircan,[2] was not one to let herself become idle or melancholy, and having asked her husband for permission, she spoke to the old Lady Oisille.[3]

"Madame," she said. "you have had much experience of life, and you now occupy the position of mother in regard to the rest of us women, and it surprises me that you do not consider some pastime to alleviate the boredom and distress that we shall have to bear during our long stay here. Unless we have some amusing and virtuous way of occupying ourselves, we run the risk of [falling][4] sick."

Longarine,[5] the young widow, added, "What is worse, we'll all become miserable and disagreeable—and that's an incurable disease. There isn't a man or woman amongst us who hasn't every cause to sink into despair, if we consider all that we have lost."

Ennasuite[6] laughed and rejoined, "Not everyone's lost a husband, like you, you know. And as for losing servants, no need to despair about that—there are plenty of men ready to do service! All the same, I do agree that we ought to have something to amuse us, so that we can pass the time as pleasantly as we can."

Her companion Nomerfide[7] said that this was a very good idea, and that if she had to spend a single day without some entertainment, she would be sure to die the next.

All the men supported this, and asked the Lady Oisille if she would kindly organize what they should do.

"My children," replied Oisille, "when you ask me to show you a pastime that is capable of delivering you from your boredom and your sorrow, you are asking me to do something that I find very difficult. All my life I have searched for a remedy, and I have found only one—the reading of holy Scripture, in which one may find true and perfect spiritual joy, from which proceed health and bodily repose. And if you ask what the prescription is that keeps me happy and healthy in my old age, I will tell you. As soon as I rise in the morn-

---

1. Translated by P. A. Chilton.
2. Hircan is variously described, in the book itself and by its commentators, as brilliant, flighty, sensual, capable of sarcasm and grossness. The name is related to Hircania, an imaginary and proverbially wild region in classical literature; the root is that of *hircus*, Latin for "goat" (cf. English *hircine*: libidinous). Parlamente probably represents Marguerite, whose name can be construed as *perle amante*, "loving pearl," or as *parlementer*, which refers to eloquent speaking.
3. The oldest, most authoritative, and most evangelical of the storytellers; she seems to be named for Louise—either Louise of Savoy, Marguerite's mother, or her lady-in-waiting, Louise de Daillon.

4. Brackets indicate translator's interpolations.
5. A young and wisely talkative widow, often identified with one of Marguerite's ladies-in-waiting, who among her titles had that of lady of Langrai (hence her name, which is also interpreted as a play on *langue orine*, meaning "tongue of gold").
6. *Enna* may stand for "Anne," and *suite* means "retinue"; so the character is identifiable with Anne de Vivonne, one of the ladies in Marguerite's entourage who collaborated on the *Heptameron* project at court. Her attitude toward men can be bitter and sharply ironical.
7. The youngest member of the group, who generally views life with joyful optimism.

ing I take the Scriptures and read them. I see and contemplate the goodness of God, who for our sakes has sent His son to earth to declare the holy word and the good news by which He grants remission of all our sins, and payment of all our debts, through His gift to us of His love, His passion and His merits. And my contemplations give me such joy, that I take my psalter, and with the utmost humility, sing the beautiful psalms and hymns that the Holy Spirit has composed in the heart of David and the other authors. The contentment this affords me fills me with such well-being that whatever the evils of the day, they are to me so many blessings, for in my heart I have by faith Him who has borne these evils for me. Likewise, before supper, I withdraw to nourish my soul with readings and meditations. In the evening I ponder in my mind everything I have done during the day, so that I may ask God forgiveness of my sins, and give thanks to Him for His mercies. And so I lay myself to rest in His love, fear and peace, assured against all evils. And this, my children, is the pastime that long ago I adopted. All other ways have I tried, but none has given me spiritual contentment. I believe that if, each morning, you give one hour to reading, and then, during mass, say your prayers devoutly, you will find even in this wilderness all the beauty a city could afford. For, a person who knows God will find all things beautiful in Him, and without Him all things will seem ugly. So I say to you, if you would live in happiness, heed my advice."

Then Hircan spoke: "Madame, anyone who has read the holy Scriptures—as indeed I think we all have here—will readily agree that what you have said is true. However, you must bear in mind that we have not yet become so mortified in the flesh that we are not in need of some sort of amusement and physical exercise in order to pass the time. After all, when we're at home, we've got our hunting and hawking to distract us from the thousand and one foolish thoughts that pass through one's mind. The ladies have their housework and their needlework. They have their dances, too, which provide a respectable way for them to get some exercise. All this leads me to suggest, on behalf of the men here, that you, Madame, since you are the oldest among us, should read to us every morning about the life of our Lord Jesus Christ, and the great and wonderful things He has done for us. Between dinner and vespers I think we should choose some pastime, which, while not being prejudicial to the soul, will be agreeable to the body. In that way we shall spend a very pleasant day."

Lady Oisille replied that she herself found it so difficult to put behind her the vanities of life, that she was afraid the pastime suggested by Hircan might not be a good choice. However, the question should, she thought, be judged after an open discussion, and she asked Hircan to put his point of view first.

"Well, my point of view wouldn't take long to give," he began, "if I thought that the pastime I would really like were as agreeable to a certain lady among us as it would be to me. So I'll keep quiet for now, and abide by what the others say."

Thinking he was intending this for her, his wife, Parlamente, began to blush. "It may be, Hircan," she said, half angrily and half laughing, "that the lady you think ought to be the most annoyed at what you say would have ways and means of getting her own back, if she so desired. But let's leave on one side all pastimes that require only two participants, and concentrate on those which everybody can join in."

Hircan turned to the ladies. "Since my wife has managed to put the right interpretation on my words," he said, "and since private pastimes don't appeal to her,
I think she's in a better position than anyone to know which pastime all of us will
be able to enjoy. Let me say right now that I accept her opinion as if it were my
own."

They all concurred in this, and Parlamente, seeing that it had fallen to her to
make the choice, addressed them all as follows.

"If I felt myself to be as capable as the ancients, by whom the arts were
discovered, then I would invent some pastime myself that would meet the
requirements you have laid down for me. However, I know what lies within
the scope of my own knowledge and ability—I can hardly even remember the
clever things other people have invented, let alone invent new things myself.
So I shall be quite content to follow closely in the footsteps of other people
who have already provided for your needs. For example, I don't think there's
one of us who hasn't read the hundred tales by Boccaccio,[8] which have
recently been translated from Italian into French, and which are so highly
thought of by the [most Christian] King Francis I, by Monseigneur the Dauphin, Madame the Dauphine[9] and Madame Marguerite. If Boccaccio could
have heard how highly these illustrious people praised him, it would have
been enough to raise him from the grave. As a matter of fact, the two ladies
I've mentioned, along with other people at the court, made up their minds to
do the same as Boccaccio. There was to be one difference—that they should
not write any story that was not truthful. Together with Monseigneur the
Dauphin the ladies promised to produce ten stories each, and to get together
a party of ten people who were qualified to contribute something, excluding
those who studied and were men of letters. Monseigneur the Dauphin didn't
want their art brought in, and he was afraid that rhetorical ornament would
in part falsify the truth of the account. A number of things led to the project
being completely forgotten—the major affairs of state that subsequently
overtook the King, the peace treaty between him and the King of England,
the confinement of Madame the Dauphine and several other events of sufficient importance to keep the court otherwise occupied. However, it can now
be completed in the ten days of leisure we have before us, while we wait for
our bridge to be finished. If you so wished, we could go each afternoon
between midday and four o'clock to the lovely meadow that borders the Gave
de Pau, where the leaves on the trees are so thick that the hot sun cannot
penetrate the shade and the cool beneath. There we can sit and rest, and
each of us will tell a story which he has either witnessed himself, or which he
has heard from somebody worthy of belief. At the end of our ten days we will
have completed the whole hundred. And if, God willing, the lords and ladies
I've mentioned find our endeavors worthy of their attention, we shall make
them a present of them when we get back, instead of the usual statuettes and
beads. I'm sure they would find that preferable. In spite of all this, if any of
you is able to think of something more agreeable, I shall gladly bow to his or
her opinion."

But every one of them replied that it would be impossible to think of anything better, and that they could hardly wait for the morrow. So the day came

8. The *Decameron*.
9. The future queen Catherine de Médici.

"Monseigneur the Dauphin": the future Henry
II, nephew of Marguerite.

happily to a close with reminiscences of things they had all experienced in their time.

As soon as morning came they all went into Madame Oisille's room, where she was already at her prayers. When they had listened for a good hour to the lesson she had to read them, and then devoutly heard mass, they went, at ten o'clock, to dine, after which they retired to their separate rooms to attend to what they had to do. At midday they all went back as arranged to the meadow, which was looking so beautiful and fair that it would take a Boccaccio to describe it as it really was. Enough for us to say that a more beautiful meadow there never was seen. When they were all seated on the grass, so green and soft that there was no need for carpets or cushions, Simontaut[1] said: "Which of us shall be [the one in charge]?"

* * *

Story 8

In the county of Alès there was once a man by the name of Bornet, who had married a very decent and respectable woman. He held her honor and reputation very dear, as I am sure all husbands here hold the honor and reputation of *their* wives dear. He wanted her to be faithful to him, but was not so keen on having the rule applied to them both equally. He had become enamored of his chambermaid, though the only benefit he got from transferring his affections in this way was the sort of pleasure one gets from varying one's diet. He had a neighbor called Sendras, who was of similar station and temperament to himself—he was a tailor and a drummer. These two were such close friends that, with the exception of the wife, there was nothing that they did not share between them. Naturally he told him that he had designs on the chambermaid.

Not only did his friend wholeheartedly approve of this, but did his best to help him, in the hope that he too might get a share in the spoils.

The chambermaid herself refused to have anything to do with him, although he was constantly pestering her and in the end she went to tell her mistress about it. She told her that she could not stand being badgered by him any longer, and asked permission to go home to her parents. Now the good lady of the house, who was really very much in love with her husband, had often had occasion to suspect him, and was therefore rather pleased to be one up on him, and to be able to show him that she had found out what he was up to. So she said to her maid: "Be nice to him dear, encourage him a little bit, and then make a date to go to bed with him in my dressing-room. Don't forget to tell me which night he's supposed to be coming, and make sure you don't tell anyone else."

The maid did exactly as her mistress had instructed. As for her master, he was so pleased with himself that he went off to tell his friend about his stroke

1. Identified with François de Bourdeille, the husband of Anne of Vivonne. He is the long-standing *serviteur* to Parlamente: "According to the *serviteur*'s practice, as the *Heptameron* presents it, a married aristocratic woman has the right to maintain several devoted knights in her service. . . . Since it is supposed to be chaste, the *serviteur*'s relationship, this remnant of courtly and chivalrous love, can coexist with faithful marriage. . . . Nevertheless, there is evidently considerable anxiety about the institution as such" [From the translator's introduction]. His name punningly alludes to masculinity (*monte haut*: rises high).

of luck, whereupon the friend insisted on taking his share afterwards, since he had been in on the business from the beginning. When the appointed time came, off went the master, as had been agreed, to get into bed, as he thought, with his little chambermaid. But his wife, having abandoned her position of authority in order to serve in a more pleasurable one, had taken her maid's place in the bed. When he got in with her, she did not act like a wife, but like a bashful young girl, and he was not in the slightest suspicious. It would be impossible to say which of them enjoyed themselves more—the wife deceiving her husband, or the husband who thought he was deceiving his wife. He stayed in bed with her for some time, not as long as he might have wished (many years of marriage were beginning to tell on him), but as long as he could manage. Then he went out to rejoin his accomplice, and tell him what a good time he had had. The lustiest piece of goods he had ever come across, he declared. His friend, who was younger and more active than he was, said: "Remember what you promised?"

"Hurry up, then," replied the master, "in case she gets up, or my wife wants her for something."

Off he went and climbed into bed with the supposed chambermaid his friend had just failed to recognize as his wife. *She* thought it was her husband again, and did not refuse anything he asked for (I say "asked," but "took" would be nearer the mark, because he did not dare open his mouth). He made a much longer business of it than the husband, to the surprise of the wife, who was not used to these long nights of pleasure. However, she did not complain, and looked forward to what she was planning to say to him in the morning, and the fun she would have teasing him. When dawn came, the man got up, and fondling her as he got out of bed, pulled off a ring she wore on her finger, a ring that her husband had given her at their marriage. Now the women in this part of the world are very superstitious about such things. They have great respect for women who hang on to their wedding rings till the day they die, and if a woman loses her ring, she is dishonored, and is looked upon as having given her faith to another man. But she did not mind him taking it, because she thought it would be sure evidence against her husband of the way she had hoodwinked him.

The husband was waiting outside for his friend, and asked him how he had got on. The man said he shared the husband's opinion, and added that he would have stayed longer, had he not been afraid of getting caught by the daylight. The pair of them then went off to get as much sleep as they could. When morning came, and they were getting dressed together, the husband noticed that his friend had on his finger a ring that was identical to the one he had given his wife on their wedding day. He asked him where he had got it, and when he was told it had come from the chambermaid the night before, he was aghast. He began banging his head against the wall, and shouted: "Oh my God! Have I gone and made myself a cuckold without my wife even knowing about it?"

His friend tried to calm him down. "Perhaps your wife had given the ring to the girl to look after before going to bed?" he suggested. The husband made no reply, but marched straight out and went back to his house.

There he found his wife looking unusually gay and attractive. Had she not saved her chambermaid from staining her conscience, and had she not put her husband to the ultimate test, without any more cost to herself than a night's sleep? Seeing her in such good spirits, the husband thought to himself: "She wouldn't be greeting me so cheerfully if she knew what I'd been up to."

As they chatted, he took hold of her hand and saw that the ring, which normally never left her finger, had disappeared. Horrified, he stammered: "What have you done with your ring?"

She was pleased that he was giving her the opportunity to say what she had to say.

"Oh! You're the most dreadful man I ever met! Who do you think you got it from? You think you got it from the chambermaid, don't you? You think you got it from that girl you're so much in love with, the girl who gets more out of you than I've ever had! The first time you got into bed you were so passionate that I thought you must be about as madly in love with her as it was possible for any man to be! But when you came back the *second* time, after getting up, you were an absolute devil! Completely uncontrolled you were, didn't know when to stop! You miserable man! You must have been blinded by desire to pay such tribute to my body—after all you've had me long enough without showing much appreciation for my figure. So it wasn't because that young girl is so pretty and so shapely that you were enjoying yourself so much. Oh no! You enjoyed it so much because you were seething with some depraved pent-up lust—in short the sin of concupiscence was raging within you, and your senses were dulled as a result. In fact you'd worked yourself up into such a state that I think any old nanny-goat would have done for you, pretty or otherwise! Well, my dear, it's time you mended your ways. It's high time you were content with me for what I am—your own wife and an honest woman, and it's high time that you found *that* just as satisfying as when you thought I was a poor little erring chambermaid. I did what I did in order to save you from your wicked ways, so that when you get old, we can live happily and peacefully together without anything on our consciences. Because if you go on in the way you have been, I'd rather leave you altogether than see you destroying your soul day by day, and at the same time destroying your physical health and squandering everything you have before my very eyes! But if you will acknowledge that you've been in the wrong, and make up your mind to live according to the ways of God and His commandments, then I'll overlook all your past misbehavior, even as I hope God will forgive me *my* ingratitude to Him, and failure to love Him as I ought."

If there was ever a man who was dumbfounded and despairing, it was this poor husband. There was his wife, looking so pretty, and yet so sensible and so chaste, and he had gone and left her for a girl who did not love him. What was worse, he had had the misfortune to have gone and made her do something wicked without her even realizing what was happening. He had gone and let another man share pleasures which, rightly, were his alone to enjoy. He had gone and given himself cuckold's horns and made himself look ridiculous for evermore. But he could see she was already angry enough about the chambermaid, and he did not dare tell her about the other dirty trick he had played. So he promised that he would leave his wicked ways behind him, asked her to forgive him and gave her the ring back. He told his friend not to breathe a word to anybody, but secrets of this sort nearly always end up being proclaimed from the [roof-tops], and it was not long before the facts became public knowledge. The husband was branded as a cuckold without his wife having done a single thing to disgrace herself.

"Ladies, it strikes me that if all the men who offend their wives like that got a punishment like that, then Hircan and Saffredent ought to be feeling a bit nervous."

"Come now, Longarine," said Saffredent, "Hircan and I aren't the only married men here, you know."

"True," she replied, "but you're the only two who'd play a trick like that."

"And just when have you heard of us chasing our wives' maids?" he retorted.

"If the ladies in question were to tell us the facts," Longarine said, "then you'd soon find plenty of maids who'd been dismissed before their pay-day!"

"Really," intervened Geburon, "a fine one you are! You promise to make us all laugh, and you end up making these two gentlemen annoyed."

"It comes to the same thing," said Longarine. "As long as they don't get their swords out, their getting angry makes it all the more amusing."

"But the fact remains," said Hircan, "that if our wives were to listen to what this lady here has to say, she'd make trouble for every married couple here!"

"I know what I'm saying, and who I'm saying it to," Longarine replied. "Your wives are so good, and they love you so much, that even if you gave them horns like a stag's, they'd still convince themselves, and everybody else, that they were garlands of roses!"

Everyone found this remark highly amusing, even the people it was aimed at, and the subject was brought to a close. Dagoucin,[2] however, who had not yet said a word, could not resist saying: "When a man already has everything he needs in order to be contented, it is very unreasonable of him to go off and seek satisfaction elsewhere. It has often struck me that when people are not satisfied with what they already have, and think they can find something better, then they only make themselves worse off. And they do not get any sympathy, because inconstancy is one thing that is universally condemned."

"But what about people who have not yet found their other half?" asked Simontaut. "Would you still say it was inconstancy if they seek her wherever she may be found?"

"No man can know," replied Dagoucin, "where his other half is to be found, this other half with whom he may find a union so equal that between [the parts] there is no difference; which being so, a man must hold fast where Love constrains him and, whatever may befall him, he must remain steadfast in heart and will. For if she whom you love is your true likeness, if she is of the same will, then it will be your own self that you love, and not her alone."

"Dagoucin, I think you're adopting a position that is completely wrong," said Hircan. "You make it sound as if we ought to love women without being loved in return!"

"What I mean, Hircan, is this. If love is based on a woman's beauty, charm and favors, and if our aim is merely pleasure, ambition, or profit, then such love can never last. For if the whole foundation on which our love is based should collapse, then love will fly from us and there will be no love left in us. But I am utterly convinced that if a man loves with no other aim, no other desire, than to love truly, he will abandon his soul in death rather than allow his love to abandon his heart."

"Quite honestly, Dagoucin, I don't think you've ever really been in love," said Simontaut, "because if you had felt the fire of passion, as the rest of us have, you wouldn't have been doing what you've just been doing—describing Plato's republic, which sounds all very fine in writing, but is hardly true to experience."

2. The most philosophical member of the group, described elsewhere (story 11) as "so wise that he would rather die than say some-thing foolish." He is also the saintliest; our translator indicates that his name is "a fairly obvious pun: de goûts saints (of saintly tastes)."

"If I have loved," he replied, "I love still, and shall love till the day I die. But my love is a perfect love, and I fear lest showing it openly should betray it. So greatly do I fear this, that I shrink to make it known to the lady whose love and friendship I cannot but desire to be equal to my own. I scarcely dare think my own thoughts, lest something should be revealed in my eyes, for the longer I conceal the fire of my love, the stronger grows the pleasure in knowing that it is indeed a perfect love."

"Ah, but all the same," said Geburon, "I don't think you'd be sorry if she did return your love!"

"I do not deny it. But even if I were loved as deeply as I myself love, my love could not possibly increase, just as it could not possibly decrease if I were loved less deeply than I love."

At this point, Parlamente, who was suspicious of these flights of fancy, said: "Watch your step, Dagoucin. I've seen plenty of men who've died rather than speak what's in their minds."

"Such men as those," he replied, "I would count happy indeed."

"Indeed," said Saffredent, "and worthy to be placed among the ranks of the Innocents—of whom the Church chants 'Non loquendo, sed moriendo confessi sunt'![3] I've heard a lot of talk about these languishing lovers, but I've never seen a single one actually die. I've suffered enough from such torture, but I got over it in the end, and that's why I've always assumed that nobody else ever really dies from it either."

"Ah! Saffredent, the trouble is that you desire your love to be returned," Dagoucin replied, "and men of your opinions never die for love. But I know of many who *have* died, and died for no other cause than that they have loved, and loved perfectly."

3. "Not by speaking but by dying they confessed," a line recited during the Feast of the Holy Innocents.

MICHEL DE MONTAIGNE
1533–1592

The probing, skeptical essays of Michel Eyquem de Montaigne show a Renaissance mind exploring its own workings. The first writer to ask "Who am I?" and pursue the question with extraordinary honesty and rigor, Montaigne at times appears surprisingly modern in his outlook. He pays unflinching attention to the embarrassing realities of his own body and mind, even as he considers the most abstract questions. His radical break with traditional forms of writing and thinking is particularly striking in that Montaigne was an avid student of the classical even as he also paved the way for the modern form of the essay.

LIFE AND TIMES

Montaigne was born on February 28, 1533, in the castle of Montaigne, to a Catholic father and a Protestant mother of Spanish-Jewish descent. His father, Pierre Eyquem, was for two terms mayor of Bordeaux and had fought in Italy under Francis I. Though no man of learning, Pierre had unconventional ideas of upbringing: Michel was awakened in the morning by the sound of music and was taught Latin as his mother tongue. At six Michel went to the famous Collège de Guienne at Bordeaux; later he studied law; and in 1557 he became a member of the Bordeaux parliament. In 1565 he married Françoise de la Chassaigne, daughter of a man who, as one of Montaigne's colleagues in the Bordeaux parliament, was a member of the new legal nobility.

Perhaps because of disappointed political ambitions, Montaigne retired from politics in 1570 at the age of thirty-eight: he sold his post as magistrate and retreated to his castle of Montaigne, which he had inherited two years earlier. There he devoted himself to meditation and writing. Although Montaigne spent, as he put it, "most of his days, and most hours of the day" in his library on the third floor of a round tower, the demands of his health and France's tumultuous politics often drew him out of retirement. For the sake of his health (he suffered from gallstones), in 1580 he took a journey through Switzerland, Germany, and Italy. While in Italy he received news that he had been appointed mayor of Bordeaux, an office that he held for two terms (1581–85).

His greatest political distractions, however, concerned the Catholic and Protestant factions that violently divided the court and France itself. French politics profoundly influenced the attitudes toward warfare, political resistance, and mercy expressed in Montaigne's Essays. When Henry II died in a jousting accident in 1559 and left the fifteen-year-old Francis II to succeed him, the Huguenots (French Reformers in the tradition of John Calvin), recognized the opportunity to influence the weakened royal government. Catherine de Médicis, the queen mother, seized power when Francis II died in 1560 (his successor, Charles IX, was only ten years old). Her policy of limited religious toleration satisfied neither the Catholic nor the Huguenot factions, and from 1562 to 1598 France repeatedly fell into civil war. In the infamous St. Bartholomew's Day Massacre of August 24, 1572, noblemen, municipal authorities, and the Parisian mobs indiscriminately slaughtered the Protestants in Paris. The slaughter was imitated in other French cities, and the civil wars once again broke out.

Throughout his country's political struggles, Montaigne sympathized with the unfanatical Henry of Navarre, leader of the Protestants, but his attitude was neutral and conservative. He expressed his joy when Henry of Navarre became King Henry IV and turned Catholic to do so: "Paris," Henry memorably observed, "is well worth a Mass." Montaigne, who died on September 13, 1592, did not live to see Henry's triumphal entrance into Paris.

ESSAYS

Montaigne's Essays, which began as a collection of interesting quotations, observations, and recordings of remarkable events, slowly developed into its final form of three large books. The essays are at once highly personal and outward looking; they present a curious mind investigating history, the complex and changing sociopolitical world, and the mind's own slightly mysterious workings. To essay—from the French essayer, meaning to attempt or try out—is Montaigne's characteristic intellectual operation, as he carefully examines his topics from a variety of possible angles. The literary result of that operation is the *essay*, the common noun that, in the wake of Montaigne, describes a short piece of highly personal and exploratory writing.

Though fascinated by the complexities of self-understanding, Montaigne explores far more than his own circumstances or thoughts. "I am a man," he says, quoting the Roman playwright Terence, and "I consider nothing human to be alien to me." As an ethnographer and historian, Montaigne studies geographically and historically distant cultures, insisting that cultural norms are relative and should be free from judgment by sixteenth-century European standards. As a psychologist, he is drawn to the stranger thoughts and experiences of himself and his countrymen. His method is not didactic or moralizing, and his criticism, which he reserves for fellow Europeans, emerges largely through subtle ironies that he leaves readers to detect.

When Montaigne looks inward, he does not aggrandize or justify himself but tries to understand how the mind works. Far from prizing his capacity for reason and judgment, for example, he neutrally observes, "My judgment floats, it wanders." Montaigne is, in fact, disarmingly modest: "Reader, I am myself the subject of my book; it is not reasonable to expect you to waste your leisure on a matter so frivolous and empty." Although massively learned, he emphasizes not what he knows but rather, like his revered model, Plato's Socrates, the ways that knowledge reveals how little he truly knows.

Although he refuses certainty and mocks vanity, Montaigne's stance is skeptical, not cynical. Thus when he "essays" or probes the human capacity to act purposefully and coherently—as he does in "Of the Inconsistency of Our Actions"—he does not aim to prove that action is futile. Instead, he resists granting the mind a coherence it does not possess; to Montaigne, the

Stoic ideal of the "constant man," unmoved by emotion or circumstance, is an impoverished version of humankind. Instead, he emphasizes the strangeness and instability of the self: "There is as much difference between us and ourselves as between us and others." This idea became highly influential in Renaissance thinking and shaped such haunting insights as John Donne's observation that "ourselves are what we know not." For Renaissance thinkers who embraced Montaigne's doubt, the difficult philosophical imperative of Socrates, "know thyself," seemed unattainable.

Montaigne charts the elusive "self" through a wide range of anecdotes, both contemporary and classical. A slippery or indefinable historical character intrigues him far more than a monolithic or single-minded one. The legendary warrior Alexander the Great is rendered frighteningly transparent by his obsession with power and conquest: he wants nothing less than to be a god. Emperor Augustus, on the other hand, rewards study precisely because his character has "escaped" the willful reductions of historians bent on "fashioning a consistent and solid fabric" of his character.

Why was Montaigne so unusually able to suspend the self-interest and bias he considered ingrained in human nature in order to analyze himself, and his culture? As his life in politics indicates, the violent instability of French history taught him tolerance, skepticism about human self-interest, and hatred of dogmatic positions: "It demands a great deal of self-love and presumption, to take one's own opinions so seriously as to disrupt the peace in order to establish them, introducing so many inevitable evils, and so terrible a corruption of manners as civil wars and political revolutions with them." His hatred of political radicalism influenced much of what he saw in ancient history and in contemporary accounts of New World discovery and conquest. Alienated from his own political context, Montaigne developed a rich double perspective, both ethnographic (outward-looking and impartial) and self-critical (introspective and moral). As he reflects on the ancient and new worlds, he pays special attention to how human beings respond to adversity, oppression, and physical torture.

In the best known of the selections included here, "Of Cannibals," Montaigne compares the behavioral codes of Brazilian cannibals and those of "ourselves" (Europeans) and concludes that "each man calls barbarism whatever is not his own practice." Once he has asserted the relativity of customs, Montaigne is able to praise elements of the savages' culture that he regards as superior to Europe's. He admires the savages' courage, for instance, in which "the honor of valor consists in combating, not in beating." Moreover, he finds in the positive example of the Brazilian cannibals an implicit criticism of violence by Europeans both at home and in the New World.

As an ethnographer, Montaigne is able to grapple with a distinct and alien culture without passing judgment; but when he reflects on France, he becomes a moralist. Central to "Of Cannibals" is the invocation of the Catholics' torture and burning of fellow citizens. Montaigne juxtaposes two kinds of savagery: that which appears foreign (cannibalism) and that which has grown too familiar (religious persecution). His own country's civil strife enables him to transcend smug cultural bias, making him a powerful critic of European culture and allowing him to imagine communities other than his own. Like the world of antiquity, which also riveted his imagination, the idea of America allowed Montaigne to explore alternate worlds for their own sake and for their illumination of his own.

The genre that Montaigne inaugurated quickly made its way into the English tradition, with the *Essays* of Francis Bacon (1597). Yet its larger influence reached much further: with the advent of the Enlightenment and the rise of periodicals, the essay enabled the intellectual exchange of carefully considered, highly personal opinions in the public realm and thus shapes our own thinking and writing to this day.

FROM ESSAYS[1]

To the Reader

This book was written in good faith, reader. It warns you from the outset that in it I have set myself no goal but a domestic and private one. I have had no thought of serving either you or my own glory. My powers are inadequate for such a purpose. I have dedicated it to the private convenience of my relatives and friends, so that when they have lost me (as soon they must), they may recover here some features of my habits and temperament, and by this means keep the knowledge they have had of me more complete and alive.

If I had written to seek the world's favor, I should have bedecked myself better, and should present myself in a studied posture. I want to be seen here in my

1. Translated by Donald Frame.

simple, natural, ordinary fashion, without straining or artifice; for it is myself that I portray. My defects will here be read to the life, and also my natural form, as far as respect for the public has allowed. Had I been placed among those nations which are said to live still in the sweet freedom of nature's first laws, I assure you I should very gladly have portrayed myself here entire and wholly naked.

Thus, reader, I am myself the matter of my book; you would be unreasonable to spend your leisure on so frivolous and vain a subject.

So farewell. Montaigne, this first day of March, fifteen hundred and eighty.

Of Cannibals

When King Pyrrhus[2] passed over into Italy, after he had reconnoitered the formation of the army that the Romans were sending to meet him, he said: "I do not know what barbarians these are" (for so the Greeks called all foreign nations), "but the formation of this army that I see is not at all barbarous." The Greeks said as much of the army that Flaminius brought into their country, and so did Philip, seeing from a knoll the order and distribution of the Roman camp, in his kingdom, under Publius Sulpicius Galba.[3] Thus we should beware of clinging to vulgar opinions, and judge things by reason's way, not by popular say.

I had with me for a long time a man who had lived for ten or twelve years in that other world which has been discovered in our century, in the place where Villegaignon landed, and which he called Antarctic France.[4] This discovery of a boundless country seems worthy of consideration. I don't know if I can guarantee that some other such discovery will not be made in the future, so many personages greater than ourselves having been mistaken about this one. I am afraid we have eyes bigger than our stomachs, and more curiosity than capacity. We embrace everything, but we clasp only wind.

Plato brings in Solon,[5] telling how he had learned from the priests of the city of Saïs in Egypt that in days of old, before the Flood, there was a great island named Atlantis, right at the mouth of the Strait of Gibraltar, which contained more land than Africa and Asia put together, and that the kings of that country, who not only possessed that island but had stretched out so far on the mainland that they held the breadth of Africa as far as Egypt, and the length of Europe as far as Tuscany, undertook to step over into Asia and subjugate all the nations that border on the Mediterranean, as far as the Black Sea; and for this purpose crossed the Spains, Gaul, Italy, as far as Greece, where the Athenians checked them; but that some time after, both the Athenians and themselves and their island were swallowed up by the Flood.

It is quite likely that that extreme devastation of waters made amazing changes in the habitations of the earth, as people maintain that the sea cut off Sicily from Italy—

2. King of Epirus (in Greece) who fought the Romans in Italy in 280 B.C.E.
3. Both Titus Quinctius Flaminius and Publius Sulpicius Galba were Roman statesmen and generals who fought Philip V of Macedon in the early years of the 2nd century B.C.E.
4. In Brazil. Villegaignon landed there in 1557.
5. In his *Timaeus*.

> 'Tis said an earthquake once asunder tore
> These lands with dreadful havoc, which before
> Formed but one land, one coast
>
> VIRGIL[6]

—Cyprus from Syria, the island of Euboea from the mainland of Boeotia; and elsewhere joined lands that were divided, filling the channels between them with sand and mud:

> A sterile marsh, long fit for rowing, now
> Feeds neighbor towns, and feels the heavy plow.
>
> HORACE[7]

But there is no great likelihood that that island was the new world which we have just discovered; for it almost touched Spain, and it would be an incredible result of a flood to have forced it away as far as it is, more than twelve hundred leagues; besides, the travels of the moderns have already almost revealed that it is not an island, but a mainland connected with the East Indies on one side, and elsewhere with the lands under the two poles; or, if it is separated from them, it is by so narrow a strait and interval that it does not deserve to be called an island on that account.

It seems that there are movements, some natural, others feverish, in these great bodies, just as in our own. When I consider the inroads that my river, the Dordogne, is making in my lifetime into the right bank in its descent, and that in twenty years it has gained so much ground and stolen away the foundations of several buildings, I clearly see that this is an extraordinary disturbance; for if it had always gone at this rate, or was to do so in the future, the face of the world would be turned topsy-turvy. But rivers are subject to changes: now they overflow in one direction, now in another, now they keep to their course. I am not speaking of the sudden inundations whose causes are manifest. In Médoc, along the seashore, my brother, the sieur d'Arsac, can see an estate of his buried under the sands that the sea spews forth; the tops of some buildings are still visible; his farms and domains have changed into very thin pasturage. The inhabitants say that for some time the sea has been pushing toward them so hard that they have lost four leagues of land. These sands are its harbingers; and we see great dunes of moving sand that march half a league ahead of it and keep conquering land.

The other testimony of antiquity with which some would connect this discovery is in Aristotle, at least if that little book *Of Unheard-of Wonders* is by him. He there relates that certain Carthaginians, after setting out upon the Atlantic Ocean from the Strait of Gibraltar and sailing a long time, at last discovered a great fertile island, all clothed in woods and watered by great deep rivers, far remote from any mainland; and that they, and others since, attracted by the goodness and fertility of the soil, went there with their wives and children, and began to settle there. The lords of Carthage, seeing that their country was gradually becoming depopulated, expressly forbade anyone to go there any more, on pain of death, and drove out these new inhabitants, fearing, it is

---

6. *Aeneid* 3.414–15.
7. Horatius Flaccus (65–8 B.C.E.), great poet of Augustan Rome; *Art of Poetry*, lines 65–66.

said, that in course of time they might come to multiply so greatly as to supplant their former masters and ruin their state. This story of Aristotle does not fit our new lands any better than the other.

This man I had was a simple, crude fellow—a character fit to bear true witness; for clever people observe more things and more curiously, but they interpret them; and to lend weight and conviction to their interpretation, they cannot help altering history a little. They never show you things as they are, but bend and disguise them according to the way they have seen them; and to give credence to their judgment and attract you to it, they are prone to add something to their matter, to stretch it out and amplify it. We need a man either very honest, or so simple that he has not the stuff to build up false inventions and give them plausibility; and wedded to no theory. Such was my man; and besides this, he at various times brought sailors and merchants, whom he had known on that trip, to see me. So I content myself with his information, without inquiring what the cosmographers say about it.

We ought to have topographers who would give us an exact account of the places where they have been. But because they have over us the advantage of having seen Palestine, they want to enjoy the privilege of telling us news about all the rest of the world. I would like everyone to write what he knows, and as much as he knows, not only in this, but in all other subjects; for a man may have some special knowledge and experience of the nature of a river or a fountain, who in other matters knows only what everybody knows. However, to circulate this little scrap of knowledge, he will undertake to write the whole of physics. From this vice spring many great abuses.

Now, to return to my subject, I think there is nothing barbarous and savage in that nation, from what I have been told, except that each man calls barbarism whatever is not his own practice; for indeed it seems we have no other test of truth and reason than the example and pattern of the opinions and customs of the country we live in. *There* is always the perfect religion, the perfect government, the perfect and accomplished manners in all things. Those people are wild, just as we call wild the fruits that Nature has produced by herself and in her normal course; whereas really it is those that we have changed artificially and led astray from the common order, that we should rather call wild. The former retain alive and vigorous their genuine, their most useful and natural, virtues and properties, which we have debased in the latter in adapting them to gratify our corrupted taste. And yet for all that, the savor and delicacy of some uncultivated fruits of those countries is quite as excellent, even to our taste, as that of our own. It is not reasonable that art should win the place of honor over our great and powerful mother Nature. We have so overloaded the beauty and richness of her works by our inventions that we have quite smothered her. Yet wherever her purity shines forth, she wonderfully puts to shame our vain and frivolous attempts:

> Ivy comes readier without our care;
> In lonely caves the arbutus grows more fair;
> No art with artless bird song can compare.
> **PROPERTIUS**[8]

8. *Elegies* 1.2.10–12.

All our efforts cannot even succeed in reproducing the nest of the tiniest little bird, its contexture, its beauty and convenience; or even the web of the puny spider. All things, says Plato,[9] are produced by nature, by fortune, or by art; the greatest and most beautiful by one or the other of the first two, the least and most imperfect by the last.

These nations, then, seem to me barbarous in this sense, that they have been fashioned very little by the human mind, and are still very close to their original naturalness. The laws of nature still rule them, very little corrupted by ours; and they are in such a state of purity that I am sometimes vexed that they were unknown earlier, in the days when there were men able to judge them better than we. I am sorry that Lycurgus[1] and Plato did not know of them; for it seems to me that what we actually see in these nations surpasses not only all the pictures in which poets have idealized the golden age and all their inventions in imagining a happy state of man, but also the conceptions and the very desire of philosophy. They could not imagine a naturalness so pure and simple as we see by experience; nor could they believe that our society could be maintained with so little artifice and human solder. This is a nation, I should say to Plato, in which there is no sort of traffic, no knowledge of letters, no science of numbers, no name for a magistrate or for political superiority, no custom of servitude, no riches or poverty, no contracts, no successions, no partitions, no occupations but leisure ones, no care for any but common kinship, no clothes, no agriculture, no metal, no use of wine or wheat.[2] The very words that signify lying, treachery, dissimulation, avarice, envy, belittling, pardon—unheard of. How far from this perfection would he find the republic that he imagined: *Men fresh sprung from the gods* [Seneca].[3]

> These manners nature first ordained.
>   VIRGIL[4]

For the rest, they live in a country with a very pleasant and temperate climate, so that according to my witnesses it is rare to see a sick man there; and they have assured me that they never saw one palsied, bleary-eyed, toothless, or bent with age. They are settled along the sea and shut in on the land side by great high mountains, with a stretch about a hundred leagues wide in between. They have a great abundance of fish and flesh which bear no resemblance to ours, and they eat them with no other artifice than cooking. The first man who rode a horse there, though he had had dealings with them on several other trips, so horrified them in this posture that they shot him dead with arrows before they could recognize him.

Their buildings are very long, with a capacity of two or three hundred souls; they are covered with the bark of great trees, the strips reaching to the ground at one end and supporting and leaning on one another at the top, in the manner of some of our barns, whose covering hangs down to the ground and acts as a side. They have wood so hard that they cut with it and make of it their

---

9. See his *Laws*.
1. The half-legendary Spartan lawgiver (9th century B.C.E.).
2. This passage is always compared with Shakespeare's *The Tempest* 2.1.147 ff.

3. Roman tragedian (ca. 4 B.C.E.–65 C.E.), philosopher, and political leader, *Epistles* 90.
4. *Georgics* 2.20.

swords and grills to cook their food. Their beds are of a cotton weave, hung from the roof like those in our ships, each man having his own; for the wives sleep apart from their husbands.

They get up with the sun, and eat immediately upon rising, to last them through the day; for they take no other meal than that one. Like some other Eastern peoples, of whom Suidas[5] tells us, who drank apart from meals, they do not drink then; but they drink several times a day, and to capacity. Their drink is made of some root, and is of the color of our claret wines. They drink it only lukewarm. This beverage keeps only two or three days; it has a slightly sharp taste, is not at all heady, is good for the stomach, and has a laxative effect upon those who are not used to it; it is a very pleasant drink for anyone who is accustomed to it. In place of bread they use a certain white substance like preserved coriander. I have tried it; it tastes sweet and a little flat.

The whole day is spent in dancing. The younger men go to hunt animals with bows. Some of the women busy themselves meanwhile with warming their drink, which is their chief duty. Some one of the old men, in the morning before they begin to eat, preaches to the whole barnful in common, walking from one end to the other, and repeating one single sentence several times until he has completed the circuit (for the buildings are fully a hundred paces long). He recommends to them only two things: valor against the enemy and love for their wives. And they never fail to point out this obligation, as their refrain, that it is their wives who keep their drink warm and seasoned.

There may be seen in several places, including my own house, specimens of their beds, of their ropes, of their wooden swords and the bracelets with which they cover their wrists in combats, and of the big canes, open at one end, by whose sound they keep time in their dances. They are close shaven all over, and shave themselves much more cleanly than we, with nothing but a wooden or stone razor. They believe that souls are immortal, and that those who have deserved well of the gods are lodged in that part of heaven where the sun rises, and the damned in the west.

They have some sort of priests and prophets, but they rarely appear before the people, having their home in the mountains. On their arrival there is a great feast and solemn assembly of several villages—each barn, as I have described it, makes up a village, and they are about one French league[6] from each other. The prophet speaks to them in public, exhorting them to virtue and their duty; but their whole ethical science contains only these two articles: resoluteness in war and affection for their wives. He prophesies to them things to come and the results they are to expect from their undertakings, and urges them to war or holds them back from it; but this is on the condition that when he fails to prophesy correctly, and if things turn out otherwise than he has predicted, he is cut into a thousand pieces if they catch him, and condemned as a false prophet. For this reason, the prophet who has once been mistaken is never seen again.

Divination is a gift of God; that is why its abuse should be punished as imposture. Among the Scythians, when the soothsayers failed to hit the mark, they were laid, chained hand and foot, on carts full of heather and drawn by oxen, on which they were burned. Those who handle matters subject to the control of human capacity are excusable if they do the best they can. But these

---

5. A Byzantine lexicographer.   **6.** About 2.49 miles.

others who come and trick us with assurances of an extraordinary faculty that is beyond our ken, should they not be punished for not making good their promise, and for the temerity of their imposture?

They have their wars with the nations beyond the mountains, further inland, to which they go quite naked, with no other arms than bows or wooden swords ending in a sharp point, in the manner of the tongues of our boar spears. It is astonishing what firmness they show in their combats, which never end but in slaughter and bloodshed; for as to routs and terror, they know nothing of either.

Each man brings back his trophy the head of the enemy he has killed, and sets it up at the entrance to his dwelling. After they have treated their prisoners well for a long time with all the hospitality they can think of, each man who has a prisoner calls a great assembly of his acquaintances. He ties a rope to one of the prisoner's arms, by the end of which he holds him, a few steps away, for fear of being hurt, and gives his dearest friend the other arm to hold in the same way; and these two, in the presence of the whole assembly, kill him with their swords. This done, they roast him and eat him in common and send some pieces to their absent friends. This is not, as people think, for nourishment, as of old the Scythians used to do; it is to betoken an extreme revenge. And the proof of this came when they saw the Portuguese, who had joined forces with their adversaries, inflict a different kind of death on them when they took them prisoner, which was to bury them up to the waist, shoot the rest of their body full of arrows, and afterward hang them. They thought that these people from the other world, being men who had sown the knowledge of many vices among their neighbors and were much greater masters than themselves in every sort of wickedness, did not adopt this sort of vengeance without some reason, and that it must be more painful than their own; so they began to give up their old method and to follow this one.

I am not sorry that we notice the barbarous horror of such acts, but I am heartily sorry that, judging their faults rightly, we should be so blind to our own. I think there is more barbarity in eating a man alive than in eating him dead; and in tearing by tortures and the rack a body still full of feeling, in roasting a man bit by bit, in having him bitten and mangled by dogs and swine (as we have not only read but seen within fresh memory, not among ancient enemies, but among neighbors and fellow citizens, and what is worse, on the pretext of piety and religion),[7] than in roasting and eating him after he is dead.

Indeed, Chrysippus and Zeno, heads of the Stoic sect, thought there was nothing wrong in using our carcasses for any purpose in case of need, and getting nourishment from them; just as our ancestors,[8] when besieged by Caesar in the city of Alesia, resolved to relieve their famine by eating old men, women, and other people useless for fighting.

> The Gascons once, 'tis said, their life renewed
> By eating of such food.
>
> JUVENAL[9]

7. The allusion is to the spectacles of religious warfare that Montaigne himself had witnessed in his time and country.
8. The Gauls.

9. Decimus Junius Juvenal (fl. early 2nd century C.E.), last great Roman satirist; *Satires* 15.93–94.

And physicians do not fear to use human flesh in all sorts of ways for our health, applying it either inwardly or outwardly. But there never was any opinion so disordered as to excuse treachery, disloyalty, tyranny, and cruelty, which are our ordinary vices.

So we may well call these people barbarians, in respect to the rules of reason, but not in respect to ourselves, who surpass them in every kind of barbarity.

Their warfare is wholly noble and generous, and as excusable and beautiful as this human disease can be; its only basis among them is their rivalry in valor. They are not fighting for the conquest of new lands, for they still enjoy that natural abundance that provides them without toil and trouble with all necessary things in such profusion that they have no wish to enlarge their boundaries. They are still in that happy state of desiring only as much as their natural needs demand; anything beyond that is superfluous to them.

They generally call those of the same age, brothers; those who are younger, children; and the old men are fathers to all the others. These leave to their heirs in common the full possession of their property, without division or any other title at all than just the one that Nature gives to her creatures in bringing them into the world.

If their neighbors cross the mountains to attack them and win a victory, the gain of the victor is glory, and the advantage of having proved the master in valor and virtue; for apart from this they have no use for the goods of the vanquished, and they return to their own country, where they lack neither anything necessary nor that great thing, the knowledge of how to enjoy their condition happily and be content with it. These men of ours do the same in their turn. They demand of their prisoners no other ransom than that they confess and acknowledge their defeat. But there is not one in a whole century who does not choose to die rather than to relax a single bit, by word or look, from the grandeur of an invincible courage; not one who would not rather be killed and eaten than so much as ask not to be. They treat them very freely, so that life may be all the dearer to them, and usually entertain them with threats of their coming death, of the torments they will have to suffer, the preparations that are being made for the purpose, the cutting up of their limbs, and the feast that will be made at their expense. All this is done for the sole purpose of extorting from their lips some weak or base word, or making them want to flee, so as to gain the advantage of having terrified them and broken down their firmness. For indeed, if you take it the right way, it is in this point alone that true victory lies:

> It is no victory
> Unless the vanquished foe admits your mastery.
> CLAUDIAN[1]

The Hungarians, very bellicose fighters, did not in olden times pursue their advantage beyond putting the enemy at their mercy. For having wrung a confession from him to this effect, they let him go unharmed and unransomed, except, at most, for exacting his promise never again to take up arms against them.

We win enough advantages over our enemies that are borrowed advantages, not really our own. It is the quality of a porter, not of valor, to have sturdier

1. *Of the Sixth Consulate of Honorius*, lines 248–49.

arms and legs; agility is a dead and corporeal quality; it is a stroke of luck to make our enemy stumble, or dazzle his eyes by the sunlight; it is a trick of art and technique, which may be found in a worthless coward, to be an able fencer. The worth and value of a man is in his heart and his will; there lies his real honor. Valor is the strength, not of legs and arms, but of heart and soul; it consists not in the worth of our horse or our weapons, but in our own. He who falls obstinate in his courage, *if he has fallen, he fights on his knees* [Seneca].[2] He who relaxes none of his assurance, no matter how great the danger of imminent death; who, giving up his soul, still looks firmly and scornfully at his enemy—he is beaten not by us, but by fortune; he is killed, not conquered.

The most valiant are sometimes the most unfortunate. Thus there are triumphant defeats that rival victories. Nor did those four sister victories, the fairest that the sun ever set eyes on—Salamis, Plataea, Mycale, and Sicily[3]—ever dare match all their combined glory against the glory of the annihilation of King Leonidas and his men at the pass of Thermopylae.[4]

Who ever hastened with more glorious and ambitious desire to win a battle than Captain Ischolas to lose one? Who ever secured his safety more ingeniously and painstakingly than he did his destruction? He was charged to defend a certain pass in the Peloponnesus against the Arcadians. Finding himself wholly incapable of doing this, in view of the nature of the place and the inequality of the forces, he made up his mind that all who confronted the enemy would necessarily have to remain on the field. On the other hand, deeming it unworthy both of his own virtue and magnanimity and of the Lacedaemonian name to fail in his charge, he took a middle course between these two extremes, in this way. The youngest and fittest of his band he preserved for the defense and service of their country, and sent them home; and with those whose loss was less important, he determined to hold this pass, and by their death to make the enemy buy their entry as dearly as he could. And so it turned out. For he was presently surrounded on all sides by the Arcadians, and after slaughtering a large number of them, he and his men were all put to the sword. Is there a trophy dedicated to victors that would not be more due to these vanquished? The role of true victory is in fighting, not in coming off safely; and the honor of valor consists in combating, not in beating.

To return to our story. These prisoners are so far from giving in, in spite of all that is done to them, that on the contrary, during the two or three months that they are kept, they wear a gay expression; they urge their captors to hurry and put them to the test; they defy them, insult them, reproach them with their cowardice and the number of battles they have lost to the prisoners' own people.

I have a song composed by a prisoner which contains this challenge, that they should all come boldly and gather to dine off him, for they will be eating at the same time their own fathers and grandfathers, who have served to feed and nourish his body. "These muscles," he says, "this flesh and these veins are your own, poor fools that you are. You do not recognize that the substance of your ancestors' limbs is still contained in them. Savor them well; you will find in them the taste of your own flesh." An idea that certainly does not smack of

2. *Of Providence* 2.
3. References to the famous Greek victories against the Persians and (at Himera, Sicily) against the Carthaginians in or about 480 B.C.E.

4. The Spartan king Leonidas's defense here also took place in 480 B.C.E., during the war against the Persians.

barbarity. Those that paint these people dying, and who show the execution, portray the prisoner spitting in the face of his slayers and scowling at them. Indeed, to the last gasp they never stop braving and defying their enemies by word and look. Truly here are real savages by our standards; for either they must be thoroughly so, or we must be; there is an amazing distance between their character and ours.

The men there have several wives, and the higher their reputation for valor the more wives they have. It is a remarkably beautiful thing about their marriages that the same jealousy our wives have to keep us from the affection and kindness of other women, theirs have to win this for them. Being more concerned for their husbands' honor than for anything else, they strive and scheme to have as many companions as they can, since that is a sign of their husbands' valor.

Our wives will cry "Miracle!" but it is no miracle. It is a properly matrimonial virtue, but one of the highest order. In the Bible, Leah, Rachel, Sarah, and Jacob's wives gave their beautiful handmaids to their husbands; and Livia seconded the appetites of Augustus to her own disadvantage; and Stratonice, the wife of King Deiotarus,[5] not only lent her husband for his use a very beautiful young chambermaid in her service, but carefully brought up her children, and backed them up to succeed to their father's estates.

And lest it be thought that all this is done through a simple and servile bondage to usage and through the pressure of the authority of their ancient customs, without reasoning or judgment, and because their minds are so stupid that they cannot take any other course, I must cite some examples of their capacity. Besides the warlike song I have just quoted, I have another, a love song, which begins in this vein: "Adder, stay; stay, adder, that from the pattern of your coloring my sister may draw the fashion and the workmanship of a rich girdle that I may give to my love; so may your beauty and your pattern be forever preferred to all other serpents." This first couplet is the refrain of the song. Now I am familiar enough with poetry to be a judge of this: not only is there nothing barbarous in this fancy, but it is altogether Anacreontic.[6] Their language, moreover, is a soft language, with an agreeable sound, somewhat like Greek in its endings.

Three of these men, ignorant of the price they will pay some day, in loss of repose and happiness, for gaining knowledge of the corruptions of this side of the ocean; ignorant also of the fact that of this intercourse will come their ruin (which I suppose is already well advanced: poor wretches, to let themselves be tricked by the desire for new things, and to have left the serenity of their own sky to come and see ours!)—three of these men were at Rouen, at the time the late King Charles IX was there. The king talked to them for a long time; they were shown our ways, our splendor, the aspect of a fine city. After that, someone asked their opinion, and wanted to know what they had found most amazing. They mentioned three things, of which I have forgotten the third, and I am very sorry for it; but I still remember two of them. They said that in the first place they thought it very strange that so many grown men, bearded, strong, and armed, who were around the king (it is likely that they were talking about the Swiss of his guard) should submit to obey a child, and that one of them was

5. Tetrarch of Galatia, in Asia Minor.
6. Worthy of Anacreon (572?–488? B.C.E.), major Greek writer of amatory lyrics.

not chosen to command instead. Second (they have a way in their language of speaking of men as halves of one another), they had noticed that there were among us men full and gorged with all sorts of good things, and that their other halves were beggars at their doors, emaciated with hunger and poverty; and they thought it strange that these needy halves could endure such an injustice, and did not take the others by the throat, or set fire to their houses.

I had a very long talk with one of them; but I had an interpreter who followed my meaning so badly, and who was so hindered by his stupidity in taking in my ideas, that I could get hardly any satisfaction from the man. When I asked him what profit he gained from his superior position among his people (for he was a captain, and our sailors called him king), he told me that it was to march foremost in war. How many men followed him? He pointed to a piece of ground, to signify as many as such a space could hold; it might have been four or five thousand men. Did all this authority expire with the war? He said that this much remained, that when he visited the villages dependent on him, they made paths for him through the underbrush by which he might pass quite comfortably.

All this is not too bad—but what's the use? They don't wear breeches.

Of the Inconsistency of Our Actions

Those who make a practice of comparing human actions are never so perplexed as when they try to see them as a whole and in the same light; for they commonly contradict each other so strangely that it seems impossible that they have come from the same shop. One moment young Marius is a son of Mars, another moment a son of Venus.[7] Pope Boniface VIII, they say, entered office like a fox, behaved in it like a lion, and died like a dog. And who would believe that it was Nero, that living image of cruelty, who said, when they brought him in customary fashion the sentence of a condemned criminal to sign: "Would to God I had never learned to write!" So much his heart was wrung at condemning a man to death!

Everything is so full of such examples—each man, in fact, can supply himself with so many—that I find it strange to see intelligent men sometimes going to great pains to match these pieces; seeing that irresolution seems to me the most common and apparent defect of our nature, as witness that famous line of Publilius, the farce writer:

> Bad is the plan that never can be changed.
> PUBLILIUS SYRUS[8]

There is some justification for basing a judgment of a man on the most ordinary acts of his life; but in view of the natural instability of our conduct and

---

7. Goddess of love. "Marius": the nephew of the older and better-known Marius. Montaigne's source is Plutarch's *Life of Marius*.

"Mars": the god of war.
8. *Apothegms (Sententiae)*, line 362.

opinions, it has often seemed to me that even good authors are wrong to insist on fashioning a consistent and solid fabric out of us. They choose one general characteristic, and go and arrange and interpret all a man's actions to fit their picture; and if they cannot twist them enough, they go and set them down to dissimulation. Augustus has escaped them; for there is in this man throughout the course of his life such an obvious, abrupt, and continual variety of actions that even the boldest judges have had to let him go, intact and unsolved. Nothing is harder for me than to believe in men's consistency, nothing easier than to believe in their inconsistency. He who would judge them in detail and distinctly, bit by bit, would more often hit upon the truth.

In all antiquity it is hard to pick out a dozen men who set their lives to a certain and constant course, which is the principal goal of wisdom. For, to comprise all wisdom in a word, says an ancient [Seneca], and to embrace all the rules of our life in one, it is "always to will the same things, and always to oppose the same things."[9] I would not deign, he says, to add "provided the will is just"; for if it is not just, it cannot always be whole.

In truth, I once learned that vice is only unruliness and lack of moderation, and that consequently consistency cannot be attributed to it. It is a maxim of Demosthenes, they say, that the beginning of all virtue is consultation and deliberation; and the end and perfection, consistency. If it were by reasoning that we settled on a particular course of action, we would choose the fairest course—but no one has thought of that:

> He spurns the thing he sought, and seeks anew
> What he just spurned; he seethes, his life's askew.
> HORACE[1]

Our ordinary practice is to follow the inclinations of our appetite, to the left, to the right, uphill and down, as the wind of circumstance carries us. We think of what we want only at the moment we want it, and we change like that animal which takes the color of the place you set it on. What we have just now planned, we presently change, and presently again we retrace our steps: nothing but oscillation and inconsistency:

> Like puppets we are moved by outside strings.
> HORACE[2]

We do not go; we are carried away, like floating objects, now gently, now violently, according as the water is angry or calm:

> Do we not see all humans unaware
> Of what they want, and always searching everywhere,
> And changing place, as if to drop the load they bear?
> LUCRETIUS[3]

9. *Epistles* 20.
1. *Epistles* 1.1.98–99.

2. *Satires* 2.7.82.
3. *On the Nature of Things* 3.1057–59.

Every day a new fancy, and our humors shift with the shifts in the weather:

> Such are the minds of men, as is the fertile light
> That Father Jove himself sends down to make earth bright.
> HOMER[4]

We float between different states of mind; we wish nothing freely, nothing absolutely, nothing constantly. If any man could prescribe and establish definite laws and a definite organization in his head, we should see shining throughout his life an evenness of habits, an order, and an infallible relation between his principles and his practice.

Empedocles noticed this inconsistency in the Agrigentines, that they abandoned themselves to pleasures as if they were to die on the morrow, and built as if they were never to die.[5]

This man would be easy to understand, as is shown by the example of the younger Cato:[6] he who has touched one chord of him has touched all; he is a harmony of perfectly concordant sounds, which cannot conflict. With us, it is the opposite: for so many actions, we need so many individual judgments. The surest thing, in my opinion, would be to trace our actions to the neighboring circumstances, without getting into any further research and without drawing from them any other conclusions.

During the disorders of our poor country,[7] I was told that a girl, living near where I then was, had thrown herself out of a high window to avoid the violence of a knavish soldier quartered in her house. Not killed by the fall, she reasserted her purpose by trying to cut her throat with a knife. From this she was prevented, but only after wounding herself gravely. She herself confessed that the soldier had as yet pressed her only with requests, solicitations, and gifts; but she had been afraid, she said, that he would finally resort to force. And all this with such words, such expressions, not to mention the blood that testified to her virtue, as would have become another Lucrece.[8] Now, I learned that as a matter of fact, both before and since, she was a wench not so hard to come to terms with. As the story[9] says: Handsome and gentlemanly as you may be, when you have had no luck, do not promptly conclude that your mistress is inviolably chaste; for all you know, the mule driver may get his will with her.

Antigonus,[1] having taken a liking to one of his soldiers for his virtue and valor, ordered his physicians to treat the man for a persistent internal malady that had long tormented him. After his cure, his master noticed that he was going about his business much less warmly, and asked him what had changed him so and made him such a coward. "You yourself, Sire," he answered, "by delivering me from the ills that made my life indifferent to me." A soldier of Lucullus[2] who had been robbed of everything by the enemy made a bold attack

---

4. *Odyssey* 18.135–36, 152–53 in the Fitzgerald translation.
5. From Diogenes Laertius's life of the Greek philosopher Empedocles (5th century).
6. Cato Uticensis (1st century B.C.E.), a philosopher. He is traditionally considered the epitome of moral and intellectual integrity.
7. See p. 1656, n. 7.
8. The legendary virtuous Roman who stabbed herself after being raped by King Tarquinius Superbus's son.
9. A common folktale.
1. Macedonian king (382–301 B.C.E.).
2. Roman general (1st century B.C.E.).

on them to get revenge. When he had retrieved his loss, Lucullus, having formed a good opinion of him, urged him to some dangerous exploit with all the fine expostulations he could think of,

> With words that might have stirred a coward's heart.
> HORACE[3]

"Urge some poor soldier who has been robbed to do it," he replied;

> Though but a rustic lout,
> "That man will go who's lost his money," he called out;
> HORACE[4]

and resolutely refused to go.

We read that Sultan Mohammed outrageously berated Hassan, leader of his Janissaries, because he saw his troops giving way to the Hungarians and Hassan himself behaving like a coward in the fight. Hassan's only reply was to go and hurl himself furiously—alone, just as he was, arms in hand—into the first body of enemies that he met, by whom he was promptly swallowed up; this was perhaps not so much self-justification as a change of mood, nor so much his natural valor as fresh spite.

That man whom you saw so adventurous yesterday, do not think it strange to find him just as cowardly today: either anger, or necessity, or company, or wine, or the sound of a trumpet, had put his heart in his belly. His was a courage formed not by reason, but by one of these circumstances; it is no wonder if he has now been made different by other, contrary circumstances.

These supple variations and contradictions that are seen in us have made some imagine that we have two souls, and others that two powers accompany us and drive us, each in its own way, one toward good, the other toward evil; for such sudden diversity cannot well be reconciled with a simple subject.

Not only does the wind of accident move me at will, but, besides, I am moved and disturbed as a result merely of my own unstable posture; and anyone who observes carefully can hardly find himself twice in the same state. I give my soul now one face, now another, according to which direction I turn it. If I speak of myself in different ways, that is because I look at myself in different ways. All contradictions may be found in me by some twist and in some fashion. Bashful, insolent; chaste, lascivious; talkative, taciturn; tough, delicate; clever, stupid; surly, affable; lying, truthful; learned, ignorant; liberal, miserly, and prodigal: all this I see in myself to some extent according to how I turn; and whoever studies himself really attentively finds in himself, yes, even in his judgment, this gyration and discord. I have nothing to say about myself absolutely, simply, and solidly, without confusion and without mixture, or in one word. *Distinguo*[5] is the most universal member of my logic.

---

3. *Epistles* 2.2.36.
4. *Epistles* 2.2.39–40.

5. I distinguish (Latin)—that is, I separate into its components.

1664 | MICHEL DE MONTAIGNE

Although I am always minded to say good of what is good, and inclined to interpret favorably anything that can be so interpreted, still it is true that the strangeness of our condition makes it happen that we are often driven to do good by vice itself—were it not that doing good is judged by intention alone.

Therefore one courageous deed must not be taken to prove a man valiant; a man who was really valiant would be so always and on all occasions. If valor were a habit of virtue, and not a sally, it would make a man equally resolute in any contingency, the same alone as in company, the same in single combat as in battle; for, whatever they say, there is not one valor for the pavement and another for the camp. As bravely would he bear an illness in his bed as a wound in camp, and he would fear death no more in his home than in an assault. We would not see the same man charging into the breach with brave assurance, and later tormenting himself, like a woman, over the loss of a lawsuit or a son. When, though a coward against infamy, he is firm against poverty; when, though weak against the surgeons' knives, he is steadfast against the enemy's swords, the action is praiseworthy, not the man.

Many Greeks, says Cicero, cannot look at the enemy, and are brave in sickness; the Cimbrians and Celtiberians, just the opposite; *for nothing can be uniform that does not spring from a firm principle* [Cicero].[6]

There is no more extreme valor of its kind than Alexander's; but it is only of one kind, and not complete and universal enough. Incomparable though it is, it still has its blemishes; which is why we see him worry so frantically when he conceives the slightest suspicion that his men are plotting against his life, and why he behaves in such matters with such violent and indiscriminate injustice and with a fear that subverts his natural reason. Also superstition, with which he was so strongly tainted, bears some stamp of pusillanimity. And the excessiveness of the penance he did for the murder of Clytus[7] is also evidence of the unevenness of his temper.

Our actions are nothing but a patchwork—*they despise pleasure, but are too cowardly in pain; they are indifferent to glory, but infamy breaks their spirit* [Cicero][8]—and we want to gain honor under false colors. Virtue will not be followed except for her own sake; and if we sometimes borrow her mask for some other purpose, she promptly snatches it from our face. It is a strong and vivid dye, once the soul is steeped in it, and will not go without taking the fabric with it. That is why, to judge a man, we must follow his traces long and carefully. If he does not maintain consistency for its own sake, *with a way of life that has been well considered and preconcerted* [Cicero];[9] if changing circumstances makes him change his pace (I mean his path, for his pace may be hastened or slowed), let him go: that man goes before the wind, as the motto of our Talbot[1] says.

It is no wonder, says an ancient [Seneca], that chance has so much power over us, since we live by chance.[2] A man who has not directed his life as a

6. Marcus Tullius Cicero (106–43 B.C.E.), Roman orator; *Tusculan Disputations* 2.27.
7. A commander in Alexander's army who was killed by him during an argument, an act Alexander immediately and bitterly regretted, as related by Plutarch in his *Life of Alexander*,

chaps. 50–52.
8. *On Duties (De officiis)* 1.21.
9. *Paradoxes* 5.
1. An English captain who fought in France and died there in 1453.
2. *Epistles* 71.

whole toward a definite goal cannot possibly set his particular actions in order. A man who does not have a picture of the whole in his head cannot possibly arrange the pieces. What good does it do a man to lay in a supply of paints if he does not know what he is to paint? No one makes a definite plan of his life; we think about it only piecemeal. The archer must first know what he is aiming at, and then set his hand, his bow, his string, his arrow, and his movements for that goal. Our plans go astray because they have no direction and no aim. No wind works for the man who has no port of destination.

I do not agree with the judgment given in favor of Sophocles, on the strength of seeing one of his tragedies, that it proved him competent to manage his domestic affairs, against the accusation of his son. Nor do I think that the conjecture of the Parians sent to reform the Milesians was sufficient ground for the conclusion they drew. Visiting the island, they noticed the best-cultivated lands and the best-run country houses, and noted down the names of their owners. Then they assembled the citizens in the town and appointed these owners the new governors and magistrates, judging that they, who were careful of their private affairs, would be careful of those of the public.

We are all patchwork, and so shapeless and diverse in composition that each bit, each moment, plays its own game. And there is as much difference between us and ourselves as between us and others. *Consider it a great thing to play the part of one single man* [Seneca].[3] Ambition can teach men valor, and temperance, and liberality, and even justice. Greed can implant in the heart of a shop apprentice, brought up in obscurity and idleness, the confidence to cast himself far from hearth and home, in a frail boat at the mercy of the waves and angry Neptune; it also teaches discretion and wisdom. Venus herself supplies resolution and boldness to boys still subject to discipline and the rod, and arms the tender hearts of virgins who are still in their mothers' laps:

> Furtively passing sleeping guards, with Love as guide,
> Alone by night the girl comes to the young man's side.
>   TIBULLUS[4]

In view of this, a sound intellect will refuse to judge men simply by their outward actions; we must probe the inside and discover what springs set men in motion. But since this is an arduous and hazardous undertaking, I wish fewer people would meddle with it.

---

3. *Epistles* 120.   4. *Elegies* 2.1.75–76.

MIGUEL DE CERVANTES
1547–1616

Often described as the first novel, Miguel de Cervantes' *Don Quixote* uses the conventions of fiction to question the accepted truths of his own society. What happens when readers take books at their word, or try to live out ideal versions of the world around them, as does the would-be knight Don Quixote? How does life in early modern Spain fall short of the wishful fictional version? In *Don Quixote*, the narrative breaks off and leaves the reader hanging, characters reflect on what it means to exist in print, and a complicated cast of antagonistic narrators all quarrel over the *real* truth, as Cervantes ironically surveys his world while examining the nature of fiction.

LIFE

The author of Don Quixote's extravagant adventures himself had a most unusual and adventurous life. As a student, soldier, captive, and tax-collector, he witnessed his contemporaries at their best and at their worst. His skeptical, ironic perspective on both the literary and political pieties of his day is combined in his works with a profound sympathy for human striving. The son of an apothecary, Miguel de Cervantes Saavedra was born in Alcalá de Henares, a university town near Madrid. Almost nothing is known of his childhood and early education. Only in 1569 is he mentioned as a favorite pupil by a Madrid humanist, Juan López. Records indicate that by the end of that year he had left Spain and was living in Rome, for a time in the service of a future cardinal. He enlisted in the Spanish fleet under the command of Don John of Austria and took part in the struggle of the allied forces of Christendom against the Ottomans. He was at the crucial Battle of Lepanto (1571), where in spite of fever he fought valiantly and received three gunshot wounds, one of which permanently impaired the use of his left hand, "for the greater glory of the right." After further military action at Palermo and Naples, he and his brother Rodrigo, bearing testimonials from Don John and from the viceroy of Sicily, began the journey back to Spain, where Miguel hoped to obtain a captaincy. In September 1575 their ship was captured near Marseille by Barbary pirates, and the two brothers were taken as prisoners to Algiers. Cervantes' captors, considering him a person of some consequence because of the letters he carried, held him as a slave for a high ransom. His daring and fortitude as he attempted repeatedly to escape excited the admiration of Hassan Pasha, the viceroy of Algiers, who bought him for five hundred crowns after five years of captivity.

Cervantes was finally ransomed on September 15, 1580, and reached Madrid in December of that year. There his literary career began rather inauspiciously; he wrote some ten to twenty plays, with middling success, and in 1585 published *Galatea*, a pastoral romance that anticipates the formal experimentation of *Don Quixote* but ends inconclusively. None of these established his reputation or, more important, allowed him to live from his writing. At about this time he had a daughter with Ana Franca de Rojas, and during the same period married Catalina de Salazar, who was eighteen years his junior.

Seeking nonliterary employment, he obtained a position in the navy, requisitioning and collecting supplies for the "Invincible Armada." Irregularities in his administration, for which he was held responsible if not directly guilty, caused him to spend more time in prison. In 1590 he was denied colonial employment in the New World. Later he served as tax collector in the province of Granada but was dismissed from government service in 1597.

The following years of Cervantes' life are the most obscure; there is a legend that *Don Quixote* was first conceived and planned while its author was in prison in Seville. In 1604 he was in Valladolid, then the temporary capital of Spain, living in sordid surroundings with the numerous women of his family (his wife, daughter, niece, and two sisters). It was in Valladolid, in late 1604, that he obtained the official license for the publication of *Don Quixote* (part I). The book appeared in 1605 and was a popular success. Cervantes followed the Spanish court when it returned to Madrid, where he continued to live poorly in spite of a popularity with readers that quickly made proverbial figures of his heroes. A false sequel to his book appeared, prompting him to write his own continuation, *Don Quixote*, part II, published in 1615. His *Exemplary Novellas* had appeared in 1613. He died on April 23, 1616. *Persiles and Sigismunda*, his last novel, was published posthumously in 1617.

TIMES

Cervantes' Spain was a great empire, with huge possessions in the New World, in Italy, and in Flanders, sustained by an equally enormous army of disciplined soldiers organized in infantry battalions—the famous *tercios españoles*. It was ruled by Philip II, the devout Habsburg monarch who became known as "the prudent king" for his careful administration. In 1580, Philip II annexed the Portuguese crown and its commercial empire in Asia, Africa, and the New World, rendering Spain a truly universal power. At the same time, the enormous influx of gold from the Americas led to inflation and widespread poverty, and to the perception that everything and everyone could be bought. As the vivacious gypsy Preciosa jokes to an impoverished official in one of Cervantes' novellas, if he only took bribes as everyone expects him to do, he would not be so poor. Both as a tax-collector and as a convict, Cervantes had ample experience of a down-and-out, picaresque Spain that held the law in small regard, a world depicted in colorful detail in the earthier episodes of *Don Quixote*.

Overburdened with military expenses and foreign debt, the Crown experienced repeated bankruptcies despite the heavy taxes it imposed on its subjects. In 1588, it suffered the added indignity of the Armada's defeat against England, and Spain entered a long period of decline and disillusion. Philip II's death in 1598 signaled the end of an era. Cervantes marked the occasion with a devastating sonnet on the king's funerary monument. Its greatness, the poem suggests, is but an illusion: as soon as the admiring glances of the impressionable viewers wander, king, reign, and monument are reduced to nothingness.

Meanwhile, the Counter-Reformation led to an increased emphasis on religious orthodoxy, and heightened suspicions of the humanist reform traditions that had shaped Cervantes' thought. Increasingly, his society scrutinized not only people's religious practices but also their roots, stigmatizing them for Jewish or Muslim forebears and holding all *conversos* and *Moriscos* (converts from Judaism and Islam, respectively) suspect. Cervantes' own fortunes may have been complicated by his origins: we cannot be sure whether he came from a line of *conversos*, but his family connections to the medical profession, the denial of his request for New World employment, and the refusal of the authorities to reward his heroic military service and captivity with any real preferment all suggest a striking disregard for his services. If he was in fact descended from Jews, Cervantes would have been barred from many honors and privileges in his time, however sincere his own Christian faith. Cervantes mocked the Inquisitorial and popular anxiety about origins in his dramatic interlude *The Miracle Show*. In this satire of Spanish obsessions with honor, legitimacy, and "blood purity," rascally entertainers trick village notables by convincing them that only those who are legitimate and free of the Jewish "taint" can actually see their marvelous show. In his version of "The Emperor's New Clothes," Cervantes holds up a sly theatrical mirror to his own society's prejudices.

During Cervantes' life, Spain faced challenges to both its political power and its religious orthodoxy. Protestants across Europe and humanist reformers within the Catholic Church constantly defied the strictures of the Counter-Reformation. The Ottoman Empire, which encroached on Italy, the Mediterranean, and North Africa, represented the greatest geopolitical threat to Spain, and also the religious threat of Islam as a competing faith. In its own territories, Spain struggled to incorporate the descendants of its Muslim subjects. Though this population had been forcibly converted to Christianity, their place and that of their descendants within a belligerently Christian nation was increasingly threatened. Their customs and language were forbidden by law, in an attempt to enforce acculturation. Beginning in 1609, the Moriscos,

Title page of the 1620 English translation (by Thomas Shelton) of *Don Quixote*.

though Christians, were forcibly expelled from Spain, in a move that was widely condemned by Church authorities across Europe. Cervantes comments directly on the situation of the Moriscos in *Don Quixote*, in two sections not included in this anthology: in "The Captive's Tale" of part I, he considers how Spanish society might receive a hugely sympathetic young woman, a fresh convert from Islam, who had saved a Spanish captive much like the author himself. In part II, published after the expulsions, Sancho Panza, Don Quixote's earthy sidekick, runs into his Morisco former neighbor, Ricote, now back in Spain disguised as a German pilgrim. They proceed to share a communal meal, with plenty of wine to go around. Thus Cervantes turns again and again to his own experience of captivity and to the Morisco problem within Spain, to explore how a newly unified and forcibly homogenized nation might include those it had led to Christianity.

DON QUIXOTE

The Ingenious Gentleman Don Quixote de la Mancha was a popular success from the time part I was published in 1605, although it was only later recognized as an important work of literature. This delay was due partly to the fact that in a period of established and well-defined literary genres such as the epic, the tragedy, and the pastoral romance (Cervantes himself had tried his hand at some of these forms), the unconventional combination of elements in *Don Quixote* resulted in a work of considerable novelty, with the serious aspects hidden under a mocking surface.

The proclaimed purpose of the book was to satirize the romances of chivalry. In those long yarns—based on the Carolingian and Arthurian legends, and full of supernatural deeds of valor, implausible and complicated adventures, duels, and enchantments—the literature that had expressed the medieval spirit of chivalry and romance had become conventional and formulaic (much as, in our day, certain literary conventions have become "pulp" fiction and film melodrama). Up to a point, then, what Cervantes set out to do was to produce a parody, a caricature of a hugely popular literary type. But he did not limit himself to such a relatively simple and direct undertaking. To expose the silliness of the romances of chivalry, he showed to what extraordinary consequences they would lead a man insanely infatuated with them, once this man set out to live "now" according to their patterns of action and belief. While the anachronism of Don Quixote makes him a figure of fun, it also allows Cervantes to examine the realities of his own time: an impoverished Spain full of underemployed noblemen; an overextended empire burdened by too many modern, impersonal wars; widespread anxiety about religious and political conformity, as well as genealogical "purity."

So what we have is not mere parody or caricature; for there is a great deal of difference between presenting a remote and more-or-less imaginary world and presenting an individual deciding to live by the standards of that world in a modern and realistic context. The first consequence is a mingling of genres. Don Quixote sees the world through the lens of medieval chivalry as its authors had portrayed it, and often the narrator echoes his vision, albeit in an ironic mode. The chivalric world is continuously jostled by elements of contemporary life evoked by the narrator—the realities of landscape and speech, peasants and nobles, inns and highways. The hero attempting to recreate the world of the romances is not, as we know, a cavalier; he is an impoverished country gentleman who embraces that code in the "modern" world. His squire, the peasant Sancho Panza, is only too happy to point out Don Quixote's delusions. Nevertheless, he too becomes invested in the quest, in search of material wealth and aggrandizement. The exchanges between Don Quixote and Sancho pit a gentleman against a peasant, yet more often than not the two find common ground in their conviction that they can improve their lot through their own actions.

Don Quixote soon finds that he is not the only one modeling his life after books. Other characters follow their own idealizing genres, such as the pastoral romance to which Don Quixote and his friends will turn at the end. All must make their peace with the reality of the world that surrounds them. That debased world, in turn, produces its own stories, such as the picaresque "life" that the rascally Ginés de Pasamonte has written in prison.

Along the way, Cervantes casts doubt on the possibility of reconstructing history from written sources. The facts about Don Quixote are never fully available to the primary narrator, who confesses to the many gaps in his knowledge and keeps losing track of the story. While the prologue describes the text as the author's "child," the narrator is not even certain of his protagonist's name. More spectacularly, the first part of the novel breaks off entirely at the end of chapter 8, leaving both characters and readers in suspense. The problem of finding more text then leads to one of Cervantes' most interesting narrative games: a second author, Cid Hamete Benengeli, who just happens to be an "Arabic historian," and whose disheveled account must be translated from a forbidden language by a "Spanish-speaking Moor," i.e., a Morisco. The entire story from this point forth is thus supposedly written by a Moor, the traditional enemy of a Spanish knight, and translated by a marginalized contemporary Morisco. Don Quixote and his narrator both worry about the implications of such authorship for the story on which they are embarked: will the Moorish author distort Don Quixote's adventures, or diminish his greatness? These narrative games are fully fleshed out in part II, when Don Quixote and Sancho, now famous from part I, must confront their own celebrity and grapple with the selves that the printing press has given them, while the authorial voice of Cide Hamete intervenes more and more frequently to make sure that the reader gets the "right" story.

Generally speaking, the encounters between the ordinary world and Don Quixote confront reality with illusion, and reason with imagination. Among the first adventures are some that have most contributed to the popularity of the Don Quixote legend: he sees windmills and decides they are giants, country inns become castles, and flocks of sheep become armies. Though the conclusions of such episodes often have the ludicrousness of slapstick comedy, there is a powerfully imposing quality about Don Quixote's insanity; his madness always has method, a commanding persistence and coherence. And there is perhaps an inevitable sense of moral grandeur in the spectacle of anyone remaining so unflinchingly faithful to his or her own vision. The world of "reason" may win in point of fact, but we come to wonder whether from a moral point of view Quixote is not the victor.

Yet at the same time the novel explores the deterioration of the chivalric ideals that inspire its protagonist—for instance, the notion of love as devoted "service." Don Quixote loves a purely fantastic lady, Dulcinea, so remote and unattainable that she does not even exist. Other plots interwoven through the text, and not included in our selection, show lovers struggling with problems of class and religious difference, and pervasive sexual jealousy. Don Quixote also examines the anachronism of individual heroics: new forms of warfare had rendered knights passé in more than the literary sense— battles are now fought with artillery and squadrons of infantry. The episode of the lions (part II, chapter 17) features the knight, crowned with cottage cheese, seeking a challenge at all costs. That challenge comes in the ironic form of a caged animal being sent to the King, and who has no intention of engaging in battle. Unwilling to confront the futility of the knight in an age of gunpowder, Don Quixote will take what he can get in the form of challenges. The ridiculousness of the situation is counterbalanced by the basic seriousness of Quixote's motives; his notion of courage for its own sake appears, and is recognized, as singularly noble, a sort of generous display of integrity in a world usually ruled by lower standards. Thus the distinction between reason and madness, truth and illusion, becomes, to say the least, ambiguous. The hero's delusions are indeed exposed when they come up against hard facts, but the authority of such facts is seen to be morally questionable. A similar ambiguity colors an earlier episode where he frees a group of thuggish galley slaves (part I, chapter 22). Don Quixote, comically anachronistic, ignores the existence of a centralized state with its own justice system, which has tried the men and found them guilty. Yet his intervention and his determination to hear out the prisoners raises more basic questions of social justice, and insists on the imagination, however anachronistic, as a basic tool for rethinking the status quo.

Don Quixote has been intensely read and reread since its first publication, for its broad humor and its slippery ironies alike. Both parts of the novel were immediately translated across Europe, giving rise to such rewritings and imitations as the Jacobean comedy *The Knight of the Burning Pestle* (1607), the early feminist novel *The Female Quixote* (1752), and, more recently, the Broadway musical *Man of la Mancha* (1964). In Spain, *Don Quixote* was long embraced as the symbol of a kind of national idealism; the philosopher Miguel de Unamuno in his *The Life of Don Quixote and Sancho* (1905) argued that the novel was the true "Spanish Bible," a degree of respect that might well have amused the more irreverent Cervantes.

FROM DON QUIXOTE[1]

From Part I

Prologue

Idling reader, you may believe me when I tell you that I should have liked this book, which is the child of my brain, to be the fairest, the sprightliest, and the cleverest that could be imagined; but I have not been able to contravene the law of nature which would have it that like begets like. And so, what was to be expected of a sterile and uncultivated wit such as that which I possess if not an offspring that was dried up, shriveled, and eccentric: a story filled with thoughts that never occurred to anyone else, of a sort that might be engendered in a prison where every annoyance has its home and every mournful sound its habitation?[2] Peace and tranquility, the pleasures of the countryside, the serenity of the heavens, the murmur of fountains, and ease of mind can do much toward causing the most unproductive of muses to become fecund and bring forth progeny that will be the marvel and delight of mankind.

It sometimes happens that a father has an ugly son with no redeeming grace whatever, yet love will draw a veil over the parental eyes which then behold only cleverness and beauty in place of defects, and in speaking to his friends he will make those defects out to be the signs of comeliness and intellect. I, however, who am but Don Quixote's stepfather, have no desire to go with the current of custom, nor would I, dearest reader, beseech you with tears in my eyes as others

---

1. Translated by Samuel Putnam.
2. Cervantes was imprisoned in Seville in 1597 and 1602.

do to pardon or overlook the faults you discover in this book; you are neither relative nor friend but may call your soul your own and exercise your free judgment. You are in your own house where you are master as the king is of his taxes, for you are familiar with the saying, "Under my cloak I kill the king."[3] All of which exempts and frees you from any kind of respect or obligation; you may say of this story whatever you choose without fear of being slandered for an ill opinion any more than you will be rewarded for a good one.

I should like to bring you the tale unadulterated and unadorned, stripped of the usual prologue and the endless string of sonnets, epigrams, and eulogies such as are commonly found at the beginning of books. For I may tell you that, although I expended no little labor upon the work itself, I have found no task more difficult than the composition of this preface which you are now reading. Many times I took up my pen and many times I laid it down again, not knowing what to write. On one occasion when I was thus in suspense, paper before me, pen over my ear, elbow on the table, and chin in hand, a very clever friend of mine came in. Seeing me lost in thought, he inquired as to the reason, and I made no effort to conceal from him the fact that my mind was on the preface which I had to write for the story of Don Quixote, and that it was giving me so much trouble that I had about decided not to write any at all and to abandon entirely the idea of publishing the exploits of so noble a knight.

"How," I said to him, "can you expect me not to be concerned over what that venerable legislator, the Public, will say when it sees me, at my age, after all these years of silent slumber, coming out with a tale that is as dried as a rush, a stranger to invention, paltry in style, impoverished in content, and wholly lacking in learning and wisdom, without marginal citations or notes at the end of the book when other works of this sort, even though they be fabulous and profane, are so packed with maxims from Aristotle and Plato and the whole crowd of philosophers as to fill the reader with admiration and lead him to regard the author as a well read, learned, and eloquent individual? Not to speak of the citations from Holy Writ! You would think they were at the very least so many St. Thomases[4] and other doctors of the Church; for they are so adroit at maintaining a solemn face that, having portrayed in one line a distracted lover, in the next they will give you a nice little Christian sermon that is a joy and a privilege to hear and read.

"All this my book will lack, for I have no citations for the margins, no notes for the end. To tell the truth, I do not even know who the authors are to whom I am indebted, and so am unable to follow the example of all the others by listing them alphabetically at the beginning, starting with Aristotle and closing with Xenophon, or, perhaps, with Zoilus or Zeuxis, notwithstanding the fact that the former was a snarling critic, the latter a painter. This work will also be found lacking in prefatory sonnets by dukes, marquises, counts, bishops, ladies, and poets of great renown; although if I were to ask two or three colleagues of mine, they would supply the deficiency by furnishing me with productions that could not be equaled by the authors of most repute in all Spain.

"In short, my friend," I went on, "I am resolved that Señor Don Quixote shall remain buried in the archives of La Mancha until Heaven shall provide him

---

3. I.e., the king does not own your body.
4. Thomas Aquinas (1225–1274), Italian philosopher and theologian.

with someone to deck him out with all the ornaments that he lacks; for I find myself incapable of remedying the situation, being possessed of little learning or aptitude, and I am, moreover, extremely lazy when it comes to hunting up authors who will say for me what I am unable to say for myself. And if I am in a state of suspense and my thoughts are woolgathering, you will find a sufficient explanation in what I have just told you."

Hearing this, my friend struck his forehead with the palm of his hand and burst into a loud laugh.

"In the name of God, brother," he said, "you have just deprived me of an illusion. I have known you for a long time, and I have always taken you to be clever and prudent in all your actions; but I now perceive that you are as far from all that as Heaven from the earth. How is it that things of so little moment and so easily remedied can worry and perplex a mind as mature as yours and ordinarily so well adapted to break down and trample underfoot far greater obstacles? I give you my word, this does not come from any lack of cleverness on your part, but rather from excessive indolence and a lack of experience. Do you ask for proof of what I say? Then pay attention closely and in the blink of an eye you shall see how I am going to solve all your difficulties and supply all those things the want of which, so you tell me, is keeping you in suspense, as a result of which you hesitate to publish the history of that famous Don Quixote of yours, the light and mirror of all knight-errantry."

"Tell me, then," I replied, "how you propose to go about curing my diffidence and bringing clarity out of the chaos and confusion of my mind?"

"Take that first matter," he continued, "of the sonnets, epigrams, or eulogies, which should bear the names of grave and titled personages: you can remedy that by taking a little trouble and composing the pieces yourself, and afterward you can baptize them with any name you see fit, fathering them on Prester John of the Indies or the Emperor of Trebizond, for I have heard tell that they were famous poets; and supposing they were not and that a few pedants and bachelors of arts should go around muttering behind your back that it is not so, you should not give so much as a pair of maravedis[5] for all their carping, since even though they make you out to be a liar, they are not going to cut off the hand that put these things on paper.

"As for marginal citations and authors in whom you may find maxims and sayings that you may put in your story, you have but to make use of those scraps of Latin that you know by heart or can look up without too much bother. Thus, when you come to treat of liberty and slavery, jot down:

Non bene pro toto libertas venditur auro.[6]

And then in the margin you will cite Horace or whoever it was that said it. If the subject is death, come up with:

Pallida mors aequo pulsat pede pauperum tabernas
Regumque turres.[7]

5. Coin worth a thirty-fourth of a *real*; that is, even two *maravedís* were worth very little.
6. Freedom is not bought by gold (Latin); from the anonymous *Aesopian Fables* 3.14.

7. Pale death knocks at the cottages of the poor and the palaces of kings with equal foot (Latin); Horace, *Odes* 1.4.13–14.

If it is friendship or the love that God commands us to show our enemies, then is the time to fall back on the Scriptures, which you can do by putting yourself out very little; you have but to quote the words of God himself:

Ego autem dico vobis: diligite inimicos vestros.[8]

If it is evil thoughts, lose no time in turning to the Gospels:

De corde exeunt cogitationes malae.[9]

If it is the instability of friends, here is Cato for you with a distich:

Donec eris felix multos numerabis amicos;
Tempora si fuerint nubila, solus eris.[1]

With these odds and ends of Latin and others of the same sort, you can cause yourself to be taken for a grammarian, although I must say that is no great honor or advantage these days.

"So far as notes at the end of the book are concerned, you may safely go about it in this manner: let us suppose that you mentioned some giant, Goliath let us say; with this one allusion which costs you little or nothing, you have a fine note which you may set down as follows: *The giant Golias or Goliath. This was a Philistine whom the shepherd David slew with a mighty cast from his sling-shot in the valley of Terebinth,*[2] according to what we read in the Book of Kings, chapter so-and-so where you find it written.

"In addition to this, by way of showing that you are a learned humanist and a cosmographer, contrive to bring into your story the name of the River Tagus, and there you are with another great little note: *The River Tagus was so called after a king of Spain; it rises in such and such a place and empties into the ocean, washing the walls of the famous city of Lisbon; it is supposed to have golden sands,* etc. If it is robbers, I will let you have the story of Cacus,[3] which I know by heart. If it is loose women, there is the Bishop of Mondoñedo,[4] who will lend you Lamia, Laïs, and Flora, an allusion that will do you great credit. If the subject is cruelty, Ovid will supply you with Medea; or if it is enchantresses and witches, Homer has Calypso and Vergil Circe. If it is valorous captains, Julius Caesar will lend you himself, in his *Commentaries,* and Plutarch will furnish a thousand Alexanders. If it is loves, with the ounce or two of Tuscan that you know you may make the acquaintance of Leon the Hebrew,[5] who will satisfy you to your heart's content. And in case you do not care to go abroad, here in your own house you have Fonseca's *Of the Love of God,*[6] where you will encounter in condensed form all that the most imaginative person could wish upon this subject. The short of the matter is, you have but to allude to these

8. But I say unto you, love your enemies (Latin); Matthew 5.44.
9. For out of the heart proceed evil thoughts (Latin); Matthew 15.19.
1. As long as you are happy, you will count many friends, but if times become clouded, you will be alone (Latin); Ovid, *Sorrows* 1.9.5–6.
2. 1 Samuel 17.48–49.

3. Gigantic thief in *Aeneid* 8, defeated by Hercules.
4. Father Anthony of Guevara.
5. Leone Ebreo, Neoplatonic author of the *Dialogues of Love* (1535).
6. Cristóbal de Fonseca, *Treatise of the Love of God* (1592).

names or touch upon those stories that I have mentioned and leave to me the business of the notes and citations; I will guarantee you enough to fill the margins and four whole sheets at the back.

"And now we come to the list of authors cited, such as other works contain but in which your own is lacking. Here again the remedy is an easy one; you have but to look up some book that has them all, from A to Z as you were saying, and transfer the entire list as it stands. What if the imposition is plain for all to see? You have little need to refer to them, and so it does not matter; and some may be so simple-minded as to believe that you have drawn upon them all in your simple unpretentious little story. If it serves no other purpose, this imposing list of authors will at least give your book an unlooked-for air of authority. What is more, no one is going to put himself to the trouble of verifying your references to see whether or not you have followed all these authors, since it will not be worth his pains to do so.

"This is especially true in view of the fact that your book stands in no need of all these things whose absence you lament; for the entire work is an attack upon the books of chivalry of which Aristotle never dreamed, of which St. Basil has nothing to say, and of which Cicero had no knowledge; nor do the fine points of truth or the observations of astrology have anything to do with its fanciful absurdities; geometrical measurements, likewise, and rhetorical argumentations serve for nothing here; you have no sermon to preach to anyone by mingling the human with the divine, a kind of motley in which no Christian intellect should be willing to clothe itself.

"All that you have to do is to make proper use of imitation in what you write, and the more perfect the imitation the better will your writing be. Inasmuch as you have no other object in view than that of overthrowing the authority and prestige which books of chivalry enjoy in the world at large and among the vulgar, there is no reason why you should go begging maxims of the philosophers, counsels of Holy Writ, fables of the poets, orations of the rhetoricians, or miracles of the saints; see to it, rather, that your style flows along smoothly, pleasingly, and sonorously, and that your words are the proper ones, meaningful and well placed, expressive of your intention in setting them down and of what you wish to say, without any intricacy or obscurity.

"Let it be your aim that, by reading your story, the melancholy may be moved to laughter and the cheerful man made merrier still; let the simple not be bored, but may the clever admire your originality; let the grave ones not despise you, but let the prudent praise you. And keep in mind, above all, your purpose, which is that of undermining the ill-founded edifice that is constituted by those books of chivalry, so abhorred by many but admired by many more; if you succeed in attaining it, you will have accomplished no little."

Listening in profound silence to what my friend had to say, I was so impressed by his reasoning that, with no thought of questioning them, I decided to make use of his arguments in composing this prologue. Here, gentle reader, you will perceive my friend's cleverness, my own good fortune in coming upon such a counselor at a time when I needed him so badly, and the profit which you yourselves are to have in finding so sincere and straightforward an account of the famous Don Quixote de la Mancha, who is held by the inhabitants of the Campo de Montiel region to have been the most chaste lover and the most valiant knight that had been seen in those parts for many a year. I have no

desire to enlarge upon the service I am rendering you in bringing you the story
of so notable and honored a gentleman; I merely would have you thank me for
having made you acquainted with the famous Sancho Panza, his squire, in
whom, to my mind, is to be found an epitome of all the squires and their drolleries scattered here and there throughout the pages of those vain and empty
books of chivalry. And with this, may God give you health, and may He be not
unmindful of me as well. VALE.[7]

["I Know Who I Am, and Who I May Be, If I Choose"]

CHAPTER I

*Which treats of the station in life and the pursuits of the famous gentleman,
Don Quixote de la Mancha.*

In a village of La Mancha[1] the name of which I have no desire to recall, there
lived not so long ago one of those gentlemen who always have a lance in the
rack, an ancient buckler, a skinny nag, and a greyhound for the chase. A stew
with more beef than mutton in it, chopped meat for his evening meal, scraps
for a Saturday, lentils on Friday, and a young pigeon as a special delicacy for
Sunday, went to account for three-quarters of his income. The rest of it he laid
out on a broadcloth greatcoat and velvet stockings for feast days, with slippers
to match, while the other days of the week he cut a figure in a suit of the finest
homespun. Living with him were a housekeeper in her forties, a niece who was
not yet twenty, and a lad of the field and market place who saddled his horse
for him and wielded the pruning knife.

This gentleman of ours was close on to fifty, of a robust constitution but with
little flesh on his bones and a face that was lean and gaunt. He was noted for
his early rising, being very fond of the hunt. They will try to tell you that his
surname was Quijada or Quesada—there is some difference of opinion among
those who have written on the subject—but according to the most likely conjectures we are to understand that it was really Quejana. But all this means
very little so far as our story is concerned, providing that in the telling of it we
do not depart one iota from the truth.

You may know, then, that the aforesaid gentleman, on those occasions when
he was at leisure, which was most of the year around, was in the habit of reading books of chivalry with such pleasure and devotion as to lead him almost
wholly to forget the life of a hunter and even the administration of his estate.
So great was his curiosity and infatuation in this regard that he even sold many
acres of tillable land in order to be able to buy and read the books that he loved,
and he would carry home with him as many of them as he could obtain.

Of all those that he thus devoured none pleased him so well as the ones that
had been composed by the famous Feliciano de Silva,[2] whose lucid prose style
and involved conceits were as precious to him as pearls; especially when he

7. Farewell (Latin).
1. Efforts at identifying the village have
proved inconclusive. La Mancha is a section
of Spain south of Madrid.

2. Author of romances (16th century); the
lines that follow are from his *Don Florisel de
Niguea.*

came to read those tales of love and amorous challenges that are to be met with in many places, such a passage as the following, for example: "The reason of the unreason that afflicts my reason, in such a manner weakens my reason that I with reason lament me of your comeliness." And he was similarly affected when his eyes fell upon such lines as these: ". . . the high Heaven of your divinity divinely fortifies you with the stars and renders you deserving of that desert your greatness doth deserve."

The poor fellow used to lie awake nights in an effort to disentangle the meaning and make sense out of passages such as these, although Aristotle himself would not have been able to understand them, even if he had been resurrected for that sole purpose. He was not at ease in his mind over those wounds that Don Belianís[3] gave and received; for no matter how great the surgeons who treated him, the poor fellow must have been left with his face and his entire body covered with marks and scars. Nevertheless, he was grateful to the author for closing the book with the promise of an interminable adventure to come; many a time he was tempted to take up his pen and literally finish the tale as had been promised, and he undoubtedly would have done so, and would have succeeded at it very well, if his thoughts had not been constantly occupied with other things of greater moment.

He often talked it over with the village curate, who was a learned man, a graduate of Sigüenza,[4] and they would hold long discussions as to who had been the better knight, Palmerin of England or Amadis of Gaul; but Master Nicholas, the barber of the same village, was in the habit of saying that no one could come up to the Knight of Phoebus,[5] and that if anyone *could* compare with him it was Don Galaor, brother of Amadis of Gaul, for Galaor was ready for anything—he was none of your finical knights, who went around whimpering as his brother did, and in point of valor he did not lag behind him.

In short, our gentleman became so immersed in his reading that he spent whole nights from sundown to sunup and his days from dawn to dusk in poring over his books, until, finally, from so little sleeping and so much reading, his brain dried up and he went completely out of his mind. He had filled his imagination with everything that he had read, with enchantments, knightly encounters, battles, challenges, wounds, with tales of love and its torments, and all sorts of impossible things, and as a result had come to believe that all those fictitious happenings were true; they were more real to him than anything else in the world. He would remark that the Cid Ruy Díaz had been a very good knight, but there was no comparison between him and the Knight of the Flaming Sword, who with a single backward stroke had cut in half two fierce and monstrous giants. He preferred Bernardo del Carpio, who at Roncesvalles had slain Roland despite the charm the latter bore, availing himself of the stratagem which Hercules employed when he strangled Antaeus,[6] the son of Earth, in his arms.

---

3. The allusion is to a romance by Jerónimo Fernández.
4. Ironical, for Sigüenza was the seat of a minor and discredited university.
5. Or Knight of Sun. Heroes of romances customarily adopted emblematic names and also changed them according to circumstances.

"Palmerin . . . Amadis": each a hero of a very famous romance of chivalry.
6. The mythological Antaeus was invulnerable as long as he maintained contact with his mother, Earth. Hercules killed him while holding him raised in his arms. "Charm": the magic gift of invulnerability.

He had much good to say for Morgante;[7] who, though he belonged to the haughty, overbearing race of giants, was of an affable disposition and well brought up. But, above all, he cherished an admiration for Rinaldo of Montalbán,[8] especially as he beheld him sallying forth from his castle to rob all those that crossed his path, or when he thought of him overseas stealing the image of Mohammed which, so the story has it, was all of gold. And he would have liked very well to have had his fill of kicking that traitor Galalón,[9] a privilege for which he would have given his housekeeper with his niece thrown into the bargain.

At last, when his wits were gone beyond repair, he came to conceive the strangest idea that ever occurred to any madman in this world. It now appeared to him fitting and necessary, in order to win a greater amount of honor for himself and serve his country at the same time, to become a knight-errant and roam the world on horseback, in a suit of armor; he would go in quest of adventures, by way of putting into practice all that he had read in his books; he would right every manner of wrong, placing himself in situations of the greatest peril such as would redound to the eternal glory of his name. As a reward for his valor and the might of his arm, the poor fellow could already see himself crowned Emperor of Trebizond at the very least; and so, carried away by the strange pleasure that he found in such thoughts as these, he at once set about putting his plan into effect.

The first thing he did was to burnish up some old pieces of armor, left him by his great-grandfather, which for ages had lain in a corner, moldering and forgotten. He polished and adjusted them as best he could, and then he noticed that one very important thing was lacking: there was no closed helmet, but only a morion, or visorless headpiece, with turned up brim of the kind foot soldiers wore. His ingenuity, however, enabled him to remedy this, and he proceeded to fashion out of cardboard a kind of half-helmet, which, when attached to the morion, gave the appearance of a whole one. True, when he went to see if it was strong enough to withstand a good slashing blow, he was somewhat disappointed; for when he drew his sword and gave it a couple of thrusts, he succeeded only in undoing a whole week's labor. The ease with which he had hewed it to bits disturbed him no little, and he decided to make it over. This time he placed a few strips of iron on the inside, and then, convinced that it was strong enough, refrained from putting it to any further test; instead, he adopted it then and there as the finest helmet ever made.

After this, he went out to have a look at his nag; and although the animal had more *cuartos*, or cracks, in its hoof than there are quarters in a real,[1] and more blemishes than Gonela's steed which *tantum pellis et ossa fuit*,[2] it nonetheless looked to its master like a far better horse than Alexander's Bucephalus or the Babieca of the Cid.[3] He spent all of four days in trying to think up a name for

---

7. In Pulci's *Morgante maggiore*, a comic-epic poem of the Italian Renaissance.
8. Roland's cousin. In Boiardo's *Roland in Love* (*Orlando Innamorato*) and Ariosto's *Roland Mad* (*Orlando Furioso*), romantic and comic-epic poems of the Italian Renaissance.
9. Ganelón, the villain in the Charlemagne legend who betrayed the French at Roncesvalles.
1. A coin (about five cents). "*Cuarto*": one-eighth of a *real*.
2. Was so much skin and bones (Latin).
3. The chief (Spanish)—that is, Ruy Díaz, celebrated hero of *Poema del Cid* (12th century).

his mount; for—so he told himself—seeing that it belonged to so famous and worthy a knight, there was no reason why it should not have a name of equal renown. The kind of name he wanted was one that would at once indicate what the nag had been before it came to belong to a knight-errant and what its present status was; for it stood to reason that, when the master's worldly condition changed, his horse also ought to have a famous, high-sounding appellation, one suited to the new order of things and the new profession that it was to follow.

After he in his memory and imagination had made up, struck out, and discarded many names, now adding to and now subtracting from the list, he finally hit upon "Rocinante," a name that impressed him as being sonorous and at the same time indicative of what the steed had been when it was but a hack, whereas now it was nothing other than the first and foremost of all the hacks[4] in the world.

Having found a name for his horse that pleased his fancy, he then desired to do as much for himself, and this required another week, and by the end of that period he had made up his mind that he was henceforth to be known as Don Quixote, which, as has been stated, has led the authors of this veracious history to assume that his real name must undoubtedly have been Quijada, and not Quesada as others would have it. But remembering that the valiant Amadis was not content to call himself that and nothing more, but added the name of his kingdom and fatherland that he might make it famous also, and thus came to take the name Amadis of Gaul, so our good knight chose to add his place of origin and become "Don Quixote de la Mancha"; for by this means, as he saw it, he was making very plain his lineage and was conferring honor upon his country by taking its name as his own.

And so, having polished up his armor and made the morion over into a closed helmet, and having given himself and his horse a name, he naturally found but one thing lacking still: he must seek out a lady of whom he could become enamored; for a knight-errant without a lady-love was like a tree without leaves or fruit, a body without a soul.

"If," he said to himself, "as a punishment for my sins or by a stroke of fortune I should come upon some giant hereabouts, a thing that very commonly happens to knights-errant, and if I should slay him in a hand-to-hand encounter or perhaps cut him in two, or, finally, if I should vanquish and subdue him, would it not be well to have someone to whom I may send him as a present, in order that he, if he is living, may come in, fall upon his knees in front of my sweet lady, and say in a humble and submissive tone of voice, 'I, lady, am the giant Caraculiambro, lord of the island Malindrania, who has been overcome in single combat by that knight who never can be praised enough, Don Quixote de la Mancha, the same who sent me to present myself before your Grace that your Highness may dispose of me as you see fit'?"

Oh, how our good knight reveled in this speech, and more than ever when he came to think of the name that he should give his lady! As the story goes, there was a very good-looking farm girl who lived near by, with whom he had once been smitten, although it is generally believed that she never knew or suspected it.

4. In Spanish, *rocín*.

Her name was Aldonza Lorenzo, and it seemed to him that she was the one upon whom he should bestow the title of mistress of his thoughts. For her he wished a name that should not be incongruous with his own and that would convey the suggestion of a princess or a great lady; and, accordingly, he resolved to call her "Dulcinea del Toboso," she being a native of that place. A musical name to his ears, out of the ordinary and significant, like the others he had chosen for himself and his appurtenances.

CHAPTER 2

Which treats of the first sally that the ingenious Don Quixote made from his native heath.

Having, then, made all these preparations, he did not wish to lose any time in putting his plan into effect, for he could not but blame himself for what the world was losing by his delay, so many were the wrongs that were to be righted, the grievances to be redressed, the abuses to be done away with, and the duties to be performed. Accordingly, without informing anyone of his intention and without letting anyone see him, he set out one morning before daybreak on one of those very hot days in July. Donning all his armor, mounting Rocinante, adjusting his ill-contrived helmet, bracing his shield on his arm, and taking up his lance, he sallied forth by the back gate of his stable yard into the open countryside. It was with great contentment and joy that he saw how easily he had made a beginning toward the fulfillment of his desire.

No sooner was he out on the plain, however, than a terrible thought assailed him, one that all but caused him to abandon the enterprise he had undertaken. This occurred when he suddenly remembered that he had never formally been dubbed a knight, and so, in accordance with the law of knighthood, was not permitted to bear arms against one who had a right to that title. And even if he had been, as a novice knight he would have had to wear white armor, without any device on his shield, until he should have earned one by his exploits. These thoughts led him to waver in his purpose, but, madness prevailing over reason, he resolved to have himself knighted by the first person he met, as many others had done if what he had read in those books that he had at home was true. And so far as white armor was concerned, he would scour his own the first chance that offered until it shone whiter than any ermine. With this he became more tranquil and continued on his way, letting his horse take whatever path it chose, for he believed that therein lay the very essence of adventures.

And so we find our newly fledged adventurer jogging along and talking to himself. "Undoubtedly," he is saying, "in the days to come, when the true history of my famous deeds is published, the learned chronicler who records them, when he comes to describe my first sally so early in the morning, will put down something like this: 'No sooner had the rubicund Apollo spread over the face of the broad and spacious earth the gilded filaments of his beauteous locks, and no sooner had the little singing birds of painted plumage greeted with their sweet and mellifluous harmony the coming of the Dawn, who, leaving the soft couch of her jealous spouse, now showed herself to mortals at all the doors and balconies of the horizon that bounds La Mancha—no sooner had this happened than the famous knight, Don Quixote de la Mancha, forsaking his own downy bed and mounting his famous steed, Rocinante, fared forth and began riding over the ancient and famous Campo de Montiel.'"[5]

And this was the truth, for he was indeed riding over that stretch of plain.

"O happy age and happy century," he went on, "in which my famous exploits shall be published, exploits worthy of being engraved in bronze, sculptured in marble, and depicted in paintings for the benefit of posterity. O wise magician, whoever you be, to whom shall fall the task of chronicling this extraordinary history of mine! I beg of you not to forget my good Rocinante, eternal companion of my wayfarings and my wanderings."

Then, as though he really had been in love: "O Princess Dulcinea, lady of this captive heart! Much wrong have you done me in thus sending me forth with your reproaches and sternly commanding me not to appear in your beauteous presence. O lady, deign to be mindful of this your subject who endures so many woes for the love of you."

And so he went on, stringing together absurdities, all of a kind that his books had taught him, imitating insofar as he was able the language of their authors. He rode slowly, and the sun came up so swiftly and with so much heat that it would have been sufficient to melt his brains if he had had any. He had been on the road almost the entire day without anything happening that is worthy of being set down here; and he was on the verge of despair, for he wished to meet someone at once with whom he might try the valor of his good right arm. Certain authors say that his first adventure was that of Puerto Lápice, while others state that it was that of the windmills; but in this particular instance I am in a position to affirm what I have read in the annals of La Mancha; and that is to the effect that he went all that day until nightfall, when he and his hack found themselves tired to death and famished. Gazing all around him to see if he could discover some castle or shepherd's hut where he might take shelter and attend to his pressing needs, he caught sight of an inn not far off the road along which they were traveling, and this to him was like a star guiding him not merely to the gates, but rather, let us say, to the palace of redemption. Quickening his pace, he came up to it just as night was falling.

By chance there stood in the doorway two lasses of the sort known as "of the district"; they were on their way to Seville in the company of some mule drivers who were spending the night in the inn. Now, everything that this adventurer of ours thought, saw, or imagined seemed to him to be directly out of one of the storybooks he had read, and so, when he caught sight of the inn, it at once became a castle with its four turrets and its pinnacles of gleaming silver, not to speak of the drawbridge and moat and all the other things that are commonly supposed to go with a castle. As he rode up to it, he accordingly reined in Rocinante and sat there waiting for a dwarf to appear upon the battlements and blow his trumpet by way of announcing the arrival of a knight. The dwarf, however, was slow in coming, and as Rocinante was anxious to reach the stable, Don Quixote drew up to the door of the hostelry and surveyed the two merry maidens, who to him were a pair of beauteous damsels or gracious ladies taking their ease at the castle gate.

5. The scene of a battle in 1369.

And then a swineherd came along, engaged in rounding up his drove of hogs—for, without any apology, that is what they were. He gave a blast on his horn to bring them together, and this at once became for Don Quixote just what he wished it to be: some dwarf who was heralding his coming; and so it was with a vast deal of satisfaction that he presented himself before the ladies in question, who, upon beholding a man in full armor like this, with lance and buckler, were filled with fright and made as if to flee indoors. Realizing that they were afraid, Don Quixote raised his pasteboard visor and revealed his withered, dust-covered face.

"Do not flee, your Ladyships," he said to them in a courteous manner and gentle voice. "You need not fear that any wrong will be done you, for it is not in accordance with the order of knighthood which I profess to wrong anyone, much less such highborn damsels as your appearance shows you to be."

The girls looked at him, endeavoring to scan his face, which was half hidden by his ill-made visor. Never having heard women of their profession called damsels before, they were unable to restrain their laughter, at which Don Quixote took offense.

"Modesty," he observed, "well becomes those with the dower of beauty, and, moreover, laughter that has not good cause is a very foolish thing. But I do not say this to be discourteous or to hurt your feelings; my only desire is to serve you."

The ladies did not understand what he was talking about, but felt more than ever like laughing at our knight's unprepossessing figure. This increased his annoyance, and there is no telling what would have happened if at that moment the innkeeper had not come out. He was very fat and very peaceably inclined; but upon sighting this grotesque personage clad in bits of armor that were quite as oddly matched as were his bridle, lance, buckler, and corselet, mine host was not at all indisposed to join the lasses in their merriment. He was suspicious, however, of all this paraphernalia and decided that it would be better to keep a civil tongue in his head.

"If, Sir Knight," he said, "your Grace desires a lodging, aside from a bed—for there is none to be had in this inn—you will find all else that you may want in great abundance."

When Don Quixote saw how humble the governor of the castle was—for he took the innkeeper and his inn to be no less than that—he replied, "For me, Sir Castellan,[6] anything will do, since

> Arms are my only ornament,
> My only rest the fight, etc."

The landlord thought that the knight had called him a castellan because he took him for one of those worthies of Castile, whereas the truth was, he was an Andalusian from the beach of Sanlúcar, no less a thief than Cacus[7] himself, and as full of tricks as a student or a page boy.

"In that case," he said,

> "Your bed will be the solid rock,
> Your sleep: to watch all night.

6. The Spanish, castellano, means both "castellan" and "Castilian."
7. In Roman mythology he stole some of Her-

cules' cattle, concealing the theft by having them walk backward into his cave; Cacus was finally discovered and slain.

This being so, you may be assured of finding beneath this roof enough to keep you awake for a whole year, to say nothing of a single night."

With this, he went up to hold the stirrup for Don Quixote, who encountered much difficulty in dismounting, not having broken his fast all day long. The knight then directed his host to take good care of his steed, as it was the best piece of horseflesh in all the world. The innkeeper looked it over, and it did not impress him as being half as good as Don Quixote had said it was. Having stabled the animal, he came back to see what his guest would have and found the latter being relieved of his armor by the damsels, who by now had made their peace with the new arrival. They had already removed his breastplate and backpiece but had no idea how they were going to open his gorget or get his improvised helmet off. That piece of armor had been tied on with green ribbons which it would be necessary to cut, since the knots could not be undone, but he would not hear of this, and so spent all the rest of that night with his headpiece in place, which gave him the weirdest, most laughable appearance that could be imagined.

Don Quixote fancied that these wenches who were assisting him must surely be the chatelaine and other ladies of the castle, and so proceeded to address them very gracefully and with much wit:

> Never was knight so served
> By any noble dame
> As was Don Quixote
> When from his village he came,
> With damsels to wait on his every need
> While princesses cared for his hack . . .

"By hack," he explained, "is meant my steed Rocinante, for that is his name, and mine is Don Quixote de la Mancha. I had no intention of revealing my identity until my exploits done in your service should have made me known to you; but the necessity of adapting to present circumstances that old ballad of Lancelot has led to your becoming acquainted with it prematurely. However, the time will come when your Ladyships shall command and I will obey and with the valor of my good right arm show you how eager I am to serve you."

The young women were not used to listening to speeches like this and had not a word to say, but merely asked him if he desired to eat anything.

"I could eat a bite of something, yes," replied Don Quixote. "Indeed, I feel that a little food would go very nicely just now."

He thereupon learned that, since it was Friday, there was nothing to be had in all the inn except a few portions of codfish, which in Castile is called *abadejo*, in Andalusia *bacalao*, in some places *curadillo*, and elsewhere *truchuella* or small trout. Would his Grace, then, have some small trout, seeing that was all there was that they could offer him?

"If there are enough of them," said Don Quixote, "they will take the place of a trout, for it is all one to me whether I am given in change eight reales or one piece of eight. What is more, those small trout may be like veal, which is better than beef, or like kid, which is better than goat. But however that may be, bring them on at once, for the weight and burden of arms is not to be borne without inner sustenance."

Placing the table at the door of the hostelry, in the open air, they brought the guest a portion of badly soaked and worse cooked codfish and a piece of bread as black and moldy as the suit of armor that he wore. It was a mirth-provoking sight to see him eat, for he still had his helmet on with his visor fastened, which made it impossible for him to put anything into his mouth with his hands, and so it was necessary for one of the girls to feed him. As for giving him anything to drink, that would have been out of the question if the inn-keeper had not hollowed out a reed, placing one end in Don Quixote's mouth while through the other end he poured the wine. All this the knight bore very patiently rather than have them cut the ribbons of his helmet.

At this point a gelder of pigs approached the inn, announcing his arrival with four or five blasts on his horn, all of which confirmed Don Quixote in the belief that this was indeed a famous castle, for what was this if not music that they were playing for him? The fish was trout, the bread was the finest, the wenches were ladies, and the innkeeper was the castellan. He was convinced that he had been right in his resolve to sally forth and roam the world at large, but there was one thing that still distressed him greatly, and that was the fact that he had not as yet been dubbed a knight; as he saw it, he could not legitimately engage in any adventure until he had received the order of knighthood.

CHAPTER 3

Of the amusing manner in which Don Quixote had himself dubbed a knight.

Wearied of his thoughts, Don Quixote lost no time over the scanty repast which the inn afforded him. When he had finished, he summoned the landlord and, taking him out to the stable, closed the doors and fell on his knees in front of him.

"Never, valiant knight," he said, "shall I arise from here until you have cour-teously granted me the boon I seek, one which will redound to your praise and to the good of the human race."

Seeing his guest at his feet and hearing him utter such words as these, the innkeeper could only stare at him in bewilderment, not knowing what to say or do. It was in vain that he entreated him to rise, for Don Quixote refused to do so until his request had been granted.

"I expected nothing less of your great magnificence, my lord," the latter then continued, "and so I may tell you that the boon I asked and which you have so generously conceded me is that tomorrow morning you dub me a knight. Until that time, in the chapel of this your castle, I will watch over my armor, and when morning comes, as I have said, that which I so desire shall then be done, in order that I may lawfully go to the four corners of the earth in quest of adventures and to succor the needy, which is the chivalrous duty of all knights-errant such as I who long to engage in deeds of high emprise."

The innkeeper, as we have said, was a sharp fellow. He already had a suspi-cion that his guest was not quite right in the head, and he was now convinced of it as he listened to such remarks as these. However, just for the sport of it, he determined to humor him; and so he went on to assure Don Quixote that he was fully justified in his request and that such a desire and purpose was only natural on the part of so distinguished a knight as his gallant bearing plainly showed him to be.

He himself, the landlord added, when he was a young man, had followed the same honorable calling. He had gone through various parts of the world seeking adventures, among the places he had visited being the Percheles of Málaga, the Isles of Riarán, the District of Seville, the Little Market Place of Segovia, the Olivera of Valencia, the Rondilla of Granada, the beach of Sanlúcar, the Horse Fountain of Cordova, the Small Taverns of Toledo,[8] and numerous other localities where his nimble feet and light fingers had found much exercise. He had done many wrongs, cheated many widows, ruined many maidens, and swindled not a few minors until he had finally come to be known in almost all the courts and tribunals that are to be found in the whole of Spain.

At last he had retired to his castle here, where he lived upon his own income and the property of others; and here it was that he received all knights-errant of whatever quality and condition, simply out of the great affection that he bore them and that they might share with him their possessions in payment of his good will. Unfortunately, in this castle there was no chapel where Don Quixote might keep watch over his arms, for the old chapel had been torn down to make way for a new one; but in case of necessity, he felt quite sure that such a vigil could be maintained anywhere, and for the present occasion the courtyard of the castle would do; and then in the morning, please God, the requisite ceremony could be performed and his guest be duly dubbed a knight, as much a knight as anyone ever was.

He then inquired if Don Quixote had any money on his person, and the latter replied that he had not a cent, for in all the storybooks he had never read of knights-errant carrying any. But the innkeeper told him he was mistaken on this point: supposing the authors of those stories had not set down the fact in black and white, that was because they did not deem it necessary to speak of things as indispensable as money and a clean shirt, and one was not to assume for that reason that those knights-errant of whom the books were so full did not have any. He looked upon it as an absolute certainty that they all had well-stuffed purses, that they might be prepared for any emergency; and they also carried shirts and a little box of ointment for healing the wounds that they received.

For when they had been wounded in combat on the plains and in desert places, there was not always someone at hand to treat them, unless they had some skilled enchanter for a friend who then would succor them, bringing to them through the air, upon a cloud, some damsel or dwarf bearing a vial of water of such virtue that one had but to taste a drop of it and at once his wounds were healed and he was as sound as if he had never received any.

But even if this was not the case, knights in times past saw to it that their squires were well provided with money and other necessities, such as lint and ointment for healing purposes; and if they had no squires—which happened very rarely—they themselves carried these objects in a pair of saddlebags very cleverly attached to their horses' croups in such a manner as to be scarcely noticeable, as if they held something of greater importance than that, for among the knights-errant saddlebags as a rule were not favored. Accordingly, he would advise the novice before him, and inasmuch as the latter was soon to be his godson, he might even command him, that henceforth he should not go

8. All reputed to be haunts of robbers and rogues.

without money and a supply of those things that have been mentioned, as he would find that they came in useful at a time when he least expected it.

Don Quixote promised to follow his host's advice punctiliously; and so it was arranged that he should watch his armor in a large barnyard at one side of the inn. He gathered up all the pieces, placed them in a horse trough that stood near the well, and, bracing his shield on his arm, took up his lance and with stately demeanor began pacing up and down in front of the trough even as night was closing in.

The innkeeper informed his other guests of what was going on, of Don Quixote's vigil and his expectation of being dubbed a knight; and, marveling greatly at so extraordinary a variety of madness, they all went out to see for themselves and stood there watching from a distance. For a while the knight-to-be, with tranquil mien, would merely walk up and down; then, leaning on his lance, he would pause to survey his armor, gazing fixedly at it for a considerable length of time. As has been said, it was night now, but the brightness of the moon, which well might rival that of Him who lent it, was such that everything the novice knight did was plainly visible to all.

At this point one of the mule drivers who were stopping at the inn came out to water his drove, and in order to do this it was necessary to remove the armor from the trough.

As he saw the man approaching, Don Quixote cried out to him, "O bold knight, whoever you may be, who thus would dare to lay hands upon the accouterments of the most valiant man of arms that ever girded on a sword, look well what you do and desist if you do not wish to pay with your life for your insolence!"

The muleteer gave no heed to these words—it would have been better for his own sake had he done so—but, taking it up by the straps, tossed the armor some distance from him. When he beheld this, Don Quixote rolled his eyes heavenward and with his thoughts apparently upon his Dulcinea exclaimed, "Succor, O lady mine, this vassal heart in this my first encounter; let not your favor and protection fail me in the peril in which for the first time I now find myself."

With these and other similar words, he loosed his buckler, grasped his lance in both his hands, and let the mule driver have such a blow on the head that the man fell to the ground stunned; and had it been followed by another one, he would have had no need of a surgeon to treat him. Having done this, Don Quixote gathered up his armor and resumed his pacing up and down with the same calm manner as before. Not long afterward, without knowing what had happened—for the first muleteer was still lying there unconscious—another came out with the same intention of watering his mules, and he too was about to remove the armor from the trough when the knight, without saying a word or asking favor of anyone, once more adjusted his buckler and raised his lance, and if he did not break the second mule driver's head to bits, he made more than three pieces of it by dividing it into quarters. At the sound of the fracas everybody in the inn came running out, among them the innkeeper; whereupon Don Quixote again lifted his buckler and laid his hand on his sword.

"O lady of beauty," he said, "strength and vigor of this fainting heart of mine! Now is the time to turn the eyes of your greatness upon this captive knight of yours who must face so formidable an adventure."

By this time he had worked himself up to such a pitch of anger that if all the mule drivers in the world had attacked him he would not have taken one step backward. The comrades of the wounded men, seeing the plight those two were in, now began showering stones on Don Quixote, who shielded himself as best he could with his buckler, although he did not dare stir from the trough for fear of leaving his armor unprotected. The landlord, meanwhile, kept calling for them to stop, for he had told them that this was a madman who would be sure to go free even though he killed them all. The knight was shouting louder than ever, calling them knaves and traitors. As for the lord of the castle, who allowed knights-errant to be treated in this fashion, he was a lowborn villain, and if he, Don Quixote, had but received the order of knighthood, he would make him pay for his treachery.

"As for you others, vile and filthy rabble, I take no account of you; you may stone me or come forward and attack me all you like; you shall see what the reward of your folly and insolence will be."

He spoke so vigorously and was so undaunted in bearing as to strike terror in those who would assail him; and for this reason, and owing also to the persuasions of the innkeeper, they ceased stoning him. He then permitted them to carry away the wounded, and went back to watching his armor with the same tranquil, unconcerned air that he had previously displayed.

The landlord was none too well pleased with these mad pranks on the part of his guest and determined to confer upon him that accursed order of knighthood before something else happened. Going up to him, he begged Don Quixote's pardon for the insolence which, without his knowledge, had been shown the knight by those of low degree. They, however, had been well punished for their impudence. As he had said, there was no chapel in this castle, but for that which remained to be done there was no need of any. According to what he had read of the ceremonial of the order, there was nothing to this business of being dubbed a knight except a slap on the neck and one across the shoulder, and that could be performed in the middle of a field as well as anywhere else. All that was required was for the knight-to-be to keep watch over his armor for a couple of hours, and Don Quixote had been at it more than four. The latter believed all this and announced that he was ready to obey and get the matter over with as speedily as possible. Once dubbed a knight, if he were attacked one more time, he did not think that he would leave a single person in the castle alive, save such as he might command be spared, at the bidding of his host and out of respect to him.

Thus warned, and fearful that it might occur, the castellan brought out the book in which he had jotted down the hay and barley for which the mule drivers owed him, and, accompanied by a lad bearing the butt of a candle and the two aforesaid damsels, he came up to where Don Quixote stood and commanded him to kneel. Reading from the account book—as if he had been saying a prayer—he raised his hand and, with the knight's own sword, gave him a good thwack upon the neck and another lusty one upon the shoulder, muttering all the while between his teeth. He then directed one of the ladies to gird on Don Quixote's sword, which she did with much gravity and composure; for it was all they could do to keep from laughing at every point of the ceremony, but the thought of the knight's prowess which they had already witnessed was sufficient to restrain their mirth.

"May God give your Grace much good fortune," said the worthy lady as she attached the blade, "and prosper you in battle."

Don Quixote thereupon inquired her name, for he desired to know to whom it was he was indebted for the favor he had just received, that he might share with her some of the honor which his strong right arm was sure to bring him. She replied very humbly that her name was Tolosa and that she was the daughter of a shoemaker, a native of Toledo who lived in the stalls of Sancho Bicnaya.[9] To this the knight replied that she would do him a very great favor if from then on she would call herself Doña Tolosa, and she promised to do so. The other girl then helped him on with his spurs, and practically the same conversation was repeated. When asked her name, she stated that it was La Molinera and added that she was the daughter of a respectable miller of Antequera. Don Quixote likewise requested her to assume the "don" and become Doña Molinera and offered to render her further services and favors.

These unheard-of ceremonies having been dispatched in great haste, Don Quixote could scarcely wait to be astride his horse and sally forth on his quest for adventures. Saddling and mounting Rocinante, he embraced his host, thanking him for the favor of having dubbed him a knight and saying such strange things that it would be quite impossible to record them here. The innkeeper, who was only too glad to be rid of him, answered with a speech that was no less flowery, though somewhat shorter, and he did not so much as ask him for the price of a lodging, so glad was he to see him go.

CHAPTER 4

Of what happened to our knight when he sallied forth from the inn.

Day was dawning when Don Quixote left the inn, so well satisfied with himself, so gay, so exhilarated, that the very girths of his steed all but burst with joy. But remembering the advice which his host had given him concerning the stock of necessary provisions that he should carry with him, especially money and shirts, he decided to turn back home and supply himself with whatever he needed, and with a squire as well; he had in mind a farmer who was a neighbor of his, a poor man and the father of a family but very well suited to fulfill the duties of squire to a man of arms. With this thought in mind he guided Rocinante toward the village once more, and that animal, realizing that he was homeward bound, began stepping out at so lively a gait that it seemed as if his feet barely touched the ground.

The knight had not gone far when from a hedge on his right hand he heard the sound of faint moans as of someone in distress.

"Thanks be to Heaven," he at once exclaimed, "for the favor it has shown me by providing me so soon with an opportunity to fulfill the obligations that I owe to my profession, a chance to pluck the fruit of my worthy desires. Those, undoubtedly, are the cries of someone in distress, who stands in need of my favor and assistance."

Turning Rocinante's head, he rode back to the place from which the cries appeared to be coming. Entering the wood, he had gone but a few paces when he saw a mare attached to an oak, while bound to another tree was a lad of

9. An old square in Toledo.

fifteen or thereabouts, naked from the waist up. It was he who was uttering the cries, and not without reason, for there in front of him was a lusty farmer with a girdle who was giving him many lashes, each one accompanied by a reproof and a command, "Hold your tongue and keep your eyes open"; and the lad was saying, "I won't do it again, sir; by God's Passion, I won't do it again. I promise you that after this I'll take better care of the flock."

When he saw what was going on, Don Quixote was very angry. "Discourteous knight," he said, "it ill becomes you to strike one who is powerless to defend himself. Mount your steed and take your lance in hand"—for there was a lance leaning against the oak to which the mare was tied—"and I will show you what a coward you are."

The farmer, seeing before him this figure all clad in armor and brandishing a lance, decided that he was as good as done for. "Sir Knight," he said, speaking very mildly, "this lad that I am punishing here is my servant; he tends a flock of sheep which I have in these parts and he is so careless that every day one of them shows up missing. And when I punish him for his carelessness or his roguery, he says it is just because I am a miser and do not want to pay him the wages that I owe him, but I swear to God and upon my soul that he lies."

"It is you who lie, base lout," said Don Quixote, "and in my presence; and by the sun that gives us light, I am minded to run you through with this lance. Pay him and say no more about it, or else, by the God who rules us, I will make an end of you and annihilate you here and now. Release him at once."

The farmer hung his head and without a word untied his servant. Don Quixote then asked the boy how much his master owed him. For nine months' work, the lad told him, at seven reales the month. The knight did a little reckoning and found that this came to sixty-three reales; whereupon he ordered the farmer to pay over the money immediately, as he valued his life. The cowardly bumpkin replied that, facing death as he was and by the oath that he had sworn—he had not sworn any oath as yet—it did not amount to as much as that; for there were three pairs of shoes which he had given the lad that were to be deducted and taken into account, and a real for two blood-lettings when his servant was ill.

"That," said Don Quixote, "is all very well; but let the shoes and the blood-lettings go for the undeserved lashings which you have given him; if he has worn out the leather of the shoes that you paid for, you have taken the hide off his body, and if the barber let a little blood for him when he was sick,[1] you have done the same when he was well; and so far as that goes, he owes you nothing."

"But the trouble is, Sir Knight, that I have no money with me. Come along home with me, Andrés, and I will pay you real for real."

"I go home with him!" cried the lad. "Never in the world! No, sir, I would not even think of it; for once he has me alone he'll flay me like a St. Bartholomew."

"He will do nothing of the sort," said Don Quixote. "It is sufficient for me to command, and he out of respect will obey. Since he has sworn to me by the order of knighthood which he has received, I shall let him go free and I will guarantee that you will be paid."

1. Barbers were also surgeons.

"But look, your Grace," the lad remonstrated, "my master is no knight; he has never received any order of knighthood whatsoever. He is Juan Haldudo, a rich man and a resident of Quintanar."

"That makes little difference," declared Don Quixote, "for there may well be knights among the Haldudos, all the more so in view of the fact that every man is the son of his works."

"That is true enough," said Andrés, "but this master of mine—of what works is he the son, seeing that he refuses me the pay for my sweat and labor?"

"I do not refuse you, brother Andrés," said the farmer. "Do me the favor of coming with me, and I swear to you by all the orders of knighthood that there are in this world to pay you, as I have said, real for real, and perfumed at that."

"You can dispense with the perfume," said Don Quixote; "just give him the reales and I shall be satisfied. And see to it that you keep your oath, or by the one that I myself have sworn I shall return to seek you out and chastise you, and I shall find you though you be as well hidden as a lizard. In case you would like to know who it is that is giving you this command in order that you may feel the more obliged to comply with it, I may tell you that I am the valorous Don Quixote de la Mancha, righter of wrongs and injustices; and so, God be with you, and do not fail to do as you have promised, under that penalty that I have pronounced."

As he said this, he put spurs to Rocinante and was off. The farmer watched him go, and when he saw that Don Quixote was out of the wood and out of sight, he turned to his servant, Andrés.

"Come here, my son," he said. "I want to pay you what I owe you as that righter of wrongs has commanded me."

"Take my word for it," replied Andrés, "your Grace would do well to observe the command of that good knight—may he live a thousand years; for as he is valorous and a righteous judge, if you don't pay me then, by Rocque,[2] he will come back and do just what he said!"

"And I will give you my word as well," said the farmer; "but seeing that I am so fond of you, I wish to increase the debt, that I may owe you all the more." And with this he seized the lad's arm and bound him to the tree again and flogged him within an inch of his life. "There, Master Andrés, you may call on that righter of wrongs if you like and you will see whether or not he rights this one. I do not think I have quite finished with you yet, for I have a good mind to flay you alive as you feared."

Finally, however, he unbound him and told him he might go look for that judge of his to carry out the sentence that had been pronounced. Andrés left, rather down in the mouth, swearing that he would indeed go look for the brave Don Quixote de la Mancha; he would relate to him everything that had happened, point by point, and the farmer would have to pay for it seven times over. But for all that, he went away weeping, and his master stood laughing at him.

Such was the manner in which the valorous knight righted this particular wrong. Don Quixote was quite content with the way everything had turned out; it seemed to him that he had made a very fortunate and noble beginning with his deeds of chivalry, and he was very well satisfied with himself as he jogged

---

2. The origin of this oath is unknown.

along in the direction of his native village, talking to himself in a low voice all the while.

"Well may'st thou call thyself fortunate today, above all other women on earth, O fairest of the fair, Dulcinea del Toboso! Seeing that it has fallen to thy lot to hold subject and submissive to thine every wish and pleasure so valiant and renowned a knight as Don Quixote de la Mancha is and shall be, who, as everyone knows, yesterday received the order of knighthood and this day has righted the greatest wrong and grievance that injustice ever conceived or cruelty ever perpetrated, by snatching the lash from the hand of the merciless foeman who was so unreasonably flogging that tender child."

At this point he came to a road that forked off in four directions, and at once he thought of those crossroads where knights-errant would pause to consider which path they should take. By way of imitating them, he halted there for a while; and when he had given the subject much thought, he slackened Rocinante's rein and let the hack follow its inclination. The animal's first impulse was to make straight for its own stable. After they had gone a couple of miles or so Don Quixote caught sight of what appeared to be a great throng of people, who, as was afterward learned, were certain merchants of Toledo on their way to purchase silk at Murcia. There were six of them altogether with their sunshades, accompanied by four attendants on horseback and three mule drivers on foot.

No sooner had he sighted them than Don Quixote imagined that he was on the brink of some fresh adventure. He was eager to imitate those passages at arms of which he had read in his books, and here, so it seemed to him, was one made to order. And so, with bold and knightly bearing, he settled himself firmly in the stirrups, couched his lance, covered himself with his shield, and took up a position in the middle of the road, where he paused to wait for those other knights-errant (for such he took them to be) to come up to him. When they were near enough to see and hear plainly, Don Quixote raised his voice and made a haughty gesture.

"Let everyone," he cried, "stand where he is, unless everyone will confess that there is not in all the world a more beauteous damsel than the Empress of La Mancha, the peerless Dulcinea del Toboso."

Upon hearing these words and beholding the weird figure who uttered them, the merchants stopped short. From the knight's appearance and his speech they knew at once that they had to deal with a madman; but they were curious to know what was meant by that confession that was demanded of them, and one of their number who was somewhat of a jester and a very clever fellow raised his voice.

"Sir Knight," he said, "we do not know who this beauteous lady is of whom you speak. Show her to us, and if she is as beautiful as you say, then we will right willingly and without any compulsion confess the truth as you have asked of us."

"If I were to show her to you," replied Don Quixote, "what merit would there be in your confessing a truth so self-evident? The important thing is for you, without seeing her, to believe, confess, affirm, swear, and defend that truth. Otherwise, monstrous and arrogant creatures that you are, you shall do battle with me. Come on, then, one by one, as the order of knighthood prescribes; or all of you together, if you will have it so, as is the sorry custom of those of your breed. Come on, and I will await you here, for I am confident that my cause is just."

"Sir Knight," responded the merchant, "I beg your Grace, in the name of all the princes here present, in order that we may not have upon our consciences the burden of confessing a thing which we have never seen nor heard, and one, moreover, so prejudicial to the empresses and queens of Alcarria and Estremadura,[3] that your Grace will show us some portrait of this lady, even though it be no larger than a grain of wheat, for by the thread one comes to the ball of yarn; and with this we shall remain satisfied and assured, and your Grace will likewise be content and satisfied. The truth is, I believe that we are already so much of your way of thinking that though it should show her to be blind of one eye and distilling vermilion and brimstone from the other, nevertheless, to please your Grace, we would say in her behalf all that you desire."

"She distills nothing of the sort, infamous rabble!" shouted Don Quixote, for his wrath was kindling now. "I tell you, she does not distill what you say at all, but amber and civet[4] wrapped in cotton; and she is neither one-eyed nor hunchbacked but straighter than a spindle that comes from Guadarrama. You shall pay for the great blasphemy which you have uttered against such a beauty as is my lady!"

Saying this, he came on with lowered lance against the one who had spoken, charging with such wrath and fury that if fortune had not caused Rocinante to stumble and fall in mid-career, things would have gone badly with the merchant and he would have paid for his insolent gibe. As it was, Don Quixote went rolling over the plain for some little distance, and when he tried to get to his feet, found that he was unable to do so, being too encumbered with his lance, shield, spurs, helmet, and the weight of that ancient suit of armor.

"Do not flee, cowardly ones," he cried even as he struggled to rise. "Stay, cravens, for it is not my fault but that of my steed that I am stretched out here."

One of the muleteers, who must have been an ill-natured lad, upon hearing the poor fallen knight speak so arrogantly, could not refrain from giving him an answer in the ribs. Going up to him, he took the knight's lance and broke it into bits, and then with a companion proceeded to belabor him so mercilessly that in spite of his armor they milled him like a hopper[5] of wheat. The merchants called to them not to lay on so hard, saying that was enough and they should desist, but the mule driver by this time had warmed up to the sport and would not stop until he had vented his wrath, and, snatching up the broken pieces of the lance, he began hurling them at the wretched victim as he lay there on the ground. And through all this tempest of sticks that rained upon him Don Quixote never once closed his mouth nor ceased threatening Heaven and earth and these ruffians, for such he took them to be, who were thus mishandling him.

Finally the lad grew tired, and the merchants went their way with a good story to tell about the poor fellow who had had such a cudgeling. Finding himself alone, the knight endeavored to see if he could rise; but if this was a feat that he

---

3. Ironical, because both were known as particularly backward regions.
4. A musky substance used in perfume, imported
from Africa in cotton packings.
5. Funnel-shaped container for grain.

could not accomplish when he was sound and whole, how was he to achieve it when he had been thrashed and pounded to a pulp? Yet nonetheless he considered himself fortunate; for as he saw it, misfortunes such as this were common to knights-errant, and he put all the blame upon his horse; and if he was unable to rise, that was because his body was so bruised and battered all over.

CHAPTER 5

In which is continued the narrative of the misfortune that befell our knight.

Seeing, then, that he was indeed unable to stir, he decided to fall back upon a favorite remedy of his, which was to think of some passage or other in his books; and as it happened, the one that he in his madness now recalled was the story of Baldwin and the Marquis of Mantua, when Carloto left the former wounded upon the mountainside,[6] a tale that is known to children, not unknown to young men, celebrated and believed in by the old, and, for all of that, not any truer than the miracles of Mohammed. Moreover, it impressed him as being especially suited to the straits in which he found himself; and, accordingly, with a great show of feeling, he began rolling and tossing on the ground as he feebly gasped out the lines which the wounded knight of the wood is supposed to have uttered:

> "Where art thou, lady mine,
> That thou dost not grieve for my woe?
> Either thou art disloyal,
> Or my grief thou dost not know."

He went on reciting the old ballad until he came to the following verses:

> "O noble Marquis of Mantua,
> My uncle and liege lord true!"

He had reached this point when down the road came a farmer of the same village, a neighbor of his, who had been to the mill with a load of wheat. Seeing a man lying there stretched out like that, he went up to him and inquired who he was and what was the trouble that caused him to utter such mournful complaints. Thinking that this must undoubtedly be his uncle, the Marquis of Mantua, Don Quixote did not answer but went on with his recitation of the ballad, giving an account of the Marquis' misfortunes and the amours of his wife and the emperor's son, exactly as the ballad has it.

The farmer was astounded at hearing all these absurdities, and after removing the knight's visor which had been battered to pieces by the blows it had received, the good man bathed the victim's face, only to discover, once the dust was off, that he knew him very well.

"Señor Quejana," he said (for such must have been Don Quixote's real name when he was in his right senses and before he had given up the life of a quiet country gentleman to become a knight-errant), "who is responsible for your Grace's being in such a plight as this?"

---

6. The allusion is to an old ballad about Charlemagne's son Charlot (Carloto) wounding Baldwin, nephew of the Marquis of Mantua.

But the knight merely went on with his ballad in response to all the questions asked of him. Perceiving that it was impossible to obtain any information from him, the farmer as best he could relieved him of his breastplate and backpiece to see if he had any wounds, but there was no blood and no mark of any sort. He then tried to lift him from the ground, and with a great deal of effort finally managed to get him astride the ass, which appeared to be the easier mount for him. Gathering up the armor, including even the splinters from the lance, he made a bundle and tied it on Rocinante's back, and, taking the horse by the reins and the ass by the halter, he started out for the village. He was worried in his mind at hearing all the foolish things that Don Quixote said, and that individual himself was far from being at ease. Unable by reason of his bruises and his soreness to sit upright on the donkey, our knight-errant kept sighing to Heaven, which led the farmer to ask him once more what it was that ailed him.

It must have been the devil himself who caused him to remember those tales that seemed to fit his own case; for at this point he forgot all about Baldwin and recalled Abindarráez, and how the governor of Antequera, Rodrigo de Narváez, had taken him prisoner and carried him off captive to his castle. Accordingly, when the countryman turned to inquire how he was and what was troubling him, Don Quixote replied with the very same words and phrases that the captive Abindarráez used in answering Rodrigo, just as he had read in the story *Diana* of Jorge de Montemayor,[7] where it is all written down, applying them very aptly to the present circumstances as the farmer went along cursing his luck for having to listen to such a lot of nonsense. Realizing that his neighbor was quite mad, he made haste to reach the village that he might not have to be annoyed any longer by Don Quixote's tiresome harangue.

"Señor Don Rodrigo de Narváez," the knight was saying, "I may inform your Grace that this beautiful Jarifa of whom I speak is not the lovely Dulcinea del Toboso, in whose behalf I have done, am doing, and shall do the most famous deeds of chivalry that ever have been or will be seen in all the world."

"But, sir," replied the farmer, "sinner that I am, cannot your Grace see that I am not Don Rodrigo de Narváez nor the Marquis of Mantua, but Pedro Alonso, your neighbor? And your Grace is neither Baldwin nor Abindarráez but a respectable gentleman by the name of Señor Quijana."

"I know who I am," said Don Quixote, "and who I may be, if I choose: not only those I have mentioned but all the Twelve Peers of France and the Nine Worthies[8] as well; for the exploits of all of them together, or separately, cannot compare with mine."

With such talk as this they reached their destination just as night was falling; but the farmer decided to wait until it was a little darker in order that the badly battered gentleman might not be seen arriving in such a condition and mounted on an ass. When he thought the proper time had come, they entered the village

---

7. The reference is to the tale of the love of Abindarráez, a captive Moor, for the beautiful Jarifa, included in the second edition of Jorge de Montemayor's *Diana*, a pastoral romance.
8. In a tradition originating in France, the Nine Worthies consisted of three biblical, three classical, and three Christian figures (David, Hector, Alexander, Charlemagne, and so on). In French medieval epics, the Twelve Peers (Roland, Oliver, and so on) were warriors all equal in rank, forming a kind of guard of honor around Charlemagne.

and proceeded to Don Quixote's house, where they found everything in confusion. The curate and the barber were there, for they were great friends of the knight, and the housekeeper was speaking to them.

"Señor Licentiate Pero Pérez," she was saying, for that was the manner in which she addressed the curate, "what does your Grace think could have happened to my master? Three days now, and not a word of him, nor the hack, nor the buckler, nor the lance, nor the suit of armor. Ah, poor me! I am as certain as I am that I was born to die that it is those cursed books of chivalry he is always reading that have turned his head; for now that I recall, I have often heard him muttering to himself that he must become a knight-errant and go through the world in search of adventures. May such books as those be consigned to Satan and Barabbas,[9] for they have sent to perdition the finest mind in all La Mancha."

The niece was of the same opinion. "I may tell you, Señor Master Nicholas," she said, for that was the barber's name, "that many times my uncle would sit reading those impious tales of misadventure for two whole days and nights at a stretch; and when he was through, he would toss the book aside, lay his hand on his sword, and begin slashing at the walls. When he was completely exhausted, he would tell us that he had just killed four giants as big as castle towers, while the sweat that poured off him was blood from the wounds that he had received in battle. He would then drink a big jug of cold water, after which he would be very calm and peaceful, saying that the water was the most precious liquid which the wise Esquife, a great magician and his friend, had brought to him. But I blame myself for everything. I should have advised your Worships of my uncle's nonsensical actions so that you could have done something about it by burning those damnable books of his before things came to such a pass; for he has many that ought to be burned as if they were heretics."

"I agree with you," said the curate, "and before tomorrow's sun has set there shall be a public *auto da fé*, and those works shall be condemned to the flames that they may not lead some other who reads them to follow the example of my good friend."

Don Quixote and the farmer overheard all this, and it was then that the latter came to understand the nature of his neighbor's affliction.

"Open the door, your Worships," the good man cried. "Open for Sir Baldwin and the Marquis of Mantua, who comes badly wounded, and for Señor Abindarráez the Moor whom the valiant Rodrigo de Narváez, governor of Antequera, brings captive."

At the sound of his voice they all ran out, recognizing at once friend, master, and uncle, who as yet was unable to get down off the donkey's back. They all ran up to embrace him.

"Wait, all of you," said Don Quixote, "for I am sorely wounded through fault of my steed. Bear me to my couch and summon, if it be possible, the wise Urganda to treat and care for my wounds."

"There!" exclaimed the housekeeper. "Plague take it! Did not my heart tell me right as to which foot my master limped on? To bed with your Grace at

---

9. The thief whose release, rather than that of Jesus, the crowd requested when Pilate, conforming to Passover custom, was ready to have one prisoner set free.

once, and we will take care of you without sending for that Urganda of yours. A curse, I say, and a hundred other curses, on those books of chivalry that have brought your Grace to this."

And so they carried him off to bed, but when they went to look for his wounds, they found none at all. He told them it was all the result of a great fall he had taken with Rocinante, his horse, while engaged in combating ten giants, the hugest and most insolent that were ever heard of in all the world.

"Tut, tut," said the curate. "So there are giants in the dance now, are there? Then, by the sign of the cross, I'll have them burned before nightfall tomorrow."

They had a thousand questions to put to Don Quixote, but his only answer was that they should give him something to eat and let him sleep, for that was the most important thing of all; so they humored him in this. The curate then interrogated the farmer at great length concerning the conversation he had had with his neighbor. The peasant told him everything, all the absurd things their friend had said when he found him lying there and afterward on the way home, all of which made the licentiate more anxious than ever to do what he did the following day,[1] when he summoned Master Nicholas and went with him to Don Quixote's house.

[Fighting the Windmills and a Choleric Biscayan]

CHAPTER 7

Of the second sally of our good knight, Don Quixote de la Mancha.

* * * After that he remained at home very tranquilly for a couple of weeks, without giving sign of any desire to repeat his former madness. During that time he had the most pleasant conversations with his two old friends, the curate and the barber, on the point he had raised to the effect that what the world needed most was knights-errant and a revival of chivalry. The curate would occasionally contradict him and again would give in, for it was only by means of this artifice that he could carry on a conversation with him at all.

In the meanwhile Don Quixote was bringing his powers of persuasion to bear upon a farmer who lived near by, a good man—if this title may be applied to one who is poor—but with very few wits in his head. The short of it is, by pleas and promises, he got the hapless rustic to agree to ride forth with him and serve him as his squire. Among other things, Don Quixote told him that he ought to be more than willing to go, because no telling what adventure might occur which would win them an island, and then he (the farmer) would be left to be the governor of it. As a result of these and other similar assurances, Sancho Panza forsook his wife and children and consented to take upon himself the duties of squire to his neighbor.

Next, Don Quixote set out to raise some money, and by selling this thing and pawning that and getting the worst of the bargain always, he finally scraped together a reasonable amount. He also asked a friend of his for the loan of a

---

1. He and the barber burned most of Don Quixote's library.

buckler and patched up his broken helmet as well as he could. He advised his squire, Sancho, of the day and hour when they were to take to the road and told him to see to laying in a supply of those things that were most necessary, and, above all, not to forget the saddlebags. Sancho replied that he would see to all this and added that he was also thinking of taking along with him a very good ass that he had, as he was not much used to going on foot.

With regard to the ass, Don Quixote had to do a little thinking, trying to recall if any knight-errant had ever had a squire thus asininely mounted. He could not think of any, but nevertheless he decided to take Sancho with the intention of providing him with a nobler steed as soon as occasion offered; he had but to appropriate the horse of the first discourteous knight he met. Having furnished himself with shirts and all the other things that the inn-keeper had recommended, he and Panza rode forth one night unseen by any-one and without taking leave of wife and children, housekeeper or niece. They went so far that by the time morning came they were safe from discovery had a hunt been started for them.

Mounted on his ass, Sancho Panza rode along like a patriarch, with saddle-bags and flask, his mind set upon becoming governor of that island that his master had promised him. Don Quixote determined to take the same route and road over the Campo de Montiel that he had followed on his first journey; but he was not so uncomfortable this time, for it was early morning and the sun's rays fell upon them slantingly and accordingly did not tire them too much.

"Look, Sir Knight-errant," said Sancho, "your Grace should not forget that island you promised me; for no matter how big it is, I'll be able to govern it right enough."

"I would have you know, friend Sancho Panza," replied Don Quixote, "that among the knights-errant of old it was a very common custom to make their squires governors of the islands or the kingdoms that they won, and I am resolved that in my case so pleasing a usage shall not fall into desuetude. I even mean to go them one better; for they very often, perhaps most of the time, waited until their squires were old men who had had their fill of serving their masters during bad days and worse nights, whereupon they would give them the title of count, or marquis at most, of some valley or province more or less. But if you live and I live, it well may be that within a week I shall win some kingdom with others dependent upon it, and it will be the easiest thing in the world to crown you king of one of them. You need not marvel at this, for all sorts of unforeseen things happen to knights like me, and I may readily be able to give you even more than I have promised."

"In that case," said Sancho Panza, "if by one of those miracles of which your Grace was speaking I should become king, I would certainly send for Juana Gutiérrez, my old lady, to come and be my queen, and the young ones could be infantes."

"There is no doubt about it," Don Quixote assured him.

"Well, I doubt it," said Sancho, "for I think that even if God were to rain kingdoms upon the earth, no crown would sit well on the head of Mari Gutiérrez,[2] for I am telling you, sir, as a queen she is not worth two maravedis. She would do better as a countess, God help her."

2. Sancho's wife, Juana Gutiérrez.

"Leave everything to God, Sancho," said Don Quixote, "and he will give you whatever is most fitting; but I trust you will not be so pusillanimous as to be content with anything less than the title of viceroy."

"That I will not," said Sancho Panza, "especially seeing that I have in your Grace so illustrious a master who can give me all that is suitable to me and all that I can manage."

CHAPTER 8

Of the good fortune which the valorous Don Quixote had in the terrifying and never-before-imagined adventure of the windmills, along with other events that deserve to be suitably recorded.

At this point they caught sight of thirty or forty windmills which were standing on the plain there, and no sooner had Don Quixote laid eyes upon them than he turned to his squire and said, "Fortune is guiding our affairs better than we could have wished; for you see there before you, friend Sancho Panza, some thirty or more lawless giants with whom I mean to do battle. I shall deprive them of their lives, and with the spoils from this encounter we shall begin to enrich ourselves; for this is righteous warfare, and it is a great service to God to remove so accursed a breed from the face of the earth."

"What giants?" said Sancho Panza.

"Those that you see there," replied his master, "those with the long arms some of which are as much as two leagues in length."

"But look, your Grace, those are not giants but windmills, and what appear to be arms are their wings which, when whirled in the breeze, cause the millstone to go."

"It is plain to be seen," said Don Quixote, "that you have had little experience in this matter of adventures. If you are afraid, go off to one side and say your prayers while I am engaging them in fierce, unequal combat."

Saying this, he gave spurs to his steed Rocinante, without paying any heed to Sancho's warning that these were truly windmills and not giants that he was riding forth to attack. Nor even when he was close upon them did he perceive what they really were, but shouted at the top of his lungs, "Do not seek to flee, cowards and vile creatures that you are, for it is but a single knight with whom you have to deal!"

At that moment a little wind came up and the big wings began turning.

"Though you flourish as many arms as did the giant Briareus,"[3] said Don Quixote when he perceived this, "you still shall have to answer to me."

He thereupon commended himself with all his heart to his lady Dulcinea, beseeching her to succor him in this peril; and, being well covered with his shield and with his lance at rest, he bore down upon them at a full gallop and fell upon the first mill that stood in his way, giving a thrust at the wing, which was whirling at such a speed that his lance was broken into bits and both horse and horseman went rolling over the plain, very much battered indeed. Sancho upon his donkey came hurrying to his master's assistance as fast as he could, but when he reached the spot, the knight was unable to move, so great was the shock with which he and Rocinante had hit the ground.

3. Mythological giant with a hundred arms.

"God help us!" exclaimed Sancho, "did I not tell your Grace to look well, that those were nothing but windmills, a fact which no one could fail to see unless he had other mills of the same sort in his head?"

"Be quiet, friend Sancho," said Don Quixote. "Such are the fortunes of war, which more than any other are subject to constant change. What is more, when I come to think of it, I am sure that this must be the work of that magician Frestón, the one who robbed me of my study and my books,[4] and who has thus changed the giants into windmills in order to deprive me of the glory of overcoming them, so great is the enmity that he bears me; but in the end his evil arts shall not prevail against this trusty sword of mine."

"May God's will be done," was Sancho Panza's response. And with the aid of his squire the knight was once more mounted on Rocinante, who stood there with one shoulder half out of joint. And so, speaking of the adventure that had just befallen them, they continued along the Puerto Lápice highway; for there, Don Quixote said, they could not fail to find many and varied adventures, this being a much traveled thoroughfare. The only thing was, the knight was exceedingly downcast over the loss of his lance.

"I remember," he said to his squire, "having read of a Spanish knight by the name of Diego Pérez de Vargas, who, having broken his sword in battle, tore from an oak a heavy bough or branch and with it did such feats of valor that day, and pounded so many Moors, that he came to be known as Machuca,[5] and he and his descendants from that day forth have been called Vargas y Machuca. I tell you this because I too intend to provide myself with just such a bough as the one he wielded, and with it I propose to do such exploits that you shall deem yourself fortunate to have been found worthy to come with me and behold and witness things that are almost beyond belief."

"God's will be done," said Sancho. "I believe everything that your Grace says; but straighten yourself up in the saddle a little, for you seem to be slipping down on one side, owing, no doubt, to the shaking-up that you received in your fall."

"Ah, that is the truth," replied Don Quixote, "and if I do not speak of my sufferings, it is for the reason that it is not permitted knights-errant to complain of any wound whatsoever, even though their bowels may be dropping out."

"If that is the way it is," said Sancho, "I have nothing more to say; but, God knows, it would suit me better if your Grace did complain when something hurts him. I can assure you that I mean to do so, over the least little thing that ails me—that is, unless the same rule applies to squires as well."

Don Quixote laughed long and heartily over Sancho's simplicity, telling him that he might complain as much as he liked and where and when he liked, whether he had good cause or not; for he had read nothing to the contrary in the ordinances of chivalry. Sancho then called his master's attention to the fact that it was time to eat. The knight replied that he himself had no need of food at the moment, but his squire might eat whenever he chose. Having been granted this permission, Sancho seated himself as best he could upon his beast, and, taking out from his saddlebags the provisions that he had stored

4. Don Quixote had promptly attributed the ruin of his library to magical intervention (see p. 1696, n. 1).

5. "The Crusher," the hero of a folk ballad.

there, he rode along leisurely behind his master, munching his victuals and taking a good, hearty swig now and then at the leather flask in a manner that might well have caused the biggest-bellied tavernkeeper of Málaga to envy him. Between draughts he gave not so much as a thought to any promise that his master might have made him, nor did he look upon it as any hardship, but rather as good sport, to go in quest of adventures however hazardous they might be.

The short of the matter is, they spent the night under some trees, from one of which Don Quixote tore off a withered bough to serve him as a lance, placing it in the lance head from which he had removed the broken one. He did not sleep all night long for thinking of his lady Dulcinea; for this was in accordance with what he had read in his books, of men of arms in the forest or desert places who kept a wakeful vigil, sustained by the memory of their ladies fair. Not so with Sancho, whose stomach was full, and not with chicory water. He fell into a dreamless slumber, and had not his master called him, he would not have been awakened either by the rays of the sun in his face or by the many birds who greeted the coming of the new day with their merry song.

Upon arising, he had another go at the flask, finding it somewhat more flaccid than it had been the night before, a circumstance which grieved his heart, for he could not see that they were on the way to remedying the deficiency within any very short space of time. Don Quixote did not wish any breakfast; for, as has been said, he was in the habit of nourishing himself on savorous memories. They then set out once more along the road to Puerto Lápice, and around three in the afternoon they came in sight of the pass that bears that name.

"There," said Don Quixote as his eyes fell upon it, "we may plunge our arms up to the elbow in what are known as adventures. But I must warn you that even though you see me in the greatest peril in the world, you are not to lay hand upon your sword to defend me, unless it be that those who attack me are rabble and men of low degree, in which case you may very well come to my aid; but if they be gentlemen, it is in no wise permitted by the laws of chivalry that you should assist me until you yourself shall have been dubbed a knight."

"Most certainly, sir," replied Sancho, "your Grace shall be very well obeyed in this; all the more so for the reason that I myself am of a peaceful disposition and not fond of meddling in the quarrels and feuds of others. However, when it comes to protecting my own person, I shall not take account of those laws of which you speak, seeing that all laws, human and divine, permit each one to defend himself whenever he is attacked."

"I am willing to grant you that," assented Don Quixote, "but in this matter of defending me against gentlemen you must restrain your natural impulses."

"I promise you I shall do so," said Sancho. "I will observe this precept as I would the Sabbath day."

As they were conversing in this manner, there appeared in the road in front of them two friars of the Order of St. Benedict, mounted upon dromedaries— for the she-mules they rode were certainly no smaller than that. The friars wore travelers' spectacles and carried sunshades, and behind them came a coach accompanied by four or five men on horseback and a couple of muleteers on foot. In the coach, as was afterwards learned, was a lady of Biscay, on her way to Seville to bid farewell to her husband, who had been appointed to some high post in the Indies. The religious were not of her company although they were going by the same road.

The instant Don Quixote laid eyes upon them he turned to his squire. "Either I am mistaken or this is going to be the most famous adventure that ever was seen; for those black-clad figures that you behold must be, and without any doubt are, certain enchanters who are bearing with them a captive princess in that coach, and I must do all I can to right this wrong."

"It will be worse than the windmills," declared Sancho. "Look you, sir, those are Benedictine friars and the coach must be that of some travelers. Mark well what I say and what you do, lest the devil lead you astray."

"I have already told you, Sancho," replied Don Quixote, "that you know little where the subject of adventures is concerned. What I am saying to you is the truth, as you shall now see."

With this, he rode forward and took up a position in the middle of the road along which the friars were coming, and as soon as they appeared to be within earshot he cried out to them in a loud voice, "O devilish and monstrous beings, set free at once the highborn princesses whom you bear captive in that coach, or else prepare at once to meet your death as the just punishment of your evil deeds."

The friars drew rein and sat there in astonishment, marveling as much at Don Quixote's appearance as at the words he spoke. "Sir Knight," they answered him, "we are neither devilish nor monstrous but religious of the Order of St. Benedict who are merely going our way. We know nothing of those who are in that coach, nor of any captive princesses either."

"Soft words," said Don Quixote, "have no effect on me. I know you for what you are, lying rabble!" And without waiting for any further parley he gave spur to Rocinante and, with lowered lance, bore down upon the first friar with such fury and intrepidity that, had not the fellow tumbled from his mule of his own accord, he would have been hurled to the ground and either killed or badly wounded. The second religious, seeing how his companion had been treated, dug his legs into his she-mule's flanks and scurried away over the countryside faster than the wind.

Seeing the friar upon the ground, Sancho Panza slipped lightly from his mount and, falling upon him, began stripping him of his habit. The two mule drivers accompanying the religious thereupon came running up and asked Sancho why he was doing this. The latter replied that the friar's garments belonged to him as legitimate spoils of the battle that his master Don Quixote had just won. The muleteers, however, were lads with no sense of humor, nor did they know what all this talk of spoils and battles was about; but, perceiving that Don Quixote had ridden off to one side to converse with those inside the coach, they pounced upon Sancho, threw him to the ground, and proceeded to pull out the hair of his beard and kick him to a pulp, after which they went off and left him stretched out there, bereft at once of breath and sense.

Without losing any time, they then assisted the friar to remount. The good brother was trembling all over from fright, and there was not a speck of color in his face, but when he found himself in the saddle once more, he quickly spurred his beast to where his companion, at some little distance, sat watching and waiting to see what the result of the encounter would be. Having no curiosity as to the final outcome of the fray, the two of them now resumed their journey, making more signs of the cross than the devil would be able to carry upon his back.

Meanwhile Don Quixote, as we have said, was speaking to the lady in the coach.

"Your beauty, my lady, may now dispose of your person as best may please you, for the arrogance of your abductors lies upon the ground, overthrown by this good arm of mine; and in order that you may not pine to know the name of your liberator, I may inform you that I am Don Quixote de la Mancha, knight-errant and adventurer and captive of the peerless and beauteous Doña Dulcinea del Toboso. In payment of the favor which you have received from me, I ask nothing other than that you return to El Toboso and on my behalf pay your respects to this lady, telling her that it was I who set you free."

One of the squires accompanying those in the coach, a Biscayan,[6] was listening to Don Quixote's words, and when he saw that the knight did not propose to let the coach proceed upon its way but was bent upon having it turn back to El Toboso, he promptly went up to him, seized his lance, and said to him in bad Castilian and worse Biscayan, "Go, *caballero*, and bad luck go with you; for by the God that created me, if you do not let this coach pass, me kill you or me no Biscayan."

Don Quixote heard him attentively enough and answered him very mildly, "If you were a *caballero*,[7] which you are not, I should already have chastised you, wretched creature, for your foolhardiness and your impudence."

"Me no *caballero*," cried the Biscayan. "Me swear to God, you lie like a Christian. If you will but lay aside your lance and unsheath your sword, you will soon see that you are carrying water to the cat![8] Biscayan on land, gentleman at sea, but a gentleman in spite of the devil, and you lie if you say otherwise."

"'You shall see as to that presently,' said Agrajes,"[9] Don Quixote quoted. He cast his lance to the earth, drew his sword, and, taking his buckler on his arm, attacked the Biscayan with intent to slay him. The latter, when he saw his adversary approaching, would have liked to dismount from his mule, for she was one of the worthless sort that are let for hire and he had no confidence in her; but there was no time for this, and so he had no choice but to draw his own sword in turn and make the best of it. However, he was near enough to the coach to be able to snatch a cushion from it to serve him as a shield; and then they fell upon each other as though they were mortal enemies. The rest of those present sought to make peace between them but did not succeed, for the Biscayan with his disjointed phrases kept muttering that if they did not let him finish the battle then he himself would have to kill his mistress and anyone else who tried to stop him.

The lady inside the carriage, amazed by it all and trembling at what she saw, directed her coachman to drive on a little way; and there from a distance she watched the deadly combat, in the course of which the Biscayan came down with a great blow on Don Quixote's shoulder, over the top of the latter's shield,

6. From the Basque region.
7. Knight, gentleman (Spanish).
8. An inversion of a proverbial phrase: "carry-ing the cat to the water."

9. A violent character in the romance *Amadis de Gaul*. His challenging phrase is the conventional opener of a fight.

and had not the knight been clad in armor, it would have split him to the waist.

Feeling the weight of this blow, Don Quixote cried out, "O lady of my soul, Dulcinea, flower of beauty, succor this your champion who out of gratitude for your many favors finds himself in so perilous a plight!" To utter these words, lay hold of his sword, cover himself with his buckler, and attack the Biscayan was but the work of a moment; for he was now resolved to risk everything upon a single stroke.

As he saw Don Quixote approaching with so dauntless a bearing, the Biscayan was well aware of his adversary's courage and forthwith determined to imitate the example thus set him. He kept himself protected with his cushion, but he was unable to get his she-mule to budge to one side or the other, for the beast, out of sheer exhaustion and being, moreover, unused to such childish play, was incapable of taking a single step. And so, then, as has been stated, Don Quixote was approaching the wary Biscayan, his sword raised on high and with the firm resolve of cleaving his enemy in two; and the Biscayan was awaiting the knight in the same posture, cushion in front of him and with uplifted sword. All the bystanders were trembling with suspense at what would happen as a result of the terrible blows that were threatened, and the lady in the coach and her maids were making a thousand vows and offerings to all the images and shrines in Spain, praying that God would save them all and the lady's squire from this great peril that confronted them.

But the unfortunate part of the matter is that at this very point the author of the history breaks off and leaves the battle pending, excusing himself upon the ground that he has been unable to find anything else in writing concerning the exploits of Don Quixote beyond those already set forth. It is true, on the other hand, that the second author[1] of this work could not bring himself to believe that so unusual a chronicle would have been consigned to oblivion, nor that the learned ones of La Mancha were possessed of so little curiosity as not to be able to discover in their archives or registry offices certain papers that have to do with this famous knight. Being convinced of this, he did not despair of coming upon the end of this pleasing story. * * *

CHAPTER 9

In which is concluded and brought to an end the stupendous battle between the gallant Biscayan and the valiant Knight of La Mancha.

* * * We left the valorous Biscayan and the famous Don Quixote with swords unsheathed and raised aloft, about to let fall furious slashing blows which, had they been delivered fairly and squarely, would at the very least have split them in two and laid them wide open from top to bottom like a pomegranate; and it was at this doubtful point that the pleasing chronicle came to a halt and broke off, without the author's informing us as to where the rest of it might be found.

I was deeply grieved by such a circumstance, and the pleasure I had had in reading so slight a portion was turned into annoyance as I thought of how

---

1. Cervantes himself, adopting here—with tongue in cheek—a device used in the romances of chivalry to create suspense.

difficult it would be to come upon the greater part which it seemed to me must still be missing. It appeared impossible and contrary to all good precedent that so worthy a knight should not have had some scribe to take upon himself the task of writing an account of these unheard-of exploits; for that was something that had happened to none of the knights-errant who, as the saying has it, had gone forth in quest of adventures, seeing that each of them had one or two chroniclers, as if ready at hand, who not only had set down their deeds, but had depicted their most trivial thoughts and amiable weaknesses, however well concealed they might be. The good knight of La Mancha surely could not have been so unfortunate as to have lacked what Platir and others like him had in abundance. And so I could not bring myself to believe that this gallant history could have remained thus lopped off and mutilated, and I could not but lay the blame upon the malignity of time, that devourer and consumer of all things, which must either have consumed it or kept it hidden.

On the other hand, I reflected that inasmuch as among the knight's books had been found such modern works as *The Disenchantments of Jealousy* and *The Nymphs and Shepherds of Henares*, his story likewise must be modern, and that even though it might not have been written down, it must remain in the memory of the good folk of his village and the surrounding ones. This thought left me somewhat confused and more than ever desirous of knowing the real and true story, the whole story, of the life and wondrous deeds of our famous Spaniard, Don Quixote, light and mirror of the chivalry of La Mancha, the first in our age and in these calamitous times to devote himself to the hardships and exercises of knight-errantry and to go about righting wrongs, succoring wid-ows, and protecting damsels—damsels such as those who, mounted upon their palfreys and with riding-whip in hand, in full possession of their virginity, were in the habit of going from mountain to mountain and from valley to valley; for unless there were some villain, some rustic with an ax and hood, or some mon-strous giant to force them, there were in times past maiden ladies who at the end of eighty years, during all which time they had not slept for a single day beneath a roof, would go to their graves as virginal as when their mothers had borne them.

If I speak of these things, it is for the reason that in this and in all other respects our gallant Quixote is deserving of constant memory and praise, and even I am not to be denied my share of it for my diligence and the labor to which I put myself in searching out the conclusion of this agreeable narrative; although if heaven, luck, and circumstance had not aided me, the world would have had to do without the pleasure and the pastime which anyone may enjoy who will read this work attentively for an hour or two. The manner in which it came about was as follows:

I was standing one day in the Alcaná, or market place, of Toledo when a lad came up to sell some old notebooks and other papers to a silk weaver who was there. As I am extremely fond of reading anything, even though it be but the scraps of paper in the streets, I followed my natural inclination and took one of the books, whereupon I at once perceived that it was written in characters which I recognized as Arabic. I recognized them, but reading them was another thing; and so I began looking around to see if there was any Spanish-speaking Moor near by who would be able to read them for me. It was not very hard to find such an interpreter, nor would it have been even if the tongue in question had been an older and a better one.[2] To make a long story short, chance brought a fellow my way; and when I told him what it was I wished and placed the book in his hands, he opened it in the middle and began reading and at once fell to laughing. When I asked him what the cause of his laughter was, he replied that it was a note which had been written in the margin.

I besought him to tell me the content of the note, and he, laughing still, went on, "As I told you, it is something in the margin here: 'This Dulcinea del Toboso, so often referred to, is said to have been the best hand at salting pigs of any woman in all La Mancha.'"

No sooner had I heard the name Dulcinea del Toboso than I was astonished and held in suspense, for at once the thought occurred to me that those notebooks must contain the history of Don Quixote. With this in mind I urged him to read me the title, and he proceeded to do so, turning the Arabic into Castilian upon the spot: *History of Don Quixote de la Mancha, Written by Cid Hamete Benengeli*[3] Arabic Historian. It was all I could do to conceal my satisfaction and, snatching them from the silk weaver, I bought from the lad all the papers and notebooks that he had for half a real; but if he had known or suspected how very much I wanted them, he might well have had more than six reales for them.

The Moor and I then betook ourselves to the cathedral cloister, where I requested him to translate for me into the Castilian tongue all the books that had to do with Don Quixote, adding nothing and subtracting nothing; and I offered him whatever payment he desired. He was content with two arrobas of raisins and two fanegas[4] of wheat and promised to translate them well and faithfully and with all dispatch. However, in order to facilitate matters, and also because I did not wish to let such a find as this out of my hands, I took the fellow home with me, where in a little more than a month and a half he translated the whole of the work just as you will find it set down here.

In the first of the books there was a very lifelike picture of the battle between Don Quixote and the Biscayan, the two being in precisely the same posture as described in the history, their swords upraised, the one covered by his buckler, the other with his cushion. As for the Biscayan's mule, you could see at the distance of a crossbow shot that it was one for hire. Beneath the Biscayan there was a rubric which read: "Don Sancho de Azpeitia," which must undoubtedly have been his name; while beneath the feet of Rocinante was another inscription: "Don Quixote." Rocinante was marvelously portrayed: so long and lank, so lean and flabby, so extremely consumptive-looking that one could well understand the justness and propriety with which the name of "hack" had been bestowed upon him.

Alongside Rocinante stood Sancho Panza, holding the halter of his ass, and below was the legend: "Sancho Zancas." The picture showed him with a big belly, a short body and long shanks, and that must have been where he got the names of Panza y Zancas[5] by which he is a number of times called in the

2. I.e., Hebrew.
3. Citing some ancient chronicle as the author's source and authority is very much in the tradition of the romances. "*Benengeli*":
eggplant (Arabic).
4. About fifty pounds. "Two arrobas": three bushels.
5. Paunch and Shanks (Spanish).

course of the history. There are other small details that might be mentioned, but they are of little importance and have nothing to do with the truth of the story—and no story is bad so long as it is true.

If there is any objection to be raised against the veracity of the present one, it can be only that the author was an Arab, and that nation is known for its lying propensities; but even though they be our enemies, it may readily be understood that they would more likely have detracted from, rather than added to, the chronicle. So it seems to me, at any rate; for whenever he might and should deploy the resources of his pen in praise of so worthy a knight, the author appears to take pains to pass over the matter in silence; all of which in my opinion is ill done and ill conceived, for it should be the duty of historians to be exact, truthful, and dispassionate, and neither interest nor fear nor rancor nor affection should swerve them from the path of truth, whose mother is history, rival of time, depository of deeds, witness of the past, exemplar and adviser to the present, and the future's councilor. In this work, I am sure, will be found all that could be desired in the way of pleasant reading; and if it is lacking in any way, I maintain that this is the fault of that hound of an author rather than of the subject.

But to come to the point, the second part, according to the translation, began as follows:

As the two valorous and enraged combatants stood there, swords upraised and poised on high, it seemed from their bold mien as if they must surely be threatening heaven, earth, and hell itself. The first to let fall a blow was the choleric Biscayan, and he came down with such force and fury that, had not his sword been deflected in mid-air, that single stroke would have sufficed to put an end to this fearful combat and to all our knight's adventures at the same time; but fortune, which was reserving him for greater things, turned aside his adversary's blade in such a manner that, even though it fell upon his left shoulder, it did him no other damage than to strip him completely of his armor on that side, carrying with it a good part of his helmet along with half an ear, the headpiece clattering to the ground with a dreadful din, leaving its wearer in a sorry state.

Heaven help me! Who could properly describe the rage that now entered the heart of our hero of La Mancha as he saw himself treated in this fashion? It may merely be said that he once more reared himself in the stirrups, laid hold of his sword with both hands, and dealt the Biscayan such a blow, over the cushion and upon the head, that, even so good a defense proving useless, it was as if a mountain had fallen upon his enemy. The latter now began bleeding through the mouth, nose, and ears; he seemed about to fall from his mule, and would have fallen, no doubt, if he had not grasped the beast about the neck, but at that moment his feet slipped from the stirrups and his arms let go, and the mule, frightened by the terrible blow, began running across the plain, hurling its rider to the earth with a few quick plunges.

Don Quixote stood watching all this very calmly. When he saw his enemy fall, he leaped from his horse, ran over very nimbly, and thrust the point of his sword into the Biscayan's eyes, calling upon him at the same time to surrender or otherwise he would cut off his head. The Biscayan was so bewildered that he was unable to utter a single word in reply, and things would have gone badly with him, so blind was Don Quixote in his rage, if the ladies of the coach, who up to then had watched the struggle in dismay, had not come up to him at this point and begged him with many blandishments to do them the very great favor of sparing their squire's life.

To which Don Quixote replied with much haughtiness and dignity, "Most certainly, lovely ladies, I shall be very happy to do that which you ask of me, but upon one condition and understanding, and that is that this knight promise me that he will go to El Toboso and present himself in my behalf before Doña Dulcinea, in order that she may do with him as she may see fit."

Trembling and disconsolate, the ladies did not pause to discuss Don Quixote's request, but without so much as inquiring who Dulcinea might be they promised him that the squire would fulfill that which was commanded of him.

"Very well, then, trusting in your word, I will do him no further harm, even though he has well deserved it."

CHAPTER 10

*Of the pleasing conversation that took place between Don Quixote
and Sancho Panza, his squire.*

By this time Sancho Panza had got to his feet, somewhat the worse for wear as the result of the treatment he had received from the friars' lads. He had been watching the battle attentively and praying God in his heart to give the victory to his master, Don Quixote, in order that he, Sancho, might gain some island where he could go to be governor as had been promised him. Seeing now that the combat was over and the knight was returning to mount Rocinante once more, he went up to hold the stirrup for him; but first he fell on his knees in front of him and, taking his hand, kissed it and said, "May your Grace be pleased, Señor Don Quixote, to grant me the governorship of that island which you have won in this deadly affray; for however large it may be, I feel that I am indeed capable of governing it as well as any man in this world has ever done."

To which Don Quixote replied, "Be advised, brother Sancho, that this adventure and other similar ones have nothing to do with islands; they are affairs of the crossroads in which one gains nothing more than a broken head or an ear the less. Be patient, for there will be others which will not only make you a governor, but more than that."

Sancho thanked him very much and, kissing his hand again and the skirt of his cuirass, he assisted him up on Rocinante's back, after which the squire bestraddled his own mount and started jogging along behind his master, who was now going at a good clip. Without pausing for any further converse with those in the coach, the knight made for a near-by wood, with Sancho following as fast as his beast could trot; but Rocinante was making such speed that the ass and its rider were left behind, and it was necessary to call out to Don Quixote to pull up and wait for them. He did so, reining in Rocinante until the weary Sancho had drawn abreast of him.

"It strikes me, sir," said the squire as he reached his master's side, "that it would be better for us to take refuge in some church; for in view of the way you have treated that one with whom you were fighting, it would be small wonder if they did not lay the matter before the Holy Brotherhood[6] and have us arrested; and faith, if they do that, we shall have to sweat a-plenty before we come out of jail."

"Be quiet," said Don Quixote. "And where have you ever seen, or read of, a knight being brought to justice no matter how many homicides he might have committed?"

"I know nothing about omecils,"[7] replied Sancho, "nor ever in my life did I bear one to anybody; all I know is that the Holy Brotherhood has something to say about those who go around fighting on the highway, and I want nothing of it."

"Do not let it worry you," said Don Quixote, "for I will rescue you from the hands of the Chaldeans, not to speak of the Brotherhood. But answer me upon your life: have you ever seen a more valorous knight than I on all the known face of the earth? Have you ever read in the histories of any other who had more mettle in the attack, more perseverance in sustaining it, more dexterity in wounding his enemy, or more skill in overthrowing him?"

"The truth is," said Sancho, "I have never read any history whatsoever, for I do not know how to read or write; but what I would wager is that in all the days of my life I have never served a more courageous master than your Grace; I only hope your courage is not paid for in the place that I have mentioned. What I would suggest is that your Grace allow me to do something for that ear, for there is much blood coming from it, and I have here in my saddlebags some lint and a little white ointment."

"We could well dispense with all that," said Don Quixote, "if only I had remembered to bring along a vial of Fierabrás's[8] balm, a single drop of which saves time and medicines."

"What vial and what balm is that?" inquired Sancho Panza.

"It is a balm the receipt[9] for which I know by heart; with it one need have no fear of death nor think of dying from any wound. I shall make some of it and give it to you; and thereafter, whenever in any battle you see my body cut in two—as very often happens—all that is necessary is for you to take the part that lies on the ground, before the blood has congealed, and fit it very neatly and with great nicety upon the other part that remains in the saddle, taking care to adjust it evenly and exactly. Then you will give me but a couple of swallows of the balm of which I have told you, and you will see me sounder than an apple in no time at all."

"If that is so," said Panza, "I herewith renounce the governorship of the island you promised me and ask nothing other in payment of my many and faithful services than that your Grace give me the receipt for this wonderful potion, for I am sure that it would be worth more than two reales the ounce anywhere, and that is all I need for a life of ease and honor. But may I be so bold as to ask how much it costs to make it?"

6. A tribunal instituted by Ferdinand and Isabella at the end of the 15th century to punish highway robbers.
7. In Spanish a wordplay on *homecidio-omecillo*. Not to bear an *omecillo* to anybody means not to bear a grudge, and good-natured Sancho does not.
8. A giant Saracen healer in the medieval epics of the Twelve Peers (see p. 1694, n. 8).
9. Recipe.

"For less than three reales you can make something like six quarts," Don Quixote told him.

"Sinner that I am!" exclaimed Sancho. "Then why does your Grace not make some at once and teach me also?"

"Hush, my friend," said the knight, "I mean to teach you greater secrets than that and do you greater favors; but, for the present, let us look after this ear of mine, for it is hurting me more than I like."

Sancho thereupon took the lint and the ointment from his saddlebags; but when Don Quixote caught a glimpse of his helmet, he almost went out of his mind and, laying his hand upon his sword and lifting his eyes heavenward, he cried, "I make a vow to the Creator of all things and to the four holy Gospels in all their fullness of meaning that I will lead from now on the life that the great Marquis of Mantua did after he had sworn to avenge the death of his nephew Baldwin: not to eat bread of a tablecloth, not to embrace his wife, and other things which, although I am unable to recall them, we will look upon as understood—all this until I shall have wreaked an utter vengeance upon the one who has perpetrated such an outrage upon me."

"But let me remind your Grace," said Sancho when he heard these words, "that if the knight fulfills that which was commanded of him, by going to present himself before my lady Dulcinea del Toboso, then he will have paid his debt to you and merits no further punishment at your hands, unless it be for some fresh offense."

"You have spoken very well and to the point," said Don Quixote, "and so I annul the vow I have just made insofar as it has to do with any further vengeance, but I make it and confirm it anew so far as leading the life of which I have spoken is concerned, until such time as I shall have obtained by force of arms from some other knight another headpiece as good as this. And do not think, Sancho, that I am making smoke out of straw; there is one whom I well may imitate in this matter, for the same thing happened in all literalness in the case of Mambrino's helmet[1] which cost Sacripante so dear."

"I wish," said Sancho, "that your Grace would send all such oaths to the devil, for they are very bad for the health and harmful for the conscience as well. Tell me, please; supposing that for many days to come we meet no man wearing a helmet, then what are we to do? Must you still keep your vow in spite of all the inconveniences and discomforts, such as sleeping with your clothes on, not sleeping in any town, and a thousand other penances contained in the oath of that old madman of a Marquis of Mantua, an oath which you would now revive? Mark you, sir, along all these roads you meet no men of arms but only muleteers and carters, who not only do not wear helmets but quite likely have never heard tell of them in all their livelong days."

"In that you are wrong," said Don Quixote, "for we shall not be at these crossroads for the space of two hours before we shall see more men of arms than came to Albraca to win the fair Angélica."[2] "Very well, then," said Sancho,

---

1. The enchanted helmet of Mambrino, a Moorish king, is stolen by Rinaldo in Boiardo's *Roland in Love.*

2. Another allusion to *Roland in Love.*

"so be it, and pray God that all turns out for the best so that I may at last win that island that is costing me so dearly, and then let me die."

"I have already told you, Sancho, that you are to give no thought to that; should the island fail, there is the kingdom of Denmark or that of Sobradisa, which would fit you like a ring on your finger, and you ought, moreover, to be happy to be on *terra firma*.[3] But let us leave all this for some other time, while you look and see if you have something in those saddlebags for us to eat, after which we will go in search of some castle where we may lodge for the night and prepare that balm of which I was telling you, for I swear to God that my ear is paining me greatly."

"I have here an onion, a little cheese, and a few crusts of bread," said Sancho, "but they are not victuals fit for a valiant knight like your grace."

"How little you know about it!" replied Don Quixote. "I would inform you, Sancho, that it is a point of honor with knights-errant to go for a month at a time without eating, and when they do eat, it is whatever may be at hand. You would certainly know that if you had read the histories as I have. There are many of them, and in none have I found any mention of knights eating unless it was by chance or at some sumptuous banquet that was tendered them; on other days they fasted. And even though it is well understood that, being men like us, they could not go without food entirely, any more than they could fail to satisfy the other necessities of nature, nevertheless, since they spent the greater part of their lives in forest and desert places without any cook to prepare their meals, their diet ordinarily consisted of rustic viands such as those that you now offer me. And so, Sancho my friend, do not be grieved at that which pleases me, nor seek to make the world over, nor to unhinge the institution of knight-errantry."

"Pardon me, your Grace," said Sancho, "but seeing that, as I have told you I do not know how to read or write, I am consequently not familiar with the rules of the knightly calling. Hereafter, I will stuff my saddlebags with all manner of dried fruit for your Grace, but inasmuch as I am not a knight, I shall lay in for myself a stock of fowls and other more substantial fare."

"I am not saying, Sancho, that it is incumbent upon knights-errant to eat only those fruits of which you speak; what I am saying is that their ordinary sustenance should consist of fruit and a few herbs such as are to be found in the fields and with which they are well acquainted, as am I myself."

"It is a good thing," said Sancho, "to know those herbs, for, so far as I can see, we are going to have need of that knowledge one of these days."

With this, he brought out the articles he had mentioned, and the two of them ate in peace, and most companionably. Being desirous, however, of seeking a lodging for the night, they did not tarry long over their humble and unsavory repast. They then mounted and made what haste they could that they might arrive at a shelter before nightfall but the sun failed them, and with it went the hope of attaining their wish. As the day ended they found themselves beside some goatherds' huts, and they accordingly decided to

3. Solid earth (Latin, literal trans.), here Firm Island, an imaginary final destination for the squires of knights-errant. "Sobradisa": an imaginary realm.

spend the night there. Sancho was as much disappointed at their not having reached a town as his master was content with sleeping under the open sky; for it seemed to Don Quixote that every time this happened it merely provided him with yet another opportunity to establish his claim to the title of knight-errant.

[*Of Goatherds, Roaming Shepherdesses, and Unrequited Loves*]

CHAPTER II

Of what happened to Don Quixote in the company of certain goatherds.

He was received by the herders with good grace, and Sancho having looked after Rocinante and the ass to the best of his ability, the knight, drawn by the aroma, went up to where some pieces of goat's meat were simmering in a pot over the fire. He would have liked then and there to see if they were done well enough to be transferred from pot to stomach, but he refrained in view of the fact that his hosts were already taking them off the fire. Spreading a few sheepskins on the ground, they hastily laid their rustic board and invited the strangers to share what there was of it. There were six of them altogether who belonged to that fold, and after they had urged Don Quixote, with rude politeness, to seat himself upon a small trough which they had turned upside down for the purpose, they took their own places upon the sheep hides round about. While his master sat there, Sancho remained standing to serve him the cup, which was made of horn. When the knight perceived this, he addressed his squire as follows.

"In order, Sancho, that you may see the good that there is in knight-errantry and how speedily those who follow the profession, no matter what the nature of their service may be, come to be honored and esteemed in the eyes of the world, I would have you here in the company of these good folk seat yourself at my side, that you may be even as I who am your master and natural lord, and eat from my plate and drink from where I drink; for of knight-errantry one may say the same as of love that it makes all things equal."

"Many thanks!" said Sancho. "But if it is all the same to your Grace, providing there is enough to go around, I can eat just as well, or better, standing up and alone as I can seated beside an emperor. And if the truth must be told, I enjoy much more that which I eat in my own corner without any bowings and scrapings, even though it be only bread and onions, that I do a meal of roast turkey where I have to chew slowly, drink little, be always wiping my mouth, and can neither sneeze nor cough if I feel like it, nor do any of those other things that you can when you are free and alone.

"And so, my master," he went on, "these honors that your Grace would confer upon me as your servant and a follower of knight-errantry—which I am, being your Grace's squire—I would have you convert, if you will, into other things that will be of more profit and advantage to me; for though I hereby acknowledge them as duly received, I renounce them from this time forth to the end of the world."

"But for all that," said Don Quixote, "you must sit down, for whosoever humbleth himself, him God will exalt." And, laying hold of his squire's arm, he compelled him to take a seat beside him.

The goatherds did not understand all this jargon about squires and knights-errant; they did nothing but eat, keep silent, and study their guests, who very dexterously and with much appetite were stowing away chunks of meat as big as your fist. When the meat course was finished, they laid out upon the sheepskins a great quantity of dried acorns and half a cheese, which was harder than if it had been made of mortar. The drinking horn all this while was not idle but went the rounds so often—now full, now empty, like the bucket of a water wheel—that they soon drained one of the two wine bags that were on hand. After Don Quixote had well satisfied his stomach, he took up a handful of acorns and, gazing at them attentively, fell into a soliloquy.

"Happy the age and happy those centuries to which the ancients gave the name of golden, and not because gold, which is so esteemed in this iron age of ours, was then to be had without toil, but because those who lived in that time did not know the meaning of the words 'thine' and 'mine.' In that blessed year all things were held in common, and to gain his daily sustenance no labor was required of any man save to reach forth his hand and take it from the sturdy oaks that stood liberally inviting him with their sweet and seasoned fruit. The clear-running fountains and rivers in magnificent abundance offered him palatable and transparent water for his thirst; while in the clefts of the rocks and the hollows of the trees the wise and busy honeymakers set up their republic so that any hand whatever might avail itself, fully and freely, of the fertile harvest which their fragrant toil had produced. The vigorous cork trees of their own free will and grace, without the asking, shed their broad, light bark with which men began to cover their dwellings, erected upon rude stakes merely as a protection against the inclemency of the heavens.

"All then was peace, all was concord and friendship; the crooked plowshare had not as yet grievously laid open and pried into the merciful bowels of our first mother, who without any forcing on man's part yielded her spacious fertile bosom on every hand for the satisfaction, sustenance, and delight of her first sons. Then it was that lovely and unspoiled young shepherdesses, with locks that were sometimes braided, sometimes flowing, went roaming from valley to valley and hillock to hillock with no more garments than were needed to cover decently that which modesty requires and always had required should remain covered. Nor were their adornments such as those in use today—of Tyrian purple and silk worked up in tortured patterns; a few green leaves of burdock or of ivy, and they were as splendidly and as becomingly clad as our ladies of the court with all the rare and exotic tricks of fashion that idle curiosity has taught them.

"Thoughts of love, also, in those days were set forth as simply as the simple hearts that conceived them, without any roundabout and artificial play of words by way of ornament. Fraud, deceit, and malice had not yet come to mingle with truth and plain-speaking. Justice kept its own domain, where favor and self-interest dared not trespass, dared not impair her rights, becloud, and persecute her as they now do. There was no such thing then as arbitrary judgments, for the reason that there was no one to judge or be judged. Maidens in all their modesty, as I have said, went where they would and unattended; whereas in this hateful age of ours none is safe, even though she go to hide and shut herself up in some new labyrinth like that of Crete; for in spite of all her seclusion, through chinks and crevices or borne upon the air, the amorous plague with all its cursed importunities will find her out and lead her to her ruin.

"It was for the safety of such as these, as time went on and depravity increased, that the order of knights-errant was instituted, for the protection of damsels, the aid of widows and orphans, and the succoring of the needy. It is to this order that I belong, my brothers, and I thank you for the welcome and the kindly treatment that you have accorded to me and my squire. By natural law, all living men are obliged to show favor to knights-errant, yet without being aware of this you have received and entertained me; and so it is with all possible good will that I acknowledge your own good will to me."

This long harangue on the part of our knight—it might very well have been dispensed with—was all due to the acorns they had given him, which had brought back to memory the age of gold; whereupon the whim had seized him to indulge in this futile harangue with the goatherds as his auditors. They listened in open-mouthed wonderment, saying not a word, and Sancho himself kept quiet and went on munching acorns, taking occasion very frequently to pay a visit to the second wine bag, which they had suspended from a cork tree to keep it cool.

It took Don Quixote much longer to finish his speech than it did to put away his supper; and when he was through, one of the goatherds addressed him.

"In order that your Grace may say with more truth that we have received you with readiness and good will, we desire to give you solace and contentment by having one of our comrades, who will be here soon, sing for you. He is a very bright young fellow and deeply in love, and what is more, you could not ask for anything better than to hear him play the three-stringed lute."

Scarcely had he done saying this when the sound of a rebec was heard, and shortly afterward the one who played it appeared. He was a good-looking youth, around twenty-two years of age. His companions asked him if he had had his supper, and when he replied that he had, the one who had spoken to Don Quixote said to him, "Well, then, Antonio, you can give us the pleasure of hearing you sing, in order that this gentleman whom we have as our guest may see that we of the woods and mountains also know something about music. We have been telling him how clever you are, and now we want you to show him that we were speaking the truth. And so I beg you by all means to sit down and sing us that lovesong of yours that your uncle the prebendary composed for you and which the villagers liked so well."

"With great pleasure," the lad replied, and without any urging he seated himself on the stump of an oak that had been felled and, tuning up his rebec, soon began singing, very prettily, the following ballad:

The Ballad That Antonio Sang

I know well that thou dost love me,
My Olalla, even though
Eyes of thine have never spoken—
Love's mute tongues—to tell me so.
   Since I know thou knowest my passion,   5
Of thy love I am more sure:
No love ever was unhappy
When it was both frank and pure.
   True it is, Olalla, sometimes
Thou a heart of bronze hast shown,   10
And it seemed to me that bosom,
White and fair, was made of stone.
   Yet in spite of all repulses
And a chastity so cold,
It appeared that I Hope's garment   15
By the hem did clutch and hold.
   For my faith I ever cherished;
It would rise to meet the bait;
Spurned, it never did diminish;
Favored, it preferred to wait.   20
   Love, they say, hath gentle manners:
Thus it is it shows its face;
Then may I take hope, Olalla,
Trust to win a longed for grace.
   If devotion hath the power   25
Hearts to move and make them kind,
Let the loyalty I've shown thee
Plead my cause, be kept in mind.
   For if thou didst note my costume,
More than once thou must have seen,   30
Worn upon a simple Monday
Sunday's garb so bright and clean.
   Love and brightness go together.
Dost thou ask the reason why
I thus deck myself on Monday?   35
It is but to catch thine eye.
   I say nothing of the dances
I have danced for thy sweet sake;
Nor the serenades I've sung thee
Till the first cock did awake.   40
   Nor will I repeat my praises
Of that beauty all can see;
True my words but oft unwelcome—
Certain lasses hated me.
   One girl there is, I well remember—   45
She's Teresa on the hill—
Said, "You think you love an angel,
But she is a monkey still.
   "Thanks to all her many trinkets
And her artificial hair   50

And her many aids to beauty,
Love's own self she would ensnare."
    She was lying, I was angry,
And her cousin, very bold,
Challenged me upon my honor;   55
What ensued need not be told.
    Highflown words do not become me;
I'm a plain and simple man.
Pure the love that I would offer,
Serving thee as best I can.   60
    Silken are the bonds of marriage,
When two hearts do intertwine;
Mother Church the yoke will fasten;
Bow your neck and I'll bow mine.
    Or if not, my word I'll give thee,   65
From these mountains I'll come down—
Saint most holy be my witness—
Wearing a Capuchin gown.

With this the goatherd brought his song to a close, and although Don Quixote begged him to sing some more, Sancho Panza would not hear of this as he
was too sleepy for any more ballads.

"Your Grace," he said to his master, "would do well to find out at once where
his bed is to be, for the labor that these good men have to perform all day long
does not permit them to stay up all night singing."

"I understand, Sancho," replied Don Quixote. "I perceive that those visits to
the wine bag call for sleep rather than music as a recompense."

"It tastes well enough to all of us, God be praised," said Sancho.

"I am not denying that," said his master; "but go ahead and settle yourself
down wherever you like. As for men of my profession, they prefer to keep vigil.
But all the same, Sancho, perhaps you had better look after this ear, for it is
paining me more than I like."

Sancho started to do as he was commanded, but one of the goatherds, when
he saw the wound, told him not to bother, that he would place a remedy upon
it that would heal it in no time. Taking a few leaves of rosemary, of which there
was a great deal growing thereabouts, he mashed them in his mouth and, mixing them with a little salt, laid them on the ear, with the assurance that no
other medicine was needed; and this proved to be the truth.

CHAPTER 12

Of the story that one of the goatherds told to Don Quixote and the others.

Just then, another lad came up, one of those who brought the goatherds their
provisions from the village.

"Do you know what's happening down there, my friends?" he said.

"How should we know?" one of the men answered him.

"In that case," the lad went on, "I must tell you that the famous student and
shepherd known as Grisóstomo died this morning, muttering that the cause of
his death was the love he had for that bewitched lass of a Marcela, daughter of

the wealthy Guillermo—you know, the one who's been going around in these parts dressed like a shepherdess."

"For love of Marcela, you say?" one of the herders spoke up.

"That is what I'm telling you," replied the other lad. "And the best part of it is that he left directions in his will that he was to be buried in the field, as if he were a Moor, and that his grave was to be at the foot of the cliff where the Cork Tree Spring is; for, according to report, and he is supposed to have said so himself, that is the place where he saw her for the first time. There were other provisions, which the clergy of the village say cannot be carried out, nor would it be proper to fulfill them, seeing that they savor of heathen practices. But Grisóstomo's good friend, the student Ambrosio, who also dresses like a shepherd, insists that everything must be done to the letter, and as a result there is great excitement in the village.

"Nevertheless, from all I can hear, they will end by doing as Ambrosio and Grisóstomo's other friends desire, and tomorrow they will bury him with great ceremony in the place that I have mentioned. I believe it is going to be something worth seeing; at any rate, I mean to see it, even though it is too far for me to be able to return to the village before nightfall."

"We will all do the same," said the other goatherds. "We will cast lots to see who stays to watch the goats."

"That is right, Pedro," said one of their number, "but it will not be necessary to go to the trouble of casting lots. I will take care of the flocks for all of us; and do not think that I am being generous or that I am not as curious as the rest of you; it is simply that I cannot walk on account of the splinter I picked up in this foot the other day."

"Well, we thank you just the same," said Pedro.

Don Quixote then asked Pedro to tell him more about the dead man and the shepherd lass; to which the latter replied that all he knew was that Grisóstomo was a rich gentleman who had lived in a near-by village. He had been a student for many years at Salamanca and then had returned to his birthplace with the reputation of being very learned and well read; he was especially noted for his knowledge of the science of the stars and what the sun and moon were doing up there in the heavens, "for he would promptly tell us when their clips was to come."

"*Eclipse*, my friend, not *clips*," said Don Quixote, "is the name applied to the darkening-over of those major luminaries."

But Pedro, not pausing for any trifles, went on with his story. "He could also tell when the year was going to be plentiful or estil—"

"*Sterile*, you mean to say, friend—"

"*Sterile* or *estil*," said Pedro, "it all comes out the same in the end. But I can tell you one thing, that his father and his friends, who believed in him, did just as he advised them and they became rich; for he would say to them, 'This year, sow barley and not wheat'; and again, 'Sow chickpeas and not barley'; or, 'This season there will be a good crop of oil[4] but the three following ones you will not get a drop.'"

"That science," Don Quixote explained, "is known as astrology."

4. Olive oil.

"I don't know what it's called," said Pedro, "but he knew all this and more yet. Finally, not many months after he returned from Salamanca, he appeared one day dressed like a shepherd with crook and sheepskin jacket; for he had resolved to lay aside the long gown that he wore as a scholar, and in this he was joined by Ambrosio, a dear friend of his and the companion of his studies. I forgot to tell you that Grisóstomo was a great one for composing verses; he even wrote the carols for Christmas Eve and the plays that were performed at Corpus Christi by the lads of our village, and everyone said that they were the best ever.

"When the villagers saw the two scholars coming out dressed like shepherds, they were amazed and could not imagine what was the reason for such strange conduct on their part. It was about that time that Grisóstomo's father died and left him the heir to a large fortune, consisting of land and chattels, no small quantity of cattle, and a considerable sum of money, of all of which the young man was absolute master; and, to tell the truth, he deserved it, for he was very sociable and charitably inclined, a friend to all worthy folk, and he had a face that was like a benediction. Afterward it was learned that if he had changed his garments like this, it was only that he might be able to wander over the waste-lands on the trail of that shepherdess Marcela of whom our friend was speaking, for the poor fellow had fallen in love with her. And now I should like to tell you, for it is well that you should know, just who this lass is; for it may be—indeed, there is no maybe about it—you will never hear the like in all the days of your life, though you live to be older than Sarna."

"You should say *Sarah*," Don Quixote corrected him; for he could not bear hearing the goatherd using the wrong words all the time.[5]

"The itch," said Pedro, "lives long enough; and if, sir, you go on interrupting me at every word, we'll never be through in a year."

"Pardon me, friend," said Don Quixote, "it was only because there is so great a difference between Sarna and Sarah that I pointed it out to you; but you have given me a very good answer, for the itch does live longer than Sarah; and so go on with your story, and I will not contradict you any more."

"I was about to say, then, my dear sir," the goatherd went on, "that in our village there was a farmer who was richer still than Grisóstomo's father. His name was Guillermo, and, over and above his great wealth, God gave him a daughter whose mother, the most highly respected woman in these parts, died in bearing her. It seems to me I can see the good lady now, with that face that rivaled the sun and moon; and I remember, above all, what a friend she was to the poor, for which reason I believe that her soul at this very moment must be enjoying God's presence in the other world.

"Grieving for the loss of so excellent a wife, Guillermo himself died, leaving his daughter Marcela, now a rich young woman, in the custody of one of her uncles, a priest who holds a benefice in our village. The girl grew up with such beauty as to remind us of her mother, beautiful as that lady had been. By the time she was fourteen or fifteen no one looked at her without giving thanks to God who had created such comeliness, and almost all were hopelessly in love with her. Her uncle kept her very closely shut up, but, for all of that, word of

5. Actually in this case the goatherd is not really wrong, for *sarna* means "itch" and "older than the itch" was a proverbial expression.

her great beauty spread to such an extent that by reason of it, as much as on account of the girl's wealth, her uncle found himself besought and importuned not only by the young men of our village, but by those for leagues around who desired to have her for a wife.

"But he, an upright Christian, although he wished to marry her off as soon as she was of age, had no desire to do so without her consent, not that he had any eye to the gain and profit which the custody of his niece's property brought him while her marriage was deferred. Indeed, this much was said in praise of the good priest in more than one circle of the village; for I would have you know, Sir Knight, that in these little places everything is discussed and becomes a subject of gossip; and you may rest assured, as I am for my part, that a priest must be more than ordinarily good if his parishioners feel bound to speak well of him, especially in the small towns."

"That is true," said Don Quixote, "but go on. I like your story very much, and you, good Pedro, tell it with very good grace."

"May the Lord's grace never fail me, for that is what counts. But to go on: Although the uncle set forth to his niece the qualities of each one in particular of the many who sought her hand, begging her to choose and marry whichever one she pleased, she never gave him any answer other than this: that she did not wish to marry at all, since being but a young girl she did not feel that she was equal to bearing the burdens of matrimony. As her reasons appeared to be proper and just, the uncle did not insist but thought he would wait until she was a little older, when she would be capable of selecting someone to her taste. For, he said, and quite right he was, parents ought not to impose a way of life upon their children against the latters' will. And then, one fine day, lo and behold, there was the finical Marcela turned shepherdess; and without paying any attention to her uncle or all those of the village who advised against it, she set out to wander through the fields with the other lasses, guarding flocks as they did.

"Well, the moment she appeared in public and her beauty was uncovered for all to see, I really cannot tell you how many rich young bachelors, gentlemen, and farmers proceeded to don a shepherd's garb and go to make love to her in the meadows. One of her suitors, as I have told you, was our deceased friend, and it is said that he did not love but adored her. But you must not think that because Marcela chose so free and easy a life, and one that offers little or no privacy, that she was thereby giving the faintest semblance of encouragement to those who would disparage her modesty and prudence; rather, so great was the vigilance with which she looked after her honor that of all those who waited upon her and solicited her favors, none could truly say that she had given him the slightest hope of attaining his desire.

"For although she does not flee nor shun the company and conversation of the shepherds, treating them in courteous and friendly fashion, the moment she discovers any intentions on their part, even though it be the just and holy one of matrimony, she hurls them from her like a catapult. As a result, she is doing more damage in this land than if a plague had fallen upon it; for her beauty and graciousness win the hearts of all who would serve her, but her disdain and the disillusionment it brings lead them in the end to despair, and then they can only call her cruel and ungrateful, along with other similar epithets that reveal all too plainly the state of mind that prompts them. If you were to stay here some time, sir, you would hear these uplands and valleys echo with the laments of those who have followed her only to be deceived.

"Not far from here is a place where there are a couple of dozen tall beeches, and there is not a one of them on whose smooth bark Marcela's name has not been engraved; and above some of these inscriptions you will find a crown, as if by this her lover meant to indicate that she deserved to wear the garland of beauty above all the women on the earth. Here a shepherd sighs and there another voices his lament. Now are to be heard amorous ballads, and again despairing ditties. One will spend all the hours of the night seated at the foot of some oak or rock without once closing his tearful eyes, and the morning sun will find him there, stupefied and lost in thought. Another, without giving truce or respite to his sights, will lie stretched upon the burning sands in the full heat of the most exhausting summer noontide, sending up his complaint to merciful Heaven.

"And, meanwhile, over this one and that one, over one and all, the beauteous Marcela triumphs and goes her own way, free and unconcerned. All those of us who know her are waiting to see how far her pride will carry her, and who will be the fortunate man who will succeed in taming this terrible creature and thus come into possession of a beauty so matchless as hers. Knowing all this that I have told you to be undoubtedly true, I can readily believe this lad's story about the cause of Grisóstomo's death. And so I advise you, sir, not to fail to be present tomorrow at his burial; it will be well worth seeing, for he has many friends, and the place is not half a league from here."

"I will make a point of it," said Don Quixote, "and I thank you for the pleasure you have given me by telling me so delightful a tale."

"Oh," said the goatherd, "I do not know the half of the things that have happened to Marcela's lovers; but it is possible that tomorrow we may meet along the way some shepherd who will tell us more. And now it would be well for you to go and sleep under cover, for the night air may not be good for your wound, though with the remedy that has been put on it there is not much to fear."

Sancho Panza, who had been sending the goatherd to the devil for talking so much, now put in a word with his master, urging him to come and sleep in Pedro's hut. Don Quixote did so; and all the rest of the night was spent by him in thinking of his lady Dulcinea, in imitation of Marcela's lovers. As for Sancho, he made himself comfortable between Rocinante and the ass and at once dropped off to sleep, not like a lovelorn swain but, rather, like a man who has had a sound kicking that day.

CHAPTER 13

In which is brought to a close the story of the shepherdess Marcela, along with other events.

Day had barely begun to appear upon the balconies of the east when five or six goatherds arose and went to awaken Don Quixote and tell him that if he was still of a mind to go see Grisóstomo's famous burial they would keep him company. The knight, desiring nothing better, ordered Sancho to saddle at once, which was done with much dispatch, and then they all set out forthwith.

They had not gone more than a quarter of a league when, upon crossing a footpath, they saw coming toward them six shepherds clad in black sheepskins and with garlands of cypress and bitter rosebay on their heads. Each of them carried a thick staff made of the wood of the holly, and with them came two gentlemen on horseback in handsome traveling attire, accompanied by three lads on foot. As the two parties met they greeted each other courteously, each inquiring as to the other's destination, where upon they learned that they were all going to the burial, and so continued to ride along together.

Speaking to his companion, one of them said, "I think, Señor Vivaldo, that we are going to be well repaid for the delay it will cost us to see this famous funeral; for famous it must surely be, judging by the strange things that these shepherds have told us of the dead man and the homicidal shepherdess."

"I think so too," agreed Vivaldo. "I should be willing to delay our journey not one day, but four, for the sake of seeing it."

Don Quixote then asked them what it was they had heard of Marcela and Grisóstomo. The traveler replied that on that very morning they had fallen in with those shepherds and, seeing them so mournfully trigged out, had asked them what the occasion for it was. One of the fellows had then told them of the beauty and strange demeanor of a shepherdess by the name of Marcela, her many suitors, and the death of this Grisóstomo, to whose funeral they were bound. He related, in short, the entire story as Don Quixote had heard it from Pedro.

Changing the subject, the gentleman called Vivaldo inquired of Don Quixote what it was that led him to go armed in that manner in a land that was so peaceful.

"The calling that I profess," replied Don Quixote, "does not permit me to do otherwise. An easy pace, pleasure, and repose—those things were invented for delicate courtiers; but toil, anxiety, and arms—they are for those whom the world knows as knights-errant, of whom I, though unworthy, am the very least."

No sooner had they heard this than all of them immediately took him for a madman. By way of assuring himself further and seeing what kind of madness it was of which Don Quixote was possessed, Vivaldo now asked him what was meant by the term knights-errant.

"Have not your Worships read the annals and the histories of England that treat of the famous exploits of King Arthur, who in our Castilian balladry is always called King Artús? According to a very old tradition that is common throughout the entire realm of Great Britain, this king did not die, but by an act of enchantment was changed into a raven; and in due course of time he is to return and reign once more, recovering his kingdom and his scepter; for which reason, from that day to this, no Englishman is known to have killed one of those birds. It was, moreover, in the time of that good king that the famous order of the Knights of the Round Table was instituted; and as for the love of Sir Lancelot of the Lake and Queen Guinevere, everything took place exactly as the story has it, their confidante and go-between being the honored matron Quintañona; whence comes that charming ballad that is such a favorite with us Spaniards:

> Never was there a knight
> So served by maid and dame
> As the one they call Sir Lancelot
> When from Britain he came—

to carry on the gentle, pleasing course of his loves and noble deeds.

"From that time forth, the order of chivalry was passed on and propagated from one individual to another until it had spread through many and various parts of the world. Among those famed for their exploits was the valiant Amadis of Gaul, with all his sons and grandsons to the fifth generation; and there was also the brave Felixmarte of Hircania, and the never sufficiently praised Tirant lo Blanch; and in view of the fact that he lived in our own day, almost, we came near to seeing, hearing, and conversing with that other courageous knight, Don Belianís of Greece.

"And that, gentlemen, is what it means to be a knight-errant, and what I have been telling you of is the order of chivalry which such a knight professes, an order to which, as I have already informed you, I, although a sinner, have the honor of belonging; for I have made the same profession as have those other knights. That is why it is you find me in these wild and lonely places, riding in quest of adventure, being resolved to offer my arm and my person in the most dangerous undertaking fate may have in store for me, that I may be of aid to the weak and needy."

Listening to this speech, the travelers had some while since come to the conclusion that Don Quixote was out of his mind, and were likewise able to perceive the peculiar nature of his madness, and they wondered at it quite as much as did all those who encountered it for the first time. Being endowed with a ready wit and a merry disposition and thinking to pass the time until they reached the end of the short journey which, so he was told, awaited them before they should arrive at the mountain where the burial was to take place, Vivaldo decided to give him a further opportunity of displaying his absurdities.

"It strikes me, Sir Knight-errant," he said, "that your Grace has espoused one of the most austere professions to be found anywhere on earth—even more austere, if I am not mistaken, than that of the Carthusian monks."

"Theirs may be as austere as ours," Don Quixote replied, "but that it is as necessary I am very much inclined to doubt. For if the truth be told, the soldier who carries out his captain's order does no less than the captain who gives the order. By that I mean to say that the religious, in all peace and tranquility, pray to Heaven for earth's good, but we soldiers and knights put their prayers into execution by defending with the might of our good right arms and at the edge of the sword those things for which they pray; and we do this not under cover of a roof but under the open sky, beneath the insufferable rays of the summer sun and the biting cold of winter. Thus we become the ministers of God on earth, and our arms the means by which He executes His decrees. And just as war and all the things that have to do with it are impossible without toil, sweat, and anxiety, it follows that those who have taken upon themselves such a profession must unquestionably labor harder than do those who in peace and tranquility and at their ease pray God to favor the ones who can do little in their own behalf.

"I do not mean to say—I should not think of saying—that the state of knight-errant is as holy as that of the cloistered monk; I merely would imply, from what I myself endure, that ours is beyond a doubt the more laborious and arduous calling, more beset by hunger and thirst, more wretched, ragged, and ridden with lice. It is an absolute certainty that the knights-errant of old experienced much misfortune in the course of their lives; and if some by their might and valor came to be emperors, you may take my word for it, it cost them dearly in blood and sweat, and if those who rose to such a rank had lacked enchanters and magicians to aid them, they surely would have been cheated of their desires, deceived in their hopes and expectations."

"I agree with you on that," said the traveler, "but there is one thing among others that gives me a very bad impression of the knights-errant, and that is the fact that when they are about to enter upon some great and perilous adventure in which they are in danger of losing their lives, they never at that moment think of commending themselves to God as every good Christian is obliged to do under similar circumstances, but, rather, commend themselves to their ladies with as much fervor and devotion as if their mistresses were God himself; all of which to me smacks somewhat of paganism."

"Sir," Don Quixote answered him, "it could not by any means be otherwise; the knight-errant who did not do so would fall into disgrace, for it is the usage and custom of chivalry that the knight, before engaging in some great feat of arms, shall behold his lady in front of him and shall turn his eyes toward her, gently and lovingly, as if beseeching her favor and protection in the hazardous encounter that awaits him, and even though no one hears him, he is obliged to utter certain words between his teeth, commending himself to her with all his heart; and of this we have numerous examples in the histories. Nor is it to be assumed that he does not commend himself to God also, but the time and place for that is in the course of the undertaking."

"All the same," said the traveler, "I am not wholly clear in this matter; for I have often read of two knights-errant exchanging words until, one word leading to another, their wrath is kindled; whereupon, turning their steeds and taking a good run up the field, they whirl about and bear down upon each other at full speed, commending themselves to their ladies in the midst of it all. What commonly happens then is that one of the two topples from his horse's flanks and is run through and through with the other's lance; and his adversary would also fall to the ground if he did not cling to his horse's mane. What I do not understand is how the dead man would have had time to commend himself to God in the course of this accelerated combat. It would be better if the words he wasted in calling upon his lady as he ran toward the other knight had been spent in paying the debt that he owed as a Christian. Moreover, it is my personal opinion that not all knights-errant have ladies to whom to commend themselves, for not all of them are in love."

"That," said Don Quixote, "is impossible. I assert there can be no knight-errant without a lady; for it is as natural and proper for them to be in love as it is for the heavens to have stars, and I am quite sure that no one ever read a story in which a loveless man of arms was to be met with, for the simple reason that such a one would not be looked upon as a legitimate knight but as a bastard one who had entered the fortress of chivalry not by the main gate, but over the walls, like a robber and a thief."

"Nevertheless," said the traveler, "if my memory serves me right, I have read that Don Galaor, brother of the valorous Amadis of Gaul, never had a special lady to whom he prayed, yet he was not held in any the less esteem for that but was a very brave and famous knight."

Once again, our Don Quixote had an answer. "Sir, one swallow does not make a summer. And in any event, I happen to know that this knight was secretly very much in love. As for his habit of paying court to all the ladies that caught his fancy, that was a natural propensity on his part and one that he was unable to resist. There was, however, one particular lady whom he had made the mistress of his will and to whom he did commend himself very frequently and privately; for he prided himself upon being a reticent knight."

"Well, then," said the traveler, "if it is essential that every knight-errant be in love, it is to be presumed that your Grace is also, since you are of the profession. And unless it be that you pride yourself upon your reticence as much as did Don Galaor, then I truly, on my own behalf and in the name of all this company, beseech your Grace to tell us your lady's name, the name of the country where she resides, what her rank is, and something of the beauty of her person, that she may esteen herself fortunate in having all the world know that she is loved and served by such a knight as your Grace appears to me to be."

At this, Don Quixote heaved a deep sigh. "I cannot say," he began, "as to whether or not my sweet enemy would be pleased that all the world should know I serve her. I can only tell you, in response to the question which you have so politely put to me, that her name is Dulcinea, her place of residence El Toboso, a village of La Mancha. As to her rank, she should be at the very least a princess, seeing that she is my lady and my queen. Her beauty is superhuman, for in it are realized all the impossible and chimerical attributes that poets are accustomed to give their fair ones. Her locks are golden, her brow the Elysian Fields, her eyebrows rainbows, her eyes suns, her cheeks roses, her lips coral, her teeth pearls, her neck alabaster, her bosom marble, her hands ivory, her complexion snow-white. As for those parts which modesty keeps covered from the human sight, it is my opinion that, discreetly considered, they are only to be extolled and not compared to any other."

"We should like," said Vivaldo, "to know something as well of her lineage, her race and ancestry."

"She is not," said Don Quixote, "of the ancient Roman Curtii, Caii, or Scipios, nor of the modern Colonnas and Orsini, nor of the Moncades and Requesenses of Catalonia, nor is she of the Rebellas and Villanovas of Valencia, or the Palafoxes, Nuzas, Rocabertis, Corellas, Lunas, Alagones, Urreas, or Gurreas of Aragon, the Cerdas, Manriques, Mendozas, or Guzmanes of Castile, the Alencastros, Pallas, or Menezes of Portugal; but she is of the Tobosos of La Mancha, and although the line is a modern one, it well may give rise to the most illustrious families of the centuries to come. And let none dispute this with me, unless it be under the conditions which Zerbino has set forth in the inscription beneath Orlando's arms:

> These let none move
> Who dares not with Orlando his valor prove."[6]

"Although my own line," replied the traveler, "is that of the Gachupins of Laredo, I should not venture to compare it with the Tobosos of La Mancha, in view of the fact that, to tell you the truth, I have never heard the name before."

6. From Ludovico Ariosto's *Orlando Furioso*, canto 24, stanza 57.

"How does it come that you have never heard it!" exclaimed Don Quixote.

The others were listening most attentively to the conversation of these two, and even the goatherds and shepherds were by now aware that our knight of La Mancha was more than a little insane. Sancho Panza alone thought that all his master said was the truth, for he was well acquainted with him, having known him since birth. The only doubt in his mind had to do with the beauteous Dulcinea del Toboso, for he knew of no such princess and the name was strange to his ears, although he lived not far from that place.

They were continuing on their way, conversing in this manner, when they caught sight of some twenty shepherds coming through the gap between two high mountains, all of them clad in black woolen garments and with wreaths on their heads, some of the garlands, as was afterward learned, being of cypress, others of yew. Six of them were carrying a bier covered with a great variety of flowers and boughs.

"There they come with Grisóstomo's body," said one of the goatherds, "and the foot of the mountain yonder is where he wished to be buried."

They accordingly quickened their pace and arrived just as those carrying the bier had set it down on the ground. Four of the shepherds with sharpened picks were engaged in digging a grave alongside the barren rock. After a courteous exchange of greetings, Don Quixote and his companions turned to look at the bier. Upon it lay a corpse covered with flowers, the body of a man dressed like a shepherd and around thirty years of age. Even in death it could be seen that he had had a handsome face and had been of a jovial disposition. Round about him upon the bier were a number of books and many papers, open and folded.

Meanwhile, those who stood gazing at the dead man and those who were digging the grave—everyone present, in fact—preserved an awed silence, until one of the pallbearers said to another. "Look well, Ambrosio, and make sure that this is the place that Grisóstomo had in mind, since you are bent upon carrying out to the letter the provisions of his will."

"This is it," replied Ambrosio; "for many times my unfortunate friend told me the story of his misadventure. He told me that it was here that he first laid eyes upon that mortal enemy of the human race, and it was here, also, that he first revealed to her his passion, for he was as honorable as he was lovelorn; and it was here, finally, at their last meeting, that she shattered his illusions and showed him her disdain, thus bringing to an end the tragedy of his wretched life. And here, in memory of his great misfortune, he wished to be laid in the bowels of eternal oblivion."

Then, turning to Don Quixote and the travelers, he went on, "This body, gentlemen, on which you now look with pitying eyes was the depository of a soul which heaven had endowed with a vast share of its riches. This is the body of Grisóstomo, who was unrivaled in wit, unequaled in courtesy, supreme in gentleness of bearing, a model of friendship, generous without stint, grave without conceit, merry without being vulgar—in short, first in all that is good and second to none in the matter of misfortunes. He loved well and was hated, he adored and was disdained; he wooed a wild beast, importuned a piece of marble, ran after the wind, cried out to loneliness, waited upon ingratitude, and his reward was to be the spoils of death midway in his life's course—a life that was brought to an end by a shepherdess whom he sought to immortalize that she might live on in the memory of mankind, as those papers that you see there would very plainly show if he had not commanded me to consign them to the flames even as his body is given to the earth."

"You," said Vivaldo, "would treat them with greater harshness and cruelty than their owner himself, for it is neither just nor fitting to carry out the will of one who commands what is contrary to all reason. It would not have been a good thing for Augustus Caesar to consent to have them execute the behests of the divine Mantuan in his last testament.[7] And so, Señor Ambrosio, while you may give the body of your friend to the earth, you ought not to give his writings to oblivion. If out of bitterness he left such an order, that does not mean that you are to obey it without using your own discretion. Rather, by granting life to these papers, you permit Marcela's cruelheartedness to live forever and serve as an example to the others in the days that are to come in order that they may flee and avoid such pitfalls as these.

"I and those that have come with me know the story of this lovesick and despairing friend of yours; we know the affection that was between you, and what the occasion of his death was, and the things that he commanded be done as his life drew to a close. And from this lamentable tale anyone may see how great was Marcela's cruelty; they may behold Grisóstomo's love, the loyalty that lay in your friendship, and the end that awaits those who run headlong, with unbridled passion, down the path that doting love opens before their gaze. Last night we heard of your friend's death and learned that he was to be buried here, and out of pity and curiosity we turned aside from our journey and resolved to come see with our own eyes that which had aroused so much compassion when it was told to us. And in requital of that compassion, and the desire that has been born in us to prevent if we can a recurrence of such tragic circumstances, we beg you, O prudent Ambrosio!—or, at least, I for my part implore you—to give up your intention of burning these papers and let me carry some of them away with me."

Without waiting for the shepherd to reply he put out his hand and took a few of those that were nearest him.

"Out of courtesy, sir," said Ambrosio when he saw this, "I will consent for you to keep those that you have taken; but it is vain to think that I will refrain from burning the others."

Vivaldo, who was anxious to find out what was in the papers, opened one of them and perceived that it bore the title "Song of Despair."

Hearing this, Ambrosio said, "That is the last thing the poor fellow wrote; and in order, sir, that you may see the end to which his misfortunes brought him, read it aloud if you will, for we shall have time for it while they are digging the grave."

"That I will very willingly do," said Vivaldo.

And since all the bystanders had the same desire, they gathered around as he in a loud clear voice read the following poem.

---

7. Virgil (born near Mantua) had left instructions that his Roman epic, the *Aeneid*, should be burned.

CHAPTER 14

*In which are set down the despairing verses of the deceased shepherd,
with other unlooked-for happenings.*

Grisóstomo's Song

Since thou desirest that thy cruelty
Be spread from tongue to tongue and land to land,
The unrelenting sternness of thy heart
Shall turn my bosom's hell to minstrelsy
That all men everywhere may understand   5
The nature of my grief and what thou art.
And as I seek my sorrows to impart,
Telling of all the things that thou hast done,
My very entrails shall speak out to brand
Thy heartlessness, thy soul to reprimand,   10
Where no compassion ever have I won.
Then listen well, lend an attentive ear;
This ballad that thou art about to hear
Is not contrived by art; 'tis a simple song
Such as shepherds sing each day throughout the year—   15
Surcease of pain for me, for thee a prong.
        Then let the roar of lion, fierce wolf's cry,
The horrid hissing of the scaly snake,
The terrifying sound of monsters strange,
Ill-omened call of crow against the sky,   20
The howling of the wind as it doth shake
The tossing sea where all is constant change,
Bellow of vanquished bull that cannot range
As it was wont to do, the piteous sob
Of the widowed dove as if its heart would break,   25
Hoot of the envied owl,[8] ever awake,
From hell's own choir the deep and mournful throb—
Let all these sounds come forth and mingle now.
For if I'm to tell my woes, why then, I vow,
I must new measures find, new modes invent,   30
With sound confusing sense, I may somehow
Portray the inferno where my days are spent.
        The mournful echoes of my murmurous plaint
Father Tagus shall not hear as he rolls his sand,
Nor olive-bordered Betis;[9] my lament shall be   35
To the tall and barren rock as I acquaint
The caves with my sorrow; the far and lonely strand
No human foot has trod shall hear from me
The story of thine inhumanity
As told with lifeless tongue but living word.   40
I'll tell it to the valleys near at hand
Where never shines the sun upon the land;

---

8. Envied by other birds as the only one that
witnessed the Crucifixion.

9. The Guadalquivir. "Father Tagus": the river
Tagus.

By venomous serpents shall my tale be heard
On the low-lying, marshy river plain.
And yet, the telling will not be in vain; 45
For the reverberations of my plight,
Thy matchless austerity and this my pain,
Through the wide world shall go, thee to indict.
   Disdain may kill; suspicion false or true
May slay all patience; deadliest of all 50
Is jealousy; while absence renders life
Worse than a void; Hope lends no roseate hue
Against forgetfulness or the dread call
Of death inevitable, the end of strife.
Yet—unheard miracle!—with sorrows rife, 55
My own existence somehow still goes on;
The flame of life with me doth rise and fall.
Jealous I am, disdained; I know the gall
Of those suspicions that will not be gone,
Which leave me not the shadow of a hope, 60
And, desperate, I will not even grope
But rather will endure until the end,
And with despair eternally I'll cope,
Knowing that things for me will never mend.
   Can one both hope and fear at the same season? 65
Would it be well to do so in any case,
Seeing that fear, by far, hath the better excuse?
Confronting jealousy, is there any reason
For me to close my eyes to its stern face,
Pretend to see it not? What is the use, 70
When its dread presence I can still deduce
From countless gaping wounds deep in my heart?
When suspicion—bitter change!—to truth gives place,
And truth itself, losing its virgin grace,
Becomes a lie, is it not wisdom's part 75
To open wide the door to frank mistrust?
When disdain's unveiled, to doubt is only just.
O ye fierce tyrants of Love's empery!
Shackle these hands with stout cord, if ye must.
My pain shall drown your triumph—woe is me! 80
   I die, in short, and since nor life nor death
Yields any hope, to my fancy will I cling.
That man is freest who is Love's bond slave:
I'll say this with my living-dying breath,
And the ancient tyrant's praises I will sing. 85
Love is the greatest blessing Heaven e'er gave.
What greater beauty could a lover crave
Than that which my fair enemy doth show
In soul and body and in everything?
E'en her forgetfulness of me doth spring 90
From my own lack of grace, that I well know.
In spite of all the wrongs that he has wrought,
Love rules his empire justly as he ought.

Throw all to the winds and speed life's wretched span
By feeding on his self-deluding thought.   95
No blessing holds the future that I scan.
    Thou whose unreasonableness reason doth give
For putting an end to this tired life of mine,
From the deep heart wounds which thou mayest plainly see,
Judge if the better course be to die or live.   100
Gladly did I surrender my will to thine,
Gladly I suffered all thou didst to me;
And now that I'm dying, should it seem to thee
My death is worth a tear from thy bright eyes,
Pray hold it back, fair one, do not repine,   105
For I would have from thee no faintest sign
Of penitence, e'en though my soul thy prize.
Rather, I'd have thee laugh, be very gay,
And let my funeral be a festive day—
But I am very simple! knowing full well   110
That thou art bound to go thy blithesome way,
And my untimely end thy fame shall swell.
    Come, thirsting Tantalus from out Hell's pit;
Come, Sisyphus with the terrifying weight
Of that stone thou rollest; Tityus, bring   115
Thy vulture and thine anguish infinite;
Ixion[1] with thy wheel, be thou not late;
Come, too, ye sisters ever laboring;[2]
Come all, your griefs into my bosom fling,
And then, with lowered voices, intone a dirge,   120
If dirge be fitting for one so desperate,
A body without a shroud, unhappy fate!
And Hell's three-headed gateman,[3] do thou emerge
With a myriad other phantoms, monstrous swarm,
Beings infernal of fantastic form,   125
Raising their voices for the uncomforted
In a counterpoint of grief, harmonious storm.
What better burial for a lover dead?
    Despairing song of mine, do not complain,
Nor let our parting cause thee any pain,   130
For my misfortune is not wholly bad,
Seeing her fortune's bettered by my demise.
Then, even in the grave, be thou not sad.

Those who had listened to Grisóstomo's poem liked it well enough, but the one who read it remarked that it did not appear to him to conform to what had been told him of Marcela's modesty and virtue, seeing that in it the author

---

1. In Greek myth, all four are proverbial images of mortals punished by the Gods with different forms of torture: *Tantalus*, craving water and fruit which he always fails to reach; *Sisyphus*, forever vainly trying to roll a stone upward to the top of a hill; *Tityus*, having his liver devoured by a vulture; and *Ixion*, being bound to a revolving wheel.
2. In classical mythology the three Fates (Moerae to the Greeks, Parcae to the Romans), spinners of man's destiny.
3. Cerberus, a doglike three-headed monster, the mythological guardian of Hell.

complains of jealousy, suspicion, and absence, all to the prejudice of her good name. To this Ambrosio, as one who had known his friend's most deeply hidden thoughts, replied as follows:

"By way of satisfying, sir, the doubt that you entertain, it is well for you to know that when the unfortunate man wrote that poem, he was by his own volition absent from Marcela, to see if this would work a cure; but when the enamored one is away from his love, there is nothing that does not inspire in him fear and torment, and such was the case with Grisóstomo, for whom jealous imaginings, fears, and suspicions became a seeming reality. And so, in this respect, Marcela's reputation for virtue remains unimpaired; beyond being cruel and somewhat arrogant, and exceedingly disdainful, she could not be accused by the most envious of any other fault."

"Yes, that is so," said Vivaldo.

He was about to read another of the papers he had saved from the fire when he was stopped by a marvelous vision—for such it appeared—that suddenly met his sight; for there atop the rock beside which the grave was being hollowed out stood the shepherdess Marcela herself, more beautiful even than she was reputed to be. Those who up to then had never seen her looked on in silent admiration, while those who were accustomed to beholding her were held in as great a suspense as the ones who were gazing upon her for the first time.

No sooner had Ambrosio glimpsed her than, with a show of indignation, he called out to her, "So, fierce basilisk[4] of these mountains, have you perchance come to see if in your presence blood will flow from the wounds of this poor wretch whom you by your cruelty have deprived of life?[5] Have you come to gloat over your inhuman exploits, or would you from that height look down like another pitiless Nero upon your Rome in flames and ashes?[6] Or perhaps you would arrogantly tread under foot this poor corpse, as an ungrateful daughter did that of her father Tarquinius?[7] Tell us quickly why you have come and what it is that you want most; for I know that Grisóstomo thoughts never failed to obey you in life, and though he is dead now, I will see that all those who call themselves his friends obey you likewise."

"I do not come, O Ambrosio, for any of the reasons that you have mentioned," replied Marcela. "I come to defend myself and to demonstrate how unreasonable all those persons are who blame me for their sufferings and for Grisóstomo's death. I therefore ask all present to hear me attentively. It will not take long and I shall not have to spend many words in persuading those of you who are sensible that I speak the truth.

"Heaven made me beautiful, you say, so beautiful that you are compelled to love me whether you will or no; and in return for the love that you show me,

---

4. A mythical lizardlike creature whose look and breath were supposed to be lethal.
5. According to folklore, the corpse of a murdered person was supposed to bleed in the presence of the murderer.
6. The Roman emperor Nero is supposed, in tale and proverb, to have been singing while from a tower he observed the burning of Rome

in 64 C.E.
7. The inaccurate allusion is to Tullia, actually the wife of the last of the legendary kings of early Rome, Tarquinius; she let the wheel of her carriage trample over the body of her father—the previous king Servius Tullius—whom her husband Tarquinius had liquidated.

you would have it that I am obliged to love you in return. I know, with that natural understanding that God has given me, that everything beautiful is lovable; but I cannot see that it follows that the object that is loved for its beauty must love the one who loves it. Let us suppose that the lover of the beautiful were ugly and, being ugly, deserved to be shunned; it would then be highly absurd for him to say, 'I love you because you are beautiful; you must love me because I am ugly.'

"But assuming that two individuals are equally beautiful, it does not mean that their desires are the same; for not all beauty inspires love, but may sometimes merely delight the eye and leave the will intact. If it were otherwise, no one would know what he wanted, but all would wander vaguely and aimlessly with nothing upon which to settle their affections; for the number of beautiful objects being infinite, desires similarly would be boundless. I have heard it said that true love knows no division and must be voluntary and not forced. This being so, as I believe it is, then why would you compel me to surrender my will for no other reason than that you say you love me? But tell me: supposing that Heaven which made me beautiful had made me ugly instead, should I have any right to complain because you did not love me? You must remember, moreover, that I did not choose this beauty that is mine; such as it is, Heaven gave it to me of its grace, without any choice or asking on my part. As the viper is not to be blamed for the deadly poison that it bears, since that is a gift of nature, so I do not deserve to be reprehended for my comeliness of form.

"Beauty in a modest woman is like a distant fire or a sharp-edged sword: the one does not burn, the other does not cut, those who do not come near it. Honor and virtue are the adornments of the soul, without which the body is not beautiful though it may appear to be. If modesty is one of the virtues that most adorn and beautify body and soul, why should she who is loved for her beauty part with that virtue merely to satisfy the whim of one who solely for his own pleasure strives with all his force and energy to cause her to lose it? I was born a free being, and in order to live freely I chose the solitude of the fields; these mountain trees are my company, the clear-running waters in these brooks are my mirror, and to the trees and waters I communicate my thoughts and lend them of my beauty.

"In short, I am that distant fire, that sharp-edged sword, that does not burn or cut. Those who have been enamored by the sight of me I have disillusioned with my words; and if desire is sustained by hope, I gave none to Grisóstomo or any other, and of none of them can it be said that I killed them with my cruelty, for it was rather their own obstinacy that was to blame. And if you reproach me with the fact that his intentions were honorable and that I ought for that reason to have complied with them, I will tell you that when, on this very spot where his grave is now being dug, he revealed them to me, I replied that it was my own intention to live in perpetual solitude and that only the earth should enjoy the fruit of my retirement and the spoils of my beauty; and if he with all this plain-speaking was still stubbornly bent upon hoping against hope and sailing against the wind, is it to be wondered at if he drowned in the gulf of his own folly?

"Had I led him on, it would have been falsely; had I gratified his passion, it would have been against my own best judgment and intentions; but, though I had disillusioned him, he persisted, and though I did not hate him, he was driven to despair. Ask yourselves, then, if it is reasonable to blame me for his woes! Let him who has been truly deceived complain; let him despair who has been cheated of his promised hopes; if I have enticed any, let him speak up; if I have accepted the attentions of any, let him boast of it; but let not him to whom I have promised nothing, whom I have neither enticed nor accepted, apply to me such terms as cruel and homicidal. It has not as yet been Heaven's will to destine me to love any man, and there is no use expecting me to love of my own free choice.

"Let what I am saying now apply to each and every one of those who would have me for their own, and let it be understood from now on that if any die on account of me, he is not to be regarded as an unfortunate victim of jealousy, since she that cares for none can give to none the occasion for being jealous; nor is my plain-speaking to be taken as disdain. He who calls me a wild beast and a basilisk, let him leave me alone as something that is evil and harmful; let him who calls me ungrateful cease to wait upon me; let him who finds me strange shun my acquaintance; if I am cruel, do not run after me; in which case this wild beast, this basilisk, this strange, cruel, ungrateful creature will not run after them, seek them out, wait upon them, nor endeavor to know them in any way.

"The thing that killed Grisóstomo was his impatience and the impetuosity of his desire; so why blame my modest conduct and retiring life? If I choose to preserve my purity here in the company of the trees, how can he complain of my unwillingness to lose it who would have me keep it with other men? I, as you know, have a worldly fortune of my own and do not covet that of others. My life is a free one, and I do not wish to be subject to another in any way. I neither love nor hate anyone; I do not repel this one and allure that one; I do not play fast and loose with any. The modest conversation of these village lasses and the care of my goats is sufficient to occupy me. Those mountains there represent the bounds of my desire, and should my wishes go beyond them, it is but to contemplate the beauty of the heavens, that pathway by which the soul travels to its first dwelling place."

Saying this and without waiting for any reply, she turned her back and entered the thickest part of a near-by wood, leaving all present lost in admiration of her wit as well as her beauty. A few—those who had felt the powerful dart of her glances and bore the wounds inflicted by her lovely eyes—were of a mind to follow her, taking no heed of the plainly worded warning they had just had from her lips; whereupon Don Quixote, seeing this and thinking to himself that here was an opportunity to display his chivalry by succoring a damsel in distress, laid his hand upon the hilt of his sword and cried out, loudly and distinctly, "Let no person of whatever state or condition he may be dare to follow the beauteous Marcela under pain of incurring my furious wrath. She has shown with clear and sufficient reasons that little or no blame for Grisóstomo's death is to be attached to her; she has likewise shown how far she is from acceding to the desires of any of her suitors, and it is accordingly only just that in place of being hounded and persecuted she should be honored and esteemed by all good people in this world as the only woman in it who lives with such modesty and good intentions."

Whether it was due to Don Quixote's threats or because Ambrosio now told them that they should finish doing the things which his good friend had desired should be done, no one stirred from the spot until the burial was over and Grisóstomo's papers had been burned. As the body was laid in the grave, many tears were shed by the bystanders. Then they placed a heavy stone upon it until the slab which Ambrosio was thinking of having made should be ready, with an epitaph that was to read:

> Here lies a shepherd by love betrayed,
> His body cold in death,
> Who with his last and faltering breath
> Spoke of a faithless maid.
> He died by the cruel, heartless hand   5
> Of a coy and lovely lass,
> Who by bringing men to so sorry a pass
> Love's tyranny doth expand.

They then scattered many flowers and boughs over the top of the grave, and, expressing their condolences to the dead man's friend, Ambrosio, they all took their leave, including Vivaldo and his companions. Don Quixote now said good-by to the travelers as well, although they urged him to come with them to Seville, assuring him that he would find in every street and at every corner of that city more adventures than are to be met with anywhere else. He thanked them for the invitation and the courtesy they had shown him in offering it, but added that for the present he had no desire to visit Seville, not until he should have rid these mountains of the robbers and bandits of which they were said to be full.

Seeing that his mind was made up, the travelers did not urge him further but, bidding him another farewell, left him and continued on their way; and the reader may be sure that in the course of their journey they did not fail to discuss the story of Marcela and Grisóstomo as well as Don Quixote's madness. As for the good knight himself, he was resolved to go seek the shepherdess and offer her any service that lay in his power; but things did not turn out the way he expected. * * *

[Fighting the Sheep]

CHAPTER 18

In which is set forth the conversation that Sancho Panza had with his master, Don Quixote, along with other adventures deserving of record.

* * * Don Quixote caught sight down the road of a large cloud of dust that was drawing nearer.

"This, O Sancho," he said, turning to his squire, "is the day when you shall see the boon that fate has in store for me; this, I repeat, is the day when, as well as on any other, shall be displayed the valor of my good right arm. On this day I shall perform deeds that will be written down in the book of fame for all centuries to come. Do you see that dust cloud rising there, Sancho? That is the dust stirred up by a vast army marching in this direction and composed of many nations."

"At that rate," said Sancho, "there must be two of them, for there is another one just like it on the other side."

Don Quixote turned to look and saw that this was so. He was overjoyed by the thought that these were indeed two armies about to meet and clash in the middle of the broad plain; for at every hour and every moment his imagination was filled with battles, enchantments, nonsensical adventures, tales of love, amorous challenges, and the like, such as he had read of in the books of chivalry, and every word he uttered, every thought that crossed his mind, every act he performed, had to do with such things as these. The dust clouds he had sighted were raised by two large droves of sheep coming along the road in opposite directions, which by reason of the dust were not visible until they were close at hand, but Don Quixote insisted so earnestly that they were armies that Sancho came to believe it.

"Sir," he said, "what are we to do?"

"What are we to do?" echoed his master. "Favor and aid the weak and needy. I would inform you, Sancho, that the one coming toward us is led and commanded by the great emperor Alifanfarón, lord of the great isle of Trapobana. This other one at my back is that of his enemy, the king of the Garamantas, Pentapolín of the Rolled-up Sleeve, for he always goes into battle with his right arm bare."

"But why are they such enemies?" Sancho asked.

"Because," said Don Quixote, "this Alifanfarón is a terrible pagan and in love with Pentapolín's daughter, who is a very beautiful and gracious lady and a Christian, for which reason her father does not wish to give her to the pagan king unless the latter first abjures the law of the false prophet, Mohammed, and adopts the faith that is Pentapolín's own."

"Then, by my beard," said Sancho, "if Pentapolín isn't right, and I am going to aid him all I can."

"In that," said Don Quixote, "you will only be doing your duty; for to engage in battles of this sort you need not have been dubbed a knight."

"I can understand that," said Sancho, "but where are we going to put this ass so that we will be certain of finding him after the fray is over? As for going into battle on such a mount, I do not think that has been done up to now."

"That is true enough," said Don Quixote. "What you had best do with him is to turn him loose and run the risk of losing him; for after we emerge the victors we shall have so many horses that even Rocinante will be in danger of being exchanged for another. But listen closely to what I am about to tell you, for I wish to give you an account of the principal knights that are accompanying these two armies; and in order that you may be the better able to see and take note of them, let us retire to that hillock over there which will afford us a very good view."

They then stationed themselves upon a slight elevation from which they would have been able to see very well the two droves of sheep that Don Quixote took to be armies if it had not been for the blinding clouds of dust. In spite of this, however, the worthy gentleman contrived to behold in his imagination what he did not see and what did not exist in reality.

Raising his voice, he went on to explain, "That knight in the gilded armor that you see there, bearing upon his shield a crowned lion crouched at the feet of a damsel, is the valiant Laurcalco, lord of the Silver Bridge; the other with the golden flowers on his armor, and on his shield three crowns argent on an azure field, is the dread Micocolembo, grand duke of Quirocia. And that one on Micocolembo's right hand, with the limbs of a giant, is the ever undaunted Brandabarbarán de Boliche, lord of the three Arabias. He goes armored in a serpent's skin and has for shield a door which, so report has it, is one of those from the temple that Samson pulled down, that time when he avenged himself on his enemies with his own death.

"But turn your eyes in this direction, and you will behold at the head of the other army the ever victorious, never vanquished Timonel de Carcajona, prince of New Biscay, who comes with quartered arms—azure, vert, argent, and or—and who has upon his shield a cat or on a field tawny, with the inscription *Miau*, which is the beginning of his lady's name; for she, so it is said, is the peerless Miulina, daughter of Alfeñquén, duke of Algarve. And that one over there, who weights down and presses the loins of that powerful charger, in a suit of snow-white armor with a white shield that bears no device whatever—he is a novice knight of the French nation, called Pierres Papin, lord of the baronies of Utrique. As for him you see digging his iron spurs into the flanks of that fleet-footed zebra courser and whose arms are vairs azure, he is the mighty duke of Nervia, Espartafilardo of the Wood, who has for device upon his shield an asparagus plant with a motto in Castilian that says '*Rastrea mi suerte.*'"[8]

In this manner he went on naming any number of imaginary knights on either side, describing on the spur of the moment their arms, colors, devices, and mottoes; for he was completely carried away by his imagination and by this unheard-of madness that had laid hold of him.

Without pausing, he went on, "This squadron in front of us is composed of men of various nations. There are those who drink the sweet waters of the famous Xanthus; woodsmen who tread the Massilian plain; those that sift the fine gold nuggets of Arabia Felix; those that are so fortunate as to dwell on the banks of the clear-running Thermodon, famed for their coolness; those who in many and diverse ways drain the golden Pactolus; Numidians, whose word is never to be trusted; Persians, with their famous bows and arrows; Medes and Parthians, who fight as they flee; Scythians, as cruel as they are fair of skin; Ethiopians, with their pierced lips; and an infinite number of other nationalities whose usages I see and recognize although I cannot recall their names.

"In this other squadron come those that drink from the crystal currents of the olive-bearing Betis; those that smooth and polish their faces with the liquid of the ever rich and gilded Tagus; those that enjoy the beneficial waters of the divine Genil; those that roam the Tartessian plains with their abundant pasturage; those that disport themselves in the Elysian meadows of Jerez; the men of La Mancha, rich and crowned with golden ears of corn; others clad in iron garments, ancient relics of the Gothic race; those that bathe in the Pisuerga, noted for the mildness of its current; those that feed their herds in the wide-spreading pasture lands along the banks of the winding Guadiana, celebrated for its underground course;[9] those that shiver from the cold of the wooded Pyrenees or dwell amid the white peaks of the lofty Apennines—in short, all those whom Europe holds within its girth."

---

8. Probably a pun on *rastrear*. The meaning of the motto may be either "On Fortune's track" or "My Fortune creeps."

9. The Guadiana does run underground part of the way through La Mancha.

So help me God! How many provinces, how many nations did he not mention by name, giving to each one with marvelous readiness its proper attributes; for he was wholly absorbed and filled to the brim with what he had read in those lying books of his! Sancho Panza hung on his words, saying nothing, merely turning his head from time to time to have a look at those knights and giants that his master was pointing out to him; but he was unable to discover any of them.

"Sir," he said, "may I go to the devil if I see a single man, giant, or knight of all those that your Grace is talking about. Who knows? Maybe it is another spell, like last night."[1]

"How can you say that?" replied Don Quixote. "Can you not hear the neighing of the horses, the sound of trumpets, the roll of drums?"

"I hear nothing," said Sancho, "except the bleating of sheep."

And this, of course, was the truth; for the flocks were drawing near.

"The trouble is, Sancho," said Don Quixote, "you are so afraid that you cannot see or hear properly; for one of the effects of fear is to disturb the senses and cause things to appear other than what they are. If you are so craven as all that, go off to one side and leave me alone, and I without your help will assure the victory to that side to which I lend my aid."

Saying this, he put spurs to Rocinante and, with his lance at rest, darted down the hillside like a flash of lightning.

As he did so, Sancho called after him, "Come back, your Grace, Señor Don Quixote; I vow to God those are sheep that you are charging. Come back! O wretched father that bore me! What madness is this? Look you, there are no giants, nor knights, nor cats, nor shields either quartered or whole, nor vairs azure or bedeviled. What is this you are doing, O sinner that I am in God's sight?"

But all this did not cause Don Quixote to turn back. Instead, he rode on, crying out at the top of his voice, "Ho, knights, those of you who follow and fight under the banners of the valiant Pentapolín of the Rolled-up Sleeve; follow me, all of you, and you shall see how easily I give you revenge on your enemy, Alifanfarón of Trapobana."

With these words he charged into the middle of the flock of sheep and began spearing at them with as much courage and boldness as if they had been his mortal enemies. The shepherds and herdsmen who were with the animals called to him to stop; but seeing it was no use, they unloosed their slings and saluted his ears with stones as big as your fist.

Don Quixote paid no attention to the missiles and, dashing about here and there, kept crying, "Where are you, haughty Alifanfarón? Come out to me; for here is a solitary knight who desires in single combat to test your strength and deprive you of your life, as a punishment for that which you have done to the valorous Pentapolín Garamanta."

At that instant a pebble from the brook struck him in the side and buried a couple of ribs in his body. Believing himself dead or badly wounded, and remembering his potion, he took out his vial, placed it to his mouth, and began to swallow the balm; but before he had had what he thought was enough, there

1. The inn where they had spent the previous night had been pronounced by Don Quixote to be an enchanted castle.

came another almond, which struck him in the hand, crushing the tin vial and carrying away with it a couple of grinders from his mouth, as well as badly mashing two of his fingers. As a result of these blows the poor knight tumbled from his horse. Believing that they had killed him, the shepherds hastily collected their flock and, picking up the dead beasts, of which there were more than seven, they went off down the road without more ado.

Sancho all this time was standing on the slope observing the insane things that his master was doing; and as he plucked savagely at his beard he cursed the hour and minute when luck had brought them together. But when he saw him lying there on the ground and perceived that the shepherds were gone, he went down the hill and came up to him, finding him in very bad shape though not unconscious.

"Didn't I tell you, Señor Don Quixote," he said, "that you should come back, that those were not armies you were charging but flocks of sheep?"

"This," said Don Quixote, "is the work of that thieving magician, my enemy, who thus counterfeits things and causes them to disappear. You must know, Sancho, that it is very easy for them to make us assume any appearance that they choose; and so it is that malign one who persecutes me, envious of the glory he saw me about to achieve in this battle, changed the squadrons of the foe into flocks of sheep. If you do not believe me, I beseech you on my life to do one thing for me, that you may be undeceived and discover for yourself that what I say is true. Mount your ass and follow them quietly, and when you have gone a short way from here, you will see them become their former selves once more; they will no longer be sheep but men exactly as I described them to you in the first place. But do not go now, for I need your kind assistance; come over here and have a look and tell me how many grinders are missing, for it feels as if I did not have a single one left."

["To Right Wrongs and Come to the Aid of the Wretched"]

CHAPTER 22

Of how Don Quixote freed many unfortunate ones who, much against their will, were being taken where they did not wish to go.

Cid Hamete Benengeli, the Arabic and Manchegan;[2] author, in the course of this most grave, high-sounding, minute, delightful, and imaginative history, informs us that, following the remarks that were exchanged between Don Quixote de la Mancha and Sancho Panza, his squire, . . . the knight looked up and saw coming toward them down the road which they were following a dozen or so men on foot, strung together by their necks like beads on an iron chain and all of them wearing handcuffs. They were accompanied by two men on horseback and two on foot, the former carrying wheel-lock muskets while the other two were armed with swords and javelins.

"That," said Sancho as soon as he saw them, "is a chain of galley slaves, people on their way to the galleys where by order of the king they are forced to labor."

2. Of La Mancha.

"What do you mean by 'forced'?" asked Don Quixote. "Is it possible that the king uses force on anyone?"

"I did not say that," replied Sancho. "What I did say was that these are folks who have been condemned for their crimes to forced labor in the galleys for his Majesty the King."

"The short of it is," said the knight, "whichever way you put it, these people are being taken there by force and not of their own free will."

"That is the way it is," said Sancho.

"Well, in that case," said his master, "now is the time for me to fulfill the duties of my calling, which is to right wrongs and come to the aid of the wretched."

"But take note, your Grace," said Sancho, "that justice, that is to say, the king himself, is not using any force upon, or doing any wrong to, people like these, but is merely punishing them for the crimes they have committed."

The chain of galley slaves had come up to them by this time, whereupon Don Quixote very courteously requested the guards to inform him of the reason or reasons why they were conducting these people in such a manner as this. One of the men on horseback then replied that the men were prisoners who had been condemned by his Majesty to serve in the galleys, whither they were bound, and that was all there was to be said about it and all that he, Don Quixote, need know.

"Nevertheless," said the latter, "I should like to inquire of each one of them, individually, the cause of his misfortune." And he went on speaking so very politely in an effort to persuade them to tell him what he wanted to know that the other mounted guard finally said, "Although we have here the record and certificate of sentence of each one of these wretches, we have not the time to get them out and read them to you; and so your Grace may come over and ask the prisoners themselves, and they will tell you if they choose, and you may be sure that they will, for these fellows take a delight in their knavish exploits and in boasting of them afterward."

With this permission, even though he would have done so if it had not been granted him, Don Quixote went up to the chain of prisoners and asked the first whom he encountered what sins had brought him to so sorry a plight. The man replied that it was for being a lover that he found himself in that line.

"For that and nothing more?" said Don Quixote. "And do they, then, send lovers to the galleys? If so, I should have been rowing there long ago."

"But it was not the kind of love that your Grace has in mind," the prisoner went on. "I loved a wash basket full of white linen so well and hugged it so tightly that, if they had not taken it away from me by force, I would never of my own choice have let go of it to this very minute. I was caught in the act, there was no need to torture me, the case was soon disposed of, and they supplied me with a hundred lashes across the shoulders and, in addition, a three-year stretch in the *gurapas*, and that's all there is to tell."

"What are *gurapas*?" asked Don Quixote.

"*Gurapas* are the galleys," replied the prisoner. He was a lad of around twenty-four and stated that he was a native of Piedrahita.

The knight then put the same question to a second man, who appeared to be very downcast and melancholy and did not have a word to say. The first man answered for him.

"This one, sir," he said, "is going as a canary—I mean, as a musician and singer."

"How is that?" Don Quixote wanted to know. "Do musicians and singers go to the galleys too?"

"Yes, sir; and there is nothing worse than singing when you're in trouble."

"On the contrary," said Don Quixote, "I have heard it said that he who sings frightens away his sorrows."

"It is just the opposite," said the prisoner; "for he who sings once weeps all his life long."

"I do not understand," said the knight.

One of the guards then explained. "Sir Knight, with this *non sancta*[3] tribe, to sing when you're in trouble means to confess under torture. This singer was put to the torture and confessed his crime, which was that of being a *cuatrero*, or cattle thief, and as a result of his confession he was condemned to six years in the galleys in addition to two hundred lashes which he took on his shoulders; and so it is he is always downcast and moody, for the other thieves, those back where he came from and the ones here, mistreat, snub, ridicule, and despise him for having confessed and for not having had the courage to deny his guilt. They are in the habit of saying that the word *no* has the same number of letters as the word *sí*, and that a culprit is in luck when his life or death depends on his own tongue and not that of witnesses or upon evidence; and, in my opinion, they are not very far wrong."

"And I," said Don Quixote, "feel the same way about it." He then went on to a third prisoner and repeated his question.

The fellow answered at once, quite unconcernedly. "I'm going to my ladies, the *gurapas*, for five years, for the lack of five ducats."

"I would gladly give twenty," said Don Quixote, "to get you out of this."

"That," said the prisoner, "reminds me of the man in the middle of the ocean who has money and is dying of hunger because there is no place to buy what he needs. I say this for the reason that if I had had, at the right time, those twenty ducats your Grace is now offering me, I'd have greased the notary's quill and freshened up the attorney's wit with them, and I'd now be living in the middle of Zocodover Square in Toledo instead of being here on this highway coupled like a greyhound. But God is great; patience, and that's enough of it."

Don Quixote went on to a fourth prisoner, a venerable-looking old fellow with a white beard that fell over his bosom. When asked how he came to be there, this one began weeping and made no reply, but a fifth comrade spoke up in his behalf.

"This worthy man," he said, "is on his way to the galleys after having made the usual rounds clad in a robe of state and on horseback."[4]

"That means, I take it," said Sancho, "that he has been put to shame in public."

"That is it," said the prisoner, "and the offense for which he is being punished is that of having been an ear broker, or, better, a body broker. By that I mean to say, in short, that the gentleman is a pimp, and besides, he has his points as a sorcerer."

3. Unholy (Latin).
4. After having been flogged in public, with all the ceremony that accompanied that punishment.

"If that point had not been thrown in," said Don Quixote, "he would not deserve, for merely being a pimp, to have to row in the galleys, but rather should be the general and give orders there. For the office of pimp is not an indifferent one; it is a function to be performed by persons of discretion and is most necessary in a well-ordered state; it is a profession that should be followed only by the wellborn, and there should, moreover, be a supervisor or examiner as in the case of other offices, and the number of practitioners should be fixed by law as is done with brokers on the exchange. In that way many evils would be averted that arise when this office is filled and this calling practiced by stupid folk and those with little sense, such as silly women and pages or mountebanks with few years and less experience to their credit, who, on the most pressing occasions, when it is necessary to use one's wits, let the crumbs freeze between their hand and their mouth and do not know which is their right hand and which is the left.

"I would go on and give reasons why it is fitting to choose carefully those who are to fulfill so necessary a state function, but this is not the place for it. One of these days I will speak of the matter to someone who is able to do something about it. I will say here only that the pain I felt at seeing those white hairs and this venerable countenance in such a plight, and all for his having been a pimp, has been offset for me by the additional information you have given me, to the effect that he is a sorcerer as well; for I am convinced that there are no sorcerers in the world who can move and compel the will, as some simple-minded persons think, but that our will is free and no herb or charm can force it.[5] All that certain foolish women and cunning tricksters do is to compound a few mixtures and poisons with which they deprive men of their senses while pretending that they have the power to make them loved, although, as I have just said, one cannot affect another's will in that manner."

"That is so," said the worthy old man; "but the truth is, sir, I am not guilty on the sorcery charge. As for being a pimp, that is something I cannot deny. I never thought there was any harm in it, however, my only desire being that everyone should enjoy himself and live in peace and quiet, without any quarrels or troubles. But these good intentions on my part cannot prevent me from going where I do not want to go, to a place from which I do not expect to return; for my years are heavy upon me and an affection of the urine that I have will not give me a moment's rest."

With this, he began weeping once more, and Sancho was so touched by it that he took a four-real piece from his bosom and gave it to him as an act of charity.

Don Quixote then went on and asked another what his offense was. The fellow answered him, not with less, but with much more, briskness than the preceding one had shown.

"I am here," he said, "for the reason that I carried a joke too far with a couple of cousins-german of mine and a couple of others who were not mine, and I ended by jesting with all of them to such an extent that the devil himself would never be able to straighten out the relationship. They proved everything on me,

---

5. Here Don Quixote despises charms and love potions, although often elsewhere, in his own vision of himself as a knight-errant, he accepts enchantments and spells as part of his world of fantasy.

there was no one to show me favor, I had no money, I came near swinging for it, they sentenced me to the galleys for six years, and I accepted the sentence as the punishment that was due me. I am young yet, and if I live long enough, everything will come out all right. If, Sir Knight, your Grace has anything with which to aid these poor creatures that you see before you, God will reward you in Heaven, and we here on earth will make it a point to ask God in our prayers to grant you long life and good health, as long and as good as your amiable presence deserves."

This man was dressed as a student, and one of the guards told Don Quixote that he was a great talker and a very fine Latinist.

Back of these came a man around thirty years of age and of very good appearance, except that when he looked at you his eyes were seen to be a little crossed. He was shackled in a different manner from the others, for he dragged behind a chain so huge that it was wrapped all around his body, with two rings at the throat, one of which was attached to the chain while the other was fastened to what is known as a keep-friend or friend's foot, from which two irons hung down to his waist, ending in handcuffs secured by a heavy padlock in such a manner that he could neither raise his hands to his mouth nor lower his head to reach his hands.

When Don Quixote asked why this man was so much more heavily chained than the others, the guard replied that it was because he had more crimes against him than all the others put together, and he was so bold and cunning that, even though they had him chained like this, they were by no means sure of him but feared that he might escape from them.

"What crimes could he have committed," asked the knight, "if he has merited a punishment no greater than that of being sent to the galleys?"

"He is being sent there for ten years," replied the guard, "and that is equivalent to civil death. I need tell you no more than that this good man is the famous Ginés de Pasamonte, otherwise known as Ginesillo de Parapilla."

"Señor Commissary," spoke up the prisoner at this point, "go easy there and let us not be so free with names and surnames. My just name is Ginés and not Ginesillo; and Pasamonte, not Parapilla as you make it out to be, is my family name. Let each one mind his own affairs and he will have his hands full."

"Speak a little more respectfully, you big thief, you," said the commissary, "unless you want me to make you be quiet in a way you won't like."

"Man goes as God pleases, that is plain to be seen," replied the galley slave, "but someday someone will know whether my name is Ginesillo de Parapilla or not."

"But, you liar, isn't that what they call you?"

"Yes," said Ginés, "they do call me that; but I'll put a stop to it, or else I'll skin their you-know-what. And you, sir, if you have anything to give us, give it and may God go with you, for I am tired of all this prying into other people's lives. If you want to know anything about my life, know that I am Ginés de Pasamonte whose life story has been written down by these fingers that you see here."

"He speaks the truth," said the commissary, "for he has himself written his story, as big as you please, and has left the book in the prison, having pawned it for two hundred reales."

"And I mean to redeem it," said Ginés, "even if it costs me two hundred ducats."

"Is it as good as that?" inquired Don Quixote.

"It is so good," replied Ginés, "that it will cast into the shade *Lazarillo de Tormes*[6] and all others of that sort that have been or will be written. What I would tell you is that it deals with facts, and facts so interesting and amusing that no lies could equal them."

"And what is the title of the book?" asked Don Quixote.

"The Life of Ginés de Pasamonte."

"Is it finished?"

"How could it be finished," said Ginés, "when my life is not finished as yet? What I have written thus far is an account of what happened to me from the time I was born up to the last time that they sent me to the galleys."

"Then you have been there before?"

"In the service of God and the king I was there four years, and I know what the biscuit and the cowhide are like. I don't mind going very much, for there I will have a chance to finish my book. I still have many things to say, and in the Spanish galleys I shall have all the leisure that I need, though I don't need much, since I know by heart what it is I want to write."

"You seem to be a clever fellow," said Don Quixote.

"And an unfortunate one," said Ginés; "for misfortunes always pursue men of genius."

"They pursue rogues," said the commissary.

"I have told you to go easy, Señor Commissary," said Pasamonte, "for their Lordships did not give you that staff in order that you might mistreat us poor devils with it, but they intended that you should guide and conduct us in accordance with his Majesty's command. Otherwise, by the life of—But enough. It may be that someday the stains made in the inn will come out in the wash. Meanwhile, let everyone hold his tongue, behave well, and speak better, and let us be on our way. We've had enough of this foolishness."

At this point the commissary raised his staff as if to let Pasamonte have it in answer to his threats, but Don Quixote placed himself between them and begged the officer not to abuse the man; for it was not to be wondered at if one who had his hands so bound should be a trifle free with his tongue. With this, he turned and addressed them all.

"From all that you have told me, my dearest brothers," he said, "one thing stands out clearly for me, and that is the fact that, even though it is a punishment for offenses which you have committed, the penalty you are about to pay is not greatly to your liking and you are going to the galleys very much against your own will and desire. It may be that the lack of spirit which one of you displayed under torture, the lack of money on the part of another, the lack of influential friends, or, finally, warped judgment on the part of the magistrate, was the thing that led to your downfall; and, as a result, justice was not done you. All of which presents itself to my mind in such a fashion that I am at this moment engaged in trying to persuade and even force myself to show you what the purpose was for which Heaven sent me into this world, why it was it led me to adopt the calling of knighthood which I profess and take the knightly vow to favor the needy and aid those who are oppressed by the powerful.

---

6. A picaresque or rogue novel, published anonymously about the middle of the 15th century.

"However, knowing as I do that it is not the part of prudence to do by foul means what can be accomplished by fair ones, I propose to ask these gentlemen, your guards, and the commissary to be so good as to unshackle you and permit you to go in peace. There will be no dearth of others to serve his Majesty under more propitious circumstances; and it does not appear to me to be just to make slaves of those whom God created as free men. What is more, gentlemen of the guard, these poor fellows have committed no offense against you. Up there, each of us will have to answer for his own sins; for God in Heaven will not fail to punish the evil and reward the good; and it is not good for self-respecting men to be executioners of their fellow-men in something that does not concern them. And so, I ask this of you, gently and quietly, in order that, if you comply with my request, I shall have reason to thank you; and if you do not do so of your own accord, then this lance and this sword and the valor of my arm shall compel you to do it by force."

"A fine lot of foolishness!" exclaimed the commissary. "So he comes out at last with this nonsense! He would have us let the prisoners of the king go free, as if we had any authority to do so or he any right to command it! Be on your way, sir, at once; straighten that basin that you have on your head, and do not go looking for three feet on a cat."[7]

"You," replied Don Quixote, "are the cat and the rat and the rascal!" And, saying this, he charged the commissary so quickly that the latter had no chance to defend himself but fell to the ground badly wounded by the lance blow. The other guards were astounded by this unexpected occurrence; but, recovering their self-possession, those on horseback drew their swords, those on foot leveled their javelins, and all bore down on Don Quixote, who stood waiting for them very calmly. Things undoubtedly would have gone badly for him if the galley slaves, seeing an opportunity to gain their freedom, had not succeeded in breaking the chain that linked them together. Such was the confusion that the guards, now running to fall upon the prisoners and now attacking Don Quixote, who in turn was attacking them, accomplished nothing that was of any use.

Sancho for his part aided Ginés de Pasamonte to free himself, and that individual was the first to drop his chains and leap out onto the field, where, attacking the fallen commissary, he took away that officer's sword and musket; and as he stood there, aiming first at one and then at another, though without firing, the plain was soon cleared of guards, for they had taken to their heels, fleeing at once Pasamonte's weapon and the stones which the galley slaves, freed now, were hurling at them. Sancho, meanwhile, was very much disturbed over this unfortunate event, as he felt sure that the fugitives would report the matter to the Holy Brotherhood, which, to the ringing of the alarm bell, would come out to search for the guilty parties. He said as much to his master, telling him that they should leave at once and go into hiding in the near-by mountains.

"That is all very well," said Don Quixote, "but I know what had best be done now." He then summoned all the prisoners, who, running riot, had by this time despoiled the commissary of everything that he had, down to his skin, and as they gathered around to hear what he had to say, he addressed them as follows:

7. Looking for the impossible ("five feet" is the more usual form of the proverb).

"It is fitting that those who are wellborn should give thanks for the benefits they have received, and one of the sins with which God is most offended is that of ingratitude. I say this, gentlemen, for the reason that you have seen and had manifest proof of what you owe to me; and now that you are free of the yoke which I have removed from about your necks, it is my will and desire that you should set out and proceed to the city of El Toboso and there present yourselves before the lady Dulcinea del Toboso and say to her that her champion, the Knight of the Mournful Countenance, has sent you; and then you will relate to her, point by point, the whole of this famous adventure which has won you your longed-for freedom. Having done that, you may go where you like, and may good luck go with you."

To this Ginés de Pasamonte replied in behalf of all of them, "It is absolutely impossible, your Grace, our liberator, for us to do what you have commanded. We cannot go down the highway all together but must separate and go singly, each in his own direction, endeavoring to hide ourselves in the bowels of the earth in order not to be found by the Holy Brotherhood, which undoubtedly will come out to search for us. What your Grace can do, and it is right that you should do so, is to change this service and toll that you require of us in connection with the lady Dulcinea del Toboso into a certain number of Credos and Hail Marys which we will say for your Grace's intention, as this is something that can be accomplished by day or night, fleeing or resting, in peace or in war. To imagine, on the other hand, that we are going to return to the fleshpots of Egypt, by which I mean, take up our chains again by setting out along the highway for El Toboso, is to believe that it is night now instead of ten o'clock in the morning and is to ask of us something that is the same as asking pears of the elm tree."

"Then by all that's holy!" exclaimed Don Quixote, whose wrath was now aroused, "you, Don Son of a Whore, Don Ginesillo de Parapilla, or whatever your name is, you shall go alone, your tail between your legs and the whole chain on your back."

Pasamonte, who was by no means a long-suffering individual, was by this time convinced that Don Quixote was not quite right in the head, seeing that he had been guilty of such a folly as that of desiring to free them; and so, when he heard himself insulted in this manner, he merely gave the wink to his companions and, going off to one side, began raining so many stones upon the knight that the latter was wholly unable to protect himself with his buckler, while poor Rocinante paid no more attention to the spur than if he had been made of brass. As for Sancho, he took refuge behind his donkey as a protection against the cloud and shower of rocks that was falling on both of them, but Don Quixote was not able to shield himself so well, and there is no telling how many struck his body, with such force as to unhorse and bring him to the ground.

No sooner had he fallen than the student was upon him. Seizing the basin from the knight's head, he struck him three or four blows with it across the shoulders and banged it against the ground an equal number of times until it was fairly shattered to bits. They then stripped Don Quixote of the doublet which he wore over his armor, and would have taken his hose as well, if his greaves had not prevented them from doing so, and made off with Sancho's greatcoat, leaving him naked; after which, dividing the rest of the battle spoils amongst themselves, each of them went his own way, being a good deal more concerned with eluding the dreaded Holy Brotherhood than they were with burdening themselves with a chain or going to present themselves before the lady Dulcinea del Toboso.

They were left alone now—the ass and Rocinante, Sancho and Don Quixote: the ass, crestfallen and pensive, wagging its ears now and then, being under the impression that the hurricane of stones that had raged about them was not yet over; Rocinante, stretched alongside his master, for the hack also had been felled by a stone; Sancho, naked and fearful of the Holy Brotherhood; and Don Quixote, making wry faces at seeing himself so mishandled by those to whom he had done so much good.

[*"Set Free at Once That Lovely Lady"*]

CHAPTER 52

Of the quarrel that Don Quixote had with the goatherd, together with the rare adventure of the penitents, which the knight by the sweat of his brow brought to a happy conclusion.[8]

All those who had listened to it were greatly pleased with the goatherd's story, especially the canon,[9] who was more than usually interested in noting the manner in which it had been told. Far from being a mere rustic herdsman, the narrator seemed rather a cultured city dweller; and the canon accordingly remarked that the curate had been quite right in saying that the mountain groves bred men of learning. They all now offered their services to Eugenio, and Don Quixote was the most generous of any in this regard.

"Most assuredly, brother goatherd," he said, "if it were possible for me to undertake any adventure just now, I would set out at once to aid you and would take Leandra out of that convent, where she is undoubtedly being held against her will, in spite of the abbess and all the others who might try to prevent me, after which I would place her in your hands to do with as you liked, with due respect, however, for the laws of chivalry, which command that no violence be offered to any damsel. But I trust in God, Our Lord, that the power of one malicious enchanter is not so great that another magician may not prove still more powerful, and then I promise you my favor and my aid, as my calling obliges me to do, since it is none other than that of succoring the weak and those who are in distress."

The goatherd stared at him, observing in some astonishment the knight's unprepossessing appearance.

8. Last chapter of part I. Through various devices, including the use of Don Quixote's own belief in enchantments and spells, the curate and the barber have persuaded the knight to let himself be taken home in an ox cart.
9. A canon from Toledo who has joined Don Quixote and his guardians on the way; conversing about chivalry with the knight, he has

had cause to be "astonished at Don Quixote's well-reasoned nonsense." Eugenio, a very literate goatherd met on the way, has just told them the story of his unhappy love for Leandra. The girl, instead of choosing one of her local suitors, had eloped with a flashy and crooked soldier; robbed and abandoned by him, she had been put by her father in a convent.

"Sir," he said, turning to the barber who sat beside him, "who is this man who looks so strange and talks in this way?"

"Who should it be," the barber replied, "if not the famous Don Quixote de la Mancha, righter of wrongs, avenger of injustices, protector of damsels, terror of giants, and champion of battles?"

"That," said the goatherd, "sounds to me like the sort of thing you read of in books of chivalry, where they do all those things that your Grace has mentioned in connection with this man. But if you ask me, either your Grace is joking or this worthy gentleman must have a number of rooms to let inside his head."

"You are the greatest villain that ever was!" cried Don Quixote when he heard this. "It is you who are the empty one; I am fuller than the bitch that bore you ever was." Saying this, he snatched up a loaf of bread that was lying beside him and hurled it straight in the goatherd's face with such force as to flatten the man's nose. Upon finding himself thus mistreated in earnest, Eugenio, who did not understand this kind of joke, forgot all about the carpet, the tablecloth, and the other diners and leaped upon Don Quixote. Seizing him by the throat with both hands, he would no doubt have strangled him if Sancho Panza, who now came running up, had not grasped him by the shoulders and flung him backward over the table, smashing plates and cups and spilling and scattering all the food and drink that was there. Thus freed of his assailant, Don Quixote then threw himself upon the shepherd, who, with bleeding face and very much battered by Sancho's feet, was creeping about on his hands and knees in search of a table knife with which to exact a sanguinary vengeance, a purpose which the canon and the curate prevented him from carrying out. The barber, however, so contrived it that the goatherd came down on top of his opponent, upon whom he now showered so many blows that the poor knight's countenance was soon as bloody as his own.

As all this went on, the canon and the curate were laughing fit to burst, the troopers[1] were dancing with glee, and they all hissed on the pair as men do at a dog fight. Sancho Panza alone was in despair, being unable to free himself of one of the canon's servants who held him back from going to his master's aid. And then, just as they were all enjoying themselves hugely, with the exception of the two who were mauling each other, the note of a trumpet fell upon their ears, a sound so mournful that it caused them all to turn their heads in the direction from which it came. The one who was most excited by it was Don Quixote; who, very much against his will and more than a little bruised, was lying pinned beneath the goatherd.

"Brother Demon," he now said to the shepherd, "for you could not possibly be anything but a demon, seeing that you have shown a strength and valor greater than mine, I request you to call a truce for no more than an hour; for the doleful sound of that trumpet that we hear seems to me to be some new adventure that is calling me."

---

1. Law officers from the Holy Brotherhood. They had wanted to arrest Don Quixote for his attempt to liberate the galley slaves, but had been persuaded not to do so because of the knight's insanity.

Tired of mauling and being mauled, the goatherd let him up at once. As he rose to his feet and turned his head in the direction of the sound, Don Quixote then saw, coming down the slope of a hill, a large number of persons clad in white after the fashion of penitents; for, as it happened, the clouds that year had denied their moisture to the earth, and in all the villages of that district processions for prayer and penance were being organized with the purpose of beseeching God to have mercy and send rain. With this object in view, the good folk from a near-by town were making a pilgrimage to a devout hermit who dwelt on these slopes. Upon beholding the strange costumes that the penitents wore, without pausing to think how many times he had seen them before, Don Quixote imagined that this must be some adventure or other, and that it was for him alone as a knight-errant to undertake it. He was strengthened in this belief by the sight of a covered image that they bore, as it seemed to him this must be some highborn lady whom these scoundrelly and discourteous brigands were forcibly carrying off; and no sooner did this idea occur to him than he made for Rocinante, who was grazing not far away.

Taking the bridle and his buckler from off the saddletree, he had the bridle adjusted in no time, and then, asking Sancho for his sword, he climbed into the saddle, braced his shield upon his arm, and cried out to those present, "And now, valorous company, you shall see how important it is to have in the world those who follow the profession of knight-errantry. You have but to watch how I shall set at liberty that worthy lady who there goes captive, and then you may tell me whether or not such knights are to be esteemed."

As he said this, he dug his legs into Rocinante's flanks, since he had no spurs, and at a fast trot (for nowhere in this veracious history are we ever told that the hack ran full speed) he bore down on the penitents in spite of all that the canon, the curate, and the barber could do to restrain him—their efforts were as vain as were the pleadings of his squire.

"Where are you bound for, Señor Don Quixote?" Sancho called after him. "What evil spirits in your bosom spur you on to go against our Catholic faith? Plague take me, can't you see that's a procession of penitents and that lady they're carrying on the litter is the most blessed image of the Immaculate Virgin? Look well what you're doing, my master, for this time it may be said that you really do not know."

His exertions were in vain, however, for his master was so bent upon having it out with the sheeted figures and freeing the lady clad in mourning that he did not hear a word, nor would he have turned back if he had, though the king himself might have commanded it. Having reached the procession, he reined in Rocinante, who by this time was wanting a little rest, and in a hoarse, excited voice he shouted, "You who go there with your faces covered, out of shame, it may be, listen well to what I have to say to you."

The first to come to a halt were those who carried the image; and then one of the four clerics who were intoning the litanies, upon beholding Don Quixote's weird figure, his bony nag, and other amusing appurtenances, spoke up in reply.

"Brother, if you have something to say to us, say it quickly, for these brethren are engaged in macerating their flesh, and we cannot stop to hear any thing, nor is it fitting that we should, unless it is capable of being said in a couple of words."

"I will say it to you in one word," Don Quixote answered, "and that word is the following: 'Set free at once that lovely lady whose tears and mournful countenance show plainly that you are carrying her away against her will and that you have done her some shameful wrong. I will not consent to your going one step farther until you shall have given her the freedom that should be hers.'"

Hearing these words, they all thought that Don Quixote must be some madman or other and began laughing heartily; but their laughter proved to be gunpowder to his wrath, and without saying another word he drew his sword and fell upon the litter. One of those who bore the image, leaving his share of the burden to his companions, then sallied forth to meet the knight, flourishing a forked stick that he used to support the Virgin while he was resting; and upon this stick he now received a mighty slash that Don Quixote dealt him, one that shattered it in two, but with the piece about a third long that remained in his hand he came down on the shoulder of his opponent's sword arm, left unprotected by the buckler, with so much force that the poor fellow sank to the ground sorely battered and bruised.

Sancho Panza, who was puffing along close behind his master, upon seeing him fall cried out to the attacker not to deal another blow, as this was an unfortunate knight who was under a magic spell but who had never in all the days of his life done any harm to anyone. But the thing that stopped the rustic was not Sancho's words; it was, rather, the sight of Don Quixote lying there without moving hand or foot. And so, thinking that he had killed him, he hastily girded up his tunic and took to his heels across the countryside like a deer.

By this time all of Don Quixote's companions had come running up to where he lay; and the penitents, when they observed this, and especially when they caught sight of the officers of the Brotherhood with their crossbows, at once rallied around the image, where they raised their hoods and grasped their whips as the priests raised their tapers aloft in expectations of an assault; for they were resolved to defend themselves and even, if possible, to take the offensive against their assailants, but, as luck would have it, things turned out better than they had hoped. Sancho, meanwhile, believing Don Quixote to be dead, had flung himself across his master's body and was weeping and wailing in the most lugubrious and, at the same time, the most laughable fashion that could be imagined; and the curate had discovered among those who marched in the procession another curate whom he knew, their recognition of each other serving to allay the fears of all parties concerned. The first curate then gave the second a very brief account of who Don Quixote was, whereupon all the penitents came up to see if the poor knight was dead. And as they did do, they heard Sancho Panza speaking with tears in his eyes.

"O flower of chivalry,"[2] he was saying, "the course of whose well-spent years has been brought to an end by a single blow of a club! O honor of your line,

---

2. Note how Sancho has absorbed some of his master's speech mannerisms.

honor and glory of all La Mancha and of all the world, which, with you absent
from it, will be full of evil-doers who will not fear being punished for their
deeds! O master more generous than all the Alexanders, who after only eight
months of service presented me with the best island that the sea washes and
surrounds! Humble with the proud, haughty with the humble, brave in facing
dangers, long-suffering under outrages, in love without reason, imitator of the
good, scourge of the wicked, enemy of the mean—in a word, a knight-errant,
which is all there is to say."

At the sound of Sancho's cries and moans, Don Quixote revived, and the first
thing he said was, "He who lives apart from thee, O fairest Dulcinea, is subject
to greater woes than those I now endure. Friend Sancho, help me onto that
enchanted cart, as I am in no condition to sit in Rocinante's saddle with this
shoulder of mine knocked to pieces the way it is."

"That I will gladly do, my master," replied Sancho, "and we will go back to
my village in the company of these gentlemen who are concerned for your welfare, and there we will arrange for another sally and one, let us hope, that will
bring us more profit and fame than this one has."

"Well spoken, Sancho," said Don Quixote, "for it will be an act of great prudence to wait until the present evil influence of the stars has passed."

The canon, the curate, and the barber all assured him that he would be wise
in doing this; and so, much amused by Sancho Panza's simplicity, they placed
Don Quixote upon the cart as before, while the procession of penitents re-
formed and continued on its way. The goatherd took leave of all of them, and
the curate paid the troopers what was coming to them, since they did not wish
to go any farther. The canon requested the priest to inform him of the outcome
of Don Quixote's madness, as to whether it yielded to treatment or not; and
with this he begged permission to resume his journey. In short, the party broke
up and separated, leaving only the curate and the barber, Don Quixote and
Panza, and the good Rocinante, who looked upon everything that he had seen
with the same resignation as his master. Yoking his oxen, the carter made the
knight comfortable upon a bale of hay, and then at his customary slow pace
proceeded to follow the road that the curate directed him to take. At the end of
the six days they reached Don Quixote's village, making their entrance at noon
of a Sunday, when the square was filled with a crowd of people through which
the cart had to pass.

They all came running to see who it was, and when they recognized their
townsman, they were vastly astonished. One lad sped to bring the news to the
knight's housekeeper and his niece, telling them that their master had returned
lean and jaundiced and lying stretched out upon a bale of hay on an ox-cart. It
was pitiful to hear the good ladies' screams, to behold the way in which they
beat their breasts, and to listen to the curses which they once more heaped
upon those damnable books of chivalry, and this demonstration increased as
they saw Don Quixote coming through the doorway.

At news of the knight's return, Sancho Panza's wife had hurried to the scene,
for she had some while since learned that her husband had accompanied him
as his squire; and now, as soon as she laid eyes upon her man, the first question she asked was if all was well with the ass, to which Sancho replied that the
beast was better off than his master.

"Thank God," she exclaimed, "for all his blessings! But tell me now, my dear, what have you brought me from all your squirings? A new cloak to wear? Or shoes for the young ones?"

"I've brought you nothing of the sort, good wife," said Sancho, "but other things of greater value and importance."

"I'm glad to hear that," she replied. "Show me those things of greater value and importance, my dear. I'd like a sight of them just to cheer this heart of mine which has been so sad and unhappy all the centuries that you've been gone."

"I will show them to you at home, wife," said Sancho. "For the present be satisfied that if, God willing, we set out on another journey in search of adventures, you will see me in no time a count or the governor of an island, and not one of those around here, but the best that is to be had."

"I hope to Heaven it's true, my husband, for we certainly need it. But tell me, what is all this about islands? I don't understand."

"Honey," replied Sancho, "is not for the mouth of an ass. You will find out in good time, woman; and you're going to be surprised to hear yourself called 'my Ladyship' by all your vassals."

"What's this you are saying, Sancho, about ladyships, islands, and vassals?" Juana Panza insisted on knowing—for such was the name of Sancho's wife, although they were not blood relatives, it being the custom in La Mancha for wives to take their husbands' surnames.

"Do not be in such a hurry to know all this, Juana," he said. "It is enough that I am telling you the truth. Sew up your mouth, then; for all I will say, in passing, is that there is nothing in the world that is more pleasant than being a respected man, squire to a knight-errant who goes in search of adventures. It is true that most of the adventures you meet with do not come out the way you'd like them to, for ninety-nine out of a hundred will prove to be all twisted and crosswise. I know that from experience, for I've come out of some of them blanketed and out of others beaten to a pulp. But, all the same, it's a fine thing to go along waiting for what will happen next, crossing mountains, making your way through woods, climbing over cliffs, visiting castles, and putting up at inns free of charge, and the devil take the maravedi that is to pay."

Such was the conversation that took place between Sancho Panza and Juana Panza, his wife, as Don Quixote's housekeeper and niece were taking him in, stripping him, and stretching him out on his old-time bed. He gazed at them blankly, being unable to make out where he was. The curate charged the niece to take great care to see that her uncle was comfortable and to keep close watch over him so that he would not slip away from them another time. He then told them of what it had been necessary to do in order to get him home, at which they once more screamed to Heaven and began cursing the books of chivalry all over again, praying God to plunge the authors of such lying nonsense into the center of the bottomless pit. In short, they scarcely knew what to do, for they were very much afraid that their master and uncle would give them the slip once more, the moment he was a little better, and it turned out just the way they feared it might.

From Part II

Prologue

TO THE READER

God bless me, gentle or, it may be, plebeian reader, how eagerly you must be awaiting this prologue, thinking to find in it vengeful scoldings and vituperations directed against the author of the second Don Quixote—I mean the one who, so it is said, was begotten in Tordesillas and born in Tarragona.[1] The truth is, however, that I am not going to be able to satisfy you in this regard; for granting that injuries are capable of awakening wrath in the humblest of bosoms, my own must be an exception to the rule. You would, perhaps, have me call him an ass, a crackbrain, and an upstart, but it is not my intention so to chastise him for his sin. Let him eat it with his bread and have done with it.

What I cannot but resent is the fact that he describes me as being old and one-handed, as if it were in my power to make time stand still for me, or as if I had lost my hand in some tavern instead of upon the greatest occasion that the past or present has ever known or the future may ever hope to see.[2] If my wounds are not resplendent in the eyes of the chance beholder, they are at least highly thought of by those who know where they were received. The soldier who lies dead in battle has a more impressive mien than the one who by flight attains his liberty. So strongly do I feel about this that even if it were possible to work a miracle in my case, I still would rather have taken part in that prodigious battle than be today free of my wounds without having been there. The scars that the soldier has to show on face and breast are stars that guide others to the Heaven of honor, inspiring them with a longing for well-merited praise. What is more, it may be noted that one does not write with gray hairs but with his understanding, which usually grows better with the years.

I likewise resent his calling me envious; and as though I were some ignorant person, he goes on to explain to me what is meant by envy; when the truth of the matter is that of the two kinds, I am acquainted only with that which is holy, noble, and right-intentioned.[3] And this being so, as indeed it is, it is not likely that I should attack any priest, above all, one that is a familiar of the Holy Office.[4] If he made this statement, as it appears that he did, on behalf of a certain person, then he is utterly mistaken; for the person in question is one whose genius I hold in veneration and whose works I admire, as well as his constant industry and powers of application. But when all is said, I wish to thank this gentlemanly author for observing that my *Novels*[5] are more satirical than exemplary, while admitting at the same time that they are good; for they could not be good unless they had in them a little of everything.

---

1. A continuation of *Don Quixote* was published by a writer who gave himself the name of Avellaneda and claimed to come from Tordesillas. The mood of the second prologue is grim in comparison to the optimistic and witty prologue to Part I.
2. The Battle of Lepanto in 1571.
3. *Jealousy* and *zealousness* are etymologically related.
4. An allusion to the Spanish playwright Lope de Vega, who had been made a priest and appointed an official of the Spanish Inquisition. Avellaneda accused Cervantes of envying Lope's enormous popularity.
5. *Exemplary Tales.*

You will likely tell me that I am being too restrained and overmodest, but it is my belief that affliction is not to be heaped upon the afflicted, and this gentleman must be suffering greatly, seeing that he does not dare to come out into the open and show himself by the light of day, but must conceal his name and dissemble his place of origin, as if he had been guilty of some treason or act of lese-majeste. If you by chance should come to know him, tell him on my behalf that I do not hold it against him; for I know what temptations the devil has to offer, one of the greatest of which consists in putting it into a man's head that he can write a book and have it printed and thereby achieve as much fame as he does money and acquire as much money as he does fame; in confirmation of which I would have you, in your own witty and charming manner, tell him this tale.

There was in Seville a certain madman whose madness assumed one of the drollest forms that ever was seen in this world. Taking a hollow reed sharpened at one end, he would catch a dog in the street or somewhere else; and, holding one of the animal's legs with his foot and raising the other with his hand, he would fix his reed as best he could in a certain part, after which he would blow the dog up, round as a ball. When he had it in this condition he would give it a couple of slaps on the belly and let it go, remarking to the bystanders, of whom there were always plenty, "Do your Worships think, then, that it is so easy a thing to inflate a dog?" So you might ask, "Does your Grace think that it is so easy a thing to write a book?" And if this story does not set well with him, here is another one, dear reader, that you may tell him. This one, also, is about a madman and a dog.

The madman in this instance lived in Cordova. He was in the habit of carrying on his head a marble slab or stone of considerable weight, and when he met some stray cur he would go up alongside it and drop the weight full upon it, and the dog in a rage, barking and howling, would then scurry off down three whole streets without stopping. Now, it happened that among the dogs that he treated in this fashion was one belonging to a capmaker, who was very fond of the beast. Going up to it as usual, the madman let the stone fall on its head, whereupon the animal set up a great yowling, and its owner, hearing its moans and seeing what had been done to it, promptly snatched up a measuring rod and fell upon the dog's assailant, flaying him until there was not a sound bone left in the fellow's body; and with each blow that he gave him he cried, "You dog! You thief! Treat my greyhound like that, would you? You brute, couldn't you see it was a greyhound?" And repeating the word "greyhound" over and over, he sent the madman away beaten to a pulp.

Profiting by the lesson that had been taught him, the fellow disappeared and was not seen in public for more than a month, at the end of which time he returned, up to his old tricks and with a heavier stone than ever on his head. He would go up to a dog and stare at it, long and hard, and without daring to drop his stone, would say, "This is a greyhound; beware." And so with all the dogs that he encountered: whether they were mastiffs or curs, he would assert that they were greyhounds and let them go unharmed.

The same thing possibly may happen to our historian; it may be that he will not again venture to let fall the weight of his wit in the form of books which, being bad ones, are harder than rocks.

As for the threat he has made to the effect that through his book he will deprive me of the profits on my own,[6] you may tell him that I do not give a rap. Quoting from the famous interlude, *La Perendenga*,[7] I will say to him in reply, "Long live my master, the Four-and-twenty,[8] and Christ be with us all." Long live the great Count of Lemos, whose Christian spirit and well-known liberality have kept me on my feet despite all the blows an unkind fate has dealt me. Long life to his Eminence of Toledo, the supremely charitable Don Bernardo de Sandoval y Rojas.[9] Even though there were no printing presses in all the world, or such as there are should print more books directed against me than there are letters in the verses of *Mingo Revulgo*,[1] what would it matter to me? These two princes, without any cringing flattery or adulation on my part but solely out of their own goodness of heart, have taken it upon themselves to grant me their favor and protection, in which respect I consider myself richer and more fortunate than if by ordinary means I had attained the peak of prosperity. The poor man may keep his honor, but not the vicious one. Poverty may cast a cloud over nobility but cannot wholly obscure it. Virtue of itself gives off a certain light, even though it be through the chinks and crevices and despite the obstacles of adversity, and so comes to be esteemed and as a consequence favored by high and noble minds.

Tell him no more than this, nor do I have anything more to say to you, except to ask you to bear in mind that this *Second Part of Don Quixote*, which I herewith present to you, is cut from the same cloth and by the same craftsman as Part I. In this book I give you Don Quixote continued and, finally, dead and buried, in order that no one may dare testify any further concerning him, for there has been quite enough evidence as it is. It is sufficient that a reputable individual should have chronicled these ingenious acts of madness once and for all, without going into the matter again; for an abundance even of good things causes them to be little esteemed, while scarcity may lend a certain worth to those that are bad.

I almost forgot to tell you that you may look forward to the *Persiles*, on which I am now putting the finishing touches, as well as Part Second of the *Galatea*.[2]

["*Put into a Book*"]

CHAPTER 3

Of the laughable conversation that took place between Don Quixote, Sancho Panza, and the bachelor Sansón Carrasco.

Don Quixote remained in a thoughtful mood as he waited for the bachelor Carrasco,[1] from whom he hoped to hear the news as to how he had been put into a book, as Sancho had said. He could not bring himself to believe that any

6. Avellaneda asserted that his second part would earn the profits Cervantes might have expected from a continuation of his own.
7. No interlude by this name has survived.
8. Council of the town hall at Andalucía.
9. Archbishop of Toledo, uncle of the duke of Lerma, and patron of Cervantes.
1. Long verse satire.
2. Never published.

1. The bachelor of arts Sansón Carrasco, an important new character who appears at the beginning of Part II and will play a considerable role in the story with his attempts at "curing" Don Quixote. Just now he has been telling Sancho about a book relating the adventures of Don Quixote and his squire, by which the two have been made famous; the book is, of course, *Don Quixote*, part I.

such history existed, since the blood of the enemies he had slain was not yet dry on the blade of his sword; and here they were trying to tell him that his high deeds of chivalry were already circulating in printed form. But, for that matter, he imagined that some sage, either friend or enemy, must have seen to the printing of them through the art of magic. If the chronicler was a friend, he must have undertaken the task in order to magnify and exalt Don Quixote's exploits above the most notable ones achieved by knights-errant of old. If an enemy, his purpose would have been to make them out as nothing at all, by debasing them below the meanest acts ever recorded of any mean squire. The only thing was, the knight reflected, the exploits of squires never were set down in writing. If it was true that such a history existed, being about a knight-errant, then it must be eloquent and lofty in tone, a splendid and distinguished piece of work and veracious in its details.

This consoled him somewhat, although he was a bit put out at the thought that the author was a Moor, if the appellation "Cid" was to be taken as an indication,[2] and from the Moors you could never hope for any word of truth, seeing that they are all of them cheats, forgers, and schemers. He feared lest his love should not have been treated with becoming modesty but rather in a way that would reflect upon the virtue of his lady Dulcinea del Toboso. He hoped that his fidelity had been made clear, and the respect he had always shown her, and that something had been said as to how he had spurned queens, empresses, and damsels of every rank while keeping a rein upon those impulses that are natural to a man. He was still wrapped up in these and many other similar thoughts when Sancho returned with Carrasco.

Don Quixote received the bachelor very amiably. The latter, although his name was Sansón, or Samson, was not very big so far as bodily size went, but he was a great joker, with a sallow complexion and a ready wit. He was going on twenty-four and had a round face, a snub nose, and a large mouth, all of which showed him to be of a mischievous disposition and fond of jests and witticisms. This became apparent when, as soon as he saw Don Quixote, he fell upon his knees and addressed the knight as follows:

"O mighty Don Quixote de la Mancha, give me your hands; for by the habit of St. Peter that I wear[3]—though I have received but the first four orders—your Grace is one of the most famous knights-errant that ever have been or ever will be anywhere on this earth. Blessings upon Cid Hamete Benengeli who wrote down the history of your great achievements, and upon that curious-minded one who was at pains to have it translated from the Arabic into our Castilian vulgate for the universal entertainment of the people."

Don Quixote bade him rise. "Is it true, then," he asked, "that there is a book about me and that it was some Moorish sage who composed it?"

"By way of showing you how true it is," replied Sansón, "I may tell you that it is my belief that there are in existence today more than twelve thousand copies of that history. If you do not believe me, you have but to make inquiries in Portugal, Barcelona, and Valencia, where editions have been brought out, and there is even a report to the effect that one edition was printed at Antwerp. In

2. The allusion is to Cid Hamete Benengeli (see p. 1705, n. 3). The word *cid* is of Arabic derivation.

3. The dress of one of the minor clerical orders.

short, I feel certain that there will soon not be a nation that does not know it or a language into which it has not been translated."

"One of the things," remarked Don Quixote, "that should give most satisfaction to a virtuous and eminent man is to see his good name spread abroad during his own lifetime, by means of the printing press, through translations into the languages of the various peoples. I have said 'good name,' for if he has any other kind, his fate is worse than death."

"If it is a matter of good name and good reputation," said the bachelor, "your Grace bears off the palm from all the knights-errant in the world; for the Moor in his tongue and the Christian in his have most vividly depicted your Grace's gallantry, your courage in facing dangers, your patience in adversity and suffering, whether the suffering be due to wounds or to misfortunes of another sort, and your virtue and continence in love, in connection with that platonic relationship that exists between your Grace and my lady Doña Dulcinea del Toboso."

At this point Sancho spoke up. "Never in my life," he said, "have I heard my lady Dulcinea called 'Doña,' but only 'la Señora Dulcinea del Toboso'; so on that point, already, the history is wrong."

"That is not important," said Carrasco.

"No, certainly not," Don Quixote agreed. "But tell me, Señor Bachelor, what adventures of mine as set down in this book have made the deepest impression?"

"As to that," the bachelor answered, "opinions differ, for it is a matter of individual taste. There are some who are very fond of the adventure of the windmills—those windmills which to your Grace appeared to be so many Briareuses and giants. Others like the episode at the fulling mill. One relishes the story of the two armies which took on the appearance of droves of sheep, while another fancies the tale of the dead man whom they were taking to Segovia for burial. One will assert that the freeing of the galley slaves is the best of all, and yet another will maintain that nothing can come up to the Benedictine giants and the encounter with the valiant Biscayan."

Again Sancho interrupted him. "Tell me, Señor Bachelor," he said, "does the book say anything about the adventure with the Yanguesans, that time our good Rocinante took it into his head to go looking for tidbits in the sea?"

"The sage," replied Sansón, "has left nothing in the inkwell. He has told everything and to the point, even to the capers which the worthy Sancho cut as they tossed him in the blanket."

"I cut no capers in the blanket," objected Sancho, "but I did in the air, and more than I liked."

"I imagine," said Don Quixote, "that there is no history in the world, dealing with humankind, that does not have its ups and downs, and this is particularly true of those that have to do with deeds of chivalry, for they can never be filled with happy incidents alone."

"Nevertheless," the bachelor went on, "there are some who have read the book who say that they would have been glad if the authors had forgotten a few of the innumerable cudgelings which Señor Don Quixote received in the course of his various encounters."

"But that is where the truth of the story comes in," Sancho protested.

"For all of that," observed Don Quixote, "they might well have said nothing about them; for there is no need of recording those events that do not alter the veracity of the chronicle, when they tend only to lessen the reader's respect for the hero. You may be sure that Aeneas was not as pious as Vergil would have us believe, nor was Ulysses as wise as Homer depicts him."

"That is true enough," replied Sansón, "but it is one thing to write as a poet and another as a historian. The former may narrate or sing of things not as they were but as they should have been; the latter must describe them not as they should have been but as they were, without adding to or detracting from the truth in any degree whatsoever."

"Well," said Sancho, "if this Moorish gentleman is bent upon telling the truth, I have no doubt that among my master's thrashings my own will be found; for they never took the measure of his Grace's shoulders without measuring my whole body. But I don't wonder at that; for as my master himself says, when there's an ache in the head the members have to share it."

"You are a sly fox, Sancho," said Don Quixote. "My word, but you can remember things well enough when you choose to do so!"

"Even if I wanted to forget the whacks they gave me," Sancho answered him, "the welts on my ribs wouldn't let me, for they are still fresh."

"Be quiet, Sancho," his master admonished him, "and do not interrupt the bachelor. I beg him to go on and tell me what is said of me in this book."

"And what it says about me, too," put in Sancho, "for I have heard that I am one of the main presonages in it—"

"*Personages*, not *presonages*, Sancho my friend," said Sansón.

"So we have another one who catches you up on everything you say," was Sancho's retort. "If we go on at this rate, we'll never be through in a lifetime."

"May God put a curse on *my* life," the bachelor told him, "if you are not the second most important person in the story; and there are some who would rather listen to you talk than to anyone else in the book. It is true, there are those who say that you are too gullible in believing it to be the truth that you could become the governor of that island that was offered you by Señor Don Quixote, here present."

"There is still sun on the top of the wall," said Don Quixote, "and when Sancho is a little older, with the experience that the years bring, he will be wiser and better fitted to be a governor than he is at the present time."

"By God, master," said Sancho, "the island that I couldn't govern right now I'd never be able to govern if I lived to be as old as Methuselah. The trouble is, I don't know where that island we are talking about is located; it is not due to any lack of noddle on my part."

"Leave it to God, Sancho," was Don Quixote's advice, "and everything will come out all right, perhaps even better than you think; for not a leaf on the tree stirs except by His will."

"Yes," said Sansón, "if it be God's will, Sancho will not lack a thousand islands to govern, not to speak of one island alone."

"I have seen governors around here," said Sancho, "that are not to be compared to the sole of my shoe, and yet they call them 'your Lordship' and serve them on silver plate."

"Those are not the same kind of governors," Sansón informed him. "Their task is a good deal easier. The ones that govern islands must at least know grammar."

"I could make out well enough with the *gram*," replied Sancho, "but with the *mar* I want nothing to do, for I don't understand it at all. But leaving this business of the governorship in God's hands—for He will send me wherever I can best serve Him—I will tell you, Señor Bachelor Sansón Carrasco, that I am very much pleased that the author of the history should have spoken of me in such a way as does not offend me; for, upon the word of a faithful squire, if he had said anything about me that was not becoming to an old Christian, the deaf would have heard of it."

"That would be to work miracles," said Sansón.

"Miracles or no miracles," was the answer, "let everyone take care as to what he says or writes about people and not be setting down the first thing that pops into his head."

"One of the faults that is found with the book," continued the bachelor, "is that the author has inserted in it a story entitled *The One Who Was Too Curious for His Own Good.* It is not that the story in itself is a bad one or badly written; it is simply that it is out of place there, having nothing to do with the story of his Grace, Señor Don Quixote."[4]

"I will bet you," said Sancho, "that the son of a dog has mixed the cabbages with the baskets."[5]

"And I will say right now," declared Don Quixote, "that the author of this book was not a sage but some ignorant prattler who at haphazard and without any method set about the writing of it, being content to let things turn out as they might. In the same manner, Orbaneja,[6] the painter of Ubeda, when asked what he was painting would reply, 'Whatever it turns out to be.' Sometimes it would be a cock, in which case he would have to write alongside it, in Gothic letters, 'This is a cock.' And so it must be with my story, which will need a commentary to make it understandable."

"No," replied Sansón, "that it will not; for it is so clearly written that none can fail to understand it. Little children leaf through it, young people read it, adults appreciate it, and the aged sing its praises. In short, it is so thumbed and read and so well known to persons of every walk in life that no sooner do folks see some skinny nag than they at once cry, 'There goes Rocinante!' Those that like it best of all are the pages; for there is no lord's antechamber where a *Don Quixote* is not to be found. If one lays it down, another will pick it up; one will pounce upon it, and another will beg for it. It affords the pleasantest and least harmful reading of any book that has been published up to now. In the whole of it there is not to be found an indecent word or a thought that is other than Catholic."

"To write in any other manner," observed Don Quixote, "would be to write lies and not the truth. Those historians who make use of falsehoods ought to be burned like the makers of counterfeit money. I do not know what could have led the author to introduce stories and episodes that are foreign to the subject matter when he had so much to write about in describing my adventures. He must, undoubtedly, have been inspired by the old saying, 'With straw or with hay[7] . . .' For, in truth, all he had to do was to record my thoughts, my

---

4. The story, a tragic tale about a jealousy-ridden husband, occupies several chapters of part I. Here, as elsewhere in this chapter, Cervantes echoes criticism currently aimed at his book.

5. Has jumbled together things of different kinds.
6. Unidentified.
7. The proverb concludes either "the mattress is filled" or "I fill my belly."

sighs, my tears, my lofty purposes, and my undertakings, and he would have had a volume bigger or at least as big as that which the works of El Tostado[8] would make. To sum the matter up, Señor Bachelor, it is my opinion that, in composing histories or books of any sort, a great deal of judgment and ripe understanding is called for. To say and write witty and amusing things is the mark of great genius. The cleverest character in a comedy is the clown, since he who would make himself out to be a simpleton cannot be one. History is a near-sacred thing, for it must be true, and where the truth is, there is God. And yet there are those who compose books and toss them out into the world as if they were no more than fritters."

"There is no book so bad," opined the bachelor, "that there is not some good in it."

"Doubtless that is so," replied Don Quixote, "but it very often happens that those who have won in advance a great and well-deserved reputation for their writings, lose it in whole or in part when they give their works to the printer."

"The reason for it," said Sansón, "is that, printed works being read at leisure, their faults are the more readily apparent, and the greater the reputation of the author the more closely are they scrutinized. Men famous for their genius, great poets, illustrious historians, are almost always envied by those who take a special delight in criticizing the writings of others without having produced anything of their own."

"That is not to be wondered at," said Don Quixote, "for there are many theologians who are not good enough for the pulpit but who are very good indeed when it comes to detecting the faults or excesses of those who preach."

"All of this is very true, Señor Don Quixote," replied Carrasco, "but, all the same, I could wish that these self-appointed censors were a bit more forbearing and less hypercritical; I wish they would pay a little less attention to the spots on the bright sun of the work that occasions their fault-finding. For if *aliquando bonus dormitat Homerus*,[9] let them consider how much of his time he spent awake, shedding the light of his genius with a minimum of shade. It well may be that what to them seems a flaw is but one of those moles which sometimes add to the beauty of a face. In any event, I insist that he who has a book printed runs a very great risk, inasmuch as it is an utter impossibility to write it in such a manner that it will please all who read it."

"This book about me must have pleased very few," remarked Don Quixote.

"Quite the contrary," said Sansón, "for just as *stultorum infinitus est numerus*,[1] so the number of those who have enjoyed this history is likewise infinite. Some, to be sure, have complained of the author's forgetfulness, seeing that he neglected to make it plain who the thief was who stole Sancho's gray;[2] for it is not stated there, but merely implied, that the ass was stolen; and, a little further on, we find the knight mounted on the same beast, although it has not made its reappearance in the story. They also say that the author forgot to tell us what Sancho did with those hundred crowns that he found in the valise on the Sierra Morena, as nothing more is said of them and there are many who would like to know how he disposed of the money or how he spent it. This is one of the serious omissions to be found in the work."

8. Alonso de Madrigal, bishop of Ávila, a prolific author of devotional works.
9. Good Homer sometimes nods too (Latin);

Horace, *Art of Poetry*, line 359.
1. Infinite is the number of fools (Latin).
2. In part I, chapter 23.

To this Sancho replied, "I, Señor Sansón, do not feel like giving any account or accounting just now; for I feel a little weak in my stomach, and if I don't do something about it by taking a few swigs of the old stuff, I'll be sitting on St. Lucy's thorn.[3] I have some of it at home, and my old woman is waiting for me. After I've had my dinner, I'll come back and answer any questions your Grace or anybody else wants to ask me, whether it's about the loss of the ass or the spending of the hundred crowns."

And without waiting for a reply or saying another word, he went on home. Don Quixote urged the bachelor to stay and take potluck with him, and Sansón accepted the invitation and remained. In addition to the knight's ordinary fare, they had a couple of pigeons, and at table their talk was of chivalry and feats of arms.

[A Victorious Duel]

CHAPTER 12

Of the strange adventure that befell the valiant Don Quixote with the fearless Knight of the Mirrors.[4]

The night following the encounter with Death was spent by Don Quixote and his squire beneath some tall and shady trees,[5] the knight having been persuaded to eat a little from the stock of provisions carried by the gray.

"Sir," said Sancho, in the course of their repast, "how foolish I'd have been if I had chosen the spoils from your Grace's first adventure rather than the foals from the three mares.[6] Truly, truly, a sparrow in the hand is worth more than a vulture on the wing."[7]

"And yet, Sancho," replied Don Quixote, "if you had but let me attack them as I wished to do, you would at least have had as spoils the Empress's gold crown and Cupid's painted wings;[8] for I should have taken them whether or no and placed them in your hands."

"The crowns and scepters of stage emperors," remarked Sancho, "were never known to be of pure gold; they are always of tinsel or tinplate."

"That is the truth," said Don Quixote, "for it is only right that the accessories of a drama should be fictitious and not real, like the play itself. Speaking of

3. I shall be weak and exhausted.
4. Until he earns this title (in chapter 15), he will be referred to as the Knight of the Wood.
5. Don Quixote and his squire are now in the woody region around El Toboso, Dulcinea's town. Sancho has been sent to look for his knight's lady and has saved the day by pretending to see the beautiful damsel in a "village wench, and not a pretty one at that, for she was round-faced and snub-nosed." But by his imaginative lie he has succeeded, as he had planned, in setting in motion Don Quixote's belief in spells and enchantments: enemy magicians, envious of him, have hidden his lady's splendor only from his sight. While the knight was still under the shock of this experience, farther along their way he and his squire have met a group of itinerant players dressed in their proper costumes for a religious play, The Parliament of Death.
6. Don Quixote has promised them to Sancho as a reward for bringing news of Dulcinea.
7. I.e., a bird in the hand is worth two in the bush.
8. The Empress and Cupid were characters in The Parliament of Death.

that, Sancho, I would have you look kindly upon the art of the theater and, as a consequence, upon those who write the pieces and perform in them, for they all render a service of great value to the State by holding up a mirror for us at each step that we take, wherein we may observe, vividly depicted, all the varied aspects of human life; and I may add that there is nothing that shows us more clearly, by similitude, what we are and what we ought to be than do plays and players.

"Tell me, have you not seen some comedy in which kings, emperors, pontiffs, knights, ladies, and numerous other characters are introduced? One plays the ruffian, another the cheat, this one a merchant and that one a soldier, while yet another is the fool who is not so foolish as he appears, and still another the one of whom love has made a fool. Yet when the play is over and they have taken off their players' garments, all the actors are once more equal."

"Yes," replied Sancho, "I have seen all that."

"Well," continued Don Quixote, "the same thing happens in the comedy that we call life, where some play the part of emperors, others that of pontiffs—in short, all the characters that a drama may have—but when it is all over, that is to say, when life is done, death takes from each the garb that differentiates him, and all at last are equal in the grave."

"It is a fine comparison," Sancho admitted, "though not so new but that I have heard it many times before. It reminds me of that other one, about the game of chess. So long as the game lasts, each piece has its special qualities, but when it is over they are all mixed and jumbled together and put into a bag, which is to the chess pieces what the grave is to life."

"Every day, Sancho," said Don Quixote, "you are becoming less stupid and more sensible."

"It must be that some of your Grace's good sense is sticking to me," was Sancho's answer. "I am like a piece of land that of itself is dry and barren, but if you scatter manure over it and cultivate it, it will bear good fruit. By this I mean to say that your Grace's conversation is the manure that has been cast upon the barren land of my dry wit; the time that I spend in your service, associating with you, does the cultivating; and as a result of it all, I hope to bring forth blessed fruits by not departing, slipping, or sliding, from those paths of good breeding which your Grace has marked out for me in my parched understanding."

Don Quixote had to laugh at this affected speech of Sancho's, but he could not help perceiving that what the squire had said about his improvement was true enough; for every now and then the servant would speak in a manner that astonished his master. It must be admitted, however, that most of the time when he tried to use fine language, he would tumble from the mountain of his simple-mindedness into the abyss of his ignorance. It was when he was quoting old saws and sayings, whether or not they had anything to do with the subject under discussion, that he was at his best, displaying upon such occasions a prodigious memory, as will already have been seen and noted in the course of this history.

With such talk as this they spent a good part of the night. Then Sancho felt a desire to draw down the curtains of his eyes, as he was in the habit of saying when he wished to sleep, and, unsaddling his mount, he turned him loose to graze at will on the abundant grass. If he did not remove Rocinante's saddle, this was due to his master's express command; for when they had taken the field and were not sleeping under a roof, the hack was under no circumstances to be stripped. This was in accordance with an old and established custom which knights-errant faithfully observed; the bridle and saddlebow might be removed, but beware of touching the saddle itself! Guided by this precept, Sancho now gave Rocinante the same freedom that the ass enjoyed.

The close friendship that existed between the two animals was a most unusual one, so remarkable indeed that it has become a tradition handed down from father to son, and the author of this veracious chronicle even wrote a number of special chapters on the subject, although, in order to preserve the decency and decorum that are fitting in so heroic an account, he chose to omit them in the final version. But he forgets himself once in a while and goes on to tell us how the two beasts when they were together would hasten to scratch each other, and how, when they were tired and their bellies were full, Rocinante would lay his long neck over that of the ass—it extended more than a half a yard on the other side—and the pair would then stand there gazing pensively at the ground for as much as three whole days at a time, or at least until someone came for them or hunger compelled them to seek nourishment.

I may tell you that I have heard it said that the author of this history, in one of his writings, has compared the friendship of Rocinante and the gray to that of Nisus and Euryalus and that of Pylades and Orestes;[9] and if this be true, it shows for the edification of all what great friends these two peace-loving animals were, and should be enough to make men ashamed, who are so inept at preserving friendship with one another. For this reason it has been said:

> There is no friend for friend,
> Reeds to lances turn[1] . . .

And there was the other poet who sang:

> Between friend and friend the bug[2] . . .

Let no one think that the author has gone out of his way in comparing the friendship of animals with that of men; for human beings have received valuable lessons from the beasts and have learned many important things from them. From the stork they have learned the use of clysters; the dog has taught them the salutary effects of vomiting as well as a lesson in gratitude; the cranes have taught them vigilance, the ants foresight, the elephants modesty, and the horse loyalty.[3]

Sancho had at last fallen asleep at the foot of a cork tree, while Don Quixote was slumbering beneath a sturdy oak. Very little time had passed when the knight was awakened by a noise behind him, and, starting up, he began looking about him and listening to see if he could make out where it came from. Then he caught sight of two men on horseback, one of whom, slipping down from the saddle, said to the other, "Dismount, my friend, and unbridle the horses; for there seems to be plenty of grass around here for them and sufficient silence and solitude for my amorous thoughts."

9. Famous examples of friendship in Virgil's *Aeneid* and in Greek tradition and drama.
1. From a popular ballad.
2. The Spanish "a bug in the eye" implies keeping a watchful eye on somebody.
3. All folkloristic beliefs about the virtues of animals.

Saying this, he stretched himself out on the ground, and as he flung himself down the armor that he wore made such a noise that Don Quixote knew at once, for a certainty, that he must be a knight-errant. Going over to Sancho, who was still sleeping, he shook him by the arm and with no little effort managed to get him awake.

"Brother Sancho," he said to him in a low voice, "we have an adventure on our hands."

"God give us a good one," said Sancho. "And where, my master, may her Ladyship, Mistress Adventure, be?"

"Where, Sancho?" replied Don Quixote. "Turn your eyes and look, and you will see stretched out over there a knight-errant who, so far as I can make out, is not any too happy; for I saw him fling himself from his horse to the ground with a certain show of despondency, and as he fell his armor rattled."

"Well," said Sancho, "and how does your Grace make this out to be an adventure?"

"I would not say," the knight answered him, "that this is an adventure in itself, but rather the beginning of one, for that is the way they start. But listen; he seems to be tuning a lute or guitar, and from the way he is spitting and clearing his throat he must be getting ready to sing something."

"Faith, so he is," said Sancho. "He must be some lovesick knight."

"There are no knights-errant that are not lovesick," Don Quixote informed him. "Let us listen to him, and the thread of his song will lead us to the yarn-ball of his thoughts; for out of the abundance of the heart the mouth speaketh."

Sancho would have liked to reply to his master, but the voice of the Knight of the Wood, which was neither very good nor very bad, kept him from it; and as the two of them listened attentively, they heard the following:

Sonnet

Show me, O lady, the pattern of thy will,
That mine may take that very form and shape;
For my will in thine own I fain would drape,
Each slightest wish of thine I would fulfill.
If thou wouldst have me silence this dead ill   5
Of which I'm dying now, prepare the crape!
Or if I must another manner ape,
Then let Love's self display his rhyming skill.
Of opposites I am made, that's manifest:
In part soft wax, in part hard-diamond fire;   10
Yet to Love's laws my heart I do adjust,
And, hard or soft, I offer thee this breast:
Print or engrave there what thou may'st desire,
And I'll preserve it in eternal trust.[4]

With an *Ay!* that appeared to be wrung from the very depths of his heart, the Knight of the Wood brought his song to a close, and then after a brief pause began speaking in a grief-stricken voice that was piteous to hear.

---

4. The poem intentionally follows affected conventions of the time.

"O most beautiful and most ungrateful woman in all the world!" he cried, "how is it possible, O most serene Casildea de Vandalia,[5] for you to permit this captive knight of yours to waste away and perish in constant wanderings, amid rude toils and bitter hardships? Is it not enough that I have compelled all the knights of Navarre, all those of León, all the Tartessians and Castilians, and, finally, all those of La Mancha, to confess that there is no beauty anywhere that can rival yours?"

"That is not so!" cried Don Quixote at this point. "I am of La Mancha, and I have never confessed, I never could nor would confess a thing so prejudicial to the beauty of my lady. The knight whom you see there, Sancho, is raving; but let us listen and perhaps he will tell us more."

"That he will," replied Sancho, "for at the rate he is carrying on, he is good for a month at a stretch."

This did not prove to be the case, however; for when the Knight of the Wood heard voices near him, he cut short his lamentations and rose to his feet.

"Who goes there?" he called in a loud but courteous tone. "What kind of people are you? Are you, perchance, numbered among the happy or among the afflicted?"

"Among the afflicted," was Don Quixote's response.

"Then come to me," said the one of the Wood, "and, in doing so, know that you come to sorrow's self and the very essence of affliction."

Upon receiving so gentle and courteous an answer, Don Quixote and Sancho as well went over to him, whereupon the sorrowing one took the Manchegan's arm.

"Sit down here, Sir Knight," he continued, "for in order to know that you are one of those who follow the profession of knight-errantry, it is enough for me to have found you in this place where solitude and serenity keep you company, such a spot being the natural bed and proper dwelling of wandering men of arms."

"A knight I am," replied Don Quixote, "and of the profession that you mention; and though sorrows, troubles, and misfortunes have made my heart their abode, this does not mean that compassion for the woes of others has been banished from it. From your song a while ago I gather that your misfortunes are due to love—the love you bear that ungrateful fair one whom you named in your lamentations."

As they conversed in this manner, they sat together upon the hard earth, very peaceably and companionably, as if at daybreak they were not going to break each other's heads.

"Sir Knight," inquired the one of the Wood, "are you by any chance in love?"

"By mischance I am," said Don Quixote, "although the ills that come from well-placed affection should be looked upon as favors rather than as misfortunes."

"That is the truth," the Knight of the Wood agreed, "if it were not that the loved one's scorn disturbs our reason and understanding; for when it is excessive scorn appears as vengeance."

"I was never scorned by my lady," said Don Quixote.

---

5. The Knight of the Wood's counterpart to Don Quixote's Dulcinea del Toboso.

"No, certainly not," said Sancho, who was standing near by, "for my lady is gentle as a ewe lamb and soft as butter."

"Is he your squire?" asked the one of the Wood.

"He is," replied Don Quixote.

"I never saw a squire," said the one of the Wood, "who dared to speak while his master was talking. At least, there is mine over there; he is as big as your father, and it cannot be proved that he has ever opened his lips while I was conversing."

"Well, upon my word," said Sancho, "I have spoken, and I will speak in front of any other as good—but never mind; it only makes it worse to stir it."

The Knight of the Wood's squire now seized Sancho's arm. "Come along," he said, "let the two of us go where we can talk all we like, squire fashion, and leave these gentlemen our masters to come to lance blows as they tell each other the story of their loves; for you may rest assured, daybreak will find them still at it."

"Let us, by all means," said Sancho, "and I will tell your Grace who I am, so that you may be able to see for yourself whether or not I am to be numbered among the dozen most talkative squires."

With this, the pair went off to one side, and there then took place between them a conversation that was as droll as the one between their masters was solemn.

CHAPTER 13

In which is continued the adventure of the Knight of the Wood,
together with the shrewd, highly original, and amicable
conversation that took place between the two squires.

The knights and the squires had now separated, the latter to tell their life stories, the former to talk of their loves; but the history first relates the conversation of the servants and then goes on to report that of the masters. We are told that, after they had gone some little distance from where the others were, the one who served the Knight of the Wood began speaking to Sancho as follows:

"It is a hard life that we lead and live, *Señor mio*, those of us who are squires to knights-errant. It is certainly true that we eat our bread in the sweat of our faces, which is one of the curses that God put upon our first parents."[6]

"It might also be said," added Sancho, "that we eat it in the chill of our bodies, for who endures more heat and cold than we wretched ones who wait upon these wandering men of arms? It would not be so bad if we did eat once in a while, for troubles are less where there is bread; but as it is, we sometimes go for a day or two without breaking our fast, unless we feed on the wind that blows."

"But all this," said the other, "may very well be put up with, by reason of the hope we have of being rewarded; for if a knight is not too unlucky, his squire after a little while will find himself the governor of some fine island or prosperous earldom."

6. Cf. Genesis 3.19: "In the sweat of thy face shalt thou eat bread, till thou return unto the ground."

"I," replied Sancho, "have told my master that I would be satisfied with the governorship of an island, and he is so noble and so generous that he has promised it to me on many different occasions."

"In return for my services," said the Squire of the Wood, "I'd be content with a canonry. My master has already appointed me to one—and what a canonry!"

"Then he must be a churchly knight," said Sancho, "and in a position to grant favors of that sort to his faithful squire; but mine is a layman, pure and simple, although, as I recall, certain shrewd and, as I see it, scheming persons did advise him to try to become an archbishop. However, he did not want to be anything but an emperor. And there I was, all the time trembling for fear he would take it into his head to enter the Church, since I was not educated enough to hold any benefices. For I may as well tell your Grace that, though I look like a man, I am no more than a beast where holy orders are concerned."

"That is where you are making a mistake," the Squire of the Wood assured him. "Not all island governments are desirable. Some of them are misshapen bits of land, some are poor, others are gloomy, and, in short, the best of them lays a heavy burden of care and trouble upon the shoulders of the unfortunate one to whose lot it falls. It would be far better if we who follow this cursed trade were to go back to our homes and there engage in pleasanter occupations, such as hunting or fishing, for example; for where is there in this world a squire so poor that he does not have a hack, a couple of greyhounds, and a fishing rod to provide him with sport in his own village?"

"I don't lack any of those," replied Sancho. "It is true, I have no hack, but I do have an ass that is worth twice as much as my master's horse. God send me a bad Easter, and let it be the next one that comes, if I would make a trade, even though he gave me four fanegas[7] of barley to boot. Your Grace will laugh at the price I put on my gray—for that is the color of the beast. As to greyhounds, I shan't want for them, as there are plenty and to spare in my village. And, anyway, there is more pleasure in hunting when someone else pays for it."

"Really and truly, Sir Squire," said the one of the Wood, "I have made up my mind and resolved to have no more to do with the mad whims of these knights; I intend to retire to my village and bring up my little ones—I have three of them, and they are like oriental pearls."

"I have two of them," said Sancho, "that might be presented to the Pope in person, especially one of my girls that I am bringing up to be a countess, God willing, in spite of what her mother says."

"And how old is this young lady that is destined to be a countess?"

"Fifteen," replied Sancho, "or a couple of years more or less. But she is tall as a lance, fresh as an April morning, and strong as a porter."

"Those," remarked the one of the Wood, "are qualifications that fit her to be not merely a countess but a nymph of the verdant wildwood. O whore's daughter of a whore! What strength the she-rogue must have!"

Sancho was a bit put out by this. "She is not a whore," he said, "nor was her mother before her, nor will either of them ever be, please God, so long as I live. And you might speak more courteously. For one who has been brought up among knights-errant, who are the soul of courtesy, those words are not very becoming."

7. About 1.6 bushels.

"Oh, how little your Grace knows about compliments, Sir Squire!" the one of the Wood exclaimed. "Are you not aware that when some knight gives a good lance thrust to the bull in the plaza, or when a person does anything remarkably well, it is the custom for the crowd to cry out, 'Well done, whoreson rascal!' and that what appears to be vituperation in such a case is in reality high praise? Sir, I would bid you disown those sons or daughters who do nothing to cause such praise to be bestowed upon their parents."

"I would indeed disown them if they didn't," replied Sancho, "and so your Grace may go ahead and call me, my children, and my wife all the whores in the world if you like, for everything that they say and do deserves the very highest praise. And in order that I may see them all again, I pray God to deliver me from mortal sin, or, what amounts to the same thing, from this dangerous calling of squire, seeing that I have fallen into it a second time, decoyed and deceived by a purse of a hundred ducats that I found one day in the heart of the Sierra Morena.[8] The devil is always holding up a bag full of doubloons in front of my eyes, here, there—no, not here, but there—everywhere, until it seems to me at every step I take that I am touching it with my hand, hugging it, carrying it off home with me, investing it, drawing an income from it, and living on it like a prince. And while I am thinking such thoughts, all the hardships I have to put up with serving this crackbrained master of mine, who is more of a madman than a knight, seem to me light and easy to bear."

"That," observed the Squire of the Wood, "is why it is they say that avarice bursts the bag. But, speaking of madmen, there is no greater one in all this world than my master; for he is one of those of whom it is said, 'The cares of others kill the ass.' Because another knight has lost his senses, he has to play mad too[9] and go hunting for that which, when he finds it, may fly up in his snout."

"Is he in love, maybe?"

"Yes, with a certain Casildea de Vandalia, the rawest[1] and best-roasted lady to be found anywhere on earth; but her rawness is not the foot he limps on, for he has other and greater schemes rumbling in his bowels, as you will hear tell before many hours have gone by."

"There is no road so smooth," said Sancho, "that it does not have some hole or rut to make you stumble. In other houses they cook horse beans, in mine they boil them by the kettleful.[2] Madness has more companions and attendants than good sense does. But if it is true what they say, that company in trouble brings relief, I may take comfort from your Grace, since you serve a master as foolish as my own."

"Foolish but brave," the one of the Wood corrected him, "and more of a rogue than anything else."

"That is not true of my master," replied Sancho. "I can assure you there is nothing of the rogue about him; he is as open and aboveboard as a wine pitcher and would not harm anyone but does good to all. There is no malice in his

8. When Don Quixote retired there in part I, chapter 23.
9. In the Sierra Morena, Don Quixote had decided to imitate Amadis de Gaul and Ariosto's Roland "by playing the part of a desperate and raving madman" as a consequence of love.
1. The Spanish has a pun on *crudo*, meaning both "raw" and "cruel."
2. Meaning that his misfortunes always come in large quantities.

make-up, and a child could make him believe it was night at midday. For that very reason I love him with all my heart and cannot bring myself to leave him, no matter how many foolish things he does."

"But, nevertheless, good sir and brother," said the Squire of the Wood, "with the blind leading the blind, both are in danger of falling into the pit. It would be better for us to get out of all this as quickly as we can and return to our old haunts; for those that go seeking adventures do not always find good ones."

Sancho kept clearing his throat from time to time, and his saliva seemed rather viscous and dry; seeing which, the woodland squire said to him, "It looks to me as if we have been talking so much that our tongues are cleaving to our palates, but I have a loosener over there, hanging from the bow of my saddle, and a pretty good one it is." With this, he got up and went over to his horse and came back a moment later with a big flask of wine and a meat pie half a yard in diameter. This is no exaggeration, for the pasty in question was made of a hutch-rabbit of such a size that Sancho took it to be a goat, or at the very least a kid.

"And are you in the habit of carrying this with you, Señor?" he asked.

"What do you think?" replied the other. "Am I by any chance one of your wood-and-water[3] squires? I carry better rations on the flanks of my horse than a general does when he takes the field."

Sancho ate without any urging, gulping down mouthfuls that were like the knots on a tether, as they sat there in the dark.

"You are a squire of the right sort," he said, "loyal and true, and you live in grand style as shown by this feast, which I would almost say was produced by magic. You are not like me, poor wretch, who have in my saddlebags only a morsel of cheese so hard you could crack a giant's skull with it, three or four dozen carob beans, and a few nuts. For this I have my master to thank, who believes in observing the rule that knights-errant should nourish and sustain themselves on nothing but dried fruits and the herbs of the field."

"Upon my word, brother," said the other squire, "my stomach was not made for thistles, wild pears, and woodland herbs. Let our masters observe those knightly laws and traditions and eat what their rules prescribe; I carry a hamper of food and a flask on my saddlebow, whether they like it or not. And speaking of that flask, how I love it! There is scarcely a minute in the day that I'm not hugging and kissing it, over and over again."

As he said this, he placed the wine bag in Sancho's hands, who put it to his mouth, threw his head back, and sat there gazing up at the stars for a quarter of an hour. Then, when he had finished drinking, he let his head loll on one side and heaved a deep sigh.

"The whoreson rascal!" he exclaimed, "that's a fine vintage for you!"

"There!" cried the Squire of the Wood, as he heard the epithet Sancho had used, "do you see how you have praised this wine by calling it 'whoreson'?"

"I grant you," replied Sancho, "that it is no insult to call anyone a son of a whore so long as you really do mean to praise him. But tell me, sir, in the name of what you love most, is this the wine of Ciudad Real?"[4]

---

3. Of low quality.
4. The main town in La Mancha and the center of a wine region.

"What a winetaster you are! It comes from nowhere else, and it's a few years old, at that."

"Leave it to me," said Sancho, "and never fear, I'll show you how much I know about it. Would you believe me, Sir Squire, I have such a great natural instinct in this matter of wines that I have but to smell a vintage and I will tell you the country where it was grown, from what kind of grapes, what it tastes like, and how good it is, and everything that has to do with it. There is nothing so unusual about this, however, seeing that on my father's side were two of the best winetasters La Mancha has known in many a year, in proof of which, listen to the story of what happened to them.

"The two were given a sample of wine from a certain vat and asked to state its condition and quality and determine whether it was good or bad. One of them tasted it with the tip of his tongue while the other merely brought it up to his nose. The first man said that it tasted of iron, the second that it smelled of Cordovan leather. The owner insisted that the vat was clean and that there could be nothing in the wine to give it a flavor of leather or of iron, but, nevertheless, the two famous winetasters stood their ground. Time went by, and when they came to clean out the vat they found in it a small key attached to a leather strap. And so your Grace may see for yourself whether or not one who comes of that kind of stock has a right to give his opinion in such cases."

"And for that very reason," said the Squire of the Wood, "I maintain that we ought to stop going about in search of adventures. Seeing that we have loaves, let us not go looking for cakes, but return to our cottages, for God will find us there if He so wills."

"I mean to stay with my master," Sancho replied, "until he reaches Saragossa, but after that we will come to an understanding."

The short of the matter is, the two worthy squires talked so much and drank so much that sleep had to tie their tongues and moderate their thirst, since to quench the latter was impossible. Clinging to the wine flask, which was almost empty by now, and with half-chewed morsels of food in their mouths, they both slept peacefully; and we shall leave them there as we go on to relate what took place between the Knight of the Wood and the Knight of the Mournful Countenance.

CHAPTER 14

Wherein is continued the adventure of the Knight of the Wood.

In the course of the long conversation that took place between Don Quixote and the Knight of the Wood, the history informs us that the latter addressed the following remarks to the Manchegan:

"In short, Sir Knight, I would have you know that my destiny, or, more properly speaking, my own free choice, has led me to fall in love with the peerless Casildea de Vandalia. I call her peerless for the reason that she has no equal as regards either her bodily proportions or her very great beauty. This Casildea, then, of whom I am telling you, repaid my worthy affections and honorable intentions by forcing me, as Hercules[5] was forced by his stepmother, to incur

---

5. Son of Zeus and Alcmena; he was persecuted by Zeus's wife, Hera.

many and diverse perils; and each time as I overcame one of them she would promise me that with the next one I should have that which I desired; but instead my labors have continued, forming a chain whose links I am no longer able to count, nor can I say which will be the last one, that shall mark the beginning of the realization of my hopes.

"One time she sent me forth to challenge that famous giantess of Seville, known as La Giralda,[6] who is as strong and brave as if made of brass, and who without moving from the spot where she stands is the most changeable and fickle woman in the world. I came, I saw, I conquered her, I made her stand still and point in one direction only, and for more than a week nothing but north winds blew. Then, there was that other time when Casildea sent me to lift those ancient stones, the mighty Bulls of Guisando,[7] an enterprise that had better have been entrusted to porters than to knights. On another occasion she commanded me to hurl myself down into the Cabra chasm[8]—an unheard-of and terribly dangerous undertaking—and bring her back a detailed account of what lay concealed in that deep and gloomy pit. I rendered La Giralda motionless, I lifted the Bulls of Guisando, and I threw myself into the abyss and brought to light what was hidden in its depths; yet my hopes are dead—how dead!—while her commands and her scorn are as lively as can be.

"Finally, she commanded me to ride through all the provinces of Spain and compel all the knights-errant whom I met with to confess that she is the most beautiful woman now living and that I am the most enamored man of arms that is to be found anywhere in the world. In fulfillment of this behest I have already traveled over the greater part of these realms and have vanquished many knights who have dared to contradict me. But the one whom I am proudest to have overcome in single combat is that famous gentleman, Don Quixote de la Mancha; for I made him confess that my Casildea is more beautiful than his Dulcinea, and by achieving such a conquest I reckon that I have conquered all the others on the face of the earth, seeing that this same Don Quixote had himself routed them. Accordingly, when I vanquished him, his fame, glory, and honor passed over and were transferred to my person.

> The brighter is the conquered one's lost crown,
> The greater is the conqueror's renown.[9]

Thus, the innumerable exploits of the said Don Quixote are now set down to my account and are indeed my own."

Don Quixote was astounded as he listened to the Knight of the Wood, and was about to tell him any number of times that he lied; the words were on the tip of his tongue, but he held them back as best he could, thinking that he would bring the other to confess with his own lips that what he had said was a lie. And so it was quite calmly that he now replied to him.

"Sir Knight," he began, "as to the assertion that your Grace has conquered most of the knights-errant in Spain and even in all the world, I have nothing to say, but that you have vanquished Don Quixote de la Mancha, I am inclined to

6. Actually a statue on the Moorish belfry of the cathedral at Seville.
7. Statues representing animals and supposedly marking a place where Caesar defeated Pompey.

8. Possibly an ancient mine in the Sierra de Cabra near Cordova.
9. From Alonso de Ercilla y Zúñiga's *Araucana*, a poem about the Spanish struggle against the Araucanian Indians of Chile.

doubt. It may be that it was someone else who resembled him, although there are very few that do."

"What do you mean?" replied the one of the Wood. "I swear by the heavens above that I did fight with Don Quixote and that I overcame him and forced him to yield. He is a tall man, with a dried-up face, long, lean legs, graying hair, an eagle-like nose somewhat hooked, and a big, black, drooping mustache. He takes the field under the name of the Knight of the Mournful Countenance, he has for squire a peasant named Sancho Panza, and he rides a famous steed called Rocinante. Lastly, the lady of his heart is a certain Dulcinea del Toboso, once upon a time known as Aldonza Lorenzo, just as my own lady, whose name is Casildea and who is an Andalusian by birth, is called by me Casildea de Vandalia. If all this is not sufficient to show that I speak the truth, here is my sword which shall make incredulity itself believe."

"Calm yourself, Sir Knight," replied Don Quixote, "and listen to what I have to say to you. You must know that this Don Quixote of whom you speak is the best friend that I have in the world, so great a friend that I may say that I feel toward him as I do toward my own self; and from all that you have told me, the very definite and accurate details that you have given me, I cannot doubt that he is the one whom you have conquered. On the other hand, the sight of my eyes and the touch of my hands assure me that he could not possibly be the one, unless some enchanter who is his enemy—for he has many, and one in particular who delights in persecuting him—may have assumed the knight's form and then permitted himself to be routed, by way of defrauding Don Quixote of the fame which his high deeds of chivalry have earned for him throughout the known world. To show you how true this may be, I will inform you that not more than a couple of days ago those same enemy magicians transformed the figure and person of the beauteous Dulcinea del Toboso into a low and mean village lass, and it is possible that they have done something of the same sort to the knight who is her lover. And if all this does not suffice to convince you of the truth of what I say, here is Don Quixote himself who will maintain it by force of arms, on foot or on horseback, or in any way you like."

Saying this, he rose and laid hold of his sword, and waited to see what the Knight of the Wood's decision would be. That worthy now replied in a voice as calm as the one Don Quixote had used.

"Pledges," he said, "do not distress one who is sure of his ability to pay. He who was able to overcome you when you were transformed, Señor Don Quixote, may hope to bring you to your knees when you are your own proper self. But inasmuch as it is not fitting that knights should perform their feats of arms in the darkness, like ruffians and highwaymen, let us wait until it is day in order that the sun may behold what we do. And the condition governing our encounter shall be that the one who is vanquished must submit to the will of his conqueror and perform all those things that are commanded of him, provided they are such as are in keeping with the state of knighthood."

"With that condition and understanding," said Don Quixote, "I shall be satisfied."

With this, they went off to where their squires were, only to find them snoring away as hard as when sleep had first overtaken them. Awakening the pair, they ordered them to look to the horses; for as soon as the sun was up the two knights meant to stage an arduous and bloody single-handed combat. At this news Sancho was astonished and terrified, since, as a result of what the other squire had told him of the Knight of the Wood's prowess, he was led to fear for his master's safety. Nevertheless, he and his friend now went to seek the mounts without saying a word, and they found the animals all together, for by this time the two horses and the ass had smelled one another out. On the way the Squire of the Wood turned to Sancho and addressed him as follows:

"I must inform you, brother, that it is the custom of the fighters of Andalusia, when they are godfathers in any combat, not to remain idly by, with folded hands, while their godsons fight it out. I tell you this by way of warning you that while our masters are settling matters, we, too, shall have to come to blows and hack each other to bits."

"The custom, Sir Squire," replied Sancho, "may be all very well among the fighters and ruffians that you mention, but with the squires of knights-errant it is not to be thought of. At least, I have never heard my master speak of any such custom, and he knows all the laws of chivalry by heart. But granting that it is true and that there is a law which states in so many words that squires must fight while their masters do, I have no intention of obeying it but rather will pay whatever penalty is laid on peaceable-minded ones like myself, for I am sure it cannot be more than a couple of pounds of wax,[1] and that would be less expensive than the lint which it would take to heal my head—I can already see it split in two. What's more, it's out of the question for me to fight since I have no sword nor did I ever in my life carry one."

"That," said the one of the Wood, "is something that is easily remedied. I have here two linen bags of the same size. You take one and I'll take the other and we will fight that way, on equal terms."

"So be it, by all means," said Sancho, "for that will simply knock the dust out of us without wounding us."

"But that's not the way it's to be," said the other squire. "Inside the bags, to keep the wind from blowing them away, we will put a half-dozen nice smooth pebbles of the same weight, and so we'll be able to give each other a good pounding without doing ourselves any real harm or damage."

"Body of my father!" cried Sancho, "just look, will you, at the marten and sable and wads of carded cotton that he's stuffing into those bags so that we won't get our heads cracked or our bones crushed to a pulp. But I am telling you, *Señor mio*, that even though you fill them with silken pellets, I don't mean to fight. Let our masters fight and make the best of it, but as for us, let us drink and live; for time will see to ending our lives without any help on our part by way of bringing them to a close before they have reached their proper season and fall from ripeness."

"Nevertheless," replied the Squire of the Wood, "fight we must, if only for half an hour."

"No," Sancho insisted, "that I will not do. I will not be so impolite or so ungrateful as to pick any quarrel however slight with one whose food and drink I've shared. And, moreover, who in the devil could bring himself to fight in cold blood, when he's not angry or vexed in any way?"

"I can take care of that, right enough," said the one of the Wood. "Before we begin, I will come up to your Grace as nicely as you please and give you three

1. In some confraternities, penalties were paid in wax, presumably to make church candles.

or four punches that will stretch you out at my feet; and that will surely be enough to awaken your anger, even though it's sleeping sounder than a dormouse."

"And I," said Sancho, "have another idea that's every bit as good as yours. I will take a big club, and before your Grace has had a chance to awaken my anger I will put yours to sleep with such mighty whacks that if it wakes at all it will be in the other world; for it is known there that I am not the man to let my face be mussed by anyone, and let each look out for the arrow.[2] But the best thing to do would be to leave one's anger to its slumbers, for no one knows the heart of any other, he who comes for wool may go back shorn, and God bless peace and curse all strife. If a hunted cat when surrounded and cornered turns into a lion, God knows what I who am a man might not become. And so from this time forth I am warning you, Sir Squire, that all the harm and damage that may result from our quarrel will be upon your head."

"Very well," the one of the Wood replied, "God will send the dawn and we shall make out somehow."

At that moment gay-colored birds of all sorts began warbling in the trees and with their merry and varied songs appeared to be greeting and welcoming the fresh-dawning day, which already at the gates and on the balconies of the east was revealing its beautiful face as it shook out from its hair an infinite number of liquid pearls. Bathed in this gentle moisture, the grass seemed to shed a pearly spray, the willows distilled a savory manna, the fountains laughed, the brooks murmured, the woods were glad, and the meadows put on their finest raiment. The first thing that Sancho Panza beheld, as soon as it was light enough to tell one object from another, was the Squire of the Wood's nose, which was so big as to cast into the shade all the rest of his body. In addition to being of enormous size, it is said to have been hooked in the middle and all covered with warts of a mulberry hue, like eggplant; it hung down for a couple of inches below his mouth, and the size, color, warts, and shape of this organ gave his face so ugly an appearance that Sancho began trembling hand and foot like a child with convulsions and made up his mind then and there that he would take a couple of hundred punches before he would let his anger be awakened to a point where he would fight with this monster.

Don Quixote in the meanwhile was surveying his opponent, who had already adjusted and closed his helmet so that it was impossible to make out what he looked like. It was apparent, however, that he was not very tall and was stockily built. Over his armor he wore a coat of some kind or other made of what appeared to be the finest cloth of gold, all bespangled with glittering mirrors that resembled little moons and that gave him a most gallant and festive air, while above his helmet were a large number of waving plumes, green, white, and yellow in color. His lance, which was leaning against a tree, was very long and stout and had a steel point of more than a palm in length. Don Quixote took all this in, and from what he observed concluded that his opponent must be of tremendous strength, but he was not for this reason filled with fear as Sancho Panza was. Rather, he proceeded to address the Knight of the Mirrors, quite boldly and in a highbred manner.

---

2. A proverbial expression from archery: let each one take care of his or her own arrow. Other obviously proverbial expressions follow, as is typical of Sancho's speech.

"Sir Knight," he said, "if in your eagerness to fight you have not lost your courtesy, I would beg you to be so good as to raise your visor a little in order that I may see if your face is as handsome as your trappings."

"Whether you come out of this emprise the victor or the vanquished, Sir Knight," he of the Mirrors replied, "there will be ample time and opportunity for you to have a sight of me. If I do not now gratify your desire, it is because it seems to me that I should be doing a very great wrong to the beauteous Casildea de Vandalia by wasting the time it would take me to raise my visor before having forced you to confess that I am right in my contention, with which you are well acquainted."

"Well, then," said Don Quixote, "while we are mounting our steeds you might at least inform me if I am that knight of La Mancha whom you say you conquered."

"To that our[3] answer," said he of the Mirrors, "is that you are as like the knight I overcame as one egg is like another; but since you assert that you are persecuted by enchanters, I should not venture to state positively that you are the one in question."

"All of which," said Don Quixote, "is sufficient to convince me that you are laboring under a misapprehension; but in order to relieve you of it once and for all, let them bring our steeds, and in less time than you would spend in lifting your visor, if God, my lady, and my arm give me strength, I will see your face and you shall see that I am not the vanquished knight you take me to be."

With this, they cut short their conversation and mounted, and, turning Rocinante around, Don Quixote began measuring off the proper length of field for a run against his opponent as he of the Mirrors did the same. But the Knight of La Mancha had not gone twenty paces when he heard his adversary calling to him, whereupon each of them turned halfway and he of the Mirrors spoke.

"I must remind you, Sir Knight," he said, "of the condition under which we fight, which is that the vanquished, as I have said before, shall place himself wholly at the disposition of the victor."

"I am aware of that," replied Don Quixote, "not forgetting the provision that the behest laid upon the vanquished shall not exceed the bounds of chivalry."

"Agreed," said the Knight of the Mirrors.

At that moment Don Quixote caught sight of the other squire's weird nose and was as greatly astonished by it as Sancho had been. Indeed, he took the fellow for some monster, or some new kind of human being wholly unlike those that people this world. As he saw his master riding away down the field preparatory to the tilt, Sancho was alarmed; for he did not like to be left alone with the big-nosed individual, fearing that one powerful swipe of that protuberance against his own nose would end the battle so far as he was concerned and he would be lying stretched out on the ground, from fear if not from the force of the blow.

He accordingly ran after the knight, clinging to one of Rocinante's stirrup straps, and when he thought it was time for Don Quixote to whirl about and bear down upon his opponent, he called to him and said, "*Señor mio*, I beg your Grace, before you turn for the charge, to help me up into that cork tree

3. Note the dignified, "majestic" plural form.

yonder where I can watch the encounter which your Grace is going to have with this knight better than I can from the ground and in a way that is much more to my liking."

"I rather think, Sancho," said Don Quixote, "that what you wish to do is to mount a platform where you can see the bulls without any danger to yourself."

"The truth of the matter is," Sancho admitted, "the monstrous nose on that squire has given me such a fright that I don't dare stay near him."

"It is indeed of such a sort," his master assured him, "that if I were not the person I am, I myself should be frightened. And so, come, I will help you up."

While Don Quixote tarried to see Sancho ensconced in the cork tree, the Knight of the Mirrors measured as much ground as seemed to him necessary and then, assuming that his adversary had done the same, without waiting for sound of trumpet or any other signal, he wheeled his horse, which was no swifter nor any more impressive-looking than Rocinante, and bore down upon his enemy at a mild trot; but when he saw that the Manchegan was busy helping his squire, he reined in his mount and came to a stop midway in his course, for which his horse was extremely grateful, being no longer able to stir a single step. To Don Quixote, on the other hand, it seemed as if his enemy was flying, and digging his spurs with all his might into Rocinante's lean flanks he caused that animal to run a bit for the first and only time, according to the history, for on all other occasions a simple trot had represented his utmost speed. And so it was that, with an unheard-of fury, the Knight of the Mournful Countenance came down upon the Knight of the Mirrors as the latter sat there sinking his spurs all the way up to the buttons without being able to persuade his horse to budge a single inch from the spot where he had come to a sudden standstill.

It was at this fortunate moment, while his adversary was in such a predicament, that Don Quixote fell upon him, quite unmindful of the fact that the other knight was having trouble with his mount and either was unable or did not have time to put his lance at rest. The upshot of it was, he encountered him with such force that, much against his will, the Knight of the Mirrors went rolling over his horse's flanks and tumbled to the ground, where as a result of his terrific fall he lay as if dead, without moving hand or foot.

No sooner did Sancho perceive what had happened than he slipped down from the cork tree and ran up as fast as he could to where his master was. Dismounting from Rocinante, Don Quixote now stood over the Knight of the Mirrors, and undoing the helmet straps to see if the man was dead, or to give him air in case he was alive, he beheld—who can say what he beheld without creating astonishment, wonder, and amazement in those who hear the tale? The history tells us that it was the very countenance, form, aspect, physiognomy, effigy, and image of the bachelor Sansón Carrasco!

"Come, Sancho," he cried in a loud voice, "and see what is to be seen but is not to be believed. Hasten, my son, and learn what magic can do and how great is the power of wizards and enchanters."

Sancho came, and the moment his eyes fell on the bachelor Carrasco's face he began crossing and blessing himself a countless number of times. Meanwhile, the overthrown knight gave no signs of life.

"If you ask me, master," said Sancho, "I would say that the best thing for your Grace to do is to run his sword down the mouth of this one who appears to be the bachelor Carrasco; maybe by so doing you would be killing one of your enemies, the enchanters."

"That is not a bad idea," replied Don Quixote, "for the fewer enemies the better." And, drawing his sword, he was about to act upon Sancho's advice and counsel when the Knight of the Mirrors' squire came up to them, now minus the nose which had made him so ugly.

"Look well what you are doing, Don Quixote!" he cried. "The one who lies there at your feet is your Grace's friend, the bachelor Sansón Carrasco, and I am his squire."

"And where is your nose?" inquired Sancho, who was surprised to see him without that deformity.

"Here in my pocket," was the reply. And, thrusting his hand into his coat, he drew out a nose of varnished pasteboard of the make that has been described. Studying him more and more closely, Sancho finally exclaimed, in a voice that was filled with amazement, "Holy Mary preserve me! And is this not my neighbor and crony, Tomé Cecial?"

"That is who I am!" replied the de-nosed squire, "your good friend Tomé Cecial, Sancho Panza. I will tell you presently of the means and snares and falsehoods that brought me here. But, for the present, I beg and entreat your master not to lay hands on, mistreat, wound, or slay the Knight of the Mirrors whom he now has at his feet; for without any doubt it is the rash and ill-advised bachelor Sansón Carrasco, our fellow villager."

The Knight of the Mirrors now recovered consciousness, and, seeing this, Don Quixote at once placed the naked point of his sword above the face of the vanquished one.

"Dead you are, knight," he said, "unless you confess that the peerless Dulcinea del Toboso is more beautiful than your Casildea de Vandalia. And what is more, you will have to promise that, should you survive this encounter and the fall you have had, you will go to the city of El Toboso and present yourself to her in my behalf, that she may do with you as she may see fit. And in case she leaves you free to follow your own will, you are to return to seek me out— the trail of my exploits will serve as a guide to bring you wherever I may be— and tell me all that has taken place between you and her. These conditions are in conformity with those that we arranged before our combat and they do not go beyond the bounds of knight-errantry."

"I confess," said the fallen knight, "that the tattered and filthy shoe of the lady Dulcinea del Toboso is of greater worth than the badly combed if clean beard of Casildea, and I promise to go to her presence and return to yours and to give you a complete and detailed account concerning anything you may wish to know."

"Another thing," added Don Quixote, "that you will have to confess and believe is that the knight you conquered was not and could not have been Don Quixote de la Mancha, but was some other that resembled him, just as I am convinced that you, though you appear to be the bachelor Sansón Carrasco, are another person in his form and likeness who has been put here by my enemies to induce me to restrain and moderate the impetuosity of my wrath and make a gentle use of my glorious victory."

"I confess, think, and feel as you feel, think, and believe," replied the lamed knight. "Permit me to rise, I beg of you, if the jolt I received in my fall will let me do so, for I am in very bad shape."

DON QUIXOTE, PART II, CH. 15 | 1775

Don Quixote and Tomé Cecial the squire now helped him to his feet. As for Sancho, he could not take his eyes off Tomé but kept asking him one question after another, and although the answers he received afforded clear enough proof that the man was really his fellow townsman, the fear that had been aroused in him by his master's words—about the enchanters' having transformed the Knight of the Mirrors into the bachelor Sansón Carrasco—prevented him from believing the truth that was apparent to his eyes. The short of it is, both master and servant were left with this delusion as the other ill-errant knight and his squire, in no pleasant state of mind, took their departure with the object of looking for some village where they might be able to apply poultices and splints to the bachelor's battered ribs.

Don Quixote and Sancho then resumed their journey along the road to Saragossa, and here for the time being the history leaves them in order to give an account of who the Knight of the Mirrors and his long-nosed squire really were.

CHAPTER 15

*Wherein is told and revealed who the Knight of the Mirrors
and his squire were.*

Don Quixote went off very happy, self-satisfied, and vainglorious at having achieved a victory over so valiant a knight as he imagined the one of the Mirrors to be, from whose knightly word he hoped to learn whether or not the spell which had been put upon his lady was still in effect; for, unless he chose to forfeit his honor, the vanquished contender must of necessity return and give an account of what had happened in the course of his interview with her. But Don Quixote was of one mind, the Knight of the Mirrors of another, for, as has been stated, the latter's only thought at the moment was to find some village where plasters were available.

The history goes on to state that when the bachelor Sansón Carrasco advised Don Quixote to resume his feats of chivalry, after having desisted from them for a while, this action was taken as the result of a conference which he had held with the curate and the barber as to the means to be adopted in persuading the knight to remain quietly at home and cease agitating himself over his unfortunate adventures. It had been Carrasco's suggestion, to which they had unanimously agreed, that they let Don Quixote sally forth, since it appeared to be impossible to prevent his doing so, and that Sansón should then take to the road as a knight-errant and pick a quarrel and do battle with him. There would be no difficulty about finding a pretext, and then the bachelor knight would overcome him (which was looked upon as easy of accomplishment), having first entered into a pact to the effect that the vanquished should remain at the mercy and bidding of his conqueror. The behest in this case was to be that the fallen one should return to his village and home and not leave it for the space of two years or until further orders were given him, it being a certainty that, once having been overcome, Don Quixote would fulfill the agreement, in order not to contravene or fail to obey the laws of chivalry. And it was possible that in the course of his seclusion he would forget his fancies, or they would at least have an opportunity to seek some suitable cure for his madness.

Sansón agreed to undertake this, and Tomé Cecial, Sancho's friend and neighbor, a merry but featherbrained chap, offered to go along as squire. Sansón then proceeded to arm himself in the manner that has been described, while Tomé disguised his nose with the aforementioned mask so that his crony would not recognize him when they met. Thus equipped, they followed the same route as Don Quixote and had almost caught up with him by the time he had the adventure with the Cart of Death. They finally overtook him in the wood, where those events occurred with which the attentive reader is already familiar; and if it had not been for the knight's extraordinary fancies, which led him to believe that the bachelor was not the bachelor, the said bachelor might have been prevented from ever attaining his degree of licentiate, as a result of having found no nests where he thought to find birds.

Seeing how ill they had succeeded in their undertaking and what an end they had reached, Tomé Cecial now addressed his master.

"Surely, Señor Sansón Carrasco," he said, "we have had our deserts. It is easy enough to plan and embark upon an enterprise, but most of the time it's hard to get out of it. Don Quixote is a madman and we are sane, yet he goes away sound and laughing while your Grace is left here, battered and sorrowful. I wish you would tell me now who is the crazier: the one who is so because he cannot help it, or he who turns crazy of his own free will?"

"The difference between the two," replied Sansón, "lies in this: that the one who cannot help being crazy will be so always, whereas the one who is a madman by choice can leave off being one whenever he so desires."

"Well," said Tomé Cecial, "since that is the way it is, and since I chose to be crazy when I became your Grace's squire, by the same reasoning I now choose to stop being insane and to return to my home."

"That is your affair," said Sansón, "but to imagine that I am going back before I have given Don Quixote a good thrashing is senseless; and what will urge me on now is not any desire to see him recover his wits, but rather a thirst for vengeance; for with the terrible pain that I have in my ribs, you can't expect me to feel very charitable."

Conversing in this manner they kept on until they reached a village where it was their luck to find a bonesetter to take care of poor Sansón. Tomé Cecial then left him and returned home, while the bachelor meditated plans for revenge. The history has more to say of him in due time, but for the present it goes on to make merry with Don Quixote.

CHAPTER 16

Of what happened to Don Quixote upon his meeting with a prudent gentleman of La Mancha.

With that feeling of happiness and vainglorious self-satisfaction that has been mentioned, Don Quixote continued on his way, imagining himself to be, as a result of the victory he had just achieved, the most valiant knight-errant of the age. Whatever adventures might befall him from then on he regarded as already accomplished and brought to a fortunate conclusion. He thought little now of enchanters and enchantments and was unmindful of the innumerable beatings he had received in the course of his knightly wanderings, of the volley of pebbles that had knocked out half his teeth, of the ungratefulness of the galley slaves and the audacity of the Yanguesans whose poles had fallen upon his body like rain. In short, he told himself, if he could but find the means, manner, or way of freeing his lady Dulcinea of the spell that had been put upon her, he would not envy the greatest good fortune that the most fortunate of knights-errant in ages past had ever by any possibility attained.

He was still wholly wrapped up in these thoughts when Sancho spoke to him.

"Isn't it strange, sir, that I can still see in front of my eyes the huge and monstrous nose of my old crony, Tomé Cecial?"

"And do you by any chance believe, Sancho, that the Knight of the Mirrors was the bachelor Sansón Carrasco and that his squire was your friend Tomé?"

"I don't know what to say to that," replied Sancho. "All I know is that the things he told me about my home, my wife and young ones, could not have come from anybody else; and the face, too, once you took the nose away, was the same as Tomé Cecial's, which I have seen many times in our village, right next door to my own house, and the tone of voice was the same also."

"Let us reason the matter out, Sancho," said Don Quixote. "Look at it this way: how can it be thought that the bachelor Sansón Carrasco would come as a knight-errant, equipped with offensive and defensive armor, to contend with me? Am I, perchance, his enemy? Have I given him any occasion to cherish a grudge against me? Am I a rival of his? Or can it be jealousy of the fame I have acquired that has led him to take up the profession of arms?"

"Well, then, sir," Sancho answered him, "how are we to explain the fact that the knight was so like the bachelor and his squire like my friend? And if this was a magic spell, as your Grace has said, was there no other pair in the world whose likeness they might have taken?"

"It is all a scheme and a plot," replied Don Quixote, "on the part of those wicked magicians who are persecuting me and who, foreseeing that I would be the victor in the combat, saw to it that the conquered knight should display the face of my friend the bachelor, so that the affection which I bear him would come between my fallen enemy and the edge of my sword and might of my arm, to temper the righteous indignation of my heart. In that way, he who had sought by falsehood and deceits to take my life, would be left to go on living. As proof of all this, Sancho, experience, which neither lies nor deceives, has already taught you how easy it is for enchanters to change one countenance into another, making the beautiful ugly and the ugly beautiful. It was not two days ago that you beheld the peerless Dulcinea's beauty and elegance in its entirety and natural form, while I saw only the repulsive features of a low and ignorant peasant girl with cataracts over her eyes and a foul smell in her mouth. And if the perverse enchanter was bold enough to effect so vile a transformation as this, there is certainly no cause for wonderment at what he has done in the case of Sansón Carrasco and your friend, all by way of snatching my glorious victory out of my hands. But in spite of it all, I find consolation in the fact that, whatever the shape he may have chosen to assume, I have laid my enemy low."

"God knows what the truth of it all may be," was Sancho's comment. Knowing as he did that Dulcinea's transformation had been due to his own scheming and plotting, he was not taken in by his master's delusions. He was at a loss for a reply, however, lest he say something that would reveal his own trickery.

As they were carrying on this conversation, they were overtaken by a man who, following the same road, was coming along behind them. He was mounted on a handsome flea-bitten mare and wore a hooded greatcoat of fine green cloth trimmed in tawny velvet and a cap of the same material, while the trappings of his steed, which was accoutered for the field, were green and mulberry in hue, his saddle being of the *jineta*[4] mode. From his broad green and gold shoulder strap there dangled a Moorish cutlass, and his half-boots were of the same make as the baldric. His spurs were not gilded but were covered with highly polished green lacquer, so that harmonizing as they did with the rest of his apparel, they seemed more appropriate than if they had been of purest gold. As he came up, he greeted the pair courteously and, spurring his mare, was about to ride on past when Don Quixote called to him.

"Gallant sir," he said. "If your Grace is going our way and is not in a hurry, it would be a favor to us if we might travel together."

"The truth is," replied the stranger, "I should not have ridden past you if I had not been afraid that the company of my mare would excite your horse."

"In that case, sir," Sancho spoke up, "you may as well rein in, for this horse of ours is the most virtuous and well mannered of any that there is. Never on such an occasion has he done anything that was not right—the only time he did misbehave, my master and I suffered for it aplenty. And so, I say again, your Grace may slow up if you like; for even if you offered him your mare on a couple of platters, he'd never try to mount her."

With this, the other traveler drew rein, being greatly astonished at Don Quixote's face and figure. For the knight was now riding along without his helmet, which was carried by Sancho like a piece of luggage on the back of his gray, in front of the packsaddle. If the green-clad gentleman stared hard at his new-found companion, the latter returned his gaze with an even greater intensity. He impressed Don Quixote as being a man of good judgment, around fifty years of age, with hair that was slightly graying and an aquiline nose, while the expression of his countenance was half humorous, half serious. In short, both his person and his accoutrements indicated that he was an individual of some worth.

As for the man in green's impression of Don Quixote de la Mancha, he was thinking that he had never before seen any human being that resembled this one. He could not but marvel at the knight's long neck, his tall frame, and the leanness and the sallowness of his face, as well as his armor and his grave bearing, the whole constituting a sight such as had not been seen for many a day in those parts. Don Quixote in turn was quite conscious of the attentiveness with which the traveler was studying him and could tell from the man's astonished look how curious he was; and so, being very courteous and fond of pleasing everyone, he proceeded to anticipate any questions that might be asked him.

"I am aware," he said, "that my appearance must strike your Grace as being very strange and out of the ordinary, and for that reason I am not surprised at your wonderment. But your Grace will cease to wonder when I tell you, as I am telling you now, that I am a knight, one of those

> Of whom it is folks say,
> They to adventures go.

4. It has a high pommel and short stirrups.

I have left my native health, mortgaged my estate, given up my comfortable life, and cast myself into fortune's arms for her to do with me what she will. It has been my desire to revive a knight-errantry that is now dead, and for some time past, stumbling here and falling there, now throwing myself down headlong and then rising up once more, I have been able in good part to carry out my design by succoring widows, protecting damsels, and aiding the fallen, the orphans, and the young, all of which is the proper and natural duty of knights-errant. As a result, owing to my many valiant and Christian exploits, I have been deemed worthy of visiting in printed form nearly all the nations of the world. Thirty thousand copies of my history have been published, and, unless Heaven forbid, they will print thirty million of them.

"In short, to put it all into a few words, or even one, I will tell you that I am Don Quixote de la Mancha, otherwise known as the Knight of the Mournful Countenance. Granted that self-praise is degrading, there still are times when I must praise myself, that is to say, when there is no one else present to speak in my behalf. And so, good sir, neither this steed nor this lance nor this buckler nor this squire of mine, nor all the armor that I wear and arms I carry, nor the sallowness of my complexion, nor my leanness and gauntness, should any longer astonish you, now that you know who I am and what the profession is that I follow."

Having thus spoken, Don Quixote fell silent, and the man in green was so slow in replying that it seemed as if he was at a loss for words. Finally, however, after a considerable while, he brought himself to the point of speaking.

"You were correct, Sir Knight," he said, "about my astonishment and my curiosity, but you have not succeeded in removing the wonderment that the sight of you has aroused in me. You say that, knowing who you are, I should not wonder any more, but such is not the case, for I am now more amazed than ever. How can it be that there are knights-errant in the world today and that histories of them are actually printed? I find it hard to convince myself that at the present time there is anyone on earth who goes about aiding widows, protecting damsels, defending the honor of wives, and succoring orphans, and I should never have believed it had I not beheld your Grace with my own eyes. Thank Heaven for that book that your Grace tells me has been published concerning your true and exalted deeds of chivalry, as it should cast into oblivion all the innumerable stories of fictitious knights-errant with which the world is filled, greatly to the detriment of good morals and the prejudice and discredit of legitimate histories."

"As to whether the stories of knights-errant are fictitious or not," observed Don Quixote, "there is much that remains to be said."

"Why," replied the gentleman in green, "is there anyone who can doubt that such tales are false?"

"I doubt it," was the knight's answer, "but let the matter rest there. If our journey lasts long enough, I trust with God's help to be able to show your Grace that you are wrong in going along with those who hold it to be a certainty that they are not true."

From this last remark the traveler was led to suspect that Don Quixote must be some kind of crackbrain, and he was waiting for him to confirm the impression by further observations of the same sort; but before they could get off on another subject, the knight, seeing that he had given an account of his own station in life, turned to the stranger and politely inquired who his companion might be.

"I, Sir Knight of the Mournful Countenance," replied the one in the green-colored greatcoat, "am a gentleman, and a native of the village where, please God, we are going to dine today. I am more than moderately rich, and my name is Don Diego de Miranda. I spend my life with my wife and children and with my friends. My occupations are hunting and fishing, though I keep neither falcon nor hounds but only a tame partridge[5] and a bold ferret or two. I am the owner of about six dozen books, some of them in Spanish, others in Latin, including both histories and devotional works. As for books of chivalry, they have not as yet crossed the threshold of my door. My own preference is for profane rather than devotional writings, such as afford an innocent amusement, charming us by their style and arousing and holding our interest by their inventiveness, although I must say there are very few of that sort to be found in Spain.

"Sometimes," the man in green continued, "I dine with my friends and neighbors, and I often invite them to my house. My meals are wholesome and well prepared and there is always plenty to eat. I do not care for gossip, nor will I permit it in my presence. I am not lynx-eyed and do not pry into the lives and doings of others. I hear mass every day and share my substance with the poor, but make no parade of my good works lest hypocrisy and vainglory, those enemies that so imperceptibly take possession of the most modest heart, should find their way into mine. I try to make peace between those who are at strife. I am the devoted servant of Our Lady, and my trust is in the infinite mercy of God Our Savior."

Sancho had listened most attentively to the gentleman's account of his mode of life, and inasmuch as it seemed to him that this was a good and holy way to live and that the one who followed such a pattern ought to be able to work miracles, he now jumped down from his gray's back and, running over to seize the stranger's right stirrup, began kissing the feet of the man in green with a show of devotion that bordered on tears.

"Why are you doing that, brother?" the gentleman asked him. "What is the meaning of these kisses?"

"Let me kiss your feet," Sancho insisted, "for if I am not mistaken, your Grace is the first saint riding *jineta* fashion that I have seen in all the days of my life."

"I am not a saint," the gentleman assured him, "but a great sinner. It is you, brother, who are the saint; for you must be a good man, judging by the simplicity of heart that you show."

Sancho then went back to his packsaddle, having evoked a laugh from the depths of his master's melancholy and given Don Diego fresh cause for astonishment.

Don Quixote thereupon inquired of the newcomer how many children he had, remarking as he did so that the ancient philosophers, who were without a true knowledge of God, believed that mankind's greatest good lay in the gifts of nature, in those of fortune, and in having many friends and many and worthy sons.

5. Used as a decoy.

"I, Señor Don Quixote," replied the gentleman, "have a son without whom I should, perhaps, be happier than I am. It is not that he is bad, but rather that he is not as good as I should like him to be. He is eighteen years old, and for six of those years he has been at Salamanca studying the Greek and Latin languages. When I desired him to pass on to other branches of learning, I found him so immersed in the science of Poetry (if it can be called such) that it was not possible to interest him in the Law, which I wanted him to study, nor in Theology, the queen of them all. My wish was that he might be an honor to his family; for in this age in which we are living our monarchs are in the habit of highly rewarding those forms of learning that are good and virtuous, since learning without virtue is like pearls on a dunghill. But he spends the whole day trying to decide whether such and such a verse of Homer's *Iliad* is well conceived or not, whether or not Martial is immodest in a certain epigram, whether certain lines of Vergil are to be understood in this way or in that. In short, he spends all of his time with the books written by those poets whom I have mentioned and with those of Horace, Persius, Juvenal, and Tibullus. As for our own moderns, he sets little store by them, and yet, for all his disdain of Spanish poetry, he is at this moment racking his brains in an effort to compose a gloss on a quatrain that was sent him from Salamanca and which, I fancy, is for some literary tournament."

To all this Don Quixote made the following answer:

"Children, sir, are out of their parents' bowels and so are to be loved whether they be good or bad, just as we love those that gave us life. It is for parents to bring up their offspring, from the time they are infants, in the paths of virtue, good breeding, proper conduct, and Christian morality, in order that, when they are grown, they may be a staff to the old age of the ones that bore them and an honor to their own posterity. As to compelling them to study a particular branch of learning, I am not so sure as to that, though there may be no harm in trying to persuade them to do so. But where there is no need to study *pane lucrando*[6]—where Heaven has provided them with parents that can supply their daily bread—I should be in favor of permitting them to follow that course to which they are most inclined; and although poetry may be more pleasurable than useful, it is not one of those pursuits that bring dishonor upon those who engage in them.

"Poetry in my opinion, my dear sir," he went on, "is a young and tender maid of surpassing beauty, who has many other damsels (that is to say, the other disciplines) whose duty it is to bedeck, embellish, and adorn her. She may call upon all of them for service, and all of them in turn depend upon her nod. She is not one to be rudely handled, nor dragged through the streets, nor exposed at street corners, in the market place, or in the private nooks of palaces. She is fashioned through an alchemy of such power that he who knows how to make use of it will be able to convert her into the purest gold of inestimable price. Possessing her, he must keep her within bounds and not permit her to run wild in bawdy satires or soulless sonnets. She is not to be put up for sale in any manner, unless it be in the form of heroic poems, pity-inspiring tragedies, or pleasing and ingenious comedies. Let mountebanks keep hands off her, and the ignorant mob as well, which is incapable of recognizing or appreciating the

6. Earning one's bread (Latin).

treasures that are locked within her. And do not think, sir, that I apply that term 'mob' solely to plebeians and those of low estate; for anyone who is ignorant, whether he be lord or prince, may, and should, be included in the vulgar herd.

"But," Don Quixote continued, "he who possesses the gift of poetry and who makes the use of it that I have indicated, shall become famous and his name shall be honored among all the civilized nations of the world. You have stated, sir, that your son does not greatly care for poetry written in our Spanish tongue, and in that I am inclined to think he is somewhat mistaken. My reason for saying so is this: the great Homer did not write in Latin, for the reason that he was a Greek, and Vergil did not write in Greek since he was a Latin. In a word, all the poets of antiquity wrote in the language which they had imbibed with their mother's milk and did not go searching after foreign ones to express their loftiest conceptions. This being so, it would be well if the same custom were to be adopted by all nations, the German poet being no longer looked down upon because he writes in German, nor the Castilian or the Basque for employing his native speech.

"As for your son, I fancy, sir, that his quarrel is not so much with Spanish poetry as with those poets who have no other tongue or discipline at their command such as would help to awaken their natural gift; and yet, here, too, he may be wrong. There is an opinion, and a true one, to the effect that 'the poet is born,' that is to say, it is as a poet that he comes forth from his mother's womb, and with the propensity that has been bestowed upon him by Heaven, without study or artifice, he produces those compositions that attest the truth of the line: '*Est deus in nobis*,'[7] etc. I further maintain that the born poet who is aided by art will have a great advantage over the one who by art alone would become a poet, the reason being that art does not go beyond, but merely perfects, nature; and so it is that, by combining nature with art and art with nature, the finished poet is produced.

"In conclusion, then, my dear sir, my advice to you would be to let your son go where his star beckons him; for being a good student as he must be, and having already successfully mounted the first step on the stairway of learning, which is that of languages, he will be able to continue of his own accord to the very peak of humane letters, an accomplishment that is altogether becoming in a gentleman, one that adorns, honors, and distinguishes him as much as the miter does the bishop or his flowing robe the learned jurisconsult. Your Grace well may reprove your son, should he compose satires that reflect upon the honor of other persons; in that case, punish him and tear them up. But should he compose discourses in the manner of Horace, in which he reprehends vice in general as that poet so elegantly does, then praise him by all means; for it is permitted the poet to write verses in which he inveighs against envy and the other vices as well, and to lash out at the vicious without, however, designating any particular individual. On the other hand, there are poets who for the sake of uttering something malicious would run the risk of being banished to the shores of Pontus.[8]

"If the poet be chaste where his own manners are concerned, he would likewise be modest in his verses, for the pen is the tongue of the mind, and

7. There is a god in us (Latin); Ovid's *Fasti* 6.5.   8. As Ovid was by Augustus in 8 C.E.

whatever thoughts are engendered there are bound to appear in his writings. When kings and princes behold the marvelous art of poetry as practiced by prudent, virtuous, and serious-minded subjects of their realm, they honor, esteem, and reward those persons and crown them with the leaves of the tree that is never struck by lightning[9]—as if to show that those who are crowned and adorned with such wreaths are not to be assailed by anyone."

The gentleman in the green-colored greatcoat was vastly astonished by this speech of Don Quixote's and was rapidly altering the opinion he had previously held, to the effect that his companion was but a crackbrain. In the middle of the long discourse, which was not greatly to his liking, Sancho had left the highway to go seek a little milk from some shepherds who were draining the udders of their ewes near by. Extremely well pleased with the knight's sound sense and excellent reasoning, the gentleman was about to resume the conversation when, raising his head, Don Quixote caught sight of a cart flying royal flags that was coming toward them down the road and, thinking it must be a fresh adventure, began calling to Sancho in a loud voice to bring him his helmet. Whereupon Sancho hastily left the shepherds and spurred his gray until he was once more alongside his master, who was now about to encounter a dreadful and bewildering ordeal.

["For I Well Know the Meaning of Valor"]

CHAPTER 17

Wherein Don Quixote's unimaginable courage reaches its highest point, together with the adventure of the lions and its happy ending.

The history relates that, when Don Quixote called to Sancho to bring him his helmet, the squire was busy buying some curds from the shepherds and, flustered by his master's great haste, did not know what to do with them or how to carry them. Having already paid for the curds, he did not care to lose them, and so he decided to put them into the headpiece, and, acting upon this happy inspiration, he returned to see what was wanted of him.

"Give me that helmet," said the knight; "for either I know little about adventures or here is one where I am going to need my armor."

Upon hearing this, the gentleman in the green-colored greatcoat looked around in all directions but could see nothing except the cart that was approaching them, decked out with two or three flags which indicated that the vehicle in question must be conveying his Majesty's property. He remarked as much to Don Quixote, but the latter paid no attention, for he was always convinced that whatever happened to him meant adventures and more adventures.

"Forewarned is forearmed," he said. "I lose nothing by being prepared, knowing as I do that I have enemies both visible and invisible and cannot tell when or where or in what form they will attack me."

Turning to Sancho, he asked for his helmet again, and as there was no time to shake out the curds, the squire had to hand it to him as it was. Don Quixote

9. The laurel.

took it and, without noticing what was in it, hastily clapped it on his head; and forthwith, as a result of the pressure on the curds, the whey began running down all over his face and beard, at which he was very much startled.

"What is this, Sancho?" he cried. "I think my head must be softening or my brains melting, or else I am sweating from head to foot. If sweat it be, I assure you it is not from fear, though I can well believe that the adventure which now awaits me is a terrible one indeed. Give me something with which to wipe my face, if you have anything, for this perspiration is so abundant that it blinds me."

Sancho said nothing but gave him a cloth and at the same time gave thanks to God that his master had not discovered what the trouble was. Don Quixote wiped his face and then took off his helmet to see what it was that made his head feel so cool. Catching sight of that watery white mass, he lifted it to his nose and smelled it.

"By the life of my lady Dulcinea del Toboso!" he exclaimed. "Those are curds that you have put there, you treacherous, brazen, ill-mannered squire!"

To this Sancho replied, very calmly and with a straight face, "If they are curds, give them to me, your Grace, so that I can eat them. But no, let the devil eat them, for he must be the one who did it. Do you think I would be so bold as to soil your Grace's helmet? Upon my word, master, by the understanding that God has given me, I, too, must have enchanters who are persecuting me as your Grace's creature and one of his members, and they are the ones who put that filthy mess there to make you lose your patience and your temper and cause you to whack my ribs as you are in the habit of doing. Well, this time, I must say, they have missed the mark; for I trust my master's good sense to tell him that I have neither curds nor milk nor anything of the kind, and if I did have, I'd put it in my stomach and not in that helmet."

"That may very well be," said Don Quixote.

Don Diego was observing all this and was more astonished than ever, especially when, after he had wiped his head, face, beard, and helmet, Don Quixote once more donned the piece of armor and, settling himself in the stirrups, proceeded to adjust his sword and fix his lance.

"Come what may, here I stand, ready to take on Satan himself in person!" shouted the knight.

The cart with the flags had come up to them by this time, accompanied only by a driver riding one of the mules and a man seated up in front.

"Where are you going, brothers?" Don Quixote called out as he placed himself in the path of the cart. "What conveyance is this, what do you carry in it, and what is the meaning of those flags?"

"The cart is mine," replied the driver, "and in it are two fierce lions in cages which the governor of Oran is sending to court as a present for his Majesty. The flags are those of our lord the King, as a sign that his property goes here."

"And are the lions large?" inquired Don Quixote.

It was the man sitting at the door of the cage who answered him. "The largest," he said, "that ever were sent from Africa to Spain. I am the lionkeeper and I have brought back others, but never any like these. They are male and female. The male is in this first cage, the female in the one behind. They are hungry right now, for they have had nothing to eat today; and so we'd he obliged if your Grace would get out of the way, for we must hasten on to the place where we are to feed them."

"Lion whelps against me?" said Don Quixote with a slight smile. "Lion whelps against me? And at such an hour? Then, by God, those gentlemen who sent them shall see whether I am the man to be frightened by lions. Get down, my good fellow, and since you are the lionkeeper, open the cages and turn those beasts out for me; and in the middle of this plain I will teach them who Don Quixote de la Mancha is, notwithstanding and in spite of the enchanters who are responsible for their being here."

"So," said the gentleman to himself as he heard this, "our worthy knight has revealed himself. It must indeed be true that the curds have softened his skull and mellowed his brains."

At this point Sancho approached him. "For God's sake, sir," he said, "do something to keep my master from fighting those lions. For if he does, they're going to tear us all to bits."

"Is your master, then, so insane," the gentleman asked, "that you fear and believe he means to tackle those fierce animals?"

"It is not that he is insane," replied Sancho, "but, rather, foolhardy."

"Very well," said the gentleman, "I will put a stop to it." And going up to Don Quixote, who was still urging the lionkeeper to open the cages, he said, "Sir Knight, knights-errant should undertake only those adventures that afford some hope of a successful outcome, not those that are utterly hopeless to begin with; for valor when it turns to temerity has in it more of madness than of bravery. Moreover, these lions have no thought of attacking your Grace but are a present to his Majesty, and it would not be well to detain them or interfere with their journey."

"My dear sir," answered Don Quixote, "you had best go mind your tame partridge and that bold ferret of yours and let each one attend to his own business. This is my affair, and I know whether these gentlemen, the lions, have come to attack me or not." He then turned to the lionkeeper. "I swear, Sir Rascal, if you do not open those cages at once, I'll pin you to the cart with this lance!"

Perceiving how determined the armed phantom was, the driver now spoke up. "Good sir," he said, "will your Grace please be so kind as to let me unhitch the mules and take them to a safe place before you turn those lions loose? For if they kill them for me, I am ruined for life, since the mules and cart are all the property I own."

"O man of little faith!" said Don Quixote. "Get down and unhitch your mules if you like, but you will soon see that it was quite unnecessary and that you might have spared yourself the trouble."

The driver did so, in great haste, as the lionkeeper began shouting, "I want you all to witness that I am being compelled against my will to open the cages and turn the lions out, and I further warn this gentleman that he will be responsible for all the harm and damage the beasts may do, plus my wages and my fees. You other gentlemen take cover before I open the doors; I am sure they will not do any harm to me."

Once more Don Diego sought to persuade his companion not to commit such an act of madness, as it was tempting God to undertake anything so foolish as that; but Don Quixote's only answer was that he knew what he was doing. And when the gentleman in green insisted that he was sure the knight was laboring under a delusion and ought to consider the matter well, the latter cut him short.

"Well, then, sir," he said, "if your Grace does not care to be a spectator at what you believe is going to turn out to be a tragedy, all you have to do is to spur your flea-bitten mare and seek safety."

Hearing this, Sancho with tears in his eyes again begged him to give up the undertaking, in comparison with which the adventure of the windmills and the dreadful one at the fulling mills—indeed, all the exploits his master had ever in the course of his life undertaken—were but bread and cakes.

"Look, sir," Sancho went on, "there is no enchantment here nor anything of the sort. Through the bars and chinks of that cage I have seen a real lion's claw, and judging by the size of it, the lion that it belongs to is bigger than a mountain."

"Fear, at any rate," said Don Quixote, "will make him look bigger to you than half the world. Retire, Sancho, and leave me, and if I die here, you know our ancient pact: you are to repair to Dulcinea—I say no more."

To this he added other remarks that took away any hope they had that he might not go through with his insane plan. The gentleman in the green-colored greatcoat was of a mind to resist him but saw that he was no match for the knight in the matter of arms. Then, too, it did not seem to him the part of wisdom to fight it out with a madman; for Don Quixote now impressed him as being quite mad in every way. Accordingly, while the knight was repeating his threats to the lionkeeper, Don Diego spurred his mare, Sancho his gray, and the driver his mules, all of them seeking to put as great a distance as possible between themselves and the cart before the lions broke loose.

Sancho already was bewailing his master's death, which he was convinced was bound to come from the lions' claws, and at the same time he cursed his fate and called it an unlucky hour in which he had taken it into his head to serve such a one. But despite his tears and lamentations, he did not leave off thrashing his gray in an effort to leave the cart behind them. When the lionkeeper saw that those who had fled were a good distance away, he once more entreated and warned Don Quixote as he had warned and entreated him before, but the answer he received was that he might save his breath as it would do him no good and he had best hurry and obey. In the space of time that it took the keeper to open the first cage, Don Quixote considered the question as to whether it would be well to give battle on foot or on horseback. He finally decided that he would do better on foot, as he feared that Rocinante would become frightened at sight of the lions; and so, leaping down from his horse, he fixed his lance, braced his buckler, and drew his sword, and then advanced with marvelous daring and great resoluteness until he stood directly in front of the cart, meanwhile commending himself to God with all his heart and then to his lady Dulcinea.

Upon reaching this point, the reader should know, the author of our veracious history indulges in the following exclamatory passage:

"O great-souled Don Quixote de la Mancha, thou whose courage is beyond all praise, mirror wherein all the valiant of the world may behold themselves, a new and second Don Manuel de León,[1] once the glory and the honor of Spanish knighthood! With what words shall I relate thy terrifying exploit, how

1. Don Manuel Ponce de León, a paragon of gallantry and courtesy, from the time of Ferdinand and Isabella.

render it credible to the ages that are to come? What eulogies do not belong to thee of right, even though they consist of hyperbole piled upon hyperbole? On foot and singlehanded, intrepid and with greathearted valor, armed but with a sword, and not one of the keen-edged Little Dog[2] make, and with a shield that was not of gleaming and polished steel, thou didst stand and wait for the two fiercest lions that ever the African forests bred! Thy deeds shall be thy praise, O valorous Manchegan; I leave them to speak for thee, since words fail me with which to extol them."

Here the author leaves off his exclamations and resumes the thread of the story.

Seeing Don Quixote posed there before him and perceiving that, unless he wished to incur the bold knight's indignation there was nothing for him to do but release the male lion, the keeper now opened the first cage, and it could be seen at once how extraordinarily big and horribly ugly the beast was. The first thing the recumbent animal did was to turn round, put out a claw, and stretch himself all over. Then he opened his mouth and yawned very slowly, after which he put out a tongue that was nearly two palms in length and with it licked the dust out of his eyes and washed his face. Having done this, he stuck his head outside the cage and gazed about him in all directions. His eyes were now like live coals and his appearance and demeanor were such as to strike terror in temerity itself. But Don Quixote merely stared at him attentively, waiting for him to descend from the cart so that they could come to grips, for the knight was determined to hack the brute to pieces, such was the extent of his unheard-of madness.

The lion, however, proved to be courteous rather than arrogant and was in no mood for childish bravado. After having gazed first in one direction and then in another, as has been said, he turned his back and presented his hind parts to Don Quixote and then very calmly and peaceably lay down and stretched himself out once more in his cage. At this, Don Quixote ordered the keeper to stir him up with a stick in order to irritate him and drive him out.

"That I will not do," the keeper replied, "for if I stir him, I will be the first one he will tear to bits. Be satisfied with what you have already accomplished, Sir Knight, which leaves nothing more to be said on the score of valor, and do not go tempting your fortune a second time. The door was open and the lion could have gone out if he had chosen; since he has not done so up to now, that means he will stay where he is all day long. Your Grace's stout-heartedness has been well established; for no brave fighter, as I see it, is obliged to do more than challenge his enemy and wait for him in the field; his adversary, if he does not come, is the one who is disgraced and the one who awaits him gains the crown of victory."

"That is the truth," said Don Quixote. "Shut the door, my friend, and bear me witness as best you can with regard to what you have seen me do here. I would have you certify: that you opened the door for the lion, that I waited for him and he did not come out, that I continued to wait and still he stayed there, and finally went back and lay down. I am under no further obligation. Away with enchantments, and God uphold the right, the truth, and true chivalry! So

---

2. The trademark of a famous armorer of Toledo and Saragossa.

close the door, as I have told you, while I signal to the fugitives in order that they who were not present may hear of this exploit from your lips."

The keeper did as he was commanded, and Don Quixote, taking the cloth with which he had dried his face after the rain of curds, fastened it to the point of his lance and began summoning the runaways, who, all in a body with the gentleman in green bringing up the rear, were still fleeing and turning around to look back at every step. Sancho was the first to see the white cloth.

"May they slay me," he said, "if my master hasn't conquered those fierce beasts, for he's calling to us."

They all stopped and made sure that the one who was doing the signaling was indeed Don Quixote, and then, losing some of their fear, they little by little made their way back to a point where they could distinctly hear what the knight was saying. At last they returned to the cart, and as they drew near Don Quixote spoke to the driver.

"You may come back, brother, hitch your mules, and continue your journey. And you, Sancho, may give each of them two gold crowns to recompense them for the delay they have suffered on my account."

"That I will, right enough," said Sancho. "But what has become of the lions? Are they dead or alive?"

The keeper thereupon, in leisurely fashion and in full detail, proceeded to tell them how the encounter had ended, taking pains to stress to the best of his ability the valor displayed by Don Quixote, at sight of whom the lion had been so cowed that he was unwilling to leave his cage, though the door had been left open quite a while. The fellow went on to state that the knight had wanted him to stir the lion up and force him out, but had finally been convinced that this would be tempting God and so, much to his displeasure and against his will, had permitted the door to be closed.

"What do you think of that, Sancho?" asked Don Quixote. "Are there any spells that can withstand true gallantry? The enchanters may take my luck away, but to deprive me of my strength and courage is an impossibility."

Sancho then bestowed the crowns, the driver hitched his mules, and the lion-keeper kissed Don Quixote's hands for the favor received, promising that, when he reached the court, he would relate this brave exploit to the king himself.

"In that case," replied Don Quixote, "if his Majesty by any chance should inquire who it was that performed it, you are to say that it was the Knight of the Lions; for that is the name by which I wish to be known from now on, thus changing, exchanging, altering, and converting the one I have previously borne, that of Knight of the Mournful Countenance; in which respect I am but following the old custom of knights-errant, who changed their names whenever they liked or found it convenient to do so."

With this, the cart continued on its way, and Don Quixote, Sancho, and the gentleman in the green-colored greatcoat likewise resumed their journey. During all this time Don Diego de Miranda had not uttered a word but was wholly taken up with observing what Don Quixote did and listening to what he had to say. The knight impressed him as being a crazy sane man and an insane one on the verge of sanity. The gentleman did not happen to be familiar with the first part of our history, but if he had read it he would have ceased to wonder at such talk and conduct, for he would then have known what kind of madness this was. Remaining as he did in ignorance of his companion's malady, he took him now for a sensible individual and now for a madman, since what Don Quixote said was coherent, elegantly phrased, and to the point, whereas his actions were nonsensical, foolhardy, and downright silly. What greater madness could there be, Don Diego asked himself, than to don a helmet filled with curds and then persuade oneself that enchanters were softening one's cranium? What could be more rashly absurd than to wish to fight lions by sheer strength alone? He was roused from these thoughts, this inward soliloquy, by the sound of Don Quixote's voice.

"Undoubtedly, Señor Don Diego de Miranda, your Grace must take me for a fool and a madman, am I not right? And it would be small wonder if such were the case, seeing that my deeds give evidence of nothing else. But, nevertheless, I would advise your Grace that I am neither so mad nor so lacking in wit as I must appear to you to be. A gaily caparisoned knight giving a fortunate lance thrust to a fierce bull in the middle of a great square makes a pleasing appearance in the eyes of his king. The same is true of a knight clad in shining armor as he paces the lists in front of the ladies in some joyous tournament. It is true of all those knights who, by means of military exercises or what appear to be such, divert and entertain and, if one may say so, honor the courts of princes. But the best showing of all is made by a knight-errant who, traversing deserts and solitudes, crossroads, forests, and mountains, goes seeking dangerous adventures with the intention of bringing them to a happy and successful conclusion, and solely for the purpose of winning a glorious and enduring renown.

"More impressive, I repeat, is the knight-errant succoring a widow in some unpopulated place than a courtly man of arms making love to a damsel in the city. All knights have their special callings: let the courtier wait upon the ladies and lend luster by his liveries to his sovereign's palace; let him nourish impoverished gentlemen with the splendid fare of his table; let him give tourneys and show himself truly great, generous, and magnificent and a good Christian above all, thus fulfilling his particular obligations. But the knight-errant's case is different.

"Let the latter seek out the nooks and corners of the world; let him enter into the most intricate of labyrinths; let him attempt the impossible at every step; let him endure on desolate highlands the burning rays of the midsummer sun and in winter the harsh inclemencies of wind and frost; let no lions inspire him with fear, no monsters frighten him, no dragons terrify him, for to seek them out, attack them, and conquer them all is his chief and legitimate occupation. Accordingly, I whose lot it is to be numbered among the knights-errant cannot fail to attempt anything that appears to me to fall within the scope of my duties, just as I attacked those lions a while ago even though I knew it to be an exceedingly rash thing to do, for that was a matter that directly concerned me.

"For I well know the meaning of valor: namely, a virtue that lies between the two extremes of cowardice on the one hand and temerity on the other. It is, nonetheless, better for the brave man to carry his bravery to the point of rashness than for him to sink into cowardice. Even as it is easier for the prodigal to become a generous man than it is for the miser, so is it easier for the foolhardy to become truly brave than it is for the coward to attain valor. And in this matter of adventures, you may believe me, Señor Don Diego, it is better to lose by a card too many than a card too few, and 'Such and such a knight is temerarious and overbold' sounds better to the ear than 'That knight is timid and a coward.'"

"I must assure you, Señor Don Quixote," replied Don Diego, "that everything your Grace has said and done will stand the test of reason; and it is my opinion that if the laws and ordinances of knight-errantry were to be lost, they would be found again in your Grace's bosom, which is their depository and store-house. But it is growing late; let us hasten to my village and my home, where your Grace shall rest from your recent exertions; for if the body is not tired the spirit may be, and that sometimes results in bodily fatigue."

"I accept your offer as a great favor and an honor, Señor Don Diego," was the knight's reply. And, by spurring their mounts more than they had up to then, they arrived at the village around two in the afternoon and came to the house that was occupied by Don Diego, whom Don Quixote had dubbed the Knight of the Green-colored Greatcoat.

[Last Duel]

CHAPTER 64

Which treats of the adventure that caused Don Quixote the most sorrow of all those that have thus far befallen him.

* * * One morning, as Don Quixote went for a ride along the beach,[3] clad in full armor—for, as he was fond of saying, that was his only ornament, his only rest the fight, and, accordingly, he was never without it for a moment—he saw approaching him a horseman similarly arrayed from head to foot and with a brightly shining moon blazoned upon his shield.

As soon as he had come within earshot the stranger cried out to Don Quixote in a loud voice. "O illustrious knight, the never to be sufficiently praised Don Quixote de la Mancha, I am the Knight of the White Moon whose incomparable exploits you will perhaps recall. I come to contend with you and try the might of my arm, with the purpose of having you acknowledge and confess that my lady, whoever she may be, is beyond comparison more beautiful than your own Dulcinea del Toboso. If you will admit the truth of this fully and freely, you will escape death and I shall be spared the trouble of inflicting it upon you. On the other hand, if you choose to fight and I should overcome you, I ask no other satisfaction than that, laying down your arms and seeking no further adventures, you retire to your own village for the space of a year, during which time you are not to lay hand to sword but are to dwell peacefully and tranquilly, enjoying a beneficial rest that shall redound to the betterment of your worldly fortunes and the salvation of your soul. But if you are the victor, then my head shall be at your disposal, my arms and steed shall be the spoils, and the fame of my exploits shall go to increase your own renown. Consider well which is the

---

3. Don Quixote and Sancho, after number-less encounters and experiences (of which the most prominent have been Don Quixote's descent into the cave of Montesinos and their residence at the castle of the playful ducal couple who give Sancho the "governorship of an island" for ten days), are now in Barcelona. Famous as they are, they meet the viceroy and the nobles; their host is Don Antonio Moreno, "a gentleman of wealth and discernment who was fond of amusing himself in an innocent and kindly way."

better course and let me have your answer at once, for today is all the time I have for the dispatching of this business."

Don Quixote was amazed at the knight's arrogance as well as at the nature of the challenge, but it was with a calm and stern demeanor that he replied to him.

"Knight of the White Moon," he said, "of whose exploits up to now I have never heard, I will venture to take an oath that you have not once laid eyes upon the illustrious Dulcinea; for I am quite certain that if you had beheld her you would not be staking your all upon such an issue, since the sight of her would have convinced you that there never has been, and never can be, any beauty to compare with hers. I do not say that you lie, I simply say that you are mistaken; and so I accept your challenge with the conditions you have laid down, and at once, before this day you have fixed upon shall have ended. The only exception I make is with regard to the fame of your deeds being added to my renown, since I do not know what the character of your exploits has been and am quite content with my own, such as they are. Take, then, whichever side of the field you like, and I will take up my position, and may St. Peter bless what God may give."

Now, as it happened, the Knight of the White Moon was seen by some of the townspeople, who informed the viceroy that he was there, talking to Don Quixote de la Mancha. Believing this to be a new adventure arranged by Don Antonio Moreno or some other gentleman of the place, the viceroy at once hastened down to the beach, accompanied by a large retinue, including Don Antonio, and they arrived just as Don Quixote was wheeling Rocinante to measure off the necessary stretch of field. When the viceroy perceived that they were about to engage in combat, he at once interposed and inquired of them what it was that impelled them thus to do battle all of a sudden.

The Knight of the White Moon replied that it was a matter of beauty and precedence and briefly repeated what he had said to Don Quixote, explaining the terms to which both parties had agreed. The viceroy then went up to Don Antonio and asked him if he knew any such knight as this or if it was some joke that they were playing, but the answer that he received left him more puzzled than ever; for Don Antonio did not know who the knight was, nor could he say as to whether this was a real encounter or not. The viceroy, accordingly, was doubtful about letting them proceed, but inasmuch as he could not bring himself to believe that it was anything more than a jest, he withdrew to one side, saying, "Sir Knights, if there is nothing for it but to confess or die, and if Señor Don Quixote's mind is made up and your Grace, the Knight of the White Moon, is even more firmly resolved, then fall to it in the name of God and may He bestow the victory."

The Knight of the White Moon thanked the viceroy most courteously and in well-chosen words for the permission which had been granted them, and Don Quixote did the same, whereupon the latter, commending himself with all his heart to Heaven and to his lady Dulcinea, as was his custom at the beginning of a fray, fell back a little farther down the field as he saw his adversary doing the same. And then, without blare of trumpet or other war-like instrument to give them the signal for the attack, both at the same instant wheeled their steeds about and returned for the charge. Being mounted upon the swifter horse, the Knight of the White Moon met Don Quixote two-thirds of the way and with such tremendous force that, without touching his opponent with his lance (which, it seemed, he deliberately held aloft) he brought both Rocinante and his rider to the ground in an

1792 | MIGUEL DE CERVANTES

exceedingly perilous fall. At once the victor leaped down and placed his lance at Don Quixote's visor.

"You are vanquished, O knight! Nay, more, you are dead unless you make confession in accordance with the conditions governing our encounter."

Stunned and battered, Don Quixote did not so much as raise his visor but in a faint, wan voice, as if speaking from the grave, he said, "Dulcinea del Toboso is the most beautiful woman in the world and I the most unhappy knight upon the face of this earth. It is not right that my weakness should serve to defraud the truth. Drive home your lance, O knight, and take my life since you already have deprived me of my honor."

"That I most certainly shall not do," said the one of the White Moon. "Let the fame of my lady Dulcinea del Toboso's beauty live on undiminished. As for me, I shall be content if the great Don Quixote will retire to his village for a year or until such a time as I may specify, as was agreed upon between us before joining battle."

The viceroy, Don Antonio, and all the many others who were present heard this, and they also heard Don Quixote's response, which was to the effect that, seeing nothing was asked of him that was prejudicial to Dulcinea, he would fulfill all the other conditions like a true and punctilious knight. The one of the White Moon thereupon turned and with a bow to the viceroy rode back to the city at a mild canter. The viceroy promptly dispatched Don Antonio to follow him and make every effort to find out who he was; and, in the meanwhile, they lifted Don Quixote up and uncovered his face, which held no sign of color and was bathed in perspiration. Rocinante, however, was in so sorry a state that he was unable to stir for the present.

Brokenhearted over the turn that events had taken, Sancho did not know what to say or do. It seemed to him that all this was something that was happening in a dream and that everything was the result of magic. He saw his master surrender, heard him consent not to take up arms again for a year to come as the light of his glorious exploits faded into darkness. At the same time his own hopes, based upon the fresh promises that had been made him, were whirled away like smoke before the wind. He feared that Rocinante was maimed for life, his master's bones permanently dislocated—it would have been a bit of luck if his madness also had been jolted out of him.[4]

Finally, in a hand litter which the viceroy had them bring, they bore the knight back to town. The viceroy himself then returned, for he was very anxious to ascertain who the Knight of the White Moon was who had left Don Quixote in so lamentable a condition.

CHAPTER 65

Wherein is revealed who the Knight of the White Moon was.

The Knight of the White Moon was followed not only by Don Antonio Moreno, but by a throng of small boys as well, who kept after him until the doors of one of the city's hostelries had closed behind him. A squire came out to meet him and remove his armor, for which purpose the victor proceeded to shut himself up

---

4. The Spanish has an untranslatable pun on *deslocado*, which means "out of joint" ("dislocated") and also "cured of madness" (from *loco*, "mad").

in a lower room, in the company of Don Antonio, who had also entered the inn and whose bread would not bake until he had learned the knight's identity. Perceiving that the gentleman had no intention of leaving him, he of the White Moon then spoke.

"Sir," he said, "I am well aware that you have come to find out who I am; and, seeing that there is no denying you the information that you seek, while my servant here is removing my armor I will tell you the exact truth of the matter. I would have you know, sir, that I am the bachelor Sansón Carrasco from the same village as Don Quixote de la Mancha, whose madness and absurdities inspire pity in all of us who know him and in none more than me. And so, being convinced that his salvation lay in his returning home for a period of rest in his own house, I formed a plan for bringing him back.

"It was three months ago that I took to the road as a knight-errant, calling myself the Knight of the Mirrors, with the object of fighting and overcoming him without doing him any harm, intending first to lay down the condition that the vanquished was to yield to the victor's will. What I meant to ask of him—for I looked upon him as conquered from the start—was that he should return to his village and not leave it for a whole year, in the course of which time he might be cured. Fate, however, ordained things otherwise; for he was the one who conquered me and overthrew me from my horse, and thus my plan came to naught. He continued on his wanderings, and I went home, defeated, humiliated, and bruised from my fall, which was quite a dangerous one. But I did not for this reason give up the idea of hunting him up once more and vanquishing him as you have seen me do today.

"Since he is the soul of honor when it comes to observing the ordinances of knight-errantry, there is not the slightest doubt that he will keep the promise he has given me and fulfill his obligations. And that, sir, is all that I need to tell you concerning what has happened. I beg you not to disclose my secret or reveal my identity to Don Quixote, in order that my well-intentioned scheme may be carried out and a man of excellent judgment be brought back to his senses—for a sensible man he would be, once rid of the follies of chivalry."

"My dear sir," exclaimed Don Antonio, "may God forgive you for the wrong you have done the world by seeking to deprive it of its most charming madman! Do you not see that the benefit accomplished by restoring Don Quixote to his senses can never equal the pleasure which others derive from his vagaries? But it is my opinion that all the trouble to which the Señor Bachelor has put himself will not suffice to cure a man who is so hopelessly insane; and if it were not uncharitable, I would say let Don Quixote never be cured, since with his return to health we lose not only his own drolleries but also those of his squire, Sancho Panza, for either of the two is capable of turning melancholy itself into joy and merriment. Nevertheless, I will keep silent and tell him nothing, that I may see whether or not I am right in my suspicion that Señor Carrasco's efforts will prove to have been of no avail."

The bachelor replied that, all in all, things looked very favorable and he hoped for a fortunate outcome. With this, he took his leave of Don Antonio, after offering to render him any service that he could; and, having had his armor tied up and placed upon a mule's back, he rode out of the city that same day on the same horse on which he had gone into battle, returning to his native province without anything happening to him that is worthy of being set down in this veracious chronicle.

1794 | MIGUEL DE CERVANTES

[Homecoming and Death]

Of the omens that Don Quixote encountered upon entering his village, with other incidents that embellish and lend credence to this great history.

As they entered the village, Cid Hamete informs us, Don Quixote caught sight of two lads on the communal threshing floor who were engaged in a dispute.

"Don't let it worry you, Periquillo," one of them was saying to the other; "you'll never lay eyes on it again as long as you live."

Hearing this, Don Quixote turned to Sancho. "Did you mark what that boy said, my friend?" he asked. "'You'll never lay eyes on it[5] again . . .'"

"Well," replied Sancho, "what difference does it make what he said?"

"What difference?" said Don Quixote. "Don't you see that, applied to the one I love, it means I shall never again see Dulcinea."

Sancho was about to answer him when his attention was distracted by a hare that came flying across the fields pursued by a large number of hunters with their greyhounds. The frightened animal took refuge by huddling down beneath the donkey, whereupon Sancho reached out his hand and caught it and presented it to his master.

"*Malum signum, malum signum,*"[6] the knight was muttering to himself. "A hare flees, the hounds pursue it, Dulcinea appears not."

"It is very strange to hear your Grace talk like that," said Sancho. "Let us suppose that this hare *is* Dulcinea del Toboso and the hounds pursuing it are those wicked enchanters that transformed her into a peasant lass; she flees, I catch her and turn her over to your Grace, you hold her in your arms and caress her. Is that a bad sign? What ill omen can you find in it?"

The two lads who had been quarreling now came up to have a look at the hare, and Sancho asked them what their dispute was about. To this the one who had uttered the words "You'll never lay eyes on it again as long as you live," replied that he had taken a cricket cage from the other boy and had no intention of returning it ever. Sancho then brought out from his pocket four cuartos and gave them to the lad in exchange for the cage, which he placed in Don Quixote's hands.

"There, master," he said, "these omens are broken and destroyed, and to my way of thinking, even though I may be a dunce, they have no more to do with what is going to happen to us than the clouds of yesteryear. If I am not mistaken, I have heard our curate say that sensible persons of the Christian faith should pay no heed to such foolish things, and you yourself in the past have given me to understand that all those Christians who are guided by omens are fools. But there is no need to waste a lot of words on the subject; come, let us go on and enter our village."

The hunters at this point came up and asked for the hare, and Don Quixote gave it to them. Continuing on their way, the returning pair encountered the curate and the bachelor Carrasco, who were strolling in a small meadow on

---

5. The same as *her* in the Spanish, because the reference is to a cricket cage, which is a feminine noun. Hence Don Quixote's inference con-

cerning Dulcinea.
6. Meeting a hare is considered an ill omen (Latin)—that is, a bad sign.

the outskirts of the town as they read their breviaries. And here it should be mentioned that Sancho Panza, by way of sumpter cloth, had thrown over his gray and the bundle of armor it bore the flame-covered buckram robe in which they had dressed the squire at the duke's castle, on the night that witnessed Altisidora's[7] resurrection; and he had also fitted the miter over the donkey's head, the result being the weirdest transformation and the most bizarrely appareled ass that ever were seen in this world. The curate and the bachelor recognized the pair at once and came forward to receive them with open arms. Don Quixote dismounted and gave them both a warm embrace; meanwhile, the small boys (boys are like lynxes in that nothing escapes them), having spied the ass's miter, ran up for a closer view.

"Come, lads," they cried, "and see Sancho Panza's ass trigged out finer than Mingo,[8] and Don Quixote's beast is skinnier than ever!"

Finally, surrounded by the urchins and accompanied by the curate and the bachelor, they entered the village and made their way to Don Quixote's house, where they found the housekeeper and the niece standing in the doorway, for the news of their return had preceded them. Teresa Panza, Sancho's wife, had also heard of it, and, half naked and disheveled, dragging her daughter Sanchica by the hand, she hastened to greet her husband and was disappointed when she saw him, for he did not look to her as well fitted out as a governor ought to be.

"How does it come, my husband," she said, "that you return like this, tramping and footsore? You look more like a vagabond than you do like a governor."

"Be quiet, Teresa," Sancho admonished her, "for very often there are stakes where there is no bacon. Come on home with me and you will hear marvels. I am bringing money with me, which is the thing that matters, money earned by my own efforts and without harm to anyone."

"You just bring along the money, my good husband," said Teresa, "and whether you got it here or there, or by whatever means, you will not be introducing any new custom into the world."

Sanchica then embraced her father and asked him if he had brought her anything, for she had been looking forward to his coming as to the showers in May. And so, with his wife holding him by the hand while his daughter kept one arm about his waist and at the same time led the gray, Sancho went home, leaving Don Quixote under his own roof in the company of niece and housekeeper, the curate and the barber.

Without regard to time or season, the knight at once drew his guests to one side and in a few words informed them of how he had been overcome in battle and had given his promise not to leave his village for a year, a promise that he meant to observe most scrupulously, without violating it in the slightest degree, as every knight-errant was obliged to do by the laws of chivalry. He accordingly meant to spend that year as a shepherd,[9] he said, amid the solitude of

7. A girl in the duke's castle, where Don Quixote and Sancho were guests for a time. She dramatically pretended to be in love with Don Quixote.
8. The allusion is to the opening lines of *Mingo Revulgo* (15th century), a satire.
9. Because the knight-errant's life has been forbidden him by his defeat, Don Quixote for a time plans to live according to another and no less "literary" code, that of the pastoral. The following paragraphs, especially through the bachelor Carrasco, refer humorously to some of the conventions of pastoral literature.

the fields, where he might give free rein to his amorous fancies as he practiced the virtues of the pastoral life; and he further begged them, if they were not too greatly occupied and more urgent matters did not prevent their doing so, to consent to be his companions. He would purchase a flock sufficiently large to justify their calling themselves shepherds; and, moreover, he would have them know, the most important thing of all had been taken care of, for he had hit upon names that would suit them marvelously well. When the curate asked him what these names were, Don Quixote replied that he himself would be known as "the shepherd Quixotiz," the bachelor as "the shepherd Carrascón," the curate as "the shepherd Curiambro," and Sancho Panza as "the shepherd Pancino."

Both his listeners were dismayed at the new form which his madness had assumed. However, in order that he might not go faring forth from the village on another of his expeditions (for they hoped that in the course of the year he would be cured), they decided to fall in with his new plan and approve it as being a wise one, and they even agreed to be his companions in the calling he proposed to adopt.

"What's more," remarked Sansón Carrasco, "I am a very famous poet, as everyone knows, and at every turn I will be composing pastoral or courtly verses or whatever may come to mind, by way of a diversion for us as we wander in those lonely places; but what is most necessary of all, my dear sirs, is that each one of us should choose the name of the shepherd lass to whom he means to dedicate his songs, so that we may not leave a tree, however hard its bark may be, where their names are not inscribed and engraved as is the custom with lovelorn shepherds."

"That is exactly what we should do," replied Don Quixote, "although, for my part, I am relieved of the necessity of looking for an imaginary shepherdess, seeing that I have the peerless Dulcinea del Toboso, glory of these brookside regions, adornment of these meadows, beauty's mainstay, cream of the Graces—in short, one to whom all praise is well becoming however hyperbolical it may be."

"That is right," said the curate, "but we will seek out some shepherd maids that are easily handled, who if they do not square with us will fit in the corners."

"And," added Sansón Carrasco, "if we run out of names we will give them those that we find printed in books the world over: such as Fílida, Amarilis, Diana, Flérida, Galatea, and Belisarda; for since these are for sale in the market place, we can buy them and make them our own. If my lady, or, rather, my shepherdess, should by chance be called Ana, I will celebrate her charms under the name of Anarda; if she is Francisca, she will become Francenia; if Lucía, Luscinda; for it all amounts to the same thing. And Sancho Panza, if he enters this confraternity, may compose verses to his wife, Teresa Panza, under the name of Teresaina."

Don Quixote had to laugh at this, and the curate then went on to heap extravagant praise upon him for his noble resolution which did him so much credit, and once again he offered to keep the knight company whenever he could spare the time from the duties of his office. With this, they took their leave of him, advising and beseeching him to take care of his health and to eat plentifully of the proper food.

As fate would have it, the niece and the housekeeper had overheard the conversation of the three men, and as soon as the visitors had left they both descended upon Don Quixote.

"What is the meaning of this, my uncle? Here we were thinking your Grace had come home to lead a quiet and respectable life, and do you mean to tell us you are going to get yourself involved in fresh complications—

> Young shepherd, thou who comest here,
> Young shepherd, thou who goest there . . .[1]

For, to tell the truth, the barley is too hard now to make shepherds' pipes of it."[2]

"And how," said the housekeeper, "is your Grace going to stand the midday heat in summer, the winter cold, the howling of the wolves out there in the fields? You certainly cannot endure it. That is an occupation for robust men, cut out and bred for such a calling almost from their swaddling clothes. Setting one evil over against another, it is better to be a knight-errant than a shepherd. Look, sir, take my advice, for I am not stuffed with bread and wine when I give it to you but am fasting and am going on fifty years of age: stay at home, attend to your affairs, go often to confession, be charitable to the poor, and let it be upon my soul if any harm comes to you as a result of it."

"Be quiet, daughters," said Don Quixote. "I know very well what I must do. Take me up to bed, for I do not feel very well; and you may be sure of one thing: whether I am a knight-errant now or a shepherd to be, I never will fail to look after your needs as you will see when the time comes."

And good daughters that they unquestionably were, the housekeeper and the niece helped him up to bed, where they gave him something to eat and made him as comfortable as they could.

CHAPTER 74

Of how Don Quixote fell sick, of the will that he made, and of the manner of his death.

Inasmuch as nothing that is human is eternal but is ever declining from its beginning to its close, this being especially true of the lives of men, and since Don Quixote was not endowed by Heaven with the privilege of staying the downward course of things, his own end came when he was least expecting it. Whether it was owing to melancholy occasioned by the defeat he had suffered, or was, simply, the will of Heaven which had so ordained it, he was taken with a fever that kept him in bed for a week, during which time his friends, the curate, the bachelor, and the barber, visited him frequently, while Sancho Panza, his faithful squire, never left his bedside.

Believing that the knight's condition was due to sorrow over his downfall and disappointment at not having been able to accomplish the disenchantment and liberation of Dulcinea, Sancho and the others endeavored to cheer him up in every possible way. The bachelor urged him to take heart and get up from bed that he might begin his pastoral life, adding that he himself had already composed an eclogue that would cast in the shade all that Sannazaro[3] had ever written, and had purchased with his own money from a herdsman of Quintanar two fine dogs to guard the flock, one of them named Barcino and the other Butrón. All this, however, did not serve to relieve Don Quixote's sadness; whereupon his friends called in the doctor, who took his pulse and was not very well satisfied

---

1. From a ballad.
2. A proverb.
3. Jacopo Sannazaro (1456–1530), Italian poet whose *Arcadia* is one of the milestones in the pastoral tradition.

with it. In any case, the physician told them, they should attend to the health of his soul as that of his body was in grave danger.

Don Quixote received this news calmly enough, but not so his housekeeper, niece, and squire, who began weeping bitterly, as if he were already lying dead in front of them. It was the doctor's opinion that melancholy and depression were putting an end to his patient's life. The knight then requested them to leave him alone as he wished to sleep a little, and they complied. He slept for more than six hours at a stretch, as the saying is, and so soundly that the housekeeper and niece thought he would never wake.

At last he did, however, and at once cried out in a loud voice, "Blessed be Almighty God who has given me so many blessings! Truly His mercy is boundless and is not limited or restrained by the sins of men."

The niece listened carefully to what her uncle said, and it seemed to her that he was speaking more rationally than was his wont, at least during his illness.

"Sir," she said to him, "what does your Grace mean? Has something occurred that we know nothing about? What is this talk of mercy and sins?"

"The mercy that I speak of," replied Don Quixote, "is that which God is showing me at this moment—in spite of my sins, as I have said. My mind now is clear, unencumbered by those misty shadows of ignorance that were cast over it by my bitter and continual reading of those hateful books of chivalry. I see through all the nonsense and fraud contained in them, and my only regret is that my disillusionment has come so late, leaving me no time to make any sort of amends by reading those that are the light of the soul. I find myself, niece, at the point of death, and I would die in such a way as not to leave the impression of a life so bad that I shall be remembered as a madman; for even though I have been one, I do not wish to confirm it on my deathbed. And so, my dear, call in my good friends: the curate, the bachelor Sansón Carrasco, and Master Nicholas the barber; for I want to confess my sins and make my last will and testament."

The niece, however, was relieved of this errand, for the three of them came in just then.

"I have good news for you, kind sirs," said Don Quixote the moment he saw them. "I am no longer Don Quixote de la Mancha but Alonso Quijano, whose mode of life won for him the name of 'Good.' I am the enemy of Amadis of Gaul and all his innumerable progeny; for those profane stories dealing with knight-errantry are odious to me, and I realize how foolish I was and the danger I courted in reading them; but I am in my right senses now and I abominate them."

Hearing this, they all three were convinced that some new kind of madness must have laid hold of him.

"Why, Señor Don Quixote!" exclaimed Sansón. "What makes you talk like that, just when we have received news that my lady Dulcinea is disenchanted? And just when we are on the verge of becoming shepherds so that we may spend the rest of our lives in singing like a lot of princes, why does your Grace choose to turn hermit? Say no more, in Heaven's name, but be sensible and forget these idle tales."

"Tales of that kind," said Don Quixote, "have been the truth for me in the past, and to my detriment, but with Heaven's aid I trust to turn them to my profit now that I am dying. For I feel, gentlemen, that death is very near; so, leave all jesting aside and bring me a confessor for my sins and a notary to draw up my will. In such straits as these a man cannot trifle with his soul. Accordingly, while the Señor Curate is hearing my confession, let the notary be summoned."

Amazed at his words, they gazed at one another in some perplexity, yet they could not but believe him. One of the signs that led them to think he was dying was this quick return from madness to sanity and all the additional things he had to say, so well reasoned and well put and so becoming in a Christian that none of them could any longer doubt that he was in full possession of his faculties. Sending the others out of the room, the curate stayed behind to confess him, and before long the bachelor returned with the notary and Sancho Panza, who had been informed of his master's condition, and who, finding the housekeeper and the niece in tears, began weeping with them. When the confession was over, the curate came out.

"It is true enough," he said, "that Alonso Quijano the Good is dying, and it is also true that he is a sane man. It would be well for us to go in now while he makes his will."

At this news the housekeeper, niece, and the good squire Sancho Panza were so overcome with emotion that the tears burst forth from their eyes and their bosoms heaved with sobs; for, as has been stated more than once, whether Don Quixote was plain Alonso Quijano the Good or Don Quixote de la Mancha, he was always of a kindly and pleasant disposition and for this reason was beloved not only by the members of his household but by all who knew him.

The notary had entered along with the others, and as soon as the preamble had been attended to and the dying man had commended his soul to his Maker with all those Christian formalities that are called for in such a case, they came to the matter of bequests, with Don Quixote dictating as follows:

"ITEM. With regard to Sancho Panza, whom, in my madness, I appointed to be my squire, and who has in his possession a certain sum of money belonging to me: inasmuch as there has been a standing account between us, of debits and credits, it is my will that he shall not be asked to give any accounting whatsoever of this sum, but if any be left over after he has had payment for what I owe him, the balance, which will amount to very little, shall be his, and much good may it do him. If when I was mad I was responsible for his being given the governorship of an island, now that I am of sound mind I would present him with a kingdom if it were in my power, for his simplicity of mind and loyal conduct merit no less."

At this point he turned to Sancho. "Forgive me, my friend," he said, "for having caused you to appear as mad as I by leading you to fall into the same error, that of believing that there are still knights-errant in the world."

"Ah, master," cried Sancho through his tears, "don't die, your Grace, but take my advice and go on living for many years to come; for the greatest madness that a man can be guilty of in this life is to die without good reason, without anyone's killing him, slain only by the hands of melancholy. Look you, don't be lazy but get up from this bed and let us go out into the fields clad as shepherds as we agreed to do. Who knows but behind some bush we may come upon the lady Dulcinea, as disenchanted as you could wish. If it is because of worry over your defeat that you are dying, put the blame on me by saying that the reason for your being overthrown was that I had not properly fastened Rocinante's girth. For the matter of that, your Grace knows from reading your books of chivalry that it is a common thing for certain knights to overthrow others, and he who is vanquished today will be the victor tomorrow."

"That is right," said Sansón, "the worthy Sancho speaks the truth."

"Not so fast, gentlemen," said Don Quixote. "In last year's nests there are no birds this year. I was mad and now I am sane; I was Don Quixote de la Mancha, and now I am, as I have said, Alonso Quijano the Good. May my repentance and the truth I now speak restore to me the place I once held in your esteem. And now, let the notary proceed:

"ITEM. I bequeath my entire estate, without reservation, to my niece Antonia Quijana, here present, after the necessary deductions shall have been made from the most available portion of it to satisfy the bequests that I have stipulated. The first payment shall be to my housekeeper for the wages due her, with twenty ducats over to buy her a dress. And I hereby appoint the Señor Curate and the Señor Bachelor Sansón Carrasco to be my executors.

"ITEM. It is my will that if my niece Antonia Quijana should see fit to marry, it shall be to a man who does not know what books of chivalry are; and if it shall be established that he is acquainted with such books and my niece still insists on marrying him, then she shall lose all that I have bequeathed her and my executors shall apply her portion to works of charity as they may see fit.

"ITEM. I entreat the aforementioned gentlemen, my executors, if by good fortune they should come to know the author who is said to have composed a history now going the rounds under the title of *Second Part of the Exploits of Don Quixote de la Mancha*, to beg his forgiveness in my behalf, as earnestly as they can, since it was I who unthinkingly led him to set down so many and such great absurdities as are to be found in it; for I leave this life with a feeling of remorse at having provided him with the occasion for putting them into writing."

The will ended here, and Don Quixote, stretching himself at length in the bed, fainted away. They all were alarmed at this and hastened to aid him. The same thing happened very frequently in the course of the three days of life that remained to him after he had made his will. The household was in a state of excitement, but with it all the niece continued to eat her meals, the housekeeper had her drink, and Sancho Panza was in good spirits; for this business of inheriting property effaces or mitigates the sorrow which the heir ought to feel and causes him to forget.

Death came at last for Don Quixote, after he had received all the sacraments and once more, with many forceful arguments, had expressed his abomination of books of chivalry. The notary who was present remarked that in none of those books had he read of any knight-errant dying in his own bed so peacefully and in so Christian a manner. And thus, amid the tears and lamentations of those present, he gave up the ghost; that is to say, he died. Perceiving that their friend was no more, the curate asked the notary to be a witness to the fact that Alonso Quijano the Good, commonly known as Don Quixote, was truly dead, this being necessary in order that some author other than Cid Hamete Benengeli might not have the opportunity of falsely resurrecting him and writing endless histories of his exploits.

Such was the end of the Ingenious Gentleman of La Mancha, whose birthplace Cid Hamete was unwilling to designate exactly in order that all the towns and villages of La Mancha might contend among themselves for the right to adopt him and claim him as their own, just as the seven cities of Greece did in the case of Homer. The lamentations of Sancho and those of Don Quixote's niece and his housekeeper, as well as the original epitaphs that were composed for his tomb, will not be recorded here, but mention may be made of the verses by Sansón Carrasco:

> Here lies a gentleman bold
> Who was so very brave
> He went to lengths untold,
> And on the brink of the grave
> Death had on him no hold.
> By the world he set small store—
> He frightened it to the core—
> Yet somehow, by Fate's plan,
> Though he'd lived a crazy man,
> When he died he was sane once more.

WILLIAM SHAKESPEARE
1564–1616

Hamlet portrays the doubts and fears of a conflicted prince whose dead father places on him the most burdensome of obligations: to avenge the king's murder by none other than his brother, Hamlet's uncle Claudius, who has married the recently widowed queen, Gertrude. Hamlet's personal tragedy is also that of Denmark, a state left rudderless by the domestic and familial conflicts of the play. Rich though it may be in plot, the most striking thing about *Hamlet* is its representation of the main character's interiority. Balancing the public and the private, Shakespeare gives the audience intimate access to the prince's mind, by transforming his thoughts into powerful dialogue and unprecedented soliloquies. Using older dramatic forms such as revenge tragedy, Shakespeare forged an entirely new type of play that depicts the inner doubts and hesitations of his quintessential protagonist.

LIFE AND TIMES

William Shakespeare was born in the rural community of Stratford-upon-Avon in Warwickshire. His father, John Shakespeare, was a glover and, when William was born, prominent in the town's government. Little is known of Shakespeare's early life, although it is likely that he received an education at the good local grammar school. He married Anne Hathaway, about seven years his senior, when he was eighteen. The couple had three children, Susanna (1583) and the twins Judith and Hamnet (1585).

Shakespeare lived in a period of great nationalist fervor. Under Queen Elizabeth I (1533–1603, ruled 1558–1603), a successful and much beloved ruler, England solidified its sense of itself as a small but heroic Protestant nation valiantly resisting the encroachment of Spain and other enemies. In 1587, fearing a Catholic conspiracy, Elizabeth put to death her cousin, Mary Queen of Scots, who had sought refuge in England in 1568. Even after a powerful storm scattered the Spanish Armada, the fleet sent to invade England in 1588, the nation continued to fear Spanish invasion and Catholic plots against Elizabeth. The sense of a state under siege in *Hamlet* would thus have echoed powerfully for the English, just as they would have recognized the public tragedy of a nation undone by its rulers' outsized appetites for power. The play's reliance on the truth spoken by a ghost trapped in Purgatory—Catholic notions rejected by Protestantism—is also striking in a period that saw both the strong official repudiation of Catholicism and an enduring popular attachment to its rituals.

After a youth spent in the provinces, by 1592 Shakespeare had made his way to the burgeoning city of London. There he rapidly became the "greatest shake-scene" around, in the irritated words of a rival who envied Shakespeare's ability to impress audiences despite his lack of a university education. Shakespeare soon became a shareholder in a prominent players' company that claimed the Lord Chamberlain as patron and the tragic actor Richard Burbage and the comedian Will Kempe as members. Shakespeare's company originally performed at the theatre, north of the city of London, where its actor-owner, James Burbage,

A detail from Claes Jansz Visscher's engraved panorama of London, *Londinum Florentissima Britanniae Urbs* (1616). The Globe Theater is in the center foreground.

faced steady opposition from puritanical city officials who sought to close the theaters, which they considered to be hotbeds of immorality. Burbage conceived of a means to escape civic legislation against theatrical performances, and secretly moved the boards of his playhouse across the river Thames to the south bank; with these planks he constructed the Globe, the theater most often associated with Shakespeare's name.

The Globe was open to all social classes: anyone who wished could enter the theater by paying a penny, and at the cost of another, get a bench, cushion, and protection (in the boxes) from inclement weather. This mixing of social classes in his audience was echoed in Shakespeare's plays: rather than submitting to the stricter forms of classical drama, Shakespeare mixed comic routines with tragic soliloquies, the speech of common soldiers and bawds with the elegant language of the court. The Globe used almost no scenery and few stage props, so Shakespeare had to evoke the

scene through language and deploy stage props sparingly. Only the costumes were lavish and constituted one of the most valuable possessions of the company. Shakespeare knew the theater inside out and his plays used its resources to the fullest, including sudden entrances and concealed eavesdroppers, brutal sword-fights and touching love scenes, and witty asides and striking double entendres.

Although he began his career as a player, Shakespeare found his calling as a playwright and his fortune as a shareholder in his company. His financial successes enabled him to purchase the title of gentleman for his father, a purchase that made Shakespeare himself officially a "gentleman born," and a fine house in Stratford to which he eventually retired. Despite the unparalleled success of his plays, Shakespeare seems to have valued them only in performance, and never sought to have them printed. Early versions of the plays were often published in unauthorized versions, in some cases on the basis of actors' recollections of their lines. After Shakespeare's death in 1616, his friends published most of his plays in the collection we know as the "First Folio" (1623), the basis for most later editions.

HAMLET

Shakespeare's plays constitute the most important body of dramatic work in the modern world, and no character in literature is more familiar to audiences around the globe than Hamlet. Beyond the impact of the protagonist, *Hamlet* has commanded a leading place in our literary heritage for juxtaposing political obligation and human limitations, idealized virtue and actual experience. Though it is a drama about characters of superior station and the conflicts and problems associated with men and women of high degree, it reveals these problems in a particular family, but presents the domestic conflict within the larger world of politics—like the plays of antiquity that deal with the Theban myth, such as **Oedipus** or *Antigone*. Shakespeare underscores the humanity and frailty of rulers, providing a window into their interiority, whether it be the portrayal of a villainous king in *Richard III* or of a frail and diminished one in *King Lear*. The vulnerability of Hamlet, the disproportion between the heroism demanded of him and the response he can muster, and his acute awareness of how he fails all make him a singularly compelling figure. Leavened with odd moments of black humor, the portrayal of Hamlet's exquisitely self-conscious dilemma amid the increasingly dangerous and opaque machinations of his uncle's court is gripping and casts doubt on dynastic rule itself.

Based on a medieval Scandinavian legend, Shakespeare's play brings the figure of the hero who feigns madness much closer to his own time. In spite of the Danish locale and the relatively remote period of the action, the setting of *Hamlet* is plainly a Renaissance court. There is a ruler holding power, and much of the action is related to questions concerning the nature of that power—the way in which he had acquired it and the ways in which it can be preserved. Around the king are several courtiers, among whom Hamlet, the heir apparent, is only the most prominent. The sense of outside dangers and internal disruption everywhere frames the personal story of Hamlet, of his revenge, and of Claudius's crime. These individual stories are signs of a general societal breakdown. The play charts a kingdom and a society going to pieces, and the realization by its most privileged subjects that it has already crumbled. Lurking behind it all is a sense of the vanity of those forms of human endeavor and power of which the kingdom and the court are symbols.

The tone Shakespeare wants to establish is evident from the opening scenes: the night air is full of premonitions; sentinels turn their eyes toward the threatening outside world; meanwhile, the Ghost has already made his appearance, a sinister omen. The kingdom is presented in terms that are an almost point-by-point reversal of the ideal. Claudius, whether we believe the Ghost's indictment or not (Hamlet does not necessarily, and some of his famous indecision has been attributed to his seeking evidence of the Ghost's truthfulness before acting), has by marrying the queen committed an act that by Elizabethan standards is incestuous. There is an overwhelming sense of disintegration in the body of the state, evident in the first court assembly and in all subsequent ones. Instead of supporting the throne, the two most promising courtiers, Hamlet and Laertes, are restless presences, contemplating departure from a troubled scene.

Decadent and overwrought, the court is marked by semblance instead of substance. Thus Polonius, who after

Hamlet is the major figure in the king's retinue, is presented satirically in his empty formalities and conventional behavior. Often, as with the minor figure of Osric, manners are replaced by mannerisms. Courtly life as depicted in the play suggests always the hollow, the fractured, and the crooked. The traditional forms and institutions of gentle living and all the pomp and solemnity of the court are marred by corruption and distortion. Courtship and love are reduced to Hamlet's mockery of Ophelia, and all but undone by the punning undercurrents of bawdiness. In the famous play-within-the-play, the theater, a traditional institution of court life, is used by the hero as a device to expose the king's crime. There are elements of macabre caricature in Shakespeare's treatment of the solemn theme of death, as in the black comedy of Polonius's death, or the clownish talk of the gravediggers. Finally, the arms tournament, the typical occasion for the display of courtiers' gallantry in front of their king, is here turned by the scheming of the king himself into an almost farcical scene of carnage.

This sense of corruption and decadence dominates the temper of the play and situates Hamlet, his indecision, and his sense of vanity and disenchantment with the world in which he must live. In Hamlet the relationship between thought and deed, intent and realization, is confused, while all around him the norms and institutions that regulate a well-ordered court have been replaced by duplicity and dissimulation. He and the king are "mighty opposites," and it can be argued that against Hamlet's indecision and negativism the king presents a more positive scheme of action, at least in the purely Machiavellian sense, at the level of practical power politics. On various occasions the king shows a high and competent conception of his office: a culminating instance is the courageous and cunning way in which he confronts and handles Laertes' wrath. Since his life is obviously threatened by Hamlet (who was seeking to kill him when by mistake he killed Polonius instead), one might argue that the king acts within a legitimate pattern of politics in wanting to have Hamlet liquidated. Yet this argument cannot be carried so far as to demonstrate that he represents a fully positive attitude toward life and the world, even in the strictly amoral terms of political technique. For in fact his action is corroded by the vexations of his own conscience. Despite his energy and his extrovert qualities, he too becomes part of the negative picture of disruption and lacks concentration of purpose. The images of decay and putrescence that characterize his court extend to his own speech: his "offense," in his own words, "smells to heaven."

Hamlet as a Renaissance tragedy presents a world particularly "out of joint," a world that, having long ago lost the sense of a grand timeless design that was so important in medieval times (to Hamlet the thought of the afterlife is even more puzzling and dark than that of this life), looks with an even greater sense of disenchantment at the temporal world symbolized by the kingdom and the court. They could have given individual action a purposeful meaning. Yet now their order has been destroyed, and ideals that once had power and freshness have lost their vigor under the impact of satiety, doubt, and melancholy.

Because communal values are so degraded, it is natural to ask in the end whether some alternative attempt at a settlement could be imagined, with Hamlet—like other Renaissance heroes—adopting an individual code of conduct, however extravagant. On the whole, Hamlet seems too steeped in his own hopelessness and in the courtly mechanism to which he inevitably belongs to be able to find personal intellectual and moral compromise or his own version of escape. Still, the tone of his brooding and often moralizing speech, his melancholy and dissatisfaction, his very desire for revenge imply a nostalgia for a world—associated with his father—of loyal allegiances and ideals of honor. Yet in *Hamlet* the political world turns out to offer no protection for the values—friendship, loyalty, and honesty—that Hamlet himself most cherishes. This is perhaps the reason why Hamlet has struck many later readers as a representative modern, someone forced to make his way in a world no longer ordered by traditional institutions.

The influence of Shakespeare's plays on the course of English literature is matched only by the King James translation of the Bible. In his time,

Shakespeare garnered the interest of two British monarchs (Elizabeth I and James I), the love of popular audiences, and the respect of such tough critics as the poet and playwright Ben Jonson, who saw him as "the Soule of the Age" yet recognized that he was "Not of an age, but for all time!" *Hamlet* has always been one of Shakespeare's best loved and most widely produced plays. A tantalizing window into an inscrutable interiority, the play has fascinated thinkers and writers from Sigmund Freud, who offered it as an example of the Oedipal complex, to Tom Stoppard, who portrayed the absurdity of the minor characters with great humor in his *Rosencrantz and Guildenstern Are Dead* (1966).

Hamlet, Prince of Denmark

CHARACTERS

CLAUDIUS, *king of Denmark*
HAMLET, *son to the late, and nephew to the present king*
POLONIUS, *lord chamberlain*
HORATIO, *friend to Hamlet*
LAERTES, *son of Polonius*
PRIEST
MARCELLUS, } *officers*
BERNARDO,
FRANCISCO, *a soldier*
REYNALDO, *servant to Polonius*
PLAYERS
TWO CLOWNS, *grave-diggers*
FORTINBRAS, *prince of Norway*
CAPTAIN

VOLTIMAND,
CORNELIUS,
ROSENCRANTZ,
GUILDENSTERN, } *courtiers*
OSRIC,
GENTLEMAN,
ENGLISH AMBASSADORS
GERTRUDE, *queen of Denmark, and mother to Hamlet*
OPHELIA, *daughter of Polonius*
LORDS, LADIES, OFFICERS, SOLDIERS, SAILORS, MESSENGERS, *and* OTHER ATTENDANTS
GHOST OF HAMLET'S FATHER

[SCENE: *Denmark.*]

Act 1

SCENE I

[SCENE: *Elsinore. A platform before the castle.*]

    [FRANCISCO *at his post. Enter to him* BERNARDO.]
BERNARDO Who's there?
FRANCISCO Nay, answer me: stand, and unfold yourself.

BERNARDO Long live the king!

FRANCISCO Bernardo?

BERNARDO He.   5

FRANCISCO You come most carefully upon your hour.

BERNARDO 'Tis now struck twelve; get thee to bed, Francisco.

FRANCISCO For this relief much thanks: 'tis bitter cold,
And I am sick at heart.

BERNARDO Have you had quiet guard?

FRANCISCO   Not a mouse stirring.   10

BERNARDO Well, good night.
If you do meet Horatio and Marcellus,
The rivals[1] of my watch, bid them make haste.

FRANCISCO I think I hear them. Stand, ho! Who is there?
        [*Enter* HORATIO *and* MARCELLUS.]

HORATIO Friends to this ground.

MARCELLUS   And liegemen to the Dane.[2]   15

FRANCISCO Give you good night.

MARCELLUS   O, farewell, honest soldier:
Who hath relieved you?

FRANCISCO   Bernardo hath my place.
Give you good night.
        [*Exit.*]

MARCELLUS   Holla! Bernardo!

BERNARDO   Say,
What, is Horatio there?

HORATIO   A piece of him.

BERNARDO Welcome, Horatio; welcome, good Marcellus.   20

MARCELLUS What, has this thing appeared again to-night?

BERNARDO I have seen nothing.

MARCELLUS Horatio says 'tis but our fantasy,
And will not let belief take hold of him
Touching this dreaded sight, twice seen of us: 25
Therefore I have entreated him along
With us to watch the minutes of this night,
That if again this apparition come,
He may approve our eyes[3] and speak to it.

HORATIO Tush, tush, 'twill not appear.

BERNARDO   Sit down a while;   30
And let us once again assail your ears,
That are so fortified against our story,
What we have two nights seen.

HORATIO   Well, sit we down,
And let us hear Bernardo speak of this.

BERNARDO Last night of all,   35
When yond same star that's westward from the pole
Had made his course to illume that part of heaven

1. Partners.   3. Confirm what we saw.
2. The king of Denmark.

Where now it burns, Marcellus and myself,
The bell then beating one,—

     [*Enter* GHOST.]

Ghost enters

MARCELLUS   Peace, break thee off; look, where it comes again!   40
BERNARDO   In the same figure, like the king that's dead.
MARCELLUS   Thou art a scholar; speak to it, Horatio.
BERNARDO   Looks it not like the king? mark it, Horatio.
HORATIO   Most like it: it harrows me with fear and wonder.
BERNARDO   It would be spoke to.
MARCELLUS   Question it, Horatio.   45
HORATIO   What art thou, that usurp'st this time of night,
   Together with that fair and warlike form
   In which the majesty of buried Denmark
   Did sometimes[4] march? by heaven I charge thee, speak!
MARCELLUS   It is offended.
BERNARDO   See, it stalks away!   50
HORATIO   Stay! speak, speak! I charge thee, speak!

     [*Exit* GHOST.]

MARCELLUS   'Tis gone, and will not answer.
BERNARDO   How now, Horatio! you tremble and look pale:
   Is not this something more than fantasy?
   What think you on't?   55
HORATIO   Before my God, I might not this believe
   Without the sensible and true avouch
   Of mine own eyes.
MARCELLUS   Is it not like the king?

Ghost is wearing same armor

HORATIO   As thou art to thyself:
   Such was the very armor he had on   60
   When he the ambitious Norway[5] combated;
   So frown'd he once, when, in an angry parle,
   He smote the sledded[6] Polacks on the ice.
   'Tis strange.
MARCELLUS   Thus twice before, and jump[7] at this dead hour,   65
   With martial stalk hath he gone by our watch.

a sign of something to come

HORATIO   In what particular thought to work I know not;
   But, in the gross and scope of my opinion,[8]
   This bodes some strange eruption to our state.
MARCELLUS   Good now, sit down, and tell me, he that knows,   70
   Why this same strict and most observant watch
   So nightly toils the subject[9] of the land,
   And why such daily cast of brazen cannon,
   And foreign mart for implements of war;
   Why such impress of shipwrights, whose sore task   75
   Does not divide the Sunday from the week;

---

4. Formerly, "Denmark": the king of Denmark.
5. The king of Norway (the elder Fortinbras).
6. They travel in sledges. "Parle": parley.
7. Just.

8. Taking a general view.
9. The people.
1. Ship carpenters. "Mart": trading. "Impress": pressing into service.

What might be toward,[2] that this sweaty haste
Doth make the night joint-laborer with the day:
Who is't that can inform me?

HORATIO   That can I;
At least the whisper goes so. Our last king,
Whose image even but now appear'd to us,   80
Was, as you know, by Fortinbras of Norway,
Thereto pricked on by a most emulate pride,
Dared to the combat; in which our valiant Hamlet—
For so this side of our known world esteem'd him—   85
Did slay this Fortinbras; who by a seal'd compact
Well ratified by law and heraldry,[3]
Did forfeit, with his life, all those his lands
Which he stood seized of, to the conqueror:
Against the which, a moiety competent   90
Was gagèd[4] by our king; which had returned
To the inheritance of Fortinbras,
Had he been vanquisher; as, by the same covenant
And carriage[5] of the article design'd,
His fell to Hamlet. Now, sir, young Fortinbras,   95
Of unimprovèd metal hot and full,
Hath in the skirts[6] of Norway here and there
Shark'd up a list of lawless resolutes,
For food and diet, to some enterprise
That hath a stomach in't:[7] which is no other—   100
As it doth well appear unto our state—
But to recover of us, by strong hand
And terms compulsatory, those foresaid lands
So by his father lost: and this, I take it,
Is the main motive of our preparations,   105
The source of this our watch and the chief head
Of this post-haste and romage[8] in the land.

BERNARDO   I think it be no other but e'en so:
Well may it sort,[9] that this portentous figure
Comes armèd through our watch, so like the king   110
That was and is the question of these wars.

HORATIO   A mote it is to trouble the mind's eye.
In the most high and palmy state of Rome,
A little ere the mightiest Julius fell,
The graves stood tenantless, and the sheeted dead   115
Did squeak and gibber in the Roman streets:
As stars with trains of fire and dews of blood,
Disasters in the sun; and the moist star,

---

2. Impending.
3. Duly ratified and proclaimed through heralds.
4. Pledged. "Seized": possessed. "Moiety competent": equal share.
5. Purport.

6. Outskirts, border regions. "Unimprovèd": untested.
7. Calls for courage.
8. Bustle. "Head": origin, cause.
9. Fit with the other signs of war.

Upon whose influence Neptune's empire stands,[1]
Was sick almost to doomsday with eclipse: 120
And even the like precurse[2] of fierce events,
As harbingers preceding still the fates
And prologue to the omen coming on,
Have heaven and earth together demonstrated
Unto our climatures[3] and countrymen.   125
   [*Re-enter* GHOST.]
But soft, behold! lo, where it comes again!
I'll cross it, though it blast me. Stay, illusion!
If thou hast any sound, or use of voice,
Speak to me:
If there be any good thing to be done,   130
That may to thee do ease and grace to me,
Speak to me:
If thou art privy to thy country's fate,
Which, happily, foreknowing may avoid,
O, speak!   135
Or if thou hast uphoarded in thy life
Extorted treasure in the womb of earth,
For which, they say, you spirits oft walk in death,
Speak of it: stay, and speak! [*The cock crows.*] Stop it, Marcellus.
MARCELLUS Shall I strike at it with my partisan?   140
HORATIO Do, if it will not stand.
BERNARDO   'Tis here!
HORATIO   'Tis here!
   [*Exit* GHOST.]
MARCELLUS 'Tis gone!
We do it wrong, being so majestical,
To offer it the show of violence;
For it is, as the air, invulnerable,   145
And our vain blows malicious mockery.
BERNARDO It was about to speak, when the cock crew.
HORATIO And then it started like a guilty thing
Upon a fearful summons. I have heard
The cock, that is the trumpet to the morn,   150
Doth with his lofty and shrill-sounding throat
Awake the god of day, and at his warning,
Whether in sea or fire, in earth or air,
The extravagant[4] and erring spirit hies
To his confine: and of the truth herein   155
This present object made probation.[5]
MARCELLUS It faded on the crowing of the cock.
Some say that ever 'gainst[6] that season comes

---

1. The moon (*moist star*) regulates the sea's tides. "Disasters": ill omens.
2. Foreboding.
3. Regions.
4. Wandering out of its confines.
5. Gave proof.
6. Just before.

Wherein our Saviour's birth is celebrated,
The bird of dawning singeth all night long: 160
And then, they say, no spirit dare stir abroad,
The nights are wholesome, then no planets strike,
No fairy takes nor witch hath power to charm,
So hallowed and so gracious[7] is the time.
HORATIO   So have I heard and do in part believe it. 165
But look, the morn, in russet mantle clad,
Walks o'er the dew of yon high eastward hill:
Break we our watch up; and by my advice,
Let us impart what we have seen to-night
Unto young Hamlet; for, upon my life, 170
This spirit, dumb to us, will speak to him:
Do you consent we shall acquaint him with it,
As needful in our loves, fitting our duty?
MARCELLUS   Let's do't, I pray; and I this morning know
Where we shall find him most conveniently. 175
      [*Exeunt.*]

SCENE 2

[SCENE: *A room of state in the castle.*]

      [*Flourish. Enter the* KING, QUEEN, HAMLET, POLONIUS, LAERTES,
      VOLTIMAND, CORNELIUS, LORDS, *and* ATTENDANTS.]
KING   Though yet of Hamlet our dear brother's death
The memory be green, and that it us befitted
To bear our hearts in grief and our whole kingdom
To be contracted in one brow of woe,
Yet so far hath discretion[8] fought with nature 5
That we with wisest sorrow think on him,
Together with remembrance of ourselves.
Therefore our sometime sister, now our queen,
The imperial jointress to this warlike state,
Have we, as 'twere with a defeated joy,— 10
With an auspicious and a dropping eye,
With mirth in funeral and with dirge in marriage,
In equal scale weighing delight and dole,—
Taken to wife: nor have we herein barr'd[9]
Your better wisdoms, which have freely gone 15
With this affair along. For all, our thanks.
Now follows, that[1] you know, young Fortinbras,
Holding a weak supposal of our worth,
Or thinking by our late dear brother's death
Our state to be disjoint and out of frame, 20
Colleaguèd with this dream[2] of his advantage,

---

7. Full of blessing. "Strike": exercise evil influence (compare *moonstruck*). "Fairy takes": bewitches.
8. Restraint (on grief).
9. Ignored. "Dole": grief.
1. What.
2. Combined with this fantastic notion.

He hath not failed to pester us with message,
Importing the surrender of those lands
Lost by his father, with all bonds of law,
To our most valiant brother. So much for him   25
Now for ourself, and for this time of meeting:
Thus much the business is: we have here writ
To Norway, uncle of young Fortinbras,—
Who, impotent and bed-rid, scarcely hears
Of this his nephew's purpose,—to suppress   30
His further gait herein; in that the levies,
The lists and full proportions,[3] are all made
Out of his subject: and we here dispatch
You, good Cornelius, and you, Voltimand,
For bearers of this greeting to old Norway,   35
Giving to you no further personal power
To business with the king more than the scope
Of these delated[4] articles allow.
Farewell, and let your haste commend your duty.

CORNELIUS }
VOLTIMAND } In that and all things will we show our duty. 40

KING We doubt it nothing: heartily farewell.
        [*Exeunt* VOLTIMAND *and* CORNELIUS.]
And now, Laertes, what's the news with you?
You told us of some suit; what is't, Laertes?
You cannot speak of reason to the Dane,
And lose your voice: what wouldst thou beg, Laertes,   45
That shall not be my offer, not thy asking?
The head is not more native to[5] the heart,
The hand more instrumental to the mouth,
Than is the throne of Denmark to thy father.
What wouldst thou have, Laertes?

LAERTES   My dread lord,   50
Your leave and favor to return to France,
From whence though willingly I came to Denmark,
To show my duty in your coronation,
Yet now, I must confess, that duty done,
My thoughts and wishes bend again toward France   55
And bow them to your gracious leave and pardon.

KING Have you your father's leave? What says Polonius?

POLONIUS He hath, my lord, wrung from me my slow leave
By laborsome petition, and at last
Upon his will I sealed my hard consent: 60
I do beseech you, give him leave to go.

KING Take thy fair hour, Laertes; time be thine,
And thy best graces spend it at thy will!
But now, my cousin Hamlet, and my son,—

---

3. Amounts of forces and supplies. "Gait":   **4.** Detailed.
proceeding.   **5.** Naturally bound to.

HAMLET [*Aside.*]   A little more than kin, and less than kind.   65
KING   How is it that the clouds still hang on you?
HAMLET   Not so, my lord; I am too much i' the sun.[6]
QUEEN   Good Hamlet, cast thy nighted color off,
    And let thine eye look like a friend on Denmark.
    Do not for ever with thy vailèd[7] lids   70
    Seek for thy noble father in the dust:
    Thou know'st 'tis common; all that lives must die,
    Passing through nature to eternity.
HAMLET   Aye, madam, it is common.
QUEEN   If it be,
    Why seems it so particular with thee?   75
HAMLET   Seems, madam! nay, it is; I know not "seems."
    'Tis not alone my inky cloak, good mother,
    Nor customary suits of solemn black,
    Nor windy suspiration of forced breath,
    No, nor the fruitful river in the eye,   80
    Nor the dejected havior of the visage,
    Together with all forms, moods, shapes of grief,
    That can denote me truly: these indeed seem,
    For they are actions that a man might play:
    But I have that within which passeth show;   85
    These but the trappings and the suits of woe.
KING   'Tis sweet and cómmendàble in your nature, Hamlet,
    To give these mourning duties to your father:
    But, you must know, your father lost a father,
    That father lost, lost his, and the survivor bound   90
    In filial obligation for some term
    To do obsequious[8] sorrow: but to persevere
    In obstinate condolement is a course
    Of impious stubbornness; 'tis unmanly grief:
    It shows a will most incorrect[9] to heaven,   95
    A heart unfortified, a mind impatient,
    An understanding simple and unschool'd:
    For what we know must be and is as common
    As any the most vulgar thing to sense,
    Why should we in our peevish opposition   100
    Take it to heart? Fie! 'tis a fault to heaven,
    A fault against the dead, a fault to nature,
    To reason most absurd, whose common theme
    Is death of fathers, and who still hath cried,
    From the first corse till he that died to-day,   105
    "This must be so." We pray you, throw to earth
    This unprevailing[1] woe, and think of us

6. The cue to Hamlet's irony is given by the King's "my cousin . . . my son" (line 64). Hamlet is punning on *son*.
7. Downcast.
8. Dutiful, especially concerning funeral rites (obsequies).
9. Not subdued.
1. Useless.

As of a father: for let the world take note,
You are the most immediate to our throne,
And with no less nobility of love   110
Than that which dearest father bears his son
Do I impart toward you. For your intent
In going back to school in Wittenberg,
It is most retrograde[2] to our desire:
And we beseech you, bend you to remain   115
Here in the cheer and comfort of our eye,
Our chiefest courtier, cousin and our son.
QUEEN   Let not thy mother lose her prayers, Hamlet:
    I pray thee, stay with us; go not to Wittenberg.
HAMLET   I shall in all my best obey you, madam.   120
KING   Why, 'tis a loving and a fair reply:
    Be as ourself in Denmark. Madam, come;
    This gentle and unforced accord of Hamlet
    Sits smiling to my heart: in grace whereof,
    No jocund health that Denmark drinks to-day,   125
    But the great cannon to the clouds shall tell,
    And the king's rouse the heaven shall bruit[3] again,
    Re-speaking earthly thunder. Come away.
        [Flourish. Exeunt all but HAMLET.]
HAMLET   O, that this too too sullied flesh would melt,
    Thaw and resolve itself into a dew!   130
    Or that the Everlasting had not fixed
    His canon[4] 'gainst self-slaughter! O God! God!
    How weary, stale, flat and unprofitable
    Seem to me all the uses of this world!
    Fie on't! ah fie! 'tis an unweeded garden,   135
    That grows to seed; things rank and gross in nature
    Possess it merely. That it should come to this!
    But two months dead! nay, not so much, not two:
    So excellent a king; that was, to this,
    Hyperion to a satyr: so loving to my mother,   140
    That he might not beteem[5] the winds of heaven
    Visit her face too roughly. Heaven and earth!
    Must I remember? why, she would hang on him,
    As if increase of appetite had grown
    By what it fed on: and yet, within a month—   145
    Let me not think on't—Frailty, thy name is woman!—
    A little month, or ere those shoes were old
    With which she followed my poor father's body,
    Like Niobe,[6] all tears:—why she, even she,—

2. Opposed. "Wittenberg": the seat of a university; at the peak of fame in Shakespeare's time because of its connection with Martin Luther.
3. Proclaim, echo. "Rouse": carousal, revel.
4. Law.
5. Allow. "Hyperion": the sun god.

6. A proud mother who boasted of having more children than Leto; her seven sons and seven daughters were slain by Apollo and Artemis, children of Leto. The grieving Niobe was changed by Zeus into a continually weeping stone.

O God! a beast that wants discourse[7] of reason   150
Would have mourned longer,—married with my uncle,
My father's brother, but no more like my father
Than I to Hercules: within a month;
Ere yet the salt of most unrighteous tears
Had left the flushing in her gallèd[8] eyes,   155
She married. O, most wicked speed, to post
With such dexterity to incestuous sheets![9]
It is not, nor it cannot come to good:
But break, my heart, for I must hold my tongue!
      [*Enter* HORATIO, MARCELLUS, *and* BERNARDO.]
HORATIO   Hail to your lordship!
HAMLET   I am glad to see you well: 160
  Horatio,—or I do forget myself.
HORATIO   The same, my lord, and your poor servant ever.
HAMLET   Sir, my good friend; I'll change[1] that name with you:
  And what make you from Wittenberg, Horatio?
  Marcellus?   165
MARCELLUS   My good lord?
HAMLET   I am very glad to see you. [*To* BERNARDO.] Good even, sir.
  But what, in faith, make you from Wittenberg?
HORATIO   A truant disposition, good my lord.
HAMLET   I would not hear your enemy say so,   170
  Nor shall you do my ear that violence,
  To make it truster of your own report
  Against yourself: I know you are no truant.
  But what is your affair in Elsinore?
  We'll teach you to drink deep ere you depart.   175
HORATIO   My lord, I came to see your father's funeral.
HAMLET   I pray thee, do not mock me, fellow-student;
  I think it was to see my mother's wedding.
HORATIO   Indeed, my lord, it followed hard upon.
HAMLET   Thrift, thrift, Horatio! the funeral baked-meats   180
  Did coldly furnish forth the marriage tables.
  Would I had met my dearest[2] foe in heaven
  Or ever I had seen that day, Horatio!
  My father!—methinks I see my father.
HORATIO   O where, my lord?
HAMLET   In my mind's eye, Horatio.   185
HORATIO   I saw him once; he was a goodly king.
HAMLET   He was a man, take him for all in all,
  I shall not look upon his like again.
HORATIO   My lord, I think I saw him yesternight.
HAMLET   Saw? who?   190

7. Lacks the faculty.
8. Inflamed.
9. According to principles that Hamlet accepts,

marrying one's brother's widow is incest.
1. Exchange.
2. Bitterest.

HORATIO   My lord, the king your father.
HAMLET   The king my father!
HORATIO   Season your admiration[3] for a while
  With an attent ear, till I may deliver,
  Upon the witness of these gentlemen,
  This marvel to you.
HAMLET   For God's love, let me hear.   195
HORATIO   Two nights together had these gentlemen,
  Marcellus and Bernardo, on their watch,
  In the dead vast and middle of the night,
  Been thus encountered. A figure like your father,
  Armed at point exactly, cap-a-pe,[4]   200
  Appears before them, and with solemn march
  Goes slow and stately by them: thrice he walked
  By their oppressed and fear-surprisèd eyes,
  Within his truncheon's length; whilst they, distilled
  Almost to jelly with the act of fear,   205
  Stand dumb, and speak not to him. This to me
  In dreadful secrecy impart they did;
  And I with them the third night kept the watch:
  Where, as they had delivered, both in time,
  Form of the thing, each word made true and good,   210
  The apparition comes: I knew your father;
  These hands were not more like.
HAMLET   But where was this?
MARCELLUS   My lord, upon the platform where we watched.
HAMLET   Did you not speak to it?
HORATIO   My lord, I did.
  But answer made it none: yet once methought   215
  It lifted up its head and did address
  Itself to motion, like as it would speak:
  But even then the morning cock crew loud,
  And at the sound it shrunk in haste away
  And vanished from our sight.
HAMLET   'Tis very strange.   220
HORATIO   As I do live, my honored lord, 'tis true,
  And we did think it writ down in our duty
  To let you know of it.
HAMLET   Indeed, indeed, sirs, but this troubles me.
  Hold you the watch to-night?
MARCELLUS ⎫
BERNARDO ⎬   We do, my lord.   225
HAMLET   Armed, say you?
MARCELLUS ⎫
BERNARDO ⎬   Armed, my lord.

3. Restrain your astonishment.   4. From head to foot. "At point": completely.

HAMLET   From top to toe?

MARCELLUS⎫
BERNARDO ⎭   My lord, from head to foot.

HAMLET   Then saw you not his face?

HORATIO   O, yes, my lord; he wore his beaver⁵ up.

HAMLET   What, looked he frowningly?   230

HORATIO   A countenance more in sorrow than in anger.

HAMLET   Pale, or red?

HORATIO   Nay, very pale.

HAMLET   And fixed his eyes upon you?

HORATIO   Most constantly.

HAMLET   I would I had been there.

HORATIO   It would have much amazed you.   235

HAMLET   Very like, very like. Stayed it long?

HORATIO   While one with moderate haste might tell⁶ a hundred.

MARCELLUS⎫
BERNARDO ⎭ Longer, longer.

HORATIO   Not when I saw't.

HAMLET   His beard was grizzled?⁷ no?

HORATIO   It was, as I have seen it in his life,   240
A sable silvered.⁸

HAMLET   I will watch to-night;
Perchance 'twill walk again.

HORATIO   I warrant it will.

HAMLET   If it assume my noble father's person,
I'll speak to it, though hell itself should gape
And bid me hold my peace. I pray you all,   245
If you have hitherto concealed this sight,
Let it be tenable in your silence still,⁹
And whatsoever else shall hap to-night,
Give it an understanding, but no tongue:
I will requite your loves. So fare you well: 250
Upon the platform, 'twixt eleven and twelve,
I'll visit you.

ALL   Our duty to your honor.

HAMLET   Your loves, as mine to you: farewell.
    [*Exeunt all but* HAMLET.]
My father's spirit in arms! all is not well;
I doubt¹ some foul play: would the night were come!   255
Till then sit still, my soul: foul deeds will rise,
Though all the earth o'erwhelm them, to men's eyes.
    [*Exit.*]

5. Visor.   8. Black and white.
6. Count.   9. Consider it still a secret.
7. Gray.   1. Suspect.

SCENE 3

[SCENE: *A room in Polonius's house.*]

     [*Enter* LAERTES *and* OPHELIA.]
LAERTES   My necessaries are embarked: farewell:
  And, sister, as the winds give benefit
  And convoy² is assistant, do not sleep,
  But let me hear from you.
OPHELIA   Do you doubt that?
LAERTES   For Hamlet, and the trifling of his favor,   5
  Hold it a fashion, and a toy in blood,
  A violet in the youth of primy nature,
  Forward,³ not permanent, sweet, not lasting,
  The perfume and suppliance of a minute;
  No more.   10
OPHELIA   No more but so?
LAERTES   Think it no more:
  For nature crescent does not grow alone
  In thews and bulk; but, as this temple⁴ waxes,
  The inward service of the mind and soul   15
  Grows wide withal. Perhaps he loves you now;
  And now no soil nor cautel⁵ doth besmirch
  The virtue of his will: but you must fear,
  His greatness weighed,⁶ his will is not his own;
  For he himself is subject to his birth: 20
  He may not, as unvalued persons do,
  Carve for himself, for on his choice depends
  The safety and health of this whole state,
  And therefore must his choice be circumscribed
  Unto the voice and yielding⁷ of that body   25
  Whereof he is the head. Then if he says he loves you,
  It fits your wisdom so far to believe it
  As he in his particular act and place
  May give his saying deed; which is no further
  Than the main voice of Denmark goes withal.⁸   30
  Then weigh what loss your honor may sustain,
  If with too credent ear you list his songs,
  Or lose your heart, or your chaste treasure open
  To his unmastered importunity.
  Fear it, Ophelia, fear it, my dear sister,   35
  And keep you in the rear of your affection,
  Out of the shot and danger of desire.
  The chariest maid is prodigal enough

2. Conveyance, means of transport.
3. Early. "Fashion": passing mood. "Primy": early, young.
4. The body. "Crescent": growing.
5. No foul or deceitful thoughts.
6. When you consider his rank. "Will": desire.
7. Assent.
8. Goes along with, agrees. "Main": powerful.

If she unmask her beauty to the moon:
Virtue itself 'scapes not calumnious strokes: 40
The canker galls the infants of the spring
Too oft before their buttons be disclosed,
And in the morn and liquid dew of youth
Contagious blastments[9] are most imminent.
Be wary then; best safety lies in fear: 45
Youth to itself[1] rebels, though none else near.

OPHELIA   I shall the effect of this good lesson keep,
As watchman to my heart. But, good my brother,
Do not, as some ungracious pastors do,
Show me the steep and thorny way to heaven,   50
Whilst, like a puffed and reckless libertine,
Himself the primrose path of dalliance treads
And recks not his own rede.[2]

LAERTES   O, fear me not.
I stay too long; but here my father comes.
        [*Enter* POLONIUS.]
A double blessing is a double grace;   55
Occasion smiles upon a second leave.

POLONIUS   Yet here, Laertes! Aboard, aboard, for shame!
The wind sits in the shoulder of your sail,
And you are stayed for. There; my blessing with thee!
And these few precepts in thy memory   60
See thou character.[3] Give thy thoughts no tongue,
Nor any unproportioned[4] thought his act.
Be thou familiar, but by no means vulgar.
Those friends thou hast, and their adoption tried,
Grapple them to thy soul with hoops of steel,   65
But do not dull thy palm[5] with entertainment
Of each new-hatched unfledged comrade. Beware
Of entrance to a quarrel; but being in,
Bear't, that the opposèd may beware of thee.
Give every man thy ear, but few thy voice: 70
Take each man's censure,[6] but reserve thy judgment.
Costly thy habit as thy purse can buy,
But not expressed in fancy; rich, not gaudy:
For the apparel oft proclaims the man;
And they in France of the best rank and station   75
Are of a most select and generous chief[7] in that.
Neither a borrower nor a lender be:
For loan oft loses both itself and friend,
And borrowing dulls the edge of husbandry.[8]
This above all: to thine own self be true,   80

9. Blights.
1. Against its better self.
2. Does not follow his own advice.
3. Engrave in your memory.
4. Unsuitable.

5. Make the palm of your hand callous (by the indiscriminate shaking of hands).
6. Opinion.
7. Preeminence.
8. Thriftiness.

And it must follow, as the night the day,
Thou canst not then be false to any man.
Farewell: my blessing season[9] this in thee!
LAERTES   Most humbly do I take my leave, my lord.
POLONIUS   The time invites you; go, your servants tend.[1]   85
LAERTES   Farewell, Ophelia, and remember well
   What I have said to you.
OPHELIA   'Tis in my memory locked,
   And you yourself shall keep the key of it.
LAERTES   Farewell.
         [Exit.]
POLONIUS   What is't, Ophelia, he hath said to you?
OPHELIA   So please you, something touching the Lord Hamlet.   90
POLONIUS   Marry, well bethought:
   'Tis told me, he hath very oft of late
   Given private time to you, and you yourself
   Have of your audience been most free and bounteous:
   If it be so—as so 'tis put on me,   95
   And that in way of caution—I must tell you,
   You do not understand yourself so clearly
   As it behoves my daughter and your honor.
   What is between you? give me up the truth.
OPHELIA   He hath, my lord, of late made many tenders   100
   Of his affection to me.
POLONIUS   Affection! pooh! you speak like a green girl,
   Unsifted[2] in such perilous circumstance.
   Do you believe his tenders, as you call them?
OPHELIA   I do not know, my lord, what I should think.   105
POLONIUS   Marry, I'll teach you: think yourself a baby,
   That you have ta'en these tenders for true pay,
   Which are not sterling. Tender[3] yourself more dearly;
   Or—not to crack the wind of the poor phrase,
   Running it thus—you'll tender me a fool.[4]   110
OPHELIA   My lord, he hath importuned me with love
   In honorable fashion,
POLONIUS   Aye, fashion you may call it; go to, go to.
OPHELIA   And hath given countenance[5] to his speech, my lord,
   With almost all the holy vows of heaven.   115
POLONIUS   Aye, springes to catch woodcocks. I do know,
   When the blood burns, how prodigal the soul
   Lends the tongue vows: these blazes, daughter,
   Giving more light than heat, extinct in both,
   Even in their promise, as it is a-making,   120
   You must not take for fire. From this time
   Be something scanter of your maiden presence;

9. Ripen.   3. Regard.
1. Wait.   4. You'll furnish me with a fool (a foolish
2. Untested.   daughter).
                                   5. Authority.

Set your entreatments⁶ at a higher rate
Than a command to parley. For Lord Hamlet,
Believe so much in him, that he is young,   125
And with a larger tether may he walk
Than may be given you: in few, Ophelia,
Do not believe his vows; for they are brokers,
Not of that dye which their investments⁷ show,
But mere implorators of unholy suits,   130
Breathing like sanctified and pious bawds,
The better to beguile. This is for all:
I would not, in plain terms, from this time forth,
Have you so slander any moment⁸ leisure,
As to give words or talk with the Lord Hamlet.   135
Look to't, I charge you: come your ways.
OPHELIA   I shall obey, my lord.
    [*Exeunt.*]

SCENE 4

[SCENE: *The platform.*]

    [*Enter* HAMLET, HORATIO, *and* MARCELLUS.]
HAMLET   The air bites shrewdly; it is very cold.
HORATIO   It is a nipping and an eager⁹ air.
HAMLET   What hour now?
HORATIO   I think it lacks of twelve.
MARCELLUS   No, it is struck.
HORATIO   Indeed? I heard it not: it then draws near the season   5
    Wherein the spirit held his wont to walk.
    [*A flourish of trumpets, and ordnance shot off within.*]
    What doth this mean, my lord?
HAMLET   The king doth wake to-night, and takes his rouse,
    Keeps wassail, and the swaggering up-spring reels;
    And as he drains his draughts of Rhenish¹ down,   10
    The kettle-drum and trumpet thus bray out
    The triumph of his pledge.²
HORATIO   Is it a custom?
HAMLET   Aye, marry, is't:
    But to my mind, though I am native here
    And to the manner born, it is a custom   15
    More honored³ in the breach than the observance.
    This heavy-headed revel east and west
    Makes us traduced and taxed of other nations:
    They clepe us drunkards, and with swinish phrase
    Soil our addition;⁴ and indeed it takes   20

---

6. Conversation, company.
7. Clothes. "Brokers": procurers, panders.
8. Use badly any momentary.
9. Sharp.

1. Rhine wine. "Up-spring reels": wild dances.
2. In downing the cup in one draught.
3. Honorable.
4. Reputation. "Taxed": blamed. "Clepe": call.

From our achievements, though performed at height,[5]
The pith and marrow of our attribute.[6]
So, oft it chances in particular men,
That for some vicious mole of nature in them,
As, in their birth,—wherein they are not guilty,   25
Since nature cannot choose his origin,—
By the o'ergrowth of some complexion,[7]
Oft breaking down the pales and forts of reason,
Or by some habit that too much o'er-leavens[8]
The form of plausive[9] manners, that these men,—   30
Carrying, I say, the stamp of one defect,
Being nature's livery, or fortune's star,—
Their virtues else[1]—be they as pure as grace,
As infinite as man may undergo—
Shall in the general censure take corruption   35
From that particular fault: the dram of evil
Doth all the noble substance often dout
To his own scandal.[2]
    [*Enter* GHOST.]
HORATIO   Look, my lord it comes!
HAMLET   Angels and ministers of grace defend us!
Be thou a spirit of health or goblin damned,   40
Bring with thee airs from heaven or blasts from hell,
Be thy intents wicked or charitable,
Thou comest in such a questionable shape
That I will speak to thee: I'll call thee Hamlet,
King, father, royal Dane: O, answer me!   45
Let me not burst in ignorance; but tell
Why thy canónized bones, hearsèd in death,
Have burst their cerements; why the sepulchre,
Wherein we saw thee quietly inurned,
Hath oped his ponderous and marble jaws,   50
To cast thee up again. What may this mean,
That thou, dead corse, again, in complete steel,
Revisit'st thus the glimpses of the moon,
Making night hideous; and we fools of nature
So horridly to shake our disposition   55
With thoughts beyond the reaches of our souls?
Say, why is this? Wherefore? what should we do?
    [GHOST *beckons* HAMLET.]
HORATIO   It beckons you to go away with it,
As if it some impartment did desire
To you alone.   60
MARCELLUS   Look, with what courteous action
It waves you to a more removèd ground:

---

5. Done in the best possible manner.
6. Reputation.
7. Excess in one side of their temperament.
8. Modifies, as yeast changes dough.

9. Agreeable.
1. The rest of their qualities.
2. To its own harm. "Dout": extinguish, nullify.

But do not go with it.
HORATIO   No, by no means.
HAMLET   It will not speak; then I will follow it.
HORATIO   Do not, my lord.
HAMLET   Why, what should be the fear?   65
I do not set my life at a pin's fee;
And for my soul, what can it do to that,
Being a thing immortal as itself?
It waves me forth again: I'll follow it.
HORATIO   What if it tempt you toward the flood, my lord,   70
Or to the dreadful summit of the cliff
That beetles o'er[3] his base into the sea,
And there assume some other horrible form,
Which might deprive your sovereignty of reason
And draw you into madness? think of it: 75
The very place puts toys[4] of desperation,
Without more motive, into every brain
That looks so many fathoms to the sea
And hears it roar beneath.
HAMLET   It waves me still.
Go on; I'll follow thee.   80
MARCELLUS   You shall not go, my lord.
HAMLET   Hold off your hands.
HORATIO   Be ruled; you shall not go.
HAMLET   My fate cries out,
And makes each petty artery in this body
As hardy as the Nemean lion's nerve.[5]
Still am I called, unhand me, gentlemen;   85
By heaven, I'll make a ghost of him that lets[6] me:
I say, away! Go on; I'll follow thee.
        [*Exeunt* GHOST *and* HAMLET.]
HORATIO   He waxes desperate with imagination.
MARCELLUS   Let's follow; 'tis not fit thus to obey him.
HORATIO   Have after. To what issue will this come?   90
MARCELLUS   Something is rotten in the state of Denmark.
HORATIO   Heaven will direct it.
MARCELLUS   Nay, let's follow him.
        [*Exeunt.*]

SCENE 5

[SCENE: *Another part of the platform.*]

        [*Enter* GHOST *and* HAMLET.]
HAMLET   Whither wilt thou lead me? speak; I'll go no further.
GHOST   Mark me.
HAMLET   I will.

3. Juts over.
4. Fancies.
5. Sinew, muscle. "Nemean lion": slain by
Hercules as one of his twelve labors.
6. Hinders.

GHOST   My hour is almost come,
   When I to sulphurous and tormenting flames[7]
   Must render up myself.
HAMLET   Alas, poor ghost!
GHOST   Pity me not, but lend thy serious hearing   5
   To what I shall unfold.
HAMLET   Speak; I am bound to hear.
GHOST   So art thou to revenge, when thou shalt hear.
HAMLET   What?
GHOST   I am thy father's spirit;
   Doomed for a certain term to walk the night,   10
   And for the day confined to fast in fires,
   Till the foul crimes done in my days of nature
   Are burnt and purged away. But that I am forbid
   To tell the secrets of my prison-house,
   I could a tale unfold whose lightest word   15
   Would harrow up thy soul, freeze thy young blood,
   Make thy two eyes, like stars, start from their spheres,[8]
   Thy knotted and combinèd locks to part
   And each particular hair to stand on end,
   Like quills upon the fretful porpentine: 20
   But this eternal blazon[9] must not be
   To ears of flesh and blood. List, list, O, list!
   If thou didst ever thy dear father love—
HAMLET   O God!
GHOST   Revenge his foul and most unnatural murder.   25
HAMLET   Murder!
GHOST   Murder most foul, as in the best it is,
   But this most foul, strange, and unnatural.
HAMLET   Haste me to know't, that I, with wings as swift
   As meditation or the thoughts of love,   30
   May sweep to my revenge.
GHOST   I find thee apt;
   And duller shouldst thou be than the fat weed
   That roots itself in ease on Lethe[1] wharf,
   Wouldst thou not stir in this. Now, Hamlet, hear:
   'Tis given out that, sleeping in my orchard,   35
   A serpent stung me; so the whole ear of Denmark
   Is by a forgèd process of my death
   Rankly abused: but know, thou noble youth,
   The serpent that did sting thy father's life
   Now wears his crown.
HAMLET   O my prophetic soul!   40
   My uncle!

---

7. Of purgatory.
8. Transparent revolving shells in each of which, according to Ptolemaic astronomy, a planet or other heavenly body was placed.

9. Publication of the secrets of the other world (of eternity). "Porpentine": porcupine.
1. The river of forgetfulness in Hades.

GHOST Aye, that incestuous, that adulterate beast,
With witchcraft of his wit, with traitorous gifts,—
O wicked wit and gifts, that have the power
So to seduce!—won to his shameful lust   45
The will of my most seeming-virtuous queen:
O Hamlet, what a falling-off was there!
From me, whose love was of that dignity
That it went hand in hand even with the vow
I made to her in marriage; and to decline   50
Upon a wretch, whose natural gifts were poor
To those of mine!
But virtue, as it never will be moved,
Though lewdness court it in a shape of heaven,[2]
So lust, though to a radiant angel linked,   55
Will sate itself in a celestial bed
And prey on garbage.
But, soft! methinks I scent the morning air;
Brief let me be. Sleeping within my orchard,
My custom always of the afternoon.   60
Upon my secure hour thy uncle stole,
With juice of cursed hebenon[3] in a vial,
And in the porches of my ears did pour
The leperous distilment; whose effect
Holds such an enmity with blood of man   65
That swift as quicksilver it courses through
The natural gates and alleys of the body;
And with a sudden vigor it doth posset
And curd, like eager[4] droppings into milk,
The thin and wholesome blood: so did it mine;   70
And a most instant tetter barked about,[5]
Most lazar-like,[6] with vile and loathsome crust,
All my smooth body.
Thus was I, sleeping, by a brother's hand
Of life, of crown, of queen, at once dispatched: 75
Cut off even in the blossoms of my sin,
Unhouseled, disappointed, unaneled;[7]
No reckoning made, but sent to my account
With all my imperfections on my head:
O, horrible! O, horrible! most horrible!   80
If thou hast nature in thee, bear it not;
Let not the royal bed of Denmark be
A couch for luxury and damned incest.
But, howsoever thou pursuest this act,
Taint not thy mind, nor let thy soul contrive   85

2. A heavenly, angelic form.
3. Henbane, a poisonous herb.
4. Sour. "Posset": coagulate.
5. The skin immediately became thick like the bark of a tree.

6. Leper-like (from the beggar Lazarus, "full of sores," in Luke 16.20).
7. Without sacrament, unprepared, without extreme unction.

Against thy mother aught: leave her to heaven,
And to those thorns that in her bosom lodge,
To prick and sting her. Fare thee well at once!
The glow-worm shows the matin to be near,
And 'gins to pale his uneffectual fire: 90
Adieu, adieu, adieu! remember me.
    [*Exit.*]
HAMLET   O all you host of heaven! O earth! what else?
And shall I couple hell? O, fie! Hold, hold, my heart;
And you, my sinews, grow not instant old,
But bear me stiffly up. Remember thee!   95
Aye, thou poor ghost, while memory holds a seat
In this distracted globe. Remember thee!
Yea, from the table[8] of my memory
I'll wipe away all trivial fond records,
All saws of books, all forms, all pressures past,   100
That youth and observation copied there:
And thy commandment all alone shall live
Within the book and volume of my brain,
Unmixed with baser matter: yes, by heaven!
O most pernicious woman!   105
O villain, villain, smiling, damnèd villain!
My tables,—meet it is I set it down,
That one may smile, and smile, and be a villain;
At least I'm sure it may be so in Denmark.
    [*Writing.*]
So, uncle, there you are. Now to my word;   110
It is "Adieu, adieu! remember me."
I have sworn't.
HORATIO
MARCELLUS   } [*Within.*] My lord, my lord!
    [*Enter* HORATIO *and* MARCELLUS.]
MARCELLUS   Lord Hamlet!
HORATIO   Heaven
                            secure him!
HAMLET   So be it!
MARCELLUS   Illo,[9] ho, ho, my lord!   115
HAMLET   Hillo, ho, ho, boy! come, bird, come.
MARCELLUS   How is't, my noble lord?
HORATIO   What news, my lord?
HAMLET   O, wonderful!
HORATIO   Good my lord, tell it.
HAMLET   No; you will reveal it.
HORATIO   Not I, my lord, by heaven.

---

8. Writing tablet; used in the same sense in   9. A falconer's call.
line 107. "Globe": head.

MARCELLUS   Nor I, my lord.   120
HAMLET   How say you, then; would heart of man once think it?
  But you'll be secret?
HORATIO   ⎫
MARCELLUS   ⎭   Aye, by, heaven, my lord.
HAMLET   There's ne'er a villain dwelling in all Denmark
  But he's an arrant knave.
HORATIO   There needs no ghost, my lord, come from the grave   125
  To tell us this.
HAMLET   Why, right; you are i' the right;
  And so, without more circumstance¹ at all,
  I hold it fit that we shake hands and part:
  You, as your business and desire shall point you;
  For every man hath business and desire,   130
  Such as it is; and for my own poor part,
  Look you, I'll go pray.
HORATIO   These are but wild and whirling words, my lord.
HAMLET   I'm sorry they offend you, heartily;
  Yes, faith, heartily.
HORATIO   There's no offense, my lord.   135
HAMLET   Yes, by Saint Patrick, but there is, Horatio,
  And much offense too. Touching this vision here,
  It is an honest² ghost, that let me tell you:
  For your desire to know what is between us,
  O'ermaster't as you may. And now, good friends,   140
  As you are friends, scholars and soldiers,
  Give me one poor request.
HORATIO   What is't, my lord? we will.
HAMLET   Never make known what you have seen tonight.
MARCELLUS   ⎫
HORATIO   ⎭   My lord, we will not.
HAMLET   Nay, but swear't.
HORATIO   In faith,
  My lord, not I.
MARCELLUS   Nor I, my lord, in faith.   145
HAMLET   Upon my sword.
MARCELLUS   We have sworn, my lord, already.
HAMLET   Indeed, upon my sword, indeed.
GHOST [*Beneath.*]   Swear.
HAMLET   Ah, ha, boy! say'st thou so? art thou there, true-penny?³
  Come on: you hear this fellow in the cellarage:
  Consent to swear.
HORATIO   Propose the oath, my lord.   150

1. Ceremony.   3. Honest fellow.
2. Genuine.

HAMLET   Never to speak of this that you have seen,
   Swear by my sword.
GHOST [*Beneath.*]   Swear.
HAMLET   Hic et ubique?⁴ then we'll shift our ground.
   Come hither, gentlemen,   155
   And lay your hands again upon my sword:
   Never to speak of this that you have heard,
   Swear by my sword.
GHOST [*Beneath.*]   Swear.
HAMLET   Well said, old mole! canst work i' the earth so fast?   160
   A worthy pioner!⁵ Once more remove, good friends.
HORATIO   O day and night, but this is wondrous strange!
HAMLET   And therefore as a stranger give it welcome.
   There are more things in heaven and earth, Horatio,
   Than are dreamt of in your philosophy.   165
   But come;
   Here, as before, never, so help you mercy,
   How strange or odd soe'er I bear myself,
   As I perchance hereafter shall think meet
   To put an antic⁶ disposition on,   170
   That you, at such times seeing me, never shall,
   With arms encumbered⁷ thus, or this head-shake,
   Or by pronouncing of some doubtful phrase,
   As "Well, well, we know," or "We could, an if we would,"
   Or "If we list to speak," or "There be, an if they might,"   175
   Or such ambiguous giving out, to note
   That you know aught of me: this not to do,
   So grace and mercy at your most need help you,
   Swear.
GHOST [*Beneath.*]   Swear.   180
HAMLET   Rest, rest, perturbèd spirit!
     [*They swear.*]
   So, gentlemen,
   With all my love I do commend⁸ me to you:
   And what so poor a man as Hamlet is
   May do, to express his love and friending to you,   185
   God willing, shall not lack. Let us go in together;
   And still your fingers on your lips, I pray,
   The time is out of joint: O cursèd spite,
   That ever I was born to set it right!
   Nay, come, let's go together.   190
     [*Exeunt.*]

---

4. Here and everywhere (Latin).
5. Miner.
6. Odd, fantastic.

7. Folded.
8. Entrust.

Act 2

[SCENE: *A room in Polonius's house.*]

   [*Enter* POLONIUS *and* REYNALDO.]
POLONIUS Give him this money and these notes, Reynaldo.
REYNALDO I will, my lord.
POLONIUS You shall do marvelous wisely, good Reynaldo,
 Before you visit him, to make inquire
 Of his behavior.
REYNALDO   My lord, I did intend it.   5
POLONIUS Marry, well said, very well said. Look you, sir,
 Inquire me first what Danskers are in Paris,
 And how, and who, what means, and where they keep,⁹
 What company, at what expense, and finding
 By this encompassment¹ and drift of question   10
 That they do know my son, come you more nearer
 Than your particular demands will touch it:
 Take you, as 'twere, some distant knowledge of him,
 As thus, "I know his father and his friends,
 And in part him": do you mark this, Reynaldo?   15
REYNALDO Aye, very well, my lord.
POLONIUS "And in part him; but," you may say, "not well:
 But if 't be he I mean, he's very wild,
 Addicted so and so"; and there put on him
 What forgeries you please; marry, none so rank   20
 As may dishonor him; take heed of that;
 But, sir, such wanton, wild and usual slips
 As are companions noted and most known
 To youth and liberty.
REYNALDO   As gaming, my lord.
POLONIUS Aye, or drinking, fencing, swearing, quarreling, 25
 Drabbing:² you may go so far.
REYNALDO My lord, that would dishonor him.
POLONIUS Faith, no; as you may season it in the charge.³
 You must not put another scandal on him,
 That he is open to incontinency;   30
 That's not my meaning: but breathe his faults so quaintly⁴
 That they may seem the taints of liberty,
 The flash and outbreak of a fiery mind,
 A savageness in unreclaimèd blood,
 Of general assault.⁵
REYNALDO   But, my good lord,—   35
POLONIUS Wherefore should you do this?

9. Dwell. "Danskers": Danes.
1. Roundabout way.
2. Whoring.
3. Qualify it in making the accusation.
4. Delicately, skillfully. "Incontinency": extreme sensuality.
5. Assailing all. "Unreclaimèd": untamed.

REYNALDO   Aye, my lord,
  I would know that.
POLONIUS   Marry, sir, here's my drift,
  And I believe it is a fetch of warrant:[6]
  You laying these slight sullies on my son,
  As 'twere a thing a little soiled i' the working,   40
  Mark you,
  Your party in converse, him you would sound,
  Having ever seen in the prenominate[7] crimes
  The youth you breathe of guilty, be assured
  He closes with you in this consequence;[8]   45
  "Good sir," or so, or "friend," or "gentleman,"
  According to the phrase or the addition[9]
  Of man and country.
REYNALDO   Very good, my lord.
POLONIUS   And then, sir, does he this—he does—what was I about to
  say? By the mass, I was about to say something: where did I leave?   50
REYNALDO   At "closes in the consequence," at "friend or so," and
  "gentleman."
POLONIUS   At "closes in the consequence," aye, marry;
  He closes with you thus: "I know the gentleman;
  I saw him yesterday, or t' other day,   55
  Or then, or then, with such, or such, and, as you say,
  There was a' gaming, there o'ertook in 's rouse,[1]
  There falling out at tennis": or perchance,
  "I saw him enter such a house of sale,"
  Videlicet,[2] a brothel, or so forth.   60
  See you now;
  Your bait of falsehood takes this carp of truth:
  And thus do we of wisdom and of reach,[3]
  With windlasses and with assays of bias,[4]
  By indirections find directions out: 65
  So, by my former lecture and advice,
  Shall you my son. You have me, have you not?
REYNALDO   My lord, I have.
POLONIUS   God be wi' ye; fare ye well.
REYNALDO   Good my lord!
POLONIUS   Observe his inclination in yourself.[5]   70
REYNALDO   I shall, my lord.
POLONIUS   And let him ply his music.
REYNALDO   Well, my lord.

---

6. Allowable stratagem.
7. Aforementioned. "Having ever": if he has
ever.
8. You may be sure he will agree in this
conclusion.
9. Title.
1. Intoxicated in his reveling.

2. Namely.
3. Wise and far-sighted.
4. Sending the ball indirectly (in bowling),
devious attacks. "Windlasses": winding ways,
round-about courses.
5. Ways of procedure by yourself.

POLONIUS   Farewell!
       [*Exit* REYNALDO.—*Enter* OPHELIA.]
   How now, Ophelia! what's the matter?
OPHELIA   O, my lord, I have been so affrighted!   75
POLONIUS   With what, i' the name of God?
OPHELIA   My lord, as I was sewing in my closet,
   Lord Hamlet, with his doublet[6] all unbraced,
   No hat upon his head, his stockings fouled,
   Ungartered and down-gyvèd[7] to his ankle;   80
   Pale as his shirt, his knees knocking each other,
   And with a look so piteous in purport
   As if he had been loosèd out of hell
   To speak of horrors, he comes before me.
POLONIUS   Mad for thy love?
OPHELIA   My lord, I do not know,   85
   But truly I do fear it.
POLONIUS   What said he?
OPHELIA   He took me by the wrist and held me hard;
   Then goes he to the length of all his arm,
   And with his other hand thus o'er his brow,
   He falls to such perusal of my face   90
   As he would draw it. Long stayed he so;
   At last, a little shaking of mine arm,
   And thrice his head thus waving up and down,
   He raised a sigh so piteous and profound
   As it did seem to shatter all his bulk   95
   And end his being: that done, he lets me go:
   And with his head over his shoulder turned,
   He seemed to find his way without his eyes;
   For out o' doors he went without their help,
   And to the last bended their light on me.   100
POLONIUS   Come, go with me: I will go seek the king.
   This is the very ecstasy of love;
   Whose violent property fordoes itself[8]
   And leads the will to desperate undertakings
   As oft as any passion under heaven   105
   That does afflict our natures. I am sorry.
   What, have you given him any hard words of late?
OPHELIA   No, my good lord, but, as you did command,
   I did repel his letters and denied
   His access to me.
POLONIUS   That hath made him mad.   110
   I am sorry that with better heed and judgment
   I had not quoted him: I fear'd he did but trifle
   And meant to wreck thee; but beshrew my jealousy![9]

---

6. Jacket. "Closet": private room.
7. Pulled down like fetters on a prisoner's leg.
8. Which, when violent, destroys itself. "Ecstasy":

madness.
9. Curse my suspicion. "Quoted": noted.

By heaven, it is as proper to our age
To cast beyond ourselves[1] in our opinions   115
As it is common for the younger sort
To lack discretion. Come, go we to the king:
This must be known; which, being kept close, might move
More grief to hide than hate to utter love.[2]
Come.   120

    [*Exeunt.*]

SCENE 2

[SCENE: *A room in the castle.*]

    [*Flourish. Enter* KING, QUEEN, ROSENCRANTZ, GUILDENSTERN, *and*
    ATTENDANTS.]

KING   Welcome, dear Rosencrantz and Guildenstern!
  Moreover that we much did long to see you,
  The need we have to use you did provoke
  Our hasty sending. Something have you heard
  Of Hamlet's transformation; so call it,   5
  Sith[3] nor the exterior nor the inward man
  Resembles that it was. What it should be,
  More than his father's death, that thus hath put him
  So much from the understanding of himself,
  I cannot dream of: I entreat you both,   10
  That, being of so young days brought up with him
  And sith so neighbored to his youth and behavior,
  That you vouchsafe your rest[4] here in our court
  Some little time: so by your companies
  To draw him on to pleasures, and to gather   15
  So much as from occasion you may glean,
  Whether aught to us unknown afflicts him thus,
  That opened[5] lies within our remedy.
QUEEN   Good gentlemen, he hath much talked of you,
  And sure I am two men there are not living   20
  To whom he more adheres.[6] If it will please you
  To show us so much gentry[7] and good will
  As to expend your time with us awhile
  For the supply and profit of our hope,
  Your visitation shall receive such thanks   25
  As fits a king's remembrance.
ROSENCRANTZ   Both your majesties
  Might, by the sovereign power you have of us,
  Put your dread pleasures more into[8] command

---

1. Overshoot, go too far.
2. If Hamlet's love is revealed. "To hide": if kept hidden.
3. Since.
4. Consent to stay.
5. Once revealed.
6. Is more attached.
7. Courtesy.
8. Give your sovereign wishes the form of.

Than to entreaty.

GUILDENSTERN   But we both obey,
  And here give up ourselves, in the full bent[9]   30
  To lay our service freely at your feet,
  To be commanded.

KING   Thanks, Rosencrantz and gentle Guildenstern.

QUEEN   Thanks, Guildenstern and gentle Rosencrantz:
  And I beseech you instantly to visit   35
  My too much changéd son. Go, some of you,
  And bring these gentlemen where Hamlet is.

GUILDENSTERN   Heavens make our presence and our practices
  Pleasant and helpful to him!

QUEEN   Aye, amen!
    [*Exeunt* ROSENCRANTZ, GUILDENSTERN, *and some* ATTENDANTS.—*Enter*
    POLONIUS.]

POLONIUS   The ambassadors from Norway, my good lord,   40
  Are joyfully returned.

KING   Thou still[1] hast been the father of good news.

POLONIUS   Have I, my lord? I assure my good liege,
  I hold my duty as I hold my soul,
  Both to my God and to my gracious king: 45
  And I do think, or else this brain of mine
  Hunts not the trail of policy so sure
  As it hath used to do, that I have found
  The very cause of Hamlet's lunacy.

KING   O, speak of that; that do I long to hear.   50

POLONIUS   Give first admittance to the ambassadors;
  My news shall be the fruit to that great feast.

KING   Thyself do grace[2] to them, and bring them in.
    [*Exit* POLONIUS.]
  He tells me, my dear Gertrude, he hath found
  The head and source of all your son's distemper.   55

QUEEN   I doubt it is no other but the main;
  His father's death and our o'erhasty marriage.

KING   Well, we shall sift him.
    [*Re-enter* POLONIUS, *with* VOLTIMAND *and* CORNELIUS.]
                     Welcome, my good friends!
  Say, Voltimand, what from our brother Norway?

VOLTIMAND   Most fair return of greetings and desires.   60
  Upon our first,[3] he sent out to suppress
  His nephew's levies, which to him appeared
  To be a preparation 'gainst the Polack,
  But better looked into, he truly found
  It was against your highness: whereat grieved,   65
  That so his sickness, age and impotence

---

9. Bent (as a bow) to the limit.
1. Always.

2. Honor. "Fruit": dessert.
3. As soon as we made the request.

Was falsely borne in hand,[4] sends out arrests
On Fortinbras; which he, in brief, obeys,
Receives rebuke from Norway, and in fine[5]
Makes vow before his uncle never more   70
To give the assay[6] of arms against your majesty.
Whereon old Norway, overcome with joy,
Gives him three thousand crowns in annual fee
And his commission to employ those soldiers,
So levied as before, against the Polack: 75
With an entreaty, herein further shown,
  [*Giving a paper.*]
That it might please you to give quiet pass
Through your dominions for this enterprise,
On such regards of safety and allowance
As therein are set down.
KING   It likes us well,   80
And at our more considered time we'll read,
Answer, and think upon this business.
Meantime we thank you for your well-took labor:
Go to your rest; at night we'll feast together:
Most welcome home!
  [*Exeunt* VOLTIMAND *and* CORNELIUS.]
POLONIUS   This business is well ended.   85
My liege, and madam, to expostulate
What majesty should be, what duty is,
Why day is day, night night, and time is time,
Were nothing but to waste night, day and time.
Therefore, since brevity is the soul of wit   90
And tediousness the limbs and outward flourishes,
I will be brief. Your noble son is mad:
Mad call I it; for, to define true madness,
What is 't but to be nothing else but mad?
But let that go.
QUEEN   More matter, with less art.   95
POLONIUS   Madam, I swear I use no art at all.
That he is mad, 'tis true: 'tis true 'tis pity,
And pity 'tis 'tis true: a foolish figure;[7]
But farewell it, for I will use no art.
Mad let us grant him then: and now remains   100
That we find out the cause of this effect,
Or rather say, the cause of this defect,
For this effect defective comes by cause:
Thus it remains and the remainder thus.
Perpend.[8]   105
I have a daughter,—have while she is mine,—

---

4. Deceived, deluded.   7. Of speech.
5. Finally.   8. Consider.
6. Test.

Who in her duty and obedience, mark,
Hath given me this: now gather and surmise.
[*Reads.*] "To the celestial, and my soul's idol, the most beautified
Ophelia,"—That's an ill phrase, a vile phrase; "beautified" is a vile   110
phrase; but you shall hear. Thus:
     [*Reads.*] "In her excellent white bosom, these," &c.
QUEEN   Came this from Hamlet to her?
POLONIUS   Good madam, stay awhile; I will be faithful.
        [*Reads.*] "Doubt thou the stars are fire;   115
             Doubt that the sun doth move;
             Doubt truth to be a liar;
             But never doubt I love.
"O dear Ophelia, I am ill at these numbers;[9] I have not art to reckon
my groans: but that I love thee best, O most best, believe it. Adieu.   120
          "Thine evermore, most dear lady, whilst this
              machine is to him,[1] HAMLET."
This in obedience hath my daughter shown me;
And more above,[2] hath his solicitings,
As they fell out by time, by means and place,   125
All given to mine ear.
KING   But how hath she
Received his love?
POLONIUS   What do you think of me?
KING   As of a man faithful and honorable.
POLONIUS   I would fain prove so. But what might you think,
When I had seen this hot love on the wing,—   130
As I perceived it, I must tell you that,
Before my daughter told me,—what might you,
Or my dear majesty your queen here, think,
If I had played the desk or table-book,[3]
Or given my heart a winking,[4] mute and dumb,   135
Or looked upon this love with idle sight;
What might you think? No, I went round[5] to work,
And my young mistress thus I did bespeak:
"Lord Hamlet is a prince, out of thy star;[6]
This must not be:" and then I prescripts gave her,   140
That she should lock herself from his resort,
Admit no messengers, receive no tokens.
Which done, she took the fruits of my advice;
And he repulsed, a short tale to make,
Fell into a sadness, then into a fast,   145
Thence to a watch, thence into a weakness,
Thence to a lightness,[7] and by this declension
Into the madness wherein now he raves

9. Verses.
1. Body is attached.
2. Moreover.
3. If I had acted as a desk or notebook (in keeping the matter secret).

4. Shut my heart's eye.
5. Straight.
6. Sphere.
7. Light-headedness. "Watch": insomnia.

And all we mourn for.

KING Do you think this?

QUEEN   It may be, very like.   150

POLONIUS Hath there been such a time, I'd fain know that,
   That I have positively said "'tis so,"
   When it proved otherwise?

KING   Not that I know.

POLONIUS [*Pointing to his head and shoulder.*] Take this, from this,
      if this be otherwise: 155
   If circumstances lead me, I will find
   Where truth is hid, though it were hid indeed
   Within the center.[8]

KING   How may we try it further?

POLONIUS You know, sometimes he walks for hours together
   Here in the lobby.

QUEEN   So he does, indeed.   160

POLONIUS At such a time I'll loose my daughter to him:
   Be you and I behind an arras then;
   Mark the encounter: if he love her not,
   And be not from his reason fall'n thereon,[9]
   Let me be no assistant for a state,   165
   But keep a farm and carters.

KING   We will try it.

QUEEN But look where sadly the poor wretch comes reading.

POLONIUS Away, I do beseech you, both away:
   I'll board him presently.[1]

      [*Exeunt* KING, QUEEN, *and* ATTENDANTS.—*Enter* HAMLET, *reading.*]

   O, give me leave: how does my good Lord Hamlet?   170

HAMLET Well, God-a-mercy.

POLONIUS Do you know me, my lord?

HAMLET Excellent well; you are a fishmonger.[2]

POLONIUS Not I, my lord.

HAMLET Then I would you were so honest a man.   175

POLONIUS: Honest, my lord!

HAMLET Aye, sir; to be honest, as this world goes, is to be one man
   picked out of ten thousand.

POLONIUS That's very true, my lord.

HAMLET For if the sun breed maggots in a dead dog, being a good   180
   kissing carrion[3]—Have you a daughter?

POLONIUS I have, my lord.

HAMLET Let her not walk i' the sun: conception is a blessing; but as
   your daughter may conceive,—friend, look to 't.

POLONIUS [*Aside.*] How say you by that? Still harping on my daughter: 185
   yet he knew me not at first; he said I was a fishmonger: he is far
   gone: and truly in my youth I suffered much extremity for love; very

---

8. Of the earth.
9. For that reason.
1. Approach him at once.

2. Fish seller but also slang for procurer.
3. Good bit of flesh for kissing.

near this. I'll speak to him again.—What do you read, my lord?
HAMLET   Words, words, words.
POLONIUS   What is the matter,⁴ my lord?   190
HAMLET   Between who?
POLONIUS   I mean, the matter that you read, my lord.
HAMLET   Slanders, sir: for the satirical rogue says here that old men
   have gray beards, that their faces are wrinkled, their eyes purging
   thick amber and plum-tree gum, and that they have a plentiful lack   195
   of wit, together with most weak hams: all which, sir, though I most
   powerfully and potently believe, yet I hold it not honesty to have it
   thus set down; for yourself, sir, shall grow old as I am, if like a crab
   you could go backward.
POLONIUS [Aside.]   Though this be madness, yet there is method in   200
   't.—Will you walk out of the air, my lord?
HAMLET   Into my grave.
POLONIUS   Indeed, that's out of the air.
      [Aside.]
   How pregnant sometimes his replies are! a happiness⁵ that often
   madness hits on, which reason and sanity could not so prosperously   205
   be delivered of. I will leave him, and suddenly contrive the means of
   meeting between him and my daughter.—My honorable lord, I will
   most humbly take my leave of you.
HAMLET   You cannot, sir, take from me any thing that I will more will-
   ingly part withal: except my life, except my life, except my life.   210
POLONIUS   Fare you well, my lord.
HAMLET   These tedious old fools.
      [Re-enter ROSENCRANTZ and GUILDENSTERN.]
POLONIUS   You go to seek the Lord Hamlet; there he is.
ROSENCRANTZ [To POLONIUS.]   God save you, sir!
      [Exit POLONIUS.]
GUILDENSTERN   My honored lord!   215
ROSENCRANTZ   My most dear lord!
HAMLET   My excellent good friends! How dost thou, Guildenstern? Ah,
   Rosencrantz! Good lads, how do you both?
ROSENCRANTZ   As the indifferent⁶ children of the earth.
GUILDENSTERN   Happy, in that we are not over-happy;   220
   On Fortune's cap we are not the very button.⁷
HAMLET   Nor the soles of her shoe?
ROSENCRANTZ   Neither, my lord.
HAMLET   Then you live about her waist, or in the middle of her
   favors?   225
GUILDENSTERN   Faith, her privates⁸ we.
HAMLET   In the secret parts of Fortune? O, most true; she is a strumpet.
   What's the news?

4. The subject matter of the book. Hamlet responds as if he referred to the subject of a quarrel.
5. Aptness of expression.
6. Average.
7. Top.
8. Ordinary men (with obvious play on the sexual term private parts).

ROSENCRANTZ   None, my lord, but that the world's grown honest.

HAMLET   Then is doomsday near: but your news is not true. Let
me question more in particular: what have you, my good friends, 230
deserved at the hands of Fortune, that she sends you to prison
hither?

GUILDENSTERN   Prison, my lord!

HAMLET   Denmark's a prison.

ROSENCRANTZ   Then is the world one. 235

HAMLET   A goodly one; in which there are many confines, wards[9] and
dungeons, Denmark being one o' the worst.

ROSENCRANTZ   We think not so, my lord.

HAMLET   Why, then, 'tis none to you; for there is nothing either good
or bad, but thinking makes it so: to me it is a prison. 240

ROSENCRANTZ   Why, then your ambition makes it one; 'tis too narrow
for your mind.

HAMLET   O God, I could be bounded in a nut-shell and count myself
a king of infinite space, were it not that I have bad dreams.

GUILDENSTERN   Which dreams indeed are ambition; for the very sub- 245
stance of the ambitious is merely the shadow of a dream.

HAMLET   A dream itself is but a shadow.

ROSENCRANTZ   Truly, and I hold ambition of so airy and light a quality
that it is but a shadow's shadow.

HAMLET   Then are our beggars bodies, and our monarchs and out- 250
stretched heroes the beggars' shadows. Shall we to the court? for,
by my fay, I cannot reason.

ROSENCRANTZ   ⎫
            ⎬   We'll wait upon you.
GUILDENSTERN   ⎭

HAMLET   No such matter: I will not sort you[1] with the rest of my
servants; for, to speak to you like an honest man, I am most dreadfully 255
attended. But, in the beaten way of friendship, what make you at
Elsinore?

ROSENCRANTZ   To visit you, my lord; no other occasion.

HAMLET   Beggar that I am, I am even poor in thanks; but I thank you:
and sure, dear friends, my thanks are too dear a halfpenny.[2] Were 260
you not sent for? Is it your own inclining? Is it a free visitation?
Come, deal justly[3] with me: come, come; nay, speak.

GUILDENSTERN   What should we say, my lord?

HAMLET   Why, any thing, but to the purpose. You were sent for; and
there is a kind of confession in your looks, which your modesties 265
have not craft enough to color: I know the good king and queen
have sent for you.

ROSENCRANTZ   To what end, my lord?

HAMLET   That you must teach me. But let me conjure you, by the
rights of our fellowship, by the consonancy of our youth, by the 270
obligation of our ever-preserved love, and by what more dear

---

9. Cells. "Confines": places of confinement.   2. If priced at a halfpenny.
1. Put you together.   3. Honestly.

a better proposer[4] could charge you withal, be even and direct
with me, whether you were sent for, or no.

ROSENCRANTZ [*Aside to* GUILDENSTERN.] What say you?

HAMLET [*Aside.*] Nay then, I have an eye of[5] you.—If you love me,   275
hold not off.

GUILDENSTERN My lord, we were sent for.

HAMLET I will tell you why; so shall my anticipation prevent your
discovery,[6] and your secrecy to the king and queen moult no feather.
I have of late—but wherefore I know not—lost all my mirth, forgone   280
all custom of exercises; and indeed it goes so heavily with my
disposition that this goodly frame, the earth, seems to me a sterile
promontory; this most excellent canopy, the air, look you, this brave
o'erhanging firmament, this majestical roof fretted[7] with golden fire,
why, it appears no other thing to me than a foul and pestilent congre-   285
gation of vapors. What a piece of work is a man! how noble in
reason! how infinite in faculty! in form and moving how express[8] and
admirable! in action how like an angel! in apprehension how like a
god! the beauty of the world! the paragon of animals! And yet, to me,
what is this quintessence of dust? man delights not me; no, nor wom-   290
an neither, though by your smiling you seem to say so.

ROSENCRANTZ My lord, there was no such stuff in my thoughts.

HAMLET Why did you laugh then, when I said "man delights not me"?

ROSENCRANTZ To think, my lord, if you delight not in man, what
lenten entertainment the players shall receive from you: we coted[9]   295
them on the way; and hither are they coming, to offer you service.

HAMLET He that plays the king shall be welcome; his majesty shall
have tribute of me; the adventurous knight shall use his foil and
target; the lover shall not sigh gratis; the humorous[1] man shall end   300
his part in peace; the clown shall make those laugh whose lungs are
tickle o' the sere,[2] and the lady shall say her mind freely, or the blank
verse shall halt for 't. What players are they?

ROSENCRANTZ Even those you were wont to take such delight in, the
tragedians of the city.   305

HAMLET How chances it they travel? their residence, both in reputation
and profit, was better both ways.

ROSENCRANTZ I think their inhibition comes by means of the late
innovation.[3]

HAMLET Do they hold the same estimation they did when I was in the   310
city? are they so followed?

ROSENCRANTZ No, indeed, are they not.

HAMLET How comes it? do they grow rusty?

ROSENCRANTZ Nay, their endeavor keeps in the wonted pace: but

4. Speaker.
5. On.
6. Precede your disclosure.
7. Adorned.
8. Precise.
9. Overtook.

1. Eccentric, whimsical.
2. Ready to shoot off at a touch.
3. The introduction of the children (line 315),
as Rosencrantz explains in his subsequent replies
to Hamlet. "Inhibition": prohibition.

there is, sir, an eyrie of children, little eyases,[4] that cry out on the 315
top of question[5] and are most tyrannically clapped for 't: these are
now the fashion, and so berattle[6] the common stages—so they call
them—that many wearing rapiers are afraid of goose-quills,[7] and
dare scarce come thither.

HAMLET   What, are they children? who maintains 'em? how are they 320
escoted? Will they pursue the quality[8] no longer than they can sing?
will they not say afterwards, if they should grow themselves to
common players—as it is most like, if their means are no better,—
their writers do them wrong, to make them exclaim against their
own succession?[9] 325

ROSENCRANTZ   Faith, there has been much to-do on both sides, and
the nation holds it no sin to tarre[1] them to controversy: there was
for a while no money bid for argument unless the poet and the player
went to cuffs in the question.[2]

HAMLET   Is 't possible? 330

GUILDENSTERN   O, there has been much throwing about of brains.

HAMLET   Do the boys carry it away?[3]

ROSENCRANTZ   Aye, that they do, my lord; Hercules and his load too.[4]

HAMLET   It is not very strange; for my uncle is king of Denmark,
and those that would make mows[5] at him while my father lived, give 335
twenty, forty, fifty, a hundred ducats a-piece, for his picture in little.
'Sblood, there is something in this more than natural, if philosophy
could find it out.

[Flourish of trumpets within.]

GUILDENSTERN   There are the players.

HAMLET   Gentlemen, you are welcome to Elsinore. Your hands, come 340
then: the appurtenance of welcome is fashion and ceremony: let me
comply with you in this garb, lest my extent[6] to the players, which,
I tell you, must show fairly outwards, should more appear like
entertainment[7] than yours. You are welcome: but my uncle-father
and aunt-mother are deceived.

GUILDENSTERN   In what, my dear lord? 345

HAMLET   I am but mad north-north-west: when the wind is southerly
I know a hawk from a handsaw.[8]

[Re-enter POLONIUS.]

POLONIUS   Well be with you, gentlemen!

HAMLET   Hark you, Guildenstern; and you too: at each ear a hearer: 350

---

4. Nestling hawks. "Eyrie": nest.
5. Above others on matter of dispute.
6. Berate.
7. Gentlemen are afraid of pens (that is, of poets satirizing the "common stages").
8. Profession of acting. "Escoted": financially supported.
9. Recite satiric pieces against what they are themselves likely to become, common players.
1. Incite.
2. No offer to buy a plot for a play if it did not

contain a quarrel between poet and player on that subject.
3. Win out.
4. The sign in front of the Globe Theater showed Hercules bearing the world on his shoulders.
5. Faces, grimaces.
6. Welcoming behavior. "Garb": style.
7. Welcome.
8. A hawk from a heron as well as a kind of ax from a handsaw.

that great baby you see there is not yet out of his swaddling clouts.[9]

ROSENCRANTZ   Happily he's the second time come to them; for they
say an old man is twice a child.

HAMLET   I will prophesy he comes to tell me of the players; mark it.
You say right, sir: o' Monday morning; 'twas so, indeed.[1]   355

POLONIUS   My lord, I have news to tell you.

HAMLET   My lord, I have news to tell you. When Roscius[2] was an actor
in Rome,—

POLONIUS   The actors are come hither, my lord.

HAMLET   Buz, buz![3]   360

POLONIUS   Upon my honor,—

HAMLET   Then came each actor on his ass,—

POLONIUS   The best actors in the world, either for tragedy, comedy,
history, pastoral, pastoral-comical, historical-pastoral, tragical-
historical, tragical-comical-historical-pastoral, scene individable,   365
or poem unlimited:[4] Seneca cannot be too heavy, nor Plautus too
light. For the law of writ and the liberty,[5] these are the only men.

HAMLET   O Jephthah,[6] judge of Israel, what a treasure hadst thou!

POLONIUS   What a treasure had he, my lord?

HAMLET   Why,   370
"One fair daughter, and no more,
The which he lovèd passing well."[7]

POLONIUS [Aside.]   Still on my daughter.

HAMLET   Am I not i' the right, old Jephthah?

POLONIUS   If you call me Jephthah, my lord, I have a daughter that I   375
love passing well.

HAMLET   Nay, that follows not.

POLONIUS   What follows, then, my lord?

HAMLET   Why,
"As by lot, God wot."
and then you know,   380
"It came to pass, as most like it was,"—
the first row of the pious chanson will show you more; for look, where
my abridgment[8] comes.

[Enter four or five PLAYERS.]

You are welcome, masters; welcome, all. I am glad to see thee well.
Welcome, good friends. O, my old friend! Why thy face is valanced[9]   385
since I saw thee last; comest thou to beard me in Denmark? What,
my young lady and mistress! By'r lady, your ladyship is nearer to

9. Clothes.
1. Hamlet, for Polonius's sake, pretends he is deep in talk with Rosencrantz.
2. A famous Roman comic actor (ca. 126–62 B.C.E.).
3. An expression used to stop the teller of a stale story.
4. For plays governed and those not governed by classical rules.
5. Possibly, for both written and extemporized

plays. Seneca (after 4 B.C.E.–65 C.E.) was a Roman who wrote tragedies. Plautus (ca. 254–184 B.C.E.) was a Roman who wrote comedies.
6. Who was compelled to sacrifice a dearly beloved daughter (Judges 11).
7. From an old ballad about Jephthah.
8. That is, the players interrupting him. "Row": stanza. "Chanson": song.
9. Draped (with a beard).

heaven than when I saw you last, by the altitude of a chopine. Pray
God, your voice, like a piece of uncurrent gold, be not cracked within
the ring.[1] Masters, you are all welcome. We'll e'en to 't like French   390
falconers, fly at any thing we see: we'll have a speech straight: come,
give us a taste of your quality; come, a passionate speech.

FIRST PLAYER   What speech, my good lord?

HAMLET   I heard thee speak me a speech once, but it was never acted;
or, if it was, not above once; for the play, I remember, pleased not   395
the million; 'twas caviare to the general:[2] but it was—as I received
it, and others, whose judgments in such matters cried in the top of
mine[3]—an excellent play, well digested in the scenes, set down with
as much modesty as cunning. I remember, one said there were no
sallets in the lines to make the matter savory, nor no matter in the   400
phrase that might indict the author of affection;[4] but called it an
honest method, as wholesome as sweet, and by very much more
handsome than fine.[5] One speech in it I chiefly loved: 'twas Æneas'
tale to Dido; and thereabout of it especially, where he speaks of
Priam's slaughter:[6] it live in your memory, begin at this line; let me   405
see, let me see;
"The rugged Pyrrhus, like th' Hyrcanian beast,"[7]—
It is not so: it begins with "Pyrrhus."
"The rugged Pyrrhus, he whose sable arms,
Black as his purpose, did the night resemble   410
When he lay couchèd in the ominous horse,[8]
Hath now this dread and black complexion smeared
With heraldry more dismal: head to foot
Now is he total gules; horridly tricked[9]
With the blood of fathers, mothers, daughters, sons,   415
Baked and impasted with the parching streets,
That lend a tyrannous[1] and a damnèd light
To their lord's murder: roasted in wrath and fire,
And thus o'er-sizèd[2] with coagulate gore,
With eyes like carbuncles, the hellish Pyrrhus   420
Old grandsire Priam seeks."
So, proceed you.

POLONIUS   'Fore God, my lord, well spoken, with good accent and
good discretion.

FIRST PLAYER   'Anon he finds him   425
Striking too short at Greeks; his antique sword,
Rebellious to his arm, lies where it falls,

1. A pun on the *ring* of the voice and the *ring* around the king's head on a coin. "Chopine": a thick-soled shoe. "Uncurrent": unfit for currency.
2. A delicacy wasted on the general public.
3. Were louder (more authoritative than) mine.
4. Affectation. "Sallets": salads (that is, relish, spicy passages).
5. More elegant than showy.

6. The story of the fall of Troy, told by Aeneas to Queen Dido. Priam was the king of Troy.
7. Tiger. "Pyrrhus": Achilles' son (also called Neoptolemus).
8. The wooden horse in which Greek warriors were smuggled into Troy.
9. Adorned. "Gules": heraldic term for red.
1. Savage.
2. Glued over.

Repugnant to command: unequal matched,
Pyrrhus at Priam drives; in rage strikes wide;
But with the whiff and wind of his fell sword   430
The unnervèd father falls. Then senseless Ilium,[3]
Seeming to feel this blow, with flaming top
Stoops to his base, and with a hideous crash
Takes prisoner Pyrrhus's ear: for, lo! his sword,
Which was declining on the milky[4] head   435
Of reverend Priam seemed i' the air to stick:
So, as a painted tyrant, Pyrrhus stood,
And like a neutral to his will and matter,
Did nothing.
But as we often see, against some storm,   440
A silence in the heavens, the rack[5] stand still,
The bold winds speechless and the orb below
As hush as death, anon the dreadful thunder
Doth rend the region, so after Pyrrhus's pause
Aroused vengeance sets him new a-work;   445
And never did the Cyclops'[6] hammers fall
On Mars's armor, forged for proof[7] eterne,
With less remorse than Pyrrhus's bleeding sword
Now falls on Priam.
Out, thou strumpet, Fortune! All you gods,   450
In general synod take away her power,
Break all the spokes and fellies from her wheel,
And bowl the round nave[8] down the hill of heaven
As low as to the fiends!
POLONIUS   This is too long.   455
HAMLET   It shall to the barber's, with your beard. Prithee, say on: he's
   for a jig[9] or a tale of bawdry, or he sleeps: say on: come to Hecuba.
FIRST PLAYER   "But who, O, who had seen the mobled[1] queen—"
HAMLET   "The mobled queen?"
POLONIUS   That's good; "mobled queen" is good.   460
FIRST PLAYER   "Run barefoot up and down, threatening the flames
   With bisson rheum; a clout[2] upon that head
   Where late the diadem stood; and for a robe,
   About her lank and all o'er-teemèd loins,[3]
   A blanket, in the alarm of fear caught up: 465
   Who this had seen, with tongue in venom steeped
   'Gainst Fortune's state[4] would treason have pronounced:
   But if the gods themselves did see her then,
   When she saw Pyrrhus make malicious sport

3. Troy's citadel.
4. White-haired.
5. Clouds. "Against": just before.
6. The gigantic workmen of Hephaestus (Vulcan), god of blacksmiths and fire.
7. Protection.
8. Hub. "Fellies": rims.

9. Ludicrous sung dialogue, short farce.
1. Muffled.
2. Cloth. "Bisson rheum": blinding moisture, tears.
3. Worn out by childbearing.
4. Government.

In mincing with his sword her husband's limbs,   470
The instant burst of clamor that she made,
Unless things mortal move them[5] not at all,
Would have made milch the burning eyes of heaven[6]
And passion in the gods."

POLONIUS   Look, whether he has not turned his color and has tears in   475
's eyes. Prithee, no more.

HAMLET   'Tis well; I'll have thee speak out the rest of this soon. Good
my lord, will you see the players well bestowed?[7] Do you hear, let
them be well used, for they are the abstracts and brief chronicles
of the time: after your death you were better have a bad epitaph than   480
their ill report while you live.

POLONIUS   My lord, I will use them according to their desert.

HAMLET   God's bodykins,[8] man, much better: use every man after his
desert, and who shall 'scape whipping? Use them after your own
honor and dignity: the less they deserve, the more merit is in your   485
bounty. Take them in.

POLONIUS   Come, sirs.

HAMLET   Follow him, friends: we'll hear a play to-morrow. [*Exit*
POLONIUS *with all the* PLAYERS *but the first.*] Dost thou hear me, old
friend; can you play the Murder of Gonzago?   490

FIRST PLAYER   Aye, my lord.

HAMLET   We'll ha 't to-morrow night. You could, for a need, study a
speech of some dozen or sixteen lines, which I would set down and
insert in 't, could you not?

FIRST PLAYER   Aye, my lord.   495

HAMLET   Very well. Follow that lord; and look you mock him not.
[*Exit* FIRST PLAYER.] My good friends, I'll leave you till night: you are
welcome to Elsinore.

ROSENCRANTZ   Good my lord!

HAMLET   Aye, so, God be wi' ye! [*Exeunt* ROSENCRANTZ *and* GUIL-   500
DENSTERN.] Now I am alone.
O, what a rogue and peasant slave am I!
Is it not monstrous that this player here,
But in a fiction, in a dream of passion,
Could force his soul so to his own conceit   505
That from her[9] working all his visage wanned;
Tears in his eyes, distraction in 's aspect,
A broken voice, and his whole function[1] suiting
With forms to his conceit? and all for nothing!
For Hecuba![2]   510
What's Hecuba to him, or he to Hecuba,
That he should weep for her? What would he do,

---

5. The gods.
6. The stars. "Milch": moist (milk-giving).
7. Taken care of, lodged.
8. By God's little body.

9. His soul's.
1. Bodily action.
2. Queen of Troy, Priam's wife. "Conceit":
imagination, conception of the role played.

Had he the motive and the cue for passion
That I have? He would drown the stage with tears
And cleave the general air with horrid speech,   515
Make mad the guilty and appal the free,
Confound the ignorant, and amaze indeed
The very faculties of eyes and ears.
Yet I,
A dull and muddy-mettled rascal, peak,[3]   520
Like John-a-dreams, unpregnant of my cause,[4]
And can say nothing; no, not for a king,
Upon whose property and most dear life
A damn'd defeat was made. Am I a coward?
Who calls me villain? breaks my pate across?   525
Plucks off my beard, and blows it in my face?
Tweaks me by the nose? gives me the lie i' the throat,
As deep as to the lungs? who does me this?
Ha!
'Swounds, I should take it: for it cannot be   530
But I am pigeon-livered and lack gall
To make oppression bitter, or ere this
I should have fatted all the region kites[5]
With this slave's offal: bloody, bawdy villain!
Remorseless, treacherous, lecherous, kindless[6] villain!   535
O, vengeance!
Why, what an ass am I! This is most brave,
That I, the son of a dear father murdered,
Prompted to my revenge by heaven and hell,
Must, like a whore, unpack my heart with words,   540
And fall a-cursing, like a very drab,
A scullion!
Fie upon 't! About,[7] my brain! Hum, I have heard
That guilty creatures, sitting at a play,
Have by the very cunning of the scene   545
Been struck so to the soul that presently
They have proclaimed their malefactions;
For murder, though it have no tongue, will speak
With most miraculous organ. I'll have these players
Play something like the murder of my father   550
Before mine uncle: I'll observe his looks;
I'll tent him to the quick: if he but blench,[8]
I know my course. The spirit that I have seen
May be the devil; and the devil hath power

3. Mope. "Muddy mettled": of poor metal
(spirit, temper), dull-spirited.
4. Not really conscious of my cause, unquick-
ened by it. "John-a-dreams": a dreamy, absent-
minded character.

5. Kites (hawks) of the air.
6. Unnatural.
7. To work!
8. Flinch. "Tent": probe.

To assume a pleasing shape; yea, and perhaps   555
Out of my weakness and my melancholy,
As he is very potent with such spirits,
Abuses me to damn me. I'll have grounds
More relative⁹ than this. The play's the thing
Wherein I'll catch the conscience of the king.   560
     [*Exit.*]

Act 3

SCENE I

[SCENE: *A room in the castle.*]

    [*Enter* KING, QUEEN, POLONIUS, OPHELIA, ROSENCRANTZ, *and*
    GUILDENSTERN.]
KING   And can you, by no drift of circumstance,¹
  Get from him why he puts on this confusion,
  Grating so harshly all his days of quiet
  With turbulent and dangerous lunacy?
ROSENCRANTZ   He does confess he feels himself distracted,   5
  But from what cause he will by no means speak.
GUILDENSTERN   Nor do we find him forward to be sounded;
  But, with a crafty madness, keeps aloof,
  When we would bring him on to some confession
  Of his true state.
QUEEN   Did he receive you well?   10
ROSENCRANTZ   Most like a gentleman.
GUILDENSTERN   But with much forcing of his disposition.
ROSENCRANTZ   Niggard of question, but of our demands
  Most free in his reply.
QUEEN   Did you assay² him
  To any pastime?   15
ROSENCRANTZ   Madam, it so fell out that certain players
  We o'er-raught³ on the way. of these we told him,
  And there did seem in him a kind of joy
  To hear of it: they are about the court,
  And, as I think, they have already order   20
  This night to play before him.
POLONIUS   'Tis most true:
  And he beseeched me to entreat your majesties
  To hear and see the matter.
KING   With all my heart; and it doth much content me
  To hear him so inclined.   25
  Good gentlemen, give him a further edge,⁴
  And drive his purpose on to these delights.

---

9. Relevant.   3. Overtook.
1. Turn of talk, or roundabout way.   4. Incitement.
2. Try to attract him.

ROSENCRANTZ   We shall, my lord.
    [*Exeunt* ROSENCRANTZ *and* GUILDENSTERN.]
KING   Sweet Gertrude, leave us too;
  For we have closely[5] sent for Hamlet hither,
  That he, as 'twere by accident, may here   30
  Affront Ophelia:
  Her father and myself, lawful espials,
  Will so bestow[6] ourselves that, seeing unseen,
  We may of their encounter frankly judge,
  And gather by him, as he is behaved,   35
  If't be the affliction of his love or no
  That thus he suffers for.
QUEEN   I shall obey you:
  And for your part, Ophelia, I do wish
  That your good beauties be the happy cause
  Of Hamlet's wildness: so shall I hope your virtues   40
  Will bring him to his wonted way again,
  To both your honors.
OPHELIA   Madam, I wish it may.
    [*Exit* QUEEN.]
POLONIUS   Ophelia, walk you here. Gracious, so please you,
  We will bestow ourselves. [*To* OPHELIA.] Read on this book;
  That show of such an exercise may color[7]   45
  Your loneliness. We are oft to blame in this,—
  'Tis too much proved—that with devotion's visage
  And pious action we do sugar o'er
  The devil himself.
KING [*Aside.*]   O, 'tis too true!
  How smart a lash that speech doth give my conscience!   50
  The harlot's cheek, beautied with plastering art,
  Is not more ugly to the thing that helps it
  Than is my deed to my most painted word:
  O heavy burthen!
POLONIUS   I hear him coming: let's withdraw, my lord.   55
    [*Exeunt* KING *and* POLONIUS.—*Enter* HAMLET.]
HAMLET   To be, or not to be: that is the question:
  Whether 'tis nobler in the mind to suffer
  The slings and arrows of outrageous fortune,
  Or to take arms against a sea of troubles,
  And by opposing end them. To die: to sleep;   60
  No more; and by a sleep to say we end
  The heart-ache, and the thousand natural shocks
  That flesh is heir to, 'tis a consummation[8]
  Devoutly to be wished. To die, to sleep;
  To sleep: perchance to dream: aye, there's the rub;[9]   65

[Handwritten marginalia: "a sign of guilt possibly"; "Most famous lines"]

---

5. Privately.   8. Final settlement.
6. Place. "Affront": confront. "Espials": spies.   9. The impediment (a bowling term).
7. Excuse.

For in that sleep of death what dreams may come,
When we have shuffled off this mortal coil,[1]
Must give us pause: there's the respect
That makes calamity of so long life;[2]
For who would bear the whips and scorns of time,   70
The oppressor's wrong, the proud man's contumely,
The pangs of despisèd love, the law's delay,
The insolence of office, and the spurns
That patient merit of the unworthy takes,
When he himself might his quietus make   75
With a bare bodkin? who would fardels[3] bear,
To grunt and sweat under a weary life,
But that the dread of something after death,
The undiscovered country from whose bourn[4]
No traveler returns, puzzles the will,   80
And makes us rather bear those ills we have
Than fly to others that we know not of?
Thus conscience does make cowards of us all,
And thus the native hue of resolution
Is sicklied o'er with the pale cast of thought,   85
And enterprises of great pitch[5] and moment
With this regard their currents turn awry
And lose the name of action. Soft you now!
The fair Ophelia! Nymph, in thy orisons[6]
Be all my sins remembered.
OPHELIA   Good my lord,   90
How does your honor for this many a day?
HAMLET   I humbly thank you: well, well, well.
OPHELIA   My lord, I have remembrances of yours,
That I have longed to re-deliver;
I pray you, now receive them.
HAMLET   No, not I;   95
I never gave you aught.
OPHELIA   My honored lord, you know right well you did;
And with them words of so sweet breath composed
As made the things more rich: their perfume lost,
Take these again; for to the noble mind   100
Rich gifts wax poor when givers prove unkind.
There, my lord.
HAMLET   Ha, ha! are you honest?
OPHELIA   My lord?   105
HAMLET   Are you fair?
OPHELIA   What means your lordship?
HAMLET   That if you be honest and fair, your honesty should admit no
discourse to your beauty.

1. Have rid ourselves of the turmoil of mortal   4. Boundary.
life.   5. Height.
2. So long-lived. "Respect": consideration.   6. Prayers.
3. Burdens. "Bodkin": poniard, dagger.

OPHELIA   Could beauty, my lord, have better commerce[7] than with   110
honesty?

HAMLET   Aye, truly; for the power of beauty will sooner transform
honesty from what it is to a bawd than the force of honesty can
translate beauty into his[8] likeness: this was sometime a paradox,
but now the time gives it proof.[9] I did love you once.

OPHELIA   Indeed, my lord, you made me believe so.   115

HAMLET   You should not have believed me; for virtue cannot so
inoculate our old stock, but we shall relish[1] of it: I loved you not.

OPHELIA   I was the more deceived.

HAMLET   Get thee to a nunnery: why wouldst thou be a breeder of
sinners? I am myself indifferent honest; but yet I could accuse me   120
of such things that it were better my mother had not borne me: I
am very proud, revengeful, ambitious; with more offenses at my
beck than I have thoughts to put them in, imagination to give them
or time to act them in. What should such fellows as I do crawling
shape, between heaven and earth! We are arrant knaves all; believe   125
none of us. Go thy ways to a nunnery. Where's your father?

OPHELIA   At home, my lord.

HAMLET   Let the doors be shut upon him, that he may play the fool
no where but in 's own house. Farewell.

OPHELIA   O, help him, you sweet heavens!   130

HAMLET   If thou dost marry, I'll give thee this plague for thy dowry:
be thou as chaste as ice, as pure as snow, thou shalt not escape
calumny. Get thee to a nunnery, go: farewell. Or, if thou wilt needs
marry, marry a fool; for wise men know well enough what monsters[2]
you make of them. To a nunnery, go; and quickly too. Farewell.   135

OPHELIA   O heavenly powers, restore him!

HAMLET   I have heard of your paintings too, well enough; God hath
given you one face, and you make yourselves another: you jig, you
amble, and you lisp, and nick-name God's creatures, and make your
wantonness your ignorance.[3] Go to, I'll no more on 't; it hath made   140
me mad. I say, we will have no more marriages: those that are
married already, all but one, shall live; the rest shall keep as they are.
To a nunnery, go.
          [*Exit.*]

OPHELIA   O, what a noble mind is here o'erthrown!
The courtier's, soldier's, scholar's, eye, tongue, sword: 145
The expectancy and rose of the fair state,
The glass of fashion and the mould of form.[4]
The observed of all observers, quite, quite down!
And I, of ladies most deject and wretched,
That sucked the honey of his music vows,   150

---

7. Intercourse.
8. Its.
9. In his mother's adultery.
1. Retain the flavor of. "Inoculate": graft itself
onto.
2. Cuckolds bear imaginary horns and "a horned

man's a monster" (*Othello* 4.1).
3. Misname (out of affectation) the most natural things, and pretend that this is due to
ignorance instead of affectation.
4. The mirror of fashion and the model of
behavior.

Now see that noble and most sovereign reason,
Like sweet bells jangled, out of tune and harsh;
That unmatched form and feature of blown⁵ youth
Blasted with ecstasy: O, woe is me,
To have seen what I have seen, see what I see!   155
        [*Re-enter* KING *and* POLONIUS.]
KING   Love! his affections do not that way tend;
    Nor what he spake, though it lacked form a little,
    Was not like madness. There's something in his soul
    O'er which his melancholy sits on brood,
    And I do doubt⁶ the hatch and the disclose   160
    Will be some danger: which for to prevent,
    I have in quick determination
    Thus set it down:—he shall with speed to England,
    For the demand of our neglected tribute:
    Haply the seas and countries different   165
    With variable objects shall expel
    This something-settled matter in his heart,
    Whereon his brains still beating puts him thus
    From fashion of himself.⁷ What think you on 't?
POLONIUS   It shall do well: but yet do I believe   170
    The origin and commencement of his grief
    Sprung from neglected love. How now, Ophelia!
    You need not tell us what Lord Hamlet said;
    We heard it all. My lord, do as you please;
    But, if you hold it fit, after the play,   175
    Let his queen mother all alone entreat him
    To show his grief: let her be round⁸ with him;
    And I'll be placed, so please you, in the ear
    Of all their conference. If she find him not,
    To England send him, or confine him where   180
    Your wisdom best shall think.
KING   It shall be so:
    Madness in great ones must not unwatched go.
        [*Exeunt.*]

SCENE 2

[SCENE: *A hall in the castle.*]

        [*Enter* HAMLET *and* PLAYERS.]   actors from play
HAMLET   Speak the speech, I pray you, as I pronounced it to you,
    trippingly on the tongue: but if you mouth it, as many of your players
    do, I had as lief the town-crier spoke my lines. Nor do not saw
    the air too much with your hand, thus; but use all gently: for in the
    very torrent, tempest, and, as I may say, whirlwind of your passion,   5

---

5. In full bloom.   7. Makes him behave unusually.
6. Fear.   8. Direct.

you must acquire and beget a temperance that may give it smoothness. O, it offends me to the soul to hear a robustious periwig-pated fellow tear a passion to tatters, to very rags, to split the ears of the groundlings,[9] who, for the most part, are capable of nothing but inexplicable dumb-shows and noise: I would have such a fellow whipped for o'er doing Termagant;[1] it out-herods Herod: pray you, avoid it.

FIRST PLAYER   I warrant your honor.

HAMLET   Be not too tame neither, but let your own discretion be your tutor: suit the action to the word, the word to the action; with this special observance, that you o'erstep not the modesty[2] of nature: for anything so overdone is from the purpose of playing, whose end, both at the first and now, was and is, to hold, as 'twere, the mirror up to nature; to show virtue her own feature, scorn her own image, and the very age and body of the time his form and pressure.[3] Now this overdone or come tardy off, though it make the unskillful laugh, cannot but make the judicious grieve; the censure of the which one must in your allowance o'erweigh a whole theater of others. O, there be players that I have seen play, and heard others praise, and that highly, not to speak it profanely,[4] that neither having the accent of Christians nor the gait of Christian, pagan, nor man, have so strutted and bellowed, that I have thought some of nature's journeymen had made men, and not made them well, they imitated humanity so abominably.

FIRST PLAYER   I hope we have reformed that indifferently[5] with us, sir.

HAMLET   O, reform it altogether. And let those that play your clowns speak no more than is set down for them: for there be of them that will themselves laugh, to set on some quantity of barren[6] spectators to laugh too, though in the mean time some necessary question of the play be then to be considered: that's villainous, and shows a most pitiful ambition in the fool that uses it. Go, make you ready.

    [*Exeunt* PLAYERS. —*Enter* POLONIUS, ROSENCRANTZ, *and* GUILDENSTERN.]

How now, my lord! will the king hear this piece of work?

POLONIUS   And the queen too, and that presently.

HAMLET   Bid the players make haste.

    [*Exit* POLONIUS.]

Will you two help to hasten them?

ROSENCRANTZ
GUILDENSTERN   } We will, my lord.

    [*Exeunt* ROSENCRANTZ *and* GUILDENSTERN.]

HAMLET   What ho! Horatio!

    [*Enter* HORATIO.]

HORATIO   Here, sweet lord, at your service.

---

9. Spectators in the pit, where admission was cheapest.
1. God of the Muslims in old romances and morality plays; he was portrayed as being noisy and excitable.
2. Moderation.

3. Impress, shape. "Feature": form. "His": its.
4. Hamlet apologizes for the profane implication that there could be men not of God's making.
5. Pretty well.
6. Silly.

HAMLET   Horatio, thou art e'en as just a man
  As e'er my conversation coped withal.[7]   45
HORATIO   O, my dear lord,—
HAMLET   Nay, do not think I flatter;
  For what advancement may I hope from thee,
  That no revenue hast but thy good spirits,
  To feed and clothe thee? Why should the poor be flattered?
  No, let the candied tongue lick absurd pomp,   50
  And crook the pregnant hinges of the knee
  Where thrift may follow fawning.[8] Dost thou hear?
  Since my dear soul was mistress of her choice,
  And could of men distinguish, her election
  Hath sealed thee for herself: for thou hast been   55
  As one, in suffering all, that suffers nothing;
  A man that fortune's buffets and rewards
  Hast ta'en with equal thanks: and blest are those
  Whose blood and judgment[9] are so well commingled
  That they are not a pipe for fortune's finger   60
  To sound what stop she please.[1] Give me that man
  That is not passion's slave, and I will wear him
  In my heart's core, ay, in my heart of heart,
  As I do thee. Something too much of this.
  There is a play to-night before the king;   65
  One scene of it comes near the circumstance
  Which I have told thee of my father's death:
  I prithee, when thou sees that act a-foot,
  Even with the very comment of thy soul[2]
  Observe my uncle: if his occulted guilt   70
  Do not itself unkennel in one speech
  It is a damned ghost that we have seen,
  And my imaginations are as foul
  As Vulcan's stithy.[3] Give him heedful note;
  For I mine eyes will rivet to his face,   75
  And after we will both our judgments join
  In censure of his seeming.[4]
HORATIO   Well, my lord:
  If he steal aught the whilst this play is playing,
  And 'scape detecting, I will pay the theft.
HAMLET   They are coming to the play: I must be idle:[5]   80
  Get you a place.
        [*Danish march. A flourish. Enter* KING, QUEEN, POLONIUS, OPHELIA,
        ROSENCRANTZ, GUILDENSTERN, *and other* LORDS *attendant, with the*
        GUARD *carrying torches.*]

7. As I ever associated with.
8. Material profit may be derived from cringing. "Pregnant hinges": supple joints.
9. Passion and reason.
1. For Fortune to put her finger on any windhole of the pipe she wants.
2. With all your powers of observation.
3. Smithy.
4. To judge his behavior.
5. Crazy.

KING   How fares our cousin Hamlet?

HAMLET   Excellent, i' faith; of the chameleon's dish: I eat the air,[6] promise-crammed: you cannot feed capons so.

KING   I have nothing with this answer, Hamlet; these words are not mine.[7]   85

HAMLET   No, nor mine now. [*To* POLONIUS.] My lord, you played once i' the university, you say?

POLONIUS   That did I, my lord, and was accounted a good actor.

HAMLET   What did you enact?   90

POLONIUS   I did enact Julius Caesar: I was killed i' the Capitol; Brutus killed me.

HAMLET   It was a brute part of him to kill so capital a calf there. Be the players ready?

ROSENCRANTZ   Aye, my lord: they stay upon your patience.   85 → 95

QUEEN   Come hither, my dear Hamlet, sit by me.

HAMLET   No, good mother, here's metal more attractive.

POLONIUS [*To the* KING.]   O, ho! do you mark that?

HAMLET   Lady, shall I lie in your lap? [*Lying down at* OPHELIA's *feet.*]

OPHELIA   No, my lord.   100

HAMLET   I mean, my head upon your lap?

OPHELIA   Aye, my lord.

HAMLET   Do you think I meant country matters?

OPHELIA   I think nothing, my lord.

HAMLET   That's a fair thought to lie between maids' legs.   105

OPHELIA   What is, my lord?

HAMLET   Nothing.[8]

OPHELIA   You are merry, my lord.

HAMLET   Who, I?

OPHELIA   Aye, my lord.   110

HAMLET   O God, your only jig-maker.[9] What should a man do but be merry? for, look you, how cheerfully my mother looks, and my father died within 's two hours.

OPHELIA   Nay, 'tis twice two months, my lord.

HAMLET   So long? Nay then, let the devil wear black, for I'll have a   115
suit of sables.[1] O heavens! die two months ago, and not forgotten
yet? Then there's hope a great man's memory may outlive his life
half a year: but, by 'r lady, he must build churches then; or else shall
he suffer not thinking on, with the hobby-horse,[2] whose epitaph is,
"For, O, for, O, the hobby-horse is forgot."   120

> [*Hautboys play. The dumb-show enters. —Enter a King and a Queen very lovingly; the Queen embracing him and he her. She kneels, and makes show of protestation unto him. He takes her up, and declines his head upon her neck; lays him down upon a bank of flowers: she, seeing him asleep,*]

---

6. The chameleon was supposed to feed on air.

7. Have nothing to do with my question.

8. A sexual pun: no thing.

9. Maker of comic songs.

1. Hamlet notes sarcastically the lack of mourning for his father in the fancy dress of court and king.

2. A figure in the old May Day games and Morris dances.

leaves him. Anon comes in a fellow, takes off his crown, kisses it, and pours poison in the King's ears, and exits. The Queen returns; finds the King dead, and makes passionate action. The Poisoner, with some two or three Mutes comes in again, seeming to lament with her. The dead body is carried away. The Poisoner woos the Queen with gifts: she seems loath and unwilling awhile, but in the end accepts his love. —Exeunt.]

OPHELIA   What means this, my lord?

HAMLET   Marry, this is miching mallecho;[3] it means mischief.

OPHELIA   Belike this show imports the argument of the play.

[*Enter* PROLOGUE.]

HAMLET   We shall know by this fellow: the players cannot keep counsel;[4]
they'll tell all.   125

OPHELIA   Will he tell us what this show meant?

HAMLET   Aye, or any show that you'll show him: be not you ashamed
to show, he'll not shame to tell you what it means.

OPHELIA   You are naught,[5] you are naught: I'll mark the play.

PROLOGUE   For us, and for our tragedy,   130
            Here stooping to your clemency,
            We beg your hearing patiently.

HAMLET   Is this a prologue, or the posy[6] of a ring?

OPHELIA   'Tis brief, my lord.

HAMLET   As woman's love.   135

[*Enter two* PLAYERS, KING *and* QUEEN.]

PLAYER KING   Full thirty times hath Phœbus's cart[7] gone round
Neptune's salt wash and Tellus's orbed ground,
And thirty dozen moons with borrowed sheen
About the world have times twelve thirties been,
Since love our hearts and Hymen did our hands   140
Unite commutual in most sacred bands.

PLAYER QUEEN   So many journeys may the sun and moon
Make us again count o'er ere love be done!
But, woe is me, you are so sick of late,
So far from cheer and from your former state,   145
That I distrust you.[8] Yet, though I distrust,
Discomfort you, my lord, it nothing must:
For women's fear and love holds quantity,[9]
In neither aught, or in extremity.
Now, what my love is, proof hath made you know,   150
And as my love is sized, my fear is so:
Where love is great, the littlest doubts are fear,
Where little fears grow great, great love grows there.

PLAYER KING   Faith, I must leave thee, love, and shortly too;
My operant powers their functions leave[1] to do: 155
And thou shalt live in this fair world behind,

3. Sneaking misdeed.
4. A secret.
5. Naughty, improper.
6. Motto, inscription.

7. The chariot of the sun.
8. I am worried about you.
9. Maintain mutual balance.
1. Cease.

Honored, beloved; and haply one as kind
For husband shalt thou—
PLAYER QUEEN   O, confound the rest!
   Such love must needs be treason in my breast:
   In second husband let me be accurst!   160
   None wed the second but who killed the first.
HAMLET [*Aside.*]   Wormwood, wormwood.
PLAYER QUEEN   The instances that second marriage move
   Are base respects of thrift,[2] but none of love:
   A second time I kill my husband dead,   165
   When second husband kisses me in bed.
PLAYER KING   I do believe you think what now you speak,
   But what we do determine oft we break.
   Purpose is but the slave to memory,
   Of violent birth but poor validity: 170
   Which now, like fruit unripe, sticks on the tree,
   But fall unshaken when they mellow be.
   Most necessary 'tis that we forget
   To pay ourselves what to ourselves is debt:
   What to ourselves in passion we propose,   175
   The passion ending, both the purpose lose.
   The violence of either grief or joy
   Their own enactures[3] with themselves destroy:
   Where joy most revels, grief doth most lament;
   Grief joys, joy grieves, on slender accident.   180
   This world is not for aye, nor 'tis not strange
   That even our loves should with our fortunes change,
   For 'tis a question left us yet to prove,
   Whether love lead fortune or else fortune love.
   The great man down, you mark his favorite flies;   185
   The poor advanced makes friends of enemies:
   And hitherto doth love on fortune tend;
   For who not needs shall never lack a friend,
   And who in want a hollow friend doth try
   Directly seasons[4] him his enemy.   190
   But, orderly to end where I begun,
   Our wills and fates do so contrary run,
   That our devices still are overthrown,
   Our thoughts are ours, their ends none of our own:
   So think thou wilt no second husband wed,   195
   But die thy thoughts when thy first lord is dead.
PLAYER QUEEN   Nor earth to me give food nor heaven light!
   Sport and repose lock from me day and night!
   To desperation turn my trust and hope!
   An anchor's cheer in prison be my scope!   200
   Each opposite, that blanks[5] the face of joy,

---

2. Considerations of material profit. "Instances": motives.
3. Their own fulfillment in action.
4. Matures.
5. Makes pale. "Anchor's cheer": hermit's, or anchorite's, fare.

Meet what I would have well and it destroy!
Both here and hence pursue me lasting strife,
If, once a widow, ever I be wife!
HAMLET   If she should break it now!   205
PLAYER KING 'Tis deeply sworn. Sweet, leave me here a while;
My spirits grow dull, and fain I would beguile
The tedious day with sleep.
        [*Sleeps.*]
PLAYER QUEEN   Sleep rock thy brain;
And never come mischance between us twain!
        [*Exit.*]
HAMLET   Madam, how like you this play?   210
QUEEN   The lady doth protest[6] too much, methinks.
HAMLET   O, but she'll keep her word.
KING   Have you heard the argument?[7] Is there no offense in 't?
HAMLET   No, no, they do but jest, poison in jest; no offense i' the   215
world.
KING   What do you call the play?
HAMLET   The Mouse-Trap. Marry, how? Tropically.[8] This play is the
image of a murder done in Vienna: Gonzago is the duke's name; his
wife, Baptista: you shall see anon; 'tis a knavish piece of work; but   220
what o' that? your majesty, and we that have free souls, it touches
us not: let the galled jade wince, our withers are unwrung.[9]
        [*Enter LUCIANUS.*]
This is one Lucianus, nephew to the king.
OPHELIA   You are as good as a chorus, my lord.
HAMLET   I could interpret[1] between you and your love, if I could see   225
the puppets dallying.
OPHELIA   You are keen,[2] my lord, you are keen.
HAMLET   It would cost you a groaning to take off my edge.
OPHELIA   Still better and worse.
HAMLET   So you must take[3] your husbands. Begin, murderer; pox,   230
leave thy damnable faces, and begin. Come: the croaking raven doth
bellow for revenge.
LUCIANUS   Thoughts black, hands apt, drugs fit, and time agreeing;
Confederate season, else no creature seeing;
Thou mixture rank, of midnight weeds collected,   235
With Hecate's ban[4] thrice blasted, thrice infected,
Thy natural magic and dire property,
On wholesome life usurp immediately.
        [*Pours the poison into the sleeper's ear.*]
HAMLET   He poisons him i' the garden for his estate. His name's

---

6. Promise.
7. Plot of the play in outline.
8. By a trope, figuratively.
9. Not wrenched. "Galled jade": injured horse.
"Withers": the area between a horse's shoulders.
1. Act as interpreter (regular feature in puppet shows).

2. Bitter, but Hamlet chooses to take the word sexually.
3. That is, for better or for worse, as in the marriage service—but in fact you "mis-take," deceive them.
4. Goddess of witchcraft's curse. "Confederate": favorable.

Gonzago: the story is extant, and written in very choice Italian: you   240
shall see anon how the murderer gets the love of Gonzago's wife.
OPHELIA   The king rises.
HAMLET   What, frighted with false fire!⁵
QUEEN   How fares my lord?
POLONIUS   Give o'er the play.   245
KING   Give me some light. Away!
POLONIUS   Lights, lights, lights!
      [*Exeunt all but* HAMLET *and* HORATIO.]
HAMLET   Why, let the stricken deer go weep,
          The hart ungallèd play;
      For some must watch, while some must sleep: 250
          Thus runs the world away.
Would not this, sir, and a forest of feathers—if the rest of my fortunes
turn Turk with me—with two Provincial roses on my razed shoes,
get me a fellowship in a cry⁶ of players, sir?
HORATIO   Half a share.   255
HAMLET   A whole one, I.
      For thou dost know, O Damon dear,
          This realm dismantled was
      Of Jove himself; and now reigns here
          A very, very—pajock.   260
HORATIO   You might have rhymed.⁷
HAMLET   O good Horatio, I'll take the ghost's word for a thousand
pound. Didst perceive?
HORATIO   Very well, my lord.
HAMLET   Upon the talk of the poisoning?   265
HORATIO   I did very well note him.
HAMLET   Ah, ha! Come, some music! come, the recorders!
      For if the king like not the comedy,
      Why then, belike, he likes it not, perdy.⁸
Come, some music!
      [*Re-enter* ROSENCRANTZ *and* GUILDENSTERN.]   270
GUILDENSTERN   Good my lord, vouchsafe me a word with you.
HAMLET   Sir, a whole history.
GUILDENSTERN   The king, sir—
HAMLET   Aye, sir, what of him?
GUILDENSTERN   Is in his retirement marvelous distempered.   275
HAMLET   With drink, sir?
GUILDENSTERN   No, my lord, rather with choler.⁹
HAMLET   Your wisdom should show itself more richer to signify this to
the doctor; for, for me to put him to his purgation would perhaps
plunge him into far more choler.   280
GUILDENSTERN   Good my lord, put your discourse into some frame,
and start not so wildly from my affair.

5. Blank shot.
6. Company; a term generally used with hounds. "Turk with": betray. "Razed shoes": sometimes worn by actors.
7. *Ass* would have rhymed. "Pajock": peacock.
8. By God (*per Dieu*).
9. Bile, anger.

HAMLET   I am tame, sir: pronounce.

GUILDENSTERN   The queen, your mother, in most great affliction of
spirit, hath sent me to you.   285

HAMLET   You are welcome.

GUILDENSTERN   Nay, good my lord, this courtesy is not of the right
breed. If it shall please you to make me a wholesome[1] answer, I will
do your mother's commandment: if not, your pardon and my return
shall be the end of my business.   290

HAMLET   Sir, I cannot.

GUILDENSTERN   What, my lord?

HAMLET   Make you a wholesome answer; my wit's diseased: but, sir,
such answer as I can make, you shall command; or rather, as you
say, my mother: therefore no more, but to the matter: my mother,   295
you say,—

ROSENCRANTZ   Then thus she says; your behavior hath struck her into
amazement and admiration.[2]

HAMLET   O wonderful son, that can so astonish a mother! But is there
no sequel at the heels of this mother's admiration? Impart.   300

ROSENCRANTZ   She desires to speak with you in her closet, ere you go
to bed.

HAMLET   We shall obey, were she ten times our mother. Have you any
further trade with us?

ROSENCRANTZ   My lord, you once did love me.   305

HAMLET   So I do still, by these pickers and stealers.[3]

ROSENCRANTZ   Good my lord, what is your cause of distemper? you do
surely bar the door upon your own liberty, if you deny your griefs to
your friend.

HAMLET   Sir, I lack advancement.[4]   310

ROSENCRANTZ   How can that be, when you have the voice of the king
himself for your succession in Denmark?

HAMLET   Aye, sir, but "while the grass grows,"[5]—the proverb is something musty.

    [*Re-enter* PLAYERS *with recorders.*]

O, the recorders! let me see one. To withdraw with you:—why do   315
you go about to recover the wind of me, as if you would drive me
into a toil?[6]

GUILDENSTERN   O, my lord, if my duty be too bold, my love is too
unmannerly.

HAMLET   I do not well understand that. Will you play upon this pipe?   320

GUILDENSTERN   My lord, I cannot.

HAMLET   I pray you.

GUILDENSTERN   Believe me, I cannot.

HAMLET   I do beseech you.

1. Sensible.
2. Confusion and surprise.
3. The hands.
4. Hamlet pretends that the cause of his "distemper" is frustrated ambition.

5. The proverb ends: "oft starves the silly
steed."
6. Snare. "Withdraw": retire, talk in private.
"Recover the wind of": get to the windward.

GUILDENSTERN I know no touch of it, my lord.   325

HAMLET It is as easy as lying: govern these ventages[7] with your fingers
and thumb, give it breath with your mouth, and it will discourse most
eloquent music. Look you, these are the stops.

GUILDENSTERN But these cannot I command to any utterance of
harmony; I have not the skill.   330

HAMLET Why, look you now, how unworthy a thing you make of me!
You would play upon me; you would seem to know my stops; you
would pluck out the heart of my mystery; you would sound me from
my lowest note to the top of my compass: and there is much music,
excellent voice, in this little organ; yet cannot you make it speak.   335
'Sblood, do you think I am easier to be played on than a pipe? Call
me what instrument you will, though you can fret[8] me, yet you cannot
play upon me.
        [Re-enter POLONIUS.]
God bless you, sir!

POLONIUS My lord, the queen would speak with you, and presently.   340

HAMLET Do you see yonder cloud that's almost in shape of a camel?

POLONIUS By the mass, and 'tis like a camel, indeed.

HAMLET Methinks it is like a weasel.

POLONIUS It is backed like a weasel.

HAMLET Or like a whale?   345

POLONIUS Very like a whale.

HAMLET Then I will come to my mother by and by. They fool me to
the top of my bent. I will come by and by.

POLONIUS I will say so.
        [Exit POLONIUS.]

HAMLET "By and by" is easily said. Leave me, friends.   350
        [Exeunt all but HAMLET.]
'Tis now the very witching time of night,
When churchyards yawn, and hell itself breathes out
Contagion to this world: now could I drink hot blood,
And do such bitter business as the day
Would quake to look on. Soft! now to my mother.   355
O heart, lose not thy nature; let not ever
The soul of Nero[9] enter this firm bosom:
Let me be cruel, not unnatural:
I will speak daggers to her, but use none;
My tongue and soul in this be hypocrites;   360
How in my words soever she be shent,
To give them seals[1] never, my soul, consent!
        [Exit.]

---

7. Windholes.
8. Vex, with a pun on *frets*, the ridges placed
across the finger board of a guitar to regulate
the fingering.

9. A Roman emperor (37–68 C.E.) who murdered his mother.
1. Ratify them by action. "Shent": reproached.

SCENE 3

[SCENE: *A room in the castle.*]
        [*Enter* KING, ROSENCRANTZ, *and* GUILDENSTERN.]
KING   I like him not, nor stands it safe with us
   To let his madness range. Therefore prepare you;
   I your commission will forthwith dispatch,
   And he to England shall along with you:
   The terms of our estate² may not endure   5
   Hazard so near us as doth hourly grow
   Out of his lunacies.
GUILDENSTERN   We will ourselves provide:
   Most holy and religious fear it is
   To keep those many many bodies safe
   That live and feed upon your majesty.   10
ROSENCRANTZ   The single and peculiar³ life is bound
   With all the strength and armor of the mind
   To keep itself from noyance; but much more
   That spirit upon whose weal depends and rests
   The lives of many. The cease⁴ of majesty   15
   Dies not alone, but like a gulf doth draw
   What 's near it with it; it is a massy wheel,
   Fixed on the summit of the highest mount,
   To whose huge spokes ten thousand lesser things
   Are mortised⁵ and adjoined; which, when it falls,   20
   Each small annexment, petty consequence,
   Attends the boisterous ruin. Never alone
   Did the king sigh, but with a general groan.
KING   Arm you, I pray you, to this speedy voyage,
   For we will fetters put about this fear,   25
   Which now goes too free-footed.
ROSENCRANTZ
                          } We will haste us.
GUILDENSTERN
        [*Exeunt* ROSENCRANTZ *and* GUILDENSTERN.—*Enter* POLONIUS.]
POLONIUS   My lord, he's going to his mother's closet:
   Behind the arras I'll convey myself,
   To hear the process: I'll warrant she'll tax him home:⁶   30
   And, as you said, and wisely was it said
   'Tis meet that some more audience than a mother,
   Since nature makes them partial, should o'erhear
   The speech, of vantage.⁷ Fare you well, my liege:
   I'll call upon you ere you go to bed,   35
   And tell you what I know.
KING   Thanks, dear my lord.
        [*Exit* POLONIUS.]
   O, my offense is rank, it smells to heaven;

---

2. My position as king.
3. Individual.
4. Decease, extinction.

5. Fastened.
6. Take him to task thoroughly.
7. From a vantage point.

It hath the primal eldest curse[8] upon 't,
A brother's murder. Pray can I not,
Though inclination be as sharp as will: 40
My stronger guilt defeats my strong intent,
And like a man to double business bound,
I stand in pause where I shall first begin,
And both neglect. What if this cursed hand
Were thicker than itself with brother's blood,   45
Is there not rain enough in the sweet heavens
To wash it white as snow? Whereto serves mercy
But to confront the visage of offense?[9]
And what's in prayer but this twofold force,
To be forestalled ere we come to fall,   50
Or pardoned being down? Then I'll look up;
My fault is past. But O, what form of prayer
Can serve my turn? "Forgive me my foul murder?"
That cannot be, since I am still possessed
Of those effects for which I did the murder,   55
My crown, mine own ambition and my queen.
May one be pardoned and retain the offense?[1]
In the corrupted currents of this world
Offense's gilded hand may shove by justice,
And oft 'tis seen the wicked prize itself   60
Buys out the law:[2] but 'tis not so above;
There is no shuffling, there the action lies
In his[3] true nature, and we ourselves compelled
Even to the teeth and forehead of our faults
To give in evidence. What then? what rests?[4]   65
Try what repentance can: what can it not?
Yet what can it when one can not repent?
O wretched state! O bosom black as death!
O limèd soul, that struggling to be free
Art more engaged! Help, angels! make assay![5]   70
Bow, stubborn knees, and, heart with strings of steel,
Be soft as sinews of the new-born babe!
All may be well.
        [*Retires and kneels.—Enter* HAMLET.]
HAMLET   Now might I do it pat,[6] now he is praying
And now I'll do 't: and so he goes to heaven: 75
And so am I revenged. That would be scanned;[7]
A villain kills my father; and for that,
I, his sole son, do this same villain send
To heaven.

---

8. The curse of Cain.
9. Guilt.
1. The things obtained through the offense.
2. The wealth unduly acquired is used for bribery.
3. Its.

4. What remains?
5. Make the attempt! "Limèd": caught as with birdlime.
6. Conveniently.
7. Would have to be considered carefully.

O, this is hire and salary, not revenge. 80
He took my father grossly, full of bread,
With all his crimes broad blown, as flush as May;
And how his audit[8] stands who knows save heaven?
But in our circumstance and course of thought,
'Tis heavy with him: and am I then revenged, 85
To take him in the purging of his soul,
When he is fit and seasoned[9] for his passage?
No.
Up, sword, and know thou a more horrid hent:[1]
When he is drunk asleep, or in his rage, 90
Or, in the incestuous pleasure of his bed;
At game, a-swearing, or about some act
That has no relish of salvation in 't;
Then trip him, that his heels may kick at heaven
And that his soul may be as damned and black 95
As hell, whereto it goes. My mother stays:
This physic but prolongs thy sickly days.
        [*Exit.*]
KING [*Rising.*]   My words fly up, my thoughts remain below:
    Words without thoughts never to heaven go.
        [*Exit.*]

SCENE 4

[SCENE: *The Queen's closet.*]

    [*Enter* QUEEN *and* POLONIUS.]
POLONIUS   He will come straight. Look you lay home to him:
    Tell him his pranks have been too broad[2] to bear with,
    And that your grace hath screen'd and stood between
    Much heat and him. I'll sconce me even here.
    Pray you, be round[3] with him.
HAMLET [*Within.*]   Mother, mother, mother! 5
QUEEN   I'll warrant you; fear me not. Withdraw,
    I hear him coming.
        [POLONIUS *hides behind the arras.—Enter* HAMLET.]
HAMLET   Now, mother, what's the matter?
QUEEN   Hamlet, thou hast thy father much offended.
HAMLET   Mother, you have my father much offended. 10
QUEEN   Come, come, you answer with an idle tongue.
HAMLET   Go, go, you question with a wicked tongue.
QUEEN   Why, how now, Hamlet!
HAMLET   What's the matter now?
QUEEN   Have you forgot me?
HAMLET   No, by the rood,[4] not so:
    You are the queen, your husband's brother's wife; 15

8. Account. "Broad blown": in full bloom.
9. Ripe, ready.
1. Grip.
2. Unrestrained. "Lay home": give him a stern
lesson.
3. Straightforward.
4. Cross.

And—would it were not so!—you are my mother.
QUEEN   Nay, then, I'll set those to you that can speak.
HAMLET   Come, come, and sit you down; you shall not budge:
  You go not till I set you up a glass[5]
  Where you may see the inmost part of you.   20
QUEEN   What wilt thou do? thou wilt not murder me?
  Help, help, ho!
POLONIUS [*Behind.*]   What, ho! help, help, help!
HAMLET [*Drawing.*]   How now! a rat? Dead, for a ducat, dead!
    [*Makes a pass through the arras.*]
POLONIUS [*Behind.*]   O, I am slain!
    [*Falls and dies.*]
QUEEN   O me, what hast thou done?   25
HAMLET   Nay, I know not: is it the king?
QUEEN   O, what a rash and bloody deed is this!
HAMLET   A bloody deed! almost as bad, good mother,
  As kill a king, and marry with his brother.
QUEEN   As kill a king!
HAMLET   Aye, lady, 'twas my word.   30
    [*Lifts up the arras and discovers* POLONIUS.]
  Thou wretched, rash, intruding fool, farewell!
  I took thee for thy better: take thy fortune;
  Thou find'st to be too busy[6] is some danger.
  Leave wringing of your hands: peace! sit you down,
  And let me wring your heart: for so I shall,   35
  If it be made of penetrable stuff;
  If damned custom have not brassed it so,
  That it be proof and bulwark against sense.[7]
QUEEN   What have I done, that thou darest wag thy tongue
  In noise so rude against me?
HAMLET   Such an act   40
  That blurs the grace and blush of modesty,
  Calls virtue hypocrite, takes off the rose
  From the fair forehead of an innocent love,
  And sets a blister there; makes marriage vows
  As false as dicers' oaths: O, such a deed   45
  As from the body of contraction[8] plucks
  The very soul, and sweet religion makes
  A rhapsody of words: heaven's face doth glow;[9]
  Yea, this solidity and compound mass,
  With tristful visage, as against the doom,[1]   50
  Is thought-sick at the act.
QUEEN   Aye me, what act,
  That roars so loud and thunders in the index?[2]
HAMLET   Look here, upon this picture, and on this,
  The counterfeit presentment[3] of two brothers.   55

5. Mirror.
6. Too much of a busybody.
7. Feeling.
8. Duty to the marriage contract.

9. Blush with shame.
1. Doomsday. "Tristful": sad.
2. Prologue, table of contents.
3. Portrait.

See what a grace was seated on this brow;
Hyperion's curls, the front of Jove himself,
An eye like Mars, to threaten and command;
A station[4] like the herald Mercury
New-lighted on a heaven-kissing hill;   60
A combination and a form indeed,
Where every god did seem to set his seal
To give the world assurance of a man:
This was your husband. Look you now, what follows:
Here is your husband; like a mildewed ear,[5]   65
Blasting his wholesome brother. Have you eyes?
Could you on this fair mountain leave to feed,
And batten[6] on this moor? Ha! have you eyes?
You cannot call it love, for at your age
The hey-day in the blood is tame, it's humble,   70
And waits upon[7] the judgment: and what judgment
Would step from this to this? Sense sure you have,
Else could you not have motion: but sure that sense
Is apoplexed: for madness would not err,
Nor sense to ecstasy was ne'er so thralled   75
But it reserved some quantity of choice,
To serve in such a difference. What devil was 't
That thus hath cozened you at hoodman-blind?[8]
Eyes without feeling, feeling without sight,
Ears without hands or eyes, smelling sans[9] all,   80
Or but a sickly part of one true sense
Could not so mope.[1]
O shame! where is thy blush? Rebellious hell,
If thou canst mutine in a matron's bones,
To flaming youth let virtue be as wax   85
And melt in her own fire: proclaim no shame
When the compulsive ardor gives the charge,[2]
Since frost itself as actively doth burn,
And reason panders[3] will.
QUEEN   O Hamlet, speak no more:
Thou turn'st mine eyes into my very soul,   90
And there I see such black and grained spots
As will not leave their tinct.[4]
HAMLET   Nay, but to live
In the rank sweat of an enseamèd[5] bed,
Stew'd in corruption, honeying and making love
Over the nasty sty,—
QUEEN   O, speak to me no more;   95
These words like daggers enter in my ears;

4. Posture.
5. Of corn.
6. Gorge, fatten. "Leave": cease.
7. Is subordinated to.
8. Blindman's buff. "Cozened": tricked.
9. Without.

1. Be stupid.
2. Attack.
3. Becomes subservient to.
4. Lose their color. "Grained": dyed in.
5. Greasy.

No more, sweet Hamlet!
HAMLET   A murderer and a villain;
A slave that is not twentieth part the tithe[6]
Of your precédent lord; a vice of kings;
A cutpurse[7] of the empire and the rule,   100
That from a shelf the precious diadem stole
And put it in his pocket!
QUEEN   No more!
HAMLET   A king of shreds and patches—
        [Enter GHOST.]
Save me, and hover o'er me with your wings,
You heavenly guards! What would your gracious figure?   105
QUEEN   Alas, he's mad!
HAMLET   Do you not come your tardy son to chide,
That, lapsed in time and passion, lets go by
The important acting of your dread command?
O, say!   110
GHOST   Do not forget: this visitation
Is but to whet thy almost blunted purpose.
But look, amazement on thy mother sits:
O, step between her and her fighting soul:
Conceit[8] in weakest bodies strongest works:
Speak to her, Hamlet.
HAMLET   How is it with you, lady?   115
QUEEN   Alas, how is 't with you,
That you do bend your eye on vacancy
And with the incorporal air do hold discourse?
Forth at your eyes your spirits wildly peep;
And, as the sleeping soldiers in the alarm,   120
Your bedded hairs, like life in excrements,[9]
Start up and stand on end. O gentle son,
Upon the heat and flame of thy distemper
Sprinkle cool patience. Whereon do you look?
HAMLET   On him, on him! Look you how pale he glares!   125
His form and cause conjoined, preaching to stones,
Would make them capable.[1] Do not look upon me,
Lest with this piteous action you convert
My stern effects:[2] then what I have to do
Will want true color; tears perchance for[3] blood.   130
QUEEN   To whom do you speak this?
HAMLET   Do you see nothing there?
QUEEN   Nothing at all; yet all that is I see.
HAMLET   Nor did you nothing hear?
QUEEN   No, nothing but ourselves.
HAMLET   Why, look you there! look, how it steals away!

6. Tenth.
7. Pickpocket. "Vice": clown, from the custom in the old morality plays of having a buffoon take the part of Vice or of a particular vice.
8. Imagination.
9. Outgrowths. "Alarm": call to arms.
1. Of feeling.
2. You make me change my purpose.
3. Instead of.

My father, in his habit as he lived! 135
Look, where he goes, even now, out at the portal!
    [*Exit* GHOST.]
QUEEN   This is the very coinage of your brain:
This bodiless creation ecstasy
Is very cunning in.
HAMLET   Ecstasy!
My pulse, as yours, doth temperately keep time, 140
And makes as healthful music: it is not madness
That I have uttered: bring me to the test,
And I the matter will re-word, which madness
Would gambol from. Mother, for love of grace,
Lay not that flattering unction to your soul, 145
That not your trespass but my madness speaks:
It will but skin and film the ulcerous place,
Whiles rank corruption, mining all within,
Infects unseen. Confess yourself to heaven;
Repent what's past, avoid what is to come, 150
And do not spread the compost on the weeds,
To make them ranker. Forgive me this my virtue,
For in the fatness of these pursy[4] times
Virtue itself of vice must pardon beg.
Yea, curb[5] and woo for leave to do him good. 155
QUEEN   O Hamlet, thou hast cleft my heart in twain.
HAMLET   O, throw away the worser part of it,
And live the purer with the other half.
Good night: but go not to my uncle's bed;
Assume a virtue, if you have it not. 160
That monster, custom, who all sense doth eat,
Of habits devil, is angel yet in this,
That to the use of actions fair and good
He likewise gives a frock or livery,
That aptly is put on.[6] Refrain to-night, 165
And that shall lend a kind of easiness
To the next abstinence; the next more easy;
For use almost can change the stamp[7] of nature,
And either curb the devil, or throw him out
With wondrous potency. Once more, good night: 170
And when you are desirous to be blest,
I'll blessing beg of you. For this same lord,
    [*Pointing to* POLONIUS.]
I do repent: but heaven hath pleased it so,
To punish me with this, and this with me,
That I must be their scourge and minister. 175
I will bestow[8] him, and will answer well
The death I gave him. So, again, good night.

---

4. Swollen from pampering.
5. Bow.
6. I.e., habit, although like a devil in establishing evil ways in us, is like an angel in doing
the same for virtues. "Aptly": easily.
7. Cast, form. "Use": habit.
8. Stow away. "Minister": agent of punishment.

I must be cruel, only to be kind:
Thus bad begins, and worse remains behind.
One word more, good lady.

QUEEN   What shall I do?   180

HAMLET   Not this, by no means, that I bid you do:
Let the bloat⁹ king tempt you again to bed;
Pinch wanton on your cheek, call you his mouse;
And let him, for a pair of reechy¹ kisses,
Or paddling in your neck with his damned fingers,   185
Make you to ravel all this matter out,
That I essentially am not in madness,
But mad in craft.² 'Twere good you let him know;
For who, that's but a queen, fair, sober, wise,
Would from a paddock, from a bat, a gib,   190
Such dear concernings³ hide? who would do so?
No, in despite of sense and secrecy,
Unpeg the basket on the house's top,
Let the birds fly, and like the famous ape,⁴
To try conclusions, in the basket creep   195
And break your own neck down.

QUEEN   Be thou assured, if words be made of breath
And breath of life, I have no life to breathe
What thou hast said to me.

HAMLET   I must to England; you know that?

QUEEN   Alack,   200
I had forgot: 'tis so concluded on.

HAMLET   There's letters sealed: and my two schoolfellows,
Whom I will trust as I will adders fanged,
They bear the mandate; they must sweep my way,
And marshal me to knavery. Let it work;   205
For 'tis the sport to have the enginer
Hoist with his own petar:⁵ and 't shall go hard
But I will delve one yard below their mines,
And blow them at the moon: I, 'tis most sweet
When in one line two crafts directly meet.   210
This man shall set me packing:
I'll lug the guts into the neighbor room.
Mother, good night. Indeed this councillor
Is now most still, most secret and most grave,⁶
Who was in life a foolish prating knave.   215
Come, sir, to draw toward an end with you.
Good night, mother.

       [*Exeunt severally*; HAMLET *dragging in* POLONIUS.]

9. Bloated with drink.
1. Fetid.
2. Simulation.
3. Matters with which one is closely concerned. "Paddock": toad. "Gib": tomcat.
4. The ape in the unidentified animal fable to which Hamlet alludes; apparently the animal saw birds fly out of a basket and drew the conclusion that by placing himself in a basket he could fly, too.
5. Petard, a variety of bomb. "Marshal": lead. "Enginer": military engineer. "Hoist": blow up.
6. Hamlet is punning on the word.

Act 4

SCENE I

[SCENE: *A room in the castle.*]

       [*Enter* KING, QUEEN, ROSENCRANTZ, *and* GUILDENSTERN.]
KING   There's matter in these sighs, these profound heaves:
  You must translate: 'tis fit we understand them.
  Where is your son?
QUEEN   Bestow this place on us[7] a little while.
       [*Exeunt* ROSENCRANTZ *and* GUILDENSTERN.]
  Ah, mine own lord, what have I seen to-night!   5
KING   What, Gertrude? How does Hamlet?
QUEEN   Mad as the sea and wind, when both contend
  Which is the mightier: in his lawless fit,
  Behind the arras hearing something stir,
  Whips out his rapier, cries "A rat, a rat!"   10
  And in this brainish apprehension[8] kills
  The unseen good old man.
KING   O heavy deed!
  It had been so with us, had we been there:
  His liberty is full of threats to all,
  To you yourself, to us, to every one.   15
  Alas, how shall this bloody deed be answered?
  It will be laid to us, whose providence
  Should have kept short,[9] restrained and out of haunt,
  This mad young man: but so much was our love,
  We would not understand what was most fit,   20
  But, like the owner of a foul disease,
  To keep it from divulging, let it feed
  Even on the pith of life. Where is he gone?
QUEEN   To draw apart the body he hath killed:
  O'er whom his very madness, like some ore   25
  Among a mineral[1] of metals base,
  Shows itself pure; he weeps for what is done.
KING   O Gertrude, come away!
  The sun no sooner shall the mountains touch,
  But we will ship him hence: and this vile deed   30
  We must, with all our majesty and skill,
  Both countenance[2] and excuse. Ho, Guildenstern!
       [*Re-enter* ROSENCRANTZ *and* GUILDENSTERN.]
  Friends both, go join you with some further aid:
  Hamlet in madness hath Polonius slain,
  And from his mother's closet hath he dragged him: 35
  Go seek him out; speak fair, and bring the body
  Into the chapel. I pray you, haste in this.
       [*Exeunt* ROSENCRANTZ *and* GUILDENSTERN.]

7. Leave us alone.   1. Mine. "Ore": gold.
8. Imaginary notion.   2. Recognize.
9. Under close watch.

Come, Gertrude, we'll call up our wisest friends;
And let them know, both what we mean to do,
And what's untimely done. . . .[3]   40
Whose whisper o'er the world's diameter
As level as the cannon to his blank[4]
Transports his poisoned shot, may miss our name
And hit the woundless air. O, come away!
My soul is full of discord and dismay.   45
     [*Exeunt.*]

SCENE 2

[SCENE: *Another room in the castle.*]

     [*Enter* HAMLET.]
HAMLET   Safely stowed.
ROSENCRANTZ } [*Within.*] Hamlet! Lord Hamlet!
GUILDENSTERN
HAMLET   But soft, what noise? who calls on Hamlet?
  O, here they come.
     [*Enter* ROSENCRANTZ *and* GUILDENSTERN.]
ROSENCRANTZ   What have you done, my lord, with the dead body?   5
HAMLET   Compounded[5] it with dust, whereto 'tis kin.
ROSENCRANTZ   Tell us where 'tis, that we may take it thence
  And bear it to the chapel.
HAMLET   Do not believe it.
ROSENCRANTZ   Believe what?   10
HAMLET   That I can keep your counsel and not mine own. Besides, to
  be demanded of a sponge! what replication[6] should be made by the
  son of a king?
ROSENCRANTZ   Take you me for a sponge, my lord?
HAMLET   Aye, sir; that soaks up the king's countenance,[7] his rewards,   15
  his authorities. But such officers do the king best service in the end:
  he keeps them, like an ape, in the corner of his jaw; first mouthed,
  to be last swallowed: when he needs what you have gleaned, it is but
  squeezing you, and sponge, you shall be dry again.
ROSENCRANTZ   I understand you not, my lord.   20
HAMLET   I am glad of it: a knavish speech sleeps in a foolish ear.
ROSENCRANTZ   My lord, you must tell us where the body is, and go
  with us to the king.
HAMLET   The body is with the king, but the king is not with the body.
  The king is a thing—   25
GUILDENSTERN   A thing, my lord?
HAMLET   Of nothing: bring me to him. Hide fox, and all after.[8]
     [*Exeunt.*]

---

3. This gap in the text has been guessingly filled
in with "So envious slander."
4. His target.
5. Mixed.

6. Formal reply. "Demanded": questioned by.
7. Favor.
8. A children's game.

SCENE 3

[SCENE: *Another room in the castle.*]

[*Enter* KING, *attended.*]

KING   I have sent to seek him, and to find the body.
How dangerous is it that this man goes loose!
Yet must not we put the strong law on him:
He's loved of the distracted multitude,
Who like not in their judgment, but their eyes;   5
And where 'tis so, the offender's scourge is weighed,
But never the offense. To bear⁹ all smooth and even,
This sudden sending away must seem
Deliberate pause: diseases desperate grown
By desperate appliance¹ are relieved,   10
Or not at all.

[*Enter* ROSENCRANTZ.]

       How now! what hath befall'n?

ROSENCRANTZ   Where the dead body is bestowed, my lord,
We cannot get from him.

KING   But where is he?

ROSENCRANTZ   Without, my lord; guarded, to know your pleasure.

KING   Bring him before us.   15

ROSENCRANTZ   Ho, Guildenstern! bring in my lord.

[*Enter* HAMLET *and* GUILDENSTERN.]

KING   Now, Hamlet, where's Polonius?

HAMLET   At supper.

KING   At supper! where?

HAMLET   Not where he eats, but where he is eaten: a certain convocation   20
of public worms are e'en at him. Your worm is your only emperor for
diet:² we fat all creatures else to fat us, and we fat ourselves for
maggots: your fat king and your lean beggar is but variable service,³
two dishes, but to one table: that's the end.

KING   Alas, alas!   25

HAMLET   A man may fish with the worm that hath eat of a king, and
eat of the fish that hath fed of that worm.

KING   What dost thou mean by this?

HAMLET   Nothing but to show you how a king may go a progress⁴
through the guts of a beggar.   30

KING   Where is Polonius?

HAMLET   In heaven; send thither to see: if your messenger find him
not there, seek him i' the other place yourself. But indeed, if you
find him not within this month, you shall nose⁵ him as you go up
the stairs into the lobby.   35

KING   [*To some* ATTENDANTS.] Go seek him there.

HAMLET   He will stay till you come.

---

9. Conduct. "Scourge": punishment.
1. Treatment. "Deliberate pause": the result
of careful argument.
2. Possibly a punning reference to the Diet

(assembly) of the Holy Roman Empire at Worms.
3. That is, the service varies, not the food.
4. Royal state journey.
5. Smell.

[*Exeunt* ATTENDANTS.]

KING   Hamlet, this deed, for thine especial safety,
　Which we do tender,⁶ as we dearly grieve
　For that which thou hast done, must send thee hence   40
　With fiery quickness: therefore prepare thyself;
　The bark is ready and the wind at help,
　The associates tend, and every thing is bent
　For England.
HAMLET　　　　For England?
KING　　　　　　　　　Aye, Hamlet.
HAMLET　　　　　　　　　　　　Good.
KING   So is it, if thou knew'st our purposes.   45
HAMLET   I see a cherub that sees them. But, come; for England!
　Farewell, dear mother.
KING   Thy loving father, Hamlet.
HAMLET   My mother: father and mother is man and wife; man and
　wife is one flesh, and so, my mother. Come, for England!   50
　　　[*Exit.*]
KING   Follow him at foot;⁷ tempt him with speed aboard;
　Delay it not; I'll have him hence to-night:
　Away! for every thing is sealed and done
　That else leans on⁸ the affair: pray you, make haste.
　　　[*Exeunt* ROSENCRANTZ *and* GUILDENSTERN.]
　And, England,⁹ if my love thou hold'st at aught—   55
　As my great power thereof may give thee sense,
　Since yet thy cicatrice looks raw and red
　After the Danish sword, and thy free awe
　Pays homage to us—thou mayst not coldly set¹
　Our sovereign process; which imports at full,   60
　By letters conjuring² to that effect,
　The present death of Hamlet. Do it, England;
　For like the hectic³ in my blood he rages,
　And thou must cure me; till I know 'tis done,
　Howe'er my haps, my joys were ne'er begun.   65
　　　[*Exit.*]

SCENE 4

[SCENE: *A plain in Denmark.*]

　　　[*Enter* FORTINBRAS, *a* CAPTAIN *and* SOLDIERS, *marching.*]
FORTINBRAS   Go, captain, from me greet the Danish king;
　Tell him that by his license Fortinbras
　Craves the conveyance⁴ of a promised march
　Over his kingdom. You know the rendezvous.
　If that his majesty would aught with us,   5

6. Care for.
7. At his heels.
8. Pertains to.
9. The king of England.

1. Regard with indifference.
2. Enjoining.
3. Fever.
4. Convoy.

We shall express our duty in his eye;[5]
And let him know so.
CAPTAIN   I will do 't, my lord.
FORTINBRAS   Go softly on.
        [*Exeunt* FORTINBRAS *and* SOLDIERS.—*Enter* HAMLET, ROSENCRANTZ,
        GUILDENSTERN, *and others.*]
HAMLET   Good sir, whose powers[6] are these?
CAPTAIN   They are of Norway, sir.   10
HAMLET   How purposed, sir, I pray you?
CAPTAIN   Against some part of Poland.
HAMLET   Who commands them, sir?
CAPTAIN   The nephew to Old Norway, Fortinbras.
HAMLET   Goes it against the main[7] of Poland, sir,   15
Or for some frontier?
CAPTAIN   Truly to speak, and with no addition,
We go to gain a little patch of ground
That hath in it no profit but the name.
To pay five ducats, five, I would not farm it;   20
Nor will it yield to Norway or the Pole
A ranker rate, should it be sold in fee.[8]
HAMLET   Why, then the Polack never will defend it.
CAPTAIN   Yes, it is already garrisoned.
HAMLET   Two thousand souls and twenty thousand ducats   25
Will not debate the question of this straw!
This is the imposthume[9] of much wealth and peace,
That inward breaks, and shows no cause without
Why the man dies. I humbly thank you, sir.
CAPTAIN   God be wi' you, sir.
        [*Exit.*]
ROSENCRANTZ   Will 't please you go, my lord?   30
HAMLET   I'll be with you straight. Go a little before.
        [*Exeunt all but* HAMLET.]
How all occasions do inform against[1] me,
And spur my dull revenge! What is a man,
If his chief good and market[2] of his time
Be but to sleep and feed? a beast, no more.   35
Sure, he that made us with such large discourse,[3]
Looking before and after, gave us not
That capability and god-like reason
To fust[4] in us unused. Now, whether it be
Bestial oblivion, or some craven scruple   40
Of thinking too precisely on the event,[5]—
A thought which, quartered, hath but one part wisdom
And ever three parts coward,—I do not know
Why yet I live to say "this thing's to do,"

5. Presence.   1. Denounce.
6. Armed forces.   2. Payment for, reward.
7. The whole of.   3. Reasoning power.
8. For absolute possession. "Ranker": higher.   4. Become moldy, taste of the cask.
9. Ulcer.   5. Outcome.

Sith I have cause, and will, and strength, and means,   45
To do 't. Examples gross as earth exhort me:
Witness this army, of such mass and charge,[6]
Led by a delicate and tender prince,
Whose spirit with divine ambition puffed
Makes mouths[7] at the invisible event,   50
Exposing what is mortal and unsure
To all that fortune, death, and danger dare,
Even for an egg-shell. Rightly to be great
Is not to stir without great argument,
But greatly to find quarrel in a straw   55
When honor's at the stake. How stand I then,
That have a father killed, a mother stained,
Excitements of my reason and my blood,
And let all sleep, while to my shame I see
The imminent death of twenty thousand men,   60
That for a fantasy and trick[8] of fame
Go to their graves like beds, fight for a plot
Whereon the numbers cannot try the cause,[9]
Which is not tomb enough and continent[1]
To hide the slain? O, from this time forth,   65
My thoughts be bloody, or be nothing worth!
    [*Exit.*]

SCENE 5

[SCENE: *Elsinore. A room in the castle.*]

    [*Enter* QUEEN, HORATIO, *and a* GENTLEMAN.]
QUEEN   I will not speak with her.
GENTLEMAN   She is importunate, indeed distract:
  Her mood will needs be pitied.
QUEEN   What would she have?
GENTLEMAN   She speaks much of her father, says she hears
  There's tricks i' the world, and hems and beats her heart,   5
  Spurns enviously at straws;[2] speaks things in doubt,
  That carry but half sense: her speech is nothing,
  Yet the unshapèd use of it doth move
  The hearers to collection; they aim[3] at it,
  And botch[4] the words up fit to their own thoughts;   10
  Which, as her winks and nods and gestures yield them,
  Indeed would make one think there might be thought,
  Though nothing sure, yet much unhappily.
HORATIO   'Twere good she were spoken with, for she may strew
  Dangerous conjectures in ill-breeding minds.[5]   15

---

6. Cost.
7. Laughs at.
8. Trifle.
9. So small that it cannot hold the men who fight for it.
1. Container.

2. Gets angry at trifles.
3. Guess. "Collection": gathering up her words and trying to make sense of them.
4. Patch.
5. Minds breeding evil thoughts.

QUEEN   Let her come in.
          [*Exit* GENTLEMAN.]
     [*Aside.*] To my sick soul, as sin's true nature is,
     Each toy seems prologue to some great amiss:
     So full of artless jealousy[6] is guilt,
     It spills itself in fearing to be spilt.   20
          [*Re-enter* GENTLEMAN, *with* OPHELIA.]
OPHELIA   Where is the beauteous majesty of Denmark?
QUEEN   How now, Ophelia!
OPHELIA [*Sings.*]   How should I your true love know
                      From another one?
                  By his cockle hat and staff   25
                      And his sandal shoon.[7]

QUEEN   Alas, sweet lady, what imports this song?
OPHELIA   Say you? nay, pray you, mark.
     [*Sings.*]   He is dead and gone, lady,
                      He is dead and gone;   30
                  At his head a grass-green turf,
                      At his heels a stone.
     Oh, oh!
QUEEN   Nay, but Ophelia,—
OPHELIA   Pray you, mark.
     [*Sings.*]   White his shroud as the mountain snow,—   35
               [*Enter* KING.]
QUEEN   Alas, look here, my lord.
OPHELIA [*Sings.*]   Larded[8] with sweet flowers;
                  Which bewept to the grave did—not—go
                      With true-love showers.

KING   How do you, pretty lady?   40
OPHELIA   Well, God 'ild[9] you! They say the owl was a baker's daughter.
     Lord, we know what we are, but know not what we may be.[1] God be
     at your table!
KING   Conceit upon her father.
OPHELIA   Pray you, let's have no words of this; but when they ask you   45
     what it means, say you this:
     [*Sings.*]   To-morrow is Saint Valentine's day
                  All in the morning betime,
                  And I a maid at your window,
                      To be your Valentine.
               Then up he rose, and donned his clothes,   50
                  And dupped[2] the chamber-door;
               Let in the maid, that out a maid
                  Never departed more.

6. Uncontrolled suspicion. "Toy": trifle. "Amiss": misfortune.
7. Shoes. These are all typical signs of pilgrims traveling to places of devotion.
8. Garnished.
9. Yield—that is, repay.
1. An allusion to a folk tale about a baker's daughter changed into an owl for having shown no charity to those in need.
2. Opened.

KING   Pretty Ophelia!

OPHELIA   Indeed, la, without an oath, I'll make an end on 't: 55
    [*Sings.*]   By Gis[3] and by Saint Charity,
              Alack, and fie for shame!
          Young men will do 't, if they come to 't;
              By Cock,[4] they are to blame.
          Quoth she, before you tumbled me,   60
              You promised me to wed.

    He answers:

          So would I ha' done, by yonder sun,
              An thou hadst not come to my bed.

KING   How long hath she been thus?   65

OPHELIA   I hope all will be well. We must be patient: but I cannot
    choose but weep, to think they should lay him i' the cold ground.
    My brother shall know of it: and so I thank you for your good counsel.
    Come, my coach! Good night, ladies; good night, sweet ladies; good
    night, good night.   70
        [*Exit.*]

KING   Follow her close; give her good watch, I pray you.
        [*Exit* HORATIO.]
    O, this is the poison of deep grief; it springs
    All from her father's death. O Gertrude, Gertrude,
    When sorrows come, they come not single spies,
    But in battalions! First, her father slain: 75
    Next, your son gone; and he most violent author
    Of his own just remove: the people muddied,[5]
    Thick and unwholesome in their thoughts and whispers,
    For good Polonius' death; and we have done but greenly
    In hugger-mugger[6] to inter him: poor Ophelia   80
    Divided from herself and her fair judgment,
    Without the which we are pictures, or mere beasts:
    Last, and as much containing as all these,
    Her brother is in secret come from France,
    Feeds on his wonder,[7] keeps himself in clouds,   85
    And wants not buzzers[8] to infect his ear
    With pestilent speeches of his father's death;
    Wherein necessity, of matter beggared,[9]
    Will nothing stick our person to arraign[1]
    In ear and ear. O my dear Gertrude, this,   90
    Like to a murdering-piece,[2] in many places
    Gives me superfluous death.

3. By Jesus.
4. Corruption of *God*, but with a sexual undermeaning.
5. Confused, their thoughts made turbid (as water by mud).
6. Hasty secrecy. "Greenly": foolishly.
7. Broods, keeps wondering.
8. Lacks not tale-bearers.
9. The necessity to build up a story without the materials for doing so.
1. Will not hesitate to accuse me.
2. A variety of cannon that scattered its shot in many directions.

[*A noise within.*]

QUEEN   Alack, what noise is this?

KING   Where are my Switzers?[3] Let them guard the door.

      [*Enter another* GENTLEMAN.]

   What is the matter?

GENTLEMAN   Save yourself, my lord:

   The ocean, overpeering of his list,[4]   95

   Eats not the flats with more impetuous haste

   Than young Laertes, in a riotous head,[5]

   O'erbears your officers. The rabble call him lord;

   And, as the world were now but to begin,

   Antiquity forgot, custom not known,   100

   The ratifiers and props of every word,

   They cry "Choose we; Laertes shall be king!"

   Caps, hands and tongues applaud it to the clouds,

   "Laertes shall be king, Laertes king!"

QUEEN   How cheerfully on the false trail they cry!   105

   O, this is counter,[6] you false Danish dogs!

      [*Noise within.*]

KING   The doors are broke.

      [*Enter* LAERTES, *armed;* DANES *following.*]

LAERTES   Where is this king? Sirs, stand you all without.

DANES   No, let's come in.

LAERTES   I pray you, give me leave.

DANES   We will, we will.   110

      [*They retire without the door.*]

LAERTES   I thank you: keep the door. O thou vile king,

  Give me my father!

QUEEN   Calmly, good Laertes.

LAERTES   That drop of blood that's calm proclaims me bastard;

  Cries cuckold to my father; brands the harlot

  Even here, between the chaste unsmirchèd brows   115

  Of my true mother.

KING   What is the cause, Laertes,

  That thy rebellion looks so giant-like?

  Let him go, Gertrude; do not fear[7] our person

  There's such divinity doth hedge a king,

  That treason can but peep to what it would,[8]   120

  Acts little of his[9] will. Tell me, Laertes,

  Why thou art thus incensed: let him go, Gertrude

  Speak, man.

LAERTES   Where is my father?

KING   Dead.

QUEEN   But not by him.

KING   Let him demand his fill.   125

---

3. Swiss guards.
4. Overflowing above the high-water mark.
5. Group of rebels.
6. Following the scent in the wrong direction.

7. Fear for.
8. Look from a distance at what it desires.
9. Its.

LAERTES   How came he dead? I'll not be juggled with
  To hell, allegiance! vows, to the blackest devil!
  Conscience and grace, to the profoundest pit
  I dare damnation: to this point I stand,
  That both the worlds I give to negligence,[1]   130
  Let come what comes; only I'll be revenged
  Most thoroughly for my father.
KING   Who shall stay you?
LAERTES   My will, not all the world
  And for my means, I'll husband them so well,
  They shall go far with little.
KING   Good Laertes,   135
  If you desire to know the certainty
  Of your dear father's death, is 't writ in your revenge
  That, swoopstake,[2] you will draw both friend and foe,
  Winner and loser?
LAERTES   None but his enemies.
KING   Will you know them then?   140
LAERTES   To his good friends thus wide I'll ope my arms;
  And, like the kind life-rendering pelican,[3]
  Repast them with my blood.
KING   Why, now you speak
  Like a good child and a true gentleman.
  That I am guiltless of your father's death,   145
  And am most sensibly in grief for it,
  It shall as level to your judgment pierce
  As day does to your eye.
DANES [*Within.*]   Let her come in.
LAERTES   How now! what noise is that?
        [*Re-enter* OPHELIA.]
  O heat, dry up my brains! tears seven times salt,   150
  Burn out the sense and virtue[4] of mine eye!
  By heaven, thy madness shall be paid with weight,
  Till our scale turn the beam. O rose of May!
  Dear maid, kind sister, sweet Ophelia!
  O heavens! is 't possible a young maid's wits   155
  Should be as mortal as an old man's life?
  Nature is fine in love, and where 'tis fine
  It sends some precious instance[5] of itself
  After the thing it loves.
OPHELIA [*Sings.*]   They bore him barefaced on the bier   160
              Hey non nonny, nonny, hey nonny
              And in his grave rained many a tear,—
  Fare you well, my dove!

1. I don't care what may happen to me in either this world or the next.
2. Without making any distinction, as the winner takes the whole stake in a card game.
3. In myth, the pelican is supposed to feed its young with its own blood.
4. Power, faculty.
5. Sample, token. "Fine": refined.

LAERTES   Hadst thou thy wits, and didst persuade revenge,
   It could not move thus.   165

OPHELIA [*Sings.*]   You must sing down a-down,
               An you call him a-down-a.
   O, how the wheel becomes it! It is the false steward,[6] that stole his
   master's daughter.

LAERTES   This nothing's more than matter.[7]   170

OPHELIA   There's rosemary, that's for remembrance: pray you, love,
   remember: and there is pansies, that's for thoughts.

LAERTES   A document[8] in madness; thoughts and remembrance fitted.

OPHELIA   There's fennel for you, and columbines: there's rue for you:
   and here's some for me: we may call it herbs of grace o' Sundays: O,   175
   you must wear your rue with a difference. There's a daisy: I would
   give you some violets,[9] but they withered all when my father died:
   they say he made a good end,—
   [*Sings.*]   For bonnie sweet Robin is all my joy.

LAERTES   Thought and affliction, passion, hell itself,   180
   She turns to favor[1] and to prettiness.

OPHELIA [*Sings.*]   And will he not come again?
               And will he not come again?
                  No, no, he is dead,
                  Go to thy death-bed,   185
               He never will come again.
               His beard was as white as snow,
               All flaxen was his poll
                  He is gone, he is gone,
                  And we cast away moan   190
               God ha' mercy on his soul!
   And of all Christian souls, I pray God. God be wi' you.
     [*Exit.*]

LAERTES   Do you see this, O God?

KING   Laertes, I must commune with your grief,
   Or you deny me right. Go but apart,   195
   Make choice of whom your wisest friends you will.
   And they shall hear and judge 'twixt you and me:
   If by direct or by collateral hand
   They find us touched,[2] we will our kingdom give,
   Our crown, our life, and all that we call ours,   200
   To you in satisfaction; but if not,
   Be you content to lend your patience to us,
   And we shall jointly labor with your soul
   To give it due content.

---

6. An allusion (probably to a lost ballad) further expressing Ophelia's preoccupation with betrayal, lost love, and death. "How the wheel becomes it": that is, how well the refrain fits.
7. This nonsense is more indicative than sane speech.
8. Lesson. Traditionally, flowers and herbs have symbolic meanings. Here rosemary is the symbol for remembrance and pansies symbolize thoughts.
9. Violets symbolize faithfulness. Fennel stands for flattery, columbines for cuckoldom, and rue for sorrow and repentance (compare the verb *rue*).
1. Charm.
2. Involved (in the murder). "Collateral": indirect.

1878 | WILLIAM SHAKESPEARE

LAERTES   Let this be so;
  His means of death, his obscure funeral,   205
  No trophy, sword, nor hatchment³ o'er his bones,
  No noble rite nor formal ostentation,
  Cry to be heard, as 'twere from heaven to earth,
  That I must call 't in question.
KING   So you shall;
  And where the offense is let the great axe fall.   210
  I pray you, go with me.
     [Exeunt.]

SCENE 6

[SCENE: *Another room in the castle.*]

     [Enter HORATIO *and a* SERVANT.]
HORATIO   What are they that would speak with me?
SERVANT   Sea-faring men, sir: they say they have letters for you.
HORATIO   Let them come in.
     [Exit SERVANT.]
  I do not know from what part of the world
  I should be greeted, if not from Lord Hamlet.   5
     [Enter SAILORS.]
FIRST SAILOR   God bless you, sir.
HORATIO   Let him bless thee too.
FIRST SAILOR   He shall, sir, an 't please him.
  There's a letter for you, sir; it comes from the ambassador that was
  bound for England; if your name be Horatio, as I am let to know   10
  it is.
HORATIO [*Reads.*] "Horatio, when thou shalt have overlooked⁴ this,
  give these fellows some means to the king: they have letters for him.
  Ere we were two days old at sea, a pirate of very warlike appointment
  gave us chase. Finding ourselves too slow of sail, we put on a compelled   15
  valor, and in the grapple I boarded them: on the instant they
  got clear of our ship; so I alone became their prisoner. They have
  dealt with me like thieves of mercy:⁵ but they knew what they did; I
  am to do a good turn for them. Let the king have the letters I have
  sent; and repair thou to me with as much speed as thou wouldst fly   20
  death. I have words to speak in thine ear will make thee dumb; yet
  are they much too light for the bore⁶ of the matter. These good
  fellows will bring thee where I am. Rosencrantz and Guildenstern
  hold their course for England: of them I have much to tell thee.
  Farewell.   25
     "He that thou knowest thine, HAMLET."
  Come, I will make you way for these your letters;
  And do 't the speedier, that you may direct me
  To him from whom you brought them.
     [Exeunt.]

---

3. Coat of arms.   5. Merciful.
4. Read over.   6. Caliber, that is, importance.

SCENE 7

[SCENE: *Another room in the castle.*]

[*Enter* KING *and* LAERTES.]

KING   Now must your conscience my acquittance seal,
And you must put me in your heart for friend,
Sith you have heard, and with a knowing ear,
That he which hath your noble father slain
Pursued my life.
LAERTES   It well appears: but tell me   5
Why you proceeded not against these feats,
So crimeful and so capital in nature,
As by your safety, wisdom, all things else,
You mainly[7] were stirred up.
KING   O, for two special reasons,
Which may to you perhaps seem much unsinewed,[8]   10
But yet to me they're strong. The queen his mother
Lives almost by his looks; and for myself—
My virtue or my plague, be it either which—
She's so conjunctive[9] to my life and soul,
That, as the star moves not but in his sphere,   15
I could not but by her. The other motive,
Why to a public count I might not go,
Is the great love the general gender[1] bear him;
Who, dipping all his faults in their affection,
Would, like the spring that turneth wood to stone,   20
Convert his gyves[2] to graces; so that my arrows,
Too slightly timber'd for so loud a wind,
Would have reverted to my bow again
And not where I had aim'd them.
LAERTES   And so have I a noble father lost;   25
A sister driven into desperate terms,
Whose worth, if praises may go back again,
Stood challenger on mount of[3] all the age
For her perfections: but my revenge will come.
KING   Break not your sleeps for that: you must not think   30
That we are made of stuff so flat and dull
That we can let our beard be shook with danger
And think it pastime. You shortly shall hear more:
I loved your father, and we love ourself;
And that, I hope, will teach you to imagine—   35
[*Enter a* MESSENGER, *with letters.*]
How now! what news?
MESSENGER   Letters, my lord, from Hamlet:
This to your majesty; this to the queen.

7. Powerfully.
8. Weak.
9. Closely joined.

1. Common people. "Count": accounting, trial.
2. Leg irons (shames).
3. Above. "Go back": to what she was before her madness.

KING   From Hamlet! who brought them?

MESSENGER   Sailors, my lord, they say; I saw them not:
    They were given me by Claudio; he received them   40
    Of him that brought them.

KING   Laertes, you shall hear them.
    Leave us.
        [Exit MESSENGER.]
    [Reads.] "High and mighty, you shall know I am set naked on your
    kingdom. To-morrow shall I beg leave to see your kingly eyes: when
    I shall, first asking your pardon thereunto, recount the occasion of   45
    my sudden and more strange return.   HAMLET.
    What should this mean? Are all the rest come back?
    Or is it some abuse, and no such thing?[4]

LAERTES   Know you the hand?

KING   'Tis Hamlet's character.[5] "Naked!"   50
    And in a postscript here, he says "alone."
    Can you advise me?

LAERTES   I'm lost in it, my lord. But let him come;
    It warms the very sickness in my heart,
    That I shall live and tell him to his teeth,   55
    "Thus diddest thou."

KING   If it be so, Laertes,—
    As how should it be so? how otherwise?—
    Will you be ruled by me?

LAERTES   Aye, my lord;
    So you will not o'errule me to a peace.

KING   To thine own peace. If he be now returned,   60
    As checking[6] at his voyage, and that he means
    No more to undertake it, I will work him
    To an exploit now ripe in my device,
    Under the which he shall not choose but fall:
    And for his death no wind of blame shall breathe;   65
    But even his mother shall uncharge the practice,[7]
    call it accident.

LAERTES   My lord, I will be ruled;
    The rather, if you could devise it so
    That I might be the organ.[8]

KING   It falls right.
    You have been talked of since your travel much,   70
    And that in Hamlet's hearing, for a quality
    Wherein, they say, you shine; your sum of parts[9]
    Did not together pluck such envy from him,
    As did that one, and that in my regard
    Of the unworthiest siege.[1]

LAERTES   What part is that, my lord?   75

4. A delusion, not a reality.
5. Handwriting.
6. Changing the course of, refusing to
continue.

7. Not recognize it as a plot.
8. Instrument.
9. The sum of your gifts.
1. Seat, that is, rank.

KING   A very riband in the cap of youth,
      Yet needful too; for youth no less becomes[2]
      The light and careless livery that it wears
      Than settled age his sables and his weeds,[3]
      Importing health and graveness. Two months since   80
      Here was a gentleman of Normandy:—
      I've seen myself, and served against, the French,
      And they can well on horseback: but this gallant
      Had witchcraft in 't; he grew unto his seat,
      And to such wondrous doing brought his horse   85
      As had he been incorpsed and demi-natured[4]
      With the brave beast: so far he topped my thought
      That I, in forgery of shapes and tricks,[5]
      Come short of what he did.
LAERTES   A Norman was 't?
KING   A Norman.   90
LAERTES   Upon my life, Lamord.
KING   The very same.
LAERTES   I know him well: he is the brooch[6] indeed
      And gem of all the nation.
KING   He made confession of you,
      And gave you such a masterly report,   95
      For art and exercise in your defense,[7]
      And for your rapier most especial,
      That he cried out, 'twould be a sight indeed
      If one could match you: the scrimers[8] of their nation,
      He swore, had neither motion, guard, nor eye,   100
      If you opposed them. Sir, this report of his
      Did Hamlet so envenom with his envy
      That he could nothing do but wish and beg
      Your sudden coming o'er, to play with him.
      Now, out of this—
LAERTES   What out of this, my lord?   105
KING   Laertes, was your father dear to you?
      Or are you like the painting of a sorrow,
      A face without a heart?
LAERTES   Why ask you this?
KING   Not that I think you did not love your father,
      But that I know love is begun by time,   110
      And that I see, in passages of proof,[9]
      Time qualifies[1] the spark and fire of it.
      There lives within the very flame of love
      A kind of wick or snuff[2] that will abate it;

2. Is the appropriate age for. "Riband":
ribbon, ornament.
3. Furs (also meaning "blacks," dark colors)
and robes.
4. Incorporated and split his nature in two.
5. In imagining methods and skills of horsemanship.

6. Ornament.
7. Report of your mastery in the theory and
practice of fencing.
8. Fencers.
9. Instances that prove it.
1. Weakens.
2. Charred part of the wick.

And nothing is at a like goodness still, 115
For goodness, growing to a plurisy,[3]
Dies in his own too much: that we would do
We should do when we would; for this "would" changes
And hath abatements and delays as many
As there are tongues, are hands, are accidents, 120
And then this "should" is like a spendthrift sigh,
That hurts by easing.[4] But, to the quick o' the ulcer:
Hamlet comes back: what would you undertake,
To show yourself your father's son in deed
More than in words?
LAERTES   To cut his throat i' the church. 125
KING   No place indeed should murder sanctuarize;
Revenge should have no bounds. But, good Laertes,
Will you do this, keep close within your chamber.
Hamlet returned shall know you are come home:
We'll put on[5] those shall praise your excellence 130
And set a double varnish on the fame
The Frenchman gave you; bring you in fine together
And wager on your heads: he, being remiss,[6]
Most generous and free from all contriving,
Will not peruse[7] the foils, so that with ease, 135
Or with a little shuffling, you may choose
A sword unbated, and in a pass of practice[8]
Requite him for your father.
LAERTES   I will do 't;
And for that purpose I'll anoint my sword.
I bought an unction of a mountebank,[9] 140
So mortal that but dip a knife in it,
Where it draws blood no cataplasm so rare,
Collected from all simples[1] that have virtue
Under the moon, can save the thing from death
That is but scratched withal: I'll touch my point 145
With this contagion, that, if I gall[2] him slightly,
It may be death.
KING   Let's further think of this;
Weigh what convenience both of time and means
May fit us to our shape: if this should fail,
And that our drift look through[3] our bad performance, 150
'Twere better not assayed: therefore this project
Should have a back or second, that might hold
If this did blast in proof.[4] Soft! let me see:

3. Excess. "Still": constantly.
4. A sigh that gives relief but is harmful (according to an old notion that it draws blood from the heart).
5. Instigate.
6. Careless. "In fine": finally.
7. Examine closely.
8. Treacherous thrust. "Unbated": not blunted

(as a rapier for exercise ordinarily would be).
9. Ointment of a peddler of quack medicines.
1. Healing herbs. "Cataplasm": plaster.
2. Scratch.
3. Our design should show through. "Shape": plan.
4. Burst (like a new firearm) once it is put to the test.

We'll make a solemn wager on your cunnings:
I ha 't: 155
When in your motion you are hot and dry—
As make your bouts more violent to that end—
And that he calls for drink, I'll have prepared him
A chalice for the nonce;[5] whereon but sipping,
If he by chance escape your venomed stuck,[6]   160
Our purpose may hold there. But stay, what noise?
        [*Enter* QUEEN.]
How now, sweet queen!
QUEEN   One woe doth tread upon another's heel,
    So fast they follow: your sister's drowned, Laertes.
LAERTES   Drowned! O, where?   165
QUEEN   There is a willow grows aslant[7] a brook,
    That shows his hoar leaves in the glassy stream;
    There with fantastic garlands did she come
    Of crow-flowers, nettles, daisies, and long purples,
    That liberal shepherds give a grosser name,   170
    But our cold maids do dead men's fingers call them:
    There, on the pendent boughs her coronet weeds
    Clambering to hang, an envious sliver[8] broke;
    When down her weedy trophies and herself
    Fell in the weeping brook. Her clothes spread wide,   175
    And mermaid-like a while they bore her up:
    Which time she chanted snatches of old tunes,
    As one incapable of[9] her own distress,
    Or like a creature native and indued[1]
    Unto that element: but long it could not be   180
    Till that her garments, heavy with their drink,
    Pulled the poor wretch from her melodious lay
    To muddy death.
LAERTES   Alas, then she is drowned!
QUEEN   Drowned, drowned.
LAERTES   Too much of water hast thou, poor Ophelia,   185
    And therefore I forbid my tears: but yet
    It is our trick;[2] nature her custom holds,
    Let shame say what it will: when these are gone,
    The woman[3] will be out. Adieu, my lord:
    I have a speech of fire that fain would blaze,   190
    But that this folly douts[4] it.
        [*Exit.*]
KING   Let's follow, Gertrude:
    How much I had to do to calm his rage!
    Now fear I this will give it start again;

---

5. For that particular occasion.
6. Thrust.
7. Across.
8. Malicious bough.
9. Insensitive to.

1. Adapted, in harmony with.
2. Peculiar trait.
3. The softer qualities, the woman in me.
4. Extinguishes.

Therefore let's follow.
[*Exeunt.*]

Act 5

SCENE I

[SCENE: *A churchyard.*]

[*Enter two* CLOWNS, *with spades, etc.*]

FIRST CLOWN   Is she to be buried in Christian burial that willfully seeks
her own salvation?

SECOND CLOWN   I tell thee she is; and therefore make her grave
straight: the crowner[5] hath sat on her, and finds it Christian burial.

FIRST CLOWN   How can that be, unless she drowned herself in her own   5
defense?

SECOND CLOWN   Why, 'tis found so.

FIRST CLOWN   It must be "se offendendo";[6] it cannot be else. For here
lies the point: if I drown myself wittingly, it argues an act: and an
act hath three branches; it is, to act, to do, to perform: argal,[7] she   10
drowned herself wittingly.

SECOND CLOWN   Nay, but hear you, goodman delver.

FIRST CLOWN   Give me leave. Here lies the water; good: here stands
the man; good: if the man go to this water and drown himself, it is,
will he, nill he,[8] he goes; mark you that; but if the water come to   15
him and drown him, he drowns not himself: argal, he that is not
guilty of his own death shortens not his own life.

SECOND CLOWN   But is this law?

FIRST CLOWN   Aye, marry, is 't; crowner's quest[9] law.

SECOND CLOWN   Will you ha' the truth on 't? If this had not been a   20
gentlewoman, she should have been buried out o' Christian burial.

FIRST CLOWN   Why, there thou say'st: and the more pity that great folk
should have countenance[1] in this world to drown or hang themselves,
more than their even[2] Christian. Come, my spade. There is
no ancient gentlemen but gardeners, ditchers and gravemakers: they   25
hold up Adam's profession.

SECOND CLOWN   Was he a gentleman?

FIRST CLOWN   A' was the first that ever bore arms.

SECOND CLOWN   Why, he had none.

FIRST CLOWN   What, art a heathen? How dost thou understand the   30
Scripture? The Scripture says Adam digged: could he dig without
arms? I'll put another question to thee: if thou answerest me not to
the purpose, confess thyself—

SECOND CLOWN   Go to.

FIRST CLOWN   What is he that builds stronger than either the mason,   35
the shipwright, or the carpenter?

---

5. Coroner. "Straight": right away.
6. The Clown's blunder for *se defendendo*: "in
self-defense" (Latin).
7. Blunder for *ergo*: "therefore" (Latin).

8. Willy-nilly.
9. Inquest.
1. Sanction.
2. Fellow.

SECOND CLOWN   The gallows-maker; for that frame outlives a thousand tenants.

FIRST CLOWN   I like thy wit well, in good faith: the gallows does well; but how does it well? it does well to those that do ill: now, thou dost ill to say the gallows is built stronger than the church: argal, the gallows may do well to thee. To 't again, come.   40

SECOND CLOWN   "Who builds stronger than a mason, a shipwright, or a carpenter?"

FIRST CLOWN   Aye, tell me that, and unyoke.[3]   45

SECOND CLOWN   Marry, now I can tell.

FIRST CLOWN   To 't.

SECOND CLOWN   Mass, I cannot tell.

[Enter HAMLET and HORATIO, afar off.]

FIRST CLOWN   Cudgel thy brains no more about it, for your dull ass will not mend his pace with beating, and when you are asked this question next, say "a grave-maker": the houses that he makes last till doomsday. Go, get thee to Yaughan; fetch me a stoup[4] of liquor.   50

[Exit SECOND CLOWN.—FIRST CLOWN digs and sings.]

>   In youth, when I did love, did love,
>   Methought it was very sweet,
>   To contract, O, the time, for-a my behove,   55
>   O, methought, there-a was nothing-a meet.[5]

HAMLET   Has this fellow no feeling of his business that he sings at grave-making?

HORATIO   Custom hath made it in him a property of easiness.[6]

HAMLET   'Tis e'en so: the hand of little employment hath the daintier[7] sense.   60

FIRST CLOWN [Sings.]   But age, with his stealing steps,
>   Hath clowed me in his clutch,
>   And hath shipped me intil[8] the land,
>   As if I had never been such.   65

[Throws up a skull.]

HAMLET   That skull had a tongue in it, and could sing once: how the knave jowls it to the ground, as if it were Cain's jaw-bone, that did the first murder! It might be the pate of a politician,[9] which this ass now o'er-reaches;[1] one that would circumvent God, might it not?

HORATIO   It might, my lord.   70

HAMLET   Or of a courtier, which could say, "Good morrow, sweet lord! How dost thou, sweet lord?" This might be my lord such-a-one, that praised my lord such-a-one's horse, when he meant to beg it; might it not?

HORATIO   Aye, my lord.   75

HAMLET   Why, e'en so: and now my Lady Worm's; chapless, and knocked about the mazzard[2] with a sexton's spade: here's fine revolution,

3. Call it a day.
4. Mug. "Yaughan": apparently a tavern keeper's name.
5. Fitting. "Contract": shorten. "Behove": profit.
6. Has made it a matter of indifference to him.
7. Finer sensitivity. "Of little employment": that does little labor.
8. Into.
9. In a pejorative sense. "Jowls": knocks. "First murder": possibly an allusion to the legend that Cain slew Abel with an ass's jawbone.
1. Outwits.
2. Pate. "Chapless": the lower jawbone missing.

an we had the trick to see 't. Did these bones cost no more
the breeding, but to play at loggats[3] with 'em? mine ache to think
on 't.   80

FIRST CLOWN [*Sings.*]   A pick-axe, and a spade, a spade,
                            For a shrouding sheet:
                            O, a pit of clay for to be made
                            For such a guest is meet.
            [*Throws up another skull.*]

HAMLET   There's another: why may not that be the skull of a lawyer?   85
Where be his quiddities now, his quillets, his cases, his tenures,[4] and
his tricks? why does he suffer this rude knave now to knock him
about the sconce with a dirty shovel, and will not tell him of his
action of battery?[5] Hum! This fellow might be in 's time a great buyer
of land, with his statutes, his recognizances,[6] his fines, his double   90
vouchers, his recoveries: is this the fine[7] of his fines and the recovery
of his recoveries, to have his fine pate full of fine dirt? will his vouchers
vouch him no more of his purchases, and double ones too, than the
length and breadth of a pair of indentures? The very conveyances[8] of
his lands will hardly lie in this box; and must the inheritor himself   95
have no more, ha?

HORATIO   Not a jot more, my lord.

HAMLET   Is not parchment made of sheep-skins?

HORATIO   Aye, my lord, and of calf-skins too.

HAMLET   They are sheep and calves which seek out assurance[9] in that.   100
I will speak to this fellow. Whose grave's this, sirrah?

FIRST CLOWN   Mine, sir.
      [*Sings.*]   O, a pit of clay for to be made
                   For such a guest is meet.

HAMLET   I think it be thine indeed, for thou liest in 't.   105

FIRST CLOWN   You lie out on 't, sir, and therefore 'tis not yours: for my
part, I do not lie in 't, and yet it is mine.

HAMLET   Thou dost lie in 't, to be in 't and say it is thine: 'tis for the dead,
not for the quick;[1] therefore thou liest.

FIRST CLOWN   'Tis a quick lie, sir; 'twill away again, from me to you.   110

HAMLET   What man dost thou dig it for?

FIRST CLOWN   For no man, sir.

HAMLET   What woman then?

FIRST CLOWN   For none neither.

HAMLET   Who is to be buried in 't?   115

FIRST CLOWN   One that was a woman, sir; but, rest her soul, she's dead.

HAMLET   How absolute the knave is! we must speak by the card,[2] or
equivocation will undo us. By the Lord, Horatio, these three years I

---

3. A game resembling bowls. "Trick": faculty.
4. Real estate holdings. "Quiddities": subtle
definitions. "Quillets": quibbles.
5. Assault. "Sconce": head.
6. Varieties of bonds. This passage contains
legal terms relating to the transfer of estates.
7. End. Hamlet is punning on the legal and
nonlegal meanings of the word.
8. Deeds. "Indentures": contracts drawn in

duplicate on the same piece of parchment; the
two copies were separated by an indented
line.
9. Security; another pun, because the word is
also a legal term.
1. Living.
2. By the chart, that is, exactness. "Absolute":
positive.

have taken note of it; the age is grown so picked[3] that the toe of the
peasant comes so near the heel of the courtier, he galls his kibe.[4] How   120
long hast thou been a grave-maker?

FIRST CLOWN   Of all the days i' the year, I came to 't that day that our
last King Hamlet o'ercame Fortinbras.

HAMLET   How long is that since?

FIRST CLOWN   Cannot you tell that? every fool can tell that: it was that   125
very day that young Hamlet was born: he that is mad, and sent into
England.

HAMLET   Aye, marry, why was he sent into England?

FIRST CLOWN   Why, because a' was mad; a' shall recover his wits there:
or, if a' do not, 'tis no great matter there.   130

HAMLET   Why?

FIRST CLOWN   'Twill not be seen in him there; there the men are as mad
as he.

HAMLET   How came he mad?

FIRST CLOWN   Very strangely, they say.   135

HAMLET   How "strangely?"

FIRST CLOWN   Faith, e'en with losing his wits.

HAMLET   Upon what ground?

FIRST CLOWN   Why, here in Denmark: I have been sexton here, man and
boy, thirty years.   140

HAMLET   How long will a man lie i' the earth ere he rot?

FIRST CLOWN   I' faith, if a' be not rotten before a' die—as we have many
pocky corses now-a-days, that will scarce hold the laying in[5]—
a' will last you some eight year or nine year: a tanner will last you
nine year.   145

HAMLET   Why he more than another?

FIRST CLOWN   Why, sir, his hide is so tanned with his trade that a' will
keep out water a great while; and your water is a sore decayer of
your whoreson dead body. Here's a skull now: this skull has lain in
the earth three and twenty years.   150

HAMLET   Whose was it?

FIRST CLOWN   A whoreson mad fellow's it was: whose do you think it
was?

HAMLET   Nay, I know not.

FIRST CLOWN   A pestilence on him for a mad rogue! a' poured a flagon   155
of Rhenish on my head once. This same skull, sir, was Yorick's skull,
the king's jester.

HAMLET   This?

FIRST CLOWN   E'en that.

HAMLET   Let me see. [Takes the skull.] Alas, poor Yorick! I knew him,   160
Horatio: a fellow of infinite jest, of most excellent fancy: he hath
borne me on his back a thousand times; and now how abhorred in
my imagination it is! my gorge rises at it. Here hung those lips that
I have kissed I know not how oft. Where be your gibes now? your
gambols? your songs? your flashes of merriment, that were wont to   165

3. Choice, fastidious.
4. Hurts the chilblain on the courtier's heel.
5. Hold together till they are buried. "Pocky": with marks of disease (from "pox").

set the table on a roar? Not one now, to mock your own grinning? quite chop-fallen?[6] Now get you to my lady's chamber, and tell her, let her paint an inch thick, to this favor[7] she must come; make her laugh at that. Prithee, Horatio, tell me one thing.

HORATIO   What's that, my lord?   170

HAMLET   Dost thou think Alexander looked o' this fashion i' the earth?

HORATIO   E'en so.

HAMLET   And smelt so? pah!
    [Puts down the skull.]

HORATIO   E'en so, my lord.

HAMLET   To what base uses we may return, Horatio! Why may not imagi-   175
nation trace the noble dust of Alexander, till he find it stopping a bung-
hole?

HORATIO   'Twere to consider too curiously, to consider so.

HAMLET   No, faith, not a jot; but to follow him thither with modesty
enough[8] and likelihood to lead it: as thus: Alexander died, Alexander   180
was buried, Alexander returneth into dust; the dust is earth; of earth
we make loam; and why of that loam, whereto he was converted, might
they not stop a beer-barrel?
    Imperious Caesar, dead and turned to clay,
    Might stop a hole to keep the wind away: 185
    O, that that earth, which kept the world in awe,
    Should patch a wall to expel the winter's flaw!
But soft! but soft! aside: here comes the king.
    [Enter PRIESTS *etc., in procession; the Corpse of* OPHELIA, LAERTES
      and MOURNERS *following;* KING, QUEEN, *their trains, etc.]*
The queen, the courtiers: who is this they follow?
And with such maimèd rites?[9] This doth betoken   190
The corse they follow did with desperate hand
Fordo its own life: 'twas of some estate.[1]
Couch we awhile, and mark.
    [Retiring with HORATIO.]

LAERTES   What ceremony else?

HAMLET   That is Laertes, a very noble youth: mark.   195

LAERTES   What ceremony else?

FIRST PRIEST   Her obsequies have been as far enlarged
As we have warranty: her death was doubtful;
And, but that great command o'ersways the order[2]
She should in ground unsanctified have lodged   200
Till the last trumpet; for[3] charitable prayers,
Shards, flints and pebbles should be thrown on her:
Yet here she is allowed her virgin crants,
Her maiden strewments and the bringing home[4]
Of bell and burial.   205

6. The lower jaw fallen down, hence dejected.
7. Appearance.
8. Without exaggeration.
9. Incomplete, mutilated ritual.
1. Rank. "Fordo": destroy.
2. The king's command prevails against ordi-

nary rules. "Doubtful": of uncertain cause
(that is, accident or suicide).
3. Instead of.
4. Laying to rest. "Crants": garlands. "Strewments": strews the grave with flowers.

LAERTES   Must there no more be done?
FIRST PRIEST   No more be done:
   We should profane the service of the dead
   To sing a requiem and such rest to her
   As to peace-parted souls.
LAERTES   Lay her i' the earth:
   And from her fair and unpolluted flesh   210
   May violets spring! I tell thee, churlish priest,
   A ministering angel shall my sister be,
   When thou liest howling.
HAMLET   What, the fair Ophelia!
QUEEN [*Scattering flowers.*]   Sweets to the sweet: farewell!
   I hoped thou shouldst have been my Hamlet's wife;   215
   I thought thy bride-bed to have decked, sweet maid,
   And not have strewed thy grave.
LAERTES   O, treble woe
   Fall ten times treble on that cursed head
   Whose wicked deed thy most ingenious sense
   Deprived thee of! Hold off the earth a while,   220
   Till I have caught her once more in mine arms.
      [*Leaps into the grave.*]
   Now pile your dust upon the quick and dead,
   Till of this flat a mountain you have made
   To o'ertop old Pelion[5] or the skyish head
   Of blue Olympus.
HAMLET [*Advancing.*]   What is he whose grief   225
   Bears such an emphasis? whose phrase of sorrow
   Conjures the wandering stars and makes them stand
   Like wonder-wounded hearers? This is I,
   Hamlet the Dane.
      [*Leaps into the grave.*]
LAERTES   The devil take thy soul!   230
      [*Grappling with him.*]
HAMLET   Thou pray'st not well.
   I prithee, take thy fingers from my throat;
   For, though I am not splenitive[6] and rash,
   Yet have I in me something dangerous,
   Which let thy wisdom fear. Hold off thy hand.
KING   Pluck them asunder.
QUEEN   Hamlet, Hamlet!
ALL   Gentlemen,—   235
HORATIO   Good my lord, be quiet.
      [*The* ATTENDANTS *part them, and they come out of the grave.*]
HAMLET   Why, I will fight with him upon this theme
   Until my eyelids will no longer wag.
QUEEN   O my son, what theme?   240

---

5. The mountain on which the Aloadae, two
rebellious giants in Greek mythology, piled
up Mount Ossa in their attempt to reach

Olympus.
6. Easily moved to anger.

HAMLET   I loved Ophelia: forty thousand brothers
  Could not, with all their quantity of love,
  Make up my sum. What wilt thou do for her?
KING   O, he is mad, Laertes.
QUEEN   For love of God, forbear him.   245
HAMLET   'Swounds, show me what thou 'lt do:
  Woo't weep? woo't fight? woo't fast? woo't tear thyself?
  Woo't drink up eisel?[7] eat a crocodile?
  I'll do't. Dost thou come here to whine?
  To outface me with leaping in her grave?   250
  Be buried quick with her, and so will I:
  And, if thou prate of mountains, let them throw
  Millions of acres on us, till our ground,
  Singeing his pate against the burning zone,
  Make Ossa like a wart! Nay, an thou 'lt mouth,   255
  I'll rant as well as thou.
QUEEN   This is mere madness:
  And thus a while the fit will work on him;
  Anon, as patient as the female dove
  When that her golden couplets are disclosed,[8]
  His silence will sit drooping.
HAMLET   Hear you, sir;   260
  What is the reason that you use me thus?
  I loved you ever: but it is no matter;
  Let Hercules himself do what he may,
  The cat will mew, and dog will have his day.
     [Exit.]
KING   I pray thee, good Horatio, wait upon him.   265
     [Exit HORATIO.]
  [To LAERTES.] Strengthen your patience in our last night's speech;
  We'll put the matter to the present push.[9]
  Good Gertrude, set some watch over your son.
  This grave shall have a living monument:
  An hour of quiet shortly shall we see;   270
  Till then, in patience our proceeding be.
     [Exeunt.]

SCENE 2

[SCENE: *A hall in the castle.*]

     [*Enter* HAMLET *and* HORATIO.]
HAMLET   So much for this, sir: now shall you see the other;
  You do remember all the circumstance?
HORATIO   Remember it, my lord?
HAMLET   Sir, in my heart there was a kind of fighting,
  That would not let me sleep: methought I lay   5

7. Vinegar (the bitter drink given to Christ).   8. Twins are hatched.
"Woo't": wilt thou.   9. We'll push the matter on immediately.

Worse than the mutines in the bilboes.[1] Rashly,
And praised be rashness for it, let us know,
Our indiscretion sometime serves us well
When our deep plots do pall;[2] and that should learn us
There's a divinity that shapes our ends,   10
Rough-hew them how we will.
HORATIO   That is most certain.
HAMLET   Up from my cabin,
My sea-gown scarfed about me, in the dark
Groped I to find out them; had my desire,
Fingered their packet, and in fine withdrew   15
To mine own room again; making so bold,
My fears forgetting manners, to unseal
Their grand commission; where I found, Horatio,—
O royal knavery!—an exact command,
Larded with many several sorts of reasons,   20
Importing[3] Denmark's health and England's too,
With, ho! such bugs and goblins in my life,
That, on the supervise, no leisure bated,[4]
No, not to stay the grinding of the axe,
My head should be struck off.
HORATIO   Is't possible?   25
HAMLET   Here's the commission: read it at more leisure.
But wilt thou hear now how I did proceed?
HORATIO   I beseech you.
HAMLET   Being thus be-netted round with villainies,—
Ere I could make a prologue to my brains,   30
They had begun the play,—I sat me down;
Devised a new commission; wrote it fair:
I once did hold it, as our statists[5] do,
A baseness to write fair, and labored much
How to forget that learning; but, sir, now   35
It did me yeoman's service:[6] wilt thou know
The effect of what I wrote?
HORATIO   Aye, good my lord.
HAMLET   An earnest conjuration from the king,
As England was his faithful tributary,
As love between them like the palm might flourish,   40
As peace should still her wheaten garland wear
And stand a comma[7] 'tween their amities,
And many such-like "As"es of great charge,[8]
That, on the view and knowing of these contents,
Without debatement further, more or less,   45

1. Mutineers in iron fetters.
2. Become useless.
3. Concerning.
4. As soon as the message was read, with no
time subtracted for leisure. "Bugs": imaginary
horrors to be expected if I lived.

5. Statesmen.
6. Excellent service.
7. Connecting element.
8. "'As'es": a pun on *as* and *ass*, which extends
to "of great charge," signifying both "moral
weight" and "ass's burden."

He should the bearers put to sudden death,
Not shriving-time[9] allowed.

HORATIO   How was this sealed?

HAMLET   Why, even in that was heaven ordinant.[1]
I had my father's signet in my purse,
Which was the model of that Danish seal: 50
Folded the writ up in the form of the other;
Subscribed it; gave 't the impression;[2] placed it safely,
The changeling never known. Now, the next day
Was our sea-fight; and what to this was sequent
Thou know'st already.   55

HORATIO   So Guildenstern and Rosencrantz go to 't.

HAMLET   Why, man, they did make love to this employment;
They are not near my conscience; their defeat
Does by their own insinuation[3] grow:
'Tis dangerous when the baser nature comes   60
Between the pass and fell[4]-incensèd points
Of mighty opposites.

HORATIO   Why, what a king is this!

HAMLET   Does it not, think'st thee, stand me now upon[5]—
He that hath killed my king, and whored my mother;
Popped in between the election and my hopes;   65
Thrown out his angle for my proper life,[6]
And with such cozenage—is't not perfect conscience,
To quit[7] him with this arm? and is't not to be damned,
To let this canker of our nature come
In further evil?   70

HORATIO   It must be shortly known to him from England
What is the issue of the business there.

HAMLET   It will be short: the interim is mine;
And a man's life's no more than to say "One."
But I am very sorry, good Horatio,   75
That to Laertes I forgot myself;
For, by the image of my cause, I see
The portraiture of his: I'll court his favors:
But, sure, the bravery[8] of his grief did put me
Into a towering passion.

HORATIO   Peace! who comes here?   80

   [*Enter* OSRIC.]

OSRIC   Your lordship is right welcome back to Denmark.

HAMLET   I humbly thank you, sir. Dost know this waterfly?

HORATIO   No, my good lord.

HAMLET   Thy state is the more gracious, for 'tis a vice to know him. He
hath much land, and fertile: let a beast be lord of beasts, and his crib   85

9. Time for confession and absolution.
1. Ordaining.
2. Of the seal.
3. Meddling. "Defeat": destruction.
4. Fiercely. "Baser": lower in rank than the

king and Prince Hamlet. "Pass": thrust.
5. Is it not my duty now?
6. An angling line for my own life.
7. Pay back.
8. Ostentation, bravado.

shall stand at the king's mess: 'tis a chough,[9] but, as I say, spacious in the possession of dirt.

OSRIC   Sweet lord, if your lordship were at leisure, I should impart a thing to you from his majesty.

HAMLET   I will receive it, sir, with all diligence of spirit. Put your bonnet   90
to his right use; 'tis for the head.

OSRIC   I thank your lordship, it is very hot.

HAMLET   No, believe me, 'tis very cold; the wind is northerly.

OSRIC   It is indifferent[1] cold, my lord, indeed.

HAMLET   But yet methinks it is very sultry and hot, or my complexion—   95

OSRIC   Exceedingly, my lord; it is very sultry, as 'twere,—I cannot tell how. But, my lord, his majesty bade me signify to you that he has laid a great wager on your head: sir, this is the matter—

HAMLET   I beseech you, remember—   100
        [HAMLET *moves him to put on his hat.*]

OSRIC   Nay, good my lord; for mine ease, in good faith. Sir, here is newly come to court Laertes; believe me, an absolute gentleman, full of most excellent differences, of very soft society and great showing:[2] indeed, to speak feelingly of him, he is the card or calendar of gentry,[3] for you shall find in him the continent of what part[4] a gentleman would   105
see.

HAMLET   Sir, his definement suffers no perdition in you; though, I know, to divide him inventorially would dizzy the arithmetic[5] of memory, and yet but yaw neither, in respect of his quick sail.[6] But in the verity of extolment, I take him to be a soul of great article, and his   110
infusion[7] of such dearth and rareness, as, to make true diction of him, his semblable is his mirror, and who else would trace him, his umbrage,[8] nothing more.

OSRIC   Your lordship speaks most infallibly of him.

HAMLET   The concernancy, sir? why do we wrap the gentleman[9] in our   115
more rawer breath?

OSRIC   Sir?

HORATIO   Is 't not possible to understand in another tongue?[1] You will do 't, sir, really.

HAMLET   What imports the nomination of this gentleman?   120

OSRIC   Of Laertes?

HORATIO   His purse is empty already; all's golden words are spent.

HAMLET   Of him, sir.

OSRIC   I know you are not ignorant—

9. Jackdaw. "Mess": table.
1. Fairly.
2. Agreeable company, handsome in appearance. "Differences": distinctions.
3. Chart and model of gentlemanly manners.
4. Whatever quality. "Continent": container.
5. Arithmetical power. "Definement": definition. "Perdition": loss. "Inventorially": make an inventory of his virtues.
6. And yet would only be able to steer unsteadily (unable to catch up with the *sail* of Laertes's virtues).
7. The virtues infused into him. "Verify of extolments": to prize Laertes truthfully. "Article": importance.
8. Keep pace with him, his shadow.
9. Laertes. "Concernancy": meaning.
1. In a less affected jargon or in the same jargon when spoken by another (that is, Hamlet's) tongue.

HAMLET   I would you did, sir; yet, in faith, if you did, it would not much   125
approve me.[2] Well, sir?

OSRIC   You are not ignorant of what excellence Laertes is—

HAMLET   I dare not confess that, lest I should compare with him in
excellence; but, to know a man well, were to know himself.[3]

OSRIC   I mean, sir, for his weapon; but in the imputation laid on him by   130
them, in his meed he's unfellowed.[4]

HAMLET   What's his weapon?

OSRIC   Rapier and dagger.

HAMLET   That's two of his weapons: but, well.

OSRIC   The king, sir, hath wagered with him six Barbary horses: against   135
the which he has imponed, as I take it, six French rapiers and poniards,
with their assigns,[5] as girdle, hanger, and so: three of the carriages,
in faith, are very dear to fancy, very responsive[6] to the hilts, most
delicate carriages, and of very liberal conceit.[7]

HAMLET   What call you the carriages?   140

HORATIO   I knew you must be edified by the margent[8] ere you had
done.

OSRIC   The carriages, sir, are the hangers.

HAMLET   The phrase would be more germane to the matter if we could
carry a cannon by our sides:[9] I would it might be hangers till then.   145
But, on: six Barbary horses against six French swords, their assigns,
and three liberal-conceited carriages; that's the French bet against
the Danish. Why is this "imponed," as you call it?

OSRIC   The king, sir, hath laid, sir, that in a dozen passes between
yourself and him, he shall not exceed you three hits: he hath laid on   150
twelve for nine; and it would come to immediate trial, if your lordship
would vouchsafe the answer.[1]

HAMLET   How if I answer "no"?

OSRIC   I mean, my lord, the opposition of your person in trial.

HAMLET   Sir, I will walk here in the hall: if it please his majesty, it is the   155
breathing time[2] of day with me; let the foils be brought, the gentleman
willing, and the king hold his purpose, I will win for him an I can; if
not, I will gain nothing but my shame and the odd hits.

OSRIC   Shall I redeliver you e'en so?[3]

HAMLET   To this effect, sir, after what flourish your nature will.   160

OSRIC   I commend my duty to your lordship.

HAMLET   Yours, yours. [Exit OSRIC] He does well to commend it himself;
there are no tongues else for's turn.

HORATIO   This lapwing[4] runs away with the shell on his head.

2. Be to my credit.
3. To know others one has to know oneself.
4. In the reputation given him by his weapons,
his merit is unparalleled.
5. Appendages. "Imponed": wagered.
6. Closely matched. "Carriages": ornamented
straps by which the rapiers hung from the belt.
"Very dear to fancy": agreeable to the taste.
7. Elegant design.
8. Instructed by the marginal note.

9. Hamlet is playfully criticizing Osric's affected application of the term *carriage*, more
properly used to mean "gun carriage."
1. The terms of this wager have never been
satisfactorily clarified.
2. Time for exercise.
3. Is that the reply you want me to carry
back?
4. A bird supposedly able to run as soon as it
is out of its shell.

HAMLET   He did comply with his dug before he sucked it. Thus has he—   165
and many more of the same breed that I know the drossy⁵ age dotes
on—only got the tune of the time and outward habit of encounter; a
kind of yesty⁶ collection, which carries them through and through the
most fond and winnowed opinions;⁷ and do but blow them to their
trial, the bubbles are out.   170

    [*Enter a* LORD.]

LORD   My lord, his majesty commended him⁸ to you by young Osric,
who brings back to him, that you attend him in the hall: he sends to
know if your pleasure hold to play with Laertes, or that you will take
longer time.

HAMLET   I am constant to my purposes; they follow the king's pleasure: 175
if his fitness speaks, mine is ready; now or whensoever, provided I be
so able as now.

LORD   The king and queen and all are coming down.

HAMLET   In happy time.

LORD   The queen desires you to use some gentle entertainment⁹ to   180
Laertes before you fall to play.

HAMLET   She well instructs me.

    [*Exit* LORD.]

HORATIO   You will lose this wager, my lord.

HAMLET   I do not think so; since he went into France, I have been in
continual practice; I shall win at the odds. But thou wouldst not think   185
how ill all's here about my heart: but it is no matter.

HORATIO   Nay, good my lord,—

HAMLET   It is but foolery; but it is such a kind of gaingiving¹ as would
perhaps trouble a woman.

HORATIO   If your mind dislike anything, obey it. I will forestall their   190
repair² hither, and say you are not fit.

HAMLET   Not a whit; we defy augury: there is special providence in the
fall of a sparrow. If it be now, 'tis not to come; if it be not to come, it
will be now; if it be not now, yet it will come: the readiness is all; since
no man has aught of what he leaves, what is't to leave betimes?³   195
Let be.

    [*Enter* KING, QUEEN, LAERTES, *and* LORDS, OSRIC *and other* ATTENDANTS
    with foils and gauntlets; a table and flagons of wine on it.]

KING   Come, Hamlet, come, and take this hand from me.

    [*The* KING *puts* LAERTES's *hand into* HAMLET's.]

HAMLET   Give me your pardon, sir: I've done you wrong;
But pardon't, as you are a gentleman.
This presence⁴ knows,   200
And you must needs have heard, how I am punished
With sore distraction. What I have done,

---

5. Degenerate. "Comply": use ceremony.
6. Frothy.
7. Makes them pass the test of the most refined judgment.
8. Sent his regards.
9. Kind word of greeting.

1. Misgiving.
2. Coming.
3. What is wrong with dying early (leaving *betimes*), because man knows nothing of life (*what he leaves*)?
4. Audience.

That might your nature, honor and exception[5]
Roughly awake, I here proclaim was madness.
Was't Hamlet wronged Laertes? Never Hamlet: 205
If Hamlet from himself be ta'en away,
And when he's not himself does wrong Laertes,
Then Hamlet does it not, Hamlet denies it.
Who does it then? His madness: if't be so,
Hamlet is of the faction that is wronged;   210
His madness is poor Hamlet's enemy.
Sir, in this audience,
Let my disclaiming from a purposed evil
Free me so far in your most generous thoughts,
That I have shot mine arrow o'er the house,   215
And hurt my brother.
LAERTES   I am satisfied in nature,
Whose motive, in this case, should stir me most
To my revenge: but in my terms of honor[6]
I stand aloof, and will no reconcilement,
Till by some elder masters of known honor   220
I have a voice and precedent of peace,
To keep my name ungored.[7] But till that time
I do receive your offered love like love
And will not wrong it.
HAMLET   I embrace it freely,
And will this brother's wager frankly play.   225
Give us the foils. Come on.
LAERTES   Come, one for me.
HAMLET   I'll be your foil,[8] Laertes: in mine ignorance
Your skill shall, like a star i' the darkest night,
Stick fiery off[9] indeed.
LAERTES   You mock me, sir.
HAMLET   No, by this hand.   230
KING   Give them the foils, young Osric. Cousin Hamlet,
You know the wager?
HAMLET   Very well, my lord;
Your grace has laid the odds o' the weaker side.
KING   I do not fear it; I have seen you both:
But since he is bettered, we have therefore odds.   235
LAERTES   This is too heavy; let me see another.
HAMLET   This likes me well. These foils have all a length?
        [*They prepare to play.*]
OSRIC   Aye, my good lord.

---

5. Objection.
6. Laertes answers separately each of the two
points brought up by Hamlet in line 86. "Nature"
is Laertes' natural feeling toward his father.
"Honor" is the code of honor with its conventional rules.

7. Unwounded. "A voice and": an opinion
based on.
8. A pun, because "foil" means both "rapier"
and "a thing that sets off another to advantage" (as gold leaf under a jewel).
9. Stand out brilliantly.

KING   Set me the stoups[1] of wine upon that table.
    If Hamlet give the first or second hit,   240
    Or quit in answer of the third exchange,[2]
    Let all the battlements their ordnance fire;
    The king shall drink to Hamlet's better breath;
    And in the cup an union[3] shall he throw,
    Richer than that which four successive kings   245
    In Denmark's crown have worn. Give me the cups;
    And let the kettle[4] to the trumpet speak,
    The trumpet to the cannoneer without,
    The cannons to the heavens, the heaven to earth,
    "Now the king drinks to Hamlet." Come, begin;   250
    And you, the judges, bear a wary eye.
HAMLET   Come on, sir.
LAERTES   Come, my lord.
       [*They play.*]
HAMLET   One.
LAERTES   No.
HAMLET   Judgment.
OSRIC   A hit, a very palpable hit.
LAERTES   Well; again.
KING   Stay; give me drink. Hamlet, this pearl is thine;
    Here's to thy health.
       [*Trumpets sound, and cannon shot off within.*]
                 Give him the cup.   255
HAMLET   I'll play this bout first; set it by awhile.
    Come. [*They play.*] Another hit; what say you?
LAERTES   A touch, a touch, I do confess.
KING   Our son shall win.
QUEEN   He's fat and scant of breath.
    Here, Hamlet, take my napkin,[5] rub thy brows: 260
    The queen carouses to thy fortune, Hamlet.
HAMLET   Good madam!
KING   Gertrude, do not drink.
QUEEN   I will, my lord; I pray you, pardon me.
KING [*Aside.*]   It is the poisoned cup; it is too late.
QUEEN   Come, let me wipe thy face.   265
LAERTES   My lord, I'll hit him now.
KING   I do not think't.
LAERTES [*Aside.*]   And yet it is almost against my conscience.
HAMLET   Come, for the third, Laertes: you but dally;
    I pray you, pass with your best violence;
    I am afeard you make a wanton[6] of me.   270
LAERTES   Say you so? come on.
       [*They play.*]

1. Cups.
2. Requite, or repay (by scoring a hit) on the third bout.
3. A large pearl.
4. Kettledrum.
5. Handkerchief. "Fat": sweaty, or soft, because out of training.
6. Weakling, spoiled child.

OSRIC   Nothing, neither way.

LAERTES   Have at you now!

> [LAERTES *wounds* HAMLET; *then, in scuffling, they change rapiers, and* HAMLET *wounds* LAERTES.]

KING   Part them; they are incensed.

HAMLET   Nay, come, again.

> [*The* QUEEN *falls.*]

OSRIC   Look to the queen there, ho!

HORATIO   They bleed on both sides. How is it, my lord?

OSRIC   How is't, Laertes?   275

LAERTES   Why, as a woodcock to mine own springe,[7] Osric;
   I am justly killed with mine own treachery.

HAMLET   How does the queen?

KING   She swounds to see them bleed.   280

QUEEN   No, no, the drink, the drink,—O my dear Hamlet,—
   The drink, the drink! I am poisoned.

> [*Dies.*]

HAMLET   O villainy! Ho! let the door be locked:
   Treachery! seek it out.

> [LAERTES *falls.*]

LAERTES   It is here, Hamlet: Hamlet, thou art slain;   285
   No medicine in the world can do thee good,
   In thee there is not half an hour of life;
   The treacherous instrument is in thy hand,
   Unbated and envenomed: the foul practice[8]
   Hath turned itself on me; lo, here I lie,   290
   Never to rise again: thy mother's poisoned:
   I can no more: the king, the king's to blame.

HAMLET   The point envenomed too!
   Then, venom, to thy work.

> [*Stabs the* KING.]

ALL   Treason! treason!   295

KING   O, yet defend me, friends; I am but hurt.

HAMLET   Here, thou incestuous, murderous, damnèd Dane,
   Drink off this potion: is thy union here?
   Follow my mother.

> [KING *dies.*]

LAERTES   He is justly served;
   It is a poison tempered[9] by himself.   300
   Exchange forgiveness with me, noble Hamlet:
   Mine and my father's death come not upon thee,
   Nor thine on me!

> [*Dies.*]

HAMLET   Heaven make thee free of it! I follow thee.
   I am dead, Horatio. Wretched queen, adieu!   305
   You that look pale and tremble at this chance,

---

7. Snare.   9. Compounded.
8. Plot.

That are but mutes or audience to this act,
Had I but time—as this fell sergeant, death,
Is strict in his arrest—O, I could tell you—
But let it be. Horatio, I am dead;   310
Thou livest; report me and my cause aright
To the unsatisfied.
HORATIO   Never believe it:
I am more an antique Roman than a Dane:
Here's yet some liquor left.
HAMLET   As thou'rt a man,
Give me the cup: let go; by heaven, I'll have 't.   315
O good Horatio, what a wounded name,
Things standing thus unknown, shall live behind me!
If thou didst ever hold me in thy heart,
Absent thee from felicity a while,
And in this harsh world draw thy breath in pain,   320
To tell my story.
        [*March afar off, and shot within.*]
                            What warlike noise is this?
OSRIC   Young Fortinbras, with conquest come from Poland,
To the ambassadors of England gives
This warlike volley.
HAMLET   O, I die, Horatio;
The potent poison quite o'er-crows¹ my spirit: 325
I cannot live to hear the news from England;
But I do prophesy the election lights
On Fortinbras: he has my dying voice;
So tell him, with the occurrents, more and less,
Which have solicited.² The rest is silence.   330
        [*Dies.*]
HORATIO   Now cracks a noble heart. Good night sweet prince,
And flights of angels sing thee to thy rest;
        [*March within.*]
Why does the drum come hither?
        [*Enter FORTINBRAS, and the ENGLISH AMBASSADORS, with drum, colors, and*
        ATTENDANTS.]
FORTINBRAS   Where is this sight?
HORATIO   What is it you would see?
If aught of woe or wonder, cease your search.   335
FORTINBRAS   This quarry cries on havoc.³ O proud death,
What feast is toward⁴ in thine eternal cell,
That thou so many princes at a shot
So bloodily hast struck?
FIRST AMBASSADOR   The sight is dismal;
And our affairs from England come too late: 340
The ears are senseless that should give us hearing,

1. Overcomes.   3. This heap of corpses proclaims a carnage.
2. Which have brought all this about. "Occur-   4. Imminent.
rents": occurrences.

To tell him his commandment is fulfilled,
That Rosencrantz and Guildenstern are dead:
Where should we have our thanks?
HORATIO   Not from his mouth
  Had it the ability of life to thank you: 345
  He never gave commandment for their death.
  But since, so jump upon[5] this bloody question,
  You from the Polack wars, and you from England
  Are here arrived, give order that these bodies
  High on a stage be placèd to the view;   350
  And let me speak to the yet unknowing world
  How these things came about; so shall you hear
  Of carnal, bloody and unnatural acts,
  Of accidental judgments, casual slaughters,
  Of deaths put on[6] by cunning and forced cause,   355
  And, in this upshot, purposes mistook
  Fall'n on the inventors' heads: all this can I
  Truly deliver.
FORTINBRAS   Let us haste to hear it,
  And call the noblest to the audience.
  For me, with sorrow I embrace my fortune: 360
  I have some rights of memory in this kingdom,
  Which now to claim my vantage[7] doth invite me.
HORATIO   Of that I shall have also cause to speak,
  And from his mouth whose voice will draw on more:[8]
  But let this same be presently performed,   365
  Even while men's minds are wild; lest more mischance
  On[9] plots and errors happen.
FORTINBRAS   Let four captains
  Bear Hamlet, like a soldier, to the stage;
  For he was likely, had he been put on,[1]
  To have proved most royal: and, for his passage,[2]   370
  The soldiers' music and the rites of war
  Speak loudly for him.
  Take up the bodies: such a sight as this
  Becomes the field, but here shows much amiss.
  Go, bid the soldiers shoot.   375
     *[A dead march. Exeunt, bearing off the bodies: after which a peal
     of ordnance is shot off.]*

---

5. So immediately on.
6. Prompted. "Casual": chance.
7. Advantageous position, opportunity. "Have some rights of memory": am still remembered.
8. More voices.

9. Following on.
1. Tried (as a king).
2. Death.

s.Catherina Ins

THE ENCOUNTER OF EUROPE
AND THE NEW WORLD

As it dawned on Europeans that Christopher Columbus's voyages had led him not to the East Indies but to a continent previously unknown to them, the enormity of his "discovery" shattered the certainties of the medieval world, introducing a new era of extensive exploration around the globe and increased skepticism about received knowledge. Both the "brave new world" (in Shakespeare's phrase) and its inhabitants produced in the Europeans a sense that reality had been decisively altered and could never revert to older, familiar ways. Europe, with its traditions rooted in the medieval and ancient eras, seemed almost magically transformed into the Old World by its encounter with the New World. Columbus's initial forays into the Caribbean were soon followed by multiple expeditions to present-day Brazil, Central America, Mexico, and Peru, as the European presence gradually spread over the American continent. Portuguese, Dutch, French, and English explorers all set sail in an attempt to emulate the Spanish conquests and establish colonial outposts.

Wonder at radically different cultures and landscapes permeates the early Spanish and Portuguese accounts of the New World. The Europeans idealize the native peoples for their artlessness and generosity, while keeping a sharp eye on the commercial and extractive possibilities that such innocence enables. "Of

A 1592 engraving by Theodore de Bry that depicts the encounter between the Spanish and native people at the Río de San Francisco in Brazil, 1549.

anything they have, if it be asked for, they never say no," Columbus exclaims, yet he also reveals that he has taken some Indians "by force" to train them as interpreters, while leaving a group of his men behind in a well-armed fort. Columbus reads his surroundings largely by denying all evidence of culture: a cursory glance tells him that the Indians have no clothing, no religion, no guile, even as he confesses that he can barely communicate with them.

The contradictions in Columbus's letter to Ferdinand and Isabella regarding his first voyage are magnified in later texts that relate the conquest of the powerful Aztec Empire for Spain by Hernán Cortés, as wonder gives way to military calculation. The conquest of Mexico forever changed the stakes of New World exploration, as other European nations were forced to grapple with the enormous power and riches that it granted Spain. The immediate consequence of the fall of Tenochtitlán (now Mexico City) was the dismantling of the Aztec Empire, which had stretched from the Gulf Coast to the Pacific and from what is now the state of San Luis Potosí in central Mexico eastward to just within the present boundary of Guatemala. In due course, Tenochtitlán became the base from which Spain launched further conquests, ultimately reaching to the upper Rio Grande Valley and deep into Central America. Cortés's example inspired a generation of opportunistic intruders, notably Francisco Pizarro, whose conquest of the Inca Empire of Peru was completed in 1533. Exploration by other European nations, including Britain and Portugal, had begun even

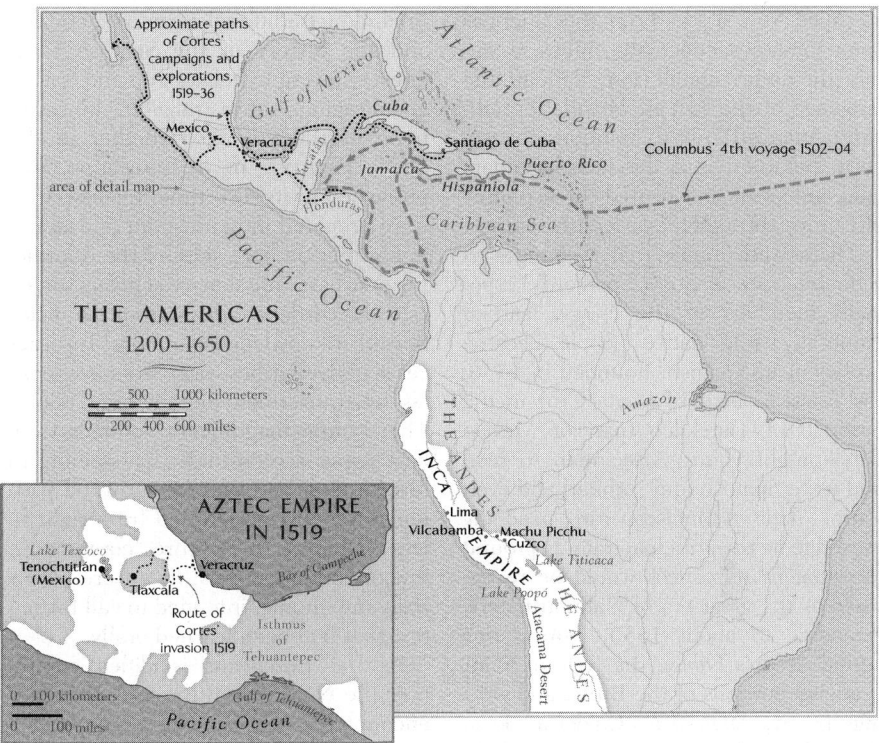

before Cortés, and within a hundred years of the initial contact, European outposts would be implanted all along the rim of the Americas.

With Spain's huge empire came administrative and moral dilemmas. Spain established vice-royalties in Mexico (1535) and Peru (1542) that ruled over impossibly large territories. As Indian labor proved insufficient for the colonists' needs, Spain and other nations began importing enslaved Africans into the New World. The conquest remained a work in progress, as Spaniards were forced to confront native hierarchies that complicated any allegiance to Spain, religious beliefs that seemed quite capable of surviving the forcible teaching of Christianity, and a bewildering admixture of populations. All these made the conquest a long and complex process.

While Spain's European rivals eagerly circulated reports of Spanish cruelty and greed (a war of words known as the "black legend"), the Spaniards themselves embarked on a vigorous internal debate about the legitimacy of the conquest and the status of indigenous subjects. The most famous advocate for the Indians was Bartolomé de las Casas, who loudly denounced Spanish excesses in an effort to reform the colonial administration. Las Casas persuaded the Spanish Crown to pass laws protecting the Indians, but exploitation of the native population in mines and other forms of forced labor was intractable.

Devastating to native people and permanently disruptive to long-established cultures, the conquests nevertheless prepared the way for exchange. Wheat, livestock, horses, and firearms entered the so-called New World. From the Americas came tomatoes, chocolate, chilies, avocados (the names are all from Nahuatl, the language of the Aztecs: *tomatl, xocolatl, chilli, ahuacatl*), not to mention tobacco, corn, potatoes, and the near-legendary gold and silver that heated the economy of Europe through the sixteenth century.

There were intellectual exchanges as well. In Aztec territory Spaniards, especially members of the clergy, learned Nahuatl, while native people became proficient in Spanish. Founded in 1536, the Royal College of Santa Cruz in the borough of Tlatelolco (part of Mexico City) taught young Aztec men to read and write Spanish and Nahuatl and even Latin. This Franciscan-run academy proved to be the principal training ground for what in retrospect would be recognized as the great era of Nahuatl letters, extending to about 1650. During this period Aesop's *Fables*, the "Life of Saint Francis," portions of the **Bible**, and writings by **St. Augustine**, Calderón de la Barca, Lope de Vega, and other authors were translated into Nahuatl and recorded in the alphabetic script used by Europeans (the Aztecs had used a pictographic and ideographic recording system rather than a standardized written language). At the same time, the Spaniards published grammars of many of the native languages that they encountered, as part of their efforts to convert indigenous peoples.

During these years, works of Aztec poetry and history were recorded for posterity and, in some cases, translated into Spanish. Among the most noteworthy is the massive *Florentine Codex* (including traditional narratives, oratory, and the history of the Spanish Conquest). Owing to censorship and fear of encouraging native religion, however, none of these works, whether in the native language or in translation, was published in its own time. Instead, they were prepared in manuscript and stored in libraries on both sides of the Atlantic. In some cases missionary-scholars served as the recorders, writing from the dictation of a knowledgeable elder. In other cases native scribes wrote from live recitals or transcribed old pictorial books. These often magnificent volumes were bark-paper screen-folds that opened to form a lengthy streamer, crowded with illustrations typically read from right to left. Although the pictures contained a few phonetic features, they were essentially mnemonic, intended to call forth a text that had been learned orally.

As the Europeans solidified control over the New World, the texts that they encountered and in some cases helped produce—the **Popol Vuh**, the *Huarochiri Manuscript*, the *Florentine Codex*—made it clear that this world was new only to Europeans and that it had its own origin myths and revered ancients. These texts make the point that New World cultures had carefully charted their own histories, political organization, and belief systems, however much Columbus idealized their material and religious innocence. The European project of collecting and preserving information about the cultures they encountered, in a kind of early ethnography, contrasts markedly with the violence and rapacity of the conquest.

POPOL VUH

transcribed 1554–58

A compendium of stories cherished by the ancient, the colonial, and even the modern Quiché Maya people of Guatemala, the sixteenth-century Popol Vuh has been compared to the *Odyssey* of the Greeks and the *Mahābhārata* of India. Woven together, its stories form an epic narrative that leads from the creation of the world and of humankind to the time of the text's writing, amid the violence of the Spanish Conquest. Inevitably, following the conquest of Mexico in 1521, Spanish imperialism cast its eye toward Guatemala, and in 1524, after a brief struggle, Quiché fell to Spanish and Mexican troops under the command of Pedro de Alvarado (called "the sun" by native people). By the 1530s, Quiché scribes, presumably including the Popol Vuh author, were being trained to use alphabetic writing. The book thus represents the cultural and intellectual mix born of the encounter: it is written in the Quiché language but in the Roman alphabet, and translates into book form what may have been an earlier text. In the narrative itself the anonymous author hints at the existence of a certain "council book" (*popol vuh*), presumably a pre-Columbian screen-fold that served him as a source. The Maya were the only civilization in the New World to have developed a full writing system, based on an elaborate system of glyphs.

The sixteenth-century Quiché were well acquainted with "council books," some dating from the classic period of Maya culture (100–900 C.E.), which saw the rise of such imposing centers as Tikal, Copán, and Palenque. By the time of European contact those important sites, abandoned in the mysterious collapse of Maya civilization ca. C.E. 900, lay in ruins. But Maya learning survived in southern Guatemala among the Quiché and their neighbors, and in the northern part of the Yucatán peninsula. Mayanists conclude that although the Popol Vuh is not an actual transcription of ancient screenfolds, it no doubt borrows from them. The modern text survives thanks to a copy made by a Dominican friar in the early eighteenth century, but it may have lost accompanying illustrations or hieroglyphs, which were standard for Mayan writings.

Stylistically, the text is fascinated by numbers, as evidenced in the pairing, tripling, and quadrupling of phrases. Major characters and deities also are paired, occasionally tripled, with a strong suggestion that they are the same. The work has a repeating structure, fitted to a traditional pattern of four successive worlds, or creations: the first three are said to have ended in failure; our own is the fourth. Yet against the background of this formal pattern, the hero-gods appear as light-hearted boys, even as tricksters. Their adventures, which are sometimes quite bawdy, have a playful, anecdotal quality.

As the author plainly states in the preamble that begins part 1, "We shall write about this now amid the preaching of God, in Christendom now." Admittedly, then, the Popol Vuh is written after the conquest, but the question of how much of it was influenced by Christian missionaries is not easy to settle. Most critics have assumed that the account of the Earth's creation that immediately follows the preamble owes something to the **Book of Genesis**. If so, the material has been thoroughly assimilated to the Maya pantheon and to the Native American concept of primordial water. The text may be as easily compared to Aztec accounts of creation, in which the gods deliberate, then place the Earth on the surface of a preexisting sea, as to Genesis.

Part 1 continues with a description of the first three efforts at creating humans, in line with a widespread pattern shared by Aztec and other Mesoamerican traditions. As part 1 ends, the narrative moves on to the exploits of the divine heroes Hunahpu and Xbalanque. The work of these two heroes may be said to prepare the world for society and for the well-being of individuals within society when they bring low the overproud Seven Macaw, while part 3, the most celebrated portion of the Popol Vuh, confronts the scourge of death.

In the cycle of tales that comprises part 3, Hunahpu and Xbalanque vanquish the lords of the Maya underworld, called Xibalba (a term of obscure etymology, provisionally translated "place of fright"). This material is quintessentially Mayan: scenes from the story are preserved on painted vases of the classic period, recovered by archaeologists from Maya burial chambers. The story told here must have aided the Maya in their journey through the realms of death somewhat as the *Book of the Dead* comforted the ancient Egyptians. Parts 4 and 5 complete the vast epic, relating the connected stories of the origin of humans, the discovery of corn, the birth of the sun, and the history of the Quiché tribes and their royal lineages down to the time of the Spanish Conquest and, subsequently, to the 1550s.

Old as the stories are, they are also new. Narratives of the origin and destruction of early humans can still be heard in traditional Maya storytelling sessions. The tale of the discovery of corn continues to be widely told; and the exploits of the trickster Zipacna and the hero twins also persist in shorter versions. Beyond the native community, knowledge of the Popol Vuh among Central Americans is not only widespread but taken for granted. For the Salvadoran novelist Manlio Argueta (*Cuzcatlán*, 1986) the story of the origin of humans from corn as told in the Popol Vuh is a reminder, in Argueta's words, that "the species will not perish." The theme appears also in the 1949 novel *Men of Maize* by the Guatemalan Nobel laureate Miguel Angel Asturias, inspired by the same source.

In the translation printed here, wherever the text solidifies into a string of three or more couplets, the passage is set apart as though it were a poem. This is a device of the translator. It is not meant to imply that the lines were chanted but rather to show off the more pronounced moments of formalism in a prose that borders on oratory.

From Popol Vuh[1]

FROM PART I

[*Prologue, Creation*]

THIS IS THE BEGINNING OF THE ANCIENT WORD, here in this place called Quiché. Here we shall inscribe, we shall implant the Ancient Word, the potential and source for everything done in the citadel of Quiché, in the nation of Quiché people.

1. Translated by Dennis Tedlock.

And here we shall take up the demonstration, revelation, and account of how things were put in shadow and brought to light by

> the Maker, Modeler,
> named Bearer, Begetter,
> Hunahpu Possum, Hunahpu Coyote,
> Great White Peccary,
> Sovereign Plumed Serpent,
> Heart of the Lake, Heart of the Sea,
> plate shaper,
> bowl shaper,[2] as they are called,
> also named, also described as
> the midwife, matchmaker
> named Xpiyacoc, Xmucane,
> defender, protector,[3]
> twice a midwife, twice a matchmaker,

as is said in the words of Quiché. They accounted for everything—and did it, too—as enlightened beings, in enlightened words. We shall write about this now amid the preaching of God, in Christendom now. We shall bring it out because there is no longer

> a place to see it, a Council Book,
> a place to see "The Light That Came from
>   Beside the Sea,"
> the account of "Our Place in the Shadows,"
> a place to see "The Dawn of Life,"

as it is called. There is the original book and ancient writing, but the one who reads and assesses it has a hidden identity.[4] It takes a long performance and account to complete the lighting of all the sky-earth:

> the fourfold siding, fourfold cornering,
> measuring, fourfold staking,
> halving the cord, stretching the cord
> in the sky, on the earth,
> the four sides, the four corners,[5]
> by the Maker, Modeler,
> mother-father of life, of humankind,

2. All thirteen names refer to the Creator or to a company of creators, a designation applicable clearly to the first four names and *Sovereign Plumed Serpent. Heart of the Lake* and *Heart of the Sea* also apply, since the creators will later be described as "in the water," and somewhat obscurely, so does the last pair of names (*plate* and *bowl* may be read as "earth" and "sky," respectively). *Hunahpu Possum, Hunahpu Coyote, Great White Peccary,* and *Coati* refer specifically to the grandpar-

ents of the gods, usually called Xpiyacoc and Xmucane.

3. Four names for Xpiyacoc and Xmucane.

4. The hieroglyphic source (*Council Book*) was suppressed by missionaries; it was said to have been brought to Quiché in ancient times from the far side of a lagoon (*Sea*). The reader hides his identity to avoid the missionaries.

5. As though a farmer were measuring and staking a cornfield.

> giver of breath, giver of heart,
> bearer, upbringer in the light that lasts
> of those born in the light, begotten in the light;
> worrier, knower of everything, whatever there is:
> sky-earth, lake-sea.

THIS IS THE ACCOUNT, here it is:

Now it still ripples, now it still murmurs, ripples, it still sighs, still hums, and it is empty under the sky.

Here follow the first words, the first eloquence:

There is not yet one person, one animal, bird, fish, crab, tree, rock, hollow, canyon, meadow, forest. Only the sky alone is there; the face of the earth is not clear. Only the sea alone is pooled under all the sky; there is nothing whatever gathered together. It is at rest; not a single thing stirs. It is held back, kept at rest under the sky.

Whatever there is that might be is simply not there: only the pooled water, only the calm sea, only it alone is pooled.

Whatever might be is simply not there: only murmurs, ripples, in the dark, in the night. Only the Maker, Modeler alone, Sovereign Plumed Serpent, the Bearers, Begetters are in the water, a glittering light. They are there, they are enclosed in quetzal feathers, in blue-green.

Thus the name, "Plumed Serpent." They are great knowers, great thinkers in their very being.

And of course there is the sky, and there is also the Heart of Sky. This is the name of the god, as it is spoken.

And then came his word, he came here to the Sovereign Plumed Serpent, here in the blackness, in the early dawn. He spoke with the Sovereign Plumed Serpent, and they talked, then they thought, then they worried. They agreed with each other, they joined their words, their thoughts. Then it was clear, then they reached accord in the light, and then humanity was clear, when they conceived the growth, the generation of trees, of bushes, and the growth of life, of humankind, in the blackness, in the early dawn, all because of the Heart of Sky, named Hurricane. Thunderbolt Hurricane comes first, the second is Newborn Thunderbolt, and the third is Sudden Thunderbolt.[6]

So there were three of them, as Heart of Sky, who came to the Sovereign Plumed Serpent, when the dawn of life was conceived:

"How should the sowing be, and the dawning? Who is to be the provider, nurturer?"[7]

"Let it be this way, think about it: this water should be removed, emptied out for the formation of the earth's own plate and platform, then should come the sowing, the dawning of the sky-earth. But there will be no high days and no

---

6. Alternate names for Heart of Sky, the deity who cooperates with Sovereign Plumed Serpent. The triple naming adapts the Christian trinity to native theology, perhaps more in the spirit of defiant preemption than of conciliation.

7. That is, humanity, which alone is capable of *nurturing* the gods with sacrifices.

bright praise for our work, our design, until the rise of the human work, the human design," they said.

And then the earth arose because of them, it was simply their word that brought it forth. For the forming of the earth they said "Earth." It arose suddenly, just like a cloud, like a mist, now forming, unfolding. Then the mountains were separated from the water, all at once the great mountains came forth. By their genius alone, by their cutting edge[8] alone they carried out the conception of the mountain-plain, whose face grew instant groves of cypress and pine.

And the Plumed Serpent was pleased with this:

"It was good that you came, Heart of Sky, Hurricane, and Newborn Thunderbolt, Sudden Thunderbolt. Our work, our design will turn out well," they said.

And the earth was formed first, the mountain-plain. The channels of water were separated; their branches wound their ways among the mountains. The waters were divided when the great mountains appeared.

Such was the formation of the earth when it was brought forth by the Heart of Sky, Heart of Earth, as they are called, since they were the first to think of it. The sky was set apart, and the earth was set apart in the midst of the waters.

Such was their plan when they thought, when they worried about the completion of their work.[9]

FROM PART 2

[The Twins Defeat Seven Macaw]

HERE IS THE BEGINNING OF THE DEFEAT AND DESTRUCTION OF THE DAY OF SEVEN MACAW by the two boys, the first named Hunahpu and the second named Xbalanque.[1] Being gods, the two of them saw evil in his attempt at self-magnification before the Heart of Sky.

* * *

This is the great tree of Seven Macaw, a nance,[2] and this is the food of Seven Macaw. In order to eat the fruit of the nance he goes up the tree every day. Since Hunahpu and Xbalanque have seen where he feeds, they are now hiding beneath the tree of Seven Macaw, they are keeping quiet here, the two boys are in the leaves of the tree.

8. ...Refers to the cutting of flesh with a knife....In the present context, it implies that "the mountains were separated from the water" through an act resembling the extraction of the heart (or other organs) from a sacrifice [translator's note].

9. That is, the creation of humans; an account of the first three, unsuccessful, attempts at creating humans occupies the remainder of part 1.

1. First mention of the twin hero gods (their origin is recounted in part 3). Here they confront the false god Seven Macaw, who has arisen during the time of primordial darkness, boasting, "My eyes are of metal; my teeth just glitter with jewels, and turquoise as well....I am like the sun and the moon." Note that all the characters in parts 1, 2, and 3 are supernatural; humans are not created until part 4.

2. A pickle tree (Byrsonima crassifolia).

And when Seven Macaw arrived, perching over his meal, the nance, it was then that he was shot by Hunahpu. The blowgun shot went right to his jaw, breaking his mouth. Then he went up over the tree and fell flat on the ground. Suddenly Hunahpu appeared, running. He set out to grab him, but actually it was the arm of Hunahpu that was seized by Seven Macaw. He yanked it straight back, he bent it back at the shoulder. Then Seven Macaw tore it right out of Hunahpu. Even so, the boys did well: the first round was not their defeat by Seven Macaw.

And when Seven Macaw had taken the arm of Hunahpu, he went home. Holding his jaw very carefully, he arrived:

"What have you got there?" said Chimalmat, the wife of Seven Macaw.

"What is it but those two tricksters! They've shot me, they've dislocated my jaw.[3] All my teeth are just loose, now they ache. But once what I've got is over the fire—hanging there, dangling over the fire—then they can just come and get it. They're real tricksters!" said Seven Macaw, then he hung up the arm of Hunahpu.

Meanwhile Hunahpu and Xbalanque were thinking. And then they invoked a grandfather, a truly white-haired grandfather, and a grandmother, a truly humble grandmother—just bent-over, elderly people. Great White Peccary is the name of the grandfather, and Great White Coati is the name of the grandmother.[4] The boys said to the grandmother and grandfather:

"Please travel with us when we go to get our arm from Seven Macaw; we'll just follow right behind you. You'll tell him:

'Do forgive us our grandchildren, who travel with us. Their mother and father are dead, and so they follow along there, behind us. Perhaps we should give them away, since all we do is pull worms out of teeth.' So we'll seem like children to Seven Macaw, even though *we're* giving *you* the instructions," the two boys told them.

"Very well," they replied.

After that they approached the place where Seven Macaw was in front of his home. When the grandmother and grandfather passed by, the two boys were romping along behind them. When they passed below the lord's house, Seven Macaw was yelling his mouth off because of his teeth. And when Seven Macaw saw the grandfather and grandmother traveling with them:

"Where are you headed, our grandfather?" said the lord.

"We're just making our living, your lordship," they replied.

"Why are you working for a living? Aren't those your children traveling with you?"

"No, they're not, your lordship. They're our grandchildren, our descendants, but it is nevertheless *we* who take pity on *them*. The bit of food they get is the portion we give them, your lordship," replied the grandmother and grandfather. Since the lord is getting done in by the pain in his teeth, it is only with great effort that he speaks again:

"I implore you, please take pity on me! What sweets can you make, what poisons[5] can you cure?" said the lord.

---

3. This is the origin of the way a macaw's beak looks, with a huge upper mandible and a small, retreating lower one [translator's note].
4. Animal names of the divine grandparents, Xpiyacoc and Xmucane, who are also the twins' genealogical grandparents.
5. Play on words as *qui* is translated as both "sweet" and "poison."

"We just pull the worms out of teeth, and we just cure eyes. We just set bones, your lordship," they replied.

"Very well, please cure my teeth. They really ache, every day. It's insufferable! I get no sleep because of them—and my eyes. They just shot me, those two tricksters! Ever since it started I haven't eaten because of it. Therefore take pity on me! Perhaps it's because my teeth are loose now."

"Very well, your lordship. It's a worm, gnawing at the bone.[6] It's merely a matter of putting in a replacement and taking the teeth out, sir."

"But perhaps it's not good for my teeth to come out—since I am, after all, a lord. My finery is in my teeth—and my eyes."

"But then we'll put in a replacement. Ground bone will be put back in." And this is the "ground bone": it's only white corn.

"Very well. Yank them out! Give me some help here!" he replied.

And when the teeth of Seven Macaw came out, it was only white corn that went in as a replacement for his teeth—just a coating shining white, that corn in his mouth. His face fell at once, he no longer looked like a lord. The last of his teeth came out, the jewels that had stood out blue from his mouth.

And when the eyes of Seven Macaw were cured, he was plucked around the eyes, the last of his metal came off.[7] Still he felt no pain; he just looked on while the last of his greatness left him. It was just as Hunahpu and Xbalanque had intended.

And when Seven Macaw died, Hunahpu got back his arm. And Chimalmat, the wife of Seven Macaw, also died.

Such was the loss of the riches of Seven Macaw: only the doctors got the jewels and gems that had made him arrogant, here on the face of the earth. The genius of the grandmother, the genius of the grandfather did its work when they took back their arm: it was implanted and the break got well again. Just as they had wished the death of Seven Macaw, so they brought it about. They had seen evil in his self-magnification.

After this the two boys went on again. What they did was simply the word of the Heart of Sky.

FROM PART 3

[Victory over the Underworld]

AND NOW WE SHALL NAME THE NAME OF THE FATHER OF HUNAHPU AND XBAL-ANQUE. Let's drink to him, and let's just drink to the telling and accounting of the begetting of Hunahpu and Xbalanque. We shall tell just half of it, just a part of the account of their father. Here follows the account.

These are the names: One Hunahpu and Seven Hunahpu,[8] as they are called.

*   *   *

6. The present-day Quiché retain the notion that a toothache is caused by a worm gnawing at the bone [translator's note].

7. This is clearly meant to be the origin of the large white and completely featherless eye patches and very small eyes of the scarlet macaw [translator's note].

8. Twin sons of Xpiyacoc and Xmucane; the elder of these twins, One Hunahpu, will become the father of Hunahpu and Xbalanque. "As for Seven Hunahpu," according to the text, "he has no wife. He's just a partner and just secondary; he just remains a boy."

AND ONE AND SEVEN HUNAHPU WENT INSIDE DARK HOUSE.[9]

And then their torch was brought, only one torch, already lit, sent by One and Seven Death, along with a cigar for each of them, also already lit, sent by the lords. When these were brought to One and Seven Hunahpu they were cowering, here in the dark. When the bearer of their torch and cigars arrived, the torch was bright as it entered; their torch and both of their cigars were burning. The bearer spoke:

"'They must be sure to return them in the morning—not finished, but just as they look now. They must return them intact,' the lords say to you," they were told, and they were defeated. They finished the torch and they finished the cigars that had been brought to them.

And Xibalba is packed with tests, heaps and piles of tests.

This is the first one: the Dark House, with darkness alone inside.

And the second is named Rattling House, heavy with cold inside, whistling with drafts, clattering with hail. A deep chill comes inside here.

And the third is named Jaguar House, with jaguars alone inside, jostling one another, crowding together, with gnashing teeth. They're scratching around; these jaguars are shut inside the house.

Bat House is the name of the fourth test, with bats alone inside the house, squeaking, shrieking, darting through the house. The bats are shut inside; they can't get out.

And the fifth is named Razor House, with blades alone inside. The blades are moving back and forth, ripping, slashing through the house.

These are the first tests of Xibalba, but One and Seven Hunahpu never entered into them, except for the one named earlier, the specified test house.

And when One and Seven Hunahpu went back before One and Seven Death, they were asked:

"Where are my cigars? What of my torch? They were brought to you last night!"

"We finished them, your lordship."

"Very well. This very day, your day is finished, you will die, you will disappear, and we shall break you off. Here you will hide your faces: you are to be sacrificed!" said One and Seven Death.

And then they were sacrificed and buried. They were buried at the Place of Ball Game Sacrifice,[1] as it is called. The head of One Hunahpu was cut off; only his body was buried with his younger brother.

"Put his head in the fork of the tree that stands by the road," said One and Seven Death.

And when his head was put in the fork of the tree, the tree bore fruit. It would not have had any fruit, had not the head of One Hunahpu been put in the fork of the tree.

This is the calabash tree, as we call it today, or "the skull of One Hunahpu," as it is said.

9. The first of the "test" houses in Xibalba (the underworld) to which One and Seven Hunahpu, avid ballplayers, have been lured by the underworld lords, One and Seven Death; the lords have promised them a challenging ball game. The Mesoamerican ball game, remotely com- parable to both basketball and soccer, was played on a rectangular court, using a ball of native rubber.
1. Probably not a place name, but rather a name for the altar where losing ball players were sacrificed [translator's note].

And then One and Seven Death were amazed at the fruit of the tree. The fruit grows out everywhere, and it isn't clear where the head of One Hunahpu is; now it looks just the way the calabashes look. All the Xibalbans see this, when they come to look.

The state of the tree loomed large in their thoughts, because it came about at the same time the head of One Hunahpu was put in the fork. The Xibalbans said among themselves:

"No one is to pick the fruit, nor is anyone to go beneath the tree," they said. They restricted themselves; all of Xibalba held back.

It isn't clear which is the head of One Hunahpu; now it's exactly the same as the fruit of the tree. Calabash came to be its name, and much was said about it. A maiden heard about it, and here we shall tell of her arrival.

AND HERE IS THE ACCOUNT OF A MAIDEN, the daughter of a lord named Blood Gatherer.[2]

And this is when a maiden heard of it, the daughter of a lord. Blood Gatherer is the name of her father, and Blood Moon is the name of the maiden.

And when he heard the account of the fruit of the tree, her father retold it. And she was amazed at the account:

"I'm not acquainted with that tree they talk about. '"Its fruit is truly sweet!" they say,' I hear," she said.

Next, she went all alone and arrived where the tree stood. It stood at the Place of Ball Game Sacrifice:

"What? Well! What's the fruit of this tree? Shouldn't this tree bear something sweet? They shouldn't die, they shouldn't be wasted. Should I pick one?" said the maiden.

And then the bone spoke; it was here in the fork of the tree:

"Why do you want a mere bone, a round thing in the branches of a tree?" said the head of One Hunahpu when it spoke to the maiden. "You don't want it," she was told.

"I do want it," said the maiden.

"Very well. Stretch out your right hand here, so I can see it," said the bone.

"Yes," said the maiden. She stretched out her right hand, up there in front of the bone.

And then the bone spit out its saliva, which landed squarely in the hand of the maiden.

And then she looked in her hand, she inspected it right away, but the bone's saliva wasn't in her hand.

"It is just a sign I have given you, my saliva, my spittle. This, my head, has nothing on it—just bone, nothing of meat. It's just the same with the head of a great lord: it's just the flesh that makes his face look good. And when he dies, people get frightened by his bones. After that, his son is like his saliva, his spittle, in his being, whether it be the son of a lord or the son of a craftsman, an orator. The father does not disappear, but goes on being fulfilled. Neither dimmed nor destroyed is the face of a lord, a warrior, craftsman, orator. Rather, he will leave his daughters and sons. So it is that I have done likewise through you. Now go up there on the face of the earth; you will not die. Keep

---

2. Fourth-ranking lord of Xibalba, whose commission is to draw blood from people.

the word. So be it," said the head of One and Seven Hunahpu—they were of one mind when they did it.

This was the word Hurricane, Newborn Thunderbolt, Sudden Thunderbolt had given them. In the same way, by the time the maiden returned to her home, she had been given many instructions. Right away something was generated in her belly, from the saliva alone, and this was the generation of Hunahpu and Xbalanque.

And when the maiden got home and six months had passed, she was found out by her father. Blood Gatherer is the name of her father.

* * *

AND THEY CAME TO THE LORDS.[3] Feigning great humility, they bowed their heads all the way to the ground when they arrived. They brought themselves low, doubled over, flattened out, down to the rags, to the tatters. They really looked like vagabonds when they arrived.

So then they were asked what their mountain[4] and tribe were, and they were also asked about their mother and father:

"Where do you come from?" they were asked.

"We've never known, lord. We don't know the identity of our mother and father. We must've been small when they died," was all they said. They didn't give any names.

"Very well. Please entertain us, then. What do you want us to give you in payment?" they were asked.

"Well, we don't want anything. To tell the truth, we're afraid," they told the lord.

"Don't be afraid. Don't be ashamed. Just dance this way: first you'll dance to sacrifice yourselves, you'll set fire to my house after that, you'll act out all the things you know. We want to be entertained. This is our heart's desire, the reason you had to be sent for, dear vagabonds. We'll give you payment," they were told.

So then they began their songs and dances, and then all the Xibalbans arrived, the spectators crowded the floor, and they danced everything: they danced the Weasel, they danced the Poorwill,[5] they danced the Armadillo. Then the lord said to them:

"Sacrifice my dog, then bring him back to life again," they were told.

"Yes," they said.

> When they sacrificed the dog
>   he then came back to life.
> And that dog was really happy
>   when he came back to life.
> Back and forth he wagged his tail
>   when he came back to life.

---

3. Forced to flee the underworld the maiden (Blood Moon) finds refuge on earth with Xmucane. There she gives birth to the twins, who, like their father and uncle, become ballplayers and are enticed to the underworld. Surviving the Dark House and other tests, they disguise themselves as vagabonds and earn a reputation as clever entertainers among the denizens of Xibalba; as such they are summoned to entertain the high lords.

4. A metonym for almost any settlement, but especially a fortified town or citadel, located on a defensible elevation [translator's note].

5. The goatsucker. The dances apparently were imitations of these animals and birds.

And the lord said to them:

"Well, you have yet to set my home on fire," they were told next, so then they set fire to the home of the lord. The house was packed with all the lords, but they were not burned. They quickly fixed it back again, lest the house of One Death be consumed all at once, and all the lords were amazed, and they went on dancing this way. They were overjoyed.

And then they were asked by the lord:

"You have yet to kill a person! Make a sacrifice without death!" they were told.

"Very well," they said.

And then they took hold of a human sacrifice.

And they held up a human heart on high.

And they showed its roundness to the lords.

And now One and Seven Death admired it, and now that person was brought right back to life. His heart was overjoyed when he came back to life, and the lords were amazed:

"Sacrifice yet again, even do it to yourselves! Let's see it! At heart, that's the dance we really want from you," the lords said now.

"Very well, lord," they replied, and then they sacrificed themselves.

AND THIS IS THE SACRIFICE OF HUNAHPU BY XBALANQUE. One by one his legs, his arms were spread wide. His head came off, rolled far away outside. His heart, dug out, was smothered in a leaf,[6] and all the Xibalbans went crazy at the sight.

So now, only one of them was dancing there: Xbalanque.

"Get up!" he said, and Hunahpu came back to life. The two of them were overjoyed at this—and likewise the lords rejoiced, as if they were doing it themselves. One and Seven Death were as glad at heart as if they themselves were actually doing the dance.

And then the hearts of the lords were filled with longing, with yearning for the dance of little Hunahpu and Xbalanque, so then came these words from One and Seven Death:

"Do it to us! Sacrifice us!" they said. "Sacrifice both of us!" said One and Seven Death to Hunahpu and Xbalanque.

"Very well. You ought to come back to life. What is death to you?[7] And aren't we making you happy, along with the vassals of your domain?" they told the lords.

And this one was the first to be sacrificed; the lord at the very top, the one whose name is One Death, the ruler of Xibalba.

And with One Death dead, the next to be taken was Seven Death. They did not come back to life.

And then the Xibalbans were getting up to leave, those who had seen the lords die. They underwent heart sacrifice there, and the heart sacrifice was performed on the two lords only for the purpose of destroying them.

As soon as they had killed the one lord without bringing him back to life, the other lord had been meek and tearful before the dancers. He didn't consent, he didn't accept it:

"Take pity on me!" he said when he realized. All their vassals took the road to the great canyon, in one single mass they filled up the deep abyss. So they piled

6. As a tamale is wrapped. In the typical Meso-american heart sacrifice, the victim's arms and legs were stretched wide and the heart was excised and offered to a deity.

7. Evident sarcasm.

up there and gathered together, countless ants, tumbling down into the canyon, as if they were being herded there. And when they arrived, they all bent low in surrender, they arrived meek and tearful.

Such was the defeat of the rulers of Xibalba. The boys accomplished it only through wonders, only through self-transformation.

* * *

Such was the beginning of their disappearance and the denial of their worship.

> Their ancient day was not a great one,
> these ancient people only wanted conflict,
> their ancient names are not really divine,
> but fearful is the ancient evil of their faces.
>
> They are makers of enemies, users of owls,[8]
> they are inciters to wrongs and violence,
> they are masters of hidden intentions as well,
> they are black and white,[9]
> masters of stupidity, masters of perplexity,

as it is said. By putting on appearances they cause dismay.

Such was the loss of their greatness and brilliance. Their domain did not return to greatness. This was accomplished by little Hunahpu and Xbalanque.

FROM PART 4

[Origin of Humanity, First Dawn]

AND HERE IS THE BEGINNING OF THE CONCEPTION OF HUMANS, and of the search for the ingredients of the human body. So they spoke, the Bearer, Begetter, the Makers, Modelers named Sovereign Plumed Serpent:

"The dawn has approached, preparations have been made, and morning has come for the provider, nurturer, born in the light, begotten in the light. Morning has come for humankind, for the people of the face of the earth," they said. It all came together as they went on thinking in the darkness, in the night, as they searched and they sifted, they thought and they wondered.

And here their thoughts came out in clear light. They sought and discovered what was needed for human flesh. It was only a short while before the sun, moon, and stars were to appear above the Makers and Modelers. Split Place, Bitter Water Place is the name: the yellow corn, white corn came from there.

And these are the names of the animals who brought the food: fox, coyote, parrot, crow. There were four animals who brought the news of the ears of yellow corn and white corn. They were coming from over there at Split Place, they showed the way to the split.[1]

And this was when they found the staple foods.

---

8. The lords had used owls as messengers to lure the ballplayers to Xibalba.
9. Contradictory, duplicitous.
1. In the widespread Mesoamerican story of the discovery of corn, one or more animals reveal that corn and other foods are hidden within a rock or a mountain, accessible through a cleft; in some versions the mountain is split apart by lightning.

And these were the ingredients for the flesh of the human work, the human design, and the water was for the blood. It became human blood, and corn was also used by the Bearer, Begetter.

And so they were happy over the provisions of the good mountain, filled with sweet things, thick with yellow corn, white corn, and thick with pataxte and cacao, countless zapotes, anonas, jocotes, nances, matasanos,[2] sweets—the rich foods filling up the citadel named Split Place, Bitter Water Place. All the edible fruits were there: small staples, great staples, small plants, great plants. The way was shown by the animals.

And then the yellow corn and white corn were ground, and Xmucane did the grinding nine times. Corn was used, along with the water she rinsed her hands with, for the creation of grease; it became human fat when it was worked by the Bearer, Begetter, Sovereign Plumed Serpent, as they are called.

After that, they put it into words:

> the making, the modeling of our first mother-father,
> with yellow corn, white corn alone for the flesh,
> food alone for the human legs and arms,
> for our first fathers, the four human works.

It was staples alone that made up their flesh.

THESE ARE THE NAMES OF THE FIRST PEOPLE WHO WERE MADE AND MODELED.

> This is the first person: Jaguar Quitze.
> And now the second: Jaguar Night.
> And now the third: Not Right Now.
> And the fourth: Dark Jaguar.[3]

And these are the names of our first mother-fathers.[4] They were simply made and modeled, it is said; they had no mother and no father. We have named the men by themselves. No woman gave birth to them, nor were they begotten by the builder, sculptor, Bearer, Begetter. By sacrifice alone, by genius alone they were made, they were modeled by the Maker, Modeler, Bearer, Begetter, Sovereign Plumed Serpent. And when they came to fruition, they came out human:

> They talked and they made words.
> They looked and they listened.
> They walked, they worked.

They were good people, handsome, with looks of the male kind. Thoughts came into existence and they gazed; their vision came all at once. Perfectly they saw, perfectly they knew everything under the sky, whenever they looked. The moment they turned around and looked around in the sky, on the earth, everything was seen without any obstruction. They didn't have to walk around before they could see what was under the sky; they just stayed where they were.

As they looked, their knowledge became intense. Their sight passed through trees, through rocks, through lakes, through seas, through mountains, through

2. Quincelike fruits of the tree *Casimiroa edulis.* Pataxte (*Theobroma bicolor*) is a species of cacao that is inferior to cacao proper (*T. cacao*). Zapotes are fruits of the sapota tree (*Lucuma mammosa*). Anonas are custard apples (genus *Anona*). Jocotes are yellow plumlike fruits of the tree *Spondias purpurea.*
3. The four original Quiché males.
4. That is, parents, although only the first three founded lineages; Dark Jaguar had no son.

plains. Jaguar Quitze, Jaguar Night, Not Right Now, and Dark Jaguar were truly gifted people.

And then they were asked by the builder and mason:

"What do you know about your being? Don't you look, don't you listen? Isn't your speech good, and your walk? So you must look, to see out under the sky. Don't you see the mountain-plain clearly? So try it," they were told.

And then they saw everything under the sky perfectly. After that, they thanked the Maker, Modeler:

> "Truly now,
> double thanks, triple thanks
> that we've been formed, we've been given
> our mouths, our faces,
> we speak, we listen,
> we wonder, we move,
> our knowledge is good, we've understood
> what is far and near,
> and we've seen what is great and small
> under the sky, on the earth.
> Thanks to you we've been formed,
> we've come to be made and modeled,
> our grandmother, our grandfather,"

they said when they gave thanks for having been made and modeled. They understood everything perfectly, they sighted the four sides, the four corners in the sky, on the earth, and this didn't sound good to the builder and sculptor:

"What our works and designs have said is no good:

'We have understood everything, great and small,' they say." And so the Bearer, Begetter took back their knowledge:

"What should we do with them now? Their vision should at least reach nearby, they should see at least a small part of the face of the earth, but what they're saying isn't good. Aren't they merely 'works' and 'designs' in their very names? Yet they'll become as great as gods, unless they procreate, proliferate at the sowing, the dawning, unless they increase."

"Let it be this way: now we'll take them apart just a little, that's what we need. What we've found out isn't good. Their deeds would become equal to ours, just because their knowledge reaches so far. They see everything," so said

> the Heart of Sky, Hurricane,
> Newborn Thunderbolt, Sudden Thunderbolt,
> Sovereign Plumed Serpent,
> Bearer, Begetter,
> Xpiyacoc, Xmucane,
> Maker, Modeler,

as they are called. And when they changed the nature of their works, their designs, it was enough that the eyes be marred by the Heart of Sky. They were blinded as the face of a mirror is breathed upon. Their vision flickered. Now it was only from close up that they could see what was there with any clarity.

And such was the loss of the means of understanding, along with the means of knowing everything, by the four humans. The root was implanted.

And such was the making, modeling of our first grandfather, our father, by the Heart of Sky, Heart of Earth.

AND THEN THEIR WIVES AND WOMEN CAME INTO BEING. Again, the same gods thought of it. It was as if they were asleep when they received them, truly beautiful women were there with Jaguar Quitze, Jaguar Night, Not Right Now, and Dark Jaguar. With their women there they really came alive. Right away they were happy at heart again, because of their wives.

Red Sea Turtle is the name of the wife of Jaguar Quitze.

Prawn House is the name of the wife of Jaguar Night.

Water Hummingbird is the name of the wife of Not Right Now.

Macaw House is the name of the wife of Dark Jaguar.

So these are the names of their wives, who became ladies of rank, giving birth to the people of the tribes, small and great.

* * *

AND HERE IS THE DAWNING AND SHOWING OF THE SUN, MOON, AND STARS. And Jaguar Quitze, Jaguar Night, Not Right Now, and Dark Jaguar were overjoyed when they saw the sun carrier.[5] It came up first. It looked brilliant when it came up, since it was ahead of the sun.

After that they unwrapped their copal[6] incense, which came from the east, and there was triumph in their hearts when they unwrapped it. They gave their heartfelt thanks with three kinds at once:

Mixtam Copal is the name of the copal brought by Jaguar Quitze.

Cauiztan Copal, next, is the name of the copal brought by Jaguar Night.

Godly Copal, as the next one is called, was brought by Not Right Now.

The three of them had their copal, and this is what they burned as they incensed the direction of the rising sun. They were crying sweetly as they shook their burning copal,[7] the precious copal.

After that they cried because they had yet to see and yet to witness the birth of the sun.

And then, when the sun came up, the animals, small and great, were happy. They all came up from the rivers and canyons; they waited on all the mountain peaks. Together they looked toward the place where the sun came out.

So then the puma and jaguar cried out, but the first to cry out was a bird, the parrot by name. All the animals were truly happy. The eagle, the white vulture, small birds, great birds spread their wings, and the penitents and sacrificers knelt down.

5. The morning star.
6. Resin used as incense.

7. Note that the Mesoamerican pottery censer must be shaken or swayed back and forth to keep the incense burning.

FROM PART 5

[*Prayer for Future Generations*]

AND THIS IS THE CRY OF THEIR HEARTS, HERE IT IS:

"Wait! On this blessed day,
thou Hurricane, thou Heart of the Sky-Earth,
thou giver of ripeness and freshness,
and thou giver of daughters and sons,
spread thy stain, spill thy drops
of green and yellow;[8]
give life and beginning
to those I bear and beget,
that they might multiply and grow,
nurturing and providing for thee,
calling to thee along the roads and paths,
on rivers, in canyons,
beneath the trees and bushes;
give them their daughters and sons.

"May there be no blame, obstacle, want or misery;
let no deceiver come behind or before them,
may they neither be snared nor wounded,
nor seduced, nor burned,
nor diverted below the road nor above it;
may they neither fall over backward nor stumble;
keep them on the Green Road, the Green Path.

"May there be no blame or barrier for them
through any secrets or sorcery of thine;
may thy nurturers and providers be good
before thy mouth and thy face,
thou, Heart of Sky; thou, Heart of Earth;
thou, Bundle of Flames;[9]
and thou, Tohil, Auilix, Hacauitz,[1]
under the sky, on the earth,
the four sides, the four corners;
may there be only light, only continuity within,
before thy mouth and thy face, thou god."

---

8. The imagery, denoting human offspring, alludes to semen and plant growth.
9. A sacred relic left to the Quiché lords by Jaguar Quitze; like the sacred bundles of the North American peoples, a cloth-wrapped ark with mysterious contents [translator's note].
1. Patron deities of the Quiché lineages.

CHRISTOPHER COLUMBUS

Born in Italy, most likely in Genoa, Columbus (1450–1506) became a sailor on the Mediterranean and the Atlantic oceans, eventually establishing himself also as a navigator and mapmaker. While most thinkers of his day agreed that the Earth was spherical, there was considerable disagreement over its size and the habitability of its various zones. Convinced that he was led by Providence, Columbus persuaded the Spanish King Ferdinand and Queen Isabella to fund an expedition in 1492 that he hoped would find a shorter route to the East Indies and its lucrative spice trade by sailing west. In this sense, the discovery of the New World was an accident, and Columbus continued to believe for some time that he had reached Asia, hence the pervasive misnomer "Indians" that he uses for the peoples he encounters. In Hispaniola (present-day Haiti and the Dominican Republic), he found what seemed to him an earthly paradise, filled with an inexhaustible variety of flowers and fruits, and gentle natives who, in his telling, denied him nothing.

Columbus's letter about his first voyage is a public version of the more sensitive information that he sent his patrons, and emphasizes the potential utility of the islands as a source of gold and other commodities. Columbus also envisions the island's population as future converts, introducing the theme of evangelization that was to be an important justification for the conquest, or as docile laborers. Although it idealizes the islands, the letter also reveals the difficulties that attended the encounter, and the threat of violence that overshadows the idyll. Excited at the promise of gold on the next island beyond the horizon, he disregards both the actual scarcity of treasure and the Indians' urgent insistence that he move on to search elsewhere.

Later voyages were to prove far less idyllic: Columbus returned to Hispaniola to find the fort he had left there destroyed and his men lost, and a great deal more hostility from the Indians who had suffered their depredations. In Spain, meanwhile, he faced strong opposition to his demands for reward and recognition, and increasing skepticism as gold remained elusive in the Caribbean. For the Taínos, the native inhabitants of the Caribbean islands, the contact with Europeans proved fatal: through a combination of war, smallpox, and the violent exploitation of their labor by the Spanish, their population was decimated by the mid-sixteenth century. Although Columbus's early accounts cannot envision such dire outcomes, the tremendous destruction wrought on this population has tainted the legacy of his voyages over the centuries.

Letter Concerning the First Voyage[1]

Sir: As I know that you will have pleasure from the great victory which our Lord hath given me in my voyage, I write you this, by which you shall know that in thirty-three days I passed over to the Indies with the fleet which the most illustrious King and Queen, our Lords, gave me; where I found very many islands peopled

1. Translated by Sir Clements R. Markham.

with inhabitants beyond number. And, of them all, I have taken possession for their Highnesses, with proclamation and the royal standard displayed; and I was not gainsaid. To the first which I found, I gave the name Sant Salvador, in commemoration of His High Majesty, who marvellously hath given all this: the Indians call it Guanaham. The second I named the Island of Santa Maria de Concepcion, the third Ferrandina, the fourth, Fair Island, the fifth La Isla Juana; and so for each one a new name. When I reached Juana, I followed its coast westwardly, and found it so large that I thought it might be mainland, the province of Cathay. And as I did not thus find any towns and villages on the sea-coast, save small hamlets with the people whereof I could not get speech, because they all fled away forthwith, I went on further in the same direction, thinking I should not miss of great cities or towns. And at the end of many leagues, seeing that there was no change, and that the coast was bearing me northwards, whereunto my desire was contrary, since the winter was already confronting us, I formed the purpose of making from thence to the South, and as the wind also blew against me, I determined not to wait for other weather and turned back as far as a port agreed upon; from which I sent two men into the country to learn if there were a king, or any great cities. They traveled for three days, and found innumerable small villages and a numberless population, but nought of ruling authority; wherefore they returned. I understood sufficiently from other Indians whom I had already taken, that this land, in its continuousness, was an island; and so I followed its coast eastwardly for a hundred and seven leagues as far as where it terminated; from which headland I saw another island to the east, eighteen leagues distant from this, to which I at once gave the name La Española. And I proceeded thither, and followed the northern coast, as with La Juana, eastwardly for a hundred and eighty-eight great leagues in a direct easterly course, as with La Juana. The which, and all the others, are most fertile to an excessive degree, and this extremely so. In it, there are many havens on the sea-coast, incomparable with any others that I know in Christendom, and plenty of rivers so good and great that it is a marvel. The lands thereof are high, and in it are very many ranges of hills, and most lofty mountains incomparably beyond the island of Tenerife, all most beautiful in a thousand shapes, and all accessible, and full of trees of a thousand kinds, so lofty that they seem to reach the sky. And I am assured that they never lose their foliage; as may be imagined, since I saw them as green and as beautiful as they are in Spain during May. And some of them were in flower, some in fruit, some in another stage according to their kind. And the nightingale was singing, and other birds of a thousand sorts, in the month of November, there where I was going. There are palm-trees of six or eight species, wondrous to see for their beautiful variety; but so are the other trees, and fruits, and plants therein. There are wonderful pine-groves, and very large plains of verdure, and there is honey, and many kinds of birds, and many various fruits. In the earth there are many mines of metals; and there is a population of incalculable number. Española is a marvel; the mountains and hills, and plains, and fields, and the soil, so beautiful and rich for planting and sowing, for breeding cattle of all sorts, for building of towns and villages. There could be no believing, without seeing, such harbors as are here, as well as the many and great rivers, and excellent waters, most of which contain gold. In the trees and fruits and plants, there are great diversities from those of Juana. In this, there are many spiceries, and great mines of gold and other metals. The people of this island, and of all the others that I have found and seen, or not seen, all go naked, men and women, just as their mothers bring them forth;

although some women cover a single place with the leaf of a plant, or a cotton something which they make for that purpose. They have no iron or steel, nor any weapons; nor are they fit thereunto; not because they be not a well-formed people and of fair stature, but that they are most wondrously timorous. They have no other weapons than the stems of reeds in their seeding state, on the end of which they fix little sharpened stakes. Even these, they dare not use; for many times has it happened that I sent two or three men ashore to some village to parley, and countless numbers of them sallied forth, but as soon as they saw those approach, they fled away in such wise that even a father would not wait for his son. And this was not because any hurt had ever been done to any of them:—on the contrary, at every headland where I have gone and been able to hold speech with them, I gave them of everything which I had, as well cloth as many other things, without accepting aught therefore;—but such they are, incurably timid. It is true that since they have become more assured, and are losing that terror, they are artless and generous with what they have, to such a degree as no one would believe but him who had seen it. Of anything they have, if it be asked for, they never say no, but do rather invite the person to accept it, and show as much lovingness as though they would give their hearts. And whether it be a thing of value, or one of little worth, they are straightway content with whatsoever trifle of whatsoever kind may be given them in return for it. I forbade that anything so worthless as frag-ments of broken platters, and pieces of broken glass, and strap buckles, should be given them; although when they were able to get such things, they seemed to think they had the best jewel in the world, for it was the hap of a sailor to get, in exchange for a strap, gold to the weight of two and a half castellanos, and others much more for other things of far less value; while for new blancas they gave everything they had, even though it were [the worth of] two or three gold castel-lanos, or one or two arrobas of spun cotton. They took even pieces of broken barrel-hoops, and gave whatever they had, like senseless brutes; insomuch that it seemed to me bad. I forbade it, and I gave gratuitously a thousand useful things that I carried, in order that they may conceive affection, and furthermore may become Christians; for they are inclined to the love and service of their High-nesses and of all the Castilian nation, and they strive to combine in giving us things which they have in abundance, and of which we are in need. And they knew no sect, nor idolatry; save that they all believe that power and goodness are in the sky, and they believed very firmly that I, with these ships and crews, came from the sky; and in such opinion, they received me at every place where I landed, after they had lost their terror. And this comes not because they are ignorant: on the contrary, they are men of very subtle wit, who navigate all those seas, and who give a marvelously good account of everything, but because they never saw men wearing clothes nor the like of our ships. And as soon as I arrived in the Indies, in the first island that I found, I took some of them by force, to the intent that they should learn [our speech] and give me information of what there was in those parts. And so it was, that very soon they understood [us] and we them, what by speech or what by signs; and those [Indians] have been of much service. To this day I carry them [with me] who are still of the opinion that I come from Heaven [as appears] from much conversation which they have had with me. And they were the first to proclaim it wherever I arrived; and the others went running from house to house and to the neighboring villages, with loud cries of "Come! come to see the people from Heaven!" Then, as soon as their minds were reassured about us, every one came, men as well as women, so that there remained none behind, big or little; and they all brought something to eat and drink, which they gave with wondrous lovingness. They have in all the islands very many *canoas*, after the manner of rowing-galleys, some larger, some smaller; and a good many are larger than a galley of eighteen benches. They are not so wide, because they are made of a single log of timber, but a galley could not keep up with them in rowing, for their motion is a thing beyond belief. And with these, they navigate through all those islands, which are numberless, and ply their traffic. I have seen some of those *canoas* with seventy and eighty men in them, each one with his oar. In all those islands, I saw not much diversity in the looks of the people, nor in their manners and language; but they all understand each other, which is a thing of singular advantage for what I hope their Highnesses will decide upon for converting them to our holy faith, unto which they are well disposed. I have already told how I had gone a hundred and seven leagues, in a straight line from West to East, along the sea-coast of the Island of Juana; according to which itinerary, I can declare that that island is larger than England and Scotland combined; as, over and above those hundred and seven leagues, there remain for me, on the western side, two provinces whereto I did not go—one of which they call Avan, where the people are born with tails—which provinces cannot be less in length than fifty or sixty leagues, according to what may be understood from the Indians with me, who know all the islands. This other, Española, has a greater circumference than the whole of Spain from Col[ibre in Catal]unya, by the sea-coast, as far as Fuente Ravia in Biscay; since, along one of its four sides, I went for a hundred and eighty-eight great leagues in a straight line from west to east. This is [a land] to be desired,—and once seen, never to be relinquished—in which (although, indeed, I have taken possession of them all for their Highnesses, and all are more richly endowed than I have skill and power to say, and I hold them all in the name of their Highnesses who can dispose thereof as much and as completely as of the kingdoms of Castile) in this Española, in the place most suitable and best for its proximity to the gold mines, and for traffic with the mainland both on this side and with that over there belonging to the Great Can, where there will be great commerce and profit, I took possession of a large town which I named the city of Navidad. And I have made fortification there, and a fort (which by this time will have been completely finished) and I have left therein men enough for such a purpose, with arms and artillery, and provisions for more than a year, and a boat, and a [man who is] master of all seacraft for making others; and great friendship with the king of that land, to such a degree that he prided himself on calling and holding me as his brother. And even though his mind might change towards attacking those men, neither he nor his people know what arms are, and go naked. As I have already said, they are the most timorous creatures there are in the world, so that the men who remain there are alone sufficient to destroy all that land, and the island is without personal danger for them if they know how to behave themselves. It seems to me that in all those islands, the men are all content with a single wife; and to their chief or king they give as many as twenty. The women, it appears to me, do more work than the men. Nor have I been able to learn whether they held personal property, for it seemed to me that whatever one had, they all took share of, especially of eatable things. Down to the present, I have not found in those islands any monstrous men, as many expected, but on the contrary all the people are very comely; nor are they black like those in Guinea, but have flowing hair; and they are not begotten where there is an excessive violence of the rays of the sun. It is true that the sun is there very strong, although it is twenty-six degrees distant from the equinoctial line. In those islands, where there are lofty mountains, the cold was very keen there, this winter; but they endure it by being accustomed thereto, and by the help of the meats which they eat with many and inordinately hot spices. Thus I have not found, nor had any information of monsters, except of an island which is here the second in the approach to the Indies, which is inhabited by a people whom, in all the islands, they regard as very ferocious, who eat human flesh. These have many canoes with which they run through all the islands of India, and plunder and take as much as they can. They are no more ill-shapen than the others, but have the custom of wearing their hair long, like women; and they use bows and arrows of the same reed stems, with a point of wood at the top, for lack of iron which they have not. Among those other tribes who are excessively cowardly, these are ferocious; but I hold them as nothing more than the others. These are they who have to do with the women of Matinino—which is the first island that is encountered in the passage from Spain to the Indies—in which there are no men. Those women practise no female usages, but have bows and arrows of reed such as above mentioned; and they arm and cover themselves with plates of copper of which they have much. In another island, which they assure me is larger than Española, the people have no hair. In this there is incalculable gold; and concerning these and the rest I bring Indians with me as witnesses. And in conclusion, to speak only of what has been done in this voyage, which has been so hastily performed, their Highnesses may see that I shall give them as much gold as they may need, with very little aid which their Highnesses will give me; spices and cotton at once, as much as their Highnesses will order to be shipped, and as much as they shall order to be shipped of mastic,—which till now has never been found except in Greece, in the island of Xio, and the Seignory sells it for what it likes; and aloe-wood as much as they shall order to be shipped; and slaves as many as they shall order to be shipped,—and these shall be from idolators. And I believe that I have discovered rhubarb and cinnamon, and I shall find that the men whom I am leaving there will have discovered a thousand other things of value; as I made no delay at any point, so long as the wind gave me an opportunity of sailing, except only in the town of Navidad till I had left things safely arranged and well established. And in truth I should have done much more if the ships had served me as well as might reasonably have been expected. This is enough; and [thanks to] Eternal God our Lord who gives to all those who walk His way, victory over things which seem impossible; and this was signally one such, for although men have talked or written of those lands, it was all by conjecture, without confirmation from eyesight, amounting only to this much that the hearers for the most part listened and judged that there was more fable in it than anything actual, however trifling. Since thus our Redeemer has given to our most illustrious King and Queen, and to their famous kingdoms, this victory in so high a matter, Christendom should have rejoicing therein and make great festivals, and give solemn thanks to the Holy Trinity for the great exaltation they shall have by the conversion of so many peoples to our holy faith; and next for the temporal benefit which will bring hither refreshment and profit, not only to Spain, but to all Christians. This briefly, in accordance with the facts. Dated, on the caravel, off the Canary Islands, the 15 February of the year 1493.

At your command,

THE ADMIRAL.

HERNÁN CORTÉS

The heroism and brutality of conquest are the main themes in the life of Hernán Cortés (1485–1547). As he encountered in the Aztec Empire the untold riches that had eluded Christopher Columbus in the Caribbean, Cortés was forced to negotiate a formidable and sophisticated enemy that he barely understood. Yet he proved remarkably astute at harnessing local discontent with Aztec rule, establishing alliances with native peoples who also served as interpreters and spies. Despite the evasiveness of the Aztec ruler Moctezuma, Cortés and his men took him prisoner, and he died while in their custody. After many setbacks and the destruction of Tenochtitlán, chief city of the Aztecs, Cortés succeeded in his conquest—an astonishing achievement given the slender resources with which he faced the massive and well-organized Aztec Empire.

Cortés had disobeyed his superiors' explicit orders in pressing on to the land he would name New Spain. His letters to the Spanish ruler Charles V must therefore make the case that his spectacular achievements far outweighed his transgressions. Cortés foregrounds his heroic role as wise military leader, conveying the magnificence of the defeated empire while carefully justifying his own violent acts. "The manner of living among the people is very similar to that in Spain," he states, recognizing the sophistication of Aztec civilization even as he destroys it. Religion plays an important role in Cortés's effort to justify his military actions and the authority he had already claimed for himself in Mexico. Emphasizing his own efforts to convert the Aztecs to Christianity, he suggests to both Moctezuma and to Charles V that the Aztecs met their downfall because they refused to give up their devotion to their local gods. In Cortés's account, certain religious and sexual practices (human sacrifice and sodomy) of the Aztecs become mandates for the conquest. Finally, the Aztecs' belief that the Spanish conquerors were ancestral gods returning to claim their vassals is ably harnessed by Cortés: although he neither accepts nor denies the identification, it serves him as proof of Aztec idolatry and as sanction for the Spanish conquest of Mexico.

From The Second Letter[1]

On the following day I set out again and after half a mile entered upon a causeway which crosses the middle of the lake arriving finally at the great city of Tenochtitlán[2] which is situated at its center. This causeway was as broad as two lances and very stoutly made such that eight horsemen could ride along it abreast, and in these two leagues either on the one hand or the other we met with three cities all containing very fine buildings and towers, especially the houses of the chief men and the mosques and little temples in which they keep

1. Translated by J. Bayard Morris.
2. The capital of the Aztec Empire, site of present-day Mexico City.

their idols. In these towns there is quite a brisk trade in salt which they make from the water of the lake and what is cast up on the land that borders it; this they cook in a certain manner and make the salt into cakes which they sell to the inhabitants and neighboring tribes. I accordingly proceeded along this causeway and half a league from the city of Tenochtitlán itself, at the point where another causeway from the mainland joins it, I came upon an extremely powerful fort with two towers, surrounded by a six foot wall with a battlement running round the whole of the side abutting on the two causeways, and having two gates and no more for going in and out. Here nearly a thousand of the chief citizens came out to greet me, all dressed alike and, as their custom is, very richly; on coming to speak with me each performed a ceremony very common among them, to wit, placing his hand on the ground and then kissing it, so that for nearly an hour I stood while they performed this ceremony. Now quite close to the city there is a wooden bridge some ten paces broad, which cuts the causeway and under which the water can flow freely, for its level in the two parts of the lake is constantly changing: moreover it serves as a fortification to the city, for they can remove certain very long and heavy beams which form the bridge whenever they so desire; and there are many such bridges throughout the city as your Majesty will see from that which I shall presently relate.

When we had passed this bridge Moctezuma himself came out to meet us with some two hundred nobles, all barefoot and dressed in some kind of uniform also very rich, in fact more so than the others. They came forward in two long lines keeping close to the walls of the street, which is very broad and fine and so straight that one can see from one end of it to the other, though it is some two-thirds of a league in length and lined on both sides with very beautiful, large houses, both private dwellings and temples. Moctezuma himself was borne along in the middle of the street with two lords one on his right hand and one on his left. * * * All three were dressed in similar fashion except that Moctezuma wore shoes whereas the others were barefoot. The two lords bore him along each by an arm, and as he drew near I dismounted and advanced alone to embrace, but the two lords prevented me from touching him, and they themselves made me the same obeisance as did their comrades, kissing the earth. * * * After he had spoken to me all the other lords who were in the two long lines came up likewise in order one after the other, and then re-formed in line again. And while speaking to Moctezuma I took off a necklace of pearls which I was wearing and threw it round his neck; whereupon having proceeded some little way up the street a servant of his came back to me with two necklaces wrapped up in a napkin, made from the shells of sea snails, which are much prized by them; and from each necklace hung eight prawns fashioned very beautifully in gold some six inches in length. The messenger who brought them put them round my neck and we then continued up the street in the manner described until we came to a large and very handsome house which Moctezuma had prepared for our lodging. There he took me by the hand and led me to a large room opposite the patio by which we had entered, and seating me on a daïs very richly worked, for it was intended for royal use, he bade me await him there, and took his departure. After a short time, when all my company had found lodging, he returned with many various ornaments of gold, silver and featherwork, and some five or six thousand cotton clothes, richly dyed and embroidered in various ways, and having made me a present of them he seated himself on another low bench which was placed next to mine, and addressed me in this manner:

"Long time have we been informed by the writings of our ancestors that neither myself nor any of those who inhabit this land are natives of it, but rather strangers who have come to it from foreign parts. We likewise know that from those parts our nation was led by a certain lord (to whom all were subject), and who then went back to his native land, where he remained so long delaying his return that at his coming those whom he had left had married the women of the land and had many children by them and had built themselves cities in which they lived, so that they would in no wise return to their own land nor acknowledge him as lord; upon which he left them. And we have always believed that among his descendants one would surely come to subject this land and us as rightful vassals. Now seeing the regions from which you say you come, which is from where the sun rises, and the news you tell of this great king and ruler who sent you hither, we believe and hold it certain that he is our natural lord: especially in that you say he has long had knowledge of us. Wherefore be certain that we will obey you and hold you as lord in place of that great lord of whom you speak, in which service there shall be neither slackness nor deceit: and throughout all the land, that is to say all that I rule, you may command anything you desire, and it shall be obeyed and done, and all that we have is at your will and pleasure. And since you are in your own land and house, rejoice and take your leisure from the fatigues of your journey and the battles you have fought; for I am well informed of all those that you have been forced to engage in on your way here from Potonchan, as also that the natives of Cempoal and Tlascala have told you many evil things of me; but believe no more than what you see with your own eyes, and especially not words from the lips of those who are my enemies, who were formerly my vassals and on your coming rebelled against me and said these things in order to find favor with you: I am aware, moreover, that they have told you that the walls of my houses were of gold as was the matting on my floors and other household articles, even that I was a god and claimed to be so, and other like matters. As for the houses, you see that they are of wood, stones and earth." Upon this he lifted his clothes showing me his body, and said: "and you see that I am of flesh and blood like yourself and everyone else, mortal and tangible."

Grasping with his hands his arms and other parts of his body, he continued: "You see plainly how they have lied. True I have a few articles of gold which have remained to me from my forefathers, and all that I have is yours at any time that you may desire it. I am now going to my palace where I live. Here you will be provided with all things necessary for you and your men, and let nothing be done amiss seeing that you are in your own house and land."

I replied to all that he said, satisfying him in those things which seemed expedient, especially in having him believe that your Majesty was he whom they had long expected, and with that he bade farewell. On his departure we were very well regaled with great store of chickens, bread, fruit, and other necessities, particularly household ones. And in this wise I continued six days very well provided with all that was necessary and visited by many of the principal men of the city.

I have already related, most catholic Lord, how at the time when I departed from the town of Vera Cruz in search of this ruler Moctezuma, I left in it a hundred and fifty men to finish the fortress which I had already begun: like-wise how that I had left many neighboring towns and strongholds under the dominion of your royal Majesty, and the natives very peaceably disposed and loyal subjects of your Majesty. Being in the city of Cholula I received letters from the officer whom I left in Vera Cruz, by which I learnt that Qualpopoca, the native ruler of Almería, had sent in messengers to say that he desired to become a vassal of your Majesty, the reason for his delay being that enemy country lay between him and Vera Cruz and he had been chary of passing through it, but that if four Spaniards would return to his land, the enemies through whose country they would have to pass would refrain from molesting them and he would come forthwith to make his submission. The officer, think-ing the message to have been sent in good faith, for many others had done the same, sent four Spaniards as requested. But Qualpopoca having once received them into his house ordered them to be killed . . . and two of them thus died.

* * *

Having passed six days, then, in the great city of Tenochtitlán, invincible Prince, and having seen something of its marvels, though little in comparison with what there was to be seen and examined, I considered it essential both from my observation of the city and the rest of the land that its ruler should be in my power and no longer entirely free; to the end that he might in nowise change his will and intent to serve your Majesty, more especially as we Span-iards are somewhat intolerant and stiff-necked, and should he get across with us he would be powerful enough to do us great damage, even to blot out all memory of us in the land; and in the second place, could I once get him in my power all the other provinces subject to him would come more promptly to the knowledge and service of your Majesty, as indeed afterward happened. I decided to capture him and place him in the lodging where I was, which was extremely strong.

* * *

But before beginning to relate the wonders of this city and people, their rights and government, I should perhaps for a better understanding say something of the state of Mexico itself which contains this city and the others of which I have spoken, and is the principal seat of Moctezuma. The province is roughly circular in shape and entirely surrounded by very lofty and rocky mountains, the level part in the middle being some seventy leagues[3] in circumference and containing two lakes which occupy it almost entirely, for canoes travel over fifty leagues in making a circuit of them. One of the lakes is of fresh water, the other and larger one of salt. A narrow but very lofty range of mountains cuts across the valley and divides the lakes almost completely save for the western end where they are joined by a narrow strait no wider than a sling's throw which runs between the mountains. Commerce is carried on between the two lakes and the cities on their banks by means of canoes, so that land traffic is avoided. Moreover, since the salt lake rises and falls with the tide sea water pours from it at high tide into the fresh water lake with the rapidity of a mountain torrent, and likewise at low tide flows back from the fresh to the salt.

3. Cortés's estimations of distance are approximate; a Spanish league is about three to four miles.

The great city of Tenochtitlán is built in the midst of this salt lake, and it is two leagues from the heart of the city to any point on the mainland. Four causeways lead to it, all made by hand and some twelve feet wide. The city itself is as large as Seville or Córdova. The principal streets are very broad and straight, the majority of them being of beaten earth, but a few and at least half the smaller thoroughfares are waterways along which they pass in their canoes. Moreover, even the principal streets have openings at regular distances so that the water can freely pass from one to another, and these openings which are very broad are spanned by great bridges of huge beams, very stoutly put together, so firm indeed that over many of them ten horsemen can ride at once. Seeing that if the natives intended any treachery against us they would have every opportunity from the way in which the city is built, for by removing the bridges from the entrances and exits they could leave us to die of hunger with no possibility of getting to the mainland, I immediately set to work as soon as we entered the city on the building of four brigs, and in a short space of time had them finished, so that we could ship three hundred men and the horses to the mainland whenever we so desired.

The city has many open squares in which markets are continuously held and the general business of buying and selling proceeds. One square in particular is twice as big as that of Salamanca and completely surrounded by arcades where there are daily more than sixty thousand folk buying and selling. Every kind of merchandise such as may be met with in every land is for sale there, whether of food and victuals, or ornaments of gold and silver, or lead, brass, copper, tin, precious stones, bones, shells, snails and feathers; limestone for building is likewise sold there, stone both rough and polished, bricks burnt and unburnt, wood of all kinds and in all stages of preparation. There is a street of game where they sell all manner of birds that are to be found in their country, including hens, partridges, quails, wild duck, fly-catchers, widgeon, turtle doves, pigeons, little birds in round nests made of grass, parrots, owls, eagles, vulcans, sparrow-hawks and kestrels; and of some of these birds of prey they sell the skins complete with feathers, head, bill and claws. They also sell rabbits, hares, deer and small dogs which they breed especially for eating. There is a street of herb-sellers where there are all manner of roots and medicinal plants that are found in the land. There are houses as it were of apothecaries where they sell medicines made from these herbs, both for drinking and for use as ointments and salves. There are barbers' shops where you may have your hair washed and cut. There are other shops where you may obtain food and drink. There are street porters such as we have in Spain to carry packages. There is a great quantity of wood, charcoal, braziers made of clay and mats of all sorts, some for beds and others more finely woven for seats, still others for furnishing halls and private apartments. All kinds of vegetables may be found there, in particular onions, leeks, garlic, cresses, watercress, borage, sorrel, artichokes, and golden thistles. There are many different sorts of fruits including cherries and plums very similar to those found in Spain. They sell honey obtained from bees, as also the honeycomb and that obtained from maize plants which are as sweet as sugar canes; they also obtain honey from plants which are known both here and in other parts as *maguey*,[4] which is preferable to grape juice; from

4. Mexican aloe.

maguey in addition they make both sugar and a kind of wine, which are sold in their markets. All kinds of cotton thread in various colors may be bought in skeins, very much in the same way as in the great silk exchange of Granada, except that the quantities are far less. They have colors for painting of as good quality as any in Spain, and of as pure shades as may be found anywhere. There are leathers of deer both skinned and in their natural state, and either bleached or dyed in various colors. A great deal of chinaware is sold of very good quality and including earthen jars of all sizes for holding liquids, pitchers, pots, tiles and an infinite variety of earthenware all made of very special clay and almost all decorated and painted in some way. Maize is sold both as grain and in the form of bread and is vastly superior both in the size of the ear and in taste to that of all the other islands or the mainland. Pasties made from game and fish pies may be seen on sale, and there are large quantities of fresh and salt water fish both in their natural state and cooked ready for eating. Eggs from fowls, geese and all the other birds I have described may be had, and likewise omelettes ready made. There is nothing to be found in all the land which is not sold in these markets, for over and above what I have mentioned there are so many and such various other things that on account of their very number and the fact that I do not know their names, I cannot now detail them. Each kind of merchandise is sold in its own particular street and no other kind may be sold there: this rule is very well enforced. All is sold by number and measure, but up till now no weighing by balance has been observed. A very fine building in the great square serves as a kind of audience chamber where ten or a dozen persons are always seated, as judges, who deliberate on all cases arising in the market and pass sentence on evildoers. In the square itself there are officials who continually walk among the people inspecting goods exposed for sale and the measures by which they are sold, and on certain occasions I have seen them destroy measures which were false.

There are a very large number of mosques or dwelling places for their idols throughout the various districts of this great city, all fine buildings, in the chief of which their priests live continuously, so that in addition to the actual temples containing idols there are sumptuous lodgings. These pagan priests are all dressed in black and go habitually with their hair uncut; they do not even comb it from the day they enter the order to that on which they leave. Chief men's sons, both nobles and distinguished citizens, enter these orders at the age of six or seven and only leave when they are of an age to marry, and this occurs more frequently to the first-born who will inherit their fathers' estates than to others. They are denied all access to women, and no woman is ever allowed to enter one of the religious houses. Certain foods they abstain from and more so at certain periods of the year than at others. Among these temples there is one chief one in particular whose size and magnificence no human tongue could describe. For it is so big that within the lofty wall which entirely circles it one could set a town of fifteen thousand inhabitants.

Immediately inside this wall and throughout its entire length are some admirable buildings containing large halls and corridors where the priests who live in this temple are housed. There are forty towers at the least, all of stout construction and very lofty, the largest of which has fifty steps leading up to its base: this chief one is indeed higher than the great church of Seville. The workmanship both in wood and stone could not be bettered anywhere, for all the stonework within the actual temples where they keep their idols is cut into ornamental borders of flowers, birds, fishes and the like, or trelliswork, and the woodwork is likewise all in relief highly decorated with monsters of very various device. The towers all serve as burying places for their nobles, and the little temples which they contain are all dedicated to a different idol to whom they pay their devotions.

There are three large halls in the great mosque where the principal idols are to be found, all of immense size and height and richly decorated with sculptured figures both in wood and stone, and within these halls are other smaller temples branching off from them and entered by doors so small that no daylight ever reaches them. Certain of the priests but not all are permitted to enter, and within are the great heads and figures of idols, although as I have said there are also many outside. The greatest of these idols and those in which they placed most faith and trust I ordered to be dragged from their places and flung down the stairs, which done I had the temples which they occupy cleansed for they were full of the blood of human victims who had been sacrificed, and placed in them the image of Our Lady and other saints, all of which made no small impression upon Moctezuma and the inhabitants. They at first remonstrated with me, for should it be known, they said, by the people of the country they would rise against me, believing as they did that to these idols were due all temporal goods, and that should they allow them to be ill used they would be wroth against them and would give them nothing, denying them the fruits of the earth, and thus the people would die of starvation. I instructed them by my interpreters how mistaken they were in putting their trust in idols made by their own hands from unclean things, and that they must know that there was but one God, Lord of all, Who created the sky, the earth and all things, Who made both them and ourselves, Who was without beginning and immortal, Whom alone they had to adore and to believe in, and not in any created thing whatsoever: I told them moreover all things else that I knew of touching this matter in order to lead them from their idolatry and bring them to the knowledge of Our Lord: and all, especially Moctezuma, replied that they had already told me that they were not natives of this land but had come to it long time since, and that therefore they were well prepared to believe that they had erred somewhat from the true faith during the long time since they had left their native land, and I as more lately come would know more surely the things that it was right for them to hold and believe than they themselves: and that hence if I would instruct them they would do whatever I declared to be best. Upon this Moctezuma and many of the chief men of the city went with me to remove the idols, cleanse the chapels, and place images of the saints therein, and all with cheerful faces. I forbade them moreover to make human sacrifice to the idols as was their wont, because besides being an abomination in the sight of God it is prohibited by your Majesty's laws which declare that he who kills shall be killed. From this time henceforth they departed from it, and during the whole time that I was in the city not a single living soul was known to be killed and sacrificed.

* * *

Finally, to avoid prolixity in telling all the wonders of this city, I will simply say that the manner of living among the people is very similar to that in Spain, and considering that this is a barbarous nation shut off from a knowledge of the true God or communication with enlightened nations, one may well marvel at the orderliness and good government which is everywhere maintained.

* * *

On the day of Saint John after having heard mass I entered the city about midday, seeing few people about, and certain doors at the crossroads and turnings taken down, which appeared to be a bad sign, although I considered that it was done out of fright for what had already occurred and that my entrance would serve to calm them. I went straight to the fortress and the great temple next to it in which my men had taken up their quarters, and where they received us with such joy as if we had given them back their lives which they counted already lost: and so we remained there very much at ease throughout the rest of that day and night, thinking that all disturbance had settled down. Next day after hearing mass I despatched a messenger to Vera Cruz giving them the good news that I had entered the city to find the Christians alive and the city now quiet. But in half an hour he returned all covered with bruises and wounds, crying that the whole populace of the city was advancing in war dress and all the bridges were raised. And immediately behind him came a multitude of people from all parts so that the streets and house-roofs were black with natives; all of whom came on with the most frightful yells and shouts it is possible to imagine.

The stones from their slings came down on us within the fortress as if they were raining from the sky; the arrows and darts fell so thickly that the walls and courtyards were full of them and one could hardly move without treading on them. I made sallies in one or two parts and they fought against us with tremendous fury; one of my officers led two hundred men out by another door and before he could retire they had killed four of them and wounded both him and many others. I myself and many of my men were also wounded. We killed but few of them for they were waiting for us on the other side of the bridges, and did us much damage from the flat housetops with stones: some of these flat roofs we gained possession of and burnt the houses. But there were so many and so strongly fortified, being held by such numbers of natives and all so well provided with stones and other missiles, that we were not numerous enough to take all of them nor to hold what we had taken, for they could attack us at their pleasure.

The fight went on so fiercely in the fortress itself that they succeeded in setting fire to it in many parts, and actually burnt a large portion, without our being able to stop the flames until at last we broke down a stretch of wall and thus prevented it from spreading further. Indeed, had it not been for the strong guard I placed there of musketeers, crossbowmen and guns they would have entered under our eyes without our being able to stop them. We continued thus fighting all day until night was well come, though even then the yelling and commotion did not cease. During the night I ordered the doorways which had suffered by the fire to be repaired and all other places of the fortress which seemed to me weak. I decided upon the squads that were to defend the various parts of the fortress on the morrow and also the one that was to sally out with me to attack the Indians outside: I also ordered the wounded to be looked to, who numbered more than eighty.

As soon as it was day the enemy began to attack us with greater fury even than the day before: they came on in such numbers that the gunners had no need to take aim but simply poured their shot into the mass. Yet in spite of the damage done by the guns, for there were three arquebuses[5] without counting muskets and crossbows, they made so little impression that their effect could hardly be perceived, for wherever a shot carried away ten or a dozen men, the gap closed up with others so that it seemed as if no damage had been done. Upon this, leaving such suitable guard as I could in the fortress I sallied out and got possession of a few houses, killing many of those who were defending them: but their numbers were so great that although we had done still greater damage it would have had but slight effect. Moreover, whereas we had to continue fighting all the day they could fight for several hours and then give way to others, for their forces were amply sufficient. They again wounded as many as fifty to seventy Spaniards that day, although no one was killed, and so we fought on till nightfall when we had to retire worn out to the fortress.

Seeing then the great damage that our enemies did us, and that they could wound and kill us almost unhurt themselves, we spent the whole of that night and next day in making three wooden engines, each one of which would protect twenty men when they had got inside it: the engines were covered with boards to protect the men from the stones which were thrown from the house-tops; and those chosen to go inside were crossbowmen and musketeers together with others provided with pickaxes, hoes and iron bars to burrow under the houses and tear down the barricades which they had erected in the streets. All the while these wooden affairs were being made fighting did not cease for a moment, in such wise that as we prepared to make a sally[6] out of the fortress they attempted to force an entrance, and it was as much as we could do to resist them. Moctezuma, who was still a prisoner together with his son and many other nobles who had been taken on our first entering the city, requested to be taken out on to the flat roof of the fortress, where he would speak to the leaders of the people and make them stop fighting. I ordered him to be brought forth and as he mounted a breast-work that extended beyond the fortress, wishing to speak to the people who were fighting there, a stone from one of their slings struck him on the head so severely that he died three days later: when this happened I ordered two of the other Indian prisoners to take out his dead body on their shields to the people, and I know not what became of it; save only this that the fighting did not cease but rather increased in intensity every day.

The day that Moctezuma was wounded they called out to me from the place where he had been struck down saying that some of the native captains wished to speak to me; and thither I went and spent much time talking with them, begging them to cease fighting against me, for they had no reason to do so, and should consider that I had always treated them very well. They replied that I should depart and abandon their land when they would immediately stop fighting; but otherwise they were of a mind to kill us, or die themselves to a man. This they said, as it appeared, in order to persuade me to leave the fortress, when they would fall upon us at their pleasure between the bridges as we left

5. A heavy but portable gun of the 15th century.

6. A rush made by the defense on an attacking army.

the city. I replied that they were not to think that I besought them for peace because I feared them in any way, but because I was grieved at the damage I was doing them and should have to do them, and in order not to destroy so fine a city: to which they still replied that they would not cease fighting until I should leave the city.

* * *

They forced their way almost to the inner towers and succeeded in taking the temple, the chief tower of which was quickly filled with as many as five hundred Indians, all seemingly of high rank. Forthwith they proceeded to carry up large stores of bread, water and other food, together with plentiful supplies of stones. Most of them, moreover, were armed with long lances with heads of flint broader but no whit less sharp than our own; and from their position they did great damage to my men within the fortress for they were very close. The Spaniards two or three times attacked this tower and attempted to mount it, but as it was very tall and steep, having more than a hundred steps, and those above were well provided with stones and arms and moreover protected to a certain extent since we had been unable to take the neighboring roofs, they were forced to descend every time they attempted, and suffered many casualties; whereupon the natives in other parts of the city were so encouraged as to rush on the fortress without any signs of fear. Seeing that if our enemies were allowed to hold the tower they would not only do us much damage but would encourage the rest, I sallied out from the fortress, though disabled in the left hand from a wound received in the first day's fighting. Tying my shield on to my arm, however, I made for the tower followed by certain others and we surrounded it entirely at its base; this was done with no great difficulty, although not without danger, since my men had to deal with the enemy who were rushing up on all sides to support their comrades. I myself with a few behind me began to mount the staircase of the tower. And although they defended themselves very furiously, so much so that three or four Spaniards were knocked spinning downstairs, nevertheless with the help of God and our Gracious Mother, to whose honor the building had been dedicated and crowned with her statue, we finally got up the tower, and fought with them on top so fiercely that they were forced to leap down on to certain flat roofs, between which and the tower there was a gap of about a yard. There were about three or four of these all about eighteen feet below the top of the tower. Some fell right to the ground and were either broken by the fall or dispatched by the Spaniards who were below. Those who escaped on to the flat roofs continued to fight with extreme bravery so that it was more than three hours before we finished with them, and then there was not a man left alive. And your Majesty may well believe that had not God broken their ranks twenty of them might have stopped a thousand men from mounting the tower. Nevertheless those who died fought very valiantly. When it was all over I set fire to this tower and the other towers of the temple, having already abandoned them and removed all the images of the saints which we had placed there.

They lost somewhat of their pride on our taking this stronghold from them; so much so that on all sides their attack slackened, on which I returned to the housetop and spoke to the captains with whom I had already held speech and who were somewhat dismayed by what they had seen. On their approach I bade them note that they could not help themselves, that each day we should do them great hurt and kill many of them; already we were burning and destroying their city and would have to continue so to do until nothing of it or of them remained. To which they replied that they plainly perceived this but were determined to die to a man, if need be, to finish with us. And they bade me observe that the streets, squares and rooftops were all packed full of people, and that they had reckoned that if twenty-five thousand of them were to die for every one of us yet we should perish sooner, for we were few and they were many; and they gave me to know that all the bridges in the streets had been removed, as was indeed the case excepting a single one. We had therefore no way of escape except by water. Moreover, they knew well that we had but slight store of food and drinking water so that we could not hold out long without dying of hunger, even if they should not kill us themselves. And in truth they were perfectly right: for had we no other foes than hunger and general short-ness of provisions, we were like to die in a short time. Many other arguments were put forward each supporting his own position.

After nightfall I went out with a few Spaniards and taking them off their guard succeeded in capturing a whole street in which we burnt more than three hundred houses. So soon as the natives had rushed there I returned by another street where I likewise set fire to many houses, especially to certain ones with low flat roofs lying close to the fortress from which they had inflicted great dam-age upon us. What was done that night inspired them with great terror. * * *

THE FLORENTINE CODEX

Compiled over three decades (1547–79), the encyclopedic *Florentine Codex* represents the joint effort of the Franciscan missionary-ethnographer Bernardino de Sahagún and the knowledgeable Aztec elders and scribes who labored with him to produce a permanent record of Aztec culture. There had never been a document quite like this, and there have been few since. In view of its linguistic precision, its scope, and its objectivity, it can be considered the first work of modern anthropology. The name *Florentine Codex* is merely a latter-day scholar's designation for the most finished version of a corpus properly known as *General History of the Things of New Spain.* Several versions of the *History* have survived. But the manuscript now at the Laurentian Library in Florence, although it lacks some texts preserved in the so-called Madrid codices, is the copy that best deserves to be called complete.

Written in paired columns, with Nahuatl on the left and a Spanish paraphrase on the right, the Codex's twelve books begin with descriptions of the pre-conquest gods and ceremonies, followed by detailed expositions of native astronomy, botany, zoology, commerce, industry, medicine, time counting, prophecy, and other topics. The final book is devoted to a native history of the Spanish Conquest.

The excerpt reproduced here relates the initial Aztec encounter with the Spaniards: messengers relay the news of the strangers' extraordinary appearance and weapons to Moctezuma, as terror takes hold of the land. It shows **Cortés** taking advantage of native alliances and enmities, while the Indians also arguably take advantage of him, as when the Tlaxcallans use the Spaniards to destroy their enemies, the Cholulans, in an infa-mous massacre in a temple courtyard. The eventual meeting between Mocte-zuma and Cortés is described in all its magnificence, with the emperor receiv-ing the conqueror as the embodiment of the prophecy that gods would return from the east. The text recognizes the important role played by the female interpreter Malintzin (known as Doña Marina or La Malinche to the Span-iards), who advised and guided Cortés.

From The Florentine Codex[1]

BOOK 12, THE CONQUEST OF MEXICO

What the messengers who had gone to see the boats told Moctezuma.

And when this was done, they thereupon reported to Moctezuma; so they told him how they had gone marveling, and they showed him what [the Spaniards'] food was like.

And when he had so heard what the messengers reported, he was terrified, he was astounded. And much did he marvel at their food.

Especially did it cause him to faint away when he heard how the gun, at [the Spaniards'] command, discharged [the shot]; how it resounded as if it thun-dered when it went off. It indeed bereft one of strength; it shut off one's ears. And when it discharged, something like a round pebble came forth from within. Fire went showering forth; sparks went blazing forth. And its smoke smelled very foul; it had a fetid odor which verily wounded the head. And when [the shot] struck a mountain, it was as if it were destroyed, dissolved. And a tree was pulverized; it was as if it vanished; it was as if someone blew it away.

All iron was their war array. In iron they clothed themselves. With iron they covered their heads. Iron were their swords. Iron were their crossbows. Iron were their shields. Iron were their lances.

And those which bore them upon their backs, their deer, were as tall as roof terraces.

And their bodies were everywhere covered; only their faces appeared. They were very white; they had chalky faces; they had yellow hair, though the hair of some was black. Long were their beards; they also were yellow. They were yellow-bearded. [The Negroes' hair] was kinky, it was curly.

And their food was like fasting food—very large, white; not heavy like [tortil-las]; like maize stalks, good-tasting as if of maize stalk flour; a little sweet, a little honeyed. It was honeyed to eat; it was sweet to eat.

And their dogs were very large. They had ears folded over; great dragging jowls. They had fiery eyes—blazing eyes; they had yellow eyes—fiery yellow

1. Translated by Arthur J. O. Anderson and Charles E. Dibble.

eyes. They had thin flanks—flanks with ribs showing. They had gaunt stomachs. They were very tall. They were nervous; they went about panting, with tongues hanging. They were spotted like ocelots; they were varicolored.

And when Moctezuma so heard, he was much terrified. It was as if he fainted away. His heart saddened; his heart failed him.

* * *

How Moctezuma wept, and [how] the Mexicans wept, when they knew that the Spaniards were very powerful.

And Moctezuma loudly expressed his distress. He felt distress, he was terrified, he was astounded; he expressed his distress because of the city.

And indeed everyone was greatly terrified. There were terror, astonishment, expressions of distress, feelings of distress. There were consultations. There were formations of groups; there were assemblies of people. There was weeping— there was much weeping, there was weeping for others. There was only the hanging of heads, there was dejection. There were tearful greetings, there were tearful greetings given others. There was the encouragement of others; there was mutual encouragement. There was the smoothing of the hair; the hair of small boys was smoothed. Their fathers said: "Alas, O my beloved sons! How can what is about to come to pass have befallen you?" And their mothers said: "My beloved sons, how will you marvel at what is about to befall you?"

And it was told, declared, shown, announced, made known to Moctezuma, it was fixed in his heart, that a woman from among us people here brought them here; she interpreted for them. Her name was Marina.[2] Her home was Teticpac. There on the coast they had first come to take her.

And then at that time [this] began—that no more was there the placing of themselves at [the Spaniards'] feet. The emissaries, those who had interceded for them for everything, everywhere, that they might need, just went, turning their backs.

And at just this same time [the Spaniards] came enquiring about Moctezuma: "What sort [of man is he]? Is he perchance a youth? Is he perchance mature? Is he perchance already old? Is he perchance already advanced in years? Is he perchance an able old man? Is he perchance already an aged man? Is he perchance already white-headed?" And they answered the gods, the Spaniards: "He is a mature man, not fat but rather slender; thin—rather thin."

And when Moctezuma had thus heard that he was much enquired about, that he was much sought, [that] the gods wished to look upon his face, it was as if his heart was afflicted; he was afflicted. He would flee; he wished to flee; he needed to flee; he would take himself hence. He would hide himself; he needed to hide himself; he would hide himself—he wished to take refuge from the gods. And he was determining for himself in secret, he determined for himself in secret; he was imagining to himself, he imagined to himself; he was inventing, he invented; he thus was consulting within his heart, he consulted within his heart; he was saying to himself, he secretly said to himself that he would somewhere enter a cave. And of those whom he much unburdened himself to, confided in, held especially easy conversation with, some told what they knew; they said: "[Some] know where Mictlan is, and Tonatiuh ichan, and

2. The Spanish name for Malintzin.

Tlalocan, and Cincalco,[3] that one may be benefited. [Determine] in what place indeed is thy need."

And indeed he wished, he desired [to go] there to Cincalco. So was it well known; it was so rumored.

But this he could not do. He could not hide. He could not take refuge. No longer had he strength; no longer was there any use; no longer had he energy. No longer were verified, no longer could be accomplished the words of the soothsayers by which they had changed his mind, had misled him, had troubled him. Thus they were taking vengeance upon him when they were feigning to be wise in knowing [the way] there [to places] named.

[Moctezuma] only awaited [the Spaniards]; he made himself resolute; he put forth great effort; he quieted, he controlled his heart; he submitted himself entirely to whatsoever he was to see, at which he was to marvel.

* * *

How the Spaniards arrived in Tlaxcalla.

[The Tlaxcallans] went guiding them. They accompanied them there; they guided them there in order to go to leave them, to quarter them, in their palaces. They made very much of them. They gave them whatsoever they required; they attended to them. And then they gave them their maidens.

Then [the Spaniards] asked them: "Where is Mexico? What manner of place is it? Is it yet distant?"

[The Tlaxcallans] answered them: "It is by no means distant now; it may be reached in perhaps but three days. It is a very good place. And [the Mexicans] are very strong, very brave. They are conquerors; they go everywhere."

And the Tlaxcallans had formerly been at enmity with the Cholulans. There was regarding with rage, there was regarding with hatred; there was detesting. They were disgusted; they could have nothing to do with them. Wherefore they incited [the Spaniards] against them, so that they might harm them.

They said to them: "They are very wicked. They are our foes. The Cholulan is as strong as the Mexican. He is the Mexican's friend."

When the Spaniards had so heard, they then went to Cholula. The Tlaxcallans and the Cempoallans accompanied them. They went arrayed for war. When they went arriving, thereupon there was calling out, there was shouting [that] all the noblemen, the lords, those who led one, the brave warriors and the commoners should come. There was crowding into the temple courtyard. And when all had come together, then [the Spaniards and their allies] closed off each of the entrances—as many places as there was entrance.

There was thereupon the stabbing, the slaying, the beating of the people. The Cholulan had suspected nothing; neither with arrows nor with shields had he contended against the Spaniards. Just so were they treacherously slain, deceitfully slain, unknowingly slain. For in truth the Tlaxcallans had incited [the Spaniards] against them.[4]

And of all which had come to pass, they gave, told, related all the account to Moctezuma. And all the messengers who arrived here all departed; they just

3. Lands to the north, east, south, and west, respectively.
4. The Tlaxcallans, like the neighboring Cempoallans, were indigenous groups that allied with the Spaniards against the Aztecs, and used them in their own rivalries with other groups, in this case the Cholulans.

went fleeing. No longer did there remain listening anyone to hear the news which was to be heard. And indeed everyone among the commoners went about overwrought; often they rose in revolt. It was just as if the earth moved; just as if the earth rebelled; just as if all revolved before one's eyes. There was terror.

And when there had been death in Cholula,[5] then [the Spaniards] started forth in order already to come to Mexico. They came grouped, they came assembled, they came raising dust. Their iron lances, their halberds seemed to glisten, and their iron swords were wavy, like a water [course]. Their cuirasses, their helmets seemed to resound. And some came all in iron; they came turned into iron; they came gleaming. Hence they went causing great astonishment; hence they went causing great fear; hence they were regarded with fear; hence they were dreaded.

And their dogs came leading; they came preceding them. They kept coming at their head; they remained coming at their head. They came panting; their foam came dripping [from their mouths].

* * *

How Moctezuma sent emissaries to the Spaniards.

And Moctezuma thereupon sent [and] charged the noblemen, whom Tziuac-popocatzin led, and many others besides of his officials, to go to meet [Cortés] between Popocatepetl and Iztac tepetl, there in Quauhtechcac.[6] They gave them golden banners, precious feather streamers, and golden necklaces.

And when they had given them these, they appeared to smile; they were greatly contented, gladdened. As if they were monkeys they seized upon the gold. It was as if there their hearts were satisfied, brightened, calmed. For in truth they thirsted mightily for gold; they stuffed themselves with it; they starved for it; they lusted for it like pigs.

And they went about lifting on high the golden banners; they went moving them back and forth; they went taking them to themselves. It was as if they babbled. What they said was gibberish.

* * *

How Moctezuma went peacefully to meet the Spaniards.

And when this had happened, when [the Spaniards] had come to reach Xoloco,[7] when already matters were at this conclusion, had come to this point, thereupon Moctezuma arrayed himself, attired himself, in order to meet them, and also a number of great lords [and] princes, his ruling men, his noblemen [arrayed themselves]. Thereupon they went to meet them. In gourd supports they set out precious flowers—helianthus, talauma,[8] in the midst of which went standing popcorn flowers, yellow tobacco flowers, cacao blossoms, wreaths for the head, garlands of flowers. And they bore golden necklaces, necklaces with pendants, plaited neck bands.

---

5. The massacre at Cholula was one of the key events in the conquest of Mexico, and one of the most violent.
6. A nearby town. "Popocatepetl and Iztac tepetl": two peaks southeast of Tenochtitlán.

7. A locality on the outskirts of Tenochtitlán, to the south.
8. Mexican magnolia, a flower reserved for the nobility.

And already Moctezuma met them there in Uitzillan.[9] Thereupon he gave gifts to the commandant, the commander of soldiers; he gave him flowers, he bejeweled him with necklaces, he hung garlands about him, he covered him with flowers, he wreathed his head with flowers. Thereupon he had the golden necklaces laid before him—all the kinds of gifts of greeting, with which the meeting was concluded. On some he hung necklaces.

Then [Cortés] said to Moctezuma: "Is this not thou? Art thou not he? Art thou Moctezuma?"

Moctezuma replied: "Indeed yes; I am he."

Thereupon he arose; he arose to meet him face to face. He inclined his body deeply. He drew him close. He arose firmly.

Thus he besought him: he said to him: "O our lord, thou hast suffered fatigue, thou hast endured weariness. Thou hast come to arrive on earth. Thou hast come to govern thy city of Mexico; thou hast come to descend upon thy mat, upon thy seat, which for a moment I have watched for thee, which I have guarded for thee. For thy governors are departed—the rulers Itzcoatl, Moctezuma the Elder, Axayacatl, Tizoc, Auitzotl, who yet a very short time ago had come to stand guard for thee, who had come to govern the city of Mexico. Under their protection thy common folk came. Do they yet perchance know it in their absence? O that one of them might witness, might marvel at what to me now hath befallen, at what I see quite in the absence of our lords. I by no means merely dream, I do not merely see in a dream, I do not see in my sleep; I do not merely dream that I see thee, that I look into thy face. I have been afflicted for some time. I have gazed at the unknown place whence thou hast come—from among the clouds, from among the mists. And so this. The rulers departed maintaining that thou wouldst come to visit thy city, that thou wouldst come to descend upon thy mat, upon thy seat. And now it hath been fulfilled; thou hast come; thou hast endured fatigue, thou hast endured weariness. Peace be with thee. Rest thyself. Visit thy palace. Rest thy body. May peace be with our lords."

And when Moctezuma's address which he directed to the Marquis was ended, Marina then interpreted it, she translated it to him. And when the Marquis had heard Moctezuma's words, he spoke to Marina; he spoke to them in a barbarous tongue; he said in his barbarous tongue:

"Let Moctezuma put his heart at ease; let him not be frightened. We love him much. Now our hearts are indeed satisfied, for we know him, we hear him. For a long time we have wished to see him, to look upon his face. And this we have seen. Already we have come to his home in Mexico. At his leisure he will hear our words."

Thereupon [the Spaniards] grasped [Moctezuma] by the hand. Already they went leading him by it. They caressed him with their hands to make their love known to him.

And the Spaniards looked at him; they each looked at him thoroughly. They were continually active on their feet; they continually mounted, they continually dismounted in order to look at him.

And the rulers who had gone with him were, first, Cacamatzin, ruler of Texcoco; second, Tetlepanquetzatzin, ruler of Tlacopan; third, the *tlacochcalcatl*[1] Itzquauhtzin, ruler of Tlatilulco; fourth, Topantemoctzin, Moctezuma's

9. Cortés describes this as a large and beautiful building.

1. High general.

storekeeper in Tlatilulco. These went. And still other noblemen of Tenochtitlan were Atlixcatzin, the *tlacateccatl*; Tepeuatzin, the *tlacochcalcatl*; Quetzalaztatzin, the *tiçociauacatl*;[2] Totomotzin, Ecatenpatiltzin, Quappiatzin. When Moctezuma was made captive, they not only hid themselves, took refuge, [but] they abandoned him in anger.

How the Spaniards took Moctezuma with them when they went to enter the great palace, and what there happened.

And when they had gone to arrive in the palace, when they had gone to enter it, at once they firmly seized Moctezuma. They continually kept him closely under observation; they never let him from their sight. With him was Itzquauhtzin. But the others just came forth [unimpeded].

And when this had come to pass, then each of the guns shot off. As if in confusion there was going off to one side, there was scattering from one's sight, a jumping in all directions. It was as if one had lost one's breath; it was as if for the time there was stupefaction, as if one were affected by mushrooms, as if something unknown were shown one. Fear prevailed. It was as if everyone had swallowed his heart. Even before it had grown dark, there was terror, there was astonishment, there was apprehension, there was a stunning of the people.

And when it dawned, thereupon were proclaimed all the things which [the Spaniards] required: white tortillas, roasted turkey hens, eggs, fresh water, wood, firewood, charcoal, earthen bowls, polished vessels, water jars, large water pitchers, cooking vessels, all manner of clay articles. This had Moctezuma indeed commanded.

But when he summoned forth the noblemen, no longer did they obey him. They only grew angry. No longer did they come to him, no longer did they go to him. No longer was he heeded. But nevertheless he was not therefore neglected; he was given all that he required—food, drink, and water [and] fodder for the deer.

And when [the Spaniards] were well settled, they thereupon inquired of Moctezuma as to all the city's treasure—the devices, the shields. Much did they importune him; with great zeal they sought gold. And Moctezuma thereupon went leading the Spaniards. They went surrounding him, scattered about him; he went among them, he went in their lead; they went each holding him, each grasping him. And when they reached the storehouse, a place called Teocalco, thereupon were brought forth all the brilliant things; the quetzal feather head fan, the devices, the shields, the golden discs, the devils' necklaces, the golden nose crescents, the golden leg bands, the golden arm bands, the golden forehead bands.

Thereupon was detached the gold which was on the shields and which was on all the devices. And as all the gold was detached, at once they ignited, set fire to, applied fire to all the various precious things [which remained]. They all burned. And the gold the Spaniards formed into separate bars. And the green stone, as much as they saw to be good they took. But the rest of the green stone the Tlaxcallans just stole. And the Spaniards walked everywhere; they went everywhere taking to pieces the hiding places, storehouses, storage places. They took all, all that they saw which they saw to be good.

2. A great lord. "*Tlacateccatl*": general.

Selected Bibliographies

I. Ancient Mediterranean and Near Eastern Literature

On the early history of writing, an excellent starting point is Walter Ong, *Orality and Literacy: Technologizing of the Word* (1982), which teases out the cultural and psychological implications of the shift from an oral to a literate culture. Those with a particular interest in Near Eastern cultures can begin with James Pritchard's classic anthology of texts in translation, containing many illustrations: *The Ancient Near East: An Anthology of Texts and Pictures* (reissued 2010). A good illustrated survey of Greek and Roman culture by a number of different specialists is John Boardman, Jasper Griffin, and Oswyn Murray, *The Oxford History of the Classical World* (1986). Introductory texts that combine discussion of Greek, Roman, and Near Eastern cultures include *An Introduction to the Ancient World* (2008), by Lukas de Blois and R. J. van der Spek, and the less scholarly but lively *The History of the Ancient World: From the Earliest Accounts to the Fall of Rome*, by Susan Wise Bauer (2007). Reliable general introductions to Greek and Roman literature include Albin Lesky, *Greek Literature* (reissued 1996), and G. B. Conte, *Latin Literature: A History* (reissued 1999). For more information about the ancient world, including images of ancient art, architecture, and artifacts, as well as ancient Greek and Roman texts, a wonderful resource is Tufts University's website *Perseus* (www.perseus.tufts.edu).

Ancient Athenian Drama

A good introduction to the genre of Athenian tragedy, which includes discussions of all the extant plays and is particularly strong on social context, is Edith Hall, *Greek Tragedy: Suffering under the Sun* (2010). Marianne McDonald and J. Michael Walton, eds., *Cambridge Companion to Greek and Roman Theatre* (2007), includes essays on both tragedy and comedy, and also has some discussion of staging. Another fine collection of introductory essays, on tragedy, comedy, and satyr plays, is Ian C. Storey and Arlene Allan, *A Guide to Ancient Greek Drama* (2005). Further information on performance contexts, in the fifth century and also in modern revivals, can be found in David Wiles, *Mask and Performance in Greek Tragedy: From Ancient Festival to Modern Experimentation* (2007). Many pieces of visual evidence of Greek theater, including vase paintings, statues, and photographs of remaining theater sites, are collected in Richard Green and Eric Handley, *Images of the Greek Theater* (1995).

Ancient Egyptian Literature

The material and cultural background to ancient Egyptian civilization is presented in John Baines and Jaromir Malek, *Cultural Atlas of Ancient Egypt* (2000). Ian Shaw, ed., *The Oxford History of Ancient Egypt* (2000), is a useful treatment with broad cultural coverage for some periods. Marc van de Mieroop, *A History of Ancient Egypt* (2011), is the most up-to-date and reliable history. Alan K. Bowman, *Egypt after the Pharaohs, 332 BC–AD 642: From Alexander to the Arab Conquest* (1996), is an excellent presentation of the post-Pharaonic period. Two reliable surveys of Egyptian religion are Byron E. Shafer, ed., *Religion in Ancient Egypt: Gods, Myths, and Personal Practice* (1991), and Stephen Quirke, *Ancient Egyptian Religion* (1995). Donald B. Redford, ed., *The Oxford Encyclopedia of Ancient Egypt*, 3 vols. (2001), has articles on most major topics relating to ancient Egypt. The *UCLA Encyclopedia of Egyptology* (www.uee.ucla.edu) is an online resource that will gradually supersede print materials in its area.

There is no broad, general study of all periods of ancient Egyptian literature, but the works detailed in this paragraph have introductions setting the ancient works in context, in addition to prefatory remarks and notes on the individual texts. The largest and richest collection of translations is Miriam Lichtheim, *Ancient Egyptian Literature: A Book of Readings* (1973–80; reprinted with new forewords, 2006), 3 vols. A one-volume work that concentrates on fictional texts is William Kelly Simpson, ed., *The Literature of Ancient Egypt* (3rd ed., 2003). R. B. Parkinson, *Voices from Ancient Egypt* (1991), gives an excellent, more diverse selection from the Middle Kingdom. Parkinson has also provided an outstanding full translation of Middle Kingdom texts, The Tale of Sinuhe *and Other Ancient Egyptian Poems, 1940–1640* BC (1998), and his *Reading Ancient Egyptian Poetry: Among Other Histories* (2009) is a detailed study of the context and background of the principal Middle Kingdom tales and includes questions of performance and new translations of the oldest surviving manuscripts.

For those wishing to explore Egyptian literature in relation to other Near Eastern literatures, William W. Hallo and K. Lawson Younger, eds., *The Context of Scripture: Canonical Compositions, Monumental Inscriptions, and Archival Documents from the Biblical World* (2003), 3 vols., is a rich resource. Susan Walker and Peter Higgs, eds., *Cleopatra of Egypt: From History to Myth* (2001), places *Stela of Taimhotep* in the context of the art and religion of its period (184–87).

Catullus

A good general literary introduction is Charles Martin, *Catullus* (1992). An important study of Catullus's masculine, macho persona is David Wray, *Catullus and the Poetics of Roman Manhood* (2001). To know more about Clodia, on whom Lesbia may have been based, read Cicero's *Pro Caelio*, which is included in Michael Grant, trans., *Selected Political Speeches* (1977). Maria Wyke, *The Roman Mistress: Ancient and Modern Representations* (2002), mostly focuses on authors later than Catullus, but has important implications for interpretation of the Lesbia poems; Wyke reads the poet's girlfriend as a literary creation and stresses that she need not be based on any real person.

Creation and the Cosmos

A useful survey of ancient Near Eastern literature is J. M. Sasson, *Civilizations of the Ancient Near East* (1995), vol. 4, a large part of which is dedicated to the literatures of Egypt. In Markham J. Geller and Mineke Schipper, eds., *Imagining Creation* (2008), W. G. Lambert's article "Mesopotamian Creation Stories" (15–59) includes a general survey of Mesopotamian creation myths and a new translation of the *Enuma Elish*. Introductions to Sumerian and Akkadian literature can also be found in J. Black et al., *The Literature of Ancient Sumer* (2004), and B. R. Foster, *Before the Muses* (2005). Martin West's introduction to his prose translation of *Theogony* and *Works and Days* (1999), draws useful parallels between Hesiodic and Near Eastern myths. Jenny Strauss Clay, *Hesiod's Cosmos* (2003), is an intelligent literary account of Greek myth. Catherine Osborne, *Presocratic Philosophy: A Very Short Introduction* (2004), gives a good overview of Thales and the other pre-Socratics and points the reader to further secondary sources. Stuart Gillespie and Philip Hardie, eds., *The Cambridge Companion to Lucretius* (2007), contains essays by prominent Lucretius scholars on both literary and philosophical questions.

Euripides

A good collection of scholarly essays on Euripides is Judith Mossman, ed., *Euripides* (2003). For representations of "barbarians" in tragedy, including in *Medea*, see Edith Hall, *Inventing the Barbarian: Greek Self-Definition through Tragedy* (1989). Ruby Blondell, ed., *Women on the Edge: Four Plays* (1999), includes a translation of *Medea* and three other Euripides plays focused on women, as well as a useful introduction that discusses representations of gender in these plays. A good general introduction to Euripides, with brief discussions of all nineteen extant plays and a focus on their reception after ancient times is Michael Walton, *Euripides Our Contemporary* (2010). William Allan, *Euripides: Medea* (2002), surveys the most important literary themes of the play.

Gilgamesh

The most recent scholarly translations of *The Epic of Gilgamesh* are Stephanie Delany, *Myths from Mesopotamia: Creation, the Flood, Gilgamesh, and Others* (1989); Maureen Kovacs, *The Epic of Gilgamesh* (1989); Andrew George, *The Epic of Gilgamesh: The Babylonian Epic Poem and Other Texts in Akkadian and Sumerian* (1999) and *The Babylonian Gilgamesh Epic: Introduction, Critical Edition, and Cuneiform Texts* (2003); and Benjamin Foster, *The Epic of Gilgamesh* (2001). They contain ample commentary and important introductory articles that aid in the interpretation of the epic. The poet Stephen Mitchell's *Gilgamesh: A New English Version* (2004) is a smooth verse retelling of the epic. David Ferry, *Gilgamesh: A New Rendering into English Verse* (1992) is also recommended. For a study of the evolution of the story over time, see Geffrey Tigay, *The Evolution of the Gilgamesh Epic* (1982). Alexander Heidel shows the importance of *Gilgamesh* for biblical studies in *The Gilgamesh Epic and Old Testament Parallels* (1963). Rivkah Harris, *Gender and Aging in Mesopotamia: The Gilgamesh Epic and Other Ancient Literature* (2000), discusses the gender dynamic in the epic in the light of other ancient texts. John Maier, *Gilgamesh: A Reader* (1997), contains seminal articles on *Gilgamesh* and an extensive bibliography. David Damrosch, *The Buried Book: The Loss and Rediscovery of the Great Epic of Gilgamesh* (2007), tells the story of the colonial adventurers, scholars, and contemporary writers involved in the rediscovery of *Gilgamesh*.

For those wishing to discover the riches of Mesopotamian literature beyond *Gilgamesh*, Benjamin Foster's voluminous *Before the Muses: An Anthology of Akkadian Literature* (1993, 2005) and *From Distant Days: Myths, Tales, and Poetry of Ancient Mesopotamia* (1995) contain a wealth of material. Jack Sasson et al., *Civilizations of the Ancient Near East* (1995), vol. 4, is devoted to languages and literatures of the region. For vivid presentations of Mesopotamian civilization, see Jean Bottéro, *Mesopotamia: Writing, Reasoning, and the Gods* (1992); J. N. Postgate, *Early Mesopotamia: Society and Economy at the Dawn of History* (1992); and Benjamin Foster and Karen Polinger Foster, *Civilizations of Ancient Iraq* (2009).

The Hebrew Bible

Richard Elliott Friedman, *Who Wrote the Bible?* (1987), is a clear introduction to the idea that each of the first books of the Bible is composed from several narrative strands (the "documentary hypothesis"). The *Anchor Bible*, in multiple volumes, has useful introductions and notes to each book of the Bible, including historical information. More on the historicity of the Bible can be found in Ronald Hendel, *Remembering Abraham: Culture, History and Memory in Ancient Israel* (2004). Robert Alter and Frank Kermode, eds., *The Literary Guide to the Bible* (1987), has useful essays on approaching the stylistic and narrative structures of the Bible. James L. Crenshaw, *Defending God: Biblical Responses to the Problem of Evil* (2005), is an interesting attempt to grapple with the central moral problems raised by the Hebrew Bible.

Homer

The first chapter of Erich Auerbach's *Mimesis: The Representation of Reality in Western Literature* (1953), trans. Willard Trask, gives a stimulating account of how Homeric narrative technique might differ from that of the Hebrew Bible. Essential works on the relation of the Homeric poems to the Greek oral tradition include Albert Lord, *The Singer of Tales* (1960), and Milman Parry, *The Making of Homeric Verse* (1973). Jenny Strauss Clay, *The Wrath of Athena: Gods and Men in the Odyssey* (1983), provides a useful overview of the gods in the epic. Female characters, human and divine, are discussed in Beth Cohen, ed., *The Distaff Side: Representing the Female in Homer's Odyssey* (1995). A good collection of classic essays on the *Odyssey* is Seth Schein, ed., *Reading the Odyssey: Selected Interpretive Essays* (1996). Those interested in the history of Homeric Greece will find useful information in M. I. Finley, *Early Greece: The Bronze and Archaic Ages* (1981). James Tatum, *The Mourner's Song: War and Remembrance from the Iliad to Vietnam* (2003), is a moving account of the *Iliad* in the context of later representations of war. Sheila Murnaghan's introductory essays to Stanley Lombardo's translations of the *Odyssey* (2000) and the *Iliad* (1997) provide rich interpretations of important literary themes, such as disguise, hospitality, heroism, and death.

Ovid

Sarah Mack, *Ovid* (1988), is a good general introduction, with a long chapter on the *Metamorphoses*. Philip Hardie, *Ovid's Poetics of Illusion* (2002), is an important guide to Ovid's poetic technique; metapoetic aspects are also discussed in R. A. Smith, *Poetic Allusion and Poetic Embrace in Ovid and Virgil* (1997), which includes a fine reading of the Pygmalion episode. Garth Tissol, *The Face of Nature* (1997), provides a useful close reading of the poem, including discussion of Ovid's puns, and looks in particular at the Myrrha episode. Charles Martindale, *Ovid Renewed: Ovidian Influences on Literature and Art from the Middle Ages to the Twentieth Century* (1988), gives some idea of the importance of Ovid for later literature.

Sappho

A useful collection of scholarly essays is Ellen Greene, ed., *Reading Sappho: Contemporary Approaches* (1996). Marguerite Johnson, *Sappho* (2007), is a clear, short introduction to some important literary themes in the poet's work. Sappho is read alongside two male, contemporary lyric poets in A. P. Burnett, *Three Archaic Poets: Archilochus, Alcaeus, Sappho* (1983). The reception of Sappho is particularly interesting; Margaret Reynolds, ed., *The Sappho Companion* (2000), is a collection of translations, imitations, and adaptations of Sappho's poems by postclassical poets and writers.

Sophocles

A good literary introduction to Sophocles, which draws on psychoanalytic and anthropological ideas to emphasize pairs of concepts (such as civilization versus wildness) is Charles Segal, *Tragedy and Civilization: An Interpretation of Sophocles* (1981). Important essays by various scholars on *Oedipus the King*, including a classic article by E. R. Dodds on common student misinterpretations of the play, are collected in Michael O'Brien, ed., *Twentieth-Century Interpretations of* Oedipus Rex (1968). Mary Blundell, *Helping Friends and Harming Enemies* (1989), reads Sophocles through the maxim of Greek popular morality alluded to in its title; one chapter is devoted to *Antigone*. The city of Thebes in Greek tragedy in general, and in these plays in particular, is discussed by Froma Zeitlin in her essay in Zeitlin and John J. Winkler, eds.,

Nothing to Do with Dionysos? (1990). In two editions of the plays in Greek, scholars have written introductions that are accessible and useful even to the nonspecialist reader: R. D. Dawe on *Oedipus Tyrannos*, and Mark Griffith on *Antigone* (1982 and 1999 respectively). The political dimensions of the plays are particularly difficult for modern readers to grasp; an interesting attempt to apply the specifics of Athenian political history to the plays is Michael Vickers, *Sophocles and Alcibiades: Athenian Politics in Ancient Greek Literature* (2008). Both plays have been adapted in many different ways for the modern stage; one important example is Seamus Heaney's version of *Antigone*, set in Northern Ireland, *The Burial at Thebes* (2004).

Speech, Writing, Poetry

Walter Ong, *Orality and Literacy: The Technologizing of the Word* (2002), is essential reading. On the social contexts of scribal life in Mesopotamia, see L. E. Pearce, "The Scribes and Scholars of Ancient Mesopotamia," in J. M. Sasson et al., eds., *Civilizations of the Ancient Near East* (1995). More ancient Greek and Roman texts expressing ideas about speech, literacy, and literature can be found in D. Russell and M. Winterbottom, eds. and trans., *Ancient Literary Criticism* (1972). An important close reading of Aristotle's *Poetics* is S. Halliwell, *Aristotle's* Poetics (1986); see also his translation with commentary (1987). An introduction to the *Ars Poetica* is Bernard Frischer, *Shifting Paradigms: New Approaches to Horace's* Ars poetica (1991). Andrew Ford, *The Origins of Criticism* (2002), is an important account of how literary criticism came into being. A groundbreaking discussion of ancient modes of reading, including the importance of allegorical reading, is Peter Struck, *Birth of the Symbol* (2004). A. Richard Hunter, *Critical Moments in Classical Literature: Studies in the Ancient View of Literature and Its Uses* (2009), also offers insights into how the ancient Greeks and Romans imagined their literature.

Virgil

The structure of the whole poem is discussed in David O. Ross, *Virgil's Aeneid: A Reader's Guide* (2007). S. Harrison, ed., *Oxford Readings in Virgil's* Aeneid (1990) has useful articles on many aspects of the poem. A good literary introduction to the whole poem is Michael C. J. Putnam, *Virgil's Aeneid: Interpretation and Influence* (1995). Yasmin Syed, *Virgil's* Aeneid *and the Roman Self* (2005), gives an interesting account of how the poem participated in, and formed, Roman cultural values. A good short discussion of Virgilian allusion to earlier literature, why it works and why it matters, is R. O. A. M. Lyne, *Further Voices in Virgil's* Aeneid (1987). S. Quinn, ed., *Why Virgil?* (2000), includes literary essays and some examples of modern literature imitating or responding to Virgil. David Quint, *Epic and Empire* (1993), provides an important model for reading Virgil and later epics in terms of the losers and winners of history.

II. Ancient India

Burton Stein, *A History of India* (1998), and Stanley Wolpert, *A New History of India* (2008), offer good, complementary historical overviews of ancient India; Upinder Singh, *A History of Ancient and Early Medieval India* (2009), provides a more detailed, up-to-date account. Romila Thapar, *Cultural Pasts: Essays in Early Indian History* (2000), contains the best critical analyses of specific aspects of the ancient period. Thomas R. Trautmann, *The Aryan Debate* (2005), surveys recent controversies on India's prehistory, and includes a selection of important texts from the eighteenth century onward. Patrick Olivelle, *Upaniṣads* (1996), provides an excellent overview of Vedic religion, with translations of some canonical texts; Gavin Flood, *An Introduction to Hinduism* (1996), explains both early and later forms of the religion. Peter Harvey, *An Introduction to Buddhism* (1990), covers history, doctrine, and practice, with a focus on Mahayana Buddhism; Joseph M. Kitagawa and Mark D. Cummings, *Buddhism and Asian History* (1989), offers greater depth as well as a broader sweep, with specialist essays by many scholars.

The Bhagavad-gītā
Among the world's canonical religious texts, the *Bhagavad-gītā* is second only to the Bible in the number of times it has been translated, and the range of languages into which it has been rendered. Of the many modern translations available in English, Barbara Stoler Miller, *The* Bhagavad-gītā: *Krishna's Counsel in Time of War* (1986), is one of the most reliable and accessible. R. C. Zaehner, *The Bhagavad-gītā* (1969), includes the original Sanskrit text in English transcription, along with a literal rendering, a more polished version, and a commentary on each verse. The most useful Indian translation into English is S. Radhakrishnan's older *The Bhagavad-gītā*—1948 and later editions. For a discussion of Indian interpretations of the poem, see Robert Minor, *Modern Interpreters of the* Bhagavadgītā (1986); and for an account of its reception in the West, consult Eric Sharpe, *The Universal Gītā: Western Images of the* Bhagavad Gītā, *a Bicentennial Survey* (1985).

The Rāmāyaṇa of Vālmīki
The Rāmāyaṇa of Vālmīki: An Epic of Ancient India (1984–), translated, annotated, and introduced by various scholars led by Robert Goldman, is the best recent version in English; five volumes, representing books 1 through 5, have appeared so far. Swami Venkatesananda, *The Concise* Rāmāyaṇa (1988), the source of our text, is a condensed prose version, which emphasizes the religious message of Vālmīki's epic, interpreted from a conservative modern perspective. A particularly readable literary prose rendering of Kamban's twelfth-century Tamil version of the poem appears in R. K. Narayan, *The* Rāmāyaṇa (1972). Important scholarly essays on most aspects of "the story of Rāma" are collected in Paula Richman, *Many Rāmāyaṇas: The Diversity of a Narrative Tradition in South Asia* (1991).

III. Early Chinese Literature and Thought

Jacques Gernet, *A History of Chinese Civilization* (1982), is a commanding survey history of China. Patricia Ebrey, Anne Walthall, and James Palais, *Pre-Modern East Asia to 1800: A Cultural, Social and Political History* (2009), is an excellent shorter account of Chinese history in the broader context of East Asia. Michael Loewe and Edward Shaughnessy, eds., *The Cambridge History of Ancient China* (1999), is a comprehensive reference work for early Chinese history and culture. For a vivid account of thought and society in early imperial China, see Mark Lewis, *The Early Chinese Empires: Qin and Han* (2007).

For those wishing to explore more early Chinese texts, Stephen Owen, *Anthology of Chinese Literature, Beginnings to 1911* (1996), presents a rich selection of Chinese literature with ample introductory material and commentary. Cyril Birch, *Anthology of Chinese Literature* (1965), and Victor Mair, *The Columbia Anthology of Traditional Chinese Literature* (1994), which is organized by genre and not chronology, are also recommended. For early Chinese thought and religion, see William Theodore de Bary, *Sources of Chinese Tradition* (2nd ed. 1999), a two-volume anthology covering a broad variety of original texts in translation from the beginnings to the modern period.

For broader explorations of Chinese Masters Literature, see Benjamin Schwartz, *The World of Thought in Ancient China* (1985); A. C. Graham, *Disputers of the Tao: Philosophical Argument in Ancient China* (1989); Chad Hansen, *A Daoist Theory of Chinese Thought: A Philosophical Interpretation* (1992); and Wiebke Denecke, *The Dynamics of Masters Literature: Early Chinese Thought from Confucius to Han Feizi* (2010). To explore comparisons between Ancient Greece and China, see Lisa Raphals, *Knowing Words: Wisdom and Cunning in the Classical Traditions of China and Greece* (1992), and Steven Shankman and Stephen Durrant, *The Siren and the Sage: Knowledge and Wisdom in Ancient Greece and China* (2000).

Classic of Poetry

Other translations for comparison include Arthur Waley, *The Book of Songs* (1937), and Ezra Pound, *The Classic Anthology Defined by Confucius* (1954). Anecdotes by the Han Dynasty scholar Han Ying (fl. 150 B.C.E.) that show how poems from the *Classic of Poetry* were applied to concrete situations and moral questions can be found in James R. Hightower, *Han Shih Wai Chuan: Han Ying's Illustrations of the Didactic Application of the Classic of Songs* (1952). For stimulating studies of the anthology and its interpretation, see Steven Van Zoeren, *Poetry and Personality: Reading, Exegesis and Hermeneutics in Traditional China* (1991), and Haun Saussy, *The Problem of a Chinese Aesthetic* (1993). Pauline Yu, *The Reading of Imagery in the Chinese Poetic Tradition* (1987), is a compelling study of imagery in the *Classic of Poetry* and other Chinese texts.

Confucius

There are many translations of the *Analects*. The selections in this anthology are from Simon Leys's complete translation, *The Analects of Confucius* (1997). Arthur Waley's resonant translation of 1938 has recently been reprinted with an explanatory introduction by Sarah Allan (2000). D. C. Lau, *Analects* (1979), is a solid translation and contains a lucid introduction to Confucius and his ideas. Roger T. Ames and Henry Rosemont, *The Analects of Confucius: A Philosophical Translation* (1998), provides the classical Chinese text alongside an English version. Herbert Fingarette, *Confucius—The Secular as Sacred* (1972), remains one of the most persuasive accounts of the appeal of the *Analects*. David L. Hall and Roger T. Ames, *Thinking through Confucius* (1987), is an innovative reading of the *Analects* inspired by American pragmatic philosophy. John Makeham, *Transmitters and*

Creators: Chinese Commentators and Commentaries on the Analects (2003), gives insight into later commentators' understanding of the *Analects*. For a compelling account of early Confucianism, see Robert Eno, *The Confucian Creation of Heaven: Philosophy and the Defense of Ritual Mastery* (1990). Thomas A. Wilson, *On Sacred Grounds: Culture, Society, Politics, and the Formation of the Cult of Confucius* (2002), is a collection of articles about the religious dimensions of Confucianism and the Confucius cult. Lionel Jensen, *Manufacturing Confucianism: Chinese Traditions and Universal Civilization* (1997), discusses how the image of Confucianism created by European missionaries working in China during the sixteenth and seventeenth centuries has influenced modern understandings. John Makeham, *Lost Soul: "Confucianism" in Contemporary Chinese Academic Discourse* (2008), surveys the significance of Confucianism in today's intellectual debates.

Daodejing

Among the many translations of the *Daodejing*, D. C. Lau, *Tao Te Ching* (1963); Roger Ames and David L. Hall, *Daodejing—Making This Life Significant—A Philosophical Translation* (2003); and Red Pine, *Lao-tzu's Taoteching: With Selected Commentaries of the Past 2000 Years* (1997), are especially recommended. Robert G. Henricks, *Lao-Tzu's Tao Te Ching: A New Translation Based on the Recently Discovered Ma-wang-tui Texts* (1989) and *Lao Tzu's Tao Te Ching: A Translation of the Startling New Documents Found at Guodian* (2000), are based on excavated manuscripts of the *Daodejing* and are interesting to compare to the received text.

For a broader view on the *Daodejing* within the context of Early Chinese intellectual debates, see the chapters on the *Daodejing* in the books on Chinese Masters Literature indicated in the regional introduction to "Early Chinese Thought and Literature." Arthur Waley, *The Way and Its Power: A Study of the Tao Te Ching and Its Place in Chinese Thought* (1958), is still a classic study of the *Daodejing*. Michael LaFargue, *Tao and Method: A Reasoned Approach to the Tao Te Ching* (1994), is a compelling reconstruction of what the text might have meant to its earliest readers. For interpretations of one of the most influential

commentators of the *Daodejing*, see Rudolf Wagner, *The Craft of the Chinese Commentator: Wang Bi on the* Laozi (2000) and *A Chinese Reading of the* Daodejing: *Wang Bi's Commentary on the* Laozi *with Critical Text and Translation* (2003). For views on the *Daodejing* and its relation to the *Laozi* and Daoism, see Livia Kohn and Michael LaFargue, *Lao-tzu and the* Tao-te-ching (1998), and Mark Csikszentmihalyi and Philip J. Ivanhoe, *Religious and Philosophical Aspects of the* Laozi (1999).

Speech, Writing, and Poetry in Early China

Mark Lewis, *Writing and Authority* (1999), is an extensive exploration of the role of writing in early Chinese society. To explore Chinese writing and the languages of China, see John DeFrancis, *The Chinese Language: Fact and Fantasy* (1984); S. Robert Ramsey, *The Languages of China* (1987); Jerry Norman, *Chinese* (1988); and Xigui Qiu, *Chinese Writing* (2000). Steven van Zoeren, *Poetry and Personality: Reading, Exegesis and Hermeneutics in Traditional China* (1991), surveys the interpretation of the *Classic of Poetry*. For witty anecdotes about early Chinese persuaders and strategists, see J. I. Crump, *Legends of the Warring States: Persuasions, Romances, and Stories from Chan-kuo ts'e* (1999). Lisa Raphals, *Knowing Words: Wisdom and Cunning in the Classical Traditions of China and Greece* (1992), compares Chinese and Ancient Greek cultures of persuasion, as does Xing Lu, *Rhetoric in Ancient China, Fifth to Third Century B.C.E.: A Comparison with Classical Greek Rhetoric* (1998).

Zhuangzi

There are a number of good English translations, including Burton Watson, *The Complete Works of Chuang Tzu* (1968); A. C. Graham, *Chuang-tzu: The Inner Chapters* (1981); Sam Hamill and J. P. Seaton, *The Essential Chuang Tzu* (1998); and Brook Ziporyn, *Zhuangzi: The Essential Writings with Selections from Traditional Commentaries* (2009). For situating *Zhuangzi* in the context of early Chinese intellectual debates see the chapters on *Zhuangzi* in the books on Chinese Masters Literature indicated in the regional introduction to "Early Chinese thought and literature." *Zhuangzi* has inspired many interpretive essays and personal reflections, some of which can be found in Roger T. Ames, *Wandering at Ease in the* Zhuangzi (1998); Paul Kjellberg and Philip J. Ivanhoe, *Essays on Skepticism, Relativism and Ethics in the* Zhuangzi (1996); and Victor H. Mair, *Experimental Essays on Chuang-tzu* (1983).

IV. Circling the Mediterranean: Europe and the Islamic World

On the idea of the Mediterranean, see the classic 1949 study by Fernand Braudel, *The Mediterranean and the Mediterranean World in the Age of Philip II*, trans. Siân Reynolds (1972–1973; rpt., 1996), as well as the increasingly influential work of Peregrine Horden and Nicholas Purcell, *The Corrupting Sea: A Study of Mediterranean History* (2000). On late antiquity and the early Middle Ages, see Peter Brown, *The World of Late Antiquity: From Marcus Aurelius to Muhammad* (1989), and Averil Cameron, *The Mediterranean World in Late Antiquity*, A.D. 395–600 (1993).

For an overview of medieval Islamic history, see John Esposito, *Oxford History of Islam* (2000); Albert Hourani, *A History of the Arab Peoples* (2002); Seyyed Hossein Nasr, *Islam: Religion, History and Civilization* (2003). Information on almost any subject can be found in P. J. Bearman et al., eds., *Encyclopaedia of Islam*, 12 vols. (2nd ed., 1960–2005). A useful account of Persian poetics is offered by Julie Scott Meisami, *Medieval Persian Court Poetry* (1987).

For a survey of Europe's history from the fall of Rome to the beginnings of the Renaissance, three classic and still valuable studies are R. W. Southern, *The Making of the Middle Ages* (1953); Charles Homer Haskins, *The Renaissance of the Twelfth Century* (1927); and J. W. Huizinga, *The Autumn of the Middle Ages* (1919), trans. Rodney J. Payton and Ulrich Mammitzsch (1996). For information on almost any topic pertaining to medieval Europe, see *The Dictionary of the Middle Ages*, gen. ed. Joseph Strayer, 13 vols. (1989), with *Supplement 1*, ed. William Chester Jordan (2003).

Classic overviews of medieval European literary history and its place within the discipline of world literature can be found in Ernst Robert Curtius, *European Literature and the Latin Middle Ages* (1948), trans. Willard Trask (1953), and Erich Auerbach, *Mimesis: The Representation of Reality in Western Literature* (1946), trans. Willard Trask (1953; rpt., 2003). On the literary interactions of the Islamic world and medieval Europe, see María Rosa Menocal, *The Arabic Role in Medieval Literary History* (1987), and the reappraisal of Menocal's work in *A Sea of Languages: Literature and Culture in the Pre-modern Mediterranean*, ed. Suzanne Conklin Akbari and Karla Mallette (2011).

Augustine

A wonderful introduction and detailed notes can be found in the translation by Henry Chadwick (1991) and also the 3-volume edition and commentary by James J. O'Donnell (1992), both titled *Confessions*. O'Donnell's text is available online from the Stoa Consortium in cooperation with the Perseus Project at www.stoa.org/hippo/. For an account of Augustine's life by the foremost historian of early Christianity in the Roman Empire, see Peter Brown, *Augustine of Hippo: A Biography* (1967; 2nd ed., 2000). A provocative and engaging life of the bishop and saint appears in James J. O'Donnell, *Augustine: A New Biography* (2005). On Augustine's own reading practices and the reading communities that formed in his wake, see Brian Stock, *Augustine the Reader: Meditation, Self-Knowledge and the Ethics of Interpretation* (1996).

Beowulf

See the invaluable guide to the poem by Andy Orchard, *A Critical Companion to 'Beowulf'* (2003). A useful collection of essays is Robert Bjork and John Niles, eds., *A Beowulf Hand-*

book (1997). For a broad view of Anglo-Saxon literature and culture, see Malcolm Godden and Michael Lapidge, eds., *The Cambridge Companion to Old English Literature* (1991).

The Christian Bible

A full text with useful notes can be found in *The New Oxford Annotated Bible: New Revised Standard Version*, ed. Michael D. Coogan, Marc Z. Brettler, Carol Newsom, and Pheme Perkins (4th ed., 2010). For a brief overview of the historical background of the Bible and the diverse reading communities that have made it their own, see John Riches, *The Bible: A Very Short Introduction* (2000). The poetic and artistic qualities of scripture are on view in *The Literary Guide to the Bible*, ed. Robert Alter and Frank Kermode (1987). A more idiosyncratic reading of the Bible, rooted in a deep knowledge of history but with the profound inquisitiveness of a science fiction writer, appears in Isaac Asimov, *Asimov's Guide to the Bible: The Old and New Testaments* (1981; rpt., 1988). An intriguing interpretation of the Bible as graphic novel is Siku's *The Manga Bible: From Genesis to Revelation* (2008).

Geoffrey Chaucer

The most complete edition of Chaucer's poetry, with authoritative notes and commentary, is *The Riverside Chaucer*, ed. Larry D. Benson (3rd ed., 1987). An engaging portrait of Chaucer and his times can be found in Donald R. Howard, *Chaucer: His Life, His Works, His World* (1987). On the manuscript history of the *Canterbury Tales* in historical context, see Derek Pearsall, *The Canterbury Tales* (1985), and for an art-historical perspective focused on the poem's interlocking structure, see V. A. Kolve, *Chaucer and the Imagery of Narrative: The First Five Canterbury Tales* (1984). On Chaucer's role in the premodern invention of the subject, see Lee Patterson, *Chaucer and the Subject of History* (1991). On sexuality and gender, including influential readings of the Wife of Bath and the Pardoner, see Carolyn Dinshaw, *Chaucer's Sexual Poetics* (1989).

Dante Alighieri

Charles Singleton's annotated translation of Dante's *Divine Comedy*, with facing-page Italian text, is unsurpassed (6 vols., 1970–1975; rpt., 1990–1991). See also Singleton's ground-breaking and still stimulating short studies *Commedia: Elements of Structure* (1954) and *Journey to Beatrice* (1958). Short articles on a range of topics appear in *The Dante Encyclopedia*, gen. ed. Richard Lansing (2000), and a synoptic view of the encyclopedic quality of the *Comedy* is given in Giuseppe Mazzotta, *Dante's Vision and the Circle of Knowledge* (1993). The influence of Singleton remains strong in recent generations of Dante scholarship. Robert Pogue Harrison responds to Singleton's *Journey* in his *Body of Beatrice* (1988), while Teodolinda Barolini pushes back against the theologizing impulse of Singleton's work in *The Undivine Comedy: Detheologizing Dante* (1992). On Dante's relationship to his poetic forebears, from Virgil to the Occitan troubadours, see Teodolinda Barolini, *Dante's Poets: Textuality and Truth in the "Comedy"* (1984).

Abolqasem Ferdowsi

A complete version of the *Shahnameh* with an excellent introduction can be found in Abolqasem Ferdowsi, *Shahnameh: The Persian Book of Kings*, trans. Dick Davis (2006); for a fuller analysis of how the epic poem fits into Persian political history, see Davis, *Epic and Sedition: The Case of Ferdowsi's "Shahnameh"* (1992). A summary of Ferdowsi's life appears in Djalal Khaleghi-Motlagh, "Ferdowsi, Abu'l-Qasem: i. Life," in *Encyclopaedia Iranica*, ed. Ehsan Yarshater, vol. 9 (1999). For a broad overview of the place of Ferdowsi's epic in the traditions of oral poetry, see Olga Davidson, *Poet and Hero in the Persian Book of Kings* (1994), and Kumiko Yamamoto, *The Oral Background of Persian Epics: Storytelling and Poetry* (2003). On the interrelation of poetry and history writing in medieval Persia, viewed comparatively against medieval European literature, see Julie Scott Meisami, *Medieval Persian Court Poetry* (1987). See also Meisami, *Persian Historiography to the End of the Twelfth Century* (1999), especially her discussion of the *Shahnameh* itself; more generally, she provides a very useful framework for understanding the practice of writing history in medieval Persia.

Marie de France

A full collection of Marie's lais appears in Robert Hanning and Joan Ferrante, trans., *The Lais of Marie de France* (1978; reprint, 1995). A still useful overview of her work is Emanuel J. Mickel, Jr., *Marie de France* (1974); for an insightful reading of Marie within the framework of medieval gender categories, see R. Howard Bloch, *The Anonymous Marie de France* (2003).

The Qur'an

An extraordinarily readable translation of the Qur'an with good annotations is M. A. S. Abdel Haleem, *The Qur'an: A New Translation* (2004). See also his *Understanding the Qur'an: Themes and Style* (1999). A scholarly collection of essays appears in Jane Dammen McAuliffe, ed., *The Cambridge Companion to the Qur'an* (2009); for detailed information on specific topics, see also McAuliffe, ed., *The Encyclopaedia of the Qur'an*, 5 vols. (2001–2006). A useful overview is W. Montgomery Watt and Richard Bell, *Introduction to the Qur'an* (rev. ed., 2001). To get a sense of the rhythm and musicality of Qur'anic recitation, see Michael Sells, "Sound, Spirit, and Gender in the Qur'an" (1991), reprinted as an appendix to his *Approaching the Qur'an: The Early Revelations* (2nd ed., 2007), which includes a CD.

Song of Roland

An edition of the poem with facing-page English translation, plus a separate volume of commentary, can be found in Gerald J. Brault, *The Song of Roland: An Analytical Edition*, 2 vols. (1978). For a well-written introduction to the epic with emphasis on the role of narratology, see Eugene Vance, *Reading the Song of Roland* (1970). On the context of emergent French nationalism and feudal politics, see Peter Haidu, *The Subject of Violence: The "Song of Roland" and the Birth of the State* (1993). For a reading of the *Song of Roland* in terms of European views of Islam, with a special focus on gender, see Sharon Kinoshita, *Medieval Boundaries: Rethinking Difference in Old French Literature* (2006), especially chap. 4. On the interrelation of the genres of epic and romance, see the lively analysis of Sarah Kay, *The Chansons de geste in the Age of Romance* (1995).

The Thousand and One Nights

The best short overview of the history of the *Nights'* composition and translation is Dwight F. Reynolds, "A Thousand and One Nights: A History of the Text and Its Reception," in *Arabic Literature in the Post-classical Period*, ed. Roger Allen and D. S. Richards (2006). The novelist Robert Irwin has published a widely available (but not always consistently reliable) guide called *The Arabian Nights: A Companion* (1994; rpt., 2004). The two best collections on the *Nights* focus respectively on the formation of the work and on its reception. The first is *The Arabian Nights Reader*, ed. Ulrich Marzolph (2006), which includes many of the crucial, groundbreaking scholarly articles on the *Nights* by such authors as Muhsin Mahdi, the modern editor of the Arabic text, and Nabia Abbott, the discoverer of the ninth-century manuscript fragment that is the first evidence of the work; the second, which offers some very useful correctives to Irwin, is *The Arabian Nights in Historical Context: Between East and West*, ed. Saree Makdisi and Felicity Nussbaum (2008).

Fruitful literary analyses of the *Nights* include Sandra Naddaff, *Arabesque: Narrative Structure and the Aesthetics of Repetition in the 1001 Nights* (1991), which features a comparative and theoretical literary analysis of the Porter and the Three Ladies group of tales, and David Pinault, *Story-telling Techniques in the Arabian Nights* (1992), which offers an excellent comparative analysis of the Syria and Cairo compilations of the *Nights* and their historical contexts. Provocative food for thought on the *Nights'* role in modern fiction, especially in magical realism, can be found in Jorge Luis Borges, "The Translators of *The Thousand and One Nights*" (1934), trans. Esther Allen, in *Selected Non-fictions* (in paperback as *The Total Library: Non-fiction, 1922–86*), ed. Eliot Weinberger (1999), and in *The Translation Studies Reader*, ed. Lawrence Venuti (2nd ed., 2004). Finally, http://journalofthenights. blogspot.com/ provides an appropriately abundant and fertile overview of everything imaginable responding to the *Nights*—adaptations (music, opera, theatre, film, video games, toys, etc.), recently published studies and articles, new translations, political issues (especially censorship), et cetera.

V. India's Classical Age

Daniel H. H. Ingalls's *An Anthology of Sanskrit Court Poetry* (1965) still offers the best critical introduction to the classical lyric tradition; it also contains a complete, annotated translation of Vidyākara's eleventh-century *Subhāṣitaratnakośa*. *Theater of Memory: The Plays of Kālidāsa*, ed. Barbara Stoler Miller, (1984), and J. A. B.

van Buitenen's *Tales of Ancient India* (1959) provide similar overviews of the classical dramatic and narrative genres, with translations of representative texts. A. Berridale Keith's *A History of Sanskrit Literature* (1928) remains a useful source of information. Sheldon Pollock's *The Language of the Gods in the World of Men: Sanskrit, Culture, and Power in Premodern India* (2006), which is more advanced, is the most comprehensive, up-to-date, and stimulating account of the world of Sanskrit literature and culture. Edward Dimock et al., *The Literatures of India: An Introduction* (1974), and Sheldon Pollock, *Literary Cultures in History: Reconstructions from South Asia* (2003), include excellent discussions of the classical period in the context of other Indian literatures. General historical background is provided in Burton Stein, *A History of India* (1998), and Stanley Wolpert, *A New History of India* (8th ed., 2008); and a more detailed analysis appears in Upinder Singh, *A History of Ancient and Early Medieval India: From the Stone Age to the 12th Century* (2009).

Classical Sanskrit Lyric

Daniel H. H. Ingalls's *An Anthology of Sanskrit Court Poetry* (1965) provides the most balanced introduction to the classical Sanskrit lyric, containing a complete, annotated translation of Vidyākara's eleventh-century collection, *Subhāṣitaratnakośa*, and an excellent critical discussion. Barbara Stoler Miller's *Bhartṛhari: Poems* (1967) focuses on the multifaceted work of a single poet, translating 200 poems from his fifth-century *Satakatrayam*. J. Moussaieff Masson and W. S. Merwin's *Sanskrit Love Poetry* (1977), an unusual collaboration between an American scholar of Sanskrit and an American poet, provides a more panoramic view, offering memorable examples from the second to the sixteenth century. Edward Dimock et al., *The Literatures of India: An Introduction* (1974), contains stimulating analyses by several scholars on the aesthetic, cultural, and historical dimensions of Sanskrit poetry. Martha Ann Selby, *Grow Long, Blessed Night: Love Poems from Classical India* (2000), compares the Sanskrit lyric to the lyric in early Prakrit and classical Tamil by presenting poems on a common theme.

Somadeva

C. H. Tawney's *The Kathá Sarit Ságara: or, Ocean of the Streams of Story*, 2 vols. (1880–1884), provides a complete translation, later edited with additional notes by N. M. Penzer (10 vols., 1924–1928; rpt., 1968). A selection of the stories, together with a critical discussion, is included in J. A. B. van Buitenen, *Tales of Ancient India* (1959). A new partial rendering, with an updated, contemporary perspective on Somadeva's classic, appears in Sir James Mallinson, *The Ocean of the Rivers of Story*, 2 vols. (2007–2009).

VI. Medieval Chinese Literature

Two books by Mark Lewis, *China Between Empires: The Northern and Southern Dynasties* (2009) and *China's Cosmopolitan Empire: The Tang Dynasty* (2009), provide lively depictions of China's medieval world. Edward H. Schafer's *The Golden Peaches of Samarkand: A Study of T'ang Exotics* (1963) vividly evokes the multiethnic atmosphere of Tang culture.

For a general survey of medieval literature, see the relevant chapters in *The Cambridge History of Chinese Literature*, ed. Stephen Owen and Kang-i Sun Chang, 2 vols. (2010). On medieval poetry in particular, see Stephen Owen, *The Making of Early Chinese Classical Poetry* (2006); Kang-i Sun Chang, *Six Dynasties Poetry* (1986); and Kōjirō Yoshikawa, *An Introduction to Sung Poetry*, trans. Burton Watson (1967). Xiaofei Tian's *Beacon Fire and Shooting Star: The Literary Culture of the Liang (502–557)* (2008) is a compelling study of literary court culture in the South during the Period of Disunion.

Li Qingzhao

Chapter 4 of *The Red Brush: Writing Women of Imperial China* (2004) by Idema Wilt and Beata Grant is devoted to Li Qingzhao's life and work. Pinqing Hu gives a portrait of her life in *Li Ch'ing-chao* (1966). A discussion of her "Afterword" can be found in Stephen Owen's *Remembrances: The Experience of the Past in Classical Chinese Literature* (1986). For a discussion of the development of the song lyric, see Kang-i Sun Chang's *The Evolution of Chinese Tz'u Poetry: From Late T'ang to Northern Sung* (1980). For more translations of Li Qingzhao's song lyrics, see James Cryer's *Plum Blossom: Poems of Li Ch'ing-chao* (1984), Sam Hamill's *The Lotus Lovers: Poems and Songs* (by Li Ye and Li Qingzhao) (1985), and Kenneth Rexroth and Ling Chung's *Li Ch'ing-chao: Complete Poems* (1979).

Tang Poetry

Stephen Owen's *Traditional Chinese Poetry and Poetics: Omen of the World* (1985) provides a general introduction to Chinese poetry. For an anthology of guided readings in various genres of Chinese poetry, see Zongqi Cai's *How to Read Chinese Poetry: A Guided Anthology* (2008). To further explore the breadth and development of Tang poetry, see Stephen Owen's four magisterial studies: *The Poetry of the Early T'ang* (1977), *The Great Age of Chinese Poetry: The High T'ang* (1981), *The End of the Chinese 'Middle Ages': Essays in Mid-Tang Literary Culture* (1996), and *The Late Tang: Chinese Poetry of the Mid-Ninth Century (827–860)* (2006).

For translations of Wang Wei's poetry, see Pauline Yu's *The Poetry of Wang Wei: New Translations and Commentary* (1980), G. W. Robinson's *Poems of Wang Wei* (1973), and Vikram Seth's *Three Chinese Poets: Translations of Poems by Wang Wei, Li Bai, and Du Fu* (1992). For studies that explore Wang Wei's life, and his penchant for painting and Buddhism, see Marsha Wagner, *Wang Wei* (1981); Lewis Calvin and Dorothy Brush Walmsley, *Wang Wei, the Painter-Poet* (1968); and Jing-qing Yang, *The Chan Interpretations of Wang Wei's Poetry: A Critical Review* (2007).

For translations of Li Bo's poetry, see Vikram Seth's *Three Chinese Poets: Translations of Poems by Wang Wei, Li Bai, and Du Fu* (1992). Paul Kroll's *Studies in Medieval Taoism and the Poetry of Li Po* (2009) and Paula Varsano's *Tracking the Banished Immortal: The Poetry of Li Bo and Its Critical Reception* (2003)

are compelling studies of the poetry; Arthur Waley's *The Poetry and Career of Li Po, 701–762 A.D.* (1950) is a biography.

Among translations of Du Fu, David Hawkes's *A Little Primer of Tu Fu* (1967), an introductory bilingual edition of a few of the poems, is particularly recommended. See also Burton Watson's *The Selected Poems of Du Fu* (2002). For studies of Du Fu's life and legacy see David McCraw's *Du Fu's Laments from the South* (1992) and Eva Shan Chou's *Reconsidering Tu Fu: Literary Greatness and Cultural Context* (1995).

For Bo Juyi's poetry, see Howard S. Levy's *Translations from Po Chü-i's Collected Works* (1978), David Hinton's *The Selected Poems of Po Chü-i* (1999), and Burton Watson's *Po Chü-i: Selected Poems* (2000). Arthur Waley's *The Life and Times of Po Chü-i* (1949) is a vivid evocation of Bo Juyi's life in his literary context.

Tao Qian

A. R. Davis's *T'ao Yüan-ming, A.D. 365–427, His Works and their Meaning*, 2 vols. (1984), and James Robert Hightower's *The Poetry of T'ao Ch'ien* (1970) provide complete translations of Tao Qian's poetry. Because his works circulated only in manuscript form for centuries before the advent of print, there are many different versions of his poems; Xiaofei Tian's *Tao Yuanming & Manuscript Culture: The Record of a Dusty Table* (2005) is a compelling study of how early editors adapted Tao Qian's pieces, based on their own image of him. Robert Ashmore's *The Transport of Reading: Text and Understanding in the World of Tao Qian (365–427)* (2010) discusses cultures of reading and interpretation in Tao Qian's work and time. Wendy Swartz's *Reading Tao Yuanming: Shifting Paradigms of Historical Reception (427–1900)* (2008) traces the changing images of Tao Qian from his death up until the twentieth century.

Yuan Zhen

You can read more Tang tales in Yang Xianyi and Gladys Yang's *Tang Dynasty Stories* (1986) and William H. Nienhauser Jr.'s *Tang Dynasty Tales: A Guided Reader* (2010). Stephen Owen's *The End of the Chinese 'Middle Ages': Essays in Mid-Tang Literary Culture* (1996) contains an excellent chapter on "The Story of Yingying." For a translation of the *Romance of the Western Chamber*, see Stephen H. West and Wilt L. Idema, *The Story of the Western Wing* (1995).

VII. Japan's Classical Age

To further explore early and medieval Japanese history see Conrad Schirokauer, David Lurie, and Suzanne Gay's *A Brief History of Japanese Civilization* (2nd ed., 2006) For a shorter treatment of Japanese history in the context of East Asia, Patricia Bückley Ebrey, Anne Walthall, and James B. Palais, *East Asia: A Cultural, Social, and Political History* (2nd ed., 2009), is recommended.

Traditional Japanese Literature: An Anthology, Beginnings to 1600, ed. Haruo Shirane (2007), and Donald Keene's *Anthology of Japanese Literature: From the Earliest Era to the Mid-Nineteenth Century* (1955) are great treasure troves of original early and medieval Japanese texts in English translation; see also *Traditional Japanese Poetry: An Anthology*, trans. Steven D. Carter (1991), and *Classical Japanese Prose: An Anthology*, ed. Helen Craig McCullough (1990). Lovers of travel literature will appreciate Donald Keene's *Travelers of a Hundred Ages: The Japanese As Revealed Through 1,000 Years of Diaries* (rev. ed., 1999). Keene presents a sweeping history of premodern Japanese literature in *Seeds in the Heart: Japanese Literature from Earliest Times to the Late Sixteenth Century* (1993).

Earl Miner, Hiroko Odagiri, and Robert E. Morrell's *The Princeton Companion to Classical Japanese Literature* (1985) is a reliable reference work to the world of Japanese literature. Groundbreaking studies of the interplay between Chinese and Japanese cultural traditions in Japanese literature include David Pollack, *The Fracture of Meaning: Japan's Synthesis of China from the Eighth Through the Eighteenth Centuries* (1986); Thomas LaMarre, *Uncovering Heian Japan: An Archaeology of Sensation and Inscription* (2000); and Atsuko Sakaki, *Obsessions with the Sino-Japanese Polarity in Japanese Literature* (2005). Tomiko Yoda's *Gender and National Literature: Heian Texts in the Constructions of Japanese Modernity* (2004) is a compelling study of how Heian texts have influenced modern Japanese identity and self-understanding.

The Man'yōshū

Good partial translations include Nippon Gakujutsu Shinkōkai's *The Manyōshū*, ed. Donald Keene (1965), Ian Hideo Levy's *The Ten Thousand Leaves* (1981), and Edwin Cranston's evocative translations in *A Waka Anthology*, vol. 1, *The Gem-Glistening Cup* (1993). Levy has also produced a detailed study of one poet, *Hitomaro and the Birth of Japanese Lyricism* (1984). Robert H. Brower and Earl Miner's *Japanese Court Poetry* (1961) contains a general study of the anthology, and Gary L. Ebersole's *Ritual Poetry and the Politics of Death in Early Japan* (1989) explores the religious and historical context of the anthology's poems on death and mourning.

Murasaki Shikibu

This anthology uses a new translation by Dennis Washburn; the three previous English translations of *The Tale of Genji* all have their partisans. The first English translation was published by Arthur Waley in installments between 1925 and 1933. Edward G. Seidensticker's *The Tale of Genji* (1976) is a beautiful translation, more faithful than Waley's. The translation by Royall Tyler (2001) is sparkling.

For a glimpse into the life of the author, see *Murasaki Shikibu Her Diary and Poetic Memoirs*, trans. Richard Bowring (1982). Ivan Morris, *The World of the Shining Prince: Court Life in Ancient Japan*, with a new introduction by Barbara Ruch (1964; rpt., 1994), is a colorful account of the world that Murasaki and her characters inhabit.

The best brief introduction to the tale is Richard Bowring, *Murasaki Shikibu: "The Tale of Genji"* (1988). Two excellent longer studies are Norma Field, *The Splendor of Longing in the "Tale of Genji"* (1987), and Haruo Shirane, *The Bridge of Dreams: A Poetics of "The Tale of Genji"* (1987). *Envisioning "The Tale of Genji": Media, Gender, and Cultural Production* (2008), a collection of articles edited by Shirane, gives fascinating glimpses of how *The Tale of Genji* influenced later literature, art, and popular culture.

Poetry of the Heian Court

Robert Borgen's *Sugawara no Michizane and the Early Heian Court* (1986) is a detailed biography of Michizane and contains many translations from his poetry. For further translations of his poetry and of the Chinese-style imperial anthologies of the ninth century, see Judith N. Rabinovitch and Timothy R. Bradstock's *Dance of the Butterflies: Chinese Poetry from the Japanese Court Tradition* (2005) and Burton Watson's *Japanese Literature in Chinese*, 2 vols. (1975–1976).

Two complete translations of *The Kokinshū* are available in English: Helen Craig McCullough's *Kokin Wakashū: The First Imperial Anthology of Japanese Poetry*, with *"Tosa Nikki"* and *"Shinsen Waka"* (1985) and Laura Rasplica Rodd and Mary Catherine Henkenius's *Kokinshū: A Collection of Poems Ancient and Modern* (1984); Edwin A. Cranston's *A Waka Anthology*, vol. 2, *Grasses of Remembrance* (2006), contains selections from *The Kokinshū* with ample commentary. *Brocade by Night: "Kokin Wakashū" and the Court Style in Japanese Classical Poetry* (1985), McCullough's companion volume to her translation of the anthology, is a detailed study of the Chinese influences on Kokinshū poetry. On the interplay of poetry and politics at the Heian court, see Gustav Heldt's study *The Pursuit of Harmony: Poetry and Power in Early Heian Japan* (2008). Robert H. Brower and Earl Miner, *Japanese Court Poetry* (1961), is still the standard account of the development of the *waka* tradition in premodern Japan.

Ki No Tsurayuki

Complete translations of *Tosa Diary* include Helen Craig McCullough's *Kokin Wakashū: The First Imperial Anthology of Japanese Poetry, with "Tosa Nikki" and "Shinsen Waka"* (1985) and Earl Miner's *The Tosa Diary*, in his *Japanese Poetic Diaries* (1969).

McCullough's *Brocade by Night: "Kokin Wakashū" and the Court Style in Japanese Classical Poetry* (1985) focuses on *The Kokinshū* but also outlines the broader context of Tsurayuki's literary activities, and includes a discussion of *Tosa Diary*. Lynne Miyake, "The *Tosa Diary*: In the Interstices of Gender and Criticism," in *The Woman's Hand: Gender and Theory in Japanese Women's Writing*, ed. Paul Gordon Schalow and Janet A. Walker (1996), discusses Tsurayuki's diary in the context of gender.

Zeami Motokiyo

A basic introduction to the dramatic genres of Japan and important pieces of the repertoire can be found in Karen Brazell and James T. Araki's *Traditional Japanese Theater: An Anthology of Plays* (1998). A valuable introduction to Noh is Donald Keene's *Nō: The Classical Theatre of Japan* (1973). Zeami's theories of drama are available in English in J. Thomas Rimer and Yamazaki Masakazu's *On the Art of Nō Drama: The Major Treatises of Zeami* (1894); they are discussed by Makoto Ueda in "Zeami and the Art of the Nō Drama: Imitation, Yugen and Sublimity," in Nancy G. Hulme, ed., *Japanese Aesthetics and Culture: A Reader* (1998) and Benito Ortolani and Samuel L. Leiter, eds., *Zeami and the Nō Theatre in the World* (1998). Two excellent technical works are P. G. O'Neill's *Early Nō Drama* (1974) and Thomas Blenman Hare's *Zeami's Style: The Noh Plays of Zeami Motokiyo* (1986). Other collections of translations include Arthur Waley's *The Nō Plays of Japan* (1921); Donald Keene's *Twenty Plays of the Nō Theatre* (1970); Nippon Gakujutsu Shinkōkai, *The Noh Drama* (1973); Kenneth Yasuda's *Masterworks of the Nō Theatre* (1989); and Royall Tyler's *Japanese Nō Dramas* (1992).

VIII. Encounters with Islam

The most comprehensive reference for the Ottoman Empire for years to come will be *The Cambridge History of Turkey*, which includes contributions on all aspects of land, state, society, and culture: *Volume 1, Byzantium to Turkey, 1071–1453*, ed. by Kate Fleet, appeared in 2009; *Volume 3, The Later Ottoman Empire, 1603–1839*, ed. by Suraiya Faroqhi, in 2006. *Volume 2, The Ottoman Empire as a World Power, 1453–1603*, ed. by Faroqhi and Fleet, is due to appear in 2011. Faroqhi's *Subjects of the Sultans* (2000) is a very readable overview of Ottoman cultural history. Fleet and Ebru Boyar give a vivid picture of life in Istanbul, the center of the Ottoman universe: *A Social History of Ottoman Istanbul* (2010). The most original, and most engaging, work on Ottoman literature in society is Walter Andrews and Mehmed Kalpakli, *The Age of Beloveds: Love and the Beloved in Early-Modern Ottoman and European Culture and Society* (2005).

David Conrad's *Empires of Medieval West Africa* (rev. ed. 2010) provides a broad introduction to West Africa, as does Nehemia Levtzion's *Ancient Ghana and Mali* (1980). Levtzion and J. F. P. Hopkins's *Corpus of Early Arabic Sources for West African History* (1981) is an excellent source book for the study of the region. For the history of Islam in West Africa, consult Levtzion and R. L. Pouwels's *The History of Islam in Africa* (2000) and Levtzion and Jay Spaulding's *Medieval West Africa: Views from Arab Scholars and Merchants* (2003).

Stanley Wolpert's *A New History of India* (2008) places Islam's multifaceted impact on South Asia in its historical and political contexts; Ira M. Lapidus's *A History of Islamic Societies* (1988) analyzes that impact in a global and comparative perspective. Richard M. Eaton's *The Rise of Islam and the Bengal Frontier, 1204– 1760* (1993), though more specialized, provides an excellent historical, social, and political account of the arrival and spread of Islam in India. On many specific aspects of Muslim India, see David Waines's *An Introduction to Islam* (1995); and on the transformation of Indian literature under Muslim influence, see Vinay Dharwadker's *Kabir: The Weaver's Songs* (2003). Excellent essays by many scholars on the Delhi Sultanate and the Mughal Empire are included in Irfan Habib's *Medieval India* (1992) and *Akbar and His India* (1997); and in Muzaffar Alam and Sanjay Subrahmanyam's *The Mughal State, 1526–1750* (1998).

Evliya Çelebi

No complete English translation of the *Book of Travels* has been undertaken; a rich array of the most colorful passages is found in *An Ottoman Traveller. Selections from the* Book of Travels *of Evliya Çelebi*, trans. and ed. by Robert Dankoff & Sooyong Kim (2010). Dankoff's *Evliya Çelebi—An Ottoman Mentality* 2nd ed. (2006) is the best introduction to the person and work of Evliya. Dankoff's *The Intimate Life of an Ottoman Statesman, Melek Ahmed Pasha (1588–1662): As Portrayed In Evliya Çelebi's Book of Travels (Seyahat-name)* (1991) offers further details of the lives of Evliya and his most important patron. Both works translate extensively from the *Book of Travels*. The background of the Vienna episode is studied in Karl Teply's *Türkische Sagen und Legenden um die Kaiserstadt Wien* (1980).

Indian Poetry after Islam

A. K. Ramanujan's *Speaking of Siva* (1973) offers the best English translations of the Virasaiva poets in Kannada, including Basavanna and Mahadeviyakka, as well as an excellent introduction to the *bhakti* movement, especially in southern India. The most reliable and

poetic translations of a representative selection of Kabir's poetry, accompanied by an extensive commentary on the Hindi and northern Indian *bhakti* traditions, are available in Vinay Dharwadker's *Kabir: The Weaver's Songs* (2003). John Stratton Hawley and Mark Juergensmeyer's *Songs of the Saints of India* (1988) provides basic selections of poems and introductions to several northern Indian *bhakti* figures, including Kabir and Mirabai; Hawley's *Three Bhakti Voices: Mirabai, Surdas, and Kabir in Their Time and Ours* (2005) contains more recent translations and scholarly accounts of the poets. Vinay Dharwadker's "Poems of Tukaram," in Donald Lopez's *Religions of India in Practice* (1996) offers a handy overview of the poet's life and work. Christian Noetzke, *Religion and Public Memory: A Cultural History of Saint Namdev in India* (2008), provides a wider perspective on *bhakti* in Marathi literature and culture.

Sunjata

Musical performances involving the singing of stories and praises about Sunjata are called *Sunjata fasa*, and the prose narrative in its many versions is known as *Manden maana*, or *Manden tariku*. The version excerpted here was collected and translated by David C. Conrad; his *Sunjata* (2004) offers a detailed introduction. Conrad's *Epic Ancestors of the Sunjata Era: Oral Tradition from the Maninka of Guinea* collects seven variants of the Sunjata epic. Laye Camara's *The Guardian of the Word* (1984) is a prose variant in novel form, based on the narrative by Babu Condé of Fadama, Guinea, recorded in 1963. But it was another prose variant, Djibril Tamsir Niane's *Sundiata: An Epic of Old Mali* (1965) that first drew worldwide attention to this epic. The three versions edited by Gordon Innes in *Sunjata* (1974) were narrated in the Mandinka dialect of the Gambia, and the one published by John Johnson in 1986 as *Son-Jara* third edition (2003) represents the Kita region of Mali. Eric Charry's *Mande Music* (2000) describes the musical instruments involved in performing the epic, while Stephen Belcher, *Epic Traditions of Africa* (1999), and Marloes Janson, *The Best Hand is the Hand that Always Gives: Griottes and their Profession in Eastern Gambia* (2002), provide broad context and analytical insight.

IX. Europe and the New World

Eugene Rice with Anthony Grafton, *The Foundations of Early Modern Europe*, second edition (1994), is the finest introduction to the contexts in which Renaissance or early modern literature was produced. William Bouwsma, *A Usable Past: Essays in European Cultural History* (1990), especially the chapter "Anxiety and the Formation of Early Modern Culture," also offers illuminating perspectives on the intellectual character of the period. Constance Jordan, *Renaissance Feminism: Literary Texts and Political Models* (1990), is a recommended study of the place of women in history and political thought. William Kerrigan and Gordon Braden, *The Idea of the Renaissance* (1989), offers a helpful and direct analysis of the critical construction of the Renaissance as a concept. Harry Berger Jr., *Second World and Green World: Studies in Renaissance Fiction-Making* (1988), especially the title essay, is a dense but recommended study of the aims of fiction making. Stephen Greenblatt, *Renaissance Self-Fashioning* (1980), describes the construction of identity in the period. J. H. Elliott's *The Old World and the New: 1492–1650* (1992) and *Imperial Spain: 1492–1716*, second edition (2002) provide good introductions.

Miguel de Cervantes
William Byron, *Cervantes: A Biography* (1978), is thorough. Ruth El Saffar, ed., *Critical Essays on Cervantes* (1986), and Anne Cruz and Carroll Johnson, eds., *Cervantes and his Postmodern Constituencies* (1998) offer interesting essays by eminent scholars. Vladimir Nabokov, *Lectures on Don Quixote* (1983), presents an elegant engagement with Cervantes' fiction. More technical studies include Carroll Johnson, *Cervantes and the Material World* (2000) and David Quint, *Cervantes' Novel of Modern Times: A New Reading of* Don Quixote (2003).

Niccolò Machiavelli
Peter E. Bondanella focuses on the literary aspects of Machiavelli's works in *Machiavelli and the Art of Renaissance History* (1973).

Sebastian de Grazia, *Machiavelli in Hell* (1989), on politics in *The Prince*, contains indexes and a bibliography. J. R. Hale's biography, *Machiavelli and Renaissance Italy* (1972), places Machiavelli in a historical perspective. A political analysis is provided by Anthony Parel in *The Political Calculus: Essays on Machiavelli's Political Philosophy* (1972). Roberto Ridolfi, *The Life of Niccolò Machiavelli* (1963), is still considered the best and most accurate biography. Silvia Ruffo-Fiore, *Niccolò Machiavelli* (1982), is a useful comprehensive guide for the beginning student. Victoria Kahn, *Machiavellian Rhetoric: From the Counter-Reformation to Milton* (1994), and Wayne A. Rebhorn, *Foxes and Lions: Machiavelli's Confidence Men* (1988), are recommended.

Marguerite de Navarre

P. A. Chilton's justly praised translation of the *Heptameron* (1984) has an excellent introduction. John D. Lyons and Mary B. McKinley, eds., *Critical Tales: New Studies of the Heptameron and Early Modern Culture* (1993), contains useful essays on the *Heptameron*. B. J. Davis, *The Storytellers in Marguerite de Navarre's Heptameron* (1978), presents detailed discussions of the narrators. Timothy Hampton, *Literature and Nation in the Sixteenth Century: Inventing Renaissance France* (2001) offers a historical reading of story 10. Samuel Putnam, *Marguerite de Navarre* (1935), is an informative and readable biography. Barbara M. Stephenson, *The Power and Patronage of Marguerite de Navarre* (2004), uses Marguerite's letters to trace her involvement in politics and in religious reform.

Michel de Montaigne

Hugo Friedrich, *Montaigne* (1991), is a careful historical study of the author. David Quint, *Montaigne and the Quality of Mercy* (1998) analyzes the political and ethical goals of the *Essays*. Judith Shklar, *Ordinary Vices* (1984), and Edwin Duval, "Lessons of the New World: Design and Meaning in Montaigne's 'Des Cannibales' (I:31) and 'Des coches' (III:6)," in *Montaigne: Essays in Reading*, ed. Gerard Defaux, *Yale French Studies* 64 (1983): 95–112, provide excellent studies of Montaigne that include, but are not limited to, his New World contexts. Marcel Tetel, *Montaigne*, updated edition (1990), and Richard Sayce, *The Essays of Montaigne: A Critical Exploration* (1972), are excellent introductions designed for the general reader.

Petrarch

Ernest Hatch Wilkins' biography, *Life of Petrarch* (1961), is informative, but tends to take Petrarch's autobiographical writings at face value. Giuseppe Mazzotta, *The Worlds of Petrarch* (1993), is an encyclopedic introduction to Petrarch's work and times. Victoria Kirkham and Armando Maggi have compiled the useful *Petrarch: A Critical Guide to the Complete Works* (2009). Robert Durling's introduction to *Petrarch's Lyric Poems* (1976) provides a rich overview of his poetry. Diana Vickers, "Diana Described: Scattered Woman and Scattered Rhyme," *Writing and Sexual Difference*, ed. Elizabeth Abel (1982), is the central feminist reading of Petrarch's lyric. In *Unrequited Conquests* (2000), Roland Greene reads Petrarchism in relation to early modern imperialism.

Popol Vuh

Dennis Tedlock's translation, satisfyingly annotated, is published as *Popol Vuh: The Mayan Book of the Dawn of Life* (1985; revised 1996). The text in this volume is from the 1996 edition. Older translations with useful introductions are Adrián Recinos, Delia Goetz, and Sylvanus Morley, *Popol Vuh: The Sacred Book of the Ancient Quiché Maya* (1950); and Munro S. Edmonson. *The Book of Counsel: The Popol Vuh of the Quiché Maya of Guatemala* (1971). Edmonson's is the only Quiché-English edition. Essays on the Popol Vuh and related topics are in Tedlock's *The Spoken Word and the Work of Interpretation* (1983).

William Shakespeare

Recent biographies placing Shakespeare in his social and intellectual context include Stephen Greenblatt, *Will in the World: How Shakespeare Became Shakespeare* (2004) and Jonathan Bate, *Soul of the Age: A Biography of the Mind of William Shakespeare* (2009). Marjorie Garber, *Shakespeare After All* (2005), provides a lively introduction, with individual essays on all the plays. Paul Arthur Cantor, *Shakespeare, "Hamlet"* (1989), is an in-depth study of the tragedy. Valuable studies are to be found in Harry Levin, *The Question of "Hamlet"* (1959) and Margreta de Grazia, *"Hamlet" without Hamlet* (2007).

TIMELINE *for*

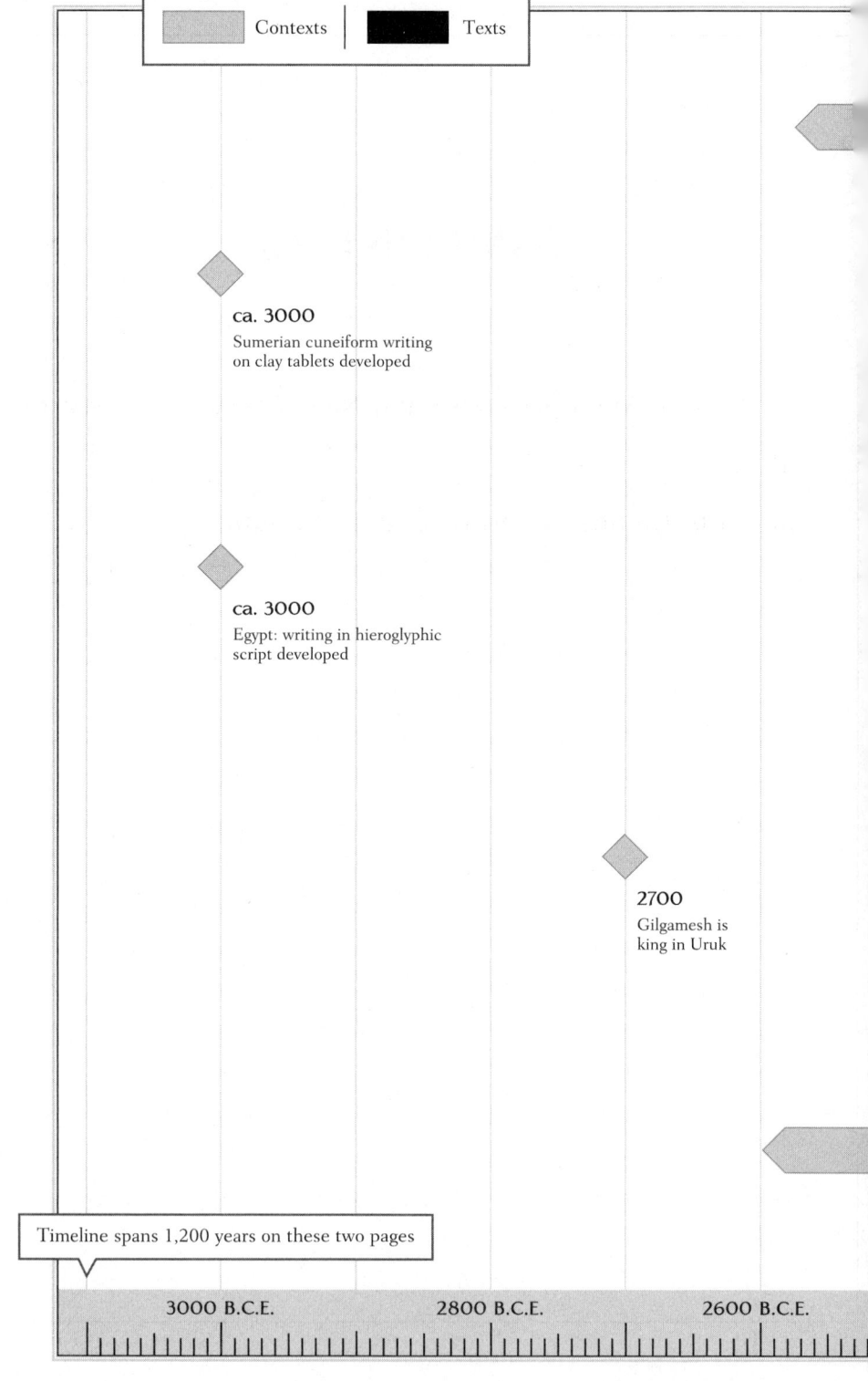

Contexts │ Texts

ca. 3000
Sumerian cuneiform writing
on clay tablets developed

ca. 3000
Egypt: writing in hieroglyphic
script developed

2700
Gilgamesh is
king in Uruk

Timeline spans 1,200 years on these two pages

3000 B.C.E.   2800 B.C.E.   2600 B.C.E.

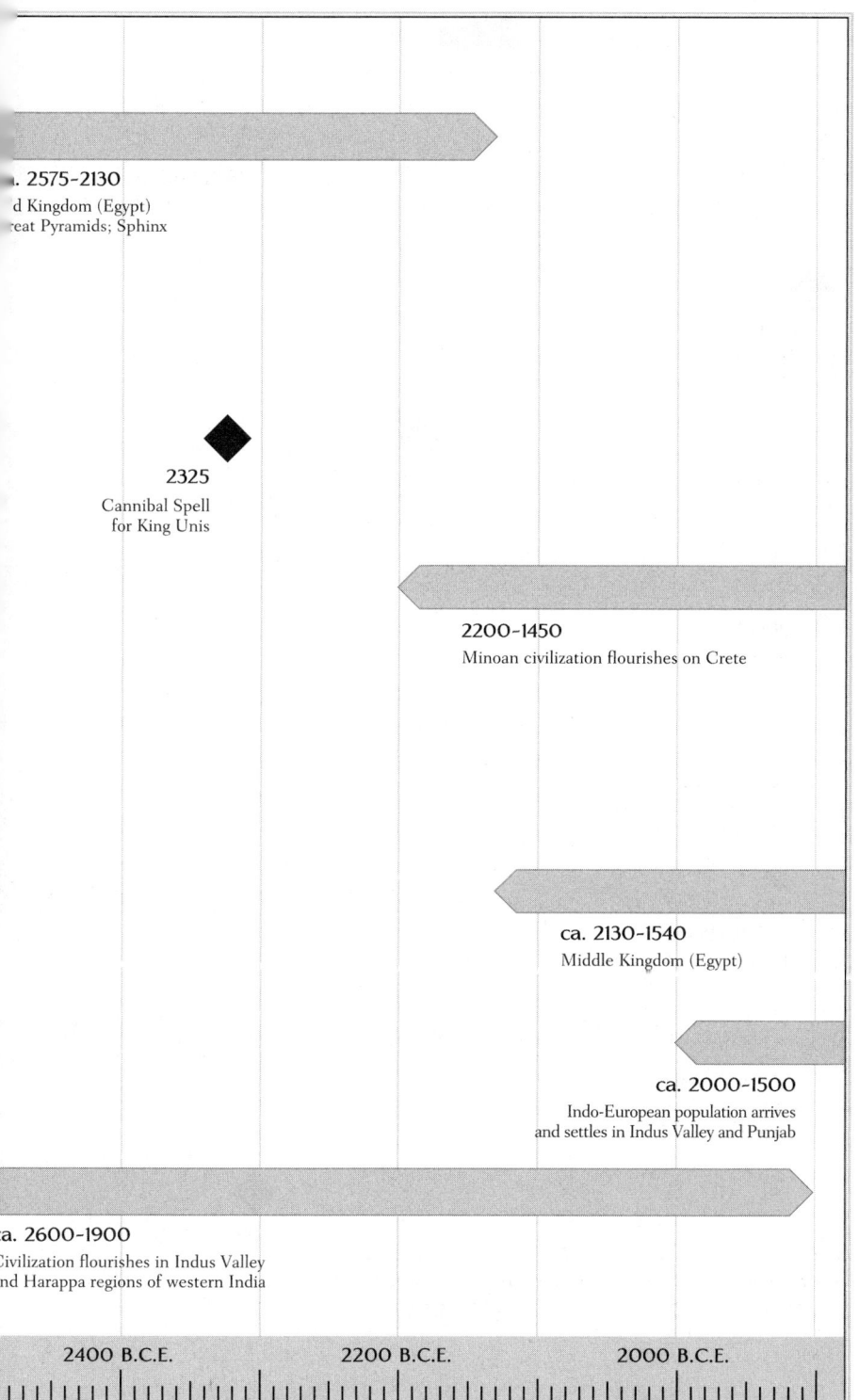

.. 2575–2130
d Kingdom (Egypt)
reat Pyramids; Sphinx

2325
Cannibal Spell
for King Unis

2200–1450
Minoan civilization flourishes on Crete

ca. 2130–1540
Middle Kingdom (Egypt)

ca. 2000–1500
Indo-European population arrives
and settles in Indus Valley and Punjab

ca. 2600–1900
Civilization flourishes in Indus Valley
and Harappa regions of western India

2400 B.C.E.   2200 B.C.E.   2000 B.C.E.

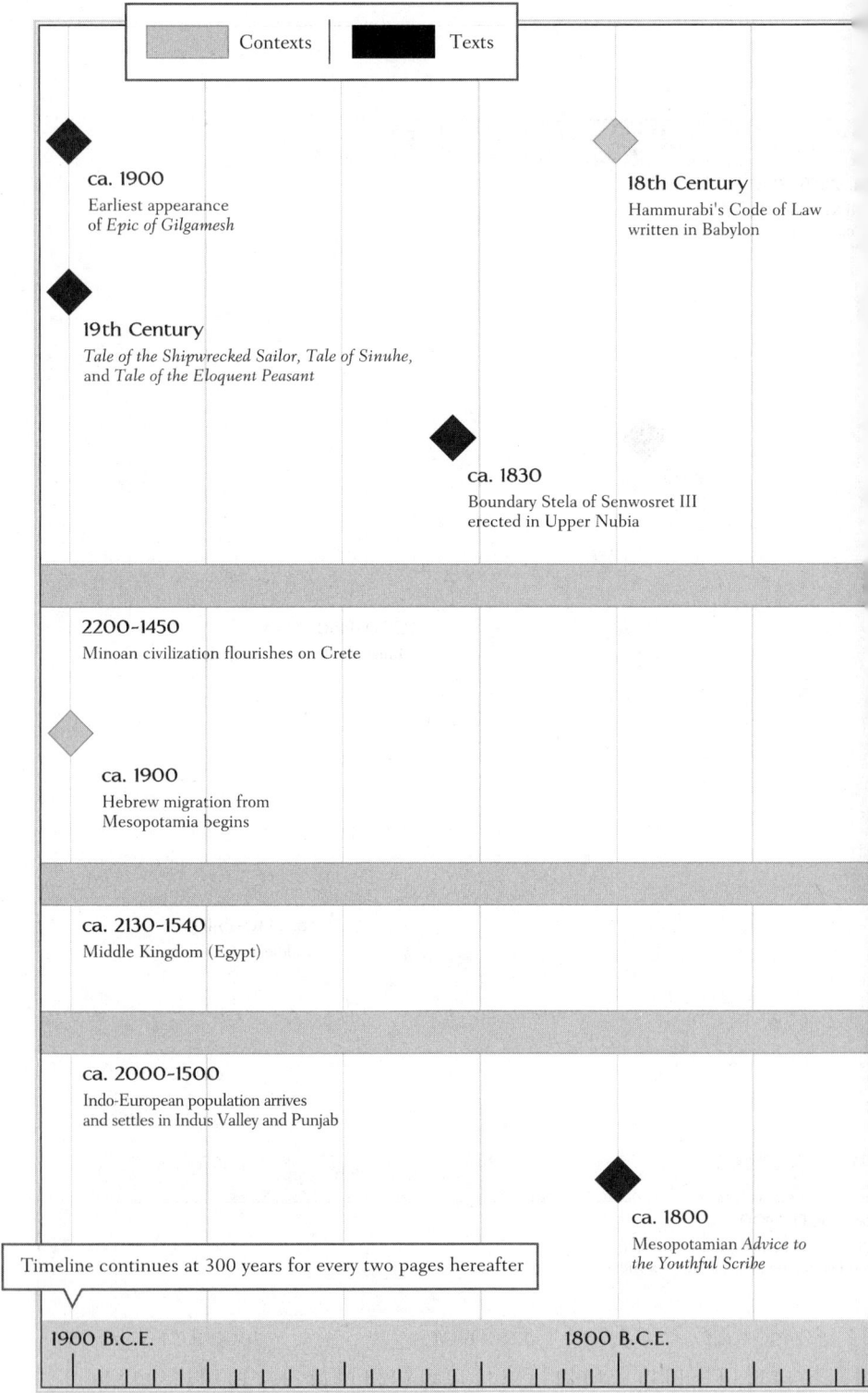

Contexts | Texts

ca. 1900
Earliest appearance
of *Epic of Gilgamesh*

18th Century
Hammurabi's Code of Law
written in Babylon

19th Century
Tale of the Shipwrecked Sailor, Tale of Sinuhe,
and *Tale of the Eloquent Peasant*

ca. 1830
Boundary Stela of Senwosret III
erected in Upper Nubia

2200-1450
Minoan civilization flourishes on Crete

ca. 1900
Hebrew migration from
Mesopotamia begins

ca. 2130-1540
Middle Kingdom (Egypt)

ca. 2000-1500
Indo-European population arrives
and settles in Indus Valley and Punjab

ca. 1800
Mesopotamian *Advice to
the Youthful Scribe*

Timeline continues at 300 years for every two pages hereafter

1900 B.C.E.   1800 B.C.E.

1700 B.C.E.

1600 B.C.E.

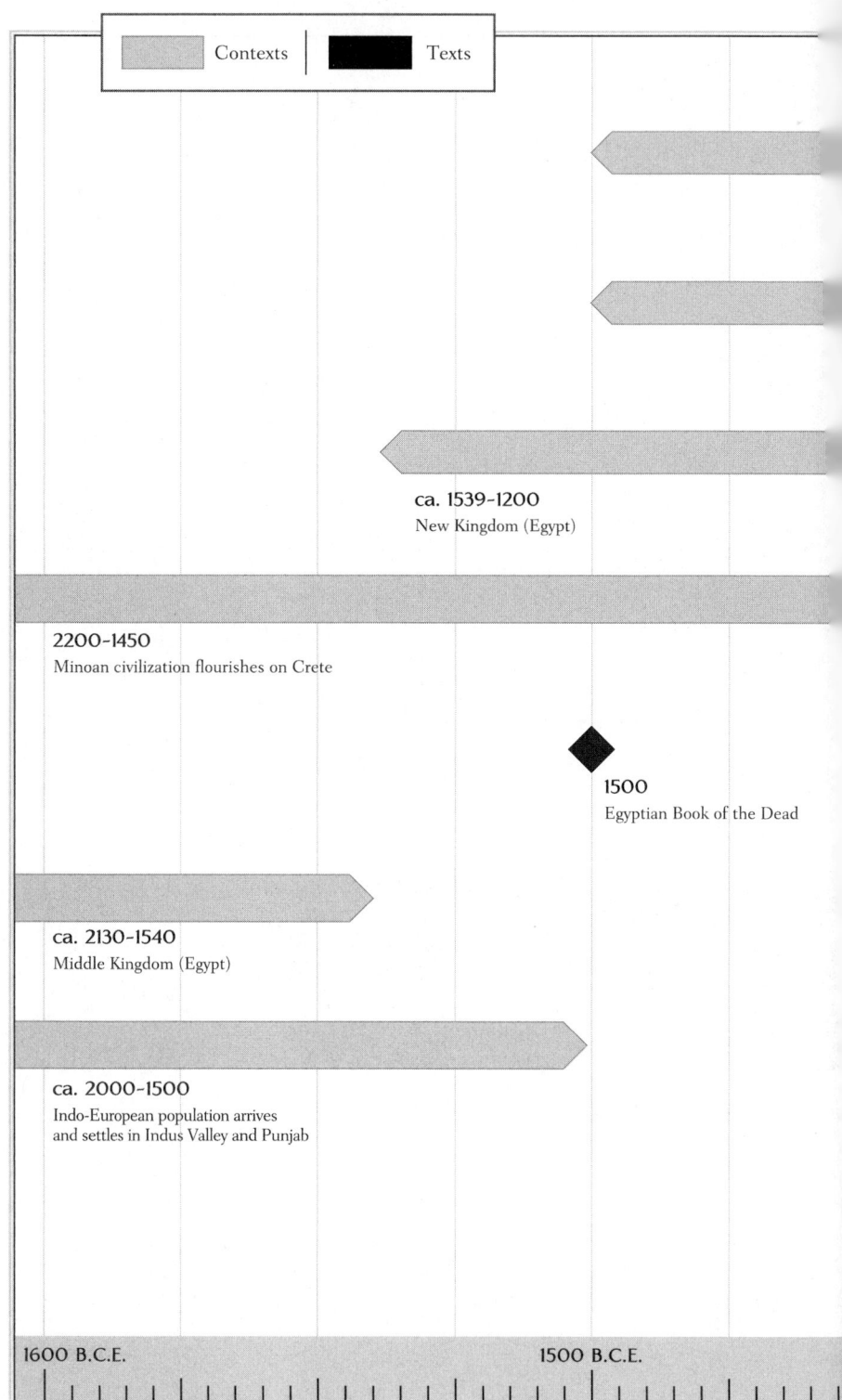

Contexts | Texts

ca. 1539-1200
New Kingdom (Egypt)

2200-1450
Minoan civilization flourishes on Crete

1500
Egyptian Book of the Dead

ca. 2130-1540
Middle Kingdom (Egypt)

ca. 2000-1500
Indo-European population arrives
and settles in Indus Valley and Punjab

1600 B.C.E.   1500 B.C.E.

, 1500–1200
liest form of Sanskrit developed

, 1500–1200
Indo-European settlers establish agrarian
age society in northwestern India

ca. 1350
Akhenaten's *Great
Hymn to Aten*

ca. 1450
Mycenaeans from mainland
Greece occupy Crete

ca. 1375–1354
Egyptian king Akhenaten dedicates
his capital to Aten, the sun god

1400 B.C.E.   1300 B.C.E.

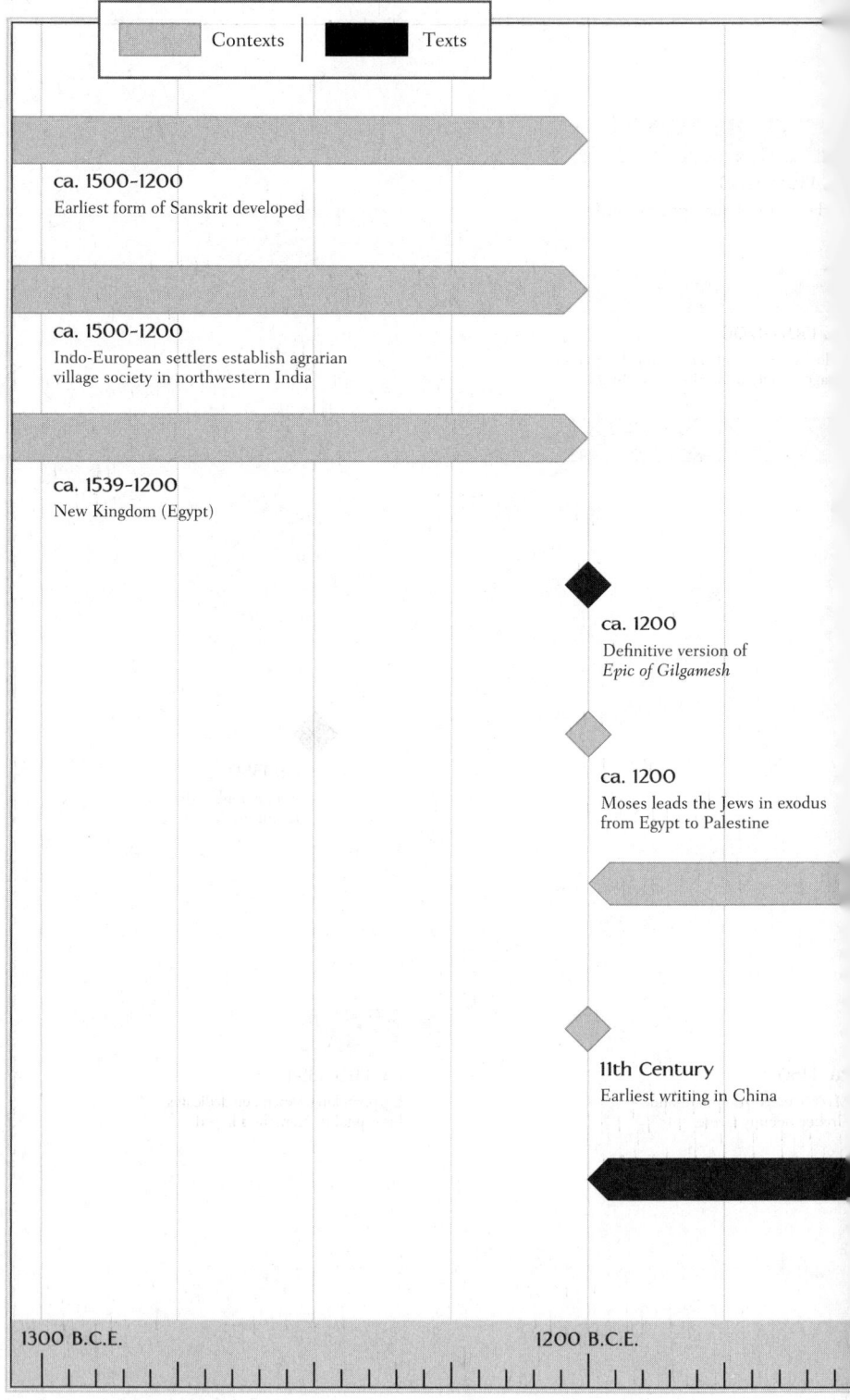

Contexts | Texts

ca. 1500–1200
Earliest form of Sanskrit developed

ca. 1500–1200
Indo-European settlers establish agrarian
village society in northwestern India

ca. 1539–1200
New Kingdom (Egypt)

ca. 1200
Definitive version of
Epic of Gilgamesh

ca. 1200
Moses leads the Jews in exodus
from Egypt to Palestine

11th Century
Earliest writing in China

1300 B.C.E.   1200 B.C.E.

1045
King Wen and King Wu
found the Zhou Dynasty
in China

. 1200-900
~ergence of Hindu beliefs and
uals in India. Caste system develops

a. 1200-700
he Vedas (Hindu scripture) and early Upaniṣads (philosophical
d mystical texts) composed in the Punjab region of India

1100 B.C.E.   **1000 B.C.E.**

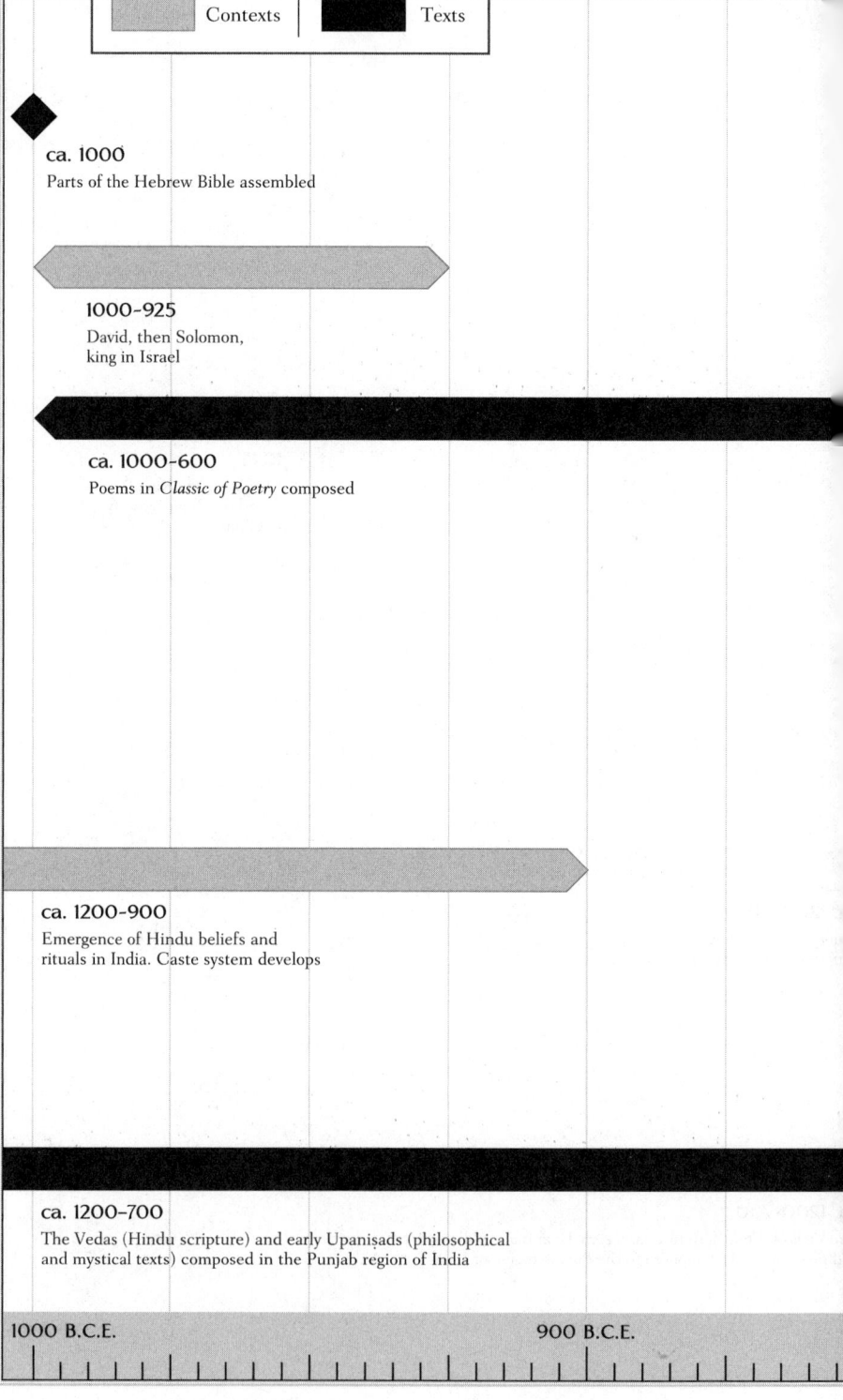

Contexts | Texts

ca. 1000
Parts of the Hebrew Bible assembled

1000–925
David, then Solomon,
king in Israel

ca. 1000–600
Poems in *Classic of Poetry* composed

ca. 1200–900
Emergence of Hindu beliefs and
rituals in India. Caste system develops

ca. 1200–700
The Vedas (Hindu scripture) and early Upaniṣads (philosophical
and mystical texts) composed in the Punjab region of India

1000 B.C.E.   900 B.C.E.

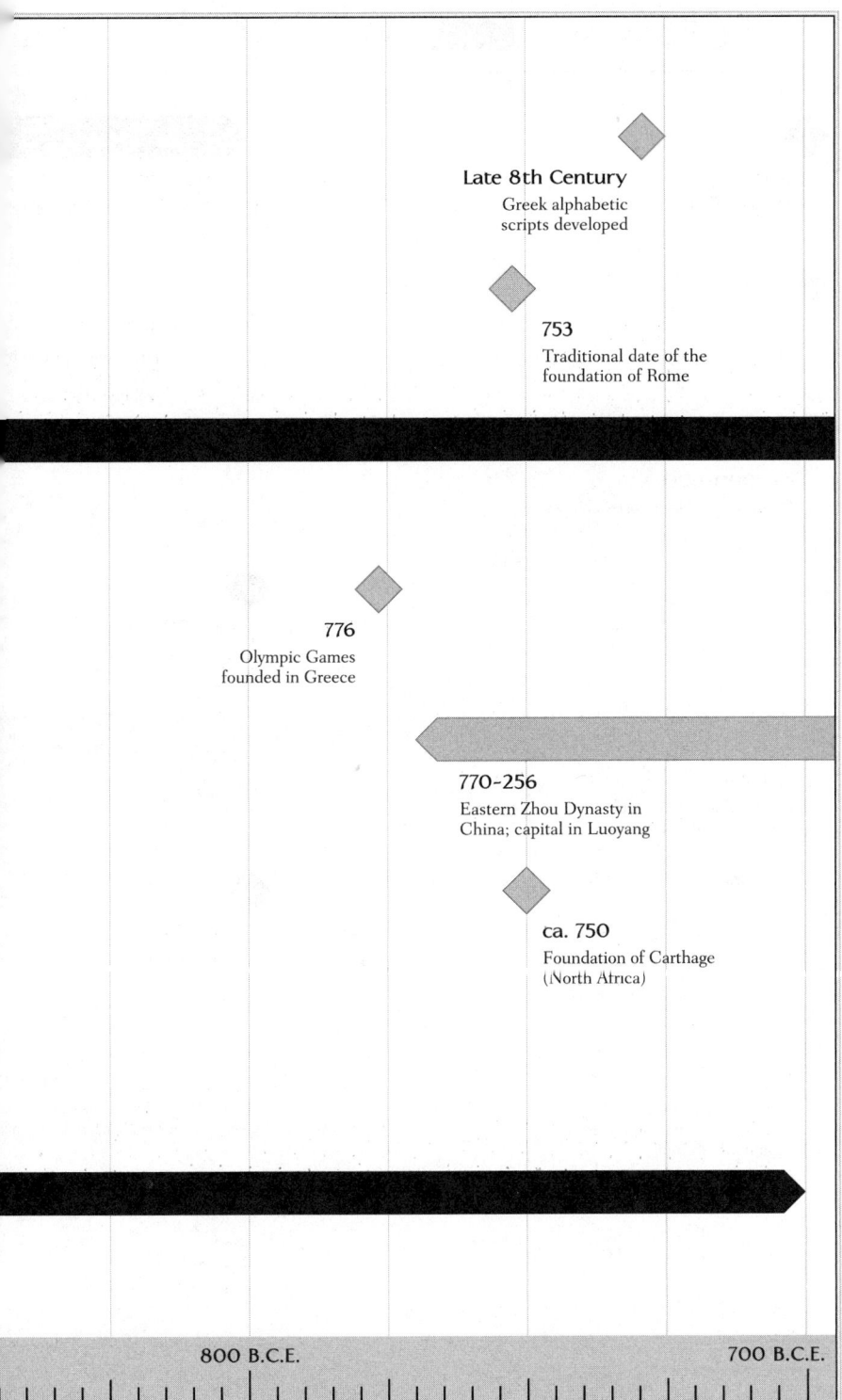

Late 8th Century
Greek alphabetic
scripts developed

753
Traditional date of the
foundation of Rome

776
Olympic Games
founded in Greece

770–256
Eastern Zhou Dynasty in
China; capital in Luoyang

ca. 750
Foundation of Carthage
(North Africa)

800 B.C.E.   700 B.C.E.

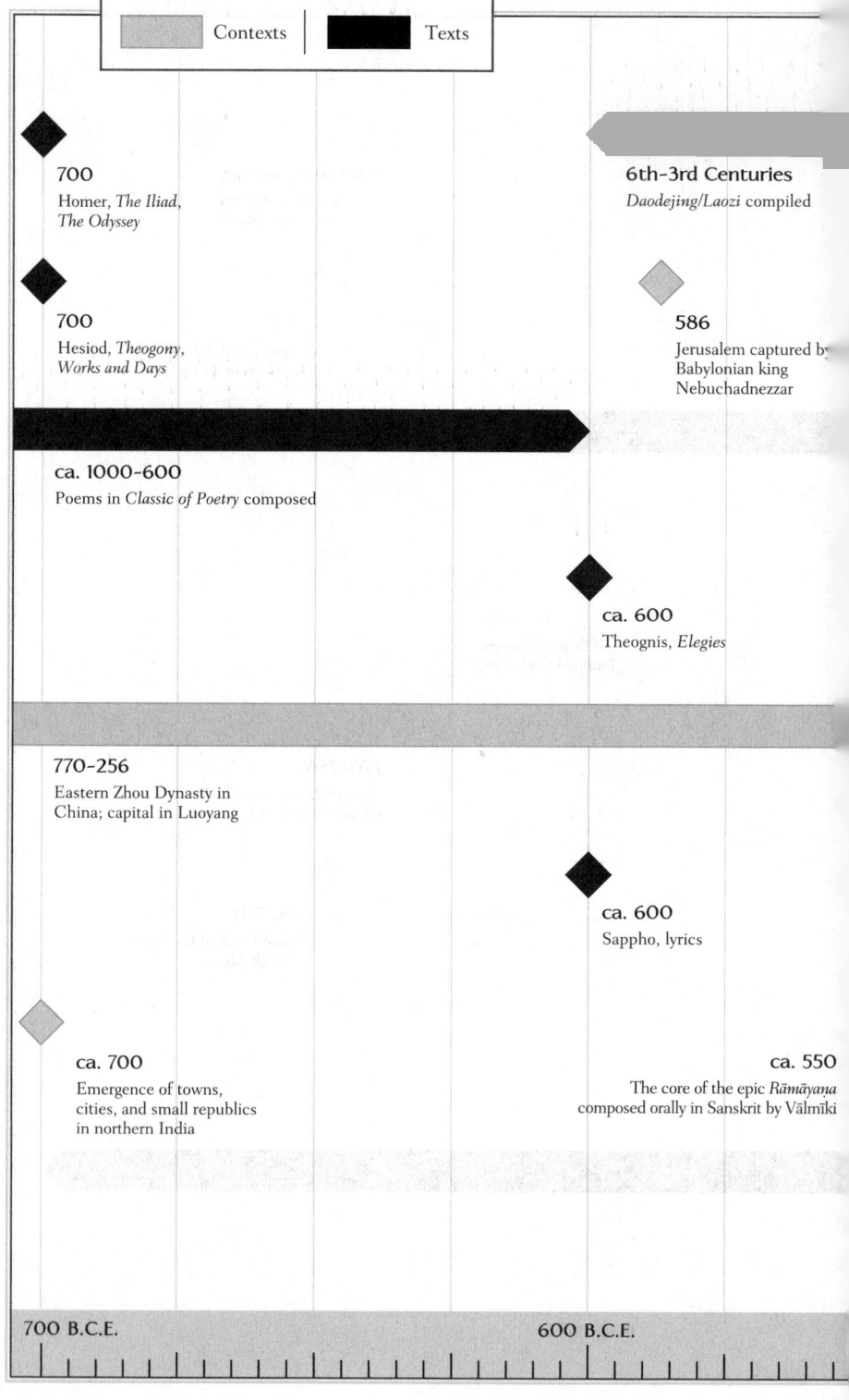

| Contexts | Texts |

700
Homer, *The Iliad*,
The Odyssey

700
Hesiod, *Theogony*,
Works and Days

ca. 1000–600
Poems in *Classic of Poetry* composed

6th–3rd Centuries
Daodejing/Laozi compiled

586
Jerusalem captured by
Babylonian king
Nebuchadnezzar

ca. 600
Theognis, *Elegies*

770–256
Eastern Zhou Dynasty in
China; capital in Luoyang

ca. 600
Sappho, lyrics

ca. 700
Emergence of towns,
cities, and small republics
in northern India

ca. 550
The core of the epic *Rāmāyaṇa*
composed orally in Sanskrit by Vālmīki

700 B.C.E.   600 B.C.E.

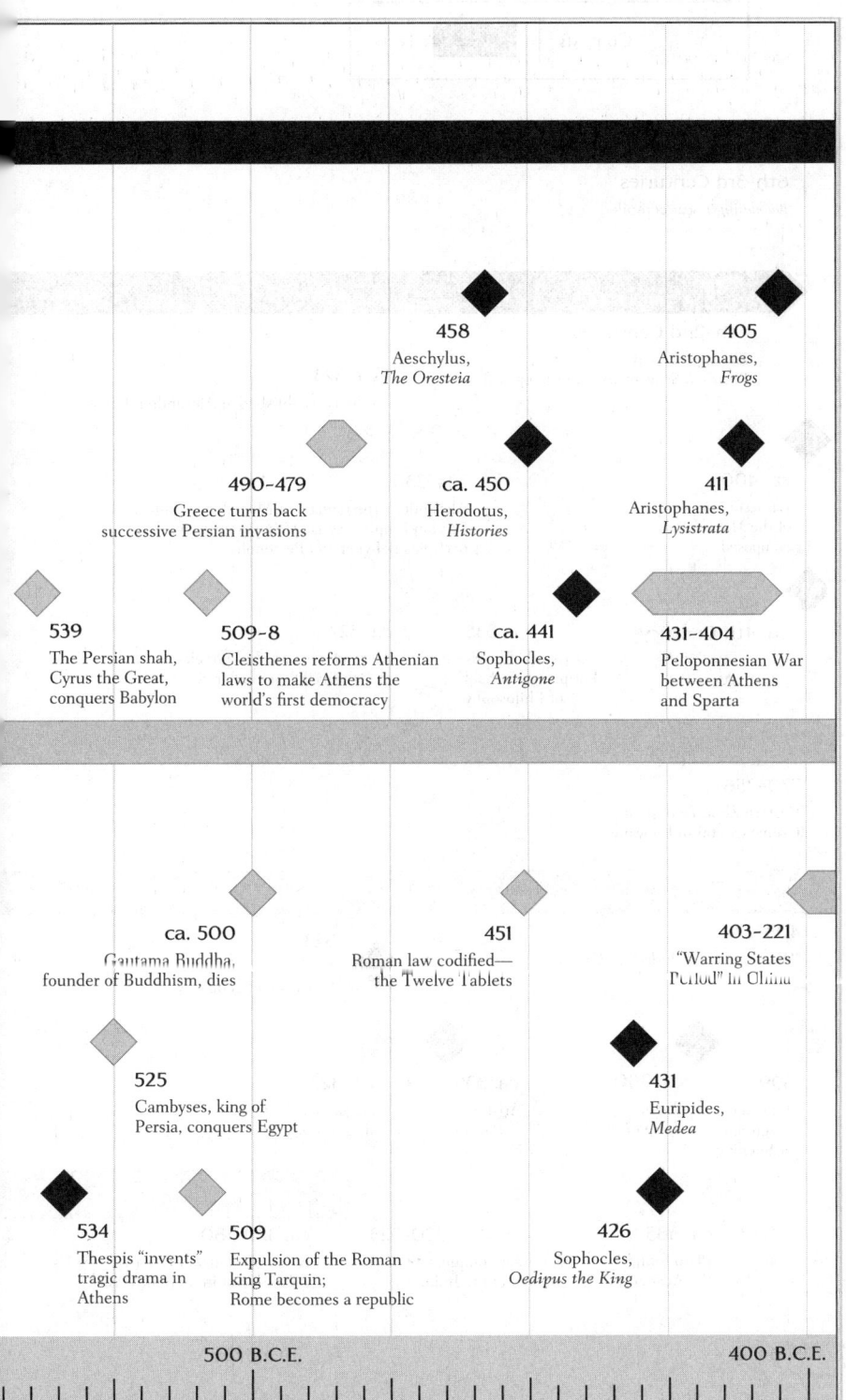

458

Aeschylus,
The Oresteia

405

Aristophanes,
Frogs

490–479

Greece turns back
successive Persian invasions

ca. 450

Herodotus,
Histories

411

Aristophanes,
Lysistrata

539

The Persian shah,
Cyrus the Great,
conquers Babylon

509–8

Cleisthenes reforms Athenian
laws to make Athens the
world's first democracy

ca. 441

Sophocles,
Antigone

431–404

Peloponnesian War
between Athens
and Sparta

ca. 500

Gautama Buddha,
founder of Buddhism, dies

451

Roman law codified—
the Twelve Tablets

403–221

"Warring States
Period" in China

525

Cambyses, king of
Persia, conquers Egypt

431

Euripides,
Medea

534

Thespis "invents"
tragic drama in
Athens

509

Expulsion of the Roman
king Tarquin;
Rome becomes a republic

426

Sophocles,
Oedipus the King

500 B.C.E.

400 B.C.E.

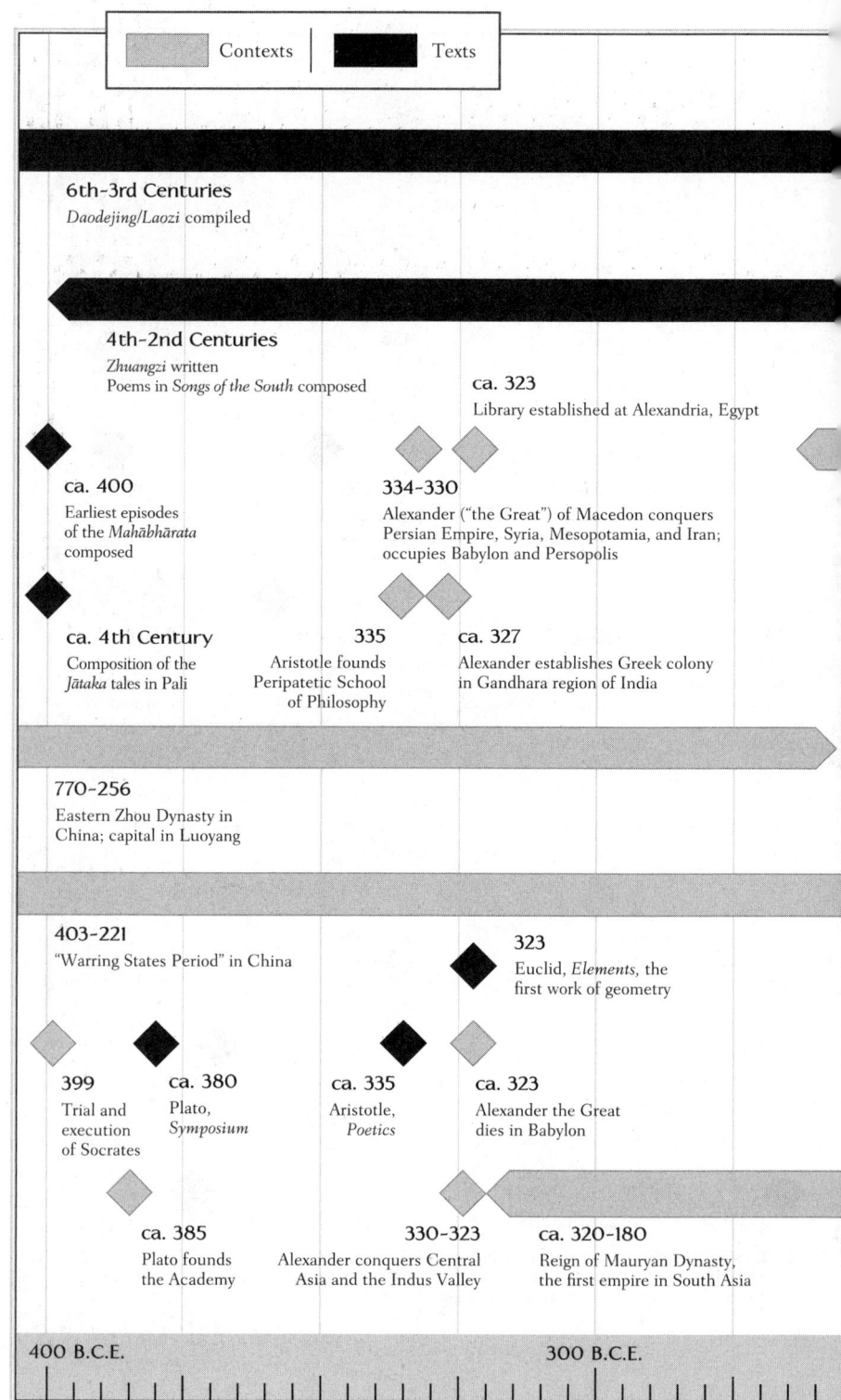

Contexts | Texts

6th-3rd Centuries
Daodejing/Laozi compiled

4th-2nd Centuries
Zhuangzi written
Poems in *Songs of the South* composed

ca. 323
Library established at Alexandria, Egypt

ca. 400
Earliest episodes
of the *Mahābhārata*
composed

334-330
Alexander ("the Great") of Macedon conquers
Persian Empire, Syria, Mesopotamia, and Iran;
occupies Babylon and Persopolis

ca. 4th Century
Composition of the
Jātaka tales in Pali

335
Aristotle founds
Peripatetic School
of Philosophy

ca. 327
Alexander establishes Greek colony
in Gandhara region of India

770-256
Eastern Zhou Dynasty in
China; capital in Luoyang

403-221
"Warring States Period" in China

323
Euclid, *Elements,* the
first work of geometry

399
Trial and
execution
of Socrates

ca. 380
Plato,
Symposium

ca. 335
Aristotle,
Poetics

ca. 323
Alexander the Great
dies in Babylon

ca. 385
Plato founds
the Academy

330-323
Alexander conquers Central
Asia and the Indus Valley

ca. 320-180
Reign of Mauryan Dynasty,
the first empire in South Asia

400 B.C.E.

300 B.C.E.

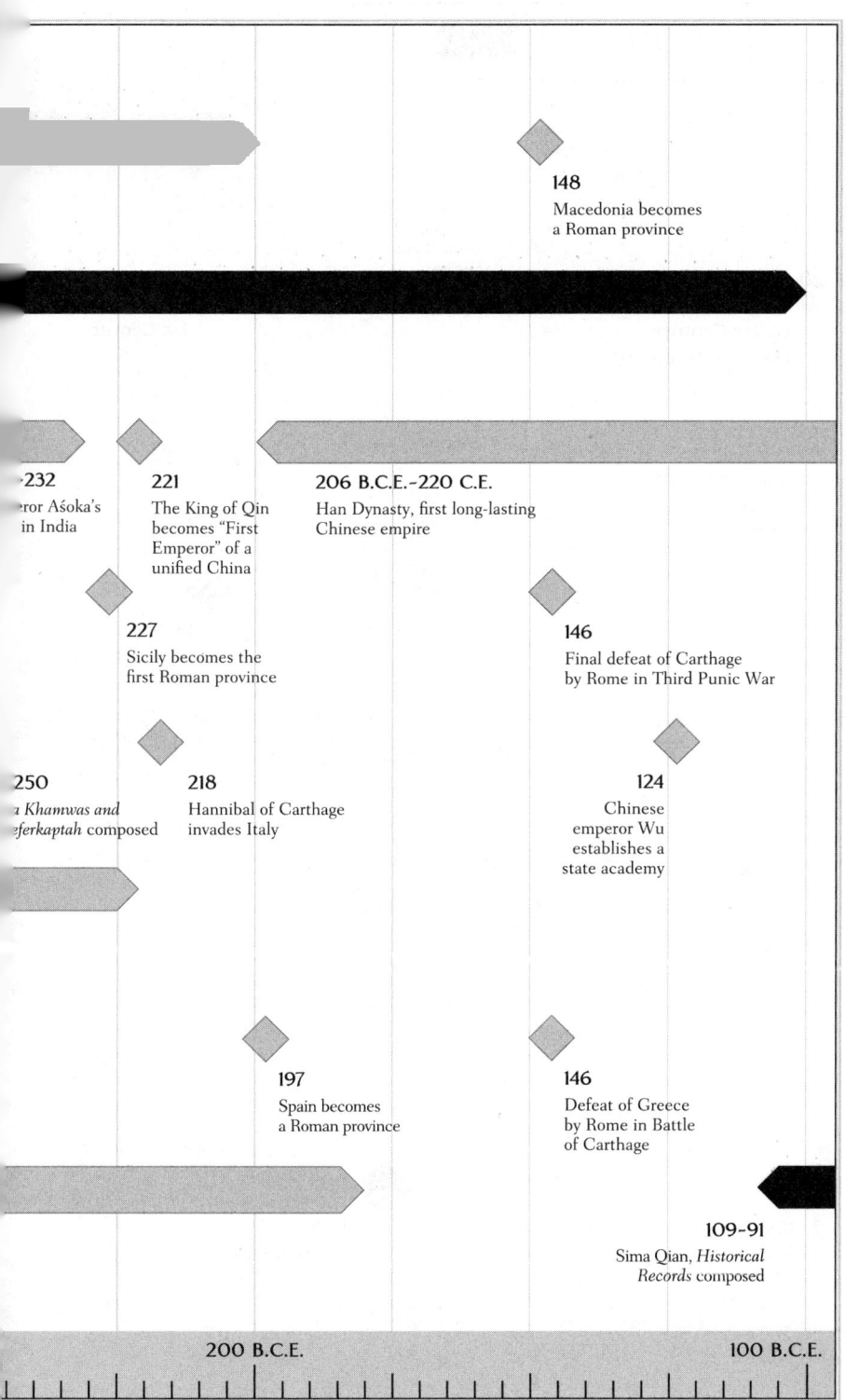

148
Macedonia becomes
a Roman province

232
eror Aśoka's
in India

221
The King of Qin
becomes "First
Emperor" of a
unified China

206 B.C.E.–220 C.E.
Han Dynasty, first long-lasting
Chinese empire

227
Sicily becomes the
first Roman province

146
Final defeat of Carthage
by Rome in Third Punic War

250
a Khamwas and
eferkaptah composed

218
Hannibal of Carthage
invades Italy

124
Chinese
emperor Wu
establishes a
state academy

197
Spain becomes
a Roman province

146
Defeat of Greece
by Rome in Battle
of Carthage

109–91
Sima Qian, *Historical*
Records composed

200 B.C.E.   **100 B.C.E.**

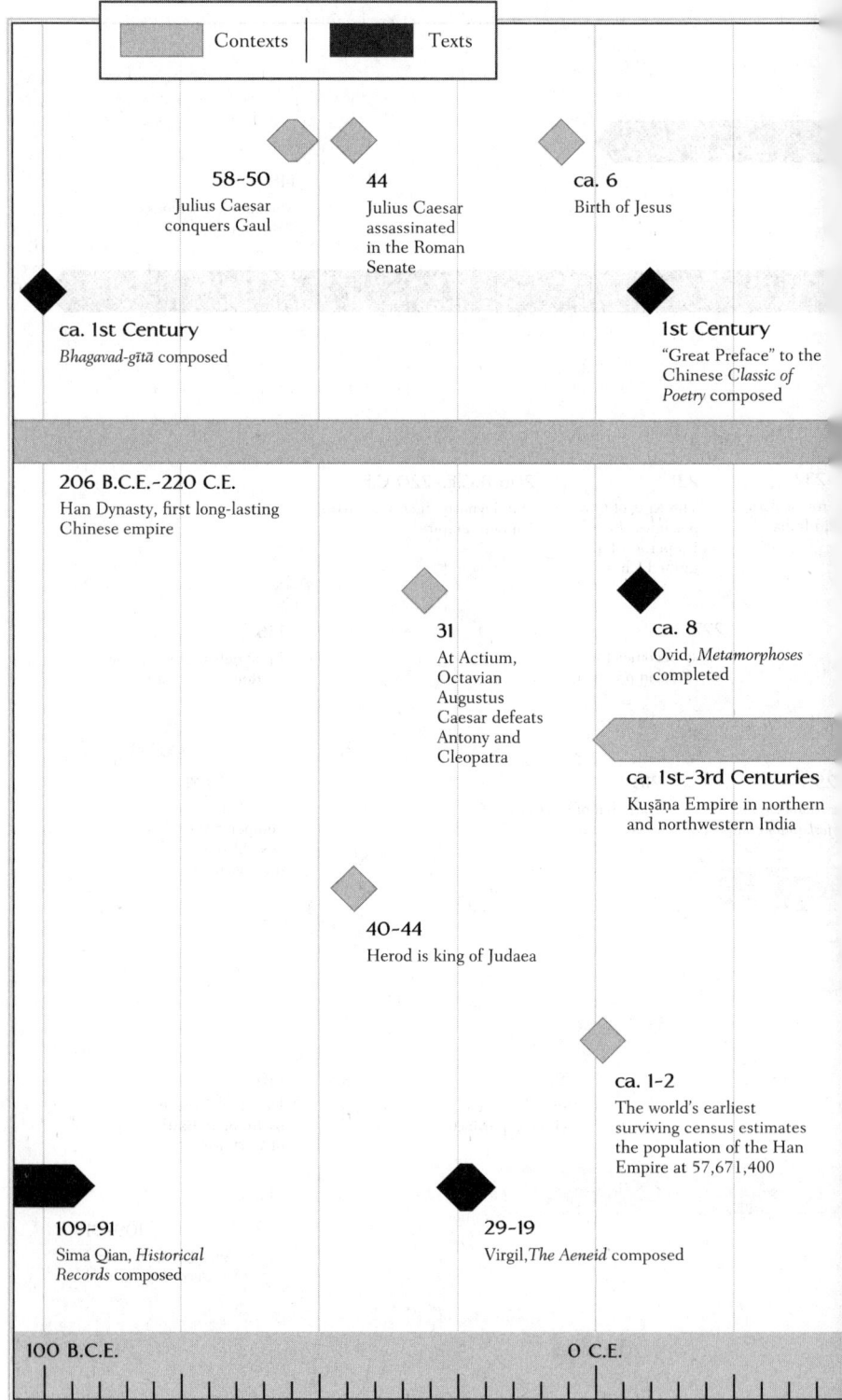

Contexts | Texts

58–50
Julius Caesar conquers Gaul

44
Julius Caesar assassinated in the Roman Senate

ca. 6
Birth of Jesus

ca. 1st Century
Bhagavad-gītā composed

1st Century
"Great Preface" to the Chinese *Classic of Poetry* composed

206 B.C.E.–220 C.E.
Han Dynasty, first long-lasting Chinese empire

31
At Actium, Octavian Augustus Caesar defeats Antony and Cleopatra

ca. 8
Ovid, *Metamorphoses* completed

ca. 1st–3rd Centuries
Kuṣāṇa Empire in northern and northwestern India

40–44
Herod is king of Judaea

ca. 1–2
The world's earliest surviving census estimates the population of the Han Empire at 57,671,400

109–91
Sima Qian, *Historical Records* composed

29–19
Virgil, *The Aeneid* composed

100 B.C.E.

0 C.E.

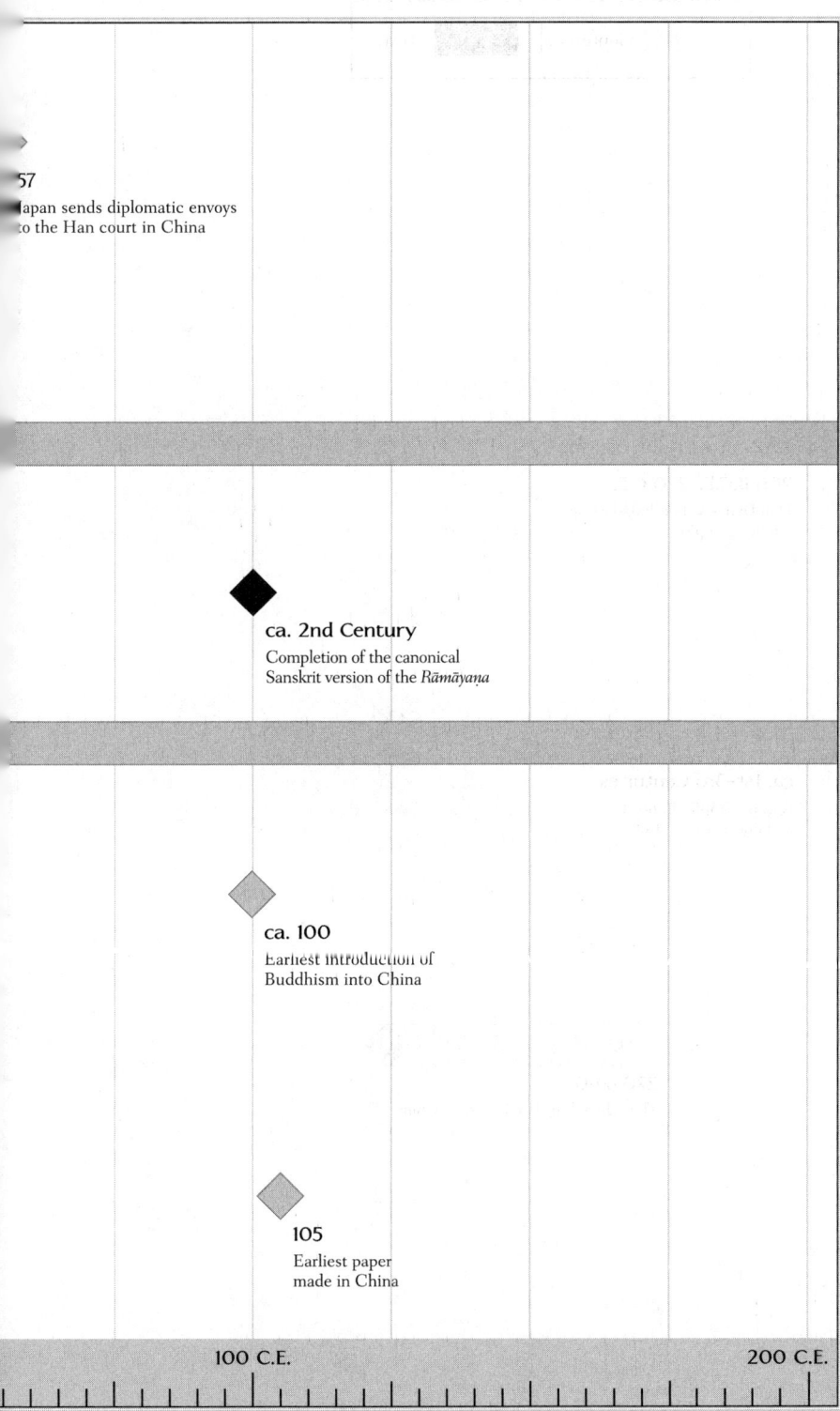

57
Japan sends diplomatic envoys
to the Han court in China

ca. 2nd Century
Completion of the canonical
Sanskrit version of the *Rāmāyaṇa*

ca. 100
Earliest introduction of
Buddhism into China

105
Earliest paper
made in China

100 C.E.

200 C.E.

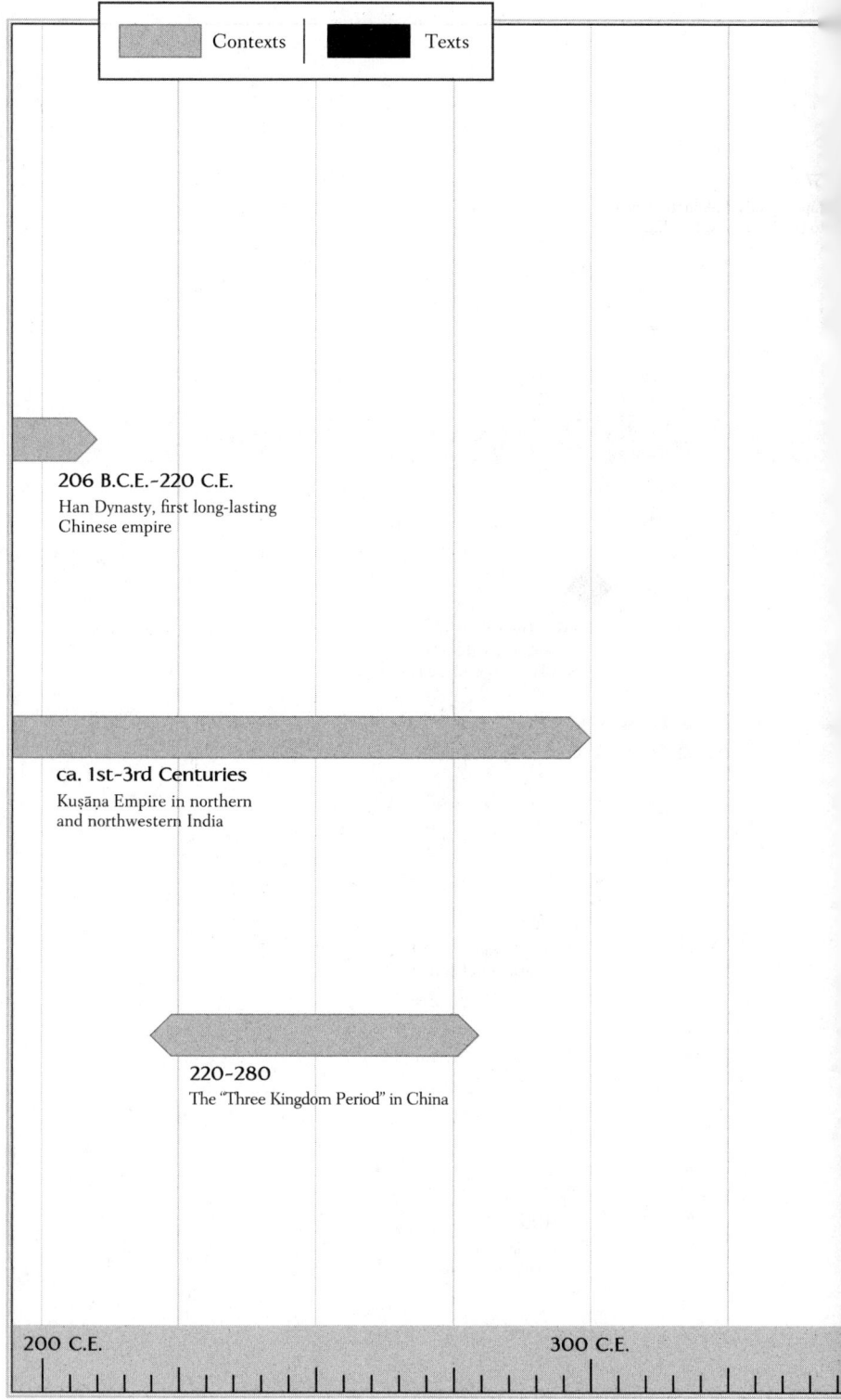

Contexts | Texts

206 B.C.E.–220 C.E.
Han Dynasty, first long-lasting
Chinese empire

ca. 1st–3rd Centuries
Kuṣāṇa Empire in northern
and northwestern India

220–280
The "Three Kingdom Period" in China

200 C.E.   300 C.E.

ca. 400

Completion of the canonical Sanskrit
version of the *Mahābhārata*

400 C.E.   500 C.E.

TIMELINE *for*

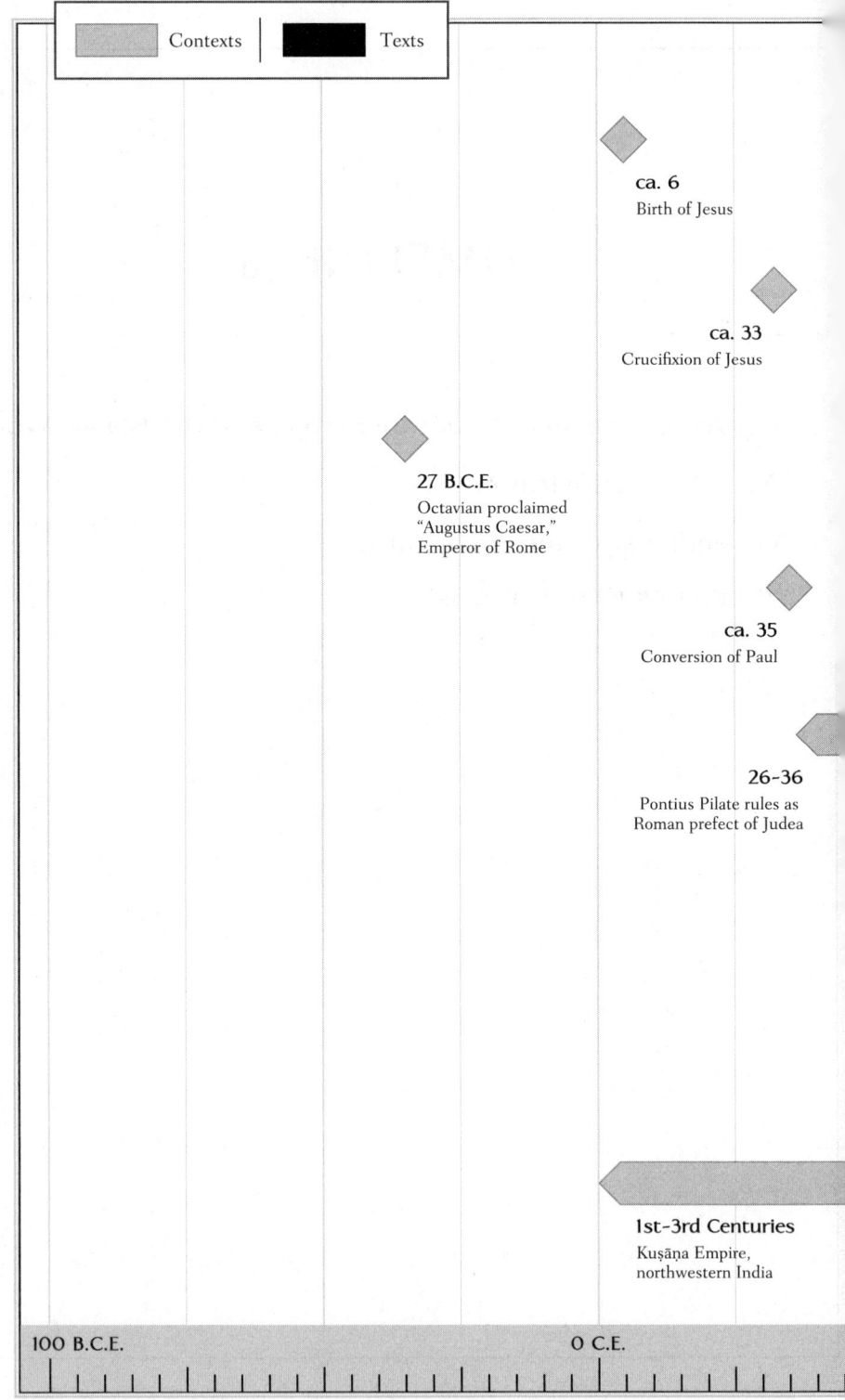

Contexts | Texts

ca. 6
Birth of Jesus

ca. 33
Crucifixion of Jesus

27 B.C.E.
Octavian proclaimed
"Augustus Caesar,"
Emperor of Rome

ca. 35
Conversion of Paul

26–36
Pontius Pilate rules as
Roman prefect of Judea

1st–3rd Centuries
Kuṣāṇa Empire,
northwestern India

100 B.C.E.   0 C.E.

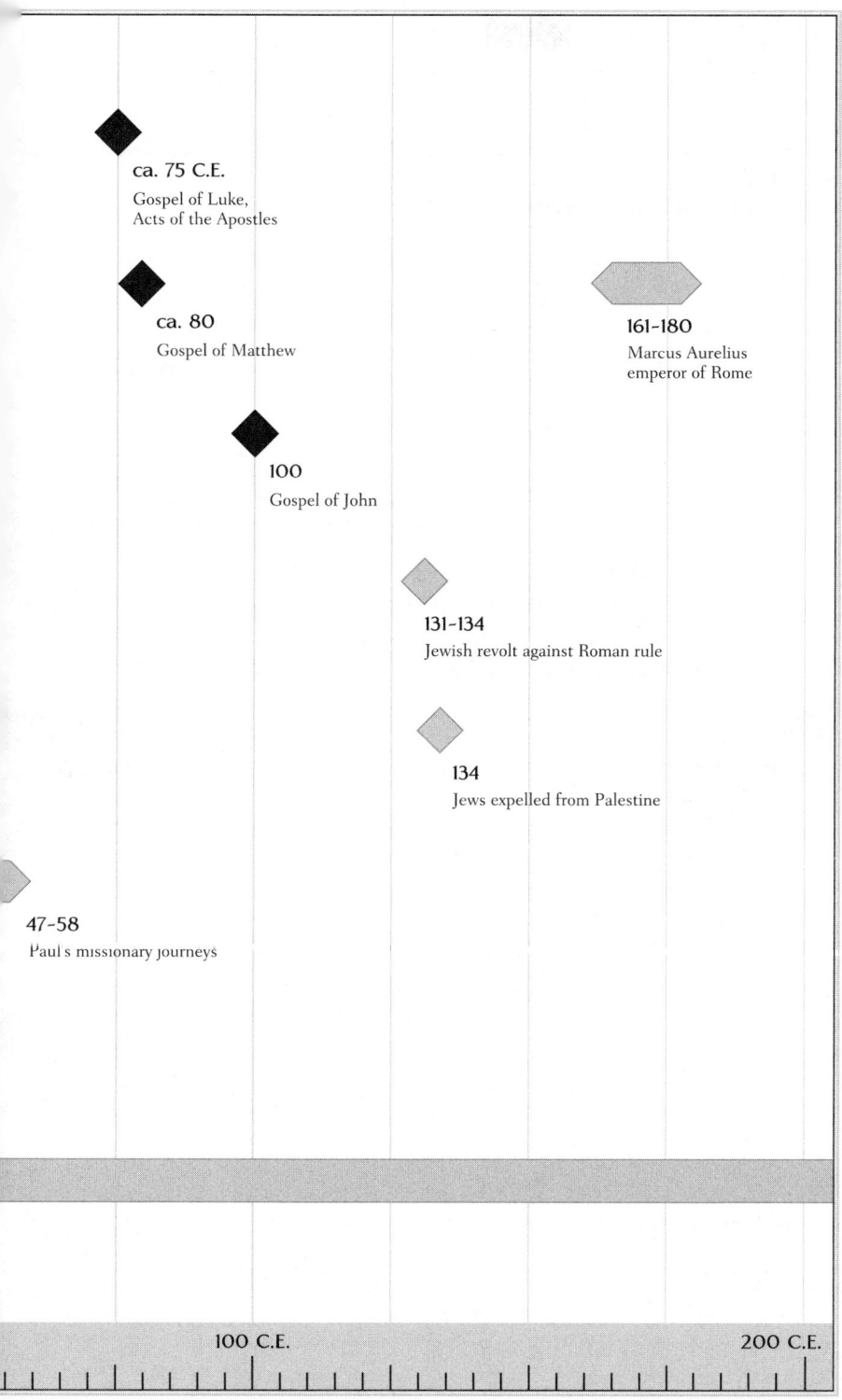

ca. 75 C.E.
Gospel of Luke,
Acts of the Apostles

ca. 80
Gospel of Matthew

161–180
Marcus Aurelius
emperor of Rome

100
Gospel of John

131–134
Jewish revolt against Roman rule

134
Jews expelled from Palestine

47–58
Paul's missionary journeys

100 C.E.

200 C.E.

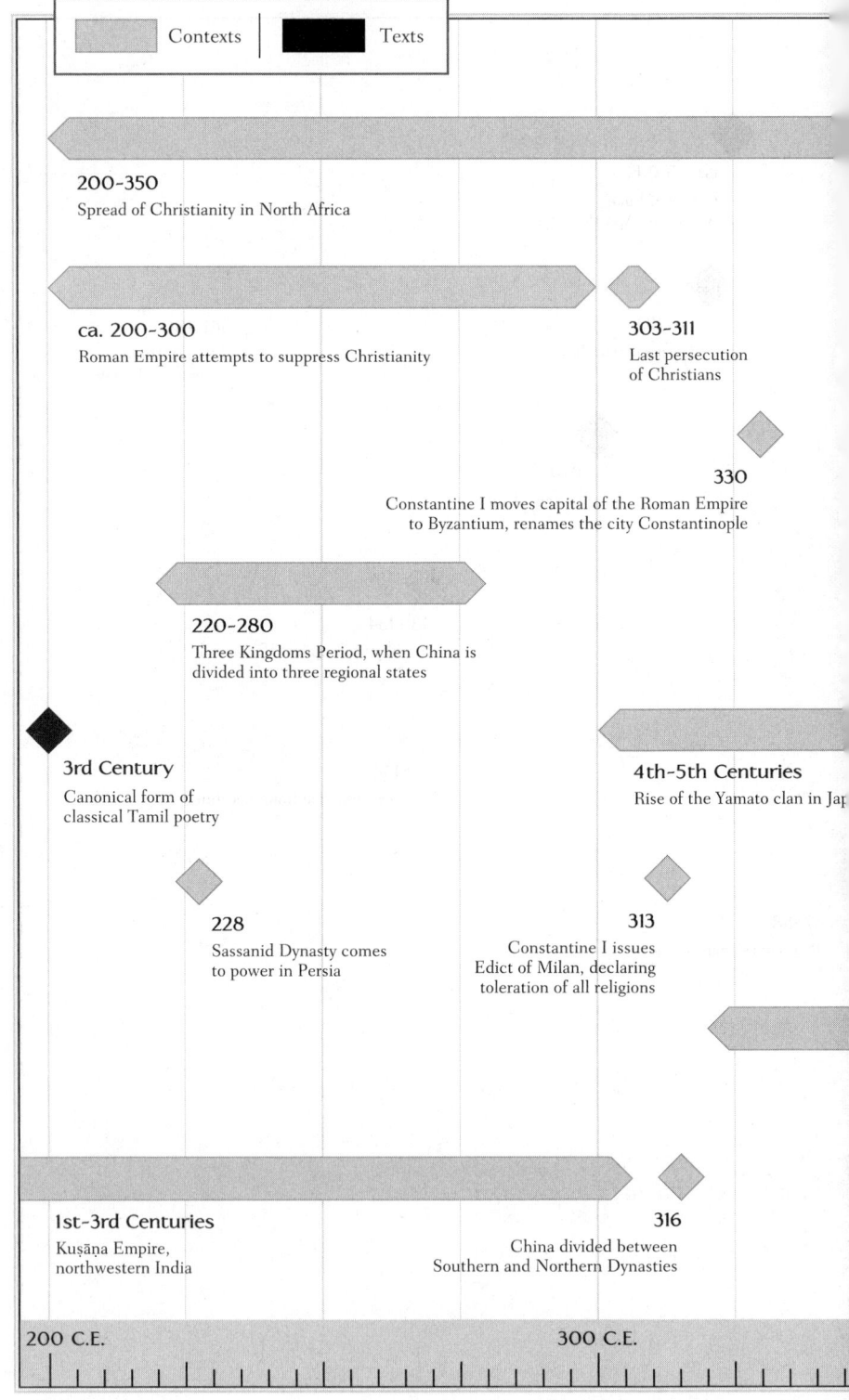

Contexts | Texts

200–350
Spread of Christianity in North Africa

ca. 200–300
Roman Empire attempts to suppress Christianity

303–311
Last persecution
of Christians

330
Constantine I moves capital of the Roman Empire
to Byzantium, renames the city Constantinople

220–280
Three Kingdoms Period, when China is
divided into three regional states

3rd Century
Canonical form of
classical Tamil poetry

4th–5th Centuries
Rise of the Yamato clan in Jap

228
Sassanid Dynasty comes
to power in Persia

313
Constantine I issues
Edict of Milan, declaring
toleration of all religions

1st–3rd Centuries
Kuṣāṇa Empire,
northwestern India

316
China divided between
Southern and Northern Dynasties

200 C.E.   300 C.E.

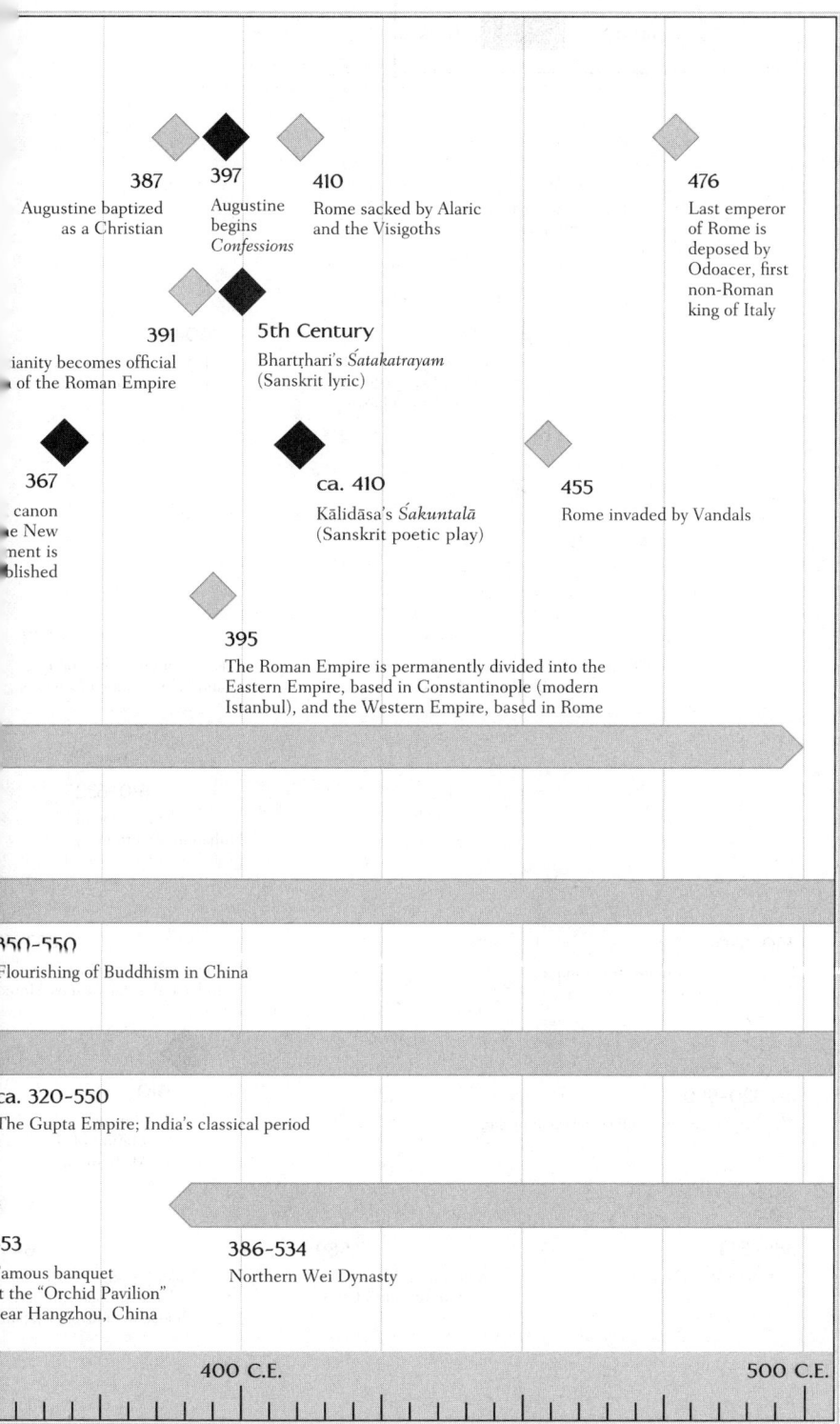

387

Augustine baptized as a Christian

397

Augustine begins *Confessions*

410

Rome sacked by Alaric and the Visigoths

476

Last emperor of Rome is deposed by Odoacer, first non-Roman king of Italy

391

ianity becomes official ... of the Roman Empire

5th Century

Bhartṛhari's *Śatakatrayam* (Sanskrit lyric)

367

canon ... ...e New ...ment is ...blished

ca. 410

Kālidāsa's *Śakuntalā* (Sanskrit poetic play)

455

Rome invaded by Vandals

395

The Roman Empire is permanently divided into the Eastern Empire, based in Constantinople (modern Istanbul), and the Western Empire, based in Rome

350-550

Flourishing of Buddhism in China

ca. 320-550

The Gupta Empire; India's classical period

353

Famous banquet at the "Orchid Pavilion" near Hangzhou, China

386-534

Northern Wei Dynasty

400 C.E.

500 C.E.

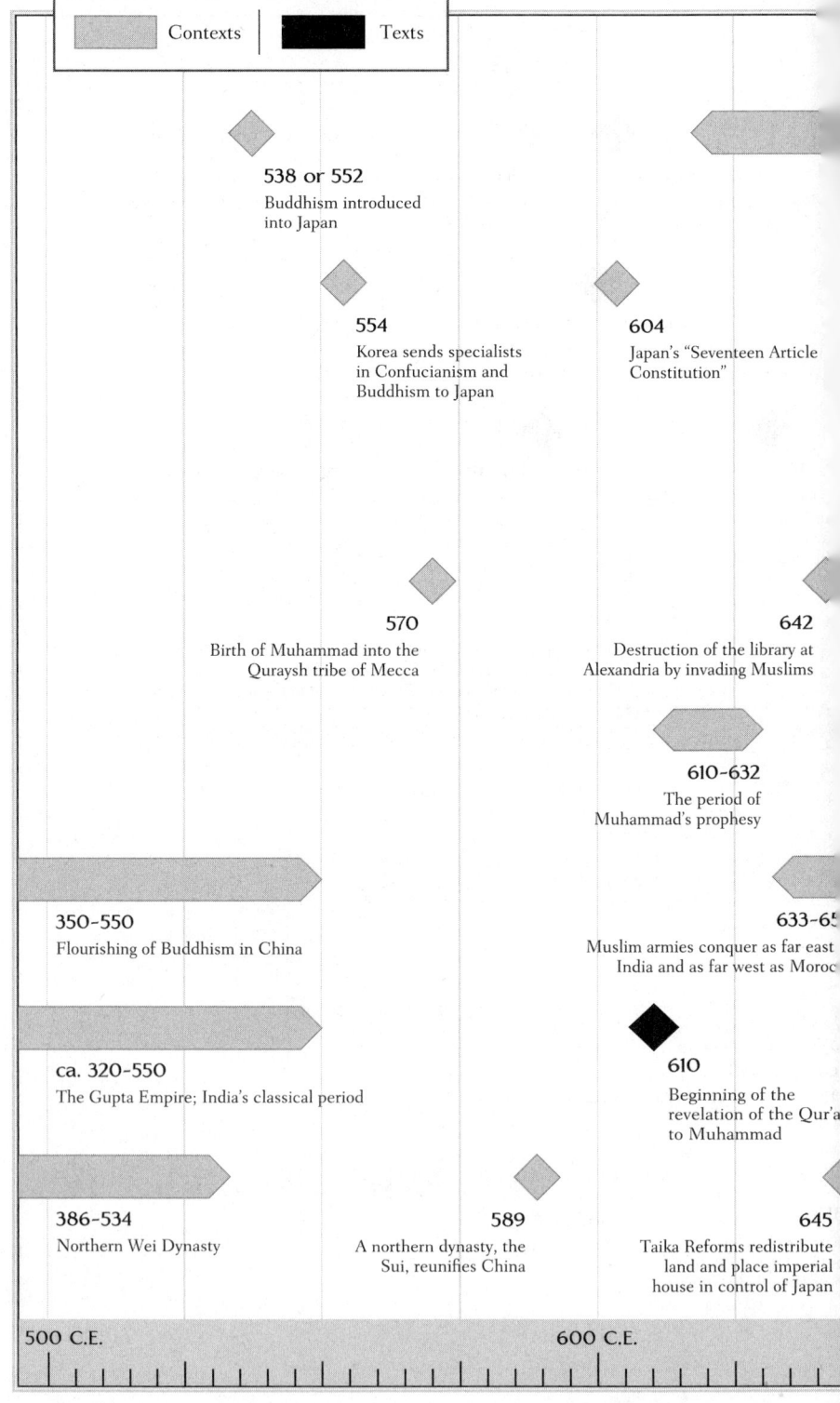

Contexts | Texts

538 or 552
Buddhism introduced into Japan

554
Korea sends specialists in Confucianism and Buddhism to Japan

604
Japan's "Seventeen Article Constitution"

570
Birth of Muhammad into the Quraysh tribe of Mecca

642
Destruction of the library at Alexandria by invading Muslims

610-632
The period of Muhammad's prophesy

350-550
Flourishing of Buddhism in China

633-6!
Muslim armies conquer as far east India and as far west as Moroc

ca. 320-550
The Gupta Empire; India's classical period

610
Beginning of the revelation of the Qur'a to Muhammad

386-534
Northern Wei Dynasty

589
A northern dynasty, the Sui, reunifies China

645
Taika Reforms redistribute land and place imperial house in control of Japan

500 C.E.   600 C.E.

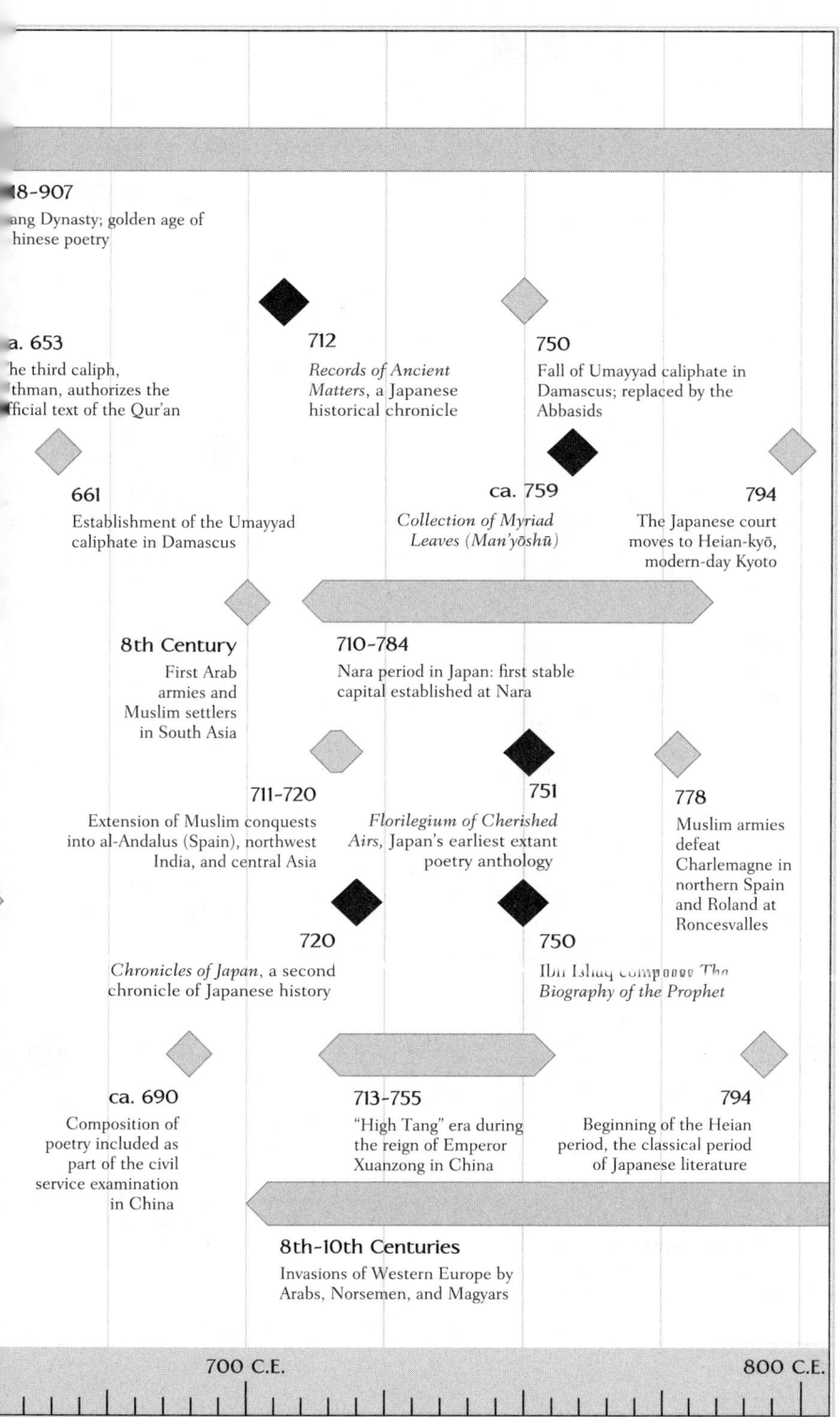

18–907

ang Dynasty; golden age of
hinese poetry

a. 653

he third caliph,
'thman, authorizes the
fficial text of the Qur'an

712

*Records of Ancient
Matters,* a Japanese
historical chronicle

750

Fall of Umayyad caliphate in
Damascus; replaced by the
Abbasids

661

Establishment of the Umayyad
caliphate in Damascus

ca. 759

*Collection of Myriad
Leaves (Man'yōshū)*

794

The Japanese court
moves to Heian-kyō,
modern-day Kyoto

8th Century

First Arab
armies and
Muslim settlers
in South Asia

710–784

Nara period in Japan: first stable
capital established at Nara

711–720

Extension of Muslim conquests
into al-Andalus (Spain), northwest
India, and central Asia

751

*Florilegium of Cherished
Airs,* Japan's earliest extant
poetry anthology

778

Muslim armies
defeat
Charlemagne in
northern Spain
and Roland at
Roncesvalles

720

Chronicles of Japan, a second
chronicle of Japanese history

750

Ibn Ishaq composes *The
Biography of the Prophet*

ca. 690

Composition of
poetry included as
part of the civil
service examination
in China

713–755

"High Tang" era during
the reign of Emperor
Xuanzong in China

794

Beginning of the Heian
period, the classical period
of Japanese literature

8th–10th Centuries

Invasions of Western Europe by
Arabs, Norsemen, and Magyars

700 C.E.

800 C.E.

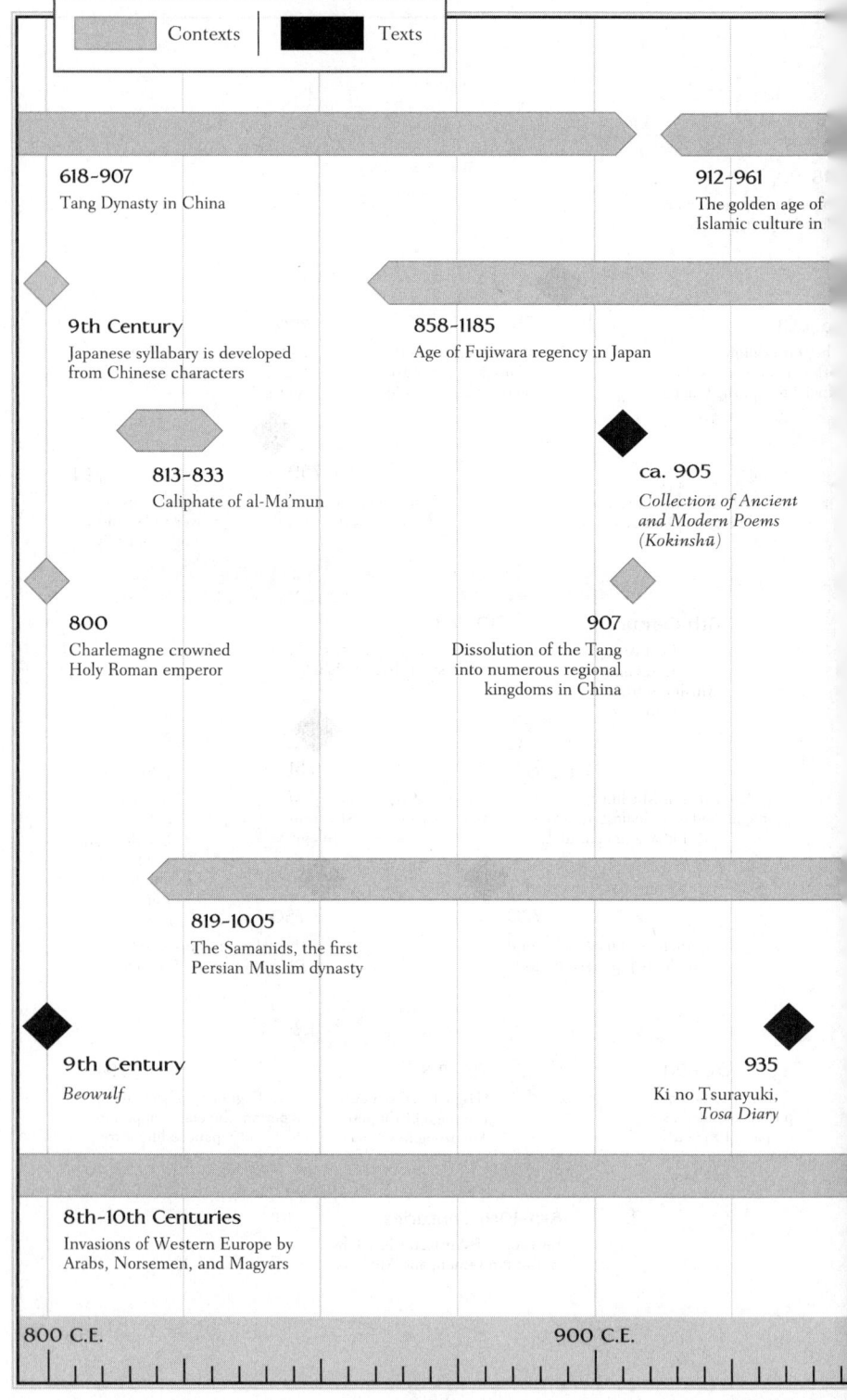

Contexts | Texts

618-907
Tang Dynasty in China

912-961
The golden age of
Islamic culture in

9th Century
Japanese syllabary is developed
from Chinese characters

858-1185
Age of Fujiwara regency in Japan

813-833
Caliphate of al-Ma'mun

ca. 905
*Collection of Ancient
and Modern Poems
(Kokinshū)*

800
Charlemagne crowned
Holy Roman emperor

907
Dissolution of the Tang
into numerous regional
kingdoms in China

819-1005
The Samanids, the first
Persian Muslim dynasty

9th Century
Beowulf

935
Ki no Tsurayuki,
Tosa Diary

8th-10th Centuries
Invasions of Western Europe by
Arabs, Norsemen, and Magyars

800 C.E.

900 C.E.

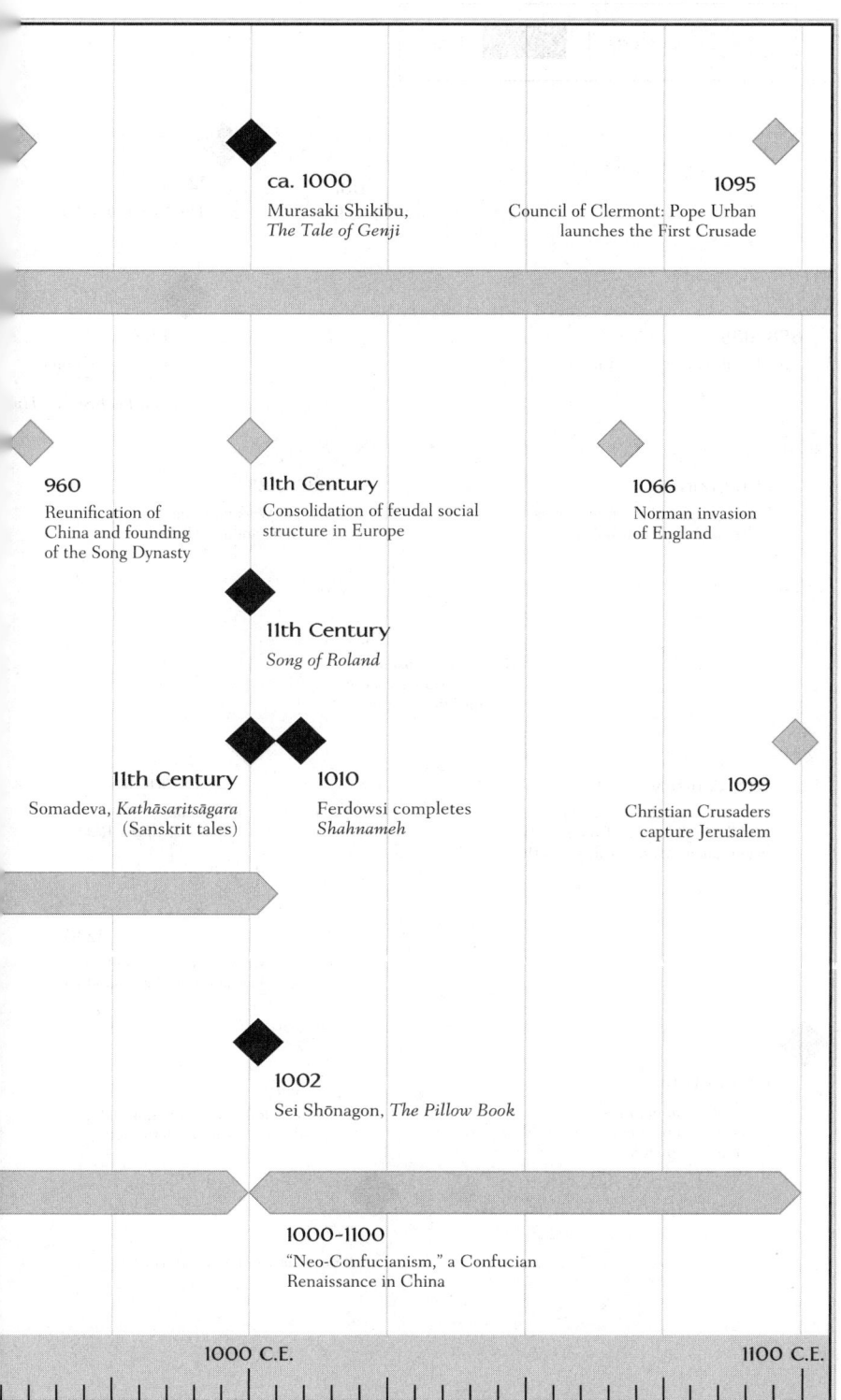

ca. 1000
Murasaki Shikibu,
The Tale of Genji

1095
Council of Clermont: Pope Urban
launches the First Crusade

960
Reunification of
China and founding
of the Song Dynasty

11th Century
Consolidation of feudal social
structure in Europe

1066
Norman invasion
of England

11th Century
Song of Roland

11th Century
Somadeva, *Kathāsaritsāgara*
(Sanskrit tales)

1010
Ferdowsi completes
Shahnameh

1099
Christian Crusaders
capture Jerusalem

1002
Sei Shōnagon, *The Pillow Book*

1000–1100
"Neo-Confucianism," a Confucian
Renaissance in China

1000 C.E.

1100 C.E.

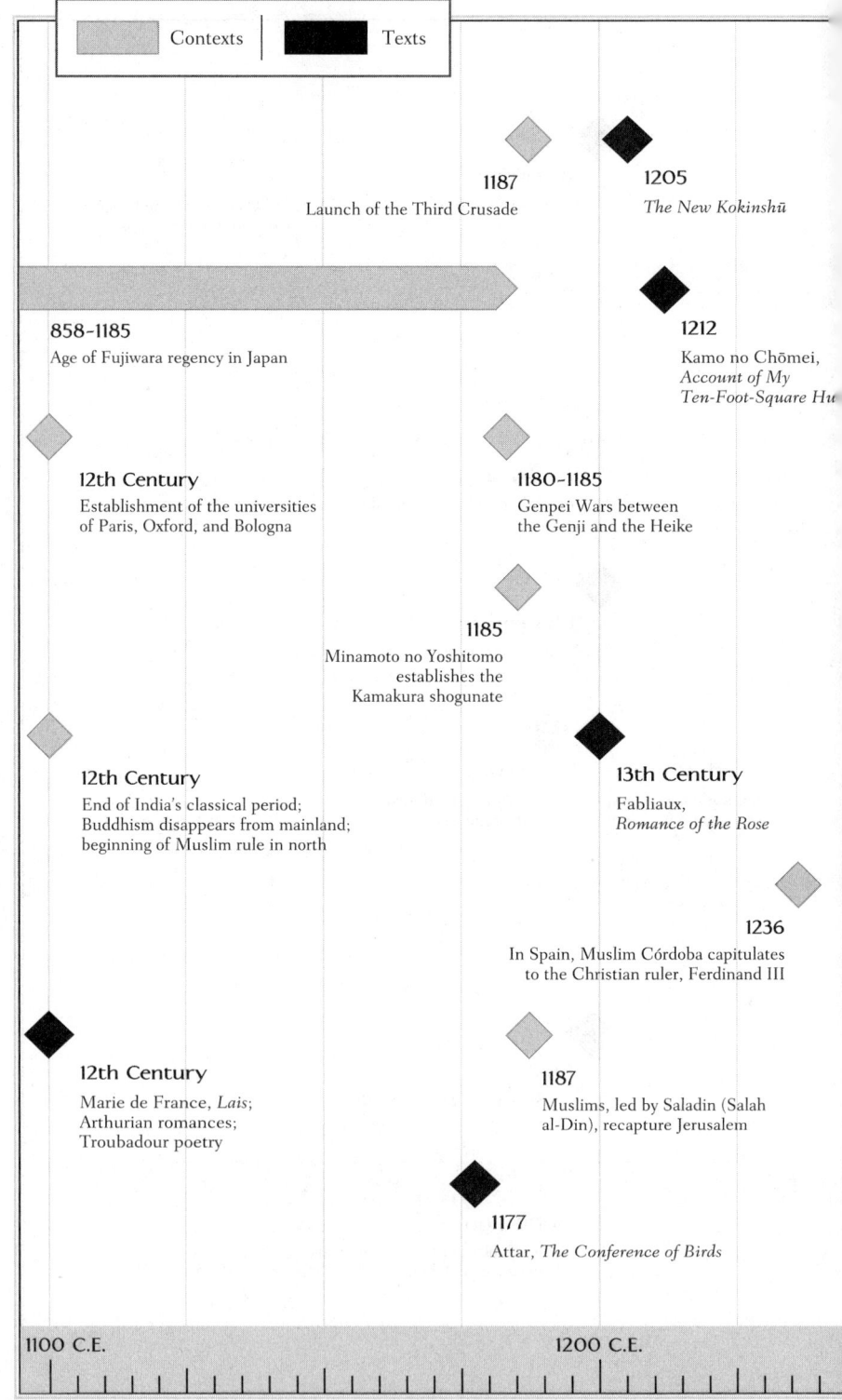

Contexts | Texts

1187
Launch of the Third Crusade

1205
The New Kokinshū

858–1185
Age of Fujiwara regency in Japan

1212
Kamo no Chōmei,
*Account of My
Ten-Foot-Square Hu*

12th Century
Establishment of the universities
of Paris, Oxford, and Bologna

1180–1185
Genpei Wars between
the Genji and the Heike

1185
Minamoto no Yoshitomo
establishes the
Kamakura shogunate

12th Century
End of India's classical period;
Buddhism disappears from mainland;
beginning of Muslim rule in north

13th Century
Fabliaux,
Romance of the Rose

1236
In Spain, Muslim Córdoba capitulates
to the Christian ruler, Ferdinand III

12th Century
Marie de France, *Lais*;
Arthurian romances;
Troubadour poetry

1187
Muslims, led by Saladin (Salah
al-Din), recapture Jerusalem

1177
Attar, *The Conference of Birds*

1100 C.E.   1200 C.E.

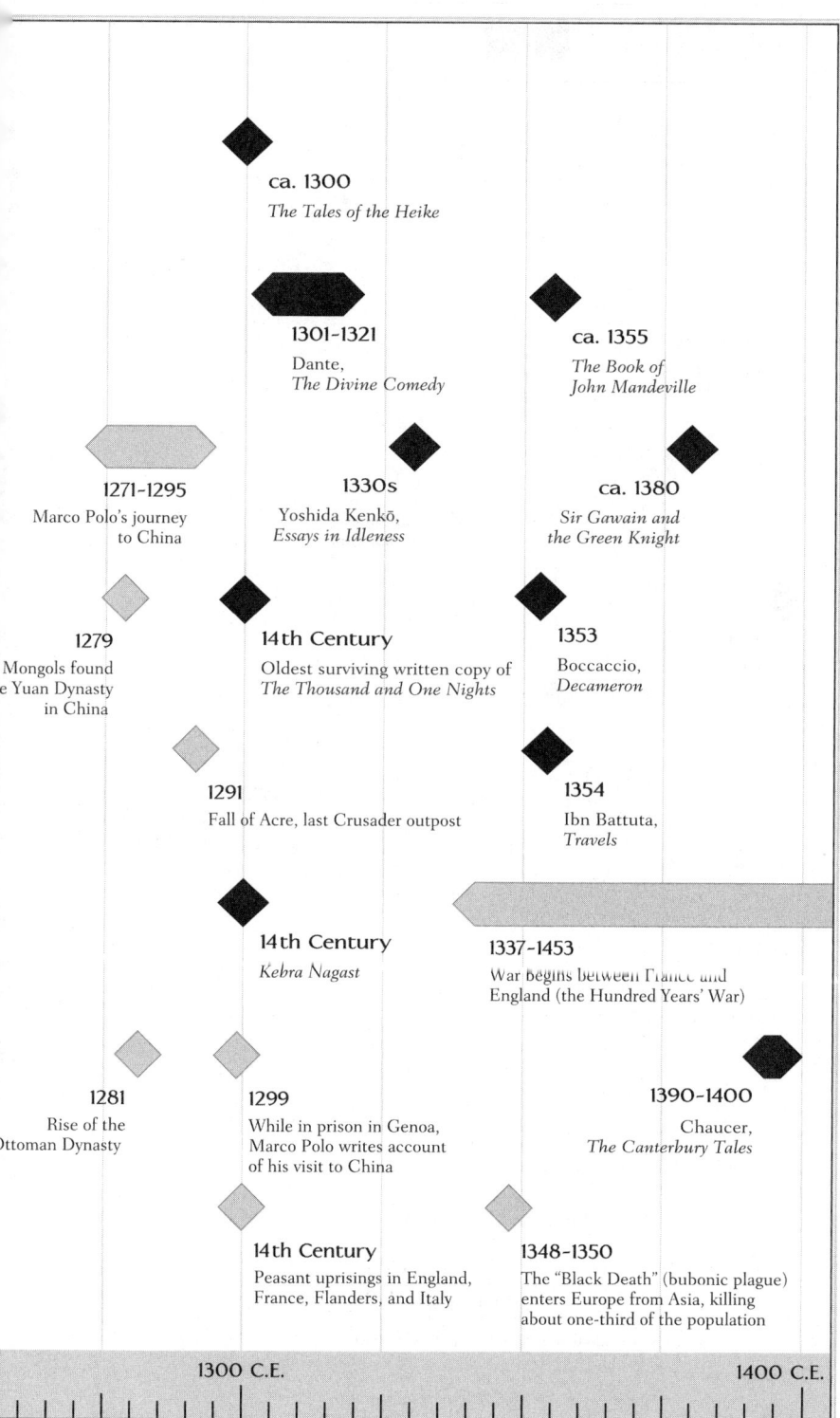

ca. 1300
The Tales of the Heike

1301-1321
Dante,
The Divine Comedy

ca. 1355
*The Book of
John Mandeville*

1271-1295
Marco Polo's journey
to China

1330s
Yoshida Kenkō,
Essays in Idleness

ca. 1380
*Sir Gawain and
the Green Knight*

1279
Mongols found
the Yuan Dynasty
in China

14th Century
Oldest surviving written copy of
The Thousand and One Nights

1353
Boccaccio,
Decameron

1291
Fall of Acre, last Crusader outpost

1354
Ibn Battuta,
Travels

14th Century
Kebra Nagast

1337-1453
War begins between France and
England (the Hundred Years' War)

1281
Rise of the
Ottoman Dynasty

1299
While in prison in Genoa,
Marco Polo writes account
of his visit to China

1390-1400
Chaucer,
The Canterbury Tales

14th Century
Peasant uprisings in England,
France, Flanders, and Italy

1348-1350
The "Black Death" (bubonic plague)
enters Europe from Asia, killing
about one-third of the population

1300 C.E.

1400 C.E.

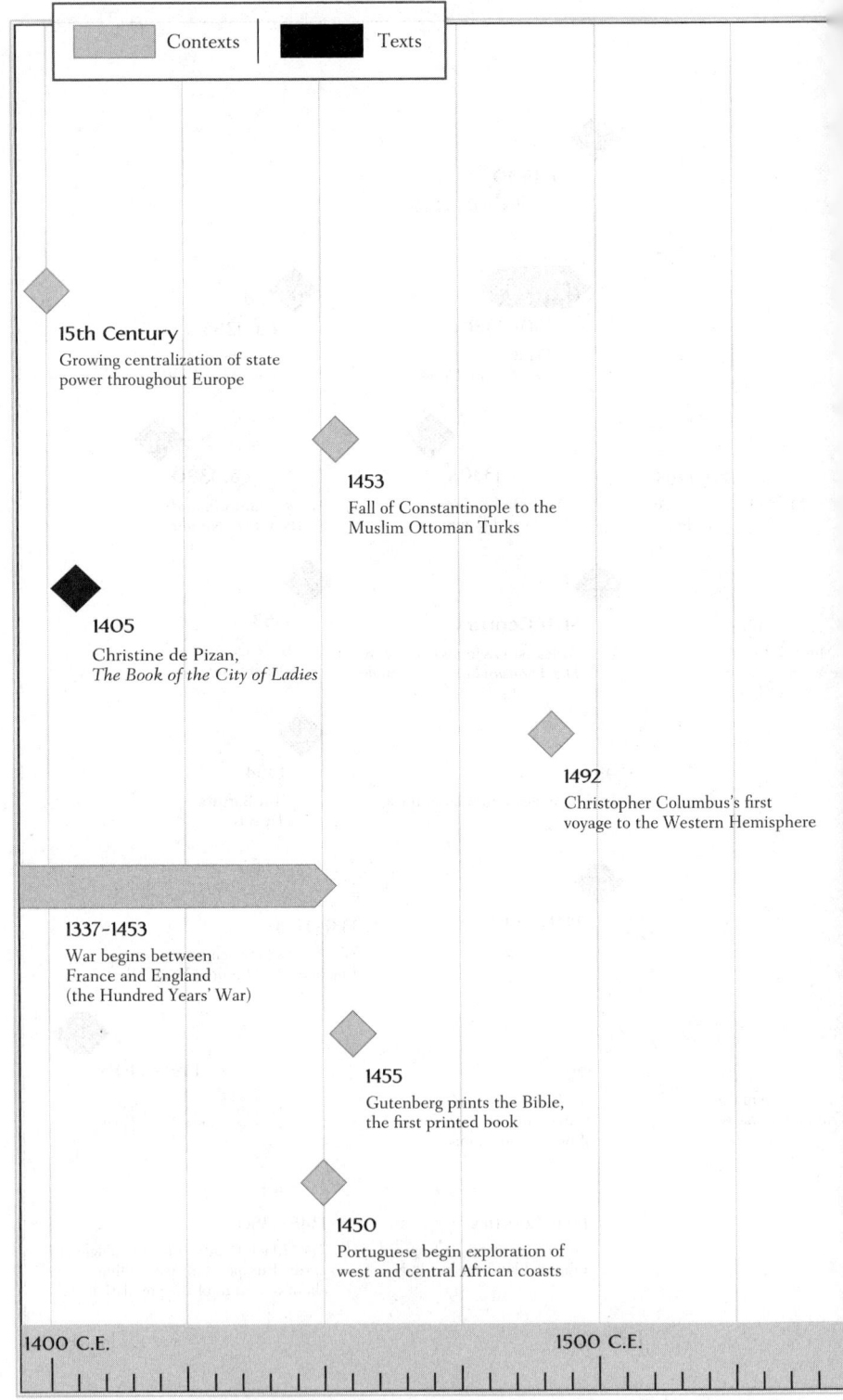

Contexts | Texts

15th Century
Growing centralization of state
power throughout Europe

1453
Fall of Constantinople to the
Muslim Ottoman Turks

1405
Christine de Pizan,
The Book of the City of Ladies

1492
Christopher Columbus's first
voyage to the Western Hemisphere

1337–1453
War begins between
France and England
(the Hundred Years' War)

1455
Gutenberg prints the Bible,
the first printed book

1450
Portuguese begin exploration of
west and central African coasts

1400 C.E.   1500 C.E.

1600 C.E.

1700 C.E.

TIMELINE *for*

| Contexts | Texts |

6th-8th Centuries

South Indian *bhakti*
poets compose hymns to
Śiva

ca. 1035

Sanhaja chief Yahya Ibn
Ibrahim makes
pilgrimage to Mecca

8th Century

Stone inscriptions–the
first monuments of
literature in Turkish

ca. 8th Century

The Songhay kingdom of Gao
becomes an important terminus for
trans-Saharan trade with Muslim
North Africa

ca. 1042-4

Founding of the Almoravi
movement in the Wester
Sahara by Ibn Yaci

Timeline spans 500 years on these two pages

800 C.E.   900 C.E.   1000 C.E.

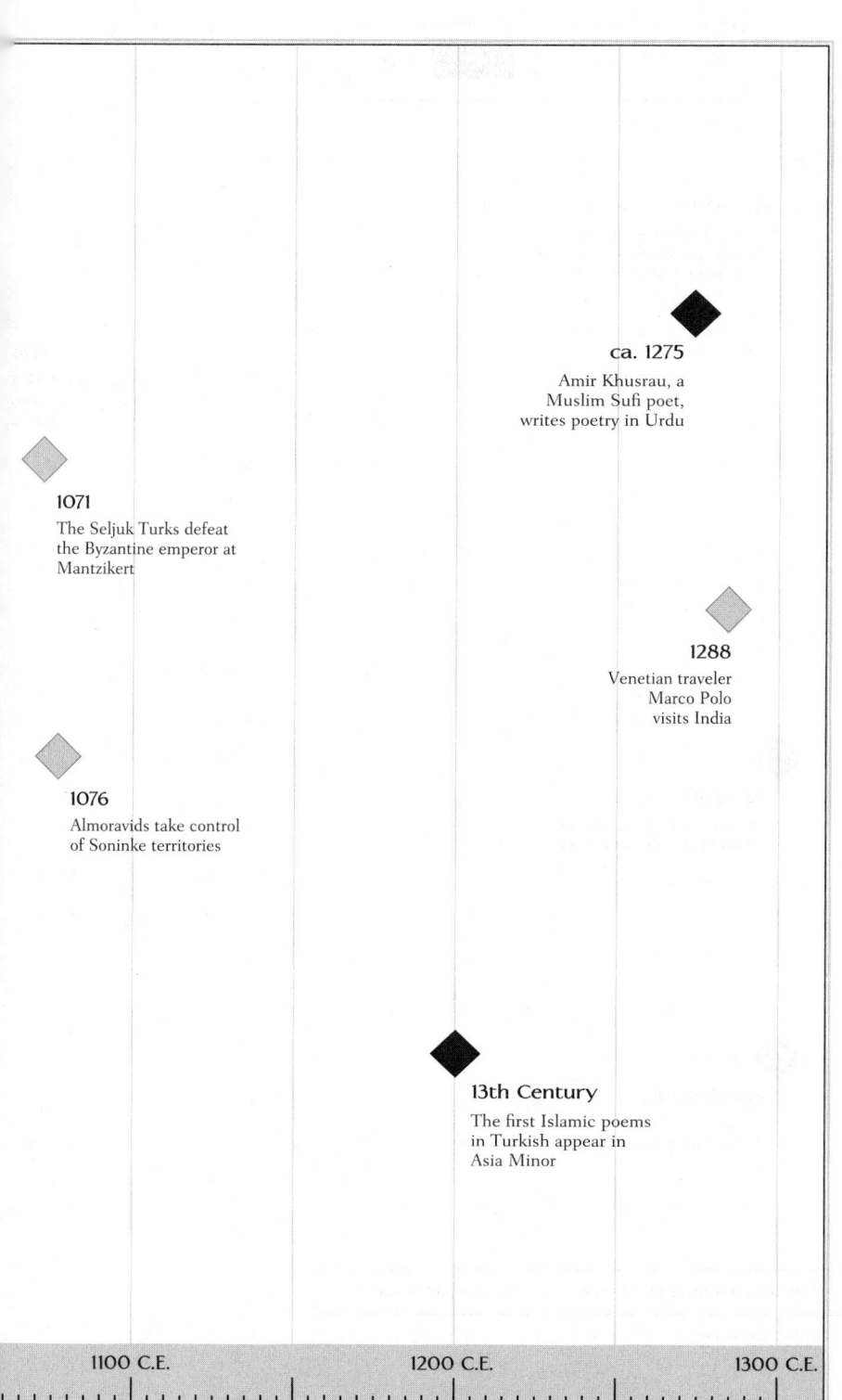

ca. 1275

Amir Khusrau, a
Muslim Sufi poet,
writes poetry in Urdu

1071

The Seljuk Turks defeat
the Byzantine emperor at
Mantzikert

1288

Venetian traveler
Marco Polo
visits India

1076

Almoravids take control
of Soninke territories

13th Century

The first Islamic poems
in Turkish appear in
Asia Minor

1100 C.E.   1200 C.E.   1300 C.E.

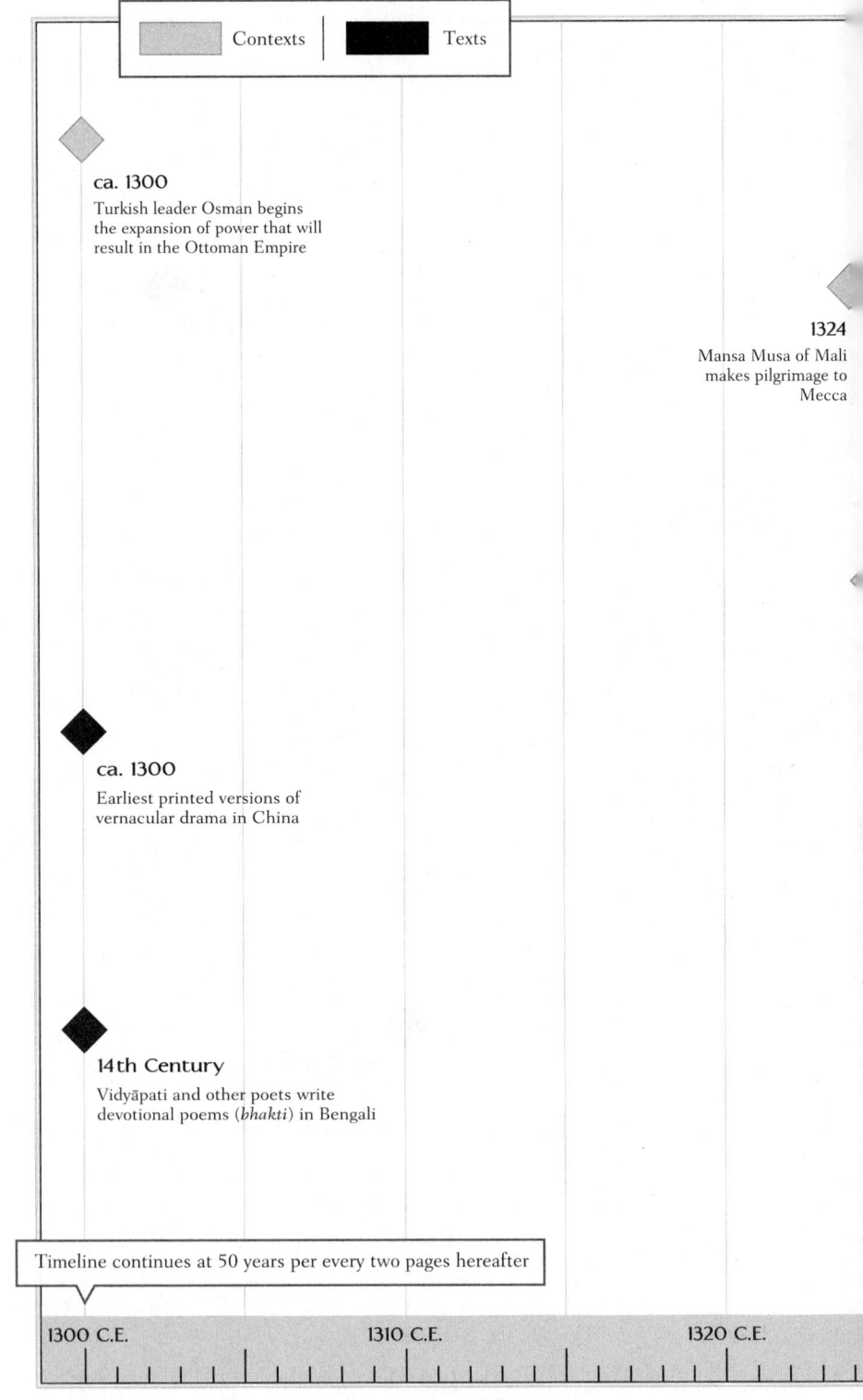

Contexts | Texts

ca. 1300
Turkish leader Osman begins
the expansion of power that will
result in the Ottoman Empire

1324
Mansa Musa of Mali
makes pilgrimage to
Mecca

ca. 1300
Earliest printed versions of
vernacular drama in China

14th Century
Vidyāpati and other poets write
devotional poems (*bhakti*) in Bengali

Timeline continues at 50 years per every two pages hereafter

1300 C.E.   1310 C.E.   1320 C.E.

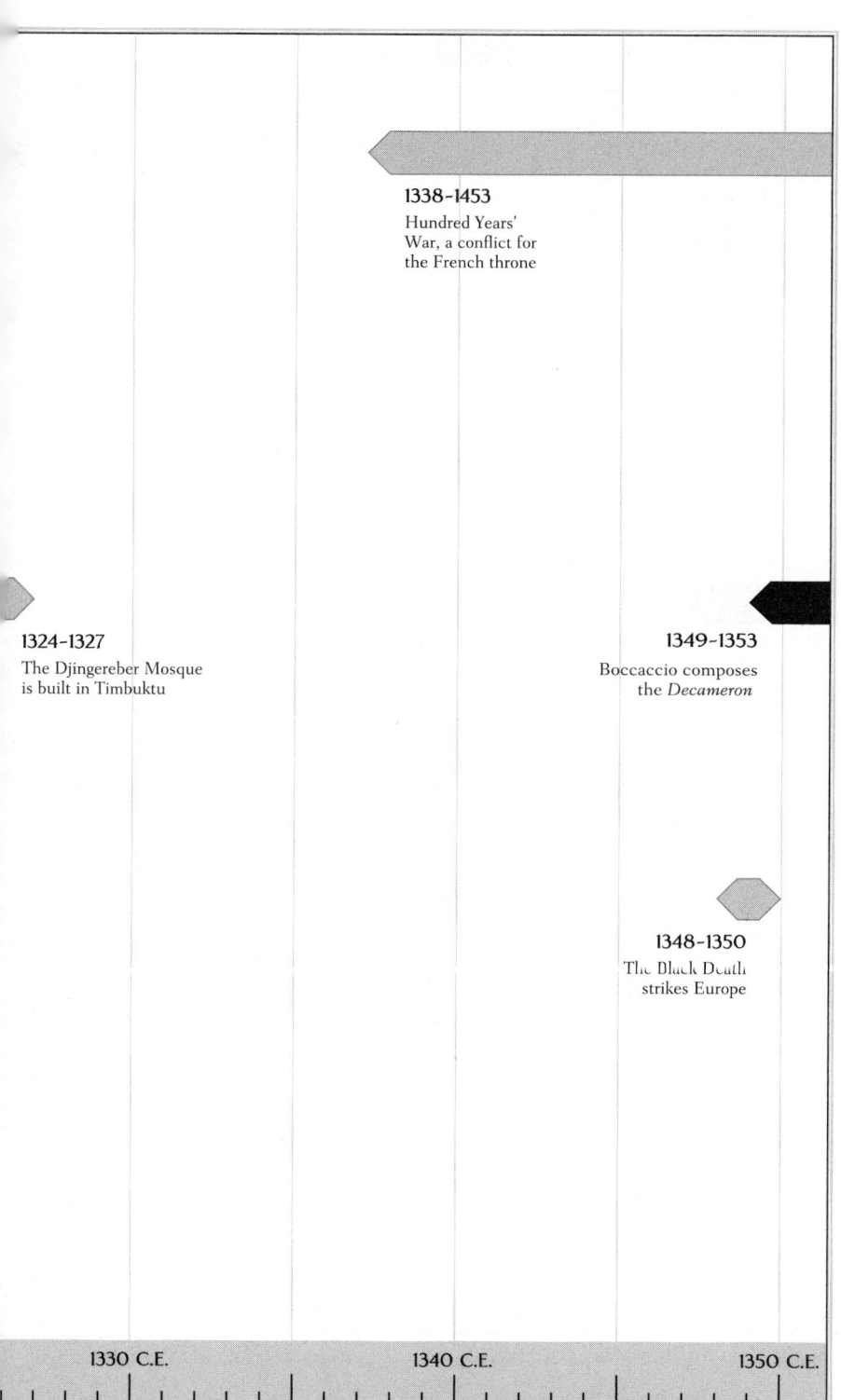

1338-1453

Hundred Years'
War, a conflict for
the French throne

1324-1327

The Djingereber Mosque
is built in Timbuktu

1349-1353

Boccaccio composes
the *Decameron*

1348-1350

The Black Death
strikes Europe

1330 C.E.   1340 C.E.   1350 C.E.

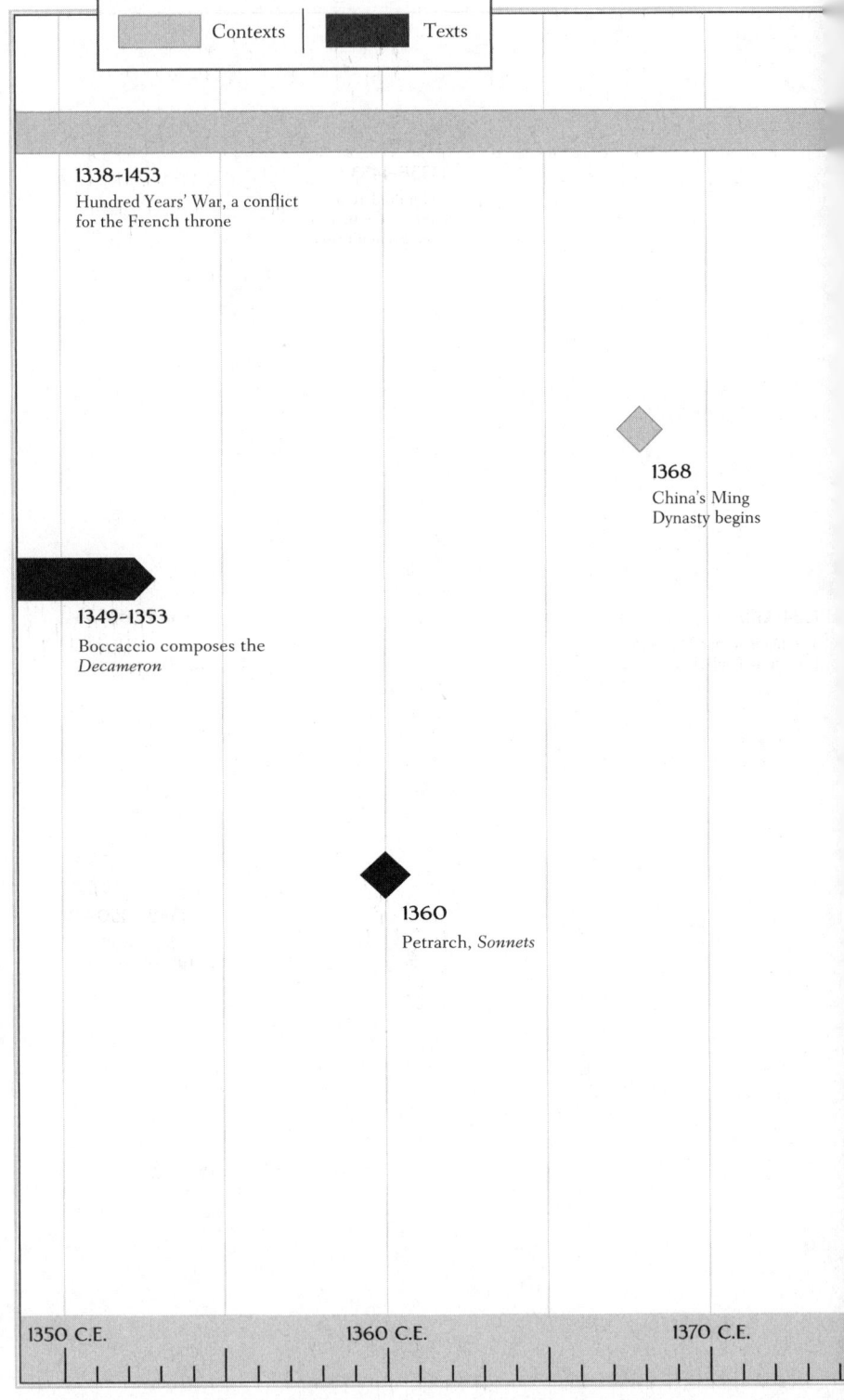

Contexts | Texts

1338–1453
Hundred Years' War, a conflict
for the French throne

1368
China's Ming
Dynasty begins

1349–1353
Boccaccio composes the
Decameron

1360
Petrarch, *Sonnets*

1350 C.E.   1360 C.E.   1370 C.E.

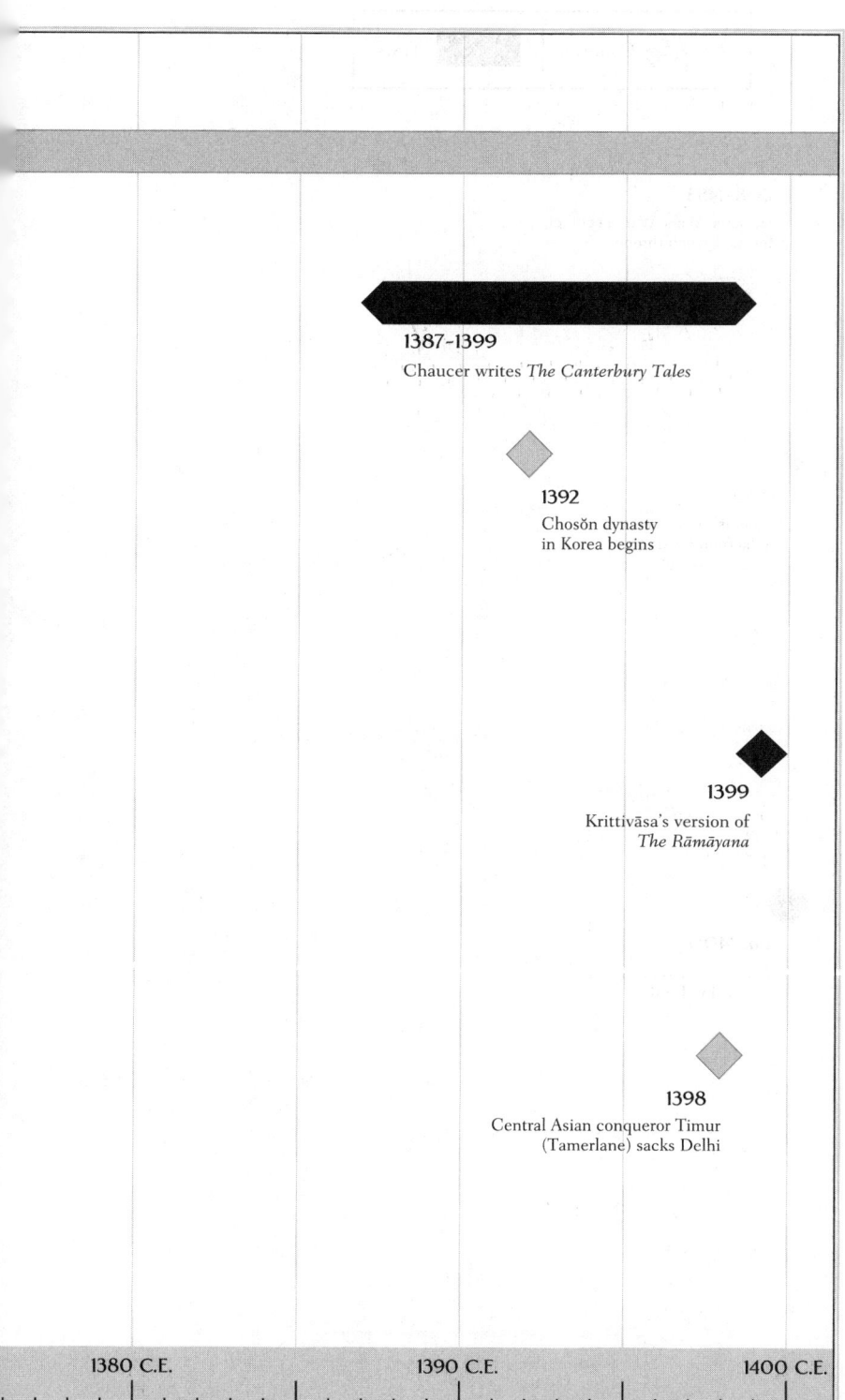

1387–1399
Chaucer writes *The Canterbury Tales*

1392
Chosŏn dynasty
in Korea begins

1399
Krittivāsa's version of
The Rāmāyana

1398
Central Asian conqueror Timur
(Tamerlane) sacks Delhi

1380 C.E.   1390 C.E.   1400 C.E.

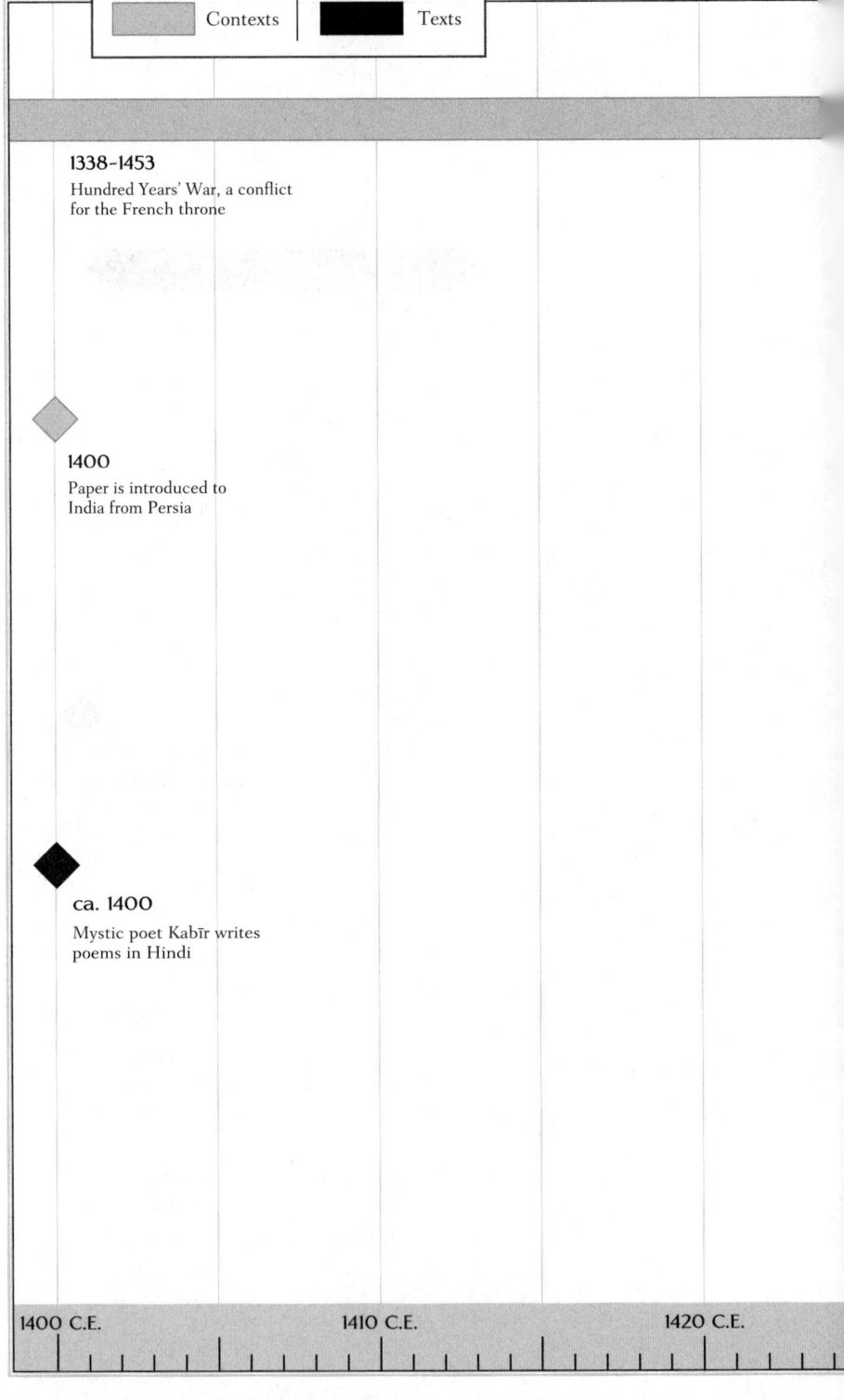

Contexts | Texts

1338–1453
Hundred Years' War, a conflict
for the French throne

1400
Paper is introduced to
India from Persia

ca. 1400
Mystic poet Kabīr writes
poems in Hindi

1400 C.E.   1410 C.E.   1420 C.E.

1446

King Sejong of Korea promulgates Hangul, a native alphabet

1430 C.E.   1440 C.E.   1450 C.E.

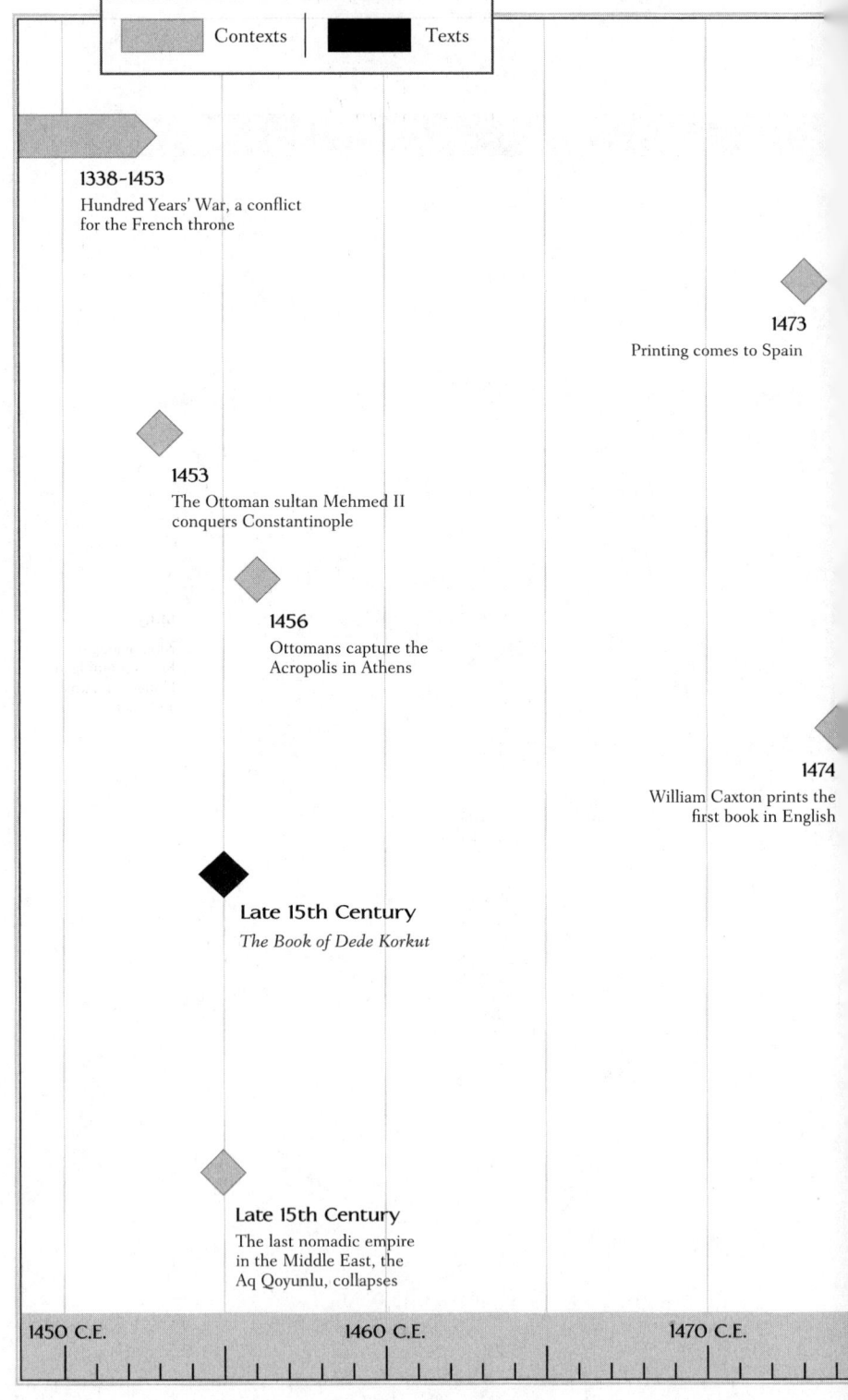

Contexts | Texts

1338-1453
Hundred Years' War, a conflict
for the French throne

1473
Printing comes to Spain

1453
The Ottoman sultan Mehmed II
conquers Constantinople

1456
Ottomans capture the
Acropolis in Athens

1474
William Caxton prints the
first book in English

Late 15th Century
The Book of Dede Korkut

Late 15th Century
The last nomadic empire
in the Middle East, the
Aq Qoyunlu, collapses

1450 C.E.   1460 C.E.   1470 C.E.

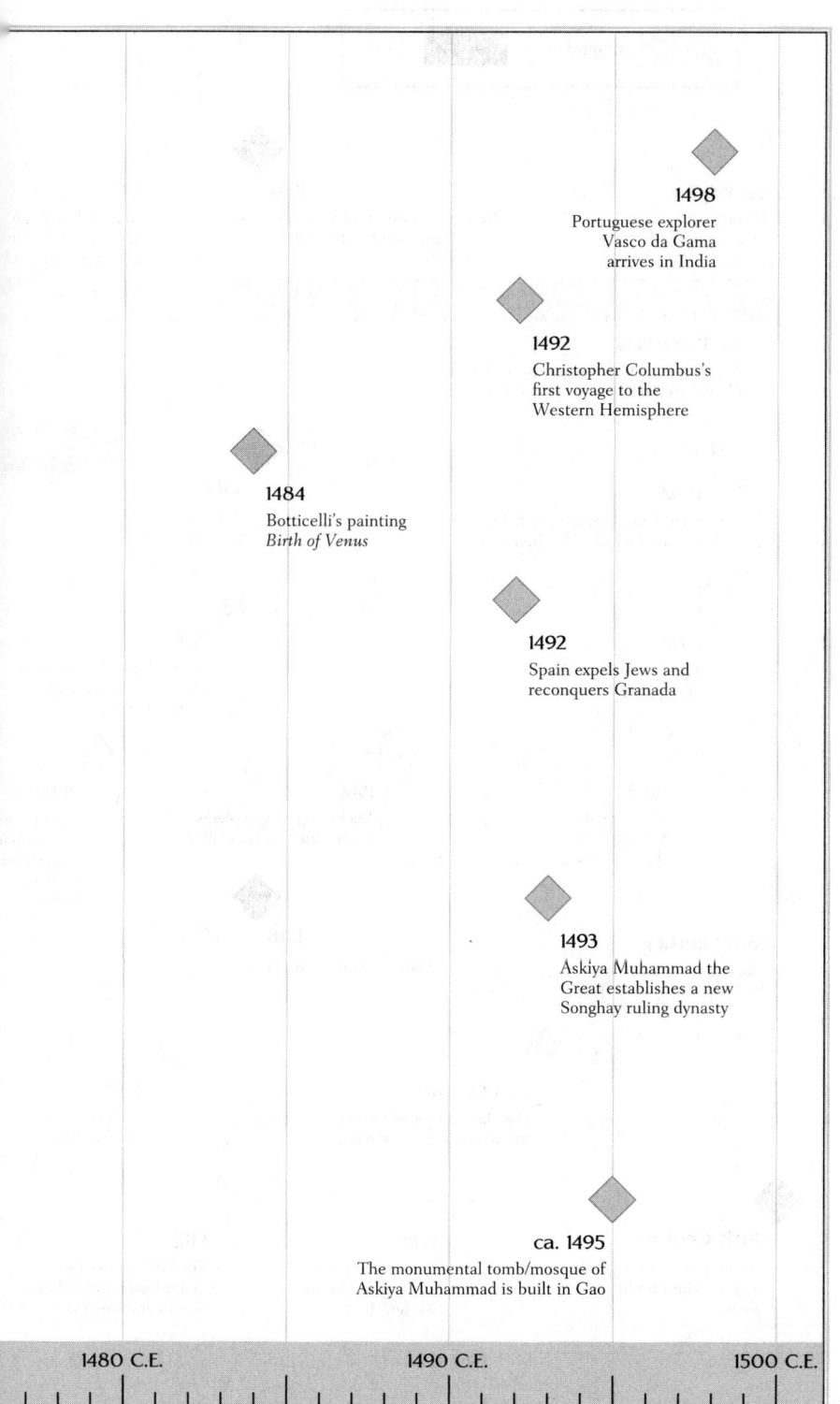

1498
Portuguese explorer
Vasco da Gama
arrives in India

1492
Christopher Columbus's
first voyage to the
Western Hemisphere

1484
Botticelli's painting
Birth of Venus

1492
Spain expels Jews and
reconquers Granada

1493
Askiya Muhammad the
Great establishes a new
Songhay ruling dynasty

ca. 1495
The monumental tomb/mosque of
Askiya Muhammad is built in Gao

1480 C.E.   1490 C.E.   1500 C.E.

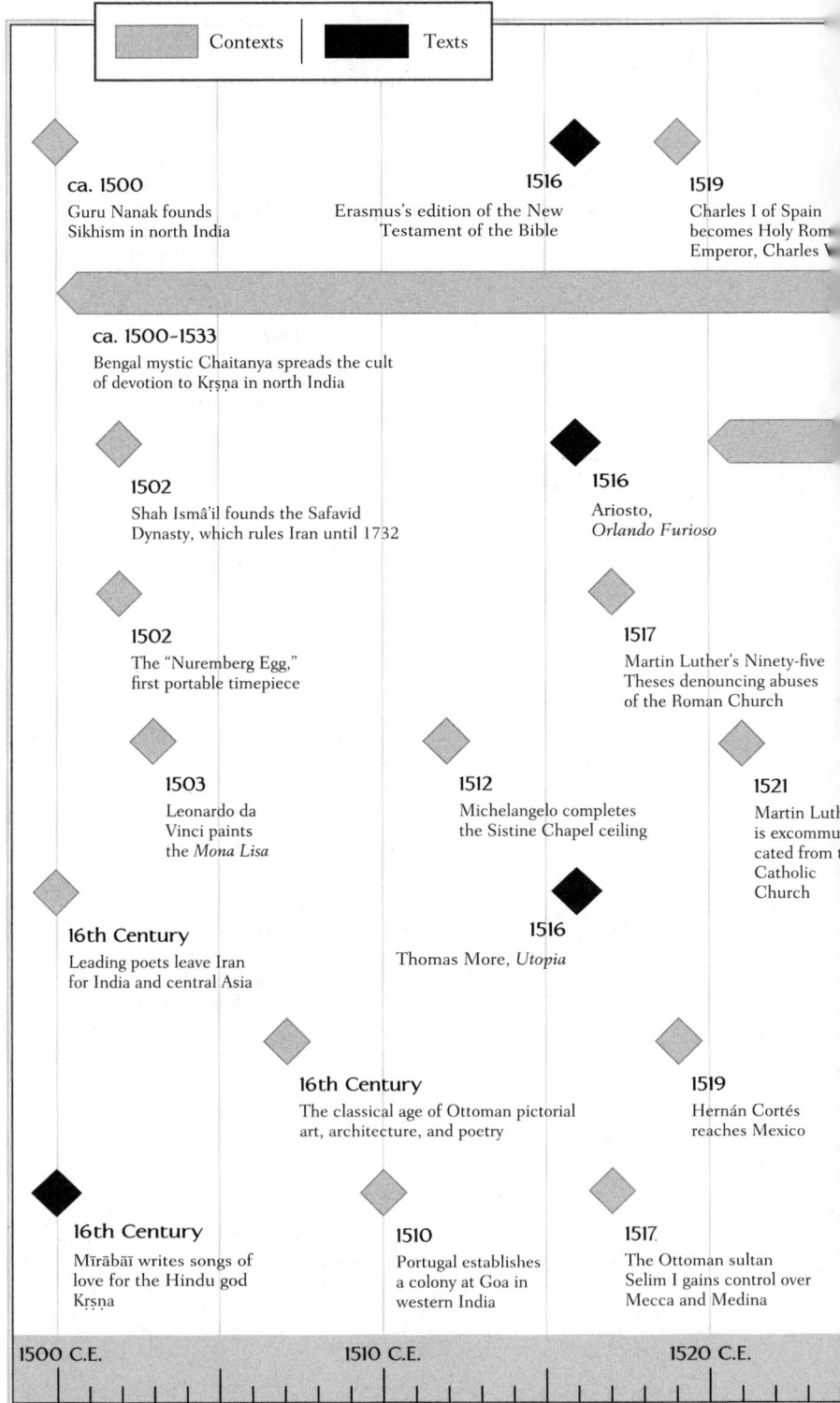

Contexts | Texts

ca. 1500
Guru Nanak founds
Sikhism in north India

1516
Erasmus's edition of the New
Testament of the Bible

1519
Charles I of Spain
becomes Holy Rom
Emperor, Charles V

ca. 1500–1533
Bengal mystic Chaitanya spreads the cult
of devotion to Kṛṣṇa in north India

1502
Shah Ismâ'il founds the Safavid
Dynasty, which rules Iran until 1732

1516
Ariosto,
Orlando Furioso

1502
The "Nuremberg Egg,"
first portable timepiece

1517
Martin Luther's Ninety-five
Theses denouncing abuses
of the Roman Church

1503
Leonardo da
Vinci paints
the *Mona Lisa*

1512
Michelangelo completes
the Sistine Chapel ceiling

1521
Martin Luth
is excommu
cated from
Catholic
Church

1516
Thomas More, *Utopia*

16th Century
Leading poets leave Iran
for India and central Asia

16th Century
The classical age of Ottoman pictorial
art, architecture, and poetry

1519
Hernán Cortés
reaches Mexico

16th Century
Mīrābāī writes songs of
love for the Hindu god
Kṛṣṇa

1510
Portugal establishes
a colony at Goa in
western India

1517
The Ottoman sultan
Selim I gains control over
Mecca and Medina

1500 C.E.   1510 C.E.   1520 C.E.

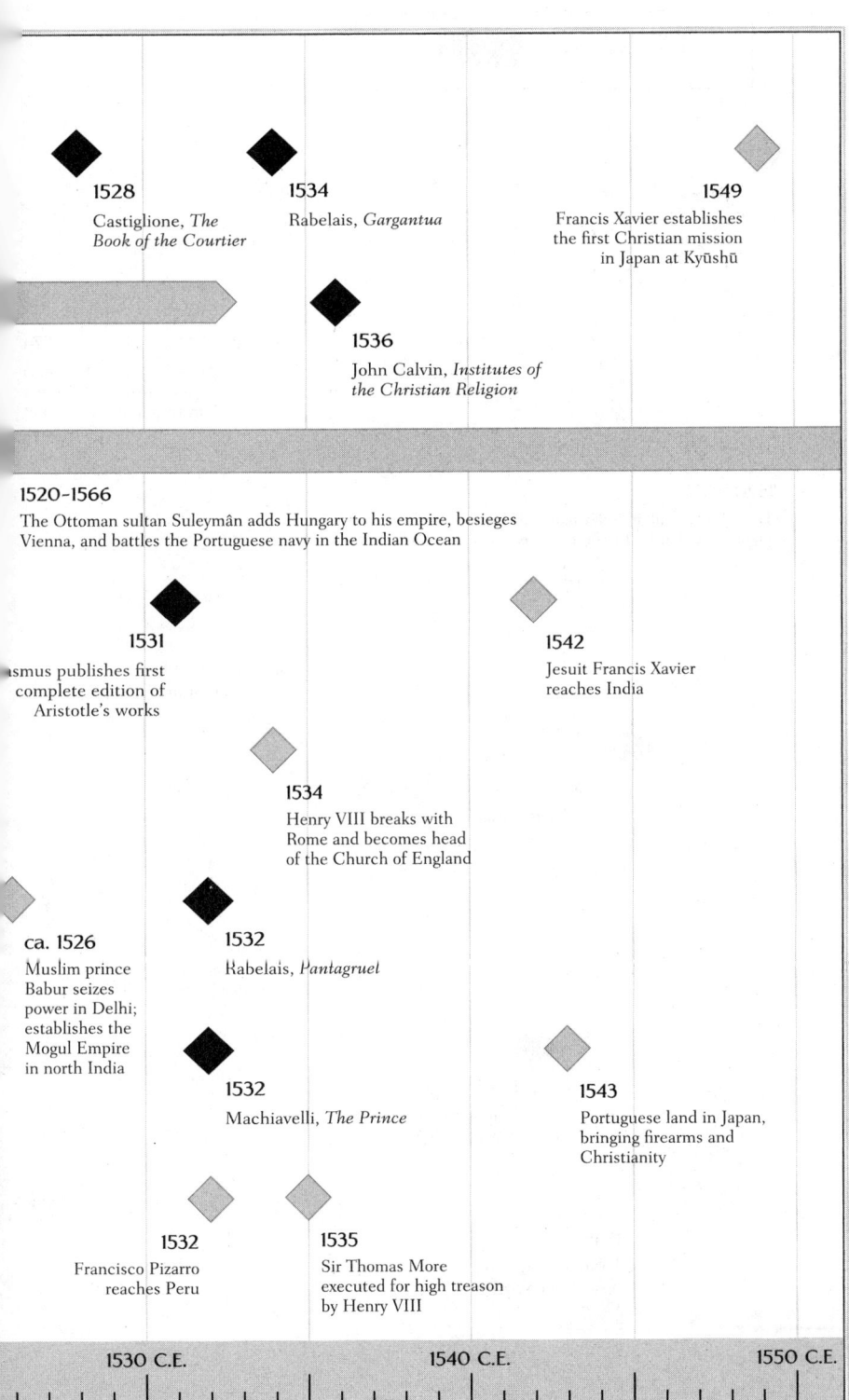

1528

Castiglione, *The Book of the Courtier*

1534

Rabelais, *Gargantua*

1549

Francis Xavier establishes the first Christian mission in Japan at Kyūshū

1536

John Calvin, *Institutes of the Christian Religion*

1520–1566

The Ottoman sultan Suleymân adds Hungary to his empire, besieges Vienna, and battles the Portuguese navy in the Indian Ocean

1531

...smus publishes first complete edition of Aristotle's works

1542

Jesuit Francis Xavier reaches India

1534

Henry VIII breaks with Rome and becomes head of the Church of England

ca. 1526

Muslim prince Babur seizes power in Delhi; establishes the Mogul Empire in north India

1532

Rabelais, *Pantagruel*

1532

Machiavelli, *The Prince*

1543

Portuguese land in Japan, bringing firearms and Christianity

1532

Francisco Pizarro reaches Peru

1535

Sir Thomas More executed for high treason by Henry VIII

1530 C.E.   1540 C.E.   1550 C.E.

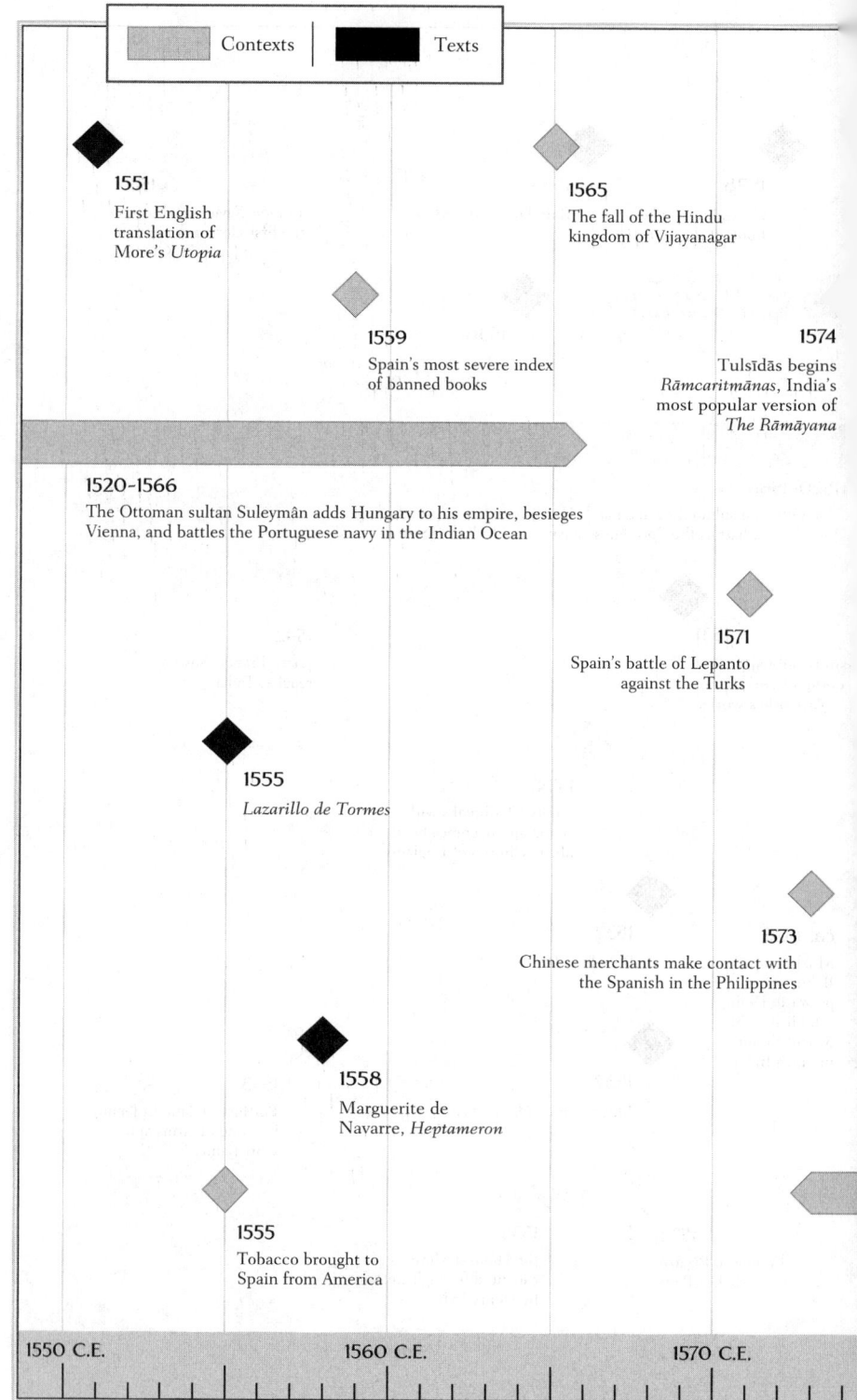

Contexts | Texts

1551

First English translation of More's *Utopia*

1565

The fall of the Hindu kingdom of Vijayanagar

1559

Spain's most severe index of banned books

1574

Tulsīdās begins *Rāmcaritmānas*, India's most popular version of *The Rāmāyana*

1520–1566

The Ottoman sultan Suleymân adds Hungary to his empire, besieges Vienna, and battles the Portuguese navy in the Indian Ocean

1571

Spain's battle of Lepanto against the Turks

1555

Lazarillo de Tormes

1573

Chinese merchants make contact with the Spanish in the Philippines

1558

Marguerite de Navarre, *Heptameron*

1555

Tobacco brought to Spain from America

1550 C.E.　　　　　1560 C.E.　　　　　1570 C.E.

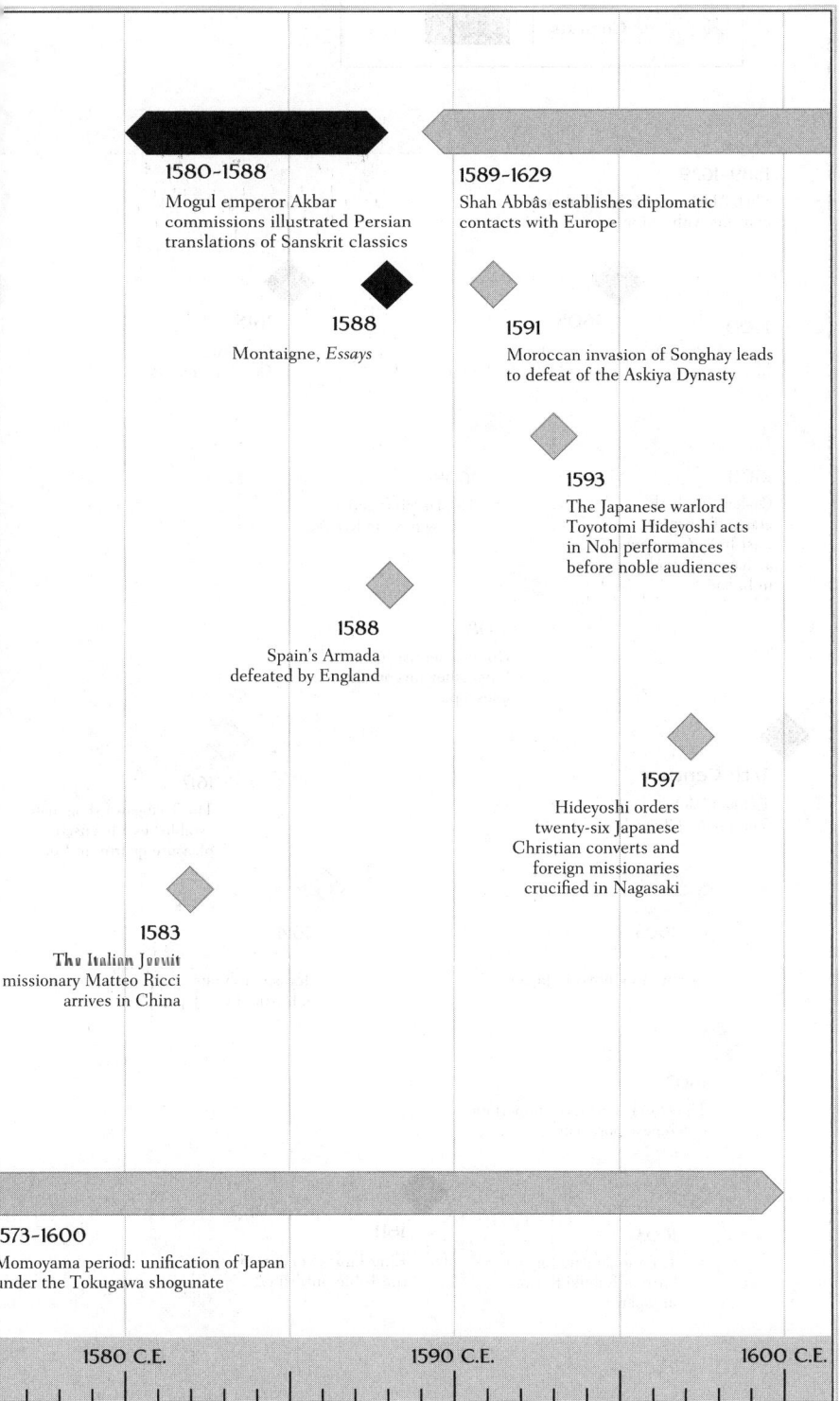

1580-1588

Mogul emperor Akbar commissions illustrated Persian translations of Sanskrit classics

1589-1629

Shah Abbâs establishes diplomatic contacts with Europe

1588

Montaigne, *Essays*

1591

Moroccan invasion of Songhay leads to defeat of the Askiya Dynasty

1593

The Japanese warlord Toyotomi Hideyoshi acts in Noh performances before noble audiences

1588

Spain's Armada defeated by England

1597

Hideyoshi orders twenty-six Japanese Christian converts and foreign missionaries crucified in Nagasaki

1583

The Italian Jesuit missionary Matteo Ricci arrives in China

1573-1600

Momoyama period: unification of Japan under the Tokugawa shogunate

1580 C.E.   1590 C.E.   1600 C.E.

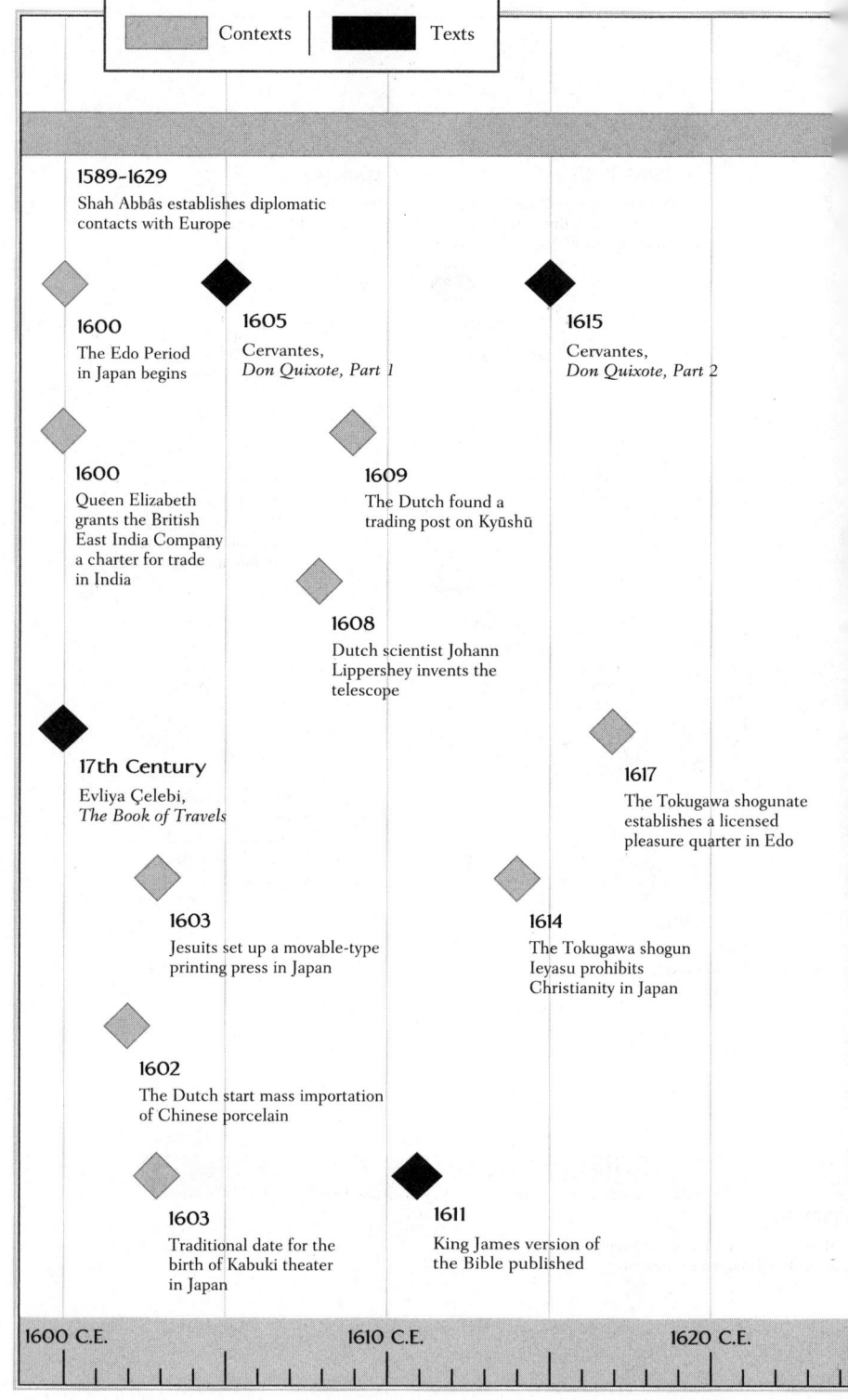

Contexts | Texts

1589–1629
Shah Abbâs establishes diplomatic
contacts with Europe

1600
The Edo Period
in Japan begins

1605
Cervantes,
Don Quixote, Part 1

1615
Cervantes,
Don Quixote, Part 2

1600
Queen Elizabeth
grants the British
East India Company
a charter for trade
in India

1609
The Dutch found a
trading post on Kyūshū

1608
Dutch scientist Johann
Lippershey invents the
telescope

17th Century
Evliya Çelebi,
The Book of Travels

1617
The Tokugawa shogunate
establishes a licensed
pleasure quarter in Edo

1603
Jesuits set up a movable-type
printing press in Japan

1614
The Tokugawa shogun
Ieyasu prohibits
Christianity in Japan

1602
The Dutch start mass importation
of Chinese porcelain

1603
Traditional date for the
birth of Kabuki theater
in Japan

1611
King James version of
the Bible published

1600 C.E.   1610 C.E.   1620 C.E.

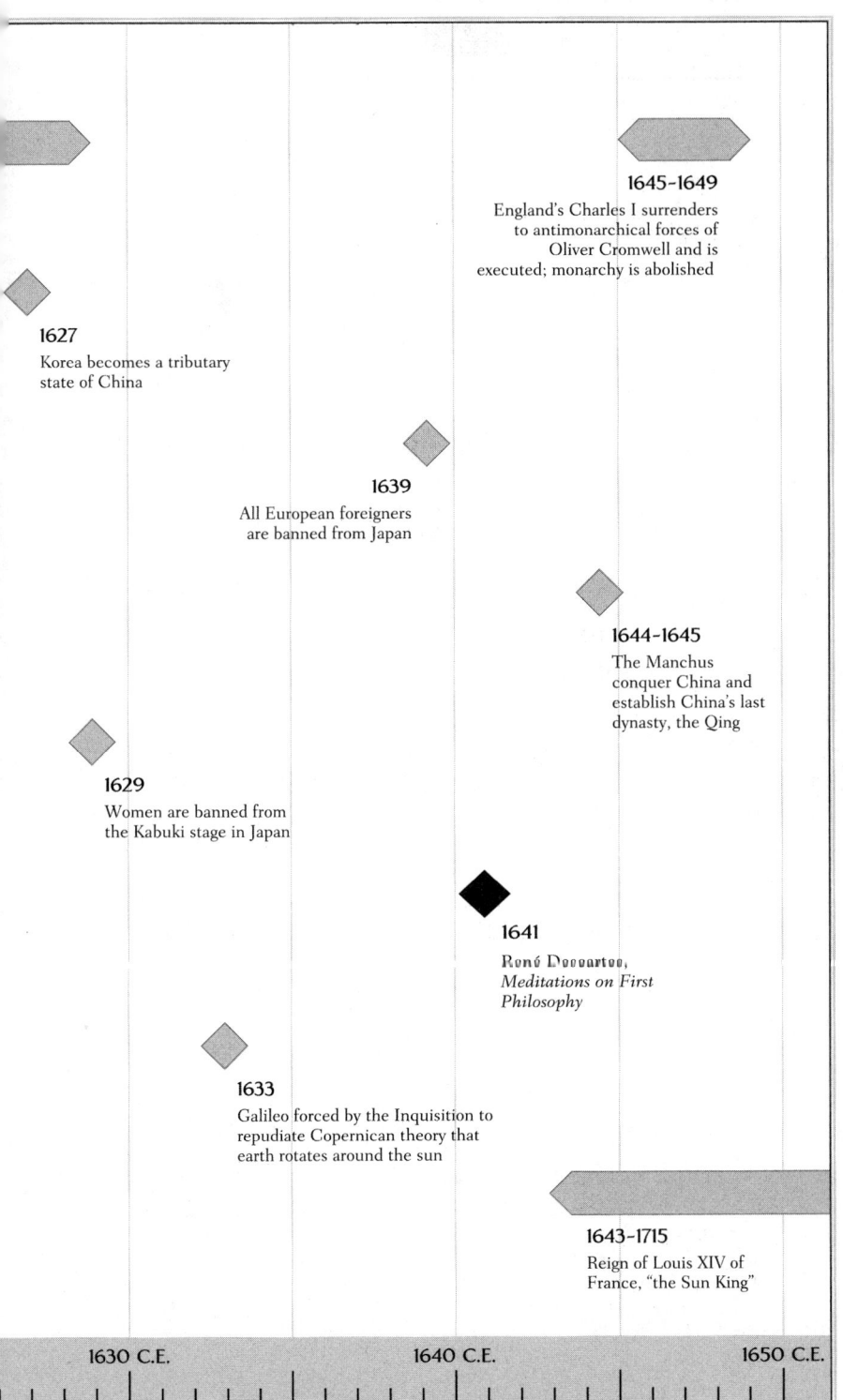

1645–1649
England's Charles I surrenders
to antimonarchical forces of
Oliver Cromwell and is
executed; monarchy is abolished

1627
Korea becomes a tributary
state of China

1639
All European foreigners
are banned from Japan

1644–1645
The Manchus
conquer China and
establish China's last
dynasty, the Qing

1629
Women are banned from
the Kabuki stage in Japan

1641
René Descartes,
*Meditations on First
Philosophy*

1633
Galileo forced by the Inquisition to
repudiate Copernican theory that
earth rotates around the sun

1643–1715
Reign of Louis XIV of
France, "the Sun King"

1630 C.E.   1640 C.E.   1650 C.E.

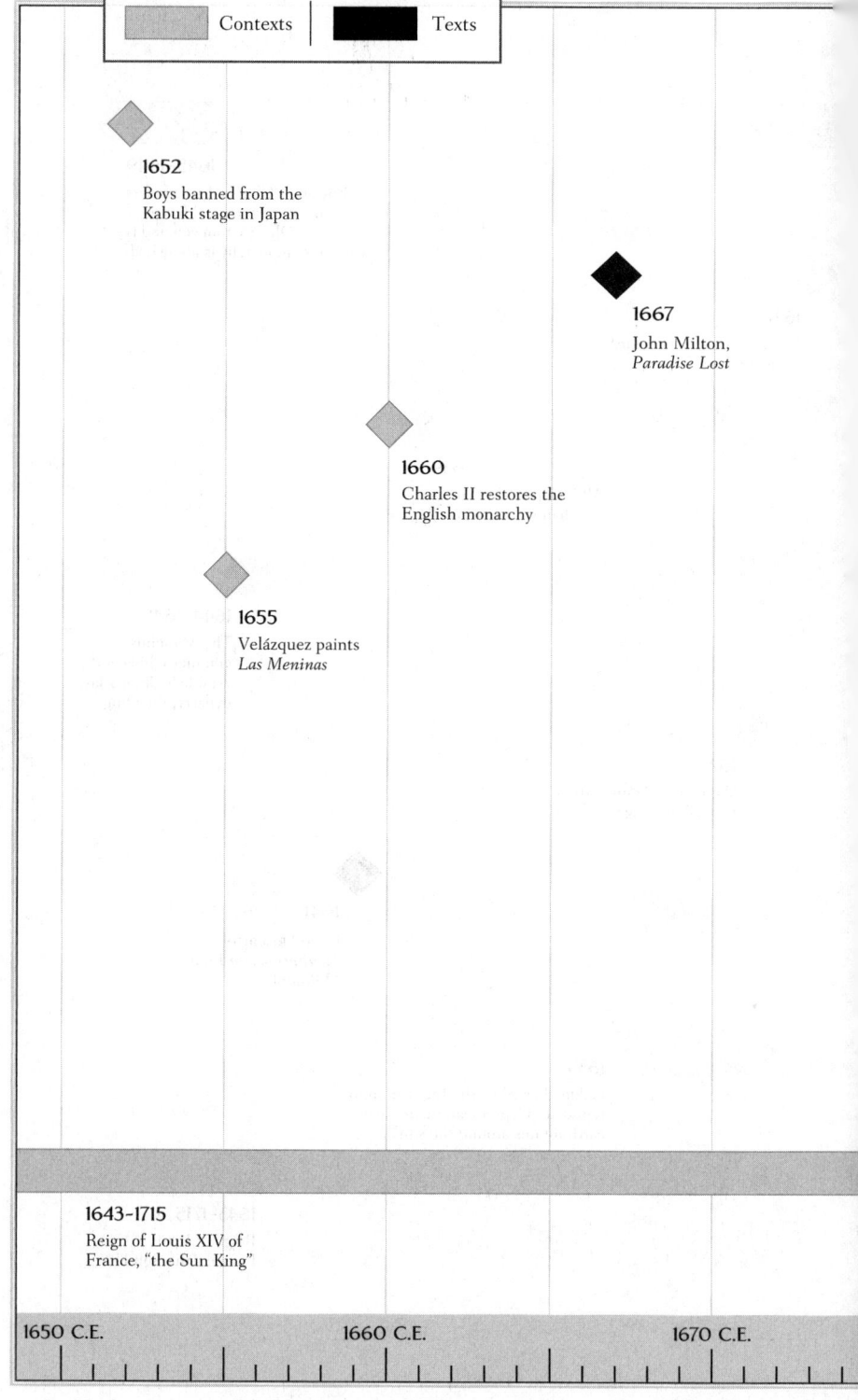

Contexts | Texts

1652
Boys banned from the
Kabuki stage in Japan

1667
John Milton,
Paradise Lost

1660
Charles II restores the
English monarchy

1655
Velázquez paints
Las Meninas

1643–1715
Reign of Louis XIV of
France, "the Sun King"

1650 C.E.   1660 C.E.   1670 C.E.

1683
The second unsuccessful siege
of Vienna marks the limits of
Ottoman power in Europe

1699

Kong Shangren,
The Peach Blossom Fan

1680 C.E.   1690 C.E.   1700 C.E.

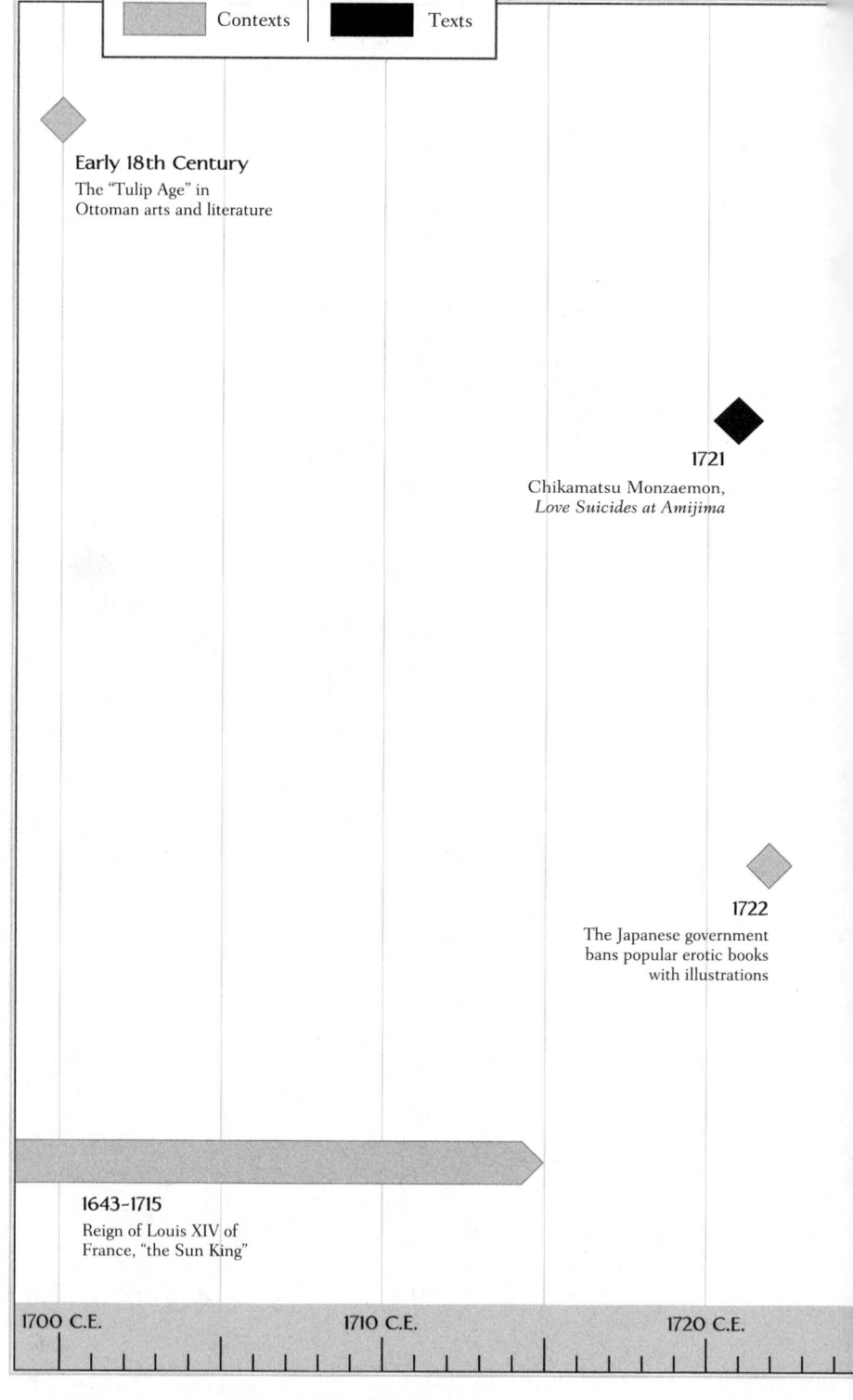

Contexts | Texts

Early 18th Century
The "Tulip Age" in
Ottoman arts and literature

1721
Chikamatsu Monzaemon,
Love Suicides at Amijima

1722
The Japanese government
bans popular erotic books
with illustrations

1643–1715
Reign of Louis XIV of
France, "the Sun King"

1700 C.E.   1710 C.E.   1720 C.E.

1726

Nader Shah, founder of
the Afshar dynasty, defeats
the Safavids in Persia

1729

Nader Shah sacks Delhi,
further weakening the
Mughals

1729

Arabic books set from
movable type are printed
in the Ottoman Empire

1730 C.E.   1740 C.E.   1750 C.E.

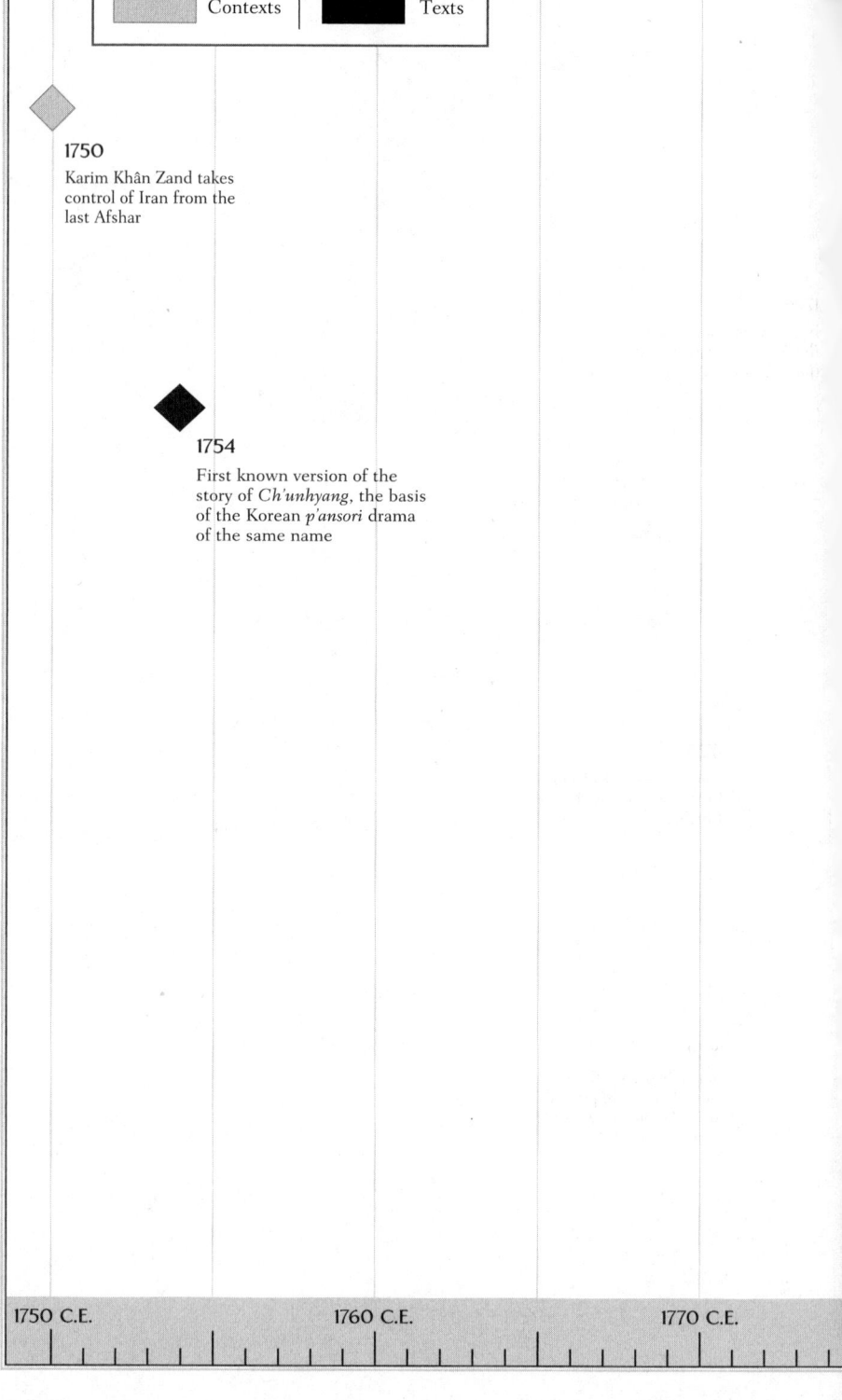

Contexts | Texts

1750
Karim Khân Zand takes
control of Iran from the
last Afshar

1754
First known version of the
story of *Ch'unhyang*, the basis
of the Korean *p'ansori* drama
of the same name

1750 C.E.   1760 C.E.   1770 C.E.

1798

Napoleon Bonaparte
invades Egypt

1779–1924

The Qajars gradually take
control of Iran from the Zands

1780 C.E.   1790 C.E.   1800 C.E.

Permissions Acknowledgments

Dharmakīrti: Translations by Vinay Dharwadker from THE COLUMBIA BOOK OF SOUTH ASIAN POETRY to be published by Columbia University Press. Reprinted with permission of the publisher.

Du Fu: "Qiang Village 1," translated by Paul W. Kroll. is reprinted by permission of Paul W. Kroll. "Thoughts While Traveling at Night" from THREE CHINESE POETS: TRANSLATIONS OF POEMS BY WANG WEI, LI BAI, AND DU FU (1992), trans. by Vikram Seth. Copyright © 1992 by Vikram Seth. Reprinted by permission of David Godwin Associates Ltd. "My Thatched Roof is Ruined by the Autumn Wind" and "Spending the Night in a Tower by the River," trans. by Stephen Owen from THE GREAT AGE OF CHINESE POETRY. Copyright © 1981 by Yale University. Reprinted by permission of Yale University Press. "Moonlight Night," "Spring Prospect," "Ballad of the Firewood Vendors," and "Autumn Meditations IV" from SELECTED POEMS OF DU FU, trans. by Burton Watson. Copyright © 2003 by Columbia University Press. Reprinted by permission of the publisher. "Painted Hawk" and "I Stand Alone" from AN ANTHOLOGY OF CHINESE LITERATURE: BEGINNINGS TO 1911, ed. and trans. by Stephen Owen. Copyright © 1996 by Stephen Owen and The Council for Cultural Planning and Development of the Executive Yuan of the Republic of China. Used by permission of W.W. Norton & Company, Inc.

Egyptian Love Poems: From THE SONG OF SONGS AND THE ANCIENT EGYPTIAN LOVE SONGS by Michael V. Fox (The University of Wisconsin Press 2005) is reprinted by permission of the translator.

Euripides: MEDEA from ALCESTIS, MEDEA, HIPPOLYTUS, trans. D. Arnson Svarlien. Copyright © 2008 by Hackett Publishing Company, Inc. All rights reserved. Reprinted by permission of Hackett Publishing Company, Inc.

Abolqasem Ferdowsi: "The Story of Darab and the Fuller," "Sekandar's Conquest of Persia," "The Reign of Sekandar," ed. and condensed from SHAHNAMEH: THE PERSIAN BOOK OF KINGS by Abolqasem Ferdowsi, foreword by Azar Nafisi, trans. by Dick Davis. Copyright © 1997, 2000, 2004 by Mage Publishers Inc. Used by permission of Viking Penguin, a division of Penguin Group (USA) Inc.

Florentine Codex: From Book 12 "The Conquest of Mexico" from FLORENTINE CODEX: GENERAL HISTORY OF THE THINGS OF NEW SPAIN, ed. and trans. by Arthur J.O. Anderson and Charles E. Dibble. Used by permission of the University of Utah Press.

Gilgamesh: From THE EPIC OF GILGAMESH, trans. by Benjamin R. Foster. Copyright © 2001 by W.W. Norton & Company, Inc. Used by permission of W.W. Norton & Company, Inc.

The Hebrew Bible: From THE FIVE BOOKS OF MOSES: A TRANSLATION WITH COMMENTARY, trans. by Robert Alter, translated by Robert Alter. Copyright © 2004 by Robert Alter. Used by permission of W.W. Norton & Company, Inc. Visual adaptation of Genesis, Chapter 25, from THE BOOK OF GENESIS ILLUSTRATED by Robert Crumb. Copyright © 2009 by Robert Crumb, with text from GENESIS: TRANSLATION AND COMMENTARY, trans. by Robert Alter. Copyright © 1996 by Robert Alter. Used by permission of W.W. Norton & Company, Inc.

Homer: THE ODYSSEY trans. by Stanley Lombardo, copyright © 2000 by Hackett Publishing Company, Inc. Reprinted by permission of Hackett Publishing Company, Inc. All rights reserved. From THE ILIAD trans. by Stanley Lombardo. Copyright © 1997 by Hackett Publishing Company, Inc. All rights reserved. Reprinted by permission of Hackett Publishing Company, Inc.

Kabir: Poems from KABIR: THE WEAVER'S SONGS trans. by Vinay Dharwadker are reprinted by permission of Penguin Group (India).

Ki no Tsurayuki: "Kanajo," "The Japanese Preface" by Ki no Tsurayuki, trans. by Laurel Rasplica Rodd from KOKINSHU: A COLLECTION OF POEMS ANCIENT AND MODERN, trans. and annotated by Laurel Rasplica Rodd with Mary Catherine Henkenius, copyright © 1996 by Cheng & Tsui Company, Inc. Used by permission of Cheng & Tsui Company, Inc.

Kokinshū: Poems from A WAKA ANTHOLOGY: Vol. 2 THE GEM-GLISTENING CUP by Edwin Cranston. Copyright © 1993 by the Board of Poems from A WAKA ANTHOLOGY: GRASSES OF REMEMBRANCE by Edwin Cranston. Copyright © 2006 by the Board of Trustees of the Leland Stanford Jr. University. All rights reserved. Used with the permission of Stanford University Press, www.sup.org. Translation by Edwin Cranston of [When pressed with longing] first appeared in "The Dark Path: Images of Longing in Japanese Love Poetry" in the *Harvard Journal of Asiatic Studies*, Vol. 35, 1975, p. 60-100. Poems from TRADITIONAL JAPANESE LITERATURE, trans. by Lewis Cook, ed. by Haruo Shirane, copyright © 2007 by Columbia University Press. Reprinted by permission of the publisher.

Laozi: From TAO TE CHING by Lao Tzu, trans. with an introduction by D.C. Lau (Penguin Classics 1963). Copyright © 1963 by D.C. Lau. Reproduced by permission of Penguin Books Ltd.

Li Bo: "Question and Answer in the Mountains," "Drinking Alone with the Moon," and "In the Quiet Night" from THREE CHINESE POETS: TRANSLATIONS OF POEMS BY WANG WEI, LI BAI, AND DU FU (1992), trans. by Vikram Seth. Copyright © 1992 by Vikram Seth. Reprinted by permission of David Godwin Associates Ltd. "The Sun Rises and Sets," "Bring in the Wine," "Summer Day in the Mountains," and "Sitting Alone by Jingting Mountain," trans. by Stephen Owen from THE GREAT AGE OF CHINESE POETRY. Copyright © 1981 by Yale University. Reprinted by

Sophocles: Translation by Robert Bagg of OEDIPUS THE KING from THE COMPLETE PLAYS OF SOPHOCLES: TRANSLATIONS by Robert Bagg and James Scully. Copyright © 2011 by Robert Bagg and James Scully. Reprinted by permission of HarperCollins Publishers.

Sunjata: From SUNJATA: A WEST AFRICAN EPIC OF THE MANDE PEOPLES, ed. and trans. by David Conrad. Copyright © 2004 by the Hackett Publishing Company, Inc. All rights reserved. Reprinted with the permission of Hackett Publishing Company, Inc.

Tao Qian: "Biography of Master Five Willows" is reprinted by permission of the publisher from REMEMBRANCES: THE EXPERIENCE OF THE PAST IN CLASSICAL CHINESE LITERATURE by Stephen Owen. Cambridge, Mass.: Harvard university Press. Copyright © 1986 by the President and Fellows of Harvard College. Poems from THE POETRY OF T'ao Ch'ien, trans. by James Robert Hightower (1970) are reprinted by permission of Oxford University Press.

The Thousand and One Nights: From THE ARABIAN NIGHTS: THE THOUSAND AND ONE NIGHTS, trans. by Husain Haddawy. Copyright © 1990 by W.W. Norton & Company, Inc. Used by permission of W.W. Norton & Company, Inc. [The Third Old Man's Tale], trans. by Jerome W. Clinton is reprinted by permission of the translator.

Tukaram: Poems trans. by Vinay Dharwadker from RELIGIONS OF INDIA IN PRACTICE, ed. Donald S. Lopez, Jr. Copyright © 1995 Princeton University Press. Reprinted by permission of Princeton University Press.

Vidyā: Reprinted by permission of the publisher from AN ANTHOLOGY OF SANSKRIT COURT POETRY: VIDYAKARA'S SUBHSITARATNAKOSA, trans. by Daniel H. Ingalls (Harvard Oriental Series, 44). Cambridge, Mass.: Harvard University Press. Copyright © 1965 by the President and Fellows of Harvard College.

Vikaṭanitambā: Reprinted by permission of the publisher from AN ANTHOLOGY OF SANSKRIT COURT POETRY: VIDYAKARA'S SUBHSITARATNAKOSA, trans. by Daniel H. Ingalls (Harvard Oriental Series, 44). Cambridge, Mass.: Harvard University Press. Copyright © 1965 by the President and Fellows of Harvard College.

Virgil: From VIRGIL: THE AENEID, trans. by Robert Fagles, copyright © 2006 by Robert Fagles. Used by permission of Viking Penguin, a division of Penguin Group (USA) Inc.

Wang Wei: From THE POETRY OF WANG WEI, tr. Pauline Yu. Copyright © 1980 by Pauline Ruth Yu. Reprinted with permission of Indiana University Press.

Yogeśvara: Reprinted by permission of the publisher from AN ANTHOLOGY OF SANSKRIT COURT POETRY: VIDYAKARA'S SUBHSITARATNAKOSA, trans. by Daniel H. Ingalls (Harvard Oriental Series, 44). Cambridge, Mass.: Harvard University Press. Copyright © 1965 by the President and Fellows of Harvard College.

Yuan Zhen: "The Story of Ying-ying," trans. by James R. Hightower, from TRADITIONAL CHINESE STORIES: THEMES AND VARIATIONS, edited by Y.W. Ma and Joseph S.M. Lau, copyright © 1978 by Columbia University Press, is reprinted by permission of Joseph S.M. Lau.

Zeami Motokiyo: "Atsumori" from JAPANESE NO DRAMAS, ed. and trans. by Royall Tyler (Penguin Classics 1992). Selection, translation, and notes copyright © 1992 by Royall Tyler. Reproduced by permission of Penguin Books Ltd.

Zhuangzi: From THE COMPLETE WORKS OF CHUANG TZU, trans. by Burton Watson. Copyright © 1968 by Columbia University Press. Reprinted with permission of the publisher.

IMAGES

2–3 bpk, Berlin / Antikensammlung, Staatliche Museen / Art Resource, NY; **4** © The Metropolitan Museum of Art / Art Resource, NY; **5** Erich Lessing / Art Resource, NY; **6** Gianni Dagli Orti/Corbis; **8** Marie Mauzy / Art Resource, NY; **9** DEA/Getty Images; **12** DEA/Getty Images; **14** Vanni / Art Resource, NY; **15** HIP / Art Resource, NY; **18** Gianni Dagli Orti/Corbis; **19** DEA/Gianni Dagli Orti/Getty Images; **35** Werner Forman / Art Resource, NY; **107–10** From The Book of Genesis © 2009 by Robert Crumb; **125** © The Trustees of the British Museum / Art Resource, NY; **476** Museo Archeologico Nazionale, Naples, Italy / Scala / Art Resource, NY; **477** Marie Mauzy / Art Resource, NY; **478** Theater and Playhouse by Richard and Helen Leacroft, Methuen Publishing, Ltd; **576** Réunion des Musées Nationaux / Art Resource, NY; **651** Andrea Jemolo / Scala / Art Resource, NY; **676–77** © The Metropolitan Museum of Art / Art Resource, NY; **680** Victoria & Albert Museum, London / Art Resource, NY; **680** © The Trustees of the British Museum / Art Resource, NY; **683** Werner Forman / Art Resource, NY; **689** Angelo Hornak / Corbis; **746–47** The Granger Collection, NY; **749 top** Réunion des Musées Nationaux / Art Resource, NY; **749 bottom** Bridgeman-Giraudon / Art Resource, NY; **753** HIP / Art Resource, NY; **767** AKG-images; **800–1** bpk, Berlin / Bodleian Library, Oxford UK/Hermann Buresch. / Art Resource, NY; **802** Giraudon / Art Resource, NY; **804** Erich Lessing / Art Resource, NY; **808** SSPL/Science Museum / Art Resource, NY; **812** Wikimedia Commons; **813** HIP / Art Resource, NY; **1250–51** Art Resource, NY; **1255** Borromeo / Art Resource, NY; **1257** © Rubin Museum of Art / Art Resource, NY; **1280–81** © The Metropolitan Museum of Art / Art Resource, NY; **1283** Allen Lee Taylor / Getty

Images; **1285** HIP / Art Resource, NY; **1290** © The Metropolitan Museum of Art / Art Resource, NY; **1344–45** © Corbis; **1348** Sakamoto Photo Research Laboratory/ Corbis; **1350** Wikimedia Commons; **1353** Burstein Collection/Corbis; **1380** The Art Archive / Private Collection Paris / Gianni Dagli Orti; **1495** Digital Image © 2009 Museum Associates / LACMA / Art Resource, NY; **1504–5** Giraudon / Art Resource, NY; **1510** Gavin Hellier/JAI/Corbis; **1515 top** Photo by David C. Conrad; **1515 middle** Photo by David C. Conrad; **1515 bottom** Photo by David C. Conrad; **1606–7** National Gallery, London / Art Resource, NY; **1608** World History Archive / Alamy; **1611** Giraudon / Art Resource, NY; **1616** Bildarchiv Preussischer Kulturbesitz / Art Resource, NY; **1617** The Trustees of The British Museum / Art Resource, NY; **1668** HIP / Art Resource, NY; **1802** Snark/Art Resource, NY; **1901** Bildarchiv Preussischer Kulturbesitz / Art Resource, NY.

COLOR INSERT

Egyptian Statue of Seated Scribe. Gianni Dagli Orti/Corbis; **Clay tablet with cuneiform letter.** The Trustees of the British Museum / Art Resource, NY; **Shang dynasty oracle bone.** Royal Ontario Museum/Corbis; **Detail of Book of the Dead of Maiherperi.** Sandro Vannini/ Corbis; **Ostrakon. Greek potsherd.** Scala / Art Resource, NY; **Pillar edict of Emperor Asoka.** The Trustees of The British Museum / Art Resource, NY; **Portrait of girl, Roman fresco.** Vanni / Art Resource, NY; **Battle scene from Homer's Iliad.** Heritage Images/Corbis; **Ibe Ezra.** Scala / Art Resource; **Diamond Sutra.** HIP / Art Resource; **Koran fragment.** bpk, Berlin / Art Resource, NY; **Text from "Beowulf."** HIP / Art Resource, NY; **Servants at Work.** Burstein Collection/Corbis; **Page from Gutenberg's Bible.** Lebrecht Music & Arts/Corbis; **The Printer's Workshop.** The Trustees of the British Museum / Art Resource; **Nushirvan Receives an Embassy.** LACMA / Art Resource, NY; **Panel from the Codex Fejervary-Mayer.** © Werner Forman / Art Resource, NY; **Medieval concept of the earth as the center of the universe.** bpk, Berlin / Art Resource, NY; **Antoine du Four, The Lives of Famous Women.** DeA Picture Library / Art Resource, NY; **Map of Venice, by Piri Reis.** bpk, Berlin / Art Resource, NY; **The Reader.** Scala/White Images / Art Resource, NY; **Illustration from Rasik Priya.** bpk, Berlin / Art Resource, NY; **Title page, Shakespeare's first folio.** Nathan Benn/Corbis; **Velazquez: The Court Jester.** Erich Lessing / Art Resource, NY.

Index